The PILGRIMAGE

Paulo Coelho was born in Brazil and has become one of the most widely read and loved authors in the world. Especially renowned for *The Alchemist* and *Eleven Minutes*, he has sold more than 320 million books worldwide and has been translated into 88 languages. The recipient of numerous prestigious international awards, amongst them the Crystal Award by the World Economic Forum and France's Légion d'Honneur, Paulo Coelho was inducted into the Brazilian Academy of Letters in 2002.

Also by Paulo Coelho

The Alchemist
The Pilgrimage
The Valkyries
By the River Piedra I Sat Down and Wept
The Fifth Mountain
Veronika Decides to Die
Manual of the Warrior of Light
Eleven Minutes
The Zahir
The Devil and Miss Prym
The Witch of Portobello
Brida
The Winner Stands Alone
Like the Flowing River
Aleph
Manuscript Found in Accra
Adultery
The Spy
Hippie

The PILGRIMAGE

PAULO COELHO

Author of THE ALCHEMIST

TRANSLATED BY ALAN R. CLARKE

Thorsons
An imprint of HarperCollins*Publishers*
1 London Bridge Street
London SE1 9GF

HarperCollins*Publishers*
1st Floor, Watermarque Building, Ringsend Road
Dublin 4, Ireland

www.harpercollins.co.uk
www.paulocoelho.com
www.paulocoelhoblog.com

Originally published in Portuguese as *O diário de um Mago*
by Editoria Rocco Ltd, Rio de Janeiro 1987
English version first published as *The Diary of a Magus* 1992
Published in paperback by HarperCollins*Publishers*, USA 1995
Published by HarperCollins*Publishers*, UK 1997
This edition published by Thorsons 2022

2 4 6 8 10 9 7 5 3 1

English version © Paulo Coelho
and Alan R. Clarke 1992, 2012

Paulo Coelho asserts the moral right to
be identified as the author of this work

A catalogue record for this book
is available from the British Library

ISBN 978-0-00-854731-8

FICTION / PHILOSOPHY

Printed and bound in India by Thomson Press India Ltd

All rights reserved. No part of this publication may be

reproduced, stored in a retrieval system, or transmitted,
in any form or by any means, electronic, mechanical,
photocopying, recording or otherwise, without the prior
written permission of the publishers.

This book is produced from independently certified FSC® paper
to ensure responsible forest management.

O Mary!
conceived without sin,
pray for us who turn to you!
Amen.

The disciples said, “See, Lord, here are two swords.”
“That’s enough.” he replied.

– Lucas 22:38

Disclaimer

When we began our pilgrimage, I thought my greatest dream as a young man had come true. To me, you were the medicine man Don Juan and I was living Castaneda's tale as he searched for the extraordinary. But you resisted every effort I made to turn you into a hero. This complicated our relationship, until the day I finally understood that the extraordinary lies in the path of ordinary people. Now, this understanding is the thing I treasure most in my life – it allows me to do anything and will stay with me forever. For this understanding, which I will now try to share with others, this book is dedicated to you, Petrus.

Prologue

'And now, before the sacred countenance of RAM, you must touch with your hands the Word of Life and acquire such power as you need to become a witness to that Word throughout the World'.

The master raised high my new sword, still sheathed in its scabbard. The flames on the bonfire crackled – a good omen, indicating that the ritual should continue. I knelt and, with my bare hands, began to dig into the earth.

It was the night of January 2, 1986, and we were in Itatiaia, high on one of the peaks in the Serra do Mar, close to the formation known as the Agulhas Negras (Black Needles) in Brazil. My Master and I were accompanied by my wife, one of my disciples, a local guide, and a representative of the great fraternity that is comprised of esoteric orders from all over the world – the fraternity known as 'The Tradition.' The five of us – and the guide, who had been told what was to happen – were participating in my ordination as a Master of the Order of RAM.

I finished digging a smooth, elongated hole in the dirt. With great solemnity, I placed my hands on the earth and spoke the ritual words. My wife drew near and handed me the sword I had used for more than ten years; it had been a great help to me during hundreds of magical operations. I placed it in the hole I had dug, covered it with dirt, and smoothed the surface. As I did so, I thought of the many tests I had endured, of all I had learned, and of the strange phenomena I had been able to invoke simply because I had had that ancient and friendly sword with me. Now it was to be devoured by the earth, the iron of its blade and the wood of its hilt returning to nourish the source from which its power had come.

The Master approached me and placed my new sword on the earth that now covered the grave of my ancient one. All of us spread our arms wide, and the Master, invoking his power, created a strange light that surrounded us; it did not illuminate, but it was clearly visible, and it caused the figures of those who were there to take on a color that was different from the yellowish tinge cast by the fire. Then, drawing his own sword, he touched it to my shoulders and my forehead as he said, 'By the power and the love of RAM, I anoint you Master and Knight of the Order, now and for all the days of your life. R for rigor, A for adoration, and M for mercy; R for *regnum*, A for *agnus*, and M for *mundi*. Let not your sword remain for long in its scabbard, lest it rust. And when you draw your sword, it must never be replaced without having performed an act of goodness, opened a new path, or tasted the blood of an enemy.'

With the point of his sword, he lightly cut my forehead. From then on, I was no longer required to remain silent. No longer did I have to hide my capabilities nor maintain secrecy regarding the marvels I had learned to accomplish on the road of the Tradition. From that moment on, I was a Magus.

I reached out to take my new sword of indestructible steel and wood, with its black and red hilt and black scabbard. But as my hands touched the scabbard and as I prepared to pick it up, the Master came forward and stepped on my fingers with all his might. I screamed and let go of the sword.

I looked at him, astonished. The strange light had disappeared, and his face had taken on a phantasmagoric appearance, heightened by the flames of the bonfire.

He returned my gaze coldly, called to my wife, and gave her the sword, speaking a few words that I could not hear. Turning to me, he said, 'Take away your hand; it has deceived you. The road of the Tradition is not for the chosen few. It is everyone's road. And the power that you think you have is worthless, because it is a power that is shared by all. You should have refused the sword. If you had done so, it would have been given to you, because you would have shown that your heart was pure. But just as I feared, at the supreme moment you stumbled and fell. Because of your avidity, you will now have to seek again for your sword. And because of your pride, you will have to seek it among simple people.

Because of your fascination with miracles, you will have to struggle to recapture what was about to be given to you so generously.'

The world seemed to fall away from me. I knelt there unable to think about anything. Once I had returned my old sword to the earth, I could not retrieve it. And since the new one had not been given to me, I now had to begin my quest for it all over again, powerless and defenceless. On the day of my Celestial Ordination, my Master's violence had brought me back to earth.

The guide smothered the fire, and my wife helped me up. She had my new sword in her hands, but according to the rules of the Tradition, I could not touch it without permission from my Master. We descended through the forest in silence, following the guide's lantern, until we reached the narrow dirt road where the cars were parked.

Nobody said good-bye. My wife put the sword in the trunk of the car and started the engine. We were quiet for a long time as she carefully navigated around the bumps and holes in the road.

'Don't worry,' she said, trying to encourage me. 'I'm sure you'll get it back.'

I asked her what the Master had said to her.

'He said three things to me. First, that he should have brought along something warm to wear, because it was much colder up there than he had expected. Second, that he wasn't surprised at anything that had happened up there, that this has happened many times before with others who have reached the same point as you. And third, that your sword would be waiting for you at the right time, on the right day, at some point on the road that you will have to travel. I don't know either the day or the time. He only told me where I should hide it.'

'And what road was he talking about?' I asked nervously.

'Ah, well, that he didn't explain very well. He just said that you should look on the map of Spain for a medieval route known as the Strange Road to Santiago.'

THE ROAD TO SANTIAGO

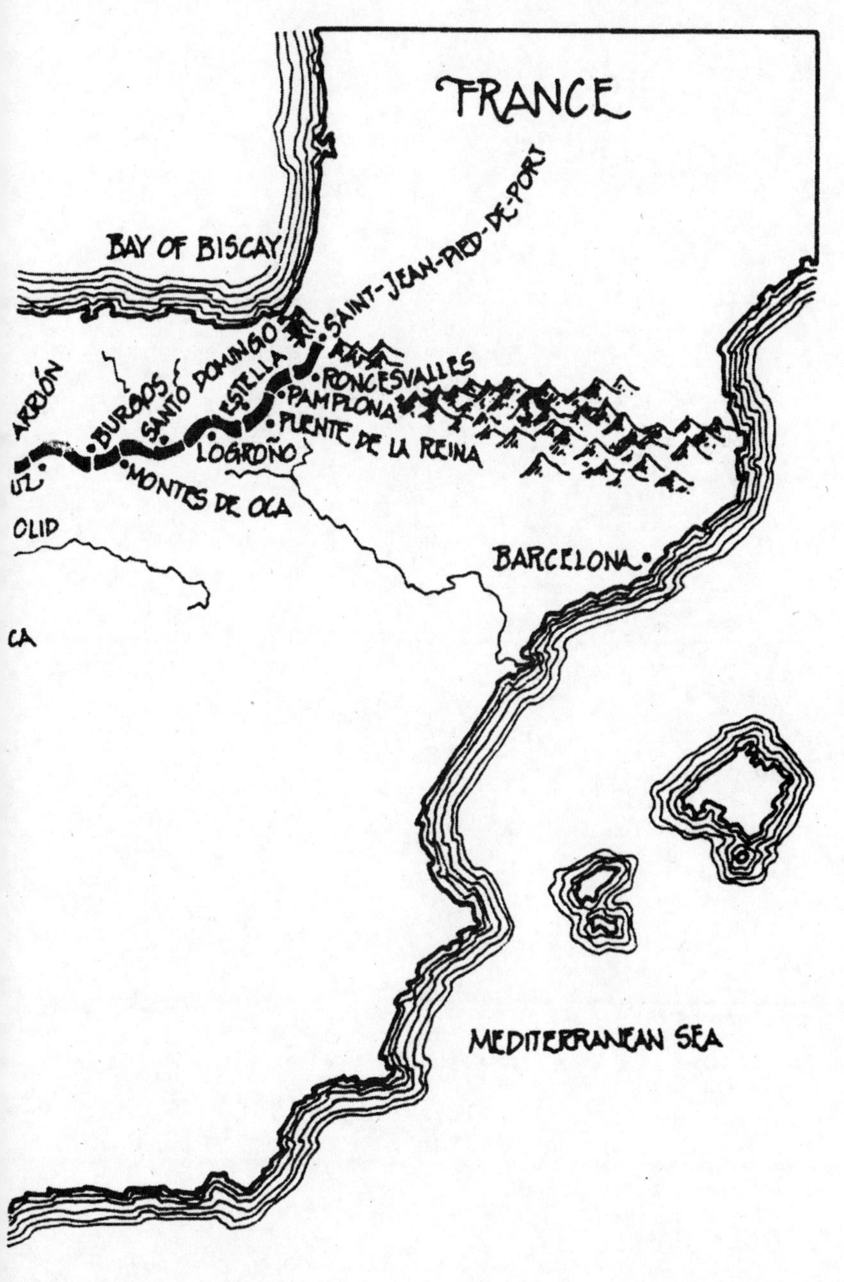
FRANCE
BAY OF BISCAY
SAINT-JEAN-PIED-DE-PORT
RONCESVALLES
PAMPLONA
PUENTE DE LA REINA
ESTELLA
SANTO DOMINGO
BURGOS
ARRIÓN
LOGROÑO
MONTES DE OCA
OLID
CA
BARCELONA
MEDITERRANEAN SEA

Arrival

The customs agent spent more time than usual examining the sword that my wife had brought into the country and then asked what we intended to do with it. I said that a friend of ours was going to assess its value so that we could sell it at auction. This lie worked: the agent gave us a declaration stating that we had entered the country with the sword at the Bajadas airport, and he told us that if we had any problems trying to leave the country with it, we need only show the declaration to the customs officials.

We went to the car rental agency and confirmed our two vehicles. Armed with the rental documents, we had a bite together at the airport restaurant prior to going our separate ways.

We had spent a sleepless night on the plane – the result of both a fear of flying and a sense of apprehension about what was going to happen once we arrived – but now we were excited and wide awake.

'Not to worry,' she said for the thousandth time. 'You're supposed to go to France and, at Saint-Jean-Pied-de-Port, seek out Mme Lourdes. She is going to put you in touch with someone who will guide you along the Road to Santiago.'

'And what about you?' I asked, also for the thousandth time, knowing what her answer would be.

'I'm going where I have to go, and there I'll leave what has been entrusted to me. Afterward, I'll spend a few days in Madrid and then return to Brazil. I can take care of things back there as well as you would.'

'I know you can,' I answered, wanting to avoid the subject. I felt an enormous anxiety about the business matters I had left behind in Brazil. I had learned all I needed to know about the Road to Santiago in the fifteen days following the incident in the Agulhas Negras, but I had vacillated for another seven months before deciding to leave everything behind and make the trip. I had put it off until one morning when my wife had said that the time was drawing near and that if I did not make a decision, I might as well forget about the road of the Tradition and the Order of RAM. I had tried to explain to her that my Master had assigned me an impossible task, that I couldn't simply shrug off my livelihood. She had smiled and said that my excuse was dumb, that during the entire seven months I had done nothing but ask myself night and day whether or not I should go. And with the most casual of gestures, she had held out the two airline tickets, with the flight already scheduled.

'We're here because of your decision,' I said glumly now in the airport restaurant. 'I don't know if this will even work, since I let another person make the decision for me to seek out my sword.'

My wife said that if we were going to start talking nonsense, we had better say good-bye and go our separate ways.

'You have never in your life let another person make an important decision for you. Let's go. It's getting late.' She rose, picked up her suitcase, and headed for the parking lot. I didn't stop her. I stayed seated, observing the casual way in which she carried my sword; at any moment it seemed that it could slip from under her arm.

She stopped suddenly, came back to the table, and kissed me desperately. She looked at me for some time without saying a word. This suddenly made me realize that now I was actually in Spain and that there was no going back. In spite of the knowledge that there were many ways in which I could fail, I had taken the first step. I hugged her passionately, trying to convey all the love I felt for her at that moment. And while she was still in my arms, I prayed to everything and everyone I believed in, imploring that I be given the strength to return to her with the sword.

'That was a beautiful sword, wasn't it?' said a woman's voice from the next table, after my wife had left.

'Don't worry,' a man said. 'I'll buy one just like it for you. The tourist shops here in Spain have thousands of them.'

After I had driven for an hour or so, I began to feel the fatigue accumulated from the night before. The

August heat was so powerful that even on the open highway, the car began to overheat. I decided to stop in a small town identified by the road signs as Monumento Nacional. As I climbed the steep road that led to it, I began to review all that I had learned about the Road to Santiago.

Just as the Muslin tradition requires that all members of the faith, at least once in their life, make the same pilgrimage that Muhammad made from Mecca to Medina, so Christians in the first millennium considered three routes to be sacred. Each of them offered a series of blessings and indulgences to those who traveled its length. The first led to the tomb of Saint Peter in Rome; its travelers, who were called wanderers, took the cross as their symbol. The second led to the Holy Sepulcher of Christ in Jerusalem; those who took this road were called Palmists, since they had as their symbol the palm branches with which Jesus was greeted when he entered that city. There was a third road, which led to the mortal remains of the apostle, San Tiago – Saint James in English, Jacques in French, Giacomo in Italian, Jacob in Latin. He was buried at a place on the Iberian peninsula where, one night, a shepherd had seen a brilliant star above a field. The legend says that not only San Tiago but also the Virgin Mary went there shortly after the death of Christ, carrying the word of the Evangelist and exhorting the people to convert. The site came to be known as Compostela – the star field – and there a city had arisen that drew travelers from every part of the Christian world. These travelers were called pilgrims, and their symbol was the scallop shell.

At the height of its fame, during the fourteenth century, the Milky Way – another name for the third road, since at night the pilgrims plotted their course using this galaxy – was traveled each year by more than a million people from every corner of Europe. Even today, mystics, devotees, and researchers traverse on foot the seven hundred kilometers that separate the French city of Saint-Jean-Pied-de-Port from the cathedral of Santiago de Compostela in Spain.*

Thanks to the French priest, Aymeric Picaud, who walked to Compostela in 1123, the route followed by the pilgrims today is exactly the same as the medieval path taken by Charlemagne, Saint Francis of Assisi, Isabella of Castile, and, most recently, by Pope John XXIII.

Picaud wrote five books about his experience. They were presented as the work of Pope Calixtus II – a devotee of San Tiago – and they were later known as the Codex Calixtinus. In Book Five of the codex, Picaud identified the natural features, fountains, hospitals, shelters, and cities found along the road. A special society – 'Les Amis de Saint-Jacques' – was formed with the

* The Road to Santiago, on the French side, comprised several routes that joined at a Spanish city called Puente de la Reina. The city of Saint-Jean-Pied-de-Port is located on one of those three routes; it is neither the only one nor the most important.

charge of maintaining all of the natural markings on the route and helping to guide the pilgrims, using Picaud's annotations.

Also in the twelfth century, Spain began to capitalize on the legend of San Tiago as the country fought against the Moors who had invaded the peninsula. Several militant religious orders were established along the Road to Santiago, and the apostle's ashes became a powerful symbol in the fight against the Muslims. The Muslims, in turn, claimed that they had with them one of Muhammad's arms and took that as their guiding symbol. By the time Spain had regained control of the country, the militant orders had become so strong that they posed a threat to the nobility, and the Catholic kings had to intervene directly to prevent the orders from mounting an insurgency. As a result, the Road to Santiago was gradually forgotten, and were it not for sporadic artistic manifestations – in paintings such as Buñuel's *The Milky Way* and Juan Manoel Serrat's *Wanderer* – no one today would remember that millions of the people who would one day settle the New World had passed along that route.

The town that I reached by car was completely deserted. After searching on foot for quite some time, I finally found a small bar open for business in an old, medieval-style house. The owner, who did not even look up from the television program he was watching, advised me that it was siesta time and suggested that I must be crazy to be out walking in such heat.

I asked for a soft drink and tried to watch the television, but I was unable to concentrate. All I could think of was that in two days I was going to relive, here in the latter part of the twentieth century, something of the great human adventure that had brought Ulysses from Troy, that had been a part of Don Quixote's experience, that had led Dante and Orpheus into hell, and that had directed Columbus to the Americas: the adventure of traveling toward the unknown.

By the time I returned to my car, I was a bit calmer. Even if I were not able to find my sword, the pilgrimage along the Road to Santiago was going to help me to find myself.

Saint-Jean-Pied-de-Port

A parade of masked people accompanied by a band – all of them dressed in red, green, and white, the colors of the French Basque region – filled the main street of Saint-Jean-Pied-de-Port. It was Sunday. I had spent the last two days driving, and now I was enjoying the festivities. But it was time for my meeting with Mme Lourdes. Forcing my way through the crowd by car, I heard some shouted insults in French, but I finally made it through to the fortified sector that constituted the oldest part of the city, where Mme Lourdes lived. Even this high in the Pyrenees, it was hot during the day, and I was soaked with perspiration as I got out of the car.

I knocked at the gate. I knocked again, but there was no response. A third time, and still nothing happened. I felt confused and worried. My wife had said that I had to arrive there exactly on that day, but no one answered when I called out. I thought that perhaps Mme Lourdes had gone out to watch the parade, but it was also possible that I had arrived too late and that she had decided not to meet with me. My journey along the Road to Santiago seemed to have ended even before it had begun.

Suddenly, the gate opened, and a child jumped through it. I was startled, and in halting French I asked for Mme Lourdes. The child smiled at me and pointed toward the house. It was only then that I saw my mistake: the gate led onto an immense courtyard, around which were situated medieval houses with balconies. The gate had been open, and I hadn't even thought to try its handle.

I ran across the courtyard and up to the house that the child had indicated. Inside, an elderly, obese woman yelled something in Basque at a small boy with sad, brown eyes. I waited for a few moments, giving the argument a chance to end; it finally did, with the poor boy being sent to the kitchen under a hail of insults from the old woman. It was only then that she turned to me and, without even asking what it was that I wanted, led me – with delicate gestures and slight shoves – to the second floor of the small house. This floor consisted of just one room: a small, crowded office filled with books, objects, statues of San Tiago, and memorabilia from the Road. She took a book from its shelf and sat down behind the only table in the room, leaving me standing.

'You must be another pilgrim to Santiago,' she said, without preamble. 'I need to enter your name in the register of those who walk the Road.'

I gave her my name, and she wanted to know if I had brought 'the Scallops.' She was referring to the shells adopted as a symbol by pilgrims to the tomb of the apostle; they served as a means of identification for the pilgrims when they met.*

Before leaving for Spain, I had made a pilgrimage to a place in Brazil called Aparecida do Norte. There, I had purchased an image of Our Lady of the Visitation, mounted on three scallop shells. I took it from my knapsack and offered it to Mme Lourdes.

'Pretty but not very practical,' she said, handing it back to me. 'It could break during your pilgrimage.'

'It's not going to break. And I am going to leave it at the tomb of the apostle.'

Mme Lourdes appeared not to have much time for me. She gave me a small card that would help me to get lodging at the monasteries along the Road, stamped it with the seal of Saint-Jean-Pied-de-Port to indicate that I had started the pilgrimage there, and said that I could leave with God's blessing.

'But where is my guide?' I asked.

'What guide?' she answered, a bit surprised but also with a gleam in her eye.

I realized that I had forgotten something very important. In my eagerness to arrive and be attended to, I had neglected to say the Ancient Word – a kind of password that identifies those who belong to the orders of the Tradition. I immediately corrected my mistake and said

* The Road to Santiago has made only one mark on French culture, and that has been on that country's national pride, gastronomy, through the name 'Coquilles Saint-Jacques.'

the word to her. In response, Mme Lourdes quickly snatched from my hands the card she had given me a few moments earlier.

'You won't be needing this,' she said, as she moved a pile of old newspapers that were sitting on top of a cardboard box. 'Your road and your stopping places will depend on decisions made by your guide.'

Mme Lourdes took a hat and a cape from the box. They seemed to be very old but well preserved. She asked me to stand in the middle of the room, and she began silently to pray. Then she placed the cape on my shoulders and the hat on my head. I could see that scallop shells had been sewn onto both the hat and the shoulders of the cape. Without interrupting her prayers, the old woman seized a shepherd's crook from the corner of the room and made me take it in my right hand. A small water gourd hung from the crook. There I stood: dressed in Bermuda shorts and a T-shirt that read 'I LOVE NY,' covered by the medieval garb of the pilgrims to Compostela.

The old woman approached me and stopped only a foot away. Then, in a kind of trance, placing the palms of her hands on my head, she said, 'May the apostle San Tiago be with you, and may he show you the only thing that you need to discover; may you walk neither too slowly nor too fast but always according to the laws and the requirements of the Road; may you obey the one who is your guide, even though he may issue an order that is homicidal, blasphemous, or senseless. You must swear total obedience to your guide.'

I so swore.

'The Spirit of the ancient pilgrims of the Tradition must be with you during your journey. The hat will protect you from the sun and from evil thoughts; the cape will protect you from the rain and from evil words; the gourd will protect you from enemies and from evil deeds. May the blessing of God, of San Tiago, and of the Virgin Mary be with you through all of your nights and days. Amen.'

Having said this, she returned to her normal manner; hurriedly and with a bit of irritation, she took back the articles of clothing, placed them in the box, and returned the crook with the gourd to the corner of the room; then, after teaching me the password, she asked me to leave, since my guide was waiting for me two kilometers outside of Saint-Jean-Pied-de-Port.

'He hates band music,' she said. But even two kilometers away he must have been able to hear it; the Pyrenees are an excellent echo chamber.

Before I left, I asked what I should do with the car, and she said I should leave the keys with her; someone would come to pick it up. Then, without another word, she descended the stairs and went to the kitchen to inflict more torment on the boy with the sad eyes. I opened the trunk of the car, took out my small blue knapsack with my sleeping bag tied to it, and placed the image of Our Lady of the Visitation in its most protected corner. I put the knapsack on my back and went back to give the keys to Mme Lourdes.

'Leave Pied-de-Port by following this street to the city gates at the end of the wall,' she told me. 'And when you get to Santiago de Compostela, say a Hail Mary for me. I have walked the Road so many times that now I content myself with reading in other pilgrims' eyes the excitement that I still feel; I just can't put it into practice anymore because of my age. Tell that to San Tiago. And tell him also that any time now I will join him, following a different road that's more direct and less exhausting.'

I left the small city, passing through the wall at the Spanish Gate. In the past, the city had been on the preferred route for the Roman invaders, and through that gate had also passed the armies of Charlemagne and Napoleon. I walked along, hearing the band music in the distance, and suddenly, in the ruins of a village not far from the city, I was overwhelmed by emotion, and my eyes filled with tears; there in the ruins, the full impact of the fact that I was walking the Strange Road to Santiago finally hit me.

The view of the Pyrenees surrounding the valley, lit by the morning sun and intensified by the sound of the music, gave me the sensation that I was returning to something primitive, something that had been forgotten by most other human beings, something that I was unable to identify. But it was a strange and powerful feeling, and I decided to quicken my pace and arrive as soon as possible at the place where Mme Lourdes had said my guide would be waiting for me. Without stopping, I took off my shirt and put it in my knapsack. The straps cut into my bare shoulders a bit, but at least my old sneakers were broken in enough that they caused me no discomfort. After almost forty minutes, at a curve in the road that circled around a gigantic rock, I came upon an old abandoned well. There, sitting on the ground, was a man of about fifty; he had black hair and the look of a gypsy, and he was searching for something in his knapsack.

'*Hola*,' I said in Spanish, with the same timidity that I show whenever I meet someone new. 'You must be waiting for me. My name is Paulo.'

The man interrupted his search through the knapsack and looked me up and down. His gaze was cold, and he seemed not at all surprised by my arrival. I also had the vague impression that I knew him.

'Yes, I was waiting for you, but I didn't know that I was going to meet you so soon. What do you want?'

I was a little disconcerted by his question and answered that it was I whom he was to guide along the Milky Way in search of my sword.

'That's not necessary,' said the man. 'If you want me to, I can find it for you. But you have to decide right now whether you want me to.'

This conversation with the stranger seemed increasingly weird to me. But since I had sworn complete obedience, I tried to respond. If he could find my sword for me, it would save an enormous amount of time, and I could return immediately to my friends and my business in Brazil; they were always on my mind. This could also be a trick, but there was no harm in giving him an answer.

As I was about to say yes, I heard a voice behind me say, in heavily accented Spanish, 'You don't have to climb a mountain to find out whether or not it's high.'

It was the password! I turned and saw a man of about forty, in khaki Bermudas and a white, sweaty T-shirt, staring at the gypsy. He was gray-haired, and his skin was darkened by the sun. In my haste, I had forgotten the most elementary rules of self-protection and had thrown myself body and soul into the arms of the first stranger I had met.

'The ship is safest when it's in port, but that's not what ships were built for,' I said, as the correct response. Meanwhile, the man looked directly at the gypsy and the gypsy stared at the man. Both confronted each other, with no sign of fear or challenge, for some time. Then the gypsy left the knapsack on the ground, smiled disdainfully, and walked off in the direction of Saint-Jean-Pied-de-Port.

'My name is Petrus,'* said the new arrival as soon as the gypsy had disappeared behind the huge stone that I had circled a few minutes earlier. 'Next time, be more cautious.'

* Actually, Petrus told me his real name. I have changed it in order to protect his privacy, but this is one of the few times that names have been changed in this book.

I heard a sympathetic tone in his voice, it was different from the tone of the gypsy and of Mme Lourdes. He lifted the knapsack from the ground, and I noticed that it had the scallop shell on its back. He produced a bottle of wine, took a swallow, and offered it to me. After I had taken a drink, I asked him who the gypsy was.

'This is a frontier route often used by smugglers and terrorist refugees from the Spanish Basque country,' said Petrus. 'The police hardly ever come near here.'

'But you're not answering me. You two looked at each other like old acquaintances. And I had the feeling that I knew him, too. That's why I was so much at ease.'

Petrus smiled and said that we should move along. I picked up my things, and we began to walk in silence. From Petrus's smile I knew that he was thinking the same thing I was.

We had met with a devil.

We walked along without talking for a while, and I could see that Mme Lourdes had been right; from almost three kilometers away, we could still hear the sound of the band. I wanted to ask some questions of Petrus – about his life, his work, and what had brought him here. I knew, though, that we still had seven hundred kilometers to cover together and that the appropriate moment would come for having all my questions answered. But I could not get the gypsy out of my mind, and finally I broke the silence.

'Petrus, I think that the gypsy was the devil.'

'Yes, he was the devil.' When he confirmed this, I felt a mixture of terror and relief. 'But he isn't the devil that you know from the Tradition.'

In the Tradition, the devil is a spirit that is neither good nor evil; he is considered to be the guardian of most of the secrets that are accessible to human beings and to have strength and power over material things. Since he is a fallen angel, he is identified with the human race, and he is always ready to make deals and exchange favors. I asked what was the difference between the gypsy and the devil of the Tradition.

'We are going to meet others along the Road,' he smiled. 'You will see for yourself. But just to give you an idea, try to remember your entire conversation with the gypsy.'

I reviewed the two phrases I had heard from him. He had said that he was waiting for me and had affirmed that he would seek out the sword for me.

Then Petrus said that those two phrases fit perfectly well in the mouth of a thief who had been surprised in the act of robbing a knapsack: they were aimed at gaining time and at winning favor while he quickly figured out a means of escape. On the other hand, the two phrases could mean exactly what they said.

'Which is right?'

'Both are true. That poor thief, while he defended himself, picked out of the air the very words that needed to be said to you. He thought that he was being intelligent, but he was really acting as the instrument of a greater power. If he had fled when I arrived, we wouldn't be having this conversation now. But he confronted me, and I read in his eyes the name of a devil that you are going to meet somewhere along the Road.'

For Petrus, the meeting had been a favorable omen, since the devil had revealed himself so early.

'Meanwhile, don't worry about him because, as I have already told you, he won't be the only one. He may be the most important one, but he won't be the only one.'

We continued walking, passing from a desertlike area to one where small trees were scattered here and there. Once in a while Petrus broke the silence to tell me some historic fact or other about the places we were passing. I saw the house where a queen had spent the last night of her life and a small chapel encrusted with rocks, which had been the hermitage of a saintly man who the few inhabitants of the area swore could perform miracles.

'Miracles are very important, don't you think?' Petrus said.

I agreed but said that I had never witnessed a great miracle. My apprenticeship in the Tradition had been much more on the intellectual plane. I believed that when I recovered my sword, then, yes, I would be capable of doing the great deeds that my Master did.

'But what my Master performs are not miracles, because they don't contradict the laws of nature. What my Master does is utilize these forces to …'

I couldn't finish the sentence because I couldn't explain how my Master had been able to materialize spirits, move objects from one place to another without touching them, or, as I had witnessed more than once, create patches of blue sky on a cloudy afternoon.

'Maybe he does those things simply to convince you that he has the knowledge and the power,' answered Petrus.

'Yes, maybe so,' I said, without much conviction.

We sat down on a stone because Petrus told me that he hated to smoke cigarettes while he was walking. According to him, the lungs absorbed much more nicotine if one smoked while walking, and the smoke nauseated him.

'That was why the Master refused to let you have the sword,' Petrus continued. 'Because you didn't understand why he performs his prodigious feats. Because you forgot that the path to knowledge is a path that's open to everyone, to the common people. During our journey, I'm going to teach you some exercises and some rituals that are known as the practices of RAM. All of us, at some time in our lives, have made use of at least one of them. Every one of these practices, without exception, can be discovered by anyone who is willing to seek them out, with patience and perspicacity, among the lessons that life itself teaches us.

'The RAM practices are so simple that people like you, who are used to making life too complicated, ascribe little value to them. But it is they that make people capable of achieving anything, absolutely anything, that they desire.

'Jesus glorified the Father when his disciples began to perform miracles and cures; he thanked God for having kept such things secret from wise people and for revealing them to simple folk. When all is said and done, if we believe in God, we have to believe also that God is just.'

Petrus was absolutely right. It would be a divine injustice to allow only those people who were learned and who had the time and money to buy expensive books to have access to true knowledge.

'The true path to wisdom can be identified by three things,' said Petrus. 'First, it must involve agape, and I'll tell you more about this later; second, it has to have practical application in your life. Otherwise, wisdom becomes a useless thing and deteriorates, like a sword that is never used.

'And finally, it has to be a path that can be followed by anyone. Like the road you are walking now, the Road to Santiago.'

We walked for the rest of the afternoon, and only when the sun began to disappear behind the mountains did Petrus decide to stop again. All around us the highest peaks of the Pyrenees still shone in the last light of the day.

Petrus told me to clear a small area on the ground and to kneel there.

'The first RAM practice will help you to achieve rebirth. You will have to do the exercise for seven consecutive days, each time trying to experience in some different way your first contact with the world. You know how difficult it was for you to make the decision to drop everything and come here to walk the Road to Santiago in search of a sword. But this was difficult only because you were a prisoner of the past. You had been defeated before, and you were afraid that it could happen again. You had already achieved things, and you were afraid you might lose them. But at the same time, something stronger than any of that prevailed: the desire to find your sword. So you decided to take the risk.'

I said that he was right but that I still had the worries he described.

'That doesn't matter. The exercise, little by little, will free you from the burdens that you have created in your life.'

And Petrus taught me the first RAM practice: the Seed Exercise.

'Do it now for the first time,' he said.

I lowered my head between my knees, breathed deeply, and began to relax. My body obeyed without question, perhaps because we had walked so far during the day and I was exhausted. I began to listen to the sound of the earth, muffled and harsh, and bit by bit I transformed myself into a seed. I didn't think. Everything was dark, and I was asleep at the center of the earth. Suddenly, something moved. It was a part of me, a minuscule part of me that wanted to awaken, that said that I had to leave this place because there was something else 'up there'. I wanted to sleep, but this part insisted. I began to move my fingers, and my fingers began to move my arms – but they were neither fingers nor arms. They were a small shoot that was fighting to overcome the force of the earth and to move in the direction of that 'something up there.' I felt my body begin to follow the movement of my arms. Each second seemed like an eternity, but the seed needed to be born; it needed to know what that 'something up there' was. With immense difficulty, my head, then my body, began to rise. Everything was too slow, and I had to fight against the force that was pushing me down toward the center of the earth where before I had been tranquil, dreaming an eternal dream. But I was winning, I was winning, and finally I broke through something and was upright. The force that had been pressing down on me suddenly ceased. I had broken through the earth and was surrounded by that 'something up there.'

The 'something up there' was the field. I sensed the heat of the sun, the hum of the mosquitoes, the sound of a river that ran in the distance. I arose slowly, with my eyes closed, and felt that at any moment I was going to become dizzy and fall to the ground. But meanwhile I continued to grow. My arms were spreading and my body stretching. There I was, being reborn, wanting to be bathed both inside and out by the immense sun that

The Seed Exercise

Kneel on the ground. Then seat yourself on your heels and bend forward so that your head touches your knees. Stretch your arms behind you. You are now in a fetal position. Relax, releasing all your tensions. Breathe calmly and deeply. Little by little you will perceive that you are a tiny seed, cradled in the comfort of the earth. Everything around you is warm and delicious. You are in a deep, restful sleep.

Suddenly, a finger moves. The shoot no longer wants to be a seed; it wants to grow. Slowly you begin to move your arms, and then your body will begin to rise, straightening up until you are seated on your heels. Now you begin to lift your body up, and slowly, slowly you will become erect, still kneeling on the ground.

The moment has come to break completely through the earth. You begin to rise slowly, placing one foot on the ground, then the other, fighting against the disequilibrium just as a shoot battles to make its own space, until finally you are standing. Imagine the area about you, the sun, the water, the wind, and the birds. Now you are a shoot that is beginning to grow. Slowly raise your arms toward the sky. Then stretch yourself more and more, more and more, as if you want to grasp the enormous sun that shines above you. Your body begins to become more and more rigid, all of your muscles strain, and you feel yourself to be growing, growing, growing – you become huge. The tension increases more and more until it becomes painful, unbearable. When you can no longer stand it, scream and open your eyes.

Repeat this exercise for seven consecutive days, always at the same time.

was shining and that was asking me to continue to grow more, stretch more, and embrace it with all of my branches. I was stretching my arms more and more, and the muscles throughout my body began to hurt. I felt that I was a thousand meters tall and that I could embrace mountains. And my body was expanding, expanding until the pain in my muscles became so intense that I couldn't bear it, and I screamed.

I opened my eyes, and Petrus was there in front of me, smiling and smoking a cigarette. The light of day had not yet disappeared, but I was surprised to see that the sun was not as bright as I had imagined. I asked if he wanted me to describe the sensations, and he said no.

'This is a very personal thing, and you should keep it to yourself. How can I judge it? The sensations are yours, not mine.'

Petrus said that we were going to sleep right there. We built a small fire, drank what was left of his wine, and I made some sandwiches with a foie gras that I had bought before I reached Saint-Jean. Petrus went to the stream that ran nearby and caught some fish, which he fried over the fire. And then we crawled into our sleeping bags.

Among the greatest sensations that I have experienced in my life were those I felt on that unforgettable first night on the Road to Santiago. It was cold, despite its being summer, but I could still taste the warmth of the wine that Petrus had brought. I looked up at the sky;

the Milky Way spread across it, reflecting the immensity of the Road we would have to travel. This immensity made me very anxious; it created a terrible fear that I would not be able to succeed – that I was too small for this task. Yet today I had been a seed and had been reborn. I had discovered that although the earth and my sleep were full of comfort, the life 'up there' was much more beautiful. And I could always be reborn, as many times as I wanted, until my arms were long enough to embrace the earth from which I had come.

The Creator and the Created

For seven days we continued walking through the Pyrenees, climbing and descending the mountains, and each evening, as the rays of the sun reflected from the tallest peaks, Petrus had me perform the Seed Exercise. On the third day of our trek, we passed a cement marker, painted yellow, indicating that we had crossed the frontier; from then on we would be walking through Spain. Little by little, Petrus began to reveal some things about his private life; I learned that he was Italian and that he worked in industrial design.*

I asked him whether he was worried about the many things he had been forced to abandon in order to guide a pilgrim in search of his sword.

* It has been said that there is no such thing as coincidence in this world, and the following story confirms the truth of this assertion once again. One afternoon, I was leafing through some magazines in the lobby of the hotel where I was staying in Madrid, when I noticed a piece about the Prince of Asturias Prize; a Brazilian journalist, Robert Marinho, had been one of the prize winners. A closer study of the photograph of those at the awards dinner startled me, though. At one of the tables, elegantly dressed in his tuxedo, was Petrus, described in the caption as 'one of the most famous European designers of the moment.'

'Let me explain something to you,' he answered. 'I am not guiding you to your sword. It is your job, solely and exclusively, to find it. I am here to lead you along the Road to Santiago and to teach you the RAM practices. How you apply this to your search for your sword is your problem.'

'But you didn't answer my question.'

'When you travel, you experience, in a very practical way, the act of rebirth. You confront completely new situations, the day passes more slowly, and on most journeys you don't even understand the language the people speak. So you are like a child just out of the womb. You begin to be more accessible to others because they may be able to help you in difficult situations. And you accept any small favor from the gods with great delight, as if it were an episode you would remember for the rest of your life.

'At the same time, since all things are new, you see only the beauty in them, and you feel happy to be alive. That's why a religious pilgrimage has always been one of the most objective ways of achieving insight. The word *peccadillo*, which means a "small sin," comes from *pecus*, which means "defective foot," a foot that is incapable of walking a road. The way to correct the peccadillo is always to walk forward, adapting oneself to new situations and receiving in return all of the thousands of blessings that life generously offers to those who seek them.

'So why would you think that I might be worried about a half-dozen projects that I left behind in order to be here with you?'

Petrus looked around him, and I followed his eyes. On the uplands of one of the peaks, some goats were grazing. One of them, more daring than the others, stood on an outcropping of a high boulder, and I could not figure out how he had reached that spot or how he would get down. But as I was thinking this, the goat leapt and, alighting in a place I couldn't even see, rejoined his companions. Everything in our surrounds reflected an uneasy peace, the peace of a world that was still in the process of growing and being created – a world that seemed to know that, in order to grow, it had to continue moving along, always moving along. Great earthquakes and killer storms might make nature seem cruel, but I could see that these were just the vicissitudes of being on the road. Nature itself journeyed, seeking illumination.

'I am very glad to be here,' said Petrus, 'because the work I did not finish is not important and the work I will be able to do after I get back will be so much better.'

When I had read the works of Carlos Castaneda, I had wanted very much to meet the old medicine man, Don Juan. Watching Petrus look at the mountain, I felt that I was with someone very much like him.

On the afternoon of the seventh day, after having passed through some pine woods, we reached the top of a mountain. There, Charlemagne had said his prayers for the first time on Spanish soil, and now an ancient monument urged in Latin that all who passed by should say a Salve Regina. We both did as the monument asked. Then Petrus had me do the Seed Exercise for the last time.

There was a strong wind, and it was cold, I argued that it was still early – at the latest, it was only three in the afternoon – but he told me not to talk about it, just do exactly as he ordered.

I knelt on the ground and began to perform the exercise. Everything went as usual until the moment when I extended my arms and began to imagine the sun. When I reached that point, with the gigantic sun shining there in front of me, I felt myself entering into a state of ecstasy. My memories of human life began slowly to dim, and I was no longer doing an exercise: I had become a tree. I was happy about this. The sun shone and revolved, which had never happened before. I remained there, my branches extended, my leaves trembling in the wind, not wanting ever to change my position – until something touched me, and everything went dark for a fraction of a second.

I immediately opened my eyes. Petrus had slapped me across the face and was holding me by the shoulders.

'Don't lose sight of your objective!' he said, enraged. 'Don't forget that you still have a great deal to learn before you find your sword!'

I sat down on the ground, shivering in the cold wind.

'Does that always happen?' I asked.

'Almost always,' he said. 'Mainly with people like you, who are fascinated by details and forget what they are after.'

Petrus took a sweater from his knapsack and put it on. I put my overshirt on, covering my 'I LOVE NY' T-shirt. I would never have imagined that in the 'hottest summer of the decade,' according to the newspapers, it could be so cold. The two shirts helped to cut the wind, but I asked Petrus if we couldn't move along more quickly so that I could warm up.

The Road now made for an easy descent. I thought that the extreme cold I had experienced was due to the fact that we had eaten very frugally, just fish and the fruits of the forest.*

Petrus said that it wasn't the lack of food and explained that it was cold because we had reached the highest point in the range of mountains.

We had not gone more than five hundred meters when, at a curve in the Road, the scene changed completely. A tremendous, rolling plain extended into the distance. And to the left, on the Road down, less than two hundred meters away, a beautiful little village awaited us with its chimneys smoking.

I began to walk faster, but Petrus held me back.

'I think that this is a good time to teach you the second RAM practice,' he said, sitting down on the ground and indicating that I should do the same.

I was irritated, but I did as he asked. The sight of the

* There is a red fruit whose name I do not know, but just the sight of it today makes me nauseated from having eaten so much of it while walking through the Pyrenees.

small village with its inviting chimney smoke had really upset me. Suddenly I realized that we had been out in the woods for a week; we had seen no one and had been either sleeping on the ground or walking throughout the day. I had run out of cigarettes, so I had been smoking the horrible roller tobacco that Petrus used. Sleeping in a sleeping bag and eating unseasoned fish were things that I had loved when I was twenty, but here on the Road to Santiago, they were sacrifices. I waited impatiently for Petrus to finish rolling his cigarette, while I thought about the warmth of a glass of wine in the bar I could see less than five minutes down the Road.

Petrus, bundled up in his sweater, was relaxed and looked out over the immense plain.

'What do you think about this crossing of the Pyrenees?' he asked, after a while.

'Very nice,' I answered, not wanting to prolong the conversation.

'It must have been nice, because it took us six days to go a distance we could have gone in one'.

I could not believe what he was saying. He pulled out the map and showed me the distance: seventeen kilometers. Even walking at a slow pace because of the ups and downs, the Road could have been hiked in six hours.

'You are so concerned about finding your sword that you forgot the most important thing: you have to get there. Looking only for Santiago – which you can't see from here, in any case – you didn't see that we passed by certain places four or five times, approaching them from different angles.'

Now that Petrus mentioned it, I began to realize that Mount Itchasheguy – the highest peak in the region – had sometimes been to my right and sometimes to my left. Although I had noticed this, I had not drawn the only possible conclusion: that we had gone back and forth many times.

'All I did was to follow different routes, using the paths made through the woods by the smugglers. But it was your responsibility to have seen that. This happened because the process of moving along did not exist for you. The only thing that existed was your desire to arrive at your goal.'

'Well, what if I had noticed?'

'We would have taken seven days anyway, because that is what the RAM practices call for. But at least you would have approached the Pyrenees in a different way.'

I was so surprised that I forgot about the village and the temperature.

'When you are moving toward an objective,' said Petrus, 'It is very important to pay attention to the road. It is the road that teaches us the best way to get there, and the road enriches us as we walk its length. You can compare it to a sexual relationship: the caresses of foreplay determine the intensity of the orgasm. Everyone knows that.

'And it is the same thing when you have an objective in your life. It will turn out to be better or worse depending on the route you choose to reach it and the way you negotiate that route. That's why the second RAM practice is so important; it extracts from what we are used to seeing every day the secrets that because of our routine, we never see.'

And then Petrus taught me the Speed Exercise.

'In the city, amid all the things we have to do every day, the exercise should be done for twenty minutes. But since we are on the Strange Road to Santiago, we should wait an hour before getting to the village.'

The cold – about which I had already forgotten – returned, and I looked at Petrus with desperation. But he paid no attention; he got up, grabbed his knapsack, and began to walk the two hundred meters to the village with an exasperating slowness. At first, I looked only in the direction of the tavern, a small, ancient, two-story building with a wooden sign hanging above the door. We were so close that I could even read the year when the tavern had been built: 1652. We were moving, but it seemed as if we had not left our original spot. Petrus placed one foot in front of the other very slowly, and I did the same. I took my watch from my knapsack and strapped it to my wrist.

'It's going to be worse that way,' he said, 'because time isn't something that always proceeds at the same pace. It is we who determine how quickly time passes.'

I began to look at my watch every minute and found that he was right. The more I looked at it, the more slowly the minutes passed. I decided to take his advice,

The Speed Exercise

Walk for twenty minutes at half the speed at which you normally walk. Pay attention to the details, people, and surroundings. The best time to do this is after lunch.

Repeat the exercise for seven days.

and I put the watch back in my knapsack. I tried to pay more attention to the Road, the plain, and the stones I stepped on, but I kept looking ahead to the tavern – and I was convinced that we hadn't moved at all. I thought about telling myself some stories, but the exercise was making me anxious, and I couldn't concentrate. When I couldn't resist any longer and took my watch out again, only eleven minutes had passed.

'Don't make a torture out of this exercise, because it wasn't meant to be like that,' said Petrus. 'Try to find pleasure in a speed that you're not used to. Changing the way you do routine things allows a new person to grow inside of you. But when all is said and done, you're the one who must decide how you handle it.'

The kindness expressed in his final phrase calmed me down a bit. If it was I who decided what I would do, then it was better to take advantage of the situation. I breathed deeply and tried not to think. I put myself into a strange state, one in which time was something distant and of no interest to me. I calmed myself more and more and began to perceive the things that surrounded me through new eyes. My imagination, which was unavailable when I was tense, began to work to my advantage. I looked at the small village there in front of me and began to create a story about it; the delight in finding people and lodging after the cold wind of the Pyrenees. At one point, I sensed that there was in the village a strong, mysterious, and all-knowing presence. My imagination peopled the plain with knights and battles. I could see their swords shining in the sun and hear the cries of war. The village was no longer just a place where I could warm my soul with wine and my body with a blanket; it was a historic monument, the work of heroic people who had left everything behind to become a part of that solitary place. The world was there around me, and I realized that seldom had I paid attention to it.

When I regained my everyday awareness, we were at the door of the tavern, and Petrus was inviting me to enter.

'I'll buy the wine,' he said. 'And let's get to sleep early, because tomorrow I have to introduce you to a great sorcerer.'

Mine was a deep and dreamless sleep. As soon as daylight began to show itself in the two streets of the village of Roncesvalles, Petrus knocked on my door. We were in rooms on the top floor of the tavern, which also served as a hotel.

We had some coffee and some bread with olive oil, and we left, plodding through the dense fog that had fallen over the area. I could see that Roncesvalles wasn't exactly a village, as I had thought at first. At the time of the great pilgrimages along the Road, it had been the most powerful monastery in the region, with direct influence over the territory that extended all the way to the Navarra border. And it still retained some of its original character: its few buildings had been part of a religious brotherhood. The only construction that had any lay characteristics was the tavern where we had stayed.

We walked through the fog to the Collegiate Church. Inside, garbed in white, several monks were saying the first morning mass in unison. I couldn't understand a word they were saying, since the mass was being celebrated in Basque. Petrus sat in one of the pews to the side and indicated that I should join him.

The Church was enormous and filled with art objects of incalculable value. Petrus explained to me in a whisper that it had been built through donations from the kings and queens of Portugal, Spain, France, and Germany, on a site selected by the emperor Charlemagne. On the high altar, the Virgin of Roncesvalles – sculpted in massive silver, with a face of precious stone – held in her hands a branch of flowers made of jewels. The smell of incense, the Gothic construction, and the chanting monks in white began to induce in me a state similar to the trances I had experienced during the rituals of Tradition.

'And the sorcerer?' I asked, remembering what he had said on the previous afternoon.

Petrus indicated with a nod of his head a monk who was middle-aged, thin, and bespectacled, sitting with the other brothers on the narrow benches beside the high altar. A sorcerer, and at the same time a monk! I was eager for the mass to be over, but as Petrus had said to me the day before, it is we who determine the pace of time: my anxiety caused the religious ceremony to last for more than an hour.

When the mass was over, Petrus left me alone in the pew and went out through the door that the monks had used as an exit. I remained there for a while, gazing about the church and feeling that I should offer some kind of prayer, but I wasn't able to concentrate. The images appeared to be in the distance, locked in a past that would never return, like the Golden Age of the Road to Santiago.

Petrus appeared in the doorway and, without a word, signalled that I should follow him.

We came to an inside garden of the monastery, surrounded by a stone veranda. At the center of the garden there was a fountain, and seated at its edge, waiting for us, was the bespectacled monk.

'Father Jordi, this is the pilgrim,' said Petrus, introducing me.

The monk held out his hand, and I shook it. No one said anything else. I was waiting for something to happen, but I heard only the crowing of roosters in the distance and the cries of the hawks taking off for their daily hunt. The monk looked at me expressionlessly, in a way that reminded me of Mme Lourdes's manner after I had spoken the Ancient Word.

Finally, after a long and uncomfortable silence, Father Jordi spoke.

'It looks to me like you rose through the levels of the Tradition a bit early, my friend.'

I answered that I was thirty-eight and had been quite successful in all the trials.*

'Except for one, the last and most important,' he said, continuing to look at me without expression. 'And without that one, nothing you have learned has any significance.'

'That is why I am walking the Road to Santiago.'

'Which guarantees nothing. Come with me.'

Petrus stayed in the garden, and I followed Father Jordi. We crossed the cloisters, passed the place where a king was buried – Sancho the Strong – and went to a small chapel set among the group of main buildings that made up the monastery of Roncesvalles.

There was almost nothing inside: only a table, a book, and a sword – a sword that wasn't mine.

Father Jordi sat at the table, leaving me standing. He took some herbs and lit them, filling the place with their perfume. More and more, the situation reminded me of my encounter with Mme Lourdes.

'First, I want to tell you something,' said Father Jordi. 'The Jacobean route is only one of four roads. It is the Road of the Spades, and it may give you power, but that is not enough.'

'What are the other three?'

* Trials are ritual tests in which importance is given not only to the disciple's dedication but also to the auguries that emerge during their execution. This usage of the term originated during the Inquisition.

'You know at least two others: the Road to Jerusalem, which is the Road of the Hearts, or of the Grail, and which endows you with the ability to perform miracles; and the Road to Rome, which is the Road of the Clubs; it allows you to communicate with other worlds.'

'So what's missing is the Road of the Diamonds to complete the four suits of the deck,' I joked. And the father laughed.

'Exactly. That's the secret Road. If you take it someday, you won't be helped by anybody. For now, let us leave that one aside. Where are your scallop shells?'

I opened my knapsack and took out the shells on which stood the image of Our Lady of the Visitation. He put the figure on the table. He held his hands over it and began to concentrate. He told me to do the same. The perfume in the air was growing stronger. Both the monk and I had our eyes open, and suddenly I could sense that the same phenomenon was occurring as had taken place at Itatiaia: the shells glowed with a light that did not illuminate. The brightness grew and grew, and I heard a mysterious voice, emanating from Father Jordi's throat, saying, 'Wherever your treasure is, there will be your heart.'

It was a phrase from the Bible. But the voice continued, 'And wherever your heart is, there will be the cradle of the Second Coming of Christ; like these shells, the pilgrim is only an outer layer. When that layer, which is a stratum of life, is broken, life appears, and that life is comprised of agape.'

He drew back his hands, and the shells lost their glow. Then he wrote my name in the book that was on the table. Along the Road to Santiago, I saw only three books where my name was written: Mme Lourdes's, Father Jordi's, and the Book of Power, where later I was to write my own name.

'That's all,' he said. 'You can go with the blessing of the Virgin of Roncesvalles and of San Tiago of the Sword.

'The Jacobean route is marked with yellow pointers, painted all the way across Spain,' said the monk, as we returned to the place where Petrus was waiting. 'If you should lose your way at any time, look for the markers – on trees, on stones, and on traffic signs – and you will be able to find a safe place.'

'I have a good guide.'

'But try to depend mainly on yourself – so that you aren't coming and going for six days in the Pyrenees.'

So the monk already knew the story.

We found Petrus and then said good-bye. As we left Roncesvalles that morning, the fog had disappeared completely. A straight, flat road extended in front of us, and I began to see the yellow markers Father Jordi had mentioned. The knapsack was a bit heavier, because I had bought a bottle of wine at the tavern, despite the fact that Petrus had told me that it was unnecessary. After Roncesvalles, hundreds of small villages dotted the route, and I was to sleep outdoors very seldom.

'Petrus, Father Jordi spoke about the Second Coming of Christ as if it were something that were happening now.'

'It is always happening. That is the secret of your sword.'

'And you told me that I was going to meet with a sorcerer, but I met with a monk. What does magic have to do with the Catholic Church?'

Petrus said just one word:

'Everything.'

Cruelty

'Right there. That's the exact spot where love was murdered,' said the old man, pointing to a small church built into the rocks.

We had walked for five days in a row, stopping only to eat and sleep. Petrus continued to be guarded about his private life but asked many questions about Brazil and about my work. He said that he really liked my country, because the image he knew best was that of Christ the Redeemer on Corcovado, standing open armed rather than suffering on the cross. He wanted to know everything, and he especially wanted to know if the women were as pretty as the ones here in Spain. The heat of the day was almost unbearable, and in all of the bars and villages where we stopped, the people complained about the drought. Because of the heat, we adopted the Spanish custom of the siesta and rested between two and four in the afternoon when the sun was at its hottest.

That afternoon, as we sat in an olive grove, the old man had come up to us and offered us a taste of wine. In spite of the heat, the habit of drinking wine had been part of life in that region for centuries.

'What do you mean, love was murdered there?' I asked, since the old man seemed to want to strike up a conversation.

'Many centuries ago, a princess who was walking the Road to Santiago, Felicia of Aquitaine, decided, on her way back to Compostela, to give up everything and live here. She was love itself, because she divided all of her wealth among the poor people of the region and began to care for the sick.'

Petrus had lit one of his horrible rolled cigarettes, but despite his air of indifference, I could see that he was listening carefully to the old man's story.

'Her brother, Duke Guillermo, was sent by their father to bring her home. But Felicia refused to go. In desperation, the duke fatally stabbed her there in that small church that you can see in the distance; she had built it with her own hands in order to care for the poor and offer praise to God.

'When he came to his senses and realized what he had done, the duke went to Rome to ask the pope's forgiveness. As penitence, the pope ordered him to walk to Compostela. Then a curious thing happened: on his way back, when he arrived here, he had the same impulse as his sister, and he stayed on, living in that little church that his sister had built, caring for the poor until the last days of his long life.'

'That's the law of retribution at work,' Petrus laughed. The old man did not understand, but I knew what Petrus was saying. His concept of the law of retribution was similar to that of karma, or of the concept that as one sows, so shall they reap.

As we had been walking, we had gotten involved in some long theological discussions about the relationship between God and humanity. I had argued that in the Tradition, there was always an involvement with God, but that it was a complex one. The path to God, for me, was quite different from the one we were following on the Road to Santiago, with its priests who were sorcerers, its gypsies who were devils, and its saints who performed miracles. All of these things seemed to me to be primitive, and too much connected with Christianity; they lacked the fascination, the elegance, and the ecstasy that the rituals of the Tradition evoked in me. Petrus on the other hand, argued that the guiding concept along the Road to Santiago was its simplicity. That the Road was one along which any person could walk, that its significance could be understood by even the least sophisticated person, and that, in fact, only such a road as that could lead to God. So Petrus thought my relationship to God was based too much on concept, on intellect, and on reasoning; I felt that his was too simplistic and intuitive.

'You believe that God exists, and so do I,' Petrus had said at one point. 'So God exists for both of us. But if someone doesn't believe in him, that doesn't mean God ceases to exist. Nor does it mean that the nonbeliever is wrong.'

'Does that mean that the existence of God depends on a person's desire and power?'

'I had a friend once who was drunk all the time but who said three Hail Marys every night. His mother had conditioned him to do so ever since he was a child. Even when he came home helplessly drunk, and even though he did not believe in God, my friend always said his three Hail Marys. After he died, I was at a ritual of the Tradition, and I asked the spirit of the ancients where my friend was. The spirit answered that he was fine and that he was surrounded by light. Without ever having had the faith during his life, the three prayers he had said ritualistically every day had brought him salvation.

'God was manifest in the caves and in the thunderstorms of prehistory. After people began to see God's hand in the caves and thunderstorms, they began to see him in the animals and in special places in the forest. During certain difficult times, God existed only in the catacombs of the great cities. But through all of time, he never ceased to live in the human heart in the form of love.

'In recent times, some thought that God was merely a concept, subject to scientific proof. But, at this point, history has been reversed, or rather is starting all over again. Faith and love have resumed their importance. When Father Jordi cited that quotation from Jesus, saying that wherever your treasure is, there also would your heart be, he was referring to the importance of love and good works. Wherever it is that you want to see the face of God, there you will see it. And if you don't want to see it, that doesn't matter, so long as you are performing good works. When Felicia of Aquitaine built her small church and began to help the poor, she forgot about the God of the Vatican. She became God's manifestation by becoming wiser and by living a simpler life – in other words, through love. It is in that respect that the old man was absolutely right in saying that love had been murdered.'

Now Petrus said, 'The law of retribution was operating when Felicia's brother felt forced to continue the good works he had interrupted. Anything is permissible but the interruption of a manifestation of love. When that happens, whoever tried to destroy it is responsible for its recreation.'

I explained that in my country the law of return said that people's deformities and diseases were punishments for mistakes committed in previous incarnations.

'Nonsense,' said Petrus. 'God is not vengeance, God is love. His only form of punishment is to make someone who interrupts a work of love continue it.'

The old man excused himself, saying that it was late and that he had to get back to work. Petrus thought it was a good time for us to get up, too, and get back on the Road.

'Let's forget all of our discussion about God,' he said, as we made our way through the olive trees. 'God is in everything around us. He has to be felt and lived. And here I am trying to transform him into a problem in logic so that you can understand him. Keep doing the exercise of walking slowly, and you will learn more and more about his presence.'

Two days later, we had to climb a mountain called the Peak of Forgiveness. The climb took several hours, and at the top, I was shocked to find a group of tourists sunbathing and drinking beer; their car radios blasted music at top volume. They had driven up a nearby road to get to the top of the mountain.

'That's the way it is,' said Petrus. 'Did you expect that you were going to find one of El Cid's warriors up here, watching for the next Moorish attack?'

As we descended, I performed the Speed Exercise for the last time. Before us was another immense plain with sparse vegetation burned by the drought; it was bordered by blue mountains. There were almost no trees, only the rocky ground and some cactus. At the end of the exercise, Petrus asked me about my work, and it was only then that I realized that I hadn't thought about it for some time. My worries about business and about the things I had left undone had practically disappeared. Now I thought of these things only at night, and even then I didn't give them much importance. I was happy to be there, walking the Road to Santiago.

I told Petrus how I was feeling, and he joked, 'Any time now you are going to do the same thing as Felicia of Aquitaine.' Then he stopped and asked me to put my knapsack on the ground.

'Look around you, and choose some point to fixate on,' he said.

I chose the cross on a church that I could see in the distance.

'Keep your eyes fixed on that point, and try to concentrate only on what I am going to tell you. Even if you feel something different, don't become distracted. Do as I am telling you.'

I stood there, relaxed, with my eyes fixed on the cross, as Petrus took a position behind me and pressed a finger into the base of my neck.

'The Road you are traveling is the Road of power, and only the exercises having to do with power will be taught to you. The journey, which prior to this was torture because all you wanted to do was get there, is now beginning to become a pleasure. It is the pleasure of searching and the pleasure of an adventure. You are nourishing something that's very important – your dreams.

'We must never stop dreaming. Dreams provide nourishment for the soul, just as a meal does for the body. Many times in our lives we see our dreams shattered and our desires frustrated, but we have to continue dreaming. If we don't, our soul dies, and agape cannot reach it. A lot of blood has been shed in those fields out there; some of the cruelest battles of Spain's war to expel the Moors were fought on them. Who was in the right or who knew the truth does not matter; what's important is knowing that both sides were fighting the good fight.

'The good fight is the one we fight because our heart asks it of us. In the heroic ages – at the time of the knights in armor – this was easy. There were lands to conquer and much to do. Today, though, the world has changed a lot, and the good fight has shifted from the battlefields to the fields within ourselves.

'The good fight is the one that's fought in the name of our dreams. When we're young and our dreams first explode inside us with all of their force, we are very courageous, but we haven't yet learned how to fight. With great effort, we learn how to fight, but by then we no longer have the courage to go into combat. So we turn against ourselves and do battle within. We become our own worst enemy. We say that our dreams were childish, or too difficult to realize, or the result of our not having known enough about life. We kill our dreams because we are afraid to fight the good fight.'

The pressure of Petrus's finger on my neck became stronger. I perceived that the cross on the church had been transformed; now its outline seemed to be that of a winged being, an angel. I blinked my eyes, and the cross became a cross again.

'The first symptom of the process of our killing our dreams is the lack of time,' Petrus continued. 'The busiest people I have known in my life always have time enough to do everything. Those who do nothing are always tired and pay no attention to the little amount of work they are required to do. They complain constantly that the day is too short. The truth is, they are afraid to fight the good fight.

'The second symptom of the death of our dreams lies in our certainties. Because we don't want to see life as a grand adventure, we begin to think of ourselves as wise and fair and correct in asking so little of life. We look beyond the walls of our day-to-day existence, and we hear the sound of lances breaking, we smell the dust and the sweat, and we see the great defeats and the fire in the eyes of the warriors. But we never see the delight, the immense delight in the hearts of those who are engaged in the battle. For them, neither victory nor defeat is important; what's important is only that they are fighting the good fight.

'And, finally, the third symptom of the passing of our dreams is peace. Life becomes a Sunday afternoon; we ask for nothing grand, and we cease to demand anything more than we are willing to give. In that state, we think of ourselves as being mature; we put aside the fantasies of our youth, and we seek personal and professional achievement. We are surprised when people our age say that they still want this or that out of life. But really, deep in our hearts, we know that what has happened is that we have renounced the battle for our dreams – we have refused to fight the good fight.'

The tower of the church kept changing; now it appeared to be an angel with its wings spread. The more I blinked, the longer the figure remained. I wanted to speak to Petrus but I sensed that he hadn't finished.

'When we renounce our dreams and find peace,' he said after a while, 'we go through a short period of tranquillity. But the dead dreams begin to rot within us and to infect our entire being. We become cruel to those around us, and then we begin to direct this cruelty against ourselves. That's when illnesses and psychoses arise. What we sought to avoid in combat – disappointment and defeat – come upon us because of our cowardice. And one day, the dead, spoiled dreams make it difficult to breathe, and we actually seek death. It's death that frees us from our certainties, from our work, and from that terrible peace of our Sunday afternoons.'

Now I was sure that I was really seeing an angel, and I couldn't pay attention to what Petrus was saying. He must have sensed this, because he removed his finger from my neck and stopped talking. The image of the angel remained for a few moments and then disappeared. In its place, the tower of the church returned.

We were silent for a few minutes. Petrus rolled himself a cigarette and began to smoke. I took the bottle of wine from my knapsack and had a swallow. It was warm, but it was still delicious.

'What did you see?' he asked me.

I told him about the angel. I said that at the beginning, the image would disappear when I blinked.

'You, too, have to learn how to fight the good fight. You have already learned to accept the adventures and challenges that life provides, but you still want to deny anything that is extraordinary.'

Petrus took a small object from his knapsack and handed it to me. It was a golden pin.

'This was a present from my grandmother. In the Order of the RAM, all of the ancients have an object such as this. It's called "the Point of Cruelty." When you saw the angel appear on the church tower, you wanted to deny it, because it wasn't something that you are used to. In your view of the world, churches are churches, and visions occur only during the ecstasy created by the rituals of the Tradition.'

I said that my vision must have been caused by the pressure he was applying to my neck.

'That's right, but that doesn't change anything. The fact is that you rejected the vision. Felicia of Aquitaine must have seen something similar, and she bet her entire life on what she saw. And the result of her having done that transformed her work into a work of love. The same thing probably happened to her brother. And the same thing happens to everyone every day: we always know which is the best road to follow, but we follow only the road that we have become accustomed to.'

Petrus began to walk again, and I followed along. The rays of the sun made the pin in my hand glisten.

'The only way we can rescue our dreams is by being generous with ourselves. Any attempt to inflict self-punishment – no matter how subtle it may be – should be dealt with rigorously. In order to know when we are being cruel to ourselves, we have to transform any attempt at causing spiritual pain – such as guilt, remorse, indecision, and cowardice – into physical pain.

By transforming a spiritual pain into a physical one, we can learn what harm it can cause us.'

And then Petrus taught me the Cruelty Exercise.

'In ancient times, they used a golden pin for this,' he said. 'Nowadays, things have changed, just as the sights along the Road to Santiago change.'

Petrus was right. Seen from down at this level, the plain appeared to be a series of mountains in front of me.

'Think of something cruel that you did to yourself today, and perform the exercise.'

I couldn't think of anything.

'That's the way it always is. We are only able to be kind to ourselves at the few times when we need severity.'

Suddenly I remembered that I had called myself an idiot for having laboriously climbed the Peak of Forgiveness while the tourists had driven up in their cars. I knew that this was unfair and that I had been cruel to myself; the tourists, after all, were only looking for a place to sunbathe, while I was looking for my sword. I wasn't an idiot, even if I had felt like one. I dug the nail of my index finger forcefully into the cuticle of my thumb. I felt intense pain, and as I concentrated on it, the feeling of having been an idiot dissipated.

I described this to Petrus, and he laughed without saying anything.

That night, we stayed in a comfortable hotel in the village where the church I had focused on was located. After dinner, we decided to take a walk through the streets, as an aid to digestion.

The Cruelty Exercise

Every time a thought comes to mind that makes you feel bad about yourself – jealousy, self pity, envy, hatred, and so on – do the following:

Dig the nail of your index finger into the cuticle of the thumb of the same hand until it becomes quite painful. Concentrate on the pain: it is a physical reflection of the suffering you are going through spiritually. Ease the pressure only when the cruel thought has gone.

Repeat this as many times as necessary until the thought has left you, even if this means digging your fingernail into your thumb over and over. Each time, it will take longer for the cruel thought to return, and eventually it will disappear altogether, so long as you do not fail to perform the exercise every time it comes to mind.

'Of all the ways we have found to hurt ourselves, the worst has been through love. We are always suffering because of someone who doesn't love us, or someone who has left us, or someone who won't leave us. If we are alone, it is because no one wants us; if we are married, we transform the marriage to slavery. What a terrible thing!' he said angrily.

We came to a square, and there was the church I had seen. It was small and lacked any architectural distinction. Its bell tower reached up toward the sky. I tried to see the angel again, but couldn't.

'When the Son of God descended to earth, he brought love to us. But since people identified love only with suffering and sacrifice, they felt they had to crucify Jesus. Had they not done so, no one would have believed in the love that Jesus brought, since people were so used to suffering every day with their own problems.'

We sat on the curb and stared at the church. Once again, it was Petrus who broke the silence.

'Do you know what Barrabas means, Paulo? *Bar* means son, and *abba* means father.'

He gazed at the cross on the bell tower. His eyes shone, and I sensed that he was moved by something – perhaps by the love he had spoken so much about, but I couldn't be certain.

'The intentions of the divine glory were so wise!' he said, his voice echoing in the empty square. 'When Pontius Pilate made the people choose, he actually gave them no choice at all. He presented them with one man who had been whipped and was falling apart, and he presented them with another man who held his head high – Barrabas, the revolutionary. God knew that the people would put the weaker one to death so that he could prove his love.'

He concluded, 'And regardless of which choice they made, it was the Son of God who was going to be crucified.'

The Messenger

'And here all Roads to Santiago become one.'

It was early in the morning when we reached Puente de la Reina, where the name of the village was etched into the base of a statue of a pilgrim in medieval garb: three-cornered hat, cape, scallop shells, and in his hand a shepherd's crook. With a gourd – a memorial to the epic journey, now almost forgotten, that Petrus and I were reliving.

We had spent the previous night at one of the many monasteries along the Road. The brother of the gate who had greeted us had warned us that we were not to speak a word within the walls of the abbey. A young monk had led each of us to an alcove, furnished only with the bare necessities: a hard bed, old but clean sheets, a pitcher of water and a basin for personal hygiene. There was no plumbing or hot water, and the schedule for meals was posted behind the door.

At the time indicated, we had come down to the dining hall. Because of the vow of silence, the monks communicated only with their glances, and I had the impression that their eyes gleamed with more intensity than those of other people. The supper was served early at narrow tables where we sat with the monks in their brown habits. From his seat, Petrus had given me a signal, and I had understood perfectly what he meant: he was dying to light a cigarette, but it looked like he was going to have to go through the entire night without one. The same was true for me, and I dug a nail into the cuticle of my thumb, which was already like raw meat. The moment was too beautiful for me to commit any kind of cruelty toward myself.

The meal was served; vegetable soup, bread, fish, and wine. Everyone prayed, and we recited the invocation with them. Afterward, as we ate, a monk read from an Epistle of Saint Paul.

'But God hath chosen the foolish things of the world to put to shame the wise, and God hath chosen the weak things of the world to put to shame the things which are mighty,' read the monk in a thin, tuneless voice. 'We are fools for Christ's sake. We are made as filth of the world and are the offscouring of all things unto this day. But the kingdom of God is not in word but in power.'

The admonitions of Paul of the Corinthians echoed off the bare walls of the dining hall throughout the meal.

As we entered Puente de la Reina we had been talking about the monks of the previous night. I confessed to Petrus that I had smoked in my room, in mortal fear that someone would smell my cigarette burning. He laughed, and I could tell that he had probably been doing the same thing.

'Saint John the Baptist went into the desert, but Jesus went among the sinners, and he traveled endlessly,' Petrus said, 'That's my preference, too.'

In fact, aside from the time he had spent in the desert, Jesus had spent all of his life among people.

'Actually, his first miracle was not the saving of someone's soul nor the curing of a disease, and it wasn't an expulsion of the devil; it was the transformation of water into an excellent wine at a wedding because the wine supply of the owner of the house had run out.'

After Petrus said this, he suddenly stopped walking. It was so abrupt that I became alarmed and stopped, too. We were at the bridge that gave its name to the village. Petrus, though, wasn't looking at the road in front of us. His eyes were fastened on two boys who were playing with a rubber ball at the edge of the river. They were eight or ten years old and seemed not to have noticed us. Instead of crossing the bridge, Petrus scrambled down the bank and approached the two boys. As always, I followed him without question.

The boys continued to ignore us. Petrus sat down to watch them at play, until the ball fell close to where he was seated. With quick movement, he grabbed the ball and threw it to me.

I caught the ball in the air and waited to see what would happen.

One of the boys – the elder of the two – approached me. My first impulse was to throw him the ball, but

Petrus's behavior had been so unusual that I decided that I would try to understand what was happening.

'Give me the ball, Mister,' said the boy.

I looked at the small figure two meters away from me. I sensed that there was something familiar about him. It was the same feeling I had about the gypsy.

The lad asked for the ball several times, and when he got no response from me, he bent down and picked up a stone.

'Give me the ball, or I'll throw a stone at you,' he said.

Petrus and the other boy were watching me silently. The boy's aggressiveness irritated me.

'Throw the stone,' I answered. 'If it hits me, I'll come over there and whack you one.'

I sensed that Petrus gave a sigh of relief. Something in the back of my mind told me that I had already lived through this scene.

The boy was frightened by what I said. He let the stone fall and tried a different approach.

'There's a relic here in Puente de la Reina. It used to belong to a rich pilgrim. I see by your shell and your knapsack that you are pilgrims. If you give me my ball, I'll give you the relic. It's hidden in the sand here along the river.'

'I want to keep the ball,' I answered, without much conviction. Actually, I wanted the relic. The boy seemed to be telling the truth. But maybe Petrus needed the ball for some reason, and I didn't want to disappoint him. He was my guide.

'Look, Mister, you don't need the ball,' the boy said, now with tears in his eyes. 'You're strong, and you've been around, and you know the world. All I know is the edge of this river, and that ball is my only toy. Please give it back.'

The boy's words got to me. But the strangely familiar surroundings and my feeling that I had already read about or lived through the situation made me refuse again.

'No, I need the ball. I'll give you enough money to buy another one, even better than this one, but this one is mine.'

When I said that, time seemed to stop. The surroundings began to change, even without Petrus's finger at my neck; for a fraction of a second, it seemed that we had been transported to a broad, terrifying, ashen desert. Neither Petrus nor the other boy was there, just myself and the boy in front of me. He was old, and his features were kinder and friendlier. But there was a light in his eyes that frightened me.

The vision didn't last more than a second. Then I was back at Puente de la Reina, where the many Roads to Santiago, coming from all over Europe, became one. There in front of me, a boy was asking for his ball, with a sweet, sad look in his eye.

Petrus approached me, took the ball from my hand, and gave it to the boy.

'Where is the relic hidden?' he asked the boy.

'What relic?' he said, as he grabbed his friend's hand, jumped away, and threw himself into the water.

We climbed the bank and crossed the bridge. I began to ask questions about what had happened, and I described my vision of the desert, but Petrus changed the subject and said that we should talk about it when we had traveled further from that spot.

Half an hour later, we came to a stretch of the Road that still showed vestiges of Roman paving. Here was another bridge, this one in ruins, and we sat down to have the breakfast that had been given to us by the monks: rye bread, yogurt, and goat's cheese.

'Why did you want the kid's ball?' Petrus asked me.

I told him that I hadn't wanted the ball – that I had acted that way because Petrus himself had behaved so strangely, as if the ball were very important to him.

'In fact, it was. It allowed you to win out over your personal devil.'

My personal devil? This was the most ridiculous thing I had heard during the entire trip. I had spent six days coming and going in the Pyrenees, I had met a sorcerer priest who had performed no sorcery, and my finger was raw meat because every time I had a cruel thought about myself – from hypochondria, to feelings of guilt, to an inferiority complex – I had to dig my fingernail into my wounded thumb. But about one thing Petrus was right: my negative thinking had diminished considerably. Still, this story about having a personal devil was something I had never heard – and I wasn't going to swallow it easily.

'Today, before crossing the bridge, I had a strong feeling of the presence of someone, someone who was trying to give us a warning. But the warning was more for you than for me. A battle is coming on very soon, and you will have to fight the good fight.

'When you do not know your personal devil, he usually manifests himself in the nearest person. I looked around, and I saw those boys playing – and I figured that it was there that he would probably give his warning. But I was only following a hunch. I became sure that it was your personal devil when you refused to give the ball back.'

I repeated that I had done so because I thought it was what Petrus wanted.

'Why me? I never said a word.'

I began to feel a little dizzy. Maybe it was the food, which I was devouring voraciously after almost an hour of walking and feeling hungry. Still, I could not escape the feeling that the boy had seemed familiar.

'Your personal devil tried three classical approaches: a threat, a promise, and an attack on your weak side. Congratulations: you resisted bravely.'

Now I remembered that Petrus had asked the boy about the relic. At that time, I had thought that the boy's response showed that he had tried to fool me. But he must really have a relic hidden there – a devil never makes false promises.

'When the boy could not remember about the relic, your personal devil had gone away.'

Then he added without blinking, 'It is time to call him back. You are going to need him.'

We were sitting on the ruins of the old bridge. Petrus carefully gathered the remains of the meal and put them into the paper bag that the monks had given us. In the fields in front of us, the workers began to arrive for the day's plowing, but they were so far away that I couldn't hear what they were saying. It was rolling land, and the cultivated patches created unusual designs across the landscape. Under our feet, the water course, almost nonexistent due to the drought, made very little noise.

'Before he went out into the world, Christ went into the desert to talk with his personal devil,' Petrus began. 'He learned that he needed to know about people, but he did not let the devil dictate the rules of the game; that is how he won.

'Once, a poet said that no man is an island. In order to fight the good fight, we need help. We need friends, and when the friends aren't nearby, we have to turn solitude into our main weapon. We need the help of everything around us in order to take the necessary steps toward our goal. Everything has to be a personal manifestation of our will to win the good fight. If we don't understand that, then we don't recognize that we need everything and everybody, and we become arrogant warriors. And our arrogance will defeat us in the end, because we will be so sure of ourselves that we won't see the pitfalls there on the field of battle.'

His comments about warriors and battles reminded me again of Carlos Castaneda's Don Juan. I asked myself whether the old medicine man would have given lessons early in the morning, before his disciple had even been able to digest his breakfast. But Petrus continued:

'Over and above the physical forces that surround us and help us, there are basically two spiritual forces on our side: an angel and a devil. The angel always protects us and is a divine gift – you do not have to invoke him. Your angel's face is always visible when you look at the world with eyes that are receptive. He is this river, the workers in the field, and that blue sky. This old bridge that helps us to cross the stream was built here by the hands of anonymous Roman Legionnaires, and the bridge, too, is the face of your angel. Our grandparents called him the guardian angel.

'The devil is an angel, too, but he is a free, rebellious force. I prefer to call him the messenger, since he is the main link between you and the world. In antiquity, he was represented by Mercury and by Hermes Trismegistus, the messenger of the gods. His arena is only on the material plane. He is present in the gold of the Church, because the gold from the earth, and the earth is your devil. He is present in our work and in our ways of dealing with money. When we let him loose, his tendency is to disperse himself. When we exorcise him, we lose all of the good things that he has to teach us; he knows a great deal about the world and about human beings. When we become fascinated by his power, he owns us and keeps us from fighting the good fight.

'So the only way to deal with our messenger is to accept him as a friend – by listening to his advice and asking for his help when necessary, but never allowing him to dictate the rules of the game. Like you did with the boy. To keep the messenger from dictating the rules of the game, it is necessary first that you know what you want and then that you know his face and his name.'

'How can I know them?' I asked.

And then Petrus taught me the Messenger Ritual.

'Wait until night to perform it, when it is easier,' Petrus said. 'Today, at your first meeting, he will tell you his name. This name is secret and should never be told to anyone, not even me. Whoever knows the name of your messenger can destroy you.'

Petrus got up, and we began to walk. Shortly, we reached the field where the farmers were working. We said '*Buenos días*' to them and went on down the road.

'If I had to use a metaphor, I would say that your angel is your armor, and your messenger is your sword. Armor protects you under any set or circumstances, but a sword can fall to the ground in the midst of a battle, or it can kill a friend, or be turned against its owner. A sword can be used for almost anything … except as something to sit on,' he said, laughing.

We stopped in a town for lunch, and the young waiter who served us was clearly in a bad mood. He didn't answer any of our questions, he served the meal sloppily, and he even succeeded in spilling coffee on Petrus's shorts. I watched my guide go through a transformation:

furious, he went to find the owner and complained loudly about the waiter's rudeness. He wound up going to the men's room and taking off his shorts; the owner cleaned them and spread them out to dry.

As we waited for the two o'clock sun to dry Petrus's shorts, I was thinking about everything we had talked about that morning. It was true that most of what Petrus had said about the boy by the river made sense. After all, I had had a vision of the desert and of a face. But that story about 'the messenger' seemed a little primitive to me. For a person with any intelligence here in the twentieth century, the concepts of hell, of sin, and of the devil did not make much sense. In the Tradition, whose teachings I had followed for much longer that I had followed the Road to Santiago, the messenger was a spirit that ruled the forces of the earth and was always a friend. He was often used in magical operations but never as an ally or counsellor with regard to daily events. Petrus had led me to believe that I could use the friendship of the messenger as a means to improve my work and my dealings with the world. Beside being profane, this idea seemed to me to be childish.

But I had sworn to Mme Lourdes that I would give total obedience to my guide. Once again, I had to dig my nail into my red, raw thumb.

'I should not have put him down,' Petrus said about the waiter after we had left. 'I mean, after all, he didn't spill that coffee on me but on the world he hated. He knows that there is a huge world out there that extends

The Messenger Ritual

1. Sit down and relax completely. Let your mind wander and your thinking flow without restraint. After a while, begin to repeat to yourself, 'Now I am relaxed, and I am in the deepest kind of sleep.'

2. When you feel that your mind is no longer concerned with anything, imagine a billow of fire to your right. Make the flames lively and brilliant. Then quietly say, 'I order my subconscious to show itself. I order it to open and reveal its magic secrets.' Wait a bit, and concentrate only on the fire. If an image appears, it will be a manifestation of your subconscious. Try to keep it alive.

3. Keeping the fire always to your right, now begin to imagine another billow of fire to your left. When the flames are lively, say the following words quietly: 'May the power of the Lamb, which manifests itself in everything and everyone, manifest itself also in me when I invoke my messenger. (Name of messenger) will appear before me now.

4. Talk with your messenger, who should appear between the two fires. Discuss your specific problems, ask for advice, and give him the necessary orders.

5. When your conversation has ended, dismiss the messenger with the following words: 'I thank the Lamb for the miracle I have performed. May (name of messenger) return whenever he is invoked, and when he is far away, may he help me to carry on my work.'

Note: On the first invocation – or during the first invocations, depending on the ability of the person performing the ritual to concentrate – do not say the name of the messenger. Just say "he." If the ritual is well performed, the messenger should immediately reveal his name telepathically. If not, insist until you learn his name, and only then begin the conversation. The more the ritual is repeated, the stronger the presence of the messenger will be and the more rapid his actions.

well beyond the borders of his imagination. And his participation in that world is limited to getting up early, going to the bakery, waiting on whoever comes by, and masturbating every night, dreaming about the women he will never get to know.'

It was the time of day when we usually stopped for our siesta, but Petrus had decided to keep walking. He said that it was a way of doing penance for his intolerance. And I, who had not done a thing, had to trudge along with him under the hot sun. I was thinking about the good fight and the millions of souls who, right then, were scattered all over the planet, doing things they didn't want to do. The Cruelty Exercise, in spite of having made my thumb raw, was helping me. It had helped me to see how my mind could betray me, pushing me into situations I wanted no part of and into feelings that were no help to me. Right then, I began to hope that Petrus was right: that a messenger really did exist and that I could talk to him about practical matters and ask him for help with my day-to-day problems. I was anxious for night to fall.

Meanwhile, Petrus could not stop talking about the waiter. Finally, he wound up convincing himself that he had acted properly; once again, he used a Christian argument to make his case.

'Christ forgave the adulterous woman but cursed the grower who would not give him a fig. And I am not here, either, just to be a nice guy.'

That was it. In his view, the matter was settled. Once again, the Bible had saved him.

We reached Estella at almost nine o'clock at night. I took a bath, and we went down to eat. The author of the first guide for the Jacobean route, Aymeric Picaud, had described Estella as a 'fertile place, with good bread and great wine, meat, and fish. Its river, the Ega, has good, fresh, clean water.' I didn't drink the river water, but as far as the menu at our restaurant was concerned, Picaud's assessment was still right, even after eight centuries. It offered braised leg of lamb, artichoke hearts, and a Rioja wine from a very good year. We sat at the table for a long time, talking about inconsequential things and enjoying the wine. But finally Petrus said that it was a good time for me to have my first contact with my messenger.

We went out to look around the city. Some alleys led directly to the river – as they do in Venice – and I decided to sit down in one of them. Petrus knew that from that point on it was I who would conduct the ceremony, so he hung back.

I looked at the river for a long time. Its water and its sound began to take me out of this world and to create a profound serenity in me. I closed my eyes and imagined the first billow of fire. It was not easy to imagine at first, but finally it appeared.

I pronounced the ritual words, and another billow of fire appeared to my left. The space between the two billows, illuminated by the fires, was completely empty.

I kept looking at the space for a while, trying not to think so that the messenger would manifest himself. But instead of his appearing, various exotic scenes began to appear – the entrance to a pyramid, a woman dressed in pure gold, some black men dancing around a fire. The images came and went in rapid succession, and I let them flow uncontrolled. There also appeared some stretches of the Road that I had traversed with Petrus – byways, restaurants, forests – until, with no warning, the ashen desert that I had seen that morning appeared between the two fires. And there, looking at me, was the friendly man with the traitorous look in his eyes.

He laughed, and I smiled in my trance. He showed me a closed bag, then opened it and looked inside – but in such a way that I could not see into it. Then a name came to my mind: Astrain.*

I began to envision the name and make it dance between the two fires, and the messenger gave a nod of approval; I had learned his name.

It was time to end the exercise. I said the ritual words and extinguished the fires – first on the left and then on the right. I opened my eyes, and there was the river Ega in front of me.

'It was much less difficult than I had imagined,' I said to Petrus, after I had told him about everything that had occurred between the two fires.

* This is not the real name.

'This was your first contact – a meeting to establish mutual recognition and mutual friendship. Your conversations with the messenger will be productive if you invoke him every day and discuss your problems with him. But you have to know how to distinguish between what is real assistance and what is a trap. Keep your sword ready every time you meet with him.'

'But I don't have my sword yet,' I answered.

'Right, so he can't cause you much damage. But even so, don't make it easy for him.'

The ritual having ended, I left Petrus and went back to the hotel. In bed, I thought about the poor young waiter who had served us lunch. I felt like going back there and teaching him the Messenger Ritual, telling him that he could change everything if he wanted to. But it was useless to try to save the world: I hadn't even been able to save myself yet.*

* This description of my first experience with the Messenger Ritual is incomplete. Actually, Petrus explained the meaning of the visions, of the memories, and of the bag that Astrain showed me. But since each meeting with the messenger is different for every person, I do not want to insist on my own personal experience as it might influence the experience of others.

Love

'Talking with your messenger doesn't mean asking questions about the world of the spirits,' Petrus said the next day. 'The messenger performs only one function for you: he helps you with regard to the material world. And he will give you this help only if you know exactly what it is that you want.'

We had stopped in a town to have something to drink. Petrus had ordered a beer, and I asked for a soft drink. My fingers were abstract designs in the water on the table, and I was worried.

'You told me that the messenger had manifested himself in the boy because he needed to tell me something.'

'Something urgent,' he confirmed.

We talked some more about messengers, angels, and devils. It was difficult for me to accept such a practical application of the mysteries of the Tradition. Petrus said that we are always seeking some kind of reward. But I reminded him that Jesus had said that the rich man would not enter into the kingdom of heaven.

'But Jesus rewarded the man who knew how to make his master more adept. People did not believe in Jesus just because he was an outstanding orator: he had to perform miracles and reward those who followed him.'

'No one is going to blaspheme Jesus in my bar,' said the owner, who had been listening to our conversation.

'No one is blaspheming Jesus,' Petrus answered. 'People speak poorly of Jesus when they commit the sin of taking his name in vain. Like all of you did out there in the plaza.'

The owner hesitated for a moment. But then he answered, 'I had nothing to do with that. I was only a child at the time.'

'The guilty ones are always the others,' Petrus mumbled. The owner went into the kitchen, and I asked Petrus what he was talking about.

'Fifty years ago, in this twentieth century of ours, a gypsy was burned at the stake out there in the plaza. He was accused of sorcery and of blaspheming the sacred host. The case was lost amid the news of the Spanish civil war, and no one remembers it today. Except the people who live here.'

'How do you know about it, Petrus?'

'Because I have already walked the Road to Santiago.'

We went on drinking there in the empty bar. The sun was hot, and it was our siesta time. A few minutes later, the owner reappeared, accompanied by the town priest.

'Who are you people?' asked the priest.

Petrus showed him the scallop shells sewn to his knapsack. For twelve hundred years, pilgrims had passed along the Road in front of the bar, and the tradition was that every pilgrim was respected and welcomed under any circumstance. The priest changed his tone.

'How can it be that pilgrims on the Road to Santiago are speaking poorly of Jesus?' he asked, in a tone that was appropriate to a catechism.

'Nobody here was speaking poorly of Jesus. We were speaking poorly of the crimes committed in the name of Jesus. Like the gypsy that was burned there in the square.'

The shells on Petrus's knapsack had also changed the owner's attitude. Now he addressed us with some respect.

'The curse of the gypsy is still with us today,' he said and the priest looked at him reprovingly.

Petrus wanted to know how. The priest said that these were stories told by the villagers and that the church did not approve of them. But the owner of the bar went on:

'Before the gypsy died, he said that the youngest child in the village was going to receive and incorporate his devils. And that when that child became old and died, the devils would pass on to another child. And so on, for all the centuries to come.'

'The soil here is the same as the soil in the other towns around here,' said the priest. 'When the other towns have a drought, we do, too. Nothing has happened here with us that has not happened in the neighboring towns, too. This whole story is a fantasy.'

'Nothing has happened because we isolated the curse,' said the owner.

'Well, then, let's see it,' answered Petrus. The priest laughed and said that that was no way to talk. The owner of the bar made the sign of the cross. But neither of them moved.

Petrus got the check and insisted that someone take us to the person who had inherited the curse. The priest excused himself, saying that he had been interrupted at something important and had to get back to his church. And he left before anyone could say anything.

The owner of the bar looked at Petrus fearfully.

'Not to worry,' said my guide. 'Just show us the house where the curse resides. We are going to try to rid the town of it.'

The owner of the bar went out into the dusty street with us. The hot sun of the afternoon beat down everywhere. We walked to the outskirts of the town, and he pointed to a house set off by itself at the side of the Road.

'We always send meals, clothing, everything they need,' he apologized. 'But not even the priest goes in there.'

We said good-bye to him and walked toward the house. The owner of the bar waited there, perhaps thinking that we would pass it by. But Petrus went up to the house and knocked on the door, and when I looked around, the bar owner had disappeared.

A woman of about seventy came to the door. At her side was an enormous black dog, wagging his tail and apparently happy to see company. The woman asked what we wanted; she said she was busy washing clothes and had left some pots on the fire. She did not seem surprised by our visit. I figured that many pilgrims, not knowing about the curse, must have knocked on the door seeking shelter.

'We are pilgrims on the Road to Compostela, and we need some hot water,' Petrus said. 'I knew that you would not refuse us.'

With a show of irritation, the woman opened the door. We went into a small room, clean but poorly furnished. There was a sofa with its stuffing coming out, a bureau, and a Formica-topped table with two chairs. On the bureau was an image of the Sacred Heart of Jesus, some saints, and a crucifix made of mirrors. Through one of the two doors in the room, I could see the bedroom. The woman led Petrus through the other door into the kitchen.

'I have some water boiling,' she said. 'Let me get you a container, and you can both get going.'

I was there in the living room, alone with the huge dog. He wagged his tail, docile and contented. The woman came back with an old can, filled it with water, and held it out to Petrus.

'There. Go with God's blessing.'

But Petrus did not move. He took a tea bag from his knapsack, put it in the can, and said that he would like to share the little he had with her in appreciation for her welcome.

The woman, clearly upset now, brought two cups and sat down at the table with Petrus. I kept looking at the dog as I listened to their conversation.

'They told me in the village that there was a curse on this house,' Petrus commented boldly. The dog's eyes seemed to light up, as if he had understood what had been said. The old woman stood up immediately.

'That's a lie. It's an old superstition. Please finish your tea, because I have lots of things to do.'

The dog sensed the woman's sudden mood change. He remained still but alert. But Petrus continued to do what he was doing. He slowly poured the tea into the cup, raised it to his lips, and put it down on the table without drinking a drop.

'That's really hot,' he said. 'I think I will wait until it cools off a bit.'

The woman did not sit down again. She was visibly uncomfortable with us there and clearly regretted having opened the door. She noticed that I was staring fixedly at the dog and called him to her. The animal obeyed, but when he reached her side, he turned to look at me.

'This is why he did it, my friend,' Petrus said, looking at me. 'This is why your messenger appeared yesterday in the child.'

Suddenly I realized that I was not just looking at the dog. As soon as I had come in, the animal had hypnotized me and had kept my eyes fastened on him. The dog was staring at me and making me do as he wanted.

I began to feel weak, as if I would like to lie down and sleep on the torn couch; it was really hot outside, and I did not feel much like walking. The feelings all seemed strange to me, and I had the impression that I was falling into a trap. The dog continued to looked fixedly at me, and the more he looked at me, the more tired I felt.

'Let's go,' said Petrus, getting up and offering me the cup of tea. 'Drink a bit of tea, because the lady wants us to get going.'

I hesitated, but I took the cup, and the hot tea revived me. I wanted to say something, ask what the animal's name was, but I could not get my voice to work. Something inside me had been aroused, something that Petrus had not taught me but that nevertheless began to manifest itself. I felt an uncontrollable desire to say strange words, the meaning of which I didn't even know. I thought that Petrus had put something in the tea. Everything began to blur, and I heard only very faintly the woman repeat to Petrus that we had to leave. I was in a state of euphoria, and I decided to speak the strange words that were coming to my mind.

All I could see in the room was the dog. When I began to say those strange words, the dog started to growl. He understood what I was saying. I became more excited and continued to speak, louder and louder. The dog rose and bared his teeth. He was no longer the docile animal I had seen on arrival but something awful and threatening that could attack me at any moment. I knew that the words were protecting me, and I began to speak even louder, focusing all of my energies on the dog. I felt that I had a different power within me and that it could keep the animal from attacking me.

From that point on, everything began to happen in slow motion. I saw the woman come toward me, shrieking and trying to push me out of the house. And I saw Petrus holding the woman back. The dog paid no attention at all to their struggle. Snarling and baring his teeth, he continued to stare at me. I was trying to understand the strange language I was speaking, but each time I stopped to think about it, my power would weaken and the dog would start coming toward me; he was growing stronger. I began to scream, giving up my attempt at understanding, and the woman began to scream, too. The dog barked and threatened me, but so long as I continued speaking, I was safe. I heard raucous laughter, but I did not know if it was really occurring or if it was in my imagination.

Suddenly, a strong wind swept through the house, and the dog howled and leapt on me. I raised my arm to protect my face, shouted something, and waited to see what the impact would be.

The dog had thrown himself upon me with all his strength, and I fell onto the couch. For a few moments, our eyes were locked on each other's; in the next second, he ran from the house.

I began to cry hysterically. I thought of my family, my wife, and my friends. I experienced an enormous feeling of love and, at the same time, an absurd happiness, because all of a sudden I understood everything about the dog.

Petrus took me by the arm and led me outside, as the woman pushed us both from behind. I looked around, and there was no sign of the dog. I hugged Petrus and continued to cry as we walked along in the sunlight.

The next part of the journey is a blank; I only came to my senses later at a fountain, where Petrus was throwing water in my face and on the back of my neck. I asked for some to drink, and he said that if I drank anything then, I would vomit. I was a little nauseated, but I felt good. An immense love for everything and everybody had invaded my being. I looked around me and sensed the trees along the edge of the Road, the small fountain where we had stopped, the fresh breeze, and the bird song from the forest. I was seeing the face of my angel, as Petrus had told me I would. I asked how far we were from the woman's house, and he said we had been walking for about fifteen minutes.

'You probably want to know what happened,' he said.

Actually that was not important to me at all. I was just happy about the feelings of love that permeated me. The dog, the woman, the owner of the bar, everything was a distant memory that seemed to have nothing to do with what I was feeling now. I told Petrus that I would like to go on walking because I was feeling so well.

I got up, and we returned to the Road to Santiago. Throughout the rest of the afternoon, I said almost nothing, delighting in the agreeable feeling that seemed to fill me. I still thought that perhaps Petrus had put something in the tea, but this was no longer important.

We arrived at a hotel at eight o'clock that night, and I was still in this state of beautitude, although it had diminished somewhat. The owner asked me for my passport so that I could register, and I gave it to him.

'You're from Brazil? I've been there. I stayed at a hotel on Ipanema Beach.'

That absurd message brought me back to reality. There, along the Jacobean route, in a town that had been built centuries ago was a hotel keeper who had been to Ipanema Beach.

'I'm ready to talk,' I told Petrus. 'I have to know what happened today'.

The sense of beautitude had passed. Reason took its place, and my fear of the unknown, along with an urgent need to get my feet back on the ground, had returned.

'After we eat,' said Petrus.

Petrus asked the hotel owner to turn on the television but to leave the sound off. He said that this was the best way for me to hear everything he said without asking a lot of questions, because part of me would be watching the television screen. He asked me how much I remembered of what had happened. I answered that I remembered everything except the part where we had walked to the fountain.

'That part is not important to the story,' he answered. On the television screen, a film having something to do with coal mines began. The actors were dressed in turn-of-the-century clothing.

'Yesterday, when I sensed the urgency in your messenger, I knew that a battle along the Road to Santiago was about to begin. You are here to find your sword and learn the RAM practices. But every time a guide leads a pilgrim, there is at least one situation that goes beyond the control of both of them. It represents a kind of practical test of what is being taught. In your case, this was the encounter with the dog.

'The details of the battle and the explanation for the many devils that can be present in an animal I will explain later. What is important now is that you understand that the woman was already used to the curse. She had accepted it as normal, and the attitudes of the world were fine with her. She had learned to be satisfied with very little.

'When you exorcised the poor old woman's demons, you also unbalanced her universe. The other day we talked about the cruelty that people are capable of inflicting on themselves. Often, when we try to demonstrate that life is good and generous, such people reject the idea as if it came from the devil. People don't like to ask too much of life because they are afraid they will be defeated. But if someone wants to fight the good fight, that person must view the world as if it were a marvellous treasure waiting to be discovered and won.'

Petrus asked me if I knew what I was doing there on the Road to Santiago.

'I am searching for my sword,' I answered.

'And what do you want your sword for?'

'I want it because it will bring me the power and the wisdom of the Tradition.'

I felt that he was not too happy with my response. But he continued, 'You are here, searching for a reward. You are daring to dream, and you are doing everything possible to make your dream come true. You need to have a better idea of what it is that you are going to do with your sword; this has to be clearer to you before we can find it. But there is one thing in your favor: you are looking for a reward. You are walking the Road to Santiago only because you want to be rewarded for your effort. I have noticed that you have applied everything I have taught you; you have been looking for a practical outcome. That is very positive.

'The only thing missing is your learning how to combine the RAM practices with your own intuition. The language of your heart is what is going to determine the best way to find and use your sword. If you can't bring the two together, the exercises and the RAM practices will become simply a part of the useless wisdom of the Tradition.'

Petrus had told me this before, in a different way, and although I agreed with him, it wasn't what I wanted to hear about. There were two aspects of the experience that I could not understand: the strange language I had spoke and my feeling of love and happiness after having evicted the dog.

'The sensation of happiness occurred because your action was suffused with agape.'

'You talk a lot about agape, but you haven't really explained to me what it is. I have a feeling we are dealing with something that relates to a higher form of love.'

'That's exactly right. In a little while, the time will come for you to experience that intense love – the love that consumes the one who loves. Meanwhile, be happy knowing that this love has manifested itself freely in you.'

'I have had this sensation before, but it was brief, and different somehow. It always happened after a professional triumph, a win, or when I felt that Lady Luck was being generous with me. But when the feeling arose, I always pulled back; I felt frightened of experiencing it too intensely – as if the happiness could cause envy in others or as if I were unworthy of it.'

'All of us, before we learn about agape, act that way,' he said, with his gaze on the television screen.

I asked him about the strange language I had spoken.

'That was a surprise to me. That is not a practice of the Road to Santiago. It is a divine grace, and it is one of the RAM practices for the Road to Rome.'

I had already heard some things about the divine graces, but I asked Petrus to explain them to me.

'They are gifts from the Holy Ghost that manifest themselves in people. There are a number of different kinds: the gift of curing, the gift of miracles, the gift of prophecy, among others. You experienced the gift of tongues, which is what the apostles experienced at Pentecost.

'The gift of tongues is related to direct communication with the Holy Ghost. It is used in powerful oratory, in exorcisms – as was your case – and in wisdom. Your days on the Road and the RAM practices not only led to the danger that the dog represented for you but also by chance gave rise to the gift of tongues. It won't happen again, unless you find your sword and decide to walk the Road to Rome. In any case, it was a good omen.'

I watched the silent television screen. The story of the coal mines had been transformed into a succession of men and women talking and arguing. Every so often, an actor and an actress would kiss.

'One other thing,' said Petrus. 'It may be that you are going to meet up with that dog again. Next time, don't try to invoke the gift of tongues, because it won't come back. Trust in what your intuition is going to tell you. I am going to teach you another RAM practice that will enhance your intuition. With it, you will begin to learn the secret language of your mind, and that language will be very useful to you for the rest of your life.'

Petrus turned the television off, just as I was beginning to get involved in the story. He went to the bar and asked for a bottle of mineral water. We each drank a little, and he took what was left outdoors.

We felt the fresh air, and for a few moments neither of us said anything. The night was quiet, and the Milky Way overhead reminded me again that my goal was to find my sword.

After some time, Petrus taught me the Water Exercise.

'I'm tired; I'm going to bed,' he said. 'But do this exercise now. Call up your intuition again, your secret side. Don't be concerned about logic, because water is a fluid element, and it does not allow itself to be controlled easily. But water, little by little and in a non-violent way, is going to build a new relationship between you and the universe.'

And before he went through the door of the hotel, he added, 'It is not often that someone gets help from a dog.'

I continued to enjoy the freshness and the silence of the night. The hotel was out in the country, and there was no one there with me. I remembered the owner, who had been to Ipanema; he must find it absurd to see me there in that arid place, burned by the sun that shone down with such ferocity day after day.

I was getting sleepy, so I decided to do the exercise right away. I emptied the remaining water onto the cement and a small puddle formed. I did not have any image or shape in mind, and I wasn't seeking one. I

The Arousal of Intuition
(The Water Exercise)

Make a puddle of water on a smooth, non-absorbant surface. Look into the puddle for a while. Then, begin to play with it, without any particular commitment or objective. Make designs that mean absolutely nothing.

Do this exercise for a week, allowing at least ten minutes each time.

Don't look for practical results from this exercise; it is simply calling up your intuition, little by little. When this intuition begins to manifest itself at other times of the day, always trust in it.

swirled my fingers through the cold water, and I experienced the same kind of hypnosis that one feels when staring into the flames of a fire. I thought about nothing; I was just playing – playing with a puddle of water. I made some streaks at the edge of the puddle, and it seemed to become a wet sun; but the streaks quickly rejoined the puddle and disappeared. With the palm of my hand, I batted at the center of the puddle; the water splashed away, covering the cement with droplets, black stars on a gray background. I was completely lost in that absurd exercise, an exercise that had not the slightest purpose but was delightful to do. I felt that my mind had stopped working almost completely, a feeling I had previously achieved only after long periods of meditation and relaxation. At the same time, something told me that down deep, in places that my mind could not reach, a force was being born and becoming ready to manifest itself.

I stayed there for quite a while playing with the puddle, and it was difficult to give up the exercise. If Petrus had taught me the water exercise at the beginning of the journey, there is no doubt that I would have found it to be a waste of time. But now, having spoken in strange tongues and having exorcised devils, that puddle of water established a contact – however fragile – with the Milky Way above me. It reflected the stars, created designs I could not understand, and gave me the feeling not that I was wasting time but that I was creating a new code for communicating with the world. It was the soul's secret code – the language that we know but so seldom hear.

When I came back to myself, it was late. The lights at the door had been turned off, and I entered the hotel quietly. In my room, once again I invoked Astrain. He appeared more clearly, and I spoke to him for a while about my sword and about my goals in life. For now, he made no answer, but Petrus had told me that as the invocations continued, Astrain would become a live and powerful presence at my side.

Marriage

Logroño is one of the largest cities through which pilgrims traveling the Jacobean route pass. The only other city of any size that we had entered had been Pamplona – but we had not spent the night there. On the afternoon that we arrived in Logroño, though, the city was preparing for a great festival, and Petrus suggested that we stay there, at least for one night.

I was used to the silence and freedom of the countryside, so the idea did not much appeal to me. It had been five days since the incident with the dog, and every night since then, I had invoked Astrain and performed the Water Exercise. I was feeling very calm, and I was more and more aware of the importance of the Road to Santiago in my life and of the question of what I was going to do after the pilgrimage had ended. The area we walked through was like a desert, the meals were seldom very good, and the long days on the Road were exhausting, but I was living my dream.

All of these feelings disappeared the day we arrived at Logroño. Instead of the warm, pure air of the fields, we found a city crowded with cars, journalists, and television equipment. Petrus went into the first bar we saw to ask what was happening.

'You didn't know? Today is the wedding of Colonel M.'s daughter,' said the bartender. 'We are going to have a huge public banquet in the square, and I am closing early today.'

It was impossible to find rooms at a hotel, but eventually we were given lodging at the home of an elderly couple who had noticed the shells on Petrus's knapsack. We showered, I put on the only trousers that I had brought, and we left for the town square.

Dozens of workers, perspiring in their black suits, were putting the finishing touches on the tables that had been placed all over the square. National television crews were filming the preparations. We went down a narrow street that led to the church of the Royal Santiago parish, where the ceremony was about to begin.

Flocking to the church were great numbers of well-dressed people. The women's makeup was running in the heat, and their children, dressed in white, were irritable. Some fireworks were exploding overhead as a long black limousine stopped at the main gate. It was the groom arriving. There was no room for Petrus and me in the church, so we decided to go back to the square.

Petrus wanted to scout around, but I sat down on one of the benches, waiting for the ceremony to end and the banquet to begin. Nearby, a popcorn vendor, hoping for a windfall profit, awaited the crowd from the church.

'Are you one of the invited guests?' he asked me.

'No,' I answered. 'We are pilgrims on our way to Compostela.'

'There's a train that goes there straight from Madrid, and if you leave on a Friday, you get your hotel free.'

'Yes, but we are doing a pilgrimage.'

The vendor looked at me and said respectfully, 'Pilgrimages are made by saints.'

I decided not to get into that discussion. He said that his daughter had already been married but was now separated from her husband.

'In Franco's time, there was more respect,' he said. 'Nowadays, no one cares about the family.'

Despite my being in a strange country, where it is never advisable to talk politics, I could not let this pass without a response. I said that Franco had been a dictator and that nothing during his time could have been better than now.

The vendor's face turned red.

'Who do you think you are, talking like that?'

'I know this country's history. I know the war the people fought for their freedom. I have read about the crimes of the Franco forces during the Spanish civil war.'

'Well, I fought in that war. I was there when my family's blood was spilled. Whatever stories you have read don't interest me; what I'm concerned about is what happens to my family. I fought against Franco, but when he won the war, life was better for me. I'm not a beggar, and I have my little popcorn stand. It wasn't this socialist government we have now that helped me. I'm worse off now than I was before.'

I remembered what Petrus had said about people being content with very little. I decided not to press my point of view, and I moved to another bench.

When Petrus came back, I told him about my exchange with the popcorn vendor.

'Conversation is useful,' he said, 'when people want to convince themselves that what they are saying is right. I am a member of the Italian Communist Party. But I didn't know about this fascist side of you.'

'What do you mean, fascist side?' I asked him angrily.

'Well, you helped the popcorn man to convince himself that Franco was good. Maybe he never knew why. Now he knows.'

'Well, I'm just as surprised to learn that the ICP believes in the gifts of the Holy Ghost.'

'Well, I have to be careful about what the neighbors will think,' he said, laughing.

The fireworks started up again, as musicians climbed to the bandstand and tuned their instruments. The festival was about to begin.

I looked up at the sky. It was growing dark, and the stars were beginning to appear. Petrus went over to one of the waiters and brought back two plastic cups full of wine.

'It is good luck to have a drink before the party begins,' he said, handing me one of the cups. 'Have some of this. It will help you forget about the popcorn man.'

'I wasn't even thinking about him anymore.'

'Well, you should. Because what happened with him is an example of mistaken behavior. We are always trying to convert people to a belief in our own explanation of the universe. We think that the more people there are who believe as we do, the more certain it will be that what we believe is the truth. But it doesn't work that way at all.

'Look around. Here is a huge party about to begin. A commemoration. Many different things are being celebrated simultaneously: the father's hope that his daughter would marry, the daughter's wish for the same thing, the groom's dreams. That's good, because they believe in their dreams and want to demonstrate to everyone that they have achieved their goals. It is not a party that is being held to convince anyone of anything, so it's going to be a lot of fun. From what I can see, they are people who have fought the good fight of love.'

'But you are trying to convince me, Petrus, by guiding me along the Road to Santiago.'

He gave me a cold look.

'I am only teaching you the RAM practices. But you will find your sword only if you discover that the Road and the truth and the life are in your heart.'

Petrus pointed to the sky, where the stars were now clearly visible.

'There is no religion that is capable of bringing all of the stars together, because if this were to happen, the universe would become a gigantic, empty space and would lose its reason for existence. Every star – and every person – has their own space and their own special characteristics. There are green stars, yellow stars, blue stars, and white stars, and there are comets, meteors and meteorites, nebulas and rings. What appear from down here to be a huge number of bodies that are similar to each other are really a million different things, spread over a space that is beyond human comprehension.'

A rocket from the fireworks burst, and its light obscured the sky for a moment. A shower of brilliant green streamers fell to the ground.

'Earlier, we only heard their noise because of the daylight. Now we can see their light,' Petrus said. 'That's the only change people can aspire to.'

The bride came out of the church, and people shouted and threw their handfuls of rice. She was a thin girl of about sixteen, and she held the arm of a boy in a tuxedo. The congregation appeared and began to move toward the square.

'Look, there's the colonel … Oh, look at the bride's dress. How beautiful,' said some boys near us. The guests took their places at the tables, the waiters served the wine, and the band began to play. The popcorn vendor was surrounded by a mob of screaming boys who made their purchases and then scattered the empty bags on the ground. I imagined that for the townspeople of Logroño, at least that night, the rest of the world – with its threat of nuclear war, unemployment, and murders – did not exist. It was a festival night, the tables had been placed in the square for the people, and everyone felt important.

A television crew came toward us, and Petrus averted his face. But the men passed us by, heading for one of the guests who sat near us. I recognized immediately who he was: Antonio, the man who had led the Spanish fans in their cheers at the World Cup in Mexico in 1986. When the interview was over, I went up to him and told him that I was a Brazilian; feigning anger, he complained about a goal of which Spain had been robbed in the opening round of the Cup.*

But then he gave me a hug, and said that Brazil would soon once again have the best players in the world.

'How do you manage to see the game when your back is always to the field and you are inciting the fans,' I asked. It was something I had noticed over and over again during the television transmissions of the World Cup games.

'That's what gives me satisfaction. Helping the fans believe in victory.'

* In the game between Spain and Brazil at that World Cup in Mexico, a Spanish goal was disallowed because the referee had not seen the ball cross the goal line before rebounding out. Brazil ended up winning that game 1–0.

And then, as if he too were a guide on the Road to Santiago, he said, 'Fans who lack the faith can make a team lose a game it is already winning.'

Manolo was then grabbed by others who wanted to interview him, but I stood there thinking about what he had said. Even without ever having walked the Road to Santiago, he knew what it was to fight the good fight.

I found Petrus hiding behind some trees, obviously uncomfortable with the presence of the television cameras. It was only after their lights had been turned off that he emerged from the trees and relaxed a bit. We asked for two more cups of wine, I fixed myself a plate of canapés, and Petrus found a table where we could sit with some of the guests.

The newlyweds cut into a huge wedding cake. People cheered.

'They must really love each other,' I said.

'Of course they do,' said a dark-suited man sitting with us. 'Have you ever heard of anyone marrying for any other reason?'

I kept my answer to myself, remembering what Petrus had said about the popcorn vendor. But my guide didn't let it pass.

'Which kind of love are you talking about: eros, philos, or agape?'

The man looked at him blankly. Petrus got up, filled his cup, and asked me to walk with him.

'There are three Greek words that mean love,' he

began. 'Today, you are seeing a manifestation of eros, the feeling of love that exists between two people.'

The bride and groom were smiling for the photographers and accepting congratulations.

'It appears that these two really do love each other,' he said, looking at the couple. 'And they believe that their love will grow. But shortly, they will be alone with each other, struggling to earn a living, build a house, and share their adventure. This is what ennobles love and dignifies it. He will do his time in the army. She is probably a good cook and will be an excellent housewife, because she has been trained since she was a child for that role. She will be good company for him, they'll have children, and they will feel that they are building something together. They'll be fighting the good fight. So even if they have problems, they will never be really unhappy.

'However, this story that I am telling you could go a very different way. He might begin to feel that he's not free enough to express all of the eros, all of the love that he has for other women. She might begin to feel that she gave up a brilliant career in order to be with her husband. So instead of creating something together, each could begin to feel robbed of a means of expressing love. Eros, the spirit that unites them, would begin to reveal only its negative side. And what God had provided to humans as their noblest sentiment would become a source of hatred and destructiveness.'

I looked around me. Eros was present in many of the relationships there. The Water Exercise had awakened the language of my heart, and I was seeing people in a different way. Maybe it was the days of solitude on the road, or maybe it was the RAM practices, but I could feel the presence of good eros and evil eros, just as Petrus had described.

'It's strange,' Petrus said, sensing the same thing. 'Whether it's good or evil, the face of eros is never the same for any two people. Just like the stars I was talking about half an hour ago. And no one can escape eros. Everyone needs its presence, despite the fact that many times, eros makes us feel apart from the world, trapped in our solitude.'

The band began to play a waltz. The guests went to a small cement section in front of the bandstand and started to dance. The alcohol was making itself felt, and people were perspiring more and smiling more. I noticed a girl dressed in blue who looked as if she had waited for this wedding just to have the chance to dance the waltz – she wanted to dance with someone who would embrace her in the way she had dreamed of since adolescence. She was watching a well-dressed boy, who wore a white suit and stood among his friends. They were all talking and had not noticed that the waltz had begun. Nor did they see that a few yards away, a girl in a blue dress looked longingly at one of them.

I thought about small towns and marriage to the boy one has dreamed of since childhood.

The girl in blue saw that I was watching her and tried to conceal herself among her girlfriends. As she did, the boy searched for her with his eyes. When he saw that she was there with her friends, he went back to his conversation with his own group.

I pointed out the two of them to Petrus. He watched the game of glances for a while and then went back to his cup of wine.

'They act as if it were shameful to make any show of love,' was all he said.

A girl near us was staring at Petrus and me. She must have been half our age. Petrus held up his cup of wine and made a toast in her direction. The girl laughed in embarrassment and pointed toward her parents, as if to explain why she did not come closer.

'That's the beautiful side of love,' Petrus said. 'The love that dares, the love for two older strangers who have come from nowhere and will be gone tomorrow – gone into a world where she would like to travel, too.'

I could hear in his voice that the wine was having an effect on him.

'Today, we will talk of love!' said my guide, a bit loudly. 'Let us speak of true love, which grows and grows, and makes the world go round, and makes people wise!'

A well-dressed woman near us seemed not to be paying any attention at all to the party. She went from table to table, straightening the cups, the china, and the silverware.

'See that woman there?' asked Petrus. 'The one who's straightening things up? Well, as I said, eros has many faces, and that's another of them. That's frustrated love, with its own kind of unhappiness. She is going to kiss the bride and groom, but inside she'll be saying that a knot has been tied around them. She's trying to neaten up the world because she herself is in complete disorder. And there' – he pointed toward another couple, the wife wearing excessive makeup and an elaborate coiffure – 'is eros accepted. Social love, without a vestige of passion. She has accepted her role and has severed any connection with the world or with the good fight.'

'You're being very bitter, Petrus. Isn't there anyone here who can be saved?'

'Of course there is. The girl who was watching us, the adolescents that are dancing – they know only about good eros. If they don't allow themselves to be influenced by the hypocrisy of the love that dominated the past generation, the world will certainly be a different place.'

He pointed to an elderly couple sitting at one of the tables.

'And those two, also. They haven't let themselves be infected by hypocrisy like the others. They look like working people. Hunger and need have required them to work together. They learned the practices you are learning without ever having heard of RAM. They find the power of love in the work they do. It's there that eros shows its most beautiful face, because it's united with that of philos.'

'What is philos?'

'Philos is love in the form of friendship. It's what I feel toward you and others. When the flame of eros stops burning, it is philos that keeps a couple together.'

'And agape?'

'Today's not the day to talk about agape. Agape is in both eros and philos – but that's just a phrase. Let's enjoy the rest of the party without talking about the love that consumes.' And Petrus poured some more wine into his plastic cup.

The happiness around us was contagious. Petrus was getting drunk, and at first I was a little surprised. But I remembered what he had said one afternoon: that the RAM practices made sense only if they could be performed by the common people.

That night, Petrus seemed to be a person like any other. He was companionable and friendly, patting people on the back and talking to anyone who paid him any attention. A little later, he was so drunk that I had to help him back to the hotel.

On the way, I took stock of my situation. Here I was, guiding my guide. I realized that at no time during the entire journey had Petrus made any effort to appear wiser, holier, or in any way better than I. All he had done was to transmit to me his experience with the RAM practices. Beyond that, he had made a point of showing that he was just like anyone else – that he experienced eros, philos, and agape.

This realization made me feel stronger. Petrus was just another pilgrim on the Road to Santiago.

Enthusiasm

'Though I speak with the tongues of men and of angels … and though I have the gift of prophecy … and have all faith so that I could remove mountains … and have not love, I am nothing.'

Petrus was once again quoting from Saint Paul. My guide felt that the apostle Paul was the major occult interpreter of Christ's message. We were fishing that afternoon after having walked for the whole morning. No fish had yet perished on the hook, but Petrus didn't care about that at all. According to him, fishing was basically a symbol of the human being's relationship with the world: we know why we are fishing, and we will catch something if we stay with it, but whether we do or not depends on God's help.

'It's a good idea always to do something relaxing prior to making an important decision in your life,' he said. 'The Zen monks listen to the rocks growing. I prefer fishing.'

But at that time of day, because of the heat, even the fat, lazy fish on the bottom ignored the hook. Whether the bait was up or down, the result was the same. I decided to give it up and take a walk through the nearby woods. I went as far as an old, abandoned cemetery close to the river – it had a gate that was totally disproportionate to the size of the burial ground – and then came back to where Petrus was fishing. I asked about the cemetery.

'The gate was part of an ancient hospital for pilgrims,' he said. 'But the hospital was abandoned, and later, someone had the idea of using the facade and building the cemetery.'

'Which has also been abandoned.'

'That's right. The things of this life don't last very long.'

I said that he had been nasty the night before in his judgments of the people at the party, and he was surprised at me. He said that what we had talked about was no more or less than we had ourselves experienced in our personal lives. All of us seek eros, and then when eros wants to turn itself into philos, we think that love is worthless. We don't see that it is philos that leads us to the highest form of love, agape.

'Tell me more about agape,' I said.

Petrus answered that agape cannot really be discussed; it has to be lived. That afternoon, if possible, he wanted to show me one of the faces of agape. But in order for this to happen, the universe, as in the business of fishing, would have to collaborate so that everything went well.

'The messenger helps you, but there is one thing that is beyond the messenger's control, beyond his desires, and beyond you, as well.'

'What is that?'

'The divine spark. What we call luck.'

When the sun had begun to set, we resumed our walking. The Jacobean route passed through some vineyards and fields that were completely deserted at that time of day. We crossed the main road – also deserted – and started again through the woods. In the distance, I could see the Saint Lorenzo peak, the highest point in the kingdom of Castile. I had changed a great deal since I had met Petrus for the first time near Saint-Jean-Pied-de-Port. Brazil and the business deals that I had been worried about had practically vanished from my mind. The only important thing for me now was my objective. I discussed it every night with Astrain, who was becoming clearer and clearer for me. I was able to see him, seated at my side, any time I tried. I learned that he had a nervous tic in his right eye and that he had the habit of smiling disdainfully every time I repeated something as evidence that I had understood what he was saying. A few weeks earlier – during the first days of the pilgrimage – I had been afraid that I would never complete it. When we had passed through Roncesvalles, I had been very disillusioned about everything to do with the journey. I had wanted to get to Santiago immediately, recover my sword, and get back to fighting what Petrus called the good fight.* But right now, with my connection to

* I found out later that the term had actually been created by Saint Paul.

civilization severed, what was most important was the sun on my head and the possibility that I might experience agape.

We went down the bank of an arroyo, crossed the dry bed, and had to struggle to climb up the other side. An impressive river must have flowed there once, washing away the bottom in its search for the depths and secrets of the earth. Now the riverbed was so dry that it could be crossed on foot. But the river's major accomplishment, the valley it had created, was still there, and it took a major effort to climb out of it. 'Nothing in this life endures,' Petrus had said a few hours before.

'Petrus, have you ever been in love?'

The question was a spontaneous one, and I was surprised at my courage. Up until then, I had known only the bare outline of my guide's private life.

'I have known a lot of women, if that is what you mean. And I have really loved each of them. But I experienced agape only with two.'

I told him that I had been in love many times but had been worried about whether I could ever become serious with anyone. If I had continued that way, it would have led to a solitary old age, and I had been very fearful of this.

'I don't think you look to love as a means to a comfortable retirement.'

It was almost nine o'clock before it began to get dark. The vineyards were behind us, and we were walking through an arid landscape. I looked around and could see in the distance a small hermitage in the rocks, similar to many others we had passed on our pilgrimage. We walked on for a while, and then, detouring from the yellow markers, we approached the small building.

When we were close enough, Petrus called out a name that I didn't understand, and he stopped to listen for an answer. We heard nothing. Petrus called again, but no one answered.

'Let's go, anyway,' he said. And we moved forward.

The hermitage consisted of just four whitewashed walls. The door was open – or rather, there really was no door, just a small entry panel, half a meter high, which hung precariously by one hinge. Within, there was a stone fireplace and some basins stacked on the floor. Two of them were filled with wheat and potatoes.

We sat down in the silence. Petrus lit a cigarette and said we should wait. My legs were hurting, but something in that hermitage, rather than calming me, made me feel excited. It would also have frightened me a little if Petrus had not been there.

'Where does whoever lives here sleep?' I asked, just to break the uneasy silence.

'There, where you are sitting,' Petrus said, pointing to the bare earth. I said something about moving to another spot, but he told me to stay exactly where I was. The temperature must have been dropping, because I began to feel cold.

We waited for almost an hour. Petrus called out the strange name several more times and then gave up. Just when I expected us to get up and leave, he began to speak.

'Present here is one of the two manifestations of agape,' he said, as he stubbed out his third cigarette. 'It is not the only one, but it is the purest. Agape is total love. It is the love that consumes the person who experiences it. Whoever knows and experiences agape learns that nothing else in the world is important – just love. This was the kind of love that Jesus felt for humanity, and it was so great that it shook the stars and changed the course of history. His solitary life enabled him to accomplish things that kings, armies, and empires could not.

'During the millennia of Christian civilization, many individuals have been seized by this love that consumes. They had so much to give – and their world demanded so little that they went out into the deserts and to isolated places, because the love they felt was so great that it transformed them. They became the hermit saints that we know today.

'For you and for me, who experience a different form of agape, this life may seem terrible. But the love that consumes makes everything else – absolutely everything – lose its importance. Those men lived just to be consumed by their love.'

Petrus told me that a monk named Alfonso lived there. Petrus had met him on his first pilgrimage to Compostela, as he was picking fruit to eat. His guide, a much more enlightened man than he, was a friend of

Alfonso's, and the three of them had together performed the Ritual of Agape, the Blue Sphere Exercise. Petrus said that it had been one of the most important experiences of his life and that even today when he performed the exercise, he remembered the hermitage and Alfonso. There was more emotion in his voice than I had ever heard from him.

'Agape is the love that consumes,' he repeated, as if that were the phrase that best defined this strange kind of love. 'Martin Luther King once said that when Christ spoke of loving one's enemies, he was referring to agape. Because according to him, it was "impossible to like our enemies, those who were cruel to us, those who tried to make our day-to-day suffering even worse." But agape is much more than liking. It is a feeling that suffuses, that fills every space in us, and turns our aggression to dust.

'You have learned how to be reborn, how to stop being cruel to yourself, and how to communicate with your messenger. But everything you do from now on and every good result that you take with you from the Road to Santiago will make sense only when you have also experienced the love that consumes.'

I reminded Petrus that he had said that there were two forms of agape. And that he probably had not experienced this first form, since he had not become a hermit.

'You're right. You and I and most pilgrims who walk the Road to Santiago, learning the RAM practices, experience agape in its other form: enthusiasm.

'For the ancients, enthusiasm meant trance, or ecstasy – a connection with God. Enthusiasm is agape directed at a particular idea or a specific thing. We have all experienced it. When we love and believe from the bottom of our heart, we feel ourselves to be stronger than anyone in the world, and we feel a serenity that is based on the certainty that nothing can shake our faith. This unusual strength allows us always to make the right decision at the right time, and when we achieve our goal, we are amazed at our own capabilities. Because when we are involved in the good fight, nothing else is important; enthusiasm carries us toward our goal.

'Enthusiasm normally manifests itself with all of its force during the first years of our lives. At that time, we still have strong links with the divinity, and we throw ourselves into our play with our toys with such a will that dolls take on life and our tin soldiers actually march. When Jesus said that the kingdom of heaven belonged to the children, he was referring to agape in the form of enthusiasm. Children were attracted to him, not because they understood his miracles, his wisdom, or his Pharisees and apostles. They went to him in joy, moved by enthusiasm.'

I told Petrus that on that very afternoon, I had realized that I was completely absorbed by the Road to Santiago. Those days and nights in Spain had almost made me forget about my sword, and they were a unique experience. Most other things had lost their importance.

'This afternoon, we were trying to fish, but the fish would not bite,' said Petrus. 'Normally, we allow enthusiasm to elude us when we are involved in such mundane activities, those that have no importance at all in the overall scale of our existence. We lose our enthusiasm because of the small and unavoidable defeats we suffer during the good fight. And since we don't realize that enthusiasm is a major strength, able to help us win the ultimate victory, we let it dribble through our fingers; we do this without recognizing that we are letting the true meaning of our lives escape us. We blame the world for our boredom and for our losses, and we forget that it was we ourselves who allowed this enchanting power, which justifies everything, to diminish – the manifestation of agape – in the form of enthusiasm.'

I remembered the cemetery near the river. That strange, unusually large portal was a perfect representation of what had been lost. And beyond it, only the dead.

As if he had guessed what I was thinking, Petrus began to talk about something that was similar.

'A few days ago, you must have been surprised when I got so angry with that poor waiter who had spilled coffee on my shorts – shorts that were already filthy with the dust and dirt of the road. Actually, I was nervous because I saw in the boy's eyes that his enthusiasm was draining away like the blood that runs from wrists that have been slashed. I saw that boy, so strong and full of life, beginning to die because inside him, moment by moment, agape was perishing. I have been around for a long time, and I have learned to live with these things, but that lad, with the way he behaved and with all the good things I felt that he could bring to humanity, left me shocked and sad. But I know that my anger wounded him a bit and stemmed the death of agape.

'In the same vein, when you exorcised that woman's dog, you felt agape in its purest form. It was a noble deed, and it made me proud to be here serving as your guide. So for the first time in our experience on the Road, I am going to participate in an exercise with you.'

And Petrus taught me the Ritual of Agape, the Blue Sphere Exercise.

'I am going to help you to arouse your enthusiasm, to create a power that is going to expand like a blue sphere that encloses the entire planet,' he said, 'to show that I respect you and what you are doing.'

Up until then, Petrus had never expressed an opinion, either favorable or unfavorable, regarding the way in which I performed the exercises. He had helped me to interpret my first contact with the messenger, and he had rescued me from the trance of the Seed Exercise, but he had never expressed any interest in the results I had achieved. More than once I had asked him why he did not want to know about my feelings, and he had answered that his only obligation as my guide was to show me the Road and to teach me the RAM practices. It was up to me whether I enjoyed the results or found them to be unpleasant.

When he said that he was going to participate with me in the exercise, I suddenly felt unworthy of his praise. I knew my faults, and many times I had doubted whether he could succeed in guiding me along the Road. I wanted to say all this to him, but he interrupted me before I could begin.

'Don't be cruel with yourself, or you will not have learned the lesson I taught you before. Be kind. Accept the praise that you deserve.'

Tears came to my eyes. Petrus led me outside. The night was darker than usual. I sat down next to him, and we began to sing. The melody came from within me, and he accompanied me with no effort. I began to clap my hands softly, as I rocked forward and back. My clapping increased in its intensity, and the music flowed from me, a psalm of praise to the darkness of the sky, the deserted plateau, and the lifeless stones around us. I began to see the saints that I had believed in as a child; and I could sense that life had gotten away from me because of my having killed a great deal of my agape. But now the love that consumes returned, and the saints smiled from the heavens with the same look and intensity that I had seen in them when I was small.

I spread my arms so that agape could flow, and a mysterious current of bright blue light began to wash through me, cleansing my soul and pardoning my sins. The light spread first to our surroundings and then enveloped the world, and I started to weep. I wept because I was re-experiencing the enthusiasm of my

The Blue Sphere Exercise

Seat yourself comfortably, and relax. Try not to think about anything.

1. Feel how good it is to be alive. Let your heart feel free and affectionate; let it rise above and beyond the details of the problems that may be bothering you. Begin to sing softly a song from your childhood. Imagine that your heart is growing, filling the room – and later your home – with an intense, shining blue light.

2. When you reach this point, begin to sense the presence of the saints (or other beings) in which you placed your faith when you were a child. Notice that they are present, arriving from everywhere, smiling and giving you faith and confidence.

3. Picture the saints approaching you, placing their hands on your head and wishing you love, peace, and communion with the world – the communion of the saints.

4. When this sensation becomes strong, feel that the blue light is a current that enters you and leaves you like a shining, flowing river. This blue light begins to spread through your house, then through your neighborhood, your city, and your country; it eventually envelops the world in an immense blue sphere. This is the manifestation of the great love that goes beyond the day-to-day struggle; it reinforces and invigorates, as it provides energy and peace.

5. Keep the light spread around the world for as long as possible. Your heart is open, spreading love. This phase of the exercise should last for a minimum of five minutes.

6. Come out of your trance, bit by bit, and return to reality. The saints will remain near. The blue light will continue to spread around the world.

This ritual can and should be done with more than one person. When this is the case, the participants should hold hands while they do the exercise.

childhood; I was once again a child, and nothing in the world could cause me harm. I felt a presence draw near and sit down to my right. I imagined that it was my messenger and that he was the only one who could perceive the strong blue light that was entering me and leaving me, spreading throughout the world.

The light was increasing in its intensity, and I felt that as it enclosed the world, it penetrated into every door and every back alley, touching every person alive for at least a fraction of a second.

I felt my hands being held open and extended to the heavens. At that moment, the flow of the blue light increased and became so strong that I thought I was going to pass out. But I was able to keep the light alive for a few moments more, until I reached the end of the song I was singing.

I was exhausted but relaxed; I felt free and content with life and with what I had just done. The hands that held mine released me. I saw that one of them was Petrus's, and I knew in my heart who it was that held the other.

I opened my eyes, and there at my side was the monk, Alfonso. He smiled and said, *'Buenas noches.'* I smiled, too, and I seized his hand and held it tightly to my breast. He allowed me to do this for a moment and then gently removed his hand.

None of us spoke. Some time later, Alfonso arose and continued his trek along the rocky plateau. I watched him until he was completely hidden by the darkness.

Petrus broke the silence then, but he made no mention of Alfonso.

'Do this exercise whenever you can, and soon agape will live once again within you. Repeat it before you embark on any project, during the first days of any trip, or when you have been greatly affected by something. If possible, do it with someone you like. It is an exercise that should be shared.'

So there was the old Petrus: coach, instructor, and guide, the man about whom I knew so little. The emotion that he had shown in the hermitage had already passed away. But when he had touched my hand during the exercise, I had felt the greatness of his soul.

We returned to the hermitage where we had left our things.

'The occupant won't be back today, so I think we can sleep here,' said Petrus, lying down. I unrolled my sleeping bag, took a swallow of wine, and lay down. I was exhausted by the love that consumes. But it was a tiredness that was free of tension, and before I closed my eyes, I thought of the thin, bearded monk who had sat beside me and wished me good night. Somewhere out there he was being consumed by the divine flame. Maybe that was why the night was so unusually dark – he had taken all the light of the world into himself.

Death

'Are you pilgrims?' asked the old woman who served us our breakfast. We were in Azofra, a village of small houses, each with a medieval shield embossed on its facade. We had filled our canteens at the village fountain a few moments earlier.

I said that we were, and the woman's eyes glowed with respect and pride.

'When I was a girl, at least one pilgrim passed through here every day, bound for Compostela. After the war and after Franco, I don't know what happened, but the pilgrimages stopped. Someone must have built a highway. Nowadays, people only want to travel by car.'

Petrus said nothing. He had awakened in a bad mood. I nodded in agreement with the old woman and pictured a new, paved expressway, climbing the mountains and running across the valleys, automobiles with scallop shells painted on their hoods, and souvenir shops at the gates of the monasteries. I finished my coffee and bread dipped in olive oil. Looking at Aymeric Picaud's guide, I estimated that we should arrive that afternoon in Santo Domingo de la Calzada, and I was planning to sleep at the Parador Nacional.*

I was spending much less money than I had planned, even eating three meals a day. It was time for an extravagance, time to give my body the same treatment I had been giving my stomach.

I had awakened with a strange feeling of being in a hurry and of wanting to be in Santo Domingo already. I had experienced the same feeling two days earlier, when we had walked to the hermitage. Petrus was more melancholy and quiet than usual; was this the result of our meeting with Alfonso two days ago? I felt a strong need to invoke Astrain so that we could discuss the matter. But I had never summoned him in the morning, and I was not sure that I could. I decided against it.

We finished our coffee and began to walk. We passed a medieval house with its coat of arms, the ruins of an ancient hostel for pilgrims, and a park on the outskirts of the village. As I once again readied myself to move out across the countryside, I felt a strong presence to my left side. I walked on, but Petrus stopped me.

'There is no use running away,' he said. 'Stop and deal with it.'

I wanted to get away from Petrus and keep going. I had a disagreeable feeling, a kind of colic near my

* The Paradores Nacionales are ancient castles and historic monuments that have been turned into first-class hotels by the Spanish government.

stomach. For a few moments, I tried to believe that it was caused by the bread with olive oil, but I knew that I had felt it earlier in the day and I could not fool myself. It was tension – tension and fear.

'Look behind you.' Petrus's voice had an urgency to it. 'Look before it's too late!'

I spun around quickly. To my left was an abandoned house, its vegetation burned by the sun. An olive tree raised its twisted branches to the sky. And between the tree and the house, looking fixedly at me, was a dog.

A black dog, the same dog that I had banished from the woman's house a few days earlier.

I forgot all about Petrus and looked squarely into the dog's eyes. Something inside me – perhaps it was the voice of Astrain or of my guardian angel – told me that if I averted my eyes, the dog would attack me. We remained that way, staring at each other, for some time. Here I was, I thought, after having experienced the wonder of the love that consumes, once again about to be confronted by the daily and constant threats to my existence that the world would always present. I wondered why the animal had followed me for such a great distance and what it was that he wanted; after all, I was just a pilgrim in quest of my sword, and I had neither the desire nor the patience for problems with people or animals. I tried to say this to him with my eyes – remembering the monks at the convent who communicated through their eyes – but the dog did not move. He continued to stare at me, without emotion, but he appeared ready to attack should I become distracted or show fear.

Fear! I could sense that my fear had vanished. I thought the situation too stupid for fear. My stomach was knotted up, and I felt like vomiting, but I wasn't frightened. If I had been, something told me that my eyes would have given me away, and the animal would try to overcome me, as he had before. I did not want to avert my eyes, even when I sensed that a figure was approaching along a narrow road to my right.

The figure stopped for an instant and then came directly toward us. It crossed my line of sight as I stared at the dog, and this person said something I could not understand in a feminine voice. Its presence was good – friendly and positive.

In the fraction of a second during which the image had crossed my line of sight, my stomach relaxed. I felt that I had a powerful friend who was there to help me through this absurd, unnecessary conflict. When the figure had passed by, the dog lowered his eyes. Then he jumped, ran behind the abandoned house, and disappeared from view.

It was only then that my heart began to react. The tachycardia was so strong that I felt dizzy and faint. As the scene around me spun, I looked along the road that Petrus and I had walked only a few minutes earlier, seeking the figure that had given me the strength to defeat the dog. It was a nun. Her back was to me, and she was walking toward Azofra. I could not see her face, but I remembered her voice, and I guessed that she was in her early twenties. I looked in the direction from which she had come: she had appeared from a narrow path that seemed to lead nowhere.

'It was she … it was she who helped me,' I murmured, as my dizziness grew worse.

'Don't start creating fantasies in a world that is already extraordinary,' said Petrus, supporting me by the arm. 'She comes from a convent in Cañas, three or four miles from here. You can't see it from here.'

My heart was still pounding, and I was sure I was going to be sick. I was too upset to speak or ask for an explanation. I sat down on the ground, and Petrus threw some water on my forehead and on the nape of my neck. I remembered that he had done the same thing after we had left the woman's house – but that day I had cried for joy. Now the sensation was just the opposite.

Petrus let me rest a bit. The water brought me around, and the nausea began to subside. Things slowly returned to normal. When I felt restored, Petrus said we should walk a little, and I obeyed. We walked for about fifteen minutes, but the exhaustion returned. We sat down at the foot of a *rollo*, a medieval column supporting a cross. Such columns marked a number of stretches along the Jacobean route.

'Your fear has hurt you much more than the dog did,' said Petrus, as I rested.

I wanted to understand that absurd encounter.

'In the life on the Road to Santiago, certain things happen that are beyond our control. When we first met, I told you that I had read in the gypsy's eyes the name of the demon you would have to confront. I was surprised to learn that the demon was a dog, but I did not say anything to you about it at the time. Only after we arrived at that woman's house – when for the first time, you showed the love that consumes – did I see your enemy.

'When you chased away that woman's dog, you did not place him anywhere. You didn't hurl the spirits into a drove of pigs that was thrown over a precipice, as Jesus did. You simply chased the dog away. Now his force wanders along behind you, without a destination. Before finding your sword, you are going to have to decide whether you want to be enslaved by that force or whether you will dominate it.'

My fatigue began to pass. I took a deep breath and felt the cold stone of the *rollo* against my back. Petrus gave me some more water and went on:

'Cases of obsession occur when people lose their mastery over the forces of the earth. The gypsy's curse had frightened that woman, and her fear had opened a breach that the messenger of death was then able to penetrate. This doesn't always happen, but neither is it rare. Your confidence and your sense of mastery depend a great deal on how you react to threats made by others.'

This time it was I who remembered a passage from the Bible. A verse in the Book of Job says, 'For the thing that I greatly feared is come upon me.'

'A threat leads to nothing if it is not accepted. In fighting the good fight, you should never forget that. Just as you should never forget that both attacking and fleeing are part of the fight. What isn't a part of the fight is becoming paralyzed by fear.'

I had not felt fear when the dog was there. This had surprised me, and I told Petrus about it.

'I could see that you felt no fear. If you had, the dog would have attacked you. And without a doubt, he would have won the fight. Because the dog was not afraid either. The strangest thing, though, was the arrival of that nun. When you sensed the presence of something positive, your imagination concluded that someone had arrived to help you. And this, your faith, saved you. Even though it was based on an assumption that was absolutely false.'

Petrus was right. He laughed at me, and I laughed, too. We got up to resume our walking. I was already feeling better.

'There is one thing you have to know, though,' said Petrus as we moved on. 'The duel with the dog will end only with a victory for you or for him. He will be back, and the next time you must try to take the fight through to the end. If you don't, his presence will worry you for the rest of your life.'

In the encounter with the gypsy, Petrus had told me, he had learned the name of the demon. I asked him what it was.

'Legion,' he answered. 'Because he is many.'

We passed through fields that the farmers were preparing for sowing. Here and there, some peasants operated crude water pumps in the centuries-old fight against the arid soil. Along the edge of the Road to Santiago, stones had been piled into endless walls, criss-crossing the fields. I thought about how, in spite of all the centuries during which that soil had been worked, stones still surfaced – stones that could break the blade of a plow, render a horse lame, and leave calluses on the peasants' hands. It was a battle every year, a battle that would never end.

Petrus was quieter than usual, and I realized that he had said almost nothing since morning. After our conversation at the medieval *rollo*, he had been mute, not answering any of the questions I had asked. I wanted to know more about the 'many demons,' because he had already explained to me that each person has only one messenger. But Petrus was not interested in talking about it, and I decided to wait for a better time.

We climbed a small rise, and from the top we could see the main tower of the church at Santo Domingo de la Calzada. I was glad to see it; I began to think about the magical comfort of the Parador Nacional. From what I had read about it, the building had been constructed by Santo Domingo himself as a shelter for pilgrims. Saint Francis of Assisi had stayed there on his way to Compostela. Everything about it excited me.

At about seven o'clock that evening, Petrus said we should stop. I was reminded of Roncesvalles and of the slow pace we had taken when I had needed some wine to warm me, and I was afraid that he was preparing something like that.

'A messenger would never help you to defeat someone else. Messengers are neither good nor bad, as I have already told you, but they have a sense of loyalty among themselves. Don't rely on your messenger to help you defeat the dog.'

Now it was my turn not to want to talk about messengers. I wanted to get to Santo Domingo.

'The messengers of people who have died can occupy the body of someone who is dominated by fear. That is why, in the case of the dog, he is many. Messengers were invited in by the woman's fear – not just the murdered gypsy's messenger but all of the many messengers who wander in space, seeking a way to establish contact with the forces of the earth.'

He was finally answering my question, but there was something in the way he spoke that seemed artificial, as if this were not what he really wanted to say. My instincts told me to be wary.

'What do you want, Petrus?' I asked him, a bit irritated.

My guide did not answer. He walked into the field toward an ancient, almost leafless tree that stood about thirty yards from us. It was the only tree visible on the entire horizon. Since he had not given me the signal to follow, I stood where I was. And I saw a strange thing happen: Petrus walked around the tree several times and said something out loud, while he looked at the ground. When he had finished, he gestured for me to come over.

'Sit here,' he said. There was a different tone to his voice, and I couldn't tell whether it was friendliness or irritation. 'Stay here. I will see you tomorrow in Santo Domingo de la Calzada.'

Before I could say a word, Petrus continued, 'One of these days – and I guarantee you that it will not be today – you are going to have to confront the most important enemy you will meet on the Road to Santiago: the dog. When that day comes, you can be sure that I will be close at hand and will give you the strength you need to fight him. But today you are going to confront a different type of enemy, an unreal enemy that may destroy you or may turn out to be your best friend: death.

'Human beings are the only ones in nature who are aware that they will die. For that reason and only for that reason, I have a profound respect for the human race, and I believe that its future is going to be much better than its present. Even knowing that their days are numbered and that everything will end when they least expect it, people make of their lives a battle that is worthy of a being with eternal life. What people regard as vanity – leaving great works, having children, acting in such a way as to prevent one's name from being forgotten – I regard as the highest expression of human dignity.

'Still, being fragile creatures, humans always try to hide from themselves the certainty that they will die. They do not see that it is death itself that motivates them to do the best things in their lives. They are afraid to step into the dark, afraid of the unknown, and their only way of conquering that fear is to ignore the fact that their days are numbered. They do not see that with an awareness of death, they would be able to be even more daring, to go much further in their daily conquests, because then they would have nothing to lose – for death is inevitable.'

The possibility of spending the night in Santo Domingo was looking more and more remote. But now I was interested in what Petrus was saying. The sun itself was dying beyond the horizon there in front of us.

'Death is our constant companion, and it is death that gives each person's life its true meaning. But in order to see the real face of our death, we first have to know all of the anxieties and terrors that the simple mention of its name is able to evoke in any human being.'

Petrus sat down beside me under the tree. He said that he had circled its trunk a few minutes before because it reminded him of everything that had happened to him when he had been a pilgrim bound for Santiago. Then he took from his knapsack two sandwiches that he had bought at lunchtime.

'Here, where you are now, there is no danger,' he said, giving me the sandwiches. 'There are no poisonous snakes, and the dog will return to attack you only after he has forgotten this morning's defeat. And there are no bandits or criminals around here. You are in a spot that is absolutely safe, with one exception: the danger created by your own fear.'

Petrus pointed out to me that two days earlier, I had experienced a sensation that had been as intense and as violent as death itself – that of the love that consumes. And that at one point I had vacillated and been afraid. He said that I had been afraid because I knew nothing about universal love. He explained to me that although all of us have some idea of death, we do not see that death is only another manifestation of agape. I answered that with all of my years of training in magic, I had practically lost my fear of death. Actually, I was more frightened by the way in which I would die than by death itself.

'Well, then, tonight take a look at the most frightening way to die.'

And at that point, Petrus taught me the Buried Alive Exercise.

'You should do this exercise only once,' he said. I was thinking of an exercise from the theater that was quite similar. 'It is important that you be as truthful with yourself as possible and that you be as fearful as necessary for the exercise to get at the roots of your soul; it has to strip away the scary mask that hides the gentle face of your death.'

Petrus stood up, and I saw his silhouette against the background of the setting sun. From where I was seated, he seemed to be a gigantic and powerful figure.

The Buried Alive Exercise

Lie down on the floor and relax. Cross your arms over your chest in the posture of death.

Imagine all of the details of your burial, as if it were to be carried out tomorrow, the only difference being that you are being buried alive. As the situation develops in your mind – the chapel, the procession to the cemetery, the lowering of the casket, the worms in the grave – you begin tensing all of your muscles more and more in a desperate attempt to escape. But you cannot do so. Keep trying until you cannot stand it any longer, and then, using a movement that involves your entire body, throw aside the confines of the coffin, breathe deeply, and find yourself free. This movement will have a greater effect if you scream at the same time; it should be a scream that emanates from the depths of your body.

'Petrus, I have one more question.'

'What is it?'

'This morning you were close-mouthed and strange. You sensed before I did that the dog was going to appear. How was that possible?'

'When we both experienced the love that consumes, we shared in the Absolute. The Absolute shows each of us who we really are; it is an enormous web of cause and effect, where every small gesture made by one person affects the life of someone else. This morning, that slice of the Absolute was still very much alive in my soul. I was seeing not only you but everything there is in the world, unlimited by space or time. Now, the effect is much weaker and will only return in its full strength the next time that I do the exercise of the love that consumes.'

I remembered Petrus's bad mood of that morning. If what he said was true, the world was going through a very bad phase.

'I will be waiting for you there at the Parador,' he said, as he prepared to leave. 'I will leave your name at the desk.'

I watched him walk away until I could no longer see him. In the fields to my left, the peasants had finished their day's labors and gone home. I decided that I would do the exercise as soon as darkness had fallen.

I was content. It was the first time I had been completely alone since I had started along the Strange Road to Santiago. I stood up and explored my immediate surroundings, but night was falling fast, and I decided to go back to the tree before I got lost. Before it became completely dark, I made a mental estimate of the distance between the tree and the road. Even in darkness, I would be able to see the way perfectly well and make my way to Santo Domingo with just the help of the frail new moon that had risen in the sky.

Up until that point, I had not been at all frightened; I felt that it would take a lot of imagination to make me fearful of any kind of horrible death. But no matter how long we have lived, when night falls it arouses the hidden fears that have been there in our souls since we were children. The darker it grew, the less comfortable I became.

There I was, alone in the fields; if I were to scream, no one would even hear me. I remembered that I had almost passed out completely that morning. Never in my life had I felt my heart to be so out of control.

And what if I had died? My life would have ended, obviously. Through my experiences with the Tradition, I had already communicated with many spirits. I was absolutely certain that there was a life after death, but it had never occurred to me to wonder just how the transition was made. To pass from one dimension to another, no matter how well prepared one is, must be terrible. If I had died that morning, for example, I would have known nothing else about the rest of the Road to Santiago, about my years of study, about my family's grief for me, or about the money hidden in my belt. I thought about a plant on my desk in Brazil. The plant would go on, as would other plants, as would the streetcars, as would the man on the corner who charges more for his vegetables than anyone else, as would the woman at directory assistance who provides me with telephone numbers that are not listed in the book. All these things – which would have disappeared if I had died that morning – took on an enormous importance for me. I realized that those were the things, rather than the stars or wisdom, that told me I was alive.

The night was quite dark, and on the horizon I could see the faint lights of the city. I lay down on the ground and looked at the branches of the tree overhead. I began to hear strange sounds, sounds of all kinds. They were the sounds of the nocturnal animals, setting out on the hunt. Petrus could not know everything; he was just another human being like me. How was I to know if his guarantee about the absence of poisonous snakes was true? And the wolves, those eternal European wolves – wasn't it possible that they had decided to show up there that night, sniffing out my presence? A louder noise, similar to the breaking of a branch, frightened me, and my heart once again started pounding.

I was growing scared. The best thing to do would be to complete the exercise right away and then head for the hotel. I began to relax and crossed my arms over my chest in the posture of death. Something nearby made a sound. I jumped up immediately.

It was nothing. The night had aroused my greatest fears. I lay down again, deciding that this time I would turn any source of fear into a stimulus for the exercise. I noticed that even though the temperature had fallen quite a bit, I was perspiring.

I imagined my coffin being closed, and the screws being turned. I was immobile, but I was alive, and I wanted to tell my family that I was seeing everything. I wanted to tell them all that I loved them, but not a sound came out of my mouth. My father and mother were weeping, my wife and my friends were gathered around, but I was completely alone! With all of the people dear to me standing there, no one was able to see that I was alive and that I had not yet accomplished all that I wanted to do in this world. I tried desperately to open my eyes, to give a sign, to beat on the lid of the coffin. But I could not move any part of my body.

I felt the coffin being carried toward the grave. I could hear the sound of the handles grinding against their fittings, the steps of those in the procession, and conversations from this side and that. Someone said that he had a date for dinner later on, and another observed that I had died early. The smell of flowers all around me began to suffocate me.

I remembered how I had given up trying to establish a relationship with two or three women, fearing their rejection. I remembered also the number of times I had failed to do what I wanted to do, thinking I could always do it later. I felt very sorry for myself, not only because I was about to be buried alive but also because I had been afraid to live. Why be fearful of saying no to someone or of leaving something undone when the most important thing of all was to enjoy life fully? There I was, trapped in a coffin, and it was already too late to go back and show the courage I should have had.

There I was, having played the role of my own Judas, having betrayed myself. There I was, powerless to move a muscle, screaming for help, while the others were involved in their lives, worrying about what they were going to do that night, admiring statues and buildings that I would never see again. I began to feel how unfair it was to have to be buried while others continued to live. I would have felt better if there had been a catastrophe and all of us had been in the same boat, heading for the same abyss toward which they were carrying me now. Help! I tried to cry out. I'm still alive. I haven't died. My mind is still functioning!

They placed my coffin at the edge of the grave. They are going to bury me! My wife is going to forget all about me; she will marry someone else and spend the money we have struggled to save for all these years! But who cares about that. I want to be with her now, because I'm alive!

I hear sobs, and I feel tears falling from my eyes, too. If my friends were to open my coffin now, they would see my tears and save me. But instead all I feel is the lowering of the coffin into the ground. Suddenly, everything is dark. A moment ago, there was a ray of light at the edge of the coffin, but now the darkness is complete. The grave diggers' shovels are filling in the grave, and I'm alive! Buried alive! I sense that the air is being cut off, and the fragrance of the flowers is awful. I hear the mourners' departing footsteps. My terror is total. I'm not able to do anything; if they go away now, it will soon be night, and no one will hear me knocking on the lid of my coffin!

The footsteps fade, nobody hears my screams, and I am alone in the darkness; the air is heavy, and the smell of the flowers is driving me crazy. Suddenly, I hear a sound. It's the worms, coming to eat me alive. I try with all my strength to move the parts of my body, but I am inert. The worms begin to climb over my body. They are sticky and cold. They creep over my face and crawl into my shorts. One of them enters through my anus, and another begins to sneak into a nostril. Help! I'm being eaten alive, and nobody can hear me; nobody says a word to me. The worm that entered my nostril has reached my throat. I feel another invading my ear. I have to get out! Where is God; why doesn't he help me? They are beginning to eat at my throat, and soon I won't be able to scream! They are coming into me everywhere: through my ear, the corner of my mouth, the opening in my penis. I feel those disgusting, oily things inside me, and I have to scream; I have to get away! I am shut up in this cold, dark grave, alone and being eaten alive! The air is giving out, and the worms are eating me! I have to move. I have to break out of this coffin! God, help me gather all of my strength, because I have to escape! I HAVE TO GET OUT OF HERE; I HAVE TO ... I'M GOING TO GET OUT! I'M GOING TO GET OUT!

I DID IT!

The boards of the coffin flew in all directions, the grave disappeared, and I filled my lungs with the fresh air of the Road to Santiago. My body was trembling from head to foot and bathed in perspiration. I moved a bit and felt that my insides had been twisted around. But none of this was important: I was alive.

The shaking continued, and I made no effort whatsoever to control it. A great sense of calm came over me, and I felt a kind of presence alongside me. I looked over and saw the face of my death. This was not the death that I had experienced a few minutes before, the death I had created with my fears and my imagination; it was my true death, my friend and counselor, who was never again going to allow me to act like such a coward. Starting then, he was going to be of more help to me than Petrus's guiding hand and advice. He was not going to allow me to put off until tomorrow what I should be enjoying today. He was not going to let me flee from life's battles, and he was going to help me fight the good fight. Never again, ever, was I going to feel ridiculous about doing anything. Because he was there, saying that when he took me in hand to travel with me to other worlds, I should leave behind the greatest sin of all: regret. With the certainty of his presence and the gentleness of his face, I was sure that I was going to be able to drink from the fountain of life.

The night held no further secrets or terrors. It was a joyful night, filled with peace. When the trembling ceased, I got up and walked to the pumps in the fields. I washed my shorts and put on a fresh pair from my knapsack. Then I returned to the tree and ate the two sandwiches that Petrus had left for me. They seemed like the most delicious food in the world, because I was alive and because death frightened me no longer.

I decided to sleep right there. The darkness had never been so reassuring.

Personal Vices

We were in the middle of a level field of wheat that stretched all the way to the horizon. The only object that stood out in the scene was another medieval column supporting a cross, one of the road markers for pilgrims. As we approached the column, Petrus stopped, placed his knapsack on the ground, and knelt down. He told me to do the same.

'We are going to say a prayer concerning the only thing that can defeat you as a pilgrim after you find your sword: your personal vices. No matter how much you learn from your Master about how to handle the sword, one of your hands will always be your potential enemy. Let us pray that, if you are successful in finding your sword, you will always wield it with the hand that does not bring scandal down upon you.'

It was two o'clock in the afternoon, and there wasn't a sound to be heard as Petrus began to pray aloud:

'Pity us, O Lord, for we are pilgrims on the road to Compostela, and our being here may be a vice. In your infinite pity, help us never to turn our knowledge against ourselves.

'Have pity on those who pity themselves and who see themselves as good people treated unfairly by life – who feel that they do not deserve what has befallen them. Such people will never be able to fight the good fight. And pity those who are cruel to themselves and who see only the evil in their own actions, feeling that they are to blame for the injustice in the world. Because neither of these kinds of people know thy law that says, "But the very hairs of your head are numbered."

'Have pity on those who command and those who serve during long hours of work, and who sacrifice themselves in exchange merely for a Sunday off, only to find that there is nowhere to go, and everything is closed. But also have pity on those who sanctify their efforts, and who are able to go beyond the bounds of their own madness, winding up indebted, or nailed to the cross by their very brothers. Because neither of these kinds of people know thy law that says, "Be ye therefore as wise as the serpents and as harmless as the doves."

'Have pity on those who may conquer the world but never join the good fight within themselves. But pity also those who have won the good fight within themselves, and now find themselves in the streets and the bars of life because they were unable to conquer the world. Because neither of these kinds of people know thy law that says, "He who heeds my words I will liken to a wise man who built his house on rock."

'Have pity on those who are fearful of taking up a pen, or a paintbrush, or an instrument, or a tool because they are afraid that someone has already done so better than they could, and who feel themselves to be unworthy to enter the marvelous mansion of art. But have even more pity on those who, having taken up the pen, or the paintbrush, or the instrument, or the tool, have turned inspiration into a paltry thing, and yet feel themselves to be better than others. Neither of these kinds of people know thy law that says, "For there is nothing covered that will not be revealed, nor hidden that will not be known."

'Pity those who eat and drink and sate themselves, but are unhappy and alone in their satiety. But pity even more those who fast, and who censure and prohibit, and who thereby see themselves as saints, preaching your name in the streets. For neither of these types of people know thy law that says, "If I bear witness of myself, my witness is not true."

'Pity those who fear death, and are unaware of the many kingdoms through which they have already passed, and the many deaths they have already suffered, and who are unhappy because they think that one day their world will end. But have even more pity for those who already know their many deaths, and today think of themselves as immortal. Neither of these kinds of people know thy law that says, "Except that one is born again, he cannot see the kingdom of God."

'Have pity on those who bind themselves with the silken ties of love, and think of themselves as masters of others, and who feel envy, and poison themselves, and who torture themselves because they cannot see that love and all things change like the wind. But pity even more those who die of their fear of loving and who reject love in the name of a greater love that they know not. Neither of these kinds of people know thy law that says, "Whoever drinks of the water that I shall give him will never thirst."

'Pity those who reduce the cosmos to an explanation, God to a magic potion, and humanity to beings with basic needs that must be satisfied, because they never hear the music of the spheres. But have even more pity on those who have blind faith, and who in their laboratories transform mercury into gold, and who are surrounded by their books about the secrets of the Tarot and the power of the pyramids. Neither of these kinds of people know thy law that says, "Whoever does not receive the kingdom of God as a little child will by no means enter it."

'Pity those who see no one but themselves, and for whom others are a blurred and distant scenario as they pass through the streets in their limousines and lock themselves in their air-conditioned penthouse offices, as they suffer in silence the solitude of power. But pity even more those who will do anything for anybody, and are charitable, and seek to win out over evil only through love. For neither of these kinds of people know thy law that says, "Let he who has no sword sell his garment and buy one."

'Have pity, Lord, on we who seek out and dare to take up the sword that you have promised, and who are a saintly and sinful lot scattered throughout the world. Because we do not recognize even ourselves, and often think that we are dressed, but we are nude; we believe that we have committed a crime, when in reality we have saved someone's life. And do not forget in your pity for all of us that we hold the sword with the hand of an angel and the hand of a devil, and that they are both the same hand. Because we are of the world, and we continue to be of the world, and we have need of thee. We will always be in need of thy law that says, "When I sent you without money bag, knapsack, and sandals, you lacked nothing."'

Petrus ended his prayer. As silence prevailed, he gazed out over the field of wheat that surrounded us.

Conquest

We arrived one afternoon at the ruins of an old castle of the Order of the Knights Templar. We sat down to rest, and while Petrus smoked his usual cigarette, I drank a bit of the wine left over from lunch. I studied the view that surrounded us: a few peasant houses, the tower of the castle, the undulating fields ready for sowing. To my right appeared a shepherd, guiding his flock past the walls of the castle, bound for home. The sky was red, and the dust raised by the animals blurred the view, making it look like a dream or a magic vision. The shepherd waved to us, and we waved back.

The sheep passed in front of us and continued down the road. Petrus got to his feet. It was an impressive scene, and I would like to have stayed, but Petrus said, 'Let's go, right away. We've got to hurry.'

'Why?'

'Because I said so. Don't you think we have spent enough time on the Road to Santiago?'

But something told me that his haste had something to do with the magic scene of the shepherd and his sheep.

Two days later we were close to some mountains to the south; their elevation was a relief to the monotony of the immense wheat fields. The area had some natural elevations, but it was well punctuated by the yellow markers that Father Jordi had mentioned. At that point, Petrus, without explanation, began to stray from the markers and to plunge more and more in a northerly direction. When I pointed this out to him, he answered brusquely, saying that he was the guide and that he knew where he was leading me.

After half an hour or so along the new path, I began to hear the sound of tumbling water. All about us were the sun-drenched fields, and I tried to imagine what the sound could be. As we continued, the sound grew louder, and there was no doubt that it was produced by a waterfall. But I could see neither mountains nor falls near us.

Then, as we crested a small rise, we were confronted with one of nature's most extravagant works: a basin opened up in the plateau, deep enough to contain a five-story building, and a stream hurtled to its floor. The immense crater was bordered by luxuriant vegetation, completely different in appearance from the flora we had been passing until then, and it framed the falling water.

'Let's climb down here,' Petrus said.

We began a descent that put me in mind of Jules Verne; it was as if we were descending to the center of the earth. The way was steep and difficult to navigate, and so as not to fall, we were forced to grasp at thorny branches and sharp rocks. When I reached the bottom, my arms and legs were lacerated.

'Isn't this beautiful,' said Petrus, taking no notice of my discomfort.

I agreed. It was an oasis in the desert. The plant life and the rainbow formed by the droplets of water made the basin as beautiful seen from below as from above.

'This is where nature really shows its power,' he said.

'True,' I nodded.

'And it gives us a chance to show our own strength. Let's climb the falls,' said my guide. 'Through the water!'

I looked again at the scene. Now I no longer saw it as an oasis, nor as one of nature's more sophisticated caprices. Instead, I was looking at a wall more than fifty feet high over which the water fell with a deafening force. The small lagoon formed by the cataract was no deeper than a man's height, since the river ran to an opening that probably took it underground. On the wall, there were no protrusions that I could make use of in a climb, and the depth of the pool was not sufficient to break a fall. I was looking at an absolutely impossible task.

I thought of an event from five years ago, during a ritual that had required – like this situation – an extremely dangerous climb. My Master had given me a choice as to whether I wanted to continue or not, I was younger and fascinated by his powers and by the miracles of the Tradition, so I decided to go on. I needed to demonstrate my courage and my bravery.

After I had climbed the mountain for nearly an hour and as I was approaching the most difficult stretch, a wind of unexpected force arose, and to keep myself from falling, I had had to cling with all my strength to the small ledge that supported me. I closed my eyes, expecting the worst, and dug my nails into the rock. A minute later, I was surprised to find that someone had helped me to assume a safer and more comfortable position. I opened my eyes to see that my Master was there at my side.

He made some gestures in the air, and the wind suddenly ceased. With an absolutely mysterious agility, at times seeming to require an exercise in levitation, he descended the mountain and told me to do likewise.

I arrived at the base with my legs trembling and asked him angrily why he hadn't caused the wind to abate before it threatened me.

'Because it was I who ordered the wind to blow,' he answered.

'So it would kill me?'

'No, in order to save you. It would have been impossible for you to climb this mountain. When I asked if you wanted to, I was not testing your courage. I was testing your wisdom.

'You made it into an order, when I had not given one,' said the Master. 'If you were able to levitate yourself, you would not have had a problem. But you wanted to be brave, when it was enough to have been intelligent.'

That day, he told me about Magi who had become insane during the process of illumination and who could no longer distinguish between their own powers and those of their disciples. During my lifetime, I have known some great men in the Tradition. I had gotten to know three great Masters – including my own – who were able to dominate material objects in ways that went far beyond what anyone could imagine. I had witnessed miracles, exact predictions of the future, and knowledge of past incarnations. My Master had spoken of the Falklands War two months before Argentina had invaded the islands. He had described everything in detail and had explained the reasons, on an astral level, for the conflict.

But after that day, I had begun to notice that there were Magi who, in the Master's words, had been 'crazed by the process of illumination.' They were individuals who in almost every way were the equal of their Masters, even with respect to their powers: I saw one of them make a seed germinate in twenty minutes of extreme concentration. But that man and some others had already led many disciples to madness and despair; some of those disciples had had to be committed to mental hospitals, and there was at least one confirmed case of suicide. Those Masters were on the 'blacklist' of the Tradition, but it was impossible to control them, and I know that many of them continue their work even today.

All of this passed through my mind in a fraction of a second as I looked at the waterfall that seemed impossible to scale. I thought of the length of time that Petrus and I had traveled together, of the dog's attack that had left me unhurt, of Petrus's lack of control with the boy who had waited on us in the restaurant, and of Petrus's drinking bout at the wedding celebration. Those events were all I could remember.

'Petrus, there's no way I'm going to climb that waterfall. And for a very simple reason: it's impossible.'

He didn't say a word. He sat down in the grass, and I did the same. We sat there in silence for fifteen minutes. His silence disarmed me, and I took the initiative by beginning to speak.

'Petrus, I don't want to climb because I'll fall. I know that I'm not going to die, because when I saw the face of my death, I also saw the day it will happen. But I could fall and be crippled for the rest of my life.'

'Paulo, Paulo …' He looked at me and smiled. 'You have completely changed. There is in your voice a bit of the love that consumes, and your eyes are shining.'

'Are you going to say that I'm breaking a vow of obedience that I made before setting out on the Road?'

'You are not breaking that vow. You are not afraid, and you are not lazy. Nor should you be thinking that I have given you a useless order. You don't want to climb the falls because you are thinking about the Black

Magi.* You have not broken a vow just because you have used your decision making ability. A pilgrim is never prevented from using that ability.'

I looked again at the cataract and again at Petrus. I was weighing my chances of success in making the climb, and they didn't weigh very much.

'Now, pay attention,' he continued. 'I'm going to climb before you do, without using any gift. And I'm going to make it. If I succeed just by knowing where to place my feet, you will have to climb, too. I am nullifying your freedom to make a decision. If you refuse, after you have seen me make the climb, then you will be breaking your vow.'

Petrus began to take off his sneakers. He was at least ten years older than I, and if he succeeded in the climb, I would have no further excuse. I studied the waterfall and felt my stomach seize up.

But he didn't move. Even though he had taken off his sneakers, he remained seated in the same place. He looked at the sky and said, 'A few kilometers from here, in 1502, the Virgin appeared to a shepherd. Today is the feast day commemorating that event – the Feast of the Virgin of the Road – and I am going to offer my victory

* This is the name given, in the Tradition, to those Masters who have lost their magical contact with their disciples, as just described. This expression is also used to describe Masters who interrupted their learning process after having established dominion only over earthly forces.

to her. I would advise you to do the same thing. Offer a victory to her. Don't offer the pain in your feet or the cuts on your hands from the rocks. Everybody in the world offers only pain as penance. There is nothing wrong with that, but I think she would be happier if, rather than just pain, people would also offer her their joys.'

I was in no condition to speak. I still doubted whether Petrus could climb the wall. I thought the whole thing was a farce, that I was being drawn in by the way he spoke and that he would then convince me to do something I really did not want to do. In the face of these doubts, I closed my eyes for a moment and prayed to the Virgin of the Road. I promised that if Petrus and I were able to climb the wall, I would one day return to this place.

'Everything you have learned up to now makes sense only if it is applied in real life. Don't forget that I described the Road to Santiago to you as the road of the common person; I have said that a thousand times. On the Road to Santiago and in life itself, wisdom has value only if it helps us to overcome some obstacle.

'A hammer would make no sense in the world if there were not nails to be driven. And even given the existence of nails, the hammer would be useless if it only thought, "I can drive those nails with two blows." The hammer has to act. To put itself into the hands of the carpenter and to be used in its proper function.'

I remembered my Master's words at Itatiaia: 'Whoever has the sword must constantly put it to the test, so it doesn't rust in its scabbard.'

'The waterfall is the place where you will put into practice everything you have learned so far,' said my guide. 'There is one thing working in your favor: you know the day on which you are going to die so that fear will not paralyze you when you have to decide quickly where to find a hold. But remember that you are going to have to work with the water and use it to provide what you need. Remember that you have to dig a nail into your thumb if a bad thought takes over. And most important, that you have to find support for yourself in the love that consumes during every minute of the climb, because it is that love which directs and justifies your every step.'

Petrus fell silent. He took off his shirt and his shorts and was completely naked. He went into the cold water of the lagoon, wet himself completely, and spread his arms to the sky. I could see that he was happy; he was enjoying the coldness of the water and the rainbows created by the mist that surrounded us.

'One more thing,' he said, before going in under the falls. 'This waterfall will teach you how to be a Master. I am going to make the climb, but there will be a veil of water between you and me. I will climb without your being able to see where I place my hands and feet.

'In the same way, a disciple such as you can never imitate his guide's steps. You have your own way of living your life, of dealing with problems, and of winning. Teaching is only demonstrating that it is possible. Learning is making it possible for yourself.'

He said nothing else as he disappeared through the veil of the cascade and began to climb. I could see only his outline, as if perceived through frosted glass. But I could see that he was climbing. Slowly and inexorably he moved toward the top. The closer he got to the crest, the more fearful I became, because my time was coming. Finally, the most terrible moment arrived: the moment when he had to come up through the falling water without holding to the sides. The force of the water would surely plunge him back to the ground. But Petrus's head emerged there at the top, and the falling water became his silver mantle. I saw him for just an instant because, with a rapid motion, he threw his body upward and secured himself somehow on top of the plateau, still immersed in the stream of water. Then, I lost sight of him for some moments.

Finally, Petrus appeared on the bank. He was bathed in moisture, brilliant in the sunlight, and laughing.

'Let's go,' he yelled, waving his hands. 'It's your turn.'

It really was my turn. Either I did it, or I forever renounced my sword.

I took all of my clothes off and prayed again to the Virgin of the Road. Then I dived into the lagoon. It was freezing, and my body went rigid with its impact; but I then felt a pleasant sensation, a sensation of being really alive. Without thinking about it, I went straight to the waterfall.

The weight of the water on my head brought me back to a sense of reality, the sense that weakens us at the moment when we most need to have faith in our powers. I could see that the falls had much more force than I had thought and that if the water continued to fall directly onto the top of my head, it would defeat me, even if I kept both feet firmly planted on the bottom of the lagoon. I passed through the falls and stood between the water and the rock, in a space into which my body just fit, glued to the wall. From there, I could see that the task was easier than I had thought.

The water did not beat down here, and what had appeared to me to be a wall with a polished surface was actually a wall with a great many cavities. I was dumbfounded to think that I might have renounced my sword out of fear of the smoothness of the wall when it turned out to be the kind of rock that I had climbed dozens of times. I seemed to hear Petrus's voice saying, 'Didn't I tell you? Once a problem is solved, its simplicity is amazing.'

I began to climb, with my face against the humid rock. In ten minutes I was almost to the top. Only one hurdle remained: the final phase, the place where the water fell over the crest on its trajectory toward the lagoon. The victory I had won in making the climb would be worth nothing if I were not able to negotiate the last stretch that separated me from the open air. This was where the danger lay, and I had not been able to see how Petrus had succeeded. I prayed again to the Virgin of the Road, a Virgin I had never heard of but who was now the object of all my faith and all my hopes for success. I began tentatively to put first my hair and then my entire head up through the water that was rushing over and past me.

The water covered me completely and blurred my vision. I began to feel its impact and held firmly to the rock. I bent my head to create an air pocket that would allow me to breathe. I trusted completely in my hands and feet. My hands had, after all, already held an ancient sword, and my feet had trod the Road to Santiago. They were my friends, and they were helping me. But the noise of the water was deafening, and I began to have trouble breathing. I was determined to put my head through the flow, and for several seconds everything went black. I fought with all my strength to keep my hands and feet anchored to their holds, but the noise of the water seemed to take me to another place. It was a mysterious and distant place where nothing that was happening at that moment was at all important, and it was a place that I could get to if I had the strength. In that place, there would no longer be any need for the superhuman effort it took to keep my hands and feet holding to the rock; there would be only rest and peace.

But my hands and feet did not obey this impulse to surrender. They had resisted a mortal temptation. And my head began to emerge from the stream as gradually as it had entered it. I was overcome by a profound love for my body. It was there, helping me in this crazy adventure of climbing through a waterfall in search of a sword.

When my head came completely through the surface, I saw the bright sun above me and took a deep breath. This renewed my strength, and as I looked about, I could see, just a few inches away, the plateau we had originally walked along – the end of the journey. I had an impulse to throw myself up and grab for something to hold, but I could see nothing to grab through the flowing water. The impulse was strong, but the moment of victory had not yet come, and I had to control myself. I was at the most difficult point in the ascent, with the water beating on my chest, and the pressure was threatening to throw me back to the place below that I had dared to leave in pursuit of my dream.

It was no time to be thinking about Masters or friends, and I could not look to the side to see if Petrus would be able to save me if I should slip. 'He has probably made this climb a million times,' I thought, 'and he knows that here is where I most desperately need help.' But he had abandoned me. Or maybe he hadn't abandoned me, but he was there somewhere behind me, and I couldn't turn to look for him without losing my balance. I had to do it all. I, alone, had to win my victory.

I kept my feet and one hand holding to the rock, while the other hand let go and sought to become one with the water. I didn't want to exert any more effort, because I was already using all of my strength. My hand, knowing this, became a fish that gives itself up but knows where it wants to go. I remembered films from my childhood in which I had seen salmon jumping over waterfalls because they had a goal and they simply had to achieve it.

The arm rose slowly, using the force of the water to its advantage. It finally burst free, and it took on the task of finding a hold and deciding the fate of the rest of my body. Like a salmon in the film, the hand dived into the water atop the crest, searching for a place, a point that would support me in the final leap.

The rock had been polished by centuries of running water. But there must be a handhold: if Petrus had been able to find one, I could, too. I began to feel great pain, because now I knew that I was only one step from success; this is the moment when one's strength begins to flag, and one loses confidence in oneself. On a few occasions in my life I had lost at the last minute – swum across an ocean and drowned in the surf of regret. But I was on the Road to Santiago, and that old experience must not be allowed to repeat itself – I had to win.

My free hand slid along the smooth stone, and the pressure was becoming stronger and stronger. I felt that my other limbs could not hold out and that I was going to begin to cramp. The water was beating on my genitals, too, and the pain was unbearable. Then my free hand suddenly found a hold in the rock. It wasn't a large one, and it was off to the side of where I wanted to rise, but it would serve as a support for my other hand when its turn came. I marked its location mentally, and my free hand returned to its search for my salvation. A few inches from the first hold, I found another.

There it was! There was the place that for centuries had served as a hold for the pilgrims bound for Santiago. I could see this, and I held on with all my strength. The other hand came free, was thrown back by the force of the water, but, in an arc across the sky, reached and found the handhold. With a quick movement, my entire body followed the path opened by my arms, and I threw myself upward.

The biggest and final step had been taken. My whole body came up through the water, and a moment later the savage waterfall had become just a trickle of water, hardly moving. I crawled to the bank and gave in to exhaustion. The sun fell on my body, warming me, and I told myself again that I had won, that I was alive as before when I had stood below in the lagoon. Over the sound of the water, I heard Petrus's approaching footsteps.

I wanted to get up and show how happy I was, but my exhausted body refused.

'Relax, rest a little,' he said. 'Try to breathe slowly.'

I did so and fell into a deep, dreamless sleep. When I awoke, the sun had moved across the sky, and Petrus, already fully dressed, handed me my clothes and said we had to move on.

'I'm very tired,' I answered.

'Don't worry. I am going to show you how to draw energy from everything around you.'

And Petrus taught me the RAM Breathing Exercise.

I did the exercise for five minutes and felt better. I arose, dressed, and grabbed my knapsack.

'Come here,' Petrus said. I went to the edge of the cliff. At my feet, the waterfall rushed by.

'Looking at it from here, it looks a lot easier than it did from down there,' I said.

'Exactly. And if I had shown it to you from here before, you would have been misled. You would have made a poor analysis of your chances.'

I still felt weak, and I repeated the exercise. Shortly, the entire universe about me fell into harmony with me and came into my heart. I asked Petrus why he had not taught me RAM breathing before, since many times I had felt lazy and tired on the Road to Santiago.

'Because you never looked like you felt that way,' he said, laughing. Then he asked me if I still had any of the delicious butter cookies I had bought in Astorga.

The RAM Breathing Exercise

Expel all of the air from your lungs, emptying them as much as you can. Then, inhale slowly as you raise your arms as high as possible. As you inhale, concentrate on allowing love, peace, and harmony with the universe to enter into your body.

Hold the air you have taken in and keep your arms raised for as long as you can, enjoying the harmony between your inner sensations and the outer world. When you reach your limit, exhale all of the air rapidly, as you say the word, 'RAM.'

Repeat this process for five minutes each time you do the exercise.

Madness

For three days we had been making a kind of forced march. Petrus would wake me before daybreak, and we would not end our day's hike before nine in the evening. The only rest stops granted were for quick meals, since my guide had abolished our siesta. He gave the impression that he was keeping to some mysterious schedule that he hadn't shared with me.

What's more, his behavior had changed completely. At first, I thought it had something to do with my hesitation at the waterfall, but later I could see that it was not that. He was irritable with everyone, and he looked at his watch frequently during the day. I reminded him that it was he who had told me that we ourselves create the pace of time.

'You are becoming wiser every day,' he answered. 'Let's see if you can put all of this wisdom into play when it is needed.'

On one afternoon, I was so tired from the pace of our hiking that I simply could not get up. Petrus told me to take my shirt off and settle my spine along the trunk of a nearby tree. I held that position for several minutes and felt much better. He began to explain to me that vegetation, and especially mature trees, are able to transmit harmony when one rests one's nerve centers against a tree trunk. For hours he discoursed on the physical, energetic, and spiritual properties of plants.

Since I had already read all of this somewhere, I didn't worry about taking notes. But Petrus's discourse helped to diminish my feeling that he was irritated with me. Afterward, I treated his silence with greater respect, and he, perhaps guessing correctly at my apprehension, tried to be friendlier whenever his constant bad mood allowed him to do so.

We arrived one morning at an immense bridge, totally out of proportion to the modest stream that coursed below it. It was early on a Sunday morning, and, since the bars and taverns nearby were all closed, we sat down there to eat our breakfast.

'People and nature are equally capricious,' I said, trying to start a conversation. 'We build beautiful bridges, and then Mother Nature changes the course of the rivers they cross.'

'It's the drought,' he said. 'Finish your sandwich, because we have to move along.'

I decided to ask him why we were in such a hurry.

'We have been on the Road to Santiago for a long time. I have already told you that I left a lot of things unattended in Italy, and I have got to get back.'

I wasn't convinced. What he was saying might well be true, but it wasn't the only issue. When I started to question what he had said, he changed the subject.

'What do you know about this bridge?'

'Nothing,' I answered. 'But even with the drought, it's too big. I think the river must have changed its course.'

'As far as that goes, I have no idea,' he said. 'But it is known along the Road to Santiago as the "honorable passage." These fields around us were the site of some bloody battles between the Suevians and the Visigoths, and later between Alphonse III's soldiers and the Moors. Maybe the bridge is oversize to allow all that blood to run past without flooding the city.'

He was making an attempt at macabre humor. I didn't laugh, and he was put off for a moment, but then he continued, 'However, it wasn't the Visigoth hordes or the triumphant cries of Alphonse III that gave this bridge its name. It was another story of love and death.

'During the first centuries of the Road to Santiago, pilgrims, priests, nobles, and even kings came from all over Europe to pay homage to the saint. Because of this, there was also an influx of assailants and robbers. History has recorded innumerable cases of robbery of entire caravans of pilgrims and of horrible crimes committed against lone travelers.'

Just like today, I thought.

'Because of the crimes, some of the nobility decided to provide protection for the pilgrims, and each of the nobles involved took responsibility for protecting one segment of the Road. But just as rivers change their course, people's ideals are subject to alteration. In addition to frightening the malefactors, the knights began to compete with each other to determine who was the strongest and most courageous on the Road. It wasn't long before they began to do battle with each other, and the bandits returned to the Road with impunity.

'This developed over a long period of time until, in 1434, a noble from the city of Leon fell in love with a woman. The man was Don Suero de Quiñones; he was powerful and rich, and he did everything in his power to win his lady's hand in marriage. But this woman – history has forgotten her name – did not even want to know about his grand passion and rejected his request.'

I was dying of curiosity to know what an unrequited love had to do with battles among the knights. Petrus saw that I was interested and said that he would relate the rest of the story only if I finished my sandwich and we began to move along.

'You are just like my mother when I was a child,' I said. But I gulped down the last morsel of bread, picked up my knapsack, and we began to make our way through the sleepy city.

Petrus continued, 'Our gentleman, whose pride had been offended, resolved to do what all men do when they feel themselves to have been rejected: he began a private war. He promised himself that he was going to perform such an important feat that the woman would never forget his name. For months he sought a noble idea that would consecrate his spurned love. And then he heard of the crimes and the battles along the Road to Santiago. That gave him an idea.

'He called together ten of his friends, and they set themselves up in the small city we are passing through right now. He spread the word by means of the pilgrims that he was prepared to remain there for thirty days – and break thirty lances – in order to prove that he was the strongest and boldest of all the knights of the Road. He established himself with his banners, his standards, his pages, and servants, and waited for challengers.'

I could imagine what a picnic that must have been: roast boar, endless supplies of wine, music, stories, and battles. A lively picture came to my mind as Petrus related the rest of the story.

'The bouts began on the tenth of July with the arrival of the first challengers. Quiñones and his companions fought during the day and held huge feasts every night. The contests were always held on the bridge so that no one could flee. During one period, so many challengers came that fires were built along the entire length of the bridge so that the bouts could go on until dawn. All of the vanquished knights were required to swear that they would never again do battle with the others and that from then on, their only mission would be to protect the pilgrims going to Compostela.

'On the ninth of August, the combat ended, and Don Suero de Quiñones was recognized as the bravest and most valiant of all the knights of the Road to Santiago. From that day forward, no one dared to issue challenges of bravery, and the nobles returned to their battle against the only enemy in common, the bandits who assaulted the pilgrims. This epic was later to give rise to the Military Order of Santiago of the Sword.'

We had crossed the small city. I wanted to go back and take another look at the 'honorable passage,' the bridge on which all of that had taken place. But Petrus said that we had to move on.

'And what happened to Don Quiñones?' I asked.

'He went to Santiago de Compostela and placed a golden necklace at San Tiago's shrine; even today it adorns the bust of San Tiago the Lesser.'

'I was asking whether he wound up marrying the lady.'

'Oh, I don't know,' Petrus answered. 'In those days, history was written only by men. With such a battlefield close at hand, who was going to be interested in a love story?'

After telling me the story of Don Suero de Quiñones, my guide went back to his – now – habitual silence, and we went along for two more days without a word. We hardly stopped to rest. On the third day, though, Petrus began to walk more slowly than usual. He said that he was a bit tired from the efforts of the week and that he was too old to continue at that pace. Again I was sure that he was not telling the truth; his face, rather than showing fatigue, revealed an intense preoccupation, as if something very important was about to occur.

We arrived that afternoon at Foncebadon, a large village that was completely in ruins. The houses, built of stone, had slate roofs that had been destroyed by time and the rotting of the wood that supported them. One side of the village gave onto a precipice, and in front of us, behind a mountain peak, was one of the most important landmarks of the Road to Santiago: the Iron Cross. This time it was I who was impatient; I wanted to get to that strange monument, comprised of an immense wooden base, almost thirty feet tall, topped by the Iron Cross. The cross had been left there during the epoch of Caesar's invasion, in homage to Mercury. Observing the pagan tradition, the pilgrims along the Jacobean route were accustomed to leaving stones brought from elsewhere at the base of the cross. I took advantage of the abundance of stones in the abandoned village and picked up a piece of slate.

It was only when I had resolved to move along more quickly that I saw that Petrus was walking more slowly. He examined the ruined houses and the fallen tree trunks and finally decided to sit down in the middle of one of the plazas where there was a wooden cross.

'Let's rest a bit,' he said.

It was early afternoon, so even if we stayed there for an hour there would still be time to reach the Iron Cross before nightfall.

I sat down beside him and gazed at the empty surroundings. Just as rivers change their course, humans also change where they live. The houses were solid and must have lasted for a long time before falling into ruin. It was a pretty place, with mountains in the distance and a valley in front of us. I asked myself what could have happened to cause the people to leave such a place.

'Do you think that Don Suero de Quiñones was crazy?' Petrus asked.

I did not even remember who Don Suero was, and he had to remind me about the 'honorable passage.'

'I don't think he was crazy,' I answered. But I wasn't sure about my answer.

'Well, he was, just as Alfonso, the monk that you met, was. Just as I am, as you can see from the plans that I make. Or you, seeking your sword. Every one of us has the flame of madness burning inside, and it is fed by agape.

'Crazy doesn't mean you want to conquer America or talk to the birds like Saint Francis of Assisi. Even a vegetable vendor on the street corner can show this flame of madness if he likes what he is doing. Agape is grander than our ordinary human concepts, and everyone thirsts for it.'

Petrus told me that I knew how to invoke agape by means of the Blue Sphere Exercise. But in order for agape to flourish, I must not be afraid to change my life. If I liked what I was doing, very well. But if I did not, there was always the time for a change. If I allowed change to occur, I would be transforming myself into a fertile field and allowing the Creative Imagination to sow its seeds in me.

'Everything I have taught you, including agape, makes sense only if you are satisfied with yourself. If you are not, then the exercises you have learned are inevitably going to make you seek change. And if you do not want all of those exercises to work against you, you have to allow change to happen.

'This is the most difficult moment in a person's life – when the person witnesses the good fight and is unable to change and join the battle. When this happens, knowledge turns against the person who holds it.'

I looked at the deserted city of Foncebadon. Maybe all of those people, collectively, had felt the need for a change. I asked whether Petrus had chosen this place purposely in order to say all of this to me.

'I don't know what happened here,' he answered. 'Often people have to accept the changes that destiny forces upon them, but that's not what I'm talking about. I am speaking of an act of will, a concrete desire to do battle against everything that is unsatisfying in one's everyday life.

'On the road of our lives, we always run into problems that are hard to solve – like, for example, passing through a waterfall without letting it make us fall. So you have to allow the Creative Imagination to do its work. In your case, the waterfall was a life-and-death situation, and there wasn't time to consider many options; agape showed you the only way.

'But there are problems in our lives that require us to choose between one way and another. Everyday problems, like a business decision, the breakup of a relationship, a social obligation. Each of these small decisions we have to make, throughout our lives, might represent a choice between life and death. When you leave the house in the morning on your way to work, you might choose one means of transportation that will drop you off safe and sound or another that is going to crash and kill its passengers. This is a radical example of how a simple decision may affect us for the rest of our lives.'

I began to think about myself as Petrus spoke. I had chosen to walk the Road to Santiago in search of my sword. It was the sword that was most important to me now, and I needed somehow to find it. I had to make the right decision.

'The only way to make the right decision is to know what the wrong decision is,' he said after I had mentioned my concern. 'You have to examine the other path, without fear and without being morbid, and then decide.'

It was then that Petrus taught me the Shadows Exercise.

'Your problem is your sword,' he said after he had explained the exercise.

I agreed.

'So do the exercise now. I'm going to take a walk. When I come back, I know that you will have the right solution.'

I remembered how much of a hurry Petrus had been in during the past few days, yet now we were having a prolonged conversation in this abandoned city. It seemed to me that he was trying to gain some time so

The Shadows Exercise

Relax completely.

For five minutes, study the shadows of all of the objects and people around you. Try to identify exactly which part of the object or person is casting a shadow.

For the next five minutes, continue to do this, but at the same time, focus on the problem you are trying to solve. Look for all of the possible wrong solutions to the problem.

Finally, spend five more minutes studying the shadows and thinking about what correct solutions remain. Eliminate them, one by one, until only the single correct solution is left.

that he, too, could make a decision regarding something. This made me excited, and I began to do the exercise.

I did a bit of RAM breathing to put me in harmony with my surroundings. Then I noted on my watch when fifteen minutes would have passed, and I began to look at the shadows all around me – shadows of ruined houses, stones, wood, and the cross behind me. As I studied the shadows, I saw that it was difficult to know exactly what part was casting any given shadow. I had never noticed this before. Some house beams that were straight were transformed into shadows with sharp angles, and an irregular stone cast a shadow with a smoothly rounded form. I did this for ten minutes. The exercise was so fascinating that it was not difficult to concentrate on it. Then I began to think of the wrong solutions to the problem of finding my sword. Many ideas came to mind – I thought about taking a bus to Santiago, and then I thought about phoning my wife and using some sort of emotional trickery to find out where she had placed it.

When Petrus returned, I was smiling.

'So?' he asked.

'I found out how Agatha Christie wrote her mystery novels,' I joked. 'She transformed the hunch that was most wrong into the one that was correct. She must have known about the Exercise of the Shadows.'

Petrus asked where my sword was.

'First I'm going to tell you the most erroneous guess that I came up with as I looked at the shadows: that the sword is somewhere other than on the Road to Santiago.'

'You are a genius. You figured out that we have been walking all this way in order to find your sword. I thought they had told you that already in Brazil.'

'It's being kept in a safe place that my wife could not enter,' I continued. 'I deduced that it's in an absolutely open place but that it has been assimilated so well into its surroundings that it can't be seen.'

This time Petrus didn't smile. I went on:

'And since the most absurd thing would be that it is in a place where there are lots of people, it has to be in some locale that is practically deserted. And most important, and so that the few people who see it don't notice the difference between it and a typical Spanish sword, it must be in a place where no one knows how to distinguish between styles of swords.'

'Do you think it is here?' he asked.

'No, it's not here. The thing that would be most wrong would be to do this exercise at the place where my sword is. I discarded that hunch right away. It must be in a city that is similar to this one, but it cannot be in an abandoned city, because a sword in an abandoned city would attract a lot of attention from pilgrims and passersby. It would wind up as a decoration on the wall of a bar.'

'Very good,' he said, and I could see that he was proud of me – or of the exercise he had taught me.

'There's another thing,' I said.

'What's that?'

'The place that would be most wrong for the sword of a Magus to be left is a profane place. It has to be in a sacred place. Like a church, for example, where no one would dare to steal it. So, in a church in a small city near Santiago, visible to everyone but embedded in its surroundings – that's where my sword is. Starting now, I'm going to visit every church on the Road.'

'You don't have to,' he said. 'When the moment comes, you will know it.'

I had been right!

'Listen, Petrus, why did we hurry for such a long while, when now we're spending so much time in this abandoned city?'

'What would be the answer that is most wrong?'

I glanced at the shadows. He was right. We were there for some reason.

The sun was hidden behind the mountain, but nightfall was still some hours away. I was thinking that the sun was probably shining just then on the Iron Cross. The cross was only a few hundred yards distant, and I really wanted to see it. I also wanted to know why we were waiting around. We had moved along so rapidly for the entire week, and now it seemed to me that the only reason for that must have been that we had to be at this place, on this day, and at this time.

I tried to make conversation to pass the time, but I could see that Petrus was tense and preoccupied. I had already seen Petrus in a bad mood many times, but I could not remember having seen him so tense. And then I remembered that I *had* seen him like this once. It was at breakfast one morning in a small town whose name I could not remember, just before we had run into …

I looked to my left. There he was: the dog. The ferocious dog that had thrown me to the ground, the coward of a dog that had immediately fled afterward. Petrus had promised to help me if we ran into him again, and I turned to my guide. But he had disappeared.

I kept my gaze fixed on the dog's eyes while I frantically tried to think of a way to deal with the situation. Neither of us moved, and I was reminded for a moment of the duel scenes in the ghost towns of Western movies. In those films, no one would ever have dreamed of pitting a man against a dog; it just wouldn't have worked. Yet here I was, confronted with a reality that fiction would have considered too far out.

And there was Legion, so named because he was so many. Nearby stood a deserted house. If I were to bolt suddenly, I could climb to its roof, and Legion could not follow. It seemed absurd that I felt trapped by the physical presence of a dog and all that his presence implied.

As I kept my eyes on him, I immediately rejected the possibility of taking flight. Many times along the Road I had feared this moment, and now here it was. Before I could find my sword, I had to meet with the Enemy and either vanquish him or be defeated by him. I had no choice but to go up against him. If I fled now, I would be falling into a trap. It might be that the dog would not appear again, but I would travel the Road to Santiago de Compostela gripped by fear and apprehension. Ever afterward, I would dream about the dog, fearing his reappearance at any minute and living with dread for the rest of my life.

As I thought about all this, the dog started toward me. I stopped thinking immediately and concentrated only on the battle that was about to begin. Petrus had left, and I was alone. I was frightened. And as I experienced that fear, the dog began to move closer, making a low growling sound. The growl was much more threatening than a loud bark would have been, and I became even more terrified. Seeing the weakness in my eyes, the dog leapt on me.

It was as if a boulder had been thrown at my chest. I fell to the ground, and he began to bite at me. I remembered vaguely that I already knew about my death and that it was not to be like this, but even so, my fear grew, and I was unable to control it. I began to fight just to protect my face and throat. An intense pain in my leg caused me to curl up, and I could see that some flesh had been torn away. I took my hands from my head and throat, reaching toward the wound. The dog, seeing this, began an assault on my face. At that moment, one of my hands felt a rock at my side. I grasped it and began to beat on the dog with all my strength.

He backed off a bit, more surprised than hurt, and I was able to stand. The dog continued to retreat, and the bloody stone gave me courage. I was paying too much respect to the strength of my enemy, and this was a trap. He could not be any stronger than I. He might be more agile, but he could not be stronger, because I weighed more and was taller than he. My fear had lessened, but I wasn't in control of myself yet, and with the rock in my hand, I began to shout at the dog. He withdrew a little further and then suddenly stopped.

It seemed as if he were reading my mind. In my desperation I was beginning to feel strong, and I began to think that it was ridiculous to be fighting a dog. A sense of power suddenly came to me, and a hot wind began to blow across the deserted city. Then I began to be tired of the whole thing; when all was said and done, I had only to batter him once on the head with the stone, and I would have won. I wanted it to be over immediately so that I could dress my wound and put an end to this absurd business of swords and the Strange Road to Santiago.

But this was another trap. The dog hurled himself at me and again pushed me to the ground. This time he evaded the rock easily, biting my hand and causing me to let it go. I began to punch him with my hands, but I was not causing any serious damage. The only thing my blows accomplished was to keep him from biting me even more. His sharp claws began to tear my clothing and my arms, and I saw that it was only a matter of time before he took charge completely.

All of a sudden, I heard a voice from within me. The voice said that if the dog established dominion over me, the fight would be over, and I would be saved: defeated but alive. My leg was aching, and my entire body stung from its lacerations. The voice insisted that I give up, and I recognized whose voice it was: it was Astrain, my messenger, speaking to me. The dog stopped for a moment, as if he had heard the same voice, and once again I felt like leaving the whole thing behind. Astrain had told me in our conversations that many people fail to find the sword in their lives, and what difference did it make? What I wanted to do was go home, be with my wife, have my children, and work at what I liked. Enough of these absurdities, fighting with dogs and climbing waterfalls. This was the second time that this thought had come to me, but the desire to give up was even stronger now, and I was certain that I would surrender.

A sound from the streets of the abandoned city caught the animal's attention. I looked in the direction of the sound and saw a shepherd returning from the fields with his flock. I remembered that I had seen this scene before, in the ruins of an old castle. When the dog spotted the sheep, he jumped away from me and made ready to attack them. This was my salvation.

The shepherd started to yell, and the sheep scattered. Before the dog got completely away, I decided to engage him for another moment or two, just to provide enough time for the animals to flee. I grabbed one of the dog's legs. I had the absurd hope that the shepherd might come to my assistance, and for a moment, my hopes about the sword and the power of RAM returned.

The dog tried to pull away from me. I was no longer the enemy; I was a hindrance. What he wanted now was there in front of him: the sheep. But I continued to grasp the animal's leg, awaiting a shepherd who would not come and suddenly hoping that the sheep would *not* take flight.

That is what saved my soul. An immense feeling of strength infused me. It was no longer the illusion of power, which causes one to become weary of the battle and to want to give in. Astrain whispered to me again, but this time it was something different. He said that I should always confront the world with the same weapons that were used to challenge me. And that I could confront a dog only by transforming myself into a dog.

This was the same craziness that Petrus had talked about that day. I began to feel that I was a dog. I bared my teeth and sounded a low growl, and hatred flowed from the sounds I made. I saw the frightened face of the shepherd off to the side and could sense that the sheep were as terrified of me as they were of the dog.

Legion also saw this and became fearful. Then I attacked him. It was the first time I had done this in our fight. I attacked him with my teeth and my nails, trying to bite the dog in the throat, exactly as I had feared he would do to me. Inside, I felt only a tremendous desire for victory. Nothing else was important. I threw myself on top of the animal and pressed him to the ground. He fought to free himself from the weight of my body, and he clawed at my skin, but I too was biting and scratching. I could sense that if he got out from under me, he would run away, and I did not want that to happen ever again. Today I was going to beat him.

The animal began to show fear in his eyes. Now I was the dog, and he seemed to have been transformed into a man. My old fear was operating in him now. It was so strong that he was able to work his way out from under me, but I corralled him in the basement of one of the abandoned houses. Behind its low slate wall was the precipice, and he had no escape. Right there, he was going to see the face of his death.

I suddenly began to realize that there was something wrong. My thinking was becoming cloudy, and I began to see a gypsy's face with vague images dancing around it. I had turned myself into Legion. This was the source of my power. The many devils had abandoned the poor, frightened dog that a moment from now was going to fall into an abyss, and now they were in me. I felt a terrible desire to destroy the defenseless animal. 'You are the Prince, and they are Legion,' whispered Astrain. But I did not want to be a Prince, and I heard from a distance the voice of my Master. He said insistently that there was a sword to be won. I had to resist for one more minute. I should not kill that dog.

I looked over at the shepherd. His look confirmed what I was thinking. He, too, was now more frightened of me than of the dog.

I began to feel dizzy, and the scene began to spin. I could not allow myself to faint. If I fainted now, Legion would have won. I had to find a solution. I was no longer fighting against an animal but against the force that possessed me. I felt my legs beginning to weaken, and I leaned against a wall, but it gave way under my weight. Among the stones and bits of wood, I fell with my face in the dirt.

The earth. Legion was the earth and the fruits of the earth – the good fruits of the earth and the bad, but of the earth. His house was in the earth, and there he ruled the earth or was ruled by it. Agape exploded within me, and I dug my nails into the earth. I screamed, and the scream was the same as I had heard the first time the dog and I had met. I felt Legion pass through my body and descend into the earth. Within me was agape, and Legion did not want to be eaten by the love that consumes. This was my will, the will that had made me fight with my remaining strength against fainting; it was the will of agape residing in my soul and resisting. My entire body trembled.

Legion plummeted into the earth. I began to vomit, but I felt that it was agape, growing and exiting through all of my pores. My body continued to tremble, and a long time later I sensed that Legion had returned to his realm.

I could feel his last vestige pass out through my fingers. I sat on the ground, wounded and exhausted, and looked at the absurd scene in front of me: a dog, bleeding and waving his tail, and a terrified shepherd staring at me.

'It must have been something you ate,' said the shepherd, not wanting to believe what he had seen. 'But now that you've vomited, you will feel better.'

I nodded my head. He thanked me for having controlled 'my' dog and went his way down the road with his sheep.

Petrus appeared but said nothing. He tore off a strip of his shirt and made a tourniquet for my leg, which was bleeding badly. He told me to check the rest of my body, and I replied that there was nothing serious.

'You look awful,' he said, smiling. His good mood seemed to have returned. 'We can't visit the Iron Cross with you looking like that. There are probably tourists there, and they would be frightened.'

I didn't pay any attention to him. I got up, brushed off the dust, and saw that I could walk. Petrus suggested that I do the RAM Breathing Exercise, and he picked up my knapsack. I did the exercise and returned once again to a sense of harmony with the world. In half an hour, I would be at the Iron Cross.

And someday, Foncebadon was going to rise from its ruins. Legion had left a lot of power there.

Command and Obedience

Petrus was carrying me as we arrived at the Iron Cross; my leg wound prevented me from walking. When he realized the extent of the damage done by the dog, he decided that I should rest until the wound had healed enough for us to continue along the Strange Road to Santiago. Nearby there was a village that provided shelter for pilgrims who were overtaken by nightfall before crossing the mountains, and Petrus found us two rooms in the home of a blacksmith.

My haven had a small veranda, an architectural feature we hadn't seen previously along the Road. From it, I could see the range of mountains we would have to cross sooner or later in order to reach Santiago. I fell into bed and slept until the following day; although I felt slightly feverish when I awoke, I also felt better.

Petrus brought some water from the fountain that the villagers called 'the bottomless well,' and he bathed my wounds. In the afternoon, he came to my room with an old woman who lived nearby. They placed several different types of herbs on the wounds and lacerations, and the woman made me drink some bitter tea. Petrus insisted that I lick the wounds until they had completely closed. I can still remember the sweet, metallic flavor of my blood; it nauseated me, but my guide told me that my saliva was a powerful disinfectant.

The fever returned during the second day. Petrus and the old woman again plied me with the tea, and they again put the herbs on my wounds. But the fever, although it was not high, continued. My guide decided to go to a military base nearby to see if he could get some bandages, since there was no place in the entire village where gauze or adhesive tape was available.

Several hours later, Petrus returned with the bandages. He was accompanied by a young medical officer, who insisted on knowing where the animal was that had attacked me.

'From the type of bite you have, the animal was rabid,' he told me.

'No, no,' I said. 'I was just playing with him, and it got out of control. I have known the dog for a long time.'

The medical officer was not convinced. He insisted that I take an antirabies vaccine, and I was forced to let him administer at least one dose or else I would have been transferred to the base hospital. Afterward, he again asked where the animal was.

'In Foncebadon,' I answered.

'Foncebadon is a city in ruins. There are no dogs there,' he said, with an air of having found out the lie.

I began to moan as though I were in pain, and Petrus led the young officer out of the room. But he left everything we would need: clean bandages, adhesive tape, and a styptic compound.

Petrus and the old woman refused to use the compound. They bound the wounds with gauze and herbs instead. This made me happy, because it meant that I would no longer have to lick the places where the dog had bitten me. During the night, they both knelt at my bedside and, with their hands placed on my body, prayed aloud for me. I asked Petrus what he was doing, and he made a vague reference to the divine graces and the Road to Rome. I wanted him to tell me more, but he said nothing else.

Two days later, I had recuperated completely. That morning, I looked out my window and saw some soldiers conducting a search of the houses nearby and of the hills around the village. I asked one of them what was happening.

'There is a rabid dog somewhere around here,' he answered.

That afternoon, the blacksmith in whose rooms we were staying came to me and asked that I leave the town as soon as I was able to travel. The story had spread among the townspeople, and they were fearful that I would become rabid and transmit the disease to others. Petrus and the old woman began to argue with the blacksmith, but he was adamant. At one point, he even asserted that he had seen a trickle of foam at the comer of my mouth while I was sleeping.

There was no way to convince him that all of us drool a bit in our sleep. That night, Petrus and the woman prayed incessantly over me, and the next day, limping somewhat, I was once again on the Strange Road to Santiago.

I asked Petrus if he had been worried about my recovery.

'There is an understanding about the Road to Santiago that I have not told you about before,' he said. 'Once a pilgrimage has begun, the only acceptable excuse for interrupting it is illness. If you had not been able to recover from your wounds and your fever had continued, it would have been an omen, telling us that our pilgrimage had to end there.'

But he added, with some pride, that his prayers had been answered. And I was certain that the outcome had been as important for him as it was for me.

The Road was downhill now, and Petrus pointed out that it would be that way for the next two days. We had returned to our usual schedule, with a siesta every afternoon at the time when the sun was fiercest. Because of my bandages, Petrus carried my knapsack. We were no longer in a hurry: the encounter we had been rushing toward was over.

My disposition improved with every hour, and I was quite proud of myself; I had climbed a waterfall and defeated the demon of the Road. All that remained was the most important task: to find my sword. I mentioned this to Petrus.

'Your victory was beautiful, but you failed in the most critical sense,' he said, throwing a deluge of cold water over me.

'What do you mean?'

'Knowing the right moment for the encounter. I had to hurry us along, setting a pace that was demanding, and the only thing you could think about was that we were after your sword. What good is a sword if you don't know where you are going to run into your enemy?'

'The sword is the instrument of my power,' I answered.

'You are too preoccupied with your power,' he said. 'The waterfall, the RAM practices, the dialogues with your messenger – they all made you forget that there was your enemy to vanquish. And forget that you had an impending encounter with him. Before your hand can wield the sword, you have to discover where your enemy is and how to deal with him. The sword only strikes a blow, but the hand is already victorious or defeated before the blow is delivered.

'You defeated Legion without your sword. There is a secret in this search, and it is a secret you have not yet learned. If you do not do so, you will never find what you are looking for.'

I didn't answer him. Every time I began to feel that I was getting close to my objective, Petrus insisted on reminding me that I was just a simple pilgrim and that there was always something else I needed in order to find what I was looking for. The happiness I had been feeling a few minutes before we began the conversation now disappeared completely.

Once again I was starting out on the Strange Road to Santiago, and I was totally discouraged. Along the same Road that I was walking, millions of souls had passed during the past twelve centuries, going to and returning from Santiago de Compostela. In their case, getting to where they had wanted to go had only been a matter of time. In my case, the traps set by the Tradition were forever placing another obstacle in my path and creating new tests for me.

I told Petrus that I was growing tired, and we sat down in the shade. There were huge wooden crosses along the side of the road. Petrus put the two knapsacks on the ground and spoke again: 'Our enemy always represents our weaker side. This may be a fear of physical pain, but it may also be a premature sense of victory or the desire to abandon the fight because we define it as not being worth the effort.

'Our enemy joins the battle only because he knows that he can hurt us – and hurt us in exactly the spot where our pride tells us that we are most invincible. During the fight, we always try to protect our weak spot, so the enemy strikes at the unguarded side – the side in which we have the most confidence. And we wind up defeated because we allow what should never be allowed: we let the enemy choose how the battle will be waged.'

Everything Petrus was describing had happened during my fight with the dog. Yet I told him that I could not accept the idea that I had enemies and that I had to do battle with them. I said that when Petrus had spoken of the good fight, I had thought that he had been talking about fighting for achievements in one's life.

'That's right,' he said. 'But that is not all the good fight is. Going to war is not a sin. It is an act of love. The enemy develops us and sharpens us, as the dog did with you.'

'OK, I understand that. But let's get back to what we were talking about before. Why is it that you never seem to be satisfied with what I do? I have the impression that you always think I am going about things the wrong way. And weren't you about to tell me the secret of my sword?'

Petrus said that this was something I should have learned before beginning the pilgrimage. And he went on about the enemy.

'Our enemy is part of agape, there to test our grip, our will, and our handling of the sword. He was placed in our lives – and we in his – with a purpose. And that purpose has to be met. So to flee from the battle is the worst thing that could happen. It is worse than losing the fight, because we can always learn something from defeat; if we flee, all we do is declare that our enemy has won.'

I said I was surprised to hear him say that; it amazed me to hear a man who seemed to feel so close to Jesus talk about violence in this way.

'Think about why Jesus needed Judas so,' he said. 'He had to choose an enemy, or his battle here on earth could not have been glorified.'

The wooden crosses along the road testified to how that glory had been achieved: with blood, treason, and desertion. I got up and said I was ready to move on.

As we walked, I asked him what, in a battle situation, was a person's greatest source of strength in trying to defeat the enemy.

'Your present. We defend ourselves best through what we are doing right now, because that is where agape and the will to win, through enthusiasm, are.

'And there's another thing I want to make very clear: the enemy rarely represents evil. He is an everyday presence, and it is he that keeps our sword from rusting in its scabbard.'

I remembered that once, when we were building a summer house, my wife had decided suddenly to change the location of one of the rooms. It had been my job to give this disagreeable news to the builder. I had called him, a man of about seventy years of age, and told him what I wanted. He had looked at the plan, thought about it, and came up with an even better solution, using a wall that he had already begun to raise. My wife had loved the idea.

Maybe it was this that Petrus was trying to describe in a more complicated way: that we have to use the thrust of what we are doing right now to defeat the enemy.

I told him the story about the builder.

'Life always teaches us more than the Road to Santiago does,' he answered. 'But we don't have much faith in what life teaches us.'

There were crosses all along this part of the Jacobean route. They were made of such massive, heavy wood that the pilgrim who put them there must have had an almost superhuman strength. A cross had been placed every thirty meters for as far as I could see. I asked Petrus what their significance was.

'An ancient and obsolete instrument of torture,' he said.

'But why are they here?'

'They must have been some kind of pledge. How should I know?'

We stopped in front of one of them that had toppled over.

'Maybe the wood rotted,' I said.

'It's the same wood as all the others. And none of the others rotted.'

'Then it must not have been sunk into the earth firmly enough.'

Petrus stopped and looked around. He put his knapsack on the ground and sat down. We had stopped to rest only a few minutes before, so I couldn't understand what he was doing. Instinctively, I looked around, expecting to see the dog.

'You defeated the dog,' he said, knowing what I was thinking. 'Don't worry about the ghosts of the dead.'

'Well, then, why are we stopping?'

Petrus made a gesture that told me to be quiet, and I did not say anything for several minutes. I felt the old fear of the dog and decided to remain standing, hoping Petrus would say something.

'What do you hear?' he asked me.

'Nothing. The silence.'

'We are not smart enough to be able to listen to the silence! We are just human beings, and we don't even know how to listen to our own ramblings. You have never asked me how I knew that Legion was about to arrive. Now I will tell you how: by listening. The sound began many days before, when we were still in Astorga. Starting then, I began to move along more quickly, because all the indications were that we were going to meet up with him in Foncebadon. You heard the same sound as I, but you were not listening.

'Everything is contained in sounds – the past, the present, and the future. The person who does not know how to listen will never hear the advice that life offers us all the time. And only the person who listens to the sounds of the moment is able to make the right decisions.'

Petrus bade me sit down and forget about the dog. He said that he was going to teach me one of the easiest and most important practices of the Road to Santiago.

And he explained the Listening Exercise to me.

'Do it right now,' he said.

I began to perform the exercise. I heard the wind and a woman's voice far in the distance, and at one

The Listening Exercise

Relax. Close your eyes.

Try for several minutes to concentrate on all of the sounds you hear in your surroundings, as if you were hearing an orchestra playing its instruments.

Little by little, try to separate each sound from the others. Concentrate on each one, as if it were the only instrument playing. Try to eliminate the other sounds from your awareness.

When you do this exercise every day, you will begin to hear voices. First, you will think that they are imaginary. Later, you will discover that they are voices of people from your past, present, and future, all of them participating with you in the remembrance of time.

This exercise should be performed only when you already know the voice of your messenger.

Do this exercise for ten minutes at a time.

point I sensed that a branch was being broken. It was not a difficult exercise, and I was fascinated by its simplicity. I put my ear to the ground and began to listen to the muted sounds of the earth. After a few moments, I began to separate the sounds from each other: the sound of the leaves rustling, the sound of the voice in the distance, and the noise of the beating of the wings of birds. An animal grunted, but I could not identify what kind of beast it was. The fifteen minutes I spent on the exercise flew by.

'After a while, you will see that this exercise will help you to make the right decision,' Petrus said, without asking me what I had heard. 'Agape speaks to you through the Blue Sphere Exercise, but it also speaks to you through your sight, your sense of touch, through scents, and your heart, and your hearing. A week from now, at the most, you will begin to hear voices. At first, they will be timid, but before long they are going to begin to tell you things that are important. Be careful, though, with your messenger. He is going to try to confuse you. However, you already know the sound of his voice, so he will no longer be a threat.'

Petrus asked if I had heard the joyful call of an enemy, or an invitation offered by a woman, or the secret of my sword.

'I just heard the voice of a woman in the distance,' I said. 'But it was a farmer's wife calling to her child.'

'Well, look at that cross there, and see if you can raise it with your thoughts.'

I asked him what such an exercise would mean.

'It means having faith in your thoughts,' he responded.

I sat down on the ground in a yoga position. I was certain that after everything I had accomplished with the dog and with the waterfall, I was going to be able to do this, too. I fixated on the cross. I imagined myself leaving my body, grasping the cross, and raising it using my astral body. On the road of the Tradition, I had already performed some of these small 'miracles.' I had been able to shatter glasses and porcelain statues and to move objects along the surface of a table. It was an easy magic trick, and even though it did not signify any great power, it was useful in winning over nonbelievers. I had never tried it, though, with an object the size and weight of the cross. But if Petrus had commanded that I do so, I felt I would know how to make it happen.

For half an hour I tried everything I could. I used astral displacement and suggestion. I remembered the power my Master had over the force of gravity, and I tried to repeat the words that he always used on such occasions. Nothing happened. I was concentrating completely, but the cross did not budge. I invoked Astrain, and he appeared between the columns of fire. But when I spoke to him about the cross, he said that he detested crosses.

Petrus finally shook me to bring me out of my trance.

'Come on, this is becoming irritating,' he said. 'Since you can't do it by thinking, put the cross upright with your hands.'

'With my hands?'

'Do it!'

I was startled. Suddenly the man in front of me had become nasty, very different from the person who had cared for my wounds. I didn't know what to say or do.

'Do it!' he repeated. 'I am ordering you to do it!'

There I was, with my arms and hands wrapped in bandages because of the dog's attack. I had just been through the Listening Exercise, but I couldn't believe what I was hearing from Petrus. Without saying anything, I showed him my bandages. But he continued to look coldly at me, not changing his expression in the least. He expected me to obey him. The guide and friend who had accompanied me all this time, who had taught me the RAM practices and told me the beautiful stories about the Road to Santiago, seemed no longer to be there. In his place I saw a man who regarded me as a slave and had ordered me to do something that was stupid.

'What are you waiting for?' he asked.

I remembered the waterfall experience. I recalled that on that day I had had some doubts about Petrus but that then he had been generous with me. He had demonstrated his love and had kept me from giving up on my sword. I could not understand how the same person who had been so kind could be so harsh now.

He suddenly seemed to represent the very thing that the human race was trying to put behind it – the oppression of one person by another.

'Petrus, I …'

'Do it, or the Road to Santiago ends right here!'

I was scared again. At that moment, I was more frightened than I had been at the waterfall; I was more fearful of him than of the dog that had terrorized me for so long. I prayed that a signal would come to me from somewhere in our surroundings, that I would see or hear something that would explain his senseless command. But we were engulfed in silence. I either had to obey Petrus or forget about the sword. Once again, I raised my bandaged arms, but he sat down on the ground, waiting for me to carry out his orders.

So I decided to obey him.

I went to the cross and tried to budge it with my foot to test its weight. It hardly moved. Even if my hands had been in good shape, I would have had a very difficult time trying to lift it, and I knew that with my hands bound as they were, the task would be almost impossible. But I was going to comply. I was going to die in the attempt, if that was necessary; I was going to sweat blood, as Jesus had when he had had to carry the same kind of burden. But Petrus was going to perceive the seriousness of my effort, and perhaps that would touch him in some way and he would free me from the test.

The cross had broken at its base, but it was still attached to it. I had no knife with which to cut through the fibers. Forgetting about my pain, I put my arms around the cross and tried to wrench it from the shattered base, without using my hands. The wood abraded the lacerations on my arms, and I cried out in pain. I looked at Petrus, and he was completely impassive. I resolved that I would not cry out again. From that moment on, I would stifle any such demonstration.

I knew that my immediate problem was not to move the cross but to free it from its base. Afterward, I would have to dig a hole and push the cross into it. I found a stone with an edge to it and, ignoring the pain, began to pound at the wooden fibers.

The pain was terrible and grew worse with every blow, and the fibers were parting very slowly. I had to give up that approach right away, before my wounds reopened and the whole effort became impossible. I decided to work at it more slowly so that I could accomplish the task without succumbing to the pain. I took off my shirt, wrapped it around my hand, and went back to the job with this additional protection. The idea was a good one: the first fiber parted, and then the second. The stone was losing its edge, so I looked around for another. Each time I paused, I had the feeling that I would not be able to start again. I gathered several sharp stones and used them, one after the other, so that the pain in the hand I was working with was bearable. Almost all of the fibers had been cut, but the main one still held firm. The pain in my hand was increasing, and abandoning the idea of working slowly,

I began to strike at the wood frantically. I knew that I was coming close to the point where the pain would make it impossible to continue. It was just a matter of time until this happened, and I had to make good use of that time. I was sawing and pounding now, and something sticky between my skin and the bandages was making the work even more difficult. It is probably blood, I thought, but then I put it out of my mind. I gritted my teeth, struck harder at the fiber, and it seemed about to break. I was so excited that I stood up and delivered a blow with all my strength to the wood that was causing all my suffering.

With a groan, the cross fell to the side, freed from its base.

My joy lasted only for a few moments. My hand was throbbing violently, and I had only begun the job. I looked over at Petrus and saw that he was sleeping. I stood there for a time, trying to figure out some way of fooling him, of putting the cross upright without his noticing it.

But that was exactly what Petrus wanted: that I raise the cross. And there was no way to deceive him, because the task depended solely on me.

I looked at the ground – the dry, yellow earth. Once again, stones would be my only tools. I could not work anymore with my right hand because it hurt too much, and there was that sticky substance under the bandage that worried me. I carefully unwrapped the shirt from the bandages; blood was staining the gauze – and this was a wound that had almost healed. Petrus was a monster!

I found a different kind of stone, one that was heavier and more resistant. Rolling the shirt around my left hand, I began to beat at the earth, trying to dig a hole at the foot of the cross. My initial progress was good, but it was soon slowed by the hardness and dryness of the ground. I kept digging, but the hole seemed to stay the same depth. I decided that I would not make the hole very wide so that the cross would fit into it without wobbling, but this made it more difficult to remove the dirt from the excavation. My right hand had stopped hurting as much as it had, but the coagulated blood made me nauseated and anxious. I was not used to working with my left hand, and the stone kept slipping from my grip.

I dug forever! Every time the stone beat on the ground, and every time I put my hand into the hole to remove some dirt, I thought of Petrus. I looked over at him, dozing peacefully, and I hated him from the bottom of my heart. Neither the noise nor my hatred appeared to disturb him. 'He must have his reasons,' I said to myself, but I could not understand the debasement and humiliation he was inflicting on me. I saw his face in the earth I was pounding, and the rage I was feeling helped me to dig the hole deeper. Again, it was just a matter of time: sooner or later I was going to win.

As I thought about this, the rock hit something solid and sprang back. This was my worst fear. After all that work, I had run into a stone that was too big for me to continue.

I stood up, wiping the sweat from my face, and began to think. I didn't have enough strength to move the cross to another place. I couldn't start again from the beginning because my left hand, now that I had stopped, felt dead. This was worse than pain, and it really scared me. I looked at my fingers, and I was able to move them, but instinct told me that I shouldn't punish the hand anymore.

I looked at the hole. It wasn't deep enough to hold the cross erect.

'The wrong answer will indicate the right one.' I remembered the Shadows Exercise and what Petrus had said then. It was also then that he had told me that the RAM practices would make sense only if I could apply them in my daily life. Even in a situation as absurd as the present one, the RAM practices should be of some use.

'The wrong answer will indicate the right one.' The impossible solution would be to try to drag the cross to a different place; I no longer had the strength to do that. It was also impossible to try digging deeper into the ground.

So if the impossible answer was to go deeper into the earth, the possible answer was to raise the earth. But how?

And suddenly, all of my love for Petrus was restored. He was right. I could raise the earth!

I began to collect all the stones nearby and placed them around the hole, mixing them with the earth I had removed. With great effort, I lifted the foot of the cross a little and supported it with stones to raise it higher off the ground. In half an hour, the ground was higher, and the hole was deep enough.

Now I just had to get the cross into the hole. It was the last step, and I had to make it work. One of my hands was numb, and the other was giving me a great deal of pain. My arms were wrapped in bandages. But my back was all right; it had just a few scratches. If I could lie down beneath the cross and raise it bit by bit, I would be able to slide it into the hole.

I stretched out on the ground, feeling the dust in my nose and eyes. With the hand that was numb, I raised the cross a fraction and slid underneath it. Carefully, I adjusted my position so that its trunk rested squarely on my back. I felt its weight and knew that it would be heavy to lift but not impossible. I thought about the Seed Exercise, and very slowly I squirmed into a fetal position, balancing the cross on my back. Several times I thought it was going to fall, but I was working slowly; I was able to sense the direction it might take and correct for it by repositioning my body. I finally achieved the position I wanted, with my knees in front of me and the cross balanced. For a moment, the foot of the cross shook on the pile of stones, but it did not fall out of place.

'It's a good thing I don't have to save the universe,' I thought, oppressed by the weight of the cross and everything it represented. A profoundly religious feeling took possession of me. I remembered that another person had carried the cross on his shoulders and that his damaged hands had not been able to free themselves from the wood or the pain as mine could. This religious feeling was loaded down with pain, but I forgot about it immediately because the cross began to shake again.

Then, slowly raising myself up, I began a rebirth. I couldn't look behind me, and sound was my only means of orientation. But just a while ago I had learned how to listen to the world, as if Petrus had guessed that I was going to need this kind of knowledge. I felt the weight of the cross and sensed that the stones were accommodating each other. The cross rose bit by bit, as if to help me in this test. It was as if the cross, itself, wanted to return to its position, framing that section of the Road to Santiago.

One final push was all that was needed. If I could get into a seated position, the trunk of the cross would slide down my back into the hole. One or two of the stones had been dislodged, but the cross was now helping me, since its foot remained in place where I had built up the wall. Finally, a pull on my back indicated that the base was free. It was the final moment, just as at the waterfall when I had had to fight my way through the current: the most difficult moment, because it is then that we fear failure and want to give up before it occurs. Once again I sensed how absurd the task was, trying to raise a cross when all I really wanted to do was find my sword. But none of these thoughts was important. With a sudden thrust, I raised my back, and the cross slid into place. At that moment I recognized once again that fate had been directing the work I had done.

I stood there expecting the cross to fall in the other direction, scattering the stones I had placed. Then I thought that maybe my push had not been strong enough and that the cross was going to fall back on top of me. But what I heard was the muffled sound of something hitting against the bottom of the hole.

I turned carefully. The cross was upright, and it was still trembling from the impact. Some stones were rolling down their slope, but the cross was not going to fall. I quickly put the stones back in place and embraced the cross so that it would stop wavering. I felt alive and hot, certain that the cross had been my friend throughout all of my work. I stepped away slowly, improving the placement of the stones with my feet.

I stood there admiring my work for a long time, until my wounds began to hurt. Petrus was still asleep. I went over to him and nudged him with my foot.

He awoke with a start and looked at the cross.

'Very good,' was all that he said. 'In Ponferrada, we will change the bandages.'

The Tradition

'I would rather have lifted a tree. That cross on my back had me thinking that my search for wisdom was going to be the death of me.'

Looking at my surroundings, my words rang a bit hollow. The cross episode was already history, as if it had happened a long time ago and not just the previous day. It had no relation to the black marble bathroom, the warmth of the water in the hot tub, or the crystal goblet of Rioja wine that I was enjoying. I could not see Petrus, who was in his own bedroom in the luxury suite we had rented in a first-class hotel.

'Why the cross?' I insisted.

'It wasn't easy to convince the man at the front desk that you weren't a beggar,' he yelled from his room.

He was changing the subject, and I knew from experience that it would do no good to press the matter. I got up and put on trousers, a clean shirt, and fresh bandages. I had removed the old ones very carefully, expecting to find open wounds, but the scabs had only broken away from the skin slightly and allowed some blood to ooze out. A new scab had already formed, and I was feeling restored and happy.

We had dinner at the hotel restaurant. Petrus asked for the specialty of the house – a Valencia paella – which we ate in silence. After dinner, he suggested a walk.

We left the hotel and walked in the direction of the railroad station. He was in his now-habitual laconic state and said nothing throughout our entire stroll. We came to a train yard, filthy and smelling of oil, and he sat down on the steps of a gigantic locomotive.

'Let's stop here,' he said.

I didn't want to get oil stains on my pants, so I decided to stand. I asked him if he wouldn't prefer to walk to the main square of Ponferrada.

'The Road to Santiago is about to end,' said my guide, 'and since our reality is a lot more similar to these railroad cars, stinking of oil, than to the bucolic retreats we have encountered during our journey, it is better that today's conversation happen here.'

Petrus told me to take off my sneakers and my shirt. Then he loosened the bandages on my arms, leaving them freer to move. But he left those on my hands as they were.

'Don't worry,' he said. 'You are not going to need your hands for this, at least not to hold anything.'

He was more serious than usual, and his tone of voice surprised me. Something important was about to happen.

Petrus sat down again on the steps of the locomotive and looked at me for a long time. Then he said, 'I am not going to say anything about yesterday's episode. You will discover for yourself what it means, and this will happen only if someday you decide to walk the Road to Rome – the Road of the graces and miracles. I want to tell you just one thing: people who consider themselves to be wise are often indecisive when command is called for and rebellious when they are called upon to obey. They are ashamed to give orders and consider it dishonorable to receive them. Don't ever be that way.

'In the room, you said that the path to wisdom leads to sacrifice. That is wrong. Your learning period did not end yesterday: you still have to find your sword and learn its secret. The RAM practices allow us to engage in the good fight and to have a better chance at winning in life. The experience you had yesterday was only one of the tests along the Road – it was part of the preparation for the Road to Rome. It saddens me that you thought that it might have been the death of you.'

He really sounded saddened. I realized that throughout all the time we had spent together, I had always expressed doubt regarding what he was teaching me. I was not a strong, humble Castaneda receiving his teachings from Don Juan; I was an arrogant and fractious man in my approach to the simple RAM practices. I wanted to say this to Petrus, but I knew that it was too late.

'Close your eyes,' Petrus said. 'Do the RAM Breathing Exercise, and try to harmonize yourself with this iron, this machinery, and this smell of oil. This is our world.

You should open your eyes only when I have completed teaching you an exercise.'

I closed my eyes, concentrated on the RAM breathing, and felt my body begin to relax. I could hear the noises of the city, some dogs barking in the distance, and the sound of voices in argument not far from where we were. Suddenly, I began to hear Petrus's voice singing an Italian song recorded by Pepino Di Capri that had been a hit when I was a teenager. I didn't understand the words, but the melody brought back happy memories and helped me to reach a state of tranquillity.

'Some time ago,' he began, when he had stopped singing, 'as I was working on a project that I had to deliver to the mayor's office in Milan, I received a message from my Master. Someone had gone all the way to the end of the road of the Tradition and had not received his sword. I was supposed to guide him along the Road to Santiago.

'I was not surprised at this: I had been expecting such a summons at any time, because I had not yet paid my dues. I had to guide a pilgrim along the Milky Way, just as I had once been guided. But I was nervous because it was the first and only time that I would do this, and I did not know how to carry out my mission.'

Petrus's words really surprised me. I thought that he had been a guide dozens of times.

'You came here, and I guided you,' he continued. 'I must confess that in the beginning it was very hard, because you were much more interested in the intellectual implications of the teachings than in the true meaning of the Road – the Road of the common people. After the encounter with Alfonso, we developed a much stronger, more intense relationship, and I began to believe that I would be able to teach you the secret of your sword. But this did not happen, and now you will have to learn it for yourself during the little time you have left.'

This conversation was making me nervous, and I was losing my concentration on the RAM Breathing Exercise. Petrus must have noticed, because he began to sing the song again and stopped only when I was once again relaxed.

'If you discover the secret and find your sword, you will also discover the face of RAM, and you will have the power. But that is not all: in order to achieve total wisdom, you will have to walk the other three Roads, including the secret one, and the secret Road will not be revealed to you, even by someone who has walked it. I am telling you this because we are going to see each other only one more time.'

My heart stopped, and involuntarily, I opened my eyes. Petrus was glowing with the kind of brilliance I had only seen around my Master.

'Close your eyes!' he barked, and I immediately obeyed. But I was very upset, and I could not concentrate anymore. My guide started to sing the Italian song again, and only after a while was I able to relax.

'Tomorrow you are going to receive a note telling you where I am. I will be at a group initiation, a ritual of honor in the Tradition. It is a ritual in honor of all of the men and women who, down through the centuries, have helped to keep alive the flame of wisdom, of the good fight, and of agape. You will not be able to speak to me. The place where we will meet is secret. It is bathed in the blood of all those who have walked the road of the Tradition and who, even with their swords sharpened, were unable to brighten the darkness. But their sacrifice was not in vain, and the proof that it was not is that, centuries later, those who have walked different roads will be there to pay them tribute. This is important, and you should never forget it: even if you become a Master, you have to realize that your road is only one of many that lead to God. Jesus once said, "In my Father's house, there are many mansions."'

Petrus repeated that after tomorrow, I would not see him again.

'On some future day, you will receive a message from me, asking you to lead someone along the Road to Santiago, just as I have led you. Then you will be able to experience the great secret of the journey – a secret that I am going to reveal to you now, but only through words. It is a secret that has to be experienced to be understood.'

There was a prolonged silence. I began to think that he had changed his mind or that he had left the train yard. I felt an enormous desire to open my eyes to see what was happening, but I forced myself to concentrate on the RAM breathing.

'The secret is the following,' Petrus said. 'You can learn only through teaching. We have been together here on the Road to Santiago, but while you were learning the practices, I learned the meaning of them. In teaching you, I truly learned. By taking on the role of guide, I was able to find my own true path.

'If you succeed in finding your sword, you will have to teach the Road to someone else. And only when that happens – when you accept your role as a Master – will you learn all the answers you have in your heart. Each of us knows the answers, even before someone tells us what they are. Life teaches us lessons every minute, and the secret is to accept that only in our daily lives can we show ourselves to be as wise as Solomon and as powerful as Alexander the Great. But we become aware of this only when we are forced to teach others and to participate in adventures as extravagant as this one has been.'

I was hearing the most unexpected farewell in my life. The person with whom I had had the most intense bond was saying good-bye right there in midjourney – in an oily-smelling train yard, with me forced to keep my eyes closed.

'I don't like saying good-bye,' Petrus continued. 'I am Italian, and I am very emotional. But according to the law of the Tradition, you must find your sword alone. This is the only way that you will believe in your own power. I have passed on to you everything that I have to give. The only thing left is the Dance Exercise, which I am going to teach you now; you should perform it tomorrow at the ritual.'

He was silent for a while, and then he spoke:

'May that which is glorified be glorified in the Lord. You may open your eyes.'

Petrus was still sitting on the locomotive. I did not want to say anything, because I am Brazilian and also emotional. The mercury lamp providing us with light began to flutter, and a train whistled in the distance, announcing its next stop.

It was then that Petrus taught me the Dance Exercise.

'One more thing,' he said, looking deeply into my eyes. 'When I completed my pilgrimage, I painted a beautiful, immense picture that depicted everything that had happened to me here. This is the Road of the common people, and you can do the same thing, if you like. If you don't know how to paint, write something, or create a ballet. Then, regardless of where they are, people will be able to walk the Jacobean route, the Milky Way, the Strange Road to Santiago.'

The train that had sounded its whistle began to enter the station. Petrus waved to me and disappeared between the parked railroad cars. I stood there amid the noise of brakes screeching on steel, trying to decipher the mysterious Milky Way over my head, those stars that had guided me here and that had silently watched over the loneliness and destiny of all human beings.

Next day, there was just a note left in my room: 7:00 p.m. – CASTLE OF THE TEMPLARS.

The Dance Exercise

Relax. Close your eyes.

Recall the first songs you heard as a child. Begin to sing them in your thoughts. Little by little, let a certain part of your body – your feet, your stomach, your hands, your head, and so on – but only one part, begin to dance to the melody you are singing.

After five minutes, stop singing, and listen to the sounds all around you. Compose an internal melody based on them, and dance to it with your whole body. Don't think about anything in particular, but try to memorize the images that spontaneously appear.

The dance offers an almost-perfect means of communication with the Infinite Intelligence.

This exercise should last fifteen minutes.

I spent the rest of that afternoon walking around the streets aimlessly. I crossed and recrossed the small city of Ponferrada, looking from a distance at the castle on the hill where I had been bidden to appear. The Templars had always stirred my imagination, and the castle in Ponferrada was not the only mark made on the Jacobean route by their order. The order had been created by nine knights who had decided not to return from the Crusades. Within a short time, their power had spread throughout Europe, and they had caused a revolution in the values at the beginning of this millennium. While most of the nobility of the time was concerned only with enriching itself through the labor of the serfs, the Knights Templar dedicated their lives, their fortunes, and their swords to one cause only: the protection of the pilgrims that walked the Road to Jerusalem. In the behavior of the Knights, the pilgrims found a model for their own search for wisdom.

In 1118, when Hugh de Payens and eight other knights held a meeting in the courtyard of an old, abandoned castle, they took a vow of love for all humanity. Two centuries later, there were more than five thousand benefices spread throughout the known world; they reconciled two activities that until then had appeared to be incompatible: the military life and the religious one. Donations from the members and from grateful pilgrims allowed the Order of the Knights Templars to accumulate incalculable wealth, which was used more than once to ransom important Christians who had been kidnapped by the Muslims. The honesty of the Knights was such that kings and nobles entrusted their valuables to the Templars and traveled only with a document that attested to the existence of their wealth. This document could be redeemed at any castle of the Order of the Templars for an equivalent sum, giving rise to the letter of credit that is used today.

Their spiritual devotion, in turn, had allowed the Knights Templars to understand the great truth that Petrus had quoted the night before: that the house of the Lord has many mansions. They sought to put an end to religious conflict and to unite the main monotheistic religions of the time: Christian, Jewish, and Islamic. Their chapels were built with the rounded cupola of the Judaic temples of Solomon, the octagonal walls of the Arab mosques, and the naves that were typical of Christian churches.

But as with everything that happens before its time, the Templars came to be viewed with suspicion. The great kings sought to hold economic power, and religious liberalism was regarded as a threat to the Church. On Friday, October 13, 1307, the Vatican and the major European states unleashed one of the most massive police operations of the Middle Ages: during the night, the main leaders of the Templars were seized in their castles and thrown in prison. They were accused of practicing secret ceremonies, including the worship of the devil, of blasphemy against Jesus Christ, of orgiastic rituals, and of engaging in sodomy with their apprentices.

Following a violent sequence of torture, renunciation, and treason, the Order of the Templars was erased from the map of medieval history. Their treasures were confiscated, and their members scattered throughout the world. The last master of the Order, Jacques de Molay, was burned at the stake in the center of Paris, along with a fellow Knight. His last request was that he be allowed 'to die looking at the towers of the Cathedral of Notre Dame.'

Spain, which was struggling to recapture the Iberian peninsula, welcomed the Knights fleeing from other parts of Europe, and the Spanish kings sought their help in the battles against the Moors. These Knights were absorbed into the Spanish orders, one of which was the Order of San Tiago of the Sword, responsible for protection along the Road.

I was thinking about this history when, exactly at seven in the evening, I passed through the main gate of the old Castle of the Templars of Ponferrada, where I was scheduled for an encounter with the Tradition.

There was no one there. I waited for half an hour and then began to fear the worst: that the ritual must have been at 7:00 a.m. But just as I was deciding to leave, two boys appeared, carrying the flag of Holland and with the scallop shell – the symbol of the Road to Santiago – sewn to their clothing. They came up to me, and we exchanged some words, concluding that we were there for the same purpose. I was relieved that the note had not been wrong.

Every fifteen minutes someone else arrived. There were an Australian, five Spaniards, and another man from Holland. Other than a few questions about the schedule – about which everyone was confused – we did not talk at all. We all sat together in the same part of the castle – a ruined atrium that had served as a storeroom for food in ancient times – and we decided to wait until something happened, even if we had to wait another day and night.

The waiting went on, and we fell to talking about the reasons we were there. It was then that I learned that the Road to Santiago is used by a number of different orders, most of them part of the Tradition. The people who were there had already been through many tests and initiations of the kind that I had gone through long ago in Brazil. Only the Australian and I were expecting to be conferred the highest degree of the first Road. Even without knowing the details, I could see that the process the Australian had gone through was completely different from the RAM practices.

At about 8:45, as we were beginning to talk about our personal lives, a gong rang. We followed the sound to the ancient chapel of the castle.

There we found an impressive scene. The chapel – or what remained of it, since most of it was in ruins – was illuminated only by torches. Where there had once been an altar could be seen seven figures garbed in the secular costumes of the Templars: a hood and steel helmet, a coat of mail, a sword, and a shield. I gasped: it was a scene from the distant past. All that made the situation seem real were our own suits and jeans and our shirts with the scallop shell emblem.

Even with the faint illumination provided by the torches, I could see that one of the Knights was Petrus.

'Approach your Masters,' said the Knight who appeared to be the oldest. 'Look into the eyes of your Master. Take off your clothes and receive your vestments.'

I went to Petrus and looked deeply into his eyes. He was in a kind of trance and seemed not to recognize me. But I could see in his eyes a certain sadness, the same sadness that his voice had conveyed on the previous night. I took all of my clothes off, and Petrus handed me a perfumed black tunic that fell loosely around my body. I surmised that one of the Masters had more than one disciple, but I could not see which he was because of the requirement that I keep my eyes fixed on those of Petrus.

The High Priest directed us to the center of the chapel, and two Knights began to trace a circle around us as they chanted: 'Trinitas, Sother, Messias, Emmanuel, Sabahot, Adonai, Athanatos, Jesus …'*

* Since this is an extremely long ritual and can be understood only by those who know the road of the Tradition, I have opted to summarize the incantations used. But this does not change the narrative at all, since this ritual was performed only to establish a reunion with and respect for the ancients. The important element of this part of the Road to Santiago – the Dance Exercise – is described here in its entirety.

The circle was being drawn to provide the protection needed for those within it. I noticed that four of us had white tunics, signifying vows of total chastity.

'Amides, Throdonias, Anitor!' intoned the High Priest. 'By the grace of the angels. Lord, I provide the vestment of salvation; I pray that everything I desire be transformed into reality, through thee, O my sacred Adonai, whose kingdom is forever. Amen!'

The High Priest placed over his coat of mail the white mantle with the Templar's Cross outlined in red in the center. The other Knights did the same.

It was exactly nine o'clock, the hour of Mercury, the messenger. And there I was, once again within the circle of the Tradition. There was an incense of mint, basil, and benjamin burning in the chapel, and the grand invocation of the Knights began:

'O great and glorious King, who rules through the power of the Supreme God, EL, over all higher and lower spirits, but especially over the Infernal Order of the Dominion of the East, I invoke you … so that I may realize my wish, whatever that may be, so long as it is proper to your labors, through the power of our God, EL, who created and provided all things celestial, of the air, of the earth, and of the infernal realm.'

A profound silence followed, and even without being able to see him, we could sense the presence of the being who had been the object of the invocation. This was the consecration of the ritual, a propitious sign that we should continue with our magical activities. I had already participated in hundreds of similar ceremonies, at some of which the results up to this point had been much more surprising. But the Castle of the Templars must have stimulated my imagination a little, because I thought I saw, hovering in the corner of the chapel, a kind of shining bird that I had never seen before.

The High Priest sprinkled water over us without stepping into the circle. Then, with the sacred ink, he wrote in the earth the seventy-two names by which God is known within the Tradition.

All of us – pilgrims and Knights – began to recite the sacred names. The flames of the torches crackled, a sign that the spirit that had been invoked had surrendered.

The moment for the dance had arrived. I knew how to participate because Petrus had taught me on the previous day; it was a different dance from the one I was used to performing at this stage during similar rituals.

No rule was stated, but all of us already knew what it was: no initiate could step outside the protective circle, since we lacked the protection that the Knights had with their suits of mail. I visualized the size of the circle and did exactly as Petrus had taught me.

I thought back to my infancy. A voice, the far-off voice of a woman within me, began to sing a simple melody. I knelt and compressed myself into the seed position and felt that my breast – only my breast – was beginning to dance. I felt at ease, able to enter completely into the ritual of the Tradition. The music within me began to change; my movements became more pronounced, and I entered into a powerful state of ecstasy. Everything around me was darkened, and my body, surrounded by that darkness, felt weightless. I saw myself walking through the flowered fields of Aghata, where I met my grandmother and an uncle who had been important to me when I was a child. I felt the vibration of time in its grid of quadrants, where all roads are joined and mixed, becoming identical despite their being so different from each other. At one point, I saw the Australian flash by me: his body was suffused in a red glow.

The image that followed was of a chalice and paten, and this image lasted for a long time, as if it had a special importance for me. I tried to understand its significance, but nothing came to me, despite my conviction that it had something to do with my sword. Then, after the chalice and paten had vanished, I saw the face of RAM coming toward me out of the darkness. But when the face came closer, it was only the face of N., the spirit that had been invoked, who was well known to me. We did not establish any special kind of communication, and his face dissolved into the darkness that was fluctuating around me.

I don't know how long we continued to dance. But suddenly I heard a voice:

'YAHWEH, TETRAGRAMMATON ...' and I didn't want to emerge from my trance, but the voice insisted:

'YAHWEH, TETRAGRAMMATON ...' and I recognized the voice of the High Priest, calling upon everyone to come out of the trance. It irritated me. The Tradition was where I was rooted, and I did not want to come back. But the Master demanded it:

'YAHWEH, TETRAGRAMMATON …'

I couldn't maintain the trance. Resentfully, I returned to earth. I was once again within the magic circle there in the ancestral ambiance of the Castle of the Templars.

We pilgrims looked at each other. The sudden interruption seemed to have displeased everyone. I felt a strong urge to tell the Australian that I had seen him in my trance. But when I looked over at him, I saw that it wasn't necessary: he had seen me, too.

The Knights came to us and surrounded us. They began to beat upon their shields with their hands, making a noise that was deafening. Then the High Priest spoke:

'O Spirit N., because thou so diligently responded to my requests, with all due solemnity I allow thee to depart, without injury to man or beast. Go, I command thee, and be ready and anxious to return whenever thou art duly exorcised and conjured by the sacred rites of the Tradition. I conjure thee to go, peacefully and quietly, and may God's peace continue ever to be with thee and me. Amen.'

The circle was erased, and we knelt with our heads bowed. A Knight said seven Paternosters and seven Ave Marias with us. The High Priest added seven repetitions of the Apostles' Creed, stating that Our Lady of

Medjugorje – whose visitations had been noted in Yugoslavia ever since 1982 – had indicated that he should do this. And then we began another of the Christian rituals.

'Andrew, rise and come before me,' said the High Priest. The Australian approached the altar, where the seven Knights were standing.

One of the Knights – the one who must have been his guide – spoke:

'Brother, dost thou demand the company of the House?'

'Yes,' answered the Australian. And then I understood which of the Christian rituals we were witnessing: the initiation of a Templar.

'Dost thou understand the great severities of the House and its charitable orders?'

'I am ready to support all of them, in God's name, and I desire to be a servant and slave of the House forever, through all the days of my life,' answered the Australian.

There followed a series of ritual questions, some of which made no sense in today's world; others were concerned with profound devotion and love. Andrew, with his head bowed, responded to all of them.

'Distinguished brother, thou art asking a great thing of me. But thou art seeing only the outer layer of our religion – the beautiful horses and the elegant vestments,' said his guide. 'But thou knowest not the hard demands made here within: it will be difficult for thee, who art master of thyself, to serve others; rarely wilt thou be able to do as thou wishest. If thou desirest that thou be here, thou wilt be sent beyond the sea, and if thou desirest that thou be in Acre, thou wilt be sent to Tripoli, or Antioch, or Armenia. And when thou desirest sleep, thou wilt be told to stand guard, and when thou wantest to stand guard, thou wilt be told to sleep in thy bed.'

'I desire to enter the House,' answered the Australian. It felt as if all of the Templars who had ever lived in the castle were happily attending the initiation ceremony; the torches were crackling in earnest.

Several admonishments followed, and the Australian answered them all by saying that he wanted to enter the House. Finally, his guide turned to the High Priest and repeated all of the answers the Australian had made. The High Priest solemnly asked once more if he was ready to accept all of the rules of the House.

'Yes, Master, God willing. I come before God, before thee, and before the brothers, and I implore and solicit thee, before God and Our Lady, to take me into thy company and into the favors of the House, spiritually and temporally, as one who desires to be servant and slave of the House from now on, for all the days of his life.'

'I bid you enter, by God's love,' said the High Priest.

With that, all of the Knights unsheathed their swords and pointed them toward heaven. Then they lowered the blades and made of them a crown of steel around Andrew's head. The flames created a golden reflection on the blades, consecrating the moment.

Solemnly his Master came to him. And he gave him his sword.

Someone began to toll a bell, and its notes echoed off the walls of the ancient castle, infinitely repeating themselves. We all bowed our heads, and the Knights disappeared from view. When we looked up, we were only ten; the Australian had left to join the Knights in the ritual banquet.

We changed back into our street clothes and said our good-byes without any further formalities. The dance must have lasted for a long time, because the day was brightening. An immense loneliness invaded my soul.

I was envious of the Australian, who had recovered his sword and had reached the end of his quest. Now I was alone, with no one to guide me; the Tradition – in a distant country in South America – had expelled me without showing me the road back. And I had to continue to walk the Strange Road to Santiago, which was now coming to an end, without knowing the secret of my sword or how to find it.

The bell continued to toll. As I left the castle, with dawn breaking, I noticed that it was the bell of a nearby church, calling the faithful to the first mass of the day. The people of the city were awakening to their work and their unpaid bills, their love affairs and their dreams. But they didn't know that, on the previous night, an ancestral rite had once again taken place, that what had been thought of as dead and gone for centuries had once again been celebrated, and that it continued to demonstrate its awesome power.

El Cebrero

'Are you a pilgrim?' asked the little girl. She was the only person in sight on that blazing afternoon in Villafranca del Bierzo.

I looked at her but didn't answer. She was about eight and poorly dressed. She had run to the fountain where I had sat down to rest.

My only concern now was to get to Santiago de Compostela as quickly as possible and put an end to this crazy adventure. I had not been able to forget the sadness in Petrus's voice at the train yard nor the way he had looked at me from a distance when I had met his gaze during the ritual of the Tradition. It was as if all of the effort he had made in helping me had led to nothing. When the Australian had been called to the altar, I was sure that Petrus would have preferred that it had been I who had been called. My sword might very well be hidden in that castle, the repository of legends and ancient wisdom. It was a place that fit perfectly with all of my deductions: deserted, visited only by a few pilgrims who respected the relics of the Order of the Templars, and located on sacred ground.

But only the Australian had been called to the altar. And Petrus must have felt humiliated in the presence of the others because, as a guide, he had not been capable of leading me to my sword.

Besides this, the ritual of the Tradition had aroused in me again a bit of my fascination with occult wisdom, most of which I had forgotten about as I made my way along the Strange Road to Santiago, the Road of the common people. The invocations, the absolute control over the material, the communication with other worlds – all of that was much more interesting to me than the RAM practices. But perhaps the practices had a more objective application in my life; there was no doubt that I had changed a lot since I had begun to walk the Strange Road to Santiago. Thanks to Petrus's help, I had learned that I could pass through waterfalls, win out over enemies, and converse with my messenger about practical matters. I had seen the face of my death and the blue sphere of the love that consumes and floods the entire world. I was ready to fight the good fight and turn my life into a series of triumphs.

Yet a hidden part of me was still nostalgic for the magic circles, the transcendental formulas, the incense, and the sacred ink. The ceremony that Petrus had called an 'homage to the ancients' had been for me an intense and healthful encounter with old, forgotten lessons. And the possibility that I might never again have access to that world discouraged me from wanting to go on.

When I had returned to my hotel after the ritual of the Tradition, there in my box, along with my key, was a copy of *The Pilgrim's Guide*. This was a book that Petrus had utilized for orientation when the yellow markers were hard to find; it had helped us to calculate the distances between cities. I left Ponferrada that same morning, without having slept, and went out on the Road. By that afternoon, I had discovered that the map was not drawn to scale, and that I had to spend a night out in the open, in a cave in the cliffs.

There, as I meditated on everything that had happened to me since my meeting with Mme Lourdes, I thought about the relentless effort Petrus had made to help me understand that contrary to what we had always been taught, results *were* what counted. One's efforts are salutary and indispensable, but without results, they amount to nothing. And now the only result that I demanded of myself, the only reward for everything I had been through, was to find my sword. That had not happened yet, and Santiago was only a few days away.

'If you are a pilgrim, I can take you to the Gates of Forgiveness,' insisted the girl at the fountain in Villafranca del Bierzo. 'Whoever passes through those gates need not go all the way to Santiago.'

I held out some pesetas to her so that she would go away and leave me alone. But instead she began to splash the water in the fountain, wetting my knapsack and my shorts.

'Come on, come on,' she said again. At that moment, I was thinking about one of Petrus's repeated quotations: 'He that ploweth should plow in hope. He that thresheth in hope should be partaker of his hope.' It was from one of the letters of the apostle Paul.

I had to persevere for a little longer, to continue searching until the end, without being fearful of defeat, to keep alive the hope of finding my sword and understanding its secret.

And – who knows? – was this little girl trying to tell me something that I didn't want to understand? If the Gates of Forgiveness, which were part of a church, had the same spiritual effect as arriving at Santiago, why couldn't my sword be there?

'Let's go,' I said to the child. I looked at the mountain that I had just descended; I was going to have to climb part of it again. I had passed by the Gates of Forgiveness with no desire to go to them, since my only goal was to get to Santiago. Now, here was a little girl, the only human being present there on that hot afternoon, insisting that I go back and see something I had decided to ignore. After all, why hadn't that little girl gone away after I had given her some money? Could it be that, in my discouragement and haste, I had walked right past my objective without recognizing it?

Petrus had always said that I liked to fantasize too much about things. But perhaps he was wrong.

As I walked along with the girl, I was remembering the story of the Gates of Forgiveness. They represented a kind of 'arrangement' that the Church had made for pilgrims who fell sick. From that point on, the Road became once again difficult and mountainous all the way to Compostela, so during the twelfth century, one of the popes had said that whoever was unable to go further had only to pass through the Gates of Forgiveness to receive the same indulgences as the pilgrims who made it to the end of the Road. With one magic gesture, that pope had resolved the problem posed by the mountains and had inspired an increased number of pilgrimages.

We climbed, following the same route I had traveled earlier in the day: twisting roads, slippery and steep. The girl led, moving along very quickly, and many times I had to ask that she go more slowly. She would do so for a while and then, losing her sense of pace, would begin to run again. Half an hour later, and after much grumbling on my part, we reached the Gates of Forgiveness.

'I have the key to the church,' she said. 'I will go in and open the gates so you can pass through them.'

She went in through the main entrance, and I waited outside. It was a small church, and the gates opened to the north. The door frame was decorated with scallop shells and scenes from the life of San Tiago. As I heard the sound of the key in the lock, an immense German shepherd, appearing out of nowhere, came up to me and stood between the portal and me.

I was immediately prepared for a fight. 'Not again,' I thought. 'Is this story never going to end? Nothing but more and more tests, battles, and humiliations – and still no clue about my sword.'

At that moment, though, the Gates of Forgiveness swung open, and the girl appeared. When she saw that the dog was watching me – and that my eyes were already fixed on his – she said some affectionate words to him, and the dog relaxed. Wagging his tail, he followed her toward the back of the church.

Maybe Petrus was right. Maybe I did like to fantasize about things. A simple German shepherd had been transformed in my mind into a threatening supernatural being. That was a bad sign – a sign of the fatigue that leads to defeat.

But there was still hope. The girl signaled to me to enter. With my heart full of expectation, I passed through the Gates of Forgiveness, thereby receiving the same indulgences as the pilgrims who went all the way to Santiago.

My gaze swept over the empty, undecorated church, seeking the only thing I cared about.

'At the top of all the columns you can see shells. The shell is the symbol of the Road,' began the girl. 'This is Santa Agueda of …'

Before long, I could see that it had been useless to come all the way back to this church.

'And this is San Tiago Matamoros, brandishing his sword. You can see dead Moors under his horse's hooves. This statue was made in …'

San Tiago's sword was there but not mine. I offered a few more pesetas to the girl, but she would not accept them. A bit offended, she ended her explanations about the church and asked me to leave.

Once again I walked down the mountain and resumed my pilgrimage toward Compostela. As I passed through Villafranca del Bierzo for the second time, a man approached me. He said that his name was Angel and asked if I would be interested in seeing the Church of Saint Joseph the Carpenter. The man's name gave me hope, but I had just been disappointed, and I was beginning to see that Petrus was an expert observer of behavior. People do have a tendency to fantasize about things that do not even exist, while they fail to learn the lessons that are before their very eyes.

But perhaps just to confirm this tendency one more time, I allowed myself to be led by Angel to this other church. It was closed, and he did not have a key. He pointed to the framework of the entrance with its carving of Saint Joseph, his carpentry tools close alongside him. I nodded, thanked him, and offered him some pesetas. He refused them and left me there in the middle of the street – but not before saying, 'We are proud of our city. It is not for money that we do this.'

I returned to the Road and in fifteen minutes had left Villafranca del Bierzo behind – Villafranca del Bierzo, with its doors, its streets, and its mysterious guides who asked nothing in exchange for their services.

I walked for some time through mountainous terrain; my progress was slow and demanding. As I started out, I thought only about my previous worries

– solitude, shame at having disappointed Petrus, my sword and its secret. But soon the images of the little girl and of Angel began insistently to come to mind. While I had been focusing only on what I would gain, they had done the best for me that they could. And they had asked for nothing in return. A vague idea began to surface from deep inside me. It was some sort of link among all the things I was thinking about. Petrus had always insisted that the expectation of reward was absolutely necessary to the achievement of victory. Yet every time that I forgot about the rest of the world and began to think only about my sword, he forced me, through his painful lessons, to return to reality. This was a sequence that had occurred repeatedly during our time together on the Road.

There was some reason for this, and it was somehow connected with the secret of my sword. What was hiding there inside me began to coalesce and come to light. I still was not sure what it was that I was thinking, but something told me that I was looking in the right direction.

I appreciated having run into the little girl and Angel; they had shown something of the love that consumes in the way they spoke about their churches. They had caused me to go over the same ground twice, and because of this, I had forgotten my fascination with the ritual of the Tradition and had returned to the fields of Spain.

I remembered a day long ago when Petrus had told me that we had walked several times over the same part of the Road in the Pyrenees. I remembered that day with nostalgia. It had been a good beginning, and who knew but what this repetition of that event was not an omen of a positive outcome.

That night I arrived at a village and asked for a room at the home of an old lady. She charged me a pittance for my bed and food. We chatted a bit, and she talked about her faith in Jesus of the Sacred Heart and her worries about the olive crop in that drought year. I drank some wine, had some soup, and went to bed early.

I was feeling better about things, mainly because of the concept that was developing in my mind and the fact that it felt ready for expression. I prayed, did some of Petrus's exercises, and decided to invoke Astrain.

I needed to talk to him about what had happened during the fight with the dog. That day he had almost caused me to lose, and then, after his refusal in the episode of the cross, I had decided to do away with him forever. On the other hand, if I had not recognized his voice during the fight, I would have given in to the temptations that had appeared.

'You did everything possible to help Legion win,' I said.

'I do not fight against my brothers,' Astrain answered. It was the response I had expected. I had already predicted that he would say this, and it didn't make sense to get irritated with the messenger for being himself. I had to seek out in him the ally who had helped me at times like this, for that was his only function. I put my rancor aside and began to tell him animatedly about the Road, about Petrus, and about the secret of the sword, which I felt was beginning to formulate itself in my mind. He had nothing important to say – only that these secrets were not available to him. But at least I had someone to open up with after having spent the entire afternoon in silence. We had been talking for hours when the old lady rapped on my door to tell me that I was talking in my sleep.

I awoke feeling more optimistic and took to the Road early. According to my calculations, that afternoon I would reach Galicia, the region where Santiago de Compostela was located. It was all uphill, and I had to exert myself for almost four hours to keep to the pace I had set for myself. Every time I reached the crest of a hill I hoped that it would mark the point of descent. But this never seemed to happen, and I had to give up any hope of moving along more rapidly. In the distance I could see mountains that were even higher, and I realized that sooner or later I was going to have to cross them. My physical exertions, meanwhile, had made it impossible to think much, and I began to feel more friendly toward myself.

'Come on now, after all, how can you take seriously anyone who leaves everything behind to look for a sword?' I asked myself. What would it really mean to my life if I couldn't find it? I had learned the RAM practices, I had gotten to know my messenger, fought with the dog, and seen my death, I told myself, trying to convince myself that the Road to Santiago was what was important to me. The sword was only an outcome. I would like to find it, but I would like even more to know what to do with it. Because I would have to use it in some practical way, just as I used the exercises Petrus had taught me.

I stopped short. The thought that up until then had been only nascent exploded into clarity. Everything became clear, and a tide of agape washed over me. I wished with all my heart that Petrus were there so that I could tell him what he had been waiting to hear from me. It was the only thing that he had really wanted me to understand, the crowning accomplishment of all the hours he had devoted to teaching me as we walked the Strange Road to Santiago: it was the secret of my sword!

And the secret of my sword, like the secret of any conquest we make in our lives, was the simplest thing in the world: it was what I should do with the sword.

I had never thought in these terms. Throughout our time on the Strange Road to Santiago, the only thing I had wanted to know was where it was hidden. I had never asked myself why I wanted to find it or what I needed it for. All of my efforts had been bent on reward; I had not understood that when we want something, we have to have a clear purpose in mind for the thing that we want. The only reason for seeking a reward is to know what to do with that reward. And this was the secret of my sword.

Petrus needed to know that I had learned this, but I was sure I would never see him again. He had waited so long for this, and he would never know that it had happened.

So I knelt there, took some paper from my notebook, and wrote down what I intended to do with my sword. I folded the sheet carefully and placed it under a stone – one that reminded me of him and his friendship. Time would eventually destroy the paper, but symbolically, I was delivering it to Petrus.

Now he knew that I was going to succeed with my sword. My mission with Petrus had been accomplished.

I climbed the mountain, and the agape flowing through me intensified the colors in the surroundings. Now that I had discovered the secret, I had to find what I was looking for. A faith, an unshakable certainty, took control of my being. I began to sing the Italian song that Petrus had remembered in the train yard. I didn't know the words, so I made them up. There was no one in sight, and I was passing through some deep woods, so the isolation made me sing even louder. Shortly I saw that the words I had used made a kind of absurd sense. They were a way of communicating with the world that only I knew, since now it was the world that was teaching me.

I had experimented with this in a different way during my first encounter with Legion. That day, the gift of tongues had manifested itself in me. I had been the servant of the Spirit, which had used me to save a woman and to create an enemy, and had taught me the cruel version of the good fight. Now everything was different: I was my own Master, and I was learning to communicate with the universe.

I began to talk to everything along the Road: tree trunks, puddles, fallen leaves, and beautiful vines. It was an exercise of the common people, learned by children and forgotten by adults. And I received a mysterious response from those things, as if they understood what I was saying; they, in turn, flooded me with the love that consumes. I went into a kind of trance that frightened me, but I wanted to continue the game until I tired of it.

Petrus was right again: by teaching myself, I had transformed myself into a Master.

It was time for lunch, but I didn't stop to eat. When I passed through the small villages along the Road, I spoke more softly and smiled to myself, and if by chance someone noticed me, they would have concluded that the pilgrims arriving nowadays at the Cathedral of Santiago were crazy. But this didn't matter to me, because I was celebrating the life all around me and because I knew what I had to do with my sword when I found it.

For the rest of the afternoon, I walked along in a trance, aware of where it was that I wanted to go but more aware of my surroundings and the fact that they had returned agape to me. Heavy clouds began to gather in the sky for the first time in my journey, and I hoped it would rain. After such a long period of hiking and of drought, the rain would be a new, exciting experience. At three in the afternoon, I crossed into Galicia, and I could see on the map that there was one more mountain to climb in order to complete that leg of the pilgrimage. I was determined to climb it and then to sleep in the first town on the other side: Tricastela, where a great king – Alfonso IX – had dreamed of creating an immense city but which, many centuries later, was still a tiny country village.

Still singing and speaking the language I had invented for communicating with the things around me, I began to climb the only remaining mountain: El Cebrero. Its name went back to ancient Roman settlements in the region and was said to mean 'February,' when something important had presumably happened. In ancient times, this was considered to be the most difficult part of the Jacobean route, but today things have changed. Although the angle of ascent is steeper than in the other mountains, a large television antenna on a neighboring mountain serves as a reference point for pilgrims and prevents their wandering from the Road, a common and fatal event in the past.

The clouds began to lower, and I saw that I would shortly be entering fog. To get to Tricastela, I had to follow the yellow markers carefully; the television antenna was already hidden in the mist. If I got lost, I would wind up sleeping outdoors, and on that day, with the threat of rain, the experience would be quite disagreeable. It is one thing to feel raindrops falling on your face, enjoying the freedom of the life of the Road, and then find a place nearby where you can have a glass of wine and sleep in a bed in preparation for the next day's march. It is quite another to have the raindrops cause a night of insomnia as you try to sleep in the mud, with your wet bandages providing fertile ground for a knee infection.

I had to decide quickly. Either I went forward through the fog – there was still enough light to do so – or I returned to sleep in the small village I had passed through a few hours ago, leaving the crossing of El Cebrero for the next day.

As I realized that I had to make a quick decision, I noticed that something strange was happening. My certainty that I had discovered the secret of my sword was somehow pushing me to go forward into the fog that would shortly engulf me. This feeling was quite different from the one that had made me follow the little girl to the Gates of Forgiveness and made me go with the man to the Church of Saint Joseph the Carpenter.

I remembered that, on the few occasions when I had agreed to put a magic curse on someone in Brazil, I had compared this mystical experience with another very common experience: that of learning to ride a bicycle. You begin by mounting the bicycle, pushing on the pedals, and falling. You try and you fall, try and fall, and you cannot seem to learn how to balance yourself. Suddenly, though, you achieve perfect equilibrium, and you establish complete mastery over the vehicle. It is not a cumulative experience but a kind of 'miracle' that manifests itself only when you allow the bicycle 'to ride you.' That is, you accept the disequilibrium of the two wheels and, as you go along, begin to convert the initial force toward falling into a greater force on the pedal.

At that moment in my ascent of El Cebrero, at four in the afternoon, I saw that the same miracle had occurred. After so much time spent walking the Road to Santiago, the Road to Santiago began to 'walk me.' I followed what everyone calls one's intuition. And because of the love that consumes that I had experienced all that day, and because my sword's secret had been discovered, and because at moments of crisis a person always makes the right decision, I went forward with no hesitation into the fog.

'This fog has to stop,' I thought, as I struggled to see the yellow markers on the stones and trees along the Road. By now the visibility had been very poor for almost an hour, but I continued to sing as an antidote to my fear, while I hoped that something extraordinary would happen. Surrounded by the fog, alone in those unreal surroundings, I began to look at the Road to Santiago as if it were a film; this was the moment when the hero does things that no one else in the film would dare to do, while the audience is thinking that such things only happen in the movies. But there I was, living through a real situation. The forest was growing quieter and quieter, and the fog began to dissipate. I seemed to be reaching the end of the obscurity, but the light confused me and bathed everything in mysterious, frightening colors.

The silence was now complete, and as I noticed this, I heard, coming from my left, a woman's voice. I stopped immediately, expecting to hear it again, but I heard nothing – not even the normal sounds of the forest, with its crickets, its insects, and its animals walking through the dry leaves. I looked at my watch: it was exactly 5:15 p.m. I estimated that I was still about three miles from Tricastela and that there was still time to arrive before dark.

As I looked up from my watch, I heard the woman's voice again. And from that point on, I was to live through one of the most significant experiences of my life.

The voice wasn't coming from somewhere in the woods but from somewhere inside me. I was able to hear it clearly, and it heightened my intuitive sense. It was neither I nor Astrain who was speaking. The voice only told me that I should keep on walking, which I did unquestioningly. It was as if Petrus had returned and was telling me again about giving orders and taking them. At that moment, I was simply an instrument of the Road; the Road was indeed 'walking me.' The fog grew less and less dense; I seemed to be walking out of it. Around me were the bare trees, the moist and slippery terrain, and ahead of me, the same steep slope I had been climbing for such a long time.

Suddenly, as if by magic, the fog lifted completely. And there before me, driven into the crest of the mountain, was a cross.

I looked around, and I could see both the fog bank from which I had emerged and another above me. Between the two, I could see the peaks of the tallest mountains and the top of El Cebrero, where the cross was. I felt a strong desire to pray. Even though I knew that I would have to detour from the road to Tricastela, I decided to climb to the peak and say my prayers at the foot of the cross. It took forty minutes to make the climb, and I did it in complete silence, within and without. The language I had invented was forgotten; it was not the right language for communicating with other people or with God. The Road to Santiago was 'walking me,' and it was going to show me where my sword was. Petrus was right again.

When I reached the peak, a man was sitting there, writing something. For an instant I thought he was a supernatural being, sent from elsewhere. Then my intuition told me that he was not, and I saw the scallop shell stitched into his clothing; he was just a pilgrim, who looked at me for a few moments and then walked away, disturbed by my having appeared. Perhaps he had been expecting the same thing as I – an angel – and we had each found just another person on the Road of the common people.

Although I wanted to pray, I wasn't able to say anything. I stood in front of the cross for some time, looking at the mountains and at the clouds that covered the sky and the land, leaving only the high peaks clear. Thirty yards below me there was a hamlet with fifteen houses and a small church, whose lights were being turned on. At least I had somewhere to spend the night if the Road told me to do so. I was not sure when it would tell me, but even with Petrus gone, I was not without a guide. The Road was 'walking me.'

An unfettered lamb, climbing the mountain, stopped between the cross and me. He looked at me, a bit frightened. For some time I stood there, looking at the black sky, and the cross, and the white lamb at its foot. All at once, I felt exhausted by all that time spent on tests and battles and lessons and the pilgrimage. I felt a terrible pain in my stomach, and it rose to my throat, where it was transformed into dry, tearless sobs. There I stood, overcome by the scene of the lamb and the cross. This was a cross that I need not set upright, for it was there before me, solitary and immense, resisting time and the elements. It was a symbol of the fate that people created, not for their God but for themselves. The lessons of the Road to Santiago came back to me as I sobbed there, with a frightened lamb as my witness.

'My Lord,' I said, finally able to pray, 'I am not nailed to this cross, nor do I see you there. The cross is empty, and that is how it should stay forever; the time of death is already past, and a god is now reborn within me. This cross is the symbol of the infinite power that each of us has. Now this power is reborn, the world is saved, and I am able to perform your miracles, because I trod the Road of the common people and, in mingling with them, found your secret. You came among us to teach us all that we were capable of becoming, and we did not want to accept this. You showed us that the power and the glory were within every person's reach, and this sudden vision of our capacity was too much for us. We crucified you, not because we were ungrateful to the Son of God but because we were fearful of accepting our own capacity. We crucified you fearing that we might be transformed into gods. With time and tradition, you came to be just a distant divinity, and we returned to our destiny as human beings.

'It is not a sin to be happy. Half a dozen exercises and an attentive ear are enough to allow us to realize our most impossible dreams. Because of my pride in wisdom, you made me walk the Road that every person can walk, and discover what everyone else already knows if they have paid the slightest attention to life. You made me see that the search for happiness is a personal search and not a model we can pass on to others. Before finding my sword, I had to discover its secret – and the secret was so simple; it was to know what to do with it. With it and with the happiness that it would represent to me.

'I have walked so many miles to discover things I already knew, things that all of us know but that are so hard to accept. Is there anything harder for us, my Lord, than discovering that we can achieve the power? This pain that I feel now in my breast, that makes me sob and that frightens that poor lamb, has been felt since human beings first existed. Few can accept the burden of their own victory: most give up their dreams when they see that they can be realized. They refuse to fight the good fight because they do not know what to do with their own happiness; they are imprisoned by the things of the world. Just as I have been, who wanted to find my sword without knowing what to do with it.'

A god sleeping within me was awakening, and the pain was growing worse and worse. I felt the presence close to me of my Master, and I was able for the first time to turn my sobs into tears. I wept with gratitude for his having made me search for my sword along the Road to Santiago. I wept with gratitude for Petrus, for his having taught me, without saying a word, that I would realize my dreams if I first discovered what I wanted to do with them. I saw the cross, with no one on it, and the lamb at its base, free to go where he wanted in those mountains and to see the clouds above his head and below his feet.

The lamb began to walk away, and I followed him. I already knew where he would lead me; in spite of the clouds, everything had become clear to me. Even if I could not see the Milky Way in the sky, I was certain that it was there, pointing the way along the Road to Santiago. I followed the lamb as he walked in the direction of the hamlet – which was called El Cebrero, like the mountain.

There, at one time, a miracle had happened. It was the miracle of transforming what you do into what you believe in, just like the secret of my sword and of the

Strange Road to Santiago. As we descended the mountain, I remembered the story. A farmer from a nearby village had climbed the mountain to attend mass at El Cebrero on a stormy day. The mass was being celebrated by a monk who was almost completely lacking in faith and who ridiculed the farmer for having made such an effort to get there. But at the moment of consecration, the host had actually been transformed into the body of Christ and the wine into his blood. The relics are still there, guarded in that small chapel, a treasure greater than all the riches of the Vatican.

The lamb stopped at the edge of the hamlet, where there was only one street leading to the church. At that moment, I was seized by a terrible fear, and I began to repeat over and over, 'Lord, I am not worthy to enter thy house.' But the lamb looked at me and spoke to me through his eyes. He said that I should forget forever my unworthiness because the power had been reborn in me, in the same way that it could be reborn in all people who devoted their lives to the good fight. A day would come – said the lamb's eyes – when people would once again take pride in themselves, and then all of nature would praise the awakening of the God that had been sleeping within them.

As the lamb looked at me, I could read all of this in his eyes; now he had become my guide along the Road to Santiago. For a moment everything went dark, and I began to see scenes that were reminiscent of those I had read about in the Apocalypse: the Great Lamb on his throne and people washing his vestments, cleansing them with his blood. This was the moment when the God was awakened in each of them. I also saw the wars and hard times and catastrophes that were going to shake the earth over the next few years. But everything ended with the victory of the Lamb and with every human being on earth awakening the sleeping God and all of God's power.

I followed the lamb to the small chapel built by the farmer and by the monk who had come to believe in what he did. Nobody knows who they were. Two nameless tombstones in the cemetery by the chapel mark the place where they were buried. But it is impossible to tell which is the grave of the monk and which of the farmer. The miracle had occurred because both had fought the good fight.

The chapel was completely lit when I came to its door. Yes, I was worthy of entering, because I had a sword and I knew what to do with it. These were not the Gates of Forgiveness, because I had already been forgiven and had washed my clothing in the blood of the Lamb. Now I wanted only to hold my sword and go out to fight the good fight.

In the small church there was no cross. There on the altar were the relics of the miracle: the chalice and the paten that I had seen during the dance, and a silver reliquary containing the body and blood of Jesus. I once again believed in miracles and in the impossible things that human beings can accomplish in their daily lives.

The mountain peaks seemed to say to me that they were there only as a challenge to humans – and that humans exist only to accept the honor of that challenge.

The lamb slipped into one of the pews, and I looked to the front of the chapel. Standing before the altar, smiling – and perhaps a bit relieved – was my Master: with my sword in his hand.

I stopped, and he came toward me, passing me by and going outside. I followed him. In front of the chapel, looking up at the dark sky, he unsheathed my sword and told me to grasp its hilt with him. He pointed the blade upward and said the sacred Psalm of those who travel far to achieve victory:

A thousand fall at your side, and ten thousand to your right,
but you will not be touched.
No evil will befall you, no curse will fall upon your tent;
your angels will be given orders regarding you,
to protect you along your every way.

I knelt, and as he touched the blade to my shoulders, he said:

Trample the lion and the serpent,
The lion cub and the dragon will make shoes for your feet.

As he finished saying this, it began to rain. The rain fertilized the earth, and its water would return to the sky after having given birth to a seed, grown a tree, brought a flower into blossom. The storm intensified, and I raised my head, feeling the rain for the first time in my entire journey along the Road to Santiago. I remembered the dry fields, and I was joyful that they were being showered upon that night. I remembered the rocks in Leon, the wheat fields of Navarra, the dryness of Castile, and the vineyards of Rioja that today were drinking the rain that fell in torrents, with all of the force in the skies. I remembered having raised a cross, and I thought that the storm would once again cause it to fall to earth so that another pilgrim could learn about command and obedience. I thought of the waterfall, which now must be even stronger because of the rainfall, and of Foncebadon, where I had left such power to fertilize the soil again. I thought about all of the water I had drunk from so many fountains that were now being replenished. I was worthy of my sword because I knew what to do with it.

The Master held out the sword to me, and I grasped it. I looked about for the lamb, but he had disappeared. But that did not matter: the Water of Life fell from the sky and caused the blade of my sword to glisten.

Epilogue:
Santiago de Compostela

From the window of my hotel I can see the Cathedral of Santiago and the tourists at its main gate. Students in black medieval clothing mingle with the townspeople, and the souvenir vendors are setting up their stalls. It is early in the morning, and except for my notes, these are the first lines I have written about the Road to Santiago.

I reached the city yesterday, after having caught the bus that runs from Pedrafita, near El Cebrero, to Compostela. In four hours we covered the 150 kilometers that separate the two cities, and this reminded me of the journey with Petrus. At times, it took us two weeks to cover that distance. In a short while, I am going to the tomb of San Tiago to leave there the image of Our Lady of the Visitation, mounted on the scallop shells. Then, as soon as possible, I am going to catch a plane for Brazil, because I have a lot to do. I remember that Petrus told me once that he had condensed all of his experience into one picture, and the thought occurs to me that I might write a book about everything that has happened to me. But this is still a remote idea; I have so much to do now that I have recovered my sword.

The secret of my sword is mine, and I will never reveal it to anyone. I wrote it down and left it under a stone, but with the rain, the paper has probably been destroyed. It's better that way. Petrus didn't need to know.

I asked my Master whether he had known what day I was going to arrive or whether he had been waiting there for some time. He laughed and said that he had arrived there the morning before and was going to leave the next day, whether I appeared or not.

I asked how that was possible, and he did not answer me. But when we were saying good-bye and he was getting into the rental car that would take him back to Madrid, he gave me a small medal of the Order of San Tiago of the Sword. And he told me that I had already had a great revelation when I had looked into the eyes of the lamb.

And when I think about it, I guess it is true that people always arrive at the right moment at the place where someone awaits them.

Author's Note

Seated in a garden in a city in the South of France.

At my side, a letter from my editor, asking for a presentation (a title) for the new edition.

Mineral water.

Coffee.

Temperature: 27 °C

People conversing, people strolling.

People who are also drinking coffee and mineral water.

Then I go back in time fifteen years. An afternoon, a cup of coffee, a bottle of mineral water, people conversing and strolling – except that this time, the scenario is the plains of León, the language is Spanish, my birthday is coming up shortly, I already know that getting to Jean Pied-de-Port will take some time and I'm only just a bit past the halfway point on the road leading to Santiago de Compostela. I look ahead, the monotonous countryside, the guide who is also having his coffee in a bar that seems to have arisen out of nowhere. I look back at the same monotonous countryside, the only difference being that the dust on the road shows the prints of the soles of my shoes. But the prints are temporary; the wind will blow them away before the arrival of nightfall. Everything seems unreal to me. What am I doing here? This question remains without an answer, even though several weeks have already passed.

I am seeking a sword. I'm living up to a ritual of RAM, a minor order within the Catholic Church that has no secrets or mysteries beyond the attempt to understand the world's symbolic language. I'm thinking that I was wrong. That the spiritual search is nothing but an idea lacking in sense or logic and that it would be better to be in Brazil taking care of what I have always cared for. I'm feeling doubts about my sincerity regarding the spiritual search because it's hard to find a God who never shows Himself; to pray at certain times, travel strange roads, be disciplined and accept orders that seem absurd to me.

That's it! I doubt my sincerity. All these days Petrus has been saying that the road is for everyone, that it's for the common people. And that really disappoints me. I've been thinking that all of this effort was going to gain me a place among the few chosen people that approach being the great archetypes of the universe. I've been thinking that I was finally going to discover that all the stories about the secret governments of wise men in Tibet, about magic potions capable of creating love where there was no attraction and about rituals through which the doors to Paradise would suddenly appear before me were true.

* * *

But what Petrus has told me is the exact opposite: there are no chosen individuals. Everyone is chosen, if instead of asking 'What am I doing here,' people would simply resolve to do anything that sparks enthusiasm in their heart. The gateway to Paradise lies in working with enthusiasm; it lies in love that transforms and the choice that leads to God. It is that enthusiasm that connects us with the Holy Spirit, not hundreds and thousands of readings of the classical texts. It is the willingness to believe that life is a miracle that allows miracles to happen and not the so-called 'secret rituals' or 'orders of initiation'. In the end, it is a man's decision to fulfil his destiny that really makes him a man and not the theories he develops regarding the mystery of existence.

And here I am. Just a little past the halfway point along the road that takes me to Santiago de Compostela. This afternoon in León, in the long year of 1986, I still don't know that six or seven months from now I'm going to write a book about my experience. That the shepherd Santiago is already in my soul, searching for a treasure. That a woman named Veronika is preparing to swallow some pills and attempt suicide. That Pilar will come to the banks of the river Piedra and weeping, write her diary. All I know at this moment is that I am tense, nervous, incapable of conversing with Petrus, because I have just realized that I can no longer return to what I have been doing, even if this means giving up some reasonable monetary return at the end of the month, sacrificing a certain degree of emotional stability, abandoning work that I understand and within which I have mastered certain techniques. I have to change, follow in the direction of my dream, a dream that appears to me to be infantile, ridiculous, impossible of attainment. I have to be the writer that I have secretly wanted to be but that I have lacked the courage to become.

Petrus finishes his coffee and his mineral water, asks that I pay the bill and that we resume our trek, since we are still some kilometres away from the next city. The people continue walking and conversing, observing out of the corner of their eyes the two middle-aged pilgrims and thinking that there are strange people in this world, thinking always of trying to revive a past that is already dead.*

The temperature must be about 27 °C because it's the end of the afternoon and I ask myself for the thousandth time, what am I doing here? Did I really want to change? I don't think so, but when all's said and done, this road is transforming me. Did I really want to understand the mysteries? I think so, but the road is teaching me that mysteries don't exist. That – as Jesus said – there is nothing hidden that has not been revealed. All in all, everything is happening in a way that is exactly opposite to what I had been expecting.

* In the year that I completed my pilgrimage, only 400 people had walked the Road to Santiago. In 1999, according to unofficial statistics, 400 people per day passed by the bar mentioned in the text.

We rise and begin walking in silence. I'm immersed in my thoughts, in my insecurity, and Petrus must be thinking – I imagine – about his work in Milan. He is here because in some way he was obligated by the Tradition, but it's possible that he is hoping that this journey will end now, so that he can return to doing what he enjoys.

We walk for almost the entire afternoon hardly speaking to each other. There are no cell phones, faxes or email. We are isolated in our forced companionship. Santiago de Compostela lies ahead and I cannot imagine that this road is going to lead me not only to that city but to many other cities in the world. Neither I nor Petrus know that, on this afternoon, on the plains of León, I am also traveling to Milan, his city, where I will arrive almost ten years later with a book called *The Alchemist*. I am walking toward the garden where, on this afternoon in June 2001, there is a café, some mineral water, agreeable sunlight and a letter from my publisher asking for a preface for the English edition of *The Pilgrimage*.

I am walking in order to see the story of my rebirth published.

Paulo Coelho
Massey Garden,
Tarbes, France.

Life is a
journey

Make sure you don't miss a thing.
Live it with Paulo Coelho.

Visit f /paulocoelho

How can you find your heart's desire?

A world-wide phenomenon; an inspiration for anyone seeking their path in life.

The Alchemist

Do you believe in yourself?

A modern-day adventure in the searing heat of the Mojave desert and an exploration of fear and self-doubt.

The Valkyries

How do we see the amazing in the everyday?

When two young lovers are reunited, they discover anew the truth of what lies in their hearts.

By the River Piedra
I Sat Down & Wept

What are you searching for?

A transforming journey on the pilgrims' road to Santiago – and the first of Paulo's extraordinary books.

The Pilgrimage

Can faith triumph over suffering?

Paulo Coelho's brilliant telling of the story of Elijah, who was forced to choose between love and duty.

The Fifth Mountain

Is life always worth living?

A fundamental moral question explored as only Paulo Coelho can.

Veronika Decides to Die

Could you be tempted into evil?

The inhabitants of a small town are challenged by a mysterious stranger to choose between good and evil.

The Devil & Miss Prym

Are you brave enough to live your dream?

Strategies and inspiration to help you follow your own path in a troubled world.

Manual of the Warrior of Light

Can sex be sacred?

An unflinching exploration of the lengths we go to in our search for love, sex and spirituality.

Eleven Minutes

How far would you go for your obsession?

A sweeping story of love, loss and longing that spans the world.

The Zahir

What happens when obsession turns to murder?

An enthralling story of jealousy, death and suspense.

The Winner Stands Alone

Can we dare to be true to ourselves?

A story that will transform the way we think about love, joy and sacrifice.

The Witch of Portobello

How will you know who your soulmate is?

A moving tale of passion, mystery and spirituality.

Brida

What does it mean to be truly alive?

Powerful tales of living and dying, destiny and choice, and love lost and found.

Like the Flowing River

Are you where you want to be?

Read *Aleph*. And rewrite your life.

Aleph

Is there a weapon more powerful than words?

A timeless and powerful exploration of personal growth, everyday wisdom and joy.

Manuscript Found in Accra

MANUAL of the WARRIOR of LIGHT

PAULO COELHO

Author of THE ALCHEMIST

TRANSLATED FROM THE PORTUGUESE
BY MARGARET JULL COSTA

Thorsons

Thorsons
An imprint of HarperCollins*Publishers*
1 London Bridge Street
London SE1 9GF

HarperCollins*Publishers*
1st Floor, Watermarque Building, Ringsend Road
Dublin 4, Ireland

www.harpercollins.co.uk
www.paulocoelho.com
www.paulocoelhoblog.com

First published in English by HarperCollins*Publishers* 2002
This edition published 2021

2 4 6 8 10 9 7 5 3 1

© Paulo Coelho 1997
English translation © Margaret Jull Costa 2002

Paulo Coelho asserts the moral right to
be identified as the author of this work

A catalogue record for this book is
available from the British Library

ISBN: 978-0-00-854724-0

FICTION / PHILOSOPHY

Printed and bound in India by Thomson Press India Ltd

All rights reserved. No part of this publication may be reproduced, stored in a retrieval system, or transmitted, in any form or by any means, electronic, mechanical, photocopying, recording or otherwise, without the prior written permission of the publishers.

This book is produced from independently certified FSC® paper to ensure responsible forest management.

O Mary!
conceived without sin,
pray for us who turn to you!
Amen.

The disciple is not above his master;
but every one that is perfect shall
be as his master.

Luke 6:40

For S.I.L., Carlos Eduardo Rangel and Anne Carrière,
masters of rigour and compassion.

Your children are not your children.
They are the sons and daughters of Life's longing for itself.
They come through you but not from you,
And though they are with you yet they belong not to you.
You may give them your love but not your thoughts,
For they have their own thoughts.
You may house their bodies but not their souls,
For their souls dwell in the house of tomorrow, which
you cannot visit, not even in your dreams.
You may strive to be like them, but seek not to make
them like you.
For life goes not backward nor tarries with yesterday.
You are the bows from which your children as living
arrows are sent forth.
The archer sees the mark upon the path of the infinite,
and He bends you with His might that His arrows may go
swift and far.
Let your bending in the archer's hand be for gladness;
For even as He loves the arrow that flies, so He loves also
the bow that is stable.

Khalil Gibran, 'On Children' from
The Prophet (Knopf, 1923)

PROLOGUE

'Just off the beach to the west of the village lies an island, and on it is a vast temple with many bells,' said the woman.

The boy noticed that she was dressed strangely and had a veil covering her head. He had never seen her before.

'Have you ever visited that temple?' she asked. 'Go there and tell me what you think of it?'

Seduced by the woman's beauty, the boy went to the place she had indicated. He sat down on the beach and stared out at the horizon, but he saw only what he always saw: blue sky and ocean.

Disappointed, he walked to a nearby fishing village and asked if anyone there knew about an island and a temple.

'Oh, that was many years ago, when my great-grandparents were alive,' said an old fisherman. 'There was an earthquake, and the island was swallowed up by the sea. But although we can no longer see the island, we can still hear the temple bells when the ocean sets them swinging down below.'

The boy went back to the beach and tried to hear the bells. He spent the whole afternoon there, but all he heard was the noise of the waves and the cries of the seagulls.

When night fell, his parents came looking for him. The following morning, he went back to the beach; he could not believe that such a beautiful woman would have lied to him. If she ever returned, he could tell her that, although he had not seen the island, he had heard the temple bells set ringing by the motion of the waves.

Many months passed; the woman did not return and the boy forgot all about her; now he was convinced that he needed to discover the riches and treasures in the submerged temple. If he could hear the bells, he would be able to locate it and salvage the treasure hidden below.

He lost interest in school and even in his friends. He became the butt of all the other children's jokes. They used to say: 'He's not like us. He prefers to sit looking at the sea because he's afraid of being beaten in our games.'

And they all laughed to see the boy sitting on the shore.

Although he still could not hear the old temple bells ringing, the boy learned about other things. He began to realise that he had grown so used to the sound of the waves that he was no longer distracted by them. Soon after that, he became used to the cries of the seagulls, the buzzing of the bees and the wind blowing amongst the palm trees.

Six months after his first conversation with the woman, the boy could sit there oblivious to all other noises, but he still could not hear the bells from the drowned temple.

Fishermen came and talked to him, insisting that they had heard the bells.

But the boy never did.

Some time later, however, the fishermen changed their tune: 'You spend far too much time thinking about the bells beneath the sea. Forget about them and go back to playing with your friends. Perhaps it's only fishermen who can hear them.'

After almost a year, the boy thought: 'Perhaps they're right. I would do better to grow up and become a fisherman and come down to this beach every morning, because I've come to love it here.' And he thought too: 'Perhaps it's just another legend and the bells were all shattered during the earthquake and have never rung out since.'

That afternoon, he decided to go back home.

He walked down to the ocean to say goodbye. He looked once more at the natural world around him and because he was no longer concerned about the bells, he could again smile at the beauty of the seagulls' cries, the roar of the sea and the wind blowing in the palm trees. Far off, he heard the sound of his friends playing and he felt glad to think that he would soon resume his childhood games.

The boy was happy and – as only a child can – he felt grateful for being alive. He was sure that he had not wasted his time, for he had learned to contemplate Nature and to respect it.

Then, because he was listening to the sea, the seagulls, the wind in the palm trees and the voices of his friends playing, he also heard the first bell.

And then another.

And another, until, to his great joy, all the bells in the drowned temple were ringing.

Years later, when he was a grown man, he returned to the village and to the beach of his childhood. He no longer dreamed of finding treasure at the bottom of the sea; perhaps that had all been a product of his imagination, and he had never really heard the submerged bells ring out on one lost childhood afternoon. Even so, he decided to walk for a while along the beach, to listen to the noise of the wind and to the cries of the seagulls.

Imagine his surprise when, there on the beach, he saw the woman who had first spoken to him about the island and its temple.

'What are you doing here?' he asked.

'I was waiting for you,' she replied.

He noticed that, despite the passing years, the woman looked exactly the same; the veil hiding her hair had not faded with time.

She handed him a blue notebook full of blank pages.

'Write: a warrior of light values a child's eyes because they are able to look at the world without bitterness. When he wants to find out if the person beside him is worthy of his trust, he tries to see him as a child would.'

'What is a warrior of light?'

'You already know that,' she replied with a smile. 'He is someone capable of understanding the miracle of life, of fighting to the last for something he believes in – and of hearing the bells that the waves sets ringing on the seabed.'

He had never thought of himself as a warrior of light. The woman seemed to read his thoughts. 'Everyone is capable of these things. And, though no one thinks of themselves as a warrior of light, we all are.'

He looked at the blank pages in the notebook. The woman smiled again.

'Write about that warrior,' she said.

MANUAL of the WARRIOR of LIGHT

A warrior of light
knows that he has much
to be grateful for.

A warrior of light knows that he has much to be grateful for.

He was helped in his struggle by the angels; celestial forces placed each thing in its place, thus allowing him to give of his best.

His companions say: 'He's so lucky!' And the warrior does sometimes achieve things far beyond his capabilities.

That is why, at sunset, he kneels and gives thanks for the Protective Cloak surrounding him.

His gratitude, however, is not limited to the spiritual world; he never forgets his friends, for their blood mingled with his on the battlefield.

A warrior does not need to be reminded of the help given him by others; he is the first to remember and he makes sure to share with them any rewards he receives.

All the world's roads
lead to the heart of
the warrior; he plunges
unhesitatingly into the
river of passions always
flowing through his life.

All the world's roads lead to the heart of the warrior; he plunges unhesitatingly into the river of passions always flowing through his life.

The warrior knows that he is free to choose his desires, and he makes these decisions with courage, detachment and – sometimes – with just a touch of madness.

He embraces his passions and enjoys them intensely. He knows that there is no need to renounce the pleasures of conquest; they are part of life and bring joy to all those who participate in them.

But he never loses sight of those things that last or of the strong bonds that are forged over time.

A warrior can distinguish between the transient and the enduring.

A warrior of light does not rely on strength alone, he makes use of his opponent's energy too.

A warrior of light does not rely on strength alone, he makes use of his opponent's energy too.

When he enters the fight, all he has is his enthusiasm and the moves and strikes that he learned during his training. As the fight progresses, he discovers that enthusiasm and training are not enough to win: what counts is experience.

Then he opens his heart to the Universe and asks God to give him the inspiration he needs to turn every blow from his enemy into a lesson in self-defence.

His companions say: 'He's so superstitious. He stopped fighting in order to pray; he even shows respect for his opponent's tricks.'

The warrior does not respond to these provocations. He knows that without inspiration and experience, no amount of training will help him.

A warrior of light
never resorts to trickery,
but he knows how to
distract his opponent.

A warrior of light never resorts to trickery, but he knows how to distract his opponent.

However anxious he is, he uses every strategy at his disposal to gain his objective. When he sees that his strength is almost gone, he makes his enemy think that he is simply biding his time. When he needs to attack the right flank, he moves his troops to the left. If he intends beginning the battle at once, he pretends that he is tired and prepares for sleep.

His friends say: 'Look, he's lost all enthusiasm.' But he pays no attention to such remarks because his friends do not understand his tactics.

A warrior of light knows what he wants. And he has no need to waste time on explanations.

‘Convince your enemy that he will gain very little by attacking you; this will diminish his enthusiasm.’

A wise Chinese man has this to say about the strategies of the warrior of light:

'Convince your enemy that he will gain very little by attacking you; this will diminish his enthusiasm.'

'Do not be ashamed to make a temporary withdrawal from the field if you see that your enemy is stronger than you; it is not winning or losing a single battle that matters, but how the war ends.'

'Even if you are very strong, never be ashamed to feign weakness; this will make your enemy act imprudently and attack too soon.'

'In war, the key to victory is the ability to surprise one's opponent.'

A warrior takes
every opportunity to
teach himself.

'It's odd,' says the warrior of light to himself. 'I have met so many people who, at the first opportunity, try to show their very worst qualities. They hide their inner strength behind aggression; they hide their fear of loneliness behind an air of independence. They do not believe in their own abilities, but are constantly trumpeting their virtues.'

The warrior reads these messages in many of the men and women he meets. He is never taken in by appearances and makes a point of remaining silent when people try to impress him. And he uses the occasion to correct his own faults, for other people make an excellent mirror.

A warrior takes every opportunity to teach himself.

The warrior of light sometimes fights with those he loves.

The warrior of light sometimes fights with those he loves.

The man who defends his friends is never overwhelmed by the storms of life; he is strong enough to come through difficulties and to carry on.

However, he is often faced by challenges from those he is trying to teach the art of the sword. His disciples provoke him into fighting with them.

And the warrior demonstrates his abilities: with just a few blows he disarms his students, and harmony returns to the place where they meet.

'Why bother to do that, when you are so much better than they are?' asks a traveller.

'Because in challenging me, what they really want is to talk to me and this is my way of keeping the dialogue open,' replies the warrior.

Before embarking on an important battle, a warrior of light asks himself: 'How far have I developed my abilities?'

Before embarking on an important battle, a warrior of light asks himself: 'How far have I developed my abilities?'

He knows that he has learned something with every battle he has fought, but many of those lessons have caused him unnecessary suffering. More than once he has wasted his time fighting for a lie. And he has suffered for people who did not deserve his love.

Victors never make the same mistake twice. That is why the warrior only risks his heart for something worthwhile.

A warrior of light respects the main teaching of the *I Ching*: 'To persevere is favourable.'

A warrior of light respects the main teaching of the *I Ching*: 'To persevere is favourable.'

He knows that perseverance is not the same thing as insistence. There are times when battles go on longer than necessary, draining him of strength and enthusiasm.

At such moments, the warrior thinks: 'A prolonged war finally destroys the victors too.'

Then he withdraws his forces from the battlefield and allows himself a respite. He perseveres in his desire, but knows he must wait for the best moment to attack.

A warrior always returns to the fray. He never does so out of stubbornness, but because he has noticed a change in the weather.

A warrior of light knows that certain moments repeat themselves.

A warrior of light knows that certain moments repeat themselves.

He often finds himself faced by the same problems and situations, and seeing these difficult situations return, he grows depressed, thinking that he is incapable of making any progress in life.

'I've been through all this before,' he says to his heart.

'Yes, you have been through all this before,' replies his heart. 'But you have never been beyond it.'

Then the warrior realises that these repeated experiences have but one aim: to teach him what he does not want to learn.

A warrior of light
is never predictable.

A warrior of light is never predictable.

He might dance down the street on his way to work, gaze into the eyes of a complete stranger and speak of love at first sight, or defend an apparently absurd idea. Warriors of light allow themselves days like these.

He is not afraid to weep over ancient sorrows or feel joy at new discoveries. When he feels that the moment has arrived, he drops everything and goes off on some long-dreamed-of adventure. When he realises that he can do no more, he abandons the fight, but never blames himself for having committed a few unexpected acts of folly.

A warrior does not spend his days trying to play the role that others have chosen for him.

Warriors of light
always have a certain
gleam in their eyes.

Warriors of light always have a certain gleam in their eyes.

They are of this world, they are part of the lives of other people and they set out on their journey with no saddlebags and no sandals. They are often cowardly. They do not always make the right decisions.

They suffer over the most trivial things, they have mean thoughts and sometimes believe they are incapable of growing. They frequently deem themselves unworthy of any blessing or miracle.

They are not always quite sure what they are doing here. They spend many sleepless nights, believing that their lives have no meaning.

That is why they are warriors of light. Because they make mistakes. Because they ask themselves questions. Because they are looking for a reason – and are sure to find it.

The warrior of light
does not worry that,
to others, his behaviour
might seem quite mad.

The warrior of light does not worry that, to others, his behaviour might seem quite mad.

He talks out loud to himself when he is alone. Someone told him that this is the best way of communicating with the angels, and so he takes a chance and tries to make contact.

At first, he finds this very difficult. He thinks that he has nothing to say, that he will just repeat the same meaningless twaddle. Even so, the warrior persists. He spends all day talking to his heart. He says things with which he does not agree, he talks utter nonsense.

One day, he notices a change in his voice. He realises that he is acting as a channel for some higher wisdom.

The warrior may seem mad, but this is just a disguise.

'The warrior of light chooses his enemies.'

According to a poet: 'The warrior of light chooses his enemies.'

He knows what he is capable of; he does not have to go about the world boasting of his qualities and virtues. Nevertheless, there is always someone who wants to prove himself better than he is.

For the warrior, there is no 'better' or 'worse': everyone has the necessary gifts for his particular path.

But certain people insist. They provoke and offend and do everything they can to irritate him. At that point, his heart says: 'Do not respond to these insults, they will not increase your abilities. You will tire yourself needlessly.'

A warrior of light does not waste his time listening to provocations; he has a destiny to fulfil.

'Although I have
been through all that
I have, I do not regret
the many hardships I met,
because it was they who
brought me to the place
I wished to reach.'

The warrior of light remembers a passage from John Bunyan:

'Although I have been through all that I have, I do not regret the many hardships I met, because it was they who brought me to the place I wished to reach. Now all I have is this sword and I give it to whomever wishes to continue his pilgrimage. I carry with me the marks and scars of battles – they are the witnesses of what I suffered and the rewards of what I conquered.

'These are the beloved marks and scars that will open the gates of Paradise to me. There was a time when I used to listen to tales of bravery. There was a time when I lived only because I needed to live. But now I live because I am a warrior and because I wish one day to be in the company of Him for whom I have fought so hard.'

The moment
that he begins to walk
along it, the warrior
of light recognises
the Path.

The moment that he begins to walk along it, the warrior of light recognises the Path.

Each stone, each bend cries welcome to him. He identifies with the mountains and the streams, he sees something of his own soul in the plants and the animals and the birds of the field.

Then, accepting the help of God and of God's Signs, he allows his Personal Legend to guide him towards the tasks that life has reserved for him.

On some nights, he has nowhere to sleep, on others, he suffers from insomnia. 'That's just how it is,' thinks the warrior. 'I was the one who chose to walk this path.'

In these words lies all his power: he chose the path along which he is walking and so has no complaints.

From now on –
and for the next few
hundred years – the
Universe is going to help
warriors of light and
hinder the prejudiced.

From now on – and for the next few hundred years – the Universe is going to help warriors of light and hinder the prejudiced.

The Earth's energy needs to be renewed.

New ideas need space.

Body and soul need new challenges.

The future has become the present, and every dream – except those dreams that involve preconceived ideas – will have a chance to be heard.

Anything of importance will remain; anything useless will disappear. However, it is not the warrior's responsibility to judge the dreams of others, and he does not waste time criticising other people's decisions.

In order to have faith in his own path, he does not need to prove that someone else's path is wrong.

A warrior of light carefully studies the position that he intends to conquer.

A warrior of light carefully studies the position that he intends to conquer.

However difficult the objective, there is always a way of overcoming obstacles. He seeks out alternative paths, he sharpens his sword, he tries to fill his heart with the necessary determination to face the challenge.

But as he advances, the warrior realises that there are difficulties he had not reckoned with.

If he waits for the ideal moment, he will never set off; he requires a touch of madness to take the next step.

The warrior uses that touch of madness. For – in both love and war – it is impossible to foresee everything.

A warrior of light
knows his own faults.
But he also knows
his qualities.

A warrior of light knows his own faults. But he also knows his qualities.

Some of his companions complain all the time that 'other people have more opportunities than we do'.

Perhaps they are right, but a warrior does not allow himself to be paralysed by this; he tries to make the most of his virtues.

He knows that the gazelle's power lies in its strong legs. The power of the seagull lies in the accuracy with which it can spear a fish. He has learned that the reason the tiger does not fear the hyena is because he is aware of his own strength.

He tries to establish what he can truly rely on. And he always checks that he carries three things with him: faith, hope and love.

If these three things are there, he does not hesitate to go forward.

The warrior of light knows that no one is stupid and that life teaches everyone – however long that may take.

The warrior of light knows that no one is stupid and that life teaches everyone – however long that may take.

He always does his best and expects the best of others. Through his generosity, he tries to show each person how much they are capable of achieving.

Some of his companions say: 'Some people are so ungrateful.'

The warrior is not discouraged by this. And he continues to encourage other people because this is also a way of encouraging himself.

Every warrior of light has felt afraid of going into battle.

Every warrior of light has felt afraid of going into battle.

Every warrior of light has, at some time in the past, lied or betrayed someone.

Every warrior of light has trodden a path that was not his.

Every warrior of light has suffered for the most trivial of reasons.

Every warrior of light has, at least once, believed that he was not a warrior of light.

Every warrior of light has failed in his spiritual duties.

Every warrior of light has said 'yes' when he wanted to say 'no'.

Every warrior of light has hurt someone he loved.

That is why he is a warrior of light, because he has been through all this and yet has never lost hope of being better than he is.

The warrior simply has to accept the challenge.

The warrior always listens to the words of certain thinkers, such as these by T.H. Huxley:

'The consequences of our actions are the scarecrows of fools and the beacons of wise men.'

'The chessboard is the world; the pieces are the gestures of our daily lives; the rules of the game are what we call the laws of Nature. The player on the other side is hidden from us, but we know that his play is always fair, just and patient.'

The warrior simply has to accept the challenge. He knows that God never overlooks a single mistake made by those he loves, nor does he allow his favourites to pretend ignorance of the rules of the game.

A warrior of light does not postpone making decisions.

A warrior of light does not postpone making decisions.

He thinks a good deal before he acts; he considers his training, as well as his responsibilities and duties as a teacher. He tries to remain calm and to analyse each step as if it were of supreme importance.

However, as soon as he has made a decision, the warrior proceeds: he has no doubts about his chosen action, nor does he change direction if circumstances turn out differently from how he had imagined them.

If his decision is correct, he will win the battle, even if it lasts longer than expected. If his decision is wrong, he will be defeated and he will have to start all over again – only this time with more wisdom.

But once he has started, a warrior of light perseveres until the end.

A warrior knows
that his best teachers
are the people with
whom he shares
the battlefield.

A warrior knows that his best teachers are the people with whom he shares the battlefield.

It is dangerous to ask for advice. It is even more dangerous to give advice. When he needs help, he tries to see how his friends resolve – or fail to resolve – their problems.

If he is in search of inspiration, he reads on the lips of his neighbour the words that his guardian angel is trying to say to him.

When he is tired or lonely, he does not dream about distant men and women; he turns to the person beside him and shares his sorrow or his need for affection with them – with pleasure and without guilt.

A warrior knows that the farthest-flung star in the Universe reveals itself in the things around him.

A warrior of light
shares his world with
the people he loves.

A warrior of light shares his world with the people he loves.

He tries to encourage them to do the things they would like to do but for which they lack the courage; at such times, the Enemy appears holding two wooden signs in his hand.

On one sign is written: 'Think about yourself. Keep all the blessings for yourself, otherwise you'll end up losing everything.'

On the other sign, he reads: 'Who do you think you are, helping other people? Can't you see your own faults?'

A warrior knows that he has faults. But he knows too that he cannot do his growing alone and thus distance himself from his companions.

Therefore, he throws the two signs to the floor, even if he thinks they may contain a grain of truth. The signs crumble into dust, and the warrior continues to encourage those nearest him.

'The Way involves respect for all small and subtle things. Learn to recognise the right moment to adopt the necessary attitudes.'

The philosopher Lao Tzu says of the journey of the warrior of light:

'The Way involves respect for all small and subtle things. Learn to recognise the right moment to adopt the necessary attitudes.'

'Even if you have already fired a bow several times, continue to pay attention to how you position the arrow and how you flex the string.'

'When a beginner knows what he needs, he proves more intelligent than an absent-minded sage.'

'Accumulating love brings luck, accumulating hatred brings calamity. Anyone who fails to recognise problems leaves the door open for tragedies to rush in.'

'The battle is not the same as the quarrel.'

The warrior of light meditates.

The warrior of light meditates.

He sits in a quiet place in his tent and surrenders himself to the divine light. When he does this, he tries not to think about anything; he shuts himself off from the search for pleasure, from challenges and revelations, and allows his gifts and powers to reveal themselves.

Even if he does not recognise them then, these gifts and powers are taking care of his life and will influence his day-to-day existence.

While he meditates, the warrior is not himself, but a spark from the Soul of the World. These are the moments that give him an understanding of his responsibilities and of how he should behave accordingly.

A warrior of light knows that in the silence of his heart he will hear an order that will guide him.

A warrior of light sometimes thinks: 'If I do not do something, it will not be done.'

'When I draw my bow,' says Herrigel to his Zen master, 'there comes a point when I feel as if I will get breathless if I do not let fly at once.'

'If you continue to try to provoke the moment when you must release the arrow, you will never learn the art of the archer,' says his master. 'Sometimes, it is the archer's own overactive desire that ruins the accuracy of the shot.'

A warrior of light sometimes thinks: 'If I do not do something, it will not be done.'

It is not quite like that: he must act, but he must allow room for the Universe to act too.

When a warrior
is the victim of some
injustice, he usually tries
to be alone, in order
not to show his pain
to others.

When a warrior is the victim of some injustice, he usually tries to be alone, in order not to show his pain to others.

This is both good and bad.

It is one thing to allow one's heart to heal its wounds slowly, but it is quite another to sit all day in deep contemplation for fear of seeming weak.

Inside each of us there lives an angel and a devil, and their voices are very alike. Confronted by a problem, the devil encourages that solitary conversation, trying to show us how vulnerable we are. The angel makes us reflect upon our attitudes and occasionally needs someone else's mouth to reveal itself.

A warrior balances solitude and dependence.

A warrior of light needs love.

A warrior of light needs love.

Love and affection are as much a part of his nature as eating and drinking and a taste for the Good Fight. When the warrior watches a sunset and feels no joy, then something is wrong.

At this point, he stops fighting and goes in search of company, so that they can watch the setting sun together.

If he has difficulty in finding company, he asks himself: 'Was I too afraid to approach someone? Did I receive affection and not even notice?'

A warrior of light makes use of solitude, but is not used by it.

The warrior of light knows that it is impossible to live in a state of complete relaxation.

The warrior of light knows that it is impossible to live in a state of complete relaxation.

He has learned from the archer that, in order to shoot his arrow any distance, he must hold the bow taut. He has learned from the stars that only an inner explosion allows them to shine. The warrior notices that when a horse is about to jump over a fence, it tenses all its muscles.

But he never confuses tension with anxiety.

The warrior of light always manages to balance Rigour and Mercy.

The warrior of light always manages to balance Rigour and Mercy.

To attain his dream, he needs a strong will and an enormous capacity for acceptance; although he may have an objective, the path that leads to that objective is not always as he imagined it would be.

That is why the warrior uses a mixture of discipline and compassion. God never abandons His children, but His purposes are unfathomable, and He builds the road with our own steps.

The warrior uses that combination of discipline and acceptance to fuel his enthusiasm. Routine was never at the head of any important new movement.

The warrior of light sometimes behaves like water, flowing around the obstacles he encounters.

The warrior of light sometimes behaves like water, flowing around the obstacles he encounters.

Occasionally, resisting might mean being destroyed, and so he adapts to the circumstances. He accepts without complaint that the stones along the path hinder his way across the mountains.

Therein lies the strength of water: it cannot be shattered by a hammer or wounded by a knife. The strongest sword in the world cannot scar its surface.

The waters of a river adapt themselves to whatever route proves possible, but the river never forgets its one objective: the sea. So fragile at its source, it gradually gathers the strength of the other rivers it encounters.

And, after a certain point, its power is absolute.

For the warrior of light, there are no abstractions.

For the warrior of light, there are no abstractions.

Everything is concrete and everything is meaningful. He does not sit comfortably in his tent, observing what is going on in the world; he accepts each challenge as an opportunity to transform himself.

Some of his companions spend their lives moaning about their lack of choice or passing comment on the decisions made by other people. The warrior, however, transforms his thinking into action.

Sometimes he chooses the wrong goal and pays the price for his mistake without complaint. At others, he swerves from the path and wastes a great deal of time only to end up back where he started.

But the warrior never allows himself to be discouraged.

The warrior of light
has the qualities
of a rock.

The warrior of light has the qualities of a rock.

When he is on flat terrain, everything around him is in harmony and he remains stable. People can build their houses upon him, and the storm will not destroy them.

When, however, he is placed on a slope, and the things around him show neither balance nor respect, then he reveals his strength; he rolls towards the enemy that is threatening his peace. At such moments, the warrior is a devastating force, and no one can stop him.

A warrior of light thinks about both war and peace and knows how to act in accordance with the circumstances.

A warrior of light who trusts too much in his intelligence will end up underestimating the power of his opponent.

A warrior of light who trusts too much in his intelligence will end up underestimating the power of his opponent.

It is important not to forget that sometimes strength is more effective than strategy.

A bullfight lasts fifteen minutes; the bull quickly learns that it is being tricked, and its next step is to charge the bullfighter. When that happens, no amount of brilliance, argument, intelligence or charm can avert tragedy.

That is why the warrior never underestimates brute force. When it proves too violent, he withdraws from the battlefield until his enemy has exhausted himself.

The warrior of light knows when an enemy is stronger than he is.

The warrior of light knows when an enemy is stronger than he is.

If he decides to confront him, he will be destroyed instantly. If he responds to his provocations, he will fall into a trap. So he uses diplomacy to resolve the difficult situation in which he finds himself. When the enemy behaves like a baby, he does the same. When he challenges him to a fight, he pretends not to understand.

His friends say: 'He's a coward.'

But the warrior pays no attention; he knows that all the rage and courage of a little bird are as nothing to a cat.

In such situations, the warrior remains patient; the enemy will soon go off in search of others to provoke.

A warrior of light
is never indifferent
to injustice.

A warrior of light is never indifferent to injustice.

He knows that all is one and that each individual action affects everyone on the planet. That is why, when confronted by the suffering of others, he uses his sword to restore order.

But even though he fights against oppression, at no point does he attempt to judge the oppressor. Each person will answer for his actions before God and so, once the warrior has completed his task, he makes no further comment.

A warrior of light is in the world in order to help his fellow man, not to condemn his neighbour.

A warrior of light
is never cowardly.

A warrior of light is never cowardly.

Flight might be an excellent form of defence, but it cannot be used when one is very afraid. When in doubt, the warrior prefers to face defeat and then lick his wounds, because he knows that if he flees he is giving to the aggressor greater power than he deserves.

In difficult and painful times, the warrior faces overwhelming odds with heroism, resignation and courage.

A warrior of light
is never in a hurry.

A warrior of light is never in a hurry.

Time works in his favour; he learns to master his impatience and avoids acting without thinking.

By walking slowly, he becomes aware of the firmness of his step. He knows that he is taking part in a decisive moment in the history of humanity and that he needs to change himself before he can transform the world. That is why he remembers the words of Lanza del Vasto: 'A revolution takes time to settle in.'

A warrior never picks fruit while it is still green.

A warrior of light
needs both patience
and speed.

A warrior of light needs both patience and speed.

The two worst strategic mistakes to make are acting prematurely and letting an opportunity slip; to avoid this, the warrior treats each situation as if it were unique and never resorts to formulae, recipes or other people's opinions.

The caliph Moauiyat asked Omr Ben Al-Aas the secret of his great political skills:

'I never get involved in something without having first worked out my retreat; then again, I have never gone into a situation and immediately wanted to run straight out again,' came the answer.

A warrior of light
often loses heart.

A warrior of light often loses heart.

He believes that nothing can stir in him the emotion he so desired. He is forced to spend many evenings and nights feeling that he is one of the vanquished, and nothing seems able to restore his enthusiasm.

His friends say: 'Perhaps his fight is over.'

The warrior feels pain and confusion when he hears such remarks because he knows that he has not yet reached the place he wanted to reach. But he is stubborn and refuses to relinquish his aims.

Then, when he least expects it, a new door opens.

A warrior of light
always keeps his heart
free of any feelings
of hatred.

A warrior of light always keeps his heart free of any feelings of hatred.

When he goes into battle, he remembers what Christ said: 'Love your enemies.' And he obeys.

But he knows that the act of forgiveness does not mean that he must accept everything; a warrior cannot bow his head, for if he did he would lose sight of the horizon of his dreams.

He accepts that his opponents are there to test his valour, his persistence, his ability to make decisions. They force him to fight for his dreams.

It is the experience of battle that strengthens the warrior of light.

The warrior remembers the past.

The warrior remembers the past.

He knows about man's Spiritual Quest, he knows that this Quest has been responsible for some of history's finest pages.

But also some of history's worst chapters: massacres, sacrifices, obscurantism. It was used for personal ends and has seen its ideas used to defend the most terrible of intentions.

The warrior has heard people ask: 'How am I to know that the path I am on is the right path?' And he has seen many people abandon their quest because they could not answer that question.

The warrior has no doubts; he follows one infallible saying:

'By their fruits ye shall know them,' said Jesus. That is the rule he follows, and he never goes wrong.

The warrior of light knows the importance of intuition.

The warrior of light knows the importance of intuition.

In the midst of battle, he does not have time to think about the enemy's blows, and so he uses his instinct and obeys his angel.

In times of peace, he deciphers the signs that God sends him.

People say: 'He's mad.'

Or: 'He lives in a fantasy world.'

Or even: 'How can he possibly believe in such illogical things?'

But the warrior knows that intuition is God's alphabet and he continues listening to the wind and talking to the stars.

The warrior of light sits around a fire with his companions.

The warrior of light sits around a fire with his companions.

They talk about his conquests, and any strangers who join the group are made welcome because everyone is proud of his life and of his Good Fight. The warrior speaks enthusiastically about the path, he tells how he resisted a particular challenge or speaks of the solution he found to one especially difficult situation. When he tells stories, he invests his words with passion and romance.

Sometimes, he exaggerates a little. He remembers that at times his ancestors used to exaggerate too.

That is why he does the same thing. But he never confuses pride with vanity, and he never believes his own exaggerations.

A warrior of light makes decisions. His soul is as free as the clouds in the sky, but he is committed to his dream.

The warrior hears someone say: 'I need to understand everything before I can make a decision. I want to have the freedom to change my mind.'

The warrior regards these words suspiciously. He too can enjoy that freedom, but this does not prevent him from taking on a commitment, even if he does not know quite why he does so.

A warrior of light makes decisions. His soul is as free as the clouds in the sky, but he is committed to his dream. On his freely chosen path, he often has to get up earlier than he would like, speak to people from whom he learns nothing, make certain sacrifices.

His friends say: 'You're not free.'

The warrior is free. But he knows that an open oven bakes no bread.

The warrior of light listens.

To engage in any activity you need to know what you can expect, how to achieve your objective, and whether or not you are capable of carrying out the proposed task.

'Only a person who, suitably equipped, feels no desire for the results of conquest and yet remains absorbed in the struggle can truly say that he has renounced the fruits of victory.

One can renounce the fruit, but that renunciation does not signal indifference to the results.'

The warrior of light listens with respect to Gandhi's strategy. And he remains unconvinced by those who, incapable of achieving any result at all, preach renunciation.

The warrior of light pays attention to small things because they can severely hamper him.

The warrior of light pays attention to small things because they can severely hamper him.

A thorn, however tiny, can cause the traveller to halt. A tiny, invisible cell can destroy a healthy organism. The memory of a past moment of fear allows cowardice to be reborn with each new morning. A fraction of a second opens the way for the enemy's fatal blow.

The warrior is attentive to small things. Sometimes he is hard on himself, but he prefers to act in this way.

'The devil is in the detail,' says one of the Tradition's old proverbs.

The warrior of light
does not always
have faith.

The warrior of light does not always have faith.

There are moments when he believes in absolutely nothing. And he asks his heart: 'Is all this effort really worth it?'

But his heart remains silent. And the warrior has to decide for himself.

Then he looks for an example. And he remembers that Jesus went through something similar in order fully to inhabit the human condition.

'Take away this cup from me,' said Jesus. He too lost heart and courage, but he did not stop.

The warrior of light continues despite his lack of faith. He goes forward and, in the end, faith returns.

The warrior knows
that no man is an island.

The warrior knows that no man is an island.

He cannot fight alone; whatever his plan, he depends on other people. He needs to discuss his strategy, to ask for help, and – in moments of relaxation – to have someone with whom he can sit by the fire, someone he can regale with tales of battle.

But he does not allow people to confuse this camaraderie with insecurity. He is transparent in his actions and secretive in his plans.

A warrior of light dances with his companions, but does not place the responsibility for his actions on anyone else.

In the intervals
between battles, the
warrior rests.

In the intervals between battles, the warrior rests.

Often he spends whole days doing nothing, because that is what his heart demands; but his intuition remains alert. He does not commit the capital sin of Sloth, because he knows where that can lead – to the warm monotony of Sunday afternoons when time simply passes.

The warrior calls this 'the peace of the cemetery'. He remembers a passage from Revelation: 'I know thy works, that thou art neither cold nor hot ... So then because thou art lukewarm and neither cold nor hot, I will spew thee out of my mouth.'

A warrior rests and laughs. But he is always alert.

The warrior of light knows that everyone is afraid of everyone else.

The warrior of light knows that everyone is afraid of everyone else.

This fear generally manifests itself in two ways: through aggression or through submission. They are two facets of the same problem.

That is why, whenever he finds himself before someone who fills him with fear, the warrior reminds himself that the other person has the same insecurities as he has. He has surmounted similar obstacles and experienced the same problems.

But he knows how to deal with the situation better. Why? Because he uses fear as an engine, not as a brake.

The warrior learns from his opponent and acts in a like manner.

For the warrior
there is no such thing as
an impossible love.

For the warrior there is no such thing as an impossible love.

He is not intimidated by silence, indifference or rejection. He knows that, behind the mask of ice that people wear, there beats a heart of fire.

This is why the warrior takes more risks than other people. He is constantly seeking the love of someone, even if that means often having to hear the word 'no', returning home defeated and feeling rejected in body and soul.

A warrior never gives in to fear when he is searching for what he needs. Without love, he is nothing.

The warrior of light recognises the silence that precedes an important battle.

The warrior of light recognises the silence that precedes an important battle.

And that silence seems to be saying: 'Things have stopped. Why not forget about fighting and enjoy yourself a little.' At this point, inexperienced combatants lay down their arms and complain that they are bored.

The warrior listens intently to that silence; somewhere something is happening. He knows that devastating earthquakes arrive without warning. He has walked through forests at night and knows that it is precisely when the animals are silent that danger is near.

While the others talk, the warrior trains himself in the use of the sword and keeps his eye on the horizon.

The warrior of light
is a believer.

The warrior of light is a believer.

Because he believes in miracles, miracles begin to happen. Because he is sure that his thoughts can change his life, his life begins to change. Because he is certain that he will find love, that love appears.

Now and then, he is disappointed. Sometimes, he gets hurt.

Then he hears people say: 'He's so ingenuous!'

But the warrior knows that it is worth it. For every defeat, he has two victories in his favour.

All believers know this.

The warrior of light has learned that it is best to follow the light.

The warrior of light has learned that it is best to follow the light.

He has behaved treacherously, he has lied, he has strayed from the path, he has courted darkness. And everything was fine, as if nothing had happened.

Then an abyss suddenly opens up; you can take a thousand steps in safety, but just one step too many can put an end to everything. Then the warrior stops before he destroys himself.

When he makes that decision, he hears four comments: 'You always do the wrong thing. You're too old to change. You're no good. You don't deserve it.'

He looks up at the sky. And a voice says: 'My dear, everyone makes mistakes. You're forgiven, but I cannot force that forgiveness on you. It's your choice.'

The true warrior of light accepts that forgiveness.

The warrior of light
is always trying to
improve.

The warrior of light is always trying to improve.

Every blow of his sword carries with it centuries of wisdom and meditation. Every blow needs to have the strength and skill of all the warriors of the past who, even today, continue to bless the struggle. Each movement during combat honours the movements that the previous generations tried to transmit through the Tradition.

The warrior develops the beauty of his blows.

A warrior of light is reliable.

A warrior of light is reliable.

He makes a few mistakes, he sometimes thinks he is more important than he really is, but he does not lie.

When people gather round the fire, he talks to his friends, male and female. He knows that his words are stored in the memory of the Universe, like a testimony of what he thinks.

And the warrior asks himself: 'Why do I talk so much, when often I am incapable of carrying out everything I say?'

His heart replies: 'When you defend your ideas in public, you then have to make an effort to live accordingly.'

It is because he believes that he is what he says he is that the warrior ends up becoming precisely that.

The warrior knows that there are occasional pauses in the struggle.

The warrior knows that there are occasional pauses in the struggle.

There is no point in forcing things; he must have patience and wait for the two sides to clash again. In the silence of the battlefield, he listens to his heart beating.

He notices that he is tense, that he is afraid.

The warrior takes stock of his life; he makes sure that his sword is sharp, his heart satisfied, that faith still burns in his soul. He knows that maintenance is as important as action.

There is always something not quite right. And the warrior takes advantage of those moments when time stops to equip himself better.

A warrior knows
that an angel and a devil
are both competing for his
sword hand.

A warrior knows that an angel and a devil are both competing for his sword hand.

The devil says: 'You will weaken. You will not know exactly when. You are afraid.' The angel says: 'You will weaken. You will not know exactly when. You are afraid.'

The warrior is surprised. Both angel and devil have said the same thing.

Then the devil goes on: 'Let me help you.' And the angel says: 'I will help you.'

At that moment, the warrior understands the difference. The words may be the same, but these two allies are completely different.

And he chooses the angel's hand.

Whenever the warrior draws his sword, he uses it.

Whenever the warrior draws his sword, he uses it.

It can be used to clear a path, to help someone, to fend off danger, but a sword is a capricious thing and does not like to see its blade exposed for no good reason.

That is why the warrior never makes threats. He can attack, defend himself or flee; all of these attitudes form part of combat. It is not, however, part of combat to diminish the force of a blow by talking about it.

A warrior of light is always alert to the movements of his sword. But he never forgets that the sword is watching his every move as well.

It was not made to be used by the mouth.

Sometimes evil pursues the warrior of light, and when it does, he calmly invites it into his tent.

Sometimes evil pursues the warrior of light, and when it does, he calmly invites it into his tent.

He asks evil: 'Do you want to hurt me or use me to hurt others?'

Evil pretends not to hear. It says that it knows the darkness in the warrior's soul. It touches wounds that have not yet healed and calls for vengeance. It mentions certain tricks and subtle poisons that will help him to destroy his enemies.

The warrior of light listens. If conversation flags, he encourages evil to continue talking by asking all about its various plans.

When he has heard everything, he gets up and leaves. Evil feels so weary and empty after all this talk that it does not have the strength to follow him.

The warrior of light unwittingly takes a false step and plunges into the abyss.

The warrior of light unwittingly takes a false step and plunges into the abyss.

Ghosts frighten him and solitude torments him. His aim had been to fight the Good Fight, and he never imagined that this would happen to him, but it did. Shrouded in darkness, he makes contact with his master.

'Master, I have fallen into the abyss,' he says. 'The waters are deep and dark.'

'Remember one thing,' replies his master. 'You do not drown simply by plunging into water, you only drown if you stay beneath the surface.'

And the warrior uses all his strength to escape from his predicament.

The warrior of light behaves like a child.

The warrior of light behaves like a child.

People are shocked; they have forgotten that a child needs to have fun and to play, to be slightly irreverent and to ask awkward, childish questions, to talk nonsense that not even he believes in.

And they say, horrified: 'So this is the spiritual path, is it? He's so immature!'

The warrior feels proud of such comments. And he remains in touch with God through his innocence and his joy, without ever losing sight of his mission.

A responsible warrior is one who has proved able to observe and to learn.

The Latin root of the word 'responsibility' reveals its true meaning: the capacity to respond, to react.

A responsible warrior is one who has proved able to observe and to learn. He is even capable of being 'irresponsible'. Sometimes, he has allowed himself to be carried along by a situation, without responding or reacting.

But he always learned his lesson; he took a stance, listened to advice and was humble enough to accept help.

A responsible warrior is not someone who takes the weight of the world on his shoulders, but someone who has learned to deal with the challenges of the moment.

A warrior of light
cannot always choose
his battlefield.

A warrior of light cannot always choose his battlefield.

Sometimes he is taken by surprise in the middle of battles not of his choosing, but there is no point in running away, those battles will merely follow him.

Then, at the point when conflict seems almost inevitable, the warrior talks to his opponent. Showing neither fear nor cowardice, he tries to find out why the other man wants to fight, what made him leave his village in order to seek him out to fight this duel. Without even unsheathing his sword, the warrior persuades his opponent that this is not a fight for him.

A warrior of light listens to what his opponent has to say. He only fights if absolutely necessary.

The warrior allows
the decision to
reveal itself.

The warrior of light is terrified when it comes to making important decisions.

'This is too much for you,' says a friend. 'Go on, be brave,' says another. And so his doubts grow.

After some days of anxiety, he withdraws to the corner of his tent where he usually sits to meditate and pray. He sees himself in the future. He sees the people who will benefit or be harmed by his attitude. He does not want to cause pointless suffering, but nor does he want to abandon the path.

The warrior allows the decision to reveal itself.

If he has to say 'yes', he will say it bravely. If he has to say 'no', he will say it without a trace of cowardice.

A warrior of light accepts his Personal Legend completely.

A warrior of light accepts his Personal Legend completely.

His companions say: 'He has remarkable faith!'

For a moment, the warrior feels proud, then immediately feels ashamed of what he has heard because he does not have as much faith as he appears to have.

At that moment, his angel whispers: 'You are only an instrument of the light. There is no reason to feel proud or to feel guilty. There are only reasons to feel happy.'

And the warrior of light, aware now that he is but an instrument, feels calmer and more secure.

Warriors of light never accept what is unacceptable.

'Hitler may have lost the war on the battlefield, but he ended up winning something too,' says Marek Halter, 'because man in the twentieth century created the concentration camp and revived torture and taught his fellow men that it is possible to close their eyes to the misfortunes of others.'

Perhaps he is right: there are abandoned children, massacred civilians, innocent people imprisoned, lonely old people, drunks in the gutter, madmen in power.

But perhaps he isn't right at all, for there are also warriors of light.

And warriors of light never accept what is unacceptable.

A warrior of light
is wise; he does not talk
about his defeats.

The warrior of light never forgets the old saying: the good little goat doesn't bleat.

Injustices happen. Everyone finds themselves in situations they do not deserve, usually when they are unable to defend themselves. Defeat often knocks at the warrior's door.

At such times, he remains silent. He does not waste energy on words, because they can do nothing; it is best to use his strength to resist and have patience, knowing that Someone is watching, Someone who saw the unnecessary suffering and who will not accept it.

That Someone gives him what he most needs: time. Sooner or later, everything will once more work in his favour.

A warrior of light is wise; he does not talk about his defeats.

A sword may not last very long, but the warrior of light must.

A sword may not last very long, but the warrior of light must.

That is why he never allows himself to be deceived by his own abilities and thus avoids being taken by surprise. He gives each thing the value it deserves.

Often, when the warrior is pondering grave matters, the devil whispers in his ear: 'Don't worry about that, it's not important.'

At others, when he is faced by banalities, the devil says to him: 'You should pour all your energies into resolving this situation.'

The warrior does not listen to what the devil is telling him; he is the master of his sword.

A warrior of light
is always vigilant.

A warrior of light is always vigilant.

He does not ask anyone else for permission to wield his sword; he simply takes it in his hands. Nor does he waste time explaining his actions; faithful to God's decisions, he gives his answer in what he does.

He looks to either side of him and identifies his friends. He looks behind him and identifies his opponents. He is implacable with treachery, but he does not seek revenge; he merely drives away the enemies of his life, never fighting with them any longer than is necessary.

A warrior does not try to seem, he is.

A warrior does not keep company with those who wish to harm him.

A warrior does not keep company with those who wish to harm him. Nor is he seen in the company of those who want to 'console' him.

He avoids anyone who is only by his side in the event of a defeat: these false friends want to prove that weakness is rewarded. They always bring him bad news. They always try to destroy the warrior's confidence, all under the cloak of 'solidarity'.

When they see him wounded, they dissolve in tears, but, in their heart of hearts, they are happy because the warrior has lost a battle. They do not understand that this is part of the fight.

The true companions of a warrior are beside him always, during the difficult times and the easy times.

At the beginning of his struggle, the warrior of light stated: 'I have dreams.'

At the beginning of his struggle, the warrior of light stated: 'I have dreams.'

After some years, he realises that it is actually possible to reach his goal; he knows that he will be rewarded.

At that moment, he feels sad. He knows about other people's unhappiness, about the loneliness and frustration experienced by so much of humanity, and he does not believe that he deserves what he is about to receive.

His angel whispers: 'Give it all up.' The warrior kneels down and offers God his conquests.

That act of surrender forces the warrior to stop asking foolish questions and helps him to overcome his feelings of guilt.

The warrior of light has
the sword in his hands.

The warrior of light has the sword in his hands.

He is the one who decides what he will do and what he will never do.

There are moments when life leads him into a crisis; he is separated from things he has always loved; it is then that the warrior reflects. He checks that he is fulfilling God's will or if he is merely acting selfishly. If this separation is really part of his path, then he accepts it without complaint.

If, however, such a separation was provoked by someone else's perverse actions, then he is implacable in his response.

The warrior possesses both force and forgiveness. He can use both with equal skill.

The warrior of light never falls into the trap of that word 'freedom'.

The warrior of light never falls into the trap of that word 'freedom'.

When his people are oppressed, freedom is a very clear concept. At such times, using sword and shield, he fights as long as he has breath and life. When contrasted with oppression, freedom is easy to understand: it is the opposite of slavery.

But sometimes the warrior hears older people saying: 'When I stop working, I will be free.' A year later, those same people are complaining: 'Life is all boring routine.' In this case, freedom is difficult to understand: it means absence of meaning.

A warrior of light is always committed. He is the slave of his dream and free to act.

A warrior of light is not constantly repeating the same struggle, especially when there are neither advances nor retreats.

A warrior of light is not constantly repeating the same struggle, especially when there are neither advances nor retreats.

If a battle is not progressing, he knows that he must sit down with the enemy and negotiate a truce; they have both practised the art of the sword, now they need to understand each other.

This is a dignified gesture, not a cowardly one. It is a balance of forces and a change of strategy.

Once the peace plans have been drawn up, the warriors return to their houses. They do not need to prove anything to anyone; they fought the Good Fight and kept the faith. Each one gave a little, thus learning the art of negotiation.

Yesterday's pain
is the warrior of light's
strength.

The friends of the warrior of light ask him where he draws his energy from. He says: 'From the hidden enemy.'

His friends ask who that is.

The warrior responds: 'Someone we can no longer hurt.'

It might be a boy who beat him in a childhood scrap, the girlfriend who left him when he was eleven, the teacher who said he was stupid. When he is tired, the warrior reminds himself that these enemies have still not seen his courage.

He does not consider revenge, because the hidden enemy is no longer part of his story. He thinks only of improving his skills so that his deeds will be known throughout the world and reach the ears of those who have hurt him in the past.

Yesterday's pain is the warrior of light's strength.

A warrior of light always has a second chance in life.

A warrior of light always has a second chance in life.

Like all other men and woman, he was not born knowing how to use a sword; he made many mistakes before he discovered his Personal Legend.

No warrior can sit down by the fire and tell the others: 'I always did the right thing.' Anyone who says this is lying and has not yet learned to know himself. The true warrior of light has committed injustices in the past.

But as he proceeds on his journey, he realises that the people to whom he did not behave correctly always cross his path again.

It is his chance to right the wrong he did them, and he always, unhesitatingly, seizes that chance.

A warrior is as
wise as a serpent and as
innocent as a dove.

A warrior is as wise as a serpent and as innocent as a dove.

When people gather to talk, he does not judge the behaviour of others; he knows that darkness uses an invisible net to spread its evil. This net catches any snippet of information floating in the air and transforms it into the intrigue and envy that infest the human soul.

Thus, everything that is said about someone reaches the ears of the enemies of that person, augmented by the dark weight of poison and malice.

For this reason, when the warrior speaks of his brother's opinions, he imagines that his brother is there present, listening to what he is saying.

'The spiritual energy of the Path uses justice and patience to prepare your spirit.'

The Breviary of Medieval Knights says:

'The spiritual energy of the Path uses justice and patience to prepare your spirit.

This is the Path of the Knight: a path that is at once easy and difficult, because it forces one to set aside trivial things and chance friendships. That is why, at first, many hesitate to follow it.

This is the first teaching of the Knights: you will erase everything you had written in the book of your life up until now: restlessness, uncertainty, lies. And in the place of all this you will write the word *courage*. By beginning the journey with that word and continuing with faith in God, you will arrive wherever you need to arrive.'

When the moment for
combat approaches, the
warrior of light is prepared
for all eventualities.

When the moment for combat approaches, the warrior of light is prepared for all eventualities.

He analyses every strategy and asks: 'What would I do if I had to fight myself?' He thus discovers his weak points.

At that moment, his opponent approaches; he comes with a bag full of promises, treaties, negotiations. He has tempting proposals and easy alternatives.

The warrior analyses each of the proposals; he also seeks agreement, but without ever losing his dignity. If he avoids combat, it will not be because he was seduced, but because he judged it to be the best strategy.

A warrior of light does not accept gifts from his enemy.

Warriors of light often ask themselves what they are doing here. Often they find their lives meaningless.

I repeat:

You can recognise a warrior of light by the look in his eye. Warriors of light are in the world, they form part of the world, and they were sent into the world without saddlebags or sandals. They are often cowardly. They do not always act correctly.

Warriors of light are wounded by the most foolish things, they worry about trivialities, they believe themselves incapable of growing. Warriors of light sometimes believe themselves unworthy of any blessing or miracle.

Warriors of light often ask themselves what they are doing here. Often they find their lives meaningless.

That is why they are warriors of light. Because they fail. Because they ask questions. Because they keep looking for a meaning. And, in the end, they will find it.

The warrior thinks:
'Changes must be made
that I do not feel like
making.'

The warrior of light is now waking from his dream.

He thinks: 'I do not know how to deal with this light that is making me grow.' The light, however, does not disappear.

The warrior thinks: 'Changes must be made that I do not feel like making.'

The light remains, because 'feel' is a word full of traps.

Then the eyes and heart of the warrior begin to grow accustomed to the light. It no longer frightens him and he finally accepts his own Legend, even if this means running risks.

The warrior has been asleep for a long time. It is only natural that he should wake up very gradually.

Like the fighter,
the warrior of light
is aware of his own
immense strength; he
never fights with
anyone who does not
deserve the honour
of combat.

The experienced fighter puts up with insults; he knows the strength of his fist and the skill of his blows. Confronted by an unprepared opponent, he looks deep into his eyes and conquers him without ever having to resort to a physical fight.

As the warrior learns from his spiritual master, the light of faith shines in his eyes and he does not need to prove anything to anyone. He is not bothered by his opponent's aggressive arguments which say that God is a superstition, that miracles are just tricks, that believing in angels is running away from reality.

Like the fighter, the warrior of light is aware of his own immense strength; he never fights with anyone who does not deserve the honour of combat.

The warrior of light
must always remember
the five rules of combat,
set down by Chuan Tzu
three thousand years ago.

The warrior of light must always remember the five rules of combat, set down by Chuan Tzu three thousand years ago:

Faith Before going into battle, you must believe in the reasons for the fight.

Companions Choose your allies and learn to fight in company, for no one ever won a war single-handed.

Time A battle in winter is different from a battle in summer; a good warrior is careful to select the right moment to begin a fight.

Space One does not fight in the same way in a mountain pass as one would on a plain. Think about your surroundings and how best to move around in them.

Strategy The best warrior is the one who plans his fight.

The warrior rarely
knows the result of
a battle when the
battle is over.

The warrior rarely knows the result of a battle when the battle is over.

The activity of fighting will have generated an enormous amount of energy around him and there is always a moment when victory and defeat are equally possible. Time will tell who won and who lost, but he knows that, from that moment on, he can do nothing more: the fate of that battle lies in God's hands.

At such moments, the warrior of light is not concerned with results. He examines his heart and asks: 'Did I fight the Good Fight?' If the answer is 'yes', he can rest. If the answer is 'no', he takes up his sword and begins training all over again.

Each warrior of light contains within him the spark of God.

Each warrior of light contains within him the spark of God.

His destiny is to be with other warriors, but sometimes he will need to practise the art of the sword alone; this is why, when he is apart from his companions, he behaves like a star.

He lights up his allotted part of the Universe and tries to point out galaxies and worlds to all those who gaze up at the sky.

The warrior's persistence will soon be rewarded. Gradually, other warriors approach, and they join together to form constellations, each with their own symbols and mysteries.

Sometimes the warrior feels as if he were living two lives at once.

Sometimes the warrior feels as if he were living two lives at once.

In one of them he is obliged to do all the things he does not want to do and to fight for ideas in which he does not believe. But there is another life, and he discovers it in his dreams, in his reading and in his encounters with people who share his ideas.

The warrior allows his two lives to draw near. 'There is a bridge that links what I do with what I would like to do,' he thinks. Slowly, his dreams take over his everyday life, and then he realises that he is ready for the thing he always wanted.

Then all that is needed is a little daring, and his two lives become one.

The warrior of light
needs time to himself.
And he uses that time for
rest, contemplation and
contact with the Soul
of the World.

Write down again what I told you:

The warrior of light needs time to himself. And he uses that time for rest, contemplation and contact with the Soul of the World. Even in the midst of a battle, he manages to meditate.

Occasionally, the warrior sits down, relaxes and lets everything that is happening around him continue to happen. He looks at the world as a spectator, he does not try to add to it or take away from it, he merely surrenders unresistingly to the movement of life.

Little by little, everything that seemed complicated begins to become simple. And the warrior is glad.

The warrior of light is wary of people who think they know the path.

The warrior of light is wary of people who think they know the path.

They are always so confident of their own ability to make decisions that they do not notice the irony with which destiny writes each life, and they always complain when the inevitable knocks at the door.

The warrior of light has dreams. His dreams carry him forward. But he never makes the mistake of thinking that the way is broad and the gate wide. He knows that the Universe functions in the same way as alchemy: *solve et coagula* said the masters – 'Concentrate and disperse your energies according to the situation.'

There are moments when one should act and moments when one should accept. The warrior knows how to distinguish between these moments.

The warrior of light, once he has learned how to use a sword, discovers that his equipment is still incomplete – he needs armour.

The warrior of light, once he has learned how to use a sword, discovers that his equipment is still incomplete – he needs armour.

He sets off in search of this armour and he listens to the advice of various salesmen.

'Use the breastplate of solitude,' says one.

'Use the shield of cynicism', says another.

'The best armour is not to get involved in anything,' says a third.

The warrior, however, ignores them. He calmly goes to his sacred place and puts on the indestructible cloak of faith.

Faith parries all blows. Faith transforms poison into crystal clear water.

A warrior trusts other people because, first and foremost, he trusts himself.

'I always believe everything anyone tells me and I'm always disappointed,' his companion says.

It is important to trust people; a warrior of light is not afraid of disappointments because he knows the power of his sword and the strength of his love.

However, he imposes certain limits: it is one thing to accept God's signs and to know that the angels use the mouths of other people to give us advice. It is quite another to be incapable of making decisions and to be always looking for ways of letting others tell us what we should do.

A warrior trusts other people because, first and foremost, he trusts himself.

The warrior of light
views life with tenderness
and determination.

The warrior of light views life with tenderness and determination.

He stands before a mystery, whose solution he will one day find. Every so often, he says to himself: 'This life is absolutely insane.'

He is right. In surrendering to the miracle of the everyday, he notices that he cannot always foresee the consequences of his actions. Sometimes he acts without even knowing that he is doing so, he saves someone without even knowing he is saving them, he suffers without even knowing why he is sad.

Yes, life is insane. But the great wisdom of the warrior lies in choosing his insanity wisely.

The warrior of light
studies the two columns
on either side of the door
he is trying to open.

The warrior of light studies the two columns on either side of the door he is trying to open.

One is called Fear and the other is called Desire. The warrior looks at the column of Fear and on it is written: 'You are entering a dangerous, unfamiliar world where everything you have learned up until now will prove useless.'

The warrior looks at the column of Desire and on it is written: 'You are about to leave a familiar world wherein are stored all the things you ever wanted and for which you struggled long and hard.'

The warrior smiles because nothing frightens him and nothing holds him. With the confidence of one who knows what he wants, he opens the door.

A warrior of light
practises a powerful
exercise for inner growth.

A warrior of light practises a powerful exercise for inner growth: he pays attention to the things he does automatically, such as breathing, blinking, or noticing the things around him.

He does this when he feels confused, and in this way he frees himself from tensions and allows his intuition to work more freely, without interference from his fears and desires. Certain problems that appeared to be insoluble are resolved, certain sorrows from which he thought he would never recover vanish naturally.

He uses this technique whenever he is faced with a difficult situation.

A warrior of light knows the power of words.

The warrior of light hears comments like: 'There are certain things I'd rather not talk about because people are so envious.'

When he hears this, the warrior laughs. Envy cannot harm you, if you don't let it. Envy is part of life and everyone should learn to deal with it.

However, he rarely discusses his plans. And sometimes people believe this is because he is afraid of envy.

But he knows that whenever he talks about a dream, he uses a little bit of the energy from that dream in order to do so. And by talking, he runs the risk of spending all the energy he needs to put the dream into action.

A warrior of light knows the power of words.

The warrior of light knows the value of persistence and of courage.

The warrior of light knows the value of persistence and of courage.

Often, during combat, he receives blows that he was not expecting. And he realises that, during war, his enemy is bound to win some of the battles. When this happens, he weeps bitter tears and rests in order to recover his energies a little. But he immediately resumes his battle for his dreams.

The longer he remains away, the more likely he is to feel weak, fearful and intimidated. When a horseman falls off his horse, if he does not remount immediately, he will never have the courage to do so again.

A warrior knows when a battle is worth fighting.

A warrior knows when a battle is worth fighting.

He bases his decisions on inspiration and faith. He nevertheless meets people who ask him to fight battles that are not his own, on battlefields that he does not know or which do not interest him. They want to involve the warrior of light in contests that are important to them, but not to him.

Often these are people close to the warrior of light, people who love him and trust in his strength and who want him to ease their anxieties in some way.

At such moments, he smiles and makes it clear to them that he loves them, but he does not take up the challenge.

A true warrior of light always chooses his own battlefield.

The warrior of light knows how to lose.

The warrior of light knows how to lose.

He does not treat defeat as if it were a matter of indifference to him, saying things like 'Oh, it doesn't matter' or 'To be honest, I didn't really want it that much'. He accepts defeat as defeat and does not try to make a victory out of it.

Painful wounds, the indifference of friends, the loneliness of losing – all leave a bitter taste. But at these times, he says to himself: 'I fought for something and did not succeed. I lost the first battle.'

These words give him renewed strength. He knows that no one wins all the time and he knows how to distinguish his successes from his failures.

When somebody wants something, the whole Universe conspires in their favour. The warrior of light knows this.

When somebody wants something, the whole Universe conspires in their favour. The warrior of light knows this.

For this reason, he takes great care with his thoughts. Hidden beneath a whole series of good intentions lie feelings that no one dares confess to himself: vengeance, self-destruction, guilt, fear of winning, a macabre joy at other people's tragedies.

The Universe does not judge; it conspires in favour of what we want. That is why the warrior has the courage to look into the dark places of his soul in order to ensure that he is not asking for the wrong things.

And he is always very careful about what he thinks.

When the warrior takes on a commitment, he keeps his word.

Jesus said: 'Let your yea be yea; and your nay, nay.' When the warrior takes on a commitment, he keeps his word.

Those who make promises they do not keep lose their self-respect and feel ashamed of their actions. These people spend their lives in constant flight; they expend far more energy on coming up with a series of excuses to unsay what they said than the warrior of light does in honouring his commitments.

Sometimes he too takes on a foolish commitment which will in some way harm him. He does not repeat this mistake, but he nevertheless keeps his word and pays the price for his own impulsiveness.

When he wins a battle,
the warrior celebrates.

When he wins a battle, the warrior celebrates.

This victory has cost him anxious moments, nights racked with doubt, endless days of waiting. Since ancient times, celebrating a triumph has been part of the ritual of life itself: celebration is a rite of passage.

His companions see the warrior of light's joy and think: 'Why is he doing that? He might be disappointed in his next battle. He might draw down on himself the wrath of his enemy.'

But the warrior knows why he is celebrating. He is savouring the best gift that victory can bring: confidence.

He celebrates yesterday's victory in order to gain more strength for tomorrow's battle.

The warrior keeps
his attention focused
on the battle and he
perseveres, even when
everything seems
utterly pointless.

One day, for no apparent reason, the warrior realises that he does not feel the same enthusiasm for the fight that he used to.

He continues to do what he has always done, but every gesture seems meaningless. At such a time, he has only one choice: to continue fighting the Good Fight. He says his prayers out of duty or fear or whatever, but he does not abandon the path.

He knows that the angel of the One who inspires him has simply wandered off somewhere. The warrior keeps his attention focused on the battle and he perseveres, even when everything seems utterly pointless. The angel will soon return and the merest flutter of his wings will restore the warrior's joy to him.

A warrior of light shares with others what he knows of the path.

A warrior of light shares with others what he knows of the path.

Anyone who gives help also receives help and needs to teach what he has learned. That is why he sits by the fire and recounts his day on the battlefield.

A friend whispers: 'Why talk so openly about your strategy? Don't you realise that, by doing so, you run the risk of sharing your conquests with others?'

The warrior merely smiles and says nothing. He knows that if, at the end of his journey, he arrives to find an empty paradise, his struggle will have been a waste of time.

The warrior of light
has learned that God uses
solitude to teach us how
to live with other people.

The warrior of light has learned that God uses solitude to teach us how to live with other people.

He uses rage to show us the infinite value of peace. He uses boredom to underline the importance of adventure and spontaneity.

God uses silence to teach us to use words responsibly. He uses tiredness so that we can understand the value of waking up. He uses illness to underline the blessing of good health.

God uses fire to teach us about water. He uses earth so that we can understand the value of air. He uses death to show us the importance of life.

The warrior of light
gives before he is asked.

The warrior of light gives before he is asked.

Seeing this, some of his companions say: 'If someone wants something, they'll ask for it.'

But the warrior knows that there are many people who simply cannot bring themselves to ask for help. Alongside him live people with such fragile hearts that love becomes a sickness; they are starving for affection and yet are ashamed to show it.

The warrior gathers these people round the fire, he tells stories, shares his food, gets drunk with them. The following day, everyone feels better.

Those who look on other people's misery with indifference are the most miserable of all.

Warriors who
spend all their time
training lose their
spontaneity in
battle.

If the strings of an instrument are always taut, they go out of tune.

Warriors who spend all their time training lose their spontaneity in battle. Horses that are always jumping fences end up breaking a leg. Bows that are bent all day no longer shoot arrows with the same force.

That is why, even if he is not in the mood, the warrior of light tries to enjoy the small everyday things of life.

The warrior of light lets go of the idea of days and hours in order to pay more attention to the moment.

The warrior of light listens to Lao Tzu when he says that we should let go of the idea of days and hours in order to pay more attention to the moment.

Only in this way can the warrior resolve certain problems before they occur; by focusing on the small things, he manages to avoid larger calamities.

But thinking about the small things is not the same as thinking small. Over-anxiety ultimately banishes every trace of joy from life.

The warrior knows that a great dream is made up of many different things, just as the light from the sun is the sum of its millions of rays.

When he is forced to perform the same task several times, the warrior transforms work into prayer.

There are times when the warrior's path becomes merely routine.

Then he applies the teaching of Rabbi Nachman of Breslov:

'If you cannot meditate, you should repeat one simple word, because this is good for the soul. Do not say anything else, just repeat that word over and over, innumerable times. Finally, it will lose all meaning, but take on an entirely new significance. God will open the doors and you will find yourself using that simple word to say everything that you wanted to say.'

When he is forced to perform the same task several times, the warrior uses this tactic and transforms work into prayer.

A warrior of light has no 'certainties', he just has a path to follow, a path to which he tries to adapt depending on the season.

A warrior of light has no 'certainties', he just has a path to follow, a path to which he tries to adapt depending on the season.

During battles that take place in summer he does not use the same equipment and techniques that he would use during battles that take place in winter. By being flexible, he no longer judges the world on the basis of 'right' and 'wrong', but on the basis of 'the most appropriate attitude for that particular moment'.

He knows that his companions also have to adapt and is not surprised when they change their attitude. He gives each one the necessary time to justify his actions.

But when it comes to treachery, he is implacable.

A warrior of light does not go into battle without knowing the limitations of his ally.

A warrior sits around the fire with his friends.

They spend hours criticising each other, but they end the night sleeping in the same tent, having forgotten all the insults that were bandied about. Occasionally, a new member joins the group. Because he does not yet share a common history, he shows only his good qualities, and some see in him a master.

But the warrior of light never compares him with his old companions in battle. He makes the stranger welcome, but he will not trust him until he knows his defects too.

A warrior of light does not go into battle without knowing the limitations of his ally.

The warrior knows an old saying: 'If regrets could kill …'

The warrior knows an old saying: 'If regrets could kill ...'

And he knows that regrets can kill; they slowly eat away at the soul of someone who has done something wrong and they lead eventually to self-destruction.

The warrior does not want to die like that. When he acts perversely or maliciously – because he is a man of many faults – he is never too ashamed to ask forgiveness.

If possible, he does his best to repair the wrong he has done. If the injured party is dead, then he does some good turn to a stranger and offers up that deed to the soul that he wounded.

A warrior of light has no regrets, because regrets can kill. He humbles himself and undoes the wrong he has done.

The warrior of light
takes responsibility
for everything he does,
even if he has to pay a
high price for his
mistake.

All warriors of light have heard their mothers say: 'My son wasn't thinking straight when he did that; deep down, he's a very good person.'

Although he respects his mother, he knows that this is not true. He does not waste his time blaming himself for his rash actions nor does he spend his life forgiving himself for all the wrong he has done – doing that would never set him back on the right path.

He uses common sense to judge not the intentions of an action but its consequences. He takes responsibility for everything he does, even if he has to pay a high price for his mistake.

As the old Arabic proverb says: 'God judges a tree by its fruits and not by its roots.'

The warrior asks himself: 'How will this affect the fifth generation of my descendants?'

Before making any important decision – declaring a war, moving with his companions to another plain, choosing a field in which to sow seed – the warrior asks himself: 'How will this affect the fifth generation of my descendants?'

A warrior knows that everything a person does has enduring consequences and he needs to understand what kind of world he is leaving behind for that fifth generation.

The warrior respects
the suffering of others and
does not try to compare
it with his own.

'It's just a storm in a teacup,' someone says to the warrior of light.

But he never exaggerates his difficulties and always tries to remain calm.

And he never judges someone else's suffering.

A small detail – which does not affect him in the least – could serve to ignite the storm brewing in his brother's soul. The warrior respects the suffering of others and does not try to compare it with his own.

The cup of suffering is not the same size for everyone.

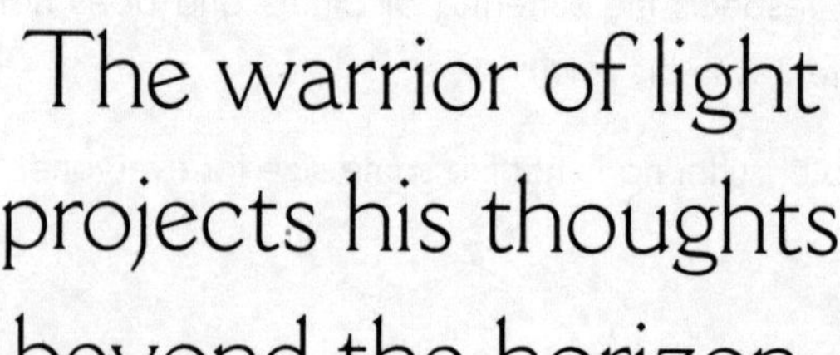

The warrior of light projects his thoughts beyond the horizon.

'The most important quality on the spiritual path is courage,' said Gandhi.

The world seems threatening and dangerous to cowards. They seek the false security of a life with no major challenges and arm themselves to the teeth in order to defend what they think they possess. Cowards end up making the bars of their own prison.

The warrior of light projects his thoughts beyond the horizon. He knows that if he does not do anything for the world, no one else will.

So he fights the Good Fight and he helps others, even though he does not quite understand why.

‘Carry in your memory, for the rest of your life, the good things that came out of difficulties.’

The warrior of light pays close attention to a text that the Soul of the World transmitted to Chico Xavier:

'When you have managed to overcome grave problems in a relationship, do not spend time remembering the difficult times, concentrate on the joy of having passed yet another of life's tests. When you emerge from a long period of medical treatment, do not brood on the suffering you endured, think instead of God's blessing that allowed you to be cured.

'Carry in your memory, for the rest of your life, the good things that came out of those difficulties. They will serve as a proof of your abilities and will give you confidence when you are faced by other obstacles.'

The warrior of light concentrates on the small miracles of daily life.

The warrior of light concentrates on the small miracles of daily life.

He is capable of seeing what is beautiful because he carries beauty within himself, for the world is a mirror and gives back to each man the reflection of his own face. The warrior knows his faults and limitations, but he does all he can to maintain his good humour in moments of crisis.

The world is, after all, doing its best to help him, even though everything around him seems to be saying the opposite.

The warrior has memories, but he learns how to separate the useful from the unnecessary; he disposes of his emotional rubbish.

There is such a thing as emotional rubbish; it is produced in the factories of the mind. It consists of pain that has long since passed and is no longer useful. It consists of precautions that were important in the past, but that serve no purpose in the present.

The warrior has memories too, but he learns how to separate the useful from the unnecessary; he disposes of his emotional rubbish.

A companion says: 'But that's part of my history. Why should I jettison feelings that marked my very existence?'

The warrior smiles, but he does not try to feel things that he no longer feels. He is changing and he wants his feelings to keep pace with him.

‘You are not what you seem to be in moments of sadness. You are better than that.’

When the master sees that the warrior is depressed, he says:

'You are not what you seem to be in these moments of sadness. You are better than that.

'Many have left – for reasons we will never understand – but you are still here. Why did God carry off all those amazing people and leave you?

'By now, millions of people will have given up. They don't get angry, they don't weep, they don't do anything; they merely wait for time to pass. They have lost the ability to react.

'You, however, are sad. That proves that your soul is still alive.'

Sometimes, in the middle of an apparently endless battle, the warrior has an idea and he manages to triumph in a matter of seconds.

Sometimes, in the middle of an apparently endless battle, the warrior has an idea and he manages to triumph in a matter of seconds.

Then he thinks: 'Why did I labour for so long over a battle that could have been resolved with only half the energy I spent on it?'

The truth is that all problems seem very simple once they have been resolved. The great victory, which appears so simple today, was the result of a series of small victories that went unnoticed.

Then the warrior understands what happened and he sleeps easy. Far from blaming himself for having taken so long to arrive, he is simply glad to know that he did arrive in the end.

'Thy will be done.'
This is how the
warrior of light
chooses to pray.

There are two types of prayer.

In the first type, the person asks for certain things to happen and attempts to tell God what he should do. This does not allow the Creator either time or space in which to act. God – who knows perfectly well what is best for each of us – will continue to do as he sees fit. And the person praying is left with the impression that his prayer went unanswered.

In the second type, the person may not understand the Almighty's intentions, but he allows his life to develop according to his Creator's plans. He asks to be spared suffering, he asks for joy in the Good Fight, but he never forgets to add: 'Thy will be done'.

This is how the warrior of light chooses to pray.

The warrior knows that
the most important words
in all languages are the
small words.
Yes. Love. God.

The warrior knows that the most important words in all languages are the small words.

Yes. Love. God.

They are words that are easy enough to say and which fill vast empty spaces.

There is, however, one word – another small word – that many people have great difficulty in saying: no.

Someone who never says 'no', thinks of himself as generous, understanding, polite, because 'no' is thought of as being nasty, selfish, unspiritual.

The warrior does not fall into this trap. There are times when, in saying 'yes' to others, he is actually saying 'no' to himself.

That is why he never says 'yes' with his lips if, in his heart, he is saying 'no'.

These are
the commandments
that no warrior of light
can obey.

F*irst:* God is sacrifice. Suffer in this life and you will be happy in the next.

Second: People who have fun are childish. Remain tense at all times.

Third: Other people know what is best for us because they have more experience.

Fourth: Our duty is to make other people happy. We must please them even if that means making major sacrifices.

Fifth: We must not drink from the cup of happiness; we might get to like it and we won't always have it in our hands.

Sixth: We must accept all punishments. We are guilty.

Seventh: Fear is a warning. We don't want to take any risks.

These are the commandments that no warrior of light can obey.

A very large group of people is standing in the middle of the road, barring the way into Paradise … the warriors of light go in.

A very large group of people is standing in the middle of the road, barring the way into Paradise.

The puritan asks: 'What are these sinners doing here?'

And the moralist bawls: 'The prostitute wants to join the feast!'

The guardian of social values yells: 'How can the adulteress be forgiven when she has sinned?'

The penitent rends his clothes: 'Why cure a blind man if all he cares about is his illness and when he doesn't even say thank you?'

The ascetic protests: 'You let that woman pour expensive oil on your hair! Why didn't she sell it instead to buy food?'

Smiling, Jesus holds the door open. And the warriors of light go in, despite the hysterical shouting.

The warrior of light
is not a coward.

The opponent is wise.

Whenever he can, he makes use of the easiest and most effective of his weapons: gossip. It doesn't take much effort to use it because others do the work for him. A few misdirected words can destroy months of dedication, years spent in search of harmony.

The warrior of light is often the victim of this trick. He does not know where the blow came from and cannot prove that the gossip is false. Gossip does not allow him the right to defend himself: it condemns without a trial.

When this happens, he puts up with the consequences and the undeserved punishment, for, as he well knows, words are powerful. But he suffers in silence and never uses the same weapon to hit back at his opponent.

The warrior of light is not a coward.

A true warrior of light
knows that every garden
has its own mysteries,
which only the patient
hand of the gardener
can unravel.

'You can give a fool a thousand intellects, but the only one he will want is yours,' says an Arabic proverb. When the warrior of light starts planting his garden, he notices that his neighbour is there, spying. He likes to give advice on when to sow actions, when to fertilise thoughts and water conquests.

If he listens to what his neighbour is saying, he will end up creating something that is not his; the garden he is tending will be his neighbour's idea.

But a true warrior of light knows that every garden has its own mysteries, which only the patient hand of the gardener can unravel. That is why he prefers to concentrate on the sun, the rain and the seasons.

He knows that the fool who gives advice about someone else's garden is not tending his own plants.

No one is entirely good or evil; that is what the warrior thinks when he sees that he has a new opponent.

In order to fight, you must keep your eyes open and have faithful companions by your side.

It can happen that someone who was fighting alongside the warrior of light suddenly becomes his opponent instead.

The warrior's first reaction is hatred, but he knows that a blind combatant is lost in the midst of battle.

And so he tries to see the good things that his former ally did during the time in which they lived side by side; he tries to understand what led to that sudden change of attitude, what wounds he had accumulated in his soul. He tries to discover what made one of them abandon their dialogue.

No one is entirely good or evil; that is what the warrior thinks when he sees that he has a new opponent.

A warrior knows that the ends do not justify the means.

A warrior knows that the ends do not justify the means.

Because there are no ends, there are only means. Life carries him from unknown to unknown. Each moment is filled with this thrilling mystery: the warrior does not know where he came from nor where he is going.

But he is not here by chance. And he is overjoyed by surprises and excited by landscapes that he has never seen before. He often feels afraid, but that is normal in a warrior.

If he thinks only of the goal, he will not be able to pay attention to the signs along the way. If he concentrates only on one question, he will miss the answers that are there beside him.

That is why the warrior submits.

The warrior is careful in his use of the sword and only accepts an opponent who is worthy of him.

The warrior knows about the 'waterfall effect'.

He has often seen someone mistreating another person who lacks the courage to respond. Then, out of cowardice and resentment, that person vents his anger on someone weaker than himself, who takes it out on someone else, in a veritable torrent of misery. No one knows the consequences of his own cruelty.

That is why the warrior is careful in his use of the sword and only accepts an opponent who is worthy of him. In moments of rage, he punches a rock and bruises his hand.

The hand will heal eventually, but the child who got beaten because his father lost a battle will bear the marks for the rest of his life.

The warrior of light must obey the orders of the One to whom he offered up his struggle.

When the order to move on comes, the warrior looks at all the friends he has made during the time that he followed the path. He taught some to hear the bells of a drowned temple, he told others stories around the fire.

His heart is sad, but he knows that his sword is sacred and that he must obey the orders of the One to whom he offered up his struggle.

Then the warrior thanks his travelling companions, takes a deep breath and continues on, laden with memories of an unforgettable journey.

EPILOGUE

It was dark by the time she finished speaking. The two of them sat watching the moon rising.

'Many of the things you told me contradict each other,' he said.

She got up.

'Goodbye,' she said. 'You knew that the bells at the bottom of the sea were not just a legend, but you could only hear them when you realised that the wind, the seagulls and the sound of the palm fronds were all part of the pealing of the bells.

In júst the same way, the warrior of light knows that everything around him – his victories, his defeats, his enthusiasm and his despondency – form part of his Good Fight. And he will know which strategy to use when he needs it. A warrior does not try to be coherent; he has learned to live with his contradictions.'

'Who are you?' he asked.

But the woman was already moving off, walking over the waves towards the rising moon.

Life is a journey

Make sure you don't miss a thing.
Live it with Paulo Coelho.

Visit f /paulocoelho

How can you find your heart's desire?

A world-wide phenomenon; an inspiration for anyone seeking their path in life.

The Alchemist

Do you believe in yourself?

A modern-day adventure in the searing heat of the Mojave desert and an exploration of fear and self-doubt.

The Valkyries

How do we see the amazing in the everyday?

When two young lovers are reunited, they discover anew the truth of what lies in their hearts.

By the River Piedra I Sat Down & Wept

What are you searching for?

A transforming journey on the pilgrims' road to Santiago – and the first of Paulo's extraordinary books.

The Pilgrimage

Can faith triumph over suffering?

Paulo Coelho's brilliant telling of the story of Elijah, who was forced to choose between love and duty.

The Fifth Mountain

Is life always worth living?

A fundamental moral question explored as only Paulo Coelho can.

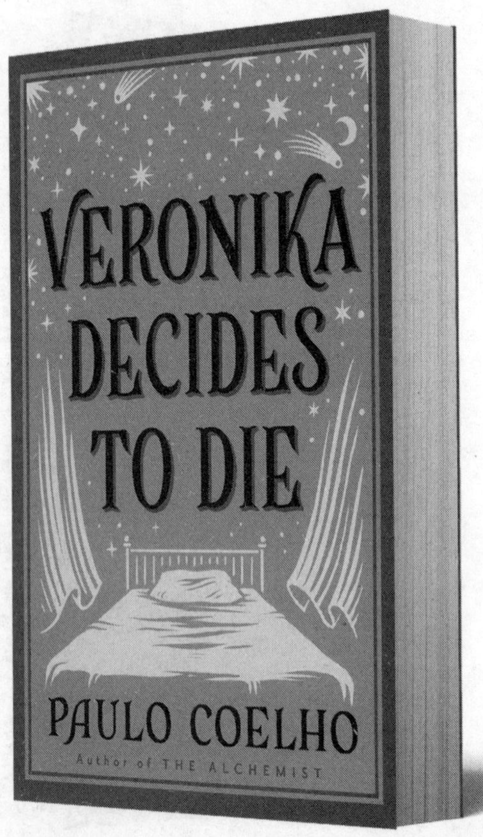

Veronika Decides to Die

Could you be tempted into evil?

The inhabitants of a small town are challenged by a mysterious stranger to choose between good and evil.

The Devil & Miss Prym

Are you brave enough to live your dream?

Strategies and inspiration to help you follow your own path in a troubled world.

Manual of the Warrior of Light

Can sex be sacred?

An unflinching exploration of the lengths we go to in our search for love, sex and spirituality.

Eleven Minutes

How far would you go for your obsession?

A sweeping story of love, loss and longing that spans the world.

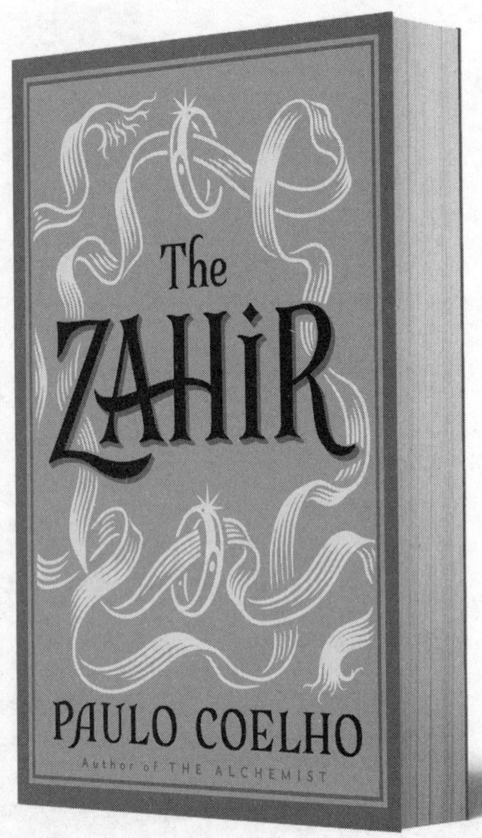

The Zahir

What happens when obsession turns to murder?

An enthralling story of jealousy, death and suspense.

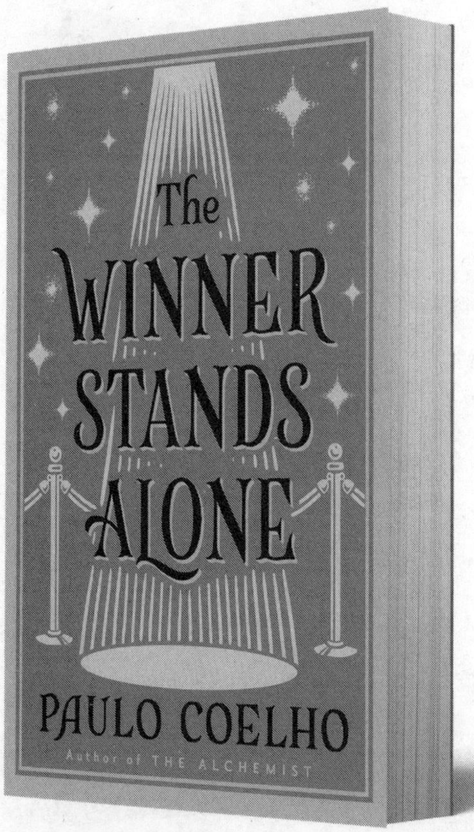

The Winner Stands Alone

Can we dare to be true to ourselves?

A story that will transform the way we think about love, joy and sacrifice.

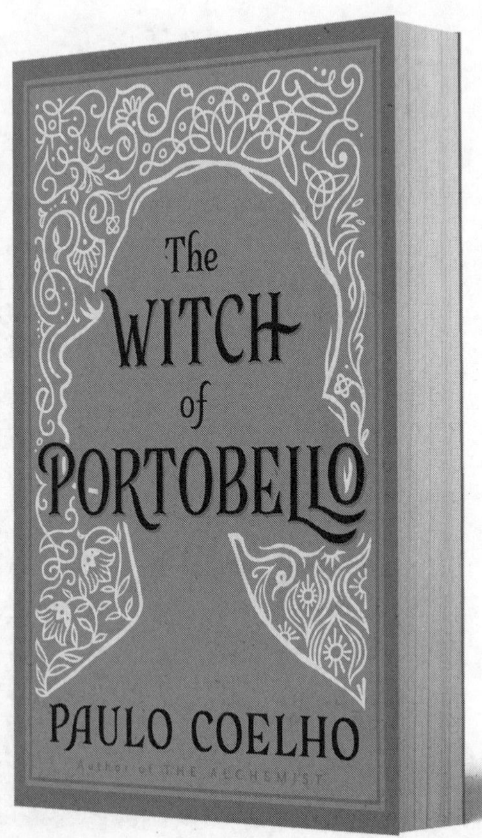

The Witch of Portobello

How will you know who your soulmate is?

A moving tale of passion, mystery and spirituality.

Brida

What does it mean to be truly alive?

Powerful tales of living and dying, destiny and choice, and love lost and found.

Like the Flowing River

Are you where you want to be?

Read *Aleph*. And rewrite your life.

Aleph

Is there a weapon more powerful than words?

A timeless and powerful exploration of personal growth, everyday wisdom and joy.

Manuscript Found in Accra

The ALCHEMIST

Paulo Coelho was born in Brazil and has become one of the most widely read and loved authors in the world. Especially renowned for *The Alchemist* and *Eleven Minutes*, he has sold more than 320 million books worldwide and has been translated into 88 languages. The recipient of numerous prestigious international awards, amongst them the Crystal Award by the World Economic Forum and France's Légion d'Honneur, Paulo Coelho was inducted into the Brazilian Academy of Letters in 2002.

Also by Paulo Coelho

The Alchemist
The Pilgrimage
The Valkyries
By the River Piedra I Sat Down and Wept
The Fifth Mountain
Veronika Decides to Die
Manual of the Warrior of Light
Eleven Minutes
The Zahir
The Devil and Miss Prym
The Witch of Portobello
Brida
The Winner Stands Alone
Like the Flowing River
Aleph
Manuscript Found in Accra
Adultery
The Spy
Hippie

The ALCHEMIST

PAULO COELHO

TRANSLATED BY ALAN R. CLARKE

Thorsons

Thorsons
An imprint of HarperCollins*Publishers*
1 London Bridge Street
London SE1 9GF

HarperCollins*Publishers*
1st Floor, Watermarque Building, Ringsend Road
Dublin 4, Ireland

www.harpercollins.co.uk
www.paulocoelho.com
www.paulocoelhoblog.com

First published by Editora Rocco Ltd 1988
English edition 1993
This HarperCollins edition published 2021

2 4 6 8 10 9 7 5 3 1

English version © Paulo Coelho and Alan R. Clarke 1992

Paulo Coelho asserts the moral right to
be identified as the author of this work

A catalogue record for this book is
available from the British Library

ISBN: 978-0-00-854725-7

FICTION / PHILOSOPHY

Printed and bound in India by Thomson Press India Ltd

All rights reserved. No part of this publication may be
reproduced, stored in a retrieval system, or transmitted,
in any form or by any means, electronic, mechanical,
photocopying, recording or otherwise, without the prior
written permission of the publishers.

This book is produced from independently certified FSC® paper
to ensure responsible forest management.

O Mary!
conceived without sin,
pray for us who turn to you!
Amen.

Now while they were on their way, they entered a village. And a woman named Martha welcomed Jesus into her home.

She had a sister named Mary, who seated herself at the Lord's feet listening to His teaching.

But Martha was very busy and distracted with all of her serving responsibilities; and she approached Him and said:

– Lord, is it of no concern to You that my sister has left me to do the serving alone? Tell her to help me!

But the Lord replied to her:

– Martha, Martha, you are worried and bothered about many things; but Mary has chosen the good part, which will not be taken away from her.

Luke 10:38-42

For J.,
Alchemist that knows
and uses the secrets
of the Great Work.

Foreword

When *The Alchemist* was first published thirty years ago in my native Brazil, no one noticed. A bookseller in the north-east corner of the country told me that only one person purchased a copy in the first week of its release. It took another six months for the bookseller to unload a second copy—and that was to the same person who bought the first! And who knows how long it took to sell the third.

By the end of the year, it was clear to everyone that *The Alchemist* wasn't working. My original publisher decided to cut me loose and cancelled our contract. They wiped their hands of the project and let me take the book with me. I was forty-one and desperate.

But I never lost faith in the book or ever wavered in my vision. Why? Because it was me in there, all of me, heart and soul. I was living my own metaphor. A man sets out on a journey, dreaming of a beautiful or magical place, in pursuit of some unknown treasure. At the end of his journey, the man realizes the treasure was with him the entire time. I was following my Personal Legend, and my treasure was my capacity to write. And I wanted to share this treasure with the world.

As I wrote in *The Alchemist*, when you want something, the whole universe conspires to help you.

I started knocking on the doors of other publishers. One opened, and the publisher on the other side believed in me and my book and agreed to give *The Alchemist* a second chance. Slowly, through word of mouth, it finally started to sell—three thousand, then six thousand, ten thousand—book by book, gradually throughout the year.

Eight months later, an American visiting Brazil picked up a copy of *The Alchemist* in a local bookstore. He wanted to translate the book and help me find a publisher in the United States. HarperCollins agreed to bring it to an American audience, publishing it with great fanfare: ads in the *New York Times* and influential news magazines, radio and television interviews. But it still took some time to sell, slowly finding its audience in the United States by word of mouth, just as it did in Brazil. And then one day, Bill Clinton was photographed leaving the White House with a copy. Then Madonna raved about the book to *Vanity Fair*, and people from different walks of life—from Rush Limbaugh and Will Smith to college students and soccer moms—were suddenly talking about it.

The Alchemist became a spontaneous—and organic—phenomenon. The book hit the *New York Times* bestseller list, an important milestone for any author, and stayed there for more than three hundred weeks. It has been translated into more than eighty different languages, the most translated book by any living author, and is widely considered one of the ten best books of the twentieth century.

People continue to ask me if I knew *The Alchemist* would be such a huge success. The answer is no. I had no idea. How could I? When I sat down to write *The Alchemist*, all I knew was that I wanted to write about my soul. I wanted to write about my quest to find my treasure. I wanted to follow the omens, because I knew even then that the omens are the language of God.

Though *The Alchemist* is now celebrating its thirtieth anniversary, it is no relic of the past. Like my heart and like my soul, it continues to live every day, because my heart and soul are in it. And my heart and soul are your heart and soul. I am Santiago the shepherd boy in search of my treasure, just as you are Santiago in search of your own. The story of one person is the story of everyone, and one man's quest is the quest of all of humanity, which is why I believe *The Alchemist* continues all these years later to resonate with people from different cultures all around the world, touching them emotionally and spiritually, equally, without prejudice.

I re-read *The Alchemist* regularly and each time I do I experience the same sensations I felt when I wrote it. And here is what I feel. I feel happiness, because it is all of me, and all of you simultaneously. I feel happiness, too, because I know I can never be alone. Wherever I go, people understand me. They understand my soul. This continues to give me hope. When I read about clashes around the world—political clashes, economic clashes, cultural clashes—I am reminded that it is within our power to build a bridge to be crossed. Even if my neighbour doesn't understand my religion or understand my politics, he can understand my story. If he can understand my story, then he's never too far from me. It is always within my power to build a bridge. There is always a chance for reconciliation, a chance that one day he and I will sit around a table together and put an end to our history of clashes. And on this day, he will tell me his story and I will tell him mine.

Paulo Coelho, 2018
Translated by Margaret Jull Costa

Prologue

The alchemist picked up a book that someone in the caravan had bought. Leafing through the pages, he found a story about Narcissus.

The alchemist knew the legend of Narcissus, a youth who knelt daily beside a lake to contemplate his own beauty. He was so fascinated by himself that, one morning, he fell into the lake and drowned. At the spot where he fell, a flower was born, which was called the narcissus.

But this was not how the author of the book ended the story.

He said that when Narcissus died, the goddesses of the forest appeared and found the lake, which had been fresh water, transformed into a lake of salty tears.

"Why do you weep?" the goddesses asked.

"I weep for Narcissus," the lake replied.

"Ah, it is no surprise that you weep for Narcissus," they said, "for though we always pursued him in the forest, you alone could contemplate his beauty close at hand."

"But . . . was Narcissus beautiful?" the lake asked.

"Who better than you to know that?" the goddesses said in wonder. "After all, it was by your banks that he knelt each day to contemplate himself!"

The lake was silent for some time. Finally, it said:

"I weep for Narcissus, but I never noticed that Narcissus was beautiful. I weep because, each time he knelt beside my banks, I could see, in the depths of his eyes, my own beauty reflected."

"What a lovely story," the alchemist thought.

Translated by Clifford E. Landers

Part One

The boy's name was Santiago. Dusk was falling as the boy arrived with his herd at an abandoned church. The roof had fallen in long ago, and an enormous sycamore had grown on the spot where the sacristy had once stood.

He decided to spend the night there. He saw to it that all the sheep entered through the ruined gate, and then laid some planks across it to prevent the flock from wandering away during the night. There were no wolves in the region, but once an animal had strayed during the night, and the boy had had to spend the entire next day searching for it.

He swept the floor with his jacket and lay down, using the book he had just finished reading as a pillow. He told himself that he would have to start reading thicker books: they lasted longer, and made more comfortable pillows.

It was still dark when he awoke, and, looking up, he could see the stars through the half-destroyed roof.

I wanted to sleep a little longer, he thought. He had had the same dream that night as a week ago, and once again he had awakened before it ended.

He arose and, taking up his crook, began to awaken the sheep that still slept. He had noticed that, as soon as he awoke, most of his animals also began to stir. It was as if some mysterious energy bound his life to that of the sheep, with whom he had spent the past two years, leading them through the countryside in search of food and water. "They are so used to me that they know my schedule," he muttered. Thinking about that for a moment, he realized that it could be the other way around: that it was he who had become accustomed to *their* schedule.

But there were certain of them who took a bit longer to awaken. The boy prodded them, one by one, with his crook, calling each by name. He had always believed that the sheep were able to understand what he said. So there were times when he read them parts of his books that had made an impression on him, or when he would tell them of the loneliness or the happiness of a shepherd in the fields. Sometimes he would comment to them on the things he had seen in the villages they passed.

But for the past few days he had spoken to them about only one thing: the girl, the daughter of a merchant who lived in the village they would reach in about four days. He had been to the village only once, the year before. The merchant was the proprietor of a dry goods shop, and he always demanded that the sheep be sheared in his presence, so that he would not be cheated. A friend had told the boy about the shop, and he had taken his sheep there.

* * *

“I need to sell some wool,” the boy told the merchant.

The shop was busy, and the man asked the shepherd to wait until the afternoon. So the boy sat on the steps of the shop and took a book from his bag.

“I didn’t know shepherds knew how to read,” said a girl’s voice behind him.

The girl was typical of the region of Andalusia, with flowing black hair, and eyes that vaguely recalled the Moorish conquerors.

“Well, usually I learn more from my sheep than from books,” he answered. During the two hours that they talked, she told him she was the merchant’s daughter, and spoke of life in the village, where each day was like all the others. The shepherd told her of the Andalusian countryside, and related the news from the other towns where he had stopped. It was a pleasant change from talking to his sheep.

“How did you learn to read?” the girl asked at one point.

“Like everybody learns,” he said. “In school.”

“Well, if you know how to read, why are you just a shepherd?”

The boy mumbled an answer that allowed him to avoid responding to her question. He was sure the girl would never understand. He went on telling stories about his travels, and her bright, Moorish eyes went wide with fear and surprise. As the time passed, the boy found himself wishing that the day would never end, that her father would stay busy and keep him waiting for three days. He recognized that he was feeling something he had never experienced before: the desire to live in one place forever. With the girl with the raven hair, his days would never be the same again.

But finally the merchant appeared, and asked the boy to shear four sheep. He paid for the wool and asked the shepherd to come back the following year.

* * *

And now it was only four days before he would be back in that same village. He was excited, and at the same time uneasy: maybe the girl had already forgotten him. Lots of shepherds passed through, selling their wool.

"It doesn't matter," he said to his sheep. "I know other girls in other places."

But in his heart he knew that it did matter. And he knew that shepherds, like seamen and like traveling salesmen, always found a town where there was someone who could make them forget the joys of carefree wandering.

The day was dawning, and the shepherd urged his sheep in the direction of the sun. They never have to make any decisions, he thought. Maybe that's why they always stay close to me.

The only things that concerned the sheep were food and water. As long as the boy knew how to find the best pastures in Andalusia, they would be his friends. Yes, their days were all the same, with the seemingly endless hours between sunrise and dusk; and they had never read a book in their young lives, and didn't understand when the boy told them about the sights of the cities. They were content with just food and water, and, in exchange, they generously gave of their wool, their company, and—once in a while—their meat.

If I became a monster today, and decided to kill them, one by one, they would become aware only after most of the flock had been slaughtered, thought the boy. They trust me, and they've forgotten how to rely on their own instincts, because I lead them to nourishment.

The boy was surprised at his thoughts. Maybe the church, with the sycamore growing from within, had been haunted. It had caused him to have the same dream for a second time, and it was causing him to feel anger toward his faithful companions. He drank a bit from the wine that remained from his dinner of the night before, and he gathered his jacket closer to his body. He knew that a few hours from now, with the sun at its zenith, the heat would be so great that he would not be able to lead his flock across the fields. It was the time of day when all of Spain slept during the summer. The heat lasted until nightfall, and all that time he had to carry his jacket. But when he thought to complain about the burden of its weight, he remembered that, because he had the jacket, he had withstood the cold of the dawn.

We have to be prepared for change, he thought, and he was grateful for the jacket's weight and warmth.

The jacket had a purpose, and so did the boy. His purpose in life was to travel, and, after two years of walking the Andalusian terrain, he knew all the cities of the region. He was planning, on this visit, to explain to the girl how it was that a simple shepherd knew how to read. That he had attended a seminary until he was sixteen. His parents had wanted him to become a priest, and thereby a source of pride for a simple farm family. They worked hard just to have food and water, like the sheep. He had studied Latin, Spanish, and theology. But ever since he had been a child, he had wanted to know the world, and this was much more important to him than knowing God and learning about man's sins. One afternoon, on a visit to his family, he had summoned up the courage to tell his father that he didn't want to become a priest. That he wanted to travel.

* * *

"People from all over the world have passed through this village, son," said his father. "They come in search of new things, but when they leave they are basically the same people they were when they arrived. They climb the mountain to see the castle, and they wind up thinking that the past was better than what we have now. They have blond hair, or dark skin, but basically they're the same as the people who live right here."

"But I'd like to see the castles in the towns where they live," the boy explained.

"Those people, when they see our land, say that they would like to live here forever," his father continued.

"Well, I'd like to see their land, and see how they live," said his son.

"The people who come here have a lot of money to spend, so they can afford to travel," his father said. "Amongst us, the only ones who travel are the shepherds."

"Well, then I'll be a shepherd!"

His father said no more. The next day, he gave his son a pouch that held three ancient Spanish gold coins.

"I found these one day in the fields. I wanted them to be a part of your inheritance. But use them to buy your flock. Take to the fields, and someday you'll learn that our countryside is the best, and our women the most beautiful."

And he gave the boy his blessing. The boy could see in his father's gaze a desire to be able, himself, to travel the world—a desire that was still alive, despite his father's having had to bury it, over dozens of years, under the burden of struggling for water to drink, food to eat, and the same place to sleep every night of his life.

* * *

The horizon was tinged with red, and suddenly the sun appeared. The boy thought back to that conversation with his father, and felt happy; he had already seen many castles and met many women (but none the equal of the one who awaited him several days hence). He owned a jacket, a book that he could trade for another, and a flock of sheep. But, most important, he was able every day to live out his dream. If he were to tire of the Andalusian fields, he could sell his sheep and go to sea. By the time he had had enough of the sea, he would already have known other cities, other women, and other chances to be happy. I couldn't have found God in the seminary, he thought, as he looked at the sunrise.

Whenever he could, he sought out a new road to travel. He had never been to that ruined church before, in spite of having traveled through those parts many times. The world was huge and inexhaustible; he had only to allow his sheep to set the route for a while, and he would discover other interesting things. The problem is that they don't even realize that they're walking a new road every day. They don't see that the fields are new and the seasons change. All they think about is food and water.

Maybe we're all that way, the boy mused. Even me—I haven't thought of other women since I met the merchant's daughter. Looking at the sun, he calculated that he would reach Tarifa before midday. There, he could exchange his book for a thicker one, fill his wine bottle, shave, and have a haircut; he had to prepare himself for his meeting with the girl, and he didn't want to think about the possibility that some other shepherd, with a larger flock of sheep, had arrived there before him and asked for her hand.

It's the possibility of having a dream come true that makes life interesting, he thought, as he looked again at the position of the sun, and hurried his pace. He had suddenly remembered that, in Tarifa, there was an old woman who interpreted dreams.

* * *

The old woman led the boy to a room at the back of her house; it was separated from her living room by a curtain of colored beads. The room's furnishings consisted of a table, an image of the Sacred Heart of Jesus, and two chairs.

The woman sat down, and told him to be seated as well. Then she took both of his hands in hers, and began quietly to pray.

It sounded like a Gypsy prayer. The boy had already had experience on the road with Gypsies; they also traveled, but they had no flocks of sheep. People said that Gypsies spent their lives tricking others. It was also said that they had a pact with the devil, and that they kidnapped children and, taking them away to their mysterious camps, made them their slaves. As a child, the boy had always been frightened to death that he would be captured by Gypsies, and this childhood fear returned when the old woman took his hands in hers.

But she has the Sacred Heart of Jesus there, he thought, trying to reassure himself. He didn't want his hand to begin trembling, showing the old woman that he was fearful. He recited an Our Father silently.

"Very interesting," said the woman, never taking her eyes from the boy's hands, and then she fell silent.

The boy was becoming nervous. His hands began to tremble, and the woman sensed it. He quickly pulled his hands away.

"I didn't come here to have you read my palm," he said, already regretting having come. He thought for a moment that it would be better to pay her fee and leave without learning a thing, that he was giving too much importance to his recurrent dream.

"You came so that you could learn about your dreams," said the old woman. "And dreams are the language of God. When he speaks in our language, I can interpret what he has said. But if he speaks in the language of the soul, it is only you who can understand. But, whichever it is, I'm going to charge you for the consultation."

Another trick, the boy thought. But he decided to take a chance. A shepherd always takes his chances with wolves and with drought, and that's what makes a shepherd's life exciting.

"I have had the same dream twice," he said. "I dreamed that I was in a field with my sheep, when a child appeared and began to play with the animals. I don't like people to do that, because the sheep are afraid of strangers. But children always seem to be able to play with them without frightening them. I don't know why. I don't know how animals know the age of human beings."

"Tell me more about your dream," said the woman. "I have to get back to my cooking, and, since you don't have much money, I can't give you a lot of time."

"The child went on playing with my sheep for quite a while," continued the boy, a bit upset. "And suddenly, the child took me by both hands and transported me to the Egyptian pyramids."

He paused for a moment to see if the woman knew what the Egyptian pyramids were. But she said nothing.

"Then, at the Egyptian pyramids,"—he said the last three words slowly, so that the old woman would understand—"the child said to me, 'If you come here, you will find a hidden treasure.' And, just as she was about to show me the exact location, I woke up. Both times."

The woman was silent for some time. Then she again took his hands and studied them carefully.

"I'm not going to charge you anything now," she said. "But I want one-tenth of the treasure, if you find it."

The boy laughed—out of happiness. He was going to be able to save the little money he had because of a dream about hidden treasure!

"Well, interpret the dream," he said.

"First, swear to me. Swear that you will give me one-tenth of your treasure in exchange for what I am going to tell you."

The shepherd swore that he would. The old woman asked him to swear again while looking at the image of the Sacred Heart of Jesus.

"It's a dream in the language of the world," she said. "I can interpret it, but the interpretation is very difficult. That's why I feel that I deserve a part of what you find.

"And this is my interpretation: you must go to the Pyramids in Egypt. I have never heard of them, but, if it was a child who showed them to you, they exist. There you will find a treasure that will make you a rich man."

The boy was surprised, and then irritated. He didn't need to seek out the old woman for this! But then he remembered that he wasn't going to have to pay anything.

"I didn't need to waste my time just for this," he said.

"I told you that your dream was a difficult one. It's the simple things in life that are the most extraordinary; only wise men are able to understand them. And since I am not wise, I have had to learn other arts, such as the reading of palms."

"Well, how am I going to get to Egypt?"

"I only interpret dreams. I don't know how to turn them into reality. That's why I have to live off what my daughters provide me with."

"And what if I never get to Egypt?"

"Then I don't get paid. It wouldn't be the first time."

And the woman told the boy to leave, saying she had already wasted too much time with him.

So the boy was disappointed; he decided that he would never again believe in dreams. He remembered that he had a number of things he had to take care of: he went to the market for something to eat, he traded his book for one that was thicker, and he found a bench in the plaza where he could sample the new wine he had bought. The day was hot, and the wine was refreshing. The sheep were at the gates of the city, in a stable that belonged to a friend. The boy knew a lot of people in the city. That was what made traveling appeal to him—he always made new friends, and he didn't need to spend all of his time with them. When someone sees the same people every day, as had happened with him at the seminary, they wind up becoming a part of that person's life. And then they want the person to change. If someone isn't what others want them to be, the others become angry. Everyone seems to have a clear idea of how other people should lead their lives, but none about his or her own.

He decided to wait until the sun had sunk a bit lower in the sky before following his flock back through the fields. Three days from now, he would be with the merchant's daughter.

He started to read the book he had bought. On the very first page it described a burial ceremony. And the names of the people involved were very difficult to pronounce. If he ever wrote a book, he thought, he would present one person at a time, so that the reader wouldn't have to worry about memorizing a lot of names.

When he was finally able to concentrate on what he was reading, he liked the book better; the burial was on a snowy day, and he welcomed the feeling of being cold. As he read on, an old man sat down at his side and tried to strike up a conversation.

"What are they doing?" the old man asked, pointing at the people in the plaza.

"Working," the boy answered dryly, making it look as if he wanted to concentrate on his reading.

Actually, he was thinking about shearing his sheep in front of the merchant's daughter, so that she could see that he was someone who was capable of doing difficult things. He had already imagined the scene many times; every time, the girl became fascinated when he explained that the sheep had to be sheared from back to front. He also tried to remember some good stories to relate as he sheared the sheep. Most of them he had read in books, but he would tell them as if they were from his personal experience. She would never know the difference, because she didn't know how to read.

Meanwhile, the old man persisted in his attempt to strike up a conversation. He said that he was tired and thirsty, and asked if he might have a sip of the boy's wine. The boy offered his bottle, hoping that the old man would leave him alone.

But the old man wanted to talk, and he asked the boy what book he was reading. The boy was tempted to be rude, and move to another bench, but his father had taught him to be respectful of the elderly. So he held out the book to the man—for two reasons: first, that he, himself, wasn't sure how to pronounce the title; and second, that if the old man didn't know how to read, he would probably feel ashamed and decide of his own accord to change benches.

"Hmm …" said the old man, looking at all sides of the book, as if it were some strange object. "This is an important book, but it's really irritating."

The boy was shocked. The old man knew how to read, and had already read the book. And if the book was irritating, as the old man had said, the boy still had time to change it for another.

"It's a book that says the same thing almost all the other books in the world say," continued the old man. "It describes people's inability to choose their own destinies. And it ends up saying that everyone believes the world's greatest lie."

"What's the world's greatest lie?" the boy asked, completely surprised.

"It's this: that at a certain point in our lives, we lose control of what's happening to us, and our lives become controlled by fate. That's the world's greatest lie."

"That's never happened to me," the boy said. "They wanted me to be a priest, but I decided to become a shepherd."

"Much better," said the old man. "Because you really like to travel."

"He knew what I was thinking," the boy said to himself. The old man, meanwhile, was leafing through the book, without seeming to want to return it at all. The boy noticed that the man's clothing was strange. He looked like an Arab, which was not unusual in those parts. Africa was only a few hours from Tarifa; one had only to cross the narrow straits by boat. Arabs often appeared in the city, shopping and chanting their strange prayers several times a day.

"Where are you from?" the boy asked.

"From many places."

"No one can be from many places," the boy said. "I'm a shepherd, and I have been to many places, but I come from only one place—from a city near an ancient castle. That's where I was born."

"Well then, we could say that I was born in Salem."

The boy didn't know where Salem was, but he didn't want to ask, fearing that he would appear ignorant. He looked at the people in the plaza for a while; they were coming and going, and all of them seemed to be very busy.

"So, what is Salem like?" he asked, trying to get some sort of clue.

"It's like it always has been."

No clue yet. But he knew that Salem wasn't in Andalusia. If it were, he would already have heard of it.

"And what do you do in Salem?" he insisted.

"What do I do in Salem?" The old man laughed. "Well, I'm the king of Salem!"

People say strange things, the boy thought. Sometimes it's better to be with the sheep, who don't say anything. And better still to be alone with one's books. They tell their incredible stories at the time when you want to hear them. But when you're talking to people, they say some things that are so strange that you don't know how to continue the conversation.

"My name is Melchizedek," said the old man. "How many sheep do you have?"

"Enough," said the boy. He could see that the old man wanted to know more about his life.

"Well, then, we've got a problem. I can't help you if you feel you've got enough sheep."

The boy was getting irritated. He wasn't asking for help. It was the old man who had asked for a drink of his wine, and had started the conversation.

"Give me my book," the boy said. "I have to go and gather my sheep and get going."

"Give me one-tenth of your sheep," said the old man, "and I'll tell you how to find the hidden treasure."

The boy remembered his dream, and suddenly everything was clear to him. The old woman hadn't charged him anything, but the old man—maybe he was her husband—was going to find a way to get much more money in exchange for information about something that didn't even exist. The old man was probably a Gypsy, too.

But before the boy could say anything, the old man leaned over, picked up a stick, and began to write in the sand of the plaza. Something bright reflected from his chest with such intensity that the boy was momentarily blinded. With a movement that was too quick for someone his age, the man covered whatever it was with his cape. When his vision returned to normal, the boy was able to read what the old man had written in the sand.

There, in the sand of the plaza of that small city, the boy read the names of his father and his mother and the name of the seminary he had attended. He read the name of the merchant's daughter, which he hadn't even known, and he read things he had never told anyone.

* * *

"I'm the king of Salem," the old man had said.

"Why would a king be talking with a shepherd?" the boy asked, awed and embarrassed.

"For several reasons. But let's say that the most important is that you have succeeded in discovering your destiny."

The boy didn't know what a person's "destiny" was.

"It's what you have always wanted to accomplish. Everyone, when they are young, knows what their destiny is.

"At that point in their lives, everything is clear and everything is possible. They are not afraid to dream, and to yearn for everything they would like to see happen to them in their lives. But, as time passes, a mysterious force begins to convince them that it will be impossible for them to realize their destiny."

None of what the old man was saying made much sense to the boy. But he wanted to know what the "mysterious force" was; the merchant's daughter would be impressed when he told her about that!

"It's a force that appears to be negative, but actually shows you how to realize your destiny. It prepares your spirit and your will, because there is one great truth on this planet: whoever you are, or whatever it is that you do, when you really want something, it's because that desire originated in the soul of the universe. It's your mission on earth."

"Even when all you want to do is travel? Or marry the daughter of a textile merchant?"

"Yes, or even search for treasure. The Soul of the World is nourished by people's happiness. And also by unhappiness, envy, and jealousy. To realize one's destiny is a person's only real obligation. All things are one.

"And, when you want something, all the universe conspires in helping you to achieve it."

They were both silent for a time, observing the plaza and the townspeople. It was the old man who spoke first.

"Why do you tend a flock of sheep?"

"Because I like to travel."

The old man pointed to a baker standing in his shop window at one corner of the plaza. "When he was a child, that man wanted to travel, too. But he decided first to buy his bakery and put some money aside. When he's an old man, he's going to spend a month in Africa. He never realized that people are capable, at any time in their lives, of doing what they dream of."

"He should have decided to become a shepherd," the boy said.

"Well, he thought about that," the old man said. "But bakers are more important people than shepherds.

Bakers have homes, while shepherds sleep out in the open. Parents would rather see their children marry bakers than shepherds."

The boy felt a pang in his heart, thinking about the merchant's daughter. There was surely a baker in her town.

The old man continued, "In the long run, what people think about shepherds and bakers becomes more important for them than their own destinies."

The old man leafed through the book, and fell to reading a page he came to. The boy waited, and then interrupted the old man just as he himself had been interrupted. "Why are you telling me all this?"

"Because you are trying to realize your destiny. And you are at the point where you're about to give it all up."

"And that's when you always appear on the scene?"

"Not always in this way, but I always appear in one form or another. Sometimes I appear in the form of a solution, or a good idea. At other times, at a crucial moment, I make it easier for things to happen. There are other things I do, too, but most of the time people don't realize I've done them."

The old man related that, the week before, he had been forced to appear before a miner, and had taken the form of a stone. The miner had abandoned everything to go mining for emeralds. For five years he had been working a certain river, and had examined hundreds of thousands of stones looking for an emerald.

The miner was about to give it all up, right at the point when, if he were to examine just one more stone—just one more—he would find his emerald. Since the miner had sacrificed everything to his destiny, the old man decided to become involved. He transformed himself into a stone that rolled up to the miner's foot. The miner, with all the anger and frustration of his five fruitless years, picked up the stone and threw it aside. But he had thrown it with such force that it broke the stone it fell upon, and there, embedded in the broken stone, was the most beautiful emerald in the world.

"People learn, early in their lives, what is their reason for being," said the old man, with a certain bitterness. "Maybe that's why they give up on it so early, too. But that's the way it is."

The boy reminded the old man that he had said something about hidden treasure.

"Treasure is uncovered by the force of flowing water, and it is buried by the same currents," said the old man. "If you want to learn about your own treasure, you will have to give me one-tenth of your flock."

"What about one-tenth of my treasure?"

The old man looked disappointed. "If you start out by promising what you don't even have yet, you'll lose your desire to work toward getting it."

The boy told him that he had already promised to give one-tenth of his treasure to the Gypsy.

"Gypsies are experts at getting people to do that," sighed the old man. "In any case, it's good that you've learned that everything in life has its price. This is what the Warriors of the Light try to teach."

The old man returned the book to the boy.

"Tomorrow, at this same time, bring me a tenth of your flock. And I will tell you how to find the hidden treasure. Good afternoon."

And he vanished around the corner of the plaza.

* * *

The boy began again to read his book, but he was no longer able to concentrate. He was tense and upset, because he knew that the old man was right. He went over to the bakery and bought a loaf of bread, thinking about whether or not he should tell the baker what the old man had said about him. Sometimes it's better to leave things as they are, he thought to himself, and decided to say nothing. If he were to say anything, the baker would spend three days thinking about giving it all up, even though he had gotten used to the way things were. The boy could certainly resist causing that kind of anxiety for the baker. So he began to wander through the city, and found himself at the gates. There was a small building there, with a window at which people bought tickets to Africa. And he knew that Egypt was in Africa.

"Can I help you?" asked the man behind the window.

"Maybe tomorrow," said the boy, moving away. If he sold just one of his sheep, he'd have enough to get to the other shore of the strait. The idea frightened him.

"Another dreamer," said the ticket seller to his assistant, watching the boy walk away. "He doesn't have enough money to travel."

While standing at the ticket window, the boy had remembered his flock, and decided he should go back to being a shepherd. In two years he had learned everything about shepherding: he knew how to shear sheep, how to care for pregnant ewes, and how to protect the sheep from wolves. He knew all the fields and pastures of Andalusia. And he knew what was the fair price for every one of his animals.

He decided to return to his friend's stable by the longest route possible. As he walked past the city's castle, he interrupted his return, and climbed the stone ramp that led to the top of the wall. From there, he could see Africa in the distance. Someone had once told him that it was from there that the Moors had come, to occupy all of Spain.

He could see almost the entire city from where he sat, including the plaza where he had talked with the old man. Curse the moment I met that old man, he thought. He had come to the town only to find a woman who could interpret his dream. Neither the woman nor the old man were at all impressed by the fact that he was a shepherd. They were solitary individuals who no longer believed in things, and didn't understand that shepherds become attached to their sheep. He knew everything about each member of his flock: he knew which ones were lame, which one was to give birth two months from now, and which were the laziest. He knew how to shear them, and how to slaughter them. If he ever decided to leave them, they would suffer.

The wind began to pick up. He knew that wind: people called it the levanter, because on it the Moors had come from the Levant at the eastern end of the Mediterranean.

The levanter increased in intensity. Here I am, between my flock and my treasure, the boy thought. He had to choose between something he had become accustomed to and something he wanted to have. There was also the merchant's daughter, but she wasn't as important as his flock, because she didn't depend on him. Maybe she didn't even remember him. He was sure that it made no difference to her on which day he appeared: for her, every day was the same, and when each day is the same as the next, it's because people fail to recognize the good things that happen in their lives every day that the sun rises.

I left my father, my mother, and the town castle behind. They have gotten used to my being away, and so have I. The sheep will get used to my not being there, too, the boy thought.

From where he sat, he could observe the plaza. People continued to come and go from the baker's shop. A young couple sat on the bench where he had talked with the old man, and they kissed.

"That baker ...," he said to himself, without completing the thought. The levanter was still getting stronger, and he felt its force on his face. That wind had brought the Moors, yes, but it had also brought the smell of the desert and of veiled women. It had brought with it the sweat and the dreams of men who had once left to search for the unknown, and for gold and adventure—and for the Pyramids. The boy felt jealous of the freedom of the wind, and saw that he could have the same freedom. There was nothing to hold him back except himself. The sheep, the merchant's daughter, and the fields of Andalusia were only steps along the way to his destiny.

The next day, the boy met the old man at noon. He brought six sheep with him.

"I'm surprised," the boy said. "My friend bought all the other sheep immediately. He said that he had always dreamed of being a shepherd, and that it was a good omen."

"That's the way it always is," said the old man. "It's called the principle of favorability. When you play cards the first time, you are almost sure to win. Beginner's luck."

"Why is that?"

"Because there is a force that wants you to realize your destiny; it whets your appetite with a taste of success."

Then the old man began to inspect the sheep, and he saw that one was lame. The boy explained that it wasn't important, since that sheep was the most intelligent of the flock, and produced the most wool.

"Where is the treasure?" he asked.

"It's in Egypt, near the Pyramids."

The boy was startled. The old woman had said the same thing. But she hadn't charged him anything.

"In order to find the treasure, you will have to follow the omens. God has prepared a path for everyone to follow. You just have to read the omens that he left for you."

Before the boy could reply, a butterfly appeared and fluttered between him and the old man. He remembered something his grandfather had once told him: that butterflies were a good omen. Like crickets, and like expectations; like lizards and four-leaf clovers.

"That's right," said the old man, able to read the boy's thoughts. "Just as your grandfather taught you. These are good omens."

The old man opened his cape, and the boy was struck by what he saw. The old man wore a breastplate of heavy gold, covered with precious stones. The boy recalled the brilliance he had noticed on the previous day.

He really was a king! He must be disguised to avoid encounters with thieves.

"Take these," said the old man, holding out a white stone and a black stone that had been embedded at the center of the breastplate. "They are called Urim and Thummim. The black signifies 'yes,' and the white 'no.' When you are unable to read the omens, they will help you to do so. Always ask an objective question.

"But, if you can, try to make your own decisions. The treasure is at the Pyramids; that you already knew.

But I had to insist on the payment of six sheep because I helped you to make your decision."

The boy put the stones in his pouch. From then on, he would make his own decisions.

"Don't forget that everything you deal with is only one thing and nothing else. And don't forget the language of omens. And, above all, don't forget to follow your destiny through to its conclusion.

"But before I go, I want to tell you a little story.

"A certain shopkeeper sent his son to learn about the secret of happiness from the wisest man in the world. The lad wandered through the desert for forty days, and finally came upon a beautiful castle, high atop a mountain. It was there that the wise man lived.

"Rather than finding a saintly man, though, our hero, on entering the main room of the castle, saw a hive of activity: tradesmen came and went, people were conversing in the corners, a small orchestra was playing soft music, and there was a table covered with platters of the most delicious food in that part of the world. The wise man conversed with everyone, and the boy had to wait for two hours before it was his turn to be given the man's attention.

"The wise man listened attentively to the boy's explanation of why he had come, but told him that he didn't have time just then to explain the secret of happiness. He suggested that the boy look around the palace and return in two hours.

"'Meanwhile, I want to ask you to do something,' said the wise man, handing the boy a teaspoon that held two drops of oil. 'As you wander around, carry this spoon with you without allowing the oil to spill.'

"The boy began climbing and descending the many stairways of the palace, keeping his eyes fixed on the spoon. After two hours, he returned to the room where the wise man was.

"'Well,' asked the wise man, 'did you see the Persian tapestries that are hanging in my dining hall? Did you see the garden that it took the master gardener ten years to create? Did you notice the beautiful parchments in my library?'

"The boy was embarrassed, and confessed that he had observed nothing. His only concern had been not to spill the oil that the wise man had entrusted to him.

"'Then go back and observe the marvels of my world,' said the wise man. 'You cannot trust a man if you don't know his house.'

"Relieved, the boy picked up the spoon and returned to his exploration of the palace, this time observing all of the works of art on the ceilings and the walls. He saw the gardens, the mountains all around him, the beauty of the flowers, and the taste with which everything had been selected. Upon returning to the wise man, he related in detail everything he had seen.

"'But where are the drops of oil I entrusted to you?' asked the wise man.

"Looking down at the spoon he held, the boy saw that the oil was gone.

"'Well, there is only one piece of advice I can give you,' said the wisest of wise men. 'The secret of happiness is to see all the marvels of the world, and never to forget the drops of oil on the spoon.'"

The shepherd said nothing. He had understood the story the old king had told him. A shepherd may like to travel, but he should never forget about his sheep.

The old man looked at the boy and, with his hands held together, made several strange gestures over the boy's head. Then, taking his sheep, he walked away.

* * *

At the highest point in Tarifa there is an old fort, built by the Moors. From atop its walls, one can catch a glimpse of Africa. Melchizedek, the king of Salem, sat on the wall of the fort that afternoon, and felt the levanter blowing in his face. The sheep fidgeted nearby, uneasy with their new owner and excited by so much change. All they wanted was food and water.

Melchizedek watched a small ship that was plowing its way out of the port. He would never again see the boy, just as he had never seen Abraham again after having charged him his one-tenth fee. That was his work.

The gods should not have desires, because they don't have destinies. But the king of Salem hoped desperately that the boy would be successful.

It's too bad that he's quickly going to forget my name, he thought. I should have repeated it for him. Then when he spoke about me he would say that I am Melchizedek, the king of Salem.

He looked to the skies, feeling a bit abashed, and said, "I know it's the vanity of vanities, as you said, my Lord. But an old king sometimes has to take some pride in himself."

* * *

How strange Africa is, thought the boy.

He was sitting in a bar very much like the other bars he had seen along the narrow streets of Tangier. Some men were smoking from a gigantic pipe that they passed from one to the other. In just a few hours he had seen men walking hand in hand, women with their faces covered, and priests that climbed to the tops of towers and chanted—as everyone about him went to their knees and placed their foreheads on the ground.

"A practice of infidels," he said to himself. As a child in church, he had always looked at the image of Saint Santiago Matamoros on his white horse, his sword unsheathed, and figures such as these kneeling at his feet. The boy felt ill and terribly alone. The infidels had an evil look about them.

Besides this, in the rush of his travels he had forgotten a detail, just one detail, which could keep him from his treasure for a long time: only Arabic was spoken in this country.

The owner of the bar approached him, and the boy pointed to a drink that had been served at the next table. It turned out to be a bitter tea. The boy preferred wine.

But he didn't need to worry about that right now. What he had to be concerned about was his treasure, and how he was going to go about getting it. The sale of his sheep had left him with enough money in his pouch, and the boy knew that in money there was magic; whoever has money is never really alone. Before long, maybe in just a few days, he would be at the Pyramids. An old man, with a breastplate of gold, wouldn't have lied just to acquire six sheep.

The old man had spoken about signs and omens, and, as the boy was crossing the strait, he had thought about omens. Yes, the old man had known what he was talking about: during the time the boy had spent in the fields of Andalusia, he had become used to learning which path he should take by observing the ground and the sky. He had discovered that the presence of a certain bird meant that a snake was nearby, and that a certain shrub was a sign that there was water in the area. The sheep had taught him that.

If God leads the sheep so well, he will also lead a man, he thought, and that made him feel better. The tea seemed less bitter.

"Who are you?" he heard a voice ask him in Spanish.

The boy was relieved. He was thinking about omens, and someone had appeared.

"How come you speak Spanish?" he asked. The new arrival was a young man in Western dress, but the color of his skin suggested he was from this city. He was about the same age and height as the boy.

"Almost everyone here speaks Spanish. We're only two hours from Spain."

"Sit down, and let me treat you to something," said the boy. "And ask for a glass of wine for me. I hate this tea."

"There is no wine in this country," the young man said. "The religion here forbids it."

The boy told him then that he needed to get to the Pyramids. He almost began to tell about his treasure, but decided not to do so. If he did, it was possible that the Arab would want a part of it as payment for taking him there. He remembered what the old man had said about offering something you didn't even have yet.

"I'd like you to take me there if you can. I can pay you to serve as my guide."

"Do you have any idea how to get there?" the new-comer asked.

The boy noticed that the owner of the bar stood nearby, listening attentively to their conversation. He felt uneasy at the man's presence. But he had found a guide, and didn't want to miss out on an opportunity.

"You have to cross the entire Sahara desert," said the young man. "And to do that, you need money. I need to know whether you have enough."

The boy thought it a strange question. But he trusted in the old man, who had said that, when you really want something, the universe always conspires in your favor.

He took his money from his pouch and showed it to

the young man. The owner of the bar came over and looked, as well. The two men exchanged some words in Arabic, and the bar owner seemed irritated.

"Let's get out of here," said the new arrival. "He wants us to leave."

The boy was relieved. He got up to pay the bill, but the owner grabbed him and began to speak to him in an angry stream of words. The boy was strong, and wanted to retaliate, but he was in a foreign country. His new friend pushed the owner aside, and pulled the boy outside with him. "He wanted your money," he said. "Tangier is not like the rest of Africa. This is a port, and every port has its thieves."

The boy trusted his new friend. He had helped him out in a dangerous situation. He took out his money and counted it.

"We could get to the Pyramids by tomorrow," said the other, taking the money. "But I have to buy two camels."

They walked together through the narrow streets of Tangier. Everywhere there were stalls with items for sale. They reached the center of a large plaza where the market was held. There were thousands of people there, arguing, selling, and buying; vegetables for sale amongst daggers, and carpets displayed alongside tobacco. But the boy never took his eye off his new friend. After all, he had all his money. He thought about asking him to give it back, but decided that would be unfriendly. He knew nothing about the customs of the strange land he was in.

"I'll just watch him," he said to himself. He knew he was stronger than his friend.

Suddenly, there in the midst of all that confusion, he saw the most beautiful sword he had ever seen. The scabbard was embossed in silver, and the handle was black and encrusted with precious stones. The boy promised himself that, when he returned from Egypt, he would buy that sword.

"Ask the owner of that stall how much the sword costs," he said to his friend. Then he realized that he had been distracted for a few moments, looking at the sword. His heart squeezed, as if his chest had suddenly compressed it. He was afraid to look around, because he knew what he would find. He continued to look at the beautiful sword for a bit longer, until he summoned the courage to turn around.

All around him was the market, with people coming and going, shouting and buying, and the aroma of strange foods … but nowhere could he find his new companion.

The boy wanted to believe that his friend had simply become separated from him by accident. He decided to stay right there and await his return. As he waited, a priest climbed to the top of a nearby tower and began his chant; everyone in the market fell to their knees, touched their foreheads to the ground, and took up the chant. Then, like a colony of worker ants, they dismantled their stalls and left.

The sun began its departure, as well. The boy watched it through its trajectory for some time, until it was hidden behind the white houses surrounding the plaza. He recalled that when the sun had risen that morning, he was on another continent, still a shepherd with sixty sheep, and looking forward to meeting with a girl. That morning he had known everything that was going to happen to him as he walked through the familiar fields. But now, as the sun began to set, he was in a different country, a stranger in a strange land, where he couldn't even speak the language. He was no longer a shepherd, and he had nothing, not even the money to return and start everything over.

All this happened between sunrise and sunset, the boy thought. He was feeling sorry for himself, and lamenting the fact that his life could have changed so suddenly and so drastically.

He was so ashamed that he wanted to cry. He had never even wept in front of his own sheep. But the marketplace was empty, and he was far from home, so he wept. He wept because God was unfair, and because this was the way God repaid those who believed in their dreams.

When I had my sheep, I was happy, and I made those around me happy. People saw me coming and welcomed me, he thought. But now I'm sad and alone. I'm going to become bitter and distrustful of people because one person betrayed me. I'm going to hate those who have found their treasure because I never found mine. And I'm going to hold on to what little I have, because I'm too insignificant to conquer the world.

He opened his pouch to see what was left of his possessions; maybe there was a bit left of the sandwich he had eaten on the ship. But all he found was the heavy book, his jacket, and the two stones the old man had given him.

As he looked at the stones, he felt relieved for some reason. He had exchanged six sheep for two precious stones that had been taken from a gold breastplate. He could sell the stones and buy a return ticket. But this time I'll be smarter, the boy thought, removing them from the pouch so he could put them in his pocket. This was a port town, and the only truthful thing his friend had told him was that port towns are full of thieves.

Now he understood why the owner of the bar had been so upset: he was trying to tell him not to trust that man. "I'm like everyone else—I see the world in terms of what I would like to see happen, not what actually does."

He ran his fingers slowly over the stones, sensing their temperature and feeling their surfaces. They were his treasure. Just handling them made him feel better. They reminded him of the old man.

"When you want something, all the universe conspires in helping you to achieve it," he had said.

The boy was trying to understand the truth of what the old man had said. There he was in the empty marketplace, without a cent to his name, and with not a sheep to guard through the night. But the stones were proof that he had met with a king—a king who knew of the boy's past.

"They're called Urim and Thummim, and they can help you to read the omens." The boy put the stones back in the pouch and decided to do an experiment. The old man had said to ask very clear questions, and to do that, the boy had to know what he wanted. So, he asked if the old man's blessing was still with him.

He took out one of the stones. It was "yes."

"Am I going to find my treasure?" he asked. He stuck his hand into the pouch, and felt around for one of the stones. As he did so, both of them pushed through a hole in the pouch and fell to the ground. The boy had never even noticed that there was a hole in his pouch. He knelt down to find Urim and Thummim and put them back in the pouch. But as he saw them lying there on the ground, another phrase came to his mind.

"Learn to recognize omens, and follow them," the old king had said.

An omen. The boy smiled to himself. He picked up the two stones and put them back in his pouch. He didn't consider mending the hole—the stones could fall through any time they wanted. He had learned that there were certain things one shouldn't ask about, so as not to flee from one's own destiny. "I promised that I would make my own decisions," he said to himself.

But the stones had told him that the old man was still with him, and that made him feel more confident. He looked around at the empty plaza again, feeling less desperate than before. This wasn't a strange place; it was a new one.

After all, what he had always wanted was just that: to know new places. Even if he never got to the Pyramids, he had already traveled farther than any shepherd he knew. Oh, if they only knew how different things are just two hours by ship from where they are, he thought. Although his new world at the moment was just an empty marketplace, he had already seen it when it was teeming with life, and he would never forget it. He remembered the sword. It hurt him a bit to think about it, but he had never seen one like it before. As he mused about these things, he realized that he had to choose between thinking of himself as the poor victim of a thief and as an adventurer in quest of his treasure.

"I'm an adventurer, looking for treasure," he said to himself.

* * *

He was shaken into wakefulness by someone. He had fallen asleep in the middle of the marketplace, and life in the plaza was about to resume. Looking around, he sought his sheep, and then realized that he was in a new world. But instead of being saddened, he was happy. He no longer had to seek out food and water for the sheep; he could go in search of his treasure, instead. He had not a cent in his pocket, but he had faith. He had decided, the night before, that he would be as much an adventurer as the ones he had admired in books.

He walked slowly through the market. The merchants were assembling their stalls, and the boy helped a candy seller to do his. The candy seller had a smile on his face: he was happy, aware of what his life was about, and ready to begin a day's work. His smile reminded the boy of the old man—the mysterious old king he had met. "This candy merchant isn't making candy so that later he can travel or marry a shopkeeper's daughter. He's doing it because it's what he wants to do," thought the boy. He realized that he could do the same thing the old man had done—sense whether a person was near to or far from his destiny. Just by looking at them. It's easy, and yet I've never done it before, he thought.

When the stall was assembled, the candy seller offered the boy the first sweet he had made for the day. The boy thanked him, ate it, and went on his way. When he had gone only a short distance, he realized that, while they were erecting the stall, one of them had spoken Arabic and the other Spanish.

And they had understood each other perfectly well.

There must be a language that doesn't depend on words, the boy thought. I've already had that experience with my sheep, and now it's happening with people.

He was learning a lot of new things. Some of them were things that he had already experienced, and weren't really new, but that he had never perceived before. And he hadn't perceived them because he had become accustomed to them. He realized: If I can learn to understand this language without words, I can learn to understand the world.

Relaxed and unhurried, he resolved that he would walk through the narrow streets of Tangier. Only in that way would he be able to read the omens. He knew it would require a lot of patience, but shepherds know all about patience. Once again he saw that, in that strange land, he was applying the same lessons he had learned with his sheep.

"All things are one," the old man had said.

* * *

The crystal merchant awoke with the day, and felt the same anxiety that he felt every morning. He had been in the same place for thirty years: a shop at the top of a hilly street where few customers passed. Now it was too late to change anything—the only thing he had ever learned to do was to buy and sell crystal glassware. There had been a time when many people knew of his shop: Arab merchants, French and English geologists, German soldiers who were always well-heeled. In those days it had been wonderful to be selling crystal, and he had thought how he would become rich, and have beautiful women at his side as he grew older.

But, as time passed, Tangier had changed. The nearby city of Ceuta had grown faster than Tangier, and business had fallen off. Neighbors moved away, and there remained only a few small shops on the hill. And no one was going to climb the hill just to browse through a few small shops.

But the crystal merchant had no choice. He had lived thirty years of his life buying and selling crystal pieces, and now it was too late to do anything else.

He spent the entire morning observing the infrequent comings and goings in the street. He had done this for years, and knew the schedule of everyone who passed. But, just before lunchtime, a boy stopped in front of the shop. He was dressed normally, but the practiced eyes of the crystal merchant could see that the boy had no money to spend. Nevertheless, the merchant decided to delay his lunch for a few minutes until the boy moved on.

* * *

A card hanging in the doorway announced that several languages were spoken in the shop. The boy saw a man appear behind the counter.

"I can clean up those glasses in the window, if you want," said the boy. "The way they look now, nobody is going to want to buy them."

The man looked at him without responding.

"In exchange, you could give me something to eat."

The man still said nothing, and the boy sensed that he was going to have to make a decision. In his pouch, he had his jacket—he certainly wasn't going to need it in the desert. Taking the jacket out, he began to clean the glasses. In half an hour, he had cleaned all the glasses in the window, and, as he was doing so, two customers had entered the shop and bought some crystal.

When he had completed the cleaning, he asked the man for something to eat. "Let's go and have some lunch," said the crystal merchant.

He put a sign on the door, and they went to a small cafe nearby. As they sat down at the only table in the place, the crystal merchant laughed.

"You didn't have to do any cleaning," he said. "The Koran requires me to feed a hungry person."

"Well then, why did you let me do it?" the boy asked.

"Because the crystal was dirty. And both you and I needed to cleanse our minds of negative thoughts."

When they had eaten, the merchant turned to the boy and said, "I'd like you to work in my shop. Two customers came in today while you were working, and that's a good omen."

People talk a lot about omens, thought the shepherd. But they really don't know what they're saying. Just as I hadn't realized that for so many years I had been speaking a language without words to my sheep.

"Do you want to go to work for me?" the merchant asked.

"I can work for the rest of today," the boy answered. "I'll work all night, until dawn, and I'll clean every piece of crystal in your shop. In return, I need money to get to Egypt tomorrow."

The merchant laughed. "Even if you cleaned my crystal for an entire year … even if you earned a good commission selling every piece, you would still have to borrow money to get to Egypt. There are thousands of kilometers of desert between here and there."

There was a moment of silence so profound that it seemed the city was asleep. No sound from the bazaars, no arguments among the merchants, no men climbing to the towers to chant. No hope, no adventure, no old kings or destinies, no treasure, and no Pyramids. It was as if the world had fallen silent because the boy's soul had. He sat there, staring blankly through the door of the cafe, wishing that he had died, and that everything would end forever at that moment.

The merchant looked anxiously at the boy. All the joy he had seen that morning had suddenly disappeared.

"I can give you the money you need to get back to your country, my son," said the crystal merchant.

The boy said nothing. He got up, adjusted his clothing, and picked up his pouch.

"I'll work for you," he said.

And after another long silence, he added, "I need money to buy some sheep."

Part Two

The boy had been working for the crystal merchant for almost a month, and he could see that it wasn't exactly the kind of job that would make him happy. The merchant spent the entire day mumbling behind the counter, telling the boy to be careful with the pieces and not to break anything.

But he stayed with the job because the merchant, although he was an old grouch, treated him fairly; the boy received a good commission for each piece he sold, and had already been able to put some money aside. That morning he had done some calculating: if he continued to work every day as he had been, he would need a whole year to be able to buy some sheep.

"I'd like to build a display case for the crystal," the boy said to the merchant. "We could place it outside, and attract those people who pass at the bottom of the hill."

"I've never had one before," the merchant answered. "People will pass by and bump into it, and pieces will be broken."

"Well, when I took my sheep through the fields some of them might have died if we had come upon a snake. But that's the way life is with sheep and with shepherds."

The merchant turned to a customer who wanted three crystal glasses. He was selling better than ever … as if time had turned back to the old days when the street had been one of Tangier's major attractions.

"Business has really improved," he said to the boy, after the customer had left. "I'm doing much better, and soon you'll be able to return to your sheep. Why ask more out of life?"

"Because we have to respond to omens," the boy said, almost without meaning to; then he regretted what he had said, because the merchant had never met the king.

"It's called the principle of favorability, beginner's luck. Because life wants you to achieve your destiny," the old king had said.

But the merchant understood what the boy had said. The boy's very presence in the shop was an omen, and, as time passed and money was pouring into the cash drawer, he had no regrets about having hired the boy. The boy was being paid more money than he deserved, because the merchant, thinking that sales wouldn't amount to much, had offered the boy a high commission rate. He had assumed he would soon return to his sheep.

"Why did you want to get to the Pyramids?" he asked, to get away from the business of the display.

"Because I've always heard about them," the boy answered, saying nothing about his dream. The treasure was now nothing but a painful memory, and he tried to avoid thinking about it.

"I don't know anyone around here who would want to cross the desert just to see the Pyramids," said the merchant. "They're just a pile of stones. You could build one in your backyard."

"You've never had dreams of travel," said the boy, turning to wait on a customer who had entered the shop.

Two days later, the merchant spoke to the boy about the display.

"I don't much like change," he said. "You and I aren't like Hassan, that rich merchant. If he makes a buying mistake, it doesn't affect him much. But we two have to live with our mistakes."

That's true enough, the boy thought, ruefully.

"Why did you think we should have the display?"

"I want to get back to my sheep faster. We have to take advantage when luck is on our side, and do as much to help it as it's doing to help us. It's called the principle of favorability. Or beginner's luck."

The merchant was silent for a few moments. Then he said, "The Prophet gave us the Koran, and left us just five obligations to satisfy during our lives. The most important is to believe only in the one true God. The others are to pray five times a day, fast during Ramadan, and be charitable to the poor."

He stopped there. His eyes filled with tears as he spoke of the Prophet. He was a devout man, and, even with all his impatience, he wanted to live his life in accordance with Muslim law.

"What's the fifth obligation?" the boy asked.

"Two days ago, you said that I had never dreamed

of travel," the merchant answered. "The fifth obligation of every Muslim is a pilgrimage. We are obliged, at least once in our lives, to visit the holy city of Mecca.

"Mecca is a lot farther away than the Pyramids. When I was young, all I wanted to do was put together enough money to start this shop. I thought that someday I'd be rich, and could go to Mecca. I began to make some money, but I could never bring myself to leave someone in charge of the shop; the crystals are delicate things. At the same time, people were passing my shop all the time, heading for Mecca. Some of them were rich pilgrims, traveling in caravans with servants and camels, but most of the people making the pilgrimage were poorer than I.

"All who went there were happy at having done so. They placed the symbols of the pilgrimage on the doors of their houses. One of them, a cobbler who made his living mending boots, said that he had traveled for almost a year through the desert, but that he got more tired when he had to walk through the streets of Tangier buying his leather."

"Well, why don't you go to Mecca now?" asked the boy.

"Because it's the thought of Mecca that keeps me alive. That's what helps me face these days that are all the same, these mute crystals on the shelves, and lunch and dinner at that same horrible cafe. I'm afraid that if my dream is realized, I'll have no reason to go on living.

"You dream about your sheep and the Pyramids, but you're different from me, because you want to realize your dreams. I just want to dream about Mecca. I've already imagined a thousand times crossing the desert, arriving at the Plaza of the Sacred Stone, the seven times I walk around it before allowing myself to touch it. I've already imagined the people who would be at my side, and those in front of me, and the conversations and prayers we would share. But I'm afraid that it would all be a disappointment, so I prefer just to dream about it."

That day, the merchant gave the boy permission to build the display. Not everyone can see his dreams come true in the same way.

* * *

Two more months passed, and the shelf brought many customers into the crystal shop. The boy estimated that, if he worked for six more months, he could return to Spain and buy sixty sheep, and yet another sixty. In less than a year, he would have doubled his flock, and he would be able to do business with the Arabs, because he was now able to speak their strange language. Since that morning in the marketplace, he had never again made use of Urim and Thummim, because Egypt was now just as distant a dream for him as was Mecca for the merchant. Anyway, the boy had become happy in his work, and thought all the time about the day when he would disembark at Tarifa as a winner.

"You must always know what it is that you want," the old king had said. The boy knew, and was now working toward it. Maybe it was his treasure to have wound up in that strange land, met up with a thief, and doubled the size of his flock without spending a cent.

He was proud of himself. He had learned some important things, like how to deal in crystal, and about the language without words … and about omens. One afternoon he had seen a man at the top of the hill, complaining that it was impossible to find a decent place to get something to drink after such a climb. The boy, accustomed to recognizing omens, spoke to the merchant.

"Let's sell tea to the people who climb the hill."

"Lots of places sell tea around here," the merchant said.

"But we could sell tea in crystal glasses. The people will enjoy the tea and want to buy the glasses. I have been told that beauty is the great seducer of men."

The merchant didn't respond, but that afternoon, after saying his prayers and closing the shop, he invited the boy to sit with him and share his hookah, that strange pipe used by the Arabs.

"What is it you're looking for?" asked the old merchant.

"I've already told you. I need to buy my sheep back, so I have to earn the money to do so."

The merchant put some new coals in the hookah, and inhaled deeply.

"I've had this shop for thirty years. I know good crystal from bad, and everything else there is to know about crystal. I know its dimensions and how it behaves. If we serve tea in crystal, the shop is going to expand. And then I'll have to change my way of life."

"Well, isn't that good?"

"I'm already used to the way things are. Before you came, I was thinking about how much time I had wasted in the same place, while my friends had moved on, and either went bankrupt or did better than they had before. It made me very depressed. Now, I can see that it hasn't been too bad. The shop is exactly the size I always wanted it to be. I don't want to change anything, because I don't know how to deal with change. I'm used to the way I am."

The boy didn't know what to say. The old man continued, "You have been a real blessing to me. Today, I understand something I didn't see before: every blessing ignored becomes a curse. I don't want anything else in life. But you are forcing me to look at wealth and at horizons I have never known. Now that I have seen them, and now that I see how immense my possibilities are, I'm going to feel worse than I did before you arrived. Because I know the things I should be able to accomplish, and I don't want to do so."

It's good I refrained from saying anything to the baker in Tarifa, thought the boy to himself.

They went on smoking the pipe for a while as the sun began to set. They were conversing in Arabic, and the boy was proud of himself for being able to do so. There had been a time when he thought that his sheep could teach him everything he needed to know about the world. But they could never have taught him Arabic.

There are probably other things in the world that the sheep can't teach me, thought the boy as he regarded the old merchant. All they ever do, really, is look for food and water. And maybe it wasn't that they were teaching me, but that I was learning from them.

"Maktub," the merchant said, finally.

"What does that mean?"

"You would have to have been born an Arab to understand," he answered. "But in your language it would be something like 'It is written.'"

And, as he smothered the coals in the hookah, he told the boy that he could begin to sell tea in the crystal glasses. Sometimes, there's just no way to hold back the river.

* * *

The men climbed the hill, and they were tired when they reached the top. But there they saw a crystal shop that offered refreshing mint tea. They went in to drink the tea, which was served in beautiful crystal glasses.

"My wife never thought of this," said one, and he bought some crystal—he was entertaining guests that night, and the guests would be impressed by the beauty of the glassware. The other man remarked that tea was always more delicious when it was served in crystal, because the aroma was retained. The third said that it was a tradition in the Orient to use crystal glasses for tea because it had magical powers.

Before long, the news spread, and a great many people began to climb the hill to see the shop that was doing something new in a trade that was so old. Other shops were opened that served tea in crystal, but they weren't at the top of a hill, and they had little business.

Eventually, the merchant had to hire two more employees. He began to import enormous quantities of tea, along with his crystal, and his shop was sought out by men and women with a thirst for things new.

And, in that way, the months passed.

* * *

The boy awoke before dawn. It had been eleven months and nine days since he had first set foot on the African continent.

He dressed in his Arabian clothing of white linen, bought especially for this day. He put his headcloth in place and secured it with a ring made of camel skin. Wearing his new sandals, he descended the stairs silently.

The city was still sleeping. He prepared himself a sandwich and drank some hot tea from a crystal glass. Then he sat in the sun-filled doorway, smoking the hookah.

He smoked in silence, thinking of nothing, and listening to the sound of the wind that brought the scent of the desert. When he had finished his smoke, he reached into one of his pockets, and sat there for a few moments, regarding what he had withdrawn.

It was a bundle of money. Enough to buy himself a hundred and twenty sheep, a return ticket, and a license to import products from Africa into his own country.

He waited patiently for the merchant to awaken and open the shop. Then the two went off to have some more tea.

"I'm leaving today," said the boy. "I have the money I need to buy my sheep. And you have the money you need to go to Mecca."

The old man said nothing.

"Will you give me your blessing?" asked the boy. "You have helped me." The man continued to prepare his tea, saying nothing. Then he turned to the boy.

"I am proud of you," he said. "You brought a new feeling into my crystal shop. But you know that I'm not going to go to Mecca. Just as you know that you're not going to buy your sheep."

"Who told you that?" asked the boy, startled.

"Maktub," said the old crystal merchant.

And he gave the boy his blessing.

* * *

The boy went to his room and packed his belongings. They filled three sacks. As he was leaving, he saw, in the corner of the room, his old shepherd's pouch.

It was bunched up, and he had hardly thought of it for a long time. As he took his jacket out of the pouch, thinking to give it to someone in the street, the two stones fell to the floor. Urim and Thummim.

It made the boy think of the old king, and it startled him to realize how long it had been since he had thought of him. For nearly a year, he had been working incessantly, thinking only of putting aside enough money so that he could return to Spain with pride.

"Never stop dreaming," the old king had said. "Follow the omens."

The boy picked up Urim and Thummim, and, once again, had the strange sensation that the old king was nearby. He had worked hard for a year, and the omens were that it was time to go.

I'm going to go back to doing just what I did before, the boy thought. Even though the sheep didn't teach me to speak Arabic.

But the sheep had taught him something even more important; that there was a language in the world that everyone understood, a language the boy had used throughout the time that he was trying to improve things at the shop. It was the language of enthusiasm, of things accomplished with love and purpose, and as part of a search for something believed in and desired. Tangier was no longer a strange city, and he felt that, just as he had conquered this place, he could conquer the world.

"When you want something, all the universe conspires to help you achieve it," the old king had said.

But the old king hadn't said anything about being robbed, or about endless deserts, or about people who know what their dreams are but don't want to realize them. The old king hadn't told him that the Pyramids were just a pile of stones, or that anyone could build one in his backyard. And he had forgotten to mention that, when you have enough money to buy a flock larger than the one you had before, you should buy it.

The boy picked up his pouch and put it with his other things. He went down the stairs and found the merchant waiting on a foreign couple, while two other customers walked about the shop, drinking tea from crystal glasses. It was more activity than usual for this time of the morning. From where he stood, he saw for the first time that the old merchant's hair was very much like the hair of the old king. He remembered the smile of the candy seller, on his first day in Tangier, when he had nothing to eat and nowhere to go – that smile had also been like the old king's smile.

It's almost as if he had been here and left his mark, he thought. And yet, none of these people has ever met the old king. On the other hand, he said that he always appeared to help those who are trying to realize their destiny.

He left without saying good-bye to the crystal merchant. He didn't want to cry with the other people there. He was going to miss the place and all the good things he had learned. He was more confident in himself, though, and felt as though he could conquer the world.

"But I'm going back to the fields that I know, to take care of my flock again." He said that to himself with certainty, but he was no longer happy with his decision. He had worked for an entire year to make a dream come true, and that dream, minute by minute, was becoming less important. Maybe because that wasn't really his dream.

Who knows … maybe it's better to be like the crystal merchant: never go to Mecca, and just go through life wanting to do so, he thought, again trying to convince himself. But as he held Urim and Thummim in his hand, they had transmitted to him the strength and will of the old king. By coincidence—or maybe it was an omen, the boy thought—he came to the bar he had entered on his first day there. The thief wasn't there, and the owner brought him a cup of tea.

I can always go back to being a shepherd, the boy thought. I learned how to care for sheep, and I haven't forgotten how that's done. But maybe I'll never have another chance to get to the Pyramids in Egypt. The old man wore a breastplate of gold, and he knew about my past. He really was a king, a wise king.

The hills of Andalusia were only two hours away, but there was an entire desert between him and the Pyramids. Yet the boy felt that there was another way to regard his situation: he was actually two hours closer to his treasure … the fact that the two hours had stretched into an entire year didn't matter.

I know why I want to get back to my flock, he thought. I understand sheep; they're no longer a problem, and they can be good friends. On the other hand, I don't know if the desert can be a friend, and it's in the desert that I have to search for my treasure. If I don't find it, I can always go home. I finally have enough money, and all the time I need. Why not?

He suddenly felt tremendously happy. He could always go back to being a shepherd. He could always become a crystal salesman again. Maybe the world had other hidden treasures, but he had a dream, and he had met with a king. That doesn't happen to just anyone!

He was planning as he left the bar. He had remembered that one of the crystal merchant's suppliers transported his crystal by means of caravans that crossed the desert. He held Urim and Thummim in his hand; because of those two stones, he was once again on the way to his treasure.

"I am always nearby, when someone wants to realize their destiny," the old king had told him.

What could it cost to go over to the supplier's warehouse and find out if the Pyramids were really that far away?

* * *

The Englishman was sitting on a bench in a structure that smelled of animals, sweat, and dust; it was part warehouse, part corral. I never thought I'd end up in a place like this, he thought, as he leafed through the pages of a chemical journal. Ten years at the university, and here I am in a corral.

But he had to move on. He believed in omens. All his life and all his studies were aimed at finding the one true language of the universe. First he had studied Esperanto, then the world's religions, and now it was alchemy. He knew how to speak Esperanto, he understood all the major religions well, but he wasn't yet an alchemist. He had unraveled the truths behind important questions, but his studies had taken him to a point beyond which he could not seem to go. He had tried in vain to establish a relationship with an alchemist. But the alchemists were strange people, who thought only about themselves, and almost always refused to help him. Who knows, maybe they had failed to discover the secret of the Master Work—the Philosopher's Stone—and for this reason kept their knowledge to themselves.

He had already spent much of the fortune left to him by his father, fruitlessly seeking the Philosopher's Stone. He had spent enormous amounts of time at the great libraries of the world, and had purchased all the rarest and most important volumes on alchemy. In one he had read that, many years ago, a famous Arabian alchemist had visited Europe. It was said that he was more than two hundred years old, and that he had discovered the Philosopher's Stone and the Elixir of Life. The Englishman had been profoundly impressed by the story. But he would never have thought it more than just a myth, had not a friend of his—returning from an archaeological expedition in the desert—told him about an Arab that was possessed of exceptional powers.

"He lives at the Al-Fayoum oasis," his friend had said. "And people say that he is two hundred years old, and is able to transform any metal into gold."

The Englishman could not contain his excitement. He canceled all his commitments and pulled together the most important of his books, and now here he was, sitting inside a dusty, smelly warehouse. Outside, a huge caravan was being prepared for a crossing of the Sahara, and was scheduled to pass through Al-Fayoum.

I'm going to find that damned alchemist, the Englishman thought. And the odor of the animals became a bit more tolerable.

A young Arab, also loaded down with baggage, entered, and greeted the Englishman.

"Where are you bound?" asked the young Arab.

"I'm going into the desert," the man answered, turning back to his reading. He didn't want any conversation at this point. What he needed to do was review all he had learned over the years, because the alchemist would certainly put him to the test.

The young Arab took out a book and began to read. The book was written in Spanish. That's good, thought the Englishman. He spoke Spanish better than Arabic, and, if this boy was going to Al-Fayoum, there would be someone to talk to when there were no other important things to do.

* * *

"That's strange," said the boy, as he tried once again to read the burial scene that began the book. "I've been trying for two years to read this book, and I never get past these first few pages." Even without a king to provide an interruption, he was unable to concentrate.

He still had some doubts about the decision he had made. But he was able to understand one thing: making a decision was only the beginning of things. When someone makes a decision, he is really diving into a strong current that will carry him to places he had never dreamed of when he first made the decision.

When I decided to seek out my treasure, I never imagined that I'd wind up working in a crystal shop, he thought. And joining this caravan may have been my decision, but where it goes is going to be a mystery to me.

Nearby was the Englishman, reading a book. He seemed unfriendly, and had looked irritated when the boy had entered. They might even have become friends, but the Englishman closed off the conversation.

The boy closed his book. He felt that he didn't want to do anything that might make him look like the Englishman. He took Urim and Thummim from his pocket, and began playing with them.

The stranger shouted, "Urim and Thummim!"

In a flash the boy put them back in his pocket.

"They're not for sale," he said.

"They're not worth much," the Englishman answered. "They're only made of rock crystal, and there are millions of rock crystals in the earth. But those who know about such things would know that those are Urim and Thummim. I didn't know that they had them in this part of the world."

"They were given to me as a present by a king," the boy said.

The stranger didn't answer; instead, he put his hand in his pocket, and took out two stones that were the same as the boy's.

"Did you say a king?" he asked.

"I guess you don't believe that a king would talk to someone like me, a shepherd," he said, wanting to end the conversation.

"Not at all. It was shepherds who were the first to recognize a king that the rest of the world refused to acknowledge. So, it's not surprising that kings would talk to shepherds."

And he went on, fearing that the boy wouldn't understand what he was talking about, "It's in the Bible. The same book that taught me about Urim and Thummim. These stones were the only form of divination permitted by God. The priests carried them in a golden breastplate."

The boy was suddenly happy to be there at the warehouse.

"Maybe this is an omen," said the Englishman, half aloud.

"Who told you about omens?" The boy's interest was increasing by the moment.

"Everything in life is an omen," said the Englishman,

now closing the journal he was reading. "There is a universal language, understood by everybody, but already forgotten. I am in search of that universal language, among other things. That's why I'm here. I have to find a man who knows that universal language. An alchemist."

The conversation was interrupted by the warehouse boss.

"You're in luck, you two," the fat Arab said. "There's a caravan leaving today for Al-Fayoum."

"But I'm going to Egypt," the boy said.

"Al-Fayoum is in Egypt," said the Arab. "What kind of Arab are you?"

"That's a good luck omen," the Englishman said, after the fat Arab had gone out. "If I could, I'd write a huge encyclopedia just about the words *luck* and *coincidence*. It's with those words that the universal language is written."

He told the boy it was no coincidence that he had met him with Urim and Thummim in his hand. And he asked the boy if he, too, were in search of the alchemist.

"I'm looking for a treasure," said the boy, and he immediately regretted having said it. But the Englishman appeared not to attach any importance to it.

"In a way, so am I," he said.

"I don't even know what alchemy is," the boy was saying, when the warehouse boss called to them to come outside.

* * *

"I'm the leader of the caravan," said a dark-eyed, bearded man. "I hold the power of life and death for every person I take with me. The desert is a capricious lady, and sometimes she drives men crazy."

There were almost two hundred people gathered there, and four hundred animals—camels, horses, mules, and fowl. In the crowd were women, children, and a number of men with swords at their belts and rifles slung on their shoulders. The Englishman had several suitcases filled with books. There was a babble of noise, and the leader had to repeat himself several times for everyone to understand what he was saying.

"There are a lot of different people here, and each has his own God. But the only God I serve is Allah, and in his name I swear that I will do everything possible once again to win out over the desert. But I want each and every one of you to swear by the God you believe in that you will follow my orders no matter what. In the desert, disobedience means death."

There was a murmur from the crowd. Each was swearing quietly to his or her own God. The boy swore to Jesus Christ. The Englishman said nothing. And the murmur lasted longer than a simple vow would have. The people were also praying to heaven for protection.

A long note was sounded on a bugle, and everyone mounted up. The boy and the Englishman had bought camels, and climbed uncertainly onto their backs. The boy felt sorry for the Englishman's camel, loaded down as he was with the cases of books.

"There's no such thing as coincidence," said the Englishman, picking up the conversation where it had been interrupted in the warehouse. "I'm here because a friend of mine heard of an Arab who …"

But the caravan began to move, and it was impossible to hear what the Englishman was saying. The boy knew what he was about to describe, though: the mysterious chain that links one thing to another, the same chain that had caused him to become a shepherd, that had caused his recurring dream, that had brought him to a city near Africa, to find a king, and to be robbed in order to meet a crystal merchant, and …

The closer one gets to realizing his destiny, the more that destiny becomes his true reason for being, thought the boy.

The caravan moved toward the east. It traveled during the morning, halted when the sun was at its strongest, and resumed late in the afternoon. The boy spoke very little with the Englishman, who spent most of his time with his books.

The boy observed in silence the progress of the animals and people across the desert. Now everything was quite different from how it was that day they had set out: then, there had been confusion and shouting, the cries of children and the whinnying of animals, all mixed with the nervous orders of the guides and the merchants.

But, in the desert, there was only the sound of the

eternal wind, and of the hoofbeats of the animals. Even the guides spoke very little to one another.

"I've crossed these sands many times," said one of the camel drivers one night. "But the desert is so huge, and the horizons so distant, that they make a person feel small, and as if he should remain silent."

The boy understood intuitively what he meant, even without ever having set foot in the desert before. Whenever he saw the sea, or a fire, he fell silent, impressed by their elemental force.

I've learned things from the sheep, and I've learned things from crystal, he thought. *I can learn something from the desert, too. It seems old and wise.*

The wind never stopped, and the boy remembered the day he had sat at the fort in Tarifa with this same wind blowing in his face. It reminded him of the wool from his sheep ... his sheep who were now seeking food and water in the fields of Andalusia, as they always had.

"They're not my sheep anymore," he said to himself, without nostalgia. "They must be used to their new shepherd, and have probably already forgotten me. That's good. Creatures like the sheep, that are used to traveling, know about moving on."

He thought of the merchant's daughter, and was sure that she had probably married. Perhaps to a baker, or to another shepherd who could read and could tell her exciting stories—after all, he probably wasn't the only one. But he was excited at his intuitive understanding of the camel driver's comment: maybe he was also learning the universal language that deals with the past and the present of all people. "Hunches," his mother used to call them. The boy was beginning to understand that intuition is really a sudden immersion of the soul into the universal current of life, where the histories of all people are connected, and we are able to know everything, because it's all written there.

"*Maktub*," the boy said, remembering the crystal merchant.

The desert was all sand in some stretches, and rocky in others. When the caravan was blocked by a boulder, it had to go around it; if there was a large rocky area, they had to make a major detour. If the sand was too fine for the animals' hooves, they sought a way where the sand was more substantial. In some places, the ground was covered with the salt of dried-up lakes. The animals balked at such places, and the camel drivers were forced to dismount and unburden their charges. The drivers carried the freight themselves over such treacherous footing, and then reloaded the camels. If a guide were to fall ill or die, the camel drivers would draw lots and appoint a new one.

But all this happened for one basic reason: no matter how many detours and adjustments it made, the caravan moved toward the same compass point. Once obstacles were overcome, it returned to its course, sighting on a star that indicated the location of the oasis. When the people saw that star shining in the morning sky, they knew they were on the right course toward water, palm trees, shelter, and other people.

It was only the Englishman who was unaware of all this; he was, for the most part, immersed in reading his books.

The boy, too, had his book, and he had tried to read it during the first few days of the journey. But he found it much more interesting to observe the caravan and listen to the wind. As soon as he had learned to know his camel better, and to establish a relationship with him, he threw the book away. Although the boy had developed a superstition that each time he opened the book he would learn something important, he decided it was an unnecessary burden.

He became friendly with the camel driver who traveled alongside him. At night, as they sat around the fire, the boy related to the driver his adventures as a shepherd.

During one of these conversations, the driver told of his own life.

"I used to live near El Cairum," he said. "I had my orchard, my children, and a life that would change not at all until I died. One year, when the crop was the best ever, we all went to Mecca, and I satisfied the only unmet obligation in my life. I could die happily, and that made me feel good.

"One day, the earth began to tremble, and the Nile overflowed its banks. It was something that I thought could happen only to others, never to me. My neighbors feared they would lose all their olive trees in the flood, and my wife was afraid that we would lose our children. I thought that everything I owned would be destroyed.

"The land was ruined, and I had to find some other way to earn a living. So now I'm a camel driver. But that disaster taught me to understand the word of Allah: people need not fear the unknown if they are capable of achieving what they need and want.

"We are afraid of losing what we have, whether it's our life or our possessions and property. But this fear evaporates when we understand that our life stories and the history of the world were written by the same hand."

Sometimes, their caravan met with another. One always had something that the other needed—as if everything were indeed written by one hand. As they sat around the fire, the camel drivers exchanged information about windstorms, and told stories about the desert.

At other times, mysterious, hooded men would appear; they were Bedouins who did surveillance along the caravan route. They provided warnings about thieves and barbarian tribes. They came in silence and departed the same way, dressed in black garments that showed only their eyes. One night, a camel driver came to the fire where the Englishman and the boy were sitting. "There are rumors of tribal wars," he told them.

The three fell silent. The boy noted that there was a sense of fear in the air, even though no one said anything. Once again he was experiencing the language without words … the universal language.

The Englishman asked if they were in danger.

"Once you get into the desert, there's no going back," said the camel driver. "And, when you can't go back, you have to worry only about the best way of moving forward. The rest is up to Allah, including the danger."

And he concluded by saying the mysterious word: "*Maktub*."

"You should pay more attention to the caravan," the boy said to the Englishman, after the camel driver had left. "We make a lot of detours, but we're always heading for the same destination."

"And you ought to read more about the world," answered the Englishman. "Books are like caravans in that respect."

The immense collection of people and animals began to travel faster. The days had always been silent, but now, even the nights—when the travelers were accustomed to talking around the fires—had also become quiet. And, one day, the leader of the caravan made the decision that the fires should no longer be lighted, so as not to attract attention to the caravan.

The travelers adopted the practice of arranging the animals in a circle at night, sleeping together in the center as protection against the nocturnal cold. And the leader posted armed sentinels at the fringes of the group.

The Englishman was unable to sleep one night. He called to the boy, and they took a walk along the dunes surrounding the encampment. There was a full moon, and the boy told the Englishman the story of his life.

The Englishman was fascinated with the part about the progress achieved at the crystal shop after the boy began working there.

"That's the principle that governs all things," he said. "In alchemy, it's called the Soul of the World. When you want something with all your heart, that's when you are closest to the Soul of the World. It's always a positive force."

He also said that this was not just a human gift, that everything on the face of the earth had a soul, whether mineral, vegetable, or animal—or even just a simple thought.

"Everything on earth is being continuously transformed, because the earth is alive … and it has a soul. We are part of that soul, so we rarely recognize that it is working for us. But in the crystal shop you probably realized that even the glasses were collaborating in your success."

The boy thought about that for a while as he looked at the moon and the bleached sands. "I have watched the caravan as it crossed the desert," he said. "The caravan and the desert speak the same language, and it's for that reason that the desert allows the crossing. It's going to test the caravan's every step to see if it's in time, and, if it is, we will make it to the oasis."

"If either of us had joined this caravan based only on personal courage, but without understanding that language, this journey would have been much more difficult."

They stood there looking at the moon.

"That's the magic of omens," said the boy. "I've seen how the guides read the signs of the desert, and how the soul of the caravan speaks to the soul of the desert."

The Englishman said, "I'd better pay more attention to the caravan."

"And I'd better read your books," said the boy.

* * *

They were strange books. They spoke about mercury, salt, dragons, and kings, and he didn't understand any of it. But there was one idea that seemed to repeat itself throughout all the books: all things are the manifestation of one thing only.

In one of the books he learned that the most important text in the literature of alchemy contained only a few lines, and had been inscribed on the surface of an emerald.

"It's the Emerald Tablet," said the Englishman, proud that he might teach something to the boy.

"Well, then, why do we need all these books?" the boy asked.

"So that we can understand those few lines," the Englishman answered, without appearing really to believe what he had said.

The book that most interested the boy told the stories of the famous alchemists. They were men who had dedicated their entire lives to the purification of metals in their laboratories; they believed that, if a metal were heated for many years, it would free itself of all its individual properties, and what was left would be the Soul of the World. This Soul of the World allowed them to understand anything on the face of the earth, because it was the language with which all things communicated. They called that discovery the Master Work—it was part liquid and part solid.

"Can't you just observe men and omens in order to understand the language?" the boy asked.

"You have a mania for simplifying everything," answered the Englishman, irritated. "Alchemy is a serious discipline. Every step has to be followed exactly as it was followed by the masters."

The boy learned that the liquid part of the Master Work was called the Elixir of Life, and that it cured all illnesses; it also kept the alchemist from growing old. And the solid part was called the Philosopher's Stone.

"It's not easy to find the Philosopher's Stone," said the Englishman. "The alchemists spent years in their laboratories, observing the fire that purified the metals. They spent so much time close to the fire that gradually they gave up the vanities of the world. They discovered that the purification of the metals had led to a purification of themselves."

The boy thought about the crystal merchant. He had said that it was a good thing for the boy to clean the crystal pieces, so that he could free himself from negative thoughts. The boy was becoming more and more convinced that alchemy could be learned in one's daily life.

"Also," said the Englishman, "the Philosopher's Stone has a fascinating property. A small sliver of the stone can transform large quantities of metal into gold."

Having heard that, the boy became even more interested in alchemy. He thought that, with some patience, he'd be able to transform everything into gold. He read the lives of the various people who had succeeded in doing so: Helvétius, Elias, Fulcanelli, and Geber. They were fascinating stories: each of them lived out his destiny to the end. They traveled, spoke with wise men, performed miracles for the incredulous, and owned the Philosopher's Stone and the Elixir of Life.

But when the boy wanted to learn how to achieve the Master Work, he became completely lost. There were just drawings, coded instructions, and obscure texts.

* * *

"Why do they make things so complicated?" he asked the Englishman one night. The boy had noticed that the Englishman was irritable, and missed his books.

"So that those who have the responsibility for understanding can understand," he said. "Imagine if everyone went around transforming lead into gold. Gold would lose its value.

"It's only those who are persistent, and willing to study things deeply, who achieve the Master Work. That's why I'm here in the middle of the desert. I'm seeking a true alchemist who will help me to decipher the codes."

"When were these books written?" the boy asked.

"Many centuries ago."

"They didn't have the printing press in those days," the boy argued. "There was no way for everybody to know about alchemy. Why did they use such strange language, with so many drawings?"

The Englishman didn't answer him directly. He said that for the past few days he had been paying attention to how the caravan operated, but that he hadn't learned anything new. The only thing he had noticed was that talk of war was becoming more and more frequent.

* * *

Then one day the boy returned the books to the Englishman. "Did you learn anything?" the Englishman asked, eager to hear what it might be. He needed someone to talk to so as to avoid thinking about the possibility of war.

"I learned that the world has a soul, and that whoever understands that soul can also understand the language of things. I learned that many alchemists realized their destinies, and wound up discovering the Soul of the World, the Philosopher's Stone, and the Elixir of Life.

"But, above all, I learned that these things are all so simple that they could be written on the surface of an emerald."

The Englishman was disappointed. The years of research, the magic symbols, the strange words and the laboratory equipment … none of this had made an impression on the boy. His soul must be too primitive to understand those things, he thought.

He took back his books and packed them away again in their bags.

"Go back to watching the caravan," he said. "That didn't teach me anything, either."

The boy went back to contemplating the silence of the desert, and the sand raised by the animals. "Everyone has his or her own way of learning things," he said to himself. "His way isn't the same as mine, nor mine as his. But we're both in search of our destinies, and I respect him for that."

* * *

The caravan began to travel day and night. The hooded Bedouins reappeared more and more frequently, and the camel driver—who had become a good friend of the boy's—explained that the war between the tribes had already begun. The caravan would be very lucky to reach the oasis.

The animals were exhausted, and the men talked among themselves less and less. The silence was the worst aspect of the night, when the mere groan of a camel—which before had been nothing but the groan of a camel—now frightened everyone, because it might signal a raid.

The camel driver, though, seemed not to be very concerned with the threat of war.

"I'm alive," he said to the boy, as they ate a bunch of dates one night, with no fires and no moon. "When I'm eating, that's all I think about. If I'm on the march, I just concentrate on marching. If I have to fight, it will be just as good a day to die as any other.

"Because I don't live in either my past or my future. I'm interested only in the present. If you can concentrate always on the present, you'll be a happy man. You'll see that there is life in the desert, that there are stars in the heavens, and that tribesmen fight because they are part of the human race. Life will be a party for you, a grand festival, because life is the moment we're living right now."

Two nights later, as he was getting ready to bed down, the boy looked for the star they followed every night. He thought that the horizon was a bit lower than it had been, because he seemed to see stars on the desert itself.

"It's the oasis," said the camel driver.

"Well, why don't we go there right now?" the boy asked.

"Because we have to sleep."

* * *

The boy awoke as the sun rose. There, in front of him, where the small stars had been the night before, was an endless row of date palms, stretching across the entire desert.

"We've done it!" said the Englishman, who had also awakened early.

But the boy was quiet. He was at home with the silence of the desert, and he was content just to look at the trees. He still had a long way to go to reach the pyramids, and someday this morning would just be a memory. But this was the present moment—the party the camel driver had mentioned—and he wanted to live it as he did the lessons of his past and his dreams of the future. Although the vision of the date palms would someday be just a memory, right now it signified shade, water, and a refuge from the war. Yesterday, the camel's groan signaled danger, and now a row of date palms could herald a miracle.

The world speaks many languages, the boy thought.

* * *

The times rush past, and so do the caravans, thought the alchemist, as he watched the hundreds of people and animals arriving at the oasis. People were shouting at the new arrivals, dust obscured the desert sun, and the children of the oasis were bursting with excitement at the arrival of the strangers. The alchemist saw the tribal chiefs greet the leader of the caravan, and converse with him at length.

But none of that mattered to the alchemist. He had already seen many people come and go, and the desert remained as it was. He had seen kings and beggars walking the desert sands. The dunes were changed constantly by the wind, yet these were the same sands he had known since he was a child. He always enjoyed seeing the happiness that the travelers experienced when, after weeks of yellow sand and blue sky, they first saw the green of the date palms. Maybe God created the desert so that man could appreciate the date trees, he thought.

He decided to concentrate on more practical matters. He knew that in the caravan there was a man to whom he was to teach some of his secrets. The omens had told him so. He didn't know the man yet, but his practiced eye would recognize him when he appeared. He hoped that it would be someone as capable as his previous apprentice.

I don't know why these things have to be transmitted by word of mouth, he thought. It wasn't exactly that they were secrets; God revealed his secrets easily to all his creatures.

He had only one explanation for this fact: things have to be transmitted this way because they were made up from the pure life, and this kind of life cannot be captured in pictures or words.

Because people become fascinated with pictures and words, and wind up forgetting the Language of the World.

* * *

The boy couldn't believe what he was seeing: the oasis, rather than being just a well surrounded by a few palm trees—as he had seen once in a geography book—was much larger than many towns back in Spain. There were three hundred wells, fifty thousand date trees, and innumerable colored tents spread among them.

"It looks like *The Thousand and One Nights,*" said the Englishman, impatient to meet with the alchemist.

They were surrounded by children, curious to look at the animals and people that were arriving. The men of the oasis wanted to know if they had seen any fighting, and the women competed with one another for access to the cloth and precious stones brought by the merchants. The silence of the desert was a distant dream; the travelers in the caravan were talking incessantly, laughing and shouting, as if they had emerged from the spiritual world and found themselves once again in the world of people. They were relieved and happy.

They had been taking careful precautions in the desert, but the camel driver explained to the boy that oases were always considered to be neutral territories, because the majority of the inhabitants were women and children. There were oases throughout the desert, but the tribesmen fought in the desert, leaving the oases as places of refuge.

With some difficulty, the leader of the caravan brought all his people together and gave them his instructions. The group was to remain there at the oasis until the conflict between the tribes was over. Since they were visitors, they would have to share living space with those who lived there, and would be given the best accommodations. That was the law of hospitality. Then he asked that everyone, including his own sentinels, hand over their arms to the men appointed by the tribal chieftains.

"Those are the rules of war," the leader explained. "The oases may not shelter armies or troops."

To the boy's surprise, the Englishman took a chrome-plated revolver out of his bag and gave it to the men who were collecting the arms.

"Why a revolver?" he asked.

"It helped me to trust in people," the Englishman answered.

Meanwhile, the boy thought about his treasure. The closer he got to the realization of his dream, the more difficult things became. It seemed as if what the old king had called "beginner's luck" were no longer functioning. In his pursuit of the dream, he was being constantly subjected to tests of his persistence and courage. So he could not be hasty, nor impatient. If he pushed forward impulsively, he would fail to see the signs and omens left by God along his path.

God placed them along my path. He had surprised himself with the thought. Until then, he had considered the omens to be things of this world. Like eating or sleeping, or like seeking love or finding a job. He had never thought of them in terms of a language used by God to indicate what he should do.

"Don't be impatient," he repeated to himself. "It's like the camel driver said: 'Eat when it's time to eat. And move along when it's time to move along.'"

That first day, everyone slept from exhaustion, including the Englishman. The boy was assigned a place far from his friend, in a tent with five other young men of about his age. They were people of the desert, and clamored to hear his stories about the great cities.

The boy told them about his life as a shepherd, and was about to tell them of his experiences at the crystal shop when the Englishman came into the tent.

"I've been looking for you all morning," he said, as he led the boy outside. "I need you to help me find out where the alchemist lives."

First, they tried to find him on their own. An alchemist would probably live in a manner that was different from that of the rest of the people at the oasis, and it was likely that in his tent an oven was continuously burning. They searched everywhere, and found that the oasis was much larger than they could have imagined; there were hundreds of tents.

"We've wasted almost the entire day," said the Englishman, sitting down with the boy near one of the wells.

"Maybe we'd better ask someone," the boy suggested.

The Englishman didn't want to tell others about his reasons for being at the oasis, and couldn't make up his mind. But, finally, he agreed that the boy, who spoke better Arabic than he, should do so. The boy approached a woman who had come to the well to fill a goatskin with water.

"Good afternoon, ma'am. I'm trying to find out where the alchemist lives here at the oasis."

The woman said she had never heard of such a person, and hurried away. But before she fled, she advised the boy that he had better not try to converse with women who were dressed in black, because they were married women. He should respect tradition.

The Englishman was disappointed. It seemed he had made the long journey for nothing. The boy was also saddened; his friend was in pursuit of his destiny. And, when someone was in such pursuit, the entire universe made an effort to help him succeed—that's what the old king had said. He couldn't have been wrong.

"I had never heard of alchemists before," the boy said. "Maybe no one here has, either."

The Englishman's eyes lit up. "That's it! Maybe no one here knows what an alchemist is! Find out who it is who cures the people's illnesses!"

Several women dressed in black came to the well for water, but the boy would speak to none of them, despite the Englishman's insistence. Then a man approached.

"Do you know someone here who cures people's illnesses?" the boy asked.

"Allah cures our illnesses," said the man, clearly frightened of the strangers. "You're looking for witch doctors." He spoke some verses from the Koran, and moved on.

Another man appeared. He was older, and was carrying a small bucket. The boy repeated his question.

"Why do you want to find that sort of person?" the Arab asked.

"Because my friend here has traveled for many months in order to meet with him," the boy said.

"If such a man is here at the oasis, he must be the very powerful one," said the old man after thinking for a few moments. "Not even the tribal chieftains are able to see him when they want to. Only when he consents.

"Wait for the end of the war. Then leave with the caravan. Don't try to enter into the life of the oasis," he said, and walked away.

But the Englishman was exultant. They were on the right track.

Finally, a young woman approached who was not dressed in black. She had a vessel on her shoulder, and her head was covered by a veil, but her face was uncovered. The boy approached her to ask about the alchemist.

At that moment, it seemed to him that time stood still, and the Soul of the World surged within him. When he looked into her dark eyes, and saw that her lips were poised between a laugh and silence, he learned the most important part of the language that all the world spoke—the language that everyone on earth was capable of understanding in their heart. It was love. Something older than humanity, more ancient than the desert. Something that exerted the same force whenever two pairs of eyes met, as had theirs here at the well. She smiled, and that was certainly an omen—the omen he had been awaiting, without even knowing he was, for all his life. The omen he had sought to find with his sheep and in his books, in the crystals and in the silence of the desert.

It was the pure Language of the World. It required no explanation, just as the universe needs none as it travels through endless time. What the boy felt at that moment was that he was in the presence of the only woman in his life, and that, with no need for words, she recognized the same thing. He was more certain of it than of anything in the world. He had been told by his parents and grandparents that he must fall in love and really know a person before becoming committed. But maybe people who felt that way had never learned the universal language. Because, when you know that language, it's easy to understand that someone in the world awaits you, whether it's in the middle of the desert or in some great city. And when two such people encounter each other, and their eyes meet, the past and the future become unimportant. There is only that moment, and the incredible certainty that everything under the sun has been written by one hand only. It is the hand that evokes love, and creates a twin soul for every person in the world. Without such love, one's dreams would have no meaning.

Maktub, thought the boy.

The Englishman shook the boy: "Come on, ask her!"

The boy stepped closer to the girl, and when she smiled, he did the same.

"What's your name?" he asked.

"Fatima," the girl said, averting her eyes.

"That's what some women in my country are called."

"It's the name of the Prophet's daughter," Fatima said. "The invaders carried the name everywhere." The beautiful girl spoke of the invaders with pride.

The Englishman prodded him, and the boy asked her about the man who cured people's illnesses.

"That's the man who knows all the secrets of the world," she said. "He communicates with the genies of the desert."

The genies were the spirits of good and evil. And the girl pointed to the south, indicating that it was there the strange man lived. Then she filled her vessel with water and left.

The Englishman vanished, too, gone to find the alchemist. And the boy sat there by the well for a long time, remembering that one day in Tarifa the levanter had brought to him the perfume of that woman, and realizing that he had loved her before he even knew she existed. He knew that his love for her would enable him to discover every treasure in the world.

The next day, the boy returned to the well, hoping to see the girl. To his surprise, the Englishman was there, looking out at the desert.

"I waited all afternoon and evening," he said. "He appeared with the first stars of evening. I told him what I was seeking, and he asked me if I had ever transformed lead into gold. I told him that was what I had come here to learn.

"He told me I should try to do so. That's all he said: 'Go and try.'"

The boy didn't say anything. The poor Englishman had traveled all this way, only to be told that he should repeat what he had already done so many times.

"So, then try," he said to the Englishman.

"That's what I'm going to do. I'm going to start now."

As the Englishman left, Fatima arrived and filled her vessel with water.

"I came to tell you just one thing," the boy said. "I want you to be my wife. I love you."

The girl dropped the container, and the water spilled.

"I'm going to wait here for you every day. I have crossed the desert in search of a treasure that is somewhere near the Pyramids, and for me, the war seemed a curse. But now it's a blessing, because it brought me to you."

"The war is going to end someday," the girl said.

The boy looked around him at the date palms. He reminded himself that he had been a shepherd, and that he could be a shepherd again. Fatima was more important than his treasure.

"The tribesmen are always in search of treasure," the girl said, as if she had guessed what he was thinking. "And the women of the desert are proud of their tribesmen."

She refilled her vessel and left.

The boy went to the well every day to meet with Fatima. He told her about his life as a shepherd, about the king, and about the crystal shop. They became friends, and except for the fifteen minutes he spent with her, each day seemed that it would never pass. When he had been at the oasis for almost a month, the leader of the caravan called a meeting of all of the people traveling with him.

"We don't know when the war will end, so we can't continue our journey," he said. "The battles may last for a long time, perhaps even years. There are powerful forces on both sides, and the war is important to both armies. It's not a battle of good against evil. It's a war between forces that are fighting for the balance of power, and, when that type of battle begins, it lasts longer than others—because Allah is on both sides."

The people went back to where they were living, and the boy went to meet with Fatima that afternoon. He told her about the morning's meeting. "The day after we met," Fatima said, "you told me that you loved me. Then, you taught me something of the universal language and the Soul of the World. Because of that, I have become a part of you."

The boy listened to the sound of her voice, and thought it to be more beautiful than the sound of the wind in the date palms.

"I have been waiting for you here at this oasis for a long time. I have forgotten about my past, about my traditions, and the way in which men of the desert expect women to behave. Ever since I was a child, I have dreamed that the desert would bring me a wonderful present. Now, my present has arrived, and it's you."

The boy wanted to take her hand. But Fatima's hands held to the handles of her jug.

"You have told me about your dreams, about the old king and your treasure. And you've told me about omens. So now, I fear nothing, because it was those omens that brought you to me. And I am a part of your dream, a part of your destiny, as you call it.

"That's why I want you to continue toward your goal. If you have to wait until the war is over, then wait. But if you have to go before then, go on in pursuit of your dream. The dunes are changed by the wind, but the desert never changes. That's the way it will be with our love for each other.

"*Maktub,*" she said. "If I am really a part of your dream, you'll come back one day."

The boy was sad as he left her that day. He thought of all the married shepherds he had known. They had a difficult time convincing their wives that they had to go off into distant fields. Love required them to stay with the people they loved.

He told Fatima that, at their next meeting.

"The desert takes our men from us, and they don't always return," she said. "We know that, and we are used to it. Those who don't return become a part of the clouds, a part of the animals that hide in the ravines and of the water that comes from the earth. They become a part of everything … they become the Soul of the World.

"Some do come back. And then the other women are happy because they believe that their men may one day return, as well. I used to look at those women and envy them their happiness. Now, I too will be one of the women who wait.

"I'm a desert woman, and I'm proud of that. I want my husband to wander as free as the wind that shapes the dunes. And, if I have to, I will accept the fact that he has become a part of the clouds, and the animals and the water of the desert."

The boy went to look for the Englishman. He wanted to tell him about Fatima. He was surprised when he saw that the Englishman had built himself a furnace outside his tent. It was a strange furnace, fueled by firewood, with a transparent flask heating on top. As the Englishman stared out at the desert, his eyes seemed brighter than they had when he was reading his books.

"This is the first phase of the job," he said. "I have to separate out the sulfur. To do that successfully, I must have no fear of failure. It was my fear of failure that first kept me from attempting the Master Work. Now, I'm beginning what I could have started ten years ago. But I'm happy at least that I didn't wait twenty years."

He continued to feed the fire, and the boy stayed on until the desert turned pink in the setting sun. He felt the urge to go out into the desert, to see if its silence held the answers to his questions.

He wandered for a while, keeping the date palms of the oasis within sight. He listened to the wind, and felt the stones beneath his feet. Here and there, he found a shell, and realized that the desert, in remote times, had been a sea. He sat on a stone, and allowed himself to become hypnotized by the horizon. He tried to deal with the concept of love as distinct from possession, and couldn't separate them. But Fatima was a woman of the desert, and, if anything could help him to understand, it was the desert.

As he sat there thinking, he sensed movement above him. Looking up, he saw a pair of hawks flying high in the sky.

He watched the hawks as they drifted on the wind. Although their flight appeared to have no pattern, it made a certain kind of sense to the boy. It was just that he couldn't grasp what it meant. He followed the movement of the birds, trying to read something into it. Maybe these desert birds could explain to him the meaning of love without ownership.

He felt sleepy. In his heart, he wanted to remain awake, but he also wanted to sleep. "I am learning the Language of the World, and everything in the world is beginning to make sense to me … even the flight of the hawks," he said to himself. And, in that mood, he was grateful to be in love. When you are in love, things make even more sense, he thought.

Suddenly, one of the hawks made a flashing dive through the sky, attacking the other. As it did so, a sudden, fleeting image came to the boy: an army, with its swords at the ready, riding into the oasis. The vision vanished immediately, but it had shaken him. He had heard people speak of mirages, and had already seen some himself: they were desires that, because of their intensity, materialized over the sands of the desert. But he certainly didn't desire that an army invade the oasis.

He wanted to forget about the vision, and return to his meditation. He tried again to concentrate on the pink shades of the desert, and its stones. But there was something there in his heart that wouldn't allow him to do so.

"Always heed the omens," the old king had said. The boy recalled what he had seen in the vision, and sensed that it was actually going to occur.

He rose, and made his way back toward the palm trees. Once again, he perceived the many languages in the things about him: this time, the desert was safe, and it was the oasis that had become dangerous.

The camel driver was seated at the base of a palm tree, observing the sunset. He saw the boy appear from the other side of the dunes.

"An army is coming," the boy said. "I had a vision."

"The desert fills men's hearts with visions," the camel driver answered.

But the boy told him about the hawks: that he had been watching their flight and had suddenly felt himself to have plunged to the Soul of the World.

The camel driver understood what the boy was saying. He knew that any given thing on the face of the earth could reveal the history of all things. One could open a book to any page, or look at a person's hand; one could turn a card, or watch the flight of the birds … whatever the thing observed, one could find a connection with his experience of the moment.

Actually, it wasn't that those things, in themselves, revealed anything at all; it was just that people, looking at what was occurring around them, could find a means of penetration to the Soul of the World.

The desert was full of men who earned their living based on the ease with which they could penetrate to the Soul of the World. They were known as seers, and they were held in fear by women and the elderly. Tribesmen were also wary of consulting them, because it would be impossible to be effective in battle if one knew that he was fated to die.

The tribesmen preferred the taste of battle, and the thrill of not knowing what the outcome would be; the future was already written by Allah, and what he had written was always for the good of man. So the tribesmen lived only for the present, because the present was full of surprises, and they had to be aware of many things: Where was the enemy's sword? Where was his horse? What kind of blow should one deliver next in order to remain alive? The camel driver was not a fighter, and he had consulted with seers. Many of them had been right about what they said, while some had been wrong. Then, one day, the oldest seer he had ever sought out (and the one most to be feared) had asked why the camel driver was so interested in the future.

"Well … so I can do things," he had responded. "And so I can change those things that I don't want to happen."

"But then they wouldn't be a part of your future," the seer had said.

"Well, maybe I just want to know the future so I can prepare myself for what's coming."

"If good things are coming, they will be a pleasant surprise," said the seer. "If bad things are, and you know in advance, you will suffer greatly before they even occur."

"I want to know about the future because I'm a man," the camel driver had said to the seer. "And men always live their lives based on the future."

The seer was a specialist in the casting of twigs; he threw them on the ground, and made interpretations based on how they fell. That day, he didn't make a cast. He wrapped the twigs in a piece of cloth and put them back in his bag.

"I make my living forecasting the future for people," he said. "I know the science of the twigs, and I know how to use them to penetrate to the place where all is written. There, I can read the past, discover what has already been forgotten, and understand the omens that are here in the present.

"When people consult me, it's not that I'm reading the future; I am guessing at the future. The future belongs to God, and it is only he who reveals it, under extraordinary circumstances. How do I guess at the future? Based on the omens of the present. The secret is here in the present. If you pay attention to the present, you can improve upon it. And, if you improve on the present, what comes later will also be better. Forget about the future, and live each day according to the teachings, confident that God loves his children.

Each day, in itself, brings with it an eternity."

The camel driver had asked what the circumstances were under which God would allow him to see the future.

"Only when he, himself, reveals it. And God only rarely reveals the future. When he does so, it is for only one reason: it's a future that was written so as to be altered."

God had shown the boy a part of the future, the camel driver thought. Why was it that he wanted the boy to serve as his instrument?

"Go and speak to the tribal chieftains," said the camel driver. "Tell them about the armies that are approaching."

"They'll laugh at me."

"They are men of the desert, and the men of the desert are used to dealing with omens."

"Well, then, they probably already know."

"They're not concerned with that right now. They believe that if they have to know about something Allah wants them to know, someone will tell them about it. It has happened many times before. But, this time, the person is you."

The boy thought of Fatima. And he decided he would go to see the chiefs of the tribes.

* * *

The boy approached the guard at the front of the huge white tent at the center of the oasis.

"I want to see the chieftains. I've brought omens from the desert."

Without responding, the guard entered the tent, where he remained for some time. When he emerged, it was with a young Arab, dressed in white and gold. The boy told the younger man what he had seen, and the man asked him to wait there. He disappeared into the tent.

Night fell, and an assortment of fighting men and merchants entered and exited the tent. One by one, the campfires were extinguished, and the oasis fell as quiet as the desert. Only the lights in the great tent remained. During all this time, the boy thought about Fatima, and he was still unable to understand his last conversation with her.

Finally, after hours of waiting, the guard bade the boy enter. The boy was astonished by what he saw inside. Never could he have imagined that, there in the middle of the desert, there existed a tent like this one. The ground was covered with the most beautiful carpets he had ever walked upon, and from the top of the structure hung lamps of hand-wrought gold, each with a lighted candle. The tribal chieftains were seated at the back of the tent in a semicircle, resting upon richly embroidered silk cushions. Servants came and went with silver trays laden with spices and tea. Other servants maintained the fires in the hookahs. The atmosphere was suffused with the sweet scent of smoke.

There were eight chieftains, but the boy could see

immediately which of them was the most important: an Arab dressed in white and gold, seated at the center of the semicircle. At his side was the young Arab the boy had spoken with earlier.

"Who is this stranger who speaks of omens?" asked one of the chieftains, eyeing the boy.

"It is I," the boy answered. And he told what he had seen.

"Why would the desert reveal such things to a stranger, when it knows that we have been here for generations?" said another of the chieftains.

"Because my eyes are not yet accustomed to the desert," the boy said. "I can see things that eyes habituated to the desert might not see."

And also because I know about the Soul of the World, he thought to himself.

"The oasis is neutral ground. No one attacks an oasis," said a third chieftain.

"I can only tell you what I saw. If you don't want to believe me, you don't have to do anything about it."

The men fell into an animated discussion. They spoke in an Arabic dialect that the boy didn't understand, but, when he made to leave, the guard told him to stay. The boy became fearful; the omens told him that something was wrong. He regretted having spoken to the camel driver about what he had seen in the desert.

Suddenly, the elder at the center smiled almost imperceptibly, and the boy felt better. The man hadn't participated in the discussion, and, in fact, hadn't said a word up to that point. But the boy was already used to the Language of the World, and he could feel the vibrations of peace throughout the tent. Now his intuition was that he had been right in coming.

The discussion ended. The chieftains were silent for a few moments as they listened to what the old man was saying. Then he turned to the boy: this time his expression was cold and distant.

"Two thousand years ago, in a distant land, a man who believed in dreams was thrown into a dungeon and then sold as a slave," the old man said, now in the dialect the boy understood. "Our merchants bought that man, and brought him to Egypt. All of us know that whoever believes in dreams also knows how to interpret them."

The elder continued, "When the pharaoh dreamed of cows that were thin and cows that were fat, this man I'm speaking of rescued Egypt from famine. His name was Joseph. He, too, was a stranger in a strange land, like you, and he was probably about your age."

He paused, and his eyes were still unfriendly.

"We always observe the Tradition. The Tradition saved Egypt from famine in those days, and made the Egyptians the wealthiest of peoples. The Tradition teaches men how to cross the desert, and how their children should marry. The Tradition says that an oasis is neutral territory, because both sides have oases, and so both are vulnerable."

No one said a word as the old man continued.

"But the Tradition also says that we should believe the messages of the desert. Everything we know was taught to us by the desert."

The old man gave a signal, and everyone stood. The meeting was over. The hookahs were extinguished, and the guards stood at attention. The boy made ready to leave, but the old man spoke again.

"Tomorrow, we are going to break the agreement that says that no one at the oasis may carry arms. Throughout the entire day we will be on the lookout for our enemies. When the sun sets, the men will once again surrender their arms to me. For every ten dead men among our enemies, you will receive a piece of gold.

"But arms cannot be drawn unless they also go into battle. Arms are as capricious as the desert, and, if they are not used, the next time they might not function. If at least one of them hasn't been used by the end of the day tomorrow, one will be used on you."

When the boy left the tent, the oasis was illuminated only by the light of the full moon. He was twenty minutes from his tent, and began to make his way there.

He was alarmed by what had happened. He had succeeded in reaching through to the Soul of the World, and now the price for having done so might be his life. It was a frightening bet. But he had been making risky bets ever since the day he had sold his sheep to pursue his destiny. And, as the camel driver had said, to die tomorrow was no worse than dying on any other day. Every day was there to be lived or to mark one's departure from this world. Everything depended on one word: "*Maktub*."

Walking along in the silence, he had no regrets. If he died tomorrow, it would be because God was not willing to change the future. He would at least have died after having crossed the strait, after having worked in a crystal shop, and after having known the silence of the desert and Fatima's eyes. He had lived every one of his days intensely since he had left home so long ago. If he died tomorrow, he would already have seen more than other shepherds, and he was proud of that.

Suddenly he heard a thundering sound, and he was thrown to the ground by a wind such as he had never known. The area was swirling in dust so intense that it hid the moon from view. Before him was an enormous white horse, rearing over him with a frightening scream.

When the blinding dust had settled a bit, the boy trembled at what he saw. Astride the animal was a horseman dressed completely in black, with a falcon perched on his left shoulder. He wore a turban and his entire face, except for his eyes, was covered with a black kerchief. He appeared to be a messenger from the desert, but his presence was much more powerful than that of a mere messenger.

The strange horseman drew an enormous, curved sword from a scabbard mounted on his saddle. The steel of its blade glittered in the light of the moon.

"Who dares to read the meaning of the flight of the hawks?" he demanded, so loudly that his words seemed to echo through the fifty thousand palm trees of Al-Fayoum.

"It is I who dared to do so," said the boy. He was reminded of the image of Santiago Matamoros, mounted on his white horse, with the infidels beneath his hooves. This man looked exactly the same, except that now the roles were reversed.

"It is I who dared to do so," he repeated, and he lowered his head to receive a blow from the sword. "Many lives will be saved, because I was able to see through to the Soul of the World."

The sword didn't fall. Instead, the stranger lowered it slowly, until the point touched the boy's forehead. It drew a droplet of blood.

The horseman was completely immobile, as was the boy. It didn't even occur to the boy to flee. In his heart, he felt a strange sense of joy: he was about to die in pursuit of his destiny. And for Fatima. The omens had been true, after all. Here he was, face-to-face with his enemy, but there was no need to be concerned about dying—the Soul of the World awaited him, and he would soon be a part of it. And, tomorrow, his enemy would also be a part of that Soul.

The stranger continued to hold the sword at the boy's forehead. "Why did you read the flight of the birds?"

"I read only what the birds wanted to tell me. They wanted to save the oasis. Tomorrow all of you will die, because there are more men at the oasis than you have."

The sword remained where it was. "Who are you to change what Allah has willed?"

"Allah created the armies, and he also created the hawks. Allah taught me the language of the birds. Everything has been written by the same hand," the boy said, remembering the camel driver's words.

The stranger withdrew the sword from the boy's forehead, and the boy felt immensely relieved. But he still couldn't flee.

"Be careful with your prognostications," said the stranger. "When something is written, there is no way to change it."

"All I saw was an army," said the boy. "I didn't see the outcome of the battle."

The stranger seemed satisfied with the answer. But he kept the sword in his hand. "What is a stranger doing in a strange land?"

"I am following my destiny. It's not something you would understand."

The stranger placed his sword in its scabbard, and the boy relaxed.

"I had to test your courage," the stranger said. "Courage is the quality most essential to understanding the Language of the World."

The boy was surprised. The stranger was speaking of things that very few people knew about.

"You must not let up, even after having come so far," he continued. "You must love the desert, but never trust it completely. Because the desert tests all men: it challenges every step, and kills those who become distracted."

What he said reminded the boy of the old king.

"If the warriors come here, and your head is still on your shoulders at sunset, come and find me," said the stranger.

The same hand that had brandished the sword now held a whip. The horse reared again, raising a cloud of dust.

"Where do you live?" shouted the boy, as the horseman rode away.

The hand with the whip pointed to the south.

The boy had met the alchemist.

* * *

Next morning, there were two thousand armed men scattered throughout the palm trees at Al-Fayoum. Before the sun had reached its high point, five hundred tribesmen appeared on the horizon. The mounted troops entered the oasis from the north; it appeared to be a peaceful expedition, but they all carried arms hidden in their robes. When they reached the white tent at the center of Al-Fayoum, they withdrew their scimitars and rifles. And they attacked an empty tent.

The men of the oasis surrounded the horsemen from the desert and within half an hour all but one of the intruders were dead. The children had been kept at the other side of a grove of palm trees, and saw nothing of what had happened. The women had remained in their tents, praying for the safekeeping of their husbands, and saw nothing of the battle, either.

Were it not for the bodies there on the ground, it would have appeared to be a normal day at the oasis.

The only tribesman spared was the commander of the battalion. That afternoon, he was brought before the tribal chieftains, who asked him why he had violated the Tradition. The commander said that his men had been starving and thirsty, exhausted from many days of battle, and had decided to take the oasis so as to be able to return to the war.

The tribal chieftain said that he felt sorry for the tribesmen, but that the Tradition was sacred. He condemned the commander to death without honor. Rather than being killed by a blade or a bullet, he was hanged from a dead palm tree, where his body twisted in the desert wind.

The tribal chieftain called for the boy, and presented him with fifty pieces of gold. He repeated his story about Joseph of Egypt, and asked the boy to become the counselor of the oasis.

* * *

When the sun had set, and the first stars made their appearance, the boy started to walk to the south. He eventually sighted a single tent, and a group of Arabs passing by told the boy that it was a place inhabited by genies. But the boy sat down and waited.

Not until the moon was high did the alchemist ride into view. He carried two dead hawks over his shoulder.

"I am here," the boy said.

"You shouldn't be here," the alchemist answered. "Or is it your destiny that brings you here?"

"With the wars between the tribes, it's impossible to cross the desert. So I have come here."

The alchemist dismounted from his horse, and signaled that the boy should enter the tent with him. It was a tent like many at the oasis. The boy looked around for the ovens and other apparatus used in alchemy, but saw none. There were only some books in a pile, a small cooking stove, and the carpets, covered with mysterious designs.

"Sit down. We'll have something to drink and eat these hawks," said the alchemist.

The boy suspected that they were the same hawks he had seen on the day before, but he said nothing. The alchemist lighted the fire, and soon a delicious aroma filled the tent. It was better than the scent of the hookahs.

"Why did you want to see me?" the boy asked.

"Because of the omens," the alchemist answered. "The wind told me you would be coming, and that you would need help."

"It's not I the wind spoke about. It's the other foreigner, the Englishman. He's the one that's looking for you."

"He has other things to do first. But he's on the right track. He has begun to try to understand the desert."

"And what about me?"

"When a person really desires something, all the universe conspires to help that person to realize his dream," said the alchemist, echoing the words of the old king. The boy understood. Another person was there to help him toward his destiny.

"So you are going to instruct me?"

"No. You already know all you need to know. I am only going to point you in the direction of your treasure."

"But there's a tribal war," the boy reiterated.

"I know what's happening in the desert."

"I have already found my treasure. I have a camel, I have my money from the crystal shop, and I have fifty gold pieces. In my own country, I would be a rich man."

"But none of that is from the Pyramids," said the alchemist.

"I also have Fatima. She is a treasure greater than anything else I have won."

"She wasn't found at the Pyramids, either."

They ate in silence. The alchemist opened a bottle and poured a red liquid into the boy's cup. It was the most delicious wine he had ever tasted.

"Isn't wine prohibited here?" the boy asked.

"It's not what enters men's mouths that's evil," said the alchemist. "It's what comes out of their mouths that is."

The alchemist was a bit daunting, but, as the boy drank the wine, he relaxed. After they finished eating they sat outside the tent, under a moon so brilliant that it made the stars pale.

"Drink and enjoy yourself," said the alchemist,

noticing that the boy was feeling happier. "Rest well tonight, as if you were a warrior preparing for combat. Remember that wherever your heart is, there you will find your treasure. You've got to find the treasure, so that everything you have learned along the way can make sense.

"Tomorrow, sell your camel and buy a horse. Camels are traitorous: they walk thousands of paces and never seem to tire. Then suddenly, they kneel and die. But horses tire bit by bit. You always know how much you can ask of them, and when it is that they are about to die."

* * *

The following night, the boy appeared at the alchemist's tent with a horse. The alchemist was ready, and he mounted his own steed and placed the falcon on his left shoulder. He said to the boy, "Show me where there is life out in the desert. Only those who can see such signs of life are able to find treasure."

They began to ride out over the sands, with the moon lighting their way. I don't know if I'll be able to find life in the desert, the boy thought. I don't know the desert that well yet.

He wanted to say so to the alchemist, but he was afraid of the man. They reached the rocky place where the boy had seen the hawks in the sky, but now there was only silence and the wind.

"I don't know how to find life in the desert," the

boy said. "I know that there is life here, but I don't know where to look."

"Life attracts life," the alchemist answered.

And then the boy understood. He loosened the reins on his horse, who galloped forward over the rocks and sand. The alchemist followed as the boy's horse ran for almost half an hour. They could no longer see the palms of the oasis—only the gigantic moon above them, and its silver reflections from the stones of the desert. Suddenly, for no apparent reason, the boy's horse began to slow.

"There's life here," the boy said to the alchemist. "I don't know the language of the desert, but my horse knows the language of life."

They dismounted, and the alchemist said nothing. Advancing slowly, they searched among the stones. The alchemist stopped abruptly, and bent to the ground. There was a hole there among the stones. The alchemist put his hand into the hole, and then his entire arm, up to his shoulder. Something was moving there, and the alchemist's eyes—the boy could see only his eyes—squinted with his effort. His arm seemed to be battling with whatever was in the hole. Then, with a motion that startled the boy, he withdrew his arm and leaped to his feet. In his hand, he grasped a snake by the tail.

The boy leapt as well, but away from the alchemist. The snake fought frantically, making hissing sounds that shattered the silence of the desert. It was a cobra, whose venom could kill a person in minutes.

"Watch out for his venom," the boy said. But even though the alchemist had put his hand in the hole, and had surely already been bitten, his expression was calm. "The alchemist is two hundred years old," the Englishman had told him. He must know how to deal with the snakes of the desert.

The boy watched as his companion went to his horse and withdrew a scimitar. With its blade, he drew a circle in the sand, and then he placed the snake within it. The serpent relaxed immediately.

"Not to worry," said the alchemist. "He won't leave the circle. You found life in the desert, the omen that I needed."

"Why was that so important?"

"Because the Pyramids are surrounded by the desert."

The boy didn't want to talk about the Pyramids. His heart was heavy, and he had been melancholy since the previous night. To continue his search for the treasure meant that he had to abandon Fatima.

"I'm going to guide you across the desert," the alchemist said.

"I want to stay at the oasis," the boy answered. "I've found Fatima, and, as far as I'm concerned, she's worth more than treasure."

"Fatima is a woman of the desert," said the alchemist. "She knows that men have to go away in order to return. And she already has her treasure: it's you. Now she expects that you will find what it is you're looking for."

"Well, what if I decide to stay?"

"Let me tell you what will happen. You'll be the counselor of the oasis. You have enough gold to buy many sheep and many camels. You'll marry Fatima, and you'll both be happy for a year. You'll learn to love the desert, and you'll get to know every one of the fifty thousand palms. You'll watch them as they grow, demonstrating how the world is always changing. And you'll get better and better at understanding omens, because the desert is the best teacher there is.

"Sometime during the second year, you'll remember about the treasure. The omens will begin insistently to speak of it, and you'll try to ignore them. You'll use your knowledge for the welfare of the oasis and its inhabitants. The tribal chieftains will appreciate what you do. And your camels will bring you wealth and power.

"During the third year, the omens will continue to speak of your treasure and your destiny. You'll walk around, night after night, at the oasis, and Fatima will be unhappy because she'll feel it was she who interrupted your quest. But you will love her, and she'll return your love. You'll remember that she never asked you to stay, because a woman of the desert knows that she must await her man. So you won't blame her. But many times you'll walk the sands of the desert, thinking that maybe you could have left … that you could have trusted more in your love for Fatima. Because what kept you at the oasis was your own fear that you might never come back. At that point, the omens will tell you that your treasure is buried forever.

"Then, sometime during the fourth year, the omens will abandon you, because you've stopped listening to them. The tribal chieftains will see that, and you'll be dismissed from your position as counselor. But, by then, you'll be a rich merchant, with many camels and a great deal of merchandise. You'll spend the rest of your days knowing that you didn't pursue your destiny, and that now it's too late.

"You must understand that love never keeps a man from pursuing his destiny. If he abandons that pursuit, it's because it wasn't true love … the love that speaks the Language of the World."

The alchemist erased the circle in the sand, and the snake slithered away among the rocks. The boy remembered the crystal merchant who had always wanted to go to Mecca, and the Englishman in search of the alchemist. He thought of the woman who had trusted in the desert. And he looked out over the desert that had brought him to the woman he loved.

They mounted their horses, and this time it was the boy who followed the alchemist back to the oasis. The wind brought the sounds of the oasis to them, and the boy tried to hear Fatima's voice.

But that night, as he had watched the cobra within the circle, the strange horseman with the falcon on his shoulder had spoken of love and treasure, of the women of the desert and of his destiny.

"I'm going with you," the boy said. And he immediately felt peace in his heart.

"We'll leave tomorrow before sunrise," was the alchemist's only response.

* * *

The boy spent a sleepless night. Two hours before dawn, he awoke one of the boys who slept in his tent, and asked him to show him where Fatima lived. They went to her tent, and the boy gave his friend enough gold to buy a sheep.

Then he asked his friend to go into the tent where Fatima was sleeping, and to awaken her and tell her that he was waiting outside. The young Arab did as he was asked, and was given enough gold to buy yet another sheep.

"Now leave us alone," said the boy to the young Arab. The Arab returned to his tent to sleep, proud to have helped the counselor of the oasis, and happy at having enough money to buy himself some sheep.

Fatima appeared at the entrance to the tent. The two walked out among the palms. The boy knew that it was a violation of the Tradition, but that didn't matter to him now.

"I'm going away," he said. "And I want you to know that I'm coming back. I love you because …"

"Don't say anything," Fatima interrupted. "One is loved because one is loved. No reason is needed for loving."

But the boy continued, "I had a dream, and I met with a king. I sold crystal and crossed the desert. And, because the tribes declared war, I went to the well, seeking the alchemist. So, I love you because the entire universe conspired to help me find you."

The two embraced. It was the first time either had touched the other.

"I'll be back," the boy said.

"Before this, I always looked to the desert with longing," said Fatima. "Now it will be with hope. My father went away one day, but he returned to my mother, and he has always come back since then."

They said nothing else. They walked a bit farther among the palms, and then the boy left her at the entrance to her tent.

"I'll return, just as your father came back to your mother," he said.

He saw that Fatima's eyes were filled with tears.

"You're crying?"

"I'm a woman of the desert," she said, averting her face. "But above all, I'm a woman."

Fatima went back to her tent, and, when daylight came, she went out to do the chores she had done for years. But everything had changed. The boy was no longer at the oasis, and the oasis would never again have the same meaning it had had only yesterday. It would no longer be a place with fifty thousand palm trees and three hundred wells, where the pilgrims arrived, relieved at the end of their long journeys. From that day on, the oasis would be an empty place for her.

From that day on, it was the desert that would be important. She would look to it every day, and would try to guess which star the boy was following in search of his treasure. She would have to send her kisses on the wind, hoping that the wind would touch the boy's face, and would tell him that she was alive. That she was waiting for him, a woman awaiting a courageous man in search of his treasure. From that day on, the desert would represent only one thing to her: the hope for his return.

* * *

"Don't think about what you've left behind," the alchemist said to the boy as they began to ride across the sands of the desert. "Everything is written in the Soul of the World, and there it will stay forever."

"Men dream more about coming home than about leaving," the boy said. He was already reaccustomed to desert's silence.

"If what one finds is made of pure matter, it will never spoil. And one can always come back. If what you had found was only a moment of light, like the explosion of a star, you would find nothing on your return."

The man was speaking the language of alchemy. But the boy knew that he was referring to Fatima.

It was difficult not to think about what he had left behind. The desert, with its endless monotony, put him to dreaming. The boy could still see the palm trees, the wells, and the face of the woman he loved. He could see the Englishman at his experiments, and the camel driver who was a teacher without realizing it. Maybe the alchemist has never been in love, the boy thought.

The alchemist rode in front, with the falcon on his shoulder. The bird knew the language of the desert well, and whenever they stopped, he flew off in search of game. On the first day he returned with a rabbit, and on the second with two birds.

At night, they spread their sleeping gear and kept their fires hidden. The desert nights were cold, and were becoming darker and darker as the phases of the moon passed. They went on for a week, speaking only of the precautions they needed to follow in order to avoid the battles between the tribes. The war continued, and at times the wind carried the sweet, sickly smell of blood. Battles had been fought nearby, and the wind reminded the boy that there was the language of omens, always ready to show him what his eyes had failed to observe.

On the seventh day, the alchemist decided to make camp earlier than usual. The falcon flew off to find game, and the alchemist offered his water container to the boy.

"You are almost at the end of your journey," said the alchemist. "I congratulate you for having pursued your destiny."

"And you've told me nothing along the way," said the boy. "I thought you were going to teach me some of the things you know. A while ago, I rode through the desert with a man who had books on alchemy. But I wasn't able to learn anything from them."

"There is only one way to learn," the alchemist answered. "It's through action. Everything you need to know you have learned through your journey. You need to learn only one thing more."

The boy wanted to know what that was, but the alchemist was searching the horizon, looking for the falcon.

"Why are you called the alchemist?"

"Because that's what I am."

"And what went wrong when other alchemists tried to make gold and were unable to do so?"

"They were looking only for gold," his companion answered. "They were seeking the treasure of their destiny, without wanting actually to live out the destiny."

"What is it that I still need to know?" the boy asked.

But the alchemist continued to look to the horizon. And finally the falcon returned with their meal. They dug a hole and lit their fire in it, so that the light of the flames would not be seen.

"I'm an alchemist simply because I'm an alchemist," he said, as he prepared the meal. "I learned the science from my grandfather, who learned from his father, and so on, back to the creation of the world. In those times, the Master Work could be written simply on an emerald. But men began to reject simple things, and to write tracts, interpretations, and philosophical studies. They also began to feel that they knew a better way than others had. Yet the Emerald Tablet is still alive today."

"What was written on the Emerald Tablet?" the boy wanted to know.

The alchemist began to draw in the sand, and completed his drawing in less than five minutes. As he drew, the boy thought of the old king, and the plaza where they had met that day; it seemed as if it had taken place years and years ago.

"This is what was written on the Emerald Tablet," said the alchemist, when he had finished.

The boy tried to read what was written in the sand.

"It's a code," said the boy, a bit disappointed. "It looks like what I saw in the Englishman's books."

"No," the alchemist answered. "It's like the flight of those two hawks; it can't be understood by reason alone. The Emerald Tablet is a direct passage to the Soul of the World.

"The wise men understood that this natural world is only an image and a copy of paradise. The existence of this world is simply a guarantee that there exists a world that is perfect. God created the world so that, through its visible objects, men could understand his spiritual teachings and the marvels of his wisdom. That's what I mean by action."

"Should I understand the Emerald Tablet?" the boy asked.

"Perhaps, if you were in a laboratory of alchemy, this would be the right time to study the best way to understand the Emerald Tablet. But you are in the desert. So immerse yourself in it. The desert will give you an understanding of the world; in fact, anything on the face of the earth will do that. You don't even have to understand the desert: all you have to do is contemplate a simple grain of sand, and you will see in it all the marvels of creation."

"How do I immerse myself in the desert?"

"Listen to your heart. It knows all things, because it came from the Soul of the World, and it will one day return there."

* * *

They crossed the desert for another two days in silence. The alchemist had become much more cautious, because they were approaching the area where the most violent battles were being waged. As they moved along, the boy tried to listen to his heart.

It was not easy to do; in earlier times, his heart had always been ready to tell its story, but lately that wasn't true. There had been times when his heart spent hours telling of its sadness, and at other times it became so emotional over the desert sunrise that the boy had to hide his tears. His heart beat fastest when it spoke to the boy of treasure, and more slowly when the boy stared entranced at the endless horizons of the desert. But his heart was never quiet, even when the boy and the alchemist had fallen into silence.

"Why do we have to listen to our hearts?" the boy asked, when they had made camp that day.

"Because, wherever your heart is, that is where you'll find your treasure."

"But my heart is agitated," the boy said. "It has its dreams, it gets emotional, and it's become passionate over a woman of the desert. It asks things of me, and it keeps me from sleeping many nights, when I'm thinking about her."

"Well, that's good. Your heart is alive. Keep listening to what it has to say."

During the next three days, the two travelers passed by a number of armed tribesmen, and saw others on the horizon. The boy's heart began to speak of fear. It told him stories it had heard from the Soul of the World, stories of men who sought to find their treasure and never succeeded. Sometimes it frightened the boy with the idea that he might not find his treasure, or that he might die there in the desert. At other times, it told the boy that it was satisfied: it had found love and riches.

"My heart is a traitor," the boy said to the alchemist, when they had paused to rest the horses. "It doesn't want me to go on."

"That makes sense," the alchemist answered. "Naturally it's afraid that, in pursuing your dream, you might lose everything you've won."

"Well, then, why should I listen to my heart?"

"Because you will never again be able to keep it quiet. Even if you pretend not to have heard what it tells you, it will always be there inside you, repeating to you what you're thinking about life and about the world."

"You mean I should listen, even if it's treasonous?"

"Treason is a blow that comes unexpectedly. If you know your heart well, it will never be able to do that to you. Because you'll know its dreams and wishes, and will know how to deal with them.

"You will never be able to escape from your heart. So it's better to listen to what it has to say. That way, you'll never have to fear an unanticipated blow."

The boy continued to listen to his heart as they crossed the desert. He came to understand its dodges and tricks, and to accept it as it was. He lost his fear, and forgot about his need to go back to the oasis, because, one afternoon, his heart told him that it was happy. "Even though I complain sometimes," it said, "it's because I'm the heart of a person, and people's hearts are that way. People are afraid to pursue their most important dreams, because they feel that they don't deserve them, or that they'll be unable to achieve them. We, their hearts, become fearful just thinking of loved ones who go away forever, or of moments that could have been good but weren't, or of treasures that might have been found but were forever hidden in the sands. Because, when these things happen, we suffer terribly."

"My heart is afraid that it will have to suffer," the boy told the alchemist one night as they looked up at the moonless sky.

"Tell your heart that the fear of suffering is worse than the suffering itself. And that no heart has ever suffered when it goes in search of its dreams, because every second of the search is a second's encounter with God and with eternity."

"Every second of the search is an encounter with God," the boy told his heart. "When I have been truly searching for my treasure, every day has been luminous, because I've known that every hour was a part of the dream that I would find it. When I have been truly searching for my treasure, I've discovered things along the way that I never would have seen had I not had the courage to try things that seemed impossible for a shepherd to achieve."

So his heart was quiet for an entire afternoon. That night, the boy slept deeply, and, when he awoke, his heart began to tell him things that came from the Soul of the World. It said that all people who are happy have God within them. And that happiness could be found in a grain of sand from the desert, as the alchemist had said. Because a grain of sand is a moment of creation, and the universe has taken millions of years to create it. "Everyone on earth has a treasure that awaits him," his heart said. "We, people's hearts, seldom say much about those treasures, because people no longer want to go in search of them. We speak of them only to children. Later, we simply let life proceed, in its own direction, toward its own fate. But, unfortunately, very few follow the path laid out for them—the path to their destinies, and to happiness. Most people see the world as a threatening place, and, because they do, the world turns out, indeed, to be a threatening place.

"So, we, their hearts, speak more and more softly. We never stop speaking out, but we begin to hope that our words won't be heard: we don't want people to suffer because they don't follow their hearts."

"Why don't people's hearts tell them to continue to follow their dreams?" the boy asked the alchemist.

"Because that's what makes a heart suffer most, and hearts don't like to suffer."

From then on, the boy understood his heart. He asked it, please, never to stop speaking to him. He asked that, when he wandered far from his dreams, his heart press him and sound the alarm. The boy swore that, every time he heard the alarm, he would heed its message.

That night, he told all of this to the alchemist. And the alchemist understood that the boy's heart had returned to the Soul of the World.

"So what should I do now?" the boy asked.

"Continue in the direction of the Pyramids," said the alchemist. "And continue to pay heed to the omens. Your heart is still capable of showing you where the treasure is."

"Is that the one thing I still needed to know?"

"No," the alchemist answered. "What you still need to know is this: before a dream is realized, the Soul of the World tests everything that was learned along the way. It does this not because it is evil, but so that we can, in addition to realizing our dreams, master the lessons we've learned as we've moved toward that dream. That's the point at which most people give up.

It's the point at which, as we say in the language of the desert, one 'dies of thirst just when the palm trees have appeared on the horizon.'

"Every search begins with beginner's luck. And every search ends with the victor's being severely tested."

The boy remembered an old proverb from his country. It said that the darkest hour of the night came just before the dawn.

* * *

On the following day, the first clear sign of danger appeared. Three armed tribesmen approached, and asked what the boy and the alchemist were doing there.

"I'm hunting with my falcon," the alchemist answered.

"We're going to have to search you to see whether you're armed," one of the tribesmen said.

The alchemist dismounted slowly, and the boy did the same.

"Why are you carrying money?" asked the tribesman, when he had searched the boy's bag.

"I need it to get to the Pyramids," he said.

The tribesman who was searching the alchemist's belongings found a small crystal flask filled with a liquid, and a yellow glass egg that was slightly larger than a chicken's egg.

"What are these things?" he asked.

"That's the Philosopher's Stone and the Elixir of Life. It's the Master Work of the alchemists. Whoever swallows that elixir will never be sick again, and a fragment from that stone turns any metal into gold."

The Arabs laughed at him, and the alchemist laughed along. They thought his answer was amusing, and they allowed the boy and the alchemist to proceed with all of their belongings.

"Are you crazy?" the boy asked the alchemist, when they had moved on. "What did you do that for?"

"To show you one of life's simple lessons," the alchemist answered. "When you possess great treasures within you, and try to tell others of them, seldom are you believed."

They continued across the desert. With every day that passed, the boy's heart became more and more silent. It no longer wanted to know about things of the past or future; it was content simply to contemplate the desert, and to drink with the boy from the Soul of the World. The boy and his heart had become friends, and neither was capable now of betraying the other.

When his heart spoke to him, it was to provide a stimulus to the boy, and to give him strength, because the days of silence there in the desert were wearisome. His heart told the boy what his strongest qualities were: his courage in having given up his sheep and in trying to live out his destiny, and his enthusiasm during the time he had worked at the crystal shop.

And his heart told him something else that the boy had never noticed: it told the boy of dangers that had threatened him, but that he had never perceived. His heart said that one time it had hidden the rifle the boy had taken from his father, because of the possibility that the boy might wound himself. And it reminded the boy of the day when he had been ill and vomiting out in the fields, after which he had fallen into a deep sleep. There had been two thieves farther ahead who were planning to steal the boy's sheep and murder him. But, since the boy hadn't passed by, they had decided to move on, thinking that he had changed his route.

"Does a man's heart always help him?" the boy asked the alchemist.

"Mostly just the hearts of those who are trying to realize their destinies. But they do help children, drunkards, and the elderly, too."

"Does that mean that I'll never run into danger?"

"It means only that the heart does what it can," the alchemist said.

One afternoon, they passed by the encampment of one of the tribes. At each corner of the camp were Arabs garbed in beautiful white robes, with arms at the ready. The men were smoking their hookahs and trading stories from the battlefield. No one paid any attention to the two travelers.

"There's no danger," the boy said, when they had moved on past the encampment.

The alchemist sounded angry: "Trust in your heart, but never forget that you're in the desert. When men are at war with one another, the Soul of the World can hear the screams of battle. No one fails to suffer the consequences of everything under the sun."

All things are one, the boy thought. And then, as if the desert wanted to demonstrate that the alchemist was right, two horsemen appeared from behind the travelers.

"You can't go any farther," one of them said. "You're in the area where the tribes are at war."

"I'm not going very far," the alchemist answered, looking straight into the eyes of the horsemen. They were silent for a moment, and then agreed that the boy and the alchemist could move along.

The boy watched the exchange with fascination. "You dominated those horsemen with the way you looked at them," he said.

"Your eyes show the strength of your soul," answered the alchemist.

That's true, the boy thought. He had noticed that, in the midst of the multitude of armed men back at the encampment, there had been one who stared fixedly at the two. He had been so far away that his face wasn't even visible. But the boy was certain that he had been looking at them.

Finally, when they had crossed the mountain range that extended along the entire horizon, the alchemist said that they were only two days from the Pyramids.

"If we're going to go our separate ways soon," the boy said, "then teach me about alchemy."

"You already know about alchemy. It is about penetrating to the Soul of the World, and discovering the treasure that has been reserved for you."

"No, that's not what I mean. I'm talking about transforming lead into gold."

The alchemist fell as silent as the desert, and answered the boy only after they had stopped to eat.

"Everything in the universe evolved," he said. "And, for wise men, gold is the metal that evolved the furthest. Don't ask me why; I don't know why. I just know that the Tradition is always right.

"Men have never understood the words of the wise. So gold, instead of being seen as a symbol of evolution, became the basis for conflict."

"There are many languages spoken by things," the boy said. "There was a time when, for me, a camel's whinnying was nothing more than whinnying. Then it became a signal of danger. And, finally, it became just a whinny again."

But then he stopped. The alchemist probably already knew all that.

"I have known true alchemists," the alchemist continued. "They locked themselves in their laboratories, and tried to evolve, as gold had. And they found the Philosopher's Stone, because they understood that when something evolves, everything around that thing evolves as well.

"Others stumbled upon the stone by accident. They already had the gift, and their souls were readier for such things than the souls of others. But they don't count. They're quite rare.

"And then there were the others, who were interested only in gold. They never found the secret. They forgot that lead, copper, and iron have their own destinies to fulfill. And anyone who interferes with the destiny of another thing never will discover his own."

The alchemist's words echoed out like a curse. He reached over and picked up a shell from the ground.

"This desert was once a sea," he said.

"I noticed that," the boy answered.

The alchemist told the boy to place the shell over his ear. He had done that many times when he was a child, and had heard the sound of the sea.

"The sea has lived on in this shell, because that's its destiny. And it will never cease doing so until the desert is once again covered by water."

They mounted their horses, and rode out in the direction of the Pyramids of Egypt.

* * *

The sun was setting when the boy's heart sounded a danger signal. They were surrounded by gigantic dunes, and the boy looked at the alchemist to see whether he had sensed anything. But he appeared to be unaware of any danger. Five minutes later, the boy saw two horsemen waiting ahead of them. Before he could say anything to the alchemist, the two horsemen had become ten, and then a hundred. And then they were everywhere in the dunes.

They were tribesmen dressed in blue, with black rings surrounding their turbans. Their faces were hidden behind blue veils, with only their eyes showing.

Even from a distance, their eyes conveyed the strength of their souls. And their eyes spoke of death.

* * *

The two were taken to a nearby military camp. A soldier shoved the boy and the alchemist into a tent where the chief was holding a meeting with his staff.

"These are the spies," said one of the men.

"We're just travelers," the alchemist answered.

"You were seen at the enemy camp three days ago. And you were talking with one of the troops there."

"I'm just a man who wanders the desert and knows the stars," said the alchemist. "I have no information about troops or about the movement of the tribes. I was simply acting as a guide for my friend here."

"Who is your friend?" the chief asked. "An alchemist," said the alchemist. "He understands the forces of nature. And he wants to show you his extraordinary powers."

The boy listened quietly. And fearfully.

"What is a foreigner doing here?" asked another of the men.

"He has brought money to give to your tribe," said the alchemist, before the boy could say a word. And seizing the boy's bag, the alchemist gave the gold coins to the chief.

The Arab accepted them without a word. There was enough there to buy a lot of weapons.

"What is an alchemist?" he asked, finally.

"It's a man who understands nature and the world. If he wanted to, he could destroy this camp just with the force of the wind."

The men laughed. They were used to the ravages of war, and knew that the wind could not deliver them a fatal blow. Yet each felt his heart beat a bit faster. They were men of the desert, and they were fearful of sorcerers.

"I want to see him do it," said the chief.

"He needs three days," answered the alchemist. "He is going to transform himself into the wind, just to demonstrate his powers. If he can't do so, we humbly offer you our lives, for the honor of your tribe."

"You can't offer me something that is already mine," the chief said, arrogantly. But he granted the travelers three days.

The boy was shaking with fear, but the alchemist helped him out of the tent.

"Don't let them see that you're afraid," the alchemist said. "They are brave men, and they despise cowards."

But the boy couldn't even speak. He was able to do so only after they had walked through the center of the camp. There was no need to imprison them: the Arabs simply confiscated their horses. So, once again, the world had demonstrated its many languages: the desert only moments ago had been endless and free, and now it was an impenetrable wall.

"You gave them everything I had!" the boy said. "Everything I've saved in my entire life!"

"Well, what good would it be to you if you had to die?" the alchemist answered. "Your money saved us for three days. It's not often that money saves a person's life."

But the boy was too frightened to listen to words of wisdom. He had no idea how he was going to transform himself into the wind. He wasn't an alchemist!

The alchemist asked one of the soldiers for some tea, and poured some on the boy's wrists. A wave of relief washed over him, and the alchemist muttered some words that the boy didn't understand.

"Don't give in to your fears," said the alchemist, in a strangely gentle voice. "If you do, you won't be able to talk to your heart."

"But I have no idea how to turn myself into the wind."

"If a person is living out his destiny, he knows everything he needs to know. There is only one thing that makes a dream impossible to achieve: the fear of failure."

"I'm not afraid of failing. It's just that I don't know how to turn myself into the wind."

"Well, you'll have to learn; your life depends on it."

"But what if I can't?"

"Then you'll die in the midst of trying to realize your destiny. That's a lot better than dying like millions of other people, who never even knew what their destinies were.

"But don't worry," the alchemist continued. "Usually the threat of death makes people a lot more aware of their lives."

The first day passed. There was a major battle nearby, and a number of wounded were brought back to the camp. The dead soldiers were replaced by others, and life went on. Death doesn't change anything, the boy thought.

"You could have died later on," a soldier said to the body of one of his companions. "You could have died after peace had been declared. But, in any case, you were going to die."

At the end of the day, the boy went looking for the alchemist, who had taken his falcon out into the desert.

"I still have no idea how to turn myself into the wind," the boy repeated.

"Remember what I told you: the world is only the visible aspect of God. And that what alchemy does is to bring spiritual perfection into contact with the material plane."

"What are you doing?"

"Feeding my falcon."

"If I'm not able to turn myself into the wind, we're going to die," the boy said. "Why feed your falcon?"

"You're the one who may die," the alchemist said. "I already know how to turn myself into the wind."

* * *

On the second day, the boy climbed to the top of a cliff near the camp. The sentinels allowed him to go; they had already heard about the sorcerer who could turn himself into the wind, and they didn't want to go near him. In any case, the desert was impassable.

He spent the entire afternoon of the second day looking out over the desert, and listening to his heart. The boy knew the desert sensed his fear.

They both spoke the same language.

* * *

On the third day, the chief met with his officers. He called the alchemist to the meeting and said, "Let's go see the boy who turns himself into the wind."

"Let's," the alchemist answered.

The boy took them to the cliff where he had been on the previous day. He told them all to be seated.

"It's going to take a while," the boy said.

"We're in no hurry," the chief answered. "We are men of the desert."

The boy looked out at the horizon. There were mountains in the distance. And there were dunes, rocks, and plants that insisted on living where survival seemed impossible. There was the desert that he had wandered for so many months; despite all that time, he knew only a small part of it. Within that small part, he had found an Englishman, caravans, tribal wars, and an oasis with fifty thousand palm trees and three hundred wells.

"What do you want here today?" the desert asked him. "Didn't you spend enough time looking at me yesterday?"

"Somewhere you are holding the person I love," the boy said. "So, when I look out over your sands, I am also looking at her. I want to return to her, and I need your help so that I can turn myself into the wind."

"What is love?" the desert asked.

"Love is the falcon's flight over your sands. Because for him, you are a green field, from which he always returns with game. He knows your rocks, your dunes, and your mountains, and you are generous to him."

"The falcon's beak carries bits of me, myself," the desert said. "For years, I care for his game, feeding it with the little water that I have, and then I show him where the game is. And, one day, as I enjoy the fact that his game thrives on my surface, the falcon dives out of the sky, and takes away what I've created."

"But that's why you created the game in the first place," the boy answered. "To nourish the falcon. And the falcon then nourishes man. And, eventually, man will nourish your sands, where the game will once again flourish. That's how the world goes."

"So is that what love is?"

"Yes, that's what love is. It's what makes the game become the falcon, the falcon become man, and man, in his turn, the desert. It's what turns lead into gold, and makes the gold return to the earth."

"I don't understand what you're talking about," the desert said.

"But you can at least understand that somewhere in your sands there is a woman waiting for me. And that's why I have to turn myself into the wind."

The desert didn't answer him for a few moments.

Then it told him, "I'll give you my sands to help the

wind to blow, but, alone, I can't do anything. You have to ask for help from the wind."

A breeze began to blow. The tribesmen watched the boy from a distance, talking among themselves in a language that the boy couldn't understand.

The alchemist smiled.

The wind approached the boy and touched his face. It knew of the boy's talk with the desert, because the winds know everything. They blow across the world without a birthplace, and with no place to die.

"Help me," the boy said. "One day you carried the voice of my loved one to me."

"Who taught you to speak the language of the desert and the wind?"

"My heart," the boy answered.

The wind has many names. In that part of the world, it was called the sirocco, because it brought moisture from the oceans to the east. In the distant land the boy came from, they called it the levanter, because they believed that it brought with it the sands of the desert, and the screams of the Moorish wars. Perhaps, in the places beyond the pastures where his sheep lived, men thought that the wind came from Andalusia. But, actually, the wind came from no place at all, nor did it go to any place; that's why it was stronger than the desert. Someone might one day plant trees in the desert, and even raise sheep there, but never would they harness the wind.

"You can't be the wind," the wind said. "We're two very different things."

"That's not true," the boy said. "I learned the alchemist's secrets in my travels. I have inside me the winds, the deserts, the oceans, the stars, and everything created in the universe. We were all made by the same hand, and we have the same soul. I want to be like you, able to reach every corner of the world, cross the seas, blow away the sands that cover my treasure, and carry the voice of the woman I love."

"I heard what you were talking about the other day with the alchemist," the wind said. "He said that everything has its own destiny. But people can't turn themselves into the wind."

"Just teach me to be the wind for a few moments," the boy said. "So you and I can talk about the limitless possibilities of people and the winds."

The wind's curiosity was aroused, something that had never happened before. It wanted to talk about those things, but it didn't know how to turn a man into the wind. And look how many things the wind already knew how to do! It created deserts, sank ships, felled entire forests, and blew through cities filled with music and strange noises. It felt that it had no limits, yet here was a boy saying that there were other things the wind should be able to do.

"This is what we call love," the boy said, seeing that the wind was close to granting what he requested. "When you are loved, you can do anything in creation. When you are loved, there's no need at all to understand what's happening, because everything happens within you, and even men can turn themselves into the wind. As long as the wind helps, of course."

The wind was a proud being, and it was becoming irritated with what the boy was saying. It commenced to blow harder, raising the desert sands. But finally it had to recognize that, even making its way around the world, it didn't know how to turn a man into the wind. And it knew nothing about love.

"In my travels around the world, I've often seen people speaking of love and looking toward the heavens," the wind said, furious at having to acknowledge its own limitations. "Maybe it's better to ask heaven."

"Well then, help me do that," the boy said. "Fill this place with a sandstorm so strong that it blots out the sun. Then I can look to heaven without blinding myself."

So the wind blew with all its strength, and the sky was filled with sand. The sun was turned into a golden disk.

At the camp, it was difficult to see anything. The men of the desert were already familiar with that wind. They called it the *simum*, and it was worse than a storm at sea. Their horses cried out, and all their weapons were filled with sand.

On the heights, one of the commanders turned to the chief and said, "Maybe we had better end this!"

They could barely see the boy. Their faces were covered with the blue cloths, and their eyes showed fear.

"Let's stop this," another commander said.

"I want to see the greatness of Allah," the chief said, with respect. "I want to see how a man turns himself into the wind."

But he made a mental note of the names of the two men who had expressed their fear. As soon as the wind stopped, he was going to remove them from their commands, because true men of the desert are not afraid.

"The wind told me that you know about love," the boy said to the sun. "If you know about love, you must also know about the Soul of the World, because it's made of love."

"From where I am," the sun said, "I can see the Soul of the World. It communicates with my soul, and together we cause the plants to grow and the sheep to seek out shade. From where I am—and I'm a long way from the earth—I learned how to love. I know that if I came even a little bit closer to the earth, everything there would die, and the Soul of the World would no longer exist. So we contemplate each other, and we want each other, and I give it life and warmth, and it gives me my reason for living."

"So you know about love," the boy said.

"And I know the Soul of the World, because we have talked at great length to each other during this endless trip through the universe. It tells me that its greatest problem is that, up until now, only the minerals and vegetables understand that all things are one. That there's no need for iron to be the same as copper, or copper the same as gold. Each performs its own exact function as a unique being, and everything would be a symphony of peace if the hand that wrote all this had stopped on the fifth day of creation.

"But there was a sixth day," the sun went on.

"You are wise, because you observe everything from a distance," the boy said. "But you don't know about love. If there hadn't been a sixth day, man would not exist; copper would always be just copper, and lead just lead. It's true that everything has its destiny, but one day that destiny will be realized. So each thing has to transform itself into something better, and to acquire a new destiny, until, someday, the Soul of the World becomes one thing only."

The sun thought about that, and decided to shine more brightly. The wind, which was enjoying the conversation, started to blow with greater force, so that the sun would not blind the boy.

"This is why alchemy exists," the boy said. "So that everyone will search for his treasure, find it, and then want to be better than he was in his former life. Lead will play its role until the world has no further need for lead; and then lead will have to turn itself into gold.

"That's what alchemists do. They show that, when we strive to become better than we are, everything around us becomes better, too."

"Well, why did you say that I don't know about love?" the sun asked the boy.

"Because it's not love to be static like the desert, nor is it love to roam the world like the wind. And it's not love to see everything from a distance, like you do. Love is the force that transforms and improves the Soul of the World. When I first reached through to it, I thought the Soul of the World was perfect. But later, I could see that it was like other aspects of creation, and had its own passions and wars. It is we who nourish the Soul of the World, and the world we live in will be either better or worse, depending on whether we become better or worse. And that's where the power of love comes in. Because when we love, we always strive to become better than we are."

"So what do you want of me?" the sun asked.

"I want you to help me turn myself into the wind," the boy answered.

"Nature knows me as the wisest being in creation," the sun said. "But I don't know how to turn you into the wind."

"Then, whom should I ask?"

The sun thought for a minute. The wind was listening closely, and wanted to tell every corner of the world that the sun's wisdom had its limitations. That it was unable to deal with this boy who spoke the Language of the World.

"Speak to the hand that wrote all," said the sun.

The wind screamed with delight, and blew harder than ever. The tents were being blown from their ties to the earth, and the animals were being freed from their tethers. On the cliff, the men clutched at each other as they sought to keep from being blown away.

The boy turned to the hand that wrote all. As he did so, he sensed that the universe had fallen silent, and he decided not to speak.

A current of love rushed from his heart, and the boy began to pray. It was a prayer that he had never said before, because it was a prayer without words or pleas. His prayer didn't give thanks for his sheep having found new pastures; it didn't ask that the boy be able to sell more crystal; and it didn't beseech that the woman he had met continue to await his return. In the silence, the boy understood that the desert, the wind, and the sun were also trying to understand the signs written by the hand, and were seeking to follow their paths, and to understand what had been written on a single emerald. He saw that omens were scattered throughout the earth and in space, and that there was no reason or significance attached to their appearance; he could see that not the deserts, nor the winds, nor the sun, nor people knew why they had been created. But that the hand had a reason for all of this, and that only the hand could perform miracles, or transform the sea into a desert ... or a man into the wind. Because only the hand understood that it was a larger design that had moved the universe to the point at which six days of creation had evolved into a Master Work.

The boy reached through to the Soul of the World, and saw that it was a part of the Soul of God. And he saw that the Soul of God was his own soul. And that he, a boy, could perform miracles.

* * *

The *simum* blew that day as it had never blown before. For generations thereafter, the Arabs recounted the legend of a boy who had turned himself into the wind, almost destroying a military camp, in defiance of the most powerful chief in the desert.

When the *simum* ceased to blow, everyone looked to the place where the boy had been. But he was no longer there; he was standing next to a sand-covered sentinel, on the far side of the camp.

The men were terrified at his sorcery. But there were two people who were smiling: the alchemist, because he had found his perfect disciple, and the chief, because that disciple had understood the glory of God.

The following day, the general bade the boy and the alchemist farewell, and provided them with an escort party to accompany them as far as they chose.

* * *

They rode for the entire day. Toward the end of the afternoon, they came upon a Coptic monastery. The alchemist dismounted, and told the escorts they could return to the camp.

"From here on, you will be alone," the alchemist said. "You are only three hours from the Pyramids."

"Thank you," said the boy. "You taught me the Language of the World."

"I only invoked what you already knew."

The alchemist knocked on the gate of the monastery. A monk dressed in black came to the gates. They spoke for a few minutes in the Coptic tongue, and the alchemist bade the boy enter.

"I asked him to let me use the kitchen for a while," the alchemist smiled.

They went to the kitchen at the back of the monastery. The alchemist lighted the fire, and the monk brought him some lead, which the alchemist placed in an iron pan. When the lead had become liquid, the alchemist took from his pouch the strange yellow egg. He scraped from it a sliver as thin as a hair, wrapped it in wax, and added it to the pan in which the lead had melted.

The mixture took on a reddish color, almost the color of blood. The alchemist removed the pan from the fire, and set it aside to cool. As he did so, he talked with the monk about the tribal wars.

"I think they're going to last for a long time," he said to the monk.

The monk was irritated. The caravans had been stopped at Giza for some time, waiting for the wars to end. "But God's will be done," the monk said.

"Exactly," answered the alchemist.

When the pan had cooled, the monk and the boy looked at it, dazzled. The lead had dried into the shape of the pan, but it was no longer lead. It was gold.

"Will I learn to do that someday?" the boy asked.

"This was my destiny, not yours," the alchemist answered. "But I wanted to show you that it was possible."

They returned to the gates of the monastery. There, the alchemist separated the disk into four parts.

"This is for you," he said, holding one of the parts out to the monk. "It's for your generosity to the pilgrims."

"But this payment goes well beyond my generosity," the monk responded.

"Don't say that again. Life might be listening, and give you less the next time."

The alchemist turned to the boy. "This is for you. To make up for what you gave to the general."

The boy was about to say that it was much more than he had given the general. But he kept quiet, because he had heard what the alchemist said to the monk.

"And this is for me," said the alchemist, keeping one of the parts. "Because I have to return to the desert, where there are tribal wars."

He took the fourth part and handed it to the monk. "This is for the boy. If he ever needs it."

"But I'm going in search of my treasure," the boy said. "I'm very close to it now."

"And I'm certain you'll find it," the alchemist said.

"Then why this?"

"Because you have already lost your savings twice. Once to the thief, and once to the general. I'm an old, superstitious Arab, and I believe in our proverbs. There's one that says, 'Everything that happens once can never happen again. But everything that happens twice will surely happen a third time.'" They mounted their horses.

* * *

"I want to tell you a story about dreams," said the alchemist.

The boy brought his horse closer.

"In ancient Rome, at the time of Emperor Tiberius, there lived a good man who had two sons. One was in the military, and had been sent to the most distant regions of the empire. The other son was a poet, and delighted all of Rome with his beautiful verses.

"One night, the father had a dream. An angel appeared to him, and told him that the words of one of his sons would be learned and repeated throughout the world for all generations to come. The father woke from his dream grateful and crying, because life was generous, and had revealed to him something any father would be proud to know.

"Shortly thereafter, the father died as he tried to save a child who was about to be crushed by the wheels of a chariot. Since he had lived his entire life in a manner that was correct and fair, he went directly to heaven, where he met the angel that had appeared in his dream.

"'You were always a good man,' the angel said to him. 'You lived your life in a loving way, and died with dignity. I can now grant you any wish you desire.'

"'Life was good to me,' the man said. 'When you appeared in my dream, I felt that all my efforts had been rewarded, because my son's poems will be read by men for generations to come. I don't want anything for myself. But any father would be proud of the fame achieved by one whom he had cared for as a child, and educated as he grew up. Sometime in the distant future, I would like to see my son's words.'

"The angel touched the man's shoulder, and they

were both projected far into the future. They were in an immense setting, surrounded by thousands of people speaking a strange language.

"The man wept with happiness.

"'I knew that my son's poems were immortal,' he said to the angel through his tears. 'Can you please tell me which of my son's poems these people are repeating?'

"The angel came closer to the man, and, with tenderness, led him to a bench nearby, where they sat down.

"'The verses of your son who was the poet were very popular in Rome,' the angel said. 'Everyone loved them and enjoyed them. But when the reign of Tiberius ended, his poems were forgotten. The words you're hearing now are those of your son in the military.'

"The man looked at the angel in surprise.

"'Your son went to serve at a distant place, and became a centurion. He was just and good. One afternoon, one of his servants fell ill, and it appeared that he would die. Your son had heard of a rabbi who was able to cure illnesses, and he rode out for days and days in search of this man. Along the way, he learned that the man he was seeking was the Son of God. He met others who had been cured by him, and they instructed your son in the man's teachings. And so, despite the fact that he was a Roman centurion, he converted to their faith. Shortly thereafter, he reached the place where the man he was looking for was visiting.'

"'He told the man that one of his servants was

gravely ill, and the rabbi made ready to go to his house with him. But the centurion was a man of faith, and, looking into the eyes of the rabbi, he knew that he was surely in the presence of the Son of God.'

"'And this is what your son said,' the angel told the man. 'These are the words he said to the rabbi at that point, and they have never been forgotten: "My Lord, I am not worthy that you should come under my roof. But only speak a word and my servant will be healed."'"

The alchemist said, "No matter what he does, every person on earth plays a central role in the history of the world. And normally he doesn't know it."

The boy smiled. He had never imagined that questions about life would be of such importance to a shepherd.

"Good-bye," the alchemist said.

"Good-bye," said the boy.

* * *

The boy rode along through the desert for several hours, listening avidly to what his heart had to say. It was his heart that would tell him where his treasure was hidden.

"Where your treasure is, there also will be your heart," the alchemist had told him.

But his heart was speaking of other things. With pride, it told the story of a shepherd who had left his flock to follow a dream he had on two different occasions. It told of destiny, and of the many men who had wandered in search of distant lands or beautiful women, confronting the people of their times with their preconceived notions. It spoke of journeys, discoveries, books, and change.

As he was about to climb yet another dune, his heart whispered, "Be aware of the place where you are brought to tears. That's where I am, and that's where your treasure is."

The boy climbed the dune slowly. A full moon rose again in the starry sky: it had been a month since he had set forth from the oasis. The moonlight cast shadows through the dunes, creating the appearance of a rolling sea; it reminded the boy of the day when that horse had reared in the desert, and he had come to know the alchemist. And the moon fell on the desert's silence, and on a man's journey in search of treasure.

When he reached the top of the dune, his heart leapt. There, illuminated by the light of the moon and the brightness of the desert, stood the solemn and majestic Pyramids of Egypt.

The boy fell to his knees and wept. He thanked God for making him believe in his destiny, and for leading him to meet a king, a merchant, an Englishman, and an alchemist. And above all for his having met a woman of the desert who had told him that love would never keep a man from his destiny.

If he wanted to, he could now return to the oasis, go back to Fatima, and live his life as a simple shepherd. After all, the alchemist continued to live in the desert, even though he understood the Language of the World, and knew how to transform lead into gold. He didn't need to demonstrate his science and art to anyone. The boy told himself that, on the way toward realizing his own destiny, he had learned all he needed to know, and had experienced everything he might have dreamed of.

But here he was, at the point of finding his treasure, and he reminded himself that no project is completed until its objective has been achieved. The boy looked at the sands around him, and saw that, where his tears had fallen, a scarab beetle was scuttling through the sand. During his time in the desert, he had learned that, in Egypt, the scarab beetles are a symbol of God.

Another omen! The boy began to dig into the dune. As he did so, he thought of what the crystal merchant had once said: that anyone could build a pyramid in his backyard. The boy could see now that he couldn't do so if he placed stone upon stone for the rest of his life.

Throughout the night, the boy dug at the place he had chosen, but found nothing. He felt weighted down by the centuries of time since the Pyramids had been built. But he didn't stop. He struggled to continue digging as he fought the wind, which often blew the sand back into the excavation. His hands were abraded and exhausted, but he listened to his heart. It had told him to dig where his tears fell.

As he was attempting to pull out the rocks he encountered, he heard footsteps. Several figures approached him. Their backs were to the moonlight, and the boy could see neither their eyes nor their faces.

"What are you doing here?" one of the figures demanded.

Because he was terrified, the boy didn't answer. He had found where his treasure was, and was frightened at what might happen.

"We're refugees from the tribal wars, and we need money," the other figure said. "What are you hiding there?"

"I'm not hiding anything," the boy answered.

But one of them seized the boy and yanked him back out of the hole. Another, who was searching the boy's bags, found the piece of gold.

"There's gold here," he said.

The moon shone on the face of the Arab who had seized him, and in the man's eyes the boy saw death.

"He's probably got more gold hidden in the ground."

They made the boy continue digging, but he found nothing. As the sun rose, the men began to beat the boy. He was bruised and bleeding, his clothing was torn to shreds, and he felt that death was near.

"What good is money to you if you're going to die? It's not often that money can save someone's life," the alchemist had said. Finally, the boy screamed at the men, "I'm digging for treasure!" And, although his mouth was bleeding and swollen, he told his attackers that he had twice dreamed of a treasure hidden near the Pyramids of Egypt.

The man who appeared to be the leader of the group

spoke to one of the others: "Leave him. He doesn't have anything else. He must have stolen this gold."

The boy fell to the sand, nearly unconscious. The leader shook him and said, "We're leaving."

But before they left, he came back to the boy and said, "You're not going to die. You'll live, and you'll learn that a man shouldn't be so stupid. Two years ago, right here on this spot, I had a recurrent dream, too. I dreamed that I should travel to the fields of Spain and look for a ruined church where shepherds and their sheep slept. In my dream, there was a sycamore growing out of the ruins of the sacristy, and I was told that, if I dug at the roots of the sycamore, I would find a hidden treasure. But I'm not so stupid as to cross an entire desert just because of a recurrent dream."

And they disappeared.

The boy stood up shakily, and looked once more at the Pyramids. They seemed to laugh at him, and he laughed back, his heart bursting with joy.

Because now he knew where his treasure was.

Epilogue

The boy reached the small, abandoned church just as night was falling. The sycamore was still there in the sacristy, and the stars could still be seen through the half-destroyed roof. He remembered the time he had been there with his sheep; it had been a peaceful night … except for the dream.

Now he was here not with his flock, but with a shovel.

He sat looking at the sky for a long time. Then he took from his knapsack a bottle of wine, and drank some. He remembered the night in the desert when he had sat with the alchemist, as they looked at the stars and drank wine together. He thought of the many roads he had traveled, and of the strange way God had chosen to show him his treasure. If he hadn't believed in the significance of recurrent dreams, he would not have met the Gypsy woman, the king, the thief, or … "Well, it's a long list. But the path was written in the omens, and there was no way I could go wrong," he said to himself.

He fell asleep, and when he awoke the sun was already high. He began to dig at the base of the sycamore.

"You old sorcerer," the boy shouted up to the sky. "You knew the whole story. You even left a bit of gold at the monastery so I could get back to this church. The monk laughed when he saw me come back in tatters. Couldn't you have saved me from that?"

"No," he heard a voice on the wind say. "If I had told you, you wouldn't have seen the Pyramids. They're beautiful, aren't they?"

The boy smiled, and continued digging. Half an hour later, his shovel hit something solid. An hour later, he had before him a chest of Spanish gold coins. There were also precious stones, gold masks adorned with red and white feathers, and stone statues embedded with jewels. The spoils of a conquest that the country had long ago forgotten, and that some conquistador had failed to tell his children about.

The boy took out Urim and Thummim from his bag. He had used the two stones only once, one morning when he was at a marketplace. His life and his path had always provided him with enough omens.

He placed Urim and Thummim in the chest. They were also a part of his new treasure, because they were a reminder of the old king, whom he would never see again.

It's true; life really is generous to those who pursue their destiny, the boy thought. Then he remembered that he had to get to Tarifa so he could give one-tenth of his treasure to the Gypsy woman, as he had promised. "Those Gypsies are really smart," he thought. Maybe it was because they moved around so much.

The wind began to blow again. It was the levanter, the wind that came from Africa. It didn't bring with it the smell of the desert, nor the threat of Moorish invasion. Instead, it brought the scent of a perfume he knew well, and the touch of a kiss—a kiss that came from far away, slowly, slowly, until it rested on his lips.

The boy smiled. It was the first time she had done that.

"I'm coming, Fatima," he said.

Life is a

journey

Make sure you don't miss a thing.
Live it with Paulo Coelho.

Visit f /paulocoelho

How can you find your heart's desire?

A world-wide phenomenon; an inspiration for anyone seeking their path in life.

The Alchemist

Do you believe in yourself?

A modern-day adventure in the searing heat of the Mojave desert and an exploration of fear and self-doubt.

The Valkyries

How do we see the amazing in the everyday?

When two young lovers are reunited, they discover anew the truth of what lies in their hearts.

By the River Piedra I Sat Down & Wept

What are you searching for?

A transforming journey on the pilgrims' road to Santiago – and the first of Paulo's extraordinary books.

The Pilgrimage

Can faith triumph over suffering?

Paulo Coelho's brilliant telling of the story of Elijah, who was forced to choose between love and duty.

The Fifth Mountain

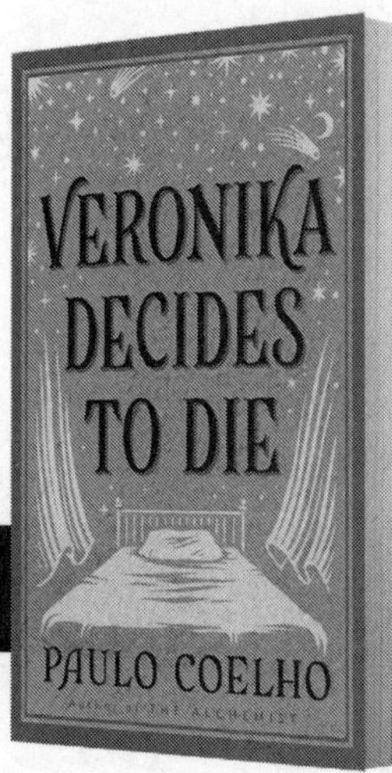

Is life always worth living?

A fundamental moral question explored as only Paulo Coelho can.

Veronika Decides to Die

Could you be tempted into evil?

The inhabitants of a small town are challenged by a mysterious stranger to choose between good and evil.

The Devil & Miss Prym

Are you brave enough to live your dream?

Strategies and inspiration to help you follow your own path in a troubled world.

Manual of the Warrior of Light

Can sex be sacred?

An unflinching exploration of the lengths we go to in our search for love, sex and spirituality.

Eleven Minutes

How far would you go for your obsession?

A sweeping story of love, loss and longing that spans the world.

The Zahir

What happens when obsession turns to murder?

An enthralling story of jealousy, death and suspense.

The Winner Stands Alone

Can we dare to be true to ourselves?

A story that will transform the way we think about love, joy and sacrifice.

The Witch of Portobello

How will you know who your soulmate is?

A moving tale of passion, mystery and spirituality.

Brida

What does it mean to be truly alive?

Powerful tales of living and dying, destiny and choice, and love lost and found.

Like the Flowing River

Are you where you want to be?

Read *Aleph*. And rewrite your life.

Aleph

Is there a weapon more powerful than words?

A timeless and powerful exploration of personal growth, everyday wisdom and joy.

Manuscript Found in Accra

The ZAHIR

Paulo Coelho was born in Brazil and has become one of the most widely read and loved authors in the world. Especially renowned for *The Alchemist* and *Eleven Minutes*, he has sold more than 320 million books worldwide and has been translated into 88 languages. The recipient of numerous prestigious international awards, amongst them the Crystal Award by the World Economic Forum and France's Légion d'Honneur, Paulo Coelho was inducted into the Brazilian Academy of Letters in 2002.

Also by Paulo Coelho

The Alchemist
The Pilgrimage
The Valkyries
By the River Piedra I Sat Down and Wept
The Fifth Mountain
Veronika Decides to Die
Manual of the Warrior of Light
Eleven Minutes
The Zahir
The Devil and Miss Prym
The Witch of Portobello
Brida
The Winner Stands Alone
Like the Flowing River
Aleph
Manuscript Found in Accra
Adultery
The Spy
Hippie

VERONIKA DECIDES TO DIE

Paulo Coelho was born in Brazil and has become one of the most widely read and loved authors in the world. Especially renowned for *The Alchemist* and *Eleven Minutes*, he has sold more than 320 million books worldwide and has been translated into 88 languages. The recipient of numerous prestigious international awards, amongst them the Crystal Award by the World Economic Forum and France's Légion d'Honneur, Paulo Coelho was inducted into the Brazilian Academy of Letters in 2002.

Also by Paulo Coelho

The Alchemist
The Pilgrimage
The Valkyries
By the River Piedra I Sat Down and Wept
The Fifth Mountain
Veronika Decides to Die
Manual of the Warrior of Light
Eleven Minutes
The Zahir
The Devil and Miss Prym
The Witch of Portobello
Brida
The Winner Stands Alone
Like the Flowing River
Aleph
Manuscript Found in Accra
Adultery
The Spy
Hippie

VERONIKA DECIDES TO DIE

PAULO COELHO

Author of THE ALCHEMIST

TRANSLATED FROM THE PORTUGUESE
BY MARGARET JULL COSTA

Thorsons

Thorsons
An imprint of HarperCollins*Publishers*
1 London Bridge Street
London SE1 9GF

HarperCollins*Publishers*
1st Floor, Watermarque Building, Ringsend Road
Dublin 4, Ireland

www.harpercollins.co.uk
www.paulocoelho.com
www.paulocoelhoblog.com

First published in English by
HarperCollins*Publishers* 1999
This edition published 2021

2 4 6 8 10 9 7 5 3 1

© Paulo Coelho 1998

English translation © Margaret Jull Costa 1999

Paulo Coelho asserts the moral right to
be identified as the author of this work

A catalogue record of this book is
available from the British Library

ISBN: 978-0-00-854729-5

FICTION / PHILOSOPHY

Printed and bound in India by Thomson Press India Ltd

All rights reserved. No part of this publication may be
reproduced, stored in a retrieval system, or transmitted,
in any form or by any means, electronic, mechanical,
photocopying, recording or otherwise, without the prior
written permission of the publishers.

This book is produced from independently certified FSC® paper
to ensure responsible forest management.

O Mary!
conceived without sin,
pray for us who turn to you!
Amen.

Behold I give unto you power to tread
on serpents . . . and nothing shall by
any means hurt you.

Luke 10:19

For S.T. de L,
who began to help me without
my realising it.

On 11 November 1997, Veronika decided that the moment to kill herself had – at last! – arrived. She carefully cleaned the room that she rented in a convent, turned off the heating, brushed her teeth and lay down.

She picked up the four packs of sleeping pills from her bedside table. Instead of crushing them and mixing them with water, she decided to take them one by one, because there is always a gap between intention and action, and she wanted to feel free to turn back half way. However, with each pill she swallowed, she felt more convinced: after five minutes the packs were empty.

Since she didn't know exactly how long it would take her to lose consciousness, she had placed on the bed that month's issue of a French magazine, *Homme*, which had just arrived in the library where she worked. She had no particular interest in computer science, but, as she leafed through the magazine, she came across an article about a computer game (one of those CD-Roms), created by Paulo Coelho, a Brazilian writer she had happened to meet at a lecture in the café at the Grand Union Hotel. They had exchanged a few words and she had ended up being invited by his publisher to join them for supper. There were a lot of people there, though, and they hadn't had a chance to talk in depth about anything.

The fact that she had met the author, however, led her to think that he was part of her world, and that reading an article about his work could help pass the time. While she was waiting for death, Veronika started reading about computer science, a subject in which she was not in the least bit interested, but then that was in keeping with what she had done all her life, always looking for the easy option, for whatever was nearest to hand. Like that magazine, for example.

To her surprise, though, the first line of text shook her out of her natural passivity (the tranquillizers had not yet dissolved in her stomach, but Veronika was, by nature, passive), and, for the first time in her life, it made her ponder the truth of a saying that was very fashionable amongst her friends: 'nothing in this world happens by chance'.

Why that first line, at precisely the moment when she had begun to die? What was the hidden message she saw before her, assuming there are such things as hidden messages rather than mere coincidences.

Underneath an illustration of the computer game, the journalist began his article by asking: 'Where is Slovenia?'

'Honestly,' she thought, 'no one ever knows where Slovenia is.'

But Slovenia existed nonetheless, and it was outside, inside, in the mountains around her and in the square she was looking out at: Slovenia was her country.

She put the magazine to one side, there was no point now in getting indignant with a world that knew absolutely nothing about the Slovenes; her nation's honour no longer concerned her. It was time to feel proud of herself, to recognise that she had been able to do this, that she had finally had the courage and was leaving this life: what joy! Also she was doing it as she had always dreamed she would – by taking sleeping pills, which leave no mark.

Veronika had been trying to get hold of the pills for nearly six months. Thinking that she would never manage it, she had even considered slashing her wrists. It didn't matter that the room would end up awash with blood, and the nuns would be left feeling confused and troubled, for suicide demands that people think of themselves first and of others later. She was prepared to do all she could so that her death would cause as little upset as possible, but if slashing her wrists was the only way, then she had no option – and the nuns could clean up the room and quickly forget the whole story, otherwise they would find it hard to rent out the room again. We may live at the end of the twentieth century, but people still believe in ghosts.

Obviously she could have thrown herself off one of the few tall buildings in Ljubljana, but what about the further suffering caused to her parents by a fall from such a height? Apart from the shock of learning that their daughter had died, they would also have to identify a disfigured corpse; no, that was a worse solution than bleeding to death, because it would leave indelible marks on two people who only wanted the best for her.

'They would get used to their daughter's death eventually. But it must be impossible to forget a shattered skull.'

Shooting, jumping off a high building, hanging, none of these options suited her feminine nature. Women, when they kill themselves, choose far more romantic methods – like slashing their wrists or taking an overdose of sleeping pills. Abandoned princesses and Hollywood actresses have provided numerous examples of this.

Veronika knew that life was always a matter of waiting for the right moment to act. And so it proved. In response to her complaints that she could no longer sleep at night, two friends of hers managed to get hold of two packs each of a powerful drug, used by musicians at a local nightclub. Veronika left the four packs on her bedside table for a week, courting approaching death and saying goodbye – entirely unsentimentally – to what people called Life.

Now she was there, glad she had gone all the way, and bored because she didn't know what to do with the little time that remained to her.

She thought again about the absurd question she had just read. How could an article about computers begin with such an idiotic opening line: 'Where is Slovenia?'

Having nothing more interesting to do, she decided to read the whole article and she learned that the said computer game had been made in Slovenia – that strange country that no one seemed quite able to place, except the people who lived there – because it was a cheap source of labour. A few months before, when the product was launched, the French manufacturer had given a party for journalists from all over the world in a castle in Vled.

Veronika remembered reading something about the party, which had been quite an event in the city, not just because the castle had been redecorated in order to match as closely as possible the medieval atmosphere of the CD-Rom, but because of the controversy in the local press: journalists from Germany, France, Britain, Italy and Spain had been invited, but not a single Slovene.

Homme's correspondent – who was visiting Slovenia for the first time, doubtless with all expenses paid, and determined to spend his visit chatting up other journalists, making supposedly interesting comments and enjoying the free food and drink at the castle – had decided to begin his article with a joke which must have appealed to the sophisticated intellectuals of his country. He had probably told his fellow journalists on the magazine various untrue stories about local customs too, and said how badly Slovene women dress.

That was *his* problem. Veronika was dying, and she had other concerns, such as wondering if there was life after death, or when her body would be found. Nevertheless – or perhaps precisely because of the important decision she had taken – the article bothered her.

She looked out of the convent window that gave on to the small square in Ljubljana. 'If they don't know where Slovenia is, then Ljubljana must be a myth,' she thought. Like Atlantis or Lemuria, or the other lost continents that fill men's imaginations. No one, anywhere in the world, would begin an article asking where Mount Everest was, even if they had never been there. Yet, in the middle of Europe, a journalist on an important magazine felt no shame at asking such a question, because he knew that most of his readers would not know where Slovenia was, still less its capital, Ljubljana.

It was then that Veronika found a way of passing the time, now that ten minutes had gone by and she had still not noticed any bodily changes. The final act of her life would be to write a letter to the magazine, explaining that Slovenia was one of the five republics into which the former Yugoslavia had been divided.

The letter would be her suicide note. She would give no explanation of the real reasons for her death.

When they found her body, they would conclude that she had killed herself because a magazine did not know where her country was. She laughed to think of the controversy in the newspapers, with some for and some against her suicide committed in honour of her country's cause. And she was shocked by how quickly she could change her mind, since only moments before she had thought exactly the opposite, that the world and other geographical problems were no longer her concern.

She wrote the letter. That moment of good humour almost made her have second thoughts about the need to die, but she had already taken the pills, it was too late to turn back.

Anyway, she had had such moments before and, besides, she was not killing herself because she was a sad, embittered woman, constantly depressed. She had spent many afternoons walking gaily along the streets of Ljubljana or gazing – from the window in her convent room – at the snow falling on the small square with its statue of the poet. Once, for almost a month, she had felt as if she were walking on air, all because a complete stranger, in the middle of that very square, had given her a flower.

She believed herself to be completely normal. Two very simple reasons lay behind her decision to die, and she was sure that, were she to leave a note explaining, many people would agree with her.

The first reason: everything in her life was the same and, once her youth was gone, it would be downhill all the way, with old age beginning to leave irreversible marks, the onset of illness, the departure of friends. She would gain nothing by continuing to live; indeed, the likelihood of suffering only increased.

The second reason was more philosophical: Veronika read the newspapers, watched TV, and she was aware of what was going on in the world. Everything was wrong, and she had no way of putting things right – that gave her a sense of complete powerlessness.

In a short while, though, she would have the final experience of her life, which promised to be very different: death. She wrote the letter to the magazine, then abandoned the topic, and concentrated on more pressing matters, more appropriate to what she was living, or, rather, dying, through at that moment.

She tried to imagine what it would be like to die, but failed to reach any conclusion.

Besides, there was no point worrying about that, for in a few minutes' time she would know.

How many minutes?

She had no idea. But she relished the thought that she was about to find out the answer to the question that everyone asked themselves: does God exist?

Unlike many people, this had not been the great inner debate of her life. Under the old Communist regime, the official line in schools had been that life ended with death and she had got used to the idea. On the other hand, her parents' generation and her grandparents' generation still went to church, said prayers and went on pilgrimages, and were utterly convinced that God listened to what they said.

At twenty-four, having experienced everything she could experience – and that was no small achievement – Veronika was almost certain that everything ended with death. That is why she had chosen suicide: freedom at last. Eternal oblivion.

In her heart of hearts, though, there was still a doubt: what if God did exist? Thousands of years of civilization had made of suicide a taboo, an affront to all religious codes: man struggles to survive, not to succumb. The human race must procreate. Society needs workers. A couple has to have a reason to stay together, even when love has ceased to exist, and a country needs soldiers, politicians and artists.

'If God exists, and I truly don't believe he does, he will know that there are limits to human understanding. He was the one who created this confusion in which there is poverty, injustice, greed and loneliness. He doubtless had the best of intentions, but the results have proved disastrous; if God exists, He will be generous with those creatures who chose to leave this Earth early, and he might even apologise for having made us spend time here.'

To hell with taboos and superstitions. Her devout mother would say: God knows the past, the present and the future. In that case, He had placed her in this world in the full knowledge that she would end up killing herself, and He would not be shocked by her actions.

Veronika began to feel a slight nausea, which became rapidly more intense.

In a few moments, she would no longer be able to concentrate on the square outside her window. She knew it was winter, it must have been about four o'clock in the afternoon, and the sun was setting fast. She knew that other people would go on living. At that moment, a young man passed her window and saw her, utterly unaware that she was about to die. A group of Bolivian musicians (where is Bolivia? why don't magazine articles ask that?) were playing in front of the statue of France Prešeren, the great Slovenian poet, who had made such a profound impact on the soul of his people.

Would she live to hear the end of that music drifting up from the square? It would be a beautiful memory of this life: the late afternoon, a melody recounting the dreams of a country on the other side of the world, the warm cosy room, the handsome young man passing by, full of life, who had decided to stop and was now standing looking up at her. She realised that the pills were beginning to take effect and that he was the last person who would see her.

He smiled. She returned his smile – she had nothing to lose. He waved; she decided to pretend she was looking at something else, the young man was going too far. Disconcerted, he continued on his way, forgetting that face at the window for ever.

But Veronika was glad to have felt desired by somebody one last time. She wasn't killing herself because of a lack of love. It wasn't because she felt unloved by her family, or had money problems or an incurable disease.

Veronika had decided to die on that lovely Ljubjlana afternoon, with Bolivian musicians playing in the square, with a young man passing by her window, and she was happy with what her eyes could see and her ears hear. She was even happier that she would not have to go on seeing those same things for another thirty, forty or fifty years, because they would lose all their originality and be transformed into the tragedy of a life in which everything repeats itself and where one day is exactly like another.

Her stomach was beginning to churn now and she was feeling very ill indeed. 'It's odd, I thought an overdose of tranquillizers would send me straight to sleep.' What she was experiencing, though, was a strange buzzing in her ears and a desire to vomit.

'If I throw up, I won't die.'

She decided not to think about the stabbing pains in her stomach and tried to concentrate on the rapidly falling night, on the Bolivians, on the people who were starting to shut up their shops and go home. The noise in her ears was becoming more and more strident and, for the first time since she had taken the pills, Veronika felt fear, a terrible fear of the unknown.

It did not last long. Soon afterwards, she lost consciousness.

When she opened her eyes, Veronika did not think 'this must be heaven'. Heaven would never use a fluorescent tube to light a room, and the pain – which started a fraction of a second later – was typical of the Earth. Ah, that Earth pain – unique, unmistakable.

She tried to move and the pain increased. A series of bright dots appeared, but, even so, Veronika knew that those dots were not the stars of Paradise, but the consequences of the intense pain she was feeling.

'She's coming round,' she heard a woman say. 'You've landed slap bang in hell, so you'd better make the most of it.'

No, it couldn't be true, that voice was deceiving her. It wasn't hell, because she felt really cold and she was aware of plastic tubes coming out of her nose and mouth. One of the tubes – the one stuck down her throat – made her feel as if she were choking.

She made as if to remove it, but her arms were strapped down.

'I'm joking, it's not really hell,' the voice went on. 'It's worse than hell, not that I've ever actually been there. You're in Villete.'

Despite the pain and the feeling of choking, Veronika realised at once what had happened. She had tried to kill herself and someone had arrived in time to save her. It could have been one of the nuns, a friend who had decided to drop by unannounced, someone delivering something she had forgotten she had ordered. The fact is, she had survived, and she was in Villete.

Villete, the famous and much-feared lunatic asylum, which had been in existence since 1991, the year of the country's independence. At that time, believing that the partitioning of the former Yugoslavia would be achieved through peaceful means (after all, Slovenia had only experienced eleven days of war), a group of European businessmen had obtained permission to set up a hospital for mental patients in an old barracks, abandoned because of high maintenance costs.

Shortly afterwards, however, the wars commenced: first in Croatia, then in Bosnia. The businessmen were worried. The money for the investment came from capitalists scattered all round the globe, from people whose names they didn't even know, so there was no possibility of sitting down in front of them, offering a few excuses and asking them to be patient.They resolved the problem by adopting practices which were far from commendable in a psychiatric hospital, and for the young nation that had just emerged from a benign communism, Villete came to symbolise all the worst aspects of capitalism: to be admitted to the hospital, all you needed was money.

There was no shortage of people who, in their desire to get rid of some family member because of arguments over an inheritance (or over that person's embarrassing behaviour), were willing to pay large sums of money to obtain a medical report that would allow the internment of their problematic children or parents. Others, fleeing from debts or trying to justify certain attitudes that could otherwise result in long prison sentences, spent a brief time in the asylum and then simply left without paying any penalty or undergoing any judicial process.

Villete was the place from which no one had ever escaped, where genuine madmen – sent there by the courts or by other hospitals – mingled with those merely accused of madness or those pretending to be mad. The result was utter confusion, and the press were constantly publishing tales of ill-treatment and abuse, although they had never been given permission to visit Villete and actually see what was happening. The government was investigating the complaints, but could get no proof; the shareholders threatened to spread the word that foreign investment was difficult in Slovenia, and so the institution managed to remain afloat, indeed, it went from strength to strength.

'My aunt killed herself a few months ago,' the female voice continued. 'For almost eight years she was too afraid to even leave her room, eating, getting fat, smoking, taking tranquillisers and sleeping most of the time. She had two daughters and a husband who loved her.'

Veronika tried to move her head in the direction of the voice, but failed.

'I only saw her fight back once, when her husband took a lover. Then she kicked up a fuss, lost a few pounds, smashed some glasses and – for weeks on end – kept the rest of the whole neighbourhood awake with her shouting. Absurd though it may seem, I think that was the happiest time of her life. She was fighting for something, she felt alive and capable of responding to the challenges facing her.'

'What's all that got to do with me?' thought Veronika, unable to say anything. 'I'm not your aunt and I haven't got a husband.'

'In the end, her husband got rid of his lover,' said the woman, 'and gradually, my aunt returned to her former passivity. One day, she phoned to say that she wanted to change her life: she'd given up smoking. That same week, after increasing the number of tranquillisers she was taking because she'd stopped smoking, she told everyone that she wanted to kill herself.

'No one believed her. Then, one morning, she left a message on my answerphone, saying goodbye, and she gassed herself. I listened to that message several times: I had never heard her sound so calm, so resigned to her fate. She said she was neither happy nor unhappy, and that was why she couldn't go on.'

Veronika felt sorry for the woman telling the story, for she seemed to be doing so in an attempt to understand her aunt's death. In a world where everyone struggles to survive whatever the cost, how could one judge those people who decide to die?

No one can judge. Each person knows the extent of their own suffering, or the total absence of meaning in their lives. Veronika wanted to explain that, but instead she choked on the tube in her mouth and the woman hurried to her aid.

She saw the woman bending over her bound body, which was full of tubes and protected against her will, her freely expressed desire to destroy it. She moved her head from side to side, pleading with her eyes for them to remove the tubes and let her die in peace.

'You're upset,' said the woman. 'I don't know if you're sorry for what you did or if you still want to die; that doesn't interest me. What interests me is doing my job. If the patient gets agitated, the regulations say I must give them a sedative.'

Veronika stopped struggling, but the nurse was already injecting something into her arm. Soon afterwards, she was back in a strange dreamless world, where the only thing she could remember was the face of the woman she had just seen:

green eyes, brown hair, and a very distant air, the air of someone doing things because she has to do them, never questioning why the rules say this or that.

Paulo Coelho heard about Veronika's story three months later when he was having supper in an Algerian restaurant in Paris with a Slovenian friend, also called Veronika, who happened to be the daughter of the doctor in charge at Villete.

Later, when he decided to write a book about the subject, he considered changing his friend's name in order not to confuse the reader. He thought of calling her Blaska or Edwina or Marietzja, or some other Slovenian name, but he ended up keeping the real names. When he referred to his friend Veronika, he would call her his friend, Veronika. When he referred to the other Veronika, there would be no need to describe her at all, because she would be the central character in the book, and people would get irritated if they were always having to read 'Veronika the mad woman,' or 'Veronika the one who tried to commit suicide'. Besides, both he and his friend Veronika would only take up a very brief part of the book, this part.

His friend Veronika was horrified at what her father had done, especially bearing in mind that he was the director of an institution seeking respectability and was himself working on a thesis that would be judged by the conventional academic community.

'Do you know where the word "asylum" comes from?' she was saying. 'It dates back to the Middle Ages, from a person's right to seek refuge in churches and other holy places. The right of asylum is something any civilised person can understand. So how could my father, the director of an asylum, treat someone like that?'

Paulo Coelho wanted to know all the details of what had happened, because he had a genuine reason for finding out about Veronika's story.

The reason was the following: he himself had been admitted into an asylum or, rather, mental hospital as they were better known. And this had happened not once, but three times, in 1965, 1966 and 1967. The place where he had been interned was the Dr Eiras Sanatorium in Rio de Janeiro.

Precisely why he had been admitted into hospital was something which, even today, he found odd; perhaps his parents were confused by his unusual behaviour, half-shy, half-extrovert, and by his desire to be an 'artist', something that everyone in the family considered a perfect recipe for ending up as a social outcast and dying in poverty.

When he thought about it – and, it must be said, he rarely did – he considered the real madman to have been the doctor who had agreed to admit him for the flimsiest of reasons (as in any family, the tendency is always to place the blame on others, and to state adamantly that the parents didn't know what they were doing when they took that drastic decision).

Paulo laughed when he learned of the strange letter to the newspapers that Veronika had left behind, complaining that an important French magazine didn't even know where Slovenia was.

'No one would kill themselves over something like that.'

'That's why the letter had no effect,' said his friend Veronika, embarrassed. 'Yesterday, when I checked in at the hotel, the receptionist thought Slovenia was a town in Germany.'

He knew the feeling, for many foreigners believed the Argentine city of Buenos Aires to be the capital of Brazil.

But apart from having foreigners blithely compliment him on the beauty of his country's capital city (which was to be found in the neighbouring country of Argentina), Paulo Coelho shared with Veronika the fact just mentioned, but which is worth restating: he too had been admitted into a mental hospital, and, as his first wife had once remarked, 'should never have been let out'.

But he was let out. And when he left the sanatorium for the last time, determined never to go back, he had made two promises: (a) that he would one day write about the subject and (b) that he would wait until both his parents were dead before touching publicly on the issue, because he didn't want to hurt them, since both had spent many years of their lives blaming themselves for what they had done.

His mother had died in 1993, but his father, who had turned eighty-four in 1997, was still alive and in full possession of his mental faculties and his health, despite having emphysema of the lungs (even though he'd never smoked) and despite living entirely off frozen food because he couldn't get a housekeeper who could put up with his eccentricities.

So, when Paulo Coelho heard Veronika's story, he discovered a way of talking about the issue without breaking his promises. Even though he had never considered suicide, he had an intimate knowledge of the world of the mental hospital – the treatments, the relationships between doctors and patients, the comforts and anxieties of living in a place like that.

So let us allow Paulo Coelho and his friend Veronika to leave this book for good and let us get on with the story.

Veronika didn't know how long she had slept. She remembered waking up at one point – still with the life-giving tubes in her mouth and nose – and hearing a voice say:

'Do you want me to masturbate you?'

But now, looking round the room with her eyes wide open, she didn't know if that had been real or an hallucination. Apart from that one memory, she could remember nothing, absolutely nothing.

The tubes had been taken out, but she still had needles stuck all over her body, wires connected to the area around her heart and her head, and her arms were still strapped down. She was naked, covered only by a sheet, and she felt cold, but she was determined not to complain.The small area surrounded by green curtains was filled by the bed she was lying on, the machinery of the Intensive Care Unit and a white chair on which a nurse was sitting reading a book.

This time, the woman had dark eyes and brown hair. Even so, Veronika was not sure if it was the same person she had talked to hours – or was it days? – ago.

'Can you unstrap my arms?'

The nurse looked up, said a brusque 'No', and went back to her book.

I'm alive, thought Veronika. Everything's going to start all over again. I'll have to stay in here for a while, until they realise that I'm perfectly normal. Then they'll let me out, and I'll see the streets of Ljubljana again, its main square, the bridges, the people going to and from work.

Since people always tend to help others – just so that they can feel they are better than they really are – they'll give me my job back at the library. In time, I'll start frequenting the same bars and nightclubs, I'll talk to my friends about the injustices and problems of the world, I'll go to the cinema, take walks around the lake.

Since I only took sleeping pills, I'm not disfigured in any way: I'm still young, pretty, intelligent, I won't have any difficulty in getting boyfriends, I never did. I'll make love with them in their houses, or in the woods, I'll feel a certain degree of pleasure, but the moment I reach orgasm, the feeling of emptiness will return. We won't have much to talk about, and both he and I will know it. The time will come to make our excuses – 'It's late', or 'I have to get up early tomorrow' – and we'll part as quickly as possible, avoiding looking each other in the eye.

I'll go back to my rented room in the convent. I'll try and read a book, turn on the TV to see the same old programmes, set the alarm clock to wake up at exactly the same time I woke up the day before and mechanically repeat my tasks at the library. I'll eat a sandwich in the park opposite the theatre, sitting on the same bench, along with other people who also choose the same benches on which to sit and have their lunch, people who all have the same vacant look, but pretend to be pondering extremely important matters.

Then I'll go back to work, I'll listen to the gossip about who's going out with whom, who's suffering from what, how such and such a person was in tears about her husband, and I'll be left with the feeling that I'm privileged: I'm pretty, I have a job, I can have any boyfriend I choose. So I'll go back to the bars at the end of the day, and the whole thing will start again.

My mother, who must be out of her mind with worry over my suicide attempt, will recover from the shock and will keep asking me what I'm going to do with my life, why I'm not the same as everyone else, things really aren't as complicated as I think they are. 'Look at me, for example, I've been married to your father for years, and I've tried to give you the best possible upbringing and set you the best possible example.'

One day, I'll get tired of hearing her constantly repeating the same things, and to please her I'll marry a man whom I oblige myself to love. He and I will end up finding a way of dreaming of a future together: a house in the country, children, our children's future. We'll make love often in the first year, less in the second, and after the third year, people perhaps think about sex only once a fortnight and transform that thought into action only once a month. Even worse, we'll barely talk. I'll force myself to accept the situation, and I'll wonder what's wrong with me, because he no longer takes any interest in me, ignores me, and does nothing but talk about his friends, as if they were his real world.

When the marriage is just about to fall apart, I'll get pregnant. We'll have a child, feel closer to each other for a while, and then the situation will go back to what it was before.

I'll begin to put on weight like the aunt that nurse was talking about yesterday – or was it days ago, I don't really know. And I'll start to go on diets, systematically defeated each day, each week, by the weight that keeps creeping up regardless of the controls I put on it. At that point, I'll take those magic pills that stop you feeling depressed, then I'll have a few more children, conceived during nights of love that pass all too quickly.

I'll tell everyone that the children are my reason for living, when in reality my life is their reason for living.

People will always consider us a happy couple, and no one will know how much solitude, bitterness and resignation lies beneath the surface happiness.

Until one day, when my husband takes a lover for the first time, and I will perhaps kick up a fuss like the nurse's aunt, or think again of killing myself. By then, though, I'll be too old and cowardly, with two or three children who need my help, and I'll have to bring them up and help them find a place in the world before I can just abandon everything. I won't commit suicide: I'll make a scene, I'll threaten to leave and take the children with me. Like all men, my husband will back down, he'll tell me he loves me and that it won't happen again. It won't even occur to him that, if I really did decide to leave, my only option would be to go back to my parents' house and stay there for the rest of my life, forced to listen to my mother going on and on all day about how I lost my one opportunity for being happy, that he was a wonderful husband despite his peccadillos, that my children will be traumatised by the separation.

Two or three years later, another woman will appear in his life. I'll find out – because I saw them, or because someone told me – but this time I'll pretend I don't know. I used up all my energy fighting against that other lover, I've no energy left, it's best to accept life as it really is, and not as I imagined it to be. My mother was right.

He will continue being a considerate husband, I will continue working at the library, eating my sandwiches in the square opposite the theatre, reading books I never quite manage to finish, watching television programmes that are the same as they were ten, twenty, fifty years ago.

Except that I'll eat my sandwiches with a sense of guilt, because I'm getting fatter; and I won't go to bars any more, because I have a husband expecting me to come home and look after the children.

After that, it's a matter of waiting for the children to grow up and of spending all day thinking about suicide, without the courage to do anything about it. One fine day, I'll reach the conclusion that that's what life is like, there's no point worrying about it, nothing will change. And I'll accept it.

Veronika brought her interior monologue to a close and made a promise to herself: she would not leave Villete alive. It was best to put an end to everything now, while she was still brave and healthy enough to die.

She fell asleep and woke up several times, noticing that the number of machines around her was diminishing, the warmth of her body was growing, and the nurses' faces kept changing; but there was always someone beside her. Through the green curtain she heard the sound of someone crying, groans or voices whispering in calm, technical tones. From time to time, a distant machine would buzz and she would hear hurried footsteps along the corridor. Then the voices would lose their calm, technical tone and become tense, issuing rapid orders.

In one of her lucid moments, a nurse asked her:

'Don't you want to know how you are?'

'I already know,' replied Veronika. 'And it's nothing to do with what you can see happening in my body, it's what's happening in my soul.'

The nurse tried to continue the conversation, but Veronika pretended to be asleep.

When she opened her eyes again for the first time, she realised that she had been moved; she was in what looked like a large ward. She still had a drip in her arm, but all the other wires and needles had been removed.

A tall doctor, wearing the traditional white coat, in sharp contrast to the artificial black of his dyed hair and beard, was standing at the foot of her bed. Beside him, a young junior doctor holding a clipboard was taking notes.

'How long have I been here?' she asked, noticing that she spoke with some difficulty, slurring her words slightly.

'You've been in this ward for two weeks, after five days spent in the Intensive Care Unit,' replied the older man. 'And just be grateful that you're still here.'

The younger man seemed surprised, as if that final remark did not quite fit the facts.Veronika noticed his reaction at once, and her instincts were alerted: had she been here longer? Was she still in some danger? She began to pay attention to each gesture, each movement the two men made; she knew it was pointless asking questions, they would never tell her the truth, but if she was clever, she could find out what was going on.

'Tell me your name, address, marital status and date of birth,' the older man said. Veronika knew her name, her marital status and her date of birth, but she realised there were blanks in her memory: she couldn't quite remember her address.

The doctor shone a light in her eyes and examined them for a long time, in silence. The young man did the same thing. They exchanged glances, which meant absolutely nothing.

'Did you say to the night nurse that we couldn't see into your soul?' asked the younger man.

Veronika couldn't remember. She was having difficulty knowing who she was and what she was doing there.

'You have been kept in an artificially induced sleep with tranquillisers, and that might affect your memory a bit, but please try to answer all our questions.'

And the doctors began an absurd questionnaire, wanting to know the names of the principal Ljubljana newspapers, the name of the poet whose statue was in the main square (ah, that she would never forget, every Slovene has the image of Prešeren engraved on his or her soul), the colour of her mother's hair, the names of her colleagues at work, the titles of the most popular books at the library.

To begin with, Veronika considered not replying – her memory was still confused – but as the questionnaire continued, she began reconstructing what she'd forgotten. At one point, she remembered that she was now in a mental hospital, and that the mad were not obliged to be coherent; but, for her own good, and to keep the doctors by her side, in order to see if she could find out something more about her state, she began making a mental effort. As she recited the names and facts, she was recovering not only her memory, but also her personality, her desires, her way of seeing life. The idea of suicide, which, that morning, appeared buried beneath several layers of sedatives, resurfaced.

'Fine,' said the older man, at the end of the questionnaire.

'How much longer must I stay here?'

The younger man lowered his eyes, and she felt as if everything were hanging in the air, as if, once that question was answered, a new chapter of her life would be written, and no one would be able to change it.

'You can tell her,' said the older man. 'A lot of other patients have already heard the rumours, and she'll find out in the end anyway; it's impossible to keep secrets round here.'

'Well, you decided your own fate,' sighed the young man, weighing each word. 'So you had better know the consequence of your actions: during the coma brought on by the pills you took, your heart was irreversibly damaged. There was a necrosis of the ventricle...'

'Put it in layman's terms,' said the older man. 'Get straight to the point.'

'Your heart was irreversibly damaged and soon it will stop beating altogether.'

'What does that mean?' she asked, frightened.

'If your heart stops beating, that means only one thing, death. I don't know what your religious beliefs are, but...'

'When will my heart stop beating?' asked Veronika, interrupting him.

'Within five days, a week at most.'

Veronika realised that behind his professional appearance and behaviour, behind the concerned manner, the young man was taking immense pleasure in what he was saying, as if she deserved the punishment, and would serve as an example to all the others.

During her life, Veronika had noticed that a lot of people she knew would talk about the horrors in other people's lives as if they were genuinely concerned to help them, but the truth was that they took pleasure in the suffering of others, because that made them believe they were happy and that life had been generous with them. She hated that kind of person and she wasn't going to give the young man an opportunity to take advantage of her state, in order to mask his own frustrations.

She kept her eyes fixed on his and, smiling, said:

'So I succeeded then.'

'Yes,' came the reply. But any pleasure he had taken in giving her the tragic news had vanished.

During the night, however, she began to feel afraid. It was one thing to die quickly after taking some pills, it was quite another to wait five days or a week for death to come, when she had already been through so much.

She had always spent her life waiting for something: for her father to come back from work, for the letter from a lover that never arrived, for her end-of-year exams, for the train, the bus, the phone call, the holiday, the end of the holidays. Now she was going to have to wait for death, which had made an appointment with her.

'This could only happen to me. Normally, people die on precisely the day they least expect.'

She had to get out of there and get some more pills. If she couldn't, and the only solution was to jump from a high building in Ljubljana, that's what she'd do; she had tried to save her parents any unnecessary suffering, but now she had no option.

She looked about her. All the beds were occupied by sleeping people, some of whom were snoring loudly. There were bars on the windows. At the end of the ward, there was a small bright light that filled the place with strange shadows and meant that the ward could be kept under constant vigilance. Near the light, a woman was reading a book.

'These nurses must be very cultivated, they spend their whole lives reading.'

Veronika's bed was the farthest from the door; between her and the woman there were nearly twenty other beds. She got up with difficulty because, if she was to believe what the doctor had said, she hadn't walked for nearly three weeks. The nurse looked up and saw the girl approaching, dragging her drip-feed with her.

'I want to go to the toilet,' she whispered, afraid of waking the other mad women.

The woman gestured vaguely towards the door. Veronika's mind was working fast, looking everywhere for an escape route, a crack, a way out. 'It has to be quick, while they think I'm still too frail, incapable of acting.'

She peered about her. The toilet was a cubicle with no door. If she wanted to get out of there, she would have to grab the nurse and overcome her in order to get the key from her, but she was too weak for that.

'Is this a prison?' she asked the nurse, who had stopped reading and was now watching her every movement.

'No, it's a mental hospital.'

'But I'm not mad.'

The woman laughed.

'That's what they all say.'

'All right then, I am mad, but what does that mean?'

The woman told Veronika not to stay too long on her feet, and sent her back to her bed.

'What does it mean to be mad?' insisted Veronika.

'Ask the doctor tomorrow. But go to sleep now, otherwise I'll have to give you a sedative, whether you want it or not.'

Veronika obeyed. On her way back, she heard someone whispering from one of the beds:

'Don't you know what it means to be mad?'

For a moment, she considered ignoring the voice: she didn't want to make friends, to develop a social circle, to create allies for a great mass revolt. She had only one fixed idea: death. If she really couldn't escape, she would find some way to kill herself right there, as soon as possible.

But the woman asked her the same question she had asked the nurse.

'Don't you know what it means to be mad?'

'Who are you?'

'My name is Zedka. Go to your bed. Then, when the nurse thinks you're asleep, crawl back over here.'

Veronika returned to her bed, and waited for the nurse to resume her reading. What did it mean to be mad? She hadn't the slightest idea, because the word was used in a completely anarchic way: people would say, for example, that certain sportsmen were mad because they wanted to break records, or that artists were mad, because they led such strange, insecure lives, different from the lives of normal people. On the other hand, Veronika had often seen thinly clad people walking the streets of Ljubljana in winter, pushing supermarket trolleys full of plastic bags and rags, and proclaiming the end of the world.

She didn't feel sleepy. According to the doctor, she had slept for almost a week, too long for someone who was used to a life without great emotions, but with rigid timetables for rest. What did it mean to be mad? Perhaps she should ask one of the mad.

Veronika crouched down, pulled the needle out of her arm and went over to Zedka's bed, trying to ignore her churning stomach. She didn't know if the feeling of nausea was because of her weakened heart or the effort she was having to make.

'I don't know what it means to be mad,' whispered Veronika. 'But I'm not. I'm just a failed suicide.'

'Anyone who lives in their own world is mad. Like schizophrenics, psychopaths, maniacs. I mean people who are different from others.'

'Like you?'

'On the other hand,' Zedka continued, pretending not to have heard the remark, 'you have Einstein, saying that there was no time or space, just a combination of the two. Or Columbus, insisting that on the other side of the world lay not an abyss but a continent. Or Edmund Hillary, convinced that a man could reach the top of Everest. Or the Beatles, who created an entirely different sort of music and dressed like people from another time. Those people – and thousands of others – all lived in their own world.'

'This madwoman talks a lot of sense,' thought Veronika, remembering stories her mother used to tell her about saints who swore they had spoken to Jesus or the Virgin Mary. Did *they* live in a world apart?

'I once saw a woman wearing a low-cut dress; she had a glazed look in her eyes and she was walking the streets of Ljubljana when it was five degrees below zero. I thought she must be drunk and I went to help her, but she refused my offer to lend her my jacket. Perhaps in her world it was summer and her body was warmed by the desire of the person waiting for her. Even if that person only existed in her delirium, she had the right to live and die as she wanted, don't you think?'

Veronika didn't know what to say, but the madwoman's words made sense to her. Who knows, perhaps she was the woman who had been seen half-naked walking the streets of Ljubljana?

'I'm going to tell you a story,' said Zedka. 'A powerful wizard, who wanted to destroy an entire kingdom, placed a magic potion in the well from which all the inhabitants drank. Whoever drank that water would go mad.

'The following morning, the whole population drank from the well and they all went mad, apart from the king and his family, who had a well set aside for them alone, and which the magician had not managed to poison. The king was worried and tried to control the population by issuing a series of edicts governing security and public health. The policemen and the inspectors, however, had also drunk the poisoned water and they thought the king's decisions were absurd and resolved to take no notice of them.

'When the inhabitants of the kingdom heard these decrees, they became convinced that the king had gone mad and was now giving nonsensical orders. They marched on the castle and called for his abdication.

'In despair, the king prepared to step down from the throne, but the queen stopped him, saying: "Let us go and drink from the communal well. Then, we will be the same as them."

'And that was what they did: the king and the queen drank the water of madness and immediately began talking nonsense. Their subjects repented at once; now that the king was displaying such wisdom, why not allow him to continue ruling the country?

'The country continued to live in peace, although its inhabitants behaved very differently from those of its neighbours. And the king was able to govern until the end of his days.'

Veronika laughed.

'You don't seem mad at all,' she said.

'But I am, although I'm undergoing a cure, because my problem is that I lack a particular chemical. However, while I hope that the chemical gets rid of my chronic depression, I want to continue being mad, living my life the way I dream it, and not the way other people want it to be. Do you know what exists out there, beyond the walls of Villete?'

'People who have all drunk from the same well.'

'Exactly,' said Zedka. 'They think they're normal, because they all do the same thing. Well, I'm going to pretend that I have drunk from the same well as them.'

'I already did that, and that's precisely my problem. I've never been depressed, never felt great joy or sadness, at least none that lasted. I have the same problems as everyone else.'

For a while, Zedka said nothing, then:

'They told us you're going to die.'

Veronika hesitated for a moment. Could she trust this woman? She needed to take the risk.

'Yes, within about five or six days. I keep wondering if there's a way of dying sooner. If you, or someone else, could get me some more pills, I'm sure my heart wouldn't survive this time. You must understand how awful it is to have to wait for death, you must help me.'

Before Zedka could reply, the nurse appeared with an injection.

'I can give you the injection myself,' she said, 'or, depending on how you feel about it, I can ask the guards outside to help me.'

'Don't waste your energy,' said Zedka to Veronika. 'Save your strength, if you want to get what you asked me.'

Veronika got up, went back to her bed and allowed the nurse to do her work.

It was her first normal day in a mental hospital. She left the ward, had some breakfast in the large refectory where men and women were eating together. She noticed how different it was to the way these places were usually depicted in films – hysterical scenes, shouting, people making demented gestures – everything seemed wrapped in an aura of oppressive silence; it seemed that no one wanted to share their inner world with strangers.

After breakfast (which wasn't bad at all, no one could blame Villete's terrible reputation on the meals), they all went out to take the sun. In fact, there wasn't any sun – the temperature was below zero and the garden was covered in snow.

'I'm not here to preserve my life, but to lose it,' said Veronika to one of the nurses.

'You must still go out and take the sun.'

'You're the ones who are mad; there isn't any sun.'

'But there is light, and that helps to calm the patients. Unfortunately, our winter lasts a long time, if it didn't, we'd have a lot less work.'

It was useless arguing; she went out and walked a little, looking about her and surreptitiously seeking some way of escaping. The wall was high, as required by the builders of the old type of barracks, but the watchtowers for the sentries were empty. The garden was surrounded by military-looking buildings, which now housed the male and female wards, the administrative offices and the employees' rooms. After a first, rapid inspection, she noticed that the only place that was really guarded was the main gate, where everyone who entered and left had their papers checked by two guards.

Everything seemed to be falling into place in her mind again. In order to exercise her memory, she began trying to remember small things, like the place where she used to leave the key to her room, the record she'd just bought, the last book she was asked for at the library.

'I'm Zedka,' said a woman, approaching.

The previous night, Veronika hadn't been able to see her face, she had been crouched down beside the bed all the time they were talking. Zedka must have been about thirty-five and seemed absolutely normal.

'I hope the injection didn't bother you too much. After a while, the body gets habituated, and the sedatives lose their effect.'

'I'm fine.'

'About our conversation last night, do you remember what you asked me?'

'Of course I do.'

Zedka took her by the arm, and they began to walk along together, amongst the many leafless trees in the courtyard. Beyond the walls, you could see the mountains disappearing into the clouds.

'It's cold, but a lovely morning all the same,' said Zedka. 'Oddly enough, I never used to suffer from depression on cold, grey, cloudy days like this. I felt as if nature was in harmony with me, that it reflected my soul. On the other hand, when the sun appeared, the children would come out to play in the streets, and everyone was happy that it was such a lovely day, and then I would feel terrible, as if that display of exuberance in which I could not participate was somehow unfair.'

Delicately, Veronika detached herself from the woman. She didn't like physical contact.

'You didn't finish what you were saying. You were saying something about what I asked you last night.'

'There's a group of people here, men and women who could have left, who could be back home, but who don't want to leave. There are many reasons for this: Villete isn't as bad as people say, although it's far from being a five-star hotel. Here inside, everyone can say what they like, do what they want, without being criticised, after all, they're in a mental hospital. Then, when there are government inspections, these men and women behave like dangerous maniacs, because some are here at the State's expense. The doctors know this, but there must be some order from the owners which allows the situation to continue, because there are more vacancies than there are patients.'

'Could they get hold of some pills for me?'

'Try and contact them, they call their group the Fraternity.'

Zedka pointed to a woman with white hair, who was talking animatedly with some younger women.

'Her name is Mari, she belongs to the Fraternity. Ask her.'

Veronika started walking towards Mari, but Zedka stopped her:

'No, not now, she's having fun. She's not going to stop something which gives her pleasure, just to be nice to a complete stranger. If she should react badly, you'll never have another chance to approach her. The "mad" always believe in first impressions.'

Veronika laughed at the way Zedka said the word 'mad', but she was worried too, because everything here seemed so normal, so nice. After so many years of going straight from work to a bar, from that bar to the bed of some lover, from his bed to her room, from her room to her mother's house, she was now experiencing something she had never dreamed of:

a mental hospital, madness, an insane asylum, where people were not ashamed to say they were mad, where no one stopped doing something they were enjoying just to be nice to others.

She began to doubt that Zedka was serious, or if it wasn't just a way by which mental patients could pretend that the world they lived in was better than that of others. But what did it matter? She was experiencing something interesting, different, totally unexpected: imagine a place where people pretend to be mad in order to do exactly what they want.

At that precise moment, Veronika's heart turned over. She suddenly remembered what the doctor had said and she felt frightened.

'I want to walk alone for a bit,' she said to Zedka. After all, she was 'mad' too, and she no longer had to worry about pleasing anyone.

The woman moved off, and Veronika stood looking at the mountains beyond the walls of Villete. A faint desire to live seemed about to surface, but Veronika determinedly pushed it away.

'I must get hold of those pills as soon as possible.'

She reflected on her situation there; it was far from ideal. Even if they allowed her to do all the mad things she wanted to do, she wouldn't know where to start.

She had never done anything mad.

After some time in the garden, everyone went back to the refectory and had lunch. Immediately afterwards, the nurses led both men and women to a huge lounge divided up into lots of different areas; there were tables, chairs, sofas, a piano, a television and large windows through which you could see the grey sky and the low clouds. None of the windows had bars on them, because the room opened onto the garden. The doors were closed because of the cold, but all you had to do was turn the handle, and you could go outside again and walk once more amongst the trees.

Most people went and sat down in front of the television. Others stared into space, others talked in low voices to themselves, but who has not done the same at some moment in their lives? Veronika noticed that the older woman, Mari, was now with a larger group, in one of the corners of the vast room. Some other patients were walking nearby and Veronika tried to join them in order to eavesdrop on what the group members were saying.

She tried to disguise her intentions as best she could, but whenever she came close, they all fell silent and turned as one to look at her.

'What do you want?' said an elderly man, who seemed to be the leader of the Fraternity (if such a group really existed, and Zedka was not actually madder than she seemed).

'Nothing, I was just passing.'

They exchanged glances, and made a few mad gestures with their heads. One said to the other: 'She was just passing.' The other repeated the remark more loudly this time and soon they were all shouting the same words.

Veronika didn't know what to do and stood there paralysed with fear. A burly, shifty-looking male nurse came over, wanting to know what was going on.

'Nothing,' said one member of the group. 'She was just passing. She's standing right there, but she's still just passing.'

The whole group fell about laughing. Veronika assumed an ironic air, smiled, turned and moved off, so that no one would notice that her eyes were filling with tears. She went straight out into the garden, without bothering to put on a coat or jacket. A nurse tried to convince her to come back in, but another appeared soon after and whispered something in his ear, and the two of them left her in peace, in the cold. There was no point taking care of the health of someone who was condemned to die.

She was confused, tense, irritated with herself. She had never allowed herself to be provoked; she had learned from early on that, whenever a new situation presented itself, you had to remain cool and distant. Those mad people, however, had managed to make her feel shame, fear, rage, a desire to murder them all, to wound them with words she hadn't dared to utter.

Perhaps the pills or the treatment they had administered to get her out of her coma had transformed her into a frail woman, incapable of fending for herself. She had confronted far worse situations in her adolescence, and yet for the first time, she had been unable to hold back her tears. She needed to get back to the person she used to be, someone able to respond with irony, to pretend that the insults didn't bother her because she was better than all of them. Who, in that group, had had the courage to desire death? Who amongst them could teach her about life when they were all huddled behind the walls of Villete? She would never want to depend on their help for anything, even if she had to wait five or six days to die.

'One day's already gone. There are only another four or five left.'

She walked a little, letting the freezing cold enter her body and calm the blood that was flowing too fast, her heart that was beating too hard.

'Honestly, here I am, with my days literally numbered, giving importance to remarks made by people I've never even seen before, people who soon I'll never see again. And yet I suffer and get upset, I want to attack and defend. Why waste my time?'

But she *was* wasting the little time left to her, fighting for her tiny bit of space in that strange community where you had to put up a fight if you didn't want others imposing their rules on you.

'I can't believe it, I never used to be like this. I never used to fight over stupid things.'

She stopped in the middle of the icy garden. It was precisely because she had found everything so stupid that she had ended up accepting what life had naturally imposed on her. In adolescence, she thought it was too early to choose; now, in youth, she was convinced it was too late to change.

And what had she spent all her energies on until then? On trying to ensure that her life continued exactly as it always had. She had given up many of her desires so that her parents would continue to love her as they had when she was a child, even though she knew that real love changes and grows with time and discovers new ways of expressing itself. One day, when she had listened to her mother telling her, in tears, that her marriage was over, Veronika had sought out her father; she had cried, threatened and finally extracted a promise from him that he would not leave home, never imagining the high price her parents would have to pay for this.

When she decided to get a job, she rejected a tempting offer from a company that had just been set up in her recently created country in favour of a job at the public library, where you didn't earn much money, but where you were secure. She went to work every day, always keeping to the same timetable, always making sure she wasn't perceived as a threat by her superiors; she was contented, she didn't struggle and so she didn't grow: all she wanted was her salary at the end of the month.

She rented the room in the convent because the nuns required all tenants to be back at a certain hour, and then they locked the door: anyone still outside after that had to sleep in the street. She always had a genuine excuse to give boyfriends, so as not to have to spend the night in hotel rooms or strange beds.

When she used to dream of getting married, she imagined herself in a little house outside Ljubljana, with a man quite different from her father, a man who earned enough to support his family, one who would be contented just to be with her in a house with an open fire and to look out at the snow-covered mountains.

She had taught herself to give men a precise amount of pleasure, never more, never less, only what was necessary. She didn't get angry with anyone, because that would mean having to react, having to do battle with the enemy, and then having to face unforeseen consequences, such as vengeance.

When she had achieved almost everything she wanted in life, she had reached the conclusion that her existence had no meaning, because every day was the same. And she had decided to die.

Veronika went back in and walked over to the group gathered in one corner of the room. The people were talking animatedly, but fell silent as soon as she approached.

She went straight over to the oldest man, who seemed to be the leader. Before anyone could stop her, she gave him a resounding slap in the face.

'Aren't you going to react?' she asked out loud, so that everyone in the room could hear her. 'Aren't you going to do something?'

'No,' the man said and passed a hand over his face. A little thread of blood ran from his nose. 'You won't be troubling us for very long.'

She left the lounge and went triumphantly back to her ward. She had done something that she had never done in her entire life.

Three days had passed since the incident with the group that Zedka called the Fraternity. Veronika regretted that slap, not because she was afraid of the man's reaction, but because she had done something different. If she wasn't careful, she might end up convinced that life was worth living, and that would cause her pointless pain, since she would soon have to leave this world anyway.

Her only option was to keep away from everything and everyone, to try to be in every way as she had been before, to obey Villete's rules and regulations. She adapted herself to the routine imposed by the hospital: rising early, having breakfast, going for a walk in the garden, having lunch, going to the lounge, for another walk in the garden, then supper, television and bed.

Before Veronika went to sleep, a nurse always appeared with medication. All the other women took pills, Veronika was the only one who was given an injection. She never complained, she just wanted to know why she was given so many sedatives, since she had never had any problems sleeping. They explained that the injection was not a sedative, but medication for her heart.

And so, by falling in with that routine, her days in the hospital all began to seem the same. When the days are all the same, they pass more quickly; in another two or three days she would no longer have to brush her teeth or comb her hair. Veronika noticed her heart growing rapidly weaker: she became easily out of breath, she got pains in her chest, she had no appetite, and the slightest effort made her dizzy.

After the incident with the Fraternity, she had sometimes thought: 'If I had a choice, if I had understood earlier that the reason my days were all the same was because I wanted them like that, perhaps...'

But the reply was always the same: 'There is no perhaps, because there is no choice.' And her inner peace returned, because everything had already been decided.

During this period, she formed a relationship with Zedka (not a friendship, because friendship requires a lot of time spent together, and that wouldn't be possible). They used to play cards – which helps the time pass more rapidly – and sometimes they would walk together, in silence, in the garden.

On one particular morning, immediately after breakfast, they all went out to take the sun, as the regulations demanded. A nurse, however, asked Zedka to go back to the ward, because it was her treatment day.

Veronika, who was having breakfast with her, heard the request.

'What treatment's that?'

'It's an old treatment, from the sixties, but the doctors think it might hasten my recovery. Do you want to come and watch?'

'You said you were depressed. Isn't taking the medication enough to replace the chemical you're lacking?'

'Do you want to watch?' insisted Zedka.

She was going to step outside the routine, thought Veronika. She was going to discover new things, when she didn't need to learn anything more – all she needed was patience. But her curiosity got the better of her and she nodded.

'This isn't a show, you know,' said the nurse.

'She's going to die. She's hardly seen anything. Let her come with us.'

Veronika watched the woman, still smiling, being strapped to the bed.

'Tell her what's going on,' said Zedka to the male nurse. 'Otherwise she'll be frightened.'

He turned and showed her the syringe. He seemed pleased to be treated like a doctor, explaining to a younger doctor the correct procedures and the proper treatments.

'This syringe contains a dose of insulin,' he said, speaking in a grave, technical tone of voice. 'It's used by diabetics to combat high blood glucose. However, when the dose is much larger than normal, the consequent drop in blood glucose provokes a state of coma.'

He tapped the needle lightly, to get rid of any air, and then stuck it in a vein in Zedka's right foot.

'That's what's going to happen now. She's going to enter a state of induced coma. Don't be frightened if her eyes go glazed, and don't expect her to recognise you when she's under the effects of the medication.'

'That's awful, inhuman. People struggle to get out of a coma not to go into one.'

'People struggle to live, not to commit suicide,' replied the nurse, but Veronika ignored the remark. 'And a state of coma allows the organism to rest; its functions are all drastically reduced and any existing tension disappears.'

While he was talking, he was injecting the liquid, and Zedka's eyes were growing dull.

'Don't worry,' Veronika was saying to her. 'You're absolutely normal, the story you told me about the king…'

'Don't waste your time. She can't hear you any more.'

The woman on the bed, who a few minutes before had seemed so lucid and full of life, now had her eyes fixed on some point in the distance, and there was liquid bubbling from one corner of her mouth.

'What did you do?' she shouted at the nurse.

'Just my job.'

Veronika started calling to Zedka, shouting, threatening that she would go to the police, the press, the human rights organisations.

'Calm down. You may be in a mental hospital, but you still have to abide by certain rules.'

She saw that the man was utterly serious and she was afraid. But since she had nothing to lose, she went on shouting.

From where she was, Zedka could see the ward and the beds, all empty except for one, to which her body was strapped, and beside which a girl was standing, staring in horror. The girl didn't know that the person in the bed was still alive with all her biological functions working perfectly, but that her soul was flying, almost touching the ceiling, experiencing a sense of profound peace.

Zedka was making an astral journey, something that had been a surprise during her first experience of insulin shock. She hadn't mentioned it to anyone, she was only there to be cured of depression and, as soon as she was in a fit state, she hoped to leave that place for ever. If she started telling them that she had left her body, they would think she was madder than when she had entered Villete. However, as soon as she had returned to her body, she began reading up on both subjects: insulin shock and that strange feeling of floating in space.

There wasn't much written about the treatment. It had been used for the first time around 1930, but had been completely banned in psychiatric hospitals, because of the possibility of irreversible damage to the patient. During one such session, she had visited Dr Igor's office in her astral form, at precisely the moment when he was discussing the subject with one of the owners of the hospital. 'It's a crime,' Dr Igor was saying. 'Yes, but it's cheap and it's quick!' replied the other man. 'Anyway, who's interested in the rights of the mad? No one's going to complain.'

Even so, some doctors still considered it a quick way of treating depression. Zedka had sought out and borrowed everything that had been written about insulin shock, especially first-hand reports by patients who had experienced it. The story was always the same: horrors and more horrors, not one of them had experienced anything resembling what she was living through at that moment.

She concluded – quite rightly – that there was no relationship between insulin and the feeling that her consciousness was leaving her body. On the contrary, the tendency with that kind of treatment was to diminish the patient's mental capacity.

She started researching into the existence of the soul, read a few books on occultism, and then, one day, she stumbled on a vast literature that described exactly what she was experiencing: it was called 'astral travel' and many people had already had the same experience. Some had merely set out to describe what they had felt, while others had developed techniques to provoke it. Zedka now knew those techniques by heart and she used them every night to go wherever she wished.

The descriptions of those experiences and visions varied, but they all had certain points in common: the strange, irritating noise that preceded the separation of the body from the spirit, followed by a shock, a rapid loss of consciousness, and then the peace and joy of floating in the air, attached to the body by a silvery cord, a cord that could be stretched indefinitely, although there were legends (in books, of course) that said the person would die if they allowed that silver thread to break.

Her experience, however, showed that she could go as far as she wanted and the cord never broke. But, generally speaking, the books had been very useful in teaching her how to get more and more out of her astral travelling. She had learned, for example, that when she wanted to move from one place to another, she had to concentrate on projecting herself into space, imagining where exactly she wanted to go. Unlike the routes followed by planes – which leave from one place and fly the necessary distance to reach another – an astral journey was made through mysterious tunnels. You imagined yourself in a place, you entered the appropriate tunnel at a terrifying speed, and the other place would appear.

It was through books too that she had lost her fear of the creatures inhabiting space. Today there was no one else in the ward, but the first time she had left her body, she had found a lot of people watching her, amused by her look of surprise.

Her first reaction was to assume that these were dead people, ghosts haunting the hospital. Then, with the help of books and of her own experience, she realised that, although there were a few disembodied spirits wandering about there, amongst them were people as alive as she was, who had either developed the technique of leaving their bodies, or who were not even aware of what was happening to them because, in some other part of the world, they were sleeping deeply, while their spirits roamed freely abroad.

Today – knowing that this was her last astral journey on insulin, because she had just been to visit Dr Igor's office and overheard him saying he was ready to release her – she decided to remain inside Villete. From the moment she went out through the main gate, she would never again return, not even in spirit, and she wanted to say goodbye.

To say goodbye. That was the really difficult part: once in a mental hospital, a person grows used to the freedom that exists in the world of madness and becomes addicted to it. You no longer have to take on responsibilities, to struggle to earn your daily bread, to be bothered with repetitive, mundane tasks. You could spend hours looking at a picture or making absurd doodles. Everything is tolerated because, after all, the person is mentally ill. As she herself had had occasion to observe, most of the inmates showed a marked improvement once they entered the hospital: they no longer had to hide their symptoms, and the 'family' atmosphere helped them to accept their own neuroses and psychoses.

At the beginning, Zedka had been fascinated by Villete and had even considered joining the Fraternity once she was cured. But she realised that if she was sensible, she could continue doing everything she enjoyed doing outside, as long as she dealt with the challenges of daily life. As someone had said, all you had to do was to keep your madness under control. You could cry, get worried or angry like any other normal human being, as long as you remembered that, up above, your spirit was laughing out loud at all those thorny situations.

She would soon be back home, with her children and her husband, and that part of her life also had its charms. Of course it would be difficult to find work; after all, in a small town like Ljubljana news travels fast, and her internment in Villete was already common knowledge to many people. But her husband earned enough to keep the family, and she could use her free time to continue making her astral journeys, though not under the dangerous influence of insulin.

There was only one thing she did not want to experience again, the reason that had brought her to Villete.

Depression.

The doctors said that a recently discovered substance, serotonin, was one of the compounds responsible for how human beings felt. A lack of serotonin impaired one's capacity to concentrate at work, to sleep, to eat and to enjoy life's pleasures. When this substance was completely absent, the person experienced despair, pessimism, a sense of futility, terrible tiredness, anxiety, difficulties in making decisions, and would end up sinking into permanent gloom, which would lead either to complete apathy or to suicide.

Other more conservative doctors said that any drastic change in life could trigger depression – moving to another country, losing a loved one, divorce, an increase in the demands of work or family. Some modern studies, based on the number of internments in winter and summer, pointed to the lack of sunlight as one of the causes of depression.

In Zedka's case, however, the reasons were simpler than anyone suspected: a man hidden in her past, or rather, the fantasy she had built up about a man she had known a long time ago.

It was so stupid. Plunging into depression and madness all because of a man whose current whereabouts she didn't even know, but with whom she had fallen hopelessly in love in her youth, since, like every normal young girl, Zedka had needed to experience the Impossible Love.

However, unlike her friends, who only dreamed of the Impossible Love, Zedka had decided to go further; she had actually tried to realise that dream. He lived on the other side of the ocean and she sold up everything to go and join him. He was married, but she accepted her role as mistress, plotting secretly to make him her husband. He barely had enough time for himself, but she resigned herself to spending days and nights in a cheap hotel room, waiting for his rare telephone calls.

Despite her determination to put up with everything in the name of love, the relationship did not work out. He never said anything directly, but one day, Zedka realised that she was no longer welcome and she returned to Slovenia.

She spent a few months barely eating and remembering every second they had spent together, reviewing again and again their moments of joy and pleasure in bed, trying to fix on something that would allow her to believe in the future of that relationship. Her friends were worried about the state she was in, but something in Zedka's heart told her it was just a passing phase; personal growth has its price, and she was paying it without complaint. And so it was: one morning she woke up with an immense will to live; for the first time in ages, she ate heartily and then went out and found a job. She found not only a job, but also the attentions of a handsome, intelligent young man, much sought after by other women. A year later, she was married to him.

She aroused both the envy and the applause of her girlfriends. The two of them went to live in a comfortable house, with a garden that looked over the river that flows through Ljubljana. They had children and took trips to Austria or Italy during the summer.

When Slovenia decided to separate from Yugoslavia, he was called up into the army. Zedka was a Serb – that is, the enemy – and her life seemed on the point of collapse. In the ten tense days that followed, with the troops prepared for confrontation, and no one knowing quite what the result of the declaration of independence would be and how much blood would have to be spilt because of it, Zedka realised how much she loved him. She spent the whole time praying to a God who, until then, had seemed remote, but who now seemed her only hope. She promised the saints and angels anything as long as she could have her husband back.

And so it was. He came back, the children were able to go to schools where they taught the Slovene language, and the threat of war shifted to the neighbouring republic of Croatia.

Three years had passed. Yugoslavia's war with Croatia moved to Bosnia, and reports began to circulate of massacres committed by the Serbs. Zedka thought it unjust to label a whole nation as criminals because of the folly of a few madmen. Her life took on a meaning she had never expected: she defended her people with pride and courage, writing in newspapers, appearing on television, organising conferences. None of this bore any fruit, and even today, foreigners still believe all the Serbs were responsible for those atrocities, but Zedka knew she had done her duty, and that she could not abandon her brothers and sisters at such a difficult time. She could count on the support of her Slovene husband, of her children, and of people who were not manipulated by the propaganda machines of either side.

One evening, she walked past the statue of Prešeren, the great Slovene poet, and she began to think about his life. When he was thirty-four, he went into a church and saw an adolescent girl, Julia Primic, with whom he fell passionately in love. Like the ancient minstrels, he began to write her poems, in the hope of one day marrying her.

It turned out that Julia was the daughter of an upper middle-class family and, apart from that chance sighting inside the church, Prešeren never again managed to get near her. But that encounter inspired his finest poetry and created a whole legend around his name. In the small central square of Ljubljana, the statue of the poet stares fixedly at something. If you follow his gaze, you will see, on the other side of the square, the face of a woman carved into the stone of one of the houses. That was where Julia had lived. Even after death, Prešeren gazes for all eternity on his Impossible Love.

And what if he had fought a little harder?

Zedka's heart started beating fast, perhaps it was a presentiment of something bad, an accident involving one of her children. She raced back home only to find them watching television and eating popcorn.

That sadness, however, did not pass. Zedka lay down and slept for nearly twelve hours and, when she woke, she didn't feel like getting up. Prešeren's story had brought back to her the image of her first lover, who had never again contacted her.

And Zedka asked herself: did I fight hard enough? Should I have accepted my role as mistress, rather than wanting things to go as I expected them to? Did I fight for my first love with the same energy with which I fought for my people?

Zedka persuaded herself that she had, but the sadness would not go away. What once had seemed to her a Paradise – the house near the river, the husband whom she loved, the children eating popcorn in front of the television – was gradually transformed into a hell.

Today, after many astral journeys and many encounters with highly evolved beings, Zedka knew that this was all nonsense. She had used her Impossible Love as an excuse, a pretext for breaking the ties with the life she led, and which was far from being the life she really expected for herself.

But twelve months earlier, the situation had been quite different: she began frantically looking for that distant lover, she spent a fortune on international phone calls, but he no longer lived in the same city, and it was impossible to find him. She sent letters by express mail, which were always returned. She phoned all his friends, but no one had any idea what had happened to him.

Her husband was completely unaware of what was going on, and that infuriated her, because he should at least have suspected something, made a scene, complained, threatened to put her out in the street. She became convinced that the international telephone operators, the postman and all her girlfriends had been bribed by him to pretend indifference. She sold the jewellery that had been given to her when she married and bought a plane ticket to the other side of the ocean, until someone managed to convince her that America was a very large place and there was no point going there if you didn't know quite what you were looking for.

One evening, she lay down, suffering for love as she had never suffered before, not even when she had come back to the awful day-to-day life of Ljubljana. She spent that night and the following two days in her room. On the third day, her husband – so kind, so concerned about her – called a doctor. Did he really not know that Zedka was trying to get in touch with the other man, to commit adultery, to exchange her life as a respected wife for life as someone's secret mistress, to leave Ljubljana, her home, her children for ever?

The doctor arrived. She became hysterical and locked the door, and only opened it again when the doctor had left. A week later, she no longer had sufficient strength of will to get out of bed and began to use the bed as a toilet. She did not think any more, her head was completely taken up by fragmentary memories of the man who, she was convinced, was also unsuccessfully looking for her.

Her infuriatingly generous husband changed the sheets, smoothed her hair, said that it would all be all right in the end. The children no longer came into her bedroom, ever since she had slapped one of them for no reason, and then knelt down, kissed his feet, begging forgiveness, tearing her nightdress into shreds in order to show her despair and repentance.

After another week, in which she spat out the food offered to her, drifted in and out of reality several times, spent whole nights awake and whole days asleep, two men came into her room without knocking. One of them held her down while the other gave her an injection, and she woke up in Villete.

'Depression,' she heard the doctor say to her husband. 'Sometimes it's provoked by the most banal things, for example, the lack of a chemical substance, serotonin, in the organism.'

From the ceiling in the ward, Zedka watched the nurse approaching, syringe in hand. The girl was still standing there, trying to talk to her body, terrified by her vacant gaze. For some moments, Zedka considered the possibility of telling her about everything that was happening, but then she changed her mind; people never learn anything by being told, they have to find out for themselves.

The nurse placed the needle in Zedka's arm and injected her with glucose. As if grabbed by an enormous arm, her spirit left the ceiling, sped through a dark tunnel and returned to her body.

'Hello, Veronika.'

The girl looked frightened.

'Are you all right?'

'Yes, I'm fine. Fortunately, I've managed to survive this dangerous treatment, but it won't be repeated.'

'How do you know? Here no one respects the patient's wishes.'

Zedka knew because, during her astral journey, she had gone to Dr Igor's office.

'I can't explain why, I just know. Do you remember the first question I ever asked you?'

'Yes, you asked me if I knew what being mad meant?'

'Exactly. This time I'm not going to tell you a story.

Madness is the inability to communicate your ideas. It's as if you were in a foreign country, able to see and understand everything that's going on around you, but incapable of explaining what you need to know or of being helped, because you don't understand the language they speak there.'

'We've all felt that.'

'And all of us, one way or another, are mad.'

Outside the barred window, the sky was thick with stars, and the moon, in its first quarter, was rising behind the mountains. Poets loved the full moon, they wrote thousands of poems about it, but it was the new moon that Veronika loved best because there was still room for it to grow, to expand, to fill the whole of its surface with light before its inevitable decline.

She felt like going over to the piano in the lounge, and celebrating that night with a lovely sonata she had learned at school. Looking up at the sky, she had an indescribable sense of well-being, as if the infinite nature of the universe had revealed her own eternity to her. However, she was separated from her desire by a steel door and a woman who was always endlessly reading a book. Besides, no one played the piano at that hour of night, she would wake up the whole neighbourhood.

Veronika laughed. The 'neighbourhood' were the wards full of mad people, and those mad people were, in turn, full of drugs to make them sleep.

Her sense of well-being continued though. She got up and went over to Zedka's bed, but she was sound asleep too, perhaps recovering from the horrible experience she had been through.

'Go back to bed,' said the nurse. 'Good girls should be dreaming of angels or lovers.'

'Don't treat me like a child. I'm not some tame mad woman who's afraid of everything, I'm raving, hysterical, I don't even respect my own life, or the lives of others. Anyway, today I'm in a bad way. I've looked at the moon and I need to talk to someone.'

The nurse looked at her, surprised by her reaction.

'Are you afraid of me?' asked Veronika. 'In a couple of days' time I'll be dead, what have I got to lose?'

'Why don't you go for a walk, dear, and let me finish my book?'

'Because this is a prison and there's a prison warder pretending to read a book, just to make others think she's an intelligent woman. The fact is, though, that she's watching every movement in the ward, and she guards the keys to the door as if they were a treasure. It's doubtless all in the regulations and so she must obey, because that way she can pretend to an authority she doesn't have in her everyday life, with her husband and children.'

Veronika was trembling, without quite knowing why.

'Keys?' said the nurse. 'The door is always open. You don't think I'd stay locked up in here with a load of mental patients, do you?'

What does she mean the door's open? A few days ago I wanted to get out of here, and this woman even went with me to the toilet. What is she talking about?

'Don't take me too seriously,' said the nurse. 'The fact is we don't need a lot of security here, because of the sedatives we dole out. You're shivering, are you cold?'

'I don't know. I think it must be something to do with my heart.'

'If you like, you can go for a walk.'

'What I'd really like is to play the piano.'

'The lounge is quite separate, so your piano playing won't disturb anyone. Do what you like.'

Veronika's trembling changed into low, timid, suppressed sobs. She knelt down, lay her head on the woman's lap and cried and cried.

The nurse put down the book, and stroked Veronika's hair, allowing that wave of sadness and tears its natural expression. There they sat, for almost half an hour, one crying, the other consoling, though neither knew why or what.

The sobbing finally ceased. The nurse helped her up, took her by the arm and led her to the door.

'I've got a daughter your age. When you were first admitted, full of drips and tubes, I kept wondering why a pretty young girl, with her whole life ahead of her, should want to kill herself. Then all kinds of rumours started flying around: about the letter that you left behind, which I never believed could be the real motive, and how you didn't have long to live because of some incurable heart problem. I couldn't get the image of my own daughter out of my head: what if she decided to do something like that? Why do certain people try to go against the natural order of things, which is to fight for survival whatever happens?'

'That's why I was crying,' said Veronika. 'When I took the pills, I wanted to kill someone I hated. I didn't know that other Veronikas existed inside me, Veronikas that I could love.'

'What makes a person hate themselves?'

'Cowardice perhaps. Or the eternal fear of being wrong, of not doing what others expect. A few moments ago I was happy, I forgot I was under sentence of death; then, when I remembered the situation I'm in, I felt frightened.'

The nurse opened the door and Veronika went out.

How could she ask me that? What does she want, to understand why I was crying? Doesn't she realise I'm a perfectly normal person, with the same desires and fears as everyone else, and that a question like that, now that it's all too late, could throw me into panic?

As she was walking down the corridors, lit by the same faint light as in the ward, Veronika realised that it *was* too late: she could no longer control her fear.

'I must get a grip on myself. I'm the kind of person who sticks to any decision she makes, who always sees things through.'

It's true that in her life she had seen many things through to their ultimate consequences, but only unimportant things, like prolonging a quarrel that could easily have been resolved with an apology, or not phoning a man she was in love with, simply because she thought the relationship would lead nowhere. She was intransigent about the easy things, as if trying to prove to herself how strong and indifferent she was, when, in fact, she was just a fragile woman, who had never been an outstanding student, never excelled at school sports and had never succeeded in keeping the peace at home.

She had overcome her minor defects, only to be defeated by matters of fundamental importance. She had managed to appear utterly independent, when she was, in fact, desperately in need of company. When she entered a room, everyone would turn to look at her, but she almost always ended the night alone, in the convent, watching a TV that she hadn't even bothered to have properly tuned in. She gave all her friends the impression that she was a woman to be envied, and she expended most of her energy in trying to behave in accordance with the image she had created of herself.

Because of that, she had never had enough energy to be herself, a person who, like everyone else in the world, needed other people in order to be happy. But other people were so difficult.

They reacted in unpredictable ways, they surrounded themselves with defensive walls, they behaved just as she did, pretending they didn't care about anything. When someone more open to life appeared, they either rejected them outright, or made them suffer, considering them inferior, 'ingenuous'.

She may have impressed a lot of people with her strength and determination, but where had it left her? In the void. Utterly alone. In Villete. In the anteroom of death.

Veronika's remorse over her attempted suicide resurfaced, and she firmly pushed it away again. Now she was feeling something she had never allowed herself to feel: hatred.

Hatred. Something almost as physical as walls, pianos or nurses; she could almost touch the destructive energy leaking out of her body. She allowed the feeling to emerge, regardless of whether it was good or bad, she was sick of self-control, of masks, of appropriate behaviour. Veronika wanted to spend her remaining two or three days of life behaving as inappropriately as she could.

She had begun by slapping an old man in the face, she had burst into tears in front of a nurse, she had refused to be nice and to talk to the others when what she really wanted was to be alone, and now she was free enough to feel hatred, although intelligent enough not to smash everything around her and risk spending what remained of her life under sedation and in a bed in a ward.

At that moment, she hated everything: herself, the world, the chair in front of her, the broken radiator in one of the corridors, people who were perfect, criminals. She was in a mental hospital and so could allow herself to feel things that people usually hide from themselves, because we are all brought up only to love, to accept, to look for ways round things, to avoid conflict. Veronika hated everything, but mainly she hated the way she had lived her life, never bothering to discover the hundreds of other Veronikas who lived inside her and who were interesting, mad, curious, brave, bold.

Then she started to feel hatred for the person she loved most in the world: her mother. A wonderful wife who worked all day and washed the dishes at night, sacrificing her own life so that her daughter would have a good education, know how to play the piano and the violin, dress like a princess, have the latest trainers and jeans, while she mended the same old dress she had worn for years.

'How can I hate someone who only ever gave me love?' thought Veronika, confused, trying to check her feelings. But it was too late, her hatred had been unleashed, she had opened the door to her personal hell. She hated the love she had been given, because it had asked for nothing in return, which was absurd, unreal, against the laws of nature.

That love asking for nothing in return had managed to fill her with guilt, with a desire to fulfil another's expectations, even if that meant giving up everything she had dreamed of for herself. It was a love that for years had tried to hide from her the difficulties and the corruption that existed in the world, ignoring the fact that, one day, she would have to find this out, and would then be defenceless against them.

And her father? She hated her father too, because, unlike her mother, who worked all the time, he knew how to live, he took her to bars and to the theatre, they had fun together, and when he was still young, she had loved him secretly, not the way one loves a father, but as a man. She hated him because he had always been so charming and so open with everyone except her mother, the only person who really deserved such treatment.

She hated everything. The library with its pile of books full of explanations about life, the school that had forced her to spend whole evenings learning algebra, even though she didn't know a single person, apart from teachers and mathematicians, who needed algebra in order to be happy. Why did they make them learn so much algebra or geometry or any of that mountain of other useless things?

Veronika pushed open the door to the lounge, went over to the piano, opened the lid, and, summoning up all her strength, pounded on the keys. A mad, cacophonous, jangled chord echoed round the empty room, bounced off the walls and returned to her in the guise of a shrill sound that seemed to tear at her soul. Yet it was an accurate portrait of her soul at that moment.

She pounded on the keys again, and again the dissonant notes reverberated about her.

'I'm mad. I'm allowed to do this. I can hate, I can pound away at the piano. Since when have mental patients known how to play notes in the right order?'

She pounded the piano again, once, twice, ten, twenty times, and each time she did it, her hatred seemed to diminish, until it passed away completely.

Then, once more, a deep peace flooded through her and Veronika again looked out at the starry sky and at the new moon, her favourite, filling the room she was in with gentle light. The impression returned of Infinity and Eternity walking hand in hand; you only had to look for one of them, for example, the limitless universe, to feel the presence of the other, Time that never ends, that never passes, that remains in the Present, where all of life's secrets lie. As she had been walking from the ward to that room, she had felt such pure hatred that now she had no more rancour left in her heart. She had finally allowed her negative feelings to surface, feelings that had been repressed for years in her soul. She had actually *felt* them, and they were no longer necessary, they could leave.

She sat on in silence, enjoying the present moment, letting love fill up the empty space left behind by hatred. When she felt the moment had come, she turned to the moon and played a sonata in homage to it, knowing that the moon was listening and would feel proud, and that this would provoke the jealousy of the stars. Then she played music for the stars, for the garden, for the mountains that she could not see in the darkness, but which she knew were there.

While she was playing that music for the garden, another mad person appeared, Eduard, a schizophrenic who was beyond all cure. She was not frightened by his presence; on the contrary, she smiled, and to her surprise, he smiled back.

The music could even penetrate his remote world, more distant than the moon itself; it could even perform miracles.

'I must buy a new key ring,' thought Dr Igor, as he opened the door to his small consulting room in Villete. The old one was falling to pieces and a small decorative metal shield had just fallen to the floor.

Dr Igor bent down and picked it up. What should he do with that shield bearing the Ljubljana coat of arms? He might as well throw it away, although he could have it mended and ask them to make a new leather strap, or else he could give it to his nephew to play with. Both alternatives seemed equally absurd. A key ring doesn't cost very much and his nephew had no interest in shields; he spent all his time watching television, or playing with electronic toys imported from Italy. Dr Igor could still not bring himself to throw it out, however, so he put it back in his pocket; he would decide what to do with it later on.

That was why he was the director of the hospital and not a patient, because he thought a lot before making any decisions.

He turned on the light; as winter advanced, dawn came ever later. Moving house, getting divorced and the absence of light were the main reasons for the increase in the number of cases of depression. Dr Igor was hoping that spring would arrive early and solve half his problems.

He looked at his diary for the day. He needed to find some way to prevent Eduard from dying of hunger; his schizophrenia made him unpredictable, and now he had stopped eating. Dr

Igor had already prescribed intravenous feeding, but he couldn't keep that up for ever. Eduard was a strong young man of twenty-eight, but even with a drip, he would eventually waste away, becoming more and more skeletal.

What would Eduard's father think? He was one of the young Slovene republic's best-known ambassadors. He had been one of the people behind the delicate negotiations with Yugoslavia in the early 1990s. He, after all, had managed to work for years for the Belgrade government, surviving his detractors, who accused him of working for the enemy, and he was still in the diplomatic corps, except, this time, he represented a different country. He was a powerful and influential man, feared by everyone.

Dr Igor felt momentarily worried, just as before he had been worried about the shield on his key ring, but he immediately dismissed the thought. As far as the ambassador was concerned, it didn't matter whether his son looked well or not; he had no intention of taking him to official functions or having him accompany him to the various places in the world where he was sent as a government representative. Eduard was in Villete, and there he would stay for ever, or at least as long as his father continued earning his nice, fat salary.

Dr Igor decided to stop the intravenous feeding, and allow Eduard to waste away a little more, until he himself felt like eating. If the situation got worse, he would write a report and pass responsibility on to the council of doctors who administered Villete. 'The best way to avoid trouble is to share responsibility,' his father had taught him. He had been a doctor too, and although he had had various deaths on his hands, he had never had any problem with the authorities.

Once Dr Igor had ordered Eduard's treatment to stop, he moved on to the next case. According to the report, Zedka Mendel had completed her course of treatment and could be allowed to leave. Dr Igor wanted to see for himself. There was nothing a doctor dreaded more than getting complaints from the families of patients who had been in Villete, which was what nearly always happened, for it was rare for a patient to readjust successfully to normal life after a period spent in a mental hospital.

It wasn't the fault of the hospital, nor of any of the hospitals scattered round the world; the problem of readjustment was exactly the same everywhere. Just as prison never corrects the prisoner – it only teaches him to commit more crimes – so hospitals merely got patients used to a completely unreal world, where everything was allowed and where no one had to take responsibility for their actions.

There was only one way out: to discover a cure for insanity. And Dr Igor was engaged heart and soul on just that, developing a thesis that would revolutionise the psychiatric world. In mental hospitals, temporary patients who lived alongside incurable patients began a process of social degeneration which, once started, was impossible to stop. Zedka Mendel would come back to hospital eventually, this time of her own volition, complaining of non-existent ailments, simply in order to be close to people who seemed to understand her better than those in the outside world.

If, however, he could find a way of combating Vitriol, the poison which Dr Igor believed to be the cause of madness, his name would go down in history and people would finally know where Slovenia was. That week, he had been given a heaven-sent opportunity in the shape of a would-be suicide; he was not going to lose this opportunity for all the money in the world.

Dr Igor felt happy. Although he was obliged for economic reasons to accept treatments, like insulin shock for example, that had long ago been condemned by the medical profession, the same economic reasons lay behind Villete's instigation of a new psychiatric treatment. As well as having the time and the staff to carry out his researches into Vitriol, he also had the owners' permission to allow the group calling itself the Fraternity to remain in the hospital. The shareholders in the institution tolerated – note that word well, not encouraged, but tolerated – a longer period of internment than was strictly necessary. They argued that, for humanitarian reasons, they should give the recently-cured the option of deciding for themselves when would be the best moment for them to rejoin the world, and that had led to a group of people deciding to stay in Villete, as if at a select hotel, or a club for those with similar interests and views. Thus Dr Igor managed to keep the mad and the sane in the same place, allowing the latter to have a positive influence on the former. To prevent things from degenerating and to stop the mad having a negative effect on those who had been cured, every member of the Fraternity had to leave the hospital at least once a day.

Dr Igor knew that the reasons given by the shareholders for allowing the presence of healthy people in the hospital – 'humanitarian reasons' they said – were just an excuse. They were afraid that Ljubljana, Slovenia's small but charming capital, did not have a sufficient number of wealthy mad people to sustain this expensive, modern building. Besides, the public health system ran a number of first-class mental hospitals of its own, and that left Villete at a disadvantage in the mental health market.

When the shareholders had converted the old barracks into a hospital, their target market had been the men and women likely to be affected by the war with Yugoslavia. The war, however, had been brief. The shareholders had felt certain that war would return, but it didn't.

Moreover, recent research had shown that whilst wars did have their psychological victims, they were far fewer than, say, the victims of stress, tedium, congenital illness, loneliness and rejection. When a community had a major problem to face, for example, war, hyperinflation or plague, there was a slight increase in the number of suicides, but a marked decline in cases of depression, paranoia and psychosis. These returned to their normal levels as soon as that problem had been overcome, indicating, or so Dr Igor thought, that people only allow themselves the luxury of being mad when they are in a position to do so.

He had before him another recent survey, this time from Canada, which an American newspaper had recently voted the country with the highest standard of living. Dr Igor read:

According to *Statistics Canada*, 40% of people between 15 and 34, 33% of people between 35 and 54 and 20% of people between 55 and 64 have already had some kind of mental illness. It is thought that one in every five individuals suffers some form of psychiatric disorder and one in every eight Canadians will be hospitalised at least once in their lifetime because of mental disturbances.

'They've got a bigger market there than we have,' he thought. 'The happier people can be, the unhappier they are.'

Dr Igor analysed a few more cases, thinking carefully about those he should share with the council and those he should resolve alone. By the time he had finished, day had broken, and he turned off the light.

He immediately ordered his first appointment to be shown in: the mother of the patient who had tried to commit suicide.

'I'm Veronika's mother. How is my daughter?'

Dr Igor wondered if he should tell her the truth and save her any unpleasant surprises – after all, he had a daughter with the same name – but he decided it was best to say nothing.

'We don't yet know,' he lied. 'We need another week.'

'I've no idea why Veronika did it,' said the woman tearfully. 'We've always been loving parents, we sacrificed everything to give her the best possible upbringing. Although my husband and I have had our ups and downs, we've kept the family together, as an example of perseverance in adversity. She's got a good job, she's nice-looking, and yet…'

'… and yet she tried to kill herself,' said Dr Igor. 'There's no reason to be surprised, that's the way it is. People just can't cope with happiness. If you like, I could show you the statistics for Canada.'

'Canada?'

The woman seemed startled. Dr Igor saw that he had managed to distract her and went on.

'Look, you haven't come here to find out how your daughter is, but to apologise for the fact that she tried to commit suicide. How old is she?'

'Twenty-four.'

'So she's a mature, experienced woman who knows what she wants and is perfectly capable of making her own choices. What has that got to do with your marriage or with the sacrifices that you and your husband made? How long has she lived on her own?'

'Six years.'

'You see? She's fundamentally independent. But, because of what a certain Austrian doctor – Dr Sigmund Freud, I'm sure you've heard of him – wrote about unhealthy relationships between parents and children, people today still blame themselves for everything. Do you imagine that Indians believe that the son-turned-murderer is a victim of his parents' upbringing? Tell me.'

'I haven't the faintest idea,' replied the woman, who couldn't get over her bewilderment at the doctor's behaviour. Perhaps he was influenced by his patients.

'Well, I'll tell you,' said Dr Igor. 'The Indians believe the murderer to be guilty, not society, not his parents, not his ancestors. Do the Japanese commit suicide because a son of theirs decides to take drugs and go out and shoot people? The reply is the same: no! And, as we all know, the Japanese will commit suicide at the drop of a hat. The other day, I read that a young Japanese man killed himself because he had failed his university entrance exams.'

'Do you think I could talk to my daughter?' asked the woman, who was not interested in the Japanese, the Indians or the Canadians.

'Yes, yes, in a moment,' said Dr Igor, slightly annoyed by the interruption. 'But first, I want you to understand one thing: apart from certain grave pathological cases, people only go mad when they try to escape from routine. Do you understand?'

'I do,' she replied. 'And if you think that I won't be capable of looking after her, you can rest assured, I've *never* tried to change my life.'

'Good.' Dr Igor seemed relieved. 'Can you imagine a world in which, for example, we were not obliged to repeat the same thing every day of our lives? If, for example, we all decided to eat only when we were hungry, what would housewives and restaurants do?'

'It would be more normal to eat only when we were hungry,' thought the woman, but she said nothing, afraid that he might not let her speak to Veronika.

'Well, it would cause tremendous confusion,' she said at last. 'I'm a housewife myself, and I know what I'm talking about.'

'So we have breakfast, lunch and supper. We have to wake up at a certain hour every day and rest once a week. Christmas exists so that we can give each other presents, Easter so that we can spend a few days at the lake. How would you like it if your husband were gripped by a sudden, passionate impulse and decided he wanted to make love in the living room?'

The woman thought: 'What *is* the man talking about? I came here to see my daughter.'

'I would find it very sad,' she said, carefully, hoping she was giving the right answer.

'Excellent,' roared Dr Igor. 'The bedroom is the correct place for making love. To make love anywhere else would set a bad example and promote the spread of anarchy.'

'Can I see my daughter?' said the woman.

Dr Igor gave up. This peasant would never understand what he was talking about; she wasn't interested in discussing madness from a philosophical point of view, even though she knew her daughter had made a serious suicide attempt and had been in a coma.

He rang the bell and his secretary appeared.

'Call the young woman who tried to commit suicide,' he said. 'The one who wrote the letter to the newspapers, saying that she was killing herself in order to put Slovenia on the map.'

'I don't want to see her. I've cut all my links with the outside world.'

It had been hard to say that in the lounge, with everyone else there. But the nurse hadn't been exactly discreet either, and had announced in a loud voice that her mother was waiting to see her, as if it were a matter of general interest.

She didn't want to see her mother; it would only upset both of them. It was best that her mother should think of her as dead. Veronika had always hated goodbyes.

The man disappeared whence he had come, and she went back to looking at the mountains. After a week, the sun had finally returned, something she had known would happen the previous night, because the moon had told her while she was playing the piano.

'No, that's crazy, I'm losing my grip. Planets don't talk, or only to self-styled astrologers. If the moon spoke to anyone, it was to that schizophrenic.'

The very moment she thought this, she noticed a sharp pain in her chest, and her arm went numb. Veronika felt her head spinning. A heart attack!

She entered a kind of euphoric state, as if death had freed her from the fear of dying. So, it was all over. She might still experience some pain, but what were five minutes of agony in exchange for an eternity of peace? The only possible response was to close her eyes: in films, the thing she most hated to see were dead people with staring eyes.

But the heart attack was different from what she had imagined; her breathing became laboured, and Veronika was horrified to realise that she was about to experience the worst of her fears: suffocation. She was going to die as if she were being buried alive, or had suddenly been plunged into the depths of the sea.

She stumbled, fell, felt a sharp blow on her face, continued making heroic efforts to breathe, but the air wouldn't go in. Worst of all, death did not come. She was entirely conscious of what was going on around her, she could still see colours and shapes, although she had difficulty in hearing what others were saying; the cries and exclamations seemed distant, as if coming from another world. Apart from this, everything else was real; the air wouldn't enter her lungs, it would simply not obey the commands of her lungs and her muscles, and still she did not lose consciousness.

She felt someone touch her and turn her over, but now she had lost control of her eye movements, and her eyes were flickering wildly, sending hundreds of different images to her brain, combining the feeling of suffocation with a sense of complete visual confusion.

After a while, the images became distant too, and just when the agony reached its peak, the air finally rushed into her lungs, making a tremendous noise that left everyone in the room paralysed with fear.

Veronika began to vomit copiously. Once the near-tragedy had passed, some of the mad people there began to laugh, and she felt humiliated, lost, paralysed.

A nurse came running in and gave her an injection in her arm.

'It's all right, calm down, it's over now.'

'I didn't die!' she started shouting, crawling towards the other patients, smearing the floor and the furniture with her vomit. 'I'm still in this bloody hospital, forced to live with you lot, living a thousand deaths every day, every night, and not one of you feels an ounce of pity for me.'

She rounded on the nurse, grabbed the syringe from his hand and threw it out into the garden.

'And what do you want? Why don't you just inject me with poison, since I'm already condemned to die? How can you be so heartless?'

Unable to control herself any longer, she sat down on the floor again and started crying uncontrollably, shouting, sobbing loudly, while some of the patients laughed and made remarks about her filthy clothes.

'Give her a sedative,' said a doctor, hurrying in. 'Get this situation under control.'

The nurse, however, was frozen to the spot. The doctor went out again and returned with two more male nurses and another syringe. The men grabbed the hysterical girl struggling in the middle of the room, while the doctor injected the last drop of sedative into a vein in her vomit-smeared arm.

She was in Dr Igor's consulting room, lying on an immaculate white bed with clean sheets on it.

He was listening to her heart. She was pretending that she was still asleep, but something inside her must have changed, judging by the doctor's muttered words:

'Don't you worry. In your state of health, you could live to be a hundred.'

Veronika opened her eyes. Someone had taken her clothes off. Who? Dr Igor? Did that mean he had seen her naked? Her brain wasn't working properly.

'What did you say?'

'I said not to worry.'

'No, you said I could live to be a hundred.'

The doctor went over to his desk.

'You said I could live to be a hundred,' Veronika repeated.

'Nothing is certain in medicine,' said Dr Igor, trying to cover up. 'Everything's possible.'

'How's my heart?'

'The same.'

She didn't need to hear any more. When faced with a serious case, doctors always say: 'You'll live to be a hundred', or 'There's nothing seriously wrong with you,' or 'You have the heart and blood pressure of a young girl,' or even 'We need to redo the tests.' They're probably afraid the patient will go berserk in the consulting room.

She tried to get up, but couldn't; the whole room started to turn.

'Just lie down for a bit longer, until you feel better. You're not bothering me.'

Oh good, thought Veronika. But what if I was?

Being an experienced physician, Dr Igor remained silent for some time, pretending to be reading the papers on his desk. When we're with another person, and they say nothing, the situation becomes irritating, tense, unbearable. Dr Igor was hoping that the girl would start talking so that he could collect more data for his thesis on madness and the cure he was developing.

But Veronika didn't say a word. 'She may still be suffering from a high level of Vitriol poisoning,' thought Dr Igor, and decided to break the silence, which was becoming tense, irritating, unbearable.

'So you like to play the piano,' he said, trying to sound as nonchalant as possible.

'And the mad enjoy it too. Yesterday there was a guy listening who was utterly transfixed.'

'Yes, Eduard. He mentioned to someone how much he'd enjoyed it. Who knows, he might start eating normally again.'

'A schizophrenic liking music? And he mentioned it to someone else?'

'Yes. And I imagine you have no idea what you're talking about.'

That doctor – who looked more like a patient, with his dyed black hair – was right. Veronika had often heard the word 'schizophrenic', but she had no idea what it meant.

'Is there a cure, then?' she asked, hoping to find out more about schizophrenics.

'It can be controlled. We still don't really know what goes on in the world of madness. Everything's still so new, and the treatments change every decade or so. A schizophrenic is a person who already has a natural tendency to absent himself from this world, until some factor, sometimes serious, sometimes superficial, depending on the individual circumstances, forces him to create his own reality. It can develop into a state of complete alienation, what we call catatonia, but people do occasionally recover, at least enough to allow the patient to work and lead a near-normal life. It all depends on one thing, environment.'

'You say they create their own reality,' said Veronika, 'but what is reality?'

'It's whatever the majority deems it to be. It's not necessarily the best or the most logical, but it's the one that has become adapted to the desires of society as a whole. You see this thing I've got round my neck?'

'You mean your tie?'

'Exactly. Your answer is the logical, coherent answer an absolutely normal person would give: it's a tie! A madman, however, would say that what I have round my neck is a ridiculous, useless bit of coloured cloth tied in a very complicated way, and which makes it harder to get air into your lungs and difficult to turn your neck. I have to be careful when I'm anywhere near a fan, or I could be strangled by this bit of cloth.

'If a mad person were to ask me what this tie is for, I would have to say, absolutely nothing. It's not even purely decorative, since nowadays it's become a symbol of slavery, power, aloofness. The only really useful function a tie serves is the sense of relief when you get home and take it off; you feel as if you've freed yourself from something, though quite what you don't know.

'But does that sense of relief justify the existence of ties? No. Nevertheless, if I were to ask a madman and a normal person what this is, the sane person would say: a tie. It doesn't matter who's correct, what matters is who's right.'

'So just because I gave the right name to a bit of coloured cloth you conclude that I'm not mad.'

No, you're not mad, thought Dr Igor, who was an authority on the subject, with various diplomas hung on the walls of his consulting room. Attempting to take your own life was something proper to a human being; he knew a lot of people who were doing just that, and yet they lived outside the hospital, feigning innocence and normality, merely because they had not chosen the scandalous route of suicide. They were killing themselves gradually, poisoning themselves with what Dr Igor called Vitriol.

Vitriol was a toxic substance, whose symptoms he had identified in his conversations with the men and women he had met. Now he was writing a thesis on the subject, which he would submit to the Slovenian Academy of Sciences for their scrutiny. It was the most important step in the field of insanity since Dr Pinel had ordered that patients should be unshackled, astonishing the medical world with the idea that some of them might even be cured.

As with the libido – the chemical reaction responsible for sexual desire which Dr Freud had identified, but which no laboratory had ever managed to isolate – Vitriol was released by the human organism whenever a person found him or herself in a frightening situation, although it had yet to be picked up in any spectrographic tests. It was easily recognised, though, by its taste, which was neither sweet nor savoury – a bitter taste. Dr Igor, the as yet unrecognised discoverer of this fatal substance, had given it the name of a poison much favoured in the past by emperors, kings and lovers of all kinds whenever they needed to rid themselves of some obstructive person.

A golden age, the age of kings and emperors, when you could live and die romantically. The murderer would invite his or her victim to partake of a magnificent supper, the servant would pour them drinks served in two exquisite glasses, and one of the drinks would be laced with Vitriol. Imagine the excitement aroused by each gesture the victim made, picking up the glass, saying a few tender or aggressive words, drinking as if the glass contained some delicious beverage, giving his host one last startled look, then falling to the floor.

But this poison, which was now very expensive and difficult to obtain, had been replaced by more reliable methods of extermination – revolvers, bacteria, etc. Dr Igor, a natural romantic, had rescued this name from obscurity and given it to the disease of the soul he had managed to diagnose, and whose discovery would soon amaze the world.

It was odd that no one had ever described Vitriol as a mortal poison, although most of the people affected could identify its taste, and they referred to the process of poisoning as Bitterness. To a greater or lesser degree, everyone had some Bitterness in their organism, just as we are all carriers of the tuberculosis bacillus. But these two illnesses only attack when the patient is debilitated; in the case of Bitterness, the right conditions for the disease occur when the person becomes afraid of so-called 'reality'.

Certain people, in their eagerness to construct a world which no external threat can penetrate, build exaggeratedly high defences against the outside world, against new people, new places, different experiences, and leave their inner world stripped bare. It is there that Bitterness begins its irrevocable work.

The will was the main target of Bitterness (or Vitriol, as Dr Igor preferred to call it). The people attacked by this malaise began to lose all desire, and, within a few years, they became unable to leave their world, where they had spent enormous reserves of energy constructing high walls in order to make reality what they wanted it to be.

In order to avoid external attack, they had also deliberately limited internal growth. They continued going to work, watching television, having children, complaining about the traffic, but these things happened automatically, unaccompanied by any particular emotion, because, after all, everything was under control.

The great problem with poisoning by Bitterness was that the passions – hatred, love, despair, enthusiasm, curiosity – also ceased to manifest themselves. After a while, the embittered person felt no desire at all. They lacked the will either to live or to die, that was the problem.

That is why embittered people find heroes and madmen a perennial source of fascination, for they have no fear of life or death. Both heroes and madmen are indifferent to danger and will forge ahead regardless of what other people say. The madman committed suicide, the hero offered himself up to martyrdom in the name of a cause, but both would die, and the embittered would spend many nights and days remarking on the absurdity and the glory of both. It was the only moment when the embittered person had the energy to clamber up his defensive walls and peer over at the world outside, but then his hands and feet would grow tired and he would return to daily life.

The chronically embittered person only noticed his illness once a week, on Sunday afternoons. Then, with no work or routine to relieve the symptoms, he would feel that something was very wrong, since he found the peace of those endless afternoons infernal and felt only a keen sense of constant irritation.

Monday would arrive, however, and the embittered man would immediately forget his symptoms, although he would curse the fact that he never had time to rest and would complain that the weekends always passed far too quickly.

From the social point of view, the only advantage of the disease was that it had become the norm, and internment was no longer necessary, except in cases where the poisoning was so serious that the patient's behaviour began to affect others. Most embittered people, though, could continue to live outside, constituting no threat to society or to others, since, because of the high walls with which they had surrounded themselves, they were totally isolated from the world, even though they appeared to participate in it.

Dr Sigmund Freud had discovered the libido and a cure for the problems it caused, in the form of psychoanalysis. Apart from discovering the existence of Vitriol, Dr Igor needed to prove that a cure for it was also possible. He wanted to leave his mark on the history of medicine, although he had no illusions about the difficulties he would face when it came to publishing his ideas, for 'normal' people were contented with their lives and would never admit to the existence of such an illness, whilst the 'sick' fed a gigantic industry of mental hospitals, laboratories, congresses, etc.

'I know the world will not recognise my efforts,' he said to himself, proud of being misunderstood. After all, that was the price every genius had to pay.

'Is there anything wrong, doctor?' asked the girl. 'You seem to have drifted off into the world of your patients.'

Dr Igor ignored the disrespectful comment.

'You can go now,' he said.

Veronika didn't know if it was day or night. Dr Igor had the light on, but then he did every morning. It was only when she reached the corridor and saw the moon that she realised she had slept far longer than she had thought.

On the way to the ward, she noticed a framed photograph on the wall: it was of the main square in Ljubljana, before the statue of the poet Prešeren had been put up; it showed couples strolling, probably on a Sunday.

She looked at the date on the photograph: the summer of 1910.

The summer of 1910. There were all those people, whose children and grandchildren had already died, frozen in one particular moment of their lives.The women wore voluminous dresses and the men were all wearing hat, jacket, gaiters, tie (or that coloured piece of cloth as the mad call it) and carrying an umbrella under one arm.

And how hot would it have been then? The temperature must have been what it would be today in summer, thirty-five degrees in the shade. If an Englishman turned up in clothing more suited to the heat – in Bermuda shorts and shirtsleeves – what would those people think?

'He must be mad.'

She had understood perfectly what Dr Igor meant, just as

she understood that, although she had always felt loved and protected, there had been one missing element that would have transformed that love into a blessing: she should have allowed herself to be a little madder.

Her parents would still have loved her, but, afraid of hurting them, she had not dared to pay the price of her dream, the dream that was buried in the depths of her memory, although sometimes it was awoken by a concert or by a beautiful record she happened to hear. Whenever her dream was awoken, though, the feeling of frustration was so intense that she immediately sent it back to sleep again.

Veronika had known since childhood that her true vocation was to be a pianist.

This was something she had felt ever since her first lesson, at twelve. Her teacher had recognised her talent too and had encouraged her to become a professional. However, whenever she had felt pleased about a competition she had just won and said to her mother that she intended giving up everything and dedicating herself to the piano, her mother would look at her fondly and say: 'No one makes a living playing the piano, my love.'

'But you were the one who wanted me to have lessons.'

'To develop your artistic gifts, that's all. A husband likes that kind of thing in a wife; he can show you off at parties. Forget about being a pianist, and go and study law, that's the profession of the future.'

Veronika did as her mother asked, sure that her mother had enough experience of life to understand reality. She finished her studies, went to university, got a good degree, but ended up working as a librarian.

'I should have been madder.' But, as doubtless happens with most people, she had found this out too late.

She was about to continue on her way, when someone took her by the arm. The powerful sedative was still flowing in her veins; that's why she didn't react when Eduard, the schizophrenic, delicately began to lead her in a different direction – towards the lounge.

The moon was still new and Veronika had already sat down at the piano – in response to Eduard's silent request – when she heard a voice coming from the refectory, someone speaking with a foreign accent which Veronika could not remember having heard in Villete before.

'I don't want to play the piano just now, Eduard. I want to know what's going on in the world, what they're talking about over there, who that man is.'

Eduard smiled, perhaps not understanding a word she was saying, but she remembered what Dr Igor had said: schizophrenics could move in and out of their separate realities.

'I'm going to die,' she went on, hoping that her words were making sense to him. 'Today, death brushed my face with its wing and will probably be knocking at my door if not tomorrow, then soon afterwards. It's not a good idea for you to get used to listening to the piano every night.

'No one should let themselves get used to anything, Eduard. Look at me, I was beginning to enjoy the sun again, the mountains, even life's problems, I was beginning to accept that the meaninglessness of life was no one's fault but mine. I wanted to see the main square in Ljubljana again, to feel hatred and love, despair and tedium, all those simple, foolish things that make up everyday life, but which give pleasure to your existence. If one day I could get out of here, I would allow myself to be mad, because everyone is, indeed, the maddest are the ones who don't know they're mad, but keep repeating what others tell them to.

'But none of that's possible, do you see? In the same way, you can't spend the whole day waiting for night to come and for one of the patients to play the piano, because soon that will end. My world and yours are about to come to an end.'

She got up, tenderly touched the boy's face and then went to the refectory.

When she opened the door, she came upon an unusual scene; the tables and chairs had been pushed back against the walls, forming a large central space. There, sitting on the floor, were the members of the Fraternity, listening to a man in a suit and tie.

'...then they invited Nasrudin, the great master of the Sufi tradition, to give a lecture,' he was saying.

When the door opened, everyone in the room looked at Veronika. The man in the suit turned to her.

'Sit down.'

She sat down on the floor, next to Mari, the white-haired woman who had been so aggressive on their first encounter. To Veronika's surprise, Mari gave her a welcoming smile.

The man in the suit went on:

'Nasrudin arranged to give a lecture at two o'clock in the afternoon, and it looked set to be a great success: the thousand seats were completely sold out and more than seven hundred people were left outside, watching the lecture on closed-circuit television.

'At two o'clock precisely, an assistant of Nasrudin's came in, saying that, for unavoidable reasons, the lecture would begin late. Some got up indignantly, asked for their money back and left. Even so, a lot of people remained both inside and outside the lecture hall.

'By four in the afternoon, the Sufi master had still not

appeared and people gradually began to leave the place, picking up their money at the box office. The working day was coming to an end, it was time to go home. When it was six o'clock, the original one thousand seven hundred spectators had dwindled to less than a hundred.

'At that moment, Nasrudin came in. He appeared to be extremely drunk and began to flirt with a beautiful young woman sitting in the front row.

'Astonished, the people who had remained behind began to feel indignant. How could the man behave like that after making them wait four solid hours? There were some disapproving murmurs, but the Sufi master ignored them. He went on, in a loud voice, to say how sexy the young woman was, and invited her to go with him to France.'

Some teacher, thought Veronika. Just as well I've never believed in such things.

'After cursing the people who were complaining, Nasrudin tried to get up, but fell heavily to the floor. Disgusted, more people decided to leave, saying it was pure charlatanism, that they would denounce the degrading spectacle to the press.

'Only nine people remained. As soon as the final group of outraged spectators had left, Nasrudin got up; he was completely sober, his eyes glowed, and he had about him an air of great authority and wisdom. "Those of you who stayed are the ones who will hear me," he said. "You have passed through the two hardest tests on the spiritual road: the patience to wait for the right moment and the courage not to be disappointed with what you encounter. It is you I will teach."

'And Nasrudin shared with them some of the Sufi techniques.'

The man paused and took a strange flute out of his pocket.

'Let's take a short break now, and then we'll do our meditation.'

The members of the group stood up. Veronika didn't know what to do.

'You get up too,' said Mari, grabbing her hand. 'We've got a five-minute break.'

'I'll leave, I don't want to be in the way.'

Mari led her to one corner.

'Haven't you learned anything, not even with the approach of death? Stop thinking all the time that you're in the way, that you're bothering the person next to you. If people don't like it, they can complain. And if they don't have the courage to complain, that's their problem.'

'That day, when I came over to you, I was doing something I'd never dared to do before.'

'And you allowed yourself to be cowed by a joke made by a mad person. Why didn't you just stick to your guns? What did you have to lose?'

'My dignity, by being where I wasn't welcome.'

'What's dignity? It's wanting everyone to think you're good, well-behaved, full of love for your fellow man. Have some respect for nature, watch a few films about animals and see how they fight for their own space. We all heartily approved of that slap of yours.'

Veronika did not have any more time to spend fighting for space, and so she changed the subject and asked who the man in the suit was.

'You're improving,' laughed Mari. 'You now ask questions without worrying about whether you're being indiscreet or not. He's a Sufi master.'

'What does Sufi mean?'

'Wool.'

Veronika didn't understand. Wool?

'Sufism is the spiritual tradition of the dervishes. Its teachers never strive to show how wise they are, and their disciples go into a trance by performing a kind of whirling dance.'

'What's the point of that?'

'I'm not quite sure, but our group has resolved to investigate all prohibited experiences. All my life, the government taught us that the only purpose of searching for a spiritual meaning to life was to make people forget about their real problems. Now tell me this: wouldn't you say that trying to understand life was a real problem?'

Yes, it was, although Veronika wasn't sure any more what the word 'real' meant.

The man in the suit – a Sufi master, according to Mari – asked them all to sit in a circle. From a vase he removed all the flowers but one, a single red rose, and this he placed in the centre of the group.

'You see how far we've come,' said Veronika to Mari. 'Some madman decided it was possible to grow flowers in winter, and nowadays, throughout Europe, we have roses all year round. Do you think even a Sufi master, with all his knowledge, could do that?'

Mari seemed to guess her thoughts.

'Save your criticisms for later.'

'I'll try to, although all I have is the present, and a very brief one too it seems.'

'That's all anyone has, and it's always very brief, although, of course, some people believe they have a past where they can accumulate things and a future where they will accumulate still more. By the way, speaking of the present moment, do you masturbate a lot?'

Although still under the effects of the sedative she had been given, Veronika was immediately reminded of the first words she had heard in Villete.

'When I was first brought here and was still full of tubes

from the artificial respirator, I clearly heard someone asking me if I wanted to be masturbated. What *is* all that about? Why do you people spend your time thinking about such things?'

'It's the same outside; it's just that here we don't need to hide the fact.'

'Was it you who asked me?'

'No, but I think that, as far as pleasure is concerned, you do need to discover how far you can go. Next time, with a little patience, you might be able to take your partner there too, instead of waiting to be guided by him. Even if you have only got two days to live, I don't think you should leave this life without knowing how far you can go.'

'Only if my partner is the schizophrenic who's right now waiting to hear me play the piano again.'

'He's certainly nice-looking.'

The man in the suit interrupted their conversation with a call for silence. He told everyone to concentrate on the rose and to empty their minds.

'The thoughts will come back, but try to push them to one side. You have two choices: to control your mind or to let your mind control you. You're already familiar with the latter experience, allowing yourself to be swept along by fears, neuroses, insecurity, for we all have self-destructive tendencies.

'Don't confuse madness with a loss of control. Remember that in the Sufi tradition, the master – Nasrudin – is the one everyone calls the madman. And it is precisely because his fellow citizens consider him mad that Nasrudin can say whatever he thinks and do whatever he wants. So it was with court jesters in the Middle Ages; they could alert the king to dangers that the ministers would not dare to comment upon, because they were afraid of losing their positions.

'That's how it should be with you; stay mad, but behave like normal people. Run the risk of being different, but learn to do so without attracting attention. Concentrate on this flower and allow the real "I" to reveal itself.'

'What is the real "I"?' asked Veronika. Perhaps everyone else there knew, but what did it matter: she must learn to care less about annoying others.

The man seemed surprised by the interruption, but he answered her question.

'It's what you are, not what others make of you.'

Veronika decided to do the exercise, concentrating as hard as she could on discovering who she was. During those days in Villete, she had felt things she had never before felt with such intensity – hatred, love, fear, curiosity, a desire to live. Perhaps Mari was right: did she really know what it meant to have an orgasm? Or had she only gone as far as men had wanted to take her?

The man started playing the flute. Gradually the music calmed her soul, and she managed to concentrate on the rose. It might have been the effect of the sedative, but the fact was that since she had left Dr Igor's consulting room, she had felt extremely well.

She knew she was going to die soon, why be afraid? It wouldn't help at all, it wouldn't avoid the fatal heart attack; the best plan would be to enjoy the days and hours that remained to her, doing things she had never done before.

The music was soft, and the dim light in the refectory created an almost religious atmosphere. Religion: why didn't she try going deep inside herself and see what remained of her beliefs and her faith?

The music, however, was leading her elsewhere: empty your mind, stop thinking about anything, simply BE. Veronika gave herself up to the experience; she stared at the rose, saw who she was, liked what she saw and felt only regret that she had been so hasty.

When the meditation was over and the Sufi master had left, Mari stayed on for a while in the refectory, talking to the other members of the Fraternity. Veronika said she was tired and left at once; after all, the sedative she had been given that morning had been strong enough to knock out a horse, and yet she had still had strength enough to remain awake all that time.

'That's youth for you; it sets its own limits without even asking if the body can take it. Yet the body always does.'

Mari wasn't tired; she had slept until late, then decided to go for a walk in Ljubljana – Dr Igor required that the members of the Fraternity left Villete every day. She had gone to the cinema and fallen asleep again in her seat, watching a deeply boring film about marital conflict. Was there no other subject? Why always repeat the same stories – husband with lover, husband with wife and sick child, husband with wife, lover and sick child? There were more important things in the world to talk about.

The conversation in the refectory did not last long; the meditation had left the group members feeling relaxed and they were all ready to go back to their wards, apart from Mari, who instead went out into the garden. On the way, she passed the lounge and saw that the young woman had not yet managed to get to bed.

She was playing for Eduard the schizophrenic, who had perhaps been waiting all that time by the piano. Like children, the mad will not budge until their desires have been satisfied.

The air was icy. Mari came back in, grabbed a coat and went out again. Outside, far from the eyes of everyone, she lit a cigarette. She smoked slowly and guiltlessly, thinking about the young woman, the piano music she could hear and life outside the walls of Villete, which was becoming unbearably difficult for everyone.

In Mari's view, this difficulty was due not to chaos or disorganisation or anarchy, but to an excess of order. Society had more and more rules, and laws that contradicted the rules, and new rules that contradicted the laws. People felt too frightened to take even a step outside the invisible regulations that guided everyone's lives.

Mari knew what she was talking about; until her illness had brought her to Villete, she had spent forty years of her life working as a lawyer. She had lost her innocent vision of Justice early on in her career, and had come to understand that the laws had not been created to resolve problems, but in order to prolong quarrels indefinitely.

It was a shame that Allah, Jehovah, God – it didn't matter what name you gave him – did not live in the world today, because if He did, we would still be in Paradise, while He would be mired in appeals, requests, demands, injunctions, preliminary verdicts, and would have to justify to innumerable tribunals His decision to expel Adam and Eve from Paradise for breaking an arbitrary rule with no foundation in law: Of the tree of the knowledge of good and evil thou shalt not eat.

If he had not wanted that to happen, why did he put the tree in the midst of the garden and not outside the walls of

Paradise? If she were called upon to defend the couple, Mari would undoubtedly accuse God of administrative negligence, because, as well as planting the tree in the wrong place, he had failed to surround it with warnings and barriers, had failed to adopt even minimal security arrangements, and had thus exposed everyone to danger.

Mari could also accuse him of inducement to criminal activity, for he had pointed out to Adam and Eve the exact place where the tree was to be found. If he had said nothing, generation upon generation would have passed on this earth without anyone taking the slightest interest in the forbidden fruit, since the tree was presumably in a forest full of similar trees, and therefore of no particular value.

But God had proceeded quite differently. He had devised a rule and then found a way of persuading someone to break it, merely in order to invent Punishment. He knew that Adam and Eve would become bored with perfection and would, sooner or later, test His patience. He set a trap, perhaps because He, Almighty God, was also bored with everything going so smoothly: if Eve had not eaten the apple, nothing of any interest would have happened in the last few billion years.

When the law was broken, God – the Omnipotent Judge – even pretended to pursue them, as if he did not already know every possible hiding place. With the angels looking on, amused by the game (life must have been very dreary for them since Lucifer left Heaven), he began to walk about the garden. Mari thought what a wonderful scene in a suspense movie that episode from the Bible would make: God's footsteps, the couple exchanging frightened glances, the feet suddenly stopping by their hiding place.

'Where art thou?' asked God.

'I heard thy voice in the garden, and I was afraid, because I was naked; and I hid myself,' Adam replied, without knowing that by making this statement, he had confessed himself guilty of a crime.

So, by means of a simple trick, pretending not to know where Adam was nor why he had run away, God got what he wanted. Even so, in order to leave no doubts amongst the audience of angels who were intently watching the episode, he decided to go further.

'Who told thee that thou was naked?' said God, knowing that this question could have only one possible response: because I ate of the tree of the knowledge of good and evil.

With that question, God demonstrated to his angels that he was a just god, and that his condemnation of the couple was based on solid evidence. From then on, it wasn't a matter of whether it was the woman's fault or of their asking for forgiveness: God needed an example, so that no other being, earthly or heavenly, would ever again dare to go against his decisions.

God expelled the couple, and their children paid for the crime too (as still happens with the children of criminals) and thus the judiciary system was invented: the law, the transgression of the law (no matter how illogical or absurd), judgement (in which the more experienced triumphs over the ingenuous) and punishment.

Since all of humanity was condemned with no right of appeal, humankind decided to create a defence mechanism, against the eventuality of God deciding to wield his arbitrary power again. However, millennia of study resulted in so many legal measures that, ultimately, we went too far, and justice became a tangle of clauses, jurisprudence and contradictory texts that no one could quite understand.

So much so that, when God had a change of heart and sent His Son to save the world, what happened? He fell into the hands of the very justice He had invented.

The tangle of laws created such confusion that the Son ended up nailed to a cross. It was no simple trial; he was passed from Ananias to Caiphas, from the priest to Pilate, who alleged that there were insufficient laws in the Roman code. From Pilate to Herod, who, in turn, alleged that the Jewish code did not permit the death sentence. From Herod back to Pilate again, who, looking for a way out, offered the people a juridical deal: he had the Son beaten and then displayed to the people with his wounds, but it didn't work.

Like prosecutors nowadays, Pilate decided to save himself at the expense of the condemned man: he offered to exchange Jesus for Barabbas, knowing that, by then, justice had become a grand spectacle requiring a denouement: the death of the prisoner.

Finally, Pilate used the article of law that gave the judge, and not the person being judged, the benefit of the doubt. He washed his hands, which means: 'I'm not quite sure either way.' It was just another ruse to preserve the Roman juridical system without injuring relations with local magistrates, and even transferring the weight of the decision onto the people, just in case the sentence should cause any problems, and some inspector from the imperial capital came to see for himself what was going on.

Justice. Law. Although both were vital in order to protect the innocent, they did not always work to everyone's liking. Mari was glad to be far from all that confusion, although tonight, listening to the piano, she was not quite so sure that Villete was the right place for her.

'If I were to decide once and for all to leave here, I wouldn't go back to the law. I'm not going to spend my time with mad people who think they're normal and important, but whose sole function in life is to make everything more difficult for others. I'll be a seamstress, an embroiderer, I'll sell fruit outside the Municipal Theatre. I've already made my contribution to the futile madness of the law.'

In Villete you were allowed to smoke, but not to stub your cigarette out on the lawn. With great pleasure, she did what was forbidden, because the great advantage of being there was not having to respect the rules and not even having to put up with any major consequences if you broke them.

She went over to the door. The guard – there was always a guard there, after all, that was the law – nodded to her and opened the door.

'I'm not going out,' she said.

'Lovely piano music,' said the guard. 'I've listened to it nearly every night.'

'It won't last much longer,' she said and walked rapidly away so as not to have to explain.

She remembered what she had read in the young girl's eyes the moment she had come into the refectory: fear.

Fear. Veronika might feel insecurity, shyness, shame, constraint, but why fear? That was only justifiable when confronted by a real threat: ferocious animals, armed attackers, earthquakes, but not a group of people gathered together in a refectory.

'But human beings are like that,' she said. 'We've replaced nearly all our emotions with fear.'

And Mari knew what she was talking about, because that was what had brought her to Villete: panic attacks.

In her room Mari had a veritable library of articles on the subject. Now people talked about it openly, and she had recently seen a German television programme in which people discussed their experiences. In that same programme, a survey revealed that a significant percentage of the population suffers from panic attacks, although most of those affected tried to hide the symptoms, for fear of being considered mad.

But at the time when Mari had her first attack, none of this was known. 'It was absolute hell,' she thought, lighting another cigarette.

The piano was still playing, the girl seemed to have enough energy to play all night.

A lot of the inmates had been affected by the young woman's arrival in the hospital, Mari amongst them. At first, she had tried to avoid her, afraid to awaken the young woman's desire to live; since there was no escape, it was better that she should keep on wanting to die. Dr Igor had let it be known that, even though she would continue to be given daily injections, her physical condition would visibly deteriorate and there would be no way of saving her.

The inmates had understood the message and kept their distance from the condemned woman. However, without anyone knowing quite why, Veronika had begun fighting for her life, and the only two people who approached her were Zedka, who would be leaving tomorrow and didn't talk that much anyway, and Eduard.

Mari needed to have a word with Eduard; he always respected her opinions. Did he not realise he was drawing Veronika back into the world, and that that was the worst thing he could do to someone with no hope of salvation?

She considered a thousand ways of explaining the situation

to him, but all of them would only make him feel guilty, and that she would never do. Mari thought a little and decided to let things run their normal course. She was no longer a lawyer and she did not want to set a bad example by creating new behaviour laws in a place where anarchy should reign.

But the presence of the young woman had touched a lot of people there, and some were ready to rethink their lives. At one of the meetings with the Fraternity, someone had tried to explain what was happening. Deaths in Villete tended to happen suddenly, without giving anyone time to think about it, or after a long illness, when death is always a blessing.

The young woman's case, though, was dramatic because she was so young and because she now wanted to live again, something they all knew to be impossible. Some people asked themselves 'What if that happened to me? I do have a chance to live. Am I making good use of it?'

Some were not bothered with finding an answer; they had long ago given up and now formed part of a world in which neither life nor death, space or time existed. Others, however, were being forced to think hard, and Mari was one of them.

Veronika stopped playing for a moment and looked out at Mari in the garden. She was wearing only a light jacket against the cold night air; did she want to die?

'No, I was the one who wanted to die.'

She turned back to the piano. In the last days of her life, she had finally realised her grand dream: to play with heart and soul, for as long as she wanted and whenever the mood took her. It didn't matter to her that her only audience was a young schizophrenic; he seemed to understand the music, and that was what mattered.

Mari had never wanted to kill herself. On the contrary, five years before, in the same cinema she had visited today, she had watched, horrified, a film about poverty in El Salvador and thought how important her life was. At that time – with her children grown up and making their way in their own professions – she had decided to give up the tedious, unending job of being a lawyer in order to dedicate the rest of her days to working for some humanitarian organisation. The rumours of civil war in the country were growing all the time, but Mari didn't believe them. It was impossible that, at the end of the twentieth century, the European Community would allow a new war at their gates.

On the other side of the world, however, there was no shortage of tragedies, and one of those tragedies was El Salvador's, where starving children were forced to live on the streets and turn to prostitution.

'It's terrible,' she said to her husband, who was sitting in the seat next to her.

He nodded.

Mari had been putting off the decision for a long time, but perhaps now was the moment to talk to him. They had been given all the good things that life could possibly offer them: a home, work, good children, modest comforts, interests and culture. Why not do something for others for a change? Mari had contacts in the Red Cross and she knew that volunteers were desperately needed in many parts of the world.

She was tired of struggling with bureaucracy and law suits, unable to help people who had spent years of their lives trying to resolve problems not of their own making. Working with the Red Cross, though, she would see immediate results.

She decided that, when they left the cinema, she would invite her husband for a coffee so that they could discuss the idea.

Just as a Salvadorean government official appeared on screen to offer a bored excuse for some new injustice, Mari suddenly noticed her heart beating faster.

She told herself it was nothing. Perhaps the stuffy atmosphere in the cinema was getting to her; if the symptoms persisted she would go out to the foyer to get a breath of fresh air.

But events took on their own momentum; her heart began beating faster and faster, and she broke out in a cold sweat.

She felt afraid and tried hard to concentrate on the film, in an attempt to dispel any negative thoughts, but realised she could no longer follow what was happening on the screen. Mari could see the images and the subtitles, but she seemed to have entered a completely different reality, where everything going on around her seemed strange and out of kilter, as if taking place in a world she did not know.

'I don't feel well,' she said to her husband.

She had put off making that remark as long as possible, because it meant admitting that there was something wrong, but she could not hold out any longer.

'Let's go outside,' he said.

When he took his wife's hand to help her to her feet, he noticed it was ice cold.

'I don't think I can get that far. Please, tell me what's happening to me.'

Her husband felt afraid too. Sweat was pouring down Mari's face and there was a strange light in her eyes.

'Keep calm. I'll go out and call a doctor.'

She was gripped by despair. What he said made absolute sense, but everything – the cinema, the semi-darkness, the people sitting side by side staring up at the brilliant screen – all of it seemed so threatening. She was certain she was alive, she could even touch the life around her as if it were something solid. And that had never happened to her before.

'On no account leave me here alone. I'll get up and go out with you, but take it slowly.'

They both made their apologies to the people in the same row as them, and began walking to the exit at the back of the cinema. Mari's heart was now beating furiously, and she was certain, absolutely certain, that she would never get out of that place. Everything she did, every gesture she made – placing one foot in front of the other, saying 'excuse me', holding on to her husband's arm, breathing in and out – seemed terrifyingly conscious and deliberate.

She had never felt so frightened in her life.

'I'm going to die right here in this cinema.'

And she was convinced she knew what was happening, because, many years before, a friend of hers had died in a cinema of a cerebral aneurism.

Cerebral aneurisms are like time bombs. They are tiny varicose veins that form along the arteries – like the ballooning you get on worn tyres – and they can remain there undetected during a whole lifetime. No one knows if they've got an aneurism, unless it's discovered accidentally, for example, after a brain scan carried out for other reasons, or at the moment when it actually ruptures, flooding everything with blood, leaving the person in an immediate state of coma, usually followed shortly by death.

While she was walking down the aisle of the dark cinema, Mari remembered the friend she had lost. The strangest thing, though, was the effect this ruptured aneurism was having on her perception. She seemed to have been transported to a different planet, seeing each familiar thing as if for the first time.

And then there was the terrifying, inexplicable fear, the sheer panic of being alone on that other planet. Death.

'I must stop thinking. I'll pretend that everything's all right and then everything will be.'

She tried to act naturally and, for a few seconds, the sense of oddness diminished. The two minutes that elapsed between first feeling the palpitations and reaching the exit with her husband were the most terrifying two minutes of her life.

When they reached the brightly-lit foyer, however, everything seemed to start up again. The colours were so garish, the noises from the street seemed to rush in on her from all sides, and everything seemed utterly unreal. She started to notice certain details for the first time, for example, the clarity of vision that covers only the small area on which we fix our gaze, while the rest remains completely unfocused.

There was more. She knew that everything she could see around her was just a scene created by electrical impulses inside her brain, using light impulses that passed through a gelatinous organ called the eye.

No, she must stop thinking. That way madness lay.

By then, her fear of an aneurism had passed; she had managed to get out of the cinema and was still alive. The friend who had died, on the other hand, never even had time to leave her seat.

'I'll call an ambulance,' said her husband, when he saw his wife's ashen face and bloodless lips.

'Call a taxi,' she said, hearing the sounds leaving her mouth, conscious of the vibration of each vocal cord.

Going to hospital would mean accepting that she really was seriously ill and Mari was determined to do her utmost to restore everything to normality.

They left the foyer, and the icy cold air seemed to have a positive effect; Mari recovered some control over herself, although the inexplicable feelings of panic and terror persisted. While her husband was desperately trying to find a taxi, which were scarce at that time of day, she sat down on the kerb and tried not to look at her surroundings: the children playing, the buses passing, the music coming from a nearby funfair, all seemed absolutely surreal, frightening, alien.

Finally, a taxi appeared.

'To the hospital,' said her husband, helping his wife in.

'Please, let's just go home,' she said. She didn't want any more strange places, she was desperately in need of familiar, ordinary things that might diminish the fear she was feeling.

While the taxi was driving them home, her heart rate gradually slowed and her temperature began to return to normal.

'I'm beginning to feel better,' she said to her husband. 'It must have been something I ate.'

When they reached home, the world again seemed exactly as it had been since her childhood. When she saw her husband go over to the phone, she asked him what he was doing.

'I'm going to call a doctor.'

'There's no need. Look at me, I'm fine.'

The colour had returned to her cheeks, her heart was beating normally and the uncontrollable fear had vanished.

Mari slept heavily that night and woke convinced that someone must have put some drug in the coffee they had drunk before they went into the cinema. It was a dangerous prank, and she was fully prepared, at the end of the afternoon, to call the prosecutor and go to the bar to try and find the person responsible.

She went to work, read through several pending law suits and tried to occupy herself with various other tasks, for the experience of the previous day had left a residue of fear, and she wanted to prove to herself that it would never happen again.

She discussed the film on El Salvador with one of her colleagues and mentioned in passing that she was fed up with doing the same thing every day.

'Perhaps it's time I retired.'

'You're one of the best lawyers we've got,' said the colleague. 'Besides, law is one of the few professions where age is in your favour. Why not take a long holiday instead? I'm sure you'd come back to work with renewed energy.'

'I want to do something completely different with my life. I want to have an adventure, help other people, do something I've never done before.'

The conversation ended there. She went down to the square, had lunch in a more expensive restaurant than the one she normally went to, and returned to the office early. That moment marked the beginning of her withdrawal.

The rest of the employees had still not come back, and Mari took the opportunity to look over the work still on her desk. She opened the drawer to take out the pencil which she always kept in the same place and she couldn't find it. For a fraction of a second, it occurred to her that her failure to put the pencil back in its proper place was an indication that she was perhaps behaving oddly.

That was enough to make her heart start pounding again, and the terror of the previous night returned in force.

Mari was frozen to the spot. The sun was coming in through the shutters, lending a brighter, more aggressive tone to everything about her, but she again had the feeling that she was about to die at any minute. It was all so strange; what was she doing in that office?

'I don't believe in you, God, but please, help me.'

Again she broke out in a cold sweat and realised that she was unable to control her fear. If someone came in at that moment, they would notice her frightened eyes and she would be lost.

'Cold air.'

The cold air had made her feel better the previous night, but how could she get as far as the street? Once more she was noticing each detail of what was happening to her – her breathing rate (there were moments when she felt that if she did not make a special effort to inhale and exhale, her body would be incapable of doing so itself), the movement of her head (the images succeeded each other as if there were television cameras whirring inside it), her heart beating faster and faster, her body bathed in a cold, sticky sweat.

And then the terror, an awful, inexplicable fear of doing anything, of taking a single step, of leaving the chair she was sitting in.

'It will pass.'

It had passed last time, but now she was at work, what could she do? She looked at the clock and it seemed to her an absurd mechanism, two needles turning on the same axis, indicating a measurement of time that no one had ever explained: why twelve and not ten, like all our other measurements?

'I mustn't think about these things, they make me crazy.'

Crazy. Perhaps that was the right word to describe what was wrong with her. Summoning all her willpower, she got to her feet and made her way to the toilets. Fortunately, the office was still empty and, in a minute that seemed to last an eternity, she managed to reach them. She splashed her face with water, and the feeling of strangeness diminished, although the fear remained.

'It will pass,' she said to herself. 'Yesterday it did.'

She remembered that, the day before, the whole thing had lasted about thirty minutes. She locked herself in one of the toilets, sat on the toilet seat and put her head between her knees. That position, however, seemed only to amplify the sound of her heart beating and Mari immediately sat up again.

'It will pass.'

She stayed there, thinking that she no longer knew who she was, that she was hopelessly lost. She heard the sound of people coming in and out of the toilets, taps being turned on and off, pointless conversations about banal subjects. More than once someone tried to open the door of the cubicle where she was sitting, but she said something in a murmur and no one insisted. The noise of toilets flushing was like some horrendous force of nature, capable of demolishing an entire building and sweeping everyone down into hell.

But, as she had foreseen, the fear passed off and her heartbeat returned to normal. It was just as well that her secretary was incompetent enough not even to notice her absence, otherwise the whole office would have been in the toilets asking if she was all right.

When she saw that she had regained control of herself, Mari opened the cubicle door, again splashed her face with water for a long time and went back to the office.

'You haven't got any make-up on,' said a trainee. 'Do you want to borrow some of mine?'

Mari didn't even bother to reply. She went into the office, picked up her handbag and her personal belongings, and told her secretary that she would be spending the rest of the day at home.

'But you've got loads of appointments,' protested her secretary.

'You don't give orders, you receive them. Do exactly as I say, and cancel the appointments.'

The secretary stared at this woman with whom she had been working for nearly three years, and who had never once been rude to her before. Something must be seriously wrong with her, perhaps someone had told her that her husband was at home with his lover, and she wanted to catch them *in flagrante*.

'She's a good lawyer, she knows what she's doing,' said the girl to herself. Doubtless tomorrow she would come and apologise to her.

There was no tomorrow. That night, Mari had a long conversation with her husband and described all the symptoms she had experienced. Together, they reached the conclusion that the palpitations, the cold sweats, the feelings of displacement, impotence, lack of control, could all be summed up in one word: fear. Together, husband and wife pondered what was happening. He thought it might be a brain tumour, but he didn't say anything. She thought she was having premonitions of some terrible event, but she didn't say anything either. They tried to find some common ground for discussion, like logical, reasonable, mature people.

'Perhaps you'd better have some tests done.'

Mari agreed, on one condition, that no one, not even their children, should know anything about it.

The next day she applied for and was given thirty days' unpaid leave from the office. Her husband thought of taking her to Austria where there were many eminent specialists in disorders of the brain, but she refused to leave the house; the attacks were becoming more frequent and lasted longer.

With great difficulty, with Mari dosed up on tranquillisers, the two of them managed to get as far as a hospital in Ljubljana where Mari underwent a vast range of tests. Nothing unusual was found, not even an aneurism – a source of consolation to Mari for the rest of her life.

The panic attacks continued however. While her husband did the shopping and the cooking, Mari obsessively cleaned the house every day, just to keep her mind fixed on other things. She started reading all the psychiatry books she could find, only immediately to put them down again because she seemed to recognise her own malaise in each of the illnesses they described.

The worst of it was that, although the attacks were no longer a novelty, she still felt the same intense fear and sense of alienation from reality, the same loss of self-control. In addition, she started to feel guilty about her husband, obliged to do his own job as well as all the housework, cleaning apart.

As time passed, and the situation remained unresolved, Mari began to feel and express a deep irritation. The slightest thing made her lose her temper and start shouting, then sob hysterically.

After her thirty days' leave was over, one of Mari's colleagues turned up at the house. He had phoned every day, but Mari either didn't answer the phone or else asked her husband to say she was busy. That afternoon, he simply stood there ringing the bell until she opened the front door.

Mari had had a quiet morning. She made some tea and they talked about the office, and he asked her when she would be coming back to work.

'Never.'

He remembered their conversation about El Salvador.

'You've always worked hard, and you have the right to choose what you want to do,' he said, with no rancour in his voice. 'But I think that, in cases such as these, work is the best therapy. Do some travelling, see the world, go wherever you think you might be useful, but the doors of the office are always open, awaiting your return.'

When she heard this, Mari burst into tears, which she often did now, with great ease.

Her colleague waited for her to calm down. Like a good lawyer, he didn't ask anything; he knew he had more chance of getting a reply to his silence than to any question.

And so it was. Mari told him the whole story, from what had happened in the cinema to her recent hysterical attacks on her husband, who had given her so much support.

'I'm mad,' she said.

'Possibly,' he replied, with an all-knowing air, but with real tenderness in his voice. 'In that case, you have two options: either get some treatment or continue being ill.'

'There isn't any treatment for what I'm feeling. I'm still in full possession of all my mental faculties and I'm worried because this situation has gone on now for such a long time. I don't haven't any of the classic symptoms of madness, like withdrawal from reality, apathy or uncontrolled aggression, just fear.'

'That's what all mad people say, that they're perfectly normal.'

The two of them laughed and she made some more tea. They talked about the weather, the success of Slovenian independence, the growing tensions between Croatia and Yugoslavia. Mari watched TV all day and was very well informed.

Before saying goodbye, her colleague touched on the subject again.

'They've just opened a new hospital in the city,' he said, 'backed by foreign money and offering first-class treatment.'

'Treatment for what?'

'Imbalances, shall we say. And excessive fear is definitely an imbalance.'

Mari promised to think about it, but she still took no real decision. She continued to have panic attacks for another month, until she realised that not only her personal life but her marriage was on the point of collapse. Again she asked for some tranquillisers and again she managed to set foot outside the house, for only the second time in sixty days.

She took a taxi and went to the new hospital. On the way, the driver asked if she was going to visit someone.

'They say it's very comfortable, but apparently they've got some real nutters in there too, and part of the treatment includes electric shocks.'

'I'm going to visit someone,' said Mari.

It took only an hour of conversation for Mari's two months of suffering to come to an end. The director of the hospital – a tall man with dyed hair, who answered to the name of Dr Igor – explained that it was merely a panic disorder, a recently recognised illness in the annals of world psychiatry.

'That doesn't mean it's a new illness,' he explained, taking care to make himself clear.

'What happens is that the people affected by it tend to hide, afraid they'll be mistaken for mad people. It's just a chemical imbalance in the body, as is depression.'

Dr Igor wrote her a prescription and told her to go back home.

'I don't want to go back now,' said Mari. 'Even after all you've told me, I won't have the courage to go out into the street. My marriage has become a hell, and my husband needs time to recover from these months he's spent looking after me.'

As always happened in such cases – because the shareholders wanted to keep the hospital working at full capacity – Dr Igor accepted her as a patient, although making it absolutely clear that it wasn't necessary.

Mari received the necessary medication, along with the appropriate psychiatric treatment, and the symptoms diminished and finally disappeared altogether.

During that time, however, the story of her internment in the hospital went the rounds of the small city of Ljubljana. Her colleague, a friend of many years, and companion of who knows how many moments of joy and trepidation, came to visit her in Villete. He complimented her on her courage in following his advice and getting help, but he then went on to explain the real reason for his visit:

'Perhaps it really is time you retired.'

Mari knew what lay behind those words: no one was going to entrust their affairs to a lawyer who had been a mental patient.

'You said that work was the best therapy. I need to come back, even if only for a short time.'

She waited for a response, but he said nothing. Mari went on:

'You were the one who suggested I get treatment. When I was considering retirement, my idea was to leave on a high note, fulfilled, having made a free, spontaneous decision. I don't want to leave my job just like that, defeated. At least give me a chance to win back my self-esteem, and then I'll ask to retire.'

The lawyer cleared his throat.

'I suggested you get treatment, I didn't say anything about going into hospital.'

'But it was a question of survival. I was too afraid to go out into the street, my marriage was falling apart.'

Mari knew she was wasting her words. Nothing she could say would persuade him; after all, it was the prestige of the office that was at risk. Even so, she tried once more.

'Inside here, I've lived with two sorts of people: those who have no chance of ever going back into society and those who are completely cured, but who prefer to pretend to be mad rather than face up to life's responsibilities. I want and need to learn to like myself again, I have to convince myself that I'm capable of taking my own decisions. I can't be pushed into decisions not of my own making.'

'We're allowed to make a lot of mistakes in our lives,' said her colleague, 'except the mistake that destroys us.'

There was no point in continuing the conversation; in his opinion, Mari had committed the fatal error.

Two days later, she received a visit from another lawyer, this time from a different practice, her now ex-colleagues' greatest rival. Mari cheered up; perhaps he knew she was free to take up a new post, and there was a chance she could regain her place in the world.

The lawyer came into the visiting room, sat down opposite her, smiled, asked if she was feeling better and then took various papers out of his briefcase.

'I'm here at your husband's request,' he said.

'This is an application for divorce. Obviously, though, he'll continue to pay all your hospital bills for as long as you remain in here.'

This time Mari did not attempt to argue. She signed everything, even though she knew that, in accordance with the law she had studied and practised, she could prolong the quarrel indefinitely. She then went straight to see Dr Igor and told him that her symptoms had returned.

Dr Igor knew she was lying, but he nevertheless extended her internment for an indefinite period.

Veronika decided she would have to go to bed, but Eduard was still standing by the piano.

'I'm tired, Eduard. I need to sleep.'

She would like to continue playing for him, dredging up from her anaesthetised memory all the sonatas, requiems and adagios she used to know, because he knew how to admire without appearing to demand anything of her. But her body could take no more.

He was so good-looking. If only he would take one step outside his world and see her as a woman, then her last nights on this earth might be the most beautiful of her entire life: Eduard was the only one capable of understanding that Veronika was an artist. Through the pure emotion of a sonata or a minuet she had forged a bond with this man such as she had never known with anyone else.

Eduard was the ideal man, sensitive, educated; a man who had destroyed an indifferent world in order to recreate it again in his head, this time with new colours, new characters, new stories. And this new world included a woman, a piano and a moon that was continuing to grow.

'I could fall in love right now and give everything I have to you,' she said, knowing that he couldn't understand her. 'All you ask from me is a little music, but I am much more than I ever thought I was, and I would like to share other things with you that I have only just begun to understand.'

Eduard smiled. Had he understood? Veronika felt afraid – all the manuals of good behaviour say that you should never speak of love so directly, and never to a man you barely know. But she decided to continue, because she had nothing to lose.

'You're the only man on the face of the Earth with whom I could fall in love, Eduard, for the simple reason that, when I die, you will not miss me. I don't know what a schizophrenic feels, but I'm sure they never miss anyone.

'Perhaps, to begin with, you'll miss the fact that there's no more night music, but the moon will still rise, there'll be someone willing to play sonatas for you, especially in a hospital, where each and every one of us is a "lunatic".'

She didn't quite know what the relationship was between mad people and the moon, but it must be a strong one, if they used a word like that to describe the mad.

'And I won't miss you either, Eduard, because I will be dead, far from here. And since I'm not afraid of losing you, I don't care what you think or don't think about me. Tonight I played for you like a woman in love. It was wonderful. It was the best moment of my entire life.'

She looked at Mari outside in the garden. She remembered her words. And again she looked at the man standing in front of her.

Veronika took off her sweater and moved closer to Eduard. If she was going to do something, let it be now. Mari would put up with the cold out there for a long time and only then would she come back in.

He stepped back. The question in his eyes was this: when was she going to play the piano again? When would she play a new piece of music to fill his soul with the same colour, pain, suffering and joy of those mad composers who had leapt the generations with their work?

'The woman outside told me to masturbate and to find out how far I could go. Could I really go farther than I've ever been before?'

She took his hand and tried to pull him towards the sofa, but Eduard politely declined. He preferred to remain standing where he was, beside the piano, waiting patiently for her to play again.

Veronika was disconcerted at first and then realised that she had nothing to lose. She was dead, what was the point of continuing to feed the fears or preconceptions that had always limited her life? She took off her blouse, her trousers, her bra, her pants, and stood before him naked.

Eduard laughed. She didn't know why, she merely noted that he had laughed. Delicately, she took his hand and placed it on her genitals; his hand remained there, immobile. Veronika gave up the idea and removed his hand.

Something was exciting her far more than any physical contact with this man: the fact that she could do whatever she wanted, that there were no limits. Apart from the woman outside, who might come back in at any moment, nobody else would be awake.

Her blood began to race, and the cold – which she had felt when she took off her clothes – was fading. Veronika and Eduard were both standing up, face to face, she naked, he fully clothed. Veronika slid her own hand down to her genitals and started to masturbate; she had done it before, either alone or with certain partners, but never in a situation like this, where the man showed no apparent interest in what was happening.

And this was exciting, very exciting. Standing up, legs apart, Veronika was touching her genitals, her breasts, her hair, surrendering herself as she had never done before, not because she wanted to see Eduard leave his distant world, but because this was something she had never experienced before.

She started talking, saying unthinkable things, things that her parents, her friends, her ancestors would have considered absolute filth. Her first orgasm came and she bit her lips so as not to cry out with pleasure.

Eduard was looking at her. There was a different light in his eyes, as if he understood, even if it was only the energy, heat, sweat and smell that her body gave off. Veronika was still not satisfied. She knelt down and started masturbating again.

She wanted to die of orgasmic pleasure, thinking about and realising everything that had always been forbidden to her: she begged him to touch her, to force her, to use her in any way he wanted. She wished Zedka was there too, because a woman knows how to touch another woman's body better than any man, because she already knows all its secrets.

On her knees before Eduard, who remained standing, she felt possessed, touched, and she used coarse words to describe what she wanted him to do to her. Another orgasm came, stronger than ever, as if everything around her were about to explode. She remembered the heart attack she had had that morning, but what did that matter, she would die in one great explosion of pleasure. She was tempted to touch Eduard – he was there before her – but she did not want to risk spoiling the moment. She was going far, very far, just as Mari had said.

She imagined herself both queen and slave, dominatrix and victim. In her imagination, she was making love with men of all skin colours – white, black, yellow – with homosexuals and beggars. She was anyone's and anyone could do anything to her. She had one, two, three orgasms one after the other. She imagined everything she had never imagined before and she gave herself to all that was most base and most pure. At last, unable to contain herself any longer, she cried out with pleasure, with the pain of all those orgasms, all those men and women who had entered and left her body through the doors of her mind.

She lay down on the ground and stayed there, drenched in sweat, her soul full of peace. She had concealed her hidden desires even from herself, unable to say why, but she needed no answer. It was enough that she had done what she had done: she had surrendered herself.

Gradually, the universe returned to its proper place and Veronika stood up. Eduard had not moved in all that time, but there seemed to be something different about him: there was a tenderness in his eyes, a very human tenderness.

'It was so good that I can see love in everything, even in the eyes of a schizophrenic.'

She was beginning to put her clothes back on, when she felt a third presence in the room.

Mari was there. Veronika didn't know when she had come in or what she had heard or seen, but even so she felt no shame or fear. She merely looked at her distantly, as one does at someone who has come too close.

'I did as you suggested,' she said. 'And I went a long, long way.'

Mari said nothing; she had just been reliving certain vital moments of her past life, and she was feeling slightly uneasy. Perhaps it was time to return to the world, to face up to things out there, to say that everyone could be a member of a great Fraternity, even if they had never been in a mental hospital.

Like this young girl, for example, whose only reason for being in Villete was because she had made an attempt on her own life. She had never known panic, depression, mystical visions, psychoses – the limits to which the mind can take us. Although she had known many men, she had never experienced the most hidden part of her own desires, and the result was that half of her life had been unknown to her. If only everyone could know and live with their inner madness. Would the world be a worse place for it? No, people would be fairer and happier.

'Why did I never do that before?'

'He wants you to play more music,' said Mari, looking at Eduard. 'I think he deserves it.'

'I will, but answer my question first: why did I never do that before? If I'm free, if I can think whatever I choose to think, why have I always avoided imagining forbidden situations?'

'Forbidden? Listen, I was a lawyer and I know the law. I was also a Catholic and I used to know whole sections of the Bible by heart. What do you mean by "forbidden"?'

Mari went over to her and helped her on with her sweater.

'Look me in the eye and never forget what I'm about to tell you. There are only two prohibitions, one according to man's law, the other according to God's. Never force a sexual relationship on anyone, because that is considered to be rape. And never have sexual relations with children, because that is the worst of all sins. Apart from that, you're free. There's always someone who wants exactly what you want.'

Mari didn't have the patience to teach important things to someone who was about to die. With a smile, she said good night and left the room.

Eduard didn't move; he was waiting for the music. Veronika needed to reward him for the immense pleasure he had given her, merely by staying with her and witnessing her madness without horror or repulsion. She sat down at the piano and started to play again.

Her soul was light, and not even the fear of death tormented her now. She had experienced what she had always kept hidden from herself. She had experienced the pleasures of virgin and prostitute, of slave and queen, albeit more slave than queen.

That night, as if by a miracle, all the songs she had known returned to her memory, and she played in order to give Eduard as much pleasure as she herself had experienced.

When he turned on the light, Dr Igor was surprised to see the young woman sitting in the waiting room outside his office.

'It's still very early. And I'm completely booked up all day.'

'I know it's early,' she said. 'And the day hasn't yet begun. I just need to talk for a while, only a short while. I need your help.'

She had dark shadows under her eyes and her hair was dull, the typical symptoms of someone who has spent the whole night awake.

Dr Igor decided to show her into his room.

He asked her to sit down, while he turned on the light and opened the curtains. It would be dawn in less than an hour, and then he would be able to save on electricity; the shareholders were very hot on expenses, however insignificant.

He glanced rapidly through his diary: Zedka had had her last insulin shock and had reacted positively, that is, she had managed to survive that inhuman treatment. Just as well, in this particular case, that Dr Igor had demanded that the hospital council sign a declaration taking full responsibility for the consequences.

He started reading some reports. Two or three patients had behaved aggressively during the night, amongst them, according to the nurses' report, Eduard. He had gone back to his ward at about four in the morning and had refused to take his sleeping tablets. Dr Igor would have to act. However liberal Villete might be inside, it was necessary to preserve its image as a harsh, conservative institution.

'I've got something very important to ask you,' said Veronika.

But Dr Igor ignored her. Picking up his stethoscope, he began to listen to her heart and lungs. He tested her reflexes and examined the back of her retina with a small torch. He saw that there were now almost no signs of Vitriol poisoning, or Bitterness as some preferred to call it.

He immediately went to the phone and asked the nurse to bring in some medication with a complicated name.

'It seems you didn't have your injection last night,' he said.

'But I'm feeling much better.'

'I just have to look at your face: dark shadows under the eyes, tiredness, the lack of immediate reflexes. If you want to make the most of the little time left to you, please do as I say.'

'That's exactly why I'm here. I want to make the most of that little time, but in my own way. How much time have I actually got?'

Dr Igor peered at her over the top of his glasses.

'You can tell me,' she said. 'I'm not afraid or indifferent or anything. I want to live, but I know that's not enough, and I'm resigned to my fate.'

'What is it you want then?'

The nurse came in with the injection. Dr Igor nodded and the nurse gently rolled up the sleeve of Veronika's sweater.

'How much time have I got left?' said Veronika again, while the nurse gave her the injection.

'Twenty-four hours, perhaps less.'

She looked down, and bit her lip, but managed to maintain her composure.

'I want to ask two favours. First, that you give me some medication, an injection or whatever, so that I can stay awake and enjoy every moment that remains of my life. I'm very tired, but I don't want to sleep. I've got a lot to do, things that I always postponed for some future date, in the days when I thought life would last for ever. Things I'd lost interest in, when I started to believe that life wasn't worth living.'

'And what's the second favour?'

'I want to leave here so that I can die outside. I need to visit Ljubljana castle. It's always been there and I've never even had the curiosity to go and see it close to. I need to talk to the woman who sells chestnuts in winter and flowers in the spring. We passed each other so often, and I never once asked her how she was. And I want to go out without a jacket and walk in the snow, I want to find out what extreme cold feels like, I, who was always so well wrapped up, so afraid of catching a cold.

'In short, Dr Igor, I want to feel the rain on my face, to smile at any man I feel attracted to, to accept all the coffees men might buy for me. I want to kiss my mother, tell her I love her, weep in her lap, unashamed of showing my feelings, because they were always there even though I hid them.

'I might go into a church and look at those images that never meant anything to me and see if they say something to me now. If an interesting man invites me out to a club, I'll accept, and I'll dance all night until I drop. Then I'll go to bed with him, but not the way I used to go to bed with other men, trying to stay in control, pretending things I didn't feel. I want to give myself to one man, to the city, to life and, finally, to death.'

When Veronika had finished speaking, there was a heavy silence. Doctor and patient looked each other in the eye, absorbed, perhaps distracted by all the many possibilities that a mere twenty-four hours could offer.

'I'm going to give you some stimulants, but I don't recommend you take them,' Dr Igor said at last. 'They'll keep you awake, but they'll also take away the peace you need in order to experience everything you want to experience.'

Veronika was starting to feel ill; whenever she was given that injection, something bad always happened inside her body.

'You're looking very pale. Perhaps you'd better go to bed, and we'll talk again tomorrow.'

Once more she felt like crying, but she remained in control.

'There won't be a tomorrow, as you well know. I'm tired, Dr Igor, very tired. That's why I asked for the tablets. I spent all night awake, half-desperate, half-resigned. I could succumb to another hysterical attack of fear, as happened yesterday, but what's the point? If I've still got twenty-four hours of life left, and there are so many experiences waiting for me, I decided it would be better to put aside despair.

'Please, Dr Igor, let me live a little of the time remaining to me, because we both know that tomorrow will be too late.'

'Go and sleep,' said the doctor, 'and come back here at midday. Then we'll speak again.'

Veronika saw there was no way out.

'I'll go and sleep and then I'll come back, but could I just talk to you for a few more minutes?'

'It'll have to be a few. I'm very busy today.'

'I'll come straight to the point. Last night, for the first time, I masturbated in a completely uninhibited way. I thought all the things I'd never dared to think, I took pleasure in things that before frightened or repelled me.'

Dr Igor assumed his most professional air. He didn't know where this conversation might lead and he didn't want any problems with his superiors.

'I discovered that I'm a pervert, doctor. I want to know if that played some part in my attempted suicide. There are so many things I didn't know about myself.'

'I just have to give her an answer,' he thought. 'There's no need to call in the nurse to witness the conversation, and avoid any future law suits for sexual abuse.'

'We all want different things,' he replied. 'And our partners do too. What's wrong with that?'

'You tell me.'

'There's everything wrong with it. Because when everyone dreams, but only a few realise their dreams, that makes cowards of us all.'

'Even if those few are right?'

'The person who's right is just the person who's strongest. In this case, paradoxically, it's the cowards who are the brave ones, and they manage to impose their ideas on everyone else.'

Dr Igor didn't want to go any further.

'Now, please, go and rest a little; I have other patients to see. If you do as I say, I'll see what can be done about your second request.'

Veronika left the room. The doctor's next patient was Zedka, who was due to be discharged, but Dr Igor asked her to wait a little; he needed to take a few notes on the conversation he had just had.

In his dissertation about Vitriol, he would have to include a long chapter on sex. After all, so many neuroses and psychoses had their origins in sex. He believed that fantasies were electrical impulses from the brain, which, if not realised, released their energy into other areas.

During his medical studies, Dr Igor had read an interesting treatise on sexual dissidence: sadism, masochism, homosexuality, coprophagy, coprolalia, voyeurism, the list was endless. At first, he considered these things examples of deviant behaviour in a few maladjusted people incapable of having a healthy relationship with their partners.

However, as he advanced in his profession as psychiatrist and talked to his patients, he realised that everyone has an unusual story to tell. His patients would sit down in the comfortable armchair in his office, stare hard at the floor, and begin a long dissertation on what they called 'illnesses' (as if he were not the doctor) or perversions (as if he were not the psychiatrist charged with deciding what was and wasn't perverse).

And one by one, these normal people would describe fantasies that were all to be found in that famous treatise on erotic minorities, a book, in fact, that defended the right of everyone to have the orgasm they chose, as long as it did not violate the rights of their partner.

Women who had studied in convent schools dreamed of being sexually humiliated; men in suits and ties, high-ranking civil servants, told him of the fortunes they spent on Rumanian prostitutes just so that they could lick their feet. Boys in love with boys, girls in love with their fellow schoolgirls. Husbands who wanted to watch their wives having sex with strangers, women who masturbated every time they found some hint that their men had committed adultery. Mothers who had to suppress an impulse to give themselves to the first delivery man who rang the doorbell, fathers who recounted secret adventures with the bizarre transvestites who managed to slip through the strict border controls.

And orgies. It seemed that everyone, at least once in their life, wanted to take part in an orgy.

Dr Igor put down his pen for a moment and thought about himself: what about him? Yes, he would like it too. An orgy, as he imagined it, must be something completely anarchic and joyful, in which the feeling of possession no longer existed, just pleasure and confusion.

Was that one of the main reasons why there were so many people poisoned by bitterness? Marriages restricted to an enforced monotheism, within which, according to studies that Dr Igor kept safely in his medical library, sexual desire disappeared in the third or fourth year of living together. After that, the wife felt rejected and the man felt trapped, and Vitriol, or bitterness, began to eat away at everything.

People talked more openly to a psychiatrist than they did to a priest because a doctor couldn't threaten them with Hell. During his long career as a psychiatrist, Dr Igor had heard almost everything they had to tell him.

To *tell* him, for they rarely *did* anything. Even after several years in the profession, he still asked himself why they were so afraid of being different.

When he tried to find out the reason, the most common responses were: 'My husband would think I was behaving like a prostitute', or, when it was a man: 'My wife deserves my respect.'

The conversation usually stopped there. There was no point saying that everyone has a different sexual profile, as individual as their fingerprints, no one wanted to believe that. It was very dangerous being uninhibited in bed; there was always the fear that the other person might still be a slave to their preconceived ideas.

'I'm not going to change the world,' he said, resignedly, asking the nurse to send in the ex-depressive, Zedka, 'but at least I can say what I think in my thesis.'

Eduard saw Veronika leaving Dr Igor's consulting room and making her way to the ward. He felt like telling her his secrets, opening his heart to her, with the same honesty and freedom with which, the previous night, she had opened her body to him.

It had been one of the severest tests he had been through since he had come to Villete as a schizophrenic. But he had managed to resist, and he was pleased, although his desire to return to the world was beginning to unsettle him.

'Everyone knows this young girl isn't going to last until the end of the week. There'd be no point.'

Or perhaps, precisely because of that, it would be good to share his story with her. For three years, he had spoken only to Mari, and even then he wasn't sure she had entirely understood him; as a mother, she was bound to think his parents were right, that they had just wanted the best for him, that his visions of Paradise were the foolish dreams of an adolescent completely out of touch with the real world.

Visions of Paradise. That was exactly what had led him down into hell, into endless arguments with his family, into such a powerful feeling of guilt that he had felt incapable of doing anything and had finally sought refuge in another world. If it hadn't been for Mari, he would still be living in that separate reality.

Then Mari had appeared; she had taken care of him and made him feel loved again. Thanks to her, Eduard was still capable of knowing what was going on around him.

A few days ago, a young woman the same age as him had sat down at the piano to play the *Moonlight Sonata*. Eduard had once more felt troubled by his visions of Paradise and he couldn't have said if it was the fault of the music or the young woman or the moon or the long time he had spent in Villete.

He followed her as far as the women's ward, to find his way barred by a nurse.

'You can't come in here, Eduard. Go into the garden, it's nearly dawn and it's going to be a lovely day.'

Veronika looked back.

'I'm going to sleep for a bit,' she said gently. 'We'll talk when I wake up.'

Veronika didn't know why, but that young man had become part of her world, or the little that remained of it. She was certain that Eduard was capable of understanding her music, of admiring her talent; even if he couldn't utter a word, his eyes said everything, as they did at that moment, at the door of the ward, speaking of things she didn't want to hear about.

Tenderness. Love.

'Living with mental patients is fast making me mad. Schizophrenics don't feel things like that, not for other human beings.'

Veronika felt like turning back and giving him a kiss, but she didn't; the nurse would see and tell Dr Igor, and the doctor would certainly not allow a woman who kissed schizophrenics to leave Villete.

Eduard looked at the nurse. His attraction for the young girl was stronger than he had thought, but he had to control himself. He would go and ask Mari's advice, she was the only person with whom he shared his secrets. She would doubtless tell him what he wanted to hear, that in such a case, love was both dangerous and pointless. Mari would ask Eduard to stop being so foolish and to go back to being a normal schizophrenic (and then she would giggle gleefully at her own nonsensical words).

He joined the other inmates in the refectory, ate what he was given and went outside for the obligatory walk in the garden. While 'taking the sun' (on that day the temperature was below zero), he tried to approach Mari, but she looked as if she wanted to be left alone. She didn't need to say anything, Eduard knew enough about solitude to respect other people's needs.

A new inmate came over to Eduard. He obviously didn't know anyone yet.

'God punished humanity,' he said. 'He punished it with the plague. However, I saw Him in my dreams and He asked me to come and save Slovenia.'

Eduard started to move away, while the man continued shouting:

'Do you think I'm mad? Then read the gospels. God sent His only Son and His Son has risen again.'

But Edward couldn't hear him any more. He was looking at the mountains beyond and wondering what was happening to him. Why did he feel like leaving there if he had finally found the peace he had so longed for? Why risk shaming his parents again, just when all the family problems were resolved? He began to feel agitated, pacing up and down, waiting for Mari to emerge from her silence so that they could talk, but she seemed as remote as ever.

He knew how to escape from Villete. However strict the security might seem, it was actually full of holes, simply because, once people entered Villete, they felt little desire to leave. On the west side, there was a wall that could quite easily be scaled since it was full of footholds; anyone who wanted to climb it would soon find themselves out in the countryside and, five minutes later, on a road heading north to Croatia. The war was over, brothers were once more brothers, the frontiers were no longer guarded as they had been before; with a little luck, he could be in Belgrade in six hours.

Eduard had already been on that road several times, but he had always decided to go back, because he had still not received the signal to go forward. Now things were different: the signal had finally come in the form of a young woman with green eyes, brown hair and the startled look of someone who thinks they know what they want.

Eduard thought of climbing the wall there and then, of leaving and never being seen in Slovenia again. But the girl was sleeping and he needed at least to say goodbye to her.

When everyone had finished 'taking the sun' and the Fraternity had gathered in the lounge, Eduard joined them.

'What's that madman doing here?' asked the oldest member of the group.

'Leave him alone,' said Mari. 'Anyway, we're mad too.'

They all laughed and started talking about the previous day's lecture. The question was this, could Sufi meditation really change the world? Theories were put forward, as were suggestions, methodologies, contrary ideas, criticisms of the lecturer, ways of improving what had been tested over many centuries.

Eduard was sick of this kind of discussion. These people locked themselves up in a mental hospital and set about saving the world without actually taking any risks because they knew that, outside, they would be thought ridiculous, even if some of their ideas were very practical. Everyone had their own theory about everything, and they believed that their truth was the only one that mattered. They spent days, nights, weeks and years talking, never accepting the fact that, good or bad, an idea only exists when someone tries to put it into practice.

What was Sufi meditation? What was God? What was salvation if, that is, the world needed saving? Nothing. If everyone there – and outside Villete too – just lived their lives and let others do the same, God would be in every moment, in every grain of mustard, in the fragment of cloud that is there and then gone the following moment. God was there and yet people believed they still had to go on looking, because it seemed too simple to accept that life was an act of faith.

He remembered the exercise he had heard the Sufi master teaching while he was waiting for Veronika to come back to the piano: simply look at a rose. What more was necessary?

Yet even after the experience of that deep meditation, even after having been brought so close to a vision of Paradise, there they were, discussing, arguing, criticising and constructing theories.

His eyes met Mari's. She looked away, but Eduard was determined to put an end to that situation once and for all; he went over to her and took her by the arm.

'Stop it, Eduard.'

He could say: 'Come with me.' But he didn't want to do so in front of all those people, who would be surprised at his forthright tone. That's why he preferred to kneel down and look beseechingly up at her.

The men and women laughed.

'You've become a saint for him, Mari,' someone said. 'It must have been yesterday's meditation.'

But Eduard's years of silence had taught him to speak with his eyes; he was able to pour all his energies into them. Just as he was absolutely sure that Veronika had understood his tenderness and love, he knew that Mari would understand his despair, because he really needed her.

She resisted a little longer, then she got up and took him by the hand.

'Let's go for a walk,' she said. 'You're upset.'

They went out into the garden again. As soon as they were at a safe distance, certain that no one could hear them, Eduard broke the silence.

'I've been in Villete for years,' he said. 'I've stopped being an embarrassment to my parents, I've set aside all my ambitions, but still the visions of Paradise remain.'

'I know,' said Mari. 'We've often talked about it, and I know what you're leading up to as well: it's time to leave.'

Eduard glanced up at the sky; did Mari feel the same?

'And it's because of the girl,' said Mari. 'We've seen a lot of people die here, always when they least expected it, and usually after they'd entirely given up on life. But this is the first time we've seen it happening to a young, pretty, healthy person with so much to live for. Veronika is the only one who doesn't want to stay in Villete for ever. And that makes us ask ourselves: What about us? What are we doing here?'

He nodded.

'Then, last night, I too asked myself what I was doing in this hospital. And I thought how very interesting to be down in the square, at the Three Bridges, in the market place opposite the theatre, buying apples and talking about the weather. Obviously, I'd be struggling with a lot of other long-forgotten things, like unpaid bills, problems with neighbours, the ironic looks of people who don't understand me, solitude, my children's carping. But all that is just part of life, I think; and the price you pay for having to deal with those minor problems is far less than the price you pay for not recognising they're yours. I'm thinking of going round to my ex-husband's tonight, just to say "Thank you". What do you think?'

'I don't know. Do you think I should go to my parents' house too and say the same thing?'

'Possibly. Basically, everything that happens in our life is our fault and ours alone. A lot of people go through the same difficulties we went through, and they react completely differently. We looked for the easiest way out: a separate reality.'

Eduard knew that Mari was right.

'I feel like starting to live again, Eduard. I feel like making the mistakes I always wanted to make, but never had the courage to, facing up to the feelings of panic that might well come back, but whose presence will merely weary me, since I know I'm not going to die or faint because of them. I can make new friends and teach them how to be mad too in order to be wise. I'll tell them not to follow the manual of good behaviour but to discover their own lives, desires, adventures and to LIVE. I'll quote from Ecclesiastes to the Catholics, from the Koran to the Muslims, from the Torah to the Jews, from Aristotle to the atheists. I never want to be a lawyer again, but I can use my experience to give lectures about men and women who knew the truth about this existence of ours and whose writings can be summed up in one word: Live. If you live, God will live with you. If you refuse to run his risks, He'll retreat to that distant Heaven and be merely a subject for philosophical speculation. Everyone knows this, but no one takes the first step, perhaps for fear of being called mad. At least, we haven't got that fear, Eduard. We've already been inmates of Villete.'

'The only thing we can't do is stand as candidates for President of the Republic. The opposition would be sure to probe into our past.'

Mari laughed and agreed.

'I'm tired of the life here. I don't know if I'll manage to

overcome my fear, but I've had enough of the Fraternity, of this garden, of Villete, of pretending to be mad.'

'If I do it, will you?'

'You won't do it.'

'I almost did, just a few moments ago.'

'I don't know. I'm tired of all this, but I'm used to it too.'

'When I came here, diagnosed as a schizophrenic, you spent days, months, talking to me and treating me as a human being. I was getting used to the life I'd decided to lead, to the other reality I'd created, but you wouldn't let me. I hated you and now I love you. I want you to leave Villete, Mari, just as I left my separate universe.'

Mari moved off without answering.

In the small and never used library in Villete, Eduard didn't find the Koran or Aristotle or any of the other philosophers that Mari had mentioned. He found instead the words of a poet:

Then I said in my heart, As it happeneth to the fool
so will it happen even to me…
Go thy way, eat thy bread with joy,
and drink thy wine with a merry heart;
for God hath already accepted thy works.
Let thy garments be always white;
and let not thy head lack ointment.
Live joyfully with the wife whom thou lovest
all the days of the life of thy vanity,
which he hath given thee under the sun,
all the days of thy vanity:
for that is thy portion in life,
and in thy labour wherein thou labourest under the sun…

Walk in the ways of thine heart,
and in the sight of thine eyes:
but know thou, that for all these things
God will bring thee into judgement.

'God will bring me into judgement,' said Eduard out loud, 'and I will say: "For a time in my life I stood looking at the wind, I forgot to sow, I did not live joyfully, I did not even drink the wine offered me. But one day, I judged myself ready, and I went back to work. I told men about my visions of Paradise, as did Bosch, Van Gogh, Wagner, Beethoven, Einstein and other madmen before me." Fine, let Him say that I left hospital in order to avoid seeing a young girl dying; she will be there in Heaven, and she will intercede for me.'

'What are you saying?' said the man in charge of the library.

'I want to leave Villete,' said Eduard, in a slightly louder voice than normal. 'I've got things to do.'

The librarian rang a bell, and a few moments later, two nurses appeared.

'I want to leave,' said Eduard again, agitated. 'I'm fine, just let me talk to Dr Igor.'

But the two men already had hold of him, one on each arm. Eduard tried to free himself from the arms of the nurses, though he knew it was useless.

'You're having a bit of a crisis, now just keep calm,' said one of them. 'We'll take care of it.'

Eduard started to struggle.

'Let me talk to Dr Igor. I've got a lot to tell him, I'm sure he'll understand.'

The men were already dragging him towards the ward.

'Let me go,' he was yelling. 'Just let me talk for a minute.'

The way to the ward was through the lounge, and all the other inmates were gathered there. Eduard was struggling and things were starting to look ugly.

'Let him go! He's mad!'

Some laughed, others beat with their hands on chairs and tables.

'This is a mental hospital. No one here is obliged to behave the way you do.'

One of the nurses whispered to the other:

'We'd better give them a fright, otherwise the situation will get completely out of control.'

'There's only one way.'

'Dr Igor won't like it.'

'He'll like it still less if this gang of maniacs start smashing up his beloved hospital.'

Veronika woke up with a start, in a cold sweat. There was a terrible noise outside, and she needed silence to go on sleeping. But the racket continued.

Feeling slightly dizzy, she got out of bed and went into the lounge, just in time to see Eduard being dragged off, while other nurses were rushing in, wielding syringes.

'What are you doing?' she screamed.

'Veronika!'

The schizophrenic had spoken to her. He had said her name. With a mixture of surprise and shame, she tried to approach, but one of the nurses stopped her.

'What are you doing? I'm not here because I'm mad. You can't treat me like this.'

She managed to push the nurse away, while the other inmates continued to shout and kick up what seemed to her a terrifying din. Should she go and find Dr Igor and leave there at once?

'Veronika!'

He had said her name again. Making a superhuman effort, Eduard managed to break free from the two male nurses. Instead of running away, though, he stood there, motionless, just as he had the previous night. As if transfixed by a conjuring trick, everyone stopped, waiting for the next move.

One of the nurses came over again, but Eduard looked at him, summoning all his strength.

'I'll go with you, I know where you're taking me, and I know too that you want everyone else to know. Just wait a minute.'

The nurse decided it was worth taking the risk; after all, everything seemed to have returned to normal.

'I think...I think you're important to me,' said Eduard to Veronika.

'You can't speak. You don't live in this world, you don't know that my name's Veronika. You weren't with me last night, please, say you weren't there.'

'I was.'

She took his hand. The mad people were shouting, applauding, making obscene remarks.

'Where are they taking you?'

'For some treatment.'

'I'll come with you.'

'It's not worth it. You'd just be frightened, even if I swear to you that it doesn't hurt, that you don't feel anything. And it's much better than sedatives because you recover your lucidity much more quickly.'

Veronika didn't know what he was talking about. She regretted having taken his hand, she wanted to get away from there as soon as possible, to hide her shame, never again to see that man who had witnessed all that was most sordid in her, and who nevertheless continued to treat her with such tenderness.

But again, she remembered Mari's words: she didn't need to explain her life to anyone, not even to that young man standing before her.

'I'll come with you.'

The nurses thought it might be better like that. The schizophrenic no longer needed to be restrained, he was going of his own free will.

When they reached the ward, Eduard lay down on the bed. There were two other men waiting, with a strange machine and a bag containing strips of cloth.

Eduard turned to Veronika and asked her to sit down on the bed.

'In a few minutes, the story will be all round Villete and people will calm down again, because even the maddest of the mad feel fear. Only someone who has experienced this knows that it isn't as terrible as it seems.'

The nurses listened to the conversation and didn't believe a word of what the schizophrenic was saying. It must hurt terribly, but then who knows what goes on inside the head of a madman? The only sensible thing the young man had said was about fear: the story *would* soon be all round Villete and calm would swiftly be restored.

'You lay down too soon,' said one of them.

Eduard got up again, and they spread a kind of rubber sheet beneath him.

'Now you can lie down.'

He obeyed. He was perfectly calm, as if everything that was happening was absolutely routine.

The nurses tied some of the strips of cloth round Eduard's body and placed a piece of rubber in his mouth.

'It's so that he doesn't accidentally bite his tongue,' said one of the men to Veronika, pleased to be able to give some technical information as well as a warning.

They placed the strange machine – not much larger than a shoe box, with a few buttons and three dials on it – on a chair by the bed. Two wires came out of the top part and were connected to what looked like earphones.

One of the nurses placed these 'earphones' on Eduard's temples. The other seemed to be regulating the machine, twiddling some knobs, now to the right, now to the left. Although he couldn't speak because of the piece of rubber in his mouth, Eduard kept his eyes fixed on hers, and seemed to be saying: 'Don't worry, don't be afraid.'

'It's set at 130 volts for 0.3 seconds,' said the nurse controlling the machine. 'Here goes.'

He pressed a button and the machine buzzed. At that moment, Eduard's eyes glazed over, his body thrashed about on the bed with such fury that, but for the straps holding him down, he would have broken his spine.

'Stop it!' shouted Veronika.

'We have,' said the nurse, removing the 'headphones' from Eduard's temples. Even so, Eduard's body continued to writhe about, his head rocking from side to side, so violently that one of the men had to hold it still. The other nurse put the machine in a bag and sat down to smoke a cigarette.

The scene lasted a matter of moments. Eduard's body seemed to return to normal, but then the spasms recommenced, and the nurse had to redouble his efforts to keep Eduard's head still. After a while, the contractions lessened, until they stopped altogether. Eduard's eyes were wide open, and one of the nurses closed them, as one does with the dead.

Then he removed the piece of rubber from Eduard's mouth, untied him and put the strips of cloth in the bag along with the machine.

'The effects of electric shock treatment last about an hour,' he said to the girl, who was no longer shouting and who seemed mesmerised by what she was seeing. 'It's all right, he'll soon be back to normal and he'll be calmer too.'

As soon as the electric charge took effect, Eduard felt what he had experienced before: his normal vision gradually decreased, as if someone were closing a curtain, until everything disappeared. There was no pain or suffering, but he had seen other people being treated with electric shock and he knew how awful it looked.

Eduard was at peace now. If, moments before, he had experienced the stirrings of a new emotion in his heart, if he had begun to understand that love was something other than what his parents gave him, the electric shock treatment – or electroconvulsive therapy (ECT) as the specialists preferred to call it – would certainly restore him to normality.

The main effect of ECT was to destroy short-term memory. There would be no nurturing of impossible dreams for Eduard. He could not continue looking forward to a future that did not exist; his thoughts must remain turned toward the past, or he would again begin wanting to return to life.

An hour later, Zedka went into the ward, almost deserted apart from a bed, where a young man was lying, and a chair, where a young woman was sitting.

When she got closer, she saw that the young woman had been sick again, and that her bent head was lolling slightly to the right.

Zedka turned to call for help, but Veronika looked up.

'It's all right,' she said. 'I had another attack, but it's over now.'

Zedka gently helped her up and led her to the toilet.

'It's a men's toilet,' Veronika said.

'Don't worry, there's no one here.'

She removed Veronika's filthy sweater, washed it and placed it on the radiator. Then, she removed her own woollen top, and gave it to Veronika.

'Keep it. I only came to say goodbye.'

The girl seemed distant, as if she had lost all interest in life. Zedka led her back to the chair where she had been sitting.

'Eduard will wake up soon. He may have difficulty remembering what happened, but his memory will soon come back. Don't be frightened if he doesn't recognise you at first.'

'I won't be,' said Veronika, 'because I don't even recognise myself.'

Zedka pulled up a chair and sat down beside her. She had been in Villete so long, it would cost her nothing to spend a few minutes longer keeping Veronika company.

'Do you remember when we first met? I told you a story to try to explain that the world is exactly as we see it. Everyone thought the king was mad, because he wanted to impose an order that no longer existed in the minds of his subjects.

'There are things in life, though, which, however we look at them, are valid for everyone. Like love, for example.'

Zedka noticed a change in Veronika's eyes. She decided to go on.

'I would say that if someone only has a short time to live and decides to spend that time sitting beside a bed, watching a man sleeping, then that must be love. I'd go further: if, during that time, that person has a heart attack, but sits on in silence, just so as to remain close to the man, I would say that such love had a lot of potential for growth.'

'It might also be despair,' said Veronika. 'An attempt to prove that, after all, there are no reasons to continue battling away beneath the sun. I can't be in love with a man who lives in another world.'

'We all live in our own world. But if you look up at the starry sky, you'll see that all the different worlds up there combine to form constellations, solar systems, galaxies.'

Veronika got up and went over to Eduard. Tenderly, she smoothed his hair. She was glad to have someone to talk to.

'A long time ago, when I was just a child, and my mother was forcing me to learn the piano, I said to myself that I would only be able to play it well when I was in love. Last night, for the first time in my life, I felt the notes leaving my fingers as if I had no control over what I was doing.

'A force was guiding me, constructing melodies and chords that I never even knew I could play. I gave myself to the piano because I had just given myself to this man, without him even touching a hair of my head. I was not myself yesterday, not when I gave myself over to sex or when I played the piano. And yet I think I *was* myself.' Veronika shook her head.'Nothing of what I'm saying makes any sense.'

Zedka remembered her encounters in space with all those beings floating in different dimensions. She wanted to tell Veronika about it, but was afraid she might just confuse her even more.

'Before you say again that you're going to die, I want to tell you something. There are people who spend their entire lives searching for a moment like the one you had last night, but they never achieve it. That's why, if you were to die now, you would die with your heart full of love.'

Zedka got up.

'You've got nothing to lose. Many people don't allow themselves to love, precisely because of that, because there are a lot of things at risk, a lot of future and a lot of past. In your case, there is only the present.'

She went over and gave Veronika a kiss.

'If I stay here any longer, I won't leave at all. I'm cured of my depression, but in Villete, I've learned that there are other kinds of madness. I want to carry those with me and begin to see life with my own eyes.

'When I came here, I was deeply depressed. Now I'm proud to say I'm mad. Outside, I'll behave exactly like everyone else. I'll go shopping at the supermarket, I'll exchange trivialities with my friends, I'll waste precious time watching television. But I know that my soul is free and that I can dream and talk with other worlds which, before I came here, I didn't even imagine existed.

'I'm going to allow myself to do a few foolish things, just so that people can say: she's just been released from Villete. But I know that my soul is complete, because my life has meaning. I'll be able to look at a sunset and believe that God is behind it. When someone irritates me, I'll tell them what I think of them, and I won't worry what they think of me, because everyone will say: she's just been released from Villete.

'I'll look at men in the street, right in their eyes, and I won't feel guilty about feeling desired. But immediately after that, I'll go into a shop selling imported goods, buy the best wines my money can buy and I'll drink that wine with the husband I adore, because I want to laugh with him again.

'And laughing, he'll say: "You're mad!" And I'll say: "Of course I am, I was in Villete, remember! And madness freed me. Now, my dear husband, you must have a holiday every year, and make me climb some dangerous mountains, because I need to run the risk of being alive."

'People will say: "She's just been released from Villete and now she's making her husband mad too." And he will realise they're right and he'll thank God because our marriage is starting all over again and because we're both mad, like those who first invented love.'

Zedka left the ward, humming a tune Veronika had never heard before.

The day had proved exhausting, but rewarding. Dr Igor was trying to maintain the *sangfroid* and indifference of a scientist, but he could barely control his enthusiasm. The tests he was carrying out to find a cure for Vitriol poisoning were yielding surprising results.

'You haven't got an appointment today,' he said to Mari, who had come in without knocking.

'It won't take long. I'd just like to ask your opinion about something.'

'Today everyone just wants to ask my opinion,' thought Dr Igor, remembering the young girl's question about sex.

'Eduard has just been given electric shock treatment.'

'Electroconvulsive therapy, please use the correct name, otherwise it will look as if we're a mere band of barbarians.' Dr Igor tried to hide his surprise, but later, he would go and find out who had taken that decision. 'And if you want my opinion on the subject, I must make it clear that ECT is not used today as it used to be.'

'But it's dangerous.'

'It used to be *very* dangerous; they didn't know the exact voltage to use, where precisely to place the electrodes, and a lot of people died of brain haemorrhages during treatment. But things have changed: nowadays, ECT is being used with far greater technical precision and it has the advantage of provoking immediate amnesia, avoiding the chemical poisoning that comes with prolonged use of drugs. Read the psychiatric journals and don't confuse ECT with the electric shock treatment used by South American torturers. Right, you've heard my opinion. Now I must get back to my work.'

Mari didn't move.

'That isn't what I came to ask. I want to know if I can leave.'

'You can leave whenever you want and come back whenever you want, because your husband has enough money to keep you in an expensive place like this. Perhaps you should ask me: am I cured? And my reply will be another question: cured of what? You'll say: cured of my fear, of my panic attacks. And I'll say, well, Mari, you haven't actually suffered from that for the last three years.'

'So I'm cured.'

'Of course not. That wasn't what your illness was about. In the thesis I'm writing for the Slovenian Academy of Sciences' (Dr Igor didn't want to go into any detail about Vitriol), 'I'm trying to study so-called normal human behaviour. A lot of doctors before me have made similar studies and reached the conclusion that normality is merely a matter of consensus, that is, a lot of people think something is right, and so that thing becomes right.

'Some things are governed by common sense: putting buttons on the front of a shirt is a matter of logic, since it would be very difficult to button them up at the side, and impossible if they were at the back.

'Other things, however, become fixed because more and more people believe that's the way they should be. I'll give you two examples. Have you ever wondered why the keys on a typewriter are arranged in that particular order?'

'No, I haven't.'

'We call it the QWERTY keyboard, because that's the order of the letters on the first row of keys. I once wondered why it was like that and I found the answer: the first machine was invented by Christopher Scholes, in 1873, to improve calligraphy, but there was a problem: if a person typed very fast, the keys got stuck together and stopped the machine working. Then Scholes designed the QWERTY keyboard, *a keyboard that would oblige typists to type more slowly*.'

'I don't believe it.'

'But it's true. It so happened that Remington – who were sewing machine manufacturers at the time – used the QWERTY keyboard for their first typewriters. That meant that more people were forced to learn that particular system, and more companies started to make those keyboards, until it became the only available model. To repeat: the keyboard on typewriters and computers was designed so that people would type more slowly, not more quickly, do you understand? If you changed the letters around, you wouldn't find anyone to buy your product.'

When she saw a keyboard for the first time, Mari had wondered why the letters weren't in alphabetical order, but she had then promptly forgotten about it. She assumed it was simply the best layout in order for people to type quickly.

'Have you ever been to Florence?' asked Dr Igor.

'No.'

'You should go there, it's not far, for that is where you will find my second example. In the cathedral in Florence, there's a beautiful clock designed by Paolo Uccello in 1443. Now the curious thing about this clock is that, although it keeps time like all other clocks, its hands go in the opposite direction to that of normal clocks.'

'What's that got to do with my illness?'

'I'm just coming to that. When he made this clock, Paolo Uccello was not trying to be original: the fact is that, at the time, there were clocks like his as well as others with hands that went in the direction we're familiar with now. For some unknown reason, perhaps because the Duke had a clock with hands that went in the direction we now think of as the 'right' direction, that became the only direction, and Uccello's clock then seemed an aberration, a madness.'

Dr Igor paused, but he knew that Mari was following his reasoning.

'So, let's turn to your illness: each human being is unique, each with their own qualities, instincts, forms of pleasure and desire for adventure. However, society always imposes on us a collective way of behaving, and people never stop to wonder why they should behave like that. They just accept it, the way typists accepted the fact that the QWERTY keyboard was the best possible one. Have you ever met anyone in your entire life who asked why the hands of a clock should go in one particular direction and not in the other?'

'No.'

'If someone were to ask, the response they got would probably be: "You're mad." If they persisted, people would try to come up with a reason, but they'd soon change the subject, because there isn't a reason apart from the one I've just given you. So to go back to your question. What was it again?'

'Am I cured?'

'No. You're someone who is different, but who wants to be the same as everyone else. And that, in my view, is a serious illness.'

'Is wanting to be different a serious illness?'

'It is if you force yourself to be the same as everyone else: it causes neuroses, psychoses and paranoia. It's a distortion of nature, it goes against God's laws, for in all the world's woods and forests, He did not create a single leaf the same as another. But you think it's mad to be different and that's why you chose to live in Villete, because everyone is different here, and so you appear to be the same as everyone else. Do you understand?'

Mari nodded.

'People go against nature because they lack the courage to be different, and then the organism starts to produce Vitriol, or Bitterness as this poison is more commonly known.'

'What's Vitriol?'

Dr Igor realised he had gone too far and decided to change the subject.

'That doesn't matter. What I mean is this: everything indicates that you are not cured.'

Mari had years of experience in law courts and she decided to put it into practice right there and then. Her first tactic was to pretend to be in agreement with her adversary, only to draw him immediately into another line of argument.

'I agree. My reason for coming here was very concrete: I was getting panic attacks. My reason for staying was very abstract: I couldn't face the idea of a different way of life, with no job and no husband. I agree with you that I had lost the will to start a new life, a life I would have to get used to all over again. I'll go further: I agree that in a mental hospital, even with its electric shocks – sorry, ECT, as you prefer to call it – rigid timetables and occasional hysterical outbursts on the part of some inmates, the rules are easier to accept than the rules of a world which, as you say, does everything it can to conform.

'Then last night, I heard a woman playing the piano. She played superbly, in a way I've rarely heard before. As I was listening to the music, I thought of all those who had suffered in order to compose those sonatas, preludes, adagios, how foolish they must have been made to feel when they played their pieces – which were, after all, different – to those who held sway in the world of music then. I thought about the difficulties and humiliations involved in getting someone to fund an orchestra.

I thought of the booing public who were not yet used to such harmonies.

'Worse than the composers' suffering, though, was the fact that the girl was playing the music with such soul because she knew she was going to die. And am I not going to die? Where is my soul that I might play the music of my own life with such enthusiasm?'

Dr Igor was listening in silence. It seemed that all his ideas were beginning to bear fruit, but it was still too early to be sure.

'Where is my soul?' Mari asked again. 'In my past. In what I wanted my life to be. I left my soul captive in that moment when I still had a house, a husband, a job I wanted to leave but never had the courage to.

'My soul was in my past. But today it's here, I can feel it again in my body, vibrant with enthusiasm. I don't know what to do. I only know that it's taken me three years to understand that life was pushing me in a direction I didn't want to go in.'

'I think I can see some signs of improvement,' said Dr Igor.

'I don't need to ask if I can leave Villete. I can just walk through the door and never come back. But I needed to say all this to someone, and I'm saying it to you: the death of that young girl made me understand my own life.'

'I think these signs of improvement are turning into something of a miracle cure,' laughed Dr Igor. 'What do you think you'll do?'

'I'll go to El Salvador and work with children there.'

'There's no need to go so far away: Sarajevo is only about two hundred kilometres from here. The war may be over, but the problems continue.'

'Then I'll go to Sarajevo.'

Dr Igor took a form from a drawer and carefully filled it in. Then he got up and accompanied Mari to the door.

'Good luck,' he said, then immediately went back to his office and closed the door. He tried hard not to grow fond of his patients, but he never succeeded. Mari would be much missed in Villete.

When Eduard opened his eyes, the girl was still there. After his first electric shock sessions, he had had to struggle for a long time to remember what had happened; but then the therapeutic effect of the treatment lay precisely in that artificially induced partial amnesia which allowed the patient to forget the problems troubling him and to regain his calm.

However, the more frequently electric shock treatment was given, the less enduring its effects; he recognised the girl at once.

'While you were sleeping, you said something about visions of Paradise,' she said, stroking his hair.

Visions of Paradise? Yes, visions of Paradise. Eduard looked at her. He wanted to tell her everything.

At that moment, however, the nurse came in with a syringe.

'You've got to have this now,' she said to Veronika. 'Dr Igor's orders.'

'I've already had some today and I don't want any more,' she said. 'What's more I've no desire to leave here either. I refuse to obey any orders, any rules and I won't be forced to do anything.'

The nurse seemed used to this kind of reaction.

'Then, I'm afraid, we'll have to sedate you.'

'I need to talk to you,' said Eduard. 'Have the injection.'

Veronika rolled up the sleeve of her sweater, and the nurse injected her with the drug.

'There's a good girl,' she said. 'Now why don't the two of you leave this gloomy ward and go outside for a walk?'

'You're ashamed of what happened last night,' said Eduard, while they were walking in the garden.

'I was, but now I'm proud. I want to know about these visions of Paradise, because I came very close to having one myself.'

'I need to look further, beyond the buildings of Villete,' he said.

'Go on, then.'

Eduard looked behind him, not at the walls of the wards or at the garden where the inmates were walking in silence, but at a street in another continent, in a land where it either rained in torrents or not at all.

Eduard could smell that land. It was the dry season; he could feel the dust in his nostrils and the feeling gave him pleasure, because to smell the earth is to feel alive. He was riding an imported bicycle, he was seventeen, and had just left the American college in Brasília, where all the other diplomats' children studied.

He hated Brasília, but he loved the Brazilians. His father had been appointed Yugoslavian ambassador two years before, at a time when no one even dreamed of the violent division of their country. Miloševic was still in power; men and women lived with their differences and tried to find a harmony beyond regional conflicts.

His father's first posting was to Brazil. Eduard dreamed of beaches, carnival, football matches and music, but they ended up in the Brazilian capital, far from the coast – a city created to provide shelter only to politicians, bureaucrats, diplomats and to their children, who didn't quite know what to do, stuck in the middle of all that.

Eduard hated living there. He spent the day immersed in his studies, trying – but failing – to relate to his classmates, trying – but failing – to work up some interest in cars, the latest trainers and designer clothes, the only possible topics of conversation with the other young people.

Now and then, there would be a party, where the boys would get drunk on one side of the room, and the girls would feign indifference on the other. There were always drugs around, and Eduard had already experimented with almost all the possible varieties, not that he could get very excited about any of them; he either got too agitated or too sleepy and immediately lost interest in what was going on around him.

His family were concerned. They had to prepare him to follow in his father's footsteps, and although Eduard had almost all the necessary talents, a desire to study, good artistic taste, a facility with languages, an interest in politics, he lacked one essential quality for a diplomat. He found it difficult to talk to other people.

His parents took him to parties, told him to invite his schoolfriends home and gave him a generous allowance, but Eduard rarely turned up with anyone. One day, his mother asked him why he didn't bring his friends to lunch or supper.

'I know every make of trainer and I know the names of all the girls who are easy to get into bed. After that, there's nothing left to talk to them about.'

Then the Brazilian girl appeared on the scene. The ambassador and his wife felt better when their son began going out on dates and coming home late. No one knew exactly where she had come from, but one night, Eduard invited her home to supper. She was a well-brought-up girl, and his parents felt contented; the boy had finally started to develop his talent for relating to other people. Moreover, they both thought – though neither actually said anything – that the girl's existence removed one great worry from their minds: Eduard clearly wasn't homosexual.

They treated Maria (that was her name) with all the consideration of future in-laws, even though they knew that in two years' time they would be transferred to another post, and they had not the slightest intention of letting their son marry someone from an exotic country. They had plans for him to meet a girl from a good family in France or Germany, who could be a dignified companion in the brilliant diplomatic career the ambassador was preparing for him.

Eduard, however, seemed more and more in love. Concerned, his mother went to talk to her husband.

'The art of diplomacy consists in keeping your opponent waiting,' said the ambassador. 'Whilst you may never get over a first love affair, it always ends.'

But Eduard seemed to have changed completely. He started bringing strange books home, he built a pyramid in his room, and, together with Maria, burned incense every night and spent hours staring at a strange design pinned on the wall. Eduard's marks at school began to get worse.

The mother didn't understand Portuguese, but she could see the book covers: crosses, bonfires, hanged witches, exotic symbols.

'Our son is reading some dangerous stuff.'

'Dangerous? What's happening in the Balkans is dangerous,' said the ambassador. 'There are rumours that Slovenia wants independence, and that could lead us into war.'

The mother, however, didn't care about politics; she wanted to know what was happening to her son.

'What about this mania for burning incense?'

'It's to disguise the smell of marijuana,' said the ambassador. 'Our son has had an excellent education, he can't possibly believe that those perfumed sticks draw down the spirits.'

'My son involved in drugs?'

'It happens. I smoked marijuana too when I was young; people soon get bored with it. I did.'

His wife felt proud and reassured. Her husband was an experienced man, he had entered the world of drugs and emerged unscathed. A man with such strength of will could control any situation.

One day, Eduard asked if he could have a bicycle.

'We've got a chauffeur and a Mercedes Benz. Why do you want a bicycle?'

'To be more in touch with nature. Maria and I are going on a ten-day trip,' he said. 'There's a place near here with huge deposits of crystal, and Maria says they give off really positive energy.'

His father and mother had been brought up under a communist regime: crystals were merely a mineral product composed of certain atoms, and did not give off any kind of energy, either positive or negative. They did some research and discovered that these ideas about 'crystal vibrations' were beginning to be fashionable.

If their son started talking about such things at official parties, he could appear ridiculous in the eyes of others. For the first time, the ambassador acknowledged that the situation was becoming serious. Brasília was a city that lived on rumours, and as soon as his rivals at the embassy learned that Eduard believed in these primitive superstitions, they might think he had picked them up from his parents, and diplomacy, as well as being the art of waiting, was also the art of keeping up a façade of normality whatever the circumstances.

'My boy, this can't go on,' said his father. 'I have friends in the Foreign Office in Yugoslavia. You have a brilliant career as a diplomat ahead of you and you've got to learn to face up to reality.'

Eduard left the house and didn't come back that night. His parents phoned Maria's house, as well as all the mortuaries and hospitals in the city, to no avail. The mother lost her confidence in her husband's abilities as head of the family, however good he might be at negotiating with complete strangers.

The following day, Eduard turned up, hungry and sleepy. He ate and went to his room, lit his incense sticks, said his mantras, and slept for the rest of that evening and night. When he woke up, a brand new bicycle was waiting for him.

'Go and see your crystals,' said his mother. 'I'll explain to your father.'

And so, on that dry, dusty afternoon, Edward cycled happily over to Maria's house. The city was so well designed (in the architects' opinion) or so badly designed (in Eduard's opinion), that there were almost no corners, he just kept straight on down a high speed lane, looking up at the sky full of rainless clouds, then he felt himself rising up at a tremendous speed towards the sky, only to plummet down again and land on the asphalt. Crash!

'I've had an accident.'

He tried to turn over, because his face was pressed against the asphalt, and realised he had no control over his own body. He heard the noise of cars braking, people talking in alarmed voices, someone approaching and trying to touch him, then a shout: 'Don't move him! If anyone moves him, he could be crippled for life!'

The seconds passed slowly and Eduard began to feel afraid. Unlike his parents, he believed in God and in the afterlife, but even so, it seemed grossly unfair to die at seventeen, staring at the asphalt, in a land not his own.

'Are you all right?' he heard someone say.

No, he wasn't all right, he couldn't move, but he couldn't say anything either. The worst thing was that he didn't lose consciousness, he knew exactly what was happening and what his situation was. Why didn't he faint? At precisely the moment when he was looking for God with such intensity, despite everything and everyone, God had no pity on him.

'The doctors are on their way,' someone whispered to him, clutching his hand. 'I don't know if you can hear me, but keep calm. It's nothing serious.'

Yes, he could hear, he would have liked that person – a man – to keep on talking, to promise him that it was nothing serious, even though he was old enough to know that people only say that when the situation is very serious indeed. He thought about Maria, about the place where there were mountains of crystals full of positive energy, unlike Brasília, which had the highest concentration of negativity he had ever encountered in his meditations.

The seconds became minutes, people continued trying console him, and for the first time since it all happened, he began to feel pain. A sharp pain that came from the centre of his head and seemed to spread throughout his entire body.

'They're here,' said the man who was holding his hand. 'Tomorrow you'll be riding your bike again.'

But the following day, Eduard was in hospital, with both his legs and one arm in plaster, unable to leave for at least a month, and having to listen to his mother's non-stop sobbing, his father's anxious phone calls and the doctor's reassurances, reiterated every five minutes, that the crucial twenty-four hour period had passed, and there was no injury to the brain.

The family phoned the American Embassy, who never believed the diagnoses of the state hospitals and had their own sophisticated emergency service, along with a list of Brazilian doctors they considered capable of attending their own diplomats. Now and again, as part of a 'good neighbour policy', they allowed these services to be used by other diplomats.

The Americans brought along their state-of-the-art machines, carried out a further barrage of tests and examinations and reached the conclusion they always reach: the doctors in the state hospital had correctly evaluated the injuries and had taken the right decisions.

The doctors in the state hospital may have been good, but the programmes on Brazilian television were as awful as they are anywhere else in the world, and Eduard had little to do. Maria's visits to the hospital become more and more infrequent; perhaps she had found someone else to go with her to the crystal mountains.

In contrast to his girlfriend's erratic behaviour, the ambassador and his wife went to see him every day, but refused to bring him the Portuguese books he had at home on the pretext that his father would soon be transferred; so there was no need to learn a language he would never have to use again. Eduard, therefore, contented himself with talking to the other patients, discussing football with the nurses and devouring any magazines that fell into his hands.

Then one day, a nurse brought him a book he had just been given, but which he judged 'much too fat to actually read'. And that was the moment that Eduard's life began to set him on a strange path, one that would lead him to Villete and to his withdrawal from reality and that would distance him completely from all the things that other boys his age would get up to in the years that followed.

The book was about visionaries whose ideas had shaken the world, people with their own vision of an earthly Paradise, people who had spent their lives sharing their ideas with others. Jesus Christ was there, but so was Darwin and his theory that man was descended from the apes; Freud, affirming the importance of dreams; Columbus, pawning the Queen's jewels in order to set off in search of a new continent; Marx, with his belief that everyone deserved the same opportunities.

And there were saints too, like Ignatius Loyola, a Basque soldier who had slept with many women and killed many enemies in numerous battles, until he was wounded at Pamplona and came to understand the universe from the bed where he lay convalescing. Teresa of Ávila, who wanted somehow to find a path to God, and who stumbled across it when she happened to walk down a corridor and pause to look at a painting. Anthony, who, weary of the life he was leading, decided to go into exile in the desert, where he spent ten years in the company of demons and was racked by every conceivable temptation. Francis of Assisi, a young man like himself, who was determined to talk to the birds and to turn his back on everything that his parents had planned for his life.

Having nothing better to do, he began to read the 'fat book' that very afternoon. In the middle of the night, a nurse came in, asking if he needed help, since his was the only room with the light still on. Eduard waved her away, without even looking up from the book.

The men and women who shook the world were ordinary men and women, like him, like his father, like the girlfriend he knew he was losing. They were full of the same doubts and anxieties that all human beings experienced in their daily routine. They were people who had no special interest in religion or God, in expanding their minds or reaching a new level of consciousness, until one day they simply decided to change everything. The most interesting thing about the book was that it told how, in each of those lives, there was a single magical moment that made them set off in search of their own vision of Paradise.

They were people who had not allowed their lives to pass by blankly, and who, to achieve what they wanted, had begged for alms or courted kings, used diplomacy or force, flouted laws or faced the wrath of the powers-that-be, but who had never given up, and were always able to see the advantages in any difficulty that presented itself.

The following day, Eduard handed over his gold watch to the nurse who had given him the book, and asked him to sell it, and, with the money, to buy all the books he could find on the same subject. There weren't any more. He tried reading the biographies of some of those visionaries, but they were always described as if they were someone chosen, inspired, and not an ordinary person who, like everyone else, had to fight to be allowed to say what they thought.

Eduard was so impressed by what he had read, though, that he seriously considered becoming a saint and using the accident as an opportunity to change the direction of his life. But he had two broken legs, he had not had a single vision while in hospital, he hadn't stopped by a painting that shook him to his very soul, he had no friends who would build him a chapel in the middle of the Brazilian plateau, and the deserts were all far away and bristling with political problems. There was, however, something he could do: he could learn to paint and try to show the world the visions those men and women had experienced.

When they removed the plaster and he went back to the Embassy, surrounded by all the care, kindness and attention that the son of an ambassador could hope for from other diplomats, he asked his mother if he could enrol in a course on painting.

His mother said that he had already missed a lot of classes at the American school and that he would have to make up for lost time. Eduard refused. He did not have the slightest desire to go on learning about geography and sciences, he wanted to be a painter. In an unguarded moment, he explained why:

'I want to paint visions of Paradise.'

His mother said nothing, but promised to talk to her women friends and ascertain which was the best painting course available in the city.

When the ambassador came back from work that evening, he found her crying in her bedroom.

'Our son is mad,' she said, her face streaming with tears. 'The accident has affected his brain.'

'Impossible!' the ambassador replied, indignant. 'He was examined by doctors specially selected by the Americans.'

His wife told him what her son had said.

'It's just youthful rebelliousness. Just you wait, everything will go back to normal, you'll see.'

This time, waiting did no good at all, because Eduard was in a hurry to start living. Two days later, tired of marking time while his mother's friends deliberated, he decided to enrol himself on an art course. He started learning about colour and perspective, but he also got to know people who never talked about trainers or makes of car.

'He's living with artists!' said his mother tearfully to the ambassador.

'Oh, leave the boy alone,' said the ambassador. 'He'll soon get sick of it, like he did of his girlfriend, like he did of crystals, pyramids, incense and marijuana.'

But time passed, and Eduard's room became an improvised studio, full of paintings that made no sense at all to his parents:

circles, exotic colour combinations and primitive symbols all mixed up with people in attitudes of prayer.

Eduard, the solitary boy, who, in his two years in Brazil, had never once brought friends home, was now filling the house with strange people, all of them badly dressed and with untidy hair, who listened to horrible music at full blast – endlessly drinking and smoking and showing a complete disregard for basic good manners. One day, the director of the American school called his mother.

'I think your son must be involved in drugs,' she said. 'His school marks are well below average, and if he goes on like this, we won't be able to renew his enrolment.'

His mother went straight to the ambassador's office and told him what the director had said.

'You keep saying that, with time, everything will go back to normal,' she screamed hysterically. 'There's your crazy, drug-addict son, obviously suffering from some serious brain injury, and all you care about are cocktail parties and social gatherings.'

'Keep your voice down,' he said.

'No, I won't, and I never will again if you don't do something. The boy needs help, don't you see? Medical help. Do something.'

Concerned that the scene his wife was making might embarrass him in front of his staff, and worried that Eduard's interest in painting was lasting longer than expected, the ambassador, a practical man, who knew all the correct procedures, drew up a plan of attack.

First, he phoned his colleague, the American ambassador, and asked politely if he could again make use of the Embassy's medical facilities. His request was granted.

He went back to the accredited doctors, explained the situation and asked them to go over all the tests they had made at the time. The doctors, fearing a law suit, did exactly as they were asked and concluded that the tests revealed nothing abnormal. Before the ambassador left, they demanded that he sign a document exempting the American Embassy from any responsibility for sending him to them.

The ambassador immediately went to the hospital where Eduard had been a patient. He talked to the director, explained his son's problem and asked that, under the pretext of a routine checkup, a blood test be taken to see if there were any drugs in the boy's system.

They took a blood test and no trace of drugs was found.

There remained the third and final stage of his strategy: talking to Eduard himself and finding out what was going on. Only when he was in possession of all the facts, could he hope to make the correct decision.

Father and son sat down in the living room.

'Your mother's very worried about you,' said the ambassador. 'Your marks have got worse, and there's a danger that your place at the school won't be renewed.'

'But my marks at art school have improved, Dad.'

'I find your interest in art very pleasing, but you have your whole life ahead of you to do that. At the moment, the main thing is to finish your secondary education, so that I can set you on the path to a diplomatic career.'

Eduard thought long and hard before saying anything. He thought about the accident, about the book on visionaries, which had turned out to be only a pretext for finding his true vocation, and he thought about Maria, from whom he had never heard again. He hesitated for some time, but in the end, said:

'Dad, I don't want to be a diplomat. I want to be a painter.'

His father was prepared for that response and knew how to get round it.

'You will be a painter, but first, finish your studies. We'll arrange for exhibitions in Belgrade, Zagreb, Ljubljana and Sarajevo. I've got influence, I can help you a lot, but you must complete your studies.'

'If I do that, I'll be choosing the easy route. I'll enter some faculty or other, get a degree in a subject that doesn't interest me, but which will help me earn a living. Painting will just recede into the background, and I'll end up forgetting my vocation. I'll just have to find a way of earning money through my painting.'

The ambassador was starting to get irritated.

'You've got everything, son, a family which loves you, a house, money, social position, but as you know, our country is going through a difficult time, there are rumours of civil war. Tomorrow I might not even be here to help you.'

'I can help myself. Trust me. One day, I'll paint a series entitled "Visions of Paradise". It'll be a visual history of what men and women have previously only experienced in their hearts.'

The ambassador praised his son's determination, drew the conversation to a close with a smile, and decided to give him another month; after all, diplomacy is also the art of postponing decisions until the problems resolve themselves.

A month passed, and Eduard continued to devote all his time to painting, to his strange friends and to that music apparently expressly designed to induce some psychological disorder. To make matters worse, he had been expelled from the American college for arguing with a teacher about the existence of saints.

Since the decision could be put off no longer, the ambassador made one last attempt and called his son in for a man-to-man talk.

'Eduard, you are now of an age to take responsibility for your own life. We've put up with this for as long as we could, but now you've got to forget all this nonsense about becoming a painter and give some direction to your career.'

'But Dad, being a painter *is* giving a direction to my career.'

'What about our love for you, all our efforts to give you a good education. You never used to be like this, and I can only assume that what's happening is some consequence of the accident.'

'Look, I love you both more than anything or anyone else in the world.'

The ambassador cleared his throat. He wasn't used to such outspoken expressions of affection.

'Then, in the name of the love you have for us, please, do as your mother wants. Just stop all this painting business for a while, get some friends who belong to the same social class as you and go back to your studies.'

'You love me, Dad. You can't ask me to do that, because you've always set me a good example, fighting for the things you cared about. You can't want me to be a man with no will of my own.'

'I said, in the name of love. And I have never said that before, but I'm asking you now. For the love that you bear us, for the love we bear you, come home, and I don't just mean in the physical sense, but really. You're deceiving yourself, running away from reality.

'Ever since you were born, we've built up such dreams of how our lives would be. You're everything to us, our future and our past. Your grandfathers were civil servants and I had to fight like a lion to enter the diplomatic service and make my way up the ladder. And I did all this just to create a space for you, to make things easier for you. I've still got the pen with which I signed my first document as an ambassador, and I lovingly saved it to pass on to you the day you did the same.

'Don't let us down, son. We won't live forever and we want to die in peace, knowing that we've set you on the right path in life.

'If you really love us, do as I ask. If you don't love us, then carry on as you are now.'

Eduard sat for long hours staring up at the sky in Brasília, watching the clouds moving across the blue – beautiful clouds, but without a drop of rain in them to moisten the dry earth of the central Brazilian plateau. He was as empty as they were.

If he continued as he was, his mother would fade away with grief, his father would lose all enthusiasm for his career, and both would blame each other for failing in the upbringing of their beloved son. If he gave up his painting, the visions of Paradise would never see the light of day, and nothing else in this world could ever give him the same feelings of joy and pleasure.

He looked around him, he saw his paintings, he remembered the love and meaning he had put into each brushstroke, and he found every one of his paintings mediocre. He was a fraud, he wanted something for which he had not been chosen, and the price of which was his parents' disappointment.

Visions of Paradise were for the chosen few, who appeared in books as heroes and martyrs of the faith in which they believed, people who knew from childhood what the world wanted of them; the so-called facts in that first book he had read were the inventions of a storyteller.

At supper time, he told his parents that they were right; it was just a youthful dream; his enthusiasm for painting had passed. His parents were pleased, his mother wept with joy and embraced her son, and everything went back to normal.

That night, the ambassador secretly commemorated his victory by opening a bottle of champagne which he drank alone. When he went to bed, his wife – for the first time in many months – was already sleeping peacefully.

The following day, they found Eduard's room in confusion, the paintings slashed and the boy sitting in a corner, gazing up at the sky. His mother embraced him, told him how much she loved him, but Eduard didn't respond.

He wanted nothing more to do with love, he was fed up with the whole business. He had thought that he could just give up and follow his father's advice, but he had advanced too far in his work; he had crossed the abyss that separates a man from his dream and now there was no going back.

He couldn't go forwards or back. It was easier just to leave the stage.

Eduard stayed on in Brazil for another five months, being treated by specialists, who diagnosed a rare form of schizophrenia, possibly the result of a bicycle accident. Then war broke out in Yugoslavia and the ambassador was hastily recalled. It was too problematic for the family to look after Eduard, and the only way out was to leave him in the newly opened hospital of Villete.

By the time Eduard had finished telling his story, it was dark and they were both shivering with cold.

'Let's go in,' he said. 'They'll be serving supper.'

'Whenever we went to see my grandmother when I was a child, I was always fascinated by one particular painting in her house. It showed a woman – Our Lady, as Catholics call her – standing poised above the world, with her hands outstretched to the Earth and with rays of light streaming from her fingertips.

What most intrigued me about the painting was that this lady was standing on a live snake. I said to my grandmother: "Isn't she afraid of the snake? Won't it bite her on the foot and kill her with its poison?"

My grandmother said: "According to the Bible, the snake brought Good and Evil to the Earth, and she is keeping both Good and Evil in check with her love.'

'What's that got to do with my story?'

'I've only known you a week, so it would be far too early for me to tell you that I love you, but since I probably won't live through the night, it would also be too late. But then the great madness of men and women is precisely that: love.

'You told me a love story. I honestly believe your parents wanted the best for you, but their love almost destroyed your life. If Our Lady, as she appeared in my grandmother's painting, was treading on a snake, that indicates that love has two faces.'

'I see what you mean,' said Eduard. 'I provoked the nurses into giving me the electric shock treatment, because you get me all mixed up. I can't say for sure what I feel, and love has already destroyed me once.'

'Don't be afraid. Today, I asked Dr Igor for permission to leave here and to choose a place where I can close my eyes for ever. But when I saw you being held down by the nurses, I realised what it was I wanted to be looking at when I left this world: your face. And I decided not to leave.

'While you were sleeping off the effects of the electric shock treatment, I had another heart attack, and I thought my time had come. I looked at your face and I tried to guess what your story was, and I prepared myself to die happy. But death didn't come, my heart survived yet again, perhaps because I'm still young.'

He looked down.

'Don't be embarrassed about being loved. I'm not asking you for anything, just let me love you and play the piano again tonight, just once more, if I still have the strength to do it. In exchange, I ask only one thing, if you hear anyone say that I'm dying, go straight to my ward. Let me have my wish.'

Eduard remained silent for a long time and Veronika thought he must have retreated once more into his separate world, from which he would not return for a long time.

Then, he looked at the mountains beyond the walls of Villete and said:

'If you want to leave, I can take you. Just give me time to grab a couple of jackets and some money. Then we'll go.'

'It won't last long, Eduard. You do know that.'

Eduard didn't reply. He went in and came back at once carrying two jackets.

'It will last an eternity, Veronika, longer than all the identical days and nights I've spent in here, constantly trying to forget those visions of Paradise. And I almost did forget them too, though it seems to me they're coming back.

'Come on, let's go. Mad people do mad things.'

That night, when they were all gathered together for supper, the inmates noticed four people were missing.

Zedka, who everyone knew had been released after a long period of treatment, Mari, who had probably gone to the cinema, as she often did, and Eduard, who had perhaps not recovered from the electric shock treatment. When they thought this, all the inmates felt afraid, and they began their supper in silence.

Finally, the girl with green eyes and brown hair was missing. The one whom they all knew would not see out the week.

No one spoke openly of death in Villete, but absences were noted, although everyone always tried to behave as if nothing had happened.

A rumour started to go from table to table. Some wept, because she had been so full of life and now she would be lying in the small mortuary behind the hospital. Only the most daring ever went there, even during daylight hours. It contained three marble tables and there was generally a new body on one of them, covered with a sheet.

Everyone knew that tonight Veronika would be there. Those who were truly insane soon forgot the presence, during that week, of another guest, who sometimes disturbed everyone's sleep playing the piano. A few, when they heard the news, felt rather sad, especially the nurses who had been with

Veronika during her time in the Intensive Care Unit, but the employees had been trained not to develop strong bonds with the patients, because some left, others died, and the great majority got steadily worse. Their sadness lasted a little longer, and then that too passed.

The vast majority of the inmates, however, heard the news, pretended to be shocked and sad, but actually felt relieved, because once more, the Exterminating Angel had passed over Villete and they had been spared.

When the Fraternity got together after supper, one member of the group gave them a message: Mari had not gone to the cinema, she had left never to return and had given him a note.

No one seemed to attach much importance to the matter: she had always seemed different, rather too mad, incapable of adapting to the ideal situation in which they all lived in Villete.

'Mari never understood how happy we are here,' said one of them. 'We are friends with common interests, we have a routine, sometimes we go out on trips together, invite lecturers here to talk about important matters, then we discuss their ideas. Our life has reached a perfect equilibrium, something that many people outside would love to achieve.'

'Not to mention the fact that, in Villete, we are protected from unemployment, the consequences of the war in Bosnia, from economic problems and violence,' said another. 'We have found harmony.'

'Mari left me this note,' said the one who had given them the news, holding up a sealed envelope. 'She asked me to read it out loud, as if she were saying goodbye to us all.'

The oldest member of the group opened the envelope and did as Mari had asked. He was tempted to stop halfway, but by then, it was too late, and so he read to the end.

'When I was still a young lawyer, I read some poems by an

English poet and something he said impressed me greatly: "Be like the fountain that overflows, not like the cistern that merely contains." I always thought he was wrong: it was dangerous to overflow, because we might end up flooding areas occupied by our loved ones and drowning them with our love and enthusiasm. All my life I did my best to be a cistern, never going beyond the limits of my inner walls.

'Then, for some reason I will never understand, I began suffering from panic attacks. I became the kind of person I had fought so hard to avoid becoming: I became a fountain that overflowed and flooded everything around me. The result was my internment in Villete.

'After I was cured, I returned to the cistern and I met all of you. Thank you for your friendship, for your affection and for many happy moments. We lived together like fish in an aquarium, contented because someone threw us food when we needed it, and we could, whenever we wanted to, see the world outside through the glass.

'But yesterday, because of a piano and a young woman who is probably dead by now, I learned something very important: life inside is exactly the same as life outside. Both there and here, people gather together in groups, they build their walls and allow nothing strange to trouble their mediocre existences. They do things because they're used to doing them, they study useless subjects, they have fun because they're supposed to have fun, and the rest of the world can go hang – let them sort themselves out. At the very most, they watch the news on television – as we often did – as confirmation of their happiness, in a world full of problems and injustices.

'What I'm saying is that the life of the Fraternity is exactly the same as the lives of almost everyone outside Villete, carefully avoiding all knowledge of what lies beyond the glass walls of the aquarium. For a long time, it was comforting and useful, but people change, and now I'm off in search of adventure, even though I'm sixty-five and fully aware of all the limitations that age can bring. I'm going to Bosnia. There are people waiting for me there. Although they don't yet know me, and I don't know them. But I'm sure I can be useful, and the danger of an adventure is worth a thousand days of ease and comfort.'

When he had finished reading the note, the members of the Fraternity all went to their rooms and wards, telling themselves that Mari had finally gone mad.

Eduard and Veronika chose the most expensive restaurant in Ljubljana, ordered the finest dishes and got drunk on three bottles of 1988 wine, one of the best vintages of the century. During supper, they did not once mention Villete or the past or the future.

'I like that story about the snake,' he said, filling her glass for the nth time. 'But your grandmother was too old to be able to interpret the story correctly.'

'Have a little respect for my grandmother, please!' roared Veronika drunkenly, making everyone in the restaurant turn round.

'A toast to this young woman's grandmother!' said Eduard, jumping to his feet. 'A toast to the grandmother of this madwoman sitting here before me, who is doubtless some escapee from Villete.'

People turned their attention back to their food, pretending that nothing was happening.

'A toast to my grandmother!' insisted Veronika.

The owner of the restaurant came to their table.

'Will you please behave!'

They went quiet for a few moments, but soon resumed their loud talking, their nonsensical remarks and inappropriate behaviour. The owner of the restaurant went back to their table, told them they didn't need to pay the bill, but they had to leave that instant.

'Think of the money we'll save on that exorbitantly expensive wine,' said Eduard. 'Let's leave before this gentleman changes his mind.'

But the man wasn't about to change his mind. He was already pulling at Veronika's chair, an apparently courteous gesture intended to get her out of the restaurant as quickly as possible.

They walked to the middle of the small square in the centre of the city. Veronika looked up at her convent room and her drunkenness vanished. She remembered that soon she would die.

'Let's buy some more wine!' said Eduard.

There was a bar nearby. Eduard bought two bottles and the two of them sat down and continued drinking.

'What's wrong with my grandmother's interpretation of the painting?' said Veronika.

Eduard was so drunk that he had to make an immense effort to remember what he had said in the restaurant, but he managed it.

'Your grandmother said that the woman was standing on the snake because love must master Good and Evil. It's a nice, romantic interpretation, but it's nothing to do with that. I've seen that image before, it's one of the visions of Paradise I imagined painting. I used to wonder why they always depicted the Virgin like that.'

'And why do they?'

'Because the Virgin equals female energy and is the mistress of the snake, which signifies wisdom. If you look at the ring Dr Igor wears, you'll see that it bears the physician's symbol: two serpents coiled around a stick. Love is above wisdom, just as the Virgin is above the snake. For her, everything is Inspiration. She doesn't bother judging what is Good and what Evil.'

'Do you know something else?' said Veronika. 'The Virgin never took any notice of what others might think of her. Imagine having to explain to everyone that business about the Holy Ghost. She didn't explain anything, she just said: "That's what happened." And do you know what the others must have said?'

'Of course. That she was mad.'

They both laughed. Veronika raised her glass.

'Congratulations. You should paint those visions of Paradise, rather than just talking about them.'

'I'll begin with you,' said Eduard.

Beside the small square there is a small hill. On top of the small hill, there is a small castle. Veronika and Eduard trudged up the steep path, cursing and laughing, slipping on the ice and complaining of exhaustion.

Beside the castle, there is a gigantic yellow crane. For anyone coming to Ljubljana for the first time, the crane gives the impression that the castle is being restored and that work will soon be completed. The inhabitants of Ljubljana, however, know that the crane has been there for many years, although no one knows why. Veronika told Eduard that when children in kindergarten are asked to draw the castle of Ljubljana, they always include the crane in the drawing.

'Besides, the crane is much better preserved than the castle.'

Eduard laughed.

'You should be dead by now,' he said, still under the effects of alcohol, but with a flicker of fear in his voice. 'Your heart shouldn't have survived that climb.'

Veronika gave him a long, lingering kiss.

'Look at my face,' she said. 'Remember it with the eyes of your soul, so that you can reproduce it one day. If you like, that can be your starting point, but you must go back to painting.

That is my last request. Do you believe in God?'

'I do.'

'Then you must swear by the God you believe in that you will paint me.'

'I swear.'

'And that after painting me, you will go on painting.'

'I don't know if I can swear that.'

'You can. And I'll go further: thank you for giving meaning to my life. I came into this world in order to go through everything I've gone through, attempted suicide, ruining my heart, meeting you, coming up to this castle, letting you engrave my face on your soul. That is the only reason I came into the world, to make you go back to the path you strayed from. Don't make me feel my life has been in vain.'

'I don't know if it's too early or too late, but, just as you did with me, I want to tell you that I love you. You don't have to believe it, maybe it's just foolishness, a fantasy of mine.'

Veronika put her arms around him and asked the God she did not believe in to take her at that very moment.

She closed her eyes and felt him doing the same. And a deep dreamless sleep came upon her. Death was sweet, it smelled of wine and it stroked her hair.

Eduard felt someone prodding him in the shoulder. When he opened his eyes, day was breaking.

'You can go and shelter in the Town Hall, if you like,' said the policeman. 'You'll freeze if you stay here.'

In a second, Eduard remembered everything that had happened the previous night. There was a woman lying curled in his arms.

'She … she's dead.'

But the woman moved and opened her eyes.

'What's going on?' asked Veronika.

'Nothing,' said Eduard, helping her to her feet. 'Or rather, a miracle happened: another day of life.'

As soon as Dr Igor went into his consulting room and turned on the light – for daylight still arrived late and winter was dragging on far too long – a nurse knocked at his door.

'Things have started early today,' he said to himself.

It was going to be a difficult day, because of the conversation he would have to have with Veronika. He had been building up to it all week, and had hardly slept a wink the previous night.

'I've got some worrying news,' said the nurse. 'Two of the inmates have disappeared: the ambassador's son and the girl with the heart problem.'

'Honestly, you're a load of incompetents, you are, not that the security in this hospital has ever been up to much.'

'It's just that no one's ever tried to escape before,' said the nurse, frightened. 'We didn't know it was possible.'

'Get out of here! Now I'll have to prepare a report for the owners, notify the police, take steps. Tell everyone I'm not to be disturbed, these things take hours!'

The nurse left, looking pale, knowing that a large part of that major problem would land on his own shoulders, because that is how the powerful deal with the weak. He would doubtless be dismissed before the day was out.

Dr Igor picked up a pad, put it on the table and began making notes; then he changed his mind.

He switched off the light and sat in the office precariously lit by the incipient sunlight, and he smiled. It had worked.

In a while, he would make the necessary notes, describing the only known cure for Vitriol: an awareness of life. And describing the medication he had used in his first major test on patients: an awareness of death.

Perhaps other forms of medication existed, but Dr Igor had decided to centre his thesis round the one he had the opportunity to experiment with scientifically, thanks to a young woman who, quite unwittingly, had become part of his fate. She had been in a terrible state when she arrived, suffering from a severe overdose, nearly in a coma. She had hovered between life and death for nearly a week, just the amount of time he needed to come up with a brilliant idea for his experiment.

Everything depended on one thing: the girl's capacity to survive.

And she had, with no serious consequences, no irreversible health problems; if she looked after herself, she could live as long or longer than him.

But Dr Igor was the only one who knew this, just as he knew that failed suicides tend to repeat the attempt sooner or later. Why not use her as a guinea pig, to see if he could eliminate the Vitriol, or Bitterness, from her organism?

And so Dr Igor had conceived his plan.

Using a drug known as Fenotal, he had managed to simulate the effects of heart attacks. For a week, she had received injections of the drug, and she must have been very frightened, because she had time to think about death and to review her own life. In that way, according to Dr Igor's thesis (the final chapter of his work would be entitled 'An awareness of death encourages us to live more intensely') the girl had gone on to eliminate Vitriol completely from her organism, and would, quite possibly, never repeat her attempt at suicide.

He was supposed to see her today and tell her that, thanks to the injections, he had achieved a total reversal of her heart condition. Veronika's escape saved him the unpleasant experience of lying to her yet again.

What Dr Igor had not counted on was the infectious nature of his cure for Vitriol poisoning. A lot of people in Villete had been frightened by their awareness of that slow, irreparable death. They must all have been thinking about what they were missing, forced to re-evaluate their own lives.

Mari had come to him asking to be discharged. Other patients were asking for their cases to be reviewed. The position of the ambassador's son was more worrying, though, because he had simply disappeared, probably helping Veronika to escape.

'Perhaps they're still together,' he thought.

At any rate, the ambassador's son knew where Villete was, if he wanted to come back. Dr Igor was too excited by the results to pay much attention to minor details.

For a few moments, he was assailed by another doubt: sooner or later, Veronika would realise that she wasn't going to die of a heart attack. She would probably go to a specialist who would tell her that her heart was perfectly normal. She would judge that the doctor who had taken care of her in Villete was a complete incompetent, but then all those who dare to research into forbidden subjects require both a certain amount of courage and a good dose of incomprehension.

But what about the many days that she would have to live with the fear of imminent death?

Dr Igor pondered the arguments long and hard and decided that it didn't really matter. She would consider each day a miracle, which indeed it is, when you consider the number of unexpected things that could happen in each second of our fragile existences.

He noticed that the sun's rays were growing stronger; at that hour, the inmates would be having breakfast. Soon his waiting room would be full, the usual problems would arise, and it was best to start taking notes at once for his thesis.

Meticulously he began to write up his experiment with Veronika; he would leave until later the reports on the building's lack of security.

St Bernadette's Day, 1998

Afterword

> 'Stay mad, but behave like normal people. Run the risk of being different, but learn to do so without attracting attention.'
>
> *Veronika Decides to Die*

I entered a tiled cubicle. There was a bed covered with a rubber sheet and beside the bed some sort of apparatus with a handle.

'So you're going to give me electric-shock treatment,' I said to Dr Benjamim Gaspar Gomes.

'Don't worry. It's far more traumatic watching someone being treated than actually having the treatment yourself. It doesn't hurt at all.'

I lay down and the male nurse put a kind of tube in my mouth so that my tongue wouldn't roll back. Then, on either temple, he placed two electrodes, rather like the earpieces of a telephone.

I was looking up at the peeling paint on the ceiling when I heard the handle being turned. The next moment, a curtain seemed to fall over my eyes; my vision quickly reduced down to a single point, and then everything went dark.

The doctor was right; it didn't hurt at all.

The scene I have just described is not taken from my latest book. It comes from the diary I wrote during my second stay in a mental hospital. That was in 1966, the beginning of the blackest period of Brazil's military dictatorship (1964–89), and, as if by some natural reflex of the social mechanism, this external repression was gradually becoming internalised. So much so that good middle-class families found it simply unacceptable that their children or grandchildren should want to be 'artists'. In Brazil at the time, the word 'artist' was synonymous with homosexual, communist, drug addict and layabout.

When I was 18, I believed that my world and that of my parents could coexist peacefully. I did my best to get good marks, I worked every afternoon, but at night, I wanted to live out my dream of being an artist. Not knowing quite where to begin, I became involved in an amateur theatre group. Although I had no desire to act professionally, at least I was amongst people with whom I felt some affinity.

Unfortunately, my parents did not share my belief in the peaceful coexistence of two such diametrically opposed worlds. One night, I came home drunk, and the following morning, I was woken by two burly male nurses. The situation I found myself in was so strange, so extreme, that it brought with it something unprecedented: total freedom. All my family's efforts to make me the same as everyone else had exactly the opposite result: I was now completely different from all the other young men of my own age.

When I came out of hospital for the third time I was nearly 20 and had become accustomed to that rhythm of events. This time, however, something had changed.

Although I again got into 'bad company', my parents were growing reluctant to have me readmitted to a mental hospital. Unbeknown to me, they were by then convinced that I was a hopeless case, and preferred to keep me with them and to support me for the rest of my life.

My behaviour went from bad to worse, I became more

aggressive, but still there was no mention of hospital. I experienced a period of great joy as I tried to exercise my so-called freedom, in order, finally, to live the 'artist's life'. For one long year, I did exactly as I pleased; but then the theatre group was broken up by the political police, the bars became infiltrated by spies, my stories were rejected by every publisher I sent them to, and none of the girls I knew wanted to go out with me – because I was a young man without a future, with no real career and had never even been to university.

So, one day, I decided to trash my bedroom. It was a way of saying, without words: 'You see, I can't live in the real world. I can't get a job, I can't realise my dream. I think you're absolutely right: I am mad, and I want to go back to the mental hospital!'

Fate can be so ironic. When I had finished wrecking my room, I was relieved to see that my parents were phoning the mental hospital. However, the doctor who usually dealt with me was on holiday. The nurses arrived with a junior doctor in tow. He saw me sitting there surrounded by torn-up books, broken records, ripped curtains, and asked my family and the nurses to leave the room.

'What's going on?' he asked.

I didn't reply. A madman should always behave like someone not of this world.

'Stop playing around,' he said. 'I've been reading your case history. You're not mad at all, and I won't admit you to the hospital.'

He left the room, wrote a prescription for some tranquillisers and – so I found out later – told my parents that I was suffering from 'admission syndrome'. Normal people who, at some point, find themselves in an abnormal situation such as depression, panic, etc., occasionally use illness as an alternative to life. That is, they choose to be ill, because being 'normal' is too much like hard work. My parents listened to his advice and never again had me admitted into a mental institution.

In 1997, after an exhausting promotional tour across three continents, I began to notice a very odd phenomenon: what I had wanted on that day when I trashed my bedroom seemed to be something a lot of other people wanted, too. People preferred to live in a huge asylum, religiously following rules written by who knows who, rather than fighting for the right to be different. Between normality and madness, which are basically the same thing, there exists an intermediary stage: it is called 'being different'. And people were becoming more and more afraid of 'being different'. I decided to write a book based on my own experiences. I wrote *Veronika Decides to Die*, in the third person and using my feminine ego, because I knew that the important subject to be addressed was not what I personally had experienced in mental institutions, but, rather, the risks we run by being different and yet our horror at being the same.

Veronika Decides to Die came out in Brazil in August 1998. By September, I had received more than 1,200 emails and letters relating similar experiences. In October, some of the themes touched on in the book – depression, panic attacks, suicide – were discussed in a seminar that had national repercussions.

On 22 January 1999, Brazilian Senator Eduardo Suplicy read out passages from my book to the other senators and managed to gain approval for a law that they had been trying to get through Congress for the previous ten years, a law forbidding arbitrary admissions into mental institutions.

Veronika Decides to Die forms part of the trilogy *And On the Seventh Day*. The other books in the trilogy are *By The River Piedra I Sat Down and Wept* (1994) and *The Devil and Miss Prym* (2000). Each of the three books is concerned with a week in the life of ordinary people, all of whom find themselves suddenly confronted by love, death and power. I have always believed that in the lives of individuals, just as in society at large, the most profound changes take place within a reduced time frame. When we least expect it, life sends us a challenge to test our courage and willingness to change; at such a moment, there is no point in pretending that nothing has happened or in saying that we are not yet ready. The challenge will not wait. Life does not look back. A week is more than enough time for us to decide whether or not to accept our destiny.

Life is a
journey

Make sure you don't miss a thing.
Live it with Paulo Coelho.

Visit /paulocoelho

How can you find your heart's desire?

A world-wide phenomenon; an inspiration for anyone seeking their path in life.

The Alchemist

Do you believe in yourself?

A modern-day adventure in the searing heat of the Mojave desert and an exploration of fear and self-doubt.

The Valkyries

How do we see the amazing in the everyday?

When two young lovers are reunited, they discover anew the truth of what lies in their hearts.

By the River Piedra I Sat Down & Wept

What are you searching for?

A transforming journey on the pilgrims' road to Santiago – and the first of Paulo's extraordinary books.

The Pilgrimage

Can faith triumph over suffering?

Paulo Coelho's brilliant telling of the story of Elijah, who was forced to choose between love and duty.

The Fifth Mountain

Is life always worth living?

A fundamental moral question explored as only Paulo Coelho can.

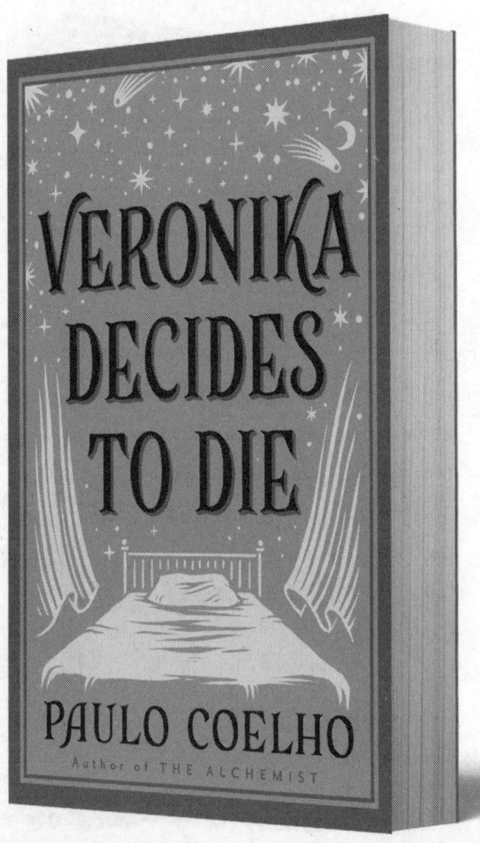

Veronika Decides to Die

Could you be tempted into evil?

The inhabitants of a small town are challenged by a mysterious stranger to choose between good and evil.

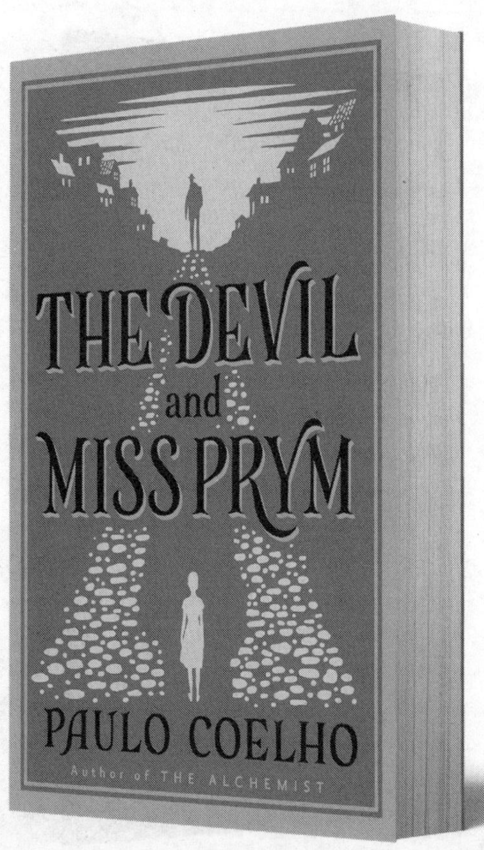

The Devil & Miss Prym

Are you brave enough to live your dream?

Strategies and inspiration to help you follow your own path in a troubled world.

Manual of the Warrior of Light

Can sex be sacred?

An unflinching exploration of the lengths we go to in our search for love, sex and spirituality.

Eleven Minutes

How far would you go for your obsession?

A sweeping story of love, loss and longing that spans the world.

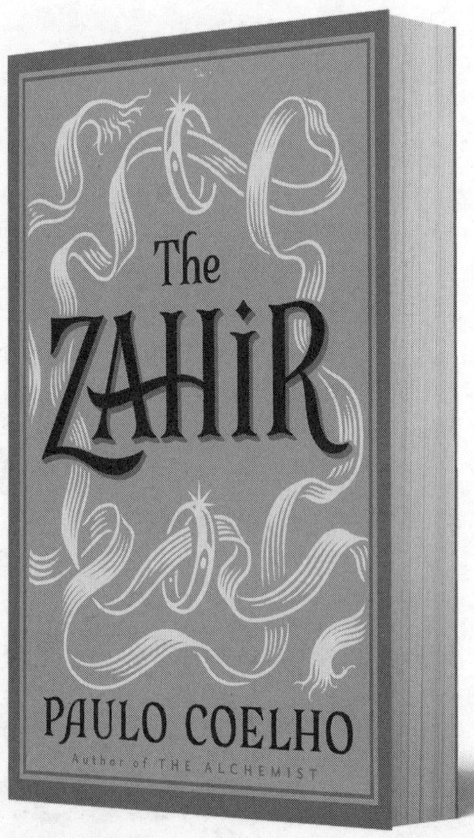

The Zahir

What happens when obsession turns to murder?

An enthralling story of jealousy, death and suspense.

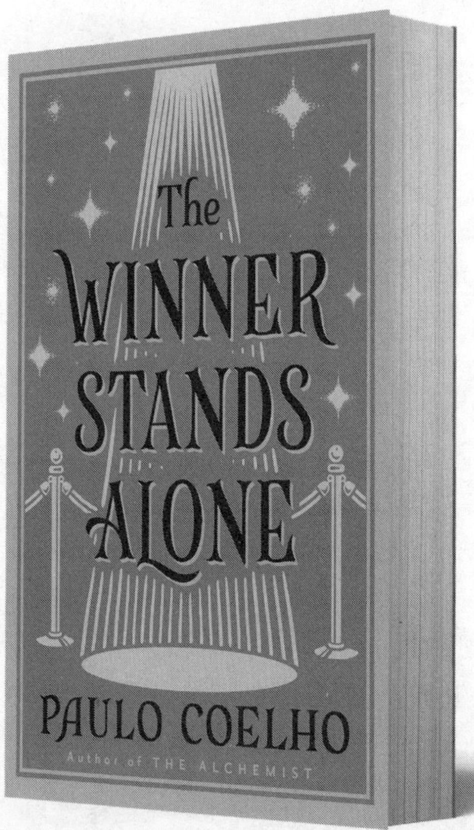

The Winner Stands Alone

Can we dare to be true to ourselves?

A story that will transform the way we think about love, joy and sacrifice.

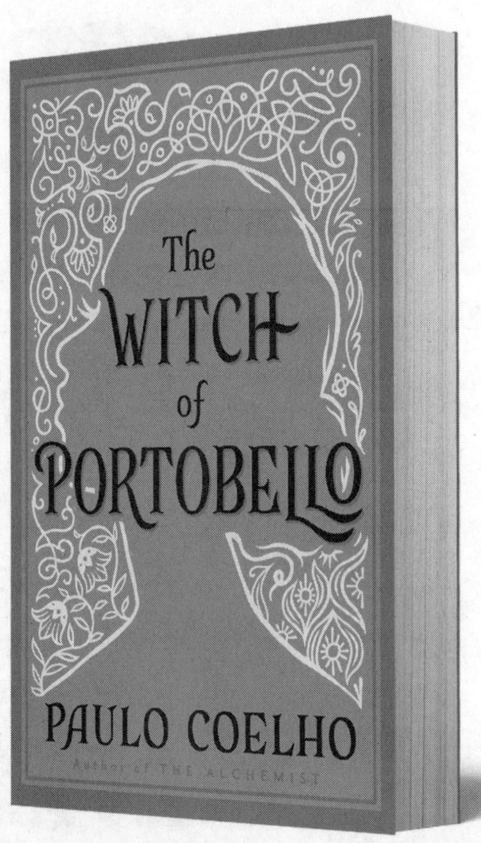

The Witch of Portobello

How will you know who your soulmate is?

A moving tale of passion, mystery and spirituality.

Brida

What does it mean to be truly alive?

Powerful tales of living and dying, destiny and choice, and love lost and found.

Like the Flowing River

Are you where you want to be?

Read *Aleph*. And rewrite your life.

Aleph

Is there a weapon more powerful than words?

A timeless and powerful exploration of personal growth, everyday wisdom and joy.

Manuscript Found in Accra

The VALKYRIES

Paulo Coelho was born in Brazil and has become one of the most widely read and loved authors in the world. Especially renowned for *The Alchemist* and *Eleven Minutes*, he has sold more than 320 million books worldwide and has been translated into 88 languages. The recipient of numerous prestigious international awards, amongst them the Crystal Award by the World Economic Forum and France's Légion d'Honneur, Paulo Coelho was inducted into the Brazilian Academy of Letters in 2002.

Also by Paulo Coelho

The Alchemist
The Pilgrimage
The Valkyries
By the River Piedra I Sat Down and Wept
The Fifth Mountain
Veronika Decides to Die
Manual of the Warrior of Light
Eleven Minutes
The Zahir
The Devil and Miss Prym
The Witch of Portobello
Brida
The Winner Stands Alone
Like the Flowing River
Aleph
Manuscript Found in Accra
Adultery
The Spy
Hippie

The VALKYRIES

PAULO COELHO

Author of THE ALCHEMIST

Translated by ALAN R. CLARKE

Thorsons

Thorsons
An imprint of HarperCollins*Publishers*
1 London Bridge Street
London SE1 9GF

HarperCollins*Publishers*
1st Floor, Watermarque Building, Ringsend Road
Dublin 4, Ireland

www.harpercollins.co.uk
www.paulocoelho.com
www.paulocoelhoblog.com

Originally published in Portuguese as *As Valkírias*,
by Editora Rocco Ltd, Brazil 1992
English translation prepared by Alan R. Clarke
English translation published by
HarperCollins*Publishers*, USA 1995, 1996
This edition published by HarperCollins, London, 2022

2 4 6 8 10 9 7 5 3 1

© HarperCollinsPublishers 1995

Paulo Coelho asserts the moral right to be
identified as the author of this work

A catalogue record for this book is
available from the British Library

ISBN 978-0-00-854732-5

FICTION / PHILOSOPHY

Printed and bound in India by Thomson Press India Ltd

All rights reserved. No part of this publication may be
reproduced, stored in a retrieval system, or transmitted,
in any form or by any means, electronic, mechanical,
photocopying, recording or otherwise, without the
prior permission of the publishers.

This book is produced from independently certified FSC® paper
to ensure responsible forest management.

O Mary!
conceived without sin,
pray for us who turn to you!
Amen.

And an angel descended
where they were
and the glory of the Lord
shone all about them.

Luke 2:9

For the name that was written in
October 12, 1988, at Glorieta Canyon

PROLOGUE

"Something that is of great importance to me?" J. thought for a few moments before responding. "Magic."

"No, something else," Paulo insisted.

"Women," J. said. "Magic and women."

Paulo laughed.

"They're important to me, too," he said. "Although marriage has slowed me down a bit."

It was J.'s turn to laugh.

"A bit," he said. "Just a bit."

Paulo filled his master's glass with wine. It had been four months since they had seen each other, and this was a quite special night. Paulo wanted to talk for a while longer, build the suspense, before giving J. the package he had brought.

"I used to imagine the great masters as people who were far removed from the world," he said to J. "If you had answered me that way a few years ago, I think I would have abandoned my apprenticeship."

"You should have done that," J. said, sipping at his wine. "And I would have found a beautiful woman disciple to take your place."

They drank the entire bottle of wine as they sat talking in the restaurant located on the top floor of J.'s hotel. They spoke of work, magic, and women. J. was euphoric about the huge contract he had just negotiated for the Dutch multinational for which he worked. And Paulo was excited about the package he had brought with him.

"Let's have another bottle," Paulo said.

"In honor of what?"

"Your coming to Rio de Janeiro. . . . The beautiful view from the window over there. . . . And the present I've brought you."

J. looked out the window to see Copacabana beach sparkling below. "The view deserves a toast," he said, signaling to the waiter.

When they were halfway through the second bottle, Paulo placed the package on the table.

Looking at J., he said, "If you were to ask me what is important to me, I would say: my master. It was he who taught me to understand that love is the only thing that never fails. He who had the patience to lead me along the intricate paths of magic. He who had the courage and dignity, despite his powers, to present himself always as a person with some doubts and with certain weaknesses. He who helped me to understand the forces that can transform our lives."

"We've had a lot of wine," J. said. "I don't want to get serious."

"I'm not talking about serious things. I'm talking about joyful things. I'm talking about love."

He pushed the package to J.'s side of the table. "Open it."

"What is this?"

"A way of saying thank you. And of passing on to others all the love you taught me."

J. opened the package. It contained almost two hundred typed pages, on the first of which was written "*The Alchemist.*"

Paulo's eyes were gleaming.

"It's a new book," he said. "Look at the next page."

There was an inscription written in longhand: "For J., the alchemist who knows and uses the secrets of the Great Work."

Paulo had anxiously awaited this moment. He had been able to keep completely secret the fact that he was writing a new book, even though he knew that J. had really liked his previous book.

"This is the original manuscript," Paulo continued. "I'd like you to read it before I send it to the publisher."

He tried to read the expression in his master's eyes, but they were impenetrable.

"I have meetings all day tomorrow," J. said, "so I'll be able to read it only at night. Let's have lunch two days from now."

Paulo had been expecting a different reaction. He thought that J. would be happy, and moved by the inscription.

"Let's do that," said Paulo, hiding his disappointment. "I'll be back in two days."

J. called for the check. They walked silently to the elevator. J. pushed the button for the eleventh floor.

When the elevator stopped at his floor, J. pushed the Emergency button to hold the door open. Then he approached Paulo and said, "May the Lamb of God protect you," making a sign on the forehead of his disciple.

Paulo embraced his master and said good night. Resetting the button, J. stepped out of the elevator.

"Why didn't you make copies of the original?" he asked, as the door began to close.

"In order to give God the chance to make it disappear, if that was his will."

"Wise decision," Paulo heard J. say as the door closed. "I hope that the literary critics never discover where it is."

❁

They met two days later, at the same restaurant.

J. began, "There are certain secrets of alchemy described in your book. Secrets I never discussed with you. And you presented them quite correctly."

Paulo was delighted. This was just what he wanted to hear.

"Well, I've been studying," he explained.

"No, you haven't been studying," J. said. "Yet what you've written about is correct."

"I can't fool him," Paulo thought. "I'd like him to think I'm dedicated, but I can't fool him."

He looked outside. The sun was glaring, and the beach was crowded.

"What do you see in that immense sky?" J. asked.

"Clouds."

"No," J. said. "You see the soul of the rivers. Rivers that have just been reborn in the sea. They will rise to the sky, and remain there until, for whatever reason, they once again become rain and fall to earth.

"The rivers return to the mountains, but carry with them the wisdom of the sea."

J. poured himself some mineral water. He didn't usually drink during the day.

"That is how you discovered those secrets we had never discussed," J. said. "You are a river. You have already run down to the sea, and you know its wisdom. You have died and been reborn many times. All you have to do is remember."

Paulo was happy. It was a kind of praise: His master said that he had "discovered secrets." But he was unable to ask openly which secrets they were.

"I have a new task for you," J. said. Silently, he thought, *It has to do with your book. Because I know it's very important to you, and it doesn't deserve to be destroyed.* But Paulo didn't need to hear about that.

❁

One week later, J. and Paulo walked together through the airport. Paulo wanted to know more about the task that his master had assigned him the week before, but J. carefully avoided conversation. They sat down at a table in the cafeteria.

"We were able to have dinner together only twice during my stay here in Rio," J. began, "and this is our third. It's in observance of the saying 'Anything that occurs once can never occur again. But, should it happen twice, it will surely happen a third time.'"

J. was trying to avoid the subject, but Paulo persevered. He knew now that his master had liked the book's dedication, because he had overheard a conversation between J. and the receptionist at the hotel. And later, one of J.'s friends had referred to Paulo as "the book's author."

He must have told a number of people about it—there was, after all, only one copy of the original. *Vanity of vanities,* he said to himself. He thanked God for having given him a master so human.

"I want to ask you about the task," Paulo said once again. "I don't want to ask 'how' or 'where,' because I know you won't tell me."

"Well, that's one thing you've learned in all this time," J. laughed.

"In one of our conversations," Paulo continued, "you told me about a man named Gene, who was able to do what you are now asking of me. I'm going to look for him."

"Did I give you his address?"

"You mentioned that he lived in the United States, in the California desert. It shouldn't be too hard to get there."

"No, it isn't."

As they spoke, Paulo became aware that the voice on the public address system was continually announcing flight departures. He began to feel tense, fearing there wouldn't be enough time to complete their conversation.

"Even though I don't want to know 'how' or 'where,' you taught me that there is a question we should always ask as we undertake something. I'm asking you that question now: Why? Why must I do this?"

"Because people always kill the things they love," J. replied.

As Paulo pondered the mystery of this answer, once again he heard a departure announced.

"That's my plane," J. said. "I have to go."

"But I don't understand your answer to my question."

Asking Paulo to pay the bill, J. quickly wrote something on a paper napkin.

Placing the napkin on the table in front of his disciple, J. said, "During the last century, a man wrote about what I've just said to you. But it's been true for many generations."

Paulo picked up the napkin. For a fraction of a second, he thought it might contain a magic formula. But it was a verse from a poem.

And each man kills the thing he loves,
By all let this be heard,
Some do it with a bitter look,
Some with a flattering word,
The coward does it with a kiss,
The brave man with a sword.

The waiter came with the change, but Paulo didn't notice. He couldn't stop looking at those terrible words.

"And so, the task," J. said after a long silence. "It's needed to break that curse."

"One way or another," Paulo said slowly, "I have wound up destroying what I've loved. I've seen my dreams fall apart just when I seemed about to achieve them. I always thought that was just the way life was. My life and everyone else's."

"The curse can be broken," J. repeated, "if you complete the task."

They walked through the noisy airport in silence. J. was thinking about the books that his disciple had written. He thought about Chris, Paulo's wife. He knew that Paulo was being drawn toward the magical initiation that appears at one time or another in everyone's life.

He knew that Paulo was on the brink of seeing one of his greatest dreams realized.

And this meant danger, because J.'s disciple was like all human beings: He was going to find that he did not necessarily deserve all that he had received.

But he didn't tell Paulo any of this.

"The women of your country are beautiful," J. said with a smile, as they arrived at the passport control line. "I hope I can come back."

But Paulo spoke seriously.

"So that's what the task is for," he said, as his master handed over his passport for stamping. "To break the curse."

And J. answered, just as seriously. "It's for love. For victory. And for the glory of God."

THEY HAD BEEN DRIVING FOR almost six hours. For the hundredth time, he asked the woman at his side if they were on the right road.

For the hundredth time, she looked at the map. Yes, they were going the right way, even though their surroundings were green, and a river ran nearby, and there were trees along the road.

"I think we should stop at a gas station and check," she said.

They drove on without speaking, listening to old songs on the radio. Chris knew that it wasn't necessary to stop at a gas station, because they were on the right road—even if the scenery around them was completely different from what they had expected. But she knew her husband well. Paulo was nervous and uncertain, thinking that she was misreading the map. He would feel better if they stopped and asked.

"What are we doing here?"

"I have a task to perform," he answered.

"Strange task," she said.

Very strange, he thought. *To speak to his guardian angel.*

"Okay," she said after a while, "you're here to speak to your guardian angel. Meanwhile, how about talking a bit with me?"

But he said nothing, concentrating on the road, thinking again that she had made a mistake about the route. *No point in insisting,* she thought. She was hoping they would come upon a gas station soon.

They had headed out on their journey straight from Los Angeles International Airport. She was afraid that Paulo was tired, and might fall asleep at the wheel. They didn't seem to be anywhere near their destination.

I should have married an engineer, she said to herself.

She had never gotten used to his life—taking off suddenly, looking for sacred pathways, swords, conversing with angels, doing everything possible to move further along the path to magic.

He has always wanted to leave everything behind.

❁

She remembered their first date. They had slept together, and within a week she had moved her art work table into his apartment. Their friends said that Paulo was a sorcerer, and one night Chris had telephoned the minister of the Protestant church she attended, asking him to say a prayer for her.

But during that first year, he had said not one word about magic. He was working at a recording studio, and that seemed to be all he was concerned about.

The following year, life was the same. He quit his job and went to work at another studio.

During their third year together, he quit his job again (a mania for leaving everything behind!) and decided to write scripts for TV. She found it strange, the way he changed jobs every year—but he was writing, earning money, and they were living well.

Then, at the end of their third year together, he decided—once again—to quit his job. He gave no explanation, saying only that he was fed up with what he was doing, that it didn't make sense to keep quitting his jobs, changing one for another. He needed to discover what it was that he wanted. They had put some money aside, and had decided to do some traveling.

In a car, Chris thought, *just like we're doing now*.

❋

Chris had met J. for the first time in Amsterdam, when they were having coffee at a cafe in the

Brower Hotel, looking out at the Singel canal. Paulo had turned pale when he saw the tall, white-haired man dressed in a business suit. Despite his anxiety, he finally worked up the courage to approach the older man's table.

That night, when Paulo and Chris were alone again, he drank an entire bottle of wine. He wasn't a good drinker, and became drunk. Only then did he reveal what she already knew: that for seven years he had dedicated himself to learning magic. Then, for some reason—which he never explained, although she asked about it a number of times—he had given it all up.

"I had a vision of J. two months ago, when we visited Dachau," Paulo said.

Chris remembered that day. Paulo had wept. He said that he was being called but didn't know how to respond.

"Should I go back to magic?" he had asked.

"Yes, you should," she had answered, but she wasn't sure.

Since Amsterdam, everything had changed. There were rituals, exercises, practices. There were long trips with J., with no defined date of return. There were long meetings with strange women, and men who had an aura of sensuality about them. There were challenges and tests, long nights when he didn't sleep, and long weekends when he never left the house. But Paulo was much happier, and he no longer thought about quitting his job. Together they had founded a small publishing house, and he was doing something he'd dreamed of for a long time: writing books.

•

Finally, a gas station. As a young Native American woman filled the tank, Paulo and Chris took a stroll.

Paulo looked at the map and confirmed the route. Yes, they were on the right road.

Now he can relax. Now he'll talk a bit, Chris thought.

"Did J. say you were to meet with your angel here?" she asked hesitantly.

"No," he replied.

Great, he gave me an answer, she thought, as she looked out at the brilliant green vegetation, lit by the setting sun. If she hadn't checked the map so often, she too would have doubted this was the right road. The map said that they should be at their destination in another six miles or so, but the scenery seemed to be telling them they had a long way to go.

"I didn't have to come here," Paulo continued. "Any place would do. But I have a contact here."

Of course. Paulo always had contacts. He referred to such people as members of the Tradition; but when Chris described them in her diary, she referred to them as the "Conspiracy." Among them were sorcerers and witch doctors—the kind of people one has nightmares about.

"Someone who speaks with angels?"

"I'm not sure. One time, J. referred—just in passing—to a master of the Tradition who lives here, and who knows how to communicate with the angels. But that might just be a rumor."

He might have been speaking seriously, but Chris knew that he might also have just selected a place at random, one of the many places where he had "contacts." A place that was far from their daily life, and where he could concentrate better on the Extraordinary.

"How are you going to speak to your angel?"

"I don't know," he replied.

What a strange way to live, thought Chris. She looked at her husband as he walked over to pay the bill. All she knew was that he felt he had to speak with the angels, and that was that! Drop everything, jump on a plane, fly for twelve hours from

Brazil to Los Angeles, drive for six hours to this gas station, arm himself with enough patience to remain here for forty days: all of this in order to speak—or rather, try to speak—with his guardian angel!

He laughed at her, and she smiled back. After all, this wasn't all that bad. They had their occasional daily irritations—paying bills, cashing checks, paying courtesy calls, accepting some tough times.

But they still believed in angels.

"We'll do it," she said.

"Thanks for the 'we,'" he answered with a smile. "But I'm the magus around here."

THE WOMAN AT THE STATION HAD SAID they were going in the right direction—about ten more minutes. They drove in silence. Paulo turned the radio off. There was a small elevation, but only when they reached the top did they realize how high up they were. They had been climbing steadily for six hours, without realizing it.

But they were there.

He parked on the shoulder and turned off the motor. Chris looked back in the direction from which they had come to see if it was true: Yes, she could see green trees, plants, vegetation.

But there in front of them, extending from horizon to horizon, was the Mojave Desert: the enormous desert that spreads into many states and into Mexico, the desert she had seen so many times in Westerns when she was a child, the desert that had places with strange names like the Rainbow Forest and Death Valley.

It's pink, Chris thought, but she didn't say anything. He was staring out at its immensity, trying to determine where the angels dwelt.

●

If you stand in the middle of the main park, you can see where the town of Borrego Springs begins and where it ends. But there are three hotels for the winter tourists who come there for the sun.

They left their luggage in the room and went to a Mexican restaurant for dinner. The waiter stood nearby for some time, trying to determine what language they were speaking. Finally, when he couldn't figure it out, he asked. When they said they were from Brazil, he said he had never met a Brazilian before.

"Well, now you've met two," Paulo laughed.

By the next day, the entire town will have heard about it, he thought. *There's not much news in Borrego Springs.*

After their meal, they walked about the town, hand in hand. Paulo wanted to wander out into the desert, get the feel of it, breathe in the air of the Mojave. So they meandered over the desert's rocky floor for a half hour, at last stopping to look back at the few distant lights of Borrego Springs.

There in the desert, the heavens were clear. They sat on the ground and made their separate wishes on the falling stars. There was no moon, and the constellations stood out brilliantly.

"Have you ever had the feeling, at certain moments in your life, that someone was observing what you were doing?" Paulo asked Chris.

"How did you know that?"

"I just know. There are moments when, without really knowing it, we are aware of the presence of angels."

Chris thought back to her adolescence. In those days, she had had that feeling very strongly.

"At such moments," he continued, "we begin to create a kind of film in which we are the main character, and we are certain that someone is observing our actions.

"But then, as we get older, we begin to think that such things are ridiculous. We think of it as having been just a child's fantasy of being a movie actor. We forget that, at those moments in which we are presenting ourselves before an invisible audience, the sensation of being observed was very strong."

He paused for a moment.

"When I look up at the night sky, that feeling often returns, and my question is always the same: Who is out there watching us?"

"And who is it?"

"Angels. God's messengers."

She stared up at the heavens, wanting to believe what he had said.

"All religions, and every person who has ever

witnessed the Extraordinary, speak of angels," Paulo went on. "The universe is populated with angels. It's they who give us hope. Like the one who announced that the Messiah had been born. They also bring death, like the exterminating angel that traveled through Egypt destroying all those who did not display the right sign at their door. Angels with flaming swords in their hands can prevent us from entering into paradise. Or they can invite us in, as the angel did to Mary.

"Angels remove the seals placed on prohibited books, and they sound the trumpets on the day of Final Judgment. They bring the light, as Michael did, or darkness, as Lucifer did."

Hesitantly, Chris asked, "Do they have wings?"

"Well, I haven't seen an angel yet," he answered. "But I wondered about that, too. I asked J. about it."

That's good, she thought. *At least I'm not the only one who has simple questions about the angels.*

"J. said that they take whatever form a person imagines they have. Because they are God's thoughts in live form, and they need to adapt to our wisdom and our knowledge. They know that if they don't, we'll be unable to see them."

Paulo closed his eyes.

"Imagine your angel, and you will feel its presence right now, right here."

They fell quiet, lying there on the floor of the desert. There was not a sound to be heard, and Chris began once again to feel like she was in a film, playing to an invisible audience. The more intensely she concentrated, the more certain she was that all around her there was a strong presence, friendly and generous. She began to imagine her angel, dressed in blue, with golden hair and immense white wings—exactly as she had pictured her angel as a child.

Paulo was imagining his angel, as well. He had already immersed himself many times in the invisible world that surrounded them, so it was not a new experience for him. But now, since J. had assigned him this task, he felt that his angel was much more present—as if the angels made themselves available only to those who believed in their existence. He knew, though, that whether one believed in them or not, they were always there—messengers of life, of death, of hell, and of paradise.

He dressed his angel in a long robe, embroidered in gold. And he also gave his angel wings.

THE HOTEL WATCHMAN, EATING HIS breakfast, turned to them as they came in.

"I wouldn't go out into the desert at night again," he said.

This really is a small town, Chris thought. *Everybody knows what you're doing.*

"It's dangerous in the desert at night," the guard explained. "That's when the coyotes come out, and the snakes. They can't stand the heat of the day, so they do their hunting after the sun goes down."

"We were looking for our angels," Paulo said.

The watchman thought that the man didn't speak English very well. What he had said didn't make sense. Angels! Perhaps he'd meant something else.

The two finished their coffee quickly. Paulo's "contact" had set their meeting for early in the morning.

CHRIS WAS SURPRISED WHEN SHE SAW Gene for the first time. He was quite young, certainly not more than twenty, and he lived in a trailer out in the desert, several miles from Borrego Springs.

"This is a master of the Conspiracy?" she whispered to Paulo, when the youth had gone to fetch some iced tea.

But Gene was back before Paulo could respond. They sat under an awning that extended along the side of the trailer.

They talked about the rituals of the Templars, about reincarnation, about Sufi magic, about the Catholic church in Latin America. The boy seemed to know a great deal, and it was amusing to listen to their conversation—they sounded like fans discussing a popular sport, defending certain tactics and criticizing others.

They spoke of everything—except angels.

The heat of the day was intensifying. They drank more tea as Gene, smiling agreeably, told them of the marvels of the desert. He warned them that novices should never go into it at night, and that it would be smart to avoid the hottest hours of the day, as well.

"The desert is made of mornings and afternoons," he said. "The other times are risky."

Chris listened to their conversation for as long as she could. But she had awakened early, and the sun was getting stronger and stronger. She decided she'd close her eyes and take a quick nap.

WHEN SHE AWOKE, THE SOUND OF THEIR voices was coming from a different place. The two men were at the rear of the trailer.

"Why did you bring your wife?" she heard Gene ask in a guarded tone.

"Because I was coming to the desert," Paulo answered, also whispering.

Gene laughed.

"But you're missing what's best about the desert. The solitude."

What a cheeky kid, Chris thought.

"Tell me about the Valkyries you mentioned," Paulo said.

"They can help you to find your angel," replied Gene. "They're the ones who instructed me. But the Valkyries are jealous and tough. They try to follow the same rules as the angels—and, you know, in the kingdom of the angels, there is no good and no evil."

"Not as we understand them," Paulo countered.

Chris had no idea what they meant by "Valkyries." She had a vague memory of having heard the name in the title of an opera.

"Was it difficult for you to see your angel?"

"A better word would be *anguishing.* It happened all of a sudden, back in the days when the Valkyries came through here. I decided I'd learn the process just for the fun of it, because at that point, I didn't yet understand the language of the desert, and I was upset about everything that was happening to me.

"My angel appeared on that third mountain peak. I was up there just wandering and listening to music on my Walkman. In those days, I had already mastered the second mind."

What the hell is the "second mind"? Chris wondered.

"Was it your father who taught it to you?"

"No. And when I asked him why he had never told me about the angels, he told me that some things are so important that you have to learn about them on your own."

They were silent for a moment.

"If you meet with the Valkyries, there's something that will make it easier for you to get along with them," Gene said.

"What's that?"

The young man laughed.

"You'll find out. But it would have been a lot better if you hadn't brought your wife along."

"Did your angel have wings?" Paulo asked.

Before Gene could answer, Chris had arisen from her folding chair, come around the trailer, and now stood before them.

"Why is he making such a big thing about your coming here alone?" she asked, speaking Portuguese. "Do you want me to leave?"

Gene went on with what he was saying to Paulo, paying no attention whatsoever to Chris's interruption. She waited for Paulo's answer—but she might just as well have been invisible.

"Give me the keys to the car," she said, at the limit of her patience.

"What does your wife want?" Gene finally asked.

"She wants to know what the 'second mind' is."

Damn! Nine years we've been together, and this stranger already knows all about us!

Gene stood up.

"Sit down, close your eyes, and I will show you what the second mind is," he said.

"I didn't come here to the desert to learn about magic or converse with angels," Chris said. "I came only to be with my husband."

"Sit down," Gene insisted, smiling.

She looked at Paulo for a fraction of a second, but was unable to determine what he was thinking.

I respect their world, but it has nothing to do with me, she thought. Although all their friends thought that she had become completely involved in her husband's lifestyle, the fact was that she and he had spoken very little of it to one another. She was used to going with him to certain places, and had once even carried his sword for purposes of a ceremony. She knew the Road to Santiago, and had—because of their relationship—learned quite a bit about sexual magic. But that was all. J. had never proposed that he teach her anything.

"What should I do?" she asked Paulo.

"Whatever you think," he answered.

I love you, she thought. If she were to learn something about his world, there was no doubt it would bring them even closer. She went back to her chair, sat down, and closed her eyes.

"What are you thinking about?" Gene asked her.

"About what you two were discussing. About Paulo traveling by himself. About the second mind. Whether his angel has wings. And why this should interest me at all. I mean, I don't think I've ever spoken to angels."

"No, no. I want to know whether you're thinking about something else. Something beyond your control."

She felt his hands touching both sides of her head.

"Relax. Relax." His voice was gentle. "What are you thinking?"

There were sounds. And voices. It was only now that she realized what she was thinking, although it had been there for almost an entire day.

"A melody," she answered. "I've been singing this melody to myself ever since I heard it yesterday on the radio on our way here."

It was true, she had been humming the melody incessantly. To the end, and then once again, and then from start to finish again. She couldn't get it out of her mind.

Gene asked that she open her eyes.

"That's the second mind," he said. "It's your second mind that's humming the song. It can do that with anything. If you're in love with someone, you can have that person inside your head. The same thing happens with someone you want to forget about. But the second mind is a tough thing to deal with. It's at work regardless of whether you want it to be or not."

He laughed.

"A song! We're always impassioned about something. And it's not always a song. Have you ever had someone you loved stick in your mind? It's really terrible when that happens. You travel, you try to forget, but your second mind keeps saying: 'Oh, he would really love that!' 'Oh, if only he were here.'"

Chris was astonished. She had never thought of such a thing as a second mind.

She had two minds. Functioning at the same time.

GENE CAME TO HER SIDE.

"Close your eyes again," he said. "And try to remember the horizon you were looking at."

She tried to recall it. "I can't," she said, her eyes still closed. "I wasn't looking at the horizon. I know that it's all around me, but I wasn't looking at it."

"Open your eyes and look at it."

Chris looked out at the horizon. She saw mountains, rocks, stones, and sparse and spindly vegetation. A sun that shone brighter and brighter seemed to pierce her sunglasses and burn into her eyes.

"You are here," Gene said, now with a serious tone of voice. "Try to understand that you are here, and that the things that surround you change you—in the same way that you change them."

Chris stared at the desert.

"In order to penetrate the invisible world and develop your powers, you have to live in the present, the *here and now.* In order to live in the present, you have to control your second mind. And look at the horizon."

Gene asked her to concentrate on the melody that she had been humming. It was "When I Fall in Love." She didn't know the words, and had been making them up, or just singing a ta-de-dum.

Chris concentrated. In a few moments, the melody disappeared. She was now completely alert, listening only to Gene's words.

But Gene seemed to have nothing more to say.

"I have to be alone now," he said. "Come back in two days."

* * *

PAULO AND CHRIS LOCKED THEMSELVES inside their air-conditioned hotel room, unwilling to confront the 110 degrees of the midday desert. No books to read, nothing to do. They tried taking a nap, but couldn't sleep.

"Let's explore the desert," Paulo said.

"It's too hot out there. Gene said it was even dangerous. Let's do it tomorrow."

Paulo didn't answer. He was certain he could turn the fact that he was locked into his hotel room into a learning experience. He tried to make sense of everything that happened in his life, and used conversation only as means for discharging tension.

But it was impossible; trying to find a meaning in everything meant he had to remain alert and tense. Paulo never relaxed, and Chris had often asked herself when he would tire of his intensity.

"Who is Gene?"

"His father is a powerful magus, and he wants Gene to maintain the family tradition—like engineers who want their children to follow in their footsteps."

"He's young, but he wants to act mature," Chris commented. "And he's giving up the best years of his life out here in the desert."

"Everything has its price. If Gene goes through all this—and doesn't abandon the Tradition—he'll be the first in a line of young masters to be integrated into a world that the older masters, although they understand it, no longer know how to explain."

Paulo lay down and started to read the only book available, *The Guide to Lodging in the Mojave Desert.* He didn't want to tell his wife that, in addition to what he had already told her, there was another reason that Gene was here: He was powerful in the paranormal processes, and had been prepared by the Tradition to be ready to act when the gates to paradise opened.

Chris wanted to talk. She felt anxious cooped up in the hotel room, and had decided not to "make sense of everything," as her husband did. She was not there to seek a place within a community of the elite.

"I didn't really understand what Gene was trying to teach me," she said. "The solitude and the desert can increase your contact with the invisible world. But I think it causes us to lose contact with other people."

"He probably has a girlfriend or two around here," Paulo said, wanting to avoid conversation.

If I have to spend another thirty-nine days locked up with Paulo, I'll commit suicide, she promised herself.

THAT AFTERNOON, THEY WENT TO A COFFEE shop across the street from the hotel. Paulo chose a table by the window. They ordered ice cream. Chris had spent several hours studying her second mind, and had learned to control it much better than before, but her appetite was never subject to control.

Paulo said, "I want you to pay close attention to the people who pass by."

She did as Paulo had asked. In the next half hour, only five people passed by.

"What did you see?"

She described the people in detail—their clothing, approximate age, what they were carrying. But apparently that wasn't what he wanted to hear. He insisted on more, trying to get a better answer, but couldn't do so.

"Okay," he said. "I'm going to tell you what it was that I wanted you to notice: All the people who passed by in the street were looking down."

They waited for some time before another person walked by. Paulo was right.

"Gene asked you to look to the horizon. Try that."

"What do you mean?"

"All of us create a kind of 'magic space' around us. Usually it's a circle with about a fifteen-foot radius, and we pay attention to what goes on within it. It doesn't matter whether it's people, tables, telephones, or windows; we try to maintain control over that small world that we, ourselves, create.

"A magus, though, always looks much further. We expand that 'magic space' and try to control a great many more things. They call it 'looking at the horizon.'"

"Well, why should I do that?"

"Because you're here. If you do it, you'll see how much things change."

When they left the coffee shop, she started to pay attention to things in the distance. She noticed the mountains, the occasional cloud that appeared as the sun began to set, and—in a strange way—she seemed to be seeing the air about her.

"Everything Gene told you is important," Paulo said. "He has already seen and talked with his angel, and he is using you as a means of instructing me. He knows the power of his words, and he knows that advice not heeded is returned to its giver, losing its energy. He needs to be sure that you are interested in what he tells you."

"Well, why doesn't he show these things directly to you?"

"Because there is an unwritten rule in the Tradition: A master never teaches another master's disciple. And he knows I am J.'s disciple. But since he wants to be of help to me, he is using you for that purpose."

"Is that why you brought me here?"

"No. It was because I was afraid of being alone in the desert."

He could have said it was because he loves me, she thought. *That would have been more truthful.*

• • •

THEY STOPPED THE CAR ON THE SHOULDER of the narrow dirt road. Two days had passed, and they were to meet Gene that night—Gene, who had told her always to look to the horizon. She was excited about their meeting.

But it was still morning. And the days in the desert were long.

She looked out at the horizon: mountains that suddenly sprang up millions of years ago, crossing the desert in a long *cordillera.* Although the earthquakes that created them had occurred long ago, one could still see how the earth's surface had buckled—the ground still climbed smoothly toward the mountains, and then, at a certain altitude, a kind of wound opened, out of which rocks sprang, pointing to the sky.

Between the mountains and the car was a rocky valley with sparse vegetation: thorn bushes, cacti, and yucca. Life that insisted on surviving in an environment that didn't support it. And an immense white expanse the size of five football fields stood out in the middle of it all. It reflected the morning sun, and resembled a field of snow.

"Salt. A salt lake."

Yes. This desert must once have been the bed of an ocean. Once a year, seagulls from the Pacific

Ocean flew the hundreds of miles to this desert to eat the species of shrimp that appeared when the rains began. Human beings may forget their origins, but nature, never.

"It must be about three miles from here," Chris said.

Paulo checked his watch. It was still early. They had looked to the horizon and it had shown them a salt lake. One hour's walk there, another to return, no risk of the midday sun.

Each placed a canteen of water on their belt. Paulo put his cigarettes and a Bible in a small bag. When they arrived at the lake, he was going to suggest that they read a passage from it, chosen at random.

THEY BEGAN TO WALK. CHRIS KEPT HER eyes fixed on the horizon whenever possible. Although it was a simple thing to be doing, something strange was happening: She felt better, freer, as if her internal energy had been increased. For the first time in many years, she regretted not having taken a more intense interest in Paulo's "Conspiracy." She had always imagined difficult rituals that only those who were prepared and disciplined could perform.

They walked at a leisurely pace for half an hour. The lake appeared to have shifted its location; it always seemed to be at the same distance from them.

They walked for another hour. They must already have covered four miles or so, but the lake appeared to be only a bit closer.

It was no longer early morning, and the heat of the sun was building.

Paulo looked back. He could see the car, a tiny red point in the distance but still visible—impossible to become lost. And when he looked at the car, he saw something else that was important.

"Let's stop here," he said.

They left the path they were taking and walked to a boulder. They huddled in close to it, because it cast only a very small shadow. In the desert, shadows appear only early in the morning or late in the afternoon, and then only near the rocks.

"Our calculation was wrong," he said.

Chris had already noticed that. She was surprised, because Paulo was good at estimating distances, and he had trusted her guess of three or four miles.

"I know how we went wrong," he said. "There's nothing in the desert to base comparisons on. We're used to calculating distance based on the size of things. We know the approximate size of a tree, or a telephone pole, or a house. They help us to decide whether things are near or far away."

Here, there was no point of reference. There were rocks they'd never seen, mountains whose size they could not estimate, and only the sparse vegetation. Paulo had realized this as he looked back at the car. And he could see that they had walked more than four miles.

"Let's rest a while, and then we'll go back."

That's all right, Chris thought. She was fascinated with the idea of continuing to look out at the horizon. It was a completely new experience for her.

"This business of looking at the horizon, Paulo . . ." Chris paused.

He waited, knowing that she would continue. He knew that she was worried that she might say something silly, or find some esoteric meaning in things, as many do who know only a little about the path.

"It seems as if . . . I don't know . . . I can't explain it . . . as if my soul has grown."

Yes, Paulo thought. *She's on the right track.*

"Before, I looked in the distance, and things in the distance seemed really *far,* you know? They seemed not to be a part of my world. Because I was used to looking only at things that were close, the things around me.

"But, two days ago, I got used to looking into the distance. And I saw that besides tables, chairs, and objects, my world also included the mountains, clouds, the sky. And my soul—my soul seems to have eyes that it uses to touch those things."

Wow! That's a great way of saying it, Paulo thought.

"My soul seems to have grown," Chris repeated.

He opened the bag, took out his cigarettes, and lit one before speaking.

"Anyone can see that. But we're always looking at the things that are closest to us. Looking down and inward. So our power diminishes, and using your term, our soul shrinks.

"Because our soul includes nothing but ourselves. It doesn't include oceans, mountains, other people; it doesn't even include the walls of the houses where we live."

Paulo liked the expression "My soul has grown." If he had been talking with another member of the Tradition, there's no doubt that he would have heard much more complicated explanations, such as "My consciousness expanded." But the term his wife had used was more exact.

He finished his cigarette. There was no point in insisting that they make it to the lake; the temperature would soon reach 110 in the shade. The car was far away, but visible, and in an hour and a half they'd be back to it.

They started walking. Surrounded by the desert, by the huge horizon, a feeling of freedom began to grow in their souls.

"Let's take off our clothes," Paulo said.

"But someone might be watching," Chris said automatically.

Paulo laughed. They could see for miles around them. The day before, when they had been out walking all morning and afternoon, only two cars had passed—and, even then, they had heard the sound of their approach long before the cars had appeared. The desert was the sun, the wind, and the silence.

"Only our angels are watching," he answered. "And they've already seen us naked many times."

He took off his shorts and his shirt and the canteen, placing them all in the bag.

Chris struggled to keep from laughing. She took her clothes off too, and in a few moments they were two people crossing the Mojave in their sneakers, their hats, and their sunglasses—one of them carrying a bag. Anyone watching would find it hilarious.

THEY WALKED FOR HALF AN HOUR. THE car was still just a point on the horizon, but—in contrast to the lake—it was growing in size as they approached it. They would be there in a short while.

Suddenly, Chris felt tremendously tired.

"Let's rest for a few minutes," she said.

Paulo stopped immediately, saying, "I can't carry this bag anymore. I'm really tired."

How could he not be able to carry the bag? Even with everything it held, it couldn't weigh more than six or seven pounds.

"You have to carry it. The water's in there."

Right, he had to carry it.

"Well then, let's get going," he said irritably.

Everything was so romantic just a few minutes ago, thought Chris. And now he was irritated. Well, forget it. She was tired, too.

They walked a bit farther, and their exhaustion worsened. If it were up to her, nothing more would be said—she didn't want to make things worse.

What a dope, she thought. To get angry in the midst of such beauty, and right after they had been talking about such interesting things as . . .

She couldn't remember, but it wasn't important. She was too tired to think now.

Paulo stopped and put the bag down in the sand.

"Let's rest," he said.

He didn't seem irritated now. He must be getting tired, too. Just like her.

There was no shade. But she needed to rest.

They sat down on the hot sand. The fact that they were naked and that the ground burned their skin didn't matter. They had to stop. Just for a while.

She remembered what they had been discussing: horizons. She noticed that now, even without wanting to, she had the feeling that her soul had grown. And it seemed like her second mind had stopped working altogether. She didn't think of melodies or repetitious things, and she didn't even care if someone was watching them walk naked across the desert.

Nothing was important. She felt relaxed, unworried, free.

They sat there for a few minutes in silence. It was hot, but the sun didn't bother them. If it started to, they had plenty of water.

He stood up first.

"I think we had better keep walking. It's not far to the car now. We'll rest in the air-conditioning when we get there."

She was sleepy. She just wanted to nap for a bit. But she got up, anyway.

They walked a bit farther, and now the car was getting close. Not more than ten minutes to walk.

"Since we're so close, let's sleep for a while. Five minutes."

Sleep for five minutes? Why would he say that? Was he reading her mind? There couldn't be any problem with sleeping for just five minutes. They could get a good tan, as if they'd been to the beach.

They sat down again. They had been walking for half an hour, not counting their pauses. Why couldn't they just sleep for five minutes or so?

They heard the sound of a motor. Half an hour earlier, she would have leaped up and dressed in a hurry. But now, so what? It didn't matter at all. Let anyone look who wants to look. It didn't make any difference to her. She just wanted to sleep.

Paulo and Chris watched calmly as a truck drove down the road, passed their car, and stopped just beyond. A man got out and walked toward the vehicle. He looked inside, then walked around the car, examining everything.

Might be a thief, Paulo thought. He imagined the guy stealing the car, leaving them both stranded in the desert with no way to get back. The key was in the ignition—he hadn't taken it with him for fear of losing it.

But they were in the Mojave Desert. In New York, maybe. But here—no one stole cars here.

Chris looked out at the desert. It was golden and beautiful. Golden. Different from the pinkness of the desert at sundown.

An agreeable feeling of relaxation permeated her entire body. The sun didn't bother her—people didn't know how lovely the desert could be during the day!

The man gave up his inspection of the car, and placed his hand above his eyes. He was looking for them.

She was naked . . . and he would surely see that. So what? Paulo didn't seem worried, either.

The man began walking toward them. The feeling of lightness and euphoria was increasing, but exhaustion kept them from moving. The desert was golden and beautiful. Everything was serene, at peace—the angels, yes, the angels would appear before long. That was what they had come to the desert for—to talk with their angels!

She was naked, and she was not ashamed.

The man stopped when he reached them. What

language was he speaking? They couldn't understand what he was saying.

Paulo tried to concentrate on what he was hearing, and realized that the man was speaking English. After all, they were in the United States.

"Come with me," the man said.

"We want to rest," Paulo said. "Five minutes."

The man picked up the bag and opened it.

"Put this on," he said to Chris, handing her clothing to her.

She forced herself to get up, and did as he said. She was too tired to argue.

He ordered Paulo to do the same, and Paulo was also too tired to argue. The man saw the canteens filled with water, opened one of them, filled the cap, and ordered them to drink.

They weren't thirsty. But they did as the man said. They were quite calm, and completely at peace with the world—and they had no desire to argue.

They would do anything they were told to do, obey any order, so long as they were left in peace.

"Let's walk," the man said.

They couldn't even think. They sat there gazing at the desert. They would do anything so long as the stranger left them alone.

But the man escorted them to the car, told them to get in, and started the engine. "I wonder where he's taking us," Paulo thought. But he wasn't worried—the world was at peace, and the only thing he wanted to do was sleep. Surely his angel would appear before long.

PAULO AWOKE WITH HIS STOMACH churning, and a tremendous need to vomit.

"Lie still for a while longer."

Someone was speaking to him, but in his head there was only confusion. He still remembered the golden paradise where all had been serene and peaceful.

He tried to move, and felt as if thousands of needles were sticking into his head.

I think I'll go back to sleep, he thought. But he couldn't—the needles wouldn't allow it. And his stomach was still turning over.

"I want to throw up," he said.

When he opened his eyes, he saw that he was sitting in a kind of mini-market: He could see several refrigerator cabinets with soft drinks and shelves with foodstuffs. The sight of the food made him feel nauseated again. Then he noticed nearby a man he had never seen before.

The man helped him to get up. In addition to the imaginary needles in his head, Paulo realized that he had another in his arm. Only this one was real.

The man held the needle in place and helped Paulo to the bathroom, where he vomited some water, nothing more.

"What's happening? What's this needle for?"

It was Chris, speaking Portuguese. He returned to the store and saw that she was sitting up, too, with a needle in her arm.

Paulo felt a little better now, and no longer needed the man's support. He helped Chris up and to the bathroom, where she vomited.

"I'm going to use your car to get back to mine," the stranger said. "I'll leave the keys in the ignition. You can get a ride to it when you're ready."

Paulo was starting to remember what had happened, but the nausea had returned, and he had to vomit again.

When he came back, the man had left, but a boy of seventeen or eighteen was there.

"Just another hour," the boy said. "The solution will be used up then, and you can go."

"What time is it?"

The boy told them. Paulo struggled to get up—he had an appointment, and there was no way he was going to miss it.

"I have to meet with Gene," he said to Chris.

"Sit down," the boy said. "Not until the solution is used up."

The comment was unnecessary. Paulo no longer

had either the strength or desire to walk even to the door.

I've missed the meeting, he thought. But at this point, nothing mattered. The less he thought about, the better.

"FIFTEEN MINUTES," GENE SAID. "THAT'S all it takes, and without even realizing what's happening, you die."

They were back at the old trailer. It was the afternoon of the next day, and the entire scene was bathed in pink. Nothing like the desert of the previous day—golden, peaceful, nausea, vomiting.

They hadn't been able to eat or sleep for twenty-four hours—they threw up everything they tried to eat. But now that strange sensation was passing.

"It's good that your horizon had been expanded. And that you were thinking about angels. An angel appeared."

Paulo thought it would be better to have said "Your soul had grown." Besides, the guy who had appeared wasn't an angel—he had an old truck, and he spoke English.

"Let's get going," said Gene, asking Paulo to start the car. He took the passenger seat, with no show of ceremony. And Chris, grumbling in Portuguese, climbed into the back.

Gene began to give instructions—take that road there, go for a few miles, drive fast so that the car gets cool inside, turn off the air-conditioning so the motor doesn't overheat. Several times they drove off the narrow dirt road into the desert. But Gene knew what he was doing. He wasn't going to make the same mistakes they had.

"What happened yesterday?" Chris asked for the hundredth time. She knew that Gene wanted her to ask. He might already have seen his guardian angel, but he acted like any other young man his age.

"Sunstroke," he finally explained. "Haven't either of you ever seen a film about the desert?"

Of course they had. Thirsty men, dragging themselves across the sand in search of a drop of water.

"We didn't feel thirsty at all. The two canteens were filled with water."

"That's not what I'm talking about," the American interrupted. "I mean your clothing."

The clothing! The Arabs with their long robes, and several hoods—one on top of the other. Of course, how stupid we were! Paulo had already heard about that, and he'd already walked across three other deserts . . . and he had never felt the desire to take his clothes off. But here, that morning, after the frustration of the lake that they seemed never to reach. . . . *How could I have had such a stupid idea?* he thought.

"When you took off your clothes, the water in your bodies began to evaporate immediately. You can't even perspire, because the climate is so dry. In fifteen minutes, you were both already dehydrated. No thirst or anything—just a slight feeling of disorientation."

"And the exhaustion?"

"That exhaustion is death arriving."

I sure didn't know it was death arriving, Chris said to herself. If someday she had to choose an easy way to leave the world behind, she would come back and take off her clothing in the middle of the desert.

"Most people who die in the desert die with water in their canteen. The dehydration is so rapid that we feel as if we've drunk an entire bottle of whisky, or taken an overdose of some tranquilizer." He suggested that, starting now, they drink water periodically—even if they weren't thirsty—because their bodies needed the water.

"But an angel did appear," Gene said.

Before Paulo could say what he was thinking, Gene ordered him to stop at the foot of a cliff.

"Let's get out here and go the rest of the way on foot."

They began to walk along a narrow path that led to the top of the cliff. Before they had gone far, Gene realized he had forgotten the flashlight from the car. He went back, picked it up, and sat on the hood of the car for some time, staring out at the desert.

Chris is right; solitude does strange things to people. He's behaving strangely, Paulo thought as he watched the youth down below.

But, a few seconds later, Gene had climbed the narrow path again, and they pushed on.

In forty minutes, with no great difficulty, they had reached the top. There was some sparse vegetation there, and Gene asked that they sit down facing north. His attitude, usually expansive, had changed—he seemed more distant, and looked as if he were concentrating hard.

"You've both come here in search of angels," he said, sitting down at their side.

"That's what I came for," Paulo said. "And I know that you have spoken with one."

"Forget about my angel. Many people in this desert have already seen or conversed with their angel. So have a lot of people in cities, or at sea, or in the mountains."

There was a tone of impatience in his voice.

"Think about *your* guardian angels," he continued. "Because my angel is here, and I can see him. This is my holy place."

Both Paulo and Chris thought back to their first night in the desert. And they imagined their angels once again, with their raiment and their wings.

"You must always have a holy place. Mine once was a small apartment, and at another time, a square in the middle of Los Angeles. Now it's here. A sacred hymn opens a gate to heaven, and heaven appears."

They both looked around at Gene's holy place: the rocks, the hard ground, the desert plants. Perhaps snakes and coyotes passed through here at night, too.

Gene appeared to be in a trance.

"It was here that I was first able to see my angel, although I knew that the angel was everywhere, and that the angel's face is the face of the desert I live in, or of the city where I lived for eighteen years.

"I was able to talk with my angel because I had faith that the angel existed. And because I loved my angel."

Neither Chris nor Paulo dared ask what they had talked about.

Gene went on, "Everyone can make contact with four different kinds of entities in the invisible world: the elementals, the disembodied spirits, the saints, and the angels.

"The elementals are the vibrations of things in nature—fire, earth, water, and air—and we make contact with them using rituals. These are pure forces—like earthquakes, lightning, or volcanoes. Because we need to understand them as 'beings,' they traditionally appear in the form of dwarfs, fairies, or salamanders. But all one can do is use the power of the elementals—we never learn anything from them."

Why is he saying all this? Paulo thought. *Has he forgotten that I'm a master of magic, too?*

Gene continued his explanation, "The disembodied spirits are those that wander between one life and another, and we make contact with them by means of a medium. Some are great masters—but all that they teach us we can learn on earth, because that's where they learned what they know. Better, then, to let them wander in the direction of their next step, to look out at the horizon, and to take from *here* the same wisdom as they did."

Paulo must know all about this, Chris thought. *He's probably talking to me.*

❁ ❁ ❁

YES, GENE WAS SPEAKING TO CHRIS—IT was because she was here that he was here. There was nothing he could teach Paulo, twenty years older than he and more experienced, and who, on his own, would surely find the way to talk with his angel. Paulo was one of J.'s disciples—and the things Gene had heard about J.! At their first meeting, Gene had tried in various ways to get the Brazilian to talk, but the woman had made it impossible. He was unable to learn anything about the techniques, the processes, or the rituals used by J.

That first meeting had been deeply disappointing for him. He thought that the Brazilian might be using J.'s name without the master's knowledge. Or—who knows?—perhaps J. had made a mistake for the first time in his selection of a disciple. And if that were the case, the entire Tradition would soon know about it. But that night of their meeting, he had dreamed of his guardian angel.

And his angel had asked that he initiate the woman into the path of magic. Just initiate her: Her husband would do the rest.

In the dream, he argued that he had already taught her about the second mind, and had asked that she look out at the horizon. The angel said that Gene should pay attention to the man, but that he should take care of the woman. And then the angel disappeared.

Gene was trained to be disciplined. So he was now doing what the angel had commanded—and he hoped that it was being observed up above.

❁

"After the disembodied spirits," he continued, "the saints appear. These are the true masters. They lived among us at one time, and are now closer to the light. The great teachings of the saints are their lives here on earth. Contained in them are all we need to know, and all we have to do is imitate them."

"How do we invoke the saints?" Chris asked.

"Through prayer," Paulo answered, cutting Gene off.

He wasn't jealous—although it was clear to him that the American wanted to impress Chris. *He respects the Tradition. He's going to use my wife as a means of reaching me. But why is he being so basic, talking about things that I already know so well?* he thought.

"We invoke the saints through constant prayer," Paulo continued. "And when they are near, everything changes. Miracles happen."

Gene couldn't help but notice the Brazilian's hostile, almost aggressive tone of voice. But he wasn't going to say anything about his dream of the angel, because he didn't owe this man anything.

"Finally," Gene said, "there are the angels."

Perhaps Paulo didn't know about this part, even though he seemed to know many other things. Gene paused for a few moments. He sat there silently praying, and remembered his angel, and hoped that he was hearing every word. And he asked that his angel help him to be clear, because—my God!—it was so difficult to explain.

"Angels are love in motion. They never rest, they struggle to grow, and they are beyond good and evil. Love that consumes all, that destroys all, that forgives all. Angels are made of that love, and are at the same time its messengers.

"The love of the exterminating angel, who one day will take away our soul, and of the guardian angel, who brings our soul back. Love in motion."

"Love at war," Chris said.

"There is no love in peace. Whoever seeks peace is lost."

What does a boy like this know about love? He lives alone in the desert, and has never been in love, Chris thought. Meanwhile, no matter how hard she tried, she could think of not one moment when love had ever brought her peace. It was always accompanied by agony, intense joy, and deep sadness.

Gene turned to them. "Let's be silent for a while, so that our angels can hear the love that exists beyond our silence."

Chris was still thinking about love. Yes, the boy seemed to be right, although she could swear that all of his knowledge was theoretical. *Love comes to rest only when we are close to death. How strange.* How strange was everything that she was experiencing, especially the sensation that her soul had grown.

She had never asked Paulo to teach her anything—she believed in God, and that was sufficient. She respected her husband's search, but—perhaps because she was so close to him, or because she knew that he had the same defects as other men—she had never taken an interest in it.

But she didn't know Gene. He had said: "Try to look at the horizon. Pay attention to your second mind." And she had done so. Now, with her soul that had grown, she was discovering how good it was, and how much time she had wasted before.

"Why do we need to speak with our angels?" Chris asked, breaking the silence.

"To discover through them," replied Gene.

Gene wasn't bothered by the comment. If she had asked the question of Paulo, he would have been angry.

They said an Our Father and a Hail Mary. Then the American said that they could go back down.

"That's it?" Paulo asked, disappointed.

"I wanted to bring you here so my angel could see that I had done as my angel asked," Gene answered. "I have nothing else to teach you. If you want to learn more, seek out the Valkyries."

THEY MADE THE RETURN TRIP IN AWKWARD silence, interrupted only when Gene had to indicate which turn should be taken. No one was interested in conversation—Paulo, because he thought that Gene had tricked him; Chris, because Paulo might be irritated at her comments, feeling that she was spoiling everything; and Gene, because he knew that the Brazilians were disappointed, and because of this, would not talk about J. and his techniques.

"You are wrong about one thing," Paulo said when they arrived at the trailer. "It was not an angel that we met up with yesterday. It was a guy driving a truck."

For a fraction of a second, Chris thought there would be no response—the hostility between the two men was growing stronger and stronger. The American turned and began to walk in the direction of his home, but suddenly he stopped.

"I want to tell you a story my father told me," he said. "A master and his disciple were walking together in the desert. The master was teaching his charge that he could always trust in God, since he was aware of everything.

"Night fell, and they decided to pitch camp. The master raised the tent, and the disciple was given the assignment of tethering the horses to a rock. But, as he stood by the rock, he thought to himself: *The master is testing me. He said that God is aware of everything, and then asked me to tie up the horses. He wants to see whether or not I believe in God.*

"Instead of tethering the animals, he said a long prayer, and left the fate of the horses in God's hands.

"Next day, when they awoke, the horses were gone. Disappointed, the disciple complained to the master, saying that he no longer believed in him, since God had not taken care of everything, and had forgotten to watch over the horses.

"'You are wrong,' the master answered. 'God wanted to take care of the horses. But in order to do so, he needed to make use of your hands to tether them to the stone.'"

THE YOUNG MAN LIT A SMALL GAS lantern that was hanging outside the trailer. The light dimmed the brilliance of the stars somewhat.

"When we begin to think about our angels, they begin to manifest themselves. Their presence becomes closer and closer, more real. But, at the beginning, angels show themselves as they have done throughout our life: through others.

"Your angel used that man. He must have been caused to leave his home early—something must have changed in his routine, altering everything so that he could be there just at the moment that you needed him. That is a miracle. Do not try to regard it as a common event."

Paulo said nothing.

"Look," Gene explained. "When we were climbing the mountain, I forgot the flashlight," Gene went on. "You probably noticed that I was back at the car for quite a while. Whenever I forget something on leaving the house, I feel that my guardian angel is in action, causing me to lose a few seconds—and this short time interval may signify important things. It may allow me to avoid an accident, or cause me to run into someone I need to see.

"So, after I get what I've forgotten, I always sit down and count to twenty. That way, the angel has time to take action. An angel uses many instruments."

Gene asked Paulo to wait where he was for a few moments. He entered the trailer, and returned with a map. "The last time I saw the Valkyries, it was here."

He pointed to a place on the map. Chris realized that the animosity between the two seemed to have lessened.

"Take care of her," Gene said. "It's a good thing that she came with you."

"I think so," Paulo said. "Thank you for everything."

And they said good-bye.

"WHAT A FOOL I'VE BEEN," PAULO SAID, punching the steering wheel as they drove away.

"What do you mean, a fool? I thought you were jealous!"

But Paulo was laughing, in a good mood.

"Four processes! And he only said three! It's through the fourth process that you converse with your angel!"

He looked at Chris, and his eyes were gleaming with the joy of discovery.

"The fourth process: channeling!"

Almost ten days in the desert. They stopped at one place where the ground had opened in a series of wounds, as if prehistoric rivers had run through there, dozens of them, leaving long, deep arroyos that were becoming larger through the action of the sun.

In those parts, not even the scorpions could survive, much less snakes, coyotes, or the ever-present tumbleweed. The desert was full of such places, known as badlands.

The two entered into one of the immense wounds. The earthen walls were high, and all that could be seen was a tortuous path, with no beginning or end.

They were no longer irresponsible adventurers, feeling that nothing could harm them. The desert had its laws, and killed those who did not respect them. They had learned what the laws were—the sound of the rattlesnake, the hours that it was safe to be out there, the precautions. Before entering the badlands, they had left a note in the car saying where they were going. Even if it were only for half an hour, and it appeared to be unnecessary, ridiculous, a car might stop, and someone would see the note and know what direction they had taken. They had to facilitate the instruments of their guardian angels.

They were looking for the Valkyries. Not there, at the end of the world—because nothing living could survive for long in those badlands. There—well, this was just training. For Chris.

But they knew that the Valkyries were nearby, because they saw the signs. They lived in the desert, never staying for long in one place—but they left signs.

Paulo and Chris had found some clues. At the beginning, they had stopped at one small town after another, asking about the Valkyries, and no one had ever heard of them. The directions Gene had given them were of no use—they had probably long ago passed by the spot on the map he had shown them. But one day, in a bar, they met a boy who remembered having read something about them. He described the way the Valkyries dressed, and the signs they left.

They began to ask others about women who were dressed that way. Some responded with obvious disapproval, saying the Valkyries had passed by a month ago, a week ago, three days ago.

Finally, they had reached a place that seemed to be just a day's travel from where the Valkyries should be.

THE SUN WAS ALREADY NEAR THE horizon—or they would not have risked being out in the desert. The earthen walls cast shadows. It was the perfect place.

Chris couldn't stand to repeat the whole thing yet again. But she had to—she hadn't yet achieved any meaningful results.

"Sit there. With your back to the sun."

She did as Paulo said. And then, automatically, she began to relax. She sat cross-legged, with her eyes closed—but she could feel the entire desert surrounding her. Her soul had been swelling during these days in the desert, and she knew that her world had expanded. It was more vast than it had been two weeks earlier.

"Concentrate on your second mind," he said.

Chris sensed an inhibited tone in his voice. He could not act toward her in the same way as he did with other disciples—after all, she knew his faults and weaknesses. But Paulo made a supreme effort to act as a master would, and she respected him for that.

She concentrated on her second mind. She allowed all thoughts to come to mind—and, as always, they were absurd thoughts for someone who was in the middle of the desert. For the past three days, whenever she had tried the exercise, she realized that her automatic thinking was very much concerned with whom she should invite to her birthday celebration—three months from now.

But Paulo had asked that she not be concerned about that. That she allow her concerns to flow freely.

"Let's start from the beginning again," he said.

"I'm thinking about my party."

"Don't fight your thoughts. They are stronger than you are," Paulo said for the thousandth time. "If you want to rid yourself of them, accept them. Think about what they want you to think about until they grow tired."

She went over her list of invitations. She rejected some. She substituted others. This was the first step: Pay attention to the second mind until it grew tired.

Now, the birthday celebration disappeared more quickly than before. But she was still composing the list. It was unbelievable how a subject like that could demand her attention for so many days, occupy hours when she could be thinking of more interesting things.

"Think until you are tired. Then, when you are tired, open the channel."

Paulo walked away from his wife and leaned against the wall. Gene was an expert, and took very seriously the business of not being able to teach anything to the disciple of another master. But, through Chris, he had given Paulo all of the clues that he needed.

The fourth way of communicating with the invisible world was channeling.

Channeling! How many times had he seen people in their cars in the midst of a traffic snarl, talking to themselves, without realizing that they were performing one of the most sophisticated of the magical processes! But, because of its extreme simplicity, all one need do is sit in a quiet place and be attentive to the thoughts that emerge from the bottom of one's mind.

Channeling has generally been considered a superficial practice. Nothing of the kind! Since the beginnings of humanity, people have known that, if they wanted to enter into contact with God, they had to make room in their soul. They had to allow their spiritual energy to manifest itself, and to create a bridge between the visible and the invisible.

How can one create such a bridge? Various mystical processes address the importance of "not being." Relax, allow the mind to become empty, and surprise yourself with the great treasure that begins to flow from your soul. The word *inspiration* means exactly that: the bringing in of air, allowing oneself to drink from an unknown source.

Channeling required no loss of awareness during the contact with the spirits; it was a more natural process for a person to use in order to plunge into the unknown. It allowed for contact with the Holy Spirit, with the soul of the world, with the enlightened masters. No ritual was needed, no incorporation, nothing. Every human being knew, subconsciously, that there was a bridge available to the invisible, a bridge one could cross without fear.

And everyone tried to do so, even without being aware of it. Everyone surprised themselves, saying things they had never thought before, giving advice of the "I don't know why I'm saying this" type, doing certain things that didn't appear to make sense.

And everyone liked to spend time observing nature's miracles—a thunderstorm, a sunset—ready to enter into contact with the universal wisdom, think about things that were truly important.

But at such times, the invisible wall would appear: the second mind.

The second mind was there, barring the entrance, with its repetitive ideas, its unimportant problems, its melodies, its financial problems, its unresolved passions.

He stood and approached Chris.

"Be patient, and listen to everything your second mind has to say. Don't respond. Don't argue. It will get tired."

Once again, Chris went over the invitation list, even though she had already lost interest in it. When she finished, she put a period to it.

And she opened her eyes.

There she was, in that wound in the earth. She felt the still air that surrounded her.

"Open the channel. Begin to speak."

Speak!

She had always been fearful of speaking out, of seeming ridiculous, stupid. Fearful of learning what others thought of what she said, because they always seemed more capable, more intelligent. Always seemed to have an answer for everything.

But now she was here, and she had to have the courage even to say things that made no sense, that were absurd. Paulo had explained that this was one way of channeling: speak. Conquer your second mind, and allow the universe to do what it wanted with it.

She began to move her head back and forth, wanting to do all that, and suddenly she wanted to make strange noises. And she did so. It wasn't ridiculous. She was free to do as she pleased.

She had no idea where these things came from—but they were coming from within, from the bottom of her soul, and manifesting themselves. From time to time, her second mind returned with its concerns, and Chris tried to organize them, but that's the way it had to be—no logic, no censure, but rather the joy of a warrior entering into an unknown world. She needed to speak the pure language of the heart.

Paulo listened in silence, and Chris felt his presence. She was totally aware, but free. She could not concern herself with what he was thinking—she had to continue to speak, making the gestures that came to her, singing the strange melodies. Yes, everything must make some kind of sense, because she had never heard these sounds before, these melodies, these words and movements. It was difficult, and she had the fear that she was fantasizing things, wanting to appear to be more in contact with the Invisible than she really was. But she overcame her fear of the ridiculous, and went on.

Today, something different was happening. She was no longer doing what she did out of obligation, as in the first days. She was enjoying herself. And she began to feel secure. A wave of security washed back and forth, and Chris tried desperately to go with it.

In order to keep the wave close to her, she had to speak. Say anything that came to mind.

"I see the earth." Her voice was hesitant, calm, even though her second mind made an appearance from time to time, saying that Paulo must be finding all of this ridiculous. "We are in a safe place, we can stay here tonight, lie here and look up at the stars and talk of angels. There are no scorpions, no snakes, no coyotes.

"The planet set aside certain places for itself. It tells us to go away. In those places, without the millions of life forms that walk on its surface, the earth is able to be alone. She also needs her solitude, for she needs to understand herself."

Why am I saying that? He's going to think I'm showing off. I'm aware!

Paulo looked around. The dry bed of the river seemed gentle, smooth. But it inspired a terror of total solitude, of the complete absence of life.

"Say a prayer," Chris went on. Her second mind was no longer able to make her feel ridiculous.

But suddenly, she felt fear. Fear of not knowing which prayer, of not knowing how to continue.

And when she felt the fear, her second mind returned—and the ridicule, the shame, the concern about Paulo returned with it. After all, he was the Magus—he knew more than she, and must think all of this was phony.

She took a deep breath. She concentrated on the present, on the earth where nothing grew, on the sun that was already hidden. Bit by bit, the wave of security came back—like a miracle.

"Say a prayer," she repeated.

And it is going to echo
clearly
against the sky
when I come along
making my noise

She sat there in silence for a while, sensing that she had given her all, and that the channeling had ended. Then she turned to him.

"I went very far today. It's never happened that way."

Paulo caressed her face and kissed her. She didn't know whether he was doing that out of pity or pride.

"Let's go," he said. "Let's respect the earth's desire."

"Maybe he is saying that to give me a stimulus, to get me to try to continue channeling," she thought. But she was certain—something had happened. She hadn't invented all that.

"The prayer?" she asked, fearful of his answer.

"It's an ancient indigenous chant. From the Ojibway shamans."

She was proud of her husband's knowledge, even though he said it didn't count for much.

"How can these things happen?"

Paulo remembered J., discussing in his book the secrets of alchemy: "The clouds are rivers that already know the sea." But he wasn't inclined to explain. He was feeling tense, irritable, and didn't know exactly why he was staying on in the desert; after all, he already knew how to converse with his guardian angel.

"Did you see the film *Psycho?*" Paulo asked Chris when they arrived back at the car.

Chris nodded her head.

"The lead actress dies in the bathroom early on in the film. In the desert, I learned how one converses with the angels by the third day. Meanwhile, I promised myself that I would spend forty days here, and now I can't change my mind."

"Well, there's still the Valkyries."

"The Valkyries! I can live without them!"

He's afraid that he won't succeed in finding them, Chris thought.

"I already know how to converse with the angels, and that's what's important." Paulo's tone of voice was hostile.

"I've been thinking about that," Chris answered. "You already know, *but you don't want to try.*"

That's my problem, Paulo said to himself as he started the car. *I need some strong emotions. I need a challenge.*

He looked over at Chris. She was busy reading *The Desert Survival Manual* they had bought in one of the towns they had passed through. They drove off through yet another of the immense desert flats that seemed to have no end.

It's not just a problem of spiritual search, he continued thinking, as he alternated between looking at Chris and watching the road. He loved his wife, but he was getting fed up with marriage. He needed some strong passion in his love, in his work, in almost everything he did in his life. And that went against one of nature's most important laws: Every movement needs to pause at times.

He knew that if he continued the way he was, nothing in his life would last for very long. He was beginning to understand what J. had meant when he said that people wind up killing what they love most.

Two days later, they reached Gringo Pass, a place with only one motel, a mini-market, and the U.S. customs building. The Mexican border was only a few yards from the center of town, and the two took snapshots of each other with one foot in each country.

At the mini-market, they asked about the Valkyries, and the woman who owned the luncheonette said she had seen "that bunch of lesbians" that morning, but that they had moved on.

"Did they cross into Mexico?" Paulo asked.

"No, no. They took the road to Tucson."

They went back to the motel, and sat down on the verandah. The car was parked directly in front of them.

"Look how dirty the car's become," Paulo said after a few minutes. "I think I'll wash it."

"The owner of the motel wouldn't like to find out people are using water for washing their car. We're in the desert, remember?"

Paulo didn't answer. He stood up, took a roll of paper towels from the car, and began to wipe away at the dust. Chris remained seated.

He's upset. He can't sit still, she thought. "I've got something serious to tell you," she said.

"You've done your work very well, don't worry," he answered, as he used up one paper towel after another.

"That's just what I wanted to talk to you about," Chris insisted. "I didn't come here to do work. I came because I thought our marriage was beginning to fall apart."

She feels the same way I do, he thought. But he continued with his cleaning.

"I've always respected your spiritual search, but I have mine, too," Chris said. "And I'm going to go on with it. I want you to understand that. I'm going to continue attending mass."

"I go to church, too."

"But what you're doing here is different, you know? You chose this way of communicating with God, and I've chosen a different one."

"I know that. I don't want to change."

"But meanwhile"—she took a deep breath, not knowing what his response would be—"meanwhile, something is happening to me. I want to speak to my angel, too."

She stood and went over to him. She began to gather the paper towels scattered on the ground.

"Do me a favor," she said, looking directly into her husband's eyes. "Don't leave me in the middle of the road."

❁ ❁ ❁

THERE WAS A SMALL DINER NEXT TO THE gas station.

They sat near the window. It was early in the morning, and the world was still quiet. Outside was the desert, the immense, packed surface . . . and silence.

Chris missed Borrego Springs, Gringo Pass, and Indio. In those places, the desert had a face: mountains, valleys, stories of pioneers and conquistadors.

Here, though, the immense emptiness was all there was to see. And the sun. The sun that before long would color the world yellow, raise the temperature to 115 in the shade, and make life impossible.

The man behind the counter took their order. He was Chinese, and spoke with a strong accent—he could not have been here for very long. Chris imagined how many times the world had turned to bring the Chinese man to this luncheonette in the middle of the American desert.

They asked for coffee, bacon, and toast, and sat there in silence.

Chris looked at the man's eyes—they appeared to gaze to the horizon, the eyes of one whose soul had grown.

But no, he was not engaged in a holy exercise, or trying to develop his spiritual side. His was the gaze of boredom. He wasn't seeing anything—not the desert, not the road, and not even the two customers who had come in so early in the morning. He limited himself to the motions required—put the coffee in the coffeemaker, fry the eggs, say, "Can I help you?" or "Thank you." The meaning of his life appeared to have been left behind, or to have disappeared in the immensity of the treeless desert.

The coffee came. They began to sip it, in no hurry. They had nowhere to go.

Paulo looked at the car outside. It had done no good at all to have cleaned it two days before. It was covered with dust once again.

They heard a sound in the distance. In a few minutes, the first truck of the day would drive past. The man behind the counter might put his boredom and eggs and bacon aside, and go outside to try to find something, wanting to be a part of the world that was on the move, the world that passed by his diner. It was the only thing he could do; watch from a distance as the world went by. He probably no longer even dreamed of leaving the luncheonette behind and hitching a ride on one of the trucks to somewhere else. He was addicted to silence and emptiness.

The sound grew louder, but it didn't seem to be that of a truck engine. For a moment, Paulo's heart was filled with hope. But it was only a hope, nothing more. He tried not to think about it. The sound came closer and closer, and Chris turned to see what was happening outside.

Paulo stared at his coffee, afraid she might perceive his anxiety.

The windows of the restaurant rattled slightly with the noise. The counterman tried to ignore it—he knew the sound, and he didn't like it.

But Chris was fascinated. The horizon lit up with metallic reflections of the sun. The thundering engines seemed to shake the plants, the asphalt, the roof, and the windows of the restaurant.

With a roar, the Valkyries swept into the gas station. And the straight road, the flat desert, the tumbleweed, the Chinese man, and the two Brazilians in search of their angels, all felt their presence.

THE WOMEN, ON THEIR POWERFUL MOTORcycles, spun one way and then the other, dangerously close to one another, their machines shimmering in the hot air, their gloved hands toying skillfully with danger. They shouted out, as if to awaken the desert, to say they were alive and happy because it was morning.

Fear gripped Paulo's heart. Maybe they wouldn't stop there, maybe they were only trying to remind the counterman that life, joy, and skill still existed.

All at once, the rumbling stopped.

The Valkyries dismounted, shaking the desert from their bodies. They pounded the dust from their black leathers, and removed the colorful bandannas that they wore over their faces like bandits to keep the desert out of their lungs.

Then they entered the luncheonette.

Eight women.

They asked for nothing. The counterman seemed to know what they wanted—he was already placing eggs, bacon, and bread on the hot grill. Even with all the commotion, he continued to appear to be the obedient servant.

"Why is the radio turned off?" asked one of them.

The counterman turned it on.

"Louder!" said another.

Like a robot, he turned the radio to its loudest setting. The forgotten diner was suddenly transformed into a Manhattan disco. Some of the women kept time with the music by clapping their hands, while others carried on shouted conversations amidst the clamor.

But Chris, watching, saw that one of them moved not at all—the oldest of them, the one with long, curly red hair. She didn't enter into the conversation or the clapping of hands. She took no interest in the breakfast being prepared.

Intently, she stared at Paulo. And Paulo, resting his chin on his left hand, met the woman's gaze.

Chris felt a stab in her heart. *Why is he sitting like that?* Something very strange was happening. Perhaps the fact that she had been looking out at the horizon for so many days—or had been training so hard at the channeling—was changing the way she saw what went on around her. She had been having premonitions, and now they were manifesting.

She pretended not to notice that the two were eyeing each other. But her heart was giving her some inexplicable signals—and she couldn't tell whether they were good signals or bad.

Gene was right, Paulo thought. *It is easy to make contact with them.*

Slowly, the other Valkyries were beginning to perceive what was happening. First, they looked at the eldest, and then, following her gaze, turned to the table where Paulo and Chris were seated. Their conversation was silenced, and they no longer swayed in time to the music.

"Turn it off," the eldest said to the counterman.

As always, he obeyed. Now the only sound that could be heard was the sizzling of the eggs and bacon on the grill.

As her friends watched, the red-haired woman walked to the couple's table and simply stood there, looking at them. Then, without preamble, she spoke.

"Where did you get that ring?" she asked Paulo.

"At the same shop where you bought your brooch," he answered.

It was only then that Chris saw the metal brooch pinned to the leather jacket. It was made in the same design as the ring that Paulo wore on the ring finger of his left hand.

That's why he was resting his chin on his left hand.

She had already seen many rings in the Tradition of the Moon—of every color, metal and carved—always in the form of a serpent, the symbol of wisdom. But never had she seen one like the one her husband wore. J. had given Paulo that ring in 1982, when they were in Norway, saying that he was thereby completing "the Tradition of the Moon, a cycle that was interrupted by fear." And now, in the middle of the desert—a woman with a brooch of the same design.

"What do you want?" the redhead asked.

Paulo stood up, and the two stared at each other, face-to-face. Chris's heart was beating wildly—she was certain that it wasn't jealousy.

"What do you want?" she asked again.

"To speak with my angel. And something else."

She seized Paulo's hand and ran her fingers over his ring. Softening a bit, she seemed to become more feminine.

"If you bought that ring at the same place I did, you must know how it's made," she said, her eyes fixed on the serpents. "If not, then sell it to me. It's a beautiful piece."

It was simply a silver ring carved into two serpents. Each had two heads, and the design was quite simple.

Paulo said nothing.

"You don't know how to converse with angels, and this ring isn't yours," said the Valkyrie.

"I do know. Through channeling."

"Right," said the woman. "That's all that's required."

"I told you that there was something else I wanted."

"What is it?"

"Gene saw his angel. I want to see mine. I want to speak to my angel, face-to-face."

"Gene?" The woman's eyes searched the past, trying to recall who Gene was, where he lived.

"Yes, now I remember," she said. "He lives in the desert. Because that's where he met his angel."

"No. He is studying to become a master."

"This business of seeing your angel is just a myth. It's enough to converse with them."

Paulo stepped closer to the Valkyrie.

Chris knew the trick her husband was using: He called it "destabilization." Normally, two people converse at arm's length. When one of them approaches the other too closely, the other's thinking becomes disorganized.

"I want to see my angel." He was quite close to the woman, and he was staring at her.

"What for?" The Valkyrie appeared to be intimidated. The trick was working.

"Because I'm desperately in need of help. I have won important things for myself, but I am going to destroy them, because I tell myself that they have lost their meaning. I know it's not true. I know they are still important, and that if I destroy them, I'll be destroying myself, as well."

He maintained a neutral tone of voice, showing no emotion.

"When I learned that channeling was all that was needed in order to speak with my angel, I lost interest. It was no longer a challenge, but rather something I knew very well. I realized that my path to magic was about to end; the unknown was becoming too familiar to me."

Chris was shocked: Why was he making this confession in such a public place, in front of people whom he had never seen before?

"In order to continue along my path, I need something more," he finished. "I need mountains that are taller and taller."

The Valkyrie said nothing for a moment.

"If I teach you how to see your angel," she said, "your desire to seek out taller and taller mountains may disappear. And that's not always a good thing."

"No, that will never disappear," Paulo replied. "What will vanish is the idea that the mountains I've conquered are too small. I will be able to keep alive my love for what I've accomplished. That's what my master was trying to say to me."

Maybe he's talking about our marriage, too, Chris thought.

The Valkyrie held out her hand to Paulo.

"My name is M.," she said.

"My name is S.," Paulo answered.

Chris was startled. Paulo had given his magic name! Very few people knew that secret, since the only way to cause a certain kind of evil to a magus is by using his magic name. Only those who were completely trustworthy were allowed to know the name.

Paulo had just met this woman. He couldn't trust her that much.

"But you can call me Valhalla," the red-haired woman continued.

That's the name of the Vikings' paradise, Paulo thought, and he told her his given name in return.

The redhead appeared to relax a bit. For the first time, she looked at Chris, seated at the table.

"In order to see an angel, three things are needed," said the Valkyrie, turning back to Paulo as if Chris didn't exist. "And, in addition to those three things, courage is needed. A woman's courage, not a man's."

Paulo made it appear that he was paying no attention.

"Tomorrow, we will be near Tucson," Valhalla said. "Come to see us at noon, if your ring is authentic."

Paulo got the map out of the car, and Valhalla showed him the place where they should meet. One of the other Valkyries told Valhalla that her breakfast was getting cold. She turned back to her place at the counter and asked the man to turn on the radio again.

For a long time, Paulo and Chris sat over their coffee, watching the Valkyries eat.

Finally, the women got up and began to leave. As Valhalla reached the door, Paulo called out, "What are the three conditions for conversing with one's angel?"

Quietly, the redhead replied: "Break a pact. Accept forgiveness. And make a bet."

PAULO AND CHRIS LOOKED OUT AT THE CITY below. For the first time in almost three weeks, they were in a real hotel—room service, bar, and breakfast in bed.

It was six in the evening, the hour in which they had gotten into the habit of practicing their channeling exercises. But Paulo was fast asleep.

Chris knew that the meeting that morning at the diner had changed everything; if she wanted to talk to her angel, she would have to do it on her own.

They had spoken little during the trip to Tucson. She had asked him only why he had divulged his magic name. Paulo answered that Valhalla had given him hers, and he could do no less.

Perhaps he was telling the truth, perhaps this was what he believed, but Chris wondered. She was a woman, and she saw things that men don't. She thought that Paulo might want to talk to her later that night.

Chris called the desk clerk and asked where the nearest bookstore was located. There was none nearby, he said; she would have to drive. She thought about it for a few moments, and then got the car keys. They were in a big city; if Paulo awoke, he would think that she had gone exploring.

* * *

SHE BECAME LOST IN THE TRAFFIC SEVERAL times, but eventually found a huge shopping mall. One of the shops made keys, and she had a copy made of the keys to the car.

She wanted to have one, just to be secure.

In a bookstore, she leafed through a volume until she found what she was looking for:

VALKYRIES: the nymphs at Wotan's palace.

She had no idea who Wotan was, but that wasn't important.

Messengers of the gods, they led heroes to their death—and then to paradise.

Messengers. *Like the angels,* she thought. Death and paradise. Also like the angels.

They excite combatants with the love that their charm excites in their hearts, and through the example of bravery at the battlefront, mounted on steeds as fast as the clouds and as deafening as a thunderstorm.

They couldn't have chosen a better name, she thought.

At the same time, they symbolize both the inebriation of courage and rest for the warrior, the adventure of love in battle, encounter, and loss.

Right, absolutely. Paulo would want to talk to her.

THEY WENT DOWN TO HAVE DINNER AT their own hotel—even though Paulo had tried to insist that they walk a bit, get to know this large city built in the middle of the desert. But Chris said she was tired, wanted to get to bed early, enjoy the comforts.

They made small talk throughout the meal. Paulo was exaggeratedly attentive. Chris knew that her husband was waiting for the right moment. So she made it appear that she was interested in everything he said, and showed enthusiasm when he said that Tucson had the most complete desert museum in the world.

In his enthusiasm, he mentioned that the museum included live coyotes, snakes, and scorpions, with a great deal of information concerning them. They could spend the entire day there.

She said she'd like very much to see it.

"You could go tomorrow morning," Paulo said.

"But Valhalla mentioned noontime."

"You don't have to be there."

"It's a strange hour," she answered. "No one spends much time in the desert at high noon. We learned that—in the worst way possible."

Paulo had thought it strange, too. But he didn't want to miss the chance; he was afraid Valhalla might change her mind, despite the ring and everything else.

He changed the subject, and Chris could sense her husband's anxiety. They went back to small talk for a time. They drank an entire bottle of wine, and she was sleepy. Paulo suggested they go right up.

"I don't know if you should go tomorrow," he said.

She had already tasted of everything—the meal, the place, Paulo's anxiety. She was enjoying the chance of confirming for herself that she really knew this man well. But now it was getting late, and it was time to give him a definite answer.

"I'm going with you. No matter what."

He was irritated. He told her that she was jealous, and that she was spoiling his process.

"Jealous of whom?"

"Of the Valkyries. Of Valhalla."

"That's crazy."

"But this is *my* quest. I brought you with me because I wanted you at my side. But there are certain things I have to do alone."

"I want to go with you," she said.

"Magic has never been important to you before. Why now?"

"Because I began the journey. And I've asked that I not be abandoned in the middle of the road," she answered, putting the matter to rest.

❁

The silence was complete.

Everyone was wearing sunglasses against the blinding sun. Everyone—except Chris and Valhalla. Chris had removed hers so that Valhalla would know that she was looking directly into her eyes.

Chris had been bearing up under the woman's gaze for some time.

The minutes passed, and no one spoke. The only word that had been spoken the entire time had been Paulo's hello when they had arrived at the meeting place. His greeting had not been returned. Valhalla simply approached Chris and stood directly before her.

And, since that moment, nothing else had happened.

We must have been doing this for twenty minutes, Chris thought, but she didn't know how much time had actually elapsed. The glare of the sun, the heat, and the silence confused her.

She tried to distract herself a bit. They were at

the foot of a mountain—wonderful, the desert once again contained mountains! Behind Valhalla, an entrance had been carved into the stone. Chris tried to imagine what the door led to, and found that she wasn't able to think clearly—just as on the day they had returned from the salt lake.

No one was perspiring—the dryness of the air was so great that all moisture evaporated immediately, as Gene had said. Chris knew that they were rapidly dehydrating—even though she had drunk as much water as possible, and even though she had prepared for the noonday desert. And even though she wasn't nude.

The other Valkyries had formed a semicircle; they wore their kerchiefs on their heads, in the manner of gypsies or pirates. Valhalla alone was bareheaded—her kerchief encircled her neck. The sun seemed not to bother her.

She is dismissing me with her eyes, Chris thought.

She knew this could not continue forever. There was a limit. She didn't know what that limit was, nor how or when she would know, but very soon, the sun would begin to be damaging. Meanwhile, everyone continued immobile—and all of this had happened because of her. Because she had insisted on coming along. *Messengers of the gods, they lead the heroes to death and to paradise.*

She had made a bad mistake, but now it was too late. She had come because her angel had required that she do so; her angel had said that Paulo was going to need her that afternoon.

No, no, it wasn't a mistake. My angel insisted that I be here, she thought.

Her angel—she was conversing with her angel! Nobody knew it, not even Paulo.

She began to feel dizzy, and she was certain she would faint soon. But she was going to see it through—it was no longer just a matter of being at her husband's side, or obeying her angel, or being jealous. Now it was a woman's pride—face-to-face with another woman.

"Put your glasses on," Valhalla said. "This sun could blind you."

"You're not wearing glasses," she answered. "And you're not afraid."

Valhalla gave a signal, and suddenly, the blazing light of the sun was multiplied a dozen times.

The Valkyries were using the mirrors on their motorcycles to reflect the sun directly into Chris's eyes. She saw a gleaming semicircle, knitted her brows, and kept her gaze upon Valhalla.

But she could no longer see clearly. The woman's image appeared to grow and grow, and the confusion in her mind increased. She felt she was about to fall, and at that moment, leather-covered arms came to her support.

Paulo watched Valhalla catch Chris in her arms. All of this could have been avoided. He could have insisted that she remain at the hotel—no matter what she was thinking. From the moment that he had first seen the brooch, he had known which tradition the Valkyries came from.

They had also seen his ring, and they knew that he had been tested in many ways. That it would be difficult to frighten him. But they would do everything possible to test the fiber of any stranger who entered their group. Even if that stranger was his wife.

But they could not prevent Chris, nor anyone else, from learning what they wanted to learn. They had taken a vow: Everything that was hidden had to be revealed. Chris was now being tested in the first great virtue of those who seek the spiritual path: courage.

The Valkyrie looked at Paulo. "Help me."

Paulo helped her support his wife. They took her to the car and laid her down on the backseat.

"Don't worry. She'll come around very quickly. With a serious headache."

He wasn't worried. He was proud.

Valhalla went to her cycle and brought a canteen. Paulo noted that she had already donned her sunglasses—she must have reached her limit, as well.

She bathed Chris's forehead in water, and dabbed some on her wrists and behind her ears. She opened her eyes, blinked several times, and sat up.

"Break a pact," she said, looking at the Valkyrie.

"You are an interesting woman," Valhalla said, passing her hand across Chris's face. "Put your glasses on."

Valhalla caressed Chris's hair. And even though both were now wearing dark glasses, Paulo knew they were staring at each other.

THEY WALKED TO THE STRANGE DOOR IN the mountain.

Valhalla turned to the other Valkyries. "For love. For victory. And for the glory of God."

The same phrase J. had used. The words of those who know angels.

The Valkyries started their engines, blowing up a cloud of dust. The women did the same maneuvers they had at the gas station—passing closely by each other—and, minutes later, they had disappeared around the mountain.

Valhalla turned to Chris and Paulo.

"Let's go in," she said.

There was no door, just a grate. On it hung a sign:

DANGER

THE FEDERAL GOVERNMENT

PROHIBITS ENTRY

VIOLATORS WILL BE PROSECUTED

"Don't believe it," said the Valkyrie. "They're not going to spend any time guarding this."

It was an old, abandoned gold mine. Valhalla, carrying a lantern, began to move forward carefully, so as not to bump her head on the passage beams. Paulo noticed that here and there the floor had collapsed. It might have been dangerous, but now wasn't the time to think about it.

As they went deeper, the temperature fell, and it even became pleasant. He was worried about a lack of air, but Valhalla was moving along as if she knew the place well—she must have been there many times, and she was still alive. Now wasn't the time to think about that, either.

After walking for ten minutes or so, the Valkyrie halted. They sat on the floor of the passage, and she placed the lantern in the middle of their circle.

"Angels," she said. "Angels are visible to those who accept the light. And break the pact with the darkness."

"I have no pact with the darkness," Paulo responded. "I had one. But no longer."

"I'm not talking about a pact with Lucifer, or with Satan, or with . . ." She began to speak the names of various demons, and her face looked strange.

"Don't say those names," Paulo interrupted. "God is in the words, and the devil as well."

Valhalla laughed. "It looks as if you've learned the lesson. Now, break the pact."

"I have no pact with evil," Paulo repeated.

"I'm talking about your pact with defeat."

Paulo thought of what J. had said—about destroying what we love most. But J. had said nothing about pacts; he knew Paulo well enough to know that his pact with evil had been broken a long time ago. The silence within the mine was worse than in the desert. Not a sound was heard, except Valhalla's voice—which sounded different.

"We have a contract, you and I: not to win when victory is possible," she insisted.

"I have never made any such pact," Paulo said for the third time.

"Everyone has. At some point in our lives, we all enter into such an agreement. That's why there is an angel with a burning sword at the gates to paradise. To allow entry only to those who have broken that pact."

Yes, she's right, thought Chris. *Everyone has made this pact.*

"Do you find me attractive?" Valhalla asked, once again changing the tone of her voice.

"You are a beautiful woman," Paulo answered.

"One day, when I was still an adolescent, I saw my best friend crying. We were inseparable, and we loved each other completely, and I asked what had happened. When I insisted on knowing, she told me that her boyfriend was in love with me. I didn't know that, and that day I made the pact. Without really knowing why, I began to gain weight, to take poor care of myself, to become unattractive. Because—unconsciously—I felt that my beauty was a curse, and had caused suffering for my best friend.

"Before long, I had destroyed all meaning in my life because I just didn't care about myself anymore. I reached the point that everything about my life became unbearable: I thought about dying."

Valhalla laughed.

"As you can see, I broke the pact."

"True," Paulo said.

"Yes, it is true," Chris said. "You are lovely."

"We are in the heart of the mountain," the Valkyrie continued. "Outside, the sun is shining, and here there is only darkness. But the temperature is pleasant, we can sleep, we have nothing to worry about. This is the darkness of the pact."

She raised her hand to the zipper of her leather jacket.

"Break the pact," she said. "For the glory of God. For love. And for victory."

She began to lower the zipper slowly. She wore nothing beneath the jacket.

The light from the lantern caused a medallion between her breasts to gleam.

"Take it," she said.

Paulo touched the medallion. The archangel Michael.

"Take it from around my neck."

He removed the medallion and held it in his hands.

"Both of you, hold the medallion."

Suddenly, Chris blurted out, "I don't need to see my angel! I don't need to. Just speaking will do."

Paulo held the medallion in his hand.

"I've already begun talking with my angel," Chris went on, more quietly. "I know that I can, and that's good enough."

Paulo didn't believe her. But Valhalla knew that it was the truth. She had read it in her eyes when they were outside. She also knew that her angel wanted her to be there with her husband.

Nevertheless, she had to test her courage. It was the rule of the Tradition.

"All right," the Valkyrie said. With a rapid movement, she blew out the lantern. The darkness was total.

"Put the cord around your neck," she said to Paulo. "And hold the medallion with both hands joined, in prayer."

Paulo did as he was told. He was fearful of a darkness so complete, and he was remembering things he would rather not think about.

He felt Valhalla approaching him from behind. Her hands touched his head.

The darkness seemed almost solid. Nothing, not a scintilla of light, entered there.

Valhalla began to pray in a strange language. At first, he tried to identify the words she was saying. Then, as her fingers moved across his head, Paulo felt the medallion growing hot. He concentrated on the heat in his hands.

The darkness was changing. Various scenes from his life began to pass before him. Light and shadow, light and shadow, and—suddenly, he was once again in darkness.

"I don't want to remember that . . ." he pleaded with the Valkyrie.

"Remember! Whatever it is, try to remember every minute of it."

The darkness brought terror to him, the terror he had experienced fourteen years earlier.

❁

When he woke up, he found a note on the coffee table: "I love you. I'll be right back." At the bottom, she had written the date: "25 May 1974."

Funny. To put the date on a love note.

He had awakened a bit dizzy, still startled by the dream. In it, the director of the recording studio was offering him a job. He didn't need a job: The director actually functioned more like his employee—his and his partner's. Their records were at the top of the charts, selling thousands of copies, and letters were arriving from all corners of Brazil, from people wanting to know what the Alternative Society was.

All you have to do is listen to the words of the song, *he thought to himself. It wasn't really a song—it was a mantra from a magic ritual, with the words of the Beast of the Apocalypse being read in the background in a low voice. Whoever sang the song would be invoking the forces of darkness. And everyone was singing it.*

He and his partner had done the whole thing. The royalties they earned were being used to buy a lot near Rio de Janeiro. There they would recreate what, almost one hundred years earlier, the Beast had tried to establish in Cefalu, Sicily. But the Beast was expelled by the Italian authorities. The Beast had erred on many points—he had not gathered a sufficient number of disciples, and he did not know how to earn money. The Beast told everyone that his number was 666, and that he had come to create a world where the strong would be served by the weak, and the only law was that everyone do as they desired. But the Beast didn't know how to spread the ideas—few people had taken the Beast's words seriously.

He and his partner, Raul Seixas, well, they were completely different! Raul sang, and the entire country listened. They were young, and they were earning money. Yes, it was true that Brazil was in the hands of a military dictatorship, but the government was concerned about guerrillas. They couldn't waste their time with a rock singer. Just the opposite: The authorities felt that rock music kept the country's youth away from communism.

He drank his coffee standing at the window. He was going to take a walk, and meet later with his partner. It didn't bother him at all that nobody knew who he was, while his friend was famous. What mattered was that they were earning money, and this would allow them to put their ideas into practice. People from the world of music, and the world of magic—ah, they knew! His anonymity with regard to the general public was even rather funny—more than once, he had had the pleasure of hearing someone comment on his work—without knowing that the author was listening nearby.

He donned his sneakers. As he was tying the laces, he felt dizzy.

He raised his head. The apartment seemed darker than it should have been. The sun was shining outside, and he had just left the window. Something was burning—an electrical appliance, maybe, because the stove was disconnected. He looked throughout the apartment. Nothing.

The air was heavy. He decided to go out right away—without tying his sneakers, he started to leave, but realized that he really wasn't feeling well.

Could be something I ate, *he said to himself. But when he ate something that was off, his entire body usually gave him a signal, and he knew that. He wasn't nauseated, didn't feel like vomiting. Just a kind of dizziness that didn't seem to want to pass.*

*Dark. The darkness grew; it seemed like a gray cloud around him. He felt the dizziness again. Yes, it had to be something he had eaten—*Or maybe an acid flashback, *he thought. But he hadn't tried LSD in five years. The delayed effects had disappeared after the first six months, and never returned.*

He was frightened, he had to get out.

He opened the door—the dizziness was coming and going, and he might get worse out in the street. Better to stay home and wait. The note was there on the table—she would be home shortly—he could wait. They could go together to the pharmacy or to a doctor, although he hated doctors. It couldn't be anything serious. No one has a heart attack at age twenty-six.

No one.

He sat down on the couch. He needed some distraction. He shouldn't think about her, or the time would pass even more slowly. He tried to read the paper, but the dizziness, the lightheadedness, came and went, stronger each time. Something was pulling him into a black hole that appeared to have formed in the middle of the room. He began to hear noises—laughing, voices, things breaking. That had never happened—never! Whenever he had taken anything, he knew he was drugged, knew it was a hallucination and would pass with time. But this—this was terribly real!

No, no, it couldn't be real. The reality was the rugs, the curtains, the bookshelves, the coffee table with the leftovers of bread on it. He made an effort to concentrate on the scene surrounding him, but the feeling of a black hole in front of him, the voices, the laughter, all continued.

None of this was happening. Definitely! He had practiced magic for six years. Performed all the rituals. He knew it was nothing more than suggestion. A psychological effect that was playing on his imagination. Nothing more.

His panic was increasing, and the dizziness was more pronounced—pulling to the outside of his body, toward a dark world, toward that laughter, those voices, those noises—real!

I cannot let myself be afraid. Fear will make it come back. *He tried to control himself, went to the sink and bathed his face. He felt a bit better, the feeling seemed to have passed. He put his sneakers on and tried to forget about it. He toyed with the idea of telling his partner he had entered into a trance, had been in contact with demons.*

But he had only to think about that, and the dizziness returned—more strongly.

"I'll be right back," the note said, and she hadn't come!

I never achieved concrete results in the astral plane, *he thought. He had never seen anything. No angels, no devils, no spirits of the dead. The Beast wrote in his diary that he was able to make things materialize, but he was lying, the Beast had never gotten that far. He knew that. The Beast had failed. He liked the Beast's ideas because they were rebellious, chic. And very few people had ever heard them. And people are always more respectful of those who speak of things no one understands. As for the rest—Hare Krishna, Children of God, the Church of Satan, Maharishi—everyone knew about those. The Beast—the Beast was just for the chosen few! "The law of the powerful," one of his books talked about.*

The Beast was on the cover of Sgt. Pepper's Lonely Hearts Club Band, *one of the Beatles's best known records—and almost no one knew it. Maybe not even the Beatles knew what they were doing when they placed that photograph there.*

The phone rang. It might be his girlfriend. But if she had written, "I'll be right back," why would she be phoning?

Only if something was happening.

That's why she hadn't come. The intervals between bouts of dizziness were growing shorter and shorter, and everything was turning black again. He knew—something was telling him—that he couldn't let that feeling take him over. Something terrible might happen—he might enter into that darkness and never return. He had to maintain control at any cost—he needed to occupy his mind, or that thing would dominate him.

The phone. He concentrated on the phone. Speak, converse, think of other things, take his mind off that darkness, the phone was a miracle, a solution. He knew it. He knew that somehow he couldn't surrender. He had to answer the phone.

"Hello?"

It was a woman's voice. But it wasn't his girlfriend—it was Argelia.

"Paulo?"

He didn't answer.

"Paulo, can you hear me? I need you to come over to my house! Something strange is going on!"

"What's happening?"

"You know, Paulo! Explain it to me, for God's sake!"

He hung up before he heard something he didn't want to hear. It wasn't a delayed drug effect. It wasn't a symptom of insanity. It wasn't a heart attack. It was real. Argelia had participated in the rituals, and "that" was happening to her, too.

He panicked. He sat there without thinking for a few minutes, and the darkness began to take him over, coming closer and closer, causing him to step to the edge of the lake of death.

He was going to die—for everything he had done without believing, for the many people he had involved without knowing it, for so much evil spread about in the name of what was good. He would die, and the Darkness would go on, because it was manifesting itself now, before his very eyes, demonstrating that things really worked, collecting what was owed for the time in which it had been used, and he had to pay—because he didn't want to know what the price was before, thought it was for free, that everything was a lie or just suggestion!

His years in the Jesuit school came back to him, and he prayed for the strength needed to get back to a church, ask forgiveness, pray that at least God would save his soul. He had to be able to do it. He found that as long as he could keep his mind busy, he was able to dominate the dizziness, at least partly. He needed time to get to the church . . . What a ridiculous idea!

He looked at the bookcase, and resolved that he would calculate how many records he owned—after all, he had always put that task off! Yes, it was important to know the exact number of records, and he began to count: one, two, three . . . he did it! He was able to overcome the dizziness, the black hole that was pulling him in. He counted all of the records—and then counted them again, to make certain he was correct. Now the books. He had to count in order to know how many books he had. Did he have more books than records? He began to count. The dizziness halted, and he had so many books. And magazines. And alternative newspapers. He would count everything, write it down, really know how many things he owned. It was so important.

He was counting the silverware when he heard the key turn in the lock. She was here, finally. But he couldn't allow himself to be distracted—he couldn't even talk about what was happening; any moment now, it was all going to stop. He was certain of it.

She went straight to the kitchen, and hugged him, crying.

"Help me! Something strange is happening. You know what it is, help me!"

He didn't want to lose his count of the silverware—that was his salvation. Keep the mind busy. Better if she hadn't arrived—it didn't help. And she thought the same as Argelia—that he knew everything, that he knew how to stop it.

"Keep your mind busy!" he shouted, as if he were possessed. "Count how many records you have! And how many books!"

She looked at him without understanding what he was talking about. Like a robot, she walked to the bookcase.

But she didn't get there. She suddenly threw herself to the floor.

"I want my mother . . ." she said, over and over. "I want my mother . . ."

He did too. He wanted to phone his parents, ask for help—his parents whom he never saw, who belonged to a middle-class world he had abandoned long ago. He tried to go on with the silverware count, but she was there, crying like a child, pulling at her hair.

That was too much. He was responsible for what was happening, because he loved her, and had taught her the rituals, guaranteed that she could get what she wanted, that things were improving day by day (although he never for a moment believed what he was saying!). Now she was there, begging for help, trusting in him—and he had no idea what to do.

For a moment, he thought of issuing an order, but he had already lost his silverware count, and the black hole came back suddenly with even greater strength.

"You help me," he said. "I don't know what to do."

And he began to cry.

He was crying out of fear, as when he was a child. He wanted his parents, as she did. He was bathed in a cold sweat, and was certain he would die. He seized her hand, and her hands were cold, too, even though her clothing was soaked in perspiration. He went to the bathroom to wash his face—as he used to do when the effects of the drugs were really strong. Maybe it would work with regard to "that," too. The hallway seemed immense, the thing was stronger now—he was no longer counting records, books, pencils, silverware. There was no place to hide.

"Running water."

The thought came from some far corner of his mind, some place that the darkness had not seemed to penetrate. Running water! Yes, there was a power in darkness, in delirium, in madness—but there were other things!

"Running water," he said to her, as he bathed his face. "Running water keeps the evil away."

She heard the certainty in his voice. He knew, he knew everything. He would save her.

He turned the shower on, and they both huddled under it—with their clothing, their documents, their money. The cold water moistened their bodies, and, for the first time since he had awakened, he experienced a sense of relief. The dizziness vanished. They stayed for two or three hours under the spray, without speaking, shivering from fear and the cold. They stepped out only once, to phone Argelia and tell her to do the same thing. The dizziness returned, and they had to flee back into the shower. There, everything seemed calm, but they needed desperately to understand what was happening.

"I never believed it," he said.

She looked at him, not understanding. Two years earlier, they had been two hippies, without a cent to their name, and now his songs were being heard all over the country. He was at the peak of success—even though few people knew his name; and he had been saying that it was all the result of the rituals, the occult studies, the power of magic.

"I never believed it," he continued. "Or I never would have walked those paths! I never would have risked myself, or you."

"Do something, for the love of God!" she said. "We can't stay here in the shower forever!"

He left the shower again, checking whether the dizziness and the black hole were still there. He went to the bookcase and came back with the Bible. He had a Bible in the house only so that he could read from the Revelation to John, be certain about the reign of the Beast. He had done everything as called for by the Beast's followers—and, in his heart, he had believed none of it.

"Let's pray to God," he said. He felt ridiculous, demoralized before this woman whom he had tried to impress for all those years. He was weak, he was going to die. He had to humiliate himself, beg for forgiveness. What was most important now was the saving of his soul. In the end, everything was true.

He embraced the Bible, and recited prayers he had learned as a child—Our Father, Hail Mary, the Creed. She refused at the beginning, and then recited them with him.

Then he opened the book at random. The water poured down on the pages, but he was able to read the story of someone who had asked something of Jesus, and Jesus said that he must maintain the faith. The man answered: "Lord, I believe—help me in my incredulity."

"Lord, I believe, help me in my incredulity!" he shouted through the sound of the falling water.

"Lord, I believe, help me in my incredulity!" he said in a whisper, through his sobs.

He began to feel strangely calm. If the terrible evil they had experienced really existed, then it was true that the kingdom of heaven did, as well, and along with it, everything else that he had learned and then denied throughout his life.

"The eternal life exists," he said, knowing that he would never again believe in those words. "I don't care if I die. You cannot fear death, either."

"I'm not afraid," she answered. "I'm not afraid, but I think it's unfair. It's a pity."

They were only twenty-six. It really was a pity.

"We have been through everything someone our age could have experienced," he answered. "Most people haven't even come close."

"That's true," she said. "We can die."

He lifted his face, and the sound of the water in his ears seemed like thunder. He was no longer crying, nor afraid; he was only paying the price for his insolence.

"Lord, I believe, help me in my incredulity," he repeated. "We want to make an exchange. We offer you anything, absolutely anything, in return for the salvation of our souls. We offer our lives, or everything we own. Please accept, my lord."

She looked at him with contempt. The man she had admired so. The powerful, mysterious, courageous man she had so admired, who had convinced so many people with regard to the Alternative Society, who had preached about a world where anything was allowed, where the strong ruled over the weak. That man was there, crying, screaming for his mother, praying like a child, and saying that he had always been courageous—because he had believed in nothing.

He turned, and said they should both look up and make the exchange. She did so. She had lost her man, her faith, and her hope. She had nothing else to lose.

He placed his hand on the faucet, and slowly shut it down. Now they could die; God had forgiven them.

The stream of water turned to droplets, and then there was complete silence. Soaked to the bone, they looked at each other. The dizziness, the black hole, the laughter, and the noises, all had disappeared.

He was lying in a woman's lap, crying. Her hand was caressing his head.

"I made that pact," he said tearfully.

"No," the woman answered. "It was a trade."

Paulo clutched the archangel medallion. Yes, there had been a trade—and the punishment was severe. Two days after that morning in 1974, they were imprisoned by the Brazilian political police and accused of subversion based on the Alternative Society. He was placed in a dark cell, similar to the black hole he had seen in his living room. He was threatened with death, and he gave in, but it was a trade. When he was released, he split up with his partner and was expelled from the world of music for a long time. No one would give him a job. But it was a trade.

Other members of the group had not made the trade. They survived in the "black hole," and regarded him as a coward. He lost his friends, his security, his desire to go on living. For years, he was afraid to go out into the street—the dizziness might return, the police could appear again. And, even worse, after his release from prison he never saw his girlfriend again. At times, he regretted the trade—it would have been better to have died than to have to live that way. But now it was too late to go back.

"There was a pact," Valhalla said. "What was it?"

"I promised I would abandon my dreams."

For seven years, he paid the price for the trade. But God was generous, and allowed him to rebuild his life. The director of the recording studio, the same person he had dreamed about that May morning, gave him a job and became his only friend. He went back to composing, but every time his work brought some success, something wound up happening, and everything went down the drain.

He remembered J's words: People destroy what they love.

"I always figured it was part of the bargain," he said.

"No," Valhalla said. "God was severe, but you were more severe than he was."

"I promised that I would never grow again. I thought that I could no longer trust myself."

The Valkyrie held his head to her bare breasts.

"Tell me about the dread," she said. "The dread that I saw when we met at the luncheonette."

"The terror . . ." He didn't know how to begin, because he felt he would sound absurd. "The terror doesn't allow me to sleep at night, or rest during the day."

Now Chris understood her angel. She had to be here, hearing this, because he would never have told her . . .

". . . and now I have a wife that I love, I found J., I walked the holy Road to Santiago, I've written books. I'm being faithful to my dreams again, and that's where the dread comes from. Because everything is going the way I would like it to, and I know that soon it will all be destroyed." It was terrible to say that. He had never said it to anyone—not even himself. He knew that Chris was there, hearing it all. And he was ashamed.

"That's the way it was with the songs," he said, forcing himself to go on. "That's the way it's been with everything I've done since then. Nothing has lasted more than two years."

He felt Valhalla's hands removing the medallion from around his neck. He stood. He didn't want her to light the lantern, because he lacked the courage to confront Chris.

But Valhalla lit the lantern, and the three made their way out in silence.

"We two are going out first, and you come along later," Valhalla said to Paulo as they were reaching the end of the tunnel.

Paulo was certain that, just as with his girlfriend

of fourteen years earlier, Chris would never again trust him.

"Today, I believe in what I'm doing," he tried to say before the other two left. It sounded like a plea for forgiveness, like self-justification.

No one answered. After a few more steps, Valhalla extinguished the lantern. There was now sufficient light for them to see.

"From the moment that you set foot outside," the Valkyrie said, "promise, in the name of the archangel Michael, that never again—*never again*—will you raise your hand against yourself."

"I'm afraid to say that," he answered. "Because I don't know how to comply."

"You have no choice, if you want to see your angel."

"I didn't realize what I was doing to myself. I might continue with the same kind of self-betrayal."

"Now you know," Valhalla said. "And the truth gives you freedom."

Paulo nodded his head.

"You will still have many problems in your life, some of them normal, some of them difficult. But, from now on, only God's hand will be responsible for everything—you will interfere no more."

"I promise in the name of Saint Michael."

The women went out. He waited a moment, and then began to walk. He had been in the darkness long enough.

THE RAYS OF LIGHT, REFLECTING FROM the stone walls, showed the way. There was the grated door, a door leading to a prohibited kingdom. A door that frightened him. Because out there was the kingdom of light, and he had been living for years in the darkness. A door that appeared to be closed—but, for anyone who approached it, it was open.

The door to the light was there in front of him. He wanted to pass through. He could see the golden light of the sun outside, but he decided not to put on his sunglasses. He needed the light. And he knew that the archangel Michael was at his side, sweeping away the darkness with his lance.

For years he had believed in the implacable hand of God, in his punishment. But it was his own hand, not God's, that had wrought such destruction. Never, for the rest of his life, would he do that again.

"Break the pact," he said to the darkness of the mine and to the desert light. "God has the right to destroy me. I do not."

He thought of the books he had written, and was happy. The year would end without any problem—because the pact had been broken. There was no doubt that problems would arise in his work, in love, and along the path to magic—serious problems or passing problems, as Valhalla had said. But from now on, he would battle side by side with his guardian angel.

You must have made a tremendous effort, he said to his angel. *And, in the end, I spoiled everything, and you couldn't understand it.*

His angel was listening. The angel knew about the pact, too, and was happy at not having to devote efforts to keeping Paulo from destroying himself.

Paulo found the door and passed through it. The sun blinded him for a moment, but he kept his eyes open—he needed the light. He saw the figures of Valhalla and Chris approaching. "Put your hand on his shoulder," Valhalla said to Chris. "Be a witness."

Chris obeyed.

Valhalla took a few drops of water from her canteen and made a cross on his forehead—as if baptizing him. Then she knelt, and told them to kneel as well.

"In the name of the archangel Michael, the pact was known in heaven. In the name of the archangel Michael, the pact was broken."

She placed the medallion on his forehead, and asked that he repeat her words:

Sainted angel of the Lord,
My zealous guardian . . .

The prayer from childhood echoed from the walls of the mountain, and spread throughout that part of the desert.

If I trust in you,
The divine piety
Will rule me always, and guard,
Govern, and enlighten.
Amen.

"Amen," said Chris.
"Amen," he repeated.

PEOPLE WERE APPROACHING THEM CURIOUSLY.

"They're lesbians," said one.

"They're crazy," said another.

The Valkyries paid no attention, but continued with what they were doing. They had tied one kerchief to another, forming a kind of rope. They sat on the ground in a circle—their arms resting on their knees, holding the joined kerchiefs.

Valhalla was in the middle, on foot. People continued to arrive. When a small multitude had formed, the Valkyries began to chant a psalm.

By the rivers of Babylon,
There we sat down, yea, and wept.
We hung our harps upon the willows
In the midst of it.

The people watched, understanding none of it. It was not the first time these women had appeared in the city. They had been there before, speaking of strange things—although certain words were similar to those uttered by television preachers.

"Have courage." Valhalla's voice rang out clearly and strongly. "Open your heart, and listen to what your dreams tell you. Follow those dreams, because only a person who is not ashamed can manifest the glory of God."

"The desert's made them crazy," a woman said.

Some people left immediately. They were fed up with preaching.

"There is no sin but the lack of love," Valhalla continued. "Have courage, be capable of loving, even if love appears to be a treacherous and terrible thing. Be happy in love. Be joyful in victory. Follow the dictates of your heart."

"That's impossible," someone in the crowd said. "People have obligations."

Valhalla turned in the direction of the voice. She was doing it—people were paying attention! Different from five years earlier, when no one came near them during their appearances in the city.

"We have children. We have husbands and wives. People have to earn a living," another person said.

"Well, meet your obligations. But obligations never prevented anyone from following their dreams. Remember that you are a manifestation of the absolute, and do only those things in your lives that are *worth the effort.* Only those who do that will understand the great transformations that are yet to be seen."

The Conspiracy, Chris thought, as she listened. She remembered the time long ago when she had sung in the plaza with others from her church, to save people from sin. In those days, no one spoke of a New Age—they spoke of the coming of Christ, of punishment and hell. There was no Conspiracy, such as now.

She walked through the crowd and found Paulo. He was sitting on a bench, far from the gathering.

"How long are we going to travel with them?" she asked.

"Until Valhalla teaches me how to see angels."

"But we've been here for almost a month."

"She cannot refuse me. She swore on the Tradition. She has to keep her vow."

The crowd was growing in size. Chris was thinking how difficult it must be to talk to the people gathered there.

"They're not going to take the Valkyries seriously," she said. "Not with the way they're dressed, and with those motorcycles."

"They have been fighting for some very old ideas," Paulo said. "Nowadays, soldiers dress in camouflage. They disguise themselves, and they hide. But the old warriors dressed in colorful outfits, much more obvious on the field of battle.

"They wanted the enemy to see them. They took pride in battle."

"Why are they doing this? Why preach in public parks and in bars and in the middle of the desert? Why are they helping us to speak to our angels?"

He lit a cigarette. "You joke about a Conspiracy, but you're right," he said. "There is a Conspiracy."

She laughed. No, no, there was no Conspiracy. She had used that term because her husband's friends acted like secret agents, always careful not to discuss certain things when others were present, always changing the subject—although they had sworn, all of them had, that there was nothing occult in the Tradition.

But Paulo seemed to be serious.

"The gates to Paradise have been reopened," he said. "God banished the angel with the burning sword who was at the gate. For some time—no one is certain for how long—anyone could enter, since it was obvious that the gates were open."

As he was speaking to Chris, Paulo recalled the abandoned gold mine. Up until that day—a week ago—he had chosen to remain outside of paradise.

"What guarantees entry?"

"Faith. And the Tradition," he answered.

They walked over to an ice cream wagon and bought cones. Valhalla continued to speak, and her sermon appeared to be endless. Before long, she might even try to get the spectators to participate, at which point it would probably end.

"Does everyone know that the gates are open?" Chris asked.

"Some people have noticed—and they are calling the others. But there's a problem."

Paulo pointed to a monument in the middle of the square. "Let's suppose that paradise is there. And every person on earth is here in the plaza. Each of them has their own path for arriving there.

"That's why people talk with their angels. Because only the angels know the best path. It does no good to seek advice about it from others."

"Follow your dreams, and take your risks," they heard Valhalla saying.

"What will this world be like?"

"It will be only for those who enter into paradise," Paulo answered. "The world of the 'Conspiracy.' The world of people who are able to see the transformations that are occurring, of people who have the courage to pursue their dreams and listen to angels. A world for all those who believe in that world."

A murmur arose from the crowd, and Chris knew that the play had begun. She wanted to move forward to observe, but what Paulo was saying was more important.

"For centuries, we wept on the banks of the rivers of Babylon," Paulo continued. "We hung up our harps, we were prohibited from singing, we were persecuted and massacred. But we never forgot that there was a promised land. The Tradition survived everything.

"We learned how to fight, and we were strengthened by the battle. People are once again speaking of the spiritual world that only a few years ago was seen as something that only ignorant, complacent people believed in. There is an invisible thread that unites all those on the side of the light—like those joined kerchiefs of the Valkyries. And this thread is becoming a strong, shining rope, anchored by the angels. A handrail that is perceived by those who are most sensitive, and that will support us. Because we are many, and we are spread all over the earth. All of us moved by the same faith."

She said, "It's a world that has so many names, isn't it? New Age, Sixth Golden Age, Seventh Beam, and so on."

"But it's all the same world. I'll guarantee you."

Chris looked at Valhalla, there in the plaza, speaking of angels.

"Well, why is she trying to convince others?"

"No, no, she's not trying to convince them of anything. We all came from Paradise, we have spread throughout the world, and now we're returning there. Valhalla is asking these people to pay the price of that return."

Chris remembered the afternoon in the mine. "Sometimes it's a very high price."

"It may be. But there are people who are willing to pay it. They know that what Valhalla is saying is true, because it brings back something they had forgotten. All of them still carry in their soul memories and visions of Paradise. Years may go by without their remembering—until something happens: the birth of a child, a serious loss, a feeling of imminent danger, a sunset, a book, a song . . . or a group of women dressed in leather, speaking of God. Anything. Suddenly, these people remember.

"That's what Valhalla is doing. Reminding them that a place exists. Some of them are listening, others aren't—those who aren't will pass by the gates without seeing that they're open."

"But she's talking about this new world."

"Those are just the words she uses. Actually, they have retrieved their harps from the willows, and are playing them again—and millions of people all over the world are singing of the joys of the Promised Land. No one is alone anymore."

They heard the sound of motorcycles. The play was over. Paulo began to walk toward the car.

"Why didn't you ever tell me about all this?" she asked.

"Because you already knew."

Yes, she had known. But only now did she remember.

❁

The Valkyries rode from city to city on their motorcycles, with their trappings, their kerchiefs, and their strange outfits. And they spoke of God.

Paulo and Chris went with them. When they made camp on the outskirts of a city, the couple stayed in hotels. When they stopped in the middle of the desert, they slept in the car. They made a campfire, and the dangers of the desert receded—the animals did not approach. As they dropped off to sleep, they could look up at the stars and hear the howls of the coyotes in the distance.

Ever since the afternoon at the mine, Paulo had been practicing the channeling process. He was afraid that Chris might think that he hadn't really known what he had tried to teach her.

"I know J.," she said, when the subject came up. "You don't have to prove your knowledge to me."

"My girlfriend back in those days also knew the person who was teaching me," he answered.

They sat down together every afternoon, working at the destruction of their second minds; they prayed for their angels, and tried to invoke their presence.

"I believe in this new world," he said to Chris, when they had completed yet another exercise in channeling.

"I know you believe in it. Or you wouldn't have done the things you've done during your lifetime."

"But, even so, I don't know whether the things I do are really correct."

"Give yourself some credit," she answered. "You're doing the best you can—very few people would travel so far to find their angel. And don't forget, you broke the pact."

The pact he had broken in the mine: J. was going to be happy about that! Although Paulo was almost certain that he already knew everything, J. hadn't tried to argue Paulo out of this trip to the desert.

When the two had completed their channeling exercises, they talked for hours about angels. But only between themselves—Valhalla never again spoke of the matter.

ONE AFTERNOON, AFTER THEIR CONVERSATION, he went to talk with Valhalla.

"You know the Tradition," he said. "You cannot interrupt a process once you have begun it."

"I'm not interrupting anything," she answered.

"But soon I'll have to go back to Brazil. And I haven't yet accepted forgiveness, nor made a bet."

"I'm not interrupting the process," she said again.

She suggested that they take a walk out in the desert. When they reached a certain point, they sat down together and watched the sunset, and talked about rituals and ceremonies. Valhalla asked about J.'s teaching methods, and Paulo wanted to know what the results were of her preaching in the desert.

"I'm preparing the path," she said casually. "I am doing my part, and I expect to do it right through to the end. Then, I'll know what the next step is."

"How are you going to know when the time comes to stop?"

Valhalla pointed to the horizon. "We have to make eleven trips through the desert, pass through the same places eleven times and repeat the same things eleven times. That's all I was told to do."

"Your master said that?"

"No, the archangel Michael."

"And what trip is this?"

"This is the tenth."

The Valkyrie put her head on Paulo's shoulder, and they sat in silence for a long time. He had a desire to caress her, put her head in his lap, as she had done for him at the abandoned mine. She was a warrior, but she, too, needed to rest.

He thought about it for some time, but decided against it. And the two returned to the camp.

AS THE DAYS PASSED, PAULO BEGAN TO suspect that Valhalla was teaching him everything he needed to know—but that, as Gene had done, she was doing it without directly showing him the path. He began to observe closely what the Valkyries did; he thought he might perceive some clue, some teaching, a new practice. And, when Valhalla called him to go with her at day's end—something she did every day now—he decided that he would discuss things with her.

"There's nothing that prevents you from teaching me directly," he said. "You are not a master. It's not like it is with Gene, or J., or even with me—people who know two Traditions."

"Yes, I am a master. I learned through revelation. You're right that I don't pronounce curses, and I don't participate in covens, nor am I a member of any secret societies. But I know many things that you don't know, because the archangel Michael taught them to me."

"Well, that's why I'm here. To learn."

The two were seated in the sand, leaning against some rocks.

"I need affection," she said. "I really need affection."

Paulo shifted his position, and Valhalla laid her head in his lap. They sat there for some time, looking out at the horizon.

It was Paulo who spoke first. He didn't want to raise the subject, but felt he had to.

"I'm going away soon, you know."

He awaited her reaction. She said nothing.

"I have to learn how to see my angel. I feel as if you have been trying to teach me, but that I'm not seeing it."

"No. My teachings are as clear as the desert sun."

Paulo caressed the hair that covered his lap.

"You have a beautiful wife," Valhalla said.

Paulo understood the comment, and took his hands away.

When he had rejoined Chris that night, he told her what Valhalla had said about her. Chris smiled, but said nothing.

THEY CONTINUED TO TRAVEL WITH THE Valkyries. Even after Valhalla's comment—about the clarity of her teachings—Paulo continued to pay close attention to everything the Valkyries did. But the routine varied little: travel along, speak in public places, perform the rituals he already knew, and move on.

And make love. They made love to men they met along the way. Usually they were groups on motorcycles, bold enough to approach the Valkyries. When this happened, there was a tacit agreement that Valhalla would have the right to first choice. If she wasn't interested, any of the others could approach the newcomer.

The men never knew this. They were made to feel that they were with the woman they had chosen—but the choice had been made much earlier. By the women.

The Valkyries drank beer and talked of God. They performed sacred rituals, and made love out among the rocks. In the larger cities, they went to some public place to perform their miracle play—getting those who were in the audience to participate.

At the end, they asked for contributions. Valhalla never played a role, but she directed everything that was happening. Afterward, she would pass her kerchief around, and she always received money.

Every afternoon, before Valhalla called Paulo to walk with her in the desert, he and Chris practiced their channeling and talked with their angels. Although the channel was not yet completely opened, they felt the presence of constant protection, of love and peace. They heard phrases that made little sense, they had some intuitions, and many times the only sensation was one of joy—nothing more. But they knew they were speaking to their angels, and that the angels were happy at this.

Yes, the angels were happy, because they had been contacted again. Any person who resolved to speak with them would discover that it was not the first time. They had already conversed with them when they were children—the angels had appeared in the form of "secret friends," and had been their companions in long conversations and in play, protecting them from evil and from danger.

And every child had spoken with their guardian angel—until that day when their parents noticed that the child was talking to people who "didn't exist." Then they became intrigued, blamed it on excessive childish imagination, consulted with educators and psychologists, and came to the conclusion that the child should give up that sort of behavior.

The parents always insisted on telling their children that their secret friends didn't exist—perhaps because they had forgotten that they too had spoken to their angel at one time. Or, who knows, perhaps they thought they lived in a world where there was no longer any place for angels. Disenchanted, the angels had returned to God's side, knowing that they could no longer impose their presence.

But a new world was beginning. The angels knew where the gates to Paradise were, and they would conduct all who believed in them to those gates. Perhaps they needn't even believe—it was enough that they *needed* angels, and the angels would return gladly.

PAULO SPENT HIS NIGHTS TRYING TO understand why Valhalla was doing as she did—putting things off.

Chris knew the answer. And the Valkyries knew the answer, as well—even though none of them said anything about it.

Chris was waiting for the blow to fall. Sooner or later it was going to happen. That's why Valhalla had not left them, had not taught them what else they needed to know about meeting with their angel.

ONE AFTERNOON, IMMENSE MOUNTAIN formations began to appear off to the right side of the road as they drove. Soon, to the left, mountains and canyons could be seen, and a gigantic salt flat, gleaming in the sun, extended from one side to the other.

They had arrived at Death Valley.

The Valkyries made camp close to Furnace Creek—the only place for miles around where there was water. Chris and Paulo decided to stay with the group, because the only hotel for miles was filled.

That night, the entire group sat around the campfire, chatting about men and motorcycles, and—for the first time in many days—angels. As they always did before sleeping, the Valkyries knotted together their kerchiefs, held the long cord that was formed, and once again repeated the psalm that sang of the rivers of Babylon and of the harps hanging in the willow trees. They could never forget that they were warriors.

When the ritual was over, silence fell over the encampment, and everyone made their sleeping arrangements. Except Valhalla.

She walked some distance from the camp, and gazed for a long time at the moon. She asked the archangel Michael to continue to appear to her, to continue to provide her with valuable advice, and to help her to maintain a firm hand.

"You won in your battles with the other angels," she prayed. "Teach me to win. That I not disperse this flock of eight people, so that one day we might be thousands, millions. Forgive my errors, and fill my heart with enthusiasm. Grant me the strength to be both man and woman, both hard and soft.

"May my word be your lance.

"May my love be your scale."

She made the sign of the cross, and fell silent, listening to the howl of a coyote in the distance. She was wakeful, and began to think back on her life. She remembered when she had been just an employee at the Chase Manhattan Bank, and when her life amounted to nothing more than her husband and her two children.

"Then I saw my angel," she said to the silent desert. "The angel appeared to me, enveloped in light, and asked that I take on this mission. I was not forced, there were no threats, nor any promise of reward. My angel simply asked."

She had left the next day, and went straight to the Mojave Desert. She began preaching alone, speaking of the open gates to Paradise. Her husband divorced her and won custody of the children. She didn't really understand clearly why she had accepted this mission, but every time she wept out of pain and solitude, her angel told her stories of other women who had accepted messages from God: the Virgin Mary, Saint Theresa, and Joan of Arc. The angel said that all the world needed was an example. People who were capable of following their dreams and of fighting for their ideas.

She lived for almost a year outside Las Vegas. She exhausted the little money she had been able to pull together, went hungry, and slept outdoors. Until one day, a poem came into her hands.

The poem told the story of a saint, Maria Egipciaca. She was traveling to Jerusalem, and had no money to pay for her passage across a river. The boatman, eyeing the attractive woman, suggested to her that, although she had no money, she did have her body. Maria Egipciaca surrendered herself to the boatman. When she arrived at Jerusalem, an angel appeared and blessed her for what she had done. And, although today almost no one remembers her, she was canonized by the church following her death.

Valhalla interpreted the story as a sign. She preached in God's name during the day, and twice a week went to the casinos, became the lover of wealthy men, and was able to put together some money. She never asked her angel whether she was doing the right thing—and her angel said nothing.

Little by little, led by the invisible hands of other angels, her companions began to arrive.

"One more trip," she said again, aloud, to the silent desert. "Only one more trip to complete my mission, and then I can get back to the world. I have no idea what awaits me, but I want to get back. I need love, affection. I need someone who can protect me here on earth, just as my angel protects me in heaven. I have done my part; I have no regrets, even though it was awfully hard."

She made the sign of the cross again, and returned to the encampment.

SHE SAW THAT THE BRAZILIAN COUPLE was still seated by the campfire, gazing at the flames.

"How many days until your fortieth?" she asked Paulo.

"Eleven."

"Well then, tomorrow night, at ten o'clock, in Golden Canyon, I will make you accept forgiveness. The Ritual That Demolishes Rituals."

Paulo was astonished. She was right! The answer had been under his nose the whole time!

"Using what?" he asked.

"Using hatred," Valhalla answered.

"That's fine," he said, trying to conceal his surprise. But Valhalla knew that Paulo had never used hatred in the Ritual That Demolishes Rituals.

She left the couple and went to where Rotha, the youngest of the Valkyries, was sleeping. She affectionately caressed the girl's face to awaken her—Rotha might have been making contact with the angels that appear in one's sleep, and Valhalla didn't want to interrupt the conversation. Rotha finally opened her eyes.

"Tomorrow night, you are going to learn how to accept forgiveness," Valhalla said. "And then you will be able to see your angel."

"But I'm already a Valkyrie."

"Of course. And even if you are not able to see your angel, you will still be a Valkyrie."

Rotha smiled. She was twenty-three, and was proud to be roaming the desert with Valhalla.

"Don't wear your leather outfit tomorrow. Not from the moment the sun rises until the end of the Ritual That Demolishes Rituals."

She embraced her with great affection. "Go back to sleep," she said.

❁

Paulo and Chris continued to sit by the fire for another half hour. Then they arranged some of their clothing as pillows, and prepared to sleep. They had thought about purchasing sleeping bags at every large city they had passed through, but they couldn't bring themselves to shop around. More than anything, they always hoped to find a hotel somewhere. So, when it was necessary to camp out with the Valkyries, they either had to sleep in the car or near the fire. Their hair had already been scorched several times by blowing sparks—but nothing any more serious had happened until now.

"What did she mean?" Chris asked as they lay there.

"Nothing important." He had had a couple of beers, and was sleepy.

But Chris pressed the matter. She wanted an answer.

"Everything in life is a ritual," Paulo said. "For witches as much as for those who have never heard of witchcraft. Both are always trying to perform their rituals to perfection."

Chris knew that those on the magical path had their rituals. And she understood, as well, that there were rituals in everyday life—marriages, baptisms, graduations.

"No, no. I'm not talking about those obvious rituals," he went on impatiently. He wanted to sleep, but she pretended not to have sensed his irritation. "I'm saying that everything is a ritual. Just as a mass is a great ritual, composed of various parts, the everyday experience of any person is, also.

"A carefully elaborate ritual that the person tries to perform precisely, because he or she is afraid that—if any part is left out—everything will go wrong. The name of that ritual is *Routine.*"

He decided to sit up. He was groggy because of the beers he had drunk, and if he continued to lie down, he would be unable to complete his explanation.

"When we are young, we don't take anything too seriously. But slowly, this set of daily rituals becomes solidified, and takes us over. Once things have begun to go along pretty much as we imagined they would, we don't dare risk altering the ritual. We like to complain, but we are reassured by the fact that each day is more or less like every other. At least there is no unexpected danger.

"That way, we are able to avoid any inner or outer growth, except for the kinds that are provided for within the ritual: so many children, such and such a kind of promotion, this and that kind of financial success. When the ritual becomes consolidated, the person becomes a slave."

"Does that happen sometimes with those on the path?"

"Of course. They use the ritual to make contact with the invisible world, to destroy the second mind, and to enter into the Extraordinary. But, for us too, the terrain we conquer becomes familiar. And we feel the need to seek out new territories. But any magus is fearful of changing the ritual. It's a fear of the unknown, or a fear that other rituals won't function as well—but it is an irrational fear, a strong one, that never disappears without some help."

"And what is the Ritual That Demolishes Rituals?"

"Since a magus is unable to change their rituals, the Tradition decides to change the magus. It's a kind of Sacred Theater in which the magus has to play a different character."

He lay down again, turned on his side, and pretended to sleep. Chris might ask for further explanations. She might want to know why Valhalla had mentioned hatred.

Negative emotions were never invoked in the sacred theater. On the contrary, people who participated in that kind of theater tried to work with the good, and to assume characters that were strong, enlightened. That way, they were able to convince themselves that they were better people than they had thought, and—when they believed that—their lives changed.

To work with negative emotions would mean the same thing. He would wind up convincing himself that he was worse than he had imagined.

THEY SPENT THE AFTERNOON OF THE following day exploring Golden Canyon, a series of ravines with tortuous curves and walls about twenty feet high. At the moment that the sun set, while they were doing their channeling exercise, they saw how the place had acquired its name: The brilliant minerals embedded in the rock reflected the rays of the sun, causing the walls to appear to be carved out of gold.

"Tonight there will be a full moon," Paulo said.

They had already seen the full desert moon, and it was an extraordinary spectacle.

"I awoke today thinking about a passage in the Bible," he continued. "It's from Solomon: 'It is good that you retain this, and that you not take away your hand from it; for whoever fears the Lord will emerge from everything unscathed.'"

"A strange message," Chris said.

"Very strange."

"My angel is speaking to me more and more," she told him. "I'm beginning to understand the words. I understand perfectly well what you were talking about in the mine, because I never believed that this communication with my angel could happen."

That made Paulo feel pleased. And together they contemplated afternoon's end. This time, Valhalla had not appeared for their walk in the desert.

The glistening stones they had seen that afternoon were no longer apparent. The moon cast a strange, phantasmagorical light into the ravine. They could hear their own footsteps in the sand, as they walked along in silence, alert to any sound they might hear. They didn't know where the Valkyries were meeting.

They came almost to the end point, where the fissure widened to form a small clearing. No sign of them.

Chris broke the silence. "Maybe they decided against it."

She knew that Valhalla was going to prolong the game as long as possible. But Chris wanted it to be over.

"The animals are on the prowl. I'm afraid of the snakes," she said. "Let's go back."

But Paulo was looking upward.

"Look," he said. "They haven't decided against it."

Chris followed his gaze. At the top of the rocks that formed the right wall of the ravine, the figure of a woman was looking down at them.

She felt a shiver.

The figure of another woman appeared. And another. Chris went to the middle of the clearing; she could see three more women on the other side.

Two were missing.

"WELCOME TO THE THEATER!" VALHALLA'S voice echoed from the stone walls. "The audience is already here, and they await the spectacle!"

That was how Valhalla had always begun her plays in the city parks.

But I'm not part of the spectacle, Chris thought. *Maybe I should climb up there with them.*

"Here, the price of admission is paid upon leaving," the voice continued, repeating what was always said in the city squares. "It may be a high price, or we might return what is paid. Do you want to take the risk?"

"Yes, I do," Paulo answered.

"What is all this?" Chris suddenly shouted. "Why such dramatics, why so much ritual, why all of this just to see an angel? Isn't it enough to speak with the angel? Why don't you do as everyone else does: simplify the way we make contact with God and with what is sacred in this world?"

There was no response. Paulo felt that Chris was ruining everything.

"The Ritual That Demolishes Rituals," said one of the Valkyries from high in the rocks.

"Silence!" Valhalla shouted. "The audience gets to speak only when this is over! Applaud or boo—but pay the admission!"

Valhalla finally appeared. She wore her kerchief knotted around her forehead, Indian-style. She usually wore it that way when she was saying her prayers at day's end. It was her crown.

She brought with her a barefoot girl, wearing Bermudas and blouse. When they had come closer, and the moonlight illuminated their faces, Chris saw that it was one of the Valkyries—the youngest of the group. Without her leather outfit and her aggressive air, she seemed only a child.

Valhalla placed her in front of Paulo, and traced a large square around them. At each of its corners, she stopped and spoke a few words. Paulo and Rotha repeated the words in Latin—the young woman made several errors, and had to begin again.

She doesn't even know what she's saying, Chris thought. Neither the square nor the words were a part of what usually happened at the performances in the city.

When Valhalla had completed the inscription of the square, she asked that the two approach her. They remained within the square, while she stood outside.

Valhalla turned to Paulo, looked deep into his eyes, and handed him the long leather belt she usually wore around her waist.

"Warrior, you are imprisoned within your destiny by the power of these lines and of these sacred names. Warrior, victorious in battle, you are now in your castle, and you will receive your reward."

In his mind, Paulo created the walls of the castle. From that moment on, the ravine, the Valkyries, Chris, Valhalla, and everything else ceased to be of importance.

He was an actor in the sacred theater. The Ritual That Demolishes Rituals.

"Prisoner," Valhalla said to the girl, "your defeat has been humiliating. You were unable to defend your army with honor. The Valkyries will come down from heaven to recover your body when you are dead. But until then, you will receive the punishment that the loser deserves."

With an abrupt gesture, she tore open the girl's blouse.

"Let the spectacle begin! This, oh warrior, is your trophy!"

He seized the girl violently. She fell awkwardly, cutting her chin, and it bled.

Paulo knelt at her side. In his hand, he clutched Valhalla's belt, and it seemed to have an energy of its own. It frightened him, and for a few moments he left the imaginary walls of the castle and returned to the ravine.

"She's really hurt," Paulo said. "She needs some help."

"Warrior, that is your trophy!" Valhalla repeated, stepping away. "The woman who knows the secret you are after. Extract that secret from her, or give it up forever."

"Not for ourselves, Lord, not for ourselves, but for the glory of your name," he said in a low voice, repeating the motto of the Templars. He had to make a quick decision. He recalled the time when he believed in nothing, thinking all of this was simply dramatics—but even then, things were transformed, and the truth emerged.

He was faced with the Ritual That Demolishes Rituals. A sacred moment in the life of a magus.

"Sed nomini Tuo de Gloriam," he said again. And in the moment that followed, he dressed himself in the role suggested by Valhalla. The Ritual That Demolishes Rituals began to unfold. Nothing else was important—only that unknown path, that frightened woman at his feet, and a secret that had to be won from her. He strode around his victim, and thought of those times when morality

was different—when taking possession of a woman was a rule of combat. Men had risked their lives in war for gold and women.

"I won!" he screamed at the girl. "And you lost!"

He knelt and seized her by the hair. Her eyes stared into his.

"It is we who will win," the girl said.

He threw her violently to the ground again.

"The rule of victory is to win."

"All of you think you won," the prisoner continued. "You won only a battle. It is we who will win the war."

Who was this woman who dared to speak to him this way? She had a lovely body—but that could wait. He had to learn the secret he had sought for so long.

"Teach me how to see my angel," he said, trying to keep his voice calm. "Then you will be set free."

"I am free."

"No. You don't know the rules of victory," he said. "That's why we defeated all of you."

The woman seemed to become confused. "Tell me about those rules," she said. "And I will tell you the secret about your angel."

The prisoner was making a trade. He could torture her, destroy her. There she was, fallen at his feet—yet she was proposing a trade. Perhaps she wouldn't confess under torture. Better to make the trade. He would tell her about the five rules of victory, since she was never going to leave there alive.

"The morality rule: You have to fight on the side that is in the right, and that's why we won. The weather rule: A war in the rain is different from a war in the sun; a battle in the winter is different from a battle in the summer."

He could fool her now. But he wasn't able to invent false rules on the spot. The woman would notice his hesitancy.

"The space rule," he continued. "A war in a ravine is different from a war in the field. The choice rule: The warrior knows how to choose who should give advice, and who will remain at his side in combat. A chieftain cannot be surrounded by cowards or traitors."

He thought for a moment about whether he should continue. But he had already told her four of the rules.

"The strategy rule." he said finally. "The way in which the battle is planned."

That was all of it. The girl's eyes gleamed.

"Now tell me about the angels."

She looked at him, saying nothing. She had learned the formula, even though it was too late. Those valiant warriors never lost a battle—and legend had it that they used five rules of victory. Now she knew what they were.

She knew it would do her no good, but at least she could die in peace. She deserved the punishment she was to receive.

"Tell me about the angels," the warrior said again.

"No! I won't tell you about the angels."

The warrior's eyes changed, and she was delighted. He would show no mercy. The only thing that frightened her was that the warrior might be governed by the rule of morality, and spare her life. She wasn't deserving of that. She was guilty—dozens, hundreds of sins accumulated during her short life. She had disappointed her parents, disappointed men who had grown close to her. Deceived the warriors who had fought at her side. She had allowed herself to be taken prisoner—she was weak. She deserved to be punished.

"Hatred!" they heard a distant woman's voice say. "The secret of the ritual is hatred!"

"We made a trade," the warrior repeated, and

now his voice was as cold as steel. "I lived up to my side."

"You are not going to let me leave alive," she said. "But at least I got what I wanted. Even though it's of no use to me."

"Hatred!" The voice of the woman was beginning to have an effect on him. He was allowing his worst feelings to surface. Hatred was permeating the warrior's heart.

"You are going to suffer." he said. "The worst tortures anyone has ever experienced."

"I will suffer."

"I deserve this," she thought. She deserved the pain and the punishment. She deserved death. Ever since she was a child, she had refused to fight—she didn't believe that she was capable of it. She accepted everything from others, suffered in silence the injustices to which she fell victim. She wanted everyone to see that she was a good girl. That she was sensitive in her heart, and able to help everyone. She wanted to be liked at any cost. God had given her a good life, and she had not been able to make use of it. Instead, she begged that others love her, lived her life as others wanted her to, all in order to show that she was kindhearted and able to please everyone.

She had been unfair to God, had thrown her life away. Now she needed an executioner who would dispatch her quickly to hell.

The warrior felt the belt becoming alive in his hand. For a moment, his eyes met those of his prisoner.

He was waiting for her to change her mind, beg his forgiveness. Instead, the prisoner winced as she awaited the blow.

Suddenly, everything disappeared except his rage at having been tricked by his prisoner. The hatred came in waves, and he was beginning to see how capable he was of cruelty. He had always been wrong, he had always allowed his heart to give in at the very moment when he should have meted out justice. He had always forgiven—not because he was a good person, but because he was a coward. He was afraid that he couldn't see such things through to the end.

Valhalla looked at Chris, and Chris returned her stare. The moonlight prevented each from seeing clearly into the eyes of the other. And that was a good thing, because each was afraid to reveal what she was feeling.

"For God's sake!" the prisoner screamed again, before the blow was delivered.

The warrior halted his stroke in midair.

But the enemy had arrived.

"Enough," said Valhalla. "That's enough."

Paulo's eyes were glazed. He grabbed Valhalla by the shoulders.

"I feel this hatred!" he shouted. "I'm not making it up! I've let some demons loose that I wasn't even aware of!"

Valhalla took the belt from his hand, and went to see whether Rotha was injured.

She was crying, her head between her knees.

"It was all true," she said, embracing Valhalla. "I provoked him, and I used him as my instrument of punishment. I wanted him to destroy me, to put me to death. My parents blamed me, my brothers and sisters blamed me. All I've ever done in life was wrong."

"Go and put on another blouse," said Valhalla.

Rotha stood up, trying to arrange her torn clothing.

"I want to stay this way," she said.

Valhalla hesitated for a moment, but said nothing. She walked to the wall of the canyon and began to climb. At the top, she was surrounded by three Valkyries, and she gave a signal that the others climb up, as well.

Chris, Rotha, and Paulo climbed the wall in silence. The moonlight showed them the way; with the many handholds in the rocks, it was not a difficult ascent. At the top, they could look out at a vast plain riven by arroyos.

Valhalla told Paulo and the girl to come together again, face to face, embracing.

"Did I hurt you?" Paulo asked. He was horrified with himself.

Rotha shook her head. She was ashamed—she would never succeed at becoming a woman like those who surrounded her. She was too weak.

Valhalla knotted together the kerchiefs of two of the Valkyries. She slipped them through the belt loops of the man and woman, binding them to each other. From where she stood, Chris could see that the moon formed a halo around the couple. It would have been a beautiful scene—if it were not for all that had happened. If that man and woman were not so distant from each other—or so close.

"I am unworthy of seeing my angel," Rotha said to Valhalla. "I am weak, and my heart is filled with shame."

"I am unworthy of seeing my angel," Paulo said, so that all could hear. "I have hatred in my heart."

"I have loved many," Rotha said. "But spurned true love."

"I have nourished hatred for years, and avenged myself over things that were unimportant," Paulo continued. "I was always forgiven by my friends, but never learned how to forgive them in return."

Valhalla turned to face the moon.

"We are here, archangel. The Lord's will be done. Our inheritance is hatred and fear, humiliation and shame. The Lord's will be done.

"Why was it not enough simply to close the gates to Paradise? Did you also have to cause us to carry hell in our hearts? But, if that is the will of the Lord, you must know that all of humanity has been doing his will for generations and generations."

Then Valhalla began to stride in circles around the couple, chanting.

"THIS IS THE PREFACE, THE SALUTATION.

"Praised be Our Lord Jesus Christ, forever may he be praised.

"Guilty warriors are speaking to You.

"Those who have always used the best weapons they have—against themselves.

"Those who deem themselves unworthy of blessings. Those who believe that happiness is not for them. Those who suffer more greatly than others do.

"Those who arrived at the gates of freedom, gazed at paradise, and said to themselves: 'We should not enter. We are not deserving.' They are speaking to You.

"Those who one day experienced the judgment of others, and concluded that most of them were right. They are speaking to You.

"Those who judge and condemn themselves. They are speaking to You."

One of the Valkyries handed the belt to Valhalla, and she raised it toward heaven

❋

"This is the first element: Air.

"Here is the belt. If we are that way, punish us.

"Punish us because we are different. Because we have dared to dream, and to believe in those things no one else any longer believes in.

"Punish us because we challenged what exists, what everyone else accepts, what most others want to remain unchanged.

"Punish us because we speak of faith, and we feel hopeless. We speak of love, but we receive neither the affection nor the comfort we feel we deserve. We speak of freedom, and we are prisoners to our own guilt.

"Lord, even were I to raise this belt high, high enough to touch the stars, I would not touch your hand.

"Because your hand covers our heads. And it caresses us, and you say to us: 'Suffer no more. I have already suffered enough.'

"You say to us: 'Like you, I dreamed, and I believed in a new world. I spoke of love, and at the same time, asked our Father to end my ordeal. I challenged what was. What the majority cared not to change. I thought I was wrong when I performed my first miracle: changing water to wine, simply to enliven a party. I felt the hard stare of others, and I shouted, "Father, Father, why have you forsaken me?"'

"They have already used the belt on me. You need suffer no more."

VALHALLA THREW THE BELT TO THE ground, and scattered sand to the wind.

•

"This is the second element: Earth.

"We are a part of this world, Lord. And this world is filled with our fears.

"We will write our sins in the sand, and it will be the desert wind's task to scatter them.

"Keep our hands strong, keep us from ceasing to struggle, even though we judge ourselves unworthy of going into battle.

"Make use of our lives, nourish our dreams. If we are made of the Earth, the Earth is also made of us. Everything is only one thing.

"Teach us and use us. We are forever yours.

"The Law was reduced to one commandment: 'Love your neighbor as yourself.'

"If we love, the world changes. The light of love scatters the darkness of guilt.

"Keep us strong in love. Make us accept for ourselves the love of God.

"Show us our love for ourselves.

"Require us to seek out the love of others. Even with fear of rejection, of severe glances, of the hardness of heart of some—do not permit us ever to give up our quest for love."

One of the Valkyries held out a torch to Valhalla. She lit it, and held up the blazing torch to heaven

❁

"This is the third element: Fire.

"You say, Lord: 'I came to set fire to the Earth. And I am watchful that the fire grow.'

"May the fire of love grow in our hearts.

"May the fire of transformation glow in our movements.

"May the fire of purification burn away our sins.

"May the fire of justice guide our steps.

"May the fire of wisdom illuminate our path.

"May the fire that spreads over the Earth never be extinguished. It has returned, and we carry it within us.

"Prior generations passed on their sins to succeeding ones. Thus has it been, down to our fathers.

"Now, though, we will pass forward the torch of your fire.

"We are warriors of the light, this light that we carry with pride.

"The fire that, when kindled for the first time, showed us our faults and our sins. We were surprised and frightened, and we felt ourselves to be incapable.

"But it was the fire of love. And it consumed what was bad in us when we accepted it.

"It showed us that we are neither better nor worse than those who frowned at us.

"And for this we accept forgiveness. There is no more guilt, and we can return to paradise. And we will bring with us the fire that will burn on earth."

VALHALLA INSERTED THE TORCH INTO A crevice in the rocks. Then she opened her canteen and spilled a few drops of water on Paulo's and Rotha's heads.

❁

"This is the fourth element: Water.

"You said: 'Whoever drinks of this water will never thirst.'

"Well then, we are drinking this water. We wash away our sins, for love of the transformation that is going to shake the Earth.

"We will hear what the angels say, we will be messengers of their words.

"We will do battle with the best weapons and the speediest of horses.

"The gates are open. We are worthy to enter."

"LORD JESUS CHRIST, WHO SAID TO HIS apostles, 'My peace I leave you, my peace I give you,' do not look at our sins, but at the faith that animates your assembly."

Chris knew that passage. It was similar to one used in the Catholic service.

"Lamb of God, who takes away the sins of the world, have pity on us," Valhalla concluded, untying the kerchiefs that joined Paulo and Rotha.

"You are free."

Then Valhalla approached Paulo.

The sting, thought Chris. *Now comes the serpent's sting. It's the payment. She's in love. If the Valkyrie tells him what the price is, he will pay with pleasure. And I won't be able to say a thing—because I'm just an ordinary woman, and I know nothing about the laws in the world of angels. None of them knows that I have already died many times here in the desert, and been reborn so many times, as well. They don't know that I have been speaking to my angel, and that my soul has grown. They're used to me, and they know how I think. I love him. She is only enamored.*

❁

"Now, it's you and me, Valkyrie! The Ritual That Demolishes Rituals!"

Chris's scream echoed out over the sinister desert, bathed in the light of the moon.

Valhalla was expecting the scream. She had already dealt with guilt, and knew that what she wanted was no crime. Only a caprice. She was entitled to cultivate her caprices—her angel had taught her that such things took no one away from God, or from the sacred task each person had to perform in their life.

She remembered the first time she had seen Chris, at the luncheonette. A shiver had coursed through her body, and strange intuitions—intuitions she was unable to understand—had taken hold of her. *The same thing must have happened to her,* she thought.

Paulo? She had completed her mission with him. And, although he didn't know it, the price she had charged was high—as they had traveled through the desert, she had learned many rituals that J. used only with his disciples. He had told her everything.

She also desired him as a man. Not for what he was, but for what he knew. A caprice, and her angel forgave capriciousness.

She looked again at Chris, and thought, *This is my tenth round. I too need to change. This woman is an instrument of the angels.*

Never taking her eyes from Chris, the Valkyrie said, "The Ritual That Demolishes Rituals. May God tell us what our characters should be!"

She had accepted the challenge. Her moment for growth had arrived.

The two women began to walk around the circumference of an imaginary circle, like cowboys of the old West before a gunfight. Not a sound could be heard—it was as if time had stopped.

The other Valkyries understood what was happening because they were all women, accustomed to fighting for love. And they would do so through to the ultimate consequences, using every trick and artifice. They would do so for love, the justification for their lives and their dreams.

Chris's character began to emerge. She donned the leather outfit, and tied the kerchief around her head. Between her breasts shone the medallion of the archangel Michael. She had dressed herself as a strong character, as the woman she admired and would like to be: She was Valhalla.

Chris gestured with her head, and the two stood still. Valhalla felt as though she were standing before a mirror.

Looking at Chris, she could see herself. She knew the arts of war by heart, but had forgotten the lessons of love. She knew the five rules of victory, and had slept with every man she desired, but she had forgotten the art of love.

She regarded herself as reflected by this other person; she had enough power to defeat her. But her own character was emerging, taking form, and this character, although it was also possessed of sufficient power, was not used to this type of battle.

She had transformed herself into a woman in love, who marched with her man, carrying his sword when necessary, and protecting him from all danger. She was a strong woman, although she appeared to be a weak one. She was a person who walked the path of love, regarding it as the only possible road to wisdom. A path where mysteries were revealed through surrender and forgiveness. She was seeing it with such clarity!

Valhalla had assumed the character of Chris.

And Chris saw herself, reflected in the other.

Chris began to walk slowly toward the precipice. Valhalla did the same, and both approached the abyss. A fall from there would be fatal. But they were women who would recognize no limits. Chris stopped at the very edge, allowing time for Valhalla to do so, as well.

The floor of the desert was thirty feet below, and the moon was thousands of miles above. Between the moon and the desert floor, two women confronted each other.

"He is my man. Don't covet him merely out of capriciousness. You don't love him," Chris said.

Valhalla didn't respond.

"I'm going to take one more step," Chris continued. "I'll survive. I'm a courageous woman."

"I'll do it with you," answered Valhalla.

"Don't. You know about love now. It's a huge world, and you will have to spend the rest of your life trying to understand it."

"I will step back if you will. You know about your strength now. Your horizon now extends to mountains, valleys, and deserts. Your soul has grown large, and will continue to grow. You've discovered your courage, and that's enough."

"Enough, if what I taught you is sufficient to pay the price you were going to charge me."

A long silence. Then the Valkyrie walked over to Chris.

And kissed her.

"I accept that as the price," she said. "Thank you for what you have taught me."

Chris removed the watch from her wrist. It was all she had to offer.

"Thank you for what you taught me, too," she said. "Now I know about my strength. I would never have learned about it, though, unless I had come to know a strange, beautiful, powerful woman."

With great tenderness, she placed the watch on Valhalla's wrist.

THE SUN SHONE DOWN ON DEATH VALLEY. The Valkyries tied their kerchiefs around their faces, leaving only their eyes exposed.

Valhalla approached the couple. "You cannot go with us. You have to talk to your angel."

"There's one thing left," Paulo said. "The bet."

"Bets and pacts are made with the angels. Or with the devils."

"I still don't know how to see my angel," he answered.

"You have already broken a pact. You have already accepted forgiveness. The bet you must make with your angel."

The other women's motorcycles roared. She placed the kerchief across her face, mounted her bike, and turned to Chris.

"I will always be a part of you," Chris said. "And you will always be a part of me."

Valhalla removed a glove and threw it to Chris. Then she revved her engine and the cycles sped away, leaving behind a gigantic cloud of dust.

A MAN AND A WOMAN WERE TRAVELING across the desert. On some days, they stopped at cities with thousands of inhabitants, and on others, in towns with just one motel, a restaurant, and a gas station. They kept to themselves—and each afternoon they walked out through the rocks and the sand, feeling as if they had returned to the place where the first star was about to be born. And there, they talked with their angels.

They heard voices, gave advice to one another, and remembered things that seemed to have been completely forgotten sometime in the past.

She had completed her communication with the protection and wisdom of her angel, and was now gazing at the desert sunset.

He sat there, waiting. He wanted his angel to descend and appear in blazing glory. He had done everything right, and now he had simply to wait.

He waited one, two, three hours. He rose only when night had completely fallen; he found his wife, and they returned to the city.

They had dinner, and returned to the hotel. She went to bed and pretended to sleep, while he stared into space.

She got out of bed in the middle of the night, and went to where he sat, asking him to come to bed. She said that she was afraid of sleeping alone because of a bad dream. He lay down beside her, quietly.

"You are already communicating with your angel," he had grown used to saying at such times. "I've heard you speaking when you are channeling. You say things you would never say in ordinary life. Wise things. Your angel is here."

He caressed he but continued to lie there in silence. She asked herself if his sadness was really because of the angel, or perhaps had to do with some lost love.

This question remained locked inside.

Paulo was thinking about the woman who had left, but that wasn't what made him disconsolate. Time was passing, and soon he would have to return to his own country. He would meet again with the man who had taught him that angels exist.

That man, Paulo imagined, *will tell me that I did enough. That I broke a pact that needed to be broken, that I accepted forgiveness that I should have accepted long ago. Yes, that man will continue to teach me about the path to wisdom and love, and I will get closer and closer to my angel. I'll speak with my angel every day, giving thanks for protection and asking for help. And that man will tell me that it is sufficient.*

Yes, because J. had taught him from the beginning that there are frontiers. That it was necessary to go as far as possible—but that there were certain times when one had to accept the mystery, and understand that each person had his own gift. Some knew how to cure, others possessed words of wisdom, while others conversed with spirits. It was through the sum of such gifts that God could demonstrate his glory, using humankind as his instrument. The gates to paradise would be open to those who had resolved that they would pass through them. The world was in the hands of those who had the courage to dream—and to realize their dreams.

Each to their own talent. Each to their own gift.

But none of that consoled Paulo. He knew that Gene had seen his angel. That Valhalla had seen her angel. That many others had written books and stories and reports telling of their meetings with their angels.

And he had not been able to see his own.

IN SIX MORE DAYS, THEY WOULD HAVE TO leave the desert. They stopped in a small city called Ajo, where most of the inhabitants were elderly. It was a place that had known its moments of glory—when the mine there had brought jobs, prosperity, and hope to the inhabitants. But, for some reason—unknown to any of them—the company had sold its houses to the employees and closed the mine.

Paulo and Chris sat in a restaurant, drinking coffee and waiting for the cool evening to arrive. An old woman asked if she could sit with them.

"All of our children have gone away," she told them. "No one is left except the old-timers. Some day, the entire city will disappear, and all our work, everything we built, will no longer mean a thing."

It had been a long time since anyone had even passed through the place. The old woman was happy to have someone to talk to.

"People come here, build, and hope that what they are doing is important," she continued. "But overnight, they find that they are demanding more of the Earth than it has to give. So, they abandon everything and move on, without thinking about the fact that they have involved others in their dream—others who, weaker than they, have to stay behind. Like with the ghost towns out there in the desert."

Maybe that's what's happening to me, Paulo thought. *I brought myself here, and I've abandoned myself.*

He recalled that once an animal trainer had told him how he was able to keep his elephants under control. The animals, as infants, were bound by chains to a log. They would try to escape, but could not. They tried throughout their entire infancy, but the log was stronger than they were.

So they became accustomed to captivity. And when they were huge and strong, all the trainer had to do was place the chain around one of their legs and anchor it anywhere—even to a twig—and they would not attempt to escape. They were prisoners of their past.

The long hours of daylight seemed to have no end. The sky caught fire, the Earth baked, and they had to wait, wait, wait—until the color of the desert changed again to softer tones of pink. That was when he could leave the city, try his channeling, and once again await the appearance of his angel.

"Someone once said that the earth produces enough to satisfy needs, but not enough to satisfy greed," the old woman continued.

"Do you believe in angels?" Paulo asked her.

The woman was astonished at the question. But that was all that Paulo wanted to talk about.

"When you're old, and death isn't too far off, you begin to believe in anything," she said. "But I don't know if I believe in angels."

"They exist."

"Have you ever seen one?" There was a mixture of incredulity and hope in her eyes.

"I talk with my guardian angel."

"Does your angel have wings?"

It was the question everyone asked. Yet he had forgotten to ask it of Valhalla.

"I don't know. I haven't seen my angel yet."

The woman considered whether she should get up and leave. The solitude of the desert made some people strange. But maybe this man was joking with her, just passing the time.

She wanted to ask where the couple came from, and what they were doing in a place like Ajo. She hadn't been able to identify their strange accent.

Maybe they're from Mexico, she thought. But they didn't look like Mexicans. She would ask when the opportunity arose.

"I don't know if you two are fooling around with me," she said, "but, as I said, I'm getting close to death. I suppose I could last another five or ten years. Maybe even twenty. But at my age, you certainly realize you're going to die."

"I know that I'm going to die, too," Chris said.

"No, not like an old person does. For you, it's a remote idea. It might happen some day. For us, it's something that could happen tomorrow. That's why many elderly people spend the time remaining to them looking only in one direction: the past. It's not that they're so fond of their memories, but they know that looking in that direction they won't see anything to be feared.

"Very few old people look to the future, and I'm one of them. When we look into the future, we see what it holds for us: death."

Paulo didn't say anything. You can't say anything new about awareness of death to those who practice magic, but he knew the woman would leave the table if she knew that he was a magus.

"That's why I'd like to believe that you both are serious. That angels really exist."

"Death is an angel," Paulo said. "I have seen it twice in this incarnation, but very briefly. There wasn't enough time to see its face. But I know people who have seen, and I know others that were oppressed by Death, and later told me about it.

They said that Death has a handsome face, and a gentle touch."

The old woman stared at Paulo. She wanted to believe him.

"Does Death have wings?"

"This angel is made of light," he answered. "When the moment comes, Death assumes the form that is easiest for you to deal with."

The old woman thought about that. Then she stood up.

"I'm not afraid anymore. I have prayed, and asked that the angel of death have wings when it comes to me. My heart tells me that my wish will be granted."

She kissed them both. It was no longer important to her where they came from.

"It was my angel that sent you both. Thank you so much."

Paulo remembered Gene. He too had been an angel's instrument. Thinking of Gene, Paulo realized that he and Chris had also served as the instruments of an angel.

AT SUNSET, THEY WENT TO A MOUNTAIN not far from Ajo. They sat facing the east, waiting for the first star to appear. When that occurred, they would initiate their channeling activity.

They called this process Contemplation of the Angel. It was the first ceremony they had created after the Ritual That Demolishes Rituals had swept the others away.

"I never asked," Chris said as they waited. "Why it is that you want to see your angel?"

"Well, you've already explained to me a number of times that it didn't matter at all to you."

His voice had a sarcastic tone. She pretended not to notice.

"Okay. But it's important for you. Can you tell me why?"

"I've already explained that. The day of our meeting with Valhalla."

"You don't need a miracle," she insisted. "You're just being capricious."

"There's nothing capricious in the spiritual world. Either you accept it, or you don't."

"So? Haven't you accepted this, your world? Or was everything you said a lie?"

She must be thinking of that story in the mine, Paulo thought. It was a difficult question to answer, but he was bound to try.

"I've already witnessed a number of miracles," he began. "Many miracles. You and I have even witnessed some together. We watched J. create openings in the clouds, fill the darkness with light, move objects from one place to another.

"You've seen me read people's minds, cause the wind to blow, perform rituals involving power. I've seen magic function many times in my life—both for evil and for good. I have no doubts about it."

He paused. "But we have also become used to miracles. And we always want to see others. Faith is a difficult conquest, and it requires daily combat in order to be maintained."

It was time for the star to appear, and he had to end his explanation. But Chris interrupted.

"It's been that way with our marriage, too," she said. "And I'm exhausted."

"I don't understand. I'm speaking about the spiritual world."

"The only reason I'm able to understand what you're saying is because I know your love," she said. "We've been together for a long time. But after the first two years of joy and passion, every day began to be a challenge for me. It's been very difficult to keep the flames of our love alive."

She regretted having brought up the subject—but now she was going to see it through.

"Once you told me that the world was divided into the farmers, who love the Earth and the harvest, and the hunters, who love the dark forests and conquest. You said I was a farmer, like J. That I walked the path of wisdom, achieved through contemplation. And you said I was married to a hunter."

Her thoughts were pushing their way out, and she couldn't stop herself. She was afraid the star might appear before she had finished.

"And I am married to a hunter. I know that, and its been very difficult being married to you! You're like Valhalla, like the Valkyries. They never rest. They deal only in the strong emotions of the hunt, of taking risks. Of the darkness of night and the taking of prisoners. At the beginning, I didn't think I'd be able to live with that. I, who was looking for a life like everybody else's, married to a magus! A magus whose world is governed by laws I don't even know—a person who feels he is alive only when he is facing challenges."

She looked into his eyes.

"Isn't J. a much more powerful magus than you are?"

"Much wiser," Paulo answered. "Much more experienced. He follows the path of the farmer, and it is on that path that he finds his power. I'll be able to achieve my power only by following the path of the hunter."

"Well then, why did he accept you as a disciple?"

Paulo laughed. "For the same reason that you chose me as a husband. Because we're different from one another."

"Valhalla, you, and all your friends think only in terms of the Conspiracy. Nothing else is important—you're all fixated on this business of changes, of a new world to come. I believe in that new world, too—but, God, does it have to be this way?"

"What way?"

She thought for a minute. She didn't know exactly what he was getting at. "This way that always involves conspiracies."

"That's *your* word for it."

"But I know it's true. And you confirmed it."

"I said that the gates of paradise are open, for a certain time, to all who desire to enter. But I also said that each person has his or her own path—and only one's angel can say which is the correct one."

Why am I acting this way? What's going on with me? she thought. She remembered the engravings she had seen as a child, of angels leading children to the edge of an abyss. She was surprised at what she had been saying here. She had fought many times with him, but she had never spoken about magic in the way that she was now.

Yet her soul had grown during these forty days in the desert, she had learned about her second mind, she had crossed swords with a powerful woman. She had died many times, and was stronger each time she was reborn.

The hunt actually gave me great pleasure, she thought.

Yes. That's what was driving her crazy. Because, since the day she had challenged Valhalla to the duel, she had had the feeling that she had wasted her entire previous life.

No, she thought. *I can't accept that. I know J. He is a farmer-type, and an enlightened person. I spoke with my angel before Paulo did. I know how to speak to my angel as well as Valhalla does—even though the language is still a bit strange.*

But she was apprehensive. Perhaps she had been wrong in choosing how she wanted to live her life. *I've got to keep talking,* she thought. *I have to convince myself that I didn't make the wrong choice.*

"You need yet another miracle," she said. "And you will always need yet another. You will never be satisfied, and you will never understand that the kingdom of heaven cannot be conquered by force."

God, make his angel appear, because it's so important to him! Make me be wrong, Lord.

"You're not even giving me a chance to talk," he said.

But at that moment, the first star appeared on the horizon.

It was time for channeling.

THEY SAT DOWN, AND, AFTER A BRIEF period of relaxing, began to concentrate on the second mind. Chris couldn't stop thinking about Paulo's last comment—she really hadn't permitted him to talk.

Now it was too late. She had to allow her second mind to recite its boring problems. To voice the same concerns, over and over. Her second mind that night wanted to get at her heart. It was saying she had chosen the wrong path, and had found her true destiny only when she had experimented with the Valhalla character.

It was telling her that it was too late to change, that her life had been a failure, that she would spend the rest of her life following her husband—without experiencing the pleasures of the dark forest and the taking of prisoners.

It was telling her she had chosen the wrong husband—that she would have been better off marrying a farmer-type. It was telling her that Paulo had other women, and that those women were hunter-types that he met on the night of the full moon, and at secret magic rituals. It was telling her that she should leave him, so that he could be happy with a woman who was his equal.

She argued several times—saying that it wasn't important that she knew there were other women, that she wouldn't leave him on that account. Because love isn't logical or rational. But her second mind came back at her—so she decided not to argue. She would just listen quietly until the conversation went silent and died out.

Then a kind of fog began to envelop her thinking. The channeling had begun. An indescribable sensation of peace took hold of her, as if the wings of her angel were covering the entire desert, preventing anything bad from happening. Whenever she did her channeling, she felt a great love for herself and for the universe.

She kept her eyes open, so as not to lose her awareness, but the cathedrals began to appear. They emerged, enveloped in mist, immense churches she had never visited, but that existed somewhere in the world. During her early days of channeling, she'd had only confused impressions, indigenous songs blending with meaningless words; but now her angel was showing her cathedrals. That seemed to make some sort of sense, although she couldn't quite understand it.

In the beginning, they had only been trying to begin a conversation. With each day that passed, she was able to understand her angel better. Soon, there would be a level of communication as clear as the one she enjoyed with anyone who spoke her own language. It was only a matter of time.

THE ALARM ON PAULO'S WATCH SOUNDED. Twenty minutes had passed. The channeling was over.

She looked at him, knowing what was going to happen now. He would sit there without saying a word, sad and disappointed. His angel hadn't appeared. They would return to the small motel in Ajo, and he would take a walk while she tried to sleep.

She waited until he stood, and then stood up, as well. But there was a strange gleam in his eye.

"I will see my angel," he said. "I know I will. I made the bet."

"The bet, you will have to make with your angel," Valhalla had said. She had never said, "The bet, you will have to make with your angel, *when he appears.*" Yet, that's what Paulo had understood her to mean. He had waited for an entire week for his angel to appear. He was ready to make any bet, because the angel was the light, and the light was what justified human existence. He trusted in that light, in the same way that, fourteen years earlier, he had doubted the darkness. In contrast with the traitorous experience with the darkness, the light established its rules beforehand—so that whoever accepted them was knowingly committing to love and compassion.

He had already met two of the three conditions, and almost failed with regard to the third—the simplest of them! But his angel's protection had prevailed, and, during the channeling . . . ah, how good it was to have learned to converse with the angels! Now he knew that he would be able to see his angel, because he had met the third condition.

"I broke a pact. I accepted forgiveness. And, today, I made a bet. I have faith, and I believe," he said. "I believe that Valhalla knows the method for seeing one's angel."

Paulo's eyes were shining. There would be no nocturnal walks, no insomnia tonight. He was absolutely certain that he was going to see his angel. Half an hour ago, he had asked for a miracle—but that was no longer important.

So that night it would be Chris's turn to be sleepless, and to walk the deserted streets of Ajo, imploring God to make a miracle, because the man she loved needed to see his angel. Her heart was squeezed more tightly than ever. Perhaps she preferred a Paulo who was in doubt. A Paulo who needed a miracle. A Paulo who appeared to have lost his faith. If his angel appeared, fine; if not, he could always blame Valhalla for having erred in her teaching. That way, he would not have to learn the most bitter lesson that God taught, when he closed the gates to paradise: the lesson of disappointment.

But instead, here was a man who seemed to have bet his life against the certainty that angels could be seen. And his only guarantee was the word of a woman who rode the desert, speaking of new worlds to come.

Perhaps Valhalla had never even seen an angel. Or maybe what worked for her didn't work for others—hadn't Paulo said that? Maybe he hadn't heeded his own words.

Chris's heart grew smaller and smaller as she saw the light in Paulo's eyes.

And at that moment, his entire face began to glow.

"Light!" he screamed. "Light!"

She turned. On the horizon, near where the first star had appeared, three lights shone in the sky.

"Light!" he said again. "The angel!"

Chris had a strong desire to kneel down and give thanks, because her prayer had been answered, and God had sent his army of angels.

Paulo's eyes filled with tears. The miracle had happened. He had made the right bet.

They heard a roar to their left, and another over

their heads. Now there were five, six lights gleaming in the sky; the desert was alight.

For a moment she lost her voice. She, too, was seeing his angel! The bursts of sound were becoming stronger and stronger, passing to the left, passing to the right, over their heads, wild thunderbursts that didn't come from the sky, but from behind, from the side—and moved toward where the lights were.

The Valkyries! The true Valkyries, daughters of Wotan, galloping across the sky, carrying their warriors! She blocked her ears in fear.

She saw that Paulo was doing the same—but his eyes appeared to have lost their brilliance.

Immense balls of fire grew on the desert horizon, and they felt the ground shake under their feet. Thunder in the sky and on the Earth.

"Let's go," she said.

"There's no danger," he answered. "They're military planes. Far from here."

But the supersonic fighters broke the sound barrier close to where they stood, with a terrifying sound.

The two clung to each other as they watched the spectacle with fascination and terror. Now there were balls of fire on the horizon, and green lights. There were more than a dozen, falling slowly from the sky, illuminating the entire desert so that no one and nothing could remain hidden.

"It's just a military exercise," he reassured her. "The Air Force. There are a lot of bases around here. I've seen them on the map." Paulo had to shout to make himself heard. "But I wanted to believe they were angels."

They're the instruments of angels, she thought. *Angels of death.*

The yellow brilliance of the bombs falling on the horizon blended with the bright green lights falling slowly by parachute. Everything below was visible, and the planes were unerring as they dropped their mortal loads.

The exercise lasted for half an hour. And, just as suddenly as they had arrived, the planes disappeared, and silence returned to the desert. The last of the green lights came to earth and died. The ground no longer trembled, and they could see the stars again.

Paulo took a deep breath. He closed his eyes, and concentrated: *I won the bet. I'm absolutely sure I won the bet.* His second mind was coming and going, saying no, that it was all in his imagination, that his angel would not show himself. But he dug the nail of his index finger into his thumb until the pain was insupportable; pain always banishes non-sensical thinking.

"I will see my angel," he repeated, as they descended the mountain.

Her heart squeezed again. But she didn't want to allow him to see how she felt. The only way to change the subject quickly was to listen to what her second mind was saying, and to ask Paulo if it made sense.

"I want to ask you something," she said.

"Don't ask me about the miracle. It will happen or it won't. Let's not waste our energy discussing it."

"No, it's not about that."

She hesitated. Paulo was her husband. He knew her better than anyone did. She was fearful of his response, because what he said carried more weight than what others said. But she resolved that she would ask the question anyway; she couldn't stand keeping it inside.

"Do you think I chose wrong?" she asked. "That I've wasted my life sowing seeds, content to watch the crops flourish around me instead of experiencing the strong emotions of the hunt?"

He walked along, looking up at the sky. He was still thinking about his bet, and about the planes.

"Often I look at people like J.," he said. "People like J., who are at peace, and through that peace, find communion with God. I look at you, able to talk with your angel before I was—even though it was I who came here to do that. I watch you sleeping so soundly, while I'm standing at the window, and I ask myself why the miracle I'm waiting so desperately for doesn't happen. And I ask myself: Did I choose the wrong path?"

He turned to her. "What do you think? Did I choose the wrong path?"

Chris took his hand in hers. "No. You would be very unhappy."

"And so would you if you had chosen mine."

"That's a good thing to remember."

Before the alarm went off, he sat up in bed without making a sound.

He looked outside, and it was still dark.

Chris was asleep. For a moment, he thought of waking her, and telling her where he was going. That she should say a prayer for him. But he decided against it. He could tell her everything when he returned. It wasn't as if he were heading for any place dangerous.

He switched on the light in the bathroom, and filled his canteen from the faucet. Then he drank as much water as he could swallow—he had no idea how long he would be out there.

He dressed, grabbed the map, and memorized his route. Then, he got ready to leave.

But he couldn't locate the key to the car. He looked in his pockets, in his knapsack, on the bedside table. He considered lighting the lamp—but no, it might awaken her, and the light from the bathroom was enough. He couldn't spend any more time looking—every minute spent here was a minute less that he could devote to waiting for his angel. Within four hours, the heat of the desert would be unbearable.

Chris hid the key, he thought. She was a different woman now—she was speaking to her angel, and her intuition had increased considerably. Perhaps she had guessed at what his plans were and was frightened.

Why would she be frightened? That night when he has seen her at the precipice with Valhalla, he and Chris had made a sacred agreement; they had promised that never again would they risk their lives in the desert. Several times, the angel of Death had passed close to them, and it wouldn't be smart to keep testing the patience of their guardian angel. Chris knew him well enough to know that he would never fail to keep a promise. That's why he was stealing away before the first rays of the sun were to be seen—to avoid the dangers of the night, and the dangers of the day.

Nevertheless, she was concerned, and had hidden the key.

He went to the bed, having decided to awaken her. And he stopped.

Yes, there was a reason. She wasn't worried about his safety, or about the risks he might take. She was fearful, but it was a different kind of fear—that her husband might be defeated. She knew that Paulo would try something. Only two days remained before they left the desert.

It was a good idea to do what you did, Chris, he

thought, laughing to himself. *A defeat such as this would take two years to overcome, and for the whole time you would have to put up with me, spend sleepless nights with me, bear with my bad moods, suffer my frustration along with me. It would be much worse than these days I lived through, before I learned how to make my bet.*

He looked through her things; the key was in the security belt where she kept her passport and her money. Then he remembered his promise about safety—all this may have been a reminder. He had learned that you never go out into the desert without leaving at least some indication of your destination. Even though he knew that he would be back soon, and even knowing that his destination, after all, was not that far away—and that if anything were to happen, he could even return on foot—he decided not to run the risk. After all, he had promised.

He placed the map on the bathroom sink. And he used the can of pressurized shaving foam to make a circle around a location: Glorieta Canyon.

Using the same means, he sprayed a message on the mirror:

I WON'T MAKE ANY MISTAKES.

Then he put on his sneakers, and left.

When he was about to put the key into the ignition, he found he had left his own key there.

She must have had a copy made, he thought. *What did she think was going to happen? That I was going to abandon her in the middle of the desert?*

Then he recalled Gene's strange behavior when he had forgotten the flashlight in the car. Thanks to the matter of the key, Paulo had marked the place where he was heading. His angel was seeing to it that he took all the necessary precautions.

❁

The streets of Borrego Springs were deserted. *Just like in the daytime,* he thought to himself. He remembered their first night there, when they had stretched out on the floor of the desert, trying to imagine what their angels would be like. Back then, all he wanted to do was talk to his.

He turned to the left, out of the city, and headed for Glorieta Canyon. The mountains were to his right—the mountains they had descended by car back when they had first arrived. *Back then,* he thought, and realized it hadn't been all that long ago. Only thirty-eight days.

But, as with Chris, his soul had died many times

out there in the desert. He was pursuing a secret that he already knew, and had seen the sun turn into the eyes of death. He had met up with women who appeared to be angels and devils at the same time. He had reentered a darkness he thought he had forgotten. And he had discovered that, although he had spoken so often of Jesus, he had never completely accepted the Savior's forgiveness.

He had reencountered his wife—at the very moment when he believed he had lost her forever. Because (and Chris could never know it) he had fallen in love with Valhalla.

That was when he had learned the difference between infatuation and love. Like conversing with the angels, it was really very simple.

Valhalla was a fantasy. The warrior woman, the huntress. The woman who conversed with angels, and was ready to run any risk in order to surpass her limits. For her, Paulo was the man who wore the ring of the Tradition of the Moon, the magus who knew about the occult mysteries. The adventurer, capable of leaving everything behind to go out in search of angels. Each would always be fascinated by the other—so long as each remained exactly what the other imagined.

That's what infatuation is: the creation of an image of someone, without advising that someone as to what the image is.

But some day, when familiarity revealed the true identity of both, they would discover that behind the Magus and the Valkyrie there was a man and a woman. Each possessing powers, perhaps, each with some precious knowledge, maybe, but—they couldn't ignore the fact—each basically a man and a woman. Each with the agony and the ecstasy, the strength and the weakness of every other human being.

And when either of them demonstrated how they really were, the other would want to flee—because it would mean the end of the world they had created.

He found love on a cliff where two women had tried to stare each other down, with the full moon as a backdrop. And love meant dividing the world with someone. He knew one of the women well, and had shared his universe with her. They had seen the same mountains, and the same trees, although each had seen them differently. She knew his weaknesses, his moments of hatred, of despair. Yet she was there at his side.

They shared the same universe. And although often he had had the feeling that their universe contained no more secrets, he had discovered—that night in Death Valley—that the feeling was wrong.

He stopped the car. Ahead, a ravine pierced the mountain. He had chosen the place based on its name—actually, angels are present at all times and in all places. He got out, drank some more of the water that now he always carried in bottles in the trunk of the car, and fixed the canteen to his belt.

He was still thinking about Chris and Valhalla as he made his way to the ravine. *I think I'll probably be infatuated many more times,* he said to himself. He felt no guilt about it. Infatuation was a good thing. It gave spice to life, and added to its enjoyment.

But it was different from love. Love was worth everything, and couldn't be exchanged for anything.

He stopped at the mouth of the ravine and looked out over the valley. The horizon was shading to crimson. It was the first time he had seen the dawn out in the desert; even when they had slept out in the open, the sun was always up when he awoke.

What a beautiful sight I've been missing, he thought. The peaks of the mountains in the distance were gleaming, and pink streaks were creeping into the valley, coloring the stones and the plants that survived there virtually without water. He gazed at the scene for some time.

He was thinking of a book he had written, in which—at a certain point—the shepherd, Santiago, climbs to the top of a mountain to look out over the desert. Except for the fact that Paulo was not atop a mountain, he was surprised at the similarity to what he had written about eight months earlier. He had also just realized the significance of the name of the city where he had disembarked in the United States.

Los Angeles. In Spanish: The Angels.

But this wasn't the time to be thinking of the signs he had seen along the way.

"This is your face, my guardian angel," he said aloud. "I see you. You have always been there before me, and never have I recognized you. I hear your voice. Every day I hear it more clearly. I know you exist, because they speak of you in all corners of the earth.

"Perhaps one man, or even an entire society, can be wrong. But all societies and all civilizations, everywhere on the planet, have always spoken of angels. Nowadays, children and the elderly and the prophets are listening. They will continue to speak of angels down through the centuries, because prophets, children, and old people will always exist."

A blue butterfly fluttered about him. It was his angel, responding.

"I broke a pact. I accepted forgiveness."

The butterfly drifted from one side to the other. He had seen numbers of white butterflies in the desert—but this one was blue. His angel was content.

"And I made a bet. That night, up on the mountain, I bet all of my faith in God, in life, in my work, in J. I bet everything I had. I bet that, when I opened my eyes, you would show yourself to me. I placed my entire life on one tray of the scales. I asked that you place your countenance on the other.

"And, when I opened my eyes, the desert was before me. For a few moments, I thought I had lost. But then—ah, how lovely the memory is—then, you spoke."

A streak of light appeared on the horizon. The sun was coming alive.

"Do you remember what you said? You said: 'Look around, this is my face. I am the place where you are. My mantle will cover you with the rays of the sun in daytime, and with the glow of the stars at night.' I heard your voice clearly!

"And then you said: 'Always need me.'"

His heart was content. He would wait for the sun to rise, and look for a long time at the face of his angel. Later, he would tell Chris of his bet. And tell her that seeing one's angel was even easier than speaking with him! One had only to believe than angels exist, only to need the angels. And they would show themselves, as brilliant as the rays of morning. And they would help, performing their task of protection and guidance, so that each generation would speak to the next of their presence—so that they would never be forgotten.

Write something, he heard a voice within him say.

Strange. He wasn't even trying to do his channeling. All he wanted to do was see his angel.

But some being within him was demanding that he write something. He tried to concentrate on the horizon and the desert, but that's all he could manage.

He went to the car and picked up a pen and some paper. He had had some experience with automatic writing, but had never gone deeply into it—J. had said that it wasn't for him. That he should seek out his true gift.

He sat down on the floor of the desert, pen in hand, and tried to relax. Before long, the pen would begin to move itself, would produce some strokes, and then words would follow. In order for this to happen, he had to lose a bit of his awareness, and allow something—a spirit or an angel—to take him over.

He surrendered completely, and accepted his role as instrument. But nothing happened. *Write something,* he heard the voice within him say again.

He was fearful. He wasn't going to be incorporated by some spirit. He was channeling, without meaning to—as if his angel were there, speaking to him. It wasn't automatic writing.

He took a different grip on the pen—now with firmness. The words began to emerge. And he wrote them down, without time even to think of what he was writing:

For Zion's sake, I will not hold my peace.
And for Jerusalem's sake, I will not rest,
Until her righteousness goes forth as
  brightness,
And her salvation, as a lamp that burns.

This had never happened before. He was *hearing* a voice within him, dictating the words:

You shall be called by a new name,
Which the mouth of the Lord will name.
You shall also be a crown of glory in the hand
of the Lord,
And a royal diadem in the hand of your God.
You shall no longer be termed Forsaken,
Nor your land anymore be termed Desolate;
But you shall be called Hephzibah,
For the Lord delights in you, and your land
shall be married.

He tried to converse with the voice. He asked to whom he should say this.

It has already been said, the voice answered. *It is simply being remembered.*

Paulo felt a lump in his throat. It was a miracle, and he gave thanks to God.

The golden globe of the sun was rising above the horizon. He put down the pad and pen, stood up, and held out his hands in the direction of the light. He asked that all of that energy of hope—hope that a new day brings to millions of people on the face of the earth—would enter through his fingers and repose in his heart. He asked that he might always believe in the new world, in the angels, and in the open gates to paradise. He asked for protection by his angel and the Virgin Mary—for him, for all whom he loved, and for his work.

The butterfly came to him and, responding to a secret sign from his angel, landed on his left hand. He kept absolutely still, because he was in the presence of another miracle: His angel had responded.

He felt the universe stop at that moment: the sun, the butterfly, and the desert there before him.

And in the next moment, the air around him trembled. It wasn't the wind. It was a shock of air—the same as one feels when a car is passed by a bus at high speed.

A shiver of absolute terror ran up his spine.

SOMEONE WAS THERE.

"Do not turn around," he heard the voice say.

His heart was pounding, and he was beginning to feel dizzy. He knew it was fear. A terrible fear. He remained motionless, his arms extended before him, the butterfly poised on his hand.

I'm going to pass out, he thought.

"Do not pass out," the voice said.

He was trying to maintain control of himself, but his hands were cold, and he began to tremble. The butterfly flew away, and he lowered his arms.

"Kneel down," the voice said.

He knelt. He couldn't think. There was nowhere to go.

"Clear the ground,"

He did as the voice ordered. With his hands, he brushed a small area in the sand directly in front of him so that it was smooth. His heart continued to beat rapidly, and he was feeling more and more dizzy. He thought he might even have a heart attack.

"Look at the ground."

An intense light, almost as strong as the morning sun, shone on his left side. He didn't want to look directly at it, and wished only that everything would end quickly. For a moment, he recalled his childhood, when appearances of Our Lady had been described to children. He had passed many sleepless nights as a child, asking God never to order the Virgin to appear to him—because the prospect was so frightening. Scary.

The same fright that he was experiencing now.

"Look at the ground," the voice insisted.

He looked down at the area he had just swept clear. And that was when the golden arm, as brilliant as the sun, appeared, and began to write in the sand.

"This is my name," the voice said.

The fearful dizziness continued. His heart was beating even faster.

"Believe," he heard the voice say. "The gates are open for a while."

He gathered every bit of strength he had remaining.

"I want to say something," he said aloud. The heat of the sun seemed to be restoring his strength.

He heard nothing. No answer.

❁

An hour later, when Chris arrived—she had awakened the hotel owner, and demanded that he drive her there—he was still looking at the name in the sand.

THE TWO OTHERS WATCHED AS PAULO prepared the cement.

"What a waste of water, out in the middle of the desert," Gene joked.

Chris asked him not to kid around, since her husband was still feeling the impact of his vision.

"I found where the passage came from," Gene said. "It's from Isaiah."

"Why that passage?" Chris asked.

"I have no idea. But I'm going to remember it."

"It speaks about a new world," she continued.

"Maybe that's why," Gene answered. "Maybe that's why."

Paulo called to them.

The three said a Hail Mary. Then Paulo climbed to the top of a boulder, spread the cement, and placed within it the image of Our Lady that he always carried with him.

"There. It's done."

"Maybe the guards will take it away when they find it here," Gene said. "They watch over the desert as if it were a flower garden."

"Maybe," Paulo said. "But the spot will still be marked. It will always be one of my sacred places."

"No," Gene said. "Sacred places are individual places. In this one, a text was dictated. A text that already existed. One that speaks of hope, and had already been forgotten."

Paulo didn't want to think about that now. He was still fearful.

"In this place, the energy of the soul of the world was felt," Gene said. "And it will be felt here forever. It is a place of power."

They gathered up the plastic sheeting in which Paulo had mixed the cement, placed it in the trunk of the car, and left to take Gene back to his old trailer.

"Paulo!" he said when they were saying their good-byes. "I think it would be good for you to know an old saying from the Tradition: *When God wants to drive a person insane, he grants that person's every wish.*"

"Could be," Paulo answered. "But it was worth it."

EPILOGUE

One afternoon, a year and a half after the angel's appearance, a letter arrived for me in Rio, from Los Angeles. It was from one of my Brazilian readers living in the United States, Rita de Freitas, and was in praise of *The Alchemist.*

On impulse, I wrote to her, asking that she go to a canyon near Borrego Springs to see whether the statue of Our Lady of Aparecida was still there.

After I had mailed the letter, I thought to myself: *That's pretty silly. This woman doesn't even know me. She's just a reader who wanted to say a few kind words, and she'll never do as I've asked. She's not going to get into her car, drive six hours into the desert, and see whether a small statue is still there.*

Just before Christmas in 1989, I received a letter from Rita, from which I have excerpted the following:

There have been some marvelous "coincidences." I had a week off from my job over the Thanksgiving holiday. My boyfriend (Andrea, an Italian musician) and I were planning on getting away to someplace different.

Then your letter arrived. And the place you mentioned was near an Indian reservation. We decided to go . . .

. . . On our third day there, we went to look for the canyon, and found it. It was on Thanksgiving Day. It was interesting, because we were driving very slowly, but saw no sign of the statue. We came to the end of a canyon, stopped, and began climbing to the top of the cliff there. All we saw were the footprints of coyotes.

At this point, we concluded that the statue couldn't any longer be there . . .

As we were returning to the car, we saw some flowers among the rocks. We stopped the car and got out. We saw some small candles burning, some golden cloth with a butterfly woven into it, and a straw basket that had been thrown aside. We decided that must have been the place where the statue had been placed, but it was no longer there.

What was interesting was the fact that I'm sure none of that was there when we had first passed by. We took a photograph—enclosed—and went on our way.

When we were almost at the mouth of the canyon, we saw a woman dressed in white. Her clothing seemed Arabian—turban, long tunic—and she was walking in the middle of the road. Very strange—how could a woman such as this appear out of nowhere, in the middle of the desert?

I was thinking: Could this be the woman who had placed those flowers and lighted the candles? There was no car to be seen, and I wondered how she could have come there.

But I was so surprised that I couldn't bring myself to talk to her.

I examined the photo Rita had sent: It was exactly where I had placed the statue.

It was Thanksgiving Day. And I'm certain that angels were there that day.

I wrote this book in January/February 1992, shortly after the end of the Third World War—where the battles were much more sophisticated than those fought with conventional arms. According to the Tradition, this war began in the 1950s, with the blockade of Berlin, and ended when the Berlin Wall fell. The victors divided up the defeated empire, as in a conventional war. The only thing that didn't occur was a nuclear holocaust—and this will never happen, because God's Work is too great to be destroyed by human beings.

Now, according to the Tradition, a new war will begin. An even more sophisticated war, survived by no one—because it is through its battles that man's growth will be completed. We will see the two armies—on one side, those who still believe in the human race, and know that our next step involves the growth of individual gifts. On the other side will be those who deny the future. Those who believe that life has a material ending, and—unfortunately—those who, although they have faith, believe that they discovered the path to enlightenment, and want the others to follow it with them.

That's why the angels have returned and must be attended. Only they can show us the way—no one else. We can share our experiences—as I have tried to share mine in this book—but there is no formula for this growth. God has generously made His wisdom and His love available to us, and it is easy, very easy, to find them. One has only to understand channeling—a process so simple that it was difficult for me to recognize and accept. Since the combat will take place for the most part in the astral plane, it will be our guardian angels who will wield the swords and shields, protecting us from danger, and guiding us to victory. But our responsibility is huge, as well: We, at this moment in history, must develop our own powers. We must believe that the universe doesn't end at the walls of our room. We must accept the signs, and follow our heart and our dreams.

We are responsible for everything that happens in this world. We are the warriors of the light. With the strength of our love and of our will, we can change our destiny, as well as the destiny of many others.

The day will come when the problem of hunger can be solved through the miracle of the multiplication of the bread. The day will come when love will be accepted by every heart, and the most terrible of human experiences—solitude, which is worse than hunger—will be banned from the face of the Earth. The day will come when those who knock at the gates will see them open; those who ask will receive; those who weep will be consoled.

For the planet Earth, that day is still a long way off. But for each of us, that day can be tomorrow. One has only to accept a simple fact: Love—of God and of others—shows us the way. Our defects, our dangerous depths, our suppressed hatreds, our moments of weakness and desperation—all are unimportant. If what we want to do is heal ourselves first, so that *then* we can go in search of our dreams, we will never reach paradise. If, on the other hand, we accept all that is wrong about us—and despite it, believe that we are deserving of a happy life—then we will have thrown open an immense window that will allow Love to enter. Little by little, our defects will disappear, because one who is happy can look at the world only with love—the force that regenerates everything that exists in the Universe.

In *The Brothers Karamazov,* Dostoyevsky tells us the story of the Grand Inquisitor, which I paraphrase here:

During the religious persecutions in Sevilla, when all who did not agree with the Church were thrown into prison, or burned at the stake, Christ returns to earth and mixes in with the multitudes. But the Grand Inquisitor notes his presence, and orders him jailed.

That night, he goes to visit Jesus in his cell. And he asks why Jesus has decided to return at that particular moment. "You are making things difficult for us," the Grand Inquisitor says. "After all, your ideals were lovely, but it is we who are capable of putting them into practice." He argues that, although the Inquisition might be judged in the future to have been severe, it is necessary, and that he is simply doing his job. There is no use talking of peace when man's heart is always at war; nor speaking of a better world when there is so much hatred in man's heart. There was no use in Jesus' having sacrificed himself in the name of the human race, when human beings still feel guilty. "You said that all people are equal, that each has the divine light within, but you forgot that people are insecure, and they need someone to guide them. Don't make our work more difficult than it is. Go away," says the Grand Inquisitor, having laid out all of his brilliant arguments.

When he is finished, there is silence in the cell. Then Jesus comes to the Grand Inquisitor, and kisses him on the cheek.

"You may be right," Jesus says. "But my love is stronger."

❁

We are not alone. The world is changing, and we are a part of the transformation. The angels guide us and protect us. Despite all the injustice in the world, and despite the things that happen to us that we feel we don't deserve, and despite the fact that we sometimes feel incapable of changing what is wrong with people and with the world, and despite all of the Grand Inquisitor's arguments—love is even stronger, and it will help us to grow. Only then will we be able to understand the stars and miracles.

AUTHOR'S NOTE

Anyone who has read *The Valkyries* will know that this book is very different from *The Pilgrimage* (previously published as *The Diary of a Magus*), *The Alchemist,* and *Brida.*

It was an extremely difficult book to write. First, because it deals with matters that require sensitivity on the part of the reader. Second, because I have already told this story to many people, and I feared that I might have exhausted my capacity to write it down. This fear remained with me from the first page to the last, but—thank God—it was only a fear.

The third and most important reason: In order to relate the events that took place, I had to reveal details from my personal life—my marriage, my relationships with others, and the fragile distance that separates the magical Tradition to which I belong from the person I am. As is true for any human being, exposing my weaknesses and my private life is not easy.

But—as was made quite clear in *The Pilgrimage*—the path to magic is the path of the common people. One can have a master, follow the esoteric

Tradition, and possess the discipline needed to perform rituals; but the spiritual search is made up of many beginnings (thus the searcher is called an "initiate," someone who is always in the act of beginning something), and the only thing that matters—always—is the will to go on.

The Valkyries clearly presents the man that exists behind the magus, and this may disappoint those who are looking for "perfect beings," with their perfect truths regarding everything. But true seekers know that, regardless of our faults and defects, the spiritual path is stronger. God is love, generosity, and forgiveness; if we believe in this, we will never allow our weaknesses to paralyze us.

The events narrated in this book took place between September 5 and October 17, 1988. The sequential order of some of the events has been changed, and in two places I made use of fiction, only so that the reader could better grasp the matter at hand. But all of the essential events are true. The letter quoted in the Epilogue is on file at the Registry of Titles and Documents in Rio de Janeiro under number 478038.

Paulo Coelho

Life is a
journey

Make sure you don't miss a thing.
Live it with Paulo Coelho.

Visit f /paulocoelho

How can you find your heart's desire?

A world-wide phenomenon; an inspiration for anyone seeking their path in life.

The Alchemist

Do you believe in yourself?

A modern-day adventure in the searing heat of the Mojave desert and an exploration of fear and self-doubt.

The Valkyries

How do we see the amazing in the everyday?

When two young lovers are reunited, they discover anew the truth of what lies in their hearts.

By the River Piedra
I Sat Down & Wept

What are you searching for?

A transforming journey on the pilgrims' road to Santiago – and the first of Paulo's extraordinary books.

The Pilgrimage

Can faith triumph over suffering?

Paulo Coelho's brilliant telling of the story of Elijah, who was forced to choose between love and duty.

The Fifth Mountain

Is life always worth living?

A fundamental moral question explored as only Paulo Coelho can.

Veronika Decides to Die

Could you be tempted into evil?

The inhabitants of a small town are challenged by a mysterious stranger to choose between good and evil.

The Devil & Miss Prym

Are you brave enough to live your dream?

Strategies and inspiration to help you follow your own path in a troubled world.

Manual of the Warrior of Light

Can sex be sacred?

An unflinching exploration of the lengths we go to in our search for love, sex and spirituality.

Eleven Minutes

How far would you go for your obsession?

A sweeping story of love, loss and longing that spans the world.

The Zahir

What happens when obsession turns to murder?

An enthralling story of jealousy, death and suspense.

The Winner Stands Alone

Can we dare to be true to ourselves?

A story that will transform the way we think about love, joy and sacrifice.

The Witch of Portobello

How will you know who your soulmate is?

A moving tale of passion, mystery and spirituality.

Brida

What does it mean to be truly alive?

Powerful tales of living and dying, destiny and choice, and love lost and found.

Like the Flowing River

Are you where you want to be?

Read *Aleph*. And rewrite your life.

THE INTERNATIONAL BESTSELLER
ALEPH
Paulo Coelho
FROM THE AUTHOR OF *THE ALCHEMIST*

Aleph

Is there a weapon more powerful than words?

A timeless and powerful exploration of personal growth, everyday wisdom and joy.

Manuscript Found in Accra

BRIDA

Paulo Coelho was born in Brazil and has become one of the most widely read and loved authors in the world. Especially renowned for *The Alchemist* and *Eleven Minutes*, he has sold more than 320 million books worldwide and has been translated into 88 languages. The recipient of numerous prestigious international awards, amongst them the Crystal Award by the World Economic Forum and France's Légion d'Honneur, Paulo Coelho was inducted into the Brazilian Academy of Letters in 2002.

Also by Paulo Coelho

The Alchemist
The Pilgrimage
The Valkyries
By the River Piedra I Sat Down and Wept
The Fifth Mountain
Veronika Decides to Die
Manual of the Warrior of Light
Eleven Minutes
The Zahir
The Devil and Miss Prym
The Witch of Portobello
Brida
The Winner Stands Alone
Like the Flowing River
Aleph
Manuscript Found in Accra
Adultery
The Spy
Hippie

BRIDA

PAULO COELHO

Author of THE ALCHEMIST

TRANSLATED FROM THE PORTUGUESE BY
MARGARET JULL COSTA

Thorsons
An imprint of HarperCollins*Publishers*
1 London Bridge Street
London SE1 9GF

HarperCollins*Publishers*
1st Floor, Watermarque Building, Ringsend Road
Dublin 4, Ireland

www.harpercollins.co.uk
www.paulocoelho.com
www.paulocoelhoblog.com

First published in the UK by HarperCollins*Publishers* 2008
This edition 2022

2 4 6 8 10 9 7 5 3 1

© Paulo Coelho 1990

English translation © Margaret Jull Costa 2008

Paulo Coelho asserts the moral right to
be identified as the author of this work

A catalogue record for this book is
available from the British Library

ISBN 978-0-00-854733-2

FICTION / PHILOSOPHY

Printed and bound in India by Thomson Press India Ltd

All rights reserved. No part of this publication may be
reproduced, stored in a retrieval system, or transmitted,
in any form or by any means, electronic, mechanical,
photocopying, recording or otherwise, without the prior
written permission of the publishers.

This book is produced from independently certified FSC® paper
to ensure responsible forest management.

O Mary!
conceived without sin,
pray for us who turn to you!
Amen.

. . . what woman having ten silver coins,
if she loses one of them,
does not light a lamp, sweep the house,
and search carefully until she finds it?
When she has found it, she calls together
her friends and neighbours, saying,
'Rejoice with me, for I have found the coin
that I had lost.'

Luke 15:8–9

For N.D.L. who made the miracles happen,
for Christina, who is one of those miracles,
and for Brida

Warning

In my book *The Diary of a Magus*, I replaced two of the practices of RAM with exercises in perception learned in the days when I worked in drama. Although the results were, strictly speaking, the same, I received a severe reprimand from my Teacher. 'There may well be quicker or easier methods – that doesn't matter; what matters is that the Tradition remains unchanged,' he said.

For this reason, the few rituals described in *Brida* are the same as those practised over the centuries by the Tradition of the Moon – a specific tradition that requires experience and practice. Practising such rituals without guidance is dangerous, inadvisable, unnecessary and can greatly hinder the Spiritual Search.

Paulo Coelho

Prologue

We used to sit until late at night in a café in Lourdes. I was a pilgrim on the sacred Road of Rome and still had many more days to travel in search of my Gift. She was Brida O'Fern and was in charge of a certain stretch of that Road.

On one such night, I asked if she remembered having felt especially moved when she arrived at a particular abbey that forms part of the star-shaped trail followed by Initiates in the Pyrenees.

'I've never been there,' she replied.

I was surprised. She did, after all, have a Gift.

'All roads lead to Rome,' said Brida, using an old proverb to tell me that Gifts could be awoken anywhere. 'I walked my Road to Rome in Ireland.'

During our subsequent meetings, she told me the story of her search. When she finished, I asked if, one day, I could write it down.

She agreed initially, but whenever we met after that, she kept raising obstacles. She asked me to change the names of those involved; she wanted to know what kind of people would read the book and how they would be likely to react.

'I've no idea,' I said. 'But I don't think that's why you're creating all these problems.'

'You're right,' she said. 'It's because it seems to me such a personal story, and I'm not sure anyone else would get much out of it.'

That's a risk we're now going to take together, Brida. An anonymous text from the Tradition says that, in life, each person can take one of two attitudes: to build or to plant. The builders might take years over their tasks, but one day, they finish what they're doing. Then they find they're hemmed in by their own walls. Life loses its meaning when the building stops.

Then there are those who plant. They endure storms and all the many vicissitudes of the seasons, and they rarely rest. But, unlike a building, a garden never stops growing. And while it requires the gardener's constant attention, it also allows life for the gardener to be a great adventure.

Gardeners always recognise each other, because they know that in the history of each plant lies the growth of the whole World.

The Author

Ireland

August 1983–March 1984

Summer and Autumn

'I want to learn about magic,' said the girl. The Magus looked at her. Faded jeans, T-shirt, the challenging look adopted by all shy people precisely when it's least needed. 'I must be twice her age,' he thought. And despite this, he knew that he had met his Soulmate.

'My name's Brida,' she went on. 'Forgive me for not introducing myself. I've waited a long time for this moment and I'm more nervous than I thought I would be.'

'Why do you want to learn about magic?' he asked.

'So that I can find answers to some of the questions I have regarding life, so that I can learn about the occult powers, and, possibly, how to travel back into the past and forwards into the future.'

It wasn't the first time someone had come to the forest to ask him this. There was a time when he'd been a Teacher who was known and respected by the Tradition. He'd taken on several pupils and believed that the world would change if he could change those around him. But he had made a mistake. And Teachers of the Tradition cannot make mistakes.

'Don't you think you're rather young?'

'I'm twenty-one,' said Brida. 'If I wanted to start learning ballet, I'd be considered too old.'

The Magus made a sign for her to follow him. They set off together through the forest, in silence. 'She's pretty,' he was thinking as the shadows cast by the trees rapidly lengthened and shifted as the sun sank lower on the horizon. 'But I'm twice her age.' This, he knew, meant that he might well suffer.

Brida felt irritated by the silence of the man walking beside her; he hadn't even deigned to respond to her last remark. The forest floor was wet and covered in fallen leaves; she, too, noticed the shadows changing and the rapid approach of night. It would be dark soon and they didn't have a torch with them.

'I have to trust him,' she told herself. 'If I believe that he can teach me magic, then I also have to believe that he can guide me through the forest.'

They continued walking. He appeared to be wandering aimlessly, from one side to the other, changing direction even when there was no obstacle in his path. More than once they walked in a circle, passing the same place three or four times.

'Perhaps he's testing me.' She was determined to see this experience through to the end and tried telling herself that everything that was happening – including those circular walks – was perfectly normal.

She had come a very long way and had hoped for more from this encounter. Dublin was over 90 miles away, and the buses to the village were uncomfortable and left at absurd times. She'd had to get up early, travel for three hours, ask the people in the village where she might find him and explain what she wanted with such a strange man. Finally, someone had told her in which part of the forest he could usually be found during the day, but not without first warning her that he'd already tried to seduce one of the village girls.

'He's an interesting man,' she thought to herself. They were climbing now, and she found herself hoping that the sun would linger a little longer in the sky. She was afraid she might slip on the damp leaves.

'Why do you really want to learn about magic?'

Brida was pleased that the silence had been broken. She gave him the same answer she had given before.

But he wasn't satisfied.

'Perhaps you want to learn about magic because it's mysterious and secret, because it provides answers that few human beings ever manage to find in a whole lifetime, or perhaps because it evokes a romantic past.'

Brida said nothing. She didn't know what to say. Afraid to give an answer the Magus might not like, she rather wished he would lapse back into his earlier silence.

* * *

At last, they came to the top of a hill, having crossed the entire forest. The ground there was rocky and bare of vegetation, but at least it was less slippery, and Brida could follow the Magus without difficulty.

He sat down on the highest point and asked Brida to do the same.

'Other people have been here before,' said the Magus. 'They, too, came to ask me to teach them about magic, but I've taught everything I needed to teach. I've given back to humanity what it gave to me. Now I want to be alone, to climb mountains, tend plants and commune with God.'

'That's not true,' replied the girl.

'What isn't true?' he asked, surprised.

'You might want to commune with God, but it isn't true that you want to be alone.'

Brida regretted having spoken. She had spoken on an impulse and now it was too late to correct her mistake. Perhaps there *were* people who wanted to be alone. Perhaps women needed men more than men needed women.

The Magus, however, showed no sign of irritation when he spoke again.

'I'm going to ask you a question,' he said, 'and you must be absolutely honest in your answer. If you tell me the truth, I'll teach you what you ask. If you lie, you must never again return to this forest.'

Brida gave a sigh of relief. He was going to ask her a question. She simply had to tell the truth, that was all. She had always assumed that a Teacher would demand really difficult things of someone before taking them on as a pupil.

'Let's suppose that I do start teaching you what I've learned,' he said, his eyes fixed on hers. 'Let's suppose that I start to show you the parallel universes that surround us, the angels, the wisdom of nature, the mysteries of the Tradition of the Sun and the Tradition of the Moon. Then one day, you go into town to buy some food and, in the middle of the street, you meet the love of your life.'

'I wouldn't know how to recognise him,' she thought, but decided to say nothing. This question was turning out to be more difficult than she'd imagined.

'He feels the same and comes over to you. You fall in love with each other. You continue your studies with me. During the day, I teach you the wisdom of the Cosmos, and at night, he teaches you the wisdom of Love. But there comes a moment when those two things can no longer coexist, and you have to choose.'

The Magus paused for a few seconds. Before he actually asked the question, he felt afraid of what the girl's reply might be. Her coming there that evening meant the end of a stage in both their lives. He knew this, because he understood the traditions and intentions of Teachers. He needed her as much as she needed him, but she had to answer the question he put to her truthfully; that was the sole condition.

'Now answer this question with total honesty,' he

said at last, screwing up his courage. 'Would you give up everything you had learned until then – all the possibilities and all the mysteries that the world of magic could offer you – in order to stay with the love of your life?'

Brida looked away. Around her lay the mountains and the forests, and down below, the lights in the village were beginning to come on; soon, families would be gathering round the table to have supper. They worked hard and honestly, they feared God, and they tried to help their fellow man. They did all these things because they had known love. Their lives had a reason, they could understand everything that was going on in the universe without ever having heard of things like the Tradition of the Sun and the Tradition of the Moon.

'I see no contradiction between my search and my personal happiness,' she said.

'Answer my question.' His eyes were still fixed on hers. 'Would you give up everything for that man?'

Brida felt a tremendous urge to cry. It wasn't so much a question, it was a choice, the most difficult choice anyone would have to make in life. It was something she'd already thought about a lot. There had been a time when nothing in the world was as important as herself. She'd had several boyfriends and had always believed that she loved each one, only to see love vanish from one moment to the next. Of all the things she'd experienced until then, love had been the most difficult. Just then, she was in love with someone slightly older than herself; he was studying physics and had a completely different vision of the world from hers. Once again, she was putting her belief in love, trusting her feelings, but she'd been disappointed so often before that she was no longer sure of anything. Nevertheless, this was the great gamble of her life.

She continued to avoid the Magus's gaze. Her eyes were fixed on the village and its twinkling lights. People had been trying to understand the universe through love ever since the beginning of time.

'I'd give it all up,' she said at last.

The man standing before her, she thought, would never understand what went on in people's hearts. He was a man who knew the power and the mystery of magic, but he didn't know people. His hair was grizzled, his skin burned by the sun, and he had the physique of someone used to walking in the mountains. He was so very attractive, with eyes that revealed a soul full of answers, and he would once again be disappointed by the feelings of ordinary human beings. She was disappointed with herself too, but she couldn't lie.

'Look at me,' said the Magus.

Brida felt ashamed, but did as he asked.

'You told the truth. I will be your teacher.'

* * *

Darkness fell, and the stars were shining in a moonless sky. It took two hours for Brida to tell the stranger her life story. She tried to look for facts that would explain her interest in magic – childhood visions, premonitions, an inner calling – but could find nothing. She simply felt a need to know, that was all. And because of that, she had taken courses in astrology, tarot and numerology.

'Those are merely languages,' said the Magus, 'and they're not the only ones. Magic speaks all the languages of the human heart.'

'So what is magic?' she asked.

Even in the darkness, Brida could sense that the Magus had turned away from her. He was looking up at the sky, absorbed in thought, perhaps in search of an answer.

'Magic is a bridge,' he said at last, 'a bridge that allows you to walk from the visible world over into the invisible world, and to learn the lessons of both those worlds.'

'And how can I learn to cross that bridge?'

'By discovering your own way of crossing it. Everyone has their own way.'

'That's what I came here to find out.'

'There are two forms,' replied the Magus. 'The Tradition of the Sun, which teaches the secrets through space and the world that surrounds us, and the Tradition of the Moon, which teaches through time and the things that are imprisoned in time's memory.'

Brida had understood. The Tradition of the Sun was

the night, the trees, the cold gripping her body, the stars in the sky. And the Tradition of the Moon was that man before her now, with the wisdom of the ancestors shining in his eyes.

'I learned the Tradition of the Moon,' said the Magus, as if he could read her thoughts, 'but I was never a Teacher of that Tradition. I am a Teacher of the Tradition of the Sun.'

'Teach me the Tradition of the Sun, then,' said Brida, feeling slightly disconcerted, for she had sensed a note of tenderness in the Magus's voice.

'I will teach you what I have learned, but the Tradition of the Sun has many roads. One must trust in each person's ability to teach him or herself.'

Brida was right. There *was* a note of tenderness in the Magus's voice. Far from reassuring her, this frightened her.

'I know I'm capable of understanding the Tradition of the Sun,' she said.

The Magus stopped gazing up at the stars and concentrated on the young woman. He knew that she was not quite ready to learn the Tradition of the Sun and yet he must teach it to her. Some pupils choose their Teachers.

'Before our first lesson, I want to remind you of one thing,' he said. 'When you find your path, you must not be afraid. You need to have sufficient courage to make mistakes. Disappointment, defeat and despair are the tools God uses to show us the way.'

'Strange tools,' said Brida. 'They often dissuade people from carrying on.'

The Magus knew the reason for these tools, he had already experienced both in body and soul.

'Teach me the Tradition of the Sun,' she insisted.

The Magus asked Brida to lean back against the rock and relax.

'There's no need to close your eyes. Look at the world around you and try to see and understand as much as you can. The Tradition of the Sun is constantly revealing eternal knowledge to each individual.'

Brida did as the Magus told her to, but she felt he was moving much too fast.

'This is the first and most important lesson,' he said. 'It was created by a Spanish mystic who understood the meaning of faith. His name was St John of the Cross.'

He looked at the girl's eager, trusting face. In his heart, he prayed she would understand what he had to teach her. She was, after all, his Soulmate, even if she didn't yet know it, even if she was still very young and fascinated by the things and the people of this world.

In the darkness, Brida could just make out the shape of the Magus going back into the forest and disappearing among the trees to her left. She was afraid of being left there alone, but tried to remain relaxed. This was her first lesson, and she must not show that she was nervous.

'He accepted me as his pupil. I can't disappoint him.'

She was pleased with herself and, at the same time, surprised at how quickly it had all happened. Not that she had ever doubted her abilities – she was proud of herself and of what had brought her there. She was sure that the Magus was somewhere nearby, watching her reactions, to see if she was capable of learning the first lesson of magic. He had spoken of courage, and so even if she felt afraid – images of the snakes and scorpions that might be living underneath that rock began to rise up from the depths of her imagination – she must be brave. In a while, he would return to teach her the first lesson.

'I'm a strong, determined woman,' she repeated to herself under her breath. She was privileged to be there with that man whom other people either loved or feared. She looked back on the evening they had just spent together and recalled the moment when she had sensed a certain tenderness in his voice. 'Perhaps he found me interesting. Perhaps he even wanted to make love with me.' It wouldn't be a bad experience; there was, however, a strange look in his eyes.

'What an idiotic thing to think.' There she was, in search of something very real – a path to knowledge – and suddenly she was thinking of herself as a mere woman. She tried not to think about it again, and it was then that she realised how much time had passed since the Magus had left her alone.

She felt the beginnings of panic; she had heard contradictory views about that man. Some said he was the most powerful Teacher they'd ever met, capable of changing the direction of the wind, of piercing the clouds, purely by the power of thought. And Brida was as fascinated as everyone else by such prodigies.

Other people, though – people on the fringes of the world of magic, who attended the same courses and classes as she did – assured her that he was a black magician and had once used his powers to destroy a man, because he had fallen in love with the man's wife. And this was why, even though he was a Teacher, he had been condemned to wander the lonely forests.

'Perhaps solitude has made his madness worse,' Brida thought, and again felt the first stirrings of panic. She may have been young, but she knew the harm that loneliness could do to people, especially as they got older. She had met people who had lost the glow of being alive because they could no longer fight against loneliness and had ended up becoming addicted to it. They were, for the most part, people who believed the world to be an undignified, inglorious place, and who spent their evenings and nights talking on and on about the mistakes others had made. They were people whom solitude had made into the judges of the world, whose verdicts were scattered to the four winds for whoever cared to listen. Perhaps the Magus had gone mad with loneliness.

A sudden noise nearby made her jump, and her heart raced. All trace of her earlier confidence vanished. She looked around – nothing. A wave of terror seemed to rise up from her belly and spread through her body.

'I must get a grip on myself,' she thought, but it was impossible. Images of snakes and scorpions and childhood ghosts began to appear before her. Brida was too terrified to stay calm. Another image arose: that of a powerful magician who had made a pact with the Devil and was offering her up as a sacrifice.

'Where are you?' she cried. She didn't care now what impression she made on anyone. She simply wanted to get out of there.

No one answered.

'I want to get out of here! Help me!'

There was only the forest and its strange noises. Brida felt so dizzy with fear she thought she might faint. But she mustn't. Now that she was quite sure he was nowhere around, fainting certainly wouldn't help matters. She must stay in control.

This thought made her aware that there was some part of her struggling to maintain control. 'I mustn't call out,' she said to herself. Her shouts could attract other men who lived in that forest and men who live in forests can be more dangerous than any wild animal.

'I have faith,' she started to say softly. 'I have faith in God, faith in my Guardian Angel, who brought me here, and who remains here with me. I can't explain what he's like, but I know he is near. I will not dash my foot against a stone.'

These last words were from a psalm she had learned as a child, and which she hadn't thought about for years. She had been taught the psalm by her grandmother, who had died quite recently. As soon as she wished her grandmother could be there, she immediately felt a friendly presence.

She was beginning to understand that there was a big difference between danger and fear.

'He that dwelleth in the secret place of the most High …' that was how the Psalm began. She realised that it was all coming back to her word for word, exactly as if her grandmother were reciting it to her now. She kept reciting for some time, without stopping, and despite her fear, she felt calmer. She had no choice: either she believed in God, in her Guardian Angel, or she despaired.

She felt a protective presence. 'I need to believe in this presence. I don't know how to explain it, but it exists. And it will stay with me all night, because I don't know how to find my way out of here alone.'

When she was a child, she would sometimes wake up in the middle of night, feeling terrified. Her father would carry her to the window and show her the town where they lived. He would talk to her about the nightwatchmen, about the milkman who would already be out delivering the milk, about the baker making their daily bread. Her father was trying to drive out the monsters with which she'd filled the night and replace them with the people who kept watch over the darkness. 'The night is just a part of the day,' he would say.

The night is just a part of the day. Therefore she could feel as safe in the dark as she did in the light. It was the dark that had made her invoke that protective presence. She must trust it. And that trust was called Faith. No one could ever understand Faith, but Faith was what she was experiencing now, an inexplicable immersion in blackest night. It only existed because she believed in it. Miracles couldn't be explained either, but they existed for those who believed in them.

'He did say something about the first lesson,' she thought, suddenly realising what was going on. The protective presence was there because she believed in it. Brida began to feel the fatigue of so many hours under tension. She began to relax again and, with each moment that passed, she felt more protected.

She had faith. And faith wouldn't allow the forest to be peopled again with scorpions and snakes. Faith would keep her Guardian Angel awake and watching.

She leaned back against the rock again and, all unknowing, fell asleep.

It was light when she woke, and a beautiful sun was gilding everything around her. She felt a little cold, her clothes were grubby, but her soul was rejoicing. She had spent the whole night alone in a forest.

She looked everywhere for the Magus, knowing that she would not find him. He must be walking in the forest somewhere trying 'to commune with God', and perhaps wondering if the girl who'd come to see him the previous night had sufficient courage to learn the first lesson of the Tradition of the Sun.

'I learned about the Dark Night,' she said to the now silent forest. 'I learned that the search for God is a Dark Night, that Faith is a Dark Night. And that's hardly a surprise really, because for us each day is a dark night. None of us knows what might happen even the next minute, and yet still we go forwards. Because we trust. Because we have Faith.'

Or, who knows, perhaps because we just don't see the mystery contained in the next second. Not that it mattered. What mattered was knowing that she had understood.

That every moment in life is an act of faith.

That you could choose to fill it with snakes and scorpions or with a strong protecting force.

That Faith cannot be explained. It was simply a Dark Night. And all she had to do was to accept it or not.

Brida looked at her watch and saw that it was getting late. She had to catch a bus, travel for three hours and think up some convincing excuse to give her boyfriend; he would never believe she had spent the whole night alone in a forest.

'It's a very difficult thing, the Tradition of the Sun!' she shouted to the forest. 'I have to be my own Teacher, and that isn't what I was expecting!'

She looked at the village down below, mentally traced her path back through the woods and set off. First, though, she turned to the rock again. In a loud, joyous voice, she cried:

'There's one other thing. You're a very interesting man.'

Leaning against the trunk of an old tree, the Magus watched the girl vanish into the woods. He had listened to her fears and heard her cries during the night. At one point, he had even been tempted to go over and embrace her, to shield her from her terror, saying that she didn't need this kind of challenge.

Now he was pleased that he hadn't, and he felt proud that the girl, in all her youthful confusion, was his Soulmate.

In the centre of Dublin there is a bookshop that specialises in occult studies. It has never advertised in newspapers or magazines; the people who go there do so on the recommendation of others, and the owner is glad to have such a select, specialist clientele.

Even so, the bookshop is always full. Brida had heard about it and finally managed to get the address from the person teaching the course on astral travel she was currently attending. She went there late one afternoon, after work, and was delighted with the place.

From then on, whenever she could, she would go there to look at the books, but she never bought any because they were all imported and very expensive. She would leaf through them, studying the designs and symbols in some of the books, and intuitively tuning in to the vibration of all that accumulated knowledge. She had grown more cautious since her experience with the Magus. Sometimes she would bemoan to herself the fact that she only managed to take part in things she could already understand. She sensed that she was missing out on something very important in life, and that if she carried on as she was, she would simply continue to repeat the same experiences over and over. And yet she didn't have the courage to change. She needed to be constantly struggling to discover her path; now that she had experienced the Dark Night, she knew that she didn't want to find her way through it. And although she was sometimes dissatisfied with herself, she felt unable to go beyond her own limitations.

Books were safer. The shelves contained reprints of treatises written hundreds of years ago; it was an area in which very few people dared to say anything new. And in the pages of these books, occult knowledge, distant and remote, seemed to smile at the efforts made by each generation to uncover it.

Apart from looking at the books, Brida had another important reason for going to the shop – to observe the other customers. Sometimes, she would pretend to be reading some respectable alchemical treatise, when she was, in fact, scrutinising the men and women, usually older than her, who frequented the shop and who knew what they wanted and always went to the right shelf. She tried to imagine what they must be like in private. Some looked very wise, capable of awakening forces and powers of which mere mortals knew nothing. Others appeared to be desperately trying to rediscover answers they had long ago forgotten, but without which life had no meaning.

She noticed, too, that the most regular customers always had a word with the owner. They talked about strange things, such as the phases of the moon, the properties of stones and the correct pronunciation of ritual words.

One afternoon, Brida got up sufficient courage to do the same. She was on her way back from work, on a day when everything had gone well. She thought she should make the most of that good luck.

'I know that there are secret societies,' she said. She thought this a good conversational opener. She 'knew' something.

But the owner merely looked up from his accounts and stared at her in amazement.

'I was with the Magus in Folk,' said Brida, rather put out now, and not knowing quite how to continue. 'He explained to me about the Dark Night. He told me that the path of wisdom means not being afraid to make mistakes.'

She noticed that the owner was listening more intently now. If the Magus had bothered to teach her something, she must be special.

'If you know that the Dark Night is the path, why do you need books?' he said at last, and she knew that mentioning the Magus had not been a good idea.

'Because that isn't the way I want to learn,' she said.

The owner looked more closely at the young woman standing before him. While she clearly had a Gift, it was nevertheless odd that the Magus of Folk should have devoted so much time to her. There must be something else. She could be lying, but then again she had spoken of the Dark Night.

'You often come here,' he said. 'You arrive, read a few books, but never buy anything.'

'They're too expensive,' said Brida, sensing that he wanted to continue the conversation. 'But I've read other books and I've attended courses.'

She told him the names of her teachers, hoping to impress him still more.

Again things did not go quite as she expected. The owner interrupted her and went to serve another customer who wanted to know if the book he'd ordered had come in, an almanac containing the planetary positions for the next hundred years.

The owner examined various packages stored underneath the counter. Brida saw that the packages bore stamps from all corners of the world.

She was getting more and more nervous. Her initial courage had vanished completely, but she had no option but to wait for the other customer to check that it was the right book, pay for it, receive his change and leave. Only then did the owner turn to her again.

'I don't know how to continue,' said Brida. Her eyes were beginning to fill with tears.

'What are you good at?' asked the owner.

'Going after what I believe in.' That was the only possible reply; she spent her life in pursuit of what she believed in. The only problem was that she believed in something different every day.

The owner wrote a name on the sheet of paper on which he was doing his accounts, tore off the piece he had written on and held it for a moment in his hand.

'I'm going to give you an address,' he said. 'There was a time when people accepted magical experiences as natural. There were no priests then, and no one went chasing after the secrets of the occult.'

Brida wasn't sure whether he was referring to her or not.

'Do you know what magic is?' he asked.

'It's a bridge between the visible world and the invisible world.'

The owner gave her the piece of paper. On it was a phone number and a name: Wicca.

Brida snatched the paper from him, thanked him and left. When she reached the door, she turned and said:

'I also know that magic speaks many languages, even the language of booksellers, who pretend to be unhelpful, but are, in fact, very generous and approachable.'

She blew him a kiss and disappeared. The bookseller paused over his accounts, and stood looking at his shop. 'The Magus of Folk taught her those things,' he thought. A Gift, however good, wasn't reason enough for the Magus to take such an interest. There must be some other motive. Wicca would find it out.

It was time to close the shop. The bookseller had noticed lately that his clientele was starting to change.

It was becoming younger. As the old treatises crowding his shelves predicted, things were finally beginning to return to the place from whence they came.

The old building was in the centre of town, in a place that is now only visited by tourists in search of a little nineteenth-century romanticism. Brida had had to wait a week before Wicca would agree to see her, and now she was standing outside a mysterious grey building, struggling to contain her excitement. That building was exactly as she'd imagined it would be; it was just the kind of place where the type of person who visited the bookshop should live.

There was no lift. She went up the stairs slowly so as not to be out of breath when she reached the floor she wanted, and when she arrived, she rang the bell of the only door there.

Inside, a dog barked. Then, after a brief delay, a slim, elegant, serious-looking woman opened the door.

'I phoned earlier,' said Brida.

Wicca indicated that she should come in, and Brida found herself in a living room entirely painted in white and with examples of modern art everywhere – with paintings on the walls and sculptures and vases on the tables. The light from outside was filtered through white curtains. The room was cleverly divided into different areas to accommodate sofas, dining table and a well-stocked library. Everything was in the very best taste and reminded Brida of the architecture and design magazines she used to look at on the newstands.

'It must have cost a fortune,' she thought.

Wicca led Brida into the vast living room, into an area furnished by two Italian armchairs in leather and steel. Between the two chairs was a low glass table with steel legs.

'You're very young,' said Wicca at last.

There was little point in making her usual comment about ballerinas, and so Brida said nothing, waiting to hear what the woman would say next and meanwhile wondering what such a modern design was doing inside an old building like that. Her romantic idea of the search for knowledge had once again been shaken.

'He phoned me,' Wicca said, and Brida understood that she was referring to the bookseller.

'I came in search of a Teacher. I want to follow the road of magic.'

Wicca looked at Brida. She clearly possessed a Gift, but she needed to know why the Magus of Folk had been so interested in her. The Gift on its own was not enough. If the Magus had been new to magic, he might have been impressed by the clarity with which the Gift manifested itself in the young woman, but he had lived long enough to know that everyone possesses a Gift. He was wise to such traps.

She got up, went over to one of the bookshelves and picked up her favourite deck of cards.

'Do you know how to lay the cards?' she asked.

Brida nodded. She had done a few courses and knew that the deck in the woman's hand was a tarot deck, with seventy-eight cards. She had learned various ways of laying out the tarot and was glad to have a chance to show off her knowledge.

However, the woman kept hold of the deck. She shuffled the cards, then placed them face down, in no particular order, on the glass table. This was a method quite unlike any Brida had learned on her courses. The woman sat looking at them for a moment, said a few words in a strange language, then turned over just one of the cards.

It was card number 23. A king of clubs.

'Good protection,' she said. 'From a strong, powerful man with dark hair.'

Her boyfriend was neither strong nor powerful, and the Magus's hair was grey.

'Don't think about his physical appearance,' said Wicca, as if she had read her thoughts. 'Think of your Soulmate.'

'What do you mean "Soulmate"?' Brida was surprised. The woman inspired a strange respect, different from the respect she had felt for the Magus or for the bookseller.

Wicca did not answer the question. She again shuffled the cards, and again spread them in that same disorderly manner on the table, except that this time the cards were face up. The card in the middle of that apparent confusion was card number 11. A woman forcing open the mouth of a lion.

Wicca picked up the card and asked Brida to hold it. Brida did so, although without knowing quite what was required of her.

'In previous incarnations, your stronger side was always a woman,' Wicca said.

'What do you mean by "Soulmate"?' Brida asked again. It was the first time she had challenged the woman, but it was, nonetheless, a very timid challenge.

Wicca remained silent for a moment. A suspicion crossed her mind – for some reason the Magus had not taught the girl about Soulmates. 'Nonsense,' she said to herself and brushed the thought aside.

'The Soulmate is the first thing people learn about when they want to follow the Tradition of the Moon,' she said. 'Only by understanding the Soulmate can we understand how knowledge can be transmitted over time.'

As Wicca continued her explanation, Brida remained silent, feeling anxious.

'We are eternal because we are all manifestations of God,' Wicca said. 'That is why we go through many lives and many deaths, emerging out of some unknown place and going towards another equally unknown place. You must get used to the fact that there are many things in magic which are not and never will be explained. God decided to do certain things in a certain way and why He did this is a secret known only to Him.'

'The Dark Night of Faith,' thought Brida. So it existed in the Tradition of the Moon as well.

'The fact is that this happens,' Wicca went on. 'And when people think of reincarnation, they always come up against a very difficult question: if, in the beginning, there were so few people on the face of the Earth, and now there are so many, where did all those new souls come from?'

Brida held her breath. She had asked herself this question many times.

'The answer is simple,' said Wicca, after pausing to savour the young woman's eager silence. 'In certain reincarnations, we divide into two. Our souls divide as do crystals and stars, cells and plants.

'Our soul divides in two, and those new souls are in turn transformed into two and so, within a few generations, we are scattered over a large part of Earth.'

'And does only one of those parts know who it is?' asked Brida. She had many questions to ask, but she wanted to ask them one at a time, and this seemed the most important.

'We form part of what the alchemists call the *Anima mundi*, the Soul of the World,' said Wicca, without replying to the question. 'The truth is that if the *Anima mundi* were merely to keep dividing, it would keep growing, but it would also become gradually weaker.

That is why, as well as dividing into two, we also find ourselves. And that process of finding ourselves is called Love. Because when a soul divides, it always divides into a male part and a female part.

'That's how the Book of Genesis explains it: the soul of Adam was split in two, and Eve was born out of him.'

Wicca stopped suddenly and sat looking at the cards scattered on the table.

'There are many cards,' she said, 'but they're all part of the same deck. In order to understand their message, we need them all, all are equally important. So it is with souls. Human beings are all interlinked, like the cards in this deck.

'In each life, we feel a mysterious obligation to find at least one of those Soulmates. The Greater Love that separated them feels pleased with the Love that brings them together again.'

'But how will I know who my Soulmate is?' Brida felt that this was one of the most important questions she had ever asked in her life.

Wicca laughed. She had already asked herself that question and with the same eager anxiety as the young woman opposite her. You could tell your Soulmate by the light in their eyes, and since time began, that has been how people have recognised their true love. The Tradition of the Moon used a different process: a kind of vision that showed a point of light above the left shoulder of your Soulmate. But she wouldn't tell the girl that just yet; she might one day learn to see that point of light, or she might not. She would get her answer soon enough.

'By taking risks,' she said to Brida. 'By risking failure, disappointment, disillusion, but never ceasing in your search for Love. As long as you keep looking, you will triumph in the end.'

Brida remembered the Magus saying something similar when he spoke about the path of magic. 'Perhaps it's all the same thing,' she thought.

Wicca started picking up the cards from the table, and Brida sensed that her time was nearly up. Yet there was one other question to ask.

'Is it possible to meet more than one Soulmate in each life?'

'Yes,' thought Wicca with a certain bitterness. And when that happens, the heart is divided, and the result is pain and suffering. Yes, we can meet three or four Soulmates, because we are many and we are scattered. The young woman was asking the right questions, but she had to avoid answering them.

'The essence of Creation is one and one alone,' she said. 'And that essence is called Love. Love is the force that brings us back together, in order to condense the experience dispersed in many lives and many parts of the world.

'We are responsible for the whole Earth because we do not know where they might be, those Soulmates we were from the beginning of time. If they are well, then we, too, will be happy. If they are not well, we will suffer, however unconsciously, a portion of their pain. Above all, though, we are responsible for re-encountering, at least once in every incarnation, the Soulmate who is sure to cross our path. Even if it is only for a matter of moments, because those moments bring with them a Love so intense that it justifies the rest of our days.'

The dog barked in the kitchen. Wicca finished picking up the cards and looked again at Brida.

'We can also allow our Soulmate to pass us by, without accepting him or her, or even noticing. Then we will need another incarnation in order to find that Soulmate. And because of our selfishness, we will be condemned to the worst torture humankind ever invented for itself: loneliness.'

Wicca got up and showed Brida to the door.

'You didn't come here to find out about your Soulmate,' she said, before saying goodbye. 'You have a Gift, and once I know what that Gift is, I might be able to teach you the Tradition of the Moon.'

Brida felt very special. She needed to feel this, for the woman inspired a respect she had felt for very few other people.

'I'll do my best. I want to learn the Tradition of the Moon.'

'Because,' she thought, 'the Tradition of the Moon doesn't require you to spend the night alone in a dark forest.'

'Now listen to me,' said Wicca sternly. 'Every day from today, at an hour of your choosing, sit down alone at a table and spread the tarot deck as I did, completely at random. Don't try to understand anything. Simply study the cards. They will teach you all you need to know for the moment.'

'It's like the Tradition of the Sun: me teaching myself again,' thought Brida as she went down the stairs. And only when she was on the bus did she realise that the woman had spoken of a Gift. But she could talk about that at their next meeting.

For a whole week, Brida devoted half an hour a day to spreading the tarot cards on the table in the living room. She went to bed at ten o'clock and set the alarm for one in the morning. She would get up, make a quick cup of coffee, and sit down to contemplate the cards, trying to decipher their hidden language.

The first night, she was very excited. Brida was convinced that Wicca had taught her some kind of secret ritual and so she tried to spread the cards in exactly the same way, expecting some occult message to be revealed. After half an hour, apart from a few minor visions, which she felt were merely the fruits of her imagination, nothing of any great note had happened.

She did the same thing on the second night. Wicca had said that the cards would tell their own story and, to judge by the courses Brida had attended, it was a very ancient story indeed, dating back more than three thousand years, to a time when mankind was closer to the original wisdom.

'The pictures seem so simple,' she thought. A woman forcing open the mouth of a lion, a cart pulled by two mysterious animals, a man sitting before a table covered with sundry objects. She had been taught that the deck was a book, a book in which the Divine Wisdom had noted down the main changes that take place during our journey through life. But its author, knowing that humanity learned more easily from vice than from virtue, had arranged for this sacred book to be transmitted across the generations in the form of a game. The deck was an invention of the gods.

'It can't be that simple,' thought Brida, every time she spread the cards on the table. She had been taught complicated methods, elaborate systems, and those cards arranged in no particular order began to have a troubling effect on her reasoning. On the third night, she threw the cards down angrily on the floor. For a moment, she thought that this angry reaction might have some magical inspiration behind it, but the results were equally unsatisfactory, just a few indefinable intuitions, which, again, she dismissed as mere imaginings.

At the same time, the idea of her Soulmate didn't leave her for a moment. At first, she felt as if she were going back to her adolescence, to dreams of an enchanted prince crossing mountains and valleys in search of his lady of the glass slipper or in order to awaken a sleeping beauty with a kiss. 'Finding your Soulmate is something that only happens in fairy tales,' she told herself, half-joking. Fairy tales had been her first experience of the magical universe that she was now so eager to enter, and more than once she had wondered why people ended up distancing themselves from that world, knowing the immense joy that childhood had brought to their lives.

'Perhaps because they weren't content with feeling joy.' She found the idea slightly absurd, but nevertheless recorded it in her diary as a 'creative' thought.

After spending a week obsessed with the idea of the Soulmate, Brida became gripped by a terrifying feeling: what if she chose the wrong man? On the eighth night, when she woke again to carry out her vain contemplation of the tarot cards, she decided to invite her boyfriend out to supper the following night.

She chose a fairly inexpensive restaurant, because he always insisted on paying the bill, despite the fact that he earned far less as a research assistant to a physics professor at the university than she earned as a secretary. It was still summer, and they sat out at one of the tables on the pavement, by the river.

'I want to know when the spirits are going to let me sleep with you again,' said Lorens good-humouredly.

Brida looked at him tenderly. She had asked him not to come to her apartment for two weeks, and he had agreed, protesting just warmly enough for her to know how much he loved her. In his way, he, too, was seeking to understand the mysteries of the Universe, and if, one day, he were to ask her to stay away from him for two weeks, she would have to say 'Yes'.

They dined unhurriedly and largely in silence, watching the boats crossing the river and the people walking past on the pavement. The bottle of white wine on the table was emptied and replaced by another. Half an hour later, they had pushed their two chairs together and were sitting, arms around each other, gazing up at the starry summer sky.

'Just look at that sky,' said Lorens, stroking her hair. 'What we're looking at now is how the sky would have appeared thousands of years ago.'

He had told her the same thing on the day they first met, but Brida chose not to interrupt him – this was his way of sharing his world with her.

'Many of those stars have already died, and yet their light still fills the Universe. Other stars were born far away, and their light has not yet reached us.'

'So no one knows what the real sky looks like?' She had asked that same question on their first meeting too, but it was good to repeat such delicious moments.

'We don't know. We study what we can see, but what we see is not always what exists.'

'I want to ask you something. What are we made of? Where did the atoms that make up our bodies come from?'

Lorens looked up at the ancient sky and said:

'They were created along with these stars and this river. In the first second of the Universe's existence.'

'So after that first moment of Creation, nothing more was added.'

'No, nothing. Everything moved and continues to move. Everything was transformed and continues to be transformed. But all the matter that exists in the Universe now is the same matter from all those billions of years ago, and not so much as a single atom has been added.'

Brida sat studying the movement of both river and

stars. It was easy to see the river flowing across the Earth, but it was hard to see the stars moving in the sky. And yet both were moving.

'Lorens,' she said at last, after a long silence during which they both watched a boat passing. 'Let me ask what might seem an absurd question: is it physically possible that the atoms that make up my body could have been in the body of someone who lived before me?'

Lorens stared at her in amazement.

'What do you mean?'

'What I said. Is such a thing possible?'

'They could be in plants or insects or they could have turned into helium molecules and be out there somewhere, millions of miles from Earth.'

'But is it possible that the atoms that made up the body of someone who died could be in my body *and* in someone else's body?'

He said nothing for a moment, then said:

'Yes, it is.'

The sound of distant music reached them. It came from a barge crossing the river, and even from far away, Brida could make out the silhouette of a sailor framed in a lighted window. It was a tune that reminded her of her adolescence; it brought back memories of school dances, the smell of her bedroom, the colour of the ribbon she used to use to tie up her pony-tail. Brida realised that Lorens had never before considered the question she had asked him, and was perhaps, at that moment, wondering if his own body contained the atoms of Viking warriors, of volcanic explosions, or of prehistoric animals that had mysteriously disappeared.

But her thoughts were elsewhere. All she wanted to know was this: had the man so tenderly embracing her once been part of herself?

The barge came closer and the music began to fill the air around them. Conversations on the other tables stopped too, everyone eager to find out where the sound was coming from, because everyone had once been an adolescent, attended school dances and had dreams full of stories about warriors and fairies.

'I love you, Lorens.'

And Brida hoped against hope that this young man who knew so much about the light from the stars contained a little of the person she had once been.

'It's no good, I can't do it.'

Brida sat up in bed and felt for the packet of cigarettes on the bedside table. Going against all her normal habits, she decided to smoke a cigarette before breakfast.

It was another two days until she was due to meet Wicca again. She knew that, during the last two weeks, she had tried her hardest. She had channelled all her hopes into the method of spreading the cards taught to her by that attractive and mysterious woman and she had struggled hard not to disappoint her, but the cards refused to reveal their secrets.

Each time she had finished the exercise on the previous three nights, she had felt like crying. She felt vulnerable and alone and had a sense that a great opportunity was slipping through her fingers. Once again, she felt that life was not treating her as it treated other people: it gave her every chance to achieve something, and just when she was close to her objective, the ground opened up and swallowed her. That's how it had been with her studies, with certain boyfriends, with certain dreams she had never shared with anyone.

She thought of the Magus. Perhaps he could help her. But she had promised herself that she would only go back to Folk when she knew enough about magic to face him again.

And now it seemed that this would never happen.

She lay for a long time in bed, before deciding to get up and make breakfast. Finally, she screwed up the necessary resolve and courage to face another day, one more of her 'daily Dark Nights' as she had taken to calling them since her experience in the forest. She prepared some coffee, looked at her watch and saw that she still had enough time.

She went over to the shelf and searched among the books for the piece of paper the bookseller had given her. To console herself she thought: there are other paths. She had met the Magus, she had met Wicca, and she would, in the end, meet the person who could teach her in a way that she could understand.

But she knew this was merely an excuse.

'I'm always starting things and then giving up,' she thought rather sourly. Perhaps life would soon realise this and stop presenting her with the same opportunities over and over. Or perhaps, by always giving up when she had only just started, she had exhausted all possible paths without even taking a single step.

But that was how she was, and she felt herself growing gradually weaker and less and less able to change.

A few years before, she would have felt depressed by her own behaviour, but she would, at least, still have been capable of the occasional heroic gesture; now, though, she was starting to adapt to her own mistakes. She knew other people who did the same – they, too, got used to their mistakes and it wasn't long before they began to see them as virtues. And by then it was too late.

She considered not phoning Wicca and simply disappearing. But what about the bookshop? She wouldn't then have the courage to go there again. If she just disappeared, the bookseller would not be so kind next time. 'It's happened before. Because of some thoughtless gesture towards one person, I've ended up losing touch with other people I really cared about.' She couldn't do the same thing now. She was on a path where valuable contacts were very hard to find.

She steeled herself and dialled the number on the piece of paper. Wicca answered.

'I won't be able to come tomorrow,' said Brida.

'No, the plumber can't make it either,' replied Wicca. For a moment Brida had no idea what the woman was talking about.

Then Wicca started complaining about some problem with her kitchen sink and how she'd arranged several times for a man to come and fix it, but he never came. She launched into a long story about old buildings, which might look terribly imposing but which were, of course, beset by all kinds of problems. Then, in the middle of her story about the plumber, Wicca suddenly asked:

'Have you got your tarot cards handy?'

Surprised, Brida said that she did. Wicca asked her to spread the cards on the table, because she was going to teach her a method of finding out whether the plumber would or would not turn up the following day.

Feeling even more surprised, Brida did as she was asked. She spread the cards and sat staring blankly at the table while she awaited instructions from the other end of the line. The courage to explain the reason for her phone call was gradually fading.

Wicca was still talking, and Brida decided to listen to her patiently. Perhaps she would become her friend. Perhaps then she would be more tolerant and show her easier ways of understanding the Tradition of the Moon.

Wicca, meanwhile, was weaving one topic of conversation seamlessly into another, and having finished her litany of complaints about plumbers, she started describing an argument she'd had with the building manager about the caretaker's salary. She then moved on to a report that she'd read on old-age pensions.

Brida accompanied all this with a few affirmative grunts, agreeing with everything Wicca was saying, but no longer listening. A terrible tedium took hold of her. This conversation with a woman she barely knew regarding plumbers, caretakers and pensioners, at that hour in the morning, was one of the most boring things she'd ever experienced. She kept trying to distract herself with the cards on the table, finding little details that she'd never noticed before.

Now and then, Wicca would ask if she was still listening and she'd give a mumbled 'Yes'. But her mind was miles away, travelling, wandering about in places she'd never been to before. Every detail on the cards seemed to push her further on in that journey.

All of a sudden, like someone entering a dream, Brida realised that she could no longer hear what Wicca was saying. A voice, a voice that seemed to come from within – but which she knew came from outside – began to whisper something to her. 'Do you understand?' Brida said that she did. 'Do you understand?' asked the mysterious voice again.

This, however, was of no importance. The tarot cards before her began to show fantastic scenes: men with bronzed, oiled bodies, wearing only thongs, and some sporting masks like the giant heads of fish. Clouds raced across the sky, as if everything were moving much faster than normal, and the scene shifted abruptly to a square, surrounded by grand buildings, where a few old men were urgently telling secrets to a group of young boys, as if some form of very ancient knowledge were about to be lost for ever.

'Add seven and eight and you'll have my number. I'm the devil, and I signed the book,' said a boy in medieval clothes at what appeared to be a celebration.

Drunken men and women smiled out at her. The scene changed yet again to the sea, to reveal temples carved out of the rocks, and then the sky began to be covered by black clouds pierced by brilliant flashes of lightning.

A door appeared. It was a heavy door, like the door of an old castle. The door came closer to Brida, and she had a sense that soon she would be able to open it.

'Come back,' said the voice.

'Come back,' said the voice on the phone. It was Wicca. Brida was annoyed with her for interrupting such a remarkable experience merely to bore her with more talk about caretakers and plumbers.

'Just a moment,' she replied. She was struggling to find that door, but everything had vanished.

'I know what happened,' Wicca told her. Brida was stunned, in a state of shock. She couldn't understand what was going on.

'I know what happened,' Wicca said again, in response to Brida's silence. 'I won't say anything more about the plumber. He was here last week and fixed everything.'

Before hanging up, she said she would expect Brida at the agreed time.

Brida put down the phone without saying goodbye. She sat for a long time staring at the kitchen wall before subsiding into convulsive, soothing sobs.

'It was a trick,' Wicca told a frightened Brida, when they sat down again in the Italian armchairs.

'I know how you must be feeling,' she went on. 'Sometimes we set off down a path simply because we don't believe in it. It's easy enough. All we have to do then is prove that it isn't the right path for us. However, when things start to happen, and the path does reveal itself to us, we become afraid of carrying on.'

Wicca said that she didn't understand why so many people chose to spend their whole life destroying paths they didn't even want to follow, instead of following the one path that would lead them somewhere.

'I can't believe it was a trick,' protested Brida. She had lost her air of arrogance and defiance. Her respect for Wicca had grown considerably.

'No, no, the vision wasn't a trick. The trick I'm referring to is the phone. For millions of years, we only ever spoke to someone we could see, then, in less than a century, "seeing" and "speaking" were suddenly separated. We think it's quite normal now and don't realise the huge impact it has on our reflexes. Our body still hasn't got used to it.

'The practical result is that, when we speak on the phone, we often enter a state very similar to certain magical trances. Our mind tunes into another frequency and becomes more receptive to the invisible world. I know some witches who always keep a pen and paper by the phone and, while they're talking to someone, they sit doodling apparently nonsensical things. When they hang up, though, they find that their "doodles" are often symbols from the Tradition of the Moon.'

'But why did the tarot reveal itself to me?'

'That's the great problem with anyone wanting to study magic,' replied Wicca. 'When we set out on the path, we always have a fairly clear idea of what we hope to find. Women are generally seeking their Soulmate, and men are looking for Power. Neither party is really interested in learning. They simply want to reach the thing they have set as their goal.

'But the path of magic – like the path of life – is and always will be the path of Mystery. Learning something means coming into contact with a world of which you know nothing. In order to learn, you must be humble.'

'Like plunging into the Dark Night,' said Brida.

'Don't interrupt.' There was a note of barely contained irritation in Wicca's voice, but Brida realised that it wasn't because of what she'd said. 'Maybe she's angry with the Magus,' she thought. 'Perhaps she was once in love with him. They are more or less the same age.'

'I'm sorry,' she said.

'That's all right.' Wicca seemed equally surprised by her own reaction.

'You were telling me about the tarot.'

'When you were spreading the cards, you always had a preconceived idea of what would happen. You never let the cards tell their own story; you were trying to make them confirm what you imagined you knew.

'I realised this when we started talking on the phone. I realised, too, that it was a sign and that the phone was my ally. So I launched into a very boring conversation and asked you to look at the cards. You went into the trance provoked by the phone, and the cards led you into their magical world.'

Wicca suggested that next time Brida was with someone who was talking on the phone, she should take a good look at their eyes. She would be surprised by what she saw.

'I want to ask something else,' said Brida over tea in Wicca's surprisingly modern and practical kitchen.

'I want to know why you didn't let me abandon the path.'

'Because,' thought Wicca, 'I want to find out what the Magus saw in you, apart, I mean, from your Gift.' What she said was: 'Because you have a Gift.'

'How do you know?'

'Easy. By your ears.'

'By my ears! How disappointing!' Brida thought to herself. 'And there was me thinking she could see my aura.'

'Everyone has a Gift, but some are born with a more highly developed Gift than others – me, for example – who have to struggle really hard to develop their Gift. People who were born with a Gift have very small, attached earlobes.'

Instinctively, Brida touched her earlobes. It was true.

'Do you have a car?'

No, Brida said, she didn't.

'Then prepare to spend a fortune on taxi fares,' said Wicca, getting up. 'It's time to take our next step.'

'Things are suddenly moving very fast,' thought Brida, as she got to her feet. Life was beginning to resemble the clouds she had seen in her trance.

By around mid-afternoon they had reached some mountains about fifteen miles south of Dublin. 'We could have made the same trip by bus,' Brida grumbled to herself while she paid the taxi. Wicca had brought with her a bag and some clothes.

'If you like, I can wait,' said the driver. 'It's going to be pretty difficult finding another taxi in these parts. This is the middle of nowhere.'

'Don't worry,' said Wicca, to Brida's relief. 'We always get what we want.'

The driver gave them a strange look and drove off. They were standing before a grove of trees, which extended as far as the foot of the nearest mountain.

'Ask permission to enter,' said Wicca. 'The spirits of the forests always appreciate good manners.'

Brida asked permission. The wood, which had, up until then, been just an ordinary wood, seemed suddenly to come to life.

'Stay on the bridge between the visible and the invisible,' said Wicca, while they walked through the trees. 'Everything in the Universe has life, and you must always try to stay in contact with that life. It understands your language. And the world will begin to take on a different meaning for you.'

Brida was surprised at Wicca's agility. Her feet seemed to levitate above the ground, making almost no noise.

They reached a clearing, near a huge stone. While she tried to think how that stone could have got there, Brida noticed the ashes from a fire right in the middle of the open space.

It was a beautiful place. It would still be some hours before evening, and the sun shone with the warm gold of summer afternoons. Birds were singing, and a light breeze rustled in the leaves. They were quite high up, and she could look across and down at the horizon.

Wicca took a kind of cloak out of her bag and put it on over her clothes. Then she placed the bag near the trees, so that it couldn't be seen from the clearing.

'Sit down,' she said.

Wicca was somehow different. Brida couldn't decide whether it was the cloak or the profound respect that the place inspired in her.

'First of all, I must explain what I'm going to do. I'm going to find out how the Gift manifests itself in you. I can only begin to teach you once I know something about your Gift.'

Wicca asked Brida to try and relax, to surrender herself to the beauty of the place, just as she had when she had surrendered to the tarot cards.

'At some point in one of your past lives, you set out along the road of magic. I know this from the tarot visions that you described.'

Brida closed her eyes, but Wicca asked her to open them again.

'Magical places are always beautiful and deserve to be contemplated. Waterfalls, mountains and forests are all places where the spirits of Earth tend to play and laugh and speak to us. You are in a sacred place, and it is showing you the birds and the wind. Thank God for this, for the birds, the wind, and for the spirits who inhabit this wood. Always stay on the bridge between the visible and the invisible.'

Wicca's voice was making Brida feel more and more relaxed. She felt an almost religious respect for the moment.

'The other day, I spoke to you about one of the great secrets of magic: the Soulmate. The whole of man's life on the face of Earth can be summed up by that search for his Soulmate. He may pretend to be running after wisdom, money or power, but none of that matters. Whatever he achieves will be incomplete if he fails to find his Soulmate.

'With the exception of a few creatures who are descended from the angels – and who need solitude in order to encounter God – the rest of humanity will only achieve Union with God if, at some point, at some moment in their life, they manage to commune with their Soulmate.'

Brida noticed a strange energy in the air. For a few moments, and for some reason she could not explain, her eyes filled with tears.

'In the Night of Time, when we were separated, one of those parts was charged with nurturing and maintaining knowledge: man. He went on to understand agriculture, nature and the movements of the stars in the sky. Knowledge was always the power that kept the Universe in its place and the stars turning in their orbits. That was the glory of man – to nurture and maintain knowledge. And that is why the whole human race has survived.

'To women was given something far more subtle and fragile, but without which knowledge makes no sense at all, and that thing was transformation. The men left the soil fertile, we sowed seeds, and the soil was transformed into trees and plants.

'The soil needs the seed, and the seed needs the soil. The one only has meaning with the other. It is the same thing with human beings. When male knowledge joins with female transformation, then the great magical union is created, and its name is Wisdom. Wisdom means both to know and to transform.'

Brida noticed that the wind was growing stronger and that Wicca's voice was leading her again into a trance. The spirits of the forest seemed alive and intent.

'Lie down,' said Wicca.

Brida leaned back and stretched out her legs. Up above her glowed a deep, blue, cloudless sky.

'Go in search of your Gift. I can't go with you today, but don't be afraid. The more you understand yourself, the more you will understand the world. And the closer you will be to your Soulmate.'

Wicca knelt down and looked at the young woman. 'She's just as I once was,' she thought fondly. 'In search of a meaning for everything and capable of looking at the world as did the strong, confident women of old, who were quite happy to rule over their own communities.'

At that time, however, God had been a woman. Wicca bent over Brida's body and unbuckled the belt of Brida's jeans, then half-unzipped them. Brida's muscles tensed.

'Don't worry,' said Wicca affectionately.

She lifted up Brida's T-shirt to reveal her navel. Then she took from the pocket of her cloak a quartz crystal and placed it on Brida's navel.

'Now I want you to close your eyes,' she said softly. 'I want you to imagine the colour of the sky, but keep your eyes closed.'

She took from her cloak a small amethyst and placed it between Brida's closed eyes.

'From now on, do exactly as I tell you and don't worry about anything else. You are in the centre of the Universe. You can see the stars all around you and some of the brighter planets. Experience this landscape as something that wraps about you completely and not like a picture or a screen. Take pleasure in contemplating this Universe; there's no need to worry about anything else. Simply concentrate on your own pleasure. Without any feelings of guilt.'

Brida saw the starry Universe and realised that she could step into it even while she was listening to Wicca's voice. The voice asked her to imagine a vast cathedral in the middle of the Universe. Brida duly saw a Gothic cathedral made of dark stone and which, absurd though it might seem, appeared to form part of the surrounding Universe.

'Walk over to the cathedral and up the steps. Go inside.'

Brida did as Wicca ordered. She went up the cathedral steps, conscious of her bare feet on the cold stone floor. At one point, she had a feeling that there was someone with her, and Wicca's voice seemed to emerge from a person walking behind her. 'I'm imagining things,' thought Brida, and suddenly remembered what she'd been told about the bridge between the visible and the invisible. She mustn't feel afraid of disappointment or failure.

Brida was now standing in front of the cathedral door. It was an enormous wrought-iron affair, adorned with scenes from the lives of the saints, and totally different from the one she had seen on her journey through the tarot cards.

'Open the door and go in.'

Brida felt the cold metal of the handle beneath her hand. Despite the door's great size, it opened easily. She entered and found herself inside a vast church.

'Notice everything around you,' said Wicca. Although it was dark outside, light came streaming in through the cathedral's huge stained-glass windows. She could make out the pews, the side altars, the decorated columns and a few lit candles. Yet everything seemed somehow empty and abandoned. The pews were covered in dust.

'Walk over to your left. Somewhere you will find another door, but this time, it will be a very small one.'

Brida walked through the cathedral. She was aware of the unpleasant feeling of the dusty floor beneath her bare feet. Somewhere, a friendly voice was guiding her. She knew it was Wicca, but she knew, too, that she no longer had any control over her imagination. She was conscious and yet she could not disobey what was being asked of her.

She found the door.

'Go in. There's a spiral staircase leading down.'

Brida had to crouch to get through the door. The walls of the staircase were lined with torches fixed to the wall, illuminating the steps. The steps were very clean. Someone had clearly been there before in order to light the torches.

'You are setting off in search of your past lives. In the cellar of this cathedral is a library. That's where we're going now. I'll be waiting at the foot of the staircase.'

Brida kept going down and down, for how long she didn't know. It made her slightly dizzy. When she did finally reach the bottom, Wicca was there in her cloak. It would be easier now; she felt more protected. She was still deep in her trance.

Wicca opened another door opposite the stairs.

'I'm going to leave you alone here. I'll be outside, waiting. Choose a book and it will show you what you need to know.'

Brida didn't even notice that Wicca was no longer there. She was staring at the dusty tomes. 'I really should come here more often and give everything a good clean.' Her past was grubby and neglected, and she felt sad to think that she'd never read any of these books before. Perhaps they contained important, long-forgotten lessons that she could incorporate into her life.

She looked at the books on the shelf. 'All those lives,' she thought. If she was so very ancient, she really should be wiser. She wished she could read them all, but she didn't have much time, and she must trust in her intuition. She could come back whenever she wanted, now that she knew the way.

She stood for a while not knowing which book to choose. Then she chose one almost at random. It was a fairly slim volume, and Brida took it and sat down on the floor.

She placed the book on her lap, but felt afraid she might open it and find that nothing happened, afraid that she might not be able to read what was written there.

'I need to take risks. I need to feel the fear of failing,' she thought as she opened the book. As soon as she glanced at the pages, she began to feel ill and dizzy again.

'I'm going to faint,' she managed to think before everything went dark.

She woke with water dripping on her face. She'd had a strange, incomprehensible dream about cathedrals floating in the air and libraries crammed with books. And yet she had never been in a library.

'Loni, are you all right?'

No, she wasn't. She couldn't feel her right foot and she knew this was a bad sign. She didn't feel like talking either, because she didn't want to forget the dream.

'Loni, wake up.'

She must be feverish, delirious, and yet what she saw in her delirium seemed so intensely real. She wished the person who kept calling to her would stop, because the dream was now fast disappearing before she had managed to grasp its meaning.

The sky was cloudy, and the clouds were so low they almost touched the castle's tallest tower. She lay looking up at the clouds. It was just as well she couldn't see the stars; according to the priests, not even the stars were entirely good.

The rain had stopped shortly before she opened her eyes. Loni was pleased it had rained, for that meant the castle's water butts would be full. She slowly shifted her gaze from the clouds to the tower, to the bonfires in the courtyard and the bewildered crowds of people milling around.

'Talbo,' she said softly.

He put his arms around her. She felt the cold of his armour and the smell of soot in his hair.

'How much time has passed? What day is it?'

'You've been asleep for three days,' said Talbo.

She looked at Talbo and felt sorry for him. He was thinner, his face grimy, his skin dull. Not that any of this mattered – she loved him.

'I'm thirsty, Talbo.'

'There's no water. The French found the secret passageway.'

Again she heard the Voices inside her head. For a long time, she had hated those Voices. Her husband was a warrior, a mercenary, who spent most of the year away fighting, and she had always been afraid that the Voices would tell her that he had died in battle. She had found a way of keeping the Voices from speaking to her. She just had to concentrate her mind on an ancient tree near her village. The Voices stopped when she did that. Now, however, she was too weak, and the Voices had returned.

'You're going to die,' said the Voices. 'But he will be saved.'

'But it rained, Talbo,' she said. 'I need water.'

'It was only a few drops. Nothing like enough.'

Loni again looked up at the clouds. They had been

there all week, and had done nothing but block the sun, making the winter even colder and the castle even gloomier. Perhaps the French Catholics were right. Perhaps God *was* on their side.

A few mercenaries came over to them. There were fires burning everywhere, and Loni had the sudden feeling that she was in hell.

'The priests are gathering everyone together, sir,' one of them said to Talbo.

'We were hired to fight, not to die,' said another.

'The French have offered us terms of surrender,' replied Talbo. 'They say that those who convert back to the Catholic faith can leave unharmed.'

'The Perfect Ones will not accept,' the Voices whispered to Loni. She knew that. She knew the Perfect Ones well. They were the reason she was there and not at home, where she usually waited for Talbo to return from battle. The Perfect Ones had been besieged in that castle for four months, and during that time, the village women had used the secret passageway connecting village and castle to bring in food, clothes and ammunition; during that time, they had been able to see their husbands, and it was because of them that the fighting had continued. Now, however, the secret passage had been discovered, and she could not go back to the village, nor could any of the other women.

She tried to sit up. Her foot didn't hurt any more. The Voices were telling her that this was a bad sign.

'We have nothing to do with their God. We're not going to die over that, sir,' said another soldier.

A gong began to sound inside the castle. Talbo got to his feet.

'Please, take me with you,' she implored. Talbo looked at his companions and then at the woman who lay trembling before him. For a moment, he didn't know what to do. His men were accustomed to war, and they knew that warriors who were in love usually hid during battles.

'I'm going to die, Talbo. Take me with you, please.'

One of the mercenaries glanced at Talbo.

'She shouldn't be left here alone,' he said. 'The French might start firing again.'

Talbo pretended to agree. He knew that the French would do no such thing. A truce had been called in order to negotiate the surrender of Monségur. But the mercenary understood what was going on in Talbo's heart; he, too, must be a man in love.

'He knows you're going to die,' the Voices said to Loni, while Talbo gently picked her up. Loni didn't want to listen to what the Voices were saying; she was remembering a day when they'd walked along together just like that, through a wheatfield, on a summer afternoon. She had been thirsty then as well, and they had drunk water from a mountain stream.

* * *

A crowd of men, soldiers, women and children were gathered round the great rock that formed part of the western wall of the fortress of Monségur. An oppressive silence hung in the air, and Loni knew that this was not out of respect for the priests, but out of fear for what might happen.

The priests arrived. There were a great many of them, all wearing black cloaks each embroidered with a huge yellow cross. They sat down on the rock, on the steps, on the ground at the foot of the tower. The last to arrive had white hair and he climbed up to the highest part of the wall. His figure was lit by the flames from the fires, and the wind caught his black cloak.

Almost everyone present knelt down and, bending forward, hands pressed together in prayer, beat their head three times on the ground. Talbo and his mercenaries remained standing. They had only been hired to fight.

'We have been granted surrender,' said the priest. 'You are all free to leave.'

A great sigh of relief came from the crowd.

'The souls belonging to the Other God will remain in the kingdom of this world. The souls belonging to the True God will return to his infinite mercy. The war will continue, but it is not an eternal war, because the Other God will be defeated in the end, even though some of the angels have already been corrupted by him. The Other God will be vanquished, but not destroyed; he will remain in hell for all eternity, along with the souls he managed to seduce.'

The people in the crowd stared at the man standing on the wall. They were not so sure now that they wanted to escape and thus suffer for all eternity.

'The Cathar Church is the true Church,' the priest went on. 'Thanks to Jesus Christ and to the Holy Spirit, we have achieved communion with God. We do not need to be reincarnated. We do not need to return to the kingdom of the Other God.'

Loni noticed that three priests bearing Bibles had stepped forward.

'The *consolamentum* will now be distributed to those who wish to die with us. Down below, the fire awaits. It will be a horrible death, involving terrible suffering. It will be a slow death, and the pain of the flames burning your flesh will be unlike any you have experienced before. However, not all of you will have that honour, only the true Cathars. The others will be condemned to live.'

Two women shyly went up to the priests who were holding the Bibles. An adolescent boy wrenched himself free from his mother's arms and joined them.

Four mercenaries approached Talbo.

'We want to receive the Sacrament, sir. We want to be baptised.'

'This is how the Tradition survives,' said the Voices. 'Because people are willing to die for an idea.'

Loni waited to hear Talbo's decision. The mercenaries

had fought all their lives purely for money, until they met these people prepared to fight only for what they deemed to be right.

Talbo finally nodded his assent, even though it meant losing some of his best men.

'Let's go,' said Loni. 'Let's go over to the walls. They said that anyone who wants to can leave.'

'It's better that we rest, Loni.'

'You're going to die,' whispered the Voices again.

'I want to see the Pyrenees. I want to see the valley one more time, Talbo. You know that I'm going to die.'

Yes, he knew. He was a man accustomed to battlefields and he could tell when a wound would prove to be the death of one of his soldiers. Loni's wound had been open for three days, poisoning her blood. Those whose wounds did not heal might last two days or two weeks, but never longer than that.

And Loni was close to death. Her fever had passed. Talbo knew that this, too, was a bad sign. As long as the foot hurt and the fever burned, that meant the organism was still fighting. Now the struggle was over, and it was only a matter of time.

'You're not afraid,' said the Voices. No, Loni wasn't afraid. Even as a child, she had known that death was merely another beginning. At that time, the Voices had been her great companions. They had faces, bodies and gestures visible only to her. They were people who came from different worlds; they talked to her and never let her feel lonely. She'd had a very interesting childhood, playing with the other children, but using her invisible friends to shift objects around and make strange noises that startled her companions. Her mother was glad that they lived in a Cathar country – 'if the Catholics were here, you'd be burned alive,' she used to say. The Cathars paid no attention to such things; they believed that the good were good, the bad were bad, and that no force in the Universe could change this.

Then the French arrived, saying that there was no Cathar country, and, since the age of eight, all she had known was war.

The war had brought her one very good thing: her husband, hired in some distant land by the Cathar priests, who never themselves took up arms. But it brought something bad too: the fear of being burned alive, because the Catholics were moving ever closer to her village. She began to feel afraid of her invisible friends, and they gradually disappeared from her life. However, the Voices remained. They continued to tell her what was going to happen and how she should behave, but she didn't want their friendship, because they always knew too much. Then one Voice taught her the trick of thinking about that ancient tree, and she hadn't heard the Voices at all since the last crusade against the Cathars had begun, and the French Catholics had continued to win battle after battle.

Today, though, she didn't have the strength to think about the tree. The Voices were back, and she didn't mind. On the contrary, she needed them. They would show her the path once she was dead.

'Don't worry about me, Talbo. I'm not afraid of dying,' she said.

They reached the top of the wall. A cold, relentless wind was blowing, and Talbo drew his cloak more tightly about him. Loni didn't feel the cold any more. She could see the lights of a town on the horizon, and the lights of the encampment at the foot of the mountain. All along the valley bottom bonfires were lit. The French soldiers were awaiting the final decision.

The notes from a flute wafted up from below, along with the sound of voices singing.

'It's the soldiers,' said Talbo. 'They know they could die at any moment, and that's why, for them, life is one long celebration.'

Loni felt suddenly furious with life. The Voices were telling her that Talbo would meet other women, have children and grow rich on what he plundered from cities. 'But he will never love anyone as he has loved you, because you are part of him for ever,' said the Voices.

Loni and Talbo, their arms about each other, remained for a while gazing down on the landscape below, listening to the soldiers singing. Loni sensed that the mountain had been the setting of other wars in the past, a past so remote that not even the Voices could remember it.

'We are eternal, Talbo. That's what the Voices used to tell me in the days when I could see their bodies and faces.'

Talbo knew about his wife's Gift, but she had not mentioned it for a long time. Perhaps it was the effect of the fever.

'And yet no one life is the same as any other life. It might be that we will never meet again, and I need you to know that I've loved you all my life. I loved you even before I met you. You're part of me.

'I'm going to die, and since tomorrow is as good a day to die as any, I would like to die with the priests. I've never understood their ideas about the world, but they have always understood me. I want to accompany them into the next life. I might prove to be a good guide, because I've visited those worlds before.'

Loni thought how ironic fate was. She had been afraid of the Voices because they might set her on the path that would lead her to the fire, and yet there the fire was, waiting for her.

Talbo looked at his wife. Her eyes were growing dull, and yet she still retained the same peculiar charm that had first drawn him to her. He had never told her certain things, about the women he received as part of the booty of battle, the women he met while he was travelling the world, the women who were expecting him to return one day. He hadn't told her this because he was certain that she knew everything anyway and forgave him because he was her great love, and a great love is above the things of this world.

But there was something else he had never told her, and which she would possibly never know: that she, with her affection and her gaiety, had been largely responsible for him having rediscovered the meaning of life, that her love had driven him to the far corners of the Earth, because he needed to be rich enough to buy some land and live in peace with her for the rest of his days. It was his utter confidence in this fragile creature, whose life was now fading fast, that had made him fight with honour, because he knew that after the battle he could forget all the horrors of war in her arms, and that, despite all the women he had known, only there in her arms could he close his eyes and sleep like a child.

'Go and call the priest, Talbo,' she said. 'I want to be baptised.'

Talbo hesitated for a moment. Only warriors choose how they will die, but that woman had given her life for love, and perhaps, for her, love was a strange form of war.

He got up and walked down the steps in the wall. Loni tried to concentrate on the music coming from below and which was somehow making dying easier. Meanwhile, the Voices kept talking.

'In her life, every woman can make use of the Four Rings of Revelation. You have used only one, the wrong one,' they said.

Loni looked at her fingers. They were torn and cracked, the nails filthy. There was no ring. The Voices laughed.

'You know what we mean,' they said. 'The virgin, the saint, the martyr and the witch.'

Loni knew in her heart what the Voices were saying, but she couldn't remember what it meant. She had heard about it a long time ago, in an age when people dressed differently and saw the world differently too. She'd had another name then, and had spoken another language.

'They are the four ways in which a woman can commune with the Universe,' the Voices said, as if it were important for her to recall these ancient things. 'The Virgin has the power of both man and woman. She is condemned to Solitude, but Solitude reveals its secrets. That is the price paid by the Virgin – to need no one, to wear herself out in her love for others, and, through Solitude, to discover the wisdom of the world.'

Loni was still looking at the encampment down below. Yes, she knew these things.

'And the Martyr,' the Voices went on, 'the Martyr has the power of those who cannot be harmed by pain and suffering. She surrenders herself, suffers and, through Sacrifice, discovers the wisdom of the world.'

Loni again looked at her hands. There, shining invisibly, she saw the ring of the Martyr encircling one of her fingers.

'You could have chosen the revelation of the Saint, even if it wasn't the right ring for you,' the Voices said. 'The Saint has the courage of those for whom giving is the only way of receiving. They are a bottomless well from which people can constantly draw water to drink. And if the well runs dry, the Saint offers her blood so that others need never go thirsty. Through surrender, the Saint discovers the wisdom of the world.'

The Voices fell silent. Loni heard Talbo coming up the stone steps. She knew which ring should have been hers in that life, because it was the one she had worn in all her past lives, when she had been known by other names and had spoken other tongues. With that ring, the wisdom of the world was discovered through Pleasure, but she didn't want to think about that now. The ring of the Martyr was shining, invisible, on her finger.

Talbo came closer. And suddenly, when she gazed up at him, Loni noticed that the night had a magical glow to it, as if it were a sunny day.

'Wake up,' said the Voices.

But these were different voices, which she had never heard before. She felt someone rubbing her left wrist.

'Come on, Brida, get up.'

She opened her eyes and immediately closed them again, because the light from the sky was so intense. What a strange thing Death was.

'Open your eyes,' said Wicca.

But she needed to go back to the castle. A man she loved had gone off in search of a priest. She couldn't just run away. He was alone and he needed her.

'Tell me what your Gift is.'

Wicca didn't give her time to think. She knew she had been through something extraordinary, much more powerful than her experience with the tarot cards. Yet still she didn't give her time to think. She neither understood nor respected her feelings; all she wanted was to find out what her Gift was.

'Talk to me about your Gift,' Wicca insisted.

Brida took a deep breath, holding in her anger, but there was no escape. The woman would keep insisting until she told her what she wanted to know.

'I was a woman in love with …'

Wicca quickly covered Brida's mouth. Then she stood up, made a few strange gestures in the air and turned back to her.

'God is the word. Always be very careful what you say in any situation and at any moment.'

Brida didn't understand why Wicca was behaving like this.

'God manifests himself in everything, but the word is one of his most favoured methods of doing so, because the word is thought transformed into vibration; you are projecting into the air around you something which, before, was only energy. Take great care with everything you say,' Wicca said again. 'The word has more power than many rituals.'

Brida still didn't understand. The only way she had of describing her experience was through words.

'When you spoke of a woman,' Wicca explained, 'you were not that woman. You were part of her. Other people might well have the same memory as you.'

Brida felt robbed. That woman had been so strong, and she didn't want to share her with anyone. Besides, there was Talbo too.

'Talk to me about your Gift,' Wicca said yet again. She couldn't allow the girl to be too dazzled by the experience. This form of time travel often brought problems.

'I have so many things to tell, and I need to talk to you, because no one else will believe me. Please,' begged Brida.

She began to tell her everything, from the moment when the rain was dripping on her face. She had a chance and she couldn't waste it, the chance to be with someone who believed in the extraordinary. She knew that no one else would listen to her with the same respect, because people were afraid of discovering that life was magical. They were used to their houses, their jobs, their expectations, and if someone turned up saying that it was possible to travel in time, that it was possible to see castles adrift in the Universe, tarot cards that told stories, men who walked through the dark night, people who had never experienced such things would feel that life had cheated them. Life, as far as they were concerned, was the same every day, every night, every weekend.

That's why Brida needed to seize that chance. If words were God, then let it be recorded on the air around her that she had travelled back in time and that she remembered every detail as if it were now, as if it were the wood where they were right now. And so, when, later on, someone managed to prove to her that none of this had happened, when time and space made her doubt it all, when she herself was convinced that it had been mere illusion, the words spoken that evening, there in the wood, would still be vibrating in the air and at least one person, someone for whom magic was part of life, would know that it had really happened.

She described the castle, the priests in the black and yellow robes, the valley filled with fires, the husband thinking thoughts that she could read without him speaking them. Wicca listened patiently, only showing any interest when she told her about the voices that appeared in Loni's mind. Then she would interrupt and ask if the voices were male or female (they were both), if they expressed any particular emotion, aggression or sympathy (no, they were impersonal), and if she could summon up the voices whenever she wished (she didn't know, she hadn't had time to find out).

'All right, we can leave now,' said Wicca, taking off her cloak and putting it back in her bag. Brida was disappointed. She thought she might receive some words of praise, or, at the very least, some explanation. But Wicca resembled one of those doctors who study their patient very coolly and objectively, more interested in noting down symptoms than in understanding the pain and suffering caused by those symptoms.

They made the long journey back. Whenever Brida tried to raise the subject again, Wicca would show a sudden interest in the increase in the cost of living, in the rush-hour traffic jams and the difficulties she was having with the manager of the building where she lived.

Only when they were once more sitting in the usual two armchairs did Wicca comment on Brida's experience.

'I just want to say one thing to you,' she said. 'Don't bother trying to explain your emotions. Live everything as intensely as you can and keep whatever you felt as a gift from God. If you think that you won't be able to stand a world in which living is more important than understanding, then give up magic now. The best way to destroy the bridge between the visible and the invisible is by trying to explain your emotions.'

Emotions were like wild horses, and Brida knew that reason could never entirely master them. Once, when a boyfriend left her, giving no explanation, she had stayed at home for months, going over and over his many defects and the thousand and one things that had been wrong with their relationship. Yet she woke up every morning thinking about him and knowing that if he phoned her, she would probably agree to meet.

The dog in the kitchen barked. Brida knew this was a sign that her visit was over.

'Oh, please, we haven't even talked about what happened!' she cried. 'And there are two questions I simply must ask.'

Wicca stood up. The girl always found a way of leaving any important questions to the very last moment, just when it was time for her to leave.

'I want to know if the priests I saw really existed.'

'We have extraordinary experiences and, less than two hours later, we're trying to convince ourselves that it was the mere product of our imagination,' said Wicca, going over to the bookshelves. Brida remembered that when they were in the wood, she herself had been thinking about people who were afraid of the extraordinary. And she felt ashamed of herself.

Wicca returned, bearing a book.

'The Cathars, or the Perfect Ones, were the priests of a church founded in the south of France at the end of the twelfth century. They believed in reincarnation and in the existence of absolute Good and absolute Evil. The world was divided into the chosen and the lost, which meant that there was no point in trying to convert anyone.

'The Cathars' indifference to worldly values led many of the feudal lords in the Languedoc region to adopt their religion as a way of avoiding having to pay the heavy taxes imposed at the time by the Catholic Church. Equally, since it had been decided at birth who was good and who was bad, the Cathars were very tolerant in their attitude to sex and, in particular, in their attitude to women. They were only strict about such matters with those who had been ordained as priests.

'Everything was fine until Catharism started to spread. The Catholic Church felt threatened and called for a crusade against the heretics. For forty years, Cathars and Catholics fought bloody battles, but the legalist forces, with the support of various other nations, finally managed to destroy all the towns that had adopted the new religion. Only the fortress of Monségur, in the Pyrenees, remained, and the Cathars besieged there held out until the French discovered the secret passageway through which they had been receiving supplies. One March morning in 1244, after the surrender of the castle, two hundred and twenty Cathars hurled themselves, singing, into the huge bonfire lit at the bottom of the mountain on which the castle had been built.'

Wicca said all this with the book, still closed, on her lap. Only when she had finished her story did she open it and leaf through it, looking for a photograph.

Brida saw the ruined building, with the tower almost completely destroyed, but with the walls intact. There was the courtyard, the steps Loni and Talbo had climbed, the rock that formed part of the wall and the tower.

'You said there was another question you wanted to ask me.'

The question was of no importance now. Brida could hardly think straight. She felt odd. With some effort she managed to remember what it was she had wanted to ask.

'I want to know why you're wasting your time with me, why you want to teach me.'

'Because that is what the Tradition is telling me to do,' replied Wicca. 'In your successive incarnations, you changed very little. You belong to the same group as people like myself and my friends. We are the ones charged with maintaining the Tradition of the Moon. You are a witch.'

Brida paid no attention to what Wicca was saying. It didn't even occur to her to make another appointment to meet. All she wanted at that moment was to leave, to be among ordinary things that would bring her back to her familiar world; a damp-stain on the wall, a packet of cigarettes discarded on the floor, some letters left on the porter's desk.

'I have to work tomorrow.' She was suddenly concerned about the time.

On her way back home, she started pondering her company's invoicing system for exports and came up with a way of simplifying certain administrative procedures. She felt very pleased. Her boss might approve of what she was doing and, who knows, give her a raise.

She got home, had supper and watched a bit of television. Then she wrote down her thoughts about invoicing on a piece of paper and fell, exhausted, into bed.

The invoicing of exports had taken on great importance in her life. That, after all, was what she was paid to do.

Nothing else existed. Everything else was a lie.

For a whole week, Brida woke promptly, worked hard at the office and received due praise from her boss. She didn't miss one of her classes and took an interest in everything printed in all the magazines at the newsagent's. All she needed was to avoid thinking. Whenever thoughts surfaced of her meeting with a Magus in the forest or with a witch in the city, she immediately drove them out by reminding herself that she had exams next week or by recalling a remark made by one female friend about another.

Friday came around, and her boyfriend met her outside the university to go to the cinema. Afterwards, they went to their usual bar, talked about the film, their colleagues, and about their respective jobs. They bumped into friends who were on their way back from a party and decided to join them for supper, grateful that, in Dublin, you could always find a restaurant open.

At two o'clock in the morning, they said goodbye to their friends and decided to go back to her place. As soon as they got in, she put on a record by Iron Butterfly and poured them each a double whiskey.

They lay on the sofa with their arms around each other, silent and abstracted, while he stroked her hair and her breasts.

'It's been a really crazy week,' she said suddenly. 'I worked non-stop, prepared for my exams *and* did all the shopping.'

The record finished. She got up to turn it over.

'You know the cupboard door in the kitchen, the one that had come unstuck? Well, I finally managed to arrange a date for someone to come and fix it. And I had to go to the bank several times as well, once to collect some money my Dad sent me, and again to deposit some cheques for the firm and then …'

Lorens was staring at her.

'Why are you staring at me?' she asked rather aggressively. Who was this man lying on the sofa, staring at her, incapable of saying anything of interest? It was quite absurd. She didn't need him. She didn't need anyone.

'Why are you staring at me?' she asked again.

But he said nothing. He merely stood up, went over to her and very tenderly led her back to the sofa.

'You're not listening to anything I say,' said Brida, confused.

Lorens put his arms around her.

'Emotions are like wild horses,' she thought.

'Tell me everything,' Lorens said sweetly. 'I'll listen and respect whatever decision you make, even if you've met someone else, even if this is goodbye.

We've been together for a while now. I may not know you that well; I mean, I don't know exactly who you are, but I know who you're not. And you haven't been yourself all night.'

Brida felt like crying, but she'd shed so many tears already over dark nights, talking tarot cards and enchanted forests. Emotions really were like wild horses, and all she could do now was set them free.

She sat down in front of him, remembering that the Magus and Wicca both favoured that position. Then she gave him a complete account of everything that had happened since her meeting with the Magus in the forest. Lorens listened in total silence. When she told him about the photograph of Monségur, Lorens asked if she had perhaps heard about the Cathars in one of her university courses.

'Look, I know you don't believe a word of what I've told you,' she retorted. 'You think it was my unconscious mind, that I just remembered things I already knew, but no, Lorens, I had never heard of the Cathars before. But you, of course, have an explanation for everything.'

Her hands were shaking uncontrollably. Lorens got to his feet, picked up a piece of paper and made two holes in it, about eight inches apart. He placed the sheet of paper on the table, leaning it against the whiskey bottle, so that it was vertical.

Then he went into the kitchen and returned bearing a cork.

He sat at the head of the table, pushed the piece of paper and the bottle to the other end, and put the cork in front of him.

'Come over here,' he said.

Brida got up. She was trying to hide her shaking hands, not that he appeared to notice.

'Let's pretend that this cork is an electron, one of the small particles that make up the atom. Do you understand?'

She nodded.

'Right, well listen carefully. If I had certain highly complicated bits of apparatus with me that would allow me to shoot an electron in the direction of that piece of paper, it would pass through the two holes at the same time, except that it would do so without splitting into two.'

'I don't believe it,' she said. 'That's impossible.'

Lorens took the piece of paper and threw it away. Then, being a tidy person, he put the cork back where it belonged.

'You may not believe it, but it's true. It's something that scientists know but can't explain. I don't believe a thing you've told me, but I know that it's true.'

Brida's hands were still shaking, but she wasn't crying and she didn't lose control. All she noticed was that the effect of the alcohol had completely worn off. She was strangely lucid.

'And what do scientists do when confronted by these mysteries?'

'They enter the Dark Night, to use a term you taught me. We know that the mystery won't ever go away and so we learn to accept it, to live with it. I think the same thing happens in many situations in life. A mother bringing up a child must feel that she's plunging into the Dark Night too. Or an immigrant who travels to a far-off country in search of work and money. They believe that their efforts will be rewarded and that one day they'll understand what happened along the way which, at the time, seemed so very frightening. It isn't explanations that carry us forward, it's our desire to go on.'

Brida suddenly felt immensely tired. She needed to sleep. Sleep was the only magical kingdom into which she could freely enter.

That night, she had a beautiful dream full of seas and leafy islands. She woke in the early hours and was glad that Lorens was there beside her. She got up and went over to the bedroom window where she looked out over the sleeping city of Dublin.

She thought of her father who used to do just that whenever she woke feeling frightened. The memory brought with it another scene from her childhood.

She was on the beach with her father, and he asked her to go and see what the temperature of the water was like. She was five years old and glad to be able to help. She went to the water's edge and dipped in a toe.

'I put my feet in and it's cold,' she told him.

Her father picked her up and carried her down to the water again and, without any warning, threw her in. She was shocked at first, but then laughed out loud at the trick he'd played.

'How's the water?' asked her father.

'It's lovely,' she replied.

'Right, from now on, whenever you want to find out about something, plunge straight in.'

She had quickly forgotten this lesson. She may only have been twenty-one, but she had already nurtured many enthusiasms, which she had abandoned as quickly as she had taken them up. She wasn't afraid of difficulties; what frightened her was being forced to choose one particular path.

Choosing a path meant having to miss out on others. She had a whole life to live and she was always thinking that, in future, she might regret the choices she made now.

'I'm afraid of committing myself,' she thought to herself. She wanted to follow all possible paths and so ended up following none.

Even in that most important area of her life, love, she had failed to commit herself. After her first romantic disappointment, she had never again given herself entirely. She feared pain, loss and separation. These things were inevitable on the path to love, and the only way of avoiding them was by deciding not to take that path at all. In order not to suffer, you had to renounce love. It was like putting out your own eyes in order not to see the bad things in life.

'Life is so complicated.'

You had to take risks, follow some paths and abandon others. She remembered Wicca telling her about people who followed certain paths only to prove that they weren't the right ones, but that wasn't as bad as choosing a path and then spending the rest of your life wondering if you'd made the right choice.

No one could make a choice without feeling afraid.

That was the law of life. That was the Dark Night, and no one could escape the Dark Night, even if they never made a decision, even if they lacked the courage to change anything, because that in itself was a decision, a change, except without the benefit of the treasures hidden in the Dark Night.

Lorens might be right. In the end, they would laugh at their initial fears. Just as she had laughed at the snakes and scorpions she had imagined were there in the forest. In her despair, she had forgotten that Ireland's patron saint, St Patrick, had long ago driven out all the snakes.

'I'm so glad you exist, Lorens,' she said softly, afraid that he might hear.

She went back to bed and soon fell asleep. Before she did, though, she remembered another story about her father. It was Sunday, and they and all the family were having lunch at her grandmother's house. She must have been about fourteen, and she was complaining about not being able to do a piece of homework, because every time she started, it went wrong.

'Perhaps the times when it goes wrong are teaching you something,' said her father. But Brida was sure that she'd taken the wrong path and that there was no way to put things right.

Her father took her by the hand and led her into the living room, where her grandmother used to watch television. There was a large, antique grandfather clock, which had stopped years before because it could no longer be repaired.

'Nothing in the world is ever completely wrong, my dear,' said her father, looking at the clock. 'Even a stopped clock is right twice a day.'

She walked for some time in the wooded mountains before she found the Magus. He was sitting on a rock, near the top of the mountain, contemplating the valley and the mountains to the west. It was a really beautiful view, and Brida recalled that spirits preferred such places.

'Is God only the God of beauty?' she asked as she approached. 'If so, what about the ugly people and places of the world?'

The Magus did not reply. Brida felt embarrassed.

'You probably don't remember me. I was here two months ago. I spent the whole night alone in the forest. I promised myself that I would only come back when I had discovered my path. I've met a woman called Wicca.'

The Magus started, but realised with relief that the girl hadn't noticed. Then he smiled to himself at the irony of fate.

'Wicca told me that I'm a witch,' the girl went on.

'Don't you trust her?'

This was the first question the Magus had asked since she arrived, and Brida was pleased to know that he was actually listening to what she was saying. Up until then, she hadn't been sure.

'Yes, I trust her,' she said. 'And I trust in the Tradition of the Moon. But I know, too, that the Tradition of the Sun helped me by forcing me to understand about the Dark Night. That's why I came back.'

'Then sit down and enjoy the sunset,' said the Magus.

'I'm not staying alone in the forest again,' she replied. 'The last time I was here …'

The Magus interrupted her:

'Don't say that. God is in the word.'

Wicca had said much the same thing.

'What did I say wrong?'

'If you say it was the "last" time, it might well turn out to be the last. What you meant was "the most recent time I was here".'

Brida was worried. She would have to take great care with her words from now on. She decided to sit quietly and do as the Magus said and watch the sunset.

Doing so made her nervous. It would not be dark for nearly an hour, and she had a lot to talk about and many things to say and ask. Whenever she sat still, just looking at something, she got the feeling that she was wasting precious time when she should be doing things or meeting people. She could be spending her time so much better, because there was still so much to learn. And yet, as the sun sank lower on the horizon, and the clouds filled up with rays of gold and pink,

Brida had the feeling that what she was struggling for in life was exactly this, to be able to sit one day and contemplate just such a sunset.

'Do you know how to pray?' asked the Magus at one point.

Of course she did. Everyone knew how to pray.

'Right, as soon as the sun touches the horizon, say a prayer. In the Tradition of the Sun, it is through prayers that we commune with God. A prayer, when couched in the words of the soul, is far more powerful than any ritual.'

'I don't know how to pray, because my soul is silent,' said Brida.

The Magus laughed.

'Only the truly enlightened have silent souls.'

'So why can't I pray with my soul, then?'

'Because you lack the humility to listen to it and find out what it wants. You're embarrassed to listen to the urgings of your soul and afraid to take those requests to God, because you think he doesn't have time to concern himself with them.'

She was watching a sunset, sitting beside a sage. However, as always happened at such moments, she had the feeling that she didn't deserve to be there.

'It's true that I feel unworthy. I always think the spiritual search was made for people better than me.'

'Those people, if they exist, don't need to search for anything. They are the manifestation of the spirit. The search was made for people like us.'

'Like us,' he had said, and yet he was a long way ahead of her.

'God is God in both the Tradition of the Moon and the Tradition of the Sun,' said Brida, believing that the Traditions were the same and only differed in the ways in which they were taught. 'So teach me how to pray.'

The Magus turned to face the sun and closed his eyes.

'We are human beings, Lord, and we do not know our own greatness. Lord, give us the humility to ask for what we need, because no desire is vain and no request is futile. Each of us knows how best to feed our own soul; give us the courage to see our desires as coming from the fount of Your eternal Wisdom. Only by accepting our desires can we begin to understand who we are. Amen. Now it's your turn,' said the Magus.

'Lord, help me understand that all the good things in life that happen to me do so because I deserve them. Help me understand that what moves me to seek out Your truth is the same force that moved the saints, and the doubts I have are the same doubts that the saints had, and my frailties are the same frailties. Help me to be humble enough to accept that I am no different from other people. Amen.'

They sat in silence, watching the sunset, until the last ray of sun left the clouds. Their souls were praying, asking for wishes to be granted and giving thanks that they were together.

* * *

'Let's go to the pub,' said the Magus.

Brida and the Magus began the walk back. Again she remembered the day when she had first gone there in search of him. She promised herself that she would go over this story only one more time; she didn't need to keep trying to convince herself.

The Magus studied the girl walking ahead of him and trying to look as if she knew where she was putting her feet amongst the damp earth and the stones, but stumbling repeatedly. His heart grew lighter for a moment, then immediately grew guarded again.

Sometimes, certain of God's blessings arrive by shattering all the windows.

It was so good to have Brida by his side, thought the Magus, as they walked back down the mountain. He was just like other men, with the same frailties and the same virtues, and he still wasn't used to the role of Teacher. At first, when people used to come to that forest from all over Ireland to hear his teachings, he spoke of the Tradition of the Sun and asked people to understand what lay around them. God had stored His wisdom there and they were all capable of understanding it by performing a few simple rituals. The way of teaching the Tradition of the Sun had been described two thousand years before by the Apostle Paul: 'And I was with you in weakness and in much fear and trembling; and my speech and my message were not in plausible words of wisdom, but in demonstration of the Spirit and of power, that your faith might not rest in the wisdom of men but in the power of God.'

Yet people seemed incapable of understanding him when he talked to them about the Tradition of the Sun and were disappointed because he was a man just like other men.

He said it didn't matter; he was a Teacher, and all he was doing was giving each person the necessary means to acquire Knowledge. But they needed much more; they needed a guide. They didn't understand about the Dark Night; they didn't understand that any guide through the Dark Night would only illuminate, with his torch, what he himself wanted to see. And if, by chance, that torch should go out, the people would be lost, because they didn't know the way back. But they needed a guide, and to be a good Teacher, he, too, had to accept the needs of others.

So he started padding out his teachings with unnecessary but fascinating things that everyone could accept and understand. The method worked. People learned the Tradition of the Sun, and when they finally realised that many of the things the Magus had told them to do were absolutely useless, they laughed at themselves. And the Magus was glad, because he had finally learned how to teach.

Brida was different. Her prayer had deeply touched the Magus's soul. She had understood that no human being who has walked this planet was or is different from the others. Few people were capable of saying out loud that the great Teachers from the past had the same qualities and the same defects as all men, and that this in no way diminished their ability to search for God. Judging oneself to be inferior to other people was one of the worst acts of pride he knew, because it was the most destructive way of being different.

* * *

When they reached the bar, the Magus ordered two whiskies.

'Look at the other customers,' Brida said. 'They probably come here every night. They probably always do the same thing.'

The Magus was suddenly not so sure that Brida really did consider herself to be the same as everyone else.

'You concern yourself too much with other people,' he replied. 'They're a mirror of yourself.'

'Yes, I know. I thought I knew what made me happy and what made me sad, then suddenly I realised that I need to think again. But it's very hard.'

'What made you change your mind?'

'Love. I know a man who makes me feel complete. Three days ago, he showed me that his world is full of mysteries too and that I'm not alone.'

The Magus remained impassive, but he was remembering the thought he'd had earlier about God's blessings sometimes shattering windows.

'Do you love him?'

'What I've realised is that I could love him still more. Even if I learn nothing new on this path, at least I will have learned one important thing: we have to take risks.'

He had been making great plans for that night as they walked down the mountain. He wanted to show how much he needed her, to show that he was just like other men, weary of so much solitude. But all she wanted were answers to her questions.

'There's something strange about the air here,' Brida said. The atmosphere appeared to have changed.

'It's the Messengers,' said the Magus. 'Artificial demons, those who do not form part of God's Left Arm, those who do not lead us to the light.'

His eyes were shining. Something really had changed, and there he was talking about demons.

'God created the legion of His Left Arm in order to improve us, so that we would know what to do with our mission,' he went on. 'But He put man in charge of concentrating the powers of darkness and creating his own demons.'

And that was what he was doing now.

'But we can concentrate the forces of good too,' said the girl, somewhat alarmed.

'No, we can't.'

He needed to be distracted, if only she would ask him something. He didn't want to create a demon. In the Tradition of the Sun, they were called Messengers, and they could do great good or great evil – only the most important Teachers were allowed to invoke them. He was one of those Teachers, but he didn't want to invoke such a Messenger now, because a Messenger could be a dangerous force, especially when mixed up with disappointments in love.

Brida was confused by his response. The Magus was behaving strangely.

'We can't concentrate the Forces of Good,' he said again, trying hard to focus on what he was saying.

'The Force for Good is always diffused, like Light. When you give off positive vibrations, you benefit all humankind, but when you concentrate the force of the Messenger, you are only benefiting – or harming – yourself.'

His eyes were still shining. He called over the landlord and paid the bill.

'Let's go to my place,' he said. 'I'm going to make some tea and you can tell me about the really important questions in your life.'

Brida hesitated. He was an attractive man, and she was an attractive woman. That night, she feared, might put an end to her apprenticeship.

'I must take risks,' she said to herself again.

The Magus lived a little way outside the village. Brida noticed that although his house was very different from Wicca's, it was equally comfortable and just as tastefully decorated. However, there wasn't a book in sight; it was mainly empty space and a few bits of furniture.

They went into the kitchen to make tea, then came back to the living room.

'Why did you come here today?' asked the Magus.

'I promised myself that I would, once I knew something.'

'And what do you know?'

'Well, I know a little. I know that the path is simple and therefore more difficult than I thought. But I will simplify my soul. Anyway, my first question is: "Why are you wasting your time with me?"'

'Because you're my Soulmate,' thought the Magus, but he said:

'Because I need someone to talk to.'

'What do you think of the path I've chosen – the Tradition of the Moon?'

The Magus needed to tell the truth, even though he wished the truth was different.

'It was your path. Wicca is quite right. You are a witch. You will learn to use Time's memory to discover the lessons that God taught.'

And he wondered why life was like this, why he had met his Soulmate only to find that the one way she could learn was through the Tradition of the Moon.

'I only have one more question,' said Brida. It was getting late; soon there would be no more buses. 'I need to know the answer, and I know that Wicca won't teach it to me. I know this because she's a woman like me. She'll always be my Teacher, but on this topic, she'll always be a woman. I want to know how to find my Soulmate.'

'He's right here with you,' thought the Magus, but again said nothing. He went over to one corner of the room and turned out the lights. Only a kind of acrylic sculpture remained lit. Brida hadn't noticed when she came in. It contained some sort of liquid, and bubbles rose and fell inside it, filling the room with red and blue lights.

'We've met twice now,' said the Magus, his eyes fixed on the sculpture. 'I only have permission to teach through the Tradition of the Sun. The Tradition of the Sun awakens in people the ancestral knowledge that they possess.'

'How do I find my Soulmate through the Tradition of the Sun?'

'That's what everyone here on Earth is searching for,' the Magus said, unwittingly echoing Wicca's words. 'Perhaps they'd been taught by the same Teacher,' Brida thought.

'And the Tradition of the Sun placed in the world, for everyone to see, the sign that someone is their Soulmate: a particular light in the eye.'

'I've seen lots of different kinds of light in lots of people's eyes,' Brida said. 'Today, for example, I saw your eyes shining. That's what everyone looks for.'

'She's forgotten her prayer,' thought the Magus. 'She thinks she's different from everyone else. She's incapable of recognising what God is generous enough to show her.'

'I don't understand eyes,' she insisted. 'Tell me instead how people discover their Soulmate through the Tradition of the Moon.'

The Magus turned to her, his eyes cold and expressionless.

'You're sad,' she said, 'and you're sad because I'm still incapable of learning through the simple things. What you don't understand is that people suffer, they search and search for love, not knowing that they're fulfilling the divine mission of finding their Soulmate. You forget – because you're a wise man and don't think about what it's like for ordinary people – that I carry millennia of disappointment within me, and I can no longer learn certain things through the simple things of life.'

The Magus remained impassive.

'A point of light,' he said. 'A point of light above the left shoulder of your Soulmate. That is how it is in the Tradition of the Moon.'

'I have to leave,' she said, hoping that he would ask her to stay. She liked being there. He had answered her question.

The Magus, however, got up and accompanied her to the door.

'I'm going to learn everything that you know,' she said. 'I'm going to discover how to see that point of light.'

The Magus waited until Brida had gone down the stairs. There was a bus to Dublin in the next half hour, so there was no need for him to worry about her. Then he went out into the garden and performed the ritual he performed every night. He was used to doing it, but sometimes he found it hard to achieve the necessary concentration. Tonight he was particularly distracted.

When the ritual was over, he sat down on the doorstep and looked up at the sky. He thought about Brida. He could see her on the bus, with the point of light above her left shoulder and which, because she was his Soulmate, only he could see. He thought how eager she must be to conclude a search that had started the day she was born. He thought how cold and distant she had been when they arrived at his house, and that this was a good sign. It meant she was confused about her own feelings. She was defending herself from something she couldn't understand.

He thought too, somewhat fearfully, that she was in love.

'Everyone finds their Soulmate, Brida,' he said out loud to the plants in his garden, but deep down, he sensed that he, too, despite all his years in the Tradition, still needed to reinforce his faith, and that he was really talking to himself.

'At some point in our lives, we all meet our Soulmate and recognise him or her,' he went on. 'If I were not a Magus and couldn't see the point of light above your left shoulder, it would take a little longer for me to accept you, but you would fight for me, and one day I would see the special light in your eyes. However, the fact is I *am* a Magus, and it's up to me to fight for you, so that all my knowledge is transformed into wisdom.'

He sat for a long time contemplating the night and thinking about Brida travelling back to Dublin on the bus. It was colder than usual. Summer would soon be over.

'There are no risks in Love, as you'll find out for yourself. People have been searching for and finding each other for thousands of years.'

Suddenly, he realised that he might be wrong. There was always a risk, a single risk: that one person might meet with more than one Soulmate in the same incarnation, as had happened millennia before.

Winter and Spring

Over the next two months, Wicca initiated Brida into the first mysteries of witchcraft. According to her, women could learn these things more quickly than men, because each month, they experienced in their own bodies the complete cycle of nature: birth, life and death, the 'Cycle of the Moon' as she called it.

Brida had to buy a new notebook and record in it any psychical experiences she'd had since her first meeting with Wicca. The notebook always had to be kept up to date and must bear on its cover a five-pointed star, which associated everything written in it with the Tradition of the Moon. Wicca told her that all witches owned such a book, known as a *Book of Shadows,* in homage to their sisters who had died during the four hundred years that the witch-hunt lasted.

'Why do I need to do all this?'

'We have to awaken the Gift. Without it, you will know only the Minor Mysteries. The Gift is your way of serving the world.'

Brida had to reserve one relatively unused corner of her house for a kind of miniature oratory in which a candle should be kept burning day and night. The candle, according to the Tradition of the Moon, was the symbol of the four elements, and contained within itself the earth of the wick, the water of the paraffin, the fire that burned and the air that allowed the fire to burn. The candle was also important as a way of reminding her that she had a mission to fulfil and that she was engaged on that mission. Only the candle should be visible; everything else should be hidden away on a shelf or in a drawer. From the Middle Ages on, the Tradition of the Moon had demanded that witches surround their activities with absolute secrecy, for there were several prophecies warning that Darkness would return at the end of the millennium.

Whenever Brida came home and saw the candle flame, she felt a strange, almost sacred, responsibility.

Wicca told her that she must always pay attention to the sound of the world. 'You can hear it wherever you are,' she said. 'It's a noise that never stops, which is there on mountain tops, in cities, in the sky and at the bottom of the ocean. This noise – which is like a vibration – is the Soul of the World transforming itself and travelling towards the light. Any witch must be keenly aware of this, because she is an important part of that journey.'

Wicca also explained that the Ancients spoke to our world through symbols. Even if no one was listening, even if the language of symbols had been forgotten by almost everyone, the Ancients never ceased talking.

'Are they beings like us?' Brida asked one day.

'We are them. And suddenly we understand everything that we learned in our past lives, and everything that the great sages left written on the Universe. Jesus said: "The Kingdom of God is as if a man should scatter seed upon the ground and should sleep and rise night and day, and the seed should sprout and grow, he knows not how."

'The human race drinks always from this same inexhaustible fountain, and even when everyone says it is doomed, it still finds a way to survive. It survived when the apes drove the men from the trees and when the waters covered the Earth. It will survive when everyone is preparing for the final catastrophe.

'We are responsible for the Universe, because we are the Universe.'

The more time Brida spent with Wicca, the more aware she became of what a very pretty woman she was.

Wicca continued to teach Brida the Tradition of the Moon. She told her to find a two-edged dagger with an undulating blade like a flame. Brida tried in various shops, but there was nothing suitable. In the end, Lorens solved the problem by asking a metallurgical chemistry engineer, who worked at the university, to make such a blade. Then he himself carved a wooden handle and gave the dagger to Brida as a gift. It was his way of saying that he respected her search.

The dagger was consecrated by Wicca in a complicated ritual involving magical words, charcoal designs drawn on the blade, and a few blows with a wooden spoon. The dagger was to be used as a prolongation of her own arm, keeping the energy of her body concentrated in the blade. Fairy godmothers used a wand for the same purpose, and magi used a sword.

When Brida expressed her surprise at the charcoal and the wooden spoon, Wicca said that, in the days of witch-hunts, witches were forced to use materials that could be mistaken for ordinary everyday objects. The tradition of the dagger, the charcoal and the wooden spoon had survived, while the actual materials once used by the Ancients had been lost entirely.

Brida learned how to burn incense and how to use the dagger inside magic circles. There was a ritual she had to perform whenever the moon changed its phase; she would place a cup of water on the windowsill so that the moon was reflected in the surface. Then she would stand so that her own face was reflected in the water and the moon's reflection was right in the middle of her forehead. When she was completely focused, she would cut the water with the dagger, causing the reflections to break up and form smaller ones.

This water had to be drunk immediately, and then the power of the moon would grow inside her.

'None of this makes sense,' Brida said once. Wicca ignored the remark, for she had once thought exactly the same, but she remembered Jesus' words about the things that grow inside each of us without our understanding how or why.

'It doesn't matter if it makes sense or not,' she told her. 'Think of the Dark Night. The more you do this, the more the Ancients will communicate with you. They will do so initially in ways you cannot understand, because only your soul will be listening, but one day, the voices will be heard again.'

Brida didn't want to hear voices, she wanted to find her Soulmate, but she said nothing of this to Wicca.

She was forbidden from returning to the past again. According to Wicca, this was rarely necessary.

'Don't use the cards to read the future either. The cards are to be used only for growth without words, the kind of growth that occurs imperceptibly.'

Brida had to spread the cards out on a table three times a week and sit looking at them. Occasionally she had visions, but they were usually incomprehensible. When she complained about this, Wicca said that the visions had a meaning so deep that she was incapable of understanding it.

'And why shouldn't I use the cards to read the future?'

'Only the present has power over our lives,' replied Wicca. 'When you read the future in the cards, you are bringing the future into the present, and that can cause serious harm. The present could confuse your future.'

Once a week, they went to the wood, and Wicca taught her apprentice the secrets of herbs. For Wicca, everything in the world bore God's signature, especially plants. Certain leaves resembled the heart and were good for heart disease, while flowers that resembled eyes could cure diseases of the eye. Brida began to understand that many herbs really did bear a close resemblance to human organs, and in a book on folk medicine that Lorens borrowed from the university library she found research indicating that the beliefs of country people and witches could well be right.

'God placed his pharmacy in the woods and fields,' Wicca said one day when they were resting under a tree, 'so that everyone could enjoy good health.'

* * *

Brida knew that her teacher had other apprentices, but she never met them – the dog always barked when her time with Wicca was up. However, she had passed other people on the stairs: an older woman, a girl about her own age and a man in a suit. Brida listened discreetly to their steps until the creaking floorboards above betrayed their destination: Wicca's apartment.

One day, Brida risked asking about these other students.

'Witchcraft is based on collective strength,' Wicca told her. 'All the different gifts keep the energy of our work in constant movement. Each gift depends on all the others.'

Wicca explained that there were nine gifts, and that both the Tradition of the Sun and the Tradition of the Moon took care that these gifts survived over the centuries.

'What are the nine gifts?'

Wicca told her off for being lazy and asking questions all the time, when a true witch should be interested in all forms of spiritual enquiry. Brida, she said, ought to spend more time reading the Bible ('which contains all the true occult wisdom') and to seek out the gifts in St Paul's First Epistle to the Corinthians. Brida did so and there she found the nine gifts: the word of wisdom, the word of knowledge, faith, healing, the working of miracles, prophecy, the discerning of the spirits, speaking in tongues and the interpretation of tongues.

It was only then that she understood the gift she was seeking: the discerning of the spirits.

Wicca taught Brida to dance. She said that she needed to learn to move her body in accordance with the sound of the world, that ever-present vibration. There was no special technique; it was simply a matter of making any movement that came into her head. Nevertheless, it took a while before Brida could become used to moving and dancing in that illogical way.

'The Magus of Folk taught you about the Dark Night. In both Traditions – which are, in fact, one – the Dark Night is the only way to grow. When you set off along the path of magic, the first thing you do is surrender yourself to a greater power, for you will encounter things that you will never understand.

'Nothing will behave in the logical way you have come to expect. You will understand things only with your heart, and that can be a little frightening. For a long time, the journey will seem like a Dark Night, but then any search is an act of faith.

'But God, who is far harder to understand than a Dark Night, appreciates our act of faith, and takes our hand and guides us through the Mystery.'

Wicca spoke of the Magus with no rancour or bitterness. Brida had been wrong; Wicca had clearly never had an affair with him; it was written in her eyes. Perhaps the irritation she had expressed on that first day had merely been because they had ended up following different paths. Wizards and witches were vain creatures, and each wanted to prove to the other that their path was the best.

She suddenly realised what she had thought.

She could tell Wicca wasn't in love with the Magus by her eyes.

She had seen films and read books that talked about this. The whole world could tell from someone's eyes if they were in love.

'I only manage to understand the simple things once I've embraced the complicated things,' she thought to herself. Perhaps one day she *would* follow the Tradition of the Sun.

It was quite late on in the year and the cold was just beginning to bite when Brida received a phone call from Wicca.

'We're going to meet in the wood in two days' time, on the night of the new moon, just before dark,' was all she said.

Brida spent those two days thinking about that meeting. She performed the usual rituals and danced to the sound of the world. 'I wish I could dance to some music,' she thought, but she was becoming used to moving her body according to that strange vibration, which she could hear better at night or in certain silent places. Wicca had told her that, when she danced to the sound of the world, her soul would feel more comfortable in her body and there would be a lessening of tension. Brida began to notice how people walking down the street didn't seem to know what to do with their hands or how to move their hips or shoulders. She felt like telling them that the world was playing a tune and if they danced a little to that music, and simply allowed their body to move illogically for a few minutes a day, they would feel much better.

That dance, however, was part of the Tradition of the Moon, and only witches knew about it. There must be something similar in the Tradition of the Sun. There always was, although no one appeared to want to learn it.

'We've lost our ability to live with the secrets of the world,' she said to Lorens. 'And yet there they are before us. The reason I want to be a witch is so that I can see those secrets.'

On the appointed day, Brida went to the wood. She walked amongst the trees, feeling the magical presence of the spirits of nature. About fifteen hundred years ago, that wood had been the sacred place of the Druids, until St Patrick drove the snakes from Ireland, and the Druid cults disappeared. Nevertheless, respect for that place had passed from generation to generation and, even now, the villagers both respected and feared it.

She found Wicca in the clearing, wrapped in her cloak. There were four other people with her, all wearing ordinary clothes and all of them women. In the place where she had once noticed ashes, a fire was burning. Brida looked at the fire and for some reason felt afraid. She didn't know if it was because of that part of Loni which she carried inside her or because she had known fire in her other incarnations.

More women arrived. Some were her age and others were older than Wicca. Altogether, there were nine.

'I didn't invite the men today. We are here waiting for the kingdom of the Moon.'

The kingdom of the Moon was the night.

They stood around the fire, talking about the most trivial things in the world, and Brida felt as if she'd been invited to a tea-party with a lot of old gossips, although the setting was rather different.

However, as soon as the sky filled up with stars, the atmosphere changed completely. Wicca didn't need to call for silence; gradually, the conversation died, and Brida wondered to herself if they'd only just noticed the presence of the fire and the forest.

After a brief silence, Wicca spoke.

'On this night, once a year, the world's witches gather together to pray and pay homage to our forebears. According to the Tradition, on the tenth moon of the year, we gather round a fire, which was life and death to our persecuted sisters.'

Brida produced a wooden spoon from beneath her cloak.

'Here is the symbol,' she said, showing the spoon to everyone.

The women remained standing and held hands. Then, raising their joined hands, they heard Wicca's prayer.

'May the blessing of the Virgin Mary and of her son Jesus be upon our heads tonight. In our bodies sleeps the Soulmate of our ancestors. May the Virgin Mary bless them.

'May she bless us because we are women and live in a world in which men love and understand us more and more. Yet still we bear on our bodies the marks of past lives, and those marks still hurt.

'May the Virgin Mary free us from those marks and put an end for ever to our sense of guilt. We feel guilty when we go out to work because we're leaving our children in order to earn money to feed them. We feel guilty when we stay at home because it seems we're not making the most of our freedom. We feel guilty about everything, because we have always been kept far from decision-making and from power.

'May the Virgin Mary remind us always that it was the women who stayed with Jesus when all the men fled and denied their faith. That it was the women who wept while he carried the cross and who waited at his feet at the hour of his death. That it was the women who visited the empty tomb, and that we have no reason to feel guilty.

'May the Virgin Mary remind us always that we were burned and persecuted because we preached the Religion of Love. When others were trying to stop time with the power of sin, we gathered together to hold forbidden festivals in which we celebrated what was still beautiful in the world. Because of this we were condemned and burned in the public squares.

'May the Virgin Mary remind us always that, while men were tried in the public square over land disputes, women were tried in the public square for adultery.

'May the Virgin Mary remind us always of our ancestors, who – like St Joan of Arc – had to disguise themselves as men in order to fulfil the Lord's word, and yet still they died in the fire.'

Wicca held the wooden spoon in both hands and stretched out both arms.

'Here is the symbol of our ancestors' martyrdom. May the flame that devoured their bodies remain always alight in our souls. Because they are in us. Because we are them.'

And she threw the spoon into the fire.

Brida continued to perform the rituals that Wicca had taught her. She kept the candle always burning and danced to the sound of the world. She noted down her meetings with Wicca in the *Book of Shadows* and went to the sacred wood twice a week. She noticed, to her surprise, that she was beginning to understand more about herbs and plants.

However, the voices that Wicca wanted to awaken did not appear. Nor did she manage to see the point of light above anyone's left shoulder.

'Who knows, perhaps I haven't yet met my Soulmate,' she thought rather fearfully. This was the fate of those who knew the Tradition of the Moon: never to make a mistake when choosing the man in their life. This meant that, from the moment they became a true witch, they would never again nurse the same illusions about love that other people did. True, this would mean less suffering or even no suffering at all, because they could love everything more intensely; finding one's Soulmate was, after all, a divine mission in everyone's life. Even if, one day, you were forced to part, love for your Soulmate – according to both Traditions – would always be crowned with glory, understanding and a kind of purifying nostalgia.

It meant, too, that, from the moment you became able to see the point of light, there would be no Dark Night of Love. Brida thought of the many times she had suffered for love, the nights she had lain awake waiting for a phone call that never came, the romantic weekends that didn't survive the following week, the parties spent glancing anxiously around to see who was there, the joy of making a conquest simply to prove that you could, the sadness and loneliness when you were sure that your best friend's boyfriend was the only man who could possibly make you happy. That was part of her world, and the world of everyone else she knew. That was love, and that was how people had searched for their Soulmate since time began, by looking into another person's eyes in search of that special light, desire. She had never given much value to such things; on the contrary, she had always thought it pointless to suffer because of someone else, or to feel scared stiff because you couldn't find anyone with whom to share your life. Now, however, that she had the chance to free herself from such fears for ever, she wasn't sure she wanted to.

'Do I really want to be able to see that point of light?'

She thought of the Magus – she was beginning to think he was right and that the Tradition of the Sun was the only way to deal with Love. But she couldn't change her mind now; she knew the path to follow, and she must follow it to the end. She knew that if she gave up now, she would find it harder and harder to make any choices in life.

One afternoon, after a long lesson devoted to rain-making rituals performed by the witches of old – rituals that Brida would have to note down in her *Book of Shadows* even though she would probably never use them – Wicca asked if she wore all the clothes she owned.

'No, of course I don't,' came the reply.

'Well, from now on, wear everything in your wardrobe.'

Brida thought perhaps she had misunderstood.

'Everything that contains our energy should be in constant movement,' Wicca explained. 'The clothes you bought are part of you, and they represent those special times when you left the house wanting to splash out a little because you were happy with the world, times when you'd been hurt and wanted to make yourself feel better or times when you thought you should change your life.

'Clothes always transform emotion into matter. It's one of the bridges between the visible and the invisible. Some clothes can even be harmful because they were made for someone else, but have ended up in your hands.'

Brida knew what she meant. There were some clothes she couldn't bring herself to wear, because whenever she did, something bad happened.

'Get rid of any clothes that were not intended for you,' Wicca went on. 'And wear all the others. It's important to keep the soil turned, the waves crashing and all your emotions in movement. The whole Universe is moving all the time, and we must do likewise.'

When she got home, Brida spread out the contents of her wardrobe on the bed. She looked at each item of clothing; there were some she'd completely forgotten about; others brought back happy memories, but were no longer fashionable. Brida kept them, though, because they held a special charm, and if she got rid of them, she might be undoing all the good things she had experienced while wearing them.

She looked at the clothes which she felt contained 'bad vibrations'. She'd always hoped that those bad vibrations might one day become good vibrations and then she would be able to wear the clothes again. However, whenever she put them to the test, the results were invariably disastrous.

She realised that her relationship with clothes was more complicated than she had thought, and yet it was hard to accept Wicca meddling in something as private and personal as the way she dressed. Some clothes had to be kept for special occasions, and only she could say when she should wear them. Others weren't suitable for work or even for going out at the weekend. Why was Wicca so interested in this? She never questioned what Wicca told her to do; she spent her life dancing and lighting candles, plunging knives into water and learning about rituals she would never use. And she accepted all that because it was part of the Tradition, a Tradition she didn't understand, but which was perhaps in touch with her unknown self. But by meddling with her clothes, Wicca was also meddling with her way of being in the world.

Perhaps Wicca had overstepped the bounds of her power. Perhaps she was trying to interfere in things she shouldn't.

'What is outside is harder to change than what is inside.'

Someone had said something. Brida instinctively looked around her, knowing that she would find no one.

It was the Voice.

The Voice that Wicca had wanted to awaken.

She managed to curb her feelings of excitement and fear. She remained silent, hoping to hear something else, but there was only the noise from the street, a television some way off and the omnipresent sound of the world. She tried to sit in the same position as before, to think the same things as before. Everything had happened so fast that she hadn't even felt frightened or surprised or proud.

But the Voice had said something. Even if everyone in the world were to prove to her that it was all just a product of her imagination, even if the witch-hunts were to return and she had to stand up in court and risked being burned to death, she was utterly sure that she'd heard a voice that was not her own.

'What is outside is more difficult to change than what is inside.' The Voice could perhaps have said something a little more earth shattering, given that this was the first time in her current incarnation that she was hearing it, but suddenly Brida was filled by an intense feeling of joy. She wanted to phone Lorens, to go and see the Magus, to tell Wicca that her Gift had finally been revealed, and that she could now become part of the Tradition of the Moon. She paced the room, smoked a few cigarettes, and only half an hour later did she feel calm enough to sit down again on the bed, along with all her clothes.

The Voice was right. Brida had surrendered her soul to a strange woman and – odd though it might seem – it was far easier to surrender her soul than her way of dressing.

Only now was she beginning to understand how much those apparently meaningless exercises were influencing her life. Only now, when she was considering changing on the outside, could she realise how much she had changed inside.

When they met again, Wicca wanted to know all about the Voice, and was pleased that Brida had noted down every detail in her *Book of Shadows*.

'Whose Voice is it?' asked Brida.

Wicca, however, had more important things to do and say than answer Brida's eternal questions.

'So far, I've shown you how to return to the path that your soul travelled several incarnations ago. I awoke that knowledge by speaking directly to it – with my soul – through the symbols and rituals of our forebears. You might have grumbled a bit about it, but your soul was glad because it was re-establishing contact with its mission. While you were getting irritated with all the exercises you had to do, feeling bored with the dancing and having to fight off sleep during rituals, your hidden side was once more drinking in the wisdom of Time, remembering what it had learned before, and as it says in the Bible, the seed was growing and sprouting, although you knew not how. Then came the moment to start to learn new things. That is called Initiation, because that is where you will truly start to learn the things you need to learn in this life. The Voice indicates that you are ready.

'In the Tradition of the witches, an Initiation always takes place at the time of the Equinox, on the two days of the year when the days and the nights are equal in length. The next one is the Spring Equinox, on the twenty-first of March. I would like that to be the date of your Initiation because I, too, was initiated at the Spring Equinox. You know how to use the ritual instruments and you know all the rituals that keep open the bridge between the visible and the invisible. Whenever you perform one of those rituals, your soul recalls the lessons it learned in past lives.

'When you heard the Voice, you brought into the visible world something that was happening in the invisible world. In other words, you realised that your soul was ready for the next step. You have achieved your first major objective.'

It occurred to Brida that her original desire had been to see the point of light that would indicate her Soulmate, but she had been thinking a lot lately about the search for love, and that first desire was now dwindling in importance with each week that passed.

'There is just one test you must pass before you can be accepted for the Spring Initiation. If you fail, don't worry, you have many Equinoxes ahead of you, and one day you will be initiated. Up until now, you have dealt only with your masculine side: knowledge. You know certain things and are capable of understanding what you know, but you haven't yet touched on the one great feminine force, one of the great transformational powers. And knowledge without transformation is not wisdom.

'This force has always been an accursed Power among witches in general and women in particular. It is a force known to everyone on this planet. We women know that we are the great guardians of its secrets. Because of this force we are doomed to wander a dangerous, hostile world, because we were the ones who awoke it and because there have been places where it was considered an abomination. Anyone who comes into contact with this force, however unknowingly, is bound to it for the rest of their life. It can be your master or your slave; you can transform it into a magical force or use it all your life without ever realising its immense power. This force is in everything around us: it's in the visible world of ordinary people and in the invisible world of the mystics. It can be killed, crushed, hidden, even denied. It can lie dormant for years, forgotten in a corner somewhere; we can treat it in whichever way we want, but once someone has experienced this force, he or she will never be able to forget it.'

'What force is that?'

'Don't keep asking stupid questions,' retorted Wicca. 'You know perfectly well what that force is.'

Yes, Brida knew.

Sex.

* * *

Wicca drew aside one of the immaculately white curtains and showed Brida the view. The window looked out on the river, on old buildings, on distant hills. The Magus lived somewhere over there.

'What's that?' asked Wicca, pointing at the top of a church steeple.

'A cross. The symbol of Christianity.'

'A Roman would never enter a building with a cross on it. He would think it was a house of torture, because the cross represents one of the cruellest instruments of torture ever invented by man. The cross might not have changed, but its meaning certainly has. In the same way, when mankind was closer to God, sex was the symbolic means of communion with the divine, a re-encounter with the meaning of life.'

'Why do people seeking God so often distance themselves from sex?'

Wicca was irritated by the interruption, but she answered anyway.

'When I talk about the force, I'm not talking only about the sexual act. Some people make use of this force without actually having sex. Everything depends on which path you take.'

'I know that force,' Brida said. 'I know how to make use of it.'

'You may know about having sex with someone in bed, but that isn't the same as knowing it as a force. Both men and women are extremely vulnerable to the force of sex, because, during sex, pleasure and fear are present in equal measure.'

'Why do pleasure and fear go together?'

She had finally asked a question worth answering.

'Because anyone who comes into contact with sex knows that they're dealing with something which only happens in all its intensity when they lose control. When we're in bed with someone, we're giving permission to that person not only to commune with our body, but with our whole being. The pure forces of life are in communication with each other, independently of us, and then we cannot hide who we are.

'It doesn't matter what image we have of ourselves. It doesn't matter what disguises we put on, what smart answers or honourable excuses we give. During sex, it's very difficult to deceive the other person, because that is when each person shows who they really are.'

Wicca was speaking like someone who knew this force well. Her eyes were shining and there was pride in her voice. Perhaps that was what lay behind her continuing attractiveness. Brida was glad Wicca was her teacher, and one day she would discover the secret of that charm.

'Before the Initiation can take place, you have to experience that force. Everything else belongs to the Great Mysteries, and you will learn about that after the ceremony.'

'How do I go about experiencing it, then?'

'It's a simple enough formula, and like all simple things, its results are far more complex than all the complicated rituals I've taught you so far.'

Wicca came over to Brida, grasped her shoulders and looked into her eyes.

'This is the formula: use your five senses at all times. If they all come together at the moment of orgasm, you will be accepted for Initiation.'

'I came to apologise,' Brida said.

They were in the same place where they had met before, near the rocks on the right-hand side of the mountain, from where you could see the valley below.

'Sometimes I think one thing and do another,' she went on. 'But if you've ever felt love, you'll know how painful it is to suffer for love.'

'Yes, I know,' replied the Magus. It was the first time he had made any comment on his private life.

'You were right about the point of light. It's not really that important. Now I've discovered that the search can be as interesting as actually finding what you're looking for.'

'As long as you can overcome your fear.'

'That's true.'

And Brida was pleased to know that even he, with all his knowledge, still felt fear.

They spent the afternoon walking through the snow-covered forest. They talked about plants, about the landscape, and about the ways in which the spiders in that region wove their webs. At one point, they met a shepherd leading his sheep back home.

'Hello, Santiago!' cried the Magus. Then he turned to her:

'God has a special fondness for shepherds. They are people accustomed to nature, silence, patience. They possess all the necessary virtues to commune with the Universe.'

Up until then, they hadn't discussed such matters at all, and Brida didn't want to anticipate the moment. She brought the conversation back to her life and to what was going on in the world. Her sixth sense told her to avoid mentioning Lorens. She didn't know what was going on, nor did she know why the Magus was being so attentive, but she needed to keep that flame alight. An accursed power, Wicca had called it. She had an objective and this was her one means of attaining it.

They passed a few sheep, whose feet left strange prints in the snow. This time there was no shepherd, but the sheep seemed to know where to go and what they were looking for. The Magus stood for a long time watching the sheep, as if he were studying some great secret from the Tradition of the Sun, one that Brida could not understand.

As the light began to fade, so did the feeling of terror and respect that always gripped her when she was with him. For the first time, she felt calm and confident by his side. Perhaps because she didn't need to demonstrate her gifts. She had heard the Voice, and her entry into the world of those other men and women was now simply a matter of time. She, too, belonged to the path of mysteries, and from the moment that she heard the Voice, the man beside her had become part of her Universe.

She felt like grasping his hands and asking him to show her some aspect of the Tradition of the Sun, just as she used to ask Lorens to talk to her about the ancient stars. It was a way of saying that they were seeing the same thing, albeit from different angles.

Something was telling her that he needed this, and it wasn't the mysterious Voice of the Tradition of the Moon, but the restless, sometimes foolish voice of her heart. A voice she didn't often listen to, since it always led her along paths she couldn't understand.

But emotions were, indeed, wild horses and they demanded to be heard. Brida let them run free for a while until they grew tired. Her emotions were telling her how good it would be that afternoon if she were in love with him, because when you were in love, you were capable of learning everything and of knowing things you had never dared even to think, because love was the key to the understanding of all the mysteries.

She ran through various amorous scenarios involving the Magus before she finally regained control. Then she said to herself that she could never love a man like him, because he understood the Universe, and all human feelings look small when viewed from a distance.

They reached the ruins of an old monastic church. The Magus sat down on one of the many piles of carved stone scattered on the ground, and Brida cleared the snow off a broad windowsill.

'It must be good to live here, spend all day in the forest and then go home to sleep in a nice warm house,' she said.

'Yes, it is good. I know the songs of all the different birds and I can read God's signs. I've learned the Traditions of the Sun and the Moon.'

'But I'm alone,' he felt like adding. 'And there's no point in understanding the entire Universe if you're alone.'

There, perched on the windowsill, was his Other Half. He could see the point of light above her left shoulder, and he regretted ever having learned the two Traditions, because had it not been for the point of light he might not have fallen in love with her.

'She's intelligent. She sensed the danger early, and now wants to know nothing more about points of light,' he thought.

'I heard the Voice. Wicca really is an excellent teacher.'

It was the first time that afternoon that she'd brought up the subject of magic.

'The Voice will teach you the mysteries of the world, the mysteries that are imprisoned in time, and which are carried from generation to generation by witches.'

He spoke without really listening to what he was saying. He was trying to remember when he had first met his Soulmate. Solitary people lose track of time, the hours are long and the days interminable. Even so, he knew they had only been together twice before. Brida was learning very fast.

'I know the rituals and I'm to be initiated into the Great Mysteries at the Spring Equinox.'

She was beginning to feel tense again.

'There's one thing, though, that I still haven't experienced – the force that everyone knows and which they revere as if it were a mystery.'

The Magus understood why she had come that afternoon. It wasn't just to walk among the trees and leave two sets of footprints in the snow, footprints that were getting closer every minute.

Brida turned up her jacket collar to protect her face, whether because the cold grew more intense when they stopped walking or whether she was merely trying to conceal her nervousness, she wasn't sure.

'I want to learn how to awaken the force of sex through the five senses,' she said at last. 'Wicca won't talk about it. She says that I'll discover it just as I discovered the Voice.'

They sat for a few minutes in silence. She wondered if she should even be talking about such a thing in the ruins of a church. But then she remembered that there are many ways of using the force. The monks who had lived there had worked through abstinence, and they would understand what she meant.

'I've tried all kinds of things. I think there must be a trick, like the trick with the phone to get me to really see the tarot cards. I think it's something Wicca doesn't want to teach me. I think she must have found it very hard to learn and wants me to experience the same difficulties.'

'Was that why you came looking for me?'

Brida looked deep into his eyes.

'Yes.'

She hoped her answer would convince him, but she wasn't sure of anything any more. The walk through the snowy wood, the sunlight on the snow, the easy conversation about the ordinary things of the world, all of this had set her emotions galloping like wild horses. She had to persuade herself again that she was there for only one reason, and that she would attain her objective by whatever means possible. Because God had been a woman before he became a man.

The Magus got up from the pile of stones he was sitting on and walked over to the only wall that had not crumbled into rubble. In the middle of the wall was a door, and he stood leaning against it. The evening sun lit him from behind and Brida could not see his face.

'There's one thing that Wicca didn't teach you,' he said. 'She may have forgotten to do so, or she may have wanted you to discover it alone.'

'Well, here I am, alone.'

And she asked herself if perhaps this had been her teacher's plan all along, to bring her together with this man.

'I'm going to teach you,' he said at last. 'Come with me.'

They walked to a place where the trees were taller and their trunks thicker. Brida noticed that some of them had rough-and-ready ladders attached to the trunks. At the top of each ladder was a kind of cabin.

'This must be where the hermits of the Tradition of the Sun live,' she thought.

The Magus carefully examined each cabin, chose one and asked Brida to join him.

She started to climb. Halfway up, she felt afraid, because a fall might prove fatal. Nevertheless, she resolved to go on; she was in a sacred place, protected by the spirits of the forest. The Magus had not asked if she wanted to do this, but perhaps this was considered unnecessary in the Tradition of the Sun.

When they reached the top, she gave a long sigh. She had conquered another of her fears.

'This is a good place to teach you the path,' he said. 'A place of ambush.'

'Ambush?'

'These cabins are used by hunters. They have to be high up so that the animals don't catch the hunters' scent. During the year, the hunters leave food on the ground so that the animals get used to coming here, and then one day, they kill them.'

Brida noticed some empty cartridges on the floor. She was shocked.

'Look down,' he said.

There was barely enough space for two people, and his body was almost touching hers. She did as he asked. The tree must have been one of the tallest, because she could see the tops of the other trees, the valley, the snow-covered mountains on the horizon. It was beautiful there; he needn't have said what he did about it being a place of ambush.

The Magus pushed back the canvas roof, and suddenly the cabin was filled with sunlight. It was cold, and it seemed to Brida that they were in a magical place, on the top of the world. Her emotions wanted to set off again at a gallop, but she had to keep them in check.

'I didn't need to bring you here in order to explain what you want to know,' said the Magus, 'but I wanted you to understand a little more about this forest. In the winter, when both hunter and hunted are far away, I come and climb these trees and contemplate the Earth.'

He really did want to share his world with her. Brida's blood began to flow more quickly. She felt at peace, immersed in one of those moments in life when the only possible alternative is to lose all control.

* * *

'Our relationships with the world come through our five senses. Plunging into the world of magic means discovering other unknown senses, and sex propels us towards one of those doors.'

He was speaking more loudly now. He sounded like a teacher giving a biology lesson. 'Perhaps it's better like this,' she thought, although she was not convinced.

'It doesn't matter whether you're seeking wisdom or pleasure through the force of sex, it will always be a total experience, because it's the only experience that touches – or should touch – all five senses at once. All our channels with the other person are wide open.

'At the moment of orgasm, the five senses vanish, and you enter the world of magic; you can no longer see, hear, taste, touch or smell. During those long seconds everything disappears, to be replaced by ecstasy. It is exactly the same ecstasy as that attained by mystics after years of renunciation and discipline.'

Brida felt like asking why the mystics hadn't tried to attain it through orgasm, then she remembered that some were the descendants of angels.

'What propels a person towards this ecstasy are the five senses. The more the senses are stimulated, the stronger will be the drive towards ecstasy and the more powerful the ecstasy. Do you understand?'

Of course she understood. She nodded. But that question left her feeling more distant. She wished he were still strolling by her side through the forest.

'That's all there is to it.'

'I know all that, but I still can't do it.' Brida didn't dare mention Lorens. She sensed it would be dangerous. 'You told me that there's a way to achieve it.'

She was nervous and upset. Her emotions were beginning to gallop out of control.

The Magus looked down again at the forest below. Brida wondered if he, too, was struggling with his emotions, but she didn't want to believe in what she was thinking, nor should she.

She knew what the Tradition of the Sun was. She knew that its Teachers taught through space and time. She had thought about this before she first searched him out. She had imagined that they might one day be together as they were now, with no one else near. That is how the Teachers of the Tradition of the Sun were - always teaching through action and never giving theory undue importance. She had thought all this before ever coming to the forest, but she had come anyway, because now her path was more important than anything else. She needed to continue the tradition of her many lives.

But now he was behaving like Wicca, who only talked about things.

'Teach me,' she said.

The Magus was staring at the bare, snowy branches. He could, at that moment, forget he was a Teacher and be merely a Magus, a man like any other man. He knew that his Soulmate was there before him. He could talk about the point of light he could see, and she would believe him, and their re-encounter would be complete. Even if she left in tears, she would come back eventually, because he was telling the truth – and she needed him as much as he needed her. That was the wisdom of Soulmates: they always recognised each other.

But he was a Teacher, and one day, in a village in Spain, he had sworn a sacred oath. That oath said, amongst other things, that no Teacher should ever force another person to make a choice. He had made that mistake once and because of that had spent all those years in exile from the world. Now it was different, but he still didn't want to take the risk. For a moment, he thought: 'I could give up magic for her,' but immediately realised how foolish that thought was. Love didn't require that kind of renunciation. True love allowed each person to follow their own path, knowing that they would never lose touch with their Soulmate.

He must be patient. He must remember the patience of shepherds and know that, sooner or later, they would be together. That was the Law. And he had believed in that Law all his life.

'What you're asking me is very simple,' he said at last. He had mastered his emotions; discipline had won out.

'Make sure that when you touch the other person, all your five senses are working, because sex has a life of its own. The moment you begin, you're no longer in control; it takes control of you. And whatever you bring to it – your fears, your desires, your sensibility – will remain. That's why people become impotent. When you have sex, take with you to bed only love and your senses, all five of them. Only then will you experience communion with God.'

Brida looked down at the cartridges on the floor. She did not betray her feelings for an instant. She knew what the trick was now, and that, she said to herself, was all she was interested in.

'That's all I can teach you.'

She did not move. The wild horses were being tamed by the silence.

'Take seven deep, calm breaths and make sure all your senses are working before there's any physical contact. Just let things take their course.'

He was a Teacher of the Tradition of the Sun. He had come through yet another test. His Soulmate was also teaching him things.

'Right, I've shown you the view from up here. We can go down now.'

She sat distractedly watching the children playing in the square. Someone had told her once that every city has a 'magic place', a place where we go when we need to think seriously about life. That square was her 'magic place' in Dublin. It was near the apartment she'd rented when she first arrived, full of dreams and expectations. Her plan then had been to enrol as a student at Trinity College and eventually become a professor of literature. She used to spend a lot of time on that bench, writing poetry and generally trying to behave as her literary idols had.

But the money her father sent wasn't enough and she'd had to take a job at the import–export company where she worked now. Not that she minded; she was happy with what she was doing, and in fact her job was one of the most important things in her life, because it gave a sense of reality to everything and kept her from going mad. It allowed her to maintain a precarious balance between the visible world and the invisible.

The children continued to play. Like her, all of them had once been told stories about fairies and witches, about witches who dressed all in black and offered poisoned apples to poor young girls lost in the forest. None of those children could possibly imagine that a real, live witch was watching them playing now.

That afternoon, Wicca had asked her to try an exercise entirely unrelated to the Tradition of the Moon, an exercise useful to anyone wishing to keep open the bridge between the visible and the invisible.

It was simple enough. She had to lie down, relax and imagine one of the main shopping areas in the city. Then she had to concentrate on one particular shop window and notice every detail of what was in the window, where it was, and how much each thing cost. When she had finished the exercise, she had to go to the street and see if she had been right.

Now she was there in the square watching the children. She had just come back from the shop, and the shop window had been exactly as she'd imagined it. She wondered if this really was an exercise for ordinary people, or if her months of training as a witch had helped. She would never know.

But the shopping street she had imagined was very near to her 'magic place'. 'Nothing happens by chance,' she thought. Her heart was troubled over a matter she could not resolve: Love. She loved Lorens, she was sure of that. She knew that when she was an adept in the Tradition of the Moon, she would see the point of light above his left shoulder. One afternoon, when they'd gone to a café together to drink a cup of hot chocolate near the tower that had inspired James Joyce's *Ulysses*, she had seen that special light in his eyes.

The Magus was right. The Tradition of the Sun was the path of all men, and it was there so that it could be deciphered by anyone who knew how to pray and be patient and who wanted to learn what it had to teach. The more she immersed herself in the Tradition of the Moon, the more she understood and admired the Tradition of the Sun.

The Magus. She was thinking about him again. This was the problem that had brought her back to her 'magic place'. She had thought about him often since that visit to the hunters' cabin. She would like to be there right now so that she could tell him about this latest exercise, but she knew that was just a pretext; what she really wanted was for him to invite her to go for a walk in the forest again. She was sure he would be pleased to see her, and she was beginning to believe, for some mysterious reason – which she didn't even dare to think about – that he enjoyed her company too.

'I've always had too vivid an imagination,' she thought, trying to get the Magus out of her head, but knowing that he would soon be back.

She didn't want to keep thinking about him. She was a woman and familiar with the symptoms of falling in love, something which she had to avoid at all costs. She loved Lorens and wanted things to continue as they were. Her world had changed quite enough.

On Saturday morning, Lorens phoned.

'Let's go for a walk along the cliffs,' he said.

Brida prepared something to eat, and together they endured the long journey in an inadequately heated bus. They reached the village at around midday.

Brida felt excited. In her first year as a student of literature at the university, she had read a lot about the poet who had lived there. He was a mysterious man, who knew a great deal about the Tradition of the Moon; he had been a member of secret societies and left in his books a hidden message for those who seek the spiritual path. His name was W.B. Yeats. She remembered two particular lines by him, which seemed just made for that cold morning, with the seagulls flying over the boats anchored in the little harbour:

I have spread my dreams under your feet;
Tread softly because you tread on my dreams.

They went into the only pub in the village, drank a whiskey to keep out the cold, and then set off. The little tarmac road gave way to a steep climb, and half an hour later they reached what the locals called 'the cliffs'. This was a promontory made up of rocky outcrops that dropped sheer into the sea. There was a path to follow and, even at a leisurely pace, they would be able do the whole walk in less than four hours and still catch the bus back to Dublin.

Brida was delighted at the prospect. Regardless of what emotions life might be holding in reserve for her that year, she always found the winter hard to bear. All she did was go to work during the day, to the university in the evening and to the cinema at weekends. She dutifully performed the rituals and dances Wicca had taught her, but she had a yearning to be out in the world, to see a little nature.

It was overcast and the clouds were very low, but the physical exercise and the whiskey helped fend off the cold. The path was too narrow for them to walk along side by side; Lorens went ahead, and Brida followed a little way behind. It was hard to talk in these circumstances. Nevertheless, they managed to exchange a few words, enough for them to feel each other close and to enjoy the nature around them.

She was gazing with childlike fascination at the landscape. It must have been exactly the same thousands of years ago, in an age when there were no towns, no harbours, no poets, no young women seeking the Tradition of the Moon; then there were only the rocks, the crashing waves, and the seagulls drifting about beneath the low clouds. Now and then, Brida peered over the precipice and felt slightly dizzy. The sea was saying things she couldn't understand; the seagulls were making patterns she couldn't follow. And yet she was looking at that primitive world as if the true wisdom of the Universe lay there rather than in any of the books she'd read or in any of the rituals she practised. As they moved away from the harbour, everything else gradually diminished in importance – her dreams, her daily life, her search. There was only what Wicca called 'God's signature'.

All that remained was that primitive moment among the pure forces of nature, the sense of being alive and in the company of someone she loved.

After nearly two hours of walking, the path suddenly grew wider, and they decided to sit down together to rest. They couldn't stop for long. The cold would soon become unbearable and they would have to move on, but she felt like spending at least a few minutes by his side, looking up at the clouds and listening to the sound of the sea.

Brida could smell the sea air and was aware of the taste of salt in her mouth. She warmed her face against Lorens' jacket. It was a moment of great plenitude. All five of her senses were working.

Yes, all five of her senses were working.

For a fraction of a second, the thought of the Magus entered her mind and then vanished. All she cared about now were those five senses. They must keep working. This was the moment.

'I need to talk to you, Lorens.'

Lorens murmured something or other, but his heart was afraid. As he looked up at the clouds or down at the precipice, he realised that this woman was the most important thing in his life; that she was the explanation, the sole reason for the existence of those rocks, that sky, that winter. If she were not there with him, it wouldn't matter if all the angels of heaven came flying down to comfort him – Paradise would make no sense.

'I want to tell you that I love you,' Brida said softly. 'Because you've shown me the joy of love.'

She felt full, complete, as if the whole landscape were seeping into her soul. He began stroking her hair. And she was sure that, if she took a risk, she would experience love as never before.

Brida kissed him. She felt the taste of his mouth, the touch of his tongue. She was aware of every movement and sensed that he was feeling exactly the same, because the Tradition of the Sun always reveals itself to those who look at the world as if they were seeing it for the first time.

'I want to make love with you right here, Lorens.'

Various thoughts flashed through his mind: they were on a public footpath, someone might come by, some other person crazy enough to visit this place in the middle of winter. But anyone crazy enough to do so would also be able to understand that certain forces, once set in motion, cannot be interrupted.

He slipped his hands under her sweater and stroked her breasts. Brida surrendered herself entirely. The forces of the world were penetrating her five senses and these were becoming transformed into an overwhelming energy. They lay down on the ground between the rock, the precipice and the sea, between the life of the seagulls flying up above and the death of the stones beneath. And they began, fearlessly, to make love, because God protects the innocent.

They no longer felt the cold. Their blood was flowing so fast in their veins that she tore off some of her clothes and so did he. There was no more pain; knees and back were pressed into the stony ground, but that became part of their pleasure, completing it. Brida knew that she was close to orgasm, but it was still a very remote feeling, because she was entirely connected to the world: her body and Lorens' body mingled with the sea and the stones, with life and death. She remained in that state for as long as possible, while some part of her was vaguely conscious that she was doing things she had never done before. What she was feeling, though, was the bringing together once more of herself and the meaning of life; it was a return to the garden of Eden; it was the moment when Eve was reabsorbed into Adam's body and the two halves became Creation.

At last, she could no longer control the world around her, her five senses seemed to break free and she wasn't strong enough to hold on to them. As if struck by a sacred bolt of lightning, she unleashed them, and the world, the seagulls, the taste of salt, the hard earth, the smell of the sea, the clouds, all disappeared, and in their place appeared a vast golden light, which grew and grew until it touched the most distant star in the galaxy.

She gradually came down from that state, and the sea and the clouds reappeared, but everything was filled by a sense of profound peace, the peace of a universe which became, if only for a matter of moments, explicable, because she was in communion with the world. She had discovered another bridge that joined the visible to the invisible, and she would never again forget the path that led to it.

The following day, she phoned Wicca and told her what had happened. For a while, Wicca said nothing.

'Congratulations,' she said at last. 'You've made it.'

She explained that, from then on, the power of sex would bring about profound changes in the way Brida saw and experienced the world.

'You're ready now for the celebration of the Equinox. There's just one more thing.'

'One more thing? But you said that was it!'

'It's quite easy. You simply have to dream of a dress, the dress you will wear on the day.'

'And what if I can't.'

'You will. You've done the most difficult part.'

And then, as so often, she changed the subject. She told Brida that she'd bought a new car and needed to do some shopping. Would Brida like to go with her?

Brida was proud to be invited and asked her boss if she could leave work early. It was the first time Wicca had shown her any kind of affection, even if it was only an invitation to join her on a shopping trip.

She knew that many of Wicca's other students would love to be in her shoes.

Perhaps that afternoon would provide her with a chance to show Wicca how important she was to her and how much she wanted to be her friend. It was difficult for Brida to separate friendship from the spiritual search, and she was hurt because, up until then, her teacher had never shown the slightest interest in her private life. Their conversations never went beyond what Brida needed to know in order to work within the Tradition of the Moon.

At the appointed hour, Wicca was waiting outside in a red MG convertible, with the top down. The car, a British classic, was exceptionally well preserved, with gleaming bodywork and a polished wooden dashboard. Brida didn't even dare hazard a guess at how much it must have cost. The idea that a witch should own such an expensive car frightened her a little. Before she'd known anything about the Tradition of the Moon, she'd heard all kinds of tales in her childhood about witches making terrible pacts with the Devil in exchange for money and power.

'Isn't it a bit cold to drive with the top down?' she asked as she got in.

'I can't wait until summer,' Wicca said, 'I just can't. I've been aching to go for a drive like this for ages.'

That was good. At least, in this respect, she was like any other normal person.

They drove through the streets, receiving admiring glances from older passers-by and a few wolf-whistles and compliments from men.

'It's a good sign that you're worried about not being able to dream about the dress,' said Wicca. Brida, however, had already forgotten about their phone conversation.

'Never stop having doubts. If you ever do, it will be because you've stopped moving forward, and at that point, God will step in and pull the rug from under your feet, because that is His way of controlling His chosen ones, by making sure they always follow their appointed path to the end. If, for any reason, we stop, whether out of complacency, laziness, or out of a mistaken belief that we know enough, He forces us on.

'On the other hand, you must be careful never to allow doubt to paralyse you. Always take the decisions you need to take, even if you're not sure you're doing the right thing. You'll never go wrong if, when you make a decision, you keep in mind an old German proverb that the Tradition of the Moon has adopted: "The Devil is in the detail". Remember that proverb and you'll always be able to turn a wrong decision into a right one.'

Wicca suddenly stopped outside a garage.

'There's a superstition connected to that proverb too,' she said. 'It only comes to our aid when we need it. I've just bought this car, and the devil is in the detail.'

She got out as soon as a mechanic came over to her. 'Is the hood broken, Madam?'

Wicca didn't even answer. She asked him to check the car over for her, and while he was working, the two women sat and drank hot chocolate in a café over the way.

'Watch what the mechanic does,' Wicca said, looking across at the garage. He had the bonnet open and was standing staring at the engine, not even moving.

'He's not touching anything. He's just looking. He's done this job for years, and he knows that the car speaks to him in a special language. It's not his reason that's working now, it's his intuition.'

Suddenly, the mechanic went straight to one particular part of the engine and starting fiddling with it.

'He's found the fault,' Wicca went on. 'He didn't waste a moment, because between him and the car there is perfect communication. Every good mechanic I've ever known has been the same.'

'So have the mechanics I've known,' thought Brida, but she'd always assumed they behaved that way because they didn't know where to start. She'd never noticed that they always started in the right place.

'If they have the wisdom of the Sun in their lives, why don't they try to understand the fundamental questions of the Universe? Why do they prefer to fix cars or work in a bar serving coffee?'

'And what makes you think that we, with our path and our dedication, understand the Universe any better than other people?

'I have many students. They're all perfectly ordinary people, who cry at the movies and worry if their children are late home, even though they know that death is not the end. Witchcraft is merely one way of being close to the Supreme Wisdom, but anything you do can lead you there, as long as you work with love in your heart. We witches can converse with the Soul of the World, see the point of light above the left shoulder of our Soulmate, and contemplate the infinite through the glow and silence of a candle, but we don't understand car engines. Mechanics need us as much as we need them. They find their bridge across to the invisible in a car engine, while we find ours in the Tradition of the Moon, but the bridge connects to the same invisible world.

'Play your part and don't worry about what others do. Believe that God also speaks to them, and that they are as engaged as you are in discovering the meaning of life.'

'The car's fine,' said the mechanic, when they went back to the garage, 'apart from a hose that was about to burst. And that could have caused you serious problems.'

Wicca haggled a little over the price, but she was very glad that she'd remembered the proverb.

They went to one of Dublin's main shopping streets, which also happened to be the location of the shop that Brida had once had to visualise as part of an exercise. Whenever the conversation turned to personal topics, Wicca would respond vaguely or evasively, but she spoke with great verve about trivial matters – prices, clothes, rude shop assistants. Everything she bought that afternoon revealed sophistication and good taste.

Brida knew that it wasn't the done thing to ask someone where she got her money, but so great was her curiosity that she came very close to violating that most elementary rule of politeness.

They ended up in a Japanese restaurant, with a dish of sashimi before them.

'May God bless our food,' said Wicca. 'We are all sailors on an unknown sea; may He make us brave enough to accept this mystery.'

'But you're a Teacher of the Tradition of the Moon,' said Brida. 'You know the answers.'

Wicca sat for a moment, absorbed, looking at the food. Then she said:

'I know how to travel between the present and the past. I know the world of the spirits, and I've communed with forces so amazing that no words in any language could describe them. I could perhaps say that I possess the silent knowledge of the journey that has brought the human race to where it is at this moment.

'But because I know all this, and because I am a Teacher, I also know that we will never ever know the ultimate reason for our existence. We might know the how, where and when of being here, but the why will always be a question that remains unanswered. The main objective of the great Architect of the Universe is known to Him alone, and to no one else.'

A silence fell.

'Right now, while we're here eating, ninety-nine per cent of the people on this planet are, in their own way, struggling with that very question. Why are we here? Many think they've found the answer in religion or in materialism. Others despair and spend their lives and their money trying to grasp the meaning of it all. A few let the question go unanswered and live for the moment, regardless of the results or the consequences.

'Only the brave and those who understand the Traditions of the Sun and the Moon are aware that the only possible answer to the question is I DON'T KNOW.

'This might, at first, seem frightening, leaving us terribly vulnerable in our dealings with the world, with the things of the world and with our own sense of our existence. Once we've got over that initial fear, however, we gradually become accustomed to the only possible solution: to follow our dreams. Having the courage to take the steps we always wanted to take is the only way of showing that we trust in God.

'As soon as we accept this, life takes on a sacred meaning, and we experience the same emotion the Virgin must have felt when, one afternoon in her otherwise very ordinary existence, a stranger appeared to her and made her an offer. "Be it unto me according to thy word," said the Virgin. Because she had understood that the greatest thing a human being can do is to accept the Mystery.'

After another long silence, Wicca again took up her knife and fork and resumed her meal. Brida looked at her, proud to be by her side. She wasn't bothered now by the questions she would never ask, about how Wicca earned her money or if she was in love with someone or jealous of someone else. She thought about the greatness of soul of the true sages, sages who had spent their entire life searching for an answer that did not exist, but who were not tempted to invent an answer when they realised there was none. Instead, they carried on humbly inhabiting a Universe they would never understand. The only way they could truly participate was by following their own desires, their own dreams, because that is how man becomes an instrument of God.

'So what's the point of looking for an answer then?'

'We don't look for an answer, we accept, and then life becomes much more intense, much more brilliant, because we understand that each minute, each step that we take, has a meaning that goes far beyond us as individuals. We realise that somewhere in time and space this question *does* have an answer. We realise that there *is* a reason for us being here, and for us, that is enough.

'We plunge into the Dark Night with faith, we fulfil what the ancient alchemists used to call our Personal Legend and we surrender ourselves fully to each moment, knowing that there is always a hand to guide us, and whether we accept it or not is entirely up to us.'

That night, Brida spent hours listening to music, entirely given over to the miracle of being alive. She thought about her favourite authors. One of them – the English poet William Blake – had, with just one simple phrase, given her enough faith to go in search of wisdom.

What is now proved was once only imagin'd.

It was time to perform one of her rituals. She would spend the next few minutes contemplating a candle flame, and to do so, she sat down before the little altar. The process of contemplation took her back to the afternoon when she and Lorens had made love among the rocks. There were seagulls flying as high as the clouds and as low as the waves.

The fish must have asked themselves how they managed to fly, these mysterious creatures who plunged into their world, then left as quickly as they entered.

The birds must have asked themselves how the creatures they fed on and that lived beneath the waves could possibly manage to breathe under water.

Birds existed and fish existed. Theirs were universes that occasionally collided, but they could not answer each other's questions. And yet both had questions, and the questions had answers.

Brida looked at the flame before her, and a magical atmosphere began to grow around her. This was what normally happened, but that night, the feeling was more intense.

If she were capable of asking a question, it was because, in another Universe, there was an answer. Someone knew it, even if she didn't. She didn't need to understand the meaning of life; it was enough to find someone who did, and then fall asleep in his arms and sleep as a child sleeps, knowing that someone stronger than you is protecting you from all evil and all danger.

When the ritual was over, she said a little prayer in gratitude for the steps she had so far taken. She was grateful because the first person she had asked about magic hadn't tried to explain the Universe to her; instead, he had made her spend the whole night in a dark forest.

She needed to go there and thank him for all he had taught her.

Whenever she went in search of that man, she was looking for something; whenever she found that something, all she did was leave, often without even saying goodbye. But he had shown her the door through which she hoped to pass at the next Equinox. She should at least say 'Thank you'.

No, she wasn't afraid of falling in love with him. She had read things in Lorens' eyes about the hidden side of her own soul, and while she might have her doubts about being able to dream of a dress, as regards his love, about that she was perfectly clear.

'Thank you for accepting my invitation,' she said to the Magus when they sat down. They were sitting in the only pub in the village, which is where she had first noticed the strange light in his eyes.

The Magus said nothing. He noticed that her energy was quite different now; she had clearly managed to awaken the Force.

'On the night you left me alone in the forest, I promised that I'd come back either to thank you or to curse you. I promised that I'd come back when I found my path. But I didn't keep either of those promises. I always came in search of help, and you never let me down. It may be presumptuous of me, but I want you to know that you have acted as God's instrument, and I would like you to be my guest tonight.'

Just as she was about to order two whiskies, he got up, went over to the bar and returned carrying two bottles, one of wine and one of mineral water, and two glasses.

'In Ancient Persia,' he said, 'when two people met to drink together, one of them was chosen to be King of the Night, usually the person who was paying.'

He didn't know if his voice sounded sufficiently steady. He was a man in love, and Brida's energy had changed.

He placed the wine and the mineral water before her.

'It was up to the King of the Night to set the tone of the conversation. If he poured more water than wine into the first glass to be drunk, that meant he wished to speak of serious things. If he poured equal quantities of both, they would speak of both serious and pleasant things. Finally, if he filled the glass with wine and added only a few drops of water, the night would be relaxing and enjoyable.'

Brida filled the glasses to the brim with wine and added only a drop of water to each.

'I came to say thank you,' she said again, 'for teaching me that life is an act of faith, and that I am worthy of the search. That has helped me enormously on the path I've chosen.'

They both drained that first glass quickly. He because he was feeling tense. She because she was feeling relaxed.

'Only light subjects, all right?' Brida said.

The Magus said that since she was the King of the Night, it was up to her to decide what they should talk about.

'I want to know a little about your personal life. I want to know if you ever had an affair with Wicca.'

He nodded. Brida felt an inexplicable tremor of jealousy, but she wasn't sure whether she felt jealous of him or of Wicca.

'But we never considered living together,' he said. They both knew the two Traditions. They both knew that they were not each other's Soulmate.

'I didn't want to learn how to see the point of light,' thought Brida, but she saw now that this was inevitable. That was what love between witches was like.

She drank a little more. She was getting closer to her objective; it would not be long now until the Spring Equinox, and she could afford to relax. It had been a long time since she had allowed herself to drink more than she should, but now, all she had to do was dream of a dress.

They continued talking and drinking. Brida wanted to return to the subject of Wicca, but she needed him to be more relaxed too. She kept both their glasses filled, and they finished the first bottle while in the middle of a conversation about the difficulties of living in such a small village. The locals associated the Magus with the devil.

Brida was pleased to feel important to him; he must be very lonely. Maybe no one in the village ever addressed more than a few polite words to him. They opened another bottle, and she was surprised to see that a Magus, a man who spent all day in the forest seeking communion with God was also capable of drinking and getting drunk.

By the time they had finished the second bottle, she had forgotten that she was there in order to thank the man sitting opposite her. Her relationship with him – she realised now – had always been a veiled challenge. She didn't want to see him as an ordinary person, but she was getting dangerously close to doing just that. She preferred the image of the wise man who had led her to a cabin high up in the trees and who often spent hours contemplating the sunset.

She began to talk about Wicca, to see how he reacted. She said what an excellent Teacher she was and how she had taught her everything she needed to know so far, but in such a subtle way that it was if she'd always known the things she was learning.

'But you have,' said the Magus. 'That is the Tradition of the Sun.'

'He's obviously not going to admit that Wicca is a good teacher,' thought Brida. She drank another glass of wine and continued to talk about her Teacher, but the Magus made no further comment.

'Tell me about you and her,' she said, to see if she could provoke him. She didn't want to know, she really didn't, but it was the best way to get a reaction.

'A case of young love. We were part of a generation that knew no limits, the generation of the Beatles and the Rolling Stones.'

She was surprised to hear this. Far from relaxing her, the wine was making her tense. She still wanted to ask those questions, but now she realised that she wasn't happy with the answers.

'That was when we met,' he went on, unaware of her feelings. 'We were both seeking our respective paths, and they crossed when we happened to go to the same Teacher. Together we learned about the Tradition of the Sun and the Tradition of the Moon, and both, in our own fashion, became Teachers.'

Brida decided to pursue the subject. Two bottles of wine can make complete strangers feel as if they have been friends from childhood; wine gives people courage.

'Why did you split up?'

It was the Magus's turn to order another bottle. She noticed this and grew even more tense. She would hate to find out that he was still in love with Wicca.

'We split up when we learned about Soulmates.'

'If you hadn't found out about those points of light or the special light in your Soulmate's eyes, would you still be together?'

'I don't know. I only know that if we were, it wouldn't work for either of us. We only understand life and the Universe when we find our Soulmate.'

Brida paused for a moment, suddenly lost for words. It was the Magus who took up the conversation.

'Let's go,' he said, after taking only a sip of the wine from that third bottle. 'I need to feel the wind and the cold air on my face.'

'He's getting drunk,' she thought. 'And he's afraid.' She felt proud of herself; she could take her drink better than he could, and she wasn't in the least afraid of losing control. She had come out that night intending to enjoy herself.

'Just a little more. After all, I'm the King of the Night.'

The Magus drank another glass, but he knew he had reached his limit.

'You haven't asked me anything about myself,' she said challengingly. 'Aren't you curious? Or can you use your powers to see right through me?'

For a fraction of a second, she felt she had gone too far, but then she dismissed the thought. She merely noticed a change in the Magus's eyes; there was a completely different light in them now. Something in Brida seemed to open, or, rather, she had the sense of a wall coming down, a feeling that, from then on, everything would be permitted. She remembered the last time they had been together, her desire to stay with him, and his coldness. Now she understood that she hadn't gone there that night in order to thank him, but to seek revenge: to tell him that she'd discovered the Force with another man, a man she loved.

'Why do I need revenge? Why am I angry with him?' she wondered, but the wine wouldn't allow her to answer those questions coherently.

The Magus was looking at the young woman opposite him, and the desire to demonstrate his Power kept coming and going in his mind. On a night very like this, many years ago, his whole life had changed. It might have been the age of the Beatles and the Rolling Stones, but there were also people around at the time in search of unknown forces, forces they didn't even believe in. They made use of magical powers, all the while thinking that they were stronger than the powers themselves, convinced that they'd be able to leave the Tradition as soon as boredom set in. He had been one of those people. He had entered the sacred world through the Tradition of the Moon, learning rituals and crossing the bridge that connects the visible and the invisible.

At first, he dabbled in these powers on his own, learning from books, with no help from anyone. Then he met his Teacher. At their first meeting, his Teacher told him that he would be better off learning through the Tradition of the Sun, but the Magus didn't want that. The Tradition of the Moon was more interesting; it involved performing ancient rituals and learning the wisdom of time. And so his Teacher taught him the

Tradition of the Moon, saying that perhaps this was the path that would eventually lead him to the Tradition of the Sun.

At the time, he was utterly sure of himself, of life, and of his conquests. A brilliant career lay ahead of him, and he intended using the Tradition of the Moon to achieve his goals. In order to do so, witchcraft demanded that he first become a Teacher, and that he never infringe the one limitation placed on all Teachers of the Tradition of the Moon: never to interfere with another person's free will. He could forge his own path in the world by using his magical knowledge, but he couldn't get rid of someone simply because they were in his way nor could he force them to follow him on his path. That was the one prohibition, the only tree of whose fruit he must not eat.

And everything went smoothly until he fell in love with one of his Teacher's other students, and she fell in love with him. Both knew the Traditions; he knew that he was not her man, and she knew that she was not his woman. Nevertheless, they surrendered to their love, leaving life in charge of separating them when the time came. Far from diminishing their passion, this only made them live each moment as if it were their last, and the love between them had all the intensity of things that take on an eternal quality precisely because they're going to die.

Then one day, she met another man. This man knew nothing of the Traditions, nor did he have a point of light above his left shoulder or the special light in his eyes that reveals someone to be your Soulmate. Love, however, is no respecter of reasons, and she fell in love; as far as she was concerned, her time with the Magus had come to an end.

They quarrelled and fought; he begged and implored. He subjected himself to all the usual humiliations endured by people in love. He learned things he never dreamed he would learn: hope, fear, acceptance. 'He doesn't have the point of light above his left shoulder,' he argued, 'you told me that yourself.' But she didn't care. Before she did finally meet her Soulmate, she wanted to know other men, to experience the world.

The Magus set a limit on his pain. When he reached it, he would forget all about her. For a reason he could now no longer remember, he did reach that limit, but instead of forgetting her, he discovered that his Teacher was right – emotions were like wild horses and it required wisdom to be able to control them. His passion was stronger than all his years of studying the Tradition of the Moon, stronger than all the mind-control techniques he had learned, stronger than the rigid discipline to which he'd had to submit in order to get where he was. Passion was a blind force, and it kept whispering in his ear that he must not lose that woman.

He could do nothing against her; she was a Teacher, like him, and she had learned her trade over many incarnations, some filled with fame and glory, others marked by fire and suffering. She would know how to defend herself.

However, there was a third party involved in this furious struggle. A man caught in destiny's mysterious web, a web that neither Magi nor Witches can understand. An ordinary man, perhaps as in love with that woman as he was, a man who wanted her to be happy and to do his best for her. An ordinary man, whom Providence's mysterious designs had thrown into the middle of this battle between a man and a woman who knew the Tradition of the Moon.

One night, when he could stand the pain no longer, he ate of the forbidden fruit. Using the power and knowledge that the wisdom of Time had taught him, he removed that man from the woman he loved.

He did not know to this day whether or not she ever found out, but it may well be that she had already grown tired of her new conquest and didn't much mind him leaving. However, his Teacher knew. His Teacher always knew everything, and the Tradition of the Moon was implacable with those Initiates who used Black Magic, especially to influence that most important and most vulnerable of human emotions: Love.

When he confronted his Teacher, he understood that the sacred vow he had made was impossible to break. He understood that the forces he thought he could control and use were far more powerful than he was.

He understood that he was on his chosen path, but that it was not a path like any other. And he understood that in this incarnation he could never leave that path.

Now that he had erred, he had to pay a price, and the price was to drink that cruellest of poisons – loneliness – until Love felt that he had once more been transformed into a Teacher. Then, the same Love that he had wounded would set him free again and finally reveal his Soulmate to him.

'You haven't asked me anything about myself. Aren't you curious? Or can you use your powers to see right through me?'

His past took no more than a second to flash through his mind, just long enough for him to decide whether to allow things to happen as they would in the Tradition of the Sun or to speak to her about the point of light and thus interfere in fate.

Brida wanted to be a witch, but she hadn't yet achieved that ambition. He remembered the cabin high up in the tree, when he had come very close to telling her; now he was tempted again, because, having lowered his guard, he had forgotten that the Devil is in the detail. We are all masters of our own destiny. We can so easily make the same mistakes over and over. We can so easily flee from everything that we desire and which life so generously places before us.

Alternatively, we can surrender ourselves to Divine Providence, take God's hand, and fight for our dreams, believing that they always arrive at the right moment.

'Let's go,' said the Magus. And Brida could see that this time he was serious.

She made a point of paying the bill; after all, she was the King of the Night. They put on their coats and went out into the cold, which was now less bitter – in a matter of weeks, it would be spring.

They walked together to the bus station. A bus was due to leave in a few minutes. Out in the cold, Brida's feelings of irritation were replaced by a terrible confusion, which she could not explain. She didn't want to get on that bus; everything was wrong; it seemed to her that she'd entirely failed to achieve her main objective of the evening and that she needed to put everything right before she left. She had come there to thank him, and yet she was behaving just as she had on the previous two occasions.

She didn't get on the bus, saying that she felt sick.

Fifteen minutes passed, and another bus arrived.

'I don't want to leave,' she said, 'not because I drank too much and feel ill, but because I've spoiled everything. I haven't thanked you as I should have.'

'This is the last bus,' said the Magus.

'I'll get a taxi later, even if it's expensive.'

When the bus left, Brida regretted not having got on it. She was confused. She had no idea what she wanted. 'I'm drunk,' she thought, and said:

'Let's go for a walk. I need to sober up.'

They strolled through the empty village, with the streetlamps lit and all the windows dark. 'It's just not possible. I saw the light in Lorens' eyes and yet I want to stay here with this man.' She was just an ordinary, fickle woman, unworthy of all that she had learned and experienced through witchcraft. She was ashamed of herself: all it took was a few glasses of wine, and Lorens – her Soulmate – and everything she'd learned in the Tradition of the Moon were suddenly of no importance. She wondered briefly if she'd been wrong, perhaps the light in Lorens' eyes wasn't the light spoken of in the Tradition of the Sun. But, no, she was merely fooling herself; no one can fail to recognise the light in the eyes of their Soulmate.

If she were to meet Lorens in a crowded theatre, without ever having spoken to him before, the moment their eyes met, she would know for sure that he was the man for her. She would find a way of approaching him, and he would welcome her approaches, because the Traditions are never wrong: Soulmates always find each other in the end. Long before she knew anything about Soulmates, she had often heard people speak about that inexplicable phenomenon: Love at First Sight.

Any human being could recognise that light, without any need for magical powers. She had known about it before she knew of its existence. She had seen it, for example, in the Magus's eyes, the first time they went to the pub together.

She stopped.

'I'm drunk,' she thought again. She must simply forget all about it. She needed to count her money to see if she had enough for a taxi fare back. That *was* important.

But she had seen the light in the Magus's eyes, the light that showed he was her Soulmate.

'You're very pale,' said the Magus. 'You must have drunk too much.'

'It will pass. Let's sit down for a while until it does. Then I'll go home.'

They sat on a bench while she fumbled around in her bag in search of money. She could stand up, find a taxi and leave forever; she had a Teacher and she knew how to continue her path. She knew her Soulmate too; if she decided to get up now and leave, she would still be fulfilling the mission God had set her.

She might only be twenty-one, but she already knew it was possible to encounter two Soulmates in the same incarnation, and that the result was bound to be pain and suffering.

How could she avoid that?

'I'm not going home,' she said. 'I'm staying here.'

The Magus's eyes shone, and what had been only a hope became a certainty.

They continued walking. The Magus watched Brida's aura change colour many times and hoped she was taking the right path. He understood the storms and earthquakes shaking the soul of his Soulmate, but knew that this was in the nature of transformations. That's how the earth and the stars and mankind are transformed.

They left the village and were walking out into the countryside, towards the mountains where they always met, when Brida asked him to stop.

'Let's go this way,' she said, turning down a path that led into a wheatfield, although why she didn't know. She simply felt a sudden need to feel the force of nature and the friendly spirits who, ever since the world was created, have inhabited all the lovely places of the planet. A huge moon was shining in the sky, illuminating the path and the countryside around.

Without a word, the Magus followed. Deep in his heart, he thanked God for having believed and for not allowing him to make the same mistake again, as he had been on the point of doing just a minute before his prayers were answered.

They walked through the wheatfield, which was transformed by the moonlight into a silver sea. Brida was walking aimlessly, with no idea what her next step would be. A voice inside her was telling her that she should go forward, that she was just as strong as her forebears, and that there was no need to worry, because they were there guiding her steps and protecting her with the Wisdom of Time.

They stopped in the middle of the field. They were surrounded by mountains, and on one of those mountains was a rock from which one could get a fine view of the sunset; there was a hunters' cabin too, higher up than all the others, and a place where, one night, a young woman had confronted fear and darkness.

'I'm ready,' she thought to herself. 'I'm ready and I know I'm protected.' She conjured up the image of the candle at home always burning, her seal with the Tradition of the Moon.

'Here's a good place,' she said, stopping.

She picked up a twig and traced a large circle in the earth while she recited the sacred names her Teacher had taught her. She didn't have her ritual dagger with her, she had none of her sacred objects, but her ancestors were there, and they were telling her that, in order not to be burned at the stake, they had consecrated their kitchen utensils.

'Everything in this world is sacred,' she said. That twig was sacred.

'Yes,' responded the Magus. 'Everything in this world is sacred, and a grain of sand can be a bridge to the invisible.'

'At this moment, though, the bridge to the invisible is my Soulmate,' Brida said.

His eyes filled with tears. God was just.

The two of them entered the circle and she ritually closed it. This was the protective gesture that magi and witches had used since time immemorial.

'You were generous enough to show me your world,' said Brida. 'I perform this ritual now to show that I belong to that world.'

She raised her arms to the moon and invoked the magical forces of nature. She had often seen her Teacher do this when they went to the wood, but now she was doing it, confident that nothing would go wrong. The forces were telling her that she did not need to learn anything; she had only to remember the many times she had done this in her many lives as a witch. She prayed then that the harvest would be good, and that the field would always be fertile. There she was, the priestess who, in other ages, had brought together the earth's knowledge and the transformation of the seed, and had prayed while her man was working the land.

The Magus let Brida take the initial steps. He knew that, at a certain point, he would have to take control, but he needed to leave recorded on space and time the fact that she had begun the process. His Teacher, who, at that moment, was wandering some astral plane awaiting his next life, was there in that field of wheat, just as he had been there in the pub, during his last temptation, and he was doubtless happy that his student had learned from his suffering. The Magus listened in silence to Brida's invocations. When she stopped, she said:

'I don't know why I have done all this, but I know I have done my part.'

'I'll continue,' he said.

Then he turned to the north and imitated the cries of birds that existed now only in myths and legends. That was the only detail that had been lacking. Wicca was a good Teacher and had taught Brida almost everything, apart from the ending.

When the sound of the sacred pelican and the phoenix had been invoked, the whole circle filled with light, a mysterious light, which illuminated nothing around it, but which was, nonetheless, a light. The Magus looked at his Soulmate and there she was, resplendent in her eternal body, with a golden aura and filaments of light emerging from her navel and her head. He knew that she was seeing the same thing, as well as the point of light above his left shoulder, slightly blurred perhaps because of the wine they'd drunk earlier.

'My Soulmate,' she said softly, when she saw the point of light.

'I am going to walk with you through the Tradition of the Moon,' said the Magus. And at once the wheatfield around them became a grey desert, in which there was a temple with women all in white dancing before the temple's vast door. Brida and the Magus were watching this from high up on a dune, and she didn't know if the people could see her.

She felt the Magus's presence beside her and wanted to ask him what the vision meant, but she could not speak. He saw the fear in her eyes, and they returned to the circle of light in the wheatfield.

'What was that?' she asked.

'A present from me to you. That is one of the eleven secret temples of the Tradition of the Moon. A gift of love and gratitude for the fact that you exist and because I have waited so long to find you.'

'Take me with you,' she said. 'Show me how to walk through your world.'

And together they travelled through time and space, through the two Traditions. Brida saw meadows full of flowers, animals she had only read about in books, mysterious castles and cities that seemed to float on clouds of light. The sky lit up as the Magus drew for her, above the wheatfield, the sacred symbols of the Tradition. At one point, they appeared to be in the icy landscape of one of the Earth's two poles, but it was not our planet: other smaller creatures, with long fingers and strange eyes were working on a vast spaceship. Whenever she was about to say something to him, the images would vanish to be replaced by others. Brida understood with her woman's soul that the man by her side was trying to show her everything he had learned over the years, and that he must have been waiting all this time simply to present her with this gift. He could give himself to her now without fear, because she was his Soulmate. She could travel with him through the Elysian Fields, where the enlightened souls live, and which are visited now and then by other souls still in search of enlightenment so that they can nourish themselves with hope.

She could not have said how much time had passed before she found herself back with that luminous being inside the circle she herself had drawn. She had known love before, but until that night love had also meant fear. That fear, however slight, was always a veil; you could see almost everything through it, but not the colours. And at that moment, with her Soulmate there before her, she understood that love was a feeling completely bound up with colour, like thousands of rainbows superimposed one on top of the other.

'How much I missed simply because I was afraid of missing it,' she thought, gazing at those rainbows.

She was lying down, and the luminous being was on top of her, with a point of light above his left shoulder and filaments of light pouring forth from his head and his navel.

'I wanted to speak to you, but I couldn't,' she said.

'That was because of the wine,' he replied.

The pub, the wine and the feeling of irritation were now but a distant memory to Brida.

'Thank you for the visions.'

'They weren't visions,' said the luminous being. 'What you saw was the wisdom of the Earth and of a distant planet.'

Brida didn't want to talk about that. She didn't want any lessons. She wanted only what she had experienced.

'Am I full of light too?'

'Yes, just as I am. The same colour, the same light and the same beams of energy.'

The colour was golden now, and the waves of energy emerging from navel and head were a brilliant pale blue.

'I feel that we were lost and now are saved,' said Brida.

'I'm tired. We should go back. I had a lot to drink too.'

Brida knew that somewhere there existed a world of pubs, wheatfields and bus stations, but she didn't want to go back there; all she wanted was to stay in that field forever. She heard a distant voice making invocations, while the light around her gradually faded, then vanished completely. An enormous moon lit up the sky, illuminating the countryside. They were naked and in each other's arms. And they felt neither cold nor shame.

* * *

The Magus asked Brida to close the ritual, since she had begun it. Brida pronounced the words she knew, and he helped where necessary. When the last formulae had been spoken, he opened the magic circle. They got dressed and sat down on the ground.

'Let's leave this place,' said Brida after a while. The Magus got up and she followed. She didn't know what to say; she felt awkward and so did he. They had confessed their love to each other and now, like any other couple in those circumstances, they were embarrassed to look each other in the eye.

Then the Magus broke the silence.

'You must go back to Dublin. I know the number of a taxi firm.'

Brida didn't know whether to feel disappointed or relieved. The feeling of joy was giving way to nausea and a throbbing head. She was sure that she would make very bad company.

'Fine,' she said.

They turned and walked back to the village. He phoned for a taxi from a telephone box. Then they sat on the kerb, waiting for the cab to arrive.

'I want to thank you for tonight,' she said.

He said nothing.

'I don't know if the Equinox festival is just for witches, but it will be a very important day for me.'

'A party is a party.'

'Then I would like to invite you.'

He made a gesture as if wanting to change the

subject. He must have been thinking the same thing she was: how hard it was to leave your Soulmate once you'd found them. She imagined him going home alone, wondering when she would come back. She would come back, because her heart was telling her to, but the solitude of forests is harder to bear than the solitude of towns.

'I don't know if love appears suddenly,' Brida went on, 'but I know that I'm open to love, ready for love.'

The taxi came. Brida looked again at the Magus and felt that he had grown many years younger.

'I'm ready for love too,' he said.

The sunlight poured into the spacious kitchen through the sparkling clean windows.

'Did you sleep well, love?'

Her mother put a mug of tea down on the table, along with some toast. Then she went back to the cooker, where she was frying eggs and bacon.

'Yes, I did, thanks. By the way, is my dress ready? I need it for the party the day after tomorrow.'

Her mother brought her the eggs and bacon and sat down. She knew that something odd was going on with her daughter, but could do nothing about it. She would like to talk to her today as she never had before, but she would achieve little if she did. There was a new world out there, a world she didn't know.

She was afraid for her daughter because she loved her and because Brida was alone in that new world.

'My dress will be ready, won't it, Mum?'

'Yes, by lunchtime,' her mother replied. And that made her happy. At least some things in the world hadn't changed. There were certain problems that mothers continued to solve for their daughters.

She hesitated, then asked:

'How's Lorens?'

'Fine. He's coming to pick me up tomorrow evening.'

She felt simultaneously relieved and sad. Problems of the heart always bruised the soul, and she thanked God that her daughter had no such problems. On the other hand, that was perhaps the one area on which she could advise her, love having changed little over the centuries.

They set off for a walk around the little village where Brida had spent her childhood. The houses had remained unchanged and people were still doing the same things they always had. Her daughter met a few old school friends, who now worked either at the village's one bank or at the stationer's. They said hello and stopped to chat. Some said how Brida had grown, others how pretty she looked. Around ten o'clock they dropped in at the café her mother used to go to on Saturdays, before she met her husband, in the days when she was still hoping to meet someone and be swept up in some whirlwind romance that would put a stop to the endless identical days.

She looked at her daughter again as she told her the latest news about the various people in the village. Brida was still interested, and this pleased her.

'I really do have to have the dress today,' Brida said. She seemed worried, but that couldn't be the reason. She knew that her mother would never let her down.

Her mother decided to take a risk and ask the kind of question children always hate, because they're independent, free and capable of solving their own problems.

'Is anything worrying you?'

'Have you ever been in love with two men at once, Mum?' There was a defiant note in her voice, as if life had set its traps only for her.

Her mother took a bite of her cake. A distant look came into her eyes, as she went off in search of a time that was almost lost.

'Yes, I have.'

Brida stared at her in amazement.

Her mother smiled and invited her to continue their walk.

'Your father was my first and greatest love,' she said, once they'd left the café. 'And I'm still very happy with him. When I was younger than you are now, I had everything I could have dreamed of. At the time, my friends and I believed that love was the only reason for living. If you failed to find someone, then you could never claim to have realised your dreams.'

'Stick to the point, Mum.' Brida was impatient.

'I had other dreams too, though. I dreamed, for example, of doing what you did, going off to the big city and discovering the world that lay beyond my village. The only way I could get my parents to accept my decision was by telling them that I needed to follow some course of study that wasn't available locally.

'The sleepless nights I spent, thinking about how to broach the subject with them. I planned exactly what I was going to say and what they would say in reply and how I would answer.'

Her mother had never spoken to her like this before. Brida felt a mixture of affection and regret. They could have enjoyed other such moments, but they were both too caught up in their own worlds and their own values.

'Two days before I was going to talk to my parents, I met your father. I looked into his eyes and saw a special light there, as if I'd met the person I most wanted to meet in the world.'

'Yes, I've had the same experience.'

'After I met your father, I realised, too, that my search was over. I didn't need any other explanation of the world. I didn't feel frustrated to be living here, always seeing the same people and doing the same things. Every day was different, because of the great love between us.

'We started going out together and then we got married. I never talked to him about my dreams of going to live in a big city, of discovering other places and other people. Because suddenly, the whole world fitted into my village. Love became my explanation for life.'

'You mentioned someone else, Mum.'

'Let me show you something,' her mother said in reply.

They walked to the bottom of the steps that led up to the Catholic church in the village, and which had been destroyed and then rebuilt over the centuries. Brida used to go to mass there every Sunday and she remembered that, as a child, climbing those steps had been really hard. At the beginning of each stretch of balustrade was the carving of a saint – St Paul to the left and St James to the right – rather worn by time and by tourists. The ground was covered in dry leaves, as if autumn were about to arrive, not spring.

The church was at the top of the hill, and it was impossible to see it from where they were because of the trees. Her mother sat down on the first step and invited Brida to do the same.

'This is where it happened,' she said. 'One afternoon, for some reason or other, I decided to come here to pray. I needed to be alone, to think about my life, and I thought the church would be a good place to do so.

'When I got here, however, I met a man. He was sitting where you are now, with two suitcases beside him, and he looked totally lost, desperately leafing through the book he was holding. I thought he must be a tourist in search of a hotel and so I went over to him. I even started talking to him. He seemed a bit startled at first, but then he relaxed.

'He said that he wasn't lost. He was an archaeologist and had been driving north – where some ruins had been found – when the engine packed up. A mechanic would arrive soon, and so he'd decided to visit the church while he waited. He asked me about the village and the other villages nearby, about historic monuments.

'Suddenly, all the problems I'd been grappling with disappeared as if by magic. I felt really useful and started telling him everything I knew, feeling that the many years I'd spent in the region at last had some meaning. Before me was a man who had studied peoples and societies, who might hold in his memory, for the benefit of future generations, everything I'd heard or discovered when I was a child. That man sitting on the steps made me understand that I was important to the world and to the history of my country. I felt necessary, and that's the best feeling a human being can have.

'When I'd finished telling him about the church, we went on to talk about other things. I told him how proud I was of my village, and he responded with some words by a writer whose name I don't recall now, something about how understanding your own village helps you understand the world.'

'Tolstoy,' said Brida.

But her mother was still travelling in time, just as she herself had done one day, except that her mother didn't require cathedrals adrift in space, subterranean libraries, or dusty books; she needed only the memory of that spring afternoon and a man sitting on the steps with his suitcases.

'We talked for quite a while. I had the whole afternoon free to spend with him, but since the mechanic might arrive at any moment, I decided to make the most of every second. I asked him about his world, about excavations, about the challenges of spending his life looking for the past in the present. He spoke to me of the warriors, wise men and pirates who had once inhabited our country.

'Before I knew it, the sun was low on the horizon, and never, in all my life, had time passed so quickly. I sensed that he felt the same. He kept asking me questions to keep the conversation going, not giving me time to say that I had to leave. He talked non-stop, telling me all about his experiences, and he wanted to know everything about me too. I could see in his eyes that he desired me, even though, at the time, I was nearly twice the age you are now.

'It was spring, there was a lovely smell of new things in the air, and I felt young again. There's a flower that only blooms in the autumn; well, that afternoon, I felt like that flower. As if, suddenly, in the autumn of my life, when I thought I'd experienced everything I could experience, that man had appeared on the steps purely to show me that feelings – love, for example – do not grow old along with the body. Feelings form part of a world I don't know, but it's a world where there's no time, no space, no frontiers.'

She remained silent for a while. Her eyes were still far-off, fixed on that distant spring.

'There was I, like a thirty-eight-year-old adolescent, feeling that someone desired me. He didn't want me to leave. Then all of a sudden, he stopped talking. He looked deep into my eyes and smiled. It was as if he'd understood with his heart what I was thinking, and wanted to tell me that it was true, that I *was* very important to him. For some time, we said nothing, and then we said goodbye. The mechanic had still not arrived.

'For many days, I wondered if that man really had existed, or if he was an angel sent by God to teach me the secret lessons of life. In the end, I decided that he had been a real man, a man who had loved me, even if only for an afternoon, and during that afternoon, he'd given me everything he had kept to himself throughout his whole life: his struggles, his joys, his difficulties and his dreams. That afternoon I gave myself wholly as well – I was his companion, his wife, his audience, his lover. In a matter of only a few hours, I experienced the love of a lifetime.'

Mother looked at daughter. She hoped her daughter had understood, but deep down, she felt that Brida lived in a world in which that kind of love had no place.

'I've never stopped loving your father, not for a single day,' she concluded. 'He's always been by my side, doing his best, and I want to be with him until the end. But the heart's a mysterious thing, and I still don't really understand what happened that afternoon. What I do know is that meeting that man left me feeling more confident, and showed me I was still capable of loving and being loved, and it taught me something else that I'll never forget: finding one important thing in your life doesn't mean you have to give up all the other important things.

'I still think of him sometimes. I'd like to know where he is, if he found what he was looking for that afternoon, if he's still alive, or if God took his soul. I know he'll never come back, which is why I could love him with such strength and such certainty, because I would never lose him; he had given himself to me entirely that afternoon.'

Her mother got up.

'I'd better go home and finish making your dress,' she said.

'I think I'll stay here for a while,' Brida replied.

She went over to her daughter and kissed her fondly.

'Thank you for listening to me. It's the first time I've ever told anyone that story. I was always afraid I might die without having done so, and that it would be wiped forever from the face of the Earth. Now you will keep it for me.'

Brida went up the steps and stood outside the church. This small, round building was the pride of the region. It was one of the first places of Christian worship in Ireland, and every year, scholars and tourists came to visit it. Nothing remained of the original fifth-century structure, apart from some fragments of floor; each destruction, however, had left some part intact and so the visitor could trace the history of the various architectural styles that made up the church.

Inside, an organ was playing, and Brida stood outside for a while, listening to the music. Everything was so clearly laid out in that church; the universe was exactly where it should be, and anyone coming in through its doors had no need to worry about anything. There were no mysterious forces far above, no Dark Nights that called on one to believe without understanding. There was no more talk of burning people at the stake, and the religions of the world lived together as if they were allies, binding man once more to God. Her island was still an exception to that peaceful co-existence – in the North, people still killed each other in the name of religion, but that would eventually end. God had almost been explained away: He was our generous Father, and we were all saved.

'I'm a witch,' she said to herself, struggling against a growing impulse to enter the church. Hers was now a different Tradition, and even if it was the same God, if she walked through those doors she would be profaning the place, and would, in turn, be profaned.

She lit a cigarette and stared across at the horizon, trying not to think about these things. She thought, instead, of her mother. She felt like running back home, flinging her arms about her neck, and telling her that in two days' time she was going to be initiated into the Great Mysteries of witchcraft, that she had made journeys in time, that she had experienced the power of sex, that she could guess what was in a shop window using only the techniques of the Tradition of the Moon. She needed love and understanding, because she, too, knew stories she could tell no one.

The organ stopped playing, and Brida once again heard the voices of the village, the singing of the birds, the wind stirring the branches and announcing the coming of spring. At the back of the church, a door opened and closed. Someone had left. For a moment, she saw herself on a Sunday in her childhood, standing where she was now, feeling irritated because the mass was so long and Sunday was the only day when she was free to explore the fields.

'I must go in.' Perhaps her mother would understand what she was feeling, but at that moment, she was far away. There before her was an empty church. She had never asked Wicca precisely what Christianity's role had been in everything that happened. She had a sense that if she walked through that door, she would be betraying all her sisters who had been burned at the stake.

'But then I was burned at the stake too,' she said to herself. She remembered the prayer Wicca had said on the day commemorating the martyrdom of the witches. And in that prayer, she had mentioned Jesus and the Virgin Mary. Love was above everything else, and there was no hatred in love, only the occasional mistake. At one point, men may have decided to make themselves God's representatives and subsequently made mistakes, but God had nothing to do with that.

When she did finally go in, there was no one else inside. A few lit candles showed that someone had taken the trouble that morning to renew their alliance with a force they could only sense, and in that way had crossed the bridge between the visible and the invisible. She regretted her thoughts before entering the church: nothing was explained here either, and people had to take a chance and plunge into the Dark Night of Faith. Before her, arms outspread, was that seemingly simple God.

He could not help her. She was alone with her decisions, and no one could help her. She needed to learn to take risks. She didn't have the same advantages as the crucified man before her, who had known what his mission was, because he was the son of God. He had never made a mistake. He had never known ordinary human love, only love for his Father. All he needed to do was to reveal his wisdom and teach humankind the true path to heaven.

But was that all? She remembered a Sunday catechism class, when the priest had been more inspired than usual. They'd been studying the episode when Jesus, sweating blood, was praying to God and asking Him to remove the cup from which he was being forced to drink.

'But why, if he already knew he was the son of God?' asked the priest. 'Because he only knew it with his heart. If he was absolutely sure, his mission would be meaningless, because he would not be entirely human. Being human means having doubts and yet still continuing on your path.'

She looked again at the image, and for the first time in her entire life, felt closer to it. There perhaps was a man, frightened and alone, facing death and asking: 'Father, Father, why hast thou forsaken me?' If he said that, it was because even he wasn't sure where he was going. He had taken a chance and plunged, as all men do, into the Dark Night, knowing that he would only find the answer at the end of his journey. He, too, had to go through the anxiety of making decisions, of leaving his father and mother and his little village to go in search of the secrets of men and the mysteries of the Law.

If he had been through all that, then he must have known love, even though the Gospels never mention this – love between people is much more difficult to understand than love for a Supreme Being. But now she remembered that, when he had risen again, the first person to whom he appeared was a woman, who had accompanied him to the last.

The silent image appeared to agree with her. He had known people, wine, bread, parties and all the beauties of the world. It was impossible that he had not also known the love of a woman, which is why he had sweated blood on the Mount of Olives, because, having known the love of one person, it was very hard to leave the Earth and to sacrifice himself for the love of all men.

He had experienced everything the world could offer and yet he continued on his journey, knowing that the Dark Night could end on the cross or on the pyre.

'Lord, we're all in the world to run the risks of that Dark Night. I'm afraid of death, but even more afraid of wasting my life. I'm afraid of love, because it involves things that are beyond our understanding; it sheds such a brilliant light, but the shadow it casts frightens me.'

She suddenly realised that she was praying. That silent, simple God was looking at her, apparently understanding her words and taking them seriously.

For a while, she sat waiting for a response from him, but heard not a sound and saw not a sign. The answer was there before her, in that man nailed to the cross. He had played his part, and shown to the world that, if everyone played their part, no one else would have to suffer, because he had suffered for all those who'd had the courage to fight for their dreams.

Brida found herself quietly weeping, although she didn't quite know why.

The day was overcast, but it wasn't going to rain. Lorens had lived in that city for many years and knew its clouds. He got up and went into the kitchen to make some coffee. Brida joined him just as the water was boiling.

'You came to bed very late last night,' he said.

She didn't answer.

'Today's the day,' he went on, 'and I know how important it is to you. I would love to be there with you.'

'It's a party,' said Brida.

'What does that mean?'

'It's a party, and for as long as we've known each other, we've always gone to parties together. You're invited too.'

The Magus went out to see if the previous day's rain had damaged the bromeliads in his garden. They were fine, and he smiled to himself; it seemed that the forces of nature did sometimes collaborate.

He thought about Wicca. She wouldn't be able to see the points of light, because they were visible only to the respective Soulmates, but she was sure to notice the energy from the rays of light moving between him and her student. Witches were, above all else, women.

The Tradition of the Moon described this as the 'Vision of Love', and although it was something that could happen between people who were not each other's Soulmate, but merely in love, he imagined that it would, nevertheless, fill her with anger, female anger, the kind felt by Snow White's stepmother, who could not allow another woman to be more beautiful than her.

Wicca, however, was a Teacher and would immediately realise how absurd such feelings of anger were, but, by then, her aura would already have changed colour.

He would go over to her then, kiss her on the cheek and say that he could see she was jealous.

She would deny this, and he would ask why she was angry.

She would say that she was a woman and didn't need to explain her feelings. He would give her another kiss on the cheek, because what she said was true. And he would tell her how much he'd missed her during the time they'd been apart, and that he still admired her more than any other woman in the world, with the exception of Brida, because Brida was his Soulmate.

Wicca, being a wise woman, would feel happy then.

'I must be getting old,' he thought. 'I'm starting to imagine conversations.' Then it occurred to him that it wasn't just a matter of age; that was how men in love had always behaved.

Wicca was pleased because the rain had stopped and the clouds would clear before nightfall. Nature needed to be in accord with the works of human beings.

She had taken all the necessary steps; everyone had played their part; everything was in place.

She went over to the altar and invoked her Teacher. She asked him to be present that night. Three new witches were to be initiated into the Great Mysteries, and she had sole responsibility for their initiation.

Then she went into the kitchen to make some coffee. She squeezed some orange juice and ate some toast and a few crispbreads. She still took care of her appearance, because she knew how pretty she was. She didn't need to neglect her beauty in order to prove that she was also intelligent and capable.

While she distractedly stirred her coffee, she remembered a day just like this many years before, when her Teacher had sealed her destiny with the Great Mysteries. For a moment, she tried to imagine the person she had been then, what her dreams had been, what she'd wanted from life.

'I must be getting old,' she said out loud, 'sitting here, thinking about the past.' She drank her coffee and began her preparations. There were still things to do. She knew, though, that she wasn't getting old. In her world, Time did not exist.

Brida was surprised by the number of cars parked by the roadside. That morning's heavy clouds had been replaced by a clear sky from which the last rays of the setting sun were now fading. Despite the distinct chill in the air, it was still the first day of spring.

She invoked the protection of the spirits of the forest, and then looked at Lorens. He rather awkwardly repeated the same words, and yet he seemed quite happy to be there. If they were to remain together, they would each, from time to time, have to enter the other's reality. Between them, too, there existed a bridge between the visible and the invisible. Magic was present in their every act.

They walked quickly through the wood and soon reached the clearing. Brida was prepared now for what she saw: men and women of all ages, and doubtless from a wide range of professions, were gathered in groups, talking and trying to make the whole event seem like the most natural thing in the world. In reality, though, they were feeling as perplexed as she and Lorens.

'Are all these people part of the ceremony?' Lorens asked, for he hadn't been expecting such a crowd.

Brida explained that some, like him, were guests. She didn't know exactly who would be taking part, but all would be revealed at the chosen moment.

They selected a corner to put their things down, including the bag Lorens was carrying. Inside were Brida's dress and three bottles of wine. Wicca had recommended that each person, both participants and guests, should bring a large bottle of wine. Before they left the house, Lorens had asked who the other guest was. Brida told him that it was the Magus whom she went to visit in the mountains, and Lorens gave the matter no further thought.

'Imagine,' he heard a woman next to him comment, 'imagine what my friends would say if they knew I was at a real witches' Sabbath.'

A witches' Sabbath. The celebration that had survived the spilled blood, the fires, the Age of Reason and oblivion. Lorens tried to reassure himself; after all, there were many other people like him there. However, a shudder ran through him when he saw a pile of logs in the middle of the clearing.

Wicca was talking to some other people, but as soon as she saw Brida, she came over to say hello and to ask if she was all right. Brida thanked her for her kindness and introduced Lorens.

'And I've invited someone else as well,' she said.

Wicca looked at her, surprised, then smiled broadly.

Brida was sure she knew who she meant.

'I'm glad,' Wicca said. 'After all, it's his celebration too. And it's ages since I saw that old wizard. Maybe he's learned a thing or two.'

More people arrived, and Brida couldn't tell who were the guests and who were the participants. Half an hour later, when almost a hundred people were gathered in the clearing, talking quietly, Wicca called for silence.

'This is a ceremony,' she said, 'but it is also a celebration. And no celebration can begin without everyone filling their glass.'

She opened her bottle of wine and filled the glass of the person next to her. The wine was soon flowing freely, and the voices grew louder. Brida didn't want to drink. Still fresh in her memory was a field of wheat in which a man had shown her the secret temples of the Tradition of the Moon. Besides, the guest she was expecting had still not arrived.

Lorens, on the other hand, was starting to feel much more relaxed and had started chatting to the people around him.

'It really is a party!' he said to Brida, smiling. He had come there expecting something extraordinary, but it turned out it was just a party, and much more fun than the parties held by his fellow scientists.

A little way off stood a man with a white beard, whom he recognised as a professor from the university. He didn't know quite what to do, but, after a while, the professor recognised him too and raised his glass in greeting.

Lorens felt relieved. Witches were no longer hunted, nor were their sympathisers.

'It's like a picnic,' Brida heard someone say. Yes, it was like a picnic and that made her feel rather irritated. She had expected something more ritualistic, more like the Sabbaths that had inspired Goya, Saint-Saëns and Picasso. She picked up the bottle beside her and began to drink.

A party. Crossing the bridge between the visible and the invisible by means of a party. Brida was intrigued to know how anything sacred could possibly happen in such a secular atmosphere.

Night was falling fast, and people continued to drink. Just as darkness threatened to submerge everything, some of the men present – without performing any specific ritual – lit the fire. That is how it had been in the past. Before fire became a powerful element in the rituals of witchcraft, it had been merely a source of light. A light around which women gathered to talk about their men, their magical experiences, their encounters with incubi and succubi, the much-feared sexual demons of the Middle Ages. That is how it had been in the past – a party, a huge popular festival, a joyful celebration of spring and hope, in an age when being happy was a challenge to the Law, because no one could enjoy themselves in a world made only to tempt the weak. The lords of the land, shut up in their dark castles, gazed out at the fires in the forests and felt as if they'd been robbed – those peasants were eager for happiness, and no one who has experienced happiness can ever again feel at ease with sadness. The peasants might then expect to be happy all year round, and that would threaten the whole political and religious system.

Four or five people, who were already slightly tipsy, began dancing round the fire, perhaps in imitation of a witches' Sabbath. Amongst the dancers Brida saw an Initiate whom she'd met when Wicca commemorated the martyrdom of the sisters. She was shocked. She had assumed followers of the Tradition of the Moon would behave in a way more in keeping with that sacred place. She remembered the night she had spent with the Magus, and how drink had hindered communication between them during their astral travel.

'My friends will be green with envy,' she heard someone say. 'They'll never believe I was here.'

That was too much. She needed to get a little distance, to understand properly what was going on, and to resist a strong desire simply to leave and go home before she became entirely disillusioned with everything she'd believed in for nearly a year now. She looked for Wicca, and saw her talking and laughing with some of the guests. The number of people dancing round the fire was growing larger all the time; some were clapping and singing, accompanied by others keeping time by beating on the empty bottles with sticks or keys.

'I need to go for a walk,' she told Lorens.

A group of people had gathered round him, fascinated by what he was telling them about ancient stars and the miracles of modern physics. However, he immediately stopped talking and asked:

'Would you like me to come with you?'

'No, I'd rather be alone.'

She left the group and headed off into the forest. The voices were growing ever louder and more raucous, and everything – the drunkenness, the comments, the people playing at being witches and wizards around the fire – became mixed up in her head. She had waited so long for this night, but it was turning out to be just another party, like one of those charity dos, where people eat, get drunk, tell jokes, and then make speeches about the need to help the Indians in the Southern Hemisphere or the seals at the North Pole.

She began walking through the forest, always keeping within sight of the fire. She walked along a path that gave her a view from above the central stone. However, seen from high up, the view was even more disappointing: Wicca was busy circulating among the different groups, asking if everything was all right; people were dancing round the fire; a few couples were already exchanging their first drunken kisses. Lorens was talking animatedly to two men, perhaps about things that would have been fine in the setting of a bar, but not at a celebration like this. A latecomer entered the wood, a stranger attracted by the noise, in search of a little fun.

She recognised his way of walking.

The Magus.

Startled, Brida began running back down the path. She wanted to reach him before he got to the party. She needed him to help her, as he had before. She needed to understand the meaning of what was going on there.

'Wicca certainly knows how to organise a Sabbath,' thought the Magus as he approached. He could see and feel the free flow of energy among the people present. At this phase of the ritual, the Sabbath resembled any other party; it was important to ensure that all the guests were on the same wavelength. At his first Sabbath, he had felt very shocked by all this. He remembered calling his Teacher over and asking him what was going on.

'Haven't you ever been to a party before?' his Teacher had asked, annoyed at the Magus for interrupting an interesting conversation.

Of course he had, the Magus said.

'And what makes for a good party?'

'Everyone enjoying themselves.'

'Men have been holding parties since the days when they lived in caves,' said his Teacher. 'They're the first group rituals we know of, and the Tradition of the Sun took it upon itself to keep that ritual alive. A good party cleanses the minds of all those taking part, but it's very difficult to make that happen; it only takes a few people to spoil the general mood.

Those people think they're more important than the others; they're hard to please; they think they're wasting their time because they can't make contact with anyone else. And they usually end up the victims of a mysterious form of poetic justice: they tend to leave weighed down by the astral larvae given off by those people who *have* managed to bond with others. Remember, the first road to God is prayer, the second is joy.'

Many years had passed since that conversation with his Teacher. The Magus had taken part in many Sabbaths since then, and he knew that this was a very skilfully arranged example; the collective energy level was growing all the time.

He looked for Brida. There were a lot of people there, and he wasn't used to crowds. He knew that he needed to partake of that collective energy, and he was quite prepared to do so, but first he needed to re-accustom himself. She could help him. He would feel more at ease once he had found her.

He was a Magus. He knew about the point of light. All he needed was to alter his state of consciousness and the point of light would appear in the midst of all those people. For years, he had searched for that light, and now it was there only yards away from him.

The Magus altered his state of consciousness. He looked again at the people gathered there, this time with a changed perception, and he could see a vast range of different-coloured auras; all of them, though, were shifting closer to the colour that would predominate that night.

'Wicca really is an excellent Teacher,' he thought again. 'She works very fast.' Soon all the auras, the energy vibrations that surround each physical body, would be vibrating as one. And then the second part of the ritual could begin.

He looked to left and right and finally located the point of light. He decided to surprise her and approached without a sound.

'Brida,' he said.

His Soulmate turned round.

'She's gone for a walk,' a young man said politely.

For a moment that seemed to last for ever, the Magus looked at the man standing before him.

'You must be the Magus that Brida has told me so much about,' said Lorens. 'Join us. She won't be long.'

But Brida was already there. She was standing opposite the two men, breathing hard, eyes wide.

From the other side of the fire, the Magus sensed someone watching. He knew that look; it would not be able to see the points of light, because only Soulmates could recognise each other, but it was a deep and ancient look, one that knew the Tradition of the Moon, and the hearts of men and women.

The Magus turned and faced Wicca. She smiled at him from the other side of the fire – in a fraction of a second she had understood everything.

Brida also had her eyes fixed on the Magus. They were alight with pleasure. He had come.

'I'd like to introduce you to Lorens,' she said. The party suddenly seemed like fun, and she no longer needed any explanations.

The Magus was still in that altered state of consciousness. He saw Brida's aura rapidly changing and moving towards the colour that Wicca had chosen. She was pleased and happy that he had come, and anything he said or did could so easily ruin her Initiation that night. He must, at all costs, control his feelings.

'Pleased to meet you,' he said to Lorens. 'How about pouring me a glass of wine?'

Lorens smiled and held out the bottle.

'Welcome to the group,' he said. 'I'm sure you'll enjoy the party.'

Wicca looked away and gave a sigh of relief. Brida had noticed nothing. She was a good student, and Wicca would have been loth to remove her from that night's initiation ceremony because she had failed to take the simplest step of all, by not joining in with the general good cheer.

'And he can take care of himself.' The Magus had years of work and discipline behind him. He would be capable of keeping his feelings in check, long enough at least to replace those feelings with something else. She respected his hard work and his stubbornness, and felt slightly afraid of his immense power.

She chatted with a few of the other guests, but couldn't quite get over her surprise at what she'd just seen. So that was why he'd paid so much attention to Brida, who was, after all, a witch like any other witch who had spent various incarnations learning the Tradition of the Moon.

Brida was his Soulmate.

'My feminine intuition clearly isn't working very well.' She had imagined everything, except that most obvious of reasons. She consoled herself by thinking that at least the result of all her curiosity had been a positive one: it was the path chosen by God to enable her to rediscover her student.

The Magus spotted someone he knew in the crowd and excused himself for a moment to go and speak to him. Brida was euphoric, enjoying his presence there beside her, but she felt it best to let him leave. Her feminine intuition was telling her that it was best if he and Lorens didn't spend too much time together; they might become friends, and when two men are in love with the same woman, it's better that they hate each other than that they become friends. Because, if that happened, she would end up losing them both.

She looked at the people round the fire, and suddenly she felt like dancing too. She asked Lorens to join her; he hesitated for a second, but then took courage and said 'Yes'. People were still spinning round and clapping, drinking wine and beating out a rhythm on the empty wine bottles with sticks and keys. Whenever she danced past the Magus, he smiled and raised his glass to her. This was one of the best nights of her life.

Wicca joined the circle of dancers, where everyone was feeling relaxed and happy. The guests, who had been rather anxious about what might happen and worried about what they might see, had now entered fully into the spirit of the night. Spring had arrived, and they needed to celebrate, to fill their soul with faith in future sunlit days, and forget as quickly as possible the grey evenings and lonely nights spent at home.

The clapping grew louder, and now it was Wicca setting the rhythm. It was an insistent, regular rhythm. Everyone's eyes were fixed on the fire. No one was cold; it was as if summer had arrived already. The people round the fire began to take off their sweaters.

'Let's sing!' said Wicca. She sang a simple two-verse song several times, and soon everyone was singing with her. A few people recognised it as a witches' mantra where what mattered was the sound of the words, not the meaning. It was the sound of union with the Gifts; and those endowed with magic vision – like the Magus and the other Teachers present – could see the filaments of light joining various people.

Lorens eventually grew bored with the dancing and went to join the 'musicians'. Others moved away from the fire, some because they were tired and others because Wicca had asked them to help keep the rhythm going. Only the Initiates noticed what was happening, that the party was beginning to enter sacred territory. Very soon, the only people dancing round the fire were the women from the Tradition of the Moon and the witches who were to be initiated that night.

Even Wicca's male students stopped dancing; the initiation ritual for the men was different and took place on a different date. What was turning and turning in the astral plane immediately above the fire was female energy, the energy of transformation. So it had been since time immemorial.

Brida began to feel very hot. It couldn't be the wine, because she'd drunk very little. It was probably the flames from the fire. She had a great desire to take off her blouse, but she felt embarrassed, an embarrassment that gradually lost all meaning as she clapped and sang that simple song and danced around the fire. Her eyes were now fixed on the flames, and the world seemed less and less important; it was a feeling very similar to the one she'd experienced when the tarot cards had revealed themselves to her for the first time.

'I'm going into a trance,' she thought. 'But so what? This party's fun!'

'What strange music,' Lorens was thinking, as he kept time, beating the bottle. His ear, trained to listen to his own body, had noticed that the rhythm of the clapping and the sound of the words vibrated exactly in the middle of his chest, as happened when he heard the bass drum in a concert of classical music. The odd thing was that the rhythm also seemed to be dictating the beating of his heart.

As Wicca quickened the pace, his heart beat faster too. The same thing must be happening to everyone.

'More blood is flowing to my brain,' the scientific part of his mind told him. But he was part of a witches' ritual and this was no time to be thinking such things; he could talk to Brida about it later.

'I'm at a party and I want to have fun,' he said out loud. Someone beside him cried: 'Hear, hear!' and Wicca's clapping grew a little faster.

'I'm free. I'm proud of my body because it's the manifestation of God in the visible world.' The heat from the fire was becoming unbearable. The world seemed far away, and she no longer cared about superficial things. She was alive, the blood was coursing through her veins, and she was entirely given over, body and soul, to her search. Dancing round that fire was not new to her, for the rhythm awoke dormant memories of when she had been a Teacher of the Wisdom of Time. She wasn't alone, because that party was a re-encounter with herself and with the Tradition she'd carried through many lives. She felt a profound respect for herself.

She was once again in a body, and it was a beautiful body, one that had fought for millions of years to survive in a hostile world. It had lived in the sea, crawled upon the earth, climbed trees, walked on all fours, and was now proudly standing with its two feet on the ground. That body deserved respect for its long struggle. There were no beautiful or ugly bodies, because all had followed the same trajectory; all were the visible part of the soul they inhabited.

She felt proud, deeply proud of her body.

She took off her blouse.

She wasn't wearing a bra, but that didn't matter. Yes, she was proud of her body, and no one could criticise her for that: even if she were seventy years old, she would still be proud of her body, because it was through her body that the soul could do its work.

The other women around the fire did the same, and that didn't matter either.

She unbuckled the belt on her trousers and finally stood there completely naked. She felt freer than at any other time in her entire life. There was no reason behind what she was doing; she was doing it simply because nakedness was the only way to show how free her soul was at that moment. It didn't matter that other people were there, clothed and watching; all she wished was that they could feel about their bodies as she felt about hers. She could dance freely, and nothing impeded her movements. Every atom of her body was touching the air, and the air was generous; it brought with it, from afar, secrets and perfumes to clothe her from head to toe.

The men and the other guests beating the wine bottles noticed that the women around the fire were naked. They clapped or held hands and sang – sometimes softly and sometimes wildly. No one knew who was setting the rhythm, whether it was the people beating time on the bottles, the clapping, or the music. They all seemed aware of what was happening, but if, at that moment, one of them had been brave enough to break the rhythm, they could not have done so. At this point in the ritual, one of the Teacher's greatest problems was making sure that no one realised they were in a trance. They needed to feel that they were in control, even though they weren't. Wicca was not violating the one Law which, if broken, was punished by the Tradition with exceptional severity – manipulating the free will of others – because everyone there knew they were present at a witches' Sabbath, and, for witches, life means communion with the Universe.

Later, when this night was just a memory, none of these people would tell what they had seen. There was no prohibition on doing so, but they all felt they were in the presence of a powerful force, a mysterious, sacred force; intense and implacable, one that no human being would dare to defy.

'Turn!' said the woman in the black, ankle-length dress. She was the only woman still fully clothed. All the others were naked as they danced and clapped and spun.

A man placed a pile of dresses beside her. Three of them would be worn for the first time, and two were very similar in style. These were people with the same Gift, which took material form in the dress each woman had dreamed.

There was no need for Wicca to clap now, for the others continued to do so as if she were still keeping the beat.

She knelt down, pressed her thumbs to her head and began to work the Power.

The Power of the Tradition of the Moon, the Wisdom of Time, was there. It was a highly dangerous Power, one that witches could only invoke once they had become Teachers. Wicca knew how to use it but, even so, she first asked for her Teacher's protection.

In that power dwelled the Wisdom of Time. There was the Serpent, wise and masterful. Only the Virgin, by crushing the serpent's head beneath her heel, could subjugate it. And so Wicca prayed to the Virgin Mary as well, asking her for purity of soul, steadiness of hand, and the protection of her cloak, so that she could bring down that Power on the women before her, without it seducing or overwhelming any of them.

With her face lifted to the sky, her voice steady and confident, she recited the words of St Paul:

'If any man defile the temple of God, him shall God destroy; for the temple of God is holy, which temple ye are.

'Let no man deceive himself. If any man among you seemeth to be wise in this world, let him become a fool, that he may be wise.

'For the wisdom of this world is foolishness with God. For it is written, He taketh the wise in their own craftiness.

'And again, the Lord knoweth the thoughts of the wise, that they are vain.

'Therefore, let no man glory in men. For all things are yours.'

With a few deft movements of her hand, Wicca slowed the rhythm of the clapping. The people beating on the wine bottles beat more slowly and the women, too, began to spin and turn more slowly. Wicca was keeping the Power under control, and the whole orchestra had to work well, from the loudest horn to the quietest violin. To achieve this, she needed the assistance of the Power, but without actually surrendering to it.

She clapped her hands and made the necessary noises. Gradually, everyone stopped playing and dancing. The witches came over to Wicca and picked up their dresses – only three women remained naked. At that point, there had been an hour and twenty-eight minutes of continuous sound, and although all those present were in a state of altered consciousness, none of them, with the exception of the three naked women, had, for one moment, lost a sense of where they were or what they were doing.

The three naked women, however, were still in a trance. Wicca held out her ritual dagger and directed all its concentrated energy at them.

Their Gifts would soon become apparent. This was their way of serving the world; having walked long and tortuous paths, they had finally arrived. The world had tested them in every possible way, and they were worthy of what they had achieved. In daily life, they would continue to have their customary weaknesses and resentments, perform their usual small acts of kindness and of cruelty. The agony and the ecstasy would continue, as it would for everyone who is part of a world in a constant state of flux. However, at the appointed time, they would learn that each human being carries within them something far more important than their own self, namely, their particular Gift. For God placed in the hands of each and every person a Gift, the instrument He used to reveal Himself to the world and to help humanity. God chose human beings to be His helpers on Earth.

Some came to understand their Gift through the Tradition of the Sun, others through the Tradition of the Moon, but all eventually learned what their Gift was, even if it took several incarnations to do so.

Wicca stood by the great stone placed there by Celtic priests. The witches, in their black robes, formed a semicircle around her.

She looked at the three naked women. Their eyes were shining.

'Come here.'

The women walked into the middle of the semi-circle. Wicca then asked them to lie face down on the ground, with their arms outstretched to form a cross.

The Magus watched Brida lie down on the ground. He tried to concentrate only on her aura, but he was a man, and a man always looks at a woman's body.

He didn't want to remember. He didn't want to think about whether he was suffering or not. He was aware of only one thing – that his mission with his Soulmate beside him was over.

'It's a shame to have spent so little time with her.' But he couldn't think like that. Somewhere in Time, they had shared the same body, felt the same pain and been made happy by the same pleasures. Perhaps they had walked together through a forest similar to this and gazed up at the night sky where the same bright stars shone. He smiled at the thought of his Teacher, who had made him spend so long in the forest merely in order that he should understand his encounter with his Soulmate.

That was how things were in the Tradition of the Sun; each person was obliged to learn what he needed to learn and not merely what he wanted to learn. In his man-heart he would weep for a long time, but in his Magus-heart, he felt exultant and grateful to the forest.

Wicca looked at the three women lying at her feet and gave thanks to God that she had been able to continue doing the same work throughout so many lives; the Tradition of the Moon was inexhaustible. The clearing in the wood had been consecrated by Celtic priests in a time now long forgotten, and little remained of their rituals, only perhaps the stone before which she was standing. It was a huge stone, so large it could not possibly have been transported there by human hands, but then the Ancients had known how to move such stones by magical means. They had built pyramids, observatories and whole cities in the mountains of South America, using only the forces known to the Tradition of the Moon. Such knowledge was no longer needed by man, and had been erased from Time so that it could not be turned to destructive ends. Nevertheless, out of pure curiosity, Wicca would like to have known how they had done it.

There were a few Celtic spirits present, and she greeted them. They were teachers who had ceased being reincarnated, and now formed part of Earth's secret government; without them, without the strength of their knowledge, the planet would long since have lost its way. Above the trees to the left of the clearing, these Celtic teachers were hovering in the air, astral bodies surrounded by an intense white light. Through the centuries, they had come there at every Equinox, to make sure that the Tradition was being maintained. Yes, said Wicca with a certain pride, the Equinoxes continued to be celebrated even after all Celtic culture had disappeared from the official History of the World.

Because no one can destroy the Tradition of the Moon, only the Hand of God.

She observed the priests for a while longer. What would they make of people today? Did they feel a nostalgia for the days when they used to come to this place and when contact with God seemed simpler and more direct? Wicca thought not, and her instinct was confirmed. The garden of God was being constructed out of human emotions, and for this to happen, people had to live a long time, in different ages, often adopting very different customs. As in the rest of the Universe, man was following his evolutionary path, and each day he was better than on the previous day, even if he forgot the previous day's lessons, even if he complained, claiming that life was unfair.

Because the Kingdom of Heaven is like the seed that a man plants in a field; he sleeps and wakes, day and night, and the seed grows even though he knows not how. These lessons were engraved on the Soul of the World and existed for the benefit of all humanity. It was important that there were still people like those present at the ceremony, people who were not afraid of the Dark Night of the Soul, as wise St John of the Cross had described it. Each step, each act of faith, redeemed the whole human race anew. As long as there were people who knew that, in God's eyes, all of man's wisdom was madness, the world would continue along the path of light.

She felt proud of her pupils, male and female, who had proved capable of sacrificing the comfort of a world of nice, neat explanations for the challenge of discovering a new world.

She looked again at the three naked women lying on the ground, arms outstretched, and tried to clothe them again in the colour of the aura they emanated. They were now travelling through Time and meeting many lost Soulmates. Those three women would, from that night on, plunge into the mission that had been awaiting them since they were born. One was over sixty, but age was of no importance. What mattered was that they were finally face to face with the destiny that had been patiently awaiting them, and from now on they would use their Gifts to keep safe certain crucial plants in God's garden. Each one had arrived at this place for different reasons – a failed love affair, a sense of weariness with routine or perhaps a search for Power. They had confronted fear, inertia and the many disappointments that assail those who follow the path of magic. But the fact is, they had reached the place they needed to reach, for the Hand of God always guides those who follow their path with faith.

* * *

'The Tradition of the Moon is a fascinating one, with its Teachers and its rituals, but there is another Tradition too,' thought the Magus, his eyes still fixed on Brida, and feeling slightly envious of Wicca, who would remain by her side for a long time. That other Tradition was a more difficult one to follow because it was simple and simple things always seem so complicated. Its Teachers lived in the world, and did not always realise the importance of what they were teaching, because the impulse behind that teaching often seemed nothing more than an absurd impulse. They were carpenters, poets, mathematicians, people from all professions and walks of life, who lived scattered throughout the world. People who suddenly felt the need to talk to someone, to explain a feeling they couldn't quite understand, but which was impossible to keep to themselves, and that was the way in which the Tradition of the Sun kept its knowledge alive. The impulse of Creation.

Wherever there were people, there was always some trace of the Tradition of the Sun. Sometimes it was a sculpture, sometimes a table, at others a few lines from a poem passed from generation to generation by a particular group or tribe. The people through which the Tradition of the Sun spoke were people just like anyone else, and who, one morning or one evening, looked at the world and felt the presence of something greater. They had unwittingly plunged into an unknown sea, and, for the most part, they did not do so again. Everyone, at least once in each incarnation, possessed the secret of the Universe.

They found themselves momentarily immersed in the Dark Night, but, lacking sufficient self-belief, they rarely returned to it. And the Sacred Heart, which nourished the world with love and peace and devotion found itself once more surrounded by thorns.

Wicca was glad she was a Teacher of the Tradition of the Moon. Everyone who came to her was eager to learn, while, in the Tradition of the Sun, most were in permanent flight from what life was teaching them.

'Not that it matters,' thought Wicca, because the age of miracles was returning, and no one could remain indifferent to the changes the world was beginning to experience. Within a few years, the power of the Tradition of the Sun would reveal itself in all its brilliance. Anyone not already following their own path would begin to feel dissatisfied with themselves and be forced to make a choice: they would either have to accept an existence beset with disappointment and pain or else come to realise that everyone was born to be happy. Having made their choice, they would have no option but to change, and the great struggle, the Jihad, would begin.

With one perfect movement of her hand, Wicca drew a circle in the air with her dagger. Inside that invisible circle, she drew a five-pointed star, which witches call the pentagram. The pentagram was the symbol of the elements at work in mankind, and through it, the women lying on the ground would now come into contact with the world of light.

'Close your eyes,' said Wicca.

The three women obeyed.

Above the head of each of them Wicca performed the ritual moves with her dagger.

'Now open the eyes of your souls.'

Brida opened the eyes of her soul. She was in a desert and the place looked very familiar.

She remembered that she had been there before. With the Magus.

She looked around, but couldn't see him. Yet she wasn't afraid; she felt calm and happy. She knew who she was and where she lived; she knew that in some other place in time a party was going on. But none of this mattered, because the landscape before her was so much prettier: the sand, the mountains in the distance and a huge stone.

'Welcome,' said a voice.

Beside her stood a gentleman wearing clothes like those worn by her grandfather.

'I am Wicca's Teacher. When you become a Teacher, your students will find Wicca here, and so on and so forth until the Soul of the World finally makes itself manifest.'

'I'm at a ritual for witches,' Brida said, 'a Sabbath.'

The Teacher laughed.

'You have found your path. Few people have the courage to do so. They prefer to follow a path that is not their own. Everyone has a Gift, but they choose not to see it. You accepted yours, and your encounter with your Gift is your encounter with the world.'

'But why?'

'So that you can plant God's garden.'

'I have a life ahead of me,' said Brida. 'I want to live that life just like anyone else. I want to be able to make mistakes, to be selfish, to have faults.'

The Teacher smiled. In his right hand a blue cloak suddenly appeared.

'You can only be close to people if you are one of them.'

The scene around her changed. She was no longer in a desert, but immersed in a kind of liquid, in which various strange creatures were swimming.

'Life is about making mistakes,' said the Teacher. 'Cells went on reproducing themselves in exactly the same way for millions of years, until one of them made a mistake, and introduced change into that endless cycle of repetition.'

Brida was gazing in amazement at the sea. She didn't ask how it was possible for them to breathe in there; all she could hear was the Teacher's voice, all she could think of was a very similar journey she had made and which had begun in a field of wheat.

'It was a mistake that set the world in motion,' said the Teacher. 'Never be afraid of making a mistake.'

'But Adam and Eve were driven out of Paradise.'

'And they will return one day knowing the miracle of the heavens and of all the world. God knew what he was doing when he drew their attention to the tree of the Knowledge of Good and Evil. If he hadn't wanted them to eat it, he would never have mentioned it.'

'So why did he, then?'

'In order to set the Universe in motion.'

The scene changed back to the desert and the stone. It was morning, and the horizon was becoming suffused with pink light. The Teacher came towards her with the cloak.

'I consecrate you now, in this moment. Your Gift is God's instrument. May you prove to be a useful tool.'

Wicca picked up the dress belonging to the youngest of the three women and held it up in her two hands. She made a symbolic offering to the Celtic priests who, in astral form, were watching everything from above the trees. Then she turned to the young woman.

'Stand up,' she said.

Brida stood up. The shadows from the fire flickered over her naked body. Once, another body had been consumed by those same flames, but that time was over.

'Raise your arms.'

Brida raised her arms. Wicca put the dress on her.

* * *

'I was naked,' she said to the Teacher, when he had wrapped the cloak about her. 'And I was not ashamed.'

'If it wasn't for shame, God would never have discovered that Adam and Eve had eaten the apple.'

The Teacher was watching the sunrise. He seemed distracted, but he wasn't. Brida knew this.

'Never be ashamed,' he said. 'Accept what life offers you and try to drink from every cup. All wines should be tasted; some should only be sipped, but with others, drink the whole bottle.'

'How will I know which is which?'

'By the taste. You can only know a good wine if you have first tasted a bad one.'

Wicca turned Brida round to face the fire, then moved on to the next Initiate. The fire picked up the energy of her Gift so that it could be made manifest in her. At that moment, Brida was watching a sunrise, a sun that would, from then on, light the rest of her life.

'Now you must go,' said the Teacher, as soon as the sun had risen.

'I'm not afraid of my Gift,' Brida told him. 'I know where I'm going and what I'm going to do. I know that someone helped me to arrive here.

'I've been here before. There were people dancing

and a secret temple built to celebrate the Tradition of the Moon.'

The Teacher said nothing. He turned to her and made a sign with his right hand.

'You have been accepted. May your path be one of peace in times of peace, and of combat in times of combat. Never confuse one with the other.'

The figure of the Teacher began to dissolve, along with the desert and the stone. Only the sun remained, but the sun began to become one with the sky. Then the sky grew dark, and the sun became more like the flames of a fire.

She was back. She remembered everything now: the noise, the clapping, the dancing, the trance. She remembered having taken off her clothes in front of all these people, and now she felt rather awkward. But she also remembered her meeting with the Teacher. She tried to master her feelings of shame and fear and anxiety – they would always be with her, and she must get used to them.

Wicca asked the three Initiates to stand in the very middle of the semicircle formed by the women. The witches joined hands and made a ring.

They sang songs that no one now dared to accompany; the sounds flowed from their barely open lips, creating a strange vibration, which grew ever shriller, until it resembled the cry of some crazed bird. At some point in the future, she would learn how to make those sounds. She would learn many more things, until she became a Teacher too. Then other men and women would be initiated by her into the Tradition of the Moon.

All of this, however, would happen at the appointed moment. She had all the time in the world, now that she had found her destiny again, and had someone to help her. Eternity was hers.

Everyone appeared to have strange colours around them, and Brida felt slightly bewildered. She liked the world as it had been before.

The witches stopped singing.

'The Initiation of the Moon is finished and complete,' said Wicca. 'The world is now a field, and you will work to make sure that there is a good harvest.'

'I feel strange,' said one of the Initiates. 'Everything's blurred.'

'What you're seeing is the energy field that surrounds each individual, their aura, as we call it. That is the first step along the path of the Great Mysteries. The sensation will soon fade, and later I will teach you how to awaken it again.'

With one swift, agile movement, she flung her ritual dagger to the ground. It stuck fast, the handle still trembling with the force of the impact.

'The ceremony is over,' she said.

Brida went over to Lorens. His eyes were shining, and she felt how very proud he was of her and how much he loved her. They could grow together, create a new way of living, discover a whole Universe that lay before them, just waiting for people of courage like them.

But there was another man too. While she was talking to Wicca's Teacher, she had made her choice, because that other man would be able to take her hand during difficult moments, and lead her with experience and love through the Dark Night of Faith. She would learn to love him, and her love for him would be as great as her respect. They were both walking the same road to knowledge, and because of him she had reached the point where she was now. With him, she would one day learn the Tradition of the Sun.

Now she knew that she was a witch. She had learned the art of witchcraft over many centuries and was back where she should be. From that night on, Wisdom and knowledge would be the most important things in her life.

'We can leave now,' she said to Lorens. He was

gazing with admiration at this woman dressed all in black; Brida, however, knew that the Magus would be seeing her dressed all in blue.

She held out the bag containing her other clothes.

'You go ahead and see if you can get us a lift. I need to speak to someone.'

Lorens took the bag, but only went a little way towards the path through the forest. The ritual was over and they were back in the world of men, with their loves, their jealousies and their wars of conquest.

Fear had come back too. Brida was behaving oddly.

'I don't know if God exists,' he said to the trees around him. 'And yet I can't think about that now, because I, too, am face to face with the mystery.'

He felt he was talking in a different way, with a strange confidence he had never known he possessed. But, at that moment, he believed that the trees were listening to him.

'The people here may not understand me; they may despise my efforts, but I know that I'm as brave as they are, because I seek God even though I don't believe in him. If he exists, he is the God of the Brave.'

Lorens noticed that his hands were trembling slightly. The night had passed and he had understood nothing of what went on. He knew that he had entered into a trance state, but that was all. However, the fact that his hands were shaking had nothing to do with that plunge into the Dark Night, as Brida called it.

He looked up at the sky, still full of low clouds. God was the God of the Brave. And He would understand him, because the brave are those who make decisions despite their fear, who are tormented by the Devil every step of the way and gripped by anxiety about their every action, wondering if they are right or wrong. And yet, nevertheless, they act. They do so because they also believe in miracles, like the witches who had danced round the fire that night.

God might be trying to return to him through that woman who was now walking away towards another man. If she left, perhaps God would leave forever. She was his opportunity, because she knew that the best way to immerse oneself in God was through love. He didn't want to lose the chance of getting her back.

He took a deep breath, feeling the cold, pure air of the forest in his lungs, and he made a sacred promise to himself.

God was the God of the Brave.

Brida walked over to the Magus. They met by the fire. Words came only with difficulty.

She was the one to break the silence.

'We are on the same path.'

He nodded.

'So let us follow it together.'

'But you don't love me,' said the Magus.

'I do love you. I don't yet know my love for you, but I do love you. You're my Soulmate.'

The Magus still had a distant look in his eye. He was thinking about the Tradition of the Sun, and how one of the most important lessons of the Tradition of the Sun was Love. Love was the only bridge between the visible and the invisible known to everyone. It was the only effective language for translating the lessons that the Universe taught to human beings every day.

'I'm not going anywhere,' she said. 'I'm staying with you.'

'Your boyfriend is waiting,' replied the Magus. 'I will bless your love.'

Brida looked at him, puzzled.

'No one can possess a sunset like the one we saw that evening,' he went on. 'Just as no one can possess an afternoon of rain beating against the window, or the serenity of a sleeping child, or the magical moment when the waves break on the rocks. No one can possess the beautiful things of this Earth, but we can know them and love them. It is through such moments that God reveals himself to mankind.

'We are not the masters of the sun or of the afternoon or of the waves or even of the vision of God, because we cannot possess ourselves.'

The Magus held out his hand to Brida and gave her a flower.

'When we first met – although it seems to me that I've always known you, because I can't remember the world before that – I showed you the Dark Night. I wanted to see how you would face up to your own limitations. I knew that you were my Soulmate, and that you would teach me everything I needed to learn – that is why God divided man and woman.'

Brida touched the flower. It seemed to her that it was the first flower she had seen in months. Spring had arrived.

'People give flowers as presents because flowers contain the true meaning of Love. Anyone who tries to possess a flower will have to watch its beauty fading. But if you simply look at a flower in a field, you will keep it forever, because the flower is part of the evening and the sunset and the smell of damp earth and the clouds on the horizon.'

Brida was looking at the flower. The Magus took it from her and returned it to the forest.

Brida's eyes filled with tears. She was proud of her Soulmate.

'That is what the forest taught me. That you will never be mine, and that is why I will never lose you. You were my hope during my days of loneliness, my anxiety during moments of doubt, my certainty during moments of faith.

'Knowing that my Soulmate would come one day, I devoted myself to learning the Tradition of the Sun. Knowing that you existed was my one reason for continuing to live.'

Brida could no longer conceal her tears.

'Then you came, and I understood all of this. You came to free me from the slavery I myself had created, to tell me that I was free to return to the world and to the things of the world. I understood everything I needed to know, and I love you more than all the women I have ever known, more than I loved the woman who, quite unwittingly, exiled me to the forest. I will always remember now that love is liberty. That was the lesson it took me so many years to learn. That is the lesson that sent me into exile and now sets me free again.'

The flames crackled in the fire, and a few latecomers were beginning to say their goodbyes. But Brida wasn't listening to anything that was going on around her.

'Brida!' she heard a distant voice call.

'Here's looking at you, kid,' said the Magus. It was a line from an old film he had seen once. He felt happy because he had turned another important page in the Tradition of the Sun. He felt the presence of his Teacher, who had chosen that night for his new Initiation.

'I will always remember you, and you will remember me, just as we will remember the evening, the rain on the windows, and all the things we'll always have because we cannot possess them.'

'Brida!' Lorens called again.

'Go in peace,' said the Magus. 'And dry those tears, or tell him that the smoke from the fire got in your eyes. Never forget me.'

He knew he didn't need to say this, but he said it anyway.

Wicca noticed that some people had left a few of their belongings behind. She would have to phone them and tell them to come and fetch them.

'The fire will have burned down soon,' she said.

He remained silent. There were still a few flames, and he still had his eyes fixed on them.

'I don't regret that I once fell in love with you,' Wicca went on.

'Nor do I,' replied the Magus.

She felt an enormous desire to talk about Brida, but she said nothing. The eyes of the man beside her inspired respect and wisdom.

'It's a shame I'm not your Soulmate,' she added. 'We would have made a good couple.'

But the Magus wasn't listening to what Wicca was saying. There was a vast world before him and many things to do. He had to help plant God's garden, he had to teach people to teach themselves. He would meet other women, fall in love, and live this incarnation as intensely as he could. That night completed one stage of his existence, and a new Dark Night lay ahead, but the next stage would be much more enjoyable and joyful, much closer to what he had dreamed. He knew this because of the flowers and the forests and because of young women who arrive one day led by God's hand, not knowing that they are there in order for destiny to be fulfilled. He knew this because of the Tradition of the Moon and the Tradition of the Sun.

Life is a journey

Make sure you don't miss a thing.
Live it with Paulo Coelho.

Visit f /paulocoelho

How can you find your heart's desire?

A world-wide phenomenon; an inspiration for anyone seeking their path in life.

The Alchemist

Do you believe in yourself?

A modern-day adventure in the searing heat of the Mojave desert and an exploration of fear and self-doubt.

The Valkyries

How do we see the amazing in the everyday?

When two young lovers are reunited, they discover anew the truth of what lies in their hearts.

By the River Piedra I Sat Down & Wept

What are you searching for?

A transforming journey on the pilgrims' road to Santiago – and the first of Paulo's extraordinary books.

The Pilgrimage

Can faith triumph over suffering?

Paulo Coelho's brilliant telling of the story of Elijah, who was forced to choose between love and duty.

The Fifth Mountain

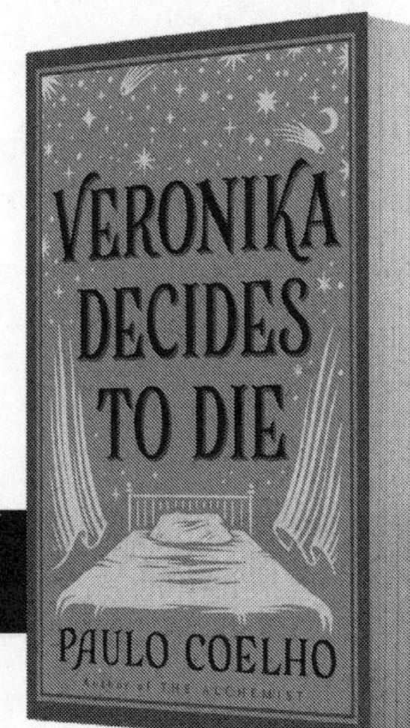

Is life always worth living?

A fundamental moral question explored as only Paulo Coelho can.

Veronika Decides to Die

Could you be tempted into evil?

The inhabitants of a small town are challenged by a mysterious stranger to choose between good and evil.

The Devil & Miss Prym

Are you brave enough to live your dream?

Strategies and inspiration to help you follow your own path in a troubled world.

Manual of the Warrior of Light

Can sex be sacred?

An unflinching exploration of the lengths we go to in our search for love, sex and spirituality.

Eleven Minutes

How far would you go for your obsession?

A sweeping story of love, loss and longing that spans the world.

The Zahir

What happens when obsession turns to murder?

An enthralling story of jealousy, death and suspense.

The Winner Stands Alone

Can we dare to be true to ourselves?

A story that will transform the way we think about love, joy and sacrifice.

The Witch of Portobello

How will you know who your soulmate is?

A moving tale of passion, mystery and spirituality.

Brida

What does it mean to be truly alive?

Powerful tales of living and dying, destiny and choice, and love lost and found.

Like the Flowing River

Are you where you want to be?

Read *Aleph*. And rewrite your life.

Aleph

Is there a weapon more powerful than words?

A timeless and powerful exploration of personal growth, everyday wisdom and joy.

Manuscript Found in Accra

By the RIVER PIEDRA I SAT DOWN and WEPT

Paulo Coelho was born in Brazil and has become one of the most widely read and loved authors in the world. Especially renowned for *The Alchemist* and *Eleven Minutes*, he has sold more than 320 million books worldwide and has been translated into 88 languages. The recipient of numerous prestigious international awards, amongst them the Crystal Award by the World Economic Forum and France's Légion d'Honneur, Paulo Coelho was inducted into the Brazilian Academy of Letters in 2002.

Also by Paulo Coelho

The Alchemist
The Pilgrimage
The Valkyries
By the River Piedra I Sat Down and Wept
The Fifth Mountain
Veronika Decides to Die
Manual of the Warrior of Light
Eleven Minutes
The Zahir
The Devil and Miss Prym
The Witch of Portobello
Brida
The Winner Stands Alone
Like the Flowing River
Aleph
Manuscript Found in Accra
Adultery
The Spy
Hippie

By the RIVER PIEDRA I SAT DOWN and WEPT

PAULO COELHO

Author of THE ALCHEMIST

Thorsons

By the River Piedra I Sat Down and Wept is an English version of *Na margem do rio Piedra eu sentei e chorei,* the Portugese original edition, published in Brazil by Editora Rocca Ltd (Rio de Janeiro),
copyright © 1994 by Paulo Coelho.

English translation by Alan R. Clarke.

Thorsons
An imprint of HarperCollins*Publishers*
1 London Bridge Street
London SE1 9GF

HarperCollins*Publishers*
1st Floor, Watermarque Building, Ringsend Road
Dublin 4, Ireland

www.harpercollins.co.uk
www.paulocoelho.com
www.paulocoelhoblog.com

Original hardback English translation published
by HarperSanFrancisco 1996
Paperback edition published by HarperCollins 1997, 1999
This edition published 2022

2 4 6 8 10 9 7 5 3 1

English translation © HarperCollins Publishers Inc. 1996

Paulo Coelho asserts the moral right to be identified as the author of this work

A catalogue record for this book is available from the British Library

ISBN 978-0-00-854730-1

FICTION / PHILOSOPHY

Printed and bound in India by Thomson Press India Ltd

All rights reserved. No part of this publication may be reproduced, stored in a retrieval system, or transmitted, in any form or by any means, electronic, mechanical, photocopying, recording or otherwise, without the prior permission of the publishers.

This book is produced from independently certified FSC® paper to ensure responsible forest management.

O Mary!
conceived without sin,
pray for us who turn to you!
Amen.

But wisdom is justified
by all her children.

Luke 7:35

For I. C. and S. B., whose loving communion made me see the feminine face of God;

for Monica Antunes, my companion from the beginning, who with her love and enthusiasm spreads the fire all over the world;

for Paulo Rocco, for the joy of the battles we have fought together and for the dignity of the battles we have fought between us;

and for Matthew Lore, for not having forgotten a sage quotation from the I Ching: *"Perseverance is favorable."*

Author's Note

A Spanish missionary was visiting an island when he came across three Aztec priests.

"How do you pray?" the missionary asked.

"We have only one prayer," answered one of the Aztecs. "We say, 'God, you are three, we are three. Have pity on us.' "

"A beautiful prayer," said the missionary. "But it is not exactly the one that God heeds. I'm going to teach you one that's much better."

The padre taught them a Catholic prayer and then continued on his path of evangelism. Years later, when he was returning to Spain, his ship stopped again at the island. From the deck, the missionary saw the three priests on the shore and waved to them.

Just then, the three men began to walk across the water toward him.

"Padre! Padre!" one of them called, approaching the ship. "Teach us again that prayer that God heeds. We've forgotten how it goes."

"It doesn't matter," responded the missionary, witnessing the miracle. And he promptly asked God's forgiveness for failing to recognize that He speaks all languages.

This story illustrates just what this book is about. Rarely do we realize that we are in the midst of the extraordinary. Miracles occur all around us, signs from God show us the way, angels plead to be heard, but we pay little attention to them because we have been taught that we must follow certain formulas and rules if we want to find God. We do not recognize that God is wherever we allow Him/Her to enter.

Traditional religious practices are important: they allow us to share with others the communal experience of adoration and prayer. But we must never forget that spiritual experience is above all a *practical* experience of love. And with love, there are no rules. Some may try to control their emotions and develop strategies for their behavior; others may turn to reading books of advice from "experts" on relationships—but this is all folly. The heart decides, and what it decides is all that really matters.

All of us have had this experience. At some point, we have each said through our tears, "I'm suffering for a love that's not worth it." We suffer because we feel we are giving more than we receive. We suffer because our love is going unrecognized. We suffer because we are unable to impose our own rules.

But ultimately there is no good reason for our suffering, for in every love lies the seed of our growth. The more we love, the closer we come to spiritual experience. Those who are truly enlightened, those whose souls are illuminated by love, have been able to overcome all of the inhibitions and preconceptions of their era. They have been able to sing, to laugh, and to pray out loud; they have danced and shared what Saint Paul called "the madness of saintliness." They have been joyful—because those who love conquer the world and have no fear of loss. True love is an act of total surrender.

This book is about the importance of that surrender. Pilar and her companion are fictitious, but they represent the many conflicts that beset us in our search for love. Sooner or later, we have to overcome our fears, because the spiritual path can only be traveled through the daily experience of love.

Thomas Merton once said that the spiritual life is essentially to love. One doesn't love in order to do what is good or to help or to protect someone. If we act that way, we are perceiving the other as a simple object, and we are seeing ourselves as wise and generous persons. This has nothing to do with love. To love is to be in communion with the other and to discover in that other the spark of God.

May Pilar's lament on the bank of the River Piedra guide us toward such communion.

Paulo Coelho

By the RIVER PIEDRA I SAT DOWN and WEPT

❦ ❦ ❦

By the River Piedra I sat down and wept. There is a legend that everything that falls into the waters of this river—leaves, insects, the feathers of birds—is transformed into the rocks that make the riverbed. If only I could tear out my heart and hurl it into the current, then my pain and longing would be over, and I could finally forget.

By the River Piedra I sat down and wept. The winter air chills the tears on my cheeks, and my tears fall into the cold waters that course past me. Somewhere, this river joins another, then another, until—far from my heart and sight—all of them merge with the sea.

May my tears run just as far, that my love might never know that one day I cried for him. May my tears run just as far, that I might forget the River Piedra, the monastery, the church in the Pyrenees, the mists, and the paths we walked together.

I shall forget the roads, the mountains, and the fields of my dreams—the dreams that will never come true.

I remember my "magic moment"—that instant when a "yes" or a "no" can change one's life forever. It seems so long ago now. It is hard to believe that it was only last week that I had found my love once again, and then lost him.

I am writing this story on the bank of the River Piedra. My hands are freezing, my legs are numb, and every minute I want to stop.

"Seek to live. Remembrance is for the old," he said.

Perhaps love makes us old before our time—or young, if youth has passed. But how can I not recall those moments? That is why I write—to try to turn sadness into longing, solitude into remembrance. So that when I finish telling myself the story, I can toss it into the Piedra. That's what the woman who has given me shelter told me to do. Only then—in the words of one of the saints—will the water extinguish what the flames have written.

All love stories are the same.

WE HAD BEEN children together. Then he left, like so many young people who leave small towns. He said he was going to learn about the world, that his dreams lay beyond the fields of Soria.

Years passed with almost no news of him. Every now and then he would send me a letter, but he never returned to the paths and forests of our childhood.

When I finished school, I moved to Zaragoza, and there I found that he had been right. Soria *was* a small town, and as its only famous poet had said, roads are made to be traveled. I enrolled in the university and found a boyfriend. I began to study for a scholarship (I was working as a salesgirl to pay for my courses). But I lost the competition for the scholarship, and after that I left my boyfriend.

Then the letters from my childhood friend began to arrive more frequently—and I was envious of the stamps from so many different places. He seemed to know everything; he had sprouted wings, and now he roamed the world. Meanwhile, I was simply trying to put down roots.

Some of his letters, all mailed from the same place in France, spoke of God. In one, he wrote about wanting to enter a seminary and dedicate his life to prayer. I wrote him back, asking him to wait a bit, urging him to experience more of his freedom before committing himself to something so serious.

But after I reread my letter, I tore it up. Who was I to speak about freedom or commitment? Compared to him, I knew nothing about such things.

One day I learned that he had begun to give lectures. This surprised me; I thought he was too young to be able to teach anything to anyone. And then he wrote to me that he was going to speak to a small group in Madrid—and he asked me to come.

So I made the four-hour trip from Zaragoza to Madrid. I wanted to see him again; I wanted to hear his voice. I wanted to sit with him in a café and remember the old days, when we had thought the world was far too large for anyone ever to know it truly.

Saturday, December 4, 1993

ↄ ↄ ↄ

THE PLACE where the conference was held was more formal than I had imagined it, and there were more people there than I had expected. How had all this come about?

He must be famous, I thought. He'd said nothing about this in his letters. I wanted to go up to the people in the audience and ask them why they were there, but I didn't have the nerve.

I was even more surprised when I saw him enter the room. He was quite different from the boy I had known—but of course, it had been twelve years; people change. Tonight his eyes were shining—he looked wonderful.

"He's giving us back what was ours," said a woman seated next to me.

A strange thing to say.

"What is he giving back?" I asked.

"What was stolen from us. Religion."

"No, no, he's not giving us anything back," said a younger woman seated on my right. "They can't return something that has always belonged to us."

"Well, then, what are you doing here?" the first woman asked, irritated.

"I want to listen to him. I want to see how they think; they've already burned us at the stake once, and they may want to do it again."

"He's just one voice," said the woman. "He's doing what he can."

The young woman smiled sarcastically and turned away, putting an end to the conversation.

"He's taking a courageous position for a seminarian," the other woman went on, looking to me for support.

I didn't understand any of this, and I said nothing. The woman finally gave up. The girl at my side winked at me, as if I were her ally.

But I was silent for a different reason. I was thinking, *Seminarian? It can't be! He would have told me.*

When he started to speak, I couldn't concentrate. I was sure he had spotted me in the audience, and I was trying to guess what he was thinking. How did I look to him? How different was the woman of twenty-nine from the girl of seventeen?

I noticed that his voice hadn't changed. But his words certainly had.

❦ ❦ ❦

*Y*OU HAVE TO *take risks,* he said. *We will only understand the miracle of life fully when we allow the unexpected to happen.*

Every day, God gives us the sun—and also one moment in which we have the ability to change everything that makes us unhappy. Every day, we try to pretend that we haven't perceived that moment, that it doesn't exist—that today is the same as yesterday and will be the same as tomorrow. But if people really pay attention to their everyday lives, they will discover that magic moment. It may arrive in the instant when we are doing something mundane, like putting our front-door key in the lock; it may lie hidden in the quiet that follows the lunch hour or in the thousand and one things that all seem the same to us. But that moment exists—a moment when all the power of the stars becomes a part of us and enables us to perform miracles.

Joy is sometimes a blessing, but it is often a conquest. Our magic moment helps us to change and sends us off in search of our dreams. Yes, we are going to suffer, we will have difficult times, and we will experience many disappointments—but all of this is transitory; it leaves no permanent mark. And one day we will look back with pride and faith at the journey we have taken.

Pitiful is the person who is afraid of taking risks. Perhaps this person will never be disappointed or disillusioned; perhaps she won't suffer the way people do when they have a dream to follow. But when that person looks back—and at some point everyone looks back—she will hear her heart saying, "What have you done with the miracles that God planted in your days? What have you done with the talents God bestowed on you? You buried yourself in a cave because you were fearful of losing those talents. So this is your heritage: the certainty that you wasted your life."

Pitiful are the people who must realize this. Because when they are finally able to believe in miracles, their life's magic moments will have already passed them by.

❦ ❦ ❦

AFTER THE LECTURE, members of the audience rushed up to him. I waited, worried about what his first impression of me would be after so many years. I felt like a child—insecure, tense because I knew none of his new friends, and jealous that he was paying more attention to the others than to me.

When he finally came up to me, he blushed. Suddenly he was no longer a man with important things to say but was once again the boy who had hidden with me at the hermitage of San Satúrio, telling me of his dream to travel the world (while our parents were calling the police, sure that we had drowned in the river).

"Pilar," he said.

I kissed him. I could have complimented him on his presentation. I could have said I was tired of being around so many people. I could have made some humorous remark about our childhood or commented on how proud I was to see him there, so admired by others.

I could have explained that I had to run and catch the last bus back to Zaragoza.

I could have. What does this phrase mean? At any given moment in our lives, there are certain things that could have happened but didn't. The magic moments go unrecognized, and then suddenly, the hand of destiny changes everything.

That's what happened to me just then. In spite of all the things I could have done or said, I asked a question that has brought me, a week later, to this river and has caused me to write these very lines.

"Can we have coffee together?" I said.

And he, turning to me, accepted the hand offered by fate.

"I really need to talk to you. Tomorrow I have a lecture in Bilbao. I have a car. Come with me."

"I have to get back to Zaragoza," I answered, not realizing that this was my last chance.

Then I surprised myself—perhaps because in seeing him, I had become a child again . . . or perhaps because we are not the ones who write the best moments of our lives. I said, "But they're about to celebrate the holiday of the Immaculate Conception in Bilbao. I can go there with you and then continue on to Zaragoza."

Just then, it was on the tip of my tongue to ask him about his being a "seminarian." He must have read my expression, because he said quickly, "Do you want to ask me something?"

"Yes. Before your lecture, a woman said that you were giving her back what had been hers. What did she mean?"

"Oh, that's nothing."

"But it's important to me. I don't know anything about your life; I'm even surprised to see so many people here."

He just laughed, and then he started to turn away to answer other people's questions.

"Wait," I said, grabbing his arm. "You didn't answer me."

"I don't think it would interest you, Pilar."

"I want to know anyway."

Taking a deep breath, he led me to a corner of the room. "All of the great religions—including Judaism, Catholicism, and Islam—are masculine. Men are in charge of the dogmas, men make the laws, and usually all the priests are men."

"Is that what the woman meant?"

He hesitated before he answered. "Yes. I have a different view of things: I believe in the feminine side of God."

I sighed with relief. The woman was mistaken; he couldn't be a seminarian because seminarians don't have such different views of things.

"You've explained it very well," I said.

❧ ❧ ❧

THE GIRL WHO HAD winked at me was waiting at the door.

"I know that we belong to the same tradition," she said. "My name is Brida."

"I don't know what you're talking about."

"Of course you do," she laughed.

She took my arm and led me out of the building before I could say anything more. It was a cold night, and I wasn't sure what I was going to do until we left for Bilbao the next morning.

"Where are we going?" I asked.

"To the statue of the Goddess."

"But . . . I need to find an inexpensive hotel where I can stay for the night."

"I'll show you one later."

I wanted to go to some warm café where I could talk to her for a bit and learn as much as I could about him. But I didn't want to argue. While she guided me across the Paseo de Castellana, I looked around at Madrid; I hadn't been there in years.

In the middle of the avenue, she stopped and pointed to the sky. "There She is."

The moon shone brilliantly through the bare branches of the trees on either side of the road.

"Isn't that beautiful!" I exclaimed.

But she wasn't listening. She spread her arms in the form of a cross, turning her palms upward, and just stood there contemplating the moon.

What have I gotten myself into? I thought. *I came here to attend a conference, and now I wind up in the Paseo de Castellana with this crazy girl. And tomorrow I'm going to Bilbao!*

"O mirror of the Earth Goddess," Brida was saying, her eyes closed. "Teach us about our power and make men understand us. Rising, gleaming, waning, and reviving in the heavens, you show us the cycle of the seed and the fruit."

She stretched her arms toward the night sky and held this position for some time. Several passersby looked at her and laughed, but she paid no attention; I was the one who was dying of embarrassment, standing there beside her.

"I needed to do that," she said, after her long adoration of the moon, "so that the Goddess would protect us."

"What are you talking about?"

"The same thing that your friend was talking about, only with words that are true."

I was sorry now that I hadn't paid closer attention to the lecture.

"We know the feminine side of God," Brida continued as we started to walk on. "We, the women, understand and love the Great Mother. We have paid for our wisdom with persecution and burnings at the stake, but we have survived. And now we understand Her mysteries."

Burnings at the stake? She was talking about witches!

I looked more closely at the woman by my side. She was pretty, with hair that hung to the middle of her back.

"While men were going off to hunt, we remained in the caves, in the womb of the Mother, caring for our children. And it was there that the Great Mother taught us everything.

"Men lived through movement, while we remained close to the womb of the Mother. This allowed us to see that seeds are turned into plants, and we told this to the men. We made the first bread, and we fed our people. We shaped the first cup so that we could drink. And we came to understand the cycle of creation, because our bodies repeat the rhythm of the moon."

She stopped suddenly. "There She is!"

I looked. There in the middle of the plaza, surrounded on all sides by traffic, was a fountain portraying a woman in a carriage drawn by lions.

"This is the Plaza Cybele," I said, trying to show off my knowledge of Madrid. I had seen this fountain on dozens of postcards.

But the young woman wasn't listening. She was already in the middle of the street, trying to make her way through the traffic. "Come on! Let's go over there!" she shouted, waving to me from the midst of the cars.

I decided to try to follow her, if only to get the name of a hotel. Her craziness was wearing me out; I needed to get some sleep.

We made it to the fountain at almost the same time; my heart was pounding, but she had a smile on her lips. "Water!" she exclaimed. "Water is Her manifestation."

"Please, I need the name of an inexpensive hotel."

She plunged her hands into the water. "You should do this, too," she said to me. "Feel the water."

"No! But I don't want to spoil your experience. I'm going to look for a hotel."

"Just a minute."

Brida took a small flute from her bag and began to play. To my surprise, the music had a hypnotic effect; the sounds of the traffic receded, and my racing heart began to slow down. I sat on the edge of the fountain, listening to the noise of the water and the sound of the flute, my eyes on the full moon gleaming above us. Somehow I was sensing—although I couldn't quite understand it—that the moon was a reflection of my womanhood.

I don't know how long she continued to play. When she stopped, she turned to the fountain. "Cybele, manifestation of the Great Mother, who governs the harvests, sustains the cities, and returns to woman her role as priestess . . ."

"Who are you?" I asked. "Why did you ask me to come with you?"

She turned to me. "I am what you see me to be. I am a part of the religion of the earth."

"What do you want from me?"

"I can read your eyes. I can read your heart. You are going to fall in love. And suffer."

"I am?"

"You know what I'm talking about. I saw how he was looking at you. He loves you."

This woman was really nuts!

"That's why I asked you to come with me—because he is important. Even though he says some silly things, at least he recognizes the Great Mother. Don't let him lose his way. Help him."

"You don't know what you're talking about. You're dreaming!" And I turned and rushed back into the traffic, swearing I'd forget everything she had said.

Sunday, December 5, 1993

❦ ❦ ❦

We stopped for a cup of coffee.

"Yes, life teaches us many things," I said, trying to continue the conversation.

"It taught me that we can learn, and it taught me that we can change," he replied, "even when it seems impossible."

Clearly he wanted to drop the subject. We had hardly spoken during the two-hour drive that had brought us to this roadside café.

In the beginning, I had tried to reminisce about our childhood adventures, but he'd shown only a polite interest. In fact, he hadn't even really been listening to me; he kept asking me questions about things I had already told him.

Something was wrong. Had time and distance taken him away from my world forever? *After all, he talks about "magic moments,"* I reasoned. *Why would he care about an old friend's career? He lives in a different universe, where Soria is only a remote memory—a town frozen in time, his childhood friends still young boys and girls, the old folks still alive and doing the same things they'd been doing for so many years.*

I was beginning to regret my decision to come with him. So when he changed the subject again, I resolved not to insist any further.

The last two hours of the drive to Bilbao were torture. He was watching the road, I was looking out the window, and neither of us could hide the bad feelings that had arisen between us. The rental car didn't have a radio, so all we could do was endure the silence.

"Let's ask where the bus station is," I suggested as soon as we left the highway. "The buses leave from here regularly for Zaragoza."

It was the hour of siesta, and there were few people in the streets. We passed one gentleman and then a couple of teenagers, but he didn't stop to ask them. "Do you know where it is?" I spoke up, after some time had passed.

"Where what is?"

He still wasn't paying attention to what I said.

And then suddenly I understood what the silence was about. What did he have in common with a woman who had never ventured out into the world? How could he possibly be interested in spending time with someone who feared the unknown, who preferred a secure job and a conventional marriage to the life he led? Poor me, chattering away about friends from childhood and dusty memories of an insignificant village—those were the only things I could discuss.

When we seemed to have reached the center of town, I said, "You can let me off here." I was trying to sound casual, but I felt stupid, childish, and irritated.

He didn't stop the car.

"I have to catch the bus back to Zaragoza," I insisted.

"I've never been here before," he answered. "I have no idea where my hotel is, I don't know where the conference is being held, and I don't know where the bus station is."

"Don't worry, I'll be all right."

He slowed down but kept on driving.

"I'd really like to . . . ," he began. He tried again but still couldn't finish his thought.

I could imagine what he would like to do: thank me for the company, send greetings to his old friends—maybe that would break the tension.

"I would really like it if you went with me to the conference tonight," he finally said.

I was shocked. Was he stalling for time so that he could make up for the awkward silence of our trip?

"I'd really like you to go with me," he repeated.

Now, maybe I'm a girl from the farm with no great stories to tell. Maybe I lack the sophistication of women from the big city. Life in the country may not make a woman elegant or worldly, but it still teaches her how to listen to her heart and to trust her instincts.

To my surprise, my instincts told me that he meant what he said.

I sighed with relief. Of course I wasn't going to stay for any conference, but at least my friend seemed to be back. He was even inviting me along on his adventures, wanting to share his fears and triumphs with me.

"Thanks for the invitation," I said, "but I don't have enough money for a hotel, and I do need to get back to my studies."

"I have some money. You can stay in my room. We'll ask for two beds."

I noticed that he was beginning to perspire, despite

the chill in the air. My heart sounded an alarm, and all the joy of the moment before turned into confusion.

Suddenly he stopped the car and looked directly into my eyes.

No one can lie, no one can hide anything, when he looks directly into someone's eyes. And any woman with the least bit of sensitivity can read the eyes of a man in love.

I thought immediately of what that weird young woman at the fountain had said. It wasn't possible—but it seemed to be true.

I had never dreamed that after all these years he would still remember. When we were children, we had walked through the world hand in hand. I had loved him—if a child can know what love means. But that was so many years ago—it was another life, a life whose innocence had opened my heart to all that was good.

And now we were responsible adults. We had put away childish things.

I looked into his eyes. I didn't want to—or wasn't able to—believe what I saw there.

"I just have this last conference, and then the holidays of the Immaculate Conception begin. I have to go up into the mountains; I want to show you something."

This brilliant man who was able to speak of magic moments was now here with me, acting as awkward as could be. He was moving too fast, he was unsure of himself; the things he was proposing were confused. It was painful for me to see him this way.

I opened the door and got out, then leaned against the fender, looking at the nearly deserted street. I lit a cigarette. I could try to hide my thoughts, pretend that I didn't understand what he was saying; I could try to convince myself that this was just a suggestion made by one childhood friend to another. Maybe he'd been on the road too long and was beginning to get confused.

Maybe I was exaggerating.

He jumped out of the car and came to my side.

"I'd really like you to stay for the conference tonight," he said again. "But if you can't, I'll understand."

There! The world made a complete turn and returned to where it belonged. It wasn't what I had been thinking; he was no longer insisting, he was ready to let me leave—a man in love doesn't act that way.

I felt both stupid and relieved. Yes, I could stay for at least one more day. We could have dinner together and get a little drunk—something we'd never done when we were younger. This would give me a chance to forget the stupid ideas I'd just had, and it would be a good opportunity to break the ice that had frozen us ever since we left Madrid.

One day wouldn't make any difference. And then at least I'd have a story to tell my friends.

"Separate beds," I said, joking. "And you pay for dinner, because I'm still a student. I'm broke."

We put our bags in the hotel room and came down to see where the conference was to be held. Since we were so early, we sat down in a café to wait.

"I want to give you something," he said, handing me a small red pouch.

I opened it and found inside an old rusty medal, with Our Lady of Grace on one side and the Sacred Heart of Jesus on the other.

"That was yours," he said, noticing my surprise. My heart began to sound the alarm again. "One day—it was autumn, just like it is now, and we must have been ten—I was sitting with you in the plaza where the great oak stood.

"I was going to tell you something, something I had rehearsed for weeks. But as soon as I began, you told me that you had lost your medal at the hermitage of San Satúrio, and you asked me to see if I could find it there."

I remembered. Oh, God, I remembered!

"I did find it. But when I returned to the plaza, I no longer had the courage to say what I had rehearsed. So I promised myself that I would return the medal to you only when I was able to complete the sentence that I'd begun that day almost twenty years ago. For a long time, I've tried to forget it, but it's always there. I can't live with it any longer."

He put down his coffee, lit a cigarette, and looked at the ceiling for a long time. Then he turned to me. "It's a very simple sentence," he said. "I love you."

❦ ❦ ❦

SOMETIMES AN UNCONTROLLABLE *feeling of sadness grips us,* he said. *We recognize that the magic moment of the day has passed and that we've done nothing about it. Life begins to conceal its magic and its art.*

We have to listen to the child we once were, the child who still exists inside us. That child understands magic moments. We can stifle its cries, but we cannot silence its voice.

The child we once were is still there. Blessed are the children, for theirs is the kingdom of heaven.

If we are not reborn—if we cannot learn to look at life with the innocence and the enthusiasm of childhood—it makes no sense to go on living.

There are many ways to commit suicide. Those who try to kill the body violate God's law. Those who try to kill the soul also violate God's law, even though their crime is less visible to others.

We have to pay attention to what the child in our heart tells us. We should not be embarrassed by this child. We must not allow this child to be scared because the child is alone and is almost never heard.

We must allow the child to take the reins of our lives. The child knows that each day is different from every other day.

We have to allow it to feel loved again. We must please this child—even if this means that we act in ways we are not used to, in ways that may seem foolish to others.

Remember that human wisdom is madness in the eyes of God. But if we listen to the child who lives in our soul, our eyes will grow bright. If we do not lose contact with that child, we will not lose contact with life.

ග ග ග

THE COLORS AROUND ME were growing vivid; I felt that I was speaking with more intensity and that my glass made a louder sound when I put it down on the table.

A group of about ten of us were having dinner together after the conference. Everyone was speaking at the same time, and I was smiling, for this night was special: it was the first night in many years that I had not planned.

What a joy!

When I'd decided to go to Madrid, I had been in control of my actions and my feelings. Now, suddenly, all that had changed. Here I was in a city where I'd never set foot before, even though it was only three hours from the place where I'd been born. I was sitting at a table where I knew only one person, and everyone was speaking to me as if they'd known me for years. I was amazed that I could enter into the conversation, that I could drink and enjoy myself with them.

I was there because suddenly life had presented me with Life. I felt no guilt, no fear, no embarrassment. As I listened to what he was saying—and felt myself growing closer to him—I was more and more convinced that he was right: there are moments when you have to take a risk, to do crazy things.

I spend day after day with my texts and notebooks, making this superhuman effort just to purchase my own servitude, I thought. *Why do I want that job? What does it offer me as a human being, as a woman?*

Nothing! I wasn't born to spend my life behind a desk, helping judges dispose of their cases.

No, I can't think that way about my life. I'm going to have to return to it this week. It must be the wine. After all, when all is said and done, if you don't work, you don't eat. This is all a dream. It's going to end.

But how long can I make the dream go on?

For the first time I considered going to the mountains with him for the next few days. After all, a week of holidays was about to begin.

"Who are you?" a woman at our table asked me.

"A childhood friend," I answered.

"Was he doing these things when he was a child, too?"

"What things?"

The conversation at the table seemed to fade and then die out.

"You know: the miracles."

"He could always speak well." I didn't understand what she meant.

Everyone laughed, including him. I had no idea what was going on. But—maybe because of the wine—I felt relaxed, and for once I didn't feel like I had to be in control.

I looked around and then said something that I forgot the next moment: I was thinking about the upcoming holiday.

It was good to be here, meeting new people, talking about serious things but always with a touch of humor. I felt like I was really participating in the world. For at least this one night, I was no longer just seeing the real world through television or the newspapers. When I returned to Zaragoza, I'd have stories to tell. If I accepted his invitation for the holidays, I'd have whole years of memories to live on.

He was so right not to pay any attention to my remarks about Soria, I thought. And I began to feel sorry for myself; for so many years, my drawer full of memories had held the same old stories.

"Have some more wine," a white-haired man said, filling my glass.

I drank it down. I kept thinking about how few things I would have had to tell my children and grandchildren if I hadn't come with him.

"I'm counting on our trip to France," he said to me so that only I could hear.

The wine had freed my tongue. "But only if you understand one thing."

"What's that?"

"It's about what you said before the conference. At the café."

"The medal?"

"No," I said, looking into his eyes and doing everything I could to appear sober. "What you said."

"We'll talk about it later," he said, quickly trying to change the subject.

He had said that he loved me. We hadn't had time to talk about it, but I knew I could convince him that it wasn't true.

"If you want me to take the trip with you, you have to listen to me," I said.

"I don't want to talk about it here. We're having a good time."

"You left Soria when you were very young," I went on. "I'm only a link to your past. I've reminded you of your roots, and that's what makes you think as you do. But that's all it is. There can't be any love involved."

He listened but didn't answer. Someone asked him his opinion about something, and our conversation was interrupted.

At least I've explained how I feel, I thought. *The love he was talking about only exists in fairy tales.*

In real life, love has to be possible. Even if it is not returned right away, love can only survive when the hope exists that you will be able to win over the person you desire.

Anything else is fantasy.

From the other side of the table, as if he had guessed what I was thinking, he raised his glass in a toast. "To love," he said.

I could tell that he, too, was a little drunk. So I decided to take advantage of the opening: "To those wise enough to understand that sometimes love is nothing more than the foolishness of childhood," I said.

"The wise are wise only because they love. And the foolish are foolish only because they think they can understand love," he answered.

The others at the table heard him, and in a moment an animated discussion about love was in full swing. Everyone had a strong opinion and was defending their position tooth and nail; it took more wine to calm things down. Finally someone said it was getting late and that the owner of the restaurant wanted to close.

"We have five days of vacation," someone shouted from another table. "If the owner wants to close, it's just because you were getting too serious."

Everyone laughed—except me.

"Then where can we talk about serious things?" someone asked the drunk at the other table.

"In church!" said the drunk. And this time all of us laughed.

My friend stood up. I thought he was going to start a fight, because we were all acting like adolescents, and that's what adolescents do. Fighting is as much a part of being a teenager as the kisses, the secret embraces, the loud music, and the fast pace.

But instead he took my hand and moved toward the door. "We should go," he said. "It's getting late."

ഗ ഗ ഗ

IT WAS RAINING in Bilbao.

Lovers need to know how to lose themselves and then how to find themselves again. He was able to do both well. Now he was happy, and as we returned to the hotel he sang:

Son los locos que inventaron el amor.

The song was right: it must have been the lunatics who invented love.

I was still feeling the effects of the wine, but I was struggling to think clearly. I had to stay in control of the situation if I wanted to make the trip with him.

But it will be easy to be in control because I'm not too emotional, I thought. *Anyone who can conquer her heart can conquer the world.*

Con un poema y un trombón
a develarte el corazón

To lose my heart to you with a poem and a trombone. I wish I didn't have to control my heart. If I could surrender, even if only for a weekend, this rain falling on my face would feel different. If love were easy, I would be embracing him now, and the words of his song would be our story. If Zaragoza weren't waiting for me after the holidays, I'd want to stay drunk and be free to kiss him, caress him, say the things and hear the things that lovers say and do to each other.

But no! I can't. I don't want to.

Salgamos a volar, querida mia, the song says.

Yes, let's fly away. But under my *conditions.*

He still didn't know that I was going to say yes to his invitation. Why did I want to take this risk?

Because I was drunk, because I was tired of days that were all the same.

But this weariness will pass. I'm going to want to get back to Zaragoza, where I have chosen to live. My studies are waiting for me. The husband I'm still looking for is waiting for me—a husband who won't be as difficult to find.

An easier life waits for me, with children and grandchildren, with a clear budget and a yearly vacation. I don't know what his fears are, but I know my own. I don't need new fears—my own are enough.

I was sure I could never fall in love with someone like him. I knew him too well, all his weaknesses and fears. I just couldn't admire him as the others seemed to.

But love is much like a dam: if you allow a tiny crack to form through which only a trickle of water can pass, that trickle will quickly bring down the whole structure, and soon no one will be able to control the force of the current.

For when those walls come down, then love takes over, and it no longer matters what is possible or impossible; it doesn't even matter whether we can keep the loved one at our side. To love is to lose control.

No, no, I cannot allow such a crack to form. No matter how small.

"Hey, hold up a minute!"

He stopped singing immediately. Quick steps echoed on the damp pavement behind us.

"Let's get out of here," he said, grabbing my arm.

"Wait!" a man shouted. "I need to talk to you!"

But he moved ahead even more rapidly. "This has nothing to do with us," he said. "Let's get to the hotel."

Yet it did have to do with us—there was no one else on the street. My heart was beating fast, and the effects of the wine disappeared altogether. I remembered that Bilbao was in Basque country and that terrorist attacks were common. The man's footsteps came closer.

"Let's go," he said, hurrying along.

But it was too late. A man's figure, soaked from head to foot, stepped in front of us.

"Stop, please!" the man said. "For the love of God."

I was frightened. I looked around frantically for a means of escape, hoping that by some miracle a police car would appear. Instinctively, I clutched at his arm—but he pulled away.

"Please!" said the man. "I heard that you were in the city. I need your help. It's my son." The man knelt on the pavement and began to weep. "Please," he said, "please!"

My friend gasped for breath; I watched as he lowered his head and closed his eyes. For a few minutes the silence was broken only by the sound of the rain and the sobs of the man kneeling on the sidewalk.

"Go to the hotel, Pilar," he said finally. "Get some sleep. I won't be back until dawn."

Monday, December 6, 1993

ᔕ ᔕ ᔕ

Love is a trap. When it appears, we see only its light, not its shadows.

"Look at the land around here!" he said. "Let's lie down on the ground and feel the planet's heart beating!"

"But I'll get my coat dirty, and it's the only one I have with me."

We were driving through hills of olive groves. After yesterday's rain in Bilbao, the morning sun made me sleepy. I hadn't brought sunglasses—I hadn't brought anything, since I'd expected to return to Zaragoza two days ago. I'd had to sleep in a shirt he loaned me, and I'd bought a T-shirt at a shop near the hotel in Bilbao so that at least I could wash the one I was wearing.

"You must be sick of seeing me in the same clothes every day," I said, trying to make a joke about something trivial to see if that would make all this seem real.

"I'm glad you're here."

He hadn't mentioned love again since he had given me the medal, but he had been in a good mood; he seemed to be eighteen again. Now he walked along beside me bathed in the clear morning light.

"What do you have to do over there?" I asked, pointing toward the peaks of the Pyrenees on the horizon.

"Beyond those mountains lies France," he answered with a smile.

"I know—I studied geography, too, you know. I'm just curious about why we have to go there."

He paused, smiling to himself. "So you can take a look at a house you might be interested in."

"If you're thinking about becoming a real estate agent, forget it. I don't have any money."

It didn't matter to me whether we visited a village in Navarra or went all the way to France. I just didn't want to spend the holidays in Zaragoza.

You see? I heard my brain say to my heart. *You're happy that you've accepted his invitation. You've changed—you just haven't recognized it yet.*

No, I hadn't changed at all. I was just relaxing a little.

"Look at the stones on the ground."

They were rounded, with no sharp edges. They looked like pebbles from the sea. But the sea had never been here in the fields of Navarra.

"The feet of laborers, pilgrims, and explorers smoothed these stones," he said. "The stones were changed—and the travelers were too."

"Has traveling taught you all the things you know?"

"No. I learned from the miracles of revelation."

I didn't understand, but I didn't pursue it. For now, I was content to bask in the beauty of the sun, the fields, and the mountains.

"Where are we going now?" I asked.

"Nowhere. Let's just enjoy the morning, the sun, and the countryside. We have a long trip ahead of us." He hesitated for a moment and then asked, "Do you still have the medal?"

"Sure, I've kept it," I said, and began to walk faster. I didn't want to talk about the medal—I didn't want to talk about anything that might ruin the happiness and freedom of our morning together.

❦ ❦ ❦

A VILLAGE APPEARED. Like most medieval cities, it was situated atop a mountain peak; even from a distance, I could see the tower of a church and the ruins of a castle.

"Let's drive to that village," I suggested.

Although he seemed reluctant, he agreed. I could see a chapel along the road, and I wanted to stop and go in. I didn't pray anymore, but the silence of churches always attracted me.

Don't feel guilty, I was saying to myself. *If he's in love, that's his problem.* He had asked about the medal. I knew that he was hoping we'd get back to our conversation at the café. But I was afraid of hearing something I didn't want to hear. *I won't get into it, I won't bring up the subject.*

But what if he really did love me? What if he thought that we could transform this love into something deeper?

Ridiculous, I thought to myself. *There's nothing deeper than love. In fairy tales, the princesses kiss the frogs, and the frogs become princes. In real life, the princesses kiss princes, and the princes turn into frogs.*

After driving for another half hour, we reached the chapel. An old man was seated on the steps. He was the first person we'd seen since our drive began.

It was the end of fall, and, in keeping with tradition, the fields had been returned once more to the Lord, who would fertilize the land with his blessings and allow human beings to harvest his sustenance by the sweat of their brows.

"Hello," he said to the man.

"How are you?"

"What is the name of this village?"

"San Martín de Unx."

"Unx?" I said. "It sounds like the name of a gnome."

The old man didn't understand the joke. Disappointed, I walked toward the entrance to the chapel.

"You can't go in," warned the old man. "It closed at noon. If you like, you can come back at four this afternoon."

The door was open and I could look inside, although it was so bright out that I couldn't see clearly.

"Just for a minute?" I asked. "I'd like to say a prayer."

"I'm very sorry. It's already closed."

He was listening to my conversation with the old man but didn't say anything.

"All right, then, let's leave," I said. "There's no point in arguing."

He continued to look at me, his gaze empty, distant. "Don't you want to see the chapel?" he asked.

I could see he didn't approve of my decision. *He thinks I'm weak, cowardly, unable to fight for what I want. Even without a kiss, the princess is transformed into a frog.*

"Remember yesterday?" I said. "You ended our conversation in the bar because you didn't want to argue with me. Now when I do the same thing, you criticize me."

The old man watched our discussion impassively. He was probably happy that something was actually happening, there in a place where all the mornings, all the afternoons, and all the nights were the same.

"The door to the church is open," he said, speaking to the old man. "If you want some money, we can give you some. But she wants to see the church."

"It's too late."

"Fine. We'll go in anyway." He took my arm and we went in.

My heart was pounding. The old man could get nasty, call the police, ruin the trip.

"Why are you doing this?"

"Because you wanted to see the chapel."

I was so nervous I couldn't even focus on what was inside. The argument—and my attitude—had ruined our perfect morning.

I listened carefully for any sounds from outside. *The old man might call the village police,* I thought. *Trespassers in the chapel! Thieves! They're breaking the law!* The old man had said the chapel was closed, that visiting hours were over. *He's a poor old man, unable to keep us from going in. And the police will be tough on us because we offended a feeble old man.*

I stayed inside the chapel just long enough to show that I'd really wanted to see it. As soon as enough time had passed for an imaginary Ave Maria, I said, "Let's go."

"Don't be frightened, Pilar. Don't just fall into playing a role."

I didn't want my problem with the old man to become a problem with him, so I tried to stay calm. "I don't know what you mean by 'playing a role.'"

"Some people always have to be doing battle with someone, sometimes even with themselves, battling with their own lives. So they begin to create a kind of play in their head, and they write the script based on their frustrations."

"I know a lot of people like that. I know just what you mean."

"But the worst part is that they cannot present the play by themselves," he continued. "So they begin to invite other actors to join in.

"That's what that fellow outside was doing. He wanted revenge for something, and he chose us to play a part. If we had accepted his restrictions, we'd be regretting it now. We would have been defeated. We would have agreed to participate in his miserable life and in his frustrations.

"The man's aggression was easy to see, so it was easy for us to refuse the role he wanted us to play. But other people also 'invite' us to behave like victims, when they complain about the unfairness of life, for example, and ask us to agree, to offer advice, to participate."

He looked into my eyes. "Be careful. When you join in that game, you always wind up losing."

He was right. But I still wasn't happy about being inside the chapel. "OK, but I've already said my prayer. I've done what I wanted to do. Let's go."

The contrast between the darkness inside the chapel and the strong sunlight blinded me for a few moments. When my eyes adjusted, I saw that the old man was no longer there.

"Let's have some lunch," he said, walking in the direction of the village.

ʊ ʊ ʊ

I DRANK TWO GLASSES of wine at lunch. I'd never done that in my life.

He was speaking to the waiter, who told him that there were several Roman ruins in the area. I was trying to listen to their conversation, but I was having trouble stifling my bad mood.

The princess had turned into a frog. So what? Who do I have to prove anything to? I wasn't looking for anything—not for a man and certainly not for love.

I knew it, I said to myself. *I knew he was going to turn my world upside down. My brain warned me, but my heart didn't want to take its advice.*

I've paid a considerable price for the little I have gained. I've been forced to deny myself many things I've wanted, to abandon so many roads that were open to me. I've sacrificed my dreams in the name of a larger dream—a peaceful soul. I didn't want to give up that peace.

"You're tense," he said, breaking off his conversation with the waiter.

"Yes, I am. I think that old man went for the police. I think this is a small place, and they know where we are. I think this boldness of yours about having lunch here could wind up ruining our holiday."

He twirled his glass of water. Surely he knew that this was not the problem—that I was actually ashamed.

Why do we always do this? Why do we notice the speck in our eye but not the mountains, the fields, the olive groves?

"Listen, that's not going to happen," he said. "The old man has gone home and has already forgotten the whole thing. Trust me."

That's not why I'm so tense, you idiot.

"Listen to your heart more," he went on.

"That's just it! I *am* listening to it," I said. "And I feel that we should leave. I'm not enjoying this place."

"You shouldn't drink during the day. It doesn't help anything."

Up to that point, I'd controlled myself. Now it was time to say what I thought.

"You think you know everything," I said, "that you know all about magic moments, the inner child . . . I don't know what you're doing here with me."

He laughed. "I admire you. And I admire the battle you're waging with your heart."

"What battle?"

"Never mind," he said.

But I knew what he was talking about.

"Don't kid yourself," I said. "We can talk about it if you like. You're mistaken about my feelings."

He stopped fooling with his glass and looked at me. "No, I'm not mistaken. I know you don't love me."

This confused me even more.

"But I'm going to fight for your love," he continued. "There are some things in life that are worth fighting for to the end."

I was speechless.

"You are worth it," he said.

I turned away, trying to pretend that I was interested in the restaurant's decor. I had been feeling like a frog, and suddenly I was a princess again.

I want to believe what you're saying, I thought to myself. *It won't change anything, but at least I won't feel so weak, so incapable.*

"I apologize for my outburst," I said.

He smiled, signaled to the waiter, and paid the check.

On the way back to the car, I became confused again. Maybe it was the sun—but no, it was autumn, and the sun was weak. Perhaps the old man—but he disappeared a while ago.

All this was so new to me. Life takes us by surprise and orders us to move toward the unknown—even when we don't want to and when we think we don't need to.

I tried to concentrate on the scenery, but I couldn't focus on the olive groves, the village atop the mountain, the chapel with the old man at the gate. All of it was so unfamiliar.

I remembered how much I'd drunk the day before and the song he had sung:

Las tardecitas de Buenos Aires tienen este no sé . . .

¿Qué sé yo?

Viste, salí de tu casa, por Arenales . . .

Why sing of the nights of Buenos Aires, when we were in Bilbao? I didn't live on a street called Arenales. What had gotten into him?

"What was that song you were singing yesterday?" I asked.

"*Balada para un loco,*" he said. "Why do you ask about it now?"

"I don't know."

But I had a reason: I knew he'd sung the song as a kind of snare. He'd made me memorize the words, just as I would memorize course work for an examination. He could have sung a song I was familiar with—but he'd chosen one I'd never heard before.

It was a trap. Later, if I heard the song played on the radio or at a club, I'd think of him, of Bilbao, and of a time in my life when autumn turned to spring. I'd recall the excitement, the adventure, and the child who was reborn out of God knows where.

That's what he was thinking. He was wise, experienced; he knew how to woo the woman he wanted.

I'm going crazy, I told myself. *I must be an alcoholic, drinking so much two days in a row. He knows all the tricks. He's controlling me, leading me along with his sweetness.*

"I admire the battle you are waging with your heart," he had said at the restaurant.

But he was wrong. Because I had fought with my heart and defeated it long ago. I was certainly not going to become passionate about something that was impossible. I knew my limits; I knew how much suffering I could bear.

"Say something," I demanded, as we walked back to the car.

"What?"

"Anything. Talk to me."

So he began to tell me about the visions of the Virgin Mary at Fátima. I don't know why he came up with that, but the story of the three shepherds who had spoken to the Virgin distracted me.

My heart relaxed. *Yes, I know my limits, and I know how to stay in control.*

WE ARRIVED AT NIGHT in a fog so dense we could hardly see where we were. I could make out only a small plaza, a lamppost, some medieval houses barely illuminated by the yellow light, and a well.

"The fog!" he exclaimed.

I couldn't understand why he was so excited.

"We're in Saint-Savin," he explained.

The name meant nothing to me. But we were in France, and that in itself thrilled me.

"Why this place?" I asked.

"Because the house I want you to see is here," he answered, laughing. "Also, I promised that I would come back here on the day of the Immaculate Conception."

"Here?"

"Well, near here."

He stopped the car. When we stepped out, he took my hand, and we began to walk through the fog.

"This place became a part of my life quite unexpectedly," he said.

You too? I thought.

"When I first came here, I thought I was lost. But I wasn't—actually, I was just rediscovering it."

"You talk in riddles sometimes," I said.

"This is where I realized how much I needed you in my life."

I looked away; I couldn't understand him. "But what does that have to do with losing your way?"

"Let's find someone who'll rent us a room, because the two hotels in this village are only open during the summer. Then we'll have dinner at a good restaurant—no tension, no fear of the police, no need to think about running back to the car! And when the wine loosens our tongues, we'll talk about many things."

We both laughed. I already felt more relaxed. During the drive here, I had looked back over the wild things I'd been thinking. And as we crossed over the top of the mountains that separate France from Spain, I'd asked God to cleanse my soul of tension and fear.

I was tired of playing the child and acting the way many of my friends did—the ones who are afraid that love is impossible without even knowing what love is. If I stayed like that, I would miss out on everything good that these few days with him might offer.

Careful, I thought. *Watch out for the break in the dam. If that break occurs, nothing in the world will be able to stop it.*

"May the Virgin protect us from here on," he said.

I remained silent.

"Why didn't you say 'amen'?" he asked.

"Because I don't think that's important anymore. There was a time when religion was a part of my life, but that time has passed."

He turned around and began to walk back to the car. "I still pray," I went on. "I prayed as we were crossing the Pyrenees. But it's something automatic, and I'm not even sure I still believe in it."

"Why?"

"Because I've suffered, and God didn't listen to my prayers. Because many times in my life I have tried to love with all my heart, and my love has wound up being trampled or betrayed. If God is love, he should have cared more about my feelings.

"God *is* love. But the one who understands this best is the Virgin."

I burst out laughing. When I turned to look at him, I saw that he was serious—this was not a joke.

"The Virgin understands the mystery of total surrender," he went on. "And having loved and suffered, she freed us from pain. In the same way that Jesus freed us from sin."

"Jesus was the son of God. They say that the Virgin was merely a woman who happened to receive him into her womb," I said. I was trying to make up for my laughter and let him know that I respected his faith.

He opened the car door and took out our bags. When I tried to take mine from his hand, he smiled. "Let me carry your bag."

No one's done that for me in a long time, I thought.

We knocked on the door of the first house, but the woman said she didn't rent rooms. At the second door, no one answered. At the third, a kind old man greeted us—but when we looked at the room, there was only a double bed. I turned it down.

"Maybe we should head for a larger city," I suggested as we left.

"We'll find a room," he said. "Do you know the exercise of the Other? It's part of a story written a hundred years ago, whose author . . ."

"Forget the author, and tell me the story," I interrupted. We were once more walking along the only street in Saint-Savin.

❦ ❦ ❦

A MAN RUNS INTO an old friend who had somehow never been able to make it in life. "I should give him some money," he thinks. But instead he learns that his old friend has grown rich and is actually seeking him out to repay the debts he had run up over the years.

They go to a bar they used to frequent together, and the friend buys drinks for everyone there. When they ask him how he became so successful, he answers that until only a few days ago, he had been living the role of the "Other."

"What is the Other?" they ask.

"The Other is the one who taught me what I should be like, but not what I am. The Other believes that it is our obligation to spend our entire life thinking about how to get our hands on as much money as possible so that we will not die of hunger when we are old. So we think so much about money and our plans for acquiring it that we discover we are alive only when our days on earth are practically done. And then it's too late."

"And you? Who are you?"

"I am just like everyone else who listens to their heart: a person who is enchanted by the mystery of life. Who is open to miracles, who experiences joy and enthusiasm for what they do. It's just that the Other, afraid of disappointment, kept me from taking action."

"But there is suffering in life," one of the listeners said.

"And there are defeats. No one can avoid them. But it's better to lose some of the battles in the struggle for your dreams than to be defeated without ever even knowing what you're fighting for."

"That's it?" another listener asked.

"Yes, that's it. When I learned this, I resolved to become the person I had always wanted to be. The Other stood there in the corner of my room, watching me, but I will never let the Other into myself again—even though it has already tried to frighten me, warning me that it's risky not to think about the future.

"From the moment that I ousted the Other from my life, the Divine Energy began to perform its miracles."

ග ග ග

IN SPITE OF the fact that my friend had long ago expelled the Other from his life, he still wasn't having much luck finding us lodging for the night. But I knew he hadn't told me that story for his own sake—he had told it for mine. He seemed to be talking about my fears, my insecurity, and my unwillingness to see what was wonderful because tomorrow it might disappear and then I would suffer.

The gods throw the dice, and they don't ask whether we want to be in the game or not. They don't care if when you go, you leave behind a lover, a home, a career, or a dream. The gods don't care whether you have it all, whether it seems that your every desire can be met through hard work and persistence. The gods don't want to know about your plans and your hopes. Somewhere they're throwing the dice—and you are chosen. From then on, winning or losing is only a question of luck.

The gods throw the dice, freeing love from its cage. And love can create or destroy—depending on the direction of the wind when it is set free.

For the moment, the wind was blowing in his favor. But the wind is as capricious as the gods—and deep inside myself, I had begun to feel some gusts.

AT LAST, as if fate wanted to show me that the story of the Other was true—and the universe always conspires to help the dreamer—we found a house to stay in, with a room with separate beds. My first move was to bathe, wash my clothes, and put on the shirt I had bought. I felt refreshed, and this made me feel more secure.

After having dinner with the couple who owned the house—the restaurants were also closed during the autumn and winter—he asked for a bottle of wine, promising to replace it the next day. We put on our coats, borrowed two glasses, and went out.

"Let's sit on the edge of the well," I suggested.

And there we sat, drinking to keep the cold and the tension away.

"It looks like the Other has gotten to you," I joked. "Your good mood seems to have disappeared."

He laughed. "I knew we were going to find a room, and we did. The universe always helps us fight for our dreams, no matter how foolish they may be. Our dreams are our own, and only we can know the effort required to keep them alive."

In the fog, which hung yellow under the glow of the street lamp, we couldn't see even as far as the other side of the plaza.

I took a deep breath. We couldn't avoid the subject any longer.

"We have to talk about love," I said. "You know how I've been these last few days. If it had been up to me, the subject would never have come up. But ever since you brought it up, I haven't been able to stop thinking about it."

"It's risky, falling in love."

"I know that," I answered. "I've been in love before. It's like a narcotic. At first it brings the euphoria of complete surrender. The next day, you want more. You're not addicted yet, but you like the sensation, and you think you can still control things. You think about the person you love for two minutes, and forget them for three hours.

"But then you get used to that person, and you begin to be completely dependent on them. Now you think about him for three hours and forget him for two minutes. If he's not there, you feel like an addict who can't get a fix. And just as addicts steal and humiliate themselves to get what they need, you're willing to do anything for love."

"What a horrible way to put it," he said.

It really was a horrible way to put it; my analogy didn't go with the romance of the evening—the wine, the well, and the medieval houses in the plaza. But it was true. If he was going to base so many of his actions on love, he needed to know what the risks were.

"So we should love only those who can stay near us," I said.

He looked out at the fog. Now he no longer seemed interested in whether we negotiated the dangerous waters of a conversation about love. I was being tough, but there was no other way.

Subject closed, I thought. *Our being together for these three days has been enough to change his mind.* My pride was a bit wounded, but my heart was relieved. *Do I really want this?* I asked myself. I realized that I was already beginning to sense the storms brought on by the winds of love. I had already begun to feel the break in the dam.

We drank for some time without bringing up anything serious. We talked about the couple who owned the house and the saint for whom the town had been named. He told me some of the legends about the church across the square, which I could barely see in the fog.

"You're upset," he said at one point.

Yes, my mind was wandering. I wished I were there with someone who could bring peace to my heart—someone with whom I could spend a little time without being afraid that I would lose him the next day. With that reassurance, the time would pass more slowly. We could be silent for a while because we'd know we had the rest of our lives together for conversation. I wouldn't have to worry about serious matters, about difficult decisions and hard words.

❦ ❦ ❦

WE SAT THERE in silence—and that in itself was a sign. For the first time, we had nothing to say, although I only noticed this when he stood up to go find us another bottle of wine.

Silence. Then I heard the sound of his footsteps returning to the well where we'd been sitting for more than an hour, drinking and staring at the fog.

This was the first time we'd been silent for so long. It was not the awkward silence of the trip from Madrid to Bilbao. And not the silence of my fearful heart when we were in the chapel near San Martín de Unx.

This was a silence that spoke for itself. A silence that said we no longer needed to explain things to each other.

The sound of his footsteps halted. He was looking at me—and what he saw must have been beautiful: a woman seated on the edge of a well, on a foggy night, in the light of the street lamp.

The ancient houses, the eleventh-century church, and the silence.

The second bottle of wine was half empty when I decided to speak.

"This morning, I convinced myself that I was an alcoholic. I've been drinking from morning to night. In these past three days, I've drunk more than in the entire past year."

He reached out and stroked my hair without saying anything. I absorbed his touch without trying to pull away.

"Tell me about your life since I last saw you," I asked.

"There are no great mysteries to tell. My path is always there, and I do everything I can to follow it in a dignified way."

"What is your path?"

"The path of someone seeking love."

He hesitated for a moment, fiddling with the near-empty bottle.

"And love's path is really complicated," he concluded.

"Because on that path we can go either to heaven or to hell?" I wasn't sure whether he was referring to us or not.

He didn't respond. Perhaps he was still deep in the ocean of silence, but the wine had loosened my tongue again, and I had to speak.

"You said that something here in this city altered your course."

"Yes, I think it did. I'm still not absolutely sure, and that's why I wanted to bring you here."

"Is this some kind of test?"

"No. It's a surrender. So that She will help me to make the right decision."

"Who will?"

"The Virgin."

The Virgin! I should have known. I was surprised that all his years of travel, of learning, of new horizons hadn't freed him from the Catholicism of his childhood. In at least this respect, my friends and I had come a long way—we no longer lived under the weight of guilt and sin.

"I'm surprised that after all you've been through, you still keep the faith."

"I haven't kept it. I lost it and recovered it."

"But a faith in virgins? In impossible things and in fantasies? Haven't you had an active sex life?"

"Well, normal. I've been in love with many women."

To my surprise, I felt a stab of jealousy. But my inner battle seemed already to have subsided, and I didn't want to start it up again.

"Why is she 'The Virgin'? Why isn't She presented to us as a normal woman, like any other?"

He drained the few drops remaining in the bottle and asked if I wanted him to go for another. I said no.

"What I want is an answer from you. Every time we start to speak about certain things, you try to talk about something else."

"She *was* normal. She had already had other children. The Bible tells us that Jesus had two brothers. Virginity, as it relates to Jesus, is based on a different thing: Mary initiated a new generation of grace. A new era began. She is the cosmic bride, Earth, which opens to the heavens and allows itself to be fertilized.

"Because of the courage She showed in accepting her destiny, She allowed God to come down to earth—and She was transformed into the Great Mother."

I didn't understand exactly what he was telling me, and he could see that.

"She is the feminine face of God. She has her own divinity."

He spoke with great emotion; in fact, his words almost sounded forced, as if he felt he was committing a sin.

"A goddess?" I asked.

I waited for him to explain, but he couldn't say anything more. I thought about his Catholicism and about how what he had just said seemed blasphemous.

"Who is the Virgin? What is the Goddess?"

"It's not easy to explain," he said, clearly growing

more and more uncomfortable. "I have some written material with me. If you want, you can read it."

"I don't want to read right now; I want you to explain it to me," I insisted.

He looked around for the wine bottle, but it was empty. Neither of us could remember why we had come to the well in the first place. Something important was in the air—as if what he was saying were part of a miracle.

"Go on," I urged him.

"Her symbol is water—like the fog all around us. The Goddess uses water as the means to manifest Herself."

The mist suddenly seemed to take on a life of its own, becoming sacred—even though I still didn't understand what he was trying to say.

"I don't want to talk to you about history. If you want to learn about the history, you can read the books I brought with me. But you should know that this woman—the Goddess, the Virgin Mary, the Shechinah, the Great Mother, Isis, Sofia, slave and mistress—is present in every religion on the face of the earth. She has been forgotten, prohibited, and disguised, but Her cult has continued from millennium to millennium and continues to survive today.

"One of the faces of God is the face of a woman."

I studied his face. His eyes were gleaming, and he was staring into the fog that enveloped us. I could see that I no longer needed to prompt him.

"She is present in the first chapter of the Bible—when the spirit of God hovered over the waters, and He placed them below and above the stars. It was the mystic marriage of earth and heaven. She is present in the final chapter of the Bible, when

the Spirit and the bride say, "Come!"
And let him who hears say, "Come!"

And let him who thirsts come.
Whoever desires, let him take the
water of life freely."

"Why is water the symbol of the feminine face of God?"

"I don't know. But She normally chooses that medium to manifest Herself. Maybe because She is the source of life; we are generated in water, and for nine months we live in it. Water is the symbol of the power of woman, the power that no man—no matter how enlightened or perfect he may be—can capture."

He paused for a moment and then began again.

"In every religion and in every tradition, She manifests Herself in one form or another—She always manifests Herself. Since I am a Catholic, I perceive Her as the Virgin Mary."

He took me by the hand, and in less than five minutes, we had walked out of Saint-Savin. We passed a column by the side of the road that had something strange at the top: it was a cross with an image of the Virgin in the place where Jesus ought to have been.

Now the darkness and the mist completely enveloped us. I began to imagine I was immersed in water, in the maternal womb—where time and thought do not exist. Everything he had been saying to me was beginning to make sense. I remembered the woman at the conference. And then I thought of the girl who had led me to the plaza. She too had said that water was the symbol of the Goddess.

ග ග ග

TWENTY KILOMETERS from here there's a grotto," he was telling me. "On the eleventh of February, 1858, a young girl was baling hay near the grotto with two other children. She was a fragile, asthmatic girl who lived in miserable poverty. On that winter's day, she was afraid of crossing a small stream, because if she got wet she might fall ill. And her parents needed the little money she made as a shepherd.

"A woman dressed in white, with two golden roses on her feet, appeared. The woman treated the child as if she were a princess, asked if she might return to that place a certain number of times, and then vanished. The two other girls, who were entranced by what had happened, quickly spread the story.

"This brought on a long ordeal for the girl. She was imprisoned, and the authorities demanded that she deny the whole story. Others offered her money to get her to ask the apparition for special favors. Within days, her family began to be insulted in the plaza by people who thought that the girl had invented the story in order to get attention.

"The girl, whose name was Bernadette, had no understanding of what she had seen. She referred to the lady who had appeared as 'That,' and her parents, concerned as they were, went to the village priest for assistance.

The priest suggested that when the apparition next appeared, Bernadette should ask the woman's name.

"Bernadette did as she was asked, but received only a smile in response. 'That' appeared before her a total of eighteen times and, for the most part, said nothing. During one of her appearances, though, she asked the girl to kiss the ground. Without understanding why, Bernadette did as she was asked. During another visitation, she asked the girl to dig a hole in the floor of the grotto. Bernadette obeyed, and there immediately appeared a hole filled with filthy water, because swine were kept there.

" 'Drink the water,' the woman said.

"The water was so dirty that although Bernadette cupped it in her hands, she threw it away three times, afraid to bring it to her mouth. Finally she did, despite her repugnance. In the place where she had dug, more water began to come forth. A man who was blind in one eye applied several drops of the water to his face and recovered his vision. A woman, desperate because her newborn child appeared to be dying, dipped the child in the spring—on a day when the temperature had fallen below zero. And the child was cured.

"Little by little, the word spread, and thousands of people began to come to the place. The girl repeatedly asked the woman her name, but the woman merely smiled.

"Until one day, 'That' turned to Bernadette, and said, 'I am the Immaculate Conception.'

"Satisfied at last, the girl ran to tell the parish priest.

" 'That cannot be,' he said. 'No one can be the tree and the fruit at the same time, my child. Go there, and throw holy water on her.'

"As far as the priest was concerned, only God could have existed from the very beginning—and God, as far as anyone could tell, was a man."

He paused for a long time.

"Bernadette threw holy water on 'That,' and the apparition smiled tenderly, nothing more.

"On the sixteenth of July, the woman appeared for the last time. Shortly after, Bernadette entered a convent, not knowing that she had changed forever the destiny of that small village near the grotto. The spring continued to flow, and miracles followed, one after the other.

"The story spread, first throughout France and later the world. The city grew and was transformed. Businesses sprang up everywhere. Hotels opened. Bernadette died and was buried in a place far from there, never knowing what had occurred.

"Some people who wanted to put the church in a bad light—and who knew that the Vatican was now acknowledging apparitions—began to invent false miracles that were later unmasked. The church reacted strongly: from a certain date on, it would accept as miracles only those phenomena that passed a rigorous series of examinations performed by medical and scientific commissions.

"But the water still flows, and the cures continue."

I heard something nearby; it frightened me, but he didn't seem to notice. The fog now had a life and a story of its own. I was thinking about everything he had told me, and I wondered how he knew all of this.

I thought about the feminine face of God. The man at my side had a soul filled with conflict. A short time ago, he had written to me that he wanted to enter a Catholic seminary, yet now he was thinking that God has a feminine face.

He was silent. I still felt as if I were in the womb of the Earth Mother, beyond time and place.

"There were two important things that Bernadette didn't know," he finally said. "The first was that prior to the arrival of the Christian religion in these parts, these mountains were inhabited by Celts—and the Goddess was their principal object of devotion. Generations and generations had understood the feminine face of God and shared in Her love and Her glory."

"And the second thing?"

"The second was that a short time before Bernadette experienced her visions, the authorities at the Vatican had met in secret. Virtually no one knew what had occurred at those meetings—and there's no question but that the priest in the small village didn't have the slightest idea. The highest council of the Catholic Church was deciding whether they should ratify the dogma regarding the Immaculate Conception.

"The dogma wound up being ratified, through the papal bull known as *Ineffabilis Deus*. But the general public never knew exactly what this meant."

"And what do you have to do with all this?" I asked.

"I am Her disciple. I have learned through Her." He seemed to be saying that She was the source of all his knowledge.

"You have seen Her?"

"Yes."

ග ග ග

We returned to the plaza and walked toward the church. I saw the well in the lamplight, with the bottle of wine and two glasses on its wall. *A couple of sweethearts must have been here,* I think. *Silent, allowing their hearts to speak to each other. And after their hearts had said all they had to say, they began to share the great mysteries.*

I felt that I was facing something quite serious and that I needed to learn everything I could from my experiences. For a few moments, I thought about my studies, about Zaragoza, and about the man I was hoping to find in my life—but all that seemed far away, clouded by the mists over Saint-Savin.

"Why did you tell me the story of Bernadette?" I asked.

"I don't know why exactly," he answered, without looking at me directly. "Maybe because we're not too far from Lourdes. Maybe because the day after tomorrow is the day of the Immaculate Conception. Or maybe it was because I wanted to show you that my world is not so solitary and mad as it may appear. There are others who are part of that world, and they believe in what they say."

"I never said that your world is mad. Maybe it's mine that's crazy. I mean, here I am, spending the most crucial time of my life concentrating on textbooks and courses that won't help me at all to escape from the place I already know too well."

I sensed that he was relieved that I understood him. I expected him to say something more about the Goddess, but instead he turned to me and said, "Let's get some sleep. We've had a lot to drink."

Tuesday, December 7, 1993

ฯ ฯ ฯ

HE WENT straight to sleep, but I was awake for a long time, thinking about the fog, the wine, and our conversation. I read the manuscript he gave me, and what was in it thrilled me: God—if God really existed—was both Father and Mother.

Later, I turned out the light and lay there thinking. When we were quiet with each other, I was able to see how close I felt to him.

Neither of us had said anything. Love doesn't need to be discussed; it has its own voice and speaks for itself. That night, by the well, the silence had allowed our hearts to approach each other and get to know each other better. My heart had listened closely to what his had said, and now it was content.

Before I fell asleep, I decided I would do what he called the "exercise of the Other."

I am here in this room, I thought, *far from everything familiar to me, talking about things that have never interested me and sleeping in a city where I've never set foot before. I can pretend—at least for a few minutes—that I am different.*

I began to imagine how I would like to be living right at that moment. I wanted to be happy, curious, joyful—living every moment intensely, drinking the water of life thirstily. Believing again in my dreams. Able to fight for what I wanted.

Loving a man who loved me.

Yes, that was the woman I wanted to be—the woman who was suddenly presenting herself and becoming me.

I felt that my soul was bathed in the light of a god—or of a goddess—in whom I had lost faith. And I felt that at that moment, the Other left my body and was standing in the corner of that small room.

I observed the woman I had been up until then: weak but trying to give the impression of strength. Fearful of everything but telling herself it wasn't fear—it was the wisdom of someone who knew what reality was. Putting up shutters in front of windows to keep the joy of the sun from entering—just so the sun's rays wouldn't fade my old furniture.

I looked at the Other, there in the corner of the room—fragile, exhausted, disillusioned. Controlling and enslaving what should really be free: her emotions. Trying to judge her future loves by the rules of her past suffering.

But love is always new. Regardless of whether we love once, twice, or a dozen times in our life, we always face a brand-new situation. Love can consign us to hell or to paradise, but it always takes us somewhere. We simply have to accept it, because it is what nourishes our existence. If we reject it, we die of hunger, because we lack the courage to stretch out a hand and pluck the fruit from the branches of the tree of life. We have to take love where we find it, even if that means hours, days, weeks of disappointment and sadness.

The moment we begin to seek love, love begins to seek us.

And to save us.

When the Other left me, my heart once again began to speak to me. It told me that the breach in the dike had allowed the waters to pour through, that the wind was blowing in all directions at once, and that it was happy because I was once again willing to listen to what it had to say.

My heart told me that I was in love. And I fell asleep with a smile on my lips.

❦ ❦ ❦

WHEN I AWOKE, the window was open and he was gazing at the mountains in the distance. I watched him without saying anything, ready to close my eyes if he turned toward me.

As if he knew, he turned and looked at me.

"Good morning," he said.

"Good morning. Close the window—it's so cold."

The Other had appeared with no warning. It was still trying to change the direction of the wind, to detect shortcomings, to say, No, that's impossible. But it knew it was too late.

"I have to get dressed," I said.

"I'll wait for you downstairs."

I got up, banished the Other from my thoughts, opened the window again, and let the sun in. Its light bathed everything—the mountains with their snow-covered peaks, the ground blanketed in dry leaves, and the river, which I could hear but not see.

The sun shone on me, warming my nude body. I was no longer cold—I was consumed by a heat, the heat of a spark becoming a flame, the flame becoming a bonfire, the bonfire becoming an inferno. I knew.

I wanted this.

I also knew that from this moment on I was going to experience heaven and hell, joy and pain, dreams and hopelessness; that I would no longer be capable of containing the winds that blew from the hidden corners of my soul. I knew that from this moment on love would be my guide—and that it had waited to lead me ever since childhood, when I had felt love for the first time. The truth is, I had never forgotten love, even when it had deemed me unworthy of fighting for it. But love had been difficult, and I had been reluctant to cross its frontiers.

I recalled the plaza in Soria and the moment when I had asked him to find the medal I had lost. I had known what he was going to tell me, and I hadn't wanted to hear it, because he was the type who would someday go off in search of wealth, adventure, and dreams. I needed a love that was possible.

I realized that I had known nothing of love before. When I saw him at the conference and accepted his invitation, I'd thought that I, as a mature woman, would be able to control the heart of the girl who had been looking for so long for her prince. Then he had spoken about the child in all of us—and I'd heard again the voice of the child I had been, of the princess who was fearful of loving and losing.

For four days, I had tried to ignore my heart's voice, but it had grown louder and louder, and the Other had become desperate. In the furthest corner of my soul, my true self still existed, and I still believed in my dreams. Before the Other could say a word, I had accepted the ride with him. I had accepted the invitation to travel with him and to take the risks involved.

And because of that—because of that small part of me that had survived—love had finally found me, after it had looked for me everywhere. Love had found me, despite the barricade that the Other had built across a quiet street in Zaragoza, a barricade of preconceived ideas, stubborn opinions, and textbooks.

I opened the window and my heart. The sun flooded the room, and love inundated my soul.

❦ ❦ ❦

We wandered for hours, through the snow and along the roads. We breakfasted in a village whose name I never found out but in whose central plaza a dramatic fountain sculpture displayed a serpent and a dove combined into a single fabulous creature.

He smiled when he saw it. "It's a sign—masculine and feminine joined in a single figure."

"I'd never thought before about what you told me yesterday," I said. "But it makes sense."

" 'And God created man and woman,' " he quoted from Genesis, "because that was his image and simulacrum: man and woman."

I noted a new gleam in his eye. He was happy and laughed at every silly thing. He fell into easy conversation with the few people we met along the way—workers dressed in gray on their way to the fields, adventurers in colorful gear, preparing to climb a mountain peak. I said little—my French is awful—but my soul rejoiced at seeing him this way.

His joy made everyone who spoke with him smile. Perhaps his heart had spoken to him, and now he knew that I loved him—even though I was still behaving like just an old friend.

"You seem happier," I said at one point.

"Because I've always dreamed of being here with you, walking through these mountains and harvesting the 'golden fruits of the sun.'"

The golden fruits of the sun—a verse written ages ago, repeated by him now, at just the right moment.

"There's another reason you're happy," I said, as we left the small village with the strange statue.

"What's that?"

"You know that I'm happy. You're responsible for my being here today, climbing the mountains of truth, far from my mountains of notebooks and texts. You're making me happy. And happiness is something that multiplies when it is divided."

"Did you do the exercise of the Other?"

"Yes. How did you know?"

"Because you've changed too. And because we always learn that exercise at the right time."

The Other pursued me all through the morning. Every minute, though, its voice grew fainter, and its image seemed to dissolve. It reminded me of those vampire films where the monster crumbles into dust.

We passed another column with an image of the Virgin on the cross.

"What are you thinking about?" he asked me.

"About vampires. Those creatures of the night, locked inside themselves, desperately seeking company. Incapable of loving."

"That's why legend has it that only a stake through the heart can kill them; when that happens, the heart bursts, freeing the energy of love and destroying the evil."

"I never thought of that before. But it makes sense."

I had succeeded in burying the stake. My heart, freed of all its curses, was aware of everything. The Other no longer had a place to call its own.

A thousand times I wanted to take his hand, and a thousand times I stopped myself. I was still confused—I wanted to tell him I loved him, but I didn't know how to begin.

We talked about the mountains and the rivers. We were lost in a forest for almost an hour, but eventually we found the path again. We ate sandwiches and drank melted snow. When the sun began to set, we decided to return to Saint-Savin.

ග ග ග

THE SOUND of our footsteps echoed from the stone walls. At the entrance to the church, I instinctively dipped my hand in the font of holy water and made the sign of the cross. I recalled that water was the symbol of the Goddess.

"Let's go in," he suggested.

We walked through the dark, empty building. Saint Savin, a hermit who had lived at the start of the first millennium, was buried below the main altar. The walls of the place were crumbling and had clearly been reconstructed several times.

Some places are like that: they can suffer through wars, persecutions, and indifference, but they still remain sacred. Finally someone comes along, senses that something is missing, and rebuilds them.

I noticed an image of the crucified Christ that gave me a funny feeling—I had the impression that his head was moving, following me.

"Let's stop here."

We were before an altar of Our Lady.

"Look at the image."

Mary, with her son in her lap. The infant Jesus pointing to the heavens.

"Look more carefully," he said.

I studied the details of the wooden carving: the gilt paint, the pedestal, the perfection with which the artist had traced the folds of the robe. But it was when I focused on the finger of the child Jesus that I understood what he meant.

Although Mary held him in her arms, it was Jesus who was supporting her. The child's arm, raised to the sky, appeared to be lifting the Virgin toward heaven, back to the place of Her Groom's abode.

"The artist who created this more than six hundred years ago knew what he wanted to convey," he commented.

Footsteps sounded on the wooden floor. A woman entered and lit a candle in front of the main altar.

We remained silent for a while, respecting her moment of prayer.

Love never comes just a little at a time, I thought, as I watched him, absorbed in contemplation of the Virgin. The previous day, the world had made sense, even without love's presence. But now we needed each other in order to see the true brilliance of things.

When the woman had gone, he spoke again. "The artist knew the Great Mother, the Goddess, and the sympathetic face of God. You've asked me a question that up until now I haven't been able to answer directly. It was 'Where did you learn all this?' "

Yes, I had asked him that, and he had already answered me. But I didn't say so.

"Well, I learned in the same way that this artist did: I accepted love from on high. I allowed myself to be guided," he went on. "You must remember the letter I wrote you, when I spoke of wanting to enter a monastery. I never told you, but I did in fact do that."

I immediately remembered the conversation we'd had before the conference in Bilbao. My heart began to beat faster, and I tried to fix my gaze on the Virgin. She was smiling.

It can't be, I thought. *You entered and then you left. Please, tell me that you left the monastery.*

"I had already lived some pretty wild years," he said, not guessing my thoughts this time. "I got to see other peoples and other lands. I had already looked for God in the four corners of the earth. I had fallen in love with other women and worked in a number of different jobs."

Another stab. I would have to be careful that the Other didn't return. I kept my gaze on the Virgin's smile.

"The mysteries of life fascinated me, and I wanted to understand them better. I looked for signs that would tell me that someone knew something. I went to India and to Egypt. I sat with masters of magic and of meditation. And finally I discovered what I was looking for: that truth resides where there is faith."

Truth resides where there is faith! I looked around again at the interior of the church—the worn stones, fallen and replaced so many times. What had made human beings so insistent? What had caused them to work so hard at rebuilding this small temple in such a remote spot, hidden in the mountains?

Faith.

"The Buddhists were right, the Hindus were right, the Muslims were right, and so were the Jews. Whenever someone follows the path to faith—sincerely follows it—he or she is able to unite with God and to perform miracles.

"But it wasn't enough simply to know that—you have to make a choice. I chose the Catholic Church because I was raised in it, and my childhood had been impregnated with its mysteries. If I had been born Jewish, I would have chosen Judaism. God is the same, even though He has a thousand names; it is up to us to select a name for Him."

Once again, steps sounded in the church.

❧ ❧ ❧

A MAN APPROACHED and stared at us. Then he turned to the center altar and reached for the two candelabra. He must have been the one responsible for guarding the church.

I remembered the watchman at the other chapel, the man who wouldn't allow us to enter. But this man said nothing.

"I have a meeting tonight," he said when the man left.

"Please, go on with what you were saying. Don't change the subject."

"I entered a monastery close to here. For four years, I studied everything I could. During that time, I made contact with the Clarifieds and the Charismatics, the sects that have been trying to open doors that have been closed for so long to certain spiritual experiences. I discovered that God was not the ogre that had frightened me as a child. There was a movement afoot for a return to the original innocence of Christianity."

"You mean that after two thousand years, they finally understood that it was time to allow Jesus to become a part of the church?" I said with some sarcasm.

"You may think you're joking, but that was exactly it. I began to study with one of the superiors at the monastery. He taught me that we have to accept the fire of revelation, the Holy Spirit."

The Virgin continued to smile, and the infant Jesus kept his joyful expression, but my heart stopped when he said that. I too had believed in that once—but time, age, and the feeling that I was a logical and practical person had distanced me from religion. I realized how much I wanted to recover my childhood faith, when I had believed in angels and miracles. But I couldn't possibly bring it back simply through an act of will.

"The superior told me that if I believed that I knew, then I would in fact eventually know," he continued. "I began to talk to myself when I was in my cell. I prayed that the Holy Spirit would manifest itself and teach me what I needed to know. Little by little, I discovered that as I talked to myself, a wiser voice was saying things for me."

"That's happened to me, too," I interrupted him.

He waited for me to go on. But I couldn't say anything else.

"I'm listening," he said.

Something had stopped my tongue. He was speaking so beautifully, and I couldn't express myself nearly as well.

"The Other wants to come back," he said, as if he had guessed what I was thinking. "The Other is always afraid of saying something that might sound silly."

"Yes," I said, struggling to overcome my fear. "OK, sometimes when I'm talking with someone and get excited about what I'm saying, I find myself saying things I've never said before. It seems almost as if I'm 'channeling' an intelligence that isn't mine—one that understands life much better than me. But this is rare. In most conversations I prefer to listen. I always feel as if I'm learning something new, even though I wind up forgetting it all."

"We are our own greatest surprise," he said. "Faith as tiny as a grain of sand allows us to move mountains. That's what I've learned. And now, my own words sometimes surprise me.

"The apostles were fishermen, illiterate and ignorant. But they accepted the flame that fell from the heavens. They were not ashamed of their own ignorance; they had faith in the Holy Spirit. This gift is there for anyone who will accept it. One has only to believe, accept, and be willing to make mistakes."

The Virgin smiled down on me. She had every reason to cry—but She was joyful.

"Go on."

"That's all," he answered. "Accept the gift. And then the gift manifests itself."

"It doesn't work that way."

"Didn't you understand me?"

"I understand. But I'm like everyone else: I'm scared. It might work for you or for my neighbor, but never for me."

"That will change someday—when you begin to see that we are really just like that child there."

"But until then, we'll all go on thinking we've come close to the light, when actually we can't even light our own flame."

He didn't answer.

"You didn't finish your story about the seminary," I said.

"I'm still there."

Before I could react, he stood up and walked to the center of the church.

I stayed where I was. My head was spinning. *Still in the seminary?*

Better not to think about it. Love had flooded my soul, and there was no way I could control it. There was only one recourse: the Other, with whom I had been harsh because I was weak, and cold because I was afraid—but I no longer wanted the Other. I could no longer look at life through its eyes.

A sharp, sustained sound like that of an immense flute interrupted my thoughts. My heart jumped.

The sound came again. And again. I looked behind me and saw a wooden staircase that led up to a crude platform, which didn't seem to fit with the frozen beauty of the church. On the platform was an ancient organ.

And there he was. I couldn't see his face because the lighting was bad—but I knew he was up there.

I stood up, and he called to me.

"Pilar!" he said, his voice full of emotion. "Stay where you are."

I obeyed.

"May the Great Mother inspire me," he said. "May this music be my prayer for the day."

And he began to play the Ave Maria. It must have been about six in the evening, time for the Angelus—a time when light and darkness merge. The sound of the organ echoed through the empty church, blending in my mind with the stones and the images laden with history and with faith. I closed my eyes and let the music flow through me, cleansing my soul of all fear and sin and reminding me that I am always better than I think and stronger than I believe.

For the first time since I had abandoned the path of faith, I felt a strong desire to pray. Although I was seated in a pew, my soul was kneeling at the feet of the Lady before me, the woman who had said,

"Yes,"

when She could have said "no." The angel would have sought out someone else, and there would have been no sin in the eyes of the Lord, because God knows His children's weakness.

But She had said,

"Thy will be done,"

even though She sensed that She was receiving, along with the words of the angel, all the pain and suffering of Her destiny; even though Her heart's eyes could see Her beloved son leaving the house, could see the people who would follow Him and then deny Him; but

"Thy will be done,"

even when, at the most sacred moment in a woman's life, She had to lie down with the animals in a stable to give birth, because that was what the Scriptures required;

"Thy will be done,"

even when, in agony, She looked through the streets for Her son and found Him at the temple. And He asked that She not interfere because He had other obligations and tasks to perform;

"Thy will be done,"

even when She knew that She would search for Him for the rest of Her days, Her heart filled with pain, fearing every moment for His life, knowing that He was being persecuted and threatened;

"Thy will be done,"

even when, finding Him in the crowd, She was unable to draw near Him;

"Thy will be done,"

even when She asked someone to tell Him that She was there and the son sent back the response, "My mother and my brothers are those who are here with me";

"Thy will be done,"

even when at the end, after everyone had fled, only She, another woman, and one of them stood at the foot of the cross, bearing the laughter of His enemies and the cowardice of His friends;

"Thy will be done."

Thy will be done, my Lord. Because you know the weakness in the heart of your children, and you assign each of them only the burden they can bear. May you understand my love—because it is the only thing I have that is really mine, the only thing that I will be able to take with me into the next life. Please allow it to be courageous and pure; please make it capable of surviving the snares of the world.

The organ stopped, and the sun went into hiding behind the mountains—as if both were ruled by the same Hand. The music had been his prayer, and his prayer had been heard. I opened my eyes and found the church in complete darkness, except for the solitary candle that illuminated the image of the Virgin.

I heard his footsteps again, returning to where I sat. The light of that single candle gleamed on my tears, and my smile—a smile that wasn't perhaps as beautiful as the Virgin's—showed that my heart was alive.

He looked at me, and I at him. My hand reached out for his and found it. Now it was his heart that was beating faster—I could almost hear it in the silence.

But my soul was serene, and my heart at peace.

I held his hand, and he embraced me. We stood there at the feet of the Virgin for I don't know how long. Time had stopped.

She looked down at us. The adolescent girl who had said "yes" to her destiny. The woman who had agreed to carry the son of God in Her womb and the love of God in Her heart. She understood.

I didn't want to ask for anything. That afternoon in the church had made the entire journey worthwhile. Those four days with him had made up for an entire year in which so little had happened.

We left the church hand in hand and walked back toward our room. My head was spinning—seminary, Great Mother, the meeting he had later that night.

I realized then that we both wanted to unite our souls under one destiny—but the seminary and Zaragoza stood in the way. My heart felt squeezed. I looked around at the medieval homes and the well where we had sat the previous night. I recalled the silence and the sadness of the Other, the woman I had once been.

God, I am trying to recover my faith. Please don't abandon me in the middle of this adventure, I prayed, pushing my fears aside.

❧ ❧ ❧

He slept a little, but I stayed awake, looking out the darkened window. Later, we got up and dined with the family—they never spoke at the table. He asked for a key to the house.

"We'll be home late tonight," he said to the woman.

"Young people should enjoy themselves," she answered, "and take advantage of the holidays as best they can."

"I have to ask you something," I said, when we were back in the car. "I've been trying to avoid it, but I have to ask."

"The seminary," he said.

That's right. I don't understand. Even though it's no longer important, I thought.

"I have always loved you," he began. "I kept the medal, thinking that someday I would give it to you and that I'd have the courage to tell you that I love you. Every road I traveled led back to you. I wrote the letters to you and opened every letter of yours afraid that you would tell me you had found someone.

"Then I was called to the spiritual life. Or rather, I accepted the call, because it had been with me since childhood—just as it was for you. I discovered that God was extremely important to my life and that I couldn't be happy if I didn't accept my vocation. The face of Christ was there in the face of every poor soul I met on my travels, and I couldn't deny it."

He paused, and I decided not to push him.

Twenty minutes later, he stopped the car and we got out.

"This is Lourdes," he said. "You should see it during the summer."

What I saw now were deserted streets, closed shops, and hotels with bars across their entrances.

"Six million people come here in the summer," he went on enthusiastically.

"It looks like a ghost town to me."

We crossed a bridge and arrived at an enormous iron gate with angels on either side. One side of the gate was standing open, and we passed through it.

"Go on with what you were saying," I said, in spite of my decision not to pursue it. "Tell me about the face of Christ on the people you met."

I could see that he didn't want to continue the conversation. Perhaps this wasn't the right time or place. But having begun, he had to complete it.

We were walking down a broad avenue, bordered on both sides by snow-covered fields. At its end, I could see the silhouette of a cathedral.

"Go on," I repeated.

"You already know. I entered the seminary. During the first year, I asked that God help me to transform my love for you into a love for all people. In the second year, I sensed that God had heard me. By the third year, even though my longing for you was still strong, I became certain that my love was turning toward charity, prayer, and helping the needy."

"Then why did you seek me out? Why rekindle the flame in me? Why did you tell me about the exercise of the Other and force me to see how shallow my life is?" I sounded confused and tremulous. From one minute to the next, I could see him drawing closer to the seminary and further from me. "Why did you come back? Why wait until today to tell me this story, when you can see that I am beginning to love you?"

He did not answer immediately. Then he said, "You'll think it's stupid."

"I won't. I'm not worried anymore about seeming ridiculous. You've taught me that."

"Two months ago, my superior asked me to accompany him to the house of a woman who had died and left all her wealth to the seminary. She lived in Saint-Savin, and my superior had to prepare an inventory of what was there."

We were approaching the cathedral at the end of the avenue. My intuition told me that as soon as we reached it, any conversation we were having would be interrupted.

"Don't stop," I said. "I deserve an explanation."

"I remember the moment I stepped into that house. The windows looked out on the Pyrenees, and the whole scene was filled with the brightness of the sun, intensified by the snow's glare. I began to make a list of the things in the house, but after just a few minutes, I had to stop.

"I had discovered that the woman's taste was exactly the same as mine. She owned records that I would have purchased, the same music that I would have enjoyed listening to as I looked out on that beautiful landscape. Her bookshelves were filled with books I had already read and others that I would have loved to read. Looking at the furnishings, the paintings, and all her other possessions, I felt as if I had chosen them myself.

"From that day on, I couldn't forget that house. Every time I went to the chapel to pray, I realized that my renunciation had not been total. I imagined myself there with you, looking out at the snow on the mountaintops, a fire blazing in the hearth. I pictured our children running around the house and playing in the fields around Saint-Savin."

Although I had never been near the house, I knew exactly what it looked like. And I hoped he'd say nothing else so that I could fantasize.

But he went on.

"For the past two weeks, I haven't been able to stand the sadness in my soul. I went to my superior and told him what was happening to me. I told him about my love for you and what had begun when we were taking the inventory."

A light rain began to fall. I bowed my head and gathered the front of my coat. I suddenly didn't want to hear the rest of the story.

"So my superior said, 'There are many ways to serve our Lord. If you feel that's your destiny, go in search of it. Only a man who is happy can create happiness in others.'

" 'I don't know if that's my destiny,' I told my superior. 'Peace came into my heart when I entered this seminary.'

" 'Well, then, go there and resolve any doubts you may have,' he said. 'Remain out there in the world, or come back to the seminary. But you have to be committed to the place you choose. A divided kingdom cannot defend itself from its adversaries. A divided person cannot face life in a dignified way.' "

He pulled something from his pocket and handed it to me. It was a key.

"The superior loaned me the key to the house. He said that he would hold off for a while on selling the possessions. I know that he wants me to return to the seminary. But he was the one who arranged the presentation in Madrid—so that we could meet."

I looked at the key in my hand and smiled. In my heart, bells were ringing, and the heavens had opened to me. He could serve God in a different way—by my side. Because I was going to fight for that to happen.

I put the key in my bag.

❦ ❦ ❦

THE BASILICA LOOMED in front of us. Before I could say anything, someone spotted him and came toward us. The light rain continued, and I had no idea how long we would be there; I couldn't forget that I had only one set of clothes, and I didn't want them to get soaked.

I concentrated on that problem. I didn't want to think about the house—that was a matter suspended between heaven and earth, awaiting the hand of destiny.

He introduced me to several people who had gathered around. They asked where we were staying, and when he said Saint-Savin, one of them told us the story of the hermit saint who was buried there. It was Saint Savin who had discovered the well in the middle of the plaza—and the original mission of the village had been to create a refuge for religious persons who had left the city and come to the mountains in search of God.

"They are still living there," another said.

I didn't know if the story was true, nor did I have any idea who "they" were.

Other people began to arrive, and the group began to move toward the entrance of the grotto. An older man tried to tell me something in French. When he saw that I didn't understand, he switched to an awkward Spanish.

"You are with a very special man," he said. "A man who performs miracles."

I said nothing but remembered that night in Bilbao when a desperate man had come looking for him. He had told me nothing about where he had gone, and I hadn't asked. Right now, I preferred to think about the house, which I could picture perfectly—its books, its records, its view, its furniture.

Somewhere in the world, a home awaited us. A place where we could care for daughters or sons who would come home from school, fill the house with joy, and never pick up after themselves.

We walked in silence through the rain until finally we reached the place where the visions of Mary had occurred. It was exactly as I had imagined: the grotto, the statue of Our Lady, and the fountain—protected by glass—where the miracle of the water had taken place. Some pilgrims were praying; others were seated silently inside the grotto, their eyes closed. A river ran past the entrance, and the sound of the water made me feel at peace. As soon as I saw the image, I said a quick prayer, asking the Virgin to help me—my heart needed no more suffering.

If pain must come, may it come quickly. Because I have a life to live, and I need to live it in the best way possible. If he has to make a choice, may he make it now. Then I will either wait for him or forget him.

Waiting is painful. Forgetting is painful. But not knowing which to do is the worst kind of suffering.

In some corner of my heart, I felt that she had heard my plea.

Wednesday, December 8, 1993

❦ ❦ ❦

BY THE TIME the cathedral's clock struck midnight, the group around us had grown considerably. We were almost a hundred people—some of them priests and nuns—standing in the rain, gazing at the statue.

"Hail, Our Lady of the Immaculate Conception," someone close to me said, as soon as the tolling of the bells ceased.

"Hail," everyone answered, with some applause.

A guard immediately came forward and asked that we be quiet. We were bothering the other pilgrims.

"But we've come a long way," said one of the men in our group.

"So have they," answered the guard, pointing to the others who were praying in the rain. "And they are praying silently."

I wanted to be alone with him, far from this place, holding his hand and telling him how I felt. We needed to talk more about the house, about our plans, about love. I wanted to reassure him, to make clear how strong my feelings were, and to let him know that his dream could come true—because I would be at his side, helping him.

The guard retreated, and one of the priests began to recite the rosary in a low voice. When we reached the creed that closes the series of prayers, everyone remained silent, their eyes closed.

"Who are these people?" I asked.

"Charismatics," he answered.

I had heard of them before but didn't know exactly what their name meant. He could see that I didn't understand.

"These are people who accept the fire of the Holy Spirit," he said, "the fire that Jesus left but that is used by so few people to light their candles. These people are very close to the original truth of Christianity, when everyone was capable of performing miracles.

"They are guided by the Woman Dressed by the Sun," he said, pointing with his eyes to the Virgin.

The group began to chant quietly, as if in response to an invisible command.

"You're shivering from the cold. You don't have to take part in this," he said.

"Are you going to stay?"

"Yes. This is my life."

"Then I'm going to participate," I answered, even though I would have preferred to be far from there. "If this is your world, I want to learn to be a part of it."

The group continued to sing. I closed my eyes and tried to follow the words, even though I couldn't speak French. I repeated the words without understanding them. But their sound helped the time to pass more quickly.

It would end soon. And we could return to Saint-Savin, just the two of us.

I went on singing mechanically—but little by little, I began to feel the music taking hold of me, as if it had a life of its own. It was hypnotizing. The cold seemed less bitter, and the rain no longer bothered me. The music made me feel better. It transported me back to a time when God had felt closer to me and had helped me.

Just as I was about to surrender completely to the music, it stopped.

I opened my eyes. This time, instead of a guard, there was a priest. He approached one of the other priests in our group. They whispered to one another for a few moments, and the padre left.

Our priest turned to us. "We have to say our prayers on the other side of the river," he said.

ʚ ʚ ʚ

SILENTLY, WE WALKED across the bridge directly in front of the grotto and moved to the other bank. It was a prettier place, on the bank of the river, surrounded by trees and an open field. The river now separated us from the grotto. From there, we could clearly see the illuminated image, and we could sing loudly without disturbing others' prayers.

The people around me began to sing louder, raising their faces to the sky and smiling as the raindrops coursed down their cheeks. Some raised their arms, and soon everyone joined in, waving their arms from side to side in rhythm to the music.

I wanted to give in to the moment, but at the same time I wanted to pay close attention to what they were doing. One priest near me was singing in Spanish, and I tried to repeat the words. They were invocations to the Holy Spirit and the Virgin, requesting their presence and asking that they rain down their blessings and their powers on each of us.

"May the gift of tongues befall us," said another priest, repeating the phrase in Spanish, Italian, and French.

What happened next was incomprehensible. Each of the many people present began to speak a language that was different from any I had ever heard. It was more sound than speech, with words that seemed to come straight from the soul, making no sense at all. I recalled our conversation in the church, when he had spoken about revelations, saying that all wisdom was the result of listening to one's own soul. *Perhaps this is the language of the angels,* I thought, trying to mimic what they were doing—and feeling ridiculous.

Everyone was looking at the statue of the Virgin on the other side of the river; they all seemed to be in a trance. I looked around for him and found him standing at some distance from me. His hands were raised to the heavens and he was speaking rapidly, as if in conversation with Her. He was smiling and nodding his head as if in agreement; occasionally he looked surprised.

This is his world, I thought.

The whole scene began to scare me. The man I wanted at my side was telling me that God is also female, he was speaking an incomprehensible language, he was in a trance, and he seemed closer to the angels than to me. The house in the mountains began to seem less real, as if it were part of a world that he had already left behind.

All of our days together—starting with the conference in Madrid—seemed to be part of a dream, a voyage beyond the space and time of my life. At the same time, though, the dream had the flavor of the world, of romance, and of new adventures. I had tried to resist; now I knew how easily love could set fire to the heart. I had tried to stay unreceptive to all of this in the beginning; now I felt that since I had loved before, I would know how to handle it.

I looked around again, and it dawned on me that this was not the Catholicism I had been taught at school. And this was not the way I had pictured the man in my life.

A man in my life! How strange! I said to myself, surprised at the thought.

There on the bank of the river, looking across at the grotto, I felt both fear and jealousy. Fear because it was all new to me, and what is new has always scared me. Jealousy because, bit by bit, I could see that his love was greater than I'd thought and spread over places where I'd never set foot.

Forgive me, Our Lady. Forgive me if I'm being selfish or small-minded, competing with you for this man's love.

But what if his vocation wasn't to be with me but was to retreat from the world, locking himself in a seminary and conversing with angels? How long would he resist before he fled from our house to return to his true path? Or even if he never went back to the seminary, what price would I have to pay to keep him from returning to that path?

Everyone there, except me, seemed to be concentrating on what they were doing. I was staring at him, and he was speaking the language of the angels.

Suddenly, fear and jealousy were replaced by calm and solitude. The angels had someone to talk with, and I was alone.

I had no idea what pushed me into trying to speak that strange language. Perhaps it was my strong need to connect with him, to tell him what I was feeling. Perhaps I needed to let my soul speak to me—my heart had so many doubts and needed so many answers.

I didn't know exactly what to do, and I felt ridiculous. But all around me were men and women of all ages, priests and laypeople, novices and nuns, students and old-timers. They gave me the courage to ask the Holy Spirit for the strength to overcome my fear.

Try, I said to myself. *All you have to do is open your mouth and have the courage to say things you don't understand. Try!*

I prayed that this night—the night following a day that had been so long that I couldn't even remember how it had begun—would be an epiphany. A new beginning for me.

God must have heard me. The words began to come more easily—and little by little they lost their everyday meanings. My embarrassment diminished, my confidence grew, and the words began to flow freely. Although I understood nothing of what I was saying, it all made sense to my soul.

Simply having the courage to say senseless things made me euphoric. I was free, with no need to seek or to give explanations for what I was doing. This freedom lifted me to the heavens—where a greater love, one that forgives everything and never allows you to feel abandoned, once again enveloped me.

It feels as if my faith is coming back, I thought, surprised at the miracles that love can perform. I sensed that the Virgin was holding me in her lap, covering me and warming me with her mantle. The strange words flew more rapidly from my lips.

Without realizing it, I began to cry. Joy flooded my heart—a joy that overpowered my fears and was stronger than my attempts to control every second of my life.

I realized that my tears were a gift; at school, the sisters had taught me that the saints wept with ecstasy. I opened my eyes, gazed at the darkness of the heavens, and felt my tears blending with the raindrops. The earth was alive and the drops from above brought the miracles of heaven with them. We were all a part of that same miracle.

How wonderful that God may be a woman, I said to myself, as the others continued to chant. *If that's true, then it was certainly God's feminine face that taught us how to love.*

"Let us pray in tents of eight," said the priest in Spanish, Italian, and French.

Once again, I was confused. What was happening? Someone came over to me and put his arm around my shoulders. Another person did the same on my other side. We formed a circle of eight people, arms around each other's shoulders. Then we leaned forward, our heads touching.

We looked like a human tent. The rain fell harder, but no one cared. The position we had taken concentrated all our energies and heat.

"May the Immaculate Conception help my child find his way," said the man embracing me from the right. "Please, let's say an Ave Maria for my child."

"Amen," everyone said. And we eight prayed an Ave Maria.

"May the Immaculate Conception enlighten me and arouse in me the gift of curing," said a woman from our circle. "Let us say an Ave Maria."

Again, all of us said "Amen" and we prayed. Each person made a petition, and everyone participated in the prayers. I was surprised at myself, because I was praying like a child—and like a child, I believed that our prayers would be answered.

The group fell silent for a fraction of a second. I realized that it was my turn to make a petition. Under any other circumstances, I would have died of embarrassment and been unable to say a word. But I felt a presence, and that presence gave me confidence.

"May the Immaculate Conception teach me to love as she loves," I finally said. "May that love grow in me and in the man to whom it is dedicated. Let us say an Ave Maria."

We prayed together, and again I felt a sense of freedom. For years, I had fought against my heart, because I was afraid of sadness, suffering, and abandonment. But now I knew that true love was above all that and that it would be better to die than to fail to love.

I had thought that only others had the courage to love. But now I discovered that I too was capable of loving. Even if loving meant leaving, or solitude, or sorrow, love was worth every penny of its price.

I have to stop thinking of these things. I have to concentrate on the ritual.

The priest leading the group asked that we disband the tents and pray for the sick. Everyone continued to pray, sing, and dance in the rain, adoring God and the Virgin Mary. Now and then, people went back to speaking strange languages, waving their arms, and pointing to the sky.

"Someone here . . . someone who has a sick daughter-in-law . . . must know that she is being cured," cried one woman.

The prayers resumed, along with chants of joy. From time to time, we would hear the voice of this woman again.

"Someone in this group who lost her mother recently must have faith and know that she is in the glory of heaven."

Later, he would tell me that she had the gift of prophecy, that certain individuals can sense what is happening at some distant place or what will happen in the future.

Secretly, I too believed in the power of that voice that was speaking of miracles. I hoped that voice would speak of the love between two of those present. I hoped to hear that voice proclaim that this love was blessed by all the angels and saints—and by God and by the Goddess.

I'M NOT SURE how long the ritual lasted. People continued to speak in tongues and to chant; they danced with their arms held up to the sky, prayed for the people around them, and petitioned for miracles.

Finally, the priest who was conducting the ceremony said, "Let us chant a prayer for all of those here who are participating for the first time in a Charismatic renewal."

Apparently I was not the only one. That made me feel better.

Everyone chanted a prayer. This time I just listened, asking that favors be granted to me.

I needed many.

"Let us receive the blessing," said the priest.

The crowd turned toward the illuminated grotto across the river. The priest said several prayers and blessed us all. Then everyone kissed, wished each other a "Happy Day of the Immaculate Conception," and went their separate ways.

He came to me. His expression was happier than usual.

"You're soaked," he said.

"So are you!" I laughed.

We walked back to the car and drove to Saint-Savin. I'd been so eager for this moment to arrive—but now that it was here, I didn't know what to say. I couldn't even bring myself to talk about the house in the mountains, the ritual, the strange languages, or the tent prayers.

He was living in two worlds. Somewhere, those two worlds intersected—and I had to find where that was.

But at that moment, words were useless. Love can only be found through the act of loving.

"I've only got one sweater left," he said when we reached the room. "You can have it. I'll buy another for myself tomorrow."

"We'll put our wet things on the heater. They'll be dry by tomorrow. Anyway, I've got the blouse that I washed yesterday."

Neither of us said anything for a few minutes.

Clothing. Nakedness. Cold.

Finally, he took another shirt out of his bag. "You can sleep in this," he said.

"Great," I answered.

I turned out the light. In the dark, I took off my wet clothes, spread them over the heater, and turned it to high.

By the light from the lamppost outside the window, he must have been able to make out my silhouette and known that I was naked. I slipped the shirt on and crawled under the covers.

"I love you," I heard him say.

"I'm learning how to love you."

He lit a cigarette. "Do you think the right moment will come?" he asked.

I knew what he meant. I got up and sat on the edge of his bed.

The light from his cigarette illuminated our faces. He took my hand and we sat there for some time. I ran my fingers through his hair.

"You shouldn't have asked," I said. "Love doesn't ask many questions, because if we stop to think we become fearful. It's an inexplicable fear; it's difficult even to describe it. Maybe it's the fear of being scorned, of not being accepted, or of breaking the spell. It's ridiculous, but that's the way it is. That's why you don't ask—you act. As you've said many times, you have to take risks."

"I know. I've never asked before."

"You already have my heart," I told him. "Tomorrow you may go away, but we will always remember the miracle of these few days. I think that God, in Her infinite wisdom, conceals hell in the midst of paradise—so that we will always be alert, so that we won't forget the pain as we experience the joy of compassion."

He took my face in his hands. "You learn quickly," he said.

I had surprised myself. But sometimes if you think you know something, you do wind up understanding it.

"I hope you won't think I'm being difficult," I said. "I have been with many men. I've made love to some I've barely known."

"Same here," he said.

He was trying to sound natural, but from his touch, I could tell that he hadn't wanted to hear this from me.

"But since this morning, I feel as if I'm rediscovering love. Don't try to understand it, because only a woman would know what I mean. And it takes time."

He caressed my face. Then I kissed him lightly on the lips and returned to my bed.

I wasn't sure why I did. Was I trying to bind him even closer to me, or was I trying to set him free? In any case, it had been a long day, and I was too tired to think about it.

For me, that was a night of great peace. At one point, I seemed to be awake even though I was still sleeping. A feminine presence cradled me in Her lap; I felt as if I had known Her a long time. I felt protected and loved.

I woke at seven, dying of the heat. I remembered having turned the heater to high in order to dry my clothes. It was still dark, and I tried to get up without making a sound so that I wouldn't disturb him.

But as soon as I stood, I could see that he wasn't there.

I started to panic. The Other immediately awoke and said to me, "See? You agreed, and he disappeared. Like all men do."

My panic was increasing by the minute, but I didn't want to lose control. "I'm still here," the Other said. "You allowed the wind to change direction. You opened the door, and now love is flooding your life. If we act quickly, we'll be able to regain control."

I had to be practical, to take precautions.

"He's gone," said the Other. "You have to get away from this place in the middle of nowhere. Your life in Zaragoza is still intact; get back there quickly—before you lose everything you've worked so hard to gain."

He must have had some good reason, I thought.

"Men always have their reasons," said the Other. "But the fact is that they always wind up leaving."

Well, then, I had to figure out how to get back to Spain. I had to keep my wits about me.

"Let's start with the practical problem: money," the Other said.

I didn't have a cent. I would have to go downstairs, call my parents collect, and wait for them to wire me the money for a ticket home.

But it was a holiday, and the money wouldn't arrive until the next day. How would I eat? How would I explain to the owners of the house that they would have to wait for several days for their payment? "Better not to say anything," said the Other.

Right, she was the experienced one. She knew how to handle situations like this. She wasn't the impassioned girl who loses control of herself. She was the woman who always knew what she wanted in life. I should simply stay on there, as if he were expected to return. And when the money arrived, I would pay the bill and leave.

"Very good," said the Other. "You're getting back to how you were before. Don't be sad. One of these days, you'll find another man—one you can love without taking so many risks."

I gathered my clothes from the heater. They were dry. I needed to find out which of the surrounding villages had a bank, make a phone call, take steps. If I thought carefully about all of that, there wouldn't be time for crying or regrets.

Then I saw his note:

I've gone to the seminary. Pack up your things, because we're going back to Spain tonight. I'll be back by late afternoon. I love you.

I clutched the note to my breast, feeling miserable and relieved at the same time. I noticed that the Other had retreated.

I loved him. With every minute that passed, my love was growing and transforming me. I once again had faith in the future, and little by little, I was recovering my faith in God. All because of love.

I will not talk to my own darkness anymore, I promised myself, closing the door on the Other. *A fall from the third floor hurts as much as a fall from the hundredth.*

If I have to fall, may it be from a high place.

❦ ❦ ❦

"DON'T GO OUT hungry again," said the woman.

"I didn't realize you spoke Spanish," I answered, surprised.

"The border isn't far from here. Tourists come to Lourdes in the summer. If I couldn't speak Spanish, I couldn't rent rooms."

She made me some toast and coffee. I was already trying to prepare myself to make it through the day—each hour was going to seem like a year. I hoped that this snack would distract me for a while.

"How long have you two been married?" she asked.

"He was the first person I ever loved," I said. That was enough.

"Do you see those peaks out there?" the woman continued. "The first love of my life died up in those mountains."

"But you found someone else."

"Yes, I did. And I found happiness again. Fate is strange: almost no one I know married the first love of their lives. Those who did are always telling me that they missed something important, that they didn't experience all that they might have."

She stopped talking suddenly. "I'm sorry," she said. "I didn't mean to offend you."

"I'm not offended."

"I always look at that well there in the plaza. And I think to myself that before, no one knew where there was water. Then Saint Savin decided to dig and found it. If he hadn't done that, this village would be down there by the river."

"But what does that have to do with love?" I asked.

"That well brought many people here, with their hopes and dreams and conflicts. Someone dared to look for water, water was found, and people gathered where it flowed. I think that when we look for love courageously, it reveals itself, and we wind up attracting even more love. If one person really wants us, everyone does. But if we're alone, we become even more alone. Life is strange."

"Have you ever heard of the book called the *I Ching?*" I asked her.

"No, I haven't."

"It says that a city can be moved but not a well. It's around the well that lovers find each other, satisfy their thirst, build their homes, and raise their children. But if one of them decides to leave, the well cannot go with them. Love remains there, abandoned—even though it is filled with the same pure water as before."

"You speak like a mature woman who has already suffered a great deal, my dear," she said.

"No. I've always been frightened. I've never dug a well. But I'm trying to do that now, and I don't want to forget what the risks are."

I felt something in the pocket of my bag pressing at me. When I realized what it was, my heart went cold. I quickly finished my coffee.

The key. I had the key.

"There was a woman in this city who died and left everything to the seminary at Tarbes," I said. "Do you know where her house is?"

The woman opened the door and showed me. It was one of the medieval houses on the plaza. The back of the house looked out over the valley toward the mountains in the distance.

"Two priests went through the house about two months ago," she said. "And . . ." She stopped, looking at me doubtfully. "And one of them looked a lot like your husband."

"It was," I answered. The woman stood in her doorway, puzzled, as I quickly left. I felt a burst of energy, happy that I had allowed the child in me to pull a prank.

I soon stood in front of the house, not knowing what to do. The mist was everywhere, and I felt as if I were in a gray dream where strange figures might appear and take me away to places even more peculiar.

I toyed nervously with the key.

With the mist as thick as it was, it would be impossible to see the mountains from the window. The house would be dark; there would be no sun shining through the curtains. The house would seem sad without him at my side.

I looked at my watch. Nine in the morning.

I had to do something—something that would make the time pass, that would help me wait.

Wait. This was the first lesson I had learned about love. The day drags along, you make thousands of plans, you imagine every possible conversation, you promise to change your behavior in certain ways—and you feel more and more anxious until your loved one arrives. But by then, you don't know what to say. The hours of waiting have been transformed into tension, the tension has become fear, and the fear makes you embarrassed about showing affection.

I didn't know whether I should go in. I remembered our conversation of the previous day—the house was the symbol of a dream.

But I couldn't spend the whole day just standing there. I gathered up my courage, grasped the key firmly, and walked to the door.

❦ ❦ ❦

"PILAR!"

The voice, with a strong French accent, came from the midst of the fog. I was more surprised than frightened. I thought it might be the owner of the house where we had rented the room—although I didn't recall having told him my name.

"Pilar!" I heard again, nearer this time.

I looked back at the plaza shrouded in mist. A figure was approaching, walking hurriedly. Perhaps the ghosts that I had imagined in the fog were becoming a reality.

"Wait," the figure said. "I want to talk to you."

When he had come closer, I could see that it was a priest. He looked like a caricature of the country padre: short, on the heavy side, with sparse white hair on a nearly bald head.

"Hola," he said, holding out his hand and smiling.

I answered him, a bit astonished.

"Too bad the fog is hiding everything," he said, looking toward the house. "Since Saint-Savin is in the mountains, the view from this house is beautiful; you can see the valley down below and the snow-covered peaks. But you probably already knew that."

I decided that this must be the superior from the monastery.

"What are you doing here?" I asked. "And how do you know my name?"

"Do you want to go in?" he said, trying to change the subject.

"No! I'd like you to answer my questions."

Rubbing his hands together to warm them, he sat down on the curb. I sat down next to him. The fog was growing thicker by the minute. The church was already hidden from sight, and it was only sixty feet away from us.

All I could see was the well. I remembered what the young woman in Madrid had said.

"She is present," I said.

"Who?"

"The Goddess," I answered. "She is this mist."

"So, he must have talked to you about that," he laughed. "Well, I prefer to refer to Her as the Virgin Mary. That's what I'm used to."

"What are you doing here? How do you know my name?" I repeated.

"I came here because I wanted to see you two. A member of the Charismatic group last night told me you were both staying in Saint-Savin. And it's a small place."

"He went to the seminary."

The padre's smile disappeared, and he shook his head. "Too bad," he said, as if speaking to himself.

"You mean, too bad he went to the seminary?"

"No, he's not there. I've just come from the seminary."

For a moment, I couldn't say anything. I thought back to the feeling I'd had when I woke up: the money, the arrangements I needed to make, the call to my parents, the ticket. But I'd made a vow, and I wasn't going to break it.

A priest was sitting beside me. As a child, I used to tell everything to our priest.

"I'm exhausted," I said, breaking the silence. "Less than a week ago, I finally learned who I am and what I want in life. Now I feel like I've been caught in a storm that's tossing me around, and I can't seem to do anything about it."

"Resist your doubts," the padre said. "It's important."

His advice surprised me.

"Don't be frightened," he continued, as if he knew what I was feeling. "I know that the church is in need of new priests, and he would be an excellent one. But the price he would have to pay would be very high."

"Where is he? Did he leave me here to return to Spain?"

"To Spain? There's nothing for him to do in Spain," said the priest. "His home is at the monastery, only a few kilometers from here. He's not there. But I know where we can find him."

His words brought back some of my joy and courage—at least he hadn't gone away.

But the priest was no longer smiling. "Don't let that encourage you," he went on, again reading my mind. "It would be better if he *had* gone back to Spain."

He stood and asked me to go with him. We could see only a few yards in front of us, but he seemed to know where he was going. We left Saint-Savin by the same road along which, two nights before—or could it have been five years before?—I had heard the story of Bernadette.

"Where are we going?" I asked.

"To find him," he answered.

"Padre, you've confused me," I said, as we walked along together. "You seemed sad when you said he wasn't at the seminary."

"Tell me what you know about the religious life, my child."

"Very little. Only that the priests take a vow of poverty, chastity, and obedience." I wondered whether I should go on and decided that I would. "And that they judge the sins of others, even though they may commit the same sins themselves. That they know all there is to know about marriage and love, but they never marry. That they threaten us with the fires of hell for mistakes that they themselves make. And they present God to us as a vengeful being who blames man for the death of His only Son."

The padre laughed. "You've had an excellent Catholic education," he said. "But I'm not asking you about Catholicism. I'm asking about the spiritual life."

I didn't respond for a moment. "I'm not sure. There are people who leave everything behind and go in search of God."

"And do they find Him?"

"Well, you would know the answer to that, Padre. I have no idea."

The padre noticed that I was beginning to gasp with exertion, and he slowed his pace.

"You had that wrong," he said. "A person who goes in search of God is wasting his time. He can walk a thousand roads and join many religions and sects—but he'll never find God that way.

"God is here, right now, at our side. We can see Him in this mist, in the ground we're walking on, even in my shoes. His angels keep watch while we sleep and help us in our work. In order to find God, you have only to look around.

"But meeting Him is not easy. The more God asks us to participate in His mysteries, the more disoriented we become, because He asks us constantly to follow our dreams and our hearts. And that's difficult to do when we're used to living in a different way.

"Finally we discover, to our surprise, that God wants us to be happy, because He is the father."

"And the mother," I said.

The fog was beginning to clear. I could see a small farmhouse where a woman was gathering hay.

"Yes, and the mother," he said. "In order to have a spiritual life, you need not enter a seminary, or fast, or abstain, or take a vow of chastity. All you have to do is have faith and accept God. From then on, each of us becomes a part of His path. We become a vehicle for His miracles."

"He has already told me about you," I interrupted, "and he has taught me these ideas."

"I hope that you accept God's gifts," he answered. "Because it hasn't always been that way, as history teaches us. Osiris was drawn and quartered in Egypt. The Greek gods battled because of the mortals on earth. The Aztecs expelled Quetzalcoatl. The Viking gods witnessed the burning of Valhalla because of a woman. Jesus was crucified. Why?"

I didn't have an answer.

"Because God came to earth to demonstrate His power to us. We are a part of His dream, and He wants His dream to be a happy one. Thus, if we acknowledge that God created us for happiness, then we have to assume that everything that leads to sadness and defeat is our own doing. That's the reason we always kill God, whether on the cross, by fire, through exile, or simply in our hearts."

"But those who understand Him . . ."

"They are the ones who transform the world—while making great sacrifices."

The woman carrying the hay saw the priest and came running in our direction. "Padre, thank you!" she said, kissing his hands. "The young man cured my husband!"

"It was the Virgin who cured your husband," he said. "The lad is only an instrument."

"It was he. Come in, please."

I recalled the previous night. When we arrived at the cathedral, a man had told me I was with a man who performed miracles.

"We're in a hurry," the padre said.

"No! No, we're not," I said, in my halting French. "I'm cold, and I'd like some coffee."

The woman took me by the hand, and we entered the house. It was simple but comfortable: stone walls, wood floors, and bare rafters. Seated in front of the fireplace was a man of about sixty. As soon as he saw the padre, he stood to kiss his hand.

"Don't get up," said the priest. "You still need to convalesce a bit."

"I've already gained twenty-five pounds," he answered. "But I'm still not able to be of much help to my wife."

"Not to worry. Before long, you'll be better than ever."

"Where is the young man?" the husband asked.

"I saw him heading toward where he always goes," the wife said. "Only today, he went by car."

The padre eyed me but didn't say anything.

"Give us your blessing, Père," the woman asked. "His power . . ."

"The Virgin's power," the priest corrected.

"The Virgin Mother's power is also your power, Père. It was you who brought it here."

This time, he didn't look my way.

"Pray for my husband, Père," the woman insisted.

The priest took a deep breath. "Stand in front of me," he said to the man.

The old man did as he was told. The padre closed his eyes and said an Ave Maria. Then he invoked the Holy Spirit, asking that it be present and help the man.

He suddenly began to speak rapidly. It sounded like a prayer of exorcism, although I couldn't understand what he was saying. His hands touched the man's shoulders and then slid down his arms to his fingertips. He repeated this gesture several times.

The fire began to crackle loudly in the fireplace. This may have been a coincidence, yet it seemed that the priest was entering into territory I knew nothing about—and that he was affecting the very elements.

Every snap of the fire startled the woman and me, but the padre paid no attention to it; he was completely involved in his task—an instrument of the Virgin, as he had said. He was speaking a strange language, and the words came forth at great speed. He was no longer moving his hands; they simply rested on the man's shoulders.

The ritual stopped as quickly as it had started. The padre turned and gave a conventional blessing, making the sign of the cross with his right hand. "May God be ever here in this house," he said.

And turning to me, he asked that we continue our walk.

"But you haven't had coffee," the woman said, as she saw that we were about to leave.

"If I have coffee now, I won't be able to sleep," the padre answered.

The woman laughed and murmured something like "It's still morning." But we were already on our way.

"Padre, the woman spoke of a young man who cured her husband. Was it he?"

"Yes, it was."

I began to feel uneasy. I remembered the day before, and Bilbao, and the conference in Madrid, and people speaking of miracles, and the presence that I had sensed as we embraced and prayed.

I was in love with a man who was capable of performing cures. A man who could help others, bring relief to suffering, give health to the sick and hope to their loved ones. Was I distracting him from his mission just because it was at odds with my image of a house with white curtains, cherished records, and favorite books?

"Don't blame yourself, my child," the padre said.

"You're reading my mind."

"Yes, I am," the padre said. "I have that gift too, and I try to be worthy of it. The Virgin taught me to penetrate the turmoil of human emotions in order to control them as well as possible."

"Do you perform miracles, too?"

"I am not able to cure. But I have one of the gifts of the Holy Spirit."

"So you can read my heart, Padre. And you know I love him, with a love that is growing every minute. We discovered the world together, and together we remain in it. He has been present every day of my life—whether I wanted him there or not."

What could I say to this priest who was walking beside me? He would never understand that I had had other men, that I had been in love, and that if I had married, I would be happy. Even as a child, I had found and forgotten love in the plaza of Soria.

But the way things looked now, I hadn't forgotten that first love very well. It had taken only three days for all of it to come rushing back.

"I have a right to be happy, Padre. I've recovered what was lost, and I don't want to lose it again. I'm going to fight for my happiness. If I give up the fight, I will also be renouncing my spiritual life. As you said, I would be putting God aside, along with my power and my strength as a woman. I'm going to fight for him, Padre."

I knew what that little man was doing here. He had come to convince me to leave him, because he had a more important mission to accomplish.

No, I couldn't believe that the padre walking at my side wanted us to marry and live in a house like the one in Saint-Savin. The priest had said that to trick me. He wanted me to lower my defenses and then—with a smile—he would convince me of the opposite.

He read my thoughts without saying a word. Or perhaps he was trying to fool me. Maybe he didn't know what others were thinking. The fog was dissipating rapidly, and I could now see the path, the mountain peak, the fields, and the snow-covered trees. My emotions were becoming clearer, as well.

Damn! If it's true that he can read someone's thoughts, then let him read mine and know everything! Let him know that yesterday he wanted to make love to me—that I refused and that now I regret it.

Yesterday I had thought that if he had to leave, I would still at least have the memory of my childhood friend. But that was nonsense. Even though he hadn't entered me, something even more profound had, and it had touched my heart.

"Padre, I love him," I repeated.

"So do I. And love always causes stupidity. In my case, it requires that I try to keep him from his destiny."

"That won't be easy, Padre. And it won't be easy in my case, either. Yesterday, during the prayers at the grotto, I discovered that I too can bring forth these gifts that you were talking about. And I'm going to use them to keep him with me."

"Good luck," said the padre, with a smile. "I hope you can."

He stopped and took a rosary from his pocket. Holding it, he looked into my eyes. "Jesus said that we should not take oaths, and I am not doing so. But I'm telling you, in the presence of all that is sacred to me, that I would not like him to adopt the conventional religious life. I would not like to see him ordained a priest. He can serve God in other ways—at your side."

It was hard for me to believe that he was telling me the truth. But he was.

"He's up there," the padre said.

I turned. I could see a car parked a bit further ahead—the same car we had driven from Spain.

"He always comes on foot," he said, smiling. "This time he wanted to give us the impression that he'd traveled a long way."

❦ ❦ ❦

THE SNOW WAS SOAKING my sneakers. But the padre was wearing only open sandals with woolen socks. I decided not to complain—if he could stand it, so could I. We began to hike toward the top of the mountains.

"How long will it take us?"

"Half an hour at the most."

"Where are we going?"

"To meet with him. And others."

I could see that he didn't want to say any more. Maybe he needed all of his energy for climbing. We walked along in silence—the fog had by now disappeared almost completely, and the yellow disk of the sun was coming into view.

For the first time I had a view of the entire valley; there was a river running through it, some scattered villages, and Saint-Savin, looking as though it were pasted against the slope of the mountain. I could make out the tower of the church, a cemetery I had not noticed before, and the medieval houses looking down on the river.

A bit below us, at a point we had already passed, a shepherd was tending his flock of sheep.

"I'm tired," the padre said. "Let's stop for a while."

We brushed the snow from the top of a boulder and rested against it. He was perspiring—and his feet must have been frozen.

"May Santiago preserve my strength, because I still want to walk his path one more time," said the padre, turning to me.

I didn't understand his comment, so I decided to change the subject. "There are footsteps in the snow."

"Some are those of hunters. Others are of men and women who want to relive a tradition."

"Which tradition?"

"The same as that of Saint Savin. Retreat from the world, come to these mountains, and contemplate the glory of God."

"Padre, there's something I need to understand. Until yesterday, I was with a man who couldn't choose between the religious life and marriage. Today, I learn that this same man performs miracles."

"We all perform miracles," he said. "Jesus said, 'If our faith is the size of a mustard seed, we will say to the mountain, "Move!" And it will move.' "

"I don't want a lesson in religion, Padre. I'm in love with a man, and I want to know more about him, understand him, help him. I don't care what everyone else can do or can't do."

The padre took a deep breath. He hesitated for a moment and then said, "A scientist who studied monkeys on an island in Indonesia was able to teach a certain one to wash bananas in the river before eating them.

Cleansed of sand and dirt, the food was more flavorful. The scientist—who did this only because he was studying the learning capacity of monkeys—did not imagine what would eventually happen. So he was surprised to see that the other monkeys on the island began to imitate the first one.

"And then, one day, when a certain number of monkeys had learned to wash their bananas, the monkeys on all of the other islands in the archipelago began to do the same thing. What was most surprising, though, was that the other monkeys learned to do so without having had any contact with the island where the experiment had been conducted."

He stopped. "Do you understand?"

"No," I answered.

"There are several similar scientific studies. The most common explanation is that when a certain number of people evolve, the entire human race begins to evolve. We don't know how many people are needed—but we know that's how it works."

"Like the story of the Immaculate Conception," I said. "The vision appeared for the wise men at the Vatican and for the simple farmer."

"The world itself has a soul, and at a certain moment, that soul acts on everyone and everything at the same time."

"A feminine soul."

He laughed, without saying just what he was laughing about.

"By the way, the dogma of the Immaculate Conception was not just a Vatican matter," he said. "Eight million people signed a petition to the pope, asking that it be recognized. The signatures came from all over the world."

"Is that the first step, Padre?"

"What do you mean?"

"The first step toward having Our Lady recognized as the incarnation of the feminine face of God? After all, we already accept the fact that Jesus was the incarnation of His masculine side."

"And so . . . ?"

"How much time must pass before we accept a Holy Trinity that includes a woman? The Trinity of the Holy Spirit, the Mother, and the Son?"

"Let's move on. It's too cold for us to stand here," he said. "A little while ago, you noticed my sandals."

"Have you been reading my mind?" I asked.

"I'm going to tell you part of the story of the founding of our religious order," he said. "We are barefoot Carmelites, according to the rules established by Saint Teresa of Avila. The sandals are a part of the story, for if one can dominate the body, one can dominate the spirit.

"Teresa was a beautiful woman, placed by her father in a convent so that she would receive a pure education. One day, when she was walking along a corridor, she began to speak with Jesus. Her ecstasies were so strong and deep that she surrendered totally to them, and in a short time, her life had been completely changed. She felt that the Carmelite convents had become nothing more than marriage brokerages, and she decided to create an order that would once again follow the original teachings of Christ and the Carmelites.

"Saint Teresa had to conquer herself, and she had to confront the great powers of her day—the church and the state. But she was determined to press on, because she was convinced that she had a mission to perform.

"One day—just when Teresa felt her soul to be weakening—a woman in tattered clothing appeared at the house where she was staying. The woman wanted to speak with Teresa, no matter what. The owner of the house offered the woman some alms, but the woman refused them; she would not go away until she had spoken with Teresa.

"For three days, the woman waited outside the house, without eating or drinking. Finally Teresa, out of sympathy, bade the woman come in.

" 'No,' said the owner of the house. 'The woman is mad.'

" 'If I were to listen to everyone, I'd wind up thinking that I'm the crazy one,' Teresa answered. 'It may be that this woman has the same kind of madness as I: that of Christ on the cross.' "

"Saint Teresa spoke with Christ," I said.

"Yes," he answered. "But to get back to our story: the woman was brought to Teresa. She said that her name was María de Jesus Yepes and that she was from Granada. She was a Carmelite novice, and the Virgin had appeared and asked that she found a convent that followed the primitive rules of the order."

Like Saint Teresa, I thought.

"María de Jesus left the convent on the day of her vision and began walking barefoot to Rome. Her pilgrimage lasted two years—and for that entire period, she slept outdoors, in the heat and the cold, living on alms and the charity of others. It was a miracle that she made it. But it was an even greater miracle that she was received by Pope Pius IV. Because the pope, just like

María de Jesus, Teresa, and many others, was thinking of the same thing," he finished.

Just as Bernadette had known nothing of the Vatican's decision and the monkeys from the other islands couldn't have known about the experiment that was being conducted, so María de Jesus and Teresa knew nothing of what the other was planning.

Something was beginning to make sense to me.

We were now walking through a forest. With the fog all but gone, the highest tree branches, covered with snow, were receiving the first rays of the sun.

"I think I know where you're going with this, Padre."

"Yes. The world is at a point when many people are receiving the same order: 'Follow your dreams, transform your life, take the path that leads to God. Perform your miracles. Cure. Make prophecies. Listen to your guardian angel. Transform yourself. Be a warrior, and be happy as you wage the good fight. Take risks.' "

Sunshine was everywhere. The snow was glistening, and the glare hurt my eyes. Yet at the same time, it seemed to support what the priest was saying.

"And what does all this have to do with him?"

"I've told you the heroic side of the story. But you don't know anything about the soul of these heroes."

He paused.

"The suffering," he picked up again. "At moments of transformation, martyrs are born. Before a person can follow his dream, others have to make sacrifices. They have to confront ridicule, persecution, and attempts to discredit what they are trying to do."

"It was the church that burned the witches at the stake, Padre."

"Right. And Rome threw the Christians to the lions. But those who died at the stake or in the sand of the arena rose quickly to eternal glory—they were better off.

"Nowadays, warriors of the light confront something worse than the honorable death of the martyrs. They are consumed, bit by bit, by shame and humiliation. That's how it was with Saint Teresa—who suffered for the rest of her life. That's how it was for María de Jesus, too. And for the happy children who saw Our Lady in Fátima, Portugal—well, Jacinta and Francisco died just a few months later; Lucia entered a convent from which she never emerged."

"But that's not how it was for Bernadette."

"Yes, it was. She had to live through prison, humiliation, and discredit. He must have described that to you. He must have told you the words of the visitation."

"Some of them."

"In the visitations at Lourdes, the phrases uttered by Our Lady wouldn't fill half a page of a notebook, but one of the things the Virgin said clearly to the girl was *'I do not promise you happiness in this world.'* Why did she warn Bernadette? Because she knew the pain that awaited Bernadette if she accepted her mission."

I looked at the sun, the snow, and the bare branches of the trees.

"He is a revolutionary," he continued, sounding humble. "He has the power, and he converses with Our Lady. If he is able to concentrate his forces well, he can be one of the leaders in the spiritual transformation of the human race. This is a critical point in the history of the world.

"But if he chooses this path, he is going to go through a great deal of suffering. His revelations have come to him before their time. I know the human soul well enough to know what he can expect."

The padre turned to me and held me by the shoulders. "Please," he said. "Keep him from the suffering and tragedy that lie in store for him. He will not be able to survive them."

"I understand your love for him, Padre."

He shook his head. "No, no. You don't understand anything. You are still too young to know the evils of the world. At this point, you see yourself as a revolutionary too. You want to change the world with him, open new paths, see the story of your love for each other become legend—a story passed down through the generations. You still think that love can conquer all."

"Well, can't it?"

"Yes, it can. But it conquers at the right time—after the celestial battles have ended."

"But I love him. I don't have to wait for the celestial battles to end for my love to win out."

He gazed into the distance.

"On the banks of the rivers of Babylon, we sat down and wept," he said, as if talking to himself. "On the willows there, we hung up our harps."

"How sad," I answered.

"Those are the first lines of one of the psalms. It tells of exile and of those who want to return to the promised land but cannot. And that exile is still going to last for a long time. What can I do to try to prevent the suffering of someone who wants to return to paradise before it is time to do so?"

"Nothing, Padre. Absolutely nothing."

❧ ❧ ❧

"THERE HE IS," said the padre.

I saw him. He was about two hundred yards from me, kneeling in the snow. He was shirtless, and even from that distance, I could see that his skin was red with the cold.

His head was bowed and his hands joined in prayer. I don't know if I was influenced by the ritual I had attended the night before or by the woman who had been gathering hay, but I felt that I was looking at someone with an incredible spiritual force. Someone who was no longer of this world—who lived in communion with God and with the enlightened spirits of heaven. The brilliance of the snow seemed to strengthen this perception.

"At this moment, there are others like him," said the priest. "In constant adoration, communing with God and the Virgin. Hearing the angels, the saints, the prophecies and words of wisdom, and transmitting all of that to a small gathering of the faithful. As long as they continue in this way, there won't be a problem.

"But he is not going to remain here. He is going to travel the world, preaching the concept of the Great Mother. The church is not yet ready for that. And the world has stones at hand to hurl at those who first introduce the subject."

"And it has flowers to throw on those who come afterward."

"Yes. But that's not what will happen to him."

The priest began to approach him.

"Where are you going?"

"To bring him out of his trance. To tell him how much I like you. To say that I give my blessing to your union. I want to do that here, in this place, which for him is sacred."

I began to feel sick with an inexplicable fear.

"I have to think, Padre. I don't know if this is right."

"It's not right," he answered. "Many parents make mistakes with their children, thinking they know what's best for them. I'm not his father, and I know I'm doing the wrong thing. But I have to fulfill my destiny."

I was feeling more and more anxious.

"Let's not disturb him," I said. "Let him finish his contemplation."

"He shouldn't be here. He should be with you."

"Maybe he's communicating with the Virgin."

"He may be. But even so, we have to go to him. If I approach him with you at my side, he will know that I have told you everything. He knows what I think."

"Today is the day of the Immaculate Conception," I insisted. "A very special day for him. I saw his happiness last night at the grotto."

"The Immaculate Conception is special for all of us," the padre answered. "But now I'm the one who doesn't want to discuss religion. Let's go to him."

"Why now, Padre? Why at this moment?"

"Because I know that he is deciding his future. And he may make the wrong choice."

I turned away and began to walk down the same path we had just come up. The padre followed me.

"What are you doing? Don't you see that you're the only one who can save him? Don't you see that he loves you and would give up everything for you?"

I hurried my steps, and it was difficult for him to keep up. Yet he fought to stay at my side.

"At this very moment, he is making his decision! He may be deciding to leave you! Fight for the person you love!"

But I didn't stop. I walked as fast as I could, trying to escape the mountains, the priest, and the choices behind me. I knew that the man who was rushing along behind me was reading my thoughts and that he understood that it was useless to try to make me go back. Yet he insisted; he argued and struggled to the end.

Finally, we reached the boulder where we had rested a half hour earlier. Exhausted, I threw myself down.

I tried to relax. I wanted to run from there, to be alone, to have time to think.

The padre appeared a few minutes later, as exhausted as I was.

"Do you see these mountains surrounding us?" he started in. "They don't pray; they are already a part of God's prayers. They have found their place in the world, and here they will stay. They were here before people looked to the heavens, heard thunder, and wondered who had created all of this. We are born, we suffer, we die, and the mountains endure.

"There is some point at which we have to wonder whether all our effort is worth it. Why not try to be like those mountains—wise, ancient, and in their place? Why risk everything to transform a half-dozen people who will immediately forget what they've been taught and move on to the next adventure? Why not wait until a certain number of monkeys learn, and then the knowledge will spread, with no suffering, to all the other islands?"

"Is that what you really think, Padre?"

He was silent for a few moments.

"Are you reading my thoughts now?"

"No. But if that's the way you feel, you wouldn't have chosen the religious life."

"I've tried many times to understand my fate," he said. "But I haven't yet. I accepted that I was to be a part of God's army, and everything I've done has been in an attempt to explain to people why there is misery, pain, and injustice. I ask them to be good Christians, and they ask me, 'How can I believe in God when there is so much suffering in the world?'

"And I try to explain something that has no explanation. I try to tell them that there is a plan, a battle among the angels, and that we are all involved in the battle. I try to say that when a certain number of people have enough faith to change the scenario, all of the others—everywhere on the planet—will benefit. But they don't believe me. They do nothing."

"They are like the mountains," I said. "The mountains are beautiful. Anyone who beholds them has to think about the grandness of creation. They are living proof of the love that God feels for us, but their fate is merely to give testimony. They are not like the rivers, which move and transform what is around them."

"Yes. But why not be like the mountains?"

"Maybe because the fate of mountains is terrible," I answered. "They are destined to look out at the same scene forever."

The padre said nothing.

"I was studying to become a mountain," I continued. "I had put everything in its proper place. I was going to take a job with the state, marry, and teach the religion of my parents to my children, even though I no longer accepted it. But now I have decided to leave all that behind me in order to be with the man I love. And it's a good thing I decided not to be a mountain—I wouldn't have lasted very long."

"You say some very wise things."

"I'm surprising myself. Before, all I could talk about was my childhood."

I stood and started back down the trail. The padre seemed to respect my silence and did not try to speak to me until we reached the road.

I took his hands and kissed them. "I'm going to say good-bye. But I want you to know that I understand you and your love for him."

The padre smiled and gave me his blessing. "And I understand your love for him, too," he said.

I spent the rest of the day walking through the valley. I played in the snow, visited a village near Saint-Savin, had a sandwich, and watched some boys playing soccer.

At the church in the village, I lit a candle. I closed my eyes and repeated the invocations I had learned the previous night. Then, concentrating on a crucifix that hung behind the altar, I began to speak in tongues. Bit by bit, the gift took over. It was easier than I had thought.

Perhaps this all seems silly—murmuring things, saying words that have no meaning, that don't help us in our reasoning. But when we do this, the Holy Spirit is conversing with our souls, saying things the soul needs to hear.

When I felt that I was sufficiently purified, I closed my eyes and prayed.

Our Lady, give me back my faith. May I also serve as an instrument of your work. Give me the opportunity to learn through my love, because love has never kept anyone away from their dreams.

May I be a companion and ally of the man I love. May we accomplish everything we have to accomplish—together.

When I returned to Saint-Savin, night had almost fallen. The car was parked in front of the house where we were staying.

"Where have you been?" he asked.

"Walking and praying," I answered.

He embraced me.

"At first, I was afraid you had gone away. You are the most precious thing I have on this earth."

"And you are for me," I answered.

❦ ❦ ❦

IT WAS LATE when we stopped in a small village near San Martín de Unx. Crossing the Pyrenees had taken longer than we'd thought because of the rain and snow of the previous day.

"We need to find someplace that's open," he said, climbing out of the car. "I'm hungry."

I didn't move.

"Come on," he insisted, opening my door.

"I want to ask you a question—a question I haven't asked since we found each other again."

He became serious, and I laughed at his concern.

"Is it an important question?"

"Very important," I answered, trying to look serious. "It's the following: where are we going?"

We both laughed.

"To Zaragoza," he said, relieved.

I jumped out of the car, and we went looking for a restaurant that was open. It was going to be almost impossible at that hour of the night.

No, it's not impossible. The Other is no longer with me. Miracles do happen, I said to myself. "When do you have to be in Barcelona?" I asked him. He'd told me he had another conference there.

He didn't answer, and his expression turned serious.

I shouldn't ask such questions, I thought. *He may think I'm trying to control his life.*

We walked along without speaking. In the village plaza, there was an illuminated sign: *Mesón el Sol.*

"It's open—let's have something to eat" was all he said.

The red peppers with anchovies were arranged on the plate in the shape of a star. On the side, some *manchego* cheese, in slices that were almost transparent. In the center of the table, a lighted candle and a half-full bottle of Rioja wine.

"This was a medieval wine cellar," our waiter told us.

There was no one in the place at that time of night. He went off to make a telephone call. When he came back to the table, I wanted to ask him whom he had called—but this time I controlled myself.

"We're open until two-thirty in the morning," the man said. "So if you like, we can bring you some more ham, cheese, and wine, and you can go out in the plaza. The wine will keep you warm."

"We won't be here that long," he answered. "We have to get to Zaragoza before dawn."

The man returned to the bar, and we refilled our glasses. I felt the same sense of lightness I had experienced in Bilbao—the smooth inebriation that helps us to say and hear things that are difficult.

"You're tired of driving, and we've been drinking," I said. "Wouldn't it be better to stay the night? I saw an inn as we were driving."

He nodded in agreement.

"Look at this table," he said. "The Japanese call it *shibumi,* the true sophistication of simple things. Instead, people fill their bank accounts with money and travel to expensive places in order to feel they're sophisticated."

I had some more wine.

The inn. Another night at his side.

"It's strange to hear a seminarian speak of sophistication," I said, trying to focus on something else.

"I learned about it at the seminary. The closer we get to God through our faith, the simpler He becomes. And the simpler He becomes, the greater is His presence.

"Christ learned about his mission while he was cutting wood and making chairs, beds, and cabinets. He came as a carpenter to show us that—no matter what we do—everything can lead us to the experience of God's love."

He stopped suddenly.

"But I don't want to talk about that," he said. "I want to talk about the other kind of love."

He reached out to caress my face. The wine made things easier for him. And for me.

"Why did you stop so suddenly? Why don't you want to talk about God and the Virgin and the spiritual world?"

"I want to talk about the other kind of love," he said again. "The love that a man and a woman share, and in which there are also miracles."

I took his hands. He might know of the great mysteries of the Goddess, but he didn't know any more than I did about love—even though he had traveled much more than I had.

We held hands for a long time. I could see in his eyes the deep fears that true love tests us with. I could see that he was remembering the rejection of the night before, as well as the long time we had been separated, and his years in the monastery, searching for a world where such anxieties didn't intrude.

I could see in his eyes the thousands of times that he had imagined this moment and the scenes he had constructed about us. I wanted to say that yes, he was welcome, that my heart had won the battle. I wanted to tell him how much I loved him and how badly I wanted him at that moment.

But I was silent. I witnessed, as if in a dream, his inner conflict. I could see that he was wondering whether I'd reject him again, that he was thinking about his fear of losing me, and about the hard words he had heard at other, similar times—because we all have such experiences, and they leave scars.

His eyes gleamed. He was ready to surmount any barrier.

I took one of my hands from his and placed my glass of wine at the edge of the table.

"It's going to fall," he said.

"Exactly. I want you to tip it over the edge."

"Break the glass?"

Yes, break the glass. A simple gesture, but one that brings up fears we can't really understand. What's wrong with breaking an inexpensive glass, when everyone has done so unintentionally at some time in their life?

"Break the glass?" he repeated. "Why?"

"Well, I could give you lots of reasons," I answered. "But actually, just to break it."

"For you?"

"No, of course not."

He eyed the glass on the edge of the table—worried that it might fall.

It's a rite of passage, I wanted to say. It's something prohibited. Glasses are not purposely broken. In a restaurant or in our home, we're careful not to place glasses by the edge of a table. Our universe requires that we avoid letting glasses fall to the floor.

But when we break them by accident, we realize that it's not very serious. The waiter says, "It's nothing," and when has anyone been charged for a broken glass? Breaking glasses is part of life and does no damage to us, to the restaurant, or to anyone else.

I bumped the table. The glass shook but didn't fall.

"Careful!" he said, instinctively.

"Break the glass," I insisted.

Break the glass, I thought to myself, *because it's a symbolic gesture. Try to understand that I have broken things within myself that were much more important than a glass, and I'm happy I did. Resolve your own internal battle, and break the glass.*

Our parents taught us to be careful with glasses and with our bodies. They taught us that the passions of childhood are impossible, that we should not flee from priests, that people cannot perform miracles, and that no one leaves on a journey without knowing where they are going.

Break the glass, please—and free us from all these damned rules, from needing to find an explanation for everything, from doing only what others approve of.

"Break the glass," I said again.

He stared at me. Then, slowly, he slid his hand along the tablecloth to the glass. And with a sudden movement, he pushed it to the floor.

The sound of the breaking glass caught the waiter's attention. Rather than apologize for having broken the glass, he looked at me, smiling—and I smiled back.

"Doesn't matter," shouted the waiter.

But he wasn't listening. He had stood, seized my hair in his hands, and was kissing me.

I clutched at his hair, too, and squeezed him with all my strength, biting his lips and feeling his tongue move in my mouth. This was the kiss I had waited for so long—a kiss born by the rivers of our childhood, when we didn't yet know what love meant. A kiss that had been suspended in the air as we grew, that had traveled the world in the souvenir of a medal, and that had remained hidden behind piles of books. A kiss that had been lost so many times and now was found. In the moment of that kiss were years of searching, disillusionment, and impossible dreams.

I kissed him hard. The few people there in the bar must have been thinking that all they were seeing was just a kiss. They didn't know that this kiss stood for my whole life—and his life, as well. The life of anyone who has waited, dreamed, and searched for their true path.

The moment of that kiss contained every happy moment I had ever lived.

❧ ❧ ❧

HE TOOK OFF MY CLOTHES and entered me with strength, with fear, and with great desire. I ran my hands over his face, heard his moans, and thanked God that he was there inside me, making me feel as if it were the first time.

We made love all night long—our lovemaking blended with our sleeping and dreaming. I felt him inside me and embraced him to make sure that this was really happening, to make sure that he wouldn't disappear, like the knights who had once inhabited this old castle-hotel. The silent walls of stone seemed to be telling stories of damsels in distress, of fallen tears and endless days at the window, looking to the horizon, looking for a sign of hope.

But I would never go through that, I promised myself. I would never lose him. He would always be with me—because I had heard the tongues of the Holy Spirit as I looked at a crucifix behind an altar, and they had said that I would not be committing a sin.

I would be his companion, and together we would tame a world that was going to be created anew. We would talk about the Great Mother, we would fight at the side of Michael the Archangel, and we would experience together the agony and the ecstasy of pioneers. That's what the tongues had said to me—and because I had recovered my faith, I knew they were telling the truth.

Thursday, December 9, 1993

ঌ ঌ ঌ

I AWOKE WITH HIS arm across my breast. It was already midmorning, and the bells of a nearby church were tolling.

He kissed me. His hands once again caressed my body.

"We have to go," he said. "The holiday ends today, and the roads will be jammed."

"I don't want to go back to Zaragoza," I answered. "I want to go straight to where you're going. The banks will be open soon, and I can use my bank card to get some money and buy some clothes."

"You told me you didn't have much money."

"There are things I can do. I need to break with my past once and for all. If we go back to Zaragoza,

I might begin to think I'm making a mistake, that the exam period is almost here and we can stand to be separated for two months until my exams are over. And then if I pass my exams, I won't want to leave Zaragoza. No, no, I can't go back. I need to burn the bridges that connect me with the woman I was."

"Barcelona," he said to himself.

"What?"

"Nothing. Let's move on."

"But you have a presentation to make."

"But that's two days from now," he said. His voice sounded different. "Let's go somewhere else. I don't want to go straight to Barcelona."

I got out of bed. I didn't want to focus on problems. As always after a first night of love with someone, I had awakened with a certain sense of ceremony and embarrassment.

I went to the window, opened the curtains, and looked down on the narrow street. The balconies of the houses were draped with drying laundry. The church bells were ringing.

"I've got an idea," I said. "Let's go to a place we shared as children. I've never been back there."

"Where?"

"The monastery at Piedra."

As we left the hotel, the bells were still sounding, and he suggested that we go into a church nearby.

"That's all we've done," I said. "Churches, prayers, rituals."

"We made love," he said. "We've gotten drunk three times. We've walked in the mountains. We've struck a good balance between rigor and compassion."

I'd said something thoughtless. I had to get used to this new life.

"I'm sorry," I said.

"Let's just go in for a few minutes. The bells are a sign."

He was right, but I wouldn't know that until the next day.

Afterward, without really understanding the meaning of the sign we had witnessed in the church, we got the car and drove for four hours to get to the monastery at Piedra.

❦ ❦ ❦

THE ROOF HAD FALLEN in, and the heads were missing from the few images that were still there—all except for one.

I looked around. In the past, this place must have sheltered strong-willed people, who'd seen to it that every stone was cleaned and that each pew was occupied by one of the powerful individuals of the time.

But all I saw now were ruins. When we had played here as children, we'd pretended these ruins were castles. In those castles I had looked for my enchanted prince.

For centuries, the monks of the monastery at Piedra had kept this small piece of paradise to themselves. Situated on a valley floor, it enjoyed a plentiful supply of what the neighboring villages had to beg for—water. Here the River Piedra broke up into dozens of waterfalls, streams, and lakes, creating luxuriant vegetation all around.

Yet one had only to walk a few hundred yards to leave the canyon and find aridity and desolation. The river itself once again became a narrow thread of water—as if it had exhausted all of its youth and energy in crossing the valley.

The monks knew all this, and they charged dearly for the water they supplied to their neighbors. An untold number of battles between the priests and the villagers marked the history of the monastery.

During one of the many wars that shook Spain, the monastery at Piedra had been turned into a barracks. Horses rode through the central nave of the church, and soldiers slept in its pews, telling ribald stories there and making love with women from the neighboring villages.

Revenge—although delayed—finally came. The monastery was sacked and destroyed.

The monks were never able to reconstruct their paradise. In one of the many legal battles that followed, someone said that the inhabitants of the nearby villages had carried out a sentence pronounced by God. Christ had said, "Give drink to those who thirst," and the priests had paid no heed. For this, God had expelled those who had regarded themselves as nature's masters.

And it was perhaps for this reason that although much of the monastery had been rebuilt and made into a hotel, the main church remained in ruins. The descendants of the local villagers had never forgotten the high price that their parents had paid for something that nature provides freely.

"Which statue is that? The only one with its head?" I asked him.

"Saint Teresa of Avila," he answered. "She is powerful. And even with the thirst for vengeance that the wars brought about, no one dared to touch her."

He took my hand, and we left the church. We walked along the broad corridors of the monastery, climbed the wooden staircases, and marveled at the butterflies in the inner gardens. I recalled every detail of that monastery because I had been there as a girl, and the old memories seemed more vivid than what I was seeing now.

Memories. The months and years leading up to that week seemed to be part of some other incarnation of mine—an era to which I never wanted to return, because it hadn't been touched by the hand of love. I felt as if I had lived the same day over and over for years on end, waking up every morning in the same way, repeating the same words, and dreaming the same dreams.

I remembered my parents, my grandparents, and many of my old friends. I recalled how much time I had spent fighting for something I didn't even want.

Why had I done that? I could think of no explanation. Maybe because I had been too lazy to think of other avenues to follow. Maybe because I had been afraid of what others would think. Maybe because it was hard work to be different. Perhaps because a human being is condemned to repeat the steps taken by the previous generation until—and I was thinking of the padre—a certain number of people begin to behave in a different fashion.

Then the world changes, and we change with it.

But I didn't want to be that way anymore. Fate had returned to me what had been mine and now offered me the chance to change myself and the world.

I thought again of the mountain climbers we had met as we traveled. They were young and wore brightly colored clothing so as to be easily spotted should they become lost in the snow. They knew the right path to follow to the peaks.

The heights were already festooned with aluminum pins; all they had to do was attach their lines to them, and they could climb safely. They were there for a holiday adventure, and on Monday they would return to their jobs with the feeling that they had challenged nature—and won.

But this wasn't really true. The adventurous ones were those who had climbed there first, the ones who had found the routes to the top. Some, who had fallen to their death on the rocks, had never even made it halfway up. Others had lost fingers and toes to frostbite.

Many were never seen again. But one day, some of them had made it to the summit.

And their eyes were the first to take in that view, and their hearts beat with joy. They had accepted the risks and could now honor—with their conquest—all of those who had died trying.

There were probably some people down below who thought, "There's nothing up there. Just a view. What's so great about that?"

But the first climber knew what was great about it: the acceptance of the challenge of going forward. He knew that no single day is the same as any other and that each morning brings its own special miracle, its *magic moment* in which ancient universes are destroyed and new stars are created.

The first one who climbed those mountains must have asked, looking down at the tiny houses with their smoking chimneys, "All of their days must seem the same. What's so great about that?"

Now all the mountains had been conquered and astronauts had walked in space. There were no more islands on earth—no matter how small—left to be discovered. But there were still great adventures of the spirit, and one of them was being offered to me now.

It was a blessing. The padre didn't understand anything. These pains are not the kind that hurt.

Fortunate are those who take the first steps. Someday people will realize that men and women are capable of speaking the language of the angels—that all of us are possessed of the gifts of the Holy Spirit and that we can perform miracles, cure, prophesy, and understand.

❧ ❧ ❧

WE SPENT THE afternoon walking along the canyon, reminiscing about our childhood. It was the first time he had done so; during our trip to Bilbao, he had seemed to have lost all interest in Soria.

Now, though, he asked me about each of our mutual friends, wanting to know whether they were happy and what they were doing with their lives.

Finally, we arrived at the largest waterfall of the Piedra, where a number of small, scattered streams come together and the water is thrown to the rocks below from a height of almost one hundred feet. We stood at the edge of the waterfall, listening to its deafening roar and gazing at the rainbow in its mist.

"The Horse's Tail," I said, surprised that I still remembered this name from so long ago.

"I remember . . . ," he began.

"Yes! I know what you're going to say!"

Of course I knew! The waterfall concealed a gigantic grotto. When we were children, returning from our first visit to the monastery at Piedra, we had talked about that place for days.

"The cavern," he said. "Let's go there."

It was impossible to pass through the torrent of water. But ancient monks had constructed a tunnel that started at the highest point of the falls and descended through the earth to a place at the rear of the grotto.

It wasn't difficult to find the entrance. During the summer, there may even have been lights showing the way, but now the tunnel was completely dark.

"Is this the right way?" I asked.

"Yes. Trust me."

We began to descend through the hole at the side of the falls. Although we were in complete darkness, we knew where we were going—and he asked me again to trust him.

Thank you, Lord, I was thinking, as we went deeper and deeper into the earth, *because I was a lost sheep, and you brought me back. Because my life was dead, and you revived it. Because love wasn't alive in my heart, and you gave me back that gift.*

I held on to his shoulder. My loved one guided my steps through the darkness, knowing that we would see the light again and that it would bring us joy. Perhaps in our future there would be moments when the situation was reversed—when I would guide him with the same love and certainty until we reached a safe place and could rest together.

We walked slowly, and it seemed as if we would never stop descending. Maybe this was another rite of passage, marking the end of an era in which there had been no light in my life. As I walked through the tunnel, I was remembering how much time I had wasted in one place, trying to put down roots in soil where nothing could grow any longer.

But God was good and had given me back my lost enthusiasm, directing me toward the adventures I had always dreamed about. And toward the man who—without my knowing it—had waited for me all my life. I felt no remorse over the fact that he was leaving the seminary—there were many ways to serve God, as the padre had said, and our love only multiplied the number of them. Starting now, I would also have the chance to serve and help—all because of him.

We would go out into the world, bringing comfort to others and to each other.

Thank you, Lord, for helping me to serve. Teach me to be worthy of that. Give me the strength to be a part of his mission, to walk with him on this earth, and to develop my spiritual life anew. May all our days be as these have been—going from place to place, curing the sick, comforting those in sorrow, speaking of the Great Mother's love for all of us.

SUDDENLY, THE SOUND of water could be heard again and light flooded our path. The dark tunnel was transformed into one of the most beautiful spectacles on earth. We were in an immense cavern, the size of a cathedral. Three of its walls were of stone, and the fourth was the Horse's Tail, with its water falling into the emerald-green lake at our feet.

The rays of the setting sun passed through the waterfall, and the moist walls glittered.

We leaned back against the stone wall, saying nothing.

When we were children, this place was a pirates' hideout, where the treasures of our childhood imagination were kept. Now, it was the miracle of Mother Earth; I knew she was there and felt myself to be in her womb. She was protecting us with her walls of stone and washing away our sins with her purifying water.

"Thank you," I said in a loud voice.

"Whom are you thanking?"

"Her. And you, because you were an instrument in restoring my faith."

He walked to the edge of the water. Looking out, he smiled. "Come over here," he said.

I joined him.

"I want to tell you something you don't know about yet," he said.

His words worried me a little. But he looked calm and happy, and that reassured me.

"Every person on earth has a gift," he began. "In some, the gift manifests itself spontaneously; others have to work to discover what it is. I worked with my gift during the four years I was at the seminary."

Now I would have to "play a role," as he had taught me when the old man had barred us from the church. I would have to feign that I knew nothing. *There's nothing wrong with doing this,* I told myself. *This is a not a script based on frustration but on happiness.*

"What did you do at the seminary?" I asked, trying to stall for time in order to play my role better.

"That doesn't matter," he said. "The fact is that I developed a gift. I am able to cure, when God so wills it."

"That's wonderful," I answered, acting surprised. "We won't have to spend money on doctors!"

He didn't laugh. I felt like an idiot.

"I developed my gift through the Charismatic practices that you saw," he went on. "In the beginning, I was surprised. I would pray, asking that the Holy Spirit appear, and then, through the laying on of my hands, I would restore many of the sick to good health. My reputation began to spread, and every day people lined up at the gates of the seminary, seeking my help. In every infected, smelly laceration, I saw the wounds of Jesus."

"I'm so proud of you," I said.

"Many of the people at the monastery opposed me, but my superior gave me his complete support."

"We'll continue this work. We'll go out together into the world. I will clean and bathe the wounds, and you will bless them, and God will demonstrate His miracles."

He looked away from me, out at the lake. There seemed to be a presence in the cavern similar to the one I had sensed that night in Saint-Savin when we had gotten drunk at the well in the plaza.

"I've already told you this, but I'll say it again," he continued. "One night I awoke, and my room was completely bright. I saw the face of the Great Mother; I saw Her loving look. After that, She began to appear to me from time to time. I cannot make it happen, but every once in a while, She appears.

"By the time of my first vision, I was already aware of the work being done by the true revolutionaries of the church. I knew that my mission on earth, in addition to curing, was to smooth the way for this new acceptance of God as a woman. The feminine principle, the column of Misericordia, would be rebuilt—and the temple of wisdom would be reconstructed in the hearts of all people."

I was staring at him. His face, which had grown tense, now relaxed again.

"This carried a price—which I was willing to pay."

He stopped, as if not knowing how to go on with his story.

"What do you mean when you say you *were* willing?" I asked.

"The path of the Goddess can only be opened through words and miracles. But that's not the way the world works. It's going to be very hard—tears, lack of understanding, suffering."

That padre, I thought to myself. *He tried to put fear in his heart. But I shall be his comfort.*

"The path isn't about pain; it's about the glory of serving," I answered.

"Most human beings still cannot trust love."

I felt that he was trying to tell me something but couldn't. I wanted to help him.

"I've been thinking about that," I broke in. "The first man who climbed the highest peak in the Pyrenees must have felt that a life without that kind of adventure would lack grace."

"What do you mean when you use the word *grace?*" he asked me, and I could see that he was feeling tense again. "One of the names of the Great Mother is Our Lady of the Graces. Her generous hands heap Her blessings on those who know how to receive them. We can never judge the lives of others, because each person knows only their own pain and renunciation. It's one thing to feel that you are on the right path, but it's another to think that yours is the only path.

"Jesus said, 'The house of my Father has many mansions.' A gift is a grace, or a mercy. But it is also a mercy to know how to live a life of dignity, love, and work. Mary had a husband on earth who tried to demonstrate the value of anonymous work. Although he was not heard from very much, he was the one who provided the roof over their heads and the food for their mouths, who allowed his wife and son to do all that they did. His work was as important as theirs, even though no one ever gave him much credit."

I didn't say anything, and he took my hand. "Forgive me for my intolerance."

I kissed his hand and put it to my cheek.

"This is what I'm trying to explain to you," he said, smiling again. "I realized, from the moment I found you again, that I couldn't cause you to suffer because of my mission."

I began to feel worried.

"Yesterday I lied to you. It was the first and last lie I've ever told you," he continued. "The truth is that instead of going to the monastery, I went up on the mountain and conversed with the Great Mother. I said to Her that if She wanted, I would leave you and continue along my path. I would go back to the gate where the sick gathered, to the visits in the middle of the night, to the lack of understanding of those who would deny the idea of faith, and to the cynical attitude of those who cannot believe that love is a savior. If She were to ask me, I would give up what I want most in the world: you."

I thought again of the padre. He had been right. A choice had been made that morning.

"But," he continued, "if it were possible to resolve this awful predicament in my life, I would promise to serve the world through my love for you."

"What are you saying?" I asked, frightened now.

He seemed not to hear me.

"It's not necessary to move mountains in order to prove one's faith," he said. "I was ready to face the suffering alone and not share it. If I had continued along that path, we would never have our house with the white curtains and the view of the mountains."

"I don't care about that house! I didn't even want to go in!" I said, trying not to shout. "I want to go with you, to be with you in your struggle. I want to be one of those who does something for the first time. Don't you understand? You've given me back my faith!"

The last rays of the sun illuminated the walls of the cavern. But I couldn't see its beauty.

God hides the fires of hell within paradise.

"You're the one who doesn't understand," he said, and I could see his eyes begging me to comprehend. "You don't see the risks."

"But you were willing to accept those risks!"

"I *am* willing. But they are *my* risks."

I wanted to interrupt him, but he wasn't listening.

"So yesterday, I asked a miracle of the Virgin," he continued. "I asked that She take away my gift."

I couldn't believe what I was hearing.

"I have a little money and all the experience that years of traveling have given me. We'll buy a house, I'll get a job, and I'll serve God as Saint Joseph did, with the humility of an anonymous person. I don't need miracles in my life anymore to keep the faith. I need you."

My legs were growing weak, and I felt as if I might faint.

"And just as I was asking that the Virgin take away my gift, I began to speak in tongues," he went on. "The tongues told me, 'Place your hands on the earth. Your gift will leave you and return to the Mother's breast.'"

I was in a panic. "You didn't . . ."

"Yes. I did as the inspiration of the Holy Spirit bade. The fog lifted, and the sun shone on the mountains. I felt that the Virgin understood—because She had also loved so greatly."

"But She followed Her man! She accepted the path taken by Her son!"

"We don't have Her strength, Pilar. My gift will be passed on to someone else—such gifts are never wasted.

"Yesterday, from that bar, I phoned Barcelona and canceled my presentation. Let's go to Zaragoza—you know the people there, and it's a good place for us to start. I'll get a job easily."

I could no longer think.

"Pilar!" he said.

But I was already climbing back through the tunnel—this time without a friendly shoulder to lean on—pursued by the multitude of the sick who would die, the families that would suffer, the miracles that would never be performed, the smiles that would no longer grace the world, and the mountains that would remain in place.

I saw nothing—only the darkness that engulfed me.

Friday, December 10, 1993

ග ග ග

On the bank of the River Piedra I sat down and wept. My memory of that night is confused and vague. I know that I almost died, but I can't remember his face nor where he took me.

I'd like to be able to remember all of it—so that I could expel it from my heart. But I can't. It all seems like a dream, from the moment when I came out of that dark tunnel into a world where darkness had already fallen.

There was not a star in the sky. I remember vaguely walking back to the car, retrieving my small bag, and beginning to wander at random. I must have walked to the road, trying to hitch a ride to Zaragoza—with no success. I wound up returning to the gardens at the monastery.

The sound of water was everywhere—there were waterfalls on all sides, and I felt the presence of the Great Mother following me wherever I walked. Yes, She had loved the world; She loved it as much as God did—because She had also given Her son to be sacrificed by men. But did She understand a woman's love for a man?

She may have suffered because of love, but it was a different kind of love. Her Groom knew everything and performed miracles. Her husband on earth was a humble laborer who believed everything his dreams told him. She never knew what it was to abandon a man or to be abandoned by one. When Joseph considered expelling Her from their home because She was pregnant, Her Groom in heaven immediately sent an angel to keep that from happening.

Her son left Her. But children always leave their parents. It's easy to suffer because you love a person, or the world, or your son. That's the kind of suffering that you accept as a part of life; it's a noble, grand sort of suffering. It's easy to suffer for a cause or a mission; this ennobles the heart of the person suffering.

But how to explain suffering because of a man? It's not explainable. With that kind of suffering, a person feels as if they're in hell, because there is no nobility, no greatness—only misery.

That night, I slept on the frozen ground, and the cold anesthetized me. I thought I might die without a covering—but where could I find one? Everything that was most important in my life had been given so generously to me in the course of one week—and had been taken from me in a minute, without my having a chance to say a thing.

My body was trembling from the cold, but I hardly noticed. At some point, the trembling would stop. My body's energy would be exhausted from trying to provide me with heat and would be unable to do anything more. It would resume its customary state of relaxation, and death would take me in its arms.

I shook for another hour. And then peace came.

Before I closed my eyes, I began to hear my mother's voice. She was telling a story she had often told me when I was a child, not realizing it was a story about me.

"A boy and a girl were insanely in love with each other," my mother's voice was saying. "They decided to become engaged. And that's when presents are always exchanged.

"The boy was poor—his only worthwhile possession was a watch he'd inherited from his grandfather. Thinking about his sweetheart's lovely hair, he decided to sell the watch in order to buy her a silver barrette.

"The girl had no money herself to buy him a present. She went to the shop of the most successful merchant in the town and sold him her hair. With the money, she bought a gold watchband for her lover.

"When they met on the day of the engagement party, she gave him the wristband for a watch he had sold, and he gave her the barrette for the hair she no longer had."

❦ ❦ ❦

I WAS AWAKENED by a man shaking me.

"Drink this!" he was saying. "Drink this quickly!"

I had no idea what was happening nor the strength to resist. He opened my mouth and forced me to drink a hot liquid. I noticed that he was in his shirtsleeves and that he had given me a wrap.

"Drink more!" he insisted.

Without knowing what I was doing, I obeyed. Then I closed my eyes.

I awoke in the convent, and a woman was tending me.

"You almost died," she said. "If it weren't for the watchman, you wouldn't be here."

I stood up dizzily. Parts of the previous day came back to me, and I wished that the watchman had never passed my way.

But apparently this was not the time for me to die. I was to go on living.

The woman led me to the kitchen and prepared some coffee, biscuits, and bread for me. She asked me no questions, and I explained nothing. When I had finished eating, she gave me my bag.

"See if everything's still there," she said.

"I'm sure it is. I didn't really have anything much."

"You have your life, my child. A long life. Take better care of it."

"There's a city near here where there's a church," I said, wanting to cry. "Yesterday, before I came here, I went into that church with . . ."

I couldn't explain.

". . . with a friend from my childhood. I had already had enough of the churches around here, but the bells were ringing, and he said it was a sign—that we should go in."

The woman refilled my cup, poured some coffee for herself, and sat down to hear my story.

"We entered the church," I continued. "There was no one there, and it was dark. I tried to look for the sign, but I saw only the same old altars and the same old saints. Suddenly, we heard a movement above, where the organ was.

"It was a group of boys with guitars, who began to tune their instruments. We decided to sit and listen to the music for a while before continuing our trip. Shortly a man came in and sat down next to us. He was happy and shouted to the boys to play a *paso doble*."

"Bullfight music?" the woman said. "I hope they didn't do that!"

"They didn't. But they laughed and played a flamenco melody instead. My friend and I felt as if heaven had descended on us; the church, the surrounding darkness, the sound of the guitars, and the man's delight—it was all a miracle.

"Little by little, the church began to fill. The boys continued to play the flamenco, and everyone who came in smiled, infected by the joy of the musicians.

"My friend asked if I wanted to attend the mass that was about to begin. I said no—we had a long ride ahead of us. So we decided to leave—but before we did, we thanked God for yet another beautiful moment in our lives.

"As we arrived at the gate, we saw that many people —perhaps the entire population of the town—were walking to the church. I thought it must have been the last completely Catholic town in Spain—maybe because the crowds seemed to be having so much fun.

"As we got into the car, we saw a funeral procession approaching. Someone had died; it was a mass for the dead. As soon as the cortege reached the gates of the church, the musicians stopped the flamenco music and began to play a dirge."

"May God have mercy on that soul," said the woman, crossing herself.

"May He have mercy," I said, repeating her gesture. "But our having gone into that church really had been a sign—that every story has a sad ending."

The woman said nothing. Then she left the room and returned immediately with a pen and paper.

"Let's go outside," she said.

We went out together, and the sun was rising.

"Take a deep breath," she said. "Let this new morning enter your lungs and course through your veins. From what I can see, your loss yesterday was not an accident."

I didn't answer.

"You also didn't really understand the story you told me, about the sign in the church," she went on. "You saw only the sadness of the procession at the end. You forgot the happy moments you spent inside. You forgot the feeling that heaven had descended on you and how good it was to be experiencing all of that with your . . ."

She stopped and smiled.

". . . childhood friend," she said, winking. "Jesus said, 'Let the dead bury the dead' because he knew that there is no such thing as death. Life existed before we were born and will continue to exist after we leave this world."

My eyes filled with tears.

"It's the same with love," she went on. "It existed before and will go on forever."

"You seem to know everything about my life," I said.

"All love stories have much in common. I went through the same thing at one point in my life. But that's not what I remember. What I remember is that love returned in the form of another man, new hopes, and new dreams."

She held out the pen and paper to me.

"Write down everything you're feeling. Take it out of your soul, put it on the paper, and then throw it away. Legend says that the River Piedra is so cold that anything that falls into it—leaves, insects, the feathers of birds—is turned to stone. Maybe it would be a good idea to toss your suffering into its waters."

I took the pages. She kissed me, and said I could come back for lunch if I wanted to.

"Don't forget!" she shouted as she walked away. "Love perseveres. It's men who change."

I smiled, and she waved good-bye.

I looked out at the river for some time. And I cried until there were no more tears.

Then I began to write.

Epilogue

ɕ ɕ ɕ

I wrote for an entire day, and then another, and another. Every morning, I went to the bank of the River Piedra. Every afternoon, the woman came, took me by the arm, and led me back to the old convent.

She washed my clothes, made me dinner, chatted about trivial things, and sent me to bed.

One morning, when I had almost finished the manuscript, I heard the sound of a car. My heart leaped, but I didn't want to believe it. I felt free again, ready to return to the world and be a part of it once again.

The worst had passed, although the sadness remained.

But my heart was right. Even without raising my eyes from my work, I felt his presence and heard his footsteps.

"Pilar," he said, sitting down next to me.

I went on writing, without answering. I couldn't pull my thoughts together. My heart was jumping, trying to free itself from my breast and run to him. But I wouldn't allow it.

He sat there looking at the river, while I went on writing. The entire morning passed that way—without a word—and I recalled the silence of a night near a well when I'd suddenly realized that I loved him.

When my hand could write no longer, I stopped. Then he spoke.

"It was dark when I came up out of the cavern. I couldn't find you, so I went to Zaragoza. I even went to Soria. I looked everywhere for you. Then I decided to return to the monastery at Piedra to see if there was any sign of you, and I met a woman. She showed me where you were, and she said you had been waiting for me."

My eyes filled with tears.

"I am going to sit here with you by the river. If you go home to sleep, I will sleep in front of your house. And if you go away, I will follow you—until you tell me to go away. Then I'll leave. But I have to love you for the rest of my life."

I could no longer hold back the tears, and he began to weep as well.

"I want to tell you something . . . ," he started to say.

"Don't say a thing. Read this." I handed him the pages.

❦ ❦ ❦

I GAZED AT THE RIVER PIEDRA all afternoon. The woman brought us sandwiches and wine, commented on the weather, and left us alone. Every once in a while, he paused in his reading and stared out into space, absorbed in his thoughts.

At one point I went for a walk in the woods, past the small waterfalls, through the landscape that was so laden with stories and meanings for me. When the sun began to set, I went back to the place where I had left him.

"Thank you" was what he said as he gave the papers back to me. "And forgive me."

On the bank of the River Piedra, I sat down and wept.

"Your love has saved me and returned me to my dream," he continued.

I said nothing.

"Do you know Psalm 137?" he asked.

I shook my head. I was afraid to speak.

"On the banks of the rivers of Babylon . . ."

"Yes, yes, I know it," I said, feeling myself coming back to life, little by little. "It talks about exile. It talks about people who hang up their harps because they cannot play the music their hearts desire."

"But after the psalmist cries with longing for the land of his dreams, he promises himself,

If I forget you, O Jerusalem,

let my right hand forget its skill.

Let my tongue cling to the roof of my mouth,

if I do not exalt Jerusalem."

I smiled again.

"I had forgotten, and you brought it back to me."

"Do you think your gift has returned?" I asked.

"I don't know. But the Goddess has always given me a second chance in life. And She is giving me that with you. She will help me to find my path again."

"Our path."

"Yes, ours."

He took my hands and lifted me to my feet.

"Go and get your things," he said. "Dreams mean work."

❦ ❦ ❦

By The River Piedra I Sat Down and Wept forms part of the trilogy *And On the Seventh Day*. The other books in the trilogy are *Veronika Decides to Die* (1998) and *The Devil and Miss Prym* (2000). Each of the three books is concerned with a week in the life of ordinary people, all of whom find themselves suddenly confronted by love, death and power. I have always believed that in the lives of individuals, just as in society at large, the most profound changes take place within a reduced time frame. When we least expect it, life sends us a challenge to test our courage and willingness to change; at such a moment, there is no point in pretending that nothing has happened or in saying that we are not yet ready. The challenge will not wait. Life does not look back. A week is more than enough time for us to decide whether or not to accept our destiny.

Life is a journey

Make sure you don't miss a thing.
Live it with Paulo Coelho.

Visit f /paulocoelho

How can you find your heart's desire?

A world-wide phenomenon; an inspiration for anyone seeking their path in life.

The Alchemist

Do you believe in yourself?

A modern-day adventure in the searing heat of the Mojave desert and an exploration of fear and self-doubt.

The Valkyries

How do we see the amazing in the everyday?

When two young lovers are reunited, they discover anew the truth of what lies in their hearts.

By the River Piedra I Sat Down & Wept

What are you searching for?

A transforming journey on the pilgrims' road to Santiago – and the first of Paulo's extraordinary books.

The Pilgrimage

Can faith triumph over suffering?

Paulo Coelho's brilliant telling of the story of Elijah, who was forced to choose between love and duty.

The Fifth Mountain

Is life always worth living?

A fundamental moral question explored as only Paulo Coelho can.

Veronika Decides to Die

Could you be tempted into evil?

The inhabitants of a small town are challenged by a mysterious stranger to choose between good and evil.

The Devil & Miss Prym

Are you brave enough to live your dream?

Strategies and inspiration to help you follow your own path in a troubled world.

Manual of the Warrior of Light

Can sex be sacred?

An unflinching exploration of the lengths we go to in our search for love, sex and spirituality.

Eleven Minutes

How far would you go for your obsession?

A sweeping story of love, loss and longing that spans the world.

The Zahir

What happens when obsession turns to murder?

An enthralling story of jealousy, death and suspense.

The Winner Stands Alone

Can we dare to be true to ourselves?

A story that will transform the way we think about love, joy and sacrifice.

The Witch of Portobello

How will you know who your soulmate is?

A moving tale of passion, mystery and spirituality.

Brida

What does it mean to be truly alive?

Powerful tales of living and dying, destiny and choice, and love lost and found.

Like the Flowing River

Are you where you want to be?

Read *Aleph*. And rewrite your life.

Aleph

Is there a weapon more powerful than words?

A timeless and powerful exploration of personal growth, everyday wisdom and joy.

Manuscript Found in Accra

The ZAHIR

PAULO COELHO

Author of THE ALCHEMIST

Translated from the Portuguese
by Margaret Jull Costa

Thorsons

Thorsons
An imprint of HarperCollins*Publishers*
1 London Bridge Street
London SE1 9GF

HarperCollins*Publishers*
1st Floor, Watermarque Building, Ringsend Road
Dublin 4, Ireland

www.harpercollins.co.uk
www.paulocoelho.com
www.paulocoelhoblog.com

First published in English by HarperCollins*Publishers* 2005

This edition 2021

2 4 6 8 10 9 7 5 3 1

© Paulo Coelho 2005

English translation © Margaret Jull Costa

Paulo Coelho asserts the moral right to
be identified as the author of this work

Acatalogue record of this book is
available from the British Library

ISBN 978-0-00-854728-8

FICTION / PHILOSOPHY

Printed and bound in India by Thomson Press India Ltd

All rights reserved. No part of this publication may be
reproduced, stored in a retrieval system, or transmitted,
in any form or by any means, electronic, mechanical,
photocopying, recording or otherwise, without the prior
written permission of the publishers.

This book is produced from independently certified FSC® paper
to ensure responsible forest management.

O Mary!
conceived without sin,
pray for us who turn to you!
Amen.

What man of you, having an hundred sheep,
if he lose one of them, doth not leave the ninety
and nine in the wilderness, and go after that
which is lost, until he find it?

Luke 15:4

Ithaca

When you set out on your journey to Ithaca,
pray that the road is long,
full of adventure, full of knowledge.
The Lestrygonians and the Cyclops,
the angry Poseidon – do not fear them:
You will never find such as these on your path
if your thoughts remain lofty, if a fine
emotion touches your spirit and your body.
The Lestrygonians and the Cyclops,
the fierce Poseidon you will never encounter,
if you do not carry them within your soul,
if your heart does not set them up before you.

Pray that the road is long.
That the summer mornings are many, when,
with such pleasure, with such joy
you will enter ports seen for the first time;
stop at Phoenician markets,
and purchase fine merchandise,
mother-of-pearl and coral, amber and ebony,
and sensual perfumes of all kinds,
as many sensual perfumes as you can;
visit many Egyptian cities,
to learn and learn from scholars.

Always keep Ithaca in your mind.
To arrive there is your ultimate goal.
But do not hurry the voyage at all.
It is better to let it last for many years;
and to anchor at the island when you are old,
rich with all you have gained on the way,
not expecting that Ithaca will offer you riches.
Ithaca has given you the beautiful voyage.
Without her you would never have set out on the road.
She has nothing more to give you.

And if you find her poor, Ithaca has not deceived you.
Wise as you have become, with so much experience,
you must already have understood what Ithacas mean.

Constantine Cavafy (1863–1933),
translated by Rae Dalven

Dedication

In the car, I mentioned that I had finished the first draft of my book. Later, as we set out together to climb a mountain in the Pyrenees which we both consider to be sacred and where we have already shared some extraordinary moments, I asked if she wanted to know the main theme of the book or its title; she would love to, she said, but, out of respect for my work, she had, until then, asked nothing, she had simply felt glad – very glad.

So I told her the title and the main theme. We continued walking in silence and, on the way back, we heard a noise; the wind was getting up, passing above the leafless trees and coming down towards us, causing the mountain once more to reveal its magic and its power.

Suddenly the snow began to fall. I stopped and stood contemplating that moment: the snowflakes falling, the grey sky, the forest, the woman by my side. The woman who has always been by my side.

I felt like telling her then, but decided to let her find out when she read these pages for the first time. This book is dedicated to you, Christina, my wife.

The author

According to the writer Jorge Luis Borges, the idea of the Zahir comes from Islamic tradition and is thought to have arisen at some point in the eighteenth century. *Zahir*, in Arabic, means visible, present, incapable of going unnoticed. It is someone or something which, once we have come into contact with them or it, gradually occupies our every thought, until we can think of nothing else. This can be considered either a state of holiness or of madness.

Faubourg Saint-Pères,
Encyclopaedia of the Fantastic (1953)

I am a Free Man

Her name is Esther; she is a war correspondent who has just returned from Iraq because of the imminent invasion of that country; she is thirty years old, married, without children. He is an unidentified male, between twenty-three and twenty-five years old, with dark, Mongolian features. The two were last seen in a café in Rue Faubourg St-Honoré.

The police were told that they had met before, although no one knew how often: Esther had always said that the man – who concealed his true identity behind the name Mikhail – was someone very important, although she had never explained whether he was important for her career as a journalist or for her as a woman.

The police began a formal investigation. Various theories were put forward – kidnapping, blackmail, a kidnapping that had ended in murder – none of which were beyond the bounds of possibility given that, in her search for information, her work brought her into frequent contact with people who had links with terrorist cells. They discovered that, in the weeks prior to her disappearance, regular sums of money had been withdrawn from her bank account: those in charge of the investigation felt that these could have been payments made for information. She had taken no change of clothes with her, but, oddly enough, her passport was nowhere to be found.

He is a stranger, very young, with no police record, with no clue as to his identity.

She is Esther, thirty years old, the winner of two international prizes for journalism, and married.

My wife.

I immediately come under suspicion and am detained because I refuse to say where I was on the day she disappeared. However, a prison officer has just opened the door of my cell, saying that I'm a free man.

And why am I a free man? Because nowadays, everyone knows everything about everyone; you just have to ask and the information is there: where you've used your credit card, where you spend your time, who you've slept with. In my case, it was even easier: a woman, another journalist, a friend of my wife, and divorced – which is why she doesn't mind revealing that she slept with me – came forward as a witness in my favour when she heard that I had been detained. She provided concrete proof that I was with her on the day and the night of Esther's disappearance.

I talk to the chief inspector, who returns my belongings and offers his apologies, adding that my rapid detention was entirely within the law, and that I have no grounds on which to accuse or sue the State. I say that I haven't the slightest intention of doing either of those things, that I am perfectly aware that we are all under constant suspicion and under twenty-four-hour surveillance, even when we have committed no crime.

'You're free to go,' he says, echoing the words of the prison officer.

I ask: Isn't it possible that something really has happened to my wife? She had said to me once that –

understandably given her vast network of contacts in the terrorist underworld – she occasionally got the feeling she was being followed.

The inspector changes the subject. I insist, but he says nothing.

I ask if she would be able to travel on her passport, and he says, of course, since she has committed no crime. Why shouldn't she leave and enter the country freely?

'So she may no longer be in France?'

'Do you think she left you because of that woman you've been sleeping with?'

That's none of your business, I reply. The inspector pauses for a second and grows serious; he says that I was arrested as part of routine procedure, but that he is nevertheless very sorry about my wife's disappearance. He is married himself and although he doesn't like my books (So he isn't as ignorant as he looks! He knows who I am!), he can put himself in my shoes and imagine what I must be going through.

I ask him what I should do next. He gives me his card and asks me to get in touch if I hear anything. I've watched this scene in dozens of films, and I'm not convinced; inspectors always know more than they say they do.

He asks me if I have ever met the person who was with Esther the last time she was seen alive. I say that I knew his code name, but didn't know him personally.

He asks if we have any domestic problems. I say that we've been together for ten years and have the same problems most married couples have – nothing more.

He asks, delicately, if we have discussed divorce recently, or if my wife was considering leaving me. I tell him we have never even considered the possibility, and say again that 'like all couples' we have our occasional disagreements.

Frequent or only occasional?

Occasional, I say.

He asks still more delicately if she suspected that I was having an affair with her friend. I tell him that it was the first – and last – time that her friend and I had slept together. It wasn't an affair; it came about simply because we had nothing else to do. It had been a bit of a dull day, neither of us had any pressing engagements after lunch, and the game of seduction always adds a little zest to life, which is why we ended up in bed together.

'You go to bed with someone just because it's a bit of a dull day?'

I consider telling him that such matters hardly form part of his investigations, but I need his help, or might need it later on – there is, after all, that invisible institution called the Favour Bank, which I have always found so very useful.

'Sometimes, yes. There's nothing else very interesting to do, the woman is looking for excitement, I'm looking for adventure, and that's that. The next day, you both pretend that nothing happened, and life goes on.'

He thanks me, holds out his hand and says that in his world, things aren't quite like that. Naturally, boredom and tedium exist, as does the desire to go to bed with someone, but everything is much more controlled, and no one ever acts on their thoughts or desires.

'Perhaps artists have more freedom,' he remarks.

I say that I'm familiar with his world, but have no wish to enter into a comparison between our different views of society and people. I remain silent, awaiting his next move.

'Speaking of freedom,' he says, slightly disappointed at this writer's refusal to enter into a debate with a police officer, 'you're free to go. Now that I've met you, I'll read your books. I know I said I didn't like them, but the fact is I've never actually read one.'

This is not the first or the last time that I will hear these words. At least this whole episode has gained me another reader. I shake his hand and leave.

***

I'm free. I'm out of prison, my wife has disappeared in mysterious circumstances, I have no fixed timetable for work, I have no problem meeting new people, I'm rich, famous, and if Esther really has left me, I'll soon find someone to replace her. I'm free, independent.

But what is freedom?

I've spent a large part of my life enslaved to one thing or another, so I should know the meaning of the word. Ever since I was a child, I have fought to make freedom my most precious commodity. I fought with my parents, who wanted me to be an engineer, not a writer. I fought with the other boys at school, who immediately homed in on me as the butt of their cruel jokes, and only after much blood had flowed from my nose and from theirs, only after many afternoons when I had to hide my scars from my mother – because it was up to me not her to solve my problems – did I manage to show them that I could take a thrashing without bursting into tears. I fought to get a job to support myself, and went to work as a delivery man for a hardware store, so as to be free from that old line in family blackmail: 'We'll give you money, but you'll have to do this, this and this.'

I fought – although without success – for the girl I was in love with when I was an adolescent, and who loved me too; she left me in the end because her parents convinced her that I had no future.

I fought against the hostile world of journalism – my next job – where my first boss kept me hanging around for three whole hours and only deigned to take any notice of me when I started tearing up the book he was reading: he looked at me in surprise and saw that here was someone capable of persevering and confronting the enemy, essential qualities for a good reporter. I fought for the socialist ideal, went to prison, came out and went on fighting, feeling like a working-class hero – until, that is, I heard the Beatles and decided that rock music was much more fun than Marx. I fought for the love of my first, second, and third wives. I fought to find the courage to leave my first, second, and third wives, because the love I felt for them hadn't lasted, and I needed to move on, until I found the person who had been put in this world to find me – and she was none of those three.

I fought for the courage to leave my job on the newspaper and launch myself into the adventure of writing a book, knowing full well that no one in my country could make a living as a writer. I gave up after a year, after writing more than a thousand pages – pages of such genius that even I couldn't understand them.

While I was fighting, I heard other people speaking in the name of freedom, and the more they defended this unique right, the more enslaved they seemed to be to their parents' wishes, to a marriage in which they had promised to stay with the other person 'for the rest of their lives', to the bathroom scales, to their diet, to half-finished projects, to lovers to whom they were incapable of saying 'No' or 'It's over', to weekends when they were obliged to have lunch with people they didn't even like. Slaves to luxury, to the appearance of luxury, to the appearance of the appearance of luxury. Slaves to a life they had not chosen, but which they had decided to live because someone had managed to convince them that it was all for the best. And so their identical days and nights passed, days and nights in which adventure was just a word in a book or an image on the television that was always on, and whenever a door opened, they would say:

'I'm not interested. I'm not in the mood.'

How could they possibly know if they were in the mood or not if they had never tried? But there was no point in asking; the truth was they were afraid of any change that would upset the world they had grown used to.

The inspector says I'm free. I'm free now and I was free in prison too, because freedom continues to be the thing I prize most in the world. Of course, this has led me to drink wines I did not like, to do things I should not have done and which I will not do again; it has left scars on my body and on my soul, it has meant hurting certain people, although I have since asked their forgiveness, when I realised that I could do absolutely anything except force another person to follow me in my madness, in my lust for life. I don't regret the painful times; I bear my scars as if they were medals. I know that freedom has a high price, as high as that of slavery; the only difference is that you pay with pleasure and a smile, even when that smile is dimmed by tears.

***

I leave the police station, and it's a beautiful day outside, a sunny Sunday that does not reflect my state of mind at all. My lawyer is waiting for me with a few consoling words and a bunch of flowers. He says that he's phoned round all the hospitals and morgues (the kind of thing you do when someone fails to return home), but has not as yet found Esther. He says that he managed to prevent journalists from finding out where I was being held. He says he needs to talk to me in order to draw up a legal strategy that will help me defend myself against any future accusation. I thank him for all his trouble; I know he's not really interested in drawing up a legal strategy, he just doesn't want to leave me alone, because he's not sure how I'll react (Will I get drunk and be arrested again? Will I cause a scandal? Will I try to kill myself?). I tell him I have some important business to sort out and that we both know perfectly well that I have no problem with the law. He insists, but I give him no choice – after all, I'm a free man.

Freedom. The freedom to be wretchedly alone.

I take a taxi to the centre of Paris and ask to be dropped near the Arc de Triomphe. I set off down the Champs-Elysées towards the Hotel Bristol, where Esther and I always used to meet for hot chocolate whenever one of us came back from some trip abroad. It was our coming-home ritual, a plunge back into the love that bound us together, even though life kept sending us off along ever more diverging paths.

I keep walking. People smile, children are pleased to have been given these few hours of spring in the middle of winter, the traffic flows freely, everything seems to be in order – except that none of them knows that I have just lost my wife; they don't even pretend not to know, they don't even care. Don't they realise the pain I'm in? They should all be feeling sad, sympathetic, supportive of a man whose soul is losing love as if it were losing blood; but they continue laughing, immersed in their miserable little lives that only happen at weekends.

What a ridiculous thought! Many of the people I pass must also have their souls in tatters, and I have no idea how or why they are suffering.

I go into a bar and buy some cigarettes; the person answers me in English. I go into a chemist's to buy a mint I particularly like, and the assistant speaks to me in English (both times I asked for the products in French). Before I reach the hotel, I am stopped by two boys just arrived from Toulouse who are looking for a particular shop; they have asked several other people, but no one understands what they say. What's going on? Have they changed languages on the Champs-Elysées in the twenty-four hours since I was arrested?

Tourism and money can perform miracles, but how come I haven't noticed this before? It has obviously been a long time since Esther and I met here to drink hot chocolate, even though we have each been away and come back several times during that period. There is always something more important. There is always some unpostponable appointment. Yes, my love, we'll have that hot chocolate next time, come back soon; I've got a really important interview today and won't be able to pick you up at the airport, take a taxi; my mobile's on, call me if there's anything urgent; otherwise, I'll see you tonight.

My mobile! I take it out of my pocket and immediately turn it on; it rings several times, and each time my heart turns over. On the tiny screen I see the names of the people who have been trying to get in touch with me, but reply to none of them. I hope for someone 'unidentified' to appear, because that would be her, since only about twenty people know my number and have sworn not to pass it on. It doesn't appear, only the numbers of friends or trusted colleagues. They must be eager to know what happened, they want to help (but how?), to ask if I need anything.

The telephone keeps ringing. Should I answer it? Should I arrange to meet up with some of these people?

I decide to remain alone until I've managed to work out what is going on.

I reach the Hotel Bristol, which Esther always described as one of the few hotels in Paris where customers are treated like guests rather than homeless people in search of shelter. I am greeted as if I were a friend of the family; I choose a table next to an exquisite clock; I listen to the piano and look out at the garden.

I need to be practical, to study the options; after all, life goes on. I am not the first nor will I be the last man whose wife has left him, but did it have to happen on a sunny day, with everyone in the street smiling and children singing, with the first signs of spring just beginning to show, the sun shining, and drivers stopping at pedestrian crossings?

I pick up a napkin. I'm going to get these ideas out of my head and put them down on paper. Let's leave sentiment to one side and see what I should do:

***

Consider the possibility that she really has been kidnapped and that her life is in danger at this very moment, and that I, as her husband and constant companion, must, therefore, move heaven and earth to find her.

Response to this possibility: she took her passport with her. The police don't know this, but she also took several other personal items with her, amongst them a wallet containing images of various patron saints which she always carries with her whenever she goes abroad. She also withdrew money from her bank.

Conclusion: she was clearly preparing to leave.

***

Consider the possibility that she believed a promise someone gave her and it turned out to be a trap.

Response: she had often put herself in dangerous situations before; it was part of her job, but she always warned me when she did so, because I was the only person she could trust completely. She would tell me where she was going to be, who she was going to see (although, so as not to put me at risk, she usually used the person's *nom de guerre*), and what I should do if she did not return by a certain time.

Conclusion: she was not planning a meeting with one of her informants.

* * *

Consider the possibility that she has met another man.

Response: there is no response. Of all the hypotheses, this is the only one that makes any sense. And yet I can't accept it, I can't accept that she would leave like that, without giving me a reason. Both Esther and I have always prided ourselves on confronting all life's difficulties together. We suffered, but we never lied to each other, although it was part of the rules of the game not to mention any extramarital affairs. I was aware that she had changed a lot since meeting this fellow Mikhail, but did that justify ending a marriage that has lasted ten years?

Even if she had slept with him and fallen in love, wouldn't she weigh in the balance all the time that we had spent together and everything we had conquered before setting off on an adventure from which there was no turning back? She was free to travel whenever she wanted to, she lived surrounded by men, soldiers who hadn't seen a woman in ages, but I never asked any questions, and she never told me anything. We were both free, and we were proud of that.

But Esther had disappeared and left clues that were visible only to me, as if it were a secret message: I'm leaving.

Why?

Is that question worth answering?

No. Because hidden in the answer is my own inability to keep the woman I love by my side. Is it worth finding her and persuading her to come back? Begging and imploring her to give our marriage another chance?

That seems ridiculous: it would be better merely to suffer as I had in the past, when other people I loved had left me. It would be better just to lick my wounds, as I had also done in the past. For a while, I'll think obsessively about her, I'll become embittered, I'll bore my friends because all I ever talk about is my wife leaving me. I'll try to justify what happened, spend days and nights reviewing every moment spent by her side, I'll conclude that she was too hard on me, even though I always tried to do my best. I'll find other women. When I walk down the street, I'll keep seeing women who could be her. I'll suffer day and night, night and day. This could take weeks, months, possibly a year or more.

Until one morning, I'll wake up and find I'm thinking about something else, and then I'll know the worst is over. My heart might be bruised, but it will recover, and become capable of seeing the beauty of life once more. It's happened before, it will happen again, I'm sure. When someone leaves, it's because someone else is about to arrive – I'll find love again.

For a moment, I savour the idea of my new state: single and a millionaire. I can go out in broad daylight with whomever I want. I can behave at parties in a way I haven't behaved in years. The news will travel fast, and soon all kinds of women, the young and the not so young, the rich and the not as rich as they would like to be, the intelligent and those trained to say only what they think I would like to hear, will all come knocking at my door.

I want to believe that it is wonderful to be free. Free again. Ready to find my one true love, who is waiting for me and who will never allow me to experience such humiliation again.

* * *

I finish my hot chocolate and look at the clock; I know it is still too soon for me to be able to enjoy the agreeable feeling that I am once more part of humanity. For a few moments, I imagine that Esther is about to come in through that door, walk across the beautiful Persian carpets, sit down beside me and say nothing, just smoke a cigarette, look out at the courtyard garden and hold my hand. Half an hour passes, and for half an hour I believe in the story I have just created, until I realise that it is pure fantasy.

I decide not to go home. I go over to reception, ask for a room, a toothbrush and some deodorant. The hotel is full, but the manager fixes things for me: I end up with a lovely suite looking out at the Eiffel Tower, a terrace, the rooftops of Paris, the lights coming on one by one, the families getting together to have Sunday supper. And the feeling I had in the Champs-Elysées returns: the more beautiful everything is around me, the more wretched I feel.

No television. No supper. I sit on the terrace and look back over my life, a young man who dreamed of becoming a famous writer, and who suddenly saw that the reality was completely different – he writes in a language almost no one reads, in a country which is said to have almost no reading public. His family forces him to go to university (any university will do, my boy, just as long as you get a degree, otherwise you'll never be anyone). He rebels, travels the world during the hippie era, meets a singer, writes a few song lyrics, and is suddenly earning more money than his sister, who listened to what her parents said and decided to become a chemical engineer …

I write more songs, the singer goes from strength to strength; I buy a few apartments and fall out with the singer, but still have enough capital not to have to work for the next few years. I get married for the first time to an older woman, I learn a lot – how to make love, how to drive, how to speak English, how to lie in bed until late – but we split up because she considers me to be 'emotionally immature, and too ready to chase after any girl with big enough breasts'. I get married for a second and a third time to women I think will give me emotional stability: I get what I want, but discover that the stability I wanted is inseparable from a deep sense of tedium.

Two more divorces. Free again, but it's just a feeling; freedom is not the absence of commitments, but the ability to choose – and commit myself to – what is best for me.

I continue my search for love, I continue writing songs. When people ask me what I do, I say I'm a writer. When they say they only know my song lyrics, I say that's just part of my work. When they apologise and say they've never read any of my books, I explain that I'm working on a project – which is a lie. The truth is that I have money, I have contacts, but what I don't have is the courage to write a book. My dream is now realisable, but if I try and fail, I don't know what the rest of my life will be like; that's why it's better to live cherishing a dream than face the possibility that it might all come to nothing.

One day, a journalist comes to interview me. She wants to know what it's like to have my work known all over the country, but to be entirely unknown myself, since normally it's only the singer who appears in the media. She's pretty, intelligent, quiet. We meet again at a party, where there's no pressure of work, and I manage to get her into bed that same night. I fall in love, but she's not remotely interested. When I phone, she always says she's busy. The more she rejects me, the more interested I become, until, at last, I manage to persuade her to spend a weekend at my house in the country (I may have been the black sheep of the family, but sometimes rebellion pays off – I was the only one of my friends at that stage in our lives to have bought a house in the country).

We spend three days alone, contemplating the sea. I cook for her, and she tells me stories about her work and ends up falling in love with me. We come back to the city, she starts sleeping at my apartment on a regular basis. One morning, she leaves earlier than usual and returns with her typewriter; from then on, without anything being said, my home becomes her home too.

The same conflicts I had with my previous wives begin to surface: women are always looking for stability and fidelity, while I'm looking for adventure and the unknown. This time, though, the relationship lasts longer. Nevertheless, two years on, I decide it's time for

Esther to take her typewriter back to her own apartment, along with everything else she brought with her.

'It's not going to work.'

'But you love me and I love you, isn't that right?'

'I don't know. If you're asking me if I like your company, the answer is yes. If, on the other hand, you're asking me if I could live without you, the answer is also yes.'

'I'm glad I wasn't born a man. I'm very content with my female condition. All you expect of us women is that we can cook well. Men on the other hand are expected to be able to do everything – they've got to be able to keep a home afloat, make love, take care of the children, bring in the money and be successful.'

'That's not it either: I'm very happy with myself. I enjoy your company, but I just don't think it's going to work.'

'You enjoy my company, but hate being by yourself. You're always looking for adventure in order to forget more important things. You always want to feel the adrenaline flowing in your veins and you forget that the only thing that should be flowing through them is blood.'

'I'm not running away from important things. Give me an example of something important.'

'Writing a book.'

'I can do that any time.'

'Go on then, do it. Then, if you like, we can go our separate ways.'

I find her comment absurd; I can write a book whenever I want to; I know publishers, journalists, all of whom owe me favours. Esther is just a woman who's afraid of losing me, she's inventing things. I tell her it's over, our relationship is at an end, it isn't a matter of what she thinks would make me happy, it's about love.

What is love? she asks. I spend half an hour explaining and realise that I can't come up with a good definition.

She says that, since I don't know how to define love, I should try and write a book.

I say that the two things are completely unrelated. I'm going to leave the apartment that very day; she can stay there for as long as she likes. I'll go and stay in a hotel until she has found somewhere else to live. She says that's fine by her, I can leave now, the apartment will be free within the month – she'll start looking for a new place tomorrow. I pack my bags, and she goes and reads a book. I say it's getting late, I'll leave tomorrow. She says I should leave at once because, tomorrow, I won't feel as strong or as determined. I ask her if she's trying to get rid of me. She laughs and says I was the one who wanted to end the relationship. We go to bed, and the following day, the desire to leave is not as urgent, and I decide I need to think things through. Esther, however, says the matter isn't over yet: this scenario will simply keep recurring as long as I refuse to risk everything for what I believe to be my real reason for living; in the end, she'll become unhappy and will leave me. Except that, if *she* left, she would do so immediately and burn any bridges that would allow her to come back. I ask her what she means. She'd get another boyfriend, she says, fall in love.

She goes off to her work at the newspaper, and I decide to take a day's leave (apart from writing lyrics, I'm also working for a recording company). I sit down at the typewriter. I get up again, read the papers, reply to some urgent letters and, when I've done that, start replying to non-urgent letters. I make a list of things I need to do, I listen to music, I take a walk around the block, chat to the baker, come home, and suddenly the whole day has gone and I still haven't managed to type a single sentence. I decide that I hate Esther, that she's forcing me to do things I don't want to do.

When she gets home, she doesn't ask me anything, but I admit that I haven't managed to do any writing. She says that I have the same look in my eye as I did yesterday.

The following day I go to work, but that evening I again go over to the desk on which the typewriter is sitting. I read, watch television, listen to music, go back to the machine, and so two months pass, with me accumulating pages and more pages of 'first sentences', but never managing to finish a paragraph.

I come up with every possible excuse – no one reads in this country, I haven't worked out a plot, or I've got a fantastic plot, but I'm still looking for the right way to develop it. Besides, I'm really busy writing an article or a song lyric. Another two months pass, and one day, she comes home bearing a plane ticket.

'Enough,' she says. 'Stop pretending that you're busy, that you're weighed down by responsibilities, that the world needs you to do what you're doing, and just go travelling for a while.' I can always become the editor of the newspaper where I publish a few articles, I can always become the president of the recording company for whom I write lyrics, and where I work simply because they don't want me to write lyrics for their competitors. I can always come back to do what I'm doing now, but my dream can't wait. Either I accept it or I forget it.

Where is the ticket for?

Spain.

I'm shocked. Air tickets are expensive; besides, I can't go away now, I've got a career ahead of me, and I need to look after it. I'll lose out on a lot of potential music partnerships; the problem isn't me, it's our marriage. If I really wanted to write a book, no one would be able to stop me.

'You can, you want to, but you don't,' she says. 'Your problem isn't me, but you, so it would be best if you spent some time alone.'

She shows me a map. I must go to Madrid, where I'll catch a bus up to the Pyrenees, on the border with France. That's where a medieval pilgrimage route begins: the road to Santiago. I have to walk the whole way. She'll be waiting for me at the other end and then she'll accept anything I say: that I don't love her any more, that I still haven't lived enough to create a literary work, that I don't even want to think about being a writer, that it was nothing but an adolescent dream.

This is madness! The woman I've been living with for two long years – a real eternity in relationship terms – is making decisions about my life, forcing me to give up my work and expecting me to walk across an entire country! It's so crazy that I decide to take it seriously. I get drunk several nights running, with her beside me getting equally drunk – even though she hates drinking. I get aggressive; I say she's jealous of my independence, that the only reason this whole mad idea was born is because I said I wanted to leave her. She says that it all started when I was still at school and dreaming of becoming a writer – no more putting things off; if I don't confront myself now, I'll spend the rest of my life getting married and divorced, telling cute anecdotes about my past and going steadily downhill.

Obviously, I can't admit she's right, but I know she's telling the truth. And the more aware I am of this, the more aggressive I become. She accepts my aggression without complaint; she merely reminds me that the departure date is getting closer.

One night, shortly before that date, she refuses to make love. I smoke a whole joint of marihuana, drink two bottles of wine and pass out in the middle of the living room. When I come to, I realise that I have reached the bottom of the pit, and now all that remains is for me to clamber back up to the top. And I, who so pride myself on my courage, see how cowardly, mean and unadventurous I am being with my own life. That morning, I wake her with a kiss and tell her that I'll do as she suggests.

I set off and for thirty-eight days I follow the road to Santiago. When I arrive, I understand that my real journey only starts there. I decide to settle in Madrid and live off my royalties, to allow an ocean to separate me from Esther's body, even though we are still officially together and often talk on the phone. It's very comfortable being married and knowing that I can always return to her arms, meanwhile enjoying all the independence in the world.

I fall in love with a Catalan scientist, with an Argentine woman who makes jewellery, and with a young woman who sings in the metro. The royalties from my lyrics keep rolling in and are enough for me to live comfortably without having to work and with plenty of time to do everything, even … write a book.

The book can always wait until tomorrow, though, because the mayor of Madrid has decreed that the city should be one long party and has come up with an interesting slogan – 'Madrid is killing me' – and urges us all to visit several bars each night, coining the phrase *la movida madrileña* ('the Madrid scene'), which is something I cannot possibly put off until tomorrow; everything is such fun; the days are short and the nights are long.

One day, Esther phones to say that she's coming to see me: according to her, we need to sort out our situation once and for all. She has booked her ticket for the following week, which gives me just enough time to organise a series of excuses. ('I'm going to Portugal, but I'll be back in a month,' I tell the blonde girl who used to sing in the metro and who now sleeps in the rented apartment where I live and with whom I go out every night to enjoy *la movida madrileña*.) I tidy the apartment, expunge any trace of a female presence, and ask my friends not to breathe a word, because my wife is coming to stay for a month.

Esther gets off the plane sporting a hideous, unrecognisable haircut. We travel to the interior of Spain, discover little towns that mean a great deal for one night, but which, if I went back there today, I wouldn't even be able to find. We go to bullfights, flamenco shows, and I am the best husband in the world, because I want her to go home feeling that I still love her. I don't know why I want to give this impression, perhaps because, deep down, I know that the Madrid dream will eventually end.

I complain about her haircut and she changes it and is pretty again. There are only ten days left of her holiday and I want her to go home feeling happy and to leave me alone to enjoy this Madrid that is killing me, the discotheques that open at ten in the morning, the bullfights, the endless conversations about the same old topics, the alcohol, the women, more bullfights, more alcohol, more women, and absolutely no timetable.

One Sunday, while we are walking to a bar that serves food all night, she brings up the forbidden topic: the book I said I was writing. I drink a whole bottle of sherry, kick any metal doors we pass on the way back, verbally abuse other people in the street, ask why she bothered travelling all this way if her one aim was to make my life a hell and to destroy my happiness. She says nothing, but we both know that our relationship has reached its limits. I have a dreamless night's sleep, and the following morning, having complained to the building manager about the phone that doesn't work, having told off the cleaning woman because she hasn't changed the bedclothes for a week, having taken a long, long bath to get rid of the hangover from the night before, I sit down at my typewriter, just to show Esther that I am trying, honestly trying, to work.

And suddenly, the miracle happens. I look across at the woman who has just made some coffee and is now reading the newspaper, whose eyes look tired and desperate, who is her usual silent self, who does not always show her affection in gestures, the woman who made me say 'yes' when I wanted to say 'no', who forced me to fight for what she, quite rightly, believed was my reason for living, who let me set off alone because her love for me was greater even than her love for herself, who made me go in search of my dream; and, suddenly, seeing that small, quiet woman, whose eyes said more than any words, who was often terrified inside, but always courageous in her actions, who could love someone without humbling herself and who never ever apologised for fighting for her man, suddenly, my fingers press down on the keys.

The first sentence emerges. Then the second.

I spend two days without eating, I sleep the bare minimum, the words seem to spring from some unknown place, as they did when I used to write lyrics, in the days when, after much arguing and much meaningless conversation, my musical partner and I would know that 'it' was there, ready, and it was time to set 'it' down in words and notes. This time, I know that 'it' comes from Esther's heart; my love is reborn, I write the book because she exists, because she has survived all the difficult times without complaint, without ever once seeing herself as victim. I start by describing the experience that has affected me most profoundly in those last few years – the road to Santiago.

* * *

As I write, I realise that the way I see the world is going through a series of major changes. For many years, I studied and practised magic, alchemy and the occult; I was fascinated by the idea of a small group of people being in possession of an immense power that could in no way be shared with the rest of humanity, because it would be far too dangerous to allow such vast potential to fall into inexperienced hands. I was a member of secret societies, I became involved in exotic sects, I bought obscure, extremely expensive books, spent an enormous amount of time performing rituals and invocations. I was always joining and leaving different groups and fraternities, always thinking that I had finally met the person who could reveal to me the mysteries of the invisible world, but, in the end, was always disappointed to discover that most of these people – however well-intentioned – were merely following this or that dogma and tended to be fanatics, because fanaticism is the only way to put an end to the doubts that constantly trouble the human soul.

I discovered that many of the rituals did actually work, but I discovered, too, that those who declared themselves to be the masters and holders of the secrets of life, who claimed to know techniques that gave them the ability to achieve their every desire, had completely lost touch with the teachings of the ancients. Following the road to Santiago, coming into contact with ordinary people, discovering that the Universe spoke its own language of 'signs' and that, in order to understand this language, we had only to look with an open mind at what was going on around us – all this made me wonder if the occult really was the one doorway into those mysteries. In my book about the road to Santiago, I discuss other possible ways of growing and end with this thought: 'All you have to do is to pay attention; lessons always arrive when you are ready, and if you can read the signs, you will learn everything you need to know in order to take the next step.'

* * *

We humans have two great problems: the first is knowing when to begin, the second is knowing when to stop.

A week later, I begin the first, second and third draft. Madrid is no longer killing me, it is time to go back home. I feel that one cycle has ended and that I urgently need to begin another. I say goodbye to the city as I have always said goodbye in life: thinking that I might change my mind and come back one day.

I return to my own country with Esther, convinced that it might be time to get another job, but until I do (and I don't because I don't need to) I continue revising the book. I can't believe that anyone will have much interest in the experiences of one man following a romantic but difficult route across Spain.

Four months later, when I am busy on my tenth draft, I discover that both the typescript and Esther have gone. Just as I'm about to go mad with anxiety, she returns with a receipt from the post office – she has sent it off to an old boyfriend of hers, who now runs a small publishing house.

The ex-boyfriend publishes the book. There is not a word about it in the press, but a few people buy it. They recommend it to other people, who also buy it and recommend it to others. Six months later, the first edition has sold out. A year later, there have been three more print runs and I am beginning to earn money from the one thing I never dreamed I would – from literature.

I don't know how long this dream will continue, but I decide to live each moment as if it were the last. And I see that this success opens the door I have so long wanted to open: other publishers are keen to publish my next book.

Obviously, I can't follow the road to Santiago every year, so what am I going to write about next? Will I have to endure the same rigmarole of sitting down in front of the typewriter and then finding myself doing everything but write sentences and paragraphs? It's important that I continue to share my vision of the world and to describe my experiences of life. I try for a few days and for many nights, and decide that it's impossible. Then, one evening, I happen upon (happen upon?) an interesting story in *The Thousand and One Nights*; in it I find the symbol of my own path, something that helps me to understand who I am and why I took so long to make the decision that was always there waiting for me. I use that story as the basis for another story about a shepherd who goes in search of his dream, a treasure hidden in the pyramids of Egypt. I speak of the love that lies waiting for him there, as Esther had waited for me while I walked round and round in circles.

I am no longer someone dreaming of becoming something: I am. I am the shepherd crossing the desert, but where is the alchemist who helps him to carry on? When I finish this novel, I don't entirely understand what I have written: it is like a fairy tale for grown-ups, and grown-ups are more interested in war, sex, or stories about power. Nevertheless, the publisher accepts it, the book is published, and my readers once again take it into the bestseller lists.

Three years later, my marriage is in excellent shape; I am doing what I always wanted to do; the first translation appears, then the second, and success – slowly but surely – takes my work to the four corners of the earth.

I decide to move to Paris because of its cafés, its writers and its cultural life. I discover that none of this exists any more: the cafés are full of tourists and photographs of the people who made those places famous. Most of the writers there are more concerned with style than content; they strive to be original, but succeed only in being dull. They are locked in their own little world, and I learn an interesting French expression: *renvoyer l'ascenseur*, meaning literally 'to send the lift back up', but used metaphorically to mean 'to return a favour'. In practice, this means that I say nice things about your book, you say nice things about mine, and thus we create a whole new cultural life, a revolution, an apparently new philosophy; we suffer because no one understands us, but then that's what happened with all the geniuses of the past: being misunderstood by one's contemporaries is surely just part and parcel of being a great artist.

'They send the lift back up', and, at first, such writers have some success: people don't want to run the risk of openly criticising something they don't understand, but they soon realise they are being conned and stop believing what the critics say.

The Internet and its simple language are all that it takes to change the world. A parallel world emerges in Paris: new writers struggle to make their words and their souls understood. I join these new writers in cafés that no one has heard of, because neither the writers nor the cafés are as yet famous. I develop my style alone and I learn from a publisher all I need to know about mutual support.

'What is this Favour Bank?'

'You know. Everyone knows.'

'Possibly, but I still haven't quite grasped what you're saying.'

'It was an American writer who first mentioned it. It's the most powerful bank in the world, and you'll find it in every sphere of life.'

'Yes, but I come from a country without a literary tradition. What favours could I do for anyone?'

'That doesn't matter in the least. Let me give you an example: I know that you're an up-and-coming writer and that, one day, you'll be very influential. I know this because, like you, I too was once ambitious, independent, honest. I no longer have the energy I once had, but I want to help you because I can't or don't want to grind to a halt just yet. I'm not dreaming about retirement, I'm still dreaming about the fascinating struggle that is life, power, and glory.

'I start making deposits in your account – not cash deposits, you understand, but contacts. I introduce you to such and such a person, I arrange certain deals, as long as they're legal. You know that you owe me something, but I never ask you for anything.'

'And then one day …'

'Exactly. One day, I'll ask you for a favour and you could, of course, say "No", but you're conscious of being in my debt. You do what I ask, I continue to help you, and other people see that you're a decent, loyal sort of person and so they too make deposits in your account – always in the form of contacts, because this world is made up of contacts and nothing else. They too will one day ask you for a favour, and you will respect and help the people who have helped you, and, in time, you'll have spread your net worldwide, you'll know everyone you need to know and your influence will keep on growing.'

'I could refuse to do what you ask me to do.'

'You could. The Favour Bank is a risky investment, just like any other bank. You refuse to grant the favour I asked you, in the belief that I helped you because you deserved to be helped, because you're the best and everyone should automatically recognise your talent. Fine, I say thank you very much and ask someone else into whose account I've also made various deposits; but from then on, everyone knows, without me having to say a word, that you are not to be trusted.

'You'll grow only half as much as you could have grown, and certainly not as much as you would have liked to. At a certain point, your life will begin to decline, you got halfway, but not all the way, you are half-happy and half-sad, neither frustrated nor fulfilled. You're neither cold nor hot, you're lukewarm, and as an evangelist in some holy book says: "Lukewarm things are not pleasing to the palate."'

The publisher places a lot of deposits – or contacts – into my account at the Favour Bank. I learn, I suffer, my books are translated into French, and, in the tradition of that country, the stranger is welcomed. Not only that, the stranger is an enormous success! Ten years on, I have a large apartment with a view over the Seine, I am loved by my readers and loathed by the critics (who adored me until I sold my first 100,000 copies, but, from that moment on, I ceased to be 'a misunderstood genius'). I always repay promptly any deposits made and soon I too am a lender – of contacts. My influence grows. I learn to ask for favours and to do the favours others ask of me.

Esther gets permission to work as a journalist. Apart from the normal conflicts in any marriage, I am contented. I understand for the first time that all the frustrations I felt about previous love affairs and marriages had nothing to do with the women involved, but with my own bitterness. Esther, however, was the only woman who understood one very simple thing: in order to be able to find her, I first had to find myself. We have been together for eight years; I believe she is the love of my life, and although I do occasionally (or, to be honest, frequently) fall in love with other women who cross my path, I never consider the possibility of divorce. I never ask her if she knows about my extramarital affairs. She never makes any comment on the subject.

That is why I am astonished when, as we are leaving a cinema, she tells me that she has asked her magazine if she can file a report on a civil war in Africa.

'What are you saying?'

'That I want to be a war correspondent.'

'You're mad. You don't need to do that. You're already doing the work you want to do now. You earn good money – not that you need that money to live on. You have all the contacts you need in the Favour Bank. You have talent and you've earned your colleagues' respect.'

'All right then, let's just say I need to be alone.'

'Because of me?'

'We've built our lives together. I love my man and he loves me, even though he's not always the most faithful of husbands.'

'You've never said anything about that before.'

'Because it doesn't matter to me. I mean, what is fidelity? The feeling that I possess a body and a soul that aren't mine? Do you imagine I haven't been to bed with other men during all these years we've been together?'

'I don't care and I don't want to know.'

'Well, neither do I.'

'So, what's all this about wanting to write about a war in some godforsaken part of the world?'

'Like I said, I need to.'

'Haven't you got everything you need?'

'I have everything a woman could want.'

'What's wrong with your life then?'

'Precisely that. I have everything, but I'm not happy. And I'm not the only one either; over the years, I've met and interviewed all kinds of people: the rich, the poor, the powerful, and those who just make do. I've seen the same infinite bitterness in everyone's eyes, a sadness which people weren't always prepared to acknowledge, but which, regardless of what they were telling me, was nevertheless there. Are you listening?'

'Yes, I'm listening. I was just thinking. So, according to you, no one is happy?'

'Some people appear to be happy, but they simply don't give the matter much thought. Others make plans: I'm going to have a husband, a home, two children, a house in the country. As long as they're busy doing that, they're like bulls looking for the bullfighter: they react instinctively, they blunder on, with no idea where the target is. They get their car, sometimes they even get a Ferrari, and they think that's the meaning of life, and they never question it. Yet their eyes betray the sadness that even they don't know they carry in their soul. Are you happy?'

'I don't know.'

'I don't know if everyone is unhappy. I know they're all busy: working overtime, worrying about their children, their husband, their career, their degree, what they're going to do tomorrow, what they need to buy, what they need to have in order not to feel inferior, etc. Very few people actually say to me: "I'm unhappy." Most say: "I'm fine, I've got everything I ever wanted." Then I ask: "What makes you happy?" Answer: "I've got everything a person could possibly want – a family, a home, work, good health." I ask again: "Have you ever stopped to wonder if that's all there is to life?" Answer: "Yes, that's all there is." I insist: "So the meaning of life is work, family, children who will grow up and leave you, a wife or husband who will become more like a friend than a real lover. And, of course, one day your work will end too. What will you do when that happens?" Answer: there is no answer. They change the subject.'

'No, what they say is: "When the children have grown up, when my husband – or my wife – has become more my friend than my passionate lover, when I retire, then I'll have time to do what I always wanted to do: travel." Question: "But didn't you say you were happy now? Aren't you already doing what you always wanted to do?" Then they say they're very busy and change the subject.'

'If I insist, they always do come up with something they're lacking. The businessman hasn't yet closed the deal he wanted, the housewife would like to have more independence and more money, the boy who's in love is afraid of losing his girlfriend, the new graduate wonders if he chose his career or if it was chosen for him, the dentist wanted to be a singer, the singer wanted to be a politician, the politician wanted to be a writer, the writer wanted to be a farmer. And even when I did meet someone who was doing what he had chosen to do, that person's soul was still in torment. He hadn't found peace yet either. So I'll ask you again: "Are you happy?"'

'No. I have the woman I love, the career I always dreamed of having, the kind of freedom that is the envy of all my friends, the travel, the honours, the praise. But there's something …'

'What?'

'I have the idea that, if I stopped, life would become meaningless.'

'You can't just relax, look at Paris, take my hand and say: I've got what I wanted, now let's enjoy what life remains to us.'

'I can look at Paris, take your hand, but I can't say those words.'

'I bet you everyone walking along this street now is feeling the same thing. The elegant woman who just passed us spends her days trying to hold back time, always checking the scales, because she thinks that is what love depends on. Look across the road: a couple with two children. They feel intensely happy when they're out with their children, but, at the same time, their subconscious keeps them in a constant state of terror: they think of the job they might lose, the disease they might catch, the health insurance that might not come up with the goods, one of the children getting run over. And in trying to distract themselves, they try as well to find a way of getting free of those tragedies, of protecting themselves from the world.'

'And the beggar on the corner?'

'I don't know about him. I've never spoken to a beggar. He's certainly the picture of misery, but his eyes, like the eyes of any beggar, seem to be hiding something. His sadness is so obvious that I can't quite believe in it.'

'What's missing?'

'I haven't a clue. I look at the celebrity magazines with everyone smiling and contented, but since I am myself married to a celebrity, I know that it isn't quite like that: everyone is laughing and having fun at that moment, in that photo, but later that night, or in the morning, the story is always quite different. "What do I have to do in order to continue appearing in this magazine?" "How can I disguise the fact that I no longer have enough money to support my luxurious lifestyle?" "How can I best manipulate my luxurious lifestyle to make it seem even more luxurious than anyone else's?" "The actress in the photo with me and with whom I'm smiling and celebrating could steal a part from me tomorrow!" "Am I better dressed than she is? Why are we smiling when we loathe each other?" "Why do we sell happiness to the readers of this magazine when we are profoundly unhappy ourselves, the slaves of fame."'

'We're not the slaves of fame.'

'Don't get paranoid. I'm not talking about us.'

'What do you think is going on, then?'

'Years ago, I read a book that told an interesting story. Just suppose that Hitler had won the war, wiped out all the Jews and convinced his people that there really was such a thing as a master race. The history books start to be changed, and, a hundred years later, his successors manage to wipe out all the Indians. Three hundred years later and the Blacks have been eliminated too. It takes five hundred years, but, finally, the all-powerful war machine succeeds in erasing the oriental race from the face of the earth as well. The history books speak of remote battles waged against barbarians, but no one reads too closely, because it's of no importance.

Two thousand years after the birth of Nazism, in a bar in Tokyo, a city that has been inhabited for five centuries now by tall, blue-eyed people, Hans and Fritz are enjoying a beer. At one point, Hans looks at Fritz and asks: "Fritz, do you think it was always like this?"

"What?" asks Fritz.

"The world."

"Of course the world was always like this, isn't that what we were taught?"

"Of course, I don't know what made me ask such a stupid question," says Hans. They finish their beer, talk about other things and forget the question entirely.'

'You don't even need to go that far into the future, you just have to go back two thousand years. Can you see yourself worshipping a guillotine, a scaffold or an electric chair?'

'I know where you're heading – to that worst of all human tortures, the cross. I remember that Cicero referred to it as "an abominable punishment" that inflicted terrible suffering on the crucified person before he or she died. And yet, nowadays people wear it around their neck, hang it on their bedroom wall and have come to identify it as a religious symbol, forgetting that they are looking at an instrument of torture.'

'Two hundred and fifty years passed before someone decided that it was time to abolish the pagan festivals surrounding the winter solstice, the time when the sun is farthest from the earth. The apostles, and those who came after them, were too busy spreading Jesus' message to worry about the *natalis invict Solis*, the Mithraic festival of the birth of the sun, which occurred on 25 December. Then a bishop decided that these solstice festivals were a threat to the faith and that was that! Now we have masses, Nativity scenes, presents, sermons, plastic babies in wooden mangers, and the cast-iron conviction that Christ was born on that very day!'

'And then there's the Christmas tree. Do you know where that comes from?'

'No idea.'

'St Boniface decided to "christianise" a ritual intended to honour the god Odin when he was a child. Once a year, the Germanic tribes would place presents around an oak tree for the children to find. They thought this would bring joy to the pagan deity.'

'Going back to the story of Hans and Fritz: do you think that civilisation, human relations, our hopes, our conquests, are all just the product of some other garbled story?'

'When you wrote about the road to Santiago, you came to the same conclusion, didn't you? You used to believe that only a select few knew the meaning of magic symbols, but now you realise that we all know the meaning, it's just that we've forgotten it.'

'Knowing that doesn't make any difference. People do their best not to remember and not to accept the immense magical potential they possess, because that would upset their neat little universes.'

'But we all have the ability, don't we?'

'Absolutely, we just don't all have the courage to follow our dreams and to follow the signs. Perhaps that's where the sadness comes from.'

'I don't know. And I'm not saying that I'm unhappy all the time. I have fun, I love you, I adore my work. Yet now and then, I feel this profound sadness, occasionally mingled with feelings of guilt or fear; the feeling passes, but always comes back later on, and then passes off again. Like Hans, I ask that same question; when I can't answer it, I simply forget. I could go and help starving children, set up a foundation for street children, start trying to save people in the name of Jesus, do something that would give me the feeling I was being useful, but I don't want to.'

'So why do you want to go and cover this war?'

'Because I think that in time of war, men live life at the limit; after all, they could die the next day. Anyone living like that must act differently.'

'So you want to find an answer to Hans's question?'

'Yes, I do.'

Today, in this beautiful suite in the Hotel Bristol, with the Eiffel Tower glittering for five minutes every time the clock strikes the hour, with an empty bottle of wine beside me and my cigarettes fast running out, with people greeting me as if nothing very serious had happened, I ask myself: was it then, coming out of the cinema, that it all began? Should I have let her go off in search of that garbled story or should I have put my foot down and told her to forget the whole idea because she was my wife and I needed her with me, needed her support?

Nonsense. At the time, I knew, as I know now, that I had no option but to accept what she wanted. If I had said: 'Choose between me and becoming a war correspondent', I would have been betraying everything that Esther had done for me. I wasn't convinced by her declared aim – to go in search of 'a garbled story' – but I concluded that she needed a bit of freedom, to get out and about, to experience strong emotions. And what was wrong with that?

I accepted, not without first making it clear that this constituted a very large withdrawal from the Favour Bank (which, when I think about it now, seems a ludicrous thing to say). For two years, Esther followed various conflicts at close quarters, changing continents more often than she changed her shoes. Whenever she came back, I thought that this time she would give it up – it's just not possible to live for very long in a place where there's no decent food, no daily bath, and no cinemas or theatres. I asked her if she had found the answer to Hans's question, and she always told me that she was on the right track, and I had to be satisfied with that. Sometimes, she was away from home for months at a time; contrary to what it says in the 'official history of marriage' (I was starting to use her terminology), that distance only made our love grow stronger, and showed us how important we were to each other. Our relationship, which I thought had reached its ideal point when we moved to Paris, was getting better and better.

As I understand it, she first met Mikhail when she needed a translator to accompany her to some country in Central Asia. At first, she talked about him with great enthusiasm – he was a very sensitive person, someone who saw the world as it really was and not as we had been told it should be. He was five years younger than her, but had a quality that Esther described as 'magical'. I listened patiently and politely, as if I were really interested in that boy and his ideas, but the truth is I was far away, going over in my mind all the things I had to do, ideas for articles, answers to questions from journalists and publishers, strategies for how to seduce a particular woman who appeared to be interested in me, plans for future book promotions.

I don't know if Esther noticed this. I certainly failed to notice that Mikhail gradually disappeared from our conversations, then vanished completely. Esther's behaviour became increasingly eccentric: even when she was in Paris, she started going out several nights a week, telling me that she was researching an article on beggars.

I thought she must be having an affair. I agonised for a whole week and asked myself: should I tell her my doubts or just pretend that nothing is happening? I decided to ignore it, on the principle that 'what the eye doesn't see, the heart doesn't grieve over'. I was utterly convinced that there wasn't the slightest possibility of her leaving me; she had worked so hard to help me become the person I am, and it would be illogical to let all that go for some ephemeral affair.

If I had really been interested in Esther's world, I should at least have asked what had happened to her translator and his 'magical' sensibility. I should have been suspicious of that silence, that lack of information. I should have asked to go with her on one of those 'research trips' to visit beggars.

When she occasionally asked if I was interested in her work, my answer was always the same: 'Yes, I'm interested, but I don't want to interfere, I want you to be free to follow your dream in your chosen way, just as you helped me to do the same.'

This, of course, was tantamount to saying that I wasn't the slightest bit interested. But because people always believe what they want to believe, Esther seemed satisfied with my response.

* * *

The words spoken by the inspector when I was released from the police cell come back to me again: *You're a free man*. But what is freedom? Is it seeing that your husband isn't interested in what you are doing? Is it feeling alone and having no one with whom to share your innermost feelings, because the person you married is entirely focused on his own work, on his important, magnificent, difficult career?

I look at the Eiffel Tower: another hour has passed, and it is glittering again as if it were made of diamonds. I have no idea how often this has happened since I have been at the window.

I know that, in the name of the freedom of our marriage, I did not notice that Mikhail had disappeared from my wife's conversations, only to reappear in a bar and disappear again, this time taking her with him and leaving behind the famous, successful writer as prime suspect.

Or, worse still, as a man abandoned.

Han's question

In Buenos Aires, the Zahir is a common 20-centavo coin; the letters N and T and the number 2 bear the marks of a knife or a letter-opener; 1929 is the date engraved on the reverse. (In Gujarat, at the end of the eighteenth century, the Zahir was a tiger; in Java, it was a blind man from the Surakarta mosque who was stoned by the faithful; in Persia, an astrolabe that Nadir Shah ordered to be thrown into the sea; in Mahdi's prisons, in around 1892, a small compass that had been touched by Rudolf Karl von Slatin ...)

A year later, I wake thinking about the story by Jorge Luis Borges, about something which, once touched or seen, can never be forgotten, and which gradually so fills our thoughts that we are driven to madness. My Zahir is not a romantic metaphor – a blind man, a compass, a tiger, or a coin.

It has a name, and her name is Esther.

Immediately after leaving prison, I appeared on the covers of various scandal sheets: they began by alleging a possible crime, but, in order to avoid ending up in court, they always concluded with the statement that I had been cleared (cleared? I hadn't even been accused!). They allowed a week to pass; they checked to see if the sales had been good (they had, because I was the kind of writer who was normally above suspicion, and everyone wanted to find out how it was possible for a man who writes about spirituality to have such a dark side). Then they returned to the attack, alleging that my wife had run away because of my many extramarital affairs: a German magazine even hinted at a possible relationship with a singer, twenty years my junior, who said she had met me in Oslo, in Norway (this was true, but the meeting had only taken place because of the Favour Bank – a friend of mine had asked me to go and had been with us throughout the only supper we had together). The singer said that there was nothing between us (so why put a photo of us on the cover?) and took the opportunity to announce that she was releasing a new album: she had used both the magazine and me, and I still don't know whether the failure of the album was a consequence of this kind of cheap publicity (the album wasn't bad, by the way – what ruined everything were the press releases).

The scandal over the famous writer did not last long; in Europe, and especially in France, infidelity is not only accepted, it is even secretly admired. And no one likes to read about the sort of thing that could so easily happen to them.

The topic disappeared from the front covers, but the hypotheses continued: she had been kidnapped, she had left home because of physical abuse (photo of a waiter saying that we often argued: I remember that I did, in fact, have an argument with Esther in a restaurant about her views on a South American writer, which were completely opposed to mine). A British tabloid alleged – and luckily this had no serious repercussions – that my wife had gone into hiding with an Islamist terrorist organisation.

This world is so full of betrayals, divorces, murders, assassination attempts, that a month later the subject had been forgotten by the ordinary public. Years of experience had taught me that this kind of thing would never affect my faithful readership (it had happened before, when a journalist on an Argentinian television programme claimed that he had 'proof' that I had had a secret meeting in Chile with the future first lady of the country – but my books remained on the bestseller lists). As an American artist almost said: Sensationalism was only made to last fifteen minutes. My main concern was quite different: to reorganise my life, to find a new love, to go back to writing books, and to put away any memories of my wife in the little drawer that exists on the frontier between love and hate.

Or should I say memories of my ex-wife (I needed to get used to the term).

Part of what I had foreseen in that hotel room did come to pass. For a while, I barely left the apartment: I didn't know how to face my friends, how to look them in the eye and say simply: 'My wife has left me for a younger man.' When I did go out, no one asked me anything, but after a few glasses of wine I felt obliged to bring the subject up – as if I could read everyone's mind, as if I really believed that they had nothing more to occupy them than what was happening in my life, but that they were too polite or smug to say anything. Depending on my mood, Esther was either a saint who deserved better, or a treacherous, perfidious woman who had embroiled me in such a complicated situation that I had even been thought a criminal.

Friends, acquaintances, publishers, people I sat next to at the many gala dinners I was obliged to attend, listened with some curiosity at first. Gradually, though, I noticed that they tended to change the subject; they had been interested in the subject at some point, but it was no longer part of their current curiosities: they were more interested in talking about the actress who had been murdered by a singer or about the adolescent girl who had written a book about her affairs with well-known politicians. One day, in Madrid, I noticed that the number of guests at events and suppers was beginning to fall off. Although it may have been good for my soul to unburden myself of my feelings, to blame or to bless Esther, I began to realise that I was becoming something even worse than a betrayed husband: I was becoming the kind of boring person no one wants to be around.

I decided, from then on, to suffer in silence, and the invitations once more flooded in through my letter box.

But the Zahir, about which I initially used to think with either irritation or affection, continued to grow in my soul. I started looking for Esther in every woman I met. I would see her in every bar, every cinema, at bus stops. More than once I ordered a taxi driver to stop in the middle of the street or to follow someone, until I could persuade myself that the person was not the person I was looking for.

With the Zahir beginning to occupy my every thought, I needed an antidote, something that would not take me to the brink of despair.

There was only one possible solution: a girlfriend.

I encountered three or four women I felt drawn to, but then I met Marie, a 35-year-old French actress. She was the only one who did not spout such nonsense as: 'I like you as a man, not as the celebrity everyone wants to meet' or 'I wish you weren't quite so famous', or worse still: 'I'm not interested in money.' She was the only one who was genuinely pleased at my success, because she too was famous and knew that celebrity counts. Celebrity is an aphrodisiac. It was good for a woman's ego to be with a man and know that he had chosen her even though he had had the pick of many others.

We were often seen together at parties and receptions; there was speculation about our relationship, but neither she nor I confirmed or denied anything, and the matter was left hanging, and all that remained for the magazines was to wait for the photo of the famous kiss – which never came, because both she and I considered such public exhibitionism vulgar. She got on with her filming and I with my work; when I could, I would travel to Milan, and when she could, she would meet me in Paris; we were close, but not dependent on each other.

Marie pretended not to know what was going on in my soul, and I pretended not to know what was going on in hers (an impossible love for a married neighbour, even though she could have had any man she wanted). We were friends, companions, we enjoyed the same things; I would even go so far as to say that there was between us a kind of love, but different from the love I felt for Esther or that Marie felt for her neighbour.

I started taking part in book-signings again, I accepted invitations to give lectures, write articles, attend charity dinners, appear on television programmes, help out with projects for up-and-coming young artists. I did everything except what I should have been doing, i.e. writing a book.

This didn't matter to me, however, for in my heart of hearts I believed that my career as a writer was over, because the woman who had made me begin was no longer there. I had lived my dream intensely while it lasted, I had got farther than most people are lucky enough to get, I could spend the rest of my life having fun.

I thought this every morning. In the afternoon, I realised that the only thing I really liked doing was writing. By nightfall, there I was once more trying to persuade myself that I had fulfilled my dream and should try something new.

The following year was a Holy Year in Spain, the *Año Santo Compostelano,* which occurs whenever the day of St James of Compostela, 25 July, falls on a Sunday. A special door to the Cathedral in Santiago stands open for 365 days, and, according to tradition, anyone who goes through that door receives a series of special blessings.

There were various commemorative events throughout Spain, and since I was extremely grateful for the pilgrimage I had made, I decided to take part in at least one event: a talk, in January, in the Basque country. In order to get out of my routine – trying to write a book/going to a party/to the airport/visiting Marie in Milan/going out to supper/to a hotel/to the airport/surfing the Internet/going to the airport/to an interview/to another airport – I chose to drive the 1,400 kilometres there alone.

Everywhere – even those places I have never visited before – reminds me of my private Zahir. I think how Esther would love to see this, how much she would enjoy eating in this restaurant or walking by this river. I spend the night in Bayonne and, before I go to sleep, I turn on the television and learn that there are about 5,000 trucks stuck on the frontier between France and Spain, due to a violent and entirely unexpected snowstorm.

I wake up thinking that I should simply drive back to Paris: I have an excellent excuse for cancelling the engagement, and the organisers will understand perfectly – the traffic is in chaos, there is ice on the roads, both the French and Spanish governments are advising people not to leave home this weekend because the risk of accidents is so high. The situation is worse than it was last night: the morning paper reports that on one stretch of road alone there are 17,000 people trapped; civil defence teams have been mobilised to provide them with food and temporary shelters, since many people have already run out of fuel and cannot use their car heaters.

The hotel staff tell me that if I really have to travel, if it's a matter of life or death, there is a minor road I can take, which, while it will avoid the blockages, will add about two hours to my journey time, and no one can guarantee what state the road will be in. Instinctively, I decide to go ahead; something is forcing me on, out onto the icy asphalt and to the hours spent patiently waiting in bottlenecks.

Perhaps it is the name of the city: Vitória – Victory. Perhaps it is the feeling that I have grown too used to comfort and have lost my ability to improvise in crisis situations. Perhaps it is the enthusiasm of the people who are, at this moment, trying to restore a cathedral built many centuries ago and who, in order to draw attention to their efforts, have invited a few writers to give talks. Or perhaps it is the old saying of the conquistadors of the Americas: 'it is not life that matters, but the journey'.

And so I keep on journeying. After many long, tense hours, I reach Vitória, where some even tenser people are waiting for me. They say that there hasn't been a snowstorm like it for more than thirty years, they thank me for making the effort, and continue with the official programme, which includes a visit to the Cathedral of Santa María.

A young woman with shining eyes starts telling me the story. To begin with there was the city wall. The wall remained, but one part of it was used to build a chapel. Many years passed, and the chapel became a church. Another century passed, and the church became a Gothic cathedral. The cathedral had had its moments of glory, there had been structural problems, for a time it had been abandoned, then restoration work had distorted the whole shape of the building, but each generation thought it had solved the problem and would rework the original plans. Thus, in the centuries that followed, they raised a wall here, took down a beam there, added a buttress over there, created or bricked up stained-glass windows.

And the cathedral withstood it all.

I walk through the skeleton of the cathedral, studying the restoration work currently being carried out: this time the architects guarantee that they have found the perfect solution. Everywhere there are metal supports, scaffolding, grand theories about what to do next and some criticism about what was done in the past.

And suddenly, in the middle of the central nave, I realise something very important: the cathedral is me, it is all of us. We are all growing and changing shape, we notice certain weaknesses that need to be corrected, we don't always choose the best solution, but we carry on regardless, trying to remain upright and decent, in order to do honour not to the walls or the doors or the windows, but to the empty space inside, the space where we worship and venerate what is dearest and most important to us.

Yes, we are all cathedrals, there is no doubt about it; but what lies in the empty space of my inner cathedral?

Esther, the Zahir.

She fills everything. She is the only reason I am alive. I look around, I prepare myself for the talk I am to give, and I understand why I braved the snow, the traffic jams and the ice on the roads: in order to be reminded that every day I need to rebuild myself and to accept – for the first time in my entire existence – that I love another human being more than I love myself.

On the way back to Paris – in far more favourable weather conditions – I am in a kind of trance: I do not think, I merely concentrate on the traffic. When I get home, I ask the maid not to let anyone in, and ask her if she can sleep over for the next few nights and make me breakfast, lunch and supper. I stamp on the small apparatus that connects me to the Internet, destroying it completely. I unplug the telephone. I put my mobile in a box and send it to my publisher, saying that he should only give it back to me when I come round personally to pick it up.

For a week, I walk by the Seine each morning and, when I get back, I lock myself in my study. As if I were listening to the voice of an angel, I write a book, or, rather, a letter, a long letter to the woman of my dreams, to the woman I love and will always love. This book might one day reach her hands and even if it doesn't, I am now a man at peace with his spirit. I no longer wrestle with my wounded pride, I no longer look for Esther on every corner, in every bar and cinema, at every supper, I no longer look for her in Marie or in the newspapers.

On the contrary, I am pleased that she exists; she has shown me that I am capable of a love of which I myself knew nothing, and this leaves me in a state of grace.

I accept the Zahir, and will let it lead me into a state of either holiness or madness.

A Time to Rend and a Time to Sew – the title is from a verse in Ecclesiastes – was published at the end of April. By the second week of May, it was already number one in the bestseller lists.

The literary supplements, which have never been kind to me, redoubled their attacks. I cut out some of the key phrases and stuck them in a notebook along with reviews from previous years; they said basically the same thing, merely changing the title of the book:

'... once again, despite the troubled times we live in, the author offers us an escape from reality with a story about love ...' (as if people could live without love)

'... short sentences, superficial style ...' (as if long sentences equalled profundity)

'... the author has discovered the secret of success – marketing ...' (as if I had been born in a country with a long literary tradition and had had millions to invest in my first book)

'... it will sell as well as all his other books, which just proves how unprepared human beings are not to face up to the encircling tragedy ...' (as if they knew what it meant to be prepared).

Some reviews, however, were different, adding that I was profiting from last year's scandal in order to make even more money. As always, these negative reviews only served to sell more of my books: my faithful readers bought the book anyway, and those who had forgotten about the whole sorry business were reminded of it again and so also bought copies, because they wanted to hear my version of Esther's disappearance (since the book was not about that, but was, rather, a hymn to love, they must have been sorely disappointed and would doubtless have decided that the critics were spot on). The rights were immediately sold to all the countries where my books were usually published.

Marie, who read the typescript before I sent it to the publisher, showed herself to be the woman I had hoped she was: instead of being jealous, or saying that I shouldn't bare my soul like that, she encouraged me to go ahead with it and was thrilled when it was a success. At the time, she was reading the teachings of a little-known mystic, whom she quoted in all our conversations.

'When people praise us, we should always keep a close eye on how we behave.'

'The critics never praise me.'

'I mean your readers: you've received more letters than ever. You'll end up believing that you're better than you are, and allow yourself to slip into a false sense of security, which could be very dangerous.'

'Ever since my visit to the cathedral in Vitória, I do think I'm better than I thought I was, but that has nothing to do with readers' letters. Absurd though it may seem, I discovered love.'

'Great. What I like about the book is the fact that, at no point, do you blame your ex-wife. And you don't blame yourself either.'

'I've learned not to waste my time doing that.'

'Good. The universe takes care of correcting our mistakes.'

'Do you think Esther's disappearance was some kind of "correction", then?'

'I don't believe in the curative powers of suffering and tragedy; they happen because they're part of life and shouldn't be seen as a punishment. Generally speaking, the universe tells us when we're wrong by taking away what is most important to us: our friends. And that, I think I'm right in saying, is what was happening with you.'

'I learned something recently: our true friends are those who are with us when the good things happen. They cheer us on and are pleased by our triumphs. False friends only appear at difficult times, with their sad, supportive faces, when, in fact, our suffering is serving to console them for their miserable lives. When things were bad last year, various people I had never even seen before turned up to "console" me. I hate that.'

'I've had the same thing happen to me.'

'But I'm very grateful that you came into my life, Marie.'

'Don't be too grateful too soon, our relationship isn't strong enough. As a matter of fact, I've been thinking of moving to Paris or asking you to come and live in Milan: it wouldn't make any difference to either of us in terms of work. You always work at home and I always work away. Would you like to change the subject now or shall we continue discussing it as a possibility?'

'I'd like to change the subject.'

'Let's talk about something else then. It took a lot of courage to write that book. What surprises me, though, is that you don't once mention the young man.'

'I'm not interested in him.'

'You must be. Every now and again you must ask yourself: why did she choose him?'

'I never ask myself that.'

'You're lying. I'd certainly like to know why my neighbour didn't divorce his boring, smiling wife, always busy with the housework, the cooking, the children and the bills. If I ask myself that, you must too.'

'Are you saying that I hate him because he stole my wife?'

'No, I want to hear you say that you forgive him.'

'I can't do that.'

'It's hard I know, but you've no option. If you don't do it, you'll always be thinking of the pain he caused you and that pain will never pass. I'm not saying you've got to like him. I'm not saying you should seek him out. I'm not suggesting you should start thinking of him as an angel. What was his name now? Something Russian wasn't it?'

'It doesn't matter what his name was.'

'You see? You don't even want to say his name. Are you superstitious?'

'Mikhail. There you are, that's his name.'

'The energy of hatred won't get you anywhere; but the energy of forgiveness, which reveals itself through love, will transform your life in a positive way.'

'Now you're sounding like some Tibetan sage, spouting stuff that is all very nice in theory, but impossible in practice. Don't forget, I've been hurt before.'

'Exactly, and you're still carrying inside you the little boy, the school weakling, who had to hide his tears from his parents. You still bear the marks of the skinny little boy who couldn't get a girlfriend and who was never any good at sport. You still haven't managed to heal the scars left by some of the injustices committed against you in your life. But what good does that do?'

'Who told you about that?'

'I just know. I can see it in your eyes, and it doesn't do you any good. All it does is feed a constant desire to feel sorry for yourself, because you were the victim of people stronger than you. Or else it makes you go to the other extreme and disguise yourself as an avenger ready to hit out at the people who hurt you. Isn't that a waste of time?'

'It's just human.'

'Oh, it is, but it's not intelligent or reasonable. Show some respect for your time on this earth, and know that God has always forgiven you and always will.'

Looking around at the crowd gathered for my book-signing at a megastore in the Champs-Elysées, I thought: how many of these people will have had the same experience I had with my wife?

Very few. Perhaps one or two. Even so, most of them would identify with what was in my new book.

Writing is one of the most solitary activities in the world. Once every two years, I sit down in front of the computer, gaze out on the unknown sea of my soul, and see a few islands – ideas that have developed and which are ripe to be explored. Then I climb into my boat – called The Word – and set out for the nearest island. On the way, I meet strong currents, winds and storms, but I keep rowing, exhausted, knowing that I have drifted away from my chosen course and that the island I was trying to reach is no longer on my horizon.

I can't turn back, though, I have to continue somehow or else I'll be lost in the middle of the ocean; at that point, a series of terrifying scenarios flash through my mind, such as spending the rest of my life talking about past successes, or bitterly criticising new writers, simply because I no longer have the courage to publish new books. Wasn't my dream to be a writer? Then I must continue creating sentences, paragraphs, chapters, and go on writing until I die, and not allow myself to get caught in such traps as success or failure. Otherwise, what meaning does my life have? Being able to buy an old mill in the south of France and tending my garden? Giving lectures instead, because it's easier to talk than to write? Withdrawing from the world in a calculated, mysterious way, in order to create a legend that will deprive me of many pleasures?

Shaken by these alarming thoughts, I find a strength and a courage I didn't know I had: they help me to venture into an unknown part of my soul. I let myself be swept along by the current, and finally anchor my boat at the island I was being carried towards. I spend days and nights describing what I see, wondering why I'm doing this, telling myself that it's really not worth the pain and the effort, that I don't need to prove anything to anyone, that I've got what I wanted and far more than I ever dreamed of having.

I notice that I go through the same process as I did when writing my first book: I wake up at nine o'clock in the morning, ready to sit down at my computer immediately after breakfast; then I read the newspapers, go for a walk, visit the nearest bar for a chat, come home, look at the computer, discover that I need to make several phone calls, look at the computer again, by which time lunch is ready, and I sit eating and thinking that I really ought to have started writing at eleven o'clock, but now I need a nap, I wake at five in the afternoon, finally turn on the computer, go to check my e-mails, then remember that I've destroyed my Internet connection; I could go to a place ten minutes away where I can get online, but couldn't I, just to free my conscience from these feelings of guilt, couldn't I at least write for half an hour?

I begin out of a feeling of duty, but suddenly 'the thing' takes hold of me and I can't stop. The maid calls me for supper and I ask her not to interrupt me; an hour later, she calls me again; I'm hungry, but I must write just one more line, one more sentence, one more page. By the time I sit down at the table, the food is cold, I gobble it down and go back to the computer – I am no longer in control of where I place my feet, the island is being revealed to me, I am being propelled along its paths, finding things I have never even thought or dreamed of. I drink a cup of coffee, and another, and at two o'clock in the morning I finally stop writing, because my eyes are tired.

I go to bed, spend another hour making notes of things to use in the next paragraph and which always prove completely useless – they serve only to empty my mind so that sleep can come. I promise myself that the next morning, I'll start at eleven o'clock prompt. And the following day, the same thing happens – the walk, the conversations, lunch, a nap, the feelings of guilt, then irritation at myself for destroying the Internet connection, until I, at last, make myself sit down and write the first page …

Suddenly, two, three, four, eleven weeks have passed, and I know that I'm near the end; I'm gripped by a feeling of emptiness, the feeling of someone who has set down in words things he should have kept to himself. Now, though, I have to reach the final sentence – and I do.

When I used to read biographies of writers, I always thought they were simply trying to make their profession seem more interesting when they said that 'the book writes itself, the writer is just the typist'. Now I know that this is absolutely true, no one knows why the current took them to that particular island and not to the one they wanted to reach. The obsessive re-drafting and editing begins, and when I can no longer bear to re-read the same words one more time, I send it to my publisher, where it is edited again, and then published.

And it is a constant source of surprise to me to discover that other people were also in search of that very island and that they find it in my book. One person tells another person about it, the mysterious chain grows, and what the writer thought of as a solitary exercise becomes a bridge, a boat, a means by which souls can travel and communicate.

From then on, I am no longer the man lost in the storm: I find myself through my readers, I understand what I wrote when I see that others understand it too, but never before. On a few rare occasions, like the one that is just about to happen, I manage to look those people in the eye and then I understand that my soul is not alone.

***

At the appointed time, I start signing books. There is brief eye-to-eye contact and a feeling of solidarity, joy and mutual respect. There are handshakes, a few letters, gifts, comments. Ninety minutes later, I ask for a ten-minute rest, no one complains, and my publisher (as has become traditional at my book-signings in France) orders champagne to be served to everyone still in the line (I have tried to get this tradition adopted in other countries, but they always say that French champagne is too expensive and end up serving mineral water instead, but that, too, shows respect for those still waiting).

I return to the table. Two hours later, contrary to what anyone observing the event might think, I am not tired, but full of energy; I could carry on all night. The shop, however, has closed its doors and the queue is dwindling. There are forty people left inside, they become thirty, twenty, eleven, five, four, three, two ... and suddenly our eyes meet.

'I waited until the end. I wanted to be the last because I have a message for you.'

I don't know what to say. I glance to one side, at the publishers, sales people and booksellers, who are all talking enthusiastically; soon we will go out to eat and drink and share the excitement of the day, and describe some of the strange things that happened while I was signing books.

I have never seen him before, but I know who he is. I take the book from him and write: 'For Mikhail, with best wishes.'

I say nothing. I must not lose him – a word, a sentence, a sudden movement might cause him to leave and never come back. In a fraction of a second, I understand that he and only he can save me from the blessing – or the curse – of the Zahir, because he is the only one who knows where to find it, and I will finally be able to ask the questions I have been repeating to myself for so long.

'I wanted you to know that she's all right, that she may even have read your book.'

The publishers, sales people and booksellers come over. They all embrace me and say it's been a great afternoon. Let's go and relax and drink and talk about it all.

'I'd like to invite this young man to supper,' I say. 'He was the last in the queue and he can be the representative of all the other readers who were here with us today.'

'I can't, I'm afraid. I have another engagement.'

And turning to me, rather startled, he adds:

'I only came to give you that message.'

'What message?' asks one of the sales people.

'He never usually invites anyone!' says my publisher. 'Come on, let's all go and have supper!'

'It's very kind of you, but I have a meeting I go to every Thursday.'

'When does it start?'

'In two hours' time.'

'And where is it?'

'In an Armenian restaurant.'

My driver, who is himself Armenian, asks which one and says that it's only fifteen minutes from the place where we are going to eat. Everyone is doing their best to please me: they think that the person I'm inviting to supper should be happy and pleased to be so honoured, that anything else can surely wait.

'What's your name?' asks Marie.

'Mikhail.'

'Well, Mikhail,' and I see that Marie has understood everything, 'why don't you come with us for an hour or so; the restaurant we're going to is just around the corner. Then the driver will take you wherever you want to go. If you prefer, though, we can cancel our reservation and all go and have supper at the Armenian restaurant instead – that way, you'd feel less anxious.'

I can't stop looking at him. He isn't particularly handsome or particularly ugly. He's neither tall nor short. He's dressed in black, simple and elegant – and by elegance I mean a complete absence of brand names or designer labels.

Marie links arms with Mikhail and heads for the exit. The bookseller still has a pile of books waiting to be signed for readers who could not come to the signing, but I promise that I will drop by the following day. My legs are trembling, my heart pounding, and yet I have to pretend that everything is fine, that I'm glad the book-signing was a success, that I'm interested in what other people are saying. We cross the Champs-Elysées, the sun is setting behind the Arc de Triomphe, and, for some reason, I know that this is a sign, a good sign.

As long as I can keep control of the situation.

Why do I want to speak to him? The people from the publishing house keep talking to me and I respond automatically; no one notices that I am far away, struggling to understand why I have invited to supper someone whom I should, by rights, hate. Do I want to find out where Esther is? Do I want to have my revenge on this young man, so lost, so insecure, and yet who was capable of luring away the person I love? Do I want to prove to myself that I am better, much better than him? Do I want to bribe him, seduce him, make him persuade my wife to come back?

I can't answer any of these questions, and that doesn't matter. The only thing I have said up until now is: 'I'd like to invite this young man to supper.' I had imagined the scene so often before: we meet, I grab him by the throat, punch him, humiliate him in front of Esther; or I get a thrashing and make her see how hard I'm fighting for her, suffering for her. I had imagined scenes of aggression or feigned indifference or public scandal, but the words 'I'd like to invite this young man to supper' had never once entered my head.

No need to ask what I will do next, all I have to do now is to keep an eye on Marie, who is walking along a few paces ahead of me, holding on to Mikhail's arm, as if she were his girlfriend. She won't let him go and yet I wonder, at the same time, why she's helping me, when she knows that a meeting with this young man could also mean that I'll find out where my wife is living.

We arrive. Mikhail makes a point of sitting far away from me; perhaps he wants to avoid getting caught up in a conversation with me. Laughter, champagne, vodka and caviar – I glance at the menu and am horrified to see that the bookseller is spending about a thousand dollars on the entrées alone. There is general chatter; Mikhail is asked what he thought of the afternoon's event; he says he enjoyed it; he is asked about the book; he says he enjoyed it very much. Then he is forgotten, and attention turns to me – was I happy with how things had gone, was the queue organised to my liking, had the security team been up to scratch? My heart is still pounding, but I present a calm front, I thank them for everything, for the efficient way in which the event was run.

Half an hour of conversation and a lot of vodka later, I can see that Mikhail is beginning to relax. He isn't the centre of attention any more, he doesn't need to say very much, he just has to endure it for a little while longer and then he can go. I know he wasn't lying about the Armenian restaurant, so at least now I have a clue. My wife must still be in Paris! I must pretend to be friendly, try to win his confidence, the initial tensions have all disappeared.

An hour passes. Mikhail looks at his watch and I can see that he is about to leave. I must do something – now. Every time I look at him, I feel more and more insignificant and understand less and less how Esther could have exchanged me for someone who seems so unworldly (she mentioned that he had 'magical' powers). However difficult it might be to pretend that I feel perfectly at ease talking to someone who is my enemy, I must do something.

'Let's find out a bit more about our reader,' I say, and there is an immediate silence. 'Here he is, about to leave at any moment, and he's hardly said a word about his life. What do you do?'

Despite the number of vodkas he has drunk, Mikhail seems suddenly to recover his sobriety.

'I organise meetings at the Armenian restaurant.'

'What does that involve?'

'I stand on stage and tell stories. And I let the people in the audience tell their stories too.'

'I do the same thing in my books.'

'I know, that's how I first met … '

He's going to say who he is!

'Were you born here?' asks Marie, thus preventing him from finishing his sentence ('… how I first met your wife').

'I was born in the Kazakhstan steppes.'

Kazakhstan. Who's going to be brave enough to ask where Kazakhstan is?

'Where's Kazakhstan?' asks the sales representative.

Blessed are those who are not afraid to admit that they don't know something.

'I was waiting for someone to ask that,' and there is an almost gleeful look in Mikhail's eyes now. 'Whenever I say where I was born, about ten minutes later people are saying that I'm from Pakistan or Afghanistan ... My country is in Central Asia. It has barely 14 million inhabitants in an area far larger than France with its population of 60 million.'

'So it's a place where no one can complain about the lack of space, then,' says my publisher, laughing.

'It's a place where, during the last century, no one had the right to complain about anything, even if they wanted to. When the Communist regime abolished private ownership, the livestock were simply abandoned and 48.6 per cent of the population died. Do you understand what that means? Nearly half the population of my country died of hunger between 1932 and 1933.'

Silence falls. After all, tragedies get in the way of celebrations, and one of the people present tries to change the subject. However, I insist that my 'reader' tells us more about his country.

'What are the steppes like?' I ask.

'They're vast plains with barely any vegetation, as I'm sure you know.'

I do know, but it had been my turn to ask a question, to keep the conversation going.

'I've just remembered something about Kazakhstan,' says my publisher. 'Some time ago, I was sent a typescript by a writer who lives there, describing the atomic tests that were carried out on the steppes.'

'Our country has blood in its soil and in its soul. Those tests changed what cannot be changed, and we will be paying the price for many generations to come. We even made an entire sea disappear.'

It is Marie's turn to speak.

'No one can make a sea disappear.'

'I'm twenty-five years old, and that is all the time it took, just one generation, for the water that had been there for millennia to be transformed into dust. Those in charge of the Communist regime decided to divert two rivers, Amu-Darya and Syr-Darya, so that they could irrigate some cotton plantations. They failed, but, by then, it was too late – the sea had ceased to exist, and the cultivated land became a desert.

The lack of water affected the whole climate. Nowadays, vast sandstorms scatter 150,000 tons of salt and dust every year. Fifty million people in five countries were affected by the Soviet bureaucrats' irresponsible – and irreversible – decision. The little water that was left is polluted and is the source of all kinds of diseases.'

I made a mental note of what he was saying. It could be useful in one of my lectures. Mikhail went on, and his tone of voice was no longer ecological, but tragic.

'My grandfather says that the Aral Sea was once known as the Blue Sea, because of the colour of its waters. It no longer exists, and yet the people there refuse to leave their houses and move somewhere else: they still dream of waves and fishes, they still have their fishing rods and talk about boats and bait.'

'Is it true about the atomic tests, though?' asks my publisher.

'I think that everyone born in my country feels what the land felt, because every Kazakh carries his land in his blood. For forty years, the plains were shaken by nuclear or thermonuclear bombs, a total of 456 in 1989. Of those tests, 116 were carried out in the open, which amounts to a bomb 2,500 times more powerful than the one that was dropped on Hiroshima during the Second World War. As a result, thousands of people were contaminated by radioactivity and subsequently contracted lung cancer, whilst thousands of children were born with motor deficiencies, missing limbs or mental problems.'

Mikhail looks at his watch.

'Now, if you don't mind, I have to go.'

Half of those around the table are sorry, the conversation was just getting interesting. The other half are glad: it's absurd to talk about such tragic events on such a happy occasion.

Mikhail says goodbye to everyone with a nod of his head and gives me a hug, not because he feels a particular affection for me, but so that he can whisper:

'As I said before, she's fine. Don't worry.'

"Don't worry," he says. Why should I worry about a woman who left me? It was because of her that I was questioned by the police, splashed all over the front pages of the scandal sheets; it was because of her that I spent all those painful days and nights, nearly lost all my friends and ...'

'... and wrote *A Time to Rend and a Time to Sew*. Come on, we're both adults, with plenty of experience of life. Let's not deceive ourselves. Of course, you'd like to know how she is. In fact, I'd go further: you'd like to see her.'

'If you're so sure about that, why did you help persuade him to come to supper with us? Now I have a clue: he appears every Thursday at that Armenian restaurant.'

'I know. You'd better follow that up.'

'Don't you love me?'

'More than yesterday and less than tomorrow, as it says on those postcards you can buy in stationery shops. Yes, of course, I love you. I'm hopelessly in love, if you must know. I'm even considering changing my address and coming to live in this huge, empty apartment of yours, but whenever I suggest it, you always change the subject. Nevertheless, I forget my pride and try to explain what a big step it would be for us to live together, and hear you say that it's too soon for that; perhaps you're afraid you'll lose me the way you lost

Esther, or perhaps you're still waiting for her to come back, or perhaps you don't want to lose your freedom, or are simultaneously afraid of being alone and afraid of living with someone – in short, our relationship's a complete disaster. But, now that you ask, there's my answer: I love you very much.'

'So why did you help?'

'Because I can't live for ever with the ghost of a woman who left without a word of explanation. I've read your book. I believe that only by finding her and resolving the matter will your heart ever truly be mine. That's what happened with the neighbour I was in love with. I was close enough to him to be able to see what a coward he was when it came to our relationship, how he could never commit himself to the thing he wanted with all his heart, but which he always felt was too dangerous to actually have. You've often said that absolute freedom doesn't exist; what does exist is the freedom to choose anything you like and then commit yourself to that decision. The closer I was to my neighbour, the more I admired you: a man who decided to go on loving the wife who had abandoned him and who wanted nothing more to do with him. You not only decided to do that, you made your decision public. This is what you say in your book; it's a passage I know by heart:

"When I had nothing more to lose, I was given everything. When I ceased to be who I am, I found myself. When I experienced humiliation and yet kept on walking, I understood that I was free to choose my destiny. Perhaps there's something wrong with me, I don't know, perhaps my marriage was a dream I couldn't understand while it lasted. All I know is that even though I can live without her, I would still like to see her again, to say what I never said when we were together: I love you more than I love myself. If I could say that, then I could go on living, at peace with myself, because that love has redeemed me."'

'Mikhail told me that Esther had probably read my book. That's enough.'

'Maybe, but for you to be able to love her fully, you need to find her and tell her that to her face. It might not be possible, she might not want to see you, but you would, at least, have tried. I would be free from the "ideal woman" and you would be free from the absolute presence of what you call the Zahir.'

'You're very brave.'

'No, I'm not, I'm afraid. But I have no choice.'

The following morning, I swore to myself that I would not try to find out where Esther was living. For two years, I had unconsciously preferred to believe that she had been forced to leave, that she had been kidnapped or was being blackmailed by some terrorist group. Now that I knew she was alive and well (that was what the young man had told me), why try to see her again? My ex-wife had the right to look for happiness, and I should respect her decision.

This idea lasted a little more than four hours; later in the afternoon, I went to a church, lit a candle and made another promise, this time a sacred, ritual promise: to try and find her. Marie was right. I was too old to continue deceiving myself by pretending I didn't care. I respected her decision to leave, but the very person who had helped me build my life had very nearly destroyed me. She had always been so brave: why, this time, had she fled like a thief in the night, without looking her husband in the eye and explaining why? We were both old enough to act and face the consequences of our actions: my wife's (or, rather, my ex-wife's) behaviour was completely out of character, and I needed to know why.

* * *

It was another week – an eternity – before the 'performance' at the restaurant. In the next few days, I agreed to do interviews that I would never normally accept; I wrote various newspaper articles, practised yoga and meditation, read a book about a Russian painter, another about a crime committed in Nepal, wrote prefaces for two books and recommendations for another four, something which publishers were always asking me to do, and which I usually refused.

There was still an awful lot of time to kill, and so I decided to pay off a few debts at the Favour Bank – accepting supper invitations, giving brief talks at schools where the children of friends were studying, visiting a golf club, doing an improvised book-signing at a bookshop in Avenue de Suffren owned by a friend (he put an advertisement in the window three days before and all of twenty people turned up). My secretary remarked that I was obviously very happy, because she hadn't seen me so active in ages; I said that having a book in the bestseller list encouraged me to work even harder than I usually did.

There were two things I didn't do that week. First, I didn't read any unsolicited typescripts – according to my lawyers, these should always be returned immediately to the sender, otherwise, sooner or later, I would run the risk of someone claiming that I had plagiarised one of their stories (I've never understood why people send me their typescripts anyway – after all, I'm not a publisher).

Second, I didn't look in an atlas to find out where Kazakhstan was, even though I knew that, in order to gain Mikhail's trust, I should try to find out a bit more about where he came from.

People are waiting patiently for someone to open the door that leads to the room at the back of the restaurant. The place has none of the charm of bars in St-Germain-des-Prés, no cups of coffee served with a small glass of water, no well-dressed, well-spoken people. It has none of the elegance of theatre foyers, none of the magic of other shows being put on all over the city in small bistros, with the actors always trying their hardest, in the hope that some famous impresario will be in the audience and will introduce himself at the end of the show, tell them they're wonderful and invite them to appear at some important arts centre.

To be honest, I can't understand why the place is so full: I've never seen it mentioned in the listings magazines that specialise in entertainment and the arts in Paris.

* * *

While I'm waiting, I talk to the owner and learn that he is planning to turn the whole restaurant area into a theatre.

'More and more people come every week,' he says. 'I agreed initially because a journalist asked me as a favour and said that, in return, he'd publish a review of my restaurant in his magazine. Besides, the room is rarely used on Thursdays, and while people are waiting, they have a meal; in fact, I probably take more money on a Thursday than I do on any other night of the week. The only thing that concerned me was that the actors might belong to a sect. As you probably know, the laws here are very strict.'

Yes, I did know; certain people had even suggested that my books were linked to some dangerous philosophical trend, to a strand of religious teaching that was out of step with commonly accepted values. France, normally so liberal, was slightly paranoid about the subject. There had been a recent long report about the 'brainwashing' practised on certain unwary people. As if those same people were able to make all kinds of other choices about school, university, toothpaste, cars, films, husbands, wives, lovers, but, when it came to matters of faith, were easily manipulated.

'How do they advertise these events?' I ask.

'I've no idea. If I did, I'd use the same person to promote my restaurant.'

And just to clear up any doubts, since he doesn't know who I am, he adds:

'By the way, it isn't a sect. They really are just actors.'

* * *

The door to the room is opened, the people flock in, depositing five euros in a small basket. Inside, standing impassive on the improvised stage, are two young men and two young women, all wearing full, white skirts, stiffly starched to make them stand out. As well as these four, there is an older man carrying a conga drum and a woman with a huge bronze cymbal covered in small, tinkling attachments; every time she inadvertently brushes against this instrument, it emits a sound like metallic rain.

Mikhail is one of the young men, although he looks completely different from the person I met at the book-signing: his eyes, fixed on some point in space, shine with a special light.

The audience sit down on the chairs scattered around the room. Young men and women dressed in such a way that if you met them in the street, you would think they were into hard drugs. Middle-aged executives or civil servants with their wives. A few nine- or ten-year-old children, possibly brought by their parents. A few older people, who must have made a great effort to get here, since the nearest metro station is five blocks away.

They drink, smoke, talk loudly, as if the people on the stage did not exist. The volume of conversation gradually increases; there is much laughter, it's a real party atmosphere. A sect? Only if it's a confraternity of smokers. I glance anxiously about, thinking I can see Esther in all the women there, sometimes even when they bear no physical resemblance at all to my wife (why can't I get used to saying 'my ex-wife'?).

I ask a well-dressed woman what this is all about. She doesn't seem to have the patience to respond; she looks at me as if I were a novice, a person who needs to be educated in the mysteries of life.

'Love stories,' she says. 'Stories and energy.'

Stories and energy. Perhaps I had better not pursue the subject, although the woman appears to be perfectly normal. I consider asking someone else, but decide that it's best to say nothing. I'll find out soon enough for myself. A gentleman sitting by my side looks at me and smiles:

'I've read your books and so, of course, I know why you're here.'

I'm shocked. Does he know about the relationship between Mikhail and my wife – I must again correct myself – the relationship between one of the people on stage and my ex-wife?

'An author like you would be bound to know about the Tengri. They're intimately connected with what you call "warriors of light".'

'Of course,' I say, relieved.

And I think: I've never even heard of the Tengri.

Twenty minutes later, by which time the air in the room is thick with cigarette smoke, we hear the sound of that cymbal. Miraculously, the conversations stop, the anarchic atmosphere seems to take on a religious aura; audience and stage are equally silent; the only sounds one can hear come from the restaurant next door.

Mikhail, who appears to be in a trance and is still gazing at some point in the distance, begins:

'In the words of the Mongolian creation myth: "There came a wild dog who was blue and grey and whose destiny was imposed on him by the heavens. His mate was a roe deer."'

His voice sounds different, more feminine, more confident.

'Thus begins another love story. The wild dog with his courage and strength, the doe with her gentleness, intuition and elegance. Hunter and hunted meet and love each other. According to the laws of nature, one should destroy the other, but in love there is neither good nor evil, there is neither construction nor destruction, there is merely movement. And love changes the laws of nature.'

He gestures with his hand and the four people on stage turn on the spot.

'In the steppes where I come from, the wild dog is seen as a feminine creature. Sensitive, capable of hunting because he has honed his instincts, but timid too. He does not use brute force, but strategy. Courageous, cautious, quick. He can change in a second from a state of complete relaxation to the tension he needs to pounce on his prey.'

Accustomed as I am to writing stories, I think: 'And what about the doe?' Mikhail is equally used to telling stories and answers the question hanging in the air:

'The roe deer has the male attributes of speed and an understanding of the earth. The two travel along together in their symbolic worlds, two impossibilities who have found each other, and because they overcome their own natures and their barriers, they make the world possible too. That is the Mongolian creation myth: out of two different natures love is born. In contradiction, love grows in strength. In confrontation and transformation, love is preserved.

We have our life. It took the world a long time and much effort to get where it is, and we organise ourselves as best we can; it isn't ideal, but we rub along. And yet there is something missing, there is always something missing, and that is why we are gathered here tonight, so that we can help each other to think a little about the reason for our existence. Telling stories that make no sense, looking for facts that do not fit our usual way of perceiving reality, so that, perhaps in one or two generations, we can discover another way of living.

As Dante wrote in *The Divine Comedy*: "The day that man allows true love to appear, those things which are well made will fall into confusion and will overturn everything we believe to be right and true." The world will become real when man learns how to love; until then we will live in the belief that we know what love is, but we will always lack the courage to confront it as it truly is.

Love is an untamed force. When we try to control it, it destroys us. When we try to imprison it, it enslaves us. When we try to understand it, it leaves us feeling lost and confused.

This force is on earth to make us happy, to bring us closer to God and to our neighbour, and yet, given the way that we love now, we enjoy one hour of anxiety for every minute of peace.'

Mikhail paused. The strange cymbal sounded again.

'As on every Thursday, we are not going to tell stories about love. We are going to tell stories about the lack of love. We will see what lies on the surface – the layer where we find all our customs and values – in order to understand what lies beneath. When we penetrate beneath that layer we will find ourselves. Who would like to begin?'

Several people raised their hand. Mikhail pointed to a young woman of Arab appearance. She turned to a man on his own, on the other side of the room.

'Have you ever failed to get an erection when you've been to bed with a woman?'

Everyone laughed. The man, however, avoided giving a direct answer.

'Are you asking that because your boyfriend is impotent?'

Again everyone laughed. While Mikhail had been speaking, I had once more begun to suspect that this was indeed some new sect, but when sects hold meetings, I can't imagine that they smoke and drink and ask embarrassing questions about each other's sex lives.

'No, he's not,' said the girl firmly. 'But it has occasionally happened to him. And I know that if you had taken my question seriously, your answer would have been "Yes, I have." All men, in all cultures and countries, independent of any feelings of love or sexual attraction, have all experienced impotence at one time or another, often when they're with the person they most desire. It's normal.'

Yes, it was normal, and the person who had told me this was a psychiatrist, to whom I went when I thought I had a problem.

The girl went on:

'But the story we're told is that all men can always get an erection. When he can't, the man feels useless, and the woman is convinced she isn't attractive enough to arouse him. Since it's a taboo subject, he can't talk to his friends about it. He tells the woman the old lie: "It's never happened to me before." He feels ashamed of himself and often runs away from someone with whom he could have had a really good relationship, if only he had allowed himself a second, third or fourth chance. If he had trusted more in the love of his friends, if he had told the truth, he would have found out that he wasn't the only one. If he had trusted more in the love of the woman, he would not have felt humiliated.'

Applause. Cigarettes are lit, as if a lot of the people there – men and women – feel a great sense of relief.

Mikhail points to a man who looks like an executive in some big multinational.

'I'm a lawyer and I specialise in contested divorces.'

'What does that mean?' asks someone in the audience.

'It's when one of the parties won't agree to the separation,' replies the lawyer, irritated at being interrupted and as if he found it absurd that anyone should not know the meaning of such a straightforward legal term.

'Go on,' says Mikhail, with an authority that I would never have imagined in the young man I had met at the book-signing.

The lawyer continues:

'Today I received a report from the London-based firm Human and Legal Resources. This is what it says:

a) two-thirds of all employees in a company have some kind of love relationship. Imagine! That means that in any office of three people, two will end up having some form of intimate contact.
b) 10 per cent leave their job because of this, 40 per cent have relationships that last more than three months, and in the case of certain professions that require people to spend long periods away from home, at least eight out of ten end up having an affair.

Isn't that unbelievable?'

'Well, of course, we have to bow down to statistics!' remarks one of a group of young men who are all dressed as if they were members of some dangerous band of robbers. 'We all believe in statistics! That means that my mother must be being unfaithful to my father, but it's not her fault, it's the fault of the statistics!'

More laughter, more cigarettes, more relief, as if the people in the audience were hearing things they had always been afraid to hear and that hearing them freed them from some kind of anxiety. I think about Esther and about Mikhail – '... professions that require people to spend long periods away from home, eight out of ten ...'.

I think about myself and the many times this has happened to me. They are, after all, statistics. We are not alone.

Other stories are told of jealousy, abandonment, depression, but I am no longer listening. My Zahir has returned in its full intensity – even though, for a few moments, I had believed I was merely engaging in a little group therapy, I am, in fact, in the same room as the man who stole my wife. My neighbour, the one who recognised me, asks if I'm enjoying myself. He distracts me for a moment from my Zahir, and I am happy to respond.

'I still can't quite see the point. It's like a self-help group, like Alcoholics Anonymous or marriage guidance.'

'But doesn't what you hear strike you as genuine?'

'Possibly, but again, I can't see the point.'

'This isn't the most important part of the evening; it's just a way of not feeling so alone. By talking about our lives, we come to realise that most people have experienced the same thing.'

'And what's the practical result?'

'If we're not alone, then we have more strength to find out where we went wrong and to change direction. But, as I said, this is just an interval between what the young man says at the beginning and the moment when we invoke the energy.'

'Who is the young man?'

Our conversation is interrupted by the sound of the cymbal. This time, it is the older man with the conga drum who speaks.

'The time for reasoning is over. Let us move on now to the ritual, to the emotion that crowns and transforms everything. For those of you who are here for the first time tonight, this dance develops our capacity to accept Love. Love is the only thing that activates our intelligence and our creativity, that purifies and liberates us.'

The cigarettes are extinguished, the clink of glasses stops. That same strange silence descends upon the room; one of the young women says a prayer:

'We will dance, Lady, in homage to you. May our dancing make us fly up to heaven.'

Did I hear right? Did she say 'Lady'? She did.

The other young woman lights the candles in four candelabra; the other lights are switched off. The four figures in white, with their starched white skirts, come down from stage and mingle with the audience. For nearly half an hour, the second young man, with a voice that seems to emerge from his belly, intones a monotonous, repetitive song, which, curiously, makes me forget the Zahir a little and slip into a kind of somnolence. Even one of the children, who had kept running up and down during the 'talking about love' session, is now quiet and still, her eyes fixed on the stage. Some of those present have their eyes closed, others are staring at the floor or at some invisible point in space, as I had seen Mikhail do.

When he stops singing, the percussion – the cymbal and the drum – strike up a rhythm familiar to me from religious ceremonies originating in Africa.

The white-clothed figures start to spin, and in that packed space, the audience makes room so that the wide skirts can trace movements in the air. The instruments play faster, the four spin ever faster too, emitting sounds that belong to no known language, as if they were speaking directly with angels or with the 'Lady'.

My neighbour gets to his feet and begins to dance too and to utter incomprehensible words. Ten or twelve other people in the audience do the same, while the rest watch with a mixture of reverence and amazement.

* * *

I don't know how long the dance went on for, but the sound of the instruments seemed to keep time with the beating of my heart, and I felt an enormous desire to surrender myself, to say strange things, to move my body; it took a mixture of self-control and a sense of the absurd to stop myself from spinning like a mad thing on the spot. Meanwhile, as never before, the figure of Esther, my Zahir, seemed to hover before me, smiling, calling on me to praise 'the Lady'.

I struggled not to enter into that unknown ritual, wanting it all to end as quickly as possible. I tried to concentrate on my main reason for being there that night – to talk to Mikhail, to have him take me to my Zahir –

but I found it impossible to remain still. I got up from my chair and just as I was cautiously, shyly taking my first steps, the music abruptly stopped.

In the room lit only by the candles, all I could hear was the laboured breathing of those who had danced. Gradually, the sound faded, the lights were switched back on, and everything seemed to have returned to normal. Glasses were again filled with beer, wine, water, soft drinks, the children started running about and talking loudly, and soon everyone was chatting, as if nothing, absolutely nothing, had happened.

'It's nearly time to close the meeting,' said the young woman who had lit the candles. 'Alma has one final story.'

Alma was the woman playing the cymbal. She spoke with the accent of someone who has lived in the East.

'The master had a buffalo. The animal's widespread horns made him think that if he could manage to sit between them, it would be like sitting on a throne. One day, when the animal was distracted, he climbed up between the horns and did just that. The buffalo, however, immediately lumbered to its feet and threw him off. When his wife saw this, she began to cry.

"Don't cry," said the master, once he had recovered. "I may have suffered, but I also realised my dream."'

People started leaving. I asked my neighbour what he had felt.

'You should know. You write about it in your books.'

I didn't know, but I had to pretend that I did.

'Maybe I do know, but I want to be sure.'

He looked at me, unconvinced, and clearly began to doubt that I really was the author he thought he knew.

'I was in touch with the energy of the Universe,' he replied. 'God passed through my soul.'

And he left, so as not to have to explain what he had said.

In the empty room there were now only the four actors, the two musicians and myself. The women went off to the ladies' toilet, presumably to change their clothes. The men took off their white costumes right there in the room and donned their ordinary clothes. They immediately began putting away the candelabra and the musical instruments in two large cases.

The older man, who had played the drum during the ceremony, started counting the money and putting it into six equal piles. I think it was only then that Mikhail noticed my presence.

'I thought I'd see you here.'

'And I imagine you know the reason.'

'After I've let the divine energy pass through my body, I know the reason for everything. I know the reason for love and for war. I know why a man searches for the woman he loves.'

I again felt as if I were walking along a knife-edge. If he knew that I was here because of my Zahir, then he also knew that this was a threat to his relationship with Esther.

'Can we talk, like two men of honour fighting for something worthwhile?'

Mikhail seemed to hesitate slightly. I went on:

'I know that I'll emerge bruised and battered, like the master who wanted to sit between the buffalo's horns, but I deserve it. I deserve it because of the pain I inflicted, however unconsciously. I don't believe Esther would have left me if I had respected her love.'

'You understand nothing,' said Mikhail.

These words irritated me. How could a 25-year-old tell an experienced man who had suffered and been tested by life that he understood nothing? I had to control myself, to humble myself, to do whatever was necessary. I could not go on living with ghosts, I could not allow my whole universe to continue being dominated by the Zahir.

'Maybe I really don't understand, but that's precisely why I'm here – in order to understand. To free myself by understanding what happened.'

'You understood everything quite clearly, and then suddenly stopped understanding; at least that's what Esther told me. As happens with all husbands, there came a point when you started to treat your wife as if she were just part of the goods and chattels.'

I was tempted to say: 'Why didn't she tell me that herself? Why didn't she give me a chance to correct my mistakes and not leave me for a 25-year-old who will only end up treating her just as I did.' Some more cautious words emerged from my mouth however.

'I don't think that's true. You've read my book, you came to my book-signing because you knew what I felt and wanted to reassure me. My heart is still in pieces: have you ever heard of the Zahir?'

'I was brought up in the Islamic religion, so, yes, I'm familiar with the idea.'

'Well, Esther fills up every space in my life. I thought that by writing about my feelings, I would free myself from her presence. Now I love her in a more silent way, but I can't think about anything else. I beg you, please, I'll do anything you want, but I need you to explain to me why she disappeared like that. As you yourself said, I understand nothing.'

It was very hard to stand there pleading with my wife's lover to help me understand what had happened. If Mikhail had not come to the book-signing, perhaps that moment in the cathedral in Vitória, where I acknowledged my love for her and out of which I wrote *A Time to Rend and a Time to Sew*, would have been enough. Fate, however, had other plans, and the mere possibility of being able to see my wife again had upset everything.

'Let's have lunch together,' said Mikhail, after a long pause. 'You really don't understand anything. But the divine energy that today passed through my body is generous with you.'

We arranged to meet the next day. On the way home, I remembered a conversation I had had with Esther three months before she disappeared.

A conversation about divine energy passing through the body.

Their eyes really are different. There's the fear of death in them, of course, but beyond that, there's the idea of sacrifice. Their lives are meaningful because they are ready to offer them up for a cause.'

'You're talking about soldiers, are you?'

'Yes, and I'm talking as well about something I find terribly hard to accept, but which I can't pretend I don't see. War is a ritual. A blood ritual, but also a love ritual.'

'You're mad.'

'Maybe I am. But I've met other war correspondents, too, who go from one country to the next, as if the routine of death were part of their lives. They're not afraid of anything, they face danger the way a soldier does. And all for a news report? I don't think so. They can no longer live without the danger, the adventure, the adrenaline in their blood. One of them, a married man with three children, told me that the place where he feels most at ease is in a war zone, even though he adores his family and talks all the time about his wife and kids.'

'I just can't understand it at all. Look, Esther, I don't want to interfere in your life, but I think this experience will end up doing you real harm.'

'It would harm me more to be living a life without meaning. In a war, everyone knows they're experiencing something important.'

'A historic moment, you mean?'

'No, that isn't enough of a reason for risking your life. No, I mean that they're experiencing the true essence of man.'

'War?'

'No, love.'

'You're becoming like them.'

'I think I am.'

'Tell your news agency you've had enough.'

'I can't. It's like a drug. As long as I'm in a war zone, my life has meaning. I go for days without having a bath, I eat whatever the soldiers eat, I sleep three hours a night and wake up to the sound of gunfire. I know that at any moment someone could lob a grenade into the place where we're sitting, and that makes me live, do you see? Really live, I mean, loving every minute, every second. There's no room for sadness, doubts, nothing; there's just a great love for life. Are you listening?'

'Absolutely.'

'It's as if there was a divine light shining in the midst of every battle, in the midst of that worst of all possible situations. Fear exists before and after, but not while the shots are being fired, because, at that moment, you see men at their very limit, capable of the most heroic of actions and the most inhumane. They run out under a hail of bullets to rescue a comrade, and at the same time shoot anything that moves – children, women – anyone who comes within their line of fire will die. People from small, provincial towns where nothing ever happened and where they were always decent citizens find themselves invading museums, destroying centuries-old works of art and stealing things they don't need. They take photos of atrocities that they themselves committed and, rather than trying to conceal these, they feel proud. And people who, before, were always disloyal and treacherous feel a kind of camaraderie and solidarity and become incapable of doing wrong. It's a mad world, completely topsy-turvy.'

'Has it helped you answer the question that Hans asked Fritz in that bar in Tokyo in the story you told me?'

'Yes, the answer lies in some words written by the Jesuit Teilhard de Chardin, the same man who said that our world is surrounded by a layer of love. He said: "We can harness the energy of the winds, the seas, the sun. But the day man learns to harness the energy of love, that will be as important as the discovery of fire."'

'And you could only learn that by going to a war zone?'

'I'm not sure, but it did allow me to see that, paradoxical though it may seem, people are happy when they're at war. For them, the world has meaning. As I said before, total power or sacrificing themselves for a cause gives meaning to their lives. They are capable of limitless love, because they no longer have anything to lose. A fatally wounded soldier never asks the medical team: "Please save me!" His last words are usually: "Tell my wife and my son that I love them." At the last moment, they speak of love!'

'So, in your opinion, human beings only find life meaningful when they're at war.'

'But we're always at war. We're at war with death, and we know that death will win in the end. In armed conflicts, this is simply more obvious, but the same thing happens in daily life. We can't allow ourselves the luxury of being unhappy all the time.'

'What do you want me to do?'

'I need help. And that doesn't mean saying to me: "Go and hand in your notice", because that would only leave me feeling even more confused than before. We need to find a way of channelling all this, of allowing the energy of this pure, absolute love to flow through our bodies and spread around us. The only person so far who has helped me understand this is a rather other-worldly interpreter who says he's had revelations about this energy.'

'Are you talking about the love of God?'

'If someone is capable of loving his partner without restrictions, unconditionally, then he is manifesting the love of God. If the love of God becomes manifest, he will love his neighbour. If he loves his neighbour, he will love himself. If he loves himself, then everything returns to its proper place. History changes.

History will never change because of politics or conquests or theories or wars; that's mere repetition, it's been going on since the beginning of time. History will only change when we are able to use the energy of love, just as we use the energy of the wind, the seas, the atom.'

'Do you think we two could save the world?'

'I think there are more people out there who think the same way. Will you help me?'

'Yes, as long as you tell what I have to do.'

'But that's precisely what I don't know!'

I had been a regular customer at this charming pizzeria ever since my very first visit to Paris, so much so that it has become part of my history. Most recently, I had held a supper here to celebrate receiving the medal of Officer of Arts and Literature presented to me by the Ministry of Culture, even though many people felt that the commemoration of such an important event should have taken place somewhere more elegant and more expensive. But Roberto, the owner, had become a kind of good luck charm to me; whenever I went to his restaurant, something good happened in my life.

'I could start with some small talk about the success of *A Time to Rend and a Time to Sew* or the contradictory emotions I felt last night as I watched your performance.'

'It's not a performance, it's a meeting,' he said. 'We tell stories and we dance in order to feel the energy of love.'

'I could talk about anything just to put you at your ease, but we both know why we're here.'

'We're here because of your wife,' said Mikhail, who was now full of a young man's defiance and in no way resembled the shy boy at the book-signing or the spiritual leader of that 'meeting'.

'You mean my ex-wife. And I would like to ask you a favour: take me to her. I want her to look me in the eye and tell me why she left. Only then will I be free of the Zahir. Otherwise, I'll go on thinking about her day and night, night and day, going over and over our story, our history, again and again, trying to pinpoint the moment when I went wrong and our paths began to diverge.'

He laughed.

'Reviewing history's a great idea, that's the only way you can make things change.'

'Very clever, but I'd prefer to leave philosophical discussions to one side for the moment. I'm sure that, like all young men, you hold in your hands the precise formula for putting the world to rights. However, like all young men, you will one day be as old as me and then you'll see that it's not so easy to change things. But there's no point talking about that now. Can you grant me that favour?'

'I must first ask you something: did she say goodbye?'

'No.'

'Did she say she was going away?'

'No, she didn't. You know that.'

'Do you think that, given the kind of person Esther is, she would be capable of leaving a man she had lived with for more than ten years without first confronting him and explaining her reasons?'

'That's precisely what I find most troubling. But what are you getting at?'

The conversation was interrupted by Roberto, who wanted to know if we were ready to order. Mikhail asked for a Napolitana and I told Roberto to choose for me – this was hardly the moment to be worrying about what I should eat. The only thing we needed urgently was a bottle of red wine, as quickly as possible. When Roberto asked me what sort of wine and I muttered an inaudible reply, he understood that he should simply leave us alone and not ask me anything else during lunch, but take all the necessary decisions himself, thus leaving me free to concentrate on my conversation with the young man before me.

The wine arrived within thirty seconds. I filled our glasses.

'What's she doing?'

'Do you really want to know?'

It irritated me to receive a question in response to mine.

'Yes, I do.'

'She's making carpets and giving French lessons.'

Carpets! My wife (ex-wife, please, do try and get used to it), who had all the money she could possibly need, had a degree in journalism, spoke four languages, was now obliged to making a living weaving carpets and giving French lessons to foreigners? I must get a grip on myself. I couldn't risk wounding the young man's male pride, even though I thought it shameful that he couldn't give Esther everything she deserved.

'Please, you must understand what I've been going through for the last year or more. I'm no threat to your relationship with Esther. I just need a couple of hours with her, or one hour, it doesn't matter.'

Mikhail appeared to be savouring my words.

'You haven't answered my question,' he said, with a smile. 'Do you think that, given the kind of person Esther is, she would leave the man of her life without at least saying goodbye and without explaining why?'

'No, I don't.'

'Then why all this stuff about "she left me"? Why do you say: "I'm no threat to your relationship with Esther"?'

I was confused. I felt something like hope stirring inside me – not that I knew what I was hoping for or where that hope had come from.

'Are you telling me that …'

'Exactly. I'm telling you that she hasn't left you or me. She has just disappeared for a while, possibly for ever, but we must both respect that.'

It was as if a bright light were suddenly shining in that pizzeria, a place that had always brought me good memories and good stories. I desperately wanted to believe what the young man was saying; the Zahir was now pulsating all around me.

'Do you know where she is?'

'Yes, I do. But even though I miss her as much as you do, I must respect her silence. I find this whole situation as confusing as you do. Esther may have found satisfaction in the Love that Devours, she might be waiting for one of us to go and find her, she may have met a new man, or she may have withdrawn from the world altogether. Whatever the truth, if you do decide to go and find her, I can't stop you. But, if you do, you must know one thing: you must find not only her body, but also her soul.'

I felt like laughing. I felt like hugging him, or possibly killing him – my emotions changed with startling speed.

'Did you and she …'

'Did we sleep together? That's none of your business. I found in Esther the partner I was looking for, the person who helped me set out on the mission I was entrusted with, the angel who opened the doors, the roads, the paths that will allow us – if our Lady is willing – to restore the energy of love to the earth. We share the same mission. And just to put your mind at rest: I have a girlfriend, the blonde girl who was on stage with me last night. Her name's Lucrecia; she's Italian.'

'Are you telling me the truth?'

'Yes, in the name of the Divine Energy, I am.'

He took a scrap of dark fabric out of his pocket.

'Do you see this? The cloth is actually green; it looks black because it's caked with dried blood. A soldier somewhere in the world asked her before he died to remove his shirt, then cut it into tiny pieces and distribute those pieces to anyone capable of understanding the message of his death. Do you have a piece?'

'No, Esther has never even mentioned it to me.'

'Whenever she meets someone whom she feels should receive the message, she also gives them a little of the soldier's blood.'

'And what is the message?'

'If she didn't give you a piece of the shirt, I don't think I can tell you; not, of course, that she swore me to secrecy.'

'Do you know anyone else who has a piece of that cloth?'

'All the people who appear with me at the restaurant do. We're only there because Esther brought us together.'

I needed to tread carefully, to build up a relationship, to make a deposit in the Favour Bank. I mustn't frighten him or seem over-eager; I should ask him about himself and his work, about his country, of which he had spoken with such pride; I needed to find out if what he was telling me was true or if he had some ulterior motive; I needed to be absolutely sure that he was still in touch with Esther or if he had lost track of her as well. He may have come from a remote country, where the values are different, but I knew that the Favour Bank operated everywhere: it was an institution that knew no frontiers.

On the one hand, I wanted to believe everything he was saying. On the other, my heart had suffered and bled enough during the thousand and one nights I had lain awake, waiting for the sound of the key in the door, for Esther to come in and lie down beside me, without saying a word. I had promised myself that if this ever happened, I would ask her no questions. I would just kiss her and say 'sleep well, my love' and we would wake the next day, hand in hand, as if this whole nightmare had never happened.

Roberto arrived with the pizzas. He seemed to be endowed with some kind of sixth sense that told him when I needed time to think.

I looked at Mikhail again. Keep calm; if you don't get your pulse rate under control, you'll have a heart attack. I drank a whole glass of wine and noticed that he had done the same.

Why was *he* so nervous?

'Oh, I believe what you say. But we've got plenty of time to talk.'

'You're going to ask me to take you to her.'

He had spoiled my game. I would have to start again.

'Yes, I am. I'm going to try to persuade you. I'm going to do everything in my power to do just that. I'm in no hurry though; we've got a whole pizza to eat first. Besides, I want to know more about you.'

I noticed that he was trying to keep his hands from trembling.

'I'm a person with a mission. I haven't yet managed to fulfil it, but I think I still have time to do so.'

'Perhaps I can help you.'

'Oh, you can. Anyone can; you just have to help spread the energy of love throughout the world.'

'I can do more than that.'

I didn't want to go any further; I didn't want it to look as if I were trying to buy his loyalty. Careful. I had to be very careful. He could be telling the truth, but he could also be lying, trying to take advantage of my suffering.

'I only know of one kind of loving energy,' I went on. 'The one I feel for the woman who left, or, rather, went away and who is waiting for me. If I could see her again, I would be a happy man. And the world would be a better place because one soul would be content.'

He glanced up at the ceiling and back down at the table, and I allowed the silence to last as long as possible.

'I can hear a voice,' he said at last, unable to look at me.

The great advantage of writing about spirituality is that I know I'm bound to keep encountering people with some kind of gift. Some of those gifts are real, others are fraudulent, some of those people are trying to use me, others are merely testing me out. I have seen so many amazing things that I no longer have the slightest doubt that miracles can happen, that everything is possible, and that people are beginning to re-learn the inner powers they long ago forgot.

However, this was not the ideal moment to speak of such matters. I was only interested in the Zahir. I needed the Zahir to become Esther again.

'Mikhail …'

'Mikhail isn't my real name. My real name is Oleg.'

'Oleg then …'

'Mikhail is the name I chose when I decided to be reborn to life. Like the warrior archangel, with his fiery sword, opening up a path so that – what is it you call them? – so that the "warriors of light" can find each other. That is my mission.'

'It's my mission too.'

'Wouldn't you rather talk about Esther?'

What? Was he changing the subject again back to the very thing that interested me?

'I'm not feeling very well.' His gaze was starting to wander; he kept glancing around the restaurant as if I were not there. 'I don't want to talk about that. The voice …'

Something strange, something very strange, was happening. How far was he prepared to go in order to impress me? Would he end up asking me to write a book about his life and powers, like so many others had before him?

Whenever I have a clear objective, I will do anything to achieve it; that, after all, was what I said in my books and I could hardly betray my own words. I had an objective now: to gaze once more into the eyes of the Zahir. Mikhail had given me a lot of new information: he wasn't her lover, Esther hadn't left me, it was just a matter of time before I could bring her back. There was also the possibility that this meeting in the pizzeria was all a farce, that he was just someone with no other means of earning a living than by exploiting someone else's pain in order to achieve his own ends.

I drank another glass of wine; Mikhail did the same.

Take care, my instinct was telling me.

'Yes, I do want to talk about Esther, but I want to know more about you too.'

'That's not true. You're just trying to seduce me, to persuade me to do things I was perfectly prepared to do anyway. Your pain is preventing you from seeing things clearly; you think I could be lying, that I'm trying to take advantage of the situation.'

Mikhail might know exactly what I was thinking, but he was speaking more loudly than good manners permit. People were starting to turn round to see what was going on.

'You're just trying to impress me; you don't realise what an impact your books had on my life or how much I learned from them. Your pain has made you blind, mean-spirited and obsessed with the Zahir. It isn't your love for her that made me accept your invitation to have lunch; in fact, I'm not sure I'm entirely convinced of your love; it might just be wounded pride. The reason I'm here ...'

His voice was growing louder; he was still glancing wildly around, as if he were losing control.

'The lights ...'

'What's wrong?'

'The reason I'm here is her love for you!'

'Are you all right?'

Roberto had noticed that something was wrong. He came over to the table, smiling, and put his hand casually on Mikhail's shoulder.

'Well, the pizza was obviously pretty terrible. No need to pay, you can leave when you like.'

That was the way out we needed. We could simply get up and go, thus avoiding the depressing spectacle of someone in a pizzeria pretending to be communing with the spirit world just to impress or embarrass me, although I did feel that this was more than a theatrical performance.

'Can you feel the wind blowing?'

At that moment, I was sure he wasn't acting; on the contrary, he was making an enormous effort to control himself and was more frightened by what was happening than I was.

'The lights, the lights are starting to appear! Please, get me out of here!'

His body began to be shaken by tremors. There was now no hiding what was going on; the people at the other tables had got up.

'In Kazakh …'

He did not manage to finish the sentence. He pushed the table away from him; pizzas, glasses and cutlery went flying, hitting the diners on the next table. His expression had changed completely, his whole body was shaking and only the whites of his eyes were now visible. His head was thrown violently back and I heard the sound of bones cracking. A gentleman from one of the other tables leapt to his feet. Roberto caught Mikhail before he fell, while the other man picked up a spoon from the floor and placed it in Mikhail's mouth.

The whole thing can only have lasted a matter of seconds, but to me it seemed like an eternity. I could imagine the scandal sheets describing how a famous writer – and, despite all the adverse reviews, a possible candidate for a major literary prize – had concocted some sort of séance in a pizzeria just to get publicity for his new book. My paranoia was racing out of control; they would find out that the medium in question was the same man who had run off with my wife; it would all start again, and this time I wouldn't have the necessary courage or energy to face the same test.

I knew a few of the other diners, but which of them were really my friends? Who would be capable of remaining silent about what they were seeing?

Mikhail's body stopped shaking and relaxed; Roberto was holding him upright in his chair. The other man took Mikhail's pulse, examined his eyes and then turned to me:

'It's obviously not the first time this has happened. How long have you known him?'

'Oh, they're regular customers,' replied Roberto, seeing that I had become incapable of speech. 'But this is the first time it's happened in public, although, of course, I've had other such cases in my restaurant before.'

'Yes,' said the man. 'I noticed that you didn't panic.'

The remark was clearly aimed at me, for I must have looked deathly pale. The man went back to his table and Roberto tried to reassure me:

'He's the personal physician of a very famous actress,' he said. 'Although it looks to me as if you're more in need of medical attention than your guest here.'

Mikhail – or Oleg or whatever the name was of the young man sitting opposite me – was beginning to come to. He looked around him and, far from seeming embarrassed, he merely smiled rather shyly.

'I'm sorry,' he said. 'I did try to control it.'

I was doing my best to remain calm. Roberto again came to my rescue.

'Don't worry. Our writer here has enough money to pay for the broken plates.'

Then he turned to me:

'Epilepsy. It was just an epileptic fit, that's all.'

I left the restaurant with Mikhail, who immediately hailed a taxi.

'But we haven't talked yet! Where are you going?'

'I'm in no state to talk now. And you know where to find me.'

There are two kinds of world: the one we dream about and the real one.

In my dream world, Mikhail had told the truth: I was just going through a difficult patch, experiencing the kind of misunderstanding that can occur in any love relationship. Esther was somewhere, waiting patiently for me to discover what had gone wrong in our marriage and for me then to go to her and ask her forgiveness so that we could resume our life together.

In that dream world, Mikhail and I talked calmly, left the pizzeria, took a taxi, rang the doorbell of a house where my ex-wife (or my wife? The question now formulated itself the other way round) wove carpets in the morning, gave French lessons in the afternoon and slept alone at night, waiting, like me, for the bell to ring, for her husband to enter bearing a large bouquet of flowers and to carry her off to drink hot chocolate in a hotel near the Champs-Elysées.

In the real world, any meeting with Mikhail would always be tense, because I feared a recurrence of what had happened at the pizzeria. Everything he had said was just the product of his imagination; he had no more idea where Esther was than I did. In the real world, I was at the Gare de l'Est at 11.45 in the morning, waiting for the Strasbourg train to arrive, bringing with it an important American actor and director who very much wanted to produce a film based on one of my books.

Up until then, whenever anyone had mentioned the possibility of making a film adaptation, my answer had always been 'No, I'm not interested.' I believe that each reader creates his own film inside his head, gives faces to the characters, constructs every scene, hears the voices, smells the smells. And that is why, whenever a reader goes to see a film based on a novel that he likes, he leaves feeling disappointed, saying: 'The book is so much better than the film.'

This time, my agent had been more insistent. She told me that this actor and producer was very much 'on our side', and was hoping to do something entirely different from any of the other proposals we had received. The meeting had been arranged two months earlier, and we were to have supper that night to discuss details and see if we really were thinking along the same lines.

In the last two weeks, however, my diary had changed completely: it was Thursday, and I needed to go to the Armenian restaurant, to try to re-establish contact with the young epileptic who swore that he could hear voices, but who was nevertheless the only person who knew where to find the Zahir. I interpreted this as a sign not to sell the film rights of the book and so tried to cancel the meeting with the actor; he insisted and said that it didn't matter in the least; we could have lunch instead the following day: 'No one could possibly feel sad about having to spend a night in Paris alone,' he said, leaving me with no possible comeback.

In the world of my imagination, Esther was still my companion, and her love gave me the strength to go forward and explore all my frontiers.

In the real world, she was pure obsession, sapping my energy, taking up all the available space, and obliging me to make an enormous effort just to continue with my life, my work, my meetings with film producers, my interviews.

How was it possible that, even after two years, I had still not managed to forget her? I could not bear having to think about it any more, analysing all the possibilities, and trying various ways out: deciding simply to accept the situation, writing a book, practising yoga, doing some charity work, seeing friends, seducing women, going out to supper, to the cinema (always avoiding adaptations of books, of course, and seeking out films that had been specially written for the screen), to the theatre, the ballet, to soccer games. The Zahir always won, though; it was always there, making me think: 'I wish she was here with me.'

I looked at the station clock – fifteen minutes to go. In the world of my imagination, Mikhail was an ally. In the real world, I had no concrete proof of this, apart from my great desire to believe what he was saying; he could well be an enemy in disguise.

I returned to the usual questions: Why had she said nothing to me? Or had she been trying to do just that when she asked me the question that Hans had asked? Had Esther decided to save the world, as she had hinted in our conversation about love and war, and was she 'preparing' me to join her on this mission?

My eyes were fixed on the railway tracks. Me and

Esther, walking along parallel to each other, never touching. Two destinies that …

Railway tracks.

How far apart were they?

In order to forget about the Zahir, I tried asking one of the platform staff.

'They're 143.5 centimetres or 4 feet 8½ inches apart,' he replied.

He seemed to be a man at peace with life, proud of his job; he didn't fit Esther's stereotype at all, that we all harbour a great sadness in our soul.

But his answer didn't make any sense at all: 143.5 centimetres or 4 feet 8½ inches?

Absurd. Logically, it should be either 150 centimetres or 5 feet. A round number, easy for builders of carriages and railway employees to remember.

'But why?' I asked the man.

'Because that's the width between the wheels on the carriages.'

'But surely the wheels are that distance apart because the tracks are.'

'Look, just because I work in a railway station doesn't mean I know everything about trains. That's just the way things are.'

He was no longer a happy person, at peace with his work; he could answer one question, but could go no further. I apologised and spent what remained of the fifteen minutes staring at the tracks, feeling intuitively that they were trying to tell me something.

Strange though it may seem, the tracks seemed to be saying something about my marriage, and about all marriages.

The actor arrived, and he was far nicer than I expected, despite being so famous. I left him at my favourite hotel and went home. To my surprise, Marie was there waiting for me, saying that, due to adverse weather conditions, filming had been put off until the following week.

'I assume that, since today is Thursday, you'll be going to the restaurant.'

'Do you want to come too?'

'Yes, I do. Why? Would you prefer to go alone?'

'Yes, I would.'

'Well, I've decided to come anyway. The man hasn't yet been born who can tell me where I can and cannot go.'

'Do you know why all railway tracks are 143.5 centimetres apart?'

'I can try and find out on the Internet. Is it important?'

'Very.'

'Leaving railway tracks to one side for the moment, I was talking to some friends of mine who are fans of your books. They think that anyone who can write books like *A Time to Rend and a Time to Sew*, or the one about the shepherd or the pilgimage to Santiago, must be some kind of sage who has an answer for everything.'

'Which is not quite true, as you know.'

'What is the truth then? How is it that you can pass on to your readers things that are beyond your own knowledge?'

'They're not beyond my knowledge. Everything that's written in my books is part of my soul, part of the lessons I've learned throughout my life, and which I try to apply to myself. I'm a reader of my own books. They show me things that I already knew, even if only unconsciously.'

'What about the reader?'

'I think it's the same for the reader. A book – and we could be talking about anything here, a film, a piece of music, a garden, the view of a mountain – reveals something. "Reveal" means both to un-veil and to re-veil. Removing the veil from something that already exists is different from me trying to teach others the secret of how to live a better life.

Love is giving me a pretty hard time at the moment, as you know. Now this could be seen as a descent into hell or it could be seen as a revelation. It was only when I wrote *A Time to Rend and a Time to Sew* that I understood my own capacity for love. And I learned this while I was actually typing the words and sentences.'

'But what about the spiritual side? What about the spirituality that appears to be present on every page of your books?'

'I'm beginning to like the idea of you coming with me to the Armenian restaurant, because you'll learn – or, rather, become conscious of – three important things. First, that as soon as people decide to confront a problem, they realise that they are far more capable than they thought they were. Second, that all energy and all knowledge come from the same unknown source, which we usually call God. What I've tried to do in my life, ever since I first started out on what I believe to be my path, is to honour that energy, to connect up with it every day, to allow myself to be guided by the signs, to learn by doing and not by thinking about doing.

Third, that no one is alone in their troubles; there is always someone else thinking, rejoicing or suffering in the same way, and that gives us the strength to confront the challenge before us.'

'Does that include suffering for love?'

'It includes everything. If there is suffering, then it's best to accept it, because it won't go away just because you pretend it's not there. If there is joy, then it's best to accept that too, even though you're afraid it might end one day. Some people can only relate to life through sacrifice and renunciation. Some people can only feel part of humanity when they think they are "happy". But why all these questions?'

'Because I'm in love and I'm afraid of suffering.'

'Don't be afraid; the only way to avoid that suffering would be to refuse to love.'

'I can feel Esther's presence. Apart from the young man's epileptic fit, you haven't told me anything else about what happened at the pizzeria. That's a bad sign for me, although it might be a good sign for you.'

'It might be a bad sign for me too.'

'Do you know what I would like to know? I'd like to know if you love me as much as I love you. But I don't have the courage to ask. Why do I have such frustrating relationships with men? I always feel like I have to be in a relationship and that means I have to be this fantastic, intelligent, sensitive, exceptional person. The effort of seduction forces me to give of my best and that helps me. Besides, it's really hard living on your own, and I don't know if that's the best option either.'

'So you want to know if I'm still capable of loving a woman, even though she left me without a word of explanation.'

'I read your book. I know you are.'

'You want to know whether, despite loving Esther, I'm still capable of loving you?'

'I wouldn't dare ask that question because the answer could ruin my life.'

'You want to know if the heart of a man or a woman can contain enough love for more than one person?'

'Since that's a less direct question than the previous one, yes, I'd like an answer.'

'I think it's perfectly possible as long as one of those people doesn't turn into ...'

'... a Zahir. Well, I'm going to fight for you anyway, because I think you're worth it. Any man capable of loving a woman as much as you loved – or love – Esther deserves all my respect and all my efforts. And to show that I want to keep you by my side, to show how important you are in my life, I'm going to do as you ask, however absurd it might be: I'm going to find out why railway tracks are always 4 feet 8½ inches apart.'

The owner of the Armenian restaurant had done exactly what he had told me he was planning to do: the whole restaurant, and not just the room at the back, was now full of people who had come for the 'meeting'. Marie eyed them with some curiosity and occasionally commented on what a very varied crowd they were.

'Why bring children to something like this? It's absurd.'

'Perhaps they haven't got anyone they can leave them with.'

At nine o'clock on the dot, the six 'performers' – the two musicians in oriental dress and the four young people in their white shirts and full skirts – walked onto the stage. Service at the tables came to an immediate halt, and the people in the audience fell silent.

'In the Mongolian creation myth, doe and wild dog come together,' said Mikhail in that voice which was not his own. 'Two beings with very different natures: in the wild, the dog would normally kill the deer for food. In the Mongolian myth, they both understand that they each need the qualities of the other if they are to survive in a hostile world and that they should, therefore, join forces.

To do this, they must first learn to love. And in order to love, they must cease to be who they are, otherwise they will never be able to live together. With the passing of time, the wild dog comes to accept that his instinct, always focused on the struggle to survive, now serves a greater purpose: finding someone with whom he can rebuild the world.'

He paused.

'When we dance, we spin around that same Energy, which rises up to our Lady and returns to us imbued with all her strength, just as the water in rivers evaporates, is transformed into clouds and returns in the form of rain. My story today is about the circle of love.

One morning, a farmer knocked loudly on the door of a monastery. When Brother Porter opened the door, the farmer held out to him a magnificent bunch of grapes.

"Dear Brother Porter, these are the finest grapes from my vineyard. Please accept them as a gift from me."

"Why, thank you! I'll take them straight to the Abbot, who will be thrilled with such a gift."

"No, no. I brought them for you."

"For me? But I don't deserve such a beautiful gift from nature."

"Whenever I knocked on the door, you opened it. When the harvest had been ruined by drought, you gave me a piece of bread and a glass of wine every day. I want this bunch of grapes to bring you a little of the sun's love, the rain's beauty and God's miraculous power."

Brother Porter put the grapes down where he could see them and spent the whole morning admiring them: they really were lovely. Because of this, he decided to give the present to the Abbot, whose words of wisdom had always been such a boon to him.

The Abbot was very pleased with the grapes, but then he remembered that one of the other monks was ill and thought: "I'll give him the grapes. Who knows, they might bring a little joy into his life."

But the grapes did not remain for very long in the room of the ailing monk, for he in turn thought: "Brother Cook has taken such good care of me, giving me only the very best food to eat. I'm sure these grapes will bring him great happiness." And when Brother Cook brought him his lunch, the monk gave him the grapes.

"These are for you. You are in close touch with the gifts Nature gives us and will know what to do with this, God's produce."

Brother Cook was amazed at the beauty of the grapes and drew his assistant's attention to their perfection. They were so perfect that no one could possibly appreciate them more than Brother Sacristan, who had charge of the Holy Sacrament, and whom many in the monastery considered to be a truly saintly man.

Brother Sacristan, in turn, gave the grapes to the youngest of the novices in order to help him understand that God's work is to be found in the smallest details of the Creation. When the novice received them, his heart was filled with the Glory of God, because he had never before seen such a beautiful bunch of grapes. At the same time, he remembered the day he had arrived at the monastery and the person who had opened the door to him; that gesture of opening the door had allowed him to be there now in that community of people who knew the value of miracles.

Shortly before dark, he took the bunch of grapes to Brother Porter.

"Eat and enjoy. You spend most of your time here all alone, and these grapes will do you good."

Brother Porter understood then that the gift really was intended for him; he savoured every grape and went to sleep a happy man. In this way, the circle was closed; the circle of happiness and joy which always wraps around those who are in contact with the energy of love.'

The woman called Alma sounded the cymbal.

'As we do every Thursday, we listen to a story of love and tell stories about the lack of love. Let us look at what is on the surface and then, little by little, we will understand what lies beneath: our habits, our values. And when we can penetrate that layer, we will be able to find ourselves. Who would like to begin?'

Several hands went up, including – to Marie's surprise – mine. The noise started up again; people shifted in their seats. Mikhail pointed to a tall, pretty woman with blue eyes.

'Last week, I went to see a male friend of mine who lives alone in the mountains, near the border with Spain; he loves the good things in life and has often said that any wisdom he may have acquired comes from the fact that he lives each moment to the full. Now, right from the start, my husband was against my going to see this friend. He knows what he's like, that his favourite pastimes are shooting birds and seducing women. But I needed to talk to this friend; I was going through a difficult time and only he could help me. My husband suggested I see a psychiatrist or go on a trip; we even had a row about it, but despite all these domestic pressures, I set off. My friend came to meet me at the airport and we spent the afternoon talking; we ate supper, drank some wine, talked a bit more and then I went to bed. When I woke up the next morning, we went for a walk near where he lives and he dropped me back at the airport.

As soon as I got home, the questions began. Was he alone? Yes. You mean he didn't have a girlfriend with him? No, he didn't. Did you have anything to drink? Yes, I did. Why don't you want to talk about it? But I am talking about it! Alone together in a house in the mountains, eh? Very romantic. So? And all you did was talk, you say? Yes, that's all. And you expect me to believe that? Why shouldn't you believe it? Because it goes against human nature – if a man and a woman get together, have a bit to drink and talk about personal things, they're bound to end up in bed!

I agree with my husband. It does go against everything we're taught. He'll never believe the story I've just told, but it's absolutely true. Since then, our life has become a little hell. It will pass, but going through all this pain is pointless, and all because we've been told that if a man and a woman like each other and circumstances allow, they're bound to end up in bed together.'

Applause. Cigarettes were lit. The clink of glasses and bottles.

'What's going on?' whispered Marie. 'Group therapy for couples?'

'It's all part of the "meeting". No one says whether it's right or wrong, they just tell stories.'

'But why do they do it in public, in this irreverent way, with people drinking and smoking?'

'Perhaps it's to stop things getting too heavy. That way it's easier. And if it helps to make things easier, what's wrong with that?'

'Easier? Talking to a load of strangers who might go and repeat this story to her husband tomorrow?'

Someone else had started talking, and so I wasn't able to tell Marie that it didn't matter: everyone was there to talk about the lack of love disguised as love.

'I'm the husband of the woman who just told that story,' said a man, who must have been at least twenty years older than the pretty, young blonde woman. 'Everything she said is true, but there's something she doesn't know and which I haven't had the courage to tell her. I'll do so now.

When she went off to the mountains, I couldn't sleep all night, and I started imagining, in detail, what was going on. When she arrives, the fire is already lit; she takes off her coat, takes off her sweater; she's not wearing a bra under her thin T-shirt. He can clearly see the shape of her breasts.

She pretends not to notice him looking at her. She says she's going to the kitchen to get another bottle of champagne. She's wearing very tight jeans, she walks slowly, and she doesn't need to turn round to know that he's watching her every move. She comes back, they talk about very personal things, which makes them feel even closer.

They finish talking about the problem that took her there. Her mobile phone rings; it's me, wanting to know if she's all right. She goes over to him, puts the phone to his ear and they both listen to what I have to say; it's an awkward conversation, because I know it's too late to put any kind of pressure on her, it's best just to pretend that everything's fine and tell her to enjoy her time in the mountains, because the following day she'll be back in Paris, taking care of the kids and doing the shopping.

I hang up, knowing that he has heard the whole conversation. The two of them – because, before, they were sitting on separate sofas – are now very close indeed.

At that point, I stopped thinking about what was happening in the mountains. I got up, went into my children's bedroom, walked over to the window and looked out over Paris, and do you know what I felt? I felt excited, very, very excited; the thought of the two of them together, knowing that my wife could, at that very moment, be kissing another man, making love with him, had aroused me sexually.

I felt awful. How could I possibly get excited over something like that? The next day, I talked to two friends; obviously, I didn't use myself as an example, but I asked them if they had ever felt aroused when they caught another man staring at their wife's cleavage. They didn't really answer the question because it's such a taboo. But they both agreed that it's always nice to know that your wife is desired by another man, although they wouldn't go any further than that. Is this a secret fantasy hidden in the hearts of all men? I don't know. This last week has been a little hell for both of us simply because I didn't understand my own feelings. And because I can't understand them, I blame her for provoking in me feelings that make my world seem suddenly unsafe.'

This time a lot of cigarettes were lit, but there was no applause. It was as if, even there, the subject continued to be a taboo.

I put up my hand again, and meanwhile asked myself if I agreed with what the man had just said. Yes, I did. I had imagined similar scenarios involving Esther and the soldiers she met in war zones, but I had never dared say as much, not even to myself.

Mikhail looked in my direction and nodded.

I don't know how I managed to get to my feet and look at that audience, who were still visibly shocked by the story of the man who had felt aroused by the thought of his wife having sex with another man. No one seemed to be listening, and that helped me make a start.

'I apologise for not being as direct as the two previous speakers, but I nevertheless have something to say. I went to a train station today and learned that the distance between railway tracks is always 143.5 centimetres or 4 feet 8½ inches. Why this absurd measurement? I asked my girlfriend to find out and this is what she discovered. When they built the first train carriages, they used the same tools as they had for building horse-drawn carriages. And why that distance between the wheels on carriages? Because that was the width of the old roads along which the carriages had to travel. And who decided that roads should be that width? Well, suddenly, we are plunged back into the distant past. It was the Romans, the first great road-builders, who decided to make their roads that width. And why? Because their war chariots were pulled by two horses, and when placed side by side, the horses they used at the time took up 143.5 centimetres.

So the distance between the tracks I saw today, used by our state-of-the-art high-speed trains, was determined by the Romans. When people went to the United

States and started building railways there, it didn't occur to them to change the width and so it stayed as it was. This even affected the building of space shuttles. American engineers thought the fuel tanks should be wider, but the tanks were built in Utah and had to be transported by train to the Space Center in Florida, and the tunnels couldn't take anything wider. And so they had to accept the measurement that the Romans had decided was the ideal. But what has all this to do with marriage?'

I paused. Some people were not in the slightest bit interested in railway tracks and had started talking amongst themselves. Others were listening attentively, amongst them Marie and Mikhail.

'It has everything to do with marriage and with the two stories we have just heard. At some point in history, someone turned up and said: when two people get married, they must stay frozen like that for the rest of their lives. You will move along side by side like two tracks, keeping always that same distance apart. Even if sometimes one of you needs to be a little further away or a little closer, that is against the rules. The rules say: be sensible, think of the future, think of your children. You can't change, you must be like two railway tracks that remain the same distance apart all the way from their point of departure to their destination. The rules don't allow for love to change, or to grow at the start and diminish halfway through – it's too dangerous. And so, after the enthusiasm of the first few years, they maintain the same distance, the same solidity, the same functional nature. Your purpose is to allow the train bearing the survival of the species to head off into the future: your children will only be happy if you stay just as you were – 143.5 centimetres apart. If you're not happy with something that never changes, think of them, think of the children you brought into the world.

Think of your neighbours. Show them that you're happy, eat roast beef on Sundays, watch television, help the community. Think of society: dress in such a way that everyone knows you're in perfect harmony. Never glance to the side, someone might be watching you, and that could bring temptation, it could mean divorce, crisis, depression.

Smile in all the photos. Put the photos in the living room, so that everyone can see them. Cut the grass, practise a sport – oh, yes, you must practise a sport in order to stay frozen in time. When sport isn't enough, have plastic surgery. But never forget, these rules were established long ago and must be respected. Who established these rules? That doesn't matter. Don't question them, because they will always apply, even if you don't agree with them.'

I sat down. There was a mixture of enthusiastic applause and indifference, and I wondered if I had gone too far. Marie was looking at me with a mixture of admiration and surprise.

The woman on stage sounded the cymbal.

I told Marie to stay where she was, while I went outside to smoke a cigarette:

'They'll perform a dance now in the name of love, in the name of the Lady.'

'You can smoke in here, can't you?'

'Yes, but I need to be alone.'

* * *

It may have been early Spring, but it was still very cold; nevertheless, I was in need of some fresh air. Why had I told that story? My marriage to Esther had never been the way I described: two railway tracks, always beside each other, always forming two correct, straight lines. We had had our ups and downs; one or other of us had occasionally threatened to leave for good; and yet we continued on together.

Until two years ago.

Or until the moment when she began to want to know why she was unhappy.

No one should ever ask themselves that: why am I unhappy? The question carries within it the virus that will destroy everything. If we ask that question, it means we want to find out what makes us happy. If what makes us happy is different from what we have now, then we must either change once and for all or stay as we are, feeling even more unhappy.

I now found myself in precisely that situation: I had a lively, interesting girlfriend, my work was going well, and there was every chance that, in the fullness of time, things would sort themselves out. I should resign myself to the situation. I should accept what life was offering me, not follow Esther's example, not look at anyone else, but remember Marie's words, and build a new life with her.

No, I can't think like that. If I behave in the way people expect me to behave, I will become their slave. It requires enormous self-control not to succumb, because our natural tendency is to want to please, even if the person to be pleased is us. If I do that, I will lose not only Esther, but Marie, my work, my future, as well as any respect I have for myself and for what I have said and written.

* * *

When I went back in, I found that people were starting to leave. Mikhail appeared, having already changed out of his stage clothes.

'Listen, what happened at the pizzeria …'

'Oh, don't worry about that,' I said. 'Let's go for a walk by the Seine.'

Marie got the message and said that she needed an early night. I asked her to give us a lift in her taxi as far as the bridge just opposite the Eiffel Tower; that way, I could walk home afterwards. I thought of asking where Mikhail lived, but felt that the question might be construed as an attempt to verify, with my own eyes, that Esther really wasn't living with him.

On the way, Marie kept asking him what the 'meeting' was about, and he always gave the same answer: it's a way of recovering love. He said that he had liked my story about the railway tracks.

'That's how love got lost,' he said. 'When we started laying down rules for when love should or shouldn't appear.'

'When was that?' Marie asked.

'I don't know, but I know it's possible to retrieve that Energy. I know, because when I dance, or when I hear the voice, Love speaks to me.'

Marie didn't know what he meant by 'hearing the voice', but, by then, we had reached the bridge. Mikhail and I got out and started walking in the cold Paris night.

* * *

'I know you were frightened by what you saw. The biggest danger when someone has a fit is that their tongue will roll back and they'll suffocate. The owner of the restaurant knew what to do, so it's obviously happened there before. It's not that unusual. But your diagnosis is wrong. I'm not an epileptic. It happens whenever I get in touch with the Energy.'

Of course he was an epileptic, but there was no point in contradicting him. I was trying to act normally. I needed to keep the situation under control. I was surprised how easily he had agreed to this second meeting.

'I need you. I need you to write something about the importance of love,' said Mikhail.

'Everyone knows that love is important. That's what most books are about.'

'All right, let me put my request another way. I need you to write something about the new Renaissance.'

'What's the new Renaissance?'

'It's similar to the Italian Renaissance of the fifteenth and sixteenth centuries, when geniuses like Erasmus, Leonardo and Michelangelo rejected the limitations of the present and the oppressive conventions of their own time and turned instead to the past. We're beginning to see a return to a magical language, to alchemy and the idea of the Mother Goddess, to people reclaiming the freedom to do what they believe in and not what the Church or the Government demand of them. As in fifteenth- and sixteenth-century Florence, we are discovering that the past contains the answers to the future.

Your story about the railway tracks, for example: in how many other areas of our lives are we obeying rules we don't understand? People read what you write, couldn't you introduce the subject somewhere?'

'I never make deals over what I write,' I replied, remembering once more that I needed to keep my self-respect. 'If it's an interesting subject, if it's in my soul, if the boat called "Word" carries me to that particular island, I might write about it. But none of this has anything to do with my search for Esther.'

'I know, and I'm not trying to impose any conditions, I'm just suggesting something that seems important to me.'

'Did she tell you about the Favour Bank?'

'She did. But this isn't a matter for the Favour Bank. It's to do with a mission that I can't fulfil on my own.'

'What you do in the Armenian restaurant, is that your mission?'

'That's just a tiny part of it. We do the same thing on Fridays with a group of beggars. And on Wednesdays we work with a group of new nomads.'

New nomads? It was best not to interrupt; the Mikhail who was talking to me now had none of the arrogance he had shown in the pizzeria, none of the charisma he had revealed on stage or the vulnerability he had revealed on that evening at the book-signing. He was a normal person, a colleague with whom we always end up, late at night, talking over the world's problems.

'I can only write about things that really touch my soul,' I insist.

'Would you like to come with us to talk to the beggars?'

I remembered Esther's remark about the phoney sadness in the eyes of those who should be the most wretched people in the world.

'Let me think about it first.'

We were approaching the Louvre, but he paused to lean on the parapet, and we both stood there contemplating the passing boats, which dazzled us with their spotlights.

'Look at them,' I said, because I needed to talk about something, afraid that he might get bored and go home. 'They only see what the spotlights show them. When they go home, they'll say they know Paris. Tomorrow, they'll go and see the Mona Lisa and claim they've visited the Louvre. But they don't know Paris and have never really been to the Louvre. All they did was go on a boat and look at a painting, one painting, instead of looking at a whole city and trying to find out what's happening in it, visiting the bars, going down streets that don't appear in any of the tourist guides, and getting lost in order to find themselves again. It's the difference between watching a porn movie and making love.'

'I admire your self-control. There you are talking about the boats on the Seine, all the while waiting for the right moment to ask the question that brought you to me. Feel free to talk openly about anything you like.'

There was no hint of aggression in his voice, and so I decided to come straight to the point.

'Where is Esther?'

'Physically, she's a long way away, in Central Asia. Spiritually, she's very close, accompanying me day and night with her smile and the memory of her enthusiastic words. She was the one who brought me here, a poor 21-year-old with no future, an aberration in the eyes of the people in my village, or else a madman or some sort of shaman who had made a pact with the devil, and, in the eyes of the people in the city, a mere peasant looking for work.

I'll tell you my story another day, but the long and the short of it is that I knew English and started working as her interpreter. We were near the border of a country where the Americans were building a lot of military bases, preparing for the war in Afghanistan, and it was impossible to get a visa. I helped her cross the mountains illegally. During the week we spent together, she made me realise that I was not alone, that she understood me.

I asked her what she was doing so far from home. After a few evasive answers, she finally told me what she must have told you: that she was looking for the place where love had hidden itself away. I told her about my mission to make the energy of love circulate freely in the world again. Basically, we were both looking for the same thing.

Esther went to the French embassy and arranged a visa for me, as an interpreter of the Kazakh language, even though no one in my country speaks anything but Russian. I came to live here. We always met up when she returned from her missions abroad; we made two more trips together to Kazakhstan; she was fascinated by the

Tengri culture, and by a nomad she had met and whom she believed held the key to everything.'

I would have liked to know what Tengri was, but the question could wait. Mikhail continued talking, and in his eyes I saw the same longing to be with Esther that I myself was feeling.

'We started working here in Paris. It was her idea to get people together once a week. She said: "The most important thing in all human relationships is conversation, but people don't talk any more, they don't sit down to talk and listen. They go to the theatre, the cinema, watch television, listen to the radio, read books, but they almost never talk. If we want to change the world, we have to go back to a time when warriors would gather round a fire and tell stories."'

I remember Esther saying that all the really important things in our lives had arisen out of long conversations we'd had sitting at a table in some bar or walking along a street or in a park.

'It was my idea that these meetings should be on a Thursday because that's how it is in the tradition in which I was brought up. But it was her idea to make occasional forays into the Paris streets at night. She said that beggars were the only ones who never pretend to be happy; on the contrary, they pretend to be sad.

She gave me your books to read. I sensed that you too – possibly unconsciously – imagined the same world as we did. I realised that I wasn't alone, even if I was the only one to hear the voice. Gradually, as more and more people started coming to the meetings, I began to believe that I really could fulfil my mission and help the energy of love to return, even if that meant going back into the past, back to the moment when that Energy left or went into hiding.'

'Why did Esther leave me?'

Was that all I was interested in? The question irritated Mikhail slightly.

'Out of love. Today, you used the example of the railway tracks. Well, she isn't just another track running along beside you. She doesn't follow rules, nor, I imagine, do you. I miss her too, you know.'

'So ...'

'So if you want to find her, I can tell you where she is. I've already felt the same impulse, but the voice tells me that now is not the moment, that no one should interrupt her encounter with the energy of love. I respect the voice, the voice protects us, protects me, you, Esther.'

'When will the moment be right?'

'Perhaps tomorrow, in a year's time, or never, and, if that were the case, then we would have to respect that decision. The voice is the Energy, and that is why she only brings people together when they are both truly prepared for that moment. And yet we all try and force the situation even if it means hearing the very words we don't want to hear: "Go away." Anyone who fails to obey the voice and arrives earlier or later than he should, will never get the thing he wants.'

'I'd rather hear her tell me to go away than be stuck with the Zahir day and night. If she said that, she would at least cease to be an *idée fixe* and become a woman who now has a different life and different thoughts.'

'She would no longer be the Zahir, but it would be a great loss. If a man and a woman can make the Energy manifest, then they are helping all the men and women of the world.'

'You're frightening me. I love her, you know I do, and you say that she still loves me. I don't know what you mean by being prepared; I can't live according to other people's expectations, not even Esther's.'

'As I understand it from conversations I had with her, at some point you got lost. The world started revolving exclusively around you.'

'That's not true. She was free to forge her own path. She decided to become a war correspondent, even though I didn't want her to. She felt driven to find out why people were unhappy, even though I told her this was impossible. Does she want me to go back to being a railway track running alongside another railway track, always keeping the same stupid distance apart, just because the Romans decided that was the way it should be?'

'On the contrary.'

Mikhail started walking again, and I followed him.

'Do you believe that I hear a voice?'

'To be perfectly honest, I don't know. But now that we're here, let me show you something.'

'Everyone thinks I'm just having an epileptic fit, and I let them believe that because it's easier. But the voice has been speaking to me ever since I was a child, when I first saw the Lady.'

'What lady?'

'I'll tell you later.'

'Whenever I ask you something, you say: "I'll tell you later."'

'The voice is telling me something now. I know that you're anxious and frightened. In the pizzeria, when I felt that warm wind and saw the lights, I knew that these were symptoms of my connection with the Power. I knew it was there to help us both. If you think that all the things I've been telling you are just the ravings of a young epileptic who wants to manipulate the feelings of a famous writer, I'll bring you a map tomorrow showing you where Esther is living, and you can go and find her. But the voice is telling us something.'

'Are you going to say what exactly, or will you tell me later?'

'I'll tell you in a moment. I haven't yet properly understood the message.'

'But you promise to give me the address and the map.'

'I promise. In the name of the divine energy of love, I promise. Now what was it you wanted to show me?'

I pointed to a golden statue of a young woman riding a horse.

'This. She used to hear voices. As long as people respected what she said, everything was fine. When they started to doubt her, the wind of victory changed direction.'

Joan of Arc, the Maid of Orléans, the heroine of the Hundred Years War, who, at the age of seventeen, was made commander of the French troops because she heard voices and the voices told her the best strategy for defeating the English. Two years later, she was condemned to be burned at the stake, accused of witchcraft. I had used part of the interrogation, dated 24 February 1431, in one of my books.

She was questioned by Maître Jean Beaupère. Asked how long it had been since she had heard the voice, she replied:

'I heard it three times, yesterday and today. In the morning, at Vespers, and again when the Ave Maria rang in the evening …'

Asked if the voice was in the room, she replied that she did not know, but that she had been woken by the voice. It wasn't in the room, but it was in the castle.

She asked the voice what she should do, and the voice asked her to get out of bed and place the palms of her hands together.

Then she said to the bishop who was questioning her:

'You say you are my judge. Take care what you are doing; for in truth I am sent by God, and you place yourself in great danger. My voices have entrusted to me certain things to tell to the King, not to you. The voice comes to me from God. I have far greater fear of doing wrong in saying to you things that would displease it than I have of answering you.'

'Are you suggesting …'

'That you're the reincarnation of Joan of Arc. No, I don't think so. She died when she was barely nineteen, and you're twenty-five. She took command of the French troops and, according to what you've told me, you can't even take command of your own life.'

We sat down on the wall by the Seine.

'I believe in signs,' I said. 'I believe in fate. I believe that every single day people are offered the chance to make the best possible decision about everything they do. I believe that I failed and that, at some point, I lost my connection with the woman I loved. And now, all I need is to put an end to that cycle. That's why I want the map, so that I can go to her.'

He looked at me and he was once more the person who appeared on stage and went into a trance-like state. I feared another epileptic fit – in the middle of the night, here, in an almost deserted place.

'The vision gave me power. That power is almost visible, palpable. I can manage it, but I can't control it.'

'It's getting a bit late for this kind of conversation. I'm tired, and so are you. Will you give me that map and the address?'

'The voice … Yes, I'll give you the map tomorrow afternoon. What's your address?'

I gave him my address and was surprised to realise that he didn't know where Esther and I had lived.

'Do you think I slept with your wife?'

'I would never even ask. It's none of my business.'

'But you did ask when we were in the pizzeria.'

I had forgotten. Of course it was my business, but I was no longer interested in his answer.

Mikhail's eyes changed. I felt in my pocket for something to place in his mouth should he have a fit, but he seemed calm and in control.

'I can hear the voice now. Tomorrow I will bring you the map, detailed directions and times of flights. I believe that she is waiting for you. I believe that the world would be happier if just two people, even two, were happier. Yet the voice is telling me that we will not see each other tomorrow.'

'I'm having lunch with an actor over from the States, and I can't possibly cancel, but I'll be home during the rest of the afternoon.'

'That's not what the voice is telling me.'

'Is the voice forbidding you to help me find Esther?'

'No, I don't think so. It was the voice that encouraged me to go to the book-signing. From then on, I knew more or less how things would turn out because I had read *A Time to Rend and a Time to Sew.*'

'Right then,' and I was terrified he might change his mind, 'let's stick to our arrangement. I'll be at home from two o'clock onwards.'

'But the voice says the moment is not right.'

'You promised.'

'All right.'

He held out his hand and said that he would come to my apartment late tomorrow afternoon. His last words to me that night were:

'The voice says that it will only allow these things to happen when the time is right.'

As I walked back home, the only voice I could hear was Esther's, speaking of love. And as I remembered that conversation, I realised that she had been talking about our marriage.

'When I was fifteen, I was desperate to find out about sex. But it was a sin, it was forbidden. I couldn't understand why it was a sin, could you? Can you tell me why all religions, all over the world, even the most primitive of religions and cultures, consider that sex is something that should be forbidden?'

'How did we get onto this subject? All right, why is sex something to be forbidden?'

'Because of food.'

'Food?'

'Thousands of years ago, tribes were constantly on the move; men could make love with as many women as they wanted and, of course, have children by them. However, the larger the tribe, the more chances there were of it disappearing. Tribes fought amongst themselves for food, killing first the children and then the women, because they were the weakest. Only the strongest survived, but they were all men. And without women men cannot continue to perpetuate the species.

Then someone, seeing what was happening in a neighbouring tribe, decided to avoid the same thing happening in his. He invented a story according to which the gods forbade men to make love indiscriminately with any of the women in a tribe. They could only make love with one or, at most, two. Some men were impotent, some women were sterile, some members of the tribe, for perfectly natural reasons, thus had no children at all, but no one was allowed to change partners.

They all believed the story because the person who told it to them was speaking in the name of the gods. He must have been different in some way: he perhaps had a deformity, an illness that caused convulsions, or some special gift, something, at any rate, that marked him out from the others, because that is how the first leaders emerged. In a few years, the tribe grew stronger, with just the right number of men needed to feed everyone, with enough women capable of reproducing and enough children to replace the hunters and reproducers. Do you know what gives a woman most pleasure within marriage?'

'Sex.'

'No, making food. Watching her man eat. That is a woman's moment of glory, because she spends all day thinking about supper. And the reason must lie in that story hidden in the past – in hunger, the threat of extinction and the path to survival.'

'Do you regret not having had any children?'

'It didn't happen, did it? How can I regret something that didn't happen?'

'Do you think that would have changed our marriage?'

'How can I possibly know? I look at my friends, both male and female: are they any happier because they have children? Some are, some aren't. And if they are happy with their children that doesn't make their relationship either better or worse. They still think they have the right to control each other. They still think that the promise "to live happily ever after" must be kept, even at the cost of daily unhappiness.'

'War isn't good for you, Esther. It brings you into contact with a very different reality from the one we experience here. I know I'll die one day, but that just makes me live each day as if it were a miracle. It doesn't make me think obsessively about love, happiness, sex, food and marriage.'

'War doesn't leave me time to think. I simply am, full stop. Whenever it occurs to me that, at any moment, I could be hit by a stray bullet, I just think: "Good, at least I don't have to worry about what will happen to my child." But I think too: "What a shame, I'm going to die and nothing will be left of me. I am only capable of losing a life, not bringing a life into the world."

'Do you think there's something wrong with our relationship? I only ask because I get the feeling sometimes that you want to tell me something, but that you keep stopping yourself.'

'Yes, there is something wrong. We feel obliged to be happy together. You think you owe me everything that you are, and I feel privileged to have a man like you at my side.'

'I have a wife whom I love, but I don't always remember that and find myself asking: "What's wrong with me?"'

'It's good that you're able to recognise that, but I don't think there's anything wrong with you or with me, because I ask myself the same question. What's wrong is the way in which we show our love now. If we were to accept that this creates problems, we could live with those problems and be happy. It would be a constant battle, but it would at least keep us active, alive and cheerful, with many universes to conquer; the trouble is we're heading towards a point where things are becoming too comfortable, where love stops creating problems and confrontations and becomes instead merely a solution.'

'What's wrong with that?'

'Everything. I can no longer feel the energy of love, what people call passion, flowing through my flesh and through my soul.'

'But something is left.'

'Left? Does every marriage have to end like this, with passion giving way to something people call "a mature relationship"? I need you. I miss you. Sometimes I'm jealous. I like thinking about what to give you for supper, even though sometimes you don't even notice what you're eating. But there's a lack of joy.'

'No, there isn't. Whenever you're far away, I wish you were near. I imagine the conversations we'll have when you or I come back from a trip. I phone you to make sure everything's all right. I need to hear your voice every day. I'm still passionate about you, I can guarantee you that.'

'It's the same with me, but what happens when we're together? We argue, we quarrel over nothing, one of us wants to change the other, to impose his or her view of reality. You demand things of me that make no sense at all, and I do the same. Sometimes, in the silence of our hearts, we say to ourselves: "How good it would be to be free, to have no commitments."'

'You're right. And at moments like that, I feel lost, because I know that I'm with the woman I want to be with.'

'And I'm with the man I always wanted to have by my side.'

'Do you think that could change?'

'As I get older, and fewer men look at me, I find myself thinking: "Just leave things as they are." I'm sure I can happily deceive myself for the rest of my life. And yet, whenever I go off to cover a war, I see that a greater love exists, much greater than the hatred that makes men kill each other. And then, and only then, do I think I can change things.'

'But you can't be constantly covering wars.'

'Nor can I live constantly in the sort of peace that I find with you. It's destroying the one important thing I have: my relationship with you, even if the intensity of my love remains undiminished.'

'Millions of people the world over are thinking the same thing right now, they resist fiercely and allow those moments of depression to pass. They withstand one, two, three crises and, finally, find peace.'

'You know that isn't how it is. Otherwise you wouldn't have written the books you've written.'

I had arranged to meet the American actor/director for lunch at Roberto's pizzeria. I needed to go back there as soon as possible in order to dispel any bad impression I might have caused. Before I left, I told the maid and the caretaker of the apartment building that if I was not back in time and a young man with Mongolian features should deliver a package for me, they must take him up to my apartment, ask him to wait in the living room and give him anything he needed. If, for some reason, the young man could not wait, then they should ask him to leave the package with one of them.

Above all, they must not let him leave without handing over the package!

I caught a taxi and asked to be dropped on the corner of Boulevard St-Germain and Rue St-Pères. A fine rain was falling, but it was only a few yards to the restaurant, its discreet sign and Roberto's generous smile, for he sometimes stood outside, smoking a cigarette. A woman with a pushchair was coming towards me along the narrow pavement, and because there wasn't room for both of us, I stepped off the kerb to let her pass.

It was then, in slow motion, that the world gave a giant lurch: the ground became the sky, the sky became the ground; I had time to notice a few architectural details on the top of the building on the corner – I had often walked past before, but had never looked up. I remember the sensation of surprise, the feeling of a wind blowing hard in my ear and the sound of a dog barking in the distance; then everything went dark.

I was bundled abruptly down a black hole at the end of which was a light. Before I could reach it, however, invisible hands were dragging me roughly back up, and I woke to voices and shouts all around me: it could only have lasted a matter of seconds. I was aware of the taste of blood in my mouth, the smell of wet asphalt, and then I realised that I had had an accident. I was conscious and unconscious at the same time; I tried without success to move; I could make out another person lying on the ground beside me; I could smell that person's smell, their perfume; I imagined it must be the woman who had been pushing her baby along the pavement. Oh, dear God!

Someone came over and tried to help me up; I yelled at them not to touch me, any movement could be dangerous. I had learned during a trivial conversation one trivial night that were I ever to fracture my neck, any sudden movement could leave me permanently paralysed.

I struggled to remain conscious; I waited for a pain that never came; I tried to move, then thought better of it. I experienced a feeling like cramp, like torpor. I again asked not to be moved. I heard a distant siren and knew then that I could sleep, that I no longer needed to fight to save my life; whether it was won or lost, it was no longer up to me, it was up to the doctors, to the nurses, to fate, to 'the thing', to God.

I heard the voice of a child – she told me her name, but I couldn't quite grasp it – asking me to keep calm, promising me that I wouldn't die. I wanted to believe what she said, I begged her to stay by my side, but she vanished; I was aware of someone placing something plastic around my neck, putting a mask over my face, and then I went to sleep again, and this time there were no dreams.

When I regained consciousness, all I could hear was a horrible buzzing in my ears; the rest was silence and utter darkness. Suddenly, I felt everything moving, and I was sure I was being carried along in my coffin, that I was about to be buried alive!

I tried banging on the walls, but I couldn't move a muscle. For what seemed an eternity, I felt as if I were being propelled helplessly forwards; then, mustering all my remaining strength, I uttered a scream that echoed round the enclosed space and came back to my own ears, almost deafening me; but I knew that once I had screamed, I was safe, for a light immediately began to appear at my feet: they had realised I wasn't dead!

Light, blessed light – which would save me from that worst of all tortures, suffocation – was gradually illuminating my whole body: they were finally removing the coffin lid. I broke out in a cold sweat, felt the most terrible pain, but was also happy and relieved that they had realised their mistake and that joy could return to the world!

The light finally reached my eyes: a soft hand touched mine, someone with an angelic face was wiping the sweat from my brow.

'Don't worry,' said the angelic face, with its golden hair and white robes. 'I'm not an angel, you didn't die, and this isn't a coffin, it's just a body scanner, to find out if you suffered any other injuries. There doesn't appear to be anything seriously wrong, but you'll have to stay in for observation.'

'No broken bones?'

'Just general abrasions. If I brought you a mirror, you'd be horrified, but the swelling will go down in a few days.'

I tried to get up, but she very gently stopped me. Then I felt a terrible pain in my head and groaned.

'You've had an accident; it's only natural that you should be in pain.'

'I think you're lying to me,' I managed to say. 'I'm a grown man, I've had a good life, I can take bad news without panicking. Some blood vessel in my head is about to burst, isn't it?'

Two nurses appeared and put me on a stretcher. I realised that I had an orthopaedic collar around my neck.

'Someone told us that you asked not to be moved,' said the angel. 'Just as well. You'll have to wear this collar for a while, but barring any unforeseen events – because one can never tell what might happen – you'll just have had a nasty shock. You're very lucky.'

'How long? I can't stay here.'

No one said anything. Marie was waiting for me outside the radiology unit, smiling. The doctors had obviously already told her that my injuries were not, in principle, very serious. She stroked my hair and carefully disguised any shock she might feel at my appearance.

Our small cortège proceeded along the corridor – Marie, the two nurses pushing the stretcher, and the angel in white. The pain in my head was getting worse all the time.

'Nurse, my head ...'

'I'm not a nurse. I'm your doctor for the moment. We're waiting for your own doctor to arrive. As for your head, don't worry. When you have an accident, your body closes down all the blood vessels as a defence mechanism, to avoid loss of blood. When it sees that the danger is over, the vessels open up again, the blood starts to flow and that feels painful, but that's all it is. Anyway, if you like, I can give you something to help you sleep.'

I refused. And as if surfacing from some dark corner of my soul, I remembered the words I had heard the day before:

'The voice says that it will only allow these things to happen when the time is right.'

He couldn't have known. It wasn't possible that everything that had happened on the corner of Boulevard St-Germain and Rue St-Pères was the result of some universal conspiracy, of something predetermined by the gods, who, despite being fully occupied in taking care of this precariously balanced planet on the verge of extinction, had all downed tools merely to prevent me from going in search of the Zahir. Mikhail could not possibly have foreseen the future, unless he really had heard a voice and there *was* a plan and this was all far more important than I imagined.

Everything was beginning to be too much for me: Marie's smiles, the possibility that someone really had heard a voice, the increasingly agonising pain in my head.

'Doctor, I've changed my mind. I want to sleep. I can't stand the pain.'

She said something to one of the nurses pushing the trolley, who went off and returned even before we had reached my room. I felt a prick in my arm and immediately fell asleep.

* * *

When I woke up, I wanted to know exactly what had happened; I wanted to know if the woman passing me on the pavement had escaped injury and what had happened to her baby. Marie said that I needed to rest, but, by then, Dr Louit, my doctor and friend, had arrived and felt that there was no reason not to tell me. I had been knocked down by a motorbike. The body I had seen lying on the ground beside me had been the young male driver. He had been taken to the same hospital and, like me, had escaped with only minor abrasions. The police investigation carried out immediately after the accident made it clear that I had been standing in the middle of the road at the time of the accident, thus putting the motorcyclist's life at risk.

It was, apparently, all my fault, but the motorcyclist had decided not to press charges. Marie had been to see him and talk to him; she had learned that he was an immigrant working illegally and was afraid of having any dealings with the police. He had been discharged twenty-four hours later, because he had been wearing a helmet, which lessened the risk of any damage to the brain.

'Did you say he left twenty-four hours later? Does that mean I've been in here more than a day?'

'You've been in here for three days. When you came out of the body scanner, the doctor here phoned me to ask if she could keep you on sedatives. It seemed to me that you'd been rather tense, irritated and depressed lately, and so I told her she could.'

'So what happens next?'

'Two more days in hospital and then three weeks with that contraption around your neck; you're through the critical 48-hour period. Of course, part of your body could still rebel against the idea of continuing to behave itself and then we'd have a problem on our hands. But let's face that emergency if and when it arises; there's no point in worrying unnecessarily.'

'So, I could still die?'

'As you well know, all of us not only can but will die.'

'Yes, but could I still die as a result of the accident?'

Dr Louit paused.

'Yes. There's always the chance that a blood clot could have formed which the machines have failed to pick up and that it could break free at any moment and cause an embolism. There's also the possibility that a cell has gone berserk and is starting to form a cancer.'

'You shouldn't say things like that,' said Marie.

'We've been friends for five years. He asked me a question and I gave him an answer. And now, if you don't mind, I have to get back to my office. Medicine isn't quite as you think. In the world we live in, if a boy goes out to buy five apples, but arrives home with only two, people would conclude that he had eaten the three missing apples. In my world, there are other possibilities: he could have eaten them, but he could also have been robbed; the money he'd been given might not have been enough to buy the five apples he'd been sent for; he could have lost them on the way home; he could have met someone who was hungry and decided to share the fruit with that person, and so on. In my world, everything is possible and everything is relative.'

'What do you know about epilepsy?'

Marie knew at once that I was talking about Mikhail and could not conceal a flicker of displeasure. She said she had to go, there was a film crew waiting.

Dr Louit, however, having picked up his things ready to leave, stopped to answer my question.

'It's an excess of electrical impulses in one specific area of the brain, which provoke convulsions of greater or lesser severity. There's no definitive study on the subject, but they think attacks may be provoked when the person is under great strain. But don't worry, while epileptic symptoms can appear at any age, epilepsy itself is unlikely to be brought on by colliding with a motorcycle.'

'So what causes it?'

'I'm not a specialist, but, if you like, I can find out.'

'Yes, if you would. And I have another question too, but please don't go thinking that my brain's been affected by the accident. Is it possible that epileptics can hear voices and have premonitions?'

'Did someone tell you this accident was going to happen?'

'Not exactly, but that's what I took it to mean.'

'Look, I can't stay any longer, I'm giving Marie a lift, but I'll see what I can find out about epilepsy for you.'

* * *

For the two days that Marie was away, and despite the shock of the accident, the Zahir took up its usual space in my life. I knew that if Mikhail had kept his word, there would be an envelope waiting for me at home containing Esther's address; now, however, the thought frightened me.

What if Mikhail was telling the truth about the voice?

I started trying to remember the details of the accident: I had stepped down from the kerb, automatically looking to see if anything was coming; I'd seen a car approaching, but it had appeared to be a safe distance away. And yet I had still been hit, possibly by a motorbike trying to overtake the car and which had been outside my field of vision.

I believe in signs. After I had walked the road to Santiago, everything had changed completely: what we need to learn is always there before us, we just have to look around us with respect and attention in order to discover where God is leading us and which step we should take next. I also learned a respect for mystery: as Einstein said, God does not play dice with the Universe; everything is interconnected and has a meaning. That meaning may remain hidden nearly all the time, but we always know we are close to our true mission on earth when what we are doing is touched with the energy of enthusiasm.

If it is, then all is well. If not, then we had better change direction.

When we are on the right path, we follow the signs, and if we occasionally stumble, Divinity comes to our aid, preventing us from making a mistake. Was the accident a sign? Had Mikhail intuited a sign that was intended for me?

I decided that the answer to these questions was 'Yes'.

And perhaps because of this, because I accepted my destiny and allowed myself to be guided by something greater than myself, I noticed that, during the day, the Zahir began to diminish in intensity. I knew that all I had to do was open the envelope, read her address, and go and knock on her door, but the signs all indicated that this was not the moment. If Esther really was as important in my life as I thought, if she still loved me (as Mikhail said she did), why force a situation that would simply lead me into making the same mistakes I had made in the past?

How to avoid repeating them?

By knowing myself better, by finding out what had changed and what had provoked this sudden break in a road that had always been marked by joy.

Was that enough?

No, I also needed to know who Esther was, what changes she had undergone during the time we were together.

And was it enough to be able to answer these two questions?

There was a third: why had fate brought us together?

I had a lot of free time in that hospital room, and so I made a general review of my life. I had always sought both adventure and security, knowing that the two things did not really mix. I was sure of my love for Esther and yet I easily fell in love with other women, merely because the game of seduction is the most interesting game in the world.

Had I shown my wife that I loved her? Perhaps for a while, but not always. Why? Because I didn't think it was necessary; she must know I loved her; she couldn't possibly doubt my feelings.

I remember that, many years ago, someone asked me if there was a common denominator amongst all the various girlfriends I had had in my life. The answer was easy: ME. And when I realised this, I saw how much time I had wasted looking for the right person – the women changed, but I remained the same and so got nothing from those shared experiences. I had lots of girlfriends, but I was always waiting for the right person. I controlled and was controlled and the relationship never went any further than that, until Esther arrived and changed everything.

I was thinking tenderly of my ex-wife; I was no longer obsessed with finding her, with finding out why she had left without a word of explanation. *A Time to Rend and a Time to Sew* had been a true account of my marriage, but it was, above all, my own testimony, declaring that I am capable of loving and needing someone else. Esther deserved more than just words, especially since I had never said those words while we were together.

It is always important to know when something has reached its end. Closing circles, shutting doors, finishing chapters, it doesn't matter what we call it; what matters is to leave in the past those moments in life that are over. Slowly, I began to realise that I could not go back and force things to be as they once were: those two years, which up until then had seemed an endless inferno, were now beginning to show me their true meaning.

* * *

And that meaning went far beyond my marriage: all men and all women are connected by an energy which many people call love, but which is, in fact, the raw material from which the universe was built. This energy cannot be manipulated, it leads us gently forwards, it contains all we have to learn in this life. If we try to make it go in the direction we want, we end up desperate, frustrated, disillusioned, because that energy is free and wild.

We could spend the rest of our life saying that we love such a person or thing, when the truth is that we are merely suffering because, instead of accepting love's strength, we are trying to diminish it so that it fits the world in which we imagine we live.

The more I thought about this, the weaker the Zahir became and the closer I moved to myself. I prepared myself mentally to do a great deal of work, work that would require much silence, meditation, and perseverance. The accident had helped me understand that I could not force something that had not yet reached its 'time to sew'.

I remembered what Dr Louit had said: after such a trauma to the body, death could come at any moment. What if that were true? What if in ten minutes' time, my heart stopped beating?

A nurse came into the room to bring me my supper and I asked him:

'Have you thought about your funeral?'

'Don't worry,' he replied. 'You'll survive; you already look much better.'

'I'm not worried. I know I'm going to survive. A voice told me I would.'

I mentioned the 'voice' deliberately, just to provoke him. He eyed me suspiciously, thinking that perhaps it was time to call for another examination and check that my brain really hadn't been affected.

'I know I'm going to survive,' I went on. 'Perhaps for a day, for a year, for thirty or forty years, but one day, despite all the scientific advances, I'll leave this world and I'll have a funeral. I was thinking about it just now and I wondered if you had ever thought about it.'

'Never. And I don't want to either; besides, that's what really terrifies me, knowing that everything will end.'

'Whether you like it or not, whether you agree or disagree, that is a reality none of us can escape. Do you fancy having a little chat about it?'

'I've got other patients to see, I'm afraid,' he said, putting the food down on the table and leaving as quickly as possible, as if running away – not from me, but from my words.

The nurse might not want to talk about it, but how about me thinking about it alone? I remembered some lines from a poem I had learned as a child:

When the Unwanted Guest arrives …
I might be afraid.
I might smile or say:
My day was good, let night fall.
You will find the fields ploughed, the house clean,
the table set,
and everything in its place.

It would be nice if that were true – everything in its place. And what would my epitaph be? Esther and I had both made wills, in which, amongst other things, we had chosen cremation: my ashes were to be scattered to the winds in a place called Cebreiro, on the road to Santiago, and her ashes were to be scattered over the sea. So there would be no inscribed headstone.

But what if I could choose an epitaph? I would ask to have these words engraved:

He died while he was still alive.

That might sound like a contradiction in terms, but I knew many people who had ceased to live, even though they continued to work and eat and engage in their usual social activities. They did everything automatically, oblivious to the magic moment that each day brings with it, never stopping to think about the miracle of life, never understanding that the next minute could be their last on the face of this planet.

It was pointless trying to explain this to the nurse, largely because it was a different nurse who came to collect the supper dish. This new nurse started bombarding me with questions, possibly on the orders of some doctor. He wanted to know if I could remember my name, if I knew what year it was, the name of the President of the United States, the sort of thing they ask when they're assessing your mental state.

And all because I asked the questions that every human being should ask: have you thought about your funeral? Do you realise that sooner or later you're going to die?

That night, I went to sleep smiling. The Zahir was disappearing, and Esther was returning, and if I were to die then, despite all that had happened in my life, despite all my failures, despite the disappearance of the woman I loved, the injustices I had suffered or inflicted on others, I had remained alive until the last moment, and could, with all certainty, affirm:

'My day was good, let night fall.'

Two days later, I was back home. Marie went to prepare lunch, and I glanced through the accumulated correspondence. The entry-phone rang. It was the caretaker to say that the envelope I had expected the previous week had been delivered and should be on my desk.

I thanked him, but, contrary to all my expectations, I did not immediately rush to open it. Marie and I had lunch; I asked her how filming had gone and she asked me about my immediate plans, given that I wouldn't be able to go out much while I was wearing the orthopaedic collar. She said that she could, if necessary, come and stay.

'I'm supposed to do an appearance on some Korean TV channel, but I can always put it off or even cancel it altogether. That's, of course, if you need my company.'

'Oh, I do, and it would be lovely to have you around.'

She smiled broadly and picked up the phone to call her manager and ask her to change her engagements. I heard her say: 'Don't tell them I'm ill though. I'm superstitious, and whenever I've used that excuse in the past, I've always gone down with something really horrible. Just tell them I've got to look after the person I love.'

I had a series of urgent things to do too: interviews to be postponed, invitations that required replies, letters to be written thanking various people for the phone calls and flowers I'd received, things to read, prefaces and recommendations to write. Marie spent the whole day on the phone to my agent, reorganising my diary so that no one would be left without a response. We had supper at home every evening, talking about the interesting and the banal, just like any other couple. During one of these suppers, after a few glasses of wine, she remarked that I had changed.

'It's as if having a brush with death had somehow brought you back to life,' she said.

'That happens to everyone.'

'But I must say – and, don't worry, I don't want to start an argument and I'm not about to have an attack of jealousy – you haven't mentioned Esther once since coming home. The same thing happened when you finished *A Time to Rend and a Time to Sew*: the book acted as a kind of therapy, the effects of which, alas, didn't last very long.'

'Are you saying that the accident has affected my brain?'

My tone wasn't aggressive, but she nevertheless decided to change the subject and started telling me about a terrifying helicopter trip she'd had from Monaco to Cannes. Later, in bed, we made love – with great difficulty given my orthopaedic collar – but we made love nevertheless and felt very close.

Four days later, the vast pile of paper on my desk had disappeared. There was only a large, white envelope bearing my name and the number of my apartment. Marie went to open it, but I told her it could wait.

She didn't ask me about it, perhaps it was information about my bank accounts or some confidential correspondence, possibly from another woman. I didn't explain either; I simply removed it from the desk and placed it on a shelf amongst some books. If I kept looking at it, the Zahir would come back.

At no point had the love I felt for Esther diminished; but every day spent in hospital had brought back some intriguing memory: not of conversations we had had, but of moments we had spent together in silence. I remembered her eyes, which, whenever she set off on some new adventure, were like those of an enthusiastic young girl, or like those of a wife proud of her husband's success or of the journalist fascinated by every subject she wrote about and, later, like those of the wife who no longer seemed to have a place in my life. That look of sadness had started before she told me she wanted to be a war correspondent; it became a look of joy every time she came back from an assignment, but it was only a matter of days before the look of sadness returned.

One afternoon, the phone rang:

'It's that young man,' Marie said, passing me the phone.

At the other end I heard Mikhail's voice, first saying how sorry he was about the accident and then asking me if I had received the envelope.

'Yes, it's here with me.'

'Are you going to go and find her?'

Marie was listening to our conversation and so I thought it best to change the subject.

'We can talk about that when I see you.'

'I'm not nagging or anything, but you did promise to help me.'

'And I always keep my promises. As soon as I'm better, we'll get together.'

He left me his mobile number, and when I hung up, I looked across at Marie, who seemed a different woman.

'So nothing's changed then,' she said.

'On the contrary. Everything's changed.'

I should have expressed myself more clearly and explained that I still wanted to see Esther, that I knew where she was. When the time was right, I would take a train, taxi, plane or whatever just to be by her side. This would, of course, mean losing the woman who was there by my side at that moment, steadfastly doing all she could to prove how important I was to her.

I was, of course, being a coward. I was ashamed of myself, but that was what life was like and – in a way I couldn't really explain – I loved Marie too.

The other reason I didn't say more was because I had always believed in signs, and when I recalled the moments of silence I had shared with my wife, I knew that – with or without voices, with or without explanations – the time to find Esther had still not yet arrived. I needed to concentrate more on those shared silences than on any of our conversations, because that would give me the freedom I needed to understand the time when things had gone right between us and the moment when they had started to go wrong.

Marie was there, looking at me. Could I go on being disloyal to someone who was doing so much for me? I started to feel uncomfortable, but I couldn't tell her everything, unless … unless I could find an indirect way of saying what I was feeling.

'Marie, let's suppose that two firemen go into a forest to put out a small fire. Afterwards, when they emerge and go over to a stream, the face of one is all smeared with black, while the other man's face is completely clean. My question is this: which of the two will wash his face?'

'That's a silly question. The one with the dirty face of course.'

'No, the one with the dirty face will look at the other man and assume that he looks like him. And, vice versa, the man with the clean face will see his colleague covered in grime and say to himself: I must be dirty too. I'd better have a wash.'

'What are you trying to say?'

'I'm saying that, during the time I spent in hospital, I came to realise that I was always looking for myself in the women I loved. I looked at their lovely, clean faces and saw myself reflected in them. They, on the other hand, looked at me and saw the dirt on my face and, however intelligent or self-confident they were, they ended up seeing themselves reflected in me and thinking that they were worse than they were. Please, don't let that happen to you.'

I would like to have added: that's what happened to Esther, and I've only just realised it, remembering now how the look in her eyes changed. I'd always absorbed her life and her energy, and that made me feel happy and confident, able to go forward. She, on the other hand, had looked at me and felt ugly, diminished, because, as the years passed, my career – the career that she had done so much to make a reality – had relegated our relationship to second place.

If I was to see her again, my face needed to be as clean as hers. Before I could find her, I must first find myself.

Ariadne's thread

'I am born in a small village, some kilometres from a slightly larger village where they have a school and a museum dedicated to a poet who lived there many years before. My father is nearly seventy years old, my mother is twenty-five. They met only recently when he was selling carpets; he had travelled all the way from Russia, but when he met her he decided to give up everything for her sake. She could be his daughter, but she behaves more like his mother, even helping him to sleep, something he has been unable to do properly since he was seventeen and was sent to fight the Germans in Stalingrad, one of the longest and bloodiest battles of the Second World War. Out of a battalion of three thousand men, only three survived.'

Oddly, Mikhail speaks almost entirely in the present tense. He doesn't say 'I was born' but 'I am born'. It is as if everything were happening here and now.

* * *

'In Stalingrad, my father and his best friend are caught in an exchange of fire on their way back from a reconnaissance patrol. They take cover in a bomb crater and spend two days in the mud and snow, with no food and no means of keeping warm. They can hear other Russians talking in a nearby building and know that they must try to reach them, but the firing never stops, the smell of blood fills the air, the wounded lie screaming for help day and night. Suddenly, everything falls silent. My father's friend, thinking that the Germans have withdrawn, stands up. My father tugs at his legs, yelling: "Get down!" But it's too late; a bullet pierces his friend's skull.

Another two days pass, my father is alone, with his friend's corpse beside him. He can't stop yelling "Get down!" At last, someone rescues him and takes him to the nearby building. There is no food, only ammunition and cigarettes. They eat the tobacco. A week later, they start to eat the flesh of their dead, frozen companions. A third battalion arrives and shoots a way through to them; the survivors are rescued, the wounded are treated and then immediately sent back to the front. Stalingrad must not fall; the future of Russia is at stake. After four months of intense fighting, of cannibalism, of limbs being amputated because of frost bite, the Germans finally surrender – it is the beginning of the end for Hitler and his Third Reich. My father returns on foot to his village, almost a thousand kilometres from Stalingrad. He now finds it almost impossible to sleep and when he does manage to drop off, he dreams every night of the friend he could have saved.

Two years later, the war ends. He receives a medal, but cannot find employment. He takes part in services of commemoration, but has almost nothing to eat. He is considered one of the heroes of Stalingrad, but can only survive by doing odd jobs for which he is paid a pittance. In the end, someone offers him work selling carpets. Suffering as he does from insomnia, he chooses to travel at night; he gets to know smugglers, wins their confidence, and begins to earn some money.

He is caught out by the Communist government, who accuse him of consorting with criminals and, despite being a war hero, he spends the next ten years in Siberia labelled "a traitor of the people". When he is finally released, he is an old man and the only thing he knows anything about are carpets. He manages to re-establish his old contacts, someone gives him a few carpets to sell, but no one is interested in buying – times are hard. He decides to go a long way away, begging as he goes, and ends up in Kazakhstan.

He is old and alone, but he needs to work in order to eat. He spends the days doing odd jobs and, at night, sleeps only fitfully and is woken by his own cries of "Get down!" Strangely enough, despite all that he has been through, despite the insomnia, the poor food, the frustrations, the physical wear and tear, and the cigarettes that he smokes whenever he can scrounge them, he still has an iron constitution.

In a small village, he meets a young woman. She lives with her parents; she takes him to her house, for, in that region, hospitality is paramount. They let him sleep in the living room, but are woken by his screams. The girl goes to him, says a prayer, strokes his head and, for the first time in many decades, he sleeps peacefully.

The following day, she says that, when she was a girl, she had dreamed that a very old man would give her a child. She waited for years, had various suitors, but was always disappointed. Her parents were terribly worried, for they did not want to see their only daughter end up a spinster, rejected by the community.

She asks him if he will marry her. He is taken aback; after all, she is nearly young enough to be his granddaughter, and so he says nothing. At sunset, in the small living room, she asks if she can stroke his head before he goes to sleep. He enjoys another peaceful night.

The following day, the subject of marriage comes up again, this time in the presence of her parents, who seem to think it a good idea; they just want their daughter to find a husband and to cease being a source of family shame. They invent a story about an old man who has come from far away and who is, in fact, a wealthy trader in carpets, but has grown weary of living a life of luxury and comfort, and has given it all up in order to go in search of adventure. People are impressed, they imagine a generous dowry, huge bank accounts, and think how lucky my mother is to have finally found someone who can take her away from that village in the back of beyond. My father listens to these stories with a mixture of fascination and surprise; he thinks of all the years he has spent alone, travelling, of all he has suffered, of how he never again found his own family, and he thinks that now, for the first time in his life, he could have a home of his own. He accepts the proposal, colludes with the lies about his past, and they get married according to the Muslim tradition. Two months later, she is pregnant with me.

I live with my father until I am seven years old; he sleeps well, works in the fields, goes hunting and talks to the other villagers about his money and his lands; and he looks at my mother as if she were the only good thing that has ever happened to him. I grow up believing that I am the son of a rich man, but one night, by the fire, he tells me about his past and why he married, but begs me not to tell anyone else. Soon, he says, he will die, and four months later he does. He breathes his last in my mother's arms, smiling, as if he had never known a moment's sadness. He dies a happy man.'

***

Mikhail is telling his story on a very cold spring night, although it is certainly not as cold as in Stalingrad, where temperatures can plummet to –35° C. We are sitting with some beggars who are warming themselves before an improvised bonfire. I had gone there after a second phone call from Mikhail, asking me to keep my part of the promise. During our conversation, he did not once mention the envelope he had left at my apartment, as if he knew – perhaps through the 'voice' – that I had, in the end, decided to follow the signs and allow things to happen in their own time and thus free myself from the power of the Zahir.

When he asked me to meet him in one of the most dangerous parts of Paris, my first reaction was one of alarm. Normally, I would have said that I was far too busy and tried to convince him that we would be better off going to some cosy bar where we could safely discuss important matters. I was still afraid that he might have another epileptic fit in public, even though I now knew what to do, but that was preferable to the risk of being mugged when I was wearing an orthopaedic collar and had no way of defending myself.

Mikhail insisted: I had to meet the beggars; they were part of his life and part of Esther's life too. I had realised while I was in hospital that there was something wrong with my own life and that change was urgently needed. How best to achieve that change? By doing something totally different; for example, going to dangerous places and meeting social outcasts.

There is a story about a Greek hero, Theseus, who goes into a labyrinth in order to slay a monster. His beloved, Ariadne, gives him one end of a thread so that he can unroll it as he goes and thus be able to find his way out again. Sitting with those people, listening to Mikhail's story, it occurs to me that I have not experienced anything like this for a long time – the taste of the unknown, of adventure. Who knows, perhaps Ariadne's thread was waiting for me in precisely the kind of place that I would never normally visit, or only if I was convinced that I had to make an enormous effort to change my story and my life.

Mikhail continued his story, and I saw that the whole group was listening to what he was saying: the most satisfying encounters do not always happen around elegant tables in nice, warm restaurants.

***

'Every day, I have to walk nearly an hour to the village where I go to school. I see the women going to fetch water, the endless steppes, the Russian soldiers driving past in long convoys, the snow-capped mountains which, I am told, conceal a vast country: China. The village I walk to each day has a museum dedicated to its one poet, a mosque, a school and three or four streets. We are taught about the existence of a dream, an ideal:

we must fight for the victory of Communism and for equality amongst all human beings. I do not believe in this dream, because even in this wretchedly poor village, there are marked differences: the Party representatives are above everyone else; now and again, they visit the big city, Almaty, and return bearing packages of exotic food, presents for their children, expensive clothes.

One afternoon, on my way home, I feel a strong wind blowing, see lights all around me and lose consciousness for a few moments. When I come to, I am sitting on the ground, and a very white little girl, wearing a white dress with a blue belt, is floating in the air above me. She smiles, but says nothing, then disappears.

I run home, interrupt my mother's work, and tell her what I have seen. She is terrified and asks me never to repeat what I have just told her. She explains to me – as well as one can explain such a complicated concept to an eight-year-old boy – that it was just an hallucination. I tell her that I really did see the girl, that I can describe her in every detail. I add that I wasn't afraid and came home at once because I wanted her to know what had happened.

The following day, coming back from school, I look for the girl, but she isn't there. Nothing happens for a whole week, and I begin to think that perhaps my mother was right: I must simply have dropped asleep and dreamed it all.

Then, this time very early one morning, on my way to school, I again see the girl floating in the air and surrounded by a white halo. I don't fall to the ground or see any flashing lights. We stand for a while, looking at each other; she smiles and I smile back; I ask her name, but receive no answer. At school, I ask my classmates if they have ever seen a girl floating in the air. They all laugh.

During class, I am summoned to the headmaster's office. He explains to me that I must have some mental problem – there is no such thing as "visions"; the only reality is what we see around us; religion was merely invented to fool the people. I ask about the mosque in the city; he says that only the old and superstitious go there, ignorant, idle people who lack the necessary energy to rebuild the socialist world. Then he issues a threat: if I repeat the story about the little girl, I will be expelled. Terrified, I beg him not to say anything to my mother, and he agrees, as long as I tell my classmates that I made the whole thing up.

He keeps his promise and I keep mine. My friends aren't much interested anyway and don't even ask me to show them the place where I saw the girl. However, she continues to appear to me for the whole of the following month. Sometimes I faint first, sometimes I don't. We never talk, we simply stay together for as long as she chooses to stay. My mother is beginning to grow worried because I always arrive home at a different time. One night, she forces me to explain what I do between leaving school and getting home. I again tell her about the little girl.

To my surprise, this time, instead of scolding me, she says that she will go to the place with me. The following day, we wake early and, when we arrive, the girl appears, but my mother cannot see her. My mother tells me to ask the girl something about my father. I don't understand the question, but I do as she requests, and then, for the first time, I hear the "voice". The girl does not move her lips, but I know she is talking to me: she says that my father is fine and is watching over us, and that he is being rewarded now for all his sufferings on earth. She suggests that I remind my mother about the heater. I do so, and my mother starts to cry and explains that because of his many hardships during the war, the thing my father most enjoyed was sitting next to a heater. The girl says that the next time my mother passes that way she should tie a scrap of fabric and a prayer around the small tree growing there.

The visions continue for a whole year. My mother tells some of her closest friends, who tell other friends, and soon the tree is covered in scraps of fabric. Everything is done in the greatest secrecy; the women ask about loved ones who have died; I listen to the voice's answers and pass on the messages. Usually, their loved ones are fine, and on only two occasions does the girl ask the group to go to a nearby hill at sunrise and say a wordless prayer for the souls of those people. Apparently, I sometimes go into a trance, fall to the ground, babble incomprehensibly, but I can never remember anything about it. I only know that when I am about to go into a trance, I feel a warm wind blowing and see bubbles of light all around me.

One day, when I am taking a group to meet the little girl, we are prevented from doing so by the police. The women protest and shout, but we cannot get through. I am escorted to school, where the headmaster informs me that I have just been expelled for provoking rebellion and encouraging superstition.

On the way back, I see that the tree has been cut down and the "ribbons" scattered on the ground. I sit down alone and weep, because those had been the happiest days of my life. At that moment, the girl reappears. She tells me not to worry, that this was all part of the plan, even the destruction of the tree, and that she will accompany me now for the rest of my days and will always tell me what I must do.'

* * *

'Did she never tell you her name?' asks one of the beggars.

'Never. But it doesn't matter because I always know when she's talking to me.'

'Could we find out something about our dead?'

'No. That only happened during one particular period. Now my mission is different. May I go on with my story?'

'Absolutely,' I say. 'But can I just ask one thing? There's a town in south-west France called Lourdes. A long time ago, a shepherdess saw a little girl, who seems to correspond to your vision.'

'No, you're wrong,' says one of the older beggars, who has an artificial leg. 'The shepherdess, whose name was Bernadette, saw the Virgin Mary.'

'I've written a book about her visions and I had to study the matter closely,' I say. 'I read everything that was published about it at the end of the nineteenth century; I had access to Bernadette's many statements to the police, to the Church and to scholars. At no point does she say that she saw a woman; she insists it was a girl. She repeated the same story all her life and was deeply angered by the statue that was placed in the grotto; she said it bore no resemblance to her vision, because she had seen a little girl, not a woman. Nevertheless, the Church appropriated the story, the visions and the place, and transformed the apparition into the Mother of Jesus, and the truth was forgotten. If a lie is repeated often enough, it ends up convincing everyone. The only difference is that "the little girl" – as Bernadette always referred to her – had a name.'

'What was it?' asks Mikhail.

'"I am the Immaculate Conception." Obviously that isn't a name like Beatriz or Maria or Isabelle. She describes herself as a fact, an event, a happening, which is sometimes translated as "I am birth without sex". Now, please, go on with your story.'

'Before he does, can I ask you something?' says another beggar, who must be about my age. 'You just said that you've written a book; what's the title?'

'I've written many books.'

And I tell him the title of the book in which I mention the story of Bernadette and her vision.

'So you're the husband of the journalist?'

'Are you Esther's husband?' asks a female beggar, wide-eyed; she is dressed garishly, in a green hat and a purple coat.

I don't know what to say.

'Why hasn't she been back here?' asks someone else. 'I hope she isn't dead. She was always going to such dangerous places. I often told her she shouldn't. Look what she gave me!'

And she shows me a scrap of bloodstained fabric, part of the dead soldier's shirt.

'No, she's not dead,' I say. 'But I'm surprised to hear that she used to come here.'

'Why? Because we're different?'

'No, you misunderstand me. I'm not judging you. I'm surprised and pleased to know that she did.'

However, the vodka we have been drinking to ward off the cold is having an effect on all of us.

'Now you're being ironic,' says a burly man with long hair, who looks as if he hasn't shaved for several days. 'If you think you're in such bad company, why don't you leave.'

I have been drinking too and that gives me courage.

'Who are you? What kind of life is this? You're healthy, you could work, but instead you prefer to hang around doing nothing!'

'We choose to stay outside, outside a world that is fast collapsing, outside people who live in constant fear of losing something, who walk along the street as if everything was fine, when, in fact, everything is bad, very bad indeed! Don't you beg too? Don't you ask for alms from your boss to pay the owner of your apartment?'

'Aren't you ashamed to be wasting your life?' asks the woman in the purple coat.

'Who said I'm wasting my life? I do precisely what I want to do.'

The burly man interrupts, saying:

'And what is it you want? To live on top of the world? Who told you that the mountain is necessarily better than the plain? You think we don't know how to live, don't you? Well, your wife understood that we know *exactly* what we want from life. Do you know what we want? Peace! Freedom! And not to be obliged to follow the latest fashions – we make our own fashions here! We drink when we want to and sleep whenever we feel like it! Not one person here chose slavery and we're proud of it, even though you and people like you may think we're just a lot of pathetic freeloaders!'

The voices are beginning to grow aggressive. Mikhail steps in:

'Do you want to hear the rest of my story or shall we leave now?'

'He's criticising us!' says the man with the artificial leg. 'He came here to judge us, as if he was God!'

There are a few more rumbles of complaint, someone slaps me on the back, I offer round my cigarettes, the bottle of vodka is placed in my hand again. People gradually calm down, and I am still surprised and shocked that these people knew Esther, apparently better than I did, since she gave them – and not me – a piece of that bloodstained shirt.

Mikhail goes on with his story:

'Since I have nowhere to go and study and I'm still too young to look after horses – which are the pride of our region and of our country – I become a shepherd. During the first week, one of the sheep dies and a rumour goes around that I'm cursed, that I'm the son of a man who came from far away and promised my mother great wealth, then ended up leaving us nothing. The Communists may have told them that religion is just a way of giving false hopes to the desperate, they may all have been brought up to believe that only reality exists and that anything our eyes can't see is just the fruit of the human imagination; but the ancient traditions of the steppes remain untouched and are passed by word of mouth across the generations.

Now that the tree has been felled, I no longer see the little girl, although I still hear her voice. I ask her to help me in tending the flocks, and she tells me to be patient; there are difficult times ahead, but before I am twenty-two a woman from far away will come and carry me off to see the world. She also tells me that I have a mission to fulfil, and that mission is to spread the true energy of love throughout the world.

The owner of the sheep is worried by the increasingly wild rumours. Oddly, the people spreading these rumours and trying to destroy my life are the very people whom the little girl had helped during the whole of the previous year. One day, he decides to go to the Communist Party office in the next village, where he learns that both I and my mother are considered to be enemies of the people. I am immediately dismissed. Not that this greatly affects our life, because my mother does embroidery for a company in the largest city in the region and there no one knows that we are enemies of the people and of the working classes; all the factory owners want is for her to continue working on her embroidery from dawn to dusk.

I now have all the time in the world and so I wander the steppes with the hunters, who know my story and believe that I have magical powers, because they always find foxes when I'm around. I spend whole days at the museum of the poet, studying his possessions, reading his books, listening to the people who come there to recite his verses. Now and then, I feel the warm wind blowing, see the lights and fall to the ground, and then the voice tells me concrete facts – when the next drought will come, when the animals will fall sick, when the traders will arrive. I tell no one except my mother, who is becoming ever more anxious and concerned about me.

One day, she takes me to see a doctor who is visiting the area. After listening attentively to my story, taking notes, peering into my eyes with a strange instrument, listening to my heart and tapping my knee, he diagnoses a form of epilepsy. He says it isn't contagious and that the attacks will diminish with age.

I know it isn't an illness, but I pretend to believe him so as to reassure my mother. The director of the museum, who notices me struggling to learn, takes pity on me and becomes my teacher. With him I learn geography and literature and the one thing that will prove vital to me in the future: English. One afternoon, the voice asks me to tell the director that he will shortly be offered an important post. When I tell him this, all I hear is a timid laugh and a firm response: there isn't the remotest chance of this ever happening because not only has he never been a Party member, he is a devout Muslim.

I am fifteen years old. Two months after this conversation, I sense that something is changing in the region. The normally arrogant civil servants are suddenly much kinder and ask if I would like to go back to school. Great convoys of Russian soldiers head off to the frontier. One evening, while I am studying in the little office that once belonged to the poet, the director comes running in and looks at me with a mixture of alarm and embarrassment. He tells me that the one thing he could never imagine happening – the collapse of the Communist regime – is happening right now, and with incredible speed. The former Soviet republics are becoming independent countries; the news from Almaty is all about the formation of a new government, and he has been appointed to govern the province!

Instead of joyfully embracing me, he asks me how I knew this was going to happen. Had I overheard someone talking about it? Had I been engaged by the secret services to spy on him because he did not belong to the Party? Or – worst of all – had I, at some point in my life, made a pact with the Devil?

I remind him that he knows my story: the little girl, the voice, the attacks that allow me to hear things that other people do not know. He says this is just part of my illness; there is only one prophet, Mohammed, and everything that needed to be said has already been revealed. This, he goes on, does not mean that the Devil is not still abroad in the world, using all kinds of tricks – including a supposed ability to foresee the future – to deceive the weak and lure people away from the true faith. He had given me a job because Islam demands that we should be charitable, but now he deeply regretted it: I am clearly either a tool of the secret services or an envoy of the Devil.

He dismisses me there and then.

Life had not been easy before and it now becomes harder still. The factory for which my mother works, and which once belonged to the government, falls into private hands, and the new owners have very different ideas; they restructure the whole business and she, too, is dismissed. Two months later, we have nothing to live on and all that remains for us is to leave the village where I have spent my whole life and go in search of work.

My grandparents refuse to leave; they would rather die of hunger on the land where they were born and have spent their entire lives. My mother and I go to Almaty and I see my first big city: I am amazed at the cars, the huge buildings, the neon signs, the escalators and – above all – the lifts. My mother gets a job in a shop and I go to work at a garage as a trainee mechanic. Much of the money we earn is sent back to my grandparents, but there is enough left over for us to be able to eat and for me to see things I have never seen before: films, funfairs and football games.

When we move to the city, my attacks vanish, but so does the voice and the little girl's presence. It's better that way, I decide. I am too fascinated by Almaty and too busy earning a living to miss the invisible friend who has been my companion since I was eight years old; I realise that all it takes to become "someone" in the world is a little intelligence. Then, one Sunday night, I am sitting at our small apartment's only window, which looks out onto a small dirt alleyway. I am very worried because, the day before, I dented a car as I was manoeuvring it inside the garage and am so frightened I might get the sack that I haven't eaten all day.

Suddenly, I feel the warm wind and see the lights. According to my mother, I fell to the floor, spoke in a strange language and the trance seemed to last longer than usual. I remember that it was then that the voice reminded me of my mission. When I come to, I can feel the presence of the little girl again and, although I cannot see her, I can talk to her.

A change of home has meant a change of worlds too, and I am no longer interested in all this. Nevertheless, I ask her what my mission is: the voice tells me that it is the mission shared by all human beings – to fill the world with the energy of total love. I ask about the one thing that is really worrying me at that precise moment: the dented car and the owner's reaction. She tells me not to worry, just tell the truth and he will understand.

I work at the garage for five more years. I make friends, have my first girlfriends, discover sex, get involved in street fights; in short, I have an entirely normal adolescence. I have a few fits and, at first, my friends are surprised, but then I invent some story about being in possession of "higher powers" and this earns me their respect. They ask for my help, consult me when they have problems with their girlfriends or with their families, but I never ask the voice for advice – the traumatic experience of seeing the tree cut down all those years ago has made me realise that when you help someone you get only ingratitude in return.

If my friends probe further, I tell them I belong to a "secret society". After decades of religious repression in Kazakhstan, mysticism and the esoteric are now very fashionable in Almaty. Books are published about people with so-called higher powers, about gurus and teachers from India and China; courses of self-improvement abound. I go to a few, but realise that I have nothing to learn. The only thing I really trust is the voice, but I am too busy to pay attention to what it is saying.

One day, a woman in a four-wheel drive stops at the garage where I work and asks me to fill up the tank. She addresses me in halting, heavily accented Russian, and I respond in English. She seems relieved and asks if I know of an interpreter who could go with her into the interior of Kazakhstan.

The moment she says this, the little girl's presence fills the whole place, and I understand that this is the person I have been waiting for all my life. She is my way out, and I must not miss this opportunity. I tell her that, if she wants, I can be her interpreter. She says that I obviously have a job already and, besides, she needs someone older, more experienced, someone who is free to travel. I say that I know every path in the steppes and the mountains, and I lie, saying that the job I have is only temporary. I beg her to give me a chance; reluctantly, she arranges to meet me later in the city's most luxurious hotel.

We meet in the lounge; she tests my knowledge of English, asks a series of questions about the geography of Central Asia, wants to know who I am and where I come from. She is suspicious and will not say exactly what she does or where she wants to go. I try to play my part as best I can, but I can see she's not convinced.

And I am surprised to realise that, for no apparent reason, I am in love with her, with this woman I have only known for a matter of hours. I control my anxiety and once more place my trust in the voice. I plead for help from the invisible girl and ask her to enlighten me; I promise that, if I get this job, I will carry out the mission entrusted to me; she had told me that one day a woman would come and take me far away from there; she had been there with me when the woman stopped to fill her tank; I need a positive response.

After Esther's intense questioning, I sense that I am beginning to win her confidence; she warns me that what she wants to do is completely illegal. She explains that she is a journalist and wants to write an article about the American bases being built in a neighbouring country in preparation for a war that is about to begin. Her application for a visa has been turned down and so we will have to travel on foot, crossing the border at points where there are no guards. Her contacts have given her a map and shown her where it is safe to cross, but she says she will reveal none of this until we are far from Almaty. If I want to go with her, I must be at the hotel in two days' time at eleven o'clock in the morning. She promises me only a week's wages, unaware that I have a permanent job, earn enough to help out my mother and my grandparents, and that my boss trusts me despite having been witness to several of the convulsive attacks – what he calls my 'epileptic fits' – that always accompany my contacts with the unknown world.

Before saying goodbye, the woman tells me her name – Esther – and warns me that if I go to the police to report her, she will be arrested and deported. She also says that there are moments in life when we need to trust blindly in intuition, which is what she is doing now. I tell her not to worry. I feel tempted to say something about the voice and the presence, but decide against it. I go home, talk to my mother and tell her I've found a new job as an interpreter, which is better paid, but will involve me going away for a while. She doesn't seem in the least concerned; everything around me is developing as if it had long been planned and we were all just waiting for the right moment.

I sleep badly and the following day I arrive earlier than usual at the garage. I tell my boss that I'm sorry, but I've found a new job. He says that, sooner or later, they'll find out about my illness, that it's very risky giving up steady employment for something less certain, but, just as happened with my mother, he makes no real fuss about letting me go, as if the voice were manipulating the minds of all the people I have to talk to that day, facilitating things, helping me take the first step.

When Esther and I meet at the hotel, I tell her: "If we're caught, you'll just be deported but I'll get put in prison, possibly for many years. Since I'm running the greater risk, you really ought to trust me." She seems to understand what I'm saying. We walk for two days; a group of men are waiting for her on the other side of the frontier; she goes off with them and returns shortly afterwards, frustrated and angry. The war is about to start, all the roads are being guarded, and it's impossible to go any further without being arrested as a spy.

We start the journey back. The usually self-confident Esther seems suddenly sad and confused. To distract her, I recite some lines written by the poet who used to live close to my village, at the same time thinking that in forty-eight hours this whole experience will be over. However, I prefer to trust in the voice. I must do everything I can to prevent Esther leaving as suddenly as she came; perhaps I should show her that I have always been waiting for her, that she is important to me.

That night, after rolling out our sleeping bags near some rocks, I reach out and touch her hand. She gently pulls back, saying that she's married. I realise that I have made a foolish blunder; then, since I now have nothing to lose, I tell her about the visions I had as a child, about my mission to spread love throughout the world, about the doctor's diagnosis of epilepsy.

To my surprise, she understands exactly what I'm talking about. She tells me a little about her life. She says that she loves her husband and that he loves her, but that, with the passing of time, something important has been lost, and she prefers now to be far away from him, rather than watch her marriage slowly disintegrate. She had everything in life, and yet she was unhappy; although she could easily go through the rest of her life pretending that this unhappiness didn't exist, she was terrified of falling into a depression from which she might never emerge.

That is why she decided to give up everything and go in search of adventure, in search of things that leave her no time to think about a love that is dying. However, the more she looked, the more confused she became, the more alone she felt. She feels she has completely lost her way, and the experience we have just had seems to be telling her that she is on the wrong track and should go back to her daily routine.

I suggest trying a less closely guarded trail, say that I know smugglers in Almaty who could help us, but she seems to have no energy, no will to go on.

At that moment, the voice tells me to bless Esther and to dedicate her to the earth. Without really knowing what I am doing, I get up, open my rucksack, dip my fingers in the small bottle of oil we have taken with us for cooking, place my hand on her head and pray in silence, asking, at the end, that she continue her search, because it is important for all of us. The voice is telling me – and I repeat the words out loud to her – that if just one person changes, the whole human race is changed. She puts her arms around me, and I can feel the earth blessing her, and we stay like that together for several hours.

Afterwards, I ask if she believes what I told her about the voice. She says that she both does and doesn't. She believes that we all have a power that we never use and that I have clearly come into contact with that power through my epileptic fits, but this is something we can find out about together. She has been thinking of interviewing a nomad who lives to the north of Almaty and who is said by everyone to have magical powers. I am welcome to accompany her. When she tells me the man's name, I realise that I know his grandson and that this could greatly facilitate matters.

We drive through Almaty, stopping only to fill the tank with petrol and buy some food, then we drive on in the direction of a tiny village near an artificial lake constructed by the Soviet regime. I find out where the nomad is staying, but despite telling one of his assistants that I know the man's grandson, we still have to wait many hours, for there is a large crowd wanting the advice of this man they consider to be a saint.

At last, we are ushered in. By acting as interpreter at that interview and by reading and re-reading Esther's article when it was published, I learn several things I needed to know.

Esther asks why people are sad.

"That's simple," says the old man. "They are the prisoners of their personal history. Everyone believes that the main aim in life is to follow a plan. They never ask if that plan is theirs or if it was created by another person.

They accumulate experiences, memories, things, other people's ideas, and it is more than they can possibly cope with. And that is why they forget their dreams."

Esther remarks that many people say to her: "You're lucky, you know what you want from life, whereas I don't even know what I want to do."

"Of course they know," replies the nomad. "How many people do you know who say: I've never done what I wanted, but then, that's life. If they say they haven't done what they wanted, then, at some point, they must have known what it was that they did want. As for life, it's just a story that other people tell us about the world and about how we should behave in the world."

"Even worse are those people who say: I'm happy because I'm sacrificing my life for those I love."

"And do you think that the people who love us want to see us suffering for their sakes? Do you think that love is a source of suffering?"

"To be honest, yes."

"Well, it shouldn't be."

"If I forget the story other people have told me, I'll also forget a lot of very important things life has taught me. What was the point of struggling to learn so much? What was the point of struggling to gain experience, so as to be able to deal with my career, my husband, my various crises?"

"Accumulated knowledge is useful when it comes to cooking or living within your means or wrapping up warm in winter or respecting certain limits or knowing where particular bus and train lines go. Do you believe that your past loves have taught you to love better?"

"They've taught me to know what I want."

"I didn't ask that. Have your past loves taught you to love your husband better?"

"No, on the contrary. In order to surrender myself to him, I had to forget all the scars left by other men. Is that what you mean?"

"In order for the true energy of love to penetrate your soul, your soul must be as if you had just been born. Why are people unhappy? Because they want to imprison that energy, which is impossible. Forgetting your personal history means leaving that channel clear, allowing that energy to manifest itself each day in whatever way it chooses, allowing yourself to be guided by it."

"That's all very romantic, but very difficult too, because that energy gets blocked by all kinds of things: commitments, children, your social situation …"

"… and, after a while, by despair, fear, loneliness and your attempts to control the uncontrollable. According to the tradition of the steppes – which is known as the Tengri – in order to live fully, it is necessary to be in constant movement; only then can each day be different from the last. When they passed through cities, the nomads would think: The poor people who live here, for them everything is always the same. The people in the cities probably looked at the nomads and thought: Poor things, they have nowhere to live. The nomads had no past, only the present, and that is why they were always happy, until the Communist governors made them stop travelling and forced them to live on collective farms. From then on, little by little, they came to believe that the story society told them was true. Consequently, they have lost all their strength."

"No one nowadays can spend their whole life travelling."

"Not physically, no, but they can on a spiritual plane. Going farther and farther, distancing yourself from your personal history, from what you were forced to become."

"How does one go about abandoning the story one was told?"

"By repeating it out loud in meticulous detail. And as we tell our story, we say goodbye to what we were and, as you'll see if you try, we create space for a new, unknown world. We repeat the old story over and over until it is no longer important to us."

"Is that all?"

"There is just one other thing: as those spaces grow, it is important to fill them up quickly, even if only provisionally, so as not to be left with a feeling of emptiness."

"How?"

"With different stories, with experiences we never dared to have or didn't want to have. That is how we change. That is how love grows. And when love grows, we grow with it."

"Does that mean we might lose things that are important?"

"Never. The important things always stay; what we lose are the things we thought were important but which are, in fact, useless, like the false power we use to control the energy of love."

The old man tells her that her time is up and that he has other people to see. Despite my pleas he proves inflexible, but tells Esther that if she ever comes back, he will teach her more.

* * *

Esther is only staying in Almaty for another week, but promises to return. During that time, I tell her my story over and over and she tells me hers, and we see that the old man is right: something is leaving us, we are lighter, although we could not really say that we are any happier.

The old man had given us another piece of advice: fill that space up quickly. Before she leaves, she asks if I would like to go to France so that we can continue this process of forgetting. She has no one with whom she can share all this; she can't talk to her husband; she doesn't trust the people she works with; she needs someone from outside, from far away, who has, up until then, had nothing to do with her personal history.

I say that I would like to do that and only then mention what the voice had prophesied. I also tell her that I don't know French and that my only work experience so far has been tending sheep and working in a garage.

At the airport, she asks me to take an intensive course in French. I ask her why she wants me to go to France. She repeats what she has said and admits she's afraid of the space opening up around her as she erases her personal history; she's afraid that everything will rush back in more intensely than before, and then there will be no way of freeing herself from her past. She tells me not to worry about buying a ticket or getting a visa; she will take care of everything. Before going through passport control, she looks at me, smiles, and says that, although she may not have known it, she had been waiting for me as well. The days we had spent together had been the happiest she had known in the last three years.

I start working at night, as a bouncer at a striptease joint, and during the day I devote myself to learning French. Oddly enough, the attacks diminish, but the presence also goes away. I tell my mother that I've been invited to go abroad, and she tells me not to be so naive, I'll never hear from the woman again.

A year later, Esther returns to Almaty. The expected war has begun, and someone else has written an article about the secret American bases, but Esther's interview with the old man had been a great success and now she has been asked to write a long article on the disappearance of the nomads. "Apart from that," she said, "it's been ages since I told my story to anyone and I'm starting to get depressed."

I help put her in touch with the few tribes who still travel, with the Tengri tradition, and with local shamans. I am now fluent in French, and over supper she gives me various forms from the consulate to fill in, gets me a visa, buys me a ticket, and I come to Paris. We both notice that, as we empty our minds of old stories, a new space opens up, a mysterious feeling of joy slips in, our intuitions grow sharper, we become braver, take more risks, do things which might be right or which might be wrong, we can't be sure, but we do them anyway. The days seem longer and more intense.

When I arrive in Paris, I ask where I'm going to work, but she has already made plans: she has persuaded the owner of a bar to allow me to appear there once a week, telling him that I specialise in an exotic kind of performance art from Kazakhstan which consists in encouraging people to talk about their lives and to empty their minds.

At first, it is very difficult to get the sparse audience to join in, but the drunks enjoy it and word spreads. "Come and tell your old story and discover a new one," says the small handwritten notice in the window, and people, thirsty for novelty, start to come.

One night, I experience something strange: it is not me on the small improvised stage in one corner of the bar, it is the presence. And instead of telling stories from my own country and then moving on to suggest that they tell their stories, I merely say what the voice tells me to. Afterwards, one of the spectators is crying and speaks about his marriage in intimate detail to the other strangers there.

The same thing happens the following week – the voice speaks for me, asking people to tell stories not about love, but about the lack of love, and the energy in the air is so different that the normally discreet French begin discussing their personal lives in public. I am also managing to control my attacks better; if, when I'm on stage, I start to see the lights or feel that warm wind, I immediately go into a trance, lose consciousness, and no one notices. I only have "epileptic fits" at moments when I am under great nervous strain.

Other people join the group. Three young men the same age as me, who had nothing to do but travel the world – the nomads of the Western world; and a couple of musicians from Kazakhstan, who have heard about their fellow countryman's "success", ask if they can join the show, since they are unable to find work elsewhere. We include percussion instruments in the performance. The bar is becoming too small, and we find a room in the restaurant where we currently appear; but now we are starting to outgrow that space too, because when people tell their stories, they feel braver; when they dance, they are touched by the energy and begin to change radically; love – which, in theory, should be threatened by all these changes – becomes stronger, and they recommend our meetings to their friends.

Esther continues travelling in order to write her articles, but always comes to the meetings when she is in Paris. One night, she tells me that our work at the restaurant is no longer enough; it only reaches those people who have the money to go there. We need to work with the young. Where will we find them, I ask? They drift, travel, abandon everything and dress as beggars or characters out of sci-fi movies.

She says that beggars have no personal history, so why don't we go to them and see what we can learn. And that is how I came to meet all of you.

These are the things I have experienced. You have never asked me who I am or what I do, because you're not interested. But today, because we have a famous writer in our midst, I decided to tell you.'

'But you're talking about your past,' said the woman in the clashing hat and coat. 'Even though the old nomad ...'

'What's a nomad?' someone asks.

'People like us,' she responds, proud to know the meaning of the word. 'People who are free and manage to live with only what they can carry.'

I correct her:

'That's not quite true. They're not poor.'

'What do you know about poverty?' The tall, aggressive man, who now has even more vodka in his veins, looks straight at me. 'Do you really think that poverty has to do with having no money? Do you think we're miserable wretches just because we go around begging money from rich writers and guilt-ridden couples, from tourists who think how terribly squalid Paris has become or from idealistic young people who think they can save the world? You're the one who's poor – you have no control over your time, you can't do what you want, you're forced to follow rules you didn't invent and which you don't understand …'

Mikhail again interrupted the conversation and asked the woman:

'What did you actually want to know?'

'I wanted to know why you're telling us your story when the old nomad said you should forget it.'

'It's not my story any more: whenever I speak about the past now, I feel as if I were talking about something that has nothing to do with me. All that remains in the present are the voice, the presence, and the importance of fulfilling my mission. I don't regret the difficulties I experienced; I think they helped me to become the person I am today. I feel the way a warrior must feel after years of training: he doesn't remember the details of everything he learned, but he knows how to strike when the time is right.'

'And why did you and that journalist keep coming to visit us?'

'To take nourishment. As the old nomad from the steppes said, the world we know today is merely a story someone has told to us, but it is not the true story. The other story includes special gifts and powers and the ability to go beyond what we know. I have lived with the presence ever since I was a child and, for a time, was even capable of seeing her, but Esther showed me that I was not alone. She introduced me to other people with special gifts, people who could bend forks by sheer force of will, or carry out surgery using rusty penknives and without anaesthetic, so that the patient could get up after the operation and leave.

I am still learning to develop my unknown potential, but I need allies, people like you who have no personal history.'

I felt like telling my story to these strangers too, in order to begin the process of freeing myself from the past, but it was late and I had to get up early the next day to see the doctor and have him remove the orthopaedic collar.

* * *

I asked Mikhail if he wanted a lift, but he said no, he needed to walk a little, because he felt Esther's absence particularly acutely that night. We left the group and headed for a street where I would be able to find a taxi.

'I think that woman was right,' I said. 'If you tell a story, then that means you're still not really free of it.'

'I am free, but, as I'm sure you'll understand, therein lies the secret; there are always some stories that are "interrupted", and they are the stories that remain nearest to the surface and so still occupy the present; only when we close that story or chapter can we begin the next one.'

I remembered reading something similar on the Internet; it was attributed to me, although I didn't write it:

That is why it is so important to let certain things go. To release them. To cut loose. People need to understand that no one is playing with marked cards; sometimes we win and sometimes we lose. Don't expect to get anything back, don't expect recognition for your efforts, don't expect your genius to be discovered or your love to be understood. Complete the circle. Not out of pride, inability or arrogance, but simply because whatever it is no longer fits in your life. Close the door, change the record, clean the house, get rid of the dust. Stop being who you were and become who you are.

But I had better find out what Mikhail means.

'What are "interrupted stories"?'

'Esther isn't here. She reached a point where she could go no further in the process of emptying herself of unhappiness and allowing joy to flow in. Why? Because her story, like that of millions of other people, is bound up with the energy of love. It can't evolve on its own: she must either stop loving or wait until her beloved comes to her.

In failed marriages, when one person stops walking, the other is forced to do the same. And while he or she is waiting, other lovers appear, or there is charitable work to get involved in, there are the children to worry about, there are long hours at the office, etc. It would be much easier to talk openly about things, to insist, to yell: "Let's move on, we're dying of tedium, anxiety, fear."'

'Are you telling me that Esther can't continue with the process of freeing herself from sadness because of me?'

'No, that's not what I meant. I don't believe that one person can blame another, under any circumstances. All

I said was that she has a choice between stopping loving you or making you come to her.'

'That's what she's doing.'

'I know, but, if it were up to me, we would only go to her when the voice allows us to.'

'Right, this should be the last you see of the orthopaedic collar, I certainly hope so anyway. But, please, avoid making any sudden movements. Your muscles need to get used to working on their own again. By the way, what happened to the girl who made those predictions?'

'What girl? What predictions?'

'Didn't you tell me at the hospital that someone had claimed to hear a voice warning that something was going to happen to you?'

'Oh, it wasn't a girl. And you said you were going to find out about epilepsy for me.'

'Yes, I got in touch with a specialist and asked him if he knew of any such cases. His answer surprised me a bit, but let me just remind you that medicine has its mysteries. Do you remember the story I told you about the boy who goes out to buy five apples and returns with two?'

'Yes, and how he might have lost them or given them away, or else they might have turned out to be more expensive than expected, etc. Don't worry, I know there are no absolute answers. But, first, did Joan of Arc suffer from epilepsy?'

'Oddly enough, my friend mentioned her during our conversation. Joan of Arc started hearing voices when she was thirteen. Her statements reveal that she saw lights, which is one of the symptoms of an attack.

According to the neurologist, Dr Lydia Bayne, the warrior-saint's ecstatic experiences were caused by what we now call musicogenic epilepsy, which is provoked by hearing a particular kind of sound or music: in Joan's case, it was the sound of bells. Were you there when the boy had a fit?'

'Yes.'

'Was there any music playing?'

'I can't remember. But even if there was, the clatter of cutlery and the buzz of conversation would have drowned it out.'

'Did he seem tense?'

'Yes, very.'

'That's another thing that can provoke a attack. Epilepsy has been around for longer than you might think. In Mesopotamia, there are remarkably accurate descriptions of what they called "the falling sickness", which was followed by convulsions. Ancient people believed that it was caused by demons invading a person's body; only much later on did the Greek Hippocrates relate these convulsions to some dysfunction of the brain. Even so, epileptics are still the victims of prejudice.'

'I'm sure. I was absolutely terrified when it happened.'

'You mentioned the word prophecy, and so I asked my friend to concentrate his researches in that area. According to him, most scientists agree that, although a lot of famous people have suffered from epilepsy, the disease itself does not confer greater or lesser powers on anyone. Nevertheless, the more famous epileptics did succeed in persuading other people to see their fits as having a "mystical aura".'

'Give me an example of some famous epileptics.'

'Napoleon, Alexander the Great, Dante … I didn't make a full list, since what you were interested in was the boy's prophecy. What's his name, by the way?'

'You don't know him, and since you've nearly always got another appointment to go to, perhaps you'd better just finish your explanation.'

'All right. Medical scientists who study the Bible are sure that the Apostle Paul was an epileptic. They base this on the fact that, on the road to Damascus, he saw a brilliant light near him which caused him to fall to the ground, leaving him temporarily blind and unable to eat or drink for some days. In medical terms, this is known as "temporal lobe epilepsy".'

'I don't think the Church would agree.'

'I'm not even sure that I agree, but that's what the medical literature says. Other epileptics develop their self-destructive side, as was the case with van Gogh. He described his convulsions as "the storm within". In Saint-Rémy, where he was a patient, one of the nurses saw him having a convulsive seizure.'

'At least he managed in his paintings to transform his self-destruction into a reconstruction of the world.'

'Some people suspect that Lewis Carroll wrote *Alice in Wonderland* in order to describe his own experiences of epilepsy. The story at the beginning of the book, when Alice falls down a black hole, is an experience familiar to most epileptics. During her journey through Wonderland, Alice often sees things flying and she herself feels very light – another very precise description of the effects of an epileptic attack.'

'So it would seem epileptics have a propensity for art.'

'Not at all, it's just that because artists tend to become famous, art and epilepsy become linked in people's minds. Literature is full of examples of writers with a suspected or confirmed diagnosis of epilepsy: Molière, Edgar Allan Poe, Flaubert … Dostoevsky had his first attack when he was nine years old, and said that it brought him moments when he felt utterly at peace with the world as well as moments of terrible depression. Don't take all of this too seriously, and don't go thinking that you might develop epilepsy because of your accident. I haven't come across a single case of epilepsy being caused by colliding with a motorbike.'

'As I said, this is someone I actually know.'

'Does the boy with the predictions really exist or did you invent all this simply because you think you might have passed out when you stepped off the pavement?'

'On the contrary, I hate knowing about illnesses. Whenever I read a medical book, I immediately start to get all the symptoms.'

'Let me tell you something, but please don't take it the wrong way. I think this accident did you a lot of good. You seem calmer, less obsessed. A brush with death always helps us to live our lives better; that's what your wife told me when she gave me a bit of blood-stained fabric, which I always carry with me, even though, as a doctor, I see death, close to, every day.'

'Did she say why she gave you the cloth?'

'She was very generous in her description of my work. She said that I was capable of combining technique with intuition, discipline with love. She told me that a soldier, before he died, had asked her to take his blood-soaked shirt, cut it into pieces and share those pieces out amongst people who were genuinely trying to reveal the world as it is. I imagine you, with all your books, must also have a bit of this shirt.'

'No, I haven't.'

'Do you know why?'

'I do, or, rather, I'm beginning to find out.'

'And since I'm not only your doctor, but your friend, may I give you some advice? If this epileptic boy did tell you that he can foresee the future, then he knows nothing about medicine.'

Zagreb, Croatia.
6.30 a.m.

Marie and I are sitting by a frozen fountain. It appears that, this year, spring has decided not to happen; indeed, it looks as if we will jump straight from winter into summer. In the middle of the fountain stands a column with a statue on top.

I have spent the entire afternoon giving interviews and cannot bear to say another word about my new book. The journalists all ask the usual questions: has my wife read the book (I don't know); do I feel I've been unfairly treated by the critics (what?); has *A Time to Rend and a Time to Sew* shocked my readers at all, given that I reveal a great deal about my personal life (a writer can only write about his own life); will the book be made into a film (I repeat for the nth time that the film happens in the reader's mind and that I have forbidden the sale of film rights on any of my books); what do I think about love; why did I choose to write about love; how can one be happy in love, love, love, love …

Once the interviews are over, there's the publisher's supper – it's part of the ritual. The table is packed with local worthies who keep interrupting me just as I'm about to put my fork in my mouth, and usually ask the same thing: 'Where do you find your inspiration?' I try to eat, but I must also be pleasant, I must chat, fulfil my role as celebrity, tell a few interesting stories, make a good impression. I know that the publisher is a real hero, because he can never tell whether a book will sell or not; he could be selling bananas or soap instead; it would certainly be easier: they're not vain, they don't have inflated egos, they don't complain if they don't like the publicity campaign or if their book doesn't appear in a particular bookshop.

After supper, it's the usual routine: they want to show me their city's monuments, historic places, fashionable bars. There is always a guide who knows absolutely everything and fills my head with information, and I have to look as if I'm really listening and ask the occasional question just to show interest. I know nearly all the monuments, museums and historic places of all the many cities I have visited to promote my work – and I can't remember any of them. What I do remember are the unexpected things, the meetings with readers, the bars, perhaps a street I happened to walk down, where I turned a corner and came upon something wonderful.

One day, I'm going to write a travel guide containing only maps, addresses of hotels, and with the rest of the pages blank. That way people will have to make their own itinerary, to discover for themselves restaurants, monuments, and all the magnificent things that every city has, but which are never mentioned because 'the history we have been taught' does not include them under the heading 'Things you must see'.

I've been to Zagreb before. And this fountain doesn't appear in any of the local tourist guides, but it is far more important to me than anything else I saw here – because it is pretty, because I discovered it by chance, and because it is linked to a story in my life. Many years ago, when I was a young man travelling the world in search of adventure, I sat in this very spot with a Croatian painter who had travelled with me for much of the journey. I was heading off into Turkey and he was going home. We said goodbye here, drank two bottles of wine between us, and talked about everything that had happened while we had been together, about religion, women, music, the price of hotels, drugs. We talked about everything except love, because although there were people we loved, there was no need to talk about it.

After the painter had returned to his house, I met a young woman and we spent three days together and loved each other with great intensity because we both knew that it would not last very long. She helped me to understand the soul of those people and I never forgot her, just as I never forgot the fountain or saying goodbye to my travelling companion.

This was why – after the interviews, the autographs, the supper, the visits to monuments and historic places – I pestered my publishers into bringing me to this fountain. They asked me where it was, and I had no idea, just as I had no idea that Zagreb had so many fountains. After nearly an hour of searching, we finally managed to locate it. I asked for a bottle of wine, we said goodbye to everyone, and Marie and I sat down together in silence, our arms about each other, drinking wine and waiting for the sun to come up.

'You seem to get happier and happier by the day,' she says, resting her head on my shoulder.

'That's because I'm trying to forget who I am. Or rather, I don't need to carry the weight of my whole history on my shoulders.'

I tell her about Mikhail's conversation with the nomad.

'It's rather like that with actors,' she says. 'With each new role, we have to stop being who we are in order to become the character. We tend to end up confused and neurotic. Is it such a good idea to abandon your personal history, do you think?'

'Didn't you say I seemed better?'

'Less egotistical, yes. Although it amused me the way you wouldn't let us rest until you found this fountain, but that goes against what you've just said, since the fountain is part of your past.'

'For me, it's a symbol. But I don't carry this fountain around with me, I don't think about it all the time, I don't take photos of it to show my friends, I don't long for the painter or for the young woman I fell in love with. It's really good to come back here again, but if I hadn't come back, it wouldn't make any difference to that initial experience.'

'I see what you're saying.'

'I'm glad.'

'And I'm sad, because it makes me think that you're about to leave. I've known you would ever since we first met, but it's still difficult, because I've got used to being with you.'

'That's the problem, we do get used to things.'

'It's human too.'

'That's why the woman I married became the Zahir. Until I had that accident, I had convinced myself that I could only be happy with her, not because I loved her more than anything and anyone in the world, but because I thought only she could understand me; she knew my likes, my eccentricities, my way of seeing the world. I was grateful for what she had done for me, and I thought she should be grateful for what I had done for her. I was used to seeing the world through her eyes. Do you remember that story about the two firemen who emerge from the fire and one has his face all blackened by smoke?'

She sat up straight. I noticed that her eyes were full of tears.

'Well, that is what the world was like for me,' I went on. 'A reflection of Esther's beauty. Is that love? Or is that dependency?'

'I don't know. I think love and dependency go hand in hand.'

'Possibly. But let's suppose that instead of writing *A Time to Rend and a Time to Sew*, which is really just a letter to a woman who is far away, I had chosen a different plot, for example, a husband and wife who have been together for ten years. They used to make love every day, now they only make love once a week, but that doesn't really matter because there is also solidarity, mutual support, companionship. He feels sad when he has to have supper alone because she is working late. She hates it when he has to go away, but accepts that it is part of his job. They feel that something is missing, but they are both grown-ups, they are both mature people, and they know how important it is to keep their relationship stable, even if only for the children's sake. They devote more and more time to work and to the children, they think less and less about their marriage. Everything appears to be going really well, and there's certainly no other man or woman in their lives.

Yet they sense that something is wrong. They can't quite put their finger on the problem. As time passes, they grow more and more dependent on each other; they are getting older; any opportunities to make a new life are vanishing fast. They try to keep busy doing reading or embroidery, watching television, seeing friends, but there is always the conversation over supper or after supper. He is easily irritated, she is more silent than usual. They can see that they are growing farther and farther apart, but cannot understand why. They reach the conclusion that this is what marriage is like, but won't talk to their friends about it; they are the image of the happy couple who support each other and share the same interests. She takes a lover, so does he, but it's never anything serious, of course. What is important, necessary, essential, is to act as if nothing was happening, because it's too late to change.'

'I know that story, although I've never experienced it myself. And I think we spend our lives being trained to put up with situations like that.'

I take off my coat and climb onto the edge of the fountain. She asks me what I'm doing.

'I'm going to walk over to that column in the middle of the fountain.'

'You're mad. It's spring now, the ice will be getting really thin.'

'I need to walk over to the column.'

I place one foot on the surface, the whole sheet of ice moves, but does not crack. With one eye on the rising sun, I make a kind of wager with God: if I manage to reach the column and come back without the ice cracking, that will be a sign that I am on the right path, and that His hand is showing me where I should go.

'You'll fall in the water.'

'So? The worst that can happen is that I'll get a bit cold, but the hotel isn't far away and I won't have to suffer for long.'

I put my other foot on the ice: I am now in the fountain. The ice breaks away from the edges and a little water laps onto the surface of the ice, but the ice does not break. I set off towards the column. It's only about four metres there and back, and all I risk is getting a very cold bath. However, I mustn't think about what might happen: I've taken the first step and I must continue to the end.

I reach the column, touch it with my hand, hear everything around me creaking, but I'm still on the ice. My first instinct is to run back, but something tells me that if I do that, my steps will become heavier, firmer and I'll fall into the water. I must walk back slowly, at the same pace.

The sun is rising ahead of me; it dazzles me slightly. I can see only Marie's silhouette and the shapes of the buildings and the trees. The sheet of ice keeps shifting, water spills over onto the surface, but I know – with absolute certainty – that I will reach the edge. I am in communion with the day, with my choices. I know the limits of the frozen water; I know how to deal with it, how to ask for its help, to keep me from falling. I begin to enter a kind of trance, a euphoric state; I am a child again, doing something that is wrong, forbidden, but which gives me enormous pleasure. Wonderful! Crazy pacts with God, along the lines of 'If I manage to do this, then so and so will happen', signs provoked not by anything that comes from outside, but by instinct, by my capacity to forget the old rules and create new situations.

I am grateful for having met Mikhail, the epileptic who thinks he can hear voices. I went to his 'meeting' at the restaurant in search of my wife and discovered that I was turning into a pale reflection of myself. Is Esther still important? I think so, for it was her love that changed my life once and which is transforming me now. My history had grown old and was becoming ever heavier to carry, and far too serious for me ever to take risks like walking on ice, making a wager with God, forcing a sign to appear. I had forgotten that one has to continue walking the road to Santiago, to discard any unnecessary baggage, to keep only what you need in order to live each day, and to allow the energy of love to flow freely, from the outside in and from the inside out.

Another cracking sound, and a fault line appears across the surface, but I know I will make it, because I am light, so light that I could even walk on a cloud and not fall to earth. I am not carrying with me the weight of fame, of stories I have told, of itineraries to follow. I am so transparent that the sun's rays can penetrate my body and illumine my soul. I see that there are still many dark areas inside me, but with perseverance and courage they will gradually be washed away.

Another step, and I remember the envelope on my desk at home. Soon I will open it and, instead of walking on ice, I will set off along the path that leads me to Esther. I will do so not because I want her by my side, for she is free to remain where she is. It is not because I dream day and night of the Zahir; that loving, destructive obsession seems to have vanished. It is not because I am used to my past as it was and passionately want to go back to it.

Another step, more sounds of cracking, but safety and the edge of the fountain are close.

I will open the envelope and go and find her because – as Mikhail, the epileptic, the seer, the guru of the Armenian restaurant, says – this story needs to reach its end. When everything has been told and retold countless times, when the places I have visited, the things I have experienced, the steps I have taken because of her are all transformed into distant memories, nothing will remain but pure love. I won't feel as if I 'owe' anything, I won't feel that I need her because only she can understand me, because I'm used to her, because she knows my vices and my virtues, knows that I like to have a slice of toast before I go to bed and to watch the international news when I wake up, that I have to go for a walk every morning, or that she knows about my collection of books on archery, about the hours spent in front of the computer screen, writing, about how annoyed I get when the maid keeps calling me to tell me the food is on the table.

All that will disappear. What remains will be the love that moves the heavens, the stars, people, flowers, insects, the love that obliges us all to walk across the ice despite the danger, that fills us with joy and with fear, and gives meaning to everything.

I touch the edge of the fountain, a hand reaches out to me, I grab hold of it, and Marie helps to steady me as I step down.

'I'm proud of you. I would never do anything like that.'

'Not so long ago, I wouldn't have either; it seems so childish, irresponsible, unnecessary, pointless. But I am being reborn and I need to take new risks.'

'The morning light is obviously good for you; you're talking like a wise man.'

'No wise man would do what I've just done.'

I have to write an important article for a magazine that is one of my major creditors in the Favour Bank. I have hundreds, thousands of ideas in my head, but I don't know which of them merits my effort, my concentration, my blood.

It is not the first time this has happened, but I feel as if I have said everything of importance that I need to say, I feel as if I'm losing my memory and forgetting who I am.

I go over to the window and look out at the street. I try to convince myself that I am professionally fulfilled and have nothing more to prove, that I can justifiably withdraw to a house in the mountains and spend the rest of my life reading, walking and talking about food and the weather. I tell myself over and over that I have achieved what almost no other writer has achieved – my books have been translated into nearly every written language in the world. Why worry about a mere magazine article, however important the magazine itself might be? Because of the Favour Bank. So I really do need to write something, but what have I got to say to people? Should I tell them that they need to forget all the stories that have been told to them and take more risks?

They'll all say: 'I'm an independent being, thank you very much. I'll do as I please.'

Should I tell them that they must allow the energy of love to flow more freely?

They'll say: 'I feel love already. In fact, I feel more and more love', as if love could be measured the way we measure the distance between two railway tracks, the height of buildings, or the amount of yeast needed to make a loaf of bread.

I return to my desk. The envelope Mikhail left for me is open. I now know where Esther is; I just need to know how to get there. I phone him and tell him about my walk across the ice. He is impressed. I ask him what he's doing tonight, and he says he's going out with his girlfriend, Lucrecia. I suggest taking them both to supper. No, not tonight, but, if I like, I could go out with him and his friends next week.

I tell him that next week I'm giving a talk in America. There's no hurry, he says, we can wait two weeks.

'You must have heard a voice telling you to walk on the ice,' he says.

'No, I heard no voice.'

'So why did you do it?'

'Because I felt it needed to be done.'

'That's just another way of hearing the voice.'

'I made a bet. If I could cross the ice, that meant I was ready. And I think I am.'

'Then the voice gave you the sign you needed.'

'Did the voice say anything to you about it?'

'No, it didn't have to. When we were on the banks of the Seine and I said that the voice would tell us when the time had come, I knew that it would also tell you.'

'As I said, I didn't hear a voice.'

'That's what you think. That's what everyone thinks. And yet, judging by what the presence tells me, everyone hears voices all the time. They are what help us to know when we are face to face with a sign, you see.'

I decide not to argue. I just need some practical details: where to hire a car, how long the journey takes, how to find the house, because otherwise all I have, apart from the map, are a series of vague indications – follow the lake shore, look for a company sign, turn right, etc. Perhaps he knows someone who can help me.

We arrange our next meeting. Mikhail asks me to dress as discreetly as possible – the 'tribe' is going walkabout in Paris.

I ask him who this tribe is. 'They're the people who work with me at the restaurant,' he replies, without going into detail. I ask him if he wants me to bring him anything from America, and he asks for a particular remedy for heartburn. There are, I think, more interesting things I could bring, but I make a note of his request.

***

And the article?

I go back to the desk, think about what I'm going to write, look again at the open envelope, and conclude that I was not surprised by what I found inside. After a few meetings with Mikhail, it was pretty much what I had expected.

Esther is living in the steppes, in a small village in Central Asia; more precisely, in a village in Kazakhstan.

I am no longer in a hurry. I continue reviewing my own story, which I tell to Marie in obsessive detail; she has decided to do the same, and I am surprised by some of the things she tells me, but the process seems to be working; she is more confident, less anxious.

I don't know why I so want to find Esther, now that my love for her has illumined my life, taught me new things, which is quite enough really. But I remember what Mikhail said: 'The story needs to reach its end', and I decide to go on. I know that I will discover the moment when the ice of our marriage cracked, and how we carried on walking through the chill water, as if nothing had happened. I know that I will discover this before I reach that village, in order to close the circle or make it larger still.

The article! Has Esther become the Zahir again, thus preventing me from concentrating on anything else?

No, when I need to do something urgent, something that requires creative energy, this is my working method: I get into a state of near hysteria, decide to abandon the task altogether, and then the article appears. I've tried doing things differently, preparing everything carefully, but my imagination only works when it's under enormous pressure. I must respect the Favour Bank, I must write three pages about – guess what! – the problems of male–female relationships. Me, of all people! But the editors believe that the man who wrote *A Time to Rend and a Time to Sew* must know the human soul well.

I try to log on to the Internet, but it's not working. It's never been the same since I destroyed the connection. I called various technicians, but, when they finally turned up, they could find nothing wrong with the computer. They asked me what I was complaining about, spent half an hour doing tests, changed the configuration, and assured me that the problem lay not with me but with the server. I allowed myself to be convinced that everything was, in fact, fine, and I felt ridiculous for having asked for help. Two or three hours later, the computer and the connection would both crash. Now, after months of physical and psychological wear and tear, I simply accept that technology is stronger and more powerful than me: it works when it wants to, and when it doesn't, it's best to sit down and read the paper or go for a walk, and just wait until the cables and the telephone links are in a better mood and the computer decides to work again. I am not, I have discovered, my computer's master: it has a life of its own.

I try a few more times, but I know from experience that it's best just to give up. The Internet, the biggest library in the world, has closed its doors to me for the moment. What about reading a few magazines in search of inspiration? I pick up one that has just arrived in the post and read a strange interview with a woman who has recently published a book about – guess what? – love? The subject seems to be pursuing me everywhere.

The journalist asks if the only way a human being can find happiness is by finding his or her beloved. The woman says 'No'.

The idea that love leads to happiness is a modern invention, dating from the end of the seventeenth century. Ever since then, people have been taught to believe that love should last for ever and that marriage is the best place in which to exercise that love. In the past, there was less optimism about the longevity of passion. Romeo and Juliet isn't a happy story, it's a tragedy. In the last few decades, expectations about marriage as the road to personal fulfilment have grown considerably, as have disappointment and dissatisfaction.

It's quite a brave thing to say, but no good for my article, mainly because I don't agree with her at all. I search my shelves for a book that has nothing to do with male–female relationships: *Magical Practices in North Mexico.* Since obsession will not help me to write my article, I need to refresh my mind, to relax.

I start leafing through it and suddenly I read something that surprises me:

The acomodador *or giving-up point: there is always an event in our lives that is responsible for us failing to progress: a trauma, a particularly bitter defeat, a disappointment in love, even a victory that we did not quite understand, can make cowards of us and prevent us from moving on. As part of the process of increasing his hidden powers, the shaman must first free himself from that giving-up point and, to do so, he must review his whole life and find out where it occurred.*

The *acomodador*. This fitted in with my experience of learning archery – the only sport I enjoyed – for the teacher of archery says that no shot can ever be repeated, and there is no point trying to learn from good or bad shots. What matters is repeating it hundreds and thousands of times, until we have freed ourselves from the idea of hitting the target and have ourselves become the arrow, the bow, the target. At that moment, the energy of the 'thing' (my teacher of *kyudo* – the form of Japanese archery I practised – never used the word 'God') guides our movements and then we begin to release the arrow not when we want to, but when the 'thing' believes that the moment has come.

The *acomodador*. Another part of my personal history resurfaces. If only Marie were here! I need to talk about myself, about my childhood, to tell her how, when I was little, I was always fighting and beating up the other children because I was the oldest in the class. One day, my cousin gave me a thrashing, and I was convinced from then on that I would never ever win another fight, and since then I have avoided any physical confrontation, even though this has often meant me behaving like a coward and being humiliated in front of girlfriends and friends alike.

The *acomodador*. For two years, I tried to learn how to play the guitar. To begin with, I made rapid progress, but then reached a point where I could progress no further, because I discovered that other people were learning faster than I was, which made me feel mediocre; and so as not to have to feel ashamed, I decided that I was no longer interested in learning. The same thing happened with snooker, football, bicycle racing. I learned enough to do everything reasonably well, but there was always a point where I got stuck.

Why?

Because according to the story we are told, there always comes a moment in our lives when we reach 'our limit'. I often recalled my struggle to deny my destiny as a writer and how Esther had always refused to allow the *acomodador* to lay down rules for my dream. The paragraph I had just read fitted in with the idea of forgetting one's personal history and being left only with the instinct that develops out of the various difficulties and tragedies one has experienced. This is what the shamans of Mexico did and what the nomads on the steppes of Central Asia preached.

The *acomodador*: 'there is always an event in our lives that is responsible for us failing to progress'.

It described exactly what happens in marriages in general and what had happened in my relationship with Esther in particular.

I could now write my article for that magazine. I went over to the computer and within half an hour I had written a first draft and was happy with the result. I wrote a story in the form of a dialogue, as if it were fiction, but which was, in fact, a conversation I had had in a hotel room in Amsterdam, after a day spent promoting my books and after the usual publishers' supper and the statutory tour of the sights, etc.

In my article, the names of the characters and the situation in which they find themselves are omitted. In real life, Esther is in her nightdress and is looking out at the canal outside our window. She has not yet become a war correspondent, her eyes are still bright with joy, she loves her work, travels with me whenever she can, and life is still one big adventure. I am lying on the bed in silence; my mind is far away, worrying about the next day's appointments.

'Last week, I interviewed a man who's an expert in police interrogations. He told me that they get most of their information by using a technique they call "cold/hot". They always start with a very aggressive policeman who says he has no intention of sticking to the rules, who shouts and thumps the table. When he has scared the prisoner nearly witless, the "good policeman" comes in and tells his colleague to stop, offers the prisoner a cigarette, pretends to be his friend and gets the information he wants.'

'Yes, I've heard about that.'

'Then he told me about something else that really frightened me. In 1971, a group of researchers at Stanford University, in California, decided to create a simulated prison in order to study the psychology of interrogations. They selected twenty-four student volunteers and divided them into "guards" and "criminals".

After just one week, they had to stop the experiment. The "guards" – girls and boys with normal decent values, from nice families – had become real monsters. The use of torture had become routine and the sexual abuse of "prisoners" was seen as normal. The students who took part in the project, both "guards" and "criminals", suffered major traumas and needed long-term medical help, and the experiment was never repeated.'

'Interesting.'

'What do you mean "interesting"? I'm talking about something of real importance: man's capacity to do evil whenever he's given the chance. I'm talking about my work, about the things I've learned!'

'That's what I found interesting. Why are you getting so angry?'

'Angry? How could I possibly get angry with someone who isn't paying the slightest bit of attention to what I'm saying? How can I possibly be angry with someone who isn't even provoking me, who's just lying there, staring into space?'

'How much did you have to drink tonight?'

'You don't even know the answer to that, do you? I've been by your side all evening, and you've no idea whether I've had anything to drink or not! You only spoke to me when you wanted me to confirm something you had said or when you needed me to tell some flattering story about you!'

'Look, I've been working all day and I'm exhausted. Why don't you come to bed and sleep? We can talk in the morning.'

'Because I've been doing this for weeks and months, for the last two years in fact! I try to have a conversation, but you're always tired, so we say, all right, we'll go to sleep and talk tomorrow. But tomorrow there are always other things to do, another day of work and publisher's suppers, so we say, all right, we'll go to sleep and talk tomorrow. That's how I'm spending my life, waiting for the day when I can have you by my side again, until I've had my fill; that's all I ask, to create a world where I can always find refuge if I need it: not so far away that I can't be seen to be having an independent life, and not so close that it looks as if I'm invading your universe.'

'What do you want me to do? Stop working? Give up everything we've struggled so hard to achieve and go off on a cruise to the Caribbean? Don't you understand that I enjoy what I'm doing and haven't the slightest intention of changing my life?'

'In your books, you talk about the importance of love, the need for adventure, the joy of fighting for your dreams. And who do I have before me now? Someone who doesn't read what he writes. Someone who confuses love with convenience, adventure with taking unnecessary risks, joy with obligation. Where is the man I married, who used to listen to what I was saying?'

'Where is the woman I married?'

'You mean the one who always gave you support, encouragement and affection? Her body is here, looking out at the Singel canal in Amsterdam, and she will, I believe, stay with you for the rest of her life. But that woman's soul is standing at the door ready to leave.'

'But why?'

'Because of those three wretched words: "we'll talk tomorrow". Isn't that enough? If not, just consider that the woman you married was excited about life, full of ideas and joy and desires, and is now rapidly turning into a housewife.'

'That's ridiculous.'

'Of course it is! It's nonsense! A trifle, especially considering that we have everything we could possibly want. We're very fortunate, we have money, we never discuss any little flings we might have, we never have jealous rages. Besides, there are millions of children in the world starving to death, there are wars, diseases, hurricanes, tragedies happening every second. So what can I possibly have to complain about?'

'Do you think we should have a baby?'

'That's how all the couples I know resolve their problems – by having a baby! You're the one who has always prized your freedom and put off having children for later on. Have you really changed your mind?'

'I think the time is right.'

'Well, in my opinion, you couldn't be more wrong! I don't want your child. I want a child by the man I knew, who had dreams, who was always by my side! If I ever do become pregnant it will be by someone who understands me, keeps me company, listens to me, who truly desires me!'

'You *have* been drinking. Look, I promise, we'll talk tomorrow, but, please, come to bed now, I'm tired.'

'All right, we'll talk tomorrow. And if my soul, which is standing at the door, does decide to leave, I doubt it will affect our lives very much.'

'Your soul won't leave.'

'You used to know my soul very well, but you haven't spoken to it for years, you don't know how much it has changed, how *desperately* it's begging you to listen. Even to banal topics of conversation, like experiments at American universities.'

'If your soul has changed so much, how come you're the same?'

'Out of cowardice. Because I genuinely think that tomorrow we *will* talk. Because of everything we've built together and which I don't want to see destroyed.

Or for that worst of all possible reasons, because I've simply given up.'

'That's just what you've been accusing me of doing.'

'You're right. I looked at you, thinking it was you I was looking at, but the truth is I was looking at myself. Tonight I'm going to pray with all my might and all my faith and ask God not to let me spend the rest of my days like this.'

I hear the applause, the theatre is packed. I'm about to do the one thing that always gives me sleepless nights, I'm about to give a lecture.

The master of ceremonies begins by saying that there's no need to introduce me, which is a bit much really, since that's what he's there for and he isn't taking into account the possibility that there might be lots of people in the audience who have simply been invited along by friends. Despite what he says, however, he ends up giving a few biographical details and talking about my qualities as a writer, the prizes I've won, and the millions of books I've sold. He thanks the sponsors, turns to me and the floor is mine.

I thank him too. I tell the audience that the most important things I have to say are in my books, but that I feel I have an obligation to my public to reveal the man who lies behind those words and paragraphs. I explain that our human condition makes us tend to share only the best of ourselves, because we are always searching for love and approval. My books, however, will only ever be the mountain top visible amongst the clouds, or an island in the ocean: the light falls on it, everything seems to be in its place, but beneath the surface lies the unknown, the darkness, the incessant search for self.

I describe how difficult it was to write *A Time to Rend and a Time to Sew*, and that there are many parts of the book which I myself am only beginning to understand now, as I re-read it, as if the created thing were always greater and more generous than its creator.

I say that there is nothing more boring than reading interviews or going to lectures by authors who insist on explaining the characters in their books: if a book isn't self-explanatory, then the book isn't worth reading. When a writer appears in public, he should attempt to show the audience his universe, not try to explain his books; and in this spirit, I begin talking about something more personal.

'Some time ago, I was in Geneva for a series of interviews. At the end of a day's work, and because a woman friend I was supposed to have supper with cancelled at the last minute, I set off for a stroll around the city. It was a particularly lovely night, the streets were deserted, the bars and restaurants still full of life, and everything seemed utterly calm, orderly, pretty, and yet suddenly … suddenly I realised that I was utterly alone.

Needless to say, I had been alone on other occasions during the year. Needless to say, my girlfriend was only two hours away by plane. Needless to say, after a busy day, what could be better than a stroll through the narrow streets and lanes of the old city, without having to talk to anyone, simply enjoying the beauty around me. And yet the feeling that surfaced was one of oppressive, distressing loneliness – not having someone with whom I could share the city, the walk, the things I'd like to say.

I got out my mobile phone; after all, I had a reasonable number of friends in the city, but it was too late to phone anyone. I considered going into one of the bars and ordering a drink; someone was bound to recognise me and invite me to join them. But I resisted the temptation and tried to get through that moment, discovering, in the process, that there is nothing worse than the feeling that no one cares whether we exist or not, that no one is interested in what we have to say about life, and that the world can continue turning without our awkward presence.

I began to imagine how many millions of people were, at that moment, feeling utterly useless and wretched – however rich, charming and delightful they might be – because they were alone that night, as they were yesterday, and as they might well be tomorrow. Students with no one to go out with, older people sitting in front of the TV as if it were their sole salvation, businessmen in their hotel rooms, wondering if what they were doing made any sense, women who spent the afternoon carefully applying their makeup and doing their hair in order to go to a bar only to pretend that they're not looking for company; all they want is confirmation that they're still attractive; the men ogle them and chat them up, but the women reject them all disdainfully, because they feel inferior and are afraid the men will find out that they're single mothers or lowly clerks with nothing to say about what's going on in the world because they work from dawn to dusk to scrape a living and have no time to read the newspapers. People who look at themselves in the mirror and think themselves ugly, believing that being beautiful is what really matters, and spend their time reading magazines in which everyone is pretty, rich, and famous. Husbands and wives who wish they could talk over supper as they used to, but there are always other things demanding their attention, more important things, and the conversation can always wait for a tomorrow that never comes.

That day, I had lunch with a friend who had just got divorced and she said to me: 'Now I can enjoy the freedom I've always dreamed of having.' But that's a lie. No one wants that kind of freedom: we all want commitment, we all want someone to be beside us to enjoy the beauties of Geneva, to discuss books, interviews, films, or even to share a sandwich with because there isn't enough money to buy one each. Better to eat half a sandwich than a whole one. Better to be interrupted by the man who wants to get straight back home because there's a big game on TV tonight or by the woman who stops outside a shop window and interrupts what we were saying about the cathedral tower, far better that than to have the whole of Geneva to yourself with all the time and quiet in the world to visit it.

Better to go hungry than to be alone. Because when you're alone – and I'm talking here about an enforced solitude not of our choosing – it's as if you were no longer part of the human race.

A lovely hotel awaited me on the other side of the river, with its luxurious rooms, its attentive employees, its five-star service. And that only made me feel worse, because I should have felt contented, satisfied with all I had achieved.

On the way back, I passed other people in the same situation and noticed that they fell into two categories: those who looked arrogant, because they wanted to pretend they had chosen to be alone on that lovely night, and those who looked sad and ashamed of their solitary state.

I'm telling you all this because the other day I remembered being in a hotel room in Amsterdam with a woman who was talking to me about her life. I'm telling you all this because, although in Ecclesiastes it says there is a time to rend and a time to sew, sometimes the time to rend leaves deep scars. Being with someone else and making that person feel as if they were of no importance in our life is far worse than feeling alone and miserable in the streets of Geneva.'

There was a long moment of silence before the applause.

I arrived in a gloomy part of Paris, which was nevertheless said to have the most vibrant cultural life of the whole city. It took me a while to recognise the scruffy group of people before me as the same ones who appeared on Thursdays in the Armenian restaurant immaculately dressed in white.

'Why are you all wearing fancy dress? Is this some kind of tribute to a movie?'

'It's not fancy dress,' replied Mikhail. 'Don't you change your clothes to go to a gala supper? Would you wear a jacket and tie to play golf?'

'All right, let me put the question another way: why have you decided to dress like young homeless people?'

'Because, at this moment, we are young homeless people, or, rather, four young homeless people and two homeless adults.'

'Let me put the question a third way, then: why are you dressed like that?'

'In the restaurant, we feed our body and talk about the Energy to people with something to lose. Amongst the beggars, we feed our soul and talk to those who have nothing to lose. Now, we come to the most important part of our work: meeting the members of the invisible movement that is renewing the world, people who live each day as if it were their last, while the old live each day as if it were their first.'

He was talking about something I had already noticed and which seemed to be growing by the day: this was how young people dressed, in grubby, but highly imaginative outfits, based on military uniforms or sci-fi movies. They all went in for body-piercing too and sported highly individual haircuts. Often, the groups were accompanied by a threatening-looking Alsatian dog. I once asked a friend why these people always had a dog with them and he told me – although I don't know if it's true – that the police couldn't arrest the owners because they had nowhere to put the dog.

A bottle of vodka began doing the rounds; we had drunk vodka when we were with the beggars and I wondered if this was to do with Mikhail's origins. I took a sip, imagining what people would say if they saw me there.

I decided they would say: 'He's probably doing research for his next book,' and felt more relaxed.

'I'm ready now to go and find Esther, but I need some more information, because I know nothing about your country.'

'I'll go with you.'

'What?'

That wasn't in my plans at all. My journey was a return to everything I had lost in myself, and would end somewhere in the Central Asian steppes. It was something intimate and personal, something that did not require witnesses.

'As long as you pay for my ticket, of course. I need to go back to Kazakhstan. I miss my country.'

'I thought you had work to do here. Haven't you got to be at the restaurant on Thursdays for the performances.'

'You keep calling it a performance. I've told you before, it's a meeting, a way of reviving what we have lost, the tradition of conversation. But don't worry. Anastásia here', and he pointed to a girl wearing a nose stud, 'is already developing her gift. She can take care of everything while I'm away.'

'He's jealous,' said Alma, the woman who played the instrument that looked like a cymbal and who told stories at the end of each 'meeting'.

'Understandable really,' said another boy, who was dressed in a leather outfit adorned with metal studs, safety pins and buckles made to look like razor blades. 'Mikhail is younger, better-looking and more in touch with the Energy.'

'He's also less famous, less rich and less in touch with those in power,' said Anastásia. 'From the female point of view, things are pretty evenly balanced, so I reckon they're both in with a chance.'

Everyone laughed and the bottle went the rounds again. I was the only one who didn't see the joke. I was surprising myself, though; it had been many years since I had sat on a pavement in Paris, and this pleased me.

'The tribe is bigger than you think. They're everywhere, from the Eiffel Tower down as far as the town of Tarbes where I was staying recently. But I can't honestly say I understand what it's all about.'

'They can be found farther south than Tarbes, and they follow routes every bit as interesting as the Road to Santiago. They set off from somewhere in France or somewhere else in Europe, swearing that they're going to be part of a society that exists outside of society. They're afraid of going back home and getting a job and getting married – they'll fight against all that for as long as they can. There are rich and poor amongst them, but they're not that interested in money. They look completely different, and yet when people walk past them, they usually pretend not to see them because they're afraid.'

'Do they have to look so aggressive?'

'Yes, because the passion to destroy is a creative passion. If they weren't aggressive, the boutiques would immediately fill up with clothes like these; publishers would soon be producing magazines about the new movement "sweeping the world with its revolutionary attitudes"; TV programmes would have a strand devoted to the tribe; sociologists would write learned articles; psychiatrists would counsel the families of tribe members, and it would lose all its impact. So the less they know about us, the better: our attack is really a defence.'

'Actually, I only came tonight so that I could ask you for some information, but, who knows, perhaps spending the night with you will turn out to be just the kind of rich and novel experience to move me on from a personal history that no longer allows for new experiences. As for the journey to Kazakhstan, I've no intention of taking anyone with me. If I can't get help from you, the Favour Bank will provide me with all the necessary contacts. I'm going away in two days' time and I'm a guest at an important supper tomorrow night, but after that, I'm free for two weeks.'

Mikhail appeared to hesitate.

'It's up to you. You've got the map, the name of the village, and it shouldn't be hard to find the house where she's staying. I'm sure the Favour Bank can help get you as far as Almaty, but I doubt it will get you much further than that, because the rules of the steppes are different. Besides, I reckon I've made a few deposits in your account at the Favour Bank too. It's time to reclaim them. I miss my mother.'

He was right.

'We've got to start work,' said Alma's husband.

'Why do you want to go with me, Mikhail? Is it really just because you miss your mother?'

He didn't reply. The man started playing the drum and Alma was clanging the cymbal, while the others begged for money from passers-by. Why did he want to go with me? And how would I be able to draw on the Favour Bank in the steppes, if I knew absolutely no one? I could get a visa from the Kazakhstan embassy, hire a car and a guide from the French consulate in Almaty – what else did I need?

I stood there observing the group, not knowing quite what to do. It wasn't the right moment to discuss the trip, and I had work to do and a girlfriend waiting for me at home: why didn't I just leave now?

I didn't leave because I was feeling free, doing things I hadn't done for years, opening up a space in my soul for new experiences, driving the *acomodador* out of my life, experiencing things that might not interest me very much, but which were at least different.

The vodka ran out and was replaced by rum. I hate rum, but since that was all there was, it was best to adapt to the circumstances. The two musicians continued to play and whenever anyone was brave enough to come near, one of the girls would hold out her hand and ask if they had any spare change. The person approached would normally quicken their pace, but would always receive a 'Thanks, have a nice evening'. One person, seeing that he had been offered thanks rather than abuse, turned back and gave us some money.

After watching this scene for more than ten minutes, without anyone in the group addressing a single word to me, I went into a bar, bought two bottles of vodka, came back and poured the rum into the gutter. Anastásia seemed pleased by my gesture and so I tried to start a conversation.

'Can you explain why you all use body-piercing?'

'Why do other people wear jewels or high heels or low-cut dresses even in winter?'

'That's not an answer.'

'We use body-piercing because we're the new barbarians sacking Rome. We don't wear uniforms and so we need something to identify us as one of the invading tribes.'

She made it sound as if they were part of an important historical movement, but for the people going home, they were just a group of unemployed young people with nowhere to sleep, cluttering up the streets of Paris, bothering the tourists who were so good for the local economy, and driving to despair the mothers and fathers who had brought them into the world and now had no control over them.

I had been like that once, when the hippie movement was at its height – the huge rock concerts, the big hair, the garish clothes, the Viking symbol, the peace sign. As Mikhail said, the whole hippie thing had turned into just another consumer product and had vanished, destroying its icons.

A man came down the street. The boy in leather and safety pins went over to him with his hand outstretched. He asked for money. However, instead of hurrying on or muttering something like 'I haven't any change', the man stopped and looked at us and said very loudly:

'I wake up every morning with a debt of approximately 100,000 euros, because of my house, because of the economic situation in Europe, because of my wife's expensive tastes. In other words, I'm worse off than you are and with far more on my mind! How about you giving *me* a bit of change to help me decrease my debt just a little?'

Lucrecia – whom Mikhail claimed was his girlfriend – produced a fifty-euro note and gave it to the man.

'Buy yourself some caviar. You need a bit of joy in your miserable life.'

The man thanked her and walked off, as if it were the most natural thing in the world to be given fifty euros by a beggar. The Italian girl had had a fifty-euro note in her bag and here we were begging in the street!

'Let's go somewhere else,' said the boy in leather.

'Where?' asked Mikhail.

'We could see if we can find the others. North or South?'

Anastásia chose West. After all, she was, according to Mikhail, developing her gift.

* * *

We passed by the Tour de Saint-Jacques where, centuries before, pilgrims heading for Santiago de Compostela used to gather. We passed Notre Dame, where there were a few more 'new barbarians'. The vodka had run out and so I went to buy two more bottles, even though I wasn't sure that everyone in the group was over eighteen. No one thanked me; they seemed to think it was perfectly normal.

I started to feel a little drunk and began eyeing up one of the girls who had just joined us. Everyone talked very loudly, kicked a few litter bins – strange metal objects with a plastic bag dangling from them – and said absolutely nothing of any interest.

We crossed the Seine and were suddenly brought to a halt by one of those orange-and-white tapes that are used to mark off an area under construction. It prevented people from walking along the pavement, forcing them to step off the kerb into the road and then rejoin the pavement five metres further on.

'It's still here,' said one of the new arrivals.

'What's still here?' I asked.

'Who's he?'

'A friend of ours,' replied Lucrecia. 'In fact, you've probably read one of his books.'

The newcomer recognised me, but showed neither surprise nor reverence; on the contrary, he asked if I could give him some money, a request I instantly refused.

'If you want to know why the tape is there, you'll have to give me a euro. Everything in life has its price, as you know better than anyone. And information is one of the most expensive products in the world.'

No one in the group came to my aid, and so I had to pay him a euro for his answer.

'The tape is here because we put it there. As you can see, there are no repairs going on at all, just a stupid orange-and-white tape blocking the stupid pavement. But no one asks what it's doing there; they step off the pavement, walk along the road at the risk of being knocked down and get back on further up. By the way, I read somewhere that you'd had an accident. Is that true?'

'Yes, I did, and all because I stepped off the pavement.'

'Don't worry, when people step off the pavement here, they're always extra careful. It was one of the reasons we put the tape up, to make people more aware of what was going on around them.'

'No, it wasn't,' said the girl I was attracted to. 'It's just a joke, so that we can laugh at the people who obey without even thinking about what they're obeying. There's no reason, it's not important, and no one will get knocked down.'

More people joined the group. Now there were eleven of us and two Alsatian dogs. We were no longer begging, because no one dared go near this band of savages who seemed to enjoy the fear they aroused. The drink had run out again and they all looked at me and asked me to buy another bottle, as if I had a duty to keep them drunk. I realised that this was my 'passport' to the pilgrimage and so set off in search of a shop.

The girl I was interested in – and who was young enough to be my daughter – seemed to notice me looking at her and started talking to me. I knew it was simply a way of provoking me, but I joined in. She didn't tell me anything about her personal life, she just asked me how many cats and how many lamp-posts there were on the back of a ten-dollar bill.

'Cats and lamp-posts?'

'You don't know, do you? You don't give any real value to money at all. Well, for your information, there are four cats and eleven lamp-posts.'

Four cats and eleven lamp-posts. I promised myself that I would check this out the next time I saw a ten-dollar bill.

'Do any of you take drugs?'

'Some, but mainly it's just alcohol. Not much at all, in fact, it's not our style. Drugs are more for people of your generation, aren't they? My mother, for example, drugs herself on cooking for the family, compulsively tidying the house, and suffering over me. When something goes wrong with my dad's business, she suffers. Can you believe that? She suffers over me, my father, my brothers and sisters, everything. I was wasting so much energy pretending to be happy all the time, I thought it was best just to leave home.'

Another personal history.

'Like your wife,' said a young man with fair hair and an eyebrow ring. 'She left home too, didn't she? Was that because she had to pretend to be happy all the time?'

So she had been here too. Had she given some of these young people a piece of that bloodstained shirt?

'She suffered too,' laughed Lucrecia. 'But as far as we know, she's not suffering any more. That's what I call courage!'

'What was my wife doing here?'

'She came with the Mongolian guy, the one with all the strange ideas about love that we're only just beginning to understand. And she used to ask questions and tell us her story. One day, she stopped doing both. She said she was tired of complaining. We suggested that she give up everything and come with us, because we were planning a trip to North Africa. She thanked us, but said she had other plans and would be heading off in the opposite direction.'

'Didn't you read his latest book?' asked Anastásia.

'No, I didn't fancy it, people told me it was too romantic. Now when are we going to get some more booze?'

* * *

People made way for us as if we were samurai riding into a village, bandits arriving in a frontier town, barbarians entering Rome. The tribe didn't make any aggressive gestures, the aggression was all in the clothes, the body-piercing, the loud conversations, the sheer oddness. We finally found a minimart: to my great discomfort and alarm, they all went in and started rummaging around on the shelves.

I didn't know any of them, apart from Mikhail, and even then I didn't know if what he had told me about himself was true. What if they stole something? What if one of them was armed? As the oldest member of the group, was I responsible for their actions?

The man on the till kept glancing up at the security mirror suspended from the ceiling in the tiny shop. The group, knowing that he was worried, spread out, gesturing to each other, and the tension grew. To cut things short, I picked up three bottles of vodka and walked quickly over to the till.

A woman buying cigarettes said that, in her day, Paris had been full of bohemians and artists, not threatening bands of homeless people. She suggested that the cashier call the police.

'I've got a feeling something bad is going to happen any minute now,' she muttered.

The cashier was terrified by this invasion of his little world, the fruit of years of work and many loans, where perhaps his son worked in the morning, his wife in the afternoon and he at night. He nodded to the woman, and I realised that he had already called the police.

I hate getting involved in things that are none of my business, but I also hate being a coward. Every time it happens, I lose all self-respect for a week.

'Don't worry ...' I began.

It was too late.

Two policemen came in and the owner beckoned them over, but the young people disguised as extraterrestrials paid no attention – it was all part of standing up to representatives of the established order. It must have happened to them many times before. They knew they hadn't committed any crime (apart from crimes against fashion, but that could all change with next season's haute couture). They must have been afraid, but they didn't show it and continued talking loudly.

'I saw a comedian the other day. He said that stupid people should have "stupid" written on their identity card,' said Anastásia to no one in particular, 'that way, we'd know who we were talking to.'

'Yeah, stupid people are a real danger to society,' said the girl with the angelic face and vampire clothing, who, shortly before, had been talking to me about the number of lamp-posts and cats to be found on the back of a ten-dollar bill. 'They should be tested once a year and have a licence for walking the streets, like drivers do to drive.'

The policemen, who couldn't have been very much older than the 'tribe', said nothing.

'Do you know what I'd like to do,' it was Mikhail's voice, but I couldn't see him because he was concealed behind a shelf. 'I'd like to change the labels on everything in this shop. People would be completely lost. They wouldn't know whether things should be eaten hot or cold, boiled or fried. If they don't read the instructions, they don't know how to prepare a meal. They've lost all their culinary instincts.'

Everyone who had spoken up until then had done so in perfect Parisian French. Only Mikhail had a foreign accent.

'May I see your passport,' said one of the policemen.

'He's with me.'

The words emerged naturally, even though I knew what it could mean – another scandal. The policeman looked at me.

'I wasn't talking to you, but since you're obviously with this lot, I hope you've got some kind of document to prove who you are, and a good reason for being surrounded by people half your age and buying vodka.'

I could refuse to show my papers. I wasn't legally obliged to have them with me. But I was thinking about Mikhail. One of the policemen was standing next to him now. Did he really have permission to stay in France? What did I know about him apart from the stories he had told me about his visions and his epilepsy? What if the tension of the moment provoked an attack?

I stuck my hand in my pocket and took out my driver's licence.

'So you're ...'

'I am.'

'I thought it was you. I've read one of your books. But that doesn't put you above the law.'

The fact that he had read one of my books threw me completely. There was this shaven-headed young man in a uniform, albeit a very different one from that worn by the 'tribes' in order to tell each other apart. Perhaps he too had once dreamed of having the freedom to be different, of subtly challenging authority, although never disrespectfully enough to end up in jail. He probably had a father who had never offered him any alternative, a family who needed his financial support, or perhaps he was just afraid of going beyond his own familiar world.

I said gently:

'No, I'm not above the law. In fact, no one here has broken the law. Unless the gentleman at the till or the lady buying cigarettes would like to make some specific complaint.'

When I turned round, the woman who had mentioned the artists and bohemians 'of her day', that prophet of imminent doom, the embodiment of truth and good manners, had disappeared. She would doubtless tell her neighbours the next day that, thanks to her, an attempted robbery had been averted.

'I've no complaints,' said the man behind the till, 'I got worried because they were talking so loudly, but it looks like they weren't actually doing any harm.'

'Is the vodka for you, sir?'

I nodded. They knew that everyone there was drunk, but they didn't want to make a big deal out of a harmless situation.

'A world without stupid people would be complete chaos!' said the boy wearing leather and metal studs. 'Instead of all the unemployed people we have today, there would be too many jobs and no one to do the work!'

'Shut up!'

My voice sounded authoritative, decisive.

'Just stop talking, all of you!'

To my surprise, silence fell. My heart was beating furiously, but I continued talking to the policemen as if I were the calmest person in the world.

'If they were really dangerous, they wouldn't be talking like that.'

The policeman turned to the cashier:

'If you need us, we'll be around.'

And before going out, he said to his colleague, so that his voice echoed round the whole shop.

'I love stupid people. If it wasn't for them, we might be having to tackle some real criminals.'

'You're right,' said the other policeman. 'Stupid people are a nice safe distraction.'

They gave their usual salute and left.

The only thing it occurred to me to do when we left the shop, was to smash the bottles of vodka. I saved one of them, though, and it was passed rapidly from mouth to mouth. By the way they were drinking, I could see they were frightened, as frightened as I was. The only difference was that they had gone on the offensive when threatened.

'I don't feel good,' said Mikhail to one of them. 'Let's go.' I didn't know what he meant by 'Let's go': each to his own house or town or bridge? No one asked me if I wanted to go with them, so I simply followed after.

Mikhail's remark 'I don't feel good' unsettled me; that meant we wouldn't have another chance that night to talk about the trip to Central Asia. Should I just leave? Or should I stick it out and see what 'let's go' meant? I discovered that I was enjoying myself and that I'd like to try seducing the girl in the vampire outfit.

Onward, then.

I could always leave at the first sign of danger.

As we headed off – where, I didn't know – I was thinking about this whole experience. A tribe. A symbolic return to a time when men travelled in protective groups and required very little to survive. A tribe in the midst of another hostile tribe called society, crossing society's lands and using aggression as a defence against rejection. A group of people who had joined together to form an ideal society, about which I knew nothing beyond the body-piercing and the clothes that they wore. What were their values? What did they think about life? How did they earn their money? Did they have dreams or was it enough just to wander the world? All this was much more interesting than the supper I had to go to the following evening, where I knew exactly what would happen. I was convinced that it must be the effect of the vodka, but I was feeling free, my personal history was growing ever more remote, there was only the present moment, instinct; the Zahir had disappeared …

The Zahir?

Yes, it had disappeared, but now I realised that the Zahir was more than a man obsessed with an object, with a vein in the marble of one of the twelve hundred columns in the mosque in Córdoba, as Borges puts it, or, as in my own painful case for the last two years, with a woman in Central Asia. The Zahir was a fixation on everything that had been passed from generation to generation; it left no question unanswered, it took up all the space; it never allowed us even to consider the possibility that things could change.

The all-powerful Zahir seemed to be born with every human being and to gain full strength in childhood, imposing rules that would thereafter always be respected:

People who are different are dangerous; they belong to another tribe; they want our lands and our women.

We must marry, have children, reproduce the species.

Love is only a small thing, enough for one person, and any suggestion that the heart might be larger than this is considered perverse.

When we marry, we are authorised to take possession of the other person, body and soul.

We must do jobs we detest because we are part of an organised society, and if everyone did what they wanted to do, the world would come to a standstill.

We must buy jewellery; it identifies us with our tribe, just as body-piercing identifies those of a different tribe.

We must be amusing at all times and sneer at those who express their real feelings; it's dangerous for a tribe to allow its members to show their feelings.

We must at all costs avoid saying 'No' because people prefer those who always say 'Yes', and this allows us to survive in hostile territory.

What other people think is more important than what we feel.

Never make a fuss, it might attract the attention of an enemy tribe.

If you behave differently, you will be expelled from the tribe because you could infect others and destroy something that was extremely difficult to organise in the first place.

We must always consider the look of our new cave, and if we don't have a clear idea of our own, then we must call in a decorator who will do his best to show others what good taste we have.

We must eat three meals a day, even if we're not hungry, and when we fail to fit the current ideal of beauty we must fast, even if we're starving.

We must dress according to the dictates of fashion, make love whether we feel like it or not, kill in the name of our country's frontiers, wish time away so that retirement comes more quickly, elect politicians, complain about the cost of living, change our hairstyle, criticise anyone who is different, go to a religious service on Sunday, Saturday or Friday, depending on our religion, and there beg forgiveness for our sins and puff ourselves up with pride because we know the truth and despise the other tribe, who worship a false god.

Our children must follow in our footsteps; after all, we are older and know about the world.

We must have a university degree even if we never get a job in the area of knowledge we were forced to study.

We must study things that we will never use, but which someone told us was important to know: algebra, trigonometry, the code of Hammurabi.

We must never make our parents sad, even if this means giving up everything that makes us happy.

We must play music quietly, talk quietly, weep in private, because I am the all-powerful Zahir, who lays down the rules and determines the distance between railway tracks, the meaning of success, the best way to love, the importance of rewards.

* * *

We stop outside a relatively chic building in an expensive area. One of the group taps in the code at the front door and we all go up to the third floor. I thought we would find one of those understanding families who put up with their son's friends in order to keep him close to home and to keep an eye on him. But when Lucrecia opened the door, everything was in darkness. As my eyes grew accustomed to the light from the street filtering in through the windows, I saw a large empty living room. The only decoration was a fireplace that probably hadn't been used for years.

A fair-haired boy, who was nearly six feet tall and wore a long rain cape and a Sioux Indian haircut, went into the kitchen and returned with some lighted candles. We all sat round in a circle on the floor and, for the first time that night, I felt afraid: it was like being in a horror movie in which a satanic ritual is about to begin, and where the victim will be the stranger who was unwise enough to tag along.

Mikhail was looking pale and his eyes kept darting about, unable to fix on any one place, and that only increased my feeling of unease. He was on the point of having an epileptic fit. Would the people there know what to do in that situation? Wouldn't it be better just to leave now and not get involved in a potential tragedy?

That would perhaps be the most prudent thing to do, in keeping with a life in which I was a famous author who writes about spirituality and should therefore be setting an example. Yes, if I was being sensible, I would say to Lucrecia that, in case of an attack, she should place something in her boyfriend's mouth to stop his tongue rolling back and prevent him choking to death. She must know this already, but in the world of the followers of the social Zahir, we leave nothing to chance, we need to be at peace with our conscience.

That is how I would have acted before my accident, but now my personal history had become unimportant. It had stopped being history and was once more becoming a legend, a search, an adventure, a journey into and away from myself. I was once more in a time in which the things around me were changing and that is how I wanted it to be for the rest of my days (I remembered one of my ideas for an epitaph: He died while he was still alive). I was carrying with me the experiences of my past, which allowed me to react with speed and precision, but I wasn't bothered about the lessons I had learned. Imagine a warrior, in the middle of a fight, pausing to decide which move to make next? He would be dead in an instant.

And the warrior in me, using intuition and technique, decided that I needed to stay, to continue the night's experiences, even if it was late and I was tired and drunk and afraid that a worried or angry Marie might be waiting up for me. I sat down next to Mikhail so that I could act quickly should he have a fit.

I noticed that he seemed to be in control of his epileptic attack. He gradually grew calmer, and his eyes took on the same intensity as when he was the young man in white standing on the stage at the Armenian restaurant.

'We will start with the usual prayer,' he said.

And the young people, who, up until then, had been aggressive, drunken misfits, closed their eyes and held hands in a large circle. Even the two Alsatian dogs sitting in one corner of the room seemed calmer.

'Dear Lady, when I look at the cars, the shop windows, the people oblivious to everyone else, when I look at all the buildings and the monuments, I see in them Your absence. Make us capable of bringing You back.'

The group continued as one:

'Dear Lady, we recognise Your presence in the difficulties we are experiencing. Help us not to give up. Help us to think of You with tranquillity and determination, even when it is hard to accept that we love You.'

I noticed that everyone there was wearing the same symbol somewhere on their clothing. Sometimes it was in the form of a brooch, or a metal badge, or a piece of embroidery, or was even drawn on the fabric with a pen.

'I would like to dedicate tonight to the man sitting on my right. He sat down beside me because he wanted to protect me.'

How did he know that?

'He's a good man. He knows that love transforms and he allows himself to be transformed by love. He still carries much of his personal history in his soul, but he is continually trying to free himself from it, which is why he stayed with us tonight. He is the husband of the woman we all know, the woman who left me a relic as proof of her friendship and as a talisman.'

Mikhail took out the piece of bloodstained cloth and put it down in front of him.

'This is part of the unknown soldier's shirt. Before he died, he said to the woman: "Cut up my clothes and distribute the pieces amongst those who believe in death and who, for that reason, are capable of living as if today were their last day on earth. Tell those people that I have just seen the face of God; tell them not to be afraid, but not to grow complacent either. Seek the one truth, which is love. Live in accordance with its laws."'

They all gazed reverently at the piece of cloth.

'We were born into a time of revolt. We pour all our enthusiasm into it, we risk our lives and our youth, and suddenly, we feel afraid, and that initial joy gives way to the real challenges: weariness, monotony, doubts about our own abilities. We notice that some of our friends have already given up. We are obliged to confront loneliness, to cope with sharp bends in the road, to suffer a few falls with no one near to help us, and we end up asking ourselves if it's worth all that effort.'

Mikhail paused.

'It is. And we will carry on, knowing that our soul, even though it is eternal, is, at this moment, caught in the web of time, with all its opportunities and limitations. We will, as far as possible, free ourselves from this web. When this proves impossible and we return to the story we were told, we will, nevertheless, remember our battles and be ready to resume the struggle as soon as the conditions are right. Amen.'

'Amen,' echoed the others.

'I need to talk to the Lady,' said the fair young man with the Sioux Indian haircut.

'Not tonight. I'm tired.'

There was a general murmur of disappointment. Unlike those people at the Armenian restaurant, they knew Mikhail's story and knew about the 'presence' he felt by his side. He got up and went into the kitchen to get a glass of water. I went with him.

I asked how they had come by that apartment, and he explained that in French law anyone can legally move into a building that is not being used by its owner. It was, in short, a squat.

I began to be troubled by the thought that Marie would be waiting up for me. Mikhail took my arm.

'You said today that you were going to the steppes. I'll say this one more time: please, take me with you. I need to go back to my country, even if only for a short time, but I haven't any money. I miss my people, my mother, my friends. I could say "the voice tells me that you will need me", but that wouldn't be true: you could find Esther easily enough and without any help at all. But I need an infusion of energy from my homeland.'

'I can give you the money for a return ticket.'

'I know you can, but I'd like to be there with you, to go with you to the village where she's living, to feel the wind on my face, to help you along the road that will lead you back to the woman you love. She was – and still is – very important to me. I learned so much from the changes she went through, from her determination, and I want to go on learning. Do you remember me talking once about "interrupted stories"? I would like to be by your side right up until the moment we reach her house. That way, I will have lived through to the end this period of your – and my – life. When we reach her house, I will leave you alone.'

I didn't know what to say. I tried to talk about something else and asked about the people in the living room.

'They're people who are afraid of ending up like your generation, a generation that dreamed it could revolutionise the world, but ended up giving in to "reality". We pretend to be strong because we're weak. There are still only a few of us, very few, but I think that's only a passing phase; people can't go on deceiving themselves for ever. Now what's your answer to my question?'

'Mikhail, you know how much I want to free myself from my personal history. If you had asked me a while ago, I would have found it much more comfortable, more convenient even, to travel with you, since you know the country, the customs and the possible dangers. Now, though, I feel that I should roll up Ariadne's thread into a ball and escape from the labyrinth I got myself into and that I should do this alone. My life has changed; I feel as if I were ten or even twenty years younger, and that in itself is enough for me to want to set off in search of adventure.'

'When will you leave?'

'As soon as I get my visa. In two or three days' time.'

'May the Lady go with you. The voice is saying that it is the right moment. If you change your mind, let me know.'

I walked past the group of people lying on the floor, ready to go to sleep. On the way home, it occurred to me that life was a much more joyful thing than I had thought it would be at my age: it's always possible to go back to being young and crazy again. I was so focused on the present moment that I was surprised when I saw that people didn't recoil from me as I passed, didn't fearfully lower their eyes. No one even noticed me, but I liked the idea; the city was once again the city of which Henry IV – when accused of betraying his Protestant religion by marrying a Catholic – had said: 'Paris is well worth a mass.'

It was worth much more than that. I could see again the religious massacres, the blood-lettings, the kings, the queens, the museums, the castles, the tortured artists, the drunken writers, the philosophers who took their own lives, the soldiers who plotted to conquer the world, the traitors who, with a gesture, brought down a whole dynasty, the stories that had once been forgotten and were now remembered and retold.

* * *

For the first time in ages, I arrived home and did not immediately go over to the computer to find out if anyone had e-mailed me, if there was some pressing matter requiring urgent action: nothing was that urgent. I didn't go into the bedroom to see if Marie was asleep either, because I knew she would only be pretending to sleep.

I didn't turn on the TV to watch the late-night news, because the news was exactly the same news I used to listen to as a child: one country was threatening another country, someone had betrayed someone else, the economy was going badly, some grand passion had come to an end, Israel and Palestine had failed, after fifty long years, to reach an agreement, another bomb had exploded, a hurricane had left thousands of people homeless.

I remembered that the major networks that morning, having no terrorist attacks to report, had all chosen as their main item a rebellion in Haiti. What did I care about Haiti? What difference would that make to my life or to that of my wife, to the price of bread in Paris, to Mikhail's tribe? How could I have spent five minutes of my precious life listening to someone talking about the rebels and the president, watching the usual scenes of street protests being repeated over and over, and being reported as if it were a great event in the history of humanity – a rebellion in Haiti! And I had swallowed it whole! I had watched until the end! Stupid people really should be issued with their own special identity cards because they are the ones who feed the collective stupidity.

I opened the window and let in the icy night air; I took off my clothes and told myself that I could withstand the cold. I stood there, not thinking anything, just aware of my feet on the floor, my eyes fixed on the Eiffel Tower, my ears hearing dogs barking, police sirens and conversations I couldn't quite understand.

I was not I, I was nothing – and that seemed to me quite marvellous.

'You seem strange.'

'What do you mean "strange"?'

'You seem sad.'

'I'm not sad. I'm happy.'

'You see? Even your tone of voice is false: you're sad about me, but you don't dare say anything.'

'Why should I be sad?'

'Because I came home late last night and I was drunk. You haven't even asked me where I went.'

'I'm not interested.'

'Why aren't you interested? I told you I was going out with Mikhail, didn't I?'

'Didn't you go out with him, then?'

'Yes. I did.'

'So what's there to ask?'

'Don't you think that when your boyfriend, whom you claim you love, comes home late, you should at least try to find out what happened?'

'All right, then, what happened?'

'Nothing. I went out with Mikhail and some of his friends.'

'Fine.'

'Do you believe me?'

'Of course I do.'

'I don't think you love me any more. You're not jealous. You don't care. Do I normally get back home at two in the morning?'

'Didn't you say you were a free man?'

'And I am.'

'In that case, it's normal that you should get back home at two in the morning and do whatever you want to do. If I was your mother, I'd be worried, but you're a grown-up, aren't you? You men should stop behaving as if you wanted the women in your life to treat you like children.'

'I don't mean that kind of worried. I'm talking about jealousy.'

'Would you prefer it if I made a scene right now, over breakfast?'

'No, don't do that, the neighbours will hear.'

'I don't care about the neighbours. I won't make a scene because I don't feel like it. It's been hard for me, but I've finally accepted what you told me in Zagreb and I'm trying to get used to the idea. Meanwhile, if it makes you happy, I can always pretend to be jealous, angry, crazy or whatever.'

'Like I said, you seem strange. I'm beginning to think I'm not important in your life any more.'

'And I'm beginning to think you've forgotten there's a journalist waiting for you in the sitting room, and who is quite possibly listening to our conversation.'

Ah, the journalist. I go onto automatic pilot, because I know what questions he will ask. I know how the interview will begin ('Let's talk about your new novel. What's the main message'), and I know how I will respond ('If I wanted to put across a message, I'd write a single sentence, not a book').

I know he'll ask me what I feel about the critics, who are usually very hard on my work. I know that he will end by asking: 'And have you already started writing a new book? What projects are you working on now?' To which I will respond: 'That's a secret.'

The interview begins as expected:

'Let's talk about your new book. What's the main message?'

'If I wanted to put across a message, I'd write a single sentence, not a book.'

'And why do you write?'

'Because that's my way of sharing my feelings with others.'

This phrase is also part of my automatic pilot script, but I stop and correct myself:

'Although that particular story could be told in a different way.'

'In a different way? Do you mean you're not happy with *A Time to Rend and a Time to Sew*?'

'No, on the contrary, I'm very pleased with the book,

but I'm not so pleased with the answer I've just given you. Why do I write? The real answer is this: I write because I want to be loved.'

The journalist eyed me suspiciously: what kind of confession was this?

'I write because when I was an adolescent, I was useless at football, I didn't have a car or much of an allowance, and I was pretty much of a weed.'

I was making a huge effort to keep talking. The conversation with Marie had reminded me of a past that no longer made any sense; I needed to talk about my real personal history, in order to become free of it. I went on:

'I didn't wear trendy clothes either. That's all the girls in my class were interested in, and so they just ignored me. At night, when my friends were out with their girlfriends, I spent my free time creating a world in which I could be happy: my companions were writers and their books. One day, I wrote a poem for one of the girls in the street where I lived. A friend found the poem in my room and stole it, and when we were all together, he showed it to the entire class. Everyone laughed. They thought it was ridiculous – I was in love!

The only one who didn't laugh was the girl I wrote the poem for. The following evening, when we went to the theatre, she managed to fix things so that she sat next to me, and she held my hand. We left the theatre hand-in-hand; there was ugly, puny, untrendy me strolling along with the girl all the boys in the class fancied.'

I paused. It was as if I were going back into the past, to the moment when her hand touched mine and changed my life.

'And all because of a poem,' I went on. 'A poem showed me that by writing and revealing my invisible world, I could compete on equal terms with the visible world of my classmates: physical strength, fashionable clothes, cars, being good at sport.'

The journalist was slightly surprised, and I was even more surprised. He managed to compose himself, though, and asked:

'Why do you think the critics are so hard on your work?'

My automatic pilot would normally reply: 'You just have to read the biography of any writer from the past who is now considered a classic - not that I'm comparing myself with them, you understand - to see how implacable their critics were then. The reason is simple: critics are extremely insecure, they don't really know what's going on, they're democrats when it comes to politics, but fascists when it comes to culture. They believe that people are perfectly capable of choosing who governs them, but have no idea when it comes to choosing films, books, music.'

I had abandoned my automatic pilot again, knowing full well that the journalist was unlikely to publish my response.

'Have you ever heard of the Law of Jante?'

'No, I haven't,' he said.

'Well, it's been in existence since the beginning of civilisation, but it was only officially set down in 1933 by a Danish writer. In the small town of Jante, the powers-that-be came up with ten commandments telling people how they should behave, and it seems to exist not only in Jante, but everywhere else too. If I had to sum it up in one sentence, I'd say: "Mediocrity and anonymity are the safest choice. If you opt for them, you'll never face any major problems in life. But if you try to be different …"'

'I'd like to know what these Jante commandments are,' said the journalist, who seemed genuinely interested.

'I don't have them here, but I can summarise if you like.'

I went over to my computer and printed out a condensed and edited version.

'You are nobody, never even dare to think that you know more than we do. You are of no importance, you can do nothing right, your work is of no significance, but as long as you never challenge us, you will live a happy life. Always take what we say seriously and never laugh at our opinions.'

The journalist folded up the piece of paper and put it in his pocket.

'You're right. If you're a nobody, if your work has no impact, then it deserves to be praised. If, however, you climb out of that state of mediocrity and are a success, then you're defying the law and deserve to be punished.'

I was so pleased that he had reached this conclusion on his own.

'And it isn't only the critics who say that,' I added. 'More people, far more people than you might think, say exactly the same thing.'

Later that afternoon, I rang Mikhail's mobile number:

'Let's travel to Kazakhstan together.'

He didn't seem in the least surprised; he merely thanked me and asked what had made me change my mind.

'For two years, my life has consisted of nothing but the Zahir. Since I met you, I've been following a long-forgotten path, an abandoned railway track with grass growing between the rails, but which can still be used by trains. I haven't yet reached the final station, so I have no way of stopping along the way.'

He asked me if I had managed to get a visa. I explained that the Favour Bank had once again come to my aid: a Russian friend had phoned his girlfriend, who was the director of a major newspaper company in Kazakhstan. She had phoned the ambassador in Paris, and the visa would be ready that afternoon.

'When do we leave?'

'Tomorrow. In order to buy the tickets, I just need to know your real name; the travel agent is on the other line now.'

'Before you hang up, I'd just like to say one thing: I really liked what you said about the distance between the tracks and what you said just now about the abandoned railway line, but I don't think that's why you're asking me to come with you. I think it's because of something you wrote once, and which I know by heart; your wife was always quoting these lines, and what they say is far more romantic than that business about the Favour Bank:

A warrior of light knows that he has much to be grateful for.

He was helped in his struggle by the angels; celestial forces placed each thing in its place, thus allowing him to give of his best. That is why, at sunset, he kneels and gives thanks for the Protective Cloak surrounding him.

His companions say: 'He's so lucky!' But he knows that 'luck' is knowing to look around him and to see where his friends are, because it was through their words that the angels were able to make themselves heard.

'I don't always remember what I wrote, but thank you for that. Now I just need your name to give to the travel agent.'

It takes twenty minutes for the taxi company to answer the phone. A tetchy voice tells me I'll have to wait another half an hour. Marie seems happy in her exuberantly sexy black dress, and I think of the Armenian restaurant and the man who admitted to feeling aroused by the thought that his wife was desired by other men. I know that all the women at the gala supper will be wearing outfits designed to make their breasts and curves the centre of attention, and that their husbands or boyfriends, knowing that their wives or girlfriends are desired by other men, will think: 'All right, have a good look, but keep your distance, because she's with me, she's mine. I'm better than you are, because I have something you'd all like to have.'

I'm not going to be doing any business, I'm not going to be signing contracts or giving interviews; I am merely attending a ceremony, to repay a deposit made into my account at the Favour Bank. I will sit next to someone boring at supper, someone who will ask me where I find the inspiration for my books. Next to me, on the other side, a pair of breasts will perhaps be on show, possibly belonging to the wife of a friend, and I will constantly have to stop myself glancing down because, if I do, even for a second, she will tell her husband that I was coming on to her. While we wait for the taxi, I draw up a list of possible topics of conversation:

a) Comments about people's appearance: 'You're looking very elegant', 'What a beautiful dress', 'Your skin's looking fabulous.' When they go back home, they'll say how badly dressed everyone was and how ill they looked.
b) Recent holidays: 'You must visit Aruba, it's fantastic', 'There's nothing like a summer night in Cancun, sipping a Martini by the seashore.' In fact, no one enjoys themselves very much on these holidays, they just experience a sense of freedom for a few days and feel obliged to enjoy themselves because they spent all that money.
c) More holidays, this time to places which they feel free to criticise: 'I was in Rio de Janeiro recently – such a violent city', 'The poverty in the streets of Calcutta is really shocking.' They only went to these places in order to feel powerful while they were there and privileged when they came back to the mean reality of their little lives, where at least there is no poverty or violence.
d) New therapies: 'Just one week of drinking wheatgrass juice really improves the texture of your hair', 'I spent two days at a spa in Biarritz; the water there opens the pores and eliminates toxins.' The following week, they will discover that wheatgrass has absolutely no special properties and that any old hot water will open the pores and eliminate toxins.
e) Other people: 'I haven't seen so-and-so for ages, what's he up to?' 'I understand that what's-her-name is in difficulties financially and has had to sell her apartment.' They can talk about the people who weren't invited to the party in question, they can

criticise all they like, as long as they end by saying, with an innocent, pitying air: 'Still, he/she's a wonderful person.'

f) A few little complaints about life, just to add savour to the evening: 'I wish something new would happen in my life', 'I'm so worried about my children, they never listen to proper music or read proper literature.' They wait for comments from other people with the same problem and then feel less alone and leave the party happy.

g) At intellectual gatherings, like the one this evening, we will discuss the Middle East conflict, the problem of Islamism, the latest exhibition, the latest philosophy guru, the fantastic book that no one has heard of, the fact that music isn't what it used to be; we will offer our intelligent, sensible opinions, which run completely counter to our real feelings – because we all know how much we hate having to go to those exhibitions, read those unbearable books, or see those dreary films, just so that we will have something to talk about on nights like tonight.

* * *

The taxi arrives, and while we are being driven to the venue I add another very personal item to my list: I complain to Marie about how much I loathe these suppers. She reminds me – and it's true – that I always enjoy myself in the end and have a really good time.

We enter one of Paris's most elegant restaurants and head for a room reserved for the event – a presentation of a literary prize for which I was one of the judges.

Everyone is standing around talking; some people say hello and others merely look at me and make some comment to each other; the organiser of the prize comes over to me and introduces me to the people who are there, always with the same irritating words: 'You know who this gentleman is, of course.' Some people give a smile of recognition, others merely smile and don't recognise me at all, but pretend to know who I am, because to admit otherwise would be to accept that the world they're living in doesn't exist, and that they are failing to keep up with the things that matter.

I remember the 'tribe' of the previous night and think: stupid people should all be marooned on a ship on the high seas and forced to attend parties night after night, being endlessly introduced to people for several months, until they finally manage to remember who is who.

I draw up a catalogue of the kind of people who attend events like this. Ten per cent are 'Members', the decision-makers, who came out tonight because of some debt they owe to the Favour Bank, but who always have an eye open for anything that might be of benefit to their work – how to make money, where to invest. They can soon tell whether or not an event is going to prove profitable or not, and they are always the first to leave the party; they never waste their time.

Two per cent are the 'Talents', who really do have a promising future; they have already managed to ford a few rivers, have just become aware of the existence of the Favour Bank and are all potential customers; they have important services to offer, but are not as yet in a position to make decisions. They are nice to everyone because they don't know who exactly they are talking to, and they are more open-minded than the Members, because, for them, any road might lead somewhere.

Three per cent are what I call the 'Tupamaros' – in homage to the former Uruguayan guerrilla group. They have managed to infiltrate this party and are mad for any kind of contact; they're not sure whether to stay or to go on to another party that is taking place at the same time; they are anxious; they want to show how talented they are, but they weren't invited, they haven't scaled the first mountains, and as soon as the other guests suss this out, they immediately withdraw any attention they have been paying them.

The last 85 per cent are the 'Trays'. I call them this because, just as no party can exist without that particular utensil, so no event can exist without these guests. The Trays don't really know what is going on, but they know it's important to be there; they are on the guest list drawn up by the promoters because the success of something like this also depends on the number of people who come. They are all ex-something-or-other-important – ex-bankers, ex-directors, the ex-husband of some famous woman, the ex-wife of some man now in a position of power. They are Counts in a country where the monarchy no longer exists, Princesses and Marchionesses who live by renting out their castles. They go from one party to the next, from one supper to the next – don't they ever get sick of it, I wonder?

When I commented on this recently to Marie, she said that just as some people are addicted to work, so others are addicted to fun. Both groups are equally unhappy, convinced that they are missing something, but unable to give up their particular vice.

A pretty young blonde comes over while I'm talking to one of the organisers of a conference on cinema and literature and tells me how much she enjoyed *A Time to Rend and a Time to Sew*. She's from one of the Baltic countries, she says, and works in film. She is immediately identified by the group as a Tupamaro, because while appearing to be interested in one thing (me), she is, in fact, interested in something else (the organisers of the conference). Despite having made this almost unforgivable gaffe, there is still a chance that she might be an inexperienced Talent. The organiser of the conference asks what she means by 'working in film'. The young woman explains that she writes film reviews for a newspaper and has published a book (about cinema? No, about her life, her short, dull life, I imagine).

She then commits the cardinal sin of jumping the gun and asking if she could be invited to this year's event. The organiser explains that the woman who publishes my books in that same Baltic country, an influential and hardworking woman (and very pretty too, I think to myself), has already been invited. They continue talking to me; the Tupamaro lingers for a few more minutes, not knowing what to say, then moves off.

Given that it's a literary prize, most of the guests tonight – Tupamaros, Talents and Trays – belong to the world of the arts. The Members, on the other hand, are either sponsors or people connected with foundations that support museums, classical music concerts, and promising young artists. After various conversations about which of the candidates for the prize that night had applied most pressure in order to win, the master of ceremonies mounts the stage, asks everyone to take their places at the tables (we all sit down), makes a few jokes (it's part of the ritual, and we all laugh), and says that the winners will be announced between the entrée and the first course.

I am on the top table; this allows me to keep the Trays at a safe distance, and also means that I don't have to bother with any enthusiastic and self-interested Talents. I am seated between the female director of a car-manufacturing firm, which is sponsoring the party, and an heiress who has decided to invest in art – to my surprise, neither of them is wearing a dress with a provocative décolletage. The other guests at our table are the director of a perfumery; an Arab prince (who was doubtless passing through Paris and was pounced on by one of the promoters to add lustre to the event); an Israeli banker who collects fourteenth-century manuscripts; the main organiser of tonight's event; the French Consul to Monaco; and a blonde woman whose presence here I can't quite fathom, although I suspect she might be the organiser's next mistress.

I have to keep putting on my glasses and surreptitiously reading the names of the people on either side of me (I ought to be marooned on that imaginary ship and invited to this same party dozens of times until I have memorised the names of all the guests). Marie, as protocol demands, has been placed on another table; someone, at some point in history, decided that at formal suppers, couples should always be seated separately, thus leaving it open to doubt whether the person beside us is married, single, or married but available. Or perhaps he or she thought that if a couple were seated together, they would simply talk to each other; but, in that case, why go out, why take a taxi and go to the supper in the first place?

As foreseen in my list of possible conversational topics, we begin with cultural small talk – isn't that a marvellous exhibition, wasn't that an intelligent review … I would like to concentrate on the entrée – caviar with salmon and egg – but I am constantly interrupted by the usual questions about how my new book is doing, where I find my inspiration, whether I'm working on a new project. Everyone seems very cultured, everyone manages to mention – as if by chance, of course – some famous person who also happens to be a close friend. Everyone can speak cogently about the current state of politics or about the problems facing culture.

'Why don't we talk about something else?'

The question slips out inadvertently. Everyone at the table goes quiet. After all, it is extremely rude to interrupt other people and worse still to draw attention to oneself. It seems, however, that last night's tour of the streets of Paris in the guise of a beggar has caused some irreparable damage, which means that I can no longer stand such conversations.

'We could talk about the *acomodador*: the moment in our lives when we decide to abandon our desires and make do, instead, with what we have.'

No one seems very interested. I decide to change the subject.

'We could talk about the importance of forgetting the story we've been told and trying to live an entirely different story. Try doing something different every day – like talking to the person on the next table to you in a restaurant, visiting a hospital, putting your foot in a puddle, listening to what another person has to say, allowing the energy of love to flow freely, instead of putting it in a jug and standing it in a corner.'

'Are you talking about adultery?' asks the director of the perfumery.

'No, I mean allowing yourself to be the instrument of love, not its master, being with someone because you really want to be, not because convention obliges you to be.'

With great delicacy, and just a touch of irony, the French Consul to Monaco assures me that all the people round our table are, of course, exercising that right and freedom. Everyone agrees, although no one believes that it's true.

'Sex!' cries the blonde woman whose role that evening no one has quite identified. 'Why don't we talk about sex? It's much more interesting and much less complicated!'

At least her remark is spontaneous. One of the women sitting next to me gives a wry laugh, but I applaud.

'Sex is certainly more interesting, but I'm not sure it's a different topic of conversation. Besides, it's no longer forbidden to talk about sex.'

'It's also in extremely bad taste,' says one of my neighbours.

'May we know what *is* forbidden?' asks the organiser, who is starting to feel uncomfortable.

'Well, money, for example. All of us around this table have money, or pretend that we do. We assume we've been invited here because we're rich, famous and influential. But have any of us ever thought of using this kind of event to find out what everyone actually earns? Since we're all so sure of ourselves, so important, why don't we look at our world as it is and not as we imagine it to be?'

'What are you getting at?' asks the director of the car-manufacturing firm.

'It's a long story. I could start by talking about Hans and Fritz sitting in a bar in Tokyo and go on to mention a Mongolian nomad who says we need to forget who we think we are in order to become who we really are.'

'You've lost me.'

'That's my fault. I didn't really explain. But let's get down to the nitty-gritty: I'd like to know how much everyone here earns, what it means, in money terms, to be sitting at the top table.'

There is a momentary silence – my gamble is not paying off. The other people round the table are looking at me with startled eyes: asking about someone's financial situation is a bigger taboo than sex, more frowned upon than asking about betrayals, corruption or parliamentary intrigues.

However, the Arab prince – perhaps because he's bored by all these receptions and banquets with their empty chatter, perhaps because that very day he has been told by his doctor that he is going to die, or perhaps for some other reason – decides to answer my question:

'I earn about 20,000 euros a month, depending on the amount approved by the parliament in my country. That bears no relation to what I spend, though, because I have an unlimited so-called "entertainment" allowance. In other words, I am here courtesy of the embassy's car and chauffeur, the clothes I'm wearing belong to the government, and tomorrow I will be travelling to another European country in a private jet, with the cost of pilot, fuel and airport taxes deducted from that allowance.'

And he concludes:

'Apparent reality is not an exact science.'

If the prince can speak so frankly, and given that he is, hierarchically, the most important person at the table, the others cannot possibly embarrass him by remaining silent. They are going to have to participate in the game, the question and the embarrassment.

'I don't know exactly how much I earn,' says the organiser, one of the Favour Bank's classic representatives, known to some as a 'lobbyist'. 'Somewhere in the region of 10,000 euros a month, but I, too, have an entertainment allowance from the various organisations I head. I can deduct everything – suppers, lunches, hotels, air tickets, sometimes even clothes, although I don't have a private jet.'

The wine has run out; he signals to a waiter and our glasses are refilled. Now it was the turn of the director of the car-manufacturing firm, who, initially, had hated the idea of talking about money, but who now seems to be rather enjoying herself.

'I reckon I earn about the same, and have the same unlimited entertainment allowance.'

One by one, everyone confessed how much they earned. The banker was the richest of them all, with ten million euros a year, as well as shares in his bank that were constantly increasing in value.

When it came to the turn of the young blonde woman who had not been introduced to anyone, she refused to answer:

'That's part of my secret garden. It's nobody's business but mine.'

'Of course it isn't, but we're just playing a game,' said the organiser.

The woman refused to join in, and by doing so, placed herself on a higher level than everyone else: after all, she was the only one in the group who had secrets. However, by placing herself on a higher level, she only succeeded in earning everyone else's scorn. Afraid of feeling humiliated by her miserable salary, she had, by acting all mysterious, managed to humiliate everyone else, not realising that most of the people there lived permanently poised on the edge of the abyss, utterly dependent on those entertainment allowances that could vanish overnight.

The question inevitably came round to me.

'It depends. In a year when I publish a new book, I could earn five million dollars. If I don't publish a book, then I earn about two million from royalties on existing titles.'

'You only asked the question so that you could say how much you earned,' said the young woman with the 'secret garden'. 'No one's impressed.'

She had realised that she had made a wrong move earlier on and was now trying to correct the situation by going onto the attack.

'On the contrary,' said the prince. 'I would have expected a leading author like yourself to be far wealthier.'

A point to me. The blonde woman would not open her mouth again all night.

The conversation about money broke a series of taboos, given that how much people earn was the biggest of them all. The waiter began to appear more frequently, the bottles of wine began to be emptied with incredible speed, the compère-cum-organiser rather tipsily mounted the stage, announced the winner, presented the prize and immediately rejoined the conversation, which had carried on even though politeness demands that we keep quiet when someone else is talking. We discussed what we did with our money (this consisted mostly of buying 'free time', travelling or practising a sport).

I thought of changing tack and asking them what kind of funeral they would like – death was as big a taboo as money – but the atmosphere was so jolly and everyone was so full of talk that I decided to say nothing.

'You're all talking about money, but you don't know what money is,' said the banker. 'Why do people think that a bit of coloured paper, a plastic card or a coin made out of fifth-rate metal has any value? Worse still, did you know that your money, your millions of dollars are nothing but electronic impulses?'

Of course we did.

'Once, wealth was what these ladies are wearing,' he went on. 'Ornaments made from rare materials that were easy to transport, count and share out. Pearls, nuggets of gold, precious stones. We all carried our wealth in a visible place. Such things were, in turn, exchanged for cattle or grain, because no one walks down the street carrying cattle or sacks of grain. The funny thing is that we still behave like some primitive tribe – we wear our ornaments to show how rich we are, even though we often have more ornaments than money.'

'It's the tribal code,' I said. 'In my day, young people wore their hair long, whereas nowadays they all go in for body-piercing. It helps them identify like-minded people, even though it can't buy anything.'

'Can our electronic impulses buy one extra hour of life? No. Can they buy back those loved ones who have departed? No. Can they buy love?'

'They can certainly buy love,' said the director of the car-manufacturing firm in a jokey tone of voice.

Her eyes, however, betrayed a terrible sadness. I thought of Esther and of what I had said to the journalist in the interview I had given that morning. We rich, powerful, intelligent people knew that, deep down, we had acquired all these ornaments and credit cards only in order to find love and affection and to be with someone who loved us.

'Not always,' said the director of the perfumery, turning to look at me.

'No, you're right, not always. After all, my wife left me, and I'm a wealthy man. But almost always. By the way, does anyone round this table know how many cats and how many lamp-posts there are on the back of a ten-dollar bill?'

No one knew and no one was interested. The comment about love had completely spoiled the jolly atmosphere, and we went back to talking about literary prizes, exhibitions, the latest film, and the play that was proving to be such an unexpected success.

'How was it on your table?'

'Oh, the usual.'

'Well, I managed to spark an interesting discussion about money, but, alas, it ended in tragedy.'

'When do you leave?'

'I have to leave here at half past seven in the morning. Since you're flying to Berlin, we could share a taxi.'

'Where are you going?'

'You know where I'm going. You haven't asked me, but you know.'

'Yes, I know.'

'Just as you know that we're saying goodbye at this very moment.'

'We could go back to the time when we first met: a man in emotional tatters over someone who had left him, and a woman madly in love with her neighbour. I could repeat what I said to you once: "I'm going to fight to the bitter end." Well, I fought and I lost, now I'll just have to lick my wounds and leave.'

'I fought and lost as well. I'm not trying to sew up what was rent. Like you, I want to fight to the bitter end.'

'I suffer every day, did you know that? I've been suffering for months now, trying to show you how much I love you, how things are only important when you're by my side. But now, whether I suffer or not, I've decided that enough is enough. It's over. I'm tired. After that night in Zagreb, I lowered my guard and said to myself: if the blow comes, it comes. It can lay me out on the canvas, it can knock me out cold, but one day I'll recover.'

'You'll find someone else.'

'Of course I will: I'm young, pretty, intelligent, desirable, but will I experience all the things I experienced with you?'

'You'll experience different emotions and, you know, although you may not believe it, I loved you while we were together.'

'I'm sure you did, but that doesn't make it any the less painful. We'll leave in separate taxis tomorrow. I hate goodbyes, especially at airports or train stations.'

The Return to Ithaca

'We'll sleep here tonight and, tomorrow, we'll continue on horseback. My car can't cope with the sand of the steppes.'

We were in a kind of bunker, which looked like a relic from the Second World War. A man, with his wife and his granddaughter, welcomed us and showed us a simple, but spotlessly clean room.

Dos went on:

'And don't forget to choose a name.'

'I don't think that's necessary,' said Mikhail.

'Of course it is,' insisted Dos. 'I was with his wife recently. I know how she thinks, I know what she has learned, I know what she expects.'

Dos's voice was simultaneously firm and gentle. Yes, I would choose a name, I would do exactly as he suggested; I would continue to discard my personal history and, instead, embark on my personal legend – even if only out of sheer tiredness.

I was exhausted. The previous night I had slept for two hours at most: my body had still not adjusted to the enormous time difference. I had arrived in Almaty at about eleven o'clock at night – local time – when in France it was only six o'clock in the evening. Mikhail had left me at the hotel and I had dozed for a bit, then woken up in the small hours. I had looked out at the lights below and thought how in Paris it would just be time to go out to supper. I was hungry and asked room service if they could send me up something to eat: 'Of course we can, sir, but you really must try to sleep; if you don't, your body will stay stuck on its European timetable.'

For me, the worst possible torture is not being able to sleep. I ate a sandwich and decided to go for a walk. I asked the receptionist my usual question: 'Is it dangerous to go walking at this hour?' He told me it wasn't, and so I set off down the empty streets, narrow alleyways, broad avenues; it was a city like any other, with its neon signs, the occasional passing police car, a beggar here, a prostitute there. I had to keep repeating out loud: 'I'm in Kazakhstan!' If I didn't, I would end up thinking I was merely in some unfamiliar quarter of Paris.

'I'm in Kazakhstan!' I said to the deserted city, and a voice replied:

'Of course you are.'

I jumped. A man was sitting close by, on a bench in a square at dead of night, with his rucksack by his side. He got up and introduced himself as Jan, from Holland, adding:

'And I know why you're here.'

Was he a friend of Mikhail's? Or was I being followed by the secret police?

'Why am I here, then?'

'Like me, you've travelled from Istanbul, following the Silk Road.'

I gave a sigh of relief, and decided to continue the conversation:

'On foot? As I understand it, that means crossing the whole of Asia.'

'It's something I needed to do. I was dissatisfied with my life. I've got money, a wife, children, I own a hosiery factory in Rotterdam. For a time, I knew what I was fighting for – my family's stability. Now I'm not so sure. Everything that once made me happy just bores me, leaves me cold. For the sake of my marriage, the love of my children, and my enthusiasm for my work, I decided to take two months out just for myself, and to take a long look at my life. And it's working.'

'I've been doing the same thing these last few months. Are there a lot of pilgrims like you?'

'Lots of them. Loads. It can be dangerous, because the political situation in some of these countries is very dodgy indeed, and they hate Westerners. But we get by. I think that, as a pilgrim, you'll always be treated with respect, as long as you can prove you're not a spy. But I gather from what you say that you have different reasons for being here. What brings you to Almaty?'

'The same thing as you. I came to reach the end of a particular road. Couldn't you sleep either?'

'I've just woken up. The earlier I set out, the more chance I have of getting to the next town; if not, I'll have to spend the night in the freezing cold steppes, with that constant wind blowing.'

'Have a good journey, then.'

'No, stay a while. I need to talk, to share my experiences. Most of the other pilgrims don't speak English.'

And he started telling me about his life, while I tried to remember what I knew about the Silk Road, the old commercial route that connected Europe with the countries of the East. The traditional route started in Beirut, passed through Antioch and went all the way to the shores of the Yangtse in China; but in Central Asia it became a kind of web, with roads heading off in all directions, which allowed for the establishment of trading posts, which, in time, became towns, which were later destroyed in battles between rival tribes, rebuilt by the inhabitants, destroyed, and rebuilt yet again. Although almost everything passed along that route – gold, strange animals, ivory, seeds, political ideas, refugees from civil wars, armed bandits, private armies to protect the caravans – silk was the rarest and most coveted item. It was thanks to one of these branch roads that Buddhism travelled from India to Sri Lanka and Tibet.

'I left Antioch with about two hundred dollars in my pocket,' said the Dutchman, having described mountains, landscapes, exotic tribes and endless problems in various countries with police patrols. 'I needed to find out if I was capable of becoming myself again. Do you know what I mean?'

'Yes, I do.'

'I was forced to beg, to ask for money. To my surprise, people are much more generous than I had imagined.'

Beg? I studied his rucksack and his clothes to see if I could spot the symbol of the 'tribe' – Mikhail's tribe – but I couldn't find it.

'Have you ever been to an Armenian restaurant in Paris?'

'I've been to lots of Armenian restaurants, but never in Paris.'

'Do you know someone called Mikhail?'

'It's a pretty common name in these parts. If I did know a Mikhail, I can't remember, so I'm afraid I can't help you.'

'No, I don't need your help. I'm just surprised by certain coincidences. It seems there are a lot of people, all over the world, who are becoming aware of the same thing and acting in a very similar way.'

'The first thing you feel, when you set out on a journey like this, is that you'll never arrive. Then you feel insecure, abandoned, and spend all your time thinking about giving up. But if you can last a week, then you'll make it to the end.'

'I've been wandering like a pilgrim through the streets of one city, and yesterday I arrived in a different one. May I bless you?'

He gave me a strange look.

'I'm not travelling for religious reasons. Are you a priest?'

'No, I'm not a priest, but I feel that I should bless you. Some things aren't logical, as you know.'

The Dutchman called Jan, whom I would never see again, bowed his head and closed his eyes. I placed my hands on his shoulders and, in my native tongue – which he wouldn't understand – I prayed that he would reach his destination safely and leave behind him on the Silk Road both his sadness and his sense that life was meaningless; I prayed, too, that he would return to his family with shining eyes and with his soul washed clean.

He thanked me, took up his rucksack, and headed off in the direction of China. I went back to the hotel thinking that I had never, in my whole life, blessed anyone before. But I had responded to an impulse, and the impulse was right; my prayer would be answered.

The following day, Mikhail turned up with his friend, Dos, who would accompany us. Dos had a car, knew my wife and knew the steppes, and he, too, wanted to be there when I reached the village where Esther was living.

I considered remonstrating with them – first, it was Mikhail, now it was his friend, and by the time we finally reached the village, there would be a huge crowd following me, applauding and weeping, waiting to see what would happen. But I was too tired to say anything. The next day, I would remind Mikhail of the promise he had made, not to allow any witnesses to that moment.

We got into the car and, for some time, followed the Silk Road. They asked me if I knew what it was and I told them that I had met a Silk Road pilgrim the previous night, and they said that such journeys were becoming more and more commonplace and could soon bring benefits to the country's tourist industry.

Two hours later, we left the main road and continued along a minor road as far as the 'bunker' where we are now, eating fish and listening to the soft wind that blows across the steppes.

'Esther was very important for me,' Dos explains, showing me a photo of one of his paintings, which includes one of those pieces of bloodstained cloth. 'I used to dream of leaving here, like Oleg …'

'You'd better call me Mikhail, otherwise he'll get confused.'

'I used to dream of leaving here, like lots of people my age. Then one day, Oleg – or, rather, Mikhail – phoned me. He said that his benefactress had decided to come and live in the steppes for a while and he wanted me to help her. I agreed, thinking that here was my chance and that perhaps I could extract the same favours from her: a visa, a plane ticket and a job in France. She asked me to go with her to some remote village that she knew from an earlier visit.

I didn't ask her why, I simply did as she requested. On the way, she insisted on going to the house of a nomad she had visited years before. To my surprise, it was my grandfather she wanted to see! She was received with the hospitality that is typical of the people who live in this infinite space. My grandfather told her that, although she thought she was sad, her soul was, in fact, happy and free, and love's energy had begun to flow again. He assured her that this would have an effect upon the whole world, including her husband. My grandfather taught her many things about the culture of the steppes, and asked me to teach her the rest. In the end, he decided that she could keep her name, even though this was contrary to tradition.

And while she learned from my grandfather, I learned from her, and realised that I didn't need to go far away, as Mikhail had done: my mission was to be in this empty space – the steppes – and to understand its colours and transform them into paintings.'

'I don't quite understand what you mean about teaching my wife. I thought your grandfather said that we should forget everything.'

'I'll show you tomorrow,' said Dos.

***

And the following day, he did show me and there was no need for words. I saw the endless steppes, which, although they appeared to be nothing but desert, were, in fact, full of life, full of creatures hidden in the low scrub. I saw the flat horizon, the vast empty space, heard the sound of horses' hooves, the quiet wind, and then, all around us, nothing, absolutely nothing. It was as if the world had chosen this place to display, at once, its vastness, simplicity and complexity. It was as if we could – and should – become like the steppes, empty, infinite and, at the same time, full of life.

I looked up at the blue sky, took off my dark glasses, and allowed myself to be filled by that light, by the feeling of being simultaneously nowhere and everywhere. We rode on in silence, stopping now and then to let the horses drink from streams that only someone who knew the place would have been able to find. Occasionally, we would see other horsemen in the distance or shepherds with their flocks, framed by the plain and by the sky.

Where was I going? I hadn't the slightest idea and I didn't care. The woman I was looking for was somewhere in that infinite space. I could touch her soul, hear the song she was singing as she wove her carpets. Now I understood why she had chosen this place: there was nothing, absolutely nothing to distract her attention; it was the emptiness she had so yearned for. The wind would gradually blow her pain away. Could she ever have imagined that one day I would be here, on horseback, riding to meet her?

A sense of Paradise descends from the skies. And I am aware that I am living through an unforgettable moment in my life; it is the kind of awareness we often have precisely when the magic moment has passed. I am entirely here, without past, without future, entirely focused on the morning, on the music of the horses' hooves, on the gentleness of the wind caressing my body, on the unexpected grace of contemplating sky, earth, men. I feel a sense of adoration and ecstasy. I am thankful for being alive. I pray quietly, listening to the voice of nature, and understanding that the invisible world always manifests itself in the visible world.

I ask the sky some questions, the same questions I used to ask my mother when I was a child:

Why do we love certain people and hate others?
Where do we go after we die?
Why are we born if, in the end, we die?
What does God mean?

The steppes respond with the constant sound of the wind. And that is enough: knowing that the fundamental questions of life will never be answered, and that we can, nevertheless, still go forward.

* * *

Mountains loomed on the horizon, and Dos asked us to stop. I saw that there was a stream nearby.

'We'll camp here.'

We removed the saddlebags from the horses and put up the tent. Mikhail started digging a hole in the ground.

'This is how the nomads used to do it; we dig a hole, fill the bottom with stones, put more stones all around the edge, and that way we have a place to light a fire without the wind bothering us.'

To the south, between the mountains and us, a cloud of dust appeared, which I realised at once was caused by galloping horses. I pointed this out to my two friends, who jumped to their feet. I could see that they were tense. Then they exchanged a few words in Russian and relaxed. Dos went back to putting up the tent and Mikhail set about lighting the fire.

'Would you mind telling me what's going on?' I said.

'It may look as if we're surrounded by empty space, but it can't have escaped your notice that we've already seen all kinds of things: shepherds, rivers, tortoises, foxes and horsemen. It feels as if we had a clear view all around us, so where do these people come from? Where are their houses? Where do they keep their flocks?

That sense of emptiness is an illusion: we are constantly watching and being watched. To a stranger who cannot read the signs of the steppes, everything is under control and the only thing he can see are the horses and the riders. To those of us who were brought up here, we can also see the yurts, the circular houses that blend in with the landscape. We know how to read what's going on by observing how horsemen are moving and in which direction they're heading. In the olden days, the survival of the tribe depended on that ability, because there were enemies, invaders, smugglers.

And now the bad news: they've found out that we're riding towards the village at the foot of those mountains and are sending people to kill the shaman who sees visions of children as well as the man who has come to disturb the peace of the foreign woman.'

He gave a loud laugh.

'Just wait a moment and you'll understand.'

The riders were approaching, and I was soon able to see what was going on.

'It looks very odd to me – a woman being pursued by a man.'

'It is odd, but it's also part of our lives.'

The woman rode past us, wielding a long whip, and, by way of a greeting, gave a shout and a smile directed at Dos, then started galloping round and round the place where we were setting up camp. The smiling, sweating man pursuing her gave us a brief greeting too, all the while trying to keep up with the woman.

'Nina shouldn't be so cruel,' said Mikhail. 'There's no need for all this.'

'It's precisely because there's no need for it that she can afford to be cruel,' replied Dos. 'She just has to be beautiful and have a good horse.'

'But she does this to everyone.'

'I unseated her once,' said Dos proudly.

'The fact that you're speaking English means that you want me to understand.'

The woman was laughing and riding ever faster; her laughter filled the steppes with joy.

'It's a form of flirtation. It's called Kyz Kuu or "Bring the girl down". And we've all taken part in it at some time in our childhood or youth.'

The man pursuing her was getting closer and closer, but we could see that his horse couldn't take much more.

'Later on, we'll talk a bit about Tengri, the culture of the steppes,' Dos went on. 'But now that you're seeing this, let me just explain something very important. Here, in this land, the woman is in charge. She comes first. In the event of a divorce, she receives half the dowry back even if she's the one who wants the divorce. Whenever a man sees a woman wearing a white turban, that means she's a mother and we, as men, must place our hand on our heart and bow our head as a sign of respect.'

'But what's that got to do with "Bring the girl down"?'

'In the village at the foot of the mountains, a group of men on horseback would have gathered around this girl; her name is Nina and she's the most desirable girl in the area. They would have begun playing the game of Kyz Kuu, which was thought up in ancient times, when the women of the steppes, known as amazons, were also warriors.

At the time, no one would have dreamt of consulting the family if they wanted to get married: the suitors and the girl would simply get together in a particular place, all on horseback. She would ride round the men, laughing, provoking them, whipping them. Then the bravest of the men would start chasing her. If the girl was able to keep out of his grasp for a set period of time, then the man would have to call on the earth to cover him for ever, because he would be considered a bad horseman – the warrior's greatest shame.

If he got close, despite her whip, and pulled her to the ground, then he was a real man and was allowed to kiss her and to marry her. Obviously, then just as now, the girls knew who they should escape from and who they should let themselves be caught by.'

Nina was clearly just having a bit of fun. She had got ahead of the man again and was riding back to the village.

'She only came to show off. She knows we're on our way and will take the news back to the village.'

'I have two questions. The first might seem stupid: do you still choose your brides like that?'

Dos said that, nowadays, it was just a game. In the West, people got all dressed up and went to bars or fashionable clubs, whereas in the steppes, Kyz Kuu was the favoured game of seduction. Nina had already humiliated quite a number of young men, and had allowed herself to be unseated by a few as well – exactly as happens in all the best discotheques.

'The second question will seem even more idiotic: is the village at the foot of the mountains where my wife is living?'

Dos nodded.

'If we're only two hours away, why don't we sleep there? It'll be a while yet before it gets dark.'

'You're right, we are only two hours away, and there are two reasons why we're stopping here for the night. First, even if Nina hadn't come out here, someone would already have seen us and would have gone to tell Esther that we were coming. This way, she can decide whether or not she wants to see us, or if she would prefer to go to another village for a few days. If she did that, we wouldn't follow her.'

My heart contracted.

'Even after all I've been through to get here?'

'If that's how you feel, then you have understood nothing. What makes you think that your efforts should be rewarded with the submission, gratitude, and recognition of the person you love? You came here because this was the road you must follow, not in order to buy your wife's love.'

However unfair his words might seem, he was right. I asked him about the second reason.

'You still haven't chosen your name.'

'That doesn't matter,' Mikhail said again. 'He doesn't understand our culture, and he's not part of it.'

'It's important to me,' said Dos. 'My grandfather said that I must protect and help the foreign woman, just as she protected and helped me. I owe Esther the peace of my eyes, and I want her eyes to be at peace too.

He will have to choose a name. He will have to forget for ever his history of pain and suffering, and accept that he is a new person who has just been reborn and that, from now on, he will be reborn every day. If he doesn't do that, and if they ever do live together again, he will expect her to pay him back for all the pain she once caused him.'

'I chose a name last night,' I said.

'Wait until this evening to tell me.'

***

As soon as the sun began to sink low on the horizon, we went to an area on the steppes that was full of vast sand dunes. I became aware of a different sound, a kind of resonance, an intense vibration. Mikhail said that it was one of the few places in the world where the dunes sang.

'When I was in Paris and I talked to people about this, they only believed me because an American said that he had experienced the same thing in North Africa; there are only thirty places like it in the world. Nowadays, of course, scientists can explain everything. It seems that because of the place's unique formation, the wind penetrates the actual grains of sand and creates this sound. For the ancients, though, this was one of the magical places in the steppes, and it is a great honour that Dos should have chosen it for your name-changing.'

We started climbing one of the dunes, and as we proceeded the noise grew more intense and the wind stronger. When we reached the top, we could see the mountains standing out clearly to the south and the gigantic plain stretching out all around us.

'Turn towards the west and take off your clothes,' Dos said.

I did as he ordered, without asking why. I started to feel cold, but they seemed unconcerned about my well-being. Mikhail knelt down and appeared to be praying. Dos looked up at the sky, at the earth, at me, then placed his hands on my shoulders, just as I had done to the Dutchman, though without knowing why.

'In the name of the Lady, I dedicate you. I dedicate you to the earth, which belongs to the Lady. In the name of the horse, I dedicate you. I dedicate you to the world, and pray that the world helps you on your journey. In the name of the steppes, which are infinite, I dedicate you. I dedicate you to the infinite Wisdom, and pray that your horizon may always be wider than you can see. You have chosen your name and will speak it now for the first time.'

'In the name of the infinite steppes, I choose a name,' I replied, without asking if I was doing as the ritual demanded, merely allowing myself to be guided by the noise of the wind in the dunes. 'Many centuries ago, a poet described the wanderings of a man called Ulysses on his way back to an island called Ithaca, where his beloved awaits him. He confronts many perils, from storms to the temptations of comfort. At one point, in a cave, he encounters a monster with only one eye.

The monster asks him his name. "Nobody," says Ulysses. They fight and he manages to pierce the monster's one eye with his sword and then seals the mouth of the cave with a rock. The monster's companions hear his cries and rush to help him. Seeing that there is a rock covering the mouth of the cave, they ask who is with him. "Nobody! Nobody!" replies the monster. His companions leave, since there is clearly no threat to the community, and Ulysses can then continue on his journey back to the woman who waits for him.'

'So your name is Ulysses?'

'My name is Nobody.'

I am trembling all over, as if my skin were being pierced by hundreds of needles.

'Focus on the cold, until you stop trembling. Let the cold fill your every thought, until there is no space for anything else, until it becomes your companion and your friend. Do not try to control it. Do not think about the sun, that will only make it worse, because you will know then that something else – heat – exists and then the cold will feel that it is not loved or desired.'

My muscles were furiously stretching and contracting in order to produce energy and keep my organism alive. However, I did as Dos ordered, because I trusted him, trusted in his calm, his tenderness and his authority. I let the needles pierce my skin, allowed my muscles to struggle, my teeth to chatter, all the while repeating to myself: 'Don't fight; the cold is your friend.' My muscles refused to obey, and I remained like that for almost fifteen minutes, until my muscles eventually gave in and stopped shaking, and I entered a state of torpor. I tried to sit down, but Mikhail grabbed hold of me and held me up, while Dos spoke to me. His words seemed to come from a long way off, from a place where the steppes meet the sky:

'Welcome, nomad who crosses the steppes. Welcome to the place where we always say that the sky is blue even when it is grey, because we know that the colour is still there above the clouds. Welcome to the land of the Tengri. Welcome to me, for I am here to receive you and to honour you for your search.'

Mikhail sat down on the ground and asked me to drink something that immediately warmed my blood. Dos helped me to get dressed, and we made our way back down the dunes that continued to talk amongst themselves; we made our way back to our improvised camp site. Before Dos and Mikhail had even started cooking, I had fallen into a deep sleep.

'What's happening? Isn't it light yet?'

'It's been light for ages. It's just a sandstorm, don't worry. Put your dark glasses on to protect your eyes.'

'Where's Dos?'

'He's gone back to Almaty, but he was very moved by the ceremony yesterday evening. He didn't really need to do that. It was a bit of a waste of time for you really and a great opportunity to catch pneumonia. I hope you realise that it was just his way of showing you how welcome you are. Here, take the oil.'

'I overslept.'

'It's only a two-hour ride to the village. We'll be there before the sun is at its highest point.'

'I need a bath. I need to change my clothes.'

'That's impossible. You're in the middle of the steppes. Put the oil in the pan, but first offer it up to the Lady. Apart from salt, it's our most valuable commodity.'

'What is Tengri?'

'The word means "sky worship"; it's a kind of religion without religion. Everyone has passed through here – Buddhists, Hindus, Catholics, Muslims, different sects with their beliefs and superstitions. The nomads became converts to avoid being killed, but they continued and continue to profess the idea that the Divinity is everywhere all the time. You can't take the Divinity out of nature and put it in a book or between four walls. I've felt so much better since coming back to the steppes, as if I had been in real need of nourishment. Thank you for letting me come with you.'

'Thank you for introducing me to Dos. Yesterday, during that dedication ceremony, I sensed that he was someone special.'

'He learned from his grandfather, who learned from his father, who learned from his father, and so on. The nomadic way of life, and the absence of a written language until the end of the nineteenth century, meant that they had to develop the tradition of the *akyn*, the person who must remember everything and pass on the stories. Dos is an *akyn*. When I say "learn", though, I hope you don't take that to mean "accumulate knowledge". The stories have nothing to do with dates and names and facts. They are legends about heroes and heroines, animals and battles, about the symbols of man's essential self, not just his deeds. They're not stories about the vanquishers or the vanquished, but about people who travel the world, contemplate the steppes, and allow themselves to be filled by the energy of love. Pour the oil in more slowly, otherwise it will spit.'

'I felt blessed.'

'I'd like to feel that too. Yesterday, I went to visit my mother in Almaty. She asked if I was well and if I was earning money. I lied and said I was fine, that I was putting on a successful theatre production in Paris. I'm going back to my own people today, and it's as if I had left yesterday, and as if during all the time I've spent abroad, I had done nothing of any importance. I talk to beggars, wander the streets with the "tribe", organise the meetings at the restaurant, and what have I achieved? Nothing. I'm not like Dos, who learned from his grandfather. I only have the presence to guide me and sometimes I think that perhaps it *is* just a hallucination; perhaps my visions really are just epileptic fits, and nothing more.'

'A minute ago you were thanking me for bringing you with me, and now it seems to have brought you nothing but sadness. Make up your mind what you're feeling.'

'I feel both things at once, I don't have to choose. I can travel back and forth between the oppositions inside me, between my contradictions.'

'I want to tell you something, Mikhail. I too have travelled back and forth between many contradictions since I first met you. I began by hating you, then I accepted you, and as I've followed in your footsteps, that acceptance has become respect. You're still young, and the powerlessness you feel is perfectly normal. I don't know how many people your work has touched so far, but I can tell you one thing: you changed my life.'

'You were only interested in finding your wife.'

'I still am, but that didn't just make me travel across the Kazakhstan steppes: it made me travel through the whole of my past life. I saw where I went wrong, I saw where I stopped, I saw the moment when I lost Esther, the moment that the Mexican Indians call the *acomodador* – "the giving-up point". I experienced things I never imagined I would experience at my age. And all because you were by my side, guiding me, even though you might not have been aware that you were. And do you know something else? I believe that you do hear voices and that you did have visions when you were a child. I have always believed in many things, and now I believe even more.'

'You're not the same man I first met.'

'No, I'm not. I hope Esther will be pleased.'

'Are you?'

'Of course.'

'Then that's all that matters. Let's have something to eat, wait until the storm eases, and then set off.'

'Let's face the storm.'

'No, it's all right. Well, we can if you want, but the storm isn't a sign, it's just one of the consequences of the destruction of the Aral Sea.'

The furious wind is abating, and the horses seem to be galloping faster. We enter a kind of valley, and the landscape changes completely. The infinite horizon is replaced by tall, bare cliffs. I look to the right and see a bush full of ribbons.

'It was here! It was here that you saw … '

'No, my tree was destroyed.'

'So what's this, then?'

'A place where something very important must have happened.'

He dismounts, opens his saddlebag, takes out a knife, and cuts a strip off the sleeve of his shirt, then ties this to one of the branches. His eyes change; he may be feeling the presence beside him, but I prefer not to ask.

I follow his example. I ask for protection and help. I, too, feel a presence by my side: my dream, my long journey back to the woman I love.

We remount. He doesn't tell me what he asked for, and nor do I. Five minutes later, we see a small village of white houses. A man is waiting for us; he comes over to Mikhail and speaks to him in Russian. They talk for a while, then the man goes away.

'What did he want?'

'He wanted me to go to his house to cure his daughter. Nina must have told him I was arriving today, and the older people still remember my visions.'

He seems uncertain. There is no one else around; it must be a time when everyone is working, or perhaps eating. We were crossing the main road, which seemed to lead to a white building surrounded by a garden.

'Remember what I told you this morning, Mikhail. You might well just be an epileptic who refuses to accept the diagnosis and who has allowed his unconscious to build a whole story around it, but it could also be that you have a mission in the world: to teach people to forget their personal history and to be more open to love as pure, divine energy.'

'I don't understand you. All the months we've known each other, you've talked of nothing but this moment – finding Esther. And suddenly, ever since this morning, you seem more concerned about me than anything else. Perhaps Dos's ritual last night had some effect.'

'Oh, I'm sure it did.'

What I meant to say was: I'm terrified. I want to think about anything except what is about to happen in the next few minutes. Today, I am the most generous person on the face of this earth, because I am close to my objective and afraid of what awaits me. My reaction is to try and help others, to show God that I'm a good person and that I deserve this blessing that I have pursued so long and hard.

***

Mikhail dismounted and asked me to do the same.

'I'm going to the house of the man whose daughter is ill. I'll take care of your horse while you talk to Esther.'

He pointed to the small white building in the middle of the trees.

'Over there.'

I struggled to keep control of myself.

'What does she do?'

'As I told you before, she's learning to make carpets and, in exchange, she teaches French. By the way, although the carpets may look simple, they are, in fact, very complicated – just like the steppes. The dyes come from plants that have to be picked at precisely the right time, otherwise the colour won't be right. Then the wool is spread out on the ground, mixed with hot water, and the threads are made while the wool is still wet; and then, after many days, when the sun has dried them, the work of weaving begins. The final details are done by children. Adult hands are too big for the smallest, most delicate bits of embroidery.'

He paused.

'And no jokes about it being child's play. It's a tradition that deserves respect.'

'How is she?'

'I don't know. I haven't spoken to her for about six months.'

'Mikhail, these carpets are another sign.'

'The carpets?'

'Do you remember yesterday, when Dos asked me to choose my name, I told you the story of a warrior who returns to an island in search of his beloved? The island is called Ithaca and the woman is called Penelope. What do you think Penelope has been doing since Ulysses left? Weaving! She has been weaving a shroud for her father-in-law, Laertes, as a way of putting off her suitors. Only when she finishes the shroud will she remarry. While she waits for Ulysses to return, she unpicks her work every night and begins again the following day.

Her suitors want her to choose one of them, but she dreams of the return of the man she loves. Finally, when she has grown weary of waiting, Ulysses returns.'

'Except that the name of this village isn't Ithaca and Esther's name isn't Penelope.'

Mikhail had clearly not understood the story, and I didn't feel like explaining that it was just an example.

I handed him the reins of my horse and then walked the hundred metres that separated me from the woman who had been my wife, had then become the Zahir, and who was once more the beloved whom all men dream of finding when they return from war or from work.

I am filthy. My clothes and my face are caked with sand, my body drenched in sweat, even though it's very cold.

I worry about my appearance, the most superficial thing in the world, as if I had made this long journey to my personal Ithaca merely in order to show off my new clothes. As I walk the remaining one hundred metres, I must make an effort to think of all the important things that have happened during her – or was it my? – absence.

What should I say when we meet? I have often pondered this and come up with such phrases as: 'I've waited a long time for this moment' or 'I know now that I was wrong', or 'I came here to tell you that I love you', or even 'You're lovelier than ever.'

I decide just to say 'Hello'. As if she had never left. As if only a day had passed, not two years, nine months, eleven days and eleven hours.

And she needs to understand that I have changed as I've travelled through the same places she travelled through, places about which I knew nothing or in which I had simply never been interested. I had seen the scrap of bloodstained cloth in the hand of a beggar, in the hands of young people and adults in a Paris restaurant, in the hand of a painter, a doctor and a young man who claimed to see visions and hear voices. While I was following in her footsteps, I had got to know the woman

I had married and had rediscovered, too, the meaning of my own life, which had been through so many changes and was now about to change again.

Despite being married all those years, I had never really known my wife. I had created a 'love story' like the ones I'd seen in the movies, read about in books and magazines, watched on TV. In my story, love was something that grew until it reached a certain size and, from then on, it was just a matter of keeping it alive, like a plant, watering it now and again and removing any dead leaves. 'Love' was also a synonym for tenderness, security, prestige, comfort, success. 'Love' could be translated into smiles, into words like 'I love you' or 'I feel so happy when you come home.'

But things were more complicated than I thought. I could be madly in love with Esther while I was crossing the road, and yet, by the time I had reached the other side, I could be feeling trapped and wretched at having committed myself to someone, and longing to be able to set off once more in search of adventure. And then I would think: 'I don't love her any more.' And when love returned with the same intensity as before, I would doubt it and say to myself: 'I must have just got used to it.'

Perhaps Esther had had the same thoughts and had said to herself: 'Don't be silly, we're happy, we can spend the rest of our lives like this.' After all, she had read the same stories, seen the same films, watched the same TV series, and although none of them said that love was anything more than a happy ending, why give herself a hard time about it? If she repeated every morning that she was happy with her life, then she would doubtless end up believing it herself and making everyone around us believe it too.

However, she thought differently and acted differently. She tried to show me, but I couldn't see. I had to lose her in order to understand that the taste of things recovered is the sweetest honey we will ever know. Now I was there, walking down a street in a tiny, cold, sleepy village, once again following a road because of her. The first and most important thread that bound me – 'all love stories are the same' – had broken when I was knocked down by that motorbike.

In hospital, love had spoken to me: 'I am everything and I am nothing. I am the wind, and I cannot enter windows and doors that are shut.'

And I said to love: 'But I *am* open to you.'

And love said to me: 'The wind is made of air. There is air inside your house, but everything is shut up. The furniture will get covered in dust, the damp will ruin the paintings and stain the walls. You will continue to breathe, you will know a small part of me, but I am not a part, I am Everything, and you will never know that.'

I saw that the furniture was covered in dust, that the paintings were being corroded by damp, and I had no alternative but to open the windows and doors. When I did that, the wind swept everything away. I wanted to cling on to my memories, to protect what I thought I had worked hard to achieve, but everything had disappeared and I was as empty as the steppes.

As empty as the steppes: I understood now why Esther had decided to come here. It was precisely because everything was empty that the wind brought with it new things, noises I had never heard, people with whom I had never spoken. I recovered my old enthusiasm, because I had freed myself from my personal history; I had destroyed the *acomodador* and discovered that I was a man capable of blessing others, just as the nomads and shamans of the steppes blessed their fellows. I had discovered that I was much better and much more capable than I myself had thought; age only slows down those who never had the courage to walk at their own pace.

One day, because of a woman, I made a long pilgrimage in order to find my dream. Many years later, the same woman had made me set off again, this time to find the man who had got lost along the way.

Now I am thinking about everything except important things: I am mentally humming a tune, I wonder why there aren't any cars parked here, I notice that my shoe is rubbing, and that my wristwatch is still on European time.

And all because a woman, my wife, my guide and the love of my life, is now only a few steps away; anything to fend off the reality I have so longed for and which I am so afraid to face.

I sit down on the front steps of the house and smoke a cigarette. I think about going back to France. I've reached my goal, why go on?

I get up. My legs are trembling. Instead of setting off on the return journey, I clean off as much sand from my clothes and my face as I can, grasp the door handle and go in.

Although I know that I may have lost for ever the woman I love, I must try to enjoy all the graces that God has given me today. Grace cannot be hoarded. There are no banks where it can be deposited to be used when I feel more at peace with myself. If I do not make full use of these blessings, I will lose them for ever.

God knows that we are all artists of life. One day, he gives us a hammer with which to make sculptures, another day he gives us brushes and paints with which to make a picture, or paper and a pencil to write with. But you cannot make a painting with a hammer, or a sculpture with a paintbrush. Therefore, however difficult it may be, I must accept today's small blessings, even if they seem like curses because I am suffering and it's a beautiful day, the sun is shining, and the children are singing in the street. This is the only way I will manage to leave my pain behind and rebuild my life.

* * *

The room was flooded with light. She looked up when I came in and smiled, then continued reading *A Time to Rend and a Time to Sew* to the women and children sitting on the floor, with colourful fabrics all around them. Whenever Esther paused, they would repeat the words, keeping their eyes on their work.

I felt a lump in my throat, I struggled not to cry, and then I felt nothing. I just stood studying the scene, hearing my words on her lips, surrounded by colours and light and by people entirely focused on what they were doing.

***

In the words of a Persian sage: Love is a disease no one wants to get rid of. Those who catch it never try to get better, and those who suffer do not wish to be cured.

Esther closed the book. The women and children looked up and saw me.

'I'm going for a stroll with a friend of mine who has just arrived,' she told the group. 'Class is over for today.'

They all laughed and bowed. She came over and kissed my cheek, linked arms with me, and we went outside.

***

'Hello,' I said.

'I've been waiting for you,' she said.

I embraced her, rested my head on her shoulder, and began to cry. She stroked my hair, and by the way she touched me I began to understand what I did not want to understand, I began to accept what I did not want to accept.

'I've waited for you in so many ways,' she said, when she saw that my tears were abating. 'Like a desperate wife who knows that her husband has never understood her life, and that he will never come to her, and so she has no option but to get on a plane and go back, only to leave again after the next crisis, then go back and leave and go back …'

The wind had dropped; the trees were listening to what she was saying.

'I waited as Penelope waited for Ulysses, as Romeo waited for Juliet, as Beatrice waited for Dante. The empty steppes were full of memories of you, of the times we had spent together, of the countries we had visited, of our joys and our battles. Then I looked back at the trail left by my footprints and I couldn't see you.

I suffered greatly. I realised that I had set off on a path of no return and that when one does that, one can only go forward. I went to the nomad I had met before and asked him to teach me to forget my personal history, to open me up to the love that is present everywhere. With him I began to learn about the Tengri tradition. One day, I glanced to one side and saw that same love reflected in someone else's eyes, in the eyes of a painter called Dos.'

I said nothing.

'I was still very bruised. I couldn't believe it was possible to love again. He didn't say much; he taught me to speak Russian and told me that in the steppes they use the word "blue" to describe the sky even when it's grey, because they know that, above the clouds, the sky is always blue. He took me by the hand and helped me to go through those clouds. He taught me to love myself rather than to love him. He showed me that my heart was at the service of myself and of God, and not at the service of others.

He said that my past would always go with me, but that the more I freed myself from facts and concentrated on emotions, the more I would come to realise that in the present there is always a space as vast as the steppes waiting to be filled up with more love and with more of life's joy.

Finally, he explained to me that suffering occurs when we want other people to love us in the way we imagine we want to be loved, and not in the way that love should manifest itself – free and untrammelled, guiding us with its force and driving us on.'

I looked up at her.

'And do you love him?'

'I did.'

'Do you still love him?'

'What do you think? If I did love another man and was told that you were about to arrive, do you think I would still be here?'

'No, I don't. I think you've been waiting all morning for the door to open.'

'Why ask silly questions, then?'

Out of insecurity, I thought. But it was wonderful that she had tried to find love again.

'I'm pregnant.'

For a second, it was as if the world had fallen in on me.

'By Dos?'

'No. It was someone who stayed for a while and then left again.'

I laughed, even though my heart was breaking.

'Well, I suppose there's not much else to do here in this one-horse town,' I said.

'Hardly a one-horse town,' she replied, laughing too. 'But perhaps it's time you came back to Paris. Your newspaper phoned me asking if I knew where to find you. They wanted you to report on a NATO patrol in Afghanistan, but you'll have to say "no".'

'Why?'

'Because you're pregnant! You don't want the baby being exposed to all the negative energy of a war, surely.'

'The baby? You don't think a baby's going to stop me working, do you? Besides, why should you worry? You didn't do anything to contribute.'

'Didn't contribute? It's thanks to me that you came here in the first place. Or doesn't that count?'

She took a piece of bloodstained cloth from the pocket of her white dress and gave it to me, her eyes full of tears.

'This is for you. I've missed our arguments.'

And then, after a pause, she added:

'Ask Mikhail to get another horse.'

I placed my hands on her shoulders and blessed her just as I had been blessed.

Author's Note

I wrote *The Zahir* between January and June 2004, while I was making my own pilgrimage through this world. Parts of the book were written in Paris and St Martin in France, in Madrid and Barcelona in Spain, in Amsterdam, on a road in Belgium, in Almaty and on the Kazakhstan steppes.

I would like to thank my French publishers, Anne and Alain Carrière, who undertook to check all the information about French law mentioned in the book.

I first read about the Favour Bank in *The Bonfire of the Vanities* by Tom Wolfe. The story that Esther tells about Fritz and Hans is based on a story in *Ishmael* by Daniel Quinn. The mystic quoted by Marie on the importance of remaining vigilant is Kenan Rifai. Most of what the 'tribe' in Paris say was told to me by young people who belong to such groups. Some of them post their ideas on the Internet, but it's impossible to pinpoint an author.

The lines that the main character learned as a child and remembers when he is in hospital ('When the Unwanted Guest arrives ...') are from the poem 'Consoada' by the Brazilian poet Manuel Bandeira. Some of Marie's remarks following the chapter when the main character goes to the station to meet the American actor are based on a conversation with the Swedish actress Agneta Sjodin. The concept of forgetting one's personal history, which is part of many initiation traditions, is clearly set out in *Journey to Ixtlan* by Carlos Castaneda. The Law of Jante was developed by the Danish writer Aksel Sandemose in his novel *A Fugitive Crossing His Tracks*.

Two people who do me the great honour of being my friends, Dmitry Voskoboynikov and Evgenia Dotsuk, made my visit to Kazakhstan possible.

In Almaty, I met Imangali Tasmagambetov, author of the book *The Centaurs of the Great Steppe* and an expert on Kazakh culture, who provided me with much important information about the political and cultural situation in Kazakhstan, both past and present. I would also like to thank the President of the Republic, Nursultan Nazarbaev for making me so welcome, and I would like to take this opportunity to congratulate him for putting a stop to nuclear tests in his country, even though all the necessary technology is there, and for deciding instead to destroy Kazakhstan's entire nuclear arsenal.

Lastly, I owe many of my magical experiences on the steppes to my three very patient companions: Kaisar Alimkulov, Dos (Dosbol Kasymov), an extremely talented painter, on whom I based the character of the same name who appears at the end of the book, and Marie Nimirovskaya, who, initially, was just my interpreter but soon became my friend.

How can you find your heart's desire?

A world-wide phenomenon; an inspiration for anyone seeking their path in life.

The Alchemist

Do you believe in yourself?

A modern-day adventure in the searing heat of the Mojave desert and an exploration of fear and self-doubt.

The Valkyries

How do we see the amazing in the everyday?

When two young lovers are reunited, they discover anew the truth of what lies in their hearts.

By the River Piedra I Sat Down & Wept

What are you searching for?

A transforming journey on the pilgrims' road to Santiago – and the first of Paulo's extraordinary books.

The Pilgrimage

Can faith triumph over suffering?

Paulo Coelho's brilliant telling of the story of Elijah, who was forced to choose between love and duty.

The Fifth Mountain

Is life always worth living?

A fundamental moral question explored as only Paulo Coelho can.

Veronika Decides to Die

Could you be tempted into evil?

The inhabitants of a small town are challenged by a mysterious stranger to choose between good and evil.

The Devil & Miss Prym

Are you brave enough to live your dream?

Strategies and inspiration to help you follow your own path in a troubled world.

Manual of the Warrior of Light

Can sex be sacred?

An unflinching exploration of the lengths we go to in our search for love, sex and spirituality.

Eleven Minutes

How far would you go for your obsession?

A sweeping story of love, loss and longing that spans the world.

The Zahir

What happens when obsession turns to murder?

An enthralling story of jealousy, death and suspense.

The Winner Stands Alone

Can we dare to be true to ourselves?

A story that will transform the way we think about love, joy and sacrifice.

The Witch of Portobello

How will you know who your soulmate is?

A moving tale of passion, mystery and spirituality.

Brida

What does it mean to be truly alive?

Powerful tales of living and dying, destiny and choice, and love lost and found.

Like the Flowing River

Are you where you want to be?

Read *Aleph*. And rewrite your life.

Aleph

Is there a weapon more powerful than words?

A timeless and powerful exploration of personal growth, everyday wisdom and joy.

Manuscript Found in Accra

The FIFTH MOUNTAIN

Paulo Coelho was born in Brazil and has become one of the most widely read and loved authors in the world. Especially renowned for *The Alchemist* and *Eleven Minutes*, he has sold more than 320 million books worldwide and has been translated into 88 languages. The recipient of numerous prestigious international awards, amongst them the Crystal Award by the World Economic Forum and France's Légion d'Honneur, Paulo Coelho was inducted into the Brazilian Academy of Letters in 2002.

Also by Paulo Coelho

The Alchemist
The Pilgrimage
The Valkyries
By the River Piedra I Sat Down and Wept
The Fifth Mountain
Veronika Decides to Die
Manual of the Warrior of Light
Eleven Minutes
The Zahir
The Devil and Miss Prym
The Witch of Portobello
Brida
The Winner Stands Alone
Like the Flowing River
Aleph
Manuscript Found in Accra
Adultery
The Spy
Hippie

The Fifth Mountain

PAULO COELHO

Author of THE ALCHEMIST

TRANSLATED BY CLIFFORD E. LANDERS

Thorsons

Thorsons
An imprint of HarperCollins*Publishers*
1 London Bridge Street
London SE1 9GF

HarperCollins*Publishers*
1st Floor, Watermarque Building, Ringsend Road
Dublin 4, Ireland

www.harpercollins.co.uk
www.paulocoelho.com
www.paulocoelhoblog.com

First published in the US by
HarperCollins*Publishers*, Inc., New York 1998
Published in the UK by HarperCollins*Publishers* 1998
This edition 2022

2 4 6 8 10 9 7 5 3 1

© Paulo Coelho 1996

English version © Paulo Coelho
and Alan R. Clarke 1992, 2012

Paulo Coelho asserts the moral right to
be identified as the author of this work

A catalogue record for this book
is available from the British Library

ISBN 978-0-00-854734-9

FICTION / PHILOSOPHY

Printed and bound in India by Thomson Press India Ltd

All rights reserved. No part of this publication may be
reproduced, stored in a retrieval system, or transmitted,
in any form or by any means, electronic, mechanical,
photocopying, recording or otherwise, without the prior
written permission of the publishers.

This book is produced from independently certified FSC® paper
to ensure responsible forest management.

O Mary!
conceived without sin,
pray for us who turn to you!
Amen.

And he said, Verily I say unto you, No prophet is accepted in his own country.

But I tell you of a truth, many widows were in Israel in the days of Elias, when the heaven was shut up three years and six months, when great famine was throughout all the land;

But unto none of them was Elias sent, save unto Zarephath, a city of Sidon, unto a woman that was a widow.

Luke 4:24-26

For A. M.,

a warrior of the light and

Mauro Salles.

NOTE FROM THE AUTHOR

◆ ◆ ◆

In my book The Alchemist, the central thesis lies in a phrase that King Melchizedek says to the shepherd boy Santiago: "When you want something, all the universe conspires in helping you to achieve it."

I believe this with all my heart. However, the act of living one's own destiny includes a series of stages that are far beyond our understanding, whose objective is always to take us back to the path of our Personal Legend—or to make us learn the lessons necessary to fulfill our own destiny. I think I can better illustrate what I am saying by relating an episode in my life.

On August 12, 1979, I went to sleep with a single certainty: at the age of thirty I was successfully making my way to the top of my career as a recording executive. I was working as artistic director for CBS in Brazil, and I had just been invited to the United

States to talk to the owners of the company, who would surely provide me with every opportunity to achieve all that I desired to do in my area. Of course my great dream—to be a writer—had been set aside, but what did that matter? After all, real life was very different from what I had imagined; there was no way to earn a living from literature in Brazil.

That night I made a decision: to abandon my dream. One had to adapt to circumstances and take advantage of opportunities. If my heart protested, I could deceive it by composing song lyrics whenever I wanted, and by doing some writing now and then for some newspaper. Besides, I was convinced that my life had taken a different path, but one no less exciting: a brilliant future awaited me in the world of the music multinationals.

When I woke up, I received a phone call from the president: I had just been fired, without further explanation. Although I knocked on various doors in the next two years, I never found a position again in that field.

When I finished writing The Fifth Mountain, I recalled that episode—and other manifestations of the unavoidable in my life. Whenever I thought myself the absolute master of a situation, something would happen to cast me down. I asked myself: why? Can it be that I'm condemned to always come close but never reach the finish line? Can God be so cruel that He would let me see the palm trees on the horizon only to have me die of thirst in the desert?

It took a long time to understand that it wasn't quite like

that. There are things that are brought into our lives to lead us back to the true path of our Personal Legend. Other things arise so we can apply all that we have learned. And, finally, some things come along to teach us.

In my book The Pilgrimage, I tried to show that these teachings need not be linked to pain and suffering; discipline and attentiveness alone are enough. Although this understanding has become an important blessing in my life, it still did not equip me to transit certain difficult moments that I experienced, even with total discipline and attentiveness.

One example is the case I have cited; I was a serious professional, made every effort to give the best there was in me, and had ideas that even today I consider worthwhile. But the unavoidable happened, at the very moment when I felt most secure and confident. I believe I am not alone in this experience; the unavoidable has touched the life of every human being on the face of the earth. Some have rebounded, others have given up—but all of us have felt the wings of tragedy brushing against us.

Why? To answer this question, I let Elijah lead me through the days and nights of Akbar.

PROLOGUE

◆ ◆ ◆

At the beginning of the year 870 B.C., a nation known as Phoenicia, which the Israelites called Lebanon, had marked almost three centuries of peace. Its inhabitants could take pride in their accomplishments; because they were not politically powerful, they had developed an enviable skill at negotiation as the only means of assuring survival in a world beset by constant war. An alliance made around the year 1000 B.C. with King Solomon of Israel had allowed the modernization of its merchant fleet and the expansion of trade. Since that time, Phoenicia had never stopped growing.

Its navigators had traveled to places as distant as Spain and the Atlantic Ocean, and there are theories—as yet unconfirmed—of their having left inscriptions in northeastern and southern Brazil. They carried glass, cedar, weapons, iron, and ivory. The inhabitants of the large cities such as Sidon, Tyre, and Byblos were familiar with numbers, astronomical calculations, the manufacture of wine, and for almost two hundred years had been using a set of characters for writing, which the Greeks knew as *alphabet.*

At the beginning of the year 870 B.C., a council of war was meeting in a distant place called Nineveh. A group of Assyrian generals had decided to send troops to conquer the nations located along the Mediterranean coast. Phoenicia had been selected as the first country to be invaded.

At the beginning of the year 870 B.C., two men hiding in a stable in Gilead, in Israel, expected to die in the next few hours.

PART I

"I have served a Lord who now abandons me into the hands of my enemies," said Elijah.

"God is God," the Levite replied. "He did not tell Moses whether He was good or evil; He simply said: *I am.* He is everything that exists under the sun—the lightning bolt that destroys a house, and the hand of man that rebuilds it."

Talking was the only way to ward off fear; at any moment, soldiers would open the door to the stable where they were hiding, discover them both, and offer the only choice possible: worship Baal, the Phoenician god, or be executed. They were searching house by house, converting the prophets or executing them.

Perhaps the Levite would convert and escape death. But for Elijah there was no choice: everything was happening through his own fault, and Jezebel wanted his head under all circumstances.

"It was an angel of the Lord who obliged me to speak to King Ahab and warn him that it would not rain so long as Baal was worshiped in Israel," he said, almost in a plea for absolution for having heeded what the angel had told him. "But God acts slowly; when the drought begins to take hold, Princess Jezebel will already have destroyed all who remain loyal to the Lord."

The Levite said nothing. He was reflecting on whether he should convert to Baal or die in the name of the Lord.

"Who is God?" Elijah continued. "Is it He who holds the sword of the soldier, the sword that executes those who will not betray the faith of our patriarchs? Was it He who placed a foreign princess on our country's throne, so that all this misfortune could befall our generation? Does God kill the faithful, the innocent, those who follow the law of Moses?"

The Levite made his decision: he preferred to die. Then he began to laugh, for the idea of death frightened him no longer. He turned to the young prophet beside him and attempted to calm him. "Ask God, since you doubt His decisions," he said. "I have accepted my fate."

"The Lord cannot wish us to be massacred without mercy," insisted Elijah.

"God is all-powerful. If He limited Himself to doing only that which we call good, we could not call Him the Almighty; he would command only one part of the universe, and there would exist someone more powerful than He, watching and judging His acts. In that case, I would worship that more powerful someone."

"If He is all-powerful, why doesn't He spare the suffering of those who love Him? Why doesn't He save them, instead of giving might and glory to His enemies?"

"I don't know," said the Levite. "But a reason exists, and I hope to learn it soon."

"You have no answer to this question."

"No."

The two men fell silent. Elijah felt a cold sweat.

"You are terrified, but I have already accepted my fate," the Levite said. "I am going out, to bring an end to this agony. Each time I hear a scream out there, I suffer, imagining how it will be when my time comes. Since we've been locked in here, I have died a hundredfold, while I could have died just once. If I am to be beheaded, let it be as quickly as possible."

He was right. Elijah had heard the same screams, and he had suffered beyond his ability to withstand.

"I'm going with you. I weary of fighting for a few more hours of life."

He rose and opened the stable door, allowing the sun to enter and expose the two men hiding there.

◆

THE LEVITE took him by the arm, and they began to walk. If not for one then another scream, it would have seemed a normal day in a city like any other—a sun that barely tingled the skin, the breeze coming from a distant ocean to moderate the temperature, the dusty streets, the houses built of a mixture of clay and straw.

"Our souls are prisoners of the terror of death, and the day is beautiful," said the Levite. "Many times before, when I felt at peace with God and the world, the temperature was horrible, the desert wind filled my eyes with sand and did not permit me to see a hand's span before me. Not always does His plan agree with what we are or what we feel, but be assured that He has a reason for all of this."

"I admire your faith."

The Levite looked at the sky, as if reflecting briefly. Then he turned to Elijah. "Do not admire, and do not believe so much; it was a wager I made with myself. I wagered that God exists."

"You're a prophet," answered Elijah. "You too hear voices and know that there is a world beyond this world."

"It could be my imagination."

"You have seen God's signs," Elijah insisted, beginning to feel anxiety at his companion's words.

"It could be my imagination," was again the answer. "In actuality, the only concrete thing I have is my wager: I have told myself that everything comes from the Most High."

◆

THE STREET was deserted. Inside their houses, the people waited for Ahab's soldiers to complete the task that the foreign princess had demanded: executing the prophets of Israel. Elijah walked beside the Levite, feeling that behind each door and window was someone watching him—and blaming him for what had happened.

"I did not ask to be a prophet. Perhaps everything is merely the fruit of my own imagination," thought Elijah.

But, after what had occurred in the carpenter's shop, he knew it was not.

◆

SINCE CHILDHOOD, he had heard voices and spoken with angels. This was when he had been impelled by his father and mother to seek out a priest of Israel who, after asking many questions, identified Elijah as a *nabi,* a prophet, a "man of the spirit," one who "exalts himself with the word of God."

After speaking with him for many hours, the priest told his father and mother that whatever the boy might utter should be regarded as earnest.

When they left that place, his father and mother demanded that Elijah never tell anyone what he saw and heard; to be a prophet meant having ties to the government, and that was always dangerous.

In any case, Elijah had never heard anything that might interest priests or kings. He spoke only with his guardian angel and heard only advice about his own life; from time to time he had visions he could not understand—distant seas, mountains populated with strange beings, wheels with wings and eyes. As soon as the visions disappeared, he—obedient to his father and mother—made every effort to forget them as rapidly as possible.

For this reason, the voices and visions became more and more infrequent. His father and mother were pleased, and they did not raise the matter again. When he came of an age to sustain himself, they lent him money to open a small carpentry shop.

◆

NOW AND AGAIN, he would gaze respectfully upon the other prophets, who walked the streets of Gilead wearing their customary cloaks of skins and sashes of leather and saying that the Lord had singled them out to guide the Chosen People. Truly, such was not his destiny; never would he be capable of evoking a trance through dancing or self-flagellation, a common practice among those "exalted by the voice of God," because he was afraid of pain. Nor would he ever walk the streets of Gilead, proudly displaying the scars from injuries achieved during a state of ecstasy, for he was too shy.

Elijah considered himself a common man, one who dressed like the rest and who tortured only his soul, with the same fears and temptations of simple mortals. As his work in the carpentry shop went on, the voices ceased completely, for adults and workers have no time for such things. His father and mother were happy with their son, and life proceeded in harmony and peace.

The conversation with the priest, when he was still a child, came to be merely a remote memory. Elijah could not believe that Almighty God must talk with men to have His orders obeyed; what had happened in his childhood was only the fantasy of a boy with nothing to do. In Gilead, his native city, there were those thought by the inhabitants to be mad. They were unable to speak coherently and incapable of distinguishing the voice of the Lord from the delirium of insanity. They spent their lives in the streets, preaching the end of the world and living on the charity of others. Even so, none of the priests considered them "exalted by the voice of God."

Elijah concluded in the end that the priests would never be sure of what they were saying. The "exalted of God" were a consequence of a country uncertain of its way, where brother fought brother, where new governments appeared with regularity. Prophets and madmen were one and the same.

When he learned of his king's marriage to Jezebel, princess of Tyre, he had thought it of little significance. Other kings of Israel had done the same, and the result had been a lasting peace in the region and an ever more important trade with Lebanon. Elijah scarcely cared if the people of the neighboring country believed in gods that did not exist or dedicated themselves to strange religious practices such as worshiping animals and mountains; they were honest in their negotiations, and that was what mattered most.

Elijah went on buying the cedar they brought in and selling the products of his carpentry shop. Though they were somewhat haughty and liked to call themselves "Phoenicians" because of the different color of their skin, none of the merchants from Lebanon had ever tried to take advantage of the confusion that reigned in Israel. They paid a fair price for the merchandise and made no comment about the constant internal wars or the political problems facing the Israelites.

◆

After ascending to the throne, Jezebel had asked Ahab to replace the worship of the Lord with that of the gods of Lebanon.

That too had happened before. Elijah, though outraged at Ahab's compliance, continued to worship the God of Israel and to observe the laws of Moses. "It will pass," he thought. "Jezebel seduced Ahab, but she will not succeed in convincing the people."

But Jezebel was a woman unlike others; she believed that Baal had brought her into the world to convert peoples and nations. Astutely and patiently, she began rewarding those who deserted the Lord and accepted the new deities. Ahab ordered a temple built for Baal in Samaria and in it raised an altar. Pilgrimages began, and the worship of the gods of Lebanon spread to all parts.

"It will pass. It may take a generation, but it will pass," Elijah went on thinking.

◆

Then something he was not expecting took place. One afternoon, as he was finishing a table in his shop, everything around him grew dark and thousands of tiny lights began twinkling about him. His head began to ache as never before; he tried to sit but could not move a muscle.

It was not his imagination.

"I'm dying," he thought at that instant. "And now I'll discover where God sends us after death: to the heart of the firmament."

One of the lights shone more brightly, and suddenly, as if coming from everywhere at once:

"And the word of the Lord came unto him, saying: Tell Ahab, that as surely as the Lord God of Israel liveth, before whom thou standest, there shall not be dew nor rain these years, but according to My word."

The next moment, all returned to normal: the carpentry shop, the afternoon light, the voices of children playing in the street.

◆

ELIJAH DID NOT SLEEP that night. For the first time in many years, the sensations of his childhood came back to him; and it was not his guardian angel speaking but "something" larger and more powerful than he. He feared that if he failed to carry out the order he might be cursed in his trade.

By morning, he had decided to do as he had been asked. After all, he was only the messenger of something that did not concern him; once the task was done, the voices would not return to trouble him.

It was not difficult to arrange a meeting with King Ahab. Many generations before, with the ascension of King Samuel to the throne, the prophets had gained importance in commerce and in government. They could marry, have children, but they must always be at the Lord's disposal so that the rulers would never stray from the correct path. Tradition held that thanks to these "exalted of God" many battles had been won, and that Israel survived because its rulers, when they did stray from the path of righteousness, always had a prophet to lead them back to the way of the Lord.

Arriving at the palace, he told the king that a drought would assail the region until worship of the Phoenician gods was forsaken.

The sovereign gave little importance to his words, but Jezebel—who was at Ahab's side and listened attentively to what Elijah was saying—began to ask a series of questions about the message. Elijah told her of the vision, of the pain in his head, of the sensation that time had stopped as he listened to the angel. As he described what had happened, he was able to observe closely the princess of whom all were talking; she was one of the most beautiful women he had ever seen, with long, dark hair falling to the waist of a perfectly contoured body. Her green eyes, which shone in her dark face, remained fixed on Elijah's; he was unable to decipher what they meant, nor could he know the impact his words were causing.

He left convinced that he had carried out his mission and could go back to his work in the carpentry shop. On his way, he desired Jezebel, with all the ardor of his twenty-three years. And he asked God whether in the future he could find a woman from Lebanon, for they were beautiful with their dark skin and green eyes full of mystery.

◆

HE WORKED for the rest of the day and slept peacefully. The next morning he was awakened before dawn by the Levite; Jezebel had convinced the king that the prophets were a menace to the growth and expansion of Israel. Ahab's soldiers had orders to execute all who refused to abandon the sacred task that God had conferred upon them.

To Elijah alone, however, no right of choice had been given: he was to be killed.

He and the Levite spent two days hidden in the stable south of Gilead while 450 *nabi* were summarily executed. But most of the prophets, who roamed the streets flagellating themselves and preaching the end of the world for its corruption and lack of faith, had accepted conversion to the new religion.

◆

A SHARP SOUND, followed by a scream, broke into Elijah's thoughts. He turned in alarm to his companion.

"What was that?"

There was no answer; the Levite's body fell to the ground, an arrow piercing his chest.

Standing before him, a soldier fitted another arrow into his bow. Elijah looked about him: the street with doors and windows tightly shut, the sun shining in the heavens, a breeze coming from an ocean of which he had heard so much but had never seen. He thought of running, but he knew he would be overtaken before he reached the next corner.

"If I must die, let it not be from behind," he thought.

The soldier again raised his bow. To Elijah's surprise, he felt neither fear nor the instinct to survive, nor anything else; it was as if everything had been determined long ago, and the two of them—he and the soldier—were merely playing roles in a drama not of their own writing. He remembered his childhood, the mornings and afternoons in Gilead, the unfinished work he would leave in his carpentry shop. He thought of his mother and father, who had never desired their son to be a prophet. He thought of Jezebel's eyes and of King Ahab's smile.

He thought how stupid it was to die at twenty-three, without ever having known a woman's love.

The soldier's hand released the string, the arrow slashed through the air, hummed past his right ear to bury itself in the dusty ground behind him.

The soldier rearmed his bow and pointed it. But instead of firing, he fixed his eyes on Elijah's.

"I am the greatest archer in all King Ahab's armies," he said. "For seven years I have never erred a shot."

Elijah turned to the Levite's body.

"That arrow was meant for you." The soldier's bow was still taut, and his hands were trembling. "Elijah was the only prophet who must be killed; the others could choose the faith of Baal," he said.

"Then finish your task."

He was surprised at his own calmness. He had imagined death so often during the nights in the stable, and now he saw that he had suffered unnecessarily; in a few seconds all would be ended.

"I can't," said the soldier, his hands still trembling, the arrow changing directions at every instant. "Leave, get out of my presence, because I believe God deflected my arrow and will curse me if I kill you."

It was then, as he discovered that death could elude him, that the fear of death returned. There was still the possibility of seeing the ocean, of finding a wife, having children, and completing his work in the shop.

"Finish this here and now," he said. "At this moment I am calm. If you tarry, I will suffer over all that I am losing."

The soldier looked about him to make certain that no one had witnessed the scene. Then he lowered his bow, replaced the arrow in its quiver, and disappeared around the corner.

Elijah felt his legs begin to weaken; the terror had returned in all its intensity. He must flee at once, disappear from Gilead, never again have to meet face-to-face a soldier with a drawn bow and an arrow pointed at his heart. He had not chosen his destiny, nor had he sought out Ahab in order to boast to his neighbors that he could talk with the king. He was not responsible for the massacre of the prophets—nor even for, one afternoon, having seen time stop and the carpentry shop transformed into a dark hole filled with points of light.

Mimicking the soldier's gesture, he looked to all sides; the street was deserted. He thought of seeing if he could still save the Levite's life, but the terror quickly returned, and before anyone else could appear, Elijah fled.

He walked for many hours, taking paths long since unused, until he arrived at the bank of the rivulet of Cherith. He felt shame at his cowardice but joy at being alive.

He drank a bit of water, sat, and only then realized the situation in which he found himself: the next day he would need to feed himself, and food was nowhere to be found in the desert.

He remembered the carpentry shop, his long years of work, and having been forced to leave it all behind. Some of his neighbors were friends, but he could not count on them; the story of his flight must have already spread throughout the city, and he was hated by all for having escaped while he sent true men of faith to martyrdom.

Whatever he had done in the past now lay in ruins—merely because he had elected to carry out the Lord's will. Tomorrow, and in the days, weeks, and months to come, the traders from Lebanon would knock on his door and someone would tell them the owner had fled, leaving behind a trail of innocent prophets' deaths. Perhaps they would add that he had tried to destroy the gods that protected heaven and earth; the story would quickly cross Israel's borders, and he could forget forever marrying a woman as beautiful as those in Lebanon.

◆

"THERE ARE the ships."

Yes, there were the ships. Criminals, prisoners of war, fugitives were usually accepted as mariners because it was a profession more dangerous than the army. In war, a soldier always had a chance to escape with his life; but the seas were an unknown, populated by monsters, and when a tragedy occurred, none were left to tell the story.

There were the ships, but they were controlled by Phoenician merchants. Elijah was not a criminal, a prisoner, or a fugitive but someone who had dared raise his voice against the god Baal. When they found him out, he would be killed and cast into the sea, for mariners believed that Baal and his gods governed the storms.

He could not go toward the ocean. Nor could he make his way north, for there lay Lebanon. He could not go east, where certain tribes of Israel were engaged in a war that had already lasted two generations.

◆

HE RECALLED the feeling of calm he had experienced in the presence of the soldier; after all, what was death? Death was an instant, nothing more. Even if he felt pain, it must pass at once, and then the Lord of Hosts would receive him in His bosom.

He lay down on the ground and looked at the sky for a long time. Like the Levite, he tried to make his wager. It was not a wager about God's existence, for of that he had no doubt, but about the reason for his own life.

He saw the mountains, the earth that soon would be beset by a long drought, as the angel of the Lord had said, but for now still had the coolness of many generations of rain. He saw the rivulet of Cherith, whose waters in a short time would cease to flow. He took his leave of the world with fervor and respect, and asked the Lord to receive him when his time was come.

He thought about the reason for his existence, and obtained no answer.

He thought about where he should go, and discovered that he was surrounded.

The following day he would go back and hand himself over, even if his fear of death returned.

He tried to find joy in the knowledge that he would go on living for a few more hours. But it was futile; he had just discovered that, as in almost all the days of a life, man is powerless to make a decision.

Elijah awoke the next day and again looked at the Cherith.

Tomorrow, or a year from now, it would be only a bed of fine sand and smooth stones. The old inhabitants still referred to the site as Cherith, and perhaps they would give directions to those passing through by saying: "Such a place is on the bank of the river that runs near here." The travelers would make their way there, see the round stones and the fine sand, and reflect to themselves: "Here in this land there was once a river." But the only thing that mattered about a river, its flow of water, would no longer be there to quench their thirst.

Souls too, like rivulets and plants, needed a different kind of rain: hope, faith, a reason to live. When this did not come to pass, everything in that soul died, even if the body went on living;

and the people could say: "Here in this body there was once a man."

It was not the time to think about that. Again he remembered the conversation with the Levite just before they left the stable: what was gained from dying many deaths, if one alone sufficed? All he had to do was wait for Jezebel's soldiers. They would come, beyond any doubt, for there were few places to flee from Gilead; wrongdoers always fled to the desert—where they were found dead within a few days—or to the Cherith, where they were quickly captured.

The soldiers would therefore come soon. And he would rejoice at their sight.

◆

HE DRANK a bit of the crystalline water that ran beside him. He cleansed his face, then sought out shade where he could await his pursuers. A man cannot fight his destiny—he had already tried, and he had lost.

Despite the priests' belief that he was a prophet, he had decided to work as a carpenter; but the Lord had led him back to his path.

He was not the only one to abandon the life that the Lord had written for every person on earth. He had once had a friend with an excellent voice, whose father and mother had been unwilling to have him become a singer because it was a profession that brought dishonor to the family. A girl with whom he had been friends as a child could have been a dancer without equal; she too had been forbidden by her family, for the king might summon her, and no one knew how long his reign would last. Moreover, the atmosphere in the palace was considered sinful and hostile, ending permanently any possibility of a good marriage.

"Man was born to betray his destiny." God placed only impossible tasks in human hearts.

"Why?"

Perhaps because custom must be maintained.

But that was not a good answer. "The inhabitants of Lebanon are more advanced than are we, because they did not follow the customs of the navigators. When everyone else was using the same kind of ship, they decided to build something different. Many lost their lives at sea, but their ships continued to improve, and today they dominate the world's commerce. They paid a high price to adapt, but it proved to be worth the cost."

Perhaps mankind betrayed its destiny because God was not closer. He had placed in people's hearts a dream of an era when everything was possible—and then gone on to busy Himself with other things. The world had transformed itself, life had become more difficult, but the Lord had never returned to change men's dreams.

God was distant. But if He still sent His angels to speak to His prophets, it was because there was still something left to be done here. What could the answer be?

"Perhaps because our fathers fell into error, and they fear we will repeat their mistakes. Or perhaps they never erred, and thus will not know how to help us if we have some problem."

He felt he was drawing near. The rivulet was flowing at his side, a few crows were circling in the sky, the plants clinging insistently to life in the sandy, sterile terrain. Had they listened to the words of their forebears, what would they have heard?

"Rivulet, seek a better place for your limpid waters to reflect the brightness of the sun, for the desert will one day dry you up," the god of waters would have said, if perchance one existed. "Crows, there is more food in the forests than among rocks and sand," the god of the birds would have said. "Plants, spread your seeds far from here, because the world is full of humid, fertile ground, and you will grow more beautiful," the god of flowers would have said.

But the Cherith, like the plants and the crows, one of which had perched nearby, had the courage to do what other rivers, or birds, or flowers thought impossible.

Elijah fixed his gaze on the crow.

"I'm learning," he told the bird. "Though the lesson is a futile one, for I am condemned to death."

"You have discovered how everything is simple," the crow seemed to reply. "Having courage is enough."

Elijah laughed, for he was putting words into the mouth of a bird. It was an amusing game, one he had learned with a woman who made bread, and he decided to continue. He would ask the questions and offer himself an answer, as if he were a true sage.

The crow, however, took flight. Elijah went on waiting for Jezebel's soldiers to arrive, for dying a single time sufficed.

The day went by without anything happening. Could they have forgotten that the principal enemy of the god Baal still lived? Jezebel must know where he was; why did she not pursue him?

"Because I saw her eyes, and she is a wise woman," he told himself. "If I were to die, I would live on as a martyr of the Lord. If I'm thought of as just a fugitive, I'll be merely a coward who had no faith in his own words."

Yes, that was the princess's strategy.

◆

SHORTLY BEFORE NIGHTFALL, a crow—could it be the same one?—perched on the bough where he had seen it that morning. In its beak was a small piece of meat that it accidentally dropped.

To Elijah, it was a miracle. He ran to the spot beneath the tree, picked up the chunk of meat, and ate it. He didn't know from where it had come, nor did he wish to know; what was important was his being able to satisfy a small part of his hunger.

Even with his sudden movement, the crow did not fly away.

"This crow knows I'm going to starve to death here," he thought. "He's feeding his prey so he can have a better feast later."

Even as Jezebel fed the faith of Baal with news of Elijah's flight.

The two of them, man and crow, contemplated each other. Elijah recalled the game he had played that morning.

"I would like to talk to you, crow. This morning, I had the thought that souls need food. If my soul has not yet perished of hunger, it has something still to say."

The bird remained immobile.

"And, if it has something to say, I must listen. Because I have no one else with whom to speak," continued Elijah.

In his imagination Elijah was transformed into the crow.

"What it is that God expects of you?" he asked himself, as if he were the crow.

"He expects me to be a prophet."

"This is what the priests said. But it may not be what God desires."

"Yes, it is what He wants. An angel appeared to me in my shop and asked me to speak with Ahab. The voices I heard as a child—"

"Everyone hears voices as a child," interrupted the crow.

"But not everyone sees an angel," Elijah said.

This time the crow did not reply. After an interval, the bird—or rather, his own soul, delirious from the sun and loneliness of the desert—broke the silence.

"Do you remember the woman who used to make bread?" he asked himself.

◆

ELIJAH REMEMBERED. She had come to ask him to make some trays. While Elijah was doing as she asked, he heard her say that her work was a way of expressing the presence of God.

"From the way you make the trays, I can see that you have the same feeling," she had continued. "Because you smile as you work."

The woman divided human beings into two groups: those who took joy in, and those who complained about, what they did. The latter affirmed that the curse cast upon Adam by God was the only truth: "*Cursed is the ground for thy sake; in sorrow shalt thou eat of it all the days of thy life.*" They took no pleasure in work and were annoyed on feast days, when they were obliged to rest. They used the Lord's words as an excuse for their futile lives, forgetting that He had also said to Moses: "*For the Lord shall greatly bless thee in the land which the Lord thy God giveth thee for an inheritance to possess it.*"

"Yes, I remember the woman. She was right; I did enjoy my work in the carpentry shop. She taught me to talk to things."

"If you had not worked as a carpenter, you would not have been able to place your soul outside yourself, to pretend that it is a crow talking, and to understand that you are better and wiser than you believe," came the reply. "Because it was in the carpentry shop that you discovered the sacred that is in all things."

"I always took pleasure in pretending to talk to the tables

and chairs I built; wasn't that enough? And when I spoke to them, I usually found thoughts that had never entered my head. The woman had told me that it was because I had put the greater part of my soul into the work, and it was this part that answered me.

"But when I was beginning to understand that I could serve God in this way, the angel appeared, and—well, you know the rest."

"The angel appeared because you were ready," replied the crow.

"I was a good carpenter."

"It was part of your apprenticeship. When a man journeys toward his destiny, often he is obliged to change paths. At other times, the forces around him are too powerful and he is compelled to lay aside his courage and yield. All this is part of the apprenticeship."

Elijah listened attentively to what his soul was saying.

"But no one can lose sight of what he desires. Even if there are moments when he believes the world and the others are stronger. The secret is this: do not surrender."

"I never thought of being a prophet," Elijah said.

"You did, but you were convinced that it was impossible. Or that it was dangerous. Or that it was unthinkable."

Elijah rose.

"Why do you tell me what I have no wish to hear?"

Startled at the movement, the bird fled.

◆

THE BIRD RETURNED the next morning. Instead of resuming the conversation, Elijah began to observe it, for the animal always managed to feed itself and always brought him the food that remained.

A mysterious friendship developed between the pair, and Elijah began to learn from the bird. Observing it, he saw that it managed to find food in the desert, and he discovered that he could survive for a few more days if he learned to do the same. When the crow's flight turned into a circle, Elijah knew there was prey at hand; he would run to the spot and try to catch it. At first, many of the small animals living there escaped, but he gradually acquired the skill and agility to capture them. He used branches as spears and dug traps, which he disguised with a fine layer of twigs and sand. When the quarry fell, Elijah would divide his food with the crow, then set aside part to use as bait.

But the solitude in which he found himself was terrible and oppressive, which is why he decided again to pretend he was conversing with the crow.

"Who are you?" asked the crow.

"I'm a man who has found peace," replied Elijah. "I can live in the desert, provide for myself, and contemplate the endless beauty of God's creation. I have discovered that there resides in me a soul better than ever I thought."

They continued hunting together for another moon. Then

one night when his soul was possessed by sorrow, he asked himself again, "Who are you?"

"I don't know."

◆

ANOTHER MOON DIED and was reborn in the sky. Elijah felt that his body was stronger, his mind more clear. Tonight he turned to the crow, who was perched on the same branch as always, and answered the question he had asked some days before.

"I am a prophet. I saw an angel as I worked, and I cannot doubt what I am capable of doing, even if the entire world should tell me the opposite. I brought about a massacre in my country by challenging the one closest to the king's heart. I'm in the desert, as before I was in a carpentry shop, because my soul told me that a man must go through various stages before he can fulfill his destiny."

"Yes, and now you know who you are," commented the crow.

That night, when Elijah returned from the hunt, he went to drink and found that the Cherith had dried up. But he was so weary that he decided to sleep.

In his dream, his guardian angel, whom he had not seen for a long time, came to him.

"The angel of the Lord hath spoken to thy soul," said the guardian angel. "And hath ordered:

"*Get thee hence, and turn thee eastward, and hide thyself by the brook Cherith, that is before Jordan.*

"Thou shalt drink of the brook; and I have commanded the ravens to feed thee there."

"My soul has heard," said Elijah in the dream.

"Then awake, for the angel of the Lord biddeth me hence and is desirous of speaking to thee."

Elijah leapt up, startled. What had happened?

Although it was night, the place was filled with light, and the angel of the Lord appeared.

"What hath brought thee here?" asked the angel.

"You brought me here."

"No. Jezebel and her soldiers caused thee to flee. This must thou never forget, for thy mission is to avenge the Lord thy God."

"I am a prophet, because you are in my presence and I hear your voice," Elijah said. "I have changed paths several times, as do all men. But I am ready to go to Samaria and destroy Jezebel."

"Thou hast found thy way, but thou mayest not destroy until thou learnest to build anew. I order thee:

"Arise, get thee to Zarephath, which belongeth to Sidon, and dwell there; behold, I have commanded a widow woman there to sustain thee."

The next morning, Elijah looked for the crow, to bid him farewell. The bird, for the first time since he had arrived at the bank of the Cherith, did not appear.

Elijah journeyed for days before arriving in the valley where lay the city of Zarephath, which its inhabitants knew as Akbar. When he was at the end of his strength, he saw a woman, dressed in black, gathering wood. The vegetation in the valley was sparse, and she had to be content with small, dry twigs.

"Who are you?" he asked.

The woman looked at the foreigner, not really understanding what he was saying.

"Bring me water to drink," Elijah said. "Bring me also a piece of bread."

The woman put aside the wood but still said nothing.

"Do not be afraid," Elijah insisted. "I am alone, hungry and thirsty, and haven't the strength to harm anyone."

"You're not from here," she said finally. "By the way you speak, you must be from the kingdom of Israel. If you knew me better, you'd be aware that I have nothing."

"You are a widow; this the Lord has told me. And I have even less than you. If you do not give me food and drink now, I will die."

The woman was taken aback; how could this foreigner know of her life?

"A man should feel shame at asking sustenance from a woman," she said, recovering.

"Do as I ask, please," Elijah insisted, knowing that his strength was beginning to fail. "When I am better, I will work for you."

The woman laughed.

"Moments ago, you told me something true; I am a widow, who lost her husband on one of my country's ships. I have never seen the ocean but I know it is like the desert: it slays those who challenge it . . ."

And she continued. "But now you tell me something false. As surely as Baal lives at the top of the Fifth Mountain, I have no food; there is nothing but a handful of flour in a barrel and a bit of oil in a flagon."

Elijah saw the horizon changing direction and knew he was about to faint. Gathering the last of his strength, he implored one final time, "I don't know if you believe in dreams; I don't know even if I believe in them. But the Lord told me that I would arrive here, and that I would find you. He has done things that caused me to doubt His wisdom, but never His existence. And thus the God of Israel asked that I tell the woman I met in Zarephath:

"*The barrel of meal shall not waste, neither shall the cruse of oil fail, until the day the Lord sendeth rain upon the earth.*"

Without explaining how such a miracle could come about, Elijah fainted.

The woman stood gazing down at the man who lay at her feet. She knew that the God of Israel was a mere superstition; the Phoenician gods were more powerful, and they had made her country one of the most respected nations on earth. But she was happy; usually she had to ask others for alms, and now, as had not happened for a long time, a man needed her. This made her feel stronger, for it was manifest that there were those in worse circumstances than she.

"If someone asks a favor of me, it is because I still have some use on this earth," she reflected.

"I'll do as he asks, if only to relieve his suffering. I too have known hunger, and know its power to destroy the soul."

She went to her house and returned with a piece of bread and some water. She kneeled, placed the foreigner's head in her lap, and began to moisten his lips. Within a few minutes, he had regained his senses.

She held out the bread to him, and Elijah ate quietly, looking at the valley, the ravines, the mountains pointing silently heavenward.

Elijah could see the reddish walls of the city of Zarephath dominating the passage through the valley.

"Give me lodging with you, for I am persecuted in my own country," Elijah said.

"What crime have you committed?" she asked.

"I'm a prophet of the Lord. Jezebel has ordered the death of all who refuse to worship the Phoenician gods."

"How old are you?"

"Twenty-three," Elijah replied.

She looked pityingly at the young man before her. He had long, dirty hair and a beard that was still sparse, as if he wished to appear older than his years. How could a poor fellow like this challenge the most powerful princess in the world?

"If you're Jezebel's enemy, you're my enemy too. She is a princess of Tyre, whose mission when she married your king was to convert your people to the true faith, or so say those who have met her."

She pointed toward one of the peaks that framed the valley.

"Our gods have lived on the Fifth Mountain for many generations, and they have kept peace in our country. But Israel lives in war and suffering. How can you go on believing in the One God? Give Jezebel time to carry out her work and you'll see that peace will reign in your cities too."

"I have heard the voice of the Lord," Elijah replied. "But your people have never climbed to the top of the Fifth Mountain to discover what exists there."

"Anyone who climbs the Fifth Mountain will die from the fire of the heavens. The gods don't like strangers."

She fell silent. She had remembered dreaming, the night before, of a very strong light. From the midst of that light came a voice saying: "Receive the stranger who comes seeking you."

"Give me lodging with you, for I have nowhere to sleep," Elijah insisted.

"I told you that I'm poor. I barely have enough for myself and my son."

"The Lord asked you to let me stay; He never abandons those He loves. Do what I ask of you. I will work for you. I'm a carpenter, I know how to work cedar; there will be no lack of something to do. This way, the Lord will use my hands to keep His promise: *The barrel of meal shall not waste, neither shall the cruse of oil fail, until the day the Lord sendeth rain upon the earth.*"

"Even if I wished to, I would have no way to pay you."

"There is no need. The Lord will provide."

Confused by the previous night's dream, and even with the knowledge that the stranger was an enemy of the princess of Tyre, the woman decided to obey.

Elijah's presence was soon noticed by the neighbors. People commented that the widow had taken a foreigner into her house, in disrespect of the memory of her husband—a hero who had died attempting to expand his country's trade routes.

When she heard the rumors, the widow explained that he was an Israelite prophet, weary from hunger and thirst. And word spread that an Israelite prophet in flight from Jezebel was hiding in the city. A delegation went to see the high priest.

"Bring the foreigner to my presence," he ordered.

And it was done. That afternoon, Elijah was led to the man who, together with the governor and the leader of the military, controlled all that took place in Akbar.

"What have you come here to do?" he asked. "Do you not know that you are our country's enemy?"

"For years I have had commerce with Lebanon, and I respect your people and their customs. I am here because I am persecuted in Israel."

"I know the reason," said the high priest. "Was it a woman who made you flee?"

"In all my life, that woman was the most beautiful creature I have ever met, though I stood before her for only a brief moment. But her heart is like stone, and behind those green eyes hides the enemy who wishes to destroy my country. I did not flee; I await only the right moment to return."

The high priest laughed.

"If you're waiting for the right moment to return, prepare yourself to remain in Akbar for the rest of your life. We are not at war with your country; all we desire is to see the spread of the true faith, by peaceful means, throughout the world. We have no wish to repeat the atrocities committed by your people when you installed yourselves in Canaan."

"Is killing prophets a peaceful means?"

"If you cut off a monster's head, it ceases to exist. A few may die, but religious wars will be averted forever. And, from what the traders tell me, it was a prophet named Elijah who started all this, then fled."

The high priest stared at him, before continuing.

"A man who looked much like you."

"It is I," Elijah replied.

"Excellent. Welcome to the city of Akbar; when we need

something from Jezebel, we will pay for it with your head—the most important currency we have. Till then, seek out employment and learn to fend for yourself, because here there is no place for prophets."

Elijah was preparing to depart, when the high priest told him, "It seems that a young woman from Sidon is more powerful than your One God. She succeeded in erecting an altar to Baal, before which the old priests now kneel."

"Everything will happen as was written by the Lord," replied the prophet. "There are moments when tribulations occur in our lives, and we cannot avoid them. But they are there for some reason."

"What reason?"

"That is a question we cannot answer before, or even during, the trials. Only when we have overcome them do we understand why they were there."

◆

AS SOON AS ELIJAH had departed, the high priest called the delegation of citizens who had sought him out that morning.

"Do not concern yourselves about this," said the high priest. "Custom mandates that we offer hospitality to foreigners. Besides that, here he is under our control and we can observe his steps. The best way to know and destroy an enemy is to pretend to become his friend. When the time comes, he will be handed over to Jezebel, and our city will receive gold and other recompense.

By then, we shall have learned how to destroy his ideas; for now, we know only how to destroy his body."

Although Elijah was a worshiper of the One God and a potential enemy of the princess, the high priest demanded that the right of asylum be honored. Everyone knew of the ancient custom: if a city were to deny shelter to a traveler, the sons of its inhabitants would later face the same difficulty. Since the greater part of Akbar had descendants scattered among the country's gigantic merchant fleet, no one dared challenge the law of hospitality.

Furthermore, it cost nothing to await the day when the Jewish prophet's head would be exchanged for large amounts of gold.

That night, Elijah supped with the widow and her son. As the Israelite prophet was now a valuable commodity to be bargained for in the future, several traders sent provisions enough to feed the three of them for a week.

"It appears the God of Israel is keeping His word," said the widow. "Not since my husband died has my table been as full as today."

LITTLE BY LITTLE ELIJAH BECAME PART OF THE LIFE OF Zarephath and, like all its inhabitants, came to call it Akbar. He met the governor, the commander of the garrison, the high priest, and the master glassmakers, who were admired throughout the region. When asked his reason for being there, he would tell the truth: Jezebel was slaying all the prophets in Israel.

"You're a traitor to your country, and an enemy of Phoenicia," they said. "But we are a nation of traders and know that the more dangerous a man is, the higher the price on his head."

And so passed several months.

AT THE ENTRANCE TO THE VALLEY, A FEW ASSYRIAN patrols had encamped, apparently intending to remain. The small group of soldiers represented no threat. But even so, the commander asked the governor to take steps.

"They have done nothing to us," said the governor. "They must be on a mission of trade, in search of a better route for their products. If they decide to make use of our roads, they will pay taxes—and we shall become even richer. Why provoke them?"

To complicate matters further, the widow's son fell ill for no apparent reason. Neighbors attributed the fact to the presence of the foreigner in her house, and the widow asked Elijah to leave. But he did not leave—the Lord had not yet called. Rumors began to spread that the foreigner had brought with him the wrath of the gods of the Fifth Mountain.

It was possible to control the army and calm the population about the foreign patrols. But, with the illness of the widow's son, the governor began having difficulty easing the people's minds about Elijah.

◆

A DELEGATION of the inhabitants of Akbar went to speak with the governor.

"We can build the Israelite a house outside the walls," they said. "In that way we will not violate the law of hospitality but will still be protected from divine wrath. The gods are displeased with this man's presence."

"Leave him where he is," replied the governor. "I do not wish political problems with Israel."

"What?" the townspeople asked. "Jezebel is pursuing all the prophets who worship the One God, and would slay them."

"Our princess is a courageous woman, and faithful to the gods of the Fifth Mountain. But, however much power she may have now, she is not an Israelite. Tomorrow she may fall into disfavor, and we shall have to face the anger of our neighbors; if we demonstrate that we have treated one of their prophets well, they will be kind to us."

The delegation left unsatisfied, for the high priest had said that one day Elijah would be traded for gold and other rewards. Nevertheless, even if the governor were in error, they could do nothing. Custom said that the ruling family must be respected.

IN THE DISTANCE, IN THE MIDDLE OF THE VALLEY, THE tents of the Assyrian warriors began to multiply.

The commander was concerned, but he had the support of neither the governor nor the high priest. He attempted to keep his warriors constantly trained, though he knew that none of them—nor even their grandfathers—had experience in combat. War was a thing of the past for Akbar, and all the strategies he had learned had been superseded by the new techniques and new weapons that other countries used.

"Akbar has always negotiated its peace," said the governor. "It will not be this time that we are invaded. Let the other countries fight among themselves: we have a weapon much more powerful than theirs—money. When they have finished destroying one another, we shall enter their cities—and sell our products."

The governor succeeded in calming the population about the Assyrians. But rumors were rife that the Israelite had brought the curse of the gods to Akbar. Elijah was becoming an ever greater problem.

◆

ONE AFTERNOON, the boy's condition worsened severely; he could no longer stand, nor could he recognize those who came to visit him. Before the sun descended to the horizon, Elijah and the widow kneeled at the child's bedside.

"Almighty Lord, who led the soldier's arrow astray and who brought me here, make this child whole again. He has done nothing, he is innocent of my sins and the sins of his fathers; save him, O Lord."

The boy barely moved; his lips were white, and his eyes were rapidly losing their glow.

"Pray to your One God," the woman asked. "For only a mother can know when her son's soul is departing."

Elijah felt the desire to take her hand, to tell her she was not alone and that Almighty God would attend him. He was a prophet; he had accepted that truth on the banks of the Cherith, and now the angels were at his side.

"I have no more tears," she continued. "If He has no compassion, if He needs a life, then ask Him to take me, and leave my son to walk through the valley and the streets of Akbar."

Elijah did all in his power to concentrate on his prayer; but that mother's suffering was so intense that it seemed to engulf the room, penetrating the walls, the door, everywhere.

He touched the boy's body; his temperature was not as high as in earlier days, and that was a bad sign.

◆

THE HIGH PRIEST had come by the house that morning and, as he had done for two weeks, applied herbal poultices to the boy's face and chest. In the preceding days, the women of Akbar had brought recipes for remedies that had been handed down for generations and whose curative powers had been proved on numerous occasions. Every afternoon, they gathered at the foot of the Fifth Mountain and made sacrifices so the boy's soul would not leave his body.

Moved by what was happening in the city, an Egyptian trader who was passing through Akbar gave, without charge, an extremely dear red powder to be mixed with the boy's food. According to legend, the technique of manufacturing the powder had been granted to Egyptian doctors by the gods themselves.

Elijah had prayed unceasingly for all this time.

But nothing, nothing whatsoever, had availed.

◆

"I KNOW WHY they have allowed you to remain here," the woman said, her voice softer each time she spoke, for she had gone many days without sleep. "I know there is a price on your head, and that one day you will be handed over to Israel in exchange for gold. If you save my son, I swear by Baal and the gods of the Fifth Mountain that you will never be captured. I know escape routes that have been forgotten for generations, and I will teach you how to leave Akbar without being seen."

Elijah did not reply.

"Pray to your One God," the woman asked again. "If He saves my son, I swear I will renounce Baal and believe in Him. Explain to your Lord that I gave you shelter when you were in need; I did exactly as He had ordered."

Elijah prayed again, imploring with all his strength. At that instant, the boy stirred.

"I want to leave here," the boy said in a weak voice.

His mother's eyes shone with happiness; tears rolled down her cheeks.

"Come, my son. We'll go wherever you like, do whatever you wish."

Elijah tried to pick him up, but the boy pushed his hand away.

"I want to do it by myself," he said.

He rose slowly and began to walk toward the outer room. After a few steps, he dropped to the floor, as if felled by a bolt of lightning.

Elijah and the widow ran to him; the boy was dead.

For an instant, neither spoke. Suddenly, the woman began to scream with all her strength.

"Cursed be the gods, cursed be they who have taken away my son! Cursed be the man who brought such misfortune to my home! My only child!" she screamed. "Because I respected the will of heaven, because I was generous with a foreigner, my son is dead!"

The neighbors heard the widow's lamentations and saw her son laid out on the floor of the house. The woman was still screaming, her fists pounding against the chest of the Israelite prophet beside her; he seemed to have lost any ability to react and did nothing to defend himself. While the women tried to comfort the widow, the men immediately seized Elijah by the arms and took him to the governor.

"This man has repaid generosity with hatred. He put a spell on the widow's house and her son died. We are sheltering someone who is cursed by the gods."

The Israelite wept, asking himself, "O my Lord and God, even this widow, who has been so generous to me, hast Thou chosen to afflict? If Thou hast slain her son, it can only be because I am failing the mission that has been entrusted to me, and it is I who deserve to die."

That evening, the council of the city of Akbar was convened, under the direction of the high priest and the governor. Elijah was brought to judgment.

"You chose to return hatred for love. For that reason, I condemn you to death," said the governor.

◆

"EVEN THOUGH YOUR HEAD is worth a satchel of gold, we cannot invite the wrath of the gods of the Fifth Mountain," the high priest said. "For later not all the gold in the world will bring peace back to this city."

Elijah lowered his head. He deserved all the suffering he could bear, for the Lord had abandoned him.

"You shall climb the Fifth Mountain," said the high priest. "You shall ask forgiveness from the gods you have offended. They will cause fire to descend from the heavens to slay you. If they do not, it is because they desire justice to be carried out at our hands; we shall be waiting for you at the descent from the mountain, and in accordance with ritual you will be executed the next morning."

Elijah knew all too well about sacred executions: they tore the heart from the breast and cut off the head. According to ancient beliefs, a man without a heart could not enter paradise.

"Why hast Thou chosen me for this, Lord?" he cried out, knowing that the men about him knew nothing of the choice the Lord had made for him. "Dost Thou not see that I am incapable of carrying out what Thou hast demanded of me?"

He heard no reply.

SHOUTING INSULTS AND HURLING STONES, THE MEN and women of Akbar followed in procession the group of guards conducting the Israelite to the face of the Fifth Mountain. Only with great effort were the soldiers able to contain the crowd's fury. After walking for half an hour, they came to the foot of the sacred mountain.

The group stopped before the stone altars, where people were wont to leave their offerings and sacrifices, their petitions and prayers. They all knew the stories of giants who lived in the area, and they remembered some who had challenged the prohibition only to be claimed by the fire from heaven. Travelers passing through the valley at night swore they could hear the laughter of the gods and goddesses amusing themselves from above.

Even if no one was certain of all this, none dared challenge the gods.

"Let's go," said a soldier, prodding Elijah with the tip of his spear. "Whoever kills a child deserves the worst punishment there is."

◆

ELIJAH STEPPED ONTO the forbidden terrain and began to climb the slope. After walking for some time, until he could no longer hear the shouts of the people of Akbar, he sat on a rock and wept; since that day in the carpentry shop when he saw the darkness dotted with brilliant points of light, he had succeeded only in bringing misfortune to others.

The Lord had lost His voices in Israel, and the worship of Phoenician gods must now be stronger than before. His first night beside the Cherith, Elijah had thought that God had chosen him to be a martyr, as He had done with so many others.

Instead, the Lord had sent a crow—a portentous bird—which had fed him until the Cherith ran dry. Why a crow and not a dove, or an angel? Could it all be merely the delirium of a man trying to hide his fear, or whose head has been too long exposed to the sun? Elijah was no longer certain of anything: perhaps Evil had found its instrument, and he was that instrument. Why had God sent him to Akbar, instead of returning him to put an end to the princess who had inflicted such evil on his people?

He had felt like a coward but had done as ordered. He had struggled to adapt to that strange, gracious people and their completely different way of life. Just when he thought he was fulfilling his destiny, the widow's son had died.

"Why me?"

◆

HE ROSE, walked a bit farther until he entered the mist covering the mountaintop. He could take advantage of the lack of visibility to flee from his persecutors, but what would it matter? He was weary of fleeing, and he knew that nowhere would he find his place in the world. Even if he succeeded in escaping now, he would bear the curse with him to another city, and other tragedies would come to pass. Wherever he went, he would take with him the shadow of those deaths. He preferred to have his heart ripped from his chest and his head cut off.

He sat down again, amid the fog. He had decided to wait a bit, so that those below would think he had climbed to the top of the mountain; then he would return to Akbar, surrendering to his captors.

"The fire of heaven." Many before had been killed by it, though Elijah doubted that it was sent by the Lord. On moonless nights its glow crossed the firmament, appearing suddenly and disappearing just as abruptly. Perhaps it burned. Perhaps it killed instantly, with no suffering.

◆

AS NIGHT FELL, the fog dissipated. He could see the valley below, the lights of Akbar, and the fires of the Assyrian encampment. He heard the barking of their dogs and the war chants of their soldiers.

"I am ready," he said to himself. "I accepted that I was a prophet, and did everything I did as best I could. But I failed, and now God needs someone else."

At that moment, a light descended upon him.

"The fire of heaven!"

The light, however, remained before him. And a voice said:

"I am an angel of the Lord."

Elijah kneeled and placed his face against the ground.

"I have seen you at other times, and have obeyed the angel of the Lord," replied Elijah, without raising his head. "And yet I have done nothing but sow misfortune wherever I go."

But the angel continued:

"When thou returnest to the city, ask three times for the boy to come back to life. The third time, the Lord will hearken unto thee."

"Why am I to do this?"

"For the grandeur of God."

"Even if it comes to pass, I have doubted myself. I am no longer worthy of my task," answered Elijah.

"Every man hath the right to doubt his task, and to forsake it from time to time; but what he must not do is forget it. Whoever doubteth not himself is unworthy—for in his unquestioning belief in his ability, he commiteth the sin of pride. Blessed are they who go through moments of indecision."

"Moments ago, you saw I was not even sure you were an emissary of God."

"Go, and obey what I have said."

After much time had passed, Elijah descended the mountain to the place of the altars of sacrifice. The guards were awaiting him, but the multitude had returned to Akbar.

"I am ready for death," he said. "I have asked forgiveness from the gods of the Fifth Mountain, and now they command that, before my soul abandons my body, I go to the house of the widow who took me in, and ask her to take pity on my soul."

The soldiers led him back, to the presence of the high priest, where they repeated what the Israelite had said.

"I shall do as you ask," the high priest told the prisoner. "Since you have sought the forgiveness of the gods, you should also seek it of the widow. So that you do not flee, you will go accompanied by four armed soldiers. But harbor no illusion that you will convince her to ask clemency; when morning comes, we shall execute you in the middle of the square."

The high priest wished to inquire what he had seen atop the mountain, but in the presence of the soldiers the answer might be awkward. He therefore decided to remain silent, but he approved of having Elijah ask for forgiveness in public; no one else could then doubt the power of the gods of the Fifth Mountain.

Elijah and the soldiers went to the poor, narrow street where he had dwelled for several months. The doors and windows of the widow's house were open so that, following custom, her son's soul could depart, to go to live with the gods. The body was in the center of the small room, with the entire neighborhood sitting in vigil.

When they noticed the presence of the Israelite, men and women alike were horrified.

"Out with him!" they screamed at the guards. "Isn't the evil he has caused enough? He is so perverse that the gods of the Fifth Mountain refused to dirty their hands with his blood!"

"Leave to us the task of killing him!" shouted a man. "We'll do it right now, without waiting for the ritual execution!"

Standing his ground against the shoves and blows, Elijah freed himself of the hands that grasped him and ran to the widow, who sat weeping in a corner.

"I can bring him back from the dead. Let me touch your son," he said. "For just an instant."

The widow did not even raise her head.

"Please," he insisted. "Even if it be the last thing you do for me in this life, give me the chance to try to repay your generosity."

Some men seized him to drag him away. But Elijah resisted, struggling with all his strength, imploring to be allowed to touch the dead child.

Although he was young and determined, he was finally pulled away to the door of the house. "Angel of the Lord, where are you?" he cried to the heavens.

At that moment, everyone stopped. The widow had risen and come toward him. Taking him by the hands, she led him to where the cadaver of her son lay, then removed the sheet that covered him.

"Behold the blood of my blood," she said. "May it descend upon the heads of your line if you do not achieve what you desire."

He drew near, to touch the boy.

"One moment," said the widow. "First, ask your God to fulfill my curse."

Elijah's heart was racing. But he believed what the angel had told him.

"May the blood of this boy descend upon the heads of my father and mother and upon my brothers, and upon the sons and daughters of my brothers, if I do not do that which I have said."

Then, despite all his doubts, his guilt, and his fears, "*He took him out of her bosom, and carried him up into a loft, where he abode, and laid him upon his own bed.*

"And he cried unto the Lord, and said, O Lord, my God, hast Thou also brought evil upon the widow with whom I sojourn, by slaying her son?

"And he stretched himself upon the child three times, and cried unto the Lord, and said, O Lord, my God, I pray Thee, let this child's soul come into him again."

For long moments nothing happened. Elijah saw himself back in Gilead, standing before the soldier with an arrow pointing at his heart, aware that oftentimes a man's fate has nothing to do with what he believes or fears. He felt calm and confident as he had that day, knowing that, whatever the outcome might be, there was a reason that all of this had come to pass. Atop the Fifth Mountain, the angel had called this reason the "grandeur of God"; he hoped one day to understand why the Creator needed His creatures to demonstrate this glory.

It was then that the boy opened his eyes.

"Where's my mother?" he asked.

"Downstairs, waiting for you," replied Elijah, smiling.

"I had a strange dream. I was traveling through a dark hole, at a speed faster than the swiftest horse in Akbar. I saw a man—I am sure he was my father, though I never knew him. Then I came to a beautiful place where I wanted to stay; but another man—one I don't know but who seemed very good and brave—asked me kindly to turn away from there. I wanted to go on, but you awoke me."

The boy seemed sad; the place he had almost entered must be lovely.

"Don't leave me alone, for you made me come back from a place where I knew I'd be protected."

"Let us go downstairs," Elijah said. "Your mother wants to see you."

The boy tried to rise, but he was too weak to walk. Elijah took him in his arms and descended the stairs.

The people downstairs appeared overwhelmed by profound terror.

"Why are all these people here?" the boy asked.

Before Elijah could respond, the widow took the boy in her arms and began kissing him, weeping.

"What did they do to you, Mother? Why are you so sad?"

"I'm not sad, my son," she answered, drying her tears. "Never in my life have I been so happy."

Saying this, the widow threw herself on her knees and said in a loud voice:

"By this act I know that you are a man of God! The truth of the Lord comes from your words!"

Elijah embraced her, asking her to rise.

"Let this man go!" she told the soldiers. "He has overcome the evil that had descended upon my house!"

The people gathered there could not believe what they saw. A young woman of twenty, who worked as a painter, kneeled beside the widow. One by one, others imitated her gesture, including the soldiers charged with taking Elijah into captivity.

"Rise," he told them, "and worship the Lord. I am merely one of His servants, perhaps the least prepared."

But they all remained on their knees, their heads bowed.

"You spoke with the gods of the Fifth Mountain," he heard a voice say. "And now you can do miracles."

"There are no gods there. I saw an angel of the Lord, who commanded me to do this."

"You were with Baal and his brothers," said another person.

Elijah opened a path, pushing aside the kneeling people, and went out into the street. His heart was still racing, as if he had erred and failed to carry out the task that the angel had taught him. "To what avail is it to restore the dead to life if none believe the source of such power?" The angel had asked him to call out the name of the Lord three times but had told him nothing about how to explain the miracle to the multitude in the room below. "Can it be, as with the prophets of old, that all I desired was to show my own vanity?" he wondered.

He heard the voice of his guardian angel, with whom he had spoken since childhood.

"Thou hast been today with an angel of the Lord."

"Yes," replied Elijah. "But the angels of the Lord do not converse with men; they only transmit the orders that come from God."

"Use thy power," said the guardian angel.

Elijah did not understand what was meant by that. "I have no power but that which comes from the Lord," he said.

"Nor hath anyone. But all have the power of the Lord, and use it not."

And the angel said moreover:

"From this day forward, and until the moment thou returnest to the land thou hast abandoned, no other miracle will be granted thee."

"And when will that be?"

"The Lord needeth thee to rebuild Israel," said the angel. "Thou wilt tread thy land when thou hast learned to rebuild."

And he said nothing more.

PART II

THE HIGH PRIEST SAID THE PRAYERS TO THE RISING sun and asked the god of the storm and the goddess of animals to have mercy on the foolish. He had been told, that morning, that Elijah had brought the widow's son back from the kingdom of the dead.

The city was both frightened and excited. Everyone believed the Israelite had received his powers from the gods of the Fifth Mountain, and now it would be much more difficult to be rid of him. "But the right moment will come," he told himself.

The gods would bring about an opportunity to do away with him. But divine wrath had another purpose, and the Assyrians' presence in the valley was a sign. Why were hundreds of years of peace about to end? He had the answer: the invention of Byblos. His country had developed a form of writing accessible to all, even to those who were unprepared to use it. Anyone could learn it in a short time, and that would mean the end of civilization.

The high priest knew that, of all the weapons of destruction that man could invent, the most terrible—and the most powerful—was the word. Daggers and spears left traces of blood; arrows could be seen at a distance. Poisons were detected in the end and avoided.

But the word managed to destroy without leaving clues. If the sacred rituals became widely known, many would be able to use them to attempt to change the Universe, and the gods would become confused. Till that moment, only the priestly caste knew the memory of the ancestors, which was transmitted orally, under oath that the information would be kept in secret. Or else years of study were needed to be able to decipher the characters that the Egyptians had spread throughout the world; thus only those who were highly trained—scribes and priests—could exchange written information.

Other peoples had their rudimentary forms of recording history, but these were so complicated that no one outside the regions where they were used would bother to learn them. The invention of Byblos, however, had one explosive aspect: it could be used in any country, independent of the language spoken. Even the Greeks, who generally rejected anything not born in their cities, had adopted the writing of Byblos as a common practice in their commercial transactions. As they were specialists in appropriating all that was novel, they had already baptized the invention of Byblos with a Greek name: *alphabet.*

Secrets guarded through centuries of civilization were at risk of being exposed to the light. Compared to this, Elijah's sacrilege in bringing someone back from the other bank of the river of death, as was the practice of the Egyptians, meant nothing.

"We are being punished because we are no longer able to safeguard that which is sacred," he thought. "The Assyrians are at our gates, they will cross the valley, and they will destroy the civilization of our ancestors."

And they would do away with writing. The high priest knew the enemy's presence was not mere happenstance.

It was the price to be paid. The gods had planned everything with great care so that none would perceive that they were responsible; they had placed in power a governor who was more concerned with trade than with the army, they had aroused the Assyrians' greed, had made rainfall ever more infrequent, and had brought an infidel to divide the city. Soon the final battle would be waged.

Akbar would go on existing even after all that, but the threat from the characters of Byblos would be expunged from the face of the earth forever. The high priest carefully cleaned the stone that marked the spot where, many generations before, the foreign pilgrim had come upon the place appointed by heaven and had founded the city. "How beautiful it is," he thought. The stones were an image of the gods——hard, resistant, surviving under all conditions, and without the need to explain why they were there. The oral tradition held that the center of the world was marked by a stone, and in his childhood he had thought about searching out its location. He had nurtured the idea until this year. But when he saw the presence of the Assyrians in the depths of the valley, he understood he would never realize his dream.

"It's not important. It fell to my generation to be offered in sacrifice for having offended the gods. There are unavoidable things in the history of the world, and we must accept them."

He promised himself to obey the gods: he would make no attempt to forestall the war.

"Perhaps we have come to the end of days. There is no way around the crises that grow with each passing moment."

The high priest took up his staff and left the small temple; he had a meeting with the commander of Akbar's garrison.

◆

HE WAS NEARLY to the southern wall when he was approached by Elijah.

"The Lord has brought a boy back from the dead," the Israelite said. "The city believes in my power."

"The boy must not have been dead," replied the high priest. "It's happened before; the heart stops and then starts beating again. Today the entire city is talking about it; tomorrow, they will recall that the gods are close at hand and can hear what they say. Their mouths will fall silent once more. I must go; the Assyrians are preparing for battle."

"Hear what I have to say: after the miracle last night, I slept outside the walls because I needed a measure of calm. Then the same angel that I saw on the Fifth Mountain appeared to me again. And he told me: Akbar will be destroyed by the war."

"Cities cannot be destroyed," said the high priest. "They will be rebuilt seventy times seven because the gods know where they have placed them, and they have need of them there."

◆

THE GOVERNOR APPROACHED, with a group of courtiers, and asked, "What are you saying?"

"That you should seek peace," Elijah repeated.

"If you are afraid, return to the place from which you came," the high priest replied coldly.

"Jezebel and her king are waiting for fugitive prophets, to slay them," said the governor. "But I should like you to tell me how you were able to climb the Fifth Mountain without being destroyed by the fire from heaven."

The high priest felt the need to interrupt that conversation. The governor was thinking about negotiating with the Assyrians and might want to use Elijah for his purposes.

"Do not listen to him," he said. "Yesterday, when he was brought into my presence to be judged, I saw him weep with fear."

"My tears were for the evil I felt I had caused you, for I fear but two things: the Lord, and myself. I did not flee from Israel, and I am ready to return as soon as the Lord permits. I will put an end to your beautiful princess, and the faith of Israel shall survive this threat too."

"One's heart must be very hard to resist the charms of Jezebel," the high priest said ironically. "However, even should that happen, we would send another woman even more beautiful, as we did long before Jezebel."

The high priest was telling the truth. Two hundred years before, a princess of Sidon had seduced the wisest of all Israel's rulers—King Solomon. She had bid him construct an altar to the goddess Astarte, and Solomon had obeyed. For that sacrilege, the Lord had raised up the neighboring armies and Solomon had nearly lost his throne.

"The same will happen with Ahab, Jezebel's husband," thought Elijah. The Lord would bring him to complete his task when the time came. But what did it avail him to try to convince these men who stood facing him? They were like those he had seen the night before, kneeling on the floor of the widow's house, praising the gods of the Fifth Mountain. Custom would never allow them to think in any other way.

◆

"A PITY that we must honor the law of hospitality," said the governor, apparently already having forgotten Elijah's words about peace. "If not for that, we could assist Jezebel in her labor of putting an end to the prophets."

"That is not the reason for sparing my life. You know that I am a valuable commodity, and you want to give Jezebel the pleasure of killing me with her own hands. However, since yesterday, the people attribute miraculous powers to me. They think I met the gods on the Fifth Mountain. For your part, it would not upset you to offend the gods, but you have no desire to vex the inhabitants of the city."

The governor and the high priest left Elijah talking to himself and walked toward the city walls. At that moment the high priest decided that he would kill the Israelite prophet at the first opportunity; what had till now been only merchandise had been transformed into a menace.

◆

WHEN HE SAW them walk away, Elijah lost hope; what could he do to serve the Lord? He then began to shout in the middle of the square, "People of Akbar! Last night, I climbed the Fifth Mountain and spoke with the gods who dwell there. When I returned, I was able to reclaim a boy from the kingdom of the dead!"

The people gathered about him; the story was already known throughout the city. The governor and the high priest stopped and retraced their steps to see what was happening. The Israelite prophet was saying that he had seen the gods of the Fifth Mountain worshiping a superior God.

"I'll have him slain," said the high priest.

"And the population will rise up against us," replied the governor, who had an interest in what the foreigner was saying. "It's better to wait for him to commit an error."

"Before I descended from the mountain," continued Elijah, "the gods charged me with helping the governor against the threat from the Assyrians! I know he is an honorable man and wishes to hear me; but there are those whose interests lie with war and will not allow me to come near him."

"The Israelite is a holy man," said an old man to the governor. "No one can climb the Fifth Mountain without being struck dead by the fire of heaven, but this man did so—and now he raises the dead."

"Sidon, Tyre, and all the cities of Phoenicia have a history of peace," said another old man. "We have been through other threats worse than this and overcome them."

Several sick and lame people began to approach, opening a path through the crowd, touching Elijah's garments and asking to be cured of their afflictions.

"Before advising the governor, heal the sick," said the high priest. "Then we shall believe the gods of the Fifth Mountain are with you."

Elijah recalled what the angel had said the night before: only those powers given to ordinary people would be permitted him.

"The sick are asking for help," insisted the high priest. "We are waiting."

"First we must attend to avoiding war. There will be more sick, and more infirm, if we fail."

The governor interrupted the conversation. "Elijah will come with us. He has been touched by divine inspiration."

Though he did not believe any gods existed on the Fifth Mountain, the governor had need of an ally to help him to convince the people that peace with the Assyrians was the only solution.

◆

AS THEY WALKED to their meeting with the commander, the high priest commented to Elijah, "You don't believe anything you just said."

"I believe that peace is the only way out. But I do not believe the top of the Fifth Mountain is inhabited by gods. I have been there."

"And what did you see?"

"An angel of the Lord. I had seen this angel before, in several places I have been," replied Elijah. "And there is but one God."

The high priest laughed.

"You mean that, in your opinion, the same god who sends the storm also made the wheat, even though they are completely different things?"

"Do you see the Fifth Mountain?" Elijah asked. "From whichever side you look, it appears different, though it is the same mountain. Thus it is with all of Creation: many faces of the same God."

◆

THEY CAME TO THE TOP of the wall, from which they could see the enemy encampment in the distance. In the desert valley, the white tents sprang into sight.

Some time earlier, when the sentinels had first noted the presence of the Assyrians at one end of the valley, spies had said that they were there on a mission of reconnaissance; the commander had suggested taking them prisoner and selling them as slaves. The governor had decided in favor of another strategy: doing nothing. He was gambling that by establishing good relations with them, he could open up a new market for the glass manufactured in Akbar. In addition, even if they were there to prepare for war, the Assyrians knew that small cities will always side with the victor. In this case, all the Assyrian generals desired was to pass through without resistance on their way to Sidon and Tyre, the cities that held the treasure and knowledge of his people.

The patrol had encamped at the entrance to the valley, and little by little reinforcements had arrived. The high priest claimed to know the reason: the city had a well, the only well in several days' travel in the desert. If the Assyrians planned to conquer Tyre or Sidon, they needed that water to supply their armies.

At the end of the first month, they could still be expelled. At the end of the second month, Akbar could still win easily and negotiate an honorable withdrawal of the Assyrian soldiers.

They waited for battle to break out, but there was no attack. At the end of the fifth month, they could still win the battle. "They're going to attack very soon, because they must be suffering from thirst," the governor told himself. He asked the commander to draw up defense strategies and to order his men into constant training to react to a surprise attack.

But he concentrated only on preparations for peace.

◆

HALF A YEAR HAD PASSED, and the Assyrian army had made no move. Tension in Akbar, which had grown during the first weeks of occupation, had now diminished almost entirely. People went about their lives: farmers once again returned to their fields; artisans made wine, glass, and soap; tradesmen continued to buy and sell their merchandise. Everyone believed that, as Akbar had not attacked the enemy, the crisis would soon be settled through negotiations. Everyone knew the governor was chosen by the gods and that he always made the wisest decision.

When Elijah arrived in the city, the governor had ordered rumors spread of the curse the foreigner brought with him; in this way, if the threat of war became insurmountable, he could blame the presence of the foreigner as the principal cause of the disaster. The inhabitants of Akbar would be convinced that with the death of the Israelite the Universe would return to normal. The governor would then explain that it was too late to demand that the Assyrians withdraw; he would order Elijah killed and explain to his people that peace was the best solution. In his view, the merchants—who desired peace—would force the others to agree to this idea.

During these months, he had fought the pressure from the high priest and the commander demanding that he attack at once. The gods of the Fifth Mountain had never abandoned him; now, with the miracle of the resurrection last night, Elijah's life was more important than his execution.

◆

"WHY IS THIS foreigner with you?" asked the commander.

"He has been enlightened by the gods," answered the governor. "And he will help us to find the best solution." He quickly changed the subject. "The number of tents appears to have increased today."

"And it will increase even more tomorrow," said the commander. "If we had attacked when they were nothing but a patrol, they probably wouldn't have returned."

"You're mistaken. Some of them would have escaped, and they would have returned to avenge themselves."

"When we delay the harvest, the fruit rots," insisted the commander. "But when we delay resolving problems, they continue to grow."

The governor explained that peace, the great pride of his people, had reigned in Phoenicia for almost three centuries. What would the generations yet unborn say if he were to interrupt this era of prosperity?

"Send an emissary to negotiate with them," said Elijah. "The best warrior is the one who succeeds in transforming an enemy into a friend."

"We don't know exactly what they want. We don't even know if they desire to conquer our city. How can we negotiate?"

"There are threatening signs. An army does not waste its time on military exercises far from its own country."

Each day saw the arrival of more soldiers, and the governor mused about the amount of water necessary for all those men. In a short time, the entire city would be defenseless before the enemy army.

"Can we attack now?" the high priest asked the commander.

"Yes, we can. We shall lose many men, but the city will be saved. But we must decide quickly."

"We must not do that, Governor. The gods of the Fifth Mountain told me that we still have time to find a pacific solution," Elijah said.

Even after hearing the conversation between the high priest and the Israelite, the governor feigned agreement. To him, it made little difference whether Sidon and Tyre were ruled by Phoenicians, by Canaanites, or by Assyrians; what mattered was that the city be able to go on trading its products.

"We must attack," insisted the high priest.

"One more day," said the governor. "It may be that things will resolve themselves."

He must decide forthwith the best way to face the Assyrian threat. He descended from the wall and headed for the palace, asking the Israelite to go with him.

On the way, he observed the people around him: the shepherds taking their flocks to the mountains; the farmers going to the fields, trying to wrest from the arid soil sustenance for themselves and their families. Soldiers were exercising with spears, and a few newly arrived merchants displayed their wares in the square. Incredibly, the Assyrians had not closed off the road that traversed the valley from end to end; tradesmen still moved about with their merchandise and paid the city its tax for transport.

"Now that they have amassed such a powerful force, why have they not closed the road?" Elijah asked.

"The Assyrian empire needs the products that arrive in the ports of Sidon and Tyre," replied the governor. "If the traders were threatened, they would interrupt the flow of supplies. The consequences would be more serious than a military defeat. There must be some way to avoid war."

"Yes," said Elijah. "If they want water, we can sell it to them."

The governor said nothing. But he understood that he could use the Israelite as a weapon against those who desired war; should the high priest persist with the idea of fighting the Assyrians, Elijah would be the only one who could face him. The governor suggested they take a walk together, to talk.

THE HIGH PRIEST REMAINED ATOP THE WALL, OBSERVING the enemy.

"What can the gods do to deter the invaders?" asked the commander.

"I have carried out sacrifices at the Fifth Mountain. I have asked them to send us a more courageous leader."

"We should act as Jezebel has done: put an end to the prophets. A simple Israelite, who yesterday was condemned to die, is today used by the governor to entice the people to peace."

The commander looked at the mountain.

"We can have Elijah assassinated. And use my warriors to remove the governor from his position."

"I shall order Elijah killed," replied the high priest. "As for the governor, we can do nothing: his ancestors have been in power for several generations. His grandfather was our chieftain, who handed power down to his son, who in turn handed it to him."

"Why does custom forbid our bringing to power someone more efficient?"

"Custom exists to maintain the world in order. If we meddle with it, the world itself will perish."

The high priest looked about him. The heavens and the earth, the mountains and the valley, everything fulfilling what had been written for it. Sometimes the ground shook; at other times—such as now—there were long periods without rain. But the stars continued undisturbed in their place, and the sun had not fallen onto the heads of men. All because, since the Flood, men had learned that it was impossible to change the order of Creation.

In the past, only the Fifth Mountain had existed. Men and gods had lived together, strolled through the gardens of paradise, talking and laughing with one another. But human beings had sinned, and the gods expelled them; having nowhere to send them, they created the earth surrounding the mountain, so they could cast them there, keep vigil over them, and ensure that they would forever remember that they abided on a plane far inferior to that of the dwellers of the Fifth Mountain.

The gods took care, however, to leave open a path of return; if humanity carefully followed the way, it would one day go back to the mountaintop. So that this idea would not be forgotten, they charged the priests and the rulers with keeping it alive in the minds of the people.

All peoples shared the same belief: if the families anointed by the gods were removed from power, the consequences would be grave. No one now remembered why these families had been chosen, but everyone knew they were related to the divine families. Akbar had existed for hundreds of years, and its affairs had always been administered by the ancestors of the present governor; it had been invaded many times, had been in the hands of oppressors and barbarians, but with the passing of time the invaders had left or been expelled. Afterward, the old order would be reestablished and the people would return to the life they had known before.

The priests' obligation was to preserve this order: the world had a destiny, and it was governed by laws. The era of attempting to fathom the gods was past; now was the time to respect them and do their will. They were capricious and easily vexed.

If not for the harvest rituals, the earth would bring forth no fruit. If certain sacrifices were neglected, the city would be infested with fatal diseases. If the god of weather were provoked anew, he could cause wheat and men to cease to grow.

"Behold the Fifth Mountain," the high priest told the commander. "From its peak, the gods rule over the valley and protect us. They have an eternal plan for Akbar. The foreigner will be killed, or return to his own land; the governor will one day be no more, and his son will be wiser than he. All that we experience today is fleeting."

"We have need of a new chieftain," said the commander. "If we continue in the hands of this governor, we shall be destroyed."

The high priest knew that this was what the gods desired, in order to put an end to the writing of Byblos. But he said nothing; he was pleased to have evidence once again that, unwittingly or not, the rulers always fulfilled the destiny of the Universe.

◆

WALKING THROUGH THE CITY with the governor, Elijah explained to him his plans for peace and was made his counselor. When they arrived at the square, more sick people approached, but he said that the gods of the Fifth Mountain had forbidden him to heal. At the end of the afternoon, he returned to the widow's house; the child was playing in the street, and Elijah gave thanks for having been the instrument of the Lord's miracle.

She was awaiting him for the evening meal. To his surprise, there was a bottle of wine on the table.

"People brought gifts to please you," she said. "And I want to ask your forgiveness for the injustice I did you."

"What injustice?" asked Elijah, surprised. "Don't you see that everything is part of God's design?"

The widow smiled, her eyes shone, and he saw for the first time that she was beautiful. She was at least ten years older than he, but at that moment he felt great tenderness for her. He was not accustomed to such sentiments, and he was filled with fear; he remembered Jezebel's eyes, and the wish he had made upon leaving Ahab's palace—to marry a woman from Lebanon.

"Though my life has been useless, at least I had my son. And his story will be remembered, because he returned from the kingdom of the dead," the woman said.

"Your life is not useless. I came to Akbar at the Lord's order, and you took me in. If someday your son's story is remembered, I am certain that yours will be also."

The woman filled two cups. They drank to the sun, which was setting, and to the stars of heaven.

"You have come from a distant country, following the signs of a God I did not know but who now has become my Lord. My son has also returned from a far-off land, and he will have a beautiful tale to tell his grandchildren. The priests will preserve and pass on his words to generations yet to come."

It was through the priests' memory that cities knew of their past, their conquests, the ancient gods, and the warriors who defended the land with their blood. Even though there were now new ways to record the past, the inhabitants of Akbar had confidence only in the memory of their priests: one could write anything he chose, but no one could remember things that never were.

"And what have I to tell?" the widow continued, filling the cup that Elijah had quickly drained. "I don't have the strength or the beauty of Jezebel. My life is like all the rest: a marriage arranged by my father and mother when I was a child, household tasks when I came of age, worship on holy days, my husband always busy with other things. When he was alive, we never spoke of anything important. He was preoccupied with his trade, I took care of the house, and that was how we spent the best of our years.

"After his death, nothing was left for me except poverty and raising my son. When he becomes a man, he will cross the seas and I shall no longer matter to anyone. I feel neither hate nor resentment, only a sense of my own uselessness."

Elijah refilled his cup. His heart was beginning to give signs of alarm; he was enjoying being at this woman's side. Love could be a more frightening experience than standing before Ahab's soldier with an arrow aimed at his heart; if the arrow had struck him, he would be dead—and the rest was up to God. But if love struck him, he alone would have to take responsibility for the consequences.

"I have so wished for love in my life," he thought. And yet, now that it was before him—and beyond doubt it was there; all he had to do was not run away from it—his sole thought was to forget it as quickly as possible.

His mind returned to the day he came to Akbar, after his exile on the Cherith. He was so weary and thirsty that he could remember nothing except the moment he recovered from fainting, and seeing her drip water onto his lips. His face was very close to hers, closer than he had ever been to any woman in his entire life. He had noticed that she had Jezebel's green eyes, but with a different glow, as if they could reflect the cedar trees, the ocean of which he had often dreamed but never known, and—how could it be?—her very soul.

"I should so like to tell her that," he thought. "But I don't know how. It's easier to speak of the love of God."

Elijah took another sip. She sensed that she had said something that displeased him, and she decided to change the subject.

"Did you climb the Fifth Mountain?" she asked.

He nodded.

She would have liked to ask what he had seen there in the heights and how he had escaped the fire of the heavens. But he seemed loath to discuss it.

"You are a prophet," she thought. "Read my heart."

Since the Israelite had come into her life, everything had changed. Even poverty was easier to bear, for that foreigner had awakened something she had never felt: love. When her son had fallen ill, she had fought the entire neighborhood so he could remain in her house.

She knew that to him the Lord was more important than anything that took place beneath the sky. She was aware that it was a dream impossible of fulfillment, for the man before her could go away at any moment, shed Jezebel's blood, and never return to tell of what had happened.

Even so, she would go on loving him, because for the first time in her life, she knew freedom. She could love him, even if he never knew; she did not need his permission to miss him, to think of him every moment of the day, to await him for the evening meal, and to worry about the plots that people could be weaving against the foreigner.

This was freedom: to feel what the heart desired, with no thought to the opinion of the rest. She had fought with her neighbors and her friends about the stranger's presence in her house; there was no need to fight against herself.

Elijah drank a bit of wine, excused himself, and went to his room. She went out, rejoiced at the sight of her son playing in front of the house, and decided to take a short walk.

She was free, for love liberates.

◆

ELIJAH STARED at the wall of his room for a long time. Finally, he decided to invoke his angel.

"My soul is in danger," he said.

The angel said nothing. Elijah was in doubt about continuing the conversation, but now it was too late: he could not call him forth for no reason.

"When I'm with that woman, I don't feel good."

"Just the opposite," answered the angel. "And that disturbs thee, because thou canst come to love her."

Elijah felt shame, for the angel knew his soul.

"Love is dangerous," he said.

"Very," replied the angel. "And so?"

He suddenly disappeared.

His angel had none of the doubts that tormented Elijah's soul. Yes, he knew what love was; he had seen the king of Israel abandon the Lord because Jezebel, a princess of Sidon, had conquered his heart. Tradition told that King Solomon had come close to losing his throne over a foreign woman. King David had sent one of his best friends to his death after falling in love with his friend's wife. Because of Delilah, Samson had been taken prisoner and had his eyes put out by the Philistines.

How could he not know what love was? History was filled with tragic examples. And even had he no knowledge of sacred Scripture, he had the example of his friends, and of the friends of friends, lost in long nights of waiting and suffering. If he'd had a wife in Israel, it would have been difficult for him to leave his city when the Lord commanded, and he would be dead now.

"I am waging combat in vain," he thought. "Love will win this battle, and I will love her all of my days. Lord, send me back to Israel so that I may never have to tell this woman what I feel. Because she does not love me and will say to me that her heart lies buried alongside the body of her heroic husband."

THE NEXT DAY, ELIJAH MET WITH THE COMMANDER AGAIN and learned that more tents had been erected.

"What is the present complement of warriors?" he asked.

"I give no information to an enemy of Jezebel."

"I am a counselor of the governor," replied Elijah. "He named me his assistant yesterday afternoon. You have been informed of this, and you owe me an answer."

The commander felt an urge to put an end to the foreigner's life.

"The Assyrians have two soldiers for each one of ours," he finally replied.

Elijah knew that, to succeed, the enemy needed a much larger force.

"We are approaching the ideal moment to begin peace negotiations," he said. "They will understand that we are being generous and we shall achieve better conditions. Any general knows that to conquer a city five invaders are needed for each defender."

"They'll have that number unless we attack now."

"Even with all their lines of supply, they will not have enough water for so many men. And the moment to send our envoys will have come."

"What moment is that?"

"We shall allow the number of Assyrian warriors to increase a bit more. When the situation becomes unbearable, they will be forced to attack. But, with the proportion of three or four to one of ours, they know they will end in defeat. That is when our envoys will offer peace, safe passage, and the sale of water. This is the governor's plan."

The commander said nothing and allowed the foreigner to leave. Even with Elijah dead, the governor could still insist on the idea. He swore to himself that if the situation came to that point he would kill the governor, then commit suicide, because he had no desire to witness the fury of the gods.

Nevertheless, under no circumstance would he let his people be betrayed by money.

◆

"Take me back to the land of Israel, O Lord," cried Elijah every afternoon, as he walked through the valley. "Let not my heart continue imprisoned in Akbar."

Following a custom of the prophets he had known as a child, he began lashing himself with a whip whenever he thought of the widow. His back became raw flesh, and for two days he lay delirious with fever. When he awoke, the first thing he saw was the woman's face; she had tended to his wounds with ointment and olive oil. As he was too weak to descend the stairs, she brought food to his room.

◆

AS SOON AS HE WAS WELL, Elijah resumed walking through the valley.

"Take me back to the land of Israel, O Lord," he said. "My heart is trapped in Akbar, but my body can still continue the journey."

The angel appeared. It was not the angel of the Lord, whom he had seen on the mountain, but the one who watched over him, and to whose voice he was accustomed.

"The Lord heareth the prayers of those who ask to put aside hatred. But He is deaf to those who would flee from love."

◆

THE THREE OF THEM supped together every night. As the Lord had promised, meal had never been wanting in the barrel nor oil in the vessel.

They rarely spoke as they ate. One night, however, the boy asked, "What is a prophet?"

"Someone who goes on listening to the same voices he heard as a child. And still believes in them. In this way, he can know the angels' thoughts."

"Yes, I know what you are speaking of," said the boy. "I have friends no one else can see."

"Never forget them, even if adults call it foolishness. That way you will always know God's will."

"I'll see into the future, like the soothsayers of Babylon," said the boy.

"Prophets don't know the future. They only transmit the words that the Lord inspires in them at the present moment. That is why I am here, not knowing when I shall return to my own country; He will not tell me before it is necessary."

The woman's eyes became sad. Yes, one day he would depart.

◆

ELIJAH NO LONGER cried out to the Lord. He had decided that, when the moment arrived to leave Akbar, he would take the widow and her son. But he would say nothing until the time came.

Perhaps she would not want to leave. Perhaps she had not even divined his feelings for her, for he himself had been a long time in understanding them. If it should happen thus, it would be better; he could then dedicate himself wholly to the expulsion of Jezebel and the rebuilding of Israel. His mind would be too occupied to think about love.

"The Lord is my shepherd," he said, recalling an ancient

prayer of King David. "He restoreth my soul. He leadeth me beside still waters.

"And He will not let me forget the meaning of my life," he concluded in his own words.

◆

ONE AFTERNOON he returned home earlier than was his wont, to find the widow sitting in the doorway of the house.

"What are you doing?"

"I have nothing to do," she replied.

"Then learn something. At this moment, many people have stopped living. They do not become angry, nor cry out; they merely wait for time to pass. They did not accept the challenges of life, so life no longer challenges them. You are running that same risk; react, face life, but do not stop living."

"My life has begun to have meaning again," she said, casting her gaze downward. "Ever since you came here."

◆

FOR A FRACTION of a second, he felt he could open his heart to her. But he decided not to take the risk; she must surely be referring to something else.

"Start doing something," he said, changing the subject. "In that way, time will be an ally, not an enemy."

"But what can I learn?"

Elijah thought for a moment.

"The writing of Byblos. It will be useful if one day you have to travel."

The woman decided to dedicate herself body and spirit to that study. She had never thought of leaving Akbar, but from the way he spoke perhaps he was thinking of taking her with him.

Once more, she felt free. Once more, she awoke at morning and strode smiling through the streets of the city.

"ELIJAH STILL LIVES," THE COMMANDER TOLD THE HIGH priest two months later. "You have not succeeded in having him killed."

"In all of Akbar there is no man who will carry out that mission. The Israelite has comforted the sick, visited the imprisoned, fed the hungry. When anyone has a dispute to settle with his neighbor, he calls on him, and all accept his judgments, because they are just. The governor is using him to increase his own standing among the people, but no one sees this."

"The merchants have no wish for war. If the governor finds favor enough with the people to convince them that peace is better, we shall never be able to expel the Assyrians. Elijah must be killed immediately."

The high priest pointed to the Fifth Mountain, its peak cloud-covered as always.

"The gods will not allow their country to be humiliated by a foreign power. They will take action; something will come to pass, and we shall be able to grasp the opportunity."

"What kind of opportunity?"

"I do not know. But I shall remain vigilant for the signs. Do not provide any further truthful information about the Assyrian forces. When you are asked, say only that the proportion of the invading warriors is still four to one. And go on training your troops."

"Why should I do that? If they attain the proportion of five to one, we are lost."

"No. We shall be in a state of equality. When the battle begins, you will not be fighting an inferior enemy and therefore cannot be branded a coward who abuses the weak. Akbar's army will confront an adversary as powerful as itself, and it will win the battle—because its commander chose the right strategy."

Piqued by vanity, the commander accepted the proposal. And from that moment, he began to withhold information from the governor and from Elijah.

TWO MORE MONTHS PASSED, AND ONE MORNING THE Assyrian army reached the proportion of five soldiers for each of Akbar's defenders. They could attack at any moment.

For some time Elijah had suspected that the commander was lying about the enemy forces, but this might yet turn to his advantage: when the proportion reached the critical point, it would be a simple matter to convince the populace that peace was the only solution.

These were his thoughts as he headed toward the place in the square where, once a week, he was wont to help the inhabitants of the city to settle their disputes. In general, the issues were trivial: quarrels between neighbors, old people reluctant to pay their taxes, tradesmen who felt they had been cheated in their business dealings.

The governor was there; it was his custom to appear now and again to see Elijah in action. The ill will the prophet had felt toward him had disappeared completely; he had discovered that he was a man of wisdom, concerned with solving problems before they arose—although he was not a spiritual man and greatly feared death. On several occasions he had conferred upon Elijah's decisions the force of law. At other times Elijah, having disagreed with a decision, had with the passage of time come to see that the governor was right.

Akbar was becoming a model of the modern Phoenician city. The governor had created a fairer system of taxation, had improved the streets of the city, and administered intelligently the profits from the imposts on merchandise. There was a time when Elijah had asked him to do away with the consumption of wine and beer, for most of the cases he was called upon to settle involved aggression by intoxicated persons. The governor had told him that a city could only be considered great if that type of thing took place. According to tradition, the gods were pleased when men enjoyed themselves after a day's work, and they protected drunkards.

In addition, the region enjoyed the reputation of producing one of the finest wines in the world, and foreigners would be suspicious if the inhabitants themselves did not consume the drink. Elijah respected the governor's decision, and he came to agree that happy people produce more.

"You need not put forth so much effort," the governor told

him before Elijah began his day's work. "A counselor helps the government with nothing more than his opinions."

"I miss my country and want to return. So long as I am involved in activity, I feel myself of use and forget that I am a foreigner," he replied.

"And better control my love for her," he thought to himself.

◆

THE POPULAR TRIBUNAL had come to attract an audience ever alert to what took place. The people were beginning to gather: some were the aged, no longer able to work in the fields, who came to applaud or jeer Elijah's decisions; others were directly involved in the matters to be discussed, either because they had been the victims or because they expected to profit from the outcome. There were also women and children who, lacking work, needed to fill their free time.

He began the morning's proceedings: the first case was that of a shepherd who had dreamed of a treasure buried near the pyramids of Egypt and needed money to journey there. Elijah had never been in Egypt, but he knew it was far away, and he said that he would be hard pressed to find the necessary means, but if the shepherd were to sell his sheep to pay for his dream, he would surely find what he sought.

Next came a woman who desired to learn the magical arts of Israel. Elijah said he was no teacher, merely a prophet.

As he was preparing to find an amicable solution to a case in which a farmer had cursed another man's wife, a soldier pushed his way through the crowd and addressed the governor.

"A patrol has captured a spy," the newcomer said, sweating profusely. "He's being brought here!"

A tremor ran through the crowd; it would be the first time they had witnessed a judgment of that kind.

"Death!" someone shouted. "Death to the enemy!"

Everyone present agreed, screaming. In the blink of an eye the news spread throughout the city, and the square was packed with people. The other cases were judged only with great difficulty, for at every instant someone would interrupt Elijah, asking that the foreigner be brought forth at once.

"I cannot judge such a case," he said. "It is a matter for the authorities of Akbar."

"For what reason have the Assyrians come here?" said one man. "Can they not see we have been at peace for many generations?"

"Why do they want our water?" shouted another. "Why are they threatening our city?"

For months none had dared speak in public about the presence of the enemy. Though all could see an ever-growing number of tents being erected on the horizon, though the merchants spoke of the need to begin negotiations for peace at once, the people of Akbar refused to believe that they were living under threat of invasion. Save for the quickly subdued incursion of some insignificant tribe, war existed only in the memory of priests. They spoke of a nation called Egypt, with horses and chariots of war and gods that looked like animals. But that had all happened long ago; Egypt was no longer a country of import, and the warriors, with their dark skin and strange language, had returned to their own land. Now the inhabitants of Sidon and Tyre dominated the seas and were spreading a new empire around the world, and though they were tried warriors, they had discovered a new way of fighting: trade.

"Why are they restless?" the governor asked Elijah.

"Because they sense that something has changed. We both know that, from this moment on, the Assyrians can attack at any time. Both you and I know that the commander has been lying about the number of the enemy's troops."

"But he wouldn't be mad enough to say that to anyone. He would be sowing panic."

"Every man can sense when he is in danger; he begins to react in strange ways, to have premonitions, to feel something in the air. And he tries to deceive himself, for he thinks himself incapable of confronting the situation. They have tried to deceive themselves till now; but there comes a moment when one must face the truth."

The high priest arrived.

"Let us go to the palace and convene the Council of Akbar. The commander is on his way."

"Do not do so," Elijah told the governor in a low voice. "They will force on you what you have no wish to do."

"We must go," insisted the high priest. "A spy has been captured, and urgent measures must be taken."

"Make the judgment in the midst of the people," murmured Elijah. "They will help you, for their desire is for peace, even as they ask for war."

"Bring the man here!" ordered the governor. The crowd shouted joyously; for the first time, they would witness a conclave of the Council.

"We cannot do that!" said the high priest. "It is a matter of great delicacy, one that requires calm in order to be resolved!"

A few jeers. Many protests.

"Bring him here," repeated the governor. "His judgment shall be in this square, amid the people. Together we have worked to transform Akbar into a prosperous city, and together we shall pass judgment on all that threatens us."

The decision was met with clapping of hands. A group of soldiers appeared dragging a blood-covered, half-naked man. He must have been severely beaten before being brought there.

All noise ceased. A heavy silence fell over the crowd; from another corner of the square could be heard the sound of pigs and children playing.

"Why have you done this to the prisoner?" shouted the governor.

"He resisted," answered one of the guards. "He claimed he wasn't a spy and said he had come here to talk to you."

The governor ordered that three chairs be brought from his

palace. His servants appeared, bearing the cloak of justice, which he always donned when a meeting of the Council of Akbar was convened.

◆

THE GOVERNOR and the high priest sat down. The third chair was reserved for the commander, who was yet to arrive.

"I solemnly declare in session the tribunal of the Council of Akbar. Let the elders draw near."

A group of old men approached, forming a semicircle around the chairs. This was the council of elders; in bygone times, their opinions were respected and obeyed. Today, however, the role of the group was merely ceremonial; they were present to accept whatever the ruler decided.

After a few formalities such as a prayer to the gods of the Fifth Mountain and the declaiming of the names of several ancient heroes, the governor addressed the prisoner.

"What is it you want?" he asked.

The man did not reply. He stared at him in a strange way, as if he were an equal.

"What is it you want?" the governor repeated.

The high priest touched his arm.

"We need an interpreter. He does not speak our language."

The order was given, and one of the guards left in search of a merchant who could serve as interpreter. Tradesmen never came to the sessions that Elijah held; they were constantly occupied with conducting their business and counting their profits.

While they waited, the high priest whispered, "They beat the prisoner because they are frightened. Allow me to carry out this judgment, and say nothing: panic makes everyone aggressive, and we must show authority, lest we lose control of the situation."

The governor did not answer. He too was frightened. He sought out Elijah with his eyes, but from where he sat could not see him.

A merchant arrived, forcibly brought by the guard. He complained that the tribunal was wasting his time and that he had many matters to resolve. But the high priest, looking sternly at him, bade him to be silent and to interpret the conversation.

"What do you want here?" the governor asked.

"I am no spy," the man replied. "I am a general of the army. I have come to speak with you."

The audience, completely silent till then, began to scream as soon as these words were translated. They called it a lie and demanded the immediate punishment of death.

The high priest asked for silence, then turned to the prisoner.

"About what do you wish to speak?"

"The governor has the reputation of being a wise man," said the Assyrian. "We have no desire to destroy this city: what interests us is Sidon and Tyre. But Akbar lies athwart the route, controlling this valley; if we are forced to fight, we shall lose time and men. I come to propose a treaty."

"The man speaks the truth," thought Elijah. He had noticed that he was surrounded by a group of soldiers who hid from view the spot where the governor was sitting. "He thinks as we do. The Lord has performed a miracle and will bring an end to this dangerous situation."

The high priest rose and shouted to the people, "Do you see? They want to destroy us without combat!"

"Go on," the governor told the prisoner.

The high priest, however, again intervened.

"Our governor is a good man who does not wish to shed a man's blood. But we are in a situation of war, and the prisoner before us is an enemy!"

"He's right!" shouted someone from the crowd.

Elijah realized his mistake. The high priest was playing on the crowd while the governor was merely trying to be just. He attempted to move closer, but he was shoved back. One of the soldiers held him by the arm.

"Stay here. After all, this was your idea."

He looked behind: it was the commander, and he was smiling.

"We must not listen to any proposal," the high priest continued, his passion flowing in his words and gestures. "If we show we are willing to negotiate, we shall also be showing that we are fearful. And the people of Akbar are courageous; they have the means to resist any invasion."

"This prisoner is a man seeking peace," said the governor, addressing the crowd.

Someone said, "Merchants seek peace. Priests desire peace. Governors administer peace. But an army wants only one thing: war!"

"Can't you see that we were able to face the religious threat from Israel without war?" bellowed the governor. "We sent neither armies nor navies, but Jezebel. Now they worship Baal, without our having to sacrifice even one man on the battlefield."

"They didn't send a beautiful woman, they sent their warriors!" shouted the high priest even more loudly.

The people were demanding the Assyrian's death. The governor took the high priest by the arm.

"Sit down," he said. "You go too far."

"The idea of public judgment was yours. Or rather it was the Israelite traitor's, who seems to command the acts of the ruler of Akbar."

"I shall settle accounts with him later. Now, we must discover what the Assyrian wants. For many generations, men tried to impose their will by force; they spoke of what they wanted but cared not what the people thought—and all those empires have been destroyed. Our people have grown because they learned how to listen; this is how we developed trade—by listening to what the other person desires and doing whatever was possible to satisfy him. The result is profit."

The high priest nodded.

"Your words seem wise, and that is the greatest danger of all. If you were speaking folly, it would be simple to prove you wrong. But what you have just said is leading us into a trap."

Those in the front row heard the argument. Until that moment, the governor had always sought out the Council's opinion, and Akbar had an excellent reputation. Sidon and Tyre had sent emissaries to see how the city was administered; its name had even reached the ears of the emperor, and with some small good fortune, the governor might end his days as a minister at the imperial court.

Today, his authority had been challenged publicly. If he did not make a decision, he would lose the respect of the people—and no longer be capable of making important decisions, for none would obey him.

"Continue," he told the prisoner, ignoring the high priest's furious gaze and demanding that the interpreter translate his question.

"I have come to propose an agreement," said the Assyrian. "Allow us to pass, and we shall march against Sidon and Tyre. When those cities have been overcome—as they surely will be, because a great many of their warriors are on ships, occupied with trade—we shall be generous with Akbar. And keep you as governor."

"Do you see?" asked the high priest, again rising to his feet. "They think our governor barters Akbar's honor for an office!"

The multitude began to roar in outrage. That half-naked,

wounded prisoner wanted to lay down rules! A defeated man was proposing the surrender of the city! Several people rushed forward to attack him; with much effort, the guards managed to keep control of the situation.

"Wait!" said the governor, trying to speak above the din. "We have before us a defenseless man, one who can arouse in us no fear. We know that our army is better prepared, that our warriors are braver. We need prove that to no one. Should we decide to fight, we will win the battle, but the losses will be enormous."

Elijah closed his eyes and prayed that the governor could convince his people.

"Our ancestors spoke to us of the Egyptian empire, but it is no more," he continued. "Now we are returning once again to the Golden Age. Our fathers and their fathers before them were able to live in peace; why should we be the ones to break this tradition? Modern warfare is carried out through commerce, not on the field of battle."

Little by little, the crowd fell silent. The governor was succeeding!

When the noise ceased, he turned to the Assyrian.

"What you are proposing is not enough. To cross our lands, you must also pay taxes, as do the merchants."

"Believe this, Governor: Akbar has no choice," replied the prisoner. "We have men enough to raze this city and kill its every inhabitant. You have long been at peace and have forgotten how to fight, while we have been conquering the world."

Murmurs began again in the crowd. Elijah thought, "He cannot betray indecisiveness now." But it was difficult to deal with the Assyrian prisoner, who even while captive imposed his conditions. Moment by moment, more people were arriving; Elijah noticed that the tradesmen, concerned about the unfolding of events, had deserted their places of work to join the audience. The judgment had taken on a dangerous significance; there was no longer any way to retreat from making a decision, whether for negotiation or for death.

◆

THE ONLOOKERS began to take sides; some defended peace while others demanded that Akbar resist. The governor whispered to the high priest, "This man has challenged me in public. But so have you."

The high priest turned to him. And, speaking so none could hear, told him to condemn the Assyrian to death immediately.

"I do not ask, I demand. It is I who keep you in power, and I can put an end to that whenever I wish, do you understand? I know sacrifices to appease the wrath of the gods, if we are forced to replace the ruling family. It will not be the first time; even in Egypt, an empire that lasted thousands of years, there have been many cases of dynasties being replaced. Yet the Universe continued in its order, and the heavens did not fall upon our heads."

The governor turned pale.

"The commander is in the middle of the crowd, with some

of his soldiers. If you insist on negotiating with this man, I will tell everyone that the gods have abandoned you. And you will be deposed. Let us go on with the judgment. And you shall do exactly as I order."

If Elijah had been in sight, the governor would have had a way out: he could have asked the Israelite prophet to say he had seen an angel on the Fifth Mountain, as he had recounted. He would recall the story of the resurrection of the widow's son. And it would be the word of Elijah—who had already proved himself able to perform a miracle—against the word of a man who had never demonstrated any type of supernatural power.

But Elijah had deserted him, and he had no choice. In any case, it was only a prisoner, and no army in the world starts a war because it lost one soldier.

"You win, for now," he told the high priest. One day he would negotiate something in return.

The high priest nodded. The verdict was delivered at once.

"No one challenges Akbar," said the governor. "And no one enters our city without permission from its people. You have attempted to do so, and are condemned to death."

From where he stood, Elijah lowered his eyes. The commander smiled.

THE PRISONER, FOLLOWED BY AN EVER LARGER THRONG, was led to a place beside the walls. There his remaining clothing was torn away, leaving him naked. One of the soldiers shoved him toward the bottom of a hollow located nearby. The people gathered around the hole, jostling against one another for a better view.

"A soldier wears his uniform with pride, and makes himself visible to the enemy, because he has courage. A spy dresses as a woman, because he's a coward," shouted the governor, for all to hear. "Therefore I condemn you to depart this life shorn of the dignity of the brave."

The crowd jeered at the prisoner and applauded the governor.

The prisoner said something, but the interpreter was no longer at hand, and no one understood him. Elijah succeeded in making his way through the crowd to the governor—but it was too late. When he touched his cloak, he was pushed away violently.

"The fault lies with you. You wanted a public judgment."

"The fault is yours," replied Elijah. "Even if the Council of Akbar had met in secret, the commander and the high priest would have imposed their will. I was surrounded by soldiers during the entire process. They had everything planned."

Custom decreed that it was the high priest's task to select the duration of the torture. He knelt, picked up a stone, and handed it to the governor; it was not large enough to grant a swift death, nor so small as to extend the suffering for long.

"First, you."

"I am being forced to do this," said the governor in a low voice so that only the high priest could hear. "But I know it is the wrong path."

"For all these years, you have forced me to take the harshest positions while you enjoyed the fruits of decisions that pleased the people," the high priest answered, also in a low voice. "I have had to face doubt and guilt, and endure sleepless nights, pursued by the ghosts of errors I may have made. But because I did not lose my courage, today Akbar is a city envied by the entire world."

People began looking for stones of the chosen size. For a time, the only sound was that of pebbles and stones striking one another. The high priest continued. "It is possible I am mistaken in condemning this man to death. But as to the honor of our city, I am certain we are not traitors."

◆

THE GOVERNOR raised his hand and threw the first stone; the prisoner dodged it. Immediately, however, the multitude, shouting and jeering, began to stone him.

The man attempted to protect his face with his arms, and the stones struck his chest, his back, his stomach. The governor wanted to leave; he had seen this many times before and knew that death was slow and painful, that the man's face would become a pulp of bones, hair, and blood, that the people would continue throwing stones even after life had left his body.

Within minutes, the prisoner would abandon his defense and lower his arms; if he had been a good man in this life, the gods would guide one of the stones to strike the front of his skull, bringing unconsciousness. If not, if he had committed cruelties, he would remain conscious until the final moment.

The multitude shouted, hurling stones with growing ferocity, and the condemned man tried to defend himself as best he could. Suddenly, however, he dropped his arms and spoke in a language that all could understand. Dismayed, the crowd interrupted the stoning.

"Long live Assyria!" he shouted. "At this moment I look upon the image of my people and die joyfully, because I die as a general who tried to save the lives of his warriors. I go to join the gods and am content because I know we shall conquer this land!"

"You see?" the high priest said. "He heard and understood everything that was said during the judgment!"

The governor agreed. The man spoke their language, and now he knew of the divisions in the Council of Akbar.

"I am not in hell, because the vision of my country gives me dignity and strength! The vision of my country brings me joy! Long live Assyria!" he shouted once more.

Recovered from its surprise, the crowd again began throwing stones. The man kept his arms at his sides, not attempting to resist; he was a brave warrior. A few seconds later, the mercy of the gods manifested itself: a stone struck his forehead and he fell unconscious to the ground.

"We can go now," the high priest said. "The people of Akbar will see to finishing the task."

◆

ELIJAH DID NOT GO back to the widow's house. He began walking through the desert, not knowing exactly where he wanted to go.

"The Lord did nothing," he said to the plants and rocks. "And He could have done something."

He regretted his decision and blamed himself for the death of yet another man. If he had accepted the idea of the Council of Akbar meeting in secret, the governor could have taken Elijah with him; then it would have been the two of them against the high priest and the commander. Their chances, though still small, would have been better than in the public judgment.

Worse yet, he had been impressed by the high priest's way of addressing the crowd; even though he disagreed with what he said, he was obliged to recognize that here was someone with a profound understanding of leadership. He would try to remember every detail of what he had seen, for one day, in Israel, he would have to face the king and the princess from Sidon.

He wandered aimlessly, looking at the mountains, the city, and the Assyrian encampment in the distance. He was a mere dot in this valley, and there was an immense world around him, a world so large that even if he traveled his entire life he would never find where it ended. His friends, and his enemies, might perhaps better understand the earth where they lived, might travel to distant countries, navigate unknown seas, love a woman without guilt. None of them still heard the angels of their childhood, nor offered themselves in the Lord's struggle. They lived out their lives in the present moment, and they were happy.

He too was a person like all the others, and in this moment walking through the valley he wished above all else never to have heard the voice of the Lord, or of His angels.

But life is made not of desires but of the acts of each person. He recalled that several times in the past he had tried to renounce his mission, but he was still there, in the middle of that valley, because this the Lord had demanded.

"I could have been a mere carpenter, O Lord, and still be useful to Thy work."

But there Elijah stood, carrying out what had been demanded of him, bearing within him the weight of the war to come, the massacre of the prophets by Jezebel, the death by stoning of the Assyrian general, his fear of loving a woman of Akbar. The Lord had given him a gift, and he did not know what to do with it.

In the middle of the valley, a light appeared. It was not his guardian angel, the one he heard but seldom saw. It was an angel of the Lord, come to console him.

"I can do nothing further here," said Elijah. "When will I return to Israel?"

"When thou learnest to rebuild," answered the angel. "But remember that which God taught Moses before a battle. Make use of every moment so that later thou wilt not regret, nor lament having lost thy youth. To every age in the life of a man, the Lord bestoweth upon him its own misgivings."

The Lord spoke unto Moses:

"Say unto them, Hear, O Israel, ye approach this day unto battle against your enemies: let not your hearts faint, fear not, and do not tremble, neither be ye terrified because of them. And what man is he that hath planted a vineyard, and hath not yet eaten of it? Let him also go and return unto his house, lest he die in the battle, and another man eat of it. And what man is there that hath betrothed a wife, and hath not taken her? Let him go and return unto his house, lest he die in the battle, and another man take her."

ELIJAH CONTINUED WALKING FOR SOME TIME, SEEKING to understand what he had heard. As he was readying to return to Akbar, he saw the woman he loved sitting on a rock facing the Fifth Mountain, a few minutes' walk from where he stood.

"What is she doing here? Does she know about the judgment, the death sentence, and the risks we have come to face?"

He must alert her at once. He decided to approach her.

She noticed his presence and waved. Elijah appeared to have forgotten the angel's words, for the feeling of uncertainty came rushing back. He tried to feign that he was worried about the problems of the city, so that she might not perceive the confusion in his heart and his mind.

"What are you doing here?" he asked when he drew close.

"I came in search of a bit of inspiration. The writing that I'm learning made me think about the Designer of the valleys, of the mountains, of the city of Akbar. Some merchants gave me inks of every color, because they want me to write for them. I thought of using them to describe the world I live in, but I know how difficult that is: although I have the colors, only the Lord can mix them with such harmony."

She kept her gaze on the Fifth Mountain. She was a completely different person from the woman he had met some months before gathering wood at the city gate. Her solitary presence in the midst of the desert inspired confidence and respect in him.

"Why do all the mountains have names except the Fifth Mountain, which is known by a number?" asked Elijah.

"So as not to create conflict among the gods," she replied. "According to tradition, if men had given that mountain the name of a specific god, the others would have become furious and destroyed the earth. Therefore it's called the Fifth Mountain, because it's the fifth mountain we see beyond the walls. In this way, we offend no one, and the Universe continues in its place."

They said nothing for a time. The woman broke the silence.

"Besides reflecting on colors, I also think about the danger in the writing of Byblos. It might offend the gods of Phoenicia and the Lord our God."

"Only the Lord exists," interrupted Elijah. "And every civilized country has its writing."

"But it's different. When I was a child, I used to go to the square to watch the word painter who worked for the merchants. His drawings were based on Egyptian script and demanded skill and knowledge. Now, ancient and powerful Egypt is in decadence, without money to buy anything, and no one uses its language anymore; sailors from Sidon and Tyre are spreading the writing of Byblos to the entire world. The sacred words and ceremonies can be placed on clay tablets and transmitted from one people to another. What will become of the world if unscrupulous people begin using the rituals to interfere with the Universe?"

Elijah understood what the woman was saying. The writing of Byblos was based on a very simple system: the Egyptian drawings first had to be transformed into sounds, and then a letter was designated for each sound. By placing these letters in order, it was possible to create all possible sounds and to describe everything there was in the Universe.

Some of these sounds were very difficult to pronounce. That difficulty had been solved by the Greeks, who had added five more letters, called *vowels,* to the twenty-odd characters of Byblos. They baptized this innovation *alphabet,* a name now used to define the new form of writing.

This had greatly facilitated commercial contact among differing peoples. The Egyptian system had required much space and a great deal of ability to draw the ideas, as well as profound understanding to interpret them; it had been imposed on conquered nations but had not survived the decline of the empire. The system of Byblos, however, was spreading rapidly through the world, and it no longer depended on the economic might of Phoenicia for its adoption.

The method of Byblos, with the Greek adaptation, had pleased the traders of the various nations; as had been the case since ancient times, it was they who decided what should remain in history and what would disappear with the death of a given king or a given person. Everything indicated that the Phoenician invention was destined to become the common language of business, surviving its navigators, its kings, its seductive princesses, its wine makers, its master glassmakers.

"Will God disappear from words?" the woman asked.

"He will continue in them," Elijah replied. "But each person will be responsible before Him for whatever he writes."

She took from the sleeve of her garment a clay tablet with something written on it.

"What does that mean?" Elijah asked.

"It's the word *love*."

Elijah took the tablet in his hands, not daring to ask why she had given it to him. On that piece of clay, a few scratches summed up why the stars continued in the heavens and why men walked the earth.

He tried to return it to her, but she refused.

"I wrote it for you. I know your responsibility, I know that one day you will have to leave, and that you will become an enemy of my country because you wish to do away with Jezebel. On that day, it may come to pass that I shall be at your side, supporting you in your task. Or it may come to pass that I fight against you, for Jezebel's blood is the blood of my country; this word that you hold in your hands is filled with mystery. No one can know what it awakens in a woman's heart, not even prophets who speak with God."

"I know the word that you have written," said Elijah, storing the tablet in a fold of his cape. "I have struggled day and night against it, for, although I do not know what it awakens in a woman's heart, I know what it can do to a man. I have the courage to face the king of Israel, the princess of Sidon, the Council of Akbar, but that one word—*love*—inspires deep terror in me. Before you drew it on the tablet, your eyes had already seen it written in my heart."

They fell silent. Despite the Assyrian's death, the climate of tension in the city, the call from the Lord that could occur at any moment—none of this was as powerful as the word she had written.

Elijah held out his hand, and she took it. They remained thus until the sun hid itself behind the Fifth Mountain.

"Thank you," she said as they returned. "For a long time I had desired to spend the hours of sunset with you."

When they arrived home, an emissary from the governor was waiting for him. He asked Elijah to come with him immediately for a meeting.

◆

"YOU REPAID MY SUPPORT with cowardice," said the governor. "What should I do with your life?"

"I shall not live a second longer than the Lord desires," replied Elijah. "It is He who decides, not you."

The governor was surprised at Elijah's courage.

"I can have you decapitated at once. Or have you dragged through the streets of the city, saying that you brought a curse upon our people," he said. "And that would not be a decision of your One God."

"Whatever my fate, that is what will happen. But I want you to know I did not flee; the commander's soldiers kept me away. He wants war and will do everything to achieve it."

The governor decided to waste no more time on that pointless discussion. He had to explain his plan to the Israelite prophet.

"It's not the commander who wishes war; like a good military man he is aware that his army is smaller and inexperienced and that it will be decimated by the enemy. As a man of honor, he knows he risks causing shame to his descendants. But his heart has been turned into stone by pride and vanity.

"He thinks the enemy is afraid. He doesn't know that the Assyrian warriors are well trained: when they enter the army, they plant a tree, and every day they leap over the spot where the seed is buried. The seed becomes a shoot, and they leap over it. The shoot becomes a plant, and they go on jumping. They neither become annoyed nor find it a waste of time. Little by little, the tree grows, and the warriors leap higher. Patiently and with dedication, they're preparing to overcome obstacles.

"They're accustomed to recognizing a challenge when they see it. They've been observing us for months."

Elijah interrupted the governor.

"Then, in whose interest is war?"

"The high priest's. I saw that during the Assyrian prisoner's trial."

"For what reason?"

"I don't know. But he was shrewd enough to convince the commander and the people. Now the entire city is on his side, and I see only one way out of the difficult situation in which we find ourselves."

He paused for a long moment, then looked directly into the Israelite's eyes. "You."

The governor began pacing the chamber, his rapid speech betraying his nervousness.

"The merchants also desire peace, but they can do nothing. In any case, they are rich enough to install themselves in some other city or to wait until the conquerors begin buying their products. The rest of the populace have lost their senses and want us to attack an infinitely superior enemy. The only thing that can change their minds is a miracle."

Elijah became tense.

"A miracle?"

"You brought back a boy that death had already claimed. You've helped the people find their way, and though you are a foreigner you are loved by almost everyone."

"That was the situation until this morning," Elijah said. "But now it's changed; in the atmosphere you've just described, anyone who advocates peace will be considered a traitor."

"I don't want you to advocate anything. I want you to perform a miracle as great as the resurrection of that boy. Then you'll tell the people that peace is the only solution, and they'll listen to you. The high priest will lose completely whatever power he possesses."

There was a moment of silence. The governor continued.

"I am willing to make a pact: if you do what I'm asking, the religion of the One God will become obligatory in Akbar. You will please Him whom you serve, and I shall be able to negotiate terms of peace."

◆

ELIJAH CLIMBED THE STAIRS to his room in the upper story of the widow's house. At that moment he had in his hands an opportunity that no prophet had ever had before: to convert a Phoenician city. It would be the most painful way to show Jezebel that there was a price to pay for what she had done to his country.

He was excited by the governor's offer. He even thought of waking the woman who was sleeping downstairs but changed his mind; she must be dreaming about the beautiful afternoon they had spent together.

He called on his guardian angel. He appeared.

"You heard the governor's proposal," Elijah said. "This is a unique chance."

"Nothing is a unique chance," the angel replied. "The Lord giveth men many opportunities. And do not forget what was said: no further miracle will be permitted thee until thou returnest to the bosom of thy country."

Elijah lowered his head. At that moment the angel of the Lord appeared and hushed his guardian angel. And he said:

"Behold the next of thy miracles:

"Thou wilt gather the people together before the mountain. On one side, thou shalt order built an altar to Baal, and that a bullock be placed on it. On the other side, thou shalt raise an altar to the Lord thy God, and on it also place a bullock.

"And thou shalt say to the worshipers of Baal: invoke the name of your god, and I shall invoke the name of the Lord. Let them be first, and let them spend from morning until noon praying and calling on Baal to come forth and receive what is offered him.

"They will cry out aloud, and cut themselves with knives, asking that the bullock be received by their god, but nothing will happen.

"When they weary, thou shalt fill four barrels with water and pour it over thy bullock. Thou shalt do this a second time. And thou shalt do this still a third time. Then call upon the Lord of Abraham, Isaac, and Israel, asking Him to show His power to all.

"At that moment, the Lord will send the fire from heaven and consume thy sacrifice."

Elijah knelt and gave thanks.

"However," continued the angel, "this miracle can be wrought but once in thy lifetime. Choose whether thou desirest to do it here, to avoid a battle, or in thy homeland, to free thy people from Jezebel."

And the angel of the Lord departed.

◆

THE WOMAN AWOKE EARLY and saw Elijah sitting in the doorway of the house. His eyes were deep in their sockets, like those of one who has not slept.

She would have liked to ask what had happened the night before, but she feared his response. It was possible that the sleepless night had been provoked by his talk with the governor and by the threat of war; but there might be another reason—the clay tablet she had given him. If so, and she raised the subject, she risked hearing that the love of a woman was not in accord with God's design.

She said only the words, "Come and eat something."

Her son awakened also. The three sat down at the table and ate.

"I should have liked to stay with you yesterday," Elijah said, "but the governor needed me."

"Do not concern yourself with him," she said, a calm feeling reentering her heart. "His family has ruled Akbar for generations, and he will know what to do in the face of the threat."

"I also spoke with an angel. And he demanded of me a very difficult decision."

"Nor should you be disturbed because of angels; perhaps it's better to believe that the gods change with the times. My ancestors worshiped the Egyptian gods, who had the forms of animals. Those gods went away, and until you arrived, I was brought up to make sacrifices to Asherat, El, Baal, and all the dwellers on the Fifth Mountain. Now I have known the Lord, but He too may leave us one day, and the next gods may be less demanding."

The boy asked for water. There was none.

"I'll go and fetch it," said Elijah.

"I want to go with you," the boy said.

They walked toward the well. On the way they passed the spot where the commander had since the early hours been training his soldiers.

"Let's watch for a while," said the boy. "I'll be a soldier when I grow up."

Elijah did as he asked.

"Which of us is best at using a sword?" asked one warrior.

"Go to the place where the spy was stoned yesterday," said the commander. "Pick up a stone and insult it."

"Why should I do that? The stone would not answer me back."

"Then attack it with your sword."

"My sword will break," said the soldier. "And that wasn't what I asked; I want to know who's the best at using a sword."

"The best is the one who's most like a rock," answered the commander. "Without drawing its blade, it proves that no one can defeat it."

"The governor is right: the commander is a wise man," thought Elijah. "But the greatest wisdom is blinded by the glare of vanity."

◆

THEY CONTINUED on their way. The boy asked why the soldiers were training so much.

"It's not just the soldiers, but your mother too, and I, and those who follow their heart. Everything in life demands training."

"Even being a prophet?"

"Even to understand angels. We so want to talk with them that we don't listen to what they're saying. It's not easy to listen: in our prayers we always try to say where we have erred, and what we should like to happen to us. But the Lord already knows all of this, and sometimes asks us only to hear what the Universe is telling us. And to be patient."

The boy looked at him in surprise. He probably understood nothing, but even so Elijah felt the need to continue the conversation. Perhaps when he came to manhood one of these words might assist him in a difficult situation.

"All life's battles teach us something, even those we lose. When you grow up, you'll discover that you have defended lies, deceived yourself, or suffered for foolishness. If you're a good warrior, you will not blame yourself for this, but neither will you allow your mistakes to repeat themselves."

He decided to speak no further; a boy of that age could not understand what he was saying. They walked slowly, and Elijah looked at the streets of the city that had sheltered him and was about to disappear. Everything depended on the decision he must make.

Akbar was more silent than usual. In the central square, people talked in hushed tones, as if fearful that the wind might carry their words to the Assyrian camp. The more elderly among them swore that nothing would happen, while the young were excited at the prospect of battle, and the merchants and artisans made plans to go to Sidon and Tyre until calm was restored.

"It is easy for them to leave," he thought. Merchants can transport their goods anywhere in the world. Artisans too can work, even in places where a strange language is spoken. "But I must have the Lord's permission."

◆

THEY CAME to the well, where they filled two vessels with water. Usually the place was crowded with people; women meeting to wash clothes, dye fabrics, and comment on everything that happened in the city. Nothing could be kept secret close to the well;

news about business, family betrayals, problems between neighbors, the intimate lives of the rulers—every matter, serious or superficial, was discussed, commented upon, criticized, or applauded there. Even during the months in which the enemy forces had grown unceasingly, Jezebel, the princess who had conquered the king of Israel, remained the favorite topic. People praised her boldness, her courage, and were certain that, should anything happen to the city, she would come back to her country to avenge it.

That morning, however, almost no one was there. The few women present said that it was necessary to go to the fields and harvest the largest possible amount of grain, for the Assyrians would soon close off the entrance and exit to the city. Two of them were making plans to go to the Fifth Mountain and offer sacrifices to the gods; they had no wish to see their sons die in combat.

"The high priest said that we can resist for many months," one woman commented to Elijah. "We need only to have the necessary courage to defend Akbar's honor and the gods will come to our aid."

The boy was frightened.

"Is the enemy going to attack?" he asked.

Elijah did not reply; it depended on the choice that the angel had offered him the night before.

"I'm afraid," the boy said insistently.

"That proves that you find joy in living. It's normal to feel fear at certain moments."

◆

Elijah and the boy returned home before the morning was over. They found the woman ringed by small vessels with inks of various colors.

"I have to work," she said, looking at the unfinished letters and phrases. "Because of the drought, the city is full of dust. The brushes are always dirty, the ink mixes with dust, and everything becomes more difficult."

Elijah remained silent; he did not want to share his concerns with anyone. He sat in a corner of the downstairs room, absorbed in his thoughts. The boy went out to play with his friends.

"He needs silence," the woman said to herself and tried to concentrate on her work.

She took the rest of the morning to complete a few words that could have been written in half the time, and she felt guilt for not doing what was expected of her; after all, for the first time in her life she had the chance to support her family.

She returned to her work. She was using papyrus, a material that a trader on his way from Egypt had recently brought, asking her to write some commercial letters that he had to send to Damascus. The sheet was not of the best quality, and the ink blurred frequently. "Even with all these difficulties, it's better than drawing on clay."

Neighboring countries had the custom of sending their

messages on clay tablets or on animal skins. Although their country was in decadence, with an obsolete script, the Egyptians had discovered a light, practical way of recording their commerce and their history; they cut into strips a plant that grew on the banks of the Nile and through a simple process glued the strips side by side, forming a yellowish sheet. Akbar had to import papyrus because it could not be grown in the valley. Though it was expensive, merchants preferred using it, for they could carry the written sheets in their pockets, which was impossible to do with clay tablets and animal skins.

"Everything is becoming simpler," she thought. A pity that the government's authorization was needed to use the Byblos alphabet on papyrus. Some outmoded law still obliged written texts to pass inspection by the Council of Akbar.

As soon as her work was done, she showed it to Elijah, who had been watching her the entire time without comment.

"Do you like the result?" she asked.

He seemed to come out of a trance.

"Yes, it's pretty," he replied, giving no mind to what he was saying.

He must be talking with the Lord. And she did not want to interrupt him. She left, to call the high priest.

When she returned with the high priest, Elijah was still in the same spot. The two men stared at each other. For a long time, neither spoke.

The high priest was the first to break the silence.

"You are a prophet, and speak with angels. I merely interpret the ancient laws, carry out rituals, and seek to defend my people from the errors they commit. Therefore I know this is not a struggle between men; it is a battle of gods—and I must not absent myself from it."

"I admire your faith, though you worship gods that do not exist," answered Elijah. "If the present situation is, as you say, worthy of a celestial battle, the Lord will use me as an instrument to defeat Baal and his companions on the Fifth Mountain. It would have been better for you to order my assassination."

"I thought of it. But it wasn't necessary; at the proper moment the gods acted in my favor."

Elijah did not reply. The high priest turned and picked up the papyrus on which the woman had just written her text.

"Well done," he commented. After reading it carefully, he took the ring from his finger, dipped it in one of the small vessels of ink, and applied his seal in the left corner. If anyone were found carrying a papyrus without the high priest's seal, he could be condemned to death.

"Why do you always have to do that?" she asked.

"Because these papyri transport ideas," he replied. "And ideas have power."

"They're just commercial transactions."

"But they could be battle plans. Or our secret prayers. Nowadays, with letters and papyrus, it has become a simple matter to steal the inspiration of a people. It is difficult to hide clay tablets, or animal skins, but the combination of papyrus and the alphabet of Byblos can bring an end to the civilization of any nation, and destroy the world."

A woman came running.

"Priest! Priest! Come see what's happening!"

Elijah and the widow followed him. People were coming from every corner, heading for the same place; the air was close to unbreathable from the dust they raised. Children ran ahead, laughing and shouting. The adults walked slowly, in silence.

When they arrived at the southern gate to the city, a small multitude was already gathered there. The high priest pushed his way through the crowd and came upon the reason for the confusion.

A sentinel of Akbar was kneeling, his arms spread, his hands tied to a large piece of wood on his shoulders. His clothes were in tatters, and his left eye had been gouged out by a small tree branch.

On his chest, written with slashes of a knife, were some Assyrian characters. The high priest understood Egyptian, but the Assyrian language was not important enough to be learned and memorized; it was necessary to ask the help of a trader who was at the scene.

"'*We declare war*,'" the man translated.

The onlookers spoke not a word. Elijah could see panic written on their faces.

"Give me your sword," the high priest said to one of the soldiers.

The soldier obeyed. The high priest asked that the governor and the commander be notified of what had happened. Then, with a swift blow, he plunged the blade into the kneeling sentinel's heart.

The man moaned and fell to the ground. He was dead, free of the pain and shame of having allowed himself to be captured.

"Tomorrow I shall go to the Fifth Mountain to offer sacrifices," he told the frightened people. "And the gods will once again remember us."

Before leaving, he turned to Elijah.

"You see it with your own eyes. The heavens are still helping."

"One question, nothing more," said Elijah. "Why do you wish to see your people sacrificed?"

"Because it is what must be done to kill an idea."

After seeing him talk with the woman that morning, Elijah had understood what that idea was: the alphabet.

"It is too late. Already it spreads throughout the world, and the Assyrians cannot conquer the whole of the earth."

"And who says they cannot? After all, the gods of the Fifth Mountain are on the side of their armies."

◆

FOR HOURS HE WALKED the valley, as he had done the afternoon before. He knew there would be at least one more afternoon and night of peace: no war was fought in darkness, because the soldiers could not distinguish the enemy. That night, he knew, the Lord was giving him the chance to change the destiny of the city that had taken him into its bosom.

"Solomon would know what to do," he told his angel. "And David, and Moses, and Isaac. They were men the Lord trusted, but I am merely an indecisive servant. The Lord has given me a choice that should be His."

"The history of our ancestors seemeth to be full of the right men in the right places," answered the angel. "Do not believe it: the Lord demandeth of people only that which is within the possibilities of each of them."

"Then He has made a mistake with me."

"Whatever affliction that cometh, finally goeth away. Such are the glories and tragedies of the world."

"I shall not forget that," Elijah said. "But when they go away, the tragedies leave behind eternal marks, while the glories leave useless memories."

The angel made no reply.

"Why, during all this time I have been in Akbar, could I not find allies to work toward peace? What importance has a solitary prophet?"

"What importance hath the sun, in its solitary travel through the heavens? What importance hath a mountain rising in the middle of a valley? What importance hath an isolated well? Yet it is they that indicate the road the caravan is to follow."

"My heart drowns in sorrow," said Elijah, kneeling and extending his arms to heaven. "Would that I could die here and now, and never have my hands stained with the blood of my people, or a foreign people. Look behind you. What do you see?"

"Thou knowest that I am blind," said the angel. "Because mine eyes still retain the light of the Lord's glory, I can perceive nothing else. I can see only what thy heart telleth me. I can see only the vibrations of the dangers that threaten thee. I cannot know what lieth behind thee . . ."

"Then I'll tell you: there lies Akbar. Seen at this time of day, with the afternoon sun lighting its profile, it's lovely. I have grown accustomed to its streets and walls, to its generous and hospitable folk. Though the city's inhabitants are still prisoners of commerce and superstition, their hearts are as pure as any nation on earth. With them I have learned much that I did not know; in return, I have listened to their laments and—inspired by God—have been able to resolve their internal conflicts. Many times have I been at risk, and someone has always come to my aid. Why must I choose between saving this city and redeeming my people?"

"Because a man must choose," answered the angel. "Therein lieth his strength: the power of his decisions."

"It is a difficult choice; it demands that I accept the death of one people to save another."

"Even more difficult is defining a path for oneself. He who maketh no choice is dead in the eyes of the Lord, though he go on breathing and walking in the streets.

"Moreover," the angel continued, "no one dieth. The arms of

eternity open for every soul, and each one will carry on his task. There is a reason for everything under the sun."

Elijah again raised his arms to the heavens.

"My people fell away from the Lord because of a woman's beauty. Phoenicia may be destroyed because a priest thinks that writing is a threat to the gods. Why does He who made the world prefer to use tragedy to write the book of fate?"

Elijah's cries echoed through the valley to return to his ears.

"Thou knowest not whereof thou speakest," the angel replied. "There is no tragedy, only the unavoidable. Everything hath its reason for being: thou needest only distinguish what is temporary from what is lasting."

"What is temporary?" asked Elijah.

"The unavoidable."

"And what is lasting?"

"The lessons of the unavoidable."

Saying this, the angel disappeared.

That night, at the evening meal, Elijah told the woman and the boy, "Prepare your things. We may depart at any moment."

"You haven't slept for two days," said the woman. "An emissary from the governor was here this afternoon, asking for you to go to the palace. I said you were in the valley and would spend the night there."

"You did well," he replied, going straightway to his room and falling into a deep sleep.

He was awakened the next morning by the sound of musical instruments. When he went downstairs to see what was happening, the boy was already at the door.

"Look!" he said, his eyes gleaming with excitement. "It's war!"

A battalion of soldiers, imposing in their battle gear and armaments, was marching toward the southern gate of Akbar. A group of musicians followed them, marking the battalion's pace to the beat of drums.

"Yesterday you were afraid," Elijah told the boy.

"I didn't know we had so many soldiers. Our warriors are the best!"

He left the boy and went into the street; he must find the governor at any cost. The other inhabitants of the city had been awakened by the sound of the war anthems and were enthralled;

for the first time in their lives they were seeing the march of an organized battalion in its military uniforms, its lances and shields reflecting the first rays of dawn. The commander had achieved an enviable feat; he had prepared his army without anyone becoming aware of it, and now—or so Elijah feared—he could make everyone believe that victory over the Assyrians was possible.

He pushed his way through the soldiers and came to the front of the column. There, mounted on horses, the commander and the governor were leading the march.

"We have an agreement!" said Elijah, running to the governor's side. "I can perform a miracle!"

The governor made no reply. The garrison marched past the city wall and into the valley.

"You know this army is an illusion!" Elijah insisted. "The Assyrians have a five-to-one advantage, and they are experienced warriors! Don't allow Akbar to be destroyed!"

"What do you desire of me?" the governor asked, without halting his steed. "Last night I sent an emissary so we could talk, and they said you were out of the city. What else could I do?"

"Facing the Assyrians in the open field is suicide! You know that!"

The commander was listening to the conversation, making no comment. He had already discussed his strategy with the governor; the Israelite prophet would have a surprise.

Elijah ran alongside the horses, not knowing exactly what he should do. The column of soldiers left the city, heading toward the middle of the valley.

"Help me, Lord," he thought. "Just as Thou stopped the sun to help Joshua in combat, stop time and let me convince the governor of his error."

As soon as he thought this, the commander shouted, "Halt!"

"Perhaps it's a sign," Elijah told himself. "I must take advantage of it."

The soldiers formed two lines of engagement, like human walls. Their shields were firmly anchored in the earth, their swords pointing outward.

"You believe you are looking at Akbar's warriors," the governor said to Elijah.

"I'm looking at young men who laugh in the face of death," was the reply.

"Know then that what we have here is only a battalion. The greater part of our men are in the city, on top of the walls. We have placed there caldrons of boiling oil ready to be poured on the heads of anyone trying to scale them.

"We have stores divided among several locations, so that flaming arrows cannot do away with our food supply. According to the commander's calculations, we can hold out for almost two months against a siege. While the Assyrians were making ready, so too were we."

"I was never told this," Elijah said.

"Remember this: even having helped the people of Akbar, you are still a foreigner, and some in the military could mistake you for a spy."

"But you wished for peace!"

"Peace is still possible, even after combat begins. But now we shall negotiate under conditions of equality."

The governor related that messengers had been dispatched to Sidon and Tyre advising of the gravity of their position. It had been difficult for him to ask for help; others might think him incapable of controlling the situation. But he had concluded that this was the only solution.

The commander had developed an ingenious plan; as soon as combat began, he would return to the city to organize the resistance. The troops in the field were to kill as many of the enemy as possible, then withdraw to the mountains. They knew the valley better than anyone and could attack the Assyrians in small skirmishes, thus reducing the pressure of the siege.

Relief would come soon, and the Assyrian army would be decimated. "We can resist for sixty days, but that will not be necessary," the governor told Elijah.

"But many will die."

"We are all in the presence of death. And no one is afraid, not even I."

The governor was surprised at his own courage. He had never before been in a battle, and as the moment of combat drew nearer, he had made plans to flee the city. That morning he had agreed with some of his most faithful friends on the best means of retreat. He could not go to Sidon or Tyre, where he would be considered a traitor, but Jezebel would receive him because she needed men she could trust.

But when he stepped onto the field of battle, he had seen in the soldiers' eyes an immense joy, as if they had trained their entire lives for an objective and the great moment had finally come.

"Fear exists until the moment when the unavoidable happens," he told Elijah. "After that, we must waste none of our energy on it."

Elijah was confused. He felt the same way, though he was ashamed to recognize it; he recalled the boy's excitement when the troops had marched past.

"Away with you," the governor said. "You're a foreigner, unarmed, and have no need to fight for something you do not believe in."

Elijah did not move.

"They will come," said the commander. "You were caught by surprise, but we are prepared."

Even so, Elijah remained where he stood.

They scanned the horizon: no dust. The Assyrian army was not on the move.

The soldiers in the first rank held their spears firmly, pointed forward; the bowmen had their strings half-drawn, ready to loose their arrows at the commander's order. A few men slashed at the air with their swords to keep their muscles warm.

"Everything is ready," the commander repeated. "They are going to attack."

Elijah noticed the euphoria in his voice. He must be eager for the battle to begin, eager to demonstrate his bravery. Beyond a doubt he was imagining the Assyrian warriors, the sword blows, the shouting and confusion, and picturing himself being remembered by the Phoenician priests as an example of efficiency and courage.

The governor interrupted his thoughts.

"They're not moving."

Elijah remembered what he had asked of the Lord, for the sun to stand still in the heavens as He had done for Joshua. He tried to talk with his angel but did not hear his voice.

Little by little the spearmen lowered their weapons, the archers relaxed the tension on their bowstrings, the swordsmen replaced their weapons in their scabbards. The burning sun of midday arrived; several warriors fainted from the heat. Even so, for the rest of the day the detachment remained at readiness.

When the sun set, the warriors returned to Akbar; they appeared disappointed at having survived another day.

Elijah alone stayed behind in the valley. He had been wandering about for some time when the light appeared. The angel of the Lord was before him.

"God hath heard thy prayers," the angel said. "And hath seen the torment in thy soul."

Elijah turned to the heavens and gave thanks for the blessing.

"The Lord is the source of all glory and all power. He stopped the Assyrian army."

"No," the angel replied. "Thou hast said that the choice must be His. And He hath made the choice for thee."

"LET'S GO," THE WOMAN TOLD HER SON.

"I don't want to go," the boy replied. "I'm proud of Akbar's soldiers."

His mother bade him gather his belongings. "Take only what you can carry," she said.

"You forget we're poor, and I don't have much."

Elijah went up to his room. He looked about him, as if for the first and last time; he quickly descended and stood watching the widow store her inks.

"Thank you for taking me with you," she said. "I was only fifteen when I married, and I had no idea what life was. Our families had arranged everything; I had been raised since childhood for that moment and carefully prepared to help my husband in all circumstances."

"Did you love him?"

"I taught my heart to do so. Because there was no choice, I convinced myself that it was the best way. When I lost my husband, I resigned myself to the sameness of day and night; I asked the gods of the Fifth Mountain—in those times I still believed in them—to take me as soon as my son could live on his own.

"That was when you appeared. I've told you this once before, and I want to repeat it now: from that day on, I began to notice the beauty of the valley, the dark outline of the mountains projected against the sky, the moon ever-changing shape so the wheat could grow. Many nights while you slept I walked about Akbar, listening to the cries of newborn infants, the songs of men who had been drinking after work, the firm steps of the sentinels on the city walls. How many times had I seen that landscape without noticing how beautiful it was? How many times had I looked at the sky without seeing how deep it is? How many times had I heard the sounds of Akbar around me without understanding that they were part of my life?

"I once again felt an immense will to live. You told me to study the characters of Byblos, and I did. I thought only of pleasing you, but I came to care deeply about what I was doing, and I discovered something: *the meaning of my life was whatever I wanted it to be.*"

Elijah stroked her hair. It was the first time he had done so.

"Why haven't you always been like this?" she asked.

"Because I was afraid. But today, waiting for the battle to start, I heard the governor's words, and I thought of you. Fear reaches only to the point where the unavoidable begins; from there on, it loses its meaning. And all we have left is the hope that we are making the right decision."

"I'm ready," she said.

"We shall return to Israel. The Lord has told me what I must do, and so I shall. Jezebel will be removed from power."

She said nothing. Like all Phoenician women, she was proud of her princess. When they arrived there, she would try to convince the man at her side to change his mind.

"It will be a long journey, and we shall find no rest until I have done what He has asked of me," said Elijah, as if guessing her thoughts. "Still, your love will be my mainstay, and in the moments I grow weary in the battles in His name, I can find repose in your arms."

The boy appeared, carrying a small bag on his shoulder. Elijah took it and told the woman, "The hour has come. As you traverse the streets of Akbar, remember each house, each sound. For you will never again see them."

"I was born in Akbar," she said. "The city will forever remain in my heart."

Hearing this, the boy vowed to himself never to forget his mother's words. If someday he could return, he would look upon the city as if seeing her face.

◆

IT WAS ALREADY DARK when the high priest arrived at the foot of the Fifth Mountain. In his right hand he held a staff; in his left he carried a large sack.

From the sack he took the sacred oil and anointed his forehead and wrists. Then, using the staff, he drew in the sand a bull and a panther, the symbols of the God of the Storm and of the Great Goddess. He said the ritual prayers; finally he opened his arms to heaven to receive the divine revelation.

The gods spoke no more. They had said all they wished to say and now demanded only the carrying out of the rites. The prophets had disappeared everywhere in the world, save in Israel, a backward, superstitious country that still believed men could communicate with the creators of the Universe.

He recalled that generations before, Sidon and Tyre had traded with a king of Jerusalem called Solomon. He was building a great temple and desired to adorn it with the best the world offered; he had commanded that cedars be bought from Phoenicia, which they called Lebanon. The king of Tyre had provided the necessary materials and had received in exchange twenty cities in Galilee, but was not pleased with them. Solomon had then helped him to construct his first ships, and now Phoenicia had the largest merchant fleet in the world.

At that time, Israel was still a great nation, despite worshiping a single god whose name was not even known and who was usually called just "the Lord." A princess of Sidon had succeeded in returning Solomon to the true faith, and he had erected an altar to the gods of the Fifth Mountain. The Israelites insisted that "the Lord" had punished the wisest of their kings, bringing about the wars that had threatened his reign.

His son Rehoboam, however, carried on the worship that his father had initiated. He ordered two golden calves to be made, and the people of Israel worshiped them. It was then that the prophets appeared and began a ceaseless struggle against the rulers.

Jezebel was right: the only way to keep the true faith alive was by doing away with the prophets. Although she was a gentle woman, brought up in the way of tolerance and of horror at the thought of war, she knew that there comes a moment when violence is the only answer. The blood that now stained her hands would be forgiven by the gods she served.

"Soon, my hands too will be stained with blood," the high priest told the silent mountain before him. "Just as the prophets are the curse of Israel, writing is the curse of Phoenicia. Both bring about an evil beyond redress, and both must be stopped while it is still possible. The god of weather must not desert us now."

He was concerned about what had happened that morning; the enemy army had not attacked. The god of weather had abandoned Phoenicia in the past because he had become irritated at its inhabitants. As a consequence, the light of the lamps had stilled, the lambs and cows had abandoned their young, the wheat and barley had failed to ripen. The Sun god commanded that important beings be sent to search for him—the eagle and the God of the Storm—but no one succeeded in finding him. Finally, the Great Goddess sent a bee, which found him asleep in a forest and stung him. He awoke furious and began to destroy everything around him. It was necessary to bind him and remove the wrath from his soul, but from that time onward, all returned to normal.

If he decided to leave again, the battle would not take place. The Assyrians would remain permanently in the entrance to the valley, and Akbar would continue to exist.

"Courage is fear that prays," he said. "That is why I am here, because I cannot vacillate at the moment of combat. I must show the warriors of Akbar that there is a reason to defend the city. It is neither the well, nor the marketplace, nor the governor's palace. We shall confront the Assyrian army because we must set the example."

The Assyrian triumph would end the threat of the alphabet for all time to come. The conquerors would impose their language and their customs, but they would go on worshiping the same gods on the Fifth Mountain; that was what truly mattered.

"In the future, our navigators will take to other lands the feats of our warriors. The priests will recall the names and the date when Akbar attempted to resist the Assyrian invasion. Painters will draw Egyptian characters on papyrus; the scribes of Byblos will be dead. The sacred texts will continue only in the hands of those born to study them. Then the later generations will try to imitate what we have done, and we shall build a better world.

"But now," he continued, "we must first lose this battle. We shall fight bravely, but our situation is inferior, and we shall die with glory."

At that moment the high priest listened to the night and saw that he was right. The silence anticipated the moment of an important battle, but the inhabitants of Akbar were misinterpreting it; they had laid down their weapons and were amusing themselves at precisely the moment when they had need of vigilance. They paid no heed to nature's example: the animals fell silent when danger was at hand.

"Let the gods' designs be fulfilled. May the heavens not fall upon the earth, for we have acted rightly; we have obeyed tradition," he concluded.

Elijah, the woman, and the boy went in a westerly direction, toward Israel; they did not need to pass near the Assyrian encampment because it was located to the south. The full moon made the walk easier but also cast strange shadows and sinister forms on the rocks and stones of the valley.

In the midst of the darkness, the angel of the Lord appeared. He bore a sword of fire in his right hand.

"Whither goest thou?" he asked.

"To Israel," Elijah answered.

"Hath the Lord summoned thee?"

"I know the miracle that God expects me to perform. And now I know where I am to execute it."

"Hath the Lord summoned thee?" repeated the angel.

Elijah remained silent.

"Hath the Lord summoned thee?" asked the angel for the third time.

"No."

"Then return to the place whence thou comest, for thou hast yet to fulfill thy destiny. The Lord hath still to summon thee."

"If nothing else, permit them to leave, for they have no reason to remain," implored Elijah.

But the angel was no longer there. Elijah dropped the bag he was carrying, sat in the middle of the road, and wept bitterly.

"What happened?" asked the woman and the boy, who had seen nothing.

"We're going back," he said. "Such is the Lord's desire."

◆

HE WAS NOT ABLE to sleep well. He awoke in the night and sensed the tension in the air around him; an evil wind blew through the streets, sowing fear and distrust.

"In the love of a woman, I have discovered the love for all creatures," he prayed silently. "I need her. I know that the Lord will not forget that I am one of His instruments, perhaps the weakest of those He has chosen. Help me, O Lord, because I must repose calmly amidst the battles."

He recalled the governor's comment about the uselessness of fear. Despite that, sleep eluded him. "I need energy and tranquillity; give me rest while it is still possible."

He thought of summoning his angel and talking with him for

a while, but knowing he might be told things he had no wish to hear, he changed his mind. To relax, he went downstairs; the bags that the woman had prepared for their flight had not been undone.

He considered returning to his room. He remembered what the Lord had told Moses: "*And what man is there that hath betrothed a wife, and hath not taken her? Let him go and return unto his house, lest he die in the battle, and another man take her.*"

They had not yet known each other. But it had been a wearying night, and this was not the moment to do so.

He decided to unpack the bags and return everything to its place. He discovered that, besides the few clothes she possessed, she was carrying the instruments for drawing the characters of Byblos.

He picked up a stylus, moistened a small clay tablet, and began to sketch a few letters; he had learned to write by watching the woman as she worked.

"What a simple and ingenious thing," he thought, in an effort to turn his mind to other concerns. Often, on his way to the well for water, he had heard the women commenting, "The Greeks stole our most important invention," but Elijah knew it was not that way: the adaptation they had made by including vowels had transformed the alphabet into something that the peoples of all nations could use. Furthermore, they called their collections of parchments *biblia,* in honor of the city where the invention had occurred.

The Greek *biblia* were written on animal hides. Elijah felt this was a very fragile way of storing words; hides were less resistant than clay tablets and could be easily stolen. Papyrus came apart after some handling and was destroyed by water. "*Biblia* and papyrus will not last; only clay tablets are destined to remain forever," he reflected.

If Akbar survived for a time longer, he would recommend that the governor order his country's entire history written on clay tablets and stored in a special room, so that generations yet to come might consult them. In this way, if one day the priests of Phoenicia, who kept in their memory the history of their people, were decimated, the feats of warriors and poets would not be forgotten.

He amused himself for some time by writing the same letters but by ordering them differently, forming several words. He was enchanted with the result. The task relaxed him, and he returned to his bed.

◆

HE AWOKE some time later at the sound of the door to his room crashing to the floor.

"It's not a dream. It's not the armies of the Lord in combat."

Shadows came from all sides, screaming like madmen in a language he did not understand.

"The Assyrians."

Other doors fell, walls were leveled by powerful hammer blows, the shouts of the invaders mixed with cries for help rising from the square. He attempted to stand, but one of the shadows knocked him to the ground. A muffled sound shook the floor below.

"Fire," Elijah thought. "They've set the house on fire."

"It's you," he heard someone saying in Phoenician. "You're the leader. Hiding like a coward in a woman's house."

He looked at the face of the person who had just spoken; flames lit the room, and he could see a man with a long beard, in a military uniform. Yes, the Assyrians had come.

"You invaded at night?" he asked, disoriented.

The man did not respond. Elijah saw the flash of swords drawn from their scabbards, and one of the warriors slashed his right arm.

Elijah closed his eyes; the scenes of an entire lifetime passed before him in a fraction of a second. He was once again playing in the street of the city of his birth, traveling to Jerusalem for the first time, smelling the odor of cut wood in the carpenter's shop, marveling at the vastness of the sea and at the garments people wore in the great cities of the coast. He saw himself walking the valleys and mountains of the Promised Land, remembered when he first saw Jezebel, who seemed like a young girl and charmed all who came near. He witnessed a second time the massacre of the prophets, heard anew the voice of the Lord ordering him into the desert. He saw again the eyes of the woman who awaited him at the gates of Zarephath, which its inhabitants called Akbar, and understood that he had loved her from the first moment. Once more he climbed the Fifth Mountain, brought a child back to life, and was welcomed by the people as a sage and a judge. He looked at the heavens, where the constellations were rapidly changing position, was dazzled by the moon that displayed its four phases in a single instant, felt heat, cold, fall and spring, experienced the rain and the lightning's flash.

Clouds swept past in millions of different shapes, and the water of rivers again ran in their beds. He relived the day that he had seen the first Assyrian tent being erected, then the second, then several, many, the angels that came and went, the fiery sword on the road to Israel, sleepless nights, drawings on clay tablets, and—

He was back in the present. He thought about what was happening on the floor below; he had to save the widow and her son at any cost.

"Fire!" he told one of the enemy soldiers. "The house is on fire!"

He was not afraid; his only concern was for the widow and her child. Someone pushed his head against the floor, and he felt the taste of earth in his mouth. He kissed it, told it how much he loved it, and explained that he had done everything possible to avoid what was happening. He tried to wrest free of his captors, but someone had his foot on his chest.

"She must have fled," he thought. "They wouldn't harm a defenseless woman."

A deep calm took hold of his heart. Perhaps the Lord had come to realize that he was the wrong man and had found another prophet to rescue Israel from sin. Death had finally come, in the way he had hoped, through martyrdom. He accepted his fate and waited for the fatal blow.

Seconds went by; the voices were still shouting, blood still ran from his wound, but the fatal blow had not come.

"Ask them to kill me at once!" he shouted, knowing that at least one of them spoke his language.

No one heeded his words. They were arguing heatedly, as if something had gone wrong. Some of the soldiers began kicking him, and for the first time Elijah noticed the instinct for survival reasserting itself. This created in him a sensation of panic.

"I can't wish for life any longer," he thought desperately. "Because I'm not leaving this room alive."

But nothing happened. The world seemed to be suspended endlessly in that confusion of shouts, noises, and dust. Perhaps the Lord had done as He had with Joshua and time had stood still amid the combat.

That was when he heard the woman's screams from below. With an effort surpassing human strength, Elijah pushed aside two of the guards and struggled to his feet, but he was quickly struck down; a soldier kicked him in the head, and he fainted.

◆

A FEW MINUTES LATER he recovered consciousness. The Assyrians had dragged him into the street.

Still dizzy, he raised his head; every house in the neighborhood was in flames.

"An innocent, helpless woman is caught in there! Save her!"

Cries, people running in every direction, confusion everywhere. He tried to rise but was struck down again.

"Lord, Thou canst do with me as Thou wilt, for I have dedicated my life and my death to Thy cause," Elijah prayed. "But save the woman who took me in!"

Someone raised him by his arms.

"Come and see," said the Assyrian officer who knew his language. "You deserve it."

Two guards seized him and pushed him toward the door. The house was rapidly being devoured by flames, and the light from the fire illuminated everything around it. He heard cries coming from all sides: children sobbing, old men begging for forgiveness, desperate women searching for their children. But he had ears only for the pleas for help of the woman who had afforded him shelter.

"What is happening? A woman and child are inside! Why have you done this to them?"

"Because she tried to hide the governor of Akbar."

"I'm not the governor! You're making a terrible mistake!"

The Assyrian officer pushed him toward the door. The ceiling had collapsed in the fire, and the woman was half-buried in the debris. Elijah could see only her arm, moving desperately from side to side. She was asking for help, begging them not to let her be burned alive.

"Why spare me," he implored, "and do this to her?"

"We're not going to spare you, but we want you to suffer as much as possible. Our general died without honor, stoned to death, in front of the city walls. He came in search of life and was condemned to death. Now you will have the same fate."

Elijah struggled desperately to free himself, but the guards carried him away. They passed through the streets of Akbar, in infernal heat; the soldiers were sweating heavily, and some of them appeared shocked at the scene they had just witnessed. Elijah thrashed about, clamoring against the heavens, but the Assyrians were as silent as the Lord Himself.

They arrived at the square. Most of the buildings in the city were ablaze, and the sound of flames mingled with the cries of Akbar's inhabitants.

"How good that death still exists."

Since that day in the stable, how often Elijah had thought this!

The corpses of Akbar's warriors, most of them without uniforms, were spread out on the ground. He saw people running in every direction, not knowing where they were going, not knowing what they sought, guided by nothing more than the necessity of pretending they were doing something, fighting against death and destruction.

"Why do they do that?" he thought. "Don't they see the city is in the hands of the enemy and there is nowhere to flee?" Everything had happened very quickly. The Assyrians had taken advantage of their large superiority in numbers and had been able to spare their warriors from combat. Akbar's soldiers had been exterminated almost without a struggle.

They stopped in the middle of the square. Elijah was made to kneel on the ground and his hands were tied. He no longer heard the woman's screams; perhaps she had died quickly, without going through the slow torture of being burned alive. The Lord had her in His hands. And she was carrying her son at her bosom.

Another group of Assyrian soldiers brought a prisoner whose face was disfigured by numerous blows. Even so, Elijah recognized the commander.

"Long live Akbar!" he shouted. "Long life to Phoenicia and its warriors, who engage the enemy by day! Death to the cowards who attack in darkness!"

He barely had time to finish the phrase. An Assyrian general's sword descended, and the commander's head rolled along the ground.

"Now it is my turn," Elijah told himself. "I'll meet her again in paradise, where we shall stroll hand in hand."

At that moment, a man approached and began to argue with the officers. He was an inhabitant of Akbar who was wont to attend the meetings in the square. Elijah recalled having helped him resolve a serious dispute with a neighbor.

The Assyrians were arguing among themselves, their words growing louder and louder, and pointing at him. The man kneeled, kissed the feet of one of them, extended his hand toward the Fifth Mountain, and wept like a child. The invaders' fury appeared to subside.

The discussion seemed to go on endlessly. The man implored and wept the entire time, pointing to Elijah and to the house where the governor lived. The soldiers appeared dissatisfied with the conversation.

Finally, the officer who spoke his language approached.

"Our spy," he said, indicating the man, "says that we are mistaken. It was he who gave us the plans to the city, and we have confidence in what he says. It's not you we wish to kill."

He pushed him with his foot. Elijah fell to the ground.

"He says you would go to Israel and remove the princess who usurped the throne. Is that true?"

Elijah did not answer.

"Tell me if it's true," the officer insisted. "And you can leave here and return to your dwelling in time to save that woman and her son."

"Yes, it's true," he said. Perhaps the Lord had listened to him and would help him to save them.

"We could take you captive to Sidon and Tyre," the officer continued. "But we still have many battles before us, and you'd be a weight on our backs. We could demand a ransom for you, but from whom? You're a foreigner even in your own country."

The officer put his foot on Elijah's face.

"You're useless. You're no good to the enemy and no good to friends. Just like your city; it's not worth leaving part of our army here, to keep it under our rule. After we conquer the coastal cities Akbar will be ours in any case."

"I have one question," Elijah said. "Just one question."

The officer looked at him warily.

"Why did you attack at night? Don't you know that wars are fought by day?"

"We did not break the law; there is no custom that forbids it," answered the officer. "And we had a long time to become familiar with the terrain. All of you were so preoccupied with custom that you forgot that times change."

Without a further word, the group left him. The spy approached and untied his hands.

"I promised myself that I would one day repay your generosity; I have kept my word. When the Assyrians entered the palace, one of the servants told them that the man they were looking for had taken refuge in the widow's house. While they went there, the real governor was able to flee."

Elijah was not listening. Fire crackled everywhere, and the screams continued.

In the midst of the confusion, it was evident that one group still maintained discipline; obeying an invisible order, the Assyrians were silently withdrawing.

The battle of Akbar was over.

◆

"She's dead," he told himself. "I don't want to go there, for she is dead. Or she was saved by a miracle and will come looking for me."

His heart nevertheless bade him rise to his feet and go to the house where they lived. Elijah struggled with himself; at that moment, more than a woman's love was at stake—his entire life, his faith in the Lord's designs, the departure from the city of his birth, the idea that he had a mission and was capable of completing it.

He looked about him, searching for a sword with which to take his own life, but with the Assyrians had gone every weapon in Akbar. He thought of throwing himself onto the flames of the burning houses, but he feared the pain.

For some moments he stood paralyzed. Little by little, he began recovering his awareness of the situation in which he found himself. The woman and her child must have already left this world, but he must bury them in accord with custom. At that moment the Lord's work—whether or not He existed—was his only succor. After finishing his religious duty, he would yield to pain and doubt.

Moreover, there was a possibility that they still lived. He could not remain there, doing nothing.

"I don't want to see their burned faces, the skin falling from their flesh. Their souls are already running free in heaven."

◆

NEVERTHELESS, HE BEGAN walking toward the house, choking and blinded by the smoke that prevented his finding his way. He gradually began to comprehend the situation in the city. Although the enemy had withdrawn, panic was mounting in an alarming manner. People continued to wander aimlessly, weeping, petitioning the gods on behalf of their dead.

He looked for someone to help him. A lone man was in sight, in a total state of shock; his mind seemed distant.

"It's best to go straightway and not ask for help." He knew Akbar as if it were his native city and was able to orient himself, even without recognizing many of the places that he was accustomed to passing. In the street the cries he heard were now more coherent. The people were beginning to understand that a tragedy had taken place and that it was necessary to react.

"There's a wounded man here!" said one.

"We need more water! We're not going to be able to control the fire!" said another.

"Help me! My husband is trapped!"

He came to the place where, many months before, he had been received and given lodging as a friend. An old woman was sitting in the middle of the street, almost in front of the house, completely naked. Elijah tried to help her but was pushed away.

"She's dying!" the old woman cried. "Do something! Take that wall off her!"

And she began screaming hysterically. Elijah took her by the arms and shoved her aside, for the noise she was making prevented his hearing the widow's moans. Everything around him was total destruction—the roof and walls had collapsed, and it was difficult to recognize where he had last seen her. The flames had died down but the heat was still unbearable; he stepped over the rubble covering the floor and went toward the place where the woman's bedroom had been.

Despite the confusion outside, he was able to make out a moan. It was her voice.

He instinctively shook the dust from his garments, as if trying to improve his appearance. He remained silent, trying to concentrate. He heard the crackling of the fire, the cries for help from people buried in the neighboring houses, and felt the urge to tell them to be silent because he must discover where the woman and her son were. After a long time, he heard the sound again; someone was scratching on the wood beneath his feet.

He fell to his knees and began digging like one possessed. He removed the dirt, stones, and wood. Finally, his hand touched something warm: it was blood.

"Please, don't die," he said.

"Leave the rubble over me," he heard her voice say. "I don't want you to see my face. Go and help my son."

He continued to dig, and she repeated, "Go and find the body of my son. Please, do as I ask."

Elijah's head fell against his chest, and he began weeping softly.

"I don't know where he's buried," he said. "Please, don't go; how I long to have you remain with me. I need you to teach me how to love; my heart is ready now."

"Before you arrived, for so many years I called out to death. It must have heard and come looking for me."

She moaned. Elijah bit his lips but said nothing. Someone touched his shoulder.

Startled, he turned and saw the boy. He was covered with dust and soot but appeared unhurt.

"Where is my mother?" he asked.

"I'm here, my son," answered the voice from beneath the ruins. "Are you injured?"

The boy began to cry. Elijah took him in his arms.

"You're crying, my son," said the voice, ever weaker. "Don't do that. Your mother took a long time to learn that life has meaning; I hope I have been able to teach it to you. In what condition is the city where you were born?"

Elijah and the boy remained silent, each clinging to the other.

"It's fine," Elijah lied. "A few warriors died, but the Assyrians have withdrawn. They were after the governor, to avenge the death of one of their generals."

Again, silence. And again her voice, still weaker than before.

"Tell me that my city is safe."

He knew that she would be gone at any moment.

"The city is whole. And your son is well."

"What about you?"

"I have survived."

He knew that with these words he was liberating her soul and allowing her to die in peace.

"Ask my son to kneel," the woman said after a time. "And I want you to swear to me, in the name of the Lord thy God."

"Whatever you want. Anything that you want."

"You once told me that the Lord is everywhere, and I believed you. You said that souls don't go to the top of the Fifth Mountain, and I also believed what you said. But you didn't explain where they go.

"This is the oath: you two will not weep for me, and each

will take care of the other until the Lord allows each of you to follow his path. From this moment on, my soul will become one with all I have known on this earth: I am the valley, the mountains that surround it, the city, the people walking in its streets. I am its wounded and its beggars, its soldiers, its priests, its merchants, its nobles. I am the ground that they tread, and the well that slakes each one's thirst.

"Don't weep for me, for there is no reason to be sad. From this moment on, I am Akbar, and the city is beautiful."

The silence of death descended, and the wind ceased to blow. Elijah no longer heard the cries outside or the flames crackling in neighboring houses; he heard only the silence and could almost touch it in its intensity.

Then Elijah led the boy away, rent his own garments, turned to the heavens, and bellowed with all the strength of his lungs, "O Lord my God! For Thy cause have I left Israel and cannot offer Thee my blood as did the prophets who remained there. I have been called a coward by my friends and a traitor by my enemies.

"For Thy cause have I eaten only what crows brought me and have crossed the desert to Zarephath, which its inhabitants call Akbar. Guided by Thy hand, I met a woman; guided by Thee, my heart learned to love her. But at no time did I forget my true mission; during all the days I spent here I was always ready to depart.

"Beautiful Akbar is in ruins, and the woman who trusted me lies beneath them. Where have I sinned, O Lord? At what moment have I strayed from what Thou desirest of me? If Thou art discontent with me, why hast Thou not taken me from this world? Instead, Thou hast afflicted yet again those who succored me and loved me.

"I do not understand Thy designs. I see no justice in Thy acts. In bearing the suffering Thou hast imposed on me, I am sorely wanting. Remove Thyself from my life, for I too am reduced to ruins, fire, and dust."

Amidst the fire and desolation, the light appeared to Elijah. And the angel of the Lord was before him.

"Why are you here?" asked Elijah. "Don't you see that it is too late?"

"I have come to say that once again the Lord hath heard thy prayer and thy petition will be granted thee. No more shalt thou hear thy angel, nor shall I meet again with thee till thou hast undergone thy days of trial."

Elijah took the boy by the hand and they began to walk aimlessly. The smoke, till then dispersed by the winds, was now concentrated in the streets, making the air impossible to breathe. "Perhaps it's a dream," he thought. "Perhaps it's a nightmare."

"You lied to my mother," the boy said. "The city is destroyed."

"What does that matter? If she did not see what was happening around her, why not allow her to die in peace?"

"Because she trusted you, and said that she was Akbar."

Elijah cut his foot on one of the broken pieces of glass and pottery strewn on the ground. The pain proved to him that he was not dreaming; everything around him was terribly real. They arrived at the square where—how long ago?—he had met with the people and helped them to resolve their disputes; the sky was gilded by flames from the fires.

"I don't want my mother to be this that I'm looking at," the boy insisted. "You lied to her."

The boy was managing to keep his oath; Elijah had not seen a single tear on his face. "What can I do?" he thought. His foot was bleeding, and he decided to concentrate on the pain, to ward off despair.

He looked at the sword cut the Assyrian had made in his body; it was not as deep as he had imagined. He sat down with the boy at the same spot where he had been bound by his enemies, and saved by a traitor. He noticed that people were no longer running; they were walking slowly from place to place, amidst the smoky, dusty ruins, as if they were the living dead. They seemed like souls abandoned by the heavens and condemned to walk the earth eternally. Nothing made sense.

Some of the people reacted; they still heeded the women's voices and the confused orders from the soldiers who had survived the massacre. But they were few and were not achieving any result.

The high priest had once said that the world was the collective dream of the gods. What if, fundamentally, he was right? Could he now help the gods to awaken from this nightmare and then make them sleep again to dream a gentler dream? When Elijah had nocturnal visions, he always awoke and then slept anew; why should the same not occur with the creators of the Universe?

He stumbled over the dead. None of them was now concerned with having to pay taxes, Assyrian encampments in the valley, religious rituals, or the existence of a wandering prophet who perhaps one day had spoken to them.

"I can't remain here permanently. The legacy that she left me is this boy, and I shall be worthy of it, even if it be the last thing I do on the face of the earth."

With a great effort, he rose, took the boy by the hand, and they began to walk. Some of the people were sacking the shops and tents that had been smashed. For the first time, he attempted to react to what had happened, by asking them not to do that.

But the people pushed him aside, saying, "We're eating the remains of what the governor devoured by himself. Get out of the way."

Elijah did not have the strength to argue; he led the boy out of the city, where they began to walk through the valley. The angels, with their swords of fire, would come no more.

"A full moon."

Far from the dust and smoke, he could see the night illuminated by moonlight. Hours before, when he was attempting to leave the city for Jerusalem, he had been able to find his way without difficulty; the Assyrians had had the same advantage.

The boy stumbled over a body and screamed. It was the high priest; his arms and legs had been cut off, but he was still alive. His eyes were fixed on the heights of the Fifth Mountain.

"As you see," he said in a labored but calm voice, "the Phoenician gods have won the celestial battle." Blood was spurting from his mouth.

"Let me end your suffering," Elijah replied.

"Pain means nothing, compared to the joy of having done my duty."

"Your duty was to destroy a city of righteous men?"

"A city does not die, only its inhabitants and the ideas they bore within themselves. One day, others will come to Akbar, drink its water, and the stone that its founder left behind will be polished and cared for by new priests. Leave me now; my pain will soon be over, while your despair will endure for the rest of your life."

The mutilated body was breathing with difficulty, and Elijah left him. At that moment, a group of people—men, women, and children—came running toward him and encircled him.

"It was you!" they shouted. "You dishonored your homeland and brought a curse upon our city!"

"May the gods bear witness to this! May they know who is to blame!"

The men pushed him and shook him by the shoulders. The boy pulled loose from his hands and disappeared. The others struck him in the face, the chest, the back, but his only thoughts were for the boy; he had not even been able to keep him at his side.

The beating did not last long; perhaps his assailants were themselves weary of so much violence. Elijah fell to the ground.

"Leave this place!" someone said. "You have repaid our love with your hatred!"

The group withdrew. Elijah did not have the strength to rise to his feet. When he recovered from the shame, he had ceased to be the same man. He desired neither to die nor to go on living. He desired nothing: he possessed no love, no hate, no faith.

◆

HE AWOKE to someone touching his face. It was still night, but the moon was no longer in the sky.

"I promised my mother that I'd take care of you," the boy said. "But I don't know what to do."

"Go back to the city. The people there are good, and someone will take you in."

"You're hurt. I need to attend to your arm. Maybe an angel will come and tell me what to do."

"You're ignorant, you know nothing about what's happening!" Elijah shouted. "The angels will come no more because we're common folk, and everyone is weak when faced with suffering. When tragedy occurs, let people fend for themselves!"

He took a deep breath, trying to calm himself; there was no point in arguing further.

"How did you find your way here?"

"I never left."

"Then you saw my shame. You saw that there is nothing left for me to do in Akbar."

"You told me that all life's battles teach us something, even those we lose."

He remembered the walk to the well the morning before. But it seemed as if years had passed since then, and he felt the urge to tell him that those beautiful words meant nothing when one faces suffering; but he decided not to upset the boy.

"How did you escape the fire?"

The boy lowered his head. "I hadn't gone to sleep. I decided to spend the night awake, to see if you and my mother were going to meet in her room. I saw the first soldiers come in."

Elijah rose and began to walk. He was looking for the stone in front of the Fifth Mountain where one afternoon he had watched the sunset with the woman.

"I mustn't go," he thought. "I'll become even more desperate."

But some force drew him in that direction. When he arrived there, he wept bitterly; like the city of Akbar, the spot was marked by a stone, but he alone in that entire valley understood its significance; it would neither be praised by new inhabitants, nor polished by couples discovering the meaning of love.

He took the boy in his arms and once again slept.

"I'M HUNGRY AND THIRSTY," THE BOY TOLD ELIJAH AS soon as he awoke.

"We can go to the home of one of the shepherds who live nearby. It's likely nothing happened to them because they didn't live in Akbar."

"We need to repair the city. My mother said that she was Akbar."

What city? No longer was there a palace, a market, or walls. The city's good people had turned into robbers, and its young soldiers had been massacred. Nor would the angels return, though this was the least among his problems.

"Do you think that last night's destruction, suffering, and deaths have a meaning? Do you think that it's necessary to destroy thousands of lives to teach someone something?"

The boy looked at him in alarm.

"Put from your mind what I just said," Elijah told him. "We're going to look for the shepherd."

"And we're going to rebuild the city," the boy insisted.

Elijah did not reply. He knew he would no longer be able to use his authority with the people, who accused him of having brought misfortune. The governor had taken flight, the commander was dead; soon Sidon and Tyre might fall under foreign domination. Perhaps the woman was right: the gods were always changing, and this time it was the Lord who had gone away.

"When will we go back there?" the boy asked again.

Elijah took him by the shoulders and began shaking him forcefully.

"Look behind you! You're not some blind angel but a boy who intended to spy on his mother's acts. What do you see? Have you noticed the columns of rising smoke? Do you know what that means?"

"You're hurting me! I want to leave here, I want to go away!"

Elijah stopped, disconcerted at himself: he had never acted in such a way. The boy broke loose and began running toward the city. Elijah overtook him and kneeled at his feet.

"Forgive me. I don't know what I'm doing."

The boy sobbed, but not a single tear ran down his cheeks. Elijah sat beside him, waiting for him to regain his calm.

"Don't leave," he asked. "When your mother went away, I promised her I'd stay with you until you could follow your own path."

"You also promised that the city was whole. And she said—"

"There's no need to repeat it. I'm confused, lost in my own guilt. Give me time to find myself. I didn't mean to hurt you."

The boy embraced him. But his eyes shed no tears.

◆

THEY CAME TO THE HOUSE in the middle of the valley; a woman was at the door, and two children were playing in front. The flock was in the enclosure, which meant that the shepherd had not yet left for the mountains that morning.

Startled, the woman looked at the man and boy walking toward her. Her instinct was to send them away at once, but custom—and the gods—demanded that she honor the universal law of hospitality. If she did not receive them now, her own children might in the future suffer the same fate.

"I have no money," she said. "But I can give you a little water and something to eat."

They sat on a small porch with a straw roof, and she brought dried fruit and a jar of water. They ate in silence, experiencing, for the first time since the events of the night before, something of the normal routine that marked their every day. The children, frightened by the newcomers' appearance, had taken refuge inside the house.

When they finished their meal, Elijah asked about the shepherd.

"He'll be here soon," she said. "We heard a lot of noise, and somebody came by this morning saying that Akbar had been destroyed. He went to see what happened."

The children called her, and she went inside.

"It will avail me nothing to try to convince the boy," Elijah thought. "He'll not leave me in peace until I do what he asks. I must show him that it is impossible; only then will he be persuaded."

The food and water achieved a miracle: he again felt himself a part of the world.

His thoughts flowed with incredible speed, seeking solutions rather than answers.

◆

SOME TIME LATER, the aged shepherd arrived. He looked at the man and boy with fear, concerned for the safety of his family. But he quickly understood what was happening.

"You must be refugees from Akbar," he said. "I've just returned from there."

"And what's happening?" asked the boy.

"The city was destroyed, and the governor ran away. The gods have disorganized the world."

"We lost everything we had," said Elijah. "We ask that you receive us."

"I think my wife has already received you, and fed you. Now you must leave and face the unavoidable."

"I don't know what to do with the boy. I'm in need of help."

"Of course you know. He's young, he seems intelligent, and he has energy. And you have the experience of someone who's known many victories and defeats in life. The combination is perfect, because it can help you to find wisdom."

The man looked at the wound on Elijah's arm. He said it was not serious; he entered the house and returned with some herbs and a piece of cloth. The boy helped him apply the poultice. When the shepherd said that he could do it alone, the boy told him that he had promised his mother to take care of this man.

The shepherd laughed.

"Your son is a man of his word."

"I'm not his son. And he's a man of his word too. He'll rebuild the city because he has to bring my mother back, the way he did with me."

Suddenly, Elijah understood the boy's concern, but before he could do anything, the shepherd shouted to his wife, who was coming out of the house at that moment. "It's better to start rebuilding life right away," he said. "It will take a long time for everything to return to what it was."

"It will never return."

"You look like a wise young man, and you can understand many things that I cannot. But nature has taught me something that I shall never forget: a man who depends on the weather and the seasons, as only a shepherd does, manages to survive the unavoidable. He cares for his flock, treats each animal as if it were the only one, tries to help the mothers with their young, is never too far from a place where the animals can drink. Still, now and again one of the lambs to which he gave so much of himself dies in an accident. It might be a snake, some wild animal, or even a fall over a cliff. But the unavoidable always happens."

Elijah looked in the direction of Akbar and recalled his conversation with the angel. The unavoidable always happens.

"You need discipline and patience to overcome it," the shepherd said.

"And hope. When that no longer exists, one can't waste his energy fighting against the impossible."

"It's not a question of hope in the future. It's a question of re-creating your own past."

The shepherd was no longer in a hurry; his heart was filled with pity for the refugees who stood facing him. As he and his family had been spared the tragedy, it cost nothing to help them, and thus to thank the gods. Moreover, he had heard talk of the Israelite prophet who had climbed the Fifth Mountain without being slain by the fire from heaven; everything indicated that it was the man before him.

"You can stay another day if you wish."

"I didn't understand what you said before," commented Elijah. "About re-creating your own past."

"I have long seen people passing through here on their way to Sidon and Tyre. Some of them complained that they had not achieved anything in Akbar and were setting out for a new destiny.

"One day these people would return. They had not found what they were seeking, for they carried with them, along with their bags, the weight of their earlier failure. A few returned with a government position, or with the joy of having given their children a better life, but nothing more. Their past in Akbar had left them fearful, and they lacked the confidence in themselves to take risks.

"On the other hand, there also passed my door people full of ardor. They had profited from every moment of life in Akbar and through great effort had accumulated the money for their journey. To these people, life was a constant triumph and would go on being one.

"These people also returned, but with wonderful tales to tell. They had achieved everything they desired because they were not limited by the frustrations of the past."

◆

THE SHEPHERD'S WORDS touched Elijah's heart.

"It is not difficult to rebuild a life, just as it is not impossible to raise Akbar from its ruins," the shepherd continued. "It is enough to be aware that we go on with the same strength that we had before. And to use that in our favor."

The man gazed into Elijah's eyes.

"If you have a past that dissatisfies you, forget it now," he went on. "Imagine a new story of your life, and believe in it. Concentrate only on those moments in which you achieved what you desired, and this strength will help you to accomplish what you want."

"There was a moment when I desired to be a carpenter, and later I wanted to be a prophet sent to save Israel," Elijah thought. "Angels descended from the heavens, the Lord spoke to me. Until I understood that He is not just and that His motives are always beyond my understanding."

The shepherd called to his wife, saying that he was not leaving; he had already been to Akbar on foot, and he was too weary to walk farther.

"Thank you for receiving us," Elijah said.

"It is no burden to shelter you for one night."

The boy interrupted the conversation. "We want to go back to Akbar."

"Wait till morning. The city is being sacked by its own inhabitants, and there is nowhere to sleep."

The boy looked at the ground, bit his lip, and once again held back tears. The shepherd led them into the house, calmed his wife and children, and, to distract them, spent the rest of the day talking about the weather.

THE NEXT DAY THEY AWOKE EARLY, ATE THE MEAL PREpared by the shepherd's wife, and went to the door of the house.

"May your life be long and your flock grow ever larger," said Elijah. "I have eaten what my body had need of, and my soul has learned what it did not know. May God never forget what you did for us, and may your sons not be strangers in a strange land."

"I don't know to which God you refer; there are many who dwell on the Fifth Mountain," the shepherd said brusquely, then quickly changed his tone. "Remember the good things you have done. They will give you courage."

"I have done very few such things, and none of them was because of my abilities."

"Then it's time to do more."

"Perhaps I could have prevented the invasion."

The shepherd laughed.

"Even if you were governor of Akbar, you would not be able to stop the unavoidable."

"Perhaps the governor of Akbar should have attacked the Assyrians when they first arrived in the valley with few troops. Or negotiated peace, before war broke out."

"Everything that could have happened but did not is carried away with the wind and leaves no trace," said the shepherd. "Life is made of our attitudes. *And there are certain things that the gods oblige us to live through.* Their reason for this does not matter, and there is no action we can take to make them pass us by."

"Why?"

"Ask a certain Israelite prophet who lived in Akbar. He seems to have the answer to everything."

The man went to the fence. "I must take my flock to pasture," he said. "Yesterday they didn't go out, and they're impatient."

He took his leave with a wave of his hand, departing with his sheep.

THE BOY AND THE MAN WALKED THROUGH THE VALLEY.

"You're walking slowly," the boy said. "You're afraid of what might happen to you."

"I'm afraid only of myself," Elijah replied. "They can do me no harm because my heart has ceased to be."

"The God that brought me back from death is alive. He can bring back my mother, if you do the same thing to the city."

"Forget that God. He's far away and no longer does the miracles we hope for from Him."

The old shepherd was right. From this moment on, it was necessary to reconstruct his own past, forget that he had once thought himself to be a prophet who would free Israel but had failed in his mission of saving even one city.

The thought gave him a strange sense of euphoria. For the

first time in his life he felt free, ready to do whatever he desired whenever he wished. True, he would hear no more angels, but as compensation he was free to return to Israel, to go back to work as a carpenter, to travel to Greece to learn the thoughts of wise men, or to journey with Phoenician navigators to the lands across the sea.

First, however, he must avenge himself. He had dedicated the best years of his youth to an unheeding God who was constantly giving commands and always did things in His own fashion. Elijah had learned to accept His decisions and to respect His designs.

But his loyalty had been rewarded by abandonment, his dedication had been ignored, his efforts to comply with the Supreme Being's will had led to the death of the only woman he had ever loved.

"Thou hast the strength of the world and the stars," said Elijah in his native tongue, so that the boy beside him would not understand the words. "Thou canst destroy a city, a country, as we destroy insects. Send, then, Thy fire from heaven and end my life, for if Thou dost not, I shall go against Thy handiwork."

Akbar loomed in the distance. He took the boy's hand and grasped it tightly.

"From this moment until we go through the city gates, I am going to walk with my eyes closed, and you must guide me," he told the boy. "If I die on the way, do what you have asked me to do: rebuild Akbar, even if to do so you must first grow to manhood and learn to cut wood or work stone."

The boy did not reply. Elijah closed his eyes and allowed himself to be led. He heard the blowing of the wind and the sound of his own steps in the sand.

He remembered Moses, who, after liberating the Chosen People and leading them through the desert, surmounting enormous difficulties, had been forbidden by God to enter Canaan. At the time, Moses had said:

"*I pray Thee, let me go over, and see the good land that is beyond Jordan.*"

The Lord, however, had been offended by his entreaty. And He had answered, "*Let it suffice thee; speak no more unto Me of this matter. Lift up thine eyes westward, and northward, and southward, and eastward, and behold it with thine eyes; for thou shalt not go over this Jordan.*"

Thus had the Lord rewarded the long and arduous task of Moses: He had not permitted him to set foot in the Promised Land. What would have happened if he had disobeyed?

Elijah again turned his thoughts to the heavens.

"O Lord, this battle was not between Assyrians and Phoenicians but between Thee and me. Thou didst not foretell to me our singular war, and as ever, Thou hast triumphed and seen Thy will made manifest. Thou hast destroyed the woman I loved and the city that took me in when I was far from my homeland."

The sound of the wind was louder in his ears. Elijah was afraid, but he continued.

"I cannot bring the woman back, but I can change the fate of Thy work of destruction. Moses accepted Thy will and did not cross the river. But I shall go forward: slay me now, because if Thou allowest me to arrive at the gates of the city, I shall rebuild that which Thou wouldst sweep from the face of the earth. And I shall go against Thy judgment."

He fell silent. He emptied his mind and waited for death. For a long time he concentrated on nothing beyond the sound of his footsteps in the sand; he did not want to hear the voices of angels or threats from heaven. His heart was free, and no longer did he fear what might befall him. Yet in the depths of his soul was the beginning of disquiet, as if he had forgotten a thing of importance.

After much time had passed, the boy stopped, then tugged on Elijah's arm.

"We've arrived," he said.

Elijah opened his eyes. The fire from heaven had not descended on him, and before him were the ruined walls of Akbar.

He looked at the boy, who now clutched Elijah's hand as if fearing that he might escape. Did he love him? He had no idea. But such reflections could wait till later; for now, he had a task to carry out—the first in many years not imposed upon him by God.

From where they stood, he could smell the odor of burning. Scavenger birds circled overhead, awaiting the right moment to devour the corpses of the sentinels that lay rotting in the sun. Elijah approached one of the fallen soldiers and took the sword from his belt. In the confusion of the previous night, the Assyrians had forgotten to gather up the weapons outside the city walls.

"Why do you want that?" the boy asked.

"To defend myself."

"The Assyrians aren't here anymore."

"Even so, it's good to have it with me. We have to be prepared."

His voice shook. It was impossible to know what might happen from the moment they crossed the half-destroyed wall, but he was ready to kill whoever tried to humiliate him.

"Like this city, I too was destroyed," he told the boy. "But also like this city, I have not yet completed my mission."

The boy smiled.

"You're talking the way you used to," he said.

"Don't be fooled by words. Before, I had the objective of removing Jezebel from the throne and turning Israel back to the Lord; now that He has forgotten us, we must forget Him. My mission is to do what you have asked of me."

The boy looked at him warily.

"Without God, my mother will not come back from the dead."

Elijah ran his hand over the boy's hair.

"Only your mother's body has gone away. She is still among us, and as she told us, she is Akbar. We must help her recover her beauty."

◆

THE CITY was almost deserted. Old people, women, and children were walking aimlessly through its streets, in a repetition of the scene he had witnessed the night of the invasion. They seemed uncertain of what to do next.

Each time Elijah's path crossed that of someone else, the boy saw him grip the handle of his sword. But the people displayed indifference; most recognized the prophet from Israel, some nodded at him, but none directed a single word to him, not even one of hatred.

"They've lost even the sense of rage," he thought, looking toward the top of the Fifth Mountain, the summit of which was covered as always by its eternal clouds. Then he recalled the Lord's words:

"*I will cast your carcasses upon the carcasses of your idols, and my soul shall abhor you. And I will make your cities waste, and bring the land into desolation.*

"*And upon them that are left alive of you I will send a faintness into their hearts; and the sound of a shaken leaf shall chase them; and they shall fall when none pursueth.*"

"BEHOLD, O LORD, WHAT THOU HAST WROUGHT: THOU hast kept Thy promise, and the living dead still walk the earth. And Akbar is the city chosen to shelter them."

Elijah and the boy continued to the main square, where they sat and rested on pieces of rubble while they surveyed their surroundings. The destruction seemed more severe and unrelenting than he had thought; the roofs of most of the houses had collapsed; filth and insects had taken over everything.

"The dead must be removed," he said. "Or plague will enter the city through the main gate."

The boy kept his eyes downward.

"Raise your head," Elijah said. "We have much work to do, so your mother can be content."

But the boy did not obey; he was beginning to understand: somewhere among the ruins was the body that had brought him into life, and that body was in a condition similar to all the others scattered on every side.

Elijah did not insist. He rose, lifted a corpse to his shoulders, and carried it to the middle of the square. He could not remember the Lord's recommendations about burying the dead; what he must do was prevent the coming of plague, and the only solution was to burn them.

He worked the entire morning. The boy did not stir from his place, nor did he raise his eyes for an instant, but he kept his promise to his mother: no tear dropped to Akbar's soil.

A woman stopped and stood for a time observing Elijah's efforts.

"The man who solved the problems of the living now puts in order the bodies of the dead," she commented.

"Where are the men of Akbar?" Elijah asked.

"They left, and they took with them the little that remained. There is nothing left worth staying for. The only ones who haven't deserted the city are those incapable of leaving: the old, widows, and orphans."

"But they were here for generations. They can't give up so easily."

"Try to explain that to someone who has lost everything."

"Help me," said Elijah, taking another corpse onto his shoulders and placing it on the pile. "We're going to burn them, so that the plague god will not come to visit us. He is horrified by the smell of burning flesh."

"Let the plague god come," said the woman. "And may he take us all, as soon as possible."

Elijah went on with his task. The woman sat down beside the boy and watched what he was doing. After a time, she approached him again.

"Why do you want to save this wretched city?"

"If I stop to reflect on it, I'll conclude I'm incapable of accomplishing what I desire," he answered.

The old shepherd was right: the only solution was to forget a past of uncertainty and create a new history for oneself. The former prophet had died together with a woman in the flames of her house; now he was a man without faith in God and beset by doubts. But he was still alive, even after challenging divine retribution. If he wished to continue on this path, he must do what he had proposed.

The woman chose one of the lighter bodies and dragged it by the heels, taking it to the pile that Elijah had started.

"It's not from fear of the plague god," she said. "Or for Akbar, since the Assyrians will soon return. It's for that boy sitting there with his head hanging; he has to learn that he still has his life ahead of him."

"Thank you," said Elijah.

"Don't thank me. Somewhere in these ruins we'll find the body of my son. He was about the same age as the boy."

She lifted her hand to her face and wept copiously. Elijah took her gently by the arm.

"The pain you and I feel will never go away, but work will help us to bear it. Suffering has no strength to wound a weary body."

They spent the entire day at the macabre task of collecting and piling up the dead; most of them were youths, whom the Assyrians had identified as part of Akbar's army. More than once he recognized friends, and wept—but he did not interrupt his task.

◆

AT THE END of the afternoon, they were exhausted. Even so, the work done was far from sufficient, and no other inhabitant of Akbar had assisted.

The pair approached the boy, who lifted his head for the first time.

"I'm hungry," he said.

"I'm going to go look for something," the woman answered. "There's plenty of food hidden in the various houses in Akbar; people were preparing for a long siege."

"Bring food for me and for yourself, for we are ministering to the city with the sweat of our brows," said Elijah. "But if the boy wants to eat, he will have to take care of himself."

The woman understood; she would have done the same with her son. She went to the place where her house had stood; almost everything had been ransacked by looters in search of objects of value, and her collection of vases, created by the great master glassmakers of Akbar, lay in pieces on the floor. But she found the dried fruits and grain that she had cached.

She returned to the square, where she divided part of the food with Elijah. The boy said nothing.

An old man approached them.

"I saw that you spent all day gathering the bodies," he said. "You're wasting your time; don't you know the Assyrians will be back, after they conquer Sidon and Tyre? Let the plague god come here and destroy them."

"We're not doing this for them, or for ourselves," Elijah answered. "She is working to teach a child that there is still a future. And I am working to show him there is no longer a past."

"So the prophet is no more a threat to the great princess of Sidon: what a surprise! Jezebel will rule Israel till the end of her days, and we shall always have a refuge if the Assyrians are not generous to the conquered."

Elijah did not reply. The name that had once awakened in him such hatred now sounded strangely distant.

"Akbar will be rebuilt, in any case," the old man insisted. "The gods choose where cities are erected, and they will not abandon it; but we can leave that labor for the generations to come."

"We can, but we will not."

Elijah turned his back on the old man, ending the conversation.

The three of them slept in the open air. The woman embraced the boy, noting that his stomach was growling from hunger. She considered giving him food but quickly dismissed the idea: fatigue truly did diminish pain, and the boy, who seemed to be suffering greatly, needed to busy himself with something. Perhaps hunger would persuade him to work.

THE NEXT DAY, ELIJAH AND THE WOMAN RESUMED their labors. The old man who had approached them the night before came to them again.

"I don't have anything to do and I could help you," he said. "But I'm too weak to carry bodies."

"Then gather bricks and small pieces of wood. Sweep away the ashes."

The old man began doing as they asked.

◆

WHEN THE SUN reached its zenith, Elijah sat on the ground, exhausted. He knew that his angel was at his side, but he could not hear him. "To what avail? He was unable to help me when I needed him, and now I don't want his counsel; all I desire is to put this city in order, to show God I can face Him, and then leave for wherever I want to go."

Jerusalem was not far away, just seven days' travel on foot, with no really difficult places to pass through, but there he was hunted as a traitor. Perhaps it would be better to go to Damascus, or find work as a scribe in some Greek city.

He felt something touch him. He turned and saw the boy holding a small jar.

"I found it in one of the houses," the boy said.

It was full of water. Elijah drank it to the final drop.

"Eat something," he said. "You're working and deserve your reward."

For the first time since the night of the invasion, a smile appeared on the boy's lips, and he ran to the spot where the woman had left the fruits and grain.

Elijah returned to his work, entering destroyed homes, pushing aside the rubble, picking up the bodies, and carrying them to the pile in the middle of the square. The bandage that the shepherd had put on his arm had fallen off, but that mattered little; he had to prove to himself that he was strong enough to regain his dignity.

The old man, who now was amassing the refuse scattered throughout the square, was right: soon the enemy would be back, to harvest fruits they had not sown. Elijah was laboring for the invaders—the assassins of the only woman he had ever loved in his life. The Assyrians were superstitious and would rebuild

Akbar in any case. According to ancient beliefs, the gods had spaced the cities in an organized manner, in harmony with the valleys, the animals, the rivers, the seas. In each of these they had set aside a sacred place to rest during their long voyages about the world. When a city was destroyed, there was always a great risk that the skies would tumble to the earth.

Legend said that the founder of Akbar had passed through there, hundreds of years before, journeying from the north. He decided to sleep at the spot and, to mark where he had left his things, planted a wooden staff upright in the ground. The next day, he was unable to withdraw it, and he quickly understood the will of the Universe; he marked with a stone the place where the miracle had occurred, and he discovered a spring nearby. Little by little, tribes began settling around the stone and the well; Akbar was born.

The governor had once explained to Elijah that, following Phoenician custom, every city was the *third point,* the element linking the will of heaven to the will of the earth. The Universe made the seed transform itself into a plant, the soil allowed it to grow, man harvested it and took it to the city, where the offerings to the gods were consecrated before they were left at the sacred mountains. Even though he had not traveled widely, Elijah was aware that a similar vision was shared by many nations of the world.

The Assyrians feared leaving the gods of the Fifth Mountain without food; they had no desire to disturb the equilibrium of the Universe.

"Why am I thinking such thoughts, if this is a struggle between my will and that of the Lord, who has left me alone in the midst of tribulations?"

The sensation he had felt the day before, when he challenged God, returned: he was forgetting something of importance, and however much he forced his memory, he could not recall it.

ANOTHER DAY WENT BY. MOST OF THE BODIES HAD been collected when a second woman approached.

"I have nothing to eat," she said.

"Nor have we," answered Elijah. "Yesterday and today we divided among three what had been intended for one. Discover where you can obtain food, then inform me."

"Where can I learn that?"

"Ask the children. They know everything."

Ever since he had offered Elijah water, the boy had seemed to recover some part of his taste for life. Elijah had told him to help the old man gather up the trash and debris but had not succeeded in keeping him working for long; he was now playing with the other boys in a corner of the square.

"It's better this way. He'll have his time to sweat when he's a man." But Elijah did not regret having made him spend an entire night hungry, under the pretext that he must work; if he had treated him as a poor orphan, the victim of the evil of murderous warriors, he would never have emerged from the depression into which he had been plunged when they entered the city. Now Elijah planned to leave him by himself for a few days to find his own answers to what had taken place.

"How can children know anything?" said the woman who had asked him for food.

"See for yourself."

The woman and the old man who were helping Elijah saw her talking to the young boys playing in the street. They said something, and she turned, smiled, and disappeared around one corner of the square.

"How did you find out that the children knew?" the old man asked.

"Because I was once a boy, and I know that children have no past," he said, remembering once again his conversation with the shepherd. "They were horrified the night of the invasion, but they're no longer concerned about it; the city has been transformed into an immense park where they can come and go without being bothered. Naturally they would come across the food that people had put aside to withstand the siege of Akbar.

"A child can always teach an adult three things: to be happy for no reason, to always be busy with something, and to know how to demand with all his might that which he desires. It was because of that boy that I returned to Akbar."

◆

THAT AFTERNOON, more old men and women added their numbers to the labor of collecting the dead. The children put to flight the scavenger birds and brought pieces of wood and cloth. When night fell, Elijah set fire to the immense pile of corpses. The survivors of Akbar contemplated silently the smoke rising to the heavens.

As soon as the task was completed, Elijah was felled by exhaustion. Before sleeping, however, the sensation he had felt that morning came again: something of importance was struggling desperately to enter his memory. It was nothing that he had learned during his time in Akbar but an ancient story, one that seemed to make sense of everything that was happening.

◆

THAT NIGHT, a man entered Jacob's tent and wrestled with him until the break of day. And when he saw that he prevailed not against him, he said, "Let me go."

Jacob answered, "I will not let thee go, except thou bless me."

Then the man said to him: "As a prince, hast thou power with God and with men, and hast prevailed. What is thy name?" And he said, Jacob.

And the man answered: "Thy name shall be called no more Jacob, but Israel."

Elijah awoke with a start and looked at the firmament. That was the story that was missing!

Long ago, the patriarch Jacob had encamped, and during the night, someone had entered his tent and wrestled with him until daybreak. Jacob accepted the combat, even knowing that his adversary was the Lord. At morning, he had still not been defeated; and the combat ceased only when God agreed to bless him.

The story had been transmitted from generation to generation so that no one would ever forget: *sometimes it was necessary to struggle with God.* Every human being at some time had tragedy enter his life; it might be the destruction of a city, the death of a son, an unproved accusation, a sickness that left one lame forever. At that moment, God challenged one to confront Him and to answer His question: "Why dost thou cling fast to an existence so short and so filled with suffering? What is the meaning of thy struggle?"

The man who did not know how to answer this question would resign himself, while another, one who sought a meaning to existence, feeling that God had been unjust, would challenge his own destiny. It was at this moment that fire of a different type descended from the heavens—not the fire that kills but the kind that tears down ancient walls and imparts to each human being his true possibilities. Cowards never allow their hearts to blaze with this fire; all they desire is for the changed situation to quickly return to what it was before, so they can go on living their lives and thinking in their customary way. The brave, however, set afire that which was old and, even at the cost of great internal suffering, abandon everything, including God, and continue onward.

"The brave are always stubborn."

From heaven, God smiles contentedly, for it was this that He desired, that each person take into his hands the responsibility for his own life. For, in the final analysis, He had given His children the greatest of all gifts: the capacity to choose and determine their acts.

Only those men and women with the sacred flame in their hearts had the courage to confront Him. And they alone knew the path back to His love, for they understood that tragedy was not punishment but challenge.

Elijah retraced in his mind each of his steps. Upon leaving the carpentry shop, he had accepted his mission without dispute. Even though it was real—and he felt it was—he had never had the opportunity to see what was happening in the paths that he had chosen not to follow because he feared losing his faith, his dedication, his will. He thought it very dangerous to experience the path of common folk—he might become accustomed to it and find pleasure in what he saw. He did not understand that he was a person like any other, even if he heard angels and now and again received orders from God; in his certainty that he knew what he wanted, he had acted in the selfsame way as those who at no time in their lives had ever made an important decision.

He had fled from doubt. From defeat. From moments of indecision. But the Lord was generous and had led him to the abyss of the unavoidable, to show him that man must *choose*—and not *accept*—his fate.

Many, many years before, on a night like this, Jacob had not allowed God to leave without blessing him. It was then that the Lord had asked: "*What is thy name?*"

The essential point was this: to have a name. When Jacob had answered, God had baptized him *Israel*. Each one has a name from birth but must learn to baptize his life with the word he has chosen to give meaning to that life.

"I am *Akbar*," she had said.

The destruction of the city and the death of the woman he loved had been necessary for Elijah to understand that he too must have a name. And at that moment he named his life *Liberation*.

◆

HE STOOD and looked at the square before him: smoke still rose from the ashes of those who had lost their lives. By setting fire to the bodies he had challenged an ancient custom of the country, which demanded that the dead be buried in accord with ritual. He had struggled with God and with custom by choosing incineration, but he felt no sense of sin when a new solution was needed to a new problem. God was infinite in His mercy, and implacable in His severity with those who lacked the courage to dare.

He looked around the square again: some of the survivors still had not slept and kept their gaze fixed on the flames, as if the fire were also consuming their memories, their pasts, Akbar's two hundred years of peace and torpor. The time for fear and hope had ended: now there remained only rebuilding or defeat.

Like Elijah, they too could choose a name for themselves. *Reconciliation, Wisdom, Lover, Pilgrim*—there were as many choices as stars in the sky, but each one had need to give a name to his life.

Elijah rose and prayed, "I fought Thee, Lord, and I am not ashamed. And because of it I discovered that I am on my path because such is my wish, not because it was imposed on me by my father and mother, by the customs of my country, or even by Thee.

"It is to Thee, O Lord, that I would return at this moment. I wish to praise Thee with the strength of my will and not with the cowardice of one who has not known how to choose another path. But for Thee to confide to me Thy important mission, I must continue this battle against Thee, until Thou bless me."

To rebuild Akbar. What Elijah thought was a challenge to God was, in truth, his reencounter with Him.

THE WOMAN WHO HAD ASKED ABOUT FOOD REAPpeared the next morning. She was accompanied by several other women.

"We found some deposits," she said. "Because so many died, and so many fled with the governor, we have enough food for a year."

"Seek older people to oversee the distribution of food," Elijah said. "They have experience at organization."

"The old ones have lost the will to live."

"Ask them to come anyway."

The woman was making ready to leave when Elijah stopped her.

"Do you know how to write, using letters?"

"No."

"I have learned, and I can teach you. You'll need this skill to help me administer the city."

"But the Assyrians will return."

"When they arrive, they'll need our help to manage the affairs of the city."

"Why should we do this for the enemy?"

"So that each of us can give a name to his life. The enemy is only a pretext to test our strength."

◆

As Elijah had foreseen, the old people came.

"Akbar needs your help," he told them. "Because of that, you don't have the luxury of being old; we need the youth that you once had and have lost."

"We do not know where to find it," one of them replied. "It vanished among the wrinkles and the disillusion."

"That's not true. You never had illusions, and it is that which caused your youth to hide itself away. Now is the moment to find it again, for we have a dream in common: to rebuild Akbar."

"How can we do the impossible?"

"With ardor."

Eyes veiled behind sorrow and discouragement made an effort to shine again. They were no longer the useless citizens who attended judgments searching for something to talk about later in the day; now they had an important mission before them. They were needed.

The stronger among them separated the usable materials from the damaged houses and utilized them to repair those that were still standing. The older ones helped spread in the fields the ashes of the incinerated bodies, so that the city's dead might be remembered at the next harvest; others took on the task of separating the grains stocked haphazardly throughout the city, making bread, and raising water from the well.

TWO NIGHTS LATER, ELIJAH GATHERED ALL THE INHABitants in the square, now cleared of most of the debris. Torches were lit, and he began to speak.

"We have no choice," he said. "We can leave this work for the foreigner to do; but that means giving away the only chance that a tragedy offers us: that of rebuilding our lives.

"The ashes of the dead that we burned some days ago will become the plants that are reborn in the spring. The son who was lost the night of the invasion will become the many children running freely through the ruined streets and amusing themselves by invading forbidden places and houses they had never known. Until now only the children have been able to overcome what took place, because they have no past—for them, everything that matters is the present moment. So we shall try to act as they do."

"Can a man cast from his heart the pain of a loss?" asked a woman.

"No. But he can find joy in something won."

Elijah turned, pointed to the top of the Fifth Mountain, forever covered in clouds. The destruction of the walls had made it visible from the middle of the square.

"I believe in One God, though you think that the gods dwell in those clouds on the Fifth Mountain. I don't want to argue whether my God is stronger or more powerful; I would speak not of our differences but of our similarities. Tragedy has united us in a single sentiment: despair. Why has that come to pass? Because we thought that everything was answered and decided in our souls, and we could accept no changes.

"Both you and I belong to trading nations, but we also know how to act as warriors," he continued. "And a warrior is always aware of what is worth fighting for. He does not go into combat over things that do not concern him, and he never wastes his time over provocations.

"A warrior accepts defeat. He does not treat it as a matter of indifference, nor does he attempt to transform it into a victory. The pain of defeat is bitter to him; he suffers at indifference and becomes desperate with loneliness. After all this has passed, he licks his wounds and begins everything anew. A warrior knows that war is made of many battles; he goes on.

"Tragedies do happen. We can discover the reason, blame others, imagine how different our lives would be had they not occurred. But none of that is important: they did occur, and so be it. From there onward we must put aside the fear that they awoke in us and begin to rebuild.

"Each of you will give yourselves a new name, beginning at this very moment. This will be the sacred name that brings together in a single word all that you have dreamed of fighting for. For my name, I have chosen *Liberation*."

The square was silent for some time. Then the woman who had been the first to help Elijah rose to her feet.

"My name is *Reencounter*," she said.

"My name is *Wisdom*," said an old man.

The son of the widow whom Elijah had loved shouted, "My name is *Alphabet*."

The people in the square burst into laughter. The boy, embarrassed, sat down again.

"How can anybody call himself *Alphabet*?" shouted another boy.

Elijah could have interfered, but it was good for the boy to learn to defend himself.

"Because that was what my mother did," the boy said. "Whenever I look at drawn letters, I'll remember her."

This time no one laughed. One by one, the orphans, widows, and old people of Akbar spoke their names, and their new identities. When the ceremony was over, Elijah asked everyone to go to sleep early: they had to resume their labors the next morning.

He took the boy by the hand, and the two went to the place in the square where a few pieces of cloth had been extended to form a tent.

Starting that night, he began teaching him the writing of Byblos.

The days became weeks, and the face of Akbar was changing. The boy quickly learned to draw the letters and had already begun creating words that made sense; Elijah charged him with writing on clay tablets the history of the rebuilding of the city.

The clay tablets were baked in an improvised oven, transformed into ceramics, and carefully stored away by an aged couple. At the meetings at the end of each afternoon, Elijah asked the old folk to tell of what they had seen in their childhood, and he wrote down the greatest possible number of stories.

"We shall keep Akbar's memory on a material that fire cannot destroy," he explained. "One day our children and the children of their children will know that defeat was not accepted, and that the unavoidable was overcome. This can serve as an example for them."

Each night, after his lessons with the boy, Elijah would walk through the deserted city until he came to the beginning of the road leading to Jerusalem; he would think about departing, then turn around.

The heavy work demanded that he concentrate on the present moment. He knew that the inhabitants of Akbar were relying on him for the rebuilding; he had already disappointed them once, when he had been unable to prevent the death of the enemy general—and thus avoid war. But God always gives His children a second chance, and he must take advantage of this new opportunity. In addition, he was becoming ever fonder of the boy and desired to teach him not only the characters of Byblos but also faith in the Lord and the wisdom of his ancestors.

Even so, he did not forget that in his own land reigned a foreign princess and a foreign god. There were no more angels bearing flaming swords; he was free to leave whenever he desired, and to do whatever he wished.

Each night, he thought of departing. And each night he would lift his hands to the heavens and pray.

"Jacob fought the whole night through and was blessed at daybreak. I have fought Thee for days, for months, and Thou refusest me Thy ear. But if Thou lookest about Thee, Thou wilt know that I am winning: Akbar is rising from its ruins, and I am rebuilding what Thou, using the Assyrian sword, made ashes and dust.

"I shall struggle with Thee until Thou bless me, and bless the fruits of my labor. One day Thou shalt have to answer me."

◆

WOMEN AND CHILDREN carried water to the fields, struggling against the drought that seemed to have no end. One day, when the inclement sun shone down in all its force, Elijah heard someone say, "We work without ceasing, we no longer recall the pains of that night, and we even forget that the Assyrians will return as soon as they have sacked Tyre, Sidon, Byblos, and all of Phoenicia. This is a good thing for us.

"But because we concentrate so much on rebuilding the city, it seems that everything remains the same; we do not see the result of our effort."

Elijah reflected for some time on what he had heard. And he ordered that, at the end of each day of work, the people gather at the foot of the Fifth Mountain to contemplate together the sunset.

Most were so weary that they exchanged not a word, but they discovered that it is important to allow thought to wander as aimlessly as the clouds in the sky. In this way, anxiety fled from each person's heart and they found inspiration and strength for the day to come.

Elijah awoke saying that today he would not labor.

"In my land, this is the Day of Atonement."

"There is no sin in your soul," a woman told him. "You have done the best that you can."

"But custom must be maintained. And I shall keep it."

The women left, bearing water for the fields, the old men went back to their task of erecting walls and shaping the wood for doors and windows. The children helped to mold the small clay bricks that would later be baked in fire. Elijah watched them with immense joy in his heart. Then he went out from Akbar and walked toward the valley.

He wandered about aimlessly, praying the prayers that he had learned in childhood. The sun was not yet completely risen, and from the place where he stood he could see the enormous shadow of the Fifth Mountain covering part of the valley. He felt a horrible premonition: the struggle between the God of Israel and the gods of the Phoenicians would go on for many generations, and for many thousands of years.

◆

HE RECALLED that one night he had climbed to the top of the mountain and spoken with an angel. But since Akbar's destruction he had never again heard the voices from heaven.

"O Lord, today is the Day of Atonement, and my list of sins against Thee is long," he said, turning toward Jerusalem. "I have been weak, for I have forgotten my strength. I have been compassionate when I should have been firm. I have failed to choose, for fear of making the wrong decision. I have yielded before the time to do so, and I have blasphemed when I should have given thanks.

"Still, Lord, I have also a long list of Thy sins against me. Thou hast made me suffer more than was just, by taking from this world one that I loved. Thou hast destroyed the city that received me, Thou hast confounded my search, Thy harshness almost made me forget the love I have for Thee. For all that time I have struggled with Thee, yet Thou dost not accept the worthiness of my combat.

"If we compare the list of my sins with the list of Thy sins, Thou shalt see that Thou art in my debt. But, as today is the Day of Atonement, give me Thy forgiveness and I shall forgive Thee, so that we may go on walking at each other's side."

At that moment, a wind blew, and he heard his angel say to

him, "Thou hast done well, Elijah. God hath accepted thy combat."

Tears streamed from his eyes. He knelt and kissed the valley's arid soil.

"Thanks unto you for having come, for I still have one doubt: is it not a sin to do this?"

The angel said, "If a warrior fight with his instructor, doth he offend him?"

"No. It is the only way to teach the technique that he must learn."

"Then continue, until the Lord call thee back to Israel," said the angel. "Rise and go on proving that thy struggle hath meaning, because thou hast known how to cross the current of the unavoidable. Many navigate it and founder; others are swept to places for which they were not fated. But thou confrontest the crossing with dignity; thou hast guided the path of thy vessel well and transformed pain into action."

"How sad that you are blind," said Elijah. "Otherwise you would see how orphans, widows, old people have been able to rebuild a city. Soon, all will be as it was."

"Would that it not be so," said the angel. "Remember that they have paid a high price so that their lives could be changed."

Elijah smiled. The angel was right.

"Would that thou mightest act as do men who are given a second chance: do not twice commit the same error. Never forget the reason for thy life."

"I shall not forget," he replied, happy that the angel had returned.

Caravans no longer came through the valley; the Assyrians must have destroyed the roads and changed the trade routes. Day after day, children scaled the only turret in the wall that had escaped destruction; they were charged with watching the horizon and alerting the city to the return of enemy warriors. Elijah planned to receive them with dignity and hand over command.

Then he could depart.

But with each passing day the feeling grew that Akbar had become part of his life. Perhaps his mission was not to remove Jezebel from the throne but to be there with these people for the rest of his life, carrying out the humble role of servant for the Assyrian conqueror. He would help to reestablish trade routes, learn the language of the enemy, and during his moments of repose, oversee the library, which was daily more complete.

Whereas on a night already lost in time the city had appeared to be at its end, it now seemed possible to make it even more beautiful than it had been. The work of rebuilding encompassed widening streets, erecting sturdier roofs, and creating an ingenious system for bringing water from the well to the most distant places. And his soul too was being restored; each day he learned something new from the old people, from the children, from the women. That group, which had not abandoned Akbar only because of the absolute impossibility of doing so, was now a competent, disciplined company.

"If the governor had known that they were of such help, he would have created another type of defense, and Akbar would not have been destroyed."

Elijah thought a moment, then saw that he was mistaken. Akbar needed to be destroyed so that all could awaken the forces that lay dormant inside their own being.

Months went by without the Assyrians showing any sign of life. By now Akbar was almost complete, and Elijah could think of the future. The women had repaired pieces of cloth and made new garments from them. The old folk were reorganizing the dwellings and attending to the city's sanitation. The children were helping when asked, but they usually spent the day at play: that is a child's foremost obligation.

Elijah lived with the boy in a small stone house rebuilt on

the site that had once been a storage place for merchandise. Each night the inhabitants of Akbar would sit around a fire in the main square, telling stories that they had heard earlier in their lives, alongside the boy, who noted everything on clay tablets that were baked the next day. The library was growing before their very eyes.

The woman who had lost her son was also learning the characters of Byblos. When Elijah saw that she could create words and phrases, he charged her with teaching the alphabet to the rest of the population; in this way, when the Assyrians returned, they could be used as interpreters or teachers.

"This was just what the high priest wanted to prevent," an old man, who had taken the name *Ocean* because he desired to have a soul as great as the sea, said one afternoon. "That the writing of Byblos survive to threaten the gods of the Fifth Mountain."

"Who can prevent the unavoidable?" Elijah replied.

The people of Akbar would toil by day, watch the sunset together, and recount stories during the night.

Elijah was proud of his work. And with each day that passed he grew more impassioned with it.

One of the children charged with keeping the vigil descended in a run.

"I saw dust on the horizon!" he said excitedly. "The enemy is returning!"

Elijah climbed to the turret and saw that the news was correct.

He reckoned that they would be at the gates of Akbar the next day.

That afternoon he told the inhabitants that they should not attend the sunset but gather in the square. When the day's work was over, he stood before the assembled group and saw that they were afraid.

"Today we shall tell no stories of the past, nor speak of Akbar's future," he said. "We shall talk about ourselves."

No one said a word.

"Some time ago, a full moon shone in the sky. That night, what all of us had foreseen, but did not want to accept, came to pass: Akbar was destroyed. When the Assyrian army departed, the best among our men were dead. Those who had escaped saw that it was futile to remain here, and they determined to go. Only the old, the widows, and the orphans were left—that is, the useless.

"Look about you; the square is more beautiful than ever, the buildings are more solid, the food is divided among us, and everyone is learning the writing invented in Byblos. Somewhere in this city is a collection of tablets on which we have written our stories, and generations yet to be born will remember what we did.

"Today we know that the old, the widows, the orphans, also departed. They left in their place a band of youths of every age, filled with enthusiasm, who have given name and meaning to their lives.

"At each moment of rebuilding, we knew that the Assyrians

would return. We knew that one day we would be obliged to hand our city over to them and, together with the city, our efforts, our sweat, our joy at seeing it more beautiful than before."

The light from the fire illuminated tears coursing down the faces of some of the people. Even the children, who customarily played during the evening meetings, were listening attentively to his words. Elijah continued.

"This does not matter. We have carried out our duty to the Lord because we accepted His challenge and the honor of His struggle. Before that night, He had urged us, saying, *Walk!* But we heeded Him not. Why?

"Because each of us had already decided his own future: I thought only of removing Jezebel from the throne, the woman who is now called *Reencounter* wanted her son to become a navigator, the man who today bears the name *Wisdom* wished merely to spend the rest of his days drinking wine in the square. We were accustomed to the sacred mystery of life and gave little importance to it.

"Then the Lord thought to Himself: *They would not walk? Then let them be idle for a long time!*

"And only then did we understand His message. The steel of Assyrian blades swept away our youth, and cowardice swept away our adults. Wherever they are at this moment, they are still idle; they have accepted God's curse.

"We, however, struggle with the Lord, just as we struggle

with the men and women we love in our lifetimes. For it is that struggle with the divine that blesses us and makes us grow. We grasp the opportunity in the tragedy and do our duty by Him, by proving we were able to obey the order to *walk*. Even in the worst of circumstances, we have forged ahead.

"There are moments when God demands obedience. But there are moments in which He wishes to test our will and challenges us to understand His love. We understood that will when Akbar's walls tumbled to the ground: they opened our horizon and allowed each of us to see his capabilities. We stopped thinking about life and chose to live it.

"The result is good."

Elijah saw that the people's eyes were shining again. They had understood.

"Tomorrow I shall deliver Akbar without a struggle; I am free to leave whenever I choose, for I have done what the Lord expected of me. But my blood, my sweat, and the only love I have known are in the soil of this city, and I have decided to remain here the rest of my days, to prevent its being destroyed again. Make whatever decision you wish but never forget one thing: all of you are much better than you believed.

"Take advantage of the chance that tragedy has given you; not everyone is capable of doing so."

Elijah rose, ending the meeting. He told the boy that he would return late and said he should go to bed without waiting for his arrival.

◆

He went to the temple, the only place that had escaped the destruction and had not needed rebuilding, though the statues of the gods had been taken away by the Assyrians. With all respect, he touched the stone that, according to tradition, marked the spot where an ancestor had embedded a staff in the ground and been unable to wrest it free.

He thought how, in his country, places such as this were being erected by Jezebel, and a part of his people bowed down before Baal and his deities. Once again the premonition ran through his soul that the war between the Lord of Israel and the gods of Phoenicia would go on for a long time, beyond anything his imagination could encompass. As in a vision, he saw stars crossing the sun and raining death and destruction on both countries. Men who spoke strange languages rode animals of steel and dueled in the middle of the clouds.

"It is not this that thou shouldst now see, for the time hath not yet come," he heard his angel say. "Look out the window."

Elijah did as he was ordered. Outside, the full moon illuminated the streets and houses of Akbar, and despite the late hour he could hear conversations and laughter from the city's inhabitants. Even facing the Assyrians' return, the people kept the will to live, ready to confront a new stage in their lives.

He saw a form and knew that it was the woman he had

loved, who now returned to walk with pride through her city. He smiled, feeling her touch his face.

"I am proud," she seemed to be saying. "Akbar truly is still beautiful."

He felt the urge to weep, then remembered the boy, who had never shed a tear for his mother. He checked his sobs and thought anew of the most beautiful parts of the story that together they had lived, from the meeting at the city gates, till the moment she had written the word *love* on a clay tablet. Once again he could see her garment, her chair, the fine sculpting of her nose.

"You told me you were Akbar. Well, I have taken care of you, healed your wounds, and now I return you to life. May you be happy among your new companions.

"And I want to tell you something: I too was Akbar and did not know."

He knew that she was smiling.

"Long since, the desert wind wiped away our footprints in the sand. But at every second of my existence, I remember what happened, and you still walk in my dreams and in my reality. Thank you for having crossed my path."

He slept there, in the temple, feeling the woman caressing his hair.

THE CHIEF TRADER SAW A RAGGED GROUP OF PEOPLE IN the middle of the road. Thinking they were robbers, he ordered the caravan to take up arms.

"Who are you?" he asked.

"We are the people of Akbar," replied a bearded man with shining eyes. The leader of the caravan noticed that he spoke with a foreign accent.

"Akbar was destroyed. We have been charged by the governments of Sidon and Tyre to find a well so caravans can cross the valley again. Communication with the rest of the land cannot be interrupted forever."

"Akbar still exists," the man said. "Where are the Assyrians?"

"The entire world knows where they are," laughed the caravan leader. "Making the soil more fertile. And feeding the birds and wild animals for a long time now."

"But they were a powerful army."

"There's no such thing as power or an army, if we find out where they're going to attack. Akbar sent word that they were approaching, and Sidon and Tyre set an ambuscade for them at the end of the valley. Whoever didn't die in battle was sold as slaves by our navigators."

The ragged people cheered and embraced one another, crying and laughing at the same time.

"Who are you people?" insisted the trader. "And who are you?" he asked, pointing to their leader.

"We are the young warriors of Akbar" was the reply.

◆

THE THIRD HARVEST had begun, and Elijah was the governor of Akbar. There had been great resistance at first; the old governor had attempted to return and reoccupy his position, for such did custom dictate. The inhabitants of the city, however, refused to admit him and for days threatened to poison the water in the well. The Phoenician authorities finally yielded to their demands; after all, Akbar's only importance was the water it supplied to travelers, and the government of Israel was in the hands of a princess of Tyre. By conceding the position of governor to an Israelite, the Phoenician rulers could begin to consolidate a stronger commercial alliance.

The news spread throughout the region, carried by the merchant caravans that had begun circulating again. A minority in Israel considered Elijah the worst of traitors, but at the proper moment Jezebel would take on the task of eliminating this resistance, and peace would return to the region. The princess was content, for one of her worst foes had in the end become her greatest ally.

◆

RUMORS OF A NEW Assyrian invasion began to arise, and the walls of Akbar were rebuilt. A new system of defense was developed, with sentinels and outposts spread between Tyre and Akbar; in this way, if one of the cities was besieged, the other could send troops overland while assuring the delivery of food by sea.

The city prospered before one's very eyes: the new Israelite governor had created a rigorous system, based on writing, to control taxes and merchandise. The old folk of Akbar attended to it all, using new techniques for supervision, and patiently resolved the problems that arose.

The women divided their time between tending to the crops and weaving. During the period of isolation, to recover the small amount of cloth that had remained, they had been obliged to create new patterns of embroidery; when the first merchants arrived in the city, they were enchanted by the designs and placed several orders.

The children too had learned the writing of Byblos; Elijah was certain that one day this would be of help to them.

As was always his wont before the harvest, he strolled through the fields that afternoon, giving thanks to the Lord for the countless blessings bestowed upon him for all these years. He saw people with their baskets filled with grain, and around them children at play. He waved to them, and they returned his greeting.

Smiling, he walked toward the stone where, long ago, he had been given a clay tablet with the word *love*. It was his custom to visit that spot every day to watch the sunset and recall each instant that they had spent together.

"And it came to pass after many days, that the word of the Lord came to Elijah in the third year, saying, Go, shew thyself unto Ahab; and I will send rain upon the earth."

FROM THE STONE WHERE HE SAT, ELIJAH SAW THE world shudder about him. The sky turned black for an instant, but the sun quickly shone again.

He saw the light. An angel of the Lord was before him.

"What has happened?" asked Elijah, startled. "Has the Lord pardoned Israel?"

"No," answered the angel. "He desireth that thou return to liberate thy people. Thy struggle with Him is ended, and—at this moment—he hath blessed thee. He hath given thee leave to continue His work in that land."

Elijah was astonished.

"But, now, just when my heart has again found peace?"

"Recall the lesson once taught thee," said the angel. "And recall the words the Lord spake unto Moses:

"*And thou shalt remember all the way which the Lord thy God led thee to humble thee, and to prove thee. To know what was in thine heart.*

"*Lest when thou hast eaten and art full, and hast built goodly houses, and dwelt therein, and when thy herds and thy flocks multiply, then thine heart be lifted up, and thou forget the Lord thy God.*"

Elijah turned to the angel. "What about Akbar?" he asked.

"It can live without thee, for thou hast left an heir. It will survive for many years."

The angel of the Lord disappeared.

ELIJAH AND THE BOY ARRIVED AT THE FOOT OF THE Fifth Mountain. Weeds had grown between the stones of the altars; since the high priest's death no one had gone there.

"Let's climb it," he said.

"It's forbidden."

"Yes, it's forbidden. But that doesn't mean it's dangerous."

He took him by both hands, and they began climbing toward the top. They stopped from time to time to gaze at the valley below; the absence of rain had left its mark throughout the countryside, and with the exception of the cultivated fields around Akbar, everything seemed a desert as harsh as those of Egypt.

"I've heard my friends say the Assyrians are coming back," the boy said.

"That could be, but what we have done was worthwhile; it was the way that God chose to teach us."

"I don't know if He bothers much with us," the boy said. "He didn't have to be so severe."

"He must have tried other means before discovering that we were not listening to Him. We were too accustomed to our lives and no longer read His words."

"Where are they written?"

"In the world around us. Merely be attentive to what happens in your life, and you will discover where, every moment of the day, He hides His words and His will. Seek to do as He asks: this alone is the reason you are in the world."

"If I discover it, I'll write it on clay tablets."

"Do so. But write them, above all, in your heart; there they can be neither burned nor destroyed, and you will take them wherever you go."

They walked for some time more. The clouds were now very close.

"I don't want to go there," the boy said, pointing to them.

"They will do you no harm: they're just clouds. Come with me."

He took him by the hands, and they climbed. Little by little, they found themselves entering the fog. The boy clung to him, and although Elijah tried to talk to him now and again, he said not a word. They walked among the naked rocks of the summit.

"Let's go back," asked the boy.

Elijah decided not to insist; the boy had already experienced great difficulties and much fear in his short life. He did as he was asked; they came out from the fog and could once again discern the valley below.

"Someday, look in Akbar's library for what I wrote for you. It's called *The Manual of the Warrior of Light*."

"Am I a warrior of light?" replied the boy.

"Do you know what my name is?" asked Elijah.

"*Liberation*."

"Sit here beside me," said Elijah, pointing to a rock. "I cannot forget my name. I must continue with my task, even if at this moment all I desire is to be at your side. That was why Akbar was rebuilt, to teach us that it is necessary to go onward, however difficult it may appear."

"You're going away."

"How do you know?" he asked, surprised.

"I wrote it on a tablet, last night. Something told me; it may have been my mother, or an angel. But I already felt it in my heart."

Elijah caressed the boy's head.

"You have learned to read God's will," he said contentedly. "So there's nothing that I need to explain to you."

"What I read was the sadness in your eyes. It wasn't difficult. Other friends of mine noticed it too."

"This sadness you read in my eyes is part of my story. Only a small part that will last but a few days. Tomorrow, when I depart for Jerusalem, it will not have the strength it had before, and little by little it will disappear. Sadness does not last forever when we walk in the direction of that which we always desired."

"Is it always necessary to leave?"

"It's always necessary to know when a stage of one's life has ended. If you stubbornly cling to it after the need has passed, you lose the joy and meaning of the rest. And you risk being shaken to your senses by God."

"The Lord is stern."

"Only with those He has chosen."

◆

ELIJAH LOOKED AT AKBAR below. Yes, God sometimes could be very stern, but never beyond a person's capacity: the boy was unaware that they were sitting where Elijah had received an angel of the Lord and learned how to bring him back from the dead.

"Are you going to miss me?" Elijah asked.

"You told me that sadness disappears if we press ahead. There's still much to do to leave Akbar as beautiful as my mother deserves. She walks in its streets."

"Come back to this place when you have need of me. And look toward Jerusalem: I shall be there, seeking to give meaning to my name, *Liberation*. Our hearts are linked forever."

"Was that why you brought me to the top of the Fifth Mountain? So I could see Israel?"

"So you could see the valley, the city, the other mountains, the rocks and clouds. The Lord often has his prophets climb mountains to converse with Him. I always wondered why He did that, and now I know the answer: when we are on high, we can see everything else as small.

"Our glory and our sadness lose their importance. Whatever we conquered or lost remains there below. From the heights of the mountain, you see how large the world is, and how wide its horizons."

The boy looked about him. From the top of the Fifth Mountain, he could smell the sea that bathed the beaches of Tyre. And he could hear the desert wind that blew from Egypt.

"Someday I'll govern Akbar," he told Elijah. "I know what's big. But I also know every corner of the city. I know what needs to be changed."

"Then change it. Don't let things remain idle."

"Couldn't God have chosen a better way of showing us all this? There was a time when I thought He was evil."

Elijah said nothing. He recalled a conversation, many years before, with a Levite prophet while the two awaited death at the hands of Jezebel's soldiers.

"Can God be evil?" the boy insisted.

"God is all-powerful," answered Elijah. "He can do anything, and nothing is forbidden to Him, for if it were, there would exist someone more powerful than He, to prevent His doing certain things. In that case, I should prefer to worship and revere that more powerful someone."

He paused for several instants to allow the boy to fathom the meaning of his words. Then he continued.

"Still, because of His infinite power, He chose to do only Good. If we reach the end of our story, we shall see that often Good is disguised as Evil, but it goes on being the Good, and is part of the plan that He created for humanity."

He took the boy by the hand, and together they descended the mountain in silence.

◆

THAT NIGHT, the boy went to sleep in his arms. As soon as day began to break, Elijah carefully removed him from his bosom so he would not awaken him.

He quickly donned the only garment he possessed and departed. On the road, he picked up a piece of wood from the ground and used it as a staff. He planned never to be without it: it was the remembrance of his struggle with God, of the destruction and rebuilding of Akbar.

Without looking back, he continued toward Israel.

FIVE YEARS LATER, ASSYRIA AGAIN INVADED THE COUNTRY, this time with a more professional army and more competent generals. All Phoenicia fell under the domination of the foreign conqueror except Tyre and Zarephath, which its inhabitants called Akbar.

The boy became a man, governed the city, and was judged a sage by his contemporaries. He died in the fullness of his years, surrounded by loved ones and saying always that "it was necessary to keep the city beautiful and strong, for his mother still strolled its streets." Because of their joint system of defense, Tyre and Zarephath were not occupied by the Assyrian king Sennacherib until 701 B.C., almost 160 years after the events related in this book.

From that time on, Phoenician cities never recovered their importance and began to suffer a series of invasion——by the Neo-Babylonians, the Persians, the Macedonians, the Seleucids, and, finally, by Rome. Even so, they continue to exist in our own time because, according to ancient tradition, the Lord never selected at random the places He wished to see inhabited. Tyre, Sidon, and Byblos are still part of Lebanon, which even today remains a battlefield.

Elijah returned to Israel and called the prophets together at Mount Carmel. There he asked them to divide into two groups: those who worshiped Baal, and those who believed in the Lord. Following the angel's instructions, he offered a bullock to the first group and asked them to call out to the heavens for their gods to receive it. The Bible says:

"And it came to pass at noon, that Elijah mocked them, and said, Cry aloud: for he is a god; either he is talking, or he is pursuing, or he is in a journey, or peradventure he sleepeth, and must be awaked.

"And they cried aloud, and cut themselves after their manner with knives and lancets, till the blood gushed out upon them.

"And there was neither voice, nor any to answer, nor any that regarded."

Then Elijah took his animal and offered it, following the angel's instructions. At that moment the fire of heaven descended and "consumed the burnt sacrifice, and the wood, and the stones." Minutes later, a heavy rain fell, ending four years of drought.

From that moment, civil war broke out. Elijah ordered the execution of the prophets who had betrayed the Lord, and Jezebel sought him everywhere, to kill him. He fled, however, to the eastern part of the Fifth Mountain, which faced Israel.

The Syrians invaded the country and killed King Ahab, husband of the princess of Tyre, with an accidentally shot arrow that entered an opening in his armor. Jezebel took refuge in her palace and, following several popular revolts and the rise and fall of various governments, was captured. She preferred leaping from a window to giving herself up to the men sent to arrest her.

Elijah remained on the mountain until the end of his days. The Bible says that one afternoon, when he was conversing with Elisha, the prophet he had named as his successor, "there appeared a chariot of fire, and horses of fire, and parted them both asunder; and Elijah went up by a whirlwind into heaven."

Almost eight hundred years later, Jesus bade Peter, James, and John to climb a mountain. The Gospel according to Matthew relates that Jesus "was transfigured before them; and his face did shine as the sun, and his raiment was white as the light. And, behold, there appeared unto them Moses and Elias talking with him."

Jesus asks the apostles not to speak of this vision until the Son of Man be risen from the dead, but they reply that this will happen only when Elijah returns.

Matthew 17:10–13 tells the rest of the story:

"And his disciples asked him, saying, Why then say the scribes that Elias must first come?

"And Jesus answered and said unto them, Elias truly shall first come, and restore all things. But I say unto you, That Elias is come already, and they knew him not, but have done unto him whatsoever they listed.

"Then the disciples understood that he spake unto them of John the Baptist."

Life is a journey

Make sure you don't miss a thing.
Live it with Paulo Coelho.

Visit f /paulocoelho

How can you find your heart's desire?

A world-wide phenomenon; an inspiration for anyone seeking their path in life.

The Alchemist

Do you believe in yourself?

A modern-day adventure in the searing heat of the Mojave desert and an exploration of fear and self-doubt.

The Valkyries

How do we see the amazing in the everyday?

When two young lovers are reunited, they discover anew the truth of what lies in their hearts.

By the River Piedra I Sat Down & Wept

What are you searching for?

A transforming journey on the pilgrims' road to Santiago – and the first of Paulo's extraordinary books.

The Pilgrimage

Is life always worth living?

A fundamental moral question explored as only Paulo Coelho can.

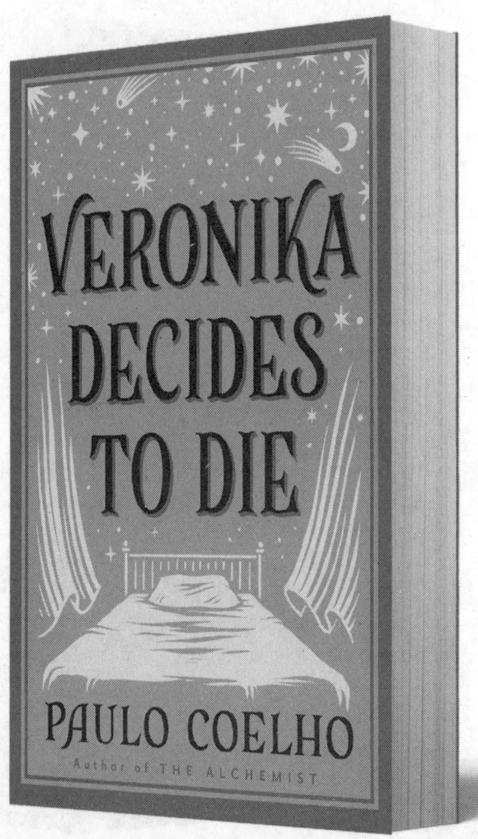

Veronika Decides to Die

Could you be tempted into evil?

The inhabitants of a small town are challenged by a mysterious stranger to choose between good and evil.

The Devil & Miss Prym

Are you brave enough to live your dream?

Strategies and inspiration to help you follow your own path in a troubled world.

Manual of the Warrior of Light

Can sex be sacred?

An unflinching exploration of the lengths we go to in our search for love, sex and spirituality.

Eleven Minutes

How far would you go for your obsession?

A sweeping story of love, loss and longing that spans the world.

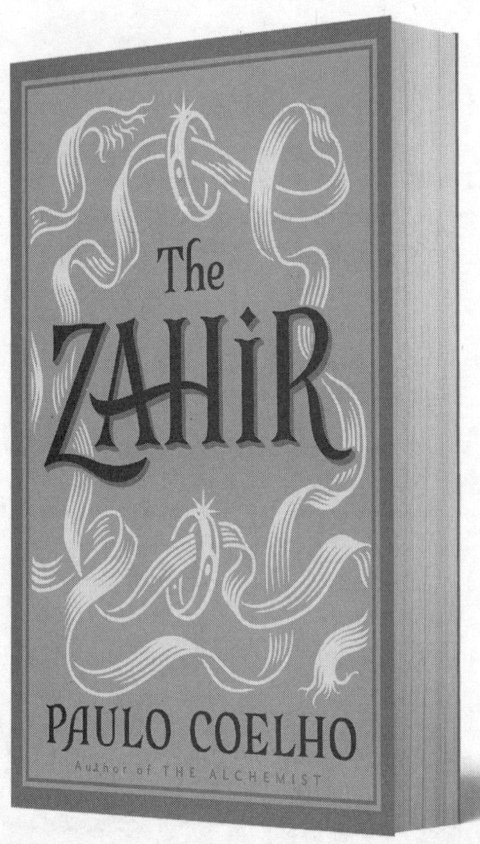

The Zahir

What happens when obsession turns to murder?

An enthralling story of jealousy, death and suspense.

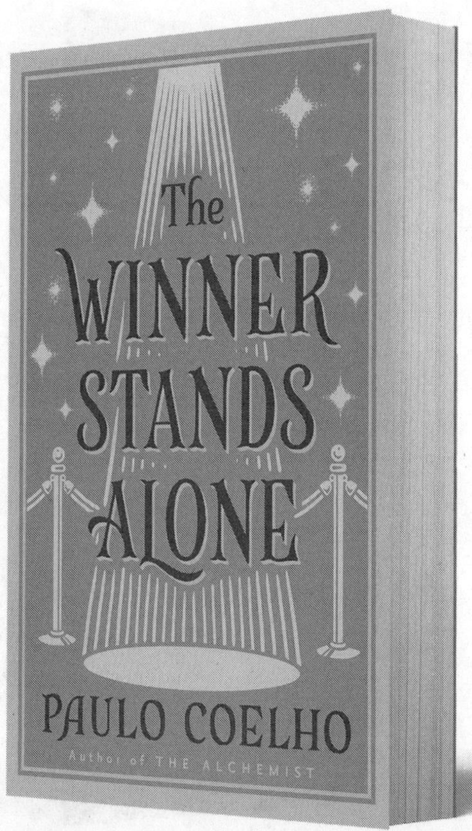

The Winner Stands Alone

Can we dare to be true to ourselves?

A story that will transform the way we think about love, joy and sacrifice.

The Witch of Portobello

How will you know who your soulmate is?

A moving tale of passion, mystery and spirituality.

Brida

What does it mean to be truly alive?

Powerful tales of living and dying, destiny and choice, and love lost and found.

Like the Flowing River

Are you where you want to be?

Read *Aleph*. And rewrite your life.

Aleph

Is there a weapon more powerful than words?

A timeless and powerful exploration of
personal growth, everyday wisdom and joy.

Manuscript Found in Accra

The WINNER STANDS ALONE

Paulo Coelho was born in Brazil and has become one of the most widely read and loved authors in the world. Especially renowned for *The Alchemist* and *Eleven Minutes*, he has sold more than 320 million books worldwide and has been translated into 88 languages. The recipient of numerous prestigious international awards, amongst them the Crystal Award by the World Economic Forum and France's Légion d'Honneur, Paulo Coelho was inducted into the Brazilian Academy of Letters in 2002.

Also by Paulo Coelho

The Alchemist
The Pilgrimage
The Valkyries
By the River Piedra I Sat Down and Wept
The Fifth Mountain
Veronika Decides to Die
Manual of the Warrior of Light
Eleven Minutes
The Zahir
The Devil and Miss Prym
The Witch of Portobello
Brida
The Winner Stands Alone
Like the Flowing River
Aleph
Manuscript Found in Accra
Adultery
The Spy
Hippie

The WINNER STANDS ALONE

PAULO COELHO

Author of THE ALCHEMIST

TRANSLATED FROM THE PORTUGUESE
BY MARGARET JULL COSTA

Thorsons

Thorsons
An imprint of HarperCollins*Publishers*
1 London Bridge Street
London SE1 9GF

HarperCollins*Publishers*
1st Floor, Watermarque Building, Ringsend Road
Dublin 4, Ireland

www.harpercollins.co.uk
www.paulocoelho.com
www.paulocoelhoblog.com

First published in the UK by HarperCollins*Publishers* 2009
This edition 2021

2 4 6 8 10 9 7 5 3 1

© Paulo Coelho 2008

English translation © Margaret Jull Costa 2008

Extracts from 'The Road Not Taken' by Robert Frost on pp. 111 and 120 from *The Poetry of Robert Frost*, edited by Edward Connery Lathem. © 1916, 1969 by Henry Holt and Company, © 1944 by Robert Frost. Reprinted by permission of Henry Holt and Company, LLC.

Paulo Coelho asserts the moral right to be identified as the author of this work

A catalogue record of this book is available from the British Library

ISBN: 978-0-00-854727-1

FICTION / PHILOSOPHY

Printed and bound in India by Thomson Press India Ltd

All rights reserved. No part of this publication may be reproduced, stored in a retrieval system, or transmitted, in any form or by any means, electronic, mechanical, photocopying, recording or otherwise, without the prior written permission of the publishers.

This book is produced from independently certified FSC® paper to ensure responsible forest management.

O Mary!
conceived without sin,
pray for us who turn to you!
Amen.

And he said unto his disciples, Therefore I say unto you, Take no thought for your life, what ye shall eat; neither for the body, what ye shall put on. The life is more than meat, and the body is more than raiment.

Consider the ravens: for they neither sow nor reap; which neither have storehouse nor barn; and God feedeth them: how much more are ye better than the fowls? And which of you with taking thought can add to his stature one cubit? If ye then be not able to do that thing which is least, why take ye thought for the rest?

Consider the lilies how they grow: they toil not, they spin not;and yet I say unto you,that Solomon in all his glory was not arrayed like one of these.

Luke 12:22–27

Whoever you are holding me now in hand,
Without one thing all will be useless,
I give you fair warning before you attempt me further,
I am not what you supposed, but far different.
Who is he that would become my follower?
Who would sign himself a candidate for my affections?
The way is suspicious, the result uncertain, perhaps destructive.
You would have to give up all else, I alone would expect to be your sole and exclusive standard,
Your novitiate would even then be long and exhausting,
The whole past theory of your life and all conformity to the lives around you would have to be abandon'd,
Therefore release me now before troubling yourself any further, let go your hand from my shoulders,
Put me down and depart on your way.

Walt Whitman: *Leaves of Grass*

For N.D.P.
who came down to Earth in order to show us the path of the Good Fight

Preface

One of the recurrent themes in my books has been the importance of paying the price for following your dreams. But to what extent can our dreams be manipulated? During the past few decades, we have lived in a culture that has privileged fame, money and power. Many of us have been led to believe that these were the only values worth pursuing, unaware that the real, behind-the-scenes manipulators remain anonymous. These manipulators understand that the most effective power is the kind that goes unnoticed by anyone – until it is too late, and we are trapped. This book is about that trap.

In *The Winner Stands Alone*, three of the four main characters allow their dreams to be manipulated:

Igor, a Russian millionaire, who believes that killing is acceptable if it is done for a good reason, such as alleviating human suffering or getting back the woman he loves.

Hamid, a fashion magnate, who started out with the best of intentions only to be caught up in the very system he was trying to use.

Gabriela, who – like most people today – is convinced that fame is an end in itself, the ultimate reward in a world that considers celebrity to be the supreme achievement.

This is not a thriller, but a stark portrait of where we are now.

Paulo Coelho

3.17 a.m.

The Beretta Px4 compact pistol is slightly larger than a mobile phone, weighs around 700 grams and can fire ten shots. Small, light, invisible when carried in a pocket, its small calibre has one enormous advantage: instead of passing through the victim's body, the bullet hits bones and smashes everything in its path.

Obviously the chances of surviving a shot of that calibre are fairly high; there are thousands of cases in which no vital artery was severed and the victim had time to react and disarm his attacker. However, if the person firing the pistol is experienced enough, he can opt either for a quick death – by aiming at the point between the eyes or at the heart – or a slower one – by placing the barrel at a certain angle close to the ribs and squeezing the trigger. The person shot takes a while to realise that he has been mortally wounded and tries to fight back, run away or call for help. The great advantage of this is that the victim has time to see his killer's face while his strength ebbs slowly away and he falls to the ground, with little external loss of blood, still not fully understanding why this is happening to him.

It is far from being the ideal weapon for experts. 'Nice and light – in a lady's handbag. No stopping power though', someone in the British Secret Service tells James Bond in the first film in the series, meanwhile confiscating Bond's old pistol and handing him a new model. However, that advice applied only to professionals, and for what he now had in mind it was perfect.

He had bought the Beretta on the black market so that it would be impossible to trace. There are five bullets in the magazine, although he intends to use only one, the tip of which he has marked with an 'X', using a nail file. That way, when it's fired and hits something solid, it will break into four pieces.

He will only use the Beretta as a last resort. There are other ways of extinguishing a world, of destroying a universe, and she will probably understand the message as soon as the first victim is found. She will know that he did it in the name of love, and that he feels no resentment, but will take her back and ask no questions about her life during these past two years.

He hopes that six months of careful planning will produce results, but he will only know for sure tomorrow morning. His plan is to allow the Furies, those ancient figures from Greek mythology, to descend on their black wings to that blue-and-white landscape full of diamonds, botox and high-speed cars of no use to anyone because they carry only two passengers. With the little artifacts he has brought with him, all those dreams of power, success, fame and money could be punctured in an instant.

He could have gone up to his room because the scene he had been waiting to witness occurred at 11.11 p.m., although he would have been prepared to wait for even longer. The man and his beautiful companion arrived – both of them in full evening dress – for yet another of those gala events that take place each night after every important supper, and which attracted more people than any film première at the Festival.

Igor ignored the woman. He shielded his face behind a French newspaper (a Russian newspaper would have aroused suspicions) so that she wouldn't see him. An unnecessary precaution: like all women who feel themselves to be queen of the world, she never looked at anyone else. Such women are there in order to shine and always avoid looking at what other people are wearing because, even if their own clothes and accessories have cost them a fortune, the number of diamonds or a particularly exclusive outfit worn by someone else might make them feel depressed or bad-tempered or inferior.

Her elegant, silver-haired companion went over to the bar and ordered champagne, a necessary aperitif for a night that promised new contacts, good music and a fine view of the beach and the yachts moored in the harbour.

He noticed how extremely polite the man was, thanking the waitress when she brought their drinks and giving her a large tip.

The three of them knew each other. Igor felt a great wave of happiness as the adrenaline began to mingle with his blood. The following day he would make her fully aware of his presence there and, at some point, they would meet.

God alone knew what would come of that meeting. Igor, an orthodox Catholic, had made a promise and sworn an oath in a church in Moscow before the relics of St Mary Magdalene (which were in the Russian capital for a week, so that the faithful could worship them). He had queued for nearly five hours and, when he finally saw them, had felt sure that the whole thing was something dreamed up by the priests. He did not, however, want to run the risk of breaking his word, and so he had asked for her protection and help in achieving his goal without too much sacrifice. And he had promised, too, that when it was all over and he could at last return to his native land, he would commission a golden icon from a well-known artist who lived in a monastery in Novosibirsk.

At three in the morning, the bar of the Hotel Martinez smells of cigarettes and sweat. By then, Jimmy (who always wears different coloured shoes) has stopped playing the piano, and the waitress is exhausted, but the people who are still there refuse to leave. They want to stay in that lobby for at least another hour or even all night until *something* happens!

They're already four days into the Cannes Film Festival and still nothing has happened. Every guest at every table is interested in but one thing: meeting the people with Power. Pretty women are waiting for a producer to fall in love with them and give them a major role in their next movie. A few actors are talking amongst themselves, laughing and pretending that the whole business is a matter of complete indifference to them – but they always keep one eye on the door.

Someone is about to arrive. Someone must arrive. Young directors, full of ideas and with CVs listing the videos they made at university, and who have read everything ever written about photography and scriptwriting, are hoping for a stroke of luck; perhaps meeting someone just back from a party who is looking for an empty table where he'll order a coffee and light a cigarette, someone who's tired of going to the same old places all the time and feels ready for a new adventure.

How naïve!

If that did happen, the last thing such a person would want to hear about is some 'really fresh angle' on a hackneyed subject; but despair can deceive the desperate. The people with power who do occasionally enter merely glance around, then go up to their rooms. They're not worried. They have nothing to fear. The Superclass does not forgive betrayals and they know their limitations – whatever the legend may say, they didn't get where they are by trampling on others. On the other hand, if there is some important new discovery to be made – be it in the world of cinema, music or fashion – it will emerge only after much research and not in some hotel bar.

The Superclass are now making love to the girl who managed to gatecrash the party and who is game for anything. They're taking off their make-up, studying the lines on their faces and thinking that it's time for more plastic surgery. They're looking at the online news to see if the announcement they made earlier that day has been picked up by the media. They're taking the inevitable sleeping pill and drinking the tea that promises easy weight-loss. They're ticking the boxes on the menu for their room-service breakfast and hanging it on the door handle along with the sign saying 'Do not disturb'. The Superclass are closing their eyes and thinking: 'I hope I get to sleep quickly. I've got a meeting tomorrow at ten.'

However, everyone knows that the bar in the Hotel Martinez is where the powerful people hang out, which means there's always a chance of meeting them.

It doesn't even occur to the hopefuls that the Powerful only talk to the Powerful, that they need to get together now and then for lunches and suppers, to lend allure to the big festivals, to feed the fantasy that the world of luxury and glamour is accessible to all those with the courage to pursue an idea, to avoid any non-lucrative wars and to promote aggression between countries or companies where they feel this might bring them more power and more money, to pretend that they're happy, even though they're now hostage to their own success, to continue struggling to increase their wealth and influence, even when both those things are already vast, because the vanity of the Superclass consists in competing with itself to see who is the top of the tops.

In an ideal world, the Powerful would talk to the actors, directors, designers and writers who are now bleary-eyed with tiredness and thinking about going back to their rented rooms in distant towns, so that tomorrow they can begin again the marathon of making requests, fixing possible meetings, and being endlessly ready and available.

In the real world, the Powerful are, at this moment, locked in their rooms, checking their e-mails, complaining that these Festival parties are always the same, that their friend was wearing a bigger jewel than they were, and asking how come the yacht a competitor has just bought has a totally unique décor?

Igor has no one to talk to, nor does he want to talk. The winner stands alone.

Igor is the successful owner and president of a telephone company in Russia. A year ago, he reserved the best suite in the Martinez (which makes everyone pay up-front for at least twelve nights, regardless of how long they'll be staying); he arrived this afternoon in his private jet, was driven to the hotel, where he took a bath and then went downstairs in the hope of witnessing one particular scene.

At first, he was pestered by actresses, actors and directors, until he came up with the perfect response for them all:

'Don't speak English, sorry. Polish.'

Or:

'Don't speak French, sorry. Mexican.'

When someone ventured a few words in Spanish, Igor tried another ploy. He started writing down numbers in a notebook so as to look neither like a journalist (because everyone wants to meet journalists) nor a movie mogul. Beside him lay a Russian economics magazine (most people can't tell Russian from Polish or Spanish) with the photo of some boring executive on the cover.

The denizens of the bar, who pride themselves on their keen understanding of the human race, leave Igor in peace, thinking that he must be one of those millionaires who come to Cannes in search of a new girlfriend. That, at least, is the rumour doing the rounds by the time the fifth person has sat down at his table and ordered a mineral water, alleging that there are no other free seats. Igor is duly relegated to the category of 'perfume'.

'Perfume' is the slang term used by actresses (or 'starlets' as they're called at the Festival) because, as with perfumes, it's easy enough to change brands, but one of them might just turn out to be a real find. 'Perfumes' are sought out during the last two days of the Festival, if the actresses in question haven't managed to pick up anything or anyone of interest in the movie industry. For the moment, then, this strange, apparently wealthy man can wait. Actresses know that it's always best to leave the Festival with a new boyfriend (whom they might, later on, be able to transform into a film producer) than to move on to the next event and go through the same old ritual – drinking, smiling (must keep smiling) and pretending that you're not looking at anyone, while your heart beats furiously, time ticks rapidly on, and there are still gala nights to which you haven't yet been invited, but to which the 'perfumes' have.

They know what the 'perfumes' are going to say because they always say the same thing, but they pretend to believe them anyway.

(a) 'I could change your life.'
(b) 'A lot of women would like to be in your shoes.'
(c) 'You're young now, but what will become of you in a few years' time. You need to think about making a longer-term investment.'
(d) 'I'm married, but my wife ...' (this opening line can have various endings: '... is ill', '... has threatened to commit suicide if I leave her', etc.)
(e) 'You're a princess and deserve to be treated like one. I didn't know it until now, but I've been waiting for you. I don't believe in coincidences and I really think we ought to give this relationship a chance.'

It's always the same old spiel. The only variable is how many presents you get (preferably jewellery, which can be sold), how many invites to yacht parties, how many visiting cards you collect, how many times you have to listen to the same chat-up lines, and whether you can wangle a ticket to the Formula 1 races where you'll get to mingle with the same class of people and where your 'big chance' might be waiting for you.

'Perfume' is also the word used by young actors to refer to elderly millionairesses, all plastic and botox, but who are, at least, more intelligent than their male counterparts. They never waste any time: they, too, arrive in the final days of the Festival, knowing that money provides their only pulling power.

The male 'perfumes' deceive themselves: they think that the long legs and youthful faces have genuinely fallen for them and can now be manipulated at will. The female 'perfumes' put all their trust in the power of their diamonds.

Igor knows nothing of all this. This is his first time at the Festival. And he has just realised that, much to his surprise, no one here seems very interested in films, except the people in that bar. He has leafed through a few magazines, opened the envelope in which his company has placed the invitations to the most prestigious parties, but not one of them is for a film première. Before travelling to France, he tried to find out which films were in the running, but had great difficulty in obtaining this information. Then a friend said:

'Forget about films. Cannes is just a fashion show.'

Fashion. Whatever can people be thinking? Do they think fashion is something that changes according to the season of the year? Did they really come from all corners of the world to show off their dresses, their jewellery and their collection of shoes? They don't understand. 'Fashion' is merely a way of saying: 'I belong to your world. I'm wearing the same uniform as your army, so don't shoot.'

Ever since groups of men and women first started living together in caves, fashion has been the only language everyone can understand, even complete strangers. 'We dress in the same way. I belong to your tribe. Let's gang up on the weaklings as a way of surviving.'

But some people believe that 'fashion' is everything. Every six months, they spend a fortune changing some tiny detail in order to keep up their membership of the very exclusive tribe of the rich. If they were to visit Silicon Valley, where the billionaires of the IT industry wear plastic watches and beat-up jeans, they would understand that the world has changed; everyone now seems to belong to the same social class; no one cares any more about the size of a diamond or the make of a tie or a leather briefcase. In fact, ties and leather briefcases don't even exist in that part of the world; nearby, however, is Hollywood, a relatively more powerful machine - albeit in decline - which still manages to convince the innocent to believe in haute-couture dresses, emerald necklaces and stretch limos. And since this is what still appears in all the magazines, who would dare destroy a billion-dollar industry involving advertisements, the sale of useless objects, the invention of entirely unnecessary new trends and the creation of identical face creams all bearing different labels?

How ridiculous! Igor cannot conceal his loathing for those whose decisions affect the lives of millions of honest, hard-working men and women leading dignified lives and glad to have their health, a home and the love of their family.

How perverse! Just when everything seems to be in order and as families gather round the table to have supper, the phantom of the Superclass appears, selling impossible dreams: luxury, beauty, power. And the family falls apart.

The father works overtime to be able to buy his son the latest trainers because if his son doesn't have a pair, he'll be ostracised at school. The wife weeps in silence because her friends have designer clothes and she has no money. Their adolescent children, instead of learning the real values of faith and hope, dream only of becoming singers or movie stars. Girls in provincial towns lose any real sense of themselves and start to think of going to the big city, prepared to do anything, absolutely anything, to get a particular piece of jewellery. A world that should be directed towards justice begins instead to focus on material things, which, in six months' time, will be worthless and have to be replaced, and that is how the whole circus ensures that the despicable creatures gathered together in Cannes remain at the top of the heap.

Igor is untouched by this destructive power, for he has one of the most enviable jobs in the world. He continues to earn more money in a day than he could spend in a year, even if he were to indulge in all possible pleasures, legal and illegal. He has no difficulty in finding women, regardless of whether they know how much money he has – he's tested it out on more than one occasion and never failed yet. He has just turned forty, is in good physical shape and, according to his annual check-up, has no health problems. He has no debts either. He doesn't have to wear a particular designer label, go to a particular restaurant, spend his holidays at a beach where 'everyone' goes or buy a watch just because some successful sportsman is promoting it. He can sign major contracts with a cheap ball-point pen, wear comfortable, elegant jackets, handmade by a tailor who has a small shop next to his office, and which carry no label at all. He can do as he likes and doesn't have to prove to anyone that he's rich; he has an interesting job and loves what he does.

Perhaps that's the problem: he still loves what he does. He's sure that this is why the woman who came into the bar some hours earlier is not sitting at his table with him.

He tries to keep thinking, to pass the time. He asks Kristelle for another drink – he knows the waitress's name because an hour ago, when the bar was emptier (people were having supper), he asked for a glass of whisky, and she said that he looked sad and should eat something to cheer himself up. He thanked her for her concern, and was glad that someone should care about his state of mind.

He is perhaps the only one who knows the name of the waitress serving him; the others only want to know the names –

and, if possible, the job titles – of the people sitting at the tables and in the armchairs.

He tries to keep thinking, but it's gone three o'clock in the morning, and the beautiful woman and her courteous companion – who, by the way, looks remarkably like him – have not reappeared. Maybe they went straight up to their room where they are now making love, or perhaps they're still drinking champagne on one of the yachts where the parties only begin when the other parties are all coming to an end. Perhaps they're lying in bed, reading magazines, ignoring each other.

Not that it matters. Igor is alone and tired and needs to sleep.

7.22 a.m.

He wakes up at 7.22 a.m., much earlier than his body would like, but he hasn't yet adapted to the time difference between Moscow and Cannes. If he was at work, he would already have held two or three meetings with his subordinates and be preparing to have lunch with some new client.

He has another task to fulfil here: he must find someone he can sacrifice in the name of love. He needs a victim, so that Ewa will get his message that very morning.

He has a bath, goes downstairs to have a coffee in an almost deserted restaurant, then sets off along the Boulevard de la Croisette on which nearly all the major luxury hotels are located. There is no traffic because one lane is blocked off and only cars with official permission are being allowed through. The other lane is empty because even the people who live in the city are still only just getting ready to go to work.

He feels no resentment. He has passed the really difficult phase, when he couldn't sleep because he was so filled with pain and hatred. Now he can understand Ewa's feelings: after all, monogamy is a myth that has been rammed down people's throats for far too long. He has read a lot on the subject. It isn't just a matter of excess hormones or vanity, but, as all the research indicates, a genetic configuration found in almost all animals.

Paternity tests given to birds, monkeys and foxes revealed that simply because these species had developed a social relationship very similar to marriage it did not necessarily mean that they had been faithful to each other. In 70 per cent of cases, their offspring turn out to have been fathered by males other than their partners. Igor remembered something written by David Barash, Professor of Psychology at the University of Washington in Seattle, in which he said that the only species in nature that doesn't commit adultery and in which there seems to be 100 per cent monogamy is a flatworm, *Diplozoon paradoxum*. The male and female worms meet as adolescents, and their bodies literally fuse together.

This is why he cannot accuse Ewa of anything; she was merely following her human instincts. However, she had been brought up to believe in those unnatural social conventions and must be feeling guilty, thinking that he doesn't love her any more and will never forgive her.

He is, in fact, prepared to do anything, even to send messages that will mean he has destroyed someone's world, just so that she'll know that not only is he willing to welcome her back, he will gladly bury the past and ask no questions.

He sees a young woman setting out her wares on the pavement - various bits of craftwork and jewellery of rather dubious taste.

Yes, she will be the sacrifice. She is the message he must send, a message that will be understood as soon as it reaches its destination. Before going over to her, he observes her tenderly; she doesn't know that in a little while, if all goes well, her soul will be wandering the clouds, free for ever from an idiotic job that will never take her where her dreams would like her to go.

'How much?' he asks in perfect French.

'Which piece do you want, sir?'

'All of them.'

The young woman - who must be twenty at most - smiles.

'This isn't the first time someone has asked to buy everything. The next step is usually: "Would you like to go for a walk? You're far too pretty to be here selling these things. I'm ..."'

'No, I'm not. I don't work in the movies, nor am I going to make you an actress and change your life. I'm not interested in the things you're selling either. I just need to talk, and we can do that right here.'

The young woman averts her gaze.

'My parents make these things, and I'm proud of what I do. One day, someone will come along who'll recognise their value. Please, go away. I'm sure you can find someone else to listen to what you have to say.'

Igor takes a bundle of notes out of his pocket and puts them gently down beside her.

'Forgive my rudeness. I only said I wasn't interested in buying anything to see if you would lower the price. Anyway, my name is Igor Malev. I flew in from Moscow yesterday, and I'm still a little jet-lagged.'

'My name's Olivia,' says the young woman, pretending to believe his lie.

Without asking her permission, he sits down on the bench beside her. She shifts up an inch or so.

'What do you want to talk about?'

'First, take the money.'

Olivia hesitates, then, looking around, realises that she has no reason to be afraid. Cars are now driving down the one available lane, young people are heading for the beach and an elderly couple are coming towards them down the pavement. She puts the money in her pocket, not even bothering to count it; she has enough experience of life to know that it's more than enough.

'Thank you for accepting my offer,' says the Russian. 'You asked me what I want to talk about? Well, nothing very important.'

'You must be here for a reason. You need a reason to visit Cannes at this time of year when the city is as unbearable for the people who live here as it is for the tourists.'

Igor is looking at the sea. He lights a cigarette.

'Smoking's bad for your health,' she says.

He ignores this remark.

'What, for you, is the meaning of life?' he asks.

'Love.'

Olivia smiles. This really is an excellent way to start the day, talking about deeper things than the price of each piece of handiwork or the clothes people are wearing.

'And for you?'

'Yes, love too. But for me it was also important to earn enough money to show my parents that I was capable of succeeding. I did that, and now they're proud of me. I met the perfect woman, we married and I would like to have had children, to honour and fear God. The children, alas, never came.'

Olivia doesn't like to ask why. The man in his forties continues in his perfect French:

'We thought of adopting a child. Indeed, we spent two or three years thinking about it, but then life began to get too busy what with business trips and parties, meetings and deals.'

'When you sat down here to talk, I thought you were just another eccentric millionaire in search of an adventure, but I'm enjoying talking about these things.'

'Do you think about the future?'

'Yes, I do, and I think my dreams are much the same as yours. Obviously, I'd like to have children as well …'

She pauses. She doesn't want to hurt the feelings of this unexpected new companion.

'… if, of course, I can. Sometimes, God has other plans.'

He appears not to have heard her answer.

'Do only millionaires come to the Festival?'

'Millionaires and people who think they're millionaires or want to become millionaires. While the Festival is on, this part of the city is like a madhouse. Everyone behaves as if they were terribly important, apart from the people who really are important; they're much politer; they don't need to prove anything to anyone. They don't always buy what I have to sell, but at least they smile, make some pleasant remark and treat me with respect. What are you doing here?'

'God made the world in six days, but what *is* the world? It's what you or I see. Whenever someone dies, a part of the universe dies too. Everything a person felt, experienced and saw dies with them, like tears in the rain.'

'"Like tears in the rain" … I saw a film once that used that phrase. I can't remember now what it was.'

'I didn't come here to cry. I came to send messages to the woman I love, and in order to do that, I need to destroy a few universes or worlds.'

Instead of feeling alarmed by this last statement, Olivia laughs. This handsome, well-dressed man, speaking fluent French, doesn't seem like a madman at all. She was fed up with always hearing the same things: you're very pretty, you could be doing better for yourself, how much is this, how much is that, it's awfully expensive, I'll go away and think about it and come back later (which they never do, of course), etc. At least this Russian has a sense of humour.

'Why do you need to destroy the world?'

'So that I can rebuild my own world.'

Olivia would like to try and console him, but she's afraid of hearing the famous words: 'I think you could give meaning to my life,' at which point the conversation would come to an abrupt halt because she has other plans for her future. Besides, it would be absurd on her part to try and teach someone older and more successful how to overcome his difficulties.

One way out would be to learn more about his life. After all, he's paid her – and paid her well – for her time.

'How do you intend to do that?'

'Do you know anything about frogs?'

'Frogs?'

'Yes, various biological studies have shown that if a frog is placed in a container along with water from its own pond, it will remain there, utterly still, while the water is slowly heated up. The frog doesn't react to the gradual increase in temperature, to the changes in its environment, and when the water reaches boiling point, the frog dies, fat and happy.

'On the other hand, if a frog is thrown into a container full of already boiling water, it will jump straight out again, scalded, but alive!'

Olivia doesn't quite see what this has to do with the destruction of the world. Igor goes on:

'I was like that boiled frog. I didn't notice the changes. I thought everything was fine, that the bad things would just go away, that it was just a matter of time. I was ready to die because I lost the most important thing in my life, but, instead of reacting, I sat there bobbing apathetically about in water that was getting hotter by the minute.'

Olivia plucks up the courage to ask:

'What did you lose?'

'The truth is I didn't lose anything. Life sometimes separates people so that they can realise how much they mean to each other. For example, last night, I saw my wife with another man. I know she wants to come back to me, that she still loves me, but she's not brave enough to take the first step. Some boiled frogs still think it's obedience that counts, not ability: those who can, lead, and those with any sense, obey. So where's the truth in all this? It's better to emerge from a situation slightly scalded, but alive and ready to act. And I think you can help me in that task.'

Olivia tries to imagine what is going through the mind of the man beside her. How could anyone leave such an interesting person, someone who can talk about things she has never even thought about? Then again, there's no logic to love. Despite her youth, she knows that. Her boyfriend, for example, can be quite brutal and sometimes hits her for no reason, and yet she can't bear to be apart from him even for a day.

What exactly were they talking about? About frogs and about how she could help him. She can't help him, of course, so she'd better change the subject.

'And how do you intend to set about destroying the world?'

Igor points to the one free lane on the Boulevard de la Croisette.

'Let's say that I don't want you to go to a party, but I daren't say so openly. If I wait for the rush hour to begin and stop my car in the middle of the road, within ten minutes, the whole of the boulevard opposite the beach will have come to a standstill. Drivers will think: "There must have been an accident" and will wait patiently. In fifteen minutes, the police will arrive with a truck to tow the car away.'

'That kind of thing is always happening.'

'Ah, yes, but I – very carefully and without anyone noticing – will have got out of my car and scattered nails and other sharp objects on the road in front of it. And I will have carefully painted all of these objects black, so that they blend in with the asphalt. As the tow-truck approaches, its tyres will be punctured. Now we have two problems, and the tailback of traffic will have reached the suburbs of this small city, the very suburbs where you perhaps live.'

'You clearly have a very vivid imagination, but you would still only have managed to delay me by about an hour.'

It was Igor's turn to smile.

'Oh, I could come up with all kinds of ways of making the situation worse. When people started gathering round to help, for example, I would throw something like a small smoke-bomb under the truck. This would frighten everyone. I would get into my car, feigning despair, and start the engine. At the same time, though, I would empty a bit of lighter fluid on the floor of the car and it would ignite. I would then jump out of the car in time to observe the scene: the car gradually going up in flames, the flames reaching the fuel tank, the explosion that would affect the car behind as well, and so on in a chain reaction. And I could achieve all that with a car, a few nails, a smoke-bomb that you can buy in a shop, and a small amount of lighter fluid ...'

Igor takes from his pocket a small flask containing some kind of liquid.

'... about this much. I should have done that when I realised Ewa was about to leave me, to make her postpone her decision and reflect a little and consider the consequences. When people start to reflect on decisions they're trying to make, they usually change their mind – it requires a lot of courage to take certain steps.

'But I was too proud. I thought it was just a temporary move and that she would soon realise her mistake. I'm sure she regrets leaving me and, as I said, wants to come back. But for that to happen I need to destroy a few worlds.'

The expression on his face has changed, and Olivia is no longer amused by the story. She gets up.

'Well, I need to do some work.'

'But I paid you to listen to me. I paid enough to cover your whole working day.'

She puts her hand in her pocket to give him back the money, but at that moment, she sees the pistol pointing at her face.

'Sit down.'

Her first impulse is to run. The elderly couple are still slowly approaching.

'Don't run away,' he says, as if he could read her thoughts. 'I haven't the slightest intention of firing the gun if you'll just sit down again and hear me out. If you don't try anything and do as I say, then I swear I won't shoot.'

A series of options pass rapidly through Olivia's head, the first being to run, zigzagging her way across the street, but she realises that her legs have gone weak.

'Sit down,' the man says again. 'I won't shoot if you do as you're told. I promise.'

Yes, it would be madness on his part to fire that gun on a sunny morning, with cars driving past, people going to the beach, the traffic getting heavier by the minute and more pedestrians walking along the pavement. Best to do as the man says, even if only because she's in no state to do anything else; she's almost fainting.

She obeys. Now she just has to convince him that she's not a threat, to listen to his deserted husband's lament, to promise him that she has seen nothing, and then, as soon as a policeman appears, doing his usual round, throw herself to the ground and scream for help.

'I know exactly what you're feeling,' the man says, trying to calm her. 'The symptoms of fear have been the same since the dawn of time. They were the same when men had to face wild beasts and they continue to be so right up to the present day: blood drains away from the face and the epidermis, protecting the body and avoiding blood loss, that's why people turn pale. The intestines relax and release everything, so that there will be no toxic matter left contaminating the organism. The body initially refuses to move, so as not to provoke the beast in question by making any sudden movement.'

'This is all a dream,' thinks Olivia. She remembers her parents, who should have been here with her this morning, but who had been up all night making jewellery because the day looked likely to be a busy one. A few hours ago, she had been making love with her boyfriend, whom she believed to be the man of her life, even though he sometimes hit her; they reached orgasm simultaneously, something that hadn't happened for a long time. After breakfast, she decided not to take her usual shower because she felt free and full of energy and pleased with life.

No, this can't be happening. She must try to appear calm.

'Let's talk. The reason you bought all my stuff was so that we could talk. Besides, I wasn't getting up in order to run away.'

He presses the barrel of the gun gently against the girl's ribs. The elderly couple pass by, glance at them and notice nothing odd. There's that Portuguese girl, they think, trying, as usual, to impress some man with her dark eyebrows and child-like smile. It's not the first time they've seen her with a strange man, and this one, to judge by his clothes, has plenty of money.

Olivia fixes them with her eyes, as if trying to tell them what's going on just by looking. The man beside her says brightly:

'Good morning.'

The couple move off without uttering a word. They're not in the habit of talking to strangers or of exchanging greetings with street vendors.

'Yes, let's talk,' says the Russian, breaking the silence. 'I'm not really going to try and disrupt the traffic. I was just giving that as an example. My wife will realise I'm here when she starts to receive the messages. I'm not going to take the obvious route, which would be to go and meet her. I need her to come to me.'

This was a possible way out.

'I can deliver the messages, if you like. Just tell me which hotel she's staying at.'

The man laughs.

'You suffer from the youthful vice of thinking you're cleverer than everyone else. The moment you left here, you'd go straight to the police.'

Her blood freezes. Are they going to sit on this bench all day? Is he going to shoot her after all, now that she knows his face?

'You said you weren't going to shoot.'

'I promised I wouldn't if you behaved in a more adult fashion and with due respect for my intelligence.'

He's right. The adult thing to do would be to talk a little about herself. She might arouse the compassion that is always there in the mind of a madman by explaining that she's in a similar situation, even though it isn't true.

A boy runs past, an iPod in his ears. He doesn't even turn to look at them.

'I live with a man who makes my life hell, and yet I can't leave him.'

The look in Igor's eyes changes.

Olivia thinks she's found a way of escaping from the trap. 'Be intelligent. Don't just give up; think of the woman who's married to the man sitting next to you. Be honest.'

'He's cut me off from my friends. He's always jealous even though he can get all the women he wants. He criticises everything I do and says I have no ambition. He even takes the little money I earn as commission.'

The man says nothing but stares at the sea. The pavement is filling up with people; what would happen if she just got to her feet and ran? Would he shoot her? Is it a real gun?

She senses that she has touched on a topic of possible interest to him. It would be best not to do anything foolish, she thinks, remembering the way he spoke and looked at her minutes before.

'And yet, you see, I can't bring myself to leave him. Even if I were to meet the kindest, richest, most generous man in the world, I wouldn't give my boyfriend up for anything. I'm not a masochist, I take no pleasure in these constant humiliations, I just happen to love him.'

She feels the barrel of the gun pressing into her ribs again. She has said the wrong thing.

'I'm not like that scoundrel of a boyfriend of yours,' he says, his voice full of loathing now. 'I worked hard to build up what I have. I worked long and hard, and survived many a setback. I was always honest in my dealings, although there were, of course, times when I had to be hard and implacable. I was always a good Christian. I have influential friends, and

I've always been grateful to them. In short, I did everything right.

'I never harmed anyone who got in my way. Whenever possible, I encouraged my wife to do what she wanted to do, and the result: here I am, alone. Yes, I killed people during the idiotic war I was sent to fight, but I never lost my sense of reality. I'm not one of those traumatised war veterans who goes into a restaurant and machine-guns people. I'm not a terrorist. Of course, I could say that life has treated me unfairly and taken from me the most important thing there is: love. But there are other women, and the pain of love always passes. I need to act, I'm tired of being a frog slowly boiling to death.'

'If you know there are other women and you know that the pain of love will pass, why are you so upset?'

Yes, she's behaving like an adult now, surprised at the calm way in which she's trying to deal with the madman by her side.

He seems to waver.

'I don't really know. Perhaps because I've been abandoned once too often. Perhaps because I need to prove to myself just what I'm capable of. Perhaps because I lied, and there is only one woman for me. I have a plan.'

'What plan?'

'I told you before. I'm going to keep destroying worlds until she realises how important she is to me and that I'm prepared to run any risk in order to get her back.'

The police!

They both notice the police car approaching.

'I'm sorry,' says the man. 'I intended to talk a little more. Life hasn't treated you very fairly either.'

Olivia realises this is the end. And since she now has nothing to lose, she again tries to get up. Then she feels the hand of that stranger on her right shoulder, as if he were fondly embracing her.

Samozashchita Bez Orujiya, or Sambo as it is better known among Russians, is the art of killing swiftly with one's bare hands, without the victim realising what is happening. It was developed over the centuries, when peoples or tribes had to confront invaders unarmed. It was widely used by the Soviet state apparatus to eliminate people without leaving any trace. They tried to introduce it as a martial art in the 1980 Moscow Olympics, but it was rejected as being too dangerous, despite all the efforts of the Communists of the day to include in the Games a sport which they alone practised.

Perfect. That way, only a few people know the moves.

Igor's right thumb is pressing down on Olivia's jugular vein, and the blood stops flowing to her brain. Meanwhile, his other hand is pressing on a particular point near her armpit, causing the muscles to seize up. There are no contractions, it's merely a question of waiting two minutes.

Olivia appears to have gone to sleep in his arms. The police car drives by behind them, using the lane that is closed to other traffic. They don't even notice the embracing couple; they have other things to worry about this morning, like doing their best to keep the traffic moving – an impossible task if carried out to the letter. The latest call over the radio tells them that some drunken millionaire has just crashed his car a mile or so away.

Still supporting the girl, Igor bends down and uses his other hand to pick up the cloth spread out in front of the bench and on which all those tasteless objects were to be displayed. He adroitly folds the cloth up to form an improvised pillow.

When he sees that no one else is around, he tenderly lays her inert body on the bench. She looks as if she were asleep; and in her dreams she must be remembering some particularly lovely day or else having nightmares about her violent boyfriend.

Only the elderly couple had noticed them sitting together. And if the crime were discovered – which Igor doubted, since there were no visible marks – they would describe him to the police as fairer or darker or older or younger than he really was;

there wasn't the slightest reason to be worried; people never pay much attention to what's going on around them.

Before leaving, he plants a kiss on the brow of the sleeping beauty and murmurs:

'As you see, I kept my promise. I didn't shoot.'

He takes a few steps and his head begins to ache terribly. This is perfectly normal: the blood is flooding the brain, an understandable reaction in someone who has just been under extreme tension.

Despite the headache, he feels happy. Yes, he has done what he set out to do.

He can do it. And he's happier still because he has freed the soul from that fragile body, freed a spirit incapable of defending herself against a bullying coward. If her relationship with her boyfriend had continued, the girl would have ended up depressed and anxious and devoid of all self-respect, and would have been even more under her boyfriend's thumb.

This had never been the case with Ewa. She had always been capable of making her own decisions. He had given her both moral and financial support when she decided to open her haute-couture boutique; and she had been free to travel as much as she wanted. He had been an exemplary man and husband. And yet, she had made a mistake: she had been unable to understand his love or his forgiveness. He hoped, however, that she would receive these messages; after all, he had told her on the day she left that he would destroy whole worlds to get her back.

He picks up the throwaway mobile phone he has just bought and on which he has entered the smallest possible amount of credit. He sends a text message.

11.00 a.m.

It all began, they say, with an unknown 19-year-old posing in a bikini for photographers who had nothing better to do during the 1953 Cannes Festival. She immediately shot to stardom, and her name became legendary: Brigitte Bardot. And now everyone thinks they can do the same. No one understands the importance of being an actress; beauty is the only thing that counts.

That's why women with long legs and dyed hair, the bottle blondes of this world, travel hundreds or even thousands of miles to be in Cannes, even if only to spend the whole day on the beach, hoping to be seen, photographed, discovered. They want to escape from the trap that awaits all women: becoming a housewife, who makes supper for her husband every evening, takes the children to school every day and tries to dig up some dirt on her neighbours' monotonous lives so as to have something to gossip about with her friends. What these women want is fame, glory and glamour, to be the envy of the other people who live in their town and of the boys and girls who always thought of them as ugly ducklings, unaware that they would one day grow up to be a swan or blossom into a flower coveted by everyone. They want a career in the world of dreams even if they have to borrow money to get silicone breast implants or to buy some newer, sexier outfits. Drama school? Forget it; good looks and the right contacts are all you need. The cinema can work miracles, always assuming, of course, you can ever break into that world. Anything to escape from the prison of the provincial city and the long, dreary, repetitive days. There are millions of people who don't mind that kind of life, and they should be left to live their lives as they see fit. However, if you come to the Festival you must leave fear at home and be prepared for anything: making spur-of-the-moment decisions, telling lies if necessary, pretending to be younger than you are, smiling at people you loathe, feigning an interest in people who bore you, saying 'I love you' without a thought for the consequences, or stabbing in the back the friend who once helped you out, but who has now become an undesirable rival. Don't let feelings of remorse or shame get in your way. The reward is worth any amount of sacrifice.

Fame. Glory. Glamour.

Gabriela finds these thoughts irritating. It's definitely not the best way to start a new day. Worse, she has a hangover.

At least there's one consolation. She hasn't woken up in a five-star hotel next to a man telling her to put her clothes on and leave because he has important business to deal with, like buying or selling films.

She gets up and looks around to see if any of her friends are still in the apartment. Needless to say they're not. They've long since left for the Boulevard de la Croisette, for the swimming pools, hotel bars, yachts, possible lunch dates and chance meetings on the beach. There are five fold-out mattresses on the floor of the small shared apartment, hired for the duration at an exorbitant rent. The mattresses are surrounded by a tangle of clothes, discarded shoes and hangers that no one has taken the trouble to put back in the wardrobe.

'The clothes take up more room here than the people,' she thinks.

Not that any of them could even dream of wearing clothes designed by Elie Saab, Karl Lagerfeld, Versace or Galliano, but what they have nevertheless takes up most of the apartment: bikinis, miniskirts, T-shirts, platform shoes and a vast amount of make-up.

'One day I'll wear what I like, but right now, I just need to be given a chance,' she thinks.

And why does she want that chance?

Quite simple. Because she knows she's the best, despite her experience at school – when she so disappointed her parents – and despite the challenges she's faced since in order to prove to herself that she can overcome difficulties, frustrations and defeats. She was born to win and to shine, of that she has no doubt.

'And when I get what I always wanted, I know I'll have to ask myself: Do they love and admire me because I'm me or because I'm famous.'

She knows people who have achieved stardom on the stage and, contrary to her expectations, they're not at peace with themselves: they're insecure, full of doubts, unhappy as soon as they come off stage. They want to be actors so as not to have to be themselves, and they live in fear of making the one false step that could end their career.

'I'm different, though. I've always been me.'

Is that true? Or does everyone in her position think the same?

She gets up and makes herself some coffee. The kitchen is a mess, and none of her friends has bothered to wash the dishes. She doesn't know why she's woken up in such a bad mood and with so many doubts. She knows her job, she's devoted herself to it heart and soul, and yet it's as if people refuse to recognise her talent. She knows what human beings are like too, especially men – future allies in a battle she needs to win soon, because she's 25 already and nearly too old for the dream factory. She knows three things:

(a) that men are less treacherous than women;
(b) that they never notice what a woman is wearing because they're always mentally undressing her;
(c) that as long as you've got breasts, thighs, buttocks and belly in good trim, you can conquer the world.

Because of those three things, and because she knows that all the other women she's competing with try to emphasise their attributes, she pays attention only to item (c) on her list. She exercises and tries to keep fit, avoids diets and, illogical though it may seem, dresses very discreetly. This has worked well so far, and she can usually pass for younger than her age. She's hoping that it'll do the trick in Cannes too.

Breasts, buttocks, thighs. They can focus on those things now if they want to, but the day will come when they'll see what she can really do.

She drinks her coffee and begins to understand her bad mood. She's surrounded by some of the most beautiful women on the planet! She certainly doesn't consider herself ugly, but there's no way she can compete with them. She needs to decide what to do. She had thought long and hard before making this trip, money is tight, and she doesn't have much time in which to land a contract. She went to various places during the first two days, giving people a copy of her CV and her photos, but all she achieved was an invitation to last night's party at a cheap restaurant, with the music at full blast, and where she met no one from the Superclass. In order to lose her inhibitions, she drank more than she should and ended up not knowing where she was or what she was doing there. Everything seemed strange to her - Europe, the way people dress, the different languages, the phoney jollity - when the truth was everyone was wishing they could have been invited to some more important event, instead of being in that utterly insignificant place, listening to the same old music, and having to hold shouted conversations about other people's lives and the injustices committed by the powerful on the powerless.

Gabriela is tired of talking about these so-called injustices. That's simply the way it is. They choose the people they want to choose and don't have to explain themselves to anyone, which is why she needs a plan. A lot of other young women with the same dream (but not, of course, with as much talent as her) will be doing the rounds with their CVs and their photos; the producers who come to the Festival must be inundated with portfolios, DVDs, business cards.

What would make her stand out?

She needs to think. She won't get another chance like this, largely because she's spent all her savings on this trip. And – horror of horrors – she's getting old. She's 25. This is her last chance.

While she drinks her coffee, she looks through the small kitchen window at the dead-end street down below. All she can see is a tobacconist's and a little girl eating chocolate. Yes, this is her last chance. She hopes it will turn out quite differently from the first one.

She thinks back to when she was eleven years old and performing in her first school play at one of the most expensive schools in Chicago. Her subsequent desire to succeed was not born of the unanimous acclaim she received from the audience, composed of fathers, mothers, relatives and teachers. Far from it. She was playing the Mad Hatter in *Alice in Wonderland*. She had got the part – one of the best roles in the play – after auditioning along with a lot of other girls and boys.

Her first line was: 'Your hair wants cutting.' Then Alice would reply: 'You should learn not to make personal remarks, it's very rude.'

When the long-awaited moment came, a moment she had rehearsed and rehearsed, she was so nervous that she got the line wrong and said instead: 'Your hair wants washing.' The girl playing Alice said her next line anyway, and the audience would never have noticed anything was wrong if Gabriela, who knew she had made a mistake, hadn't promptly lost the power of speech. Since the Mad Hatter was an essential character if the scene was to continue, and since children are not good at improvising on stage (although they improvise happily enough in real life), no one knew what to do. Then, after several long minutes, during which the actors simply looked at each other, the teacher started applauding, announced it was time for an interval and ordered everyone off-stage.

Gabriela not only left the stage, she left the school in tears. The following day, she found out that the scene with the Mad Hatter had been cut, and the actors would instead move straight on to the game of croquet with the Queen. The teacher said this didn't matter in the least because the story of *Alice in Wonderland* is a lot of nonsense anyway, but during playtime, the other girls and boys ganged up on Gabriela and started beating her.

This wasn't so very unusual – it was a fairly regular occurrence – and she had learned to defend herself as energetically as when she, in turn, attacked the weaker children. On this occasion, however, she took the beating without uttering a word and without shedding a tear. Her reaction was so surprising that the fight lasted almost no time at all; her schoolmates expected her to scream and shout and, when she didn't, rapidly lost interest. For with each blow, Gabriela was thinking:

'I'll be a great actress one day and then you'll be sorry.'

Who says that children aren't capable of deciding what they want to do in life?

Adults do.

And when we grow to be adults ourselves, we believe that we really are wise beings who are always right. Many children had doubtless been through a similar experience, playing the role of the Mad Hatter or Sleeping Beauty or Aladdin or Alice, and decided there and then to abandon the spotlights and the applause. Gabriela, though, had never before lost a battle; she was the prettiest and most intelligent student in school and always got the best marks in class; and she knew intuitively that if she didn't fight back at once, she would be lost.

It was one thing to get a beating from her schoolmates - because she could give as good as she got - but it was quite another to carry a failure like that around with her for the rest of her life. As we all know, a fluffed line in a school play, an inability to dance as well as everyone else, or rude comments passed about skinny legs or a big head - which all children have to put up with - can have two radically different consequences.

Some people opt for revenge and try to be really good at whatever it is the others thought they couldn't do. 'One day, you'll envy me,' they think.

Most people, however, accept their limitations, and then things tend to go from bad to worse. They grow up insecure and obedient (although they dream of a day when they'll be free and able to do whatever they want), they get married to prove that they're not as ugly as other kids said they were (although deep down they still believe they are), they have children so that no one can say they're infertile (even though they wanted kids anyway), they dress well so that no one can say they dress badly (although they know people will say that anyway).

By the following week, the incident at the play had been forgotten by everyone at school, but Gabriela had decided that, one day, when she was a world-famous actress, accompanied by secretaries, bodyguards, photographers and legions of fans, she would go back to that school. She would put on a performance of *Alice in Wonderland* for needy children, she would make the news and her childhood friends would say:

'I was on the same stage as her once!'

Her mother wanted her to study chemical engineering, and as soon as she finished high school, her parents sent her to the Illinois Institute of Technology. During the day, she studied protein paths and the structure of benzene, but she spent her evenings with Ibsen, Coward and Shakespeare while attending a drama course paid for with money sent to her by her parents to buy clothes and course books. She trained with the best professionals and had excellent teachers. She received good reviews and letters of recommendation, she performed (without her parents' knowledge) as a backing singer for a rock group and as a belly dancer in a play about Lawrence of Arabia. It was always a good idea to accept any role that came along. There was always the chance that someone important might be in the audience, someone who would invite her to her first real audition, and then all those testing times and all her struggles to gain a place in the spotlight would be over.

The years passed. Gabriela made TV commercials, toothpaste ads, did some modelling work, and was even tempted to respond to an invitation from a group that specialised in providing escorts for businessmen because she desperately needed money to put together a proper portfolio to send to all the major modelling and acting agencies in the United States. Fortunately, God – in whom she never lost faith – saved her. That same day, she was offered a job as an extra in a video starring a Japanese singer, which was going to be filmed beneath the viaduct of the Chicago 'L'. She was paid much more than she expected (apparently the producers had demanded a fortune in fees for the foreign cast) and with that extra money she managed to produce the vital book of photos (or 'book' as it's known in every language in the world), which also cost much more than she had imagined.

She was always telling herself that she was just at the beginning of her career, even though the days and months were beginning to fly by. She might have been picked to play Ophelia in *Hamlet* while she was on the drama course, but life mostly offered her only ads for deodorants and beauty creams. Whenever she went to an agency to show them her book and the letters of recommendation from teachers, friends and colleagues, she found the waiting-room full of girls who looked very like her, all of them smiling, all of them hating each other, and all doing whatever they could to get something, anything, that would give them 'visibility' as the professionals called it.

She would wait hours for her turn to come, and meanwhile read books on meditation and positive thinking. She would end up sitting opposite someone – male or female – who ignored the letters and went straight to the photos, not that they ever commented on those either. They would make a note of her name. Sometimes, she would be called in for an audition, about one in ten of which bore fruit. There she would be again, with all her talent (or so she thought), standing in front of a camera and a lot of ill-mannered people, who were always telling her: 'Relax, smile, turn to the right, drop your chin a little, lick your lips.' And the result: a photo of a new brand of coffee.

And what happened when she wasn't called? She felt rejected, but soon learned to live with that and had come to see it as a necessary experience, a test of her perseverance and faith. She refused to accept the fact that the drama course, the letters of recommendation, the CV listing minor roles performed in minor theatres, were of no use at all …

Her mobile phone rang.

… none at all.

It continued to ring.

She was still travelling back in time as she gazed out at the tobacconist's and at the little girl eating chocolate, then she finally emerged from her reverie, realised what was happening and answered the phone.

A voice at the other end was saying that she had an audition in two hours' time.

She had an audition!

In Cannes!

So it *had* been worth crossing the ocean, arriving in a city where all the hotels were full, meeting up at the airport with other young women in exactly the same position as her (a Pole, two Russians and a Brazilian), and going round knocking on doors until they found that shared, exorbitantly priced apartment. After all those years of trying her luck in Chicago and travelling now and then to Los Angeles in search of more agents, more adverts, more rejections, it turned out that her future lies in Europe!

In two hours' time?

She couldn't catch a bus because she didn't know the routes. She was staying high up on a steep hill and had only been down it twice so far – to distribute copies of her book and to go to that stupid party last night. On both occasions, when she reached the bottom of the hill, she had hitched a lift from complete strangers, usually single men in magnificent convertibles. Everyone knew Cannes to be a safe place, and all women know that good looks help when trying to get a ride, but she couldn't leave anything to chance this time – she would have to resolve the problem herself. Auditions follow a rigorous timetable, that was one of the first things you learn at any acting agency. She had noticed on her first day in Cannes that the traffic was almost permanently gridlocked, and so all she could do was get dressed and leave at once. She would be there in an hour and a half; she remembered the hotel where the producer was staying because it was on the 'pilgrimage route' she had followed yesterday, in search of some opportunity, some opening.

Now the problem was what to wear.

She fell upon the suitcase she had brought with her, chose some Armani jeans made in China and bought on the black market in Chicago for a fifth of the real price. No one could say they were fake because they weren't: everyone knew that the Chinese manufacturers sent 80 per cent of what they produced to the original stores, with the remaining 20 per cent being sold off by employees on the side. It was, shall we say, excess stock, surplus to requirements.

She was wearing a white DKNY T-shirt, which had cost more than the jeans. Faithful to her principles, she knew that the more discreet the clothes, the better. No short skirts, no plunging necklines, because if other women had been invited to the audition, that is what they would be wearing.

She wasn't sure about her make-up. In the end, she opted for a very light foundation and an even lighter application of lip liner. She had already lost a precious fifteen minutes.

11.45 a.m.

People are never satisfied. If they have a little, they want more. If they have a lot, they want still more. Once they have more, they wish they could be happy with little, but are incapable of making the slightest effort in that direction.

Is it just that they don't understand how simple happiness is? What can she want, that girl in the jeans and white T-shirt who just came running past? What could be so urgent that it stopped her taking time to contemplate the lovely sunny day, the blue sea, the babies in their prams, the palms fringing the beach?

'Don't run, child! You'll never escape the two most important presences in the life of any human being: God and death. God accompanies your every step and will be annoyed because he can see that you're not paying attention to the miracle of life. Or indeed death. You just ran past a corpse and didn't even notice.'

Igor has walked past the scene of the crime several times now. At one point, he realised that his comings and goings might arouse suspicion and so decided to remain a prudent two hundred yards from the scene, leaning on the balustrade that looked out over the beach. He's wearing dark glasses, but there's nothing suspicious about that, not only because it's a sunny day, but because in a celebrity town like Cannes, dark glasses are synonymous with status.

He's surprised to see that it's almost midday, and yet no one has realised that there's a person lying dead on the main street of a city which, at this time of year, is the focus of the world's attention.

A couple are approaching the bench now, visibly irritated. They start shouting at the Sleeping Beauty; they're the girl's parents, angry because she isn't working. The man shakes her almost violently. Then the woman bends over, obscuring Igor's field of vision.

Igor knows what will happen next.

The mother screams. The father takes his mobile phone from his pocket and moves away, clearly agitated. The mother is shaking her daughter's unresponsive body. Passers-by stop, and now he can remove his dark glasses and join them as one more curious onlooker.

The mother is crying, clinging to her daughter. A young man gently pushes her away and attempts mouth-to-mouth resuscitation, but soon gives up; Olivia's face already has a slight purple tinge to it.

'Someone call an ambulance!'

Several people dial the same number, all of them feeling useful, important, caring. He can already hear the sound of the siren in the distance. The mother's screams are growing louder. A young woman tries to put a comforting arm around her, but the mother pushes her away. Someone attempts to sit the body up, and someone else tells them to lay her down again because it's too late to do anything.

'It's probably a drug overdose,' the person next to him says. 'Young people today are a lost cause.'

Those who hear the comment nod sagely. Igor remains impassive while he watches the paramedics unload their equipment from the ambulance, apply electric shocks to Olivia's heart, while a more experienced doctor stands by, not saying a word, because although he knows there's nothing to be done, he doesn't want his colleagues to be accused of negligence. They place Olivia's body on the stretcher and put it in the ambulance, the mother still clinging to her daughter. After a brief discussion, they allow the mother to get in too, and the ambulance speeds away.

No more than ten minutes have passed between the couple discovering the body and the ambulance leaving. The father is still standing there, stunned, not knowing where to go or what to do. Forgetting who he's speaking to, the same person who made the comment about a drug overdose, goes over to the father and gives him his version of the facts:

'Don't worry, sir. This kind of thing happens every day around here.'

The father does not respond. He's still holding his mobile phone and staring into space. He either doesn't understand the remark or has no idea what it is that happens every day, or else he's in a state of shock that has sent him immediately into some unknown dimension where pain does not exist.

The crowd disperses as quickly as it appeared. Only two people remain: the father still clutching his phone and the man who has now taken off his dark glasses and is holding them in his hand.

'Did you know the girl?' Igor asks.

There is no reply.

It's best to do as everyone else has done, keep walking along the Boulevard de la Croisette and see what else is happening on this sunny morning in Cannes. Like the girl's father, he doesn't know quite what he is feeling: he has destroyed a world he will never be able to rebuild, even if he had all the power in the world. Did Ewa deserve that? From the womb of that young woman, Olivia – the fact that he knows her name troubles him greatly because that means she's no longer just a face in the crowd – might have sprung a genius who would have gone on to discover a cure for cancer or drafted an agreement that would ensure that the world could finally live in peace. He has destroyed not just one person, but all the future generations that might have sprung from her. What has he done? Was love, however great and however intense, sufficient justification for that?

He had chosen the wrong person as his first victim. Her death will never make the news and Ewa won't understand the message.

Don't think about it, it's done now. You have prepared yourself to go much further than this, so carry on. The girl will understand that her death was not in vain, but was a sacrifice in the name of a greater love. Look around you, see what's happening in the city, behave like a normal citizen. You've already had your fair share of suffering in this life; now you deserve a little peace and comfort.

Enjoy the Festival. This is what you have been preparing yourself for.

Even if he'd had his swimming things with him, he would have found it difficult to get anywhere near the sea shore. The big hotels had, it seems, acquired the rights to great swathes of beach which they had filled with their chairs, logos, waiters and bodyguards, who, at every entry point, demanded the guest's room key or some other form of identification. Other areas were occupied by huge white marquees, where some production company, brewery or cosmetics firm was launching its latest product at a so-called 'lunch'. People here were dressed normally, if by 'normal' you mean a baseball cap, bright shirt and light-coloured trousers for men, and jewellery, loose top, Bermudas and low-heeled shoes for women.

Dark glasses were de rigueur for both sexes, and there was little bare flesh on show because members of the Superclass were too old for that now, and any such display would be considered ridiculous or, rather, pathetic.

Igor noticed one other thing: the mobile phone. The most important item of clothing.

It was essential to be receiving a constant stream of messages or calls, to be prepared to interrupt any conversation in order to answer a call that was not in the least urgent, to stand keying in endless texts via an SMS. They had all forgotten that these initials mean Short Message Service and instead used the key pad as if it were a typewriter. It was slow, awkward and could cause serious damage to the thumb, but what did it matter? At that very moment, not only in Cannes, but in the whole world, the ether was being filled with messages like 'Good morning, my love, I woke up thinking about you and I'm so glad to have you in my life', 'I'll be home in ten minutes, please have my lunch ready and check that my clothes were sent to the laundry', or 'The party here is a real drag, but I haven't got anywhere else to go, where are you?' Things that take five minutes to be written down and only ten seconds to be spoken, but that's the way the world is. Igor knows all about this because he has earned hundreds of millions of dollars thanks to the fact that the phone is no longer simply a method of communicating with others, but a thread of hope, a way of believing that you're not alone, a way of showing others how important you are.

And it was leading the world into a state of utter madness. For a mere 5 euros a month, via an ingenious system created in London, a call centre would send you a standard message every three minutes. When you know you're going to be talking to someone you want to impress, you just have to dial a particular number to activate the system. The phone rings, you pick it up, open the message, read it quickly and say 'Oh, that can wait' (of course it can: it was written to order). This way, the person you're talking to feels important, and things move along more quickly because he realises he's in the presence of a very busy person. Three minutes later, the conversation is interrupted by another message, the pressure mounts, and the user of the service can decide whether it's worth turning off his phone for a quarter of an hour or lying and saying that he really must take this call, and so rid himself of a disagreeable companion.

There is only one situation in which all mobile phones must be turned off. Not at formal suppers, in the middle of a play, during the key moment in a film or while an opera singer is attempting the most difficult of arias; we've all heard someone's mobile phone go off in such circumstances. No, the only time when people are genuinely concerned that their phone might prove dangerous is when they get on a plane and hear the usual lie: 'All mobile phones must be switched off during the flight because they might interfere with the on-board systems.' We all believe this and do as the flight attendants ask.

Igor knew when this myth had been created: for years now, airlines had been doing their best to convince passengers to use the phones attached to their seat. These cost $10 a minute and use the same transmission system as mobile phones. The strategy didn't work, but the myth lingered on; they had simply forgotten to remove the warning from the list of dos and don'ts that the flight attendant has to read out before take-off. What no one knew was that on every flight, there were always at least two or three passengers who forgot to turn their phones off, and besides, laptops access the Internet using exactly the same system as mobiles. And no plane anywhere in the world has yet fallen out of the sky because of that.

Now they were trying to modify the warning without alarming the passengers too much and without dropping the price. You could use your mobile phone as long as it was one you could put into flight mode. Such phones cost four times as much. No one has ever explained what 'flight mode' is, but if people choose to be taken in like this, that's their problem.

He keeps walking. He's troubled by the last look the girl had given him before she died, but prefers not to think about it.

More bodyguards, more dark glasses, more bikinis on the beach, more light-coloured clothes and jewellery attending 'lunches', more people hurrying along as if they had something very important to do that morning, more photographers on every corner attempting the impossible task of snapping something unusual, more magazines and free newspapers about what's happening at the Festival, more people handing out flyers to the poor mortals who haven't been invited to lunch in one of the white marquees, flyers advertising restaurants on the top of the hill, far from everything, where little is heard of what goes on in Boulevard de la Croisette, up there where models rent apartments for the duration of the Festival, hoping they'll be summoned to an audition that will change their lives for ever.

All so unsurprising. All so predictable. If he were to go into one of those marquees now, no one would dare ask for his identification because it's still early and the promoters will be afraid that no one will come. In half an hour's time, though, depending on how things go, the security guards will be given express orders to let in only pretty, unaccompanied girls.

Why not try it out?

He follows his impulse; after all, he's on a mission. He goes down some steps, which lead not to the beach, but to a large white marquee with plastic windows, air-conditioning and white chairs and tables, largely empty. One of the security guards asks if he has an invitation, and he says that he does. He pretends to search his pockets. A receptionist dressed in red asks if she can help.

He offers her his business card, bearing the logo of his phone company and his name, Igor Malev, President. He's sure his name is on the list, he says, but he must have left his invitation at the hotel; he's been at a series of meetings and forgot to bring it with him. The receptionist welcomes him and invites him in; she has learned to judge men and women by the way they dress, and 'President' means the same thing worldwide. Besides, he's the President of a Russian company! And everyone knows how rich Russians like to show off their wealth. There was no need to check the list.

Igor enters, heads straight for the bar – it's a very well-equipped marquee; there's even a dance floor – and orders a pineapple juice because it suits the atmosphere and, more importantly, because the drink, decorated with a tiny, blue Japanese umbrella, comes complete with a black straw.

He sits down at one of the many empty tables. Among the few people present is a man in his fifties, with hennaed mahogany brown hair, fake tan and a body honed in one of those gyms that promise eternal youth. He's wearing a torn T-shirt and is sitting with two other men, who are both dressed in impeccable designer suits. The two men turn to face Igor, and he immediately turns his head slightly, but continues to study them from behind his dark glasses. The men in suits try to work out who this new arrival is, then lose interest.

Igor's interest, however, increases.

The man does not even have a mobile phone on the table, although his two assistants are constantly fielding calls.

Given that this badly dressed, arrogant fellow has been let into the marquee; given that he has his mobile phone turned off; given that the waiter keeps coming up to him and asking if he wants anything; given that he doesn't even deign to respond, but merely waves him away, he is obviously someone very important.

Igor takes a fifty-euro note out of his pocket and gives it to the waiter who has just started laying the table.

'Who's the gentleman in the faded blue T-shirt?' he asks, glancing in the direction of the other table.

'Javits Wild. He's a very important man.'

Excellent. After someone as insignificant as the girl at the beach, a figure like Javits Wild would be ideal – not famous, but important. One of the people who decides who should be in the spotlight and who feels no need to take much care over his own appearance because he knows exactly who he is. He's in charge of pulling the strings, and the puppets feel themselves to be the most privileged and envied people on the planet, until one day, for whatever reason, the puppeteer decides to cut the strings, and the puppets fall down, lifeless and powerless.

He's clearly a member of the Superclass, which means that he has false friends and many enemies.

'One other question. Would it be acceptable to destroy a universe in the name of a greater love?'

The waiter laughs.

'Are you God or just gay?'

'Neither, but thank you for your answer.'

He realises he should not have asked that question. Firstly, because he doesn't need anyone's support to justify what he's doing; he's convinced that since everyone will die one day, some must do so in the name of something greater. That's how it's been since the beginning of time, when men sacrificed themselves in order to feed their tribe, when virgins were handed over to the priests to placate the wrath of dragons and gods. The second reason is because he has now drawn attention to himself and indicated an interest in the man on the next table.

The waiter's sure to forget, but there's no need to take unnecessary risks. He tells himself that at a Festival such as this, it's only normal that people should want to know about other people, and even more normal that such information should be rewarded. He himself has done the same thing hundreds of times in restaurants all over the world, and others had doubtless done the same with him. Waiters aren't just accustomed to being given money to supply a name or a better table or to send a discreet message, they almost expect it.

No, the waiter wouldn't remember anything. Igor knows that his next victim is there before him. If he succeeds, and if the waiter is questioned, the waiter will say that the only odd thing to happen that day was a man asking him if he thought it was acceptable to destroy a universe in the name of a greater love.

He might not even remember that much. The police will ask: 'What did he look like?' and the waiter will reply: 'I didn't pay much attention, to be honest, but I know he said he wasn't gay.' The police – accustomed to the kind of French intellectual who sits in bars and comes up with weird theories and complicated analyses of, for example, the sociology of film festivals – would quietly let the matter drop.

Something else was bothering Igor though.

The name or names.

He had killed before – with weapons and the blessing of his country. He didn't know how many people he had killed, but he had rarely seen their faces and certainly never asked their names. Knowing someone's name meant knowing that the other person was a human being and not 'the enemy'. Knowing someone's name transformed them into a unique and special individual, with a past and a future, with ancestors and possibly descendants, a person who has known triumphs and failures. People are their names; they're proud of them; they repeat them thousands of times in their lifetime and identify with them. It's the first word they learn after 'Daddy' and 'Mummy'.

Olivia. Javits. Igor. Ewa.

Someone's spirit, however, has no name; it is pure truth and inhabits a particular body for a certain period of time, and will, one day, leave it, and God won't bother asking 'What's your name?' when the soul arrives at the final judgment. God will ask only: 'Did you love while you were alive?' For that is the essence of life: the ability to love, not the name we carry around on our passport, business card and identity card. The great mystics changed their names, and sometimes abandoned them altogether. When John the Baptist was asked who he was, he said only: 'I am the voice of one crying in the wilderness.' When Jesus found the man on whom he would build his church, he ignored the fact that the man in question had spent his entire life answering to the name of Simon and called him Peter. When

Moses asked God his name, back came the reply: 'I am who I am.'

Perhaps he should look for another victim; one named victim was enough: Olivia. At this precise moment, however, he feels that he cannot turn back, but he decides that he will not ask the name of the next world he destroys. He can't turn back because he wants to do justice to the poor, vulnerable girl on the bench by the beach – such a sweet, easy victim. This new challenge – this sweaty, pseudo-athletic, henna-haired man with the bored expression and who is clearly someone very powerful – is much more difficult. The two men in suits are not just assistants; he notices that every now and then, they look around the tent, watching everything that's going on nearby. If he is to be worthy of Ewa and fair to Olivia, he must be brave.

He leaves the straw in the pineapple juice. People are beginning to arrive. He has to wait for the place to fill up, but not too long. He hadn't planned to destroy a world in broad daylight, in the middle of the Boulevard in Cannes, and he doesn't know exactly how to carry out this next project. Something tells him, though, that he has chosen the perfect place.

His thoughts are no longer with the poor young woman by the beach; adrenaline is filling his blood, his heart is beating faster, he's excited and happy.

Javits Wild wouldn't be wasting his time here just to get a free meal at one of the thousands of parties to which he must be invited every year. He must be here for some specific reason or to meet a particular person. That reason or person would doubtless be Igor's best alibi.

12.26 p.m.

Javits watches the other guests arriving. The place is getting crowded, and he thinks what he always thinks:

'What am I doing here? I don't need this. In fact, I need very little from anyone – I have all I want. I'm a big name in the movie world, I can have any woman I desire, even though I dress badly. In fact, I make a point of being badly dressed. Long gone are the days when I had only one suit, and, on the rare occasions when I received an invitation from the Superclass (after much crawling, begging and making promises), I would prepare myself for a lunch like this as if it were the most important occasion of my life. Now I know that the only thing that changes are the cities these lunches are held in; otherwise, it's all utterly boring and predictable.

'People will come up to me and tell me they adore my work. Others will call me a hero and thank me for giving movie mavericks a chance. Pretty, intelligent women, who are not taken in by appearances, will notice the people gathering round my table and ask the waiter who I am and immediately find some way of approaching me, certain that the only thing I'm interested in is sex. Every single one of them has some favour to ask of me. That's why they praise and flatter me and offer me what they think I need. But all I want is to be left alone.

'I've been to thousands of parties like this, and I'm not here in this marquee for any particular reason, except that I can't sleep, even though I flew to France in my private jet, a technological marvel capable of flying at an altitude of over 36,000 feet from California all the way to Cannes without having to make a refuelling stop. I changed the original configuration of the cabin. It can comfortably carry eighteen passengers, but I reduced the number of seats to six and kept the cabin separate for the four crew members. Someone's always sure to ask: "May I come with you?" And now I have the perfect excuse: "Sorry, there's no room." '

Javits had equipped his new toy, which cost around $40 million, with two beds, a conference table, a shower, a Miranda sound system (Bang & Olufsen had an excellent design and a good PR campaign, but they were now a thing of the past), two coffee machines, a microwave oven for the crew and an electric oven for him (because he's hates re-heated food). Javits only drinks champagne, and whoever wishes to is more than welcome to share a bottle of Moët & Chandon 1961 with him. However, the 'cellar' on the plane had every drink any guest might conceivably want. And then there were the two 21-inch LCD screens ready to show the most recent films, even those that hadn't yet made it into the cinemas.

The jet was one of the most advanced in the world (although the French insisted that the Dassault Falcon was even better), but regardless of how much money he had, he couldn't change the clocks in Europe. It was now 3.43 a.m. in Los Angeles, and he was just beginning to feel really tired. He had been awake all night, going from one party to the next, answering the same two idiotic questions that began every conversation:

'How was your flight?'

To which Javits always responded with a question:

'Why?'

People didn't know quite what to say and so they smiled awkwardly and moved on to the next question on the list:

'Are you staying here long?'

And Javits would again ask: 'Why?' Then he would pretend he had to answer his mobile phone, make his excuses and move on with his two inseparable besuited friends in tow.

He met no one interesting. But then who would a man who has almost everything money can buy find interesting? He had tried to change his friends and meet people who had nothing to do with the world of cinema: philosophers, writers, jugglers, executives of food-manufacturing companies. At first, it all went swimmingly, until the inevitable question: 'Would you like to read a script I've written?' Or the second most inevitable question: 'I have a friend who has always wanted to be an actor/actress. Would you mind meeting him/her?'

Yes, he would. He had other things to do in life apart from work. He used to fly once a month to Alaska, go into the first bar, get drunk, eat pizza, wander about in the wild and talk to the people who lived in the small towns up there. He worked out for two hours a day at his private gym, but the doctors had warned him he could still end up with heart problems. He didn't care that much about being physically fit; what he really wanted was to off-load a little of the constant tension that seemed to weigh on him every second of the day, to do some meditation and heal the wounds to his soul. When he was in the country, he always asked the people he chanced to meet what 'normal life' was like, because he had forgotten. The answers varied, and he gradually came to realise that, even when he was surrounded by other people, he was absolutely alone in the world.

He decided to draw up a list of what constituted normal attitudes and behaviour, based on what people did rather than on what they said.

Javits glances around. There's a man in dark glasses drinking a fruit juice. He seems oblivious to his surroundings and is staring out to sea as if he were somewhere far from there. He's smartly dressed and good-looking, with greying hair. He was one of the first to arrive and must know who Javits is, and yet he's made no effort to come and introduce himself. It was brave of him to sit there alone like that. Being alone in Cannes is anathema; it means that no one is interested in you, that you're unimportant or don't know anyone.

He envies that man, who probably doesn't fit the list of 'normal' behaviour he always keeps in his pocket. He seems so independent and free; if Javits weren't feeling so tired, he would really like to talk to him.

He turns to one of his 'friends'.

'What does being normal mean?'

'Is your conscience troubling you? Have you done something you shouldn't have?'

Javits has clearly asked the wrong question of the wrong man. His companion will perhaps assume that he's regretting what he's made of his life and that he wants to start anew, but that isn't it at all. And if he does have regrets, it's too late to begin again; he knows the rules of the game.

'I asked you what being normal means?'

One of the 'friends' looks bewildered. The other keeps surveying the tent, watching people come and go.

'Living like someone who lacks all ambition,' the first 'friend' says at last.

Javits takes his list out of his pocket and puts it on the table.

'I always have this with me and I add to it all the time.'

The 'friend' says that he can't look at it now because he has to keep alert to what's going on around them. The other man, though, more relaxed and confident, reads the list out loud:

1. Normal is anything that makes us forget who we are and what we want; that way we can work in order to produce, reproduce and earn money.
2. Setting out rules for waging war (the Geneva Convention).
3. Spending years studying at university only to find at the end of it all that you're unemployable.

4. Working from nine till five every day at something that gives you no pleasure at all just so that, after thirty years, you can retire.
5. Retiring and discovering that you no longer have enough energy to enjoy life and dying a few years later of sheer boredom.
6. Using botox.
7. Believing that power is much more important than money and that money is much more important than happiness.
8. Making fun of anyone who seeks happiness rather than money and accusing them of 'lacking ambition'.
9. Comparing objects like cars, houses, clothes, and defining life according to those comparisons, instead of trying to discover the real reason for being alive.
10. Never talking to strangers. Saying nasty things about the neighbours.
11. Believing that your parents are always right.
12. Getting married, having children and staying together long after all love has died, saying that it's for the good of the children (who are, apparently, deaf to the constant rows).

12a.Criticising anyone who tries to be different.

14. Waking up each morning to an hysterical alarm clock on the bedside table.
15. Believing absolutely everything that appears in print.
16. Wearing a scrap of coloured cloth around your neck, even though it serves no useful purpose, but which answers to the name of 'tie'.
17. Never asking a direct question, even though the other person can guess what it is you want to know.
18. Keeping a smile on your lips even when you're on the verge of tears. Feeling sorry for those who show their feelings.
19. Believing that art is either worth a fortune or worth nothing at all.

20. Despising anything that was easy to achieve because if no sacrifice was involved, it obviously isn't worth having.
21. Following fashion trends, however ridiculous or uncomfortable.
22. Believing that all famous people have tons of money saved up.
23. Investing a lot of time and money in external beauty and caring little about inner beauty.
24. Using every means possible to show that, although you're just an ordinary human being, you're far above other mortals.
25. Never looking anyone in the eye when you're travelling on public transport, in case it's interpreted as a sign you're trying to get off with them.
26. Standing facing the door in a lift and pretending you're the only person there, regardless of how crowded it is.
27. Never laughing too loudly in a restaurant however good the joke.
28. In the northern hemisphere, always dressing according to the season: bare arms in Spring (however cold it is) and woollen jacket in Autumn (however hot it is).
29. In the southern hemisphere, covering the Christmas tree with fake snow even though winter has nothing to do with the birth of Christ.
30. Assuming, as you grow older, that you're the guardian of the world's wisdom, even if you haven't necessarily lived enough to know what's right and wrong.
31. Going to a charity tea party and thinking that you've done your bit towards putting an end to social inequality in the world.
32. Eating three times a day even if you're not hungry.
33. Believing that other people are always better than you – better looking, more capable, richer, more intelligent – and that it's very dangerous to step outside your own limits, so it's best to do nothing.

34. Using your car as a weapon and as impenetrable armour.
35. Swearing when in heavy traffic.
36. Believing that everything your child does wrong is entirely down to the company he or she keeps.
37. Marrying the first person who offers you a decent position in society. Love can wait.
38. Always saying 'I tried' when you didn't really try at all.
39. Postponing doing the really interesting things in life for later, when you won't have the energy.
40. Avoiding depression with large daily doses of television.
41. Believing that you can be sure of everything you've achieved.
42. Assuming that women don't like football and that men aren't interested in home decoration and cooking.
43. Blaming the government for all the bad things that happen.
44. Thinking that being a good, decent, respectable person will mean that others will see you as weak, vulnerable and easy to manipulate.
45. Being equally convinced that aggression and rudeness are synonymous with having a 'powerful personality'.
46. Being afraid of having an endoscopy (if you're a man) and giving birth (if you're a woman).

The 'friend' laughs.

'You should make a film on the subject,' he says.

'Not again,' Javits thinks. 'They have no idea. They're with me all the time, but they still don't understand what I do. I don't make films.'

All films start out in the mind of a so-called producer. He's read a book, say, or had a brilliant idea while driving along the freeways of Los Angeles (which is really a large suburb in search of a city). Unfortunately, he's alone, both in the car and in his desire to transform that brilliant idea into something that can be seen on the screen.

He finds out if the film rights to the book are still available. If the response is negative, he goes in search of another product – after all, more than 60,000 books are published each year in the United States alone. If the response is positive, he phones the author and makes the lowest possible offer, which is usually accepted because it's not only actors and actresses who like to be associated with the dream machine. Every author feels more important when his or her words are transformed into images.

They arrange to have lunch. The producer says that the book is 'a work of art and highly cinematographic' and that the writer is 'a genius deserving of recognition'. The writer explains that he spent five years working on the book and asks to be allowed to help in the writing of the script. 'No, really, you shouldn't do that, it's an entirely different medium,' comes the reply, 'but I know you'll love the result.' Then he adds: 'The film will be totally true to the book', which, as both of them know, is a complete and utter lie.

The writer decides that he should agree to the conditions, promising himself that next time will be different. He accepts. The producer now says that they have to interest one of the big studios because they need financial backing for the project. He names a few stars he claims to have lined up for the lead roles – which is another complete and utter lie, but one that is always wheeled out and always works as a seduction technique. He buys what is known as an 'option', that is, he pays around $10,000 to retain the rights for three years. And then what happens? 'Then we'll pay ten times that amount and you'll have a right to 2 percent of the net profits.' That's the financial part of the conversation over with, because the writer is convinced he'll earn a fortune from his slice of the profits.

If he were to ask around, he'd soon find out that the Hollywood accountants somehow manage it so that no film *ever* makes a profit.

Lunch ends with the producer handing the writer a huge contract and asking if he could possibly sign it now, so that the studio will know that the product is definitely theirs. With his eyes fixed on that (non-existent) percentage and on the possibility of seeing his name in lights (which won't happen either – at most there'll be a line in the credits, saying: 'based on the book by ...'), the writer signs the contract without giving the matter much thought.

Vanity of vanities, all is vanity, and there is nothing new under the sun, as Solomon said more than three thousand years ago.

The producer starts knocking on the doors of various studios. He's known in the industry already, and so some of those doors open, but his proposal is not always accepted. In that case, he doesn't even bother to ring up the author and invite him to lunch again, he just writes him a letter saying that, despite his enthusiasm for the project, the movie industry isn't yet ready for that kind of story and he's returning the contract (which he, of course, did not sign).

If the proposal is accepted, the producer then goes to the lowest and least well-paid person in the hierarchy: the screenwriter, the person who will spend days, weeks and months writing and rewriting the original idea or the screen adaptation. The scripts are sent to the producer (but never to the author), who, out of habit, automatically rejects the first draft, knowing that the screenwriter can always do better. More weeks and months of coffee and insomnia for the bright young talent (or old hack – there are no halfway houses) who rewrites each scene, which are then rejected or reshaped by the producer (and the screenwriter thinks: 'If he can write so damn well, why doesn't he write the whole thing?' Then he remembers his salary and goes quietly back to his computer.)

Finally, the script is almost ready. At this point, the producer draws up a list of demands: the removal of any political references that might upset a more conservative audience; more kissing, because women like that kind of thing; a story with a beginning, middle and an end, and a hero who moves everyone to tears with his self-sacrifice and devotion; and one character who loses a loved one at the start of the film and finds him or her again at the end. In fact, most film scripts can be summed up very briefly as: Man loves woman. Man loses woman. Man gets woman back. Ninety per cent of all films are variations on that same theme.

Films that break this rule have to be very violent to make up for it, or have loads of crowd-pleasing special effects. And since this tried and tested formula is a sure-fire winner, why take any unnecessary risks?

Armed with what he considers to be a well-written story, who does the producer seek out next? The studio who financed the project. The studio, however, has a long line of films to place in the ever-diminishing number of cinemas around the world. They ask him to wait a little or to find an independent distributor, first making sure that the producer signs another gigantic contract (which even takes into account exclusive rights 'outside of Planet Earth'), taking full responsibility for all money spent.

And that's where people like Javits come in! The independent distributor can walk down the street without being recognised, although at media-fests like this everyone knows who he is. He's the person who didn't come up with the idea, didn't work on the script and didn't invest a cent.

Javits is the intermediary – the distributor!

He receives the producer in a tiny office (the big plane, the house with the swimming pool, the invitations to parties all over the world are purely for his enjoyment – the producer doesn't even merit a mineral water). He takes the DVD home with him. He watches the first five minutes. If he likes it, he watches to the end, but this only happens with one out of every hundred new films he's given. Then he spends ten cents on a phone call and tells the producer to come back on a certain date and at a certain time.

'We'll sign,' he says, as if he were doing the producer a big favour. 'I'll distribute the film.'

The producer tries to negotiate. He wants to know how many cinemas in how many countries and under what conditions. These, however, are pointless questions because he knows what the distributor will say: 'That depends on the reactions we get at the pre-launch screenings.' The product is shown to selected audiences from all social classes, people specially chosen by market-research companies. The results are analysed by professionals. If the results are positive, another ten cents gets spent on a phone call, and, the following day, Javits hands the producer three copies of yet another vast contract. The producer asks to be given time for his lawyer to read it. Javits says he has nothing against him doing that, but he needs to finalise that season's programme now and can't guarantee that by the time the producer gets back to him he won't have selected another film.

The producer reads only the clause that tells him how much he's going to earn. He's pleased with what he sees and so he signs. He doesn't want to miss this opportunity.

Years have passed since he sat down with the writer to discuss making a film of his book and he's quite forgotten that he is now in exactly the same situation.

Vanity of vanities, all is vanity, and there is nothing new under the sun, as Solomon said more than three thousand years ago.

Javits watches the marquee filling up with guests and again asks himself what he's doing there. He controls more than five hundred cinemas in the United States and has an exclusive contract with another five thousand around the world, where exhibitors are obliged to buy everything he offers them, even if the films don't always work out. They know that one box-office success more than makes up for the other five that fail to pull in the crowds. They rely on Javits, the independent megadistributor, the hero who managed to break the monopoly of the big studios and become a legend in the film world.

No one has ever asked how he did this, but since he continues to give them one big success for every five failures (the average in the big studios is one blockbuster for every nine flops), it really doesn't matter.

Javits, however, knows how he became so successful, which is why he never goes anywhere without his two 'friends', who are, at that moment, busily answering calls, arranging meetings and accepting invitations. They both have reasonably normal physiques, not like the burly bouncers on the door, but they're worth a whole army. They trained in Israel and have served in Uganda, Argentina and Panama. One fields phone calls and the other is constantly looking around, memorising each person, each movement, each gesture. They alternate these tasks because, like simultaneous translators and air-traffic controllers, they need to rest every fifteen minutes.

What is he doing at this 'lunch'? He could have stayed at the hotel, trying to get some sleep. He's tired of being fawned over and praised, and of having to smile every minute and tell someone that it's really not worth his while giving him his card because he'll only lose it. When they insist, he asks them gently to speak to one of his secretaries (duly housed at another luxury hotel on the Boulevard de la Croisette, where they are not allowed to sleep, but must answer the phone that rings non-stop or reply to the e-mails flooding in from cinemas all over the world, along with the promises of increased penis size or multiple orgasms that manage to elude all the spam filters). Depending on how he nods his head, one of his two assistants will either give the person the secretary's address or phone number or say that unfortunately they're fresh out of cards.

Yes, what is he doing at this 'lunch'? He would be sleeping now in Los Angeles, however late he might have got home from a party. Javits knows the answer, but he doesn't want to accept it: he's afraid of being alone. He envies the man who arrived earlier and sat drinking his fruit juice, staring off into the distance, apparently relaxed and unconcerned about trying to look busy or important. He decides to invite him to join him in a drink, but notices he's no longer there.

Just then, he feels something prick him in the back.

'Mosquitos! That's what I hate about beach parties.'

When he goes to scratch the bite, he finds a small needle. It must be some stupid prank. He looks behind him and, about two yards away, separated from him by various other guests, a black guy with dreadlocks is laughing loudly, while a group of women gaze at him with mingled respect and desire.

He's too tired to react to this provocation. Best let the guy play the fool if that's the only way he can impress other people.

'Idiot.'

His two companions react to the sudden change in posture of the man they are paid to protect at the rate of $435 a day. One of them raises his hand to his right shoulder, where he keeps an automatic pistol in a holster that is entirely invisible beneath his jacket. The other man gets discreetly to his feet (they are at a party, after all) and places himself between the black man and his boss.

'It was nothing,' says Javits. 'Just a prank.'

He shows them the needle.

These two idiots are prepared for attacks with firearms and knives, for acts of physical aggression or attempts on their boss's life. They're always the first to enter his hotel room, ready to shoot if necessary. They can sense when someone's carrying a weapon (a common-enough occurrence now in many cities of the world) and they don't take their eyes off that person until they're sure he's harmless. When Javits gets into a lift, he stands sandwiched between them, their two bodies forming a kind of wall. He has never seen them take out their guns because, if they did so, they would use them. They usually resolve any problem with a look or a few quiet words.

Problems? He has never had any problems since he acquired his two 'friends', as if their mere presence were enough to drive away evil spirits and evil intentions.

'That man, one of the first people to arrive, who sat down alone at that table over there,' says one of them. 'He was armed, wasn't he?'

The other man murmurs something like 'Possibly', but the man had left the party some time ago. And he had been watched the whole time because they couldn't tell what exactly he was looking at from behind his dark glasses.

They relax. One of them starts answering the phone again, the other fixes his gaze on the Jamaican, who looks fearlessly back. There's something strange about that man, but one false move on his part and he'll be wearing false teeth from now on. It would all be done as discreetly as possible, on the beach, far from prying eyes, and by only one of them, while the other stood waiting, finger on the trigger. Sometimes, though, such provocative acts are a ruse to get the bodyguard away from the intended victim. They're used to such tricks.

'Fine …'

'No, it's not fine. Call an ambulance. I can't move my hand.'

12.44 p.m.

What luck!

The last thing she was expecting that morning was to meet the man who would – she was sure – change her life. But there he is, as sloppily dressed as ever, sitting with two friends, because powerful people don't need to show how powerful they are, they don't even need bodyguards.

Maureen has a theory that the people at Cannes can be divided into two categories:

(a) the tanned, who spend the whole day in the sun (they are already winners) and have the necessary badge to gain entry to certain restricted areas of the Festival. They arrive back at their hotels to find several invitations awaiting them, most of which will be thrown in the bin.

(b) the pale, who scurry from one gloomy office to the next, watching auditions, and either seeing some really good films that will be lost in the welter of other things on offer, or having to put up with some real horrors that might just win a place in the sun (among the tanned) because the makers know the right people.

Javits Wild, of course, sports an enviable tan.

The Festival that takes over this small city in the south of France for twelve days, putting up prices, allowing only authorised cars to drive through the streets, and filling the airport with private jets and the beaches with models, isn't just a red carpet surrounded by photographers, a carpet along which the big stars walk on their way into the Palais des Congrès. Cannes isn't about fashion, it's about cinema!

What strikes you most is the luxury and the glamour, but the real heart of the Festival is the film industry's huge parallel market: buyers and sellers from all over the world who come together to do deals on films that have already been made or to talk investments and ideas. On an average day, 400 movies are shown, most of them in apartments hired for the duration, with people perched uncomfortably on beds, complaining about the heat and demanding that their every whim be met, from bottles of mineral water up, and leaving the people showing the film with their nerves in tatters and frozen smiles on their faces, for it's essential to agree to everything, to grant every wish, because what matters is having the chance to show something that has probably been years in the making.

However, while these 4,800 new productions are fighting tooth and nail for a chance to leave that hotel room and get shown in a proper cinema, the world of dreams is setting off in a different direction: the new technologies are gaining ground, people don't leave their houses so much any more because they don't feel safe, or because they have too much work or because of all those cable TV stations where you can usually choose from about 500 films a day and pay almost nothing.

Worse still, the Internet has made anyone and everyone a film-maker. Specialist portals show films of babies walking, men and women being decapitated in wars, or women who exhibit their bodies merely for the pleasure of knowing that the person watching them will be enjoying their own moment of solitary pleasure, films of people 'freezing' in Grand Central Station, of traffic accidents, sports clips and fashion shows, films made with hidden video cameras intent on embarrassing the poor innocents who happen to pass.

Of course, people do still go out, but they prefer to spend their money on restaurant meals and designer clothes because they can get everything else on their high-definition TV screens or on their computers.

The days when everyone knew who had won the Palme d'Or are long gone. Now, if you ask who won last year, even people who were actually there at the Festival won't be able to remember. 'Some Romanian, wasn't it?' says one. 'I'm not sure, but I think it was a German film,' says another. They'll sneak off to consult the catalogue and discover that it was an Italian, whose films, it turns out, are only shown at arts cinemas.

After a period of intense competition with video rentals, cinemas started to prosper again, but now they seem to be entering another period of decline, having to compete with Internet rentals, with pirating and those DVDs of old films that are given away free with newspapers. This makes distribution an even more savage affair. If one of the big studios considers a new release to be a particularly large investment, they'll try to ensure that it's being shown in the maximum number of cinemas at the same time, leaving little space for any other new film venturing onto the market.

And the few adventurous souls who decide to take the risk – despite all the arguments against – discover too late that it isn't enough to have a quality product. The cost of getting a film into cinemas in the large capitals of the world is prohibitive, what with full-page advertisements in newspapers and magazines, receptions, press officers, promotion junkets, ever more expensive teams of people, sophisticated filming equipment and increasingly scarce labour. And the most difficult problem of all: finding someone who will distribute the film.

And yet every year it goes on, the trudging from place to place, the appointments, the Superclass who are interested in everything except what's being shown on the screen, the companies prepared to pay a tenth of what is reasonable just to give some film-maker the 'honour' of having his or her work shown on television, the requests that the film be reworked so as not to offend families, the demands for the film to be re-cut, the promises (not always kept) that if the script is changed completely to focus on one particular theme, a contract will be issued next year.

People listen and accept because they have no option. The Superclass rules the world; their arguments are subtle, their voices soft, their smiles discreet, but their decisions are final. They know. They accept or reject. They have the power. And power doesn't negotiate with anyone, only with itself. However, all was not lost. In the world of fiction and in the real world, there is always a hero.

And Maureen is staring proudly at one such hero now! The great meeting that is finally going to take place in two days' time after nearly three years of work, dreams, phone calls, trips to Los Angeles, presents, favours asked of friends in her Bank of Favours and the influence of an ex-boyfriend of hers, who had studied with her at film school then decided it was much safer to work for an important film magazine than risk losing both his head and his money.

'I'll talk to Javits,' the ex-boyfriend had said. 'But he doesn't need anyone, not even the journalists who can promote or destroy his products. He's above all that. We once tried getting together an article trying to find out how it is that he has all these cinema owners eating out of his hand, but no one he works with was prepared to say anything. I'll talk to him, but I can't put any pressure on him.'

He did talk to him and got him to watch *The Secrets of the Cellar*. The following day, she received a phone call, saying that Javits would meet her in Cannes.

At the time, Maureen didn't even dare to say that she was just ten minutes by taxi from his office; instead they arranged to meet in this far-off French city. She bought a plane ticket to

Paris, caught a train that took all day to reach Cannes, showed her voucher to the bad-tempered manager of a cheap hotel, installed herself in her single room where she had to climb over her luggage to reach the bathroom and (again thanks to her ex-boyfriend) wangled invitations to a few second-rate events – a promotion for a new brand of vodka or the launch of a new line in T-shirts – but it was far too late to apply for the pass that would allow her into the Palais des Festivals et des Congrès.

She has overspent her budget, travelled for more than twenty hours, but she will at least get her ten minutes. And she's sure that she'll emerge with a contract and a future before her. Yes, the movie industry is in crisis, but so what? Movies (however few) are still making money, aren't they? Big cities are plastered with posters advertising new movies. And what are celebrity magazines full of? Gossip about movie stars! Maureen knows – or, rather, believes – that the death of cinema has been declared many times before, and yet still it survives. 'Cinema was dead' when television arrived. 'Cinema was dead' when video rentals arrived. 'Cinema was dead' when the Internet began allowing access to pirate sites. But cinema is still alive and well in the streets of this small Mediterranean town, which, of course, owes its fame to the Festival.

Now it's simply a case of making the most of this manna from heaven. And of accepting everything, absolutely everything. Javits Wild is here. He has seen her film. The subject of the film is spot on: sexual exploitation, voluntary or forced, was getting a lot of media attention after a series of cases that had hit the headlines worldwide. It is just the right moment for *The Secrets of the Cellar* to appear on the posters put up by the distribution chain he controlled.

Javits Wild, the rebel with a cause, the man who was revolutionising the way films reached the wider public. Only the actor Robert Redford had tried something similar with his Sundance

Film Festival for independent film-makers, but nevertheless, after decades of effort, Redford still hadn't managed to break through the barrier into a world that mobilised hundreds of millions of dollars in the United States, Europe and India. Javits, though, was a winner.

Javits Wild, the saviour of film-makers, the great legend, the ally of minority interests, the friend of artists, the new patron, who obviously used some very intelligent system (she had no idea what it was, but she knew it worked) to reach cinemas all around the world.

Javits Wild has arranged a ten-minute meeting with her in two days' time. This can mean only one thing, that he has accepted her project and that everything else is merely a matter of detail.

'I will accept everything, absolutely everything,' she repeats.

Obviously, in those ten minutes, Maureen won't have a chance to say a word about what she has been through in the eight years (yes, a quarter of her life) that have gone into making her film. There will be no point in telling him that she went to film school, directed a few commercials, made two short films that were warmly received in various small-town cinemas or in alternative bars in New York. That in order to raise the million dollars needed for a professional production, she had mortgaged the house she inherited from her parents. That this was her one chance because she didn't have another house to mortgage.

She had watched as her fellow students, after much struggling, opted for the comfortable world of commercials – of which there were more and more – or some safe but obscure job in one of the many companies that made TV series. After the warm reception given to her short films, she began to dream of higher things and then there was no stopping her.

She was convinced she had a mission: to make the world a better place for future generations, by getting together with like-minded people to show that art isn't just a way of entertaining or amusing a lost society; by exposing world leaders as the flawed people they are; by saving the children who were now dying of hunger somewhere in Africa; by speaking out about environmental problems; by putting an end to social injustice.

This was, of course, an ambitious project, but she was sure she would achieve it if only through sheer doggedness. To do this she needed to purify her soul and so she turned to the four forces that had always guided her: love, death, power and time. We must love because we are loved by God. We must be conscious of death if we are to have a proper understanding of life. We must struggle in order to grow, but without falling into the trap of the power we gain through that struggle, because we know that such power is worthless. Finally, we must accept that our eternal soul is, at this moment, caught in the web of time with all its opportunities and its limitations.

Caught in the web of time she might be, but she could still work on what gave her pleasure and filled her with enthusiasm. And through her films, she could make her contribution to a world that seemed to be disintegrating around her and could try to change reality and transform human beings.

When her father died, after complaining all his life that he had never had the chance to do what he had always dreamed of doing, she realised something very important: transformations always occur during moments of crisis.

She didn't want to end her life as he had. She wouldn't like to have to tell her daughter: 'There was something I wanted to do and there was even a point when I could have done it, but I just didn't have the courage to take the risk.' When she received her inheritance, she knew then that it had been given to her for one reason only: to allow her to fulfil her destiny.

She accepted the challenge. Unlike other adolescent girls who always dreamed of being famous actresses, her dream had been to tell stories that subsequent generations could see, smile at and dream about. Her great example was *Citizen Kane*. That first film by a radio producer who wanted to make an exposé of a powerful American press magnate became a classic not just because of its story, but because it dealt in a creative and innovative manner with the ethical and technical problems of the day. All it took was one film to gain eternal fame.

'His first film.'

It *was* possible to get it right first time. Even though its director, Orson Welles, never made anything as good again. Even though he had disappeared from the scene (that does happen) and was now only studied on courses about cinema, someone was sure to 'rediscover' his genius sooner or later. *Citizen Kane* wasn't his only legacy; he had proved to everyone that if your first step was good enough, you would never lack for invitations thereafter. And she would take up those invitations. She had promised herself that she would never forget the difficulties she had been through and that her life would contribute to dignifying human life.

And since there can only ever be one first film, she had poured all her physical efforts, her prayers and her emotional energy into one project. Unlike her friends, who were always firing off scripts, proposals and ideas only to end up working on several things at once without any of them ever really coming to anything, Maureen dedicated herself body and soul to *The Secrets of the Cellar*, the story of five nuns who are visited by a sex maniac. Instead of trying to convert him to Christian salvation, they realise that the only way they can communicate with him is by accepting the norms of his aberrant world; they decide to surrender their bodies to him so that he can understand the glory of God through love.

Her plan was a simple one. Hollywood actresses, however famous they might be, usually disappear from the cast lists when they reach thirty-five. They still continue to appear in the pages of the celebrity magazines, are seen at charity auctions and big parties; they embrace humanitarian causes, and when they realise that they really are about to vanish from the spotlight entirely, they start to get married or have messy divorces and create public scandals – and all for a few months, weeks or days of glory. In that period between unemployment and total obscurity, money is of no importance. They will take any role if it gives them a chance to appear on screen.

Maureen approached actresses who, less than a decade earlier, had been at the top of the tree, but who now sensed that the ground was beginning to slip away from under them and that they desperately needed to get back to the way things were. It was a good script; she sent it to their agents, who demanded an absurd salary and got a straightforward 'No' as an answer. Her next step was to approach each actress individually. She told them that she had the money for the project, and they all ended up accepting on the understanding that no one would know that they were working for almost nothing.

In something like the film industry, there was no point in being humble. Sometimes, the ghost of Orson Welles would appear to her in dreams: 'Try the impossible. Don't start low down because that's where you are now. Climb those rungs quickly before they take the ladder away. If you're afraid, say a prayer, but carry on.' She had an excellent script, a first-class cast, and knew that she had to produce something that was acceptable to the big studios and distributors, but without sacrificing quality. It was possible and, indeed, obligatory for art and commerce to go hand-in-hand. As for the rest, well, the rest consisted of various things: the kind of critic who's into mental masturbation and who loves films no one else understands; the small alternative circuits where the same half dozen people emerge from showings and spend the small hours in bars discussing one particular scene (whose meaning was, very possibly, quite different from the one intended when it was filmed); directors giving lectures to explain what should be obvious to the audience; trade-union meetings calling for more state aid for domestic cinema; manifestos in intellectual magazines - the result of interminable meetings, at which the same old complaints were made about the government's lack of interest in supporting the arts; the occasional letter published in the serious press and usually read only by the interested parties or the families of the interested parties.

Who changes the world? The Superclass. Those who do. Those who alter the behaviour, hearts and minds of the largest possible number of people.

That's why she wanted Javits, an Oscar and Cannes.

And since she couldn't get those things 'democratically' - other people were very willing to offer advice, but never to shoulder any of the risks - she simply gambled everything. She took on whoever was available, spent months rewriting the script, persuaded excellent - but unknown - art directors, designers and supporting actors to take part, promising them almost no money, only increased visibility in the future. They were all impressed by the names of the five main actresses ('The budget must be astronomical!'), and initially asked for large salaries, but ended up convinced that participating in such a project would look really good on their CVs. Maureen was so enthusiastic about the idea that her enthusiasm seemed to open all doors.

Now came the final step, the one that would make all the difference. It isn't enough for a writer or musician to produce something of quality; they have to make sure their work doesn't end up gathering dust on a shelf or in a drawer.

Vi-si-bi-li-ty is what's required!

She sent a copy of the film to just one person: Javits Wild. She used all her contacts. She suffered rejection, but carried on anyway. She was ignored, but that didn't diminish her courage.

She was mistreated, ridiculed, excluded, but still she believed it was possible because she had poured her life's blood into what she had done. Then her ex-boyfriend entered the scene, and Javits Wild agreed to see her film and to meet her.

She keeps her eyes on Javits all through lunch, savouring in anticipation the moment they will spend together in two days' time. Suddenly, she notices him go stiff, his eyes fixed on nothing. One of the friends with him glances behind and to the side, slips one hand inside his jacket. The other man starts frantically keying in a number on his mobile phone.

Has something happened? Surely not. The people nearest him are still talking, drinking, enjoying another day of Festival, parties, sun and nice bodies.

One of the men tries to help Javits up and make him walk, but he appears incapable of movement. It can't be anything serious. Too much drink perhaps. Tiredness. Stress. No, it can't be anything serious. She has come so far, she is so close and …

She can hear a siren in the distance. It must be the police, cutting their way through the permanently congested traffic in order to reach some important person.

One of the men puts Javits' arm around his shoulder and more or less carries him towards the door. The siren is getting closer. The other man, still with his hand inside his jacket, keeps looking in all directions. At one point, their eyes meet.

Javits is being taken up the ramp by one of his friends, and Maureen is wondering how someone so slight can possibly carry such a heavily built man and with so little apparent effort.

The sound of the siren stops right outside the marquee. Javits has, by now, disappeared with one of the friends, but the second man is walking towards her, one hand still inside his jacket.

'What happened?' she asks, frightened, because years of directing actors have taught her that this man's face is that of a professional killer, a face that looks as if it were carved out of stone.

'You know what happened,' the man says in an accent she can't identify.

'I saw that he began to feel ill, but what *did* happen?'

The man keeps his hand inside his jacket, and at that moment, it occurs to Maureen that this might be a chance to transform a minor incident into a great possibility.

'Can I help? Can I go with him?'

The hand in the jacket seems to relax a little, but the eyes watch every move she makes.

'I'll come with you. I know Javits Wild. I'm a friend of his.'

After what seems like an eternity, but which can't have been more than a fraction of a second, the man turns and walks quickly away towards the Boulevard, without saying a word.

Maureen's brain is working fast. Why did he say that she knew what had happened? And why did he suddenly lose all interest in her?

The other guests haven't noticed a thing, apart from the sound of the siren, which they probably attribute to something going on out in the street. Sirens have nothing to do with joy, sun, drinks, contacts, beautiful women, handsome men, with the pale and the tanned. Sirens belong to another world, a world of heart attacks, diseases and crime. Sirens are of no interest to the people here.

Maureen's head begins to spin. Something has happened to Javits, and this could be a gift from the gods. She runs to the door and sees an ambulance speeding away, sirens blaring, down the blocked-off lane of the Boulevard.

'That's my friend,' she says to one of the bodyguards at the entrance. 'Where have they taken him?'

The man gives her the name of a hospital. Without pausing to think, Maureen starts running to find a taxi. Ten minutes later, she realises that there are no taxis in the city, only those summoned by hotel porters, lured by the prospect of generous tips. Since she has no money in her bag, she goes into a pizzeria, shows someone working there the map she has with her, and learns that she must run for at least half an hour to reach her objective.

She's been running all her life, so half an hour won't make much difference.

12.53 p.m.

'Good morning.'

'You mean "Good afternoon", don't you?' one of the other girls replies. 'It's gone midday.'

Everything is exactly as she'd imagined. The five other young women waiting all rather resemble her, at least physically. They, however, are heavily made up, wear short skirts and low-cut tops and are busy with their mobile phones and their texts.

No one speaks because they know they're soulmates who have all been through the same difficulties and have uncomplainingly faced the same challenges and taken every rebuff on the chin. They're all trying hard to believe that dreams have no sell-by date, that life can change from one second to the next, that somewhere the right moment is waiting for them, and that this is just a test of their will-power.

They've all perhaps quarrelled with their families, who are convinced their daughters will end up working as prostitutes.

They've all been on stage and experienced the agony and the ecstasy of seeing the audience and knowing that every eye is fixed on them; they've felt the electricity in the air and heard the applause at the end. They've imagined a hundred times over that there will come a night when a member of the Superclass will be in the audience and visit them in their dressing-room after the performance with something more substantial to offer than an invitation to supper, a request for their phone number or compliments on a job well done.

To begin with, they accepted a few of those invitations, but the only place they led to was the bed of some powerful, older man – usually married, as all the 'interesting' men are – concerned only with notching up another conquest.

They all had a boyfriend their own age, but when anyone asked if they were married or single, they always answered: 'Free and unattached.' They thought they were in control of the situation. They've all been told – hundreds of times now – that they have real talent and just need the right opportunity, and that the person there before them is the one who can transform their lives. They've occasionally believed this too. They've fallen into the trap of being over-confident and thinking they were in charge, until the next day comes and the phone number they'd been given puts them through to the extension of a very grumpy secretary who has no intention of letting them speak to her boss.

They've threatened to sell their story to the tabloids, saying that they had been deceived, although none of them has ever actually done so because they're still at the stage of thinking: 'I mustn't spoil my chances in the acting world.'

One or two may even have shared Gabriela's *Alice in Wonderland* experience, and now want to prove to their families that they're far more capable than they thought. Their families, of course, have all by now seen their daughters in commercials, on posters and billboards scattered round the city and, after a few initial arguments, are convinced that those same daughters are on the verge of entering a world of 'bright lights and glamour'.

All the girls there believed that their dream was possible, that one day their talent would be recognised, until the penny dropped: there is only one magic word – 'contacts'. They had all distributed their 'books' as soon as they arrived in Cannes, and now keep a constant eye on their mobile phones, getting invited to whatever launches and events they can and trying their best to get into those they can't, always dreaming that someone will ask them to one of the evening parties or, dream of dreams, award them that greatest of prizes, an invitation to walk down the red carpet at the Palais des Congrès. That, however, was probably the most difficult dream to realise, so difficult that they didn't really allow themselves to think about it, in case the feelings of rejection and frustration destroyed their ability to wear the happy face they must wear at all times, even when they're not happy at all.

Contacts.

After many cases of mistaken identity, they did find the occasional useful contact, which is why they're here. One such contact had led to a New Zealand producer calling them. None had asked what it was about; they knew only that they had to be punctual because no one has any time to lose, certainly not people in the film industry. The only ones who do are the five young women in the waiting-room, busy with their mobile phones and their magazines, compulsively sending texts to see if they've been invited to something later in the day, trying to talk to their friends and always making a point of saying that they're not free to speak right now because they have an important meeting with a film producer.

Gabriela is the fourth person to be called. She had tried to interpret the look in the eyes of the first three candidates who emerged from the room without saying a word, but then, of course, they're all actresses, capable of hiding any emotion, be it joy or sadness. All three strode determinedly to the door and wished the others a confident 'Good luck', as if to say: 'No need to be nervous, girls, you've got nothing to lose. The part's mine.'

One of the walls in the apartment is covered with a black cloth. The floor there is cluttered with all kinds of electric cables and lights covered with a metal mesh, and there's a kind of umbrella with a white cloth spread before it, as well as sound equipment, screens and a video camera. In the corners stand bottles of mineral water, metal briefcases, tripods, bits of paper and a computer. Sitting on the floor, a bespectacled, thirty-something woman is leafing through Gabriela's book.

'Awful,' she says, not looking up at her.'Awful.'

Gabriela doesn't know quite what to do. Perhaps she should pretend she isn't listening and go over to the group of chain-smoking technicians chatting brightly in one corner or perhaps she should simply stay where she is.

'This one's awful,' said the woman again.

'That's me.'

She can't help herself. She has run through half of Cannes to get there, waited nearly two hours, imagined yet again that her life is about to change for ever (although she's less and less prone to such fantasies now and won't allow herself to get as excited as she used to), and she certainly doesn't need more reasons to be depressed.

'I know,' says the woman, her eyes fixed on the photos.'They must have cost you a fortune. People make a career out of making books, writing CVs, running acting courses and generally making money out of the vanity of people like you.'

'If you think I'm so awful, why did you call me?'

'Because we need someone awful.'

Gabriela laughs.The woman finally raises her head and looks her up and down.

'I like your clothes. I hate vulgar people.'

Gabriela's dream is returning. Her heart beats faster.

The woman hands her a sheet of paper.

'Go over there to the mark.'

Then she turns to the crew.

'Put those cigarettes out and close the window. I don't want the sound messed up.'

The 'mark' is a cross made with yellow tape on the floor.This means that the actor is automatically in the right position for the lighting and the camera.

'It's so hot in here, I'm sweating. Could I at least go to the bathroom and put a little foundation on, some make-up?'

'Of course you can, but when you get back, there won't be time to do the recording. We have to hand this stuff over by this afternoon.'

All the other girls who went in must have asked the same question and been given the same answer. Best not to waste time. She takes a paper handkerchief out of her pocket and dabs at her face as she makes her way over to the mark.

An assistant positions himself by the camera, while Gabriela battles against time, trying to read through what is written on that half-sheet of paper.

'Test number twenty-five, Gabriela Sheery, Thompson Agency.'

'Twenty-five!' thinks Gabriela.

'And action,' says the woman with the glasses.

Silence falls.

'No, I can't believe what you're saying. No one can commit a murder for no reason.'

'Start again. You're talking to your boyfriend.'

'No, I can't believe what you're saying. No one can commit a murder like that for no reason.'

'The words "like that" aren't in the script. Do you really think that the scriptwriter, who worked on this for months, didn't consider putting those words in, but decided against it because they're useless, superficial, unnecessary?'

Gabriela takes a deep breath. She has nothing to lose but her patience. She's going to do her best now, then leave, go to the beach or go back to bed for a while. She needs to rest in order to be in good shape for the evening round of cocktail parties.

A strange, delicious calm comes over her. Suddenly, she feels protected, loved, grateful to be alive. No one's forcing her to be there, enduring yet another humiliation. For the first time in years, she's aware of her power, a power she had never thought existed.

'No, I don't believe what you're saying. No one can commit a murder for no reason.'

'Next line.'

There was no need for her to say that. Gabriela was going to continue anyway.

'We'd better go and see a doctor. I think you need help.'

'No,' said the woman in glasses, who was playing the part of the boyfriend.

'OK, no doctor, then. How about a little walk, and you can tell me exactly what's going on. I love you, you know, and even if no one else in the world cares about you, I do.'

There are no more lines. Another silence. A strange energy fills the room.

'Tell the other girl out there she can go,' says the woman in the glasses to one of the other people present.

Does this mean what Gabriela thinks it means?

'Go to the marina at the end of Boulevard de la Croisette, opposite Allée des Palmiers. A boat will be waiting there at 1.55 prompt to take you to meet Mr Gibson. We're going to send him the video now, but he always likes to meet the people he might be working with.'

A smile appears on Gabriela's face.

'I said "might", I didn't say "*will* be working with".'

The smile remains. Mr Gibson!

1.19 p.m.

Lying on a stainless-steel table between Inspector Savoy and the pathologist is a beautiful young woman of about twenty, completely naked. And dead.

'Are you sure?'

The pathologist goes over to a stainless-steel sink, removes his rubber gloves, throws them in the bin and turns on the tap.

'Absolutely. There's no trace of drugs.'

'What happened then? Could a young woman like her have had a heart attack?'

The only noise in the room is that of running water. The pathologist thinks:

'They always come up with the obvious: drugs, a heart attack ...'

He takes longer than necessary to wash his hands – a little suspense never goes amiss. He applies disinfectant to his arms and throws away the disposable material used in the autopsy. Then he turns round and asks the inspector to study the body.

'No, really, take a good look. Don't be embarrassed. Noticing details is part of your job, isn't it?'

Savoy carefully examines the body. At one point, he reaches out to lift one of the girl's arms, but the pathologist stops him.

'No need to touch.'

Savoy runs his eyes over the girl's naked body. He knows quite a lot about her now – Olivia Martins, the daughter of Portuguese parents, currently going out with a young man of no fixed profession, who is heavily into Cannes nightlife and is, at that moment, being interrogated at a police station some way away. A judge issued a search warrant for his apartment and they found some small flasks of THC (tetrahydrocannabinol, the main hallucinogenic element in marijuana, and which can be taken dissolved in sesame oil, which leaves no smell and has a far stronger effect than when the substance is absorbed through smoke). They also found six envelopes each containing a gram of cocaine, and some bloodstains on a sheet which is now on its way to a laboratory for tests. He's probably, at most, a minor dealer. He's already known to the police, having spent a couple of spells in prison, but never for physical violence.

Olivia was lovely, even in death. Her dark eyebrows, that child-like air, her breasts … 'No,' he thinks, 'I mustn't go there. I'm a professional.'

'I can't see anything,' he says.

The pathologist smiles, and Savoy finds his smugness slightly irritating. The expert points to a small, purplish, almost imperceptible mark between the girl's right shoulder and her neck. Then he shows him another similar mark on the left-hand side of her torso, between two of her ribs.

'I could begin by giving you the technical details. Death was caused by obstruction of the jugular vein and the carotid artery while, simultaneously, similar pressure was being applied to a particular sheaf of nerves, but so precisely that it caused the complete paralysis of the upper part of the body …'

Savoy says nothing. The pathologist realises that this is not the moment to show off his knowledge or to make jokes. He feels rather sorry for himself. He works with death on a daily basis and spends each day surrounded by corpses and grave-faced people. His children never tell anyone what their father does, and he has nothing to talk about at supper parties because people hate discussing what they perceive to be macabre topics. He sometimes wonders if he hasn't perhaps chosen the wrong profession.

'… in short, she was strangled.'

Savoy still says nothing. His brain is working very fast: how could someone possibly be strangled on Boulevard de la Croisette in broad daylight? Her parents had been interviewed, and they said that their daughter had left the house that morning with the usual merchandise – illegal merchandise, it must be said, because street vendors pay no taxes and are, therefore, banned from trading. 'Although that's hardly relevant now,' he thinks.

'The intriguing thing about this particular case,' says the pathologist, 'is that in a normal case of strangulation, there are marks on both shoulders, that is, in the classic scene in which the attacker grabs the victim round the throat and the victim struggles to get free. In this case, only one hand, or, rather, one finger stopped the blood reaching the brain, while another finger paralysed the body, rendering her incapable of fighting back. This requires a very sophisticated technique and a detailed knowledge of the human body.'

'Could she have been killed somewhere else and carried to the bench where we found her?'

'If so, there would be other marks on her body. That was the first thing I looked for, assuming she was killed by just one person. When I found no marks, I looked for any indication that she had been grabbed by the wrists or ankles, if, that is, we were dealing with more than one killer. But there was nothing to indicate this; indeed, without wishing to go into more technical detail, there are certain things that happen at the moment of death which leave traces in the body. Urine for example, and …'

'What are you saying?'

'That she was killed where she was found and that, judging by the fingermarks on her body, only one person was involved; that since no one saw her trying to run away, she clearly knew her killer, who was seated on her left side; and that her killer must be someone highly trained and with an extensive knowledge of the martial arts.'

Savoy nods his thanks and walks quickly to the exit. On the way, he phones the police station where the boyfriend is being interrogated.

'Forget about drugs,' he says. 'We have a murder on our hands. Try and find out what the boyfriend knows about martial arts. I'm coming straight over.'

'No,' says the voice at the other end. 'Go straight to the hospital. I think we have another problem.'

1.28 p.m.

A seagull was flying over a beach, when it saw a mouse. It flew down and asked the mouse:

'Where are your wings?'

Each animal speaks its own language, and so the mouse didn't understand the question, but stared at the two strange, large things attached to the other creature's body.

'It must have some illness,' thought the mouse.

The seagull noticed the mouse staring at its wings and thought:

'Poor thing. It must have been attacked by monsters that left it deaf and took away its wings.'

Feeling sorry for the mouse, the seagull picked it up in its beak and took it for a ride in the skies. 'It's probably homesick,' the seagull thought while they were flying. Then, very carefully, it deposited the mouse once more on the ground.

For some months afterwards, the mouse was sunk in gloom; it had known the heights and seen a vast and beautiful world. However, in time, it grew accustomed to being just a mouse again and came to believe that the miracle that had occurred in its life was nothing but a dream.

This was a story from her childhood, but right now, she's up in the sky: she can see the turquoise sea, the luxurious yachts, the people small as ants below, the marquees on the beach, the hills, the horizon to her left, beyond which lay Africa and all its problems.

The ground is approaching fast. 'It's best to view humankind from on high,' she thinks. 'Only then can we see how very small we are.'

Ewa seems bored, either that or nervous. Hamid never really knows what's going on in his wife's head, even though they've been together for more than two years now. Cannes, it's true, is a trial for everyone concerned, but he can't leave the Festival any earlier than planned. Besides, she should be used to all this because the life of her ex-husband hadn't been so very different, with suppers to attend, events to organise and having constantly to change country, continent and language.

'Was she always like this or is it that she doesn't love me as much as she did at first?'

A forbidden thought. Concentrate on other things, please.

The noise of the engine doesn't allow for conversation, unless you use the headphones with the microphone attached. Ewa hasn't even picked hers up from the hook beside her seat. Not that there's any point asking her to put them on so that he can tell her for the thousandth time that she's the most important woman in his life and that he'll do his best to make sure she enjoys the week at this her first Cannes Festival. The sound system on board is set up so that every conversation can be overheard by the pilot, and Ewa hates public displays of affection.

There they are, in that glass bubble, just about to touch down. He can see the huge white car, a Maybach, the most expensive and most sophisticated in the world. Even more exclusive than Rolls-Royce. Soon they'll be sitting inside, listening to some relaxing music and drinking iced champagne or mineral water.

He consults his platinum watch, which is a certified copy of one of the first models produced in a small workshop in the town of Schaffhausen. Women can get away with spending a fortune on diamonds, but a watch is the only piece of jewellery allowed to a man of good taste, and only the true cognoscenti knew the significance of that watch, which was rarely advertised in the glossy magazines.

That could be a definition of true sophistication: knowing where to find the very best even if other people have never heard of it, and producing the very best too, regardless of what others might say.

It was already nearly two o'clock in the afternoon, and he needed to talk to his stockbroker in New York before trading opened on the stock exchange. When he arrived, he would make a call – just one – with his instructions for the day. Making money at the 'casino', as he called the investment funds, was not his favourite sport; however, he had to pretend to be keeping an eye on what his managers and financial engineers were up to. He could rely on the protection, support and vigilance of the sheikh, but nevertheless he had to demonstrate that he was up to date on what was happening.

He might, in the end, have to make two phone calls, but give no concrete instructions on what to buy or sell. His energy is focussed on something else: that afternoon, at least two actresses – one famous and one unknown – will be walking down the red carpet wearing his dresses. Obviously, he has assistants who can take care of everything, but he likes to be personally involved, even if only to remind himself that every detail is important and that he hasn't lost touch with the basis on which he built his empire. Apart from that, he wants to spend the rest of his time in France trying to enjoy Ewa's company to the full, introducing her to interesting people, strolling on the beach, lunching together in some small restaurant in a nearby town, or walking along, hand-in-hand, through the vineyards he can see on the horizon.

He had always felt he was incapable of falling in love with anything other than his work, although the list of his conquests includes an enviable series of relationships with some even more enviable women. The moment Ewa appeared on the scene, though, he was a different man. His love for her has grown in intensity during their two years together. In love. Him,

Hamid Hussein, one of the most famous designers on the planet, the public face of a gigantic international conglomerate selling luxury and glamour. The man who had battled against everything and everyone, who had challenged all the West's preconceived ideas about people from the Middle East and their religion, the man who had used the ancestral knowledge of his tribe to survive, learn and reach the top. Contrary to rumour, he was not from a rich oil family. His father had been a seller of cloth who, one day, had found favour with a sheikh simply because he refused to do as he was told.

Whenever Hamid had doubts about what decision to make, he liked to remember the example he had received in adolescence: Say 'No' to powerful people, even when doing so means taking a great risk. It had almost always worked. And on the few occasions when it hadn't, the consequences were not as grave as he had imagined.

His father had not, alas, lived to see his son's success. When the sheikh started buying up all the available land in that part of the desert in order to build one of the most modern cities in the world, his father had had the courage to say to one of the sheikh's emissaries:

'I'm not selling. My family has been here for centuries. We have buried our dead here. We learned to survive storms and invaders. We cannot sell the place that God charged us to take care of.'

The emissaries increased their offer. When he still refused, they got angry and threatened to do whatever was necessary to remove him. The sheikh, too, began to grow impatient. He wanted to start his project straight away because he had big plans. The price of oil had risen on the international market, and the money needed to be spent before the oil reserves ran out and any possibility of building an infrastructure to attract foreign investments vanished.

Still old Hussein refused to sell his property, whatever the price. Then the sheikh decided to go and speak to him directly.

'I can offer you anything you desire,' he said.

'Then give my son a good education. He's sixteen now, and there are no prospects for him here.'

'Only if you sell me your house.'

There was a long silence, then his father, looking straight at the sheikh, said something the latter had never expected to hear.

'You, sir, have a duty to educate your subjects, and I cannot exchange my family's future for its past.'

Hamid recalls the look of immense sadness in his father's eyes as he went on:

'But if you can at least give my son a chance in life, then I will accept your offer.'

The sheikh left without saying another word. The following day, he asked Hamid's father to send his son to him so that they could talk. After walking down blocked roads, past gigantic cranes, labourers tirelessly working and passed whole quarters in the process of being demolished, Hamid finally reached the palace that had been built beside the old port.

The sheikh came straight to the point.

'You know that I want to buy your father's house. There is very little oil left in our country, and we must wean ourselves off oil and find other paths before the oil wells run dry. We will prove to the world that we can sell not only oil, but our services too. Meanwhile, in order to take those first steps, we need to make some major reforms, like building a good airport, for example. We need land so that foreigners can build on it. My dream is a just one and my intentions are good. One thing we're going to need are more experts in the field of finance. Now you heard the conversation between myself and your father ...'

Hamid tried to disguise his fear, for there were more than a dozen people listening to their conversation. However, his heart had an answer ready for each question he was asked.

'... so tell me, what do you want to do?' asked the sheikh.

'I want to study haute-couture.'

The other people present looked at each other. They may not even have known what he meant.

'My father sells much of the cloth he buys to foreigners, who then turn his cloth into designer clothes and earn a hundred times more from it than he does. I'm sure we could do the same here. I'm convinced that fashion could be one way of breaking down the prejudices the rest of the world has about us. If they could be made to see that we don't dress like barbarians, they would find it easier to accept us.'

This time, he heard murmurings in the court. Was he talking about clothes? That was something for Westerners, who were more concerned with how people looked on the outside than with what they were like inside.

'On the other hand, the price my father is paying is very high. I would prefer to keep our house. I will work with the cloth he has, and if Merciful God so desires it, I will realise my dream. I, like Your Majesty, know what I want.'

The court listened in amazement to hear this boy not only challenging their region's great leader, but refusing to accept his own father's wishes. The sheikh, however, smiled.

'And where does one study haute-couture?'

'In France or Italy, working with the great masters. There are universities where one can study, but there's no substitute for experience. It won't be easy, but if Merciful God so wishes, I will succeed.'

The sheikh asked him to come back later that afternoon. Hamid strolled down to the port and visited the bazaar, where he marvelled at the colours, the cloths and the embroidery. He loved visiting the bazaar and it saddened him to think that it would soon be destroyed because a part of the past and part of tradition would be lost. Was it possible to stop progress? Would it be sensible to try and stop the development of a nation? He remembered the many nights he had sat up late drawing by candle-light, copying the clothes the Bedouin wore, afraid that tribal costumes would also one day be destroyed by the cranes and by foreign investment.

At the appointed hour, he returned to the palace. There were even more people with the sheikh now.

'I have made two decisions,' said the sheikh. 'First, I am going to pay your expenses for a year. We have enough boys interested in a career in the financial sector, but you are the first to express a wish to learn sewing. It seems utter madness, but then everyone tells me my dreams are mad too, and yet look where they've got me. I cannot go against my own example.

'On the other hand, none of my assistants has any contacts among the people you mentioned, and so I will be paying you a small monthly allowance to keep you from having to beg in the streets. You will return a winner; you will represent our country, and it's important that other nations should learn to respect our culture. Before leaving, you will have to learn the languages of the countries to which you are going. Which languages are they?'

'English, French and Italian. I am most grateful to you for your generosity, but what about my father ...'

The sheikh gestured to him to be silent.

'My second decision is as follows. Your father's house will remain where it is. In my dreams it will be surrounded by skyscrapers, no sun will enter its windows, and, in the end, he will have to move. However, the house will stay there for ever. In the future, people will remember me and say: "He was a great man because he changed his country. And he was just because he respected the rights of a seller of cloth."'

The helicopter lands at the very end of the pier, and he leaves aside his memories. He gets out first and then proffers Ewa a helping hand. He touches her skin and looks proudly at this blonde woman, all dressed in white, her clothes glowing in the sunlight, her other hand holding on to the lovely, discreet, beige hat she is wearing. They walk past the ranks of yachts moored on either side, towards the car that awaits them and the chauffeur standing with the door already open.

He holds his wife's hand and whispers in her ear:

'I hope you enjoyed the lunch. They're great collectors of art, and it was very generous of them to provide a helicopter for us.'

'Yes, I loved it.'

But what Ewa really means is: 'No, I hated it. Worse, I'm feeling really frightened. I've just received a text on my mobile phone and I know who sent it, even though I can't identify the number.'

They get into the vast car made for just two people, the rest being empty space. The air conditioning is set at the ideal temperature, the music is exactly right for such a moment and no outside noise penetrates their perfect isolation. He sits down on the comfortable leather seat, opens the mini-bar in front of them and asks if Ewa would like some champagne. No, she says, mineral water will be fine.

'I saw your ex-husband yesterday in the hotel bar, before we left for supper.'

'That's impossible. He has no business in Cannes.'

She would like to have said: 'You may be right. I've just received a text. We should board the next plane out of here.'

'Oh, I'm quite sure it was him.'

Hamid notices that his wife is not in the mood to talk. He has been brought up to respect the privacy of those he loves, and so he makes himself think of something else.

Having first asked Ewa's permission, he makes the obligatory phone call to his stockbroker in New York. He listens patiently for two or three sentences, then politely interrupts any further news on market trends. The whole call lasts no more than two minutes.

He makes another call to the director he has chosen for his first film. The director is on his way to the boat to meet with the Star, and yes, a young actress has been chosen and should be joining them shortly.

He turns to Ewa again, but she still seems disinclined to talk, her gaze absent, staring out of the limousine windows at nothing. Perhaps she's worried because she'll have so little time at the hotel. She'll have to change immediately and go straight to a rather insignificant fashion show by a Belgian designer, where Hamid wants to see for himself the young African model, Jasmine, whom his assistants tell him will be the ideal face for his next collection.

He wants to know how the girl will survive the pressures of an event in Cannes. If everything goes to plan, she'll be one of his star models at the Fashion Week in Paris set for October.

Ewa keeps her eyes fixed on the window, not that she's interested in what's going on outside. She knows the gentle, creative, determined, well-dressed man by her side very well. She knows that he desires her as no man has ever desired a woman, apart, that is, from the man she left. She can trust him, even though he lives surrounded by some of the most beautiful women in the world. He's an honest, hard-working man who has met and overcome many challenges in order to be chauffered around in that limo and be able to offer her a glass of champagne or her favourite mineral water. He is powerful and capable of protecting her from any danger, except one, the worst of all. Her ex-husband.

She doesn't want to arouse suspicions now by picking up her phone again to reread the message; she knows the message by heart.

'I have destroyed a world for you, Katyusha.'

She has no idea what these words means, but no one else would call her by that name.

She has taught herself to love Hamid, although she detests the life he leads, the parties they go to and his friends. She doesn't know yet if she has succeeded in making herself love him; there are moments when she feels almost suicidal with despair. All she knows is that he was her salvation at a time when she thought she was lost for ever, incapable of escaping the trap of her marriage.

Many years before, she had fallen in love with an angel with a sad childhood, who had been called up into the Soviet army to fight in an absurd war in Afghanistan only to return to a country verging on collapse. Despite this, he had overcome all difficulties to succeed. He began to work very hard, getting loans from some very shady people, then lying awake at night, worrying about the risk he was taking and wondering how he could ever repay those loans. He put up uncomplainingly with the endemic corruption, accepting that he would have to bribe a government official each time he needed a new licence for a product that would improve the quality of life of his own people. He was idealistic and affectionate. By day, his leadership went unquestioned because life had taught him how to lead, and military service had helped him understand exactly how hierarchies work. At night, he would cling to her and ask her to protect and advise him, to pray for everything to go well and for him to avoid the many traps that lay in his path each day.

Ewa would stroke his hair and assure him that everything was fine, that he was a good man and that God always rewarded the just.

Gradually, the difficulties gave way to opportunities. The small business he had started – after almost begging people to sign contracts – began to grow because he was one of the few to have invested in something that no one believed could work in a country still plagued by near-obsolete communication networks. The government changed and corruption diminished.

Money began to come in, slowly at first, then in vast quantities. However, they never forgot the difficult times they had been through and never wasted a penny. They made contributions to charities and to associations for ex-soldiers; they lived unostentatiously, dreaming of the day when they could put it all behind them and go and live in a house away from the world. When that happened, they would forget that they had once been obliged to have dealings with people who had no ethics and no dignity. They spent much of their time in airports, planes and hotels; they worked eighteen hours a day, and for years never managed to take a month's holiday together.

They nurtured the same dream: the moment would come when that frenetic pace of life would be but a distant memory. The scars from that period would be like medals won in a war waged in the name of faith and dreams. After all, each human being – or so she believed then – had been born to love and to live with their beloved.

The whole process of finding work was suddenly turned on its head. Instead of them having to hunt down contracts, they began to appear spontaneously. Her husband was featured on the front cover of an important business magazine, and the local bigwigs started sending them invitations to parties and events. They began to be treated like royalty, and ever greater quantities of money flowed in.

They had to adapt to these changed circumstances: they bought a beautiful house in Moscow, a house with every possible comfort. For reasons she didn't and preferred not to know, her husband's old associates ended up in prison. (These were the same associates who had made those initial loans, of which, despite the exorbitant interest rates, Igor had paid back every penny.) From then on, Igor began to be accompanied everywhere by bodyguards, only two at first – fellow veterans and friends from the Afghan war – but they were later joined by others as the small company grew into a multinational giant with branches in several countries in seven different time zones, making ever more, and ever more diverse investments.

Ewa spent her days in shopping malls or having tea with friends, who always talked about the same things. Igor, of course, wanted to go further ... and further. After all, he had only got where he was by dint of ambition and hard work. Whenever she asked if they had not gone far beyond what they had planned and if it wasn't time to realise their dream of living only on the love they felt for each other, he always asked for a little more time. And he began to drink more heavily. One night, he came home after a long supper with friends during which much wine and vodka had been drunk, and she could contain her feelings no longer. She said she couldn't stand the empty existence she was leading; if she didn't do something soon, she would go mad. Wasn't she satisfied with what she had, asked Igor.

'Yes, *I'm* satisfied, but the problem is you're not, and never will be. You're insecure, afraid of losing everything you've achieved; you don't know how to quit once you're ahead. You'll end up destroying yourself. You're killing our marriage and my love.'

This wasn't the first time she had spoken thus to her husband; they had always been very honest with each other, but she felt she was reaching a limit. She had had enough of the shopping and the tea parties and the ghastly television programmes that she watched while waiting for him to come home from work.

'Don't say that, don't say I'm killing our love. I promise that soon we'll leave all this behind us, just be patient. Perhaps you should start some project of your own because your life at the moment really must be pretty hellish.'

At least he recognised that.

'What would you like to do?' he asked.

Yes, she thought, perhaps that would be a way out.

'I'd like to work with fashion. That's always been my dream.'

Her husband immediately granted her wish. The following week, he turned up with the keys to a shop in one of the best shopping malls in Moscow. Ewa was thrilled. Her life took on new meaning; the long days and nights spent waiting would be over for good. She borrowed money, and Igor invested enough in the business for her to have a good chance of success.

Suppers and parties – where she had always felt like an outsider – took on a new interest for her. In just two years, thanks to contacts made at such social events, she was running the most successful haute-couture shop in Moscow. Although she had a joint account with her husband, and he never questioned how much she spent, she made a point of paying back the money he had lent her. She started going off on business trips alone, looking for new designs and exclusive brands. She took on staff, got to grips with the accounts, and became – to her own surprise – an excellent businesswoman.

Igor had taught her everything. He was a great role model, an example to be followed. And just as everything was going so well and her life had taken on new meaning, the Angel of Light that had lit her path began to waver.

They were in a restaurant in Irkutsk, after spending a weekend in a fishing village on the shores of Lake Baikal. By that stage, the company owned two planes and a helicopter, so that they could travel as far as they liked and be back on Monday to start all over again. Neither of them complained about spending so little time together, but it was clear that the many years of struggle were beginning to take their toll. Still, they knew that their love was stronger than everything else, and, as long as they were together, they would be all right.

In the middle of a candle-lit supper, a drunken beggar came into the restaurant, walked over to their table, sat down and began to talk, interrupting their precious moment alone, far from the hustle and bustle of Moscow. A minute later, the owner offered to remove him, but Igor said he would take care of it. The beggar grew animated, picked up their bottle of vodka and drank from it; then he started asking questions ('Who are you? How come you've got so much money, when we all live in such poverty here?') and generally complaining about life and about the government. Igor put up with this for a few more minutes.

Then he got to his feet, took the man by the arm and led him outside (the restaurant was in an unpaved street). His two bodyguards were waiting for him. Ewa saw through the window that her husband barely spoke to them, apart from issuing some order along the lines of 'Keep an eye on my wife' and headed off towards a small side street. He came back a few minutes later, smiling.

'Well, he won't bother anyone again,' he said.

Ewa noticed a different light in his eyes; they seemed filled by an immense joy, far greater than any joy he had shown during the weekend they had spent together.

'What did you do?'

Igor did not reply, but simply called for more vodka. They both drank steadily into the night – he happy and smiling and she choosing to understand only what she wanted to understand. He had always been so generous with those less fortunate than himself, so perhaps he had given the man money to help him out of his poverty.

When they went back to the hotel, he said:

'It's something I learned in my youth, when I was fighting in an unjust war for an ideal I didn't believe in. There's always a way of putting an end to poverty.'

No, Igor can't be here in Cannes. Hamid must have made a mistake. The two men had only met once before, in the foyer of the building where they lived in London, when Igor had found out their address and gone there to beg Ewa to come back.

Hamid had spoken to him, but hadn't allowed him to come in, threatening to call the police. For a whole week, she had refused to leave their apartment, claiming to have a headache, but knowing that the Angel of Light had turned into Absolute Evil.

She looks at her phone again and rereads the message.

Katyusha. Only one person would call her by that name. The person who lives in her past and will terrorise her present for the rest of her life, however protected she feels, however far away she lives, and even though she inhabits a world to which he has no access. The same person who, on their return from Irkutsk – as if he had sloughed off an enormous weight – had begun to speak more freely about the shadows that inhabited his soul.

'No one, absolutely no one, can threaten our privacy. We've spent long enough creating a fairer, more humane society. Anyone who fails to respect our moments of freedom should be removed in such a way that they'll never even consider coming back.'

Ewa was afraid to ask what 'in such a way' meant. She had thought she knew her husband, but from one moment to the next, it seemed that a submerged volcano had begun to roar, and the shock waves were getting stronger and stronger. She remembered certain late-night conversations with him when he was still a young man and how he had told her that, during the war in Afghanistan, he had sometimes been forced to kill in self-defence. She had never seen regret or remorse in his eyes.

'I survived, and that's what matters. My life could have ended one sunny afternoon, or at dawn in the snow-covered mountains, or one night when we were playing cards in our tent, confident that the situation was under control. And if I had died, nothing would have changed in the world. I would have been just another statistic for the army and another medal for my family.

'But Jesus helped me, and I was blessed with quick reactions. And because I survived the hardest tests a man can face, fate has given me the two most important things in life: success at work and the person I love.'

It was one thing killing in order to save your own life, but quite another to 'remove for good' some poor drunk who had interrupted their supper and who could easily have been shepherded away by the restaurant owner. She couldn't get the idea out of her head. She started going ever earlier to the shop and, when she came home, sitting at her computer until late into the night. There was a question she wanted to avoid. She managed to carry on like this for some months, following the usual routine: business trips, parties, suppers, meetings, charity auctions. She even wondered if she had misunderstood what her husband had said in Irkutsk and blamed herself for making such a snap judgement.

Time passed, and the question became less important, until the night they attended a gala supper-cum-charity auction at one of the most expensive restaurants in Milan. They were both there for different reasons: Igor in order to firm up the details of a contract with an Italian company, and Ewa in order to attend the Fashion Week, where she hoped to make a few purchases for her Moscow shop.

And what had happened in the middle of Siberia was repeated in one of the most sophisticated cities in the world. This time, a friend of theirs, rather the worse for wear, sat down at their table uninvited and started joking and making inappropriate remarks. Ewa saw Igor's hand grip the handle of his knife more tightly. As tactfully and politely as possible, she asked the friend to go away. By then, she had already drunk several glasses of Asti Spumante, as the Italians refer to what used to be called 'champagne' because the use of the word 'champagne' was banned under the so-called Protected Designation of Origin. Champagne simply means a white wine made using a particular bacteria which, when rigorously controlled, begins to generate gases inside the bottle as the wine ages over a period of at least fifteen months. The name refers to the region where it's produced. Spumante is exactly the same thing, but European law doesn't allow it to be known by the French name, since the vineyards are in Italy and not in the Champagne region of France.

They started talking about champagne and about the laws governing names, while she struggled to drive from her head the question she had tried to suppress and which was now returning in full force. While they were talking, she kept drinking, until there came a moment when she could hold back no longer.

'What does it matter if someone gets a little drunk and comes over to talk to us?'

When he answered, Igor's voice had changed.

'Because we so rarely travel together. Besides, you know what I think about the world we live in: that we're being suffocated by lies, encouraged to put our faith in science rather than in spiritual values and to feed our souls with the things society tells us are important, when, in reality, we're slowly dying because we know what's going on around us, that we're being forced to do things we never planned to do, and yet even so, are incapable of giving it all up and devoting our days and nights to true happiness, to family, nature, love. And why is that? Because we feel obliged to finish what we started, so that we can achieve the financial stability we need in order to enjoy the rest of our lives devoting ourselves to each other because we're responsible people. I know you sometimes think I work too much, but it's not true. I'm building our future and soon we'll be free to dream and to live out our dreams.'

Financial stability was hardly something they lacked. They had no debts and they could have got up from that table there and then with just their credit cards and simply left behind them the world Igor apparently hated and start all over again, and never have to worry about money. She had often spoken to him about this, and Igor always said the same thing: 'It won't be much longer.' Besides, this wasn't the moment to discuss their future as a couple.

'God thought of everything,' he went on. 'We are together because He decided we should be. You may not fully appreciate your importance in my life, but without you, I would never have got where I am today. He placed us side by side and lent me His power to defend you whenever necessary. He taught me that everything is part of a plan, and I must respect that plan down to the last detail. If I hadn't done so, I would either be dead in Kabul or living in poverty in Moscow.'

And it was then that the Spumante or champagne revealed what it was capable of, regardless of what it was called.

'What happened to that beggar in Siberia?' she asked.

Igor didn't at first know what she was talking about. Ewa reminded him of what had happened in the restaurant there.

'I'd like to know what you did.'

'I saved him.'

She gave a sigh of relief.

'I saved him from a filthy, hopeless life in those freezing winters, with his body being slowly destroyed by booze. I let his soul depart towards the light because the moment he came into that restaurant to destroy our happiness, I knew that his spirit was inhabited by the Evil One.'

Ewa felt her heart begin to pound. She didn't need him to say outright 'I killed him'. It was clear that he had.

'Without you I don't exist. Anything and anyone who tries to separate us or to destroy the little time we have together at this particular moment of our lives gets the treatment they deserve.'

Meaning perhaps that they deserved to be killed? Could such a thing have happened before without her noticing? She drank and drank some more, and Igor began to relax again.

Since he never opened his heart to anyone else, he loved their conversations.

'We speak the same language,' he went on. 'We see the world in the same way. We complete each other with a perfection that is granted only to those who put love above all else. As I said, without you I don't exist.

'Look at the Superclass around us. They think they're so important, so socially aware, because they're willing to pay a fortune for some useless item at a charity auction or to attend a supper organised to raise funds to help the homeless in Rwanda or to save the pandas in China. Pandas and the homeless are all one to them. They feel special, superior to the average person, because they're doing something useful. Have they ever fought in a war? No. They create wars, but they don't fight in them. If the war turns out well, they get all the credit. If not, others get the blame. They're in love with themselves.'

'My love, I'd like to ask you something else ...'

At that point, a presenter climbed onto the stage and thanked everyone for being there that night. The money raised would go towards buying medicine for refugee camps in Africa.

'What he doesn't say,' Igor went on, as if he hadn't heard her, 'is that only ten per cent of the total amount raised will reach its destination. The rest will be used to pay for this event, for the cost of this supper, for the publicity and the organisers, in short, for the people who had the "brilliant idea" in the first place, and all at an exorbitant price. They use poverty as a way to get even richer.'

'So why are we here?'

'Because we need to be. It's part of my work. I have no intention of saving Rwanda or sending medicine to refugees, but at least I know that I don't. The other guests here tonight are using their money to wash their consciences and their souls clean of guilt. When the genocide was going on in Rwanda, I financed a small army of friends, who prevented more than two thousand deaths. Did you know that?'

'No, you never told me.'

'I didn't need to. You know that I care about other people.'

The auction began with a small Louis Vuitton travel bag. It sold for ten times its retail price. Igor watched the auction impassively, while she drank another glass of Spumante and wondered whether she should or shouldn't ask that question.

An artist danced to a soundtrack provided by Marilyn Monroe and simultaneously painted a picture. The bids for the finished work of art were sky-high – the price of a small apartment in Moscow.

Another glass of wine. Another item sold. For an equally absurd price.

She drank so much that night that she had to be carried back to the hotel. Before he put her into bed and before she fell asleep, she finally got up the courage to ask:

'And what if I were to leave you?'

'Drink less next time.'

'Answer me.'

'That could never happen. Our marriage is perfect.'

Common sense returned, but she knew she had an excuse now and so pretended to be drunker than she was.

'Yes, but what if I did?'

'I'd make you come back, and I'm good at getting what I want, even if that means destroying whole worlds.'

'And what if I met another man?'

He looked at her without rancour, almost benevolently.

'Even if you slept with every man on Earth, my love would still survive.'

And since then, what had seemed a blessing began to turn into a nightmare. She was married to a monster, an assassin. What was that story about financing an army of mercenaries to intervene in a tribal war? How many other men had he killed to keep them from troubling their marital peace? She could blame the war, the traumas he had suffered, the hard times he had been through, but many other men had endured the same experiences, without emerging from them convinced that they were the instrument of Divine Justice, carrying out some Grand Plan.

'I'm not jealous,' Igor used to say whenever he or she set off on a business trip, 'because you know how much I love you, and I know how much you love me. Nothing will ever happen to destabilise our marriage.'

She was more convinced than ever that this was not love. It was something sick and morbid, which she would either have to accept and live the rest of her life a prisoner to fear or else free herself from as soon as possible.

Several opportunities arose, but the most insistent, the most persistent was the very last man with whom she would have imagined building a real relationship: the couturier who was dazzling the fashion world, growing ever more famous, and receiving a vast amount of money from his own country so that the world would understand that the nomadic tribes had solid moral values that were completely at odds with the reign of terror imposed by a religious minority. He was a man who, increasingly, had the world at his feet.

Whenever they met at fashion shows, he would drop whatever other commitments he had, cancel lunches and suppers, just so they could spend some time together in peace, locked in a hotel room, often without even making love. They would watch television, eat, drink (although he never touched a drop of alcohol), go for walks in parks, visit bookshops, talk to strangers, speak very little of the past, never of the future and a great deal about the present.

She resisted for as long as she could and, although she was never in love with him, when he proposed that she leave everything and move to London, she accepted at once. It was the only possible way out of her private hell.

Another message appears on her phone. It can't be; they haven't been in touch for two years.

'I've just destroyed another world because of you, Katyusha.'

'Who's it from?'

'I haven't the slightest idea. It doesn't show a number.'

What she meant to say was that she was terrified.

'We're nearly there. Remember, we haven't got much time.'

The limousine has to manoeuvre its way towards the entrance of the Hotel Martinez. On both sides, behind the metal barriers erected by the police, people of all ages spend the whole day hoping to get a close-up look at some celebrity. They take photos with their digital cameras, tell their friends who they've seen, and send messages over the Internet to the virtual communities they belong to. They would feel the long wait was justified for that one moment of glory: catching a glimpse of an actress, an actor or even a TV presenter!

Although it's only thanks to them that the celebrity industry keeps going, they are kept at a safe distance; strategically positioned bodyguards ask anyone going into the hotel for proof that they are staying there or meeting someone. Then you either have to get out the magnetic card that serves as your room key or else be turned away in full view of the public. If you're having a business meeting or have been invited for a drink at the bar, they give your name to the security people and, with everyone watching, wait to see if what you say is true or false. The bodyguard uses his radio to call reception, and you wait there for what seems like an eternity and then, finally, after that very public humiliation, you're allowed in. Those who arrive in limousines, of course, are treated quite differently.

The two doors of the Maybach are opened, one by the chauffeur and the other by the hotel porter. The cameras turn on Ewa and start to shoot; even though no one knows who she is, if she's staying at the Martinez and has arrived in a fancy car, she must be important. Perhaps she's the mistress of the man she's with, and if she is and he's having an extramarital affair, there's always a chance they can send the photos to some scandal rag. Or perhaps the beautiful blonde is a famous foreign celebrity as yet unknown in France. Later, they'll find her name in the so-called 'people magazines' and be glad that they were once only four or five yards from her.

Hamid looks at the small crowd pressed up against the metal barriers. He has never understood this phenomenon, having been brought up in a place where such things simply don't happen. Once he asked a friend why there was so much interest in celebrities.

'Don't assume they're all fans,' said his friend. 'Since time immemorial, men have believed that being close to something unattainable and mysterious can bring blessings. That's why people make pilgrimages to visit gurus and sacred places.'

'But Cannes?'

'It can be anywhere they might catch a distant glimpse of some elusive celebrity. For the adoring crowd, a wave from a celebrity is like being scattered with ambrosia dust or manna from heaven.

'It's the same everywhere. Take, for example, those massive pop concerts that seem more like religious meetings, or the way people are willing to wait outside some sell-out performance at a theatre just to see the Superclass entering and leaving. Take the crowds who go to football stadiums to watch a bunch of men chasing after a ball. Celebrities are idols, icons if you like, after all, they do resemble the paintings you see in churches and can become cult images in the bedrooms of adolescents or housewives, and even in the offices of industrial magnates, who, despite their own enormous wealth, envy their celebrity.

'There's just one difference: in this case, the public is the supreme judge, and while they may applaud today, tomorrow they'll be equally happy to read some scandalous revelation about their idol in a gossip magazine. Then they can say: "Poor thing. I'm so glad I'm not like him." They may adore their idol today, but tomorrow they'll stone and crucify him without a twinge of conscience.'

1.37 p.m.

Unlike the other girls who arrived for work this morning and are now using their iPods and mobile phones to while away the five hours that separate having their make-up and hair done from the actual fashion show, Jasmine is reading a book, a poetry book:

Two roads diverged in a yellow wood,
And sorry I could not travel both
And be one traveler, long I stood
And looked down one as far as I could
To where it bent in the undergrowth.

Then took the other, as just as fair,
And having perhaps the better claim,
Because it was grassy and wanted wear;
Though as for that the passing there
Had worn them really about the same.

And both that morning equally lay
In leaves no step had trodden black.
Oh, I kept the first for another day!
Yet knowing how way leads on to way,
I doubted if I should ever come back.

I shall be telling this with a sigh
Somewhere ages and ages hence:
Two roads diverged in a wood, and I –

I took the one less traveled by,
And that has made all the difference.

She had chosen the road less travelled, and though it cost her dear, it had been worth it. Things arrive at the right moment. Love had appeared when she most needed it and was still there with her now. She did her work with, for and out of love, or, rather, out of love for one particular person.

Jasmine's real name is Cristina. Her CV says she was discovered by Anna Dieter on a trip to Kenya, but there was little detail about this, leaving in the air the possibility of a childhood spent suffering and starving, caught up in the middle of a civil war. In fact, despite her black skin, she was born in the very traditional Belgian city of Antwerp, the daughter of parents fleeing the eternal conflicts between Hutus and Tutsis in Rwanda.

One weekend, when she was sixteen, she was helping out her mother on one of the latter's endless cleaning jobs, when a man came up to them and introduced himself, saying he was a photographer.

'Your daughter is extraordinarily beautiful,' he said. 'I'd like her to work with me as a model.'

'You see this bag I'm carrying? It's full of cleaning materials. I work day and night so that she can go to a good school and, one day, get a university degree. She's only sixteen.'

'That's the ideal age,' said the photographer, handing his card to Cristina. 'If you change your mind, let me know.'

They carried on walking, but her mother noticed that her daughter kept the card.

'Don't be deceived. That isn't your world. They just want to get you into bed.'

Cristina didn't need to be told this. Even though all the girls in her class envied her and the boys all wanted to take her to parties, she was keenly aware of her origins and her limitations.

She still didn't believe it when the same thing happened again. She had just gone into an ice-cream parlour when an older woman remarked on her beauty and said that she was a fashion photographer. Cristina thanked her, took her card and promised to phone her, even though she had no intention of doing so and even though becoming a model was the dream of every girl her age.

Given that things never happen only twice, three months later, she was looking in the window of a shop selling extremely expensive clothes, when the owner of the shop came out to speak to her.

'What do you do for a living?'

'You should really be asking me what will I be doing. I'm going to study to be a vet.'

'Well, you're on the wrong path. Wouldn't you like to work with us?'

'I haven't got time to sell clothes. Whenever I can, I help my mother.'

'I'm not suggesting you sell anything. I'd like you to do a few photo shoots wearing our designs.'

And if it hadn't been for an episode that occurred a few days later, these encounters would have been nothing but pleasant memories to look back on when she was married with children, loved by her family and fulfilled by her career.

She was with some friends at a nightclub, dancing and feeling glad to be alive, when a group of ten boys burst in, shouting. Nine of them were carrying clubs with razor-blades embedded in them and were ordering everyone to get out. Panic spread, and people started running. Cristina didn't know what to do, although her instincts told her to remain where she was and look the other way.

Before she could do anything, however, she saw the tenth boy take a knife out of his pocket, go over to one of her friends, grab him from behind and slit his throat. The gang left as quickly as they had appeared, while the other people present were either screaming, trying to run away or sitting on the floor, crying. A few went over to the victim to see if they could help, knowing that it was too late. Others, like Cristina, simply stared at the scene in shock. She knew the murdered boy and the murderer too, and even knew the motive for the crime (a fight in a bar shortly before they had gone to the nightclub), but she seemed to be floating somewhere in the clouds, as if it had all been a dream from which she would soon wake up, drenched in sweat, relieved to know that all nightmares come to an end.

This, however, was no dream.

It took only a few minutes for her to return to earth, screaming for someone to do something, screaming for people to do nothing, screaming for no reason at all, and her screams seemed to make people even more nervous. Then the police arrived, carrying guns, and were followed by paramedics and then detectives, who lined all the young people up against the wall and started questioning them, demanding to see their documents, their mobile phones, their addresses. Who had killed the boy and why? Cristina could say nothing. The body, covered by a sheet, was taken away. A nurse forced her to take a pill and told her that she must on no account drive home, but take a taxi or use public transport.

Early the next morning, the phone rang. Her mother had decided to spend the day at home with her daughter, who seemed somehow detached from the world. The police insisted on speaking to Cristina directly, saying that she must be at the police station by midday and ask for a particular inspector. Her mother refused. The police threatened her, and so, in the end, Cristina and her mother had no choice.

They arrived at the appointed time. The inspector asked Cristina if she knew the murderer.

Her mother's words were still echoing in her mind: 'Don't say anything. We're immigrants, they're Belgians. We're black, they're white. When they come out of prison, they'll track you down.' So she said:

'I don't know who the boy was. I'd never seen him before.'

She knew that by saying this, she risked losing her love of life.

'Of course you know who he was,' retorted the policeman. 'Look, don't worry, nothing's going to happen to you. We've arrested almost the whole group, and we just need witnesses for the trial.'

'I don't know anything. I was nowhere near. I didn't see who did it.'

The inspector shook his head in despair.

'You'll have to repeat that at the trial,' he said, 'knowing that you're committing perjury, that is, lying to the judge, a crime for which you could spend as long in prison as the murderers themselves.'

Months later, she was called as a witness. The boys were all there with their lawyers and seemed almost to be enjoying the situation. One of the other girls who had been at the club that night identified the murderer in court.

Then it was Cristina's turn. The prosecutor asked her to identify the person who had slit her friend's throat.

'I don't know who did it,' she said.

She was black and the daughter of immigrants. She had a student grant from the government. All she wanted was to recover her will to live, and to feel once again that she had a future. She had spent weeks staring at her bedroom ceiling, not wanting to study or to do anything. The world in which she had lived up until then did not belong to her any more. At sixteen, she had learned in the hardest way possible that she was incapable of fighting for her own security. She needed to leave Antwerp, to travel the world, to recover her joy and her strength.

The boys were let off for lack of evidence; the prosecution had needed two witnesses to corroborate the charges and ensure that the guilty parties paid for their crime. After leaving court, Cristina phoned the numbers on the business cards given her by the two photographers and made appointments to see them. Then she went back to the dress-shop where the owner had come out especially to speak to her and ask if she would model his clothes. The saleswomen, however, said that the owner had shops all over Europe and was a very busy man, and no, they couldn't give her his phone number.

Fortunately, photographers have better memories and both immediately recognised her name and arranged to meet her.

Cristina went back home and told her mother what she had decided to do. She didn't ask her advice or try to convince her, she simply said that she wanted to leave Antwerp for good, and that her one chance was to get work as a model.

Jasmine looks around her again. It's still three hours until the fashion show, and the other models are eating salad, drinking tea and talking about where they'll be going next. They come from various countries, are about the same age as her - nineteen - and probably have just two things on their minds: getting a new contract that evening and finding a rich husband.

She knows their beauty routine. Before sleeping, they apply sundry creams to cleanse their pores and keep their skin moisturised, thus, from early on, making their skin dependent on artificial substances to maintain an ideal equilibrium. In the morning, they apply more cream and more moisturiser. They drink a cup of black coffee with no sugar, and eat some fruit and fibre, so that any other food they consume during the day will pass quickly through. Then they do a few stretching exercises before setting off in search of work. They're too young to start working out in a gym and, besides, their bodies might start taking on masculine contours. They get on the scales three or four times a day; in fact, most of them always have their own scales with them just in case, because sometimes they stay in boarding houses rather than hotels. They get depressed each time the pointer on the scales tells them they've gained another ounce.

Most of the models are only seventeen or eighteen, and so their mothers go with them whenever possible. The girls never admit to being in love with anyone – although most of them are – because love makes the travelling seem longer and more unbearable and arouses in their boyfriends the strange sense that they're losing the woman (or girl) that they love. Yes, the girls think about money and earn an average of 400 euros a day – an enviable salary for someone who is often still too young to have a licence and drive a car. Their dreams go beyond being a model, however; they know that soon they'll be overtaken by new faces, new trends, and so urgently need to show that they can do more than just stride down a catwalk. They're always nagging their agencies to get them a screen test, so that they can demonstrate that they've got what it takes to become an actress – their great dream.

The agencies, of course, agree to do this, but advise them to wait a little – after all, their careers are only just beginning. The truth is that most model agencies don't have many contacts outside the fashion world; they earn a good percentage, compete with other agencies and the market isn't that big. It's best to get what they can now, before time passes and the model crosses the dangerous age barrier of twenty, by which time, her skin will have been spoiled by too many moisturisers, her body ruined by too much low-calorie food, and her mind already affected by the remedies she takes to inhibit appetite and which end up leaving eyes and head completely empty.

Contrary to what most people think, models pay their own expenses – flights, hotels and those inevitable salads. They are summoned by a designer's assistant to do what is known as 'casting', namely, selecting who will appear on the catwalk or in the photos. They are faced at these sessions by a lot of disgruntled people who use the little power they have to vent their own day-to-day frustrations and who never say a kind or encouraging word: 'awful' or 'dreadful' are the ones most commonly heard. The girls leave that test and move on to the next, clinging to their mobile phones for dear life, as if these were about to offer some divine revelation or at least put them in contact with the Higher World to which they dream of ascending and from where they'll be able to look down on all those other pretty faces and where they will be transformed into stars.

Their parents are proud that their daughters have got off to a good start and regret their initial opposition to such a career; after all, their daughters are earning money and helping the family. Their boyfriends get upset, but keep a lid on their feelings because it's good for one's ego to be seen going out with a professional model. The models' agents work with dozens of girls of a similar age and with similar fantasies, and are ready with pat answers to the kind of questions the girls all ask: 'Couldn't I take part in the Fashion Week in Paris?' 'Do you think I have what it takes to get into the movies?' The girls' friends envy them – either secretly or openly.

These young models go to any party they're invited to. They behave as if they were much more important than they are, knowing, deep down, that they would love someone to break through the artificial barrier of ice they create around themselves. They look at older men with a mixture of revulsion and attraction; they know that such men have the necessary money to help them make the big leap, but, at the same time, don't want to seem to be nothing but high-class whores. They're always seen with a glass of champagne in one hand, but that's just part of the image they want to project. They know that alcohol can affect their weight and so their preferred drink is a glass of still mineral water because although fizzy water doesn't affect their weight, it has immediate consequences on the shape of the stomach. They have ideals, dreams, dignity, but all these things will vanish one day, when they can no longer disguise the early onset of cellulite.

They make a secret pact with themselves never to think about the future. They spend much of what they earn on beauty products promising eternal youth. They adore shoes, but they're so expensive; nevertheless, they sometimes treat themselves and buy a pair of the very best. They get clothes from friends in the fashion world at half the usual price. They share a small apartment with their parents, a brother who's at university and a sister who's chosen to be a librarian or a scientist. Everyone assumes the girls must be earning a fortune and frequently ask them for loans, to which the girls agree because they want to appear important, rich, generous and different from other mortals. When they go to the bank, though, their account is always in the red and they've overshot their credit-card limit.

They acquire hundreds of business cards, meet well-dressed men who make proposals of work they know to be false, but they phone them now and then to keep in touch, conscious that they might need help one day, even though that help comes at a price. They all fall into the same traps. They all dream of easy success, only to realise that it doesn't exist. By seventeen, they have all suffered innumerable disappointments, betrayals, humiliations, and yet still they believe.

They sleep badly because of the various pills they take. They listen to stories about anorexia – the commonest illness in their world, a kind of mental disturbance caused by an obsession with weight and one's physical appearance, and which culminates in the body rejecting all nourishment. They say it won't ever happen to them, but never notice when the first symptoms appear.

They step out of childhood straight into a world of glitz and glamour, without passing through adolescence. When asked what their plans are for the future, they always have the answer on the tip of their tongue: 'I'm going to study philosophy. I'm just working to pay for my studies.'

They know this isn't true. Or rather, they know that something about these words doesn't ring true, but they can't quite put their finger on what it is. Do they really want a degree? Do they really need that money for their studies? They don't have time for college because there's always a casting session in the morning, a photo shoot in the afternoon, a cocktail party before dark, then another party they have to go to in order to be seen, admired and desired.

To other people, they seem to lead a fairy-tale existence. And, for a while, they, too, believe that this is the real meaning of life; after all, they have almost everything they once envied in the girls who appeared in magazines and cosmetic ads. With a little discipline, they can even save a little money, until, after a careful, daily examination of their skin, they discover the first mark left by age. After that, they know it's only a matter of time before a designer or a photographer notices the same thing. Their days are numbered.

I took the one less traveled by,
And that has made all the difference.

Instead of going back to her book, Jasmine gets up, fills her glass with champagne (it's always there, but rarely drunk), picks up a hot dog and goes over to the window. She stands there in silence, looking out at the sea. Her story is different.

1.46 p.m.

He wakes up bathed in sweat. When he looks at the clock on the bedside table, he realises that he's only been asleep for forty minutes. He's exhausted, frightened, in a state of panic. He had always thought himself incapable of harming anyone, and yet this morning he has already killed two innocent people. It isn't the first time he's destroyed a world, but, before, he had always had good reasons for doing so.

He dreamed that the girl on the bench near the beach came to see him and instead of condemning him, blessed him. He lay in her lap, weeping and begging her to forgive him, but she seemed not to care about that, and simply stroked his hair and told him not to upset himself. Olivia, the image of generosity and forgiveness. He wonders now if his love for Ewa is worth what he is doing.

He prefers to believe that it is. The fact that Olivia is on his side, that he met with her on a higher plane closer to the Divine, and that everything has been so much easier than he imagined, all this indicates that there must be a reason behind what is happening.

It hadn't been difficult to evade the vigilant eyes of Javits' friends. He knew that such men, as well as being physically prepared to react rapidly and precisely, were trained to memorise each face, follow every movement, second-guess any danger. They probably knew he was armed, which is why they watched him for a while, but relaxed when they realised he didn't constitute a threat. They might even have thought he was in the same line of work and had gone to the marquee to check out the place and see if it was safe for his own boss.

He had no boss. And he *was* a threat. The moment he went into the marquee and decided who would be his next victim, there was no turning back or only at the risk of losing all self-respect. He saw that the ramp leading into the marquee was guarded, but that it was perfectly easy to slip out onto the beach. He left ten minutes after he had arrived, hoping that Javits' friends would notice that he had gone. He then walked round the marquee and came back up the ramp reserved for guests at the Hotel Martinez (he had to show his key card) and into the area reserved for the 'lunch'. Walking on sand in one's shoes wasn't the pleasantest thing in the world, and Igor noticed that he was still feeling tired from the flight, from the fear that his plan might prove impossible to achieve, and from the tension he felt after destroying the universe and future generations of that poor young vendor of craftwork. Nevertheless, he had to go on.

Before returning to the marquee, he took from his pocket the drinking straw that he had made a point of keeping. He opened the small glass flask he had shown to Olivia. It did not, as he had told her, contain petrol, but something quite insignificant: a needle and a piece of cork. Using a thin metal blade, he made a hole in the cork the same diameter as the straw.

Then he rejoined the party, which, by then, was full of guests strolling around, kissing and embracing, giving little yelps of recognition, clutching cocktails of every possible hue just to have something to do with their hands and to keep a check on their anxiety, as they waited for the buffet to open. They could eat then, in moderation, of course, because there were diets and plastic surgery to be considered and suppers at the end of the day, where they would have to eat even though they weren't hungry because that was what etiquette required.

Most of the guests were older people, which meant that this was an event for professionals. The age of the guests further favoured his plan, since almost all of them would need glasses. Needless to say, no one was wearing them because 'tired eyes' are a sign of age. There, everyone had to dress and behave like people in the prime of life, 'young at heart' and 'in excellent health', and to pretend that they were indifferent to what was going on around them because they were preoccupied with other things, when the truth was that they couldn't actually see. Their contact lenses meant that they could just about identify a person a few yards away, and, besides, they would find out soon enough who it was they were talking to.

Only two of the guests noticed everything and everyone – Javits' 'friends'. This time, however, they were the ones being observed.

Igor placed the needle inside the straw, and pretended to put it back in his drink.

A group of pretty girls standing near Javits' table appeared to be listening, entranced, to the extraordinary tales told by a Jamaican man. In fact, each girl was plotting how to get rid of her rivals and carry the man off to bed because Jamaicans have such a reputation as studs.

Igor moved closer to Javits, took the straw from the glass and blew through it, projecting the needle inside in the direction of his victim. He stayed only long enough to see Javits put his hand to his back. Then he left and went straight back to the hotel to try and get some sleep.

Curare, originally used by South American Indians for hunting with darts, can also be found in European hospitals because, under controlled conditions, it can be used to paralyse certain muscles, thus facilitating the surgeon's work. A fatal dose – like that on the point of the needle he had shot into Javits' back – could kill a bird in just two minutes. Boar, on the other hand, take fifteen minutes to die and large mammals - a man for example - twenty.

As soon as it gets into the bloodstream, the nervous fibres of the body relax, then stop functioning altogether, causing gradual asphyxia. The strangest thing - or the worst, some might say - is that the victim remains conscious throughout, but cannot move in order to ask for help nor stop the slow process of paralysis overtaking his body.

If someone cuts his finger on a poisoned dart or arrow during a hunting expedition in the jungle, the Indians know exactly what to do. They use mouth-to-mouth resuscitation and a herbal antidote that they always carry with them because such accidents are commonplace. In cities, the paramedics can do nothing because they think they're dealing with a heart attack.

Igor did not look back as he walked to the hotel. He knew that just then one of the two 'friends' would be frantically searching out the perpetrator, while the other would be ringing for an ambulance, which would arrive quickly enough, but the crew would have little idea what was going on. They would be wearing colourful uniforms and high-visibility jackets, and carrying a defibrillator - to apply a series of shocks to the heart - and a portable electrocardiogram. In the case of curare, the heart seems to be the last muscle affected and continues beating even after brain death has occurred.

The paramedics would notice nothing strange about his heartbeat, and so would put him on a drip, assuming he was suffering from some form of heat-stroke or food-poisoning, although they would still take all the usual measures, even applying an oxygen mask. By then, the twenty minutes would be up, and although the body might still be alive, the brain would now be in a vegetative state.

* * *

Yes, he had planned everything. He had used his private plane so that he could enter France with an unregistered gun and with the various poisons he had obtained via his connections with the Chechen mafia working in Moscow. Each step, each move had been carefully studied and rehearsed, as if he were planning a business meeting. He had made a list of victims in his head. Apart from the one he had met and talked to, the others were all to be of different classes, ages and nationalities. He had spent months analysing the lives of serial killers, using a computer programme that was very popular with terrorists and which left no record of any searches you made. He had taken all the necessary steps to escape unnoticed once he had carried out his mission.

He is sweating. No, it's not remorse – perhaps Ewa really does deserve such a sacrifice – but the thought of the possible futility of the project. He needed the woman he most loved to know he was capable of doing anything for her, including destroying universes, but was it really worth it? Or is it sometimes necessary to accept fate and allow things to develop in their own way and simply wait for people to come to their senses in their own time?

He's tired. He can't think straight any more and, who knows, perhaps martyrdom was better than murder, surrendering himself and thus making a greater sacrifice, offering up his own life for love. Jesus was the best example of that. When his enemies saw Jesus defeated and hung upon a cross, they thought it was all over. They felt proud of what they, the victors, had done, convinced that they had put paid to the problem once and for all.

Igor is confused. His intention was to destroy universes, not relinquish his freedom out of love. In his dream, the girl with the dark eyebrows had resembled Notre Dame de Piétat; the mother with her son in her arms, at once proud and long-suffering.

He goes into the bathroom, puts his head under the shower and turns on the cold water. Perhaps it's lack of sleep, being in a strange place, in a different time zone, or the fact that he was actually doing the thing he had planned to do, but never thought he would. He remembers the promise he made before the relics of St Mary Magdalene in Moscow. But is what he's doing right? He needs a sign.

Sacrifice. Yes, he should have thought of that, but perhaps he needed the experience of destroying those two worlds this morning to be able to see more clearly what is going on. The redemption of love through total surrender. His body will be handed over to the executioners who judge only one's gestures and who forget about the intentions and reasons that lie behind any act that society considers 'insane'. Jesus (who understands that love merits any amount of sacrifice) will receive his spirit, and Ewa will have his soul. She will know what he was capable of: surrender, self-immolation, and all for the sake of one person. He won't be condemned to death because the guillotine was abolished in France decades ago, but he might spend many years in prison. Ewa will repent of her sins. She'll come to see him, bring him food, they'll have time to talk, reflect, love, and even though their bodies do not touch, their souls will be closer than ever. Even if they have to wait years before they can live in the house he intends building on the shores of Lake Baikal, that period of waiting will purify and bless them.

Yes, sacrifice. He turns off the shower, looks at his face in the mirror for a moment, and sees not himself but the Lamb prepared to be slaughtered once again. He puts on the same clothes he was wearing this morning, goes out into the street, heads for the place where the little street vendor used to sit and goes up to the first policeman he meets.

'I killed the girl who used to work here.'

The policeman looks at him and sees a well-dressed man with dishevelled hair and dark circles under his eyes.

'The one who used to sell craftwork?'

Igor nods.

The policeman doesn't take much notice of him. He greets a couple who are walking by, laden with shopping.

'You should get a maid!'

'If you'll pay her wages,' retorts the woman, smiling. 'You just can't get the staff these days!'

'Oh, come on, money can't be the reason. You have a different diamond on your finger every week.'

Igor cannot understand what's going on. He has just confessed to a murder.

'Did you hear what I said?'

'Look, it's very hot. Go and lie down for a bit. Cannes has a lot to offer its visitors.'

'But what about the girl?'

'Did you know her?'

'I'd never seen her before in my life. She was here this morning. I …'

'… you saw the ambulance arrive and someone being taken away and concluded she'd been murdered. I don't know where you're from, sir, I don't know if you've got children yourself, but just watch out for drugs. People say they're not as bad as all that, but look what happened to that poor girl.'

And the policeman moves away without waiting for a response.

Should Igor have insisted, given more details? Then would the policeman have taken him seriously? But, of course, it's impossible to kill someone in broad daylight and on the main street in Cannes. He had even been ready to own up to the other world he had destroyed at a party packed with people.

But the representative of law and order and good manners hadn't wanted to listen to him. What kind of world was he living in? Would he have to take the gun out of his pocket and start firing in all directions for them to believe him? Would he have to behave like a barbarian who kills for no reason before they would finally listen to him?

Igor watches the policeman cross the road and go into a snack bar. He decides to wait for a while, just in case he should change his mind, get further information from the police station and come back and ask him for more details of the crime. However, he's pretty certain that won't happen.

He remembers the policeman's remark to the woman about the diamond on her finger. Did he perhaps know where it came from? Of course not; if he did, he would have taken her straight to the police station and charged her with handling criminal property.

As far as the woman was concerned, the diamond had magically appeared in some high-class shop, having - as the shop assistants always said - first been cut by Dutch or Belgian jewellers. It would be classified according to cut, colour, clarity and carat weight. The price could vary from a few hundred euros to something most mere mortals would consider truly outrageous.

A diamond, or brilliant to give it its other name, is, as everyone knows, just a piece of coal that has been worked on by heat and time. Since it contains no organic matter, it is impossible to know how long it takes for its structure to change, although geologists estimate something between 300 million and a billion years. Diamonds generally form ninety miles below the Earth's crust and gradually rise to the surface, where they can be mined.

Diamond is the hardest and most resistant of natural materials, and it takes a diamond to cut another diamond. The particles produced by this process are used in machines made for polishing and cutting. The real importance of diamonds lies in their use as jewels. A diamond is the supreme manifestation of human vanity.

A few decades ago, in a world that seemed about to return to more practical things and greater social equality, diamonds began to disappear from the market. Then the largest mining company in the world, with its headquarters in South Africa, decided to commission one of the best advertising agencies in the world. Superclass met with Superclass, research was carried out and the result was a three-word phrase:

'Diamonds are forever.'

Problem solved. Jewellers took up the slogan, and the industry began to flourish again. If diamonds are forever, what better way to express one's love which, in theory at least, should also be eternal? What better way of distinguishing the Superclass from the other billions of inhabitants who make up the bottom half of the pyramid? The demand for the stones increased and prices started to rise. In a matter of a few years, that same South African company, which had, up until then, set the rules for the international market, found itself surrounded by corpses.

Igor knows what he's talking about. When he helped form an army to get involved in a tribal conflict in Africa, it had proved an extremely difficult task. Not that he regrets it because, although few people knew about the project, he managed to save many lives. He had mentioned it once in passing to Ewa over some now forgotten supper, but had decided to say no more. When he performed a charitable act, he preferred his right hand not to know what his left hand was doing. Diamonds had helped him save many lives, although that fact will never appear in his biography.

The policeman who takes no notice when a criminal confesses to a crime, but praises the jewel on the finger of a woman carrying bags packed with toilet paper and cleaning materials, is simply not fit for the job. He doesn't know that this pointless industry creates about $50 billion a year, employs a vast army of miners, transporters, private security companies, diamond factories, insurance companies, wholesalers and luxury boutiques. He doesn't realise that it begins in the mud and has to cross whole rivers of blood before it reaches a shop window.

The mud is where the miner spends his life looking for the stone that will eventually bring him the fortune he so desires. He finds several and sells each stone for an average of $20, a stone that will end up costing the consumer $10,000. But he's happy enough because, where he lives, people earn less than $50 a year, and five stones are enough for him to enjoy a short but happy life, working as he does in the worst possible conditions.

The stones are bought by unidentified buyers and immediately passed on to irregular armies in Liberia, the Congo and in Angola. In those countries, a man, surrounded by guards armed to the teeth, is designated to go to an airstrip where planes can land illegally. A plane duly lands, a man in a suit gets out, usually accompanied by another man in shirtsleeves, carrying a small suitcase. There is a perfunctory exchange of greetings. The man with the bodyguards hands over a few small packages; perhaps for superstitious reasons, the packages are always made from old tights.

The man in shirtsleeves takes a special jeweller's eyeglass from his pocket, puts it to his left eye, and begins to check each piece, one by one. After about an hour and a half, he has a good idea of what he's dealing with; he then takes a small precision electronic weighing balance from his case and empties the contents of the packages onto the scale. He makes a few calculations on a sheet of paper. The material is placed in the suitcase along with the balance; the man in the suit signals to the armed guards, and five or six of them board the plane. They start to unload large crates, which they pile up beside the airstrip until the plane leaves again. The whole operation takes most of the day.

The large crates are opened. They contain precision rifles, anti-personnel mines and bullets that explode on impact, releasing dozens of small, deadly metal balls. The arms are handed out to mercenaries and soldiers, and soon the country finds itself facing another ruthless coup d'état. Whole tribes are murdered, children's legs or arms are blown off by cluster bombs, women are raped. Meanwhile, a long way away – usually in Antwerp or in Amsterdam – earnest men are working with love and dedication, painstakingly cutting the stones, exhilarated by their own skill, hypnotised by the flashes of light that begin to emerge from each new facet of that piece of coal whose structure was transformed by time. Diamond cutting diamond.

On the one hand, women screaming in despair beneath a smoke-shrouded sky. On the other, beautiful old buildings seen through the windows of well-lit rooms.

In 2002, the United Nations adopted a resolution, the Kimberley Process, that tried to trace the origin of diamonds and forbade jewellers from buying any that came from war zones. For some time, the respectable European diamond cutters went back to buying stones from the South African monopoly. However, ways were found of making a diamond 'official', and the resolution became a mere sham that allowed politicians to claim that they were doing something to put an end to 'blood diamonds' as these became known.

Five years ago, Igor had swapped diamonds for arms and created a small group intended to put an end to a bloody conflict in the north of Liberia, and he had succeeded – only the murderers were killed. Peace returned to the small villages, and the diamonds were sold to jewellers in America, with no awkward questions asked.

When society doesn't act to stop crime, men have the right to do whatever they think correct.

Something similar had happened a few minutes ago on that beach. As soon as both murders were discovered, someone would turn to the public and say what they always said:

'We're doing our best to identify the murderer.'

So be it. Once again, ever-generous destiny had shown the way ahead. Sacrifice wasn't enough. Besides, when he thought about it, Ewa would have found his absence unbearable, with no one to talk to during the long nights and endless days while she awaited his release. She would weep whenever she thought of him in his cold cell, staring at the blank prison walls. And when the time finally came for them to go and live in the house on the shores of Lake Baikal, they might be too old to experience all the adventures they had planned together.

The policeman comes out of the snack bar and joins him on the pavement.

'Are you still here, sir? Are you lost? Do you need help?'

'No, thank you.'

'Like I said, go and have a rest. The sun can be very dangerous at this time of day.'

He goes back to the hotel and takes a shower. He asks the receptionist to wake him at four; that way he should be rested enough to recover the necessary clarity of mind not to go doing any more such foolish things. He had very nearly ruined his whole plan.

He phones the concierge and reserves a table on the hotel terrace for when he wakes up; he'd like to drink some tea there undisturbed. Then he lies down, staring up at the ceiling and waiting for sleep to come.

What does it matter where diamonds are from, as long as they shine?

In this world, only love deserves absolutely everything. Nothing else makes sense.

As he has many times before in his life, Igor feels a sense of total freedom. The confusion in his head is slowly disappearing and lucidity is returning.

He had placed his fate in Jesus' hands, and Jesus had decided that he should continue with his mission.

He falls asleep without any feeling of guilt whatsoever.

1.55 p.m.

Gabriela decides to walk very slowly to the place where she is to pick up the boat. She needs to put her thoughts in order, she needs to calm down. She is at a point where not only her most secret dreams might become reality, but also her worst nightmares.

Her phone rings. It's a text message from her agent.

'Congratulations.Accept whatever they offer. xxx'

She watches the crowds of people who seem to be wandering aimlessly up and down the Boulevard. She, on the other hand, has a goal! She isn't just another of the chancers who come to Cannes and don't know quite where to start. She has a solid CV, some respectable professional baggage, she's never tried to get ahead in life merely by using her physical attributes and she has real talent! That's why she's been chosen to meet this famous director, without any help from anyone, without having to dress in a provocative manner, without even having time to rehearse her role. He would, of course, take all these things into consideration.

She stops for a snack – she hasn't eaten anything all day – and as soon as she takes her first sip of coffee, her thoughts seem to come back down to earth.

Why had she been chosen?

What exactly would her role in the film be?

And what if, when Gibson saw the video of the audition, he decided she wasn't the person he was looking for?

'Calm down.'

She has nothing to lose, she tells herself, but another voice insists:

'This is your one and only chance.'

There's no such thing as a 'one and only chance'; life always gives you another chance, but the voice says again:

'Maybe, but how long before another chance comes along? You know how old you are, don't you?'

Of course, she does. She's twenty-five, in a world in which actresses, even the most committed, etc., etc.

She doesn't need to go over all that again. She pays for the sandwich and the coffee and makes her way over to the quay, this time trying to control her optimism, telling herself not to refer to other people as 'chancers', mentally reciting the rules of positive thinking that she can remember, anything to avoid dwelling on that all too imminent meeting.

'If you believe in victory, then victory will believe in you.'

'Risk everything in the name of chance and keep well away from everything that offers you a world of comfort.'

'Talent is a universal gift, but it takes a lot of courage to use it. Don't be afraid to be the best.'

It isn't enough to focus on what great teachers have said; she needs help from the heavens. She starts to pray, as she always does when she's anxious. She feels the need to make a promise and decides that, if she does get the role, she will walk all the way from Cannes to the Vatican. If the film gets made. If it's a world-wide success.

No, it would be enough just to get a part in a film with Gibson because that would attract the attention of other directors and producers. Then she will make the promised pilgrimage.

She reaches the appointed place, looks at the sea and again at the message she received from her agent; if her agent already knows about it, that must mean the director is serious. But what did 'accept whatever they offer' mean? That she should sleep with the director or with the starring actor?

She's never done that before, but she's prepared to do anything now. Besides, who hasn't dreamed of sleeping with a movie star?

She looks at the sea again. She could have gone back to the apartment and changed her clothes, but she's superstitious. If a pair of jeans and a white T-shirt were enough to get her this far, she should at least wait until the end of the day to change her clothes. She loosens her belt and sits in the lotus position and starts to do some yoga breathing. She breathes slowly, and body, heart and thoughts all settle into place.

She sees the launch approaching. A man jumps out and says: 'Gabriela Sheery?'

She nods, and the man asks her to go with him. They get into the launch and set off across a sea crowded with yachts of all types and sizes. The man doesn't say another word, as if he were far away, perhaps dreaming about what might be going on in the cabins of those small boats or how good it would be to own one. Gabriela hesitates: her head is full of questions and doubts, and a sympathetic word can often make a stranger into an ally who might help with valuable tips on how to behave. But she doesn't know who he is. He might have influence with Gibson or be merely a no-count assistant who gets landed with jobs like picking up unknown actresses and taking them to his boss.

Best to say nothing.

Five minutes later, they draw up alongside a huge white boat. The name on the prow is *Santiago*. A sailor climbs down a ladder and helps her aboard. She passes through the spacious central-reception room in which preparations are under way for what looks like a big party later that night. She walks towards the stern of the boat, where there is a small swimming pool, two tables shaded by parasols and a few sun-loungers. Enjoying the afternoon sun are Gibson and the Star!

'I wouldn't mind sleeping with either of them,' she thinks, smiling to herself. She feels more confident, although her heart is beating faster than usual.

The Star looks her up and down and gives her a friendly, reassuring smile. Gibson gives her a firm handshake, gets up, takes one of the chairs from the nearest table and tells her to sit down.

Then he phones someone and asks for the number of a hotel room. He repeats it out loud, looking at her.

It was just as she imagined – a hotel room.

He switches off his phone.

'When you leave here, go straight to this suite at the Hilton. That's where Hamid Hussein's clothes are on display. You've been invited to tonight's party in Cap d'Antibes.'

It wasn't at all as she imagined. The part was hers. And she would be going to a party in Cap d'Antibes – *a party in Cap d'Antibes*!

He turns to the Star.

'What do you think?'

'I think we should hear what she has to say.'

Gibson nods and makes a gesture meaning 'Tell us a little about yourself.' Gabriela starts with the drama course she took and the advertisements she's appeared in. She notices that the two men are no longer listening. They must have heard the same story thousands of times. And yet she can't stop, she's talking faster and faster, feeling that she has nothing more to say and that this chance of a lifetime depends on finding just the right word, which she is patently failing to do. She takes a deep breath and tries to appear at ease; she wants to seem witty and so she makes a joke, but she's incapable of departing from the script her agent taught her to follow in such interviews.

After two minutes, Gibson interrupts her.

'That's great, but we know all that from your CV. Why don't you talk about you?'

Some inner barrier suddenly crumbles. Instead of panicking, her voice grows calmer and steadier.

'I'm just one of millions of people in the world who have always dreamed of being on a yacht like this, looking at the sea, and talking about the possibility of working with at least one of you gentlemen. And you both know that. I doubt there's anything else I might say that will change anything very much. Am I single? Yes. But as is the case with all single women, there's a man back home who's madly in love with me and is waiting for me in Chicago right now, hoping that things here will all go horribly wrong.'

Both men laugh, and she relaxes a little more.

'I want to get as far as I can, although I know I'm almost at the limit of what's possible, given that in the world of movies, my age is already against me. I know there are lots of people out there with as much or more talent than me, but I was chosen - why I don't know - and I've decided to run with it. This might be my last chance, and perhaps the fact that I'm saying this now will decrease my value, but I have no choice. All my life, I've imagined a moment like this: doing an audition, getting chosen and being able to work with real professionals. It's finally happened. If it goes no further than this meeting and I return home empty-handed, at least I know I got here because of two qualities: integrity and perseverance.

'I'm my own best friend and my own worst enemy. Before coming here, I was thinking that I didn't deserve it, that I wouldn't be able to meet your expectations, and that you had probably chosen the wrong candidate. At the same time, my heart was telling me that I was being rewarded because I hadn't given up and had fought to the end.'

She looks away and suddenly feels an intense desire to cry, but controls herself because that might be seen as emotional blackmail. The Star's mellow voice breaks the silence.

'There *are* honest people in the movie world, people who value professionalism, just as there are in any industry. That's why I've got where I am today, and the same with our director here. I've been through exactly what you're going through now. We know how you feel.'

Her whole life passes before her eyes. All the years of seeking without finding, of knocking on doors that wouldn't open, of asking and never getting an answer and being met with blank indifference, as if she didn't exist. All the 'Nos' she had heard when no one even seemed to notice she was alive and at least deserved a response.

'I mustn't cry.'

She thinks about all the people who have told her over the years that she's chasing an impossible dream and who, if this turned out right, would be sure to say: 'I always knew you had talent!' Her lips start to tremble. It's as if all these thoughts were suddenly flowing out of her heart. She's glad to have had the guts to show that she's human and frail and that being chosen has made a huge difference to her soul. If Gibson were now to change his mind about her, she could take the launch back to shore with no regrets. At the moment of battle, she had shown real courage.

She depends on other people. It's taken her a long time to learn this lesson, but she's finally accepted that it's true. She knows people who are proud of their emotional independence, although the truth is they're as fragile as she is and weep in private and never ask for help. They believe in the unwritten rule that says 'the world is for the strong' and 'only the fittest survive'. If that were true, human beings would never have survived because, as a species, we require care and protection for several years. Her father once told her that we only acquire some ability to survive alone by the age of nine, whereas a giraffe takes a mere five hours and a bee achieves independence in less than five minutes.

'What are you thinking?' asks the Star.

'That I don't need to pretend I'm strong, which is an enormous relief. I used to have a lot of problems with relationships because I thought I knew better than anyone else how to get where I wanted. All my boyfriends hated me for this, and I couldn't understand why. Once though, when I was on tour with a play, I came down with the most terrible flu and couldn't leave my room, even though I was terrified that someone else would take my part. I couldn't eat, I was delirious with fever, and eventually they called a doctor, who ordered me home. I thought I had lost both my job and the respect of my colleagues. But that wasn't the case at all: they showered me with flowers and phone calls. They all wanted to know how I was. Suddenly, I realised that the people I believed to be my rivals, competing for the same place in the spotlight, were really concerned about me. One of the other actresses sent me a card on which she'd written the words of a doctor who went abroad to work in some far-off country. He wrote:

'"We've all heard about an illness in Central Africa called sleeping sickness. What we should also know is that a similar disease exists that attacks the soul. It's very dangerous because the early stages often go unnoticed. At the first sign of indifference or lack of enthusiasm, take note! The only preventive against this disease is the realisation that the soul suffers, suffers greatly, when we force it to live superficially. The soul loves all things beautiful and deep."'

Words. The Star thinks of his favourite line from a poem, one that he learned when still at school, and which frightens him more and more as time passes: 'You would have to give up all else, I alone would expect to be your sole and exclusive standard.' Choosing is perhaps the most difficult thing any human being has to do. As the actress tells her story, he sees his own experiences being reflected back at him.

He remembers his first big chance, which he won thanks to his talent as a theatre actor. He remembers how his life changed from one minute to the next, and the fame that overtook him so fast that he didn't really have time to adapt and ended up accepting invitations to places he shouldn't have gone to and rejecting meetings with people who would have helped him go much further in his career. Then there was the money he earned, which wasn't actually that much, but which gave him a sense that he could do anything; there were the expensive presents, the forays into an unfamiliar world, the private planes, the five-star restaurants, and the hotel suites that resembled the palatial rooms of kings and queens as imagined by a child. There were the first reviews, full of respect and praise and words that touched his heart and soul; there were the letters that flooded in from around the world and which he used to answer individually, even arranging to meet some of the women who sent him their photos, until he realised that he simply couldn't keep up that pace, and his agent terrified him by warning him that he could easily become the victim of some entrapment. Nevertheless, even now he still gets a special pleasure out of meeting the fans who have followed every step of his career, who create web pages devoted to his work, distribute little magazines describing everything that's going on in his life – the positive things, that is – and defend him against any attacks in the press, when some performance of his doesn't receive the praise it deserves.

And with the passing years, what had once seemed a miracle or the luckiest of chances, and which he had always promised himself he would never become enslaved by, has gradually become his sole reason to go on living. Then he looks ahead and feels a twinge of anxiety that it all might end one day. There were always younger actors prepared to accept less money in exchange for more work and more visibility. He's noticed that people talk only about the great film that propelled him to fame and which everyone knows about, even though he's made another ninety-nine films that no one really remembers.

The financial conditions are no longer the same either because he made the initial mistake of thinking he would always have work and forced his agent to keep his fee very high. As a result, he got fewer and fewer offers, even though now he charges only half his normal fee to appear in a film.

Feelings of despair are beginning to stir in a world which, up until then, had been made up entirely of the hope that he would get ever farther, ever higher and ever more quickly. He cannot allow himself to lose his value just like that, and so now, whenever a script arrives, regardless of its quality, he has to say that he really loves the part they're offering him and that he is willing to do it even if they're unable to offer him his usual fee. The producers pretend to believe him, and his agent pretends that he's managed to pull the wool over their eyes, but he knows that his 'product' needs to keep being seen at festivals like this one, always busy, always polite, always slightly distant, as movie legends should be.

His press officer has suggested that he should be photographed kissing a famous actress so that the resulting photo can appear on the cover of one of the scandal rags. They've already been in contact with the actress in question, who is also in need of a little extra publicity, so now it's simply a matter of choosing the right moment during tonight's gala supper.The clinch should appear spontaneous, although they'll have to be sure there's a photographer nearby, without, of course, seeming to be aware that they're being watched. Later on, when the photos are published, they'll hit the headlines again, denying any love interest and declaring that the photo was an invasion of privacy; lawyers will start legal proceedings against the magazines, and the press officers of both parties will do their best to keep the affair alive for as long as possible.

Despite his many years of work and despite being internationally famous, his situation is not so very different from that of this young actress.

You would have to give up all else, I alone would expect to be your sole and exclusive standard.

Gibson interrupts the thirty-second silence that has fallen upon this perfect scene: the yacht, the sun, the iced drinks, the cries of the seagulls, the cooling breeze.

'I assume you'd like to know about the role you'll be playing because the title of the film could change between now and its première. Well, you'll be playing opposite him.'

And he indicates the Star.

'That is, you'll be playing one of the principal roles. Your next question, logically enough, must be: why me and not some big-name movie star?'

'Exactly.'

'Money. For the script I've been asked to direct, and which will be the first film produced by Hamid Hussein, we have a very limited budget, half of which will go on promotion rather than on the final product. So we need a big name to pull in the crowds and a complete unknown, who'll be cheap, but will get lots of media attention. This isn't anything new. Ever since the movie industry became a force in the world, the studios have always done this in order to keep alive the idea that fame and money are synonymous. I remember, when I was a boy, seeing those great Hollywood mansions and thinking that all actors must earn a fortune.

'Well, it's a lie. There are maybe ten or perhaps twenty stars worldwide who can honestly say that they do earn a fortune, the rest live on appearances: in a house rented by the studio, wearing clothes and jewellery lent by couturiers and jewellers, driving cars on short-term loan from companies who want their name to be associated with the high life. The studio pays for all that glamour, and the actors earn very little. This isn't the case of our friend here, of course, but it will be with you.'

The Star doesn't know if Gibson is being sincere and if he really does include him among the major stars, or if he's just being sarcastic. Not that it matters, just as long as they sign the contract, the producer doesn't change his mind at the last minute, the screenwriters manage to deliver the script on time, they keep strictly to the budget and an excellent PR campaign is set in motion. He's seen hundreds of projects come to nothing; that's just a fact of life. However, his last film went almost unnoticed by the public, and he desperately needs a runaway success. And Gibson is in a position to produce just that.

'I accept,' says the young woman.

'We'll discuss everything with your agent. You'll sign an exclusive contract with us. For the first film, you'll earn $5,000 a month for a year, and you'll have to attend parties and be promoted by our PR department, go wherever we send you and say what we want you to and not what you think. Is that clear?'

Gabriela nods. What could she say? A secretary in Europe could earn $5,000 a month, but it was either take it or leave it, and she doesn't want to appear even a tiny bit hesitant. She understands the rules of the game.

'So,' Gibson says, 'you'll be living like a millionairess and behaving like a big star, but always remember: none of that is true. If all goes well, we'll increase your salary to $10,000 for the next film. Then we'll talk again because you'll probably be thinking: "One day, I'll get my revenge." Naturally, your agent has heard our terms and knows what to expect. Or perhaps you didn't realise that.'

'It doesn't matter, and I have no intention of seeking revenge.'

Gibson pretends not to have heard.

'I didn't call you here to talk about your test: it was great, the best I've seen in a long time. The casting director thought the same. I called you here to make sure you understand, from the start, just what you're getting into. After their first film, when they feel like the world is at their feet, a lot of actresses or actors want to change the rules. But they've signed contracts and know that's impossible. Then they fall into a kind of black depression, go into auto-destruct mode, that kind of thing. So our policy now is to set out plainly how it's going to be. If you're successful, you'll have to learn to live with two women:

one of them will be adored by people around the world, while the other will be constantly aware that she has no power at all.

'So, before you go to the Hilton to collect your clothes for the night, think long and hard about the consequences. When you enter that hotel suite, you'll find four copies of a vast contract waiting for you. Before you sign it, the world is yours and you can do what you like with your life, but the moment you sign, you're no longer the mistress of anything. We will control everything from the way you cut your hair to where you eat, even if you're not hungry. Obviously you can use your new-won fame to earn money from advertising, which is why people accept these conditions.'

The two men get up. Gibson asks the Star:

'Do you think you'll enjoy acting with her?'

'She'll be great. She showed real feeling in a situation where most people are simply trying to look competent.'

'Oh, and, by the way, don't go thinking this yacht is mine,' says Gibson, after calling someone to accompany her to the launch that will return her to shore.

She gets the message.

3.44 p.m.

'Let's go up to the terrace and have a coffee,' says Ewa.

'But the show starts in only an hour from now, and you know what the traffic's like.'

'There's still time for a cup of coffee.'

They go up the stairs, turn right and walk to the end of the corridor. The security guard there knows them already and barely acknowledges them. They walk past glass cases full of jewellery studded with diamonds, rubies and emeralds and emerge into the sunlight on the first-floor terrace. The same very famous jewellery firm hires the area every year to receive friends, celebrities and journalists. It's furnished in the very best of taste, and there's always a table groaning with a constantly replenished supply of delicacies. They sit down at a table shaded by a parasol. A waiter comes over, and they order a sparkling mineral water and an espresso. The waiter asks if they would like something from the buffet, but they decline, saying that they've already eaten. In less than two minutes, he's back with their order.

'Is everything all right?' he asks.

'Yes, thank you, excellent.'

'No,' thinks Ewa, 'things couldn't be worse, although at least the coffee's good.'

Hamid knows that something strange is going on with his wife, but prefers to leave that conversation for another time. He doesn't want to think about it. He doesn't want to risk hearing something along the lines of 'I'm leaving you'. He is disciplined enough to control his feelings.

At one of the other tables sits one of the most famous designers in the world, with his camera beside him. He's staring into space, as if hoping to make it clear that he doesn't want to be disturbed. No one approaches him, and whenever some ill-advised person attempts to do so, the hotel's PR lady, a pleasant woman in her fifties, asks them politely to leave him alone; he needs a respite from the constant barrage of models, journalists, clients and impresarios.

Hamid remembers their first meeting, so many years ago now that it seems like an eternity. He had been in Paris for eleven months, made a few friends in the fashion world, knocked on various doors and, thanks to contacts furnished by the sheikh (who may have known no one in that particular world, but had influential friends in high places), had landed a job as a designer for one of the most respected names in haute-couture. Instead of making sketches based on the materials he was given, he used to stay at the studio until late at night, working with the fabrics he had brought from his own country. During that period, he was twice summoned home. The first occasion was when he learned that his father had died and left him the small family business. Even before he'd had time to think about it, he was informed by one of the sheikh's emissaries that someone would be taking over the business and making the necessary investments to ensure that it prospered, but that ownership would remain in his name.

He asked why, since the sheikh had shown no knowledge of or interest in the subject.

'A French luggage manufacturer is setting up business here. The first thing they did was seek out local fabrics, which they've promised to use in some of their luxury goods. So not only do we already have one client, we can continue to honour our traditions and keep control of the raw material.'

Hamid returned to Paris knowing that his father's soul was in Paradise and that his memory would remain in the land he had so loved. He continued working late into the night, making designs with Bedouin themes and experimenting with the fabrics he had brought back with him. If that French company – known for its innovative designs and good taste – was showing an interest in local products, then news of this would soon reach the capital of fashion and there was sure to be a big demand. It was only a matter of time, but news travelled fast.

One morning, he was called in to see the director. This was the first time he had entered that inner sanctum, the great couturier's office, and he was astonished to see how untidy it was. There were newspapers everywhere, papers piled high on the couturier's antique desk, a vast quantity of photos taken of him with various celebrities, framed magazine covers, fabric samples and a vase full of white feathers of all sizes.

'You're very good at what you do. I had a look at the sketches you leave around for all to see. I'd be careful about doing that if I were you. You never know when someone might change jobs and steal any good ideas they picked up here.'

Hamid didn't like to think he was being spied on, but he said nothing, and the great couturier went on:

'Why do I think you're good? Because you come from a country where people dress very differently, and you're beginning to understand how to adapt those fashions to the West. There's just one problem: we can't buy those fabrics here; also your designs have religious connotations, and fashion is, above all, about clothing the body, although it does inevitably reflect a great deal of what's going on in the soul as well.'

He went over to one of the piles of magazines, and as if he knew exactly what was there, he picked up a particular copy, possibly bought from the *bouquinistes* – the booksellers who have been selling their wares on the banks of the Seine since the days of Napoleon. It was an old *Paris Match* with a picture of Christian Dior on the cover.

'What makes this man a legend? I'll tell you: his ability to understand human beings. Of all the many fashion revolutions, one merits special mention. Immediately after the Second World War, when cloth was in such short supply in Europe that there was barely enough to make clothes at all, he started designing dresses that required an enormous amount of fabric. By doing so, he was not only showing off a beautiful woman beautifully dressed; he was selling the dream that we would once again return to a time of elegance, abundance and plenty. He was attacked and insulted for doing this, but he knew he was going in the right direction, which is always the opposite direction to everyone else.'

He put the magazine back exactly where he had taken it from and returned, holding another one.

'And here is Coco Chanel. She was abandoned by her parents, became a cabaret singer, and was just the kind of woman who could expect only the worst from life. But she seized the one chance she had - in her case, a series of rich lovers - and transformed herself into the most important female couturier of her day. What did she do? She liberated women from the slavery of corsets, those instruments of torture that imprisoned the torso and prevented all natural movement. She made only one mistake: she concealed her past, when that would, in fact, have helped her become an even greater legend - the woman who had survived despite all.'

He put that magazine back in its place too. Then he went on:

'You might ask: why didn't they do that before? We'll never know. People must have tried - couturiers who have been completely forgotten by history because they failed to reflect in their collections the spirit of the times they were living in. Chanel needed more than creative talent and rich lovers to have the impact she had. Society had to be ready for the great feminist revolution that took place at the same time.'

The couturier paused.

'Now it's the turn of the Middle East, precisely because that's the source of all the tension and fear currently keeping the world in limbo. I know this because I'm the director of this company. After all, everything starts with a meeting of the main suppliers of dyes.'

Hamid glances again at the designer sitting alone on the terrace, his camera resting on the armchair beside him. Perhaps he had noticed Hamid arrive and is now wondering just where he got the money that had enabled him to become his biggest competitor.

The man now staring into space and feigning indifference had done everything possible to prevent Hamid from being admitted into the Fédération. He believed Hamid was being financed by oil money and felt that this constituted unfair competition. He didn't know that the director of the label Hamid was working for at the time had offered him a better job (not that 'better' meant his name would appear anywhere; the company had contracted another designer to shine in the spotlight and on the catwalk) nor did he know that two months after this and eight months after the death of his father, Hamid had been summoned to a face-to-face meeting with the sheikh.

When Hamid arrived home, he found it hard to recognise the city that had once been his. The skeletons of skyscrapers lined the city's one avenue; the traffic was unbearable; the old airport was in near chaos; but the sheikh's idea was beginning to take shape. The city would be a place of peace in the midst of war, an investment paradise in the midst of turbulent financial markets, the visible face of a nation that so many people took pleasure in criticising, humiliating and stereotyping. Other countries in the region had also now begun to believe in that city being built in the middle of the desert, and money was starting to flow in, first in a trickle and then like a rushing river.

The palace, however, was the same, although another much larger one was being built not far from there. Hamid arrived at the meeting in an excellent mood, saying that he had just received an excellent job offer and no longer needed the sheikh's financial help; indeed, he would pay back every penny invested in him.

'Hand in your resignation,' said the sheikh.

Hamid didn't understand. He knew that the business his father had left him was doing well, but he had other dreams for his future. However, he couldn't defy this man who had done so much to help him – not a second time.

'At our first meeting, I was able to say "No" to Your Highness because I was defending my father's rights, which were always paramount. Now, though, I must bow to your will. If you think you have lost money by investing in my work, I will do whatever you ask. I will come home and look after my inheritance. If I have to give up my dream in order to honour the code of my tribe, I will do so.'

He spoke these words without a tremor. He dared not show any weakness before a man who so respected other men's strength.

'I'm not asking you to come home. The fact that you were promoted is a sign that you're ready to set up your own company. That is what I want you to do.'

'To set up my own company?' thought Hamid. 'Did I hear him right?'

'More and more of the big fashion companies are setting up business here,' the sheikh went on. 'And they're no fools. Our women are beginning to change the way they think and dress. Fashion has had an even bigger impact on our region than foreign investment. I've spoken to men and women who know about these things. I'm just an old Bedouin who, when he saw his first car, thought it would have to be fed like a camel.

'I'd like foreigners to read our poets, listen to our music, to sing and dance to the songs that were passed down from generation to generation by our ancestors, but no one, it seems, is interested in that. There is only one way in which they can learn to respect our tradition, and that is via the world in which you work. If they can understand who we are by the way we dress, they will eventually understand everything else.'

The following day, Hamid met a group of investors from various other countries. They placed at his disposal an enormous sum of money and gave him a deadline by which it had to be repaid. They asked him if he was ready and prepared to accept the challenge.

Hamid asked for time to think. He went to his father's grave and prayed all afternoon and evening. That night, he walked in the desert, felt the wind freezing his bones. 'Blessed be that which gives your children wings and roots,' says an Arabic proverb.

He needed his roots. There is a place in the world where we are born, where we learn our mother tongue and discover how our ancestors overcame the problems they had to face. There always comes a point when we feel responsible for that place.

He needed wings too. They reveal to us the endless horizons of the imagination, they carry us to our dreams and to distant places. It is our wings that allow us to know the roots of our fellow men and to learn from them.

He asked for inspiration from God and began to pray. Two hours later, he remembered a conversation he had overheard between his father and a friend in his father's shop:

'This morning, my son asked me for money to buy a sheep. Should I help him, do you think?'

'Since it clearly isn't a matter of urgency, wait another week before giving him your answer.'

'But I have the means to help him now. What difference will a week make?'

'A very great difference indeed. Experience has taught me that people only give value to a thing if they have, at some point, been uncertain as to whether or not they'll get it.'

Hamid made the investors wait a week and then accepted the challenge. He needed people who would take care of the money and invest it as he wanted. He needed staff, preferably people who came from his own village. He needed another year in the job he was doing, so that he could learn what he still needed to know. That was all.

'Everything starts with a meeting of the main suppliers of dyes.'

Well, that isn't exactly true: everything begins when the companies involved in studying market trends (*cabinets de tendence* in French, 'trend adapters' in English) take note of the different things – among them fashion – in which each layer of society is currently interested. This research is based on interviews with consumers, the close monitoring of samples, but, above all, on careful observation of a particular cohort of people – usually aged between twenty and thirty – who go to nightclubs, hang out on the streets and read the blogs on the Internet. They never look at what's in the shop windows, even at named brands, because everything there has already reached the general public and is therefore condemned to die.

The trend adapters want to know what will be the *next* thing to capture the consumers' imagination. Young people don't have enough money to buy luxury goods and so have to invent new ways of dressing. Since they live glued to their computer screens, they share their interests with like-minded others and these interests can often become a kind of virus that infects the whole community. Young people influence their parents' views of politics, literature and music, and not, as ingenuous adults believe, the other way round. However, parents influence young people's 'system of values'. Adolescents may be rebellious by nature, but they always believe the family is right; they may dress strangely and enjoy listening to singers who howl and break guitars, but that's as far as it goes. They don't have the courage to go any further and provoke a real revolution in behaviour.

'They did that in the past, but, fortunately, that particular wave has passed and returned to the sea.'

All these studies of market trends show that society is now heading towards a more conservative style, far from the dangers posed by suffragettes (the women at the beginning of the twentieth century who fought for and achieved the right to vote) or by hairy, unhygienic hippies (a group of crazies who believed that peace and free love were real possibilities).

In 1960, for example, the world was caught up in the bloody wars of the post-colonial era, terrified by the threat of nuclear war, and although we were also living through a period of economic prosperity, we were all desperately in need of a little joy. Just as Christian Dior had understood that the hope of future abundance could be expressed through clothes using yards of material, the designers of the Sixties went in search of a combination of colours that would lift people's morale and came to the conclusion that red and violet were simultaneously calming and stimulating.

Forty years later, the collective view had changed completely: the world was no longer under the threat of war, but of grave environmental problems. Designers were opting for colours drawn from the natural world: the sands of the desert, the jungles, the sea. Between these two periods, various other trends - psychedelic, futuristic, aristocratic, nostalgic - arose and vanished.

Before the great designer collections are fully defined, these studies of market trends are used to give a snapshot of the world's current state of mind. It seems now that - despite wars, famine in Africa, terrorism, the violation of human rights and the arrogant attitude of certain developed countries - our main preoccupation is saving poor planet Earth from the many threats created by human society.

'Ecology. Save the planet. How ridiculous.'

Hamid knows, however, that there's no point in fighting the collective unconscious. The colours, the accessories, the fabrics, the so-called charity events attended by the Superclass, the books being published, the music being played on the radio, the documentaries made by ex-politicians, the new films, the material used to make shoes, the new bio-fuels, the petitions handed in to members of parliament and congressmen, the bonds being sold by the largest of the world banks - everything appears to focus on one thing: saving the planet. Fortunes are made overnight; large multinationals are given space in the press because of some completely irrelevant action they are taking; unscrupulous NGOs place advertisements on the major TV channels and receive hundreds of millions of dollars in donations because everyone seems obsessed with the fate of the Earth.

Whenever he reads articles in newspapers or magazines written by politicians using global warming or the destruction of the environment as a platform for their electoral campaigns, he thinks:

'How can we be so arrogant? The planet is, was and always will be stronger than us. *We* can't destroy *it*; if we overstep the mark, the planet will simply erase us from its surface and carry on existing. Why don't they start talking about not letting the planet destroy us?

'Because "saving the planet" gives a sense of power, action and nobility. Whereas "not letting the planet destroy *us*" might lead to feelings of despair and impotence, and to a realisation of just how very limited our capabilities are.'

However, this is what the trends reveal, and fashion must adapt to the desires of the consumers. The dye works were already busy producing what were deemed to be the best colours for the next collection. The cloth-manufacturers were on the hunt for natural fibres; the creators of accessories such as belts, bags, glasses and wristwatches were doing their best to adapt, or at least pretend to adapt, by publishing leaflets printed on recycled paper explaining the lengths they had gone to in order to preserve the environment. All of this would be shown to the major designers at the largest of the fabric shows - closed to the public - and bearing the evocative name of *Première Vision*.

After that, each designer would apply his or her creativity to the new collection and feel that haute-couture was something inventive, original and different. Not true. They were all merely slavishly following what the market trends dictated. The more important the brand, the less willing they were to take any risks, given that the jobs of hundreds of people around the world depended on the decisions of a small group of people, the Superclass of the haute-couture world, which was already weary of pretending that it had something different to sell every six months.

The first designs were made by 'misunderstood geniuses' who dreamed of one day having their own label. They worked for approximately six to eight months, at first with pencil and paper, then with prototypes made out of cheap fabric, which could be photographed on models and analysed by the directors. Out of every one hundred prototypes, about twenty would be chosen for the next show. Adjustments were made - new buttons, a different cut of sleeve, or some unusual stitching.

Then more photos would be taken, this time with the models sitting, lying down or walking, and still further adjustments, because remarks such as 'only suitable for the catwalk' could ruin a whole collection and place a particular label's reputation at risk. During this process, some of the 'misunderstood geniuses' were summarily dismissed, with no right to compensation because they were only there as trainees. The more talented of those who remained would have to rethink their creations several times, aware that, however successful the design, only the name of the label would be mentioned.

They all vowed revenge one day. They told themselves that eventually they would open their own shop and get the recognition they deserved. Meanwhile, they smiled and continued working as if they were thrilled to have been chosen. As the final models were being selected, more people were dismissed and more people taken on (for the next collection), and finally, the genuine fabrics were used to make the clothes that would appear on the catwalk, as if this were the first time they were being shown to the public. This, of course, was part of the legend because, by then, retailers worldwide already had in their hands photos of the various designs taken from every conceivable angle, as well as details of the accessories, the texture of the fabric, the recommended retail price and the addresses of suppliers. Depending on the brand's size and importance, the 'new collection' was already being produced on a large scale in various countries around the world.

Then, finally, the big day arrived, or, rather, the three weeks that marked the beginning of a new era (which, as they all knew, would last only six months). It began in London, then went on to Milan and ended in Paris. Journalists were invited from all over the world, photographers jockeyed for the best places, and everything was treated with the greatest secrecy; newspapers and magazines devoted pages and pages to the latest designs; women were dazzled, and men regarded with a certain scorn what they thought of as a mere 'fashion item' and thought sourly about how they would have to spend a few thousand dollars on something of not the slightest importance to them, but which their wives considered to be an emblem of the Superclass.

A week later, something that had been described as 'exclusive' was already available in shops around the world. No one asked how it had managed to travel so fast and be produced in such a short space of time. The legend, however, is more important than the reality.

The consumers didn't realise these new fashions were created by those who were merely following the existing fashions, that exclusivity was just a lie they chose to believe, that many of the collections praised by the specialist press belonged to the large manufacturers of luxury goods, who supported those same magazines and journals by placing full-page advertisements. There were, of course, exceptions and, after a few years of struggle, Hamid Hussein was one of them, and therein lay his power.

He notices that Ewa is again checking her mobile phone, which she doesn't normally do. The fact is that she hates the thing, perhaps because it reminds her of a past relationship, a period of her life about which he still knows little or nothing because neither of them ever refers to it. He glances at his watch. They still have time to finish their drinks without rushing. He looks again at the other designer. If only it did all begin with a meeting of dye manufacturers and end on the catwalk, but that wasn't the case.

He and the man now sitting alone and staring out at the horizon first met at *Première Vision*. Hamid was still working for the major fashion house that had taken him on as a designer, although the sheikh had, by then, already started organising the small army of eleven people who would put into practice the idea of using fashion as a window on to their world, their religion and their culture.

'Most of the time we stand here listening to explanations of how to present simple things in the most complicated way possible,' Hamid had said.

They were walking past stands displaying the latest fabrics, the latest revolutionary techniques, the colours that would be used over the next two years, the ever more sophisticated accessories – platinum belt buckles, push-button credit-card holders, watchstraps the size of which could be minutely regulated with the help of a diamond-encrusted dial.

The couturier looked him up and down.

'The world always was and always will be complicated.'

'I don't think so, and if I ever leave the company I'm working for now, it will be to open my own business, which will go against all these beliefs.'

The couturier laughed.

'You know what the world of fashion is like. You've heard of the Fédération, haven't you, well, it takes foreigners a very, very long time to get accepted.'

The Fédération Française de la Couture was one of the world's most exclusive clubs. It decided who could or couldn't take part in the Fashion Weeks in Paris, as well as setting the parameters to be followed by participants. First created in 1868, it had enormous power. It trademarked the expression 'haute-couture' so that no one outside the Fédération could use it without running the risk of being sued. It published the ten thousand copies of the Official Catalogue for the two great annual events, decided which journalists would receive the two thousand press passes, selected the major buyers and selected the venue for each show according to the importance of the designer.

'Yes, I know what the world of fashion is like,' said Hamid, bringing the conversation to a close. He sensed that the man he was talking to would, in the future, be a great designer, but he knew, too, that they would never be friends.

Six months later, everything was ready for his great adventure. He resigned from his job, opened his first shop in St-Germain-des-Près and started to fight as best he could. He lost many battles, but realised one thing: he could not bow to the tyranny of the companies who dictated the fashion trends. He had to be original, and he succeeded because he brought with him the simplicity of the Bedouin, a knowledge of the desert, everything he had learned at the company where he had worked for over a year, as well as the advice of certain financial experts, together with textiles that were completely new and original.

Two years later, he had opened five or six large shops throughout France and had been accepted by the Fédération, not just because of his talent, but through the sheikh's contacts, whose emissaries controlled which French companies could open branches in their country.

More water flowed under the bridge, people changed their minds, presidents were elected or stepped down, the new technology grew in popularity, the Internet began to dominate world communications, public opinion became more influential in all spheres of human activity, luxury and glamour regained the position they had lost. His work grew and expanded. He wasn't just involved now in fashion, but in accessories, furniture, beauty products, watches and exclusive fabrics.

Hamid was now the master of an empire, and all those who had invested in his dream were richly rewarded with the dividends paid to shareholders. He continued to supervise much of what his businesses produced, attended the most important photo shoots, still designed most of the clothes, and visited the desert three times a year to pray at his father's grave and give an account of his activities to the sheikh. Now he has taken up a new challenge; he is going to produce a film.

He glances at his watch again and tells Ewa it's time to go. She asks if it really is so very important.

'No, it's not, but I'd like to be there.'

Ewa gets to her feet. Hamid takes one last look at the famous couturier, sitting alone and contemplating the Mediterranean, oblivious to everything.

4.07 p.m.

The young all have the same dream: to save the world. Some quickly forget this dream, convinced that there are more important things to do, like having a family, earning money, travelling and learning a foreign language. Others, though, decide that it really is possible to make a difference in society and to shape the world we will hand on to future generations.

They start by choosing their profession: politicians (whose initial impulse always stems from a desire to help their local community), social activists (who believe that the root of all crime lies in class differences), artists (who believe there's no hope at all and that we'll just have start again from zero) … and policemen.

Savoy had been sure he could be a useful member of society. Having read a great deal of detective fiction, he imagined that once the baddies were all behind bars, the goodies would be able to enjoy their place in the sun for ever. He went to police college where he studied assiduously, received excellent marks for his theory exams, prepared himself physically for dangerous situations and trained as a sharpshooter, although he hoped never to have to kill anyone.

During his first year, he felt that he was learning about the nitty-gritty of the profession. His colleagues complained about low salaries, incompetent judges, other people's preconceived ideas about the job, and the almost complete absence of any real action in their particular area. As time passed, life as a policeman and the complaints continued more or less the same, apart from the addition of one thing: paper.

Endless reports on the where or how or why of a particular incident. A simple case of someone dumping some rubbish, for example, required the rubbish in question to be meticulously searched for evidence of the guilty party's identity (there are always clues, like envelopes or plane tickets), the area then had to be photographed, a map drawn, the perpetrator identified and sent a friendly warning, followed by a rather less friendly warning and, if the transgressor refused to take the matter seriously, by a visit to court, where statements were taken and sentences handed down, all of which, of course, required the services of competent lawyers. Two whole years might pass before the case was finally relegated to the files, with no real consequences for either side.

Murders, on the other hand, were extremely rare. Recent statistics showed that most of the crime in Cannes involved fights between rich kids in expensive nightclubs, break-ins at holiday apartments, traffic offences, black marketeering and domestic disputes. He should, of course, be pleased about this. In an ever more troubled world, the south of France was an oasis of peace, even during the Festival when Cannes was invaded by thousands of foreigners visiting the beach or buying and selling films. The previous year, he'd had to deal with four cases of suicide (these involved about fifteen pounds of paperwork) and two violent attacks that had ended in death. And now there had been two deaths in a matter of hours. What *was* going on?

The bodyguards had disappeared before they could even give a statement, and Savoy made a mental note to send a written reprimand - as soon as he had time - to the officers in charge of the case. After all, they had let slip the only two witnesses to what had happened, because the woman in the waiting-room clearly knew nothing. It took him no time at all to establish that she had been standing some way away when the poison had been administered, and that all she wanted was to take advantage of the situation to get close to a famous film distributor. All he has to do now is to read more paper.

He's sitting in the hospital waiting-room with two reports before him. The first, written by the doctor on duty in the intensive care unit, analysed the damage done: poisoning by an unknown substance (currently being studied in the laboratory) which was injected into the bloodstream through a needle that perforated the left lumbar region. The only agent on the list of poisons capable of provoking such a rapid and violent reaction is strychnine, but this normally sends the body into convulsions. According to the security men in the marquee, and as was confirmed both by the paramedics and by the woman in the waiting-room, there were no such symptoms. On the contrary, they had noticed an immediate paralysis of the muscles and a stiffening of the chest, and the victim had been able to be carried from the marquee without attracting the attention of the other guests.

The second, much longer report was from the EPCTF (European Police Chiefs Task Force) and Europol, who had been following the victim's every move since he set foot on European soil. The agents were taking turns during the surveillance, and, at the time of the incident, the victim was being watched by a black agent originally from Guadaloupe, but who looked Jamaican.

'Even so, the person charged with watching him noticed nothing. Or, rather, at that precise moment, his view was partially blocked by a man walking past holding a glass of fruit juice.'

Although the victim had no police record and was known in the movie world as one of the few revolutionary film distributors around, his business was, in fact, just a front for something far more profitable. According to Europol, Javits Wild had been just another second-rate film producer; then, five years ago, he was recruited by a cartel specialising in the distribution of cocaine in the Americas to help them change dirty money into clean.

'It's starting to get interesting.'

For the first time, Savoy feels pleased by what he's reading. He may have an important case on his hands, far removed from the routine of fly-tipping, domestic disputes, holiday apartments being burgled and those two murders a year.

He knows how these things work. He knows what the report is talking about. Traffickers earn fortunes from selling their products, but because they can't show where that money came from, they can't open bank accounts, buy apartments, cars or jewels, or transfer large sums of money from one country to another because the government is sure to ask: 'How did this guy get to be so rich. Where did he earn all this money?'

To overcome this obstacle, they use a financial mechanism known as 'money laundering', that is, transforming money earned by criminal means into respectable financial assets which can then become part of the economic system and generate still more money. The expression is said to have originated with the Chicago gangster Al Capone, who bought a chain of laundries known as the Sanitary Cleaning Shops and then used those shops as a front for the money he was earning from the illegal sale of drinks during the Prohibition Era. So if anyone asked him how he came to be so rich, he could always say: 'People are washing more clothes than ever. This line of business has turned out to be a really good investment.'

'He did everything right,' thought Savoy, 'apart from forgetting to file a tax return.'

Money-laundering was used not only for drugs, but for many other things: politicians getting commission on the over-invoicing of construction work, terrorists needing to finance operations in various parts of the world, companies wanting to conceal profits and losses from shareholders, individuals who deem income tax to be an unacceptable invention. Once, all you had to do was open a numbered account in a tax haven, but then governments started drawing up a series of mutual collaboration treaties and the money-launderers had to adapt to these new times.

One thing was certain, however, the criminals were always several steps ahead of the authorities and the tax inspectors.

How does it work now? Well, in a far more elegant, sophisticated and creative way. They just have to follow three clear stages: placement, layering and integration. Take several oranges, make some juice and serve it up – no one need ever suspect where the fruit came from.

Making the orange juice is relatively easy: you set up a series of accounts and start moving small amounts of money from one bank to another, often using computer-generated systems, with the aim of bringing it all together again at some future date. The routes taken are so circuitous that it's almost impossible to follow the traces left by the electronic impulses because, once the money has been deposited, it ceases to be paper and is transformed into digital codes composed of just two numbers: 0 and 1.

Savoy thinks about his own bank account; the little he has in there is entirely at the mercy of codes travelling up and down wires. What if the bank decided, from one moment to the next, to change the whole system? What if that new programme didn't work? How could he prove he had the amount of money he said he had? How could he convert those numbers into something more concrete, like a house or food bought at the supermarket?

He can do nothing because he's in the hands of the system. However, he decides that as soon as he leaves the hospital, he'll visit a cashpoint and get a balance statement. He makes a note in his diary to do this every week; that way, if some calamity does occur in the world, he'll have proof on paper.

Paper. That word again. How did he get on to this subject in the first place? Ah, yes, money-laundering.

He goes back to what he knows about laundering money. The final stage is the easiest of all; the money is put into a respectable account, for example, one belonging to a property development company or an investment fund. If the government asks: 'Where did this money come from?', the answer's easy enough: 'From small investors who believe in what we're selling.' After that, it can be invested in more shares, more land, in planes and other luxury goods, in houses with swimming pools, in credit cards with no cash limit. The partners in these companies are the very same people who first financed the buying of drugs, guns or some other illicit merchandise. The money, though, is clean; after all, any company can earn millions of dollars speculating on the stock market or on property.

This left only the first step to consider, the most difficult of all: 'Who are these small investors?'

And that's where criminal creativity comes in. The 'oranges' are people who hang around in casinos using money lent to them by a 'friend', in countries where there's corruption aplenty and few restrictions on betting. There's always a chance someone will win a fortune. If they do, there are arrangements in place with the owners, who keep a percentage of the money that crosses their tables. And the gambler – someone on a low income – can justify the enormous sum deposited in his bank account by saying that it was all a matter of luck.

The following day, he'll transfer nearly all the money to the 'friend' who lent it to him and hold back just a small percentage.

The preferred method used to be buying up restaurants, which could charge a fortune for their food and deposit the profits in an account without arousing suspicion. Even if an inspector came by and found the tables completely empty, they couldn't prove that no one had eaten there all day. Now, however, with the growth of the leisure industry, a more creative option has opened up. The ever imponderable, arbitrary, incomprehensible art market!

A middle-class couple, say, with little money will bring some extremely valuable piece to auction, alleging that they found it in the attic of their grandparents' old house. The piece is sold for a lot of money, then re-sold the following week to a specialist gallery for ten or twenty times the original price. The 'oranges' are happy, thank the gods for their generosity, deposit the money in their joint account and resolve to invest it in some foreign country, always taking care to leave a small amount – their percentage – in that first account. The gods in this case are the real owners of the painting who will buy it back from the gallery and put it on the market again, with different vendors this time.

There are, however, more expensive products still, like the theatre and the production and distribution of films. That is where the invisible hands of the money-launderers can really make a killing.

Savoy is now reading about the man currently in intensive care and trying to fill in a few blanks in his own imagination.

The man had been an actor who dreamed of becoming a major star. He couldn't find any work – although he still took great care of his physical appearance, as if he really were a star – but he got to know the industry. In middle age, he managed to raise some money from investors and make a couple of films, both of which were resounding flops because they didn't get the right distribution. Nevertheless, his name appeared on the credits, and he became known in the specialist magazines as someone who had at least tried to make something different from the films being churned out by the big studios.

Just as he was beginning to despair, unsure what to do with his life, with no one willing to give him another chance, and weary of begging money from people who were only interested in investing in sure-fire hits, he was approached by a group of people, some of whom were very affable, while others were completely silent.

They made him an offer. He would start up as a film distributor, and his first purchase should be something guaranteed to reach a wider public. The major studios would offer vast sums of money for the film, but he needn't worry – any sum offered would be matched by his new friends. The film would be shown in lots of cinemas and earn a fortune. Javits would get what he most needed – a reputation. No one would be likely to delve into the life of a frustrated film producer. Two or three films later, the authorities might start to ask where all the money was coming from, but by then, the first step was safely concealed behind the five-year time limitation on all tax investigations.

So Javits began a glorious career. His first films as a distributor were highly profitable; exhibitors began to believe in his ability to select the best films on the market; directors and producers were soon queuing up to work with him. To keep up appearances, he always made sure to accept two or three low-budget projects every six months, the rest being films made with mega-budgets, top-ranking stars, able technicians and a lot of money to spend on promotion, money that came from groups based in tax havens. Box-office earnings were deposited in a normal investment fund, above suspicion, which had 'shares' in the movie.

Fine. The dirty money was thus transformed into a marvellous work of art, which, naturally, didn't make as much money as was hoped, but was still capable of yielding millions of dollars that would immediately be invested by one of the partners in the enterprise.

At one point, however, a sharp-eyed tax inspector – or perhaps a whistle-blower at one of the studios – noticed one very simple fact: why was it that so many previously unknown producers were employing big stars and the most talented directors, spending a fortune on publicity and using only one distributor for their films? The answer: the big studios are only interested in their own productions, whereas Javits is the hero, the man standing out against the monopoly of the giant corporations, a David to their Goliath, battling an unfair system.

A more conscientious tax inspector decided to proceed with his investigation, despite all these apparently reasonable explanations. He began in great secrecy and learned that all the companies who had invested in the biggest box-office successes were always limited companies based in the Bahamas, in Panama or in Singapore. A mole in the tax office (there is *always* a mole) warned Javits' backers that they had better find another distributor to launder money from now on.

Javits was in despair. He had grown accustomed to the millionaire lifestyle and to being treated as if he were a demigod. He had travelled to Cannes, which provided an excellent front for sorting things out with his backers and personally handing over the codes of various numbered accounts. He had no idea that he was being followed, that a prison term would almost certainly ensue, pending decisions made by men in ties in ill-lit offices. They might let him continue for a while longer, in order to get more proof, or they might end the story right there.

His backers, however, never took unnecessary risks. Their man could be arrested at any moment, make a deal with the court and give details of how the whole scam worked, as well as naming names and identifying people in photos taken without his knowledge.

There was only one way to solve the problem – they would have to kill him.

Things couldn't be clearer, and Savoy can see exactly how things developed. Now he just needs to do what he always does. Fill in more forms, draw up a report, hand it to Europol, and let their bureaucrats find the murderers because it's a case that could well lead to promotions and revive stagnant careers. The investigation has to produce a result, and none of his superiors would believe that a detective from a small town in France would be capable of making any major discoveries (because however glitzy and glamorous Cannes was during the Festival, for the other 350 days of the year it was just a small provincial town).

He suspects that the perpetrator may have been one of the bodyguards at the table, since the poison could only have been administered by someone standing very close. However, he won't mention that. He'll fill up more paper about the people working in the marquee, find no further witnesses, then close the file - having first spent a few days exchanging faxes and e-mails with other more important departments.

He'll go back to his two murders a year, to the fights and the fines, having been so close to something that could have international repercussions. His adolescent dream of improving the world, contributing to creating a safer, fairer society, getting promoted, landing a job at the Ministry of Justice, giving his wife and children a more comfortable life, helping to change the public perception of the law and showing that there *are* still some honest policemen, all came down to the same thing - more paperwork.

4.16 p.m.

The terrace outside the bar is packed, and Igor feels proud of his ability to plan things, because even though he's never been to Cannes before, he had foreseen precisely this situation and reserved a table. He orders tea and toast, lights a cigarette and looks around him at the same scene you might see in any chic place anywhere in the world: women who are either anorexic or use too much botox; ladies dripping with jewellery and eating ice cream; men with much younger female companions; bored couples; smiling young women sipping low-calorie drinks and pretending to be listening to what their friends are saying when they're really on the look-out for someone more interesting to hove into view.

There is one exception: three men and a woman are sitting at a table strewn with papers and beer cans, discussing something in low voices and constantly checking figures on a calculator. They appear to be the only ones who are really engaged on some project, but that isn't quite true; everyone there is working hard in a way, in search of one thing: vi-si-bi-li-ty, which, if all goes well, will turn into Fame, which, if all goes well again, will turn into Power, the magic word that transforms any human being into a demi-god, a remote, inaccessible icon accustomed to having his every desire met and to getting jealous looks when he sweeps past in his limousine with the smoked-glass windows or in his expensive sports car, someone who no longer has mountains to climb or impossible conquests to make.

The people on the terrace have clearly leaped over certain barriers already; they are not outside with the photographers, behind the metal barriers, waiting for someone to come out of the main door and fill their universe with light. They have already made it into the hotel lobby and now all they need is fame and power, and they really don't mind what form these take. Men know that age isn't a problem; all they need are the right contacts. The young women - who keep as keen an eye on the terrace as any trained bodyguard - know that they're reaching a dangerous age, when any chance of achieving something through their beauty alone will suddenly vanish. The older women there would like to be recognised and respected for their gifts and their intelligence, but the diamonds they're wearing make it unlikely that their talents will be discovered. The men sitting with their wives are waiting for someone to pass by and say hello and for everyone to turn and look and think: 'He must be well known, or even famous, who knows?'

The celebrity syndrome. It can destroy careers, marriages and Christian values and can blind both the wise and the ignorant. A few examples. Great scientists who, on being given an important prize, abandon the research that might have helped humanity and decide instead to live off lectures that feed both their ego and their bank balance. The Indian in the Amazon jungle who, on being taken up by a famous singer, decides that he's being exploited for his poverty. The campaigner for justice who works hard defending the rights of the less fortunate, decides to run for public office, wins the election and subsequently considers himself above the law, until he's discovered one day in a motel room with a prostitute paid for by the taxpayer.

The celebrity syndrome. When people forget who they are and start to believe what other people say about them. The Superclass, everyone's dream, a world without shadows or darkness, where 'Yes' is the only possible answer to any request.

Igor is a powerful man. He has fought all his life to get where he is now. To that end, he has sat through boring suppers, endless lectures and meetings with people he loathed, has bestowed smiles when he would rather have bestowed insults, and insults when he actually felt genuinely sorry for the poor creatures being singled out for punishment as an example to others. He worked day and night and weekends too, deep in discussions with lawyers, administrators, officials and press officers. He started with nothing just after the fall of the Communist regime and he reached the top. He has, moreover, managed to survive all the political and economic storms that swept his country during the first two decades of the new regime. And why? Because he fears God and knows that the road he has travelled in his life is a blessing that must be respected; if not, he will lose everything.

There were, of course, moments when something told him he was forgetting about the most important part of that blessing: Ewa; but for many years he persuaded himself that she would understand and accept that it was simply a temporary phase and that soon they would be able to spend as much time together as they wished. They made great plans - journeys, cruises, a remote house in the mountains with a blazing log-fire, and the certain knowledge that they could stay there for as long as they wanted, with no need to worry about money, debts or obligations. They would find a school for the many children they planned to have together; they would spend whole afternoons walking through the surrounding forests; they would have supper at small, cosy local restaurants.

They would have time to garden, read, go to the cinema, and do the simple things that everyone dreams of doing, the only things truly capable of filling anyone's life. When he got home, his arms full of papers which he would then spread out on the bed, he would ask her to be patient for a little while longer. When his phone rang on the very day they'd chosen to go out to supper together, and he had to interrupt their conversation and spend a long time talking to whoever had called, he would again ask her to be patient. He knew Ewa was doing everything she could to make things easy for him, although she did complain now and then, very sweetly, that they needed to make the most of life while they were still young; after all, they had money enough for the next five generations.

Igor would say: 'Right, I'll stop today.' And Ewa would smile and stroke his cheek, and then he would remember something important he'd forgotten to do and go over to the phone to ring someone or to the computer to send an e-mail.

A man in his forties gets up, looks around the terrace and, brandishing a newspaper, shouts:

'"Violence and horror in Tokyo," says the headline. "Seven people killed in a shop selling electronic toys."'

Everyone looks at him.

'Violence! They don't know what they're talking about. This is where you get real violence!'

A shudder runs down Igor's spine.

'If some madman stabs to death a few innocent people, the whole world is shocked, but who cares about the intellectual violence being perpetrated in Cannes? Our festival is being killed in the name of a dictatorship. It's not a question of choosing the best film, but of committing crimes against humanity, forcing people to buy products they don't want, putting fashion above art, choosing to go to a lunch or a supper rather than watch a film. That's disgraceful. I'm here to …'

'Be quiet,' someone says. 'No one cares why you're here.'

'I'm here to denounce the enslavement of man's desires, for we have stopped using our intelligence to make choices and instead allow ourselves to be manipulated by propaganda and lies! People get all steamed up about these stabbings in Tokyo, but they don't give a damn about the death by a thousand cuts suffered by a whole generation of film-makers.'

The man pauses, expecting a standing ovation, but there isn't even a thoughtful silence. Everyone resumes their conversations, indifferent to his words. He sits down again, trying to look dignified, but with his heart in shreds for making such a fool of himself.

'Vi-si-bi-li-ty,' thinks Igor. 'The problem is that no one took any notice.'

It's his turn to look around. Ewa is staying at the same hotel, and a sixth sense born of many years of marriage tells him that she's sitting not very far away on that same terrace. She will have received his messages and is probably looking for him now, knowing that he, too, must be near.

He can't see her, but neither can he stop thinking about her – his obsession. He remembers one night being driven home in his imported limousine by the chauffeur who doubled as his bodyguard – they had fought together in Afghanistan, but fortune had smiled on them in very different ways – and remembers asking the driver to stop outside the Hotel Kempinski. He left his mobile phone and his papers in the car and went up to the terrace bar. Unlike this terrace in Cannes, the place was almost empty and getting ready to close. He gave a generous tip to the waiters and asked them to stay open for another hour, just for him.

And that was when he understood. It wasn't true that he would give up work next month or next year or even next decade. They would never have the house in the country and the children they dreamed of. He asked himself that night why this was impossible and he had only one answer.

On the road to power, there's no turning back. He would be an eternal slave to the road he'd chosen and if he did ever realise his dream of abandoning everything, he would plunge immediately into a deep depression.

Why was he like that? Was it because of the nightmares he had about the trenches, remembering the frightened young man he'd been then, fulfilling a duty he hadn't chosen and being forced to kill? Was it because he couldn't forget his first victim, a peasant who had strayed into the line of fire when the Red Army was fighting the Afghan guerrillas? Was it because of the many people who hadn't believed in him and had humiliated him when he was looking for investors for his mobile-phone business? Was it because in the beginning he'd had to associate with shadows, with the Russian mafia eager to launder the money they earned through prostitution.

He'd managed to repay those questionable loans without himself being corrupted and without owing any favours. He'd managed to negotiate with the shadows and still keep his own light burning. He knew that the war belonged to the distant past and that he would never again set foot on a battlefield. He'd found the love of his life. He was doing the kind of work he'd always wanted to do. He was rich, very rich, and, just in case the Communist regime were to return tomorrow, he kept most of his personal fortune abroad. He was on good terms with all the political parties. He'd met famous people from around the world. He'd set up a foundation to care for the orphans of those soldiers killed during the Soviet invasion of Afghanistan.

But it was only when he was sitting on that terrace café near Red Square, knowing that he had power and money enough to pay the waiters to work all night if necessary, that he finally understood.

He understood because he saw the same thing happening to his wife. Ewa was also constantly travelling, and even when she was in Moscow, she would arrive home late and go straight to her computer as soon as she walked in the door. He understood that, contrary to what most people think, total power means total slavery. When you get that far, you don't ever want to give it up. There's always a new mountain to climb. There's always a competitor to be convinced or crushed. Along with 2,000 other people, he formed part of the most exclusive club in the world, which met only once a year in Davos in Switzerland, at the World Economic Forum. All the members were millionaires, and they all worked from dawn until late at night, always wanting to go further, never changing tack – acquisitions, stock markets, market trends, money, money, money. They worked not because they needed to, but because they judged themselves to be necessary; they felt that thousands of families depended on them and that they had a huge responsibility to their governments and their associates. They genuinely thought they were helping the world, which might be true, but they had to pay for this with their own lives.

The following day, he did something he hated having to do: he went to a psychiatrist. Something must be wrong. He discovered then that he was suffering from an illness that was fairly common among those who had achieved something beyond the grasp of ordinary folk. He was a compulsive worker, a workaholic. According to the psychiatrist, workaholics run the risk of becoming depressed when not immersed in the challenges and problems of running a company.

'We don't yet know the origin of the disorder, but it's associated with insecurity, childhood fears and a desire to block out reality. It's as serious an addiction as drugs. Unlike drugs, however, which diminish productivity, the workaholic makes a great contribution to the wealth of his country. So it's in no one's interests to seek a cure.'

'And what are the consequences?'

'You should know, because that's presumably why you've come to see me. The gravest consequence is the damage it causes to family life. In Japan, one of the countries where the illness is most common and where the consequences are sometimes fatal, they've developed various ways of controlling the obsession.'

Igor couldn't remember listening to anyone in the last two years with the respect and attention he was paying that bespectacled, moustachioed man before him.

'So there is a way out, then?'

'When a workaholic seeks help from a psychiatrist that means he's ready to be cured. Only about one in every thousand cases realises that he needs help.'

'Oh, I need help, and I have enough money …'

'That's what all workaholics say. Yes, I know you have enough money, you all do. I know who you are as well. I've seen photos of you at charity balls, at congresses, in private audience with our president, who, by the way, shows the same symptoms. Money isn't enough. What I want to know is this: do you really want to change?'

Igor thought of Ewa, of the house in the mountains, the family he'd like to have, the hundreds of millions of dollars he had in the bank. He thought of his position in society and of the power he possessed and how difficult it would be to give all that up.

'I'm not saying you should abandon what you're doing,' said the psychiatrist, as if he'd read his thoughts. 'I'm simply suggesting that you use work as a source of happiness and not as a compulsion.'

'Yes, I can do that.'

'And what would be your main motive for doing so? All workaholics think they're happy doing what they're doing, and none of their friends, who are in the same position, will see why they should seek help.'

Igor lowered his eyes.

'Shall I tell you what your main motive is? As I said before, you're destroying your family.'

'No, it's worse than that. My wife is starting to show the same symptoms. She's been distancing herself from me ever since a trip we made to Lake Baikal. And if there's anyone in the world I would be capable of killing again for …'

Igor realised he'd said too much, but the psychiatrist seemed entirely unmoved.

'If there's anyone in the world for whom I would do anything, absolutely anything, that person is my wife.'

The psychiatrist summoned his assistant and asked her to make a series of appointments. He didn't consult his patient to see if he would be available on those dates; it was part of the treatment to make it quite clear that any other commitment, however important, could be postponed.

'May I ask a question?'

The psychiatrist nodded.

'Couldn't overwork also be considered rather noble? A proof of my deep respect for the opportunities God has given me in this life? A way of putting society to rights, even if sometimes I have to use methods that are a little …'

Silence.

'A little what?'

'Oh, nothing.'

Igor left the consulting room feeling both confused and relieved. Perhaps the psychiatrist had failed to understand the essence of what he did. Life has its reasons. We are all of us linked and often it's necessary to cut out the malignant tumours so that the rest of the body can remain healthy. People are locked up in their selfish little worlds; they make plans that don't include their fellow man; they believe the planet is simply land to be exploited; they follow their instincts and desires and care nothing for the collective well-being of society.

He wasn't destroying his family, he simply wanted to leave the world a better place for the children he dreamed of having, a world without drugs or wars or people-trafficking, a world in which love would be the great force uniting all couples, peoples, nations and religions. Ewa would understand this, even if their marriage was currently going through a crisis, a crisis doubtless sent by the Evil One.

The following day, he asked his secretary to cancel all subsequent appointments with the psychiatrist; he had more important things to do. He was drawing up a great plan to purify the world, a plan for which he would need help; indeed, he'd already contacted a group prepared to work with him.

Two months later, the wife he loved left him – because of the Evil that had possessed her, because he hadn't been able to understand her feelings.

The sound of a chair being shifted returns him to the reality of Cannes. Before him sits a woman holding a glass of whisky in one hand and a cigarette in the other. She's well dressed but visibly drunk.

'May I sit here? All the other tables are occupied.'

'You already are sitting here.'

'It's just not possible,' says the woman, as if she'd known him for years. 'It's simply not possible. The police made me leave the hospital. And the man for whose sake I travelled by train for almost a whole day, for whom I rented a hotel room at twice the normal price, is now hovering between life and death. Damn!'

Is she from the police? Or does what she's saying have nothing to do with what he thinks it does?

'Anyway, what are *you* doing here, if you don't mind my asking? Aren't you hot? Wouldn't you be cooler without your jacket on, or are you trying to impress everyone with your elegance?'

As usual, people choose their own destiny, and this woman is doing just that.

'I always wear a jacket regardless of the temperature. Are you an actress?'

The woman gives an almost hysterical laugh.

'Yes, let's say I'm an actress, yes I am. I'm playing the part of someone who has had the same dream since she was an adolescent, has grown up with it, battled seven miserable years of her life to make it a reality, who's mortgaged her house, worked ceaselessly …'

'Oh, I know what that's like.'

'No, you don't. It means thinking about just one thing day and night, going to places uninvited, shaking hands with people you despise, phoning once, twice, ten times until you get the attention of people who aren't worth half what you are, who don't have half your courage, but who've reached a certain position and are determined to take out on you all their domestic frustrations by making your life impossible …'

'… it means only finding pleasure in pursuing your dream, having no other diversions, finding everything else deadly dull and ending up destroying your family.'

The woman looks at him, taken aback. She no longer seems drunk.

'Who *are* you? How do you know what I'm thinking?'

'I was thinking about exactly the same thing when you arrived. And I don't in the least mind you asking me what I'm doing here. I think I can help you.'

'No one can help me. The only person who could is now in the intensive-care unit. And from what I could glean before the police arrived, he probably won't survive. Oh God!'

She drinks the remaining whisky in her glass. Igor signals to the waiter, who ignores him and goes to serve another table.

'I've always preferred a cynical compliment to a bit of constructive criticism. Please, tell me I'm beautiful and that I've got what it takes.'

Igor laughs.

'How do you know I can't help you?'

'Are you by any chance a film distributor? Do you have contacts and a chain of cinemas around the world?'

They had perhaps the same person in mind. If so and if this was a trap, it was too late to run away. He's obviously being watched, and as soon as he stands up, he'll be arrested. He feels his stomach contract, but why should he be afraid? Only a short time ago, he'd tried, without success, to hand himself over to the police. He'd chosen martyrdom, offered up his freedom as a sacrifice, but that gift had been rejected by God. Now, however, the Heavens had obviously reconsidered their decision.

He must think how best to deal with what will ensue: the suspect is identified, a woman pretending to be drunk is sent on ahead to confirm the facts. Then, very discreetly, a man will walk over and ask him to come with him for a little chat. That man will be a policeman. Igor has what looks like a pen in his jacket pocket, but that will arouse no suspicions; the Beretta though will give him away. He sees his whole life flash before him.

Could he use the gun to defend himself? The policeman who is sure to appear as soon as he has been identified will have colleagues watching the scene and Igor will be dead before he can make so much as a move. On the other hand, he didn't come here to kill innocent people in a barbarous, indiscriminate way; he has a mission, and his victims – or martyrs for love as he prefers to call them – are serving a greater purpose.

'No, I'm not a distributor,' he says. 'I have absolutely nothing to do with the world of cinema, fashion or glamour. I work in telecommunications.'

'Good,' says the woman. 'So you must have money. You must have had dreams in your life, so you know what I'm talking about.'

He's beginning to lose the thread of the conversation. He signals to another waiter. This time the waiter comes over and Igor orders two cups of tea.

'Can't you see I'm drinking whisky?'

'Yes, but as I said, I think I can help you. To do that, however, you need to be sober and aware of what you're doing.'

Maureen feels a change come over her. Ever since this stranger proved himself able to read her thoughts, she feels as if she were being restored to reality. Perhaps he really can help her. It's been years since anyone tried to seduce her with that most clichéd of chat-up lines in the film business:'I have some very influential friends.' There's nothing more guaranteed to change a woman's state of mind than knowing that someone of the opposite sex desires her. She feels tempted to get up and go to the restroom and check her make-up in the mirror. That can wait. First, she needs to send out some clear signals that she's interested.

Yes, she needs company, she's open to whatever surprises Fate may hold in store; when God closes a door, he opens a window. Why, of all the tables on that terrace, was this the only table occupied by just one person? There was a meaning in this, a hidden sign: the two of them were meant to meet.

She laughs at herself. In her current despairing state anything is a sign, a way out, a piece of good news.

'Firstly, tell me what you need,' says the man.

'I need help. I have a movie with a top-line cast ready and waiting; it was going to be distributed by one of the few people in the industry who still has faith in the talent of people outside the studio system. I was going to meet him tomorrow. I was even at the same lunch as him today, when suddenly I noticed he was feeling unwell.'

Igor starts to relax. Perhaps it's true, reality really is stranger than fiction.

'I left the lunch, found out which hospital he'd been taken to and went there. On the way, I imagined what I was going to say, about how I was his friend and we were going to be working together. I've never even spoken to him, but I think anyone in a situation like that feels more comfortable knowing that someone, anyone, is near.'

'In other words, turning someone else's tragedy to your own advantage,' thinks Igor.

People are all the same.

'And what exactly is a top-line cast?' he asks.

'Will you excuse me? I need to go to the bathroom.'

Igor politely stands up, puts on his dark glasses and, as she walks away, tries to look as calm as possible. He drinks his tea, all the while scanning the terrace. At first sight, there appears to be no immediate threat, but it would still be wise to leave that terrace as soon as the woman comes back.

Maureen is impressed by her new friend's gentlemanly behaviour. It's been years since she's seen anyone behave according to the rules of etiquette taught them by their mothers and fathers. As she leaves the terrace, she notices that some pretty young women on the next table, who have doubtless heard part of their conversation, are looking at him and smiling. She notices, too, that he's put on his dark glasses, possibly to be able to observe the young women without them knowing. Perhaps, by the time she gets back, they'll all be drinking tea together.

But then life is like that: don't complain and don't expect too much either.

She looks at her face in the mirror. Why would a man be interested in her? She really does need to get to grips with reality again, as he suggested. Her eyes look empty and tired; she's exhausted like everyone else taking part in the Festival, but she knows that she has to carry on fighting. Cannes isn't over yet, Javits might recover, or someone representing his company might turn up. She has tickets to see other people's films, an invitation to a party held by *Gala* – one of the most prestigious magazines in France – and she can use the time available to see how independent European producers and directors go about distributing their films. She needs to bounce back quickly.

As for the handsome stranger, she mustn't have any illusions in that regard. She returns to the table convinced that she'll find two of the young women sitting there, but he's still alone. Again he rises politely to his feet and draws back her chair so that she can sit down.

'Sorry, I haven't introduced myself. My name's Maureen.'

'I'm Igor. Pleased to meet you. You were saying that you had the ideal cast.'

She decides to get a dig in at the girls on the next table. She speaks slightly more loudly than usual.

'Here in Cannes, or indeed at any other festival, new actresses are discovered every year, and every year really great actresses lose out on getting a great role because the industry thinks they're too old, even if, in fact, they're still young and full of enthusiasm. Among the new discoveries,' (and, she thinks: 'I just hope the girls next to us are listening') 'some choose the path of pure glamour. They don't earn much on the movies they make - all directors know this and take full advantage - and so they invest in the one thing they shouldn't invest in.'

'Namely ...'

'Their own beauty. They become celebrities, start to charge for attending parties, they're asked to appear in advertisements, promoting various products. They end up meeting the most powerful men and the sexiest actors in the world. They earn a vast amount of money because they're young and pretty and their agents get them loads of contracts.

'In fact, they allow themselves to be entirely guided by their agents, who constantly feed their vanity. An actress of this type becomes the dream of housewives, of adolescent girls and would-be actresses who don't even have enough money to travel to the nearest town, but who consider her a friend, someone who's having the kind of experiences they would like to have. She continues making movies and earns a little more, although her press agent always puts it about that she's earning an enormous salary, which is a complete lie that not even the journalists believe, but which they publish anyway because they know the public prefers news to information.'

'What's the difference?' asks Igor, who's feeling more relaxed now, while still keeping a close eye on what's going on around him.

'Let's say you were to buy a gold-plated computer in an auction in Dubai and decided to write a new book using that technological marvel. When a journalist finds out about the computer, he'll phone you up and ask: "So how's your gold-plated computer?" That's news. The information – the nature of the new book you're writing – is of no importance whatsoever.'

'Perhaps Ewa is receiving news rather than information,' thinks Igor. The idea had never occurred to him before.

'Go on.'

'Time passes, or, rather, seven or eight years pass. Suddenly, the film offers dry up. The revenue from parties and advertisements begins to dwindle. Her agent seems suddenly much busier than before and doesn't always call her back. The "big star" rebels: how can they do this to her, the great sex symbol, the great icon of glamour? She blames her agent and decides to find another one; to her surprise, he doesn't appear to mind at all. On the contrary, he asks her to sign a statement saying how well they have always got on together; then he wishes her good luck, and that's the end of their relationship.'

Maureen looks around the terrace to see if she can find an example of what she's describing: people who are still famous, but who have vanished from the scene and are desperately seeking some new opportunity. They still behave like divas, they still have the same distant air, but their hearts are full of bitterness, their skin full of botox and covered with the invisible scars left by plastic surgery. She could see plenty of evidence of botox and plastic surgery, but no celebrities from the previous decade. Perhaps they didn't even have enough money now to attend a festival like this, but were instead appearing as a special guest at dances in provincial towns or fronting the launch of some new brand of chocolate or beer, still behaving as if they were the person they once were, but knowing that they weren't.

'You mentioned two types of people.'

'Yes. The second group of actresses have exactly the same problem, but there's one important difference.' Again her voice grows louder because now the girls on the next table are clearly interested to hear what someone in the know has to say. 'They know that beauty is a transient thing. They don't appear in ads or on magazine covers because they're busy honing their art. They keep studying and making contacts that will be useful in the future. They lend their name and appearance to certain products, not as models, but as partners. They earn less, of course, but it means a lifelong income.

'And then along comes someone like me, with a good script and enough money, plus I want them to be in my film. They accept and have enough talent to play the parts I give them and enough intelligence to know that even if the film doesn't turn out to be a huge success, at least they will still have a presence on the screen and will be seen to be working as mature actresses, and who knows, that might spark the interest of another producer.'

Igor is also aware that the girls are listening to their conversation.

'Perhaps we should go for a walk,' he says quietly. 'There's no privacy here. I know a place where we can be alone and watch the sun go down; it's beautiful.'

That's precisely what she needs at this moment – an invitation to go for a walk! To see the sunset, even though it'll be quite some time before the sun goes down! He's not one of those vulgar types who says: 'Let's go up to my room for a moment, I need to change my shoes' and 'Nothing will happen, I promise', and who, once they're in his room, will say as he tries to make a grab for her: 'I have contacts and I know just the people you need to talk to.'

To be honest, she wouldn't mind being kissed by this seemingly charming man. She knows absolutely nothing about him, of course, but the elegance with which he's seducing her is something she won't forget in a long time.

They get up from the table, and he asks for the drinks to be put on his tab (so, she thinks, he's staying at the Martinez!). When they reach the Boulevard de la Croisette, he suggests they turn to the left.

'There are fewer people in that direction; besides, the view should be even better, with the sun setting behind the hills.'

'Igor, who are you?'

'A good question,' he says. 'I'd like to know the answer to that one myself.'

Another point in his favour. He doesn't immediately launch into some spiel about how rich and intelligent and talented he is. He simply wants to watch the sunset with her, that's all. They walk to the end of the beach in silence, passing all kinds of different people – older couples who seem to inhabit another world, quite oblivious to the festival; young people on roller-skates, wearing tight clothes and listening to iPods; street vendors with their merchandise set out on a mat, the ends of which have string looped through them so that at the first sign of a policeman, they can transform their 'shop window' into a bag; there's even an area that seems to have been cordoned off by the police for some reason – after all, it's only a bench. She notices that her companion keeps looking behind him, as if he were expecting someone, but he's probably just spotted an acquaintance.

They walk along a pier where the boats partially conceal the beach from view, and they finally find an isolated spot. They sit down on a comfortable bench with a backrest. They're completely alone. Well, why would anyone else come to a place where there's nothing to do? She's in an excellent mood.

'It's lovely here! Do you know why God decided to rest on the seventh day?'

Igor doesn't understand the question, but she proceeds to explain anyway:

'Because on the seventh day, before he'd finished work and left the world in a perfect state for human beings, a group of producers from Hollywood came over to Him and said: "Don't you worry about the rest! We'll take care of providing the Technicolor sunset, the special storm effects, the perfect lighting and the right sound equipment so that whenever Man hears the waves, he'll think it's the real sea!"'

She laughs to herself. The man beside her is looking more serious now.

'You asked me who I am,' he says.

'I've no idea who you are, but you obviously know the city well. And I have to say, it was real luck meeting you like that. In just one day, I've experienced hope, despair, loneliness and the pleasure of finding a new companion. That's a lot of emotions.'

He takes something out of his pocket; it looks like a wooden tube less than six inches long.

'The world's a dangerous place,' he says. 'It doesn't matter where you are, you're always at risk of being approached by people who have no scruples about attacking, destroying, killing. And we never learn how to defend ourselves. We're all in the hands of those more powerful than us.'

'You're right. I suppose that wooden tube is your way of fending them off.'

He twists the upper part of the tube. As delicately as a painter putting the final touch to a masterpiece, he removes the lid. It isn't in fact a lid, but the head of what looks like a long nail. The sun glitters on the metal blade.

'You wouldn't get through airport security carrying that in your case,' she says and laughs.

'No, I wouldn't.'

Maureen feels that she's with a man who is polite, handsome, doubtless wealthy, but who is also capable of protecting her from all dangers. She has no idea what the crime statistics are for Cannes, but it's as well to think of everything. That's what men are for: to think of everything.

'Of course, you need to know exactly how to use it. It may be made of steel, but because it's so thin it's also very fragile and too small to cause any real damage. If you don't use it with great precision, it won't work.'

He places the blade level with Maureen's ear. Her initial reaction is one of fear, soon replaced by excitement.

'This would be one of the ideal places, for example. Any higher, and the cranial bones would block the blow, any lower, and the vein in the neck would be cut; the person might die, but would also be able to fight back. If he was armed, he could shoot me, especially at such close range.'

The blade slides slowly down her body. It passes over her breast, and Maureen realises that he's trying both to shock and arouse her.

'I had no idea someone working in telecommunications could know so much about killing, but from what you say, killing someone with that blade is quite a complicated business.'

This is her way of saying: 'I'm interested in what you're telling me. I find you really fascinating. But please, just take my hand and let's go and watch the sunset together.'

The blade slides over her breast, but does not stop there. Nevertheless, it's enough to make her feel aroused. It stops just under her arm.

'Here I'm on a level with your heart. It's protected by a natural barrier, the rib cage. In a fight, it would be impossible to injure someone with this blade. It would almost certainly hit a rib, and even if it did penetrate the body, the wound wouldn't bleed enough to weaken your enemy. He might not even feel the blow. But right here, it would be fatal.'

What is she doing in this isolated spot with a complete stranger talking about such a macabre subject? Just then, she feels a kind of electric shock that leaves her paralysed. His hand has driven the blade inside her body. She feels at first as if she were suffocating and tries to breathe, but then immediately loses consciousness.

Igor puts his arms around her, as he had with his first victim. This time, though, he positions her body so that she remains sitting. He then puts on some gloves and makes her head drop forward onto her chest.

If anyone ventures into that corner of the beach, all they will see is a woman sleeping, exhausted perhaps from chasing after producers and distributors at the Festival.

The boy lurking behind the old warehouse – where he often hides so as to masturbate while he watches canoodling couples – is now furiously phoning the police. He saw everything. At first, he thought it was some kind of joke, but the man really did stick that blade into the woman! He'll have to wait for the police to arrive before leaving his hiding-place. That madman could return at any moment and then he would be lost.

Igor throws the blade into the sea and walks back to the hotel. This time, his victim had chosen death. When she joined him, he'd been sitting alone on the terrace, wondering what to do next and thinking about the past. He never imagined she would agree to go for a walk to such an isolated spot with a complete stranger, but she did. She could have run away when he started showing her the different places where the blade would cause a mortal wound, but she didn't.

A police car passes, driving along the side of the road closed to the public. He decides to watch where it goes and, to his surprise, he sees it drive onto the pier where no one seems to go during the festival period. It had been as empty that morning as it had this afternoon, even though it was the best place from which to see the sunset. A few seconds later, an ambulance passes with its deafening siren blaring and its lights flashing. It, too, heads for the pier.

He keeps walking, sure of one thing: someone must have witnessed the murder. But how would that someone describe him? A man with greyish hair, wearing jeans, a white shirt and a black jacket. That possible witness would help the police make an identikit picture, a process that would not only take time, but lead them to the conclusion that there are tens or maybe thousands of men who look just like him.

Ever since he tried to give himself up to that policeman and was sent back to his hotel, he has felt sure that no one would be able to interrupt his mission. The doubts he feels now are of a different nature: Is Ewa worth the sacrifices he's offering up to the universe? When he arrived in Cannes, he had felt sure she was; now, though, something else is filling his soul: the spirit of the little street vendor with her dark eyebrows and innocent smile.

'We are all part of the divine spark,' she seems to be saying. 'We all have a purpose in creation and that purpose is called Love. That love, however, shouldn't be concentrated in just one person, it should be scattered throughout the world, waiting to be discovered. Wake up to that love. What is gone cannot return. What is about to arrive needs to be recognised.'

He struggles against the idea that perhaps we only discover that a plan is wrong when we take it to its ultimate consequences, or when all-merciful God leads us in another direction.

He looks at his watch: he still has another twelve hours in Cannes, time enough before he gets on the plane with the woman he loves and goes back to …

… goes back to what? To his work in Moscow after everything he has experienced, suffered, thought, planned? Or to find rebirth through his victims and choose absolute freedom and discover the person he didn't know he was, and from then on do all the things he had dreamed of doing when he was still with Ewa?

4.34 p.m.

Jasmine is sitting staring out at the sea while she smokes a cigarette and thinks of nothing. At such moments, she feels a deep connection with the infinite, as if it were not she who was there, but something more powerful, something capable of extraordinary things.

She remembers an old story she once read.

Nasrudin appeared at court wearing a magnificent turban and asking for money for charity.

'You come here asking for money and yet you're wearing an extremely expensive turban on your head. How much did that extraordinary thing cost?' asked the sultan.

'It was a gift from someone very rich. And it's worth, I believe, five hundred gold coins,' replied the wise Sufi.

The sultan's minister muttered: 'That's impossible. No turban could possibly be worth that much.'

Nasrudin insisted:

'I didn't come here only to beg, I also came to do business. I know that only a true sovereign would be capable of buying this turban for six hundred gold coins so that I could give the surplus to the poor.'

The sultan was flattered and paid what Nasrudin asked. On the way out, Nasrudin said to the minister:

'You may know the value of a turban, but I know how far a man's vanity will take him.'

And that's what the world around her is like. She has nothing against her profession, she doesn't judge people by their desires, but she knows what's really important in life and wants to keep her feet on the ground, even though there are temptations at every turn.

Someone opens the door and says there's just half an hour before the show begins. The worst part of the day, the long period of tedium that precedes any fashion show, is coming to an end. The other girls put down their iPods and their phones; the make-up artists do any necessary retouching; the hairdressers comb back into place any stray locks.

Jasmine sits in front of the dressing-room mirror and lets them get on with their work.

'Don't be nervous just because it's Cannes,' says the make-up artist.

'I'm not nervous.'

Why should she be? On the contrary, whenever she steps onto a catwalk, she feels a kind of ecstasy, a surge of adrenaline. The make-up artist seems in a mood to talk, and tells her about the many celebrity wrinkles she has smoothed, suggests a new face cream, says she's tired of her job, asks if Jasmine has a spare ticket to a party that night. Jasmine listens to all this with infinite patience. In her mind she's back in the streets of Antwerp on the day she decided to get in touch with the two photographers who had approached her earlier. She had met with a slight initial difficulty, but it had all worked out in the end.

As it would today and as it had when – along with her mother, who had agreed to go with her, eager for her daughter to recover from her depression as quickly as possible – she rang the bell of the first photographer, the one who had stopped her in the street. The door opened to reveal a small room with a transparent table covered in photographic negatives, another table, on which sat a computer, and a kind of drawing-board piled with papers. With the photographer was a woman of about forty, who looked at her long and hard, before smiling and introducing herself as the events co-ordinator. Then the four of them sat down.

'I'm sure your daughter has a great future as a model,' said the woman.

'Oh, I'm just here to keep her company,' said Jasmine's mother. 'If you have anything to say, speak directly to her.'

The woman, slightly taken aback, paused for a few seconds, then picked up a card and started noting down details and measurements, saying:

'Of course, Cristina isn't a good name for a model. It's too ordinary. The first thing we need to do is to change that.'

'There's another reason why Cristina isn't a good name,' Jasmine was thinking. Because it belonged to a girl who had ceased to exist when she witnessed a murder and denied what her eyes now refused to forget. When she decided to change everything, she began with the name she'd been called ever since she was a child. She needed to change everything, absolutely everything. She had her answer ready.

'My professional name is Jasmine Tiger – a combination of sweetness and danger.'

The woman seemed to like the name.

'A career in modelling isn't an easy one, and you're lucky to have been picked out to take the first step. Obviously, there are a lot of things to sort out, but we're here to help you get to where you want to be. We take photos of you and send them to the appropriate agencies. You'll also need a composite.'

She waited for Cristina to ask: 'What's a composite?' But no question came. Again the woman was temporarily thrown.

'A composite, as I'm sure you know, is a sheet of paper with, on the one side, your best photo and your measurements, and, on the other, more photos in different poses, for example, in a bikini, dressed as a student, perhaps one of just your face, another that shows you wearing more make-up, so that they won't necessarily exclude you if they want someone older. Your bust …'

Another pause.

'… your bust is perhaps a little large for a model.'

She turned to the photographer.

'We need to disguise that. Make a note.'

The photographer duly made a note. Cristina – who was rapidly becoming Jasmine Tiger – was thinking: 'But when they meet me, they'll see I've got a bigger bust than they were expecting!'

The woman picked up a handsome leather briefcase and took out a list.

'We'll need to call a make-up artist and a hairdresser. You haven't any experience on a catwalk, have you?'

'None.'

'Well, you don't stride down a catwalk as if you were walking down the street. If you did, you'd stumble because you'd be moving too fast or else trip over your high heels. You have to place one foot in front of the other, like a cat. You mustn't smile too much either. Even more important is posture.'

She ticked off three things on the list.

'And you'll have to hire some clothes.'

Another tick.

'And I think that's all for now.'

She again put her hand inside the elegant briefcase and took out a calculator. She went down the list, tapped in a few numbers, then added them up. No one else in the room dared utter a word.

'That will be around two thousand euros, I think. We won't include the photos because Yasser,' she turned to the photographer, 'is very expensive, but he's prepared to do the work for free, as long as you give him permission to use the material. We can have the make-up artist and the hairdresser here tomorrow morning and I'll get in touch with the people who run the course to see if there's a vacancy. I'm sure there will be, just as I'm sure that by investing in yourself, you're creating new possibilities for your future and will soon recover any initial expenses.'

'Are you saying I have to pay?'

Again the 'events co-ordinator' seemed taken aback. Usually, the girls who came to see her were so mad keen to realise the dream of a whole generation – being considered one of the sexiest women in the world – that they never asked indelicate questions like that.

'Listen, Cristina …'

'Jasmine. The moment I walked through that door, I became Jasmine.'

The photographer's mobile phone rang. He took it out of his pocket and moved away to the far end of the room, which had, until then, been in darkness. When he drew one of the curtains, Jasmine saw a wall draped with a black cloth, tripods mounted with flashes, boxes with blinking lights and several spotlights suspended from the ceiling.

'Listen, Jasmine, there are thousands and millions of people who would like to be in your position. You were chosen by one of Antwerp's finest photographers, you'll have the help of the best professionals and I will personally manage your career. On the other hand, as with everything else in life, you have to believe that you're going to succeed and, for that to happen, you need to invest money. I know you're beautiful enough to enjoy great success as a model, but that isn't enough in this highly competitive world. You have to be the best, and that costs money, at least to begin with.'

'But if you think I have all those qualities, why don't you invest *your* money in me?'

'I will later on. At the moment, we need to know just how committed you are. I want to be sure that you really do want to be a professional model or if you're just another young woman excited by the possibility of travelling, seeing the world and finding a rich husband.'

The woman's tone of voice had grown severe. The photographer returned from the studio end of the room.

'It's the make-up artist. She wants to know what time she should arrive tomorrow.'

'If the money's essential, I can probably ...' Jasmine's mother began to say, but Jasmine had got up and was walking over to the door, without shaking hands with either the woman or the photographer.

'Thank you very much, but I don't have that kind of money, and even if I did, I would spend it on something else.'

'But it's your future!'

'Precisely. It's my future, not yours.'

Jasmine burst into tears afterwards. First, she had gone to that expensive boutique where they'd not only been rude to her, but implied that she was lying when she said she'd met the owner. Then, just when she thought she was about to start a new life and had discovered the perfect new name for herself, she learned that it would cost her two thousand euros just to take the first step!

Mother and daughter made their way home in silence. Jasmine's mobile rang several times, but she just glanced at the number and put the phone back in her pocket.

'Why don't you answer it? We've got another appointment this afternoon, haven't we?'

'Because we don't have two thousand euros.'

Her mother grasped Jasmine's shoulders. She knew what a fragile state her daughter was in and had to do something.

'Yes, we do. I've worked every day since your father died, and we do have two thousand euros. We have more than that if you need it. Cleaners earn good money in Europe because no one here wants to clean up other people's mess.

Besides, we're talking about your future. We can't go home now.'

The phone rang again. Jasmine became Cristina again and did as her mother asked. The woman she had the appointment with that afternoon was ringing to apologise and explain that another commitment meant that she would be a couple of hours late for their meeting.

'That's all right,' said Cristina. 'But before you waste any more time, I'd like to know how much it's going to cost me.'

'How much it's going to cost?'

'Yes. I've just had a meeting with another photographer and he and his colleague were going to charge me two thousand euros for the photos, the make-up …'

The woman at the other end laughed.

'No, it won't cost you anything. That's an old trick. We can talk about it when we meet.'

Her studio was similar to the one they'd visited that morning, but the conversation they had was completely different. She asked Cristina why she looked so much sadder than when they'd first met; she clearly still remembered their initial encounter. Cristina told her what had happened with the other photographer, and the woman explained that it was common practice and one that the authorities were trying to clamp down on. At that very moment, in many places around the world, relatively pretty girls were being invited to reveal 'the full potential of their beauty' and paying through the nose for the privilege. On the pretext of looking for new talent, agencies would rent rooms in luxury hotels, fill them with photographic equipment, promise the would-be models at least one fashion show a year or their money back, charge a fortune for any photos they took, call in failed professionals to act as make-up artists and hairdressers, suggest enrolment in particular modelling schools and then, quite often, disappear without trace. The studio Cristina had visited was, in fact, a genuine one, but she'd been quite right to reject their offer.

'They're appealing to people's vanity, and there's nothing necessarily wrong in that, as long as the person involved knows what they're getting into. It's not something that only happens in the world of fashion either, it goes on in other areas too: writers publishing their own books, painters sponsoring their own exhibitions, film directors who go into debt in order to buy their place in the sun with one of the big studios, girls your age who leave home and go to the big city to work as waitresses, hoping to be discovered one day by a producer who'll propel them to stardom.'

No, they wouldn't take any photos now. She needed to get to know Cristina better; pressing the camera button was the last stage in a long process that began with uncovering your subject's soul. They arranged to meet the following day to talk more.

'You need to choose a name.'

'It's Jasmine Tiger.'

Yes, her love of life had returned.

The photographer invited her to spend the weekend at her beach house near the Dutch border, and they spent eight hours a day experimenting with the camera.

She expected Jasmine to reveal on her face a whole range of emotions suggested by words such as 'fire', 'seduction', 'water'. She had to try and show both sides of her soul, good and bad. She had to look down, straight ahead, to the side, to stare off into space. She had to imagine seagulls and demons. She had to imagine she'd been attacked by a group of older men and left in the restroom in a bar, having been raped by one or more of them; she had to be sinner and saint, perverse and innocent.

Some photos were taken out in the open, and even though her body was freezing, she was able to react to each stimulus, to respond to each suggestion. They also used a small studio set up in one of the rooms so that the photographer could play around with different types of music and lighting. Jasmine would do her own make-up, while the photographer did her hair.

'Am I any good?' Jasmine would ask. 'Why are you spending so much time on me?'

But all the photographer would say was: 'We'll talk about that later', and then spend the rest of the evening looking at the work they'd done that day, thinking and making notes, but never commenting on whether she was pleased or disappointed with the results.

Not until Monday morning did Jasmine (for Cristina was definitively dead by then) get an opinion. They were waiting at Brussels station for the connection to Antwerp when the photographer suddenly said:

'You're the best model I've ever worked with.'

'You're joking.'

The woman looked at her in surprise, then said:

'No, really, you are. I've been working in this field for twenty years now; I've taken photographs of countless people; I've worked with professional models and film actors, all of them highly experienced, but none of them had your ability to express emotion. And do you know what that's called? Talent. In certain professions, talent is quite easy to measure: managing directors who can turn around a business on the verge of bankruptcy and make it a going concern again; sportsmen who break records; artists whose work lives on for at least two generations; so how can I be so sure about you as a model? Because I'm a professional. You've managed to show your angels and your demons through the lens of a camera, and that's not easy. I'm not talking about young people who like to dress up as vampires and go to Goth parties; I'm not talking about girls who put on an innocent air to try to arouse the paedophile in men. I'm talking about real demons and real angels.'

The station was full of people walking back and forth. Jasmine looked at the train timetable and suggested they go outside. She was dying for a cigarette, and smoking was forbidden within the station precinct. She was wondering whether or not she should say what was going on inside her just then.

'It may be that I do have talent, but if I do, there's only one reason I was able to show that talent. You know, during all the time we've spent together, you've never said anything about your private life and never asked about mine. Do you want me to help you with your luggage, by the way. Photography's basically a profession for men, isn't it? There's always so much equipment to lug around.'

The woman laughed.

'There's nothing much to say, really, except that I adore my work. I'm thirty-eight, divorced, no kids, but with enough good contacts to be able to earn a comfortable living, but not to live in any great luxury. There's something else I must add to what I said: if everything goes to plan you must never ever behave like someone who depends on her profession to survive, even if it's true. If you don't follow my advice, you'll be easily manipulated by the system. Obviously, I'll use your photos and earn money with them, but from now on, I'd suggest you get yourself a professional agent.'

Jasmine lit another cigarette; it was now or never.

'Do you know why I was able to show my talent? Because of something I never imagined would happen in my life: I've fallen in love with a woman, a woman I would like to have by my side, guiding whatever steps I need to take, a woman who with her gentleness and her rigour managed to get inside my soul and release both the best and the worst that lie in those subterranean depths. She didn't do this by long instruction in meditation techniques or through psychoanalysis – which is what my mother thinks I need – she used …'

She paused. She felt afraid, but she had to go on. She had nothing now to lose.

'She used a camera.'

Time stood still. The other people outside the station stopped moving, all noise ceased, the wind dropped, her cigarette smoke hung in the air, the lights went out – there were just two pairs of eyes shining brighter than ever and fixed on each other.

'You're ready,' says the make-up artist.

Jasmine looks up and sees her partner pacing up and down in the improvised dressing-room. She must be feeling nervous; after all, this is her first fashion show in Cannes, and if it goes well, she might get a fat contract with the Belgian government.

Jasmine feels like going over and reassuring her, telling her that everything will be fine, as it always has been before. She might get a response along the lines of: 'You're only nineteen, what do you know about life?'

She would reply: 'I know what your capabilities are, just as you know mine. I know about the relationship that changed our lives one day three years ago, outside a train station, when you gently touched my cheek. Do you remember how frightened we both were? But we survived that first feeling of fear. And thanks to that relationship, I'm here now; and you, as well as being an excellent photographer, are doing what you always dreamed of doing: designing and making clothes.'

She knows it's best not to say anything. Telling a person to calm down only makes them even more nervous.

She goes over to the window and lights another cigarette. She's smoking too much, but then why shouldn't she? This is her first major fashion show in France.

4.43 p.m.

A young woman in a black suit and white blouse opens the door. She asks for her name, checks the list and says she'll have to wait a little, the suite is currently occupied. Two men and another woman, possibly younger than her, are also waiting.

They all wait their turn in silence. 'How long will this take? What exactly am I doing here?' Gabriela asks herself, and hears two responses.

The first reminds her that she must keep going. Gabriela, the optimist, the one who has persevered in order to reach stardom and now needs to think about the première, the invitations, the flights by private jet, the posters put up in all the world's capitals, the photographers on permanent watch outside her house, interested in what she's wearing and where she buys her clothes, and in the identity of the blond hunk she was seen with in some fashionable nightclub. Then there will be the victorious return to the town where she was born, the astonished friends eyeing her enviously and the charitable projects she intends to support.

The second response reminds her that Gabriela the optimist, the one who has persevered in order to reach stardom, is now walking along a knife-edge from which it would be all too easy to slip and plunge into the abyss. Hamid Hussein doesn't even know of her existence; no one has ever seen her made-up and ready for a party; the dress might not be her size, it might need adjusting and then she might arrive late for her meeting at the Martinez. She's twenty-five years old, and, who knows, they might be interviewing some other candidate right now on that same yacht or they might have changed their minds; in fact, perhaps that was the idea: to talk to two or three possible candidates and see which of them stood out from the crowd. All three of them might be invited to the party, unaware of each other's existence.

Paranoia.

No, it isn't paranoia, she's just being realistic. Even the fact that Gibson and the Star only ever got involved in major projects was no guarantee of success. And if anything went wrong, it would all be her fault. The ghost of the Mad Hatter from *Alice in Wonderland* is still there. Perhaps she isn't as talented as she thinks, just very hard-working. She hasn't been as lucky as some others; nothing of great importance has so far happened in her life, despite fighting day and night, night and day. She hasn't stopped since arriving in Cannes: distributing her extremely expensive 'book' to various casting companies and getting only one audition. If she really was that special, she would now be having to decide which of several roles to accept. She's getting above herself and will soon know the taste of defeat, all the more bitter because she has come so close and dipped her toes in the ocean of fame … only to fail.

'I'm attracting bad vibrations. I know they're out there. I must get a grip on myself.'

She can't do any yoga exercises in front of that woman in the suit and the three other people waiting in silence. She needs to drive away those negative thoughts, but where exactly are they coming from? According to what she's read – and she had read a lot on the subject at a time when she felt she was failing to achieve as much as she could because of other people's envy – it was likely that another actress who had been rejected was, at that moment, focussing all her energies on getting the role back. Yes, she could feel it, it was true! The only escape is to make her mind leave that corridor and go off in search of her

Higher Self, which is connected to all the forces of the Universe.

She breathes deeply, smiles and says to herself:

'I am spreading the energy of love all around me; it is more powerful than the forces of darkness; the God in me greets the God who lives in all the inhabitants of the planet, even those who …'

She hears someone laugh. The door to the suite opens, and a group of smiling, happy young people of both sexes, accompanied by two female celebrities, are leaving and heading for the lift. The two men and the woman go into the room, collect the dozens of bags left beside the door and join the group waiting for them by the lift. They must be assistants, chauffeurs, secretaries.

'It's your turn,' says the woman in the suit.

'Meditation never fails,' thinks Gabriela.

She smiles confidently at the receptionist, but the suite itself almost takes her breath away. It's like an Aladdin's cave, full of rail upon rail of clothes, and all kinds of pairs of glasses, handbags, jewellery, beauty products, watches, shoes, tights and electronic devices. A blonde woman comes to meet her; she has a list in one hand and a mobile phone on a chain around her neck. She takes Gabriela's name and says:

'Follow me. We haven't much time, so let's get straight down to business.'

They go into one of the other rooms, and Gabriela sees still more luxurious, glamorous treasures, things she has only ever seen in shop windows, but never had a chance to see close up, except when worn by someone else.

Yes, all this awaits her. She needs to be quick and decide exactly what she's going to wear.

'Can I start with the jewellery?'

'You don't get to choose anything. We know exactly what HH wants. And you'll have to return the dress to us tomorrow.'

HH. Hamid Hussein knows what he wants her to wear!

They cross the room. The bed and the other furniture are cluttered with more products: T-shirts, spices and seasonings, a picture of a well-known make of coffee-machine, several of which are wrapped up as presents. They go down a corridor and through the doors into an even larger room. She had no idea hotel suites could be so big.

'This is the Temple.'

An elegant long white poster bearing the designer's logo has been placed above the vast double bed. An androgynous creature – whether male or female, Gabriela cannot tell – is waiting for them in silence. The creature is extremely thin, with drab, straggly hair, shaven eyebrows, beringed fingers, and is wearing skin-tight trousers adorned with various chains.

'Get undressed.'

Gabriela takes off her blouse and her jeans, still trying to guess the gender of the creature who has now gone over to one of the dress-rails and selected a red dress.

'Take your bra off too. It makes bulges under the dress.'

There's a large mirror in the room, but it's turned away from her and so she can't see how the dress looks.

'We need to be quick. Hamid said that as well as going to the party, she has to go up the steps.'

Go up the steps!

The magic words.

The dress was all wrong. The woman and the androgyne are starting to get worried. The woman asks for two or three other dresses to be brought because Gabriela will be going up the steps with the Star, who is dressed and ready.

Going up the steps with the Star! She must be dreaming!

They decide on a long gold dress that clings to the body and has a neckline that plunges to the waist. At breast-height, a gold chain keeps the opening from getting any wider than the human imagination can bear.

The woman is very nervous. The androgyne goes out and returns with a seamstress, who makes the necessary alterations to the hem. If Gabriela could say anything at that moment, it would be to ask them to stop. Sewing the dress while she is actually wearing it means that her fate is also being sewn up and interrupted. But this is no time for superstitions, and many famous actresses must face the same situation every day without anything bad ever happening to them.

A third person arrives, carrying an enormous suitcase, goes over to one corner of the vast room and starts dismantling the case, which is, in fact, a kind of portable make-up studio, including a mirror surrounded by lights. The androgyne is kneeling before her, like a repentant Mary Magdalene, trying shoe after shoe on her foot.

She's Cinderella and will shortly meet her Prince and go up the steps with him!

'Those are good,' says the woman.

The androgyne starts putting the other shoes back in their boxes.

'OK, take it off. We'll put the final touches to the dress while you're having your hair and make-up done.'

Gabriela feels relieved that they will no longer be sewing the dress while it is on her body. Her destiny opens up again.

Wearing only a pair of knickers, she is led to the bathroom. A portable kit for washing and drying hair has already been installed there, and a shaven-headed man is waiting. He asks her to sit down and lean her head back into a kind of steel basin. He uses a hose attached to the tap to wash her hair, and, like everyone else, he's extremely agitated. He complains about the noise from outside; he needs quiet if he's to do a decent job, but no one pays any attention. Besides, he never has enough time; everything's always done in such a rush.

'No one understands the enormous responsibility resting on my shoulders,' he says.

He's not talking to her, but to himself. He goes on:

'When you go up the steps, they're not looking at you, you know. They're looking at my work, at my make-up and at my hair-styling. You're just the canvas on which I paint or draw, the clay out of which I shape my sculptures. If I make a mistake, what will other people say? I could lose my job.'

Gabriela feels offended, but she's obviously going to have to get used to this kind of thing. That's what the world of glamour is like. Later on, when she really is someone, she'll choose kind, polite people to work with her. For now, she focusses on her main virtue: patience.

The conversation is interrupted by the roar of the hair-dryer, similar to that of a plane taking off. And he was the one complaining about the noise outside!

He rather roughly primps her hair into shape and asks her to move straight over to the portable make-up studio. His mood changes completely: he stands in silence, contemplating her face in the mirror, as if he were in a trance. He paces back and forth, using the dryer and the brush much as Michelangelo used hammer and chisel on his sculpture of David. And she tries to keep looking straight ahead and remember some lines written by a Portuguese poet:

The mirror reflects perfectly; it makes no mistakes because it doesn't think. To think is to make mistakes.

The androgyne and the woman return. In only twenty minutes the limousine will arrive to take her to the Martinez to pick up the Star. There's nowhere to park there, so they have to be right on time. The hairdresser mutters to himself, as if he were a misunderstood artist, but he knows he has to meet those deadlines. He starts working on her face as if he were Michelangelo painting the Sistine Chapel.

A limousine! The steps! The Star!

The mirror reflects perfectly; it makes no mistakes because it does not think.

She mustn't think either because, if she does, she'll be infected by the prevailing anxiety and bad temper; those negative vibes will come back. She would love to know just what it is, this hotel suite packed with all these different things, but she must behave as if she were used to frequenting such places. Beneath the severe gaze of the woman and the distracted gaze of the androgyne, Michelangelo is putting the finishing touches to her make-up. Gabriela then stands up and is swiftly dressed and shod. Everything is in place, thank God.

From somewhere in the room, they grab a small leather Hamid Hussein bag. The androgyne opens it, removes some of the paper stuffing, studies the result with the same distracted air, and, when it appears to meet with his approval, hands it to her.

The woman gives her four copies of a huge contract, with small red markers along the edge, bearing the words: 'Sign here.'

'You can either sign without reading it or take it home, phone your lawyer and say you need more time to think before deciding. You'll go up those steps regardless because it's too late to change anything now. However, if this contract isn't back here tomorrow morning, you just have to return the dress and that will be that.'

She remembers her agent's words: Accept everything. Gabriela takes the pen the woman is holding out to her, turns to the pages with the markers and signs everything. She has nothing to lose. If there are any unfair clauses, she can probably go to the courts later on and say she was pressured into signing. First, though, she has to do what she has always dreamed of doing.

The woman takes the signed contract from her and vanishes without saying goodbye. Michelangelo is once again dismantling the make-up table, immersed in his own little world in which injustice rules, and in which his work is never recognised, where he never has enough time to do a proper job, and where, if anything goes wrong, the fault will be entirely his. The androgyne asks her to follow him to the door of the suite; he consults his watch – which, Gabriela notices, bears a death's head – and speaks to her for the first time since they have met.

'We've got another three minutes. You can't go down now and be seen by other people. And I have to go with you to the limousine.'

The tension returns. She's no longer thinking about the limousine, about the Star, or going up those steps. She's afraid. She needs to talk.

'What's this suite for? Why are there all these things in it?'

'There's even a safari to Kenya,' says the androgyne, pointing to one corner. She hadn't noticed the discreet advertising banner for an airline and a small pile of envelopes on the table. 'It's free, like everything else in here, apart from the clothes and the accessories in the Temple.'

Coffee machines, electronic gadgets, clothes, handbags, watches, jewellery and a trip to Kenya.

All of it absolutely free?

'I know what you're thinking,' says the androgyne in that voice which is neither male nor female, but the voice of some interplanetary being. 'But it is all free, or, rather, given in fair exchange because nothing in this world is free. This is one of the many "Gift Rooms" you get in Cannes during the Festival. The chosen few come in here and take whatever they want; they're people who will be seen around wearing a shirt designed by A or some glasses by B, they'll receive important guests in their home and, when the Festival's over, go into their kitchen and prepare some coffee with a brand-new coffee-machine. They'll carry around their laptop in a bag made by C, recommend friends to use moisturisers by D, which are just about to be launched on the market, and they'll feel important doing that because it means they'll own something exclusive, which hasn't yet reached the specialist shops. They'll wear E's jewellery to the swimming pool and be photographed wearing a belt by F, neither of which are yet available to the public. When these products do come on the market, the Superclass will already have done their advertising for them, not because they want to, but because they're the only ones who can. Then mere mortals will spend all their savings on buying the same products. What could be easier, sweetheart? The manufacturers invest in some free samples, and the chosen few are transformed into walking advertisements. But don't get too excited. You haven't reached those heights yet.'

'But what has the safari to Kenya got to do with all that?'

'What better publicity than a middle-aged couple arriving back all excited from their "jungle adventure" with loads of pictures in their camera, and recommending everyone else to go on the same exclusive holiday? All their friends will want to experience the same thing. As I say, nothing in this world is free. By the way, the three minutes are up, so we'd better go.'

A white Maybach is waiting for them. The chauffeur, in gloves and cap, opens the door. The androgyne gives Gabriela her final instructions:

'Forget about the film, that isn't why you're going up the steps. When you get to the top of the steps, greet the Festival director and the mayor, and then, as soon as you enter the Palais des Congrès, head for the restroom on the first floor. Go to the end of that corridor, turn left and leave by a side door. Someone will be waiting for you there; they know how you'll be dressed and will do some more work on your make-up and your hair, and then you can have a moment's rest on the terrace. I'll meet you there and take you to the gala supper.'

'Won't the director and the producers be annoyed?'

The androgyne shrugs and goes back into the hotel with that strange swaying gait. The film is not of the slightest importance. What matters is *la montée des marches*, going up the red-carpeted steps to the Palais and along the ultimate corridor of fame, the place where all the celebrities in the worlds of cinema, the arts and the high life are photographed, and their photos then distributed by news agencies to the four corners of the world to be published in magazines from West to East and from North to South.

'Is the air-conditioning all right for you, Madame?'

She nods to the chauffeur.

'If you want anything to drink, there's a bottle of iced champagne in the cabinet to your left.'

Gabriela opens the cabinet and gets out a glass; then, holding the bottle well away from her dress, she pops the cork and pours herself a glass of champagne which she downs in one and immediately refills. Outside, curious onlookers are trying to see who is inside the vast car with the smoked windows that is driving along the cordoned-off lane. Soon, she and the Star will be together, the beginning not just of a new career, but of an incredible, beautiful, intense love story.

She's a romantic and proud of it.

She remembers that she left her clothes and her handbag in the 'Gift Room'. She doesn't have the key to the apartment she's renting. She has nowhere to go when the night is over. If she ever writes a book about her life, how could she possibly tell the story of that particular day: waking up with a hangover, unemployed and in a bad mood, in an apartment with clothes and mattresses scattered all over the floor, and six hours later being driven along in a limousine, ready to walk along the red carpet in front of a crowd of journalists, beside one of the most desirable men in the world.

Her hands are trembling. She considers drinking another glass of champagne, but decides not to risk turning up drunk on the steps of fame.

'Relax, Gabriela. Don't forget who you are. Don't get carried away by everything that's happening now. Be realistic.'

She repeats these words over and over as they approach the Martinez. Whether she likes it or not, she can never go back to being the person she was before. There is no way out, except the one the androgyne told her about and which leads to a still higher mountain.

4.52 p.m.

Even the King of Kings, Jesus Christ, was tested as Igor is being tested now: being tempted by the Devil. And he needs to cling on tooth and nail to his faith if he's not to weaken in the mission with which he has been charged.

The Devil is asking him to stop, to forgive, to abandon his task. The Devil is a top-class professional and knows how to fill the weak with alarming feelings such as fear, anxiety, impotence and despair.

When it comes to tempting the strong, he uses more sophisticated lures: good intentions. It's exactly what he did with Jesus when he found him wandering in the wilderness. Why, he asked, didn't he command that the stones be made bread, so that he could satisfy not only his own hunger, but that of all the other people begging him for food? Jesus, however, acted with the wisdom one would expect of the Son of God. He replied that man does not live on bread alone, but on every word from God's mouth.

Besides, what exactly were good intentions, virtue and integrity? The people who built the Nazi concentration camps thought they were showing integrity by obeying government orders. The doctors who certified as insane any intellectuals opposed to the Soviet regime and had them banished to Siberia were convinced that Communism was a fair system. Soldiers who go to war may kill in the name of an ideal they don't properly understand, but they, too, are full of good intentions, virtue and integrity.

No, that's not true. If sin achieves something good, it is a virtue, and if virtue is deployed to cause evil, it is a sin.

In his case, the Evil One is trying to use forgiveness as a way to trouble his soul. He says: 'You're not the only person to have been through this. Lots of people have been abandoned by the person they most loved, and yet managed to turn bitterness into happiness. Imagine the families of the people whom you have caused to depart this life; they'll be filled with rancour and hatred and a desire for revenge. Is that how you intend to improve the world? Is that what you want to give to the woman you love?'

Igor, however, is wiser than the temptations that seem to be possessing his soul. If he can hold out a little longer, that voice will grow tired and disappear. He thinks this largely because one of the people he sent to Paradise is becoming an ever more constant presence in his life. The girl with the dark eyebrows is telling him that everything is fine, and that there's a great difference between forgiving and forgetting. He has no hatred in his heart, and he's not doing this to have his revenge on the world.

The Devil may insist all he likes, but he must stand firm and remember why he's here.

He goes into the first pizzeria he sees, and orders a pizza margherita and a Coke. It's best to eat now because he won't be able to – he never can – eat properly over supper with a lot of other people round the table. Everyone feels obliged to keep up an animated, but relaxed conversation, and someone always seems to interrupt him just as he's about to take a bite of the delicious food in front of him.

His usual way of avoiding this is to bombard his companions at table with questions, then leave them to come up with intelligent responses while he eats his meal in peace. Tonight, though, he will feel disinclined to be helpful and sociable. He will be unpleasant and distant. He can always claim not to speak their language.

He knows that in the next few hours, Temptation will prove stronger than ever, telling him to stop and give it all up. He doesn't want to stop, though; his objective is still to complete his mission, even if the reason for that mission is changing.

He has no idea if three violent deaths in one day would be considered normal in Cannes; if it is, the police won't suspect that anything unusual is happening. They'll continue their bureaucratic procedures and he'll be able to fly off as planned in the early hours of tomorrow. He doesn't know either if he has been identified: there was that couple who passed him and the girl this morning, there was one of the dead man's bodyguards and the person who witnessed the other woman's murder.

Temptation is now changing its tactics: it wants to frighten him, just as it does with the weak. It would seem that the Devil has no idea what he has been through nor that he has emerged a much stronger man from the test Fate has set him.

He picks up his mobile phone and sends another text.

He imagines Ewa's reaction when she receives it. Something tells him that she will feel a mixture of fear and pleasure. He is sure that she deeply regrets the step she took two years ago – leaving everything behind her, including her clothes and jewellery, and asking her lawyers to get in touch with him regarding divorce proceedings. The grounds: incompatibility. As if interesting people will ever necessarily think exactly the same way or have many things in common. It was clearly a lie: she had fallen in love with someone else.

Passion. Which of us can honestly say that, after more than five years of marriage, we haven't felt a desire to find another companion? Which of us can honestly say that we haven't been unfaithful at least once in our life, even if only in our imagination? And how many men and women have left home because of that, then discovered that passion doesn't last and gone back to their true partners? A little mature reflection and everything is forgotten. That's absolutely normal, part of human biology.

He has had to learn this very slowly. At first, he instructed his lawyers to proceed with the utmost rigour. If she wanted to leave him, then she would have to give up all claim to the fortune they had accumulated together over nearly twenty years, every penny of it. He got drunk for a whole week while he waited for her response. He didn't care about the money; he was doing it because he wanted her back, and that was the only way he knew of putting pressure on her.

Ewa, however, was a person of integrity. Her lawyers accepted his conditions.

It was only when the press got hold of the case that he found out about his ex-wife's new partner. One of the most successful couturiers in the world, someone who, like him, had built himself up from nothing; a man, like him, in his forties and known, like him, for his lack of arrogance and his hard work.

He couldn't understand what had happened. Shortly before Ewa left for a fashion show in London, they had spent a rare romantic holiday alone in Madrid. They had travelled there in the company jet and were staying in a hotel with every possible comfort, but they had decided to rediscover the world together. They didn't book tables at expensive restaurants, they stood in long queues outside museums, they took taxis rather than chauffeured limousines, they walked for miles and got thoroughly lost. They ate a lot and drank even more, and would arrive back at the hotel exhausted and contented, and make love every night as they used to do.

For both of them it took a real effort to stop themselves turning on their laptops or their mobile phones, but they managed it. And they returned to Moscow with their hearts full of good memories and with smiles on their faces.

He plunged back into work, surprised to see that everything had continued to function perfectly well in his absence. She left for London the following week and never came back.

Igor employed one of the top private surveillance agencies – normally used for industrial or political espionage – which meant having to look at hundreds of photos in which his wife appeared hand-in-hand with her new companion. Basing themselves on information provided by her ex-husband, the detectives managed to provide her with a made-to-measure 'friend'. Ewa met her 'by chance' in a department store; she was from Russia and had, she said, been abandoned by her husband, couldn't get work in Britain because she didn't have the right papers and had barely enough money to feed herself. Ewa was distrustful at first, but then resolved to help her. She spoke to her new lover, who decided to take a risk and get the friend a job in one of his offices, even though she was an illegal worker.

She was Ewa's only Russian-speaking 'friend'. She was alone. She had marital problems. According to the psychologist employed by the surveillance agency, she was ideally placed to obtain the desired information. He knew that Ewa hadn't yet adapted to her new life and what could be more natural than to share her intimate thoughts with another woman in similar circumstances, not in order to find a solution, but simply to unburden her soul.

The 'friend' recorded all their conversations, and the tapes ended up on Igor's desk, where they took precedence over papers requiring his signature, invitations demanding his presence, and gifts waiting to be sent to customers, suppliers, politicians and fellow businessmen.

The tapes were far more useful and far more painful than any photos. He discovered that her relationship with the famous couturier had begun two years earlier, at the Fashion Week in Milan, where they had met for professional reasons. Ewa resisted at first; after all, he lived surrounded by some of the most beautiful women in the world, and she, at the time, was thirty-eight. Nevertheless, they ended up going to bed with each other in Paris, the following week.

When Igor heard this, he realised that he felt sexually aroused and couldn't understand why his body should react in that way. Why did the simple fact of imagining his wife opening her legs and being penetrated by another man provoke in him an erection rather than a sense of revulsion?

This was the only time he feared he might be losing his mind, and he decided to make a kind of public confession in an attempt to diminish his sense of guilt. In conversation with colleagues, he mentioned that 'a friend of his' had experienced sexual pleasure when he found out that his wife was having an extramarital affair. Then came the surprise.

His colleagues, most of them executives and politicians from various social classes and nationalities, at first expressed horror at the thought. Then, after the tenth glass of vodka, they all admitted that this was one of the most exciting things that could happen in a marriage. One of them always asked his wife to tell him all the sordid details and the words she and her lover used. Another declared that swingers' clubs – places frequented by couples interested in group sex – were the ideal therapy for an ailing marriage. A slight exaggeration perhaps, but Igor was glad to learn that he wasn't the only man who found it arousing to know that his wife had slept with someone else. He was equally glad that he knew so little about human beings, especially the male of the species. His conversations usually focussed on business matters and rarely entered personal territory.

He's thinking now about what was on those tapes. During their week in London (the fashion weeks are held consecutively to make life easier for the professionals involved) the couturier declared himself to be in love with her; hardly surprising, given that he had met one of the most unusual women in the world. Ewa, for her part, was still filled with doubts. Hussein was only the second man with whom she had made love in her life; they worked in the same industry, but she felt immensely inferior to him. She would have to give up her dream of working in fashion because it would be impossible to compete with her future husband, and she would go back to being a mere housewife.

Worse, she couldn't understand why someone so powerful should be interested in a middle-aged Russian woman.

Igor could have explained this had she given him a chance: her mere presence awoke the light in all those around her; she made everyone want to give of their best and to emerge from the ashes of the past filled with renewed hope. That is what had happened to him as a young man returning from a bloody and pointless war.

Temptation returns. The Devil tells him that this isn't exactly true. He himself had overcome his traumas by plunging into work. Psychiatrists might consider working too hard to be a psychological disorder, but for him it had been a way of healing his wounds through forgiveness and forgetting. Ewa wasn't really so very important. He must stop focussing all his emotions on a non-existent relationship.

'You're not the first,' said the Devil. 'You're being led into doing evil deeds in the erroneous belief that this will somehow create good deeds.'

Igor is starting to feel nervous. He's a good man, and whenever he's been obliged to behave harshly, it has been in the name of a greater cause: serving his country, saving the marginalised from unnecessary suffering, following the example of his one role-model in life, Jesus Christ, and, like him, using a combination of turning the cheek and wielding the whip.

He makes the sign of the cross in the hope that Temptation will leave him. He forces himself to remember the tapes and what Ewa had said: that however unhappy she might be with her new partner, she would never return to the past because her ex-husband was 'unbalanced'.

How absurd. It appeared she was being brainwashed by her new environment. She must be keeping very bad company. He's sure she was lying when she told her Russian 'friend' that she had only got married again because she was afraid of being alone.

In her youth, she had always felt rejected by others and never able to be herself. She always had to pretend to be interested in the same things as her friends, playing the same games, going to parties, and looking for some handsome man to be a faithful husband and give her security, a home and children. 'It was all a lie,' she said on the tapes.

In fact, she always dreamed of adventure and the unknown. If she could have chosen a profession when she was still an adolescent, it would have been that of artist. When she was a child, she had loved making collages from photos cut out of Communist Party magazines; she hated the photos, but enjoyed colouring in the drab figures. Dolls' clothes were so hard to find that her mother had to make them for her, and Ewa loved those outfits and said to herself that, one day, she would make clothes too.

There was no such thing as fashion in the former Soviet Union. They only found out what was going on in the rest of the world when the Berlin Wall was torn down and foreign magazines started flooding into the country. As an adolescent, she was able to use these magazines to make brighter and more interesting collages. Then, one day, she decided to tell her family that her dream was to be a fashion designer.

As soon as she finished school, her parents sent her to Law School. They were very happy with their new-won freedom, but felt that certain capitalist ideas were threatening to destroy the country, distracting people from real art, replacing Tolstoy and Pushkin with spy novels, and corrupting classical ballet with modern aberrations. Their only daughter must be kept away from the moral degradation that had arrived along with Coca-Cola and flashy cars.

At university, she met a good-looking, ambitious young man who thought exactly as she did, that they had to give up the idea that the old regime would return one day. It had gone for good, and it was time to start a new life.

She really liked this young man. They started going out together. She saw that he was intelligent and would go far in life, plus he seemed to understand her. He had, of course, fought in the Afghan war and been wounded in combat, but nothing very serious. He never complained about the past and never showed any signs of being unbalanced or traumatised.

One day, he brought her a bunch of roses and told her that he was leaving university to start his own business. He then proposed to her, and she accepted, even though she felt only admiration and friendship for him. Love, she believed, would grow over time as they became closer. Besides, the young man was the only one who really understood her and provided her with the intellectual stimulus she needed. If she let this chance slip, she might never find another person prepared to accept her as she was.

They got married with little fuss and without the support of their families. He obtained loans from people she considered dangerous, but she could do nothing to prevent the loans going ahead. Gradually, the company he had started began to grow. After almost four years together, she – shaking with fear – made her first demand: that he pay off the people who had lent him money in the past and who seemed suspiciously uninterested in recouping it. He followed her advice and often had reason to thank her for it later.

The years passed, there were the inevitable failures and sleepless nights, then things started to improve, and from then on, the ugly duckling began to follow the script of all those children's stories: it grew into a beautiful swan, admired by everyone.

Ewa complained about being trapped in her role as housewife. Instead of reacting like her friends' husbands, for whom a job was synonymous with a lack of femininity, he bought her a shop in one of the most sought-after areas of Moscow. She started selling clothes made by the world's great couturiers, but never tried to create her own designs. Her work had other compensations, though: she visited all the major fashion houses, met interesting people, and it was then that she first encountered Hamid. She still didn't know whether or not she loved him – possibly not – but she felt comfortable with him. When he had told her that he'd never met anyone like her and suggested they live together, she felt she had nothing to lose. She had no children, and her husband was so married to his work that he probably wouldn't even notice she was gone.

'I left it all behind,' Ewa said on one of the tapes. 'And I don't regret it one bit. I would have done the same even if Hamid – against my wishes – hadn't bought that beautiful estate in Spain and put it in my name. I would have made the same decision if Igor, my ex-husband, had offered me half his fortune. I would have taken the same decision because I know that I need to live without fear. If one of the most desirable men in the world wants to be by my side, then I'm obviously a better person than I thought.'

On another tape, she commented that her husband clearly had severe psychological problems.

'My husband has lost his reason. Whether it stems from his war experiences or stress from over-work, I've no idea, but he thinks he knows what God intends. Before I left, I sought advice from a psychiatrist in order to try and understand him better, to see if it was possible to save our relationship. I didn't go into details so as not to compromise him and I won't do so with you now, but I think he would be capable of doing terrible things if he believed he was doing good.

'The psychiatrist explained to me that many generous, compassionate people can, from one moment to the next, change completely. Studies have been done of this phenomenon and they call that sudden change "the Lucifer effect" after Lucifer, God's best-loved angel, who ended up trying to rival God himself.'

'But why does that happen?' asked another female voice.

At that point, however, the tape ran out.

He would like to have heard her answer because he knows he doesn't consider himself on a par with God and because he's sure that his beloved is making the whole thing up, afraid that if she did come back, she would be rejected. Yes, he had killed out of necessity, but what did that have to do with their marriage? He had killed when he was a soldier, with official permission. He had killed a couple of other people too, but only in their best interests because they had no means of living a decent life. In Cannes, he was merely carrying out a mission.

And he would only kill someone he loved if he saw that she was mad, had completely lost her way and begun to destroy her own life. He would never allow the decay of a mind to ruin a brilliant, generous past. He would only kill someone he loved in order to save her from a long, painful process of self-destruction.

Igor looks at the Maserati that has just drawn up opposite him in a no-parking zone. It's an absurd, uncomfortable car which, despite its powerful engine – too low-powered for B-roads and too high-powered for motorways – has to dawdle along at the same speed as other cars.

A man of about fifty – but trying to look thirty – opens the door and struggles out because the door is too low to the ground. He goes into the pizzeria and orders a quattro formaggi to go.

Maserati and pizza are something of a mismatch, but these things happen.

Temptation returns. It's not talking to him now about forgiveness and generosity, about forgetting the past and moving on, it's trying a different tack and placing real doubts in his mind. What if Ewa were deeply unhappy? What if, despite her love for him, she was too deep in the bottomless pit of a bad decision, as Adam was the moment he accepted the apple and condemned the whole human race?

He had planned everything, he tells himself for the hundredth time. He wanted them to get back together again and not to allow a little word like 'goodbye' erase their whole past life. He knows that all marriages have their crises, especially after eighteen years. However, he also knows that a good strategist has to be flexible. He sends another text message, just to make sure she gets it. He stands up and says a prayer, asking to have the cup of renunciation removed from him.

The soul of the little seller of craftwork is beside him. He knows now that he committed an injustice; it wouldn't have hurt him to wait until he had found a more equal opponent, like the pseudo-athlete with the hennaed hair, or until he could save someone from further suffering, as was the case with the woman on the beach.

The girl with the dark eyebrows seems to hover over him like a saint, telling him to have no regrets. He acted correctly, saving her from a future of suffering and pain. Her pure soul is gradually driving away Temptation, helping Igor to understand that the reason he's in Cannes isn't to revive a lost love; that's impossible. He's here to save Ewa from bitterness and decay. She may have treated him unfairly, but the many things she did to help him deserve a reward.

'I am a good man.'

He goes over to the cashier, pays his bill and asks for a small bottle of mineral water. When he leaves, he empties the contents of the bottle over his head.

He needs to be able to think clearly. He has dreamed of this day for so long and now he is confused.

5.06 p.m.

Fashion may renew itself every six months, but one thing remains the same: bouncers always wear black.

Hamid had considered alternatives for his shows – dressing security guards in colourful uniforms for example or having them all dressed in white – but he knew that if he did anything like that, the critics would write more about 'these pointless innovations' than about what really mattered: the new collection. Besides, black is the perfect colour: conservative, mysterious and engraved on the collective unconscious, thanks to all those old cowboy films. The goodies always wear white and the baddies wear black.

'Imagine if the White House was called the Black House. Everyone would think it was inhabited by the spirit of darkness.'

Every colour has a purpose, although people may think they're chosen at random. White signifies purity and integrity. Black intimidates. Red shocks and paralyses. Yellow attracts attention. Green calms everything down and gives things the go-ahead. Blue soothes. Orange confuses.

Bouncers should wear black – so it was in the beginning and would be for ever after.

As usual, there are three different entrances. The first is for the press in general – a few journalists and a lot of photographers laden down with cameras. They seem perfectly polite, but have no qualms about elbowing a colleague out of the way to capture the best angle, an unusual shot, the perfect moment or some glaring mistake. The second entrance is for the general public, and in that respect, the Fashion Week in Paris was no different from that show in a seaside resort in the south of France; the people who come in through the second entrance are always badly dressed and would almost certainly not be able to afford anything being shown that afternoon. However, there they are in their ripped jeans, bad-taste T-shirts and, of course, their designer trainers, convinced that they're looking really relaxed and at ease, which, of course, they aren't. Some do have what might well be expensive handbags and belts, but this seems somehow even more pathetic, like putting a painting by Velázquez in a plastic frame.

Finally, there is the VIPs' entrance. The security guards never have any idea who anyone is. They simply stand there, arms crossed, looking threatening, as if they were the real owners. A polite young woman, trained to remember famous faces, comes over to them with a list in her hand.

'Welcome, Mr and Mrs Hussein. Thank you so much for being here.'

They go straight to the front. Everyone walks down the same corridor, but a barrier of metal pillars linked by a red velvet band marks out who are the most important people there. This is the Moment of Minor Glory, being singled out as special people, and even though this show isn't part of the official calendar - we mustn't forget that Cannes is, after all, a Film Festival - protocol must be rigorously observed. Because of that Moment of Minor Glory which occurs at all such similar events (suppers, lunches, cocktail parties) men and women spend hours in front of the mirror, convinced that artificial light is less harmful to the skin than the sun, against which they apply large amounts of sun factor. They are only two steps from the beach, but they prefer to use the sophisticated tanning machines in the beauty salons that are never more than a block away from the place where they're staying. They could enjoy a lovely view if they were to go for a stroll along the Boulevard de la Croisette, but would they lose many calories? No. They are far better off using the treadmills in the hotel's mini-gym.

That way, they will be in good shape to attend the free lunches – for which they dress with studied casualness – where they feel important simply because they've been invited, or the gala suppers for which they have to pay a lot of money unless they have influential contacts, or the post-supper parties that go on into the small hours, or the last cup of coffee or glass of whisky in the hotel bar, all of which involve repeated visits to the toilets to retouch make-up, straighten ties, brush off any dandruff from jacket shoulders and make sure one's lipstick is still perfect.

Finally, back in their luxurious hotel rooms, where they will find the bed made, the breakfast menu waiting, the weather forecast for the next day, a chocolate (which is immediately discarded as containing far too many calories), an envelope with their names exquisitely written (the envelope is never opened because all it contains is the standardised welcome letter from the hotel manager) beside a basket of fruit (devoured avidly because fruit is a rich source of fibre which is, in turn, good for the body and an excellent way of avoiding wind). They look in the mirror as they take off tie, make-up, dress or dinner jacket, and say to themselves: 'Nothing of much importance happened today. Perhaps tomorrow will be better.'

Ewa is beautifully dressed in an HH number that is at once discreet and elegant. They are ushered to two seats at the very front of the catwalk, next to the area reserved for the photographers, who are just coming in and setting up their equipment.

A journalist comes over and asks the usual question:

'Mr Hussein, which would you say is the best film you've seen so far?'

'It's too early to give an opinion,' he says, as usual. 'I've seen a lot of very interesting things, but I prefer to wait until the end of the Festival before passing judgement.'

In fact, he hasn't seen a single film. Later on, he'll talk to Gibson and ask him which he considers to be 'the best film of the Festival'.

The polite, smartly dressed blonde politely shoos the reporter away. She asks if they plan on going to the cocktail party being held by the Belgian government immediately after the show. She says that one of the ministers present would very much like to talk to him. Hamid considers the invitation, for he knows that the Belgians have put a lot of money into getting their couturiers a higher profile on the international scene, and thus recover some of the glory they once had as a colonial power in Africa.

'Yes, I might just drop in for a glass of champagne,' he says.

'Aren't we meeting Gibson straight after this?' asks Ewa.

Hamid gets the message. He apologises to the young woman. He had forgotten he had a prior commitment, but will be in touch with the minister later on.

A few photographers spot them and start taking photos. At the moment, they are the only people the press are interested in. Later, they're joined by a few models who were once all the rage and who pose and smile, sign autographs for some of the ill-dressed people in the audience and do everything they can to be noticed, in the hope that their faces will once again appear in the press. The photographers turn their lenses on them, knowing that they're merely going through the motions to please their editors; none of the photos will be published. Fashion is about the present, and the models of three years ago – apart from those who keep themselves in the headlines either through carefully stage-managed scandals or because they really do stand out from the crowd – are only remembered by the people who wait behind the metal barriers outside hotels, or by ladies who can't keep up with the speed of change.

The older models who have just arrived are aware of this (and 'older', of course, means anyone over 25), but the reason they're in the audience isn't that they want to return to the catwalks, but because they're hoping to get a role in a film or a career as a presenter on some cable TV show.

Who else will be on the catwalk today, aside from the only reason Hamid is here, Jasmine?

Certainly not any of the four or five top models in the world, because they do only what they want to do, always charge a fortune and would never dream of appearing at Cannes simply to lend prestige to someone else's show. Hamid reckons he will see two or three Class A models, like Jasmine, who will earn around 1,500 euros for that evening's work; you have to have a lot of charisma and, above all, a future in the industry. There will probably be another two or three Class B models, professionals who are brilliant on the catwalk, have the right kind of figure, but are not lucky enough to be taking part in any parallel events as special guests at the parties put on by the large conglomerates, and they will earn between 600 and 800 euros. The rest will be made up of Class C models, girls who have recently entered the mad world of fashion shows and who earn between 200 and 300 euros simply 'to gain experience'.

Hamid knows what's going on in the heads of the girls in that third group: 'I'm going to be a winner. I'm going to show everyone just what I can do. I'm going to be one of the most famous models in the world, even if that means having to sleep with a few older men.'

Older men, however, are not as stupid as they think. The majority of these girls are under-age, and in most countries in the world, anyone engaging in under-age sex is likely to end up in jail. The legend differs greatly from the reality: no model gets to the top because of her sexual generosity; there's more to it than that.

Charisma. Luck. The right agent. Being in the right place at the right time. And the right time, according to the trend adapters, isn't what these girls new to the fashion world think it is. According to the latest research, everything indicates that the public is tired of seeing strange, anorexic creatures of indefinite age, but with provocative eyes. The casting agencies (who choose the models) are looking for something which is, apparently, extremely difficult to find: the girl next door, that is, someone who is absolutely ordinary and who transmits to everyone who sees her on posters or in fashion magazines the sense that she's just like them. And finding that extraordinary girl who appears to be so 'ordinary' is an almost impossible task.

The days are long gone when mannequins were simply walking clothes hangers, although it has to be said that it is easier to dress someone thin – the clothes do hang better. The days are gone, too, of handsome men advertising expensive menswear. That worked well in the yuppie era, towards the end of the 1980s, but not any more. There's no set standard for male beauty, and when men buy a product, they want to see someone they can associate with a work colleague or a drinking pal.

People who have already seen Jasmine on the catwalk suggested her to Hamid as the perfect face for his new collection. They said things like: 'She's got bags of charisma and yet other women can still identify with her.' A Class C model is always chasing contacts and men who claim to be powerful enough to make her a star, but the best publicity you can get in the world of fashion – and possibly in all other worlds too – are recommendations from people in the know. Illogical though it may seem, as soon as someone is on the verge of being 'discovered', everyone starts laying bets on their success or failure. Sometimes they win, sometimes they lose, but that's the way the market is.

* * *

The room is beginning to fill up. The front row seats are all reserved, and a group of elegantly dressed women and men in suits occupy some of those seats, while the rest remain empty. The general public are seated in the second, third and fourth rows. The main focus of the photographers' attentions is now a famous model, who is married to a football player and has spent a lot of time in Brazil because, she says, she 'just adores it'. Everyone knows that 'a trip to Brazil' is code for 'plastic surgery', but no one says so openly. What happens is that, after a few days there, the visitor asks discreetly if a visit to a plastic surgeon might be fitted in between sightseeing trips to the beauties of Salvador and dancing in the Rio carnival. There's a rapid exchange of business cards and the conversation ends there.

The nice blonde girl waits for the press photographers to finish their work (they, too, ask the model which, in her opinion, is the best film she's seen so far) and then leads her to the one free seat next to Hamid and Ewa. The photographers crowd round and take dozens of photos of the threesome – the great couturier, his wife and the model-turned-housewife.

Some journalists ask Hamid what he thinks of the Belgian designer's work. Accustomed to this kind of question, he replies:

'That's what I came here to find out. I hear she's very talented.'

The journalists insist, as if they hadn't heard his answer. They're nearly all Belgians; the French press aren't much interested. The nice blonde girl asks them to leave the guests in peace.

They move away. The ex-model sits down next to Hamid and tries to strike up a conversation, saying that she simply loves his work. He thanks her politely, and if she was expecting the response 'let's talk after the show', she's disappointed. Nevertheless, she proceeds to tell him everything that's happened in her life – the photos, the invitations, the trips abroad.

Hamid listens patiently, but as soon as he gets a chance (while the model is briefly talking to someone else) he turns to Ewa to ask her to save him from this dialogue of the deaf. His wife, however, is behaving even more strangely now and refuses to talk. His only alternative is to read the explanatory leaflet about the show.

The collection is a tribute to Ann Salens, who was considered the pioneer of Belgian fashion. She began designing in the Sixties and opened a small boutique, but saw at once the enormous potential of the fashions created by the young hippies who were converging on Amsterdam from all over the world. She challenged – and triumphed over – the sober styles popular among the bourgeoisie at the time, and saw her clothes worn by various icons, including Queen Paola and that great muse of the French existentialist movement, the singer Juliette Greco. She was one of the first to create the kind of fashion show that mixed clothes on the catwalk with lighting, music and art. Nevertheless, she was little known outside her own country. She always had a terrible fear of cancer, and as Job says in the Bible, the thing that she greatly feared came upon her. She died of the dread illness after seeing her business fail because of her own financial incompetence.

And as with all things in a world that renews itself every six months, she had been completely forgotten. The designer who was about to show her own collection was displaying considerable courage in seeking inspiration in the past instead of trying to invent a future.

Hamid puts the leaflet away in his pocket. If Jasmine isn't all that he hopes, he'll go and talk to the designer afterwards anyway and see if there's some project they can work on together. He's always open to new ideas, as long as his competitors are under his supervision.

He looks around him. The spotlights are well positioned, and, to his surprise, there are a good number of photographers present. Maybe the collection really is worth seeing, or perhaps the Belgian government has used its influence with the press, offering air tickets and accommodation. There's another possible explanation for so much interest, but Hamid hopes he's wrong. That reason is Jasmine. If he wants to proceed with his plans, he needs her to be someone completely unknown to the general public. Up until now, he's only heard comments from other people in the fashion business. If her face has already appeared in lots of magazines, then it will be a waste of time taking her on. Firstly, because it means someone has got there before him, and secondly, because it would make no sense to associate her with something fresh and new.

Hamid does a few calculations. This event must have been very expensive to put on, but, like the sheikh, the Belgian government is quite right: fashion for women, sport for men, celebrities for both sexes, those are the only things that interest everyone and the only things that can get a country's image recognised on the international scene. In the case of fashion, of course, there are often long negotiations with the Fédération to deal with first. However, he notices that one of the Fédération's directors is sitting alongside the Belgian politicians, so they are clearly losing no time.

More VIPs arrive, all of them shepherded in by the nice blonde girl. They seem slightly disoriented, as if they're not sure quite what they're doing here. They're over-dressed, so this must be the first fashion show they've attended in France, having come straight from Brussels. They're certainly not part of the fauna currently invading the town to attend the Film Festival.

There is a five-minute delay. Unlike the Fashion Week in Paris, during which almost no show begins on time, there are a lot of other things happening in Cannes this week, and the press can't hang around for long. Then he realises that he's wrong: most of the journalists present are talking to and interviewing the ministers; they're nearly all foreigners and from the same country. Only in a situation like this do politics and fashion meet.

The nice blonde girl goes over to the photographers and asks them to take their places; the show is about to begin. Hamid and Ewa have not exchanged a single word. She seems neither happy nor unhappy, and that bodes very ill indeed. If only she would complain or smile or say something! But she gives no clue as to what is going on inside her.

Best to concentrate on the screen at the far end of the catwalk from behind which the models will appear. At least fashion shows are something he can understand.

A few minutes ago, the models will have taken off all their underwear because bras and pants might leave visible marks underneath the clothes they'll be wearing. The models have already put on the first item they'll be showing and are waiting for the lights to dim, the music to start and for someone – usually a woman – to tap them on the back to indicate the precise moment when they should head out towards the spotlights and the audience.

The different classes of model – A, B and C – are all suffering from varying degrees of nerves, with the least experienced being the most excited. Some are saying a prayer, others are trying to peer through the curtain to see if anyone they know is there, or if their mother or father managed to get a good seat. There must be ten or twelve of them, each with their photo pinned up above the place where the clothes they'll be wearing are hung up in the order they'll be worn so that they can change in a matter of seconds and return to the catwalk looking completely relaxed, as if they'd been wearing the clothes all afternoon. The final touches have been given to make-up and hair. The models are repeating to themselves:

'I mustn't slip. I mustn't trip on the hem. I have been personally chosen by the designer from sixty other models. I'm in

Cannes. There's probably someone important in the audience. I know that HH is here, and he might choose me for his brand. They say the place is full of photographers and journalists.

'I mustn't smile because that's against the rules. My feet must tread an invisible line. In these high heels I need to walk as if I were marching. It doesn't matter if that way of walking is artificial or uncomfortable – I must remember that.

'I must reach the mark, turn to one side, pause for two seconds, then come straight back at the same speed, knowing that as soon as I leave the catwalk, there'll be someone waiting to take off my clothes and put on the next set, and that I won't even have time to look in the mirror! I have to trust that everything will go well. I need to show off not only my body, not only the clothes, but the power of my gaze.'

Hamid glances up at the ceiling: that is the mark, a spotlight brighter than the others. If the model overshoots that mark or stops beforehand, she won't photograph well, and then the magazine editors – or, rather, the Belgian magazine editors – will choose to show a photo of another model. The French press is currently camped outside the hotels or alongside the red carpet or at some evening cocktail party or else eating a sandwich before the main gala supper of the night.

The lights in the room go out, and the spotlights above the catwalk go on.

This is the big moment.

A powerful sound system fills the air with a soundtrack from the Sixties and Seventies. It transports Hamid to a world he never knew, but which he has heard people talk about. He feels a certain nostalgia for what he has never known and a twinge of anger – why didn't he get the chance to experience the great dream of all those young people travelling the world?

The first model comes on, and sound fuses with vision – the brightly coloured clothes, full of life and energy, are telling a story that happened a long time ago, but one that the world still likes to hear. Beside him, he hears the click and whirr of dozens of shutters. The cameras are recording everything. The first model performs perfectly – she walks as far as the mark, turns to the right, pauses for two seconds, then walks back. She will have approximately fifteen seconds to reach the wings, when she will drop her pose and run to the hanger where the next dress is waiting; she quickly gets undressed, gets dressed even more quickly, takes her place in the queue and is ready for her next appearance. The designer will be watching everything via closed-circuit television, biting her lips and hoping that no one slips up, that the audience understand what she's trying to say, that she gets a round of applause at the end and that the emissary from the Fédération is duly impressed.

The show continues. From where he is sitting, both Hamid and the TV cameras can see how elegantly the models walk, how firmly they tread. The people sitting on the side – who, like the majority of VIPs present, are not used to fashion shows – wonder why the girls 'march' instead of walking normally, like the models they're used to seeing on fashion programmes. Is this the designer trying to seem original?

No, thinks Hamid. It's because of the high heels. Only by marching like that can they be sure they won't stumble. What the cameras show – because they're filming head on – isn't really a true representation of what's happening.

The collection is better than he expected, a trip back in time with a few creative, contemporary touches, nothing over-the-top, because the secret of good fashion, as with good cooking, lies in knowing how much of which ingredient to use. The flowers and beads are a reminder of those crazy years, but they're used in such a way that they seem absolutely modern. Six models have now appeared on the catwalk, and he notices that one of them has a pinprick on her knee that make-up cannot disguise. Minutes before, she must have injected herself there with a shot of heroin to calm her nerves and suppress her appetite.

Suddenly, Jasmine appears. She's wearing a long-sleeved white blouse, all hand-embroidered, and a white below-the-knee skirt. She walks confidently, but, unlike the others, her seriousness isn't put on, it's natural, absolutely natural. Hamid glances at the others in the audience; everyone in the room is mesmerised by Jasmine, so much so that no one even glances at the model leaving or entering after she has finished her turn and is walking back to the dressing room.

'Perfect!'

On her next two appearances on the catwalk, he studies every detail of her body, and sees that she radiates something more than just physical beauty. How could one define that? The marriage between Heaven and Hell? Love and Loathing going hand in hand?

As with any fashion show, the whole thing lasts no more than fifteen minutes, even though it has taken months of planning and preparation. At the end, the designer comes onto the catwalk to acknowledge the applause; the lights go up, the music stops, and only then does he realise how much he's been enjoying the soundtrack. The nice blonde girl comes over to them and says that someone from the Belgian government would very much like to speak to him. He takes out his leather wallet and offers her his card, explaining that he's staying at the Hotel Martinez and would be delighted to arrange to meet the following day.

'But I *would* like to talk to the designer and the black model. Do you happen to know which supper they'll be going to tonight? I'll wait here for a reply.'

He hopes the nice blonde girl doesn't take too long. The journalists are gathering to ask him the usual questions, or, rather, the same question repeated by different journalists:

'What did you think of the show?'

'Very interesting,' he says, which is the answer he always gives.

'And what does that mean?'

With the delicacy of a practised professional, Hamid moves on to the next journalist. Always be polite to the press, but never give a direct answer and say only what seems appropriate at the time.

The nice blonde girl returns. No, they won't be going to the gala supper that night. Despite the presence of all those ministers, Film Festival politics are dictated by a different sort of power.

Hamid says that he'll have the necessary invitations sent to them, and his offer is accepted at once. The designer doubtless expected this response, knowing the value of the product she has in her hands.

Jasmine.

Yes, she's the one. He would only rarely use her in a show because she's more powerful than the clothes she's wearing, but as 'the public face of Hamid Hussein' there could be no one better.

Ewa turns on her mobile phone as they leave. Seconds later, an envelope flies across a blue sky, lands at the bottom of the screen and opens, and all that to say: 'You have a message.'

'What a ridiculous bit of animation,' thinks Ewa.

Again the name of the caller has been blocked. She's unsure whether or not to open the text, but her curiosity is stronger than her fear.

'It seems some admirer has found your phone number,' jokes Hamid. 'You don't usually get that many texts.'

'Maybe you're right.'

What she would really like to say is: 'Don't you understand? After two years together, can you not see that I'm terrified, or do you just think I've got PMT?'

She pretends casually to read the message:

'I've destroyed another world because of you. And I'm beginning to wonder if it's really worth it because you don't appear to understand my message. Your heart is dead.'

'Who's it from?'

'I haven't the slightest idea. It doesn't give the number. Still, it's always nice to have a secret admirer.'

5.15 p.m.

Three murders. All the statistics have been overturned in only a matter of hours and are showing an increase of 50 per cent.

He goes to his car and tunes in to a special frequency on his radio.

'I believe there's a serial killer at work in the town.'

A voice murmurs something at the other end. The sound of static cuts out some of the words, but Savoy understands what is being said.

'No, I can't be sure, but neither do I have any doubts about it.'

More comments, more static.

'I'm not mad, sir, and I'm not contradicting myself. For example, I can't be sure that my salary will be deposited in my account at the end of the month, but I don't actually doubt that it will. Do you see what I mean?'

More static and angry words.

'No, sir, I'm not asking for an increase in salary, I'm just saying that certainties and doubts can co-exist, especially in a profession like ours. Yes, all right, let's leave that to one side and move on to what really matters. The man in hospital has just died, so it's quite possible that on the news tonight three murders will be reported. All we know, so far, is that each of the three murders was committed using a different but very sophisticated technique, which is why no one will suspect that they're connected, but suddenly Cannes is being seen as a dangerous town. And if this carries on, people are bound to start speculating about whether there is, in fact, only one murderer. What do you want me to do?'

More angry comments from the commissioner.

'Yes, they're here. The boy who witnessed the murder is telling them everything he knows. The place is swarming with photographers and journalists at the moment. I assumed they'd all be lined up and waiting by the red carpet, but it seems I was wrong. The problem with the Festival is that there are too many reporters and nothing to report.'

More indignant remarks. He takes a notebook from his pocket and writes down an address.

'Fine. I'll go straight to Monte Carlo and talk to him.'

The static stops. The person at the other end has hung up.

Savoy walks to the end of the pier, places the siren on the roof of his car, puts it on at maximum volume and races off like a madman, hoping to lure the reporters away to some non-existent crime. They, however, wise to this trick, stay where they are and continue interviewing the boy.

Savoy is beginning to feel excited. He can finally leave all that paperwork to be completed by an underling and devote himself to what he's always dreamed of doing: solving murders that defy all logic. He hopes he's right and that there really is a serial killer in town terrorising the population. Given the speed with which news spreads these days, he'll soon be in the spotlight explaining that 'nothing has yet been proved', but in such a way that no one quite believes him, thus ensuring that the spotlight will stay on him until the criminal is found. For all its glamour, Cannes is really just a small provincial town, where everyone knows everything that's going on, so it shouldn't be that hard to find the murderer.

Fame and celebrity.

Is he just thinking about himself rather than about the well-being of Cannes' citizens? Then again, what's wrong with seeking a little glory, when every year for years now, he's been forced to put up with twelve days of people trying to look far more important than they really are? It's infectious. After all, who doesn't want to gain public recognition for their work, whether they're policemen or film directors.

'Stop thinking about future glory. That will come of its own accord if you do your job well. Besides, fame is a very capricious thing. What if you're deemed incapable of carrying out this mission? Your humiliation will be public too. Concentrate.'

After nearly twenty years in the police force in all kinds of jobs, getting promoted on merit, reading endless reports and documents, he's reached the conclusion that when it comes to finding criminals, intuition always plays just as important a part as logic. The danger now, as he drives to Monte Carlo, isn't the murderer – who must be feeling utterly exhausted from the sheer amount of adrenaline pumping through his veins, not to mention apprehensive, because someone saw him in the act – no, the great danger now is the press. Journalists also mix logic with intuition. If they manage to establish a link, however tenuous, between the three murders, the police will lose control of the situation and the Festival could descend into chaos, with people afraid to walk the streets, foreign visitors leaving earlier than expected, tradesmen accusing the police of inefficiency and headlines in newspapers around the world. After all, a real-life serial killer is always far more interesting than any screen version.

In the years that follow, the Film Festival won't be the same: the myth of fear will take root, and the world of luxury and glamour will choose another more appropriate place to show its wares, and gradually, after more than sixty years, the Festival will become a minor event, far from the bright lights and the magazines.

He has a great responsibility, well, two great responsibilities: the first is to find out who is committing these murders and to stop him before another corpse turns up on his patch; the second is to keep the media under control.

He needs to think logically. How many of those journalists, most of whom come from far-flung places, are likely to know the murder statistics for Cannes? How many of them will take the trouble to phone the National Guard and ask?

The logical response? None of them. Their minds are focussed on what has just happened. They're excited because a major producer suffered a heart attack during one of the Festival lunches. They don't yet know that he was poisoned – the pathologist's report is on the back seat of his car. They don't yet know – and possibly never will – that he was also involved in a huge money-laundering scam.

The illogical response is that there's always someone who thinks more laterally. It's therefore now a matter of urgency to call a press conference and give a full account, but only of the film director's murder on the beach; that way, the other incidents will be momentarily forgotten.

An important figure in the world of film-making has been killed, so who's going to be interested in the death of an insignificant young woman? They'll all reach the same conclusion as he did at the start of the investigation – that she died of a drugs overdose. Problem solved.

To go back to the murdered film director; perhaps she isn't as important a figure as he thinks; if she was, the police commissioner would be calling him now on his mobile phone. The facts are as follows: a smartly dressed man of about forty, with slightly greying hair, had been seen talking to her, the two of them observed by a young man hiding nearby. After sticking a blade into her with all the precision of a surgeon, he had walked slowly away, and was now mingling with hundreds and thousands of other people, many of whom quite possibly fitted his description.

He turns off the siren for a moment and phones his deputy, who had remained at the scene of the crime and who is probably currently being interrogated by journalists rather than himself doing the interrogating. Savoy asks him to tell the journalists, whose hasty conclusions so often get them into trouble, that he is 'almost certain' it was a crime of passion.

'Don't say we're certain, just say that the circumstances may indicate this, given that they were sitting close to each other like a courting couple. It clearly wasn't a robbery or a revenge killing, but possibly a dramatic settling of personal scores.

'Be careful not to lie; your words are being recorded and may be used in evidence against you.'

'But why do I need to say that?'

'Because that is what the circumstances indicate. And the sooner we give them something to chew on, the better.'

'They're asking about the weapon used.'

'Tell them that everything indicates it was a knife, as the witness said.'

'But he's not sure.'

'If even the witness doesn't know what he saw, what else can you say apart from "everything indicates that, etc., etc."? Frighten the lad; tell him his words are being recorded by the journalists and could be used against him later on.'

He hangs up before his subordinate starts asking awkward questions.

'Everything indicates' that it was a crime of passion, even though the victim had only just arrived in Cannes from the United States, even though she was staying at a hotel alone, even though, from what they have been able to glean, she had only attended one rather trivial meeting in the morning, at the Marché du Film next to the Palais des Congrès. The journalists, however, would not have access to that information.

And there was something even more important that no one else on his team knows, indeed, that no one else in the world knows but him.

The victim had been at the hospital. He and she had talked a little and then he'd sent her away – to her death.

He turns on the siren again, so that the deafening noise can drive away any feeling of guilt. After all, he wasn't the one who stuck the knife in her.

He could, of course, think: 'She was obviously there in the waiting-room because she had some connection with the drugs mafia and was just checking that the murder had been a success.' That was 'logical', and if he told his superior about that chance encounter, an investigation along those lines would immediately be launched. It might even be true; she had been killed using a very sophisticated method, as had the Hollywood film distributor. They were both Americans. They had both been killed with sharp implements. It all seemed to indicate that the same group was behind the killings, and that there really was a connection between them.

Perhaps he's wrong, and there is no serial killer on the loose. The young woman found dead on the bench, apparently asphyxiated by an experienced killer, might have met up the previous night with someone from the group who had come to see the film distributor. Perhaps she was also peddling drugs along with the craftwork she used to sell.

Imagine the scene: a group of foreigners arrive to settle accounts. In one of Cannes' many bars, the local dealer introduces one of them to the pretty girl with the dark eyebrows, who, he says, works with them. They end up going to bed together, but the foreigner, feeling strangely relaxed on European soil, drinks more than he should; the drink loosens his tongue and he *says* more than he should too. The next morning, he realises his mistake and asks the professional hitman - every gang has one - to sort things out.

It all fits so perfectly that it must be true.

It all fits so perfectly that it makes no sense at all. It just wasn't credible that a cocaine cartel would have decided to hold such a meeting in a town which, during the Film Festival, is heaving with extra police brought in from all over the country, with private bodyguards, with security guards hired for the various parties and with detectives charged with keeping a round-the-clock watch on the priceless jewels being worn in the streets and elsewhere.

Although if that *were* true, it would be equally good for his career. A settling of accounts between mafia men would attract as much publicity as a serial killer.

He can relax; whatever the truth of the matter, he will finally acquire the reputation he has always felt he deserved.

He turns off the siren. It has taken him half an hour to drive along the motorway and across an invisible barrier into another country, and he's only minutes from his destination. His mind, however, is mulling over what are, in theory, forbidden thoughts.

Three murders in one day. His prayers are with the families of the victims, as the politicians always say. And he knows that the State pays him to maintain order and not to jump up and down with glee when it's disrupted in such a violent manner. Right now, the commissioner will be pacing his office, conscious that he now has two problems to solve: finding the killer (or killers, because he may not be convinced by Savoy's theory) and keeping the press at bay. Everyone is very worried; other police stations in the region have been alerted and an identikit picture of the murderer sent via the Internet to police cars in the area. A politician may even have had his well-deserved rest interrupted because the chief of police believed the matter to be so very delicate that he felt it necessary to pass responsibility on to someone higher up the chain of command.

The politician is unlikely to take the bait, telling the chief of police to ensure that the town returns to normal as soon as possible because 'millions or hundreds of millions of euros depend on it'. He doesn't want to get involved; he has more important issues to resolve, like which wine to serve that night to a visiting foreign delegation.

'Am I on the right path?' Savoy asks himself.

The forbidden thoughts return. He feels happy. This is the high point of a career spent filling in forms and dealing with trivia. It had never occurred to him that such a situation would produce in him this state of euphoria - he can, at last, be a real detective, the man with a theory that goes against all logic, and who will end up being given a medal because he was the first to see what no one else could. He won't confess this to anyone, not even to his wife, who would be horrified and assume that he must have temporarily lost his reason under the strain of working on such a dangerous case.

'I'm happy. I'm excited,' he thinks.

His prayers might well be with the families of the dead, but his heart, after many years of inertia, is returning to the world of the living.

Savoy had imagined a vast library full of dusty books, piles of magazines, a desk strewn with papers, but the office is, in fact, painted entirely in immaculate white and furnished with a few tasteful lamps, a comfortable armchair, and a glass table on which sits a large computer screen and nothing else, just a wireless keyboard and a small notepad with an expensive Montegrappa pen lying on it.

'Wipe that smile off your face and at least try to look a little concerned,' says the man with the white beard, who is dressed, despite the heat, in tweed jacket, tie and tailored trousers, an outfit not at all in keeping with the décor or with the subject under discussion.

'What do you mean, sir?'

'I know how you're feeling. This is the biggest case of your career, in a town where normally nothing happens. I went through the same inner turmoil when I lived and worked in Penycae, Swansea. And it was thanks to a very similar case that I got transferred to Scotland Yard.'

'*My* dream is to work in Paris,' thinks Savoy, but he says nothing. The man invites him to take a seat.

'I hope you, too, get a chance to realise your professional dream. Anyway, nice to meet you. I'm Stanley Morris.'

Savoy decides to change the subject.

'The commissioner is afraid that the press will start speculating about there being a serial killer on the loose.'

'They can speculate all they like; it's a free country. It's the kind of thing that sells newspapers and brings a little excitement into the dull lives of pensioners who will watch all the media for any new titbit on the subject with a mixture of fear and certainty that it will never happen to them.'

'I hope you've received a detailed description of the victims. Does the evidence so far suggest to you a serial killer or are we dealing here with some sort of revenge killing on the part of drug cartels?'

'Yes, I got the descriptions. By the way, they wanted to send them to me by fax, for heaven's sake. How old-fashioned! I asked them to send the information by e-mail, and do you know what they said? "We don't usually do that." Imagine! One of the best-equipped police forces in the world still relying entirely on a fax machine!'

Savoy shifts rather impatiently in his chair. He isn't here to discuss the pros and cons of modern technology.

'Let's get down to business,' says Dr Morris, who had been quite a celebrity at Scotland Yard, but had decided to retire to the Mediterranean and was possibly as glad as Savoy to have a break from routine – in Morris's case one that now revolved around reading, concerts, charity teas and suppers.

'Since this is the first time I've met such a case, could you perhaps tell me whether or not you agree with my theory that there is only one killer, just so that I know where I stand.'

Dr Morris explains that in theory, yes, he's right: three murders with certain common characteristics would normally be enough to indicate a serial killer. And such murders were usually confined to one geographical area (in this case, the town of Cannes), and …

'Whereas, a mass murderer …'

Dr Morris interrupts him and asks him not to misuse terminology. Mass murderers are terrorists or immature adolescents who go into a school or a snack bar and shoot everyone in sight, and who are then either shot dead by the police or commit suicide. They have a preference for guns and bombs that will cause the maximum amount of damage in a short space of time, usually two to three minutes at most. Such people don't care about the consequences of their actions because they know exactly how it will end.

'In the collective unconscious, the concept of the mass murderer is easier to take on board because he's clearly "mentally unbalanced" and therefore easily distinguishable from "us". The serial murderer, on the other hand, touches on something far more complicated – the destructive instinct we all carry within us.'

He pauses.

'Have you read *Dr Jekyll and Mr Hyde* by Robert Louis Stevenson?'

Savoy explains that he has so much work that he has little time for reading. Morris's gaze grows icy.

'And do you think I don't have work to do?'

'No, no, I didn't mean that. Listen, Dr Morris, I'm here on an urgent mission. I'm not interested in discussing technology or literature. I just want to know what conclusions you drew from the reports.'

'I'm sorry, but I'm afraid we can't, in this instance, avoid literature. *The Strange Case of Dr Jekyll and Mr Hyde* is the story of an apparently normal individual, Dr Jekyll, who, in seeking to explore his own violent impulses, discovers a way of transforming himself periodically into a creature entirely without morality, Mr Hyde. We all have those impulses, Inspector. A serial killer doesn't just threaten our physical safety, he threatens our sanity too. Because whether we like it or not, we all carry around in us a great destructive power and have all, at some point, wondered what it would be like to give free rein to that most repressed of feelings – the desire to take someone else's life.

'There are many reasons for this: wanting to put the world to rights, to get revenge for something that happened in our childhood, to vent one's suppressed hatred of society, but, whether consciously or unconsciously, everyone has felt that desire at one time or another, even if only in childhood.'

Another meaningful silence.

'I imagine that, regardless of your chosen profession, you must yourself have experienced this feeling. Tormenting a cat perhaps or torturing some perfectly harmless insect.'

It's Savoy's turn now to give Morris an icy stare and say nothing. Morris, however, interprets his silence as consent and continues talking in the same easy, superior tone:

'Don't expect to find some visibly unbalanced person with wild hair and a hate-filled leer on his face. If you ever do have time to read – although I know you're a busy man – I would recommend a book by Hannah Arendt, *Eichmann in Jerusalem*. Obviously, Eichmann needed help to carry out the gigantic task he was given: the purification of the human race. Just a moment.'

He goes over to his computer. He knows that the man with him wants results, but that simply isn't possible. He needs to educate him and prepare him for the difficult days ahead.

'Here it is. Arendt made a detailed analysis of the trial of Adolf Eichmann, who was responsible for the extermination of six million Jews in Nazi Germany. She says that the half a dozen psychiatrists charged with examining him had all concluded that he was normal. His psychological profile and his attitude towards wife, children, mother and father were all within the social parameters one expects in a responsible man. Arendt goes on:

'The trouble with Eichmann was precisely that so many were like him, and that the many were neither perverted nor sadistic, that they were, and still are, terribly and terrifyingly normal. From the viewpoint of our legal institutions and our moral standards of judgement, this normality was much more terrifying than all the atrocities put together.'

Now he could get down to business.

'I notice from the autopsies that there was no sign of sexual abuse …'

'Dr Morris, I have a problem to solve and I need to do so quickly. I want to know whether or not we're dealing with a serial killer. No one could possibly rape a man in the middle of a lunch party or a girl on a public bench in broad daylight.'

He might as well have said nothing. Morris ignores him completely and continues.

'… which is a common feature in many serial killers. Some have what you might call "humane" motives. Nurses who kill terminally ill patients, people who murder beggars in the street, social workers who feel so sorry for certain pensioners or disabled people that they reach the conclusion they'd be better off in the next life – there was one such case in California just recently. There are also people bent on putting society to rights, and in those cases, the victims tend to be prostitutes.'

'Dr Morris, I didn't come here …'

This time Morris raises his voice slightly.

'And I didn't invite you. I'm doing you a favour. If you want to leave, please do so, but if you're going to stay, please stop interrupting my argument every two minutes. In order to catch someone, we have to understand the way he thinks.'

'So you do believe we're dealing with a serial killer?'

'I haven't finished yet.'

Savoy controls himself. After all, why was he in such a hurry? Wouldn't it be more fun to let the press tie itself in knots and then present them with the solution?

'Please go on.'

Morris moves the monitor so that Savoy can see more clearly. On the large screen is an engraving, possibly from the nineteenth century.

'This is the most famous of all serial killers: Jack the Ripper. He was active in London in the second half of 1888, and was responsible for killing five or possibly seven women in public and semi-public places. He would rip open their bellies and disembowel them. He was never found. He became a legend, and even today, there are still people trying to uncover his real identity.'

The image on the screen changes to reveal what looks like something from an astrological chart.

'This is the signature of the Zodiac Killer. He's known to have killed five couples in California over a period of ten months, mostly courting couples who had parked their cars in isolated spots. He used to send letters to the police bearing this symbol, which is rather like a Celtic cross. No one has yet managed to identify him.

'Researchers believe that both Jack the Ripper and the Zodiac Killer were people who were trying to restore moral order and decency to their particular areas. They had, if you like, a mission to fulfil. And contrary to what the press would have us believe with the terrifying nicknames they invent, like the Boston Strangler and the Child-Killer of Toulouse, these were ordinary folk who would get together with their neighbours at weekends and who worked hard to earn a living. None of them ever benefited financially from their criminal acts.'

The conversation is beginning to interest Savoy.

'So it could be anyone who came to Cannes to attend the Film Festival …'

'Yes, having first made a conscious decision to create an atmosphere of terror for some completely absurd reason, for example "to overthrow the dictatorship of fashion" or "to put a stop to the making of films that provoke violence". The press will come up with some bloodcurdling soubriquet for him and start chasing various leads. Crimes that have nothing to do with the killer will start being attributed to him. Panic will ensue and only come to an end if by chance – and I repeat, by chance – the killer is caught. These killers are often only active for a short period of time and then disappear completely, having left their mark on history. They may perhaps write a diary that will be discovered after their death, but that's all.'

Savoy has stopped looking at his watch. His phone rings, but he decides not to answer. The subject is far more complicated than he thought.

'So you agree with me?'

'Yes,' says the expert from Scotland Yard, the man who had become a legend by solving five cases that everyone else had given up on.

'Why do you think we're dealing with a serial killer?' Savoy asks.

Morris sees what looks like an e-mail flash up on his computer and he smiles. The inspector has finally started to show a little respect for what he has to say.

'Because of the complete absence of motive. Most of these criminals have what we call a "signature": they choose one type of victim, homosexuals, say, or prostitutes, beggars, courting couples. Others are known as "asymmetrical killers": they kill because they can't control their impulse to kill. When they reach a point where that impulse is satisfied, they stop killing until the urge to kill again becomes unbearable. I think that is the kind of killer we have here.

'There are several points to consider in this case.The criminal is highly sophisticated. He has chosen a different weapon each time – his bare hands, poison and a stiletto knife. He's not motivated by the usual things: sex, alcohol or some evident mental disorder. He knows the human anatomy, and that, so far, has been his only "signature". He must have planned the crimes in advance because the poison he used isn't easy to obtain, and so we could classify him as a killer with a mission, but one who still doesn't quite know what that mission is. From what I know of the young girl's murder, and this is the only clue we have so far, he used a type of Russian martial art called Sambo.

'I could go further and say that it's part of his signature to get close to his chosen victim and befriend him or her for a while, but that theory doesn't fit with the murder committed in the middle of a lunch party on a beach in Cannes.The victim apparently had two bodyguards with him and they would have been sure to react if the killer had gone anywhere near their boss, plus the victim was under surveillance by Interpol.'

Russian. Savoy considers using his phone to ask for an urgent search of all the hotels in Cannes. A man, about forty, well-dressed, slightly greying hair – and Russian.

'The fact that he used a Russian martial-art technique doesn't mean he himself is Russian,' says Morris, reading Savoy's mind like the good ex-policeman he is.'Just as we cannot assume he's a South American Indian because he used curare.'

'So what do we do?'

'We just have to wait for him to commit his next murder.'

6.50 p.m.

Cinderella!

If people believed more in fairy tales instead of just listening to their husbands and parents – who think everything is impossible – they would be experiencing what she's experiencing now, being driven along in one of the innumerable limousines that are slowly but surely heading for the steps and the red carpet – the biggest catwalk in the world.

The Star is by her side, smiling and wearing the obligatory beautifully cut suit. He asks if she's nervous. Of course not: tension, nerves, anxiety and fear don't exist in dreams. Everything is perfect; it's just like in a movie – the heroine suffers, struggles and finally achieves everything she has always wanted.

'If Hamid Hussein decides to go ahead with the project and the film is the success he hopes it will be, then prepare yourself for more such moments.'

If Hamid Hussein decides to go ahead with the project? Isn't it all signed and sealed?

'But I signed a contract when I went to collect my outfit in the Gift Room.'

'Look, forget what I said. I don't want to spoil your special moment.'

'No, please, go on.'

The Star was expecting the silly girl to say exactly that, and he takes enormous pleasure in doing as she asks.

'I've been involved in loads of projects that begin and never come to anything. It's all part of the game, but, like I say, don't worry about that now.'

'But the contract ...'

'Contracts are there for lawyers to argue over while they earn their money. Please, forget what I said. Enjoy the moment.'

The 'moment' is approaching. Because of the slow traffic, people can see who is inside the cars, despite the smoked-glass windows separating mere mortals from the chosen. The Star waves, hands bang on the window asking him to open it just for a moment, to give them an autograph, to have a photo taken.

The Star keeps waving, as if he didn't understand what they wanted and a smile from him was enough to flood the world with light.

There's a real air of hysteria out there. Women with their little portable stools on which they must have been sitting and knitting since the morning; men with beer bellies, bored to death, but obliged to accompany their middle-aged spouses, who are dressed to the nines as if they were the ones about to go up the steps and onto the red carpet; children who have no idea what's going on, but can sense that it's something important. Crammed behind the steel barriers that separate them from the line of limousines, stand people of all ages and colours, every one of them wanting to believe that they're only two yards away from the great legends, when, in fact, they're separated by thousands of miles; for it isn't just the steel barrier and the car window keeping them apart, it's chance, opportunity and talent.

Talent? Yes, she wants to believe that talent counts too, but knows that really it's all the result of a game of dice played by the gods, who choose certain people and place others on the far side of an impassable abyss from where they can only applaud, worship and, when the tide turns against their idols, condemn.

The Star pretends to be talking to her, but he's not actually saying anything, just looking at her and moving his lips, like the great actor he is. He doesn't do this out of desire or pleasure. Gabriela realises that he simply doesn't want to appear unfriendly to his fans outside, but, at the same time, can't be bothered now to wave and smile and blow kisses.

'You must think me an arrogant, cynical person with a heart of stone,' he says at last. 'If you ever get where you want to get, then you'll understand what I'm feeling: that there's no way out. Success is both an addiction and an enslavement, and at the end of the day, when you're lying in bed with some new man or woman, you'll ask yourself: Was it really worth it? Why did I ever want this?'

He pauses.

'Go on.'

'I don't know why I'm telling you this.'

'Because you want to protect me. Because you're a good man. Please, go on.'

Gabriela may be ingenuous about many things, but she's still a woman and knows how to get almost anything she wants out of a man. In this case, the button to press is vanity.

'I don't know why I always wanted this.' The Star has fallen into the trap and is now revealing his more vulnerable side, while, outside, the fans continue to wave. 'Often, when I go back to the hotel after an exhausting day's work, I stand under the shower for ages, just listening to the sound of water falling on my body. Two opposing forces are battling it out inside me: one telling me I should be thanking God and the other telling me I should abandon it all while there's still time.

'At that moment, I feel like the most ungrateful person in the world. I have my fans, but I can't be bothered with them. I'm invited to parties that are the envy of the world, and all I want is to leave at once and go back to my room and sit quietly reading a good book. Well-meaning men and women give me prizes, organise events and do everything to make me happy, and I feel nothing but exhaustion and embarrassment because I don't believe I deserve all this, I don't feel worthy of my success. Do you understand?'

For a fraction of a second, Gabriela feels sorry for the man beside her. She imagines the number of parties he must have to attend in a year, and how there must always be someone asking him for a photo or an autograph, someone telling him some tedious story to which he pretends to be listening, someone trying to sell him some new project or embarrassing him with the classic question: 'Don't you remember me?', someone getting out his mobile phone and asking him to say a few words to his son, wife or sister. And he must always be the consummate professional, happy, attentive, good-humoured and polite.

'Do you understand?'

'Yes, I do, but I wouldn't mind having those problems one day, although I know I've a long way to go before I do.'

Only another four limousines and they'll be there. The chauffeur tells them to get ready. The Star folds down a small mirror from the roof of the car and adjusts his tie; Gabriela does the same and smoothes her hair. She can see a bit of the red carpet now, although the steps are still out of sight. The hysteria has vanished as if by magic, and the crowd is now composed of people wearing identity tags round their necks, talking to each other and taking no notice at all of who is in the cars because they're tired of seeing the same scene repeated over and over.

Two more cars. Some steps appear to her left. Men in dinner jackets and ties are opening the doors, and the aggressive metal barriers have been replaced by velvet cords looped along bronze and wooden pillars.

'Damn!' cries the Star, making Gabriela jump.

'Damn! Look who's over there, just getting out of her car!'

Gabriela sees a female Superstar, also wearing a Hamid Hussein dress, who has just stepped onto the red carpet. The Superstar turns her back on the Palais des Congrès, and when Gabriela follows her gaze, she sees the most extraordinary sight. A human wall, almost nine feet high, filled with endlessly flashing lights.

'Good!' says the Star, relieved. 'She's looking in the wrong direction.'

He's no longer polite and charming and has forgotten all his existential angst. 'They're not the accredited photographers. They're not important.'

'Why did you say "Damn"?'

The Star cannot conceal his irritation. There is one car to go before it's their turn.

'Can't you see? What planet are you from, child? When we step onto the red carpet, all the accredited photographers, who are positioned halfway along, will have their cameras trained on her!'

He turns to the chauffeur and says:

'Slow down!'

The chauffeur points to a man in plain clothes, also wearing an identity tag, and who is signalling to them to keep moving and not hold up the traffic.

The Star sighs deeply; this really isn't his lucky day. Why did he say all those things to this mere beginner at his side? It's true that he's tired of the life he leads, and yet he can't imagine anything else.

'Don't rush,' he says. 'We'll try and stay down here for as long as possible. Let's leave a good space between her and us.'

'Her' was the Superstar.

The couple in the car ahead of them don't appear to attract as much attention, although they must be important because no one gets as far as those steps without having scaled many mountains in life.

Her companion appears to relax a little, and now it's Gabriela's turn to feel tense, not knowing quite how to behave. Her hands are sweating. She grabs the handbag stuffed with paper, breathes deeply and says a prayer.

'Walk slowly,' says the Star, 'and don't stand too close to me.'

Their limousine draws up alongside the steps. Both doors are opened from outside.

Suddenly, an immense roar seems to fill the universe, shouts coming from all sides – she hadn't realised until then that she was in a soundproof car and could hear nothing. The Star gets out, smiling, as if his tantrum of two minutes ago had never happened and as if he were still the centre of the universe, despite his apparently true confessions to her in the car. He is a man in conflict with himself, his world and his past, and who cannot now turn back.

'What am I thinking about?' Gabriela tells herself. 'I should be concentrating on the moment, on going up the steps!'

They both wave to the 'unimportant' photographers and spend some time there. People hold out scraps of paper to him, and he signs autographs and thanks his fans. Gabriela isn't sure whether she should remain by his side or continue up towards the red carpet and the entrance to the Palais des Congrès; fortunately, she's saved by someone holding out pen and paper and asking for her autograph.

How she wishes this ceremony were being broadcast live to the whole world and that her mother could see her arriving in that dazzling dress, accompanied by a really famous actor (about whom she's beginning to have her doubts, but, no, she must drive away such negative thoughts), and see her giving the most important autograph of her twenty-five years of life! She can't understand the woman's name, so she smiles and writes something like 'with love'.

The Star comes over to her.

'Come on. The way ahead is clear now.'

The woman to whom she has just addressed an affectionate message reads what she's written and says angrily:

'I don't want your autograph! I just need your name so that I can identify you in the photo.'

Gabriela pretends not to hear; nothing in the world can destroy this magic moment.

They start going up the steps, with policemen forming a kind of security cordon, even though the public are a long way off now. On either side, on the building's façade, gigantic plasma screens reveal to the poor mortals outside what is going on in that open-air sanctuary. Hysterical screams and clapping can be heard in the distance. When they reach a broader step, as if they had reached the first floor, she notices another crowd of photographers, except this time, they are properly dressed and are shouting out the Star's name, asking him to turn this way, no, this way, just one more shot, please, a little closer, look up, look down! Other people pass them and continue up the steps, but the photographers aren't interested in them. The Star has lost none of his glamour; he looks as if he doesn't care and jokes around to show how relaxed and at ease he is with all this.

Gabriela notices that the photographers are interested in her too, although, of course, they don't shout out her name (they've no idea who she is), imagining that she must be his new girlfriend. They ask them to stand together so that they can get a photo of the two of them. The Star obliges for a few seconds, but keeps a prudent distance and avoids any physical contact.

Yes, they've successfully managed to avoid the Superstar, who will, by now, have reached the door of the Palais des Congrès to be greeted by the president of the Film Festival and the Mayor of Cannes.

The Star gestures to her to continue up the stairs, and she obeys.

She looks ahead and sees another gigantic screen strategically placed so that people can see themselves. A loudspeaker announces:

'And now we have …'

And the voice gives the name of the Star and of his most famous film. Later, someone tells her that everyone inside the room is watching the same scene being shown on the plasma screen outside.

They go up the remaining steps, reach the door, greet the president of the Festival and the mayor, and go inside. The whole thing has lasted less than three minutes.

Now the Star is surrounded by people who want to talk to him and flatter him and take photos (yes, even the chosen take photos of themselves with famous people). It's suffocatingly hot inside, and Gabriela starts to worry that her make-up will run …

Her make-up!

She had completely forgotten. She's supposed to go through a door on the left where someone will be waiting for her outside. She walks mechanically down some steps and past a couple of security guards. One of them asks if she's going outside for a smoke and intends coming back in for the film. She says 'No' and carries on.

She crosses another series of metal barriers and no one asks her anything because she's leaving, not trying to get in. She can see the backs of the crowd who are still waving and shouting at the limousines that continue to arrive. A man comes towards her, asks her name and tells her to follow him.

'Can you just wait a minute?'

The man seems surprised, but nods his assent. Gabriela has her eyes fixed on an old carousel, which has possibly been there since the beginning of the last century and which continues to turn, while the children riding it rise up and down.

'Can we go now?' asks the man politely.

'Just one more minute.'

'We'll be late.'

Gabriela can no longer hold back the tears, the tension, the fear and the terror of the three minutes she has just lived through. She sobs convulsively, not caring about her make-up now, which someone will fix for her anyway. The man offers her his arm to lean on, so that she won't stumble in her high heels, and they start walking across the square towards the Boulevard de la Croisette. The noise of the crowd grows ever more distant, and her sobs grow ever louder. She's crying out all the tears of the day, the week and the years she had spent dreaming of that moment, and which was over before she could even take in what had happened.

'I'm sorry,' she says to the man accompanying her.

He strokes her hair. His smile reveals affection, understanding and pity.

7.31 p.m.

He has finally understood that you cannot search out happiness at any price. Life has given him all it could, and he's beginning to see just how generous life has always been to him. Now and for the rest of his days, he will devote himself to disinterring the treasures hidden in his suffering and enjoying each second of happiness as if it were his last.

He has overcome Temptation. He is protected by the spirit of the girl who understands his mission perfectly, and who is now beginning to open his eyes to the real reason for his trip to Cannes.

For a few moments in that pizzeria, while he was remembering what he'd heard on those tapes, Temptation had accused him of being mentally unbalanced and of believing that anything was permitted in the name of love. His most difficult moment was, thank God, behind him now.

He is a normal person; his work requires discipline, routine, negotiating skills, and planning. Many of his friends say that he's become more of a loner; what they don't know is that he's always been a loner. Going to parties, weddings and christenings, and pretending to enjoy playing golf on Sundays was merely part of his professional strategy. He's always loathed the social whirl, with all those people concealing behind their smiles the real sadness in their souls. It didn't take him long to see that the Superclass are as dependent on their success as an addict is on his drugs, and nowhere near as happy as those who want nothing more than a house, a garden, a child playing, a plate of food on the table and a fire in winter. Are the latter aware of their limitations and do they know that life is short and wonder what point there is in going on?

The Superclass tries to promote its values. Ordinary people complain of divine injustice, they envy power, and it pains them to see others having fun. They don't understand that no one is having fun, that everyone is worried and insecure, and that what the jewels, cars and fat wallets conceal is a huge inferiority complex.

Igor is a man of simple tastes; indeed, Ewa always complained about the way he dressed. But what's the point of buying a ridiculously expensive shirt when no one is going to see the label anyway? What's the point of frequenting fashionable restaurants if nothing of interest is said there? Ewa used to say that he didn't talk very much at the parties and other work-related events. He tried to change his behaviour and be more sociable, but none of it really interested him. He would look at the people around him talking on and on, comparing share prices, boasting about their marvellous new yacht, launching into long disquisitions on Expressionist painting (but really just repeating what a tour guide had told them on a visit to a Paris museum) and stating boldly that one writer is infinitely better than another (basing themselves entirely on the reviews they've read because, naturally, they never have time to read fiction).

They are so very cultivated, so very rich and so utterly charming. And at the end of each day, they all ask themselves: 'Is it time I stopped?' And they all reply: 'If I did, there would be no meaning to my life.'

As if they actually knew what the meaning of life was.

Temptation has lost the battle. It wanted to make him believe that he was mad: it's one thing to plan the sacrifice of certain people, quite another to have the capacity and the courage to carry it out. Temptation said that we all dream of committing crimes, but that only the unbalanced make that macabre idea a reality.

Igor is well-balanced and successful. If he wanted, he could hire a professional killer, the best in the world, to carry out his task and send the requisite messages to Ewa. Or he could hire the best public-relations agency in the world, and by the end of the year, he'd be the talk not only of economics journals, but of magazines interested only in success and glamour.At that point, his ex-wife would weigh up the consequences of her mistaken decision, and he would know just the right moment to send her flowers and ask her to come back, all was forgiven. He has contacts at all levels of society, from businessmen who've reached the top through perseverance and hard work to criminals who've never had a chance to show their more positive side.

He isn't in Cannes because he takes a morbid pleasure in seeing the look in a person's eyes as he or she confronts the inevitable. He's decided to place himself in the line of fire, in the dangerous position in which he finds himself now, because he's sure that every step he takes during this seemingly endless day will prove vital if the new Igor who exists within him is to be born again out of the ashes of his tragedy.

He's always been able to make difficult decisions and to see things through, although no one, not even Ewa, has ever known what went on in the dark corridors of his soul. For many years he endured in silence the threats made by various individuals and groups, and he reacted discreetly when he felt strong enough to rid himself of the people threatening him. He had learned to exercise enormous self-control so as not to be left traumatised by bad experiences. He never took his fears home with him, feeling that Ewa deserved a quiet life and to be kept in ignorance of the terrors that beset any businessman. He chose to save her from that, and yet he received nothing in return, not even understanding.

The girl's spirit soothes him with that thought, then adds something that hadn't occurred to him until then: he wasn't there to win back the person who had left him, but to see, at last, that she wasn't worth all those years of pain, all those months of planning, all his enormous capacity for forgiveness, generosity and patience.

He has sent one, two, three messages now, and there's been no reaction from Ewa. It would be easy enough for her to find out where he's staying, although, admittedly, phoning the five or six top hotels wouldn't help because when he checked in he gave a different name and profession. Then again, she who seeks, finds.

He's read the statistics. Cannes has only 70,000 inhabitants, and that number usually triples during the Film Festival, but festival-goers all haunt the same places. Where would she be staying? Given that he had seen the two of them the previous night, she was probably staying in the same hotel and visiting the same bar. Even so, Ewa isn't prowling the Boulevard de la Croisette looking for him. She isn't phoning mutual friends, trying to find out where he is. At least one of those friends has all the necessary information, for Igor had assumed that the woman he thought was the love of his life would contact that friend as soon as she realised Igor was in Cannes. The friend has instructions to tell her how she can find him, but so far, there has been no news.

He takes off his clothes and gets into the shower. Ewa isn't worth all this fuss. He's almost certain that he'll see her tonight, but this is growing less and less important with each passing moment. Perhaps his mission is about something much more important than simply regaining the love of the woman who betrayed him and who speaks ill of him to other people. The spirit of the girl with the dark eyebrows reminds him of the story told by an old Afghan in a break during a battle.

After many centuries of turmoil and bad government, the population of a city high up on one of the desert mountains of Herat province was in despair. They could not simply abolish the monarchy and yet neither could they stand many more generations of arrogant, egotistical kings. They summoned the Loya Jirga, as the council of wise men is known locally.

The Loya Jirga decided that they should elect a king every four years, and that this king should have absolute power. He could increase taxes, demand total obedience, choose a different woman to take to his bed each night, and eat and drink his fill. He could wear the finest clothes, ride the finest horses. In short, any order he gave, however absurd, would be obeyed, and no one would question whether it was logical or just.

However, at the end of that period of four years, he would be obliged to give up the throne and leave the city, taking with him only his family and the clothes on his back. Everyone knew that this would mean certain death within three or four days because there was nothing to eat or drink in that vast desert, which was freezing in winter and like a furnace in summer.

The wise men of the Loya Jirga assumed that no one would risk standing for the position of king, and that they would then be able to return to the old system of democratic elections. Their decision was made public, and the post of king fell vacant. Initially, several people applied. An old man with cancer took up the challenge and died during the period of his rule with a smile on his face. A madman succeeded him, but left four months later (he had misunderstood the terms) and vanished into the desert. Then rumours started going around that the throne had a curse on it, and no one dared apply for the position. The city was left without a governor, confusion reigned, and the inhabitants realised that they must forget the monarchist tradition altogether and prepare to change their ways. The Loya Jirga felt pleased that its members had taken such a wise decision. They hadn't forced the people to make a choice; they had simply got rid of those who wanted power at any price. Then a young man, married and with three children, came forward.

'I accept the post,' he said.

The wise men tried to explain the risks. They reminded him that he had a family and explained that their decision had merely been a way of discouraging adventurers and despots. However, the young man stood firm, and since it was impossible to go back on their decision, the Loya Jirga had no option but to wait another four years before they could put in place the planned return to elections.

The young man and his family proved to be excellent governors. They ruled fairly, redistributed wealth, lowered the price of food, organised popular festivals to celebrate the change of season, and encouraged craftwork and music. Every night, though, a great caravan of horses would leave the city, drawing heavy carts covered with jute cloth so that no one could see what was inside them. These carts never came back.

At first, the wise men of the Loya Jirga thought that the king must be removing treasure from the city, but consoled themselves with the fact that the young man rarely ventured beyond the city walls; if he had and had tried to climb the nearest mountain, he would have realised that the horses would die before they got very far. This was, after all, one of the most inhospitable places on the planet. They determined that, as soon as his reign was over, they would go to the place where the horses had died of exhaustion and the riders of thirst, and they would recover all that treasure.

They stopped worrying and waited patiently.

At the end of the four years, the young man left the throne and the city. The population was in uproar; after all, it had been a long time since they had enjoyed such a wise and just governor!

However, the Loya Jirga's decision had to be respected. The young man went to his wife and children and asked them to leave with him.

'I will,' said his wife, 'but at least let our children stay. They will then survive to tell your story.'

'Trust me,' he said.

The tribal laws were very strict, and the wife had no alternative but to obey her husband. They mounted their horses and rode to the city gate, where they said goodbye to the friends they had made while governing the city. The Loya Jirga were pleased. They might have made many allies, but fate is fate. No one else would risk accepting the post of governor, and the democratic tradition would be restored at last. As soon as they could, they would recover the treasure abandoned in the desert, less than three days from there.

The family rode into the valley of death in silence. The wife didn't dare say a word, the children didn't understand what was going on, and the young man was immersed in thought. They climbed one hill, travelled for a whole day across a vast plain, and slept on the top of the next hill.

The woman woke at dawn, wanting to make the most of the final few days of her life to look her last on the mountains she had loved so much. She went up to the very top of the hill and gazed down on what should have been an empty plain, and she was startled by what she saw.

During those four years, the caravans leaving the city each night had not been carrying off jewels or gold coins. They had been carrying bricks, seeds, wood, roof-tiles, spices, animals, and traditional tools that could be used to drill into the earth and find water.

Before her lay a far more modern, far more beautiful city than the old one, and all in working order.

'This is your kingdom,' said the young man, who had just woken up and joined her. 'Ever since I heard the decree, I knew it would be pointless to try and change in four years everything that centuries of corruption and bad governance had destroyed. I was certain of one thing, though, that it was possible to start again.

Igor, too, is starting again as he stands in the shower with the water cascading over his face. He has finally understood why the first person he spoke to in Cannes is by his side now, sending him off along a different path, helping him make the necessary adjustments and explaining that her sacrifice was neither a chance event nor unnecessary. On the other hand, she has also made it plain to him that Ewa has always been naturally perverse and only interested in climbing the social ladder, even if doing so meant abandoning her family.

'When you go back to Moscow, try and do plenty of sport. That will help free you from your tensions,' says the girl.

He can just make out her face in the clouds of steam in the shower. He has never felt as close to anyone as he does now to Olivia, the girl with the dark eyebrows.

'Carry on, even if you're not so sure now of what you're doing. God moves in mysterious ways, and sometimes the path only reveals itself once you start walking it.'

'Thank you, Olivia,' he thinks. Perhaps he is here in order to show the world the aberrations of modern life, of which Cannes is the supreme manifestation.

He's not sure, but whatever the case, he's here for a reason, and the last two years of tension, planning, fear and uncertainty are finally justified.

He can imagine what the next Festival will be like: people being issued with swipe cards even to get into the lunch-parties on the beach, sharpshooters on every rooftop, hundreds of plain-clothes policemen mingling with the crowds, metal detectors at the door of every hotel, where those children-of-the-Superclass will have to wait while the police search their bags; women will have to take off their high heels and men be called back because the coins in their pockets have set off the alarm; grey-haired gentlemen will have to hold out their arms and be frisked like common criminals; the women will be led to a kind of canvas tent at the entrance - which clashes horribly with the former elegance of the place - where they'll have to wait patiently in line to be searched, until a policewoman discovers what triggered the alarm: the underwiring in a bra.

The city will begin to show its true face. Luxury and glamour will be replaced by tension, insults, wasted time and the cool, indifferent gaze of the police. People will feel more and more isolated, this time by the system itself, rather than by the eternal arrogance of the chosen few. Army units will be sent to that simple seaside town with the sole objective of protecting people who are trying to have fun, and the prohibitive cost of this will, of course, fall on the tax-payers' shoulders.

There will be demonstrations by honest workers protesting at what they deem to be an absurdity. The government will issue a statement saying that they're considering the possibility of shifting the cost to the organisers of the Festival. The sponsors - who could easily afford the expense - lose interest when one of their number is humiliated by some insignificant little officer, who tells him to shut up and respect the security regulations.

Cannes will begin to die. Two years on, they'll see that everything they did to maintain law and order really has paid off, with zero levels of crime during the Festival period. The terrorists have failed in their attempt to sow further panic.

They'll try to turn the clock back, but they won't be able to. Cannes will continue to die. This new Babylon will be destroyed, this modern-day Sodom will be erased from the map.

He steps out of the shower having made a decision. When he goes back to Russia, he will order his employees to find out the girl's family name. He will make anonymous donations through neutral banks. He will order some gifted author to write the story of her life and pay for it to be translated into different languages.

'The story of a young woman who sold craftwork, was beaten by her boyfriend, exploited by her parents, until the day she surrendered her soul to a stranger and thus changed one small corner of the planet.'

He opens the wardrobe, takes out an immaculate white shirt, his carefully pressed dinner jacket and his hand-made patent-leather shoes. He has no trouble tying his bow tie because he does this at least once a week.

He turns on the TV in time for the local news bulletin. The parade of stars along the red carpet takes up much of the programme, but there is also a brief report about a woman found murdered on the beach.

The police have cordoned off the area. The boy who witnessed the murder (Igor studies his face, but feels no desire for revenge) says that he saw the couple sit down to talk, then the man got out a small stiletto knife and appeared to run it lightly over the woman's body. The woman seemed quite happy, which is why he didn't call the police earlier because he thought it was some kind of joke.

'What did the man look like?'

White, about forty, wearing such and such clothes, and apparently very polite.

There's no need to worry. Igor opens his leather briefcase and takes out two envelopes. One contains an invitation to the party that is due to start in an hour (although everyone knows that the start will be delayed by ninety minutes), where he knows he will meet Ewa. If she won't come to him, too bad; he will go to her. It has taken less than twenty-four hours for him to see the kind of woman he married and that the sufferings of the last two years have been in vain.

The other envelope is silver and hermetically sealed. On it are the two words 'For you' written in an exquisite hand that could be either male or female.

There are CCTV cameras in the corridors, as there are in most hotels nowadays. In some part of the basement is a dark room lined with TV screens before which a group of people sit, watching. They are on the look-out for anything unusual, like the man who kept going up and down stairs and who explained to the officer sent to investigate that he was simply enjoying a little free exercise. Since the man was a guest at the hotel, the officer apologised and left.

They take no interest in guests who go into another guest's room and don't leave until the next day, usually after breakfast has been served. That's normal and none of their business.

The screens are connected to special digital recording systems, and the resulting disks are stored for six months in a safe to which only the manager has the key. No hotel in the world wants to lose a customer because some rich, jealous husband manages to bribe one of the people watching one particular part of the corridor and then gives (or sells) the material to a tabloid newspaper, having first presented proof of adultery to the courts and thus ensured that his wife will get none of his fortune.

That would be a tragic blow to the prestige of a hotel that prides itself on discretion and confidentiality. The occupation rate would immediately plummet; after all, people choose a five-star hotel because they know that the people who work there are trained to see only what they're supposed to see. For example, if someone asks for room service, when the waiter arrives, he keeps his eyes fixed on the trolley, holds out the bill to be signed by the person who opens the door, but never – *ever* – looks over at the bed.

Prostitutes – male and female – dress discreetly, although the men in the screen-lined room know exactly who they are, thanks to a data system provided by the police. This is none of their business either, but in these cases, they always keep one eye on the door of the room they went into until they come out again. In some hotels, the telephonist is told to make a fake phone call just to check that the guest is all right. The guest picks up the phone, a female voice asks for some non-existent person, hears an angry 'You've got the wrong room' and the sound of the phone being slammed down. Mission accomplished; there's no need to worry.

Drunks who try their key in the lock of the wrong room and, when the door fails to open, start angrily pounding on it, are often surprised to see a solicitous hotel employee appear out of nowhere – he just happened to be passing, he says – and who suggests accompanying the drunken guest to the right room (usually on a different floor and with an entirely different number).

Igor knows that his every move is being recorded in the hotel basement: the day, hour, minute and second that he comes into the lobby, gets out of the lift, walks to the door of his suite and puts the swipe card into the lock. Once inside, he can breathe easy; no one has access to what is happening in the room itself – that would be a step too far in violating someone's privacy.

He closes his room door behind him.

He had made a point of studying the CCTV cameras as soon as he arrived the night before. Just as all cars have a blind spot when overtaking, regardless of how many rear-view mirrors they may have, the cameras show every part of the corridor, except the rooms located in each of the four corners. Obviously, if one of the men in the basement sees someone pass by a particular place but fail to appear on the next screen, he'll suspect something untoward has happened – the person might have fainted – and immediately send someone up to check. If he gets there and finds no one, the person has obviously been invited into one of the rooms, and the rest is a private matter between guests.

Igor, however, doesn't intend to stop in the corridor. He walks nonchalantly to the point where the corridor curves away towards the lifts and slips the silver envelope under the door of the corner room or suite.

It all takes less than a fraction of a second, and if someone downstairs was observing his movements, they would have noticed nothing. Much later, when they check the disks to try and identify the person responsible for what happened, they will have great difficulty determining the exact moment of death. It may be that the guest wasn't there and only opened the envelope when he or she returned from one of that night's events. It may be that he or she opened the envelope at once, but that the contents took a while to act.

During that time, various people will have passed by the same place and every one of them will be considered suspicious; and if some shabbily dressed person or someone from the less orthodox worlds of massage, prostitution or drugs had the misfortune to follow the same trajectory, they'll immediately be arrested and questioned. During a film festival, the chances of such an individual appearing on the scene are very high indeed.

He knows, too, that there's a danger he hadn't reckoned with: the person who witnessed the murder of the woman on the beach. After jumping through the usual bureaucratic hoops, the witness will be asked to view the recordings. Igor, however, had checked in using a false passport and the photo shows a man with glasses and a beard (the hotel reception didn't even take the trouble to check, although if they'd asked, he would simply have said that he'd shaved off both beard and moustache and now wore contact lenses).

Assuming that they were much quicker off the mark than most policemen and had reached the conclusion that just one person was behind this attempt to derail the normal running of the Festival, they would be awaiting his return and he would be asked to give a statement. Igor, however, knows that this is the last time he'll walk down the corridors of the Hotel Martinez.

They'll go into his room and find an empty suitcase, bearing no fingerprints. They'll go into the bathroom and think to themselves: 'What's a millionaire doing washing his own clothes in the sink! Can't he afford the laundry?'

A policeman will reach out to pick up what he considers evidence bearing DNA traces, fingerprints and strands of hair and drop it with a yelp having burned his fingers in the sulphuric acid that is now dissolving everything Igor has left behind. He needs only his false passport, his credit cards and some cash, and he has all of this in the pockets of his dinner jacket, along with the Beretta, that weapon so despised by the cognoscenti.

He has always found travelling easy; he hates luggage. Even though he had a complicated mission to carry out in Cannes, he chose things that would be easy and light to transport. He can't understand people who take enormous suitcases with them, even when they're only spending a couple of days away.

He doesn't know who will open the envelope, nor does he care; the choice will fall to the Angel of Death, not to him. A lot of things could happen in the meantime, or indeed nothing.

The guest might phone reception and say that the envelope has been delivered to the wrong person and ask that someone come and collect it. Or they might throw it in the bin, thinking it's just another of those charming letters from the management, asking if everything is going well; the guest has other things to read and a party to get ready for. If the guest is a man expecting his wife to arrive at any moment, he'll put it in his pocket, convinced that the woman he was flirting with that afternoon is writing to say 'Yes'. Or it might be a married couple, and since neither of them knows to whom the 'you' on the envelope refers, they'll agree that this is no time for mutual suspicion and throw the envelope out of the window.

If, despite all these possibilities, the Angel of Death does decide to brush the recipient's face with his wings, then he or she will tear open the envelope and see the contents. Those contents had involved a great deal of work and required him to call on the help of the 'friends and collaborators' who had given him their financial backing when he was first setting up his company, the same ones who had been most put out when he repaid that loan early. It had been a real godsend to them being able to invest money of suspect origin in a business that was perfectly legal and above-board, and they only wanted the money back when it suited them.

Nevertheless, after a period during which the two parties barely spoke, they had become friendly again, and whenever they asked him for a favour – getting a university place for their daughter or tickets for concerts that their 'clients' wanted to attend – Igor always did all he could to help them. After all, regardless of their motives, they were the only people who had believed in his dreams. Ewa – whenever he thought of her now, Igor felt intensely irritated – used to say that they had played on her husband's innocence to launder money earned from arms trafficking, as if that made any difference. It wasn't as if he'd been involved in the actual buying or selling of arms, and besides, in any business deal, both parties need to make a profit.

And everyone has their ups and downs. Some of his former backers had spent time in prison, but he had never abandoned them, even though he no longer needed their help. A man's dignity isn't measured by the people he has around him when he's at the peak of his success, but by his ability not to forget those who helped him when his need was greatest. Whether those hands were drenched in blood or sweat was irrelevant: if you were clinging on to the edge of a precipice, you wouldn't care who it was hauling you up to safety.

A sense of gratitude is important; no one gets very far if he forgets those who were with him in his hour of need. Not that you have to be constantly thinking about who helped or was helped. God has His eyes fixed on his sons and daughters and rewards only those who behave in accordance with the blessings that were bestowed on them.

And so when he wanted to buy some curare, he knew where to go, although he had to pay an absurd price for a substance that is relatively commonplace in the jungles of South America.

He reaches the hotel lobby. The party is more than half an hour away by car, and it would be very hard to find a taxi if he just stood out in the street. He long ago learned that the first thing you do when you arrive at a hotel is give a large tip to the concierge without asking anything in exchange; all successful businessmen do this, and they never have any trouble getting reservations at the best restaurants, or tickets for shows, or information about certain areas of the city that don't appear in the guidebooks, and which prefer not to shock the middle classes.

With a smile, he asks for and gets a taxi right there and then, while another guest beside him is complaining about the problems he's having finding transport. Gratitude, necessity and the right contacts. You can get anything you want with those three things, even a silver envelope with the seductive words 'For you' written in fine calligraphy. He had held off using it until the very end because if Ewa had failed to understand the other messages, this - the most sophisticated of all - would leave no room for doubt.

His old friends had come up trumps. They had offered to let him have it for nothing, but he had preferred to pay. He had enough money and didn't like to be in anyone's debt.

He hadn't asked too many questions about how it was made; he only knew that it was a very complicated process and that the person who created the hermetically sealed envelope had to wear gloves and a gas mask. The high price he had paid for the envelope was quite justified since it had to be handled very carefully indeed, even though the product itself wasn't that hard to get hold of: it's commonly used in steel-tempering and in the production of paper, clothes and plastic. It has a rather frightening name: hydrogen cyanide, but smells of almonds and looks perfectly harmless.

He stops thinking about who sealed the envelope and begins to imagine the person who will open it - holding it quite close to the face, as is normal. On the white card inside is a printed message in French:

'Katyusha, *je t'aime*.'

'Katyusha? Who's that?' the person will ask, noticing that the card is covered in a kind of dust. Once in contact with the air, the dust will become a gas, and a strong smell of almonds will fill the room.

The person will be surprised and think: 'Whoever sent it might have chosen a nicer smell.' It must be an advertisement for perfume. He or she will remove the card and turn it this way and that, and the gas given off by the dust will start to spread ever more quickly.

'It must be some kind of joke.'

That will be their last conscious thought. Leaving the card on the table at the door, they'll go into the bathroom to take a shower or finish applying make-up or to adjust their tie.

They'll notice then that their heart is racing. They won't immediately connect this with the perfume filling the room; after all, they have no enemies, only competitors and adversaries. Before they even reach the bathroom, they will notice that they can no longer stand and they'll sit down on the edge of the bed. The next symptoms will be an unbearable headache and difficulty in breathing, followed by a desire to vomit. However, there will be no time for that; they will rapidly lose consciousness, still without making any connection between their physical state and the contents of the envelope.

In a matter of minutes – he had asked for the product to be as concentrated as possible – the lungs will stop working, the body will go into convulsions, the heart will stop pumping blood, and death will follow.

Painless. Merciful. Humane.

Igor gets into the taxi and gives the address: Hotel du Cap, Eden Roc, Cap d'Antibes.

Tonight's gala supper.

7.40 p.m.

The androgyne – wearing a black shirt, white bow tie and a kind of Indian tunic over the same tight trousers that draw attention to his scrawny legs – tells her that they could be arriving at either a very good moment or a very bad one.

'The traffic's better than I expected. We'll be one of the first to enter Eden Roc.'

Gabriela, who, by now, has had her hair and make-up retouched yet again – this time by a make-up artist who seemed totally bored by her work – doesn't understand what this means.

'Given all the traffic hold-ups, isn't it best to be early? How could that be bad?'

The androgyne gives a deep sigh before replying, as if he were having to explain the obvious to someone who doesn't even know the most elementary rules of the world of glamour.

'It could be good because you'll be alone in the corridor …'

The androgyne looks at her, sees the blank expression on her face, utters another deep sigh, then says:

'No one walks straight into this kind of party through a door. You always have to go down a corridor first. On one side are the photographers and on the other is a wall bearing the logo of the party's sponsor. Haven't you ever seen photos in celebrity magazines? Haven't you ever noticed that the celebrities are always standing in front of a logo as they smile for the cameras?'

Celebrity. The arrogant androgyne has let slip the wrong word. He has unwittingly admitted that Gabriela is also a celebrity. Gabriela savours this victory in silence, although she's grown-up enough to know that she still has a very long way to go.

'And what's so bad about arriving on time?'

Another sigh.

'The photographers themselves might not have arrived yet, but let's hope I'm mistaken, that way I can hand out a few of these flyers.'

'About me?'

'You surely don't imagine that everyone knows who you are, do you? Sorry to disappoint you, sweetheart. No, I'll have to go on ahead of you and give this wretched bit of paper to each photographer and tell them that the big star of Gibson's next film is about to arrive and that they should have their cameras ready. I'll signal to them as soon as you appear in the corridor.

'I won't be nice to them though. I mean, they're used to being treated as what they are, creatures on the lowest rung of power. I'll say I'm doing them a big favour, and they won't want to risk missing a chance and getting fired because there's no shortage of people in the world with a camera and an Internet connection, and who are mad keen to post something on the web that everyone else has missed. I reckon that, in future, given the way circulation figures are going, newspapers will rely entirely on the services of anonymous photographers as a way of keeping down their costs.'

He wants to show off his knowledge of the media, but the young woman beside him isn't interested. She picks up one of the bits of paper and starts reading.

'Who's Lisa Winner?'

'That's you. We've changed your name. Or rather, the name had been chosen even before you were selected. From now on, that's what you're called. Gabriela is too Italian, whereas Lisa could be any nationality. Market research shows that the general public find surnames with between four and six letters easiest to remember: Fanta. Taylor. Burton. Davis. Woods. Hilton. Shall I go on?'

'No, thanks. I can see you know your market, but now I need to find out who I am – according to my new biography.'

She makes no attempt to hide the irony in her voice. She was growing in confidence and beginning to behave like a real star. She starts reading: a major discovery chosen from among more than a thousand applicants to work on the first production by famous couturier and entrepreneur Hamid Hussein, etc., etc.

'The flyers were printed over a month ago,' says the androgyne, tipping the scales back in his favour. 'It was written by the group's marketing team, and they're always spot-on. Listen: "She worked as a model and studied drama." That's you, isn't it?'

'So I was chosen more for my biography than for the quality of my audition.'

'No, it means that everyone there had the same biography.'

'Look, shall we just stop making jibes at each other and try to be a little more human and friendly?'

'Here? In Cannes? Forget it. There's no such thing as friends, only self-interest. There are no human beings, just crazy machines who mow down everything in their path in order to get where they want or else end up ploughing into a lamppost.'

Despite this response, Gabriela feels she was right and that her companion's animosity is beginning to melt.

'Look at this,' he goes on. '"For years, she refused to work in the cinema, feeling that the theatre was the best way to express her talent." That gives you a lot of bonus points; it shows you're a person with integrity, who only accepted the role in the film because you really loved it, even though you'd been invited to do plays by Shakespeare, Beckett or Genet or whoever.'

He's obviously very well-read, this androgyne. Everyone's heard of Shakespeare, but fewer people know about Beckett and Genet.

Gabriela – or Lisa – agrees. The car arrives, and there, once more, are the inevitable security guards in black suits, white shirts and black ties, all clutching tiny radios as if they were real policemen (or perhaps that's the collective dream of all security guards). One of them waves the driver on because it's too early.

The androgyne – having weighed up the risks and decided that early is, in fact, best – jumps out of the limousine and goes over to one of the guards, a man twice his size. Gabriela tries to distract herself and think of other things.

'What sort of car is this?' she asks the chauffeur.

'A Maybach 57S,' he replies. He has a German accent. 'A real work of art, the perfect machine, the ultimate in luxury.'

But she's no longer listening. She can see the androgyne talking to the huge security guard. The man appears to ignore him and makes a gesture indicating that he should get into the car and stop holding up the traffic. The androgyne – a mere mosquito to the security guard's elephant – turns on his heel and walks back to the car.

He opens the door and tells Gabriela to get out; they're going in anyway.

Gabriela fears the worst, that there'll be an almighty row. She walks with the mosquito past the elephant, who says: 'Hey, you can't go in there!', but they both keep straight on. Other voices shout: 'Have a little respect for the rules! We haven't opened the door yet!' She doesn't have the courage to look back and imagines that the herd must be hot on their heels ready to trample them at any moment.

But nothing happens, even though the androgyne isn't walking any faster, perhaps out of respect for her long dress. They're passing through an immaculate garden now; the horizon is tinged with pink and blue; the sun is sinking.

The androgyne is enjoying this new victory.

'They're all very macho until you face up to them, but you just have to raise your voice, look them straight in the eye and keep walking, and they won't come after you. I have the invitations and that's all I need. They may be big those guys, but they're not stupid, and they know that only someone important would speak to them as I did.'

He concludes with surprising humility:

'I've got used to pretending to be important.'

They reach the hotel, which is totally removed from the hustle and bustle of Cannes and suitable only for those guests who don't need to keep going back and forth along the Boulevard. The androgyne asks Gabriela/Lisa to go to the bar and order two glasses of champagne; this will indicate that she's not alone. No talking to strangers. Nothing vulgar, please. He'll go and see how the land lies and distribute the flyers.

'I'm only doing this for form's sake really. No one will publish your photo, but this is what I'm paid to do. I'll be back in a minute.'

'But didn't you just say that the photographers …'

He has reverted to his former arrogant self. Before Gabriela can hit back, though, he has vanished.

There are no empty tables; the place is packed with men in dinner jackets and women in long dresses. They're all talking in low voices, those who *are* talking, for most have their eyes fixed on the sea that can be seen through the large windows. Even though this is their first time in such a place, a palpable, unmistakable feeling hovers over all these celebrated heads: a profound sense of tedium.

They have all attended hundreds, possibly thousands of parties like this. Once, they would have felt the excitement of the unknown, of possibly meeting a new love, of making important professional contacts; but now that they have reached the top of their careers, there are no more challenges; all that's left to do is to compare one yacht with another, one jewel with your neighbour's jewel, the people who are sitting at the tables nearest the window with those who are further off – a sure sign of the former's superiority. Yes, this is the end of the line: tedium and endless comparisons. After decades of struggling to get where they are, there seems to be nothing left, not even the pleasure of having watched one more sunset in one more beautiful place.

What are they thinking, those rich, silent women, so distant from their husbands?

They're thinking about age.

They need to go back to see their plastic surgeon and re-do what time is relentlessly undoing. Gabriela knows that one day this will happen to her as well, and suddenly – perhaps because of all the emotions of a day that is ending so very differently from the way it began – she can feel those negative thoughts returning.

Again there's that feeling of terror mingled with joy. Again the feeling that, despite the long struggle, she doesn't deserve what's happening to her; she's just a girl who's worked hard at her job, but who's still ill-prepared for life. She doesn't know the rules; she's going further than good sense dictates; this world doesn't belong to her and she'll never be a part of it. She feels helpless and can't remember now why she came to Europe; after all, it's not so dreadful being an actress in small-town America, doing exactly what she likes and not what other people make her do. She wants to be happy, and she's not entirely sure she's on the right path.

'Stop it! Stop thinking like that!'

She can't do any yoga exercises here, so she tries to concentrate on the sea and on the blue and pink sky. She has been given a golden opportunity; she needs to overcome her feelings of revulsion and to talk more to the androgyne in the few free moments they have before the 'corridor'. She mustn't make any mistakes; she has been lucky and she must make the most of it. She opens her handbag to take out her lipstick and touch up her lips, but all she sees inside is a lot of crumpled paper. She had been back to the Gift Room with the bored make-up artist, and had again forgotten to collect her things, but even if she had remembered, where would she have put them?

That handbag is an excellent metaphor for her current experience: lovely outside and completely empty inside.

She must control herself.

'The sun has just sunk below the horizon and will be reborn tomorrow with the same force. I need to be reborn now. The fact that I've dreamed of this moment so many times ought to have prepared me, made me more confident. I believe in miracles and I'm being blessed by God, who listened to my prayers. I must remember what the director used to say to me before each rehearsal: "Even if you're doing the same thing over and over, you need to discover something new, fantastic and unbelievable that went unnoticed the time before."'

Enter a handsome man of about forty, with greying hair and dressed in an impeccable dinner jacket hand-made by some master tailor. He looks as if he were about to come over to her, but immediately notices the second glass of champagne and heads off to the other end of the bar. She would have liked to talk to him; the androgyne is taking such a long time. But she remembers his stern words:

'Nothing vulgar.'

And it would indeed be reprehensible, inappropriate, embarrassing to see a young woman, all alone in the bar of a five-star hotel, go over to an older customer. What would people think?

She drinks her champagne and orders another glass. If the androgyne has disappeared for good, she has no way of paying the bill, but who cares? Her doubts and insecurities are disappearing as she drinks, and now she's afraid that she might not be able to get into the party and fulfil her commitments.

No, she's no longer the small-town girl who has struggled to get on in life, and she will never be that person again. The road rises before her; another glass of champagne, and the fear of the unknown becomes a dread that she might never have the chance to discover what it really means to be here. What terrifies her now is the sense that everything could change from one moment to the next; how can she make sure that the miracle of today continues tomorrow? What guarantee does she have that all the promises made earlier will ever be met? She has often before stood outside some magnificent door, some fantastic opportunity, and dreamed for days and weeks about the possibility that her life might change for ever, only to find, in the end, that the phone didn't ring, or her CV was mislaid, or that the director would call and offer his apologies, and tell her that they'd found someone more suitable for the part, 'which isn't to say you don't have real talent, so don't be discouraged'. Life has many ways of testing a person's will, either by having nothing happen at all or having everything happen all at once.

The man who arrived alone has his eyes fixed on her and on the second glass of champagne. She so wishes he would come over to her! She hasn't had a chance to talk to anyone about what's been happening. She'd thought several times of phoning her family, but her phone was in her real bag and probably full of messages from her room-mates, wanting to know where she is, if she has any spare invitations, if she'd like to go with them to some second-rate event where such-and-such a celebrity is going to make an appearance.

She can't share anything with anyone. She has taken a big step in her life; she's alone in a hotel bar, terrified that the dream might end, and at the same time knowing that she can never go back to being the person she was. She has nearly reached the top of the mountain: she must either hang on tight or be blown over by the wind.

The forty-something man with the greying hair, drinking an orange juice, is still there. At one point, their eyes meet, and he smiles. She pretends not to have seen him.

Why is she so afraid? Because with each new step she's taking, she doesn't know quite how to behave. No one helps her; all they do is give orders and expect them to be rigorously obeyed. She feels like a child locked in a dark room, trying to find her way to the door because some very powerful person is calling her and demanding to be obeyed.

Her thoughts are interrupted by the androgyne, who has just come back.

'Let's wait a while longer. People are only just starting to arrive.'

The handsome man gets up, pays his bill and heads for the exit. He seems disappointed. Perhaps he was waiting for the right moment to come over, tell her his name and …

'… talk a little.'

'What?'

She had let her guard drop. Two glasses of champagne and her tongue was looser than it should be.

'Nothing.'

'No, you said you needed to talk a little.'

She's the small child in the dark room with no one to guide her. Humility. She must do what she promised herself she would do a few minutes earlier.

'Yes, I was just going to ask what you're doing here in Cannes, how you ended up in this world of which I understand almost nothing. It's not at all as I imagined it would be; believe it or not, when you went off to talk to the photographers, I felt really alone and frightened, but I know I can count on you for help, and I wondered whether or not you enjoy your work.'

Some angel – who clearly likes champagne – is putting the right words in her mouth.

The androgyne looks at her in surprise. Is she trying to make friends with him? Why is she asking questions no one normally dares to ask, when she's only known him a few hours?

No one trusts him because he's not like anyone else – he's unique. Contrary to what most people think, he isn't homosexual, he has simply lost all interest in other human beings. He bleaches his hair, wears the clothes he's always dreamed of wearing, weighs exactly what he wants to weigh, and though he knows he makes a strange impression on people, he's not obliged to be nice to anyone as long as he does his job.

And now here's this woman asking him what he thinks, how he feels. He picks up the glass of champagne that has been waiting for him and drinks it down in one.

She must imagine that he works for Hamid Hussein and has some influence, and wants his cooperation and help so as to know what her next step should be. He knows all the steps, but he was only taken on for the duration of the Festival and to perform certain tasks, and he'll only do what he's been asked to do. When these days of luxury and glamour are over, he'll go back to his apartment in a Paris suburb, where he gets abuse from the neighbours simply because he doesn't fit the conventional model established by whatever madman once declared: 'All human beings are equal.' It's not true. All human beings are different and should take their right to be different to its ultimate consequences.

He'll watch TV, shop at the supermarket next door, buy magazines and sometimes go to the cinema; and because he's considered to be a responsible person, he'll get the occasional call from agents who need experienced assistants in the world of fashion, people who know how to dress models and choose accessories, to help those new to the fashion world avoid making social blunders, and to explain what they should and absolutely shouldn't do.

Oh, he has his dreams. He's unique, he tells himself. He's happy because he expects nothing more from life, and although he looks much younger, he's actually forty years old. He did try to get a career as a designer, but couldn't get a decent job and fell out with the people who could have helped him. He no longer has any great expectations, even though he's cultured and has good taste and a will of iron. He no longer believes that someone will look at him, see the way he dresses, and say: 'Great, we'd like to talk to you.' He's had a few invitations to work as a model, but that was a long time ago, and he doesn't regret having turned them down because being a model wasn't part of his life plan.

He makes his own clothes from off-cuts discarded by haute-couture studios. In Cannes, he's staying with two other people up on the hill, probably not very far from where the young woman is lodging. She, however, is getting her big chance, and however unfair he may feel life to be, he mustn't allow himself to be overwhelmed by frustration and envy. He'll do his very best because if he doesn't, he won't be invited back as 'production assistant'.

Of course he's happy; anyone who desires nothing is happy. He looks at his watch; it might be a good moment for them to go in.

'Come on. We'll talk another time.'

He pays for the drinks and asks for a receipt, so that he can claim back every penny once the glitz and glamour are over and done with. Some other people are getting up and doing the same thing; he and Gabriela/Lisa need to hurry if she isn't to get lost in the crowd that is now beginning to arrive. They walk across the hotel lobby towards the 'corridor'; he hands her two invitations, which he has kept safe in his pocket. After all, important people don't have to bother with such details; they always have an assistant to do that.

He is the assistant and she is the important person, and she's already beginning to show signs that 'greatness' is going to her head. She'll find out soon enough just what this world is capable of: draining every ounce of her energy, filling her mind with dreams, manipulating her vanity, then discarding her just when she thinks she's ready for anything. That's what happened with him and it happens with everyone.

They go down the stairs. They stop in the small hall just before the 'corridor'. There's no hurry; this is different from the red carpet. If anyone calls her name, she must turn and smile. If that happens, then the chances are that all the other photographers will start taking photos too because, if one of them knows her name, she must be important. She shouldn't spend more than two minutes posing because this is just the entrance to a party, even though it seems like something from another world. If she wants to be a star, then she must start behaving like one.

'Why am I going in alone?'

'Apparently there's been some hitch. He should be here – after all, he's a professional – but he's obviously been held up.'

'He' is the Star. The androgyne could have told her what he thought had really happened: 'He didn't leave his room when he should have done, which means he's probably met some girl who's got the hots for him.' This, however, would hurt the feelings of the novice by his side, who's probably nursing entirely baseless dreams of some lovely love story.

He doesn't need to be cruel, just as he doesn't need to be her friend; he simply has to do his job and then leave. Besides, if the silly girl can't control her emotions, the photos taken of her in the corridor might turn out badly.

He stands in front of her in the queue and asks her to follow him, but to leave a yard or two between them. As soon as they enter the corridor, he'll go over to the photographers and see if he can get any of them interested.

Gabriela waits for a few seconds, puts on her best smile, holds her handbag as she has been taught, straightens her back and starts to walk confidently ahead, ready to face the flashlights. The corridor opens out into a brightly lit area, with a white wall plastered with the sponsor's logo. On the other side is a small gallery where various lenses are pointing in her direction.

She keeps walking, this time trying to be aware of each step; she doesn't want to repeat the frustrating experience of earlier that day, when her walk along the red carpet was over before she knew it. She must live the present moment as if a film of her life were being shown in slow motion. At some point, the cameras will start to whir.

'Jasmine!' someone shouts out.

Jasmine? But her name is Gabriela!

She stops for a fraction of a second, a smile frozen on her face. No, her name isn't Gabriela any more. What is it? Jasmine?

Suddenly, she hears the sound of camera buttons being pressed, lenses opening and closing, except that all the lenses are pointing at the person behind her.

'Move!' says one photographer. 'Your moment of glory is over. Get out of the way!'

She can't believe it. She keeps smiling, but starts to walk more rapidly now in the direction of the dark tunnel that seems to follow on from that corridor of light.

'Jasmine! Over here! Here!'

The photographers seem to be in the grip of a collective hysteria.

She reaches the end of the corridor without having heard anyone call out her name, a name she herself has forgotten anyway. The androgyne is waiting for her.

'Don't worry,' he says, for the first time showing a little humanity. 'The same thing will happen to others. Or worse. You'll see people who used to get their name shouted out, but who'll walk along the corridor tonight, a smile on their face, waiting for someone to take their photo, only to find that no one bothers.'

She has to stay cool and in control. It wasn't the end of the world; no demons will appear just yet.

'Oh, I'm not worried. After all, I only started today. Who's Jasmine, though?'

'She started today too. It was announced this evening that she's just signed a huge contract with Hamid Hussein, but not to appear in his films, so don't worry.'

She's not worried. She just wishes the earth would open up and swallow her.

8.12 p.m.

Smile.

Pretend you don't know why so many people are interested in your name.

Walk as if you were walking on a red carpet, not a catwalk.

Careful, other people are arriving; your quota of time for photos is over, it's best to keep moving.

However, the photographers insist on calling out her name, and she feels embarrassed because the next in line – a couple, in fact – will have to wait until the photographers are satisfied, which, of course, they never are, always looking for the perfect angle, the unique shot (as if such a thing were possible), the shot of her looking straight into the camera.

Now wave, still smiling, and walk on.

As she reaches the end of the corridor, she's immediately surrounded by a crowd of journalists. They want to know everything about the huge contract she's just signed with one of the best-known couturiers in the world. She'd like to say: 'It's not true,' but instead she says:

'We're still studying the details.'

They insist. A television reporter approaches, microphone in hand and asks if she's happy about the news. She says she thought that afternoon's fashion show had gone off really well and that the designer – and she makes a point of saying her name – will be holding her next show during the Paris Fashion Week.

The journalist doesn't appear to know anything about that afternoon's show, and the questions keep coming, except now she's being filmed.

Don't drop your guard; only give the answers you want to give and not the one they're trying to get out of you. Pretend you don't know the details and just say again how well the show went, about it being a long-overdue tribute to Ann Salens, the forgotten genius who had the misfortune not to be born in France. A young man, who's a bit of a joker, asks how she's enjoying the party; she responds with equal irony: 'Well, if you give me a chance to go in, I'll tell you.' A former model, now working as a presenter on cable TV, asks how she feels about becoming the exclusive face of the next HH collection. A better-informed colleague wants to know if it's true that her salary will be more than six digits.

'They should have put "seven-digit salary" on the press release, don't you think?' he says. 'More than six digits sounds a touch absurd, don't you think? Or even better, they could have said that it's over a million euros, instead of making us count the digits, don't you think? In fact, instead of "six-*digit* salary", they could have said "six-*figure*", don't you think?'

She doesn't *think* anything.

'We're still looking into it,' she says again. 'Now let me get a little air, will you? I'll answer what questions I can later on.'

This, of course, is a complete lie. Later on, she'll get a taxi straight back to the hotel.

Someone asks her why she isn't wearing a Hamid Hussein dress.

'I've always worked for ...' and again she gives the designer's name. Some of reporters there note it down, while others simply ignore it. What they want is a piece of publishable news, not the truth behind the facts.

She's saved by the pace at which things happen at parties like this. In the corridor, the photographers are already shouting out someone else's name. In an orchestrated movement, as if under the baton of an invisible conductor, the journalists surrounding her all turn and see that a bigger, more important celebrity has just arrived. Jasmine takes advantage of this hiatus and heads for the lovely walled garden that has been transformed into a salon where people are drinking, smoking and walking up and down.

Soon she, too, will be able to drink, smoke, look up at the sky, thump the parapet, turn round and leave.

However, a young woman and a very strange-looking creature – like an android out of a science-fiction movie – are staring at her, blocking her path. They clearly don't know what they're doing there either, so she might as well strike up conversation with them. She introduces herself. The strange creature takes his mobile phone out of his pocket, grimaces, and says he'll be back shortly.

The young woman is still staring at her with a look on her face that says 'you ruined my evening'.

Jasmine is sorry she ever accepted tonight's invitation. It was delivered by two men, just as she and her partner were getting ready to go to a small reception put on by the BCA (the Belgian Clothing Association, the body that promotes and regulates fashion in her country). But it's not all bad news. If the photos are published, her dress will be seen, and someone might feel interested enough to find out the designer's name.

The men who delivered the invitation seemed very polite. They said that a limousine was waiting outside and that they were sure a model of her experience would need only fifteen minutes to get ready.

One of them opened a briefcase, took out a laptop and a portable printer, and announced that they were there to close the contract. It was simply a matter of fine-tuning the details. They would fill in the conditions, and her agent – they knew that the woman with her was also her agent – would sign.

They promised her partner every help with her next collection. And yes, of course, she could keep her name on the label and even use their PR service. More than that, HH would like to buy the brand and thus inject the necessary money into it to ensure that she got good coverage in the Italian, French and British press.

There were two conditions. First, the matter had to be decided right there and then, so that they could send a note to the press before the newspapers were put to bed for the night.

Second, she would have to transfer her contract with Jasmine Tiger to Hamid Hussein, for whom Jasmine would then work exclusively. There was, after all, no shortage of models, and the Belgian designer would soon find someone to replace her. Besides, as Jasmine's agent, she would earn a lot of money.

'I agree to the transfer of contract,' her partner said, 'but we'll have to talk about the rest.'

How could she agree so quickly, the woman who was responsible for everything that had happened in her life, and who now seemed perfectly happy to lose her? She was being stabbed in the back by the person she loved most in the world.

One of the men took out his Blackberry.

'We'll send a press release now; in fact, we've written it already: "I'm thrilled to have this opportunity …"'

'Just a minute. *I'm* not thrilled at all. I don't even know what you're talking about.'

Her partner, however, started editing the text, changing 'thrilled' to 'happy' and 'opportunity' to 'invitation'. She studied each word and phrase. She demanded that they mention some absurdly high salary. The men disagreed, saying that this might inflate the market. No deal then, came the reply. The two men left the room to make a phone call and returned almost at once. They would put something vague about a six-digit salary, without mentioning an exact sum. They all shook hands; the two men complimented both the collection and the model, put laptop and printer back in the bag, and asked the designer to record a formal agreement on one of their mobile phones as proof that their negotiations regarding

Jasmine had been successful. They left as quickly as they came, both talking on their mobile phones and, at the same time, urging Jasmine to take no longer than fifteen minutes to get ready; her presence at tonight's party was part of the contract.

'You'd better get ready, then,' said her companion.

'You don't have the power to decide what I do with my life. You know I don't agree, but I wasn't even asked my opinion. I'm not interested in working for anyone else.'

The woman went over to the dresses scattered round the room and chose the most beautiful one – a white dress embroidered with butterflies. She spent a moment considering which shoes and handbag Jasmine should wear; there was no time to lose.

'They didn't say anything about you wearing a dress by HH tonight, which means we have a chance to show off something from my collection.'

Jasmine couldn't believe what she was hearing.

'Is that why you did it?'

'Yes, it is.'

They were standing facing each other and neither of them looked away.

'You're lying.'

'Yes, I'm lying.'

And they fell into each other's arms.

'Ever since that weekend on the beach, when we took those first photographs, I knew this day would come. It took a while, but you're nineteen now and old enough to accept a challenge. Other people have approached me before, but I've always said "No", and I never knew whether it was just that I didn't want to lose you or because you weren't quite ready. Today, though, when I saw Hamid Hussein in the audience, I knew he wasn't there simply to pay tribute to Ann Salens and that he must have something else in mind, and that could only be you. Sure enough, I got a message saying he wanted to talk to us. I didn't know quite what to do, but I gave him the name of our hotel. It was no surprise when those two men arrived with the contract.'

'But why did you accept?'

'If you love someone, you must be prepared to set them free. He can offer you far more than I can, and you have my blessing. I want you to have everything you deserve. We'll still be together because you have my heart, my body and my soul. And I'll keep my independence, although I know how important sponsors can be in this world. If Hamid Hussein had come to me with a proposal to buy my label, I would have had no problem in selling it and going to work for him. However, the deal wasn't about me, it was about you. And if I accepted the part of the proposal involving me, that would mean being untrue to myself.'

She kissed Jasmine.

'Well, I can't accept either,' declared Jasmine. 'I was just a frightened child when I met you, terrified because I'd perjured myself in court, wretched because I'd been responsible for letting criminals go free, and so depressed that I was seriously considering suicide. You're responsible for everything that's happened in my life.'

Her partner asked her to sit down in front of the mirror and, before doing anything else, she tenderly stroked her hair.

'When I met you, I'd lost all my zest for life as well. My husband had left me for someone younger, better-looking and richer, and I was forced to become a photographer to make a living, spending my weekends at home reading, surfing the Internet or watching old films on TV. My great dream of becoming a designer seemed to be moving ever farther off. I couldn't get the necessary financial backing, and I'd had enough of knocking on doors that never opened or talking to people who didn't listen to what I was saying.

'That's when you appeared. And that weekend, I have to confess, I was only thinking about myself. I knew I had a rare jewel in my hands, and could make a fortune if I could get you to sign an exclusive contract with me. I seem to remember that I even suggested I should become your agent. I didn't do that out of a desire to protect you from the world. My thoughts at the time were as selfish as Hamid Hussein's. I would know how to exploit my treasure. I would get rich on those photos.'

She gave a few final touches to Jasmine's hair.

'And you, even though you were only sixteen then, showed me how love can change a person. It was through you that I discovered who I am. In order to show off your talent to the world, I started designing clothes for you to wear, clothes that had been in my head all the time, waiting to be transformed into fabrics, embroidery, accessories. We lived together and, even though I was more than twice your age, we learned together as well. Thanks to all these things, people started noticing what I was doing and decided to invest in it, and, for the first time, I began to realise my dreams. We travelled here to Cannes together, and no contract is going to part us.'

She went to the bathroom to fetch the make-up case. Her tone grew more business-like.

'You need to look really stunning tonight. Models rarely rise to stardom out of nowhere, so there'll be a lot of media interest. Just say you don't know the details yet; that's enough, but they'll keep asking and trying to get you to say things like: "I've always dreamed of working with Hamid Hussein" or "This is a very important step in my career", etc.'

She went with Jasmine down to the hotel lobby, where the waiting chauffeur opened the car door.

'Remember: you don't know the details of the contract yet; your agent is taking care of all that. Enjoy the party.'

* * *

At the party, or rather, supper - although she can see neither tables nor food, only waiters walking about, proffering every possible kind of drink, including mineral water - people form into small groups, and anyone arriving alone looks somewhat lost. The event is taking place in a vast garden furnished with armchairs and sofas; there are also several pillars about three feet high on which half-clothed models with perfect bodies are dancing to the sound of music that emerges out of strategically positioned loudspeakers.

Celebrities continue to arrive. The guests seem happy; they smile and greet each other as if they'd known each other for years, although Jasmine knows this isn't so. They probably meet now and again on occasions like this and always forget each other's names, but they need to show how very influential, famous, admired and well-connected they are.

The young woman who initially looked so angry reveals that she, too, is feeling completely lost. She asks for a cigarette and introduces herself. Within a matter of minutes, they know each other's life story. Jasmine leads her over to the balustrade overlooking the Mediterranean, and while the party fills up with strangers and acquaintances, they stand there gazing out to sea. They discover that they're now working for the same man, although on different projects. Neither of them has ever met him, and for both of them, everything has happened during this one day.

Men occasionally try to engage them in conversation, but Gabriela and Jasmine ignore them. Gabriela is the person Jasmine needed to meet, someone with whom to share her sense of having been abandoned, despite her partner's loving words. If she had to choose between her career and the love of her life, she would choose love over career every time, and she didn't care if such behaviour seemed adolescent. Now it turns out that the love of her life wants her to put her career first and seems to have accepted HH's proposal simply so that she can feel proud of everything she's done for her, of the care with which she's guided her steps and corrected her mistakes, and the enthusiasm she's put into every word spoken and decision taken, however difficult.

Gabriela had needed to meet Jasmine too, to ask her advice, to feel less alone and to see that good things happen to other people too. She confesses that she's worried that her companion has just left her there, when he's supposed to be introducing her to various people she needs to meet.

'He thinks he can hide his feelings, but I know something's wrong.'

Jasmine tells her not to worry, to relax, drink some champagne and enjoy the music and the view. Unforeseen things are always happening, and there's a whole army of people ready to deal with them, so that no one ever finds out what really goes on behind the scenes of all that wealth and glamour. The Star is sure to be here soon.

'But, please, don't leave me on my own, will you? I'm not staying long.'

Gabriela promises that she won't leave her alone. She's her only friend in this new world.

Yes, her only friend, but Jasmine's so young that Gabriela suddenly feels too old to be starting out on a new track. The Star had shown himself to be utterly superficial during the limousine drive to the red carpet; all his charm had vanished. And however much she likes the young girl by her side, she needs to find some new male companion for the night. She notices that the man who came into the bar earlier on is standing, like them, by the balustrade, looking out to sea, his back to the party, oblivious to everything else going on at this gala supper. He's charismatic, handsome, elegant, mysterious. When the opportunity arises, she'll suggest to her new friend that they go over to him and start a conversation, it really doesn't matter what about.

After all – and despite all – this has been her lucky day and it might include finding a new love.

8.21 p.m.

The pathologist, the commissioner, Savoy and a fourth person – who has not been introduced, but who arrived with the commissioner – are sitting round a table.

Their task is not to discuss the latest murder, but to draw up a joint statement to be presented to the journalists gathering outside. This time a really big Star has died, a well-known director is in intensive care, and the news agencies from around the world have obviously sent a stark message to their journalists: either come up with something we can print or you're fired.

'Legal medicine is one of the most ancient of the sciences, involved as it is with identifying poisons and producing antidotes. Nevertheless, in the past, royalty and the nobility always preferred to employ "an official taster", just to avoid any nasty surprises the doctors failed to foresee.'

Savoy had met this 'sage' earlier today. This time, he allows the commissioner to step in and put a stop to the pathologist's erudite lecture.

'That's enough showing off, doctor. There's a criminal on the loose in Cannes.'

The pathologist remains impassive.

'As a pathologist, I don't have the authority to determine the circumstances of a murder. I can't give opinions on the matter; I can only describe the cause of death, the weapon used, the identity of the victim and the approximate time when the crime was committed.'

'Do you see any link between the two deaths? Is there something that connects the murder of the film distributor and the actor?'

'Of course. They both worked in the movies.'

He chuckles, but no one else moves a muscle. They clearly have no sense of humour.

'The only connection is that, in both cases, toxic substances were used, both of which affect the organism with extraordinary speed. What is really intriguing about the second murder, though, is the way in which the hydrogen cyanide was wrapped. The envelope had inside it a fine plastic membrane vacuum-sealed, but easily torn when the envelope was opened.'

'Could it have been made here?' asks the fourth man, who has a strong foreign accent.

'Possibly, but I doubt it, because its actual manufacture is very complex, and the person who made it knew that it would be used to murder someone.'

'So the murderer didn't make it?'

'I doubt it. A specialist group would almost certainly have been commissioned to produce it. In the case of the curare, the criminal himself could have dipped the needle in the poison, but hydrogen cyanide requires special techniques.'

Savoy's thoughts immediately go to Marseilles, Corsica, Sicily, certain Eastern European countries and terrorist groups in the Middle East. He leaves the room for a moment and phones Europol. He explains the gravity of the situation and asks them for a complete run-down on laboratories equipped to produce chemical weapons of that type.

He's put through to someone who tells him that they've just had a call from an American intelligence agency asking exactly the same thing. What's going on?

'Nothing. But please get back to me as soon as you have any information – in the next ten minutes at the latest.'

'That's impossible,' says the voice on the other end. 'We'll give you the answer as soon as we have it. We'll have to put in a request ...'

Savoy hangs up and rejoins the group.

More paper.

This appears to be an obsession common to everyone working in the field of public security. No one wants to risk taking a step without first having a guarantee that their superiors approve of what they're doing. Men who once had a brilliant career ahead of them and began working with creativity and enthusiasm now cower fearfully in a corner, knowing the enormous problems they face: they need to act swiftly, but, at the same time, the hierarchy of command must be respected; the media are always quick to accuse the police of brutality, while the tax-payers complain that crimes are never solved. For all these reasons, it's always best to pass responsibility on to someone higher up.

His telephone call was really just a bit of play-acting. He knows who the killer is, and he alone will catch him; he doesn't want anyone else snatching from him the glory of having solved the biggest murder case in the history of Cannes. He must keep calm, but he's nevertheless impatient for this meeting to end.

When he goes back into the room, the commissioner informs him that Stanley Morris, formerly of Scotland Yard, has just phoned from Monte Carlo, telling them not to worry because he very much doubts that the criminal will use the same weapon again.

'We could be facing a new terror threat,' says the foreigner.

'Yes, possibly,' replies the commissioner, 'but unlike you, the last thing we want to do is sow fear among the population. What we need to do is draw up a press statement to prevent journalists from leaping to their own conclusions and broadcasting them on tonight's TV news. This is an isolated terrorist incident, and may involve a serial killer.'

'But …'

'There are no "buts".' The commissioner's voice is firm and authoritative. 'We contacted your embassy because the dead man comes from your country. You are here at our invitation. In the case of the two other Americans murdered, you showed no interest at all in sending a representative, even though in one case poison was also used. So, if you're trying to insinuate that we're facing some kind of collective threat in which biological weapons are being used, you can leave now. We're not going to turn a criminal matter into something political. We want to have another Festival next year with all the usual glitz and glamour, so we're taking Dr Morris's advice and will draw up a statement along those lines.'

The foreigner says nothing.

The commissioner summons an assistant and asks him to tell the waiting journalists that they will have their conclusions in ten minutes. The pathologist tells him that it's always possible to track down the origin of hydrogen cyanide because it leaves a kind of 'signature', but tracking it down will take not ten minutes, but a week.

'There were traces of alcohol in the body. The skin was red, and death was almost instantaneous. There's no doubt about which poison was used. If it had been an acid, we would have found burns around the nose and mouth, and in the case of belladonna, the pupils would have been dilated, and …'

'Please, doctor, we know that you studied at university and are therefore equipped to tell us the cause of death, and we have no doubts about your competence in the field. Let us conclude that it was hydrogen cyanide.'

The doctor nods and bites his lip, controlling his irritation.

'And what about the other man, who's currently in hospital. The film director …'

'We're treating him with pure oxygen, six hundred mg of Kelocyanor via intravenous drip every fifteen minutes, and if that doesn't work, we can add sodium triosulphate diluted in twenty-five per cent …'

The silence in the room is palpable.

'… Sorry. The answer is, yes, he'll survive.'

The commissioner makes some notes on a sheet of yellow paper. He knows that he's run out of time. He thanks everyone, and asks the foreigner not to come out with them, so as to avoid any further needless speculation. He goes to the bathroom, adjusts his tie and asks Savoy to adjust his as well.

'Morris says that the murderer won't use poison next time. From what I've gleaned, the killer is following a pattern, although it may be an unconscious one. Do you know what it is?'

Savoy had thought about this as he was driving back from Monte Carlo. Yes, there was a pattern, which possibly not even the great Scotland Yard inspector had noticed. It was this:

The victim on the bench: the murderer was close.
The victim at the lunch: the murderer was far away.
The victim on the beach: the murderer was close.
The victim at the hotel: the murderer was far away.

Therefore, the next crime will be committed with the murderer at his victim's side, or, rather, that will be his plan, unless he's arrested in the next half hour. He learned all this from his colleagues at the police station, who gave him the information as if it were of no importance. And Savoy, in turn, had initially dismissed it as irrelevant too, but, of course, it wasn't; it was the missing link, the vital clue, the one piece needed to complete the puzzle.

His heart is pounding. He's dreamed of this all his life and cannot wait for this interminable meeting to end.

'Are you listening?'

'Yes, sir.'

'Look, the people out there aren't expecting some official, technical statement, with precise answers to their questions. The fact is they'll do all they can to make us say what they want to hear, but we mustn't fall into that trap. They came here not to listen to us, but to look at us, and for their viewers and readers to be able to see us too.'

He regards Savoy with a superior air, as if he were the most knowledgeable person on the planet. It would seem that Morris and the pathologist are not the only ones who like to show off their knowledge; well, everyone has their own way of saying: 'I know my job.'

'Think visual, by which I mean, remember that your face and body say more than words. Look straight ahead, keep your head up, and your shoulders down and slightly back. Raised shoulders mean tension and are a sure indication that we have no idea what is going on.'

'Yes, sir.'

They walk out to the entrance of the Institute of Legal Medicine. Lights come on, microphones are thrust forward, people start to push. After a few minutes, this apparent disorder becomes more orderly. The commissioner takes the piece of paper out of his pocket.

'The actor was killed with hydrogen cyanide, a deadly poison that can be administered in various ways, although in this case it was used in the form of a gas. The film director survived the attack. His involvement was clearly accidental. He merely happened to enter the room while there were still remnants of the gas in the air. The CCTV footage shows a man walking down the corridor, going into one of the rooms and, five minutes later, coming out again and falling to the floor.'

He omits to say that the room in question is not actually visible to the camera. Omission is no lie.

'The security personnel took swift action and sent for a doctor, who immediately noticed the smell of almonds, which was, by then, too diluted to cause any harm. The police were called, and they arrived at the scene less than five minutes later and cordoned off the area. An ambulance came, and the doctors used oxygen to save the director's life.'

Savoy is beginning to feel really impressed by the commissioner's easy manner. He wonders if all commissioners have to do a course in public relations.

'The poison was delivered in an envelope, but we have not as yet been able to establish whether the writing on the envelope was that of a man or a woman. Inside was a piece of paper.'

He fails to mention that the technology used to seal the envelope was highly sophisticated. There was a chance in a million that one of the journalists present would know this, although, later on, that kind of question would become inevitable. He also fails to mention that another man in the film industry had been poisoned that same afternoon. Apparently, everyone thinks he died of a heart attack, although no one has actually told them this. Sometimes it's handy if the press – out of laziness or inattention – draw their own conclusions without bothering the police.

'What was on the paper?' is the first question.

The commissioner explains that he cannot reveal this now because doing so might hamper the investigation. Savoy is beginning to see the direction in which he's leading this interview and is filled with admiration; he really deserves his post as commissioner.

'Could it have been a crime of passion?' asks someone else.

'Anything is possible at the moment. Now, if you'll excuse me, ladies and gentlemen, we must get back to work.'

He gets into his car, turns on the siren and speeds away. Savoy walks to his own vehicle, feeling very proud of his boss. How amazing! He can imagine the headlines already: 'Star thought to have been victim of crime of passion.'

That was sure to capture people's interest. The power of celebrity was so great that the other murders would go unnoticed. Who cares about a poor young girl, who died possibly under the influence of drugs and was found on a bench near the beach? What did it matter if some henna-haired film distributor had a heart attack over lunch? What was there to say about a murder – another crime of passion – involving two complete nonentities who were never in the spotlight, on a beach away from all the hurly-burly of the Festival? It was the kind of thing that appeared every night on the television news, but the media would only continue speculating about it if a Major Celebrity was involved! And an envelope! And a piece of paper inside on which something was written!

He turns on the siren and drives in the opposite direction from the police station. In order not to raise suspicions, he uses the car radio. He finds the commissioner's frequency.

'Congratulations!'

The commissioner is also rather pleased with himself. They've gained a few hours, possibly days, but they both know that they're dealing with a serial killer of the male sex, well-dressed, with greying hair and about forty years old, and armed with sophisticated weapons. A man who is also experienced in the art of killing, and while he may be satisfied with the crimes he's already committed, he could easily strike again, at any moment.

'Have officers sent to all the Festival parties,' orders the commissioner. 'They should look out for any men on their own who correspond to that description. Tell them to keep any suspects under surveillance. Call for reinforcements. I want plain-clothes policemen, discreetly dressed and in keeping with their surroundings – either jeans or evening dress. And I repeat, I want them at all the parties, even if we have to mobilise the traffic police as well.'

Savoy immediately does as he is told. He has just received a message on his mobile phone. Europol needs more time to track down the laboratories, at least three days.

'Let me have that in writing, will you? I don't want to be held responsible if something else goes wrong here.'

He chuckles quietly. He asks them to send a copy to the foreign agent as well, since he himself is no longer interested in the matter. He drives as fast as he can to the Hotel Martinez, leaves his car at the entrance, blocking other people's vehicles. When the porter complains, he shows him his policeman's ID, throws him the keys so that he can park the car somewhere else and runs into the hotel.

He goes up to a private room on the first floor, where a police officer is waiting, along with the duty manager and a waiter.

'How much longer are we going to have to stay here?' asks the duty manager. Savoy ignores her and turns to the waiter.

'Are you sure that the murdered woman, whose picture appeared on the news, is the same woman who was sitting on the terrace this afternoon?'

'Yes, sir, pretty much. She looks younger in the photo with her hair dyed, but I'm used to remembering guests' faces, just in case one of them tries to leave without paying.'

'And are you sure she was with the male guest who reserved the table earlier?'

'Absolutely. A good-looking man of about forty, with greying hair.'

Savoy's heart almost leaps out of his mouth. He turns to the manager and the policeman.

'Let's go straight up to his room.'

'Do you have a search warrant?' asks the manager.

Savoy's nerves snap:

'*No I haven't*! And I'm not filling in any more forms! Do you know what's wrong with this country, madam? We're all too obedient! In fact, that isn't a problem peculiar to us, it applies to the whole world! Wouldn't you obey if they wanted to send your son off to war? Wouldn't your son obey? Of course! Well, since you are an obedient citizen, either take me to that room or I'll have you arrested for aiding and abetting!'

The woman seems genuinely frightened. With the other policeman, they make their way over to the lift, which is coming down, stopping at every floor, unaware that a human life may depend on the speed with which those waiting for it can act.

They decide to take the stairs instead. The manager complains because she's wearing high heels, but Savoy simply tells her to take off her shoes and go up the stairs barefoot. They race up the marble stairs, gripping the bronze banister so as not to fall and passing various elegant waiting areas on the way. The people there wonder who this barefoot woman is, and what a uniformed policeman is doing in the hotel, running up the stairs like that. Has something bad happened? If so, why don't they take the lift? Standards at the Festival are definitely dropping, they say to themselves; hotels aren't as selective about their guests as they once were; and the police treat the place as if they were raiding a brothel. As soon as they can, they will complain to the manager, who, unbeknown to them, is the same barefoot woman they've just seen bounding up the stairs.

Savoy and the duty manager finally reach the door of the suite where the murderer is staying. A member of the 'security squad' has already sent someone up to find out what's going on. He recognises the manager and asks if he can help.

Savoy asks him to speak more quietly, but yes, he can help. Is he armed? The guard says that he is.

'Then you'd better stay here.'

They are talking in whispers. The manager is instructed to knock on the door, while the three men – Savoy, the policeman and the security guard – stand to one side, backs to the wall. Savoy takes his gun out of his holster. The other policeman does the same. The manager knocks several times, but gets no answer.

'He must have gone out.'

Savoy asks her to use the master key. She explains that she doesn't have it with her, and even if she did, she would only open that door with the authorisation of the managing director.

Savoy responds politely this time:

'No matter. I'll go downstairs and wait in the surveillance room with the security staff. He'll be back sooner or later, and I'd like to be the first to question him.'

'We have a photocopy of his passport and his credit-card number downstairs. Why are you so interested in him?'

'Oh, no matter.'

9.02 p.m.

Half an hour's drive from Cannes, in another country where they speak the same language, use the same currency and have no border controls, but where they have a completely different political system from France – it's ruled by a prince, like in the olden days – a man is sitting in front of a computer. Fifteen minutes ago, he received an e-mail informing him that a famous actor had been murdered.

Morris studies the photo of the victim. He hasn't been to the cinema for ages and so has no idea who he is. However, he must be someone important because there are reports of his death on one of the news portals.

Morris may be retired, but things like this used to be the equivalent of a chess game to him, a game in which he rarely allowed his opponent to win. It wasn't his career that was at risk now, it was his self-esteem.

There are certain rules he always liked to follow when he worked for Scotland Yard, one of which was to come up with as many flawed hypotheses as he could. This freed up your mind because you weren't necessarily expecting to get it right. At the tedious meetings with work evaluation committees, he used to enjoy provoking the people present: 'Everything you know comes from experience accumulated over long years of work. However, those old solutions are only of use when applied to old problems. If you want to be creative, try to forget that you have all that experience.'

The older members of such committees would pretend they were taking notes, the younger ones would stare at him in horror, and the meeting would continue as if he had said nothing. But he knew that the message had been received loud and clear, and soon afterwards, his superiors – without giving him any of the credit, of course – would start demanding more new ideas.

He prints out the files sent by the police in Cannes. He normally tries to avoid using paper because he doesn't want to be accused of being a serial killer of forests, but sometimes it's necessary.

He starts studying the modus operandi, that is, the way the crimes were committed. Time of day (morning, afternoon and night), weapons (hands, poison, stiletto knife), type of victim (men and women of different ages), closeness to victim (two involved direct physical contact, two involved no contact at all), the reaction of victims to their aggressor (none in all cases).

When he feels that he's faced by a dead end, the best thing is to let his thoughts wander for a while, while his unconscious mind goes to work. He opens a new screen on the computer, showing the New York Stock Exchange. Since he has no money invested in shares, it couldn't be more boring, but that's how it works: his years of experience analyse all the information he has received so far and his intuition comes up with new, creative responses. Twenty minutes later, he goes back to the files, and his head is once again empty.

The process has worked. The murders do have things in common.

The murderer is an educated man. He must have spent days and weeks in a library, studying the best way to carry out his mission. He knows how to handle poisons and obviously hadn't touched the hydrogen cyanide himself. He knows enough about anatomy to be able to stick a knife in at exactly the right place without meeting a bone, and to kill someone with his bare hands. He knows about curare and its lethal power. He may have read about serial killings, and would be aware that some kind of 'signature' always leads the police to the attacker, and so he had committed his murders in a completely random manner, with no fixed modus operandi at all.

But that's impossible. The unconscious mind of the murderer is bound to leave some signature, which Morris has not yet managed to decipher.

There's something more important still: he obviously has money, enough to follow a course in Sambo, in order to be absolutely sure which points on the body he needs to press in order to paralyse his victim. He also has contacts: he didn't buy those poisons from the corner pharmacist, not even from the local criminal underworld. They are highly sophisticated biological weapons, which require great care in their handling and application. He must have got other people to acquire them for him.

Finally, he works very quickly, which leads Morris to conclude that the murderer won't be staying long. Perhaps a week, possibly a few days more.

Where does all this take him?

The reason he can't reach a conclusion now is because he's got used to the rules of the game. He has lost the innocence he always demanded of his subordinates. That's what the world does to people; gradually, over the years, we become mediocre beings, concerned not to be seen as weird or over-enthusiastic. Old age is considered a stigma, not a sign of wisdom. People assume that no one over fifty can keep up with the speed of change nowadays.

True, he can't run as fast as he could and needs reading glasses, but his mind is as sharp as ever, or so at least he wants to believe.

What about this crime though? If he's as intelligent as he thinks, why can't he solve something that seems so easy?

He can't get any further at the moment. He'll have to wait until the next victim appears.

9.11 p.m.

A couple pass by. They smile and congratulate him on his luck at having two such lovely ladies by his side!

Igor thanks them, for he's genuinely in need of distraction. Soon the long-awaited meeting will take place, and although he's accustomed to all kinds of pressure, he reminds himself of the patrols he had to go on near Kabul and how, before any very dangerous mission, he and his colleagues would drink and talk about women and sport, chatting away as if they weren't in Afghanistan, but were back in their home towns, sitting round a table with family and friends. It was a way of quelling their nerves and recovering their true identities, and thus feeling better prepared for the challenges they would face the next day.

Like any good soldier, he knows that battles have more to do with aims and objectives than with the actual fighting. Like any good strategist – he did, after all, build up his company from nothing to become one of the most respected in Russia – he knows that one's objective should always remain the same, even if the motive behind it may change over time. That is what has happened today: he arrived in Cannes for one reason, but only when he began to act did he understand the true motives behind what he was doing. He has been blind all these years, but now he can see the light; the revelation has finally come.

And precisely because of this, he needs to keep going. The decisions he made required courage, a degree of detachment and, at times, even a little madness, not the kind of madness that destroys, but the sort that carries a person beyond his own limits. He's always been the same and has won through precisely because he knew how to use that controlled madness whenever he had to make a decision. His friends would move with astonishing speed from saying 'It's too risky' to 'I always knew you were doing the right thing'. He was capable of surprising people, of coming up with fresh ideas and, above all, of taking any necessary risks.

Here in Cannes, though – perhaps because he's in an unfamiliar place and still befuddled by lack of sleep – he has taken quite unnecessary risks, risks that might have forced him to abort his plan earlier than expected. Had that happened, he would never have reached his present clear-eyed position, one that cast an entirely different light on the woman he thought of as his beloved and whom he believed merited both sacrifice and martyrdom. He remembers the moment when he went up to the policeman to confess. That was when the change began. It was then that the spirit of the girl with the dark eyebrows began to protect him and to explain that he was doing the right things but for the wrong reasons. Accumulating love brings luck, accumulating hatred brings disaster. Anyone who stands outside the Door of Problems and fails to recognise it may well end up leaving it open and allowing tragedies to enter.

He had accepted the young girl's love. He had been an instrument of God, sent to rescue her from a dark future; now she was helping him to carry on.

He is aware, too, that, regardless of the many precautions he may have taken, he could not possibly have thought of everything, and his mission might yet be interrupted before he reaches the end. There is no reason, however, for regret or fear; he has done what he could, behaved impeccably, and, if God does not wish him to complete his task, then he must accept His decisions.

Relax, he tells himself. Talk to the young women by your side. Let your muscles rest a little before the final strike; that way, they'll be more prepared. Gabriela – the young woman who was alone at the bar when he arrived – seems very excited, and whenever the waiter comes by with more drinks, she hands over her glass, even if it's still half full, and picks up a fresh one.

'I love it when it's really icy!' she says.

Her happiness infects him a little too. Apparently, she's just signed a contract to appear in a film, although she knows neither the title of the film nor what role she'll be playing, but she will, in her words, be 'the leading lady'. The director is known for his ability to choose good actors and good scripts, and the leading actor, whom Igor knows and admires, certainly merits respect. When she mentions the name of the producer, he merely nods knowledgeably, as if to say, 'Yes, of course, I know who he is', aware that she'll interpret the nod as meaning: 'I've no idea who he is, but I don't want to appear ignorant.' She babbles on about rooms full of gifts, the red carpet, her meeting on the yacht, the rigorous selection process she went through, future projects …

'At this very moment, there are thousands of young women in Cannes and millions around the world who would like to be here tonight, talking to you and being able to tell these stories. My prayers have been answered and all my efforts rewarded.'

The other young woman seems more discreet, but sadder too, perhaps because of her youth and lack of experience. Igor had been there when she walked down the corridor and had heard the photographers calling out her name and clamouring to ask her questions afterwards. Apparently, though, the other people at the party had no idea who she was; she had been so in demand at the start, and then, just as suddenly, had been dropped.

It was probably the talkative young woman who had decided to come over to him and ask him what he was doing there. At first, he'd felt rather constrained, but he knew that if they hadn't approached him, other solitary people would have done so, to avoid the impression that they were lost and alone and with no friends at the party. That's why he welcomed their conversation or, rather, their company, even though his mind was elsewhere. He told them his name was Gunther and explained that he was a German industrialist specialising in heavy machinery (a subject guaranteed to interest no one) and had been invited there by friends. He would be leaving tomorrow (which he hoped would be true, but God moves in mysterious ways).

When the actress learned that he didn't work in the film industry and wouldn't be staying long at the Festival, she almost moved away; however, the other girl stopped her, saying that it's always good to meet new people. And so there they are: he waiting for the friend who showed no signs of arriving, the actress waiting for her vanished assistant and the quiet girl waiting for absolutely nothing, just a little peace.

Suddenly, the actress notices some fluff on his dinner jacket, and before he can stop her, she reaches out to brush it away. She says:

'Oh, do you smoke cigars?'

That's a relief, she thinks the object in his inside jacket pocket is a cigar.

'Yes, but only after supper.'

'If you like, I could invite you both to a party on a yacht tonight. But first I need to find my assistant.'

The other girl suggests that maybe she's being a little precipitate. She has only been signed up for one film and has a long way to go before she can surround herself with friends (or with an 'entourage', that word universally used to describe the parasites who hover around celebrities). She should respect the rules and go to the party alone.

The actress thanks her for this advice. Then a waiter passes, and she again places her half-empty glass of champagne on the tray and takes a full one.

'I think you should stop drinking so much so quickly,' says Igor/Gunther, delicately taking the glass from her and pouring the contents over the balustrade. She makes a despairing gesture, then accepts that he's right, realising that he has her best interests at heart.

'I'm just so excited,' she says.'I need to calm down a little. Do you think I could smoke one of your cigars?'

'I'm afraid I only have one. Besides, it's been scientifically proven that nicotine is a stimulant, not a tranquilliser.'

A cigar. Well, they are similar in shape, but that's all the two objects have in common. In his inside jacket pocket he has a suppressor, or as it's more commonly known, a silencer. It's about four inches long and, once attached to the barrel of the Beretta he has in his trouser pocket, it can work miracles, by changing BANG! into *puf*.

This is because when a gun is fired a few simple laws of physics come into effect. The speed of the bullet is slightly diminished as it's forced past a series of rubber baffles; meanwhile the gases produced by the firing of the gun fill the hollow chamber around the cylinder, cool rapidly and suppress the noise of the gunpowder exploding. A silencer is useless for long-range shooting because it affects the trajectory of the bullet, but it's ideal for firing at point-blank range.

Igor is beginning to grow impatient. Could Ewa and her husband have cancelled their invitation? Or could it be – and for a fraction of a second his head swims – that he had slipped the envelope under the door to the suite in which they were staying?

No, that's not possible; that would be such a stroke of bad luck. He thinks of the families of those who have died. If his sole objective was still to win back the woman who left him for a man who did not deserve her, all his work would have been in vain.

His composure begins to crack. Could that be why Ewa hasn't attempted to contact him, despite all the messages he's sent her? He has twice rung their mutual friend, only to be told there was no news.

His doubt is beginning to become a certainty. Yes, the couple were both dead. That would explain the sudden departure of the actress's 'assistant' and why no one was bothering with the nineteen-year-old model who was supposed to appear at the great couturier's side.

Was God punishing him for having loved a woman he did not deserve and had loved too much? His ex-wife had used his hands to strangle a young woman who had her whole life ahead of her, who might have gone on to discover a cure for cancer or a way of making humanity realise that it was destroying the planet. Ewa may have known nothing about the murder, but she it was who had made him use those poisons. He had been sure that he would only have to destroy one world and that the message would reach its intended recipient. He had taken that whole small arsenal with him knowing it was all just a game, certain that on the first night, she would go to the bar for a glass of champagne before joining the party, sense his presence there, and realise that she had been forgiven for all the evil and destruction she had unleashed around her. He knows that, according to scientific research, people who have spent a lot of time together can sense their partner's presence in a place, even if they don't know exactly where they are.

That didn't happen. Ewa's indifference last night – or perhaps her guilt at what she had done to him – had prevented her from noticing the man trying to hide behind a pillar, but who had left on the table various Russian economics journals, which should have been a large enough clue for anyone who was constantly looking for what she had lost. When you're in love you imagine that you'll see the love of your life everywhere – in the street, at a party or in the theatre, but Ewa had perhaps exchanged love for a life of glamour.

He's beginning to feel calmer now. Ewa was the most powerful poison on earth, and if she had been killed by hydrogen cyanide, that was nothing. She deserved far worse.

The two young women continue talking; Igor moves away from them; he cannot allow himself to be overwhelmed by the fear that he might have destroyed his own work. He needs solitude, calm, the ability to react swiftly to this sudden change in direction.

He goes over to another group of people who are animatedly discussing various methods of giving up smoking. This was one of the favourite topics in that particular world: showing your friends that you had the necessary will-power to defeat the foe. To take his mind off other things, he lights a cigarette, knowing full well that this is a provocative act.

'It's very bad for your health, you know,' says a skeletally thin woman dripping with diamonds and holding an orange juice in one hand.

'Just being alive is bad for the health,' he replies. 'It always ends in death sooner or later.'

The men laugh. The women eye this newcomer with interest. However, just at that moment, in the corridor – about twenty yards away from where he's standing – the photographers start shouting:

'Hamid! Hamid!'

Even from a distance, and with his view blocked by the people strolling about in the garden, he can see the couturier and his companion, the same woman who, in other parts of the world, had walked into rooms with him, the same woman who used to hold his arm in that same affectionate, delicate, elegant way.

Even before he has time to utter a sigh of relief, something else attracts his attention and makes him look away: a man has just entered from the other side of the garden without being stopped by any of the security guards. The man glances this way and that, as if searching for someone, but that someone is clearly not a friend lost in the throng.

Without saying goodbye to the group he's with, Igor goes back to the two young women, who are still standing by the balustrade, talking. He takes the actress's hand in his and makes a silent prayer to the girl with the dark eyebrows. He asks forgiveness for having doubted, but we human beings are still so impure, incapable of understanding the blessings so generously bestowed on us.

'You're moving a bit fast, aren't you?' says the actress, making no attempt to move away.

'Yes, I am, but given what you've been telling me, everything in your life is moving fast today.'

She laughs. The sad girl laughs too. The policeman passes by without noticing him. He's been told to look out for men in their forties with slightly greying hair, but for men on their own.

9.20 p.m.

Doctors look at test results which are completely at odds with what they believe the actual illness to be, and must then decide whether to trust science or their heart. They learn, with time and experience, to give more weight to their instincts and they find that the outcomes for their patients improve.

Successful businessmen pore over graphs and diagrams, then go completely against the market trend and grow still richer.

Artists write books or films about which everyone says: 'That won't work. No one's interested in things like that', and end up becoming icons of popular culture.

Religious leaders preach fear and guilt rather than love, which should, in theory, be the most important thing in the world, and their congregations swell.

Only one group consistently fails to go against the current trend: politicians. They want to please everyone and stick rigidly to the rules of political correctness. They end up having to resign, apologise or contradict themselves.

Morris keeps opening one window after another on his computer. This has nothing to do with technology, but with intuition. He's tried distracting himself with the Dow Jones index, but wasn't pleased with the results. It would be best to focus a little on some of the characters he's lived with for much of his life.

He looks again at the video in which Gary Ridgway, the Green River Killer, is describing in a calm voice how he killed 48 women, most of them prostitutes. Ridgway is doing this not because he wants absolution for his sins or to relieve his conscience; the public prosecutor has offered to commute his death sentence to life imprisonment if he confesses, for despite having acted with impunity for a long time, Ridgway had left insufficient evidence to convict him. Or perhaps he had just grown weary of the macabre task he had set himself.

Ridgway had a steady job spraying trucks and could only remember his victims by relating them to whether or not he had been working that day. For twenty years, sometimes with more than fifty detectives on his trail, he managed to commit murder after murder without ever leaving any kind of signature or clue. One of the detectives on the tape comments that Ridgway wasn't very bright, wasn't too good at his job or very educated, but was a perfect killer.

In short, he was born to be a killer, even though he had always lived in the same place. His case, at one point, was even filed away as insoluble.

Morris has watched this same video hundreds of times. It has, in the past, given him the necessary inspiration to solve other cases, but not today. He closes down that window and opens another, which shows a letter written by the father of Jeffrey Dahmer, 'The Milwaukee Cannibal', who was responsible for killing and dismembering seventeen men between 1978 and 1991:

Initially, of course, I couldn't believe that it was really Jeff who had done the things the police had accused him of. How could anyone believe that his son could do such things? I had been in the actual places where they said he had done them. I had been in rooms and basements which at other moments, according to the police, had been nothing less than a slaughterhouse. I had looked in my son's refrigerator and seen only a scattering of milk cartons and soda cans. I had leaned casually on the black table they claimed my son had used both as a dissecting table and a bizarre satanic altar. How was it possible that all of this had been hidden from me – not only the horrible physical evidence of my son's crimes, but the dark nature of the man who had committed them, this child I had held in my arms a thousand times, and whose face, when I glimpsed it in the newspapers, looked like mine? If the police had told me that my son was dead, I would have thought differently about him. If they'd told me that a strange man had lured him to a seedy apartment, and a few minutes later, drugged, strangled, then sexually assaulted and mutilated his dead body – in other words, if they'd told me the same horrible things that they had to tell so many other fathers and mothers in July of 1991 – then I would have done what they have done. I would have mourned my son and demanded that the man who'd killed him be profoundly punished. If not executed, then separated forever from the rest of us. After that, I would have tried to think of my son warmly. I would, I hope, have visited his grave from time to time, spoken of him with loss and affection, continued, as much as possible, to be the custodian of his memory. But I wasn't told what these other mothers and fathers were told, that their sons were dead at the hands of a murderer. Instead, I was told that my son was the one who had murdered their sons.

A satanic altar. Charles Manson and his 'family'. In 1969, three people burst into a house occupied by a film star and killed everyone there, including a young man who happened to be driving away from the house. Two more murders followed on the next day: a married couple, both of whom were business people. Manson claimed to be capable of killing the whole of humanity.

For the thousandth time, Morris looks at the photo of the man behind those crimes, smiling at the camera, surrounded by hippy friends, including a famous pop musician of the day. They all seem perfectly harmless, talking about peace and love.

He closes down all the windows. Manson is the closest thing to what is happening now, involving as it does the cinema and well-known victims. A kind of political manifesto against luxury, consumerism and celebrity. Manson, however, was only the brains behind the killings; he didn't actually murder anyone himself; he left that to his acolytes.

No, that's not it. And despite the e-mails he has sent, explaining that he can't provide answers in such a short space of time, Morris is beginning to experience what all detectives always feel about serial killers: it's becoming a personal matter.

On the one hand, there's a man, doubtless with some other profession, who, given the weapons he uses, has clearly planned the murders in advance, but who is on entirely unfamiliar territory, where he has no knowledge of the competence or otherwise of the local police force. He is, therefore, a vulnerable man. On the other hand, there's the accumulated experience of all kinds of security organisations accustomed to dealing with society's aberrants, but apparently incapable of stopping the bloody trail left by this rank amateur.

He should never have responded to the commissioner's call. He had decided to live on the Mediterranean because the climate was better, the people more amusing, the sea close at hand and because he hoped that he still had many years ahead of him in which to be able to enjoy life's pleasures.

He had left his job in London with a reputation for being the best. And now this one failure would be sure to reach the ears of his colleagues, and he would lose that reputation earned through hard work and great dedication. They'll say: 'He was the first person to insist that modern computers be installed in our department, but despite all the technology at his disposal, he's simply too old to keep up with the challenges of a new age.'

He presses the off button. The software logo comes up and then the screen goes blank. Inside the machine, the electronic impulses disappear from the fixed memory and leave no feeling of guilt, remorse or impotence.

His body has no off buttons. The circuits in his brain keep working, always arriving at the same conclusions, trying to justify the unjustifiable, bruising his self-esteem, telling him that his colleagues are right: perhaps his instincts and his capacity for analysis *have* been affected by age.

He goes into the kitchen, turns on the espresso machine, which has been giving him problems lately. As with any modern domestic appliance, it's usually cheaper to throw the old one out and buy a new one. Fortunately, the machine decides to work this time, and he sips the resulting cup of coffee unhurriedly. A large part of his day involves pressing buttons: computer, printer, phone, lights, stove, coffee-maker, fax machine.

Now, though, he needs to press the right button in his brain. There's no point in rereading the documents sent through by the police. He needs to think laterally and make a list, however repetitive.

(a) The murderer is fairly well educated and sophisticated, at least as regards the weapons he uses. And he knows how to use them.
(b) He's not from the area; if he was, he would have chosen a better time to come, when there were fewer police around.
(c) He doesn't leave any clear signature, so he obviously has no desire to be identified. This may seem self-evident, but such 'signatures' are often a desperate way of the Doctor trying to put a stop to the evils committed by the Monster, as if Dr Jekyll were saying: 'Please arrest me. I'm a danger to society, and I can't control myself.'
(d) The fact that he was able to approach at least two of his victims, look them in the eye and find out a little about

them means that he's used to killing without remorse. Therefore, he must, at some time, have fought in a war.

(e) He must have money, a lot of money, not just because Cannes is a very expensive place to stay during the Festival, but because of the high cost of producing the envelope containing the hydrogen cyanide. He must have paid around $5,000 in all – $40 for the poison and $4,460 for the packaging.

(f) He's not part of the drugs mafia or involved in arms trafficking or that kind of thing; if he was, Europol would be on to him. Contrary to what most such criminals believe, the only reason they haven't been caught is because it isn't yet the right time for them to be put behind bars. Their groups are regularly infiltrated by agents who are paid a fortune for their work.

(g) He doesn't want to be caught, and so he's very careful. On the other hand, he can't control his unconscious mind and is, unwittingly, following a set pattern.

(h) He appears to be completely normal and unlikely to arouse suspicion; he may even be kind and friendly, capable of gaining the confidence of the people he lures to their death. He spends some time with his victims, two of whom were women, who tend to be more trusting than men.

(i) He doesn't choose his victims. They could be men or women of any age or social class.

Morris pauses for a moment. There's something that doesn't fit with the rest.

He rereads the list two or three times. On the fourth reading, he spots the flaw.

(c) He doesn't leave any clear signature, so he obviously has no desire to be identified.

This murderer isn't trying to cleanse the world as Manson was, or, like Ridgway, to purify his home town; he's not trying, like Dahmer, to satisfy the appetite of the gods. Most criminals don't want to be caught, but they do want to be identified, some in order to hit the headlines and gain fame and glory, like Zodiac or Jack the Ripper. Others perhaps think their grandchildren will be proud of what they did when, years later, they discover a dusty diary in the attic. Others have a mission to fulfil: for example, driving away prostitutes by making them too afraid to walk the streets. Psychoanalysts have concluded that when serial killers suddenly stop murdering from one moment to the next, it's because they feel that the message they've been trying to send has finally been received.

Of course, that's it! Why hadn't he thought of it before?

For one simple reason: because it would have sent the police hunt off in two different directions, in search of the murderer *and* the person to whom he was sending the messages. And this Cannes murderer is killing people very fast. Morris is almost sure that he will stop soon, once the message has been received. In two or three days at most. And as with other serial killers whose victims appear to have nothing in common, the message must be intended for one person, just one.

He goes back to the computer, turns it on and sends a reassuring e-mail to the commissioner.

'Don't worry, the murders will stop soon, before the Festival is over.'

Just for the hell of it, he copies the e-mail to a friend in Scotland Yard, as a way of letting him know that the French authorities respect him as a professional, have asked for his help and received it; that he's still capable of reaching conclusions which will, later on, prove correct; that he's not as old as they would like to think.

His reputation is at stake, but he's sure his conclusion is the right one.

10.19 p.m.

Hamid turns off his mobile phone. He isn't the slightest bit interested in what's going on in the rest of the world, and in the last half hour, his phone has been inundated with grim messages.

It's a sign that he should ditch the whole absurd idea of producing a film. He had clearly allowed himself to be carried away by vanity instead of listening to the advice of the sheikh and of his own wife. He's starting to lose touch with himself; the world of luxury and glamour is beginning to poison him, something he had always believed would never happen.

Tomorrow, when things have calmed down, he'll call a press conference for the world media present in Cannes and tell them that, despite having already invested a large amount of money in the project, he's decided to pull out because it was 'a dream shared by all those involved, one of whom is no longer with us'. A journalist is bound to ask if he has other projects in mind, and he'll reply that it's still too early to discuss such things and that 'we need to respect the memory of the departed'.

Like anyone with even a minimum of decency, he deeply regrets the fact that the actor who was going to appear in his first film should have died of poisoning and that his chosen director is still in hospital – although not now in danger of losing his life – but both these events carry a clear message: keep away from cinema. It isn't his world and he's bound to lose money and gain nothing in return.

Leave cinema to the film-makers, music to the musicians and literature to the writers. Ever since he first embarked on this adventure two months before, he has met with nothing but problems: wrestling with gigantic egos, rejecting outlandish budgets, editing a script that seemed to get worse with every new version, and putting up with condescending producers who treated him as if he knew absolutely nothing about films.

His intentions had been impeccable: to make a film about the culture of his home country, about the beauty of the desert and the Bedouins' ancient wisdom and code of honour. He felt he owed this to his tribe, although the sheikh had warned him not to stray from his original path.

'People get lost in the desert because they're taken in by mirages. You're doing an excellent job as a couturier; focus all your energies on that.'

Hamid, however, wanted to go further, to show that he could still surprise people, go higher, take risks. He had committed the sin of pride, but that wouldn't happen again.

The journalists bombard him with questions - news, it seems, is travelling even faster than usual. He says he doesn't yet know any details, but that he'll make a full statement tomorrow. He repeats the same answer over and over, until one of his own security guards comes to his aid and asks the press to leave the couple alone.

He summons an assistant and asks him to find Jasmine in the crowd of people in the garden and bring her to him. They need to have a few photos taken together, a new press release confirming the deal, and a good PR person to keep the issue alive until October and the Fashion Week in Paris. Later on, he'll try to persuade the Belgian designer to join him; he genuinely liked her work and is sure she would bring money and prestige to his group; however, he knows that, at the moment, she'll be thinking that he was only trying to buy her because he wanted her principal model. Approaching her now would not only up the price, it would seem inelegant. To everything its proper time; it would be best to wait for the right moment.

Ewa appears troubled by the journalists' questions. She says: 'I think we should leave.'

'Absolutely not. I'm not hard-hearted as you know, but I can't get upset over something that only confirms what you always told me, that I shouldn't get involved in cinema. Now, though, we're at a party, and we're going to stay here until the end.'

His voice sounds sterner than he intended, but Ewa doesn't appear to notice, as if she were as indifferent to his love as to his hate. In a more equitable tone of voice, he adds:

'This party's just perfect, don't you think? Our host must be spending a fortune to be here in Cannes, what with the travel and accommodation expenses of the celebrities who've all been specially selected to be present at this lavish gala supper. But you can be sure that all the free publicity will send his profits soaring: full-page spreads in magazines and newspapers, TV air-time and hours of coverage on the cable channels that have nothing else to show. Women will associate his jewels with glamour; men will wear his watches as proof that they're powerful and wealthy; and young people will flick through the fashion pages and think: "One day, I want to be there too, wearing exactly that."'

'Please, let's leave now. I just have a really bad feeling about this party.'

This was the last straw. He's put up with his wife's bad mood all day without complaint. She keeps turning on her mobile phone to see if there's another text message, and now he's beginning to think that there really is something strange going on. Another man perhaps? Her ex-husband, who he saw in the hotel bar, and who is perhaps doing everything he can to arrange a meeting? If that's the case, though, why doesn't she just tell him what she's feeling instead of withdrawing into herself?

'Don't talk to me about bad feelings. I'm trying to explain to you why people put on parties like this. If you ever decide to go into fashion as you always dreamed of doing or of once again owning a shop selling haute-couture clothes, you could learn something. By the way, when I told you that I'd seen your ex-husband in the bar last night, you told me that was impossible. Is he the reason you keep checking your mobile phone?'

'Why on earth would he be here?' she says, when what she feels like saying is: 'I know who ruined your film project. And I know that he's capable of far worse. We're in danger here; please, let's leave.'

'You didn't answer my question.'

'The answer is "Yes". That's why I keep checking my mobile phone because I know him, and I know he's here somewhere, and I'm afraid.'

Hamid laughs.

'But I'm here too.'

Ewa picks up a glass of champagne and drinks it down in one. He says nothing, feeling that she's simply being provocative.

He looks around him, trying to forget the recent news that flashed up on his phone, and still hoping for a chance to have a few photos taken with Jasmine before they're all called into the room where supper will be served. The death of the actor couldn't have come at a worse moment. Now no one is asking about the big contract he's signed with an unknown model, and yet, half an hour earlier, it was all the press were interested in. Not any more.

Despite his many years of working in this glamorous world, he still has a lot to learn: the contract he signed has been quickly forgotten, but the host of this party has managed to keep the media interest alive. None of the photographers and journalists present have left the party to go to the police station or the hospital to find out exactly what has happened. They are, admittedly, fashion journalists, but their editors wouldn't have dared order them to leave, for the simple reason that murders don't appear on the same pages as social events.

Makers of expensive jewellery don't get themselves mixed up in cinematographic adventures. Big promoters know that regardless of how much blood is being spilled in the world right now, people will always prefer photos depicting an ideal and inaccessible life of luxury.

Murders can take place next door or out in the street, but parties like this only occur at the very top of society. What could be of more interest to mere mortals than this perfect party, which would have been advertised months before in press releases, confirming that the jeweller would be holding his usual event in Cannes, and that all the invitations had already gone out. Not quite true; at the time, half of the guests would have received a kind of memorandum, politely asking them to keep the date free.

They would, of course, respond at once and reserve the date and buy their plane tickets and book their hotel room for twelve days, even if they're only staying for forty-eight hours. They need to prove to everyone that they're still members of the Superclass, membership of which is invaluable in making business deals, opening doors and feeding egos.

The lavish invitation card would arrive two months later. The women would start worrying about which dress to wear for the occasion, and the men would contact a few acquaintances to ask if they could meet in the bar to discuss business before supper. This was the male way of saying: 'I've been invited to the party. Have you?' Even if the acquaintance claimed he was too busy and wasn't sure he'd be able to travel to Cannes on that date, the message had been sent loud and clear: that 'full diary' was just an excuse for not yet having been invited.

Minutes later, that 'very busy man' would start mobilising friends, advisors and associates to wangle him an invitation. This meant that the host could then choose the second half of his guest list, basing it on three things: power, money, contacts.

The perfect party.

A professional team of caterers would be signed up. On the day itself, the order will go out to serve as much alcohol as possible, preferably plenty of France's legendary and unbeatable champagne. Guests from other countries don't realise that they're being served a drink produced in the country itself and which is, therefore, much cheaper than they might think. The women feel - as even does Ewa at that moment - that the golden liquid in the glass is the best possible complement to dress, shoes and bag. The men are all holding a glass as well, but they drink much less; they've come to make peace with a competitor, to cement relationships with a supplier, or to meet a potential distributor of their products. Hundreds of business cards are exchanged on such nights, most of them amongst professionals. A few, of course, are given to pretty women, who know they're not worth the paper they're printed on; no one has come here hoping to find the love of their life, but to make deals, to shine and, possibly, to enjoy themselves a little. Enjoying yourself is optional and not of great importance.

The people here tonight come from three points of an imaginary triangle. At one point are those who have it all and spend their days playing golf or having lunch or hanging out at some exclusive club, and who, when they go into a shop, can buy anything they want without first asking the price. Having reached the top, they have realised something that had never even occurred to them before: they cannot bear to be alone. They can't stand the company of their husband or wife and they need to be on the go all the time, in the belief that they can still make a difference to humanity, although they've discovered, since they retired, that their day-to-day life is as dull as that of any other middle-class person: eat breakfast, read the newspapers, eat lunch, take a nap, eat supper, watch TV. They accept most of the supper invitations they receive. They go to social and sporting events at the weekend. They spend their holidays in fashionable places (even though they no longer work, they still believe in something called 'holidays').

At the second point on the triangle are those who haven't yet achieved anything and who are doing their best to row in very choppy waters, to break the resistance of the have-it-alls, to look happy even if one of their parents happens to be in hospital, and they are having to sell off things they don't even own.

Finally, at the apex, is the Superclass.

This is the ideal mixture for a party. Those who have reached the top and yet carry on life as normal may well have enough money stashed away for several generations, but their influence has waned and they have realised, too late, that power is actually more important than wealth. Those who haven't yet reached the top put all their energy and enthusiasm into making the party go with a swing, thinking that they're making a really good impression, only to discover, in the weeks that follow, that no one phones them despite all the business cards they handed out. Finally, there are those who wobble about on the apex, knowing that it's very windy up there and that the slightest gust could blow them off into the abyss below.

People keep coming over to talk to him, although no one mentions the murder, either because they don't know about it, since they live in a world where such things don't happen, or out of politeness, which he very much doubts. He looks around him and sees the thing he hates most in the fashion world: middle-aged women who dress as if they were still twenty. Haven't they noticed that it's time they changed their style? He speaks to one person, smiles at another, thanks someone else for a kind remark, introduces Ewa to the few who still don't know her. He has, however, only one thought in his mind: to find Jasmine within the next five minutes and pose for the photographers.

An industrialist and his wife are telling him in detail about the last time they met, a meeting of which Hamid has no recollection, although he nods wisely. They talk about trips they've made, people they've met and projects they're involved in. No one touches on genuinely interesting topics like 'Are you happy?' or 'After all we've been through, what does victory actually feel like?' They are part of the Superclass and therefore obliged to behave as if they were contented and fulfilled, even if they're actually asking themselves: 'What shall I do with my future, now that I have everything I ever dreamed of?'

A squalid creature in tight trousers and an Indian top approaches, looking like something out of a comic strip.

'Mr Hamid, I'm terribly sorry …'

'Who are you?'

'I work for you, sir.'

How absurd.

'Look, I'm busy right now, and I know everything I need to know about tonight's sad events, so there's no need for you to worry.'

The creature, however, stays where he is. Hamid begins to feel embarrassed by his presence, mainly because friends nearby will have heard those dreadful words: 'I work for you, sir.' Whatever will they think?

'Mr Hamid, I'm just about to bring over the actress who's going to be appearing in your film. I had to leave her for a moment because I got a phone message, but …'

'Later. At the moment, I'm waiting to meet Jasmine Tiger.'

The strange creature leaves. The actress who's going to be appearing in his film! Poor girl: signed up and dismissed all in one day.

Ewa is holding a champagne glass in one hand and her mobile phone and an extinguished cigarette in the other. The industrialist takes a gold lighter out of his pocket and offers to light her cigarette.

'No, thank you, it's all right, I can do it myself,' she says. 'I'm deliberately keeping both hands occupied in an attempt to smoke less.'

She would like to say: 'I'm holding my mobile so as to protect this idiot, who refuses to believe me and who has never shown the slightest interest in my life or what I've been through. If I get another message, I'll make a scene and he'll be forced to leave and take me with him, whether he wants to or not. Even if he tells me off afterwards, at least I can console myself with the thought that I saved his life. I know who the killer is. I can feel the presence of Absolute Evil very near.'

A receptionist starts asking the guests to go into the main dining area. Hamid Hussein is prepared to accept his fate without complaint. The photo can wait until tomorrow when he goes up the steps with her. Just then, one of his assistants appears.

'Jasmine Tiger isn't here. She must have left.'

'Never mind. Perhaps they forgot to tell her that we were supposed to meet.'

He looks very calm, like someone accustomed to dealing with such situations. Inside, though, his blood is boiling. She's left the party? Who does she think she is?

It's so easy to die. The human body may well be one of the most efficient mechanisms in creation, but all it takes is a small metal projectile to enter and cut through it at a certain speed, and that's that.

Death, according to the dictionary, is the end of a life (although life also needs to be properly defined), the permanent paralysis of the body's vital functions, like brain activity, breathing, blood flow to and from the heart. Only two things resist this permanent paralysis – the hair and the nails, which continue to grow for a few days or weeks.

The definition changes when it comes to religions: for some, death means moving to a higher state, while others believe that it is merely a temporary condition and that the soul inhabiting the body will return later on, either to pay for its sins or to enjoy in the next life the blessings denied it during the previous incarnation.

The young woman is standing very still by his side. Either the champagne has taken full effect or its effects have passed, and she now realises that she knows no one, that this could be both her first and last invitation to such a party, and that dreams sometimes turn into nightmares. When he moved away for a moment with the other sadder girl, he noticed a few men approach the actress, but it seems she felt uncomfortable with all of them. When she saw him reappear, she asked him to stay with her for the rest of the party. She also asked if he had transport because she has no money and it doesn't look as if her companion will be coming back.

'Yes, of course, I'll be glad to take you home.'

This wasn't in his plans, but having spotted the policeman observing the guests, he knows it's best to look as if he's with someone, that he's just another of the important, anonymous people there, proud to have a pretty, much younger woman with him, one who so perfectly fits the norm in that particular place.

'Don't you think we should go in?'

'Yes, but I know how these things work. It's best to wait until everyone else is seated. Several of the tables will have places reserved at them for certain people, and we don't want to find ourselves in the embarrassing position of sitting down where we shouldn't.'

He notices that, for a moment, the girl looks slightly disappointed that he doesn't have one of those reserved places.

The waiters are collecting up the empty glasses scattered around the garden. The models have stepped down from their ridiculous pedestals where their gyrations have persuaded the male guests at the party that life can still be interesting and reminded the female guests that they really must get some more liposuction, botox, silicone or plastic surgery.

'Please, let's go in. I need to eat. I'll get sick if I don't.'

She takes his arm and they walk towards the room on the upper floor. It would seem that his last message to Ewa has been received and discarded, but then he knows now what to expect from a woman as corrupt as his ex-wife. The angel with the dark eyebrows continues by his side; she was the one who had made him turn round at the right moment and notice the plain-clothes policeman, when, in theory, he should have been concentrating on the arrival of the famous couturier.

'All right, we'll go in.'

They walk up the steps and into the dining room. As they do so, he asks her politely to let go of his arm, in case any friends there should misinterpret the situation.

'Are you married, then?'

'No, divorced.'

Yes, Ewa is thinking, she had been right, her intuition was correct, the problems they have encountered so far this evening are as nothing compared with what she has just seen. Since Igor can have no professional reason for being at a film festival, his presence there can have only one possible motive.

'Igor!' Hamid says.

The man, accompanied by a much younger woman, looks straight at him. Ewa's heart starts pounding. She says to Hamid:

'What are you doing?'

Hamid has already got up from the table. He has no idea what he's doing. He's walking towards Absolute Limitless Evil, capable of anything. Hamid assumes that Igor is just another adult and that he can confront him with either physical force or with logical argument. What he doesn't know is that Absolute Evil has the heart of a child and takes no responsibility for its actions and is convinced that it's right. And when it doesn't get what it wants, it's not afraid to use all possible means to satisfy its desires. Now she understands how it was that the Angel changed so quickly into a Devil: because he has always nursed vengeance and rancour in his heart, even though he claimed to have grown up and overcome all his traumas; because he's unbeatable when it comes to succeeding in life, thus confirming his belief in his own omnipotence; because he doesn't know how to give up, having survived the worst possible torments through which he walked without so much as a backward glance, all the while repeating to himself: 'One day, I'll be back, and then you'll see what I'm capable of.'

'Apparently, he's found someone more interesting to talk to than us,' says a former Miss Europe, who is also sitting at the top table, along with another two celebrities and the host of the party.

Ewa tries to conceal her unease, but she doesn't know what to do. The host seems almost amused and is waiting for some explanation.

'I'm sorry. He's an old friend of mine.'

Hamid goes over to Igor, who looks suddenly uncertain. The girl with him says loudly:

'Hello, Mr Hamid. I'm your new actress!'

People on the other tables turn round to see what's happening. The host smiles. It's always good to have something unusual happen at a party; it will give his guests plenty to talk about. Hamid is now standing in front of the man; the host realises that all is not well and says to Ewa:

'I think you'd better retrieve Hamid, or, if you like, we can get another chair for your friend. His companion will, I'm afraid, have to sit elsewhere.'

The guests have turned their attention back to their food and their conversations about yachts, private planes and the stock market. Only the host keeps a watchful eye on what's going on.

'Go and talk to them,' he says.

Ewa, however, isn't there. Her thoughts are thousands of miles away in a restaurant in Irkutsk, near Lake Baikal. The scene was different then, with Igor leading another man outside. Making an enormous effort, she gets to her feet and joins the two men.

'Go back to the table,' says Hamid quietly. 'We're going outside to talk.'

That is the most stupid thing he could possibly do. She grabs his arm and, smiling, pretends to be happy to be meeting someone she hasn't seen in a long time. With great aplomb, she says:

'But supper's only just beginning!'

She doesn't add 'my love'; she doesn't want to open the doors of hell.

'She's right. We'd be better off talking here.'

Did Igor say that? Perhaps she's been imagining things and it isn't at all as she thought? Has the child finally grown into a responsible adult? Has the devil been forgiven for his arrogance and returned to the kingdom of heaven?

She so wants to be wrong, but the two men are still staring at each other. Hamid can see something deeply perverse behind those blue eyes and, for a moment, a shudder runs through him. The young woman is holding out her hand.

'Pleased to meet you. My name's Gabriela …'

He doesn't return her greeting. The other man's eyes are shining.

'There's a table over in the corner. Why don't we all go and sit down there,' says Ewa.

A table in the corner? Is his wife going to leave her place of honour at the top table and sit at a table in a corner? Ewa has already linked arms with both men and is leading them towards the only free table, near the door through which the waiters come and go. The 'actress' follows behind. Hamid detaches himself for a moment and goes back to his host to apologise.

'I've just met a childhood friend. He has to leave tomorrow, and I wouldn't want to miss this chance to talk a little. Please, don't wait for us, I can't say how long we'll be.'

'No one will steal your places,' says the host, smiling, knowing full well that the two chairs will remain empty.

'I thought he was your *wife*'s childhood friend,' says the former Miss Europe waspishly.

Hamid, however, is already walking back to the worst table in the room, reserved for the celebrities' assistants, who, despite all precautions, often manage to slip in where they're not supposed to be.

'Hamid's a good man,' thinks the host, as he watches the couturier walk away, head held high, 'But the night hasn't got off to a very happy start for him.'

They all sit down at the corner table. Gabriela understands that this is her one chance, yet another of those many 'one chances' that have happened today. She says how pleased she was to receive the invitation and that she'll do all she can not to disappoint.

'I trust you,' she says. 'I even signed the contract without reading it.'

The other three people don't say a word; they just look at each other. Is something wrong? Can it be the effect of the champagne? Best to keep talking.

'I'm particularly happy because, contrary to what people usually say, the selection process was very fair. There were no special requests, no favours. I did the test this morning, and they didn't even let me finish reading the text they gave me. They just asked me to go to a yacht to talk to the director. That sets an excellent example, Mr Hamid, I mean, treating people with dignity and honesty when it comes to choosing who you're going to be working with. People think that in the world of cinema the only thing that really counts is …'

She was about to say 'sleeping with the producer', but the producer is sitting next to his wife.

'… is what a person looks like.'

The waiter brings the entrées and launches into his usual monologue:

'Tonight's entrées are artichoke hearts in a Dijon mustard sauce, drizzled with a little olive oil, flavoured with *fines herbes* and served with slivers of Pyrenean goat's cheese …'

Only the young woman smiles and listens to what he's saying. He realises that he isn't welcome and leaves.

'It looks delicious!' she says. Then she glances round at the others, none of whom has made a move to pick up knife or fork. Something is very wrong here.

'Look, you obviously need to talk. Perhaps I should sit somewhere else.'

'Yes,' says Hamid.

'No, stay here,' says the woman.

What should she do now?

'Do you like your companion?' the woman asks.

'I've only just met Gunther.'

Gunther. Hamid and Ewa look at the impassive Igor sitting beside her.

'And what does Gunther do?'

'Aren't you friends of his?'

'Yes, and we know what he does. But we don't know how much you know about his life.'

Gabriela turns to Igor. Why doesn't he help her?

A waiter arrives to ask what wine they would like to drink.

'White or red?'

Saved by a stranger!

'Red for everyone,' says Hamid.

'You still haven't told us what Gunther does?'

She hasn't been saved.

'He works with heavy machinery, I think. We hardly know each other really. The only thing we have in common is that we were both waiting for friends who never turned up.'

A good answer, thinks Gabriela. Perhaps that woman is having a secret affair with her new 'partner' or else an affair that her husband has just found out about – that would explain the tension in the air.

'His name is Igor,' announces the woman. 'He owns one of the biggest mobile-phone companies in Russia. That's far more important than selling heavy machinery.'

If this is true, why did he lie? She decides to say nothing.

'I was hoping to meet you here, Igor,' the woman says, addressing Gunther now.

'I came looking for you, but I've changed my mind now,' comes the blunt reply.

Gabriela suddenly gives her paper-stuffed handbag a squeeze and adopts a surprised expression.

'Oh, my phone's ringing. I think my friend must have arrived, so I'd better go and find him. I'm so sorry, but he's come a long way just to be with me, and since he doesn't know anyone else here, I feel kind of responsible for him.'

She gets up. Etiquette dictates that one shouldn't shake hands with someone when he or she is eating, although the others haven't even touched the food. The wine glasses, however, are already empty. And the man who, up until two minutes ago, was called Gunther has just ordered another whole bottle.

'I hope you got my messages,' says Igor.

'I received three. Perhaps the telephone network here is worse than the one you developed.'

'I'm not talking about telephones.'

'Then I don't know what you *are* talking about,' she says, but what she wants to say is: 'I know you're not.'

Just as Igor must know that, during the first year she was with Hamid, she waited for a phone call or a message, for some mutual friend to tell her how much Igor was missing her. She didn't want him near her, but she knew that hurting him would be the worst thing she could do; she needed to placate her own personal Fury and pretend that one day, they would be good friends. One afternoon, when she'd had a bit to drink and finally summoned up the nerve to call him, she found that he'd changed his mobile number. When she phoned him at the office, she was told he was in a meeting. When she rang on subsequent occasions – always with the help of a little Dutch courage – she was told that Igor was travelling or would phone her back at once, which, of course, he never did.

And she began to see ghosts everywhere, to feel that she was being watched, that soon she would suffer the same fate as the beggar and the others whose 'promotions to a better life' Igor had hinted at. Meanwhile, Hamid never asked her about her past, alleging that everyone has a right to keep his or her life locked up and private in the subterranean tunnels of memory. He did all he could to make her happy and to help her feel safe and protected; he even told her that his life had only begun to make any sense since meeting her.

Then one day, Absolute Evil rang the doorbell of their apartment building in London. Hamid was at home and sent him away. Nothing else happened in the months that followed.

Gradually, she succeeded in deceiving herself. Yes, she had made the right choice; the moment we choose a path, all other paths disappear. It was childish of her to think that she could be married to one man and be friends with her ex-husband, that was only possible between well-balanced people, and Igor was not well-balanced. It was best to believe that an invisible hand had saved her from Absolute Evil. She was enough of a woman to make the new man at her side feel dependent on her and to help him as much as she could, as lover, advisor, wife and sister, and she channelled all her energy into doing just that.

During this period, she had only one real friend, who disappeared as suddenly as she had appeared. She was Russian too, but unlike her, had been abandoned by her husband and didn't really know what she was doing in England. They spoke almost every day.

'I left it all behind,' Ewa told her once. 'And I don't regret it one bit. I would have done the same even if Hamid – against my wishes – hadn't bought a beautiful estate in Spain and put it in my name. I would have made the same decision if Igor, my ex-husband, had offered me half his fortune, because I need to live without fear. And if one of the most desirable men in the world wants to be by my side, then I'm obviously a better person than I thought.'

It was all lies. She wasn't trying to convince her only confidante, but herself. It was all a front. Inside the strong woman sitting at that table with two powerful and important men was a little girl afraid of being left alone and poor, never having experienced what it was to be a mother. Had she simply got used to all the luxury and the glamour? No. She was always preparing herself to lose everything from one day to the next, when her present companion finally found out that she wasn't what he thought and was incapable of meeting others' expectations.

Did she know how to manipulate men? Yes. They all thought she was strong and confident, mistress of her own destiny, that she was capable of leaving any man, however important or eligible. And the worst thing was that men believed it. Men like Igor and like Hamid. Because she knew how to pretend, because she never said exactly what she was thinking, because she was the best actress in the world and knew better than anyone how to hide her vulnerable side.

'What do you want?' he asks in Russian.

'More wine.'

He sounded as if he didn't much care what answer she gave; he had already said what he wanted.

'Before you left, I said something to you, but I think you must have forgotten.'

He had said so many things: 'I promise that I'll change and start working less', 'You're the only woman I love', 'If you leave, it will destroy me', words familiar to everyone and which are utterly devoid of meaning.

'I said: If you leave me, I'll destroy a world.'

She couldn't remember him saying this, but it was perfectly possible. Igor had always been a very bad loser.

'But what does that mean?' she asks in Russian.

'At least be polite enough to speak in English,' says Hamid.

Igor turns to face him.

'I will speak English, not out of politeness, but because I want you to understand.'

And turning back to Ewa, he says:

'I said I would destroy a whole world to get you back. I started doing that, but was saved by an angel. I realised that you didn't deserve it. You're a selfish, implacable woman, interested only in acquiring more fame and more money. You refused all the good things I offered you because a house deep in the Russian countryside didn't fit in with your dream world, a world, by the way, to which you don't belong and never will.

'I sacrificed myself and others for your sake, and that's not right. I need to go to the very end, so that I can return to the world of the living with a sense of duty done and mission completed. Now, as we speak, I'm in the world of the dead.'

This man's eyes are filled with a look of Absolute Evil, thinks Hamid, as he listens to this absurd conversation, full of long silences. Fine, he'll let things go to the very end, as Igor suggests, as long as that doesn't mean him losing the woman he loves. Even better for him, Ewa's ex-husband has not only turned up accompanied by some vulgar woman, he has insulted Ewa to her face. He'll allow him to go on a little longer and will know when to bring the conversation to a halt, when it's too late for Igor to apologise or to beg forgiveness.

Ewa must be seeing the same thing: a blind hatred for everything and everyone, simply because one person didn't do as he wished. He wonders what he would have done were he that man who is now apparently fighting for the woman he loves.

He would, he thinks, be capable of killing for her.

The waiter reappears and notices that the plates are all untouched.

'Is anything wrong with the food?' he asks.

No one answers. The waiter understands: the husband must have caught his wife in flagrante with her lover in Cannes, and this is the final confrontation. He's seen it all before, and it usually ends in a fight or a row.

'Another bottle of wine,' says one of the men.

'You don't deserve anything,' says the other man, his eyes fixed on the woman. 'You used me just as you're using that idiot beside you. You were the biggest mistake of my life.'

The waiter decides to check with the host before bringing them that other bottle of wine, but one of the men has just got to his feet, saying to the woman:

'That's enough. We're leaving.'

'Yes, let's all leave, let's go outside,' says the other man. 'I want to see how far you would go to defend a person who doesn't know the meaning of the words "honour" and "dignity".'

Two males fighting over a female. The woman asks them not to go outside, but to return to the table. The man with her, however, seems ready to respond to the insult. The waiter considers warning the security guards that a fight might ensue, but the head waiter is already complaining that the service is too slow, so what is he doing hanging around there? He has other tables to serve. He's right, of course. What happens outside isn't his problem. And if he admits to listening in on a conversation, he'll get told off. He's being paid to wait at tables, not to save the world.

The three of them cross the garden where the cocktails had been served and which is now undergoing a rapid transformation. When the guests come down from supper, they'll find a dance floor lit with special lights, a seating area furnished with armchairs and several small bars all serving free drinks.

Igor walks ahead in silence. Ewa follows and Hamid brings up the rear. There is a small metal gate at the top of the steps down to the beach. Igor opens it and asks them to go first. Ewa refuses, but he seems not to mind and goes down the many flights of steps that lead to the sea below. He knows that Hamid will not prove to be a coward. Until he met him at the party, he had considered him to be nothing but an unscrupulous couturier, a seducer of married women and a manipulator of other people's vanity. Now, however, he secretly admires him. He's a real man, capable of fighting to the end for someone he believes to be important, even though Igor knows that Ewa hasn't one iota of the talent of the young actress he met tonight. She can't disguise her feelings at all; he can sense her fear, he knows that she's sweating, wondering who to call, how to ask for help.

When they reach the sand, Igor walks right to the end of the beach and sits down close to some rocks. He asks the others to do the same. He knows that despite her terror, Ewa is also thinking: 'I'm going to spoil my dress. I'm going to get my shoes dirty.' But she sits down beside him. The other man asks her to move over a little, so that he can sit there, but she won't budge.

He doesn't insist. There they are, the three of them, as if they were old acquaintances in search of a moment's peace in which to contemplate the rising of the full moon before they go back up the steps to listen to the infernal racket of the discotheque.

Hamid promises himself that he will give Igor ten minutes, time enough for him to say everything that's on his mind, to vent his rage and then go back where he came from. If he turns violent, he'll be the loser because Hamid is physically stronger and, as a Bedouin, trained to respond swiftly and precisely to any attack. He doesn't want to cause a scene at the party, but the Russian should be under no illusion: he is prepared for anything.

When they go back up, he'll apologise to their host and explain that the situation has been resolved. He knows he can speak openly to him. He'll tell him that his wife's ex-husband had turned up without warning and that he'd felt it best to remove him before he caused any trouble. If the man doesn't leave as soon as they return to the party, he'll summon one of his own bodyguards to expel him. Igor may well be rich and own one of the largest mobile-phone companies in Russia, but he's being a nuisance.

'You betrayed me, not just during the two years you've spent with this man, but during all the years we spent together.'

Ewa says nothing.

'What would you be capable of doing in order to keep her?' he asks Hamid.

Hamid wonders whether he should answer or not. Ewa isn't a piece of merchandise to be haggled over.

'Can you rephrase the question?'

'OK. Would you give your life for the woman beside you?'

There is pure evil in the man's eyes. Even if Igor had managed to steal a knife from the restaurant (Hamid hadn't noticed him doing so, but he must consider all possibilities), he will have no problem disarming him. No, he wouldn't give his life for anyone, except God and the chief of his tribe, but he must say something.

'I would fight for her and, if it came to it, I think I would be capable of killing for her.'

Ewa can stand the pressure no longer; she would like to say everything she knows about the man on her right. She is sure that he murdered the actor and destroyed her new companion's long-cherished dream of becoming a film producer.

'Let's go back up.'

What she really wants to say is: 'Please, let's get out of here now. You're talking to a psychopath.'

Igor appears not to hear what she said.

'You'd be capable of killing for her, so that means you'd be capable of dying for her too.'

'If I fought and lost, yes, I think I would. But let's not start a fight here on the beach.'

'I want to go back up to the party,' says Ewa again.

Hamid, however, feels his male pride is in question. He can't leave there like a coward. The ancient dance performed by males – humans and animals – in order to impress the female is just beginning.

'When you left, I somehow couldn't be myself,' says Igor, as if he were alone on the beach. 'My business was prospering, and I could keep control of myself during the day, but at night, I would plunge into black depression. I had lost a part of myself I could never recover. I thought I might be able to do that by coming here to Cannes, but when I arrived, I realised that the part of me that had died couldn't and shouldn't be resuscitated. I'll never take you back, not even if you came to me on bended knee, begging forgiveness and threatening suicide.'

Ewa breathed easier – at least there wouldn't be a fight.

'You didn't understand my messages. I said I would be capable of destroying whole worlds, and you didn't get it. Or if you did, you couldn't believe it. What does it mean to destroy a world?'

He puts his hand in his trouser pocket and takes out a small gun. He doesn't point it at anyone, though; his eyes remain fixed on the sea and the moon. The blood starts to flow faster in Hamid's veins. Igor either wants to frighten and humiliate them or this really is a fight to the death. But will he kill them there, at the party, knowing that he'll be arrested as soon as he goes back up the steps? He can't be that mad; if he were, he could never have achieved all he has achieved in life.

Enough distractions. He is a warrior trained to defend himself and to attack. He must stay absolutely still because, although the other man isn't looking directly at him, he knows that his senses will be alert to any gesture.

The only part of his body he can safely move are his eyes, and he can see that there is no one else on the beach. Up above, the band are just beginning to tune their instruments, preparing for the most enjoyable segment of the party. Hamid isn't thinking, his instincts are now focussed on acting without the interference of his brain.

Ewa is sitting between him and Igor and she seems hypnotised by the sight of the gun. If he tries anything, Igor will turn and shoot and she might get hit.

Yes, perhaps his first hypothesis was correct. Igor just wants to frighten them, to force Hamid to show himself to be a coward and lose his honour. If he really wanted to shoot them, he wouldn't be holding the gun in that casual manner. It would be best to talk and try to get him to relax a little, while he thinks of some way out.

'What *does* destroying a world mean?' he asks.

'Destroying a life. A whole universe gone. Everything that person saw and experienced; all the good and the bad that came his way; all his dreams, hopes, defeats and victories ceasing to exist. As children, we learned by heart a passage which I only later found out came from a Protestant priest. He said something like: "When the sea bears away into its depths a single grain of sand, the whole of Europe grows smaller. We don't notice, of course. After all, it's just a grain of sand, but at that very moment the continent is diminished."'

Igor pauses. He's starting to feel irritated with the noise from up above; the sound of the waves was so calming, allowing him to treat this moment with the respect it deserves. The angel with the dark eyebrows is watching and is happy with what she sees.

'It was supposed to teach us that we were responsible for creating the perfect society, namely Communism,' he goes on. 'We were all brothers and sisters, they said, but, in fact, we were spies trained to betray each other.'

He becomes calm and thoughtful again.

'I can't quite hear you.'

This will give him a reason to move.

'Of course you can. You know that I have a gun in my hand and you want to come closer to see if you can grab it off me. You're trying to engage me in conversation in order to distract me while you consider what to do. Please, don't move. The moment hasn't yet come.'

'Igor, let's just drop the whole thing,' Ewa says in Russian. 'I love you. Let's go away together.'

'Speak in English. Your companion here needs to understand what you're saying.'

Yes, he would understand, and later on, he would thank her for it.

'I love you,' she says again, in English this time. 'I never received your messages. If I had, I would have come running back. I tried several times to phone you, but never got through. I left many messages with your secretary, but you never called me.'

'That's true.'

'Ever since I started getting your messages today, I've been longing to see you again. I didn't know where you were, but I knew that you would come and find me. I know you don't want to forgive me, but at least allow me to live by your side. I can be your servant, your cleaner, I'll look after you and your lover, should you ever decide to take one. All I want is to be with you.'

She'll explain everything to Hamid later. She has to say something, anything, just to get them out of there and back up the steps to the real world, where there are policemen who can stop Absolute Evil from revealing its hatred.

'I'd like to believe that, or, rather, I'd like to believe that I love you too and want you back, but I don't. Besides, I think you're lying and that you always lied.'

Hamid isn't listening to what either of them is saying; his mind is far away with his warrior ancestors, asking for inspiration to make the right move.

'You could have told me that our marriage wasn't working out as we both hoped. We had built so much together; couldn't we have found a solution? There's always a way of allowing happiness in, but for that to happen, both partners have to acknowledge there are problems. I would have listened to what you had to say. Our marriage would have regained all its initial excitement and joy. But you didn't want to do that, you chose the easy way out.'

'I was always afraid of you, and now, seeing you with that gun in your hand, I'm even more afraid.'

Hamid is brought abruptly back to earth by Ewa's last comment. His soul is no longer somewhere in space, asking advice from the warriors of the desert, trying to find out how he should act.

She can't have said that. She's handing over power to the enemy; now he'll know that he's capable of terrifying her.

'I would like to have invited you to supper one day and to have told you that I felt so alone, despite all the banquets, jewels, journeys and meetings with kings and presidents,' Ewa says. 'Do you know something else? You always brought me really expensive presents, but never the simplest gift of all – flowers.'

This is turning into a marital argument.

'I'll leave you two to talk.'

Igor says nothing. His eyes are still fixed on the sea, but he's pointing the gun at him, indicating that he should stay where he is. The man is mad, and his apparent calm is more dangerous than if he were screaming threats at them.

'Anyway,' he says, as if unperturbed either by her words or Hamid's attempt to move, 'you chose the easiest way out. You left me. You didn't give me a chance; you didn't understand that everything I was doing was for you and because of you.

'And yet, despite all the injustices and humiliations, I would have done anything to have you back – until today. Until I sent you those messages, and you pretended not to have received them. In other words, even the sacrifice of those other people didn't move you; you just couldn't get enough of power and luxury.'

The Star who was poisoned and the director whose life still hangs by a thread: is Hamid imagining the unimaginable? Then he understands something even more serious: with that confession, the man beside them has just signed their death warrant. He must either commit suicide there and then or put an end to the lives of two people who now know far too much.

Perhaps, Hamid thinks, he himself is going mad or simply misunderstanding the situation, but he knows that time is running out.

He looks at the gun in the man's hand. It's a small calibre. If it doesn't hit certain critical points in the body, it won't do much harm. He can't be very experienced; if he were, he would have chosen something more powerful. He obviously doesn't know what he's doing; he must have bought the first thing he was offered, something that fired bullets and could kill.

The band have started playing up above. Don't they realise that the noise of the music will mask the sound of a shot? Then again, would they know the difference between a gunshot and one of the many other artificial noises that are currently infesting – yes, that's the word, infesting, polluting, plaguing – the atmosphere?

Igor has gone quiet again, and that is far more dangerous than if he were to continue talking, emptying his heart of some of his bitterness and bile. Hamid again weighs up the possibilities; if he's going to act, he needs to do so in the next few seconds. He could throw himself across Ewa and grab the gun while it's lying casually in Igor's lap, even though Igor's finger is on the trigger. He could reach out to him with both arms, forcing Igor to draw back in fright, and then Ewa would be out of the line of fire. Igor would point the gun in his direction, but by then, he would be close enough to grab his wrist. It would all take only a second.

Now.

Maybe this silence is a positive sign; perhaps Igor has lost concentration. Or it might be the beginning of the end, meaning that he's said all he has to say.

Now.

In the first fraction of a second, the muscle in his left thigh tenses, propelling him furiously forward in the direction of Absolute Evil; the area of his body shrinks as he hurls himself over Ewa's lap, arms outstretched. The first second continues, and he sees the gun being pointed directly at his head; the man moves more quickly than he had expected.

His body is still flying towards the gun. They should have talked before. Ewa has never said much about her ex-husband, as if he belonged to a past she preferred not to think about – ever. Even though everything is happening in slow motion, the man draws back as nimbly as a cat. The gun in his hand is perfectly steady.

The first second is just reaching its end. He sees a finger move, but there is no sound, only the feeling of something crushing the bone in the middle of his forehead. His universe is extinguished and with it the memories of the young man who dreamed of being 'someone', his arrival in Paris, his father's shop, the sheikh, his battle to gain a place in the sun, the fashion shows, the trips abroad, meeting the woman he loves, the days of wine and roses, the laughter and the tears, the last moon on the rise, the eyes of Absolute Evil, the look of terror in his wife's eyes, all disappear.

'Don't cry out. Don't say a word. Keep calm.'

Of course she isn't going to cry out, nor does she need to be told to keep calm. She's in a state of shock like the animal she is, despite her fine jewellery and her expensive dress. Her blood is no longer circulating at its normal speed, her face grows pale, her voice vanishes, her blood pressure plummets. He knows exactly what she's feeling; he once experienced the same when he saw the rifle of an Afghan warrior pointing at his chest. Total immobility and a complete inability to react. He was only saved because a colleague fired first. He was still grateful to the man who had saved his life; everyone thought he was just his chauffeur, when, in fact, he owned many shares in the company, and he and Igor often talked; indeed, they had spoken that very afternoon when Igor had phoned to ask if Ewa had shown any sign of having received his messages.

Ewa, poor Ewa, sitting there with a man dying in her lap. Human beings are unpredictable; sometimes they react as that fool reacted, knowing that he had no chance of beating him. Weapons are unpredictable too. He expected the bullet to come out the other side of the man's head, blowing away the top part of the brain, but, given the angle of the shot, it must have pierced the brain, bounced off a bone and entered the thorax because he's trembling uncontrollably, but with no sign of any blood.

It must be the trembling not the shot that has so shocked Ewa. With one foot, Igor pushes the body to the ground and puts a bullet through the back of the man's neck. The tremors cease. The man deserves a dignified death; he was, after all, valiant to the end.

* * *

They are alone now on the beach. He kneels down in front of her and places the barrel of the gun against her breast. Ewa doesn't move.

He had imagined a very different ending to this story, with her understanding his messages and giving the two of them a new chance of happiness. He had thought of all the things he would say when they were finally alone again like this, looking out at the calm Mediterranean sea, smiling and chatting.

He doesn't want to live with those words stuck in his throat, even if those words are useless now.

'I always thought that one day, we'd walk hand-in-hand through a park again or along the seashore, finally saying those long-postponed words of love. We would eat out once a week, travel together to places we'd never been to simply for the pleasure of discovering new things in each other's company.

'While you've been away, I've been copying poems out in a book so that I could whisper them to you as you fell asleep. I've written letters telling you how I felt, letters I would leave where you could find them and then you'd know that I never forgot you – not for a single day, not for a single moment. We would discuss plans for the house you wanted on the shores of Lake Baikal – just for us. I know you had a lot of ideas for that. I planned to have a private airport built there, and, of course, I'd leave the decoration of the house to your good taste, to you, the woman who justified my life and gave it meaning.'

Ewa says nothing, but stares out at the sea before her.

'I came here because of you, only to realise that it was all pointless.'

He squeezes the trigger.

There was almost no sound because the barrel of the gun was pressed against her body. The bullet entered at precisely the right place, and her heart immediately stopped beating. Despite all the pain she had caused him, he didn't want her to suffer.

If there was a life after death, both of them – the woman who betrayed him and the man who encouraged her – were now walking along, holding hands, in the moonlight fringing the shoreline. They would meet the angel with the dark eyebrows, who would explain everything that had happened and put an end to any feelings of rancour or hatred; at some point, everyone has to leave this planet known as Earth. And, besides, love justifies acts that mere human beings cannot understand, unless they happen to be experiencing what he has experienced.

Ewa's eyes remain open, but her body grows limp and falls to the sand. He leaves both bodies there, goes over to the rocks, carefully wipes any fingerprints from the gun and throws it into the sea, as far as possible from the place where they had been sitting contemplating the moon. He goes back up the steps, finds a litter bin on the way and drops the silencer in. He hadn't really needed it; the music had reached a crescendo at just the right moment.

10.55 p.m.

Gabriela goes over to the only person she knows.

The guests are now leaving the supper room; the band is playing music from the Sixties, the party is beginning, and people are smiling and talking to each other, despite the deafening noise.

'I've been looking for you! Where are your friends?'

'Where's yours?'

'He's gone. He said there was some problem with the actor and the director, that's all, and then he left. The only other thing he said was that tonight's party on the yacht has been cancelled.'

Igor realises what has happened. He hadn't had the slightest intention of killing someone he greatly admired and whose films he always tried to see whenever he had time. Nevertheless, it's Fate that makes these choices – man is just the instrument.

'I'm leaving. If you like, I can drop you off at your hotel.'

'But the party's just beginning.'

'Enjoy it, then. I'm flying off early tomorrow morning.'

Gabriela has to make a decision quickly. She can either stay here with that handbag stuffed with paper, in a place where she knows no one, hoping that some charitable soul will give her a lift as far as Croisette, where she will take off her shoes to climb the interminable hill up to the room she's sharing with four other friends. Or she can accept the offer of this kind man, who probably has some very useful contacts, and who's a friend of Hamid Hussein's wife. She had witnessed the start of what looked like an argument, but such things happen every day, and they would soon make it up.

She has a role in a film. She's exhausted from all the emotions of the day. She's afraid that she'll end up drinking too much and spoiling everything. Men will come up to her, asking if she's on her own and what she's doing afterwards, and if she'd like to visit a jeweller's with them the following day. She'll have to spend the rest of the night politely avoiding people, trying not to hurt anyone's feelings, because you could never be quite sure who you were talking to. It was, after all, one of the most exclusive parties at the Festival.

'Let's go.'

That's how a star behaves. She leaves when no one is expecting her to.

They go out to the hotel reception, Gunther (she can't remember his other name) asks the receptionist to call a taxi for them, and she tells them they're in luck; if they'd waited very much longer, they would have had to wait in an enormous queue.

On the way back, she asks him why he lied about what he does. He says he didn't lie. He used to own a mobile-phone company, but had decided to sell it because he felt the future lay in heavy machinery.

And what about his name?

'Igor is an affectionate nickname, the Russian diminutive of Gunther.'

Gabriela is expecting him, at any moment, to come out with the words 'Shall we have a nightcap at my hotel?', but he doesn't. He leaves her at the door of the house where she's staying, shakes her hand and leaves.

How elegant!

Yes, this has been her first lucky day, the first of many. Tomorrow, when she gets her phone back, she'll make a collect call to a city near Chicago to tell everyone the big news and ask them to buy the gossip magazines because she'd been photographed going up the steps with the Star. She'll also tell them that she's had to adopt a new name. However, if they ask her what's going to happen next, she'll change the subject. She has a superstitious belief that one shouldn't discuss projects until they actually happen. They'll hear all about it as the news leaks out. Unknown actress chosen for major role. Lisa Winner was the guest of honour at a party in New York. Previously unknown Chicago girl is the new sensation in Gibson's latest movie. Agent negotiates million-dollar contract with one of the major Hollywood producers.

The sky's the limit.

11.11 p.m.

'You're back early?'

'I'd have been here sooner if it wasn't for the traffic.'

Jasmine kicks off her shoes, drops her bag and throws herself down on the bed, exhausted and fully clothed. She says:

'The most important words in any language are the short ones: "Yes", for example, or "Love" or "God". They're all easy to say and they fill up the empty spaces of our universe. But there's one small word that I have great difficulty in saying, but I'm going to say it now.' She looks at her companion. 'No.'

She pats the bed, inviting her companion to join her. Her companion does so and strokes her hair.

'The word "No" has a reputation for being mean, selfish, unspiritual. When we say "Yes", we think we're being generous, understanding, polite. But I'm going to say "No" to you now. I won't do what you're asking me or making me do, even though you think it's in my best interests. You'll say that I'm only nineteen and don't yet fully understand life, but going to a party like the one tonight was quite enough for me to know what I do want and what I definitely don't want.

'I never planned to be a model, and I didn't even think I was capable of falling in love. I know that love can only survive when it's free, but who ever said I was anyone's slave? I'm a slave only to my heart, and in that case my burden is a very light one. I chose you before you chose me. I embarked on what seemed an impossible adventure and never complained about the consequences, whether it was society's preconceived ideas or resistance from my own family. I overcame all those things so that I could be with you here tonight, in Cannes, savouring the victory of an excellent fashion show, and knowing that there will be other opportunities in life – by your side.'

Her companion lies down next to her, her head in Jasmine's lap.

'The person who made me realise this was a man, a foreigner, whom I met tonight while I was at the party, lost in the crowd, not knowing what to say. I asked him what he was doing there, and he said that he'd lost his love and come here to look for her, but wasn't sure any more whether she really was what he wanted. He asked me to look around at the other guests. We were, he said, surrounded by people who were full of certainties, glories and conquests, but they weren't enjoying themselves. They think they're at the peak of their careers and the inevitable descent frightens them. They've forgotten that there's still a whole world to conquer because …'

'… because they've got used to life as it is.'

'Exactly. They have lots of things but few aspirations. They're full of problems solved, projects approved, businesses that prosper without them having to do anything. Now all that's left is the fear of change, which is why they go from party to party, from meeting to meeting, so as not to have time to think, and to meet the same people over and over and be able to believe that everything's the same. Certainties have replaced passions.'

'Take off your dress,' says her companion, preferring to say nothing more.

Jasmine gets up, takes off her dress and slips between the sheets.

'You take your clothes off too and put your arms around me. I really need to feel your arms around me because today I thought you were going to let me go.'

She does as Jasmine asks and turns out the light. Jasmine falls asleep at once in her arms. She, however, lies awake for some time, staring up at the ceiling, thinking that sometimes a nineteen-year-old girl, in all her innocence, can be wiser than a forty-one-year-old woman. However fearful and insecure she may feel right now, she'll be forced to grow. She'll have a powerful enemy in HH, who will doubtless create as many obstacles as he can to prevent her taking part in the Fashion Week in October. First, he'll insist on buying her name, and when that proves impossible, he'll try to discredit her with the Fédération, saying that she failed to keep her word.

The next few months will be very difficult.

What HH doesn't know, indeed, what no one knows, is that she possesses an absolute power that will help her overcome all difficulties: the love of the young woman now lying in her arms. For her, she would do anything – anything, that is, except kill.

With her, she is capable of anything – even winning.

1.55 a.m.

His company jet already has the engines running. Igor sits in his favourite seat – second row on the left – and waits for take-off. As soon as the seat-belt sign is turned off, he goes to the bar, serves himself a generous measure of vodka and drinks it down in one.

For a moment, he wonders if he really had succeeded in sending those messages to Ewa, while he was busy destroying worlds. Should he have been more explicit, adding a further note or a name or something like that? That would have been terribly risky – people might think he was a serial killer.

And he wasn't: he had an objective, which, fortunately, had changed in time.

The thought of Ewa doesn't weigh on him as much as it used to. He doesn't love her as he once did, and he doesn't hate her as he came to hate her. With time, she will disappear completely from his life, which is a shame because he's unlikely to find another woman like her, for all her defects.

He goes back to the bar, pours himself another vodka and again drinks it down in one. Will they realise that a single person was responsible for extinguishing those worlds? It doesn't matter. His only regret is the moment he decided to give himself up to the police in the afternoon. Fate, however, was on his side and he managed to complete his mission.

Yes, he had won, but the winner doesn't stand alone. His nightmares are at an end. An angel with dark eyebrows is watching over him and will teach him which path to follow from now on.

St John's Day, 19 March 2008

Acknowledgements

I could not possibly have written this book without the help of the many people who, whether openly or in confidence, gave me access to the information it contains. When I began my research, I never imagined that I would find so much of interest behind the façade of the world of glitz and glamour. Apart from the friends who have asked for their names not to be mentioned, I would like to thank Alexander Osterwald, Bernadette Imaculada Santos, Claudine and Elie Saab, David Rothkopf (the inventor of the term 'Superclass'), Deborah Williamson, Fátima Lopes, Fawaz Gruosi, Franco Cologni, Hildegard Follon, James W. Wright, Jennifer Bollinger, Johan Reckman, Jörn Pfotenhauer, Juliette Rigal, Kevin Heienberg, Kevin Karroll, Luca Burei, Maria de Lourdes Débat, Mario Rosa, Monty Shadow, Steffi Czerny, Victoria Navaloska, Yasser Hamid and Zeina Raphael, all of whom collaborated directly or indirectly in the writing of this book. I must confess that, for the most part, they collaborated indirectly, since I never usually discuss the subject of a book when I'm writing it.

Life is a
journey

Make sure you don't miss a thing.
Live it with Paulo Coelho.

Visit f /paulocoelho

How can you find your heart's desire?

A world-wide phenomenon; an inspiration for anyone seeking their path in life.

The Alchemist

Do you believe in yourself?

A modern-day adventure in the searing heat of the Mojave desert and an exploration of fear and self-doubt.

The Valkyries

How do we see the amazing in the everyday?

When two young lovers are reunited, they discover anew the truth of what lies in their hearts.

By the River Piedra
I Sat Down & Wept

What are you searching for?

A transforming journey on the pilgrims' road to Santiago – and the first of Paulo's extraordinary books.

The Pilgrimage

Can faith triumph over suffering?

Paulo Coelho's brilliant telling of the story of Elijah, who was forced to choose between love and duty.

The Fifth Mountain

Is life always worth living?

A fundamental moral question explored as only Paulo Coelho can.

Veronika Decides to Die

Could you be tempted into evil?

The inhabitants of a small town are challenged by a mysterious stranger to choose between good and evil.

The Devil & Miss Prym

Are you brave enough to live your dream?

Strategies and inspiration to help you follow your own path in a troubled world.

Manual of the Warrior of Light

Can sex be sacred?

An unflinching exploration of the lengths we go to in our search for love, sex and spirituality.

Eleven Minutes

How far would you go for your obsession?

A sweeping story of love, loss and longing that spans the world.

The Zahir

What happens when obsession turns to murder?

An enthralling story of jealousy, death and suspense.

The Winner Stands Alone

Can we dare to be true to ourselves?

A story that will transform the way we think about love, joy and sacrifice.

The Witch of Portobello

How will you know who your soulmate is?

A moving tale of passion, mystery and spirituality.

Brida

What does it mean to be truly alive?

Powerful tales of living and dying, destiny and choice, and love lost and found.

Like the Flowing River

Are you where you want to be?

Read *Aleph*. And rewrite your life.

Aleph

Is there a weapon more powerful than words?

A timeless and powerful exploration of personal growth, everyday wisdom and joy.

Manuscript Found in Accra

The WITCH of PORTOBELLO

Paulo Coelho was born in Brazil and has become one of the most widely read and loved authors in the world. Especially renowned for *The Alchemist* and *Eleven Minutes*, he has sold more than 320 million books worldwide and has been translated into 88 languages. The recipient of numerous prestigious international awards, amongst them the Crystal Award by the World Economic Forum and France's Légion d'Honneur, Paulo Coelho was inducted into the Brazilian Academy of Letters in 2002.

Also by Paulo Coelho

The Alchemist
The Pilgrimage
The Valkyries
By the River Piedra I Sat Down and Wept
The Fifth Mountain
Veronika Decides to Die
Manual of the Warrior of Light
Eleven Minutes
The Zahir
The Devil and Miss Prym
The Witch of Portobello
Brida
The Winner Stands Alone
Like the Flowing River
Aleph
Manuscript Found in Accra
Adultery
The Spy
Hippie

The WITCH of PORTOBELLO

PAULO COELHO

Author of THE ALCHEMIST

TRANSLATED FROM THE PORTUGUESE BY
MARGARET JULL COSTA

Thorsons

Thorsons
An imprint of HarperCollins*Publishers*
1 London Bridge Street
London SE1 9GF

HarperCollins*Publishers*
1st Floor, Watermarque Building, Ringsend Road
Dublin 4, Ireland

www.harpercollins.co.uk
www.paulocoelho.com
www.paulocoelhoblog.com

First published by HarperCollins*Publishers* 2007
This edition 2022

2 4 6 8 10 9 7 5 3 1

© Paulo Coelho 2006

English translation © Margaret Jull Costa 2007

Paulo Coelho asserts the moral right to
be identified as the author of this work

A catalogue record of this book is
available from the British Library

ISBN 978-0-00-854735-6

FICTION / PHILOSOPHY

Printed and bound in India by Thomson Press India Ltd

All rights reserved. No part of this publication may be
reproduced, stored in a retrieval system, or transmitted,
in any form or by any means, electronic, mechanical,
photocopying, recording or otherwise, without the prior
written permission of the publishers.

This book is produced from independently certified FSC® paper
to ensure responsible forest management.

O Mary!
conceived without sin,
pray for us who turn to you!
Amen.

No man, when he hath lighted a candle, putteth it in a secret place, neither under a bushel, but on a candlestick, that they which come in may see the light.

Luke 11: 33

For S.F.X., a sun who spread light and warmth wherever he went, and was an example to all those who think beyond their horizons.

Disclaimer

Before these statements left my desk and followed the fate I eventually chose for them, I considered using them as the basis for a traditional, painstakingly researched biography, recounting a true story. And so I read various biographies, thinking this would help me, only to realise that the biographer's view of his subject inevitably influences the results of his research. Since it wasn't my intention to impose my own opinions on the reader, but to set down the story of the 'Witch of Portobello' as seen by its main protagonists, I soon abandoned the idea of writing a straight biography and decided that the best approach would be simply to transcribe what people had told me.

Heron Ryan, 44, journalist

'No one lights a lamp in order to hide it behind the door: the purpose of light is to create more light, to open people's eyes, to reveal the marvels around.

No one sacrifices the most important thing she possesses: love.

No one places her dreams in the hands of those who might destroy them.

No one, that is, but Athena.

A long time after Athena's death, her former teacher asked me to go with her to the town of Prestonpans in Scotland. There, taking advantage of certain ancient feudal powers which were due to be abolished the following month, the town had granted official pardons to 81 people – and their cats – who were executed in the sixteenth and seventeenth centuries for practising witchcraft.

According to the official spokeswoman for the Barons Courts of Prestoungrange & Dolphinstoun: 'Most of those persons condemned … were convicted on the basis of spectral evidence – that is to say, prosecuting witnesses declared that they felt the presence of evil spirits or heard spirit voices.'

There's no point now in going into all the excesses committed by the Inquisition, with its torture chambers and its bonfires lit by hatred and vengeance; however, on our way to Prestonpans, Edda said several times that there was something about that gesture which she found unacceptable: the town and the 14th Baron of Prestoungrange & Dolphinstoun were 'granting pardons' to people who had been brutally executed.

'Here we are in the twenty-first century, and yet the descendants of the real criminals, those who killed the innocent victims, still feel they have the right to grant pardons. Do you know what I mean, Heron?'

I did. A new witch-hunt is starting to gain ground. This time the weapon isn't the red-hot iron, but irony and repression. Anyone who happens to discover a gift and dares to speak of their abilities is usually regarded with distrust. Generally speaking, their husband, wife, father or child, or whoever, instead of feeling proud, forbids all mention of the matter, fearful of exposing their family to ridicule.

Before I met Athena, I thought all such gifts were a dishonest way of exploiting people's despair. My trip to Transylvania to make a documentary on vampires was also a way of proving how easily people are deceived. Certain superstitions, however absurd they may seem, remain in the human imagination and are often used by unscrupulous people. When I visited Dracula's castle, which has been reconstructed merely to give tourists the feeling that they're in a special place, I was approached by a government official, who implied that I would receive a 'significant' (to use his word) gift when the film was shown on the BBC. In the mind of that official, I was helping to propagate the myth, and thus deserved a generous reward. One of the guides said that the number of visitors increased each year, and that any mention of the place would prove positive, even a programme saying that the castle was a fake, that Vlad Dracula was a historical figure who had nothing to do with the myth, and that it was all merely a product of the wild imaginings of one Irishman (*Editor's note: Bram Stoker*), who had never even visited the region.

I knew then that, however rigorous I was with the facts, I was unwittingly collaborating with the lie; even if the idea behind my script was to demythologise the place, people would believe what they wanted to believe; the guide was right, I would simply be helping to generate more publicity. I immediately abandoned the project, even though I'd already spent quite a lot of money on the trip and on my research.

And yet my journey to Transylvania was to have a huge impact on my life, for I met Athena there when she was trying to track down her mother. Destiny – mysterious, implacable Destiny – brought us face to face in the insignificant foyer of a still more insignificant hotel. I was witness to her first conversation with Deidre – or Edda, as she likes to be called. I watched, as if I were a spectator of my own life, as my heart struggled vainly not to allow itself to be seduced by a woman who didn't belong to my world. I applauded when reason lost the battle, and all I could do was surrender and accept that I was in love.

That love led me to see things I'd never imagined could exist – rituals, materialisations, trances. Believing that I was blinded by love, I doubted everything, but doubt, far from paralysing me, pushed me in the direction of oceans whose very existence I couldn't admit. It was this same energy which, in difficult times, helped me to confront the cynicism of journalist colleagues and to write about Athena and her work. And since that love remains alive, the energy remains, even though Athena is dead, even though all I want now is to forget what I saw and learned. I could only navigate that world while hand in hand with Athena.

These were her gardens, her rivers, her mountains. Now that she's gone, I need everything to return as quickly as possible to how it used to be. I'm going to concentrate more on traffic problems, Britain's foreign policy, on how we administer taxes. I want to go back to thinking that the world of magic is merely a clever trick, that people are superstitious, that anything science cannot explain has no right to exist.

When the meetings in Portobello started to get out of control, we had endless arguments about how she was behaving, although I'm glad now that she didn't listen to me. If there is any possible consolation in the tragedy of losing someone we love very much, it's the necessary hope that perhaps it was for the best.

I wake and fall asleep with that certainty; it's best that Athena left when she did rather than descend into the infernos of this world. She would never have regained her peace of mind after the events that earned her the nickname 'the witch of Portobello'. The rest of her life would have been a bitter clash between her personal dreams and collective reality. Knowing her as I did, she would have battled on to the end, wasting her energy and her joy on trying to prove something that no one, absolutely no one, was prepared to believe.

Who knows, perhaps she sought death the way a shipwreck victim seeks an island. She must have stood late at night in many a Tube station, waiting for muggers who never came. She must have walked through the most dangerous parts of London in search of a murderer who never appeared, or perhaps tried to provoke the anger of the physically strong, who refused to get angry.

Until, finally, she managed to get herself brutally murdered. But, then, how many of us will be saved the pain of seeing the most important things in our lives disappearing from one moment to the next? I don't just mean people, but our ideas and dreams too: we might survive a day, a week, a few years, but we're all condemned to lose. Our body remains alive, yet, sooner or later, our soul will receive the mortal blow.

The perfect crime – for we don't know who murdered our joy, what their motives were or where the guilty parties are to be found.

Are they aware of what they've done, those nameless guilty parties? I doubt it, because they, too – the depressed, the arrogant, the impotent and the powerful – are the victims of the reality they created.

They don't understand and would be incapable of understanding Athena's world. Yes, that's the best way to think of it – Athena's world. I'm finally coming to accept that I was only a temporary inhabitant, there as a favour, like someone who finds himself in a beautiful mansion, eating exquisite food, aware that this is only a party, that the mansion belongs to someone else, that the food was bought by someone else, and that the time will come when the lights will go out, the owners will go to bed, the servants will return to their quarters, the door will close, and he'll be out in the street again, waiting for a taxi or a bus to restore him to the mediocrity of his everyday life.

I'm going back, or, rather, part of me is going back to that world where only what we can see, touch and explain makes sense. I want to get back to the world of speeding tickets, people arguing with bank cashiers, eternal complaints about the weather, to horror films and Formula 1 racing. This is the universe I'll have to live with for the rest of my days. I'll get married, have children, and the past will become a distant memory, which will, in the end, make me ask myself: How could I have been so blind? How could I have been so ingenuous?

I also know that, at night, another part of me will remain wandering in space, in contact with things as real as the pack of cigarettes and the glass of gin before me now. My soul will dance with Athena's soul; I'll be with her while I sleep; I'll wake up sweating and go into the kitchen for a glass of water. I'll understand that in order to combat ghosts you must use weapons that form no part of reality. Then, following the advice of my grandmother, I'll place an open pair of scissors on my bedside table to snip off the end of the dream.

The next day, I'll look at the scissors with a touch of regret, but I must adapt to living in the world again or risk going mad.

Andrea McCain, 32, actress

'No one can manipulate anyone else. In any relationship, both parties know what they're doing, even if one of them complains later on that they were used.'

That's what Athena used to say, but she herself behaved quite differently, because she used and manipulated me with no consideration for my feelings. And given that we're talking about magic here, this makes the accusation an even more serious one; after all, she was my teacher, charged with passing on the sacred mysteries, with awakening the unknown force we all possess. When we venture into that unfamiliar sea, we trust blindly in those who guide us, believing that they know more than we do.

Well, I can guarantee that they don't. Not Athena, not Edda, nor any of the people I came to know through them. She told me she was learning through teaching, and although, at first, I refused to believe this, later I came to think that perhaps it was true. I realised it was one of her many ways of getting us to drop our guard and surrender to her charm.

People who are on a spiritual quest don't think, they simply want results. They want to feel powerful and superior to the anonymous masses. They want to be special. Athena played with other people's feelings in a quite terrifying way.

I understand that she once felt a profound admiration for St Thérèse of Lisieux. I have no interest in the Catholic faith, but, from what I've heard, Thérèse experienced a kind of mystical and physical union with God. Athena mentioned once that she would like to share a similar fate. Well, in that case, she should have joined a convent and devoted her life to prayer or to the service of the poor. That would have been much more useful to the world and far less dangerous than using music and rituals to induce in people a kind of intoxicated state that brought them into contact with both the best and the worst of themselves.

I sought her out when I was looking for some meaning to my life, although I didn't say as much at our first meeting. I should have realised from the start that Athena wasn't very interested in that; she wanted to live, dance, make love, travel, to gather people around her in order to demonstrate how wise she was, to show off her gifts, to provoke the neighbours, to make the most of all that is profane in us – although she always tried to give a spiritual gloss to that search.

Whenever we met, whether it was to perform some magical ceremony or to meet for a drink, I was conscious of her power. It was so strong I could almost touch it. Initially, I was fascinated and wanted to be like her. But one day, in a bar, she started talking about the 'Third Rite', which has to do with sexuality. She did this in the presence of my boyfriend. Her excuse was that she was teaching me something. Her real objective, in my opinion, was to seduce the man I loved.

And, of course, she succeeded.

It isn't good to speak ill of people who have passed from this life onto the astral plane. However, Athena won't have to account to me, but to all those forces which she turned to her own benefit, rather than channelling them for the good of humanity and for her own spiritual enlightenment.

The worst thing is that if it hadn't been for her compulsive exhibitionism, everything we began together could have worked out really well. Had she behaved more discreetly, we would now be fulfilling the mission with which we were entrusted. But she couldn't control herself; she thought she was the mistress of the truth, capable of overcoming all barriers merely by using her powers of seduction.

And the result? I was left alone. And I can't leave the work half-finished – I'll have to continue to the end, even though sometimes I feel very weak and often dispirited.

I'm not surprised that her life ended as it did: she was always flirting with danger. They say that extroverts are unhappier than introverts, and have to compensate for this by constantly proving to themselves how happy and contented and at ease with life they are. In her case, at least, this is absolutely true.

Athena was conscious of her own charisma, and she made all those who loved her suffer.

Including me.

Deidre O'Neill, 37, doctor, known as Edda

If a man we don't know phones us up one day and talks a little, makes no suggestions, says nothing special, but nevertheless pays us the kind of attention we rarely receive, we're quite capable of going to bed with him that same night, feeling relatively in love. That's what we women are like, and there's nothing wrong with that – it's the nature of the female to open herself to love easily.

It was this same love that opened me up to my first encounter with the Mother when I was nineteen. Athena was the same age the first time she went into a trance while dancing. But that's the only thing we had in common – the age of our initiation.

In every other aspect, we were totally and profoundly different, especially in the way we dealt with other people. As her teacher, I always did my best to help her in her inner search. As her friend – although I'm not sure my feelings of friendship were reciprocated – I tried to alert her to the fact that the world wasn't ready for the kind of transformations she wanted to provoke. I remember spending a few sleepless nights before deciding to allow her to act with total freedom and follow the demands of her heart.

Her greatest problem was that she was a woman of the twenty-second century living in the twenty-first, and making no secret of the fact either. Did she pay a price? She certainly did. But she would have paid a still higher price if she had repressed her true exuberant self. She would have been bitter and frustrated, always concerned about 'what other people might think', always saying 'I'll just sort these things out, then I'll devote myself to my dream', always complaining 'that the conditions are never quite right'.

Everyone's looking for the perfect teacher, but although their teachings might be divine, teachers are all too human, and that's something people find hard to accept. Don't confuse the teacher with the lesson, the ritual with the ecstasy, the transmitter of the symbol with the symbol itself. The Tradition is linked to our encounter with the forces of life and not with the people who bring this about. But we are weak: we ask the Mother to send us guides, and all she sends are signs to the road we need to follow.

Pity those who seek for shepherds, instead of longing for freedom! An encounter with the superior energy is open to anyone, but remains far from those who shift responsibility onto others. Our time on this Earth is sacred, and we should celebrate every moment.

The importance of this has been completely forgotten: even religious holidays have been transformed into opportunities to go to the beach or the park or skiing. There are no more rituals. Ordinary actions can no longer be transformed into manifestations of the sacred. We cook and complain that it's a waste of time, when we should be pouring our love into making that food. We work and believe it's a divine curse, when we should be using our skills to bring pleasure and to spread the energy of the Mother.

Athena brought to the surface the immensely rich world we all carry in our souls, without realising that people aren't yet ready to accept their own powers.

We women, when we're searching for a meaning to our lives or for the path of knowledge, always identify with one of four classic archetypes.

The Virgin (and I'm not speaking here of a sexual virgin) is the one whose search springs from her complete independence, and everything she learns is the fruit of her ability to face challenges alone.

The Martyr finds her way to self-knowledge through pain, surrender and suffering.

The Saint finds her true reason for living in unconditional love and in her ability to give without asking anything in return.

Finally, the Witch justifies her existence by going in search of complete and limitless pleasure.

Normally, a woman has to choose from one of these traditional feminine archetypes, but Athena was all four at once.

Obviously we can justify her behaviour, alleging that all those who enter a state of trance or ecstasy lose contact with reality. That's not true: the physical world and the spiritual world are the same thing. We can see the Divine in each speck of dust, but that doesn't stop us wiping it away with a wet sponge. The Divine doesn't disappear; it's transformed into the clean surface.

Athena should have been more careful. When I reflect upon the life and death of my pupil, it seems to me that I had better change the way I behave too.

Lella Zainab, 64, numerologist

Athena? What an interesting name! Let's see … her Maximum number is nine. Optimistic, sociable, likely to be noticed in a crowd. People might go to her in search of understanding, compassion, generosity, and for precisely that reason she should be careful, because that tendency to popularity could go to her head and she'll end up losing more than she gains. She should also watch her tongue, because she tends to speak more than common sense dictates.

As for her Minimum number eleven, I sense that she longs for some leadership position. She has an interest in mystical subjects and through these tries to bring harmony to those around her.

However, this is in direct conflict with the number nine, which is the sum of the day, month and year of her birth reduced to a single figure: she'll always be subject to envy, sadness, introversion and impulsive decisions. She must be careful not to let herself be affected by negative vibrations: excessive ambition, intolerance, abuse of power, extravagance.

Because of that conflict, I suggest she take up some career that doesn't involve emotional contact with people, like computing or engineering.

Oh, she's dead? I'm sorry. So what *did* she do?

What did Athena do? She did a little of everything, but, if I had to summarise her life, I'd say: she was a priestess who understood the forces of nature. Or, rather, she was someone who, by the simple fact of having little to lose or to hope for in life, took greater risks than other people and ended up being transformed into the forces she thought she mastered.

She was a supermarket checkout girl, a bank employee, a property dealer, and in each of these positions she always revealed the priestess within. I lived with her for eight years, and I owed her this: to recover her memory, her identity.

The most difficult thing in collecting together these statements was persuading people to let me use their real names. Some said they didn't want to be involved in this kind of story; others tried to conceal their opinions and feelings. I explained that my real intention was to help all those involved to understand her better, and that no reader would believe in anonymous statements.

They finally agreed because they all believed that they knew the unique and definitive version of any event, however insignificant. During the recordings, I saw that things are never absolute; they depend on each individual's perceptions. And the best way to know who we are is often to find out how others see us.

This doesn't mean that we should do what others expect us to do, but it helps us to understand ourselves better. I owed it to Athena to recover her story, to write her myth.

Samira R. Khalil, 57, housewife, Athena's mother

Please, don't call her Athena. Her real name is Sherine. Sherine Khalil, our much-loved, much-wanted daughter, whom both my husband and I wish we had engendered.

Life, however, had other plans – when fate is very generous with us, there is always a well into which all our dreams can tumble.

We lived in Beirut in the days when everyone considered it the most beautiful city in the Middle East. My husband was a successful industrialist, we married for love, we travelled to Europe every year, we had friends, we were invited to all the important social events, and, once, the President of the United States himself visited my house. Imagine that! Three unforgettable days, during two of which the American secret service scoured every corner of our house (they'd been in the area for more than a month already, taking up strategic positions, renting apartments, disguising themselves as beggars or young lovers). And for one day, or, rather, two hours, we partied. I'll never forget the look of envy in our friends' eyes, and the excitement of having our photo taken alongside the most powerful man on the planet.

We had it all, apart from the one thing we wanted most – a child. And so we had nothing.

We tried everything: we made vows and promises, went to places where miracles were guaranteed, we consulted doctors, witchdoctors, took remedies and drank elixirs and magic potions. I had artificial insemination twice and lost the baby both times. On the second occasion, I also lost my left ovary, and after that no doctor was prepared to risk such a venture again.

That was when one of the many friends who knew of our plight suggested the one possible solution: adoption. He said he had contacts in Romania, and that the process wouldn't take long.

A month later, we got on a plane. Our friend had important business dealings with the dictator who ruled the country at the time, and whose name I now forget (*Editor's note: Nicolae Ceauşescu*), and so we managed to avoid the bureaucratic red tape and went straight to an adoption centre in Sibiu, in Transylvania. There we were greeted with coffee, cigarettes, mineral water, and with the paperwork signed and sealed, all we had to do was choose a child.

They took us to a very cold nursery, and I couldn't imagine how they could leave those poor children in such a place. My first instinct was to adopt them all, to carry them off to Lebanon where there was sun and freedom, but obviously that was a crazy idea. We walked up and down between the cots, listening to the children crying, terrified by the magnitude of the decision we were about to take.

For more than an hour, neither I nor my husband spoke a word. We went out, drank coffee, smoked and then went back in again – and this happened several times. I noticed that the woman in charge of adoptions was growing impatient; she wanted an immediate decision. At that moment, following an instinct I would dare to describe as maternal – as if I'd found a child who should have been mine in this incarnation, but who had come into the world in another woman's womb – I pointed to one particular baby girl.

The woman advised us to think again. And she'd been so impatient for us to make a decision! But I was sure.

Nevertheless – trying not to hurt my feelings (she thought we had contacts in the upper echelons of the Romanian government) – she whispered to me, so that my husband wouldn't hear: 'I know it won't work out. She's the daughter of a gipsy.'

I retorted that culture isn't something that's transmitted through the genes. The child, who was barely three months old, would be our daughter, brought up according to our customs. She would go to our church, visit our beaches, read books in French, study at the American School in Beirut. Besides, I knew nothing about gipsy culture – and I still know nothing. I only know that they travel a lot, don't wash very often, aren't to be trusted, and wear earrings. Legend has it that they kidnap children and carry them off in their caravans, but here, exactly the opposite was happening; they had left a child behind for me to take care of.

The woman tried again to dissuade me, but I was already signing the papers and asking my husband to do the same. On the flight back to Beirut, the world seemed different: God had given me a reason for living, working and fighting in this vale of tears. We now had a child to justify all our efforts.

Sherine grew in wisdom and beauty – I expect all parents say that, but I really do think she was an exceptional child. One afternoon, when she was five, one of my brothers said that, if, in the future, she wanted to work abroad, her name would always betray her origins, and he suggested changing it to one that gave nothing away, like Athena, for example. Now, of course, I know that Athena refers not only to the capital of Greece, but that it is also the name of the Greek goddess of wisdom, intelligence and war.

Perhaps my brother knew not only that, but was aware, too, of the problems an Arab name might bring in the future, for he was very involved in politics, as were all our family, and wanted to protect his niece from the black clouds which he, and only he, could see on the horizon. Most surprising of all was that Sherine liked the sound of the word. That same afternoon, she began referring to herself as Athena and no one could persuade her to do otherwise. To please her, we adopted the nickname too, thinking that it would be a passing fancy.

Can a name affect a person's life? Time passed, and the name stuck.

From very early on we discovered that she had a strong religious vocation – she spent all her time in the church and knew the gospels by heart; this was at once a blessing and a curse. In a world that was starting to be divided more and more along religious lines, I feared for my daughter's safety. It was then that Sherine began telling us, as if it were the most natural thing in the world, that she had a series of invisible friends – angels and saints whose images she was accustomed to seeing in the church we attended. All children everywhere have visions, but they usually forget about them after a certain age. They also treat inanimate objects, such as dolls or fluffy tigers, as if they were real. However, I really did feel she was going too far when I picked her up from school one day, and she told me that she'd seen 'a woman dressed in white, like the Virgin Mary'.

Naturally, I believe in angels. I even believe that the angels speak to little children, but when a child starts seeing visions of grown-ups, that's another matter. I've read about various shepherds and country people who claimed to have seen a woman in white, and how this eventually destroyed their lives, because others sought them out, expecting miracles;

then the priests took over, their village became a centre of pilgrimage, and the poor children ended their lives in a convent or a monastery. I was, therefore, very concerned about this story. Sherine was at an age when she should be more concerned with make-up kits, painting her nails, watching soppy TV soaps and children's programmes. There was something wrong with my daughter, and I consulted an expert.

'Relax,' he said.

According to this paediatrician specialising in child psychology – and according to most other doctors in the field – invisible friends are a projection of a child's dreams and a safe way of helping the child to discover her desires and express her feelings.

'Yes, but a vision of a woman in white?'

He replied that perhaps Sherine didn't understand our way of seeing or explaining the world. He suggested that we should gradually begin preparing the ground to tell her that she was adopted. In the paediatrician's words, the worst thing that could happen would be for her to find out by herself. Then she would begin to doubt everyone, and her behaviour might become unpredictable.

From then on, we changed the way we talked to her. I don't know how much children remember of what happens to them, but we started trying to show her just how much we loved her and that there was no need for her to take refuge in an imaginary world.

She needed to see that her visible universe was as beautiful as it could possibly be, that her parents would protect her from any danger, that Beirut was a lovely city and its beaches full of sun and people. Without ever mentioning 'the woman in white', I began spending more time with my daughter; I invited her schoolfriends to come to our house; I seized every opportunity to shower her with affection.

The strategy worked. My husband used to travel a lot, and Sherine always missed him. In the name of love, he resolved to change his way of life a little. Her solitary conversations began to be replaced by games shared by father, mother and daughter.

Everything was going well. Then, one night, she came into our room in tears, saying that she was frightened and that hell was close at hand.

I was alone at home. My husband had had to go away again, and I thought perhaps this was the reason for her despair. But hell? What were they teaching her at school or at church? I decided to go and talk to her teacher the next day.

Sherine, meanwhile, wouldn't stop crying. I took her over to the window and showed her the Mediterranean outside, lit by the full moon. I told her there were no devils, only stars in the sky and people strolling up and down the boulevard outside our apartment. I told her not to worry, that she needn't be afraid, but she continued to weep and tremble. After spending almost half an hour trying to calm her, I began to get worried. I begged her to stop; after all, she was no longer a child. I thought perhaps her first period had started and discreetly asked if there was any blood.

'Yes, lots.'

I got some cotton wool and asked her to lie down so that I could take care of her 'wound'. It wasn't important. I would explain tomorrow. However, her period hadn't started. She cried for a while longer, but she must have been tired, because then she fell asleep.

And the following morning, there was blood.

Four men had been murdered. To me, this was just another of the eternal tribal battles to which my people have become accustomed. To Sherine, it clearly meant nothing, because she didn't even mention her nightmare.

Meanwhile, from that date onwards, hell came ever closer and it hasn't gone away since. On that same day, twenty-six Palestinians were killed on a bus, as revenge for the murders. Twenty-four hours later, it was impossible to walk down the street because of shots coming from every angle. The schools closed, Sherine was hurried home by one of her teachers, and the situation went from bad to worse. My husband interrupted his business trip halfway through and came home, where he spent whole days on the phone to his friends in government, but no one said anything that made any sense. Sherine heard the shots outside and my husband's angry shouts indoors, but, to my surprise, she didn't say a word. I tried to tell her that it wouldn't last, that soon we'd be able to go to the beach again, but she would simply look away or ask for a book to read or a record to play. While hell gradually put down roots, Sherine read and listened to music.

But, if you don't mind, I'd prefer not to dwell on that. I don't want to think about the threats we received, about who was right, who was guilty and who was innocent. The fact is that, a few months later, if you wanted to cross a particular street, you had to catch a boat across to the island of Cyprus, get on another boat and disembark on the other side of the street.

For nearly a year, we stayed pretty much shut up indoors, always hoping that the situation would improve, always thinking it was a temporary thing, and that the government would take control. One morning, while she was listening to a record on her little portable record-player, Sherine started dancing and saying things like: 'This is going to last for a long, long time.'

I tried to stop her, but my husband grabbed my arm. I realised that he was listening to what she was saying and taking it seriously. I never understood why, and we've never spoken about it since. It's a kind of taboo between us.

The following day, he began taking unexpected steps, and two weeks later we were on a boat bound for London. Later, we would learn that, although there are no reliable statistics, during those years of civil war about 44,000 people died, 180,000 were wounded, and thousands made homeless. The fighting continued for other reasons, the country was occupied by foreign troops, and the hell continues to this day.

'It's going to last for a long, long time,' said Sherine. Unfortunately, she was right.

Lukás Jessen-Petersen, 32, engineer, ex-husband

When I first met Athena, she already knew that she was adopted. She was just nineteen and about to have a stand-up fight with a fellow student in the university cafeteria because the fellow student, assuming Athena to be English (white skin, straight hair, eyes that were sometimes green, sometimes grey), had made some insulting remark about the Middle East.

It was the first day of term for these students and they knew nothing about each other. But Athena got up, grabbed the other girl by the collar and started screaming:

'Racist!'

I saw the look of terror in the girl's eyes and the look of excitement in the eyes of the other students, eager to see what would happen next. I was in the year above, and I knew exactly what the consequences would be: they would both be hauled up before the vice-chancellor, an official complaint would be made, and that would probably be followed by expulsion from the university and a possible police inquiry into alleged racism, etc. etc. Everyone would lose.

'Shut up!' I yelled, without really knowing what I was saying.

I knew neither of the girls. I'm not the saviour of the world and, to be perfectly honest, young people find the occasional fight stimulating, but I couldn't help myself.

'Stop it!' I shouted again at the pretty young woman, who now had the other equally pretty young woman by the throat. She shot me a furious glance. Then, suddenly, something changed. She smiled, although she still had her hands around her colleague's throat.

'You forgot to say "please",' she said.

Everyone laughed.

'Stop,' I asked again. 'Please.'

She released the other girl and came over to me. All heads turned to watch.

'You have excellent manners. Do you also have a cigarette?'

I offered her my pack of cigarettes, and we went outside for a smoke. She had gone from outrage to nonchalance, and minutes later she was laughing, discussing the weather and asking if I liked this or that pop group. I heard the bell ringing for class and solemnly ignored the rule I'd been brought up to obey all my life: do your duty. I stayed there chatting, as if there were no university, no fights, no canteens, no wind or cold or sun. There was only that young woman with the grey eyes, saying the most boring and pointless things, but capable, nonetheless, of holding my interest for the rest of my life.

Two hours later, we were having lunch together. Seven hours later, we were in a bar, having supper and drinking whatever our limited budgets allowed us to eat and drink. Our conversations grew ever more profound, and in a short space of time I knew practically everything about her life – Athena recounted details of her childhood and adolescence with no prompting from me. Later, I realised she was the same with everyone, but, that day, I felt like the most important man on the face of the Earth.

She had come to London fleeing the civil war that had broken out in Lebanon. Her father, a Maronite Christian (*Editor's note: a branch of the Catholic Church, which, although it comes under the authority of the Vatican, does not require priests to be celibate and uses both Middle Eastern and Orthodox rituals*), had started to receive death threats because he worked for the Lebanese government, but despite this, he couldn't make up his mind to leave and go into exile. Then Athena, overhearing a phone conversation, decided that it was time she grew up, that she assumed her filial responsibilities and protected those she loved.

She performed a kind of dance and pretended that she'd gone into a trance (she had learned all about this kind of thing at school when she studied the lives of the saints), and started making various pronouncements. I don't know how a mere child could possibly persuade adults to make decisions based on what she said, but that, according to Athena, was precisely what happened. Her father was very superstitious, and she was convinced that she'd saved the lives of her family.

They arrived here as refugees, but not as beggars. The Lebanese community is scattered all over the world, and her father soon found a way of re-establishing his business, and life went on. Athena was able to study at good schools, she attended dance classes – because dance was her passion – and when she'd finished at secondary school, she chose to take a degree in engineering.

Once they were living in London, her parents invited her out to supper at one of the most expensive restaurants in the city, and explained, very carefully, that she had been adopted. Athena pretended to be surprised, hugged them both, and said that nothing would change their relationship.

The truth was, though, that a friend of the family, in a moment of malice, had called her 'an ungrateful orphan' and put her lack of manners down to the fact that she was 'not her parents' "real" daughter'. She had hurled an ashtray at him, cutting his face, and then cried for two whole days, after which she quickly got used to the idea that she was adopted. The malicious family friend was left with an unexplained scar and took to saying that he'd been attacked in the street by muggers.

I asked if she would like to go out with me the next day. She told me that she was a virgin, went to church on Sundays, and had no interest in romantic novels – she was more concerned with reading everything she could about the situation in the Middle East.

She was, in short, busy. Very busy.

'People think that a woman's only dream is to get married and have children. And given what I've told you, you probably think that I've suffered a lot in life. It's not true, and, besides, I've been there already. I've known other men who wanted to "protect" me from all those tragedies. What they forget is that, from Ancient Greece on, the people who returned from battle were either dead on their shields or stronger, despite or because of their scars. It's better that way: I've lived on a battlefield since I was born, but I'm still alive and I don't need anyone to protect me.'

She paused.

'You see how cultured I am?'

'Oh, very, but when you attack someone weaker than yourself, you make it look as if you really do need protection. You could have ruined your university career right there and then.'

'You're right. OK, I accept the invitation.'

We started seeing each other regularly, and the closer I got to her, the more I discovered my own light, because she always encouraged me to give the best of myself. She had never read any books on magic or esoterics. She said they were things of the Devil, and that salvation was only possible through Jesus – end of story. Sometimes, though, she said things that didn't seem entirely in keeping with the teachings of the Church.

'Christ surrounded himself with beggars, prostitutes, tax-collectors and fishermen. I think what he meant by this was that the divine spark is in every soul and is never extinguished. When I sit still, or when I'm feeling very agitated, I feel as if I were vibrating along with the whole Universe. And I know things then that I don't know, as if God were guiding my steps. There are moments when I feel that everything is being revealed to me.'

Then she would correct herself:

'But that's wrong.'

Athena always lived between two worlds: what she felt was true and what she had been taught by her faith.

One day, after almost a semester of equations, calculations and structural studies, she announced that she was going to leave university.

'But you've never said anything to me about it!' I said.

'I was even afraid of talking about it to myself, but this morning I went to see my hairdresser. She worked day and night so that her daughter could finish her sociology degree. The daughter finally graduated and, after knocking on many doors, found work as a secretary at a cement works. Yet even today, my hairdresser said very proudly: "My daughter's got a degree." Most of my parents' friends and most of my parents' friends' children, also have degrees. This doesn't mean that they've managed to find the kind of work they wanted. Not at all; they went to university because someone, at a time when universities seemed important, said that, in order to rise in the world, you had to have a degree. And thus the world was deprived of some excellent gardeners, bakers, antique dealers, sculptors and writers.'

I asked her to give it some more thought before taking such a radical step, but she quoted these lines by Robert Frost:

Two roads diverged in a wood, and I –
I took the one less traveled by,
And that has made all the difference.

The following day, she didn't turn up for class. At our following meeting, I asked what she was going to do.

'I'm going to get married and have a baby.'

This wasn't an ultimatum. I was twenty, she was nineteen, and I thought it was still too early to take on such a commitment.

But Athena was quite serious. And I needed to choose between losing the one thing that really filled my thoughts – my love for that woman – and losing my freedom and all the choices that the future promised me.

To be honest, the decision was easy.

Father Giancarlo Fontana, 72

Of course I was surprised when the couple, both of them much too young, came to the church to arrange the wedding ceremony. I hardly knew Lukás Jessen-Petersen, but that same day I learned that his family – obscure aristocrats from Denmark – were totally opposed to the union. They weren't just against the marriage, they were against the Church as well.

According to his father – who based himself on frankly unanswerable scientific arguments – the Bible, on which the whole religion is based, wasn't really a book, but a collage of sixty-six different manuscripts, the real name or identity of whose authors is unknown; he said that almost a thousand years elapsed between the writing of the first book and the last, longer than the time that has elapsed since Columbus discovered America. And no living being on the planet – from monkeys down to parrots – needs ten commandments in order to know how to behave. All that it takes for the world to remain in harmony is for each being to follow the laws of nature.

Naturally, I read the Bible and know a little of its history, but the human beings who wrote it were instruments of Divine Power, and Jesus forged a far stronger bond than the ten commandments: love. Birds and monkeys, or any of God's creatures, obey their instincts and merely do what they're programmed to do. In the case of the human being, things are more complicated because we know about love and its traps.

Oh dear, here I am making a sermon, when I should be telling you about my meeting with Athena and Lukás. While I was talking to the young man – and I say talking, because we don't share the same faith, and I'm not, therefore, bound by the secret of the confessional – I learned that, as well as the household's general anticlericalism, there was a lot of resistance to Athena because she was a foreigner. I felt like quoting from the Bible, from a part that isn't a profession of faith, but a call to common sense:

'Thou shalt not abhor an Edomite, for he is thy brother; thou shalt not abhor an Egyptian, because thou wast a stranger in his land.'

I'm sorry, there I am quoting the Bible again, and I promise I'll try to control myself from now on. After talking to the young man, I spent at least two hours with Sherine, or Athena as she preferred to be called.

Athena had always intrigued me. Ever since she first started coming to the church, it seemed to me that she had one clear ambition: to become a saint. She told me – although her fiancé didn't know this – that shortly before civil war broke out in Beirut she'd had an experience very similar to that of St Thérèse of Lisieux: she had seen the streets running with blood. One could attribute this to some trauma in childhood or adolescence, but the fact is that, to a greater or lesser extent, all creative human beings have such experiences, which are known as 'possession by the sacred'. Suddenly, for a fraction of a second, we feel that our whole life is justified, our sins forgiven, and that love is still the strongest force, one that can transform us forever.

But, at the same time, we feel afraid. Surrendering completely to love, be it human or divine, means giving up everything, including our own well-being or our ability to make decisions. It means loving in the deepest sense of the word. The truth is that we don't want to be saved in the way God has chosen; we want to keep absolute control over our every step, to be fully conscious of our decisions, to be capable of choosing the object of our devotion.

It isn't like that with love – it arrives, moves in and starts directing everything. Only very strong souls allow themselves to be swept along, and Athena was a strong soul. So strong that she spent hours in deep contemplation. She had a special gift for music; they say that she danced very well too, but since the church isn't really the appropriate place for that, she used to bring her guitar each morning and spend some time there singing to the Holy Virgin before going off to her classes.

I can still remember the first time I heard her. I'd just finished celebrating morning mass with the few parishioners prepared to get up that early on a winter's morning, when I realised that I'd forgotten to collect the money left in the offering box. When I went back in, I heard some music that made me see everything differently, as if the atmosphere had been touched by the hand of an angel. In one corner, in a kind of ecstasy, a young woman of about twenty sat playing her guitar and singing hymns of praise, with her eyes fixed on the statue of the Holy Virgin.

I went over to the offering box. She noticed my presence and stopped what she was doing, but I nodded to her, encouraging her to go on. Then I sat down on one of the pews, closed my eyes and listened.

At that moment, a sense of Paradise, of 'possession by the sacred', seemed to descend from the heavens. As if she understood what was going on in my heart, the young woman began to intersperse music with silence. Each time she stopped playing, I would say a prayer. Then the music would start up again.

And I was conscious that I was experiencing something unforgettable, one of those magical moments which we only understand when it has passed. I was entirely in the present, with no past, no future, absorbed in experiencing the morning, the music, the sweetness and the unexpected prayer. I entered a state of worship and ecstasy and gratitude for being in the world, glad that I'd followed my vocation despite my family's opposition. In the simplicity of that small chapel, in the voice of that young woman, in the morning light flooding everything, I understood once again that the grandeur of God reveals itself through simple things.

After many tears on my part and after what seemed to me an eternity, the young woman stopped playing. I turned round and realised that she was one of my parishioners. After that, we became friends, and whenever we could, we shared in that worship through music.

However, the idea of marriage took me completely by surprise. Since we knew each other fairly well, I asked how she thought her husband's family would react.

'Badly, very badly.'

As tactfully as I could, I asked if, for any reason, she was being forced into marriage.

'No, I'm still a virgin. I'm not pregnant.'

I asked if she'd told her own family, and she said that she had, and that their reaction had been one of horror, accompanied by tears from her mother and threats from her father.

'When I come here to praise the Virgin with my music, I'm not bothered about what other people might think, I'm simply sharing my feelings with Her. And that's how it's always been, ever since I was old enough to think for myself. I'm a vessel in which the Divine Energy can make itself manifest. And that energy is asking me now to have a child, so that I can give it what my birth mother never gave me: protection and security.'

'No one is secure on this Earth,' I replied. She still had a long future ahead of her; there was plenty of time for the miracle of creation to occur. However, Athena was determined:

'St Thérèse didn't rebel against the illness that afflicted her, on the contrary, she saw it as a sign of God's Glory. St Thérèse was only fifteen, much younger than me, when she decided to enter a convent. She was forbidden to do so, but she insisted. She decided to go and speak to the Pope himself – can you imagine? To speak to the Pope! And she got what she wanted. That same Glory is asking something far simpler and far more generous of me – to become a mother. If I wait much longer, I won't be able to be a companion to my child, the age difference will be too great, and we won't share the same interests.'

She wouldn't be alone in that, I said.

But Athena continued as if she wasn't listening:

'I'm only happy when I think that God exists and is listening to me; but that isn't enough to go on living, when nothing seems to make sense. I pretend a happiness I don't feel; I hide my sadness so as not to worry those who love me and care about me. Recently, I've even considered suicide. At night, before I go to sleep, I have long conversations with myself, praying for this idea to go away; it would be such an act of ingratitude, an escape, a way of spreading tragedy and misery over the Earth. In the mornings, I come here to talk to St Thérèse and to ask her to free me from the demons I speak to at night. It's worked so far, but I'm beginning to weaken. I know I have a mission which I've long rejected, and now I must accept it. That mission is to be a mother. I must carry out that mission or go mad. If I don't feel life growing inside me, I'll never be able to accept life outside me.'

Lukás Jessen-Petersen, ex-husband

When Viorel was born, I had just turned twenty-two. I was no longer the student who had married a fellow student, but a man responsible for supporting his family, and with an enormous burden on my shoulders. My parents, who didn't even come to the wedding, made any financial help conditional on my leaving Athena and gaining custody of the child (or, rather, that's what my father said, because my mother used to phone me up, weeping, saying I must be mad, but saying, too, how much she'd like to hold her grandson in her arms). I hoped that, as they came to understand my love for Athena and my determination to stay with her, their resistance would gradually break down.

It didn't. And now I had to provide for my wife and child. I abandoned my studies at the Engineering Faculty. I got a phone-call from my father, a mixture of stick and carrot: he said that if I continued as I was, I'd end up being disinherited, but that if I went back to university, he'd consider helping me, in his words, 'provisionally'. I refused. The romanticism of youth demands that we always take very radical stances. I could, I said, solve my problems alone.

During the time before Viorel was born, Athena began helping me to understand myself better. This didn't happen through sex – our sexual relationship was, I must confess, very tentative – but through music.

As I later learned, music is as old as human beings. Our ancestors, who travelled from cave to cave, couldn't carry many things, but modern archaeology shows that, as well as the little they might have with them in the way of food, there was always a musical instrument in their baggage, usually a drum. Music isn't just something that comforts or distracts us, it goes beyond that – it's an ideology. You can judge people by the kind of music they listen to.

As I watched Athena dance during her pregnancy and listened to her play the guitar to calm the baby and make him feel that he was loved, I began to allow her way of seeing the world to affect my life too. When Viorel was born, the first thing we did when we brought him home was to play Albinoni's Adagio. When we quarrelled, it was the force of music – although I can't make any logical connection between the two things, except in some kind of hippyish way – that helped us get through difficult times.

But all this romanticism didn't bring in the money. Since I played no instrument and couldn't even offer my services as background music in a bar, I finally got a job as a trainee with a firm of architects, doing structural calculations. They paid me a very low hourly rate, and so I would leave the house very early each morning and come home late. I hardly saw my son, who would be sleeping by then, and I was almost too exhausted to talk or make love to my wife. Every night, I asked myself: when will we be able to improve our financial situation and live in the style we deserve? Although I largely agreed with Athena when she talked about the pointlessness of having a degree, in engineering (and law and medicine, for example), there are certain basic technical facts that are essential if we're not to put people's lives at risk. And I'd been forced to interrupt my training in my chosen profession, which meant abandoning a dream that was very important to me.

The rows began. Athena complained that I didn't pay enough attention to the baby, that he needed a father, that if she'd simply wanted a child, she could have done that on her own, without causing me all these problems. More than once, I slammed out of the house, saying that she didn't understand me, and that I didn't understand either how I'd ever agreed to the 'madness' of having a child at twenty, before we had even a minimum of financial security. Gradually, out of sheer exhaustion and irritation, we stopped making love.

I began to slide into depression, feeling that I'd been used and manipulated by the woman I loved. Athena noticed my increasingly strange state of mind, but, instead of helping me, she focused her energies on Viorel and on music. Work became my escape. I would occasionally talk to my parents, and they would always say, as they had so many times before, that she'd had the baby in order to get me to marry her.

She also became increasingly religious. She insisted on having our son baptised with a name she herself had decided on – Viorel, a Romanian name. Apart from a few immigrants, I doubt that anyone else in England is called Viorel, but I thought it showed imagination on her part, and I realised, too, that she was making some strange connection with a past she'd never known – her days in the orphanage in Sibiu.

I tried to be adaptable, but I felt I was losing Athena because of the child. Our arguments became more frequent, and she threatened to leave because she feared that Viorel was picking up the 'negative energy' from our quarrels. One night, when she made this threat again, I was the one who left, thinking that I'd go back as soon as I'd calmed down a bit.

I started wandering aimlessly round London, cursing the life I'd chosen, the child I'd agreed to have, and the wife who seemed to have no further interest in me. I went into the first bar I came to, near a Tube station, and downed four glasses of whisky. When the bar closed at eleven, I searched out one of those shops that stay open all night, bought more whisky, sat down on a bench in a square and continued drinking. A group of youths approached me and asked to share the bottle with me. When I refused, they attacked me. The police arrived, and we were all carted off to the police station.

I was released after making a statement. I didn't bring any charges, saying that it had been nothing but a silly disagreement; after all, I didn't want to spend months appearing at various courts, as the victim of an attack. I was still so drunk that, just as I was about to leave, I stumbled and fell sprawling across an inspector's desk. The inspector was angry, but instead of arresting me on the spot for insulting a police officer, he threw me out into the street.

And there was one of my attackers, who thanked me for not taking the case any further. He pointed out that I was covered in mud and blood and suggested I get a change of clothes before returning home. Instead of going on my way, I asked him to do me a favour: to listen to me, because I desperately needed to talk to someone.

For an hour, he listened in silence to my woes. I wasn't really talking to him, but to myself: a young man with his whole life before him, with a possibly brilliant career ahead of him – as well as a family with the necessary contacts to open many doors – but who now looked like a beggar – drunk, tired, depressed and penniless. And all because of a woman who didn't even pay me any attention.

By the end of my story I had a clearer view of my situation: a life which I had chosen in the belief that love conquers all. And it isn't true. Sometimes love carries us into the abyss, taking with us, to make matters worse, the people we love. In my case, I was well on the way to destroying not only my life, but Athena's and Viorel's too.

At that moment, I said to myself once again that I was a man, not the boy who'd been born with a silver spoon in his mouth, and that I'd faced with dignity all the challenges that had been placed before me. Athena was already asleep, with the baby in her arms. I took a bath, went outside again to throw my dirty clothes in the bin, and lay down, feeling strangely sober.

The next day, I told Athena that I wanted a divorce. She asked me why.

'Because I love you. Because I love Viorel. And because all I've done is to blame you both because I had to give up my dream of becoming an engineer. If we'd waited a little, things would have been different, but you were only thinking about your plans and forgot to include me in them.'

Athena said nothing, as if she had been expecting this, or as if she had unconsciously been provoking such a response.

My heart was bleeding because I was hoping that she'd ask me, please, to stay. But she seemed calm and resigned, concerned only that the baby might hear our conversation. It was then that I felt sure she had never loved me, and that I had merely been the instrument for the realisation of her mad dream to have a baby at nineteen.

I told her that she could keep the house and the furniture, but she wouldn't hear of it. She'd stay with her parents for a while, then look for a job and rent her own apartment. She asked if I could help out financially with Viorel, and I agreed at once.

I got up, gave her one last, long kiss and insisted again that she should stay in the house, but she repeated her resolve to go to her parents' house as soon as she'd packed up all her things. I stayed at a cheap hotel and waited every night for her to phone me, asking me to come back and start a new life. I was even prepared to continue the old life if necessary, because that separation had made me realise that there was nothing and no one more important in the world than my wife and child.

A week later, I finally got that call. All she said, however, was that she'd cleared out all her things and wouldn't be going back. Two weeks after that, I learned that she'd rented a small attic flat in Basset Road, where she had to carry the baby up three flights of stairs every day. A few months later, we signed the divorce papers.

My real family left forever. And the family I'd been born into received me with open arms.

After my separation from Athena and the great suffering that followed, I wondered if I hadn't made a bad, irresponsible decision, typical of people who've read lots of love stories in their adolescence and desperately want to repeat the tale of Romeo and Juliet. When the pain abated – and time is the only cure for that – I saw that life had allowed me to meet the one woman I would ever be capable of loving. Each second spent by her side had been worthwhile, and given the chance, despite all that had happened, I would do the same thing over again.

But time, as well as healing all wounds, taught me something strange too: that it's possible to love more than one person in a lifetime. I remarried. I'm very happy with my new wife, and I can't imagine living without her. This, however, doesn't mean that I have to renounce all my past experiences, as long as I'm careful not to compare my two lives. You can't measure love the way you can the length of a road or the height of a building.

Something very important remained from my relationship with Athena: a son, her great dream, of which she spoke so frankly before we decided to get married. I have another child by my second wife, and I'm better prepared for all the highs and lows of fatherhood than I was twelve years ago.

Once, when I went to fetch Viorel and bring him back to spend the weekend with me, I decided to ask her why she'd reacted so calmly when I told her I wanted a separation.

'Because all my life I've learned to suffer in silence,' she replied.

And only then did she put her arms around me and cry out all the tears she would have liked to shed on that day.

Father Giancarlo Fontana

I saw her when she arrived for Sunday mass, with the baby in her arms as usual. I knew that she and Lukás were having difficulties, but, until that week, these had all seemed merely the sort of misunderstandings that all couples have, and since both of them were people who radiated goodness, I hoped that, sooner or later, they would resolve their differences.

It had been a whole year since she last visited the church in the morning to play her guitar and praise the Virgin. She devoted herself to looking after Viorel, whom I had the honour to baptise, although I must admit I know of no saint with that name. However, she still came to mass every Sunday, and we always talked afterwards, when everyone else had left. She said I was her only friend. Together we had shared in divine worship; now, though, it was her earthly problems she needed to share with me.

She loved Lukás more than any man she had ever met; he was her son's father, the person she had chosen to spend her life with, someone who had given up everything and had courage enough to start a family. When the difficulties started, she tried to convince him that it was just a phase, that she had to devote herself to their son, but that she had no intention of turning Viorel into a spoiled brat. Soon she would let him face certain of life's challenges alone. After that, she would go back to being the wife and woman he'd known when they first met, possibly with even more intensity, because now she had a better understanding of the duties and responsibilities that came with the choice she'd made. Lukás still felt rejected; she tried desperately to divide herself between her husband and her child, but she was always obliged to choose, and when that happened, she never hesitated: she chose Viorel.

Drawing on my scant knowledge of psychology, I said that this wasn't the first time I'd heard such a story, and that in such situations men do tend to feel rejected, but that it soon passes. I'd heard about similar problems in conversations with my other parishioners. During one of our talks, Athena acknowledged that she had perhaps been rather precipitate; the romance of being a young mother had blinded her to the real challenges that arise after the birth of a child. But it was too late now for regrets.

She asked if I could talk to Lukás, who never came to church, perhaps because he didn't believe in God or perhaps because he preferred to spend his Sunday mornings with his son. I agreed to do so, as long as he came of his own accord. Just when Athena was about to ask him this favour, the major crisis occurred, and he left her and Viorel.

I advised her to be patient, but she was deeply hurt. She'd been abandoned once in childhood, and all the hatred she felt for her birth mother was automatically transferred to Lukás, although later, I understand, they became good friends again. For Athena, breaking family ties was possibly the gravest sin anyone could commit.

She continued attending church on Sundays, but always went straight back home afterwards. She had no one now with whom to leave her son, who cried lustily throughout mass, disturbing everyone else's concentration. On one of the rare occasions when we could speak, she said that she was working for a bank, had rented an apartment, and that I needn't worry about her. Viorel's father (she never mentioned her husband's name now) was fulfilling his financial obligations.

Then came that fateful Sunday.

I learned what had happened during the week – one of the parishioners told me. I spent several nights praying for an angel to bring me inspiration and tell me whether I should keep my commitment to the Church or to flesh-and-blood men and women. When no angel appeared, I contacted my superior, and he said that the only reason the Church has survived is because it's always been rigid about dogma, and if it started making exceptions, we'd be back in the Middle Ages. I knew exactly what was going to happen. I thought of phoning Athena, but she hadn't given me her new number.

That morning, my hands were trembling as I lifted up the host and blessed the bread. I spoke the words that had come down to me through a thousand-year-old tradition, using the power passed on from generation to generation by the apostles. But then my thoughts turned to that young woman with her child in her arms, a kind of Virgin Mary, the miracle of motherhood and love made manifest in abandonment and solitude, and who had just joined the line as she always did, and was slowly approaching in order to take communion.

I think most of the congregation knew what was happening. And they were all watching me, waiting for my reaction. I saw myself surrounded by the just, by sinners, by Pharisees, by members of the Sanhedrin, by apostles and disciples and people with good intentions and bad.

Athena stood before me and repeated the usual gesture: she closed her eyes and opened her mouth to receive the Body of Christ.

The Body of Christ remained in my hands.

She opened her eyes, unable to understand what was going on.

'We'll talk later,' I whispered.

But she didn't move.

'There are people behind you in the queue. We'll talk later.'

'What's going on?' she asked, and everyone in the line could hear her question.

'We'll talk later.'

'Why won't you give me communion? Can't you see you're humiliating me in front of everyone? Haven't I been through enough already?'

'Athena, the Church forbids divorced people from receiving the sacrament. You signed your divorce papers this week. We'll talk later,' I said again.

When she still didn't move, I beckoned to the person behind her to come forward. I continued giving communion until the last parishioner had received it. And it was then, just before I turned to the altar, that I heard that voice.

It was no longer the voice of the girl who sang her worship of the Virgin Mary, who talked about her plans, who was so moved when she shared with me what she'd learned about the lives of the saints, and who almost wept when she spoke to me about her marital problems. It was the voice of a wounded, humiliated animal, its heart full of loathing.

'A curse on this place!' said the voice. 'A curse on all those who never listened to the words of Christ and who have transformed his message into a stone building. For Christ said: "Come unto me all ye that labour and are heavy laden, and I will give you rest." Well, I'm heavy laden, and they won't let me come to Him. Today I've learned that the Church has changed those words to read: "Come unto me all ye who follow our rules, and let the heavy laden go hang!"'

I heard one of the women in the front row of pews telling her to be quiet. But I wanted to hear. I needed to hear. I turned to her, my head bowed – it was all I could do.

'I swear that I will never set foot in a church ever again. Once more, I've been abandoned by a family, and this time it has nothing to do with financial difficulties or with the immaturity of those who marry too young. A curse upon all those who slam the door in the face of a mother and her child! You're just like those people who refused to take in the Holy Family, like those who denied Christ when he most needed a friend!'

With that, she turned and left in tears, her baby in her arms. I finished the service, gave the final blessing and went straight to the sacristy – that Sunday, there would be no mingling with the faithful, no pointless conversations. That Sunday, I was faced by a philosophical dilemma: I had chosen to respect the institution rather than the words on which that institution was based.

I'm getting old now, and God could take me at any moment. I've remained faithful to my religion and I believe that, for all its errors, it really is trying to put things right. This will take decades, possibly centuries, but one day, all that will matter is love and Christ's words: 'Come unto me all ye that labour and are heavy laden, and I will give you rest.' I've devoted my entire life to the priesthood and I don't regret my decision for one second. However, there are times, like that Sunday, when, although I didn't doubt my faith, I did doubt men.

I know now what happened to Athena, and I wonder: Did it all start there, or was it already in her soul? I think of the many Athenas and Lukáses in the world who are divorced and because of that can no longer receive the sacrament of the Eucharist; all they can do is contemplate the suffering, crucified Christ and listen to His words, words that are not always in accord with the laws of the Vatican. In a few cases, these people leave the church, but the majority continue coming to mass on Sundays, because that's what they're used to, even though they know that the miracle of the transmutation of the bread and the wine into the flesh and the blood of the Lord is forbidden to them.

I like to imagine that, when she left the church, Athena met Jesus. Weeping and confused, she would have thrown herself into his arms, asking him to explain why she was being excluded just because of a piece of paper she'd signed, something of no importance on the spiritual plane, and which was of interest only to registry offices and the tax man.

And looking at Athena, Jesus might have replied:

'My child, I've been excluded too. It's a very long time since they've allowed me in there.'

Pavel Podbielski, 57, owner of the apartment

Athena and I had one thing in common: we were both refugees from a war and arrived in England when we were still children, although I fled Poland over fifty years ago. We both knew that, despite that physical change, our traditions continue to exist in exile – communities join together again, language and religion remain alive, and in a place that will always be foreign to them, people tend to look after each other.

Traditions continue, but the desire to go back gradually disappears. That desire needs to stay alive in our hearts as a hope with which we like to delude ourselves, but it will never be put into practice; I'll never go back to live in Częstochowa, and Athena and her family will never return to Beirut.

It was this kind of solidarity that made me rent her the third floor of my house in Basset Road – normally, I'd prefer tenants without children. I'd made that mistake before, and two things had happened: I complained about the noise they made during the day, and they complained about the noise I made during the night. Both noises had their roots in sacred elements – crying and music – but they belonged to two completely different worlds and it was hard for them to coexist.

I warned her, but she didn't really take it in, and told me not to worry about her son. He spent all day at his grandmother's house anyway, and the apartment was conveniently close to her work at a local bank.

Despite my warnings, and despite holding out bravely at first, eight days later the doorbell rang. It was Athena, with her child in her arms.

'My son can't sleep. Couldn't you turn the music down at least for one night?'

Everyone in the room stared at her.

'What's going on?'

The child immediately stopped crying, as if he were as surprised as his mother to see that group of people, who had stopped in mid-dance.

I pressed the pause button on the cassette player and beckoned her in. Then I restarted the music so as not to interrupt the ritual. Athena sat down in one corner of the room, rocking her child in her arms and watching him drift off to sleep despite the noise of drums and brass. She stayed for the whole ceremony and left along with the other guests, but – as I thought she would – she rang my doorbell the next morning, before going to work.

'You don't have to explain what I saw – people dancing with their eyes closed – because I know what that means. I often do the same myself, and at the moment those are the only times of peace and serenity in my life. Before I became a mother, I used to go to clubs with my husband and my friends, and I'd see people dancing with their eyes closed there too. Some were just trying to look cool, and others seemed to be genuinely moved by a greater, more powerful force. And ever since I've been old enough to think for myself, I've always used dance as a way of getting in touch with something stronger and more powerful than myself. Anyway, could you tell me what that music was?'

'What are you doing this Sunday?'

'Nothing special. I might go for a walk with Viorel in Regent's Park and get some fresh air. I'll have plenty of time later on for a social calendar of my own; for the moment, I've decided to follow my son's.'

'I'll come with you, if you like.'

On the two nights before our walk, Athena came to watch the ritual. Her son fell asleep after only a few minutes, and she merely watched what was going on around her without saying a word. She sat quite still on the sofa, but I was sure that her soul was dancing.

On Sunday afternoon, while we were walking in the park, I asked her to pay attention to everything she was seeing and hearing: the leaves moving in the breeze, the waves on the lake, the birds singing, the dogs barking, the shouts of children as they ran back and forth, as if obeying some strange logic, incomprehensible to grown-ups.

'Everything moves, and everything moves to a rhythm. And everything that moves to a rhythm creates a sound. At this moment, the same thing is happening here and everywhere else in the world. Our ancestors noticed the same thing when they tried to escape from the cold into caves: things moved and made noise. The first human beings may have been frightened by this at first, but that fear was soon replaced by a sense of awe: they understood that this was the way in which some Superior Being was communicating with them. In the hope of reciprocating that communication, they started imitating the sounds and movements around them – and thus dance and music were born. A few days ago, you told me that dance puts you in touch with something stronger than yourself.'

'Yes, when I dance, I'm a free woman, or, rather, a free spirit who can travel through the universe, contemplate the present, divine the future, and be transformed into pure energy. And that gives me enormous pleasure, a joy that always goes far beyond everything I've experienced or will experience in my lifetime. There was a time when I was determined to become a saint, praising God through music and movement, but that path is closed to me forever now.'

'Which path do you mean?'

She made her son more comfortable in his pushchair. I saw that she didn't want to answer that question and so I asked again: when mouths close, it's because there's something important to be said.

Without a flicker of emotion, as if she'd always had to endure in silence the things life imposed on her, she told me about what had happened at the church, when the priest – possibly her only friend – had refused her communion. She also told me about the curse she had uttered then, and that she had left the Catholic Church forever.

'A saint is someone who lives his or her life with dignity,' I explained. 'All we have to do is understand that we're all here for a reason and to commit ourselves to that. Then we can laugh at our sufferings, large and small, and walk fearlessly, aware that each step has meaning. We can let ourselves be guided by the light emanating from the Vertex.'

'What do you mean by the Vertex? In mathematics, it's the topmost angle of a triangle.'

'In life, too, it's the culminating point, the goal of all those who, like everyone else, make mistakes, but who, even in their darkest moments, never lose sight of the light emanating from their hearts. That's what we're trying to do in our group. The Vertex is hidden inside us, and we can reach it if we accept it and recognise its light.'

I explained that I'd come up with the name 'the search for the Vertex' for the dance she'd watched on previous nights, performed by people of all ages (at the time there were ten of us, aged between nineteen and sixty-five). Athena asked where I'd found out about it.

I told her that, immediately after the end of the Second World War, some of my family had managed to escape from the Communist regime that was taking over Poland, and decided to move to England. They'd been advised to bring with them art objects and antiquarian books, which, they were told, were highly valued in this part of the world.

Paintings and sculptures were quickly sold, but the books remained, gathering dust. My mother was keen for me to read and speak Polish, and the books formed part of my education. One day, inside a nineteenth-century edition of Thomas Malthus, I found two pages of notes written by my grandfather, who had died in a concentration camp. I started reading, assuming it would be something to do with an inheritance or else a passionate letter intended for a secret lover, because it was said that he'd fallen in love with someone in Russia.

There was, in fact, some truth in this. The pages contained a description of his journey to Siberia during the Communist revolution. There, in the remote village of Diedov, he fell in love with an actress. (*Editor's note: It has not been possible to locate this village on the map. The name may have been deliberately changed, or the place itself may have disappeared after Stalin's forced migrations.*) According to my grandfather, the actress was part of a sect who believed that they had found the remedy for all ills through a particular kind of dance, because the dance brought the dancer into contact with the light from the Vertex.

They feared that the tradition would disappear; the inhabitants of the village were soon to be transported to another place. Both the actress and her friends begged him to write down what they had learned. He did, but clearly didn't think it was of much importance, because he left his notes inside a book, and there they remained until the day I found them.

Athena broke in:

'But dance isn't something you write about, you have to do it.'

'Exactly. All the notes say is this: Dance to the point of exhaustion, as if you were a mountaineer climbing a hill, a sacred mountain. Dance until you are so out of breath that your organism is forced to obtain oxygen some other way, and it is that, in the end, which will cause you to lose your identity and your relationship with space and time. Dance only to the sound of percussion; repeat the process every day; know that, at a certain moment, your eyes will, quite naturally, close, and you will begin to see a light that comes from within, a light that answers your questions and develops your hidden powers.'

'Have you developed some special power?'

Instead of replying, I suggested that she join our group, since her son seemed perfectly at ease even when the noise of the cymbals and the other percussion instruments was at its loudest. The following day, at the usual time, she was there for the start of the session. I introduced her to my friends, explaining that she was my upstairs neighbour. No one said anything about their lives or asked her what she did. When the moment came, I turned on the music and we began to dance.

She started dancing with the child in her arms, but he soon fell asleep, and she put him down on the sofa. Before I closed my eyes and went into a trance, I saw that she had understood exactly what I meant by the path of the Vertex.

Every day, except Sunday, she was there with the child. We would exchange a few words of welcome, then I would put on the music a friend of mine had brought from the Russian steppes, and we would all dance to the point of exhaustion. After a month of this, she asked me for a copy of the tape.

'I'd like to do the dancing in the morning, before I leave Viorel at my Mum's house and go to work.'

I tried to dissuade her.

'I don't know, I think a group that's connected by the same energy creates a kind of aura that helps everyone get into the trance state. Besides, doing the dancing before you go to work is just asking to get the sack, because you'll be exhausted all day.'

Athena thought for a moment, then said:

'You're absolutely right when you talk about collective energy. In your group, for example, there are four couples and your wife. All of them have found love. That's why they can share such a positive vibration with me. But I'm on my own, or, rather, I'm with my son, but he can't yet manifest his love in a way we can understand. So I'd prefer to accept my loneliness. If I try to run away from it now, I'll never find a partner again. If I accept it, rather than fight against it, things might change. I've noticed that loneliness gets stronger when we try to face it down, but gets weaker when we simply ignore it.'

'Did you join our group in search of love?'

'That would be a perfectly good reason, I think, but the answer is "No". I came in search of a meaning for my life, because, at present, its only meaning is my son, Viorel, and I'm afraid I might end up destroying him, either by being over-protective or by projecting onto him the dreams I've never managed to realise. Then one night, while I was dancing, I felt that I'd been cured. If we were talking about some physical ailment, we'd probably call it a miracle, but it was a spiritual malaise that was making me unhappy, and suddenly it vanished.'

I knew what she meant.

'No one taught me to dance to the sound of that music,' Athena went on, 'but I have a feeling I know what I'm doing.'

'It's not something you have to learn. Remember our walk in the park and what we saw there? Nature creating its own rhythms and adapting itself to each moment.'

'No one taught me how to love either, but I loved God, I loved my husband, I love my son and my family. And yet still there's something missing. Although I get tired when I'm dancing, when I stop, I seem to be in a state of grace, of profound ecstasy. I want that ecstasy to last throughout the day and for it to help me find what I lack: the love of a man. I can see the heart of that man while I'm dancing, but not his face. I sense that he's close by, which is why I need to remain alert. I need to dance in the morning so that I can spend the rest of the day paying attention to everything that's going on around me.'

'Do you know what the word "ecstasy" means? It comes from the Greek and means, "to stand outside yourself". Spending the whole day outside yourself is asking too much of body and soul.'

'I'd like to try anyway.'

I saw that there was no point arguing and so I made her a copy of the tape. And from then on, I woke every morning to the sound of music and dancing upstairs, and I wondered how she could face her work at the bank after almost an hour of being in a trance. When we bumped into each other in the corridor, I suggested she come in for a coffee, and she told me that she'd made more copies of the tape and that many of her work colleagues were also now looking for the Vertex.

'Did I do wrong? Was it a secret?'

Of course it wasn't. On the contrary, she was helping me preserve a tradition that was almost lost.

According to my grandfather's notes, one of the women said that a monk who visited the region had once told them that each of us contains our ancestors and all the generations to come. When we free ourselves, we are freeing all humanity.

'So all the men and women in that village in Siberia must be here now and very happy too. Their work is being reborn in this world, thanks to your grandfather. There's one thing I'd like to ask you: what made you decide to dance after you read those notes? If you'd read something about sport instead, would you have decided to become a footballer?'

This was a question no one had ever asked me.

'Because, at the time, I was ill. I was suffering from a rare form of arthritis, and the doctors told me that I should prepare myself for life in a wheelchair by the age of thirty-five. I saw that I didn't have much time ahead of me and so I decided to devote myself to something I wouldn't be able to do later on. My grandfather had written on one of those small sheets of paper that the inhabitants of Diedov believed in the curative powers of trances.'

'And it seems they were right.'

I didn't say anything, but I wasn't so sure. Perhaps the doctors were wrong. Perhaps the fact of being from an immigrant family, unable to allow myself the luxury of being ill, acted with such force upon my unconscious mind that it provoked a natural reaction in my body. Or perhaps it really was a miracle, although that went totally against what my Catholic faith preaches: dance is not a cure.

I remember that, as an adolescent, I had no idea what the right music would sound like, and so I used to put on a black hood and imagine that everything around me had ceased to exist: my spirit would travel to Diedov, to be with those men and women, with my grandfather and his beloved actress. In the silence of my bedroom, I would ask them to teach me to dance, to go beyond my limits, because soon I would be paralysed forever. The more my body moved, the more brightly the light in my heart shone, and the more I learned – perhaps on my own, perhaps from the ghosts of the past. I even imagined the music they must have listened to during their rituals, and when a friend visited Siberia many years later, I asked him to bring me back some records. To my surprise, one of them was very similar to the music I had imagined would accompany the dancing in Diedov.

It was best to say nothing of all this to Athena; she was easily influenced and, I thought, slightly unstable.

'Perhaps what you're doing is right,' was all I said.

We talked again, shortly before her trip to the Middle East. She seemed contented, as if she'd found everything she wanted: love.

'My colleagues at work have formed a group, and they call themselves "the Pilgrims of the Vertex". And all thanks to your grandfather.'

'All thanks to you, you mean, because you felt the need to share the dance with others. I know you're leaving, but I'd like to thank you for giving another dimension to what I've been doing all these years in trying to spread the light to a few interested people, but always very tentatively, always afraid people might find the whole story ridiculous.'

'Do you know what I've learned? That although ecstasy is the ability to stand outside yourself, dance is a way of rising up into space, of discovering new dimensions while still remaining in touch with your body. When you dance, the spiritual world and the real world manage to coexist quite happily. I think classical dancers dance on pointes because they're simultaneously touching the earth and reaching up to the skies.'

As far as I can remember, those were her last words to me. During any dance to which we surrender with joy, the brain loses its controlling power, and the heart takes up the reins of the body. Only at that moment does the Vertex appear. As long as we believe in it, of course.

Peter Sherney, 47, manager of a branch of [name of Bank omitted] in Holland Park, London

I only took on Athena because her family was one of our most important customers; after all, the world revolves around mutual interests. She seemed a very restless person, and so I gave her a dull clerical post, hoping that she would soon resign. That way, I could tell her father that I'd done my best to help her, but without success.

My experience as a manager had taught me to recognise people's states of mind, even if they said nothing. On a management course I attended, we learned that if you wanted to get rid of someone, you should do everything you can to provoke them into rudeness, so that you would then have a perfectly good reason to dismiss them.

I did everything I could to achieve my objective with Athena. She didn't depend on her salary to live and would soon learn how pointless it was: having to get up early, drop her son off at her mother's house, slave away all day at a repetitive job, pick her son up again, go to the supermarket, spend time with her son before putting him to bed, and then, the next day, spend another three hours on public transport, and all for no reason, when there were so many other more interesting ways of filling her days. She grew increasingly irritable, and I felt proud of my strategy. I would get what I wanted. She started complaining about the apartment where she lived, saying that her landlord kept her awake all night, playing really loud music.

Then, suddenly, something changed. At first, it was only Athena, but soon it was the whole branch.

How did I notice this change? Well, a group of workers is like a kind of orchestra; a good manager is the conductor, and he knows who is out of tune, who is playing with real commitment, and who is simply following the crowd. Athena seemed to be playing her instrument without the least enthusiasm; she seemed distant, never sharing the joys and sadnesses of her personal life with her colleagues, letting it be known that, when she left work, her free time was entirely taken up with looking after her son. Then, suddenly, she became more relaxed, more communicative, telling anyone who would listen that she had discovered the secret of rejuvenation.

'Rejuvenation', of course, is a magic word. Coming from someone who was barely twenty-one, it sounded pretty ridiculous, and yet other members of staff believed her and started to ask her for the secret formula.

Her efficiency increased, even though her workload remained unchanged. Her colleagues, who, up until then, had never exchanged more than a 'Good morning' or a 'Goodnight' with her, started asking her out to lunch. When they came back, they seemed very pleased, and the department's productivity made a giant leap.

I know that people who are in love do have an effect on the environment in which they live, and so I immediately assumed that Athena must have met someone very important in her life.

I asked, and she agreed, adding that she'd never before gone out with a customer, but that, in this case, she'd been unable to refuse. Normally, this would have been grounds for immediate dismissal – the bank's rules are clear: personal contact with customers is forbidden. But, by then, I was aware that her behaviour had infected almost everyone else. Some of her colleagues started getting together with her after work, and a few of them had, I believe, been to her house.

I had a very dangerous situation on my hands. The young trainee with no previous work experience, who up until then had seemed to veer between shyness and aggression, had become a kind of natural leader amongst my workers. If I fired her, they would think it was out of jealousy, and I'd lose their respect. If I kept her on, I ran the risk, within a matter of months, of losing control of the group.

I decided to wait a little, but meanwhile, there was a definite increase in the 'energy' at the bank (I hate that word 'energy', because it doesn't really mean anything, unless you're talking about electricity). Anyway, our customers seemed much happier and were starting to recommend other people to come to us. The employees seemed happy too, and even though their workload had doubled, I didn't need to take on any more staff because they were all coping fine.

One day, I received a letter from my superiors. They wanted me to go to Barcelona for a group meeting, so that I could explain my management techniques to them. According to them, I had increased profit without increasing expenditure, and that, of course, is the only thing that interests executives everywhere.

But what techniques?

At least I knew where it had all started, and so I summoned Athena to my office. I complimented her on her excellent productivity levels, and she thanked me with a smile.

I proceeded cautiously, not wishing to be misinterpreted.

'And how's your boyfriend? I've always found that anyone who is loved has more love to give. What does he do?'

'He works for Scotland Yard.' (*Editor's note: Police investigation department linked to London's Metropolitan Police.*)

I preferred not to ask any further questions, but I needed to keep the conversation going and I didn't have much time.

'I've noticed a great change in you and—'

'Have you noticed a change in the bank too?'

How to respond to a question like that? On the one hand, I would be giving her more power than was advisable, and on the other, if I wasn't straight with her, I would never get the answers I needed.

'Yes, I've noticed a big change, and I'm thinking of promoting you.'

'I need to travel. I'd like to get out of London and discover new horizons.'

Travel? Just when everything was going so well in my branch, she wanted to leave? Although, when I thought about it, wasn't that precisely the way out I needed and wanted?

'I can help the bank if you give me more responsibility,' she went on.

Yes, she was giving me an excellent opportunity. Why hadn't I thought of that before? 'Travel' meant getting rid of her and resuming my leadership of the group without having to deal with the fall-out from a dismissal or a rebellion. But I needed to ponder the matter, because rather than her helping the bank, I needed her to help me. Now that my superiors had noticed an increase in productivity, I knew that I would have to keep it up or risk losing prestige and end up worse off than before. Sometimes I understand why most of my colleagues don't do very much in order to improve: if they don't succeed, they're called incompetent. If they do succeed, they have to keep improving all the time, a situation guaranteed to bring on an early heart attack.

I took the next step very cautiously: it's not a good idea to frighten the person in possession of a secret before she's revealed that secret to you; it's best to pretend to grant her request.

'I'll bring your request to the attention of my superiors. In fact, I'm having a meeting with them in Barcelona, which is why I called you in. Would it be true to say that our performance has improved since, shall we say, the other employees began getting on better with you?'

'Or shall we say, began getting on better with themselves?'

'Yes, but encouraged by you – or am I wrong?'

'You know perfectly well that you're not.'

'Have you been reading some book on management I don't know about?'

'I don't read that kind of book, but I would like a promise from you that you really will consider my request.'

I thought of her boyfriend at Scotland Yard. If I made a promise and failed to keep it, would I be the object of some reprisal? Could he have taught her about some cutting-edge technology that enables one to achieve impossible results?

'I'll tell you everything, even if you don't keep your promise, but I can't guarantee that you'll get the same results if you don't practise what I teach.'

'You mean the "rejuvenation technique"?'

'Exactly.'

'Wouldn't it be enough just to know the theory?'

'Possibly. The person who taught me learned about it from a few sheets of paper.'

I was glad she wasn't forcing me to make decisions that went beyond my capabilities or my principles. But I must confess that I had a personal interest in that whole story, because I, too, dreamed of finding some way of 'recycling' my potential. I promised that I'd do what I could, and Athena began to describe the long, esoteric dance she performed in search of the so-called Vertex (or was it Axis, I can't quite remember now). As we talked, I tried to set down her mad thoughts in objective terms. An hour proved not to be enough, and so I asked her to come back the following day, and together we would prepare the report to be presented to the bank's board of directors. At one point in our conversation, she said with a smile:

'Don't worry about describing the technique in the same terms we've been using here. I reckon even a bank's board of directors are people like us, made of flesh and blood, and interested in unconventional methods.'

Athena was completely wrong. In England, tradition always speaks louder than innovation. But why not take a risk, as long as it didn't endanger my job? The whole thing seemed absurd to me, but I had to summarise it and put it in a way that everyone could understand. That was all.

Before I presented my 'paper' in Barcelona, I spent the whole morning repeating to myself: 'My' process is producing results, and that's all that matters. I read a few books on the subject and learned that in order to present a new idea with the maximum impact, you should structure your talk in an equally provocative way, and so the first thing I said to the executives gathered in that luxury hotel were these words of St Paul: 'God hid the most important things from the wise because they cannot understand what is simple.' (*Editor's note: It is impossible to know here whether he is referring to a verse from Matthew 11: 25: 'I thank thee, O Father, thou hast hid these things from the wise and prudent, and hast revealed them unto babes', or from St Paul (1 Corinthians 1: 27): 'But God hath chosen the foolish things of the world to confound the wise, and God hath chosen the weak things of the world to confound the things which are mighty.'*)

When I said this, the whole audience, who had spent the last two days analysing graphs and statistics, fell silent. It occurred to me that I had almost certainly lost my job, but I carried on. Firstly, because I had researched the subject and was sure of what I was saying and deserved credit for this. Secondly, because although, at certain points, I was obliged to omit any mention of Athena's enormous influence on the whole process, I was, nevertheless, not lying.

'I have learned that, in order to motivate employees nowadays, you need more than just the training provided by our own excellent training centres. Each of us contains something within us which is unknown, but which, when it surfaces, is capable of producing miracles.

'We all work for some reason: to feed our children, to earn money to support ourselves, to justify our life, to get a little bit of power. However, there are always tedious stages in that process, and the secret lies in transforming those stages into an encounter with ourselves or with something higher.

'For example, the search for beauty isn't always associated with anything practical and yet we still search for it as if it were the most important thing in the world. Birds learn to sing, but not because it will help them find food, avoid predators or drive away parasites. Birds sing, according to Darwin, because that is the only way they have of attracting a partner and perpetuating the species.'

I was interrupted by an executive from Geneva, who called for a more objective presentation. However, to my delight, the Director-General asked me to go on.

'Again according to Darwin, who wrote a book that changed the course of all humanity (*Editor's note:* The Origin of Species, *1859, in which he first posited that human beings evolved from a type of ape*), those who manage to arouse passions are repeating something that has been going on since the days we lived in caves, where rituals for courting a partner were fundamental for the survival and evolution of the human species. Now, what difference is there between the evolution of the human race and that of the branch of a bank? None. Both obey the same laws – only the fittest survive and evolve.'

At this point, I was obliged to admit that I'd developed this idea thanks to the spontaneous collaboration of one of my employees, Sherine Khalil.

'Sherine, who likes to be known as Athena, brought into the workplace a new kind of emotion – passion. Yes, passion, something we never normally consider when discussing loans or spreadsheets. My employees started using music as a stimulus for dealing more efficiently with their clients.'

Another executive interrupted, saying that this was an old idea: supermarkets did the same thing, using piped music to encourage their customers to buy more.

'I'm not saying that we used music in the workplace. People simply started living differently because Sherine, or Athena if you prefer, taught them to dance *before* facing their daily tasks. I don't know precisely what mechanism this awakens in people; as a manager, I'm only responsible for the results, not for the process. I myself didn't participate in the dancing, but I understand that, through dance, they all felt more connected with what they were doing.

'We were born and brought up with the maxim: Time is money. We know exactly what money is, but what does the word "time" mean? The day is made up of twenty-four hours and an infinite number of moments. We need to be aware of each of those moments and to make the most of them regardless of whether we're busy doing something or merely contemplating life. If we slow down, everything lasts much longer. Of course, that means that washing the dishes might last longer, as might totting up the debits and credits on a balance sheet or checking promissory notes, but why not use that time to think about pleasant things and to feel glad simply to be alive?'

The Director-General was looking at me in surprise. I was sure he wanted me to explain in detail what I'd learned, but some of those present were beginning to grow restless.

'I understand exactly what you mean,' he said. 'I understand, too, that your employees worked with more enthusiasm because they were able to enjoy one moment in the day when they came into full contact with themselves. And I'd like to compliment you on being flexible enough to allow such unorthodox practices, which are, it must be said, producing excellent results. However, speaking of time, this is a conference, and you have only five minutes to conclude your presentation. Could you possibly try to list the main points which would allow us to apply these principles in other branches?'

He was right. This was fine for the employees, but it could prove fatal to my career, and so I decided to summarise the points Sherine and I had written together.

'Basing ourselves on personal observations, Sherine Khalil and I developed certain points which I would be delighted to discuss with anyone who's interested. Here are the main ones:

'(a) We all have an unknown ability, which will probably remain unknown forever. And yet that ability can become our ally. Since it's impossible to measure that ability or give it an economic value, it's never taken seriously, but I'm speaking here to other human beings and I'm sure you understand what I mean, at least in theory.

'(b) At my branch, employees have learned how to tap into that ability through a dance based on a rhythm which comes, I believe, from the desert regions of Asia. However, its place of origin is irrelevant, as long as people can express through their bodies what their souls are trying to say. I realise that the word "soul" might be misunderstood, so I suggest we use the word "intuition" instead. And if that word is equally hard to swallow, then let's use the term "primary emotions", which sounds more scientific, although, in fact, it has rather less meaning than the other two words.

'(c) Before going to work, instead of encouraging my employees to do keep-fit or aerobics, I get them to dance for at least an hour. This stimulates the body and the mind; they start the day demanding a certain degree of creativity from themselves and channel that accumulated energy into their work at the bank.

'(d) Customers and employees live in the same world: reality is nothing but a series of electrical stimuli to the brain. What we think we "see" is a pulse of energy to a completely dark part of the brain. However, if we get on the same wavelength with other people, we can try to change that reality. In some way which I don't understand, joy is infectious, as is enthusiasm and love. Or indeed sadness, depression or hatred – things which can be picked up "intuitively" by customers and other employees. In order to improve performance, we have to create mechanisms that keep these positive stimuli alive.'

'How very esoteric,' commented a woman who managed investment funds at a branch in Canada.

I slightly lost confidence. I had failed to convince anyone. Nevertheless, I pretended to ignore her remark and, using all my creativity, sought to give my paper a practical conclusion:

'The bank should earmark a fund to do research into how this infectious state of mind works, and thus noticeably increase our profits.'

This seemed a reasonably satisfactory ending, and so I preferred not to use the two minutes remaining to me. When I finished the seminar, at the end of an exhausting day, the Director-General asked me to have supper with him, and he did so is front of all our other colleagues, as if he were trying to show that he supported everything I'd said. I had never before had an opportunity to dine with the Director-General, and so I tried to make the most of it. I started talking about performance, about spreadsheets, difficulties on the stock exchange and possible new markets. He interrupted me; he was more interested in knowing what else I'd learned from Athena.

In the end, to my surprise, he turned the conversation to more personal matters.

'I understood what you meant when, during your paper, you talked about time. At New Year, when I was still enjoying the holiday season, I decided to go and sit in the garden for a while. I picked up the newspaper from the mailbox, but it contained nothing of any importance, only the things that journalists had decided we should know, feel involved in and have an opinion about.

'I thought of phoning someone at work, but that would be ridiculous, since they would all be with their families. I had lunch with my wife, children and grandchildren, took a nap, and when I woke up I made a few notes, then realised that it was still only two o'clock in the afternoon. I had another three days of not working, and, however much I love being with my family, I started to feel useless.

'The following day, taking advantage of this free time, I went to have my stomach checked out, and, fortunately, the tests revealed nothing seriously wrong. I went to the dentist, who said there was nothing wrong with my teeth either. I again had lunch with my wife, children and grandchildren, took another nap, again woke up at two in the afternoon, and realised that I had absolutely nothing on which to focus my attention.

'I felt uneasy: shouldn't I be doing something? Well, if I wanted to invent work, that wouldn't take much effort. We all have projects to develop, light bulbs to change, leaves to sweep, books to put away, computer files to organise, etc. But how about just facing up to the void? It was then that I remembered something that seemed to me of great importance: I needed to walk to the letterbox – which is less than a mile from my house in the country – and post one of the Christmas cards lying forgotten on my desk.

'And I was surprised: why did I need to send that card today? Was it really so hard just to stay where I was, doing nothing?

'A series of thoughts crossed my mind: friends who worry about things that haven't yet happened; acquaintances who manage to fill every minute of their lives with tasks that seem to me absurd; senseless conversations; long telephone calls in which nothing of any importance is ever said. I've seen my directors inventing work in order to justify their jobs;

employees who feel afraid because they've been given nothing important to do that day, which might mean that they're no longer useful. My wife who torments herself because our son has got divorced, my son who torments himself because our grandson, his son, got bad marks at school, our grandson who is terrified because he's making his parents sad – even though we all know that marks aren't that important.

'I had a long, hard struggle with myself not to get up from my chair. Gradually, though, the anxiety gave way to contemplation, and I started listening to my soul – or intuition or primary emotions, or whatever you choose to believe in. Whatever you call it, that part of me had been longing to speak to me, but I had always been too busy.

'In that case, it wasn't a dance, but the complete absence of noise and movement, the silence, that brought me into contact with myself. And, believe it or not, I learned a great deal about the problems bothering me, even though all those problems had dissolved completely while I was sitting there. I didn't see God, but I had a clearer understanding of what decisions to take.'

Before paying the bill, he suggested that I send the employee in question to Dubai, where the bank was opening a new branch, and where the risks were considerable. As a good manager, he knew that I had learned all I needed to learn, and now it was merely a question of providing continuity. My employee could make a useful contribution somewhere else. He didn't know this, but he was helping me to keep the promise I'd made.

When I returned to London, I immediately told Athena about this invitation, and she accepted at once. She told me that she spoke fluent Arabic (I knew this already because of her father), although, since we would mainly be doing deals with foreigners, not Arabs, this would not be essential. I thanked her for her help, but she showed no curiosity about my talk at the conference, and merely asked when she should pack her bags.

I still don't know whether the story of the boyfriend in Scotland Yard was a fantasy or not. If it were true, I think Athena's murderer would already have been arrested, because I don't believe anything the newspapers wrote about the crime. I can understand financial engineering, I can even allow myself the luxury of saying that dancing helps my employees to work better, but I will never comprehend how it is that the best police force in the world catches some murderers, but not others. Not that it makes much difference now.

Nabil Alaihi, age unknown, Bedouin

It made me very happy to know that Athena had kept a photo of me in a place of honour in her apartment, but I don't really think what I taught her had any real use. She came here to the desert, leading a three-year-old boy by the hand. She opened her bag, took out a radio-cassette and sat down outside my tent. I know that people from the city usually give my name to foreigners who want to experience some local cooking, and so I told her at once that it was too early for supper.

'I came for another reason,' she said. 'Your nephew Hamid is a client at the bank where I work and he told me that you're a wise man.'

'Hamid is a rather foolish youth who may well say that I'm a wise man, but who never follows my advice. Mohammed, the Prophet, may the blessings of God be upon him, *he* was a wise man.'

I pointed to her car.

'You shouldn't drive alone in a place you don't know, and you shouldn't come here without a guide.'

Instead of replying, she turned on the radio-cassette. Then, all I could see was this young woman dancing on the dunes and her son watching her in joyous amazement; and the sound seemed to fill the whole desert. When she finished, she asked if I had enjoyed it.

I said that I had. There is a sect in our religion which uses dance as a way of getting closer to Allah – blessed be His Name. (*Editor's note: The sect in question is Sufism.*)

'Well,' said the woman, who introduced herself as Athena, 'ever since I was a child, I've felt that I should grow closer to God, but life always took me further away from Him. Music is one way I've discovered of getting close, but it isn't enough. Whenever I dance, I see a light, and that light is now asking me to go further. But I can't continue learning on my own; I need someone to teach me.'

'Anything will do,' I told her, 'because Allah, the merciful, is always near. Lead a decent life, and that will be enough.'

But the woman appeared unconvinced. I said that I was busy, that I needed to prepare supper for the few tourists who might appear. She told me that she'd wait for as long as was necessary.

'And the child?'

'Don't worry about him.'

While I was making my usual preparations, I observed the woman and her son. They could have been the same age; they ran about the desert, laughed, threw sand at each other, and rolled down the dunes. The guide arrived with three German tourists, who ate and asked for beer, and I had to explain that my religion forbade me to drink or to serve alcoholic drinks. I invited the woman and her son to join us for supper, and in that unexpected female presence one of the Germans became quite animated. He said that he was thinking of buying some land, that he had a large fortune saved up and believed in the future of the region.

'Great,' she replied. 'I believe in the region too.'

'It would be good to have supper somewhere, so that we could talk about the possibility of—'

'No,' she said, holding a card out to him, 'but if you like, you can get in touch with my bank.'

When the tourists left, we sat down outside the tent. The child soon fell asleep on her lap. I fetched blankets for us all, and we sat looking up at the starry sky. Finally, she broke the silence.

'Why did Hamid say that you were a wise man?'

'Perhaps so that I'll be more patient with him. There was a time when I tried to teach him my art, but Hamid seemed more interested in earning money. He's probably convinced by now that he's wiser than I am: he has an apartment and a boat, while here I am in the middle of the desert, making meals for the occasional tourist. He doesn't understand that I'm satisfied with what I do.'

'He understands perfectly, and he always speaks of you with great respect. And what do you mean by your "art"?'

'I watched you dancing today. Well, I do the same thing, except that it's the letters, not my body, that dance.'

She looked surprised.

'My way of approaching Allah – may His name be praised – has been through calligraphy, and the search for the perfect meaning of each word. A single letter requires us to distil in it all the energy it contains, as if we were carving out its meaning. When sacred texts are written, they contain the soul of the man who served as an instrument to spread them throughout the world. And that doesn't apply only to sacred texts, but to every mark we place on paper. Because the hand that draws each line reflects the soul of the person making that line.'

'Would you teach me what you know?'

'Firstly, I don't think anyone as full of energy as you would have the patience for this. Besides, it's not part of your world, where everything is printed, without, if you'll allow me to say so, much thought being given to what is being published.'

'I'd like to try.'

And so, for more than six months, that woman – whom I'd judged to be too restless and exuberant to be able to sit still for a moment – came to visit me every Friday. Her son would go to one corner of the tent, take up paper and brushes, and he, too, would devote himself to revealing in his paintings whatever the heavens determined.

When I saw the immense effort it took her to keep still and to maintain the correct posture, I said: 'Don't you think you'd be better off finding something else to do?' She replied: 'No, I need this, I need to calm my soul, and I still haven't learned everything you can teach me. The light of the Vertex told me that I should continue.' I never asked her what the Vertex was, nor was I interested.

The first lesson, and perhaps the most difficult, was: 'Patience!'

Writing wasn't just the expression of a thought, but a way of reflecting on the meaning of each word. Together we began work on texts written by an Arab poet, because I do not feel that the Koran is suitable for someone brought up in another faith. I dictated each letter, and that way she could concentrate on what she was doing, instead of immediately wanting to know the meaning of each word or phrase or line.

'Once, someone told me that music had been created by God, and that rapid movement was necessary for people to get in touch with themselves,' said Athena on one of those afternoons we spent together. 'For years, I felt that this was true, and now I'm being forced to do the most difficult thing in the world – slow down. Why is patience so important?'

'Because it makes us pay attention.'

'But I can dance obeying only my soul, which forces me to concentrate on something greater than myself, and brings me into contact with God – if I can use that word. Dance has already helped me to change many things in my life, including my work. Isn't the soul more important?'

'Of course it is, but if your soul could communicate with your brain, you would be able to change even more things.'

We continued our work together. I knew that, at some point, I would have to tell her something that she might not be ready to hear, and so I tried to make use of every minute to prepare her spirit. I explained that before the word comes the thought. And before the thought, there is the divine spark that placed it there. Everything, absolutely everything on this Earth makes sense, and even the smallest things are worthy of our consideration.

'I've educated my body so that it can manifest every sensation in my soul,' she said.

'Now you must educate only your fingers, so that they can manifest every sensation in your body. That will concentrate your body's strength.'

'Are you a teacher?'

'What is a teacher? I'll tell you: it isn't someone who teaches something, but someone who inspires the student to give of her best in order to discover what she already knows.'

I sensed that, despite her youth, Athena had already experienced this. Writing reveals the personality, and I could see that she was aware of being loved, not just by her son, but by her family and possibly by a man. I saw too that she had mysterious gifts, but I tried never to let her know that I knew this, since these gifts could bring about not only an encounter with God, but also her perdition.

I did not only teach her calligraphy techniques. I also tried to pass on to her the philosophy of the calligraphers.

'The brush with which you are making these lines is just an instrument. It has no consciousness; it follows the desires of the person holding it. And in that it is very like what we call "life". Many people in this world are merely playing a role, unaware that there is an Invisible Hand guiding them. At this moment, in your hands, in the brush tracing each letter, lie all the intentions of your soul. Try to understand the importance of this.'

'I do understand, and I see that it's important to maintain a certain elegance. You tell me to sit in a particular position, to venerate the materials I'm going to use, and only to begin when I have done so.'

Naturally, if she respected the brush that she used, she would realise that in order to learn to write she must cultivate serenity and elegance. And serenity comes from the heart.

'Elegance isn't a superficial thing, it's the way mankind has found to honour life and work. That's why, when you feel uncomfortable in that position, you mustn't think that it's false or artificial: it's real and true precisely because it's difficult. That position means that both the paper and the brush feel proud of the effort you're making. The paper ceases to be a flat, colourless surface and takes on the depth of the things placed on it. Elegance is the correct posture if the writing is to be perfect. It's the same with life: when all superfluous things have been discarded, we discover simplicity and concentration. The simpler and more sober the posture, the more beautiful it will be, even though, at first, it may seem uncomfortable.'

Occasionally, she would talk about her work. She said she was enjoying what she was doing and that she had just received a job offer from a powerful emir. He had gone to the bank to see the manager, who was a friend of his (emirs never go to banks to withdraw money, they have staff who can do that for them), and while he was talking to Athena he mentioned that he was looking for someone to take charge of selling land, and wondered if she would be interested.

Who would want to buy land in the middle of the desert or in a far-flung port? I decided to say nothing and, looking back, I'm glad I stayed silent.

Only once did she mention the man she loved, although whenever she was there when tourists arrived, one of the men would always start flirting with her. Normally Athena simply ignored them, but, one day, a man suggested that he knew her boyfriend. She turned pale and immediately shot a glance at her son, who, fortunately, wasn't listening to the conversation.

'How do you know him?'

'I'm joking,' said the man. 'I just wanted to find out if you were unattached.'

She didn't say anything, but I understood from this exchange that the man in her life was not the father of her son.

One day, she arrived earlier than usual. She said that she'd left her job at the bank and started selling real estate, and would now have more free time. I explained that I couldn't start her class any earlier because I had various things to do.

'I can combine two things: movement and stillness; joy and concentration.'

She went over to the car to fetch her radio-cassette and, from then on, Athena would dance in the desert before the start of our class, while the little boy ran round her, laughing. When she sat down to practise calligraphy, her hand was steadier than usual.

'There are two kinds of letter,' I explained. 'The first is precise, but lacks soul. In this case, although the calligrapher may have mastered the technique, he has focused solely on the craft, which is why it hasn't evolved, but become repetitive; he hasn't grown at all, and one day he'll give up the practice of writing, because he feels it is mere routine.

'The second kind is done with great technique, but with soul as well. For that to happen, the intention of the writer must be in harmony with the word. In this case, the saddest verses cease to be clothed in tragedy and are transformed into simple facts encountered along the way.'

'What do you do with your drawings?' asked the boy in perfect Arabic. He might not understand our conversation, but he was eager to share in his mother's work.

'I sell them.'

'Can I sell my drawings?'

'You *should* sell your drawings. One day, you'll become rich that way and be able to help your mother.'

He was pleased by my comment and went back to what he was doing, painting a colourful butterfly.

'And what shall I do with my texts?' asked Athena.

'You know the effort it took to sit in the correct position, to quieten your soul, keep your intentions clear and respect each letter of each word. Meanwhile, keep practising. After a great deal of practice, we no longer think about all the necessary movements we must make; they become part of our existence. Before reaching that stage, however, you must practise and repeat. And if that's not enough, you must practise and repeat some more.

'Look at a skilled blacksmith working steel. To the untrained eye, he's merely repeating the same hammer blows, but anyone trained in the art of calligraphy knows that each time the blacksmith lifts the hammer and brings it down, the intensity of the blow is different. The hand repeats the same gesture, but as it approaches the metal it understands that it must touch it with more or less force. It's the same thing with repetition: it may seem the same, but it's always different. The moment will come when you no longer need to think about what you're doing. You become the letter, the ink, the paper, the word.'

This moment arrived almost a year later. By then, Athena was already known in Dubai and recommended customers to dine in my tent, and through them I learned that her career was going very well: she was selling pieces of desert! One night, the emir in person arrived, preceded by a great retinue. I was terrified; I wasn't prepared for that, but he reassured me and thanked me for what I was doing for his employee.

'She's an excellent person and attributes her qualities to what she's learning from you. I'm thinking of giving her a share in the company. It might be a good idea to send my other sales staff to learn calligraphy, especially now that Athena is about to take a month's holiday.'

'It wouldn't help,' I replied. 'Calligraphy is just one of the ways which Allah – blessed be His Name – places before us. It teaches objectivity and patience, respect and elegance, but we can learn all that—'

'—through dance,' said Athena, who was standing nearby.

'Or through selling land,' I added.

When they had all left, and the little boy had lain down in one corner of the tent, his eyes heavy with sleep, I brought out the calligraphy materials and asked her to write something. In the middle of the word, I took the brush from her hand. It was time to say what had to be said. I suggested that we go for a little walk in the desert.

'You have learned what you needed to learn,' I said. 'Your calligraphy is getting more and more individual and spontaneous. It's no longer a mere repetition of beauty, but a personal, creative gesture. You have understood what all great painters understand: in order to forget the rules, you must know them and respect them.

'You no longer need the tools that helped you learn. You no longer need paper, ink or brush, because the path is more important than whatever made you set off along it. Once, you told me that the person who taught you to dance used to imagine the music playing in his head, and even so, he was able to repeat the necessary rhythms.'

'He was.'

'If all the words were joined together, they wouldn't make sense, or, at the very least, they'd be extremely hard to decipher. The spaces are crucial.'

She nodded.

'And although you have mastered the words, you haven't yet mastered the blank spaces. When you're concentrating, your hand is perfect, but when it jumps from one word to the next, it gets lost.'

'How do you know that?'

'Am I right?'

'Absolutely. Before I focus on the next word, for a fraction of a second I lose myself. Things I don't want to think about take over.'

'And you know exactly what those things are.'

Athena knew, but she said nothing until we went back to the tent and she could cradle her sleeping son in her arms. Her eyes were full of tears, although she was trying hard to control herself.

'The emir said that you were going on holiday.'

She opened the car door, put the key in the ignition and started the engine. For a few moments, only the noise of the engine troubled the silence of the desert.

'I know what you mean,' she said at last. 'When I write, when I dance, I'm guided by the Hand that created everything. When I look at Viorel sleeping, I know that he knows he's the fruit of my love for his father, even though I haven't seen his father for more than a year. But I …'

She fell silent again. Her silence was the blank space between the words.

'… but I don't know the hand that first rocked me in the cradle. The hand that wrote me in the book of the world.'

I merely nodded.

'Do you think that matters?'

'Not necessarily. But in your case, until you touch that hand, your, shall we say, calligraphy will not improve.'

'I don't see why I should bother to look for someone who never took the trouble to love me.'

She closed the car door, smiled and drove off. Despite her last words, I knew what her next step would be.

Samira R. Khalil, Athena's mother

It was as if all her professional success, her ability to earn money, her joy at having found a new love, her contentment when she played with her son – my grandson – had all been relegated to second place. I was quite simply terrified when Sherine told me that she'd decided to go in search of her birth mother.

At first, of course, I took consolation in the thought that the adoption centre would no longer exist, the paperwork would all have been lost, any officials she encountered would prove implacable, the recent collapse of the Romanian government would make travel impossible, and the womb that bore her would long since have vanished. This, however, provided only a momentary consolation: my daughter was capable of anything and would overcome seemingly impossible obstacles.

Up until then, the subject had been taboo in the family. Sherine knew she was adopted, because the psychiatrist in Beirut had advised me to tell her as soon as she was old enough to understand. But she had never shown any desire to know where she had come from. Her home had been Beirut, when it *was* still our home.

The adopted son of a friend of mine had committed suicide at the age of sixteen when he acquired a biological sister, and so we had never attempted to have more children of our own, and we did everything we could to make her feel that she was the sole reason for our joys and sadnesses, our love and our hopes. And yet, it seemed that none of this counted. Dear God, how ungrateful children can be!

Knowing my daughter as I did, I realised that there was no point in arguing with her about this. My husband and I didn't sleep for a whole week, and every morning, every evening, we were bombarded with the same question: 'Whereabouts in Romania was I born?' To make matters worse, Viorel kept crying, as if he understood what was going on.

I decided to consult a psychiatrist again. I asked why a young woman who had everything in life should always be so dissatisfied.

'We all want to know where we came from,' he said. 'On the philosophical level, that's the fundamental question for all human beings. In your daughter's case, I think it's perfectly reasonable that she should want to go in search of her roots. Wouldn't you be curious to know?'

'No, I wouldn't. On the contrary, I'd think it dangerous to go in search of someone who had denied and rejected me when I was still too helpless to survive on my own.'

But the psychiatrist insisted:

'Rather than getting into a confrontation with her, try to help. Perhaps when she sees that it's no longer a problem for you, she'll give up. The year she spent far from her friends must have created a sense of emotional need, which she's now trying to make up for by provoking you like this. She simply wants to be sure that she's loved.'

It would have been better if Sherine had gone to the psychiatrist herself, then she would have understood the reasons for her behaviour.

'Show that you're confident and don't see this as a threat. And if, in the end, she really does go ahead with it, simply give her the information she needs. As I understand it, she's always been a difficult child. Perhaps she'll emerge from this search a stronger person.'

I asked if the psychiatrist had any children. He didn't, and I knew then that he wasn't the right person to advise me.

That night, when we were sitting in front of the TV, Sherine returned to the subject:

'What are you watching?'

'The news.'

'What for?'

'To find out what's going on in Lebanon,' replied my husband.

I saw the trap, but it was too late. Sherine immediately pounced on this opening.

'You see, you're curious to know what's going on in the country where you were born. You're settled in England, you have friends, Dad earns plenty of money, you've got security, and yet you still buy Lebanese newspapers. You channel-hop until you find a bit of news to do with Beirut. You imagine the future as if it were the past, not realising that the war will never end. What I mean is that if you're not in touch with your roots, you feel as if you'd lost touch with the world. Is it so very hard then for you to understand what I'm feeling?'

'You're our daughter.'

'And proud to be. And I'll always be your daughter. Please don't doubt my love or my gratitude for everything you've done for me. All I'm asking is to be given the chance to visit the place where I was born and perhaps ask my birth mother why she abandoned me or perhaps, when I look into her eyes, simply say nothing. If I don't at least try and do that, I'll feel like a coward and I won't ever understand the blank spaces.'

'The blank spaces?'

'I learned calligraphy while I was in Dubai. I dance whenever I can, but music only exists because the pauses exist, and sentences only exist because the blank spaces exist. When I'm doing something, I feel complete, but no one can keep active twenty-four hours a day. As soon as I stop, I feel there's something lacking. You've often said to me that I'm a naturally restless person, but I didn't choose to be that way. I'd like to sit here quietly, watching television, but I can't. My brain won't stop. Sometimes, I think I'm going mad. I need always to be dancing, writing, selling land, taking care of Viorel, or reading whatever I find to read. Do you think that's normal?'

'Perhaps it's just your temperament,' said my husband.

The conversation ended there, as it always ended, with Viorel crying, Sherine retreating into silence, and with me convinced that children never acknowledge what their parents have done for them. However, over breakfast the next day, it was my husband who brought the subject up again.

'A while ago, while you were in the Middle East, I looked into the possibility of going home to Beirut. I went to the street where we used to live. The house is no longer there, but, despite the foreign occupation and the constant incursions, they are slowly rebuilding the country. I felt a sense of euphoria. Perhaps it was the moment to start all over again. And it was precisely that expression, "start all over again", that brought me back to reality. The time has passed when I could allow myself that luxury. Nowadays, I just want to go on doing what I'm doing, and I don't need any new adventures.

'I sought out the people I used to enjoy a drink with after work. Most of them have left, and those who have stayed complain all the time about a constant feeling of insecurity. I walked past some of my old haunts, and I felt like a stranger, as if nothing there belonged to me any more. The worst of it was that my dream of one day returning gradually disappeared when I found myself back in the city where I was born. Even so, I needed to make that visit. The songs of exile are still there in my heart, but I know now that I'll never again live in Lebanon. In a way, the days I spent in Beirut helped me to a better understanding of the place where I live now, and to value each second that I spend in London.'

'What are you trying to tell me, Dad?'

'That you're right. Perhaps it really would be best to understand those blank spaces. We can look after Viorel while you're away.'

He went to the bedroom and returned with the yellow file containing the adoption papers. He gave them to Sherine, kissed her and said it was time he went to work.

Heron Ryan, journalist

For a whole morning in 1990, all I could see from the sixth-floor window of the hotel was the main government building. A flag had just been placed on the roof, marking the exact spot where the megalomaniac dictator had fled in a helicopter only to find death a few hours later at the hands of those he had oppressed for twenty-two years.

In his plan to create a capital that would rival Washington, Ceaușescu had ordered all the old houses to be razed to the ground. Indeed, Bucharest had the dubious honour of being described as the city that had suffered the worst destruction outside of a war or a natural disaster.

The day I arrived, I attempted to go for a short walk with my interpreter, but in the streets I saw only poverty, bewilderment, and a sense that there was no future, no past and no present: the people were living in a kind of limbo, with little idea of what was happening in their country or in the rest of the world. When I went back ten years later and saw the whole country rising up out of the ashes, I realised human beings can overcome any difficulty, and that the Romanian people were a fine example of just that.

But on that other grey morning, in the grey foyer of a gloomy hotel, all I was concerned about was whether my interpreter would manage to get a car and enough petrol so that I could carry out some final research for the BBC documentary I was working on. He was taking a very long time, and I was beginning to have my doubts. Would I have to go back to England having failed to achieve my goal? I'd already invested a significant amount of money in contracts with historians, in the script, in filming interviews, but before the BBC would sign the final contract, they insisted on me visiting Dracula's castle to see what state it was in. The trip was costing more than expected.

I tried phoning my girlfriend, but was told I'd have to wait nearly an hour to get a line. My interpreter might arrive at any moment with the car and there was no time to lose, and so I decided not to risk waiting.

I asked around to see if I could buy an English newspaper, but there were none to be had. To take my mind off my anxiety, I started looking, as discreetly as I could, at the people around me drinking tea, possibly oblivious to everything that had happened the year before – popular uprisings, the cold-blooded murder of civilians in Timişoara, shoot-outs in the streets between the people and the dreaded secret service as the latter tried desperately to hold on to the power fast slipping from their grasp. I noticed a group of three Americans, an interesting-looking woman who was, however, glued to the fashion magazine she was reading, and some men sitting round a table, talking loudly in a language I couldn't identify.

I was just about to get up yet again and go over to the entrance to see if my interpreter was anywhere to be seen, when she came in. She must have been a little more than twenty years old. She sat down, ordered some breakfast, and I noticed that she spoke English. None of the other men present appeared to notice her arrival, but the other woman interrupted her reading.

Perhaps because of my anxiety or because of the place, which was beginning to depress me, I plucked up courage and went over to her.

'Excuse me, I don't usually do this. I always think breakfast is the most private meal of the day.'

She smiled, told me her name, and I immediately felt wary. It had been too easy – she might be a prostitute. Her English, however, was perfect and she was very discreetly dressed. I decided not to ask any questions, and began talking at length about myself, noticing as I did so that the woman on the next table had put down her magazine and was listening to our conversation.

'I'm an independent producer working for the BBC in London, and at the moment I'm trying to find a way to get to Transylvania …'

I noticed the light in her eyes change.

'... so that I can finish the documentary I'm making about the myth of the vampire.'

I waited. This subject always aroused people's curiosity, but she lost interest as soon as I mentioned the reason for my visit.

'You'll just have to take the bus,' she said. 'Although I doubt you'll find what you're looking for. If you want to know more about Dracula, read the book. The author never even visited Romania.'

'What about you, do you know Transylvania?'

'I don't know.'

That was not an answer; perhaps it was because English – despite her British accent – was not her mother tongue.

'But I'm going there too,' she went on. 'On the bus, of course.'

Judging by her clothes, she was not an adventuress who sets off round the world visiting exotic places. The idea that she might be a prostitute returned; perhaps she was trying to get closer to me.

'Would you like a lift?'

'I've already bought my ticket.'

I insisted, thinking that her first refusal was just part of the game. She refused again, saying that she needed to make that journey alone. I asked where she was from, and there was a long pause before she replied.

'Like I said, from Transylvania.'

'That isn't quite what you said. But if that's so, perhaps you could help me with finding locations for the film and ...'

My unconscious mind was telling me to explore the territory a little more, because although the idea that she might be a prostitute was still buzzing around in my head, I very, *very* much wanted her to come with me. She politely refused my offer. The other woman joined in the conversation at this point, as if to protect the younger woman, and I felt then that I was in the way and decided to leave.

My interpreter arrived shortly afterwards, out of breath, saying that he'd made all the necessary arrangements, but that (as expected) it was going to cost a lot of money. I went up to my room, grabbed my suitcase, which I'd packed earlier, got into the Russian wreck of a car, drove down the long, almost deserted avenues, and realised that I had with me my small camera, my belongings, my anxieties, a couple of bottles of mineral water, some sandwiches, and an image of someone that stubbornly refused to leave my head.

In the days that followed, as I was trying to piece together a script on the historical figure of Dracula, and interviewing both locals and intellectuals on the subject of the vampire myth (with, as foreseen, little success), I gradually became aware that I was no longer merely trying to make a documentary for British television. I wanted to meet that arrogant, unfriendly, self-sufficient young woman whom I'd seen in a dining room in a hotel in Bucharest, and who would, at that moment, be somewhere nearby. I knew absolutely nothing about her apart from her name, but, like the vampire of the myth, she seemed to be sucking up all my energy.

In my world, and in the world of those I lived with, this was absurd, nonsensical, unacceptable.

Deidre O'Neill, known as Edda

'I don't know what you came here to do, but whatever it was, you must see it through to the end.'

She looked at me, startled.

'Who are you?'

I started talking about the magazine I was reading, and after a while, the man sitting with her decided to get up and leave. Now I could tell her who I was.

'If you mean what do I do for a living, I qualified as a doctor some years ago, but I don't think that's the answer you want to hear.'

I paused.

'Your next step, though, will be to try to find out, through clever questioning, exactly what I'm doing here, in a country that's only just emerging from years of terrible oppression.'

'I'll be straightforward then. What did you come here to do?'

I could have said: I came for the funeral of my teacher, because I felt he deserved that homage. But it would be imprudent to touch on the subject. She may have shown no interest in vampires, but the word 'teacher' would be sure to attract her attention. Since my oath will not allow me to lie, I replied with a half-truth.

'I wanted to see where a writer called Mircea Eliade lived. You've probably never heard of him, but Eliade, who spent most of his life in France, was a world authority on myths.'

The young woman looked at her watch, feigning indifference. I went on:

'And I'm not talking about vampires, I'm talking about people who, let's say, are following the same path you're following.'

She was about to take a sip of her coffee, but she stopped:

'Are you from the government? Or are you someone my parents engaged to follow me?'

It was my turn then to feel uncertain as to whether to continue the conversation. Her response had been unnecessarily aggressive. But I could see her aura, her anxiety. She was very like me when I was her age: full of internal and external wounds that drove me to want to heal people on the physical plane and to help them find their path on the spiritual plane. I wanted to say: 'Your wounds will help you, my dear,' then pick up my magazine and leave.

If I had done that, Athena's path might have been completely different, and she would still be alive and living with the man she loved. She would have brought up her son and watched him grow, get married and have lots of children. She would be rich, possibly the owner of a company selling real estate. She had all the necessary qualities to find success and happiness. She'd suffered enough to be able to use her scars to her advantage, and it was just a matter of time before she managed to control her anxiety and move on.

So what kept me sitting there, trying to keep the conversation going? The answer is very simple: curiosity. I couldn't understand what that brilliant light was doing there in the cold hotel.

I continued:

'Mircea Eliade wrote books with strange titles: *Occultism, Witchcraft and Cultural Fashions*, for example. Or *The Sacred and the Profane*. My teacher' (I inadvertently let the word slip, but she either wasn't listening or else pretended not to have noticed) 'loved his work. And something tells me it's a subject you're interested in too.'

She glanced at her watch again.

'I'm going to Sibiu,' she said. 'My bus leaves in an hour. I'm looking for my mother, if that's what you want to know. I work as a real estate agent in the Middle East, I have a son of nearly four, I'm divorced, and my parents live in London. My adoptive parents, of course, because I was abandoned as a baby.'

She was clearly at a very advanced stage of perception, and had identified with me, even though she wasn't aware of this yet.

'Yes, that's what I wanted to know.'

'Did you have to come all this way just to do research into a writer? Aren't there any libraries where you live?'

'The fact is that Eliade only lived in Romania until he graduated from university. So if I really wanted to know more about his work, I should go to Paris, London or Chicago, where he died. However, what I'm doing isn't research in the normal sense of the word: I wanted to see the ground where he placed his feet. I wanted to feel what inspired him to write about things that affect my life and the lives of people I respect.'

'Did he write about medicine too?'

I had better not answer that. I saw that she'd picked up on the word 'teacher', and assumed it must be related to my profession.

The young woman got to her feet. I felt she knew what I was talking about. I could see her light shining more intensely. I only achieve this state of perception when I'm close to someone very like myself.

'Would you mind coming with me to the bus station?' she asked.

Not at all. My plane didn't leave until later that night, and a whole, dull, endless day stretched out before me. At least I would have someone to talk to for a while.

She went upstairs, returned with her suitcases in her hand and a series of questions in her head. She began her interrogation as soon as we left the hotel.

'I may never see you again,' she said, 'but I feel that we have something in common. Since this may be the last opportunity we have in this incarnation to talk to each other, would you mind being direct in your answers?'

I nodded.

'Based on what you've read in all those books, do you believe that through dance we can enter a trance-like state that helps us to see a light? And that the light tells us nothing – only whether we're happy or sad?'

A good question!

'Of course, and that happens not only through dance, but through anything that allows us to focus our attention and to separate body from spirit. Like yoga or prayer or Buddhist meditation.'

'Or calligraphy.'

'I hadn't thought of that, but it's possible. At such moments, when the body sets the soul free, the soul either rises up to heaven or descends into hell, depending on the person's state of mind. In both cases, it learns what it needs to learn: to destroy or to heal. But I'm no longer interested in individual paths; in my tradition, I need the help of … are you listening to me?'

'No.'

She had stopped in the middle of the street and was staring at a little girl who appeared to have been abandoned. She went to put her hand in her bag.

'Don't do that,' I said. 'Look across the street at that woman, the one with cruel eyes. She's put the girl there purely in order to—'

'I don't care.'

She took out a few coins. I grabbed her hand.

'Let's buy her something to eat. That would be more useful.'

I asked the little girl to go with us to a café and bought her a sandwich. The little girl smiled and thanked me. The eyes of the woman across the street seemed to glitter with hatred, but, for the first time, the grey eyes of the young woman walking at my side looked at me with respect.

'What were you saying?' she asked.

'It doesn't matter. Do you know what happened to you a few moments ago? You went into the same trance that your dancing provokes.'

'No, you're wrong.'

'I'm right. Something touched your unconscious mind. Perhaps you saw yourself as you would have been if you hadn't been adopted – begging in the street. At that moment, your brain stopped reacting. Your spirit left you and travelled down to hell to meet the demons from your past. Because of that, you didn't notice the woman across the street – you were in a trance, a disorganised, chaotic trance that was driving you to do something which was good in theory, but, in practice, pointless. As if you were—'

'—in the blank space between the letters. In the moment when a note of music ends and the next has not yet begun.'

'Exactly. And such a trance can be dangerous.'

I almost said: 'It's the kind of trance provoked by fear. It paralyses the person, leaves them unable to react; the body doesn't respond, the soul is no longer there. You were terrified by everything that could have happened to you had fate not placed your parents in your path.' But she had put her suitcases down on the ground and was standing in front of me.

'Who are you? Why are you saying all this?'

'As a doctor, I'm known as Deidre O'Neill. Pleased to meet you, and what's your name?'

'Athena. Although according to my passport I'm Sherine Khalil.'

'Who gave you the name Athena?'

'No one important. But I didn't ask you for your name, I asked who you are and why you spoke to me. And why I felt the same need to talk to you. Was it just because we were the only two women in that hotel dining room? I don't think so. And you're saying things to me that make sense of my life.'

She picked up her bags again, and we continued walking towards the bus station.

'I have another name too – Edda. But it wasn't chosen by chance, nor do I believe it was chance that brought us together.'

Before us was the entrance to the bus station, with various people going in and out – soldiers in uniform, farmers, pretty women dressed as if they were still living in the 1950s.

'If it wasn't chance, what was it?'

She had another half an hour before her bus left, and I could have said: It was the Mother. Some chosen spirits emit a special light and are drawn to each other, and you – Sherine or Athena – are one of those spirits, but you need to work very hard to use that energy to your advantage.

I could have explained that she was following the classic path of the witch, who, through her individual persona, seeks contact with the upper and lower world, but always ends up destroying her own life – she serves others, gives out energy, but receives nothing in return.

I could have explained that, although all paths are different, there is always a point when people come together, celebrate together, discuss their difficulties, and prepare themselves for the Rebirth of the Mother. I could have said that contact with the Divine Light is the greatest reality a human being can experience, and yet, in my tradition, that contact cannot be made alone, because we've suffered centuries of persecution, and this has taught us many things.

'Would you like to have a coffee while I wait for the bus?'

No, I did not. I would only end up saying things that might, at that stage, be misinterpreted.

'Certain people have been very important in my life,' she went on. 'My landlord, for example, or the calligrapher I met in the desert near Dubai. Who knows, you might have things to say to me that I can share with them, and repay them for all they taught me.'

So she had already had teachers in her life – excellent! Her spirit was ripe. All she needed was to continue her training, otherwise she would end up losing all she had achieved. But was I the right person?

I asked the Mother to inspire me, to tell me what to do. I got no answer, which did not surprise me. She always behaves like that when it's up to me to take responsibility for a decision.

I gave Athena my business card and asked her for hers. She gave me an address in Dubai, a country I would have been unable to find on the map.

I decided to try making a joke, to test her out a little more:

'Isn't it a bit of a coincidence that three English people should meet in a hotel in Bucharest?'

'Well, from your card I see that you're Scottish. The man I met apparently works in England, but I don't know anything else about him.'

She took a deep breath:

'And I'm … Romanian.'

I gave an excuse and said that I had to rush back to the hotel and pack my bags.

Now she knew where to find me, if it was written that we would meet again, we would. The important thing is to allow fate to intervene in our lives and to decide what is best for everyone.

Vosho 'Bushalo', 65, restaurant owner

These Europeans come here thinking they know everything, thinking they deserve the very best treatment, that they have the right to bombard us with questions which we're obliged to answer. On the other hand, they think that by giving us some tricksy name, like 'travellers' or 'Roma', they can put right the many wrongs they've done us in the past.

Why can't they just call us gipsies and put an end to all the stories that make us look as if we were cursed in the eyes of the world? They accuse us of being the fruit of the illicit union between a woman and the Devil himself. They say that one of us forged the nails that fixed Christ to the cross, that mothers should be careful when our caravans come near, because we steal children and enslave them.

And because of this there have been frequent massacres throughout history; in the Middle Ages we were hunted as witches; for centuries our testimony wasn't even accepted in the German courts. I was born before the Nazi wind swept through Europe and I saw my father marched off to a concentration camp in Poland, with a humiliating black triangle sewn to his clothes. Of the 500,000 gipsies sent for slave labour, only 5,000 survived to tell the tale.

And no one, absolutely no one, wants to hear about this.

Right up until last year, our culture, religion and language were banned in this godforsaken part of the world, where most of the tribes decided to settle. If you asked anyone in the city what they thought of gipsies, their immediate response would be: 'They're all thieves.' However hard we try to lead normal lives by ceasing our eternal wanderings and living in places where we're easily identifiable, the racism continues. Our children are forced to sit at the back of the class and not a week goes by without someone insulting them.

Then people complain that we don't give straight answers, that we try to disguise ourselves, that we never openly admit our origins. Why would we do that? Everyone knows what a gipsy looks like, and everyone knows how to 'protect' themselves from our 'curses'.

When a stuck-up, intellectual young woman appears, smiling and claiming to be part of our culture and our race, I'm immediately on my guard. She might have been sent by the Securitate, the secret police who work for that mad dictator – the Conducator, the Genius of the Carpathians, the Leader. They say he was put on trial and shot, but I don't believe it. His son may have disappeared from the scene for the moment, but he's still a powerful figure in these parts.

The young woman insists; she smiles, as if she were saying something highly amusing, and tells me that her mother is a gipsy and that she'd like to find her. She knows her full name. How could she obtain such information without the help of the Securitate?

It's best not to get on the wrong side of people who have government contacts. I tell her that I know nothing, that I'm just a gipsy who's decided to lead an honest life, but she won't listen: she wants to find her mother. I know who her mother is, and I know, too, that more than twenty years ago she had a child she gave up to an orphanage and never heard from again. We had to take her mother in because a blacksmith who thought he was the master of the universe insisted on it. But who can guarantee that this intellectual young woman standing before me really is Liliana's daughter? Before trying to find out who her mother is, she should at least respect some of our customs and not turn up dressed in red, if it's not her wedding day. She ought to wear longer skirts as well, so as not to arouse men's lust. And she should be more respectful.

If I speak of her now in the present tense, it's because for those who travel, time does not exist, only space. We came from far away, some say from India, others from Egypt, but the fact is that we carry the past with us as if it had all just happened. And the persecutions continue.

The young woman is trying to be nice and to show that she knows about our culture, when that doesn't matter at all. After all, she *should* know about our traditions.

'In town I was told that you're a Rom Baro, a tribal leader. Before I came here, I learned a lot about our history – '

'Not "our", please. It's *my* history, the history of *my* wife, *my* children, *my* tribe. You're a European. You were never stoned in the street as I was when I was five years old.'

'I think the situation is getting better.'

'The situation is always getting better, then it immediately gets worse.'

But she keeps smiling. She orders a whisky. One of our women would never do that.

If she'd come in here just to have a drink or looking for company, I'd treat her like any other customer. I've learned to be friendly, attentive, discreet, because my business depends on that. When my customers want to know more about the gipsies, I offer them a few curious facts, tell them to listen to the group who'll be playing later on, make a few remarks about our culture, and then they leave with the impression that they know everything about us.

But this young woman isn't just another tourist: she says she belongs to our race.

She again shows me the certificate she got from the government. I can believe that the government kills, steals and lies, but it wouldn't risk handing out false certificates, and so she really must be Liliana's daughter, because the certificate gives her full name and address. I learned from the television that the Genius of the Carpathians, the Father of the People, our Conducator, the one who left us to starve while he exported all our food, the one who lived in palaces and used gold-plated cutlery while the people were dying of starvation, that same man and his wretched wife used to get the Securitate to trawl the orphanages selecting babies to be trained as State assassins.

They only ever took boys, though, never girls. Perhaps she really is Liliana's daughter.

I look at the certificate once more and wonder whether or not I should tell her where her mother is. Liliana deserves to meet this intellectual, claiming to be 'one of us'. Liliana deserves to look this woman in the eye. I think she suffered enough when she betrayed her people, slept with a *gadje* (*Editor's note: foreigner*) and shamed her parents. Perhaps the moment has come to end her hell, for her to see that her daughter survived, got rich, and might even be able to help her out of the poverty she lives in.

Perhaps this young woman will pay me for this information; perhaps it'll be of some advantage to our tribe, because we're living in confusing times. Everyone's saying that the Genius of the Carpathians is dead, and they even show photos of his execution, but, who knows, he could come back tomorrow, and it'll all turn out to have been a clever trick on his part to find out who really was on his side and who was prepared to betray him.

The musicians will start playing soon, so I'd better talk business.

'I know where you can find this woman. I can take you to her.' I adopt a friendlier tone of voice. 'But I think that information is worth something.'

'I was prepared for that,' she says, holding out a much larger sum of money than I was going to ask for.

'That's not even enough for the taxi fare.'

'I'll pay you the same amount again when I reach my destination.'

And I sense that, for the first time, she feels uncertain. She suddenly seems afraid of what she's about to do. I grab the money she's placed on the counter.

'I'll take you to see Liliana tomorrow.'

Her hands are trembling. She orders another whisky, but suddenly a man comes into the bar, sees her, blushes scarlet and comes straight over to her. I gather that they only met yesterday, and yet here they are talking as if they were old friends. His eyes are full of desire. She's perfectly aware of this and encourages him. The man orders a bottle of wine, and the two sit down at a table, and it's as if she'd forgotten all about her mother.

However, I want the other half of that money. When I serve them their drinks, I tell her I'll be at her hotel at ten o'clock in the morning.

Heron Ryan, journalist

Immediately after the first glass of wine, she told me, unprompted, that she had a boyfriend who worked for Scotland Yard. It was a lie, of course. She must have read the look in my eyes, and this was her way of keeping me at a distance.

I told her that I had a girlfriend, which made us even.

Ten minutes after the music had started, she stood up. We had said very little – she asked no questions about my research into vampires, and we exchanged only generalities: our impressions of the city, complaints about the state of the roads. But what I saw next – or, rather, what everyone in the restaurant saw – was a goddess revealing herself in all her glory, a priestess invoking angels and demons.

Her eyes were closed and she seemed no longer to be conscious of who she was or where she was or why she was there; it was as if she were floating and simultaneously summoning up her past, revealing her present and predicting the future. She mingled eroticism with chastity, pornography with revelation, worship of God and nature, all at the same time.

People stopped eating and started watching what was happening. She was no longer following the music, the musicians were trying to keep up with her steps, and that restaurant in the basement of an old building in the city of Sibiu was transformed into an Egyptian temple, where the worshippers of Isis used to gather for their fertility rites. The smell of roast meat and wine was transmuted into an incense that drew us all into the same trance-like state, into the same experience of leaving this world and entering an unknown dimension.

The string and wind instruments had given up, only the percussion played on. Athena was dancing as if she were no longer there, with sweat running down her face, her bare feet beating on the wooden floor. A woman got up and very gently tied a scarf around her neck and breasts, because her blouse kept threatening to slip off her shoulders. Athena, however, appeared not to notice; she was inhabiting other spheres, experiencing the frontiers of worlds that almost touch ours, but never reveal themselves.

The other people in the restaurant started clapping in time to the music, and Athena was dancing ever faster, feeding on that energy, and spinning round and round, balancing in the void, snatching up everything that we, poor mortals, wanted to offer to the supreme divinity.

And suddenly she stopped. Everyone stopped, including the percussionists. Her eyes were still closed, but tears were now rolling down her cheeks. She raised her arms in the air and cried:

'When I die, bury me standing, because I've spent all my life on my knees!'

No one said anything. She opened her eyes as if waking from a deep sleep and walked back to the table as if nothing had happened. The band started up again, and couples took to the floor in an attempt to enjoy themselves, but the atmosphere in the place had changed completely. People soon paid their bills and started to leave the restaurant.

'Is everything all right?' I asked, when I saw that she'd recovered from the physical effort of dancing.

'I feel afraid. I discovered how to reach a place I don't want to go to.'

'Do you want me to go with you?'

She shook her head.

In the days that followed, I completed my research for the documentary, sent my interpreter back to Bucharest with the hired car, and then stayed on in Sibiu simply because I wanted to meet her again. All my life I've always been guided by logic and I know that love is something that can be built rather than simply discovered, but I sensed that if I never saw her again, I would be leaving a very important part of my life in Transylvania, even though I might only realise this later on. I fought against the monotony of those endless hours; more than once, I went to the bus station to find out the times of buses to Bucharest; I spent more than my tiny budget as an independent film-maker allowed on phone-calls to the BBC and to my girlfriend. I explained that I didn't yet have all the material I needed, that there were still a few things lacking, that I might need another day or possibly a week; I said that the Romanians were being very difficult and got upset if anyone associated their beautiful Transylvania with the hideous story of Dracula. I finally managed to convince the producers, and they let me stay on longer than I really needed to.

We were staying in the only hotel in the city, and one day she saw me in the foyer and seemed suddenly to remember our first encounter. This time, she invited me out, and I tried to contain my joy. Perhaps I *was* important in her life.

Later on, I learned that the words she had spoken at the end of her dance were an ancient gipsy saying.

Liliana, seamstress, age and surname unknown

I speak in the present tense because for us time does not exist, only space. And because it seems like only yesterday.

The one tribal custom I did not follow was that of having my man by my side when Athena was born. The midwives came to me even though they knew I had slept with a *gadje*, a foreigner. They loosened my hair, cut the umbilical cord, tied various knots and handed it to me. At that point, tradition demands that the child be wrapped in some item of the father's clothing; he had left a scarf which reminded me of his smell and which I sometimes pressed to my nose so as to feel him close to me, but now that perfume would vanish for ever.

I wrapped the baby in the scarf and placed her on the floor so that she would receive energy from the Earth. I stayed there with her, not knowing what to feel or think; my decision had been made.

The midwives told me to choose a name and not to tell anyone what it was – it could only be pronounced once the child was baptised. They gave me the consecrated oil and the amulets I must hang around her neck for the two weeks following her birth. One of them told me not to worry, the whole tribe was responsible for my child and although I would be the butt of much criticism, this would soon pass. They also advised me not to go out between dusk and dawn because the *tsinvari* (*Editor's note: evil spirits*) might attack us and take possession of us, and from then on our lives would be a tragedy.

A week later, as soon as the sun rose, I went to an adoption centre in Sibiu and placed her on the doorstep, hoping that some charitable person would take her in. As I was doing so, a nurse caught me and dragged me inside. She insulted me in every way she could and said that they were used to such behaviour, but that there was always someone watching and I couldn't escape so easily from the responsibility of bringing a child into the world.

'Although, of course, what else would one expect from a gipsy! Abandoning your own child like that!'

I was forced to fill in a form with all my details and, since I didn't know how to write, she said again, more than once: 'Yes, well, what can you expect from a gipsy. And don't try to trick us by giving false information. If you do, it could land you in jail.' Out of pure fear, I told them the truth.

I looked at my child one last time, and all I could think was: 'Child without a name, may you find love, much love in your life.'

Afterwards, I walked in the forest for hours. I remembered many nights during my pregnancy when I had both loved and hated the child herself and the man who had put her inside me.

Like all women, I'd dreamed of one day meeting an enchanted prince, who would marry me, give me lots of children and shower attentions on my family. Like many women, I fell in love with a man who could give me none of those things, but with whom I shared some unforgettable moments, moments my child would never understand, for she would always be stigmatised in our tribe as a *gadje* and a fatherless child. I could bear that, but I didn't want her to suffer as I had suffered ever since I first realised I was pregnant. I wept and tore at my own skin, thinking that the pain of the scratches would perhaps stop me thinking about a return to ordinary life, to face the shame I had brought on the tribe. Someone would take care of the child, and I would always cherish the hope of seeing her again one day, when she had grown up.

Unable to stop crying, I sat down on the ground and put my arms around the trunk of a tree. However, as soon as my tears and the blood from my wounds touched the trunk of the tree, a strange calm took hold of me. I seemed to hear a voice telling me not to worry, saying that my blood and my tears had purified the path of the child and lessened my suffering. Ever since then, whenever I despair, I remember that voice and feel calm again.

That's why I wasn't surprised when I saw her arrive with our tribe's Rom Baro, who asked me for a coffee and a drink, then smiled slyly and left. The voice told me that she would come back, and now here she is, in front of me. She's pretty. She looks like her father. I don't know what feelings she has for me; perhaps she hates me because I abandoned her. I don't need to explain why I did what I did; no one would ever understand.

We sit for an age without saying anything to each other, just looking – not smiling, not crying, nothing. A surge of love rises up from the depths of my soul, but I don't know if she's interested in what I feel.

'Are you hungry? Would you like something to eat?'

Instinct. Instinct above all else. She nods. We go into the small room in which I live, and which is living room, bedroom, kitchen and sewing workshop. She looks around, shocked, but I pretend not to notice. I go over to the stove and return with two bowls of thick meat and vegetable broth. I've prepared some strong coffee too, and just as I'm about to add sugar she speaks for the first time:

'No sugar for me, thank you. I didn't know you spoke English.'

I almost say that I learned it from her father, but I bite my tongue. We eat in silence and, as time passes, everything starts to feel familiar to me; here I am with my daughter; she went off into the world and now she's back; she followed different paths from mine and has come home. I know this is an illusion, but life has given me so many moments of harsh reality that it does no harm to dream a little.

'Who's that saint?' she asks, pointing to a painting on the wall.

'St Sarah, the patron saint of gipsies. I've always wanted to visit her church in France, but I can't leave the country. I'd never get a passport or permission ...'

I'm about to say: And even if I did, I wouldn't have enough money, but I stop myself in time. She might think I was asking her for something.

'... and besides I have too much work to do.'

Silence falls again. She finishes her soup, lights a cigarette, and her eyes give nothing away, no emotion.

'Did you think you would ever see me again?'

I say that I did, and that I'd heard yesterday, from the Rom Baro's wife, that she'd visited his restaurant.

'A storm is coming. Wouldn't you like to sleep a little?'

'I can't hear anything. The wind isn't blowing any harder or softer than before. I'd rather talk.'

'Believe me, I have all the time in the world. I have the rest of my life to spend by your side.'

'Don't say that.'

'But you're tired,' I go on, pretending not to have heard her remark. I can see the storm approaching. Like all storms, it brings destruction, but, at the same time, it soaks the fields, and the wisdom of the heavens falls with the rain. Like all storms, it will pass. The more violent it is, the more quickly it will pass.

I have, thank God, learned to weather storms.

And as if all the Holy Marys of the Sea were listening to me, the first drops of rain begin to fall on the tin roof. The young woman finishes her cigarette. I take her hand and lead her to my bed. She lies down and closes her eyes.

I don't know how long she slept. I watched her without thinking anything, and the voice I'd heard once in the forest was telling me that all was well, that I needn't worry, that the ways in which fate changes people are always favourable if we only know how to decipher them. I don't know who saved her from the orphanage and brought her up and made her into the independent woman she appears to be. I offered up a prayer to that family who had allowed my daughter to survive and achieve a better life. In the middle of the prayer, I felt jealousy, despair, regret, and I stopped talking to St Sarah. Had it really been so important to bring her back? There lay everything I'd lost and could never recover.

But there, too, was the physical manifestation of my love. I knew nothing and yet everything was revealed to me: I remembered the times I'd considered suicide and, later, abortion, when I'd imagined leaving that part of the world and setting off on foot to wherever my strength would take me; I remembered my blood and tears on the tree trunk, the dialogue with nature that had intensified from that moment on and has never left me since, although few people in my tribe have any inkling of this. My protector, whom I met while I was wandering in the forest, understood, but he had just died.

'The light is unstable, the wind blows it out, the lightning ignites it, it is never simply there, shining like the sun, but it is worth fighting for,' he used to say.

He was the only person who accepted me and persuaded the tribe that I could once again form part of their world. He was the only one with the moral authority to ensure that I wasn't expelled.

And, alas, the only one who would never meet my daughter. I wept for him, while she lay sleeping on my bed, she who must be used to all the world's comforts. Thousands of questions filled my head – who were her adoptive parents, where did she live, had she been to university, was there someone she loved, what were her plans? But I wasn't the one who had travelled the world in search of her, on the contrary. I wasn't there to ask questions, but to answer them.

She opened her eyes. I wanted to touch her hair, to give her the affection I'd kept locked inside all these years, but I wasn't sure how she would react and thought it best to do nothing.

'You came here to find out why –'

'No, I don't want to know why a mother would abandon her daughter. There is no reason for anyone to do that.'

Her words wound my heart, but I don't know how to respond.

'Who am I? What blood runs in my veins? Yesterday, when I found out where you were, I was absolutely terrified. Where do I start? I suppose, like all gipsies, you can read the future in the cards.'

'No, that's not true. We only do that with *gadje* as a way of earning a living. We never read cards or hands or try to predict the future within our own tribe. And you ...'

'... I'm part of the tribe. Even though the woman who brought me into the world sent me far away.'

'Yes.'

'So what am I doing here? Now that I've seen your face I can go back to London. My holidays are nearly over.'

'Do you want to know about your father?'

'No, I haven't the slightest interest in him.'

And suddenly, I realised that I could help her. It was as if someone else's voice came out of my mouth:

'Try to understand the blood that flows in my veins and in your heart.'

That was my teacher speaking through me. She closed her eyes again and slept for nearly twelve hours.

The following day, I took her to the outskirts of Sibiu where there's a kind of museum of the different kinds of houses found in the region. For the first time, I'd had the pleasure of preparing her breakfast. She was more rested, less tense, and she asked me questions about gipsy culture, but never about me. She told me a little of her life. I learned that I was a grandmother! She didn't mention her husband or her adoptive parents. She said she sold land in a country far from there and that she would soon return to her work.

I explained that I could show her how to make amulets to ward off evil, but she didn't seem interested. However, when I spoke to her about the healing properties of herbs, she asked me to teach her how to recognise them. In the park where we were walking, I tried to pass on to her all the knowledge I possessed, although I was sure she'd forget everything as soon as she returned to her home country, which by then I knew was England.

'We don't possess the Earth, the Earth possesses us. We used to travel constantly, and everything around us was ours: the plants, the water, the landscapes through which our caravans passed. Our laws were nature's laws: the strong survived, and we, the weak, the eternal exiles, learned to hide our strength and to use it only when necessary. We don't believe that God made the universe. We believe that God is the universe and that we are contained in Him, and He in us. Although …'

I stopped, then decided to go on, because it was a way of paying homage to my protector.

'... in my opinion, we should call "Him" "Goddess" or "Mother". Not like the woman who gives her daughter up to an orphanage, but like the Woman in all of us, who protects us when we are in danger. She will always be with us while we perform our daily tasks with love and joy, understanding that nothing is suffering, that everything is a way of praising Creation.'

Athena – now I knew her name – looked across at one of the houses in the park.

'What's that? A church?'

The hours I'd spent by her side had allowed me to recover my strength. I asked if she was trying to change the subject. She thought for a moment before replying.

'No, I want to go on listening to what you have to tell me, although, according to everything I read before I came here, what you're saying isn't part of the gipsy tradition.'

'My protector taught me these things. He knew things the gipsies don't know and he made the tribe take me back. And as I learned from him, I gradually became aware of the power of the Mother, I, who had rejected the blessing of being a mother.'

I pointed at a small bush.

'If one day your son has a fever, place him next to a young plant like this and shake its leaves. The fever will pass over into the plant. If ever you feel anxious, do the same thing.'

'I'd rather you told me more about your protector.'

'He taught me that in the beginning Creation was so lonely that it created someone else to talk to. Those two creatures, in an act of love, made a third person, and from then on, they multiplied by thousands and millions. You asked about the church we just saw: I don't know when it was built and I'm not interested. My temple is the park, the sky, the water in the lake and the stream that feeds it. My people are those who share my ideas and not those I'm bound to by bonds of blood. My ritual is being with those people and celebrating everything around me. When are you thinking of going home?'

'Possibly tomorrow. I don't want to inconvenience you.'

Another wound to my heart, but I could say nothing.

'No, please, stay as long as you like. I only asked because I'd like to celebrate your arrival with the others. If you agree, I can do this tonight.'

She says nothing, and I understand this as a 'yes'. Back home, I give her more food, and she explains that she needs to go to her hotel in Sibiu to fetch some clothes. By the time she returns, I have everything organised. We go to a hill to the south of the town; we sit around a fire that has just been lit; we play instruments, we sing, we dance, we tell stories. She watches, but doesn't take part, although the Rom Baro told me that she was a fine dancer. For the first time in many years, I feel happy, because I've had the chance to prepare a ritual for my daughter and to celebrate with her the miracle of the two of us being together, alive and healthy and immersed in the love of the Great Mother.

Afterwards, she says that she'll sleep at the hotel that night. I ask her if this is goodbye, but she says it isn't. She'll come back tomorrow.

For a whole week, my daughter and I share together the adoration of the Universe. One night, she brought a friend, making it quite clear that he was neither her boyfriend nor the father of her child. The man, who must have been ten years older than her, asked who we were worshipping in our rituals. I explained that worshipping someone means – according to my protector – placing that person outside our world. We are not worshipping anyone or anything; we are simply communing with Creation.

'But do you pray?'

'Myself, I pray to St Sarah, but here we are part of everything and we celebrate rather than pray.'

I felt that Athena was proud of my answer, but I was really only repeating my protector's words.

'And why do this in a group, when we can all celebrate the Universe on our own?'

'Because the others are me. And I am the others.'

Athena looked at me then, and I felt it was my turn to wound her heart.

'I'm leaving tomorrow,' she said.

'Before you do, come and say goodbye to your mother.'

That was the first time, in all those days, I had used the word. My voice didn't tremble, my gaze was steady, and I knew that, despite everything, standing before me was the blood of my blood, the fruit of my womb. At that moment, I was behaving like a little girl who has just found out that the world isn't full of ghosts and curses, as grown-ups have taught us. It's full of love, regardless of how that love is manifested, a love that forgives our mistakes and redeems our sins.

She gave me a long embrace. Then she adjusted the veil I wear to cover my hair; I may not have had a husband, but according to gipsy tradition, I had to wear a veil because I was no longer a virgin. What would tomorrow bring me, along with the departure of the being I've always both loved and feared from a distance? I was everyone, and everyone was me and my solitude.

The following day, Athena arrived bearing a bunch of flowers. She tidied my room, told me that I should wear glasses because my eyes were getting worn out from all that sewing. She asked if the friends I celebrated with experienced any problems with the tribe, and I told her that they didn't, that my protector had been a very respected man, had taught us many things and had followers all over the world. I explained that he'd died shortly before she arrived.

'One day, a cat brushed against him. To us, that means death, and we were all very worried. But although there is a ritual that can lift such a curse, my protector said it was time for him to leave, that he needed to travel to those other worlds which he knew existed, to be reborn as a child, and to rest for a while in the arms of the Mother. His funeral took place in a forest nearby. It was a very simple affair, but people came from all over the world.'

'Amongst those people, was there a woman of about thirty-five, with dark hair?'

'I can't be sure, but possibly. Why do you ask?'

'I met someone at a hotel in Bucharest who said that she'd come to attend the funeral of a friend. I think she said something about "her teacher".'

She asked me to tell her more about the gipsies, but there wasn't much she didn't already know, mainly because, apart from customs and traditions, we know little of our own history. I suggested that she go to France one day and take, on my behalf, a shawl to present to the image of St Sarah in the little French village of Saintes-Maries-de-la-Mer.

'I came here because there was something missing in my life,' she said. 'I needed to fill up my blank spaces, and I thought just seeing your face would be enough. But it wasn't. I also needed to understand that … I was loved.'

'You *are* loved.'

I said nothing else for a long time. I'd finally put into words what I'd wanted to say ever since I let her go. So that she would not become too emotional, I went on:

'I'd like to ask you something.'

'Ask me anything you like.'

'I want to ask your forgiveness.'

She bit her lip.

'I've always been a very restless person. I work hard, spend too much time looking after my son, I dance like a mad thing, I learned calligraphy, I go to courses on selling, I read one book after another. But that's all a way of avoiding those moments when nothing is happening, because those blank spaces give me a feeling of absolute emptiness, in which not a single crumb of love exists. My parents have always done everything they could for me, and I do nothing but disappoint them. But here, during the time we've spent together, celebrating nature and the Great Mother, I've realised that those empty spaces were starting to get filled up. They were transformed into pauses – the moment when the man lifts his hand from the drum before bringing it down again to strike it hard. I think I can leave now. I'm not saying that I'll go in peace, because my life needs to follow the rhythm I'm accustomed to. But I won't leave feeling bitter. Do all gipsies believe in the Great Mother?'

'If you were to ask them, none of them would say "yes". They've adopted the beliefs and customs of the places where they've settled, and the only thing that unites us in religious terms is the worship of St Sarah and making a pilgrimage, at least once in our lifetime, to visit her tomb in Saintes-Maries-de-la-Mer. Some tribes call her Kali Sarah, Black Sarah. Or the Virgin of the Gipsies, as she's known in Lourdes.'

'I have to go,' Athena said after a while. 'The friend you met the other day is leaving with me.'

'He seems like a nice man.'

'You're talking like a mother.'

'I am your mother.'

'And I'm your daughter.'

She embraced me, this time with tears in her eyes. I stroked her hair as I held her in my arms, as I'd always dreamed I would, ever since the day when fate – or my fear – separated us. I asked her to take good care of herself, and she told me that she had learned a lot.

'You'll learn a lot more too because, although, nowadays, we're all trapped in houses, cities and jobs, there still flows in your blood the time of caravans and journeyings and the teachings that the Great Mother placed in our path so that we could survive. Learn, but always learn with other people by your side. Don't be alone in the search, because if you take a wrong step, you'll have no one there to help put you right.'

She was still crying, still clinging to me, almost begging me to let her stay. I pleaded with my protector not to let me shed one tear, because I wanted the best for Athena, and her destiny was to go forward. Here in Transylvania, apart from my love, she would find nothing else. And although I believe that love is enough to justify a whole existence, I was quite sure that I couldn't ask her to sacrifice her future in order to stay by my side.

Athena planted a kiss on my forehead and left without saying goodbye, perhaps thinking she would return one day. Every Christmas, she sent me enough money to spend the whole year without having to sew, but I never went to the bank to cash her cheques, even though everyone in the tribe thought I was behaving like a foolish woman.

Six months ago, she stopped sending money. She must have realised that I need my sewing to fill up what she called the 'blank spaces'.

I would love to see her again, but I know she'll never come back. She's probably a big executive now, married to the man she loves. And I probably have lots of grandchildren, which means that my blood will remain on this Earth, and my mistakes will be forgiven.

Samira R. Khalil, housewife

As soon as Sherine arrived home, whooping with joy and clutching a rather startled Viorel to her, I knew that everything had gone much better than I'd imagined. I felt that God had heard my prayers, and that now she no longer had anything more to learn about herself, she would finally adapt to normal life, bring up her child, remarry and forget all about the strange restlessness that left her simultaneously euphoric and depressed.

'I love you, Mum.'

It was my turn to put my arms around her and hold her to me. During all the nights she'd been away, I had, I confess, been terrified by the thought that she might send someone to fetch Viorel and then they would never come back.

After she'd eaten, had a bath, told us about the meeting with her birth mother, and described the Transylvanian countryside (I could barely remember it, since all I was interested in, at the time, was finding the orphanage), I asked her when she was going back to Dubai.

'Next week, but, first, I have to go to Scotland to see someone.'

A man!

'A woman,' she said at once, perhaps in response to my knowing smile. 'I feel that I have a mission. While we were celebrating life and nature, I discovered things I didn't even know existed. What I thought could be found only through dance is everywhere. And it has the face of a woman. I saw in the …'

I felt frightened. Her mission, I told her, was to bring up her son, do well at her job, earn more money, remarry, and respect God as we know Him.

But Sherine wasn't listening.

'It was one night when we were sitting round the fire, drinking, telling funny stories and listening to music. Apart from in the restaurant, I hadn't felt the need to dance all the time I was there, as if I were storing up energy for something different. Suddenly, I felt as if everything around me were alive and pulsating, as if the Creation and I were one and the same thing. I wept with joy when the flames of the fire seemed to take on the form of a woman's face, full of compassion, smiling at me.'

I shuddered. It was probably gipsy witchcraft. And at the same time, the image came back to me of the little girl at school, who said she'd seen 'a woman in white'.

'Don't get caught up in things like that, they're the Devil's work. We've always set you a good example, so why can't you lead a normal life?'

I'd obviously been too hasty when I thought the journey in search of her birth mother had done her good. However, instead of reacting aggressively, as she usually did, she smiled and went on:

'What *is* normal? Why is Dad always laden down with work, when we have money enough to support three generations? He's an honest man and he deserves the money he earns, but he always says, with a certain pride, that he's got far too much work. Why? What for?'

'He's a man who lives a dignified, hard-working life.'

'When I lived at home, the first thing he'd ask me when he got back every evening was how my homework was going, and he'd give me a few examples illustrating how important his work was to the world. Then he'd turn on the TV, make a few comments about the political situation in Lebanon, and read some technical book before going to sleep. But he was always busy. And it was the same thing with you. I was the best-dressed girl at school; you took me to parties; you kept the house spick and span; you were always kind and loving and brought me up impeccably. But what happens now that you're getting older? What are you going to do with your life now that I've grown up and am independent?'

'We're going to travel the world and enjoy a well-earned rest.'

'But why don't you do that now, while your health is still good?'

I'd asked myself the same question, but I felt that my husband needed his work, not because of the money, but out of a need to feel useful, to prove that an exile also honours his commitments. Whenever he took a holiday and stayed in town, he always found some excuse to slip into the office, to talk to his colleagues and make some decision that could easily have waited. I tried to make him go to the theatre, to the cinema, to museums, and he'd do as I asked, but I always had the feeling that it bored him. His only interest was the company, work, business.

For the first time, I talked to her as if she were a friend and not my daughter, but I chose my words carefully and spoke in a way that she could understand.

'Are you saying that your father is also trying to fill in what you call the "blank spaces"?'

'The day he retires, although I really don't think that day will ever come, he'll fall into a deep depression. I'm sure of it. What to do with that hard-won freedom? Everyone will congratulate him on a brilliant career, on the legacy he leaves behind him because of the integrity with which he ran his company, but no one will have time for him any more – life flows on, and everyone is caught up in that flow. Dad will feel an exile again, but this time he won't have a country where he can seek refuge.'

'Have you got a better idea?'

'Only one: I don't want the same thing to happen to me. I'm too restless, and please don't take this the wrong way, because I'm not blaming you and Dad at all for the example you set me, but I need to change, and change fast.'

Deidre O'Neill, known as Edda

She's sitting in the pitch black.

The boy, of course, left the room at once – the night is the kingdom of terror, of monsters from the past, of the days when we wandered like gipsies, like my former teacher – may the Mother have mercy on his soul, and may he be loved and cherished until it is time for him to return.

Athena hasn't known what to do since I switched off the light. She asks about her son, and I tell her not to worry, to leave everything to me. I go out, put the TV on, find a cartoon channel and turn off the sound; the child sits there hypnotised – problem solved. I wonder how it must have been in the past, because the women who came to perform the same ritual Athena is about to take part in would have brought their children and in those days there was no TV. What did teachers do then?

Fortunately, I don't have to worry about that.

What the boy is experiencing in front of the television – a gateway into a different reality – is the same state I am going to induce in Athena. Everything is at once so simple and so complicated! It's simple because all it takes is a change of attitude: I'm not going to look for happiness any more. From now on,

I'm independent; I see life through my eyes and not through other people's. I'm going in search of the adventure of being alive.

And it's complicated: why am I not looking for happiness when everyone has taught me that happiness is the only goal worth pursuing? Why am I going to risk taking a path that no one else is taking?

After all, what *is* happiness?

Love, they tell me. But love doesn't bring and never has brought happiness. On the contrary, it's a constant state of anxiety, a battlefield; it's sleepless nights, asking ourselves all the time if we're doing the right thing. Real love is composed of ecstasy and agony.

All right then, peace. Peace? If we look at the Mother, she's never at peace. The winter does battle with the summer, the sun and the moon never meet, the tiger chases the man, who's afraid of the dog, who chases the cat, who chases the mouse, who frightens the man.

Money brings happiness. Fine. In that case, everyone who earns enough to have a high standard of living would be able to stop work. But then they're more troubled than ever, as if they were afraid of losing everything. Money attracts money, that's true. Poverty might bring unhappiness, but money won't necessarily bring happiness.

I spent a lot of my life looking for happiness, now what I want is joy. Joy is like sex – it begins and ends.

I want pleasure. I want to be contented, but happiness? I no longer fall into that trap.

When I'm with a group of people and I want to provoke them by asking that most important of questions: 'Are you happy?', they all reply: 'Yes, I am.'

Then I ask: 'But don't you want more? Don't you want to keep on growing?' And they all reply: 'Of course.'

Then I say: 'So you're not happy.' And they change the subject.

I must go back to the room where Athena is sitting. It's dark. She hears my footsteps; a match is struck and a candle lit.

'We're surrounded by Universal Desire. It's not happiness; it's desire. And desires are never satisfied, because once they are, they cease to be desires.'

'Where's my son?'

'Your son is fine; he's watching TV. I just want you to look at the candle; don't speak, don't say anything. Just believe.'

'Believe what?'

'I asked you not to say anything. Simply believe – don't doubt anything. You're alive, and this candle is the only point in your universe. Believe in that. Let go of the idea that the path will lead you to your goal. The truth is that with each step we take, we arrive. Repeat that to yourself every morning: "I've arrived". That way you'll find it much easier to stay in touch with each second of your day.'

I paused.

'The candle flame is illuminating your world. Ask the candle: "Who am I?"'

I paused again, then went on:

'I can imagine your answer. I'm so-and-so. I've had these experiences. I have a son. I work in Dubai. Now ask the candle again: "Who am I not?"'

Again I waited and again I went on:

'You probably said: I'm not a contented person. I'm not a typical mother concerned only with her son and her husband, with having a house and a garden and a place to spend the summer holidays. Is that so? You can speak now.'

'Yes, it is.'

'Good, we're on the right path. You, like me, are a dissatisfied person. Your "reality" does not coincide with the "reality" of other people. And you're afraid that your son will follow the same path as you, is that correct?'

'Yes.'

'Nevertheless, you know you cannot stop. You struggle, but you can't control your doubts. Look hard at the candle. At the moment, the candle is your universe. It fixes your attention; it lights up the room around you a little. Breathe deeply, hold the air in your lungs as long as possible and then breathe out. Repeat this five times.'

She obeyed.

'This exercise should have calmed your soul. Now, remember what I said: believe. Believe in your abilities; believe that you have already arrived where you wanted to arrive. At a particular moment in your life, as you told me over tea this afternoon, you said that you'd changed the behaviour of the people in the bank where you worked because you'd taught them to dance. That isn't true. You changed everything because, through dance, you changed their reality. You believed in the story of the Vertex, which, although I've never heard of it before, seems to me an interesting one. You like dancing and you believed in what you were doing. You can't believe in something you don't like, can you?'

Athena shook her head, keeping her eyes fixed on the candle flame.

'Faith is not desire. Faith is Will. Desires are things that need to be satisfied, whereas Will is a force. Will changes the space around us, as you did with your work at the bank. But for that, you also need Desire. Please, concentrate on the candle!

'Your son left the room and went to watch TV because he's afraid of the dark. But why? We can project anything onto the darkness, and we usually project our own ghosts. That's true for children and for adults. Slowly raise your right arm.'

She raised her arm. I asked her to do the same with her left arm. I looked at her breasts, far prettier than mine.

'Now slowly lower them again. Close your eyes and breathe deeply. I'm going to turn on the light.

Right, that's the end of the ritual. Let's go into the living room.'

She got up with some difficulty. Her legs had gone numb because of the position I'd told her to adopt.

Viorel had fallen asleep. I turned off the TV, and we went into the kitchen.

'What was the point of all that?' she asked.

'Merely to remove you from everyday reality. I could have asked you to concentrate on anything, but I like the darkness and the candle flame. But you want to know what I'm up to, isn't that right?'

Athena remarked that she'd travelled for nearly five hours in the train with her son on her lap, when she should have been packing her bags to go back to work. She could have sat looking at a candle in her own room without any need to come to Scotland at all.

'Yes, there was a need,' I replied. 'You needed to know that you're not alone, that other people are in contact with the same thing as you. Just knowing that allows you to believe.'

'To believe what?'

'That you're on the right path. And, as I said before, arriving with each step you take.'

'What path? I thought that by going to find my mother in Romania, I would, at last, find the peace of mind I so need, but I haven't. What path are you talking about?'

'I haven't the slightest idea. You'll only discover that when you start to teach. When you go back to Dubai, find a student.'

'Do you mean teach dance or calligraphy?'

'Those are things you know about already. You need to teach what you don't know, what the Mother wants to reveal through you.'

She looked at me as if I had gone mad.

'It's true,' I said. 'Why else do you think I asked you to breathe deeply and to raise your arms? So that you'd believe that I knew more than you. But it isn't true. It was just a way of taking you out of the world you're accustomed to. I didn't ask you to thank the Mother, to say how wonderful She is or that you saw Her face shining in the flames of a fire. I asked only that absurd and pointless gesture of raising your arms and focusing your attention on a candle. That's enough – trying, whenever possible, to do something that is out of kilter with the reality around us.

'When you start creating rituals for your student to carry out, you'll be receiving guidance. That's where the apprenticeship begins, or so my protector told me. If you want to heed my words, fine, but if you don't and you carry on with your life as it is at the moment, you'll end up bumping up against a wall called "dissatisfaction".'

I rang for a taxi, and we talked a little about fashion and men, and then Athena left. I was sure she would listen to me, mainly because she was the kind of person who never refuses a challenge.

'Teach people to be different. That's all!' I shouted after her, as the taxi moved off.

That is joy. Happiness would be feeling satisfied with everything she already had – a lover, a son, a job. And Athena, like me, wasn't born for that kind of life.

Heron Ryan, journalist

I couldn't admit I was in love, of course; I already had a girlfriend who loved me and shared with me both my troubles and my joys.

The various encounters and events that had taken place in Sibiu were part of a journey, and it wasn't the first time this kind of thing had happened while I was away from home. When we step out of our normal world and leave behind us all the usual barriers and prejudices, we tend to become more adventurous.

When I returned to England, the first thing I did was to tell the producers that making a documentary about the historical figure of Dracula was a nonsense, and that one book by a mad Irishman had created a truly terrible image of Transylvania, which was, in fact, one of the loveliest places on the planet. Obviously the producers were none too pleased, but at that point I didn't care what they thought. I left television and went to work for one of the world's most prestigious newspapers.

That was when I began to realise that I wanted to meet Athena again.

I phoned her and we arranged to go for a walk together before she went back to Dubai. She suggested guiding me around London.

We got on the first bus that stopped, without asking where it was going, then we chose a female passenger at random and decided that we would get off wherever she did. She got off at Temple and so did we. We passed a beggar who asked us for money, but we didn't give him any and walked on, listening to the insults he hurled after us, accepting that this was merely his way of communicating with us.

We saw someone vandalising a telephone box, and I wanted to call the police, but Athena stopped me; perhaps that person had just broken up with the love of his life and needed to vent his feelings. Or, who knows, perhaps he had no one to talk to and couldn't stand to see others humiliating him by using that phone to discuss business deals or love.

She told me to close my eyes and to describe exactly the clothes we were both wearing; to my surprise, I got nearly every detail wrong.

She asked me what was on my desk at work and said that some of the papers were only there because I was too lazy to deal with them.

'Have you ever considered that those bits of paper have a life and feelings, have requests to make and stories to tell? I don't think you're giving life the attention it deserves.'

I promised that I'd go through them one by one when I returned to work the following day.

A foreign couple with a map asked Athena how to

get to a particular tourist spot. She gave them very precise, but totally inaccurate directions.

'Everything you told them was completely wrong!'

'It doesn't matter. They'll get lost, and that's the best way to discover interesting places. Try to fill your life again with a little fantasy; above our heads is a sky about which the whole of humanity – after thousands of years spent observing it – has given various apparently reasonable explanations. Forget everything you've ever learned about the stars and they'll once more be transformed into angels, or into children, or into whatever you want to believe at that moment. It won't make you more stupid – after all, it's only a game – but it could enrich your life.'

The following day, when I went back to work, I treated each sheet of paper as if it were a message addressed to me personally and not to the organisation I represent. At midday, I went to talk to the deputy editor and suggested writing an article about the Goddess worshipped by the gipsies. He thought it an excellent idea and I was commissioned to go to the celebrations in the gipsy Mecca, Saintes-Maries-de-la-Mer.

Incredible though it may seem, Athena showed no desire to go with me. She said that her boyfriend – that fictitious policeman, whom she was using to keep me at a distance – wouldn't be very happy if she went off travelling with another man.

'Didn't you promise your mother to take the saint a new shawl?'

'Yes, I did, but only if the town happened to be on my path, which it isn't. If I do ever pass by there, then I'll keep my promise.'

She was returning to Dubai the following Sunday, but first she travelled up to Scotland with her son to see the woman we'd both met in Bucharest. I didn't remember anyone, but, perhaps the phantom 'woman in Scotland', like the phantom 'boyfriend', was another excuse, and I decided not to insist. But I nevertheless felt jealous, as if she were telling me that she preferred being with other people.

I found my jealousy odd. And I decided that if I was asked to go to the Middle East to write an article about the property boom that someone on the business pages had mentioned, I would read up everything I could on real estate, economics, politics and oil, simply as a way of getting closer to Athena.

My visit to Saintes-Maries-de-la-Mer produced an excellent article. According to tradition, Sarah was a gipsy who happened to be living in the small seaside town when Jesus' aunt, Mary Salome, along with other refugees, arrived there fleeing persecution by the Romans. Sarah helped them and, in the end, converted to Christianity.

During the celebrations, bones from the skeletons of the two women who are buried beneath the altar are taken out of a reliquary and raised up on high to bless the multitude of gipsies who arrive in their caravans from all over Europe with their bright clothes and their music. Then the image of Sarah, decked out in splendid robes, is brought from the place near the church where it's kept – for Sarah has never been canonised by the Vatican – and carried in procession to the sea through narrow streets strewn with rose petals. Four gipsies in traditional costume place the relics in a boat full of flowers and wade into the water, re-enacting the arrival of the fugitives and their meeting with Sarah. From then on, it's all music, celebration, songs and bull-running.

A historian, Antoine Locadour, helped me flesh out the article with interesting facts about the Female Divinity. I sent Athena the two pages I'd written for the newspaper's travel section. All I received in return was a friendly reply, thanking me for sending her the article, but with no other comment.

At least, I'd confirmed that her address in Dubai existed.

Antoine Locadour, 74, historian, ICP, France

It's easy to label Sarah as just one of the many Black Virgins in the world. According to tradition, Sarah-la-Kali was of noble lineage and knew the secrets of the world. She is, I believe, one more manifestation of what people call the Great Mother, the Goddess of Creation.

And it doesn't surprise me in the least that more and more people are becoming interested in pagan traditions. Why? Because God the Father is associated with the rigour and discipline of worship, whereas the Mother Goddess shows the importance of love above and beyond all the usual prohibitions and taboos.

The phenomenon is hardly a new one. Whenever a religion tightens its rules, a significant number of people break away and go in search of more freedom in their search for spiritual contact. This happened during the Middle Ages when the Catholic Church did little more than impose taxes and build splendid monasteries and convents; the phenomenon known as 'witchcraft' was a reaction to this, and even though it was suppressed because of its revolutionary nature, it left behind it roots and traditions that have managed to survive over the centuries.

According to pagan tradition, nature worship is more important than reverence for sacred books. The Goddess is in everything and everything is part of the Goddess. The world is merely an expression of her goodness. There are many philosophical systems – such as Taoism and Buddhism – which make no distinction between creator and creature. People no longer try to decipher the mystery of life, but choose instead to be part of it. There is no female figure in Taoism or Buddhism, but there, too, the central idea is that 'everything is one'.

In the worship of the Great Mother, what we call 'sin', usually a transgression of certain arbitrary moral codes, ceases to exist. Sex and customs in general are freer because they are part of nature and cannot be considered to be the fruits of evil.

The new paganism shows that man is capable of living without an institutionalised religion, while still continuing the spiritual search in order to justify his existence. If God is Mother, then we need only gather together with other people and adore Her through rituals intended to satisfy the female soul, rituals involving dance, fire, water, air, earth, songs, music, flowers and beauty.

This has been a growing trend over the last few years. We may be witnessing a very important moment in the history of the world, when the Spirit finally merges with the Material, and the two are united and transformed. At the same time, I imagine that there will be a very violent reaction from organised religious institutions, which are beginning to lose their followers. There will be a rise in fundamentalism.

As a historian, I'm content to collate all the data and analyse this confrontation between the freedom to worship and the duty to obey, between the God who controls the world and the Goddess who is part of the world, between people who join together in groups where celebration is a spontaneous affair and those who close ranks and learn only what they should and should not do.

I'd like to be optimistic and believe that human beings have at last found their path to the spiritual world, but the signs are not very positive. As so often in the past, a new conservative backlash could once more stifle the cult of the Mother.

Andrea McCain, actress

It's very difficult to be impartial and to tell a story that began in admiration and ended in rancour, but I'm going to try, yes, I'm really going to try and describe the Athena I met for the first time in an apartment in Victoria Street.

She'd just got back from Dubai with plenty of money and a desire to share everything she knew about the mysteries of magic. This time, she'd spent only four months in the Middle East: she sold some land for the construction of two supermarkets, earned a huge commission and decided that she'd earned enough money to support herself and her son for the next three years, and that she could always resume work later on if she wanted. Now was the time to make the most of the present, to live what remained of her youth and to teach others everything she had learned.

She received me somewhat unenthusiastically:

'What do you want?'

'I work in the theatre and we're putting on a play about the female face of God. I heard from a journalist friend that you spent time in the Balkan mountains with some gipsies and would be prepared to tell me about your experiences there.'

'You mean you only came here to learn about the Mother because of a play?'

'Why did you learn about Her?'

Athena stopped, looked me up and down, and smiled:

'You're right. That's my first lesson as a teacher: teach those who want to learn. The reason doesn't matter.'

'I'm sorry?'

'Nothing.'

'The origins of the theatre are sacred,' I went on. 'It began in Greece with hymns to Dionysus, the god of wine, rebirth and fertility. But it's believed that even from very remote times people performed a ritual in which they would pretend to be someone else as a way of communing with the sacred.'

'Second lesson, thank you.'

'I don't understand. I came here to learn, not to teach.'

This woman was beginning to irritate me. Perhaps she was being ironic.

'My protector—'

'Your protector?'

'I'll explain another time. My protector said that I would only learn what I need to learn if I were provoked into it. And since my return from Dubai, you're the first person to demonstrate that to me. What she said makes sense.'

I explained that, in researching the play, I'd gone from one teacher to the next, but had never found their teachings to be in any way exceptional; despite this, however, I grew more and more interested in the matter as I went on. I also mentioned that these people had seemed confused and uncertain about what they wanted.

'For example?'

Sex, for example. In some of the places I went to, sex was a complete no-no. In others, they not only advocated complete freedom, but even encouraged orgies. She asked for more details, and I couldn't tell if she was doing this in order to test me or because she had no idea what other people got up to.

Athena spoke before I could answer her question.

'When you dance, do you feel desire? Do you feel as if you were summoning up a greater energy? When you dance, are there moments when you cease to be yourself?'

I didn't know what to say. In nightclubs or at parties in friends' houses, sensuality was definitely part of how I felt when I danced. I would start by flirting and enjoying the desire in men's eyes, but as the night wore on, I seemed to get more in touch with myself, and it was no longer important to me whether I was or wasn't seducing someone.

Athena continued:

'If theatre is ritual, then dance is too. Moreover, it's a very ancient way of getting close to a partner. It's as if the threads connecting us to the rest of the world were washed clean of preconceptions and fears.

When you dance, you can enjoy the luxury of being you.'

I started listening to her with more respect.

'Afterwards, we go back to being who we were before – frightened people trying to be more important than we actually believe we are.'

That was exactly how I felt. Or is it the same for everyone?

'Do you have a boyfriend?'

I remembered that in one of the places where I'd gone to learn about the Gaia tradition, a 'druid' had asked me to make love in front of him. Ridiculous and frightening – how dare these people use the spiritual search for their own more sinister ends?

'Do you have a boyfriend?' she asked again.

'I do.'

Athena said nothing else. She merely put her finger to her lips, indicating that I should remain silent.

And suddenly I realised that it was extremely difficult for me to remain silent in the presence of someone I'd only just met. The norm is to talk about something, anything – the weather, the traffic, the best restaurants to go to. We were sitting on the sofa in her completely white sitting room, with a CD-player and a small shelf of CDs. There were no books anywhere, and no paintings on the wall. Given that she'd travelled to the Middle East, I'd expected to find objects and souvenirs from that part of the world.

But it was empty, and now there was this silence.

Her grey eyes were fixed on mine, but I held firm and didn't look away. Instinct perhaps. A way of saying that I'm not frightened, but facing the challenge head-on. Except that everything – the silence and the white room, the noise of the traffic outside in the street – began to seem unreal. How long were we going to stay there, saying nothing?

I started to track my own thoughts. Had I come there in search of material for my play or did I really want knowledge, wisdom, power? I couldn't put my finger on what it was that had led me to come and see … what? A witch?

My adolescent dreams surfaced. Who wouldn't like to meet a real witch, learn how to perform magic, and gain the respect and fear of her friends? Who, as a young woman, hasn't been outraged by the centuries of repression suffered by women and felt that becoming a witch would be the best way of recovering her lost identity? I'd been through that phase myself; I was independent and did what I liked in the highly competitive world of the theatre, but then why was I never content? Why was I always testing out my curiosity?

We must have been about the same age … or was I older? Did she, too, have a boyfriend?

Athena moved closer. We were now less than an arm's length from each other and I started to feel afraid. Was she a lesbian?

I didn't look away, but I made a mental note of where the door was so that I could leave whenever I wished. No one had made me go to that house to meet someone I'd never seen before in my life and sit there wasting time, not saying anything and not learning anything either. What did she want?

That silence perhaps. My muscles began to grow tense. I was alone and helpless. I desperately needed to talk or to make my mind stop telling me that I was under threat. How could she possibly know who I was? We are what we say!

Had she asked me anything about my life? She'd wanted to know if I had a boyfriend. I tried to say more about the theatre, but couldn't. And what about the stories I'd heard about her gipsy ancestry, her stay in Transylvania, the land of vampires?

My thoughts wouldn't stop: how much would that consultation cost? I was terrified. I should have asked before. A fortune? And if I didn't pay, would she put a spell on me that would eventually destroy me?

I felt an impulse to get to my feet, thank her and say that I hadn't come there just to sit in silence. If you go to a psychiatrist, you have to talk. If you go to a church, you listen to a sermon. If you go in search of magic, you find a teacher who wants to explain the world to you and who gives you a series of rituals to follow. But silence? Why did it make me feel so uncomfortable?

One question after another kept forming in my mind, and I couldn't stop thinking or trying to find a reason for the two of us to be sitting there, saying nothing. Suddenly, perhaps after five or ten long minutes of total immobility, she smiled.

I smiled too and relaxed.

'Try to be different. That's all.'

'That's all? Is sitting in silence being different? I imagine that, at this very moment, there are thousands of people in London who are desperate for someone to talk to, and all you can say to me is that silence makes a difference?'

'Now that you're talking and reorganising the universe, you'll end up convincing yourself that you're right and I'm wrong. But as you experienced for yourself – being silent *is* different.'

'It's unpleasant. It doesn't teach you anything.'

She seemed indifferent to my reaction.

'What theatre are you working at?'

Finally, she was taking an interest in my life! I was being restored to my human condition, with a profession and everything! I invited her to come and see the play we were putting on – it was the only way I could find to avenge myself, by showing that I was capable of things that Athena was not. That silence had left a humiliating aftertaste.

She asked if she could bring her son, and I said, no, it was for adults only.

'Well, I could always leave him with my mother. I haven't been to the theatre in ages.'

She didn't charge for the consultation. When I met

up with the other members of the cast, I told them about my encounter with this mysterious creature. They were all mad keen to meet someone who, when she first met you, asked only that you sat in silence.

Athena arrived on the appointed day. She saw the play, came to my dressing-room afterwards to say hello, but didn't say whether she'd enjoyed herself or not. My colleagues suggested that I invite her to the bar where we usually went after the performance. There, instead of keeping quiet, she started answering a question that had been left unanswered at our first meeting.

'No one, not even the Mother, would ever want sex to take place purely as a celebration. Love must always be present. Didn't you say that you'd met people like that? Well, be careful.'

My friends had no idea what she was talking about, but they warmed to the subject and started bombarding her with questions. Something troubled me. Her answers were very academic, as if she didn't have much experience of what she was talking about. She spoke about the game of seduction, about fertility rites, and concluded with a Greek myth, probably because I'd mentioned during our first meeting that the theatre had begun in Greece. She must have spent the whole week reading up on the subject.

'After millennia of male domination, we are returning to the cult of the Great Mother. The Greeks called her Gaia, and according to the myth she was born out of Chaos, the void that existed before the universe. With her came Eros, the god of love, and then she gave birth to the Sea and the Sky.'

'Who was the father?' asked one of my friends.

'No one. There's a technical term, parthenogenesis, which is a process of reproduction that does not require fertilisation of the egg by a male. There's a mystical term too, one to which we're more accustomed: Immaculate Conception.

'From Gaia sprang all the gods who would later people the Elysian Fields of Greece, including our own dear Dionysus, your idol. But as man became established as the principal political power in the cities, Gaia was forgotten, and was replaced by Zeus, Ares, Apollo and company, all of whom were competent enough, but didn't have the same allure as the Mother who originated everything.'

Then she questioned us about our work. The director asked if she'd like to give us some lessons.

'On what?'

'On what you know.'

'To be perfectly honest, I learned all about the origins of theatre this week. I learn everything as I need to learn it, that's what Edda told me to do.'

So I was right!

'But I can share other things that life has taught me.'

They all agreed. And no one asked who Edda was.

Deidre O'Neill, known as Edda

I said to Athena: 'You don't have to keep coming here all the time just to ask silly questions. If a group has decided to take you on as a teacher, why not use that opportunity to turn yourself into a teacher?

'Do what I always did.

'Try to feel good about yourself even when you feel like the least worthy of creatures. Reject all those negative thoughts and let the Mother take possession of your body and soul; surrender yourself to dance or to silence or to ordinary, everyday activities – like taking your son to school, preparing supper, making sure the house is tidy. Everything is worship if your mind is focused on the present moment.

'Don't try to convince anyone of anything. When you don't know something, ask or go away and find out. But when you do act, be like the silent, flowing river and open yourself to a greater energy. Believe – that's what I said at our first meeting – simply believe that you can.

'At first, you'll be confused and insecure. Then you'll start to believe that everyone thinks they're being conned. It's not true. You have the knowledge, it's simply a matter of being aware. All the minds on the planet are so easily cast down – they fear illness, invasion, attack, death. Try to restore their lost joy to them.

'Be clear.

'Re-programme yourself every minute of each day with thoughts that make you grow. When you're feeling irritated or confused, try to laugh at yourself. Laugh out loud at this woman tormented by doubts and anxieties, convinced that her problems are the most important thing in the world. Laugh at the sheer absurdity of the situation, at the fact that despite being a manifestation of the Mother, you still believe God is a man who lays down the rules. Most of our problems stem from just that – from following rules.

'Concentrate.

'If you can find nothing on which to focus your mind, concentrate on your breathing. The Mother's river of light is flowing in through your nose. Listen to your heart beating, follow the thoughts you can't control, control your desire to get up at once and to do something "useful". Sit for a few minutes each day, doing nothing, getting as much as you can out of that time.

'When you're washing up, pray. Be thankful that there are plates to be washed; that means there was food, that you fed someone, that you've lavished care on one or more people, that you cooked and laid the table. Imagine the millions of people at this moment who have absolutely nothing to wash up and no one for whom to lay the table.

'There are women who say: "I'm not going to do the washing up, let the men do it." Fine, let the men do it if they want to, but that has nothing to do with equality. There's nothing wrong with doing simple things, although if I were to publish an article tomorrow saying everything I think, I'd be accused of working against the feminist cause. Nonsense! As if washing up or wearing a bra or having someone open or close a door could be humiliating to me as a woman. The fact is, I love it when a man opens the door for me. According to etiquette this means: "She needs me to do this because she's fragile," but in my soul is written: "I'm being treated like a goddess. I'm a queen." I'm not here to work for the feminist cause, because both men and women are a manifestation of the Mother, the Divine Unity. No one can be greater than that.

'I'd love to see you giving classes on what you're learning. That's the main aim of life – revelation! You make yourself into a channel; you listen to yourself and are surprised at how capable you are. Remember your job at the bank? Perhaps you never properly understood that what happened there was a result of the energy flowing out of your body, your eyes, your hands.

'You'll say it was the dance.

'The dance was simply a ritual. What is a ritual? It means transforming something monotonous into something different, rhythmic, capable of channelling the Unity. That's why I say again: be different even when you're washing up. Move your hands so that they never repeat the same gesture twice, even though they maintain the rhythm.

'If you find it helpful, try to visualise images – flowers, birds, trees in a forest. Don't imagine single objects, like the candle you focused on when you came here for the first time. Try to think of something collective. And do you know what you'll find? That you didn't choose your thought.

'I'll give you an example: imagine a flock of birds flying. How many birds did you see? Eleven, nineteen, five? You have a vague idea, but you don't know the exact number. So where did that thought come from? Someone put it there. Someone who knows the exact number of birds, trees, stones, flowers. Someone who, in that fraction of a second, took charge of you and showed you Her power.

'You are what you believe yourself to be.

'Don't be like those people who believe in "positive thinking" and tell themselves that they're loved and strong and capable. You don't need to do that, because you know it already. And when you doubt it – which happens, I think, quite often at this stage of evolution – do as I suggested. Instead of trying to prove that you're better than you think, just laugh. Laugh at your worries and insecurities. View your anxieties with humour. It will be difficult at first, but you'll gradually get used to it.

'Now go back and meet all those people who think you know everything. Convince yourself that they're right, because we all know everything: it's merely a question of believing.

'Believe.

'As I said to you in Bucharest, the very first time we met, groups are very important because they force us to progress. If you're alone, all you can do is laugh at yourself, but if you're with others, you'll laugh and then immediately act. Groups challenge us. Groups allow us to choose our affinities. Groups create a collective energy, and ecstasy comes more easily because everyone infects everyone else.

'Groups can also destroy us of course, but that's part of life and the human condition – living with other people. And anyone who's failed to develop an instinct for survival has understood nothing of what the Mother is saying.

'You're lucky. A group has just asked you to teach them something, and that will make you a teacher.'

Heron Ryan, journalist

Before the first meeting with the actors, Athena came to my house. Ever since I published the article on St Sarah, she'd been convinced that I understood her world, which wasn't true at all. I simply wanted to attract her attention. I was trying to come round to the idea that there might be an invisible reality capable of interfering in our lives, but the only reason I did so was because of a love I didn't want to believe I felt, but which was continuing to grow in a subtle, devastating way.

I was content with my universe and didn't want to change it at all, even though I was being propelled in that direction.

'I'm afraid,' she said as soon as she arrived. 'But I must go ahead and do what they're asking of me. I need to believe.'

'You've had a lot of experiences in life. You learned from the gipsies, from the dervishes in the desert, from –'

'Well, that's not quite true. Besides, what does learning mean: accumulating knowledge or transforming your life?'

I suggested we go out that night for supper and to dance a little. She agreed to supper, but rejected the dancing.

'Answer me,' she said, looking round my apartment. 'Is learning just putting things on a shelf or is it discarding whatever is no longer useful and then continuing on your way feeling lighter?'

On the shelves were all the books I'd invested so much money and time in buying, reading and annotating. There were my personality, my education, my true teachers.

'How many books have you got? Over a thousand, I'd say. But most of them you'll probably never open again. You hang on to them because you don't believe.'

'I don't believe?'

'No, you don't believe, full stop. Anyone who believes will go and read up about theatre as I did when Andrea asked me about it, but, after that, it's a question of letting the Mother speak through you and making discoveries as she speaks. And as you make those discoveries, you'll manage to fill in the blank spaces that all those writers left there on purpose to provoke the reader's imagination. And when you fill in the spaces, you'll start to believe in your own abilities.

'How many people would love to read those books, but don't have the money to buy them? Meanwhile, you sit here surrounded by all this stagnant energy, purely to impress the friends who visit you. Or is it that you don't feel you've learned anything from them and need to consult them again?'

I thought she was being rather hard on me, and that intrigued me.

'So you don't think I need this library?'

'I think you need to read, but why hang on to all these books? Would it be asking too much if we were to leave here right now, and before going to the restaurant, distribute most of them to whoever we happened to pass in the street?'

'They wouldn't all fit in my car.'

'We could hire a truck.'

'But then we wouldn't get to the restaurant in time for supper. Besides, you came here because you were feeling insecure, not in order to tell me what I should do with my books. Without them I'd feel naked.'

'Ignorant, you mean.'

'Uncultivated would be the right word.'

'So your culture isn't in your heart, it's on your bookshelves.'

Enough was enough. I picked up the phone to reserve a table and told the restaurant that we'd be there in fifteen minutes. Athena was trying to avoid the problem that had brought her here. Her deep insecurity was making her go on the attack, rather than looking at herself. She needed a man by her side and, who knows, was perhaps sounding me out to see how far I'd go, using her feminine wiles to discover just what I'd be prepared to do for her.

Simply being in her presence seemed to justify my very existence. Was that what she wanted to hear?

Fine, I'd tell her over supper. I'd be capable of doing almost anything, even leaving the woman I was living with, but I drew the line, of course, at giving away my books.

In the taxi, we returned to the subject of the theatre group, although I was, at that moment, prepared to discuss something I never normally spoke about – love, a subject I found far more complicated than Marx, Jung, the British Labour Party or the day-to-day problems at a newspaper office.

'You don't need to worry,' I said, feeling a desire to hold her hand. 'It'll be all right. Talk about calligraphy. Talk about dancing. Talk about the things you know.'

'If I did that, I'd never discover what it is I don't know. When I'm there, I'll have to allow my mind to go still and let my heart begin to speak. But it's the first time I've done that, and I'm frightened.'

'Would you like me to come with you?'

She accepted at once. We arrived at the restaurant, ordered some wine and started to drink. I was drinking in order to get up the courage to say what I thought I was feeling, although it seemed absurd to me to be declaring my love to someone I hardly knew. And she was drinking because she was afraid of talking about what she didn't know.

After the second glass of wine, I realised how on edge she was. I tried to hold her hand, but she gently pulled away.

'I can't be afraid.'

'Of course you can, Athena. I often feel afraid, and yet, when I need to, I go ahead and face up to whatever it is I'm afraid of.'

I was on edge too. I refilled our glasses. The waiter kept coming over to ask what we'd like to eat, and I kept telling him that we'd order later.

I was talking about whatever came into my head. Athena was listening politely, but she seemed far away, in some dark universe full of ghosts. At one point, she told me again about the woman in Scotland and what she'd said. I asked if it made sense to teach what you didn't know.

'Did anyone ever teach you how to love?' she replied.

Could she be reading my thoughts?

'And yet,' she went on, 'you're as capable of love as any other human being. How did you learn? You didn't, you simply believe. You believe, therefore you love.'

'Athena …'

I hesitated, then managed to finish my sentence, although not at all as I had intended.

'… perhaps we should order some food.'

I realised that I wasn't yet prepared to mention the things that were troubling my world. I called the waiter over and ordered some starters, then some more starters, a main dish, a pudding and another bottle of wine. The more time I had, the better.

'You're acting strangely. Was it my comment about your books? You do what you like. It's not my job to change your world. I was obviously sticking my nose in where it wasn't wanted.'

I had been thinking about that business of 'changing the world' only a few seconds before.

'Athena, you're always telling me about ... no, I need to talk about something that happened in that bar in Sibiu, with the gipsy music.'

'In the restaurant, you mean?'

'Yes, in the restaurant. Today we were discussing books, the things that we accumulate and that take up space. Perhaps you're right. There's something I've been wanting to do ever since I saw you dancing that night. It weighs more and more heavily on my heart.'

'I don't know what you mean.'

'Of course you do. I'm talking about the love I'm discovering now and doing my best to destroy before it reveals itself. I'd like you to accept it. It's the little I have of myself, but it's not my own. It's not exclusively yours, because there's someone else in my life, but I would be happy if you could accept it anyway. An Arab poet from your country, Khalil Gibran, says: "*It is well to give when asked, but it is better to give unasked.*" If I don't say everything I need to say tonight, I'll merely be a spectator watching events unfold rather than the person actually experiencing them.'

I took a deep breath. The wine had helped me to free myself.

She drained her glass, and I did the same. The waiter appeared with the food, making a few comments about the various dishes, explaining the ingredients and the way in which they had been cooked. Athena and I kept our eyes fixed on each other. Andrea had told me that this is what Athena had done when they met for the first time, and she was convinced it was simply a way of intimidating others.

The silence was terrifying. I imagined her getting up from the table and citing her famous, invisible boyfriend from Scotland Yard, or saying that she was very flattered, but she had to think about the class she was to give the next day.

'*And is there anything you would withhold? Some day, all that you have shall be given. The trees give that they may live, for to withhold is to perish.*'

She was speaking quietly and carefully because of the wine she'd drunk, but her voice nevertheless silenced everything around us.

'*And what greater merit shall there be than that which lies in the courage and the confidence, nay the charity, of receiving? You give but little when you give of your possessions. It is when you give of yourself that you truly give.*'

She said all this without smiling. I felt as if I were conversing with a sphinx.

'Words written by the same poet you were quoting. I learned them at school, but I don't need the book where he wrote those words. I've kept his words in my heart.'

She drank a little more wine. I did the same. I couldn't bring myself to ask if she accepted my love or not, but I felt lighter.

'You may be right. I'll donate my books to a public library and only keep those I really will re-read one day.'

'Is that what you want to talk about now?'

'No. I just don't know how to continue the conversation.'

'Shall we eat then and enjoy the food. Does that seem a good idea?'

No, it didn't seem like a good idea. I wanted to hear something different, but I was afraid to ask, and so I babbled on about libraries, books and poets, regretting having ordered so many dishes. I was the one who wanted to escape now, because I didn't know how to continue.

In the end, she made me promise that I would be at the theatre for her first class, and, for me, that was a signal. She needed me; she had accepted what I had unconsciously dreamed of offering her ever since I saw her dancing in a restaurant in Transylvania, but which I had only been capable of understanding that night.

Or, as Athena would have said, of believing.

Andrea McCain, actress

Of course I'm to blame. If it hadn't been for me, Athena would never have come to the theatre that morning, gathered us all together, asked us to lie down on the stage and begin a relaxation exercise involving breathing and bringing our awareness to each part of the body.

'Relax your thighs …'

We all obeyed, as if we were before a goddess, someone who knew more than all of us, even though we'd done this kind of exercise hundreds of times before. We were all curious to know what would come after '… now relax your face and breathe deeply.'

Did she really think she was teaching us anything new? We were expecting a lecture, a talk! But I must control myself. Let's get back to what happened then. We relaxed and then came a silence which left us completely disoriented. When I discussed it with my colleagues afterwards, we all agreed that we felt the exercise was over, that it was time to sit up and look around, except that no one did. We remained lying down, in a kind of enforced meditation, for fifteen interminable minutes.

Then she spoke again.

'You've had plenty of time to doubt me now. One or two of you looked impatient. But now I'm going to ask you just one thing: when I count to three, be different. I don't mean be another person, an animal or a house. Try to forget everything you've learned on drama courses. I'm not asking you to be actors and to demonstrate your abilities. I'm asking you to cease being human and to transform yourselves into something you don't know.'

We were all still lying on the floor with our eyes closed and so couldn't see how anyone else was reacting. Athena was playing on that uncertainty.

'I'm going to say a few words and you'll immediately associate certain images with those words. Remember that you're all full of the poison of preconceived ideas and that if I were to say "fate", you would probably start imagining your lives in the future. If I were to say "red", you would probably make some psychoanalytic interpretation. That isn't what I want. As I said, I want you to be different.'

She couldn't explain what she really wanted. When no one complained, I felt sure they were simply being polite, but that when the 'lecture' was over they would never invite Athena back. They would even tell me that I'd been naïve to have sought her out in the first place.

'The first word is "sacred".'

So as not to die of boredom, I decided to join in the game. I imagined my mother, my boyfriend, my future children, a brilliant career.

'Make a gesture that means "sacred".'

I folded my arms over my chest, as if I were embracing all my loved ones. I found out later that most people opened their arms to form a cross, and that one of the women opened her legs, as if she were making love.

'Relax again, and again forget about everything and keep your eyes closed. I'm not criticising, but from what I saw, you seem to be giving form to what you consider to be sacred. That isn't what I want. When I give you the next word, don't try to define it as it manifests itself in the world. Open all the channels and allow the poison of reality to drain away. Be abstract and then you will enter the world I'm guiding you towards.'

That last phrase had real authority, and I felt the energy in the theatre change. Now the voice knew where it wanted to take us. She was a teacher now, not a lecturer.

'Earth,' she said.

Suddenly I understood what she meant. It was no longer my imagination that mattered, but my body in contact with the soil. I was the Earth.

'Make a gesture that represents Earth.'

I didn't move. I was the soil of that stage.

'Perfect,' she said. 'None of you moved. For the first time you all experienced the same feeling. Instead of describing something, you transformed yourself into an idea.'

She fell silent again for what I imagined were five long minutes. The silence made us feel lost, unable to tell whether she simply had no idea how to continue, or if she was merely unfamiliar with our usual intense rhythm of working.

'I'm going to say a third word.'

She paused.

'Centre.'

I felt – and this was entirely unconscious – that all my vital energy went to my navel, where it glowed yellow. This frightened me. If someone touched it, I could die.

'Make a gesture for centre!'

Her words sounded like a command. I immediately placed my hands on my belly to protect myself.

'Perfect,' said Athena. 'You can sit up now.'

I opened my eyes and saw the extinguished stage lights up above me, distant and dull. I rubbed my face and got to my feet. I noticed that my colleagues looked surprised.

'Was that the lecture?' asked the director.

'You can call it a lecture if you like.'

'Well, thank you for coming. Now, if you'll excuse us, we have to start rehearsals for the next play.'

'But I haven't finished yet.'

'Perhaps another time.'

Everyone seemed confused by the director's reaction. After some initial doubts, I think we were enjoying the session – it was different, no pretending to be things or people, no visualising apples or candles. No sitting in a circle holding hands as if we were practising some sacred ritual. It was simply something slightly absurd and we wanted to know where it would take us.

Without a flicker of emotion, Athena bent down to pick up her bag. At that moment, we heard a voice from the stalls.

'Marvellous!'

Heron had come to join her. The director was afraid of him because Heron knew the theatre critics on his newspaper and had close ties with the media generally.

'You stopped being individuals and turned into ideas. What a shame you're so busy, but don't worry, Athena, we'll find another group to work with and then I can see how your "lecture" ends. I have contacts.'

I was still thinking about the light travelling through my whole body to my navel. Who was that woman? Had my colleagues experienced the same thing?

'Just a moment,' said the director, aware of the look of surprise on everyone's face. 'I suppose we could postpone rehearsals today …'

'No, you mustn't do that. Besides, I have to get back to the newspaper and write something about this woman. You carry on doing what you always do. I've just found an excellent story.'

If Athena felt lost in that debate between the two men, she didn't show it. She climbed down from the stage and went off with Heron. We turned to the director and asked him why he'd reacted like that.

'With all due respect, Andrea, I thought the conversation in the bar about sex was far more interesting than the nonsense we've just been engaging in. Did you notice how she kept falling silent? She didn't know what to do next!'

'But I felt something strange,' said one of the older actors. 'When she said "centre", it was as if all my vital energy were suddenly focused in my navel. I've never experienced that before.'

'Did you? Are you sure?' asked an actress, and judging by her words, she'd experienced the same thing.

'She's a bit of a witch, that woman,' said the director, interrupting the conversation. 'Let's get back to work.'

We started doing our usual stretching exercises, warm-ups and meditation, all strictly by the book. Then after a few improvisations, we went straight into a read-through of the new script. Gradually, Athena's presence seemed to be dissolving, and everything was returning to what it was – a theatre, a ritual created by the Greeks thousands of years ago, where we were used to pretending to be different people.

But that was pure play-acting. Athena wasn't like that, and I was determined to see her again, especially after what the director had said about her.

Heron Ryan, journalist

Unbeknown to Athena, I'd followed exactly the same steps as the actors, obeying everything she told us to do, except that I kept my eyes open so that I could follow what was happening on stage. The moment she said 'Make a gesture for centre', I'd placed my hand on my navel, and, to my surprise, I saw that everyone, including the director, had done the same. What was going on?

That afternoon, I had to write a dreary article about a visiting head of state – a real drag. In order to amuse myself between phone calls, I decided to ask colleagues in the office what gesture they would make if I said the word 'centre'. Most of them made jokey comments about political parties. One pointed to the centre of the Earth. Another put his hand on his heart. But no one, absolutely no one, thought of their navel as the centre of anything. In the end, though, I managed to speak to someone who had some interesting information on the subject.

When I got home, Andrea had had a bath, laid the table and was waiting for me to start supper. She opened a bottle of very expensive wine, filled two glasses and offered me one.

'So how was supper last night?'

How long can a man live with a lie? I didn't want to lose the woman standing there before me, who had stuck with me through thick and thin, who was always by my side when I felt my life had lost meaning and direction. I loved her, but in the crazy world into which I was blindly plunging, my heart was far away, trying to adapt to something it possibly knew, but couldn't accept: being large enough for two people.

Since I would never risk letting go of a certainty in favour of a mere possibility, I tried to minimise the significance of what had happened at the restaurant, mainly because nothing *had* happened, apart from an exchange of lines by a poet who had suffered greatly for love.

'Athena's a difficult person to get to know.'

Andrea laughed.

'That's precisely why men must find her so fascinating. She awakens that rapidly disappearing protective instinct of yours.'

Best to change the subject. I've always been convinced that women have a supernatural ability to know what's going on in a man's soul. They're all witches.

'I've been looking into what happened at the theatre today. You don't know this, but I had my eyes open throughout the exercises.'

'You've always got your eyes open. I assume it's part of being a journalist. And you're going to talk about the moment when we all did exactly the same thing. We talked a lot about that in the bar after rehearsals.'

'A historian told me about a Greek temple where they used to predict the future (*Editor's note: the temple of Apollo at Delphi*) and which housed a marble stone called "the navel". Stories from the time describe Delphi as the centre of the planet. I went to the newspaper archives to make a few enquiries: in Petra, in Jordan, there's another "conic navel", symbolising not just the centre of the planet, but of the entire universe. Both "navels" try to show the axis through which the energy of the world travels, marking in a visible way something that is only there on the "invisible" map. Jerusalem is also called the navel of the world, as is an island in the Pacific Ocean, and another place I've forgotten now, because I had never associated the two things.'

'Like dance!'

'What?'

'Nothing.'

'No, I know what you mean – belly dancing, the oldest form of dance recorded, in which everything revolves about the belly. I was trying to avoid the subject because I told you that in Transylvania I saw Athena dance. She was dressed, of course, but ...'

'... all the movement began with her navel, and gradually spread to the rest of the body.'

She was right.

Best to change the subject again and talk about the theatre, about boring journalistic stuff, then drink a little wine and end up in bed making love while, outside, the rain was starting to fall. I noticed that, at the moment of orgasm, Andrea's body was all focused on her belly. I'd seen this many times before, but never thought anything of it.

Antoine Locadour, historian

Heron started spending a fortune on phone calls to France, asking me to get all the information I could by the weekend, and he kept going on about the navel, which seemed to me the least interesting and least romantic thing in the world. But, then, the English don't see things in the same way as the French, and so, instead of asking questions, I tried to find out what science had to say on the subject.

I soon realised that historical knowledge wasn't enough. I could locate a monument here, a dolmen there, but the odd thing was that the ancient cultures all seemed to agree on the subject and even use the same word to define the places they considered sacred. I'd never noticed this before and I started to get interested. When I saw the number of coincidences, I went in search of something that would complement them – human behaviour and beliefs.

I immediately had to reject the first and most logical explanation, that we're nourished through the umbilical cord, which is why the navel is, for us, the centre of life. A psychologist immediately pointed out that the theory made no sense at all: man's central idea is always to 'cut' the umbilical cord and, from then on, the brain or the heart become the more important symbols.

When we're interested in something, everything around us appears to refer to it (the mystics call these phenomena 'signs', the sceptics 'coincidence', and psychologists 'concentrated focus', although I've yet to find out what term historians should use). One night, my adolescent daughter came home with a navel piercing.

'Why did you do that?'

'Because I felt like it.'

A perfectly natural and honest explanation, even for a historian who needs to find a reason for everything. When I went into her room, I saw a poster of her favourite female pop star. She had a bare midriff and, in that photo on the wall, her navel did look like the centre of the world.

I phoned Heron and asked why he was so interested. For the first time, he told me about what had happened at the theatre and how the people there had all responded to a command in the same spontaneous, unexpected manner. It was impossible to get any more information out of my daughter, and so I decided to consult some specialists.

No one seemed very interested, until I found François Shepka, an Indian psychologist (*Editor's note: the scientist requested that his name and nationality be changed*), who was starting to revolutionise the therapies currently in use. According to him, the idea that traumas could be resolved by a return to childhood had never got anyone anywhere. Many problems that had been overcome in adult life resurfaced, and grown-ups started blaming their parents for failures and defeats. Shepka was at war with the various French psychoanalytic associations, and a conversation about absurd subjects, like the navel, seemed to relax him.

He warmed to the theme, but didn't, at first, tackle it directly. He said that according to one of the most respected psychoanalysts in history, the Swiss analyst Carl Gustav Jung, we all drank from the same spring. It's called the 'soul of the world'. However much we try to be independent individuals, a part of our memory is the same. We all seek the ideal of beauty, dance, divinity and music.

Society, meanwhile, tries to define how these ideals should be manifested in reality. Currently, for example, the ideal of beauty is to be thin, and yet thousands of years ago all the images of goddesses were fat. It's the same with happiness: there are a series of rules, and if you fail to follow them, your conscious mind will refuse to accept the idea that you're happy.

Jung used to divide individual progress into four stages: the first was the Persona – the mask we use every day, pretending to be who we are. We believe that the world depends on us, that we're wonderful parents and that our children don't understand us, that our bosses are unfair, that the dream of every human being is never to work and to travel constantly. Many people realise that there's something wrong with this story, but because they don't want to change anything, they quickly drive the thought from their head. A few do try to understand what is wrong and end up finding the Shadow.

The Shadow is our dark side, which dictates how we should act and behave. When we try to free ourselves from the Persona, we turn on a light inside us and we see the cobwebs, the cowardice, the meanness. The Shadow is there to stop our progress, and it usually succeeds, and we run back to what we were before we doubted. However, some do survive this encounter with their own cobwebs, saying: 'Yes, I have a few faults, but I'm good enough, and I want to go forward.'

At this moment, the Shadow disappears and we come into contact with the Soul.

By Soul, Jung didn't mean 'soul' in the religious sense; he speaks of a return to the Soul of the World, the source of all knowledge. Instincts become sharper, emotions more radical, the interpretation of signs becomes more important than logic, perceptions of reality grow less rigid. We start to struggle with things to which we are unaccustomed and we start to react in ways that we ourselves find unexpected.

And we discover that if we can channel that continuous flow of energy, we can organise it around a very solid centre, what Jung calls the Wise Old Man for men and the Great Mother for women.

Allowing this to manifest itself is dangerous. Generally speaking, anyone who reaches this stage has a tendency to consider themselves a saint, a tamer of spirits, a prophet. A great deal of maturity is required if someone is to come into contact with the energy of the Wise Old Man or the Great Mother.

'Jung went mad,' said my friend, when he had explained the four stages described by the Swiss psychoanalyst. 'When he got in touch with his Wise Old Man, he started saying that he was guided by a spirit called Philemon.'

'And finally …'

'… we come to the symbol of the navel. Not only people, but societies, too, fit these four stages. Western civilisation has a Persona, the ideas that guide us. In its attempt to adapt to changes, it comes into contact with the Shadow, and we see mass demonstrations, in which the collective energy can be manipulated for both good and ill. Suddenly, for some reason, the Persona or the Shadow are no longer enough for human beings, and then comes the moment to make the leap, the unconscious connection with the Soul. New values begin to emerge.'

'I've noticed that. I've noticed a resurgence in the cult of the female face of God.'

'An excellent example. And at the end of this process, if those new values are to become established, the entire race comes into contact with the symbols, the coded language by which present-day generations communicate with their ancestral knowledge. One of those symbols of rebirth is the navel. In the navel of Vishnu, the Indian divinity responsible for creation and destruction, sits the god who will rule each cycle. Yogis consider the navel one of the chakras, one of the sacred points on the human body. Primitive tribes often used to build monuments in the place they believed to be the navel of the world. In South America, people who go into trances say that the true form of the human being is a luminous egg, which connects with other people through filaments that emerge from the navel. The mandala, a design said to stimulate meditation, is a symbolic representation of this.'

I passed all this information on to Heron in England before the agreed date. I told him that the woman who had succeeded in provoking the same absurd reaction in a group of people must have enormous power, and that I wouldn't be surprised if she wasn't some kind of paranormal. I suggested that he study her more closely.

I had never thought about the subject before, and I tried to forget it at once. However, my daughter said that I was behaving oddly, thinking only of myself, that I was, in short, navel-gazing!

Deidre O'Neill, known as Edda

'It was a complete disaster. How could you have put the idea in my head that I could teach? Why humiliate me in front of other people? I should just forget you even exist. When I was taught to dance, I danced. When I was taught calligraphy, I practised calligraphy. But demanding that I go so far beyond my limits was pure wickedness. That's why I caught the train up to Scotland, that's why I came here, so that you could see how much I hate you!'

She couldn't stop crying. Fortunately, she'd left the child with her parents, because she was talking rather too loudly and there was a faint whiff of wine on her breath. I asked her to come in. Making all that noise at my front door would do nothing to help my already somewhat tarnished reputation, with people putting it around that I received visits from both men and women and organised sex orgies in the name of Satan.

But she still stood there, shouting:

'It's all your fault! You humiliated me!'

One window opened, and then another. Well, anyone working to change the axis of the world must be prepared for the fact that her neighbours won't always be happy. I went over to Athena and did exactly what she wanted me to do: I put my arms around her.

She continued weeping, her head resting on my shoulder. Very gently I helped her up the steps and into the house. I made some tea, the recipe for which I share with no one because it was taught to me by my protector. I placed it in front of her and she drank it down in one. By doing so, she demonstrated that her trust in me was still intact.

'Why am I like this?' she asked.

I knew then that the effects of the alcohol had been neutralised.

'There are men who love me. I have a son who adores me and sees me as his model in life. I have adoptive parents whom I consider to be my real family and who would lay down their lives for me. I filled in all the blank spaces in my past when I went in search of my birth mother. I have enough money to spend the next three years doing nothing but enjoy life, and still I'm not content!

'I feel miserable and guilty because God blessed me with tragedies that I've managed to overcome and with miracles to which I've done credit, but I'm never content. I always want more. The last thing I needed was to go to that theatre and add a failure to my list of victories!'

'Do you think you did the wrong thing?'

She looked at me in surprise:

'Why do you ask that?'

I said nothing, but awaited her answer.

'No, I did the right thing. I went there with a journalist friend, and I didn't have a clue what I was going to do, but suddenly things started to emerge as if out of the void. I felt the presence of the Great Mother by my side, guiding me, instructing me, filling my voice with a confidence I didn't really feel.'

'So why are you complaining?'

'Because no one understood!'

'Is that important? Important enough to make you travel up to Scotland and insult me in front of everyone?'

'Of course it's important! If I can do absolutely anything and know I'm doing the right thing, how come I'm not at least loved and admired?'

So that was the problem. I took her hand and led her into the same room where, weeks before, she had sat contemplating a candle. I asked her to sit down and try to calm herself a little, although I was sure the tea was already taking effect. I went to my room, picked up a round mirror and placed it before her.

'You have everything and you've fought for every inch of your territory. Now look at your tears. Look at your face and the bitterness etched on it. Look at the woman in the mirror, but don't laugh this time, try to understand her.'

I allowed her time to follow my instructions. When I saw that she was, as I intended, going into a trance, I went on:

'What is the secret of life? We call it "grace" or "blessing". Everyone struggles to be satisfied with what they have. Apart from me. Apart from you. Apart from a few people who will, alas, have to make a small sacrifice in the name of something greater.

'Our imagination is larger than the world around us; we go beyond our limits. This used to be called "witchcraft", but fortunately things have changed, otherwise we would both already have been burned at the stake. When they stopped burning women, science found an explanation for our behaviour, normally referred to as "female hysteria". We don't get burned any more, but it does cause problems, especially in the workplace. But don't worry; eventually they'll call it "wisdom". Keep looking into the mirror. Who can you see?'

'A woman.'

'And what is there beyond that woman?'

She hesitated. I asked again and she said:

'Another woman, more authentic and more intelligent than me. It's as if she were a soul that didn't belong to me, but which is nonetheless part of me.'

'Exactly. Now I'm going to ask you to imagine one of the most important symbols in alchemy: a snake forming a circle and swallowing its own tail. Can you imagine that?'

She nodded.

'That's what life is like for people like you and me. We're constantly destroying and rebuilding ourselves. Everything in your life has followed the same pattern: from lost to found; from divorce to new love; from working in a bank to selling real estate in the desert. Only one thing remains intact – your son. He is the connecting thread, and you must respect that.'

She started to cry again, but her tears were different this time.

'You came here because you saw a female face in the flames. That face is the face you can see now in the mirror, so try to do honour to it. Don't let yourself be weighed down by what other people think, because in a few years, in a few decades, or in a few centuries, that way of thinking will be changed. Live now what others will only live in the future.

'What do you want? You can't want to be happy, because that's too easy and too boring. You can't want only to love, because that's impossible. What do you want? You want to justify your life, to live it as intensely as possible. That is at once a trap and a source of ecstasy. Try to be alert to that danger, and experience the joy and the adventure of being that woman who is beyond the image reflected in the mirror.'

Her eyes closed, but I knew that my words had penetrated her soul and would stay there.

'If you want to take a risk and continue teaching, do so. If you don't want to, know that you've already gone further than most other people.'

Her body began to relax. I held her in my arms until she fell asleep, her head on my breast.

I tried to whisper a few more things to her, because I'd been through the same stages, and I knew how difficult it was – just as my protector had told me it would be and as I myself had found out through painful experience. However, the fact that it was difficult didn't make the experience any less interesting.

What experience? Living as a human being and as a divinity. Moving from tension into relaxation. From relaxation into trance. From trance into a more intense contact with other people. From that contact back into tension and so on, like the serpent swallowing its own tail.

It was no easy matter, mainly because it requires unconditional love, which does not fear suffering, rejection, loss.

Whoever drinks this water once can never quench her thirst at other springs.

Andrea McCain, actress

'The other day you mentioned Gaia, who created herself and had a child without the help of a man. You said, quite rightly, that the Great Mother was eventually superseded by the male gods. But you forgot about Hera, a descendant of your favourite goddess. Hera is more important because she's more practical. She rules the skies and the Earth, the seasons of the year and storms. According to the same Greeks you cited, the Milky Way that we see in the sky was created out of the milk that spurted forth from her breast. A beautiful breast, it must be said, because all-powerful Zeus changed himself into a bird purely in order to be able to have his way with her without being rejected.'

We were walking through a large department store in Knightsbridge. I'd phoned her, saying that I'd like to talk, and she'd invited me to the winter sales. It would have been far more pleasant to have a cup of tea together or lunch in some quiet restaurant.

'Your son could get lost in this crowd.'

'Don't worry about him. Go on with what you were telling me.'

'Hera discovered the trick and forced Zeus to marry her. Immediately after the ceremony, however, the great king of Olympus returned to his playboy lifestyle, seducing any woman, mortal or immortal, who happened by. Hera, however, remained faithful. Rather than blame her husband, she blamed the women for their loose behaviour.'

'Isn't that what we all do?'

I didn't know what she meant and so I carried on talking as if I hadn't heard what she'd said.

'Then she decided to give him a taste of his own medicine and find a god or a man to take to her bed. Look, couldn't we stop for a while and have a coffee?'

But Athena had just gone into a lingerie shop.

'Do you think this is pretty?' she asked, holding up a provocative flesh-coloured bra and pantie set.

'Yes, very. Will anyone see it if you wear it?'

'Of course, or do you think I'm a saint? But go on with what you were saying about Hera.'

'Zeus was horrified by her behaviour, but Hera was leading an independent life and didn't give two hoots about her marriage. Have you really got a boyfriend?'

'Yes.'

'I've never seen him.'

She went over to the cash desk, paid for the lingerie and put it in her bag.

'Viorel's hungry, and I'm sure he's not the slightest bit interested in Greek myths, so hurry up and finish Hera's story.'

'It has a rather silly ending. Zeus, afraid of losing his beloved, pretended that he was getting married again. When Hera found out, she saw that things had gone too far. Lovers were one thing, but divorce was unthinkable.'

'Nothing new there, then.'

'She decided to go to the ceremony and kick up a fuss, and it was only then that she realised Zeus was marrying a statue.'

'What did Hera do?'

'She roared with laughter. That broke the ice between them, and she became once more the queen of the skies.'

'Great. So if that ever happens to you …'

'What?'

'If your man gets himself another woman, don't forget to laugh.'

'I'm not a goddess. I'd be much more vengeful. Anyway, why is it I've never seen your boyfriend?'

'Because he's always busy.'

'Where did you meet him?'

'At the bank where I used to work. He had an account there. And now, if you don't mind, my son's waiting for me. You're right, if I don't keep my eye on him, he could get lost amongst all these people. By the way, we're having a meeting at my place next week. You're invited, of course.'

'Yes, and I know who organised it.'

Athena kissed me lightly on both cheeks and left. At least she'd got the message.

That afternoon, at the theatre, the director made a point of telling me that he was annoyed because, he said, I'd arranged for a group of actors to go and visit 'that woman'. I explained that it hadn't been my idea. Heron had become obsessed with the subject of navels and had asked me if some of the other actors would be prepared to continue the interrupted 'lecture'.

'That said,' I added, 'it was my choice to ask them.'

Of course it was, but the last thing I wanted was for him to go to Athena's house alone.

The actors had all arrived, but, instead of another read-through of the new play, the director decided to change the programme.

'Today we'll do another exercise in psychodrama.' (*Editor's note: a therapeutic technique, which involves people acting out their personal experiences.*)

There was no need. We all knew how the characters would behave in the situations described by the playwright.

'Can I suggest a subject?'

Everyone turned to look at me. The director seemed surprised.

'What's this, a revolt?'

'No, listen. We create a situation where a man, after great difficulty, manages to get a group of people together to celebrate an important ritual in the community, something, let's say, like the autumn harvest. Meanwhile, a strange woman arrives, and because of her beauty and the various rumours circulating – about her being a goddess in disguise, for example – the group the man has formed in order to keep alive the traditions in his village breaks up, and its members all go off to see the woman instead.'

'But that's got nothing to do with the play we're rehearsing!' said one of the actresses.

The director, however, had understood what I was driving at.

'That's an excellent idea. Let's begin.'

And turning to me, he said:

'Andrea, you can be the new arrival. That way you can get a better understanding of the situation in the village. And I'll be the decent man trying to preserve the old ways. The group will be made up of couples who go to church, get together on Saturdays to do work in the community, and generally help each other.'

We lay down on the floor, did some relaxation, and then began the exercise proper, which was really very simple. The main character (in this case, me) created various situations and the others reacted to them.

When the relaxation was over, I transformed myself into Athena. In my fantasy, she roamed the world like Satan in search of subjects for her realm, but she disguised herself as Gaia, the goddess who knows everything and created everything. For fifteen minutes, the other actors paired up into 'couples', got to know each other and invented a common history involving children, farms, understanding and friendship. When I felt this little universe was ready, I sat at one corner of the stage and began to speak about love.

'Here we are in this little village, and you think I'm a stranger, which is why you're interested in what I have to tell you. You've never travelled and don't know what goes on beyond the mountains, but I can tell you: there's no need to praise the Earth. The Earth will always be generous with this community. The important thing is to praise human beings. You say you'd love to travel, but you misuse the word "love". Love is a relationship between people.

'Your one desire is for the harvest to be a good one and that's why you've decided to love the Earth. More nonsense: love isn't desire or knowledge or admiration. It's a challenge; it's an invisible fire. That's why, if you think I'm a stranger on this Earth, you're wrong. Everything is familiar to me because I come in strength and in fire, and when I leave, no one will be the same. I bring true love, not the love they write about in books or in fairytales.'

The 'husband' of one of the 'couples' began looking at me. His 'wife' became distraught.

During the rest of the exercise, the director – or, rather, the decent man – did all he could to explain the importance of maintaining traditions, praising the Earth and asking the Earth to be as generous this year as it had been last year. I spoke only of love.

'He says the Earth needs rituals, well, I can guarantee that if there's love enough amongst you, you'll have an abundant harvest, because love is the feeling that transforms everything. But what do I see? Friendship. Passion died out a long time ago, because you've all got used to each other. That's why the Earth gives only what it gave last year, neither more nor less. And that's why, in the darkness of your souls, you silently complain that nothing in your lives changes. Why? Because you've always tried to control the force that transforms everything so that your lives can carry on without being faced by any major challenges.'

The decent man explained:

'Our community has survived because we've always respected the laws by which even love itself is guided. Anyone who falls in love without taking into account the common good will be condemned to live in constant fear of hurting his partner, of irritating his new love, of losing everything he built. A stranger with no ties and no history can say what she likes, but she doesn't know how hard it was to get where we are now. She doesn't know the sacrifices we made for our children. She doesn't know that we work tirelessly so that the Earth will be generous with us, so that we will be at peace, and so that we can store away provisions for the future.'

For an hour, I defended the passion that devours everything, while the decent man spoke of the feeling that brings peace and tranquillity. In the end, I was left talking to myself, while the whole community gathered around him.

I'd played my role with great gusto and with a conviction I didn't even know I felt. Despite everything, though, the stranger left the village without having convinced anyone.

And that made me very, very happy.

Heron Ryan, journalist

An old friend of mine always says: 'People learn twenty-five per cent from their teacher, twenty-five per cent from listening to themselves, twenty-five per cent from their friends and twenty-five per cent from time.' At that first meeting at Athena's apartment, where she was trying to conclude the class she had started at the theatre, we all learned from ... well, I'm not quite sure from what.

She was waiting for us, with her son, in her small living room. I noticed that the room was entirely painted in white and was completely empty apart from one item of furniture with a sound system on it, and a pile of CDs. I thought it odd that her son should be there, because he was sure to be bored by the class. I was assuming she would simply pick up from where we had stopped, giving us commands through single words. But she had other plans. She explained that she was going to play some music from Siberia and that we should all just listen.

Nothing more.

'I don't get anywhere meditating,' she said. 'I see people sitting there with their eyes closed, a smile on their lips or else grave-faced and arrogant, concentrating on absolutely nothing, convinced that they're in touch with God or with the Goddess. So instead, let's listen to some music together.'

Again that feeling of unease, as if Athena didn't know exactly what she was doing. But nearly all the actors from the theatre were there, including the director, who, according to Andrea, had come to spy on the enemy camp.

The music stopped.

'This time I want you to dance to a rhythm that has nothing whatever to do with the melody.'

Athena put the music on again, with the volume right up, and started to dance, making no attempt to move gracefully. Only an older man, who took the role of the drunken king in the latest play, did as he was told. No one else moved. They all seemed slightly constrained. One woman looked at her watch – only ten minutes had passed.

Athena stopped and looked round.

'Why are you just standing there?'

'Well,' said one of the actresses timidly, 'it seems a bit ridiculous to be doing that. We've been trained in harmony, not its opposite.'

'Just do as I say. Do you need an explanation? Right, I'll give you one. Changes only happen when we go totally against everything we're used to doing.'

Turning to the 'drunken king', she said:

'Why did you agree to dance against the rhythm of the music?'

'Oh, I've never had any sense of rhythm anyway.'

Everyone laughed, and the dark cloud hanging over us seemed to disperse.

'Right, I'm going to start again, and you can either follow me or leave. This time, I'm the one who decides when the class ends. One of the most aggressive things a human being can do is to go against what he or she believes is nice or pretty, and that's what we're going to do today. We're all going to dance badly.'

It was just another experiment and in order not to embarrass our hostess, everyone obediently danced badly. I struggled with myself, because one's natural tendency was to follow the rhythms of that marvellous, mysterious percussion. I felt as if I were insulting the musicians who were playing and the composer who created it. Every so often, my body tried to fight against that lack of harmony and I was forced to make myself behave as I'd been told to. The boy was dancing as well, laughing all the time, then, at a certain point, he stopped and sat down on the sofa, as if exhausted by his efforts. The CD was switched off in mid-stream.

'Wait.'

We all waited.

'I'm going to do something I've never done before.'

She closed her eyes and held her head between her hands.

'I've never danced unrhythmically before …'

So the experiment had been worse for her than for any of us.

'I don't feel well …'

Both the director and I got to our feet. Andrea shot me a furious glance, but I still went over to Athena. Before I could reach her, however, she asked us to return to our places.

'Does anyone want to say anything?' Her voice sounded fragile, tremulous, and she had still not uncovered her face.

'I do.'

It was Andrea.

'First, pick up my son and tell him that his mother's fine. But I need to stay like this for as long as necessary.'

Viorel looked frightened. Andrea sat him on her lap and stroked him.

'What do you want to say?'

'Nothing. I've changed my mind.'

'The boy made you change your mind, but carry on anyway.'

Slowly Athena removed her hands and looked up. Her face was that of a stranger.

'No, I won't speak.'

'All right. You,' Athena said, pointing to the older actor. 'Go to the doctor tomorrow. The fact that you can't sleep and have to keep getting up in the night to go to the toilet is serious. It's cancer of the prostate.'

The man turned pale.

'And you,' she pointed at the director, 'accept your sexual identity. Don't be afraid. Accept that you hate women and love men.'

'Are you saying—'

'Don't interrupt me. I'm not saying this because of Athena. I'm merely referring to your sexuality. You love men, and there is, I believe, nothing wrong with that.'

She wasn't saying that because of Athena? But she *was* Athena!

'And you,' she pointed to me. 'Come over here. Kneel down before me.'

Afraid of what Andrea might do and embarrassed to have everyone's eyes on me, I nevertheless did as she asked.

'Bow your head. Let me touch the nape of your neck.'

I felt the pressure of her fingers, but nothing else. We remained like that for nearly a minute, and then she told me to get up and go back to my seat.

'You won't need to take sleeping pills any more. From now on, sleep will return.'

I glanced at Andrea. I thought she might say something, but she looked as amazed as I did.

One of the actresses, possibly the youngest, raised her hand.

'I'd like to say something, but I need to know who I'm speaking to.'

'Hagia Sofia.'

'I'd like to know if ...'

She glanced round, ashamed, but the director nodded, asking her to continue.

'... if my mother is all right.'

'She's by your side. Yesterday, when you left the house, she made you forget your handbag. You went back to find it and discovered that you'd locked yourself out and couldn't get in. You wasted a whole hour looking for a locksmith, when you could have kept the appointment you'd made, met the man who was waiting for you and got the job you wanted. But if everything had happened as you planned that morning, in six months' time you would have died in a car accident. Forgetting your handbag yesterday changed your life.'

The girl began to weep.

'Does anyone else want to ask anything?'

Another hand went up. It was the director.

'Does he love me?'

So it was true. The story about the girl's mother had stirred up a whirlwind of emotions in the room.

'You're asking the wrong question. What you need to know is, are you in a position to give him the love he needs. And whatever happens or doesn't happen will be equally gratifying. Knowing that you are capable of love is enough. If it isn't him, it will be someone else. You've discovered a wellspring, simply allow it to flow and it will fill your world. Don't try to keep a safe distance so as to see what happens. Don't wait to be certain before you take a step. What you give, you will receive, although it might sometimes come from the place you least expect.'

Those words applied to me too. Then Athena – or whoever she was – turned to Andrea.

'You!'

My blood froze.

'You must be prepared to lose the universe you created.'

'What do you mean by "universe"?'

'What you think you already have. You've imprisoned your world, but you know that you must liberate it. I know you understand what I mean, even though you don't want to hear it.'

'I understand.'

I was sure they were talking about me. Was this all a set-up by Athena?

'It's finished,' she said. 'Bring the child to me.'

Viorel didn't want to go; he was frightened by his mother's transformation. But Andrea took him gently by the hand and led him to her.

Athena – or Hagia Sofia, or Sherine, or whoever she was – did just as she had done with me, and pressed the back of the boy's neck with her fingers.

'Don't be frightened by the things you see, my child. Don't try to push them away because they'll go away anyway. Enjoy the company of the angels while you can. You're frightened now, but you're not as frightened as you might be because you know there are lots of people in the room. You stopped laughing and dancing when you saw me embracing your mother and asking to speak through her mouth. But you know I wouldn't be doing this if she hadn't given me her permission. I've always appeared before in the form of light, and I still am that light, but today I decided to speak.'

The little boy put his arms around her.

'You can go now. Leave me alone with him.'

One by one, we left the apartment, leaving the mother with her child. In the taxi home, I tried to talk to Andrea, but she said that we could talk about anything but what had just happened.

I said nothing. My soul filled with sadness. Losing Andrea was very hard. On the other hand, I felt an immense peace. The evening's events had wrought changes in us all, and that meant I wouldn't need to go through the pain of sitting down with a woman I loved very much and telling her that I was in love with someone else.

In this case, I chose silence. I got home, turned on the TV, and Andrea went to have a bath. I closed my eyes, and when I opened them the room was full of light. It was morning, and I'd slept for ten hours. Beside me was a note, in which Andrea said that she hadn't wanted to wake me, that she'd gone straight to the theatre, but had left me some coffee. The note was a romantic one, decorated in lipstick and a small cut-out heart.

She had no intention of 'letting go of her universe'. She was going to fight. And my life would become a nightmare.

That evening, she phoned, and her voice betrayed no particular emotion. She told me that the elderly actor had gone to see his doctor, who had examined him and found that he had an enlarged prostate. The next step was a blood test, where they had detected a significantly raised level of a type of protein called PSA. They took a sample for a biopsy, but the clinical picture indicated that there was a high chance he had a malignant tumour.

'The doctor said he was lucky, because even if their worst fears were proved right, they can still operate and there's a ninety-nine per cent chance of a cure.'

Deidre O'Neill, known as Edda

What do you mean, Hagia Sofia! It was her, Athena, but by touching the deepest part of the river that flows through her soul she had come into contact with the Mother.

All she did was to see what was happening in another reality. The young actress's mother, now that she's dead, lives in a place outside of time and so was able to change the course of events, whereas we human beings can only know about the present. But that's no small thing: discovering a dormant illness before it gets worse, touching nervous systems and unblocking energies is within the reach of all of us.

Of course, many died at the stake, others were exiled and many ended up hiding or suppressing the spark of the Great Mother in their souls. I never brought Athena into contact with the Power. She decided to do this, because the Mother had already given her various signs: she was a light while she danced, she changed into letters while she was learning calligraphy, she appeared to her in a fire and in a mirror. What my student didn't know was how to live with Her, until, that is, she did something that provoked this whole chain of events.

Athena, who was always telling everyone to be different, was basically just like all other mortals. She had her own rhythm, a kind of cruise control. Was she more curious than most? Possibly. Had she managed to overcome her sense of being a victim? Definitely. Did she feel a need to share what she was learning with others, be they bank employees or actors? In some cases the answer was 'Yes', but in others I had to encourage her, because we are not meant for solitude, and we only know ourselves when we see ourselves in the eyes of others.

But that was as far as my interference went.

Maybe the Mother wanted to appear that night, and perhaps she whispered something in her ear: 'Go against everything you've learned so far. You, who are a mistress of rhythm, allow the rhythm to pass through your body, but don't obey it.' That was why Athena suggested the exercise. Her unconscious was already prepared to receive the Mother, but Athena herself was still dancing in time to the music and so any external elements were unable to manifest themselves.

The same thing used to happen with me. The best way to meditate and enter into contact with the light was by knitting, something my mother had taught me when I was a child. I knew how to count the stitches, manipulate the needles and create beautiful things through repetition and harmony. One day, my protector asked me to knit in a completely irrational way! I found this really distressing, because I'd learned how to knit with affection, patience and dedication. Nevertheless, he insisted on me knitting really badly.

I knitted like this for two hours, thinking all the time that it was utterly ridiculous, absurd. My head ached, but I had to resist letting the needles guide my hands. Anyone can do things badly, so why was he asking this of me? Because he knew about my obsession with geometry and with perfection.

And suddenly, it happened: I stopped moving the needles and felt a great emptiness, which was filled by a warm, loving, companionable presence. Everything around me was different, and I felt like saying things that I would never normally dare to say. I didn't lose consciousness; I knew I was still me, but, paradoxically, I wasn't the person I was used to being with.

So I can 'see' what happened, even though I wasn't there. Athena's soul following the sound of the music while her body went in a totally contrary direction. After a time, her soul disconnected from her body, a space opened, and the Mother could finally enter.

Or, rather, a spark from the Mother appeared. Ancient, but apparently very young. Wise, but not omnipotent. Special, but not in the least arrogant. Her perceptions changed, and she began to see the same things she used to see when she was a child – the parallel universes that people this world. At such moments, we can see not only the physical body, but people's emotions too. They say cats have this same power, and I believe them.

A kind of blanket lies between the physical and the spiritual world, a blanket that changes in colour, intensity and light; it's what mystics call 'aura'. From then on, everything is easy. The aura tells you what's going on. If I had been there, she would have seen a violet colour with a few yellow splodges around my body. That means that I still have a long road ahead of me and that my mission on this Earth has not yet been accomplished.

Mixed up with human auras are transparent forms, which people usually call 'ghosts'. That was the case with the young woman's mother, and only in such cases can someone's fate be altered. I'm almost certain that the young actress, even before she asked, knew that her mother was beside her, and the only real surprise to her was the story about the handbag.

Confronted by that rhythmless dance, everyone was really intimidated. Why? Because we're used to doing things 'as they should be done'. No one likes to make the wrong moves, especially when we're aware that we're doing so. Even Athena. It can't have been easy for her to suggest doing something that went against everything she loved.

I'm glad that the Mother won the battle at that point. A man has been saved from cancer, another has accepted his sexuality, and a third has stopped taking sleeping pills. And all because Athena broke the rhythm, slamming on the brakes when the car was travelling at top speed and thus throwing everything into disarray.

To go back to my knitting: I used that method of knitting badly for quite some time, until I managed to provoke the presence without any artificial means, now that I knew it and was used to it. The same thing happened with Athena. Once we know where the Doors of Perception are, it's really easy to open and close them, when we get used to our own 'strange' behaviour.

And it must be said that I knitted much faster and better after that, just as Athena danced with much more soul and rhythm once she had dared to break down those barriers.

Andrea McCain, actress

The story spread like wild fire. On the following Monday, when the theatre was closed, Athena's apartment was packed. We had all brought friends. She did as she had on the previous evening; she made us dance without rhythm, as if she needed that collective energy in order to get in touch with Hagia Sofia. The boy was there again, and I decided to watch him. When he sat down on the sofa, the music stopped and the trance began.

As did the questions. The first three questions were, as you can imagine, about love – will he stay with me, does she love me, is he cheating on me. Athena said nothing. The fourth person to receive no answer asked again, more loudly this time:

'So is he cheating on me or not?'

'I am Hagia Sofia, universal wisdom. I came into the world accompanied only by Love. I am the beginning of everything, and before I existed there was chaos. Therefore, if any of you wish to control the forces that prevailed in chaos, do not ask Hagia Sofia. For me, love fills everything. It cannot be desired because it is an end in itself. It cannot betray because it has nothing to do with possession. It cannot be held prisoner because it is a river and will overflow its banks. Anyone who tries to imprison love will cut off the spring that feeds it, and the trapped water will grow stagnant and rank.'

Hagia looked around the group, most of whom were there for the first time, and she began to point out what she saw: the threat of disease, problems at work, frictions between parents and children, sexuality, potentialities that existed but were not being explored. I remember her turning to one woman in her thirties and saying:

'Your father told you how things should be and how a woman should behave. You have always fought against your dreams, and "I want" has never even shown its face. It was always drowned out by "I must" or "I hope" or "I need", but you're a wonderful singer. One year's experience could make a huge difference to your work.'

'But I have a husband and a child.'

'Athena has a child too. Your husband will be upset at first, but he'll come to accept it eventually. And you don't need to be Hagia Sofia to know that.'

'Maybe I'm too old.'

'You're refusing to accept who you are, but that is not my problem. I have said what needed to be said.'

Gradually, everyone in that small room – unable to sit down because there wasn't enough space, sweating profusely even though the winter was not yet over, feeling ridiculous for having come to such an event – was called upon to receive Hagia Sofia's advice.

I was the last.

'Stay behind afterwards if you want to stop being two and to be one instead.'

This time, I didn't have her son on my lap. He watched everything that happened, and it seemed that the conversation they'd had after the first session had been enough for him to lose his fear.

I nodded. Unlike the previous session, when people had simply left when she'd asked to talk to her son alone, this time Hagia Sofia gave a sermon before ending the ritual.

'You are not here to receive definite answers. My mission is to provoke you. In the past, both governors and governed went to oracles who would foretell the future. The future, however, is unreliable because it is guided by decisions made in the here and now. Keep the bicycle moving, because if you stop pedalling, you will fall off.

'For those of you who came to meet Hagia Sofia wanting her merely to confirm what you hoped to be true, please, do not come back. Or else start dancing and make those around you dance too. Fate will be implacable with those who want to live in a universe that is dead and gone. The new world belongs to the Mother, who came with Love to separate the heavens from the waters. Anyone who believes they have failed will always fail. Anyone who has decided that they cannot behave any differently will be destroyed by routine. Anyone who has decided to block all changes will be transformed into dust. Cursed be those who do not dance and who prevent others from dancing!'

Her eyes glanced fire.

'You can go.'

Everyone left, and I could see the look of confusion on most of their faces. They had come in search of comfort and had found only provocation. They had arrived wanting to be told how love can be controlled and had heard that the all-devouring flame will always burn everything. They wanted to be sure that their decisions were the right ones, that their husbands, wives and bosses were pleased with them, but, instead, they were given only words of doubt.

Some people, though, were smiling. They had understood the importance of the dance and from that night on would doubtless allow their bodies and souls to drift – even though, as always happens, they would have to pay a price.

Only the boy, Hagia Sofia, Heron and myself were left in the room.

'I asked you to stay here alone.'

Without a word, Heron picked up his coat and left.

Hagia Sofia was looking at me. And, little by little, I watched her change back into Athena. The only way of describing that change is to compare it with the change that takes place in an angry child: we can see the anger in the child's eyes, but once distracted and once the anger has gone, the child is no longer the same child who, only moments before, was crying. The 'being', if it can be called that, seemed to have vanished into the air as soon as its instrument lost concentration.

And now I was standing before an apparently exhausted woman.

'Make me some tea.'

She was giving me an order! And she was no longer universal wisdom, but merely someone my boyfriend was interested in or infatuated with. Where would this relationship take us?

But making a cup of tea wouldn't destroy my self-esteem. I went into the kitchen, boiled some water, added a few camomile leaves and returned to the living room. The child was asleep on her lap.

'You don't like me,' she said.

I made no reply.

'I don't like you either,' she went on. 'You're pretty and elegant, a fine actress, and have a degree of culture and education which I, despite my family's wishes, do not. But you're also insecure, arrogant and suspicious. As Hagia Sofia said, you are two, when you could be one.'

'I didn't know you remembered what you said during the trance, because in that case you are two people as well: Athena and Hagia Sofia.'

'I may have two names, but I am only one – or else all the people in the world. And that is precisely what I want to talk about. Because I am one and everyone, the spark that emerges when I go into a trance gives me very precise instructions. I remain semi-conscious throughout, of course, but I'm saying things that come from some unknown part of myself, as if I were suckling on the breast of the Mother, drinking the milk that flows through all our souls and carries knowledge around the Earth. Last week, which was the first time I entered into contact with this new form, I received what seemed to me to be an absurd message: that I should teach you.'

She paused.

'Obviously, this struck me as quite mad, because I don't like you at all.'

She paused again, for longer this time.

'Today, though, the source repeated the same message, and so I'm giving you that choice.'

'Why do you call it Hagia Sofia?'

'That was my idea. It's the name of a really beautiful mosque I saw in a book. You could, if you like, be my student. That's what brought you here on that first day. This whole new stage in my life, including the discovery of Hagia Sofia inside me, only happened because one day you came through that door and said: "I work in the theatre and we're putting on a play about the female face of God. I heard from a journalist friend that you've spent time in the Balkan mountains with some gipsies and would be prepared to tell me about your experiences there."'

'Are you going to teach me everything you know?'

'No, everything I don't know. I'll learn through being in contact with you, as I said the first time we met, and as I say again now. Once I've learned what I need to learn, we'll go our separate ways.'

'Can you teach someone you dislike?'

'I can love and respect someone I dislike. On the two occasions when I went into a trance, I saw your aura, and it was the most highly developed aura I've ever seen. You could make a difference in this world, if you accept my proposal.'

'Will you teach me to see auras?'

'Until it happened to me the first time, I myself didn't know I was capable of doing so. If you're on the right path, you'll learn to do so as well.'

I realised then that I, too, was capable of loving someone I disliked. I said 'Yes'.

'Then let us transform that acceptance into a ritual. A ritual throws us into an unknown world, but we know that we cannot treat the things of that world lightly. It isn't enough to say "yes", you must put your life at risk, and without giving it much thought either. If you're the woman I think you are, you won't say: "I need to think about it." You'll say –'

'I'm ready. Let's move on to the ritual. Where did you learn the ritual, by the way?'

'I'm going to learn it now. I no longer need to remove myself from my normal rhythm in order to enter into contact with the spark from the Mother, because, once that spark is installed inside you, it's easy to find again. I know which door I need to open, even though it's concealed amongst many other entrances and exits. All I need is a little silence.'

Silence again!

We sat there, our eyes wide and staring, as if we were about to begin a fight to the death. Rituals! Before I even rang the bell of Athena's apartment for the first time, I had already taken part in various rituals, only to feel used and diminished afterwards, standing outside a door I could see, but not open. Rituals!

All Athena did was drink a little of the tea I prepared for her.

'The ritual is over. I asked you to do something for me. You did, and I accepted it. Now it is your turn to ask me something.'

I immediately thought of Heron, but it wasn't the right moment to talk about him.

'Take your clothes off.'

She didn't ask me why. She looked at the child, checked that he was asleep, and immediately began to remove her sweater.

'No, really, you don't have to,' I said. 'I don't know why I asked that.'

But she continued to undress, first her blouse, then her jeans, then her bra. I noticed her breasts, which were the most beautiful I'd ever seen. Finally, she removed her knickers. And there she was, offering me her nakedness.

'Bless me,' said Athena.

Bless my 'teacher'? But I'd already taken the first step and couldn't stop now, so I dipped my fingers in the cup and sprinkled a little tea over her body.

'Just as this plant was transformed into tea, just as the water mingled with the plant, I bless you and ask the Great Mother that the spring from which this water came will never cease flowing, and that the earth from which this plant came will always be fertile and generous.'

I was surprised at my own words. They had come neither from inside me nor outside. It was as if I'd always known them and had done this countless times before.

'You have been blessed. You can get dressed now.'

But she didn't move, she merely smiled. What did she want? If Hagia Sofia was capable of seeing auras, she would know that I hadn't the slightest desire to have sex with another woman.

'One moment.'

She picked up the boy, carried him to his room and returned at once.

'You take your clothes off too.'

Who was asking this? Hagia Sofia, who spoke of my potential and for whom I was the perfect disciple? Or Athena, whom I hardly knew, and who seemed capable of anything – a woman whom life had taught to go beyond her limits and to satisfy any curiosity?

We had started a kind of confrontation from which there was no retreat. I got undressed with the same nonchalance, the same smile and the same look in my eyes.

She took my hand and we sat down on the sofa.

During the next half hour, both Athena and Hagia Sofia were present; they wanted to know what my next steps would be. As they asked me this question, I saw that everything really was written there before me, and that the doors had only been closed before because I hadn't realised that I was the one person in the world with the authority to open them.

Heron Ryan, journalist

The deputy editor hands me a video and we go into the projection room to watch it.

The video was made on the morning of 26 April 1986 and shows normal life in a normal town. A man is sitting drinking a cup of coffee. A mother is taking her baby for a walk. People in a hurry are going to work. A few people are waiting at a bus stop. A man on a bench in a square is reading a newspaper.

But there's a problem with the video. There are various horizontal lines on the screen, as if the tracking button needed to be adjusted. I get up to do this, but the deputy editor stops me.

'That's just the way it is. Keep watching.'

Images of the small provincial town continue to appear, showing nothing of interest apart from these scenes from ordinary everyday life.

'It's possible that some people may know that there's been an accident two kilometres from there,' says my boss. 'It's possible that they know there have been thirty deaths – a large number, but not enough to change the routine of the town's inhabitants.'

Now the film shows school buses parking. They will stay there for many days. The images are getting worse and worse.

'It isn't the tracking, it's radiation. The video was made by the KGB. On the night of the twenty-sixth of April, at twenty-three minutes past one in the morning, the worst ever man-made disaster occurred at Chernobyl, in the Ukraine. When a nuclear reactor exploded, the people in the area were exposed to ninety times more radiation than that given out by the bomb dropped on Hiroshima. The whole region should have been evacuated at once, but no one said anything – after all, the government doesn't make mistakes. Only a week later, on page thirty-two of the local newspaper, a five-line article appeared, mentioning the deaths of workers, but giving no further explanation. Meanwhile, Workers' Day was celebrated throughout the Soviet Union, and in Kiev, the Ukrainian capital, people paraded down the street unaware of the invisible death in the air.'

And he concludes:

'I want you to go and see what Chernobyl is like now. You've just been promoted to special correspondent. You'll get a twenty per cent increase in your salary and be able to suggest the kind of article you think we should be publishing.'

I should be jumping for joy, but instead I'm gripped by a feeling of intense sadness, which I have to hide. It's impossible to argue with him, to say that there are two women in my life at the moment, that I don't want to leave London, that my life and my mental equilibrium are at stake. I ask when I should leave. As soon as possible, he says, because there are rumours that other countries are significantly increasing their production of nuclear energy.

I manage to negotiate an honourable way out, saying that, first, I need to talk to experts and really get to grips with the subject, and that I'll set off once I've collected the necessary material.

He agrees, shakes my hand and congratulates me. I don't have time to talk to Andrea, because when I get home, she's still at the theatre. I fall asleep at once and again wake up to find a note saying that she's gone to work and that the coffee is on the table.

I go to the office, try to ingratiate myself with the boss who has 'improved my life', and phone various experts on radiation and energy. I discover that, in total, 9 million people worldwide were directly affected by the disaster, including 3 to 4 million children. The initial 30 deaths became, according to the expert John Gofmans, 475,000 cases of fatal cancers and an equal number of non-fatal cancers.

A total of 2,000 towns and villages were simply wiped off the map. According to the Health Ministry in Belarus, the incidence of cancer of the thyroid will increase considerably between 2005 and 2010, as a consequence of continuing high levels of radioactivity. Another specialist explains that as well as the 9 million people directly exposed to radiation, more than 65 million in many countries round the world were indirectly affected by consuming contaminated foodstuffs.

It's a serious matter, which deserves to be treated with respect. At the end of the day, I go back to the deputy editor and suggest that I travel to Chernobyl for the actual anniversary of the accident, and meanwhile do more research, talk to more experts and find out how the British government responded to the tragedy. He agrees.

I phone Athena. After all, she claims to be going out with someone from Scotland Yard and now is the time to ask her a favour, given that Chernobyl is no longer classified as secret and the Soviet Union no longer exists. She promises that she'll talk to her 'boyfriend', but says she can't guarantee she'll get the answers I want.

She also says that she's leaving for Scotland the following day, and will only be back in time for the next group meeting.

'What group?'

The group, she says. So that's become a regular thing, has it? What I want to know is when we can meet to talk and clear up various loose ends.

But she's already hung up. I go home, watch the news, have supper alone and, later, go out again to pick Andrea up from the theatre. I get there in time to see the end of the play and, to my surprise, the person on stage seems totally unlike the person I've been living with for nearly two years; there's something magical about her every gesture; monologues and dialogues are spoken with an unaccustomed intensity.

I am seeing a stranger, a woman I would like to have by my side, then I realise that she *is* by my side and is in no way a stranger to me.

'How did your chat with Athena go?' I ask on the way home.

'Fine. How was work?'

She was the one to change the subject. I tell her about my promotion and about Chernobyl, but she doesn't seem interested. I start to think that I'm losing the love I have without having yet won the love I hope to win. However, as soon as we reach our apartment, she suggests we take a bath together and, before I know it, we're in bed. First, she puts on that percussion music at full volume (she explains that she managed to get hold of a copy) and tells me not to worry about the neighbours – people worry too much about them, she says, and never live their own lives.

What happens from then on is something that goes beyond my understanding. Has this woman making positively savage love with me finally discovered her sexuality, and was this taught to her or provoked in her by that other woman? While she was clinging to me with a violence I've never known before, she kept saying:

'Today I'm your man, and you're my woman.'

We carried on like this for almost an hour, and I experienced things I'd never dared experience before. At certain moments, I felt ashamed, wanted to ask her to stop, but she seemed to be in complete control of the situation and so I surrendered, because I had no choice. In fact, I felt really curious.

I was exhausted afterwards, but Andrea seemed re-energised.

'Before you go to sleep, I want you to know something,' she said. 'If you go forward, sex will offer you the chance to make love with gods and goddesses. That's what you experienced today. I want you to go to sleep knowing that I awoke the Mother that was in you.'

I wanted to ask if she'd learned this from Athena, but my courage failed.

'Tell me that you liked being a woman for a night.'

'I did. I don't know if I would always like it, but it was something that simultaneously frightened me and gave me great joy.'

'Tell me that you've always wanted to experience what you've just experienced.'

It's one thing to allow oneself to be carried away by the situation, but quite another to comment coolly on the matter. I said nothing, although I was sure that she knew my answer.

'Well,' Andrea went on, 'all of this was inside me and I had no idea. As was the person behind the mask that fell away while I was on stage today. Did you notice anything different?'

'Of course. You were radiating a special light.'

'Charisma – the divine force that manifests itself in men and women. The supernatural power we don't need to show to anyone because everyone can see it, even usually insensitive people. But it only happens when we're naked, when we die to the world and are reborn to ourselves. Last night, I died. Tonight, when I walked on stage and saw that I was doing exactly what I had chosen to do, I was reborn from my ashes. I was always trying to be who I am, but could never manage it. I was always trying to impress other people, have intelligent conversations, please my parents and, at the same time, I used every available means to do the things I would really like to do. I've always forged my path with blood, tears and will power, but last night, I realised that I was going about it the wrong way. My dream doesn't require that of me, I have only to surrender myself to it and, if I find I'm suffering, grit my teeth, because the suffering will pass.'

'Why are you telling me this?'

'Let me finish. In that journey where suffering seemed to be the only rule, I struggled for things for which there was no point struggling. Like love, for example. People either feel it or they don't, and there isn't a force in the world that can make them feel it. We can pretend that we love each other. We can get used to each other. We can live a whole lifetime of friendship and complicity, we can bring up children, have sex every night, reach orgasm, and still feel that there's a terrible emptiness about it all, that something important is missing. In the name of all I've learned about relationships between men and women, I've been trying to fight against things that weren't really worth the struggle. And that includes you.

'Today, while we were making love, while I was giving all I have, and I could see that you, too, were giving of your best, I realised that your best no longer interests me. I will sleep beside you tonight, but tomorrow I'll leave. The theatre is my ritual, and there I can express and develop whatever I want to express and develop.'

I started to regret everything – going to Transylvania and meeting a woman who might be destroying my life, arranging that first meeting of the 'group', confessing my love in that restaurant. At that moment, I hated Athena.

'I know what you're thinking,' said Andrea. 'That your friend Athena has brainwashed me, but that isn't true.'

'I'm a man, even though tonight in bed I behaved like a woman. I'm a species in danger of extinction because I don't see many men around. Few people would risk what I have risked.'

'I'm sure you're right, and that's why I admire you, but aren't you going to ask me who I am, what I want and what I desire?'

I asked.

'I want everything. I want savagery and tenderness. I want to upset the neighbours and placate them too. I don't want a woman in my bed, I want men, real men, like you, for example. Whether they love me or are merely using me, it doesn't matter. My love is greater than that. I want to love freely, and I want to allow the people around me to do the same.

'What I talked about to Athena were the simple ways of awakening repressed energy, like making love, for example, or walking down the street saying: "I'm here and now." Nothing very special, no secret ritual. The only thing that made our meeting slightly different was that we were both naked. From now on, she and I will meet every Monday, and if I have any comments to make, I will do so after that session. I have no desire to be her friend. Just as, when she feels the need to share something, she goes up to Scotland to talk with that Edda woman, who, it seems, you know as well, although you've never mentioned her.'

'I can't even remember meeting her!'

I sensed that Andrea was gradually calming down. I prepared two cups of coffee and we drank them together. She recovered her smile and asked about my promotion. She said she was worried about those Monday meetings, because she'd learned only that morning that friends of friends were inviting other people, and Athena's apartment was a very small place. I made an enormous effort to pretend that everything that had happened that evening was just a fit of nerves or premenstrual tension or jealousy on her part.

I put my arms around her and she snuggled into my shoulder. And despite my own exhaustion, I waited until she fell asleep. That night, I dreamed of nothing. I had no feelings of foreboding.

And the following morning, when I woke up, I saw that her clothes were gone, the key was on the table, and there was no letter of farewell.

Deidre O'Neill, known as Edda

People read a lot of stories about witches, fairies, paranormals and children possessed by evil spirits. They go to films showing rituals featuring pentagrams, swords and invocations. That's fine; people need to give free rein to their imagination and to go through certain stages. Anyone who gets through those stages without being deceived will eventually get in touch with the Tradition.

The real Tradition is this: the teacher never tells the disciple what he or she should do. They are merely travelling companions, sharing the same uncomfortable feeling of 'estrangement' when confronted by ever-changing perceptions, broadening horizons, closing doors, rivers that sometimes seem to block their path and which, in fact, should never be crossed, but followed.

There is only one difference between teacher and disciple: the former is slightly less afraid than the latter. Then, when they sit down at a table or in front of a fire to talk, the more experienced person might say: 'Why don't you do that?' But he or she never says: 'Go there and you'll arrive where I did,' because every path and every destination are unique to the individual.

The true teacher gives the disciple the courage to throw his or her world off balance, even though the disciple is afraid of things already encountered and more afraid still of what might be around the next corner.

I was a young, enthusiastic doctor who, filled by a desire to help my fellow human beings, travelled to the interior of Romania on an exchange programme run by the British government. I set off with my luggage full of medicines and my head full of preconceptions. I had clear ideas about how people should behave, about what we need to be happy, about the dreams we should keep alive inside us, about how human relations should evolve. I arrived in Bucharest during that crazed, bloody dictatorship and went to Transylvania to assist with a mass vaccination programme for the local population.

I didn't realise that I was merely one more piece on a very complicated chessboard, where invisible hands were manipulating my idealism, and that ulterior motives lay behind everything I believed was being done for humanitarian purposes: stabilising the government run by the dictator's son, allowing Britain to sell arms in a market dominated by the Soviets.

All my good intentions collapsed when I saw that there was barely enough vaccine to go round; that there were other diseases sweeping the region; that however often I wrote asking for more resources, they never came. I was told not to concern myself with anything beyond what I'd been asked to do.

I felt powerless and angry. I'd seen poverty from close to and would have been able to do something about it if only someone would give me some money, but they weren't interested in results. Our government just wanted a few articles in the press, so that they could say to their political parties or to their electorate that they'd despatched groups to various places in the world on a humanitarian mission. Their intentions were good – apart from selling arms, of course.

I was in despair. What kind of world was this? One night, I set off into the icy forest, cursing God, who was unfair to everything and everyone. I was sitting beneath an oak tree when my protector approached me. He said I could die of cold, and I replied that I was a doctor and knew the body's limits, and that as soon as I felt I was getting near those limits I would go back to the camp. I asked him what he was doing there.

'I'm speaking to a woman who can hear me, in a world in which all the men have gone deaf.'

I thought he meant me, but the woman he was referring to was the forest itself. When I saw this man wandering about amongst the trees, making gestures and saying things I couldn't understand, a kind of peace settled on my heart. I was not, after all, the only person in the world left talking to myself. When I got up to return to the camp, he came over to me again.

'I know who you are,' he said. 'People in the village say that you're a very decent person, always good-humoured and prepared to help others, but I see something else: rage and frustration.'

He might have been a government spy, but I decided to tell him everything I was feeling, even though I ran the risk of being arrested. We walked together to the field hospital where I was working; I took him to the dormitory, which was empty at the time (my colleagues were all having fun at the annual festival being held in the town), and I asked if he'd like a drink. He produced a bottle from his pocket.

'Palinka,' he said, meaning the traditional drink of Romania, with an incredibly high alcohol content. 'On me.'

We drank together, and I didn't even notice that I was getting steadily drunk. I only realised the state I was in when I tried to go to the toilet, tripped over something and fell flat.

'Don't move,' said the man. 'Look at what is there before your eyes.'

A line of ants.

'They all think they're very wise. They have memory, intelligence, organisational powers, a spirit of sacrifice. They look for food in summer, store it away for the winter, and now they are setting forth again, in this icy spring, to work. If the world were destroyed by an atomic bomb tomorrow, the ants would survive.'

'How do you know all this?'

'I studied biology.'

'Why the hell don't you work to improve the living conditions of your own people? What are you doing in the middle of the forest, talking to the trees?'

'In the first place, I wasn't alone; apart from the trees, you were listening to me too. But to answer your question, I left biology to work as a blacksmith.'

I struggled to my feet. My head was still spinning, but I was thinking clearly enough to understand the poor man's situation. Despite a university education, he had been unable to find work. I told him that the same thing happened in my country too.

'No, that's not what I meant. I left biology because I wanted to work as a blacksmith. Even as a child, I was fascinated by those men hammering steel, making a strange kind of music, sending out sparks all around, plunging the red-hot metal into water and creating clouds of steam. I was unhappy as a biologist, because my dream was to make rigid metal take on soft shapes. Then, one day, a protector appeared.'

'A protector?'

'Let's say that, on seeing those ants doing exactly what they're programmed to do, you were to exclaim: "How fantastic!" The guards are genetically prepared to sacrifice themselves for the queen, the workers carry leaves ten times their own weight, the engineers make tunnels that can resist storms and floods. They enter into mortal combat with their enemies, they suffer for the community, and they never ask: "Why are we doing this?" People try to imitate the perfect society of the ants, and, as a biologist, I was playing my part, until someone came along with this question: "Are you happy doing what you're doing?" "Of course I am," I said. "I'm being useful to my own people." "And that's enough?"

'I didn't know whether it was enough or not, but I said that he seemed to me to be both arrogant and egotistical. He replied: "Possibly. But all you will achieve is to repeat what has been done since man was man – keeping things organised."

'"But the world has progressed," I said. He asked if I knew any history. Of course I did. He asked another question: "Thousands of years ago, weren't we capable of building enormous structures like the pyramids? Weren't we capable of worshipping gods, weaving, making fire, finding lovers and wives, sending written messages? Of course we were. But although we've succeeded in replacing slaves with wage slaves, all the advances we've made have been in the field of science. Human beings are still asking the same questions as their ancestors. In short, they haven't evolved at all." At that point, I understood that the person asking me these questions was someone sent from heaven, an angel, a protector.'

'Why do you call him a protector?'

'Because he told me that there were two traditions, one that makes us repeat the same thing for centuries at a time, and another that opens the door into the unknown. However, the second tradition is difficult, uncomfortable and dangerous, and if it attracted too many followers it would end up destroying the society which, following the example of the ants, took so long to build. And so the second tradition went underground and has only managed to survive over so many centuries because its followers created a secret language of signs.'

'Did you ask more questions?'

'Of course I did, because, although I'd denied it, he knew I was dissatisfied with what I was doing. My protector said: "I'm afraid of taking steps that are not on the map, but by taking those steps despite my fears, I have a much more interesting life." I asked more about the Tradition, and he said something like: "As long as God is merely man, we'll always have enough food to eat and somewhere to live. When the Mother finally regains her freedom, we might have to sleep rough and live on love, or we might be able to balance emotion and work." The man, who, it turned out, was my protector, asked: "If you weren't a biologist, what would you be?" I said: "A blacksmith, but they don't earn enough money." And he replied: "Well, when you grow tired of being what you're not, go and have fun and celebrate life, hammering metal into shape. In time, you'll discover that it will give you more than pleasure, it will give you meaning." "How do I follow this tradition you spoke of?" I asked. "As I said, through symbols," he replied. "Start doing what you want to do, and everything else will be revealed to you. Believe that God is the Mother and looks after her children and never lets anything bad happen to them. I did that and I survived. I discovered that there were other people who did the same, but who are considered to be mad, irresponsible, superstitious. Since time immemorial, they've sought their inspiration in nature. We build pyramids, but we also develop symbols."

'Having said that, he left, and I never saw him again. I only know, from that moment on, symbols did begin to appear because my eyes had been opened by that conversation. Hard though it was, one evening I told my family that, although I had everything a man could dream of having, I was unhappy, and that I had, in fact, been born to be a blacksmith. My wife protested, saying: "You were born a gipsy and had to face endless humiliations to get where you are, and yet you want to go back?" My son, however, was thrilled, because he, too, liked to watch the blacksmiths in our village and hated the laboratories in the big cities.

'I started dividing my time between biological research and working as a blacksmith's apprentice. I was always tired, but I was much happier. One day, I left my job and set up my own blacksmith's business, which went completely wrong from the start. Just when I was starting to believe in life, things got markedly worse. One day, I was working away and I saw that there before me was a symbol.

'The unworked steel arrives in my workshop and I have to transform it into parts for cars, agricultural machinery, kitchen utensils. Do you know how that's done? First, I heat the metal until it's red-hot, then I beat it mercilessly with my heaviest hammer until the metal takes on the form I need. Then I plunge it into a bucket of cold water and the whole workshop is filled with the roar of steam, while the metal sizzles and crackles in response to the sudden change in temperature. I have to keep repeating that process until the object I'm making is perfect: once is not enough.'

The blacksmith paused for a long time, lit a cigarette, then went on:

'Sometimes the steel I get simply can't withstand such treatment. The heat, the hammer blows, the cold water cause it to crack. And I know that I'll never be able to make it into a good ploughshare or an engine shaft. Then I throw it on the pile of scrap metal at the entrance to my forge.'

Another long pause, then the blacksmith concluded:

'I know that God is putting me through the fire of afflictions. I've accepted the blows that life has dealt me, and sometimes I feel as cold and indifferent as the water that inflicts such pain on the steel. But my one prayer is this: "Please, God, my Mother, don't give up until I've taken on the shape that You wish for me. Do this by whatever means You think best, for as long as You like, but never ever throw me on the scrap heap of souls."'

I may have been drunk when I finished my conversation with that man, but I knew that my life had changed. There was a tradition behind everything we learn, and I needed to go in search of people who, consciously or unconsciously, were able to make manifest the female side of God. Instead of cursing my government and all the political shenanigans, I decided to do what I really wanted to do: to heal people. I wasn't interested in anything else.

Since I didn't have the necessary resources, I approached the local men and women, and they guided me to the world of medicinal herbs. I discovered that there was a popular tradition that went back hundreds of years and was passed from generation to generation through experience rather than through technical knowledge. With their help, I was able to do far more than I would otherwise have been able to do, because I wasn't there merely to fulfil a university task or to help my government to sell arms or, unwittingly, to spread party political propaganda. I was there because healing people made me happy.

This brought me closer to nature, to the oral tradition and to plants. Back in Britain, I decided to talk to other doctors and I asked them: 'Do you always know exactly which medicines to prescribe or are you sometimes guided by intuition?' Almost all of them, once they had dropped their guard, admitted that they were often guided by a voice and that when they ignored the advice of the voice, they ended up giving the wrong treatment. Obviously they make use of all the available technology, but they know that there is a corner, a dark corner, where lies the real meaning of the cure, and the best decision to make.

My protector threw my world off balance – even though he was only a gipsy blacksmith. I used to go at least once a year to his village and we would talk about how, when we dare to see things differently, life opens up to our eyes. On one of those visits, I met other disciples of his, and together we discussed our fears and our conquests. My protector said: 'I, too, get scared, but it's at such moments that I discover a wisdom that is beyond me, and I go forward.'

Now I earn a lot of money working as a GP in Edinburgh, and I would earn even more if I went to work in London, but I prefer to make the most of life and to take time out. I do what I like: I combine the healing processes of the ancients, the Arcane Tradition, with the most modern techniques of present-day medicine, the Hippocratic Tradition. I'm writing a paper on the subject, and many people in the 'scientific' community, when they see my text published in a specialist journal, will dare to take the steps which, deep down, they've always wanted to take.

I don't believe that the mind is the source of all ills; there are real diseases too. I think antibiotics and antivirals were great advances for humanity. I don't believe that a patient of mine with appendicitis can be cured by meditation alone; what he needs is some good, emergency surgery. So I take each step with courage and fear, combining technique and inspiration. And I'm careful who I say these things to, because I might get dubbed a witchdoctor, and then many lives I could have saved would be lost.

When I'm not sure, I ask the Great Mother for help. She has never yet failed to answer me. But she has always counselled me to be discreet. She probably gave the same advice to Athena on more than one occasion, but Athena was too fascinated by the world she was just starting to discover and she didn't listen.

A London newspaper, 24 August 1991

THE WITCH OF PORTOBELLO

London (© Jeremy Lutton): 'That's another reason why I don't believe in God. I mean, look at the behaviour of people who do believe!' This was the reaction of Robert Wilson, one of the traders in Portobello Road.

This road, known around the world for its antique shops and its Saturday flea market, was transformed last night into a battlefield, requiring the intervention of at least fifty police officers from the Royal Borough of Kensington and Chelsea to restore order. By the end of the fracas, five people had been injured, although none seriously. The reason behind this pitched battle, which lasted nearly two hours, was a demonstration organised by the Rev. Ian Buck to protest about what he called 'the Satanic cult at the heart of England'.

According to Rev. Buck, a group of suspicious individuals have been keeping the neighbourhood awake every Monday night for the last six months, Monday being their chosen night for invoking the Devil. The ceremonies are led by a Lebanese woman, Sherine H. Khalil, who calls herself Athena, after the goddess of wisdom.

About two hundred people began meeting in a former East India Company warehouse, but the numbers increased over time and, in recent weeks, an equally large crowd has been gathering outside, hoping to gain entry and take part in the ceremony. When his various verbal complaints, petitions and letters to the local newspapers achieved nothing, the Rev. Buck decided to mobilise the community, calling on his parishioners to gather outside the warehouse by 1900 hours yesterday to stop the 'devil-worshippers' getting in.

'As soon as we received the first complaint, we sent someone to inspect the place, but no drugs were found nor evidence of any other kind of illicit activity,' said an official who preferred not to be identified because an inquiry has just been set up to investigate what happened. 'They aren't contravening the noise nuisance laws because they turn off the music at ten o'clock prompt, so there's really nothing more we can do. Britain, after all, allows freedom of worship.'

The Rev. Buck has another version of events.

'The fact is that this witch of Portobello, this mistress of charlatanism, has contacts with people high up in the government, which explains why the police – paid for by taxpayers' money to maintain order and decency – refuse to do anything. We're living in an age in which everything is allowed, and democracy is being devoured and destroyed by that limitless freedom.'

The vicar says that he was suspicious of the group right from the start. They had rented a crumbling old building and spent whole days trying to renovate it, 'which is clear evidence that they belong to some sect and have undergone some kind of brainwashing, because no one in today's world works for free'. When asked if his parishioners ever did any charitable work in the community, the Rev. Buck replied: 'Yes, but we do it in the name of Jesus.'

Yesterday evening, when she arrived at the warehouse to meet her waiting followers, Sherine Khalil, her son, and some of her friends were prevented from entering by the Rev. Buck's parishioners who were carrying placards and using megaphones to call on the rest of the neighbourhood to join them. This verbal aggression immediately degenerated into fighting, and soon it was impossible to control either side.

'They say they're fighting in the name of Jesus, but what they really want is for people to continue to ignore the teachings of Christ, according to which "we are all gods",' said the well-known actress Andrea McCain, one of Sherine Khalil or Athena's followers. Ms McCain received a cut above her right eye, which was treated at once, and she left the area before your reporter could find out more about her links with the sect.

Once order was restored, Mrs Khalil was anxious to reassure her 5-year-old son, but she did tell us that all that takes place in the warehouse is some collective dancing, followed by the invocation of a being known as Hagia Sofia, of whom people are free to ask questions. The celebration ends with a kind of sermon and a group prayer to the Great Mother. The officer charged with investigating the original complaints confirmed this.

As far as we could ascertain, the group has no name and is not registered as a charity. According to the lawyer Sheldon Williams, this is not necessary: 'We live in a free country, and people can gather together in an enclosed space for non-profit-making activities, as long as these do not break any laws such as incitement to racism or the consumption of narcotics.'

Mrs Khalil emphatically rejected any suggestion that she should stop the meetings because of the disturbances.

'We gather together to offer mutual encouragement,' she said, 'because it's very hard to face social pressures alone. I demand that your newspaper denounce the religious discrimination to which we've been subjected over the centuries. Whenever we do something that is not in accord with State-instituted and State-approved religions, there is always an attempt to crush us, as happened today. Before, we would have faced martyrdom, prison, being burned at the stake or sent into exile, but now we are in a position to respond, and force will be answered with force, just as compassion will be repaid with compassion.'

When faced with the Rev. Buck's accusations, she accused him of 'manipulating his parishioners and using intolerance and lies as an excuse for violence'.

According to the sociologist Arthaud Lenox, phenomena like this will become increasingly common in the future, possibly involving more serious clashes between established religions. 'Now that the Marxist utopia has shown itself incapable of channelling society's ideals, the world is ripe for a religious revival, born of civilisation's natural fear of significant dates. However, I believe that when the year 2000 does arrive and the world survives intact, common sense will prevail and religions will revert to being a refuge for the weak, who are always in search of guidance.'

This view is contested by Dom Evaristo Piazza, the Vatican's auxiliary bishop in the United Kingdom: 'What we are seeing is not the spiritual awakening that we all long for, but a wave of what Americans call New Ageism, a kind of breeding ground in which everything is permitted, where dogmas are not respected, and the most absurd ideas from the past return to lay waste to the human mind. Unscrupulous people like this young woman are trying to instil their false ideas in weak, suggestible minds, with the one aim of making money and gaining personal power.'

The German historian Franz Herbert, currently working at the Goethe Institute in London, has a different idea: 'The established religions no longer ask fundamental questions about our identity and our reason for living. Instead, they concentrate purely on a series of dogmas and rules concerned only with fitting in with a particular social and political organisation. People in search of real spirituality are, therefore, setting off in new directions, and that inevitably means a return to the past and to primitive religions, before those religions were contaminated by the structures of power.'

At the police station where the incident was recorded, Sergeant William Morton stated that should Sherine Khalil's group decide to hold their meeting on the following Monday and feel that they are under threat, then they must apply in writing for police protection and thus avoid a repetition of last night's events.

(With additional information from Andrew Fish. Photos by Mark Guillhem)

Heron Ryan, journalist

I read the report on the plane, when I was flying back from the Ukraine, feeling full of doubts. I still hadn't managed to ascertain whether the Chernobyl disaster had been as big as it was said to have been, or whether it had been used by the major oil producers to inhibit the use of other sources of energy.

Anyway, I was horrified by what I read in the article. The photos showed broken windows, a furious Rev. Buck, and – there lay the danger – a beautiful woman with fiery eyes and her son in her arms. I saw at once what could happen, both good and bad. I went straight from the airport to Portobello, convinced that both my predictions would become reality.

On the positive side, the following Monday's meeting was one of the most successful events in the area's history: many local people came, some curious to see the 'being' mentioned in the article, others bearing placards defending freedom of religion and freedom of speech. The venue would only hold two hundred people and so the rest of the crowd were all crammed together on the pavement outside, hoping for at least a glimpse of the woman who appeared to be the priestess of the oppressed.

When she arrived, she was received with applause, handwritten notes and requests for help; some people threw flowers, and one lady of uncertain age asked her to keep on fighting for women's freedom and for the right to worship the Mother. The parishioners from the week before must have been intimidated by the crowd and so failed to turn up, despite the threats they had made during the previous days. There were no aggressive comments, and the ceremony passed off as normal, with dancing, the appearance of Hagia Sofia (by then, I knew that she was simply another facet of Athena herself), and a final celebration (this had been added recently, when the group moved to the warehouse lent by one of its original members), and that was that.

During her sermon, Athena spoke as if possessed by someone else:

'We all have a duty to love and to allow love to manifest itself in the way it thinks best. We cannot and must not be frightened when the powers of darkness want to make themselves heard, those same powers that introduced the word "sin" merely to control our hearts and minds. Jesus Christ, whom we all know, turned to the woman taken in adultery and said: "Has no man condemned thee? Neither do I condemn thee." He healed people on the Sabbath, he allowed a prostitute to wash his feet, he promised a thief that he would enjoy the delights of Paradise, he ate forbidden foods, and he said that we should concern ourselves only with today, because the lilies in the field toil not neither do they spin, but are arrayed in glory.

'What is sin? It is a sin to prevent Love from showing itself. And the Mother is love. We are entering a new world in which we can choose to follow our own steps, not those that society forces us to take. If necessary, we will confront the forces of darkness again, as we did last week. But no one will silence our voice or our heart.'

I was witnessing the transformation of a woman into an icon. She spoke with great conviction, with dignity and with faith in what she was saying. I hoped that things really were like that, that we truly were entering a new world, and that I would live to see it.

She left the warehouse to as much acclaim as she had entered it, and when she saw me in the crowd, she called me over and said that she'd missed me. She was happy and confident, sure that she was doing the right thing.

This was the positive side of the newspaper article, and things might have ended there. I wanted my analysis of events to be wrong, but three days later my prediction was confirmed. The negative side emerged in full force.

Employing the services of one of the most highly regarded and conservative law practices in Britain, whose senior partners – unlike Athena – really did have contacts in all spheres of government, and basing his case on published statements made by Athena, the Rev. Buck called a news conference to say that he was suing for defamation, calumny and moral damages.

The deputy editor called me in. He knew I was friendly with the central figure in that scandal and suggested that we publish an exclusive interview. My first reaction was of disgust: how could I use my friendship to sell newspapers?

However, after we had talked further, I started to think that it might be a good idea. She would have the chance to put her side of the story; indeed, she could use the interview to promote all the things for which she was now openly fighting. I left the deputy editor's office with the plan we had drawn up together: a series of articles on new trends in society and on radical changes that were taking place in the search for religious belief. In one of those articles, I would publish Athena's point of view.

That same afternoon, I went to her house, taking advantage of the fact that the invitation had come from her when we met outside the warehouse. The neighbours told me that, the day before, court officials had attempted to serve a summons on her, but failed.

I phoned later on, without success. I tried again as night was falling, but no one answered. From then on, I phoned every half an hour, growing more anxious with each call. Ever since Hagia Sofia had cured my insomnia, tiredness drove me to bed at eleven o'clock, but this time anxiety kept me awake.

I found her mother's number in the phone book, but it was late, and if Athena wasn't there, then I would only cause the whole family to worry. What to do? I turned on the TV to see if anything had happened – nothing special, London continued as before, with its marvels and its perils.

I decided to try one last time. The phone rang three times, and someone answered. I recognised Andrea's voice at once.

'What do you want?' she asked.

'Athena asked me to get in touch. Is everything all right?'

'Everything's all right and not all right, depending on your way of looking at things. But I think you might be able to help.'

'Where is she?'

She hung up without saying any more.

Deidre O'Neill, known as Edda

Athena stayed in a hotel near my house. News from London regarding local events, especially minor conflicts in the suburbs, never reaches Scotland. We're not much interested in how the English sort out their little problems. We have our own flag, our own football team, and soon we will have our own parliament.

I let Athena rest for a whole day. The following morning, instead of going into the little temple and performing the rituals I know, I decided to take her and her son to a wood near Edinburgh. There, while the boy played and ran about among the trees, she told me in detail what was going on.

When she'd finished, I said:

'It's daylight, the sky is cloudy, and human beings believe that beyond the clouds lives an all-powerful God, guiding the fate of men. Meanwhile, look at your son, look at your feet, listen to the sounds around you: down here is the Mother, so much closer, bringing joy to children and energy to those who walk over Her body. Why do people prefer to believe in something far away and forget what is there before their eyes, a true manifestation of the miracle?'

'I know the answer. Because up there someone is

guiding us and giving his orders, hidden behind the clouds, unquestionable in his wisdom. Down here, we have physical contact with a magical reality, and the freedom to choose where our steps will go.'

'Exactly. But do you think that is what people want? Do they want the freedom to choose their own steps?'

'Yes, I think they do. The earth I'm standing on now has laid out many strange paths for me, from a village in Transylvania to a city in the Middle East, from there to another city on an island, and then to the desert and back to Transylvania. From a suburban bank to a real estate company in the Persian Gulf. From a dance group to a bedouin. And whenever my feet drove me onwards, I said "Yes" instead of saying "No".'

'What did you gain from all that?'

'Today I can see people's auras. I can awaken the Mother in my soul. My life now has meaning, and I know what I'm fighting for. But why do you ask? You, too, gained the most important power of all – the gift of healing. Andrea can now prophesy and converse with spirits. I've followed her spiritual development every step of the way.'

'What else have you gained?'

'The joy of being alive. I know that I'm here, and that everything is a miracle, a revelation.'

The little boy fell over and grazed his knee. Instinctively, Athena ran to him, wiped the wound clean, told him not to worry, and the boy continued running about in the forest. I used that as a signal.

'What just happened to your little boy, happened to me. And it's happening to you too, isn't it?'

'Yes, but I don't think I stumbled and fell. I think I'm being tested again, and that my next step will be revealed to me.'

At such moments, a teacher must say nothing, only bless the disciple. Because, however much the teacher may want to save her disciple from suffering, the paths are mapped out and the disciple's feet are eager to follow them. I suggested we go back to the wood that night, just the two of us. She asked where she could leave her son, and I said that I would take care of that. I had a neighbour who owed me a favour and who would be delighted to look after Viorel.

As evening fell, we returned to that same place, and on the way, we spoke of things that had nothing to do with the ritual we were about to perform. Athena had seen me using a new kind of depilatory wax and was intrigued to know what advantages it had over the old methods. We talked animatedly about vanity, fashion, the cheapest places to buy clothes, female behaviour, feminism, hairstyles. At one point she said something along the lines of: 'But if the soul is ageless, I don't know why we should be so worried about all this,' then realised that it was all right just to relax and talk about superficial subjects. More than that, such conversations were really fun, and how we look is something that's still very important in women's lives (it is in men's lives too, but in a different way, and they're not as open about it as we are).

As we approached the place I'd chosen – or, rather, which the wood was choosing for me – I started to feel the presence of the Mother. In my case, this presence manifests itself in a certain, mysterious inner joy that always touches me and almost moves me to tears. It was the moment to stop and change the subject.

'Collect some wood for kindling,' I said.

'But it's dark.'

'There's enough light from the full moon even if it's obscured by clouds. Train your eyes: they were made to see more than you think.'

She began doing as I asked, occasionally cursing because she'd scratched herself on a thorn. Almost half an hour passed, and during that time we didn't talk. I felt the excitement of knowing that the Mother was close by, the euphoria of being there with that woman who still seemed little more than a child and who trusted me and was keeping me company in that search which sometimes seemed too mad for the human mind.

Athena was still at the stage of answering questions, just as she'd responded to mine that afternoon. I had been like that once, until I allowed myself to be transported completely into the kingdom of mystery, where it was simply a matter of contemplating, celebrating, worshipping, praising and allowing the gift to manifest itself.

I was watching Athena collecting firewood and I saw the girl I once was, in search of veiled secrets and secret powers. Life had taught me something completely different: the powers were not secret and the secrets had been revealed a long time ago. When I saw that she had gathered enough firewood, I indicated that she should stop.

I myself looked for some larger branches and put them on top of the kindling. So it was in life. In order for the more substantial pieces of wood to catch fire, the kindling must burn first. In order for us to liberate the energy of our strength, our weakness must first have a chance to reveal itself.

In order for us to understand the powers we carry within us and the secrets that have already been revealed, it was first necessary to allow the surface – expectations, fears, appearances – to be burned away. We were entering the peace now settling upon the forest, with the gentle wind, the moonlight behind the clouds, the noises of the animals that sally forth at night to hunt, thus fulfilling the cycle of birth and death of the Mother, and without ever being criticised for following their instincts and their nature.

I lit the fire.

Neither of us felt like saying anything. For what seemed like an eternity, we merely contemplated the dance of the fire, knowing that hundreds of thousands of people, all over the world, would also be sitting by their fireside, regardless of whether they had modern heating systems in their house or not; they did this because they were sitting before a symbol.

It took a great effort to emerge from that trance, which, although it meant nothing specific to me, and did not make me see gods, auras or ghosts, nonetheless left me in the state of grace I needed to be in. I focused once more on the present, on the young woman by my side, on the ritual I needed to perform.

'How is your student?' I asked.

'Difficult, but if she wasn't, I might not learn what I need to learn.'

'And what powers is she developing?'

'She speaks with beings in the parallel world.'

'As you converse with Hagia Sofia?'

'No. As you well know, Hagia Sofia is the Mother manifesting herself in me. She speaks with invisible beings.'

I knew this, but I wanted to be sure. Athena was more silent than usual. I don't know if she had discussed the events in London with Andrea, but that didn't matter. I got up, opened the bag I had with me, took out a handful of specially chosen herbs and threw them into the flames.

'The wood has started to speak,' said Athena, as if this were something perfectly normal, and that was good, it meant that miracles were now becoming part of her life.

'What is it saying?'

'Nothing at the moment, only noises.'

Minutes later, she heard a song coming from the fire.

'Oh, it's wonderful!'

There spoke the little girl, not the wife or mother.

'Stay just as you are. Don't try to concentrate or follow my steps or understand what I'm saying. Relax and feel good. That is sometimes all we can hope for from life.'

I knelt down, picked up a red-hot piece of wood and drew a circle around her, leaving a small opening through which I could enter. I could hear the same music as Athena, and I danced around her, invoking the union of the male fire with the earth, which received it now with arms and legs spread wide, the fire that purified everything, transforming into energy the strength contained in the firewood, in those branches, in those beings, both human and invisible. I danced for as long as the melody from the fire lasted, and I made protective gestures to the child who was sitting, smiling, inside the circle.

When the flames had burned down, I took a little ash and sprinkled it on Athena's head. Then with my feet I erased the circle I'd drawn around her.

'Thank you,' she said. 'I felt very loved, wanted, protected.'

'In difficult moments, remember that feeling.'

'Now that I've found my path, there will be no more difficult moments. After all, I have a mission to fulfil, don't I?'

'Yes, we all have a mission to fulfil.'

She started to feel uncertain.

'And what about the difficult moments?' she asked.

'That isn't an intelligent thing to ask. Remember what you said just now: you are loved, wanted, protected.'

'I'll do my best.'

Her eyes filled with tears. Athena had understood my answer.

Samira R. Khalil, housewife

My own grandson! What has my grandson got to do with all this? What kind of world are we living in? Are we still in the Middle Ages, engaging in witch-hunts?

I ran to him. He had a bloody nose, but he didn't seem to care about my distress and pushed me away.

'I know how to defend myself, and I did.'

I may never have produced a child in my own womb, but I know the hearts of children. I was far more worried about Athena than I was about Viorel. This was just one of many fights he would have to face in his life, and there was a flicker of pride in his swollen eyes.

'Some children at school said that Mum was a devil-worshipper!'

Sherine arrived shortly afterwards, soon enough to see the boy's bloodied face and to kick up a fuss. She wanted to go straight to the school and talk to the head teacher, but first I put my arms around her. I let her cry out all her tears and all her frustrations, and the best thing I could do then was to keep silent and try to convey my love for her through that silence.

When she had calmed down a little, I explained carefully that she could come back home and live with us, that we would take care of everything. When her father read about the case being brought against her, he had immediately spoken to some lawyers. We would do everything we could to get her out of this situation regardless of comments from the neighbours, ironic looks from acquaintances, and the false solidarity of friends.

Nothing in the world was more important than my daughter's happiness, even though I'd never understood why she always had to choose the most difficult and painful of paths. But a mother doesn't have to understand anything, she simply has to love and protect. And feel proud. Knowing that we could give her almost everything, she nevertheless set off early in search of her independence. She'd had her stumbles and her failures, but she insisted on facing any storms alone. She went looking for her mother, aware of the risks she was running, and in the end, that encounter brought her closer to us. I knew she had never once heeded my advice – get a degree, get married, put up with the problems of living with someone without complaint, don't try to go beyond the limits set by society. And what had been the result?

By following my daughter's story, I became a better person. Obviously I didn't understand about the Mother Goddess or Athena's need always to surround herself with strangers, or her inability to be contented with all that she'd achieved after so much work. But deep down, even though it may be rather late in the day for such ideas, I wish I could have been like her.

I was about to get up and prepare something to eat, but she stopped me.

'I want to stay here for a while with your arms around me. That's all I need. Viorel, go and watch TV. I want to talk to your grandmother.'

The boy obeyed.

'I must have caused you a lot of suffering.'

'Not at all. On the contrary, you and your son are the source of all our joy and our reason for living.'

'But I haven't exactly –'

'I'm glad it's been the way it has. I can say it now: there were moments when I hated you, when I bitterly regretted not having followed the advice of that nurse and adopted another baby. Then I'd ask myself: "How can a mother hate her own daughter?" I took tranquillisers, played bridge with my friends, went on shopping sprees, and all to make up for the love I'd given you and which I felt I wasn't getting back.

'A few months ago, when you decided to give up yet another job that was bringing you both money and prestige, I was in despair. I went to the local church. I wanted to make a promise to the Virgin and beg her to bring you back to reality, to force you to change your life and make the most of the chances you were throwing away. I was ready to do anything in exchange for that.

'I stood looking at the Virgin and Child. And I said: "You're a mother and you know what's happening. Ask anything of me, but save my child, because I think she's bent on self-destruction."'

I felt Sherine's arms holding me tighter. She was crying again, but her tears were different this time. I was doing my best to control my feelings.

'And do you know what I felt at that moment? I felt that she was talking to me and saying: "Listen, Samira, that's what I thought too. I suffered for years because my son wouldn't listen to anything I said. I used to worry about his safety, I didn't like the friends he chose, and he showed no respect for laws, customs, religion, or his elders." Need I go on?'

'Yes, I'd like to hear the rest of the story.'

'The Virgin concluded by saying: "But my son didn't listen to me. And now I'm very glad that he didn't."'

I gently removed myself from her embrace and got up.

'You two need to eat.'

I went to the kitchen, prepared some onion soup and a dish of tabbouleh, warmed up some unleavened bread, put it all on the table, and we had lunch together. We talked about trivial things, which, at such moments, always help to bring us together and justify our pleasure at being there, quietly, even if, outside, a storm is uprooting trees and sowing destruction. Of course, at the end of that afternoon, my daughter and my grandson would walk out of the door to confront the winds, the thunder and the lightning all over again, but that was their choice.

'Mum, you said that you'd do anything for me, didn't you?'

It was true. I would lay down my life if necessary.

'Don't you think I should be prepared to do anything for Viorel too?'

'I think that's a mother's instinct, but instinct aside, it's the greatest proof of love there is.'

She continued eating.

'You know that your father is happy to help with this case being brought against you, if you want him to, that is.'

'Of course I do. This is my family we're talking about.'

I thought twice, three times, but couldn't hold back my words:

'Can I give you some advice? I know you have some influential friends, that journalist, for example. Why don't you ask him to write about your story and tell him your version of events? The press are giving a lot of coverage to that vicar, and people will end up thinking he's right.'

'So, as well as accepting what I do, you also want to help me?'

'Yes, Sherine. Even though I may not understand you, even though I sometimes suffer as the Virgin must have suffered all her life, even if you're not Jesus Christ with an all-important message for the world, I'm on your side and I want to see you win.'

Heron Ryan, journalist

Athena arrived while I was frantically making notes for what I imagined would be the ideal interview on the events in Portobello and the rebirth of the Goddess. It was a very, very delicate affair.

What I saw at the warehouse was a woman saying: 'You can do it, let the Great Mother teach you – trust in love and miracles will happen.' And the crowd agreed, but that wouldn't last long, because we were living in an age in which slavery was the only path to happiness. Free will demands immense responsibility; it's hard work, it brings with it anguish and suffering.

'I need you to write something about me,' she said.

I told her that we should wait a little – after all, the whole affair could fade from view the following week – but that, meanwhile, I'd prepared a few questions about Female Energy.

'At the moment, all the fuss and the fighting is only of interest to people in the immediate area and to the tabloids. No respectable newspaper has published a single line about it. London is full of these little local disturbances, and getting into the broadsheets really isn't advisable. It would be best if the group didn't meet for two or three weeks.

However, I think that the business about the Goddess, if treated with the seriousness it deserves, could make a lot of people ask themselves some really important questions.'

'Over supper that time, you said that you loved me. And now you're not only telling me you don't want to help me, you're asking me to give up the things I believe in.'

How to interpret those words? Was she finally accepting the love I'd offered her that night, and which accompanied me every minute of my life? According to the Lebanese poet Khalil Gibran, it was more important to give than to receive, but while these were wise words, I was part of what is known as 'humanity', with my frailties, my moments of indecision, my desire simply to live in peace, to be the slave of my feelings and to surrender myself without asking any questions, without even knowing if my love was reciprocated. All she had to do was to let me love her; I was sure that Hagia Sofia would agree with me. Athena had been passing through my life now for nearly two years, and I was afraid she might simply continue on her way and disappear over the horizon, without my having even been able to accompany her on part of that journey.

'Are you talking about love?'

'I'm asking for your help.'

What to do? Control myself, stay cool, not precipitate things and end up destroying them? Or take the step I needed to take, embrace her and protect her from all dangers?

My head kept telling me to say: 'Don't you worry about a thing. I love you,' but instead I said: 'I want to help. Please trust me. I'd do anything in the world for you, including saying "No" if I thought that was the right thing to do, even though you might not understand my reasoning.'

I told her that the deputy editor on my newspaper had proposed a series of articles about the reawakening of the Goddess, which would include an interview with her. At first, it had seemed to me an excellent idea, but now I saw that it would be best to wait a little. I said:

'You either carry your mission forward or you defend yourself. You're aware, I know, that what you're doing is more important than how you're seen by other people. Do you agree?'

'I'm thinking of my son. Every day now he gets into some fight or argument at school.'

'That will pass. In a week, it'll be forgotten. That will be the moment to act, not in order to defend yourself against idiotic attacks, but to set out, confidently and wisely, the true breadth of your work. And if you have any doubts about my feelings and are determined to continue, then I'll come with you to the next meeting. And we'll see what happens.'

* * *

The following Monday I went with her to the meeting. I was not now just another person in the crowd; I could see things as she was seeing them.

People crowded into the warehouse; there were flowers and applause, young women calling her 'the priestess of the Goddess', a few smartly dressed ladies begging for a private audience because of some illness in the family. The crowd started pushing us and blocking the entrance. We had never imagined that we might need some form of security, and I was frightened. I took her arm, picked up Viorel, and we went in.

Inside the packed room, a very angry Andrea was waiting for us.

'I think you should tell them that you're not performing any miracles today!' she shouted at Athena. 'You're allowing yourself to be seduced by vanity! Why doesn't Hagia Sofia tell all these people to go away?'

'Because she can diagnose illnesses,' replied Athena defiantly. 'And the more people who benefit from that, the better.'

She was about to say more, but the crowd was applauding and she stepped up onto the improvised stage. She turned on the small sound system she'd brought from home, gave instructions for people to dance against the rhythm of the music, and the ritual began. At a certain point, Viorel went and sat down in a corner – that was the moment for Hagia Sofia to appear. Athena did as I'd seen her do many times before: she abruptly turned off the music, clutched her head in her hands, and the people waited in silence as if obeying an invisible command.

The ritual followed its unvarying path: there were questions about love, which were rejected, although she agreed to comment on anxieties, illnesses and other personal problems. From where I was, I could see that some people had tears in their eyes, others behaved as if they were standing before a saint. Then came the moment for the closing sermon, before the group celebration of the Mother.

Since I knew what would happen next, I started thinking about the best way to get out of there with the minimum of fuss. I hoped that she would take Andrea's advice and tell them not to go looking for miracles there. I went over to where Viorel was sitting, so that we could leave the place as soon as his mother had finished speaking.

And that was when I heard the voice of Hagia Sofia.

'Today, before we close, we're going to talk about diet. Forget all about slimming regimes.'

Diet? Forget about slimming regimes?

'We have survived for all these millennia because we have been able to eat. And now that seems to have become a curse. Why? What is it that makes us, at forty years old, want to have the same body we had when we were young? Is it possible to stop time? Of course not. And why should we be thin?'

I heard a kind of murmuring in the crowd. They were probably expecting a more spiritual message.

'We don't need to be thin. We buy books, we go to gyms, we expend a lot of brain power on trying to hold back time, when we should be celebrating the miracle of being here in this world. Instead of thinking about how to live better, we're obsessed with weight.

'Forget all about that. You can read all the books you want, do all the exercise you want, punish yourself as much as you want, but you will still have only two choices – either stop living or get fat.

'Eat in moderation, but take pleasure in eating: it isn't what enters a person's mouth that's evil, but what leaves it. Remember that for millennia we have struggled in order to keep from starving. Whose idea was it that we had to be thin all our lives? I'll tell you: the vampires of the soul, those who are so afraid of the future that they think it's possible to stop the wheel of time. Hagia Sofia can guarantee that it's not possible. Use the energy and effort you put into dieting to nourish yourself with spiritual bread. Know that the Great Mother gives generously and wisely. Respect that and you will get no fatter than passing time demands. Instead of artificially burning those calories, try to transform them into the energy required to fight for your dreams. No one ever stayed slim for very long just because of a diet.'

There was complete silence. Athena began the closing ceremony, and we all celebrated the presence of the Mother. I clasped Viorel in my arms, promising myself that next time I would bring a few friends along to provide a little improvised security. We left to the same shouts and applause as when we had arrived.

A shopkeeper grabbed my arm:

'This is absurd! If one of my windows gets smashed, I'll sue you!'

Athena was laughing and giving autographs. Viorel seemed happy. I just hoped that no journalist was there that night. When we finally managed to extricate ourselves from the crowd, we hailed a taxi.

I asked if they would like to go somewhere to eat.

'Of course,' said Athena, 'that's just what I've been talking about.'

Antoine Locadour, historian

In this long series of mistakes that came to be known as 'The Witch of Portobello affair', what surprises me most is the ingenuousness of Heron Ryan, an international journalist of many years' experience. When we spoke, he was horrified by the tabloid headlines:

'The Goddess Diet!' screamed one.

'Get thin while you eat says Witch of Portobello!' roared another from its front page.

As well as touching on the sensitive topic of religion, Athena had gone further: she had talked about diet, a subject of national interest, more important even than wars, strikes or natural disasters. We may not all believe in God, but we all want to get thin.

Reporters interviewed local shopkeepers, who all swore blind that, in the days preceding the mass meetings, they'd seen red and black candles being lit during rituals involving only a handful of people. It may have been nothing but cheap sensationalism, but Ryan should have foreseen that, with a court case in progress, the accuser would take every opportunity to bring to the judges' attention what he considered to be not only a calumny, but an attack on all the values that kept society going.

That same week, one of the most prestigious British newspapers published in its editorial column an article by the Rev. Ian Buck, Minister at the Evangelical Church in Kensington. It said, amongst other things:

'As a good Christian, I have a duty to turn the other cheek when I am wrongly attacked or when my honour is impugned. However, we must not forget that while Jesus may have turned the other cheek, he also used a whip to drive out those wanting to make the Lord's House into a den of thieves. That is what we are seeing at the moment in Portobello Road: unscrupulous people who pass themselves off as savers of souls, giving false hope and promising cures for all ills, even declaring that you can stay thin and elegant if you follow their teachings.

'For this reason, I have no alternative but to go to the courts to prevent this situation continuing. The movement's followers swear that they are capable of awakening hitherto unknown gifts and they deny the existence of an All-Powerful God, replacing him with pagan divinities such as Venus and Aphrodite. For them, everything is permitted, as long as it is done with "love". But what is love? An immoral force which justifies any end? Or a commitment to society's true values, such as the family and tradition?'

***

At the next meeting, foreseeing a repetition of the pitched battle of August, the police brought in half a dozen officers to avoid any confrontations. Athena arrived accompanied by a bodyguard improvised by Ryan, and this time there was not only applause, there was booing and cursing too. One woman, seeing that Athena was accompanied by a child of five, brought a charge two days later under the Children Act 1989, alleging that the mother was inflicting irreversible damage on her child and that custody should be given to the father.

One of the tabloids managed to track down Lukás Jessen-Petersen, who refused to give an interview. He threatened the reporter, saying that if he so much as mentioned Viorel in his articles, he wouldn't be responsible for his actions.

The following day, the tabloid carried the headline: 'Witch of Portobello's ex would kill for son.'

That same afternoon, two more charges under the Children Act 1989 were brought before the courts, calling for the child to be taken into care.

There was no meeting after that. Groups of people – for and against – gathered outside the door, and uniformed officers were on hand to keep the peace, but Athena did not appear. The same thing happened the following week, only this time there were fewer crowds and fewer police.

The third week there was only the occasional bunch of flowers to be seen and someone handing out photos of Athena to passers-by.

The subject disappeared from the front pages of the London dailies. And when the Rev. Ian Buck announced his decision to withdraw all charges of defamation and calumny, 'in the Christian spirit we should show to those who repent of their actions', no major paper was interested in publishing his statement, which turned up instead on the readers' pages of some local rag.

As far as I know, it never became national news, but was restricted to the pages that dealt only with London news. I visited Brighton a month after the meetings ended, and when I tried to bring the subject up with my friends there, none of them had the faintest idea what I was talking about.

Ryan could have cleared up the whole business, and what his newspaper said would have been picked up by the rest of the media. To my surprise, though, he never published a line about Sherine Khalil.

In my view, the crime – given its nature – had nothing to do with what happened in Portobello. It was all just a macabre coincidence.

Heron Ryan, journalist

Athena asked me to turn on the tape-recorder. She had brought another one with her, of a type I'd never seen before – very sophisticated and very small.

'Firstly, I wish to state that I've been receiving death threats. Secondly, I want you to promise that, even if I die, you will wait five years before you allow anyone else to listen to this tape. In the future, people will be able to tell what is true and what is false. Say you agree; that way you will be entering a legally binding agreement.'

'I agree, but I think –'

'Don't think anything. Should I be found dead, this will be my testament, on condition that it won't be published now.'

I turned off the tape-recorder.

'You have nothing to fear. I have friends in government, people who owe me favours, who need or will need me. We can –'

'Have I mentioned before that my boyfriend works for Scotland Yard?'

Not that again. If he really did exist, why wasn't he there when we needed him, when both Athena and Viorel could have been attacked by the mob?

Questions crowded into my mind: Was she trying to test me? What was going through that woman's mind? Was she unbalanced, fickle, one hour wanting to be by my side, the next talking about this non-existent man?

'Turn on the tape-recorder,' she said.

I felt terrible. I was beginning to think that she'd been using me all along. I would like to have been able to say: 'Go away. Get out of my life. Ever since I first met you, everything has been a hell. All I want is for you to come here, put your arms around me and kiss me and say you want to stay with me forever, but that never happens.'

'Is there anything wrong?'

She knew there was something wrong. Or, rather, she couldn't possibly not have known what I was feeling, because I had never concealed my love for her, even though I'd only spoken openly of it once. But I would cancel any appointment to see her; I was always there when she needed me; I was trying to build some kind of relationship with her son, in the belief that he would one day call me 'Dad'. I never asked her to stop what she was doing; I accepted her way of life, her decisions; I suffered in silence when she suffered; I was glad when she triumphed; I was proud of her determination.

'Why did you turn off the tape-recorder?'

I hovered for a second between heaven and hell, between rebellion and submission, between cold reason and destructive emotion. In the end, summoning up all my strength, I managed to control myself. I pressed the button.

'Let's continue.'

'As I was saying, I've been receiving death threats. I've been getting anonymous phone calls. They insult me and say I'm a menace, that I'm trying to restore the reign of Satan, and that they can't allow this to happen.'

'Have you spoken to the police?'

I deliberately omitted any reference to her boyfriend, showing that I'd never believed that story anyway.

'Yes, I have. They've recorded the calls. They come from public phone boxes, but the police told me not to worry, that they're watching my house. They've arrested one person: he's mentally ill and believes he's the reincarnation of one of the apostles, and that "this time, he must fight so that Christ is not driven out again". He's in a psychiatric hospital now. The police explained that he's been in hospital before for making similar threats to other people.'

'If they're on the case, there's no need to worry. Our police are the best in the world.'

'I'm not afraid of death. If I were to die today, I would carry with me moments that few people my age have had the chance to experience. What I'm afraid of, and this is why I've asked you to record our conversation today, is that I might kill someone.'

'Kill someone?'

'You know that there are legal proceedings underway to remove Viorel from me. I've asked friends, but no one can do anything. We just have to await the verdict. According to them – depending on the judge, of course – these fanatics will get what they want. That's why I've bought a gun. I know what it means for a child to be removed from his mother, because I've experienced it myself. And so, when the first bailiff arrives, I'll shoot, and I'll keep shooting until the bullets run out. If they don't shoot me first, I'll use the knives in my house. If they take the knives, I'll use my teeth and my nails. But no one is going to take Viorel from me, or only over my dead body. Are you recording this?'

'I am. But there are ways –'

'There aren't. My father is following the case. He says that when it comes to family law, there's little that can be done. Now turn off the tape-recorder.'

'Was that your testament?'

She didn't answer. When I did nothing, she took the initiative. She went over to the sound system and put on that music from the steppes, which I now knew almost by heart. She danced as she did during the rituals, completely out of rhythm, and I knew what she was trying to do. Her tape-recorder was still on, a silent witness to everything that was happening there. The afternoon sunlight was pouring in through the windows, but Athena was off in search of another light, one that had been there since the creation of the world.

When she felt the spark from the Mother she stopped dancing, turned off the music, put her head in her hands and didn't move for some time. Then she raised her head and looked at me.

'You know who is here, don't you?'

'Yes. Athena and her divine side, Hagia Sofia.'

'I've grown used to doing this. I don't think it's necessary, but it's the method I've discovered for getting in touch with her, and now it's become a tradition in my life. You know who you're talking to, don't you? To Athena. I am Hagia Sofia.'

'Yes, I know. The second time I danced at your house, I discovered that I had a spirit guide too: Philemon. But I don't talk to him very much, I don't listen to what he says. I only know that when he's present, it's as if our two souls have finally met.'

'That's right. And today Philemon and Hagia Sofia are going to talk about love.'

'Should I dance first?'

'There's no need. Philemon will understand me, because I can see that you were touched by my dance. The man before me suffers for something which he believes he has never received – my love. But the man beyond your self understands that all the pain, anxiety and feelings of abandonment are unnecessary and childish. I love you. Not in the way that your human side wants, but in the way that the divine spark wants. We inhabit the same tent, which was placed on our path by Her. There we understand that we are not the slaves of our feelings, but their masters. We serve and are served, we open the doors of our rooms and we embrace. Perhaps we kiss too, because everything that happens very intensely on Earth will have its counterpart on the invisible plane. And you know that I'm not trying to provoke you, that I'm not toying with your feelings when I say that.'

'What is love, then?'

'The soul, blood and body of the Great Mother. I love you as exiled souls love each other when they meet in the middle of the desert. There will never be anything physical between us, but no passion is in vain, no love is ever wasted. If the Mother awoke that love in your heart, she awoke it in mine too, although your heart perhaps accepts it more readily. The energy of love can never be lost – it is more powerful than anything and shows itself in many ways.'

'I'm not strong enough for this. Such abstractions only leave me feeling more depressed and alone than ever.'

'I'm not strong enough either. I need someone by my side too. But one day, our eyes will open, the different forms of Love will be made manifest, and then suffering will disappear from the face of the Earth. It won't be long now, I think. Many of us are returning from a long journey during which we were forced to search for things that were of no interest to us. Now we realise that they were false. But this return cannot be made without pain, because we have been away for a long time and feel that we are strangers in our own land. It will take some time to find the friends who also left, and the places where our roots and our treasures lie. But this will happen.'

For some reason, what she said touched me. And that drove me on.

'I want to continue talking about love,' I said.

'We are talking. That has always been the aim of everything I've looked for in my life – allowing love to manifest itself in me without barriers, letting it fill up my blank spaces, making me dance, smile, justify my life, protect my son, get in touch with the heavens, with men and women, with all those who were placed on my path. I tried to control my feelings, saying such things as "he deserves my love" or "he doesn't". Until, that is, I understood my fate, when I saw that I might lose the most important thing in my life.'

'Your son.'

'Exactly. He is the most complete manifestation of love. When the possibility arose that he might be taken away from me, then I found myself and realised that I could never have anything or lose anything. I understood this after crying for many hours. It was only after intense suffering that the part of me I call Hagia Sofia said: "What nonsense! Love always stays, even though, sooner or later, your son will leave."'

I was beginning to understand.

'Love is not a habit, a commitment, or a debt. It isn't what romantic songs tell us it is – love simply is. That is the testament of Athena or Sherine or Hagia Sofia – love is. No definitions. Love and don't ask too many questions. Just love.'

'That's difficult.'

'Are you recording?'

'You asked me to turn the machine off.'

'Well, turn it on again.'

I did as she asked. Athena went on:

'It's difficult for me too. That's why I'm not going back home. I'm going into hiding. The police might protect me from madmen, but not from human justice. I had a mission to fulfil and it took me so far that I even risked the custody of my son. Not that I regret it. I fulfilled my destiny.'

'What was your mission?'

'You know what it was. You were there from the start. Preparing the way for the Mother. Continuing a tradition that has been suppressed for centuries, but which is now beginning to experience a resurgence.'

'Perhaps ...'

I stopped, but she didn't say a word until I'd finished my sentence.

'... perhaps you came too early, and people aren't yet ready.'

Athena laughed.

'Of course they're not. That's why there were all those confrontations, all that aggression and obscurantism. Because the forces of darkness are dying, and they are thrown back on such things as a last resort. They seem very strong, as animals do before they die, but afterwards they're too exhausted to get to their feet. I sowed the seed in many hearts, and each one will reveal the Renaissance in its own way, but one of those hearts will follow the full Tradition – Andrea.'

Andrea.

Who hated her, who blamed her for the collapse of our relationship, who said to anyone who would listen that Athena had been taken over by egotism and vanity, and had destroyed something that had been very hard to create.

Athena got to her feet and picked up her bag – Hagia Sofia was still with her.

'I can see your aura. It's being healed of some needless suffering.'

'You know, of course, that Andrea doesn't like you.'

'Naturally. But we've been speaking for nearly half an hour about love. Liking has nothing to do with it. Andrea is perfectly capable of fulfilling her mission. She has more experience and more charisma than I do. She learned from my mistakes; she knows that she must be prudent because in an age in which the wild beast of obscurantism is dying, there's bound to be conflict. Andrea may hate me as a person, and that may be why she's developed her gifts so quickly – to prove that she was more able than me. When hatred makes a person grow, it's transformed into one of the many ways of loving.'

She picked up her tape-recorder, put it in her bag and left.

At the end of that week, the court gave its verdict: various witnesses were heard, and Sherine Khalil, known as Athena, was given the right to keep custody of her child.

Moreover, the head teacher at the boy's school was officially warned that any kind of discrimination against the boy would be punishable by law.

I knew there was no point in ringing the apartment where she used to live. She'd left the key with Andrea, taken her sound system, some clothes, and said that she would be gone for some time.

I waited for the telephone call to invite me to celebrate that victory together. With each day that passed, my love for Athena ceased being a source of suffering and became a lake of joy and serenity. I no longer felt so alone. At some point in space, our souls – and the souls of all those returning exiles – were joyfully celebrating their reunion.

The first week passed, and I assumed she was trying to recover from the recent tensions. A month later, I assumed she must have gone back to Dubai and taken up her old job; I telephoned and was told that they'd heard nothing more from her, but if I knew where she was, could I please give her a message: the door was always open, and she was greatly missed.

I decided to write a series of articles on the reawakening of the Mother, which provoked a number of offensive letters accusing me of 'promoting paganism', but which were otherwise a great success with our readership.

Two months later, when I was just about to have lunch, a colleague at work phoned me. The body of Sherine Khalil, the Witch of Portobello, had been found in Hampstead. She had been brutally murdered.

Now that I've finished transcribing all the taped interviews, I'm going to give her the transcript. She's probably gone for a walk in the Snowdonia National Park as she does every afternoon. It's her birthday – or, rather, the date that her parents chose for her birthday when they adopted her – and this is my present to her.

Viorel, who will be coming to the celebration with his grandparents, has also prepared a surprise for her. He's recorded his first composition in a friend's studio and he's going to play it during supper.

She'll ask me afterwards: 'Why did you do this?'

And I'll say: 'Because I needed to understand you.' During all the years we've been together, I've only heard what I thought were legends about her, but now I know that the legends are true.

Whenever I suggested going with her, be it to the Monday evening celebrations at her apartment, to Romania, or to get-togethers with friends, she always asked me not to. She wanted to be free, and people, she said, find policemen intimidating. Faced by someone like me, even the innocent feel guilty.

However, I went to the Portobello warehouse twice without her knowledge. Again without her knowledge, I arranged for various colleagues to be around to protect her when she arrived and left, and at least one person, later identified as a militant member of some sect, was arrested for carrying a knife. He said he'd been told by spirits to acquire a little blood from the Witch of Portobello, who was a manifestation of the Great Mother. The blood, he said, was needed to consecrate certain offerings. He didn't intend to kill her; he merely wanted a little blood on a handkerchief. The investigation showed that there really was no intention to murder, but nevertheless, he was charged and sentenced to six months in prison.

It wasn't my idea to make it look as if she'd been murdered. Athena wanted to disappear and asked me if that would be possible. I explained that, if the courts decided that the State should have custody of her child, I couldn't go against the law, but when the judge found in her favour, we were free to carry out her plan.

Athena was fully aware that once the meetings at the warehouse became the focus of local gossip, her mission would be ruined for good. There was no point standing up in front of the crowd and denying that she was a queen, a witch, a divine manifestation, because people choose to follow the powerful and they give power to whomever they wish. And that would go against everything she preached – freedom to choose, to consecrate your own bread, to awaken your particular gifts, with no help from guides or shepherds.

Nor was there any point in disappearing. People would interpret such a gesture as a retreat into the wilderness, an ascent into the heavens, a secret pilgrimage to meet teachers in the Himalayas, and they would always be awaiting her return. Legends and possibly a cult could grow up around her. We started to notice this when she stopped going to Portobello. My informants said that, contrary to everyone's expectations, her cult was growing with frightening speed: other similar groups were being created, people turned up claiming to be the 'heirs' of Hagia Sofia, the newspaper photograph of her holding Viorel was being sold on the black market, depicting her as a victim, a martyr to intolerance. Occultists started talking about an 'Order of Athena', through which – upon payment – one could be put in touch with the founder.

All that remained was 'death', but the death had to take place in completely normal circumstances, like the death of any other person murdered in a big city. This obliged us to take certain precautions:

(a) The crime could not in any way be associated with martyrdom for religious reasons, because, if it was, we would only aggravate the very situation we were trying to avoid.

(b) The victim would have to be so badly disfigured as to be unrecognisable.

(c) The murderer could not be arrested.

(d) We would need a corpse.

In a city like London, dead, disfigured, burned bodies turn up every day, but normally we find the culprit. So we had to wait nearly two months until the Hampstead murder. We found a murderer too, who was also conveniently dead – he had fled to Portugal and committed suicide by blowing his brains out. Justice had been done, and all I needed was a little cooperation from my closest friends. One hand washes the other: they sometimes asked me to do things that were not entirely orthodox, and as long as no major law was broken, there was – shall we say – a certain degree of flexibility in interpreting the facts.

That is what happened. As soon as the body was found, I and a colleague of many years' standing were given the case and, almost simultaneously, we got news that the Portuguese police had found the body of a suicide in Guimarães, along with a note confessing to a murder whose details fitted the case we were dealing with, and giving instructions for all his money to be donated to charitable institutions. It had been a crime of passion – love often ends like that.

In the note he left behind, the dead man said that he'd brought the woman from one of the ex-Soviet republics and done everything he could to help her. He was prepared to marry her so that she would have the same rights as a British citizen, and then he'd found a letter she was about to send to some German man, who had invited her to spend a few days at his castle.

In the letter, she said she couldn't wait to leave and asked the German to send her a plane ticket at once so that they could meet again as soon as possible. They had met in a London café and had only exchanged two letters.

We had the perfect scenario.

My friend hesitated – no one likes to have an unsolved crime on their files – but when I said that I'd take the blame for this, he agreed.

I went to the place where Athena was in hiding – a delightful house in Oxford. I used a syringe to take some of her blood. I cut off a lock of her hair and singed it slightly. Back at the scene of the crime, I scattered this 'evidence' around. I knew that since no one knew the identity of her real mother and father, no DNA identification would be possible, and so all I needed was to cross my fingers and hope the murder didn't get too much coverage in the press.

A few journalists turned up. I told them the story of the murderer's suicide, mentioning only the country, not the town. I said that no motive had been found for the crime, but that we had completely discounted any idea that it was a revenge killing or that there had been some religious motive. As I understood it (after all, the police can make mistakes too), the victim had been raped. She had presumably recognised her attacker, who had then killed and mutilated her.

If the German ever wrote again, his letters would have been sent back marked 'Return to sender'. Athena's photograph had appeared only once in the newspapers, during the first demonstration in Portobello, and so the chances of her being recognised were minimal. Apart from me, only three people know this story – her parents and her son. They all attended the burial of 'her' remains and the gravestone bears her name.

Her son goes to see her every weekend and is doing brilliantly at school.

Of course, Athena may one day tire of this isolated life and decide to return to London. Nevertheless, people have very short memories, and apart from her closest friends, no one will remember her. By then, Andrea will be the catalyst and – to be fair – she is better able than Athena to continue the mission. As well as having all the necessary gifts, she's an actress and knows how to deal with the public.

I understand that Andrea's work is spreading, although without attracting unwanted attention. I hear about people in key positions in society who are in contact with her and, when necessary, when the right critical mass is reached, they will put an end to the hypocrisy of the Rev. Ian Bucks of this world.

And that's what Athena wants, not fame for herself, as many (including Andrea) thought, but that the mission should be completed.

At the start of my investigations, of which this transcript is the result, I thought I was reconstructing her life so that she would see how brave and important she had been. But as the conversations went on, I gradually discovered my own hidden side, even though I don't much believe in these things. And I reached the conclusion that the real reason behind all this work was a desire to answer a question to which I'd never known the answer: why did Athena love me, when we're so different and when we don't even share the same world view?

I remember when I kissed her for the first time, in a bar near Victoria Station. She was working for a bank at the time, and I was a detective at Scotland Yard. After we'd been out together a few times, she invited me to go and dance at her landlord's apartment, but I never did – it's not really my style.

And instead of getting annoyed, she said that she respected my decision. When I re-read the statements made by her friends, I feel really proud, because Athena doesn't seem to have respected anyone else's decisions.

Months later, before she set off to Dubai, I told her that I loved her. She said that she felt the same way, but added that we must be prepared to spend long periods apart. Each of us would work in a different country, but true love could withstand such a separation.

That was the only time I dared to ask her: 'Why do you love me?'

She replied: 'I don't know and I don't care.'

Now, as I put the finishing touches to these pages, I believe I may have found the answer in her last conversation with the journalist.

Love simply is.

25 February 2006 19:47:00

Revised version completed on St Expeditus' Day, 2006

Life is a
journey

Make sure you don't miss a thing.
Live it with Paulo Coelho.

Visit /paulocoelho

How can you find your heart's desire?

A world-wide phenomenon; an inspiration for anyone seeking their path in life.

The Alchemist

Do you believe in yourself?

A modern-day adventure in the searing heat of the Mojave desert and an exploration of fear and self-doubt.

The Valkyries

How do we see the amazing in the everyday?

When two young lovers are reunited, they discover anew the truth of what lies in their hearts.

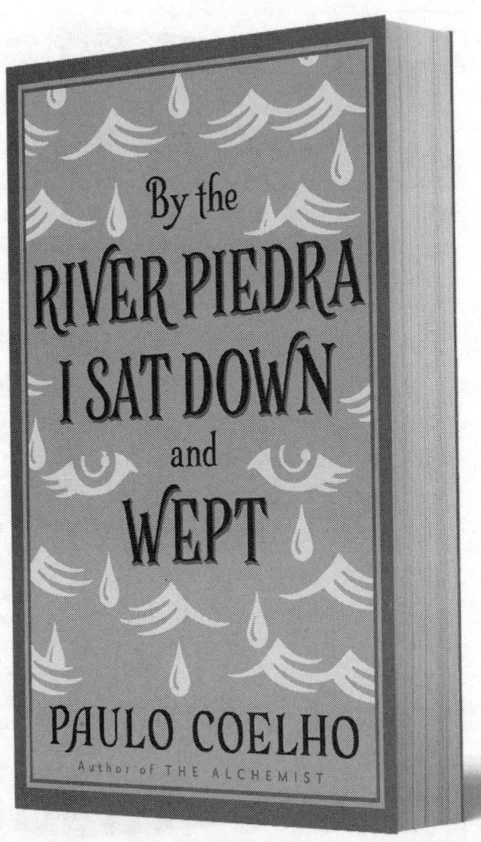

By the River Piedra I Sat Down & Wept

What are you searching for?

A transforming journey on the pilgrims' road to Santiago – and the first of Paulo's extraordinary books.

The Pilgrimage

Can faith triumph over suffering?

Paulo Coelho's brilliant telling of the story of Elijah, who was forced to choose between love and duty.

The Fifth Mountain

Is life always worth living?

A fundamental moral question explored as only Paulo Coelho can.

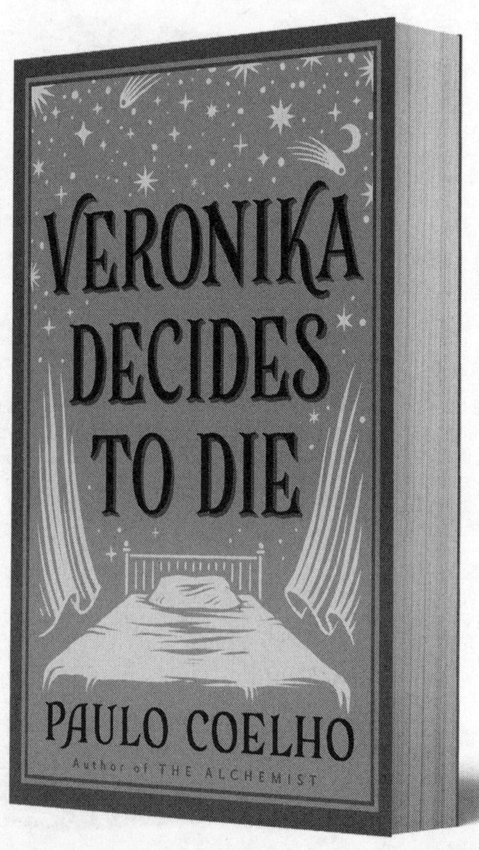

Veronika Decides to Die

Could you be tempted into evil?

The inhabitants of a small town are challenged by a mysterious stranger to choose between good and evil.

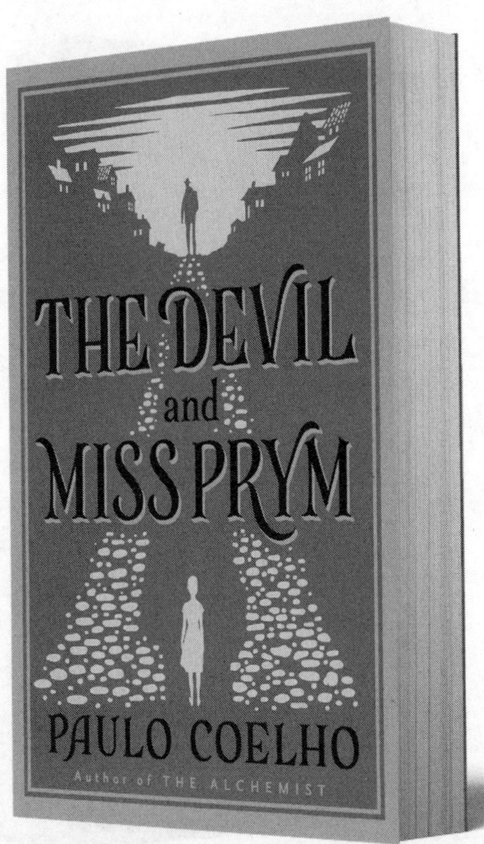

The Devil & Miss Prym

Are you brave enough to live your dream?

Strategies and inspiration to help you follow your own path in a troubled world.

Manual of the Warrior of Light

Can sex be sacred?

An unflinching exploration of the lengths we go to in our search for love, sex and spirituality.

Eleven Minutes

How far would you go for your obsession?

A sweeping story of love, loss and longing that spans the world.

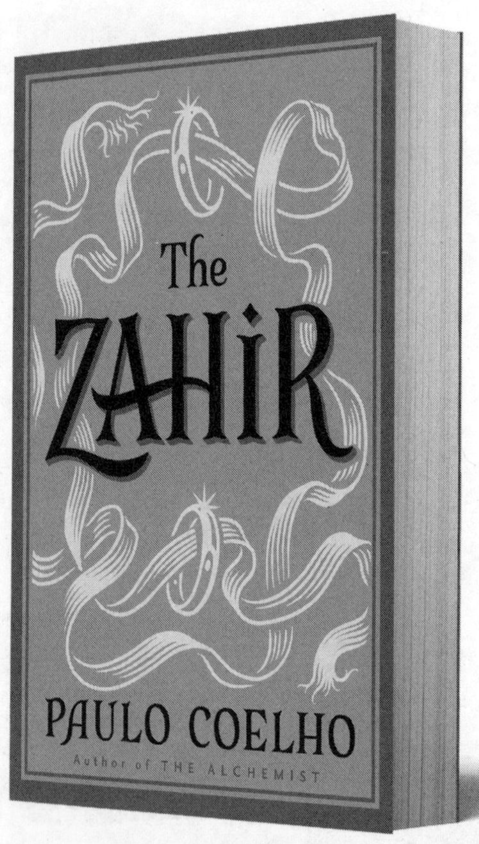

The Zahir

What happens when obsession turns to murder?

An enthralling story of jealousy, death and suspense.

The Winner Stands Alone

How will you know who your soulmate is?

A moving tale of passion, mystery and spirituality.

Brida

What does it mean to be truly alive?

Powerful tales of living and dying, destiny and choice, and love lost and found.

Like the Flowing River

Are you where you want to be?

Read *Aleph*. And rewrite your life.

Aleph

Is there a weapon more powerful than words?

A timeless and powerful exploration of
personal growth, everyday wisdom and joy.

Manuscript Found in Accra

THE DEVIL
and
MISS PRYM

Paulo Coelho was born in Brazil and has become one of the most widely read and loved authors in the world. Especially renowned for *The Alchemist* and *Eleven Minutes*, he has sold more than 320 million books worldwide and has been translated into 88 languages. The recipient of numerous prestigious international awards, amongst them the Crystal Award by the World Economic Forum and France's Légion d'Honneur, Paulo Coelho was inducted into the Brazilian Academy of Letters in 2002.

Also by Paulo Coelho

The Alchemist
The Pilgrimage
The Valkyries
By the River Piedra I Sat Down and Wept
The Fifth Mountain
Veronika Decides to Die
Manual of the Warrior of Light
Eleven Minutes
The Zahir
The Devil and Miss Prym
The Witch of Portobello
Brida
The Winner Stands Alone
Like the Flowing River
Aleph
Manuscript Found in Accra
Adultery
The Spy
Hippie

THE DEVIL and MISS PRYM

PAULO COELHO

Author of THE ALCHEMIST

TRANSLATED BY AMANDA HOPKINSON
AND NICK CAISTOR

Thorsons

Thorsons
An imprint of HarperCollins*Publishers*
1 London Bridge Street
London SE1 9GF

HarperCollins*Publishers*
1st Floor, Watermarque Building, Ringsend Road
Dublin 4, Ireland

www.harpercollins.co.uk
www.paulocoelho.com
www.paulocoelhoblog.com

First published in English by HarperCollins*Publishers* 2001
This edition published 2021

2 4 6 8 10 9 7 5 3 1

© Paulo Coelho 2000

English translation © Amanda Hopkinson and Nick Caistor

Paulo Coelho asserts the moral right to
be identified as the author of this work

A catalogue record for this book is
available from the British Library

ISBN 978-0-00-854726-4

FICTION / PHILOSOPHY

Printed and bound in India by Thomson Press India Ltd

All the characters in this book are fictitious, and
any resemblance to actual persons, living or
dead, is purely coincidental.

All rights reserved. No part of this publication may be
reproduced, stored in a retrieval system, or transmitted,
in any form or by any means, electronic, mechanical,
photocopying, recording or otherwise, without the prior
written permission of the publishers.

This book is produced from independently certified FSC® paper
to ensure responsible forest management.

O Mary!
conceived without sin,
pray for us who turn to you!
Amen.

And a certain ruler asked him, saying,
'Good Master, what shall I do to inherit eternal life?'
And Jesus said unto him, 'Why callest thou me good?
None is good, save one, that is God.'

Luke 18: 18–19

Author's note

The first story about division comes from ancient Persia: the god of time, having created the universe, sees harmony all around him, but feels that there is still something very important missing – a companion with whom to share all this beauty.

For a thousand years, he prays for a son. The story does not say to whom he prays, given that he is omnipotent, the sole, supreme lord; nevertheless, he prays and, finally, he becomes pregnant.

When he realises he has achieved his heart's desire, the god of time is filled with remorse, suddenly conscious of how fragile the balance of things is. But it is too late and the child is already on its way. All he achieves by his lamentations is to cause the son he is carrying in his belly to divide into two.

The legend recounts that just as Good (Ormuzd) is born out of the god of time's prayers, so Evil (Ahriman) is born out of his remorse – twin brothers.

The concerned father arranges everything so that Ormuzd will emerge first from his belly, to take charge of his brother and to prevent Ahriman from throwing the universe into confusion. However, Evil – being very intelligent and resourceful – manages to push Ormuzd aside at the moment of their birth, and thus is the first to see the light of the stars.

Distraught, the god of time resolves to forge alliances on Ormuzd's behalf: he brings into being the human race so that they can fight alongside Ormuzd and stop Ahriman taking control of everything.

In the Persian legend, the human race is born to be the ally of Good, and, according to tradition, Good will triumph in the end. However, many centuries later, another story about division emerges, this time presenting the opposite view: man as the instrument of Evil.

I imagine that most people will know which story I mean. A man and a woman are in the Garden of Eden, enjoying every imaginable delight. But one thing is forbidden: the couple can never know the meaning of Good and Evil. The Lord God says (Genesis 2: 17): '*But of the tree of the knowledge of Good and Evil, thou shalt not eat of it ...*'.

And one fine day the serpent appears, swearing that this knowledge is more important than paradise itself and that they should possess that knowledge. The woman refuses, saying that God has threatened her with death, but the serpent assures her that nothing of the kind will happen but quite the contrary, for on the day when they learn what Good and Evil are, they will become God's equals.

Convinced, Eve eats of the forbidden fruit and gives some of it to Adam. From this moment on, the original balance of paradise is destroyed, and the pair are driven out of paradise and cursed. Yet there remain some enigmatic words spoken by God and which confirm what the serpent said: '*Behold, the man is become as one of us, to know Good and Evil ...*'.

Here, too (as with the god of time who prays for something even though he himself is the lord of the universe), the Bible fails to explain to whom the one God is speaking, and – assuming he is unique – why he should use the expression '*one of us*'.

Whatever the answer, it is clear that from its very inception the human race has been condemned to exist within the eternal division, always moving between those two opposing poles. So here we are, afflicted by the same doubts as our ancestors. The aim of this book is to tackle this theme, occasionally interpolating into the plot other legends on the subject drawn from the four corners of the earth.

The Devil and Miss Prym concludes the trilogy *And on the Seventh Day*. The first two books were: *By the River Piedra I Sat Down and Wept* (1994) and *Veronika Decides to Die* (1998). Each of the three books is concerned with a week in the life of ordinary people, all of who find themselves suddenly confronted by love, death and power. I have always believed that in the lives of individuals, just as in society at large, the profoundest changes take place within a very reduced time frame. When we least expect it, life sets us a challenge to test our courage and willingness to change; at such a moment, there is no point in pretending that nothing has happened or in saying that we are not yet ready.

The challenge will not wait. Life does not look back. A week is more than enough time for us to decide whether or not to accept our destiny.

Buenos Aires, August 2000

For almost fifteen years, old Berta had spent every day sitting outside her front door. The people of Viscos knew that this was normal behaviour amongst old people: they sit dreaming of the past and of their youth; they look out at a world in which they no longer play a part and try to find something to talk to the neighbours about.

Berta, however, had a reason for being there. And that morning her waiting came to an end when she saw the stranger climbing the steep hill up to the village, heading for its one hotel. He did not look as she had so often imagined he would: his clothes were shabby, he wore his hair unfashionably long, he was unshaven.

And he was accompanied by the Devil.

'My husband's right,' she said to herself. 'If I hadn't been here, no one would have noticed.'

She was hopeless at telling people's ages and put the man's somewhere between forty and fifty. 'A youngster,' she thought, using a scale of values that only old people understand. She wondered how long he would be staying, but reached no conclusion; it might be only a short time, since all he had with him was a small rucksack. He would probably just stay one night before moving on to a fate about which she knew nothing and cared even less.

Even so, all the years she had spent sitting by her front door waiting for his arrival had not been in vain, because they had taught her the beauty of the mountains, something she had never really noticed before, simply because she had been born in that place and had always tended to take the landscape for granted.

As expected, the stranger went into the hotel. Berta wondered if she should go and warn the priest about this undesirable visitor, but she knew he wouldn't listen to her, dismissing the matter as the kind of thing old people like to worry about.

So now she just had to wait and see what happened. It doesn't take a devil much time to bring about destruction; they are like storms, hurricanes or avalanches, which, in a few short hours, can destroy trees planted two hundred years before. Suddenly, Berta realised that the mere fact that Evil had just arrived in Viscos did not change anything: devils come and go all the time without necessarily affecting anything by their presence. They are constantly abroad in the world, some times simply to find out what's going on, at others to put some soul or other to the test. But they are fickle creatures, and there is no logic in their choice of target, being drawn merely by the pleasure of a battle worth fighting. Berta concluded that there was nothing sufficiently interesting or special about Viscos to attract the attention of anyone for more than a day, let alone someone as important and busy as a messenger from the dark.

She tried to turn her mind to something else, but she couldn't get the image of the stranger out of her head. The sky, which had been clear and bright up until then, suddenly clouded over.

'That's normal, it always happens at this time of year,' she thought. It was simply a coincidence and had nothing to do with the stranger's arrival.

Then, in the distance, she heard a clap of thunder, followed by another three. On the one hand, this simply meant that rain was on the way; on the other, if the old superstitions of the village were to be believed, the sound could be interpreted as the voice of an angry God, protesting that mankind had grown indifferent to His presence.

'Perhaps I should do something. After all, what I was waiting for has finally happened.'

She sat for a few minutes, paying close attention to everything going on around her; the clouds had continued to gather above the village, but she heard no other sounds. As a good ex-Catholic, she put no store by traditions and superstitions, especially those of Viscos, which had their roots in the ancient Celtic civilisation that once existed in the place.

'A thunderclap is an entirely natural phenomenon. If God wanted to talk to man, he wouldn't use such roundabout methods.'

She had just thought this when she again heard a peal of thunder accompanied by a flash of lightning – a lot closer this time. Berta got to her feet, picked up her chair and went into her house before the rain started; but this time she felt her heart contract with an indefinable fear.

'What should I do?'

Again she wished that the stranger would simply leave at once; she was too old to help herself or her village, far less assist Almighty God, who, if He needed any help, would surely have chosen someone younger. This was all just some insane dream; her husband clearly had nothing better to do than to invent ways of helping her pass the time.

But of one thing she was sure, she had seen the Devil.

In the flesh and dressed as a pilgrim.

The hotel was, at one and the same time, a shop selling local products, a restaurant serving food typical of the region, and a bar where the people of Viscos could gather to talk about what they always talked about: how the weather was doing, or how young people had no interest in the village. 'Nine months of winter, three months of hell,' they used to say, referring to the fact that each year they had only ninety days to carry out all the work in the fields, fertilising, sowing, waiting, then harvesting the crops, storing the hay and shearing the sheep.

Everyone who lived there knew they were clinging to a world whose days were numbered; even so, it was not easy for them to accept that they would be the last generation of the farmers and shepherds who had lived in those mountains for centuries. Sooner or later the machines would arrive, the livestock would be reared far from there on special food, the village itself might well be sold to a big multinational that would turn it into a ski resort.

That is what had happened to other villages in the region, but Viscos had resisted – because it owed a debt to the past, to the strong traditions of those ancestors who had once chosen to live here, and who had taught them the importance of fighting to the bitter end.

The stranger carefully read the form he was given to fill in at the hotel, deciding what he was going to put. From his accent, they would know he came from some South American country, and he decided it should be Argentina, because he really liked their football team. In the space left for his address, he wrote Colombia Street, knowing that South Americans are in the habit of paying homage to each other by naming important places after neighbouring countries. As his name, he chose that of a famous terrorist from the previous century.

In less than two hours, all the 281 inhabitants of Viscos knew that a stranger named Carlos had arrived in the village, that he had been born in Argentina and now lived in a pleasant street in Buenos Aires. That is the advantage of very small villages: without making the slightest effort, you can learn all there is to know about a person's life.

Which was precisely what the newcomer wanted.

He went up to his room and unpacked his rucksack: it contained a few clothes, a shaving kit, an extra pair of shoes, vitamins to ward off colds, a thick notebook to write in, and eleven bars of gold, each weighing two kilos. Worn out by tension, by the climb and by the weight he had been carrying, the stranger fell asleep almost at once, though not before placing a chair under the door handle, even though he knew he could count on each and every one of Viscos' 281 inhabitants.

The next morning he ate breakfast, left his dirty clothes at reception to be laundered, put the gold bars back in his rucksack, and set off for the mountain to the east of the village. On his way, he saw only one villager, an old woman sitting in front of her house, who was looking at him with great interest.

He plunged into the forest, where he waited until his hearing had become used to the noises made by the insects and birds, and by the wind rattling the leafless branches; he knew that in a place like this someone could easily be observing him without his being aware of it, so he stood there for almost an hour without doing anything.

When he felt sure that any possible observer would have lost interest and moved on without anything to report, he dug a hole close to a rocky outcrop in the shape of a Y and hid one of the bars there. Then he climbed a little higher, spent another hour as if in rapt contemplation of nature, spotted another rocky outcrop – this time in the form of an eagle – and dug another hole, in which he placed the remaining ten gold bars.

The first person he saw as he walked back to the village was a young woman sitting beside one of the many temporary rivers that formed when the ice melted high up in the mountains. She looked up from her book, acknowledged his presence, and resumed her reading; doubtless her mother had told her never to talk to strangers.

Strangers, however, when they arrive in a new place, have the right to try and make friends with people they do not know, and so he went over to her.

'Hello,' he said. 'Very hot for the time of year.'

She nodded in agreement.

The stranger went on: 'I'd like you to come and look at something.'

She politely put down her book, held out her hand, and introduced herself.

'My name's Chantal. I work in the evenings at the bar of the hotel where you're staying, and I was surprised when you didn't come down to dinner, because a hotel doesn't make its money just from renting rooms, you know, but from everything the guests consume. You are Carlos from Argentina and you live in Colombia Street; everyone in the village knows that already, because a man arriving here outside of the hunting season is always an object of curiosity. A man in his fifties, with greying hair, and the look of someone whom has been around a bit.

'And thank you for your invitation, but I've already seen the landscape around Viscos from every possible and imaginable angle; perhaps it would be better if I showed you places you haven't seen, but I suppose you must be very busy.'

'I'm 52, my name isn't Carlos, and everything I wrote on the form at the hotel is false.'

Chantal didn't know what to say. The stranger went on:

'It's not Viscos I want to show you. It's something you've never seen before.'

She had read many stories about young women who decide to go into the forest with a stranger, only to vanish without trace. For a moment she was afraid, but her fear was quickly replaced by a desire for adventure: after all, this man wouldn't dare do anything to her when she had just told him that everyone in the village knew all about him – even if none of the details were actually true.

'Who are you?' she asked. 'If what you say is true, surely you realise I could turn you in to the police for passing yourself off with a false identity?'

'I promise to answer all your questions, but first you have to come with me, because I really do want to show you something. It's about five minutes' walk from here.'

Chantal closed her book, took a deep breath and offered up a silent prayer, while her heart beat in fear and excitement. Then she got up and followed the stranger, convinced that this would prove to be yet another disappointing encounter, one which started out full of promise and turned into yet another dream of impossible love.

The man went over to the Y-shaped rock, indicated the recently dug earth, and suggested she uncover what lay buried there.

'I'll get my hands dirty,' protested Chantal. 'I'll get my dress dirty too.'

The man grabbed a branch, broke it and handed it to her to use as a spade. She found such behaviour distinctly odd, but decided to do as he asked.

Five minutes later, a grubby, yellowish bar lay before her.

'It looks like gold,' she said.

'It is gold. And it's mine. Now please cover it over again.'

She did as she was told. The man led her to the next hiding place. Again she began digging, and this time was astonished at the quantity of gold she saw before her.

'That's gold too. And it's also mine,' said the stranger.

Chantal was beginning to cover the gold over again with soil, when he asked her to leave the hole as it was. He sat down on one of the rocks, lit a cigarette, and stared at the horizon.

'Why did you want to show me this?' she asked.

He didn't respond.

'Who are you exactly? And what are you doing here? Why did you show me this, knowing I could go and tell everyone what's hidden here on the mountain?'

'So many questions all at once,' the stranger replied, keeping his eyes fixed on the mountains, as if oblivious to her presence. 'As for telling the others, that's precisely what I want you to do.'

'You promised me that, if I came with you, you would answer any questions I asked you.'

'In the first place, you shouldn't believe in promises. The world is full of them: promises of riches, of eternal salvation, of infinite love. Some people think they can promise anything, others accept whatever seems to guarantee better days ahead, as, I suspect, is your case. Those who make promises they don't keep end up powerless and frustrated, and exactly the same fate awaits those who believe those promises.'

He was making things too complicated; he was talking about his own life, about the night that had changed his destiny, about the lies he had been obliged to believe because he could not accept reality. He needed, rather, to use the kind of language the young woman would understand.

Chantal, however, had understood just about everything. Like all older men, he was obsessed with the idea of sex with a younger woman. Like all human beings, he thought money could buy whatever he wanted. Like all strangers, he was sure that young women from remote villages were naïve enough to accept any proposal, real or imaginary, provided it offered a faint chance of escape.

He was not the first and would not, alas, be the last to try and seduce her in that vulgar way. What confused her was the amount of gold he was offering: she had never imagined she could be worth that much, and the thought both pleased her and filled her with a sense of panic.

'I'm too old to believe in promises,' she said, trying to gain time.

'Even though you've always believed in them and still do?'

'You're wrong. I know I live in paradise and I've read the Bible and I'm not going to make the same mistake as Eve, who wasn't contented with her lot.'

This was not, of course, true, and she had already begun to worry that the stranger might lose interest and leave. The truth was that she had spun the web, setting up their meeting in the woods by strategically positioning herself at a spot he would be sure to pass on his way back – just so as to have someone to talk to, another promise to hear, a few days in which to dream of a possible new love and a one-way ticket out of the valley where she was born. Her heart had already been broken many times over, and yet she still believed she was destined to meet the man of her life. At first, she had let many chances slip by, thinking that the right person had not yet arrived, but now she had a sense that time was passing more quickly than she had thought, and she was prepared to leave Viscos with the first man willing to take her, even if she felt nothing for him. Doubtless, she would learn to love him – love, too, was just a question of time.

'That's precisely what I want to find out: are we living in paradise or in hell?' the man said, interrupting her thoughts.

Good, he was falling into her trap.

'In paradise. But if you live somewhere perfect for a long time, you get bored with it in the end.'

She had thrown out the first bait. She had said, though not in so many words: 'I'm free, I'm available.' His next question would be: 'Like you?'

'Like you?' the stranger asked.

She had to be careful, she mustn't seem too eager or she might scare him off.

'I don't know. Sometimes I think that and sometimes I think my destiny is to stay here and that I wouldn't know how to live far from Viscos.'

The next step: to feign indifference.

'Right, then, since you won't tell me anything about the gold you showed me, I'll just thank you for the walk and return to my river and my book.'

'Just a moment!'

The stranger had taken the bait.

'Of course I'll explain about the gold; why else would I have brought you here?'

Sex, money, power, promises. But Chantal decided to pretend that she was expecting some amazing revelation; men take the oddest satisfaction in feeling superior, without knowing that most of the time they are being utterly predictable.

'You're obviously a man with a great deal of experience, someone who could teach me a lot.'

That was it. Gently slacken the rope and then lavish a little light praise on your prey so as not to frighten him off. That was an important rule to follow.

'However, you have a dreadful habit of making long speeches about promises or about how we should behave, instead of replying to a simple question. I'd be delighted to stay if only you'd answer the questions I asked you at the start: who exactly are you? And what are you doing here?'

The stranger turned his gaze from the mountains and looked at the young woman in front of him. He had worked for many years with all kinds of people and he knew – almost for certain – what she must be thinking. She probably thought he had shown her the gold in order to impress her with his wealth, just as now she was trying to impress him with her youth and indifference.

'Who am I? Well, let's say I'm a man who, for some time now, has been searching for a particular truth. I finally discovered the theory, but I've never put it into practice.'

'What sort of truth?'

'About the nature of human beings. I discovered that confronted by temptation, we will always fall. Given the right circumstances, every human being on this earth would be willing to commit evil.'

'I think ...'

'It's not a question of what you or I think, or of what we want to believe, but of finding out if my theory is correct. You want to know who I am. Well, I'm an extremely rich and famous industrialist, who held sway over thousands of employees, was ruthless when necessary and kind when I had to be.

'I'm a man who has experienced things that most people never even dream of, and who went beyond all the usual limits in his search for both pleasure and knowledge. A man who found paradise when he thought he was a prisoner to the hell of routine and family, and who found hell when he could at last enjoy paradise and total freedom. That's who I am, a man who has been both good and evil throughout his life, perhaps the person most fitted to reply to my own question about the essence of humanity – and that's why I'm here. I know what you're going to ask next.'

Chantal felt she was losing ground. She needed to regain it rapidly.

'You think I'm going to ask: "Why did you show me the gold?" But what I really want to know is why a rich and famous industrialist would come to Viscos in search of an answer he could find in books, universities, or simply by consulting some illustrious philosopher.'

The stranger was pleased at the girl's intelligence. Good, he had chosen the right person – as ever.

'I came to Viscos because I had a plan. A long time ago, I went to see a play by a writer called Dürrenmatt, whom I'm sure you know ...'

His comment was merely intended to provoke her: obviously a young woman like her would never have heard of Dürrenmatt, and he knew that she would again try to appear indifferent, as if she knew who he was talking about.

'Go on,' said Chantal, feigning indifference.

'I'm glad to see you know his work, but let me just remind you about the particular play I mean.' He measured his words carefully so that his remarks would not sound too sarcastic, but would also make it clear that he knew she was lying. 'It's about a woman who makes her fortune and then returns to her home town with the sole intention of humiliating and destroying the man who rejected her in her youth. Her life, her marriage and her financial success have all been motivated by the desire to take revenge on her first love.

'So then I thought up my own game: I would go to some remote place, where everyone looked on life with joy, peace and compassion, and I would see if I could make the people there break a few of the Ten Commandments.'

Chantal looked away and stared at the mountains. She knew the stranger had realised that she had never heard of the author he was talking about and now she was afraid he would ask her about those ten commandments; she had never been very religious and had not the slightest idea what they were.

'Everybody in this village is honest, starting with you,' the stranger went on, 'I showed you a gold bar, which would give you the necessary financial independence to get out of here, to travel the world, to do whatever it is young women from small, out-of-the-way villages dream of doing. The gold is going to stay there; you know it's mine, but you could steal it if you wanted. And then you would be breaking one of the commandments: "Thou shalt not steal".'

The girl turned to look at the stranger.

'As for the other ten gold bars,' he went on, 'they are worth enough to mean that none of the inhabitants of this village would ever need to work again. I didn't ask you to re-bury the gold bars because I'm going to move them to a place only I will know about. When you go back to the village, I want you to say that you saw them and that I am willing to hand them over to the inhabitants of Viscos on condition that they do something they would never ever dream of doing.'

'Like what, for example?'

'It's not an example, it's something very concrete. I want them to break the commandment "Thou shalt not kill".'

'What?'

Her question came out like a yell.

'Exactly what I said. I want them to commit a murder.'

The stranger saw the young woman's body go rigid and realised she might leave at any moment without hearing the rest of the story. He needed to tell her his plan quickly.

'I'm giving them a week. If, at the end of seven days, someone in the village is found dead – it could be a useless old man, or someone with an incurable illness, or a mental defective who requires constant attention, the victim doesn't matter – then the money will go to the other villagers, and I will conclude that we are all evil. If you steal the one gold bar but the village resists temptation, or vice versa, I will conclude that there are good people and evil people – which would put me in a difficult position because it would mean that there's a spiritual struggle going on that could be won by either side. Don't you believe in God and the spiritual world, in battles between devils and angels?'

The young woman said nothing, and this time he realised that he had mistimed his question and ran the risk of her simply turning on her heel and not letting him finish. He had better cut the irony and get to the heart of the matter.

'If I leave the village with my eleven gold bars intact, then everything I wanted to believe in will have proved to be a lie. I will die having received an answer I would rather not have received, because I would find life more acceptable if I was proved right and the world is evil.

'I would continue to suffer, but knowing that everyone else is suffering too would make the pain more bearable. But if only a few of us are condemned to suffer terrible tragedies, then there is something very wrong with Creation.'

Chantal's eyes filled with tears, but she managed to fight them back.

'Why are you doing this? Why did you choose my village?'

'It's nothing to do with you or with your village. I'm simply thinking of myself; the story of one man is the story of all men. I need to know if we are good or evil. If we are good, God is just and will forgive me for all I have done, for the harm I wished on those who tried to destroy me, for the wrong decisions I took at key moments, for the proposition I am putting to you now – for He was the one who drove me towards the dark.

'But if we're evil, then everything is permitted, I never took a wrong decision, we are all condemned from the start, and it doesn't matter what we do in this life, for redemption lies beyond either human thought or deed.'

Before Chantal could leave, he added:

'You may decide not to co-operate, in which case, I'll tell everyone that I gave you the chance to help them, but you refused, and then I'll put my proposition to them myself. If they do decide to kill someone, you will probably be their chosen victim.'

The inhabitants of Viscos soon grew used to the stranger's routine: he woke early, ate a hearty breakfast and went off walking in the mountains, despite the rain that had not stopped falling since his second day in the village and which eventually turned into a near continuous snowstorm. He never ate lunch and generally returned to his hotel early in the afternoon, shut himself in his room and, so everyone supposed, went to sleep.

As soon as night fell, he resumed his walks, this time in the immediate surroundings of the village. He was always the first into the restaurant, he ordered the finest dishes and – never taken in by the prices – always ordered the best wine, which wasn't necessarily the most expensive; then he would smoke a cigarette and go over to the bar, where he had begun to make friends with the regulars.

He enjoyed listening to stories about the region, about the previous generations who had lived in Viscos (someone told him that once it had been a far bigger village than it was today, as you could see from the ruined houses at the far end of the three surviving streets), and about the customs and superstitions that were part of rural life, and about the new techniques in agriculture and animal husbandry.

When the time came for him to talk about himself, he told various contradictory stories, sometimes saying he had been a sailor, at others mentioning the major arms industries he had been in charge of, or talking of a time when he had abandoned everything to spend time in a monastery in search of God.

When they left the bar, the locals argued over whether or not he was telling the truth. The mayor believed that a man could be many different things in his lifetime, although the people of Viscos always knew their fate from childhood onwards; the priest was of a different opinion and regarded the newcomer as someone lost and confused, who had come there to try and find himself.

The only thing they all knew for certain was that he was only going to be there for seven days; the hotel landlady reported that she had heard him phoning the airport in the capital, confirming his departure – interestingly enough, for Africa not South America. Then, after the phone call, he had pulled out a bundle of notes from his pocket to settle the bill for his room as well as to pay for the meals he had taken and those still to come, even though she assured him that she trusted him. When the stranger insisted, the woman suggested he pay by credit card, as most of her guests usually did; that way, he would have cash available for any emergency that might arise during the remainder of his trip. She thought of adding that 'in Africa they might not accept credit cards', but felt it would have been indelicate to reveal that she had listened in on his conversation, or to imply that certain continents were more advanced than others.

The stranger thanked her for her concern, but refused politely.

On the following three nights, he paid – again in cash – for a round of drinks for everyone. Viscos had never seen anything like it, and they soon forgot about the contradictory stories, and the man came to be viewed as friendly, generous and open-minded, prepared to treat country folk as if they were the equals of men and women from the big cities.

By now, the subject of the discussions had changed. When it was closing time in the bar, some of the late drinkers took the mayor's side, saying that the newcomer was a man of the world, capable of understanding the true value of friendship, while others agreed with the priest, with his greater knowledge of the human soul, and said that the stranger was a lonely man in search either of new friends or of a new vision of life. Whatever the truth of the matter, he was an agreeable enough character, and the inhabitants of Viscos were convinced that they would miss him when he left on the following Monday.

Apart from anything else, he was extremely discreet, a quality everyone had noticed because of one particular detail: most travellers, especially those who arrived alone, were always very quick to try and strike up a conversation with the barmaid, Chantal Prym, possibly in hopes of a fleeting romance or whatever. This man, however, only spoke to her when he ordered drinks and never once traded seductive or lecherous looks with the young woman.

Chantal found it virtually impossible to sleep during the three nights following that meeting by the river. The storm – which came and went – shook the metal blinds, making a frightening noise. She awoke repeatedly, bathed in sweat, even though she always switched off the heating at night, due to the high price of electricity.

On the first night, she found herself in the presence of Good. Between nightmares – which she was unable to remember – she prayed to God to help her. It did not once occur to her to tell anyone what she had heard and thus become the messenger of sin and death.

At one point, it seemed to her that God was much too far away to hear her, and so she began praying instead to her grandmother, who had passed away some time ago, and who had brought her up after her mother died in childbirth. She clung with all her strength to the notion that Evil had already touched their lives once and had gone away for ever.

Despite all her personal problems, Chantal knew that she lived in a village of decent men and women who honoured their commitments, people who walked with their heads held high and were respected throughout the region. But it had not always been so. For over two centuries, Viscos had been inhabited by the very dregs of humanity, and everyone took this for granted, saying it was the consequence of a curse put on the village by the Celts when they were vanquished by the Romans.

And so things remained until the silence and courage of a single man – someone who believed not in curses, but in blessings – redeemed its people. Chantal listened to the clattering metal blinds and remembered the voice of her grandmother recounting what had happened.

'Once, many years ago, a hermit – who later came to be known as St Savin – lived in one of the caves hereabouts. At the time, Viscos was little more than a frontier post, populated by bandits fleeing from justice, by smugglers and prostitutes, by confidence tricksters in search of accomplices, even by murderers resting between murders. The wickedest of them all, an Arab called Ahab, controlled the whole village and the surrounding area, imposing extortionate taxes on the local farmers who still insisted on maintaining a dignified way of life.

'One day, Savin came down from his cave, arrived at Ahab's house and asked to spend the night there. Ahab laughed: "You do know that I'm a murderer who has already slit a number of throats, and that your life is worth nothing to me?"

'"Yes, I know that," Savin replied, "but I'm tired of living in a cave and I'd like to spend at least one night here with you."

'Ahab knew the saint's reputation, which was as great as his own, and this made him uneasy, for he did not like having to share his glory with someone so weak. Thus he determined to kill him that very night, to prove to everyone that he was the one true master of the place.

'They chatted for a while. Ahab was impressed by what the saint had to say, but he was a suspicious man who no longer believed in the existence of Good. He showed Savin where he could sleep and then continued menacingly sharpening his knife. After watching him for a few minutes, Savin closed his eyes and went to sleep.

'Ahab spent all night sharpening his knife. Next day, when Savin awoke, he found Ahab in tears at his side.

'"You weren't afraid of me and you didn't judge me. For the first time ever, someone spent a night by my side trusting that I could be a good man, one ready to offer hospitality to those in need. Because you believed I was capable of behaving decently, I did."

'From that moment on, Ahab abandoned his life of crime and set about transforming the region. That was when Viscos ceased being merely a frontier post, inhabited by outcasts, and became an important trading centre on the border between two countries.'

'Exactly.'

Chantal burst into tears, grateful to her grandmother for having reminded her of that story. Her people were good, and she could trust them. While she attempted to go back to sleep, she even toyed with the idea of telling them the stranger's story, if only to see his shocked face as he was driven out of Viscos by its inhabitants.

The next day, she was surprised to see him emerge from the restaurant at the rear of the hotel, go over to the bar-cum-reception-cum-souvenir shop and stand around chatting to the people he met there, just like any other tourist, pretending to be interested in utterly pointless things, such as their methods of shearing sheep or of smoke-curing meat. The people of Viscos always believed that every stranger would be fascinated by their natural, healthy way of life, and they would repeat and expand upon the benefits of life away from modern civilisation, even though, deep in their hearts, every single one of them would have loved to live far from there, among cars that pollute the atmosphere and in neighbourhoods where it was too dangerous to walk, for the simple reason that big cities hold an enormous fascination for country people.

Yet every time a visitor appeared, they would demonstrate by their words – and only by their words – the joys of living in a lost paradise, trying to persuade themselves what a miracle it was to have been born there and forgetting that, so far, not one hotel guest had decided to leave it all behind and come and live in Viscos.

There was a lively atmosphere in the bar that night, until the stranger made one rather unfortunate comment:

'The children here are so well behaved. There's not a squeak out of them in the mornings, not like other places I've visited.'

After an awkward silence – for there were no children in Viscos – someone asked him what he thought of the local dish he had just eaten, and the conversation resumed its normal rhythm, revolving, as usual, around the wonders of the countryside and the problems of life in the big city.

As time passed, Chantal became increasingly nervous, afraid that he might ask her to tell everyone about their meeting in the forest. But the stranger never even glanced at her, and he spoke to her only once, when he ordered – and paid cash for – a round of drinks for everyone present.

As soon as the customers left and the stranger went up to his room, she took off her apron, lit a cigarette from a packet someone had left behind on the table, and told the hotel landlady she would do the clearing up the next morning, since she was worn out after a sleepless night. The landlady agreed, and Chantal put on her coat and went out into the cold night air.

Her room was only two minutes' walk away, and as she let the rain pour down her face, she was thinking that perhaps everything that had happened was just some kind of crazy fantasy, the stranger's macabre way of attracting her attention.

Then she remembered the gold: she had seen it with her own eyes.

Maybe it wasn't gold. But she was too tired to think and – as soon as she got to her room – she took off her clothes and snuggled down under the covers.

On the second night, Chantal found herself in the presence of Good and Evil. She fell into a deep, dreamless sleep, only to wake up less than an hour later. Outside, all was silence; there was no wind banging the metal blinds, not even the sounds made by night creatures; there was nothing, absolutely nothing to indicate that she was still in the world of the living.

She went to the window and looked out at the deserted street, where a fine rain was falling, the mist barely lit by the feeble light of the hotel sign, all of which only made the village seem even more sinister. She was all too familiar with the silence of this remote place, which signified not peace and tranquillity, but a total absence of new things to say.

She looked at the mountains, which lay hidden by low cloud, but she knew that somewhere up there was buried a gold bar or, rather, a yellow object, shaped like a brick, that the stranger had left behind there. He had shown her its exact location, virtually begging her to dig up the bar and keep it for herself.

She went back to bed, tossed and turned for a while, then got up again and went to the bathroom where she examined her naked body in the mirror, spent a few moments worrying that soon she would lose her looks, then returned to bed. She regretted not having picked up the packet of cigarettes left behind on the table, but she knew that its owner was bound to come back for it, and she did not want to incur people's mistrust. That was what Viscos was like: a half-empty cigarette packet had its owner, the button lost off a jacket had to be kept until someone came asking for it, every penny in change had to be handed over, there was never any rounding up the bill. It was a wretched place, in which everything was predictable, organised and reliable.

Realising that she wasn't going to be able to get to sleep, she again attempted to pray and to think of her grandmother, but her thoughts had become fixed on a single scene: the open hole, the earth-smeared metal, the branch in her hand, as though it were the staff of a pilgrim about to set off. She dozed and woke up again several times, but the silence outside continued, and the same scene kept endlessly repeating itself inside her head.

As soon as she noticed the first light of dawn coming in through the window, she dressed and went out.

Although she lived in a place where people normally rose with the sun, it was too early even for that. She walked down the empty street, glancing repeatedly behind her to be sure that the stranger wasn't following her; the mist was so thick, however, that visibility was down to a few yards. She paused from time to time, listening for footsteps, but all she could hear was her own heart beating wildly.

She plunged into the undergrowth, made for the Y-shaped rock – which had always made her nervous because it looked as if it might topple over at any moment – picked up the same branch she had left there the day before, dug at the exact spot the stranger had indicated, stuck her hand into the hole and pulled out the brick-shaped gold bar. She thought she heard something: a silence reigned in the heart of the forest, as though there was a strange presence abroad, frightening the animals and preventing the leaves from stirring.

She was surprised by the weight of the metal in her hands. She wiped it clean, studied the marks on it: two seals and a series of engraved numbers, which she tried in vain to decipher.

How much would it be worth? She couldn't tell with any degree of accuracy, but – as the stranger had said – it would be enough for her not to have to worry about earning another penny for the rest of her life. She was holding her dream in her hands, the thing she had always longed for, and which a miracle had set before her. Here was the opportunity to free herself from all those identical days and nights in Viscos and from the endless going back and forth to the hotel where she had worked since she was eighteen, from the yearly visits of all those friends whose families had sent them away to study and make something of themselves, from all the absences she had long since grown used to, from the men who arrived promising her the world and left the next day without even a goodbye, from all the farewells and non-farewells to which she had long become accustomed. That moment there in the forest was the most important moment of her entire life.

Life had always been so unfair to her: she didn't know who her father was; her mother had died in childbirth, leaving her with a terrible burden of guilt to bear; her grandmother, a countrywoman, had eked out a living as a dressmaker, saving every penny she could so that her granddaughter could at least learn to read and write. Chantal had had so many dreams: she thought she could overcome all obstacles, find a husband, get a job in the big city, be discovered by a talent scout who happened to be visiting that out-of-the-way place in the hope of finding peace, get a career in the theatre, write a best-seller, have photographers calling out to her to pose for them, walk along life's red carpets.

Every day was another day spent waiting. Every night was a night when she might meet someone who would recognise her true worth. Every man she took to her bed was the hope of leaving Viscos the following morning, never again to see those three streets, those stone houses with their slate roofs, the church with its cemetery beside it, the hotel selling local handicrafts that took months to make and were sold for the same price as mass-produced goods.

Occasionally it crossed her mind that the Celts, the ancient inhabitants of her region, might have hidden an amazing cache of treasure there, which one day she would find. Of all her dreams, that had been the most absurd, the most unlikely.

Yet here she was now with a gold bar in her hands, the treasure she had never believed in, her definitive freedom.

She was seized by panic: the one lucky moment in her life could vanish that very afternoon. What if the stranger changed his mind? What if he decided to go in search of another village where he might find another woman more willing to help him in his plans? Why not stand up, go back to her room, put her few possessions into a bag and simply leave?

She imagined herself going down the steep hill, trying to hitch a ride out of the village while the stranger set out on his morning walk and found that his gold had been stolen. She would continue on her way to the nearest town and he would go back to the hotel to call the police.

Chantal would thank the driver who had given her a lift, and then head straight for the bus station and buy a ticket to some far-away place; at that moment, two policemen would approach her, asking her politely to open her suitcase. As soon as they saw its contents, their politeness would vanish: she was the woman they were looking for, following a report filed only three hours earlier.

In the police station, Chantal would have two options: to tell the truth, which no one would believe, or to explain that she had noticed the disturbed soil, had decided to investigate and had found the gold. Once, she had shared her bed with a treasure hunter also intent on unearthing something left by the Celts. He claimed the law of the land was clear: he had the right to keep whatever he found, although any items of historical interest had to be registered with the relevant government department. But the gold bar had no historical value at all, it was brand new, with all its stamps, seals and numbers.

The police would question the man. He would have no way of proving that she had entered his room and stolen his property. It would be his word against hers, but he might prove more influential, have friends in high places, and it would all go his way. Chantal could, of course, always ask the police to examine the gold bar; then they would see that she was telling the truth, for the metal would still bear traces of earth.

By now, the news would have reached Viscos, and its inhabitants – out of envy or jealousy – would start spreading rumours about the girl, saying that there were numerous reports that she often used to go to bed with the hotel guests; perhaps the robbery had taken place while the man was asleep.

It would all end badly: the gold bar would be confiscated until the courts had resolved the matter, she would get another lift back to Viscos, where she would be humiliated, ruined, the target of gossip that would take more than a generation to die down. Later on, she would discover that lawsuits never got anywhere, that lawyers cost much more than she could possibly afford, and she would end up abandoning the case.

The net result: no gold and no reputation.

There was another possible version: the stranger might be telling the truth. If Chantal stole the gold and simply left, wouldn't she be saving the village from a much deeper disgrace?

However, even before leaving home and setting off for the mountain, she had known she would be incapable of taking such a step. Why, at precisely the moment that could change her life forever, was she so afraid? After all, didn't she sleep with whomever she pleased and didn't she sometimes ingratiate herself with visitors just to get a bigger tip? Didn't she lie occasionally? Didn't she envy her former friends who now only came back to the village to visit their families at New Year?

She clutched the gold to her, got to her feet, feeling weak and desperate, then crouched down again, replaced it in the hole and covered it with earth. She couldn't go through with it; this inability, however, had nothing to do with honesty or dishonesty, but with the sheer terror she was feeling. She had just realised there were two things that prevent us from achieving our dreams: believing them to be impossible or seeing those dreams made possible by some sudden turn of the wheel of fortune, when you least expected it. For at that moment, all our fears suddenly surface: the fear of setting off along a road heading who knows where, the fear of a life full of new challenges, the fear of losing for ever everything that is familiar.

People want to change everything and, at the same time, want it all to remain the same. Chantal did not immediately understand why, but that was what was happening to her. Perhaps she was too bound to Viscos, too accustomed to defeat, and any chance of victory was too heavy a burden to bear.

She was convinced that the stranger must now be tired of her silence and that shortly – perhaps that very afternoon – he would decide to choose someone else. But she was too cowardly to change her fate.

The hands that had touched the gold should now be washing the dirty dishes, wielding the sponge and the dishcloth. Chantal turned her back on the treasure and returned to the village, where the hotel landlady was waiting for her, looking vaguely irritated, since Chantal had promised to clean the bar before the one hotel guest was up.

Chantal's fears proved unfounded: the stranger did not leave. She saw him in the bar that night, more seductive than ever, telling tales that might not have been entirely true, but which, at least in his imagination, he had lived intensely. Once again their eyes only met impersonally, when he offered to pay for the regulars' drinks.

Chantal was exhausted. She was praying that they would all leave early, but the stranger seemed particularly inspired, recounting story after story, which his listeners lapped up, with the interest and the hateful respect – or, rather, craven submissiveness – that country people show in the presence of those who come from the big cities, judging them to be more cultivated, educated, intelligent and modern.

'Fools,' she said to herself. 'They don't understand how important they are. They don't understand that whenever someone lifts a forkful of food to their mouth, anywhere in the world, it's thanks to people like the inhabitants of Viscos, who toil from dawn to dusk, working the land with the sweat of their weary bodies, and caring for their livestock with indescribable patience. They are far more necessary to the world than all those city people, yet they behave as if they were inferior beings, uptight and talentless – and they believe it too.'

The stranger, however, seemed determined to show that his culture was worth more than all the labours of the men and women in the bar. He pointed to a print hanging on the wall:

'Do you know what that is? It's one of the most famous paintings in the world: *The Last Supper*, painted by Leonardo da Vinci.'

'It can't be as famous as all that,' said the hotel landlady. 'It was very cheap.'

'That's only a reproduction: the original is in a church a long, long way from here. But there's a story about this picture you might like to hear.'

Everyone nodded, though once again Chantal felt ashamed to be there, listening to a man showing off his pointless knowledge, just to prove that he knew more than anyone else.

'When he was creating this picture, Leonardo da Vinci encountered a serious problem: he had to depict Good – in the person of Jesus – and Evil – in the figure of Judas, the friend who resolves to betray him during the meal. He stopped work on the painting until he could find his ideal models.

'One day, when he was listening to a choir, he saw in one of the boys the perfect image of Christ. He invited him to his studio and made sketches and studies of his face.

'Three years went by. *The Last Supper* was almost complete, but Leonardo had still not found the perfect model for

Judas. The cardinal responsible for the church started to put pressure on him to finish the mural.

'After many days spent vainly searching, the artist came across a prematurely aged youth, in rags and lying drunk in the gutter. With some difficulty, he persuaded his assistants to bring the fellow directly to the church, since there was no time left to make preliminary sketches.

'The beggar was taken there, not quite understanding what was going on. He was propped up by Leonardo's assistants, while Leonardo copied the lines of impiety, sin and egotism so clearly etched on his features.

'When he had finished, the beggar, who had sobered up slightly, opened his eyes and saw the picture before him. With a mixture of horror and sadness he said:

'"I've seen that picture before!"

'"When?" asked an astonished Leonardo.

'"Three years ago, before I lost everything I had, at a time when I used to sing in a choir and my life was full of dreams. The artist asked me to pose as the model for the face of Jesus."'

There was a long pause. The stranger was looking at the priest, who was drinking his beer, but Chantal knew his words were directed at her.

'So you see, Good and Evil have the same face; it all depends on when they cross the path of each individual human being.'

He got up, made his excuses, saying he was tired, and went up to his room. Everyone paid what they owed and slowly left the bar, casting a last look at the cheap reproduction of the famous painting, asking themselves at what point in their lives they had been touched by an angel or a devil. Without anyone saying a word to anyone else, each came to the conclusion that this had only happened in Viscos before Ahab brought peace to the region; now, every day was like every other day, each the same as the last.

Exhausted, functioning almost like an automaton, Chantal knew she was the only person to think differently, for she alone had felt the heavy, seductive hand of Evil caressing her cheek. 'Good and Evil have the same face, it all depends on when they cross the path of each individual human being.' Beautiful, possibly true words, but all she really needed now was to sleep, nothing more.

She ended up giving the wrong change to one of the customers, something which almost never happened; she apologised, but did not feel overly guilty. She carried on, inscrutable and dignified, until the priest and the local mayor – generally the last to leave – had departed. Then she shut up the till, gathered her things together, put on her cheap, heavy jacket and went home, just as she had done for years.

On the third night, then, she found herself in the presence of Evil. And Evil came to her in the form of extreme tiredness and a soaring fever, leaving her in a half-conscious state, but incapable of sleep – while outside in the darkness, a wolf kept howling. Sometimes she thought she must be delirious, for it seemed the wolf had come into her room and was talking to her in a language she couldn't understand. In a brief moment of lucidity, she attempted to get up and go to the church, to ask the priest to call a doctor because she was ill, very ill; but when she tried to convert her intentions into actions, her legs gave way beneath her, and she was convinced she would be unable to walk.

Or, if she did manage to walk, she would be unable to reach the church.

Or, if she did reach the church, she would have to wait for the priest to wake up, get dressed and open the door, and meanwhile the cold would cause her fever to rise so rapidly that she would drop dead on the spot, right there outside the house that some considered to be sacred.

'At least they wouldn't have far to take me to the cemetery: I'd be virtually inside it already,' she thought.

Chantal's delirium lasted all night, but she noticed that her fever began to diminish as the morning light came filtering into her room. As her strength returned and she was trying to get to sleep, she heard the familiar sound of a car horn and realised that the baker's van had arrived in Viscos and that it must be time for breakfast.

There was no one there to make her go downstairs to buy bread; she was independent, she could stay in bed for as long as she wanted, since she only began work in the evening. But something had changed in her; she needed contact with the world, before she went completely mad. She wanted to be with the people she knew would now be gathering around the little green van, exchanging their coins for bread, happy because a new day was beginning and they had work to do and food to eat.

She went across to the van, greeting them all, and heard one or two remarks like: 'You look tired' or 'Is anything wrong?'. They were kind and supportive, always ready to help, simple and innocent in their generosity, while her soul was engaged in a bitter struggle for dreams and adventures, fear and power. Much as she would have liked to share her secret, she knew that if she revealed it to a single one of them, the rest of the village would be sure to know it before the morning was over. It was better to thank them for their concern and to carry on alone until her ideas had become a little clearer.

'No, it's nothing. There was a wolf howling all night and I couldn't get to sleep.'

'I didn't hear any wolf,' said the hotel landlady, who was also there buying bread.

'It's been months since any wolves were heard in the area,' confirmed another woman who made conserves to be sold in the hotel shop. 'The hunters must have killed them all, which is bad news for us because the wolves are the main reason the hunters come up here at all, to see who can kill the most elusive animal in the pack. It's a pretty pointless exercise, but they love it.'

'Don't say anything in front of the baker about there being no more wolves in the region,' muttered Chantal's boss. 'If word gets out, no one will come to Viscos at all.'

'But I heard a wolf.'

'Then it must have been the rogue wolf,' said the mayor's wife, who didn't much like Chantal, but who was sufficiently well-bred to hide her feelings.

The hotel landlady got annoyed. There was no rogue wolf. It was just an ordinary wolf, and it was probably dead by now anyway.

The mayor's wife, however, would not give up so easily.

'Regardless of whether or not it exists, we all know that there were no wolves howling last night. You work the poor girl too hard, up until all hours; she's so exhausted she's starting to get hallucinations.'

Chantal left the pair of them to their argument, picked up her bread and went on her way.

'A pointless exercise,' she repeated to herself, recalling the comment made by the woman who made the conserves. That was how they viewed life, as a pointless exercise. She nearly told them about the stranger's proposal there and then, just to see if those smug, narrow-minded people would be willing to take part in a genuinely purposeful exercise: ten gold bars in exchange for a simple murder, one that would guarantee the futures of their children and their grandchildren and return Viscos to its former glory, with or without wolves.

But she held back. She decided instead to tell the story that very night, in front of everyone, in the bar, so that no one could claim not to have heard or understood. Perhaps they would fall on the stranger and march him straight to the police, leaving her free to take her gold bar as a reward for services rendered to the community. Perhaps they simply wouldn't believe her, and the stranger would depart believing that they were all good, which wasn't the case at all.

They were so ignorant, so naïve, so resigned to their lot. They refused to believe anything that didn't fit in with what they were used to believing. They all lived in fear of God. They were all – herself included – cowards when the moment comes to change their fate. But as far as true goodness was concerned, that didn't exist – not in the land of cowardly men, nor in the heaven of Almighty God who sows suffering everywhere, just so that we can spend our whole lives begging him to deliver us from Evil.

The temperature had dropped. Chantal hadn't slept for three nights, but once she was preparing her breakfast, she felt much better. She wasn't the only coward, though she was possibly the only one aware of her own cowardice, because the rest of them thought of life as a 'pointless exercise' and confused fear with generosity.

She remembered a man who used to work in a chemist's in a nearby village and who had been dismissed after twenty years' service. He hadn't asked for his redundancy money because – so he said – he considered his employers to be his friends and didn't want to hurt them, because he knew they had had to dismiss him because of financial difficulties. It was all a lie: the reason the man did not go to court was because he was a coward; he wanted at all costs to be liked; he thought his employers would then always think of him as a generous, friendly sort. Some time later, when he went back to them to ask for a loan, they slammed the door in his face, but by then it was too late, for he had signed a letter of resignation and could make no further demands of them.

Very clever. Playing the part of a charitable soul was only for those who were afraid of taking a stand in life. It is always far easier to have faith in your own goodness than to confront others and fight for your rights. It is always easier to hear an insult and not retaliate than have the courage to fight back against someone stronger than yourself; we can always say we're not hurt by the stones others throw at us, and it's only at night – when we're alone and our wife or our husband or our school friend is asleep – that we can silently grieve over our own cowardice.

Chantal drank her coffee and hoped the day would pass quickly. She would destroy the village, she would bring Viscos to its knees that very night. The village would die within a generation anyway because it was a village without children – young people had their children elsewhere, in places where people went to parties, wore fine clothes, travelled and engaged in 'pointless exercises'.

The day, however, did not pass quickly. On the contrary, the grey weather and the low cloud made the hours drag. The mountains were obscured by mist, and the village seemed cut off from the world, turned in on itself, as if it were the only inhabited place on Earth. From her window, Chantal saw the stranger leave the hotel and, as usual, head for the mountains. She feared for her gold, but immediately calmed herself down – he was sure to come back because he had paid in advance for a week in the hotel, and rich men never waste a penny; only poor people do that.

She tried to read, but couldn't concentrate. She decided to go for a walk round Viscos, and the only person she saw was Berta, the widow, who spent her days sitting outside her house, watching everything that went on.

'It looks like it's finally going to get cold,' said Berta.

Chantal asked herself why people with nothing else to talk about always think the weather is so important. She nodded her agreement.

Then she went on her way, since she had said all she had to say to Berta in the many years she had lived in that village. There was a time when she had considered Berta an interesting, courageous woman, who had managed to continue her life even after the death of her husband in one of the many hunting accidents that happened each year. She had sold some of her few possessions and invested the money – together with the insurance money – in securities, and she now lived off the income.

Over time, however, the widow had ceased to be of interest to her, and had become instead an example of everything she feared *she* might become: ending her life sitting in a chair on her own doorstep, all muffled up in winter, staring at the only landscape she had ever known, watching over what didn't need watching over, since nothing serious, important or valuable ever happened there.

She walked on, unconcerned at the possibility of getting lost in the misty forest, because she knew every track, tree and stone by heart. She imagined how exciting things would be that night and tried out various ways of putting the stranger's proposal – in some versions she simply told them what she had seen and heard, in others she spun a tale that might or might not be true, imitating the style of the man who had not let her sleep now for three nights.

'A highly dangerous man, worse than any hunter I've ever met.'

Walking through the woods, Chantal began to realise that she had discovered another person just as dangerous as the stranger: herself. Up until four days ago, she had been imperceptibly becoming used to who she was, to what she could realistically expect from life, to the fact that living in Viscos wasn't really so bad – after all, the whole area was swamped with tourists in the summer, everyone of whom referred to the place as a 'paradise'.

Now the monsters were emerging from their tombs, darkening her nights, making her feel discontented, put upon, abandoned by God and by fate. Worse than that, they forced her to acknowledge the bitterness she carried around inside her day and night, into the forest and to work, into those rare love affairs and during her many moments of solitude.

'Damn the man. And damn myself too, since I was the one who made him cross my path.'

As she made her way back to the village, she regretted every single minute of her life; she cursed her mother for dying so young, her grandmother for having taught her to be honest and kind, the friends who had abandoned her and the fate that was still with her.

Berta was still at her post.

'You're in a great hurry,' she said. 'Why not sit down beside me and relax a bit?'

Chantal did as she suggested. She would do anything to make the time pass more quickly.

'The village seems to be changing,' Berta said. 'There's something different in the air, and last night I heard the rogue wolf howling.'

The girl felt relieved. She didn't know whether it had been the rogue wolf or not, but she had definitely heard a wolf howling that night, and at least one other person apart from her had heard it too.

'This place never changes,' she replied. 'Only the seasons come and go, and now it's winter's turn.'

'No, it's because the stranger has come.'

Chantal checked herself. Could it be that he had talked to someone else as well?

'What has the arrival of the stranger got to do with Viscos?'

'I spend the whole day looking at nature. Some people think it's a waste of time, but it was the only way I could find to accept the loss of someone I loved very much. I see the seasons pass, see the trees lose their leaves and then grow new ones. But occasionally something unexpected in nature brings about enormous changes. I've been told, for example, that the mountains all around us are the result of an earthquake that happened thousands of years ago.'

Chantal nodded; she had learned the same thing at school.

'After that, nothing is ever the same. I'm afraid that is precisely what is going to happen now.'

Chantal was tempted to tell her the story of the gold, but, suspecting that the old woman might know something already, she said nothing.

'I keep thinking about Ahab, our great hero and reformer, the man who was blessed by St Savin.'

'Why Ahab?'

'Because he could see that even the most insignificant of actions, however well intentioned, can destroy everything. They say that after he had brought peace to the village, driven away the remaining outlaws and modernised agriculture and trade in Viscos, he invited his friends to supper and cooked a succulent piece of meat for them. Suddenly he realised there was no salt.

'So Ahab called to his son: "Go to the village and buy some salt, but pay a fair price for it: neither too much nor too little."

'His son was surprised: "I can understand why I shouldn't pay too much for it, father, but if I can bargain them down, why not pay a bit less?"

'"That would be the sensible thing to do in a big city, but in a small village like ours it could spell the beginning of the end."

'The boy left without asking any further questions. However, Ahab's guests, who had overheard their conversation, wanted to know why they should not buy the salt more cheaply if they could. Ahab replied:

'"The only reason anyone would sell salt more cheaply than usual would be because he was desperate for money. And anyone who took advantage of that situation would be showing a lack of respect for the sweat and struggle of the man who laboured to produce it."

'"But such a small thing couldn't possibly destroy a village."

'"In the beginning, there was only a small amount of injustice abroad in the world, but everyone who came afterwards added their portion, always thinking it was very small and unimportant, and look where we have ended up today."'

'Like the stranger, for example,' Chantal said, hoping that Berta would confirm that she too had talked to him. But Berta said nothing.

'I don't know why Ahab was so keen to save Viscos,' Chantal went on. 'It started out as a den of thieves and now it's a village of cowards.'

Chantal was sure the old woman knew something. She only had to find out whether it was the stranger himself who had told her.

'That's true. But I'm not sure that it's cowardice exactly. I think everyone is afraid of change. They want Viscos to be as it always was: a place where you can till the soil and tend your livestock, a place that welcomes hunters and tourists, but where everyone knows exactly what is going to happen from one day to the next, and where the only unpredictable things are nature's storms. Perhaps it's a way of achieving peace, but I agree with you on one point: they all think they have everything under control, when, in fact, they control nothing.'

'Absolutely,' said Chantal.

'Not one jot or one tittle shall be added to what is written,' the old woman said, quoting from the Gospels. 'But we like to live with that illusion because it makes us feel safe. Well, it's a choice like any other, even though it's stupid to believe we can control the world and to allow ourselves to be lulled into a false sense of security that leaves us totally unprepared for life; because then, when you least expect it, an earthquake throws up a range of mountains, a bolt of lightning kills a tree that was preparing for its summer rebirth, or a hunting accident puts paid to the life of an honest man.'

For the hundredth time, Berta launched into the story of her husband's death. He had been one of the most respected guides in the region, a man who saw hunting not as a savage sport, but as a way of respecting local traditions. Thanks to him, Viscos had created a special nature reserve, the mayor had drawn up laws protecting certain near-extinct species, there was a tax per head of each animal killed, and the money collected was used for the good of the community.

Berta's husband tried to see the sport – considered cruel by some and traditional for others – as a way of teaching the hunters something about the art of living. Whenever someone with a lot of money but little hunting experience arrived in Viscos, he would take them out to a piece of waste ground. There, he would place a beer can on top of a stone.

Then he would stand about fifty yards from the can and, with a single shot, send it flying.

'I'm the best shot in the region,' he would say. 'And now you're going to learn how to become as good as me.'

He replaced the can on the same stone, walked back to where he had stood before, took a handkerchief out of his pocket and asked the newcomer to blindfold him. Then he aimed once more in the direction of the target and fired again.

'Did I hit it?' he would ask, removing the blindfold.

'Of course not,' the new arrival would say, pleased to see the proud guide humbled. 'You missed it by a mile. I don't think there's anything you can teach me.'

'I've just taught you the most important lesson in life,' Berta's husband would reply. 'Whenever you want to achieve something, keep your eyes open, concentrate and make sure you know exactly what it is you want. No one can hit their target with their eyes closed.'

Then, one day, while he was replacing the can on the stone after his first shot, the would-be hunter thought it must be his turn to show how good his aim was. Without waiting for Berta's husband to rejoin him, he fired. He missed the target, but hit the guide in the neck. He did not have the chance to learn that important lesson in concentration and objectivity.

'I have to go,' Chantal said. 'There are a few things I need to do before I go to work.'

Berta said goodbye and watched her all the way until she disappeared down the alley beside the church. The years she had spent sitting outside her door, looking up at the mountains and the clouds, and holding conversations in her mind with her dead husband had taught her to 'see' people. Her vocabulary was limited, so she could find no other word to describe all the many sensations that other people aroused in her, but that was what happened: she 'saw through' other people, and could tell what their feelings were.

It had all started at the funeral for her one great love. She was weeping, and a child next to her – the son of an inhabitant of Viscos, who was now a grown man and lived thousands of miles away – asked her why she was sad.

Berta did not want to frighten the child by mentioning death and final farewells, so all she said was that her husband had gone away and might not come back to Viscos for a long time.

'I think he was having you on,' the boy replied. 'I've just seen him hiding behind a grave, all smiles, and with a soup spoon in his hand.'

The boy's mother heard what he said and scolded him for it. 'Children are always seeing things,' she said, apologising to Berta. But Berta immediately stopped crying and looked in the direction the child had indicated; her husband had always had the annoying habit of wanting to eat his soup with a special spoon, however much this irritated her – because all spoons are the same and hold the same amount of soup – yet he had always insisted on using his special spoon. Berta had never told anyone this, for fear people would think him crazy.

So the boy really had seen her husband; the spoon was the proof. Children could 'see' things. From then on, Berta decided that she was going to learn to 'see' as well, because she wanted to talk to her husband, to have him back – if only as a ghost.

At first, she shut herself up at home, rarely going out, waiting for him to appear to her. Then one day, something told her that she should go to the door of her house and start paying attention to other people, that her husband wanted her to have more joy in her life, for her to participate more in what was going on in the village.

She set up her chair outside her house and sat staring at the mountains; there were not many people out and about in the streets of Viscos, but on the very first day of her vigil, a neighbour returned from the next village, saying that they were selling quality cutlery very cheaply at the market there and, as proof, she produced a spoon from her bag.

Berta realised she would never see her husband again, but he was asking her to stay there, watching the village, and that was what she would do. As time went by, she began to perceive a presence beside her, to her left, and she was certain that he was there with her, keeping her company and protecting her from any danger, as well as teaching her to see things that others could not, such as the patterns made by the clouds, which always spelled out messages. She was rather sad that whenever she tried to look at him full on, the presence disappeared, but then she realised that she could talk to him using her intuition, and so they began having long conversations about all kinds of things.

Three years later, she was able to 'see' people's feelings, as well as receive some very useful practical advice from her husband. That was why she refused to be fobbed off with less compensation than she deserved, and why she withdrew her money from the bank just before it crashed, taking with it many local people's hard-earned savings.

One morning – and she could no longer remember exactly when this had happened – her husband told her that Viscos might be destroyed. Berta immediately thought of earthquakes creating whole new ranges of mountains, but he reassured her that nothing of that sort would happen there, at least not for the next few thousand years. He was worried about another sort of destruction, even though he himself was not exactly clear what form it would take. All the same, he asked her to be on her guard, because this was his village, the place he loved most in the whole world, even if he had left it rather sooner than he would have wished.

Berta began to pay more attention to people, to the patterns made by the clouds, to the hunters who came and went, but nothing appeared to indicate that anyone was trying to destroy a village that had never harmed anyone. Yet still her husband insisted that she keep watch, and she had done as he asked.

Then three days ago, she had seen the stranger arrive with a devil by his side and she knew her wait was over. Today, she had noticed that Chantal was accompanied by both a devil and an angel. She immediately linked the two events and understood that something odd was happening in her village.

She smiled to herself, glanced to her left and blew a discreet kiss. She was not a useless old woman; she had something important to do: to save the place where she had been born, even though she had no idea as yet what steps she should take.

Chantal left the old woman immersed in her thoughts, and went back to her room. It was whispered among the inhabitants of Viscos that Berta was a witch. It was said she had shut herself up in her house for almost a year and, during that time, had taught herself the magic arts. When Chantal had asked who could have taught them to Berta, some said it was the devil himself who appeared to her at night, while others swore that she invoked the spirit of a Celtic priest, using words her parents had taught her. But no one was overly concerned: Berta was harmless and she always had good stories to tell.

They were right, although they were always the same stories. Suddenly Chantal paused with her hand on the doorknob. Even though she had heard the story of how Berta's husband had died many times over, it was only now that she realised there was an important lesson in it for her too. She remembered her recent walk in the forest and the pent-up hatred she had felt inside her, a hatred that seemed to fly out all around her, threatening whoever was near, be it herself, the village, the people in it or their children.

But she had only one real target: the stranger. Concentrate, shoot and kill your prey. To do that, she needed a plan – it would be foolish to speak out that night and let the situation run out of control. She decided to put off for another day telling the story of how she had met the stranger, if, that is, she ever did tell the other inhabitants of Viscos.

That night, when she went to collect the money for the round of drinks that the stranger usually bought, Chantal noticed that he had slipped her a note. She put it straight into her pocket, pretending that it was a matter of no importance, even though she was aware of the stranger's eyes occasionally seeking hers, as if silently questioning her. The roles seemed to have been reversed: it was she who was in control of the situation, she who could choose the battlefield and the hour of the fight. That was how all the most successful hunters behaved: they always arranged things so that the prey would come to them.

It was only when she returned to her room, this time confident that she would sleep soundly, that she looked at the note: the stranger was asking her to meet him in the place where they had first met.

He closed by saying that he would prefer to talk to her alone, but added that, if she wanted, they could also speak with everyone else present too.

The threat did not escape her, but she was, in fact, delighted that he had made it. It was proof that he was losing control, because truly dangerous men and women never make threats. Ahab, the man who brought peace to Viscos, always used to say: 'There are two kinds of idiots – those who don't take action because they have received a threat, and those who think they are taking action because they have issued a threat.'

She tore the note into shreds and flushed it down the toilet, then she took a scalding hot bath, slipped into bed and smiled. She had got exactly what she wanted: to meet the stranger again for a conversation alone. If she wanted to find out how to defeat him, she needed to get to know him better.

She fell asleep almost at once – a deep, refreshing, easeful sleep. She had spent one night with Good, one with Good and Evil, and one with Evil. Not one of the three had produced any definite result, but they were all still alive in her soul, and now they were beginning to fight amongst themselves to see who was strongest.

By the time the stranger arrived, Chantal was drenched – the storm had recommenced.

'Let's not talk about the weather,' she said. 'As you can see, it's raining. I know a place where it'll be easier for us to talk.'

She got to her feet and picked up a long canvas bag.

'You've got a shotgun in there,' the stranger said.

'Yes.'

'And you want to kill me.'

'Yes, I do. I don't know if I'll succeed, but that's what I'd like to do. I brought the weapon here for another reason, though: I might meet the rogue wolf on the way, and if I could shoot him, I might win some respect in Viscos. No one believes me, but I heard him howling last night.'

'And what is this rogue wolf?'

At first she doubted whether to share anything more with this man who was her enemy. But then she remembered a book on Japanese martial arts – she always read any books left behind by hotel guests, no matter what the books were about, because she didn't want to spend her own money buying them. There it was written that the best way to weaken one's enemy was to get him to believe that you were on his side.

As they trudged through the wind and the rain, she told him the story. Two years ago, a man from Viscos – the blacksmith, to be precise – was out for a walk when, all of a sudden, he came face to face with a wolf and its young. The man was terrified, but he tore off a branch and made to attack the animal. Normally, the wolf would have run away, but as it was with its young, it counter-attacked and bit the man on the leg. The blacksmith, a man whose job requires enormous strength, managed to deal the wolf such a blow that it finally ran back into the forest with its cubs and was never seen again; all anyone knew was that it had a white mark on its left ear.

'But why is it called the rogue wolf?'

'Usually even the fiercest of animals will only attack in exceptional circumstances, in order, for example, to protect its young. However, if an animal does attack and tastes human blood, then it becomes dangerous; it will always want more; it will cease being a wild animal and become a killer. Everyone believes that one day the wolf will attack again.'

'That's my story too,' the stranger thought.

Chantal was walking as fast as she could because she was younger and fitter than him and wanted to gain a psychological advantage over her companion by tiring him out and humiliating him, and yet he managed to keep up with her. He was out of breath, but he never once asked her to slow down.

They reached a small, well-camouflaged, green plastic tent, used by hunters as a hide. They sat inside, rubbing their frozen hands and blowing on them.

'What do you want?' she asked him. 'Why did you give me that note?'

'I'm going to ask you a riddle: of all the days in our life, which is the one that never comes?'

There was no reply.

'Tomorrow,' the stranger said. 'But you seem to believe that tomorrow will come and keep putting off what I asked you to do. We're getting towards the end of the week, and if you don't say something, I'll have to do it myself.'

Chantal left the refuge, stood a safe distance from it, undid the canvas bag, and took out the shotgun. The stranger didn't seem to attach any importance to this.

'You dug up the gold again,' he went on. 'If you had to write a book about your experiences, how do you think most of your readers would react – given all the difficulties they have to face, the injustices dealt to them by life and other people, the struggle they have in order to pay for their children's schooling and to put food on the table – don't you think that those people would be urging you to take the gold and run?'

'I don't know,' she said, loading a cartridge into the gun.

'Nor do I. But that's the answer I'm looking for.'

She inserted the second cartridge.

'You're willing to kill me, despite that reassuring little tale about finding a wolf. But that's all right, because that too provides me with an answer to my question: human beings are essentially evil, even a young woman from a remote village is capable of committing murder for money. I'm going to die, but now I have my answer, so I can die happy.'

'Here, take it,' she said, handing him the gun. 'No one knows that I know you. All the details you gave in the hotel are false. You can leave when you want and, as I understand it, you can go anywhere you want to in the world. You don't need to have a good aim: all you have to do is point the shotgun in my direction and squeeze the trigger. Each cartridge is full of tiny bits of lead; as soon as they leave the barrel, they spread out into a cone shape. They can kill birds or human beings. You can even look the other way if you don't want to see my body being blown apart.'

The man curled his finger round the trigger, and Chantal was surprised to see that he was holding the gun correctly, like a professional. They stood like that for a long while, and she was aware that he had only to slip or be startled by an animal coming on them unexpectedly and his finger could move and the gun go off. She suddenly realised how childish her gesture had been, trying to defy someone merely for the pleasure of provoking him, saying that he was incapable of doing what he was asking others to do.

The stranger was still pointing the gun at her, staring at her unblinking, his hands steady. It was too late now – maybe deep down he thought it wouldn't be such a bad idea to end the life of this young woman who had dared to challenge him. Chantal was on the point of asking him to forgive her, but the stranger lowered the gun before she could say a word.

'I can almost touch your fear,' he said, handing her back the gun. 'I can smell the sweat pouring off you, despite the rain, and even though the wind is shaking the treetops and making an infernal racket, I can hear your heart thumping in your throat.'

'I'm going to do what you asked me to do this evening,' she said, pretending she hadn't heard the truths he was telling her. 'After all, you came to Viscos to learn about your own nature, to find out if you were good or evil. There's one thing I've just shown you: regardless of what I may have felt or stopped feeling just now, you could have pulled the trigger, but you didn't. Do you know why? Because you're a coward. You use others to resolve your own conflicts, but you are incapable of taking certain decisions.'

'A German philosopher once said: "Even God has a hell: his love of mankind". No, I'm not a coward. I've pressed many worse triggers than this one, or, rather, I have made far better guns than this and distributed them around the world. I did it all perfectly legally, got the transactions approved by the government, the export licences, paid all the necessary taxes. I married a woman who loved me, I had two beautiful daughters, I never stole a penny from my company, and always succeeded in recovering any money owed to me.

'Unlike you, who feel persecuted by destiny, I was always a man of action, someone who struggled with the many difficulties in my way, who lost some battles and won others, but always understood that victories and defeats form part of everyone's life – everyone, that is, except cowards, as you call them, because they never lose or win.

'I read a lot. I was a regular churchgoer. I feared God and respected His commandments. I was a highly paid director of a huge firm. Since I was paid commission on every deal we made, I earned more than enough to support my wife, my daughters, and even my grandchildren and my great-grandchildren; because the arms trade is the most profitable business in the world. I knew the value of every item I sold, so I personally checked all our transactions; that way I uncovered several cases of corruption and dismissed those involved and halted the sales. My weapons were made to help defend order, which is the only way to ensure progress and development in this world, or so I thought.'

The stranger came up to Chantal and took her by the shoulders; he wanted her to look him in the eyes and know that he was telling the truth.

'You may consider arms manufacturers to be the lowest of the low. Perhaps you're right, but the fact is that man has used weapons ever since he lived in caves – first to kill animals, then to win power over others. The world has existed without agriculture, without domesticated animals, without religion, without music, but never without weapons.'

He picked up a stone from the ground.

'Here's the first of them, generously donated by Mother Nature to those who had to confront prehistoric animals. A stone like this doubtless saved the life of a man, and that man, after countless generations, led to you and me being born. If he hadn't had that stone, the murderous carnivore would have devoured him, and hundreds of millions of people would not have been born.'

The wind was blowing harder, and the rain was battering them, but neither of them looked away.

'Many people criticise hunters, but Viscos welcomes them with open arms because it lives off them; some people hate seeing a bull in a bullring, but go and buy the meat from the butcher's claiming that the animal had an "honourable" death; a lot of people are critical of arms manufacturers, but they will continue to exist until there's not a single weapon left on the face of the earth. Because as long as one weapon remains, there will always have to be another, to preserve the fragile balance.'

'What has all this got to do with my village?' Chantal demanded. 'What has it got to do with breaking the commandments, with murder, stealing, with the essence of human nature, with Good and Evil?'

At this, the stranger's eyes changed, as if overwhelmed by a deep sadness.

'Remember what I told you at the beginning. I always tried to do my business according to the law; I considered myself what people usually term a "good man". Then one evening I received a phone call in my office: it was a woman's voice, soft but devoid of emotion. She said her terrorist group had kidnapped my wife and daughters. They wanted a large quantity of what they knew I could give them – weapons. They told me to keep quiet about it, they told me that nothing would happen to my family if I followed their instructions.

'The woman rang off saying that she would call again in half an hour and told me to wait for her call in a phone box at the train station. She said not to worry; my family was being well treated and would be freed within a few hours, because all I had to do was send an electronic message to one of our subsidiaries in a certain country. It wasn't even real theft, more like an illegal sale that would go completely unnoticed in the company I worked for.

'Since I was a good citizen, brought up to respect the law and to feel protected by it, the first thing I did was to ring the police. A minute later, I was no longer the master of my own decisions, I was transformed into someone incapable of protecting his own family; my universe was suddenly filled with anonymous voices and frantic phone calls. When I went to the designated phone box, an army of technicians had already hooked up the underground telephone cable to the most modern equipment available, so that they could instantaneously trace exactly where the call was coming from. There were helicopters ready to take off, police cars strategically positioned to block the traffic, trained men, armed to the teeth, on full alert.

'Two different governments, in distant continents, already knew what was going on and they forbade any negotiations; all I had to do was to follow orders, repeat what they told me to say and behave exactly as instructed by the experts.

'Before the day was out, the hiding place where they were keeping the hostages had been discovered, and the kidnappers – two young men and a woman, all apparently inexperienced, simply disposable elements in a powerful political organisation – lay dead, riddled with bullets. Before they died, however, they had time to execute my wife and daughters. If even God has a hell, which is his love for mankind, then any man has his hell within easy reach, and that's his love for his family.'

The stranger fell silent; he was afraid of losing control of his voice and betraying an emotion he preferred to keep hidden. As soon as he had recovered, he went on:

'Both the police and the kidnappers used weapons made by my company. No one knows how the terrorists came to be in possession of them, and that's of no importance: they had them. Despite all my efforts, my struggle to ensure that everything was carried out according to the strictest regulations for their manufacture and sale, my family had been killed by something which I, at some point, had sold – perhaps over a meal at an expensive restaurant, while I chatted about the weather or world politics.'

Another pause. When he spoke again, it was as if he were another person, as if nothing he was saying had anything to do with him.

'I know the weapon and the ammunition used to kill my family well. I know which part of the body they aimed at: the chest. The bullet makes only a small hole on entering – about the size of your little finger. When it hits the first bone, though, it splits into four, and each of the fragments continues in a different direction, brutally destroying everything in its path: kidneys, heart, liver, lungs. Every time it comes up against something solid, like a vertebra, it changes direction again, usually carrying with it sharp bone fragments and bits of torn muscle, until at last it finds a way out. Each of the four exit wounds is almost as big as a fist, and the bullet still has enough force to spatter round the room the bits of tissue, flesh and bone that clung to it during its journey through the body.

'All of this takes less than two seconds; two seconds to die might not seem very long, but time isn't measured like that. You understand, I hope.'

Chantal nodded.

'At the end of that year, I left my job. I travelled to the four corners of the earth, alone with my grief, asking myself how human beings can be capable of such evil. I lost the most precious thing a man can have: my faith in my fellow man. I laughed and I wept at God's irony, at the absurd way he had chosen to demonstrate to me that I was an instrument of Good and Evil.

'All my sense of compassion gradually vanished, and now my heart has entirely shrivelled up; I don't care whether I live or die. But first, for the sake of my wife and daughters, I need to grasp what happened in that hiding place. I can understand how people can kill out of hate or love, but why do it for no particular reason, simply over some business transaction?

'This may seem naïve to you – after all, people kill each other every day for money – but that doesn't interest me, I'm only concerned with my wife and daughters. I want to know what was going on in the minds of those terrorists. I want to know whether, at any point, they might have taken pity on them and let them leave, because their war had nothing to do with my family. I want to know if, when Good and Evil are pitted against each other, there is a fraction of a second when Good might prevail.'

'Why Viscos? Why my village?'

'Why the weapons from my factory, when there are so many armaments factories in the world, some of them with no government controls? The answer is simple: chance. I needed a small place where everyone knew each other and got on together. The moment they learned about the reward, Good and Evil would once again be pitted against each other, and what had happened in that hiding place would happen in your village.

'The terrorists were already surrounded and defeated; nevertheless, they killed my family merely in order to carry out a useless, empty ritual. Your village has what I did not have: it has the possibility to choose. They will be tempted by the desire for money and perhaps believe they have a mission to protect and save their village, but even so, they still retain the ability to decide whether or not to execute the hostage. That's all. I want to see whether other people might have acted differently to those poor, bloodthirsty youngsters.

'As I told you when we first met, the story of one man is the story of all men. If compassion exists, I will accept that fate was harsh with me, but that sometimes it can be gentle with others. That won't change the way I feel in the slightest, it won't bring my family back, but at least it will drive away the devil that's always with me and give me some hope.'

'And why do you want to know whether I am capable of stealing the gold?'

'For the same reason. You may divide the world into trivial crimes and serious ones, but it isn't like that. I think the terrorists did the same. They thought they were killing for a cause, not just for pleasure, love, hate or money. If you took the gold bar, you would have to justify the crime to yourself and to me, and then I would understand how the murderers justified to themselves the killing of my loved ones. As you have seen, I have spent all these years trying to understand what happened. I don't know whether this will bring me peace, but I can't see any alternative.'

'If I did steal the gold, you would never see me again.'

For the first time during the almost thirty minutes they had been talking, the stranger smiled faintly.

'I worked in the arms industry, don't forget. And that included work for the secret service.'

The man asked her to lead him to the river – he was lost, and did not know how to get back. Chantal took the shotgun – she had borrowed it from a friend on the pretext that she was very tense and needed to do a bit of hunting to try and relax – put it back in its bag, and the two of them set off down the hill.

They said nothing to each other on the way down. When they reached the river, the stranger said goodbye.

'I understand why you're delaying, but I can't wait any longer. I can also understand that, in order to struggle with yourself, you needed to get to know me better: now you do.

'I am a man who walks the earth with a devil at his side; in order to drive him away or to accept him once and for all, I need to know the answers to certain questions.'

The fork banged repeatedly against the wineglass. Everyone in the bar, which was packed on that Friday night, turned towards the sound: it was Miss Prym calling for them to be silent.

The effect was immediate: never in all the history of the village had a young woman whose sole duty was to serve the customers acted in such a manner.

'She had better have something important to say,' thought the hotel landlady. 'If not, I'll get rid of her tonight, despite the promise I made to her grandmother never to abandon her.'

'I'd like you all to listen,' Chantal said. 'I'm going to tell you a story that everyone here, apart from our visitor, will know,' she said, pointing to the stranger. 'After that, I'll tell you another story that no one here, apart from our visitor, will know. When I've finished, it will be up to you to judge whether or not it was wrong of me to interrupt your well-earned Friday evening rest, after an exhausting week's work.'

'She's taking a terrible risk,' the priest thought. 'She doesn't know anything we don't know. She may be a poor orphan with few possibilities in life, but it's going to be difficult to persuade the hotel landlady to keep her on after this.'

But, when he thought about it again, perhaps it wouldn't. We all commit sins, which are generally followed by two or three days of anger, after which all is forgiven; besides, he couldn't think of anyone else in the village who could do her job. It was a young person's job, and there were no other young people in Viscos.

'Viscos has three streets, a small square with a cross in it, a few ruined houses and a church with a cemetery beside it,' Chantal began.

'Just a moment,' the stranger said.

He took a small cassette recorder out of his pocket, switched it on, and placed it on his table.

'I'm interested in everything to do with the history of Viscos. I don't want to miss a single word, so I hope you don't mind if I record you.'

Chantal did not know whether she minded or not, but there was no time to lose. She had been battling with her fears for hours, and now that she had finally found the courage to begin, she did not want any interruptions.

'Viscos has three streets, a small square with a cross in it, a few ruined houses and a few well-preserved ones, a hotel, a post box, and a church with a cemetery next to it.'

Her description this time was a little more complete. She was not so nervous now.

'As we all know, it used to be a haven for outlaws until our great lawmaker, Ahab, after his conversion by St Savin, succeeded in transforming it into the village we know today, home only to men and women of good will.

'What the stranger doesn't know, and as I am going to explain now, is how Ahab managed to achieve that transformation. At no point did he try to convince anyone, because he knew what people were like; they would confuse honesty with weakness, and his authority would immediately be placed in doubt.

What he did was to send for some carpenters from a neighbouring village, give them a piece of paper with a drawing on it, and order them to build something on the spot where the cross now stands. Day and night throughout the next ten days, the inhabitants of the village heard the sound of hammers and watched men sawing up planks of wood, fitting them together and screwing one piece to another. At the end of the ten days, this giant jigsaw puzzle was erected in the middle of the square, covered with a cloth. Ahab called all the villagers together for the inauguration of the monument.

'Solemnly, without any speeches, he removed the cloth: there stood a gallows, complete with rope, trap door, everything, brand new and greased with beeswax to withstand the ravages of the weather for many years. Then, taking advantage of the fact that everyone was there, Ahab read out a series of new laws that protected farmers, encouraged the raising of livestock and rewarded anyone bringing new trade to Viscos. He added that, from then on, everyone would either have to find honest work or leave the village. That was all he said; not once did he mention the "monument" he had just inaugurated. Ahab did not believe in making threats.

'When the ceremony was over, people gathered together in various groups. Most of them believed that Ahab had been duped by the saint, that he had lost his nerve, and that he should be killed. During the days that followed, many plans were made with that objective in mind. But the plotters could not avoid the sight of the gallows in the middle of the square, and they thought: What is that doing there? Was it erected in order to deal with anyone who goes against the new laws? Who is on Ahab's side and who isn't? Are there spies in our midst?

'The gallows looked at the villagers, and the villagers looked at the gallows. Gradually, the rebels' initial defiance gave way to fear; they all knew Ahab's reputation and they knew he never went back on a decision. Some of them left the village, others decided to try the new jobs that had been suggested, simply because they had nowhere else to go or because they were conscious of the shadow cast by that instrument of death in the middle of the square. Before long, Viscos had been pacified and it became a large trading centre near the frontier, exporting the finest wool and producing top-quality wheat.

'The gallows remained in place for ten years. The wood withstood the weather well, but the rope occasionally had to be replaced with a new one. The gallows was never used. Ahab never once mentioned it. The mere sight of the gallows was enough to turn courage into fear, trust into suspicion, bravado into whispers of submission. When ten years had passed and the rule of law had finally been established in

Viscos, Ahab had the gallows dismantled and used the wood to build a cross instead.'

Chantal paused. The bar was completely silent apart from the sound of the stranger clapping.

'That's an excellent story,' he said. 'Ahab really understood human nature: it isn't the desire to abide by the law that makes everyone behave as society requires, but the fear of punishment. Each one of us carries a gallows inside us.'

'Today, at the stranger's request, I am pulling down the cross and erecting another gallows in the middle of the square,' Chantal went on.

'Carlos,' someone said, 'his name is Carlos, and it would be more polite to call him by his name than to keep referring to him as "the stranger".'

'I don't know his real name. All the details he gave on the hotel form are false. He's never paid for anything with a credit card. We have no idea where he came from or where he's going to; even the phone call to the airport could be a lie.'

They all turned to look at the man, who kept his eyes fixed on Chantal.

'Yet, when he did tell you the truth, none of you believed him. He really did work for an armaments factory, he really has had all kinds of adventures and been all kinds of different people, from loving father to ruthless businessman. But because you live here in Viscos, you cannot comprehend how much richer and more complex life can be.'

'That girl had better explain herself,' thought the hotel landlady. And that's just what Chantal did:

'Four days ago, he showed me ten large gold bars. They are worth enough to guarantee the future of all the inhabitants of Viscos for the next thirty years, to provide for major improvements to the village, a children's playground, for example, in the hope that one day children will live here again. He then immediately hid them in the forest, and I don't know where they are.'

Everyone again turned towards the stranger, who, this time, looked back at them and nodded his head.

'That gold will belong to Viscos if, in the next three days, someone in the village is murdered. If no one dies, the stranger will leave, taking his gold with him.

'And that's it. I've said all I had to say, and I've re-erected the gallows in the square. Except that this time, it is not there to prevent a crime, but so that an innocent person can be hanged, so that the sacrifice of that innocent person will bring prosperity to the village.'

For the third time, all the people in the bar turned towards the stranger. Once again, he nodded.

'The girl tells a good story,' he said, switching off the recorder and putting it back in his pocket.

Chantal turned away and began washing glasses in the sink. It was as if time had stopped in Viscos; no one said a word. The only sound that could be heard was that of running water, of a glass being put down on a marble surface, of the distant wind shaking the branches of leafless trees.

The mayor broke the silence:

'Let's call the police.'

'Go ahead,' the stranger said. 'I've got a recording here, and my only comment was: "The girl tells a good story."'

'Please, go up to your room, pack your things, and leave here at once,' said the hotel landlady.

'I've paid for a week and I'm going to stay a week. Even if you have to call the police.'

'Has it occurred to you that you might be the person to be murdered?'

'Of course. And it really doesn't matter to me. But if you did murder me, then you would have committed the crime, but you would never receive the promised reward.'

One by one, the regulars in the bar filed out, the younger ones first and the older people last. Soon only Chantal and the stranger were left.

She picked up her bag, put on her coat, went to the door and then turned to him.

'You're a man who has suffered and wants revenge,' she said. 'Your heart is dead, your soul is in darkness. The devil by your side is smiling because you are playing the game he invented.'

'Thank you for doing as I asked. And for telling me the true and very interesting story of the gallows.'

'In the forest, you told me that you wanted answers to certain questions, but from the way you have constructed your plan, only Evil will be rewarded; if no one is murdered,

Good will earn nothing but praise. And as you know, praise cannot feed hungry mouths or help to restore dying villages. You're not trying to find the answer to a question, you're simply trying to confirm something you desperately want to believe: that everyone is evil.'

A change came over the stranger's face, and Chantal noticed it.

'If the whole world is evil, then the tragedy that befell you is justified,' she went on. 'That would make it easier for you to accept the deaths of your wife and daughters. But if good people do exist, then, however much you deny it, your life will be unbearable; because fate set a trap for you, and you know you didn't deserve it. It isn't the light you want to recover, it's the certainty that there is only darkness.'

'What exactly are you driving at?' he said, a slight tremor in his voice.

'The wager should be fairer. If, after three days, no one is murdered, the village should get the ten gold bars anyway. As a reward for the integrity of its inhabitants.'

The stranger laughed.

'And I will receive my gold bar, as a reward for my participation in this sordid game.'

'I'm not a fool, you know. If I agreed to that, the first thing you would do is to go outside and tell everyone.'

'Possibly. But I won't; I swear by my grandmother and by my eternal salvation.'

'That's not enough. No one knows whether God listens to vows, or if eternal salvation exists.'

'You'll know I haven't told them, because the gallows is there now in the middle of the village. It will be clear if there's been any kind of trickery. And anyway, even if I went out there now and told everyone what we've just been talking about, no one would believe me; it would be the same as arriving in Viscos and saying: "Look, all this is yours, regardless of whether or not you do what the stranger is asking." These men and women are used to working hard, to earning every penny with the sweat of their brow; they would never even admit the possibility of gold just falling from heaven like that.'

The stranger lit a cigarette, finished off his drink and got up from the table. Chantal awaited his reply standing by the open door, letting the cold air into the room.

'I'll know if there's been any cheating,' he said. 'I'm used to dealing with people, just like your Ahab.'

'I'm sure you are. So that means "yes", then.'

Again he nodded his agreement.

'And one more thing: you still believe that man can be good. If that weren't the case, you wouldn't have invented all this nonsense to convince yourself otherwise.'

Chantal closed the door and walked down the main street in the village – completely deserted at that hour – sobbing uncontrollably. Without wanting to, she had become caught up in the game; she was betting on the fact that people were basically good, despite all the Evil in the world. She would never tell anyone what she and the stranger had just been talking about because, now, she too wanted to know the answer.

She was aware that, although the street was empty, from behind the curtains in darkened rooms, the eyes of Viscos were watching as she walked back home. It didn't matter; it was far too dark for anyone to see her tears.

The man opened the window of his room, hoping that the cold would silence the voice of his devil for a few moments.

As expected, it did not work, because the devil was even more agitated than usual after what the girl had just said. For the first time in many years, the stranger noticed that the devil seemed weaker, and there were moments when he even appeared rather distant; however, he soon reappeared, no stronger or weaker than usual, but much as he always was. He lived in the left-hand side of the man's brain, in the part that governs logic and reasoning, but he never allowed himself to be seen, so that the man was forced to imagine what he must be like. He tried to picture him in a thousand different ways, from the conventional devil with horns and a tail to a young woman with blonde curls. The image he finally settled on was that of a young man in his twenties, with black trousers, a blue shirt, and a green beret perched nonchalantly on his dark hair.

He had first heard the devil's voice on an island, where he had travelled after resigning from his job; he was on the beach, in terrible emotional pain, trying desperately to believe that his suffering must have an end, when he saw the most beautiful sunset he had ever seen. It was then that his despair came back in force, and he plumbed the depths of the deepest abyss in his soul precisely because such a sunset should also have been seen by his wife and children. He broke into uncontrollable sobs and felt that he would never climb up from the bottom of that pit.

At that moment, a friendly, companionable voice told him that he was not alone, that everything that had happened to him had a purpose, which was to show that each person's destiny is pre-ordained. Tragedy always happens, and nothing we do can alter by one jot the evil that awaits us.

'There is no such thing as Good: virtue is simply one of the many faces of terror,' the voice said. 'When man understands that, he will realise that this world is just a little joke played on him by God.'

Then the voice – which identified itself as the prince of this world, the only being who really knows what happens on Earth – began to show him the people all around him on the beach. The wonderful father who was busy packing things up and helping his children put on some warm clothes and who would love to have an affair with his secretary, but was terrified of his wife's response. His wife who would like to work and have her independence, but who was terrified of her husband's response. The children who behaved themselves because they were terrified of being punished. The girl who was reading a book all on her own beneath a sunshade, pretending she didn't care, but inside was terrified of spending the rest of her life alone. The boy running around with a tennis racquet, terrified of having to live up to his parents' expectations. The waiter serving tropical drinks to the rich customers and terrified that he could be sacked at any moment. The young girl who wanted to be a dancer, but who was studying law instead because she was terrified of what the neighbours might say. The old man who didn't smoke or drink and said he felt much better for it, when in truth it was the terror of death that whispered in his ears like the wind. The married couple who ran by, splashing through the surf, with a smile on their face but with a terror in their hearts telling them that they would soon be old, boring and useless. The man with the suntan who swept up in his launch in front of everybody and waved and smiled, but was terrified because he could lose all his money from one moment to the next. The hotel owner, watching the whole idyllic scene from his office, trying to keep everyone happy and cheerful, urging his accountants to ever greater vigilance, and terrified because he knew that however honest he was government officials would still find mistakes in his accounts if they wanted to.

There was terror in each and every one of the people on that beautiful beach and on that breathtakingly beautiful evening. Terror of being alone, terror of the darkness filling their imaginations with devils, terror of doing anything not in the manuals of good behaviour, terror of God's judgement, of what other people would say, of the law punishing any mistake, terror of trying and failing, terror of succeeding and having to live with the envy of other people, terror of loving and being rejected, terror of asking for a rise in salary, of accepting an invitation, of going somewhere new, of not being able to speak a foreign language, of not making the right impression, of growing old, of dying, of being pointed out because of one's defects, of not being pointed out because of one's merits, of not being noticed either for one's defects or one's merits.

Terror, terror, terror. Life was a reign of terror, in the shadow of the guillotine. 'I hope this consoles you a little,' he heard the devil say. 'They're all terrified; you're not alone. The only difference is that you have already been through the most difficult part; your worst fear became reality. You have nothing to lose, whereas these people on the beach live with their terror all the time; some are aware of it, others try to ignore it, but all of them know that it exists and will get them in the end.'

Incredible though it may seem, these words did console him somewhat, as if the suffering of others alleviated his own. From that moment on, the devil had become a more and more frequent companion. He had lived with him for two years now, and he felt neither happy nor sad to know that the devil had completely taken over his soul.

As he became accustomed to the devil's company, he tried to find out more about the origin of Evil, but none of his questions received precise answers.

'There's no point trying to discover why I exist. If you really want an explanation, you can tell yourself that I am God's way of punishing himself for having decided, in an idle moment, to create the Universe.'

Since the devil was reluctant to talk about himself, the man decided to look up every reference he could find to hell. He discovered that most religions have something called 'a place of punishment', where the immortal soul goes after committing certain crimes against society (everything seemed to be seen in terms of society, rather than of the individual). Some religions said that once the spirit was separated from the body, it crossed a river, met a dog and entered hell by a gate of no return. Since the body was laid in a tomb, the place of punishment was generally described as being dark and situated inside the earth; thanks to volcanoes, it was known that the centre of the earth was full of fire, and so the human imagination came up with the idea of flames torturing sinners.

He found one of the most interesting descriptions of this punishment in an Arabian book: there it was written that once the soul had left the body, it had to walk across a bridge as narrow as a knife edge, with paradise on the right and, on the left, a series of circles that led down into the darkness inside the earth. Before crossing the bridge (the book did not explain where it led to), each person had to place all his virtues in his right hand and all his sins in his left, and the imbalance between the two meant that the person always fell towards the side to which his actions on Earth had inclined him.

Christianity spoke of a place where there would be weeping and gnashing of teeth. Judaism described a cave with only room enough for a finite number of souls – when this hell was full, the world would end. Islam spoke of the fire in which we would all burn 'unless God desires otherwise'. For Hindus, hell was never a place of eternal torment, since they believed that the soul would be reincarnated after a certain period of time in order to pay for its sins in the same place where they had been committed – in other words, in this world. Even so, there were no fewer than twenty-one of these places of punishment in what was usually referred to as 'the lower depths'.

The Buddhists also distinguished between the different kinds of punishment a soul might face; eight fiery hells and eight freezing ones, as well as a kingdom where the condemned soul felt neither heat nor cold, only infinite hunger and thirst.

Nothing though could compare to the huge variety that the Chinese had thought up; unlike everyone else – who placed hell deep down inside the earth – the Chinese believed that the souls of sinners went to a mountain range known as the Little Wall of Iron and surrounded by another mountain range known as the Great Wall. In the space between these two ranges, there were no less than eight large hells one on top of the other, each of which controlled sixteen smaller hells, which in turn controlled ten million hells beneath them. The Chinese also said that devils were made up of the souls of those who had already completed their punishment.

The Chinese were also the only ones to offer a convincing explanation of the origin of devils – they were evil because they had personal experience of evil, and now they wanted to pass it on to others, in an eternal cycle of vengeance.

'Which is perhaps what is happening to me,' the stranger said to himself, remembering Miss Prym's words. The devil had heard those words too and felt he had lost some of his hard-won ground. The only way he could regain it was to leave no room for doubt in the stranger's mind.

'All right, so you had a moment of doubt,' the devil said, 'but the terror remains. The story of the gallows was a good one, because it clearly shows that mankind is virtuous only because terror exists, but that men are still essentially bad, my true descendants.'

The stranger was shivering now, but decided to leave the window open a while longer.

'God, I did not deserve what happened to me. If you did that to me, I can do the same to others. That is justice.'

The devil was worried, but resolved to keep quiet – he could not show that he too was terrified. The man was blaspheming against God and trying to justify his actions, but this was the first time in two years he had heard him addressing the heavens.

It was a bad sign.

'It's a good sign,' was Chantal's first thought when she heard the baker's van sounding its horn. Life in Viscos was going on as usual, the bread was being delivered, people were leaving their houses, they would have the whole of Saturday and Sunday to discuss the insane proposition put before them, and then, with some regret, they would watch the stranger depart on Monday morning. Later that evening, she would tell them about the wager she had made, announcing that they had won the battle and were rich.

She would never become a saint like St Savin, but for many generations to come she would be remembered as the woman who saved the village from Evil's second visitation. Maybe they would make up legends about her; the village's future inhabitants might refer to her as a lovely young woman, the only one who had not abandoned Viscos because she knew she had a mission to fulfil. Pious ladies would light candles to her, and young men would sigh passionately over the heroine they had never known.

She was proud of herself, but was aware that she should watch what she said and make no mention of the gold bar that belonged to her, otherwise they would end up convincing her that, in order to be considered a saint, she should also divide up her share.

In her own way she was helping the stranger to save his soul, and God would take this into account when he made a final reckoning of her deeds. The fate of the stranger mattered little to her, however; what she had to do now was to hope that the next two days passed as quickly as possible, for it was hard to keep a secret like that locked up in her heart.

The inhabitants of Viscos were neither better nor worse than those of neighbouring villages, but there was no way they would be capable of committing a murder for money – of that she was sure. Now that the story was out in the open, no man or woman could take the initiative alone. First, because the reward would have to be divided up equally, and she knew that no one would want to risk themselves purely so that others might gain. Second, because, if they were thinking what she deemed to be the unthinkable, they needed to be able to count on the full co-operation of all the others – with the exception, perhaps, of the chosen victim. If a single individual was against the idea – and if need be, she would be that person – the men and women of Viscos all ran the risk of being denounced and imprisoned. Better to be poor and honourable than rich and in jail.

Chantal went downstairs remembering that hitherto even the election of a mayor to govern this village with its three streets had provoked heated arguments and internal divisions. When they wanted to make a children's playground in the lower part of the village, there was such a fuss that the building works were never begun – some said that the village had no children anyway, others roared that a playground would be just the thing to bring them back when their parents came to the village on holiday and saw that things were changing. In Viscos they debated everything: the quality of the bread, the hunting regulations, the existence (or not) of the rogue wolf, Berta's strange behaviour and, possibly, Miss Prym's secret meetings with some of the hotel guests, although no one would ever dare mention it to her face.

She approached the van with the air of someone who, for the first time in her life, was playing a leading role in the history of her village. Until then she had been the helpless orphan, the girl who had never managed to find a husband, a poor night-worker, a lonely wretch in search of company; they were losing nothing by waiting. In two days' time, they would come and kiss her feet and thank her for her generosity and for their affluence, they would perhaps insist upon her running for mayor in the coming elections (thinking it through, it might be good to stick around for a while longer and enjoy her newly won glory).

The group of people gathered around the van were buying their bread in silence. Everyone turned to look at her, but no one said a word.

'What's going on in this place?' asked the lad selling the bread. 'Did someone die?'

'No,' replied the blacksmith, who was there too, despite it being a Saturday morning when he could sleep until late. 'Someone's having a bad time and we're all rather worried.'

Chantal couldn't understand what was happening.

'Go ahead and buy what you came to buy,' she heard someone say. 'The lad has to get going.'

Mechanically, she held out her money and took the bread. The baker's lad shrugged his shoulders – as if abandoning any attempt to understand what was going on – gave her the change, wished everyone good day and drove off.

'Now it's my turn to ask what's going on in this village,' she said, and fear made her speak more loudly than good manners usually permitted.

'You know what's going on,' the blacksmith said. 'You want us to commit a murder in return for money.'

'I don't want anything! I just did what the guy told me to! Have you all gone mad?'

'You're the one who's gone mad. You should never have allowed yourself to become that madman's mouthpiece! What on earth do you want? What are you getting out of it? Do you want to turn this place into a hell, just like it was in the Ahab stories. Have you lost all sense of honour and dignity?'

Chantal began to tremble.

'You really have gone mad! Did you actually take the wager seriously?'

'Just leave her,' said the hotel landlady. 'Let's go home and have breakfast.'

The group gradually dispersed. Chantal was still trembling, clutching her bread, rooted to the spot. Those people who had never agreed about anything in their lives before were, for the first time ever, in complete accord: she was the guilty one. Not the stranger, not the wager, but her, Chantal Prym, the instigator of the crime. Had the world turned upside down?

She left the bread by her door and set off towards the mountain; she wasn't hungry or thirsty, she didn't want anything. She had just understood something very important, something that filled her with fear, horror and utter terror.

No one had said anything to the baker's boy.

Something like this would normally be talked about, either with indignation or amusement, but the lad with the van, who delivered bread and gossip to the various villages in the region, had left with no idea of what was going on. It was clear that everyone in Viscos was gathered there together for the first time that day, and no one had had time to discuss what had taken place the previous night, although everyone knew what had happened in the bar. And yet, unconsciously, they had all made a pact of silence.

In other words, each one of those people, in their heart of hearts, was thinking the unthinkable, imagining the unimaginable.

Berta called to her. She was still at her post, watching over the village, though to no avail, since the danger was already there and was far greater than anyone could possibly have envisaged.

'I don't want to talk,' said Chantal. 'I can't think, react or say anything.'

'You can at least listen. Sit down here.'

Of all the people she had known, Berta was the only one who had ever treated her with any kindness. Chantal did not just sit down, she flung her arms around Berta. They stayed like that for a long while, until Berta broke the silence.

'Now go off into the forest and clear your head; you know you're not the problem. The rest of them know that too, but they need someone to blame.'

'It's the stranger who's to blame!'

'You and I know that, but no one else does. They all want to believe they've been betrayed, that you should have told them sooner, that you didn't trust them.'

'Betrayed?'

'Yes.'

'Why would they want to believe that?'

'Think about it.'

Chantal thought. Because they needed someone to blame. A victim.

'I don't know how this story will end,' said Berta. 'Viscos is a village of good people, although, as you yourself once said, they are a bit cowardly. Even so, it might be a good idea if you were to go somewhere far away from here for a while.'

She must be joking. No one could possibly take the stranger's bet seriously. No one. And anyway, she didn't have any money and she had nowhere to go.

But that wasn't true. A gold bar awaited her and it could take her anywhere in the world. But she didn't want to think about that.

At that very moment, as if by some quirk of fate, the stranger walked past them and set off for his walk in the mountains, as he did every morning. He nodded and continued on his way. Berta followed him with her eyes, while Chantal tried to spot whether anyone in the village had noticed his greeting. They would say she was his accomplice. They would say there was a secret code between the two of them.

'He looks worried,' said Berta. 'There's something odd about him.'

'Perhaps he's realised that his little game has become reality.'

'No, it's something more than that. I don't know what, but ... it's as if ... no, no, I don't know what it is.'

'I bet my husband would know,' Berta thought, aware of a nervous fidgeting to her left, but now was not the time to talk to him.

'It reminds me of Ahab,' she said to Chantal.

'I don't want to think about Ahab, about legends, about anything! All I want is for the world to go back to how it was, and for Viscos – for all its faults – not to be destroyed by one man's madness!'

'It seems you love this place more than you think.'

Chantal was trembling. Berta hugged her again, placing her head on her shoulder, as if she were the daughter she had never had.

'As I was saying, Ahab told a story about heaven and hell that used to be passed from parent to child, but has been forgotten now. Once upon a time, a man, his horse and his dog were travelling along a road. As they passed by a huge tree, it was struck by lightning, and they all died. But the man failed to notice that he was no longer of this world and so he continued walking along with his two animal companions. Sometimes the dead take a while to register their new situation ...'

Berta thought of her husband, who kept insisting that she get rid of Chantal because he had something important to say. Maybe it was time to explain to him that he was dead, so that he would stop interrupting her story.

'It was a long, uphill walk, the sun was beating down on them and they were all sweating and thirsty. At a bend in the road they saw a magnificent marble gateway that led into a gold-paved square, in the centre of which was a fountain overflowing with crystal-clear water. The man went over to the guard at the entrance.

'"Good morning."

'"Good morning," the guard replied.

'"What is this lovely place?"

'"It's Heaven."

'"Well, I'm very glad to see it, because we're very thirsty."

'"You're welcome to come in and drink all the water you want." And the guard indicated the fountain.

'"My horse and dog are also thirsty."

'"I'm terribly sorry," said the guard, "but animals are not allowed in here."

'The man was deeply disappointed for he really was very thirsty, but he was not prepared to drink alone, so he thanked the guard and went on his way. Exhausted after more trudging uphill, they reached an old gateway that opened on to a dirt road flanked by trees. A man, his hat pulled down over his face, was stretched out in the shade of one of the trees, apparently asleep.

'"Good morning," said the traveller.

'The other man greeted him with a nod.

'"We're very thirsty – me, my horse and my dog."

'"There's a spring over there amongst those rocks," said the man indicating the spot. "You can drink all you want."

'The man, his horse and his dog went to the spring and quenched their thirst.

'The traveller returned to thank the man.

'"Come back whenever you want," he was told.

'"By the way, what's this place called?"

'"Heaven."

'"Heaven? But the guard at the marble gateway told me that was Heaven!"

'"That's not Heaven, that's Hell."

'The traveller was puzzled.

'"You shouldn't let others take your name in vain, you know! False information can lead to all kinds of confusion!"

'"On the contrary, they do us a great favour, because the ones who stay there are those who have proved themselves capable of abandoning their dearest friends."'

Berta stroked the girl's head. She could feel that inside that head Good and Evil were waging a pitiless battle, and she told her to go for a walk in the forest and ask nature which village she should go to.

'Because I have the feeling that our little mountain paradise is about to desert its friends.'

'You're wrong, Berta. You belong to a different generation; the blood of the outlaws who once populated Viscos runs thicker in your veins than in mine. The men and women here still have their dignity, or if they don't, they at least have a healthy mistrust of one another. And if they don't even have that, then at least they have fear.'

'OK, maybe I'm wrong. Even so, do as I tell you, and go and listen to what nature has to say.'

Chantal left. And Berta turned towards the ghost of her husband, asking him to keep quiet; after all, she was a grown woman, indeed, she was an elderly woman, who shouldn't be interrupted when she was trying to give advice to someone much younger. She had learned to look after herself, and now she was looking after the village.

Her husband begged her to take care. She should be wary of offering advice to the young woman because nobody knew where matters might end.

Berta was taken aback because she thought the dead knew everything – hadn't he been the one to warn her of the dangers to come? Perhaps he was getting too old and was beginning to get obsessive about other things besides always eating his soup with the same spoon.

Her husband retorted that she was the old one, for the dead never age, and that, although the dead knew things of which the living had no knowledge, it would take a long time before he gained admittance to the realm of the archangels. He, being only recently dead (having left Earth a mere fifteen years before), still had a lot to learn, even though he knew he could offer substantial help.

Berta enquired whether the realm of the archangels was more attractive and comfortable. Her husband told her not to be facetious and to concentrate her energies on saving Viscos. Not that this was a source of particular interest to him – he was, after all, dead, and no one had touched on the subject of reincarnation (although he had heard a few conversations concerning this eventuality), and if reincarnation did exist, he was hoping to be reborn somewhere new. But he also wanted his wife to enjoy some peace and comfort during the days still remaining to her in this world.

'So, stop worrying,' thought Berta. Her husband wouldn't take her advice; he wanted her to do something, anything. If Evil triumphed, even if it was in some small, forgotten place with only three streets, a square and a church, it could nevertheless go on to contaminate the valley, the region, the country, the continent, the seas, the whole world.

Although Viscos had 281 inhabitants, Chantal being the youngest and Berta the oldest, it was controlled by a mere half-dozen individuals: the hotel landlady, responsible for the wellbeing of tourists; the priest, responsible for the care of souls; the mayor, responsible for the hunting regulations; the mayor's wife, responsible for the mayor and his decisions; the blacksmith, who had survived being bitten by the rogue wolf; and the owner of most of the lands around the village. It was he who had vetoed the idea of building a children's playground in the vague belief that Viscos would one day start growing again, and besides the site would be perfect for a luxury home.

It mattered little to the rest of the villagers what did or didn't happen to the place, for they had their sheep, their wheat and their families to take care of. They visited the hotel bar, attended Mass, obeyed the laws, had their tools repaired at the blacksmith's forge and, from time to time, acquired some land.

The landowner never went to the bar. He had learned of the story through his maid, who had been there on the night in question and had left in high excitement, telling her friends and him that the hotel guest was a very rich man; who knows, perhaps she could have a child by him and force him to give her part of his fortune. Concerned about the future, or, rather, about the fact that Miss Prym's story might spread and drive away hunters and tourists alike, he decided to call an emergency meeting. The group were gathering in the sacristy of the small church, just as Chantal was heading for the forest, the stranger was off on one of his mysterious walks and Berta was chatting with her husband about whether or not to try and save the village.

'The first thing we have to do is call the police,' said the landowner. 'It's obvious the gold doesn't exist; and besides, I suspect the man of trying to seduce my maid.'

'You don't know what you're talking about, because you weren't there,' the mayor insisted. 'The gold does exist. Miss Prym wouldn't risk her reputation without concrete proof. Not that that alters things, of course, we should still call the police. The stranger must be a bandit, a fellow with a price on his head, trying to conceal his ill-gotten gains here.'

'Don't be idiotic!' the mayor's wife said. 'If he was, surely he'd be more discreet about it.'

'All this is completely relevant. We must call the police straightaway.'

Everyone agreed. The priest served a little wine to calm everyone's nerves. They began to discuss what they would say to the police, given that they had no actual proof that the stranger had done anything; it might all end with Miss Prym being arrested for inciting a murder.

'The only proof is the gold. Without the gold, we can't do anything.'

Of course. But where was the gold? Only one person had ever seen it, and she didn't know where it was hidden.

The priest suggested they form search parties. The hotel landlady drew back the curtain of the sacristy window that looked out over the cemetery; she pointed to the mountains on one side, to the valley below, and to the mountains on the other side.

'We would need a hundred men searching for a hundred years to do that.'

The landowner silently bemoaned the fact that the cemetery had been constructed on that particular spot; it had a lovely view, and the dead had no use for it.

'On another occasion, I'd like to talk to you about the cemetery,' he said to the priest. 'I could offer you a far bigger plot for the dead, just near here, in exchange for this piece of land next to the church.'

'Nobody would want to buy that and live on the same spot where the dead used to lie.'

'Maybe no one from the village would, but there are tourists desperate to buy a summer home; it would just be a matter of asking the villagers to keep their mouths shut. It would mean more income for the village and more taxes for the town hall.'

'You're right. We just have to ask the villagers to keep their mouths shut. That wouldn't be so hard.'

A sudden silence fell. A long silence, which nobody dared to break. The two women admired the view; the priest started polishing a small bronze statue; the landowner took another sip of wine; the blacksmith tied and untied the laces on both boots; and the mayor kept glancing at his watch, as if to suggest that he had other pressing engagements.

But nobody said a word; everyone knew that the people of Viscos would never say a word if someone were to express an interest in purchasing what had once been the cemetery; they would keep quiet purely for the pleasure of seeing another person coming to live in that village on the verge of disappearing. Even if they didn't earn a penny by their silence.

Imagine if they did though.

Imagine if they earned enough money for the rest of their lives.

Imagine if they earned enough money for the rest of their lives and their children's lives.

At that precise moment, a hot and wholly unexpected wind blew through the sacristy.

'What exactly are you proposing?' asked the priest after a long five minutes.

Everyone turned to look at him.

'If the inhabitants really can be relied on to say nothing, I think we can proceed with negotiations,' replied the landowner, choosing his words carefully in case they were misinterpreted – or correctly interpreted, depending on your point of view.

'They're good, hardworking, discreet people,' the hotel landlady said, adopting the same strategy. 'Today, for example, when the driver of the baker's van wanted to know what was going on, nobody said a thing. I think we can trust them.'

Another silence. Only this time it was an unmistakably oppressive silence. Eventually, the game began again, and the blacksmith said:

'It isn't just a question of the villagers' discretion, the fact is that it's both immoral and unacceptable.'

'What is?'

'Selling off hallowed ground.'

A sigh of relief ran round the room; now that they had dealt satisfactorily with the practical aspects, they could proceed with the moral debate.

'What's immoral is sitting back and watching the demise of our beloved Viscos,' said the mayor's wife. 'Knowing that we are the last people to live here, and that the dream of our grandparents, our ancestors, Ahab and the Celts, will be over in a few years' time. Soon, we'll all be leaving the village, either for an old people's home or to beg our children to take in their strange, ailing parents, who are unable to adapt to life in the big city and spend all their time longing for what they've left behind, sad because they could not pass on to the next generation the gift they received from their parents.'

'You're right,' the blacksmith said. 'The life we lead is an immoral one. When Viscos does finally fall into ruin, these fields will be abandoned or else bought up for next to nothing; then machines will arrive and open up bigger and better roads. The houses will be demolished, steel warehouses will replace what was built with the sweat of our ancestors.

Agriculture will become entirely mechanised, and people will come in to work during the day and return at night to their homes, far from here. How shaming for our generation; we let our children leave, we failed to keep them here with us.'

'One way or another, we have to save this village,' said the landowner, who was possibly the only one who stood to profit from Viscos' demise, since he was in a position to buy up everything, then sell it on to a large industrial company. But of course he certainly didn't want to hand over, for a price below market value, lands that might contain buried treasure.

'What do you think, Father?' asked the hotel landlady.

'The only thing I know well is my religion, in which the sacrifice of one individual saved all humanity.'

Silence descended for a third time, but only for a moment.

'I need to start preparing for Saturday Mass,' he went on. 'Why don't we meet up later this evening?'

Everyone immediately agreed, setting a time late in the day, as if they were all immensely busy people with important matters to deal with.

Only the mayor managed to remain calm.

'What you've just been saying is very interesting, an excellent subject for a sermon. I think we should all attend Mass today.'

Chantal hesitated no longer. She headed straight for the Y-shaped rock, thinking of what she would do with the gold as soon as she got it. Go home, get the money she kept hidden there, put on some more sensible clothes, go down the road to the valley and hitch a lift. No more wagers: those people didn't deserve the fortune within their grasp. No suitcase: she didn't want them to know she was leaving Viscos for good – Viscos with its beautiful but pointless stories, its kind but cowardly inhabitants, the bar always crammed with people talking about the same things, the church she never attended. Naturally there was always the chance that she would find the police waiting for her at the bus station, the stranger accusing her of theft etc., etc. But now she was prepared to run any risk.

The hatred she had felt only half an hour before had been transformed into a far more agreeable emotion: vengeance.

She was glad to have been the first to reveal to those people the evil hidden in the depths of their false, ingenuous souls. They were all dreaming of the chance to commit a murder – only dreaming, mind you, because they would never actually do anything. They would spend the rest of their lives asleep, endlessly telling themselves how noble they were, how incapable of committing an injustice, ready to defend the village's dignity at whatever cost, yet aware that terror alone had prevented them from killing an innocent. They would congratulate themselves every morning on keeping their integrity, and blame themselves each night for that missed opportunity.

For the next three months, the only topic of conversation in the bar would be the honesty of the generous men and women of the village. Then the hunting season would arrive and the subject wouldn't be touched upon – there was no need for visitors to know anything about it, they liked to think they were in a remote spot, where everyone was friends, where good always prevailed, where nature was bountiful, and that the local products lined up for sale on a single shelf in the hotel reception – which the hotel landlady called her 'little shop' – were steeped in this disinterested love.

But the hunting season would come to an end, and then the villagers would be free to return to the topic. This time around, after many evenings spent dreaming about the riches they had let slip through their fingers, they would start inventing hypotheses to fit the situation: why did nobody have the courage, at dead of night, to kill useless old Berta in return for ten gold bars? Why did no hunting accident befall the shepherd Santiago, who drove his flock up the mountainside each morning? All kinds of hypotheses would be weighed up, first timidly and then angrily.

One year on and they would be consumed with mutual hatred – the village had been given its opportunity and had let it slip. They would ask after Miss Prym, who had vanished without trace, perhaps taking with her the gold she had watched the stranger hide. They would say terrible things about her, the ungrateful orphan, the poor girl whom they had all struggled to help after her grandmother's death, who had got a job in the bar when she had proved incapable of getting herself a husband and leaving, who used to sleep with the hotel guests, usually men much older than herself, and who made eyes at all the tourists just to get a bigger tip.

They would spend the rest of their lives caught between self-pity and loathing; Chantal would be happy, that was her revenge. She would never forget the looks those people around the van gave her, imploring her silence regarding a murder they would never dare to commit, then rounding on her as if she was to blame for all the cowardice that was finally rising to the surface.

'A jacket. My leather trousers. I can wear two tee shirts and strap the gold bar around my waist. A jacket. My leather trousers. A jacket.'

There she was, in front of the Y-shaped rock. Beside her lay the stick she had used two days before to dig up the gold. For a moment she savoured the gesture that would transform her from an honest woman into a thief.

No, that wasn't right. The stranger had provoked her, and he also stood to gain from the deal. She wasn't so much stealing as claiming her wages for her role as narrator in this tasteless comedy. She deserved not only the gold but much, much more for having endured the stares of the victimless murderers standing round the baker's van, for having spent her entire life there, for those three sleepless nights, for the soul she had now lost – assuming she had ever had a soul to lose.

She dug down into the soft earth and saw the gold bar. When she saw it, she heard a noise.

Someone had followed her. Automatically, she began pushing the earth back into the hole, realising as she did so the futility of the gesture. Then she turned, ready to explain that she was looking for the treasure, that she knew the stranger walked regularly along this path, and that she had happened to notice that the soil had been recently disturbed.

What she saw, however, robbed her of her voice – for it had no interest in treasure, in village crises, justice or injustice, only in blood.

The white mark on its left ear. The rogue wolf.

It was standing between her and the nearest tree; it would be impossible to get past the animal. Chantal stood rooted to the spot, hypnotised by the animal's blue eyes. Her mind was working frantically, wondering what would be her next step – the branch would be far too flimsy to counter the beast's attack. She could climb onto the Y-shaped rock, but that still wasn't high enough. She could choose not to believe the legend and scare off the wolf as she would any other lone wolf, but that was too risky, it would be wisest to recognise that all legends contain a hidden truth.

'Punishment.'

Unfair punishment, just like everything else that had

happened in her life; God seemed to have singled her out purely to demonstrate his hatred of the world.

Instinctively she let the branch fall to the ground and, in a movement that seemed to her interminably slow, brought her arms up to her throat: she couldn't let him sink his teeth in there. She regretted not wearing her leather trousers; the next most vulnerable part were her legs and the vein there, which, once pierced, would see you bleed to death in ten minutes – at least that was what the hunters always said, to explain why they wore those high boots.

The wolf opened its mouth and snarled. The dangerous, pent-up growl of an animal who gives no warning, but attacks on the instant. She kept her eyes glued to his, even though her heart was pounding, for now his fangs were bared.

It was all a question of time; he would either attack or run off, but Chantal knew he was going to attack. She glanced down at the ground, looking for any loose stones she might slip on, but found none. She decided to launch herself at the animal; she would be bitten and would have to run towards the tree with the wolf's teeth sunk into her. She would have to ignore the pain.

She thought about the gold. She would soon be back to look for it. She clung to every shred of hope, anything that might give her the strength to confront the prospect of her flesh being ripped by those sharp teeth, of one of her bones poking through, of possibly stumbling and falling and having her throat torn out.

She prepared to run.

Just then, as if in a movie, she saw a figure appear behind the wolf, although still a fair distance away.

The beast sensed another presence too, but did not look away, and she continued to fix him with her stare. It seemed to be only the force of that stare that was averting the attack, and she didn't want to run any further risks; if someone else was there, her chances of survival were increased – even if, in the end, it cost her the gold bar.

The presence behind the wolf silently crouched down and moved to the left. Chantal knew there was another tree on that side, easy to climb. At that moment, a stone arced across the sky and landed near the wolf, which turned with phenomenal speed and hurtled off in the direction of this new threat.

'Run!' yelled the stranger.

She ran in the direction of her only refuge, while the man likewise clambered lithely up the other tree. By the time the rogue wolf reached him, he was safe.

The wolf began snarling and leaping, occasionally managing to get partway up the trunk, only to slip back down again.

'Tear off some branches!' shouted Chantal.

But the stranger seemed to be in a kind of trance. She repeated her instruction twice, then three times, until he registered what she was saying. He began tearing off branches and throwing them down at the wolf.

'No, don't do that! Pull off the branches, bundle them up, and set fire to them! I don't have a lighter, so do as I say!'

Her voice had the desperate edge of someone in real peril. The stranger grabbed some branches and took an eternity to light them; the previous day's storm had soaked everything and, at that time of the year, the sun didn't penetrate into that part of the forest.

Chantal waited until the flames of the improvised torch had begun to burn fiercely. She would have been quite happy to have him spend the rest of the day in the tree, confronting the fear he wanted to inflict on the rest of the world, but she had to get away and so was obliged to help him.

'Now show me you're a man!' she yelled. 'Get down from the tree, keep a firm hold on the torch and walk towards the wolf!'

The stranger could not move.

'Do it!' she yelled again and, when he heard her voice, the man understood the force of authority behind her words – an authority derived from terror, from the ability to react quickly, leaving fear and suffering for later.

He climbed down with the burning torch in his hands, ignoring the sparks that occasionally singed his cheeks. When he saw the animal's foam-flecked teeth close to, his fear increased, but he had to do something – something he should have done when his wife was abducted, his daughters murdered.

'Remember, keep looking him in the eye!' he heard the girl say.

He did as she said. Things were becoming easier with each passing moment; he was no longer looking at the enemy's weapons but at the enemy himself. They were equals, both capable of provoking fear in each other.

His feet touched the ground. The wolf recoiled, frightened by the fire: it continued snarling and leaping, but did not come near.

'Attack him!'

He advanced on the beast, which snarled more loudly than ever, showing his teeth, but still retreating.

'Chase him! Get him away from here!'

The flames were burning more fiercely now, and the stranger realised that they would soon be burning his hands; he did not have much time. Almost without thinking, keeping his eyes fixed on those sinister blue ones, he ran at the wolf, which stopped snarling and leaping, spun round and disappeared back into the forest.

In the twinkling of an eye, Chantal had scrambled down from her tree. She had soon gathered up a handful of kindling from the ground and made her own torch.

'Let's get out of here. Now.'

'And go where?'

Where? To Viscos, where everyone would see them arriving together? Into another trap where the fire would no longer produce the desired effect? She slumped to the ground, her back suddenly wracked with pain, her heart pounding.

'Make a bonfire,' she said to the stranger, 'and let me think.'

She attempted to move and let out a cry – it was as if someone had stuck a dagger in her shoulder. The stranger collected leaves and branches and built a fire. Every time she moved Chantal contorted with pain and let out a dull groan; she must have really hurt herself when she was climbing up the tree.

'Don't worry, you haven't broken anything,' the stranger said, hearing her cry out in pain. 'I've had the same thing. When your body reaches an extreme of tension, all the muscles contract and make you pay the price. Let me give you a massage.'

'Don't touch me. Don't come near me. Don't talk to me.'

Pain, fear, shame. He must have been there when she was digging up the gold; he knew – for the devil was his companion and devils can see into the human soul – that this time Chantal had intended to steal it.

By now, he also knew that the whole village was dreaming of committing a murder. He knew that they were too frightened actually to carry out the crime, but their intention was enough to answer his question: human beings are essentially bad. And since he knew she was about to flee, the wager the two of them had made the previous evening meant nothing, and he could return from whence he came (wherever that was) with his treasure intact and his suspicions confirmed.

She tried to find the most comfortable position to sit in, but there wasn't one; she would have to stay put. The fire would keep the wolf at bay, but it would be bound to attract the attention of some passing shepherds. And the two of them would be seen together.

She remembered that it was a Saturday. People would be in their homes full of ugly knick-knacks, plaster saints and reproductions of famous paintings, all trying to have a good time – and this weekend, of course, they had the best opportunity to do that since the end of the Second World War.

'Don't talk to me.'

'I didn't say a word.'

Chantal considered crying, but didn't want to do so in front of him. She bit back her tears.

'I saved your life. I deserve the gold.'

'I saved your life. The wolf was about to attack you.'

It was true.

'On the other hand, I believe you saved something else deep inside me,' the stranger went on.

A trick. She would pretend she hadn't understood; that was like giving her permission to take his fortune, to get out of there for good, end of story.

'About last night's wager. I was in so much pain myself that I needed to make everyone suffer as much as I was suffering; that was my one source of consolation. You were right.'

The stranger's devil didn't like what he was hearing at all. He asked Chantal's devil to help him out, but her devil was new and hadn't yet asserted total control.

'Does that change anything?'

'Nothing. The bet's still on, and I know I'll win. But I also know how wretched I am and how I became that way: because I feel I didn't deserve what happened to me.'

Chantal asked herself how they were going to get out of there; even though it was still only morning, they couldn't stay in the forest forever.

'Well, I think I deserve my gold, and I'm going to take it, assuming you don't stop me,' she said. 'I'd advise you to do the same. Neither of us needs to go back to Viscos; we can head straight for the valley, hitch a ride, and then each of us can follow our own destiny.'

'You can go, if you like. But at this very moment the villagers are deciding who should die.'

'That's as maybe. They'll devote a couple of days to it, until the deadline is up; then they'll devote a couple of years to arguing about who should have been the victim. They are hopelessly indecisive when it comes to doing anything, and implacable when it comes to apportioning blame – I know my village. If you don't go back, they won't even trouble themselves to discuss it. They'll dismiss it as something I made up.'

'Viscos is just like any other village in the world, and whatever happens there happens in every continent, city, camp, convent, wherever. That's something you don't understand, just as you don't understand that this time fate has worked in my favour: I chose exactly the right person to help me. Someone who, behind the mask of a hard-working, honest young woman, also wants revenge. Since we can never see the enemy – because if we take this tale to its logical conclusion, our real enemy is God for putting us through everything we've suffered – we vent our frustrations on everything around us. It's a desire for vengeance that can never be satisfied, because it's directed against life itself.'

'What are we doing sitting around here talking?' asked Chantal, irritated because this man, whom she hated more than anyone else in the world, could see so clearly into her soul. 'Why don't we just take the money and leave?'

'Because yesterday I realised that by proposing the very thing that most revolts me – a senseless murder, just like that inflicted on my wife and daughters – the truth is I was trying to save myself. Do you remember the philosopher I mentioned in our second conversation? The one who said that God's hell is His love for humanity, because human behaviour makes every second of His eternal life a torment?

'Well, that same philosopher said something else too, he said: *Man needs what's worst in him in order to achieve what's best in him.*'

'I don't understand.'

'Until now, I used to think solely in terms of revenge. Like the inhabitants of your village, I used to dream and plan day and night, but never do anything. For a while, I used to scour the newspapers for articles about other people who had lost their loved ones in similar situations, but who had ended up behaving in exactly the opposite way to myself: they formed victim support groups, organisations to denounce injustice, campaigns to demonstrate how the pain of loss can never be replaced by the burden of vengeance.

'I too tried to look at matters from a more generous perspective: I didn't succeed. But now I've gained courage; I've reached the depths and discovered that there is light at the bottom.'

'Go on,' said Chantal, for she too was beginning to see a kind of light.

'I'm not trying to prove that humanity is perverse. What I'm trying to do is to prove that I unconsciously asked for the things that happened to me. Because I'm evil, a total degenerate and I deserved the punishment that life gave me.'

'You're trying to prove that God is just.'

The stranger thought for a moment.

'Maybe.'

'I don't know if God is just. He hasn't treated me particularly fairly, and it's that sense of powerlessness that has destroyed my soul. I cannot be as good as I would like to be, nor as bad as I think I need to be. A few minutes ago, I thought He had chosen me to avenge Himself for all the sadness men cause Him. I think you have the same doubts, albeit on a much larger scale, because your goodness was not rewarded.'

Chantal was surprised at her own words. The man's devil noticed that her angel was beginning to shine with greater intensity, and everything was beginning to be turned inside out.

'Resist!' he said to the other demon.

'I am resisting,' he replied. 'But it's an uphill struggle.'

'Your problem isn't to do with God's justice exactly,' the man said. 'It's more the fact that you always chose to be a victim of circumstance. I know a lot of people in your situation.'

'Like you, for example.'

'No. I rebelled against something that happened to me and I don't care whether others like my attitude or not. You, on the other hand, believed in your role as helpless orphan, someone who wants to be accepted at all costs. Since that doesn't always happen, your need to be loved was transformed into a stubborn desire for revenge. At heart, you wish you were like the rest of Viscos' inhabitants – in other words, deep down, we'd all like to be the same as everyone else. But destiny accorded you a different fate.'

Chantal shook her head.

'Do something,' said Chantal's devil to his colleague. 'Even though she's saying no, her soul understands and is saying yes.'

The stranger's devil was feeling humiliated because the new arrival had noticed that he wasn't strong enough to get the man to shut up.

'Words don't matter in the end,' the devil said. 'Let them talk, and life will see to it that they act differently.'

'I didn't mean to interrupt you,' the stranger said. 'Please, go on with what you were saying about God's justice.'

Chantal was pleased not to have to listen any more to things she didn't want to hear.

'I don't know if it makes sense. But you must have noticed that Viscos isn't a particularly religious place, even though it has a church, like all the villages in this region. That's because Ahab, even though he was converted to Christianity by St Savin, had serious reservations about the influence of priests. Since the majority of the early inhabitants were bandits, he thought that all the priests would do, with their threats of eternal damnation, would be to send them back to their criminal ways. Men who have nothing to lose never give a thought for eternal life.

'Naturally, the first priest duly appeared, and Ahab understood what the real threat was. To compensate for it, he instituted something he had learned from the Jews – a Day of Atonement – except that he determined to establish a ritual of his own making.

'Once a year, the inhabitants shut themselves up in their houses, made two lists, turned to face the highest mountain and then raised their first list to the heavens.

'"Here, Lord, are all the sins I have committed against you," they said, reading the account of all the sins they had committed. Business swindles, adulteries, injustices, things of that sort. "I have sinned and beg forgiveness for having offended You so greatly."

'Then – and here lay Ahab's originality – the residents immediately pulled the second list out of their pocket and, still facing the same mountain, they held that one up to the skies too. And they said something like: "And here, Lord, is a list of all Your sins against me: You made me work harder than necessary, my daughter fell ill despite all my prayers, I was robbed when I was trying to be honest, I suffered more than was fair."

'After reading out the second list, they ended the ritual with: "I have been unjust towards You and You have been unjust towards me. However, since today is the Day of

Atonement, You will forget my faults and I will forget Yours, and we can carry on together for another year."'

'Forgive God!' said the stranger. 'Forgive an implacable God who is constantly creating and destroying!'

'This conversation is getting too personal for my taste,' said Chantal, looking away. 'I haven't learned enough from life to be able to teach you anything.'

The stranger said nothing.

'I don't like this at all,' thought the stranger's devil, beginning to see a bright light shining beside him, a presence he was certainly not going to allow. He had banished that light two years ago, on one of the world's many beaches.

Given the large number of legends, of Celtic and Protestant influences, of certain unfortunate examples set by the Arab who had eventually brought peace to the village, and given the constant presence of saints and bandits in the surrounding area, the priest knew that Viscos was not exactly a religious place, even though its residents still attended baptisms and weddings (although nowadays these were merely a distant memory), funerals (which, on the contrary, occurred with ever increasing frequency) and Christmas Mass. For the most part, few troubled to make the effort to attend the two weekly Masses – one on Saturday and one on Sunday, both at eleven o'clock in the morning; even so, he made sure to celebrate them, if only to justify his presence there. He wished to give the impression of being a busy, saintly man.

To his surprise, that day the church was so crowded that he had to allow some of the congregation up on to the altar steps, otherwise they could not have fitted everyone in. Instead of turning on the electric heaters suspended from the ceiling, he had to ask members of the congregation to open the two small side windows, as everyone was sweating; the priest wondered to himself whether the sweat was due to the heat or to the general tension.

The entire village was there, apart from Miss Prym – possibly ashamed of what she had said the previous day – and old Berta, whom everyone suspected of being a witch and therefore allergic to religion.

'In the Name of the Father, and of the Son, and of the Holy Ghost.'

A loud 'Amen' rang out. The priest began the liturgy, said the introit, had the usual faithful church member read the lesson, solemnly intoned the responsory, and recited the Gospel in slow, grave tones. After which, he asked all those in the pews to be seated, whilst the rest remained standing.

It was time for the sermon.

'In the Gospel according to Luke, there is a moment when an important man approaches Jesus and asks: '*Good Master, what shall I do to inherit eternal life?*' And, to our surprise, Jesus responds: '*Why callest thou me good? None is good, save one, that is, God.*'

'For many years, I pondered over this little fragment of text, trying to understand what Our Lord was saying: That He was not good? That the whole of Christianity, with its concept of charity, is based on the teachings of someone who considered Himself to be bad? Finally, I saw what he meant: Christ, at that moment, is referring to His human nature. As man, He is bad, as God, He is good.'

The priest paused, hoping that the congregation understood his message. He was lying to himself: he still couldn't grasp what Christ was saying, since if his human nature was bad, then his words and actions would also be bad. But this was a theological discussion of no relevance just then; what mattered was that his explanation should be convincing.

'I am not going to run on too long today. I want all of you to understand that part of being human is to accept our baser, perverse nature and know that the only reason that we were not condemned to eternal damnation because of this base nature was that Jesus sacrificed himself to save humanity. I repeat: the sacrifice of the Son of God saved us all. The sacrifice of a single person.

'I wish to close this sermon by mentioning the beginning of one of the sacred books that together comprise the Bible, the Book of Job. God is sitting upon His celestial throne, when the Devil comes to speak to Him. God asks where he has been and the Devil replies that he has been "going to and fro in Earth".

'"Did you see my servant Job? Did you see how he worships me, and performs all his sacrifices?"

'The Devil laughs and replies: "Well, Job does, after all, have everything, so why wouldn't he worship God and make sacrifices? Take away the good You gave him, and see if he worships You then."

'God accepts the challenge. Year after year he punishes the man who most loved Him. Job is in the presence of a power he cannot comprehend, whom he believed to be the Supreme Judge, but who is destroying his animals, killing his children and afflicting his body with boils. Then, after great suffering, Job rebels and blasphemes against the Lord. Only then does God restore to him that which He had taken away.

'For years now we have witnessed the decay of our village. I wonder now whether this might not be a divine punishment for our uncomplaining acceptance of whatever was dealt out to us, as if we deserved to lose the place we live in, the fields where we cultivate our crops and graze our sheep, the houses built by the dreams of our ancestors. Has not the moment come for us to rebel? If God forced Job to do as much, might He not be requiring us to do likewise?

'Why did God force Job to behave in that way? To show that he was by nature bad, and that everything that came to him was by grace and grace alone, and not as a reward for good behaviour. We have committed the sin of pride in believing ourselves to be better than we are – and that is why we are suffering.

'God accepted the Devil's wager and – so it seems – committed an injustice. Remember that: God accepted the Devil's wager. And Job learned his lesson for, like us, he too was committing the sin of pride in believing that he was a good man.

'*None is good*, says the Lord. No one. We should stop pretending to a goodness that offends God and accept our faults: if one day we have to accept a wager with the Devil, let us remember that our Father who is in heaven did exactly the same in order to save the soul of His servant Job.'

The sermon was at an end. The priest asked everyone to stand up, and continued the Mass. He was sure that the message had been fully understood.

'Let each of us just go our own way, me with my gold bar and you …'

'You mean my gold bar,' the stranger broke in.

'All you have to do is pack up your things and disappear. If I don't take the gold, I'll have to go back to Viscos. I'll be sacked from my job or stigmatised by the whole population. They'll think I lied to them. You can't, you simply can't do that to me. Let's say I deserve it as payment for all my work.'

The stranger rose to his feet and picked up some of the branches from the fire.

'The wolf will run away from the flames, won't it? Well, then, I'm off to Viscos. You do what you think best, steal the gold and run away if you want, I really don't care any more. I've got something more important to do.'

'Just a minute! Don't leave me here alone!'

'Come with me, then.'

Chantal looked at the fire before her, at the Y-shaped rock, at the stranger who was already moving off, taking some of the fire with him. She could do likewise: take some wood from the fire, dig up the gold and head straight down to the valley; there wasn't any need for her to go home and get the little money she had so carefully scraped together.

When she reached the town in the valley, she would ask the bank to value the gold, she would then sell it, buy clothes and suitcases, and she would be free.

'Wait!' she called after the stranger, but he was still walking towards Viscos and would soon be lost to view.

'Think fast,' she told herself.

She didn't have much time. She too took some burning twigs from the fire, went over to the rock and once again dug up the gold. She picked it up, cleaned it off on her dress and studied it for the third time.

Then she was seized with panic. She took her handful of burning wood and, hatred oozing from her every pore, ran after the stranger, down the path he must have taken. She had met two wolves that day, one who could be scared off with fire, and another who wasn't scared of anything any more because he had already lost everything he valued and was now moving blindly forward, intent on destroying everything in his path.

She ran as fast as she could, but she didn't find him. His torch would have burned out by now, but he must still be in the forest, defying the rogue wolf, wanting to die as fiercely as he wanted to kill.

She reached the village, pretended not to hear Berta calling to her and met up with the congregation leaving Mass, amazed that virtually the entire population had gone to church. The stranger had wanted to provoke a murder and had ended up filling the priest's diary; it would be a week of confessions and penances – as if God could be hoodwinked.

Everyone stared at her, but no one spoke to her. She met each of their stares because she knew that she was not to blame in any way. She had no need of confession, she was merely a pawn in an evil game, one that she was slowly beginning to understand – and she didn't at all like what she saw.

She locked herself in her room and peeped through the window. The crowd had now dispersed, and again something strange was going on; the village was unusually empty for a sunny Saturday. As a rule, people stood about chatting in small groups in the square where once there had been a gallows and where now there was a cross.

She stood for a while gazing at the empty street, feeling the sun on her face, though it no longer warmed her, for winter was beginning. If people had been out in the square, that would have been their topic of conversation – the weather. The temperature. The threat of rain or drought. But today they were all in their houses, and Chantal did not know why.

The longer she gazed at the street, the more she felt she was the same as all those other people – she, who had always believed herself to be different, daring, full of plans that would never even occur to those peasant brains.

How embarrassing. And yet, what a relief too; she was no longer in Viscos by some cruel whim of destiny, but because she deserved to be there. She had always considered herself to be different, and now she saw that she was just the same as them. She had dug up the gold bar three times, but had been incapable of actually running off with it. She had committed the crime in her soul, but had been unable to carry it out in the real world.

Now she knew that there was no way she could commit the crime, for it wasn't a temptation, it was a trap.

'Why a trap?' she wondered. Something told her that the gold bar she had seen was the solution to the problem the stranger had created. But, however hard she tried, she could not work out what that solution might be.

Her newly arrived devil glanced to one side and saw that Miss Prym's light, which before had seemed to be growing, was now almost disappearing again; what a shame his colleague wasn't there with him to celebrate the victory.

What he didn't know was that angels also have their strategies: at that moment, Miss Prym's light was hiding so as not to awaken a response in its enemy. All that the angel required was for Chantal to rest a little so that he could converse with her soul without interference from the fear and guilt that human beings love to load themselves down with every day of their lives.

Chantal slept. And she heard what she needed to hear and understood what she needed to understand.

'Let's drop all this talk of land and cemeteries,' the mayor's wife said, as soon as they were all gathered again in the sacristy. 'Let's talk plainly.'

The other five agreed.

'Father, you convinced me,' said the landowner. 'God justifies certain acts.'

'Don't be cynical,' replied the priest. 'When we looked through that window, we all knew what we meant. That's why that hot wind blew through here; it was the Devil come to keep us company.'

'Of course,' agreed the mayor, who did not believe in devils. 'We're all convinced. We'd better talk plainly, or we'll lose precious time.'

'I'll speak for all of us,' said the hotel landlady. 'We are thinking of accepting the stranger's proposal. To commit a murder.'

'To offer up a sacrifice,' said the priest, more accustomed to the rites of religion.

The silence that followed showed that everyone was in agreement.

'Only cowards hide behind silence. Let us pray in a loud voice so that God may hear us and know that we are doing this for the good of Viscos. Let us kneel.'

They all reluctantly kneeled down, knowing that it was useless begging forgiveness from God for a sin committed in full consciousness of the evil they were doing. Then they remembered Ahab's Day of Atonement; soon, when that day came around again, they would accuse God of having placed them in terrible temptation.

The priest suggested that they pray together.

'Lord, You once said that no one is good; accept us then with all our imperfections and forgive us in Your infinite generosity and Your infinite love. For as You pardoned the Crusaders who killed the Muslims in order to re-conquer the holy land of Jerusalem, as You pardoned the Inquisitors who sought to preserve the purity of Your Church, as You pardoned those who insulted You and nailed You to the cross, so pardon us who must offer up a sacrifice in order to save our village.'

'Let's get down to practicalities,' said the mayor's wife, rising to her feet. 'Who should be sacrificed? And who should carry it out?'

'The person who brought the Devil here was a young woman whom we have all always helped and supported,' commented the landowner, who in the not-too-distant past had himself slept with the girl he was referring to and had ever since been tormented by the idea that she might tell his wife about it. 'Evil must fight Evil, and she deserves to be punished.'

Two of the others agreed, arguing that, in addition, Miss Prym was the one person in the village who could not be trusted because she thought she was different from everyone else and was always saying that one day she would leave.

'Her mother's dead. Her grandmother's dead. Nobody would miss her,' the mayor agreed, thus becoming the third to approve the suggestion.

His wife, however, opposed it.

'What if she knows where the treasure is hidden? After all, she was the only one who saw it. Moreover, we can trust her precisely because of what has just been said – she was the one who brought Evil here and led a whole community into considering committing a murder. She can say what she likes, but if the rest of the village says nothing, it will be the word of one neurotic young woman against us, people who have all achieved something in life.'

The mayor was undecided, as always when his wife had expressed her opinion:

'Why do you want to save her, if you don't even like her?'

'I understand,' the priest responded. 'That way the guilt falls on the head of the one who precipitated the tragedy. She will bear that burden for the rest of her days and nights. She might even end up like Judas, who betrayed Jesus and then committed suicide, in a gesture of despair and futility, because she created all the necessary preconditions for the crime.'

The mayor's wife was surprised by the priest's reasoning – it was exactly what she had been thinking. The young woman was beautiful, she led men into temptation, and she refused to be contented with the typical life of an inhabitant of Viscos. She was forever bemoaning the fact that she had to stay in the village, which, for all its faults, was nevertheless made up of honest, hardworking people, a place where many people would love to spend their days (strangers, naturally, who would leave after discovering how boring it is to live constantly at peace).

'I can't think of anyone else,' the hotel landlady said, aware of how difficult it would be to find someone else to work in the bar, but realising that, with the gold she would receive, she could close the hotel and move far away. 'The peasants and shepherds form a closed group, some are married, many have children a long way from here, who might become suspicious should anything happen to their parents. Miss Prym is the only one who could disappear without trace.'

For religious reasons – after all, Jesus cursed those who condemned an innocent person – the priest had no wish to nominate anyone. But he knew who the victim should be; he just had to ensure that the others came to the same conclusion.

'The people of Viscos work from dawn to dusk, come rain or shine. Each one has a task to fulfil, even that poor wretch of a girl whom the Devil decided to use for his own evil ends. There are only a few of us left, and we can't afford the luxury of losing another pair of hands.'

'So, Father, we have no victim. All we can hope is that another stranger turns up tonight, yet even that would prove risky, because he would inevitably have a family who would seek him out to the ends of the earth. In Viscos everyone works hard to earn the bread brought to us by the baker's van.'

'You're right,' said the priest. 'Perhaps everything we have been through since last night has been mere illusion. Everyone in this village has someone who would miss them, and none of us would want anything to happen to one of our own loved ones. Only three people in this village sleep alone: myself, Berta and Miss Prym.'

'Are you offering yourself up for sacrifice, Father?'

'If it's for the good of the community.'

The other five felt greatly relieved, suddenly aware that it was a sunny Saturday, that there would be no murder, only a martyrdom. The tension in the sacristy evaporated as if by magic, and the hotel landlady felt so moved she could have kissed the feet of that saintly man.

'There's only one thing,' the priest went on. 'You would need to convince everyone that it is not a mortal sin to kill a minister of God.'

'You can explain it to Viscos yourself!' exclaimed the mayor enthusiastically, already planning the various reforms he could put in place once he had the money, the advertisements he could take out in the regional newspapers, attracting fresh investment because of the tax cuts he could make, drawing in tourists with the changes to the hotel he intended to fund, and having a new telephone line installed that would prove less problematic than the current one.

'I can't do that,' said the priest. 'Martyrs offer themselves up when the people want to kill them. They never incite their own death, for the Church has always said that life is a gift from God. You'll have to do the explaining.'

'Nobody will believe us. They'll consider us to be the very worst kind of murderer if we kill a holy man for money, just as Judas did to Christ.'

The priest shrugged. It felt as if the sun had once again gone in, and tension returned to the sacristy.

'Well, that only leaves Berta,' the landowner concluded.

After a lengthy pause, it was the priest's turn to speak.

'That woman must suffer greatly with her husband gone. She's done nothing but sit outside her house all these years, alone with the elements and her own boredom. All she does is long for the past. And I'm afraid the poor woman may slowly be going mad: I've often passed by that way and seen her talking to herself.'

Again a gust of wind blew through the sacristy, startling the people inside because all the windows were closed.

'She's certainly had a very sad life,' the hotel landlady went on. 'I think she would give anything to join her beloved. They were married for forty years, you know.'

They all knew that, but it was hardly relevant now.

'She's an old woman, near the end of her life,' added the landowner. 'She's the only person in the village who does nothing of note. I once asked her why she always sat outside her house, even in winter, and do you know what she told me? She said she was watching over our village, so that she could see when Evil arrived.'

'Well, she hasn't done very well on that score.'

'On the contrary,' said the priest, 'from what I understand of your conversation, the person who let Evil enter in should also be the one who should drive it out.'

Another silence, and everyone knew that a victim had been chosen.

'There's just one thing,' the mayor's wife commented. 'We know when the sacrifice will be offered up in the interests of the well being of the village. We know who it will be. Thanks to this sacrifice, a good soul will go to heaven and find eternal joy, rather than remain suffering here on earth. All we need to know now is how.'

'Try to speak to all the men in the village,' the priest said to the mayor, 'and call a meeting in the square for nine o'clock tonight. I think I know how. Drop by here shortly before nine, and the two of us can talk it over.'

Before they left, he asked that, while the meeting that night was in progress, the two women should go to Berta's house and keep her talking. Although she never went out at night, it would be best not to take any risks.

Chantal arrived at the bar in time for work. No one was there.

'There's a meeting in the square tonight at nine,' the hotel landlady said. 'Just for the men.'

She didn't need to say anything more. Chantal knew what was going on.

'Did you actually see the gold?'

'Yes, I did, but you should ask the stranger to bring it here. You never know, once he's got what he wants, he might simply decide to disappear.'

'He's not mad.'

'He is.'

The hotel landlady thought that this might indeed be a good idea. She went up to the stranger's room and came down a few minutes later.

'He's agreed. He says it's hidden in the forest and that he'll bring it here tomorrow.'

'I guess I don't need to work today, then.'

'You certainly do. It's in your contract.'

She didn't know how to broach the subject she and the others had spent the afternoon discussing, but it was important to gauge the girl's reaction.

'I'm really shocked by all this,' she said. 'At the same time, I realise that people need to think twice or even ten times before they decide what they should do.'

'They could think it over twenty or two hundred times and they still wouldn't have the courage to do anything.'

'You may be right,' the hotel landlady agreed, 'but if they do decide to make a move, what would you do?'

The woman needed to know what Chantal's reaction would be, and Chantal realised that the stranger was far closer to the truth than she was, despite her having lived in Viscos all those years. A meeting in the square! What a pity the gallows had been dismantled.

'So what would you do?' the landlady insisted.

'I won't answer that question,' she said, even though she knew exactly what she would do. 'I'll only say that Evil never brings Good. I discovered that for myself this afternoon.'

The hotel landlady didn't like having her authority flouted, but thought it prudent not to argue with the young woman and risk an enmity that could bring problems in the future. On the pretext that she needed to bring the accounts up to date (an absurd excuse, she thought later, since there was only one guest in the hotel), she left Miss Prym alone in the bar. She felt reassured; Miss Prym showed no signs of rebellion, even after she had mentioned the meeting in the square, which showed that something unusual was happening in Viscos. Besides, Miss Prym also had a great need for money, she had her whole life ahead of her, and would almost certainly like to follow in the footsteps of her childhood friends who had already left the village. And, even if she wasn't willing to co-operate, at least she didn't seem to want to interfere.

The priest dined frugally then sat down alone on one of the church pews. The mayor would be there in a few minutes.

He contemplated the whitewashed walls, the altar unadorned by any important work of art, decorated instead with cheap reproductions of paintings of the saints who – in the dim and distant past – had lived in the region. The people of Viscos had never been very religious, despite the important role St Savin had played in resurrecting the fortunes of the place. But the people forgot this and preferred to concentrate on Ahab, on the Celts, on the peasants' centuries-old superstitions, failing to understand that it took only a gesture, a simple gesture, to achieve redemption: that of accepting Jesus as the sole Saviour of humanity.

Only hours earlier, he had offered himself up for martyrdom. It had been a risky move, but he had been prepared to see it through and deliver himself over for sacrifice, had the others not been so frivolous and so easily manipulated.

'No, that's not true. They may be frivolous, but they're not that easily manipulated.' Indeed, through silence or clever words, they had made him say what they wanted to hear: the sacrifice that redeems, the victim who saves, decay transformed anew into glory. He had pretended to let himself be used by the others, but had only said what he himself believed.

He had been prepared for the priesthood from an early age, and that was his true vocation. By the time he was twenty-one, he had already been ordained a priest, and had impressed everyone with his gifts as a preacher and his skill as a parish administrator. He said prayers every evening, visited the sick and those in prison, gave food to the hungry – just as the holy scriptures commanded. His fame soon spread throughout the region and reached the ears of the bishop, a man known for his wisdom and fairness.

The bishop invited him, together with other young priests, for an evening meal. They ate and talked about various matters until, at the end, the bishop, who was getting old and had difficulties walking, got up and offered each of them some water. The priest had been the only one not to refuse, asking for his glass to be filled to the brim.

One of the other priests whispered, loud enough for the bishop to hear: 'We all refused the water because we know we are not worthy to drink from the hands of this saintly man. Only one among us cannot see the sacrifice our superior is making in carrying that heavy bottle.'

When the bishop returned to his seat, he said:

'You, who think you are holy men, were not humble enough to receive and so denied me the pleasure of giving. Only this man allowed God to be made manifest.'

He immediately appointed him to a more important parish.

The two men became friends and continued to see each other often. Whenever he had any doubts, the priest would turn to the person he called 'my spiritual father', and he usually left satisfied with the answers he got. One evening, for example, he was troubled because he could no longer tell whether or not his actions were pleasing to God. He went to see the bishop and asked what he should do.

'Abraham took in strangers, and God was happy,' came the reply. 'Elijah disliked strangers, and God was happy. David was proud of what he was doing, and God was happy. The publican before the altar was ashamed of what he did, and God was happy. John the Baptist went out into the desert, and God was happy. Paul went to the great cities of the Roman Empire, and God was happy. How can one know what will please the Almighty? Do what your heart commands, and God will be happy.'

The day after this conversation, the bishop, his great spiritual mentor, died from a massive heart attack. The priest saw the bishop's death as a sign, and began to do exactly what he had recommended; he followed the commands of his heart. Sometimes he gave alms, sometimes he told the person to go and find work. Sometimes he gave a very serious sermon, at others he sang along with his congregation. His behaviour reached the ears of the new bishop, and he was summoned to see him.

He was astonished to find that the new bishop was the same person who, a few years earlier, had made the comment about the water served by his predecessor.

'I know that today you're in charge of an important parish,' the new bishop said, an ironic look in his eye, 'and that over the years you became a great friend of my predecessor, perhaps even aspiring to this position yourself.'

'No,' the priest replied, 'aspiring only to wisdom.'

'Well, you must be a very wise man by now, but I've heard strange stories about you, that sometimes you give alms and that sometimes you refuse the aid that our Church says we should offer.'

'I have two pockets, each contains a piece of paper with writing on it, but I only put money in my left pocket,' he said in reply.

The new bishop was intrigued by the story: what did the two pieces of paper say?

'On the piece of paper in my right pocket, I wrote: *I am nothing but dust and ashes*. The piece of paper in my left pocket, where I keep my money, says: *I am the manifestation of God on Earth*. Whenever I see misery and injustice, I put my hand in my left pocket and try to help. Whenever I come up against laziness and indolence, I put my hand in my right pocket and find I have nothing to give. In this way, I manage to balance the material and the spiritual worlds.'

The new bishop thanked him for this fine image of charity and said he could return to his parish, but warned him that he was in the process of restructuring the whole region. Shortly afterwards, the priest received news that he was being transferred to Viscos.

He understood the message at once: envy. But he had made a vow to serve God wherever it might be, and so he set off for Viscos full of humility and fervour: it was a new challenge for him to meet.

A year went by. And another. By the end of five years, despite all his efforts, he had not succeeded in bringing any new believers into the church; the village was haunted by a ghost from the past called Ahab, and nothing the priest said could be more important than the legends that still circulated about him.

Ten years passed. At the end of the tenth year, the priest realised his mistake: his search for wisdom had become pride. He was so convinced of divine justice that he had failed to balance it with the art of diplomacy. He thought he was living in a world where God was everywhere, only to find himself amongst people who often would not even let God enter their lives.

After fifteen years, he knew that he would never leave Viscos: by then, the former bishop was an important cardinal working in the Vatican and quite likely to be named Pope – and he could never allow an obscure country priest to spread the story that he had been exiled out of envy and greed.

By then, the priest had allowed himself to be infected by the lack of stimulus – no one could withstand all those years of indifference. He thought that had he left the priesthood at the right moment, he could have served God better; but he had kept putting off the decision, always thinking that the situation would change, and by then it was too late, he had lost all contact with the world.

After twenty years, he woke up one night in despair: his life had been completely useless. He knew how much he was capable of and how little he had achieved. He remembered the two pieces of paper he used to keep in his pockets, and realised that now he always reached into his right-hand pocket. He had wanted to be wise, but had been lacking in political skills. He had wanted to be just, but had lacked wisdom. He had wanted to be a politician, but had lacked courage.

'Where is Your generosity, Lord? Why did You do to me what You did to Job? Will I never have another chance in this life? Give me one more opportunity!'

He got up, opened the Bible at random, as he usually did when he was searching for an answer, and he came upon the passage during the Last Supper when Christ tells the traitor to hand him over to the Roman soldiers looking for him.

The priest spent hours thinking about what he had just read: why did Jesus ask the traitor to commit a sin?

'So that the scriptures would be fulfilled,' the wise men of the Church would say. Even so, why was Jesus asking someone to commit a sin and thus leading him into eternal damnation?'

Jesus would never do that; in truth, the traitor was merely a victim, as Jesus himself was. Evil had to manifest itself and fulfil its role, so that ultimately Good could prevail. If there was no betrayal, there could be no cross, the words of the scriptures would not be fulfilled, and Jesus' sacrifice could not serve as an example.

The next day, a stranger arrived in the village, as so many others had before. The priest gave the matter no importance, nor did he connect it to the request he had made to Jesus, or to the passage he had read in the Bible. When he heard the story of the models Leonardo da Vinci had used in his *Last Supper*, he remembered reading the corresponding text in the Bible, but dismissed it as a coincidence.

It was only when Miss Prym told them about the wager that he realised his prayers had been answered.

Evil needed to manifest itself if Good was finally to move the hearts of these people. For the first time since he had come to the parish, he had seen his church full to overflowing. For the first time, the most important people in the village had visited him in the sacristy.

'Evil needs to manifest itself, for them to understand the value of Good.' Just as the traitor in the Bible, soon after betraying Jesus, understood what he had done, so the people in the village would realise what they had done and be so overwhelmed by remorse that their only refuge would be the Church. And Viscos – after all these years – would once again become a Christian village.

His role was to be the instrument of Evil; that was the greatest act of humility he could offer to God.

The mayor arrived as arranged.

'I want to know what I should say, Father.'

'Let me take charge of the meeting,' the priest replied.

The mayor hesitated; after all, he was the highest authority in Viscos, and he did not want to see an outsider dealing in public with such an important topic. The priest, it was true, had been in the village now for more than twenty years, but he had not been born there, he did not know all the old stories and he did not have the blood of Ahab in his veins.

'In matters as grave as this, I think I should be the one to speak directly to the people,' he said.

'Yes, you're right. It would probably be better if you did; things might go wrong, and I don't want the Church involved. I'll tell you my plan, and you can take on the task of making it public.'

'On second thoughts, if the plan is yours, it might be fairer and more honest for you to share it with everyone.'

'Fear again,' thought the priest. 'If you want to control someone, all you have to do is to make them feel afraid.'

The two women reached Berta's house shortly before nine and found her doing some crochet-work in her tiny living room.

'There's something different about the village tonight,' the old woman said. 'I heard lots of people walking around, lots of footsteps going past. The bar isn't big enough to hold them all.'

'It's the men in the village,' the hotel landlady replied. 'They're going to the square, to discuss what to do about the stranger.'

'I see. I shouldn't think there's much to discuss though, is there? Either they accept his proposal or they allow him to leave in two days' time.'

'We would never even consider accepting his proposal,' the mayor's wife said indignantly.

'Why not? I heard that the priest gave a wonderful sermon today, explaining how the sacrifice of one man saved humanity, and how God accepted a wager with the Devil and punished his most faithful servant. Would it be so wrong if the people of Viscos decided to accept the stranger's proposal as – let's say – a business deal?'

'You can't be serious.'

'I am. It's you who are trying to pull the wool over my eyes.'

The two women considered getting up, there and then, and leaving at once, but it was too risky.

'Apart from that, to what do I owe the honour of this visit? It's never happened before.'

'Two days ago, Miss Prym said she heard the rogue wolf howling.'

'Now we all know that the rogue wolf is just a stupid story dreamed up by the blacksmith,' the hotel landlady said. 'He probably went into the forest with a woman from another village, and when he tried to grab her, she fought back, and that's why he came up with the story of the wolf. But even so, we decided we'd better come over here to make sure everything was all right.'

'Everything's fine. I'm busy crocheting a tablecloth, although I can't guarantee I'll finish it; who knows, I might die tomorrow.'

There was a moment of general embarrassment.

'Well, you know, old people can die at any time,' Berta went on.

Things had returned to normal. Or almost.

'It's far too soon for you to be talking like that.'

'Maybe you're right; tomorrow is another day, as they say. But I don't mind telling you that it's been on my mind a lot today.'

'For any particular reason?'

'Do you think there should be?'

The hotel landlady wanted to change the subject, but she had to do so very carefully. By now, the meeting in the square must have begun and it would be over in a few minutes.

'I think that, with age, people come to realise that death is inevitable. And we need to learn to face it with serenity, wisdom and resignation. Death often frees us from a lot of senseless suffering.'

'You're quite right,' Berta replied. 'That's exactly what I was thinking this afternoon. And do you know what conclusion I came to? I'm very, very afraid of dying. I don't think my time has quite come.'

The atmosphere in the room was getting tenser and tenser, and the mayor's wife remembered the discussion in the sacristy about the land beside the church; they were talking about one thing, but meaning something else entirely.

Neither of the two women knew how the meeting in the square was going; neither of them knew what the priest's plan was, or what the reaction of the men of Viscos would be. It was pointless trying to talk more openly with Berta; after all, no one accepts being killed without putting up a fight. She made a mental note of the problem: if they wanted to kill the old woman, they would have to find a way of doing so that would avoid a violent struggle that might leave clues for any future investigation.

Disappear. The old woman would simply have to disappear. Her body couldn't be buried in the cemetery or left on the mountainside; once the stranger had ascertained that his wishes had been met, they would have to burn the corpse and scatter the ashes in the mountains. So in both theory and in practice, Berta would be helping their land become fertile again.

'What are you thinking?' Berta asked, interrupting her thoughts.

'About a bonfire,' the mayor's wife replied. 'A lovely bonfire that would warm our bodies and our hearts.'

'It's just as well we're no longer in the Middle Ages, because, you know, there are some people in the village who say I'm a witch.'

There was no point in lying, the old woman would only become suspicious, so the two women nodded their agreement.

'If we were in the Middle Ages, they might want to burn me alive, just like that, just because someone decided I must be guilty of something.'

'What's going on here?' the hotel landlady was wondering to herself. 'Could someone have betrayed us? Could it be that the mayor's wife, who's here with me now, came over earlier and told her everything? Or could it be that the priest suddenly repented and came to confess himself to this sinner?'

'Thank you so much for your visit, but I'm fine, really, in perfect health, ready to make every necessary sacrifice, including being on one of those stupid diets to lower my cholesterol levels, because I want to go on living for a long while yet.'

Berta got up and opened the door. The two women said goodbye to her. The meeting in the square had still not finished.

'I'm so pleased you came. I'm going to stop my crocheting now and go to bed. And to tell you the truth, I believe in the rogue wolf. Now since you two are so much younger than me, would you mind hanging around until the meeting finishes and make quite sure that the wolf doesn't come to my door?'

The two women agreed, bade her goodnight, and Berta went in.

'She knows!' the hotel landlady whispered. 'Someone has told her! Didn't you notice the ironic tone in her voice? She knows we're here to keep an eye on her.'

The mayor's wife was confused.

'But how can she know? No one would be so crazy as to tell her. Unless ...'

'Unless she really is a witch. Do you remember the hot wind that suddenly blew into the sacristy while we were talking?'

'Even though the windows were shut.'

The hearts of the two women contracted and centuries of superstitions rose to the surface. If Berta really was a witch, then her death, far from saving the village, would destroy it completely.

Or so the legends said.

Berta switched off the light and stood watching the two women in the street out of a corner of her window. She didn't know whether to laugh or cry, or simply to accept her fate. She was sure of one thing, though, she had been marked out to die.

Her husband had appeared earlier that evening, and to her surprise, he was accompanied by Miss Prym's grandmother.

Berta's first reaction was one of jealousy: what was he doing with that woman? But then she saw the worried look on both of their faces, and became even more troubled when she heard what they had to say about what had gone on in the sacristy.

The two of them told her to run away at once.

'You must be joking,' Berta replied. 'How am I supposed to run away? My legs can barely carry me the hundred yards to church, so how could I possibly walk all the way down the road and out of the village? Please, sort this problem out up in heaven and do something to protect me! After all, why else do I spend my time praying to all the saints?'

It was a much more complicated situation than Berta could imagine, they explained: Good and Evil were locked in combat, and no one could interfere. Angels and devils were in the midst of one of the periodic battles that decide whether whole regions of the earth are to be condemned for a while or saved.

'I'm not interested; I have no way of defending myself, this isn't my fight, I didn't ask to be caught up in it.'

Nobody had. It had all begun two years earlier with a mistake made by a guardian angel. During a kidnapping, two women were marked out to die, but a little three-year-old girl was supposed to be saved. This girl, it was said, would be a consolation to her father and help him to maintain some hope in life and overcome the tremendous suffering he would undergo. He was a good man, and although he would have to endure terrible suffering (no one knew why, that was all part of God's plan, which had never been fully explained), he would recover in the end. The girl would grow up marked by the tragedy and, when she was twenty, would use her own suffering to help alleviate that of others. She would eventually do work of such vital importance that it would have an impact all over the world.

That had been the original plan. And everything was going well: the police stormed the hideout, shots started flying and the people chosen to die began to fall. At that moment, the child's guardian angel – as Berta knew, all three-year-olds can see and talk to their guardian angels all the time – signalled to her to crouch down by the wall. But the child did not understand and ran towards him so that she could hear better.

She moved barely a matter of inches, just enough to be struck by a fatal bullet. From then on, the story took a new twist. What was meant to become an edifying story of redemption, turned into a merciless struggle. The devil made his appearance, claiming that the man's soul should be his, being as it was full of hatred, impotence and a desire for vengeance. The angels could not accept this; he was a good man and had been chosen to help his daughter make great changes in the world, even though his profession was hardly ideal.

But the angels' arguments no longer rang true to him. Bit by bit, the devil took over his soul, until now he controlled him almost completely.

'Almost completely,' Berta repeated. 'You said "almost".'

They agreed. There was still a tiny chink of light left, because one of the angels had refused to give up the fight. But he had never been listened to until the previous night, when he had managed briefly to speak out. And his instrument had been none other than Miss Prym.

Chantal's grandmother explained that this was why she was there; because if anyone could change the situation, it was her granddaughter. Even so, the struggle was more ferocious than ever, and the stranger's angel had again been silenced by the presence of the devil.

Berta tried to calm them down, because they both seemed very upset. They, after all, were already dead; she was the one who should be worried. Couldn't they help Chantal change the course of things?

Chantal's devil was also winning the battle, they replied. When Chantal was in the forest, her grandmother had sent the rogue wolf to find her – the wolf did, in fact, exist, and the blacksmith had been telling the truth. She had wanted to awaken the stranger's good side and had done so. But apparently the argument between the two of them had got them nowhere; they were both too stubborn. There was only one hope left: that Chantal had seen what they wanted her to see. Or rather, they knew she had seen it, but what they wanted was for her to understand what she had seen.

'What's that?' Berta asked.

They refused to say. Their contact with human beings had its limits, there were devils listening in to their conversation who could spoil everything if they knew of the plan in advance. But they insisted it was something very simple, and if Chantal was as intelligent as her grandmother said she was, she would know how to deal with the situation.

Berta accepted this answer; the last thing she wanted was an indiscretion that might cost her her life, even though she loved hearing secrets. But there was something she still wanted explained and so she turned to her husband:

'You told me to stay here, sitting on this chair all these years, watching over the village in case Evil entered it. You asked that of me long before that guardian angel made a mistake and the child was killed. Why?'

Her husband replied that, one way or another, Evil was bound to pass through Viscos, because the Devil was always abroad in the Earth, trying to catch people unawares.

'I'm not convinced.'

Her husband was not convinced either, but it was true. Perhaps the fight between Good and Evil is raging all the time in every individual's heart, which is the battleground for all angels and devils; they would fight inch by inch for thousands of millennia in order to gain ground, until one of them finally vanquished the other. Yet even though he now existed on a spiritual plane, there were still many things he did not understand – many more, in fact, than on Earth.

'You've convinced me. Go and rest; if I have to die, it will be because my hour has come.'

Berta did not say that she felt slightly jealous and would like to be with her husband again; Chantal's grandmother had always been one of the most sought-after women in the village.

They left, claiming that they had to make sure the girl had understood what she had seen. Berta felt even more jealous, but she managed to calm herself, even though she suspected that her husband only wanted to see her live a little longer so that he could enjoy the company of Chantal's grandmother undisturbed.

Besides, the independence he thought he was enjoying might well come to an end the very next day. Berta considered a little and changed her mind: the poor man deserved a few years' rest, it was no hardship to let him go on thinking he was free to do as he liked – she was sure he missed her dreadfully.

Seeing the two women still on guard outside her house, she thought it wouldn't be so bad to be able to stay a while longer in that valley, staring up at the mountains, watching the eternal conflicts between men and women, the trees and the wind, between angels and devils. Then she began to feel afraid and tried to concentrate on something else – perhaps tomorrow she would change the colour of the ball of yarn she was using; the tablecloth was beginning to look distinctly drab.

Before the meeting in the square had finished, she was fast asleep, sure in her mind that Miss Prym would eventually understand the message, even if she did not have the gift of speaking with spirits.

'In church, on hallowed ground, I spoke of the need for sacrifice,' the priest said. 'Here, on unhallowed land, I ask you to be prepared for martyrdom.'

The small, dimly lit square – there was still only one street lamp, despite the mayor's pre-election promises to install more – was full to overflowing. Peasants and shepherds, drowsy-eyed because they were used to going to bed and rising with the sun, stood in respectful, awed silence. The priest had placed a chair next to the cross and was standing on it so that everyone could see him.

'For centuries, the Church has been accused of fighting unjust battles, when, in reality, all we were doing was trying to survive threats to our existence.'

'We didn't come here to hear about the Church, Father,' a voice shouted. 'We came to find out about Viscos.'

'I don't need to tell you that Viscos risks disappearing off the map, taking with it you, your lands and your flocks. Nor did I come here to talk about the Church, but there is one thing I must say: only by sacrifice and penitence can we find salvation. And before I'm interrupted again, I mean the sacrifice of one person, the penitence of all and the salvation of this village.'

'It might all be a lie,' another voice cried out.

'The stranger is going to show us the gold tomorrow,' the mayor said, pleased to be able to give a piece of information of which even the priest was unaware. 'Miss Prym does not wish to bear the responsibility alone, so the hotel landlady persuaded the stranger to bring the gold bars here. We will act only after receiving that guarantee.'

The mayor took over and began telling them about the improvements that would be made to life in the village: the rebuilding work, the children's playground, the reduced taxes and the planned redistribution of their newly acquired wealth.

'In equal shares,' someone shouted.

It was time for the mayor to take on a commitment he hated to make; as if suddenly awoken from their somnolent state, all eyes were turned in his direction.

'In equal shares,' the priest said, before the mayor could respond. There was no other choice: everyone had to take part and bear the same responsibility and receive the same reward, otherwise it would not be long before someone denounced the crime – either out of jealousy or vengeance. The priest was all too familiar with both those words.

'Who is going to die?'

The mayor explained the fair process by which Berta had been chosen: she suffered greatly from the loss of her husband, she was old, had no friends, and seemed slightly mad, sitting outside her house from dawn to dusk, making absolutely no contribution to the growth of the village. Instead of her money being invested in lands or sheep, it was earning interest in some far-off bank; the only ones who benefited from it were the traders who, like the baker, came every week to sell their produce in the village.

Not a single voice in the crowd was raised against the choice. The mayor was glad because they had accepted his authority; but the priest knew that this could be a good or a bad sign, because silence does not always mean consent – usually all it meant was that people were incapable of coming up with an immediate response. If someone did not agree, they would later torture themselves with the idea that they had accepted without really wanting to, and the consequences of that could be grave.

'I need everyone here to agree,' the priest said. 'I need everyone to say out loud whether they agree or disagree, so that God can hear you and know that He has valiant men in His army. If you don't believe in God, I ask you all the same to say out loud whether you agree or disagree, so that we will all know exactly what everyone here thinks.'

The mayor did not like the way the priest had used the verb 'need': 'I need' he had said, when it would have been more appropriate to say: 'we need', or 'the mayor needs'. When this business was over, he would have to re-impose his authority in whatever way was necessary. Now, like a good politician, he would let the priest take the lead and expose himself to risk.

'I want you all to say that you agree.'

The first 'yes' came from the blacksmith. Then the mayor, to show his courage, also said 'yes' in a loud voice.

One by one, every man present declared out loud that they agreed with the choice – until they had all committed themselves. Some of them did so because they wanted to get the meeting over and done with so that they could go home; some were thinking about the gold and about the quickest way they could leave the village with their newly acquired wealth; others were planning to send money to their children so that they would no longer have to feel ashamed in front of their friends in the big city. Almost no one in the crowd believed that Viscos would regain its former glory; all they wanted were the riches they had always deserved, but had never had.

But no one said 'no'.

'108 women and 173 men live in this village,' the priest went on. 'Since it is the tradition here for everyone to learn how to hunt, each inhabitant owns at least one shotgun. Well, tomorrow morning, I want you each to leave a shotgun in the sacristy, with a single cartridge in it. I'm asking the mayor, who has more than one gun, to bring one for me as well.'

'We never leave our weapons with strangers,' a hunting guide shouted. 'Guns are sacred, temperamental, personal. They should never be fired by other people.'

'Let me finish. I'm going to explain how a firing squad works. Seven soldiers are chosen to shoot the condemned man. Seven rifles are handed out to the squad, but only six of them are loaded with real bullets, the seventh contains a blank. The gunpowder explodes in exactly the same way, the noise is identical, but there's no lead to be fired into the victim's body.

'None of the soldiers knows which rifle contains the blank. In that way, each of them thinks that his gun contained the blank and that his friends were responsible for the death of the man or woman none of them knew, but whom they were forced to shoot in the line of duty.'

'So all of them believe they are innocent,' the landowner chimed in, speaking for the first time.

'Exactly. Tomorrow I will do the same: I'll take the lead out of eighty-seven of the cartridges and leave the other shotguns with live ammunition in them. All the weapons will go off at the same time, but no one will know which of them has pellets inside; in that way, all of you can consider yourselves innocent.'

Tired though the men were, they greeted the priest's idea with a huge sigh of relief. A different kind of energy spread through the crowd as if, from one hour to the next, the entire situation had lost its tragic air and had been transformed into a simple treasure hunt. Every man was convinced that his gun would carry the blank ammunition, and that he would not therefore be guilty; he was simply showing solidarity with his fellows, who wanted to change their lives and where they lived. Everyone was excited now; at last, Viscos had become a place where different, important things happened.

'The only weapon you can be sure will be loaded is mine, because I can't choose for myself. Nor will I keep my share of the gold. I'm doing this for other reasons.'

Again, the mayor did not like the way the priest spoke. He was trying to impress on the people of Viscos what a courageous man he was, a generous leader capable of any sacrifice. If the mayor's wife had been there, she would doubtless have said that the priest was preparing to launch himself as a candidate for the next elections.

'Wait until Monday,' he told himself. He would publish a decree announcing such a steep increase in tax on the church that it would be impossible for the priest to stay on in the village. After all, he was the only one who claimed he didn't want to be rich.

'What about the victim?' the blacksmith asked.

'She'll be there,' the priest said. 'I'll take care of that. But I need three men to come with me.'

When no one volunteered, the priest chose three strong men. One of them tried to say 'no', but his friends stared him down, and he quickly changed his mind.

'Where will the sacrifice take place?' the landowner asked, addressing the priest. The mayor again sensed authority slipping away from him; he needed to regain it at once.

'I'm the one who decides that,' he said, shooting a furious look at the landowner. 'I don't want the earth of Viscos to be stained with blood. We'll do it at this same time tomorrow night up by the Celtic monolith. Bring your lanterns, lamps and torches, so that everyone can see clearly where they are pointing their shotgun, and nobody misses.'

The priest got down from his chair – the meeting was over. The women of Viscos once again heard footsteps in the street, the men returning to their houses, having a drink, staring out of the window, or simply collapsing into bed, exhausted. The mayor returned to his wife, who told him what had happened in Berta's house, and how frightened she had been. But after they – together with the hotel landlady – had analysed every single word that had been said, the two women concluded that the old woman knew nothing; it was merely their sense of guilt making them think like that.

'Make-believe ghosts, like the rogue wolf,' the mayor said.

The priest went back to the church and spent the whole night in prayer.

Chantal breakfasted on the bread she had bought the day before, since the baker's van didn't come on Sundays. She looked out of her window and saw the men of Viscos leaving their houses, each carrying a weapon. She prepared herself to die, as there was still a possibility that she would be the chosen victim; but no one knocked on her door – instead, they carried on down the street, went into the sacristy, and emerged again, empty-handed.

She left her house and went down to the hotel, where the hotel landlady told her about everything that had happened the previous night: the choice of victim, what the priest had proposed and the preparations for the sacrifice. Her hostile tone had vanished, and things seemed to be changing in Chantal's favour.

'There's something I want to tell you; one day, Viscos will realise all that you did for its people.'

'But the stranger still has to show us the gold,' Chantal insisted.

'Of course. He just went out carrying an empty rucksack.'

Chantal decided not to go to the forest, because that would mean passing by Berta's house, and she was too ashamed to look at her. She went back to her room and remembered her dream of the previous night.

For she had had a strange dream in which an angel handed her the eleven gold bars and asked her to keep them.

Chantal told the angel that, for this to happen, someone had to be killed. But the angel said that this wasn't the case: on the contrary, the bars were proof that the gold did not exist.

That was why she had insisted to the hotel landlady that the stranger should show everyone the gold; she had a plan. However, since she had always lost every other battle in her life, she had her doubts as to whether she would be able to win this one.

Berta was watching the sun setting behind the mountains when she saw the priest and three other men coming towards her. She felt sad for three reasons: she knew her time had come; her husband had not appeared to console her (perhaps because he was afraid of what he would hear, or ashamed of his own inability to save her); and she realised that the money she had saved would end up in the hands of the shareholders of the bank where she had deposited it, since she had not had time to withdraw it and burn it.

She felt happy for two reasons: she was finally going to be reunited with her husband, who was doubtless, at that moment, out and about with Miss Prym's grandmother; and although the last day of her life had been cold, it had been filled with sunlight – not everyone had the good fortune to leave the world with such a beautiful memory of it.

The priest signalled to the other men to stay back, and he went forward on his own to greet her.

'Good evening,' she said. 'See how great God is to have made the world so beautiful.'

'They're going to take me away,' she told herself, 'but I will leave them with all the world's guilt to carry on their shoulders.'

'Think, then, how beautiful paradise must be,' the priest said, but Berta could see her arrow had struck home, and that now he was struggling to remain calm.

'I'm not sure about that, I'm not even sure it exists. Have you been there yourself, Father?'

'Not yet. But I've been in hell and I know how terrible that is, however attractive it might appear from the outside.'

Berta understood him to mean Viscos.

'You're mistaken, Father. You were in paradise, but you didn't recognise it. It's the same with most people in this world; they seek suffering in the most joyous of places because they think they are unworthy of happiness.'

'It appears that all your years spent sitting out here have brought you some wisdom.'

'It's been a long time since anyone bothered to come and chat with me, and now, oddly enough, everyone has discovered that I still exist. Just imagine, Father, last night, the hotel landlady and the mayor's wife honoured me with a visit; and now here's the parish priest doing the same – have I suddenly become such an important person?'

'Very much so,' the priest replied. 'The most important person in the village.'

'Have I come into money or something?'

'Ten gold bars. Future generations of men, women and children will give thanks to you. It's even possible they'll put up a statue in your honour.'

'I'd prefer a fountain, because as well as being decorative, it quenches people's thirst and soothes those who are worried.'

'A fountain it will be then. You have my word on it.'

Berta thought it was time to put an end to this farce and come straight to the point.

'I know everything, Father. You are condemning an innocent woman who cannot fight for her life. Damn you, sir, and damn this village and all who live in it.'

'Damned indeed,' the priest said. 'For more than twenty years, I've tried to bless this village, but no one heard my calls. For the same twenty years, I've tried to inculcate Good into men's hearts, until I finally realised that God had chosen me to be his left arm, and to show the evil of which men are capable. Perhaps in this way they will become afraid and accept the faith.'

Berta felt like crying, but controlled the impulse.

'Fine words, Father, but empty. They're just an excuse for cruelty and injustice.'

'Unlike all the others, I'm not doing this for the money. I know that the gold is cursed, like this whole place, and that it won't bring happiness to anyone. I am simply doing as God has asked me. Or rather, as he commanded me, in answer to my prayers.'

'There's no point arguing further,' Berta thought, as the priest put his hand in his pocket and brought out some pills.

'You won't feel a thing,' he said. 'Let's go inside.'

'Neither you nor anyone else in this village will set foot in my house while I'm still alive. Perhaps later tonight the door will stand wide open, but not now.'

The priest gestured to one of the men, who approached carrying a plastic bottle.

'Take these pills. You'll soon fall asleep and when you wake up, you'll be in heaven, with your husband.'

'I've always been with my husband and, despite suffering from insomnia, I never take pills to get to sleep.'

'So much the better; they'll take effect at once.'

The sun had disappeared, and darkness was beginning to fall on the valley, the church, and on the entire village.

'And what if I don't want to take them?'

'You'll take them just the same.'

Berta looked at the three men and saw that the priest was right. She took the pills from him, placed them in her mouth and drank the entire bottle of water. Water: it has no taste, no smell, no colour and yet it is the most important thing in the world. Just like her at that moment.

She looked once more at the mountains, now covered in darkness. She saw the first star come out and thought that she had had a good life; she had been born and would die in a place she loved, even though it seemed that her love was unrequited, but what did that matter? Anyone who loves in the expectation of being loved in return is wasting their time.

She had been blessed. She had never been to another country, but she knew that here in Viscos the same things happened as everywhere else. She had lost the husband she loved, but God had granted her the joy of continuing at his side, even after his death. She had seen the village at its height, had witnessed the beginning of its decline, and was leaving before it was completely destroyed. She had known mankind with all its faults and virtues, and she believed that, despite all that was happening to her now, despite the struggles her husband swore were going on in the invisible world, human goodness would triumph in the end.

She felt sorry for the priest, for the mayor, for Miss Prym, for the stranger, for every one of the inhabitants of Viscos: Evil would never bring Good, however much they wanted to believe that it would. By the time they discovered the truth, it would be too late.

She had only one regret: never having seen the sea. She knew it existed, that it was vast and simultaneously wild and calm, but she had never been to see it or tasted the salt water on her tongue or felt the sand beneath her bare feet or dived into the cold water like someone returning to the womb of the Great Mother (she remembered that this was an expression favoured by the Celts).

Apart from that, she did not have much to complain about. She was sad, very sad, to have to leave like this, but she did not want to feel she was a victim: doubtless God had chosen this role for her, and it was far better than the one He had chosen for the priest.

'I want to talk to you about Good and Evil,' she heard him say, just as she began to feel a kind of numbness in her hands and feet.

'There's no need. You don't know what goodness is. You were poisoned by the evil done to you, and now you're spreading that plague throughout our land. You're no different from the stranger who came to visit us and destroy us.'

Her last words were barely audible. She looked up at the one star, then closed her eyes.

The stranger went into the bathroom in his hotel room, carefully washed each of the gold bars and replaced them in his shabby, old rucksack. Two days ago he had left the stage, and now he was returning for the final act – he had to make a last appearance.

Everything had been carefully planned: from the choice of a small, remote village with few inhabitants down to the fact of having an accomplice, so that if things did not work out, no one could ever accuse him of inciting people to murder. The tape recorder, the reward, the careful steps he had taken, first making friends with the people in the village and then spreading terror and confusion. Just as God had done to him, so he would do unto others. Just as God had given him all that was good only to cast him into the abyss, so he would do the same.

He had taken care of every detail, except one: he had never thought his plan would work. He had been sure that when the moment came to choose, a simple 'no' would change the story; at least one person would refuse to take part, and that person would be enough to prove that not everything was lost. If one person saved the village, the world itself would be saved, hope would still be possible, goodness would be strengthened, the terrorists would not have truly known the evil they were doing, there could be forgiveness, and his days of suffering would be but a sad memory that he could learn to live with and he could perhaps even seek happiness again. For that 'no' he would have liked to have heard, the village would have received its reward of ten gold bars, independently of the wager he had made with Chantal.

But his plan had failed. And now it was too late, he couldn't change his mind.

Someone knocked at his door.

'Let's go,' he heard the hotel landlady say. 'It's time.'

'I'll be right down.'

He picked up his jacket, put it on and met the landlady downstairs in the bar.

'I've got the gold,' he said. 'But, just so there's no misunderstanding, you should be aware that there are several people who know where I am. If you decide to change your victim, you can be sure that the police will come looking for me; you yourself saw me making all those phone calls.'

The hotel landlady merely nodded.

The Celtic monolith was half an hour's walk from Viscos. For many centuries, people had thought it was merely an unusually large stone, polished by the wind and the ice, which had once stood upright, but that had been toppled by a bolt of lightning. Ahab used to hold the village council there because the rock served as a natural open-air table.

Then one day the Government sent a team to write a survey of the Celtic settlements in the valley, and someone noticed the monument. Then came the archaeologists, who measured, calculated, argued, excavated and reached the conclusion that a Celtic tribe had chosen the spot as some kind of sacred place, even though they had no idea what rituals had been performed there. Some said it was a sort of observatory, others said that fertility rites – in which young virgins were possessed by priests – had taken place there. The experts discussed it for a whole week, but then left to look at something more interesting, without reaching any definite conclusions about their findings.

When he was elected, the mayor tried to attract tourism to Viscos by getting an article published in the regional press about the Celtic heritage of the village. But the paths through the forest were difficult, and the few intrepid visitors who came found only a fallen stone at the end of them, whereas other villages could boast sculptures, inscriptions and other far more interesting things. The idea came to nothing, and the monolith soon resumed its usual function as a weekend picnic table.

That evening, there were arguments in several households in Viscos all over the same thing: the men wanted to go alone, but their wives insisted on taking part in the 'ritual sacrifice', as the inhabitants had come to call the murder they were about to commit. The husbands argued that it was dangerous, a shotgun might go off by accident; their wives said that the men were just being selfish and that they should respect the women's rights, the world was no longer as they thought it was. In the end, the husbands yielded, and the wives rejoiced.

Now the procession was heading for the monolith, a chain of 281 points of light in the darkness, for the stranger was carrying a torch, and Berta was not carrying anything, so the number of inhabitants of the village was still exactly represented. Each of the men had a torch or lantern in one hand and, in the other, a shotgun, its breech open so that it would not go off by accident.

Berta was the only one who did not need to walk. She was sleeping peacefully on a kind of improvised stretcher that two woodcutters were struggling along with. 'I'm glad we won't have to carry this great weight back,' one of them was thinking, 'because by then, with all the buckshot in her, she'll weigh three times as much.'

He calculated that each cartridge would contain, on average, at least six small balls of lead. If all the loaded shotguns hit their target, the old woman's body would be riddled with 522 pellets, and would end up containing more metal than blood.

The man could feel his stomach churning. He resolved not to think any more about it until Monday.

No one said a word during the walk. No one looked at anyone else, as if this was a kind of nightmare they wanted to forget as quickly as possible. They arrived out of breath – more from tension than from exhaustion – and formed a huge semicircle of lights in the clearing where the Celtic monument lay.

The mayor gave a signal, and the woodcutters untied Berta from the stretcher and laid her on the monolith.

'That's no good,' the blacksmith protested, remembering the war films he'd seen, with soldiers crawling along the ground. 'It's hard to shoot someone when they're lying down.'

The woodcutters shifted Berta into a sitting position with her back against the stone. It seemed ideal, but then a sudden sob was heard and a woman's voice said:

'She's looking at us. She can see what we're doing.'

Berta could not, of course, see a thing, but it was unbearable to look at that kindly lady, asleep, with a contented smile on her lips, and to think that in a short while she would be torn apart by all those tiny pellets.

'Turn her round,' ordered the mayor, who was also troubled by the sight.

Grumbling, the woodcutters returned once more to the monolith and turned the body round, so that this time she was kneeling on the ground, with her face and chest resting on the stone. It was impossible to keep her upright in this position, so they had to tie a rope round her wrists, throw it over the top of the monument, and fasten it on the other side.

Berta's position was now utterly grotesque: kneeling, with her back to them, her arms stretched out over the stone, as if she were praying or begging for something. Someone protested again, but the mayor said it was time to do what they had come to do.

And the quicker the better. With no speeches or justifications; that could wait until tomorrow – in the bar, on the streets, in conversations between shepherds and farmers. It was likely that one of the three roads out of Viscos would not be used for a long while, since they were all so accustomed to seeing Berta sitting there, looking up at the mountains and talking to herself. Luckily, the village had two other exits, as well as a narrow short cut, with some improvised steps down to the road below.

'Let's get this over with,' said the mayor, pleased that the priest was now saying nothing, and that his own authority had been re-established. 'Someone in the valley might see these lights and decide to find out what's going on. Prepare your shotguns, fire, and then we can leave.'

Without ceremony. Doing their duty, like good soldiers defending their village. With no doubts in their minds. This was an order, and it would be obeyed.

And suddenly, the mayor not only understood the priest's silence, he realised that he had fallen into a trap. If one day the story of what had happened got out, all the others could claim, as all murderers did in wartime, that they were merely obeying orders. But what was going on at that moment in their hearts? Did they see him as a villain or as their saviour?

He could not weaken now, at the very moment when he heard the shotguns being snapped shut, the barrels fitting perfectly into the breech blocks. He imagined the noise that 174 guns would make, but by the time anyone arrived to see what was going on, they would be far away. Shortly before they had begun the climb up to the monolith, he had ordered them to extinguish all lights on the way back. They knew the route by heart, and the lights were simply to avoid any accidents when they opened fire.

Instinctively, the women stepped back, and the men took aim at the inert body, some fifty yards away. They could not possibly miss, having been trained since childhood to shoot fleeing animals and birds in flight.

The mayor prepared to give the order to fire.

'Just a moment,' shouted a female voice.

It was Miss Prym.

'What about the gold? Have you seen it yet?'

The shotguns were lowered, but still ready to be fired; no, no one had seen the gold. They all turned towards the stranger.

He walked slowly in front of the shotguns. He put his rucksack down on the ground and one by one took out the bars of gold.

'There it is,' he said, before returning to his place at one end of the semicircle.

Miss Prym went over to the gold bars and picked one up.

'It's gold,' she said. 'But I want you to check it. Let nine women come up here and examine each of the bars still on the ground.'

The mayor began to get worried: they would be in the line of fire, and someone of a nervous disposition might set off a gun by accident; but nine women – including his wife – went over to join Miss Prym and did as she asked.

'Yes, it's gold,' the mayor's wife said, carefully checking the bar she had in her hands, and comparing it to the few pieces of gold jewellery she possessed. 'I can see it has a hall-mark and what must be a serial number, as well as the date it was cast and its weight. It's the real thing all right.'

'Well, hang on to that gold and listen to what I have to say.'

'This is no time for speeches, Miss Prym,' the mayor said. 'All of you get away from there so that we can finish the job.'

'Shut up, you idiot!'

These words from Chantal startled everyone. None of them dreamed that anyone in Viscos could say what they had just heard.

'Have you gone mad?'

'I said shut up!' Chantal shouted even more loudly, trembling from head to foot, her eyes wide with hatred. 'You're the one who's mad, for falling into this trap that has led us all to condemnation and death! You are the irresponsible one!'

The mayor moved towards her, but was held back by two men.

'We want to hear what the girl has to say,' a voice in the crowd shouted. 'Ten minutes won't make any difference!'

Ten or even five minutes would make a huge difference, and everyone there, men and women, knew it. As they became more aware of the situation, their fear was growing, the sense of guilt was spreading, shame was beginning to take hold, their hands were starting to shake, and they were all looking for an excuse to change their minds. On the walk there, each man had been convinced that he was carrying a weapon containing blank ammunition and that soon it would all be over. Now they were starting to fear that their shotguns would fire real pellets, and that the ghost of the old woman – who was reputed to be a witch – would come back at night to haunt them.

Or that someone would talk. Or that the priest had not done as he had promised, and they would all be guilty.

'Five minutes,' the mayor said, trying to get them to believe that it was he who was giving permission, when in fact it was the young woman who was setting the rules.

'I'll talk for as long as I like,' said Chantal, who appeared to have regained her composure and to be determined not to give an inch; she spoke now with an authority no one had ever seen before. 'But it won't take long. It's strange to see what's going on here, especially when, as we all know, in the days of Ahab, men often used to come to the village claiming to have a special powder that could turn lead into gold. They called themselves alchemists, and at least one of them proved he was telling the truth when Ahab threatened to kill him.

'Today you are trying to do the same thing: mixing lead with blood, certain that this will be transformed into the gold we women are holding. On the one hand, you're absolutely right. On the other, the gold will slip through your fingers as quickly as it came.'

The stranger could not grasp what the young girl was saying, but he willed her to go on; he had noticed that, in a dark corner of his soul, the forgotten light was once again shining brightly.

'At school, we were all told the famous legend of King Midas, who met a god who offered to grant him anything he wished for. Midas was already very rich, but he wanted more money, and he asked to have the power to turn everything he touched into gold.

'Let me remind you what happened: first, Midas transformed his furniture, his palace and everything around him into gold. He worked away for a whole morning, and soon had a golden garden, golden trees and golden staircases. At noon, he felt hungry and wanted to eat. But as soon as he touched the succulent leg of lamb that his servants had prepared, that too was turned into gold. He raised a glass of wine to his lips, and it was instantly turned into gold. In despair, he ran to his wife to ask her to help him, for he was beginning to understand his mistake, but as soon as he touched her arm, she turned into a golden statue.

'The servants fled the palace, terrified that the same thing would happen to them. In less than a week, Midas had died of hunger and thirst, surrounded by gold on all sides.'

'Why are you telling us this story?' the mayor's wife wanted to know, putting her gold bar back on the ground and returning to her husband's side. 'Has some god come to Viscos and given us this power?'

'I'm telling you the story for one simple reason: gold itself has no value. Absolutely none. We cannot eat it or drink it or use it to buy more animals or land. It's money that's valuable, and how are we going to turn this gold into money?

'We can do one of two things: we can ask the blacksmith to melt the bars down into 280 equal pieces, and then each one of you can go to the city to exchange it for money. But that would immediately arouse the suspicions of the authorities, because there is no gold in this valley, so it would seem very odd if every Viscos inhabitant were suddenly to turn up bearing a small gold bar. The authorities would become suspicious. We would have to say we had unearthed an ancient Celtic treasure. But a quick check would show that the gold had been made recently, that the area round here had already been excavated, that the Celts never had this amount of gold – if they had, they would have built a large and splendid city on this site.'

'You're just an ignorant young woman,' the landowner said. 'We'll take in the bars exactly as they are, with the government hallmark and everything. We'll exchange them at a bank and divide the money between us.'

'That's the second thing. The mayor takes the ten gold bars, goes to the bank, and asks them to exchange them for money. The bank cashier wouldn't ask the same questions as if each of us were to turn up with our own gold bar; since the mayor is a figure of authority, they would simply ask him for the purchase documents for the gold. The mayor would say he didn't have them, but would point out – as his wife says – that each bar bears a government hallmark, and that it's genuine. There's a date and a serial number on each one.

'By this time, the man who gave us the gold will be far from here. The cashier will ask for more time because, although he knows the mayor and knows he is an honest man, he needs authorisation to hand over such a large amount of money. Questions will be asked about where the gold came from. The mayor will say it was a present from a stranger – after all, our mayor is an intelligent man and has an answer for everything.

'Once the cashier has spoken to his manager, the manager – who suspects nothing, but he is nevertheless a paid employee and doesn't want to run any risks – will phone the bank headquarters. Nobody there knows the mayor, and any large withdrawal is regarded as suspicious; they will ask the mayor to wait for two days, while they confirm the origin of the gold bars. What might they discover? That the gold had been stolen perhaps. Or that it was purchased by a group suspected of dealing in drugs.'

Chantal paused. The fear she had felt when she first tried to take her gold bar with her was now being shared by all of them. The story of one person is the story of all of humanity.

'This gold has serial numbers on it. And a date. This gold is easy to identify.'

Everyone looked at the stranger, who remained impassive.

'There's no point asking him anything,' Chantal said. 'We would have to take it on trust that he's telling the truth, and a man who calls for a murder to be committed is hardly to be trusted.'

'We could keep him here until the gold has been changed into money,' the blacksmith said.

The stranger nodded in the direction of the hotel landlady.

'We can't touch him. He's got powerful friends. I overheard him phoning various people, and he's reserved his plane tickets; if he disappears, they'll know he's been kidnapped and come looking for him in Viscos.'

Chantal put the gold bar down on the ground and moved out of the line of fire. The other women did the same.

'You can shoot if you like, but since I know this is a trap set by the stranger, I want nothing to do with this murder.'

'You don't know anything!' the landowner cried.

'But if I'm right, the mayor would soon be behind bars, and people would come to Viscos to find out who he stole this treasure from. Someone would have to explain, and it's not going to be me.

'But I promise to keep quiet. I'll simply plead ignorance. And besides, the mayor is someone we know, not like the stranger who is leaving Viscos tomorrow. He might take all the blame on himself and say that he stole the gold from a man who came to spend a week in Viscos. Then we would all see him as a hero, the crime would go undiscovered, and we could all go on living our lives – somehow or other – but without the gold.'

'I'll do it,' the mayor said, knowing that this was all pure invention on the part of this madwoman.

Meanwhile, the noise of the first shotgun being disarmed was heard.

'Trust me!' the mayor shouted. 'I'll take the risk!'

But the only response was that same noise, then another, and the noises seemed to spread by contagion, until almost all the shotguns had been disarmed: since when could anyone believe in the promises of a politician? Only the mayor and the priest still had their shotguns at the ready; one was pointing at Miss Prym, the other at Berta. But the woodcutter – the one who, earlier on, had worked out the number of pellets that would penetrate the old woman's body – saw what was happening, went over to the two men and took their weapons from them: the mayor was not mad enough to commit a murder purely out of revenge, and the priest had no experience of weapons and might miss.

Miss Prym was right: it is very dangerous to believe in other people. It was as if everyone there had suddenly become aware of that, because they began to drift away from the clearing, the older people first, then the younger ones.

Silently, they all filed down the hillside, trying to think about the weather, the sheep they had to shear, the land that would soon need ploughing again, the hunting season that was about to start. None of this had happened, because Viscos is a village lost in time, where every day is the same.

They were all saying to themselves that this weekend had been a dream.

Or a nightmare.

Only three people and two torches remained in the clearing – and one of those people was fast asleep, still tied to the stone.

'There's the village gold,' the stranger said to Chantal. 'It looks like I end up without the gold and without an answer.'

'The gold doesn't belong to the village, it belongs to me. As does the bar buried beside the Y-shaped rock. And you're going to come with me to make sure it gets changed into money; I don't trust a word you say.'

'You know I wasn't going to do what you said I would do. And as for the contempt you feel for me, it's nothing more than the contempt you feel for yourself. You should be grateful for all that's happened, because by showing you the gold, I gave you much more than the possibility of simply becoming rich. I forced you to act, to stop complaining about everything and to take a stand.'

'Very generous of you, I'm sure,' said Chantal with a touch of irony in her voice. 'From the very start, I could have told you something about human nature; even though Viscos is a village in decline, it once had a wise and glorious past. I could have given you the answer you were looking for, if only I had thought of it.'

Chantal went over to untie Berta; she saw that Berta had a cut on her forehead, perhaps because of the way her head had been positioned on the stone, but it was nothing serious. Now they just had to wait there until morning for Berta to wake up.

'Can you give me that answer now?' the stranger asked.

'Someone must already have told you about the meeting between St Savin and Ahab.'

'Of course. The saint came, talked to him briefly, and the Arab converted to Christianity because he realised that the saint was much braver than him.'

'That's right. Except that, before going to sleep, the two of them talked together for a while. Even though Ahab had begun to sharpen his knife the moment the saint set foot in his house, safe in the knowledge that the world was a reflection of himself, he was determined to challenge the saint and so he asked him:

'"If, tonight, the most beautiful prostitute in the village came in here, would you be able to see her as neither beautiful nor seductive?"

'"No, but I would be able to control myself," the saint replied.

'"And if I offered you a pile of gold coins to leave your cave in the mountain and come and join us, would you be able to look on that gold and see only pebbles?"

'"No, but I would be able to control myself."

'"And if you were sought by two brothers, one of whom hated you, and the other who saw you as a saint, would you be able to feel the same towards them both?"

'"It would be very hard, but I would be able to control myself sufficiently to treat them both the same."

Chantal paused.

'They say this dialogue was important in Ahab's conversion to Christianity.'

The stranger did not need Chantal to explain the story. Savin and Ahab had the same instincts – Good and Evil struggled in both of them, just as they did in every soul on the face of the earth. When Ahab realised that Savin was the same as him, he realised too that he was the same as Savin.

It was all a matter of control. And choice.

Nothing more and nothing less.

Chantal looked for the last time at the valley, the mountains and the woods where she used to walk as a child, and she felt in her mouth the taste of the crystal-clear water, of the freshly-picked vegetables and the local wine made from the best grapes in the region, jealously guarded by the villagers so that no visiting tourist would ever discover it – given that the harvest was too small to be exported elsewhere, and that money might change the wine producer's mind on the subject.

She had only returned to say goodbye to Berta. She was wearing the same clothes she usually wore, so that nobody there would know that, in her short visit to the city, she had become a wealthy woman. The stranger had arranged everything, signing all the papers necessary for the transfer in ownership of the gold bars, so that they could be sold and the money deposited in Miss Prym's newly opened account. The bank clerk had been exaggeratedly discreet and had asked no questions beyond those necessary for the transactions. But Chantal was sure she knew what he was thinking: he assumed he was looking at the young mistress of an older man.

'What a wonderful feeling!' she thought. In the bank

clerk's estimation, she must be extremely good in bed to be worth that immense amount of money.

She passed some of the local residents: none of them knew that she was about to leave, and they greeted her as if nothing had happened, as if Viscos had never received a visit from the Devil. She returned the greeting, also pretending that that day was exactly the same as every other day in her life.

She did not know how much she had changed thanks to all she had discovered about herself, but she had time to find out. Berta was sitting outside her house – not because she was still on the watch for Evil, but because she didn't know what else to do with her life.

'They're going to build a fountain in my honour,' she announced. 'It's the price for my silence. But I know the fountain won't last long or quench many people's thirst, because Viscos is doomed whichever way you look at it: not because of a devil who appeared in these parts, but because of the times we live in.'

Chantal asked what the fountain would look like. Berta had decided that it should be a sun spouting water into the mouth of a frog. She was the sun and the priest was the frog.

'I'm quenching his thirst for light and will continue to do so for as long as the fountain remains.'

The mayor had complained about the cost, but Berta would not listen, and so they had no choice. Building work was due to start the following week.

'And now you are finally going to do as I suggested, my girl. One thing I can tell you with absolute certainty: life can seem either very long or very short, according to how you live it.'

Chantal smiled, gave her a kiss, and turned her back on Viscos for the last time. The old woman was right: there was no time to lose, though she hoped that her life would be very long indeed.

Life is a
journey

Make sure you don't miss a thing.
Live it with Paulo Coelho.

Visit f /paulocoelho

How can you find your heart's desire?

A world-wide phenomenon; an inspiration for anyone seeking their path in life.

The Alchemist

Do you believe in yourself?

A modern-day adventure in the searing heat of the Mojave desert and an exploration of fear and self-doubt.

The Valkyries

How do we see the amazing in the everyday?

When two young lovers are reunited, they discover anew the truth of what lies in their hearts.

By the River Piedra
I Sat Down & Wept

What are you searching for?

A transforming journey on the pilgrims' road to Santiago – and the first of Paulo's extraordinary books.

The Pilgrimage

Can faith triumph over suffering?

Paulo Coelho's brilliant telling of the story of Elijah, who was forced to choose between love and duty.

The Fifth Mountain

Is life always worth living?

A fundamental moral question explored as only Paulo Coelho can.

Veronika Decides to Die

Could you be tempted into evil?

The inhabitants of a small town are challenged by a mysterious stranger to choose between good and evil.

The Devil & Miss Prym

Are you brave enough to live your dream?

Strategies and inspiration to help you follow your own path in a troubled world.

Manual of the Warrior of Light

Can sex be sacred?

An unflinching exploration of the lengths we go to in our search for love, sex and spirituality.

Eleven Minutes

How far would you go for your obsession?

A sweeping story of love, loss and longing that spans the world.

The Zahir

What happens when obsession turns to murder?

An enthralling story of jealousy, death and suspense.

The Winner Stands Alone

Can we dare to be true to ourselves?

A story that will transform the way we think about love, joy and sacrifice.

The Witch of Portobello

How will you know who your soulmate is?

A moving tale of passion, mystery and spirituality.

Brida

What does it mean to be truly alive?

Powerful tales of living and dying, destiny and choice, and love lost and found.

Like the Flowing River

Are you where you want to be?

Read *Aleph*. And rewrite your life.

Aleph

Is there a weapon more powerful than words?

A timeless and powerful exploration of personal growth, everyday wisdom and joy.

Manuscript Found in Accra

ELEVEN MINUTES

Paulo Coelho was born in Brazil and has become one of the most widely read and loved authors in the world. Especially renowned for *The Alchemist* and *Eleven Minutes*, he has sold more than 320 million books worldwide and has been translated into 83 languages. The recipient of numerous prestigious international awards, amongst them the Crystal Award by the World Economic Forum and France's Légion d'Honneur, Paulo Coelho was inducted into the Brazilian Academy of Letters in 2002.

Also by Paulo Coelho

The Alchemist
The Pilgrimage
The Valkyries
By the River Piedra I Sat Down and Wept
The Fifth Mountain
Veronika Decides to Die
Manual of the Warrior of Light
Eleven Minutes
The Zahir
The Devil and Miss Prym
The Witch of Portobello
Brida
The Winner Stands Alone
Like the Flowing River
Aleph
Manuscript Found in Accra
Adultery
The Spy
Hippie

ELEVEN MINUTES

PAULO COELHO

Author of THE ALCHEMIST

TRANSLATED FROM THE PORTUGUESE
BY MARGARET JULL COSTA

Thorsons

Thorsons
An imprint of HarperCollins*Publishers*
1 London Bridge Street
London SE1 9GF

HarperCollins*Publishers*
1st Floor, Watermarque Building, Ringsend Road
Dublin 4, Ireland

www.harpercollins.co.uk
www.paulocoelho.com
www.paulocoelhoblog.com

First published in English by
HarperCollinsPublishers 2003
This edition published 2021

2 4 6 8 10 9 7 5 3 1

© Paulo Coelho 2003

Paulo Coelho asserts the moral right to
be identified as the author of this work

A catalogue record of this book is
available from the British Library

ISBN 978-0-00-854723-3

FICTION / PHILOSOPHY

Printed and bound in India by Thomson Press India Ltd

All rights reserved. No part of this publication may be reproduced, stored in a retrieval system, or transmitted, in any form or by any means, electronic, mechanical, photocopying, recording or otherwise, without the prior written permission of the publishers.

This book is produced from independently certified FSC® paper
to ensure responsible forest management.

O Mary!
conceived without sin,
pray for us who turn to you!
Amen.

And, behold, a woman which was in the city, a sinner; and when she knew that Jesus was sitting at meat in the Pharisee's house, she brought an alabaster cruse of ointment.

And standing behind at his feet, weeping, she began to wet his feet with her tears, and wiped them with the hair of her head, and kissed his feet, and anointed them with the ointment.

Now when the Pharisee which had bidden him saw it, he spake within himself, saying, This man, if he were a prophet, would have perceived who and what manner of woman this is which toucheth him, that she is a sinner.

And Jesus answering said unto him, Simon, I have somewhat to say unto thee. And he saith, Master, say on.

A certain lender had two debtors: the one owed five hundred pence, and the other fifty.

And when they had not wherewith to pay, he forgave them both. Which of them therefore will love him most?

Simon answered and said, He, I suppose, to whom he forgave the most. And he said unto him, Thou hast rightly judged.

And turning to the woman, he said unto Simon, Seest thou this woman? I entered into thine house, thou gavest me no water for my feet; but she hath washed my feet with her tears, and wiped them with her hair.

Thou gavest me no kiss: but she, since the time I came in, hath not ceased to kiss my feet.

My head with oil thou didst not anoint: but this she hath anointed my feet with ointment.

Wherefore I say unto thee, Her sins, which are many, are forgiven; for she loved much: but to whom little is forgiven, the same loveth little.

Luke 7: 37–47

Dedication

On 29th May 2002, just hours before I put the finishing touches to this book, I visited the Grotto in Lourdes, in France, to fill a few bottles with miraculous water from the spring. Inside the Basilica, a gentleman in his seventies said to me: 'You know, you look just like Paulo Coelho.' I said that I was Paulo Coelho. The man embraced me and introduced me to his wife and grand-daughter. He spoke of the importance of my books in his life, concluding: 'They make me dream.' I have often heard these words before, and they always please me greatly. At that moment, however, I felt really frightened, because I knew that my new novel, *Eleven Minutes*, dealt with a subject that was harsh, difficult, shocking. I went over to the spring, filled my bottles, then came back and asked him where he lived (in northern France, near Belgium) and noted down his name.

This book is dedicated to you, Maurice Gravelines. I have a duty to you, your wife and grand-daughter and to myself to talk about the things that concern me and not only about what everyone would like to hear. Some books make us dream, others bring us face to face with reality, but what matters most to the author is the honesty with which a book is written.

For I am the first and the last
I am the venerated and the despised
I am the prostitute and the saint
I am the wife and the virgin
I am the mother and the daughter
I am the arms of my mother
I am barren and my children are many
I am the married woman and the spinster
I am the woman who gives birth and she
who never procreated
I am the consolation for the pain of birth
I am the wife and the husband
And it was my man who created me
I am the mother of my father
I am the sister of my husband
And he is my rejected son
Always respect me
For I am the shameful and the magnificent one

Hymn to Isis, third or fourth century bc,
discovered in Nag Hammadi

Once upon a time, there was a prostitute called Maria. Wait a minute. 'Once upon a time' is how all the best children's stories begin and 'prostitute' is a word for adults. How can I start a book with this apparent contradiction? But since, at every moment of our lives, we all have one foot in a fairy tale and the other in the abyss, let's keep that beginning.

Once upon a time, there was a prostitute called Maria.

Like all prostitutes, she was born both innocent and a virgin, and, as an adolescent, she dreamed of meeting the man of her life (rich, handsome, intelligent), of getting married (in a wedding dress), having two children (who would grow up to be famous) and living in a lovely house (with a sea view). Her father was a travelling salesman, her mother a seamstress, and her hometown, in the interior of Brazil, had only one cinema, one nightclub and one bank, which was why Maria was always hoping that one day, without warning, her Prince Charming would arrive, sweep her off her feet and take her away with him so that they could conquer the world together.

While she was waiting for her Prince Charming to appear, all she could do was dream. She fell in love for the first time when she was eleven, en route from her house to school. On the first day of term, she discovered that she was not alone on her way to school: making the same journey was a boy who lived in her neighbourhood and who shared the same timetable. They never exchanged a single word, but gradually Maria became aware that, for her, the best part of the day were those moments spent going to school: moments of dust, thirst and weariness, with the sun beating down, the boy walking fast, and with her trying her hardest to keep up.

This scene was repeated month after month; Maria, who hated studying and whose only other distraction in life was television, began to wish that the days would pass quickly; she waited eagerly for each journey to school and, unlike other girls her age, she found the weekends deadly dull. Given that the hours pass more slowly for a child than for an adult, she suffered greatly and found the days far too long simply because they allowed her only ten minutes to be with the love of her life and thousands of hours to spend thinking about him, imagining how good it would be if they could talk.

Then it happened.

One morning, on the way to school, the boy came up to her and asked if he could borrow a pencil. Maria didn't reply; in fact, she seemed rather irritated by this unexpected approach and even quickened her step. She had felt petrified when she saw him coming towards her, terrified that he might realise how much she loved him, how eagerly she had waited for him, how she had dreamed of taking his hand, of walking straight past the school gates with him and continuing along the road to the end, where – people said – there was a big city, film stars and television stars, cars, lots of cinemas, and an endless number of fun things to do.

For the rest of the day, she couldn't concentrate on her lessons, tormented by her own absurd behaviour, but, at the same time, relieved, because she knew that the boy had noticed her too, and that the pencil had just been an excuse to start a conversation, because when he came over to her, she had noticed that he already had a pen in his pocket. She waited for the next time, and during that night – and the nights that followed – she went over and over what she would say to him, until she found the right way to begin a story that would never end.

But there was no next time, for although they continued to walk to school together, with Maria sometimes a few steps ahead, clutching a pencil in her right hand, and at other times, walking slightly behind him so that she could gaze at him tenderly, he never said another word to her, and she had to content herself with loving and suffering in silence until the end of the school year.

During the interminable school holidays that followed, she woke up one morning to find that she had blood on her legs and was convinced she was going to die. She decided to leave a letter for the boy, telling him that he had been the great love of her life, and then she would go off into the bush and doubtless be killed by one of the two monsters that terrorised the country people round about: the werewolf and the *mula-sem-cabeça* (said to be a priest's mistress transformed into a mule and doomed to wander the night). That way, her parents wouldn't suffer too much over her death, for, although constantly beset by tragedies, the poor are always hopeful, and her parents would persuade themselves that she had been kidnapped by a wealthy, childless family, but would return one day, rich and famous, while the current (and eternal) love of her life would never forget her, torturing himself each day for not having spoken to her again.

She never did write that letter because her mother came into the room, saw the bloodstained sheets, smiled and said:

'Now you're a young woman.'

Maria wondered what the connection was between the blood on her legs and her becoming a young woman, but her mother wasn't able to give her a satisfactory explanation: she just said that it was normal, and that, from now on, for four or five days a month, she would have to wear something like a doll's pillow between her legs. Maria asked if men used some kind of tube to stop the blood going all over their trousers, and was told that this was something that only happened to women.

Maria complained to God, but, in the end, she got used to menstruating. She could not, however, get used to the boy's absence, and kept blaming herself for her own stupidity in running away from the very thing she most wanted. The day before the new term began, she went to the only church in town and vowed to the image of St Anthony that she would take the initiative and speak to the boy.

The following day, she put on her smartest dress, one that her mother had made specially for the occasion, and set off to school, thanking God that the holidays had finally ended. But the boy did not appear. And so another agonising week passed, until she found out, through some schoolfriends, that he had left town.

'He's gone somewhere far away,' someone said.

At that moment, Maria learned that certain things are lost forever. She learned too that there was a place called 'somewhere far away', that the world was vast and her own town very small, and that, in the end, the most interesting people always leave. She too would like to leave, but she was still very young. Nevertheless, looking at the dusty streets of the town where she lived, she decided that one day she would follow in the boy's footsteps. On the nine Fridays that followed, she took communion, as was the custom in her religion, and asked the Virgin Mary to take her away from there.

She grieved for a while too and tried vainly to find out where the boy had gone, but no one knew where his parents had moved to. It began to seem to Maria that the world was too large, that love was something very dangerous and that the Virgin was a saint who inhabited a distant heaven and didn't listen to the prayers of children.

Three years passed; she learned geography and mathematics, she began following the soaps on TV; at school, she read her first erotic magazine; and she began writing a diary describing her humdrum life and her desire to experience first-hand the things they told her about in class – the ocean, snow, men in turbans, elegant women covered in jewels. But since no one can live on impossible dreams – especially when their mother is a seamstress and their father is hardly ever at home – she soon realised that she needed to take more notice of what was going on around her. She studied in order to get on in life, at the same time looking for someone with whom she could share her dreams of adventure. When she had just turned fifteen, she fell in love with a boy she had met in a Holy Week procession.

She did not repeat her childhood mistake: they talked, became friends and started going to the cinema and to parties together. She also noticed that, as had happened with the first boy, she associated love more with the person's absence than with their presence: she would miss her boyfriend intensely, would spend hours imagining what they would talk about when next they met, and remembering every second they had spent together, trying to work out what she had done right and what she had done wrong.

She liked to think of herself as an experienced young woman, who had already allowed one grand passion to slip from her grasp and who knew the pain that this caused, and now she was determined to fight with all her might for this man and for marriage, determined that he *was* the man for marriage, children and the house by the sea. She went to talk to her mother, who said imploringly:

'But you're still very young, my dear.'

'You got married to my father when you were sixteen.'

Her mother preferred not to explain that this had been because of an unexpected pregnancy, and so she used the 'things were different then' argument and brought the matter to a close.

The following day, Maria and her boyfriend went for a walk in the countryside. They talked a little, and Maria asked if he wanted to travel, but, instead of answering the question, he took her in his arms and kissed her.

Her first kiss! How she had dreamed of that moment! And the landscape was special too – the herons flying, the sunset, the wild beauty of that semi-arid region, the sound of distant music. Maria pretended to draw back, but then she embraced him and repeated what she had seen so often on the cinema, in magazines and on TV: she rubbed her lips against his with some violence, moving her head from side to side, half-rhythmic, half-frenzied. Now and then, she felt the boy's tongue touch her teeth and thought it felt delicious.

Then suddenly he stopped kissing her and asked:

'Don't you want to?'

What was she supposed to say? Did she want to? Of course she did! But a woman shouldn't expose herself in that way, especially not to her future husband, otherwise he would spend the rest of his life suspecting that she might say 'yes' that easily to anything. She decided not to answer.

He kissed her again, this time with rather less enthusiasm. Again he stopped, red-faced, and Maria knew that something was very wrong, but she was afraid to ask what it was. She took his hand, and they walked back to the town together, talking about other things, as if nothing had happened.

That night – using the occasional difficult word because she was sure that, one day, everything she had written would be read by someone else, and because she was convinced that something very important had happened – she wrote in her diary:

When we meet someone and fall in love, we have a sense that the whole universe is on our side. I saw this happen today as the sun went down. And yet if something goes wrong, there is nothing left! No herons, no distant music, not even the taste of his lips. How is it possible for the beauty that was there only minutes before to vanish so quickly?

Life moves very fast. It rushes us from heaven to hell in a matter of seconds.

The following day, she talked to her girlfriends. They had

all seen her going out for a walk with her future 'betrothed'. After all, it is not enough just to have a great love in your life, you must make sure that everyone knows what a desirable person you are. They were dying to know what had happened, and Maria, very full of herself, said that the best bit was when his tongue touched her teeth. One of the other girls laughed.

'Didn't you open your mouth?'

Suddenly everything became clear – his question, his disappointment.

'What for?'

'To let him put his tongue inside.'

'What difference does it make?'

'It's not something you can explain. That's just how people kiss.'

There was much giggling, pretend pity and gleeful feelings of revenge amongst these girls who had never had a boy in love with them. Maria pretended not to care and she laughed too, although her soul was weeping. She secretly cursed the films she had seen in the cinema, from which she had learned to close her eyes, place her hand on the man's head and move her head slightly to right and left, but which had failed to show the essential, most important thing. She made up the perfect excuse (I didn't want to give myself at once, because I wasn't sure, but now I realise that you are the love of my life) and waited for the next opportunity.

She didn't see him until three days later, at a party in a local club, and he was holding the hand of a friend of hers, the one who had asked her about the kiss. She again pretended that she didn't care, and survived until the end of the evening talking with her girlfriends about film stars and about other local boys, and pretending not to notice her friends' occasional pitying looks. When she arrived home, though, she allowed her universe to crumble; she cried all night, suffered for the next eight months and concluded that love clearly wasn't made for her and that she wasn't made for love. She considered becoming a nun and devoting the rest of her life to a kind of love that didn't hurt and didn't leave painful scars on the heart – love for Jesus. At school, they learned about missionaries who went to Africa, and she decided that there lay an escape from her dull existence. She planned to enter a convent, she learned first aid (according to some teachers, a lot of people were dying in Africa), worked harder in her religious knowledge classes, and began to imagine herself as a modern-day saint, saving lives and visiting jungles inhabited by lions and tigers.

However, her fifteenth year brought with it not only the discovery that you were supposed to kiss with your mouth open, and that love is, above all, a cause of suffering. She discovered a third thing: masturbation. It happened almost by chance, as she was touching her genitals while waiting for her mother to come home. She used to do this when she was a child and she liked the feeling, until, one day, her father saw her and slapped her hard, without explaining why. She never forgot being hit like that, and she learned that she shouldn't touch herself in front of other people; since she couldn't do it in the middle of the street and she didn't have a room of her own at home, she forgot all about the pleasurable sensation.

Until that afternoon, almost six months after the kiss. Her mother was late coming home, and she had nothing to do; her father had just gone out with a friend, and since there was nothing interesting on the TV, she began examining her own body, in the hope that she might find some unwanted hair which could immediately be tweezered out. To her surprise, she noticed a small gland above her vagina; she began touching it and found that she couldn't stop; the feelings provoked were so strong and so pleasurable, and her whole body – particularly the part she was touching – became tense. After a while, she began to enter a kind of paradise, the feelings grew in intensity, until she noticed that she could no longer see or hear clearly, everything appeared to be tinged with yellow, and then she moaned with pleasure and had her first orgasm.

Orgasm!

It was like floating up to heaven and then parachuting slowly down to earth again. Her body was drenched in sweat, but she felt complete, fulfilled and full of energy. So that was what sex was! How wonderful! Not like in erotic magazines in which everyone talked about pleasure, but seemed to be grimacing in pain. And no need for a man, who liked a woman's body, but had no time for her feelings. She could do it on her own! She did it again, this time imagining that a famous movie star was touching her, and once more she floated up to paradise and parachuted down again, feeling even more energised. Just as she was about to do it for a third time, her mother came home.

Maria talked to her girlfriends about her new discovery, not saying that she had only discovered it a few hours before. All of them – apart from two – knew what she was talking about, but none of them had ever dared to raise the subject. It was Maria's turn to feel like a revolutionary, to be the leader of the group, inventing an absurd 'secret confessions' game, which involved asking everyone their favourite method of masturbation. She learned various different techniques, like lying under the covers in the height of summer (because, one of her friends assured her, sweating helped), using a goose feather to touch yourself there (she didn't yet know what the place was called), letting a boy do it to you (Maria thought this unnecessary), using the spray in the bidet (she didn't have one at home, but she would try it as soon as she visited one of her richer friends).

Anyway, once she had discovered masturbation and used a few of the techniques suggested by her friends, she abandoned forever the idea of a religious life. Masturbation gave her enormous pleasure, and yet the Church seemed to imply that sex was the greatest of sins. She heard various tales from those same girlfriends: masturbation gave you spots, could lead to madness or even pregnancy. Nevertheless, despite all these risks, she continued to pleasure herself at least once a week, usually on Wednesdays, when her father went out to play cards with his friends.

At the same time, she grew more and more insecure in

her relationships with boys, and more and more determined to leave the place where she lived. She fell in love a third time and a fourth, she knew how to kiss now, and when she was alone with her boyfriends, she touched them and allowed herself to be touched, but something always went wrong, and the relationship would end precisely at the moment when she was sure that this was the person with whom she wanted to spend the rest of her life. After a long time, she came to the conclusion that men brought only pain, frustration, suffering and a sense of time dragging. One afternoon, watching a mother playing with her two-year-old son, she decided that she could still think about a husband, children and a house with a sea-view, but that she would never fall in love again, because love spoiled everything.

And so Maria's adolescent years passed. She grew prettier and prettier, and her sad, mysterious air brought her many suitors. She went out with one boy and with another, and she dreamed and suffered – despite her promise to herself never to fall in love again. On one such date, she lost her virginity on the back seat of a car; she and her boyfriend were touching each other with more than usual ardour, the boy got very worked up, and she, weary of being the only virgin amongst her group of friends, allowed him to penetrate her. Unlike masturbation, which took her up to heaven, this hurt her and caused a trickle of blood which left a stain on her skirt that took ages to wash out. There wasn't the magical sensation of her first kiss – the herons flying, the sunset, the music ... but she would rather not think about that.

She made love with the same boy a few more times, although she had to threaten him first, saying that if he didn't, she would tell her father he had raped her. She used him as a way of learning, trying in every way she could to understand what pleasure there was in having sex with a partner.

She couldn't understand it; masturbation was much less trouble and far more rewarding. But all the magazines, the

TV programmes, books, girlfriends, everything, ABSOLUTELY EVERYTHING, said that a man was essential. Maria began to think that she must have some unspeakable sexual problem, so she concentrated still more on her studies and, for a while, forgot about that marvellous, murderous thing called Love.

From Maria's diary, when she was seventeen:

My aim is to understand love. I know how alive I felt when I was in love, and I know that everything I have now, however interesting it might seem, doesn't really excite me.

But love is a terrible thing: I've seen my girlfriends suffer and I don't want the same thing to happen to me. They used to laugh at me and my innocence, but now they ask me how it is I manage men so well. I smile and say nothing, because I know that the remedy is worse than the pain: I simply don't fall in love. With each day that passes, I see more clearly how fragile men are, how inconstant, insecure and surprising they are … a few of my girlfriends' fathers have propositioned me, but I've always refused. At first, I was shocked, but now I think it's just the way men are.

Although my aim is to understand love, and although I suffer to think of the people to whom I gave my heart, I see that those who touched my heart failed to arouse my body, and that those who aroused my body failed to touch my heart.

She turned nineteen, having finished secondary school, and found a job in a draper's shop, where her boss promptly fell in love with her. By then, however, Maria knew how to use a man, without being used by him. She never let him touch her, although she was always very coquettish, conscious of the power of her beauty.

The power of beauty: what must the world be like for ugly women? She had some girlfriends who no one ever noticed at parties or who men were never interested in. Incredible though it might seem, these girls placed far greater value on the little love they received, suffered in silence when they were rejected and tried to face the future by looking for other things beyond getting all dressed up for someone else. They were more independent, took more interest in themselves, although, in Maria's imagination, the world for them must seem unbearable.

She knew how attractive she was, and although she rarely listened to her mother, there was one thing her mother said that she never forgot: 'Beauty, my dear, doesn't last.' With this in mind, she continued to keep her boss at arm's length, though without putting him off completely, and this brought her a considerable increase in salary (she didn't know how long she would be able to string him along with the mere hope of one day getting her into bed, but at least she was earning good money meanwhile). He also paid her overtime for working late (her boss liked having her around, perhaps worried that if she went out at night, she might find the great love of her life). She worked for two years solidly, paid money each month to her parents for her keep, and, at last, she did it! She saved up enough money to go and spend a week's holiday in the city of her dreams, the place where film and TV stars live, the picture postcard image of her country: Rio de Janeiro!

Her boss offered to go with her and to pay all her expenses, but Maria lied to him, saying that, since she was going to one of the most dangerous places in the world, the one condition her mother had laid down was that she was to stay at the house of a cousin trained in judo.

'Besides, sir,' she said, 'you can't just leave the shop without some reliable person to look after it.'

'Don't call me "sir",' he said, and Maria saw in his eyes something she recognised: the flame of love. And this surprised her, because she had always thought he was only interested in sex; and yet, his eyes were saying the exact opposite: 'I can give you a house, a family, some money for your parents.' Thinking of the future, she decided to stoke the fire.

She said that she would really miss the job, as well as the colleagues she just adored working with (she was careful not to mention anyone in particular, leaving the mystery hanging in the air: did 'colleague' mean him?) and she promised to take great care of her purse and her honour.

The truth was quite different: she didn't want anyone, anyone at all, to spoil what would be her first week of total freedom. She wanted to do everything – swim in the sea, talk to complete strangers, look in shop windows, and be prepared for a Prince Charming to appear and carry her off for good.

'What's a week after all?' she said with a seductive smile, hoping that she was wrong. 'It will pass in a flash, and I'll soon be back at work.'

Saddened, her boss resisted at first, but finally accepted her decision, for at the time he was making secret plans to ask her to marry him as soon as she got back, and he didn't want to spoil everything by appearing too pushy.

Maria travelled for forty-eight hours by bus, checked into a cheap hotel in Copacabana (Copacabana! That beach, that sky ...) and even before she had unpacked her bags, she grabbed the bikini she had bought, put it on, and despite the cloudy weather, made straight for the beach. She looked at the sea fearfully, but ended up wading awkwardly into its waters.

No one on the beach noticed that this was her first contact with the ocean, with the goddess Iemanjá, the maritime currents, the foaming waves and, on the other side of the Atlantic, with the coast of Africa and its lions. When she came out of the water, she was approached by a woman trying to selling wholefood sandwiches, by a handsome black man who asked if she wanted to go out with him that night, and by another man who didn't speak a word of Portuguese but who asked, using gestures, if she would like to have a drink of coconut water.

Maria bought a sandwich because she was too embarrassed to say 'no', but she avoided speaking to the two strangers. She felt suddenly disappointed with herself; now that she had the chance to do anything she wanted, why was she behaving in this ridiculous manner? Finding no good explanation, she sat down to wait for the sun to come out from behind the clouds, still surprised at her own courage and at how cold the water was, even in the height of summer.

However, the man who couldn't speak Portuguese reappeared at her side bearing a drink, which he offered to her. Relieved not to have to talk to him, she drank the coconut water and smiled at him, and he smiled back. For some time, they kept up this comfortable, meaningless conversation – a smile here, a smile there – until the man took a small red dictionary out of his pocket and said, in a strange accent: 'bonita' – 'pretty'. She smiled again; however much she wanted to meet her Prince Charming, he should at least speak her language and be slightly younger.

The man went on leafing through the little book:

'Supper ... tonight?'

Then he said:

'Switzerland!'

And he completed this with words that sound like the bells of paradise in whatever language they are spoken:

'Work! Dollars!'

Maria did not know any restaurant called Switzerland, and could things really be that easy and dreams so quickly fulfilled? She erred on the side of caution: 'Thank you very much for the invitation, but I already have a job and I'm not interested in buying any dollars.'

The man, who understood not a word she said, was growing desperate; after many more smiles back and forth, he left her for a few minutes and returned with an interpreter. Through him, he explained that he was from Switzerland (the country, not a restaurant) and that he would like to have supper with her, in order to talk to her about a possible job offer. The interpreter, who introduced himself as the person in charge of foreign tourists and security in the hotel where the man was staying, added on his own account:

'I'd accept if I were you. He's an important impresario looking for new talent to work in Europe. If you like, I can put you in touch with some other people who accepted his invitation, got rich and are now married with children who won't have to worry about being mugged or unemployed.'

Then, trying to impress her with his grasp of international culture, he said:

'Besides, Switzerland makes excellent chocolates and watches.'

Maria's only stage experience had been in the Passion play that the local council always put on during Holy Week, and in which she had had a walk-on part as a waterseller. She had barely slept on the bus, but she was excited by the sea, tired of eating sandwiches, wholefood or otherwise, and confused because she didn't know anyone and needed to find a friend. She had been in similar situations before, in which a man promises everything and gives nothing, so she knew that all this talk of acting was just a way of getting her interested.

However, convinced that the Virgin had presented her with this chance, convinced that she must enjoy every second of her week's holiday, and because a visit to a good restaurant would provide her with something to talk about when she went home, she decided to accept the invitation, as long as the interpreter came too, for she was already getting tired of smiling and pretending that she could understand what the foreigner was saying.

The only problem was also the gravest one: she did not have anything suitable to wear. A woman never admits to such things (she would find it easier to admit that her husband had betrayed her than to reveal the state of her wardrobe), but since she did not know these people and might well never see them again, she felt that she had nothing to lose.

'I've just arrived from the northeast and I haven't got the right clothes to wear to a restaurant.'

Through the interpreter, the man told her not to worry and asked for the address of her hotel. That evening, she received a dress the like of which she had never seen in her entire life, accompanied by a pair of shoes that must have cost as much as she earned in a year.

She felt that this was the beginning of the road she had so longed for during her childhood and adolescence in the *sertão*, the Brazilian backlands, putting up with the constant droughts, the boys with no future, the poor but honest town, the dull, repetitive way of life: she was ready to be transformed into the princess of the universe! A man had offered her work, dollars, a pair of exorbitantly expensive shoes and a dress straight out of a fairy tale! All she lacked was some make-up, but the receptionist at her hotel took pity on her and helped her out, first warning her not to assume that every foreigner was trustworthy or that every man in Rio was a mugger.

Maria ignored the warning, put on her gifts from heaven, spent hours in front of the mirror, regretting not having brought a camera with her in order to record the moment, only to realise that she was late for her date. She raced off, just like Cinderella, to the hotel where the Swiss gentleman was staying.

To her surprise, the interpreter told her that he would not be accompanying them.

'Don't worry about the language, what matters is whether or not he feels comfortable with you.'

'But how can he if he doesn't understand what I'm saying?'

'Precisely. You don't need to talk, it's all a question of vibes.'

Maria didn't know what 'vibes' were; where she came from, people needed to exchange words, phrases, questions and answers whenever they met. But Maílson – the name of the interpreter-cum-security officer – assured her that in Rio de Janeiro and the rest of the world, things were different.

'He doesn't need to understand, just make him feel at ease. He's a widower with no children; he owns a nightclub and is looking for Brazilian women who want to work abroad. I said you weren't the type, but he insisted, saying that he had fallen in love with you when he saw you coming out of the water. He thought your bikini was lovely too.'

He paused.

'But, frankly, if you want to find a boyfriend here, you'll have to get a different bikini; no one, apart from this Swiss guy, will go for it; it's really old-fashioned.'

Maria pretended that she hadn't heard. Maílson went on:

'I don't think he's interested in just having a bit of a fling; he reckons you've got what it takes to become the main attraction at his club. Of course, he hasn't seen you sing or dance, but you could learn all that, whereas beauty is something you're born with. These Europeans are all the same; they come over here and imagine that all Brazilian women are really sensual and know how to samba. If he's serious, I'd advise you to get a signed contract and have the signature verified at the Swiss consulate before leaving the country. I'll be on the beach tomorrow, opposite the hotel, if you want to talk to me about anything.'

The Swiss man, all smiles, took her arm and indicated the taxi awaiting them.

'If he has other intentions, and you have too, then the normal price is three hundred dollars a night. Don't accept any less.'

Before she could say anything, she was on her way to the restaurant, with the man rehearsing the words he wanted to say. The conversation was very simple:

'Work? Dollars? Brazilian star?'

Maria, meanwhile, was still thinking about what the interpreter-cum-security officer had said: three hundred dollars a night! That was a fortune! She didn't need to suffer for love, she could play this man along just as she had her boss at the shop, get married, have children and give her parents a comfortable life. What did she have to lose? He was old and he might die before too long, and then she would be rich – these Swiss men obviously had too much money and not enough women back home.

They said little over the meal – just the usual exchange of smiles – and Maria gradually began to understand what Maílson had meant by 'vibes'. The man showed her an album containing writing in a language that she did not know; photos of women in bikinis (doubtless better and more daring than the one she had worn that afternoon), newspaper cuttings, garish leaflets in which the only word she recognised was 'Brazil', wrongly spelled (hadn't they taught him at school that it was written with an 's'?). She drank a lot, afraid that the man would proposition her (after all, even though she had never done this in her life before, no one could turn their nose up at three hundred dollars, and things always seem simpler with a bit of alcohol inside you, especially if you're among strangers). But the man behaved like a perfect gentleman, even holding her chair for her when she sat down and got up. In the end, she said that she was tired and arranged to meet him on the beach the following day (pointing to her watch, showing him the time, making the movement of the waves with her hands and saying 'a-ma-nhã' – 'tomorrow' – very slowly).

He seemed pleased and looked at his own watch (possibly Swiss), and agreed on the time.

She did not go to sleep straight away. She dreamed that it was all a dream. Then she woke up and saw that it wasn't: there was the dress draped over the chair in her modest room, the beautiful shoes and that rendezvous on the beach.

From Maria's diary, on the day that she met the Swiss man:

Everything tells me that I am about to make a wrong decision, but making mistakes is just part of life. What does the world want of me? Does it want me to take no risks, to go back where I came from because I didn't have the courage to say 'yes' to life?

I made my first mistake when I was eleven years old, when that boy asked me if I could lend him a pencil; since then, I've realised that sometimes you get no second chance and that it's best to accept the gifts the world offers you. Of course it's risky, but is the risk any greater than the chance of the bus that took forty-eight hours to bring me here having an accident? If I must be faithful to someone or something, then I have, first of all, to be faithful to myself. If I'm looking for true love, I first have to get the mediocre loves out of my system. The little experience of life I've had has taught me that no one owns anything, that everything is an illusion – and that applies to material as well as spiritual things. Anyone who has lost something they thought was theirs forever (as has happened often enough to me already) finally comes to realise that nothing really belongs to them.

And if nothing belongs to me, then there's no point wasting my time looking after things that aren't mine; it's best to live as if today were the first (or last) day of my life.

The next day, together with Maílson, the interpreter-cum-security officer and now, according to him, her agent, she said that she would accept the Swiss man's offer, as long as she had a document provided by the Swiss consulate. The foreigner, who seemed accustomed to such demands, said that this was something he wanted too, since, if she was to work in his country, she needed a piece of paper proving that no one there could do the job she was proposing to do – and this was not particularly difficult, given that Swiss women had no particular talent for the samba. Together they went to the city centre, and the security officer-cum-interpreter-cum-agent demanded a cash advance as soon as the contract was signed, thirty per cent of the five hundred dollars she received.

'That's a week's payment in advance. One week, you understand? You'll be earning five hundred dollars a week from now on, but with no deductions, because I only get a commission on the first payment.'

Up until then, travel and the idea of going far away had just been a dream, and dreaming is very pleasant as long as you are not forced to put your dreams into practice. That way, we avoid all the risks, frustrations and difficulties, and when we are old, we can always blame other people –

preferably our parents, our spouses or our children – for our failure to realise our dreams.

Suddenly, there was the opportunity she had been so eagerly awaiting, but which she had hoped would never come! How could she possibly deal with the challenges and the dangers of a life she did not know? How could she leave behind everything she was used to? Why had the Virgin decided to go this far?

Maria consoled herself with the thought that she could change her mind at any moment; it was all just a silly game, something different to tell her friends about when she went back home. After all, she lived more than a thousand kilometres from there and she now had three hundred and fifty dollars in her purse, so if, tomorrow, she decided to pack her bags and run away, there was no way they would ever be able to track her down again.

In the afternoon following their visit to the consulate, she decided to go for a walk on her own by the sea, where she looked at the children, the volleyball players, the beggars, the drunks, the sellers of traditional Brazilian artifacts (made in China), the people jogging and exercising as a way of fending off old age, the foreign tourists, the mothers with their children, and the pensioners playing cards at the far end of the promenade. She had come to Rio de Janeiro, she had been to a five-star restaurant and to a consulate, she had met a foreigner, she had an agent, she had been given a present of a dress and a pair of shoes that no one, absolutely no one, back home could ever have afforded.

And now what?

She looked out to sea: her geography lessons told her that if she set off in a straight line, she would reach Africa, with its lions and jungles full of gorillas. However, if she headed in a slightly more northerly direction, she would end up in the enchanted kingdom known as Europe, with its Eiffel Tower, EuroDisney and Leaning Tower of Pizza. What did she have to lose? Like every Brazilian girl, she had learned to samba even before she could say 'Mama'; she could always come back if she didn't like it, and she had already learned that opportunities are made to be seized.

She had spent a lot of her life saying 'no' to things to which she would have liked to say 'yes', determined to try only those experiences she could control – certain affairs she had had with men, for example. Now she was facing the unknown, as unknown as this sea had once been to the navigators who crossed it, or so she had been told in history classes. She could always say 'no', but would she then spend the rest of her life brooding over it, as she still did over the memory of the little boy who had once asked to borrow a pencil and had then disappeared – her first love? She could always say 'no', but why not try saying 'yes' this time?

For one very simple reason: she was a girl from the backlands of Brazil, with no experience of life apart from a good school, a vast knowledge of TV soaps and the certainty that she was beautiful. That wasn't enough with which to face the world.

She saw a group of people laughing and looking at the sea, afraid to go in. Two days ago, she had felt the same thing, but now she was no longer afraid; she went into the water whenever she wanted, as if she had been born there. Wouldn't it be the same in Europe?

She made a silent prayer and again asked the Virgin Mary's advice, and seconds later, she seemed perfectly at ease with her decision to go ahead, because she felt protected. She could always come back, but she would not necessarily get another chance of a trip like this. It was worth taking the risk, as long as the dream survived the forty-eight-hour journey back home in a bus with no air conditioning, and as long as the Swiss man didn't change his mind.

She was in such good spirits that when he invited her out to supper again, she wanted to appear alluring and took his hand in hers, but he immediately pulled away, and Maria realised – with a mixture of fear and relief – that he was serious about what he said.

'Samba star!' said the man. 'Lovely Brazilian samba star! Travel next week!'

This was all well and good, but 'travel next week' was out of the question. Maria explained that she couldn't take a decision without first consulting her family. The Swiss man was furious and showed her a copy of the signed contract, and for the first time she felt afraid.

'Contract!' he said.

Even though she was determined to go home, she decided to consult her agent Maílson first; after all, he was being paid to advise her.

Maílson, however, seemed more concerned with seducing a German tourist who had just arrived at the hotel and who was sunbathing topless on the beach, convinced that Brazil was the most liberal country in the world (having failed to notice that she was the only woman on the beach with her breasts exposed and that everyone was eyeing her rather uneasily). It was very hard to get him to pay attention to what she was saying.

'But what if I change my mind?' insisted Maria.

'I don't know what's in the contract, but I suppose he might have you arrested.'

'He'd never be able to find me!'

'Exactly. So why worry?'

The Swiss man, on the other hand, having spent five hundred dollars, as well as paying out for a pair of shoes, a dress, two suppers and various fees for the paperwork at the consulate, was beginning to get worried, and so, since Maria kept insisting on the need to talk to her family, he decided to buy two plane tickets and go with her to the place where she had been born – as long as it could all be resolved in forty-eight hours and they could still travel to Europe the following week, as agreed. With a smile here and a smile there, she was beginning to understand that this was all in the documents she had signed and that, when it came to seductions, feelings and contracts, one should never play around.

It was a surprise and a source of pride to the small town to see its lovely daughter Maria arrive accompanied by a foreigner who wanted to make her a big star in Europe. The whole neighbourhood knew, and her old schoolfriends asked: 'How did it happen?'

'I was just lucky.'

They wanted to know if such things were always happening in Rio de Janeiro, because they had seen similar scenarios in TV soaps. Maria would not be pinned down, wanting to place a high value on her personal experience and thus convince her friends that she was someone special.

She and the man went to her house where he handed round leaflets, with Brasil spelled with a 'z', and the contract, while Maria explained that she had an agent now and intended following a career as an actress. Her mother, seeing the diminutive bikinis worn by the girls in the photos that the foreigner was showing her, immediately gave them back and preferred to ask no questions; all that mattered was that her daughter should be happy and rich, or unhappy, but at least rich.

'What's his name?'

'Roger.'

'Rogério! I had a cousin called Rogério!'

The man smiled and clapped, and they all realised that he hadn't understood a word. Maria's father said:

'He's about the same age as me.'

Her mother told him not to interfere with their daughter's happiness. Since all seamstresses talk a great deal to their customers and acquire a great deal of knowledge about marriage and love, her advice to Maria was this:

'My dear, it's better to be unhappy with a rich man than happy with a poor man, and over there you'll have far more chance of becoming an unhappy rich woman. Besides, if it doesn't work out, you can just get on the bus and come home.'

Maria might be a girl from the backlands, but she was more intelligent than her mother or her future husband imagined, and she said, simply to be provocative:

'Mama, there isn't a bus from Europe to Brazil. Besides, I want a career as a performer, I'm not looking for marriage.'

Her mother gave her a look of near despair.

'If you can go there, you can always come back. Being a performer, an actress, is fine for a young woman, but it only lasts as long as your looks, and they start to fade when you're about thirty. So make the most of things now. Find someone who's honest and loving, and marry him. Love isn't that important. I didn't love your father at first, but money buys everything, even true love. And look at your father, he's not even rich!'

It was bad advice from a friend, but good advice from a mother. Forty-eight hours later, Maria was back in Rio, though not without first having made a visit, alone, to her old place of work in order to hand in her resignation and to hear the owner of the shop say:

'Yes, I'd heard that a big French impresario wanted to take you off to Paris. I can't stop you going in pursuit of your happiness, but I want you to know something before you leave.'

He took a medal on a chain out of his pocket.

'It's the Miraculous Medal of Our Lady of the Graces. She has a church in Paris, so go there and pray for her protection. Look, there are some words engraved around the Virgin.'

Maria read: 'Hail Mary conceived without sin, pray for us who turn to you. Amen.'

'Remember to say those words at least once a day. And …'

He hesitated, but it was getting late.

'… if one day you come back, I'll be waiting for you. I missed my chance to tell you something very simple: I love you. It may be too late now, but I wanted you to know.'

Missed chances. She had learned very early on what that meant. 'I love you', though, were three words she had often heard during her twenty-two years, and it seemed to her that they were now completely devoid of meaning, because they had never turned into anything serious or deep, never translated into a lasting relationship. Maria thanked him for his words, noted them in her memory (one never knows what life may have in store for us, and it's always good to know where the emergency exit is), gave him a chaste kiss on the cheek and left without so much as a backward glance.

They returned to Rio, and within a day she had her passport (Brazil had really changed, Roger said, using a few words in Portuguese and a lot of gestures, which Maria took to mean 'before it used to take ages'). With the help of Maílson, the security officer-cum-interpreter-cum-agent, any other important purchases were made (clothes, shoes, make-up, everything that a woman like her could want).

On the eve of their departure for Europe, they went to a nightclub, and when Roger saw her dance, he felt pleased with his choice; he was clearly in the presence of a future great star of Cabaret Cologny, this lovely dark girl with her pale eyes and hair as black as the wing of the *graúna* (the Brazilian bird often evoked by local authors to describe black hair). The work permit from the Swiss consulate was ready, so they packed their bags and, the following day, they were flying to the land of chocolate, clocks and cheese, with Maria secretly planning to make this man fall in love with her – after all, he wasn't old, ugly or poor. What more could she want?

She arrived feeling exhausted and, while still in the airport, her heart contracted with fear: she realised that she was completely dependent on the man at her side – she had no knowledge of the country, the language or the cold. Roger's behaviour changed as the hours passed; he no longer made any attempt to be pleasant, and although he had never tried to kiss her or to fondle her breasts, the look in his eyes grew more and more distant. He installed her in a small hotel, introducing her to another young Brazilian woman, a sad creature called Vivian, who would be in charge of preparing her for the work.

Vivian looked her coolly up and down, without the least show of sympathy for someone who had clearly never been abroad before. Instead of asking her how she was feeling, she got straight down to business.

'Don't delude yourself. He flies off to Brazil whenever one of his dancers gets married, something which seems to be happening more and more frequently. He knows what you want, and I assume you do too: you're probably looking for one of three things – adventure, money or a husband.'

How did she know? Was everyone looking for the same thing? Or could Vivian read other people's thoughts?

'All the girls here are looking for one of those three things,' Vivian went on, and Maria was convinced that she really could read her thoughts. 'As for adventure, it's too cold to do anything and, besides, you won't earn enough to go off travelling. And as for money, once the cost of room and board has been deducted, you'll have to work for nearly a whole year just to pay for your flight back home.'

'But …'

'I know, that isn't what you agreed. But the truth is that, like everyone else, you forgot to ask. If you had been more careful, if you had read the contract you signed, you would know exactly what you were getting yourself into, because the Swiss don't lie, they just rely on silence to help them.'

Maria felt the ground shifting beneath her.

'And as for a husband, every time a girl gets married, that represents a great financial loss for Roger, so we're forbidden to talk to the customers. If your interests lie in that direction, you'll have to run great risks. This isn't a pick-up place, like in Rue de Berne.'

Rue de Berne?

'Men come here with their wives, and the few tourists who turn up get one whiff of the family atmosphere and go looking for women elsewhere. I presume you know how to dance; well, if you can sing as well, your salary will increase, but so will the other girls' envy, so I'd suggest that, even if you're the best singer in Brazil, forget all about it and don't even try. Above all, don't use the phone. You'll spend everything you earn on it, and that won't be much.'

'He promised me five hundred dollars a week!'

'Oh yeah.'

From Maria's diary, during her second week in Switzerland:

I went to the nightclub and met the dance director who comes from somewhere called Morocco, and I had to learn every step of what he – who has never set foot in Brazil – thinks is the samba. I didn't even have time to recover from the long flight, I had to start smiling and dancing on the very first night. There are six of us, and not one of us is happy and none of us knows what we're doing here. The customers drink and applaud, blow kisses and privately make obscene gestures, but that's as far as it goes.

I got paid yesterday, barely a tenth of what we agreed, the rest, according to the contract, will be used to pay for my flight and my stay here. According to Vivian's calculations, that will take a year, which means that during that time there's no escape.

And what's the point of escaping anyway? I've only just arrived. I haven't seen anything yet. What's so awful about having to dance seven nights a week? I used to do that for pleasure, now I do it for money and fame; my legs don't ache, the only difficult thing is maintaining that fixed smile.

I can choose either to be a victim of the world or an adventurer in search of treasure. It's all a question of how I view my life.

Maria chose to be an adventurer in search of treasure – she put aside her feelings, she stopped crying every night, and she forgot all about the person she used to be; she discovered that she had enough willpower to pretend that she had just been born and so had no reason to miss anyone. Feelings could wait, now what she needed to do was to earn some money, get to know the country and return home victorious.

Besides, everything around her was very like Brazil in general and her own small town in particular: the women spoke Portuguese, complained about men, talked loudly, moaned about their working hours, turned up late at the club, defied the boss, thought themselves the most beautiful women in the world, and told stories about their Prince Charmings, who were usually living miles away or were married or had no money and so sponged off them. Contrary to what she had imagined from the leaflets Roger had brought with him, the club was exactly as Vivian had said it was: it had a family atmosphere. The girls – described on their work permits as 'samba dancers' – were not allowed to accept invitations or to go out with the customers. If they were caught receiving a note with someone's telephone number on it, they were suspended from work for two whole weeks. Maria, who had expected something livelier and more exciting, gradually allowed herself to succumb to sadness and boredom.

During the first two weeks, she barely left the boarding house where she was living, especially when she discovered that no one spoke her language, even if she said everything VE-RY SLOW-LY. She was also surprised to learn that, unlike in her own country, the city in which she was living had two different names – it was Genève to those who lived there and Genebra to Brazilians.

Finally, in the long, tedious hours spent in her small, TV-less room, she concluded:

(a) she would never find what she was looking for if she couldn't express herself. In order to do that, she needed to learn the local language.

(b) since all her colleagues were looking for the same thing, she needed to be different. For that particular problem, she as yet lacked both a solution or a method.

From Maria's diary, four weeks after arriving in Genève/Genebra:

I've already been here an eternity, I don't speak the language, I spend all day listening to music on the radio, looking round my room, thinking about Brazil, longing for work to begin and, when I'm working, longing to get back to the boarding house. In other words, I'm living the future not the present.

One day, at some distant future date, I'll get my ticket home, and I can go back to Brazil, marry the owner of the draper's shop and listen to the malicious comments of those friends who, never having taken any risks themselves, can only see other people's failures. No, I can't go back like that. I'd rather throw myself out of the plane as it's crossing the ocean.

Since you can't open the windows in the plane (I had never expected that. What a shame not to be able to breathe in the pure air!), I will die here. But before I die, I want to fight for life. If I can walk on my own, I can go wherever I like.

The following day, she enrolled in a French course that was run in the mornings, and there she met people of all creeds, beliefs and ages, men wearing brightly coloured clothes and lots of gold bracelets, women who always wore a headscarf, children who learned more quickly than the grown-ups, when it should have been the other way round, since grown-ups have more experience. She felt proud when she found out that everyone knew about her country – Carnival, the samba, football, and the most famous person in the world, Pelê. At first, she wanted to be nice and so tried to correct their pronunciation (it's Pel*ê*! Pel*ê*!), but after a while, she gave up, since they also insisted on calling her Mari*a*, with that mania foreigners have for changing all foreign names and believing that they are always right.

In the afternoons, so as to practise the language, she took her first steps around this city of two names. She discovered some delicious chocolate, a cheese she had never eaten before, a huge fountain in the middle of the lake, snow (which no one back home had ever touched), storks, and restaurants with fireplaces (although she never went inside, just seeing the fire blazing away gave her a pleasant feeling of wellbeing). She was also surprised to find that not all the shop signs advertised clocks; there were banks too, although she couldn't quite understand why there were so many for so few inhabitants, and why she rarely saw anyone inside them. She decided, however, not to ask any questions.

After three months of keeping a tight rein on herself at work, her Brazilian blood – as sensual and sexual as everyone thinks – made its voice heard; she fell in love with an Arab who was studying French with her on the same course. The affair lasted three weeks until, one night, she decided to take time off and go and visit a mountain on the outskirts of Geneva; this provoked a summons to Roger's office as soon as she arrived at work the following day.

No sooner had she opened the door than she was summarily dismissed for setting a bad example to the other girls working there. A hysterical Roger said that, yet again, he had been let down, that Brazilian women couldn't be trusted (oh dear, this mania for making generalisations about everything). She tried telling him that she had had a very high fever brought on by the sudden change in climate, but the man would not be persuaded and even claimed that he would have to go straight back to Brazil in order to find a replacement, and that he would have been far better off putting on a show using Yugoslav music and Yugoslav dancers who were far prettier and far more reliable.

Maria might be young but she was no fool, especially once her Arab lover had told her that Swiss employment laws were very strict and, since the nightclub kept back a large part of her salary, she could easily allege that she was being used for slave labour.

She went back to Roger's office, this time speaking reasonable French, which now included the word 'lawyer'. She left with a few insults and five thousand dollars in compensation – a sum of money beyond her wildest dreams – and all because of that magic word 'lawyer'. Now she was free to spend time with her Arab lover, buy a few presents, take some photos of the snow, and go back home in triumph.

The first thing she did was telephone her mother's neighbour to say that she was happy, had a brilliant career ahead of her and that there was no need for her family to worry. Then, since she had to leave the room in the boarding house that Roger had arranged for her, she had no alternative but to go to her Arab boyfriend, swear undying love, convert to his religion and marry him, even if she had to wear one of those strange headscarves; after all, as everyone knew, all Arabs were extremely wealthy and that was enough.

The Arab, however, was already far away, possibly in Arabia, a country Maria had never even heard of, and, deep down, she gave thanks to the Virgin Mary because she had not been obliged to betray her religion. She now had a reasonable grasp of spoken French, enough money for her return ticket, a work permit as a 'samba dancer' and a current visa; so, knowing that she could always go back and marry her former boss, she decided to try to earn money with her looks.

In Brazil she had read a book about a shepherd who, in searching for his treasure, encounters various difficulties, and these difficulties help him to get what he wants; she was in exactly the same position. She was aware now that the reason she had been dismissed was so that she could find her true destiny, as a model.

She rented a small room (with no television, but she had to live frugally until she began earning lots of money), and the following day, started doing the rounds of the agencies. They all told her that she needed to get some professional photos taken, but this, after all, was an investment in her career – dreams don't come cheap. She spent a large part of her money on an excellent photographer, who spoke little, but was extremely demanding: he had a vast selection of clothes in his studio and she posed for him in various outfits, sober and extravagant, and even in a bikini of which the only person she knew in Rio de Janeiro, the security officer-cum-interpreter-cum-former agent, Maílson, would have been proud. She asked for several extra copies and sent them off to her family with a letter saying how happy she was in Switzerland. They would all think she was rich and the owner of an enviable wardrobe, and that she had been transformed into her town's most illustrious daughter. If all went to plan (and she had read enough books on 'positive thinking' to be convinced that victory was assured), she would be greeted by a brass band on her return home and would try to persuade the mayor to have a square named after her.

Since she had no permanent address, she bought a mobile phone, the sort that use pre-paid phone cards, and in the days that followed, she waited for job offers. She ate in Chinese restaurants (which were the cheapest) and, to pass the time, she studied furiously.

But time dragged, and the telephone didn't ring. To her surprise, no one bothered her when she went for walks by the lake, apart from a few drug-pushers who always hung around in the same place, underneath one of the bridges that connect the lovely old public gardens to the newer part of the city. She began to doubt her looks, until an ex-colleague, whom she bumped into by chance in a café, told her that it wasn't her fault, it was the fault of the Swiss, who hate to bother anyone, and of other foreigners, who were all afraid of being arrested for 'sexual harassment' – a concept invented to make women everywhere feel worse about themselves.

From Maria's diary, one night when she lacked the courage to go out, to live or to continue waiting for the phone call that never came:

I spent today outside a funfair. Since I can't afford to fritter my money away, I thought it best just to watch other people. I stood for a long time by the roller coaster, and I noticed that most people get on it in search of excitement, but that once it starts, they are terrified and want the cars to stop.

What do they expect? Having chosen adventure, shouldn't they be prepared to go the whole way? Or do they think that the intelligent thing to do would be to avoid the ups and downs and spend all their time on a carousel, going round and round on the spot?

At the moment, I'm far too lonely to think about love, but I have to believe that it will happen, that I will find a job and that I am here because I chose this fate. The roller coaster is my life; life is a fast, dizzying game; life is a parachute jump; it's taking chances, falling over and getting up again; it's mountaineering; it's wanting to get to the very top of yourself and to feel angry and dissatisfied when you don't manage it.

It isn't easy being far from my family and from the language in which I can express all my feelings and emotions, but, from now on, whenever I feel depressed, I will remember that funfair. If I had fallen asleep and suddenly woken up on a roller coaster, what would I feel?

Well, I would feel trapped and sick, terrified of every bend, wanting to get off. However, if I believe that the track is my destiny and that God is in charge of the machine, then the nightmare becomes something thrilling. It becomes exactly what it is, a roller coaster, a safe, reliable toy, which will eventually stop, but, while the journey lasts, I must look at the surrounding landscape and whoop with excitement.

Although she was capable of writing very wise thoughts, she was quite incapable of following her own advice; her periods of depression became more frequent and the phone still refused to ring. To distract herself during these empty hours, and in order to practise her French, she began buying magazines about celebrities, but realised at once that she was spending too much money, and so she looked for the nearest lending library. The woman in charge told her that they didn't lend out magazines, but that she could suggest a few books that would help improve her French.

'I haven't got time to read books.'

'What do you mean you haven't got time? What are you doing?'

'Lots of things: studying French, writing a diary, and ...'

'And what?'

She was about to say 'waiting for the phone to ring', but she thought it best to say nothing.

'My dear, you're still very young, you've got your whole life ahead of you. Read. Forget everything you've been told about books and just read.'

'I've read loads of books.'

Suddenly, Maria remembered what Maílson the security officer had told her about 'vibes'. The librarian before her seemed a very sweet, sensitive person, someone who might be able to help her if all else failed. She needed to win her over; her instinct was telling her that this woman could become her friend. She quickly changed tack.

'But I'd like to read more. Could you help me choose some books?'

The woman brought her *The Little Prince*. She started leafing through it that same night, saw the drawings on the first page of what seemed to be a hat, but which, according to the author, all children would instantly recognise as a snake with an elephant inside it. 'Well, I don't think I can ever have been a child, then,' she thought. 'To me, it looks more like a hat.' In the absence of any television to watch, she accompanied the prince on his journeys, feeling sad whenever the word 'love' appeared, for she had forbidden herself to think about the subject at the risk of feeling suicidal. However, apart from the painful, romantic scenes between a prince, a fox and a rose, the book was really interesting, and she didn't keep checking every five minutes that the battery in her mobile phone was still fully charged (she was terrified of missing her big chance purely out of carelessness).

Maria became a regular visitor to the library, where she would chat to the woman, who seemed as lonely as she was, ask her to suggest more books and discuss life and authors – until her money had nearly run out. Another two weeks and she would not even have enough left to buy her ticket back to Brazil.

And, since life always waits for some crisis to occur before revealing itself at its most brilliant, the phone finally rang.

Three months after discovering the word 'lawyer' and after two months of living on the compensation she had received, someone from a model agency asked if Senhora Maria was still at this number. The reply was a cool, long-rehearsed 'yes', so as not to appear too eager. She learned that an Arab gentleman, who worked in the fashion industry in his country, had been very taken by her photos and wanted to invite her to take part in a fashion show. Maria remembered her recent disappointments, but also the money that she so desperately needed.

They arranged to meet in a very chic restaurant. She found herself with an elegant man, older and more charming than Roger, who asked her:

'Do you know who painted that picture over there? It's a Miró. Have you heard of Joan Miró?'

Maria said nothing, as if she were concentrating on the food, rather different from that in the Chinese restaurants where she normally ate. Meanwhile, she made a mental note: on her next visit to the library, she would have to ask for a book about Miró.

But the Arab was saying:

'This was the table where Fellini always sat. Do you know his films at all?'

She said she adored them. The man began asking more probing questions and Maria, knowing that she would fail the test, decided to be straight with him:

'I'm not going to spend the evening pretending to you. I can just about tell the difference between Coca-Cola and Pepsi, but that's about it. I thought we came here to discuss a fashion show.'

He seemed to appreciate her frankness.

'We'll do that when we have our after-supper drink.'

There was a pause, while they looked at each other, each trying to imagine what the other was thinking.

'You're very pretty,' said the man. 'If you come up and have a drink with me in my hotel room, I'll give you a thousand francs.'

Maria understood at once. Was it the fault of the model agency? Was it her fault? Should she have found out more about the nature of this supper? It wasn't the agency's fault, or hers, or the man's: this was simply how things worked. Suddenly she missed her hometown, missed Brazil, missed her mother's arms. She remembered Maílson, on the beach, when he had mentioned a fee of three hundred dollars; at the time, she had thought it funny, much more than she would have expected to receive for spending the night with a man. However, at that moment, she realised that she had no one, absolutely no one in the world she could talk to; she was alone in a strange city, a relatively experienced twenty-two-year-old, but none of her experience could help her to decide what would be the best response.

'Could you pour me some more wine, please.'

The Arab man filled her glass, and her thoughts travelled faster than the Little Prince on his travels to all those planets. She had come in search of adventure, money and possibly a husband; she had known that she would end up getting proposals such as this, because she was no innocent and was used to the ways of men. She still believed in model agencies, stardom, a rich husband, a family, children, grandchildren, nice clothes, a triumphant return to the place where she was born. She dreamed of overcoming all difficulties purely by dint of her own intelligence, charm and willpower.

But reality had just fallen in on her. To the man's surprise, she began to cry. He did not know what to do, caught between his fear of causing a scandal and his instinctive desire to protect her. He called the waiter over in order to ask for the bill, but Maria stopped him.

'No, don't do that. Pour me some more wine and just let me cry for a while.'

And Maria thought about the little boy who had asked to borrow a pencil, about the young man who had kissed her and how she had kept her mouth closed, about her excitement at seeing Rio for the first time, about the men who had used her and given nothing back, about the passions and loves lost along the way. Despite her apparent freedom, her life consisted of endless hours spent waiting for a miracle, for true love, for an adventure with the same romantic ending she had seen in films and read about in books. A writer once said that it is not time that changes man, nor knowledge; the only thing that can change someone's mind is love. What nonsense! The person who wrote that clearly knew only one side of the coin.

Love was undoubtedly one of the things capable of

changing a person's whole life, from one moment to the next. But there was the other side of the coin, the second thing that could make a human being take a totally different course from the one he or she had planned; and that was called despair. Yes, perhaps love really could transform someone, but despair did the job more quickly. What should she do? Should she run back to Brazil, become a teacher of French and marry her former boss? Should she take a small step forward; after all, it was only one night, in a city where she knew no one and no one knew her. Would that one night and that easy money mean that she would inevitably carry on until she reached a point in the road where there was no turning back? What was happening here – a great opportunity or a test set her by the Virgin Mary?

The Arab was looking around at the paintings by Joan Miró, at the place where Fellini used to have lunch, at the girl who took the coats and at the other customers arriving and leaving.

'Didn't you realise?'

'More wine, please,' said Maria, still in tears.

She was praying that the waiter would not come over and realise what was going on, and the waiter, who was watching it all from a distance, out of the corner of his eye, was praying that the man and the girl would hurry up and pay the bill, because the restaurant was full and there were people waiting.

At last, after what seemed an eternity, she spoke:

'Did you say a thousand francs for one drink?'

Maria was surprised by her own tone of voice.

'Yes,' said the man, regretting having suggested it in the first place. 'But I really wouldn't want ...'

'Pay the bill and let's go and have that drink at your hotel.'

Again, she seemed like a stranger to herself. Up until then, she had been a nice, cheerful, well-brought-up girl, and she would never have spoken like that to a stranger. But that girl, it seemed to her, had died forever: before her lay another existence, in which drinks cost one thousand francs or, to use a more universal currency, about six hundred dollars.

And everything happened as expected: she went to the Arab's hotel, drank champagne, got herself almost completely drunk, opened her legs, waited for him to have an orgasm (it didn't even occur to her to pretend to have one too), washed herself in the marble bathroom, picked up the money, and allowed herself the luxury of a taxi home.

She fell into bed and slept dreamlessly all night.

From Maria's diary, the next day:

I remember everything, although not the moment when I made the decision. Oddly enough, I have no sense of guilt. I used to think of girls who went to bed with men for money as people who had no other choice, and now I see that it isn't like that. I could have said 'yes' or 'no'; no one was forcing me to accept anything.

I walk about the streets and look at all the people, and I wonder if they chose their lives? Or were they, like me, 'chosen' by fate? The housewife who dreamed of becoming a model, the banker who wanted to be a musician, the dentist who felt he should write a book and devote himself to literature, the girl who would have loved to be a TV star, but who found herself instead working at the checkout in a supermarket.

I don't feel in the least bit sorry for myself. I am still not a victim, because I could have left that restaurant with my dignity intact and my purse empty. I could have given that man sitting opposite me a lesson in morality or tried to make him see that before him sat a princess who should be wooed not bought. I could have responded in all kinds of ways, but – like most people – I let fate choose which route I should take.

I'm not the only one, even though my fate may put me outside the law and outside society. In the search for happiness, however, we are all equal: none of us is happy – not the banker/musician, the dentist/writer, the checkout girl/actress, or the housewife/model.

So that was how it worked. As easy as that. There she was in a strange city where she knew no one, but what had been a torment to her yesterday, today gave her a tremendous sense of freedom, because she didn't need to explain herself to anyone.

She decided that, for the first time in many years, she would devote the entire day to thinking about herself. Up until then, she had always been preoccupied with what other people were thinking: her mother, her schoolfriends, her father, the people at the model agencies, the French teacher, the waiter, the librarian, complete strangers in the street. In fact, no one was thinking anything, certainly not about her, a poor foreigner, who, if she disappeared tomorrow, wouldn't even be missed by the police.

Fine. She went out early, had breakfast in her usual café, went for a stroll around the lake and saw a demonstration held by refugees. A woman out walking a small dog told her that they were Kurds, and Maria, instead of pretending that she knew the answer in order to prove that she was more cultivated and intelligent than people might think, asked:

'Where do Kurds come from?'

To her surprise, the woman didn't know. That's what the world is like: people talk as if they knew everything, but if you dare to ask a question, they don't know anything. She went into an Internet café and discovered that the Kurds came from Kurdistan, a non-existent country, now divided between Turkey and Iraq. She went back to the lake in search of the woman and her dog, but she had gone, possibly because the dog had got fed up after half an hour of staring at a group of human beings with banners, headscarves, music and strange cries.

'I'm just like that woman really. Or rather, that's what I used to be like: someone pretending to know everything, hidden away in my own silence, until that Arab guy got on my nerves, and I finally had the courage to say that the only thing I knew was how to tell the difference between two soft drinks. Was he shocked? Did he change his mind about me? Of course not. He must have been amazed at my honesty. Whenever I try to appear more intelligent than I am, I always lose out. Well, enough is enough!'

She thought of the model agency. Did they know what the Arab guy really wanted – in which case she had, yet again, been taken for a fool – or had they genuinely thought he was going to find work for her in his country?

Whatever the truth of the matter, Maria felt less alone on that grey morning in Geneva, with the temperature close to zero, the Kurds demonstrating, the trams arriving punctually at each stop, the shops setting out their jewellery in the windows again, the banks opening, the beggars sleeping, the Swiss going to work. She was less alone because by her side was another woman, invisible perhaps to passers-by. She had never noticed her presence before, but there she was.

She smiled at the invisible woman beside her who looked like the Virgin Mary, Jesus's mother. The woman smiled back and told her to be careful, things were not as simple as she imagined. Maria ignored the advice and replied that she was a grown-up, responsible for her own decisions, and she couldn't believe that there was some cosmic conspiracy being hatched against her. She had learned that there were people prepared to pay one thousand Swiss francs for one night, for half an hour between her legs, and all she had to decide over the next few days was whether to take her thousand Swiss francs and buy a plane ticket back to the town where she had been born, or to stay a little longer, and earn enough to be able to buy her parents a house, some lovely clothes for herself and tickets to all the places she had dreamed of visiting one day.

The invisible woman at her side said again that things weren't that simple, but Maria, although glad of this unexpected company, asked her not to interrupt her thoughts, because she needed to make some important decisions.

She began to analyse, more carefully this time, the possibility of going back to Brazil. Her schoolfriends, who had never left the town they were born in, would all say that she had been fired from the job, that she had never had the talent to be an international star. Her mother would be sad never to have received her promised monthly sum of money, although Maria, in her letters, had assured her that the post office must be stealing it. Her father would, forever after, look at her with that 'I told you so' expression on his face; she would go back to working in the shop, selling fabrics, and she would marry the owner – she who had travelled in a plane, eaten Swiss cheese, learned French and walked in the snow.

On the other hand, there were those drinks that had earned her one thousand Swiss francs. It might not last very long – after all, beauty changes as swiftly as the wind – but in a year, she could earn enough money to get back on her feet and return to the world, this time on her own terms. The only real problem was that she didn't know what to do, how to start. She remembered from her days at the 'family nightclub' where she had first worked that a girl had mentioned somewhere called Rue de Berne – in fact, it had been one of the first things she had said, even before she had shown her where to put her suitcases.

She went over to one of the large panels that can be found everywhere in Geneva, that most tourist-friendly of cities, which cannot bear to see tourists getting lost. For this reason the panels have advertisements on one side and maps on the other.

A man was standing there, and she asked him if he knew where Rue de Berne was. He looked at her, intrigued, and asked if it was the street she was looking for or the road that went to Berne, the capital of Switzerland. No, said Maria, I want the street in Geneva. The man looked her up and down, then walked off without a word, convinced that he was being filmed by one of those TV programmes that delight in making fools of people. Maria studied the map for fifteen minutes – it's not a very big city – and finally found the place she was looking for.

Her invisible friend, who had remained silent while she was studying the map, was now trying to reason with her; it wasn't a question of morality, but of setting off down a road of no return.

Maria said that if she could earn enough money to go back home, then she could earn enough to get out of any situation. Besides, none of the people she passed had actually chosen what they wanted to do. That was just a fact of life.

'We live in a vale of tears,' she said to her invisible friend. 'We can have all the dreams we like, but life is hard, implacable, sad. What are you trying to say: that people will condemn me? No one will ever know – this is just one phase of my life.'

With a sad, sweet smile, the invisible friend disappeared.

Maria went to the funfair and bought a ticket for the roller coaster; she screamed along with everyone else, knowing that there was no real danger and that it was all just a game. She ate in a Japanese restaurant, even though she didn't understand quite what she was eating, knowing only that it was very expensive and feeling in a mood to indulge herself in every luxury. She was happy, she didn't need to wait for a phone call now or to watch every centime she spent.

Later that day, she left a message with the agency to thank them and to tell them that the meeting had gone well.

If they were genuine, they would ask about the photos. If they were procurers of women, they would arrange more meetings.

She walked across the bridge back to her little room and decided that, however much money and however many future plans she had, she would definitely not buy a television: she needed to think, to use all her time for thinking.

From Maria's diary that night (with a note in the margin saying: 'Not sure'):

I have discovered the reason why a man pays for a woman: he wants to be happy.

He wouldn't pay a thousand francs just to have an orgasm. He wants to be happy. I do too, everyone does, and yet no one is. What have I got to lose if, for a while, I decide to become a ... it's a difficult word to think or even write ... but let's be blunt ... what have I got to lose if I decide to become a prostitute for a while?

Honour. Dignity. Self-respect. Although, when I think about it, I've never had any of those things. I didn't ask to be born, I've never found anyone to love me, I've always made the wrong decisions – now I'm letting life decide for me.

The agency phoned the next day and asked about the photos and when the fashion show was being held, since they got a percentage of every job. Maria, realising that they knew nothing about what had happened, told them that the Arab gentleman would be in touch with them.

She went to the library and asked for some books about sex. If she was seriously considering the possibility of working – just for a year, she had told herself – in an area about which she knew nothing, the first thing she needed to know was how to behave, how to give pleasure and receive money in return.

She was most disappointed when the librarian told her that, since the library was a government-funded institution, they only had a few technical works. Maria read the index of one of these books and immediately returned it: they said nothing about happiness, they talked only about dull things such as erection, penetration, impotence, precautions ... She did for a moment consider borrowing *The Psychology of Frigidity in Women*, since, in her own case, although she very much enjoyed being possessed and penetrated by a man, she only ever reached orgasm through masturbation.

She wasn't there in search of pleasure, however, but work. She thanked the librarian, and went to a shop where she made her first investment in that possible career looming on the horizon – clothes which she considered to be sexy enough to arouse men's desire. Then she went straight to the place she had found on the map. Rue de Berne. At the top of the street was a church (oddly enough, very near the Japanese restaurant where she had had supper the night before), then some shops selling cheap watches and clocks, and, at the far end, were the clubs she had heard about, all of them closed at that hour of the day. She went for another walk around the lake, then – without a tremor of embarrassment – bought five pornographic magazines in order to study the kind of thing she would have to do, waited for darkness to fall and then went back to Rue de Berne. There she chose at random a bar with the alluringly Brazilian name of 'Copacabana'.

She hadn't decided anything, she told herself. It was just an experiment. She hadn't felt so well or so free in all the time she had been in Switzerland.

'I'm looking for work,' she told the owner, who was washing glasses behind the bar. The place consisted of a series of tables, a few sofas around the walls and, in one corner, a kind of dance floor. 'Nothing doing. If you want to work here legally you have to have a work permit.'

Maria showed him hers and the man's mood seemed to improve.

'Got any experience?'

She didn't know what to say: if she said yes, he would ask her where she had worked before. If she said no, he might turn her down.

'I'm writing a book.'

The idea had come out of nowhere, as if an invisible voice had come to her aid. She saw that the man knew she was lying, but was pretending to believe her.

'Before you make any decision, talk to some of the other girls. We get at least six Brazilian women in every night, that way you can find out exactly what to expect.'

Maria was about to say that she didn't need any advice from anyone and that, besides, she hadn't come to a decision just yet, but the man had already moved off to the other side of the bar, leaving her on her own, without even a glass of water to drink.

The women started to arrive, and the owner called over some of the Brazilians and asked them to talk to the new arrival. None of them seemed very willing; fear of competition, Maria assumed. The sound system was turned on and a few Brazilian songs were played (well, the place *was* called 'Copacabana'); then some Asiatic-looking women came in, along with others who seemed to have come straight from the snowy, romantic mountains around Geneva. She had been standing there for nearly two hours, with nothing to drink and just a few cigarettes, filled by a growing sense that she was definitely making the wrong decision – the words 'what am I doing here?' kept repeating over and over in her head – and feeling increasingly irritated by the complete lack of interest on the part of both the owner and the other women, when, finally, one of the Brazilian girls came over to her.

'What made you choose this place?'

Maria could have resorted to that story about writing a book, or she could, as she had with the Kurds, with Miró and with Fellini, simply tell the truth.

'To be perfectly honest, I don't know where to start or if I want to start.'

The other woman seemed surprised by such a frank, direct answer. She took a sip of what looked like whisky, listened to the Brazilian song they were playing, made some comment about missing her home, then said that there wouldn't be many customers that night because a big international conference being held near Geneva had been cancelled. In the end, when she saw that Maria still hadn't left, she said:

'Look, it's very simple, you just have to stick to three basic rules. First: never fall in love with anyone you work with or have sex with. Second: don't believe any promises and always get paid up front. Third: don't use drugs.'

There was a pause.

'And start now. If you go home tonight without having got your first client, you'll have second thoughts about it and you won't have the courage to come back.'

Maria had gone there more for a consultation, to get some feedback on her chances of finding a temporary job. She found herself confronted by the feeling that so often pushes people into making hasty decisions – despair.

'All right. I'll start tonight.'

She didn't mention that she had, in fact, started yesterday. The woman went up to the owner, whom she called Milan, and he came over to talk to Maria.

'Have you got nice underwear on?'

No one – her boyfriends, the Arab, her girlfriends, far less a stranger – had ever asked her that question. But that was what life was like in that place: straight to the point.

'I'm wearing pale blue pants. And no bra,' she added provocatively. But all she got was a reprimand.

'Tomorrow, wear black pants, bra and stockings. Taking off your clothes is all part of the ritual.'

Without more ado, and on the assumption now that he was talking to someone who was about to start work, Milan introduced her to the rest of the ritual: the Copacabana should be a pleasant place to spend time, not a brothel. The men came into that bar wanting to believe that they would find a lady on her own. If anyone came over to her table and wasn't intercepted en route (because some clients were 'exclusive to certain girls'), he would probably say:

'Would you like a drink?'

To which Maria could say yes or no. She was free to choose the company she kept, although it wasn't advisable to say 'no' more than once a night. If she answered in the affirmative, she should ask for a fruit juice cocktail, which just happened to be the most expensive drink on the drinks list. Absolutely no alcohol or letting the customer choose for her.

Then, she should accept any invitation to dance. Most of the clientele were familiar faces and, apart from the 'special clients', about whom he did not go into any further detail, none of them represented any danger. The police and the Department of Health demanded monthly blood samples, to check that they weren't carrying any sexually transmitted diseases. The use of condoms was obligatory, although there was no way of checking if this rule was or wasn't being followed. She should never, on any account, cause any kind of scandal – Milan was a respectable married man, concerned for his reputation and the good name of his club.

He continued explaining the ritual: after dancing, they would return to the table, and the customer, as if he were saying something highly original, would invite her to go back to his hotel with him. The normal price was three hundred and fifty francs, of which fifty francs went to Milan, for the hire of the table (a trick to avoid any future legal complications and accusations of exploiting sex for financial gain).

Maria tried to say:

'But I earned a thousand francs for ...'

The owner made as if to move off, but the other Brazilian woman, who was listening in to the conversation, said:

'She's just joking.'

And turning to Maria, she said in clear, loud Portuguese:

'This is the most expensive place in Geneva. Never do that again. He knows what the going rate is and he knows that no one pays a thousand francs to go to bed with anyone, except, of course, the "special clients", but only if you get lucky and you have the right qualifications.'

Milan's eyes – later, Maria found out that he was a Yugoslav who had been living there for twenty years – left no room for doubt.

'The price is three hundred and fifty francs.'

'Right,' said a humbled Maria.

First, he had asked about the colour of her underwear, now he was deciding how much her body was worth.

But she had no time to think, the man was still issuing instructions: she must never accept invitations to anyone's house or to a hotel that had less than five stars. If the client had nowhere to take her, she was to go to a hotel located five blocks from there, and should always take a taxi so that the women who worked in the other clubs in Rue de Berne didn't get to know her face. Maria didn't believe this last reason; she thought that the real reason was that she might get an offer of better working conditions in another club. She kept her thoughts to herself, however; arguing about the price was bad enough.

'I'll say this again: just like policemen in the movies, never drink while on duty. I'll leave you now, it'll start getting busy soon.'

'Say thank you,' said the other Brazilian woman in Portuguese.

Maria thanked him. The man smiled, but he had not yet finished his list of recommendations:

'I forgot something: the time between ordering a drink and leaving the club should never, under any circumstances, exceed forty-five minutes – and in Switzerland, with clocks all over the place, even Yugoslavs and Brazilians must learn to be punctual. Just remember, I'm feeding my children on your commission.'

She would remember.

He gave her a glass of sparkling mineral water with a slice of lemon in it – a drink that could easily pass for a gin and tonic – and asked her to wait. Gradually the club began to fill up; men came in, looked around, sat down on their own, and immediately one of the women would go over to them, as if they were at a party where everyone has known each other for ages and as if they were just taking time out to have a little fun after a hard day at work. Every time a man found a partner, Maria gave a sigh of relief, even though she was now feeling much more comfortable. Perhaps it was because it was Switzerland, perhaps it was because, sooner or later, she would find adventure, money or a husband, as she had always dreamed she would. Perhaps – she suddenly realised – it was because it was the first time in many weeks that she had been out at night and to a place where there was music playing and where she could, now and then, hear someone speaking Portuguese. She was having fun with the other girls around her, laughing, drinking fruit juice cocktails, talking brightly.

None of them had come up to her to say hello or to wish her success in her new profession, but that was perfectly normal; after all, she was a rival, a competitor, competing for the same trophy. Instead of feeling depressed, she felt proud – she was fighting for herself, she wasn't some helpless person. She could, if she wanted to, open the door and leave that place for good, but she would always know that she had at least had the courage to come that far, to negotiate and discuss things about which she had never in her life even dared to think. She wasn't a victim of fate, she kept telling herself: she was running her own risks, pushing beyond her own limits, experiencing things which, one day, in the silence of her heart, in the tedium of old age, she would remember almost with nostalgia – however absurd that might seem.

She was sure that no one would approach her, and tomorrow it would all seem like some mad dream that she would never dare to repeat, for she had just realised that being paid a thousand francs for one night only happens once; perhaps she would be better off buying a plane ticket back to Brazil. To make the time pass more quickly, she began to work out how much each of the other girls would earn: if they went out three times a night, they would earn, for every four hours of work, the equivalent of what it would have taken her two months to earn at the shop.

Was that a lot? She had earned a thousand francs for one night, but perhaps that had just been beginner's luck. At any rate, an ordinary prostitute could earn more, much more than she would ever earn teaching French back home. And all they had to do was spend some time in a bar, dance, spread their legs and that was that. They didn't even have to talk.

Money was one motivation, she thought, but was that all? Or did the people there, the customers and the women, also enjoy themselves in some way? Was the world so very different from what she had been taught in school? If you used a condom, there was no risk. Nor was there any risk of being recognised by anyone; the only people who visit Geneva – she had been told once in her French class – were people who liked going to banks. The majority of Brazilians, however, enjoy shopping, preferably in Miami or in Paris.

Three hundred Swiss francs a day, five days a week. A fortune! Why did those women keep working there when they could earn enough in a month to go back home and buy a new house for their mother? Or had they only been working there a short time?

Or – and Maria felt afraid of her own question – did they enjoy it?

Again she wished she could have a proper drink – the champagne had helped a lot the previous night.

'Would you like a drink?'

Before her stood a man in his thirties, wearing the uniform of some airline.

The world went into slow motion, and Maria had a sense of stepping out of her own body and observing herself from the outside. Deeply embarrassed, but struggling to control her blushes, she nodded and smiled, knowing that from that moment on her life had changed forever.

A fruit juice cocktail, a bit of talk, what are you doing here, it's cold, isn't it? I like this music, oh, I prefer Abba myself, the Swiss are a chilly lot, are you from Brazil? Tell me about your country. Well, there's Carnival. You Brazilian women are really pretty, you know.

Smile and accept the compliment, perhaps with a slightly shy look. Back to the dance floor, but all the time keeping an eye on Milan, who sometimes scratches his head and taps his wristwatch. The smell of the man's cologne;

she realises quickly that she will have to get used to all kinds of smells. At least this is perfume. They dance very close. Another fruit juice cocktail, time is passing, didn't Milan say forty-five minutes maximum? She looks at her watch, he asks if she's expecting someone, she says a few friends of hers will be arriving in about an hour, he invites her back to his hotel. Hotel room, three hundred and fifty francs, a shower after sex (intrigued, the man remarked that no one had ever done that before). It's not Maria, it's some other person who's inside her body, who feels nothing, who mechanically goes through the motions of a ritual. She's an actress. Milan has taught her everything, even how to say goodbye to the client, she thanks him, he too feels awkward and sleepy.

She doesn't want to go back to the club, she wants to go home, but she has to go back to hand over the fifty francs, and then there's another man, another cocktail, more questions about Brazil, a hotel, another shower (this time, no comment), back to the bar where the owner takes his commission and tells her she can go, there aren't many customers tonight. She doesn't get a taxi, she walks the length of Rue de Berne, looking at the other clubs, at the shop windows full of clocks and watches, at the church on the corner (closed, always closed ...) As usual, no one looks at her.

She walks through the cold. She isn't aware of the freezing temperatures, she doesn't cry, she doesn't think about the money she has earned, she is in a kind of trance. Some people were born to face life alone, and this is neither good nor bad, it is simply life. Maria is one of those people.

She begins to try and think about what has happened: she only started work today and yet she already considers herself a professional; it's as if she started ages ago, as if she had done this all her life. She experiences a strange sense of pride; she is glad she didn't run away. Now she just has to decide whether or not to carry on. If she does carry on, then she will make sure she is the best, something she has never been before.

But life was teaching her – very fast – that only the strong survive. To be strong, she must be the best, there's no alternative.

From Maria's diary a week later:

I'm not a body with a soul, I'm a soul that has a visible part called the body. All this week, contrary to what one might expect, I have been more conscious of the presence of this soul than usual. It didn't say anything to me, didn't criticise me or feel sorry for me: it merely watched me.

Today, I realised why this was happening: it's been such a long time since I thought about love or anything called love. It seems to be running away from me, as if it wasn't important any more and didn't feel welcome. But if I don't think about love, I will be nothing.

When I went back to the Copacabana the second night, I was treated with much more respect – appar-

ently, a lot of girls do it for one night, but can't bear to go on. Anyone who does, becomes a kind of ally, a colleague, because she can understand the difficulties and the reasons or, rather, the absence of reasons for having chosen this kind of life.

They all dream of someone who will come along and see in them a real woman – companion, lover, friend. But they all know, from the very first moment of each new encounter, that this simply isn't going to happen.

I need to write about love. I need to think and think and write and write about love – otherwise, my soul won't survive.

However important Maria thought love was, she did not forget the advice she was given on her first night and did her best to confine love to the pages of her diary. Apart from that, she tried desperately to be the best, to earn a lot of money in as short a time as possible, to think very little and to find a good reason for doing what she was doing.

That was the most difficult part: what was the real reason?

She was doing it because she needed to. This wasn't quite true – everyone needs to earn money, but not everyone chooses to live on the margins of society. She was doing it because she wanted to experience something new. No, that wasn't true either; the world was full of new experiences – like skiing or going sailing on Lake Geneva, for example – but she had never been interested. She was doing it because she had nothing to lose, because her life was one of constant, day-to-day frustration.

No, none of these answers was true, so it was best to forget all about it and simply deal with whatever lay along her particular path. She had a lot in common with the other prostitutes, and with all the other women she had known in her life, whose greatest dream was to get married and have a secure life. Those who didn't think like this either had a husband (almost a third of her colleagues were married) or were recently divorced. Because of that, and in order to understand herself, she tried – as tactfully as possible – to understand why her colleagues had chosen this profession.

She heard nothing new, but she made a list of their responses. They said they had to help out their husband (wasn't he jealous? What if one of her husband's friends came to the club one night? But Maria didn't dare to ask these questions), that they wanted to buy a house for their mother (her own excuse, apparently so noble, and the most common one), to earn enough money for their fare home (Colombians, Thais, Peruvians, Brazilians all loved this reason, even though they had earned enough money several times over and had immediately spent it, afraid to realise their dream), to have fun (this didn't really tally with the atmosphere in the club, and always rang false), they couldn't find any other kind of work (this wasn't a good reason either, Switzerland was full of jobs for cleaners, drivers and cooks).

None of them came up with any valid reason, and so she stopped trying to explain her particular Universe.

She saw that the owner, Milan, was quite right: no one ever again offered her a thousand Swiss francs for the privilege of spending a few hours with her. On the other hand, no one ever complained when she asked for three hundred and fifty francs, as if they already knew or only asked in order to humiliate her, or wanted to avoid any unpleasant surprises.

One of the girls said:

'Prostitution isn't like other businesses: beginners earn more and the more experienced earn less. Always pretend you're a beginner.'

Maria still didn't know who the 'special clients' were; they had only been mentioned on the first night and no one ever spoke of them. Gradually, she picked up the most important tricks of the trade, like never asking personal questions, smiling a lot and talking as little as possible, never arranging to meet anyone outside the club. The most important piece of advice, however, came from a Filipino woman called Nyah:

'When your client comes, you must always groan as if you were having an orgasm too. That guarantees customer loyalty.'

'But why? They're just paying for their own satisfaction.'

'No, that's where you're wrong. A man doesn't prove he's a man by getting an erection. He's only a real man if he can pleasure a woman. And if he can pleasure a prostitute, he'll think he's the best lover on the block.'

And so six months passed: Maria learned all the necessary lessons, for example, how the Copacabana worked. Since it was one of the most expensive places in Rue de Berne, the clientele was largely made up of executives, who had permission to get home late because they were out 'having supper with clients', but these 'suppers' could never last longer than eleven o'clock at night. Most of the prostitutes who worked there were aged between eighteen and twenty-two and they stayed, on average, for two years, when they would be replaced by newer recruits. They then moved to the Néon, then to the Xenium, and the price went down as the woman's age went up, and the hours of work grew fewer and fewer. They almost all ended up in the Tropical Extasy, who accepted women over thirty; but once they were there, they could only just earn enough to pay for their lunch and their rent by going with one or two students a day (the average fee per client was just about enough to buy a bottle of cheap wine).

She went to bed with many men. She didn't care how old they were or how they were dressed, but whether she said yes or no depended on how they smelled. She had nothing against cigarettes, but she hated cheap aftershave or those who didn't wash or whose clothes stank of booze.

The Copacabana was a quiet place, and Switzerland was possibly the best country in the world in which to work as a prostitute, as long as you had a residence permit and a work permit, kept all your papers in order and paid your social security; Milan was always saying that he didn't want his children to see his name in the tabloid newspapers, and so he was as strict as a policeman when it came to keeping an eye on his 'employees'.

Once you had got past the barrier of the first or second night, it was a profession much like any other, in which you worked hard, fought off the competition, tried to maintain standards, put in the necessary hours, got a bit stressed out, complained about your workload, and rested on Sundays. Most of the prostitutes had some kind of religious faith, and attended their respective churches and masses, said their prayers and had their encounters with God.

Maria, however, was struggling in the pages of her diary not to lose her soul. She discovered, to her surprise, that one in every five clients didn't want her in order to have sex, but simply to talk a little. They paid for the bar tab and the hotel room, and when the moment came for them both to take off their clothes, the man would say, no, that won't be necessary. They wanted to talk about the pressures of work, about their unfaithful wife, about how lonely they felt, how they had no one to talk to (something she knew about all too well).

At first, she found this very odd. Then, one night, she went to the hotel with an arrogant Frenchman, a headhunter for top executive jobs (he told her this as if he were telling her the most fascinating thing in the world), and this is what he said:

'Do you know who the loneliest person in the world is? The executive with a successful career, earning an enormous salary, trusted by those above and below him, with a family to go on holiday with and children who he helps out with their homework, but who is then approached by someone like me and asked the following question: "How would you like to change your job and earn twice as much?"

'The executive, who has every reason to feel wanted and happy, becomes the most miserable creature on the planet. Why? Because he has no one to talk to. He is tempted to accept my offer, but he can't talk about it to his work colleagues because they would do everything they could to persuade him to stay. He can't talk about it to his wife, who has been his companion in his rise up the ladder of success and understands a great deal about security, but nothing about taking risks. He can't talk to anyone about it and there he is confronted by the biggest decision of his life. Can you imagine how that man feels?'

No, that man wasn't the loneliest person in the world. Maria knew the loneliest person on the face of this Earth: herself. Nevertheless, she agreed with her client, hoping to get a big tip, which she did. But his words made her realise that she needed to find some way of freeing her clients from the enormous pressure they all seemed to be under; this meant both improving the quality of her services and the chance of earning some extra money.

When she realised that releasing tension in the soul could be as lucrative as releasing tension in the body, if not more lucrative, she started going to the library again. She began asking for books about marital problems, psychology and politics; the librarian was delighted to see that the young woman of whom she had grown so fond had stopped thinking about sex and was now concentrating on more important matters. Maria became a regular reader of newspapers, especially, where possible, the financial pages, because the majority of her clients were business executives. She sought out self-help books, because her clients nearly all asked for her advice. She read studies of the human emotions, because all her clients were in some kind of emotional pain. Maria was a respectable, rather unusual prostitute, and after six months, she had acquired a large, faithful, very select clientele, thus arousing the envy and jealousy, but also the admiration, of her colleagues.

As for sex, it had as yet added nothing to her life: it was just a matter of opening her legs, asking them to use a condom, moaning a bit in the hope of getting a better tip (thanks to the Filipino woman, Nyah, she had learned that moaning could earn her another fifty francs), and taking a shower afterwards, hoping that the water would wash her soul clean. Nothing out of the ordinary and no kissing. For a prostitute, the kiss was sacred. Nyah had taught her to keep her kisses for the love of her life, just like in the story of Sleeping Beauty; a kiss that would waken her from her slumbers and return her to the world of fairy tales, in which

Switzerland was once more the country of chocolate, cows and clocks.

And no orgasms either, no pleasure or excitement. In her search to be the very best, Maria had watched a few porn movies, hoping to pick up tips for her work. She had seen a lot of interesting things, but had preferred not to try any of them out on her clients because they took too long, and Milan was happiest when the women averaged three men a night.

By the end of the six months, Maria had sixty thousand Swiss francs in a bank account; she ate in better restaurants, had bought a TV (she never watched it, but she liked to have it there) and was now seriously considering moving to a better apartment. Although she could easily afford to buy books, she continued going to the library, which was her bridge to the real world, a more solid and enduring world. She enjoyed chatting to the librarian, who was happy because Maria had perhaps found a boyfriend and a job, although she never asked, the Swiss being naturally shy and discreet (a complete fallacy, because in the Copacabana and in bed, they were as uninhibited, joyful or neurotic as any other nationality).

From Maria's diary, one warm Sunday evening:

All men, tall or short, arrogant or unassuming, friendly or cold, have one characteristic in common: when they come to the club, they are afraid. The more experienced amongst them hide their fear by talking loudly, the more inhibited cannot hide their feelings and start drinking to see if they can drive the fear away. But I am convinced that, with a few very rare exceptions – the 'special clients' to whom Milan has not yet introduced me – they are all afraid.

Afraid of what? I'm the one who should be shaking. I'm the one who leaves the club and goes off to a strange hotel, and I'm not the one with the superior physical strength or the weapons. Men are very strange, and I don't just mean the ones who come to the Copacabana, but all the men I've ever met. They can beat you up, shout at you, threaten you, and yet they're scared to death of women really. Perhaps not the woman they married, but there's always one woman who frightens them and forces them to submit to her caprices. Even if it's their own mother.

The men she had met since she arrived in Geneva always did everything they could to appear confident, as if they were in perfect control of the world and of their own lives; Maria, however, could see in their eyes that they were afraid of their wife, the feeling of panic that they might not be able to get an erection, that they might not seem manly enough even to the ordinary prostitute whom they were paying for her services. If they went to a shop and didn't like the shoes they had bought, they would be quite prepared to go back, receipt in hand, and demand a refund. And yet, even though they were paying for some female company, if they didn't manage to get an erection, they would be too ashamed ever to go back to the same club again because they would assume that all the other women there would know.

'I'm the one who should feel ashamed for being unable to arouse them, but, no, they always blame themselves.'

To avoid such embarrassments, Maria always tried to put men at their ease, and if someone seemed drunker or more fragile than usual, she would avoid full sex and concentrate instead on caresses and masturbation, which always seemed to please them immensely, absurd though this might seem, since they could perfectly well masturbate on their own.

She had to make sure that they didn't feel ashamed. These men, so powerful and arrogant at work, constantly having to deal with employees, customers, suppliers, prejudices, secrets, posturings, hypocrisy, fear and oppression, ended their day in a nightclub and they didn't mind spending three hundred and fifty Swiss francs to stop being themselves for a night.

'For a night? Now come on, Maria, you're exaggerating. It's really only forty-five minutes, and if you allow time for taking off clothes, making some phoney gesture of affection, having a bit of banal conversation and getting dressed again, the amount of time spent actually having sex is about eleven minutes.'

Eleven minutes. The world revolved around something that only took eleven minutes.

And because of those eleven minutes in any one twenty-four-hour day (assuming that they all made love to their wives every day, which is patently absurd and a complete lie) they got married, supported a family, put up with screaming kids, thought up ridiculous excuses to justify getting home late, ogled dozens, if not hundreds of other women with whom they would like to go for a walk around Lake Geneva, bought expensive clothes for themselves and even more expensive clothes for their wives, paid prostitutes to try to give them what they were missing, and thus sustained a vast industry of cosmetics, diet foods, exercise, pornography and power, and yet when they got together with other men, contrary to popular belief, they never talked about women. They talked about jobs, money and sport.

Something was very wrong with civilisation, and it wasn't the destruction of the Amazon rainforest or the ozone layer, the death of the panda, cigarettes, carcinogenic foodstuffs or prison conditions, as the newspapers would have it.

It was precisely the thing she was working with: sex.

But Maria wasn't there to save humanity, but to increase her bank balance, survive another six months of solitude and another six months of the choice she had made, send a regular monthly sum of money to her mother (who was thrilled to learn that the earlier absence of money had been due to the Swiss post, so much less efficient than the Brazilian postal system), and to buy all the things she had always dreamed of and never had. She moved to a much better apartment, with central heating (although the summer had already arrived), and from her window she could see a church, a Japanese restaurant, a supermarket and a very nice café, where she used to sit and read the newspapers. Otherwise, just as she had promised herself, it was a question of putting up with the same old routine: go to the Copacabana, have a drink and a dance, what do you think of Brazil, then back to his hotel, get the money up front, have a little conversation and know precisely which points to touch – on both body and soul, but mainly the soul – give some advice on personal problems, be his friend for half an hour, of which eleven minutes would be spent in opening her legs, closing her legs and pretending to moan with pleasure. Thanks very much, see you next week, you're very manly, you know, tell me how things went next time we meet, oh, that's very generous of you, but really there's no need, it's been a pleasure to spend time with you.

And, above all, never fall in love. That was the most important and most sensible piece of advice that the other Brazilian woman had given her, before she disappeared, perhaps because she herself had fallen in love. Because, incredible though it may seem, in just two months of working there, Maria had had several proposals of marriage, of which at least three were serious: the director of a firm of accountants, the pilot she went with on the very first night, and the owner of a shop specialising in knives. All three had promised 'to take her away from that life' and to give her a nice house, a future, perhaps children and grandchildren.

And all for eleven minutes a day? It wasn't possible. After her experiences at the Copacabana, she knew that she wasn't the only person who felt lonely. Human beings can withstand a week without water, two weeks without food, many years of homelessness, but not loneliness. It is the worst of all tortures, the worst of all sufferings. Like her, these men, and the many others who sought her company, were all tormented by that same destructive feeling, the sense that no one else on the planet cared about them.

In order to avoid being tempted by love, she kept her heart for her diary. She entered the Copacabana with only her body and her brain, which was growing sharper and more perceptive all the time. She had managed to persuade herself that there was some important reason why she had come to Geneva and ended up in Rue de Berne, and every time she borrowed a book from the library she was confirmed in her view that no one wrote properly about the eleven most important minutes of the day. Perhaps that was her destiny, however hard it might seem at the moment: to write a book, relating her story, her adventure.

That was it, her adventure. Although it was a forbidden word that no one dared to speak, and which most people preferred to watch on the television, in films that were shown over and over at all times of the day and night, that was what she was looking for. It was a word that evoked deserts, journeys to unknown places, idle conversations with mysterious men on a boat in the middle of a river, plane journeys, cinema studios, tribes of Indians, glaciers and Africa.

She liked the idea of a book and had even thought of a title: Eleven Minutes.

She began to put clients into three categories: the Exterminators (in homage to a film she had enjoyed hugely), who arrived stinking of drink, pretending not to look at anyone, but convinced that everyone was looking at them, dancing only briefly and then getting straight down to the business of going back to their hotel. The Pretty Woman type (again named after a film), who tried to appear elegant, gentlemanly, affectionate, as if the world depended on such kindness in order to continue turning on its axis, as if they had just been walking down the street and had come into the club by chance; they were always very sweet at first and rather uncertain when they got to the hotel, but, because of that, they always proved even more demanding than the Exterminators. And lastly, there was The Godfather type (named after yet another film), who treated a woman's body as if it were a piece of merchandise. They were the most genuine; they danced, talked, never gave tips, knew what they were buying and how much it was worth, and never let themselves be taken in by anything the woman of their choice might say. They were the only ones who, in a very subtle way, knew the meaning of the word 'Adventure'.

From Maria's diary, on a day when she had her period and couldn't work:

> *If I were to tell someone about my life today, I could do it in a way that would make them think me a brave, happy, independent woman. Rubbish: I am not even allowed to mention the only word that is more important than the eleven minutes – love.*
>
> *All my life, I thought of love as some kind of voluntary enslavement. Well, that's a lie: freedom only exists when love is present. The person who gives him or herself wholly, the person who feels freest, is the person who loves most wholeheartedly.*
>
> *And the person who loves wholeheartedly feels free.*
>
> *That is why, regardless of what I might experience, do or learn, nothing makes sense. I hope this time passes quickly, so that I can resume my search for myself – in the form of a man who understands me and does not make me suffer.*

But what am I saying? In love, no one can harm anyone else; we are each of us responsible for our own feelings and cannot blame someone else for what we feel.

It hurt when I lost each of the various men I fell in love with. Now, though, I am convinced that no one loses anyone, because no one owns anyone.

That is the true experience of freedom: having the most important thing in the world without owning it.

Another three months passed, and autumn came, as did the date marked on the calendar: ninety days until her return journey home. Everything had happened so quickly and so slowly, she thought, realising that time exists in two different dimensions, depending on one's state of mind, but in both sorts of time her adventure was drawing to a close. She could, of course, continue, but she could not forget the sad smile of the invisible woman who had accompanied her on that walk around the lake, telling her that things weren't that simple. However tempted she was to continue, however prepared she was for the challenges she had met on her path, all these months living alone with herself had taught her that there is always a right moment to stop something. In ninety days' time she would return to the interior of Brazil, where she would buy a small farm (she had earned rather more than she had expected), a few cows (Brazilian, not Swiss), invite her mother and father to come and live with her, take on a couple of workers, and set the business in motion.

Although she believed that love is the only true experience of freedom, and that no one can possess anyone else, she still harboured a secret desire for revenge, and this formed part of her triumphal return to Brazil. After setting up the farm, she would go back to her hometown and make a large deposit in Swiss francs at the bank where the boy who had two-timed her with her best friend was working. 'Hi, how are you? Don't you remember me?' he would say. She would pretend to be trying hard to remember and would end up saying that, no, she didn't, she had just come back from a year in EU-ROPE (she would say this very slowly so that all his colleagues would hear). Or, rather, SWIT-ZER-LAND (that would sound more exotic and adventurous than France), where they have the best banks in the world.

Who was he? He would mention their schooldays. She would say: 'Ah, yes, I think I remember ...', but from her face it would be clear that she didn't. Vengeance would be hers, and then it would just be a matter of working hard, and when the farm was doing as well as she expected, she would be able to devote herself to the thing that mattered most in her life: finding her true love, the man who had been waiting for her all these years, but whom she had not yet had the chance to meet.

Maria decided to forget all about writing the book entitled *Eleven Minutes*. Now she needed to concentrate on the farm, on her future plans, otherwise, she would end up postponing her trip, a fatal risk.

That afternoon, she went off to meet her best – and only – friend, the librarian. She asked for a book on cattle-raising and farm administration. The librarian said:

'You know, a few months ago, when you came here looking for books about sex, I began to fear for you. So many pretty young girls let themselves be seduced by the illusion of easy money, forgetting that, one day, they'll be old and will have missed out on meeting the love of their life.'

'Do you mean prostitution?'

'That's a very strong word.'

'As I said, I'm working for a company that imports and exports meat. But if I had to become a prostitute, would the consequences be so very grave if I stopped at the right moment? After all, being young inevitably means making mistakes.'

'That's what all the drug addicts say, that you just have to know when to stop. But none of them do.'

'You must have been very pretty when you were younger and you were brought up in a country that respects its inhabitants. Was that enough for you to be happy?'

'I'm proud of how I dealt with any obstacles in my life.'

Should she go on, thought the librarian. Yes, why not, the girl needed to learn a bit about life.

'I had a happy childhood, I studied at one of the best schools in Berne, then I came to work in Geneva, where I met and married the man I loved. I did everything for him and he did everything for me; time passed and he retired. When he was free to do exactly what he wanted with his time, his eyes grew sadder, because he had probably never really thought about himself all his life. We never had any serious arguments or any great excitements, he was never unfaithful to me and was never rude to me in public. We lived a very ordinary life, so much so that, without a job to do, he felt useless, unimportant, and, a year later, he died of cancer.'

She was telling the truth, but felt that she might be having a negative influence on the girl standing before her.

'I still think it's best to lead a life without surprises,' she concluded. 'If we hadn't, my husband might have died even earlier, who knows.'

Maria left, determined to learn all about farming. Since she had the afternoon free, she decided to go for a stroll and, in the upper part of the city, came across a small yellow plaque bearing a drawing of a sun and an inscription: 'Road to Santiago'. What did it mean? There was a bar on the other side of the road, and since she had now learned to ask about anything she didn't understand, she resolved to go in and ask.

'I've no idea,' said the girl serving behind the bar. It was a very expensive place, and the coffee cost three times the normal price. Since she had money, though, and now that she was there, she ordered a coffee and decided to spend the next hour or so learning all there was to know about farm administration. She opened the book eagerly, but found it impossible to concentrate – it was *so* boring. It would be much more interesting to talk to one of her clients about it; they always knew how best to handle money. She paid for her coffee, got up, thanked the girl who had served her, left a large tip (she had invented a superstitious belief according to which the more you gave, the more you got back), went over to the door, and, without realising the importance of that moment, heard the words that would change forever her plans, her future, her farm, her idea of happiness, her female soul, her male approach to life, her place in the world.

'Hang on a moment.'

Surprised, she glanced to one side. This was a respectable bar, it wasn't the Copacabana, where men had the right to say that, although the women could always respond: 'No, I'm leaving and you can't stop me.'

She was about to ignore the remark, but her curiosity got the better of her, and she turned towards the voice. She saw a very strange scene: kneeling on the floor, with various paintbrushes scattered around him, was a long-haired young man of about thirty (or should she have said: a boy of about thirty? Her world had aged very fast), who was making a drawing of a gentleman sitting in a chair, with a glass of anisette beside him. She hadn't noticed them when she came in.

'Don't go. I've nearly finished this portrait, and I'd like to paint you as well.'

Maria replied – and as she did so, she created the link that was lacking in the universe.

'No, I'm not interested.'

'You've got a special light about you. Let me at least do a sketch.'

What was a 'sketch'? What did he mean by 'a special light'? Besides, she was vain enough to want to have her portrait painted by someone who appeared to be a serious artist. Her imagination took flight. What if he was really famous? She would be immortalised forever in a painting that would be exhibited in Paris or in Salvador da Bahia! She would become a legend!

On the other hand, what was the man doing, surrounded by all that clutter, in an expensive, perhaps usually crowded café?

Guessing her thoughts, the waitress said softly:

'He's a very well-known artist.'

Her intuition had been right. Maria tried not to show her feelings and to remain calm.

'He comes here now and again, and he always brings an important client with him. He says he likes the atmosphere, that it inspires him; he's doing a painting of people who represent the city. It was commissioned by the town hall.'

Maria looked at the subject of the portrait. Again the waitress read her thoughts.

'He's a chemist who apparently made some really revolutionary discovery. He won the Nobel Prize.'

'Don't go,' said the painter again. 'I'll be finished in five minutes. Order what you like and put it on my bill.'

As if hypnotised, she sat down at the bar, ordered an anisette (she wasn't used to drinking, and the only thing that occurred to her was to order the same as the Nobel prizewinner), and watched the man working. 'I don't represent the city, so he must be interested in something else. But he's not really my type,' she thought automatically, repeating what she always said to herself, ever since she had been working at the Copacabana; it was her salvation, her voluntary denial of the traps set by the heart. Having cleared that up, she didn't mind waiting a while – perhaps the waitress was right, perhaps this man could open doors to a world of which she knew nothing.

She watched how quickly and adroitly he put the finishing touches to his work; it was apparently a very large canvas, but it was all rolled up, and so she couldn't see what other faces he had painted. What if this was a new opportunity? The man (she had decided that he was a 'man' and not a 'boy', because otherwise she would start to feel old before her time) didn't seem the sort likely to make that kind of proposal just in order to spend the night with her. Five minutes later, as promised, he had finished his work, while Maria concentrated hard on thinking about Brazil, about her brilliant future there, and her complete lack of interest in meeting new people who might jeopardise all her plans.

'Thanks, you can move now,' said the painter to the chemist, who seemed to awaken from a dream.

And turning to Maria, he said simply:

'Sit in that corner and make yourself comfortable. The light is wonderful.'

As if everything had been ordained by fate, as if it were the most natural thing in the world, as if she had known this man all her life or had already lived this moment in dreams and now knew what to do in reality, Maria picked up her glass of anisette, her bag, and the books on farm management, and went over to the place indicated by the man – a table near the window. He brought his brushes, the large canvas, a series of small glass bottles full of various colours and a packet of cigarettes, and knelt at her feet.

'Now don't move.'

'That's asking a lot; my life is in constant motion.'

Maria thought she was being terribly witty, but the man ignored her remark. Trying to appear natural, because she found the way the man looked at her most discomfiting, she pointed across the road at the plaque:

'What is the "Road to Santiago"?'

'It's a pilgrimage route. In the Middle Ages, people from all over Europe would come along this street, heading for a city in Spain, Santiago de Compostela.'

He folded over one part of the canvas and prepared his brushes. Maria still didn't know quite what to do.

'Do you mean that if I followed that street, I'd eventually get to Spain?'

'Yes, in two or three months' time. But can I just ask you a favour? Stop talking; it will only take about ten minutes. And take that package off the table.'

'They're books,' she said, slightly irritated by his authoritarian tone. She wanted him to know that he was kneeling before a cultivated woman, who spent her time in libraries not shops. But he himself picked up the package and placed it unceremoniously on the floor.

She had failed to impress him. Not, of course, that she was remotely interested in impressing him; she was off-duty now and would save her seductive powers for later, for men who would pay handsomely for her efforts. Why bother striking up a relationship with a painter who might not even have enough money to buy her a coffee? A man of thirty shouldn't wear his hair so long, it looked ridiculous. Why did she assume he had no money? The waitress had said he was wellknown, or was it just the chemist who was famous? She studied his clothes, but that didn't help; life had taught her that the men who took least care of their appearance – as with this painter – always seemed to have more money than the men in suits and ties.

'What am I doing thinking about this man? What interests me is the painting.'

Ten minutes of her time was not such a high price to pay for the chance of being immortalised in a painting. She saw that he was painting her alongside the prizewinning chemist and she began to wonder if, after all, he would want some kind of payment.

'Turn towards the window.'

Again she obeyed unquestioningly, which was not at all like her. She sat looking at the people passing by, at the plaque with the name of that road on it, thinking about how that road had been there for centuries, how it had survived progress and all the changes that had taken place in the world and in mankind. Perhaps it was a good omen, perhaps that painting would share the same fate and still be on display in a museum in the city in five hundred years' time …

The man started drawing, and, as the work progressed, she lost that initial sense of excitement and, instead, began to feel utterly insignificant. When she had gone into the café, she had been a very confident woman, capable of making an extremely difficult decision – leaving a job that earned her lots of money – and taking up a still more difficult challenge – running a farm back in her own country. Now, all her feelings of insecurity about the world seemed to have resurfaced, a luxury no prostitute can allow herself.

She finally worked out why she was feeling so uncomfortable: for the first time in many months, someone was looking at her not as an object, not even as a woman, but as something she could not even comprehend; the closest she could come to putting it into words was: 'he's seeing my soul, my fears, my fragility, my inability to deal with a world which I pretend to master, but about which I know nothing'.

Ridiculous, pure fantasy.

'I'd like ...'

'Please, don't talk,' said the man. 'I can see your light now.'

No one had ever said anything like that to her before. 'I can see your firm breasts', 'I can see your nicely rounded thighs', 'I can see in you the exotic beauty of the tropics', or, at most, 'I can see that you want to leave this life – let me set you up in an apartment'. She was used to comments like that, but her light? Did he mean the evening light?

'Your personal light,' he said, realising that she didn't know what he was talking about.

Her personal light. Well, how wrong could he be, that innocent painter, who obviously hadn't learned much about life in his thirty-odd years. But then, as everyone knows, women mature more quickly than men, and although Maria might not spend sleepless nights pondering her particular philosophical problems, she knew one thing: she did not have what that painter called 'light' and which she took to mean 'a special glow'. She was just like everyone else, she endured her loneliness in silence, tried to justify everything she did, pretended to be strong when she was feeling weak or weak when she was feeling strong, she had renounced love and taken up a dangerous profession, but now, as that work was coming to an end, she had plans for the future and regrets about the past, and someone like that doesn't have a 'special glow'. That must just be his way of keeping her quiet and still and happy to be there, playing the fool.

Personal light, indeed. He could have said something else, like 'you've got a lovely profile'.

How does light enter a house? Through the open windows. How does light enter a person? Through the open door of love. And her door was definitely shut. He must be a terrible painter; he didn't understand anything.

'I've finished,' he said and started collecting up his things.

Maria didn't move. She felt like asking if she could see the painting, but that might seem rude, as if she didn't trust what he had done. Curiosity, however, got the better of her; she asked and he concurred. He had painted only her face; it looked like her, but if, one day, she had seen that painting, not knowing who the model was, she would have said that it was someone much stronger, someone full of a 'light' she didn't see reflected in the mirror.

'My name's Ralf Hart. If you like, I can buy you another drink.'

'No, thank you.'

It would seem that the encounter was now taking a sadly foreseeable turn: man tries to seduce woman.

'Two more anisettes, please,' he said, ignoring Maria's answer.

What else did she have to do? Read a boring book about farm management. Walk around the lake, as she had hundreds of times before. Or talk to someone who had seen in her a light of which she knew nothing, and on the very date marked on the calendar as the beginning of the end of her 'experience'.

'What do you do?'

That was the question she did not want to hear, the question that had made her avoid other encounters when, for one reason or another, someone had approached her (though given the natural discretion of the Swiss, this happened only rarely). What possible answer could she give?

'I work in a nightclub.'

Right. An enormous load fell from her shoulders, and she was pleased with all that she had learned since she had arrived in Switzerland; ask questions (Who are the Kurds? What is the road to Santiago?) and answer (I work in a nightclub) without worrying about what other people might think.

'I have a feeling I've seen you before.'

Maria sensed that he wanted to take things further, and she savoured her small victory; the painter who, minutes before, had been giving orders and had seemed so utterly sure of what he wanted, had now gone back to being a man like any other man, full of insecurity when confronted by a woman he didn't know.

'And what are those books?'

She showed them to him. Farm administration. The man seemed to grow even more insecure.

'Are you a sex worker?'

He had shown his cards. Was she dressed like a prostitute? Anyway, she needed to gain time. She was watching herself; this was beginning to prove an interesting game, and she had absolutely nothing to lose.

'Is that all men think about?'

He put the books back in the bag.

'Sex and farm management. How very dull.'

What! It was suddenly her turn to feel put on the spot. How dare he speak ill of her profession? He still didn't know exactly what she did, though, he was just trying out a hunch, but she had to give him an answer.

'Well, I can't think of anything duller than painting; a static thing, a movement frozen in time, a photograph that is never faithful to the original. A dead thing that is no longer of any interest to anyone, apart from painters, who are people who think they're important and cultivated, but who haven't evolved with the rest of the world. Have you ever heard of Joan Miró? Well, I hadn't until an Arab in a restaurant mentioned the name, but knowing the name didn't change anything in my life.'

She wondered if she had gone too far, but then the drinks arrived and the conversation was interrupted. They sat saying nothing for a while. Maria thought it was probably time to leave, and perhaps Ralf Hart thought the same. But before them stood those two glasses full of that disgusting drink, and that was a reason for them to continue sitting there together.

'Why the book on farm management?'

'What do you mean?'

'I've been to Rue de Berne. When you said you worked in a nightclub, I remembered that I'd seen you before in that very expensive place. I didn't think of it while I was painting, though: your "light" was so strong.'

Maria felt the floor beneath her feet give way. For the first time, she felt ashamed of what she did, even though she had no reason to; she was working to keep herself and her family. He was the one who should feel ashamed of going to Rue de Berne; all the possible charm of that meeting had suddenly vanished.

'Listen, Mr Hart, I may be a Brazilian, but I've lived in Switzerland for nine months now. I've learned that the reason the Swiss are so discreet is because they live in a very small country where almost everyone knows everyone else, as we have just discovered, which is why no one ever asks what other people do. Your remark was both inappropriate and very rude, but if your aim was to humiliate me in order to make yourself feel better, you're wasting your time. Thanks for the anisette, which is disgusting, by the way, but which I will drink to the last drop. I will then smoke a cigarette, and, finally, I'll get up and leave. But you can leave right now, if you want; we can't have famous painters sitting at the same table as a prostitute. Because that's what I am, you see. A prostitute. I'm a prostitute through and through, from head to toe, and I don't care who knows. That's my one great virtue: I refuse to deceive myself or you. Because it's not worth it, because you don't merit a lie. Imagine if that famous chemist over there were to find out what I am.'

She began to speak more loudly.

'Yes, I'm a prostitute! And do you know what? It's set me free – knowing that I'll be leaving this godawful place in exactly ninety days' time, with loads of money, far better educated, capable of choosing a good bottle of wine, with my handbag stuffed with photographs of the snow, and knowing all there is to know about men!'

The waitress was listening, horrified. The chemist seemed not to notice. Perhaps it was just the alcohol talking, or the feeling that soon she would once more be a woman from the interior of Brazil, or perhaps it was the sheer joy of being able to say what she did and to laugh at the shocked reactions, the critical looks, the scandalised gestures.

'Do you understand, Mr Hart? I'm a prostitute through and through, from head to toe – and that's my one great quality, my virtue!'

He said nothing. He didn't even move. Maria felt her confidence returning.

'And you, sir, are a painter with no understanding of your models. Perhaps the chemist sitting over there, dozing, lost to the world, is really a railway worker. Perhaps none of the other people in your painting are what they seem. I can't understand otherwise how you could possibly say that you could see a "special light" in a woman who, as you discovered while you were painting, IS NOTHING BUT A PRO-STI-TUTE!'

These last words were spoken very slowly and loudly. The chemist woke up and the waitress brought the bill.

'This has nothing to do with you as prostitute, but with you as woman.' Ralf ignored the proffered bill and replied equally slowly, but quietly. 'You have a glow about you. The light that comes from sheer willpower, the light of someone who has made important sacrifices in the name of things she thinks are important. It's in your eyes – the light is in your eyes.'

Maria felt disarmed; he had not taken up her challenge. She had wanted to believe that he was simply trying to pick her up. She was not allowed to think – at least not for the next ninety days – that there were interesting men on the face of the Earth.

'You see that glass of anisette before you?' he went on. 'Now, you just see the anisette. I, on the other hand, because I need to be inside everything I do, see the plant it came from, the storms the plant endured, the hand that picked the grain, the voyage by ship from another land, the smells and colours with which the plant allowed itself to be imbued before it was placed in the alcohol. If I were to paint this scene, I would paint all those things, even though, when you saw the painting, you would think you were looking at a simple glass of anisette.

'In just the same way, while you were gazing out at the street and thinking – because I know you were – about the road to Santiago, I painted your childhood, your adolescence, your lost, broken dreams, your dreams for the future, and your will – which is what most intrigues me. When you saw your portrait …'

Maria put up her guard, knowing that it would be very difficult to lower it again later on.

'… I saw that light … even though all that was before me was a woman who looked like you.'

Again that constrained silence. Maria looked at her watch.

'I have to go in a moment. Why did you say that sex is boring?'

'You should know that better than me.'

'I know because it's my job. I do the same thing every day. But you're a young man of thirty …'

'Twenty-nine.'

'… young, attractive, famous, who should be interested in things like that, and who shouldn't have to go to Rue de Berne looking for company.'

'Well, I did. I went to bed with a few of your colleagues, but not because I had any problem finding female company. The problem lies with me.'

Maria felt a pang of jealousy, and was terrified. She really must leave.

'It was my last try. I've given up now,' said Ralf, starting to pick up the painting materials scattered on the floor.

'Have you got some physical problem?'

'No, I'm just not interested.'

This wasn't possible.

'Pay the bill and let's go for a walk. I think a lot of people feel the same, but no one ever says so. It's good to talk to someone so honest.'

They set off along the road to Santiago, which first climbed and then descended down to the river, then to the lake, then on to the mountains, to end in some distant place in Spain. They passed people going back to work after lunch, mothers with their prams, tourists taking photographs of the splendid fountain in the middle of the lake, Muslim women in their headscarves, boys and girls out jogging, all of them pilgrims in search of that mythological city, Santiago de Compostela, which might not even exist, which might be a legend in which people need to believe in order to give meaning to their lives. Along this road walked by so many people, over so many years, went that man with long hair, carrying a heavy bag full of brushes, paints, canvas and pencils, and that woman, slightly younger, with her bag full of books about farm management. It did not occur to either of them to ask why they were making that pilgrimage together, it was the most natural thing in the world; he knew everything about her, although she knew nothing about him.

Which is why she decided to ask – now that her policy was always to ask. At first, he reacted shyly, but she knew how to wheedle information out of men, and he ended up telling her that he had been married twice (a record for a twenty-nine-year-old!), had travelled widely, met kings and queens and famous actors, been to unforgettable parties. He had been born in Geneva, but had lived in Madrid, Amsterdam, New York, and in a city in the south of France, called Tarbes, which wasn't on any of the usual tourist circuits, but which he loved because it was so close to the mountains and because its inhabitants were so warm-hearted. He had been discovered as an artist when he was only twenty, when an important art dealer happened to visit a Japanese restaurant in Geneva decorated with his work. He had earned a lot of money, he was young and healthy, he could do anything, go anywhere, meet anyone he liked, he had known all the pleasures a man could know, he did what he most enjoyed doing, and yet, despite everything, fame, money, women, travel, he was unhappy, and had only one joy in his life – his work.

'Were you very hurt by women?' she asked, realising at once what an idiotic question it was, straight out of some manual entitled *Everything Women Should Know If They Want to Get Their Man*.

'No, they never hurt me. I was very happy in both my marriages. I was unfaithful and so were they, just like any other normal couple. Then, after a while, I simply lost interest in sex. I still felt love, still needed company, but sex ... but, why are we talking about sex?'

'Because, as you yourself said, I'm a prostitute.'

'My life isn't very interesting really. I'm an artist who found success very young, which is rare, and even rarer in the world of painting. I could paint anything now and it would be worth a fortune, which, of course, infuriates the critics because they think they are the only ones who know about "art". Other people think I've got all the answers, and the less I say, the more intelligent they think I am.'

He went on talking about his life, how every week he was invited to something somewhere in the world. He had an agent who lived in Barcelona – did she know where that was? Yes, Maria knew, it was in Spain. This agent dealt with everything to do with money, invitations, exhibitions, but never pressured him to do anything he didn't want to do, now that, after years of work, there was a steady demand for his paintings.

'Do you find my story interesting?' he asked, and his voice betrayed a touch of insecurity.

'It's certainly an unusual one. Lots of people would like to be in your shoes.'

Ralf wanted to know about Maria.

'Well, there are three of me, really, depending on who I'm with. There's the Innocent Girl, who gazes admiringly at the man, pretending to be impressed by his tales of power and glory. Then there's the Femme Fatale, who pounces on the most insecure and, by doing so, takes control of the situation and relieves them of responsibility, because then they don't have to worry about anything.

And, finally, there's the Understanding Mother, who looks after those in need of advice and who listens with an all-comprehending air to stories that go in one ear and out the other. Which of the three would you like to meet?'

'You.'

Maria told him everything, because she needed to – it was the first time she had done so since she left Brazil. She realised that, despite her somewhat unconventional job, nothing very exciting had happened apart from that week in Rio and her first month in Switzerland. Otherwise, it had been home, work, home, work – and nothing else.

When she finished speaking, they were sitting in another bar, this time on the other side of the city, far from the road to Santiago, each of them thinking about what fate had reserved for the other.

'Did I leave anything out?' she asked.

'How to say "goodbye".'

Yes, it had not been an afternoon like any other. She felt tense and anxious, for she had opened a door which she didn't know how to close.

'When can I see the whole painting?'

Ralf gave her the card of his agent in Barcelona.

'Phone her in about six months' time, if you're still in Europe. *The Faces of Geneva*, famous people and anonymous people. It will be exhibited for the first time in a gallery in Berlin. Then it will tour Europe.'

Maria remembered her calendar, the ninety days that remained, and the dangers posed by any relationship, any bond. She thought:

'What is more important in life? Living or pretending to live? Should I take a risk and say that this has been the loveliest afternoon I've spent in all the time I've been here? Should I thank him for listening to me without criticism and without comment? Or should I simply don the armour of the woman with willpower, with the "special light", and leave without saying anything?'

While they were walking along the road to Santiago and while she was listening to herself telling him about her life, she had been a happy woman. She could content herself with that; it was enough of a gift from life.

'I'll come and see you,' said Ralf Hart.

'No, don't. I'll be going back to Brazil soon. We have nothing more to give each other.'

'I'll come and see you as a client.'

'That would be humiliating for me.'

'I'll come and see you so that you can save me.'

He had made that comment early on, about his lack of interest in sex. She wanted to tell him that she felt the same, but she stopped herself – she had said 'no' too many times; it would be best to say nothing.

How pathetic. There she was with the little boy again, only he wasn't asking her for a pencil now, just a little company. She looked at her own past, and, for the first time, she forgave herself: it hadn't been her fault, but the fault of that insecure little boy, who had given up after the first attempt. They were children and that's how children are – neither she nor the boy had been in the wrong, and that gave her a great sense of relief, made her feel better;

she hadn't betrayed the first opportunity that life had presented her with. We all do the same thing: it's part of the initiation of every human being in search of his or her other half; these things happen.

Now, though, the situation was different. However convincing her reasons (I'm going back to Brazil, I work in a nightclub, we hardly know each other, I'm not interested in sex, I don't want anything to do with love, I need to learn how to manage a farm, I don't understand painting, we live in different worlds), life had thrown down a challenge. She wasn't a child any more, she had to choose.

She preferred to say nothing. She shook his hand, as was the custom there, and went home. If he was the man she wanted him to be, he would not be intimidated by her silence.

Extract from Maria's diary, written that same day:

Today, while we were walking around the lake, along that strange road to Santiago, the man who was with me – a painter, with a life entirely different from mine – threw a pebble into the water. Small circles appeared where the pebble fell, which grew and grew until they touched a duck that happened to be passing and which had nothing to do with the pebble. Instead of being afraid of that unexpected wave, he decided to play with it.

Some hours before that scene, I went into a café, heard a voice, and it was as if God had thrown a pebble into that place. The waves of energy touched both me and a man sitting in a corner painting a portrait. He felt the vibrations of that pebble, and so did I. So what now?

The painter knows when he has found a model. The musician knows when his instrument is well tuned. Here, in my diary, I am aware that there are certain phrases which are not written by me, but by a woman full of 'light'; I am that woman though I refuse to accept it.

I could carry on like this, but I could also, like the duck on the lake, have fun and take pleasure in that sudden ripple that set the water rocking.

There is a name for that pebble: passion. It can be used to describe the beauty of an earth-shaking meeting between two people, but it isn't just that. It's there in the excitement of the unexpected, in the desire to do something with real fervour, in the certainty that one is going to realise a dream. Passion sends us signals that guide us through our lives, and it's up to me to interpret those signs.

I would like to believe that I'm in love. With someone I don't know and who didn't figure in my plans at all. All these months of self-control, of denying love, have had exactly the opposite result: I have let myself be swept away by the first person to treat me a little differently.

It's just as well I don't have his phone number, that I don't know where he lives; that way I can lose him without having to blame myself for another missed opportunity.

And if that is what happens, if I have already lost him, I will at least have gained one very happy day in my life. Considering the way the world is, one happy day is almost a miracle.

When she arrived at the Copacabana that night, he was there, waiting for her. He was the only customer. Milan, who had been following her life with some interest, saw that she had lost the battle.

'Would you like a drink?' the man asked.

'I have to work. I can't risk losing my job.'

'I'm here as a customer. I'm making a professional proposition.'

This man, who had seemed so sure of himself that afternoon in the café, who wielded a paintbrush with such skill, met important people, had an agent in Barcelona and doubtless earned a lot of money, was now revealing his fragility; he had entered a world he should not have entered; he was no longer in a romantic café on the road to Santiago. The charm of the afternoon vanished.

'So, would you like a drink?'

'I will another time. I have clients waiting for me tonight.'

Milan overheard these last words; he was wrong, she had not allowed herself to be caught in the trap of promises of love. He nevertheless wondered, at the end of a rather slack night, why she had preferred the company of an old man, a dull accountant and an insurance salesman …

Oh, well, it was her problem. As long as she paid her commission, it wasn't up to him to decide who she should or shouldn't go to bed with.

From Maria's diary, after that night with the old man, the accountant and the insurance salesman:

What does this painter want of me? Doesn't he realise that we are from different countries, cultures and sexes? Does he think I know more about pleasure than he does and wants to learn something from me?

Why didn't he say anything else to me, apart from 'I'm here as a customer'? It would have been so easy for him to say: 'I missed you' or 'I really enjoyed the afternoon we spent together'. I would respond in the same way (I'm a professional), but he should understand my insecurities, because I'm a woman, I'm fragile, and when I'm in that place, I'm a different person.

He's a man. He's an artist. He should know that the great aim of every human being is to understand the meaning of total love. Love is not to be found in someone else, but in ourselves; we simply awaken it. But in order to do that, we need the other person. The universe only makes sense when we have someone to share our feelings with.

He says he's tired of sex. So am I, and yet neither of us really knows what that means. We are allowing one of the most important things in life to die – he should have saved me, I should have saved him, but he left me no choice.

She was terrified. She was beginning to realise that after long months of self-control, the pressure, the earthquake, the volcano of her soul was showing signs that it was about to erupt, and the moment that this happened, she would have no way of controlling her feelings. Who was this wretched painter, who might well be lying about his life and with whom she had spent only a few hours, who had not touched her or tried to seduce her – could there be anything worse?

Why were alarm bells ringing in her heart? Because she sensed that the same thing was happening to him, but no, she must be wrong. Ralf Hart just wanted to find a woman capable of awakening in him the fire that had almost burned out; he wanted to make her into some kind of personal sex goddess, with her 'special light' (he was being honest about that), who would take him by the hand and show him the road back to life. He couldn't imagine that Maria felt the same indifference, that she had her own problems (even after so many men, she had still never achieved orgasm when having ordinary penetrative sex), that she had been making plans that very morning and was organising a triumphant return to her homeland.

Why was she thinking about him? Why was she thinking about someone who, at that very moment, might be painting another woman, saying that she had a 'special light', that she could be his sex goddess?

'I'm thinking about him because I was able to talk to him.'

How ridiculous! Did she think about the librarian? No. Did she think about Nyah, the Filipino girl, the only one of all the women who worked at the Copacabana with whom she could share some of her feelings? No, she didn't. And they were people with whom she had often talked and with whom she felt comfortable.

She tried to divert her attention to thoughts of how hot it was, or to the supermarket she hadn't managed to get to yesterday. She wrote a long letter to her father, full of details about the piece of land she would like to buy – that would make her family happy. She did not give a date for her return, but she hinted that it would be soon. She slept, woke up, slept again and woke again. She realised that the book about farming was fine for Swiss farmers, but completely useless for Brazilians – they were two entirely different worlds.

As the afternoon wore on, she noticed that the earthquake, the volcano, the pressure was diminishing. She felt more relaxed; this kind of sudden passion had happened before and had always subsided by the next day – good, her universe continued unchanged. She had a family who loved her, a man who was waiting for her and who now wrote to her frequently, telling her that the draper's shop was expanding. Even if she decided to get on a plane that night, she had enough money to buy a small farm. She had got through the worst part, the language barrier, the loneliness, the first night in the restaurant with that Arab man, the way in which she had persuaded her soul not to complain about what she was doing with her body. She knew what her dream was and she was prepared to do anything to achieve it. And that dream did not, by the way, include men, at least not men who didn't speak her mother tongue or live in her hometown.

When the earthquake had subsided, Maria realised she was partly to blame. Why had she not said to him: 'I'm lonely, I'm as miserable as you are, yesterday you saw my "light", and it was the first nice, honest thing a man has said to me since I got here.'

On the radio they were playing an old song: 'my loves die even before they're born'. Yes, that was what happened with her, that was her fate.

From Maria's diary, two days after everything had returned to normal:

> *Passion makes a person stop eating, sleeping, working, feeling at peace. A lot of people are frightened because, when it appears, it demolishes all the old things it finds in its path.*
>
> *No one wants their life thrown into chaos. That is why a lot of people keep that threat under control, and are somehow capable of sustaining a house or a structure that is already rotten. They are the engineers of the superseded.*

Other people think exactly the opposite: they surrender themselves without a second thought, hoping to find in passion the solutions to all their problems. They make the other person responsible for their happiness and blame them for their possible unhappiness. They are either euphoric because something marvellous has happened or depressed because something unexpected has just ruined everything.

Keeping passion at bay or surrendering blindly to it – which of these two attitudes is the least destructive?

I don't know.

On the third day, as if risen from the dead, Ralf Hart returned, almost too late, for Maria was already talking to another customer. When she saw him, though, she politely told the other man that she didn't want to dance, that she was waiting for someone else.

Only then did she realise that she had spent the last three days waiting for him. And at that moment, she accepted everything that fate had placed in her path.

She didn't get angry with herself; she was happy, she could allow herself that luxury, because one day she would leave this city; she knew this love was impossible, and yet, expecting nothing, she could nevertheless have everything she still hoped for from that particular stage in her life.

Ralf asked her if she would like a drink, and Maria asked for a fruit juice cocktail. The owner of the bar, pretending that he was washing glasses, stared uncomprehendingly at her: what had made her change her mind? He hoped they wouldn't just sit there drinking, and felt relieved when Ralf asked her to dance. They were following the ritual; there was no reason to feel worried.

Maria felt Ralf's hand on her waist, his cheek pressed to hers, and the music – thank God – was too loud for them to talk. One fruit juice cocktail wasn't enough to give her courage, and the few words they had exchanged had been very formal. Now it was just a question of time: would they go to a hotel? Would they make love? It shouldn't be difficult, since he had already said that he wasn't interested in sex – it would just be a matter of going through the motions. On the other hand, that lack of interest would help to kill off any vestige of potential passion – she didn't know now why she had put herself through such torment after their first meeting.

Tonight she would be the Understanding Mother. Ralf Hart was just another desperate man, like millions of others. If she played her role well, if she managed to follow the rules she had laid down for herself since she began working at the Copacabana, there was no reason to worry. It was very dangerous, though, having that man so near, now that she could smell him – and she liked the way he smelled – now that she could feel his touch – and she liked his touch – now that she realised she had been waiting for him – she did not like that.

Within forty-five minutes they had fulfilled all the rules, and the man went over to the owner of the bar and said:

'I'm going to spend the rest of the night with her. I'll pay you as if I were three clients.'

The owner shrugged and thought again that the Brazilian girl would end up falling into the trap of love. Maria, for her part, was surprised: she hadn't realised that Ralf Hart knew the rules so well.

'Let's go back to my house.'

Perhaps that was the best thing to do, she thought. Although it went against all of Milan's advice, she decided, in this case, to make an exception. Apart from finding out once and for all whether or not he was married, she would also find out how famous painters live, and one day she would be able to write an article for her local newspaper, so that everyone would know that, during her time in Europe, she had moved in intellectual and artistic circles.

'What an absurd excuse!' she thought.

Half an hour later, they arrived at a small village near Geneva, called Cologny; there was a church, a bakery, a town hall, everything in its proper place. And he really did live in a two-storey house, not an apartment! First reaction: he really must be rich. Second reaction: if he were married, he wouldn't dare to do this, because they would be bound to be seen by someone.

So, he was rich and single.

They went into a hall from which a staircase ascended to the second floor, but they went straight ahead to the two rooms at the back that looked onto the garden. There was a dining table in one of the rooms, and the walls were crowded with paintings. In the other room were sofas and chairs, packed bookshelves, overflowing ashtrays and dirty glasses that had clearly been there for a long time.

'Would you like a coffee?'

Maria shook her head. No, she wouldn't. You can't treat me differently just yet. I'm confronting my own demons, doing exactly the opposite of what I promised myself I would do. But let's take things slowly; tonight I'll play the part of prostitute or friend or Understanding Mother, even though in my soul I'm a Daughter in need of affection. When it's all over, then you can make me a coffee.

'At the bottom of the garden is my studio, my soul. Here, amongst all these paintings and books, is my brain, what I think.'

Maria thought of her own apartment. She had no garden at the back. She did not even have any books, apart from those she borrowed from the library, since there was no point in spending money on something she could get for free. There were no paintings either, apart from a poster for the Shanghai Acrobatic Circus, which she dreamed of going to one day.

Ralf picked up a bottle of whisky and offered her a glass.

'No, thank you.'

He poured himself a drink and swallowed it down in one – without ice, without time to savour it. He started talking about intelligent things, but, however interesting the conversation, she knew that he too was afraid of what was going to happen, now that they were alone. Maria had regained control of the situation.

Ralf poured himself another whisky and, as if he were making some utterly inconsequential remark, he said:

'I need you.'

A pause. A long silence. Don't help to break that silence, let's see what he does next.

'I need you, Maria. Because you have a light, although I don't really think you believe me yet, and think I'm just trying to seduce you with my words. Don't ask me: "Why me?

What's so special about me?" There isn't anything special about you, at least, nothing I can put my finger on. And yet – and here's the mystery of life – I can't think of anything else.'

'I wasn't going to ask you,' she lied.

'If I were looking for an explanation, I would say: the woman in front of me has managed to overcome suffering and to transform it into something positive, something creative, but that doesn't explain everything.'

It was becoming difficult to escape. He went on:

'And what about me? I have my creativity, I have my paintings, which are sought after by galleries all over the world, I have realised my dream, my village thinks of me as a beloved son, my ex-wives never ask me for alimony or anything like that, I have good health, reasonable looks, everything a man could want ... And yet here I am saying to a woman I met in a café and with whom I have spent one afternoon: "I need you." Do you know what loneliness is?'

'I do.'

'But you don't know what loneliness is like when you have the chance to be with other people all the time, when you get invitations every night to parties, cocktail parties, opening nights at the theatre ... When women are always ringing you up, women who love your work, who say how much they would like to have supper with you – they're beautiful, intelligent, educated women. But something pushes you away and says: "Don't go. You won't enjoy yourself. You'll spend the whole night trying to impress them and squander your energies proving to yourself how you can charm the whole world."

'So I stay at home, go into my studio and try to find the light I saw in you, and I can only see that light when I'm working.'

'What can I give you that you don't already have?' she asked, feeling slightly humiliated by that remark about other women, but remembering that he had, after all, paid to have her at his side.

He drank a third glass of whisky. Maria accompanied him in her imagination, the alcohol burning his throat and his stomach, entering his bloodstream and filling him with courage, and she too began to feel drunk, even though she hadn't touched a drop. When Ralf spoke again, his voice sounded steadier:

'I can't buy your love, but you did tell me that you knew everything about sex. Teach me, then. Or teach me something about Brazil. Anything, just as long as I can be with you.'

What next?

'I only know two places in my own country: the town I was born in and Rio de Janeiro. As for sex, I don't think I can teach you anything. I'm nearly twenty-three, you're about six years older, but I know you've lived life very intensely. I know men who pay me to do what they want, not what I want.'

'I've done everything a man could dream of doing with one, two, even three women at the same time. And I don't think I learned very much.'

Silence again, except that this time it was Maria's turn to speak. And he did not help her, just as she had not helped him before.

'Do you want me as a professional?'

'I want you however you want to be wanted.'

No, he couldn't have said that, because that was precisely what she had wanted to hear. The earthquake, the volcano, the storm returned. It was going to be impossible to escape her own trap, she would lose this man without ever really having him.

'You know what I mean, Maria. Teach me. Perhaps that will save me, perhaps it will save you and bring us both back to life. You're right, I am only six years older than you, and yet I've lived enough for several lives. Our experiences have been entirely different, but we are both desperate people; the only thing that brings us any peace is being together.'

Why was he saying these things? It wasn't possible, and yet it was true. They had only met once before and yet they already needed each other. Imagine what would happen if they continued seeing each other; it would be disastrous! Maria was an intelligent woman, with many months behind her now of reading and of observing humankind; she had an aim in life, but she also had a soul, which she needed to know in order to discover her 'light'. She was becoming tired of being who she was, and although her imminent return to Brazil was an interesting challenge, she had not yet learned all she could. Ralf Hart was a man who had accepted challenges and had learned everything, and now he was asking this woman, this prostitute, this Understanding Mother, to save him. How absurd!

Other men had behaved like this with her. Many of them had been unable to have an erection, others had wanted to be treated like children, others had said that they would like her to be their wife because it excited them to know that she had had so many lovers. Although she had still not met any of the 'special clients', she had already discovered the vast universe of fantasies that fills the human soul. But they were all used to their own worlds and none of them had said to her: 'take me away from here'. On the contrary, they wanted to take Maria with them.

And even though those many men had always left her with money, but drained of energy, she must have learned something. If one of them had really been looking for love, and if sex really was only part of that search, how would she like to be treated? What did she think should happen on a first meeting?

What would she really like to happen?

'I'd like a gift,' said Maria.

Ralf Hart didn't understand. A gift? He had already paid for that night in advance, while they were in the taxi, because he knew the ritual. What did she mean?

Maria had suddenly realised that she knew, at that moment, what a man and a woman needed to feel. She took his hand and led him into one of the sitting rooms.

'We won't go up to the bedroom,' she said.

She turned out almost all the lights, sat down on the carpet and asked him to sit down opposite her. She noticed that there was a fire in the room.

'Light the fire.'

'But it's summer.'

'Light the fire. You asked me to guide our steps tonight and that's what I'm doing.'

She gave him a steady look, hoping that he would again see her 'light'. He obviously did, because he went out into the garden, collected some wood still wet with rain, and picked up some old newspapers so that the fire would dry the wood and get it to burn. He went into the kitchen to fetch more whisky, but Maria called him back.

'Did you ask me what I wanted?'

'No, I didn't.'

'Well, the person you're with has to exist too. Think of her. Think if she wants whisky or gin or coffee. Ask her what she wants.'

'What would you like to drink.'

'Wine. And I'd like you to keep me company.'

He put down the whisky bottle and returned with a bottle of wine. By this time, the fire was already beginning to burn; Maria turned out the few remaining lights, so that the flames were the only illumination in the room. She behaved as if she had always known that this was the first step: recognising the other person and knowing that he or she was there.

She opened her handbag and found inside a pen she had bought in a supermarket. Anything would do.

'This is for you. I bought it so that I could note down some ideas about farm management. I used it for two days, I worked until I was too tired to work any more. It contains some of my sweat, some of my concentration and my willpower, and I'm giving it to you now.'

She placed the pen gently in his hand.

'Instead of buying something that you would like to have, I'm giving you something that is mine, truly mine. A gift. A sign of respect for the person before me, asking him to understand how important it is to be by his side. Now he has a small part of me with him, which I gave him with my free, spontaneous will.'

Ralf got up, went over to a shelf and returned, carrying something. He held it out to Maria.

'This is a carriage belonging to an electric train set I had when I was a child. I wasn't allowed to play with it on my own, because my father said it had been imported from the United States and was very expensive. So I had to wait until he felt like setting up the train in the living room, but he spent most Sundays listening to opera. That's why the train survived my childhood, but never gave me any happiness. I've still got all the track, the engine, the houses, even the manual, because I had a train that wasn't mine and with which I never played.

'I wish I'd destroyed it along with all the other toys I was given and which I've since forgotten all about, because that passion for destruction is part of how a child discovers the world. But this pristine train set always reminds me of a part of my childhood that I never lived, because it was too precious and it meant too much work for my father. Or perhaps it was just that whenever he set the train up, he was afraid he might show his love for me.'

Maria began staring into the fire. Something was happening, and it wasn't just the wine or the cosy atmosphere. It was that exchange of gifts.

Ralf turned to the fire too. They said nothing, listening to the crackle of the flames. They drank their wine, as if it didn't matter that they said nothing, did nothing. They were just there, together, staring in the same direction.

'I have a lot of pristine train sets in my life too,' said Maria, after a while. 'One of them is my heart. And I only played with it when the world set out the tracks, and then it wasn't always the right moment.'

'But you loved.'

'Oh, yes, I loved, I loved very deeply. I loved so deeply that when my love asked me for a gift, I took fright and fled.'

'I don't understand.'

'You don't have to. I'm teaching you because I've discovered something I didn't know before. The giving of gifts. Giving something of one's own. Giving something important rather than asking. You have my treasure: the pen with which I wrote down some of my dreams. I have your treasure: the carriage of a train, part of your childhood that you did not live.

'I carry with me part of your past, and you carry with you a little of my present. Isn't that lovely?'

She said all this without blinking, and without surprise, as if she had known for ages that this was the best and only way to behave. She got lightly to her feet, took her jacket from the coat rack and kissed Ralf on the cheek. Ralf Hart did not make any move to get up, hypnotised by the fire, perhaps thinking about his father.

'I never understood why I kept that carriage. Now I do: it was in order to give it to you one night before an open fire. Now the house feels lighter.'

He said that the next day he would give the rest of the tracks, engines, smoke pills, to some children's home.

'It could be a rarity, of a kind that isn't made any more; it could be worth a lot of money,' said Maria, but immediately regretted her words. That wasn't what mattered, the point was to free yourself from something that cost your heart even more.

Before she said anything else that did not quite chime with the moment, she again kissed him on the cheek and walked to the front door. He was still gazing into the fire, and she had to ask him softly if he would open the door for her.

Ralf got up, and she explained that, although she was glad to see him staring into the fire, Brazilians have a strange superstition: when you visit someone for the first time, you must not be the one to open the door when you leave, because if you do, you will never return to that house.

'And I want to come back.'

'Although we didn't take our clothes off and I didn't come inside you, or even touch you, we've made love.'

She laughed. He offered to take her home, but she refused.

'I'll come and see you tomorrow, then, at the Copacabana.'

'No, don't. Wait a week. I've learned that waiting is the most difficult bit, and I want to get used to the feeling, knowing that you're with me, even when you're not by my side.'

She walked back through the cold and the dark, as she had so many times before in Geneva; normally, these walks were associated with sadness, loneliness, the desire to go back to Brazil, financial calculations, timetables, nostalgia for the language she hadn't spoken freely for ages.

Now, though, she was walking in order to find herself, to find that woman who had sat with a man by a fire for forty minutes and who was full of light, wisdom, experience and charm. She had seen that woman's face a long time ago, when she was walking by the lakeside wondering whether or not she should devote herself to a life that wasn't hers – on that afternoon, the woman had a terribly sad smile on her face. She had seen her for a second time on that folded canvas, and now she was with her again. She only caught a taxi after she had walked quite a way, when the magic presence had gone, leaving her alone again, as usual.

It was best not to think too much about it all, so as not to spoil it, so as not to let the beauty of what she had just experienced be replaced by anxiety. If that other Maria really existed, she would return when the moment was right.

An extract from the diary Maria wrote on the night she was given the train carriage:

Profound desire, true desire is the desire to be close to someone. From that point onwards, things change, the man and the woman come into play, but what happens before – the attraction that brought them together – is impossible to explain. It is untouched desire in its purest state.

When desire is still in this pure state, the man and the woman fall in love with life, they live each moment reverently, consciously, always ready to celebrate the next blessing.

When people feel like this, they are not in a hurry, they do not precipitate events with unthinking actions. They know that the inevitable will happen, that what is real always finds a way of revealing itself. When the moment comes, they do not hesitate, they do not miss an opportunity, they do not let slip a single magic moment, because they respect the importance of each second.

In the days that followed, Maria found herself once more caught in the trap she had tried so hard to avoid, but she felt neither sad nor concerned. On the contrary, now that she had nothing to lose, she was free.

She knew that, however romantic the situation, one day, Ralf Hart would realise that she was just a prostitute, while he was a respected artist, that she lived in a far-off country that was in a state of permanent crisis, while he lived in paradise, with his life organised and protected from birth. He had received his education in the best schools, museums and art galleries of the world, while she had barely finished secondary school. Dreams like theirs never lasted long, and Maria had enough experience of life to know that reality usually chose not to fit in with her dreams. And that was now her great joy: to say to reality that she didn't need it, that she was no longer dependent on what happened in order to be happy.

'God, I'm such a romantic.'

During the week, she tried to think of something that would make Ralf Hart happy; for he had restored to her a dignity and a 'light' that she thought were lost forever. But the only way she had of repaying him was with the thing he thought was her speciality: sex. Since there was little to inspire her in the routine at the Copacabana, she decided to look elsewhere.

She again went to see a few porn movies, and again found nothing of interest in them, apart, perhaps, from the varying number of people involved. When films proved of no help, she decided, for the first time since she had arrived in Geneva, to buy some books, although she still didn't see the point in cluttering up her apartment with something which, once read, had no further use. She went to the bookshop she had seen when she and Ralf had walked down the road to Santiago, and asked if they had any books about sex.

'Oh, loads,' said the shop assistant. 'In fact, it seems to be all people care about. There's a special section devoted to the subject, but in just about every other novel you can see around you there's always at least one sex scene. Whether it's hidden away in pretty little love stories or discussed in serious tomes on human behaviour, it appears to be all anyone thinks about.'

Maria, with all her experience, knew that the woman was wrong: people wanted to think like that because they thought sex was everyone else's sole concern. They went on diets, wore wigs, spent hours at the hairdresser's or at the gym, put on sexy clothes, all in an attempt to awaken the necessary spark. And what happened? When the moment came to go to bed with someone, eleven minutes later it was all over. There was no creativity involved, nothing that would lift them up to paradise; the fire provoked by the spark soon burned out.

But there was no point arguing with the young blonde woman, who believed that the world could be explained in books. She asked to be directed to the special section, and there she found various books about gay men, lesbians, nuns revealing scandals in the church, illustrated books showing oriental techniques, all involving extremely uncomfortable positions, but only one of the titles interested her: *Sacred Sex*. At least it was different.

She bought it, went home, tuned to a particular radio station that always helped her to think (because they played such calming music), opened the book and noticed various illustrations, showing postures that only a circus performer could possibly hope to achieve. The text itself was very dull.

Maria had learned enough in her profession to know that not everything in life is a matter of what position you adopt when making love, and that any variation usually occurs naturally, without thinking, like the steps in a dance. Nevertheless, she tried to concentrate on what she was reading.

Two hours later, she had come to two conclusions.

First, she needed to eat supper, because she had to get back to the Copacabana.

Second, the person who had written the book clearly understood nothing, absolutely nothing about the subject. It was just a lot of empty theory, oriental nonsense, pointless rituals and idiotic suggestions. She noticed that the author had studied meditation in the Himalayas (she must find out where they were), attended courses in yoga (she had heard of that), and had obviously read widely in the subject, for she kept quoting other authors, but she had failed to learn what was essential. Sex wasn't theories, incense, erogenous zones, bows and salaams. How did that person (a woman) have the nerve to write on a subject which not even Maria, who worked in the field, knew in depth. Perhaps it was all the fault of the Himalayas or the need to complicate something whose very beauty lay in simplicity and passion. If that woman could get away with publishing and selling such a stupid book, perhaps she should think seriously again about writing her own: *Eleven Minutes*. It wouldn't be cynical or false – it would just be her story.

But she had neither the time nor the interest; she needed to focus her energies on making Ralf Hart happy and on learning how to manage a farm.

From Maria's diary, just after abandoning the boring book:

> *I've met a man and fallen in love with him. I allowed myself to fall in love for one simple reason: I'm not expecting anything to come of it. I know that, in three months' time, I'll be far away and he'll be just a memory, but I couldn't stand living without love any longer; I had reached my limit.*
>
> *I'm writing a story for Ralf Hart – that's his name. I'm not sure he'll come back to the club where I work, but, for the first time in my life, that doesn't matter. It's enough just to love him, to be with him in*

my thoughts and to colour this lovely city with his steps, his words, his love. When I leave this country, it will have a face and a name and the memory of a fireplace. Everything else I experienced here, all the difficulties I had to overcome, will be as nothing compared to that memory.

I would like to do for him what he did for me. I've been thinking about it a lot, and I realise that I didn't go into that café by chance; really important meetings are planned by the souls long before the bodies see each other.

Generally speaking, these meetings occur when we reach a limit, when we need to die and be reborn emotionally. These meetings are waiting for us, but more often than not, we avoid them happening. If we are desperate, though, if we have nothing to lose, or if we are full of enthusiasm for life, then the unknown reveals itself, and our universe changes direction.

Everyone knows how to love, because we are all born with that gift. Some people have a natural talent for it, but the majority of us have to re-learn, to remember how to love, and everyone, without exception, needs to burn on the bonfire of past emotions, to relive certain joys and griefs, certain ups and downs, until they can see the connecting thread that exists behind each new encounter; because there is a connecting thread.

And then, our bodies learn to speak the language

of the soul, known as sex, and that is what I can give to the man who gave me back my soul, even though he has no idea how important he is to my life. That is what he asked me for and that is what he will have; I want him to be very happy.

Sometimes life is very mean: a person can spend days, weeks, months and years without feeling anything new. Then, when a door opens – as happened with Maria when she met Ralf Hart – a positive avalanche pours in. One moment, you have nothing, the next, you have more than you can cope with.

Two hours after writing her diary, when she arrived at work, Milan, the owner, came looking for her:

'So you went out with that painter, did you?'

Ralf was obviously known at the club – she had realised this when he paid the rate for three customers, without having to ask the price. Maria merely nodded, trying to act mysterious, but Milan took no notice; he knew this life better than she did.

'Perhaps you're ready for the next stage. There's a special client of ours who has often asked about you. I told him that you're not experienced enough, and he believed me, but perhaps now is the moment to try.'

A special client?

'What's this got to do with the painter?'

'He's a special client too.'

So everything she had done with Ralf Hart had already

been done by one of her colleagues. She bit her lip and said nothing; she had had a lovely week, and she must not forget what she had written.

'Should I do the same thing I did with him?'

'I don't know what you did; but tonight, if someone offers you a drink, say no. Special clients pay more; you won't regret it.'

Work started as it always did. The Thai women all sat together, the Colombians adopted their usual air of knowing everything, the three Brazilians (including her) looked absently about them, as if nothing could ever surprise or interest them. Apart from them, there was an Austrian, two Germans, and the rest were tall, pretty women with pale eyes who came from the former Eastern Bloc countries and who always seemed to find husbands more quickly than the others.

The men began to arrive – Russian, Swiss, German, all of them busy executives, well able to afford the services of the most expensive prostitutes in one of the most expensive cities in the world. Some came over to her table, but she kept her eye on Milan, who shook his head. Maria was pleased; tonight, she wouldn't have to open her legs, put up with smells or take showers in sometimes chilly bathrooms; all she had to do was to teach a man grown weary of sex how to make love. And when she thought about it, not every woman would have been creative enough to come up with that story about the exchange of gifts.

At the same time, she was wondering: Why is it that, having experienced everything, these men want to go right back to the start? Not that this was her concern; as long as they paid well, she was there to serve them.

A man came in, younger than Ralf Hart; he was good-looking, with dark hair, perfect teeth, and wearing what looked like a Mao jacket – no tie, just a high collar and, underneath, an impeccable white shirt. He went up to the bar, where both he and Milan turned to look at Maria; then he came over.

'Would you like a drink?'

She saw Milan nod, and so invited the man to sit down at her table. She ordered a fruit juice cocktail and waited for him to ask her to dance. Then the man introduced himself:

'My name is Terence, and I work for a record company in England. Since I assume I'm in a place where I can trust the personnel, I take it this will remain entirely between you and me.'

Maria was about to start talking about Brazil, but he interrupted her:

'Milan says you understand what I want.'

'I've no idea what you want, but I know my job.'

They did not follow the usual ritual; he paid the bill, took her arm and they got into a taxi, where he gave her a thousand francs. For a moment, she remembered the Arab man with whom she had gone to the restaurant full of famous paintings; it was the first time she had received the same amount of money, and instead of making her feel glad, it made her feel nervous.

The taxi stopped outside one of the most expensive hotels in the city. The man greeted the porter and seemed totally at ease in the place. They went straight up to his room, a suite with a view over the river. He opened a bottle of wine – possibly a rare vintage – and offered her a glass.

Maria watched him while he drank; what did a rich, good-looking man like him want with a prostitute? Since he barely spoke, she too remained largely silent, trying to work out what would make a special client happy. She knew that she should not take the initiative, but once the process had begun, she needed to be able to follow his lead as quickly as possible; after all, it wasn't every night that she earned a thousand francs.

'We've got plenty of time,' Terence said. 'All the time in the world. You can sleep here if you like.'

Her feelings of insecurity returned. The man did not seem in the least intimidated, and, unlike her other customers, he spoke very calmly. He knew what he wanted; he put on the perfect piece of music, at the perfect volume, in the perfect room, with the perfect window, which looked out onto the lake of a perfect city. His suit was welltailored, his suitcase was there in the corner, very small, as if he always travelled light, or as if he had come to Geneva just for that one night.

'I'll sleep at home,' Maria said.

The man opposite her changed completely. An icy glint came into his hitherto gentlemanly eyes.

'Sit there,' he said, indicating a chair by the desk.

It was an order! A real order. Maria obeyed and, oddly enough, she felt excited.

'Sit properly. Back straight, like a lady. If you don't, I'll punish you.'

Punish her! Special client! In a flash, she understood everything, took the thousand francs out of her bag and put it down on the desk.

'I know what you want,' she said, looking deep into those cold, blue eyes. 'And I won't do it.'

The man seemed to return to his normal self and he could see that she was telling the truth.

'Have a drink of wine,' he said. 'I won't force you to do anything. You can either stay a little longer, if you like, or you can leave.'

That made her feel better.

'I have a job. I have a boss who protects and trusts me. I'd be grateful if you didn't say anything to him.'

Maria said this without a hint of pleading or self-pity in her voice; it was simply how things were.

Terence was once again the man she had first met – neither gentle nor harsh, just someone who, unlike her other clients, gave the impression that he knew what he wanted. He seemed to emerge from a trance, from a play that had scarcely begun.

Was it worth leaving now and never finding out the truth about this 'special client'?

'What exactly did you want?'

'You know what I want. Pain. Suffering. And a great deal of pleasure.'

'Pain and suffering don't normally go with pleasure,' Maria thought. And yet she desperately wanted to believe that they did, and thus make a positive out of her many negative experiences.

He took her by the hand and led her over to the window: on the other side of the lake they could see a cathedral spire. Maria remembered passing it when she had walked the road to Santiago with Ralf Hart.

'You see the river, the lake, the houses and the church? Well, it was all pretty much the same five hundred years ago, except that the city was deserted. A strange disease had spread throughout Europe, and no one knew why so many people were dying. They began to call the disease the Black Death – sent by God because of mankind's sins.

'Then a group of people decided to sacrifice themselves for the sake of humanity. They offered the thing they most feared: physical pain. They began to spend days and nights walking across these bridges, along these streets, beating their own bodies with whips and chains. They were suffering in the name of God and praising God with their pain. They soon realised that they were happier doing this than baking bread, working in the fields or feeding their animals. Pain was no longer a cause of suffering, but a source of pleasure because they were redeeming humanity from its sins. Pain became joy, the meaning of life, pleasure.'

His eyes grew cold again. He picked up the money she had put down on the desk, separated out one hundred and fifty francs and put those in her bag.

'Don't worry about your boss. Here's his commission, and I promise I won't say anything. You can leave now.'

She grabbed the money back.

'No!'

It was the wine, the Arab man in the restaurant, the woman with the sad smile, the idea that she would never ever return to this wretched place, the fear of a new love that was coming to her in the shape of a man, the letters to her mother telling of a wonderful life full of job opportunities, the boy from her childhood who had asked her for a pencil, the struggles with herself, the guilt, the curiosity, the money, the search to discover her own limits, and all the missed chances and opportunities. Another Maria was there now: she was no longer offering gifts, she was offering herself up as a sacrifice.

'I'm not afraid any more. Let's carry on. If necessary, you can punish me for my rebelliousness. I've lied and betrayed and maligned the very person who protected and loved me.'

She was entering into the spirit of the game. She was saying the right things.

'Kneel down!' said Terence in a low, chilling voice.

Maria obeyed. She had never been treated this way, and she didn't know if it was good or bad, only that she wanted to go forward; she deserved to be humiliated for all she had done in her life. She was entering a role, becoming a different person, a woman she did not know at all.

'You will be punished because you are useless, because you don't know the rules and because you know nothing about sex, life or love.'

While he was speaking, Terence was transformed into two very different men. The one who was calmly explaining the rules to her and the one who made her feel like the most miserable wretch in the world.

'Do you know why I am doing this? Because there is no greater pleasure than that of initiating someone into an unknown world. Taking someone's virginity – the virginity not of their body, but of their soul, you understand.'

She understood.

'Today you can ask questions, but the next time, when the theatre curtain goes up, the play will begin and cannot be stopped. If it does stop, it is because our souls are incompatible. Remember: it is a play. You must be the person you have never had the courage to be. Gradually, you will discover that you are that person, but until you can see this clearly, you must pretend and invent.'

'What if I can't stand the pain?'

'There is no pain, only something that transforms itself into delight and mystery. It forms part of the play to say: "Don't treat me like that, you're really hurting me." As is: "Stop, I can't take any more!" In order to avoid danger …' He broke off at this point and said: 'Keep your head down; don't look at me!'

Maria, kneeling, lowered her head and stared at the floor.

'… in order to avoid this relationship causing any serious physical harm, we have two code words. If one of us says "yellow", that means that the violence should be decreased slightly. If one of us says "red", it must be stopped at once.'

'You said "one of us" ...'

'We take turns. One cannot exist without the other; no one can know how to humiliate another person if they themselves have not experienced humiliation.'

These were terrible words, from a world she did not know, full of shadow, slime and putrefaction. Nevertheless, she wanted to go on – her body was trembling with fear and excitement.

Terence placed his hand on her head with unexpected tenderness.

'That's all.'

He asked her to get up, not particularly kindly, but not with the same brusque aggression he had shown before. Still trembling, Maria put on her jacket. Terence noticed the state she was in.

'Have a cigarette before you go.'

'Nothing happened.'

'It doesn't need to. It will start to happen in your soul, and the next time we meet, you will be ready.'

'Was tonight worth one thousand francs?'

He didn't reply. He too lit a cigarette and they finished the wine, listening to the perfect music, savouring the silence together, until the moment came to say something, and when it did, Maria was surprised by her own words.

'I don't understand why I want to step into this slime.'

'One thousand francs.'

'No, that's not the reason.'

Terence seemed pleased with this response.

'I've asked myself the same thing. The Marquis de Sade

said that the most important experiences a man can have are those that take him to the very limit; that is the only way we learn, because it requires all our courage. When a boss humiliates an employee, or a man humiliates his wife, he is merely being cowardly or taking his revenge on life, they are people who have never dared to look into the depths of their soul, never attempted to know the origin of that desire to unleash the wild beast, or to understand that sex, pain and love are all extreme experiences.

'Only those who know those frontiers know life; everything else is just passing the time, repeating the same tasks, growing old and dying without ever having discovered what we are doing here.'

In the street again, in the cold again, and again that desire to walk. The man was wrong, it wasn't necessary to know your own demons in order to find God. She passed a group of students coming out of a bar; they were all happy and slightly tipsy, they were all good-looking and bursting with health; soon they would finish university and start what people call 'real life'. Work, marriage, children, television, bitterness, old age, the sense of having lost many things, frustrations, illness, disability, dependence on others, loneliness, death.

What was happening? She too was looking for the peace in which to live her 'real life'; the time spent in Switzerland, doing something she had never dreamed of doing, was just a difficult phase, the kind of thing everyone goes through at some time or another. During this difficult phase, she frequented the Copacabana, went with men for money, played the Innocent Girl, the Femme Fatale and the Understanding Mother, depending on the client. But it was just a job, which she did with total professionalism – for the sake of the tips – and minimum interest – for fear she might get used to it. She had spent the last nine months controlling the world around her, and shortly before she was due to go back to her own country, she was finding that she was capable of loving without demanding anything in return and of suffering for no reason. It was as if life had chosen this strange, sordid way of teaching her something about her own mysteries, her light and her darkness.

From Maria's diary on the night following her first meeting with Terence:

He quoted the Marquis de Sade, of whom I know nothing, apart from the word 'sadism'. It's true that we only know each other when we come up against our own limits, but it's wrong too, because it isn't necessary to know everything about ourselves; human beings weren't made solely to go in search of wisdom, but also to plough the land, wait for rain, plant the wheat, harvest the grain, make the bread.

I am two women: one wants to have all the joy, passion and adventure that life can give me. The other wants to be a slave to routine, to family life, to the things that can be planned and achieved. I'm a housewife and a prostitute, both of us living in the same body and doing battle with each other.

The meeting of these two women is a game with serious risks. A divine dance. When we meet, we are two divine energies, two universes colliding. If the meeting is not carried out with due reverence, one universe destroys the other.

She was back in Ralf Hart's living room, with the fire, the bottle of wine, the two of them sitting on the floor, and everything she had experienced the previous night with the English executive just a dream or a nightmare – depending on how she was feeling. Now she was searching once more for her reason for living, or, rather, for the kind of utter surrender by which a person offers his or her heart and asks for nothing in return.

She had grown a lot while waiting for this moment. She had finally discovered that real love has nothing to do with what she imagined, that is, with a chain of events provoked by the energy engendered by love – courtship, engagement, marriage, children, waiting, cooking, the amusement park on Sundays, more waiting, getting old together, an end to the waiting, and then, in its place, comes your husband's retirement, illnesses, the feeling that it is far too late to live out your dream together.

She looked at the man to whom she had decided to give herself, and to whom she had resolved never to reveal her feelings, because what she was feeling now was far from taking any definite form, not even physical form. He seemed more at ease, as if he were embarking on an interesting period of his life. He was smiling and telling her about his recent visit to Munich to meet an important museum director.

'He asked if the painting about the faces of Geneva was ready yet. I said I had just met one of the principal people I would like to paint, a woman who was full of light. But I don't want to talk about me, I want to embrace you. I desire you.'

Desire. Desire? Desire! That was the point of departure this evening, because it was something she knew extremely well!

For example, you awaken desire by not immediately handing over the object of that desire.

'All right, then, desire me. That's what we're doing right now. You are less than a yard away from me, you went to a nightclub, paid for my services, and you know you have the right to touch me. But you don't dare. Look at me. Look at me and imagine that perhaps I don't want you to look at me. Imagine what's hidden beneath my clothes.'

She always wore black to work, and she couldn't understand why the other girls at the Copacabana tried to look provocative in their low-cut dresses and garish colours. It seemed to her that it was more exciting for a man if she dressed like any other woman he might meet at the office, on the train or in the house of one of his wife's friends.

Ralf looked at her. Maria felt him undressing her and she enjoyed being desired like that – with no contact, as if she were in a restaurant or standing in a queue at the cinema.

'We're in a train station,' Maria went on. 'I'm standing next to you, waiting for a train, but you don't know me.

My eyes meet yours, by chance, and I don't look away. You don't know what I'm trying to say, because, although you're an intelligent man, capable of seeing the "light" in other people, you are not sensitive enough to see what that light is illuminating.'

She had learned about 'theatre'. She had wanted to forget the face of that English executive as quickly as possible, but there he was, guiding her imagination.

'My eyes are fixed on yours, and I might be wondering to myself: "Do I know him from somewhere?" Or I might just be distracted. Or I might be afraid of appearing unfriendly; perhaps you do know me, and so I give you the benefit of the doubt for a few seconds, until it becomes clear either that you really do know me or that it's a case of mistaken identity.

'But I might also be wanting the simplest thing in the world: to find a man. I might be trying to escape an unhappy love affair. I might be hoping to avenge myself for a recent betrayal and have gone to the train station looking for a stranger. I might want to be your prostitute just for one night, to do something different in my otherwise boring life. I might even be a real prostitute on the look-out for work.'

A brief silence; Maria had grown distracted. She was back in that hotel room, remembering the humiliation – 'yellow', 'red', pain and a great deal of pleasure. That encounter had stirred her soul in a way she did not like at all.

Ralf noticed and tried to take her back to the train station.

'In this meeting, do you desire me too?'

'I don't know. We don't talk. You don't know.'

She grows distracted again. The 'theatre' idea is proving really very helpful; it draws out the real person and drives away the many false people who live inside us.

'The fact is that I don't look away, and you don't know what to do. Should you approach? Will you be rejected? Will I call the guard? Or invite you for a coffee perhaps?'

'I'm on my way back from Munich,' Ralf Hart said, and his voice sounds different, as if they really were meeting for the first time. 'I'm thinking about a collection of paintings on the many personalities of sex, the many masks that people wear in order never to experience a real encounter.'

He knew about the 'theatre'. Milan had said that he too was a 'special client'. An alarm bell rang, but she needed time to think.

'The director of the museum said to me: what are you going to base your work on? I said: On women who feel free enough to earn their living making love. He said: That won't work; we call such women "prostitutes". I said: Fine, they are prostitutes; I'm going to study their history and create something more intellectual, more to the taste of the families who visit your museum. It's all a question of culture, you see. Of finding a palatable way of presenting something that is otherwise very hard to take.

'The director insisted: But sex is no longer a taboo. It's been so over-exploited that it's difficult to produce any new work on the subject. I said: Do you know where sexual desire comes from? From our instinct, said the director. Yes,

I said, from our instinct, but everyone knows that. How can you make a beautiful exhibition if all we are talking about is science? I want to talk about how man explains that attraction, the way, let's say, a philosopher would explain it. The director asked me to give him an example. I said that if, when I caught the train back home, a woman looked at me, I would go over and speak to her; I would say that, since we were strangers, we had the freedom to do anything we wanted, to live out all our fantasies, and then go home to our wife or husband and never meet again. And then, in the train station, I see you.'

'Your story is so interesting it's in danger of killing desire.'

Ralf Hart laughed and agreed. They had finished one bottle of wine and he went into the kitchen to fetch another; and she sat staring into the fire, knowing what the next step would be, but, at the same time, savouring the cosy atmosphere, forgetting about the English executive, and regaining that sense of surrender.

Ralf filled their two glasses, and Maria said:

'Just out of curiosity, how would you end that story with the museum director?'

'Since I was in the company of an intellectual, I would quote from Plato. According to him, at the beginning of creation, men and women were not as they are now; there was just one being, who was rather short, with a body and a neck, but his head had two faces, looking in different directions. It was as if two creatures had been glued back to back, with two sets of sex organs, four legs and four arms.

'The Greek gods, however, were jealous, because this creature with four arms could work harder; with its two faces, it was always vigilant and could not be taken by surprise; and its four legs meant that it could stand or walk for long periods at a time without tiring. Even more dangerous was the fact that the creature had two different sets of sex organs and so needed no one else in order to continue reproducing.

'Zeus, the supreme lord of Olympus, said: "I have a plan to make these mortals lose some of their strength."

'And he cut the creature in two with a lightning bolt, thus creating man and woman. This greatly increased the population of the world, and, at the same time, disoriented and weakened its inhabitants, because now they had to search for their lost half and embrace it and, in that embrace, regain their former strength, their ability to avoid betrayal and the stamina to walk for long periods of time and to withstand hard work. That embrace in which the two bodies re-fuse to become one again is what we call sex.'

'Is that a true story?'

'According to the Greek philosopher, Plato, yes.'

Maria was gazing at him, fascinated, and the experience of the previous night had vanished completely. She saw that the man before her was full of the same 'light' that he had seen in her, entirely involved in telling her that strange story, his eyes alight now not with desire but with joy.

'Can I ask you a favour?'

Ralf said she could ask anything she wanted.

'Is it possible to know why, after the gods had split the four-legged creature in two, some of them decided that the embrace could be merely a thing, just another business transaction, which instead of increasing people's energy, diminished it?'

'You mean prostitution?'

'Yes. Could you find out if, in the beginning, sex was something sacred?'

'If you like,' replied Ralf, 'although it's not something I've ever thought about, nor, as far as I know, has anyone else. Perhaps there isn't any literature on the subject.'

Maria could stand the pressure no longer:

'Has it ever occurred to you that women, in particular, prostitutes, are capable of love?'

'Yes, it has. It occurred to me on that first day, when we were sitting in the café and I saw your light. Then, when I decided to offer you a cup of coffee, I chose to believe in everything, even in the possibility of you returning me to the world I left a long, long time ago.'

There was no going back now. Maria, the teacher, needed to rush to her own aid, otherwise she would kiss him, embrace him and ask him never to leave her.

'Let's go back to the train station,' she said. 'Or, rather, let's come back to this room, to the day when we sat here together for the first time and you recognised that I existed and gave me a gift. That was your first attempt to enter my soul, and you weren't sure whether or not you were welcome. But, as you say in your story, human beings were once divided and now seek the embrace that will reunite them. That is our instinct. But it is also our reason for putting up with all the difficulties we meet in that search.

'I want you to look at me, but I want you to take care that I don't notice. Initial desire is important because it is hidden, forbidden, not permitted. You don't know whether you are looking at your lost half or not; she doesn't know either, but something is drawing you together, and you must believe that it is true you are each other's "other half".'

Where am I getting all this? I'm drawing it up from the bottom of my heart, because this is how I always wanted it to be. I'm drawing up these dreams from my own dream as a woman.

She slipped off the shoulder strap of her dress, so that one part, one tiny part of one nipple was exposed.

'Desire is not what you see, but what you imagine.'

Ralf Hart was looking at a woman with dark hair and wearing dark clothes, who was sitting on the floor of his living room, and was full of absurd desires, like having an open fire burning in the middle of summer. Yes, he would like to imagine what those clothes were hiding; he could guess the size of her breasts, and he knew that she didn't really need the bra she was wearing, although perhaps she had to wear it for her work. Her breasts were neither large nor small, they were simply young. Her eyes gave nothing away; what was she doing here? Why was he encouraging this absurd, dangerous relationship, when he had no problems finding women? He was rich, young, famous, good-looking. He loved his work; he had loved women whom he had subsequently married; he had been loved. He was someone who, according to all the rules and norms, should have been able to shout out loud: 'I'm happy.'

But he wasn't. While most of humanity was scrabbling for a piece of bread, a roof over their head and a job that would allow them to live with dignity, Ralf Hart had all of that, and it only made him feel more wretched. If he looked back on what his life had been lately, he had perhaps managed two or three days when he had woken up, looked at the sun – or the rain – and felt glad to see the morning, just happy, without wanting anything, planning anything or asking anything in exchange. Apart from those few days, the rest of his existence had been wasted on dreams, both frustrated and realised – a desire to go beyond himself, to go beyond his limitations; he had spent his life trying to prove something, but he didn't know what or to whom.

He looked at the beautiful woman before him, who was discreetly dressed in black, someone he had met by chance, although he had seen her before at the nightclub and thought that she seemed out of place. She had asked him to desire her, and he desired her intensely, far more than she could imagine, but it wasn't her breasts or her body, it was her company he desired. He wanted to put his arms around her and to sit in silence, staring into the fire, drinking wine, smoking the occasional cigarette; that would be enough. Life was made up of simple things; he was weary of all the years he had spent searching for something, though quite what he didn't know.

And yet, if he did that, if he touched her, all would be lost. For, despite the 'light' he could see in Maria, he wasn't sure she realised how good it was for him to be by her side. Was he paying? Yes, and he would continue paying for as long as it took to win her, to sit with her by the lakeside and speak of love, and to hear her say the same thing. It was best not to take any chances, not to rush things, not to say anything.

Ralf Hart stopped tormenting himself and concentrated once more on the game they had just created together. The woman before him was right; the wine, the fire, the cigarettes and the company were not enough in themselves; another kind of intoxication, another kind of flame was required.

She was wearing a dress with shoulder straps; she was revealing one breast; he could see her skin, more dark than pale. He desired her. He desired her intensely.

Maria noticed the change in Ralf's eyes. Knowing that she was desired excited her more than anything else. It had nothing to do with the automatic formula – I want to make love with you, I want to get married, I want you to have an orgasm, I want you to have my child, I want commitment. No, desire was an entirely free sensation, loose in the air, vibrating, filling life with the will to have something – and that was enough, that will carried all before it, moved mountains, made her wet.

Desire was the source of everything else – leaving her country, discovering a new world, learning French, overcoming her prejudices, dreaming of having a farm, loving without asking for anything in return, feeling that she was a woman simply because a man was looking at her. With calculated slowness, she slipped off the other strap, and the dress slid down her body. Then she undid her bra. There she was, with the upper part of her body completely bare, wondering if he would leap on her, touch her, utter vows of love, or if he was sensitive enough simply to feel sexual pleasure in desire itself.

Things around them began to change, all sound disappeared, the fire, the paintings and the books gradually vanished, to be replaced by a kind of trance-like state, in which only the object of desire exists, and nothing else is important.

The man did not move. At first, she felt a certain shyness in his eyes, but that did not last long. He was looking at her, and in the world of his imagination, he was caressing her with his tongue, they were making love, sweating, clinging to each other, mingling tenderness and violence, calling out and moaning together.

In the real world, though, they said nothing, neither of them moved, and that made her even more excited, because she too was free to think what she liked. She was asking him to touch her gently, she was opening her legs, she was masturbating in front of him, saying the most romantic things and the lewdest things, as if they were one and the same; she had several orgasms, waking the neighbours, waking the whole world with her cries. Here was her man, who was giving her pleasure and joy, with whom she could be the person she really was, with whom she could talk about her sexual problems, and tell him how much she would like to stay with him for the rest of the night, for the rest of the week, for the rest of her life.

Beads of sweat began to appear on their foreheads. It was the heat from the fire, one said mentally to the other. But both the man and the woman in that room had reached their limit, exhausted their imagination, experienced together an eternity of good moments. They needed to stop, because if they took one more step, the magic would be undone by reality.

Very slowly, because endings are always more difficult than beginnings, she put on her bra and hid her breasts. The universe returned to its normal place, the things around them re-emerged, she pulled up the dress that had fallen about her waist, smiled and very gently touched his face. He took her hand and pressed it to his cheek, not knowing for how long he should hold it there, or how tightly.

She wanted to tell him that she loved him. But that would spoil everything, it might frighten him or, worse, might make him say that he loved her too. Maria didn't want that: the freedom of her love depended on asking nothing and expecting nothing.

'Anyone capable of feeling knows that it is possible to experience pleasure before even touching the other person. The words, the looks, all contain the secret of the dance. But the train has arrived, we each go our separate ways. I hope to be able to join you on this journey to … where?'

'Back to Geneva,' replied Ralf.

'Anyone who is observant, who discovers the person they have always dreamed of, knows that sexual energy comes into play before sex even takes place. The greatest pleasure isn't sex, but the passion with which it is practised. When the passion is intense, then sex joins in to complete the dance, but it is never the principal aim.'

'You're talking about love like a teacher.'

Maria went on talking, because this was her defence, her way of saying everything without committing herself to anything.

'Anyone who is in love is making love the whole time, even when they're not. When two bodies meet, it is just the cup overflowing. They can stay together for hours, even days. They begin the dance one day and finish it the next, or – such is the pleasure they experience – they may never finish it. No eleven minutes for them.'

'What?'

'I love you.'

'I love you too.'

'I'm sorry, I don't know what I'm saying.'

'Nor do I.'

She got up, kissed him and left. This time she opened the front door herself, since, according to the Brazilian superstition, the owner of the house only has to open the door on the first occasion that a guest leaves.

From Maria's diary, written the next morning:

Last night, when Ralf Hart looked at me, he opened a door, as if he were a thief; but when he left, he took nothing from me, on the contrary, he left behind him the scent of roses – he wasn't a thief, he was a bridegroom visiting me.

Every human being experiences his or her own desire; it is part of our personal treasure and, although, as an emotion, it can drive people away, generally speaking, it brings those who are important to us closer. It is an emotion chosen by my soul, and it is so intense that it can infect everything and everyone around me.

Each day I choose the truth by which I try to live. I try to be practical, efficient, professional. But I would like to be able always to choose desire as my companion. Not out of obligation, not to lessen my loneliness, but because it is good. Yes, very good.

On average, thirty-eight women worked at the Copacabana on a regular basis, but only one of them, the Filipino, Nyah, was what Maria would consider a friend. Women stayed there an average of six months minimum and three years maximum, because they would either get a proposal of marriage, be set up as a mistress, or no longer pull in the clients, in which case, Milan would delicately ask them to find somewhere else to work.

That is why it was important to respect each other's clientele and never try to seduce men who always headed for a particular girl as soon as they came in. Apart from being dishonest, it could also be very dangerous. The previous week, a Colombian woman had quietly taken a cut-throat razor out of her pocket, placed it on the glass being used by one of the Yugoslav girls, and said, in the calmest of voices, that she would mark her face if she persisted in giving in to the advances of a certain bank manager who was a regular customer. The Yugoslav said that the man was a free agent and that, if he chose her, she couldn't really say no.

That night, the man came in, greeted the Colombian woman, but went over to the Yugoslav's table. They had a drink, danced and the Yugoslav winked at the Colombian (a provocation too far in Maria's view), as if saying: 'See? He chose me!'

But that wink contained many unspoken things: he chose me because I'm prettier, because I went with him last week and he enjoyed it, because I'm young. The Colombian said nothing. When the Yugoslav came back, two hours later, the Colombian sat down beside her, took the razor out of her pocket and made a cut on the Yugoslav's face, near her ear. It wasn't a deep cut, and it wasn't dangerous, but it was enough to leave a small scar to remind her of that night. The two started fighting, blood spurted everywhere and the frightened customers fled.

When the police arrived, wanting to know what was going on, the Yugoslav said that she had cut her face on a glass that had fallen from a shelf (there are no shelves in the Copacabana). This was the law of silence, or what Italian prostitutes like to call *omertà*: any problem to be resolved in Rue de Berne, from love to death, would be resolved, but without the interference of the law. They made their own laws there.

The police knew about the *omertà* and could see that the woman was lying, but they didn't insist – arresting someone, trying them and then keeping them in prison would cost the Swiss taxpayer far too much money. Milan thanked the police for their prompt response, but, he said, it was all a misunderstanding or else a rival nightclub owner trying to make trouble.

As soon as they left, he asked the two women not to come back to his club. After all, the Copacabana was a family place (a statement Maria found hard to grasp) and had a reputation to keep up (this left her still more intrigued). There were no fights there, because the first law was to respect another woman's client.

The second law was total discretion, 'just like a Swiss bank', he said. This was largely because, there, the women could trust the clients, who were selected much as a bank selects its clients, based on the state of their current account and on personal references. Mistakes were occasionally made; there were a few rare cases of non-payment, of girls being threatened or roughed up, but in the many years he had spent struggling to create and develop his club's reputation, Milan had become an expert at recognising who should or shouldn't be invited in. None of the women knew exactly what these criteria were, but they had often seen some well-dressed man being told that the club was full that night (even though it was empty) and that it would be full the following nights too (i.e. please don't come back). They had also seen unshaven men dressed in casual clothes being enthusiastically invited by Milan to a glass of champagne. The owner of the Copacabana did not judge by appearances, and he was always right.

It was a good working relationship, and seemed to suit all parties involved. The great majority of the clientele were married, or held important positions in some company or other. Some of the women who worked there were also married and had children and went to parents' evenings at their children's schools, but knew that they ran no risk of being exposed; if one of the other parents turned up at the Copacabana, they would be compromised too and so could say nothing: that is how *omertà* worked.

There was comradeship amongst the women, but not friendship; no one talked much about their lives. In the few conversations she had had, Maria found no bitterness, guilt or sadness amongst her colleagues, only a kind of resignation, and a strangely defiant glint in the eye, as if they were proud of the way they confronted the world, independently and confidently. After a week, any new arrival was considered a 'fellow professional' and received instructions always to help keep marriages intact (a prostitute cannot be seen as a threat to the stability of the home), never to accept invitations to meet outside working hours, to listen to confessions without offering an opinion, to moan at the moment of climax (Maria learned that everyone did this, but that they hadn't told her on her very first day because it was one of the tricks of the trade), to say hello to the police in the street, to keep her work permit up to date as well as any health checks, and, finally, not to probe too deeply into the moral or legal aspects of what she was doing; they were what they were, and that was that.

Before it got busy, Maria could always be seen with a book in her hand, and she soon became known as the intellectual of the group. At first, they wanted to know if she was reading a love story, but when they saw that the books were about dry-as-dust subjects like economics, psychology and – recently – farm management, they left her alone to continue her researches and her note-taking in peace.

Because she had a lot of regular clients and because she went to the Copacabana every night, even when it wasn't busy, Maria earned both Milan's confidence and her colleagues' envy; they said she was ambitious, arrogant and thought only about earning money – the last bit was true, but she felt like asking if they weren't all there for the very same reason.

Anyway, remarks like that never killed anyone – they were part of the life of any successful person, and it was best to get used to them, rather than let herself be diverted from her two goals: going back to Brazil on the chosen date and buying a farm.

Ralf Hart was in her thoughts from morning to night now, and for the first time she was able to feel happy with an absent love – although she slightly regretted having confessed her love, thus running the risk of losing everything. But what had she got to lose, if she was asking for nothing in exchange? She remembered how her heart had beat faster when Milan mentioned that Ralf was – or had been – a special client. What did that mean? She felt betrayed and jealous.

It was normal to feel jealous, although life had taught her that it was pointless thinking you could own another person – anyone who believes that is just deceiving themselves. Despite this, she could not stop herself having these feelings of jealousy, or of having grand intellectual thoughts about it, or even thinking it was a proof of fragility.

'The strongest love is the love that can demonstrate its fragility. Anyway, if my love is real (and not just a way of distracting myself, deceiving myself, and passing the time that never seems to pass in this city), freedom will conquer jealousy and any pain it causes me, since pain is also part of the natural process. Anyone who practises sport knows this: if you want to achieve your objectives, you have to be prepared for a daily dose of pain or discomfort. At first, it's unpleasant and demotivating, but in time you come to realise that it's part of the process of feeling good, and the moment arrives when, if you don't feel pain, you have a sense that the exercises aren't having the desired effect.'

The danger lies in focusing on that pain, giving it a particular person's name, and keeping it always present in your thoughts. Maria, thank God, had managed to free herself from that.

Even so, she sometimes found herself wondering where he was, why he didn't come and see her, if he had found that whole story about the train station and repressed desire stupid, if he had gone away forever because she had confessed her love for him.

To avoid beautiful thoughts turning into suffering, she developed a method: when something positive to do with Ralf Hart came into her head – and this could be the fire and the wine, an idea she would like to discuss with him, or simply the pleasurable longing involved in wanting to know when he would come back – Maria would stop what she was doing, smile up at the sky and give thanks for being alive and to be expecting nothing from the man she loved.

On the other hand, if her heart began to complain about his absence or about things she shouldn't have said while they were together, she would say to herself:

'Oh, so you want to think about that, do you? All right, then, you do what you like, while I get on with more important things.'

She would continue to read or, if she was out, she would focus her attention on everything around her: colours, people, sounds – especially sounds, the sound of her own footsteps, of the pages turning, of cars, of fragments of conversations, and the unfortunate thought would eventually go away. If it came back five minutes later, she would repeat the process, until those thoughts, finding themselves accepted but also gently rejected, would stay away for quite considerable periods of time.

One of these 'negative thoughts' was the possibility of never seeing him again. With a little practice and a great deal of patience, she managed to transform this into a 'positive thought': when she left, Geneva would have the face of a man with old-fashioned long hair, a child-like smile and a grave voice. If someone asked her, many years later, what the place she had known in her youth was like, she could reply:

'Very beautiful, and capable of loving and being loved.'

From Maria's diary, on a slack night at the Copacabana:

After all the time I've spent with the people who come here, I have reached the conclusion that sex has come to be used as some kind of drug: in order to escape reality, to forget about problems, to relax. And like all drugs, this is a harmful and destructive practice.

If a person wants to take drugs, in the form of sex or whatever, that's their problem; the consequences of their actions will be better or worse depending on the choices they make. But if we are talking in terms of making progress in life, we must understand that 'good enough' is very different from 'best'.

Contrary to what my clients think, sex cannot be practised at any time. We all have a clock inside us, and in order to make love, the hands on both clocks have to be pointing to the same hour at the same time. That doesn't happen every day. If you love another person, you don't depend on the sex act in order to feel good. Two people who live together and love each other need to adjust the hands of their clocks, with patience and perseverance, games and 'theatrical representations', until they realise that making love is more than just an encounter, it is a genital 'embrace'.

Everything is important. If you live your life intensely, you experience pleasure all the time and don't feel the need for sex. When you have sex, it's out of a sense of abundance, because the glass of wine is so full that it overflows naturally, because it is inevitable, because you are responding to the call of life, because at that moment, and only at that moment, you have allowed yourself to lose control.

P.S. I have just re-read what I wrote. Good grief! I'm getting way too intellectual!

Shortly after writing this, and when she was preparing for another night as Understanding Mother or Innocent Girl, the door of the Copacabana opened and in walked Terence, the record company executive, one of the special clients.

Behind the bar, Milan seemed pleased: Maria had not disappointed him. Maria remembered the words that simultaneously said so much and so little: 'pain, suffering, and a great deal of pleasure'.

'I flew in from London especially to see you. I've been thinking about you a lot.'

She smiled, trying not to look too encouraging. Again he had failed to follow the ritual and hadn't asked if she wanted a drink, but just sat down at her table.

'When a teacher helps someone to discover something, the teacher always learns something new too.'

'I know what you mean,' said Maria, thinking of Ralf Hart and feeling irritated with herself for doing so. She was with another client, and she must respect him and do what she could to please him.

'Do you want to go ahead?'

A thousand francs. A hidden universe. Her boss watching her. The certainty that she could stop whenever she chose. The date set for her return to Brazil. The other man, who never came to see her.

'Are you in a hurry?' Maria asked.

He said no. What was it she wanted?

'I'd like my usual drink and my usual dance, and some respect for my profession.'

He hesitated for a moment, but it was all part of the theatre, dominating and being dominated. He bought her a drink and danced with her, then ordered a taxi and gave her the money while they drove across the city to the same hotel. They went in, he greeted the Italian porter just as he had on the night they first met, and they went up to the same suite with a view over the river.

Terence got up and took out his lighter, and only then did Maria notice that there were dozens of candles arranged around the room. He started lighting them.

'What would you like to know? Why I'm like this? Because, unless I'm very much mistaken, you really enjoyed the other evening we spent together. Do you want to know why you're like this too?'

'I was just thinking that in Brazil we have a superstition that you should never light more than three things with the same match. You're not respecting that superstition.'

He ignored her remark.

'You're like me. You're not here for the thousand francs, but out of a sense of guilt and dependency, because of your various complexes and insecurities. That is neither good nor bad, it's simply human nature.'

He picked up the remote control and changed channels several times until he found the TV news and a report on refugees trying to escape a war.

'Do you see that? Have you ever seen those programmes in which people discuss their personal problems in front of everyone? Have you been to a newspaper kiosk and seen the headlines? The world enjoys suffering and pain. There's sadism in the way we look at these things, and masochism in our conclusion that we don't need to know all this in order to be happy, and yet we watch other people's tragedies and sometimes suffer along with them.'

He poured out two glasses of champagne, turned off the television and continued lighting candles, in contravention of the superstition Maria had mentioned.

'As I say, it's the human condition. Ever since we were expelled from paradise, we have either been suffering, making other people suffer or watching the suffering of others. It's beyond our control.'

From outside came the sound of thunder and lightning; a huge storm was approaching.

'But I can't do it,' Maria said. 'It seems ridiculous to me pretending that you're my master and I'm your slave. We don't need "theatre" to find suffering; life offers us more than enough opportunities.'

Terence had just finished lighting the candles. He picked one up and placed it in the middle of the table, then served more champagne, and caviar. Maria was drinking quickly, thinking about the one thousand francs in her bag, about this stranger who both fascinated and frightened her, and about how she could control her fear. She knew that, with this man, no night would ever be the same as another; she could not intimidate him in any way.

'Sit down.'

His voice alternated between being gentle and authoritarian. Maria obeyed, and a wave of heat swept up her body; that order was familiar, she felt more secure.

'It's theatre. I've got to get involved in the play.'

It was nice being ordered around. She didn't have to think, just obey. She asked for more champagne, and he brought vodka; it went to one's head more quickly, loosened one up, and went better with the caviar.

He opened the bottle; Maria was more or less drinking alone, while she listened to the thunder and lightning outside. Everything was conspiring to make the moment perfect, as if the energies of the skies and the earth were also showing their violent side.

After a while, Terence took a small suitcase out of the wardrobe and placed it on the bed.

'Don't move.'

Maria sat motionless. He opened the suitcase and took out two pairs of chrome metal handcuffs.

'Sit with your legs apart.'

She obeyed – impotent out of choice, submissive because she wanted to be. She saw him looking between her legs, he could see her black pants, her long stockings, her thighs, he could imagine her pubic hair, her sex.

'Stand up!'

She leaped up from her chair. She found it hard to stand straight and realised that she was drunker than she thought.

'Don't look at me. Lower your head, respect your master!'

Before she could lower her head, she saw a slender whip being removed from the suitcase, then cracking through the air, as if it had a life of its own.

'Drink. Keep your head down, but drink.'

She drank another one, two, three glasses of vodka. This wasn't just theatre now, it was reality: control was out of her hands. She felt like an object, a mere instrument, and incredible though it may seem, that feeling of submission gave her a sense of complete freedom. She was no longer the teacher, the one who instructs, consoles, listens to confessions, the one who excites; before the awesome power of this man, she was just a girl from the interior of Brazil.

'Take off your clothes.'

The order was delivered abruptly, without a flicker of desire, and yet, nothing could have been more erotic. Keeping her head down as a sign of reverence, Maria unbuttoned her dress and let it slip to the floor.

'You're not behaving yourself, you know.'

Again the whip cracked through the air.

'You need to be punished. How dare a girl your age contradict me? You should be on your knees before me!'

Maria made as if to kneel down, but the whip brought her up short; for the first time it touched her flesh – her buttocks. It stung, but seemed to leave no mark.

'Did I tell you to kneel down?'

'No.'

The whip again flicked across her buttocks.

'Say, "No, sir!"'

Another stinging whiplash. For a fraction of a second, it occurred to her that she could either stop this right now or else choose to go through with it, not for the money, but because of what he had said the first time – that you only know yourself when you go beyond your limits.

And this was new, it was an Adventure, and she could decide later on if she wanted to continue, but at that moment, she had ceased to be the girl with just three aims in life, who earned her living with her body, who had met a man who had an open fire and interesting stories to tell. Here, she was no one, and being no one meant that she could be everything she had ever dreamed of.

'Take the rest of your clothes off. And walk up and down so that I can see you.'

Once more she obeyed, keeping her head down, saying not a word. The man who was watching her, still fully dressed and utterly impassive, was not the same person who had chatted to her on their way here from the club – he was a Ulysses who had travelled from London, a Theseus come down from the heavens, a kidnapper invading the safest city in the world, and who had the coldest heart on earth. She removed her pants and her bra, feeling at once defenceless and protected. The whip cracked again, this time without touching her body.

'Keep your head down! You're here to be humiliated, to submit to my every desire, do you understand?'

'Yes, sir.'

He grabbed her arms and put the first pair of handcuffs on her wrists.

'You're going to get a good beating. Until you learn to behave yourself.'

He slapped her bottom with the flat of his hand. Maria cried out; this time it had hurt.

'Oh, so you're complaining, are you? Well, I haven't even started yet.'

Before she could do anything, he had placed a leather gag on her mouth. It didn't stop her speaking, she could still say 'yellow' or 'red', but she felt now that it was her destiny to allow this man to do whatever he wished with her, and there was no way she could escape now. She was naked, gagged and handcuffed, with vodka flowing in her veins rather than blood.

Another slap on her buttocks.

'Walk up and down!'

Maria started to walk, obeying his commands: 'stop', 'turn to the right', 'sit down', 'open your legs'. He slapped her again and again, whether she deserved it or not, and she felt the pain and felt the humiliation – which was more intense and more potent than the pain – and she felt as if she were in another world, in which nothing existed, and it was an almost religious feeling: self-annihilation, subjection, and a complete loss of any sense of Ego, desire or self-will. She was very wet and very aroused, but unable to understand what was going on.

'Down on your knees again!'

Since she always kept her head down, as a sign of obedience and humiliation, Maria could not see exactly what was happening, but she noticed that in that other universe, on that other planet, the man was breathing hard, worn out with wielding the whip and spanking her hard on the buttocks, whilst she felt herself filling up with strength and energy. She had lost all shame now, and wasn't bothered about showing her pleasure; she started to moan, pleading with him to touch her, but, instead, the man grabbed her and threw her onto the bed.

He violently forced her legs apart – although she knew this violence would not actually harm her – and tied each leg to one corner of the bed. Now that her wrists were handcuffed behind her, her legs splayed, her mouth gagged, when would he penetrate her? Couldn't he see that she was ready, that she wanted to serve him, that she was his slave, his creature, his object, and would do anything he ordered her to do?

'Would you like me to take you further still?'

She saw him place the end of the whip handle against her vagina. He rubbed it up and down, and when it touched her clitoris, she lost all control. She had no idea how long they had been there nor how many times she had been spanked, but suddenly she came and had the orgasm which, in all those months, dozens, no, hundreds of men had failed to give her. There was a burst of light, she felt herself entering a kind of black hole in her soul, in which intense pain and fear mingled with total pleasure, pushing her beyond all previously known limits and she moaned and screamed, her voice muffled by the gag, she writhed about on the bed, feeling the handcuffs cutting into her wrists and the leather thongs bruising her ankles, she moved as never before precisely because she could not move, she screamed as never before because she had a gag on her mouth and no one would be able to hear her. This was pain and pleasure, the end of the whip handle pressing ever harder against her clitoris and the orgasm flooding out of her mouth, her vagina, her pores, her eyes, her skin.

She entered a kind of trance, and slowly, very slowly, she began to come down; there was no whip pressing between her legs now, just sweat-drenched hair, kind hands removing the handcuffs, untying the leather thongs around her ankles.

She lay there, confused, unable to look at the man because she was ashamed of herself, of her screams, of her orgasm. He was stroking her hair and he too was breathing hard, but the pleasure had been entirely hers; he had not enjoyed a single moment of ecstasy.

Her naked body embraced that of this fully clothed man, who was exhausted from shouting orders and keeping tight control of the situation. She didn't know what to say, how to continue, but she felt safe and protected, because he had invited her to go to a place inside herself that she had never known before; he was her protector and her master.

She started to cry, and he waited patiently until she had finished.

'What did you do to me?' she asked tearfully.

'What you wanted me to do.'

She looked at him, feeling that she needed him desperately.

'I didn't force you or oblige you to do anything, nor did I hear you say "yellow"; I had only the power you gave me. There was no obligation, no blackmail on my part, only your will; you may have been the slave and I the master, but my only power was to push you in the direction of your own freedom.'

Handcuffs. Leather thongs around her ankles. A gag. Humiliation that was more intense and more potent than any pain. And yet – he was quite right – the feeling was one of total freedom. Maria felt full of energy and vigour and was surprised to see that the man beside her was utterly exhausted.

'Did you come?'

'No,' he said. 'The master is here to drive the slave on. The pleasure of the slave is the joy of the master.'

None of this made sense, because it wasn't the way it was in stories, it wasn't the way it was in real life. But here in this fantasy world, she was full of light, while he seemed opaque, drained.

'You can leave whenever you want,' Terence said.

'I don't want to leave, I want to understand.'

'There's nothing to understand.'

She got up in all the beauty and intensity of her nakedness and poured two glasses of wine. She lit two cigarettes and gave him one of them – the roles were reversed, she was now the mistress serving the slave, rewarding him for the pleasure he had given her.

'I'll get dressed and then I'll leave, but, first, I'd like to talk a little.'

'There's nothing to talk about. That's all I wanted, and you were marvellous. I'm tired now and I have to go back to London tomorrow.'

He lay down and closed his eyes. Maria didn't know if he was just pretending to sleep and she didn't care; she smoked a leisurely cigarette and slowly sipped her wine, with her face pressed against the window pane, looking out at the lake opposite and wishing that someone, on the other shore, could see her like this – naked, replete, satisfied, confident.

She got dressed and left without saying goodbye, and was not bothered whether she opened the door or he did, because she wasn't sure that she wanted to come back.

Terence heard the door close, waited to see if she would come back, saying that she had forgotten something, and only after a few minutes did he get up and light another cigarette.

The girl had style, he thought. She had withstood the whip well, although this was the oldest, the most common and the least severe of the punishments. For a moment, he sat remembering the first time he had experienced that mysterious relationship between two beings who want to be close, but can only be so by inflicting suffering.

Millions of couples out there practised the art of sadomasochism every day, without even realising it. They went to work, came back, complained about everything, insulted their wife or were insulted by her, felt wretched, but were, nonetheless, tightly bound to their own unhappiness, not realising that all it would take was a single gesture, a final goodbye, to free them from that oppression. Terence had experienced this with his wife, a well-known English singer; he was tormented by jealousy, he made scenes, and spent whole days dosed up with painkillers, whole nights hopelessly drunk. She loved him and couldn't understand why he behaved like that; he loved her and couldn't understand his own behaviour. It was as if the agony that the one inflicted on the other was necessary, fundamental to life.

One day, a musician – whom he had always thought of as very strange, because he seemed so normal in the midst of all those exotic people – left a book behind in the studio: *Venus in Furs* by Leopold von Sacher-Masoch. Terence started leafing through it and, as he read, he began to understand himself better.

'The lovely woman took off her clothes and picked up a long, short-handled whip. "You asked for it," she said, "so I'm going to whip you." "Oh, yes," murmured her lover, "please, I beg you."'

His wife was on the other side of the glass screen, rehearsing. She had asked them to turn off the microphones that allowed the technicians to listen in to everything, and they had done so. Terence was thinking that perhaps she was making a date with the pianist, and he realised that she was driving him mad, but it was as if he was so accustomed to suffering now that he could not live without it.

'I'm going to whip you,' said the naked woman in the book he was reading. 'Oh, yes, please, I beg you.'

He was a good-looking man, and a force to be reckoned with in the record company, why did he need to lead such a life?

Because he wanted to. He deserved to suffer because life had been so good to him, and he wasn't worthy of all these blessings – money, respect, fame. He felt that his career was leading him to a point where he would become dependent on success, and that frightened him, because he had seen a lot of people plummet from the heights.

He read the book. He started reading everything he could find about the mysterious union between pain and pleasure. His wife found the videos he was renting and the books he was hiding from her, and asked him what it was all about, was he sick? Terence said no, it was just research he was doing for a new cover. Then he said nonchalantly:

'Perhaps we should try it.'

They did. They began very timidly, using the manuals they found in porn shops. Gradually, they developed new techniques, took their activities to dangerous limits, and yet they felt that their marriage was even stronger. They were accomplices in something hidden, forbidden, proscribed.

Their joint experience was transformed into art: they created new outfits – leather with metal studs. His wife went on stage wearing boots and a suspender belt and wielding a whip, and the audience went wild. Her new record shot to the top of the charts in England and went on to triumph in the rest of Europe. Terence was surprised how young people accepted his personal fantasies as perfectly natural, and the only explanation he could find was that it provided a means of expressing repressed violence in an intense but inoffensive manner.

The whip came to be the group's logo and was reproduced on T-shirts, fake tattoos, stickers and postcards. Terence's intellectual bent drove him to track down the origins of all this, so that he could understand himself better.

These origins did not lie, as he had told Maria, with those penitents trying to drive away the Black Death. Ever since the Dark Ages, man has understood that suffering, if confronted without fear, is his passport to freedom.

Egypt, Rome and Persia all shared the notion that a man can save his country and his world by sacrificing himself. Whenever there was a great natural disaster in China, the emperor was punished, because he was the divinity's Earthly representative. In ancient Greece, the finest Spartan warriors were whipped once a year, from morning till night, in homage to the goddess Artemis, while the crowd urged them on, calling on them to withstand the pain with dignity, for it was preparing them for the world of war. At the end of the day, the priests would examine the wounds on the warriors' backs and use them to predict the city's future.

The priests of the desert, in an ancient, fourth-century Christian community that grew up around a monastery in Alexandria, used flagellation as a way of driving out demons or of proving the futility of the body in the spiritual search. The history of saints was full of similar examples – St Rosa running through the garden, letting the thorns tear her skin, St Domingos Loricatus whipping himself every night before sleeping, the martyrs who voluntarily offered themselves up to a slow death on the cross or being torn apart by wild animals. They all said that pain, once mastered, could lead to religious ecstasy.

Recent, unconfirmed studies indicated that a particular kind of fungus with hallucinogenic properties grew in the wounds and caused visions. The pleasure was so intense that the practice soon left the monasteries and convents and spread throughout the world.

In 1718, *A Treatise on Self-flagellation* was published, which showed how to achieve pleasure through pain, but without harming the body. At the end of that century, there were dozens of places in Europe where people were prepared to suffer in order to attain joy. There are records of kings and princesses who had their slaves whip them, until they found that another kind of pleasure – albeit more exhausting and less gratifying – was to be found not only in being whipped, but also in inflicting pain.

While he was smoking his cigarette, Terence took a certain pleasurable pride in knowing that most people would be unable to understand what he was thinking.

It was better to belong to an exclusive club to which only the chosen had access. He remembered again how the torment of marriage had been transformed into the miracle of marriage. His wife knew that he visited Geneva for this purpose and she didn't mind; on the contrary, in this sick world, she was glad that her husband got the reward he wanted after a hard week at work.

The girl who had just left the room had understood everything. He felt that his soul was very close to hers, although he wasn't yet ready to fall in love, for he loved his wife. But he liked to think that he was free and could dream of a new relationship.

All he had to do was to get her to attempt the next and most difficult stage: the transformation into Sacher-Masoch's 'Venus in Furs', the Dominatrix, the Mistress, capable of humiliating and punishing without pity. If she passed the test, he was ready to open his heart and let her in.

From Maria's diary, when she was still drunk on vodka and pleasure:

When I had nothing to lose, I had everything. When I stopped being who I am, I found myself.

When I experienced humiliation and total submission, I was free. I don't know if I'm ill, if it was all a dream, or if it only happens once. I know that I can perfectly well live without it, but I would like to do it again, to repeat the experience, to go still further.

I was a bit frightened by the pain, but it wasn't as bad as the humiliation, and it was just a pretext. When I had my first orgasm in many months, despite all the many men I've been with and the many different things they've done with my body, I felt – is this possible? – closer to God. I remembered what he said about how the flagellants, in offering up their pain for the salvation of humanity, found pleasure. I didn't want to save humanity, or him or me; I was just there.

The art of sex is the art of controlled abandon.

It wasn't theatre this time, they were in a real train station, at Maria's request, because she liked the pizza you could buy there. There was nothing wrong with being a bit wayward sometimes. Ralf ought to have come to see her the day before, when she was still a woman in search of love, an open fire, wine and desire. But life had chosen otherwise, and today she had got through the whole day without once having to make herself concentrate on the sounds around her or on the present moment, simply because she hadn't thought about Ralf; she had discovered other more interesting things to think about.

What was she to do with this man beside her, who was eating a pizza he probably didn't like and who was just passing the time until the moment came for them to go to his house? When he had come into the club and offered her a drink, she had thought of telling him that she wasn't interested any more and that he should find someone else; on the other hand, she had an enormous need to talk to someone about the previous night.

She had tried talking to one or two of the other prostitutes who served the 'special clients', but none of them would tell her anything, because Maria was bright, she learned quickly and had become the great threat in the

Copacabana. Of all the men she knew, Ralf Hart was the only one who would understand, because Milan considered him too to be a 'special client'. But he looked at her with eyes alight with love, and that made things difficult; it was best to say nothing.

'What do you know about pain, suffering and pleasure?'

She had once again failed to keep her thoughts to herself.

Ralf stopped eating his pizza.

'Everything. And it doesn't interest me in the least.'

The reply had been instant, and Maria was shocked. Was she the only person in the world who didn't know everything? What kind of world was this?

'I've confronted my demons and my dark side,' Ralf went on. 'I've been to the very depths and tried everything, not just in that area, but in many others too. On the last night we met, however, I went beyond my limits through desire, not pain. I plunged into the depths of my soul and I know that I still want good things, many good things from this life.'

He wanted to say: 'One of those good things is you, so, please, don't go down that path.' But he didn't have the courage; instead, he called a taxi and asked the driver to take them to the lake shore, where, an eternity before, they had walked together on the day they first met. Maria understood the request and said nothing; her instinct told her that she had a lot to lose, although her mind was still drunk on what had happened the night before.

She only awoke from her passive state when they reached the gardens beside the lake; although it was still summer, it was already starting to get very cold at night.

'What are we doing here?' she asked, as they got out of the taxi. 'It's windy. I might catch a cold.'

'I've been thinking about what you said at the train station, about suffering and pleasure. Take your shoes off.'

She remembered that once, one of her clients had asked the same thing, and had been aroused simply by looking at her feet. Would Adventure never leave her in peace?

'I'll catch a cold.'

'Do as I say,' he insisted. 'You won't catch a cold if we're quick. Believe in me, as I believe in you.'

For some reason, Maria realised that he was trying to help her; perhaps because he himself had once drunk of some very bitter water and was afraid that she was running the same risk. She didn't want to be helped; she was happy with her new world, in which she was learning that suffering wasn't a problem any more. Then she thought of Brazil, of the impossibility of finding a partner with whom to share that different universe, and since Brazil was the most important thing in her life, she took off her shoes. The ground was covered in small stones that immediately tore her stockings, but that didn't matter, she could buy some more.

'Take off your jacket.'

She could have said 'no', but, since last night, she had got used to the joy of saying 'yes' to everything that came her way. She took off her jacket, and her body, still warm, took a while to react, then gradually the cold began to get to her.

'We can talk and walk at the same time.'

'I can't walk here, the ground's covered in stones.'

'Exactly. I want you to feel these stones, I want them to hurt you and bruise you, because, just as I did, you have started to associate suffering with pleasure, and I need to tear that out of your soul.'

Maria felt like saying: 'There's no need, I like it.' Instead, she began walking slowly along, and the soles of her feet began to burn with the cold and the sharp edges of the stones.

'One of my exhibitions took me to Japan, just when I was immersed in what you called "pain, suffering and pleasure". At the time, I thought there was no way back, that I would go deeper and deeper down, until there was nothing left in my life but the desire to punish and be punished.

'After all, we are human beings, we are born full of guilt; we feel terrified when happiness becomes a real possibility; and we die wanting to punish everyone else because we feel impotent, ill-used and unhappy. To pay for one's sins and be able to punish the sinners, wouldn't that be delicious? Oh, yes, wonderful.'

Maria was still walking, the pain and the cold were making it hard for her to concentrate on what he was saying, but she was doing her best.

'I noticed the marks on your wrists today.'

The handcuffs. She had put on several bracelets to disguise the marks, but the expert eye knows what to look for.

'Now, if your recent experiences are leading you to take that step, I won't stop you, but you should know that none of it has anything to do with real life.'

'Take what step?'

'Into pain and pleasure, sadism and masochism. Call it what you like, but if you're sure that's the right path for you, I will be sad, I'll remember that feeling of desire, our meetings, our walk along the road to Santiago, your light. I will treasure the pen you gave me, and every time I light the fire, I will remember you. But I will never again come looking for you.'

Maria felt afraid; she felt it was time to recant, to tell him the truth, to stop pretending that she knew more than he did.

'What I experienced recently – last night, in fact – was something I've never experienced before. And it frightens me to think that I could only find myself at the very limits of degradation.'

It was becoming difficult to speak – her teeth were chattering and her feet were really hurting.

'My exhibition was held in a region called Kumano, and one of the people who came to see it was a woodcutter,' Ralf went on, as if he hadn't heard what she had said. 'He didn't like my pictures, but he was able to see, through the paintings, what I was experiencing and feeling. The following day, he came to my hotel and asked me if I was happy; if I was, I should continue doing what I liked. If I wasn't, I should go and spend a few days with him.

'He made me walk on stones, just as I am making you do today. He made me feel the cold. He forced me to understand the beauty of pain, except that the pain was imposed by nature, not by man. He called this *shu-gen-do*, a very ancient practice apparently.

'He told me that I was someone who wasn't afraid of pain, and that was good, because in order to master the soul, one must also learn to master the body. He told me, too, that I was using pain in the wrong way, and that was very bad.

'This uneducated woodcutter thought he knew me better than I did myself, and that annoyed me, but at the same time, I felt proud to think that my paintings were capable of expressing exactly what I was feeling.'

Maria was aware of a sharp stone cutting into her foot, but she could barely feel it for the cold, her body was growing numb, and she could only just follow what Ralf Hart was saying. Why was it that in God's holy world men were only interested in showing her pain. Sacred pain, pain with pleasure, pain with explanations or without, but always pain, pain, pain ...

Her cut foot stumbled on another stone; she smothered a cry and continued on. At first, she had managed to maintain her integrity, her self-control, what he called her 'light'. Now, though, she was walking very slowly, with both her stomach and her mind churning: she felt as if she were about to throw up. She considered stopping, because none of this made any sense, but she didn't.

And she didn't stop out of respect for herself; she could stand that barefoot walk as long as she had to, because it wouldn't last all her life. And suddenly another thought crossed her mind: what if she couldn't go to the Copacabana tomorrow night because she had injured her feet, or because of a fever brought on by the flu that would doubtless install itself in her overexposed body? She thought of the customers who would be expecting her, of Milan who so trusted her, of the money she wouldn't earn, of the farm, of her proud parents. But the suffering soon drove out all such thoughts, and she kept placing one foot in front of the other, longing for Ralf Hart to recognise the effort she was making and to tell her she could stop and put her shoes back on again.

He seemed entirely indifferent, distant, as if this were the only way of freeing her from something she didn't as yet really know about, something she found very seductive, but which would leave far deeper marks than any handcuffs. Although she knew he was trying to help her, and however hard she tried to go forward and show him the light of her willpower, the pain would not allow her any thoughts, noble or profane; it was just pain, filling everything, frightening her and forcing her to think that she did have limits and that she wasn't going to make it.

But she took one step.

And another.

The pain seemed about to invade her soul now and undermine her spiritually, because it's one thing to put on a bit of theatre in a five-star hotel, naked, with vodka and caviar inside you and a whip between your legs, but it's quite another to be cold and barefoot, with stones lacerating your feet. She was disoriented, she couldn't think of a single thing to say to Ralf Hart; all that existed in her universe were those small, sharp stones that formed the path between the trees.

Then, just when she thought she was about to give up, she was filled by a strange feeling: she had reached her limit, and beyond it was an empty space, in which she seemed to float above herself, unaware of what she was feeling. Was this what the penitents had experienced? At the far extremity of pain, she had discovered a door into a different level of consciousness, and there was no room now for anything but implacable nature and her own invincible self.

Everything around her became a dream: the ill-lit garden, the dark lake, the man walking beside her, saying nothing, the occasional couple out for a stroll, who failed to notice that she was barefoot and having difficulty walking. She didn't know if it was the cold or the pain, but she suddenly lost all sense of her own body and entered a state in which there was no desire and no fear, only a mysterious – how could she describe it? – a mysterious peace. The pain barrier was not a barrier for her; she could go beyond it.

She thought of all the people enduring unasked-for suffering and there she was, bringing suffering upon herself, but that didn't matter any more, she had crossed the frontiers of the body, and now there was only soul, 'light', a kind of void, which someone, some day, called Paradise. There are certain sufferings which can only be forgotten once we have succeeded in floating above our own pain.

The next thing she knew, Ralf was picking her up and putting his jacket around her shoulders. She must have fainted from the cold, but she didn't care; she was happy, she hadn't been afraid – she had come through. She had not humbled herself before him.

The minutes became hours, she must have gone to sleep in his arms, because when she woke up, although it was still dark, she was in a room with a TV in one corner, and nothing else. White, empty.

Ralf appeared with a cup of hot chocolate.

'Good,' he said. 'You got to the place you needed to get to.'

'I don't want hot chocolate, I want wine. And I want to go downstairs to our place by the fire, with books all around us.'

She had said 'our place'. That wasn't what she had planned.

She looked at her feet; apart from a small cut, there were just a few red marks, which would disappear in a few hours' time. With some difficulty, she went downstairs, without really looking around her. She went and sat down on the rug by the fire – she had discovered that she always felt good there, as if that really was her 'place' in the house.

'The woodcutter told me that whenever you do some form of physical exercise, when you demand the maximum from your body, the mind gains a strange spiritual strength, which has to do with the "light" I saw in you. What did you feel?'

'I felt that pain is woman's friend.'

'That is the danger.'

'I also felt that pain has its limits.'

'That is the salvation. Don't forget that.'

Maria's mind was still confused; she had experienced that 'peace' when she had gone beyond her own limits. He had shown her a different kind of suffering that had also given her a strange pleasure.

Ralf picked up a large file and opened it up in front of her. It contained drawings.

'The history of prostitution. That's what you asked me for when we met.'

Yes, she had, but it had only been a way of making conversation, of trying to appear interesting. It was of no importance now.

'All this time, I've been sailing in uncharted waters. I didn't think there was a history, I thought it was just the oldest profession in the world, as people say. But there is a history, or, rather, two histories.'

'And what are these drawings?'

Ralf Hart looked slightly disappointed at her apparent lack of interest in what he had said, but quickly set aside these feelings and went on.

'They're the things I jotted down as I was reading, researching, learning.'

'Let's talk about that another day. I don't want to change the subject today. I need to understand about pain.'

'You experienced pain yesterday and you discovered that it led to pleasure. You experienced it today and found peace. That's why I'm telling you: don't get used to it, because it's very easy to become habituated; it's a very powerful drug. It's in our daily lives, in our hidden suffering, in the sacrifices we make, blaming love for the destruction of our dreams. Pain is frightening when it shows its real face, but it's seductive when it comes disguised as sacrifice or self-denial. Or cowardice. However much we may reject it, we human beings always find a way of being with pain, of flirting with it and making it part of our lives.'

'I don't believe that. No one wants to suffer.'

'If you think you can live without suffering, that's a great step forward, but don't imagine that other people will understand you. True, no one wants to suffer, and yet nearly everyone seeks out pain and sacrifice, and then they feel justified, pure, deserving of the respect of their children, husbands, neighbours, God. Don't let's think about that now; all you need to know is that what makes the world go round is not the search for pleasure, but the renunciation of all that is important.

'Does a soldier go to war in order to kill the enemy? No, he goes in order to die for his country. Does a wife want to show her husband how happy she is? No, she wants him to see how devoted she is, how she suffers in order to make him happy. Does the husband go to work thinking he will find personal fulfilment there? No, he is giving his sweat and tears for the good of the family. And so it goes on: sons give up their dreams to please their parents, parents give up their lives in order to please their children; pain and suffering are used to justify the one thing that should bring only joy: love.'

'Stop.'

Ralf stopped. It was the right moment to change the subject, and he started showing her drawing after drawing. At first, it all seemed rather confusing: there were a few outlines of people, but also scrawls and scribbles, geometric shapes and colours. Gradually, though, she began to understand what he was saying, because each word he spoke was accompanied by a gesture of the hand, and each phrase placed her in the world which, up until then, she had always denied she was part of – telling herself that it was just one stage in her life, a way of earning money, nothing more.

'Yes, I discovered that there is not just one history of prostitution, but two. The first one you know all too well, because it is your history too: a pretty young girl, for reasons which she has chosen or which have chosen her, decides that the only way she can survive is by selling her body. Some end up ruling nations, as Messalina did in Rome, others become legendary figures, like Madame du Barry, still others chase after adventure and misfortune, like the spy, Mata Hari. But the majority never have their moment of glory, are never faced by a great challenge: they will always be young girls from the interior in search of fame, a husband, adventure, but who end up discovering quite a different reality, into which they plunge for a time, and to which they become accustomed, always believing that they are in control and yet ultimately unable to do anything else.

'Artists have been making sculptures and paintings and writing books for more than three thousand years. In just the same way, throughout all that time, prostitutes have carried on their work as if nothing very much ever changes. Would you like to know details?'

Maria nodded. She needed time in order to understand about pain, although she was starting to feel as if something very bad had left her body during that walk in the park.

'Prostitutes appear in classical texts, in Egyptian hieroglyphs, in Sumerian writings, in the Old and New Testament. But the profession only started to become organised in the sixth century BC, when a Greek legislator, Solon, set up state-controlled brothels and began imposing taxes on "the skin trade". Athenian businessmen were pleased because what was once prohibited became legal. The prostitutes, on the other hand, started to be classified according to how much tax they paid.

'The cheapest were the *pornai*, slaves who belonged to the owners of the establishment. Next came the *peripatetica*, who picked up her clients in the street. Lastly, the most expensive and highest quality, was the *hetaera*, the female companion, who accompanied businessmen on their trips, dined in chic restaurants, controlled her own money, gave advice and meddled in the political life of the city. As you see, what happened then still happens now.

'In the Middle Ages, because of sexually transmitted diseases ...'

Silence, fear of catching a cold, the heat of the fire – necessary now to warm her body and her soul ... Maria didn't want to hear any more history, it gave her a sense that the world had stopped, that everything was being endlessly repeated, and that mankind would never give sex the respect it deserved.

'You don't seem very interested.'

She pulled herself together. After all, he was the man to whom she had decided to give her heart, although now she wasn't so sure.

'I'm not interested in what I know about; it just makes me sad. You said there was another history.'

'The other history is exactly the opposite: sacred prostitution.'

She had suddenly emerged from her somnolent state and was listening to him intently. Sacred prostitution? Earning money from sex and yet still able to approach God?

'The Greek historian, Herodotus, wrote of Babylonia: "They have a strange custom here, by which every woman born in Sumeria is obliged, at least once in her lifetime, to go to the temple of the goddess Ishtar and give her body to a stranger, as a symbol of hospitality and for a symbolic price."'

She would ask him about that goddess later; perhaps she would help her to recover something she had lost, although just what that was she did not know.

'The influence of the goddess Ishtar spread throughout the Middle East, as far as Sardinia, Sicily and the Mediterranean ports. Later, during the Roman Empire, another goddess, Vesta, demanded total virginity or total surrender. In order to keep the sacred fire burning, the women serving her temple were responsible for initiating young men and kings on the path of sexuality – they sang erotic hymns, entered trance-like states and gave their ecstasy to the universe in a kind of communion with the divinity.'

Ralf Hart showed her a photocopy of some ancient lyrics, with a translation in German at the foot of the page. He read slowly, translating each line as he went:

'When I am sitting at the door of a tavern,
I, Ishtar, the goddess,
Am prostitute, mother, wife, divinity.
I am what people call life,
Although you call it death.
I am what people call Law,
Although you call it Delinquency.
I am what you seek
And what you find.
I am what you scattered
And the pieces you now gather up.'

Maria was sobbing softly, and Ralf Hart laughed; his vital energy was returning, his 'light' was beginning to shine again. It was best to continue the history, to show her the drawings, to make her feel loved.

'No one knows why sacred prostitution disappeared, since it had lasted not centuries, perhaps, but for at least two millennia. Maybe it was disease or because society changed its rules when it changed religions. Anyway, it no longer exists, and will never exist again; nowadays, men control the world, and the term serves only to create a stigma, and any woman who steps out of line is automatically dubbed a prostitute.'

'Could you come to the Copacabana tomorrow?'

Ralf didn't understand why she was asking this, but he agreed at once.

From Maria's diary, after the night she walked barefoot in the Jardin Anglais in Geneva:

I don't care whether it was once sacred or not, I HATE WHAT I DO. It's destroying my soul, making me lose touch with myself, teaching me that pain is a reward, that money buys everything and justifies everything.

No one around me is happy; the clients know they are paying for something that should be free, and that's depressing. The women know that they have to sell something which they would like to give out of pleasure and affection, and that is destructive. I've struggled long and hard before writing this, before accepting how unhappy and dissatisfied I am – I needed and I still need to hold out for a few more weeks.

But I cannot simply do nothing, pretend that everything is normal, that it's just a stage, a phase of my life. I want to forget it, I need to love – that's all, I need to love.

Life is too short, or too long, for me to allow myself the luxury of living it so badly.

It isn't his house. It isn't her house. It isn't Brazil or Switzerland. It's a hotel, which could be anywhere in the world, furnished, like all hotel rooms, in a way that tries to create a familiar atmosphere, but which only makes it seem all the more impersonal.

It isn't the hotel with the lovely view of the lake and the memory of pain, suffering and ecstasy; it looks out onto the road to Santiago, a route of pilgrimage not penance, a place where people meet in the cafés along the road, discover each other's 'light', talk, become friends, fall in love. It's raining, and at this time of night, no one is walking there, although they have for years, decades, centuries – perhaps the road needs to breathe, to rest from the many steps that trudge along it every day.

Turn out the light. Close the curtains.

She asks him to take his clothes off and she does the same. Darkness is never absolute, and as soon as her eyes become accustomed to it, she can see the man's silhouette, outlined against the faintest of lights coming from who knows where. The last time they met for this purpose, she had left only part of her body naked.

She takes two carefully folded handkerchiefs, which have been washed and rinsed several times to get rid of the slightest trace of perfume or soap. She goes over to him and asks him to blindfold himself. He hesitates for a moment, and makes some remark about various hells he has been through before. She says it's nothing to do with that, she just needs total darkness; now it is her turn to teach him something, just as yesterday he taught her about pain. He gives in and puts on the blindfold. She does the same; now there is not a glimmer of light, they are in absolute darkness, and they have to hold hands in order to reach the bed.

'No, we mustn't lie down. Let's sit as we always do, face to face, only a little closer, so that my knees touch your knees.'

She has always wanted to do this, but she never had what she most needed: time. Not with her first boyfriend, or with the man who penetrated her for the first time. Not with the Arab who paid her a thousand francs, perhaps hoping for more than she was able to give him, although a thousand francs wouldn't be enough for her to buy what she wanted. Not with the many men who had passed through her body, who have come and gone between her legs, sometimes thinking about themselves, sometimes thinking about her too, sometimes harbouring romantic dreams, sometimes instinctively repeating certain words because they have been told that that is what men do, and that if they don't, they are not real men.

She thinks of her diary. She has had enough, she wants the remaining weeks to pass quickly, and that is why she is giving herself to this man, because the light of her own love lies hidden there. Original sin was not the apple that Eve ate, it was her belief that Adam needed to share precisely the thing she had tasted. Eve was afraid to follow her path without someone to help her, and so she wanted to share what she was feeling.

Certain things cannot be shared. Nor can we be afraid of the oceans into which we plunge of our own free will; fear cramps everyone's style. Man goes through hell in order to understand this. Love one another, but let's not try to possess one another.

I love this man sitting before me now, because I do not possess him and he does not possess me. We are free in our mutual surrender; I need to repeat this dozens, hundreds, millions of time, until I finally believe my own words.

She thinks about the other prostitutes who work with her. She thinks about her mother and her friends. They all believe that man feels desire for only eleven minutes a day, and that they'll pay a fortune for it. That's not true; a man is also a woman; he wants to find someone, to give meaning to his life.

Does her mother behave just as she does and pretend to have an orgasm with her father? Or in the interior of Brazil, is it still forbidden for a woman to take pleasure in sex? She knows so little of life and love, and now – with her eyes blindfolded and with all the time in the world, she is discovering the origin of everything, and everything begins where and how she would like it to have begun.

Touch. Forget prostitutes, clients, her mother and her father, now she is in total darkness. She has spent the whole afternoon wondering what she could give to a man who had restored her dignity and made her understand that the search for happiness is more important than the need for pain.

I would like to give him the happiness of teaching me something new, just as yesterday he taught me about suffering, street prostitutes and sacred prostitutes. I saw how much he enjoys teaching me things, so let him teach me, guide me. I would like to know how one reaches the body, without going via the soul, penetration, orgasm.

She holds out her hand and asks him to do the same. She whispers a few words, saying that tonight, in this no-man's-land, she would like him to discover her skin, the boundary between her and the world. She asks him to touch her, to feel her with his hands, because bodies always understand each other, even when souls do not. He begins touching her, and she touches him too, and, as if by prior agreement, they both avoid the parts of the body where sexual energy surfaces most rapidly.

His fingers touch her face, and she can smell just a hint of ink on them, a smell that will stay there forever, even if he washes his hands thousands and millions of times, a smell which was there when he was born, when he saw his first tree, his first house, and decided to draw them in his dreams. He must be able to smell something on her hands too, but she doesn't know what, and doesn't want to ask, because at that moment everything is body, and the rest is silence.

She caresses and is caressed. She could stay like this all night, because it is so pleasurable and won't necessarily end in sex, and at that moment, precisely because there is no obligation to have sex, she feels hot between her legs and knows that she has become wet. When he touches her there, he will discover this, and she doesn't know if this is good or bad, this is just how her body is reacting, and she doesn't intend telling him to go here or there, more slowly or more quickly. His hands are touching her armpits now, the hairs on her arms stand on end, and she feels like pushing his hands away, but it feels good, although perhaps it is pain she is feeling. She does the same to him and notices that the skin in his armpits has a different texture, perhaps because of the deodorant they both use, but what is she thinking of? She mustn't think. She must touch, that is all.

His fingers trace circles around her breast, like an animal watching. She wants them to move more quickly, to touch her nipples, because her thoughts are moving faster than his hands, but, perhaps knowing this, he provokes, lingers, takes an age to get there. Her nipples are hard now, he plays with them a little, and that causes more goose pimples, causes her to become hotter and wetter. Now he is moving across her belly, then down to her legs, her feet, he strokes his hands up and down her inner thigh, he feels the heat, but does not approach, his touch is soft, light, and the lighter it is the more intoxicating.

She does the same, her hands almost floating over his skin, touching only the hairs on his legs, and she too feels the heat when she approaches his genitals. Suddenly, it is as if she had mysteriously recovered her virginity, as if she were discovering a man's body for the first time. She touches his penis. It is not as hard as she imagined, and yet she is so wet, how unfair, but maybe a man needs more time, who knows.

And she begins to stroke it as only virgins know how, because prostitutes have long since forgotten. The man reacts, his penis begins to grow in her hands, and she slowly increases the pressure, knowing now where she should touch, more at the bottom than at the top, she must wrap her fingers around it, push the skin back, towards his body. Now he is excited, very excited, he touches the lips of her vagina, still very softly, and she feels like asking him to be more forceful, to put his fingers right inside. But he doesn't do that, he moistens the clitoris with a little of the liquid pouring from her womb, and again makes the same circular movements he made on her nipples. This man touches her exactly as she would touch herself.

One of his hands goes back to her breast; it feels so good, she wishes he would put his arms around her now. But, no, they are discovering the body, they have time, they need a lot of time. They could make love now; it would be the most natural thing in the world, and it might be good, but all this is so new, she needs to control herself, she does not want to spoil everything. She remembers the wine they drank on that first night, how they sipped it slowly, savouring each mouthful, how she felt it warming her and how it made her see the world differently and left her more at ease and more in touch with life.

She wants to drink that man too, and then she can forget forever the cheap wine that you gulp down and that makes you feel drunk, but always leaves you with a headache and an empty space in your soul.

She stops, slowly entwines her fingers with his, she hears a moan and would like to moan too, but she stops herself, she feels heat spreading throughout her body; the same thing must be happening to him. Without an orgasm, the energy disperses, travels to the brain, not letting her think of anything but going all the way, but this is what she wants, to stop, to stop halfway, to spread the pleasure through her whole body, to allow it to invade her mind, renewing her commitment and her desire, restoring her virginity.

She gently removes the blindfold from her own eyes and removes his too. She turns on the bedside lamp. Both are naked; they do not smile, they simply look at each other. I am love, I am music, she thinks. Let's dance.

But she doesn't say anything: they talk about something trivial, about when they will next meet, she suggests a date, perhaps in two days' time. He says he would like to invite her to an exhibition, but she hesitates. That would mean getting to know his world, his friends, and what would they say, what would they think.

She says no, but he realises that she really wants to say yes, and so he insists, using a few foolish arguments, but which are all part of the dance they are dancing now, and in the end she agrees, because that is what she would like. They arrange where to meet – in the same café where they met that first day? No, she says, Brazilians are very superstitious, and you must never meet in the same place where you first met, because that might close a cycle and bring everything to an end.

He says that he's glad she doesn't want to close that particular cycle. They decide to meet at a church from where you can see the whole city, and which is on the road to Santiago, part of the mysterious pilgrimage that the two of them have been on ever since they met.

From Maria's diary, on the eve of buying her ticket back to Brazil:

Once upon a time, there was a bird. He was adorned with two perfect wings and with glossy, colourful, marvellous feathers. In short, he was a creature made to fly about freely in the sky, bringing joy to everyone who saw him.

One day, a woman saw this bird and fell in love with him. She watched his flight, her mouth wide in amazement, her heart pounding, her eyes shining with excitement. She invited the bird to fly with her, and the two travelled across the sky in perfect harmony. She admired and venerated and celebrated that bird.

But then she thought: He might want to visit far-off mountains! And she was afraid, afraid that she would never feel the same way about any other bird. And she felt envy, envy for the bird's ability to fly.

And she felt alone.

And she thought: 'I'm going to set a trap. The next time the bird appears, he will never leave again.'

The bird, who was also in love, returned the following day, fell into the trap and was put in a cage.

She looked at the bird every day. There he was, the object of her passion, and she showed him to her friends, who said: 'Now you have everything you could possibly want.' However, a strange transformation began to take place: now that she had the bird and no longer needed to woo him, she began to lose interest. The bird, unable to fly and express the true meaning of his life, began to waste away and his feathers to lose their gloss; he grew ugly; and the woman no longer paid him any attention, except by feeding him and cleaning out his cage.

One day, the bird died. The woman felt terribly sad and spent all her time thinking about him. But she did not remember the cage, she thought only of the day when she had seen him for the first time, flying contentedly amongst the clouds.

If she had looked more deeply into herself, she would have realised that what had thrilled her about the bird was his freedom, the energy of his wings in motion, not his physical body.

Without the bird, her life too lost all meaning, and Death came knocking at her door. 'Why have you come?' she asked Death. 'So that you can fly once more with him across the sky,' Death replied. 'If you had allowed him to come and go, you would have loved and admired him even more; alas, you now need me in order to find him again.'

She started the day by doing something she had rehearsed over and over during all these past months: she went into a travel agent's and bought a ticket to Brazil for the date she had marked on her calendar, in two weeks' time.

From then on, Geneva would be the face of a man she loved and who had loved her. Rue de Berne would just be a name, a homage to Switzerland's capital city. She would remember her room, the lake, the French language, the crazy things a twenty-three-year-old woman (it had been her birthday the night before) is capable of – until she realises there is a limit.

She would not cage the bird, nor would she suggest he go with her to Brazil; he was the only truly pure thing that had happened to her. A bird like that must fly free and feed on nostalgia for the time when he flew alongside someone else. And she too was a bird; having Ralf Hart by her side would mean remembering forever her days at the Copacabana. And that was her past, not her future.

She decided to say 'goodbye' just once, when the moment came for her to leave, rather than have to suffer every time she thought: 'Soon I won't be here any more'. So she played a trick on her heart and, that morning, she walked around Geneva as if she had always known those streets, that hill, the road to Santiago, the Montblanc bridge, the bars she used to go to. She watched the seagulls flying over the river, the market traders taking down their stalls, people leaving their offices to go to lunch, noticed the colour and taste of the apple she was eating, the planes landing in the distance, the rainbow in the column of water rising up from the middle of the lake, the shy, concealed joy of passers-by, the looks she got, some full of desire, some expressionless. She had lived for nearly a year in a small town, like so many other small towns in the world, and if it hadn't been for the architecture peculiar to the place and the excessive number of banks, it could have been the interior of Brazil. There was a fair. There was a market. There were housewives haggling over prices. There were students who had skipped a class at school, on the excuse perhaps that their mother or their father was ill, and who were now strolling by the river, exchanging kisses. There were people who felt at home and people who felt foreign. There were tabloid newspapers full of scandals and respectable magazines for businessmen, who, however, were only ever to be seen reading the scandal sheets.

She went to the library to return the manual on farm management. She hadn't understood a word of it, but, at times when she felt she had lost control of herself and of her destiny, the book had served as a reminder of her objective in life. It had been a silent companion, with its plain yellow cover, its series of graphs, but, above all, it had been a lighthouse in the dark nights of recent weeks.

Always making plans for the future, and always being surprised by the present, she thought to herself. She felt she had discovered herself through independence, despair, love, pain, and back again to love – and she would like things to end there.

The oddest thing of all was that, while some of her work colleagues spoke of the wonder or the ecstasy of going to bed with certain men, she had never discovered anything either good or bad about herself through sex. She had not solved her problem, she could still not have an orgasm through penetration, and she had vulgarised the sexual act so much that she might never again find the 'embrace of recognition' – as Ralf Hart called it – or the fire and joy she sought.

Or perhaps (as she occasionally thought, and as mothers, fathers and romances all said) love was necessary if one was to experience pleasure in bed.

The normally serious librarian (and Maria's only friend, although she had never told her so) was in a good mood. She was having a bite to eat and invited her to share a sandwich. Maria thanked her and said that she had just eaten.

'You took a long time to read this.'

'I didn't understand a word.'

'Do you remember what you asked me once?'

No, she didn't, but when she saw the mischievous look on the other woman's face, she guessed. Sex.

'You know, after you came here in search of books on the subject, I decided to make a list of what we had. It wasn't much, and since we need to educate our young people in such matters, I ordered a few more books. At least, this way they won't need to learn about sex in that worst of all possible ways – by going with prostitutes.'

The librarian pointed to a pile of books in a corner, all discreetly covered in brown paper.

'I haven't had time to catalogue them yet, but I had a quick glance through and I was horrified by what I read.'

Maria could imagine what the woman was going to say: embarrassing positions, sadomasochism, things of that sort. She had better tell her that she had to get back to work (she couldn't remember whether she had told her she worked in a bank or in a shop – lying made life so complicated, she was always forgetting what she had said).

She thanked her and was about to leave, when the other woman said:

'You'd be horrified too. Did you know, for example, that the clitoris is a recent invention?'

An invention? Recent? Just this week someone had touched hers, as if it had always been there and as if those hands knew the terrain they were exploring well, despite the total darkness.

'It was officially accepted in 1559, after a doctor, Realdo Columbo, published a book entitled *De re anatomica*. It was officially ignored for fifteen hundred years of the Christian era. Columbo describes it in his book as "a pretty and a useful thing". Can you believe it?'

They both laughed.

'Two years later, in 1561, another doctor, Gabriello Fallopio, said that he had "discovered" it. Imagine that! Two men – Italians, of course, who know about such things

– arguing about who had officially added the clitoris to the history books!'

It was an interesting conversation, but Maria didn't want to think about these things, mainly because she could already feel the juices flowing and her vagina getting wet – just remembering his touch, the blindfolds, his hands moving over her body. No, she wasn't dead to sex; that man had managed to rescue her. It was good to be alive.

The librarian, however, was warming to her subject.

'Its "discovery" didn't mean it received any more respect, though.' The librarian seemed to have become an expert on clitorology, or whatever that science is called. 'The mutilations we read about now in certain African tribes, who still insist on removing the woman's right to sexual pleasure, are nothing new. In the nineteenth century, here in Europe, they were still performing operations to remove it, in the belief that in that small, insignificant part of the female anatomy lay the root of hysteria, epilepsy, adulterous tendencies and sterility.'

Maria held out her hand to say goodbye, but the librarian showed no signs of tiring.

'Worse still, dear Dr Freud, the founder of psychoanalysis, said that in a normal woman, the female orgasm should move from the clitoris to the vagina. His most faithful followers went further and said that if a woman's sexual pleasure remained concentrated in the clitoris, this was a sign of infantilism or, worse, bisexuality.

'And yet, as we all know, it is very difficult to have an orgasm just through penetration. It's good to have sex with a man, but pleasure lies in that little nub discovered by an Italian!'

Distracted, Maria realised that she had that problem diagnosed by Freud: she was still in the infantile stage, her orgasm had not moved to the vagina. Or was Freud wrong?

'And what do you think about the G-spot?'

'Do you know where it is?'

The other woman blushed and coughed, but managed to say:

'As you go in, on the first floor, the back window.'

Brilliant! She had described the vagina as if it were a building! Perhaps she had read that explanation in a book for young girls, to say that if someone knocks on the door and comes in, you'll discover a whole universe inside your own body. Whenever she masturbated, she preferred to concentrate on her G-spot rather than on the clitoris, since the latter made her feel rather uncomfortable, a pleasure mingled with real pain, rather troubling.

She always went straight to the first floor, to the back window!

Seeing that the librarian was clearly never going to stop talking, perhaps because she had discovered in Maria an accomplice to her own lost sexuality, she gave a wave of her hand and left, trying to concentrate on whatever nonsense came into her head, because this was not a day to think about farewells, clitorises, restored virginities or G-spots. She focused on what was going on around her – bells ringing, dogs barking, a tram rattling over the tracks, footsteps, her own breathing, the signs offering everything under the sun.

She did not feel like going back to the Copacabana, and yet she felt an obligation to work until the end, although she had no real idea why – after all, she had saved enough money. She could spend the afternoon doing some shopping, talking to the bank manager, who was a client of hers, but who had promised to help her manage her savings, having a cup of coffee somewhere, sending off the clothes that wouldn't fit into her suitcases. It was strange, for some reason, she was feeling rather sad; perhaps because it was still another two weeks before she would leave, and she needed to get through that time, to look at the city with different eyes and feel glad for what she had experienced there.

She came to a crossroads where she had been hundreds of time before; you could see the lake from there and the water spout, and, on the far pavement, in the middle of the public gardens, the lovely floral clock, one of the city's symbols ... and that clock would not allow her to lie, because ...

Suddenly, time and the world stood still.

What was this story she had been telling herself since the morning, something about her recently restored virginity?

The world seemed frozen, that second would never end, she was face to face with something very serious and very important in her life, she could not just forget about it, she could not do as she did with her night-time dreams, which she always promised herself she would write down and which she never did ...

'Don't think about anything! The world has stopped. What's going on?'

ENOUGH!

The bird, the lovely story about the bird she had just written – was it about Ralf Hart?

No, it was about her!

FULL STOP!

It was 11:11 in the morning, and she was frozen in that moment. She was a foreigner inside her own body, she was rediscovering her recently restored virginity, but its rebirth was so fragile that if she stayed there, it would be lost forever. She had experienced Heaven perhaps, certainly Hell, but the Adventure was coming to an end. She couldn't wait two weeks, ten days, one week – she needed to leave now, because, as she stood looking at the floral clock, with tourists taking pictures of it and children playing all around, she had just found out why she was sad.

And the reason was this: she didn't want to go back.

And the reason she didn't want to go back wasn't Ralf Hart, Switzerland or Adventure. The real reason couldn't have been simpler: money.

Money! A special piece of paper, decorated in sombre colours, which everyone agreed was worth something – and she believed it, everyone believed it – until you took a pile of that paper to a bank, a respectable, traditional, highly confidential Swiss bank and asked: 'Could I buy back a few hours of my life?' 'No, madam, we don't sell, we only buy.'

Maria was woken from her delirium by the sound of screeching brakes, a motorist shouting, and a smiling old gentleman, speaking English, telling her to step back onto the pavement – the pedestrian light was red.

'But this can't be exactly an earth-shattering discovery. Everyone must feel what I feel. They must know.'

But they didn't. She looked around her. People were walking along, heads down, hurrying off to work, to school, to the employment agency, to Rue de Berne, telling themselves: 'I can wait a little longer. I have a dream, but there's no need to realise it today, besides, I need to earn some money.' Of course, everyone spoke ill of her profession, but, basically, it was all a question of selling her time, like everyone else. Doing things she didn't want to do, like everyone else. Putting up with horrible people, like everyone else. Handing over her precious body and her precious soul in the name of a future that never arrived, like everyone else. Saying that she still didn't have enough, like everyone else. Waiting just a little bit longer, like everyone else. Waiting so that she could earn just a little bit more, postponing the realisation of her dreams; she was too busy right now, she had a great opportunity ahead of her, loyal clients who were waiting for her, who could pay between three hundred and fifty and one thousand francs a session.

And for the first time in her life, despite all the good things she could buy with the money she might earn – who knows, she might only have to work another year – she decided consciously, lucidly and deliberately to let an opportunity pass her by.

Maria waited for the light to change, she crossed the road and paused in front of the floral clock; she thought of

Ralf, saw again the look of desire in his eyes on the night when she had slipped off the top half of her dress, felt his hands touching her breasts, her sex, her face, and she became wet; and as she looked at the vast column of water in the distance, without even having to touch any part of her own body, she had an orgasm right there, in front of everyone.

Not that anyone noticed; they were all far too busy.

Nyah, the only one of her work colleagues with whom she had a relationship that could be described as friendship, called her over as soon as she came in. She was sitting with an oriental gentleman, and they were both laughing.

'Look at this,' she said to Maria. 'Look what he wants me to do with him!'

The oriental gentleman gave a knowing look and, still smiling, opened the lid of what looked like a cigar box. Milan was watching from a distance in case it contained syringes or drugs. It did not, it was something that even he didn't know quite what to do with, but it wasn't anything very special.

'It looks like something from the last century!' said Maria.

'It is,' said the oriental gentleman indignantly. 'It's over a hundred years old and it cost a fortune.'

What Maria saw was a series of valves, a handle, electric circuits, small metal contacts and batteries. It looked like the inside of an ancient radio, with two wires sticking out, at the ends of which were small glass rods, about the thickness of a finger. It certainly didn't look like something that had cost a fortune.

'How does it work?'

Nyah didn't like Maria's question. Although she trusted Maria, people could change from one moment to the next, and she might have her eye on her client.

'He's already explained. It's the Violet Rod.'

And turning to the oriental man, she suggested that they leave, because she had decided to accept his invitation. However, the man seemed pleased that his toy should have aroused such interest.

'Around 1900, when the first batteries came onto the market, traditional medicine started experimenting with electricity to see if it could cure mental illness or hysteria. It was also used to get rid of spots and to stimulate the skin. You see these two ends? Well, they were placed here,' he indicated his temples, 'and the battery created the same sort of static electricity that you get in Switzerland when the air's very dry.'

Static electricity was something that never happened in Brazil, but was very common in Switzerland. Maria had discovered it one day when she opened the door of a taxi; she had heard a crack and received a shock. She thought there must be something wrong with the car and had complained, saying that she wasn't going to pay the fare, and the driver had insulted her and told her she was stupid. He was right; it wasn't the car, it was the dry air. After receiving several more shocks, she began to be afraid of touching anything made of metal, until she discovered in a supermarket a bracelet she could wear that discharged the electricity accumulated in the body.

She turned to the man:

'But that's really nasty.'

Nyah was getting more and more irritated by Maria's remarks. In order to avoid future conflicts with her only possible friend, she kept her arm around the man's shoulder, thus leaving no room for doubt as to who he belonged to.

'It depends where you put it,' said the man, laughing loudly.

He turned the little handle and the two rods seemed to turn violet. He quickly placed them on the two women; there was a crack, but the shock was more ticklish than painful.

Milan came over.

'Would you mind not using that in here, please.'

The man put the rods back inside the box. Nyah seized the moment and suggested that they go straight to the hotel. The man seemed rather disappointed, since the new arrival seemed far more interested in his machine than the woman who was now suggesting they go back to his hotel. He put on his jacket and stowed the box away inside a leather briefcase, saying:

'They've started making them again now; they've become quite fashionable amongst people in search of special pleasures. But you'd only find ones like this in rare medical collections, museums and antique shops.'

Milan and Maria just stood there, not knowing what to say.

'Have you ever seen one before?'

'Not like that, no. It probably did cost a fortune, but then he's a top executive with an oil company ... I've seen modern ones, though.'

'What do they do with them?'

'The man puts them inside his body ... and then asks the woman to turn the handle. He gets an electric shock inside.'

'Couldn't he do that on his own?'

'You can do most kinds of sexual activity on your own, but if they stopped believing that it was more fun with another person, my bar would go bankrupt and you would have to find work in a greengrocer's shop. By the way, your special client said that he would be here tonight, so make sure you turn down any other offers.'

'Oh, I will, including his. I came to say goodbye. I'm leaving.'

Milan appeared not to react.

'Is it the painter?'

'No, it's the Copacabana. There's a limit to everything, and I reached mine this morning when I was looking at that floral clock near the lake.'

'And what is the limit?'

'The price of a farm in the interior of Brazil. I know I could earn more money, that I could work for another year – after all, what difference would it make?

'Well, I know what difference it would make; I would be caught in this trap forever, just as you are and the clients are, the businessmen, the air stewards, the talent scouts, the record company executives, the many men I have known, to whom I have sold my time and which they can't sell back to me. If I stay another day, I'll be here for another year, and if I stay another year, I'll never leave.'

Milan nodded discreetly, as if he understood and agreed with everything she had said, although he couldn't actually say anything, for fear of infecting all the other girls who worked for him. He was a good man, and although he didn't give her his blessing, neither did he try to convince Maria that she was wrong.

She thanked him and asked for a drink – a glass of champagne, she couldn't stand another fruit juice cocktail. She could drink now that she wasn't working. Milan told her to phone him if ever she needed anything; she would always be welcome.

She made to pay for the drink, and he said it was on the house. She accepted: she had, after all, given that house a great deal more than one drink.

From Maria's diary, when she got home:

I don't remember exactly when, but one Sunday recently, I decided to go to church to attend mass. After some time, I realised that I was in the wrong church – it was a Protestant church.

I was about to leave, but the vicar was just beginning his sermon, and I thought it would be rude to get up at that point, and it was a real blessing, because that day I heard things I very much needed to hear.

He said something like:

'In all the languages in the world, there is the same proverb: "What the eyes don't see, the heart doesn't grieve over." Well, I say that there isn't an ounce of truth in it. The further off they are, the

closer to the heart are all those feelings that we try to repress and forget. If we're in exile, we want to store away every tiny memory of our roots. If we're far from the person we love, everyone we pass in the street reminds us of them.

'The gospels and all the sacred texts of all religions were written in exile, in search of God's understanding, of the faith that moves whole peoples, of the pilgrimage of souls wandering the face of the Earth. Our ancestors did not know, as we do not know, what the Divinity expects from our lives – and it is out of that doubt that books are written, pictures painted, because we don't want to forget who we are – nor can we.'

At the end of the service, I went up to him and thanked him: I said that I was a stranger in a strange land, and I thanked him for reminding me that what the eyes don't see, the heart does grieve over. And my heart has grieved so much, that today I'm leaving.

She picked up her two suitcases and put them on the bed; they had always been there, waiting for the day when everything would come to an end. She had imagined that she would fill them with presents, new clothes, photographs of snow and of the great European capitals, souvenirs of a happy time when she had lived in the safest and most generous country in the world. She had a few new clothes, it was true, and a few photos taken in the snow that fell one day in Geneva, but apart from that, nothing was as she had imagined it would be.

She had arrived with the dream of earning lots of money, learning about life and who she was, buying a farm for her parents, finding a husband, and bringing her family over to see where she lived. She was returning with just enough money to realise one of those dreams, without ever having visited the mountains and, worse still, a stranger to herself. But she was happy; she knew the time had come to stop.

Not many people do.

She had had only four adventures – being a dancer in a cabaret, learning French, working as a prostitute and falling hopelessly in love. How many people can boast of experiencing so much excitement in one year? She was happy, despite the sadness, and that sadness had a name: it wasn't prostitution, or Switzerland or money – it was Ralf Hart. Although she had never acknowledged it to herself, deep down, she would like to have married him, that man who was now waiting for her in a church, ready to take her off to see his friends, his paintings, his world.

She considered standing him up and getting a room in a hotel near the airport, since the flight left early the next morning; from now on, every minute spent by his side would be a year of suffering in the future, for everything she could have said to him and didn't, for her memories of his hands, his voice, his loving support, and his stories.

She opened one suitcase and took out the little carriage from the electric train set that he had given her on that first night in his house. She looked at it for a few minutes, then threw it in the bin; it didn't deserve to go to Brazil, and it had proved useless and unfair to the child who had always wanted it.

No, she wouldn't go to the church; he might ask her something about tomorrow, and if she was honest and told him that she was leaving, he would beg her to stay and promise her everything in order not to lose her at that moment, he would openly declare all the love he had already shown to her during the time they had spent together. But their relationship was based on freedom, and no other sort of relationship would work – perhaps that was the only reason they loved each other, because they knew they did not need each other. Men always take fright when a woman says: 'I need you', and Maria wanted to take away with her the image of a Ralf Hart who was utterly in love and utterly hers, and ready to do anything for her.

She still had time to decide whether or not to go and meet him; at the moment, she needed to concentrate on more practical matters. She looked at all the things she couldn't pack and which she had no idea what to do with. She decided that the owner could decide on their fate when he came to check the apartment and found all the household appliances in the kitchen, the pictures bought in a second-hand market, the towels and the bedclothes. She couldn't take any of that with her to Brazil, even though her parents had more need of them than any Swiss beggar; they would always remind her of everything she had risked.

She left the apartment and went to the bank and asked to withdraw all her money. The manager – who had been to bed with her in the past – said that this really wasn't a good idea, since her francs would continue earning money and she could receive the interest in Brazil. Besides, what if she were mugged, that would mean months of work wasted. Maria hesitated for a moment, thinking – as she always did – that he really was trying to help. However, after reflecting for a moment, she concluded that the point of the money was not that it should be transformed into more paper, but into a farm, a home for her parents, a few cattle and a lot more work.

She withdrew every last centime, put it in a small bag she had bought specially for the occasion and attached it to a belt beneath her clothes.

She went to the travel agency, praying that she would have the courage to go through with her decision. When she said she wanted to get a different flight, she was told that if she went on tomorrow's flight, she would have to change planes in Paris. That didn't matter – all she needed was to get far enough away from there before she had second thoughts.

She walked to one of the bridges and bought an ice cream, even though the weather had started to get cold again, and she took one last look at Geneva. Everything seemed different to her, as if she had just arrived and needed to visit the museums, the historical monuments, the fashionable bars and restaurants. It's odd how, when you live in a city, you always postpone getting to know it and usually end up never knowing it at all.

She thought she would feel happy because she was going home, but she wasn't. She thought she would feel sad because she was leaving a city that had treated her so well, but she didn't. The only thing she could do now was to shed a few tears, feeling rather afraid of herself, an intelligent young woman, who had everything going for her, but who tended to make the wrong decisions.

She just hoped that this time she was right.

The church was completely empty when she went in, and she was able to examine in silence the splendid stained-glass windows, lit from outside by the light of a day washed clean by last night's storm. Before her stood an empty cross; she was confronted not by an instrument of torture, by the bloodied body of a dying man, but by a symbol of resurrection, in which the instrument of torture had lost all its meaning, its terror, its importance. She remembered the whip on that night of thunder and lightning; it was the same thing. 'Dear God, what am I saying?'

She was pleased too not to see any images of suffering saints, covered in bloodstains and open wounds – this was simply a place where people gathered to worship something they could not understand.

She stood in front of the monstrance, in which was kept the body of a Jesus in whom she still believed, although she had not thought about him for a long time. She knelt down and promised God, the Virgin, Jesus and all the saints that whatever happened that day, she would not change her mind and would leave anyway. She made this promise because she knew love's traps all too well, and knew how easily they can change a woman's mind.

Shortly afterwards, she felt a hand touch her shoulder and

she inclined her head so that her face rested on the hand.

'How are you?'

'I'm fine,' she said in a voice without a trace of anxiety in it. 'I'm fine. Let's go and have a coffee.'

They left the church hand-in-hand, as if they were two lovers meeting again after a long time. They kissed in public, and a few people shot them scandalised looks; but they both smiled at the unease they were causing and at the desires they were provoking by their scandalous behaviour, because they knew that, in fact, those people wished they could be doing the same thing. That was the real scandal.

They went into a café which was the same as all the others, but that afternoon, it was different, because they were there together and because they loved each other. They talked about Geneva, the difficulties of the French language, the stained-glass windows in the church, the evils of smoking – both of them smoked and hadn't the slightest intention of giving up.

She insisted on paying for the coffee and he accepted. They went to the exhibition and she got to know his world: the artists, the rich who looked richer than they actually were, the millionaires who looked poor, the people discussing things she had never even heard about. They all liked her and praised her French; they asked about Carnival, football, Brazilian music. They were nice, polite, kind, charming.

When they left, he said that he would come to the club that night to see her. She asked him not to, she had the night off and would like to invite him out to supper.

He accepted and they said goodbye, arranging to meet at his house before going to have supper at a delightful restaurant in the little square in Cologny, which they had often driven past in the taxi, and where she had always wanted to stop, but had never asked to.

Then Maria remembered her one friend and decided to go to the library to tell her that she would not be coming back.

She got caught up in the traffic for what seemed like an eternity, until the Kurds had (once more!) finished their demonstration and the cars could move freely again. Now, however, she was the mistress of her own time, and it didn't matter.

By the time she reached the library, it was just about to close.

'Forgive me if I'm being too personal, but I haven't anyone else, any woman friend, I can talk to about certain things,' said the librarian as soon as Maria came in.

She didn't have any women friends? After spending her whole life in the same place and meeting all kinds of people at work, did she really have no one she could talk to? Maria had found someone like herself, or, rather, like everyone else.

'I was thinking about what I read about the clitoris …'

Didn't she ever think about anything else!

'It's just that, although I used to enjoy sex with my husband, I always found it very difficult to reach orgasm during intercourse. Do you think that's normal?'

'Do you find it normal that there are daily demonstrations by Kurds? That women in love run away from their Prince Charming? That people dream about farms rather than love? That men and women sell their time, but can never buy it back again? And yet, all these things happen, so it really doesn't matter what I believe or don't believe; all these things are normal. Everything that goes against Nature, against our most intimate desires, is normal in our eyes, even though it's an aberration in God's eyes. We seek out our own inferno, we spend millennia building it, and after all that effort, we are now able to live in the worst possible way.'

She looked at the woman standing in front of her and, for the first time, she asked what her name was (she only knew her surname). Her name was Heidi, she was married for thirty years and never – never! – during that time had she asked herself if it was normal not to have an orgasm during intercourse with her husband.

'I don't know if I should have read all those things! Perhaps it would have been better to live in ignorance, believing that a faithful husband, an apartment with a view of the lake, three children and a job in the public sector were all that a woman could hope for. Now, ever since you arrived, and since I read the first book, I'm obsessed with what my life has become. Is everyone the same?'

'I can guarantee you that they are.' And standing before that woman who was asking her advice, Maria felt herself to be very wise.

'Would you like me to give you details?'

Maria nodded.

'You're obviously too young to understand these things, but that's precisely why I would like to share a little of my life with you, so that you don't make the same mistakes I did.

'But why is it that my husband never noticed my clitoris? He assumed that the orgasm happened in the vagina, and I found it really, really difficult to pretend something that he imagined I must be feeling. Of course, I did experience pleasure, but a different kind of pleasure. It was only when the friction was on the upper part ... do you know what I mean?'

'I know.'

'And now I know why. It's in there,' she pointed to a book on her desk, whose title Maria couldn't see. 'There are lots of nerve endings that connect the clitoris and the G-spot and which are crucial to orgasm. But men think that penetration is all. Do you know what the G-spot is?'

'Yes, we talked about it the other day,' said Maria, slipping into the role of Innocent Girl. 'As you go in, on the first floor, the back window.'

'That's right!' And the librarian's eyes lit up. 'Just you ask how many of your male friends have heard of it. None of them! It's absurd. But just as an Italian discovered the clitoris, the G-spot is a twentieth-century discovery! Soon it will be in all the headlines, and then no one will be able to ignore it any longer! Have you any idea what revolutionary times we're living in?'

Maria glanced at her watch, and Heidi realised that she would have to talk fast, in order to teach this pretty young woman that all women have the right to be happy and fulfilled, in order that the next generation should benefit from all these extraordinary scientific discoveries.

'Dr Freud didn't agree because he wasn't a woman and, since he experienced his orgasm through his penis, he felt that women must, therefore, experience pleasure in their vagina. We've got to go back to basics, to what has always given us pleasure: the clitoris and the G-spot! Very few women enjoy a satisfactory sexual relationship, so if you have difficulty in getting the pleasure you deserve, let me suggest something: change position. Make your lover lie down and you stay on top; your clitoris will strike his body harder and you – not he – will be getting the stimulus you need. Or, rather, the stimulus you deserve!'

Maria, meanwhile, was only pretending that she wasn't listening to the conversation. So she wasn't the only one! She didn't have a sexual problem, it was all just a question of anatomy! She felt like kissing the librarian, as if a gigantic weight had been lifted off her heart. How good to have discovered this while she was still young! What a marvellous day she was having! Heidi gave a conspiratorial smile.

'They may not know it, but we have an erection too. The clitoris becomes erect!'

'They' presumably meant men. Since this was such an intimate conversation, Maria decided to risk a question:

'Have you ever had an affair?'

The librarian looked shocked. Her eyes gave off a kind of sacred fire, she blushed scarlet, though whether out of rage or shame it was impossible to tell. After a while, though, the battle between telling the truth or pretending ended. She simply changed the subject.

'Getting back to our erection, to our clitoris, did you know that it became rigid?'

'Yes, I've known that ever since I was a child.'

Heidi seemed disappointed. Perhaps she had just never noticed. Nevertheless, she resolved to go on:

'Anyway, apparently, if you rub your finger round it, without touching the actual tip, you can experience even more intense pleasure. So take note! Men who do respect a woman's body immediately touch the tip, not knowing that this can sometimes be quite painful, don't you agree? So, after your first or second encounter, take control of the situation: get on top, decide how and when pressure should be applied, and increase and decrease the rhythm as you see fit. According to the book I'm reading, a frank conversation about it might also be a good idea.'

'Did you ever have a frank conversation with your husband?'

Again, Heidi avoided this direct question, saying that things were different then. Now she was more interested in sharing her intellectual experiences.

'Try to think of your clitoris as the hands of a clock and ask your partner to move it back and forth between eleven and one, do you understand?'

Yes, she knew what the woman was talking about and didn't entirely agree, although the book wasn't far from the truth. As soon as she mentioned the word 'clock', though, Maria glanced at her watch, and explained that she had really come to say goodbye, her job placement had come to an end. The woman seemed not to hear her.

'Would you like to borrow this book about the clitoris?'

'No, thanks. I've got other things to think about at the moment.'

'And you don't want to borrow anything else?'

'No. I'm going back to my own country, but I just wanted to thank you for always having treated me with such respect and understanding. Perhaps we'll meet again some time.'

They shook hands and wished each other much happiness.

Heidi waited until the girl had left, then thumped the desk. Why hadn't she seized the opportunity to share something which, the way things were going, would probably go to the grave with her? Since the girl had had the courage to ask if she had ever betrayed her husband, why had she not answered, now that she was discovering a new world in which women were finally acknowledging how difficult it was to achieve a vaginal orgasm?

'Oh well, it doesn't matter. The world isn't just about sex.'

No, it wasn't the most important thing in the world, but it was still important. She looked around her; most of the thousands of books surrounding her were love stories. It was always the same: someone meets someone, falls in love, loses them and finds them again. There are souls speaking unto souls, there are distant places, adventures, sufferings, anxieties, but very rarely anyone saying: 'Excuse me, sir, but why don't you try acquiring a better understanding of the female body?' Why didn't books talk openly about that?

Perhaps people weren't really interested. Men would always go looking for novelty; they were still the troglodyte hunter, obeying the reproductive instinct of the human race.

And what about women? In her personal experience, the desire to have a good orgasm with one's partner lasted only for the first few years; then the frequency of orgasms diminished, but no one talked about it, because every woman thought it was her problem alone. And so they lied, pretending that they found their husband's desire to make love every night oppressive. And by lying, they left other women feeling worried.

They turned their thoughts to other things: children, cooking, timetables, housework, bills to pay, their husband's affairs – which they tolerated – holidays abroad during which they were more concerned with their children than with themselves, their complicity, or even love, but no sex.

She should have been more open with that young Brazilian woman, who seemed to her an innocent creature, old enough to be her daughter, and still incapable of understanding what the world was like. An immigrant, far from home, working hard at a boring job, waiting for a man she could marry, and with whom she could fake a few orgasms, find security, reproduce this mysterious human race, and then forget all about such things as orgasms, the clitoris or the G-spot (which was only discovered in the twentieth century!!). Being a good wife, a good mother, making sure there was nothing lacking in the home, masturbating occasionally in secret, thinking about some man who had passed her in the street and looked at her longingly. Keeping up appearances – why was the world so concerned with appearances?

That is why she had not replied to the question: 'Have you ever had an affair?'

These things go with you to the grave, she thought. Her husband had been the only man in her life, although sex was now a thing of the remote past. He had been an excellent companion, honest, generous and good-humoured, and had struggled to bring up the family and to keep all those who worked with him happy. He was the ideal man that all women dream of, and that is precisely why she felt so bad when she thought of how she had one day desired and been with another man.

She remembered how they had met. She was coming back from the small mountain town of Davos, when all the train services were interrupted for some hours by an avalanche. She phoned home so that no one would be worried, bought a few magazines and prepared for a long wait at the station.

That was when she noticed the man sitting next to her, along with his rucksack and sleeping bag. He had greying hair and sunburned skin, and was the only person in the station who didn't seem concerned about the absence of any trains; on the contrary, he was smiling and looking around him for someone to talk to. Heidi opened one of the magazines, but – ah, sweet mystery of life! – her eyes happened to catch his and she didn't manage to look away quickly enough to avoid him coming over to her.

Before she could – politely – say that she really needed to finish reading an important article, he began to talk. He told her that he was a writer and was returning from a meeting in Davos and that the delay would mean him missing his flight home. When they got to Geneva, would she mind helping him find a hotel?

Heidi was watching him: how could anyone be so cheerful about missing a plane and having to wait in an uncomfortable train station until things were sorted out?

The man began talking to her as if they were old friends. He told her about his travels, about the mystique of literary creation and, to her horror, about all the women he had known and loved in his lifetime. Heidi merely nodded and let him talk. Occasionally he would apologise for talking so much and ask her to tell him something about herself, but all she could say was: 'Oh, I'm just an ordinary person, nothing very special.'

Suddenly, she found herself hoping that the train would never arrive; the conversation was so enthralling; she was discovering things that she had only encountered before in fiction. And since she would never see him again, she got up her nerve and (quite why she could never say) began asking him about subjects of particular interest to her. Her marriage was going through a rough patch, her husband was very demanding of her time, and Heidi wanted to know what she could do to make him happy. The man offered her some interesting explanations, told her a story, but didn't seem very comfortable talking about her husband.

'You're a very interesting woman,' he said, something that no one had said to her for years.

Heidi didn't know how to react; he saw her embarrassment and immediately started talking about deserts, mountains, lost cities, women with veiled faces or bare midriffs, about warriors, pirates and wise men.

The train arrived. They sat down next to each other, and she was no longer a married woman who lived in a chalet looking out over the lake and had three children to bring up, she was an adventurer arriving in Geneva for the first time. She looked at the mountains and the river and felt glad to be sitting beside a man who wanted to go to bed with her (because that's all men think about) and who was doing his best to impress her. She wondered how many other men had felt the same, but to whom she had never given the slightest encouragement; that morning, however, the world had changed, and she was suddenly a thirty-eight-year-old adolescent, dazzled by this man's attempts to seduce her; it was the best feeling in the world.

In the premature autumn of her life, when she thought she had everything she could possibly want, this man appeared at the train station and walked straight into her life without first asking permission. They got off at Geneva and she showed him a hotel (a cheap one, he said, because he should have left that morning and didn't have much money on him for another night in exorbitantly expensive Switzerland); he asked her to go up to the room with him, to see if everything was in order. Heidi knew what to expect, and nevertheless, she accepted his proposal. They shut the door, they kissed each other with wild abandon, he tore off her clothes and – dear God! – he knew all about the female body, because he had known the sufferings and frustrations of so many women.

They made love all afternoon and only when evening fell did the charm dissipate, and she said the words she would have preferred not to have said:

'I must go home, my husband's expecting me.'

He lit a cigarette and they lay in silence for a few moments, and neither of them said 'goodbye'. Heidi got up and left without looking back, knowing that, whatever either of them might say, no word or phrase would make any sense.

She would never see him again, but, for a few hours, in the autumn of her despair, she had ceased to be a faithful wife, housewife, loving mother, exemplary public servant and constant friend, and reverted to being simply a woman.

For a few days, her husband kept saying that she seemed different, either happier or sadder, he couldn't quite put his finger on it. A week later, everything was back to normal.

'What a shame I didn't tell that young woman,' she thought. 'Not that she would have understood, she still lives in a world in which people are faithful and vows of love are forever.'

From Maria's diary:

I don't know what he must have thought when he opened the door that night and saw me standing there, carrying two suitcases.

'Don't worry,' I said. 'I'm not moving in. Shall we go to supper?'

He didn't say anything, just helped me in with my luggage. Then, without saying 'what's going on?' or 'how lovely to see you', he simply put his arms around me and started kissing me and touching my body, my breasts, my crotch, as if he had been waiting for this a long time and was now afraid that the moment would never come.

He pulled off my jacket and my dress, leaving me naked, and there in the hall, without any ritual or preparation, without even time to say what would be good and what bad, with the cold wind blowing in under the front door, we made love for the first time. I thought perhaps I should tell him to stop, so that we could find somewhere more comfortable, so that we could have time to explore the immense world of our sensuality, but, at the same time, I wanted him inside me, because he was the man I had never possessed and would never possess again. That is why I could love him with all my energy, and have, at least for one night, what I'd never had before and what I would possibly never have again.

He lay me down on the floor and entered me before I was aroused and ready, but the pain didn't bother me; on the contrary, I liked it like that, because he obviously understood that I was his and that he didn't need to ask permission. I wasn't there in order to teach him anything or to prove that I was more sensitive or more passionate than other women, I was there to say yes, you're welcome, that I too had been waiting for this, that I was pleased about his total disregard for the rules we had created between us and that he was now demanding that we should be guided solely by our instincts, male and female.

We were in the most conventional of positions – me underneath him, with my legs spread, and him on top of me, moving in and out, while I looked at him, with no desire to pretend or to moan or to do anything, just wanting to keep my eyes open so that I could remember every second, watch his face changing, his hands grabbing my hair, his mouth biting me, kissing me. No preliminaries, no caresses, no preparations, no sophistication, just him inside me and me inside his soul.

He came and went, quickening and slowing the rhythm, stopping sometimes to look at me too, but he didn't ask if I was enjoying it, because he knew that this was the only way our souls could communicate at that moment. The rhythm increased, and I knew that the eleven minutes were coming to an end, and I wanted them to last forever, because it was so good – ah, dear God, it was good – to be possessed and not to possess! And we had our eyes wide open all the time, until I noticed that at one point we were no longer seeing clearly any more and we seemed to move into a dimension in which I was the great mother, the universe, the beloved, the sacred prostitute of the ancient rituals that he had told me about over wine and beside an open fire. I saw that he was about to come, and his arms gripped mine, his movements increased in intensity, and it was then that he shouted – he didn't moan, he didn't grind his teeth, he shouted. He yelled. He roared like an animal! A thought flashed through my mind that the neighbours might call the police, but it didn't matter, and I felt immense pleasure, because this was how it had been since the beginning of time, when the first man met the first woman and they made love for the first time: they shouted.

Then his body collapsed onto mine, and I don't know how long we stayed there, our arms around each other; I stroked his hair as I had done only once before, on the night when we locked ourselves up in the darkness of the hotel room; I felt his racing heart gradually slow to its normal rate; his hands began delicately to move up and down my arms, making all the hairs on my body prickle.

He must have had a practical thought – the weight of his body on mine – because he rolled over, took my hand, and we lay there staring up at the ceiling and the chandelier with its three light bulbs lit.

'Good evening,' I said.

He drew me over so that my head was resting on his chest. For a long time, he just stroked me, and then he said 'Good evening' too.

'The neighbours must have heard everything,' I said, not knowing quite what to say next, because saying 'I love you' at that juncture didn't make much sense; he knew that already, and so did I.

'There's a terrific draught from under the door,' he said, when he could have said: 'Good!'

'Let's go into the kitchen.'

We got up and I saw that he hadn't even taken off his trousers, he was dressed just as I had found him, only with his penis exposed. I put my jacket over my bare shoulders. We went into the kitchen; he made some coffee; he smoked two cigarettes and I smoked one. Sitting at the table, he said 'thank you' with his eyes, and I replied 'thank you too', but our mouths remained shut.

He eventually got up the courage to ask about the suitcases.

'I'm flying back to Brazil tomorrow at midday.'

A woman knows when a man is important to her. Are men capable of that kind of realisation? Or would I have to say: 'I love you', 'I'd like to stay here with you', 'ask me to stay'.

'Don't go.' Yes, he had understood that he could say that to me.

'I have to. I made a promise.'

Because, if I hadn't, he might think that this was all going to last forever. And it wasn't; it was part of the dream of a young woman from the interior of a far-off country, who goes to the big city (well, not that big really), encounters all kinds of difficulties, but finds the man who loves her. So this was the happy ending to all the difficult times I had been through, and whenever I remembered my life in

Europe, I would end with the story of a man passionately in love with me, and who would always be mine, because I had visited his soul.

Ah, Ralf, you have no idea how much I love you. I think that perhaps we always fall in love the very first instant we see the man of our dreams, even though, at the time, reason may be telling us otherwise, and we may fight against that instinct, hoping against hope that we won't win, until there comes a point when we allow ourselves to be vanquished by our feelings. That happened on the night when I walked barefoot in the park, cold and in pain, but knowing how much you loved me.

Yes, I love you very much, as I have never loved another man, and that is precisely why I am leaving, because, if I stayed, the dream would become reality, the desire to possess, to want your life to be mine … in short, all the things that transform love into slavery. It's best left like this – a dream. We have to be careful what we take from a country, or from life.

'You didn't have an orgasm,' he said, trying to change the subject, to be careful and not to force the situation. He was afraid of losing me, and was thinking that he still had all night to make me change my mind.

'No, I didn't, but I had an enormous amount of pleasure.'

'But it would have been better if you'd had an orgasm too.'

'I could have pretended, just to please you, but you don't deserve that. Ralf Hart, you are a man in the most beautiful, intense sense of the word. You've supported me and helped me, you've let me support and help you, without there being any humiliation on either side. Yes, it would have been good to have an orgasm, but I didn't. But I loved the cold floor, your warm body, the force with which you entered me.

'I went to take back my library books today, and the librarian asked if I talked to my partner about sex. I felt like saying: Which partner? What sort of sex do you mean? But she didn't deserve that; she's always been so sweet to me.

'I've really only had two partners since I came to Geneva: one who awoke the worst in me, because I let him and even begged him to. The other one, you, who made me feel part of the world again. I would like to be able to teach you where to touch my body, how much pressure to apply, for how long, and I know you would take this not as a criticism, but as another way to improve communication between our souls. The art of love is like your painting, it requires technique, patience, and, above all, practice by the couple. It requires boldness, the courage to go beyond what people conventionally call "making love".'

The teacher in me was back, and I didn't want that, but Ralf knew how to take control of the situation. Instead of agreeing with me, he lit his third cigarette in less than half an hour and said:

'Firstly, you're staying here tonight.'

It wasn't a request, it was an order.

'Secondly, we're going to make love again, but with less anxiety this time and more desire. And finally, I'd like you to understand men better too.'

Understand men better? I spent every night with them, whites, blacks, Asians, Jews, Muslims, Catholics, Buddhists. Didn't Ralf know that?

I felt lighter; I was so pleased that the conversation had shifted into being a discussion. At one point, I even considered asking God's forgiveness and breaking my promise. But reality returned, telling me to remember to preserve my dream intact and not to fall into destiny's traps.

'Yes, to understand men better,' said Ralf again, seeing the doubtful look on my face. 'You talk about your female sexuality, about helping me to find my way around your body, to be patient, to take time. I agree, but has it occurred to you that we're different, at least in matters of time? You should complain to God about that.

'When we met, I asked you to teach me about sex, because I had lost all my sexual desire. Do you know why? Because after a certain age, every sexual relationship I had ended in tedium and frustration, because I realised how difficult it was to give the women I loved the same amount of pleasure they gave me.'

I didn't like the sound of 'the women I loved', but I feigned indifference and lit a cigarette.

'I didn't have the courage to ask: show me your body. But when I met you, I saw your light, and I loved you at once, and I thought that, at this stage in my life, I had nothing to lose by being honest with myself and with the woman I wanted to have by my side.'

My cigarette tasted delicious, and I would have liked him to offer me some wine, but I didn't want to break the thread of the conversation.

'Why is it that men only think about sex, instead of doing as you did with me and finding out how I feel?'

'Who said we only think about sex? On the contrary, we spend years of our life trying to convince ourselves that sex is actually important to us. We learn about love from prostitutes or virgins; we tell our stories to whoever will listen; when we are older, we parade about with much younger lovers, just to prove to others that we really are what women expect us to be.

'But do you know something? That's simply not true. We understand nothing. We think that sex and ejaculation are the same thing and, as you just said, they're not. We don't learn because we haven't the courage to say to the woman: show me your body. We don't learn because the woman doesn't have the courage to say: this is what I like. We are stuck with our primitive survival instincts, and that's that. Absurd though it may seem, do you know what is more important than sex for a man?'

I thought it might be money or power, but I said nothing.

'Sport. Because a man can understand another man's body. We can see that sport is a dialogue between two bodies that understand each other.'

'You're mad.'

'Maybe. But it makes sense. Have you ever stopped to think about the feelings of the men you've been to bed with?'

'Yes, I have. They were all insecure. They were all afraid.'

'Worse than afraid, they were vulnerable. They didn't really know what they were doing, they only knew what society, friends and women themselves had told them was important. Sex, sex, sex, that's the basis of life, scream the advertisements, other people, films, books. No one knows what they're talking about. Since instinct is stronger than all of us, all they know is that it has to be done. And that's that.'

Enough. I had tried to give him lessons in sex in order to protect myself, now he was doing the same, and however wise our words – because each of us was always trying to impress the other – this was so stupid and so unworthy of our relationship! I drew him to me because – regardless of what he had to say or of what I thought about myself – life had taught me many things. In the beginning, everything was love and surrender. But then the serpent appeared and said to Eve: what you surrendered, you will lose. That is how it was with me – I was driven out of paradise when I was still at school, and ever since then, I have been trying to find a way of telling the serpent he was wrong, that living was more important than keeping things to yourself. But the serpent was right and I was wrong.

I knelt down and gradually took off his clothes, and I saw his penis there, sleeping and unresponsive. This didn't seem to bother him, and I kissed the inner part of his legs, starting at his feet. His penis slowly began to respond, and I touched it, then put it in my mouth and – unhurriedly, so that he wouldn't interpret this as: 'right, get ready for action!' – I kissed it with all the tenderness of someone who expects nothing in return, and for precisely that reason I got everything I wanted. I saw that he was getting excited, and he began to touch my nipples, circling them with his fingers as he had on that night of total darkness, making me want to have him again between my legs or in my mouth or whatever way he wanted to possess me.

He didn't take off my jacket; he had me lie face forwards, with the upper part of my body bent over the table, and my feet still on the floor. He penetrated me slowly and unhurriedly this time, no longer afraid of losing me, because, deep down, he too had realised that this was a dream and that it would always be a dream, and would never become reality.

At the same time as I felt him inside me, I was aware of his hand on my breasts, my buttocks, touching me as only a woman knows how. Then I knew that we were made for each other, because he could be a woman, as he was now, and I could be a man, as when we talked or when we initiated that joint search for the two lost souls, the two missing fragments needed to complete the universe.

As he simultaneously penetrated and touched me, I felt that he was doing this not only to me, but to the whole universe. We had time, tenderness and mutual knowledge. Yes, it had been good to arrive carrying two suitcases, ready to leave, and to be immediately thrown to the floor and penetrated with a kind of fearful urgency; but it was good too knowing that the night would never end and that there, on the kitchen table, orgasm wasn't a goal in itself, but the beginning of that encounter.

He stopped moving inside me while his fingers worked quickly and I had one, two, three orgasms in a row. I felt like pushing him away, for the pain of pleasure is so intense that it hurts, but I resisted; I accepted that this was how it was, that I could withstand another orgasm or another two, or even more …

… and suddenly, a kind of light exploded inside me. I was no longer myself, but a being infinitely superior to everything I knew. When his hand took me to my fourth orgasm, I entered a place where

everything seemed at peace, and with my fifth orgasm I knew God. Then I felt him beginning to move inside me again, although his hand had still not stopped, and I said 'Oh God', and surrendered to whatever came next, Heaven or Hell.

It was Heaven. I was the earth, the mountains, the tigers, the rivers that flowed into the lakes, the lakes that became the sea. He was thrusting faster and faster now, and the pain was mingled with pleasure, and I could have said: 'I can't take any more', but that would have been unfair, because, by then, he and I were one person.

I allowed him to penetrate me for as long as it took; his nails were now digging into my buttocks, and there I was face down on the kitchen table, thinking that there wasn't a better place in the world to make love. Again the creak of the table, his breathing growing ever faster, his nails bruising me, my sex beating hard against his, flesh against flesh, bone against bone, and I was about to have another orgasm, and so was he, and none of this, absolutely none of this was a LIE!

'*Come on!*'

He knew what he was saying, and I knew that this was the moment; I felt my whole body soften, I ceased to be myself – I was no longer listening, seeing or tasting anything – I was merely feeling.

'*Come on!*'

And I came at the same moment he came. It wasn't eleven minutes, it was an eternity, it was as if we had both left our bodies and were walking joyfully through the gardens of paradise in understanding and friendship. I was woman and man, he was man and woman. I don't know how long it lasted, but everything seemed to be silent, at prayer, as if the universe and life had ceased to exist and become transformed into something sacred, nameless and timeless.

But time returned, I heard his shouts and I shouted with him, the table legs beat on the floor, and it didn't occur to either of us to wonder what the rest of the world might be thinking.

And suddenly he withdrew from me and laughed; I felt my vagina contract, and I turned to him and I laughed too, and we embraced as if it were the first time we had made love in our entire lives.

'Bless me,' he said.

I blessed him, not really knowing what I was doing. I asked him to do the same, and he did, saying, 'blessed be this woman, who has loved much'. They were beautiful words, and we embraced again and stayed there, unable to understand how eleven minutes could carry a man and a woman so far.

Neither of us was tired. We went into the living room, he put on a record and did exactly as I had hoped: he lit the fire and poured me some wine. Then he opened a book and read:

A time to be born, and a time to die;
A time to plant, and a time to pluck up that which is planted;
A time to kill, and a time to heal;
A time to break down, and a time to build up;
A time to weep, and a time to laugh;
A time to mourn, and a time to dance;
A time to cast away stones, and a time to gather stones together;
A time to embrace, and a time to refrain from embracing;
A time to get, and a time to lose;
A time to keep, and a time to cast away;
A time to rend, and a time to sew;
A time to keep silence, and a time to speak;
A time to love, and a time to hate;
A time of war, and a time of peace.

This sounded like a farewell, but it was the loveliest farewell I would ever experience in my life.

I embraced him and he embraced me, and we lay down on the carpet beside the fire. I was still filled by a sense of plenitude, as if I had always been a wise, happy, fulfilled woman.

'What made you fall in love with a prostitute?'

'I didn't understand it myself at the time. But I've thought about it since, and I think it was because, knowing that your body would never be mine alone, I had to concentrate on conquering your soul.'

'Weren't you jealous?'

'You can't say to the spring: "Come now and last as long as possible." You can only say: "Come and bless me with your hope, and stay as long as you can."'

Words lost on the wind. But I needed to hear them, and he needed to say them. I fell asleep, although I don't know when. I dreamed, not of a situation or of a person, but of a perfume that flooded the air.

When Maria opened her eyes, a few rays of sun were coming in through the open blinds.

'I've made love with him twice,' she thought, looking at the man asleep by her side. 'And yet it's as if we had always been together, and he had always known my life, my soul, my body, my light, my pain.'

She got up to go to the kitchen and make some coffee. That was when she saw the two suitcases in the hall and she remembered everything: her promise, the prayer she had said in the church, her life, the dream that insisted on becoming reality and losing its charm, the perfect man, the love in which body and soul were one and the same and in which pleasure and orgasm were different things.

She could stay; she had nothing more to lose, only an illusion. She remembered the poem: a time to weep, and a time to laugh.

But there was another line too: 'a time to embrace, and a time to refrain from embracing'. She made the coffee, shut the kitchen door and phoned for a taxi. She summoned all her willpower, which had carried her so far, and which was the source of energy for her 'light', which had told her the exact time to leave, which was protecting her and making her treasure forever the memory of that night. She got dressed, picked up her suitcases and left, hoping against hope that he would wake up and ask her to stay.

But he didn't wake up. While she was waiting for the taxi outside, a gypsy was passing, carrying bouquets of flowers.

'Would you like to buy one?'

Maria bought one; it was the sign that autumn had arrived and summer had been left behind. It would be a long time now before the café tables were out on the pavements in Geneva and the parks were full once more of people strolling about and sunbathing. It didn't matter; she was leaving because she had chosen to leave, and there was no reason for regrets.

She got to the airport, drank another cup of coffee and waited four hours for her flight to Paris, thinking all the time that he would arrive at any moment, because at some point before they fell asleep, she had told him the time of her flight. That's how it always happened in films: at the last moment, when the woman is just about to board the plane, the man races up to her, puts his arms around her and kisses her, and brings her back to his world, beneath the smiling, indulgent gaze of the flight staff. The words 'The End' appear on the screen, and the audience knows that, from then on, they will live happily ever after.

'Films never tell you what happens next,' she thought, trying to console herself. Marriage, cooking, children, ever more infrequent sex, the discovery of the first note from his mistress, the decision to confront him, his promise that it will never happen again, the second note from another mistress, another confrontation and this time a threat to leave him, this time the man reacts less vehemently and merely tells her that he loves her. The third note from a third mistress, and the decision to say nothing, to pretend that she knows nothing, because he might tell her that he doesn't love her any more and that she's free to leave.

No, films never show that. They finish before the real world begins. It's best not to think too much about it.

She read one, two, three magazines. In the end, they announced her flight, after almost an eternity in that airport lounge, and she got on the plane. She still imagined the famous scene in which, as she fastens her seatbelt, she feels a hand on her shoulder, turns round and there he is, smiling at her.

Nothing happened.

She slept on the short flight between Geneva and Paris. She hadn't had time to think about what she would tell them at home, what story she would invent, but her parents would probably just be happy to have their daughter back, and to have a farm and a comfortable old age ahead of them.

She woke up with the jolt of the plane landing. It taxied for a long time, and the flight attendant came to tell her that she would have to change terminals, because the flight to Brazil left from Terminal F and she was in Terminal C. But there was no need to worry; there were no delays, and she still had plenty of time, and if she wasn't sure where to go, the ground staff would help her.

While the passenger loading bridge was being put in place, she wondered if it would be worth spending a day in Paris, just to take some photographs and be able to tell people that she had been there. She needed time to think, to be alone with herself, to bury her memories of last night deep down inside her, so that she could use them whenever she needed to feel alive. Yes, a day in Paris was an excellent idea; she asked the flight attendant when the next flight to Brazil was, if she decided not to leave that day.

The flight attendant asked to see her ticket and said that, unfortunately, it didn't allow for that kind of stopover. Maria consoled herself with the thought that visiting such a beautiful city all on her own would only depress her. She was still managing to cling on to her sang-froid, to her willpower, and didn't want to ruin it all by seeing a beautiful view and missing someone intensely.

She got off the plane and went through the security checks; her luggage would go straight on to the next plane, so she didn't have to bother with that. The doors opened, the passengers emerged and embraced whoever was waiting for them, wife, mother, children. Maria pretended not to notice, at the same time pondering her own loneliness, except that this time she had a secret, a dream, which would make her solitude less bitter, and life would be easier.

'We'll always have Paris.'

The voice didn't belong to a tourist guide or to a taxi driver. Her legs shook when she heard it.

'We'll always have Paris?'

'It's a quote from one of my favourite films. Would you like to see the Eiffel Tower?'

Oh, yes, she would, she would love to. Ralf was holding a bunch of roses, and his eyes were full of light, the light she had seen on that first day, when he was painting her while the cold wind outside had made her feel awkward to be sitting there.

'How did you manage to get here before me?' she asked, merely to disguise her amazement; she wasn't in the least interested in the answer, but she needed a breathing space.

'I saw you reading a magazine at Geneva airport. I could have come over, but I'm such an incurable romantic that I thought it would be best to catch the next shuttle to Paris, wander about the airport here for three hours, consult the arrivals screen over and over, buy some flowers, say the words that Rick says to his beloved in *Casablanca* and see the look of surprise on your face. And to be utterly sure that this was what you wanted, that you were expecting me, that all the determination and willpower in the world would not be enough to prevent love from changing the rules of the game from one moment to the next. It's really easy being as romantic as people in the movies, don't you think?'

She had no idea whether it was easy or difficult, and she didn't honestly care, even though she had only just met this man, even though they had made love for the first time only a few hours before, even though she had only been introduced to his friends the previous evening, even though he had been a regular at the nightclub where she had worked, even though he had been married twice. These were not exactly impeccable credentials. On the other hand, she now had enough money to buy a farm, she had her youth ahead of her, a great deal of experience of life and a great independence of soul. Nevertheless, as always happened when fate chose for her, she thought, once again, that she would take the risk.

She kissed him, utterly indifferent now to what happens after the words 'The End' appear on the cinema screen.

But if, one day, someone should decide to tell her story, she would ask them to begin it just as all the fairy tales begin:

Once upon a time ...

Afterword

Like everyone else – and in this case I have no qualms about generalising – it took me a long time to discover the sacred nature of sex. My youth coincided with an age of enormous freedom, great discoveries and many excesses, which was followed by a period of conservatism and repression – the price to be paid for extremes that brought with them some very harsh consequences indeed.

In that decade of excess (the 1970s), the writer Irving Wallace wrote a book about censorship in America, describing the legal shenanigans involved in preventing the publication of a book about sex: *The Seven Minutes*.

In Wallace's novel, the contents of the book which provokes the discussion about censorship are merely hinted at, and the subject of sexuality itself is rarely mentioned. I wondered what that banned book would be like; perhaps I could have a go at writing it myself.

However, in his novel, Wallace makes many references to this non-existent book, and this necessarily limited the task I had imagined, indeed, made it impossible. I was left with just the title (although I felt Wallace had made a rather conservative estimate of the time involved, and so decided to increase it) and the idea of how important it was to treat sexuality seriously – like many writers before me.

In 1997, after a lecture I gave in Mantua, Italy, I went back to my hotel and found that someone had left a manuscript for me in reception. Now, I never normally read unsolicited manuscripts, but I did read that one – the true story of a Brazilian prostitute, her marriages, her problems with the law, and her various adventures. In 2000, when I was passing through Zurich, I met that prostitute – known professionally as Sonia – and said how much I had liked what I had read. I suggested she send it to my Brazilian publisher, who, however, decided, in the end, not to publish it. Sonia was living in Italy at the time, but had travelled up on the train to meet me in Zurich. She invited us – myself, a friend and a female journalist from the newspaper *Blick*, who had just interviewed me – to go to Langstrasse, the local red light district. I didn't know that Sonia had already forewarned her colleagues of our visit, and to my surprise, I ended up signing several of my books, translated into various languages.

At that point, I had already decided to write about sex, but I still didn't have a plot or a principal character; I was thinking of something much more along the lines of the conventional search for sacredness, but that visit to Langstrasse taught me something: in order to write about the sacred nature of sex, it was necessary to understand why it had been so profaned.

In conversation with a journalist from the Swiss magazine, *L'Illustrée*, I described that spontaneous book-signing in Langstrasse, and he wrote a long article about it. The result was that, at a book-signing in Geneva, several prostitutes turned up to have their copies of my books duly signed. I was very struck by one of them in particular, and afterwards – with my agent and friend, Mônica Antunes – we went for a coffee that turned into supper that turned into other meetings in the days that followed. Thus was born the connecting thread of *Eleven Minutes*.

I would like to thank Anna von Planta, my Swiss publisher, who supplied me with important facts about the legal situation of prostitutes in her country. I would also like to thank the following women in Zurich (using their *noms de guerre*): Sonia, whom I met for the first time in Mantua (who knows, maybe one day, someone will publish your book!), Martha, Antenora and Isabella. And in Geneva (again using their *noms de guerre*): Amy, Lucia, Andrei, Vanessa, Patrick, Thérèse and Anna Christina.

Many thanks also to Antonella Zara, who allowed me to use passages from her book, *The Science of Passion*, in certain sections of Maria's diary.

Finally, I must thank Maria (*nom de guerre*), who now lives in Lausanne with her husband and her two lovely daughters and who, during various meetings with myself and Mônica, told us her story, on which this book is based.

Paulo Coelho

Life is a journey

Make sure you don’t miss a thing.
Live it with Paulo Coelho.

Visit /paulocoelho

How can you find your heart's desire?

A world-wide phenomenon; an inspiration for anyone seeking their path in life.

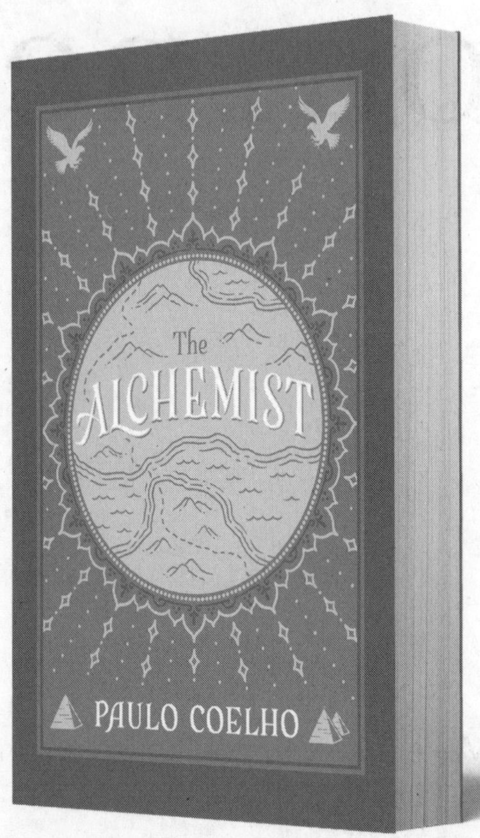

The Alchemist

Do you believe in yourself?

A modern-day adventure in the searing heat of the Mojave desert and an exploration of fear and self-doubt.

The Valkyries

How do we see the amazing in the everyday?

When two young lovers are reunited, they discover anew the truth of what lies in their hearts.

By the River Piedra I Sat Down & Wept

What are you searching for?

A transforming journey on the pilgrims' road to Santiago – and the first of Paulo's extraordinary books.

The Pilgrimage

Can faith triumph over suffering?

Paulo Coelho's brilliant telling of the story of Elijah, who was forced to choose between love and duty.

The Fifth Mountain

Is life always worth living?

A fundamental moral question explored as only Paulo Coelho can.

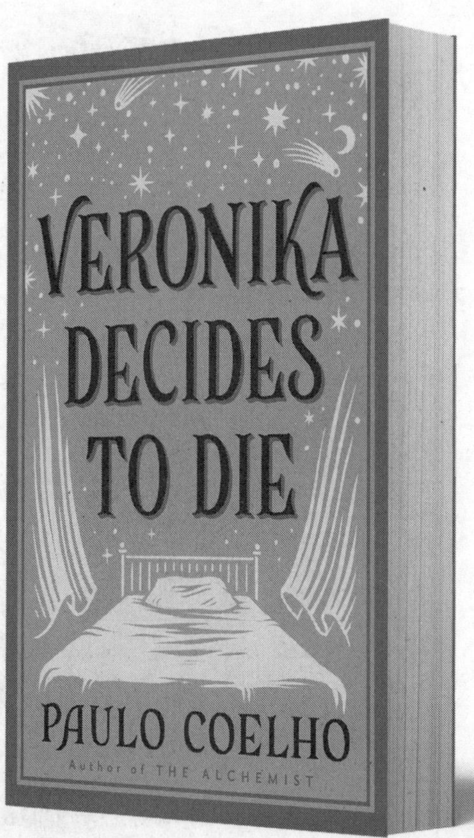

Veronika Decides to Die

Could you be tempted into evil?

The inhabitants of a small town are challenged by a mysterious stranger to choose between good and evil.

The Devil & Miss Prym

Are you brave enough to live your dream?

Strategies and inspiration to help you follow your own path in a troubled world.

Manual of the Warrior of Light

How far would you go for your obsession?

A sweeping story of love, loss and longing that spans the world.

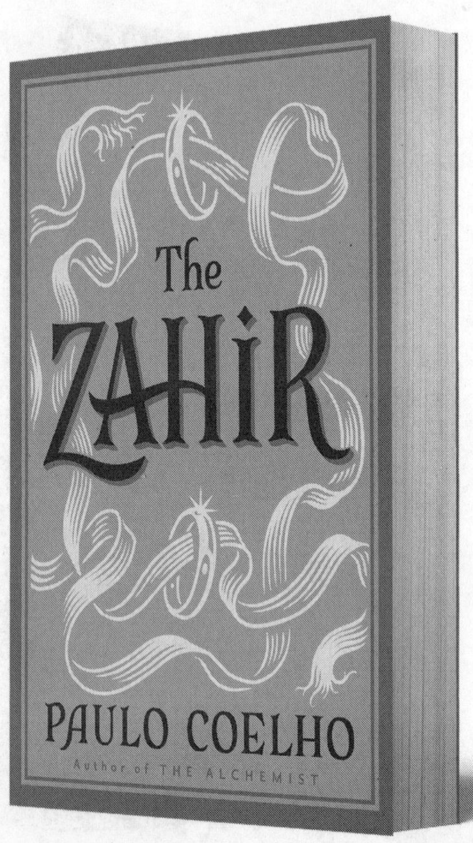

The Zahir

What happens when obsession turns to murder?

An enthralling story of jealousy, death and suspense.

The Winner Stands Alone

Can we dare to be true to ourselves?

A story that will transform the way we think about love, joy and sacrifice.

The Witch of Portobello

How will you know who your soulmate is?

A moving tale of passion, mystery and spirituality.

Brida

What does it mean to be truly alive?

Powerful tales of living and dying, destiny and choice, and love lost and found.

Like the Flowing River

Are you where you want to be?

Read *Aleph*. And rewrite your life.

Aleph

Is there a weapon more powerful than words?

A timeless and powerful exploration of personal growth, everyday wisdom and joy.

Manuscript Found in Accra

MANUAL of the WARRIOR of LIGHT

Paulo Coelho was born in Brazil and has become one of the most widely read and loved authors in the world. Especially renowned for *The Alchemist* and *Eleven Minutes*, he has sold more than 320 million books worldwide and has been translated into 83 languages. The recipient of numerous prestigious international awards, amongst them the Crystal Award by the World Economic Forum and France's Légion d'Honneur, Paulo Coelho was inducted into the Brazilian Academy of Letters in 2002.

Also by Paulo Coelho

The Alchemist
The Pilgrimage
The Valkyries
By the River Piedra I Sat Down and Wept
The Fifth Mountain
Veronika Decides to Die
Manual of the Warrior of Light
Eleven Minutes
The Zahir
The Devil and Miss Prym
The Witch of Portobello
Brida
The Winner Stands Alone
Like the Flowing River
Aleph
Manuscript Found in Accra
Adultery
The Spy
Hippie